U0063703

COLLINS 袖珍
英漢雙解詞典

COLLINS GEM
ENGLISH LEARNER'S
DICTIONARY

商務印書館

Original edition published under title *Collins Gem English Learners' Dictionary* by Collins Publishers

Collins 袖珍英漢雙解詞典

編　　者 ……	David J. Carver & Michael J. Wallace	
譯　　著 ……	廈門大學外文系	
責任編輯 ……	劉秀英	
出　　版 ……	商務印書館（香港）有限公司	
	香港筲箕灣耀興道 3 號東滙廣場 8 樓	
	http://www.commercialpress.com.hk	
發　　行 ……	香港聯合書刊物流有限公司	
	香港新界荃灣德士古道 220–248 號荃灣工業中心16樓	
印　　刷 ……	中華商務彩色印刷有限公司	
	香港新界大埔汀麗路 36 號中華商務印刷大廈	
版　　次 ……	2023 年 4 月第 17 次印刷	

© 1993 商務印書館（香港）有限公司

ISBN 978 962 07 0159 7

Printed in Hong Kong

Collins袖珍英漢雙解詞典

Contents 目　錄

Collins袖珍英漢雙解詞典

前　言

　　《Collins袖珍英漢雙解詞典》是Collins Gem English Learner's Dictionary的最新修訂本的英語和漢語雙解版。本詞典的漢語翻譯由廈門大學外文系擔當。參加的翻譯工作者都是有編纂英漢詞典經驗的教授、副教授。

　　本詞典收詞18000餘，有16000條例。提供當代英語的基本詞彙，國際音標註音。漢字以繁體字排印。在原版書的基礎上，又加了香港學生教科書中出現的語詞。

　　漢語釋義和例句的漢譯，嚴格根據英語原文。忠實於原文，且用恰當、貼切的現代漢語，力求保持原英語釋義用淺顯易懂的詞彙之特點，使全書釋義準確、簡潔，語句流暢。

　　由於有大量的例，使讀者翻開詞典查一個詞，不但弄懂詞的釋義，也可知道如何正確使用這個詞。體現了這本小小的詞典語義和語用並重，有助於讀者閱讀和翻譯英語書籍、文章，無論對初學者或有相當英語水平的人，都會有所裨益。這一突出的特點遠比同類型詞典優越。

　　商務印書館(香港)有限公司本着一貫服務社會，促進中西文化交流的業務精神，不惜重資請人翻譯，重新排版。將袖珍型英漢雙解詞典首次貢獻給讀者。

商務印書館編輯部

1993年

GUIDE TO THE DICTIONARY

本詞典使用説明

In planning and preparing this dictionary the publishers have kept firmly in mind the many virtues of the fuller Collins English Learner's Dictionary on which it is based. We have maintained the full and easy–to–understand definitions and the thousands of example sentences and phrases which help the reader build the new words he has learnt into his active vocabulary. The emphasis is again on modern up–to–date vocabulary. concentrating particularly on the 18,000 or so words and phrases which constitute the essential basis of current English usage. Such a vocabulary, already large by many accepted standards, provides a firm and sure foundation without which a fluent command of English is not possible. Once more there are hundreds of notes and labels to help the user understand the appropriateness of the vocabulary he meets.

在籌劃本詞典時，我們牢記作爲本詞典依據的《Collins英語詞典》的許多優點。我們保留其詳盡易懂的釋義和數以千計的例證，幫助讀者將所學新詞溶入其現在使用的詞彙中。本詞典仍着重現代詞彙，尤其着重構成現代英語用法基礎的18000左右個詞。這些詞按公認標準可謂豐富，它們爲讀者打下堅實的基礎，而沒有這一基礎，是不可能流利使用英語的。本詞典仍附有數百個説明和符號，以幫助本詞典使用者理解所遇到的詞彙的確切內容。

GUIDE TO THE DICTIONARY

Pronunciation

發　音

English can be spoken in a huge variety of accents and the foreign learner will want to study a type which has been widely accepted wherever English is spoken and which has been authoritatively analysed and described. The accent of standard British English which best fulfils these requirements is known as *Received Pronunciation* or *RP*, and the pronunciation of words in this dictionary has been given this accent.

英語的口音種類繁多，外國學習者都希望能學習一種各地廣泛接受而且經過權威性分析和描述的英語發音。最能滿足這些要求的是英國的標準發音（Received Pronunciation或RP），本詞典就是以這種發音標註單詞。

Pronunciation Key

發 音 符 號

Vowels

元　音

[æ] bat [bæt]

[ɑ:] farm [fɑ:m]

[e] set [set]

[ə] above [ə'bʌv]

GUIDE TO THE DICTIONARY

[ə:] fern [fə:n]

[i] pity ['piti]

[i:] green [gri:n]

[ɔ] rot [rɔt]

[ɔ:] board [bɔ:d]

[u] full [ful]

[u:] root [ru:t]

[ʌ] come [kʌm]

Diphthongs

雙 元 音

[ai] lie [lai]

[au] cow [kau]

[ei] fate [feit]

[ou] ago [ə'gou]

[ɛə] fair [fɛə*]

[iə] here [hiə*]

[ɔi] toy [tɔi]

[uə] pure [pjuə*]

Consonants

輔 音

[b] bet [bet]

[d] dime [daim]

[f] face [feis]

[g] go [gou]

[h] hit [hit]

[j] you [ju:]

[k] catch [kætʃ]

[l] lick [lik]

[m] roam [roum]

[n] nut [nʌt]

[ŋ] bank [bæŋk]

[p] pepper ['pepə*]

[r] rate [reit]

[s] sit [sit]

GUIDE TO THE DICTIONARY

[t] tell [tel]

[v] vine [vain]

[w] wine [wain]

[z] zero ['ziərou]

[ʒ] leisure ['leʒə*]

[ʃ] shame [ʃeim]

[θ] thin [θin]

[ð] this [ðis]

[x] loch [lɔx]

[tʃ] church [tʃəːtʃ]

[dʒ] judge [dʒʌdʒ]

The main stress of words is indicated by a small vertical line which appears *in front of* the syllable that is stressed. The word *insect*, for example, is written ['insekt] because the stress is on the first syllable, but the word *insist* is written [in'sist] because the stress is on the second syllable.

單詞的主重音用一小垂直綫標在該重讀音節之前。例如：insect 一詞的音標寫成 ['insekt]，因爲重讀是在第一個音節，但是 insist 一詞則寫成 [in'sist]，因爲重讀在第二個音節。

The sign * at the end of a pronunciation means that the letter *r* at the end of it is pronounced only if a vowel follows it. For example, *better* not followed by a vowel is pronounced ['betə]. but in a phrase like a *better idea*. the *r* would be pronounced.

音標末尾的星號＊表示該單詞末尾的字母 r 只在下接元音時才發音，例如 better 後面不接元音時發音是 ['betə]，但在像 better idea 這一短語中，r 要發音。

GUIDE TO THE DICTIONARY

Abbreviations used in the dictionary

本詞典所用縮畧語

adj   adjective   形容詞

adv   adverb   副詞

art   article   冠詞

attrib   attributive   定語

aux   auxiliary   助動詞

Brit   British   英國(英語)

conj   conjunction   連接詞

e.g.   for example   例如

esp.   especially   尤指

etc   et cetera   等等

fem   feminine   陰性

i.e.   that is   即

illus.   illustration   例證

interj   interjection   感嘆詞

Ir   Irish   愛爾蘭(英語)

masc   masculine   陽性

nc   countable noun   可數名詞

nu   uncountable noun   不可數名詞

nc/u   countable or
       uncountable   noun   可數名詞或不可數名詞

o.f.   old–fashioned   舊式

GUIDE TO THE DICTIONARY

opp   opposite   反義詞

past   past   tense   and   past   participle   過去式和過去分詞

past   part   past   participle   過去分詞

pl   plural   複數

pred   adj   predicative   adjective   表語形容詞

prep   preposition   介詞

pron   pronoun   代詞

pres   present   現在式

® registered trademark   註冊商標

Scot   Scottish   蘇格蘭(英語)

sing   singular   單數

US   American   美國(英語)

<u>usu.</u>   usually   通常

vt   transitive   verb   及物動詞

vi   intransitive   verb   不及物動詞

vt/i   transitive   or

   intransitive   verb   及物動詞或不及物動詞

Grammatical Points

語法要點

nc and *nu* —*nc* means countable nouns like *chair, boy, desk*. These words
   can have a plural form.

   —*nu* refers to uncountable or mass nouns, e.g. *information,*
   luggage which are seldom, or never, used in the plural form.

GUIDE TO THE DICTIONARY

Please note that the distinction between *nc* and *nu* is not always clear–cut in English, so that this classification should be taken as a general guide only.

nc 和 nu—nc 表示可數名詞，例如chair, boy, desk。這些詞可以有複數形式。

—nu表示不可數名詞或物質名詞，例如 information, luggage。這些詞很少或不用複數形式。

請注意，英語裏的可數名詞和不可數名詞之間的區別並不都是十分清楚，因此，這種分類只能作爲一般性的指導。

vi and *vt*–*vi* means intransitive verb. i.e. one which does not take an object noun or pronoun as, for example:

vi和vt—

vi表示不及物動詞，即：不能接名詞或代詞作賓語的動詞，例如：

> *The boys are running.*
>
> *He never comes here.*

–vt means transitive verb, i.e. one which takes a noun or pronoun as an object. For example:

vt 表示及物動詞，即：可帶名詞或代詞作賓語的動詞，例如：

> *The boys were kicking a ball.*
>
> *He is reading a book.*

adj–adjective. The word *good* is an adjective in the following sentences:

adj —形容詞。在下列句子裏，good 是形容詞：

> *John is a good boy.*
>
> *Exercise is good for you.*

pred adj–predicative adjective. An example would be *alive* as in *The child is still alive.* We could never say *The alive child...*

pred adj—表語形容詞：如 The child is still alive 裏的 alive，我們不能說 The alive child…

GUIDE TO THE DICTIONARY

attrib adj–attributive adjective. An example would be *utter* as in *It was an utter waste of time!* Not *The waste of time was utter!*

attrib adj–定語形容詞: 如 It was an utter waste of time! 裏的 utter.不能說 The waste of time was utter!

adv–adverb. The adverbs in the following sentences are repeated in brackets.

adv—副詞; 下列句子裏的副詞重複置於括號內。

> *He is doing well in his studies.* (well)
> *The time went quickly.* (quickly)
> *We shall have to leave now.* (now)

aux–auxiliary. The complete list (omitting past tense and changes according to person) is: *be, have, do, will, shall, may, must, ought, dare, need, used.*

aux—助動詞; 全部助動詞(畧去過去式和按人稱的變化形式)是: be, have, do, will, shall, may, must, ought, dare, need, used。

conj–conjunction, i.e. words having a joining function e.g. *and, but, either... or, neither... nor, if, when, where* etc.

conj — 連接詞, 即: 起連接作用的詞, 例如 and, but, either...or, neither...nor, if, when, where 等。

determiner–A word like *a/an, both, few, other, one, two, enough, this, these* etc, which can occur in the same position as *the* in a sentence.

determiner——限定詞, 即在句子裏的位置可以和 the 相同的詞, 如 a/an, both, few, other, one, two, enough, this, these 等

intensifier–A word like *quite, rather, awfully, fairly, much* etc which can occur in the same position as *very* in a sentence.

GUIDE TO THE DICTIONARY

intensifier—强调成分，即在句子裏的位置可以和 very 相同的詞，如 quite, rather, awfully, fairly, much 等。

interj–interjection. Words like *oh, well, really* etc as in

interj—感嘆詞; 如下列句子裏的 oh, well, really 等詞。

> *Oh, I must tell you something*
> *Well, here we are.*
> *Really! What a rude man!*

prep–preposition. A fairly large class including such words as *above, across, against, among, beneath, beside, for, from, in, on, over, round, through, to, under, up, with* etc.

prep—介詞: 這是一個相當大的詞類, 包括的詞如: above, across, against, among, beneath, beside, for, from, in, on, over, round, through, to, under, up, with 等。

pron–pronoun. Pronouns are very often used instead of repeating a noun. But this is not their only use as you will see from the examples below. Some pronouns are *I, we, he, him, who, which, that, this, whoever* etc.

pron—代詞; 代詞常用來取代重複的名詞,但這不是它們唯一的用途,從下列例句裏便可看出。一些代詞是: I, we, he, him, who, which, that, this, whoever等。

> *When I saw Mary standing there, I went*
> *and spoke to her.* (I and her)
> *Anyone can learn English.* (anyone)
> *Who is that?* (who and that)
> *He can speak twelve languages, which is*
> *most unusual.* (he and which)

GUIDE TO THE DICTIONARY

Punctuation

標 點 符 號

In keeping with the modern style of the dictionary the punctuation of abbreviations such as *nc, vt, pres part* etc has been simplified omitting full stops

爲了與現代詞典的體例一致,對諸如 nc, vt, pres part 等縮畧語加以簡化,省去句點。

A semi–colon (;) is used between separate definitions with slight shifts of meaning, and between example phrases which are not sentences. In addition, a semi–colon separates a sentence from a phrase example.

分號(;)用以隔開畧有差異的定義和非句子的例證短語;此外,還用以隔開例句和例證短語。

An oblique stroke (/) is used to show choice or variation. Examples: *vt/i* means that a verb may be either transitive or intransitive. *someone/something* means that a certain verb etc may be followed by either a person or a thing as its object.

斜綫(/)用以表示選擇或變異。例如: vt/i 表示一個動詞可以是及物的,也可以是不及物的。someone/something 表示某動詞等可以接人或事物作爲賓語。

A, a

a [ei, ə] *determiner* **1** a particular one 某一特定的: *John has bought a new car* i.e. we are referring to one particular car. 約翰買了一輛新車. 即: 某一輛特定的車. *pl* 複數: *John has bought some / several / two new cars.* 約翰買了一些／幾輛／兩輛新車. *James is a friend of mine / yours / his etc* i.e. James is one of my (your, his etc.) friends. 詹姆士是我/你/他等的一位朋友. 即: 詹姆士是我(你, 他等)的朋友之一. **2** any one 任何一個: *A new car costs a lot of money* i.e. any new car, not one in particular. 買一部新車得花很多錢. 即: 任何一部新車, 不特指哪一部. *pl* 複數: *New cars cost a lot of money.* 買新車得花好多錢. **3** one 一個: *a gallon of petrol* 一加侖汽油; *a pound of butter* 一磅黃油. *pl* 複數: *two / three etc gallons of petrol etc.* 兩／三…加侖汽油等. **4** for each one 每一: *five pence a pound* 每磅五便士. *pl* 複數: *five pence for two / three etc pounds* 五便士兩／三…磅. **5** (with the name of a person)(與人名連用) an unknown person named... 一位名叫…的不認識的人: *A Mr Smith is waiting to see you.* i.e. a man named Mr Smith whom I (or you) don't know.(not usu. *pl*) 有一位史密斯先生正等着見你. 即: 有一位我(或你)不認識的名叫史密斯的人.(通常不用複數) **6** (joined with other determiners)(與其他限定詞連用) *A few spectators were there.* 有幾名觀眾在那兒. *Give him a little milk.* 給他一點兒牛奶. *There weren't a great many people there.* 那兒沒有很

多人. *He has a lot of money.* 他有很多錢. *Note* 說明: **1** *a* is used before words beginning with a consonant sound; an [æn, ən, n] is used before words beginning with a vowel sound. Notice that although the words *honour, hour, honourable, honest* etc begin with a consonant letter, the first sound in these words is a vowel so *an* is used. In the same way, although *union, united, useful, one* etc begin with a vowel letter, the first sound in these words is a consonant so *a* is used. Some people use *an* with *hotel, historian* and a few other words which usu. begin with a consonant sound; this is old-fashioned and not recommended. a 用在以輔音開頭的詞前; an 用在以元音開頭的詞前. 注意 honour, hour, honourable, honest 等詞雖然都是以輔音字母開頭, 但是這些詞的第一個音是元音, 因此前面要用 an. 同樣地, 雖然 union, united, useful, one 等詞以元音字母開頭, 但是這些詞的第一個音是輔音, 因此前面要用 a. 有些人把 an 與 hotel, historian 以及一些其他連用的通常以輔音開頭的詞連用; 這是舊式的用法, 不可取. **2** The emphatic forms [ei] and [æn] are not often used; one is more common for emphasis (e.g. *I wanted 'one' book, not six* is more common than *I wanted 'a' book, not six*). 強調式 [ei] 和 [æn] 不常用; one 則更常用於強調(例如: I wanted 'one' book, not six 比 I wanted 'a' book, not six 更常用). **3** *many a man, many a one;* these forms are rather old-fashioned; use *many men, many etc.* many a man, many a one 這些形式是相當舊式的,現在要用 many men, many 等。

aback [ə'bæk] *adv* only in **taken aback** i.e. surprised (esp. unpleasantly)僅用於 taken aback,即:吃驚(尤指令人不愉快地): *He was taken aback at / by the news.* 這消息使他吃驚。

abacus ['æbəkəs] *nc* frame with beads sliding on wires, for doing arithmetic 算盤: *The boy used an abacus to help him solve arithmetic problems.* 那個男孩用算盤幫助他解算術題。 *pl* 複數: **abacuses** or **abaci** ['æbəsai].

abalone [æbə'louni] *nc* sea mollusc with a spiral shell lined with mother-of-pearl 鮑魚。

abandon [ə'bændən] *vt* leave, not intending to return; give up; have no more concern with 離棄;放棄;抛棄: *We had to abandon the plan we first thought of.* 我們只好放棄最初考慮的那項計劃。 *I don't think that John would abandon his friends if they were in trouble.* 我認為約翰不會在朋友有困難時棄他們。 **with abandon** in a wild and uncontrolled way 放縱地;盡情地。

abashed [ə'bæʃt] *adj* not sure what to do or say (usu. because of the behaviour or words of other people) 困窘的,侷促不安的(通常由於他人的言詞或舉止導致)(*opp* 反義詞 **unabashed**).

abate [ə'beit] *vt / i* (usu. of noise, pain, suffering, nuisance etc.) become or make less (通常指嘈雜聲,疼痛,苦難,煩擾等)減輕;減弱;減少。

abattoir ['æbətwa:*] *nc* place where animals are killed for food 屠宰場。

abbey ['æbi] *nc* **1** building(s) in which monks or nuns live 修道院。 **2** church which used to be part of an abbey (e.g. Westminster Abbey, London). (曾爲大修道院之一部份的)大教堂(例如:倫敦威斯敏斯特教堂)。

abbot ['æbət] *nc* man in charge of a monastery 男修道院院長;大寺院男住持。

abbreviate [ə'bri:vieit] *vt* make shorter (usu. a word or phrase) 簡縮,縮寫(通常指詞或短語): *'United Kingdom' can be abbreviated to 'U.K.'* 'United Kingdom' 可縮寫成爲 'U.K.'. **abbreviation** [əbri:vi'eiʃən] *nc / u* short form of a word or phrase (一個詞或短語的)縮寫式: *'U.K.' is the abbreviation of / for 'United Kingdom'.* 'U.K.' 是 'United Kingdom' 的縮寫式。

abdicate ['æbdikeit] *vt / i* leave an important position (usu. that of king or queen) 放棄重要職位(通常是王位),退位,讓位: *He abdicated the throne in favour of his brother.* 他把王位讓給弟弟。 **abdication** [æbdi'keiʃən] *nc / u.*

abdomen ['æbdəmən] *nc* part of the body containing the digestive organs 腹部。 **abdominal** [æb'dɔminl] *adj.* Note 說明: *abdomen* is best used as a medical or biological term; in ordinary use *stomach* would be better (e.g. *I have a pain in my stomach*). Medically, however, the word abdomen refers to all the digestive organs, while the stomach is only one of these organs. In medical use the word is pronounced [æb'doumən]. abdomen 最好作爲醫學或生物學的術語使用,平常使用 stomach 一詞較好。(例如: I have a pain in my stomach. 我肚子疼)。然而,從醫學角度上說,abdomen 一詞指所有的消化器官,而 stomach 僅指消化器官之一(胃)。用作醫學術語時,abdomen 讀成 [æb'doumən].

abduct [æb'dʌkt] *vt* carry somebody

away against his will (usu. by force) 拐走(通常用暴力); 綁架. **abduction** *nc / u.*

aberration [æbə'reiʃən] *nc / u* a going away from the right or usual course 偏離正道, 脫離常軌.

abeyance [ə'beiəns] *nu* (usu. in **be in / fall into abeyance**) disuse or lack of use, possibly only temporary (of a custom, law, rule etc.) (通常用於 be in / fall into abeyance) (法律, 規則等的) 中止; 不復爲人所遵循; 暫擱: *The custom has fallen into abeyance* i.e. the custom is no longer followed (but it might be brought back). 這風俗已不爲人們所遵循. 即: 現在已不再有此風俗 (但有可能恢復).

abhor [əb'hɔ:*] *vt* hate very strongly 對…深惡痛絕; 厭惡; 憎惡: *Spitting in the street is a practice I abhor.* 我很厭惡在街上吐痰的習慣. *past* 過去式和過去分詞 **abhorred.** **abhorrence** [əb'hɔrəns] *nu* feeling of strong hatred 厭惡; 憎惡.

abide [ə'baid] *vt* (usu. only with **can't** or **cannot**) like (通常僅與 can't 或 cannot 連用) 容忍, 忍受: *I can't abide that chap.* (*informal*) 我不能容忍那像伙. (非正式). **abide by** be faithful to, follow (a law, custom agreement etc.) 信守, 遵守 (法律, 習俗, 協議等): *We must abide by the- rules of the game.* 我們必須遵守比賽規則.

ability [ə'biliti] *nc / u* power or cleverness to do something 能力; 才能. (*opp* 反義詞 **inability**). see 見 **able.**

abject [æb'dʒekt] *adj* contemptible; very miserable or unhappy 可鄙的; 凄苦可憐的. *The people lived in abject poverty.* 人們過着的生活.

ablaze [ə'bleiz] *adv / pred adj* on fire; very bright; full of, overflowing with, an emotion (e.g. anger) 着火; 光亮的; 情緒 (例如: 憤怒) 激動的: *The house was ablaze with light.* 這屋燈光通明. *His followers were ablaze with enthusiasm.* 他的追隨者情緒激昂.

able ['eibl] *adj* **1** having the power or cleverness or opportunity to do something 有能力, 才幹或機會做某事的; 能: *Most children are able to walk at the age of 15 months* i.e. most children can walk at this age. 多數孩子滿十五個月就能走路了. 即: 多數孩子在這個年齡就能走路了. *Are you able to help me?* 您能幫我嗎? *When will you be able to come?* 您甚麼時候能來? (*opp* 反義詞 **unable**). **2** (of people, speech, argument etc.) doing what is intended or wanted in a very satisfactory or clever way (人, 演說, 辯論等) 出色的, 顯示才華的: *He is an able administrator.* 他是一位出色的管理人才. *The lawyer made a very able speech.* 律師做了一場十分精彩的演說. **3** (of a person) not weak, although old (人) 老而不弱的, 年老體力尚佳的: *The old woman was still quite able.* 這位老婦人還很健壯. see 見 **ability.** '**able-bodied** *adj* fit and strong 強健的, 強壯的.

abnormal [æb'nɔ:məl] *adj* not normal; strange 不正常的; 特異的. **abnormality** [æbnɔ:'mæliti] *nc / u.*

aboard [ə'bɔ:d] *adv / prep* on a ship, train, aircraft etc. 在船 (火車, 飛機等) 上.

abolish [ə'bɔliʃ] *vt* stop something (esp. by law) so that it does not start again (e.g. slavery, poverty etc or a law, custom, practice etc.) (尤指通過法律) 廢除 (例如: 奴隸制度, 貧困等或一法令、習俗慣例等): *Abraham Lincoln abolished slavery in the United States.* 亞伯拉罕·林肯廢除了美國奴隸制度. **abolition** [æbə'liʃən] *nu.*

abominable [əˈbɔminəbl] *adj* horrible, very unpleasant 令人憎惡的, 討厭的. **abominably** *adv*.

aborigine [æbəˈridʒini] *nc* (usu. *pl*) one of the first inhabitants of a country (esp. those living in Australia before it was colonized) (通常用複數) 土著居民 (尤指殖民者到達前居住在澳大利亞的土人).

abortion [əˈbɔːʃən] *nc* intentional killing of an unborn child 流產; 墮胎. **abortive** [əˈbɔːtiv] *adj* (usu. of a plan, attempt, coup etc.) ending in failure; stopped before fully developing (通常指計劃, 企圖, 政變等) 功敗垂成的; 夭折的.

abound [əˈbaund] *vi* **1** be present in great numbers 大量存在: *Wild animals abound in Africa.* 非洲野獸很多. **2** have plenty of (usu. some form of wealth or some good quality of character) 富於 (通常指財富或好品質): *Saudi Arabia abounds in oil.* 沙特阿拉伯盛產石油.

about [əˈbaut] *adv / prep* **1** on the subject of etc. 關於: *a story about a little boy* 一個小男孩的故事. *He told me about his visit to France.* 他給我講述他的法國之行. **2** in; in different parts of 在; 在…各處: *He walked about the town for a long time.* 他在城裏各處走了好久. **3** nearly or perhaps a little more 大約, 差不多: *The little boy is about six years old.* 這小男孩大約六歲. **4** near 在附近: *Is John about?* i.e. is he here? *(informal)* 約翰在嗎? 即: 他在這裏嗎? (非正式). **5** in the other direction 向相反方向: *He turned about.* 他轉過身來. **about** to just going to; on the point of 正要; 行將: *The trial is about to begin* i.e. it will begin soon. 審判就要開始了. 即: 不久就要審判. **bring something a-bout** make something take place 使某事物發生; 引起某事物; 導致某事物. **turn (and turn) about** first one, then the other, and so on 一個接一個, 依次.

above [əˈbʌv] *adv / prep* **1** higher; over; on top 高於; 在…上面; 在頂上. **2** (in a book etc.) before this point 在(書籍等的)上文, 上述. **3** in heaven 在天上, 在天空. **above all** see **all**. **above board** *adv / pred adj* honest; being what it seems to be, without hiding anything from someone 坦誠的(地); 光明正大的(地).

abrasion [əˈbreiʒən] *nc / u* rubbing away of a surface 表面磨損: *an abrasion of the skin* 皮膚的擦傷處. **abrasive** [əˈbreiziv] *adj* causing abrasion 引起磨擦的; 生硬粗暴的: *abrasive personality* i.e. annoying 暴躁的性格, 即: 招人討厭的個性.

abreast [əˈbrest] *adv* next to; by the side of 並列, 並排, 並肩. **two / three / four etc abreast** with two / three / four etc people next to each other in a line 兩/三/四…人並排. **keep / stay / be abreast of / with something** know about new ideas and events 及時瞭解新事物, 跟上形勢: *abreast of the news* 及時獲悉消息.

abridge [əˈbridʒ] *vt* make shorter (often in order to make easier to read) 刪節, 節略 (常是為了便於閱讀).

abroad [əˈbrɔːd] *adv* in or to foreign countries 在國外; 到國外.

abrupt [əˈbrʌpt] *adj* **1** sudden and unexpected 突然的; 意外的: *an abrupt change of direction* 方向的驟變; *an abrupt decision* 突然的決定. **2** rough and impolite 粗暴無禮的.

abscess [ˈæbsis] *nc* painful swelling in some part of the body, containing a thick liquid called pus or matter 膿腫.

abscond [əb'skɔnd] *vi* go away secretly (esp. in order to avoid more punishment) 逃跑，潛逃(尤指爲躲避懲罰): *The boys absconded from school after breaking the window.* 這些男孩打破窗戶後，逃學了．

absence ['æbsəns] *nc / u* 1 failure to be at or in a place 缺席，不在: *Your absence from the meeting was noticed by the chairman* i.e. the fact that you were not at the meeting was noticed. 主席已經注意到你未出席會議．即: 你不在會場之事已被注意到．2 lack of something 缺乏，缺少: *Darkness is the absence of light* i.e. when there is no light in a place, there is darkness. 黑暗就是缺少亮光．即: 如果一個地方沒有光，那裏就黑暗．

absent ['æbsənt] *adj* 1 not in or at a place 不在場的，缺席的: *John was absent from school today* 約翰今天沒來上學．2 not noticing what is happening around one 茫然的，出神的，漫不經心的．*He had an absent expression on his face.* 他臉上有種茫然的神情．

absentee [æbsən'ti:] *nc* person who is absent 缺席者，不在者: *absentee landlord* i.e. landowner who does not live on his land 在外地主，即: 不住在產權所在地的地主．**'absent-'minded** *adj* not paying attention to one's surroundings (usu. because one is thinking of something else); forgetting many things (通常因另有所思而)心不在焉的; 健忘的．

absolute ['æbsəlu:t] *adj* 1 complete; very great 完全的; 十足的: *absolute freedom / truth / stupidity* 完全自由／全部真相／十足愚蠢．2 free from any control by the law 不受法律約束的．*The Queen of England is not an absolute ruler.* 英國女王並非是不受法律約束的統治者．**absolutely** ['æbsəlu:tli]

adv 1 completely 完全地．2 [æbsə'lu:tli]quite right!, certainly!, yes! *(informal)* 一點不錯; 當然，對極了! (非正式)．

absorb [əb'zɔ:b] *vt* 1 take in (esp. a liquid) 吸收 (尤指液體): *A sponge absorbs water.* 海綿吸水．2 get full attention 使全神貫注: *The students were completely absorbed in their work.* 學生們專心致志地工作．**absorbent** *adj* (in sense 1) (用於義1)．

abstain [əb'stein] *vi* stop using something; not use something (often for the sake of one's health) 禁絕; 戒絕(常是爲了健康起見): *abstain from alcohol* 戒酒．

abstemious [əb'sti:miəs] *adj* not taking too much food, drink etc. (飲食等)有節制的．

abstention [əb'sten∫ən] *nc / u* act of abstaining 戒絕．

abstinence ['æbstinəns] *nc* practice of not taking too much food / drink etc. (飲食等方面的)節制．

abstract¹ ['æbstrækt] *adj* 1 concerned with the idea of a thing and not with actual examples (e.g. the idea of honesty rather than honest actions or honest people) 抽象的，非具體的 (例如: 誠實的概念，而不是誠實的行爲或誠實的人)．2 difficult to understand because of a concern with ideas rather than actual examples (因抽象不具體而)難以理解的，深奧的: *abstract ideas* 抽象難懂的概念; *an abstract argument* 深奧的論點．3 (with reference to some types of Western painting in the 20th century) not showing pictures of real things, but patterns, shapes and colours 抽象派的(指20世紀西方繪畫流派中不重實物而重圖形結構和色彩的)．

abstract² ['æbstrækt] *nc* summary of a

book, article, report etc. (書籍、論文、報告等的)摘要.

abstract³ [æb'strækt] *vt* take out or take away (often dishonestly) 提取，抽出;(常指不正當地);偷.

abstruse [æb'stru:s] *adj* not easy to understand 深奧的，難懂的; *a very abstruse theory* 一種很深奧的理論; *abstruse ideas* 難懂的概念.

absurd [əb'sə:d] *adj* foolish; not sensible; without a reason 愚蠢的; 荒謬的; 不合理的. **absurdity** *nc / u* (example of) foolishness, unreasonableness 愚蠢(的行為);荒謬.

abundance [ə'bʌndəns] *nu* a large amount; very much 大量，多; 豐富: *He has an abundance of good stories.* 他有許多好故事. **abundant** *adj*.

abuse¹ [æ'bju:s] **1** *nu* bad and insulting language 辱駡. **2** *nc* bad or dishonest action 陋習，弊端: *The commission of enquiry found a number of abuses in the granting of import licences.* 調查委員會發現在簽發進口許可證時有許多弊端.

abuse² [ə'bju:z] *vt* use wrongly in a way not intended 濫用，妄用: *abuse somebody's trust in oneself* i.e. act wrongly after having been trusted not to 辜負人家的信任，即:受人信賴而做不該做之事; *abuse one's health* i.e. make oneself ill by working too hard or by not taking proper care of oneself 糟蹋自己的身體，即:過度工作或不善保養而致病. **abusive** [ə'bju:siv] *adj* containing bad and insulting language 惡言謾駡的: *an abusive letter* 一封污蔑信; *abusive language* 駡人話.

abysmal [ə'bizml] *adj* very much greater than is normal (in a bad sense) 極度的(用於貶義): *abysmal ignorance* 極度的無知.

abyss [ə'bis] *nc* very deep hole (not very common use **hole, pit** etc.) 深淵，深坑(不常用，一般用 hole, pit 等).

academic [ækə'demik] *adj* **1** referring to schools, colleges etc. 學校的;學院的. **2** very theoretical, of little practical use 純理論的，不切實際的: *an idea which is of academic interest only* i.e. not concerned with things as they really are 一個僅有理論意義的想法，即:不切實際的. Also *nc* scholar; person who teaches in a university 學者;大學教師.

academy [ə'kædəmi] *nc* **1** name for some secondary schools 中等學校: *Accra Academy* 阿克拉學校; *Edinburgh Academy* 愛丁堡學校. **2** school or college for the study of certain named subjects 專科院校: *Academy of Music* 音樂學院; *Military Academy* 陸軍軍官學校;軍事學院. **3** society of learned men and women, such as scientists, writers, painters etc who try to encourage science, art, literature etc. (文藝或自然科學的)學術團體，學會.

accede [æk'si:d] *vi* agree to; say yes to 同意，答應: *He acceded to any request.* 他有求必應.

accelerate [æk'seləreit] *vt / i* (usu. with reference to a car) (make something) go faster (使)加速(通常指車輛). **acceleration** [ækselə'reiʃən] *nu* increase in speed 增速,加快. **accelerator** [ək'seləreitə*] *nc* pedal in a car which the driver presses with his foot to control the speed of the car (汽車的)加速踏板.

accent ['æksənt] *nc* **1** way of speaking which is related to the place one comes from 腔調，口音: *speak English with a London accent* 講帶有倫敦口音的英語; *speak French with an English accent* 講帶有英國口音的法語. **2**

marks written above some letters in certain languages (e.g. ´, `, ˆ in French) (加在字母上的)讀音符號(例如法語的 ´, `, ˆ). **3** special force or emphasis given to a word or syllable (e.g. in *many* the accent is on the first syllable) 重音 (例如: many 這個詞的重音在第一音節).

accentuate [æk'sentjueit] *vt* pronounce a word or syllable with special force or emphasis 以重音讀出,重讀.

accept [ək'sept] *vt* **1** take something that is offered 接受,領受: *He accepted my offer / suggestion.* 他接受我的提議 / 建議. **2** believe in or take as satisfactory something that somebody says 相信,(認爲滿意而加以)接受: *He accepted my excuse.* 他相信我的解釋. *The new theory became widely accepted* i.e. many people thought that the theory was true. 新理論被廣泛地接受了. 即: 許多人認爲這理論是正確的. **acceptable** *adj* (usu. with reference to a gift, offer, invitation etc.) pleasing, worth accepting 合意的,值得接受的(通常指禮物、建議、邀請等). (*opp* 反義詞 **unacceptable**) **acceptance** *nc / u* act of accepting what is offered 接受: *We have sent out thirty invitations and have had twenty acceptances* i.e. twenty people have agreed to come. 我們發出了三十份請帖,有二十份已被接受. 即: 二十人答應要來.

access ['ækses] *nu* **1** way to or into a place 通道: *Access to the town was across a narrow bridge.* 進入這座城鎮的通道是一座狹窄的橋. **2** opportunity or permission to use something, meet somebody etc. 使用、會面等的機會或權利,享用權: *Students have access to the library during the vacation.* 假期中學生可使用圖書館. *The prime*

minister had direct access to the king at any hour of the day. 首相在任何時刻都可以直接見到國王. **accessible** [æk'sesibl] *adj* easy to reach 容易取得的;容易達到的. *Medicine should not be kept where it is accessible to children.* 藥物不應放在容易被小孩拿到的地方. (*opp* 反義詞 **inaccessible**).

accession [æk'seʃən] **1** *nu* arriving at a position (esp. that of a ruler) 就職,就任;即位: *accession to power* 掌權.

accessory [æk'sesəri] *nc* something which is added to the main thing (esp. parts of a motorcar such as lights, windscreen wipers, radio etc; or parts of a woman's costume such as shoes, hat, handbag etc.) 附件,附屬品(尤指汽車的附件,如車燈,自動雨刷子,收音機等;或婦女裝束的配件,如鞋子,帽子,手提包等).

accident ['æksidənt] *nc* **1** harmful and unexpected happening (usu. causing damage or injury) 事故(通常引起損失或傷害): *Seventy-five people were killed in accidents at work last year.* 去年有七十五人死於工傷事故. **2** something unexpected 意外的事,偶然的事: *It was just an accident that I found the missing letter.* 我找回那封丟失的信純屬偶然. **accidental** [æksi'dentl] *adj* not intentional 偶然的,意外的. **accidentally** *adv* 'accident-'prone more likely to have accidents than other people 易出事故的. **by accident** without any intention or planning 偶然,意外地: *meet somebody by accident* 偶然遇見某人.

acclaim [ə'kleim] *vt* shout a welcome; shout approval; congratulate somebody by shouting 向…歡呼;爲…喝彩: *The crowd acclaimed the new king.* 羣眾向新國王歡呼.

acclimatize [ə'klaimətaiz] *vt / i* (Brit)

become or make somebody / something accustomed to a change of climate or surroundings（英）(使）適應；(使）服 水 土：*John soon became acclimatized to the heat in India.* 約翰很快就適應印度的炎熱. (*US* 美 **acclimate** ['æklimeit]).

accommodate [ə'kɔmədeit] *vt* have enough room for, accept people to live in 容納；提供住處；*This car accommodates six people quite comfortably.* 這輛汽車可舒舒服服坐進六個人. **accommodating** *adj* helpful; willing to make changes to help other people 肯幫忙的, 肯通融的. **accommodation** [əkɔmə'deiʃən] *nu* place to live in or sleep in (esp. for a short period only) 住處 (尤指僅供短期使用的)：*If you go to London for a holiday you will have no difficulty in finding accommodation.* 如果你去倫敦度假, 找個地方住是不難的.

accompany [ə'kʌmpəni] *vt* **1** go with somebody 陪伴, 陪同：*The Prime Minister's wife accompanied him when he visited the northern region.* 首相夫人陪同首相巡視北部地區. **2** play music while someone sings or plays on a different instrument 爲⋯伴奏：*John accompanied his wife on the piano.* 約翰爲他的妻子作鋼琴伴奏. **accompaniment** [ə'kʌmpəniment] *nc / u* part of a piece of music which fits in with the main part of the music being sung or played on a different instrument or instruments 伴奏. *Jane sang a song with a piano accompaniment by John.* 珍妮在約翰的鋼琴伴奏下唱了一首歌. **accompanist** *nc* musician who plays an accompaniment 伴奏者.

accomplice [ə'kʌmplis] *nc* person who helps somebody else to do something

(esp. something wrong) 同謀, 幫兇.

accomplish [ə'kʌmpliʃ] *vt* carry out successfully 取得 (成就), 做成功：*He accomplished a great deal during his first year.* 他在第一年裏取得很大的成就. **accomplished** *adj* able to do something well (esp. able to play music, dance, hold interesting conversations etc.) 有造詣的；有技藝的 (尤指在音樂, 舞蹈, 談吐等方面)：*Jane is a very accomplished dancer.* 珍妮是一個技巧嫻熟的舞蹈演員. **accomplishment** *nc* skill, ability of somebody who is accomplished 造詣；技藝.

accord[1] [ə'kɔːd] *nu* friendly feelings (esp. between nations) (尤指國與國之間的) 諒解.

accord[2] [ə'kɔːd] *vt* give with friendly feelings 給與, 贈與：*His friends accorded Tom their sincere thanks.* 湯姆的朋友們向他表示衷心的感謝. **of one's own accord** willingly 出於自願, 主動地：*I did it of my own accord, not because anyone asked me to do it.* 我做這事是出於自願, 而不是因爲有人要我去做. **in accordance with** in agreement with; following 與⋯一致；依照；根據：*In accordance with the law they had to pay a fine.* 根據法律, 他們得交罰金. **according to somebody / something** following what was said or written by somebody 按照某事物；根據某人所説或所寫：*According to John, there will be a meeting next week* i.e. john says so (but he may be wrong). 據約翰説, 下星期有個會議. 的；約翰是這麼説的 (但他也可能是錯的).

accordion [ə'kɔːdiən] *nc* type of portable musical instrument with keys and bellows 手風琴.

accost [ə'kɔst] *vt* go and speak to

someone one does not know (esp. in a public place and in a troublesome or unpleasant way) 跟陌生人搭訕 (尤指在公共場所進行的令人厭煩或不愉快的攀談). *A stranger accosted me in the street yesterday and asked for money.* 昨天在街上一位陌生人跟我搭訕並向我要錢.

account[1] [əˈkaunt] *vi* explain satisfactorily 解釋, 說明: *I can account for my strange behaviour last week; I was feeling ill and tired.* 我能對我上週的古怪行爲作出解釋; 當時我又累又病.

account[2] [əˈkaunt] *nc* **1** story or explanation about something that has happened 記述, 報導: *I read an account of the fire in the newspaper.* 我在報紙上讀到一篇關於那場火災的報導. **2** (often *pl*) written record of sums of money received and spent (常用複數) 帳, 帳目: *keep accounts / an account* 記帳. **3** record of goods bought at a shop for which the customer pays some time after taking the goods away (usu. at the end of the month) 賒購帳 (通常在月底付清欠款). **accountable** *adj* responsible, expected or able to explain satisfactorily if asked to do so 負有責任的; 應作解釋的; 可解釋的: *A child is not always accountable for its behaviour.* 小孩子對自己的行爲並不負有責任. **accountancy** *nu* work of keeping accounts i.e. making a record of sums of money received and spent 會計工作. **accountant** *nc* person whose work is **accountancy** 會計人員; 會計師. **on account 1** *buy something on account* i.e. to buy the goods now and paying later (usu. at the end of the month) 賒購 (通常在月底償清). **2** in part payment 做爲部份付款: *Here's five*

pounds on account i.e. the rest of the money will be paid later. 先付五英鎊. 即: 剩下部份以後付清. **on account of** because of 因爲. **on no / not on any account** for no reason 絕對不, 決不: *On no account must you touch these books.* 你切不可動這些書. **take something into account** consider; think about when making plans 考慮到, 計及: *We must take all possibilities into account when planning for next year.* 製訂明年計劃時, 我們必須考慮到所有的種種可能.

accrue [əˈkruː] *vi* increase in size or amount (esp. with reference to money) 增大; 增多 (尤指金錢): *A large sum should accrue to you by the end of the year.* 到年底你會增加一大筆收入.

accumulate [əˈkjuːmjuleit] *vt / i* **1** bring together, collect 積聚; 積累: *The old man had accumulated a lot of books / a great deal of experience during his lifetime.* 那位老人在一生中搜集了衆多書 / 積累了豐富的經驗. **2** increase; grow in number or amount 越積越多; 堆積: *If you don't clear away the rubbish regularly, it will just accumulate.* 如果不經常清理, 垃圾就會成堆. **accumulation** [əkjuːmjuˈleiʃən] *nu*.

accurate [ˈækjurit] *adj* **1** completely right; correct 精確的; 正確的. **2** never making a mistake (esp. in one's work) 從不出錯的 (尤指在工作上) (*opp* 反義詞 **inaccurate**). **accurately** *adv*. **accuracy** *nu* (*opp* 反義詞 **inaccuracy**).

accusative [əˈkjuːzətiv] *adj* usu. in **the accusative (case)** i.e. grammatical form of nouns, pronouns and adjectives in Latin and some other languages, which shows that the noun or pronoun is a direct object 通常用於

the accusative (case), 即: 在拉丁語和其他一些語言中的名詞, 代詞和形容詞的一種語法形式, 這種語法形式表示該名詞或代詞是直接賓語.

accuse [ə'kjuːz] *vt* say that somebody has done wrong 控告, 告發: *John accused his friend of stealing the money.* 約翰控告他的朋友偷錢. **accusation** [ækju:'zeiʃən] *nc*: *He made an accusation against her.* 他對她進行控告. **the accused** *n sing* or *pl* 單數或複數 the person(s) accused of a crime in a court of law 被告.

accustom [ə'kʌstəm] *vt* usu. **accustom oneself** i.e. learn to accept trouble, difficulty etc. without surprise or complaint 通常用 accustom oneself, 即: 使自己習慣於: *You must learn to accustom yourself to hard work.* 你必須學會習慣於艱苦的工作.

ace [eis] *nc* **1** playing card with the value one (紙牌上的) 么點. **2** a person who is very good at something (e.g. a pilot) 能手, 高手 (例如: 飛行員).

acetate ['æsiteit] *nu* salt or ester of acetic acid 醋酸鹽; 醋酸酯: *acetate fibre* 醋酸纖維.

acetic [ə'si:tik] *adj* of, concerning, or producing vinegar or actic acid 醋的, 醋酸的: *acetic acid* 醋酸.

ache [eik] *nc* pain which goes on for some time (連續的) 疼痛: *toothache* 牙痛; *stomach ache* 肚子痛; *headache* 頭痛. Also 亦作 *vi*: *My foot aches.* 我的腳痛.

achieve [ə'tʃiːv] *vt* get by successfully doing something 獲得, 達到: *The runner achieved his ambition of running the mile in four minutes.* 那位賽跑選手實現了他四分鐘跑完一英里的抱負. **achievement** *nc / u* something gained; act of successfully doing

something one has tried to do 成就, 成績; 完成.

acid ['æsid] *nc* **1** chemical substance containing hydrogen, which turns litmus paper red 酸 (含有氫的化合物, 能使石蕊試紙變紅). **2** sourtasting liquid (usu. also an acid in sense 1) 有酸味的液體 (通常也指義 1 中的一種酸). Also 亦作 *adj* like an acid 酸的; 酸性的. **2** sour-tasting 酸味的. **acidity** [ə'siditi] *nu*. **'acid 'test** test which finally decides the value of something (事物價值的) 決定性考驗.

acknowledge [ək'nɔlidʒ] *vt* **1** admit; say that one believes something to be true. 承認; 認以為真: *He acknowledged that he had done wrong.* 他承認他做了錯事. **2** say that one has received something (and usu. that one thanks the person who has given it) 告知收到 (通常並表示謝意): *He acknowledged the gift from his aunt.* 她告訴姑母禮物已收到. **acknowledg(e)ment** *nc / u* statement that one has received something (usu. thanking the person who has given it) 收悉通知 (通常並向對方致謝).

acne ['ækni] *nu* spots or pimples (usu. on the face of boys or girls) 粉刺; 痤瘡 (通常出現於年輕人的臉上).

acorn ['eikɔːn] *nc* nut or seed of an oak tree 橡樹果實; 橡子.

acoustic [ə'ku:stik] *adj* with reference to hearing or sound 聽覺的; 聲音的. **acoustics** *npl* makes about a building etc which make music, speeches etc in it sound clear. (建築物等的) 音響裝置.

acquaint [ə'kweint] *vt* inform, make aware, tell 告知, 使瞭解: *acquaint oneself with the facts* 摸清事實情況. **acquaintance 1** *nc* somebody one knows but not very well (contrasted with a friend) 相識的人 (以與 friend 對比). **2** *nu* small amount of knowledge 粗淺的知識: *only a slight acquaintance with mathematics* 對數學只略知一二.

acquiesce [ˌækwiˈes] *vi* accept or agree (although one is unwilling to do so) without protest or argument 勉强同意，默許: *He acquiesced in the arrangements which I had made.* 他勉强同意我所做的安排.

acquire [əˈkwaiə*] *vt* get as one's own (usu. by one's own efforts) (通常指經自己的努力而)獲得, 得到: *acquire a knowledge of German* 掌握德語. **acquisition** [ˌækwiˈziʃən] *nc / u* something gained or acquired 獲得物. **acquisitive** [əˈkwizitiv] *adj* fond of getting new things (often from other people) 好獲取的(常指對別人的財物等).

acquit [əˈkwit] *vt* **1** decide by a trial or investigation that somebody is not guilty of some crime or wrongdoing 宣判…無罪: *He was acquitted of the robbery.* 他被宣判没有犯搶劫罪. **2** do one's duty satisfactorily 履行, 完成: *He has acquitted himself very well in his new job.* 他出色地完成了他的新任務. *past* 過去式和過去分詞 **acquitted.** **acquittal** *nc* (usu. only in sense 1) (通常僅用於義1).

acre [ˈeikə*] *nc* area of 4840 square yards or approximately 4000 square metres 英畝(等於4840平方碼或約4000平方米).

acrimonious [ˌækriˈmouniəs] *adj* angry; showing personal hatred or dislike between the persons concerned 激烈的; 刻毒的: *an acrimonious argument* 激烈的争论.

acrobat [ˈækrəbæt] *nc* person who is very clever at balancing, jumping, walking on his hands etc. (esp. one who earns his living by entertaining people in this way) 雜技演員.

across [əˈkrɔs] *adv / prep* **1** from one side to the other 從一邊到另一邊; 橫過: *He walked across the bridge.* 他走過那座橋. **2** on the other side (of) 在(…的)對面: *There is a shop across the road from my house.* 我家馬路的對面有一個商店. **come across somebody / something** find or meet by accident, without meaning to do so 偶然碰見某人/找到某物.

acrylic [əˈkrilik] *adj* of a type of strong man-made material 丙烯酸的: *acrylic fibre* 丙烯酸纖維.

act¹ [ækt] *nc* **1** something done 行為; 舉動. **2** division of a stage play (戲劇的)幕. **3** *law* 法令: *act of Parliament* 議會的法令.

act² [ækt] *vi* **1** do something 做事, 行動: *We must act at once to stop this.* 我們必須立刻行動加以制止. **2** behave 舉止, 表現: *He acted very strangely.* 他舉動奇特. **3** take part in a play 扮演. **4** do some work or duty (often for somebody else) (常指代人)擔當, 擔任: *John was asked to act as chairman of the meeting because Mr. Brown was ill.* 約翰被請擔任會議的主席, 因爲布朗先生病了. **5** have an effect on 起作用, 見效: *Acids act on most metals.* 酸對大部份的金屬發生作用. **acting** *nu* art of being an actor 演技. Also 亦作 *adj* doing someone's work temporarily 代理的, 臨時的: *John was acting chairman at the meeting.* 約翰是會議的代理主席.

action [ˈækʃən] **1** *nc / u* something done 行為, 行動: *We must have action not words.* 我們必須做事而不是空談. **2** *nu* effect 作用: *the action of acid on metal* 酸對金屬所起的作用. **3** *nu* fighting in war; a battle 戰鬥; 戰事; *killed in action* 陣亡; *go into action* 開始戰鬥. **4** *nc* (legal) usu. in **take / bring an action against somebody** i.e. ask for a decision to be made in a law court against somebody; ask a judge to decide by law that somebody has done wrong to oneself (法律) 通常用作 **take / bring an action against somebody**, 即; 對某人提出訴訟. **take action** do something in order to get what one wants or in order to stop something 採取行動.

active ['æktiv] *adj* **1** busy; able to move or work 活躍的; 有活動能力的: *He is an active old man.* 他是一個活躍的老人. (*opp* 反義詞 **inactive**). **2** real; practical 現實的; 實際的: *I intend to play an active part in the society.* 我打算在社會上幹些實實在在的事. **3** (grammar) form of the verb as in *he read the book; he helped his friend* (*opp* **passive** in sense 3) (語法) 主動的; 主動語態的 (如在 *he read the book* 和 *he helped his friend* 等句子中的動詞形式) (義 3 的反義詞爲 passive).

activity [æk'tiviti] **1** *nu* state of being active 活動; 活躍. **2** *nc* (usu. *pl*) things that one does (通常用複數) 活動; 所做的事情: *He is fond of walking and other outdoor activities.* 他喜歡散步和其他各種戶外活動. *The police were investigating the activities of a number of well-known criminals.* 警務人員正在調查許多名有罪犯的活動.

activate ['æktiveit] *vt* (usu. *passive*) cause to act or move (通常用於被動語態)使活動起來.

actor ['æktə*] *nc* man who acts in plays, films, on radio or television (戲劇、電影、電台或電視的) 男演員. (*fem* 陰 **actress**).

actual ['æktjuəl] *adj* real, not imaginary

真實的; 實際的. **actually** *adv* **1** really 實際上. **2** the truth is (often with the suggestion *although it seems strange or surprising or although you do not know it*) 實際情況是 (常帶有 "說來奇怪, 但竟然這樣" 或 "儘管你不知道, 但事實如此" 的意思).

acumen ['ækjumən] *nu* ability to think clearly and quickly and to make correct decisions. 敏銳; 聰明; 才幹: *He showed great business acumen* i.e. he conducted business matters successfully. 他很有業務才幹. 即: 他業務處理得很好.

acupuncture ['ækjupʌŋktʃə*] *nu* method of treating pain or illness by sticking needles into the skin 針刺; 針刺療法.

acute [ə'kju:t] *adj* **1** strongly felt 劇烈的: *acute pain* 劇痛; *an acute illness* 急性疾病. **2** working better than or noticing more than other people 精明的; 敏銳的: *an acute sense of hearing* 敏銳的聽覺; *very acute criticism* 很尖銳的批評. **acutely** *adv*.

ad [æd] *nc* short form of **advertisement** (*informal*) advertisement 的縮寫形式(非正式).

adage ['ædidʒ] *nc* old and well-known wise saying, proverb 格言; 諺語.

adamant ['ædəmənt] *adj* determined; unwilling to change one's decision or opinion 堅定不移的; 固執的. **adamantly** *adv*.

adapt [ə'dæpt] *vt* **1** change so as to make more suitable for or cause to fit in with certain conditions 使適合, 使適應: *adapt oneself to the weather in England / to the new arrangements etc.* 使自己適應英國的天氣/新的安排等. **2** change so as to make suitable for a new purpose or for new conditions 使適用於(新用途、新情況等):

My radio has been adapted for use in the tropics. 我的收音機已改成適用於熱帶地區. **adaptable** *adj* able to adapt or be adapted 能適應的; 能適用的. (*opp* 反義詞 **unadaptable**).

adaptation [ædæp'teiʃən] *nc/u* (esp. with reference to film, play etc made from a book) process of adapting; result of adapting (尤指把另一形式的作品改成電影, 劇本等的) 改編; 改編本. *An adaptation of Heidi was broadcast on the radio.* 《海蒂》的改編本在電台上廣播了.

add [æd] *vt/i* 1 join numbers or quantities together to make a larger number or quantity 加, 加起來: *Add five to / and eighteen.* 五加十八. 2 put something with something else 添加: *Add some more milk to your coffee.* 給您的咖啡加點牛奶. 3 (usu. following direct speech) say in addition to something else (通常跟在直接引語之後) 又說, 接着又說. 4 increase 增加: *The news of John's success added to our happiness.* 約翰勝利的消息增添了我們的喜悅. **add (something) up** add (something), put numbers together 把…加起來; 合計.

adder ['ædə*] *nc* name given to various types of snake; in Europe, a small poisonous snake with V-marking on the head. Also **viper**; in America, a small and harmless snake: in Africa, a large and poisonous snake (一種產于歐洲, 頭部有 V 形斑紋的)小毒蛇(亦作 viper); (一種產于美洲的)無毒害的小蛇; (一種產于非洲的)大毒蛇.

addict ['ædikt] *nc* person who cannot stop himself from doing something or using something harmful 有癮的人: *drug addict* 吸毒上癮的人. **addiction** [ə'dikʃən] *nc/u* **addicted** [ə'diktid] *pred adj* unable to stop using some

harmful substance or to stop doing something (usu. something wrong) 上了癮的; 入了迷的(通常指壞事): *addicted to drugs* 上了毒癮的.

addition [ə'diʃən] *nc* 1 adding together 加 see 見 **add**. 2 sum of numbers to be added together; something added 添加的數目; 增加物. **additional** *adj* **in addition (to something)** besides; also; as well 另外, 此外; 又.

address [ə'dres] *nc* 1 details of street, town, district etc where a person lives 住址: *What's your address?* i.e. where exactly do you live? 您的住址是甚麼? 即: 您住在哪裏? 2 writing on letter or envelope showing where a letter is to be sent (and sometimes where it is from) (信上或信封上的)收信人地址(有時也指寄信人的地址). 3 speech made to a meeting. (*formal in sense* 3) 演說, 講話(義3為正式). Also 亦作 *vt*: *address an envelope* 在信封上寫地址; *address a public meeting* 在公開的會議上演講; 在羣衆大會上發表演說.

adept ['ædept] *adj* having great skill in doing something 熟練的; 擅長的: *He is very adept at playing games.* 他善於做游戲.

adequate ['ædikwit] *adj* enough; sufficient 足夠的; 充足的: *an adequate supply of food* 足夠的糧食供應. (*opp* 反義詞 **inadequate**). **adequately** *adv.*

adhere [əd'hiə*] *vi* 1 (with reference to mud, paste, glue, oil etc.) stick closely, firmly (指泥, 漿糊, 膠水, 油等)黏着, 附着. 2 (with reference to custom, religion, political party etc.) continue to follow or to be loyal (指習俗, 宗教, 政黨等)追隨; 遵循; 堅持.

adhesive [əd'hiːziv] *adj* sticky; able to

stick firmly 黏着的；有黏性的．Also 亦作 *nc / u* **adhesion** [ədˈhiːʒən] *nu*.

adjacent [əˈdʒeisənt] *adj* (usu. of land, rooms etc, not of numbers) next to in position (通常指土地、房屋等，不指數目) 鄰接的．

adjective [ˈædʒəktiv] *nc* (grammar) word like *black, clever, heavy, hot* which gives further information about a noun (語法) 形容詞(如用來進一步說明名詞的 black, clever, heavy, hot 等詞)．

adjoin [əˈdʒɔin] *vt / i* be next to 毗連；*His fields adjoin mine.* 他的田跟我的毗連．**adjoining** *adj*.

adjourn [əˈdʒəːn] *vt / i* stop a meeting or discussion intending to start again at another time or place 休(會)；延期討論：*Shall we adjourn the meeting for a week?* 我們要不要休會一週？

adjust [əˈdʒʌst] *vt* change something so as to make it more satisfactory or comfortable 調整，調節：*adjust a seat to one's height* 根據身高調節座位．**adjustable** *adj* able to be adjusted 可調整的，可調節的．**adjustment** *nc* act of adjusting 調整，調節．

adjutant [ˈædʒətənt] *nc* army officer who does office work for a more senior officer (軍隊的) 副官．

administer [ædˈministə*] *vt* **1** control, be in charge of 管理；支配．**2** give to those who deserve or are in need, as one's work or duty 給與；派給：*administer medicine to the sick* 給病人服藥；*administer justice* 執法．**administration** [ədminisˈtreiʃən] *nc / u* **1** government of a country 政府．**2** control of a business or other organization (企業或其他機構) 管理，經營．**administrative** [ədˈministrativ] *adj* **administrator** [ədˈministreitə*] *nc* somebody whose work is to control

the organization of a business etc. 經營管理者，管理人．

admirable [ˈædmərəbl] *adj* excellent; worthy of approval 極好的；值得讚賞的．

admiral [ˈædmərəl] *nc* officer of very senior rank in the navy; officer in charge of a fleet 海軍上將；艦隊司令．**admiralty** *nc* (Brit) government department dealing with the navy (英) 海軍部．

admire [ədˈmaiə*] *vt* look at or consider somebody / something with pleasure and approval 讚賞；羨慕．**admiration** [ædmiˈreiʃən] *nu* see 見 **admirable**.

admit [ədˈmit] *vt / i* **1** confess; agree that one has done something (usu. something wrong) 供認；承認(通常指壞事)：*admit a crime* 承認罪行．**2** allow someone inside 准許…進入，讓…進入：*admit somebody into a house.* 讓某人進入房子．*past* 過去式和過去分詞 **admitted. admission** [ədˈmiʃən] **1** *nc* confession; saying that one has done something (usu. something wrong) 供認，承認(通常指壞事)．**2** *nu* allowing to come in 准許進入：*no admission without tickets* 無票不得入場．**admittance** *nu* allowing to come in 允許進入：*gain admittance* 獲准進入．

ado [əˈduː] *nu* **without more ado** without any more delay, at once 馬上，立刻．

adolescent [ædəˈlesnt] *nc* boy or girl between the ages of about 12 and 19 青少年(約十二至十九歲)．Also 亦作 *adj* **adolescence** *nu* years during which one is changing from a child to an adult 青春期．

adopt [əˈdɔpt] *vt* **1** make by law a child of other parents part of one's own family 收養. **2** accept and use a suggestion, habit etc of somebody else 採用, 採納. **adoption** nu.

adore [ə'dɔ:*] vt **1** worship; love very much 崇拜; 敬愛. **2** like 喜愛: *I adore chocolate. (informal)* 我喜歡巧克力. (非正式). **adorable** adj **adoration** [ædə'reiʃən] nu.

adorn [ə'dɔ:n] vt make more beautiful by decorating with flowers, jewels etc. (用花朵, 珠寶等) 裝飾.

adrenalin [ə'drenəlin] nu substance produced by the body, which enables one to be active 腎上腺素.

adrift [ə'drift] adv / pred adj (usu. with reference to ships and boats) moving without human control wherever taken by the winds and tides (通常指船隻) 漂泊, 漂流.

adroit [ə'drɔit] adj clever in using one's hands or one's mind 靈巧的; 機靈的.

adult ['ædʌlt] nc **1** person who is fully grown (usu. over the age of 18) 成年人(通常爲十八歲或以上). **2** full-grown animal 發育成熟的動物. Also 亦作 adj.

adulterate [ə'dʌltəreit] vt make less pure or less good by adding something 攙雜, 攙假.

adultery [ə'dʌltəri] nc / u sexual relationship of a married person with somebody to whom he or she is not married 通姦.

advance [əd'vɑ:ns] vt / i go forward; cause to go forward; put forward (使) 前進; 提出; 提前: *He advanced twelve paces.* 他向前走了十二步. *The soldiers advanced towards the city.* 部隊向該城推進. *The general advanced his army.* 將軍命令其部隊前進. *He had no chance to advance his opinion.* 他沒有機會提出意見. *The time of the meeting was advanced by an hour*

i.e. the meeting was held earlier. 會議提前一小時召開. *He advanced rapidly in his career* i.e. he became successful. 他在事業上飛黃騰達. 即: 他成功了. Also 亦作 nc **1** movement forward 前進. **2** money paid or lent before the proper time 預付款; 貸款. **advanced** adj forward; in front 向前的; 先進的: *advanced ideas / theories* etc. i.e. ideas / theories etc which are new and not yet accepted by most people 先進的思想/理論等; 即: 尚未被多數人接受的新思想/理論等. *advanced in years* i.e. old 年長的. 即: 老. **advancement** nu development; progress 發展; 進步: *the advancement of the country's economic growth* 國家經濟的成長發展; *the advancement of learning* 學問的長進.

advantage [əd'vɑ:ntidʒ] nc / u anything which makes or is likely to make something / somebody better, luckier, happier etc than others 優點, 優勢, 有利之處. (*opp* 反義詞 **disadvantage**). **advantageous** [ædvən'teidʒəs] adj (*opp* 反義詞 **disadvantageous**). **take advantage of somebody / something** make use of somebody / something to help oneself, sometimes unfairly or by a trick (趁機) 利用某人/某物.

advent ['ædvent] nc **1** coming or arrival (*o.f.* - use **arrival**) 到來, 抵達 (舊式—現在用 arrival). **2** (**Advent**) in the Christian Church, period of devotion before Christmas 基督教會在聖誕節前的奉獻期.

adventure [əd'ventʃə*] nc unusual and exciting event (often involving danger) 冒險, 奇遇. **adventurous** adj liking or containing adventure 喜歡冒險的; 冒險的. (*opp* 反義詞 **unadventurous**).

adverb ['ædvə:b] *nc* (grammar) word like *quickly, always, there* which gives information in a sentence about *how, when, where etc.* (語法) 副詞 (如 quickly、always、there 在句子裏提供 how、when、where 等信息).

adversary ['ædvəsəri] *nc* enemy. (*formal* - use **enemy**) 敵手；敵人. (正式一 一般用 **enemy**).

adverse ['ædvə:s] *adj* unfavourable; making it difficult or impossible to do what one wants 不利的；困難的；逆的: *an adverse report* 不利的報告; *adverse winds* 逆風; *adverse circumstances* 困境. **adversity** [əd'və:si- ti] *nc/u* difficulty 困難, 逆境.

advertise ['ædvətaiz] *vt / i* **1** make known through newspapers, public notices, radio, films etc what one has to sell or offer 爲…做廣告, 登廣告. **advertisement** [əd'və:tizmənt] *nc / u* something which advertises (esp. a public notice) 廣告；公告.

advice [əd'vais] *nu* something said by somebody about the best thing for somebody else to do 勸告, 忠告: *give advice to somebody about his work* 給 某人指點工作. *Let me give you some advice.* 我來給你出出主意. *Note* 說 明: **1** there is a *pl* form which is used in business, but this form is not in general use. For plural meaning, use *some advice.* **2** the *noun* is spelled with a *c*, but the verb *advise* is spelled with an *s.* Note also the difference of pronunciation 1. 本詞有用於商業上 的複數形式, 但這種形式不常用. 要表示 複數意義用 some advice. 2. 名詞與動 詞的拼寫不同, 名詞爲 *c*, 動詞爲 *s*. 另注 意發音的不同.

advise [əd'vaiz] *vt* **1** give advice to; say what one thinks is the best thing for somebody else to do 勸告；建議. **2**

(commerce) inform (use **tell, inform** etc.) (商業上) 通知 (一般用 tell, inform 等). **advisable** *adj* for the best; to be advised 最好；合適的, 可取的: *It is not advisable to lend money to that man because he will not be able to repay it.* 最好不要借錢給那個人, 因爲他會還 不起 (*opp* 反義詞 **inadvisable**). **ill- / well-ad'vised** acting in an unwise / wise way after receiving advice (經勸 告後) (行爲) 愚蠢的/明智的.

advocate ['ædvəkeit] *vt* speak in support of something; recommend 擁護； 主張: *advocate a course of action* 擁 護某行動方針; *advocate going to see the doctor* 主張去看醫生.

aerate ['eiəreit] *vt* **1** charge (liquid) with gas 充氣於 (液體): *aerated water* 汽水. **2** expose to air, or cause air to circulate through 使暴露於空氣中, 使 通氣.

aerial ['ɛəriəl] *nc* wire used for receiving or sending radio waves (無線電) 天線. Also 亦作 *adj* in or of the air 空 中的, 空氣的: *aerial warfare* 空戰.

aerogramme ['ɛərəgræm] *nc* **1** air-mail letter written on a single sheet of light-weight paper that folds and is sealed to form an envelope 航空郵簡. **2** message sent by radio 無線電報.

aeronautic [ɛərə'nɔ:tik] *adj* of or about the science or practice of all aspects of flight through the air 航空的；航空 學的.

aeroplane ['ɛərəplein] *nc* (*Brit*) flying machine, plane (英) 飛機. (*US* 美 **airplane**).

aerosol ['ɛərəsɔl] *nc* container which squirts a spray of a substance, such as furniture polish, when a knob is pressed 噴霧罐.

aesthetic, esthetic [is'θetik] *adj* referring to what is beautiful (esp. in art, literature and music) 美的; 審美的 (尤指藝術、文學和音樂). **aesthetics, esthetics** *nu* study of beauty 美學.

afar [ə'fɑ:] *adv* at a distance; far off 在遠處; 遙遠地: *I saw him from afar.* 我從遠處看到了他.

affable [ˈæfəbl] *adj* friendly; easy to talk to 友好的; 易於交談的.

affair [əˈfɛə*] *nc* 1 something done or to be done: an event or incident (often a mysterious event) 已做或待做的)事, 事情; (神秘的)事: *We must try to get to the bottom of this affair* i.e. we must try to find out the truth. 我們必須盡量查清此事的真相. 2 (in *pl*) business, duties etc.) (用於複數) 業務, 事務: *Ministry of Foreign Affairs* i.e. Ministry which controls relations with other countries 外交部. 3 love between a man and a woman (esp. love which lasts only for a short time) (男女間的)愛戀(尤指短暫的): *have an affair with someone* 與某人有曖昧關係.

affect [əˈfekt] *vt* 1 have an effect on (often in a bad way) 影響(常指壞的方面): *His health was affected by the poor food he ate.* 他的健康因飲食不好而受影響. 2 arouse feelings of pity, sorrow etc. 激起(憐憫、悲傷等情緒), 使感動: *He was deeply affected by the news* i.e. he was made unhappy. 這消息使他深感悲傷. **affected** *adj* pretended, or not natural; put on to appear better or different from others 假裝的, 不自然的, 做作的: *an affected accent* 做作的腔調. (*opp* 反義詞 **unaffected**). **affectation** [æfek'teiʃən] *nc / u* behaviour which is affected 假裝, 做作的行為. *Note* 說明: *affect* and *effect* are often confused. 1 both words are pronounced [əˈfekt]. 2 *affect* is usu. a verb; *effect* is

noun and has the basic meaning *result of. effect* can also be a verb meaning *bring about. The members of the club effected a change in the rules.* affect 和 effect 常被混淆. 1.兩者都發[əˈfekt]音. 2. affect 通常是動詞; effect 通常是名詞, 其基本意思是"結果". effect 亦可作動詞, 其義是"實現". 如: The members of the club effected a change in the rules. (俱樂部成員修改了規則).

affection [əˈfekʃən] *nu* friendly or loving feelings 友情, 愛情: *show affection to somebody* 表現出對某人的愛. **affectionate** [əˈfekʃənit] *adj* having friendly feelings 有感情的, 熱情的. (*opp* 反義詞 **unaffectionate**). **affectionately** *adv*.

affinity [əˈfiniti] *nc / u* close connection between 密切關係: *There is an affinity between the Bantu languages.* 各種班圖語都很相近.

affirmation [æfəˈmeiʃən] *nc / u* saying, statement that something is true 斷言, 肯定. **affirmative** *adj* saying that something is true 肯定的. see 見 **negative. answer in the affirmative** say 'yes'. (*formal* - use **say yes, agree, admit** etc.) 作肯定的回答(正式——一般用 say yes, agree, admit 等).

affix [əˈfiks] *vt* 1 fasten; attach 把…固定; 貼上: *affix a stamp to an envelope* 把郵票貼在信封上. 2 add at the end 添上, 附上: *affix a postscript* 加一則附言.

afflict [əˈflikt] *vt* cause pain, disease etc. 使痛苦, 使患病: *afflict somebody with extra work* 用加班加點折磨某人; *afflicted with leprosy* 患麻瘋病. **affliction** *nc / u* suffering, or something causing it 痛苦; 痛苦的事.

affluent [ˈæfluənt] *adj* rich 富裕的, 豐富

的. **affluence** *nu*.

afford [ə'bːd] *vt* **1** find the time or money for something 抽得出(時間); 負擔得起(錢);買得起: *We can afford a new car.* 我們能夠買一輛新車. *We can afford the money for a new car.* 我們拿得出買新車的錢. **2** give; provide 給予;提供: *Reading affords him a lot of pleasure.* 讀書給他許多樂趣.

afforest [æ'fɒrist] *vt* turn (land) into forest; plant many trees on 造林於(空地); *an afforested area* 造林區. (*opp* 反義詞 **deforest**).

affront [ə'frʌnt] *nc* word or act which publicly and intentionally insults somebody 蓄意當衆侮辱. Also 亦作 *vt*: *be affronted* 當衆受辱.

afloat [ə'fləut] *adv* / *pred adj* on the sea, river etc. 在海上,在河上;漂浮的(地).

afoot [ə'fut] *adv* / *pred adj* going on; taking place 在進行中,正在發生: *Rumours / preparations were afoot.* 謠言在流傳/準備工作在進行.

afraid [ə'freid] *pred adj* feeling fear 害怕的: *The travellers were afraid that they would be robbed.* 遊客們擔心被搶劫. *The small boy was afraid of the dark.* 那小男孩怕黑暗. **be afraid (that)** way of apologising for saying something that is unpleasant for another person 恐怕(因說出的話可能使對方不悅而表示歉意): *I'm afraid (that) I don't know.* 我恐怕不知道. *I'm afraid (that) I can't help you* etc. 恐怕我不能幫你的忙等.

afresh [ə'freʃ] *adv* again 再,重新: *start afresh* 重新開始.

after ['ɑːftə*] *adv* / *conj* / *prep* **1** later in time (時間)在…以後: *after the meeting* 會後; *after they had visited him* 他們拜訪了他之後; *the day after tomorrow* 後天. **2** next in place; be-

hind (位置)其次;在…後面: *I was after him in the queue.* 我排隊排在他後面. **3** lower in rank (級別)低於: *a major comes after a general* 少校的級別低於將軍. **4** in pursuit of; in search of 追;尋求: *run after someone* 追趕某人. **'after-effect** *nc* (usu. *pl*) effect which is experienced at a later time (通常用複數)後效,副作用: *aftereffects of an illness* i.e. the effects experienced after one has recovered from the illness 後遺症. **'afterlife** life after death 來世. **after all** see 見 **all**.

aftermath ['ɑːftəmæθ] *nu* what follows something 後果,餘波: *the aftermath of war* 戰後餘殃.

afternoon ['ɑːftə'nuːn] *nc* period of the day between morning and evening (usu. between 12 or 1 p.m. and 4 or 5 p.m.) 下午(通常指十二點或下午一點至下午四,五點之間).

afterwards ['ɑːftəwədz] *adv* later 以後.

again [ə'gen] *adv* **1** one more time 再一次: *Try again.* 再試一次. **2** to the place or state in which one started etc. 回到原地或恢復原狀,又: *Come home again.* 又回家來. *Get well again soon.* 很快又好了.

against [ə'genst] *adv* / *prep* **1** in opposition to 反對,逆: *act against somebody's wishes* i.e. do what somebody does not wish one to do 違反某人的願望行事. *That is against the law* i.e. the law says that must not be done; 這是違法的; *be against war* 反戰的; *protect against the cold* 禦寒. **2** touching or in contact with 碰着,接觸,靠: *put something against the wall* 把某物靠牆放着.

agar ['eigɑː] *nu* jelly-like substance made from seaweed, used for bacterial cultures, etc. 瓊脂(取自海藻的一種膠質物,用作細菌培養基).

age¹ [eidʒ] **1** *nu* number of years somebody / something has lived or been in existence (人或物的) 年齡: *Children go to school in Britain at the age of five.* 在英國兒童五歲上學. **2** (*pl* in some phrases) period in history (某些短語裏用複數) 時代, 年代: *the Stone Age* 石器時代; *the Middle Ages* 中世紀; *the atomic age* 原子時代; *in former ages* 從前. **'age group** people between certain ages thought of as a group 同一年齡組的人. **come / be of age** see 見 **come. take ages** take a long time 用很長時間: *They took ages to mend the cooker.* (*informal*) 他們修理那個炊具花了很長時間. (非正式).

age² [eidʒ] *vi* show signs of growing old 顯得老, 變老: *He is ageing rapidly.* 他老得很快. *pres part* 現在分詞 **ageing** or **aging.** **aged** [ˈeidʒid] **1** very old 很老的: *an aged man* 老翁, 老頭. **2** [eidʒd] of the age of …歲的: *a boy aged two* 兩歲的男孩. **ageless** *adj* old but appearing to be always young or new 不顯老的.

agenda [əˈdʒendə] *nc* (usu. *sing*) paper listing what is discussed at a meeting (通常用單數) 議程; *be on the agenda* 在議程上.

agent [ˈeidʒənt] *nc* person whose work is to act for, or to manage the affairs of other people or companies 代理人, 代理商: *He is an agent for Volkswagen* i.e. he is permitted to obtain goods from the Volkswagen company and sell them to the public. 他是福克斯瓦根公司的代理商. 即: 他獲准從該公司進貨並公開銷售. **agency** *nc* business or office of somebody who acts for somebody else; permission to act for somebody else 代理業; 代理處; 代理權: *This company has the agency for Volkswagen.* 這公司代理經銷福克斯

瓦根公司的商品. see 見 **agent.**

aggravate [ˈægrəveit] *vt* **1** make worse 加劇, 使更壞. **2** annoy. (*informal* and considered an incorrect use by some people; if in doubt use **annoy**) 使煩惱; 使生氣(非正式, 有人認爲是不正確的用法; 如沒有把握, 用 annoy). **aggravation** [ˌægrəˈveiʃən] *nc / u.*

aggregate [ˈægrigit] *nc* (often with reference to points or marks scored in a game, competition or examination) total (常指比賽中得分或考試成績) 合計, 總數. Also 亦作 *adj.*

aggression [əˈgreʃən] *nc / u* attack; beginning of attack (often one made without good reason and often with reference to war made by one country against another) 攻擊; 侵犯; 侵略: *commit an act of aggression against a neighbouring country* 對鄰國採取侵略行徑. **aggressive** [əˈgresiv] *adj* fond of attacking others; attacking 好攻擊他人的; 侵略的. **aggressively** *adv* **aggressiveness** *nu.*

aggrieved [əˈgriːvd] *adj* angry and unhappy because somebody has done something wrong to one 悲傷的; 憤憤不平的; 受委屈的: *He was aggrieved at his friends' lack of interest in his success.* 他因朋友們對他的成功無動於衷而感到痛心.

agile [ˈædʒail] *adj* moving easily; able to move easily and quickly 靈活的; 敏捷的: *She was still quite agile despite her age.* 儘管地年事已高, 但行動仍然很靈快. *an agile mind* 靈活的頭腦.

agitate [ˈædʒiteit] *vt / i* ask very strongly that something should be changed and made better 強烈要求(改變或改善), 鼓動: *The workers are agitating for higher wages and better conditions.* 工人們正在極力要求提高工資和改善工作條件. **agitator** *nc* person who tries to bring about a political change by causing trouble (usu. an unfavourable word) 煽動者, 鼓動者(常帶貶義).

agnostic [æg'nɔstik] *nc* person who says that he does not know whether there is a God or not 不可知論者.

ago [ə'gou] *adv* in the past; before now 以前, 過去: *three days ago* 三天前; *long ago* 很久以前. *I left India a year ago.* 我一年前離開印度.

agony ['ægəni] *nc / u* (often *pl*) great pain (常用複數) 極大的痛苦: *He suffered agonies in hospital.* 他在醫院裏受了極大的痛苦. **agonizing** ['ægənaiziŋ] *adj* very painful 極其痛苦的.

agree [ə'griː] *vt / i* **1** say or think the same as somebody else 與某人有相同看法, 同意: *I agree with you.* 我同意你的意見. **2** allow somebody to do what he asks or suggests 同意(某人的要求或建議): *The headmaster agreed to the request for a half-term holiday.* 校長同意期中放假的要求. **3** say that one thinks something said by somebody else is true 同意(某事有道理): *I agree we ought to try again.* 我同意我們應該再試一試. **4** come to the same idea after discussion (經討論後)取得一致意見: *We agreed on a date for the next meeting.* 我們就下次會議的日期取得一致意見. **5** tell somebody else that one is willing to do something 答允(做某事): *He agreed to help me.* 他答應幫助我. **6** have a good effect on one's health; not upset (one's stomach etc.) 有益於健康; 不傷(胃等): *Pepper doesn't agree with me.* 我不宜吃辣椒. **7** (grammar) go together in the same grammatical form (語法)一致: *The verb agrees with its subject in number and person.* 那動詞與主語在數和人稱方面一致. (*opp* **disagree** ex-

cept in senses **2** and **7**) (除義2和7外, 反義詞爲 disagree). **agreement** *nc / u* (*opp* 反義詞 **disagreement**).

agreeable *adj* **1** pleasing and friendly 令人愉快的. (*opp* 反義詞 **disagreeable**). **2** willing to do something 願意的, 同意的: *If you're agreeable you can start now.* 如果你同意的話, 我們現在就可以開始. **agreeably** *adv.*

agriculture ['ægrikʌltʃə*] *nu* science or practice of farming 農業. **agricultural** [ægri'kʌltʃərəl] *adj.*

aground [ə'graund] *adv* (with reference to ships) at a place where the water has been too shallow for the ship to sail (指船隻)擱淺: *run-aground* (船)擱淺.

ahead [ə'hed] *adv* in front 在前: *Walk ahead of me.* 走在我前面.

ahoy [ə'hɔi] *interj* sound used by sailors to call somebody who is some distance away (esp. someone in another ship) 嗄嗚(船員向遠處, 尤指向另船的人的呼叫聲).

aid [eid] *nu* help (esp. help given by a rich country to a poorer one) 援助, 幫助(尤指富國對窮國). **in aid of** to help 幫助: *This money has been collected in aid of the dogs' home.* 這筆錢是募集來建無主犬收容所的.

ailment ['eilmənt] *nc* illness (often a small and unimportant one) 小病, 輕病.

aim¹ [eim] *vt / i* **1** point or throw at somebody / something (usu. intending to hurt him or it) 瞄準, 對準: *aim a blow / a gun at somebody* 對準某人打去 / 把槍對準某人; *aim a camera* i.e. point a camera intending to take a photograph 把照相機對着. **2** intend; have in one's mind as the thing one wishes to do 打算; 指望: *I aim to finish this book by next week.* 我打算下

週把這本書看完.

aim² [eim] *nc* **1** action of pointing a gun, throwing etc. 瞄準, 對準: *not a good aim* i.e. not hitting what was intended 瞄得不準, 即: 沒有打中目標. **2** intention; purpose; what one wishes to do 企圖; 目的; 目標: *His aim in life is to become rich.* 他生活的目標就是成爲富翁. **aimless** *adj* without any plan or intention 無計劃的, 無目的的. **aimlessly** *adv.*

ain't [eint] dialect pronunciation of **am not, is not, has not** or **have not** am not, is not, has not 或 have not 的方言發音. see 見 **be, have.**

air¹ [ɛə*] **1** *nu* what we breathe; invisible, tasteless gases surrounding the earth 空氣, 大氣. **2** *nu* space above the earth 天空, 空中: *fly in the air* 在空中飛行. **3** *nc* look, appearance 神態; 外表: *He has a guilty air;* 他帶着內疚的神情; *to have an air of importance* 擺架子. **'air conditioning** method of making air in a building cooler, drier (or warmer and damper) than the air outside, so as to make the people in the building more comfortable (建築物裏的)空氣調節. **'air-conditioned** *adj* (with reference to a building, room etc.) having machinery for changing the air in this way (指建築物, 房間等)有空氣調節裝置的. **'aircraft** *n sing* or *pl* 單數或複數 aeroplane(s) 飛機. **'airforce** aeroplanes and men used for war and defence 空軍. **'airgun** gun which fires a small metal object by using the pressure of air instead of gunpowder 汽槍. **'airline** company or state department whose business is to carry passengers and goods in aeroplanes 航空公司. **'airliner** *nc* large passenger plane 大型客機. **'airmail** letters etc carried

by aeroplane 航空信; 航空郵件. **'airport** place where aeroplanes carrying passengers and goods start and land (esp. such a place near a large town or city e.g. *London Airport*) 飛機場, 航空站. (尤指大城市附近的機場, 如: London Airport). **'air raid** attach from the air on a town or city 空襲. **'airsick** *adj* feeling ill as a result of travelling in an aeroplane 暈機的. **airspace** the space above a particular land area 空域, 領空. **airstrip** small piece of land cleared of vegetation and flattened for aeroplanes to land on. (An **airstrip** is a much smaller place than an **airport**) 簡易機場 (airstrip 比 airport 小得多). **'airtight** *adj* closed so that air cannot pass in or out 不透氣的, 密封的. **airway 1** passage for ventilation (esp. in a mine) 通風道(尤指礦井的風道). **2** route regularly followed by airliners 航空路線.

air² [ɛə*] *vt* leave something outside a house, near a window, uncovered etc, so that fresh air can get at it 晾(某物): *air clothes* 晾衣服. **air one's views** tell other people what one is thinking (often in order to find out what others are thinking) 發表自己的意見(常爲了知道別人的看法).

airy ['ɛəri] *adj* **1** with air moving about 通風的. **2** not serious (and often quick and happy) 不嚴肅的, 輕率的. *airy behaviour* 輕佻的行爲; *an airy manner* 輕快的樣子. **airily** *adv.*

aisle [ail] *nc* way between blocks of seats in a church, classroom, theatre etc. (教堂, 教室, 戲院等裏的)過道, 通道. *Note* 說明: the word gangway can also be used with this meaning, except for reference to a church, when *aisle* is generally the only word possible 除了指教堂外, gangway 與本詞同義, 指教堂時通常只能用 aisle.

ajar [ə'dʒɑ:*] *adv* (with reference to a door) open a little way only (門) 微開著.

alarm [ə'lɑ:m] **1** *nu* sudden fear caused by danger 驚恐, 恐懼. **2** *nc* warning of danger 警告, 警報: *He gave the alarm when the thief appeared.* 小偷出現時他發出警告. Also 亦作 *vt* frighten 使驚恐: *I was alarmed when I heard the noise.* 我聽到那聲音時很驚慌. **alarmist** *nc* one who is always giving warnings of dangers which do not really exist 危言聳聽者, 大驚小怪的人. **alarm clock** clock which rings a bell at a time at which a person wishes to wake up 鬧鐘.

alas [ə'læs] *interj* cry of unhappiness (*o.f.*) 哎呀(表示痛苦的叫聲)(舊式).

album ['ælbəm] *nc* book with blank pages to keep photographs or stamps in, or for people to write their signatures in 影集, 相片簿; 集郵簿; 簽名記念冊.

albumen ['ælbjumin] *nu* **1** white of egg 蛋白. **2** substance as in white of egg, part of animal and vegetable matter 蛋白質.

alcohol ['ælkəhɔl] *nu* liquid contained in beer, wine, whisky etc, which causes these drinks to have an effect on people's minds and bodies; the drinks themselves 酒精; 含酒精的飲料. **alcoholic** [ælkə'hɔlik] *adj* Also 亦作 *nc* person suffering from alcoholism 酗酒者. see below 見下條. **alcoholism** *nu* illness caused by drinking too much alcohol 酒精中毒.

alcove ['ælkouv] *nc* small room opening out of a bigger room, or a part of a big room divided from the main part in some way 凹室, (從大房間隔開的)

小間.

alderman ['ɔ:ldəmən] *nc* member of the local administration in England and America (英國和美國的)地方行政官員.

ale [eil] *nu* name given to various types of beer (*o.f.* - use **beer**) 啤酒(舊式—現在用 beer).

alert [ə'lə:t] *adj* ready and waiting to act as soon as is necessary; quick to notice things 警惕的, 警覺的, 機靈的. Also 亦作 *nc* warning of some danger 警報. Also 亦作 *vt* give a warning of this kind 警告, 使警覺: *The police have alerted all motorists to the need to drive carefully.* 警方已警告所有司機必須小心駕駛.

alfalfa [æl'fælfə] *nu* deep-rooted plant used for fodder and as a cover crop 苜蓿(供動物食用, 也可作爲覆蓋作物并護田、肥田作用).

alga ['ælgə] *nc* water plant of very simple structure 海藻. *pl* 複數 **algae** ['ældʒi:].

algebra ['ældʒibrə] *nu* branch of mathematics in which sums are worked out using letters for numbers which are unknown 代數.

alias ['eiliəs] *nc* name which is not one's own (often used for dishonest purposes) 化名, 假名(常用於不正當目的): *John Smith alias Tom Brown* i.e. John Smith, who is also known as Tom Brown. 約翰·史密斯化名湯姆·布朗.

alibi ['ælibai] *nc* statement or fact that one was somewhere else when a crime was committed at a certain place 不在犯罪現場的證詞或事實: *have an alibi* i.e. be able to prove that one was somewhere else when a crime was committed 有不在犯罪現場的證據; 即: 能證明在罪行發生時本人在

別處.

alien ['eiliən] *nc* person living or working in a country which is not his own. (rather *formal* - use **foreigner**). (在他國居住或工作的)外國人(頗爲正式—一般用 foreigner).

alienate ['eiliəneit] *vt* make an enemy of or lose the liking of by the way in which one behaves 使不和, 使疏遠; *He alienated his sister by his unkindness.* 由於他刻薄, 妹妹和他疏遠了. *His sister was alienated from him by his unkindness.* 他爲人刻薄, 和他妹妹疏遠了. **alienation** *nu* losing somebody's liking 疏遠.

alight¹ [ə'lait] *pred adj* burning 燒着的.

alight² [ə'lait] *vi* get out of a vehicle, come down to the ground or to a resting place 下車; 降落: *He alighted from the train.* 他從火車上下來. *past* 過去式和過去分詞 **alighted** or **alit** [ə'lit]. *Note* 說明: *alit* is found in poetry alit 用於詩歌.

align [ə'lain] *vt / i* come or bring into a straight line (使)排成一直線, (使)排齊. **alignment** *nu* arrangement in a straight line 排成直線, 列隊.

alike [ə'laik] *adv / pred adj* the same or not very different; in the same way 相同的(地), 相似的(地); 一樣的(地): *They look alike* i.e. they have the same appearance. 他們看起來很相像. 即: 他們的相貌一樣.

aliment ['ælimənt] *nu* something that nourishes; food 養料; 食物.

alimentary [æli'mentəri] *adj* connected with food or nutrition 飲食的; 營養的: *alimentary canal* 消化道.

alimony ['æliməni] *nu* regular supply of money paid under a court order by a man to a woman from whom he is divorced or separated (離婚或分居後男方依法付給女方的)贍養費.

alive [ə'laiv] *adv / pred adj* **1** not dead 活的; 活活地. **2** quick and active 活躍的. **alive with** full of living things 充滿(活東西)的, 到處是: *The kitchen was alive with ants.* 廚房裏到處是螞蟻.

alkali ['ælkəlai] *nc* (chemistry) substance which forms salts when joined to an acid, and turns litmus paper blue (化學)鹼(能使石蕊試紙變藍).

all [ɔ:l] **1** *adj / determiner* every one of, the whole of 所有的, 全部的: *all the pupils in the school* 全校學生; *all the soup* 整盆湯. *All pupils must observe the rules.* 每一學生都必須遵守這些規則. **2** *pron* everything or everybody 全部, 大家, 全體: *You'll find all you need in that box.* 你需要的東西全都在那盒子裏. *All of them are going.* 他們全體都要去. **3** *intensifier* completely 完全地: *all wrong* 全錯的; *all finished* 徹底完成的. **all right 1** correctly; well 無誤地; 好: *Do you feel all right?* i.e. are you feeling well? 你感覺好嗎? **2** (used to show agreement) yes; certainly (用以表示同意)行; 當然: *Will you do this? -All right, I'll do it.* 你願意幹這事嗎?一行, 我願意幹. **all-'rounder** man who is good at many sports, or at many parts of it particular sport 全能運動員. **all / just the same** however; in spite of that 仍然; 不管, 照樣: *He is rather boastful, but I like him all / just the same.* 他有點自誇, 但我還是照樣喜歡他. **above all** most importantly 最重要地, 首先. **after all 1** (often to introduce an excuse or reason for not doing something) when everything is considered (常引出沒有做某事的借口或理由)畢竟: *He doesn't work very hard, but after all, he is getting old.* 他幹活不怎麼賣力, 畢竟是越來越老了. **2** despite what was previously said 終究: *I went to town after all* i.e. although I had earlier said that I would not. 我終於到城裏去了. 即: 儘管我早先說過不去. **go all out** work, try etc with great effort and determination. *(informal)* 全力以赴 (非正式). **on all fours** on one's hands and knees 匍匐着, 爬着. **once and for all** for the last time 最後一次: *warn somebody once and for all.* (sometimes rather *impolite*; be careful about using this phrase) 最後一次警告某人 (有時頗不禮貌, 慎用此短語). **not at all** polite expression which one sometimes uses when someone thanks one. (It is not necessary to use this expression every time somebody thanks one) 別客氣, 沒什麼 (禮貌地回答別人感謝的用語, 但無須每謝必答).

allay [əˈlei] *vt* make less 減輕; 使和緩: *allay somebody's fear* 減輕某人的憂慮; *allay the pain of a disease* 緩和病痛.

allege [əˈledʒ] *vt* give as a fact but without proof 無根據地說, 宣稱. **allegation** [æliˈgeiʃən] *nc.*

allegiance [əˈliːdʒəns] *nu* faithfulness and duty (esp. to a leader or an association that one is a member of) 忠誠 (尤指對對領導或所屬社團).

allegory [ˈæligəri] *nc* story, intended to teach a lesson, in which either abstract ideas (such as hate, beauty, faithfulness) or animals, appear as though they were human beings 寓言, 諷喻.

allergy [ˈælədʒi] *nc* condition in which one becomes ill or uncomfortable when brought into contact with something which usu. does not affect other people (in this way) 過敏症, 過敏性反應. **allergic** [əˈləːdʒik] *adj* **1** having an allergy 患過敏症的, 有過敏性反應

的: *He is allergic to fish* i.e. he becomes ill if he eats fish. 他對魚過敏. 即: 他吃魚會生病. **2** disliking intensely. *(informal in sense 2)* 厭惡的 (義 2 爲非正式).

alleviate [əˈliːvieit] *vt* make less 減輕, 緩和: *alleviate pain* 減輕疼痛. **alleviation** [əliːviˈeiʃən] *nu.*

alley [ˈæli] *nc* narrow street in a town (often dark and dirty) 小巷, 胡同.

alliance [əˈlaiəns] *nc* joining together of countries or people in friendship 聯盟, 同盟. **allied** [ˈælaid] *adj* **1** joined together in agreement 聯合的, 同盟的. **2** connected in some way 有關聯的: *Chemistry is allied to physics.* 化學與物理有關聯. see **ally.**

alligator [ˈæligeitə*] *nc* large animal, rather like a crocodile, with long nose and sharp teeth which is found mostly in rivers in tropical America 短吻鱷 (一種主要生活在美洲熱帶河流裏的鱷魚).

alliteration [əlitəˈreiʃən] *nu* repeating the same sound at the beginning of a number of words (esp. in poetry e.g. *speak slowly and softly*) 頭韻 (一些詞的詞頭發音相同, 尤指在詩裏, 如: speak slowly and softly).

allocate [ˈæləkeit] *vt* give to someone for a purpose or as part of an arrangement 分配, (爲某目的) 把…撥給: *I have allocated this room to you.* 我已把這房間分配給你. **allocation** [æləˈkeiʃən] *nc / u.*

allot [əˈlɔt] *vt* give as a share 分配, 分給. *past* 過去式和過去分詞 **allotted.** **allotment** *nc / u* used most often with reference to a piece of land. (For other purposes **allocation** is better) (最常用於指) 分配的一塊土地. (其他義最好用 allocation).

allow [əˈlau] *vt / i* **1** say that somebody

may do what he wishes to do 准許, 允准: *He allowed his children to go to the cinema.* 他讓他的孩子們去看電影。 **2** give (esp. money) 給予 (尤指錢): *He allowed his children fifteen pence a week.* 他每週給他的孩子們十五便士。 **3** keep or be prepared to use for a special purpose 準備用: *We must allow three days for travelling from London to Hong Kong.* 我們從倫敦旅行到香港必須準備用三天時間。 **allowance** *nc* amount of money given regularly to somebody for a special purpose (定期) 津貼: *He has an allowance from the government for travelling expenses.* 他享有政府發給的旅途津貼費。 **make allowances for** remember somebody's difficulties or weakness when judging him for doing wrong, and so judge him less severely 顧及, 體諒。

alloy ['ælɔi] *nc* substance made of two or more metals 合金. Also 亦作 *vt* [ə'lɔi].

allude [ə'lu:d] *vi* talk about something without mentioning it by name 暗指, 側面提到: *You mustn't even allude to his father's illness.* 你甚至連提都不能提他父親的病. **allusion** [ə'lu:ʒən] *nc / u.*

allure [ə'ljuə*] *vt* make somebody do something (possibly something bad) by offering him something pleasant 引誘, 誘惑. Also 亦作 *nu* attraction; charm 誘惑力; 魅力. **alluring** *adj.*

alluvial [ə'lu:viəl] *adj* consisting of sand or mud left by rivers 冲積的, 淤積的: *alluvial soil* 冲積土.

alluvium [ə'lu:viəm] *nc / u* sand, mud, etc left by flowing water 冲積層; 淤積層. *pl* 複數 **alluvia** [ə'lu:viə] or **alluviums.**

ally ['ælai] *nc* person or country with

whom one is joined in friendship, often in order to fight against somebody else or another country 同盟者; 同盟國. see 見 **alliance.**

almighty [ɔ:l'maiti] *adj* having the power to do anything 全能的. **The Almighty** God 上帝.

almond ['ɑ:mənd] *nc* narrow, oval, light-brown nut 杏仁.

almoner [ə'ɑ:mənə] *nc (Brit)* hospital social worker responsible for the welfare and aftercare of patients (英) (負責爲離院後病人服務的) 醫院社會工作人員.

almost ['ɔ:lmoust] *adv* nearly 幾乎.

alms [ɑ:mz] *n sing* or *pl* 單數或複數 money or goods given to help the poor (*o.f.* — use **charity**) 救濟金, 施捨物 (舊式—現在用 charity).

alone [ə'loun] *adv / pred adj* not with anybody or anything else 單獨, 獨自: *work alone* 單獨工作: *He alone understands me;* 唯有他理解我; *leave something alone* i.e. not touch or have anything to do with it 不要動某物, 不要管某事.

along [ə'lɔŋ] *adv / prep* onward or from end to end 向前; 沿着: *walk along the road* 沿着路走. **all along** all the time 始終: *He knew the answer all along, but he kept quiet.* 他一直是知道答案的, 但他一聲不吭. **along with** together with 與⋯一起. **along-side** by the side of (usu. a ship) 在⋯旁邊 (通常指船): *come alongside* 並排靠來.

aloof [ə'lu:f] *adv / pred adj* at some distance from other people (usu. in an unfriendly way) 離開, 遠離 (通常指不友好地): *stand / hold oneself aloof from somebody* i.e. not mix or talk very much with 與某人疏遠. 即很少與之相處或談話.

aloud [ə'laud] *adv* so that one may be heard 出聲地 (以便能被聽到): *read aloud* i.e. speak the words one is reading 朗讀. (*opp* 反義語 **read to oneself** or **read silently**).

alphabet ['ælfəbet] *nc* letters used for writing a language 字 母 表. **alphabetical** [ælfə'betikl] *adj* in the order of the alphabet, A first, B second, C third etc. 依字母順序的. *Note* 說明: the letters themselves (ABC etc.) are referred to as *letters of the alphabet*. The plural *alphabets* can only be used to refer to the writing systems of various languages (e.g. *the alphabets of Russian and Greek*) 字母本身 (如 ABC 等) 稱作 letters of the alphabet. 複數 alphabets 只能用於指各種語言的書寫體系 (例如: the alphabets of Russian and Greek 俄語和希臘語的書寫體系).

alpine ['ælpain] *adj* of or like high mountains 高山的: *alpine plants* 高山植物; *alpine scenery* 高山景色.

already [ɔ:l'redi] *adv* by or before a particular moment 已經: *When we arrived, they were already there.* 我們到達時他們已經在那裏了.

alright [ɔ:l'rait] *adv* all right 行; 好; 不錯. *Note* 說明: **Alright** is very common now, but some people think all right is better English. Alright 這個詞現在已經普遍使用, 不過有人還是認爲用 all right 會比較好.

also ['ɔ:lsou] *adv* in addition; besides; too 還; 也; 亦: *John is also coming to the party.* 約翰也來參加宴會.

altar ['ɔ:ltə] *nc* table, stone or other raised object which is the most important place in a building where a religious ceremony is held 祭壇.

alter ['ɔ:ltə*] *vt / i* change; become or make different (使) 改變, (使) 變化.

alteration [ɔ:ltə'reiʃən] *nc / u*: make *alterations* i.e. make changes 作出更改.

alternate[1] [ɔ:l'tə:nit] *adj* two things in turn, one thing and then the other and then the first and so on 交替的; 間隔的: *alternate stars and circles* i.e. *o*o*o etc. 星號和圓圈相互間隔, 即: *o*o*o 等; *on alternate days* i.e. Monday, Wednesday, Friday, Sunday etc. 隔天, 如星期一、星期三、星期五、星期日等. **alternately** *adv*.

alternate[2] ['ɔ:ltə:neit] *vt / i* do a thing in turn (two people or two groups) (使) 交替, (使) 輪流: *John and his sister alternate in coming to see me* i.e. John comes on one day, and his sister on the next etc. 約翰和他妹妹輪流來看我. *John alternates hard work and / with laziness* i.e. he first shows hard work, then laziness, then hard work again etc. 約翰時而勤奮時而懶惰. **alternation** [ɔ:ltə:'neiʃən] *nc / u* **alternating current** electric current which flows first in one direction, then in the other at short, evenly timed intervals 交流電. (*opp* 反義語 **direct current**).

alternative [ɔ:l'tə:nətiv] *adj* permitting a choice 可選擇的: *an alternative route* 另一條路線. Also 亦作 *nc* one out of two or more choices (兩者或兩者以上的) 選擇; 選擇餘地: *The judge offered the criminal the alternative of a fine or six months in prison.* 法官向罪犯提供兩種選擇, 要麼罰款, 要麼坐牢六個月. *You know the alternatives, now you must choose.* 你是知道這些選擇的, 現在你必須選定. **alternatively** *adv*. *Note* 說明: some people use *alternative* only when there are two choices, not more, but many people do not follow this rule 有些人用

alternative 時只能指兩種選擇，不能多，但許多人沒有遵守這條規則.

although [ɔːlˈðou] *conj: Although the book is difficult to understand, it is interesting* i.e. the book is difficult to understand, but it is interesting. 這本書雖然不好理解，但是有趣. *Note* 說明: the difference between *although* and *though*: **1** in the phrase *as though* we cannot use *although*. **2** *though*; but not *although*, is sometimes used after a clause, to mean that what was expected did not happen. *I went to town, I didn't see John though* i.e. I expected to see him but did not. although 與 though 的區別: 1. 我們不能用 although 代替短語 as though. 2. though 有時用在從句後面，表示期望的事沒有發生，但 although 不能這樣用. 如: I went to town, I didn't see John though. 即: 我想見他，但是沒有見到.

altitude [ˈæltitjuːd] *nc* (usu. with reference to aeroplanes or mountains) height above sea level (海拔) 高度(通常指飛機或山脈): *Mt Kenya has an altitude of over 5,000 metres.* 肯尼亞山海拔高度五千公尺以上.

alto [ˈæltou] *nc* (music) (音樂) **1** highest adult male voice (above the tenor) 男聲最高音(男高音之上). **2** lowest female voice. (usu. **contralto**); person who sings with this type of voice 女低音(通常用 contralto); 女低音歌手. *pl* 複數 **altos.** Also 亦作 *adj.*

altogether [ɔːltəˈgeðəˊ] *adv* **1** completely; entirely 完全地; 全部地. *The meeting was altogether a waste of time;* 這個會議全是浪費時間. *an altogether stupid idea* 十足愚蠢的想法. **2** when all things are carefully considered 總而言之: *Your plan would be very difficult and also*

dangerous, so altogether, I think it would be better to try something else. 你的計劃實行起來會很困難也有危險，所以總的說來，我看最好還是想想其他辦法. *Note* 說明: most people would use *altogether* in the two senses given here, and *all together* with the meaning of with everybody or everything included. *He gathered his books all together. John and his friends were all together again.* 多數人用 altogether 表示上述兩義，而用 all together 表示一起或總共. 例如: He gathered his books all together (他把他的書統統收在一起). John and his friends were all together again (約翰和朋友們又聚會了).

alum [ˈæləm] *nu* white mineral salt, hard and bitter-tasting, used medically, in dyeing, etc. 明礬(用於醫藥、染色等).

aluminium [æljuˈminiəm] (*US* 美 **aluminum** [əˈluːminəm]) *nu* light, silver-coloured metal, used for making parts of aeroplanes, saucepans etc. 鋁.

always [ˈɔːlweiz] *adv* at all times; on every occasion 永遠; 總是; 老是: *I will always remember her.* 我將永遠記住她. *George is always late for school.* 喬治上課老是遲到.

amalgam [əˈmælgəm] *nu* mixture of two substances (兩種物質的)混合物.

amalgamate [əˈmælgəmeit] *vt / i* (esp. with reference to two or more businesses or companies joining together) join together .to form one thing (尤指兩個或兩個以上的商行或公司) 合併，聯合. **amalgamation** [əmælgəˈmeiʃən] *nc / u.*

amass [əˈmæs] *vt* gather together a large amount of something (usu. wealth, information etc.) 積聚(通常指財富、資料等): *In his lifetime, he* *amassed a large fortune.* 他一生積累了一大筆財產.

amateur ['æmətə*] *nc* **1** (esp. with reference to playing football or other sports, playing music, painting pictures etc.) person who does something because he enjoys doing it, and not for money or because it is his job 業餘愛好者(尤指愛好踢足球或其他運動、演奏樂曲、繪畫等). **2** person who does something badly, because it is not his real job. 外行. Also 亦作 *adj* **amateurish** ['æmətərɪʃ] *adj.*

amaze [ə'meɪz] *vt* surprise very much 使大驚, 使驚愕. **amazement** *nu* **amazing** *adj* causing great surprise 令人大爲驚異的.

ambassador [æm'bæsədə*] *nc* important government official whose work is to live in a foreign country and conduct business with the government of that country on behalf of his own government 大使, 使節.

amber ['æmbə*] *nu* **1** type of hard orange or yellow substance used for making jewellery and other ornaments 琥珀. **2** (esp. with reference to traffic lights) colour of this substance 琥珀色(尤指交通燈). Also 亦作 *adj.*

ambiguous [æm'bɪɡjuəs] *adj* **1** having two or more different meanings 有兩種或多種意思的: *The speaker gave an ambiguous reply.* 演講人作出模棱兩可的回答. **2** doubtful; not clear 含糊的, 不清楚的. (*opp* 反義詞 **unambiguous**). **ambiguity** [æmbi'ɡjuiti] *nc / u.*

ambition [æm'bɪʃən] **1** *nu* strong wish to do something (esp. to become rich, famous or successful) 雄心; 野心; 抱負 (尤指渴望發財、出名或成功). **2** *nc* thing which one wishes to have 渴望的事物: *My ambition is to be a rich*

man. 我的最大慾望是成爲富翁.

ambitious *adj* **1** having an ambition 有雄心的; 野心勃勃的. **2** needing a great deal of hard work if it is to succeed 需要巨大努力的, 大膽的: *That is a very ambitious plan, but I hope it succeeds.* 那是一項很大膽的計劃, 但我希望它會成功. (*opp* 反義詞 **unambitious**).

amble ['æmbl] *vi* (with reference to a person) walk without any hurry (指人)漫步: *We ambled along the road together.* 我們一起沿着路慢慢地走.

ambulance ['æmbjuləns] *nc* vehicle for carrying the sick or injured to hospital 救護車.

ambush ['æmbuʃ] *vt* wait in hiding until one's enemies come past and then attack them by surprise 埋伏; 伏擊: *The raiding party was ambushed in the forest.* 突擊隊在林中遭到伏擊. Also 亦作 *nc* attack made in this way 伏擊.

ameliorate [ə'miːlɪəreɪt] *vt* make better or more pleasant 改善: *ameliorate the conditions of the poor* 改善窮人的生活條件. **amelioration** [əmiːlɪə'reɪʃən] *nu.*

amen ['ɑːmen] *interj* word used at the end of a prayer, meaning 'May it be so' or 'May this prayer be granted' (祈禱的結束語)阿門(意爲"但願如此", "誠心所願".

amenable [ə'miːnəbl] *adj* willing to take advice, listen to the opinions of other people etc. 願意聽勸告的, 肯接受意見的: *The young prince was amenable to the advice of his elders.* 這年輕的王子能聽從長輩們的勸告.

amend [ə'mend] *vt / i* become or make better 改正, 修改, 改善: *The new government amended the law.* 新政府修改了法律. **amendment** *nu / u* change (usu. in a law or rule) 改善, 修正(常指法律或規則). **make amends** see 見 **make¹**.

amenity [ə'mi:niti] *nc* (usu. *pl*) something which helps to make life enjoyable (esp. in the place where one lives e.g. a cinema, a park, a library, good roads etc.) (通常用複數)令人生活愉快的東西(尤指在居住區, 如電影院, 公園, 圖書館, 良好的道路等).

americanize [ə'merikənaiz] *vt* make American or make like America in manners, style, character, etc 使美國化.

amiable ['eimiəbl] *adj* friendly and pleasant 和藹可親的, 親切的: *He is a very amiable person.* 他是一個和藹可親的人.

amicable ['æmikəbl] *adj* friendly 友好的.

amid(st) [ə'mid(st)] *prep* in the middle of 在…中.

amino [ə'mi:nou] *adj* of or containing the NH₂ radical in combination with certain organic radicals 氨基的.

amiss [ə'mis] *adv / pred adj* wrong or wrongly 錯誤的(地): *As soon as I entered the house, I felt that there was something amiss* i.e. I felt that something was wrong. 我一走進屋子, 就感到有什麼事情不對頭. **take something amiss** be angry or unhappy because of something said or done by somebody (usu. something which was not intended to have this effect) 對某事生氣或不高興, 因某事見怪(常指對他人無意中説或做的事).

ammeter ['æmitə] *nc* instrument for measuring an electric current in amperes 安培計, 電流計.

ammonia [ə'mouniə] *nu* **1** colouless, pungent gas, used in fertilizers, cleaning fluids, etc. 氨, 阿摩尼亞. **2** water

solution of this gas 氨水.

ammunition [æmju'niʃən] *nu* bullets, shells etc fired from a gun 彈藥, 軍火.

amnesia [æm'ni:ziə] *nu* illness in which a person cannot remember things 健忘症.

amnesty ['æmnisti] *nc* pardon or forgiveness given by a government to people who have broken the law 大赦, 特赦.

amoeba [ə'mi:bə] *nc* microscopic, one-celled aminal found usually in stagnant water 變形蟲, 阿米巴(生於不流動水中的極小單細胞生物). *pl* 複數 **amoebae** [ə'mi:bi:] or **amoebas.**

amok [ə'mɔk] see 見 **amuck.**

among [ə'mʌŋ] *prep* surrounded by or with other things or people 在…中間: *He lived among his own people for ten years.* 他在自己的人民中間生活了十年. **amongst** [ə'mʌŋst] *prep* among 在…中間. *Note* 說明: *among* usu. refers to more than two things or people; *between* can refer either to two or to more than two things or people. among 通常指在兩個以上的人或物之中; between 可指在兩個或兩個以上的人和物之間.

amoral [æ'mɔrl] *adj* behaving or thinking in a way which does not recognize any difference between good and bad (行爲或思想) 沒有道德觀念的. see 見 **immoral.**

amorous ['æmərəs] *adj* showing or having feelings of love; easily falling in love; concerned with love 戀愛的; 多情的; 有關愛情的. **amorously** *adv* **amorousness** *nu*.

amorphous [ə'mɔ:fəs] *adj* without definite shape, arrangement or order 無定形的; 雜亂無章的; 混亂的.

amount [ə'maunt] *nc* (esp. of money) sum, quantity 金額; 數量: *a small* *amount of money* 一小筆款項. *A large amount of damage was done in a very short time.* 在很短時間内受到很大損害. Also 亦作 *vi* 1 (esp. of money) reach the total of, add up to (尤指金額) 總數達, 合計: *The total cost of repairs amounted to sixty pounds.* 修理費共計六十英鎊. 2 be the same as; have the meaning of 相當於; 意思是: *Keeping money which you find in the street amounts to stealing.* 把在街上拾到的錢佔爲己有等於偷竊.

amp [æmp], **ampere** ['æmpεə*] *nc* unit for measuring electric current (current that one volt can send through one ohm) 安培 (計算電流的單位).

amphibious [æm'fibiəs] *adj* 1 able to live on land and in water 兩棲的. 2 by or for land and water 水陸協同的; 水陸兩用的: *amphibious attack* 水陸協同攻擊; *amphibious vehicle* 水陸兩用車輛.

amphitheatre ['æmfiθiətə] (*US* 美 **amphitheater**) *nc* round or oval building with an open space surrounded by rising rows of seats used for competitions and theatre performances 圓形(或橢圓形)劇場.

ample ['æmpl] *adj* 1 more than enough 充足的: *an ample supply of paper* 充足的紙張供應. 2 large; with plenty of space; big enough or more than big enough 大的; 寬敞的; 廣大的; 足够的: *There is ample room for twelve desks here.* 這裏足够放十二張桌子. **amply** *adv.*

amplify ['æmplifai] *vt* make louder, fuller, greater etc, give more details etc. 擴大, 放大, 增强; 詳細說明等: *The tunnel amplified the noise.* 隧道增强了響聲. **amplifier** *nc* device for making sounds louder (esp. in a record

player etc.) 擴音器.

amputate ['æmpjuteit] *vt* cut off part of the body for medical reasons (手術) 切除, 截(肢).

amuck [ə'mʌk], **amok** [ə'mɔk] in **run amuck** i.e. be overcome by madness so that one runs about killing anyone one meets; act in a wild uncontrolled way 發於 run amuck, 即: 瘋狂亂砍亂殺, 狂亂.

amuse [ə'mju:z] *vt* make somebody laugh and be happy because of something funny 逗人笑, 使高興, 使感到有趣: *The children were amused at / by the clown's jokes.* 孩子們被小丑的笑話逗樂了. **amusement** 1 *nu* state of being amused 快樂, 娛樂. 2 *nc* something which is amusing 娛樂的事物, 消遣. **amusing** *adj.*

an [æn, ən] *determiner* used before vowel sounds 用於元音之前. see 見 a.

anaemia [ə'ni:miə] (*US* 美 **anemia**) *nu* illness in which a person does not have enough red corpuscles in the blood; this makes him very tired and weak 貧血症. **anaemic** *adj.*

anaesthetic [ænis'θetik] (*US* 美 **anesthetic**) *nc* liquid or gas which makes a person unable to feel pain, either by making him become unconscious, or by affecting one part of the body only, used by a doctor or dentist before operating on a person 麻醉劑: *local anaesthetic* i.e. one which prevents pain being felt in one particular part of the body 局部麻醉劑; *general anaesthetic* 全身麻醉劑.

anagram ['ænəgræm] *nc* word or phrase made by changing the order of letters in another word or phrase (e.g. *rat* is an anagram of *art; pain* is an anagram of *a pin*) 變位字 (通過改變單詞或短語中的字母位置而組成的單詞或

短語;例如 rat 是 art 的變位字,pain 是 a pin 的變位字).

anal ['einəl] *adj* of or near the anus 肛門的; 近肛門的.

analects ['ænələkts] *npl* collected literary excerpts 文選;論集.

analogy [ə'nælədʒi] *nc / u* similarity or likeness; comparison between two things 類似, 相似; 類比: *Shakespeare makes an analogy between the citizens of a country and the parts of a person's body* 莎士比亞把一個國家的公民比作人體的各個部份.

analyse ['ænəlaiz] (*US* 美 **analyze**) *vt* examine something very carefully, and divide it into parts to see what it is made of, or what it actually is 分析, 分解: *The food was carefully analysed to see if it contained anything harmful.* 這種食物經過仔細化驗,以測定是否含有害物質. **analysis** [ə'nælisis] *nc / u* careful examination in the manner described 分析, 分解: *That newspaper has a very good analysis of the political situation.* 那家報紙對政局作了很好的分析. *pl* 複數 **analyses** [ə'næ.lisi:z].

anarchy ['ænəki] *nu* absence of law and government, so that each person does as he wishes (usu. causing harm to other people) 無政府狀態. **anarchist** *nc* somebody who has this belief 無政府主義者.

anatomy [ə'nætəmi] *nu* **1** science of the parts of the body 解剖學. **2** study of this science (usu. by medical students) by cutting up dead bodies of animals or human beings 解剖, 分析.

ancestor ['ænsestə*] *nc* person's grandparents, great-grandparents, great-great-grandparents etc. (Not usu. with reference to a person's parents) 祖先, 祖宗 (通常不指父母). **ancestral**

[æn'sestrl] *adj* coming from a person's ancestors 祖先的, 祖傳的: *They kept their ancestral customs.* 他們保留了祖傳的習俗. **ancestry** *nu* all the ancestors of a person 祖先, 列祖.

anchor ['æŋkə*] *nc* heavy piece of iron attached to a rope or chain; it is lowered from a boat or ship to the bottom of the sea in order to prevent the ship from moving 錨. Also 亦作 *vt / i*: *The ship anchored in the harbour.* 這條船在港內抛錨. **anchorage** *nc* place near the land where ships can anchor 錨地.

ancient ['einʃənt] *adj* (esp. with reference to history) very old 古代的: *history of ancient Egypt* 古埃及史; *ancient monuments* 古跡, 古址.

and [ænd, ənd, ən] *conj* word which joins two or more words, phrases or clauses 和, 與, 同, 及: *He likes books, films and plays.* 他喜歡書籍、電影和戲劇. *I like bread and butter* i.e. bread with butter on it. 我喜歡塗牛油的麵包. *He opened the door and looked round the room.* 他打開了門並四下環顧房間. *Come and sit beside me.* 過來坐在我身邊. *Come over here and I'll tell you a secret* i.e. if you come over here, I shall tell you a secret. 到這邊來,我要告訴你一個秘密. *Wait and see* i.e. if you wait you will see. 等着瞧.

anecdote ['ænikdout] *nc* short and often true story about some happening or person (usu. interesting or amusing) 簡短(而通常有趣的)真實故事, 軼事.

angel ['eindʒəl] *nc* **1** messenger of God (esp. in the Christian religion; usu. imagined as a beautiful person with wings) 天使(尤指基督教,通常想像爲帶有翅膀的美人兒). **2** any very good person. (*informal* in sense **2**) 可愛的

人. (義 2 爲非正式). **angelic** [æn'dʒelik] *adj* **1** like or of an angel 天使般的, 天使的. **2** (with reference to children) very well-behaved (指小孩) 很乖的.

anger ['æŋgə*] *nu* feeling which makes one want to fight or quarrel with somebody who has done or said something wrong or hurtful 怒, 生氣, 憤怒: *He was filled with anger.* 他滿腔怒火. Also 亦作 *vt* cause somebody to have this feeling by one's behaviour or words 使生氣, 激怒: *My explanation only angered him more.* 我的解釋只是使他更爲憤怒. see 見 **angry**.

angle¹ ['æŋgl] *nc* size of the space made by two lines which meet at a point or by two surfaces which meet along one edge 角; 角度.

angle² ['æŋgl] *vi* try to gain something without asking for it directly (usu. in a slightly deceitful or cunning way) (以間接方式)獲取(通常帶點狡詐手段): *I think he was angling for a loan.* 我看他是在想方設法要借錢. **angler** *nc* person who tries to catch fish using a rod and line, for sport 釣魚者. **angling** *nu* sport of catching fish in this way 釣魚.

Anglican ['æŋglikən] *nc* member of, belonging to, the Church of England (英國)聖公會教徒. Also 亦作 *adj*.

anglicize ['æŋglisaiz] *vt* make English or make like English 使英國化; 使英語化: *Many foreign town names are anglicized* (e.g. we say *Paris* not *Paree*). 許多外國城鎮的名稱都英語化了. (例如我們說 Paris 而不說 Paree).

Anglo- ['æŋglou] *prefix* English (e.g. *Anglo-French cooperation* i.e. cooperation between England and France) 英國的 (例如: Anglo-French coopera-

tion 即: 英法合作).

angry ['æŋgri] *adj* **1** having a feeling of anger 生氣的, 憤怒的: *Are you angry with him?* 你在生他的氣嗎? *What are you angry about?* 你爲甚麼生氣? **2** (with reference to a wound, cut etc.) red and painful-looking (指傷口等)腫痛發炎的. **angrily** *adv* see 見 **anger**.

anguish ['æŋgwiʃ] *nu* very great pain or unhappiness (esp. mental pain) (尤指精神上)極大的痛苦, 悲痛.

angular ['æŋgjulə] *adj* **1** having or forming an angle or angles 有角的; 成角的. **2** measured by an angle 用角度量的. **3** lean; bony 骨瘦如柴的: *an angular basketball player* 身材瘦削的籃球隊員. **4** awkward 生硬的; 不靈活的.

animal ['æniml] *nc* **1** living creature which is not a plant 動物. **2** living creature which is not a plant, a human, a bird, a fish, an insect or a reptile (e.g. a dog, a cat, a tiger) 獸類, 牲畜. Also 亦作 *adj*.

animate ['ænimeit] *vt* make alive; make active; make bright and lively 使活起來; 使有生氣; 使活潑: *When I showed the child a toy, curiosity animated his face.* 我給那小孩看一件玩具時, 好奇心使他喜形於色. Also 亦作 ['ænimət] *adj* alive; living 活的; 有生氣的. (opp 反義詞 **inanimate**). **animated** *adj* full of ideas and arguments 活躍的, 熱烈的: *We had an animated discussion.* 我們進行了一次熱烈的討論.

animosity [ˌæni'mɔsiti] *nu* strong hate or dislike 憎惡, 仇恨: *I think that man feels great animosity towards you.* 我想那個人對你懷有深仇大恨.

aniseed ['ænisid] *nu* seed used for flavouring 茴香子(用作調味香料).

ankle ['æŋkl] *nc* part of the body between the foot and the leg 踝, 踝節.

annals ['ænəlz] *npl* **1** written account of events year by year in chronological order 編 年 史. **2** historical records; history 歷史記載; 歷史: *the annals of warfare* 戰爭史. **3** any journal containing reports of a society, etc. (學會等的) 年報.

annex¹, annexe ['æneks] *nc* building near or joined to a bigger one, used because the bigger building is not big enough to hold all the people who want to use it 附屬建築: *build an annex to a school* 蓋學校的附屬建築.

annex² [ə'neks] *vt* take or join something to something else (often with reference to one country taking another country and ruling it) 添加, 合併(常指併吞他國).

annihilate [ə'naiəleit] *vt* destroy something entirely, so that nothing is left 摧毀, 消滅: *The raiders annihilated the village.* 入侵者毀滅了那個村莊.

anniversary [æni'və:səri] *nc* date each year on which something happened in the past (e.g. if John and his wife got married on 15 February 1955, their wedding anniversary is 15 February every year) 週年紀念日 (例如約翰和他妻子於一九五五年二月十五日結婚, 他們結婚的週年紀念日就是每年的二月十五日).

annotate ['ænouteit] *vt* write or give written notes adding more information or explaining something hard to understand 註釋, 註解: *It is usually better to buy an annotated edition of a Shakespeare play.* 買莎士比亞劇本一般最好買有註釋的版本. **annotation** [ænou'teiʃən] *nc / u*.

announce [ə'nauns] *vt* say or make known something, so that everybody can hear or read it 宣佈, 宣告; 發表: *They have announced their wedding.* 他們已經宣佈結婚. *The headmaster has announced that there will be a holiday tomorrow.* 校長宣佈明天放假.

announcement *nc / u* **announcer** *nc* person who announces (esp. a person who reads the news and makes other announcements on the radio or television, or at a railway station etc.) 宣佈者; (電台或電視的) 播音員; (火車站的) 廣播員.

annoy [ə'nɔi] *vt* do something which makes another person angry 使生氣: *Children should not annoy their parents.* 孩子們不應惹父母生氣. **annoyance** *nc / u*. **annoying** *adj* causing somebody to be annoyed 使人不高興的, 令人討厭的.

annual ['ænjuəl] *adj* **1** taking place every year 每年的, 年度的. **2** (with reference to flowers) lasting only one year (指花卉)一年生的. Also 亦作 *nc* **1** plant that lives only one year 一年生植物. **2** book of facts or stories that is sold at the same time every year 年刊; 年報; 年鑑. **annually** *adv*.

annuity [ə'nju:iti] *nc* fixed amount of money paid once a year to somebody 年金.

annul [ə'nʌl] *vt* (usu. with reference to an agreement, law, rule etc.) stop or end completely 取消, 廢除(通常指協議, 法令, 規則等). *past* 過去式和過去分詞 **annulled. annulment** *nc / u*.

anode ['ænoud] *nc* positively charged electrode 陽極, 正極.

anoint [ə'nɔint] *vt* put oil on the head or body of somebody (esp. on the head of a king or queen who is being crowned) 塗油於(某人頭上或身上) (尤指塗在被加冕的國王或女王頭上).

anomalous [ə'nɔmələs] *adj* not following the usual or regular way; different from the others of a group 不規則的,

異常的. **anomaly** *nc* something which does not follow the normal rule; something which is different 不按常規, 反常; 異常之事物: *A school with no books in it would be an anomaly these days.* 如今沒有藏書的學校是反常的.

anonymous [ə'nɔniməs] *adj* written, made etc by a person whose name is not given or is not known. 匿名的, 無名的: *He received an anonymous gift / letter / phone call etc.* 他接到匿名禮物/信件/電話等. *This poem is anonymous.* 這首詩沒有署名. **anonymity** [ænə'nimiti] *nu* state of not giving one's name, or of one's name not being known 匿名, 無名. **anon** short form of **anonymous**, written in books of poetry etc when the author of a poem is unknown. anonymous 的縮畧式, 署在詩集等作者名不明的詩上.

anorak ['ænəræk] *nc* jacket with hood, which keeps out wind and rain 帶兜帽的風雨茄克.

another [ə'nʌðə*] *adj / pron* one more; a different one 再一(個); 不同的一(個): *He ordered another drink.* 他再要了一杯酒. *I don't like this shirt; show me another one.* 我不喜歡這件襯衫, 請拿另一件給我看看.

answer[1] ['ɑ:nsə*] *vt / i* 1 say or write something in reply to what somebody else has said or written 回答, 答覆: *answer a question / a letter* 回答問題/答覆信件; *answer somebody* 回答某人. 2 be satisfactory to 適合於: *This plan will not answer our needs.* 這項計劃不符合我們的需要. **answerable** 1 able to be answered 可答覆的. (*opp* 反義詞 **unanswerable**). 2 in charge of; likely to be blamed or punished if something is found to be wrong 負責的; 應負責任的. **answer**

the door / telephone open the door when somebody knocks or rings the bell / lift the telephone when it rings 應聲開門/接電話. **answer to a description** look like the description given 看起來與描述的相符: *Have you seen anyone answering to this description?* 你有沒有看到和這個相貌特徵相像的人?

answer[2] ['ɑ:nsə*] *nc* 1 what is said, written etc when one answers somebody / something 回答, 答覆. 2 correct result of a sum or calculation 答案.

ant [ænt] *nc* small insect which can carry things heavier than itself 螞蟻.

antagonism [æn'tægənizəm] *nu* feeling of hate or dislike for an enemy or person to whom one is opposed 對抗, 反感. **antagonist** *nc* enemy or person with whom one is fighting, quarrelling 敵手, 對手. **antagonistic** [æntægə'nistik] *adj* having feelings of hate or dislike towards an enemy 敵對的, 對抗的. **antagonize** *vt* make a person dislike one 使對自己反感, 得罪: *Do not antagonize that man, he is dangerous.* 別得罪那個人, 他是個危險人物.

Antarctic [ænt'ɑ:ktik] *adj* belonging to the region round the South Pole 南極的; 南極區的. Also 亦作 *n*.

ante- ['ænti] *prefix* before (e.g. **antenatal**) 前, 在前(例如: antenatal). *Note* 說明: do not confuse with *anti-* which means *against* 別與表示 "反"、"抗"的 anti- 混淆起來.

antecedent [ænti'si:dnt] *nc* 1 something which happened before something else 發生在前的事. 2 (grammar) noun or noun clause to which a pronoun refers (語法)先行詞. 3 (*usu. pl*) past experience or history of a

person / thing（通常用複數）(個人的)
經歷,身世;（某事物的）歷史.

antelope ['æntiloup] *nc* animal with
horns, found in Africa and Asia, which
can run very fast 羚羊.

antenatal [ænti'neit] *adj* before the
birth of a baby 出生前的: *antenatal
clinic* i.e. a place where pregnant
women are given medical care 孕婦保
健診所.（*opp* 反義詞 **postnatal**).

antenna [æn'tenə] *nc* **1** one of the two
feelers on the head of an insect（昆蟲
的）觸角. **2** wire used in radio or television for sending or receiving radio
waves; aerial（無線電或電視）天線. *pl*
複數 **antennae** [æn'teni:].

anteroom ['æntirum] *nc* small room
leading into a bigger one 前室,接待
室.

anthem ['ænθəm] *nc* **1** official song or
piece of music of a country (usu.
national anthem）國歌（通常用
national anthem）. **2** any song of
praise (esp. one sung in a Christian
church with words from the Bible) 頌
歌,讚歌(尤指在基督教教堂唱的聖歌).

anther ['ænθə] *nc* the part of a stamen
that contains the pollen 花藥(花的帶
花粉部份).

anthology [æn'θɔlədʒi] *nc* book of
poems or prose passages written by
more than one author 詩集;選集.

anthropology [ænθrə'pɔlədʒi] *nu* study
of the beliefs, customs, and way of life
of human beings 人類學. **anthropo-
logist** *nc*.

anti- ['ænti] *prefix* against (e.g. **anti-
aircraft; antisocial**) 反, 抗 (例如:
anti-aircraft; antisocial). **Note** 說明:
do not confuse with *ante-* which
means *before* 別與表示"前","在前"的
ante- 混淆起來.

anti-aircraft ['ænti'ɛəkrɑːft] *adj* for use

in fighting against enemy aeroplanes
防空的: *anti-aircraft gun* 高射砲.

antibiotic ['æntibai'ɔtik] *nc* drug or
medicine which works by destroying
the germs causing an illness 抗菌素:
Penicillin is an antibiotic. 盤尼西林是
一種抗菌素.

antibody ['æntibɔdi] *nc* substance produced in the body and which fights
against disease 抗體(身體中的抗病物
質).

antic ['æntik] *nc* (usu. *pl*) funny or foolish action (usu. made to cause laugh-
ter); amusing behaviour (esp. by an
animal or a child)（通常用複數）滑稽
動作(通常用以逗笑);有趣的舉止(尤指
動物或小孩作出的): *The child's antics
made us laugh.* 這小孩有趣的動作使
得我們發笑.

anticipate [æn'tisipeit] *vt* **1** expect and
think about something before it hap-
pens 預期;預料;指望: *We did not
anticipate any trouble.* 我們預料不會
有麻煩. **2** do something before somebody else does it or asks for it 搶先
(做某事). **anticipation** [æntisi'pei-
ʃən] *nu*.

anticlimax ['ænti'klaimæks] *nc* occurrence of something foolish, unimportant, funny or unpleasant, when one
had been expecting the opposite,
something important, serious etc. 反
高潮(與所期望的重要、嚴肅的事相反而
出現可笑的、瑣細的、或令人討厭的事):
*The end of the story was an anticli-
max.* 這故事的結尾變得平平淡淡.

anticlockwise ['ænti'klɔkwaiz] *adv* in
the direction opposite to that in
which the hands of a clock move 逆時
針方向地. (*opp* 反義詞 **clockwise**).

anticyclone ['ænti'saikloun] *nc* area of
high atmospheric pressure 高氣壓;反
氣旋.

antidote ['æntidout] *nc* **1** medicine which stops the effect of a poison 解毒藥. **2** anything which stops something bad or unpleasant 除害物;解除痛苦的方法: *Hard work is an antidote for unhappiness.* 勤奮是消除悲傷的辦法.

antifreeze ['ænti'fri:z] *nu* substance added to the water in the radiator of a car to prevent freezing in cold weather 防凍劑, 抗凝劑.

antipathy [æn'tipəθi] *nu* strong and unchanging feelings of dislike 厭惡, 反感.

antiquated ['æntikweitid] *adj* (usu. with reference to objects or ideas) of no use or interest, because very old 廢棄的; 過時的; 陳舊的 (通常指物件或思想).

antique [æn'ti:k] *adj* (usu. with reference to objects) very old 古老的, 古舊的 (通常指物件). Also 亦作 *nc* very old and valuable object 古老而珍貴的東西, 古物. *Note* 說明: if we call something *antiquated* we mean that it is of no use or value; if we call it *antique* we mean that it is old and valuable 如果我們稱某物爲 antiquated, 是指它沒有用處或無價值; 如果稱它爲 antique, 則指它古老而貴重.

antiseptic [ænti'septik] *adj* preventing the growth of germs and the spread of disease 防腐的. Also 亦作 *nc* substance which has this effect 防腐劑, 抗菌劑.

antisocial [ænti'souʃl] *adj* **1** against the ideas of what is good which most people in society have agreed on (e.g. stealing, causing trouble to other people and murder are antisocial acts) 反社會常理的 (如偷竊, 損害他人和謀殺是反社會常理的行爲). **2** unfriendly, not wanting any friends 不友好的; 孤僻的.

antithesis [æn'tiθisis] *nc* opposite of something 對立, 對照: *Laughter is the antithesis of tears.* 笑聲是眼淚的反面.

antler ['æntlə*] *nc* (often *pl*) horn of a deer (常用複數) 鹿角.

anus ['einəs] *nc* part of the body from which solid waste matter is sent out 肛門.

anvil ['ænvil] *nc* large block of iron or steel on which a blacksmith shapes metal 鐵砧.

anxiety [æŋ'zaiəti] *nc / u* feeling of fear and uncertainty about what is going to happen 憂慮, 焦急.

anxious ['æŋkʃəs] *adj* **1** filled with fear and uncertainty 憂慮的, 焦急的: *He is very anxious about the results of his test.* 他很擔心他考試的成績. **2** filled with a strong wish to do something 渴望的; 急切的: *The people here are very anxious to help you.* 這裏的人們急於要幫助你. **anxiously** *adv.*

any ['eni] *determiner* **1** one, it does not matter which 任何的, 任一的: *Take any book you want to.* 你要哪一本書你就拿去吧. *Come any time you like.* 你願時都可以來. *Any kind of box will do.* 任何一種盒子都行. **2** *determiner / pron / intensifier* (esp. in *negative* and *interrogative* sentences) some (尤用在否定句和疑問句中)一些: *Have you got any children besides John?* 除了約翰你還有其他孩子嗎? *Do you want any of these?* 這些當中有你想要的嗎? *Can't this car go any faster?* 這車不能再開快些嗎? *I don't want any more.* 我不再要了. **'anybody** *pron* any person 任何人. **'anyhow** *adv* **1** in any way 無論以甚麼方式. **2** in a careless way 隨隨便便: *He leaves his books about anyhow.* 他把他的書隨便亂丟. **3** whatever happens 不管怎樣, 無論如何: *The teacher will forbid it, but you* *must do it anyhow. (informal)* 老師不會允許的, 但無論如何你必須幹. (非正式). **'anyone** *pron* any person 任何人. **'anything** *pron* any thing 任何東西, 任何事. **'anyway** *adv* whatever happens 不管怎樣, 無論如何: *I know it is dangerous but you must go there anyway.* 我知道那是危險的, 但不管怎樣你必須到那裏去. **'anywhere** *adv* in or to any place 任何地方.

apart [ə'pɑ:t] *adv* **1** in or into separate pieces or parts 分, 離; 成爲一塊塊地: *take a watch apart* 把手錶拆開. **2** away from; at a distance from other things or people 離開; 相距: *stand apart from other people* 站離其他人.

apartheid [ə'pɑ:tait] *nu* official policy of the South African government, of not allowing people of different races to work together, meet each other, have the same rights etc. (南非政府的)種族隔離(政策)

apartment [ə'pɑ:tmənt] *nc (US)* set of rooms on a single floor of a building (美)(在同一層樓的)公寓套間: *He lives in an apartment, not a house.* 他住在公寓套間, 不住在一幢房子. *(Brit* 英 **flat).**

apathy ['æpəθi] *nu* lack of interest or feeling 冷漠; 無感情. *There is too much apathy about the need for further education.* 人們普遍對深造不感興趣. **apathetic** [æpə'θetik] *adj* having no interest or feeling 冷漠的; 無感情的.

ape¹ [eip] *nc* large monkey with no tail (esp. a gorilla, chimpanzee, orangutan or gibbon) 猿, 無尾猿(尤指大猩猩、黑猩猩、長臂巨猿或長臂猿).

ape² [eip] *vt* copy somebody, do the same thing as somebody (as an ape copies the movements of human beings) 模倣, 倣效(像猿模倣人的動

作).

aperitif [ə'peritiv] *nc* drink (usu. alcoholic) which is taken before a meal to increase one's appetite 開胃酒.

aperture ['æpətjuə*] *nc* small hole (esp. one which lets light come in) (e.g. a camera has an aperture through which light passes to the film) (尤指透光線的)孔, 隙; (照相機上的)光圈.

apex ['eipeks] *nc* top (esp. of a triangle); highest point (尤指三角形的)頂點; 最高點.

apiece [ə'pi:s] *adv* for each one 每個, 各.

aplomb [ə'plɔm] *nu* self-confidence; belief in one's own abilities 自信; 自恃: *do something with aplomb* 信心十足地做某事.

apology [ə'pɔlədʒi] *nc* statement that one is sorry 道歉, 歉意. **apologize** *vi* say that one is sorry for doing wrong 道歉, 表示歉意: *He apologized for his mistake.* 他因做錯事而道歉. **apologetic** [əpɔlə'dʒetik] *adj* excusing oneself 道歉的.

apostle [ə'pɔsl] *nc* **1** one of the original twelve followers of Jesus Christ 耶穌基督的十二使徒之一. **2** any follower of a great man 偉人的跟隨者; 信徒.

apostrophe [ə'pɔstrəfi] *nc* the mark ', as in *John's book* or *I've read that book* 省字號, 撇號(即 "'") (如 John's book 或 I've read that book 裏的 "'").

appal [ə'pɔ:l] *vt* fill with a strong feeling of dislike and shock 使厭惡恐懼, 使震驚: *The number of people killed on the roads appals me.* 公路車禍死亡人數之多使我大爲震驚. *past* 過去式和過去分詞 **appalled. appalling** *adj.*

apparatus [æpə'reitəs] *nu* instruments, equipment, tools needed for a certain purpose (某種用途所需要的)儀器, 裝置, 工具.

apparel [ə'pærəl] *nu* clothing, attire 衣服, 服飾: *the new apparel for this summer* 今夏時裝.

apparent [ə'pærənt] *adj* **1** easily seen or understood 顯而易見的, 明白的: *It's quite apparent that you do not understand me.* 很顯然你不瞭解我. **2** appearing or seeming to be true (although it may not in fact be true) 表面上的, 外表的. **apparently** *adv* it seems that ... as far as one can judge etc. 似乎, 看來: *Apparently he is a good player, although I have never seen him play himself.* 看來他是個挺不錯的選手, 雖然我從未親眼看到他表演.

apparition [æpə'riʃən] *nc* appearance, or coming into sight of something (esp. a ghost or spirit) 出現, 顯現 (尤指鬼魂或幽靈).

appeal [ə'pi:l] *vi* **1** ask very earnestly or seriously to 呼籲; 要求: *The teacher appealed to John to work harder.* 老師希望約翰勤奮些. **2** ask for 請求: *The injured man appealed for help.* 那受傷的人請求幫助. *The prisoner appealed for one more chance.* 那囚犯請求再給他一次機會. **3** interest 引起興趣: *This book does not appeal to children* i.e. is not interesting to them. 這本書不投合孩子們的興趣. **4** ask somebody in a position of authority to change a decision made by somebody in a lower position 上訴: *Thousands of people appealed to the queen to pardon the condemned man.* 數千人上訴女王, 請求寬恕那個被判罪的人. Also 亦作 *nc / u*: *make an appeal to somebody* 向某人提出呼籲; *have no appeal for somebody* 對某人沒有吸引力; *make an appeal to a higher court* 向上級法院上訴.

appealing *adj* pleasing or attractive in a touching way 吸引人的, 令人喜愛的.

appear [ə'piə*] *vi* **1** come into sight; be seen 出現; 被看到: *A face suddenly appeared at the window.* 窗口突然出現一個面孔. **2** seem, look 似乎, 看起來: *He appeared to be happy* (but he may have been unhappy). 他看起來高興 (但有可能不高興). *It appears that I am wrong* i.e. it seems, I am beginning to think that I am wrong. 看來我是錯了. 即: 我開始覺得我錯了. **3** (with reference to an actor, singer, speaker etc.) perform or be seen by an audience (指演員, 歌手, 演講人等) 登台, 出場. **appearance** *nc* **1** coming into sight, being seen 出現: (*opp* 反義詞 **disappearance**). **2** what can be seen of somebody / something 外貌, 外觀. *He has a friendly appearance* i.e. he looks friendly (but in fact he may not be). 他表面看起來友好(其實未必). **3** (with reference to an actor, singer etc.) act of coming before an audience (指演員, 歌手等) 登台, 出場. **make an appearance** 登台; be seen 出現, 露面.

appease [ə'pi:z] *vt* make quiet, calm, friendly etc by giving what is wanted (給與所要的東西而) 使平靜, 使友好, 姑息: *appease somebody* i.e. make somebody friendly by giving him what he wants 姑息某人. 即: 通過給某人所想要的東西而使之友好.

appendicitis [əpendi'saitis] *nu* disease in which the appendix becomes very painful 闌尾炎, 盲腸炎. **appendix** [ə'pendiks] *nc* **1** part of the inside of the body below the stomach 闌尾, 盲腸. **2** extra information found at the end of a book 附錄. *pl* 複數 **appendixes** or **appendices** [ə'pendisi:z].

appetite ['æpitait] *nc / u* strong wish

(esp. for food) 食慾, 胃口. **appetizing** *adj* making one want to eat 促進食慾的, 開胃的: *Some very appetizing smells were coming from the kitchen.* 從廚房飄來一些令人饞涎欲滴的香味. (*opp* 反義詞 **unappetizing**). **lose one's appetite** stop wanting to eat (e.g. when one is ill) 食慾不振(例如生病時).

applaud [ə'plɔːd] *vt / i* show that one likes something / somebody (usu. by clapping the hands) 鼓掌歡迎. *applaud an actor* 向一演員鼓掌歡迎.

applause [ə'plɔːz] *nu* clapping of one's hands to show that one likes something / somebody 鼓掌歡迎.

apple ['æpl] *nc* type of round fruit with firm flesh which grows in Europe, North America, Australia etc. 蘋果. **Adam's apple** part of front of throat, a hard lump more prominent in men than women 喉結, 喉核.

appliance [ə'plaɪəns] *nc* instrument or tool 器具, 用具; 器械: *appliance for cutting holes in metal* 鑽金屬的器械.

applicable [ə'plikəbl] *adj* (esp. with reference to rules or laws) suitable to be used (尤指規則或法律)適用的: *This rule is not applicable to government employees* i.e. government employees do not have to follow this rule. 此項規定不適用於政府僱員. 即: 政府僱員不必遵照此規定. (*opp* 反義詞 **inapplicable**).

applicant ['æplikənt] *nc* person who asks for something (esp. for a post or job) 申請人(尤指求職者).

application [æpli'keiʃən] **1** *nc* asking for something 申請(書): *We have received twenty applications for this post.* 我們已經收到二十份要求這個職位的申請書. **2** *nc* putting something into use, way of using 使用, 應用; 用

法: *I don't understand the application of this word* i.e. how the word is to be used; 我不知道這個詞的用法; *application of scientific knowledge to the development of agriculture* 科學知識在農業發展中的應用. **3** *nu* act of putting something on something 施用; 敷: *application of ointment to a wound* 給傷口敷藥膏; *application of the brake* 煞車的使用. **4** *nu* hard work 勤奮, 用功: *By application to his studies he succeeded in gaining a better job.* 通過刻苦學習, 他獲得一個較好的工作.

apply [ə'plai] *vt / i* **1** ask for 申請, 請求: *Nobody applied for the reward.* 沒有人申請這筆賞金. **2** put something on 施加; 敷; 貼. *apply an ointment* 敷藥膏. **3** put something into use 使用, 應用: *He applied the brake.* 他使用煞車. *We must apply our scientific knowledge to solving the problem of mankind.* 我們必須把我們的科學知識應用於解決人類的問題. **4** be suitable to be used or considered 適用: *This rule does not apply in Scotland.* i.e. this rule is not followed in Scotland. 這項規定在蘇格蘭不適用. *What I have just said does not apply to you* i.e. I was not referring to you; I did not mean you. 我剛才說的話不是指你. **applied** *adj* put to use 應用的: *applied mathematics* 應用數學; *applied science* 應用科學. (*opp* 反義語 **pure mathematics / science** etc.). **apply oneself** work very hard 勤奮, 用功: *John applied himself to his studies.* 約翰專心致志地學習.

appoint [ə'pɔint] *vt* **1** give somebody a job or position 任命; 指派: *They appointed Mr Jones headmaster.* 他們任命瓊斯先生爲校長. **2** decide on 確定; 約定: *We must appoint a date for* *our next meeting.* 我們必須確定下次會議的日期. **appointment** *nc* **1** job or position 工作, 職務. **2** arrangement or agreement to meet somebody 約會, 約定: *John has an appointment with his housemaster today.* 約翰今天和他的舍監有個約會.

appreciable [əˈpriːʃəbl] *adj* enough to be seen, felt, noticed (often in **to make an appreciable difference** i.e. to be different enough to be seen or felt or noticed etc) 可看到的, 可覺察出的 (常用於 to make an appreciable difference, 即: 有明顯的差別).

appreciate [əˈpriːʃieit] **1** *vt* be thankful for something 感激, 感謝: *We appreciate everything that you have done for us.* 我們感謝你為我們所做的一切. **2** *vt* understand and like something (e.g. poetry, music, art) 欣賞, 鑑賞 (詩, 音樂, 藝術等): *He appreciates good music.* 他喜歡欣賞優美的音樂. **3** *vi* become more valuable 漲價, 增值: *The value of this land has appreciated greatly recently.* 這塊地的價值近日大漲. **appreciation** [əˌpriːʃiˈeiʃən] *nu* **appreciative** [əˈpriːʃiətiv] *adj* **1** showing thanks 感激的. **2** showing understanding and liking 欣賞的, 鑑賞的. (*opp* 反義詞 **unappreciative**).

apprehend [ˌæpriˈhend] *vt* arrest, take and hold (a criminal) 逮捕, 拘捕 (罪犯): *The police apprehended three men yesterday.* 警方昨天逮捕了三個男人. **apprehension** *nu* fear or worry about what will happen 害怕, 擔憂. **apprehensive** *adj* frightened; full of fear; worried about what will happen 恐懼的; 害怕的; 憂慮的: *That lady is very apprehensive about being attacked by thieves.* 那位女士很擔心被盜賊襲擊.

apprentice [əˈprentis] *nc* person (usu.

young) who works at some skilled trade or job for a number of years and receives very little money. (The apprentice is taught how to do the job properly during this time) 學徒. Also 亦作 *adj*. **apprenticeship** *nc* time during which somebody is an apprentice 學徒年限, 學徒期.

approach¹ [əˈprəutʃ] *vt / i* **1** move near (向…) 靠近; 接近. **2** ask somebody for something or offer something to somebody 與 (某人) 交涉: *He approached the headmaster with a request for some advice.* 他去找校長徵求意見.

approach² [əˈprəutʃ] *nc / u* **1** coming near 靠近; 接近. **2** asking for something or suggesting something 交涉. **3** way of beginning to learn or do something 步驟; 方法: *There is no very easy approach to mathematics.* 學數學決沒有捷徑. **approachable** *adj* able to be approached 可以接近的; 可以接近的: *The headmaster is approachable* i.e. he likes people to ask him for things, or to make suggestions to him. 校長很平易近人. (*opp* 反義詞 **unapproachable**).

appropriate¹ [əˈprəupriət] *adj* proper; suitable; correct for a particular purpose 適當的; 合適的; 正確的: *What kind of badge would be appropriate for our new school?* 我們的新學校用甚麼樣的校徽合適呢? (*opp* 反義詞 **inappropriate**). **appropriately** *adv*.

appropriate² [əˈprəuprieit] *vt* **1** keep for a certain purpose 撥出; 留作…: *We have appropriated a small amount of money for office supplies.* 我們留了少量錢作辦公費. **2** take something belonging to somebody else; steal 挪用; 盜用.

approve [əˈpruːv] *vt / i* think or say that

one is satisfied or pleased with something 贊成; 滿意: *I must say I approve of that boy's fondness for hard work.* 我得說我對這男孩的勤勉表示滿意. (*opp* 反義詞 **disapprove**). **approval** *nu* **1** feeling or showing satisfaction with something 贊成; 滿意. (*opp* 反義詞 **disapproval**). **2.** permission for a plan etc. 批准; 同意.

approximate¹ [əˈprɒksimət] *adj* not far from correct or exact; based on a guess or memory or without the need to be exactly right 大約的; 近似的. **approximately** *adv* roughly 大約地: *There were approximately 50 people there.* 那裏大約有五十個人.

approximate² [əˈprɒksimeit] *vt / i* come or be close to the correct answer, amount etc. (使) 接近; 近似; 近於. **approximation** [əprɒksiˈmeiʃən] *nc* something close to correct 大約估計; 近似.

apricot [ˈeiprikɒt] *nc* small, sweet, yellow fruit with a stone in the middle, growing in cool regions 杏.

April [ˈeiprl] *n* fourth month of the year 四月.

apron [ˈeiprn] *nc* piece of cloth or other material worn over the front of the body to keep one's clothes clean while working 圍裙.

apt [æpt] *adj* **1** likely; inclined 容易…的; 有…傾向的: *John is apt to be careless* i.e. he is often careless. 約翰經常粗心大意. **2** suitable; fitting 恰當的; 適宜的: *an apt remark* i.e. a remark which meant a lot at the time it was made 恰切的評語. **aptitude** [ˈæptitjuːd] *nu* ability to learn easily and quickly 才能; 天份: *John has an aptitude for mathematics* i.e. he learns mathematics with very little effort. 約翰有數學才能. 即: 他學數學毫不費勁.

aqualung [ˈækwəlʌŋ] *nc* apparatus which enables a swimmer to breathe under water (潛水者用的) 水中呼吸器.

aquarium [əˈkwɛəriəm] *nc* **1** glass tank or bowl in which fish and other sea creatures are kept 水族箱; 養魚缸. **2** building in a zoo etc in which fish can be seen 水族館. *pl* 複數 **aquariums** or **aquaria** [əˈkwɛəriə].

aquatic [əˈkwætik] *adj* living in or near, taking place in, water 水生的; 水邊的; 水中的: *Seals are aquatic animals.* 海豹是水生動物.

aqueduct [ˈækwidʌkt] *nc* canal or pipe for carrying water (esp. one built of stone etc carrying water on arches over a valley) 渠道, 導水管 (尤指由拱支撐, 引水越谷的石頭等渡槽).

arable [ˈærəbl] *adj* used for growing crops on 可耕的; 適於耕作的: *arable land* 可耕地; *arable farming* i.e. growing crops, rather than breeding animals 農耕業, 即: 種農作物而不飼養牲畜.

arbitrate [ˈɑːbitreit] *vt / i* act as judge; decide what is right when people are quarrelling or disagreeing (usu. at the request of the people quarrelling) 仲裁; 公斷. **arbitrator** *nc* person who arbitrates 仲裁人; 公斷人. **arbitration** [ɑːbiˈtreiʃən] *nu: The dispute between the workers and the employers went to arbitration* i.e. someone else decided between them. 勞資雙方的爭端交付仲裁. 即: 由其他人裁決. **arbiter** [ˈɑːbitə*] *nc* person given the power to judge between people who are quarrelling or disagreeing 仲裁人, 裁決者. **arbitrary** [ˈɑːbitrəri] *adj* based on somebody's wishes, feelings or opinions and not on what is just or lawful 任意的; 專橫的: *This is just an* *arbitrary decision.* 這純粹是一項隨心所欲的決定.

arc [ɑːk] *nc* part of a circle 弧.

arcade [ɑːˈkeid] *nc* passage or street covered by a roof (usu. with shops in the passage etc.) 店廊.

arch¹ [ɑːtʃ] *nc* **1** part of a building or of a bridge, with curved shape 拱; 拱門; 拱洞. **2** curved part underneath the foot 足穹.

arch² [ɑːtʃ] *vt / i* curve or bend into the shape of an arch (使)彎作拱形: *Cats arch their backs when they are angry.* 貓發怒時便拱起背. **'archway** entrance, opening or path under an arch 拱道; 拱洞.

arch-² [ɑːtʃ] *prefix* chief, first, most important (e.g. **archbishop**) 首席的, 首位的, 最重要的(如: archbishop).

archaeology, archeology [ɑːkiˈɔlədʒi] *nu* study of ancient buildings, materials, objects etc. 考古學. **archaeologist** *nc* person who studies archaeology 考古學家.

archaic [ɑːˈkeiik] *adj* very old and no longer in use 陳舊的; 古舊不用的.

archbishop [ˈɑːtʃˈbiʃəp] *nc* chief bishop 大主教.

archeology [ɑːkiˈɔlədʒi] *nu* see 見 **archaeology.**

archer [ˈɑːtʃə*] *nc* person who shoots with a bow and arrow 弓箭手. **archery** *nu* use of bows and arrows (esp. for sport or for war) 射箭, 箭術 (尤指用於體育運動或戰爭).

archipelago [ɑːkiˈpeligou] *nc* **1** group of islands 羣島. **2** sea with many islands in it 多島嶼的海. *pl* 複數 **archipelagoes.**

architect [ˈɑːkitekt] *nc* person whose work is to make the plans for buildings, bridges etc. 建築師; 設計師. **architectural** [ɑːkiˈtektʃərəl] *adj* with

reference to architecture 建築學的; 建築上的. **architecture** *nu* **1** science and art of making plans for buildings 建築學. **2** buildings of a particular type 某一式樣(或風格)的建築: *Greek architecture* i.e. the buildings of the ancient Greeks 古希臘式建築.

archives [ˈɑːkaivz] *npl* **1** place in which government documents and other official or historical papers are kept 檔案館; 檔案室. **2** documents kept in such a place 檔案.

archway [ˈɑːtʃwei] *nc* passage or entrance under an arch 拱道; 拱門.

Arctic [ˈɑːktik] *adj* **1** of or near the North Pole 北極的; 北極區的. **2** very cold 極冷的. Also 亦作 *n.*

ardent [ˈɑːdnt] *adj* full of strong feelings (usu. of love, liking, support etc.) 熱情的; 熱烈的: *He was an ardent supporter of the school football team.* 他是校足球隊的熱情支持者.

arduous [ˈɑːdjuəs] *adj* difficult and needing a lot of effort 艱苦的; 費勁的: *It must have been a very arduous task to build the pyramids.* 建築那些金字塔一定是非常艱難的工作.

area [ˈɛəriə] *nc* **1** amount of surface, measurement of the surface of something (e.g. if a field is 30 metres long and 20 metres wide it has an area of $30 \times 20 = 600$ square metres) 面積(如一田地長 30 米, 寬 20 米, 其面積為: $30 \times 20 = 600$ 平方米). **2** part of a country 地區; 地帶. **3** part of anything 領域; 方面: *area of knowledge* 知識範圍.

arena [əˈriːnə] *nc* **1** circular or oval place, surrounded by seats, for athletic competitions (圓形或橢圓形的)體育場: *sports arena* 運動場. **2** any place where people fight or compete against each other (打鬥或競賽的)競

技場.

argue ['ɑ:gju:] *vt / i* **1** talk with somebody, giving reasons for some plan or opinion, while the other person gives reasons against 辯論；爭論：*I argued with Peter all day about politics.* 我整天和彼得辯論政治問題. **2** give one's opinion about something (when somebody else disagrees) 論證：*I argued that the earth must be round since all the other planets are.* 我論證說地球應該是圓的，因爲所有其他行星都是圓的. **argument** ['ɑ:gjumənt] *nc / u* **1** discussion or conversation between people who disagree about some idea or opinion 辯論；爭論. **2** reason or opinion put forward to make somebody think in a certain way 論點；論據. **argumentative** [ɑ:gju'mentətiv] *adj* fond of arguing; unwilling to agree with other people 好爭辯的.

aria ['ɑ:riə] *nc* song for one singer in an opera (歌劇的)唱段.

arid ['ærid] *adj* dry; lacking water 乾旱的；缺水的：*The soil was very arid.* 這土地非常乾旱. **aridity** [ə'riditi] *nu.*

arise [ə'raiz] *vi* come up; appear; start; be a result of 起來；出現；發生；起因於：*This discussion arises out of what we were saying last week.* 這場爭論是因我們上星期說的話引起的. *past* 過去式 **arose** [ə'rouz]. *past part* 過去分詞 **arisen** [ə'rizn].

aristocracy [æris'tɔkrəsi] *nu* small groups of people in some countries, who are considered to be more important in society than all the rest of the people (usu. owning land and having special titles such as *Duke, Earl, Lord* etc and often a lot of money) 貴族(通常擁有土地，有特別銜頭，如公爵、伯爵、勳爵等；並常擁有大量

錢財). **aristocrat** ['æristəkræt, (*US* 美) ə'ristəkræt] *nc* member of an aristocracy 貴族的一員. **aristocratic** [æristə'krætik] *adj* of or like an aristocrat; proud and noble in appearance or behaviour 貴族的；貴族氣派的；高貴的.

arithmetic [ə'riθmətik] *nu* science of numbers i.e. addition, subtraction, multiplication and division 算術.

ark [ɑ:k] *nc* (in the Bible) **Noah's Ark** ship in which Noah and his family were saved from the great flood. (《聖經》)中挪亞及其家人在大洪水中獲救的)挪亞方舟.

arm[1] [ɑ:m] *nc* **1** part of the body extending from the shoulder 臂. **2** sleeve of a coat, dress etc. 衣袖. **3** (in *pl*) weapons, guns, swords etc. (用於複數)武器. **4** (in *pl*) (用於複數) see 見 **coat**. **5** division of military service 兵種；軍種. **'armful** *nc* as much as can be held in one arm or both arms (單臂或雙臂的)一抱. **'armchair** chair with armrests 扶手椅. **'armpit** hollow place under the top of the arm below the shoulder 腋窩.

arm[2] [ɑ:m] *vt / i* **1** get or supply weapons for fighting; prepare for war 武裝；武裝起來；備戰. (*opp* 反義詞 **disarm**). **2** supply with things which will be useful 供給，備有，裝備：*John had armed himself with an excuse before he went to see the headmaster.* 約翰去見校長前先替自己找了一個藉口.

armament ['ɑ:məmənt] *nc* **1** (often *pl*) all the military forces and equipment of a nation (常用複數)兵力，武裝力量. **2** (often *pl*) weapons and armour for defence on a warship, aircraft, etc. (常用複數)(戰艦、飛機等的)武器，軍備：*the armaments industry* 軍事工

業.

armistice ['ɑːmistis] *nc* agreement to stop fighting (usu. to discuss peace) 停戰; 休戰.

armour ['ɑːmə*] (*US* 美 **armor***) *nu* **1** metal covering for the body, formerly worn by men in battle 甲胄; 盔甲. **2** steel covering of a tank or ship (坦克或戰艦的) 裝甲. **armoured car** car which is covered by steel plates to protect people inside from bullets 裝甲車.

army ['ɑːmi] *nc* **1** soldiers or fighting men of a country 軍隊. **2** any large organized body of people 大羣, 團體: *He had an army of assistants* i.e. very many assistants. 他有一大羣助手.

aroma [ə'roumə] *nc* pleasant smell (usu. of food or herbs) (食物的) 香味; (藥草的) 芳香. **aromatic** [ærə'mætik] *adj* sweet-smelling 有香味的; 芳香的.

arose [ə'rouz] past tense of **arise**. arise 的過去式.

around [ə'raund] *adv / prep* **1** on all sides (of) 在週圍, 四面; 向四週: *He looked around.* 他四週看看了. **2** in different parts of 各處; 在各處: *We are going for a walk around the town.* 我們要去城裏到處走走. **3** in a circle about 環繞: *They sailed around the world.* 他們乘船環球航行. **4** surrounding; surrounding and closely placed to 包圍; 圍着: *cut off an enemy town by placing troops around it* 陳兵圍困敵城, 切斷其與外界聯繫; *wear a scarf around one's shoulders* 肩上圍着圍巾. **5** approximately 大約: *He earns around £4,000 a year.* 他一年約挣四千英鎊.

arouse [ə'rauz] *vt* make somebody / something be active 叫醒; 喚起, 激起: *The sleepy children were aroused by their father.* 那些打瞌睡的孩子被父親叫醒. *Her anger was aroused by his rudeness.* 她的憤怒是被他的無禮激起的.

arrange [ə'reindʒ] *vt / i* **1** put in order; make tidy 排列; 整理: *The children had to arrange their books neatly on their desks.* 孩子們必須把他們桌上的書本擺整齊. (*opp* 反義詞 **disarrange**). **2** plan something; agree to do something 計劃, 安排; 約定: *We will have to arrange another meeting.* 我們將不得不再籌備一次會議. *I must arrange to meet Peter.* 我必須約定時間見彼得. *It was arranged that John should wait behind.* 按照安排, 約翰應在後面等着. **arrangement** *nc* **1** way in which things are arranged or put in order 整理; 排列. **2** agreement 約定. **3** plan or preparation 安排; 準備: *I hope there is no change in the arrangements.* 我希望計劃沒有改變.

array [ə'rei] *n sing* 單數 collection of things arranged in order (排列整齊的) 一批, 一列.

arrears [ə'riəz] *npl* **1** amounts of money which should have been paid, but were not (過期未付的) 欠款. **2** work which should have been done, but was not 耽擱的工作. **be in arrears** late in paying, doing work etc. 拖欠; (工作等) 落在後面, 未完成進度. *be in arrears with the rent* 拖欠租金.

arrest [ə'rest] *vt* **1** take to prison; bring before a judge; take to court etc. 逮捕; 拘捕; 拘留: *The man was arrested and fined ten pounds.* 那人被拘留並罰款十英鎊. **2** stop a process 阻止; 妨礙; 抑制: *arrest the growth of a tree / natural development* etc. 妨礙樹木生長 / 自然發展等. Also 亦作 *nc / u* act of taking to prison etc. 逮捕; 拘留. **under arrest** held by the police and charged 被逮捕; 被拘留.

arrive [ə'raiv] *vi* come to a place (esp. at the end of a journey); reach a time 到達; 來到; (時間)到來: *We arrived at our hotel at nine o'clock.* 我們九點鐘到達旅館. *The moment has arrived for us to begin.* 我們開始的時刻到了.
arrival *nc / u* **1** arriving 到達; 到來. **2** person arriving 到達的人; *The new arrival entered the room.* 新來的人進入房間. **arrive at a decision** decide what to do 作出決定. *Note* 說明: notice the different constructions used with *arrive* and *reach*. *Arrive* has *at* before its object, *reach* does not. *We arrived at the village* but *We reached the village.* 注意用 arrive 和 reach 的不同結構. arrive 的賓語前有 at, 而 reach 沒有. 例如 We arrived at the village, 但是 We reached the village.

arrogant ['ærəgənt] *adj* showing very great pride; acting as though one thought that other people were much less important than oneself 驕傲自大的; 傲慢的. **arrogance** *nu*.

arrow ['ærəu] *nc* **1** stick shot from a bow 箭. **2** a sign used to draw attention to something (e.g. in a map to show the direction of something etc.) 箭號(如地圖中用以指示方向者).

arsenal ['ɑːsənl] *nc* building where guns and ammunition are stored or made (esp. for the army etc.) 軍械庫; 兵工廠.

arsenic ['ɑːsnik] *nu* type of poison 砒霜.

arson ['ɑːsn] *nu* crime of burning property (esp. buildings) 縱火(罪).

art [ɑːt] *nc / u* **1** painting, drawing, sculpture and architecture 美術(指繪畫, 雕塑, 建築). **2** any form of activity in which something of beauty is made (e.g. painting, drawing, sculpture,

music, literature, dancing etc.) 藝術(如繪畫, 雕塑, 音樂, 文學, 舞蹈等). **3** activity which needs skill 技術; 技巧: *There's an art in driving this car* i.e. it is not easy to drive this car, one must have skill. 開這輛車是要有技巧的. 即: 這輛車不好開, 要有技術才行. **4** (*in pl*) subjects such as languages, history, literature etc. (用於複數) 文科. see 見 **artist. artful** *adj* cunning; clever and dishonest 狡猾的; 欺詐的. **fine arts** painting, drawing, sculpture, architecture etc. 美術(指繪畫, 雕塑, 建築等). **work of art** something beautiful (esp. a painting, statue etc.) made by a person who has special skill 藝術品(尤指繪畫, 雕像等).

artery ['ɑːtəri] *nc* blood vessel which carries blood from the heart to the rest of the body 動脈. see 見 **vein.**

arthritis [ɑː'θraitəs] *nu* disease which attacks the joints of the body 關節炎.

article ['ɑːtikl] *nc* **1** particular thing or object 物品; 物件: *There were various articles lying around the room.* 房間裏亂七八糟地放着各種各樣的東西. **2** complete piece of writing in a magazine or newspaper (報紙或雜誌上的)文章. **3** (grammar) the words *a, an* and *the* and words in other languages which are used in the same way (語法)冠詞(指 a, an 和 the). **definite article** (grammar) 定冠詞(指 the). **indefinite article** (grammar) a, an. (語法)不定冠詞(指 a 和 an).

articulate[1] [ɑː'tikjuleit] *vt / i* **1** speak clearly 清楚地說出. **2** connect by joining together 連接, (使)接合: *articulated lorry* i.e. vehicle in which the front and back parts are joined in a flexible way 拖拉貨車. 即: 前後部份用活節連接的車輛.

articulate² [ɑːˈtikjulət] *adj* 1 clear, well-arranged, easy to understand 清楚的; 有條理的; 明白的: *He gave a very articulate account of what had happened.* 他一清二楚地講述了發生的事. 2 (with reference to a person) able to speak well and clearly, able to explain one's ideas in speech (人) 口齒伶俐的; 言語能表達思想的. (*opp* 反義詞 **inarticulate**).

artifice [ˈɑːtifis] 1 *nc* clever trick 巧計. 2 *nu* cunning; skill which is a little dishonest 狡詐; 詭計.

artificial [ɑːtiˈfiʃl] *adj* 1 not real, natural, but appearing to be real 假的; 摹擬的: *artificial flowers* 假花. 2 made by man, not natural 人造的; 非天然的: *Electricity gives us artificial light.* 電給我們人造的光. **artificial respiration** process of helping a person who is nearly dead (often by drowning) to breathe more easily by pressing on his chest or by blowing air into his lungs 人工呼吸.

artillery [ɑːˈtiləri] *nu* 1 big guns on wheels 大砲. 2 part of an army which uses big guns 砲兵.

artisan [ˈɑːtizæn] *nc* man who has been trained to work with his hands (e.g. a carpenter, a mechanic) 工匠; 技工 (例如木工, 機工).

artist [ˈɑːtist] *nc* 1 person who paints or draws pictures 美術家; 畫家. 2 person whose work is one of the arts (e.g. a musician, an architect, a dancer, a poet) 藝術家. 3 person who does any skilled work extremely well 能手. *see* 見 **art artistic** [ɑːˈtistik] *adj* 1 done with great skill and a love of art 精巧的; 藝術的. (*opp* 反義詞 **inartistic**). 2 (with reference to a person) having a love and understanding of art (指人) 愛好藝術的. **artistry**

[ˈɑːtistri] *nu* artistic skill 藝術才能; 藝術技巧.

as [æz] *adv / conj* 1 since; because 由於; 因爲: *As he was drunk we would not let him into the house.* 因爲他喝醉了, 我們不讓他進屋. 2 while; when 當; 正值: *As he pulled the rope, you could see his muscles quivering.* 當他拉繩子時, 可以看到他的肌肉在抖動. 3 in the same way as 按照; 以同樣方式: *Do as I say.* 照我說的做. **as ... as** used to express a way in which two things or people are equal 和…一樣…: *You are as strong as I (am).* 你和我一樣強壯. **as good as** nearly; almost 接近; 幾乎: *It's as good as finished.* 快完成了. *He as good as told me that I was a fool* i.e. he didn't say this, but he showed that this was what he meant. (*informal*) 他實際上等於說我是傻瓜. 即: 他沒這麼說, 但他表示出他就是這個意思. (非正式). **as it is** in fact; really 實際上; 真地. **as it were** one might say; it might be correct to say 可以說; 可說是: *The English, the Scots and the Welsh are all, as it were, members of the same family.* 英吉利人、蘇格蘭人和威爾士人可以說都是同一個家族的成員. **as long as** if, on condition that 如果; 只要: *As long as you understand, we shall say no more about it* i.e. if you understand, we shall not discuss it any more. (*informal*—use **if, since** etc.) 只要你明白, 我們對這事就不多說了. (非正式—正式用 if, since 等). **as much** so 這樣; 那樣: *I thought as much* i.e. I thought so, and now I am sure (usu. with reference to something bad). 我猜想是這麼一回事. 即: 我過去這樣想, 現在我確信了 (通常指壞事. **as a rule** usually 通常. **(just) as soon** *I would just as soon not go* i.e. I don't mind whether I go or not (or, I prefer not to go). 我還不如不去. 即: 我去不去都不在乎(或: 我寧可不去). **as well** too; also 同樣; 也. **as yet** (usu. *negative*) up to this time (通常用於否定句)到目前爲止, 迄今. *Nothing unusual has happened as yet*. 到目前爲止一切正常.

asbestos [əsˈbestəs] *nu* type of material which does not burn. It is often made into a kind of cloth which can be used for clothing, curtains etc and also for insulating 石棉.

ascend [əˈsend] *vt / i* go up; climb up 上升, 攀登; 登上. **ascent** [əˈsent] *nc* **ascension** [əˈsenʃən] *nc* act of ascending (usu. **the Ascension,** with reference to Jesus or Mary ascending to heaven) 上升, 升高 (通常爲 the Ascension, 指耶穌或聖母瑪利亞升天).

ascertain [æsəˈtein] *vt* find out; discover; make sure 查明; 證實; 確定: *The detectives are trying to ascertain the truth / how it happened.* 偵探們正在調查事件的真相/是怎樣發生的.

ascetic [əˈsetik] *nc* person who does not allow himself any pleasures or comforts (usu. for religious reasons) 苦行者, 禁慾主義者(通常出於宗教原因).

ascribe [əˈskraib] *vt* say or think that somebody / something is the cause, origin, author etc of something 把…歸於: *He ascribed his success to many years of hard work* i.e. he said the reason he was successful was that he had worked hard for many years. 他把成功歸於多年的勤奮.

ash¹ [æʃ] *nc* type of tree 梣樹.

ash² [æʃ] *nc / u* dust which is left after something has been burned 灰; 灰燼. **'ashtray** small dish for putting cigarette ash in 烟灰缸.

ashamed [əˈʃeimd] *pred adj* feeling unhappy because one has done something wrong or foolish, or because one is less clever, rich, strong etc than other people 感到羞恥的; 感到慚愧的; 不好意思的: *He was ashamed of his failure.* 他因失敗而感到羞愧. *He was ashamed of having failed.* 他失敗了感到羞愧. *He was ashamed to tell anyone that he had failed.* 他不好意思對大家說他已失敗了.

ashore [əˈʃɔː] *adv* (usu. with reference to ships and sailors) on or to the shore (通常指船和水手)在岸上; 到岸上.

aside¹ [əˈsaid] *adv* on or to one side 在一邊; 向一邊.

aside² [əˈsaid] *nc* (esp. with reference to the theatre) words which are not addressed to everyone present, which are not supposed to be heard by everyone present (尤指戲劇中的)旁白.

ask [ɑːsk] *vt / i* say that one wants something or to know something 要求; 請求; 問, 詢問: *I don't understand, so I asked.* 我不明白, 所以我問. *I asked (him) his name.* 我問他叫甚麼名字. *I asked how to mend the radio.* 我問怎樣修理收音機. *I asked him to help me.* 我請求他幫助我. **ask(ing) for trouble** act(ing) in a dangerous or foolish way. *(informal)* 自找麻煩; 自討苦吃(非正式).

askance [əsˈkɑːns] *adv* in **look askance at somebody** i.e. look at somebody as though he had done wrong or could not be trusted; disapprove of or distrust somebody 用於 look askance at somebody, 即: 用懷疑的眼光看某人; 不贊同某人; 不信任某人.

asleep [əˈsliːp] *adv / pred adj* **1** sleeping 睡着的. **2** not being able to feel properly because the blood has not been flowing freely; numb 發麻的, 麻木的: *My arm is asleep, probably because I've been lying on it.* 我的胳臂發麻, 大概是一直被身子壓住的緣故.

asparagus [əsˈpærəgəs] *nu* long, narrow pointed shoots of a particular plant, used as a vegetable 蘆筍.

aspect [ˈæspekt] *nc* 1 appearance 模樣, 外表. 2 direction in which a building faces (建築物的) 方向, 方位: *His house has a southern aspect* i.e. it faces south. 他的房子朝南. 3 part of a problem, question, difficulty etc.; way in which a problem etc can be studied or discussed (問題、困難等的) 一部份; 方面: *I'm interested in all aspects of science;* 我對科學的各個方面都感興趣; *the most important aspect of the question* 問題的最重要方面.

asphalt [ˈæsfælt] *nu* black substance used in making roads 瀝青, 柏油. Also 亦作 *vt* cover with asphalt 用瀝青舖….

asphyxiate [əsˈfiksieit] *vt* make someone die from lack of oxygen 使窒息而死. **asphyxiation** [əsfiksiˈeiʃən] *nu*.

aspirate [ˈæspərit] *nc* sound like 'h' in *hate* 送氣音 (如 hate 的 h 音). Also 亦作 [ˈæspireit] *vt* make the sound 'h' (usu. at the beginning of a word) 把…發成送氣音, 把…發成 h 音 (通常在詞首).

aspire [əsˈpaiə*] *vi* in **aspire to** i.e. be eager to reach / win something 用於 aspire to, 即: 熱望…; 追求…. **aspiration** [æspiˈreiʃən] *nc / u* hope; ambition; wish etc. 希望; 抱負; 願望.

aspirin [ˈæsprin] 1 *nu* medicine which lessens pain 阿司匹林 (減痛藥). 2 *nc* tablet or pill containing aspirin 阿司匹林藥片 (或丸).

ass [æs] *nc* 1 animal, like a small horse, with long ears 驢. 2 foolish person. *(informal)* 蠢人, 傻子(非正式).

assassinate [əˈsæsineit] *vt* murder somebody by a sudden attack (usu. for a political reason) 暗殺, 行刺(通常出於政治原因). **assassination** [əsæsiˈneiʃən] *nc / u* **assassin** *nc* person who assassinates 暗殺者, 刺客.

assault [əˈsɔːlt] *vt* attack 攻擊; 襲擊. Also 亦作 *nc* an attack 攻擊; 襲擊: *There was an assault on the town before dawn.* 天亮前對該城進行了一次攻擊.

assemble [əˈsembl] 1 *vt / i* gather together, bring together; collect in one place 集合; 聚集; 集中: *A large crowd assembled.* 一大羣人聚集在一起. 2 *vt* make by putting pieces together 裝配: *In that factory they can assemble a vehicle in less than a day.* 在那個工廠裏, 他們用不到一天就能裝配一輛車. **assembly** [əˈsembli] 1 *nc* number of people gathered together for a special purpose 集會; 集合. 2 *nc* something, such as an engine or a car, which is made of a number of parts put together 裝配物 (如引擎、汽車). 3 *nu* putting together of the parts of something 裝配. **'assembly line** row of workers and machines in a factory. The product being manufactured by the factory passes along the assembly line and at each stage a new piece is added until the product is finished (工廠裏的) 裝配線.

assent [əˈsent] *vi* agree to; say yes to 同意; 贊成: *The committee assented to our proposals.* 委員會同意我們的計劃. Also 亦作 *nu* agreement to something; permission 同意; 許可.

assert [əˈsəːt] *vt* 1 say very firmly 聲稱;

斷言: *He asserted his innocence.* 他斷言自己無罪. **2** insist on and defend 維護; 堅持: *He asserted his right to a share in the money* i.e: he believed that he ought to have a share and he asked for it very firmly. 他堅持他有權分那筆錢. 即: 他認爲應該得到一份, 而且十分堅決要拿到錢. **assertion** *nc/u* firm statement 聲稱; 斷言: *make an assertion* 斷言.

assess [ə'ses] *vt* decide how great some payment should be, or how valuable or useful something is 估定(應支付的款額); 評估(某物的價值); 確定(某事物的作用): *His taxes were assessed at £200.* 他應納的稅款定爲二百英鎊. *They sent someone to assess the value of the house.* 他們派人對那幢房屋進行估價. *It is difficult to assess the importance of the decision.* 這項決定的重要性難以確定. **assessment** *nc/u* **assessor** *nc* person whose job is to make assessments (esp. for the purpose of taxation or insurance) 評估員, 估價員(尤指評估稅款或保險費).

asset ['æset] *nc* **1** something valuable or useful which gives one an advantage 寶貴的東西; 有用的東西. **2** (in *pl*) property which one owns (用於複數)資產; 財產.

assiduous [ə'sidjuəs] *adj* working steadily and paying great attention to details 勤奮的; 專心的, 認真的.

assign [ə'sain] *vt* **1** give as a share or duty 分配: *The teacher assigned the work to John.* 老師給約翰佈置作業. **2** tell somebody to do something as his duty 分派, 指派; 要某人做某事. *The teacher assigned three boys to clean the room.* 老師指派三個男生打掃房間. **assignment** *nc/u.*

assimilate [ə'simileit] *vt/i* take in and make a part of one's body or mind; take in and make like oneself 吸收; 消化; 使相似; 變得相似: *It is difficult to assimilate a lot of information in a short time.* 很難在短時間內吸收許多知識. **assimilation** [əsimi'leiʃən] *nu.*

assist [ə'sist] *vt/i* help 幫助; 支援. *Scientists have assisted us in the stamping out of this disease.* 科學家們幫助我們消滅了這種疾病. **assistance** *nu* **assistant** *nc* person who helps 助手; 助理.

assizes [ə'saiziz] *npl* law court held in each area or county of England (英國各地區或郡的)巡迴法庭.

associate[1] [ə'souʃieit] *vt* think of something in connection with something else 聯想: *Christmas is usually associated with parties and giving presents.* 聖誕節通常使人聯想起聚會和贈送禮物.

associate[2] [ə'souʃiət] *nc* friend or partner in some activity, often in business 夥伴; 同事. **association** [əsousi'eiʃən] *nc* **1** partnership or friendship with somebody 夥伴關係; 交往. **2** connection between two or more ideas 聯想: *There is an association between Christmas and parties.* 聖誕節是和社交聚會聯繫在一起的. **3** group of people who have joined together because of some interest or purpose which they share 協會; 社團: *the Automobile Association* 汽車協會. **as'sociation 'football** see 見 **foot.**

assortment [ə'sɔ:tmənt] *nc* a number of things not all of the same kind 各種各樣的東西. **assorted** [ə'sɔ:tid] *adj* of various kinds; mixed 各種各樣的; 混合的: *assorted chocolates* i.e. chocolates of different kinds 什錦巧克力.

assume [ə'sju:m] *vt* **1** suppose; take to be true 假定; 假設: *Let us assume that you are right* i.e. Let us say that you are right (although we don't know whether you are or not). 讓我們假定你是對的. 即: 姑且說你是對的(雖然我們不知道你是否對). **2** take; begin to use 承擔; 接受; 開始使用: *The prince assumed power when he was only fifteen.* 王子才十五歲時就掌權了. *He assumed authority over the other workers.* 他對其他工人行使職權. **assumption** [əˈsʌmpʃən] *nc* **assumed** *adj* false 假的: *He lived in France under an assumed name.* 他用假名住在法國.

assure [əˈʃuə*] *vt* **1** tell somebody something very firmly so that he feels safe or certain 向⋯保證; 確告: *I assure you that I will do everything I can to help you.* 我向你保證, 我將盡我所能幫助你. *I assured him of my support for his application.* 我肯定地對他說, 我將對他的申請給予支持. **2** make certain 使肯定; 使有保證: *The only way to assure success is to work hard.* 確保成功的唯一途徑就是勤奮. **3** insure one's life 對⋯進行人壽保險. see 見 **insure. assurance 1** *nc* firm statement which is meant to make somebody feel safe or certain 保證; 斷言: *The shopkeeper gave me many assurances about the radio.* 店主再三向我保證說那部收音機的質量好. **2** *nu* feeling of strong belief 堅信, 確信. **3** *nu* feeling that one is right clever, successful etc. 自信: *He answered all my questions with complete assurance.* 他充滿自信地回答了我所有的問題. **4** *nu* insurance of one's life 人壽保險. see 見 **insure.**

asterisk [ˈæstərisk] *nc* the mark * (used to draw attention to a word in a piece of writing, and often to indicate that there is a note on the word) 星號(即 *, 用以引起對文章裏某個詞的注意, 常

表示該詞有註解).

astern [əˈstən] *adv* at or towards the back or stern of a ship 在船尾; 向船尾.

asthma [ˈæsmə] *nu* disease which causes difficulty in breathing 哮喘.

astonish [əˈstɔniʃ] *vt* fill with sudden wonder 使驚異; 使吃驚. **astonishing** *adj* **astonishment** *nu.*

astound [əˈstaund] *vt* fill with very great surprise (usu. stronger than astonish) 使大爲吃驚; 使震驚(通常比 astonish 強烈). **astounding** *adj.*

astray [əˈstrei] *adv / pred adj* away from the correct path or away from the proper course of action 迷路地(的); 脫離正軌地(的).

astride [əˈstraid] *adv / prep* with one leg on each side 跨着; 騎着: *sit astride a fence* 跨坐在柵欄上.

astrology [əˈstrɔlədʒi] *nu* science which claims to be able to say how the stars influence the way people behave and the things which happen on earth 占星學, 占星術. **astrologer** *nc.* *Note* 說明: be careful to distinguish *astrology from astronomy* 注意區別 astrology 和 astronomy.

astronaut [ˈæstrənɔ:t] *nc* person who travels in a spaceship 宇航員, 太空人.

astronomy [əˈstrɔnəmi] *nu* study of the sun, planets, stars and other objects in space 天文學. **astronomer** *nc* **astronomical** [æstrəˈnɔmikl] *adj* **1** concerned with astronomy 天文學(上)的. **2** so large that we cannot imagine it (like the distance and sizes studied by astronomers) 大得無法想像的, 極大的(像天文學家所研究的距離和體積): *an astronomical distance* 極遠的距離; *an astronomical amount* 巨大的數量. *Note* 說明: be careful to distinguish astronomy from *astrology.*

see above 注意區別 astronomy 和 astrology. 見上面.

astute [əs'tju:t] *adj* quick in deciding what is best for oneself; clever 機敏的, 精明的.

asylum [ə'sailəm] *nc* **1** hospital for insane people. (rather *o.f.* - use **mental hospital**) 精神病院. (頗爲舊式—現在用 mental hospital) **2** any place of safety 避難所.

at [æt] *prep* **1** in; on; by a place in…內; on…上; in…旁; *at my house* 在我家裏; *at school* 在學校; *at the door* 在門口. **2** with reference to condition (指狀況) in…中: *at peace* 在和平狀態中; *at war* 在交戰中; *at rest* 在休息. **3** with reference to time (指時間) 在: *at six o'clock* 在六點鐘; *at Christmas time* 在聖誕節時 .**4** doing something 在(做某事): *at work* 正在工作; *at play* 在玩耍; *at his books* 在讀書. **5** towards 向: *look at somebody* 瞧着某人; *rush at somebody* 向某人衝去; *throw a stone at somebody* 向某人扔石頭. **6** with reference to price (指價格) 以: *He is selling them at four for £1.* 他以一英鎊四個把它們出售. **what is he etc at?** what is he etc doing? 他等在幹什麼? **at once** see 見 **once. at that 1** immediately after that 緊接着: 於是. **2** as well; also 也, 又. *Note* 說明: we use at with a word referring to a place, if we think of the place as being one point rather than a large area. Such a place is often a small place, which we can think of as being one point (e.g. *he lives at a village called XY*); but if we think of XY as being a large area, we could say *he lives in a village called XY*. We normally think of large placés as being areas rather than points, and so generally say *he lives in London; his*

house is in New York etc. But if we think of the larger place as a point, for instance a point in a journey, we could say *the plane didn't stop at New York.* We would not, however, use at with names of places bigger than a city. 如果我們把某地看作一點, 而不是一大地區, 我們就用 at 與表示地方的詞連用. 這樣的地方常常是小地方, 我們可以把它看作一點, (例如: he lives at a village called XY); 但如果把 XY 看作大地區, 就可以說 he lives in a village called XY. 我們一般把大地方看作是地區, 而不是點, 因此通常說 he lives in London; his house is in New York 等. 但如果我們把較大的地方看作點, 比如旅途中的一點, 那麼我們就可以說 the plane didn't stop at New York. 然而, 至 不能與比城市大的地名連用.

ate [et, eit] past tense of **eat. eat** 的過去式 . *Note* 說明: (*Brit*) the pronunciation [et] is usual and [eit] is often thought to be wrong. (*US*) the normal pronunciation is [eit] and [et] is usu. considered wrong. (英) 一般讀音爲 [et], 而 [eit] 通常被認爲是錯的. (美)正常讀音爲 [eit], 而 [et] 通常被認爲是錯的.

atheist ['eiθiist] *nc* person who believes that there is no God 無神論者; 不信神者 . see 見 **agnostic. atheism** ['eiθiizəm] *nu* belief that there is no God 無神論; 不信神.

athlete ['æθli:t] *nc* person who is good at playing games which need strength and speed (esp. running and jumping) 運動員(尤指田徑). **athletic** [æθ'letik] *adj* **athletics** *n sing* or *pl* 單數或複數 practising for or taking part in competitions in running and jumping etc. 田徑運動; 體育運動.

atlas ['ætləs] *nc* book of maps 地圖册.

atmosphere ['ætməsfiə*] *nc* **1** the air

surrounding the earth 大氣; 大氣層. **2** the air in any place 空氣. **3** the feelings and influence on the mind which one receives from a place or from particular conditions 氣氛, 環境: *He grew up in an atmosphere of love and trust* i.e. he grew up in conditions of love and trust. 他在充滿着愛和信任的環境中長大. *There was an atmosphere of excitement in the theatre* i.e. it was possible to notice that people in the theatre were excited. 戲院裏呈現一片令人激動的氣氛.

atoll [ˈætɔl] *nc* ring-shaped island made of coral 環狀珊瑚島; 環礁.

atom [ˈætəm] *nc* **1** smallest piece or part of any substance 原子. **2** very small piece or part 微粒; 極少量.

atomic [əˈtɔmik] *adj*. **atomizer** *nc* something used to change a liquid into a spray 噴霧器. **'atom / a'tomic 'bomb** bomb which causes a very powerful explosion by splitting up atoms 原子彈.

atrocious [əˈtrouʃəs] *adj* very bad 極劣的. **atrocity** [əˈtrɔsiti] *nc* very cruel and wicked act (usu. causing pain or death to other people) 殘暴的行爲(通常使他人痛苦或死亡).

attach [əˈtætʃ] *vt* **1** fasten; join: stick to 繫住; 連接; 貼上: *He attached a rope to his car.* 他在車上繫了一條繩子. *We attached a label to his suitcase.* 我們給他的手提箱貼上一個標簽. **2** consider something to have 認爲某事有: *We didn't attach much importance to what he was saying* i.e. we didn't think that what he was saying was important. 我們不大重視他說的話. 即: 我們認爲他說的話不重要. **attachment** *nc* **1** something attached (esp. something smaller attached to a larger and more important thing) 附着物; 附件

(尤指附在較大或較重要者上的): *A sewing machine has various attachments for doing certain special stitches.* 縫紉機有各種做特殊線活的附件. **2** affection 愛慕, 情感: *He has a strong attachment for his home.* 他對自己的家懷有強烈的感情. **attaché** [əˈtæʃei] *nc* person who does certain special jobs in an embassy (e.g. *a military attaché* is responsible for any work connected with the army etc.; a *press attaché* is responsible for any work connected with the newspapers etc.) 大使館專員 (例如: military attaché 武官; press attaché 新聞專員). **be attached to something / somebody** be very fond of something / somebody; like very much 非常喜歡某事 / 某人: *He is very attached to his sister.* 他很喜歡妹妹.

attack [əˈtæk] *vt / i* go towards a person to fight him; do something to fight and hurt a person 攻擊; 抨擊: *attack the enemy* 攻擊敵人. *The newspapers attacked the government* i.e. the newspapers wrote things in opposition to the government. 報紙紛紛抨擊政府. *The team attacked their opponents' goal* i.e. they kicked the ball towards the other end of the field and tried to score a goal. 該隊進攻對方球門. 即: 他們把球踢向球場的另一方盡頭企圖射門. Also 亦作 *nc*: *an attack of malaria* 瘧疾的一次發作. **attacker** *nc*.

attain [əˈtein] *vt* gain; get something by hard work 獲得; (通過努力工作而) 得到: *He attained his ambition.* 他實現了抱負. **attainable** *adj* able to be attained 可以達到的. (*opp* 反義詞 **unattainable**). **attainment** *nc* skill or ability which has been attained; something which one does very well 成就; 造詣.

attempt [ə'tempt] *vt* try 試, 企圖: *He attempted a very difficult piece of work.* 他試圖完成一件很艱難的工作. *He attempted to find the old woman.* 他試圖找到那個老婦人. Also 亦作 *nc His attempt to become the first man to land on Mars begins tomorrow* i.e. he will try to become the first man to land on Mars. 他想成爲第一個登上火星的人, 這一嘗試於明天開始. *Note* 說明: *attempt* (noun) often refers to doing something brave or difficult. attempt (名詞) 常指做需要勇氣或艱難的事.

attend [ə'tend] *vt / i* **1** go to (esp. go to regularly) 去, 參加 (尤指經常性地): *attend school / church / a meeting* 上學 / 去教堂做禮拜 / 出席會議. **2** deal with; do something to; give attention to; listen to properly 辦理; 照顧; 注意; 傾聽: *attend to one's work* 做自己的工作. *You should attend to what your father tells you.* 你應該認真聽你爸爸的話. *I'm very busy. I can't attend to you now.* 我很忙, 現在不能接待你. **attendance** *nc / u* being present at 到場; 出席: *Attendance at school is compulsory* i.e. it is compulsory to go to school. 上學是強制性的. *There was a large attendance at the meeting* i.e. many people were there. 出席會議的人很多. **attendant**[1] *nc* person who attends upon somebody; servant; assistant or companion 侍者; 服務員; 助手; 陪從. **attendant**[2] *adj* accompanying; going with 陪同的; 伴隨的: *the weakness which is attendant upon disease* i.e. the weakness which goes with or follows disease 患病期間或病後的體弱. **attention** [ə'tenʃən] **1** *nu* act of attending; noticing something; listening carefully etc. 照顧, 關懷; 注意; 傾聽: *give one's attention to some-*

thing i.e. take careful notice of it. 注意某事. **2** *nc* (often *pl*) act of kindness or politeness (常用複數) 慇懃; 禮貌. **3** *nu* position in which somebody stands with his feet together, his arms by his sides; without moving (e.g. a soldier has to do this). 'Attention' is an order shouted by an officer etc. to make somebody stand in this position 立正 (的姿勢); "立正" (口令). **attentive** [ə'tentiv] *adj* giving attention; looking or listening carefully 慇懃的; 關心的; 注意的. (*opp* 反義詞 **inattentive**) **attentively** *adv* **attract some-one's attention** make somebody notice 引起某人注意. **pay attention to someone / something** listen carefully; notice; look at carefully etc. 傾聽某人 / 某事; 注意某人 / 某事.

attenuate [ə'tenjueit] *vt / i* become or make thin or weak (使) 變薄; (使) 變弱.

attic ['ætik] *nc* small room under the roof of a house 屋頂室, 頂樓.

attitude ['ætitjuːd] *nc* way of thinking or feeling 態度: *not a very friendly attitude* 不很友好的態度. *My attitude would be to ignore him* i.e. I would think it best to ignore him. 我的看法是不理睬他. 即: 我認爲最好是不理睬他.

attorney [ə'təːni] *nc* lawyer (*US* commoner than *Brit*) 律師 (在美國比在英國常用).

attract [ə'trækt] *vt* **1** make people notice 引 (人) 注目, 招引: *The young man was very attracted by the girl* i.e. he noticed her and liked her. 這年青人被那姑娘迷住了. *Bright colours often attract young children.* 鮮艷的色彩往往會吸引幼兒. **2** draw towards 吸引: *A magnet attracts steel* i.e. pieces of steel move towards the

magnet. 磁石會吸引鋼鐵. **attractive**
adj pleasant and interesting; good-
looking; causing attraction 令人愉快
的; 媚人的; 吸引人的. (*opp* 反義詞
unattractive). **attraction 1** *nu* act of
making people notice; act of making
something move towards one 招引; 吸
引. **2** *nc* something which attracts
(usu. something pleasant) 吸引人的東
西 (通常指令人愉快的東西): *There
are many attractions in a big city* i.e.
there are many pleasant or interesting
things. 大城市有許多誘人的東西. *What
is the attraction in collecting stamps?*
i.e. why do people like collecting
stamps? 集郵有甚麼引人之處?

attribute¹ ['ætribju:t] *nc* feeling, condition, object, sign, which is found in
somebody / something 品質; 性質; 屬
性; 特徵: *Patience is an attribute of a
good mother* i.e. a good mother is
naturally patient. 耐心是賢良母親的天
性. *Hard work is an attribute of a
successful man* i.e. a man who is successful always works hard. 成功的人
的特點是勤奮.

attribute² [ə'tribju:t] *vt* **1** say that something is the cause of something else
把…歸因於: *He attributed his success
to good luck* i.e. he said that he was
successful because of good luck. 他把
他的成功歸因於運氣好. **2** say or think
that somebody has a certain quality
認爲… 有 (某種品質): *He attributed
great cunning to his enemies* i.e. he
said or thought that his enemies were
very cunning. 他認爲他的敵人十分狡
猾. **attributive adjective** (grammar)
in English, an attributive adjective
usu. goes in front of a noun (e.g. in
'old man', 'old' is an attributive adjective) (語法) 定語形容詞 (例如 old man
中的 old 就是定語形容詞).

attrition [ə'triʃən] *nu* action which gradually makes something smaller,
weaker, less useful etc. 磨損; 消耗.

auburn ['ɔ:bən] *adj* (usu. with reference
to hair) reddish brown (通常指毛髮)
紅褐色的.

auction ['ɔ:kʃən] *nc* public sale in
which goods are sold to the person
offering the highest price 拍賣: *He
sold it by auction.* 他把它拍賣掉. Also
亦作 *vt* sell goods in this way 拍賣:
He auctioned all his old furniture. 他
把他的舊傢俱統統拍賣掉. **auctioneer**
[ɔ:kʃə'niə*] *nc* person who is in
charge of an auction 拍賣人.

audacious [ɔ:'deiʃəs] *adj* **1** brave and
ready to take a risk 大膽的. **2** impudent and without any fear of authority
放肆的; 魯莽的. **audacity** [ɔ:'dæsiti]
nc/u.

audible ['ɔ:dibl] *adj* loud enough for
somebody to hear 聽得見的. (*opp* 反
義詞 **inaudible**).

audience ['ɔ:diəns] *nc* **1** the people
watching a film or play, listening to a
concert, listening to the radio, watching television etc. 觀衆; 聽衆. **2** formal meeting with a ruler of a country
etc. 會晤; 接見: *an audience with the
Pope* 教皇的接見.

audit ['ɔ:dit] *vt* check in detail the record of money received and spent to
see that the record is correct 查 (賬).
Also 亦作 *nc* examination of this kind
審計, 查賬.

audition [ɔ:'diʃən] *nc* test given to an
actor etc before he is given a part in
a play (演員等被給予劇中角色前的) 試
演; 試聽.

auditorium [ɔ:di'tɔ:riəm] *nc* part of a
theatre, concert hall etc in which the
audience sits (戲院、音樂廳等的) 觀衆
席; 聽衆席.

augment [ɔːˈgʹment] *vt / i* become or make larger by adding something 的; *His father was a very austere man* (使)增大, (使)擴大. who punished his children whenever

augur [ˈɔːgə*] *vi* be a sign of what is going to happen in the future 成為預 兆.

August [ˈɔːgəst] *n* eighth month of the year 八月.

aunt [ɑːnt] *nc* the sister of one's father or mother, or the wife of one's father's brother 姑母; 姨母; 伯母; 舅母; 嬸母. **aunty** *nc* an informal form of **aunt.** aunt 的非正式形式.

au pair [ˈouˈpɛə*] *nc* girl from another country who lives for a time with a family and does a little work for them, in order to improve her knowledge of the language or to have a holiday 為學習語言或度假而與某家庭暫住並爲其幹些活的外國女孩. Also 亦作 *adj: She is an au-pair girl.* 她是個以工換食宿的外國女孩.

aura [ˈɔːrə] *nc* a special quality or feeling close to a person or thing (人或物的)氣味; 氣氛.

auspices [ˈɔːspisiz] *npl* usu. in **under the auspices of something** i.e. with the help and encouragement of something 通常用於 under the auspices of something, 即: 在…的贊助下, 由…主辦(或主持): *The meeting was held under the auspices of the Ministry of Education.* 這個會議是由教育部主辦召開的.

auspicious [ɔːsˈpiʃəs] *adj* giving promise that something will succeed or be good in the future 預兆成功的; 有吉兆的. (*opp* 反義詞 **inauspicious).auspiciously** *adv.*

austere [ɔsˈtiə*] *adj* **1** strict and harsh; not offering much friendship and insisting that people should behave as well as possible 嚴格的; 嚴厲的; 嚴肅

的; *His father was a very austere man who punished his children whenever they did the smallest thing wrong.* 他父親是個非常嚴厲的人, 子女一有點兒差錯他就懲罰. **2** simple; without any decoration 簡樸的; 樸素的; *an austere room, with only a table, a chair and a bed in it* 一個簡樸的房間, 裏面只有一張桌子, 一張椅子和一張床. **austerity** [ɔsˈteriti] *nu* condition of being austere (often with reference to the economic conditions of a country when goods are expensive and difficult to find, and the government wants to prevent people from spending too much money) 嚴峻; 嚴厲; 緊縮(常指國家的經濟狀況, 在價格高昂, 貨物短缺時, 政府要求人民節制花錢).

authentic [ɔːˈθentik] *adj* true; not false; reliable 真的; 真正的; 可靠的: *authentic news* i.e. news which one can believe 可靠的消息. **authenticate** [ɔːˈθentikeit] *vt* show that something is true; find out that something is genuine. 證實; 查明. **authenticity** [ɔːθenˈtisiti] *nu* condition of being true or genuine 真實性; 確實.

author [ˈɔːθə*] *nc* **1** person who writes plays, poems, novels, stories etc. 作者, 作家. **2** person who starts something 創造者; 創始人: *the author of this idea / plan / scheme / proposal* i.e. the person who first thought of this idea etc. 這種思想/計劃/方案/建議的創始人.

authority [ɔːˈθɔriti] *nu* power or right to order other people or to do something 權威; 權力: *He was given authority over the other boys* i.e. he was given the power to give orders to them. 他有權對其他男孩發號施令. *He had authority to buy more books for the library* i.e. he was allowed to do this. 他有權給圖書館增購書籍. **2** *nc* (often *pl*) person or persons who have the power or right to give orders. (常用複數) 當局; 官方: *The authorities have forbidden us to hold the meeting tomorrow.* 當局禁止我們明天開會. **3** *nc* person who is an expert on something 權威人士, 專家: *He is an authority on the history of Russia.* 他是俄國歷史權威.

authoritarian [ɔ:θɔri'teəriən] *adj* having reference to orders; based on strong rule 命令主義的; 專制的; *an authoritarian system of government* i.e. one in which the people are forced to obey the government even when they are very unwilling to do so 專制政體, 即在此政體內, 人民被迫服從政府, 即使他們很不情願這樣做. **authoritative** *adj* **1** true and to be believed in 權威的; 可信的: *He gave an authoritative account of the recent events* i.e. he told a story which seems to be true and complete. 他就最近的一些事件作了權威性的講話. 即: 他的叙述是真實而全面的. **2** giving orders or showing an ability to give orders 威嚴的; 命令式的: *He had a very authoritative manner.* 他有一種威風凜凜的樣子.

authorize ['ɔ:θəraiz] *vt* give official permission to somebody (to do something) 批准, 允許: *I am authorized to buy more books for the library.* 我獲准有權給圖書館增購書籍. **authorization** [ɔ:θərai'zeiʃən] *nu* official permission to do something 授權.

auto ['ɔ:tou] *nc (US)* car. (美)汽車.

autobiography [ɔ:toubai'ɔgrəfi] *nc / u* story of somebody's life written or told by himself. 自傳. **autobiographical** [ɔ:təbaiə'græfikl] *adj*.

autocracy [ɔ:'tɔkrəsi] *nc / u* system of government by a single person who can govern as he likes 專制政體; 獨裁. **autocratic** [ɔ:tə'krætik] *adj* **autocrat** ['ɔ:təkræt] *nc* **1** person who rules in this way 獨裁者. **2** person who always tries to make other people do what he wants, without thinking about what they may want to do 專橫霸道的人.

autograph ['ɔ:təgrɑ:f] *nc* person's name written in his own handwriting 親筆簽名.

automatic [ɔ:tə'mætik] *adj* **1** working by itself; not needing a person to attend to it 自動的; 不用人管的. **2** done without thought or intention 不經思考的, 無意識的: *Breathing is an automatic action* i.e. we breathe without having to think about what we are doing 呼吸是一種無意識的活動. 即: 我們不用想也會自己呼吸. Also 亦作 *nc* pistol or rifle in which the bullets automatically come into position for firing 自動手槍; 自動步槍. **automatically** *adv* **automation** [ɔ:tə'meiʃən] *nu* system of producing goods in a factory etc by the use of automatic machines, so that fewer workers are needed to produce the goods 自動化.

automobile ['ɔ:təməbi:l] *nc (mainly US)* motorcar (主要用於美)汽車. (Brit 英 **car** or **motorcar**).

autonomy [ɔ:'tɔnəmi] *nc* condition in which a country or part of a country governs itself, instead of being governed by another country or by the central government 自治; 自主. **autonomous** [ɔ:'tɔnəməs] *adj*.

autopsy ['ɔ:tɔpsi] *nc* examination of a dead person to find out why he died (usu. done by cutting open the body) 屍體剖檢: *perform an autopsy on somebody* i.e. do an examination of this kind 對某人解剖驗屍.

autumn ['ɔ:təm] *nc* season of the year when the leaves begin to fall from the trees and the crops are harvested; the months September, October and November in Europe 秋天, 秋季 (在歐洲爲九、十、十一月). (*US* also 美亦作 **fall**).

auxiliary [ɔ:ɡ'ziliəri] *adj* giving help 輔助的: *an auxiliary nurse* i.e. a person who helps the nurses in a hospital 助理護士; *auxiliary troops* i.e. soldiers sent to help other soldiers 援軍. Also 亦作 *nc* **auxiliary verb** (grammar) verb which helps a main verb (e.g. 'am' in I am going; 'can' in I can see him) (語法) 助動詞 (例如 I am going 裏的"am"; I can see him 裏的"can").

avail [ə'veil] *vt / i* use something for oneself; get an advantage from something 利用; 有益 (於): *He availed himself of the opportunity which he was offered.* 他利用給他提供的機會. Also 亦作 *nu* use; benefit; advantage 效用; 利益; 好處. **to no avail** uselessly; unsuccessfully 無用地; 無效地.

available [ə'veiləbl] *adj* able to be used or obtained 可利用的; 可得到的: *John is never available when I want to see him.* i.e. he is never there; I can never find him when I want him. 每當我要找約翰時他總是不在. (*opp* 反義詞 **unavailable**). **availability** [əveilə'biliti] *nu*.

avalanche ['ævəlɑ:nʃ] *nc* **1** mass of snow and ice which falls down a mountain 雪崩. **2** anything which falls on one like an avalanche 雪崩似地落下的東西: *an avalanche of questions* 連珠炮似的大量問題.

avarice ['ævəris] *nu* strong wish to get and keep something 貪婪.

ave Maria ['ɑ:veimə'riə] *nc* hail Mary (beginning of a prayer) 萬福瑪利亞 (祈禱時的開頭語).

avenge [ə'vendʒ] *vt* do something to hurt or punish somebody in return for some wrong he has done to oneself 爲…報仇: *avenge (the murder of) one's father* 報(殺)父之仇; *avenge an insult* 雪恥; *avenge oneself on the murderer of one's father* 向殺父之兇手報仇; *I can see him.* **Note** 說明: *avenge* and *revenge vt* are very similar in meaning. *Avenge* generally means to punish somebody for the harm he has done to oneself (with the idea that his punishment is a sort of unofficial justice); *revenge* generally means to hurt somebody for hurting oneself; there is not the same idea of justice in the use of this word. Do not use the person punished or hurt as the object of avenge or revenge (e.g. we cannot say *he avenged his enemy* to mean he punished his enemy; we must say *he avenged himself on his enemy* or *he avenged the murder done by his enemy*). avenge 和 revenge 作及物動詞的意思很相似. avenge 通常指因某人給自己造成損害而懲罰他 (意爲這種懲罰是一種非官方的正義行爲); revenge 通常指因某人傷害自己而傷害他, 用此詞不含上述的正義之意. 不要用被懲罰或被傷害者作賓語 (如不能說 he avenged his enemy 來表示他懲罰仇敵, 應當說 he avenged himself on his enemy 或 he avenged the murder done by his enemy).

avenue ['ævənju:] *nc* **1** road (esp. one in a town, with trees on either side) 道路; 林蔭道. **2** wide street 大街.

average ['ævəridʒ] *nc* **1** the result obtained when several numbers, quantities etc are added together and the total of this addition is divided by the number of quantities (e.g. the average of $7+8+3=(18\div3)=6$) 平均數 (例如 7、8和3的平均數是6). **2** the usual kind or standard 平常；一般水平. Also 亦作 *adj* **1** found by calculating the average 平均的. **2** normal; usual; most commonly found; neither very good nor very bad 正常的；平常的；一般的. Also 亦作 *vt* **1** calculate an average 算出…的平均數，均分. **2** produce every action, work or do something normally or usually 平均之量爲，通常幹 (…工作): *He averages forty-five hours' work a week* i.e. sometimes he does more, sometimes less, but the total is usu. near forty-five. 他每週平均工作45小時. **below / above / up to (the) average** below / above / at standard of the group, class, team etc. 低於/高於/達到一般標準. **on (the) average** usually; normally 通常地；一般地.

averse [əˈvɜːs] *adj* having a strong dislike for 厭惡的: *He is averse to hard work.* 他嫌惡艱苦的工作. **aversion** [əˈvɜːʃən] *nu: He has an aversion to / for hard work.* 他不願幹艱苦的工作.

avert [əˈvɜːt] *vt* prevent; stop from happening 防止；避免. *John's quick action averted a serious accident.* 約翰動作敏捷，避免了一次嚴重事故.

aviary [ˈeiviəri] *nc* place where many birds are kept 鳥舍；鳥類飼養場.

aviation [eiviˈeiʃən] *nu* flying in an aeroplane; art or science of flying aeroplanes; the making or production of aircraft 航空；飛行術；航空學；飛機製造業.

avid [ˈævid] *adj* with a strong wish to have 渴望的，貪婪的: *avid for money / fame / success* 貪圖金錢/追求名聲/渴望成功. **avidly** *adv*.

avocado [ævəˈkɑːdou] *nc* type of pear-shaped green or black tropical fruit

with soft pale flesh and a big stone 鱷梨(一種熱帶水果). Also 亦作 **avocado pear.** *pl* 複數 **avocados.**

avoid [əˈvoid] *vt* keep away from; move away from; act in such a way that something does not happen 避開；躲開；避免: *I tried to avoid meeting him.* 我盡量避免碰見他. *He has been avoiding me* i.e. has been staying away from me so that he does not meet me; 他一直在避開我; *avoid an accident* i.e. act in such a way that an accident does not happen 避免一次事故. **avoidance** *nu* **avoidable** *adj* able to be avoided 可避開的；可避免的. (*opp* 反義詞 **unavoidable**).

await [əˈweit] *vt* wait for; be ready for 等候；等待.

awake[1] [əˈweik] *pred adj* not asleep; conscious and noticing what is happening around one 醒着的；知道的.

awake[2] [əˈweik] *vt / i* stop sleeping or make somebody stop sleeping 醒來；喚醒. *past tense* 過去式 **awoke** [əˈwouk] *past part* 過去分詞 **awoken** or **awaked.** *Note* 說明: see also *wake*[1] which is more commonly used. 參見 wake[1],該詞更爲常用.

awaken [əˈweikən] *vt / i past* 過去式和過去分詞 **awakened.** see 見 **wake**[1].

award [əˈwɔːd] *nc* something given to somebody who has done well in some way. 獎給的東西；獎品: *an award for gaining the highest marks in the class* 班級學習優秀獎; *an award in a competition* 比賽獎. Also 亦作 *vt* give an award 獎給；授與: *They awarded the first prize to John / They awarded John the first prize.* 他們授與約翰頭獎.

aware [əˈwɛə*] *pred adj* knowing about; taking notice of; fully conscious of 知道的；注意到的；意識到的: *I am aware* *of the danger* i.e. I know about the danger. 我知道危險. *I am aware that it is dangerous.* 我意識到那是危險的.(*opp* 反義詞 **unaware**). **awareness** *nu.*

awash [ə'wɔʃ] *adv / pred adj* (esp. with reference to a ship or boat) covered by sea water (尤指船隻)被海水覆蓋的(地).

away [ə'wei] *adv* **1** at or to a distance from somebody / something 離開; 遠離: *go away* 走開; *run away* 跑掉; *away from home* 不在家; *three miles away* 三英里以外; *throw something away* 把某物扔掉. **2** out of existence; until something is finished or made smaller 不存在; 到完; …掉: *The water has boiled away* i.e. it has boiled until there is no water left. 水煮乾了. *The noises died away* i.e. they became quieter until they could no longer be heard. 那喧鬧聲逐漸消失了. **give oneself away** do something which allows a person to discover a secret which one was trying to hide 暴露出自己, 露出馬腳.

awe [ɔː] *nu* feeling which one has for somebody / something very great and powerful 畏懼; 敬畏: *The small boy felt a sense of awe when he entered the headmaster's room / when he saw the high mountains in the distance.* 這小男孩走進校長室時感到畏懼/看到遠處的高山時感到敬畏. Also 亦作 *vt* (usu. *passive*) fill with awe (通常用於被動語態) 使畏懼; 使敬畏: *The travellers were awed by the sight of the distant mountains.* 遊客們見到遠處羣山的景象時肅然起敬. **'awein-spiring** *adj* **'awesome** *adj* causing awe 使人敬畏的. **'awe-struck** *adj* filled with awe 畏懼的; 敬畏的. **'awful** *adj* very bad 極壞的: *an awful pain*

劇烈的疼痛; *an awful lot of work.* (*informal*) 許多工作(非正式). **awfully** *adv / intensifier* very much or very badly 非常; 極壞地; *thanks awfully* 非常感謝. *That's not awfully clear.* (*informal*) 不很清楚.(非正式).

awkward ['ɔːkwəd] *adj* **1** (with reference to a person or animal) not having much skill or ability in moving or doing something (指人或動物) 不靈活的: *He's a very awkward boy, he's always knocking things over.* 他是個笨手笨腳的孩子, 老是把東西打翻. **2** causing difficulty; difficult to use 不便的; 難於使用的: *an awkward shape to paint* i.e. a shape which is difficult to paint properly 難畫的形狀; *It's very awkward to use this tool;* 這工具很不好使用; *an awkward part of the road* i.e. a part of the road where it is difficult to drive properly 難於行駛的路段; *an awkward question* i.e. question which is difficult to answer, or which causes one to feel uncomfortable or unhappy 棘手的問題; 令人尷尬的問題. *I can't meet you at six o'clock, it's a very awkward time for me.* 我不能在六點鐘見你, 這個時間對我很不方便. **awkwardly** *adv* **awkwardness** *nu.*

awoke [ə'wouk] past tense of **awake**[2]. awake[2]的過去式.

axe, ax [æks] *nc* tool for cutting down trees and cutting wood into pieces 斧. Also 亦作 *vt* suddenly end or stop 突然結束; 突然停止.

axiom ['æksiəm] *nc* **1** statement which is clearly true and which needs no proof 公理. **2** rule or action which must follow if one wishes to succeed 規律; 原理. **axiomatic** [æksiə'mætik] *adj.*

axis ['æksis] *nc* real or imaginary line

through the middle of a turning object, around which the object turns 軸, 軸線. *pl* 複數 **axes** ['æksi:z].

axle ['æksl] *nc* piece of iron or other substance which joins together the centres of two wheels turning together 輪軸.

ay(e) [ai] *interj* yes (*o.f.* or dialect—use **yes**) 是 (舊式或方言一現正式用 yes). **the ayes** the people who vote 'yes' for a particular idea, proposal etc. (in a meeting) (在會上) 投贊成票者 (*opp* 反義語 **the noes).**

azalea [ə'zeiliə] *nc* shrub allied to the rhododendron, having variously coloured flowers and leaves that are usually shed in the autumn 杜鵑花.

B,b

babble ['bæbl] *nu* foolish or childish talking 愚蠢或幼稚的談話. Also 亦作 *vt / i* talk foolishly or childishly 傻里傻氣地說.

baboon [bə'bu:n] *nc* type of monkey which walks on all four legs on the ground and lives in Africa and Asia 狒狒.

baby ['beibi] *nc* infant; youngest of a group 嬰兒; 一羣人中最年幼者. Also 亦作 *adj* very small or young 很小的; 年幼的.

baby-sitter ['beibisitə*] *nc* person who stays in a house to look after children while their parents are out 臨時照看小孩的人. **baby-sit** *vi*

bachelor ['bætʃlə*] *nc* 1 unmarried man 未婚男子. (*fem* 陰 **spinster**). 2 person who has taken a first degree at a university 學士.

back¹ [bæk] *nc* 1 part of the body of a person or animal 背, 背部. 2 part of anything opposite the front; the upper part or more distant part of something 背面; 後面; 後部: *at the back of the house* 在屋後; *the back of one's hand* 手背. *He sat in the back of the car* i.e. behind the driver; 他坐在汽車裏後面的座位; *the back of a chair* i.e. the part one's back rests against 椅背; 靠背的部份. 3 (with reference to football and similar games) position of a player whose job it is to defend rather than attack (足球賽之類的) 後衛. **back-'bencher** *nc* ordinary member of Parliament who is not a minister and who does not sit on the front row in the chamber (英國議會

的) 後座議員. **'backbone** the large bone in the back 脊骨, 脊椎. **'back-cloth** see 見 **cloth**. **'back'fire** *vi* 1 (with reference to a car) make a sudden loud noise at the back caused by a fault in the engine (汽車) 發生回火. 2 (with reference to plans, ideas, schemes etc.) fail and cause harm to oneself (指計劃、主意、陰謀等)失敗反害自己: *He was punished when his evil plans backfired. (informal)* 他的罪惡勾當沒有得逞自己反遭懲罰. (非正式). **'background** 1 part of a place or picture which is in the distance or at the back 背景. 2 (with reference to the colour of something) the main colour on which there are various patterns of other colours (花色的)底子, 底色. 3 information about where a person was born, who his parents were, where he has worked etc. 家庭背景; 經歷. 4 things that have happened in the past in a story etc. 背景情況. **'backhand** *nu* stroke in tennis made with the back of the hand facing the opponent (網球的)反手擊球. Also 亦作 *adv* **'backlash** hostile or extreme reaction of some people to social or political changes which they do not like (對政治或社會變革的)對抗性反應: *The government did not pass the act because of the possible backlash.* 因可能引起強烈反應, 政府沒有通過這項法令. **'back 'number 1** copy of a magazine or newspaper which is not the latest one on sale 過期的雜誌或報紙. 2 person who was once important but is now forgotten or ignored *(informal)* 過時的人(非正式). '**back** '**pack** bag carried on the back 背包. Also 亦作 *vi* go hiking with a back pack 揹着背包徒步旅行. '**back** '**pay** payment which should have been given to somebody for the work he has done but which was in fact not given at the time 欠薪. '**back'side** part of the body on which one sits *(informal)* 屁股(非正式). '**backstroke** *nu* method of swimming while lying on one's back 仰泳. '**backwater** place or condition out of touch with new ideas *(informal)* 落後的地方; 思想閉塞的狀態.(非正式).

back² [bæk] *adv* **1** to or in an earlier position or place 回; 回原狀; 回原處: *He ran back to the house* i.e. he had left the house and now he was returning to it. 他跑回屋子. *He put the book back* i.e. the book had been taken away and now he was returning it. 他把書放回原處. *I gave back the pencil which John had lent me.* 我把約翰借給我的鉛筆還給他. *He threw the ball to me and I threw it back.* 他把球扔給我, 我又把球扔回給他. **2** to or at the back of something 往後; 在後: *We sat a long way back at the theatre* i.e. we were not near the front. 我們坐在戲院的很後面. *Sit back in your chair* i.e. rest your back against the back of the chair. 把背靠在椅背上吧. *Stand back!* i.e. keep away, do not interfere. 往後站(別干擾)! '**backbiter** *nc* person who says bad things about somebody when the person is not present 背後說人壞話的人. **backbiting** *nu*.

back³ [bæk] *vt/i* **1** (esp. with reference to a car) go, cause to go (尤指汽車)後退; 使後退: *Back the car carefully into the garage.* 把汽車小心地倒進車庫. **2** give support, help or en-couragement to 支持; 幫助; 鼓勵: *He decided to back the plan.* 他決定支持這項計劃. **3** bet money that a horse will win in a race 下賭注於(賽馬): *back a horse* 在一匹馬上下賭注. **backing** *nu* support or encourage-ment 支持; 鼓勵: *He had the backing of all his friends.* 他得到所有朋友的支持. **back out (of something)** (usu. an agreement, promise, arrangement etc.) say that one will not do some-thing, after agreeing, promising etc to do it 《事務》(通常指協議、許諾、約定等)、退出(某事)(通常指協議、許諾、約定等). 退出(某事)(通常指協議、許諾、約定等). *(informal)* 退出(某事)(非正式). **back someone (up)** give sup-port, help, encouragement etc to 支持某人; 幫助某人; 鼓勵某人.

backward ['bækwəd] *adj* **1** towards the back 向後的: *She went off without a backward glance.* 她連回頭看一下都沒有就走開了. **2** not as well-developed as others 落後的: *back-ward child* i.e. a child who is not as clever at learning as most children are 智力差的孩子. **backwards** *adv* towards the back 向後地: *walk back-wards* i.e. walk in the direction in which one's back is facing 倒退着走.

bacon ['beikən] *nu* salted and smoked meat from the back and sides of a pig 鹹肉,(用背肉或肋部肉加工的)燻豬肉.

bacteria [bæk'tiəriə] *npl* creatures which are too small to be seen by the naked eye, which live in the air, in water, in animals and plants. Some bacteria cause disease 細菌. *Note* 說明: the singular is *bacterium* [bæk'tiə-riəm] but the word is generally used in the plural 單數爲 bacterium, 但一般用複數.

bad [bæd] *adj* not good; not what it should be; unwell; unpleasant etc. 不好的; 錯的; 壞的; 不舒服的: *a bad boy* i.e. a boy who does not do what he ought to 不乖的男孩. *This egg is bad* i.e. it is rotten; it is not fit to eat. 這個蛋是壞的. 即: 臭了, 不能吃. *The light in this room is very bad* i.e. it is not easy to see well in this room; 這房間裏的光線很差; *a bad headache* i.e. a headache which is more painful than headaches usu. are 厲害的頭疼; *a bad smell* i.e. an unpleasant smell 難聞的味道. *comparative* 比較級 **worse** [wə:s]. *superlative* 最高級 **worst** [wə:st]. **badly** *adv* 1 not well 壞; 差; *badly made* 粗製濫造. 2 very much 非常; *badly hurt* 傷得厲害. *He badly needs a haircut.* 他真該理髮了.

badge [bædʒ] *nc* small piece of metal or cloth worn to show that a person is a member of a certain organization or has a certain post or occupation 徽章, 證章.

badger ['bædʒə*] *nc* type of small European animal with a white stripe on its nose, which lives in a hole in the ground and comes out at night 獾 (產於歐洲, 鼻部有一白條紋, 居地穴, 夜間出洞).

badminton ['bædmintən] *nu* game in which a shuttlecock is hit backwards and forwards across a net 羽毛球.

baffle ['bæfl] *vt* do something or be so difficult that somebody else cannot understand 使困惑, 難住: *The thief was so clever that he completely baffled the police.* 這小偷很狡猾, 把警察完全給弄糊塗了. *Question No. 7 baffled all of us.* 第七道題把我們全難住了. **baffing** *adj*.

bag[1] [bæg] *nc* 1 container made of paper, cloth or leather for carrying things in 袋, 包; *a bag of apples* 一袋蘋果. 2 the animals killed by a hunter on any one occasion 一次的獵物.

bag[2] [bæg] *vt / i* 1 put in a bag 裝進袋內. 2 kill an animal while hunting 捕殺. *past* 過去式和過去分詞 **bagged.** **baggy** *adj* (with reference to clothes) larger than necessary and rather shapeless (衣服) 寬大的.

bagpipes ['bægpaips] *npl* type of wind musical instrument found in Scotland and some other countries 風笛 (見於蘇格蘭及其他某些國家).

baggage ['bægidʒ] *nu* cases, boxes etc which somebody takes with him on a journey 行李.

bail[1] [beil] *nu* sum of money which someone accused of a crime (or a friend or relative) gives to a court of law so that he can be free until it is time for him to be put on trial. If he comes back to the court when it is time for him to be tried, the money is given back 保釋金. **bail someone out, stand / go bail for someone** deposit, promise money in this way in order to let someone out of prison (用錢)保釋某人, 爲某人作保釋人.

bail[2] [beil] *vt / i* in **bail out** i.e. throw out of a boat the water that has got into it (to prevent the boat sinking) 用於 bail out, 即: 舀掉(進入)船艙的水 (使船免於下沉). *bail out the boat / the water* 舀掉船艙的水.

bail[3] [beil] *vi* in **bail out** i.e. jump from an aeroplane with a parachute 用於 bail out, 即: 跳傘: *When the aeroplane caught fire, the pilot bailed out.* 飛機着火時, 飛行員跳傘.

bailiff ['beilif] *nc* officer of the law who assists a sheriff (郡或縣的)副司法官.

bait [beit] *nc* food or something which looks like food, used to catch a fish or an animal 餌; 假餌. Also 亦作 *vt / i* put food somewhere in order to catch a fish or an animal 裝餌(於).

bake [beik] *vt / i* **1** (esp. with reference to bread, biscuits and cakes) cook or be cooked in an oven 烘，烤(尤指麵包，餅乾和糕餅): *He baked the bread.* 他烤麵包. *The bread is still baking.* 麵包還在烘. **2** (esp. with reference to clay, pottery, soil, bricks) make very hard by heating 燒硬(尤指黏土，陶瓷，泥土，磚). **baker** *nc* person who makes or sells bread, biscuits and cakes 麵包師傅. **bakery** *nc* place where a baker works 麵包店.

balance¹ ['bæləns] **1** *vt / i* put something in such a way that it does not fall down (使)平衡: *Because he never balances them very well, the books are always falling on the floor;* 因爲他從不把書放穩，那些書老是掉到地上; *balance on one's hands* i.e. stand on one's hands with one's legs up in the air 雙手倒立. **2** *vt* usu. in **balance the books, balance the accounts** i.e. find out how much money is earned and how much is spent, and what the difference between the two sums is 通常用於 balance the books, balance the accounts, 即: 結算賬目，使收支平衡. **balanced** *adj* **1** not falling down 平穩的. **2** thoughtful and mature; completely sane (*opp* **unbalanced** esp. in sense 2) 善於思考的; 穩定的; 理智的. (反義詞 unbalanced, 尤其是義2).

balance² ['bæləns] **1** *nu* state in which something does not fall down 平衡: *John lost his balance and fell from the ladder.* 約翰失去平衡，從梯子上跌下來. **2** *nu* state in which two or more things are equal in power, strength, importance etc. 均衡，均勢: *the balance of power in the world* i.e. condition in which no country is very much stronger or richer than any other country 世界力量的均衡，即: 沒有一個國家比其他任何國家特別强大或富裕. **3** *nc* apparatus for weighing things for scientific experiments 天平. **balanced diet** all the various sorts of food which have to be eaten if one is to be healthy (有益健康的)均衡飲食.

balcony ['bælkəni] *nc* ledge outside the window of the upper floor of a house surrounded by a wall or railing 陽台.

bald [bɔːld] *adj* **1** with very little or no hair on the head 禿頂的，光禿的. **2** containing only the facts, without any disguise or pretence 無假裝的; 直率的: *a very bald account of the facts* 對事實的坦率陳述.

bale [beil] *nc* quantity tied together to be carried by ship, lorry, aeroplane etc. 大捆，貨捆.

baleful ['beilful] *adj* full of evil or wickedness 惡毒的，邪惡的.

balk, baulk [bɔːk] *vt / i* refuse or be unwilling to use something or do something 拒絕; 畏縮不前; 猶豫不決: *John balked at having to do any more work.* 約翰不情願多幹一點點活.

ball [bɔːl] *nc* **1** any round object used in playing games 球: *football, cricket ball etc.* 足球，板球等. **2** anything shaped like a ball 球狀物: *a ball of string / wool* 一團細繩/毛線. **3** large and very formal party with dancing 舞會. *Note* 說明: if the party or occasion is not formal the word *dance* is used 非正式的舞會用 dance. **'ball 'bearing 1** part of a machine which turns on small metal balls 滾珠軸承. **2** one of the metal balls used for this purpose (軸承的)滾珠. **'ballpoint 'pen** pen in which the ink comes round a small ball instead of through a metal point 圓珠筆. **'ballroom**

room in which a ball or public dance is held 舞廳.

ballad ['bæləd] *nc* type of poem or song which tells a story (usu. a traditional story) 民謠, 歌謠.

ballast ['bæləst] *nu* heavy material which is carried in a ship to keep it steady 壓艙物 (裝在船上使船平穩). Also 亦作 *vt: ballast a ship* 往船上裝壓艙物.

ballerina [bælə'ri:nə] *nc* woman ballet dancer who dances important parts 芭蕾舞女主角.

ballet ['bælei] *nc / u* play or entertainment performed by dancers in a theatre (usu. with reference to a European entertainment of this type; the word *ballet* is not usu. applied to traditional dancing or folk dancing) 芭蕾舞 (通常指歐洲式的表演, ballet 一詞通常不適用於傳統舞蹈或民間舞蹈).

ballistics [bə'listiks] *npl* (followed by *sing* verb) science of guns and bombs 彈道學 (接單數動詞).

balloon [bə'lu:n] *nc* bag made of rubber or other material, which swells when filled with air or other gas 氣球.

ballot ['bælət] *nc* process of voting in secret (usu. by marking a piece of paper and putting it into a box) 無記名投票.

balmy ['ba:mi] *adj* (esp. with reference to winds) gentle and mild (尤指風) 溫和的: *a balmy breeze* 溫和的微風.

balsa ['bɔ:lsə] *nu* type of very light wood. (Often **balsa wood**) 輕木材. (常用 balsa wood).

bamboo [bæm'bu:] *nc / u* type of tall tropical or semi-tropical plant with a hollow stem 竹. *Note* 說明: this word is usu. uncountable; for the plural use *a lot of bamboo* (for the plant) and

pieces of bamboo (for the wood). 這個單詞通常常不可數, 複數用 a lot of bamboo (指植株) 及 pieces of bamboo (指作材料的竹竿).

ban [bæn] *vt* say that something must not be done; forbid 禁止: *The police will soon ban the parking of cars in this street.* 警察不久就會禁止在這條街上停車. *past* 過去式和過去分詞 **banned**. Also 亦作 *nc* order that something must not be done 禁令, 禁止.

banal [bə'nɑ:l] *adj* very ordinary, in no way unusual or interesting 平庸的; 乏味的: *a very banal remark* 枯燥無味的話.

banana [bə'nɑ:nə] *nc* type of curved fruit, yellow in colour 香蕉.

band[1] [bænd] *nc* **1** group of musicians playing together 樂隊. *Note* 說明: the word *band* is used if the musicians are playing popular music or dance music; if they are playing classical music or serious music the word *orchestra* is normally used 演奏流行音樂或舞曲的樂隊稱 band; 演奏古典音樂或嚴肅音樂的樂隊稱 orchestra. **2** group of people joined together for some purpose (often a bad purpose) 團夥, 幫: *a band of robbers* 一夥强盜. **3** thin piece of material for tying or fastening something 帶, 箍, 條.

band[2] [bænd] *vi* join in a group for a particular purpose (爲某目的) 結合在一起: *The people banded together against the robbers.* 人民聯合起來對付强盜.

bandage ['bændidʒ] *nc* strip of cloth used for tying round a wound or injury 繃帶. Also 亦作 *vt* put a bandage on 用繃帶包紮: *bandage a wound / a person* 用繃帶包紮傷口/人.

bandit ['bændit] *nc* robber who lives in

mountains, forests or other wild places and who attacks travellers 匪徒, 盜匪.

bandy¹ ['bændi] *adj* bent outwards 向外彎曲的: *bandy-legged* i.e. having the legs bent like this 雙圈腿的.

bandy² ['bændi] *vt* exchange words when arguing with somebody 對吵: *bandy insults* 互相謾罵.

bang [bæŋ] *nc* **1** sudden loud noise 砰砰聲: *He heard a bang.* 他聽到砰的一聲. **2** sudden blow 猛然撞擊: *a bang on the head* 當頭的一擊. Also 亦作 *vt / i* make a bang (使)猛撞; (使)砰然作響. *bang the door* 砰然把門關上; *bang one's head on the wall* 把頭撞到牆壁上.

bangle ['bæŋgl] *nc* ring of metal or other substance worn round the wrist or arm as an ornament 手鐲.

banian ['bæniən] *nc* see 見 banyan.

banish ['bæniʃ] *vt* make somebody go away (esp. to make somebody leave his own country as a punishment) 放逐, 把…驅逐出境.

banister ['bænistə*] *nc* (usu. *pl*) the rail and supports for the rail at the side of a staircase (通常用複數)(樓梯的)欄杆.

banjo ['bændʒou] *nc* type of stringed musical instrument 班卓琴(一種弦樂器). *pl* 複數 **banjoes** or **banjos**.

bank¹ [bæŋk] *nc* **1** land along the side of a river, lake etc. 岸, 堤. **2** earth which is heaped up in a field or garden 田埂; 田壟; 土堆.

bank² [bæŋk] *vt / i* lean sideways when turning (使)轉彎時傾斜: *The aeroplane banked sharply before coming down to land.* 飛機着陸前作大幅度傾斜轉彎.

bank³ [bæŋk] *nc* place where money is kept and paid out, and in which busi-ness connected with money is carried on 銀行. Also 亦作 *vt / i* put money into a bank 把(錢)存入銀行: *bank one's money* 把錢存入銀行. **banker** *nc* person who is in charge of a bank or whose business is dealing in money 銀行家. **banking** *nu* the business of banks or bankers 銀行業. '**bank 'holiday** (in England) day on which the banks are closed and which is also a public holiday (在英國)銀行假日, 公假日. '**banknote** piece of paper money 鈔票.

bankrupt ['bæŋkrʌpt] *adj* officially declared by a court of law to be unable to pay one's debts '(經法院宣佈爲)無能力還債的, 破產的. Also 亦作 *nc* person who is bankrupt 破產者. **bankruptcy** *nu*.

banner ['bænə*] *nc* large piece of cloth, paper etc. (usu. fastened to two sticks, having a sign or words on it and intended to be seen by many people) 旗幟; (用兩根桿撐開的)橫幅標語旗.

banns [bænz] *npl* notice read out in a church that a certain man and woman are going to be married (在教堂宣布的)結婚預告.

banquet ['bæŋkwit] *nc* official meal, with a lot of food, at which speeches are made 宴會.

banyan, banian ['bæniən] *nc* Indian fig tree whose branches come down to the ground and take root 印度榕樹(樹枝垂入土中即可生根).

baptism ['bæptizəm] *nu* ceremony or practice of most churches, in which drops of water are put on the head of a person, or in some cases, the person is put into the water as a sign that the person has become a member of the church 洗禮儀式; 浸禮

Baptist *nc* member of the Baptist Church which believes in practising baptism only when the person is an adult. Baptism in this church is carried out by putting the person in the water 浸禮會教徒 (認爲只有對成人才施行洗禮，而且把受洗人浸在水中).

baptize [bæp'taiz] *vt* **1** give baptism to a person 給 (人) 施洗禮. **2** give a name to 命名.

bar¹ [bɑ:*] *nc* **1** (usu. with reference to iron, gold, lead etc or chocolate or soap) piece of some solid material, longer than it is wide 條、棒、桿 (通常指鐵、金、鉛等，或巧克力、肥皂). **2** anything which prevents something moving forward or developing 妨礙，障礙物: *Lack of mineral resources was a bar to the economic development of the country.* 缺乏礦物資源是該國經濟發展的障礙. **3** room or building where alcoholic drinks and other refreshments are sold; the counter at which they are sold 酒吧間; 飲食櫃台. **the Bar** all the lawyers who appear in court 律師團. **'barmaid** woman who serves drinks and other refreshments in a bar. (in sense 3) 酒吧女招待, 女侍者. **'barman** man who does this 酒吧男招待, 男侍者. **'bartender** *(US)* barman (美) 酒吧男招待, 男侍者.

bar² [bɑ:*] *vt* **1** make safe by putting in or fastening bars 閂上: *He barred all the doors and windows of his house.* 他把他房子的全部門窗都閂上. **2** prevent somebody from going in a certain direction 阻擋, 攔住: *A high wall bars the way into his garden.* 一堵高牆擋住進入他花園的路. *past* 過去式和過去分詞 **barred**.

barb [bɑ:b] *nc* sharp point projecting away from the main point of a fishhook, arrow etc. (魚鈎、箭 等的) 倒鈎.

barbarian [bɑ:ˈbɛəriən] *nc* person who behaves in a rough and bad-mannered way, and who has no respect for art, literature, education etc. 野蠻人. Also 亦作 *adj* **barbaric** [bɑ:ˈbærik] *adj* **barbarous** ['bɑ:bərəs] *adj* **barbarity** [bɑ:ˈbæriti] *nc / u.* Note 說明: *barbarian adj* means 'like a *barbarian' etc; barbaric* is often used to refer to matters of culture (e.g. *barbaric art, barbaric splendour, barbaric ornaments); barbarous* is often used to refer to cruel behaviour (e.g. *barbarous torture, barbarous insults).* 形容詞 barbarian 的含義是 "像野蠻人的" 等; barbaric 常用於指與文化有關的東西 (如: barbaric art 粗俗的藝術, barbaric splendour 粗陋的壯麗, barbaric ornaments 不優雅的裝飾品); barbarous 常用於指殘忍的行爲 (如: barbarous torture 殘酷的拷打, barbarous insults 野蠻的侮辱).

barbed wire ['bɑ:bd'waiə*] wire with sharp points on it, used for fences etc. 有刺鐵絲.

barbecue ['bɑ:bikju:] *nc* party or feast (usu. in the open air) at which the food (usu. meat) is cooked over an open fire 烤肉野餐.

barber ['bɑ:bə*] *nc* person whose job is to cut men's hair (爲男子理髮的) 理髮師. *Note* 說明: the word *hairdresser* is used for the person who cuts women's hair. hairdresser 是指爲女子理髮的人.

bare [bɛə*] *adj* **1** not covered by clothes 沒穿衣服的, 赤裸的. **2** without decoration, furniture, vegetation etc. 光禿的, 空無的, 無裝飾的: *The house looks rather bare.* 這房子看起來有點空蕩蕩的; *a bare hillside* 沒有

草木的山坡. *The trees are bare in winter.* 樹木在冬天裏光禿禿的. **3** just enough; very little 剛夠的; 很少: *He earns a bare living* i.e. he earns just enough, but he has no money to spare. 他挣的錢僅夠糊口. Also 亦作 *vt* make bare (in senses 1 and 2) 使裸露; 暴露. **bareness** *nu* **barely** *adv* **1** in a bare way 赤裸裸地, 無遮蔽地. **2** just enough and no more 僅僅, 剛剛: *barely enough money* 勉強夠的錢. **'bareback** *adj / adv* (with reference to horse riding) without a saddle (騎馬) 無鞍的(地). **'barefaced** *adj* shameless 無恥的, 不要臉的: *barefaced liar* 無恥的撒謊者. **'barefoot, barefooted** *adj* not wearing shoes, stockings etc on the feet 赤腳的.

bargain ['bɑːgin] *nc* **1** agreement with somebody to buy or sell something 買賣協議, 交易. **2** something bought or sold for less than its real value 廉價貨. **bargain for something 1** discuss the price of something in this way 爲某物討價還價. **2** expect or hope for something 預料某事, 指望某事: *more than I bargained for. (informal)* 超出我的預料 (非正式). **into the bargain** as well; in addition 而且; 加之: *That shopkeeper is a very rude man and a cheat into the bargain.* 那店主很粗魯無禮, 而且是個騙子. (非正式)

barge¹ [bɑːdʒ] *nc* large flat-bottomed boat used for carrying goods on rivers 大平底貨船, 駁船.

barge² [bɑːdʒ] *vt / i* push or enter roughly 推撞; 闖入: *He barged into the room. (informal)* 他闖進房間. (非正式)

baritone ['bæritoun] *nc* singer with a voice between tenor and bass 男中音.

barium ['bɛəriəm] *nu* silver-white, metallic chemical element 鋇: *barium meal* 鋇餐.

bark¹ [bɑːk] *nc* noise made by a dog 狗吠, 狗叫聲. Also 亦作 *vi* make this noise (狗)吠, 叫.

bark² [bɑːk] *nu* the hard outer covering of a tree 樹皮.

barley ['bɑːli] *nu* type of plant whose seeds are used to make flour or bread and in the making of beer etc. 大麥.

barn [bɑːn] *nc* building on a farm, used for storing crops or for sheltering animals 穀倉; 牲口棚.

barnacle ['bɑːnikl] *nc* small sea creature covered by a shell which attaches itself to rocks and the bottoms of ships 藤壺(附於岩石或船底上的甲殼動物).

barometer [bə'rɔmitə*] *nc* instrument which measures changes in air pressure and so can tell what changes there will be in the weather 氣壓計; 晴雨表.

baron ['bærn] *nc* title of nobility 男爵. (*fem* 陰 **baroness).**

baroque [bə'rɔk] *adj* in the style of art, architecture etc found in Europe from about 1550 to 1750; having a great deal of ornament and many curved shapes 巴羅克式的; 過份雕琢的; 多裝飾和曲面的(1550至1750年前後歐洲的藝術、建築等的風格).

barracks ['bærəks] *npl* buildings where soldiers live 兵營.

barrage ['bærɑːʒ] *nc* **1** heavy and continuous firing of big guns in battle 彈幕射擊, 火力網. **2** large dam on a river (often a dam connected with other development projects) 堰, 攔河壩(常與其他開發工程相連接).

barrel ['bærl] *nc* **1** large round container (usu. made of wood) wider in the middle than at the ends. (If the container is the same width along all its length, it is called a **drum**) 大木桶(中間比兩頭大；如果中間與兩頭一樣大的則稱爲 drum). **2** the long round part of a gun, along which the bullet or shell travels 槍管, 槍筒.

barren ['bærn] *adj* not producing any crops, flowers, fruit etc. 貧瘠的, 不毛的; 不結果實的.

barricade [,bæri'keid] *nc* anything put across a street etc in a hurry to prevent people moving along (often in times of riot or revolution) 路障(常設於暴亂或革命年代). Also 亦作 *vt* make a barricade 在…設路障: *barricade the main streets* 在主要街道設置路障. *Note* 說明: *a barricade* is hurriedly made and temporary. Something more permanent is called a *barrier*. barricade 指臨時忽促設置的路障, 較永久性的稱 barrier.

barrier ['bæriə*] *nc* **1** wall, fence, gate etc which prevents people from going forward 障牆; 柵欄; 柵門. **2** anything which prevents people from going in a certain direction or which prevents progress 障礙物; 有妨礙的東西.

barrister ['bæristə*] *nc* (in England) lawyer who speaks in a court of law, (在英國)能出庭辯護的律師. *Note* 說明: in England a lawyer who does not speak in a court of law is called a *solicitor*. In many countries all lawyers are allowed to speak in court. 在英國不能出庭辯護的律師稱 solicitor; 在許多國家裏所有律師都可以出庭辯護.

barrow ['bærou] *nc* small vehicle with one or two wheels (usu. pushed by hand) used for carrying goods (單輪或雙輪)手推車.

barter ['bɑ:tə*] *vt / i* do business without using money by exchanging goods 以物易物, 作易貨貿易: *barter rice for cotton* 以大米換取棉花.

basalt ['bæsɔ:lt] *nu* dark, tough, volcanic rock 玄武岩.

base¹ [beis] *nc* **1** the lowest part of something, on which the upper parts rest. 底座, 基部: *The refrigerator is standing on a wooden base.* 冰箱置於木製底座上. **2** the place at which the stores and senior officers etc of a section of the army, navy etc are found (esp. in time of war) 基地, 根據地.

base² [beis] *vt* place on; build on; use as a base 把…置於; 把…建立在; 以…爲基地: *He based his argument on the following fact* i.e. this fact was his main point, from which he went on to make other points. 他把以下事實作爲他的論點的依據. *This book is based on a true story* i.e. the story told in the book really happened, but some changes have been made to the original story. 這本書是根據一個真實的故事寫的.

base³ [beis] *adj* selfish; bad; dishonest; cowardly etc. 自私的; 惡劣的; 卑鄙的; 懦怯的.

baseball ['beisbɔ:l] *nu* game played in America with a bat and ball on a field with four bases 棒球運動.

basement ['beismənt] *nc* part of a building partly or completely underground, in which people live or work 地下室.

bash [bæʃ] *vt* hit very hard 重擊; 猛撞.

bashful ['bæʃful] *adj* (usu. with reference to children or young people) shy; showing great discomfort and self-consciousness in the presence of other people; not knowing what to do or say in the presence of other people 害羞的; 忸怩的; 拘謹的(通常指小孩或

年青人).

basic ['beisik] *adj* most important; on which everything else depends 首要的; 基本的. **basically** *adv*.

basin ['beisən] *nc* **1** round bowl used as a container for liquid 盆, 臉盆. **2** (geography) land from which all rainwater drains to a river and its tributaries (地理) 盆地; 流域.

basis ['beisis] *nc* main or most important part, idea, facts etc. 主要部份; 基礎; 根據. *pl* 複數 **bases** ['beisi:z].

bask [ba:sk] *vi* lie and take pleasure in warmth and light 躺着曬太陽; 取暖; *He was basking in the sun.* 他躺在陽光下取暖.

basket ['ba:skit] *nc* something made of strips of wood etc used for carrying things 籃; 筐. **'basketball** *nu* game in which two teams try to toss a ball through a ring and into a net which is shaped like a basket 籃球運動.

bass [beis] *nc* singer with lowest male voice 男低音. Also 亦作 *adj*.

bassoon [bə'su:n] *nc* (music) type of wind instrument (音樂) 巴松管, 低音管.

bastard ['ba:stəd] *nc* person whose mother and father were not married 私生子. *Note* 說明: many people consider this word impolite. 許多人認爲這個詞是不禮貌的.

baste [beist] *vt* pour hot liquid over meat which is being roasted 在(烤肉)上澆熱汁.

bastion ['bæstiən] *nc* projecting part of a wall used for defence 稜堡(牆的突出部份, 用以防禦).

bat¹ [bæt] *nc* special piece of wood used for hitting a ball in a number of games 球棒. Also 亦作 *vi* use a bat 用球棒(打球). *past* 過去式和過去分詞 **batted.**

bat² [bæt] *nc* type of small flying animal which comes out at night and which can find its way by a kind of radar 蝙蝠.

batch [bætʃ] *nc* amount or number of things / people dealt with together 一批; 一組: *He received a batch of telegrams* 他收到一批電報; *a batch of loaves in the oven* 在烤的一爐麵包.

bated ['beitid] *adj* usu. in **with bated breath** i.e. in great fear, interest, wonder, anxiety etc. 通常用於 with bated breath, 即: (在極爲恐懼、興趣、驚奇、焦慮等時)屏息地.

bath [ba:θ] *nc* **1** large container in which one can sit in order to wash the body 浴盆; 浴缸. **2** washing of the body in this way 洗澡: *have a bath* 洗澡. **3** (usu. *pl*) public building in which people can have a bath, or in which they can swim (通常用複數) (公共)澡堂. *pl* 複數 **baths** [ba:ðz]. Also 亦作 *vt / i* take or give a bath (給…)洗澡. **'bathroom** room for a bath (in sense **1**), washbasin, toilet etc. 浴室; 盥洗室.

bathe [beið] **1** *vi* swim or dip oneself in the sea, a river, lake etc. 游泳; 在海、河、湖等水中浸泡. see 參見 bath. **2** wash something (usu. a wound) carefully 浸洗(傷口). **bather** *nc* **bathing** *nu*.

baton ['bætn] *nc* stick used by the conductor of an orchestra to guide the players 指揮棒.

battalion [bə'tæliən] *nc* part of an army 營; 大隊.

batter¹ ['bætə*] *vt* hit very hard with many blows 連續重擊.

batter² ['bætə*] *nu* mixture of flour, milk, eggs etc used in cooking 牛奶麵糊(麵粉、牛奶、蛋等的混合物, 用於煮食).

battery ['bætəri] *nc* **1** device for producing an electric current 電池. **2** number of large guns used for war 砲組;砲列.

battle ['bætl] *nc* **1** fight between two or more groups of people (usu. between two armies, navies or groups of aeroplanes). 戰鬥,戰役. **2** any kind of fight or struggle. 交戰;鬥爭. Also 亦作 *vi* fight, struggle 戰鬥,鬥爭: *We must continue to battle against / with poverty and disease.* 我們必須繼續與貧窮和疾病作鬥爭. **'battlefield** place where a battle is fought 戰場. **'battleship** very large type of ship used for fighting 戰艦.

battlement ['bætlmənt] *nc* (usu. *pl*) wall at the top of a tower etc with openings through which soldiers can shoot (通常用複數)(城堡等上的)雉堞,城垛.

baulk [bɔ:k] *vt / i* see 見 balk.

bawl [bɔ:l] *vt / i* shout or cry very loudly (usu. in an impolite or unpleasant way) (通常指不禮貌或不高興地)大叫,大喊: *It is very bad manners to bawl at people in the street.* 在街上大聲叫人是很不禮貌的.

bay [bei] *nc* part of the land curved inwards at the edge of the sea or a lake 灣;海灣. **'bay 'window** type of window which projects out from a room 凸窗. **at bay** in such a position that one has to turn and face one's enemies 處於困獸之鬥的絕境.

bayonet ['beiənet] *nc* knife which can be fixed to the end of a gun (槍尖的)刺刀.

bazaar [bə'za:*] *nc* **1** (with reference to countries in Asia) street / streets containing shops (亞洲國家的)街道/集市. **2** (with reference to Britain or America) sale held for a special purpose (英、美國家的)義賣.

be [bi:] *v* infinitive form of *I am, you are, he is* etc.; exist, happen etc used with other verbs to make compound tenses and passives. I am, you are, he is 等的不定式形式;(與其他動詞組成複合時態和被動語態)存在,發生等.

beach [bi:tʃ] *nc* land at the edge of the sea or a lake (usu. consisting of sand or small stones) 海灘;湖灘. Also 亦作 *vt / i* land on a beach from a boat; land a boat (從船上)上岸;(使)船靠岸.

beacon ['bi:kən] *nc* light used to give warning of some danger (usu. to warn ships) 信號燈,燈塔(通常用於警告船隻).

bead [bi:d] *nc* **1** (usu. *pl*) small piece of glass, metal, wood etc with a hole through it, which can be put on a string and worn as an ornament (通常用複數)有孔小珠(作裝飾用). **2** something like a bead 珠狀物: *bead of sweat* i.e. a drop of sweat 汗珠,即一滴汗. *Note* 說明: the word *bead* is not used to refer to precious stones or metal worn in this way. bead 不能用來指裝飾用的寶石或貴重金屬. **beady** *adj* (with reference to eyes) small and shining (眼睛)小而亮的.

beak [bi:k] *nc* hard pointed part of a bird's mouth 鳥的嘴.

beaker ['bi:kə*] *nc* large cup or glass (esp. one used for chemical experiments) 燒杯(尤指化學實驗用的).

beam [bi:m] *nc* **1** long thick piece of wood used in a building 樑. **2** ray or line of light 光線: *A beam of sunlight was shining through a hole in the curtain.* 一束陽光透過窗簾上的小孔照射進來. **3** bright cheerful smile 笑容. Also 亦作 *vi* smile very cheerfully 很高興地微笑: *The headmaster beamed with pleasure when he saw our good* *results.* 校長看到我們的好成績時喜笑顏開.

bean [biːn] *nc* the seed of certain plants. used as food 豆, 豆類.

bear¹ [bɛə*] *vt / i* **1** carry, take the weight of, hold 承受; 負擔; 支撐: *Will this beam bear the weight of the roof?* 這根樑條承受得了這屋頂的重量嗎? **2** produce, have 產, 結(果實); 有: *These trees bear fruit twice a year.* 這些樹一年結兩次果. **3** suffer or be able to suffer 忍受; 容忍: *I didn't think I would be able to bear such pain.* 我想我無法忍受這疼痛. *past tense* 過去式 **bore** [bɔː]. *past part* 過去分詞 **borne** [bɔːn]. *Note* 說明: *borne* is the normal participle. However, when *bear* is used in the special phrase with the meaning of 'come into existence', *born* is used as the past participle. *She has borne twelve children* but *He was born in 1920.* borne 是正常的分詞, 但當 bear在特殊短語裏用來指"開始存在"時, 過去分詞用 born. 如 She has borne twelve children (她生育了十二個孩子), 但是 He was born in 1920 (他出生於1920年). **bearable** *adj* that can be endured or suffered 忍受得住的; 可忍受的. (*opp* 反義詞 **unbearable**). **bearer** *nc* **1** person who carries something 持有者; 携帶者. **2** (in Asia) house servant (用於亞洲) 僕人. **bearing 1** *nu* connection (usu. in **have a / no bearing on something**) 關係(通常用於 have a / no bearing on something): *That question has no bearing on the subject we are discussing.* 那問題與我們在討論的題目無關. **2** *nc* part of a machine or engine on which a moving part rests 軸承. **3** *nu* way of acting, walking, behaving 舉止; 姿態. **bearings** *npl* position (usu. in **take one's bearings** i.e.

find one's position, find out exactly where one is) 位置 (通常用於 take one's bearings, 即: 判別方位, 弄清準確位置). (*opp* 反義語 **lose one's bearings**). **bear with somebody** stay and listen to what somebody says although one may wish to go away (usu. in **if you will bear with me for a few more minutes, I will...**) 耐心聽某人把話說完(通常用於 if you will bear with me for a few more minutes, I will...). **bear something in mind** not forget something; remember something so as to make use of it at the proper time 不忘某事; 牢記某事. **bear right / left** (used for telling somebody how to reach a place) turn right / left (用於給人指路)向右 / 左轉. **can't bear** dislike very much 很不喜歡; 討厭: *I can't bear his singing.* 我討厭他唱歌. *She can't bear to watch a boxing match.* 她很不喜歡看拳擊比賽.

bear² [bɛə*] *nc* large, furry, meat-eating animal, many types of which sleep through the whole winter 熊.

beard [biəd] *nc* hair on the cheeks and chin of a man (兩頰和下巴上的)鬚鬍. *Note* 說明: hair on the upper lip is called a *moustache*. 上唇的小鬍子叫 moustache. **bearded** *adj*.

beast [biːst] *nc* **1** animal (esp. an animal considered simply as an animal and not as a pet or an animal which works for man) 動物, 獸(尤指野獸, 而非愛畜或牲畜). **2** cruel, unkind or unpleasant person (esp. a man or a child) 兇殘的人; 令人討厭的人(尤指男人或小孩). **beastly** *adj* unpleasant, unkind etc. 令人討厭的; 兇殘的, 殘忍的.

beat¹ [biːt] **1** *vt / i* hit several times (usu. with a stick) 打, 敲 (通常用棍

子). **2** *vt* defeat, gain a victory over, do something better than somebody. 打敗, 打贏; 勝過. **3** *vi* move regularly (有規律地) 跳動: *His heart stopped beating.* 他的心臟停止跳動. *past tense* 過去式 **beat.** *past part* 過去分詞 **beaten.** *Note* 說明: *beat* meaning 'hit' always has the sense of 'hit several times, hit repeatedly'. If only one or a few blows are involved, use *hit* instead of *beat.* beat 表示"打"總是有 "打好幾次, 連續打"的意思, 如只打一下 或幾下, 則用 hit 而不用 beat. **beater** *nc* piece of equipment used in a kitchen for mixing eggs etc. (廚房用的) 打蛋器. **beat someone up** attack someone by hitting him, kicking him etc. (*informal*) 痛毆某人 (非正式). **beat off an attack** drive away those attacking 擊退進攻. **beat about the bush** waste time by talking about something other than the most important point. (*informal*) 拐彎抹角地說話, 不着正題 (非正式). **beat time** hit something, wave one's hands etc to show how fast a piece of music is to be played 打拍子.

beat² [bi:t] *nc* **1** sound or movement of something being hit or something moving regularly (usu. in **beat of a drum; heartbeat**) 敲打聲; 敲打; 有規律的跳動(聲) (通常用於 beat of a drum; heartbeat). **2** unit of time in music 拍子, 節拍. **3** area, path, street etc where somebody regularly travels 常走的道路或地區: *The policeman was on his beat.* 警察在巡邏.

beauty ['bju:ti] *nc / u* the quality which we find pleasing to look at, hear, smell, think about etc. 美, 美麗: *We were very impressed by the beauty of the scene.* 這美景給我們留下很深的印象. **beautify** *vt* make beautiful 美化.

beautiful *adj* very pleasing to the eye, ear etc. 美麗的, 美好的; 優美的: *beautiful music.* 悦耳的音樂; *a beautiful woman* 美麗的女人. **beautifully** *adv*.

beaver ['bi:və*] *nc* type of small animal which lives both in water and on land and is known for its ability to dam up streams by using mud, twigs etc. 河狸 (生活在陸上和水中的小動物, 能用泥土、樹枝等築壩攔水).

becalm [bi'kɑ:m] *vt* (usu. *passive*) prevent a ship etc from moving through lack of wind (通常用於被動語態) 因無風而使(船等)停止不動: *The ship was becalmed for five days.* 船因無風而停了五天不能航行.

became [bi'keim] past tense of **become.** become的過去式.

because [bi'kɔz] *conj* for the reason that 因爲. *Note* 說明: if we begin with an expression such as *The reason is...* we do not usu. follow this expression with *because; that* is used instead. *The reason I am late is that I missed the bus.* 如果我們用 The reason is... 這樣的表達方式開頭, 其後通常不用 because, 而是用 that. 如: The reason I am late is that I missed the bus (我遲到是因爲趕不上公共汽車). **because of** owing to 因爲, 由於: *Our holiday was most enjoyable, mainly because of the good weather.* 我們的假日過得很愉快, 主要是因爲天氣好.

beckon ['bekən] *vt / i* make a sign with the hand用手示意: *He beckoned (to) us to follow him.* 他招手要我們跟着他. *He beckoned us nearer, forward etc.* 他用手示意我們靠近些, 向前等.

become [bi'kʌm] *vt / i* change so as to be 變得, 成爲: *He became tired easily.* 他變得容易疲倦了. *He became a* *rich man.* 他成了富翁. *past tense* 過去式 **became** [bi'keim]. *past part* 過去分詞 **become. become of** happen to 降臨; 發生於: *What became of John after he left school?* 約翰離校後情況怎樣? **becoming** *adj* suitable; pretty 合適的; 漂亮的. (*opp* 反義詞 **unbecoming**).

bed [bed] *nc* **1** piece of furniture on which one sleeps 床. **2** any place where somebody sleeps 床位; 舖. **3** ground underneath the sea, a river, lake etc. (海、湖的) 底; (河) 床. **4** piece of ground in a garden where flowers grow 花堆; 花圃. **5** material or substance on which something rests 底座; 基礎: *a bed of concrete* 混凝土底模. *Note* 說明: a person is said to be *in bed / in his bed* if he is under the blankets; if he is on top of the blankets, he is said to be *on his bed.* 如果某人在床上蓋着毯子, 就用 in bed 或 in his bed; 如果是躺在毯子上, 就用 on his bed. **bedding** *nu* sheets, blankets and pillows 被褥, 床上用品. **'bedclothes** sheets and blankets 被褥. **'bedridden** *adj* unable to get out of bed because of illness or old age (因病或年老而) 卧床不起的. **'bedroom** room in which one sleeps 卧室. **'bedside** the side of a bed 床邊: *The child's mother sat at his bedside until he recovered.* 孩子生病期間, 母親一直守在他的床邊. **'bed-'sitter, 'bed-'sitting room** room which is both a bedroom and a sitting room 卧室兼起居室. **'bedtime** time at which one goes to bed 就寢時間. **double bed** for two people 雙人床. **single bed** bed for one person 單人床. **go to bed** get into one's bed 上床, 去睡覺.

bedlam ['bedləm] *nu* place or state of noise and confusion. *(informal)* 鬧閧閧的地方; 喧鬧. (非正式).

bedraggled [bi'drægld] *adj* (usu. with reference to a person or clothes) untidy, dirty, wet etc. (通常指人或衣服) 邋遢的, 又髒又濕的.

bee [bi:] *nc* flying insect which makes honey 蜜蜂. **'beehive** box or other place in which bees live 蜂房, 蜂箱. **make a beeline for something** go by the shortest path to something 逕直朝某物走去, 直奔某物: *When he saw that I was in the room he made a beeline for the door. (informal)* 他看到我在房間就逕直朝房門走來. (非正式).

beech [bi:tʃ] *nc / u* type of tree with smooth silvery bark 山毛櫸, 櫸 (樹皮光滑, 呈銀灰色).

beef [bi:f] *nu* meat of a cow, ox or bull 牛肉.

been [bi:n] past part of **be.** be的過去分詞.

beer [biə*] *nu* alcoholic drink made from barley 啤酒.

beet [bi:t] *nc / u* name of two types of plant; one has a red root which is eaten; the other has a white root which is made into sugar 甜菜 (有兩類: 一類根紅, 供食用; 另一類根白, 供製糖用).

beetle ['bi:tl] *nc* type of insect having two hard, shiny cases which cover the wings when folded 甲蟲.

beetroot ['bi:tru:t] *nc* red root of the beet, eaten in salads 甜菜根 (紅色, 用於拌色拉).

befall [bi'fɔ:l] *vt / i* happen, happen to *(o.f.)* 發生, 降臨 (舊式) *past tense* 過去式 **befell** [bi'fel]. *past part* 過去分詞 **befallen.**

before [bi'fɔ:*] *conj / prep* **1** at an earlier time than 在 ⋯ 以前: *before six* *o'clock* 六點鐘以前; *before the end of the term* 在學期結束之前. *Haven't I met you somewhere before?* 我不是曾經在什麼地方見過你嗎? *He has never behaved like that before.* 他以前從沒有過那樣的表現. **2** in front of 在…前面: *before the king* 在國王面前. *Note* 說明: *before* in the sense of in front of is rather *o.f.*-use in front of. before 作"在…前面"解頗爲舊式, 現在用 in front of. **beforehand** *adv* before a certain time 事先; 預先: *The meal was prepared beforehand.* 這頓飯是預先準備好的.

beg [beg] *vt / i* ask (for) with great feeling 懇求; 請求: *He begged for forgiveness.* 他懇求寬恕. *He begged the judge to forgive him.* 他求法官寬恕他. **2** ask people for money (often those passing by) 乞討(錢)(常指向行人). *past* 過去式和過去分詞 **begged**. *see* 見 **beggar. beg pardon** in **1 beg your pardon** 用於 **1 beg your pardon. 1** I am sorry 對不起. **2** please say that again 請再說一遍.

began [bi'gæn] past tense of **begin.** begin的過去式.

beggar ['begə*] *nc* person who does not work to get money but asks people to give him money 乞丐.

begin [bi'gin] *vt / i* start, do something for the first time 開始; 着手: *My father began building a new house last week.* 我父親上週開始建一幢新屋. *The baby will soon begin to talk.* 這嬰兒很快就會學會講話. *The day began with rain.* 天亮時下着雨. *pres part* 現在分詞 **beginning.** past tense 過去式 **began** [bi'gæn]. *past part* 過去分詞 **begun** [bi'gʌn]. **beginning** *nc / u* **beginner** *nc* one who is beginning or learning 創始人; 初學者.

begonia [bi'gouniə] *nc* garden plant

with showy flowers and ornamental leaves 秋海棠.

begrudge [bi'grʌdʒ] *vt* **1** be unhappy because somebody else has been lucky in some way 嫉妒. **2** be unhappy about giving somebody something 捨不得給; 吝惜: *The old man begrudged his workers their wages.* 這老頭很不情願發工資給工人.

behalf [bi'haːf] for somebody / something (in **on behalf of someone / something** i.e. for somebody; in order to help somebody) 代表某人; 爲了某事(用於 on behalf of someone / something): *They are collecting on behalf of charity.* 他們正在爲慈善事業募捐. *He spoke on behalf of all the members of the society.* 他代表該協會的全體會員發言.

behave [bi'heiv] *vi* act in a certain way. (The verb by itself often means acting in a correct or good way) 舉動; 表現 (本動詞本身常有行爲得體或表現良好之意): *They behaved very badly at the party.* 他們在宴會上的舉止很不得體. *You must try to behave* i.e. you must try to act properly. 你必須盡量守規矩. *He behaved extremely well.* 他表現極佳. *How is your new car behaving?* i.e. is it running well or are you having trouble with it? 你的新車好用嗎?即: 它行駛起來好嗎或有沒有毛病? **behaviour** [bi'heivjə*] *nu* (US 美 **behavior**). **behave yourself** (usu. said to a child) act properly, be good (通常對小孩說)規矩點.

behead [bi'hed] *vt* kill by cutting somebody's head off 砍(某人的)頭, 斬(某人的)首.

behind [bi'haind] *adv / prep* **1** at / to the back of something 在(某物)後面; 向後: *He hid behind a tree.* 他躲在一棵樹後面. *He looked behind but he* *couldn't see anyone coming.* 他向後看，但看不到有人來. **2** in a lower position (usu. in school etc.) 低於，落後於 (通常指在學校等): *He was a long way behind the other boys in his class* i.e. they had done more work and knew more than he did. 他大大落後於班上的其他男生. **3** remaining (usu. after one's death) 留下 (通常指死後): *He left a large family behind when he died.* 他死後留下一大家子. Also 亦作 *nc* part of the body on which one sits. *(informal)* 屁股 (非正式). **fall behind somebody** fail to go as fast, work as hard etc as somebody else 落在某人後面: *John could not run as fast as his two friends and he soon fell behind.* 約翰跑不過他的兩個朋友，他很快就落在後面了. *He fell behind the others.* 他落後於其他人.

behold [bi'hould] *vt* notice, look at, see (*o.f.*-use **see, notice** etc). 注意，看 (舊式—現在用 **see, notice** 等). *past* 過去式和過去分詞 **beheld** [bi'held].

beige [beiʒ] *nu* pale brownishgrey colour 淺棕灰色. Also 亦作 *adj*.

being[1] ['bi:iŋ] **1** *nc* human (usu. in **human being**) 人 (通常用於 **human being**). **2** *nu* life, existence 生命；存在.

being[2] ['bi:iŋ] *pres part* of **be.** be 的現在分詞.

belch [beltʃ] **1** *vi* send out wind from the stomach through the mouth 打嗝. **2** *vt* send out with great force 噴出: *A chimney belches (out) smoke.* 煙囪冒出濃煙. Also 亦作 *nc* the act or noise of sending wind from the stomach out through the mouth 打嗝 (聲).

belfry ['belfri] *nc* tower or part of a tower in which bells are hung (esp. in a church) 鐘塔，鐘架 (尤指在教堂的).

belie [bi'lai] *vt* give a false idea of, fail to show the real thing 給人以…的錯覺；掩飾: *His happyface belied his feeling of misery.* 他那快樂的臉掩飾了痛苦的感情.

belief [bi'li:f] **1** *nu* feeling that something is true or that somebody is telling the truth 相信；信心；信任. see 見 **believe.** **2** *nc* facts about a religion etc which somebody accepts as true 信條；信仰: *The beliefs of the Christian Church* 基督教的信條.

believe [bi'li:v] having a feeling that somebody is telling the truth or that something is true 相信: *I believe your story.* 我相信你的話. *I believe him to be a good man.* 我相信他是個好人. *I believe that you are telling the truth.* 我相信你是在說真話.(opp 反義詞 **disbelieve**). **believable** *adj* causing one to believe 可信的 .(opp 反義詞 **unbelievable**). **believer** *nc* one who believes (esp. in the existence of God) 相信者 (尤指信仰上帝的人)；信徒. (opp 反義詞 **unbeliever**). **believe in someone / something 1** have a strong feeling that someone / something exists 堅信有某人／某事物；信仰某人／某事物: *I believe in God.* 我信仰上帝. **2** trust somebody 信賴某人；信任某人. **3** have a feeling that something is good 相信某事是好的: *I believe in helping other people.* 我認爲助人是件好事.

belittle [bi'litl] *vt* behave or talk, write etc as though something were small and unimportant 輕視；貶低: *We belittled the danger.* 我們不把危險看在眼裏. *Do not belittle what he has achieved.* 別小看他取得的成績.

bell [bel] *nc* **1** hollow metal vessel which makes a ringing sound when it is hit 鐘. **2** anything which makes a sound like a bell 鈴；門鈴.

belligerent [bi'lidʒərənt] *adj* fond of fighting or arguing 好戰的; 好鬥的; 好爭吵的. **belligerence** *nu*.

bellow [belou] *vi* make a deep roaring noise like a bull 牛吼; 吼叫; *When the brick fell on the man's foot, he bellowed with pain.* 磚頭掉在那個人的腳上時, 他痛得大叫.

bellows ['belouz] *npl* instrument for blowing air (e.g. used to make a fire burn more brightly) 風箱(如用於鼓風助燃).

belly[1] ['beli] *nc* lower front part of the human body (人的) 肚子, 腹部. *Note* 說明: *belly* is felt to be rather impolite-use *stomach*. belly 被認爲頗不禮貌, 禮貌的說法是 stomach.

belly[2] ['beli] *vi* (usu. with reference to sails) fill out when the wind blows (通常指船帆) 張滿; *The ship's sails bellied out in the wind.* 船帆在風中張得鼓鼓的.

belong [bi'lɔŋ] *vi* **1** be the property of 是…的財產; 屬於; *That pen belongs to me* i.e. it is my pen. 那枝鋼筆是我的. **2** be a member of 是…的一員; *He belongs to the Labour Party* i.e. he is a member of that party. 他是工黨黨員. **3** be in the proper place 適合待在某處; *These shoes don't belong in this cupboard, take them out.* 這些鞋子不應當放在這個櫥裏, 把它們拿出來. *Does this belong here?* 這東西是擱在這裏的嗎? **belongings** *npl* things which belong to somebody 所有物. *Note* 說明: *belongings* refer to personal possessions, not to houses, land, money etc. belongings 指屬個人所有的物件, 不指房屋、土地、錢財等.

beloved [bi'lʌvd] *adj* much loved 受到愛戴的; *The old man was beloved by / of everyone who knew him.* 這老人受到所有認識他的人的愛戴. Also

亦作 [bi'lʌvd] *n sing* 單數 person who is much loved 心愛的人; *He sighed for his beloved.* 他思念他心愛的人.

below [bi'lou] *adv / prep* at or to a lower place; lower than something 在下面; 在…以下; *They looked out of the aeroplane window at the sea below.* 他們從飛機的舷窗俯瞰大海. *Miners work below the surface of the earth.* 礦工在地面下勞動. *The temperature is below freezing.* 溫度在零度以下. **see below** (in a book etc) referred to later (在書本等裏的) 參見下文.

belt [belt] *nc* **1** piece of cloth, leather etc. worn round the body 腰帶, 皮帶. **2** any strip or band like a belt 帶; 帶狀物; *a belt of trees* 林帶. **con'veyor belt** type of moving belt used in factories. (The article being manufactured is placed on the moving belt, which takes it to each worker so that he can do some work on it before it moves on to the next worker.) (工廠裏的)傳送帶(正在製作的物件置於傳送帶上, 傳給各個工人以便進行部份工作後傳給後一工人).

bench [bentʃ] *nc* **1** long seat (usu. of wood and without a back) 長橙(通常爲木製、無靠背). **2** long table at which a carpenter, shoemaker etc works (木工、鞋匠等的) 工作台. **3** place where a judge sits in a court 法官席. **the Bench** the judges of a country (全體) 法官.

bend [bend] *vt / i* **1** change the shape of something straight by using force 使彎曲; *I can't ride my bicycle because I've bent the wheel.* 我沒法騎自行車了, 因爲我把輪子弄扭曲了. *He bent the knife out of shape.* 他把小刀弄彎變形了. **2** become bent in this way 彎曲; 俯身; *He bent forward to look at the picture.* 他往前傾身看那幅圖畫.

He bent himself double 他彎腰彎到頭可以觸腳. **3** turn in a new direction 轉向: *The road bends to the right when it leaves the town.* 這條路通向城外後折向右方. **past** 過去式和過去分詞 **bent.** Also 亦作 *nc.* *Note* 說明: when *bend* means 'turn in a new direction', it usu. refers to a road, path, river etc, not to a person who is travelling; we can say *The road bends to the right* but *The traveller / car turned to the right* 當 *bend* 表示 "轉向" 時通常指道路、小徑、河流等, 不指行人; 我們可以說 The road bends to the right (這路折向右方). 但應該說 The traveller / car turned to the right (那旅行者 / 汽車向右拐). **be bent on something** be determined to do something. 決心要做某事. *He is bent on becoming an engineer.* 他決心要成爲一名工程師.

beneath [bi'ni:θ] *adv / prep* below, lower than; in a lower place 在…下面, 低于; 在下方.

benediction [beni'dikʃən] *nc* **1** blessing (esp. one given by a priest in a church service) 祝福(尤指做禮拜時牧師的祝福). **2** one of the services in the Roman Catholic Church (羅馬天主教)祝福式.

benefactor ['benifæktə*] *nc* somebody who does a good or kind action to help another person / other people; somebody who gives money to an institution 行善者; 捐助人.

beneficial [beni'fiʃl] *adj* helpful, having a helpful or good effect 有助的; 有益的.

beneficiary [beni'fiʃəri] *nc* person who receives something (often money or property) 受惠者, 受益人(常指接受金錢或財產者).

benefit¹ ['benifit] *nc / u* **1** help, good effect advantage, profit 幫助; 好處; 利益: *I don't know what benefit this new arrangement will be* i.e. I don't know how the new arrangement will help anyone. 我不知道這一新安排會有甚麼好處. *I feel the benefit of this medicine already* i.e. I can feel that the medicine is curing me. 我已感到這藥有療效. **2** payment made by a government, insurance company etc to a person who is ill or unemployed (政府對有病或失業者發放的)救濟金; 保險賠償費.

benefit² ['benifit] *vt / i* be of benefit, help etc.; receive help 對…有利, 有助於; 得到幫助: *This will not benefit you.* 這對你無益. *You will not benefit by / from this.* 你不會因此事而受益. **past** 過去式和過去分詞 **benefited.**

benevolent [bə'nevələnt] *adj* kind, liking to help other people 仁慈的; 樂善好施的. **benevolence** *nu* kindness to other people 仁慈; 善行.

benign [bi'nain] *adj* (with reference to certain diseases etc.) not very harmful (疾病等) 無大害的: *a benign tumour* 良性腫瘤.

bent¹ [bent] past of **bend.** bend 的過去式和過去分詞.

bent² [bent] *nu* natural liking for or interest in 天生的喜好; 興趣: *He has a bent for engineering.* 他愛好工程學.

bequeath [bi'kwi:ð] *vt* leave to somebody (esp. after one dies) 把…留給 (尤指人死後): *He bequeathed a thousand pounds to his niece.* 他遺贈給他的姪女一千英鎊. **bequest** [bi'kwest] *nc* something which is bequeathed 遺產; 遺贈物.

bereave [bi'ri:v] *vt* (usu. *passive*) take away from something / somebody (usu. by death) (通常用被動語態)奪去, 使喪失(通常因死亡): *He was be-*

reaved of his wife and children i.e. his wife and children died. 他喪失了妻兒. 即: 他的妻子和孩子死了. *past* 過去式和過去分詞 **bereaved** or **bereft** [bi'reft]. **bereavement** *nc / u* loss of someone through death (因死亡) 喪失.

beret ['beri] *nc* small round hat with no brim 貝雷帽, 圓扁便帽 (一種圓的無沿帽).

beriberi ['beri'beri] *nu* type of tropical disease 脚氣病 (一種熱帶疾病).

berry ['beri] *nc* small round fruit (usu. containing several seeds) 漿果; 莓.

berserk [bə'zə:k] *adj / adv* so angry that one seems to be mad 狂怒的(地). **go berserk** behave in this way 狂怒: *The prisoner went berserk and wrecked the prison* 這囚犯狂怒起來, 亂毀亂砸監獄.

berth [bə:θ] *nc* **1** place on a ship or train where one sleeps (輪船或飛機上的) 卧舖. **2** place where a ship anchors in a harbour etc. 停泊地, 錨位. Also 亦作 *vt* take a ship into a berth 使(船)停泊.

beseech [bi'si:tʃ] *vt* ask for with great feeling 懇求, 哀求. *past* 過去式和過去分詞 **besought** [bi'sɔ:t].

beset [bi'set] *vt* surround so as to cause difficulty or danger to somebody 包圍; 圍困; 使陷入困境: *The expedition was beset with dangers.* 這支探險隊陷入重重危險. *pres part* 現在分詞 **besetting.** *past* 過去式和過去分詞 **beset.**

beside [bi'said] *prep* near, next to, at the side of 在…附近; 在…旁邊: *You must sit beside this boy here.* 你必須坐在這裏, 在這男孩身邊. *Put your book beside the window.* 把你的書放在窗邊. **beside oneself (with rage, anger etc.)** so angry that one has

lost control of oneself (因憤怒等) 發狂; 失常: *When he saw his enemy escaping he was beside himself with rage.* 當他看到他的仇敵逃走時, 他氣得發狂.

besides [bi'saidz] *adv / prep* in addition to, also, as well as 加之; 而且; 除…以外: *That car is in a poor state of repair, and besides, it uses too much petrol.* 那輛車修得不好, 而且很耗油. *Have you any other books besides these?* i.e. have you any more books? 除了這些書外, 你還有別的書嗎? *Note* 說明: do not confuse *beside* and *besides*. Study the meanings of these words and you will see that they are quite different. 不要把 beside 和 besides 混同. 學習這兩詞的意義, 就會明白它們大不相同.

besiege [bi'si:dʒ] *vt* **1** surround an enemy town, city etc with soldiers in order to capture it 圍困; 圍攻. **2** surround etc somebody / something for some purpose (為某目的) 困擾: *He was besieged with requests.* 他被一大堆要求弄得應接不暇.

bespectacled [bi'spektikld] *adj* wearing glasses 戴眼鏡的.

best [best] *adj / adv* superlative of **good, well.** good,well 的最高級. '**best 'man** man who helps the bridegroom at a wedding (婚禮上的) 男儐相. '**best'seller** book which sells a great many copies 暢銷書. **at best** even in the most favourable circumstances 至多, 充其量: *At best we shall have only four good players in our team* i.e. this is the most we can hope for; we might have fewer than four. 我們隊頂多只有四個好隊員. 即: 這是我們最希望的, 有可能還不到四人. **make the best of something** (often **of a bad job**) accept something bad or unsatisfactory, and try to be cheerful about it 在逆境中泰然自若；隨遇而安.

bestow [bi'stou] *vt* give in an official way 贈給.

bet [bet] *vt / i* promise to give a certain sum of money to somebody if one is wrong about something; if one is right, one is given money by the other person 打賭: *He bet five pence.* 他打賭五便士. *He bet me five pence.* 他與我打賭五便士. *He bet me that he would win.* 他認爲他會贏而與我打賭. *He bet me five pence that he would win.* 他認爲他會贏而與我打賭五便士. *pres part* 現在分詞 **betting**. *past* 過去式和過去分詞 **bet** or **betted**. Also 亦作 *nc* agreement to pay money in this way 打賭. **betting** *nu* putting of money on horses etc. (就馬等的) 打賭.

betide [bi'taid] *vt* happen to *(o.f.)* 降臨於 (舊式). **woe betide somebody** unhappiness, bad luck will come to somebody, somebody will be punished 某人將要遭殃，某人將受懲罰: *Woe betide any pupil who comes in late.* (rather *o.f.*) 哪個學生遲到就要倒霉. (頗爲舊式).

betray [bi'trei] *vt* **1** give information to an enemy, help the enemies of one's country or of one's friends 背叛，出賣: *He betrayed his friends to the enemy* i.e. he helped the enemy to capture or defeat his friends. 他將朋友出賣給敵人. 即；他幫助敵人抓住或打敗他的朋友. **2** show, be a sign of 暴露，顯示出: *His face betrayed his fear* i.e. the expression on his face showed that he was afraid. 他的面孔露出恐懼的神色. **betrayer** *nc* **betrayal** *nc / u* act of betraying 背叛 (行爲)；洩露；暴露.

better¹ [betə*] *adj / adv* comparative of **good, well.** good, well 的比較級.

better off richer, luckier, more fortunate etc. *(informal)* 較富裕；較幸運；較好 (非正式). **get the better of someone** defeat, beat, overcome someone 打敗某人；制服某人. **know better than (to) do something** have enough intelligence to avoid doing something 知道不該做某事: *You ought to know better than stay away from school.* 你本來就應該知道曠課是不行的. **think better of something** change one's mind, decide to do something other than what one first intended to do 對某事改變主意，決定不這樣做某事: *He was going to answer me back, but he thought better of it.* 他正想跟我頂嘴，但是改變了主意，沒有這樣做.

better² [betə*] *vt* improve, make better 改善，改進；使更好.

between [bi'twi:n] *adv / prep* **1** with something on either side 介於…之間. *3 comes between 2 and 4.* 3介於2和4之間. **2** joining, connecting 聯繫著…；在…之間: *a connection between smoking and lung cancer* 吸烟與肺癌的關係；*war between two countries* 兩國間的戰爭；*the journey between London and Edinburgh* 倫敦至愛丁堡之間的旅程. **3** (with reference to time or distance) later or more than the first, but earlier or less than the second (指時間或距離) 在…之間: *between four and six o'clock* 在四點到六點的時候；*between five and ten miles* 在五英里到十英里之間. **4** for two or more 在兩者或多者之間；*share something between several people* 由幾個人均分某物. see *Note* 見說明. *Note* 說明: some people consider that *between* should be used only when two people / things are involved and that *among* should be used when more than two are involved (e.g. *He divided his money between his two sons* but *He divided his money among his three sons*). However, many speakers of English do not follow this rule. 有人認為 between 只能用於兩者之間, 而 among 用於兩者以上.(例如: He divided his money between his two sons, 但是 He divided his money among his three sons). 然而, 許多講英語的人並不遵循這一規則. **between you and me** (used to introduce a secret, or something which one does not want everyone to know) I will tell you, but I would not say this to everyone 咱們私下說說, 別外傳(用於談一秘密或不想讓衆人知道的事).(Also 亦作 **between ourselves.**)

beverage ['bevəridʒ] *nc* any kind of drink 飲料.

beware [bi'wɛə*] *vt / i* (used only in *imperative* or *infinitive;* does not form tenses)(只用於祈使句和不定式, 不能組成各種時態). *Beware of falling rocks!* i.e. be careful in case a rock falls on you. 當心掉下來的石頭! *You must beware of losing your books* i.e. you must try not to lose them. 你要小心, 別把書丟了. *Beware how you do something.* 你做事要留心.

bewilder [bi'wildə*] *vt* make it difficult or impossible for somebody to understand something or to think clearly 使困惑; 使糊塗. *Most of the questions in the examination bewildered me.* 這次考試的大部份題目我都做不來. *I was bewildered by the new rules.* 我被這些新規則搞糊塗了. **bewildering** *adj* **bewilderment** *nu.*

bewitch [bi'witʃ] *vt* **1** use magic on 施魔力於. **2** attract; be so beautiful, attractive, charming etc that other people are very influenced 吸引; 使着

迷; 使銷魂: *The beautiful girl bewitched all the young men in the village.* 這美麗的姑娘使全村的年輕人都着了迷. **bewitching** *adj.*

beyond [bi'jɔnd] *adv / prep* **1** further (than), at a greater distance (than) 遠於; 再過去: *The house is beyond the village* i.e. you will come to the house after passing the village. 那房子在村莊的那一邊. 即: 你要先經過村莊才會到達那房子. **2** past, later than 超出; 遲於: *beyond help* i.e. unable to be helped 無法幫助的; *beyond belief* i.e. impossible to believe 難以置信的. *How he can tell such lies is beyond my understanding.* 我不理解他怎麽會說出這樣的謊話.

bi- [bai] *prefix* twice; every two; having two of something (e.g. **bilateral**) 二; 兩(倍); 雙(例如: **bilateral**) 二; 兩(倍); 雙(例如: **bilateral**) 二;

bias ['baiəs] *vt* make somebody come to a decision without allowing him to hear the full facts 使有偏見: *He was biassed against the plan from the beginning* i.e. he had decided that he was opposed to the plan before he had ever heard the arguments in favour of it. 他一開始就對這項計劃抱有偏見. 即: 在他未聽到贊成這項計劃的辯論之前, 就決定反對這項計劃. *The newspapers biassed their readers against the new government.* 報紙使讀者對新政府存有偏見. *He was biassed towards the plan* i.e. he was in favour of the plan before he had heard the full facts. 他偏袒該項計劃. 即: 他未聽取詳情就贊成該計劃. *past* 過去式和過去分詞 **biased** or **biassed.** Also 亦作 *nc / u* leaning, prejudice 偏見, 偏愛. **biassed** *adj. (opp* 反義詞 **unbiassed).**

bib [bib] *nc* piece of cloth or plastic which is tied round a child's neck while he is eating (小孩吃東西時圍的)圍脖.

Bible ['baibl] *nc* holy books of the Christian or Jewish religions bound in one volume (基督教或猶太教的)聖經. **biblical** ['biblikl] *adj*.

bibliography [bibli'ɔɡrəfi] *nc* list of books and other writings about a particular subject or by a particular writer (關於某一學科的)書目; (某一作家的)作品目錄.

bicarbonate [bai'kɑːbənit] *nu* acid salt of carbonic acid 碳酸氫鹽.

bicentenary [baisen'tiːnəri] *nc* celebration of something which happened 200 years ago 二百週年紀念.

biceps ['baiseps] *n sing or pl* (usu. *pl*) large muscle in the upper part of the arm (單數或複數,通常用複數)二頭肌.

bicker ['bikə*] *vi* quarrel about little things (爲小事)吵嘴,爭吵. **bickering** *nu* quarrelling of this kind 鬥嘴,爭吵.

bicycle ['baisikl] *nc* vehicle with two wheels used for riding 自行車, 腳踏車: *Everybody should learn how to ride a bicycle.* 大家都應該學騎自行車.

bid[1] [bid] *vt* make an offer of money at an auction (在拍賣場)出(價): *He bid five pounds for the chair* i.e. he offered to buy the chair for five pounds. 他出價五英鎊買那把椅子. *past* 過去式和過去分詞 **bid**. Also 亦作 *nc* an offer of this kind (拍賣)出價. **bidder** *nc* person who makes a bid 出價人,競買者. **bidding** *nu* all the bids made at an auction (拍賣時的)出價(總稱): *Was there much bidding?* i.e. did many people make bids? 很多人出價嗎?

bid[2] [bid] *vt* order, command (*o.f.*-use **order** etc.) 命令,吩咐(舊式—現在用

order 等). *past tense* 過去式 **bade** [bæd]. *past part* 過去分詞 **bidden. bidding** *nu* command, order 命令,吩咐. **bid somebody goodbye, farewell, welcome etc** say goodbye etc to somebody 向某人說再見/向某人告別/歡迎某人等.

big [big] *adj* large, not small etc. 大的,不小的. *comparative* 比較級 **bigger.** *superlative* 最高級 **biggest.** '**big-hearted** *adj* kind, generous, willing to help other people 慈善的,寬宏大量的,樂於助人的.

bigamy ['bigəmi] *nu* act of being married by the official procedure of a country or in church when already married to another person; in many countries this is a crime and a sin 重婚(在許多國家裏被視爲犯罪或不道德行爲). **bigamist** *nc*.

bigot ['bigət] *nc* person who has very strong beliefs (esp. religious beliefs) and who will not listen to other people's opinions (尤指宗教信仰)盲信者; 執拗的人. **bigoted** *adj* **bigotry** *nu*.

bike [baik] *nc* informal form of **bicycle** 自行車(bicycle 的非正式形式).

bikini [bi'kiːni] *nc* very small swimming costume for women, consisting of two pieces 比基尼式女泳裝,三點式女泳衣.

bilateral [bai'lætərl] *adj* on both sides; made by two opposing groups; having two sides 在兩邊的; 雙方的; 有兩邊的: *The two countries signed a bilateral agreement on trade.* 兩國簽署了一項雙邊貿易協定.

bile [bail] *nu* bitter liquid produced by the liver to help the digestion of food 膽汁.

bilingual [bai'liŋɡwəl] *adj* **1** speaking or knowing two languages 說(或懂)兩種語言的: *Some children educated in* *foreign countries become bilingual.* 一些在國外受教育的兒童能使用兩種語言. **2** written etc in two languages 用兩種語言寫的: *a bilingual text* 兩种文字對照的課文.

bilious ['biliəs] *adj* **1** caused by too much bile 膽汁過多引起的: *a bilous attack* i.e. a slight illness caused by too much bile. 膽汁病. 即: 膽汁過多引起的小病. **2** sickly 有病的; 病態的: *a bilious colour* 帶病的臉色.

bill¹ [bil] *nc* bird's beak 鳥嘴

bill² [bil] *nc* **1** piece of paper which lists the amounts of money one owes for goods or service which one has received (應付的)賬單. **2** law before it has been officially approved. (It is called an **act** when it has been officially approved by Parliament)爲 act). 法案. (經議會正式批准後稱爲 act). **3** (US) piece of paper money (美)紙幣, 鈔票. **'billposter** person who sticks notices on walls etc. (在牆壁等上面)張貼傳單廣告的人.

billet ['bilit] *nc* private house where a soldier lives if he does not live in a barracks (士兵不住營房時)臨時寓所.

billiards ['biliədz] *nu* game played on a big special table with ivory balls and long sticks 台球戲.

billion ['biliən] *nc* **1** (Brit) a million multiplied by a million (1,000,000,000,000) (英)萬億. **2** (US) a million multiplied by a thousand (1,000,000,000) (美)十億.

billow ['bilou] *nc* **1** large wave 巨浪: *the billows of the Pacific* 太平洋的巨浪. **2** rolling mass (as of smoke, sound, etc) like a large wave 巨浪般滾滾向前的東西(如烟火, 聲音等).

bin [bin] *nc* large container (usu. with a lid) 大箱(通常有蓋). **'dustbin** (Brit) bin for putting rubbish in (英)垃圾

箱.(US 美 **'trash can**).

binary ['bainəri] *adj* made up of two part or things; double 二; 二對的; 一雙的, 雙重的.

bind [baind] *vt* **1** use string, rope etc. to tie or fasten things together 縛, 捆, 綁, 纏: *He bound the sticks together.* 他把柴枝捆在一起. **2** make somebody do something or promise to do something (usu. by law) (通常通過法律)使做某事, 使承諾做某事; 約束: *The contract binds us to complete the work within six months.* 合同規定我們必須在六個月内完成工作. *past* 過去式和過去分詞 **bound** [baund]. **binding** *nc* covering of a book; way in which the pages of a book are fastened together (書的)封面; 裝訂.

bingo ['biŋgou] *nu* type of gambling game 賓果遊戲(一種賭博性遊戲).

binoculars [bi'nɔkjuləz] *npl* glasses which enable one to see things a long way away. (Often **a pair of binoculars**) 雙筒望遠鏡. (常用 a pair of binoculars).

binomial [bai'noumiəl] *adj* composed of two terms 二項的; 二項式的.

biochemistry ['baiou'kemistri] *nu* science of the chemistry of living things 生物化學.

biography [bai'ɔgrəfi] *nc* story of somebody's life, written by another person 傳記. see 見 **autobiography. biographical** [baiou'græfikl] *adj* biog-**rapher** *nc*.

biology [bai'ɔlədʒi] *nu* science of living things (e.g. plants and animals) 生物學. **biological** [baiə'lɔdʒikl] *adj* **biologist** *nc*.

biome ['baioum] *nc* natural community of plants and animals, its composition being largely controlled by climate conditions 生物羣落.

biotic [bai'ɔtik] *adj* of or having to do with life or living things 生命的; 生物的.

birch [bə:tʃ] *nc* type of tree having a smooth bark and thin branches 樺樹, 白樺.

bird [bə:d] *nc* 1 type of creature having wings and a beak and usu. able to fly 鳥. 2 girl, girlfriend. (*informal* in sense 2) 姑娘; 女朋友 (義2爲非正式). **'bird's-'eye 'view** view from above, covering a wide area 鳥瞰.

Biro ['bairou]* *nc* type of ballpoint pen (商標) 拜樂牌圓珠筆.

birth [bə:θ] *nc* 1 act of being born 出生, 誕生: *the birth of a baby* 嬰兒的出生. 2 beginning of something 開始, 產生: *the birth of a new political party* 一個新政黨的創立. **'birth control** various methods of ensuring that babies are born only when parents wish to have them, so as to limit the size of the family 節 (制)生育. **'birthday** date, returning each year, on which somebody was born 生日, 誕辰: *My birthday is the 22nd of April.* 我的生日是四月二十二日. **'birthmark** mark on the skin which was there when somebody was born 胎記; 胎痣. **'birthplace** town etc in which somebody was born 出生地; 故鄉. **birth rate** number of children born in one year in a country taken as a proportion of the total population (人口) 出生率. **give birth** have a baby 生; 分娩: *She gave birth to a baby boy.* 她生了一個男嬰.

biscuit ['biskit] *nc* 1 (*Brit*) type of hard, flat cake, often sweetened (英) 餅乾. 2 (*US*) type of bread made into small buns (美) 小圓麵包.

bisect [bai'sekt] *vt* divide into two parts 把…分爲二. **bisection** *nu*.

bishop ['biʃəp] *nc* clergyman of senior rank in many Christian churches (基督教的) 主教.

bit [bit] *nc* 1 small piece 小塊; 一點: *Write it on a bit of paper.* 把它寫在一張小紙片上. *I'm going to sleep for a bit* i.e. for a short time. 我要去睡一會兒. 即: 很短時間. 2 part of a drill which makes a hole 鑽頭. 3 metal bar which is placed in a horse's mouth to control it 馬嚼子, 馬啣. **bit by bit** gradually, slowly 逐漸地, 慢慢地. **not a bit** not at all 一點兒也不. **to bits** into small pieces 成碎片: *knocked to bits* 敲成碎片.

bit² [bit] *adv* rather 有點, 稍微: *This job is a bit difficult* i.e. difficult but not as difficult as it could be. 這工作有點難. 即: 困難, 但還不算頂難. *He's a bit better* i.e. better but not completely recovered from his illness. 他略有好轉. 即: 病好了些, 但未完全康復. *Note* adjs: not all *adjs* can have a *bit* in front of them. 並非所有形容詞前都可用 a bit.

bit³ [bit] past tense of **bite.** bite 的過去式.

bitch [bitʃ] *nc* 1 female dog or wolf 母狗; 母狼. 2 impolite way of referring to a woman (usu. one who is unpleasant) (*informal* in sense 2) 女人 (不禮貌的提法, 通常指其令人討厭) (義2爲非正式).

bite [bait] *vt/i* 1 use the teeth to cut or break something 咬: *He bit the apple.* 他咬蘋果. *The dog bit the man.* 狗咬了那個男人. 2 (usu. with reference to insects) sting (昆蟲) 叮: *I was bitten by a mosquito.* 我被蚊子叮了. 3 (with reference to fish) take food (called **bait**) off a hook (魚) 咬餌 (bait); (魚) 上鈎: *Are the fish biting today?* 今天魚兒上鈎嗎? *pres part* 現

在分詞 **biting**. *past tense* 過去式 **bit** [bit]. *past part* 過去分詞 **bitten.** Also 亦作 *nc* **1** act of biting 咬;叮. **2** mark left by a bite or sting 被咬(或叮)的痕跡. **3** mouthful of food 一口食物. **4** taking of food from the hook by a fish (魚)的吞餌;上鈎: *I was fishing for a long time before I had a bite.* 我釣了很久才有一條魚兒上鈎. **biting** *adj* **1** so cold as to cause pain 冷得刺痛的: *a biting wind* 刺骨的寒風. **2** causing pain to somebody 令人痛苦的: *biting remarks* 刻薄的話.

bitten ['bitn] *past part* of **bite**. bite的過去分詞.

bitter ['bitə*] *adj* **1** opposite of sweet; having a taste like beer or quinine 苦的,有苦味的. **2** causing pain or unhappiness 引起痛苦或不愉快的: *a bitter wind* i.e. a very cold wind 刺骨的寒風. *His son's behaviour has been a bitter disappointment to him.* 他兒子的行爲使他非常失望. **3** caused by or showing hate or great dislike 顯示仇恨或憎惡的;由仇恨或憎惡引起的;激烈的: *Their friendship ended with a bitter quarrel.* 他們的友誼以激烈的爭吵告終. **bitterly** *adv* **bitterness** *nu*.

bivouac ['bivuæk] *nc* soldiers' camp with no tents 軍隊的野營(無帳篷).

bizarre [bi'za:*] *adj* very strange, unnatural 奇異的,古怪的.

blab [blæb] *vt / i* talk too much (and esp. tell secrets in this way) 講過頭,亂講(話)(尤指透露秘密). *past* 過去式和過去分詞 **blabbed.** (*imformal*) (非正式).

black [blæk] **1** *nu* the colour of the print in this book 黑色. **2** *nu* (with reference to people) the colour of the Africans south of the Sahara (人的)黑色. **3** *nc* African or person of African origin 黑人. Also 亦作 *adj* dark,

gloomy, dirty, threatening黑色的;暗淡的;髒的;有兇兆的. **blacken** *vt / i* become or make black in colour (使)變黑. **blackbird** black songbird with a yellow beak related to the thrush 畫眉;燕八哥(體黑嘴黃的鳥). '**blackboard** large board (usu. black or dark in colour) in a classroom, on which the teacher writes with chalk 黑板. '**black'eye** darkcoloured bruise around the eye (被打得)發青腫脹的眼圈. '**blackhead** small pimple on the skin, having a black head 黑頭粉刺. '**blackleg** person who works when other people are on strike 罷工期間繼續幹活的工人. '**blacklist** *nc* list of people who have done wrong or who might do wrong 黑名單. Also 亦作 *vt* write someone's name on a list 把(某人的名字)列入黑名單. '**black 'magic** magic which causes harm to people; evil magic 巫術;妖術. '**blackmail** *nu* threat to tell somebody's secrets if he does not give one some money 敲詐,勒索. Also 亦作 *vt* make such a threat 敲詐,勒索. **blackmailer** *nc* 敲詐者. '**black 'mark (against somebody)** something which shows that somebody has failed to do something (對某人不利的)黑點(表示某人沒有把事情做好的符號). **(the) 'black 'market** see 見 **market.** '**blackout** *nc* **1** loss of consciousness 失去知覺,暈過去. **2** turning out all the lights 燈火熄滅. Also 亦作 *vi* lose consciousness, faint 失去知覺,昏厥. '**black 'sheep (of the family)** the person in a group or family who fails to do well or who behaves badly 敗家子;害羣之馬. '**blacksmith** man whose work is to make things out of iron (esp. horseshoes) 鐵匠(尤指做馬蹄的). **black and blue** badly bruised 青腫

的: *After the fight he was black and blue.* 他打架過後身上青一塊紫一塊的.

bladder ['blædə*] *nc* 1 bag inside the body which contains urine 膀胱. 2 rubber bag inside a football (足) 球膽.

blade [bleid] *nc* 1 part of a knife or sword which has a sharp edge or point 刀鋒; 刀口, 刀. 2 anything shaped like a knife blade 刀片狀物: *a blade of grass.* 一片草葉.

blame [bleim] *vt* say that somebody / something caused an accident or a failure of some kind 責備; 把…歸咎於: *He blamed his brother for breaking the window.* 他責備他兄弟打破窗玻璃. *He blamed the accident on his brother.* 他將這個意外事故歸咎於他的兄弟. Also 亦作 *nu* **blameless** *adj* not responsible, innocent 沒有責任的; 無罪的. **to blame** responsible 應負責的: *John is to blame for the accident* i.e. John caused the accident. 約翰應對此事故負責. 即: 約翰造成了這個事故.

blancmange [blə'mɔnʒ] *nc / u* type of sweet food made from milk and cornflour 牛奶凍(一種用牛奶和玉米粉做的甜食).

bland [blænd] *adj* 1 very gentle, too polite 很溫和的; 慇懃的. 2 (with reference to food) smooth and easily digested (and usu. without much taste) (食物)無刺激性的; 易消化的; 淡而無味的.

blank¹ [blæŋk] *adj* lacking something, without something 缺少的, 空的: *a blank piece of paper* i.e. one without any writing or drawing on it 一張白紙. *a blank wall* i.e. one without doors or windows 空牆, 即: 沒有門或窗的牆; *a blank cartridge* i.e. one without a bullet in it 空彈, 即: 沒有彈

頭的子彈. *There was a blank look on his face* i.e. his face showed no sign of thought or feeling. 他的臉上有一種茫然的神色. 即: 他的臉上沒有露出任何思想或感情. **'blank 'cheque** one which is signed but on which the sum of money to be paid is not written 空白支票.

blank² [blæŋk] *nc* 1 space in which nothing is written 空格; 空白處: *Leave a blank if you don't know the answer.* 不知道答案就空着. 2 blank cartridge. 空彈: *The soldiers were firing blanks.* 士兵們正在發射空彈. 3 emptiness or absence of something 空白; 缺乏: *His mind was a blank* i.e. he could not think of anything or remember anything. 他的腦子一片空白. 即: 他想不起或記不得任何事情. **blankly** *adv.*

blanket ['blæŋkit] *nc* 1 warm cloth (usu. made of wool) used for covering someone / something (esp. someone sleeping in a bed) 毛毯, 毛氈. 2 any thick covering 厚的覆蓋物: *a blanket of snow* 一層雪.

blare [blɛə*] *vt / i* make a loud noise like a trumpet (像喇叭般)高聲發出; 高聲吼叫. Also 亦作 *nu.*

blasé ['bla:zei] *adj* having experienced many pleasures etc and now interested in none 對享樂不再感興趣的, 玩膩了的.

blasphemy ['blæsfəmi] *nc / u* talking of God in a disrespectful or joking way 褻瀆上帝的話語. **blasphemous** *adj* **blaspheme** [blæs'fi:m] *vt / i* speak in this way (用話語)褻瀆(上帝).

blast¹ [bla:st] *nc* 1 sudden strong rush of air (esp. one caused by an explosion or by opening an oven or other place where air has been heated) 氣流(尤指爆炸、打開烤爐或其他空氣加熱處引起的): *The blast from the ex-*

plosion shattered hundreds of windows. 爆炸的氣浪震破了數百個窗戶. **2** sound made by a trumpet or other wind instrument 喇叭聲; 管樂器聲. **3** explosion 爆炸.

blast² [blɑ:st] *vt* destroy by explosion 炸毀. **blasted** *adj* damned, cursed. *(informal)* 該死的, 可惡的 (非正式).

blatant ['bleitənt] *adj* **1** not trying to hide one's bad behaviour; shameless 公然的; 無恥的; *The student showed blatant disrespect for the rules of the college.* 那個學生公然藐視學院的規章. **2** noisy and badly behaved 吵嚷的, 喧擾的.

blaze¹ [bleiz] *nc* (usu. only *sing*) (通常只用單數) **1** bright flame 熊熊火焰: *the blaze of the fire* 火焰. **2** bright light or bright colour 光亮; 絢爛的色彩; *There was a sudden blaze of light and then it became dark again.* 突然閃亮了一下後又暗下來. **3** fire which destroys a building etc. 大火, 火災; *The fireman fought the blaze for two hours before they put it out.* 消防隊員奮戰了兩小時才把大火撲滅.

blaze² [bleiz] *vi* **1** burn fiercely or quickly 熊熊燃燒; *The fire was blazing.* 火燒得很旺. **2** shine brightly 閃耀; 照耀. **3** show strong feelings 表現出激烈情緒. *His eyes were blazing with anger.* 他的眼睛閃着怒火. **blazing blaze away (at something)** fire bullets very quickly and without stopping. *(informal)* 連續 (向某物) 射擊 (非正式). **blaze a trail 1** mark trees to show the path in a forest (在森林中) 在樹上刻指路的標記. **2** do something for the first time so that other people are encouraged to do it after one 開路, 帶頭; *With his discoveries the famous scientist blazed a trail which many of his colleagues followed.* 這位著名的科學家以自己的發現開闢了道路, 他的許多同事沿着這條路前進.

blazer ['bleizə*] *nc* type of jacket, sometimes brightly coloured, worn by some schoolchildren in Britain, and by adults to show they are members of teams which play certain games (e.g. cricket, bowls etc.) 一種茄克衫, 運動上衣 (有時顏色鮮艷, 爲英國一些學童穿的; 成年人則穿此衣以表示其爲板球、滾木球等球隊的隊員).

bleach [bli:tʃ] *nu* chemical substance which takes the colour out of certain materials or which helps to make clothes clean 漂白劑. Also 亦作 *vt/i* become or make something pale or clean by using bleach, or by exposure to sunlight (使) 變白, 漂白; 脫色; 曬白; *The old curtains had been bleached by the sun.* 舊窗簾被太陽曬脫色了.

bleak [bli:k] *adj* **1** exposed to cold winds 寒風吹襲的; *The countryside here is very bleak in winter.* 在冬天, 這鄉間寒風凜冽. **2** with very little hope of happiness 沒有指望的, 慘淡的; *Without money, the future looked bleak for John.* 約翰沒有錢, 看來他的前途黯淡. **3** unhappy and unfriendly etc. 不高興的, 冷漠的; *When we arrived, we got a rather bleak welcome.* 我們到達時受到的迎接相當冷淡.

bleary ['bliəri] *adj* unable to see clearly (usu. because of tiredness) 視力模糊的 (通常由於疲倦).

bleat [bli:t] *vi* make a noise like a sheep or goat (像羊) 咩咩地叫. Also 亦作 *nc* noise made by these animals 羊的叫聲, 咩咩的叫聲.

bled [bled] past of **bleed.** bleed 的過去式和過去分詞.

bleed [bli:d] *vi* lose blood 流血; *The*

cut on his finger was bleeding. 他手指上的傷口在流血. *He was bleeding from the cut on his finger.* 血從他手指上的傷口流出來. *past* 過去式和過去分詞 **bled** [bled].

blemish ['blemiʃ] *nc* mark which makes something less beautiful or less perfect 瑕疵; 污點; 缺點: *a blemish on one's reputation* 個人名譽上的污點. Also 亦作 *vt* make something less beautiful or less perfect by adding a blemish 玷污.

blend [blend] *vt / i* **1** (esp. with reference to mixing different kinds of tea, coffee, whisky, tobacco) become, make mixed (尤指把不同種類的茶葉、咖啡、威士忌、烟草摻在一起)混合; 摻雜. **2** (with reference to different colours) be suitable for putting together; change gradually from one colour into the other (不同的顏色)相稱, 融合, 調和: *I like the way the colour of the carpet blends with the yellow curtains.* 我喜歡這地毯的顏色和黃色的窗簾相配. Also 亦作 *nc* mixture (esp. of tea, coffee, whisky or tobacco) (尤指茶葉、咖啡、威士忌或烟草的)混合物; 混成品.

bless [bles] *vt* **1** ask God's help or protection for 爲…祝福, 爲…祈禱: *The priest blessed the people.* 牧師爲人們祝福. **2** make holy 使神聖. *past* **blessed** or **blest** both pronounced/blest] 過去式和過去分詞爲 blessed 或 blest, 兩者的發音均爲[blest]. **blessing** *nc* **1** something given through the help or protection of God (上帝的)賜福, 恩賜. **2** prayer said by a priest which asks God to give help and protection to the people 祈福禱告. **3** anything which makes one happy and thankful 幸運的事: *Good health is a blessing.* 健康是件幸事. **bless you!** an ex-

clamation sometimes said by other people when somebody sneezes 百歲! (有人打噴嚏時別人說的話).

blew [blu:] past tense of **blow¹**. blow¹ 的過去式.

blight [blait] *nu* **1** disease of plants (植物的)枯萎病. **2** anything which spoils one's hopes, plans etc. 使希望、計劃等落空的事物. Also 亦作 *vt* spoil in this way 破壞; 挫折: *The accident blighted his life.* 這事故毀了他的一生.

blind¹ [blaind] *adj* **1** unable to see 瞎的, 盲的: *The old man with the white stick was blind.* 拄着白手杖的那老頭是盲人. **2** with no opening 無出口處的: *a blind alley* i.e. an alley with a wall at the end 死胡同. Also 亦作 *vt* make blind 使瞎眼. **blindly** *adv* **blindness** *nu* the blind blind people 盲人. '**blindfold** *nc* piece of cloth tied over the eyes to prevent somebody from seeing 矇眼布. Also 亦作 *vt* cover somebody's eyes in this way 把(某人的眼睛)矇住. Also 亦作 *adj / adv* with the eyes covered in this way 被矇住眼睛的(地). '**blind spot 1** small part of the eye which is not sensitive to light (眼球的)盲點. **2** prejudice against something 對某事物的偏見.

blind² [blaind] *nc* something (often cloth which can be rolled down and up) which covers a window to keep sunshine out or to stop people seeing in 窗簾; 遮陽.

blink [bliŋk] *vt / i* shut the eyes and open them again quickly 眨(眼睛).

blinkers ['bliŋkəz] *npl* pieces of leather put at the side of a horse's eyes to make it look straight ahead 馬眼罩.

bliss [blis] *nu* very great and peaceful happiness 巨大的幸福, 極樂. **blissful** *adj* **blissfully** *adv*.

blister ['blistə*] *nc* **1** small swelling on the skin filled with a watery liquid (usu. caused by rubbing or burning) (通常因皮膚擦傷或灼傷引起的)水疱. **2** swelling on painted wood, caused by heat (木器漆層的)氣泡. Also 亦作 *vt / i* get or cause blisters (使)起水疱;(使)生氣泡.

blithe [blaið] *adj* happy and cheerful (o.f.) 愉快的 (舊式). **blithely** *adv* happily, not showing any remorse, distress etc. 愉快地,無憂無慮地: *He blithely ignored me.* 他怡然自得,不理我.

blizzard ['blizəd] *nc* snowstorm with a strong wind 暴風雪.

bloated ['bloutid] *adj* too fat, fat in an unhealthy way 太胖的,病態發胖的.

blob [blɔb] *nc* small round spot or object 小斑點,小圓塊: *A blob of ice cream fell on her dress.* 一小塊冰淇淋掉在她的衣服上.

bloc [blɔk] *nc* group of people or countries who act together in certain political activities 集團(在某些政治活動中一起行動的一羣人或一些國家): *There is an Afro-Asian bloc at the United Nations.* 聯合國有個亞非集團.

block¹ [blɔk] *nc* **1** large solid piece of wood or stone etc. 大塊(木頭或石頭等). **2** *(Brit)* large tall building (英) 高樓,大廈: *They are building a new block of offices near the school.* 他們正在學校附近建一座新的辦公樓. **3** number of buildings surrounded by streets on four sides 街區(四面有街道的建築羣): *The place you're looking for is three blocks along the street.* 你要找的地方順着這條街往三個街區就到了. **4** number of seats that are together in a cinema or theatre (電影院或戲院的)座位區. **5** something which stops things moving (usu.

blockage, or if reference is to traffic, '**traffic jam** is more usual) 障礙物(通常用 blockage, 如果指交通,更常用 traffic jam). **blockage** *nc* something which prevents movement 障礙物: *There is a blockage in the pipe, and so the water is not coming through.* 因水管堵塞,水流不過來. '**block 'letters** LETTERS WRITTEN LIKE THIS. (手寫的)印刷體字母.

block² [blɔk] *vt* **1** make movement impossible 阻塞: *You can't leave the city, all the roads are blocked by snow.* 你出不了城了,所有的道路都被雪堵住了. *They will have to block up the entrance to the tunnel.* 他們將不得不封閉通往隧道的入口. **2** make it impossible for something to happen 阻擋,阻礙: *All our plans have been blocked by our opponents.* 我們的所有計劃都受到對手阻撓.

blockade [blɔ'keid] *nc* surrounding a town, country etc to prevent people or supplies getting in or out 封鎖. Also 亦作 *vt* surround a town, country etc in this way 封鎖.

blond [blɔnd] *nc* (esp. with reference to women) person having yellow or golden hair (尤指女人)黃色或金黃色頭髮的人. Also 亦作 *adj*.

blood [blʌd] *nu* red liquid in the body 血,血液. **bloody** *adj* **1** covered with blood 血污的;流血的. **2** cursed, annoying. *(informal* in sense 2) 該死的;討厭的(義2爲非正式). Note 說明: the word in sense 2 often has very little meaning. It is considered impolite except among friends. It can also be used as an *intensifier*: bloody good. 本詞義2經常幾乎無意義,被認爲是不禮貌的,只在朋友間使用;亦可作加強語氣用,如: bloody good (極好). '**blood donor** person who gives some of his blood for medical purposes 供血者, 獻血者. **'blood group** type of blood. (Everybody's blood belongs to one of four main types) 血型 (每個人的血型屬於四種主要血型之一). **'bloodhound** large dog used for tracking people who have run away (e.g. criminals) 警犬. **'blood poisoning** disease of the blood 血中毒, 敗血症: *If you don't clean that wound, you may get blood poisoning.* 要是不把傷口洗乾淨, 你可能得敗血症. **'blood pressure** pressure of the blood against the sides of the blood vessels 血壓. **'bloodshed** killing 流血; 屠殺: *The king defeated his enemies, but only after much bloodshed.* 國王經過大肆殺戮後才打敗了敵人. **'bloodshot** adj (with reference to the eyes) red (指眼睛) 充血的: *I think I must be reading too much because my eyes are rather bloodshot.* 我想我一定是看書的時間太長了, 因為我的雙眼佈滿血絲. **'bloodthirsty** adj having a liking for killing people or animals 嗜血的, 嗜殺成性的. **'blood transfusion** (medicine) taking blood from one person's veins and putting it into another's (醫學) 輸血. **'bloody-minded** adj behaving in a deliberately awkward way 故意爲難的.

bloom [blu:m] **1** nc flower 花. **2** nu time when somebody / something is most perfect 最盛期: *The girl was in the bloom of youth.* 這姑娘正當青春. Also 亦作 vi have flowers 開花: *The trees are blooming.* 樹木正在開花. **in bloom** having flowers 開着花.

blossom [ˈblɒsəm] **1** nu all the flowers on a fruit tree (一棵果樹的) 全部花朵, 花簇. **2** nc one of these flowers (果樹的) 一朵花. Also 亦作 vi have flowers 開花.

blot [blɒt] nc stain of ink on a piece of paper (紙上的) 墨跡. Also 亦作 vt **1** dry up ink with blotting paper etc. (用吸墨紙等) 弄乾. **2** make a mark with ink 沾上墨漬. past 過去式和過去分詞 **blotted.** **'blotting paper** paper used for drying ink 吸墨紙. **blot something** out hide completely; cover up; destroy; make a blot which completely hides what has been written 遮住某物; 蓋住某物; 摧毀某物; 塗去某物: *blot out a word* 塗掉一個詞.

blotch [blɒtʃ] nc large roughly-shaped mark (esp. on somebody's face) 斑 (尤指在臉上). **blotchy** adj.

blouse [blauz] nc garment covering the upper part of the body (usu. worn by women) (婦女穿的) 寬鬆上衣, 女襯衫.

blow[1] [bləu] vt / vi **1** (with reference to wind, air etc.) move or cause to move (風、空氣等) 吹; 吹動: *The wind was blowing.* 風在吹. *The wind blew my hat off.* 風颳掉我的帽子. **2** be moved or carried away by air or wind 被風或空氣吹動: *All the papers blew off his desk; the wind blew them off.* 他桌上的文件都被吹掉了; 是風把文件吹掉的. **3** (with reference to musical instruments) make, cause to make, a noise by the movement of air (樂器) 吹響; 吹奏 (樂器): *The trumpet was blowing.* 喇叭在響. *He blew the trumpet.* 他吹喇叭. **4** (with reference to a fuse) melt (保險絲) 燒斷: *If there is too much current in the circuit a fuse will blow.* 如果線路電流太強, 保險絲便會燒斷. past tense 過去式 **blew** [blu:] past part 過去分詞 **blown** [bləun]. **'blow-dry** arrange the hair after it has been washed by blowing a current of warm air onto it 熱吹 (頭髮) 做髮型 Also 亦作 n arrangement of one's hair by this means 用熱吹法做髮型. **blow**

out (with reference to a candle flame, burning match etc.) stop burning, cause to stop burning, by the movement of air (蠟火、燃着的火柴等) 熄滅; 吹滅. **'blow-out** bursting of a tyre 車胎爆裂. **blow up 1** explode, damage or destroy by an explosion. 爆炸, 炸毀: *The bomb blew up.* 炸彈爆炸. *He blew up the building.* 他炸毀大樓. **2** (with reference to a tyre, balloon etc.) fill with air 使 (輪胎、氣球等) 充氣. **blow one's nose** breathe very hard through one's nose (usu. into a handkerchief) to clear the nose of dirt 擤鼻子.

blow² [blou] *nc* **1** hard knock with the hand or a weapon (用手或武器) 用力的一擊, 打: *hit / strike somebody a blow in the eye* 照某人的眼睛猛打一拳; *give somebody a blow* 猛擊某人一下. **2** disappointment, misfortune 沮喪; 不幸: *News of John's sudden death was a great blow to his friends.* 約翰突然去世的消息對朋友們是個沉重的打擊.

blown [bloun] past part of **blow¹**. **blow¹**的過去分詞.

blubber ['blʌbə*] *nu* fat of whales and some other sea animals 鯨脂; 海生動物脂肪.

blue [blu:] *nu* colour of the sky when the sun is shining, and other colours lighter and darker than this 藍色, 青色. Also 亦作 *adj* of this colour 藍色的. **blues** *n sing or pl* 單數或複數 type of jazz music (often rather slow and sad) 布魯斯音樂 (一種節拍較慢的、感傷的爵士音樂). **'blue 'blood** the aristocracy. *(informal)* 貴族(非正式). **'bluebottle** type of large blue flying insect 青蠅. **'blueprint 1** photographic print of a plan for a building (usu. made of blue paper)

(建築物的) 藍圖. **2** any plan or scheme for work to be done 方案, 計劃大綱. **out of the blue** unexpectedly 意外地, 突然地: *The news came completely out of the blue.* (*informal*) 這消息來得完全出乎意料 (非正式).

bluff [blʌf] *vt / i* pretend to be cleverer, stronger etc than one really is in order to defeat one's enemy or to gain something 虛張聲勢嚇人; 嚇唬: *The police were bluffing when they said that they knew who had committed the crime* i.e. the police said this although they did not really know who had committed the crime. 警方説他們知道是誰犯的罪, 其實是在虛張聲勢嚇人. 即: 警方雖這麼説, 他們並不知道是誰犯的罪. Also 亦作 *nc / u* pretence of this kind; action of bluffing 虛張聲勢; 嚇唬.

blunder ['blʌndə*] *nc* a foolish (or careless) mistake 大錯; 疏忽. Also 亦作 *vi* make this kind of mistake 犯大錯; 出漏子.

blunt¹ [blʌnt] *adj* (with reference to a knife etc.) without a sharp edge or point (刀等) 鈍的, 不鋒利的. Also 亦作 *vt* make blunt 使變鈍: *blunt a knife* 把刀弄鈍.

blunt² [blʌnt] *adj* rough or direct in speech, saying what one thinks without trying to be polite or kind to other people 直率的; 不客氣的. **bluntly** *adv* **bluntness** *nu*.

blur [blə:*] *vt* make less clear or less easy to understand 使不清楚; 使模糊: *Your writing is very blurred.* 你的字跡很模糊. *Tears blurred her eyes.* 淚水模糊了她的眼睛. past 過去式和過去分詞 **blurred**. Also 亦作 *nc* condition of being blurred; something which is not seen clearly 模糊一片; 模糊不清的東西.

blurt [bləːt] in **blurt something out** i.e. say something suddenly, often without thinking first 用於 blurt something out, 即: 脫口說出某事: *blurt out a secret* 漏嘴說出了秘密.

blush [blʌʃ] *vi* become red in the face from shame or embarrassment (因羞愧或窘迫而) 臉紅. Also 亦作 *nc* reddening of the skin in this way 臉紅.

bluster [ˈblʌstə*] *vi* complain or threaten in a noisy and foolish way 大聲抱怨; 嚇橫威嚇.

blustery [ˈblʌstəri] *adj* (with reference to wind) noisy and violent 狂風大作的, 呼嘯的.

boar [bɔː*] *nc* male pig 公猪.

board[1] [bɔːd] **1** *nc* thin piece of wood much longer than broad 木板. **2** *nc* piece of wood or other material used for a special purpose (e.g. *chessboard* used for playing chess on; *noticeboard* used for pinning notices on; *blackboard* used for writing on with chalk) 板; 牌; 盤 (如下棋用的 chessboard; 釘佈告用的 noticeboard; 粉筆書寫用的 blackboard). **3** *nc* group of officials 官員團體, 委員會: *board of governors* i.e. officials in charge of school or college 董事會. 即: 管理學校或學院的行政人員. **board and lodging** food and accommodation 膳宿. **'board room** room in which the most important officials of a business or institution have meetings (董事會或委員會的) 會議室. **go by the board** (with reference to plans etc.) be lost or abandoned (計劃等) 失敗; 被放棄: *The plan for a new swimming pool had to go by the board* i.e. it is not now planned to have a new swimming pool. 興建新游泳池的計劃不得不放棄. **on board** on a boat, ship or aeroplane 在船上; 在飛機上.

board[2] [bɔːd] *vt / i* **1** get on a bus, train, ship, aeroplane etc. 上 (公共汽車、火車、船、飛機等): *board a bus etc.* 上公共汽車等. **2** cover with boards 用板覆蓋: *board up the windows* 用木板把窗封住. **boarder** *nc* **1** somebody who pays to live in the house of another person and be given food by that person 寄膳宿者. **2** pupil in a school who lives at the school during the term and not at his parent's house 寄宿生. **'boarding house 1** private house (not a hotel) where people can pay to live with the owner and be supplied with food 供膳的寄宿處. **2** house in a boarding school in which pupils live (寄宿學校的) 學生宿舍. **'boarding school** school at which some or all of the pupils live during the term 寄宿學校.

boast [bəust] *vt / i* **1** speak too much in praise of oneself, one's country, family etc. 自誇; 誇耀: *I don't like John, he is always boasting.* 我不喜歡約翰, 他老是自吹自擂. *He boasted that he was the strongest boy in the class.* 他自誇是班上最有力氣的男生. **2** be proud of having 以有…而自豪: *Our town boasts the largest secondary school in the country.* 我們市以擁有全國最大的中學而自豪. Also 亦作 *nc* **1** words used by somebody who is boasting 自誇的話. **2** something which makes one proud or think very highly of oneself 引爲自豪的事物, 值得誇耀的事物: *Until last week, it was our team's proud boast that they had not been beaten this year.* 一直到上週, 我們隊還今年保持不敗而引以自豪. **boastful** *adj.*

boat [bəut] *nc* vessel used for travelling on water 船. *Note* 說明: in general, the difference between a *ship* and a *boat* is that small vessels are called *boats* and large ones are called *ships*. The following vessels are generally called *boats*-fishing boats; sailing boats; rowing boats; motorboats; ferryboats. The following vessels are generally called *ships*— the larger vessels of a country's navy (battleships etc.); large ocean-going passenger liners. The following vessels can be called *boats* or *ships* -medium-sized vessels which carry cargo, and passengers. 一般說來，ship 和 boat的區別是：小的船稱 boats, 大的船稱 ships. 下列船隻通常稱 boats-fishing boats (漁船); sailing boats (帆船); rowing boats (划艇); motorboats (汽艇); ferryboats (渡船). 下列船隻通常稱 ships—— 國家海軍較大的艦船 (battleship等); 大型遠洋客輪, 下列船隻可稱作 boats 或 ships-medium-sized vessels (中型客輪和貨輪).

boatswain, bosun ['bousn] senior member of the crew of a ship or boat (usu. in charge of the anchor, ropes etc.) 水手長.

bob [bɔb] *vt / i* move quickly up and down (使)上下跳動: *The boats were bobbing on the water;* 那些小船在水面上隨波起伏. *bob one's head up and down* 頻頻點頭. *past* 過去式和過去分詞 **bobbed.**

bobbin ['bɔbin] *nc* object for holding thread (e.g. in a sewing machine) (縫紉機的)線軸.

bodice ['bɔdis] *nc* upper part of a woman's or child's dress or undergarment 婦女或兒童的衣服或內衣的上部; 女裝上衣; 自腰及胸之緊身衣.

body ['bɔdi] *nc* **1** the whole of a human being, animal etc considered as separate from the mind or soul (人的)身體; (動物的)軀體; 肉體(區別於 mind 或 soul). **2** the main part of a human being, animal etc without the head, legs and arms (頭、四肢除外的)軀幹. **3** the main part of anything 主體; 主要部分: *the body of the hall* i.e. the part where the audience sits 大廳的 聽衆(或觀衆)席 *the body of the work* i.e. the largest part of the work 工作的主體部分. **4** group of people 團體: *They went in a body to see the Prime Minister.* 他們全體去見首相. **bodily** *adj / adv.* **bodyguard** person / people whose job is to protect someone 保鏢; 警衛.

bog [bɔg] *nc* land which is wet and soft 沼澤地. **boggy** *adj* **bogged down** unable to move forward as though in a bog 停滯不前的; 陷入僵局的: *He was bogged down in a mass of details.* 他被一大堆細節問題拖了後腿.

boggle ['bɔgl] *vi* usu. in **The mind boggles** it is very surprising; it is a shock *(informal)* 通常用於 The mind boggles (真出乎預料, 真令人吃驚). (非正式).

bogus ['bougəs] *adj* false; untrue; pretending to be what it is not 僞造的; 假的; 假裝的.

boil¹ [bɔil] *vt / i* **1** (with reference to liquid) become or be made so hot that the liquid begins to change into gas (液體)沸騰; 煮沸: *Water boils at 100℃.* 水在攝氏100度沸騰. *He boiled the water in a saucepan.* 他用平底鍋燒開水. **2** cook in this way in boiling water 在沸水中煮: *The potatoes are boiling.* 馬鈴薯煮滾了. *He boiled the potatoes.* 他煮馬鈴薯. **boiler** *nc* container for boiling water to make steam to drive the engines of a ship 鍋爐. **boiling point** temperature at which a liquid boils 沸點: *The boiling point of water is 100℃.* 水的沸點是攝

氏100度: **come / bring to the boil**
(cookery) become or make hot until
the liquid boils 煮滾/使煮滾.

boil² [bɔil] *nc* hard swelling on the
body caused by infection 疔瘡; 癤子.

boisterous ['bɔistərəs] *adj* (of people
in their behaviour) noisy, cheerful
and rough (行爲) 喧鬧的; 狂歡的.

bold [bould] *adj* **1** without fear 勇敢的;
大膽的: *The bold young man attack-
ed the robbers*. 這勇敢的年青人揍打
強盜; *a bold attempt* 大膽的嘗試. **2**
easily seen; clear and well-marked 容
易看清的; 醒目的. **boldly** *adv* **boldness** *nu*.

bolster ['boulstə*] *nc* long pillow for a
bed stretching from one side of a bed
to the other 長枕頭. **bolster up** give
help and support to 幫助; 支持:
*John's friends had to bolster up his
courage*. 約翰的朋友不得不爲他壯膽.

bolt¹ [boult] *nc* **1** type of fastening for a
door or window 門栓; 窗栓. **2** piece
of metal used to fasten two things
together 栓, 螺栓. **3** part of a lock
which is moved by a key 鎖簧. Also
亦作 *vt* fasten or lock using a bolt (in
any of the three senses given above)
用栓拴住; 閂上; 鎖上: *He bolted the
door*. 他閂上門. *He bolted the two
pieces of metal together*. 他用螺栓把
兩片金屬拴在一起.

bolt² [boult] *vi* (usu. of horses) run
away suddenly (usu. to escape) (*informal* if applied to people) (通常指
馬) 突然逃跑(如用於指人則爲非正式用
語).

bolt³ [boult] *vt* eat food quickly 忽忙地
吃.

bomb [bɔm] *nc* metal container filled
with a substance which explodes 炸
彈. Also 亦作 *vt* use bombs as
weapons (usu. by dropping them from

an aeroplane) 投彈於, 轟炸. **bomber**
nc aeroplane used for dropping
bombs; person who uses bombs 轟炸
機; 投彈手. '**bombshell** great surprise
(often an unpleasant one) (*informal*)
令人震驚的事(常爲不愉快的) (非正
式).

bombard [bɔm'ba:d] *vt* **1** attack with
fire from big guns 砲擊, 砲轟. **2** keep
attacking 不斷抨擊: *The Members of
Parliament bombarded the Prime
Minister with questions*. 議員們連珠炮
似地向首相提出質問. **bombardment**
nc/u.

bona fide ['bounə'faidi] *adj* genuine;
real 真正的; 真實的: *He made a bona
fide enquiry* i.e. he really wanted to
know. 他真誠地提出詢問. 即: 他真想知
道.

bond [bɔnd] *nc* **1** written promise (usu.
about money) which the law forces
one to keep 契約; 票據. **2** anything
which joins or brings together 連結
物; 黏合物; 聯結: *The English language is a bond between Britain and
America*. 英語是連結英美關係的紐帶.
bondage *nu* imprisonment 監禁.

bone [boun] **1** *nc* part of the hard inner
framework of the body 骨, 骨頭. **2** *nu*
the substance of which this
framework is made 骨質物. Also 亦作
vt take the bones out of meat or fish
before it is eaten 除(肉)骨; 剔(魚)骨.
bony *adj* **1** very thin, so that the
bones show through the skin 瘦得皮
包骨的. **2** having a lot of bones (e.g.
of a fish which one is eating) 多骨的
(如餐桌上的魚). '**bone-'dry** *adj* very
dry (*informal*) 非常乾的, 乾透了的(非
正式).

bonfire ['bɔnfaiə*] *nc* fire made in the
open air 篝火, 營火.

bonnet ['bɔnit] *nc* **1** hat tied under the

chin (usu. worn by women or children) (通常婦女、兒童戴的) 有帶圓帽. **2** (*Brit*) front part of a car covering the engine or the boot (*US* 美 **hood**) (英) 汽車罩.

bonus ['bəunəs] *nc* something more than what was expected or agreed 額外的東西; 意外的收穫.

boo [bu:] *nc / interj* noise made to show dislike (usu. at a meeting) (表示厭惡的) 噓出噓噓聲 (通常指在會議上). *pl* 複數 **boos.** Also 亦作 *vt / i* make this noise 發出噓噓聲: *The crowd booed the Prime Minister.* 羣眾向首相發噓噓聲喝倒彩. *past* 過去式和過去分詞 **booed.**

booby ['bu:bi] *nc* fool, stupid person. (*informal*) 傻子, 笨蛋 (非正式). **'booby prize** prize for person who comes last in a competition 末名獎. **booby trap 1** a hidden bomb which is arranged to explode and kill somebody when he touches something or steps in a particular place 餌雷. **2** any hidden device which works in this way (usu. as a joke) 圈套; 陷阱 (通常用來開玩笑).

book¹ [buk] *nc* **1** number of sheets of paper fastened together, either containing print or to be written on 書, 書籍; 本子. **2** something fastened together like a book 冊, 本: *a book of tickets* 一本車票; *a book of stamps* 一本集郵冊. **3** (in *pl*) accounts or record of money earned and spent in business (用於複數) 賬簿, 賬冊. **booklet** *nc* thin book with soft outer pages 小冊子. **'bookcase** piece of furniture for keeping books in 書架. **'book-keeper** *nc* person who keeps a record of money in a business etc. 簿記員; 記賬人. **book-keeping** *nu* **'bookmaker** person whose work is to take bets on sporting events (esp. on

horseracing) 以體育項目賭博爲業者 (尤指賭賽馬). **'bookmark** piece of paper, leather etc placed in a book to show how far one has read 書籤. **'bookworm** person who is always reading (*informal*) 讀書迷; 書呆子(非正式). **in somebody's good / bad books** liked / disliked by somebody (*informal*) 爲某人所喜歡/厭惡(非正式).

book² [buk] *vt / i* buy or arrange to have tickets for a film, play, journey etc before the actual occasion 預定 (戲票、車船票等). **bookable** *adj* **'booking clerk** person who sells tickets (usu. at a railway station) (通常指火車站的) 售票員. **'booking office** place where one buys tickets for a play, journey etc. (戲院、車站等的) 售票處.

boom¹ [bu:m] *nc* deep, hollow, roaring noise, such as that made by a gun or a supersonic aircraft 轟轟聲; 隆隆聲. Also 亦作 *vi* make this noise 發出隆隆聲.

boom² [bu:m] *nc* sudden increase in buying and selling in business (生意) 忽然興旺; 繁榮.

boomerang ['bu:məræŋ] *nc* curved stick, used by Australian aborigines, which can be thrown so that it will return to the thrower if it does not hit something 迴飛鏢 (澳大利亞土著用的曲形木棍, 擲出後如未擊中便飛回).

boon [bu:n] *nc* advantage; help 利益, 好處; 幫助: *My new overcoat is a boon in this cold weather.* 我的新大衣在這樣冷的天氣裏很頂用.

boor [buə*] *nc* an ignorant badly-behaved person 舉止粗俗的人. **boorish** *adj.*

boost [bu:st] *vt* **1** speak favourably of, advertise (esp. in order to persuade people to buy something) 吹噓; 宣揚 (尤指爲了推銷商品). **2** push forward or up wards 往前推…; 往上推…. **3** increase the power or speed of 增強; 加速. Also 亦作 *nc*.

boot [bu:t] *nc* **1** type of covering for the foot which also covers the ankle (and sometimes also part of the leg) 長統靴. **2** *(Brit)* place in a car for luggage *(US* 美 **trunk**) (英)汽車的行李箱.

booth [bu:ð] *nc* **1** small covered place where goods are sold at a market (市場上有蓬的)貨攤. **2** place, separated off, in which one votes in an election or from which one can telephone (選舉時,間隔起來的)投票處; 電話亭. *pl* 複數 **booths**.

booty ['bu:ti] *nu* goods and money taken from the enemy in war or stolen by robbers 戰利品; 贓物.

booze [bu:z] *nu* alcoholic drink 酒. Also 亦作 *vi* drink alcoholic drinks (both *informal*) 喝酒(兩義均爲非正式).

border ['bɔ:də*] *nc* edge or side of anything (esp. the land where two neighbouring countries meet) 邊; 緣; 邊界 (尤指)國界. Also 亦作 *vt* be on a border 和…鄰接; 和…相連: *A thick forest borders the school grounds on the south side.* 校園南端連接着一片密林. **'borderline** line where two countries or districts join; division between two classes of things 國界; 邊界; 分界線. *His marks in the examination were on the borderline between a pass and a fail.* 他的考試成績剛剛及格. **border on 1** be next to, have a border with 鄰接; 與…接壤: *Scotland borders on England.* 蘇格蘭與英格蘭接壤. **2** be very near to 接近; 近似: *His behaviour sometimes borders on madness.* 他的舉止有時近乎發瘋.

bore[1] [bɔ:*] *vt* make a round hole (esp. by using a tool which keeps turning round) 鑽(孔); 挖(洞): *bore a hole in a piece of wood* 在一塊木頭上鑽孔; *bore a tunnel under the sea* 在海底鑿隧道. Also 亦作 *nc* diameter of a tube or gun barrel (管或槍筒的)口徑.

bore[2] [bɔ:*] *vt* make somebody tired and unhappy by talk, work, entertainment etc which keeps you uninteresting 使厭煩: *John always bores me when I meet him.* 每當我見到約翰時,他總是惹我厭煩. Also 亦作 *nc* somebody/something that bores people 令人討厭的人/事物: *John is a bore.* 約翰是個令人討厭的傢伙. **boredom** *nu* condition of being bored 討厭; 無趣. **boring** *adj* causing bordom 令人厭煩的; 無趣的.

bore[3] [bɔ:*] past tense of **bear**[1]. bear[1] 的過去式.

born [bɔ:n] past part of **bear**[1] only in be born i.e. come into the world. bear[1] 的過去分詞, 僅用於 be born, 即: 出生: *He was born on 25th April 1939.* 他於 1939 年 4 月 25 日出生. In other uses, past part of **bear**[1] is spelled **borne** 在其他用法上, bear[1] 的過去分詞拼作 borne. Also 亦作 *adj* natural, by nature and not by training or education 天生的, 生來的: *He is a born leader* i.e. he is naturally a leader, he did not have to learn how to lead other people. 他是個天生的領導者.

borne [bɔ:n] past part of **bear**[1]. bear[1] 的過去分詞. see **born** and *Note* on **bear**[1] 見 born 和 bear[1] 的說明.

borough ['bʌrə] *nc* town or part of a large city which governs itself (and, in England, has its own Member of Parliament) 自治的市鎭或區(在英國且擁有本市區的議員).

borrow ['bɔrou] *vt* get something from somebody with the promise that one will give it back 借: *May I borrow five pounds until Saturday?* 借給我五英鎊, 星期六還, 行嗎? *May I borrow your pen?* 可以借用一下你的鋼筆嗎? *Note* 說明: do not confuse *borrow* and *lend*. Compare *I borrowed John's dictionary* with *John lent me his dictionary*. 不要混淆 borrow 和 lend, 比較 I borrowed John's dictionary (我借來約翰的詞典) 與 John lent me his dictionary (約翰借給我他的詞典).

bosom ['buzəm] *nc* breasts of a woman (婦女的) 乳房.

boss [bɔs] *nc* chief; leader; most important person; owner of a business. (*informal*) 頭子; 領袖; 首領; 老闆. (非正式). Also 亦作 *vt* act as a boss; tell other people what to do 當…的首領; 指揮. **bossy** *adj* liking to give orders to other people 喜歡發號施令的.

bosun ['bousn] *nc* see 見 **boatswain.**

botany ['bɔtəni] *nu* study of plants 植物學. **botanical** [bə'tænikl] *adj* botan- **ist** ['bɔtənist] *nc* person who studies plants 植物學家; 研究植物的人.

botch [bɔtʃ] *vt* do work badly (esp. when repairing something) 拙劣地做 (尤指修補某物).

both [bouθ] *determiner / adv / pron* the one and the other 兩者: *both men* 兩個男人; *both John and James* 約翰和詹姆斯兩人; *both of them* 他們兩個. *You can read both these books / both of these books.* 你可以讀這兩本書. *You can read them both.* 兩本你都可以讀. *We both can go / We can both go.* 我們兩個都能去. *This machine can move both backwards and forwards.* 這台機器能往返移動. *Note* 說明: *both* is only used when two things are involved, *all* when more

than two things are involved. Do not say *all two of them;* the correct form is *both of them.* both 僅用於涉及兩者, all 用於涉及兩者以上. 不要說 all two of them; 正確的形式是 both of them.

bother ['bɔðə*] *vt / i* 1 cause trouble or disturbance to 煩擾; 打擾: *Did the noise bother you last night?* 昨晚的吵鬧聲打擾你了嗎? 2 take trouble to do something 麻煩; 費事: *Don't bother to come with me, I shall be all right by myself.* 別麻煩陪我來了, 我自個兒不會有事的. Also 亦作 *nc / u* cause of trouble or worry; state of worry 麻煩; 煩惱.

bottle ['bɔtl] *nc* container for liquids (usu. made of glass or clear plastic and narrowing at the top) (玻璃或塑料) 瓶子: *a bottle of milk* 一瓶牛奶; *a bottle of beer* 一瓶啤酒. Also 亦作 *vt* put into bottles 把…裝入瓶中. '**bottleneck** place where progress is slowed down 瓶頸; 狹口: *The narrow road through the town is a bottleneck for traffic.* 橫穿該市的狹窄的公路是交通的狹口.

bottom ['bɔtəm] *nc* 1 lowest part 底, 部: *the bottom of the page* 頁的下端; *the bottom of the sea* 海底. 2 part of the body on which one sits 屁股. Also 亦作 *adj* lowest 最低的: *the bottom shelf* 底層擱板; *the bottom rung of a ladder* 梯子最下面的一級. **bottomless** *adj* very deep 深不可測的; 很深的.

bough [bau] *nc* large branch of a tree (usu. growing out of the trunk) 大樹枝.

bought [bɔ:t] past of **buy.** buy 的過去式和過去分詞.

boulder ['bouldə*] *nc* large rock smoothed by ice, water etc. 巨石; 大

圓石.

bounce [bauns] *vt / i* **1** come up quickly (esp. after hitting against something hard), cause to come up in this way (使) 彈起; (使) 跳回: *The ball bounced in front of the goal.* 球在球門前彈回. *The boy was bouncing his ball against the wall.* 那男孩正對着牆壁打球. **2** move suddenly 突然移動; 衝: *He bounced out of the room.* 他突然衝出房間.

bound¹ [baund] *vi* move in a number of jumps 跳躍. Also 亦作 *nc* jump 跳, 躍.

bound² [baund] *vt* be on the edge of, be a border or limit to 以…爲界; 與…鄰接: *The small country of Lesotho is bounded on all sides by South Africa.* 小國萊索托的四週都與南非接壤. *England is bounded in the south by the English Channel.* 英格蘭南面濒臨英吉利海峽. Also 亦作 *nc* (usu. *pl*) limit (通常用複數) 界限. *We must keep our hopes within reasonable bounds* i.e. we must limit our hopes, we must not hope for too much. 我們所抱的希望必須合情合理. 即: 我們不能抱過份的希望. **boundless** *adj* without limit 無限的; 無窮的: *boundless ambition* 無限大的野心. **out of bounds** outside the area in which certain people (e.g. schoolchildren, soldiers) may go 禁止入內: *The two cinemas in the town are out of bounds to all junior pupils.* 市內兩家電影院一律不准低年級的小學生進場.

bound³ [baund] *adj* going to, about to go to (esp. of ships) 往…去的, (尤指船) 準備開往…的: *That ship is bound for Hong Kong.* 那船是開往香港的.

bound⁴ [baund] *pred adj* certain, sure 一定的, 肯定的: *He is bound to win* i.e. I am quite sure that he will win.

他必定會贏. 即: 我確信他會贏.

bound⁵ [baund] past of **bind.** bind 的過去式和過去分詞.

boundary ['baundəri] *nc* (esp. of land) edge or limit (尤指土地的) 邊界, 界線: *the boundary of the school playing fields* 學校運動場的界線. *Note* 說明: *boundary* (when referring to land) is generally used to refer to divisions within a country; *border* is generally used to refer to places where one country joins another. 指地界時 boundary 一般用來指國內的分界線; border 一般用來指國與國接壤的地方.

bouquet [bu'kei] *nc* bunch of flowers for carrying in the hand (e.g. at a wedding) 花束 (例如婚禮上手裏拿着的).

bout [baut] *nc* **1** contest or struggle (esp. a boxing match) 比賽, 較量, 回合 (尤指拳擊比賽). **2** period of work, exercise or illness 一段 (工作); 一次 (訓練); 一陣 (疾病): *I've just recovered from a bout of malaria.* 我患了瘧疾剛痊癒.

boutique [bu'ti:k] *nc* small shop selling fashionable clothes and other goods 時裝用品小商店.

bow¹ [bau] *vt / i* bend the body forward as a sign of greeting, respect or worship 鞠躬; 點頭 (以示招呼、尊敬或敬仰). Also 亦作 *nc* act of bending the body in a bow 鞠躬; 點頭.

bow² [bou] *nc* **1** piece of wood, bent by a cord fastened at each end, used for firing arrows 弓. **2** piece of wood with horsehair or other substance stretched along it, used for playing the violin and the stringed instruments (小提琴和其他弦樂器的) 琴弓. **3** piece of ribbon, string etc tied 蝴蝶結. **'bow-'legged** *adj* with legs bent outwards 弓形腿的, 羅圈腿的. **'bow**

'**tie** tie worn round the neck in a bow 蝴蝶結領帶.

bow³ [bau] *nc* front part of a ship or boat 船首, 船頭.

bowel ['bauəl] *nc* (usu. *pl*) (通常用複數) **1** part of the body through which waste matter from the stomach passes out of the body 腸. **2** inner part of something (usu. in **the bowels of the earth** i.e. part of the earth deep below the surface) (物的)內部 (通常用於 the bowels of the earth, 即:地殼深處).

bowl¹ [boul] *nc* **1** deep round dish generally used as a container for food or flowers 碗, 鉢. **2** deep round part of something 圓形深凹部份: *the bowl of a spoon* 湯匙的盛物部份.

bowl² [boul] *vt / i* send a ball in certain games 滾(木球). Also 亦作 *nc* heavy wooden ball used in certain games (某些遊戲用的)重木球. **bowls** *nu* game played with these balls 滾木球遊戲. **bowler** *nc* **1** person who bowls 滾木球的人. **2** type of hard, round, black hat 硬圓頂禮帽.(Also 亦作 **bowler hat**).

box¹ [bɔks] *nc* **1** container made of metal, wood, cardboard etc often rectangular in shape and with a lid 盒, 匣, 箱. **2** small compartment for a few members of the audience at a theatre (戲院的)包廂. Also 亦作 *vt* put into boxes 把…裝入箱(或盒)內. '**Boxing Day** day after Christmas Day 節禮日 (聖誕節次日). '**box office** place where tickets are sold in a theatre or cinema (戲院的)票房, 售票處. '**witness box** see 見 **witness.**

box² [bɔks] *vt / i* fight by hitting with the fists (esp. when wearing padded gloves) 用拳頭打; (尤指戴拳擊手套)拳擊. **boxer** *nc* **1** man who fights with

his fists, wearing padded gloves 拳擊手. **2** type of dog 拳師犬. **boxing** *nu* game or sport of fighting with the fists, wearing padded gloves 拳擊.

boy [bɔi] *nc* male child, up to the age of about eighteen 男孩. **boyish** *adj* like or of a boy 男孩似的, 男孩的. '**boyfriend** usual male companion of a young woman 男朋友, (男)情人. see also 參見 **scout.**

boycott ['bɔikɔt] *vt* join with other people, nations etc in an agreement to have no contact, trade etc with a person, business, nation etc or to refuse to buy a particular product 聯合抵制; 抵制(往來或貿易); 杯葛: *If they will not buy our goods, we will boycott theirs.* 如果他們不買我們的貨, 我們將聯合抵制他們的貨. Also 亦作 *nc* act of boycotting 聯合抵制; 杯葛.

bra [brɑ:] *nc* undergarment for supporting a woman's breasts (short form of **brassière)** 奶罩 (brassière的縮略式).

brace [breis] *nc* piece of metal, wood etc used to hold things together 繫縛物; 支撐物. Also 亦作 *vt* give support or strength 支住; 縛牢. **bracing** *adj* involving some kind of effort, but nevertheless refreshing 令人身心清爽的: *a bracing walk* 令人心神爽快的散步.

bracelet ['breislit] *nc* ring or chain of metal or other material worn round the wrist or arm (usu. by women) (通常婦女戴的)手鐲; 臂鐲.

braces ['breisiz] *npl* (*Brit*) straps worn over the shoulders by men, used for holding up trousers. (*US* 美 **suspenders)** (英)(男褲的)背帶, 吊帶.

bracken ['brækən] *nc* type of coarse fern; a lot of ferns together 蕨(一種植物); 一簇蕨.

bracket ['brækit] *nc* **1** one of several

signs ( ), [ ], { } etc used in writing and printing to separate something from the rest of the writing or print 括弧(指( )、[ ]、{ }等). *Note* 說明: these signs are used in pairs and the two e.g. ( ) are referred to as a bracket (*sing*) or brackets (*pl*). 這些符號成對使用, 每兩個如( ) 稱 a bracket (單數) 或 brackets (複數). **2** bent or curved piece of metal used for supporting something such as a shelf, which is fastened to a wall (固定於牆上用以支撐物件的)托架; 撐架.

brackish ['brækiʃ] *adj* **1** (of water) slightly salt (指水)稍有鹽味的. **2** distasteful; unpleasant 味道不好的; 討厭的: *a brackish personality* 使人討厭的個性.

brag [bræg] *vt / i* speak too much in praise of oneself, one's family, country etc. (often saying things that are untrue) 自誇; 吹噓: *John said that he could fight anyone but we knew that he was only bragging.* 約翰說他打得過任何人, 但我們知道他只是在吹牛罷了. *past* 過去式和過去分詞 **bragged.**

braid [breid] **1** *nc* narrow piece of material made by twisting several strands or pieces together; pieces of hair twisted together 編帶; 縧; 辮子. **2** *nu* material of this type put along the edges of clothing or used as decoration on clothing (衣服上的)縧帶; 鑲邊: *His coat was covered with braid.* 他的外套飾有縧帶.

braille [breil] *nu* system of reading and writing invented for use by the blind, in which the letters are represented by raised dots which can be read by feeling them with the fingers 布萊葉盲字(供盲人用手指摸讀、書寫的點字體系).

brain [brein] *nc* (sometimes *pl*) the matter in the head with which one thinks and feels (有時用複數)腦. **brainless** *adj* very foolish or stupid 沒有頭腦的; 愚蠢的. **brainy** *adj* very intelligent. (*informal*-use **intelligent**) 很聰明的(非正式—正式用 intelligent). **'brain-child** somebody's invention or idea 某人的發明或主意. **'brainwashing** *nu* process by which a person is made to change his ideas (esp. political ideas) by the use of continual questioning and various types of illtreatment 洗腦; 強行改變思想.

braise [breiz] *vt* cook slowly in a container with a lid on, using very little water 燉; 燜.

brake [breik] *nc* anything which makes a vehicle go more slowly or stop 煞車; 制動器. Also 亦作 *vt / i* slow down or stop by using a brake 煞(車); 制動.

branch [brɑːntʃ] *nc* **1** part of a tree growing out from the main trunk 樹枝. **2** anything growing out of the main part, like a branch of a tree; part 分支; 支部; 部份: *a branch line of a railway* 鐵路支線; *a branch of a family* 家族的一支; *a branch of learning* 學科. Also 亦作 *vi* divide into branches or parts 分支; 分部; 分門: *Keep straight on until the road branches.* 一直往前走到岔路口.

brand [brænd] *nc* **1** type or kind of manufactured product 商標; 牌子: *Smith and Co. sell three brands of tea.* 史密斯公司賣三種牌子的茶. **2** mark made on the skin with a hot piece of iron (usu. done to cattle and horses to show who owns them) 烙印(通常打在牛馬身上以示所屬). Also 亦作 *vt* mark with a hot iron 在⋯上打烙印. **'brand'new** *adj* very new 嶄新的.

brandish ['brændiʃ] *vt* wave or shake (esp. in a threatening way) 揮舞(尤指威脅性地): *The thief was brandishing a revolver.* 盜賊揮動着左輪手槍.

brandy ['brændi] *nu* type of strong alcoholic drink 白蘭地酒.

brash [bræʃ] *adj* self-confident and impolite 傲慢的; 無禮的.

brass [brɑːs] *nu* yellowish metal, an alloy of copper and zine 黃銅(銅與鋅的合金). **the brass** brass instruments, or players of these instruments, in a band or orchestra 銅管樂器; (樂隊或管弦樂隊的)銅管樂吹奏者.

brassière ['bræsiə*] *nc* see 見 **bra.**

brat [bræt] *nc* annoying or badly-behaved child. (rather *impolite*) 調皮搗蛋的孩子(頗爲不禮貌).

bravado [brə'vɑːdou] *nu* foolish courage or boldness; pretence of being brave without any real willingness to face danger or pain 虛勇; 逞能; 虛張聲勢.

brave [breiv] *adj* without fear; willing to face something dangerous or painful 勇敢的; 無畏的. Also 亦作 *vt* face danger or pain 勇敢地面對(危險或痛苦): *brave death* i.e. do something although one might be killed 冒死(做某事). **bravely** *adv* **bravery** *nu.*

bravo ['brɑː'vou] *interj* shout meaning well done! excellent! very good! etc. 妙啊! 好極了! 太好了!

brawl [brɔːl] *nc* noisy fight or quarrel, often in a public place (在公共場所的)喧鬧鬥毆; 爭吵. Also 亦作 *vi* fight or quarrel in this way 打架; 爭吵.

brawn [brɔːn] *nu* **1** size and strength of a person (often *impolite*, suggesting that the person is unintelligent) 個子, 體力(常爲不客氣的說法, 意爲此人缺乏智力). **2** pickled meat of a pig 醃豬肉.

brawny *adj* big and strong 強壯的.

bray [brei] *vi* make a sound like an ass or donkey 發出驢叫似的聲音. Also 亦作 *nc* this sound 驢叫似的聲音.

brazen ['breizn] *adj* without proper shame or respect for other people 厚顏無恥的. **brazen something out** act as though one had not done something wrong even though everybody knows that one has (*informal*) 厚着臉皮幹某事(非正式).

brazier ['breiziə*] *nc* metal framework like a basket with legs for holding burning coal or charcoal (金屬)火盆, 火缽.

breach [briːtʃ] *nc* **1** act of breaking the law or failing to do what one has promised to do (對法律的)違犯; 破壞; 毀約: *a breach of the peace* i.e. fighting or quarrelling in public 擾亂治安. 即: 在公共場所打架、爭吵; *a breach of contract* i.e. failure to do what one has agreed to do by signing a legal document 違反合同. 即: 沒有完成簽訂的合同中所同意履行的事項. **2** hole or opening made by breaking down part of a wall etc. (牆壁等的)破口; 缺口. Also 亦作 *vt* make a breach in a wall etc. 使(牆壁等)有缺口.

bread [bred] *nu* food made from flour, yeast and water, baked in an oven 麵包. **'breadwinner** person in a family who works in order to get money to support the other members of the family 負擔家庭生計的人, 養家者. **bread-and-butter** *nu* **1** slices of bread covered on one side with butter 塗上黃油的麵包. **2** food which is necessary for one to continue living. (*informal* in sense 2) 維持生活的必需食品(義2爲非正式).

breadth [bretθ] *nc* distance from one side to the other 寬度; 闊度.

break [breik] *vt / i* **1** become, cause to

become, divided into several pieces 打破；打碎；破碎：*He broke the window by throwing a stone through it.* 他扔石塊打破窗戶．*The cup broke when he dropped it.* 他失手打破了杯子．**2** become or make damaged 毀損；壞掉：*He broke the chair when he jumped on it.* 他跳上椅子時把它踩壞了．*My watch has broken.* 我的錶壞了．**3** (with reference to day or dawn) come suddenly or quickly (天)破曉；*Day was breaking when I woke up.* 我醒來時天開始亮了．**4** (with reference to arrangements) fail to do what is expected 違反；違背：*break a promise* 背約，食言；*break the law* 違法，犯法．*past tense* 過去式 **broke** [brouk]. *past part* 過去分詞 **broken** ['broukən] Also 亦作 *nc* **1** place where damage has occurred 破裂處，裂口．**2** interruption or pause 中斷；暫停：*a break in the conversation* 談話的暫停；*a break for refreshments* 休息吃點心(的時間)．**3** chance or opportunity 機會：*give me a break.* (*informal* in sense 3) 給我一次機會．(義3爲非正式)．**broken** *adj* (*opp* 反義詞 **unbroken**) **breakable** *adj* easily broken 易破碎的．(*opp* 反義詞 **unbreakable**). **breakage** *nc / u* **1** breaking; damage 破壞，損壞．**2** loss caused by breaking 破損：*All breakages must be paid for* i.e. one must pay for whatever is broken. 一切破損必須賠償．**breaker** *nc* large wave which breaks into foam 碎浪花．**'breakwater** wall or barrier built out into the sea to lessen the force of the waves 防波堤．**'breakdown** *nc* (usu. only *sing*) (通常僅用單數)．**1** failure in health through mental strain (因精神緊張而身體) 衰弱；垮；衰竭：*a nervous breakdown* 神經崩潰．**2** failure of an engine etc. (引擎等)故障；損壞；

We had a breakdown on the journey. 我們的車在旅途中抛錨了．**3** division into categories etc. 分類，分成細目：*a breakdown of the figures* 數字的細目．**break in** (usu. with reference to a thief entering a house) enter by force (常指盜賊)破門而入．**break something in** train an animal to work for one 馴服(動物)：*break in a horse* 馴服一匹馬．**break out** begin suddenly 突然開始；爆發：*A fire broke out.* 突然發生火災．**'breakthrough** *nc* **1** military attack which passes through the defence of the enemy (對敵人防線的)攻破．**2** new and important discovery in science which enables further developments to take place (科學的)重大發現，突破．**break (something) up** scatter; divide up 驅散；分開：*The two friends broke up* i.e. they decided not to continue to be friends. 這兩個朋友分手了．*The headmaster broke up the fight* i.e. he stopped the children fighting. 校長制止了這場打鬥．**break the news** tell someone something unpleasant in a gentle way 婉轉地透露不好的消息．**break a record** (usu. with reference to sport) do something faster, better etc than anyone has done it previously (通常指競賽)打破記錄：*break the record for the high jump* 打破跳高記錄．

breakfast ['brekfəst] *nc / u* first meal of the day, eaten in the early morning 早餐．

breast [brest] *nc* **1** one of the two parts of a woman's body at which a baby is fed with milk 乳房．**2** the front part of the upper body 胸部．**'breast-stroke** method of swimming in which the body is pushed forward by both arms moving through the water at the same time, followed by a strong movement with the legs 俯泳; 蛙式游泳.

breath [breθ] *nc / u* the air taken into the body and sent out again 呼吸的空氣, 氣息. **breathless** *adj* **1** without enough air in the lungs (e.g. after running fast) 喘氣的 (如快跑後): *John was breathless after running for half a mile.* 約翰跑了半英里後就氣喘吁吁. **2** causing one to be unable to breathe freely 使人屏息的: *breathless excitement* 使人喘不過氣來的激動. **breathtaking** *adj* thrilling; causing great excitement 驚險的; 令人非常激動的. **out of breath** without enough air in the lungs (e.g. after running fast) 喘不過氣來(如快跑後).

Breathalyser ['breθəlaizə*]ᴿ *nc* small device used to measure the amount of alcohol in a person's breath (測定某人氣息中酒量的) 測酒器. **'breathalyse** *vt* to test using a Breathalyser 用測酒器測驗: *The police breathalysed the motorist.* 警察用測酒器檢查駕駛汽車的人.

breathe [bri:ð] *vt / i* take air into the body and send it out again 呼吸: *He was breathing noisily.* 他正氣喘吁吁.

bred [bred] past of **breed.** breed 的過去式和過去分詞. **'well-'bred** *adj* (with reference to a person) well-behaved and from a good family (人) 有教養的, 教養良好的. (*opp* 反義詞 **ill-bred**).

breed [bri:d] *vt / i* **1** (with reference to animals) produce young (動物) 繁殖, 產仔: *Rats breed very quickly.* 老鼠繁殖很快. **2** cause animals to produce young (usu. in order to earn money) 使繁殖(通常爲了掙錢): *Many farmers breed cows and sheep.* 許多農民飼養牛羊. *past* 過去式和過去分詞 **bred** [bred]. Also 亦作 *nc* type of animal (動物的) 品種: *several different breeds of cattle* 幾個不同品種的牛; *a good breed of sheep* 良種羊. **breeder** *nc* person who breeds animals 飼養者,動物繁殖家. **breeding** *nu* production of young animals (動物的) 繁殖.

breeze [bri:z] *nc* light wind 微風. **breezy** *adj* **1** with light winds blowing 有微風的: *a very breezy day* 微風拂煦的一天. **2** (with reference to a person or his behaviour) light-hearted; cheerful; full of jokes (人或舉止) 輕鬆愉快的; 快活的; 愛說笑的.

brethren ['breðrən] *npl* (old use) brothers (舊用法) 兄弟們, 同胞.

brevity ['breviti] *nu* shortness; quality of not lasting for a long time 短; 短暫; 簡潔. see 見 **brief¹**.

brew [bru:] *vt / i* **1** make beer 釀啤酒. **2** make a drink with hot water 沖; 泡: *brew some tea* 泡些茶. **3** plan; plot; cause to happen 計劃; 圖謀; 使發生: *brew mischief* 製造麻煩; *brew mischief* 策劃惡作劇. **4** become more likely 即將來臨; 即將發生: *some trouble is brewing* 麻煩的事就要來了. Also 亦作 *nc* drink or quality of drink made by brewing (釀造的) 飲料; 釀造物的質量: *a brew of tea* 一泡茶. *The best brew of beer is made by XYZ.* 最好的啤酒是 XYZ 釀的. **brewery** *nc* place where beer is made 啤酒廠.

bribe [braib] *vt* offer money or other gifts to a person to persuade him to do something which he should not do 賄賂: *He tried to bribe the policeman not to arrest him.* 他試圖賄賂警察不要逮捕他. Also 亦作 *nc* money or other gift offered in this way 行賄物, 賄賂. **bribery** *nu* giving and taking of bribes 行賄; 受賄.

brick [brik] *nc* rectangular piece of baked clay (usu. red in colour) used in building 磚, 磚塊. **'bricklayer** *nc* person whose work is to build with bricks 泥水匠. **'brickwork** wall or other part of a building which is made of bricks 磚牆; 磚砌成的建築物.

bride [braid] *nc* woman who has just been married or who is just about to be married 新娘. **bridal** *adj* **'bridegroom** man who has just been married or who is just about to be married 新郎. **'bridesmaid** woman who helps a bride on the wedding day 女儐相.

bridge¹ [bridʒ] *nc* **1** road or path built over a river or railway line or above another road 橋, 橋樑. **2** place higher than the deck of a ship where the officer in command stands 船橋. **3** the bony part of the nose 鼻樑. Also 亦作 *vt* build a bridge across 架橋於: *bridge a river* 跨河架橋.

bridge² [bridʒ] *nu* type of card game 橋牌.

bridle ['braidl] *nc* leather straps which fit over a horse's head, used for controlling the horse 馬籠頭; 馬繮. Also 亦作 *vt/i* **1** put a bridle on 給…套籠頭: *He bridled his horse.* 他給他的馬套上馬勒. **2** control 控制: *He learned to bridle his temper.* 他學會抑制脾氣.

brief¹ [bri:f] *adj* lasting for a short time 短暫的: *a brief period of happiness* 一時的快樂; *a very brief visit* 很短暫的訪問. **briefly** *adv* **briefness** *nu* see 見 **brevity**.

brief² [bri:f] *nc* summary of the main facts about a case, used by a lawyer when speaking in court (律師在法庭上陳述的) 案情摘要. Also 亦作 *vt* **1** give a lawyer some work to do for oneself by giving him the information which he may need 向(委託律師)作案情簡介. **2** prepare somebody for a piece of work by giving him the in-

formation he may need 向(某人)作情況簡介: *Before the soldiers advanced towards the enemy, they were briefed by their commanding officer.* 士兵們向敵人推進前, 指揮官向他們下達簡要指令. **briefing** *nc* information given to somebody before he begins a piece of work 簡要指示; 情況簡介. **'brief-case** flat case for carrying papers or books 公文包. **briefs** *npl* same as **panties** but also worn by men 緊身內褲.

brigade [bri'geid] *nc* part of an army (usu. between 3,000 and 8,000 men) 旅(通常有三千至八千名士兵). **brigadier** [brigə'diə*] *nc* officer in charge of a brigade 旅長.

bright [brait] *adj* **1** shining; giving out much light 發光的, 明亮的: *a bright fire* 明亮的火; *a bright light* 亮光. **2** with colours which are easily seen; not dark (顏色) 鮮艷的; 鮮明的: *a bright-coloured dress* 一件顏色鮮艷的衣服. **3** intelligent; quick at learning 聰明的; 伶俐的: *a very bright pupil* 很聰明的小學生. **brightly** *adv* **brightness** *nu* **brighten** *vt / i* become or make bright (使)發光; (使)明亮: *The weather is brightening* i.e. it is becoming sunny. 天氣逐漸放晴.

brilliant ['briliənt] *adj* **1** shining very brightly; giving out a lot of light 明亮的, 輝煌的. **2** very intelligent; very quick at learning 很聰明的; 很伶俐的: *a very brilliant pupil* 很靈敏的小學生; *a brilliant piece of work* 一件精緻的工藝品. **brilliantly** *adv* **brilliance** *nu*.

brim [brim] *nc* **1** the edge of a cup or bowl (杯或碗的) 邊緣. **2** the edge of a hat 帽緣. **'brim'ful** *pred adj* full to the brim; so full that no more can be added 滿到邊的; 盈滿的: *The cup was brimful.* 這杯子滿滿的.

brindle ['brindl] *nc* **1** brindled animal 有斑紋的動物. **2** brindled colour 帶深色斑紋的灰色或棕色.

brindled ['brindld] *adj* having a grey or brown colour with darker bands or spots 有灰色或棕色斑紋的.

brine [brain] *nu* salty water 鹽水; 鹹水.

bring [brin] *vt* carry or lead towards 拿來; 帶來: *Bring me your book.* 把你的書拿來給我. *He brought his dog to school.* 他把他的狗帶來學校. *past* 過去式 and 及 *past* 分詞 **brought** [brɔ:t]. **bring about** cause to happen 引起, 導致: *He brought about a quarrel between his parents.* 他引起了父母的爭吵. **bring something off** succeed in 完成, 在…上獲得成功: *bring off an important business deal* 做成一筆大生意. **bring someone round 1** persuade, cause somebody to change his mind 說服某人; 使某人改變想法: *At first he didn't want to go with us, but we soon brought him round.* 起初他不願和我們一道去, 但我們很快說服了他. **2** cause to regain consciousness 使復蘇: *I was brought round by a policeman after I had been hit on the head by the thief.* 我的頭部遭盜賊猛擊後, 一個警察把我救醒過來. **bring someone / something up 1** (with reference to children) look after and train. 撫養 (孩子). **2** vomit 嘔吐: *He was so ill that he brought up everything he ate.* 他病得很重, 吃甚麼吐甚麼. **3** mention as a topic of discussion 提出 (討論的話題): *John brought up the question of giving the school an extra week's holiday.* 約翰提出學校多放一週假的問題.

brink [briŋk] *nc* **1** edge of a cliff 懸崖峭壁的邊緣. **2** edge of something dangerous or unpleasant 危險或麻煩等的邊緣: *He brought his country to the brink of war.* 他把他的國家引到戰爭的邊緣. **on the brink of** very near something dangerous or unpleasant 瀕臨 (危險或麻煩的).

brisk [briak] *adj* quick and active in behaviour or speech (舉止或講話) 輕快的; 活潑的.

bristle ['brisl] *nc* short stiff hair of an animal (動物的) 鬃毛. Also 亦作 *vi* make the hair stand up (e.g. when frightened or angry) (毛髮) 竪立(如在恐懼或憤怒時).

brittle ['britl] *adj* hard and easily broken 硬而易碎的.

broach [brəutʃ] *vt* begin to talk about 開始談論; 提出: *He broached the subject of the summer holiday.* 他談起暑假的事.

broad [brɔ:d] *adj* **1** wide; having reference to the size of something measured from one side to the other 寬的; 闊的: *a broad river* 寬闊的河流. **2** large; covering a large area 廣大的; 遼闊的: *the broad ocean* 遼闊的海洋; *very broad experience* 廣博的見識. **3** (with reference to speech) easily noticeable; strongly marked (講話) 明顯的; 顯著的: *a broad Irish accent* 很重的愛爾蘭口音. **4** general; main (usu. in **the broad outline** i.e. the main points) 概括的; 主要的 (通常用於 **broad outline**, 即: 要點, 摘要). **broadly** *adv* **broaden** *vt / i* become or make broad (使)變寬; (使)擴大. **broad 'daylight** complete daylight 大白天. **'broad'minded** *adj* not easily shocked or surprised by what others say or think 心胸開闊的; 氣量大的.

broadcast ['brɔ:dka:st] *vt / i* send out by radio or television (無線電或電視) 廣播. Also 亦作 *nc* programme sent out on radio or television (無線電或電視的) 廣播節目.

brocade [brə'keid] *nu* cloth with woven designs which are raised above the surface of the cloth 浮花布.

brochure ['brouʃuə*] *nc* small book, often paper covered, giving information about a city, country, business firm, school, government department etc. (介紹某城市、國家、公司、學校、政府部門等的)小册子.

broil [brɔil] *vt / i* cook meat by using direct heat 烤(肉), 燒(肉). **broiler** *nc* 1 pan for boiling meat in 燒肉的鍋. 2 young chicken, suitable for broiling 適合燒烤的童子鷄.

broke [brouk] 1 past tense of **break**. break的過去式. 2 *adj* short of money. (*informal in* sense 2) 沒有錢的(義 2 爲非正式).

broken ['broukən] past part of **break**. break的過去分詞. **'broken-'hearted** *adj* very unhappy 很傷心的, 心碎的.

broker ['broukə*] *nc* person who acts for other people in buying and selling shares in business 經紀人, 掮客.

bromide ['broumaid] *nu* any of several chemical compounds, used in medicine to calm excitement 溴化物(用作鎮靜劑).

bromine ['broumi:n] *nu* non-metallic element, compound of which are used in photographic and other chemicals 溴.

bronchitis [brɔŋ'kaitis] *nu* (illness caused by) inflammation of the two tubes which lead from the windpipe to the lungs 支氣管炎.

bronze [brɔnz] *nu* mixture of copper and tin 青銅(銅錫合金).

brooch [broutʃ] *nc* ornament fastened by a pin, worn on a dress etc. (別在女服上的)胸針; 飾針.

brood [bru:d] *nc* 1 young birds together in a nest 一窩幼鳥. 2 group of young creatures or children (幼小動物的)一群; (一家的)孩子們. Also 亦作 *vi* 1 (with reference to birds) sit on eggs in a nest (鳥)孵蛋. 2 sit doing nothing but thinking gloomy thoughts. 坐着悶悶不樂地沉思. **broody** *adj* used of a hen sitting on her eggs (母鷄)抱窩的, 孵蛋的. **brood on / over something.** *He brooded on / over his problem for several days.* 他對自己的問題冥思苦想了好幾天.

brook [bruk] *nc* small stream 小溪.

broom [bru:m] *nc* brush on the end of a long stick, used for sweeping the floor 掃帚.

broth [brɔθ] *nc* soup (esp. one made with meat) 湯(尤指肉湯).

brothel ['brɔθl] *nc* house where prostitutes live and do business 妓院.

brother ['brʌðə*] *nc* son of one or both of one's parents 兄弟. **brotherly** *adj* as or like a brother 兄弟般的. **brotherhood** ['brʌðəhud] *nc* group of men, joined together for a particular purpose 兄弟會; 男人團體. **'brother-in-law** brother of one's wife or husband; husband of one's sister 內兄; 內弟; 大伯; 小叔; 姊夫; 妹夫. *pl* 複數 **brothers-in-law.**

brought [brɔ:t] past of **bring.** bring的過去式和過去分詞.

brow [brau] *nc* 1 forehead 額. 2 hair on the forehead above the eye. (Often **eyebrow**) 眉, 眉毛(常用 eyebrow). 3 top of a hill 山頂.

browbeat ['braubi:t] *vt* frighten somebody in order to make him do what one wants him to do 嚇唬; 威逼. *past tense* 過去式. **browbeat.** *past part* 過去分詞 **browbeaten.**

brown [braun] *nc / u* dark colour like a very dark yellow or dark orange; skin colour of many Indian people; colour of many types of soil 深黃色;棕色;褐色. Also 亦作 *adj*.

Brownie ['brauni] *nc* young member of the Girl Guide movement. 女童子軍.

browse [brauz] *vi* read bits from different parts of a book or from different books (e.g. in a library or bookshop) 瀏覽,翻閱(如在圖書館或書店).

bruise [bruːz] *nc* dark mark on the skin made by a blow which does not break the skin 青腫;傷痕. Also 亦作 *vt / i* get or make such a mark 使青腫,使青腫;擦傷: *My skin bruises easily* i.e. if I am hit, a bruise usu. appears. 我的皮膚很容易碰傷. *The man bruised the child's arm when he hit him.* 那男人把小孩的胳臂打得青腫.

brunette [bruːˈnet] *nc* (usu. with reference to a white-skinned person) person (often a woman) with dark hair (通常指白種人中的)黑髮女子.

brunt [brʌnt] usu. in **bear the brunt of something** i.e. the main force or main part 通常用於 bear the brunt of something, 即:首當其衝;承受某事物的主要力量或主要部份.

brush [brʌʃ] *nc* **1** instrument (usu. with a short handle and with stiff bristles, wires, hairs etc for cleaning or painting etc.) 刷子;畫筆;毛筆. **2** short fight or argument 小衝突;小爭吵. **3** tail of a fox 狐狸尾巴. Also 亦作 *vt / i* **1** *He brushed the floor / his hair / his teeth etc.* 他刷地板/頭髮/牙齒等. **2** *He brushed against the door as he entered the room.* 他進入房間時,身子在房門碰擦了一下. **brush aside** ignore; refuse to take notice of 擱置;不理. **brush up** revise; improve one's knowledge of. *(informal)* 修正;溫習;複習.(非正式).

brusque [bruːsk] *adj* quick and rather impolite in behaviour or speech (舉止或言語)輕率的;魯莽的.

Brussels ['brʌsəlz] see 見 **sprout**[2].

brute [bruːt] *nc* cruel or stupid man 殘暴的人;愚蠢的人. **brutal** *adj* harsh and cruel 殘忍的;變橫的. **brutality** [bruˈtæliti] *nc / u* cruel act; cruelty 殘暴行爲;殘酷.

bubble ['bʌbl] *nc* volume of air surrounded by liquid. (Bubbles can either float in the air, or be inside or on a liquid.) 氣泡.(氣泡能飄浮在空氣中,存在於液體裏或液面上.) Also 亦作 *vi* send up bubbles, rise to the surface in the form of bubbles 冒泡,沸騰. **buck**[1] [bʌk] *nc* male deer or rabbit 雄鹿;牡兔.

buck[2] [bʌk] *vi* (with reference to a horse) jump taking all four feet off the ground (馬)跳起(騰空). **buck up 1** hurry up 趕快,加快. **2** be more cheerful 振奮起來,打起精神. **3** try harder etc. (all *informal*) 加把勁等(均爲非正式).

bucket ['bʌkit] *nc* container with a handle for carrying liquid in 水桶,提桶.

buckle[1] ['bʌkl] *nc* fastener (usu. made of metal) for fastening a belt or strap 帶扣,扣環(通常用金屬製成). Also 亦作 *vt / i* be fastened or fasten with a buckle 扣住;用扣子扣住.

buckle[2] ['bʌkl] *vi* (with reference to metal) bend under a weight (金屬受壓而)彎曲.

bud [bʌd] *nc* tightly-rolled flower or leaf before it develops 芽,蓓,蕾. Also 亦作 *vi* grow buds; grow into buds 發芽;長成芽. *past* 過去式和過去分詞 **budded. budding** *adj* developing 開始成長的: *a budding author* i.e. an author who is showing signs of becoming a good writer 初露頭角的作家.

budge [bʌdʒ] *vt / i* move or cause to move (使)移動: *He has been sitting for two hours; he won't budge.* 他坐了兩個小時，一動也不動. *This box is too heavy; I can't budge it.* 這箱子太重，我搬不動.

budgerigar [ˈbʌdʒəˈrigɑ:*] *nc* small brightly-coloured bird, often kept as a pet 虎皮鸚鵡.

budget [ˈbʌdʒit] *nc* (esp. with reference to such an estimate made by a government) statement or estimate of money which one expects to spend in the future 預算(尤指政府預算). Also 亦作 *vi* make a budget 制定預算.

buff [bʌf] *nu* pale brown colour 淡褐色, 淺棕色. Also 亦作 *adj*.

buffalo [ˈbʌfəlou] *nc* type of wild ox with a large shaggy head, found in America (美國)野牛. *pl* 複數 **buffaloes.**

buffer [ˈbʌfə*] *nc* **1** projecting pieces of metal on strong springs, placed on railway engines and at the end of railway lines, to lessen the shock if a railway engine does not stop when it should or if it is hit (機車上的)減震器; (鐵道末端的)緩衝器. **2** any object which acts in the same way 緩衝物; 緩衝者.

buffet¹ [ˈbʌfit] *nc* heavy blow (esp. one given with the hand) 重擊, 一巴掌. Also 亦作 *vt* give such a blow 用手打; 打擊: *The wind buffeted the people walking along the street.* 風吹襲着街上的行人.

buffet² [ˈbufei] *nc* **1** place where one can buy light meals and refreshments (esp. on a train or at a railway station) (尤指火車上或火車站的)餐室, 小餐店. **2** food placed on a table at a party, which one can take as one wishes, and eat standing up 自助餐.

buffoon [bʌˈfu:n] *nc* person who acts in a foolish way 小丑; 丑角.

bug [bʌg] *nc* **1** wingless insect which sucks blood 臭蟲. **2** (mainly *US*) any insect (主要用於美)蟲, 昆蟲. **3** germ which causes a disease *(informal in sense 3)* 病菌(義3爲非正式). Also 亦作 *vt* hide microphones etc in a room etc. in order to get information in⋯暗設竊聽器: *The spy bugged the room.* 密探在那房間裏偷偷地安放了竊聽器.

bugle [ˈbju:gl] *nc* type of wind musical instrument, similar to a trumpet 號角; 軍號.

build [bild] *vt / i* make by putting things together 建築; 建造; 蓋: *build a house / a ship / a wall* 建房屋／造船／築牆. *past* 過去式和過去分詞 **built** [bilt]. Also 亦作 *nu* (usu. with reference to human beings) size and shape (通常指人的)體格, 體型: *John and his brother have the same build.* 約翰和他兄弟體型相同. **builder** *nc* person whose work is to make houses and other buildings 建築者; 建築商.

building **1** *nc* thing built, in which people can live or work (e.g. a house, school, factory, shop) 建築物(如房屋、學校、工廠、商店). **2** *nu* art or skill of building 建築術. **'building society** society which lends money for people to buy houses (提供購房貸款的)房屋互助協會. **'built-in** *adj* made as part of a building (e.g. a built-in cupboard is made as part of a wall, and is not a movable piece of furniture) 與建築物連在一起的; 嵌入的 (如 a build-in cupboard 是指建在牆內的碗櫥, 嵌入式碗櫥, 不能搬動). **'built-'up 'area** area in which there are many houses 房屋密集區.

bulb [bʌlb] *nc* **1** thick, round root of

certain plants (植物的) 球莖. **2** glass object which is fixed into a source of electricity to obtain light 電燈泡.
bulbous *adj* shaped like a bulb 球莖狀的.

bulge [bʌldʒ] *vt / i* become or make large and round (使) 鼓起: *His pockets were bulging with apples.* 他的口袋因裝了蘋果而脹鼓鼓的. Also 亦作 *nc* place where something bulges 膨脹; 凸起部份: *There was a bulge in his pockets.* 他的口袋裏有個鼓鼓的東西.

bulk [bʌlk] *nu* **1** size or quantity (usu. large) 大塊; 大量. **2** largest part 絕大部份; 大半: *The bulk of the work is finished.* 絕大部份工作已經完成.
bulky *adj* large; too large 巨大的; 龐大的. **in bulk** in large quantities 大量, 大批: *buy something in bulk* 大批購買某物.

bulkhead [ˈbʌlkhed] *nc* walls inside a ship, which are built to prevent water spreading throughout the ship if the ship is damaged (船艙的) 隔牆, 艙壁.

bull [bul] *nc* **1** male of the cow family 公牛. **2** male elephant, whale, seal and other large animals 雄象; 雄鯨; 雄海豹; 雄性大動物. **'bull'seye** centre of a target 靶心. **'bullfighting** *nu* sport practised in Spain and South America, in which men on foot and horseback fight and kill a bull (流行於西班牙和南美洲的) 鬥牛.

bulldog [ˈbuldɔg] *nc* type of small but strong and brave dog 牛頭犬 (一種小而勇猛的狗).

bulldozer [ˈbuldouzə*] *nc* large vehicle for moving earth etc. 推土機.

bullet [ˈbulit] *nc* piece of metal fired from a gun (a gun which can be carried by hand) 子彈 (通常爲手槍的子彈). see 見 **shell**.

bulletin [ˈbulitin] *nc* short statement of news 簡報.

bullion [ˈbuliən] *nu* pieces or bars of gold and silver 金塊 (或條); 銀塊 (或條).

bullock [ˈbulək] *nc* castrated bull 閹牛.

bully [ˈbuli] *nc* person who hurts or frightens those weaker than himself 欺侮弱者的人, 惡棍. Also 亦作 *vt / i* behave in this way 以強凌弱; 欺侮; 威脅. **bullying** *nu*.

bulwark [ˈbulwək] *nc* **1** wall (esp. one made of earth) built to protect a against attacks 壁壘; 堡壘. **2** the side of a ship's deck (船的) 舷牆.

bum [bʌm] *nc* **1** part of the body on which one sits. (*informal and impolite*) 屁股 (非正式和不禮貌). **2** (*US*) person who travels around, doing very little work, and living by begging or stealing; a worthless or idle person. (*informal*) (美) 遊蕩者; 乞丐; 遊手好閑的人; 不中用的人. (非正式).

bumblebee [ˈbʌmblbi:] *nc* type of large bee 大黄蜂.

bump [bʌmp] *nc* **1** light blow or knock 碰; 輕撞. **2** swelling on the body made by a knock (碰撞引起的) 腫塊. **3** small lump or rise in a road (路面) 隆起的小塊. Also 亦作 *vt / i* give or receive a blow 碰; 撞; 撞傷: *bump one's head* 撞傷頭部. **bumpy** *adj* uneven; causing one to drive or move in a jerky way 崎嶇不平的; 顛簸的: *a very bumpy road* 顛簸不堪的道路.

bumper¹ [ˈbʌmpə*] *nc* (*Brit*) bar on the front or back of a car to protect the car if it hits or is hit by something (*US* 美 **fender**) (英) (汽車前後的) 保險槓.

bumper² [ˈbʌmpə*] *adj* unusually large (usu. in **a bumper crop**) 異常大的 (通常用於 a bumper crop 豐收).

bumptious ['bʌmpʃəs] *adj* having too much confidence in one's own ability 高傲的; 狂妄的.

bun [bʌn] *nc* **1** small sweet cake, often containing dried fruit 小甜麵包; 乾果甜麵包. **2** hair twisted into a knot at the back of the head 在頭後的髻.

bunch [bʌntʃ] *nc* group of things growing or fastened together 串; 束; 捆: *a bunch of grapes / of flowers / of keys* 一串葡萄/一束花/一串鑰匙.

bundle ['bʌndl] *nc* number of things tied together 捆; 束; 包: *a bundle of newspapers* 一捆報紙. Also 亦作 *vt* **1** make into a bundle 捆; 紮; 包. **2** put away in a hurry and in an untidy way 匆忙收拾; 亂七八糟地塞進: *He bundled everything into his pockets.* 他把什麼東西都亂七八糟地塞進自己的口袋.

bung [bʌŋ] *nc* piece of cork, rubber or other material, for putting in the hole in the side or end of a barrel 塞子; 桶塞.

bungalow ['bʌŋgələu] *nc* type of house (usu. with only one floor) 平房.

bungle ['bʌŋgl] *vt / i* do something or make something very badly 把(事情)做糟; 搞壞.

bunion ['bʌniən] *nc* painful swelling of the foot (esp. on the big toe) 拇趾囊腫脹.

bunk [bʌŋk] *nc* **1** narrow bed, fastened to a wall like a shelf, as in a train or boat 依壁而設的床舖(如在火車上或輪船上). **2** one of two or more narrow beds built one above the other 上舖; 中舖; 下舖.

bunker ['bʌŋkə*] *nc* **1** place for storing coal 儲煤處; 煤倉. **2** mound of earth or hollow in the ground, used as an obstacle on a golf course (高爾夫球場的)障礙; 土墩; 沙坑.

bunting ['bʌntiŋ] *nu* strips of cloth used to decorate streets and buildings for a public festival (節日裝飾街道、建築物的)布條; 彩旗.

buoy [bɔi] *nc* object which floats in the water, placed there to show hidden dangers to ships 浮標; 浮筒. **buoy something up** prevent from sinking; hold up 使浮起; 支持; 鼓勵: *buoy up somebody's hopes* 激起某人的希望.

buoyant ['bɔiənt] *adj* **1** able to float 會浮的: *Wood is buoyant, iron is not.* 木會浮, 鐵不會. **2** cheerful and full of hope 輕快的; 興致勃勃的: *a very buoyant person* 很快活的人. **buoyancy** *nu* **1** ability to float 浮力. **2** cheerfulness 快活, 輕快的心情.

burden ['bə:dn] *nc* **1** heavy load which is carried 重載; 負荷. **2** some sorrow or difficulty which somebody has to bear 負擔; 重累. Also 亦作 *vt* put a burden on 加負擔於, 使負擔.

bureau ['bju:rou] *nc* **1** office in which information is given to members of the public 提供資料的處所, 資料室. **2** type of writing desk 寫字桌. **bureaucrat** ['bju:rəkræt] *nc* civil servant; government official (esp. one who does his work in an unthinking way, following all the rules very carefully and not reallytrying to help people) 官員; 官僚. **bureaucratic** [bju:rə'krætik] *adj* **bureaucracy** [bju'rɔkrəsi] *nc / u* rule by bureaucrats 官僚統治; 官僚制度.

burette [bjuə'ret] *nc* graduated glass tube with a tap at the bottom, for measuring small quantities of liquid or gas 滴定管; 量管.

burglar ['bə:glə*] *nc* person who breaks into a building (esp. at night) in order to steal 夜盜; 竊賊. **burglary** ['bə:gləri] *nc / u* crime of doing this 夜

盜罪. **burgle** ['bə:gl] *vt* break into
and steal from 闖入…盜竊: *burgle a
house* 入屋行竊.

burial ['beriəl] *nc* act of putting a dead
body into a hole in the earth and filling up the hole 埋葬. see also **bury.**

burly ['bə:li] *adj* (with reference to a
person) big and strong (人)粗壯的; 魁
偉的.

burn [bə:n] *vt / i* **1** damage or destroy
by fire 燒壞; 燒毀: *He burned all his
old letters.* 他把他的舊信件全部燒掉.
2 be capable of being destroyed by
fire 燃燒; 點着: *Paper burns very
easily.* 紙張很容易着火. **3** hurt or
damage by heat 燙傷; 燒焦: *Hot water
will burn you.* 熱水會燙傷人. *She
burned the dinner which she was
cooking.* 她煮飯菜焦了. *past* 過去式和
過去分詞 **burned** or **burnt.** Also 亦作
nc mark or injury caused by burning
燒傷痕; 灼傷. *Note* 說明: *burnt* is
generally used as an adjective; both
burnt and *burned* are used as verbs
(*e.g. the burnt letters. He burned /
burnt the letters*). burnt一般作形容詞
用; burnt和burned都可作動詞用(例
如: the burnt letters 燒毀的信件.He
burned / burnt the letters 他燒毀信
件).

burnish ['bə:niʃ] *vt* (with reference to
metal objects) make bright by
polishing 擦亮; 磨光(金屬).

burnt [bə:nt] past of **burn.** burn的過去
式和過去分詞.

burrow ['bʌrou] *nc* hole made in the
ground as a dwelling place by certain
animals (e.g. rabbits) (某些動物, 如兔
子的)穴, 地洞. Also 亦作 *vt / i* make a
hole in this way 挖 (穴), 掘 (洞); 打地
洞.

bursary ['bə:səri] *nc* scholarship, sum
of money, given to a student to en-

able him to go on studying 獎學金.

burst [bə:st] *vt / i* **1** break into pieces or
develop a hole, so that what is inside
comes out (使)破裂: *The bag of flour
burst as I was carrying it.* 我提着麵粉
時袋子爆了. **2** explode; start suddenly; appear suddenly 爆炸; 突然開始; 突
然出現: *The bomb burst.* 炸彈爆炸.
The storm burst. 暴風雨突然襲來.
The trees were bursting into flower i.e.
the flowers on the trees were appearing in great numbers. 樹上很快地開滿了
花. *He burst into the room.* 他衝進房
間. *The building burst into flames* i.e.
it suddenly began burning. 樓房突然
起火. *past* 過去式和過去分詞 **burst.**
Also 亦作 *nc* sudden breaking, sudden
explosion; sudden appearance; sudden effort 突然破裂; 突然爆炸; 突然出
現; 突發. **burst out crying / laughing**
suddenly start crying / laughing 突然
哭/笑起來.

bury ['beri] *vt* **1** (esp. with reference to
a dead body) put into a hole in the
ground and cover with earth 埋葬(屍
體). **2** hide; cover up 隱藏; 掩蓋.
pres part 現在分詞 **burying.** *past* 過
去式和過去分詞 **buried.burial** *nc*
bury oneself in something be completely interested in something so
that one does not notice anything
else 埋頭於某事: *He buried himself in
his work.* 他埋頭工作. *He was buried
in a book.* 他埋頭看一本書.

bus [bʌs] *nc* large vehicle for carrying
people 公共汽車.

busby ['bʌzbi] *nc* tall fur hat worn by
certain soldiers 高頂皮軍帽.

bush [buʃ] *nc* small tree 灌木; 矮樹.
bushy *adj* **1** spreading wide like a
bush 灌木似的: *a bushy tail* 毛茸茸的
尾巴. **2** covered with bushes 灌木叢
生的. **the bush** *nu* wild uncultivated

land (not always with trees) (e.g. in Africa or Australia) 未開墾的荒野 (如在非洲或澳大利亞).

bushel ['buʃl] *nc* measure of dry goods (e.g. grain, fruit,vegetables) equivalent to 8 gallons or about 36 litres 蒲式耳 (穀物、水果、蔬菜的容量單位, 等於8加侖或約36公升).

business ['biznis] *nc / u* **1** work, occupation or duty 工作; 職業; 責任. **2** commercial firm or shop 商行; 商店: *He owns several businesses in this town.* 他在這城裏擁有好幾家商店. **3** (usu. only *sing*) incident or subject (通常僅用單數) 事; 題目: *We haven't had time to discuss this business until now.* 我們一直到現在才有時間討論這件事. **businesslike** *adj* doing things in the proper way, with care and attention 辦事有條理的; 認真的. (*opp* 反義詞 **unbusinesslike**). **'businessman** man whose work is buying and selling things 商人. **mind your own business / none of your business** don't ask me about this, I'm not going to tell you. (*impolite*) 少管閑事. (不禮貌).

bust [bʌst] *nc* **1** (esp. with reference to a woman) upper front part of the body (尤指女人的) 胸部. **2** statue of a person's head and shoulders 半身像, 胸像.

bustle ['bʌsl] *vt / i* move about quickly and noisily (usu. doing a lot of work) 奔忙; 喧鬧. Also 亦作 *nu* quick and noisy movement 忙碌; 喧擾.

busy ['bizi] *adj* doing a lot of work, working hard; full of work or activity 忙碌的; 繁忙的; 熱鬧的: *a busy man* 忙人; *a busy day* 忙碌的一天. *The shops are very busy.* 商店都很熱鬧. *comparative* 比較級 **busier**. *superlative* 最高級 **busiest. busily** *adv*

'busybody person who is too interested in other people's business 好管閑事的人.

but [bʌt,bət] **1** *conj* on the other hand 但是, 可是: *John is clever, but Jane is not.* 約翰聰明, 但珍妮不聰明. *John wanted to go to the party, but his wife was too tired.* 約翰想去參加舞會, 可是他妻子太累了. **2** *prep* except 除了: *I am alone here; there is no one but me.* 我獨自在這兒, 除了我別無他人. *You can tell anyone but Jane.* 除了珍妮外, 你對誰都可以說. **but for** without 沒有, 要不是: *We would have been lost but for John* i.e. John prevented us from being lost. 要不是約翰我們准迷路了. 即: 約翰使我們免於迷路. **can but** can only 只能: *You can but try.* 你只能試一試. **first / last but one / two** etc. first / last etc. except for one / two etc. 除了一/二…之外的第一個/最後一個. *You're next but one* i.e. you are after the next person. 你是再下一個. **nothing but** only 只有, 不過: *He is interested in nothing but football.* 他只對足球感興趣.

butcher ['butʃə*] *nc* person who sells meat 肉商.

butler ['bʌtlə*] *nc* chief male servant in a house 男管家.

butt¹ [bʌt] *nc* **1** large barrel 大桶. **2** thick end of something (東西的) 粗端: *a cigar butt* i.e. what is left after a cigar has been smoked 雪茄屁股; 雪茄烟吸後留下的部份. **3** (usu. *pl*) target for people to shoot at (通常用複數) 靶; 射擊目標.

butt² [bʌt] *vt / i* hit with the head 以頭頂撞: *Goats butt.* 山羊會撞人. **butt in** interrupt; interfere 插嘴; 打擾: *Don't butt in when someone else is talking.* (*informal*) 別人在講話時別插嘴. (非正式).

butter ['bʌtə*] *nu* thick yellow substance made from milk 黃油. Also 亦作 *vt* put butter on 塗黃油於…上. **'buttercup** *nc* type of small. yellow wild flower (植物)毛茛.

butterfly ['bʌtəflai] *nc* type of insect with four coloured wings 蝴蝶.

buttocks ['bʌtəks] *npl* part of the body on which one sits 臀部, 屁股.

button ['bʌtn] *nc* small object (usu. round in shape) used for holding articles of clothing together 鈕扣. Also 亦作 *vt/i* be fastened or fasten with a button 扣緊…; 扣上鈕扣. **'buttonhole 1** hole through which a button is put for fastening clothing 鈕孔, 扣眼. **2** flower fastened on a coat (usu. a man's goat, on a formal occasion such as a wedding) 別在外衣(通常指男人在正式場合如婚禮時穿的外衣)上的花. Also 亦作 *vt* stop somebody and force him to listen to what one says. 強留(某人)聽自己說的話.

buttress ['bʌtris] *nc* support for a wall 扶牆; 拱壁.

buy [bai] *vt/i* get in exchange for money 買: *buy food in the shop* 在商店裏購買食品. *past* 過去式和過去分詞 **bought** [bɔːt]. **buyer** *nc* **1** person who buys 買者. **2** person whose work is to buy goods for a large store. 採購員. **buy something up** buy as much as possible 盡量購進: *It was difficult to find flour in the shops last week because people had been buying it up.* 上週店裏很難看到麵粉, 因為人們一直在搶購.

buzz [bʌz] *nc* sound made by insects such as bees when flying; sound made by many people talking quietly (蜂等的)嗡嗡聲, 營營聲; (許多人的)喊喊喳喳聲. Also 亦作 *vi* make this sound 發嗡嗡, 發營營聲; 喊喊喳喳. **buzzer**

nc electrical device like a bell, which makes a buzzing sound 蜂音器.

buzzard ['bʌzəd] *nc* one of several types of large bird which eats small birds and animals 鵟鷹(一種食肉的大鳥).

by [bai] *adv / prep* **1** near 在…旁, 靠近; *a house by the river* 河邊的屋子. **2** along; across 沿; 經, 由: *It takes longer to get there if you go by the road.* 由公路到那裏所用的時間更長. **3** past 經過: *All the lights were out when I came by the house last night.* 我昨晚經過那房屋時, 燈全都熄了. **4** during 在…期間; *by night* 在夜間; *by day* 在白天. **5** not later than 不遲於: *I will finish the work by next week.* 我將於下週前完成這項工作. **6** through the use or agency of 用; 通過: *travel by aeroplane* 乘飛機旅行; *heat a house by electricity* 屋內用電取暖; *written by him* 由他寫的. **7** in units of 按個, 照: *buy things by the dozen* 按打購物. **by and large** generally; usually; on the whole 大體上; 通常; 總的看來. **by oneself, all by oneself** alone 獨自: *He was sitting (all) by himself.* 他獨個兒坐着. **by the way** expression used before mentioning something which is not directly connected with the main subject of conversation 順便說一下(用來提及與主要話題無關的事).

bye-bye ['bai'bai] *interj* informal form of **good-bye** 再見的非正式形式.

by-election ['baiilek∫ən] *nc* election held in one area only, to return one member to parliament or to a council (e.g. when the former Member of Parliament etc has died or resigned). (因前下院議員等死亡或辭職而只在某地舉行的)補缺選舉.

bygone ['baigɔn] *adj* belonging to the

past 過去的, 以往的: *bygone days* 往日. **let bygones be bygones** forget quarrels which happened in the past and be friendly in the future 過去的事讓它過去吧(既往不咎).

by-law ['bailɔ:] *nc* law made by a town or city or other area within a country (地方所制定的)地方法.

bypass ['baipɑːs] *nc* main road which is built to go around a town or city, instead of going through it 繞過城鎮的公路.

by-product ['baiprɔdəkt] *nc* something made while producing something else; a secondary product of an industry, not the main product 副產品.

byre ['baiə*] *nc* shed where cows are kept 牛欄.

bystander ['baistændə*] *nc* person standing near, not taking part, when something happens 旁觀者.

byword ['baiwə:d] *nc* person / thing generally disliked or laughed at for some bad quality (壞人或壞事的)代名詞; 笑柄: *His name was a byword for cruelty.* 他的名字是殘酷的代名詞.

C,c

cab [kæb] *nc* 1 taxi 出租汽車, 計程車. 2 part of a train, bus, lorry etc in which the driver sits (火車、公共汽車、卡車等的) 司機室.

cabaret ['kæbərei] *nc / u* entertainment (usu. singing and dancing) given at a club, party, dance etc. (在俱樂部、聚會、舞會等的) 娛樂性表演 (通常指歌舞).

cabbage ['kæbidʒ] *nc / u* type of vegetable with many thick leaves folded tightly on top of each other 捲心菜.

cabin ['kæbin] *nc* 1 room in a ship etc. (船等的) 艙. 2 small hut 小屋.

cabinet ['kæbinət] *nc* 1 small group of ministers or other senior officials of a government, who meet regularly with the prime minister or president 內閣. 2 piece of furniture with shelves or drawers for storing things 櫥; 櫃.

cable ['keibl] *nc* 1 type of thick rope (usu. made of many metal wires twisted together) 粗繩索; 鋼絲繩. 2 thick bundle of wires for carrying an electric current 電纜. 3 telegram carried in this way 電報. Also 亦作 *vt / i* send a message by cable 打電報; 給…發電報. '**cable-car** vehicle pulled by a moving cable (e.g. for travelling up and down a mountain) 纜車. '**cablegram** telegram sent by cable (海底) 電報.

cache [kæʃ] *nc* hiding place for supplies or food (e.g. used by travellers or explorers); supplies of food left in this way (旅行者或探險者貯藏補給品或食物的) 密藏處; 貯藏物.

cackle ['kækl] *nc / u* 1 noise made by a hen after laying an egg (母鶏下蛋後的) 咯咯叫聲. 2 laughter which sounds like this 咯咯的笑聲. Also 亦作 *vi* make this noise 咯咯地笑.

cacophony [kæ'kɔfəni] *nc* loud and unpleasant noise 刺耳的聲音.

cactus ['kæktəs] *nc* type of plant often covered with sharp points, growing in hot dry climates 仙人掌. *pl* 複數 **cacti** ['kæktai] or **cactuses.**

caddie, caddy[1] ['kædi] *nc* person whose work is to carry the clubs for a person playing golf 為打高爾夫球的人背球棍的人; 球童. Also 亦作 *vi* carry golf clubs for a player 當球童.

caddy[2] ['kædi] *nc* small box used for keeping tea in 茶葉盒, 茶葉罐.

cadet [kə'det] *nc* young man or boy receiving training to be an officer (in the army, navy, air force, police etc.) (陸海空軍軍官、警官等) 學校的學員.

cadge [kædʒ] *vt / i* beg, get without paying 乞求; 乞得: *John is always cadging meals from his friends.* 約翰老是向朋友要飯吃.

cafe ['kæfi] *nc* restaurant (esp. one which is not expensive) 餐館 (尤指便宜的餐館).

cafeteria [kæfi'tiəriə] *nc* place serving meals, in which people collect their own food and take it to their table (esp. such a place in a college, school, factory etc.) 自助餐廳 (尤指在大學、學校、工廠等內).

caffeine ['kæfi:n] *nu* drug found in coffee etc. 咖啡因.

cage [keidʒ] *nc* object made of metal bars, or place surrounded by metal bars, for keeping birds or animals in (鳥)籠; (獸)檻. Also 亦作 *vt* put in a cage 把…關進籠裏; 把…關入檻內. **cagey** *adj* secretive 保密的.

cajole [kə'dʒoul] *vt* make somebody do something by using pleasing words or false promises 哄騙.

cake [keik] *nc / u* **1** type of food made of flour, butter, eggs, sugar etc and baked in an oven 蛋糕. **2** anything made of this kind of mixture; anything like this in shape 糕餅; 餅狀物: *a fish cake* 魚餅; *a cake of soap* 一塊肥皂.

calamity [kə'læmiti] *nc* great and terrible accident or misfortune 大災禍, 極大的不幸. **calamitous** *adj.*

calcium ['kælsiəm] *nu* chemical found in chalk, milk, bones etc. (Ca)鈣.

calculate ['kælkjuleit] *vt / i* find out the answer to a problem by adding, subtracting, multiplying or dividing numbers 計算: *calculate the cost of buying a new house* 計算購買新房子的費用; *calculate the date on which the holiday will begin* 推算開始放假的日期. **calculation** [kælkju'leiʃən] *nc / u.* **calculating** *adj* careful and selfish; planning things carefully so as to be of advantage to oneself 精明的; 自私的; 為自己斤斤計較的. **calculator** machine which works out arithmetical calculations automatically 計算器.

calculus ['kælkjuləs] *nc / u* method of calculating changes in speed or rate of growth 微積分(學).

calendar ['kælində*] *nc* **1** list of the days and months of a particular year 日曆; 月曆: *a calendar for 1980* 1980年的日曆. **2** method of dividing up the year 曆法: *the Christian calendar* 基督教曆; *the Moslem calendar* 回教曆.

calf¹ [kɑːf] *nc* young of the cow,

elephant and seal families etc. 牛、象、海豹科等的幼仔. *pl* 複數 **calves** [kɑːvz]. **'calfskin** leather made from the young of the cow 小牛皮製成的革.

calf² [kɑːf] *nc* fleshy part of the leg below the back of the knee 腓, 小腿. *pl* 複數 **calves** [kɑːvz].

calibre ['kælibə*] *nc* **1** measurement across, or diameter, of a gun barrel, bullet, shell etc. (槍筒等)口徑; (子彈、炮彈等)直徑. **2** quality of mind; type of ability 器量; 能力. *He is a man of very high calibre.* 他是個極有才幹的人.

call¹ [kɔːl] *vt / i* **1** give a name to 給…取名; 稱: *They called their baby William.* 他們給自己的嬰兒取名威廉. *She called him a fool.* 她把他稱作傻瓜. **2** shout 叫, 喊: *He called for help, but nobody came.* 他呼救, 但沒有人來. **3** (esp. US) telephone to (Brit usu. **ring up, phone**) (尤美)給…打電話(英國通常用 ring up, phone). *I called you last night, but I couldn't get any reply.* 我昨晚給你打電話, 但沒有人接. **4** awaken from sleep 叫醒: *I must leave early tomorrow; will you call me at six o'clock?* 我明天必須早走, 你六點鐘叫醒我好嗎? **5** ask somebody to come in order to give a service 召喚; 請來: *He called the doctor.* 他請來醫生. *I shall call the police.* 我要叫警察了. *He called a meeting* i.e. he said that there was going to be a meeting, and he asked people to come to it. 他召集會議. 即: 他說要開會, 並請人們參加. **6** make a short visit 作短暫探訪: *Mr Smith called to see me yesterday.* 史密斯先生昨天來看我. **call for someone / something 1** get someone / something 接某人/取某物: *I'll call for you at your house at six o'clock.* 我六

點鐘到你家接你. *I've bought a new car; I shall call for it on my way home this evening.* 我買了一輛新車, 今天傍晚ї‍回家時順路去取. **2** need; require; ask for 需要; 要求; 請求: *This problem calls for very careful thought.* 這個問題需要很慎重考慮. **call something off** say or decide that something must not or will not happen 取消某事: *He called off the plan* i.e. he gave orders to stop the plan. 他取消這項計劃. *They called off the football match* i.e. they decided not to play the match. 他們取消這場足球比賽. **call on someone 1** make a short visit to someone 探訪某人. **2** ask somebody 請求某人: *If you need any help, you must call on me.* 如果你需要幫助, 就來找我. **call out** shout loudly 大聲叫喊. **call someone up** order to join the army 徵召某人入伍.

call² [kɔːl] **1** *nc* shout 喊聲: *We heard a call for help.* 我們聽到呼救聲. **2** *nc* telephone message 電話信息: *I had a call from John yesterday.* 我昨天接到約翰的電話. **3** *nc* awakening from sleep 喚醒: *Will you give me a call at six o'clock tomorrow morning?* 你明天早上六點鐘叫醒我好嗎? **4** *nc* short visit 拜訪: *I made a call on my neighbour.* 我拜訪鄰居. **callbox** see **kiosk.** **caller** *nc* person who makes a short visit to a person 訪問者. **calling** *nc* occupation or profession 職業.

calligraphy [kəˈligrəfi] *nu* handwriting 書法.

callous [ˈkæləs] *adj* having no feeling for the misfortune or suffering of others 無同情心的, 硬心腸的. **callously** *adv* **callousness** *nu.*

calm [kɑːm] *adj* quiet, not moving; not excited; not violent 靜的; 鎮定

的; 冷靜的: *a calm person* 鎮靜的人; *a calm sea* i.e. one without big waves 平靜的海面. Also 亦作 *nc* time or place where there is peace and quiet 時刻; 平靜的處所; 平靜. Also 亦作 *vt* cause to become calm 使平靜; 使鎮定; 使冷靜. **calmly** *adv* **calmness** *nu.*

calm down (usu. with reference to a person) stop being noisy, violent, angry, excited etc. (通常指人) 平靜下來; 鎮靜下來: *I told him to calm down.* 我叫他鎮靜下來.

calorie [ˈkæləri] *nc* unit for the measurement of heat (esp. for measuring the energy supplied by food) 卡(路里) (熱量單位, 尤指衡量食物所提供的熱量): *An ounce of sugar contains about a hundred calories.* 一盎司糖所含熱量約100卡.

calve [kɑːv] *vt / i* give birth to a young cow 生(小牛). see 見 **calf¹.**

calves [kɑːvz] pl of **calf.** calf 的複數.

calypso [kəˈlipsou] *nc* type of song from the West Indies, in which the singer invents the words while he is singing; the music for such a song 卡力騷曲 (一種源自西印度群島、邊唱邊編的歌曲); 卡力騷音樂. *pl* 複數 **calypsoes** or **calypsos.**

camber [ˈkæmbə*] *nc* slight rise in the middle of a surface (usu. on a road, to let the rain drain away) 翹曲(路面中間略高以排走雨水).

came [keim] past tense of **come.** come 的過去式.

camel [ˈkæml] *nc* large animal with one or two humps on its back, used for transport in the deserts of Africa and Asia 駱駝.

cameo [ˈkæmiou] *nc* piece of jewellery with a carving which is raised above the background 浮雕寶石.

camera ['kæmərə] *nc* apparatus for making pictures by photography 照相機, 攝影機. **'cameraman** man who operates the camera during the making of a motion picture 攝影師.

camouflage ['kæməflɑːʒ] *nu* (esp. with reference to the use of paint to prevent guns, tanks, ships etc from being seen by the enemy in war) anything which hides something or changes its appearance so that it is not easily seen 偽裝 (尤指用油漆塗抹槍砲、坦克、船隻等, 以防戰時被敵人發現). Also 亦作 *vt* hide something in this way 偽裝, 掩飾.

camp¹ [kæmp] *nc* **1** place where travellers, boy scouts etc live for a time in the open air (usu. in tents) 營地. **2** place where soldiers live, in tents or in huts 兵營, 營房. Also 亦作 *vi* live in a camp (esp. for a short period) 野營, 宿營: *The travellers camped in the mountains for three days.* 遊客們在山裏露營三天. **'camp-'bed** small folding bed used in a camp 行軍床. **'camping site, 'campsite** place where people camp 營地. camp out sleep in the open air 露營, 野營. **go camping** go for a holiday living in a tent 去野營.

camp² [kæmp] *adj* exaggerated in a theatrical and slightly ridiculous way. *(informal)* 做作的; 扭怩的. (非正式).

campaign [kæm'pein] *nc* series of movements or activities with some special purpose (often in war) 戰役; 運動: *The Germans were defeated in the campaign in North Africa.* 德國人在北非戰役中被打敗. *The committee began a campaign to get more members for the society.* 委員會開始一係列活動, 為該會擴充會員. Also 亦作 *vi* fight in or be active in a campaign 作

戰; 參加運動.

camphor ['kæmfə] *nu* strong-smelling white substance used medically and in the manufacture of celluloid 樟腦: *a camphor ball* 樟腦丸.

campus ['kæmpəs] *nc* the grounds on which a college or university is built 校園.

can¹ [kæn] *aux* **1** be able to 能, 會: *He can speak French.* 他會講法語. **2** have permission to 可以: *You can go home now* 你現在可以回家了. 即: 你不必再留在這裏. *past* 過去式 **could** [kud], negative 否定式 **cannot** ['kænɔt] or **can't** [kɑːnt]. *Note* 說明: **1** *can't* is more informal than *cannot*. *Can't* is generally used in spoken English and in the more informal types of writing, such as letters. **2** the use of *can* to mean 'have permission to' is considered wrong by some people, who would use *may* with this meaning. *You may go home now* i.e. you need not stay here any longer. However, the use of *can* to mean *may* is very common except in formal writing. **1.** can't 比 cannot 不正式. can't 一般用於口語和較不正式的書面語, 如信件. **2.** 有些人認爲用 can 表示"可以"是錯的, 他們用 may 表示這個意思. 如 You may go home now (你現在可以回家了). 然而, 除了正式書面語外, 用 can 表示 may 很普遍.

can² [kæn] *nc* metal container for holding food, liquid etc. 裝食品、液體等的金屬罐 (或壺等容器). Also 亦作 *vt* put into a can 把...裝入罐内. *past* 過去式和過去分詞 **canned.** *Note* 說明: *(US)* can is used for any metal container of this type (e.g. *a can of fruit; a can of milk*). *(Brit)* **tin** is more generally used, and the word *can* only for certain types of container (e.g. *an oilcan; a milk can; a can of paint)*. 在美國英語中, can 指任何這類金屬容器 (例如: a can of fruit 一罐水果; a can of milk 一罐牛奶). 在英國英語中, tin 更常用; can 僅用於某些容器 (例如: an oilcan 油壺; a milk can 牛奶罐; a can of paint 一罐油漆).

canal [kə'næl] *nc* narrow waterway through land, made by man 運河.

canary [kə'nɛəri] *nc* small yellow bird which sings sweetly, often kept as a pet 金絲雀.

cancel ['kænsl] *vt* 1 say or decide that something already arranged should not now take place 取消: *He cancelled the meeting.* 他取消會議. *They decided to cancel the agreement.* 他們決定取消一協議. 2 make a mark in something to show that something is wrong or to prevent something from being used again 劃去, 勾銷; 使作廢: *Postage stamps on letters are cancelled before the letters are delivered.* 信封上的郵票在送信前就已蓋銷. *past* 過去式和過去分詞 **cancelled**. (*US* 美 **canceled**). **cancellation** [kænsə'leiʃən] *nc/u*.

cancer ['kænsə*] *nu* illness in which a disease in part of the body grows and spreads 癌.

candid ['kændid] *adj* speaking the truth without trying to hide anything 率直的, 坦白的. **candidly** *adv* see 見 **candour**.

candidate ['kændideit] *nc* person who offers himself for some office or position 候選人; 應徵者: *In an election people are asked to choose between a number of candidates.* 選舉時要求人們在一些候選人中進行選擇.

candle ['kændl] *nc* stick of hard wax, with a thread in the middle, which is

lit to give light 蠟燭. **'candlestick** object for holding a candle upright while it is burning 燭台.

candour ['kændə*] (*US* 美 **candor**) *nu* quality of being candid; saying what one thinks or knows without trying to hide anything 直率, 坦白. see 見 **candid**.

candy ['kændi] *nc/u* 1 sugar which has been made hard by being boiled 冰糖. 2 (*US*) sweet things made from sugar (e.g. chocolate or toffee) (*Brit* 英 **sweets** or **chocolate**) (美)糖果.

cane [kein] 1 *nc* thin stick used for beating children or for helping a person to walk 笞杖; 手杖. 2 *nc/u* long stems of certain plants 莖: *bamboo cane* 竹莖; *sugar cane* 甘蔗. Also 亦作 *vt* punish by beating with a cane 用笞杖打: *He caned the boy.* 他用笞杖打那男孩.

canine ['keinain] *adj* of or like dogs 犬的; 似犬的: *canine tooth* 犬齒, 犬牙.

canister ['kænistə*] *nc* small box (esp. one for containing dry goods) (尤指裝乾貨的)小罐.

cannibal ['kænibl] *nc* person who eats human flesh 食人者. **cannibalism** *nu* practice of eating one's own kind 吃同類的肉的行爲.

cannon ['kænən] *nc* 1 old type of large gun which fired a solid metal or stone ball 火砲, 加農砲. 2 modern type of large gun 大砲.

cannot ['kænɔt] see 見 **can¹**.

canoe [kə'nu:] *nc* type of light boat moved by paddling 輕舟, 獨木舟. **canoeist** [kə'nu:ist] *nc* person who travels in a canoe 划獨木舟(旅行)的人.

canon ['kænən] *nc* 1 law of certain Christian churches (esp. Roman

Catholic) (基督教)教規(尤指羅馬天主
教). **2** officer of certain of the Christian churches 教堂裏的任職教士.
canonize ['kænənaiz] *vt* officially declare a dead person to be a saint 宣告
(死者)爲聖徒.

canopy ['kænəpi] *nc* covering (often
supported by poles and usu. made of
cloth or wood) over a throne, bed,
doorway etc. 華蓋；罩篷；天蓋；遮陽.

can't [kɑːnt] short form of **cannot**. cannot 的縮畧式. see 見 **can¹**.

cantankerous [kæn'tæŋkərəs] *adj* bad-
tempered and with the habit of being
against what other people suggest 脾
氣不好的; 愛抬槓的.

canteen [kæn'tiːn] *nc* **1** place in a factory or barracks etc where food is
provided (工廠或營房的)食堂, 餐室.
2 set of knives, forks and spoons 一套
餐具.

canter ['kæntə*] *vi* (with reference to a
horse) run slowly and easily, moving
the two front legs together and then
the two back legs and so on (馬)慢
跑.

cantilever ['kæntiliːvə*] *nc* long projecting arm of metal etc fastened at one
end only 懸臂, 伸臂.

canvas ['kænvəs] **1** *nu* strong cloth
used for tents, ships' sails etc and for
painting on with oil paints 帆布; 帳幕
布; 油畫布. **2** *nc* an oil painting 一幅
油畫. **under canvas 1** in a tent 在帳
幕裏. **2** (of a ship) with the sails
spread out (船)張滿帆的.

canvass ['kænvəs] *vt / i* go around an
area calling at houses, shops etc
asking people to vote for a particular
candidate in an election 爲某候選人走
門串户拉選票; 向…拉選票; *I've can-
vassed all the people in this street on
behalf of John Smith.* 我已經替約翰·

史密斯向這條街上所有的人爭取選票.
canvasser *nc*.

canyon ['kænjən] *nc* deep, narrow valley with sides like cliffs (esp. in America) (尤指在美洲的)峽谷.

cap [kæp] *nc* **1** type of hat (usu. worn
by schoolboys or men in uniform) 便
帽, 制服帽. **2** top of a tube, bottle etc.
(管、瓶等的)蓋, 罩.

capable ['keipəbl] *adj* able; having the
power or cleverness to do something
能; 有能力的: *He is capable of being
very unkind to people.* 他對人會很刻
薄. *He is a capable person* i.e. he is
clever, he can do what is expected of
him 他是個很能幹的人. 即: 他聰明, 需
要他幹甚麼就能幹甚麼. **capability**
[keipə'biliti] *nu.*

capacity [kə'pæsiti] *nu* **1** ability to hold
or contain a certain number or
quantity 容量; 容積: *The capacity of
this bottle is two litres* i.e. it will hold
two litres. 這瓶子的容量爲兩升. **2**
power of the mind; ability 才幹; 能力:
He has a great capacity for work i.e.
he is able to work hard. 他工作能力很
强. 即: 他能埋頭苦幹. **3** position or
office 身份; 職位: *in his capacity as a
judge* 以他的法官身份.

cape¹ [keip] *nc* type of coat without
sleeves, worn over the shoulders 披
肩; 短披風.

cape² [keip] *nc* land projecting into the
sea 岬; 海角: *the Cape of Good Hope*
好望角.

capillary [kə'piləri] *nc* tube or blood-
vessel with an opening as small as a
hair 毛細管. Also 亦作 *adj.*

capital ['kæpitl] **1** *nc* city in which the
government of a country does its
work 首都. **2** *nc* large letter 大寫字母.
A,B,C etc are capitals. A, B, C 等是大
寫字母. **3** *nu* money and property

(usu. a large amount) owned by a person or business 資本. **capitalism** ['kæpitəlizəm] *nu* system in which business and property are owned by private individuals or groups of people and not by the government or state 資本主義. **capitalist** *nc* person who owns business or property in this way 資本家. **'capital 'letter** large letter (e.g. A,B,C,D) 大寫字母(如: A、B、C、D). **'capital 'punishment** (in a legal sense) punishment by killing (法律上)死刑.

capitulate [kə'pitjuleit] *vi* agree that one's enemy has beaten one and promise to stop fighting on certain conditions (根據一定條件)投降. **capitulation** [kəpitju'leiʃən] *nu*.

capricious [kə'priʃəs] *adj* often changing in a playful or foolish way 任性的; 變化無常的.

capsize [kæp'saiz] *vt / i* (with reference to ships and boats) turn over 使(船) 傾覆; (船隻)傾覆.

capstan ['kæpstn] *nc* metal object for winding a rope (e.g. on a ship) 絞盤, 起錨機.

capsule ['kæpsju:l] *nc* **1** small container that can dissolve in water etc and that holds a certain amount of medicine (藥劑)膠囊. **2** any (small) container (esp. a spacecraft) (小)容器; 太空艙.

captain ['kæptin] *nc* **1** leader of a team in certain sports (體育項目的)隊長. **2** man in charge of a ship or aircraft 船長; (飛機)機長. Also 亦作 *vt* act as a leader 做…的首領; 任…的隊長: *John will captain the team.* 約翰將出任該隊隊長.

caption ['kæpʃən] *nc* writing below a picture in a newspaper or magazine, explaining the picture (圖畫的)文字説

明.

captivate ['kæptiveit] *vt* get the attention or interest of somebody by being beautiful or charming 迷住; 吸引.

captive ['kæptiv] *nc* prisoner (rather *o.f.*) 俘虜, 囚犯(頗爲舊式). **captivity** [kæp'tiviti] *nu* state of being a captive 被俘; 監禁.

captor ['kæptə*] *nc* person who catches somebody and holds him as a prisoner 俘虜者, 捕捉者.

capture ['kæptʃə*] *vt* **1** catch and hold as a prisoner 捕獲; 俘獲: *The policeman captured the thief as he was running away.* 那小偷正要跑掉時, 警察把他逮住. **2** take and hold as one's own property 奪取; 獲得: *The soldiers captured the town from the enemy.* 戰士們從敵人手裏奪回那座城市. Also 亦作 *nc* something captured; act of capturing 捕獲物; 戰利品; 捕獲; 俘獲.

car [kɑ:*] *nc* type of vehicle with four wheels which is driven by a petrol engine 汽車.

carafe [kə'ræf] *nc* container for wine, water etc. 酒壺; 水壺.

caramel ['kærəml] *nc / u* type of sweet substance made from sugar which has been slightly burned 焦糖.

carat ['kærət] *nc* unit for measuring the quality of gold and the weight of jewels 克拉(實石重量單位); 開(黃金成色單位).

caravan ['kærəvæn] *nc* **1** group of people travelling together (esp. in a desert country) 旅行隊(尤指在沙漠地帶). **2** (*Brit*) small house on wheels (*US* 美 **trailer**) (英)帶輪子的小屋, 活動小屋.

carbohydrate [kɑ:bou'haidreit] *nc* **1** (chemistry) substance composed of carbon, hydrogen and oxygen (化學) 碳水化合物. **2** this substance found in food, such as bread, which causes one to gain weight 糖類.

carbon ['kɑːbən] *nu* chemical element found in coal and many other substances (C) 碳. **'carbon paper** paper covered with a coloured substance, used for making copies of what one is writing by being placed between sheets of writing paper 複寫紙.

carbonate ['kɑːbənit] *nc* salt of carbonic acid 碳酸鹽.

carburettor ['kɑːbjuretə*] *nc* part of a motorcar in which petrol and air are mixed together before the petrol is burned in the engine 汽化器, 化油器.

carcass, carcase ['kɑːkəs] *nc* dead body of an animal. 動物的屍體.

card [kɑːd] *nc* flat stiff piece of paper (usu. rectangular in shape) used for various purposes 卡片. **'greetings card** card sent by post on certain occasions, to give congratulations or good wishes to somebody; the main types are *birthday cards* and *Christmas cards* (每逢節日喜慶向人祝賀致意的) 問候卡 (主要有 birthday cards 生日卡和 Christmas cards 聖誕卡). **'playing card** one of a set of (usu.) 52, used for playing various games of chance and skill 一張撲克牌. **'postcard** see 見 **post**¹. **'visiting card** see 見 **visit**. **on the cards** possible 可能的: *It's on the cards that I shall go to France next year. (informal)* 明年我可能到法國去. (非正式).

cardboard ['kɑːdbɔːd] *nu* thick, heavy type of paper, used for making boxes etc. (用以製盒子等的) 厚硬紙板.

cardiac ['kɑːdiæk] *adj* (mainly medicine) with reference to the heart (主要用於醫學上) 心臟的.

cardigan ['kɑːdigən] *nc* knitted woollen jacket, usually with long sleeves 對襟羊毛衫 (通常是長袖的).

cardinal ['kɑːdinl] *nc* one of the senior officials of the Roman Catholic Church responsible for electing a pope 紅衣主教. **cardinal number** number such as 1,2,6,10,93 used in counting. (Contrasted with *ordinal number* i.e. number such as 1st, 2nd, 6th, 10th, 93rd) 基數 (像1、2、6、10、93 一類數字, 以別於像第一、第二、第六、第十、第九十三等序數).

care¹ [keə*] *vt / i (usu. negative)* feel strongly (通常用否定結構) 老放在心上, 在乎: *When I told him that he would be punished, he said he didn't care* i.e. he was not frightened or worried. 當我對他說, 他會受處分的時候, 他說, 他不在乎. 即: 他既不怕, 也不煩惱. *I don't care what you say, I shall do it tomorrow* i.e. it does not matter what you say. 我不在乎你說甚麼, 明天我要幹這件事, 即: 你說甚麼都無所謂. **care for 1** look after; show love for and help 照顧, 愛護, 幫助: *When her mother died she was left to care for her father.* 她母親死去時候, 只剩下她照料她父親. **2** have a *liking* for 喜歡: *I don't care for modern art* i.e. I don't like it. 我不喜歡現代藝術.

care² [keə*] **1** *nu* close or serious attention 密切注意: *He gave a lot of care to his work.* 他把大量心思放在工作上. **2** *nu* protection; love; help 愛護, 幫助: *A child needs a mother's care* i.e. it needs to be loved and protected by a mother. 小孩子需要母親的愛護. *She left her children in the care of her neighbour* i.e. her neighbour looked after, protected and fea the children, while the mother was away 她請鄰居照看孩子. 即: 媽媽不在家時候, 由鄰居餵孩子、照顧他. **3** *nu* worry 憂慮: *His face showed the signs of* *care and sorrow.* 他臉上顯出憂傷的痕跡. **careful** *adj* with care; showing care 小心的. **carefully** *adv* **careless** *adj* without care 粗心的. **carelessly** *adj* **carelessness** *nu* **'carefree** *adj* free of worry; happy 無憂無慮的; 快樂的. **'caretaker** person who looks after a building when the people who work or live there are away 大樓管理員, 看管房屋的人. **take care** be careful 當心: *You must take care when you cross the road* i.e. you must make sure that no cars are coming when you cross the road. 過馬路時候, 要當心. 即: 你要斷定沒有車子正駛過來, 才橫穿走過馬路. **take care of** look after, protect; feed, clothe, love etc. 照顧; 保護; 給…吃, 穿, 溫暖等: *He took care of his younger brothers while his mother went shopping.* 媽媽上街採購時候, 他照料幾個弟弟.

career [kə'riə*] *nc* 1 work done by a person during his life 事業; 一生事跡; 職業: *He had a very successful career.* 他一生很有成就. 2 actions and experience of a person during his life 經歷, 生涯. Also 亦作 *vi* (often with **along**) move a great speed (常與along連用) 奔馳: *We were careering along in the car.* 我們乘車飛速前進.

caress [kə'res] *vt* touch gently, to express love or affection 深情地輕輕撫摸. Also 亦作 *nc* touch of this kind 愛撫.

cargo ['kɑːgou] *nc / u* the goods carried in a ship or aeroplane (船隻、飛機所載的)貨物. *pl* 複數 **cargoes.**

caricature ['kærikətjuə*] *nc* picture which makes something serious or important appear to be foolish or funny; any imitation of this kind 諷刺畫; 滑稽性的模仿.

carnal ['kɑːnl] *adj* concerned with the body (usu. in a bad sense, contrasted with **spiritual**) 肉體的(通常具有貶義, 以與 spiritual 對比): *carnal sins / desires* 姦淫/性慾; 慾念.

carnation [kɑː'neiʃ ən] *nc* type of flower with pink, white or red flowers which smell sweet 康乃馨, 荷蘭石竹.

carnival ['kɑːnivl] *nc* public celebration, with processions, games, feasts etc. (esp. in Roman Catholic countries in the period before Lent) 尤指天主教國家四旬齋前舉行的)狂歡節; 嘉年華會.

carnivorous [kɑː'nivərəs] *adj* eating meat 食肉的: *Lions and tigers are carnivorous animals.* 獅子、老虎都是食肉類動物.

carol ['kærl] *nc* religious song sung at Christmas time 聖誕頌歌.

carp[1] [kɑːp] *nc* type of freshwater fish used for food 鯉魚.

carp[2] [kɑːp] *vi* (often with **at**) make small and unnecessary criticisms; find small and unimportant faults or mistakes (常與 at 連用)找岔子, 挑剔, 吹毛求疵: *He was always carping at the arrangements made by other people.* 對於別人所作安排, 他總是愛挑剔、找毛病.

carpenter ['kɑːpintə*] *nc* person whose work is to build things from wood (but not usu. pieces of furniture) 木匠 (通常不作細木工). **carpentry** *nu* the work of a carpenter 木工, 木作.

carpet ['kɑːpit] *nc* thick heavy covering for the floor or stairs 地毯; Also 亦作 *vt* cover with a carpet 在…舖上地毯.

carriage ['kæridʒ] **1** *nc* part of a train in which a number of people sit together 火車的客車車廂. **2** *nc* vehicle pulled by a horse, for carrying passengers 馬車. **3** *nu* act or cost of carrying or moving goods by some form of transport 運輸; 運費. **'car-**

riageway road used by cars etc. 車行道.

carrier ['kæriə*] *nc* see 見 **carry**.

carrot ['kærət] *nc* plant with a long yellow or orange-red root eaten as a vegetable 胡蘿蔔, 紅蘿蔔.

carry ['kæri] *vt / i* 1 lift off the ground and move from one place to another 運載; 携帶: *The bus was carrying 28 passengers when the accident happened.* 事故發生的時候, 公共汽車上有二十八個乘客. *He always carries a small notebook in his pocket.* 他口袋裹總是帶着一本小筆記本. *He was carrying his hat* i.e. it was in his hand, not on his head. 他手上拿着帽子. *Help me carry these boxes.* 幫我提一提這些箱子. 2 (esp. with reference to parts of a building) bear the weight of something (尤指建築物各部) 支撐, 載重. 3 (usu. with reference to sound) go across a certain distance (通常指音波) 傳播, 傳送: *His voice did not carry to the back of the room.* 他講話聲音到不了房間後面那一部份. **carrier** *nc* 1 business company which carries goods or passengers from one place to another (客、貨運) 運輸行. 2 person who carries the germs of a disease to other people without having the disease himself 帶菌者. '**carrier 'bag** large bag made of paper or polythene and used for shopping 紙或聚乙烯做成的大型手提購物袋. **carry away** 1 take to another place 帶走, 運走. 2 (often *passive*) cause to have strong feelings so that one cannot think clearly (常用於被動語態) 使失常態或失去自制力; 使出神、着迷; 使忘其所: *He was so carried away by fear that he did not know what he was saying* 他大吃一驚, 嚇得話都說不清楚. **carry off** 1 take to another place

by the use of force or without the owner's permission 奪去; 不告而取. 2 (with reference to competitions, prizes etc.) win 贏得 (競賽, 錦標等): *He carried off the first prize.* 他奪得冠軍. **carry on** 1 continue 繼續: *Carry on, don't stop working.* 別停, 繼續工作. *He carried on his father's business* i.e. he worked in the business which his father had started. 他繼承父業. 2 be angry and speak loudly (*informal*) 大吵大鬧 (非正式). 3 behave badly. (*informal*) 作風不正派 (非正式). '**carry-on** *nc* fuss; troublesome procedure 麻煩事, 繁瑣的手續: *a carry-on about getting tickets. (informal)* 買票的囉嗦手續 (非正式). **carry out** do 做, 執行: *He carried out his plan* i.e. he did what he had planned; 他實現了原來的計劃; *carry out an order / threat / promise* 執行命令/實現恐嚇/履行諾言.

cart [kɑːt] *nc* vehicle pulled by a horse and used for carrying goods 用馬拉的裝貨大車. Also 亦作 *vt* carry in a cart 用馬車運送. '**cart-track** rough road suitable for carts but not for cars (不適宜於汽車行駛, 只供馬拉大車用的) 崎嶇不平的小道.

cartilage ['kɑːtilidʒ] *nc / u* strong substance like elastic in the joints of the body 體內關節間的軟質; 軟骨結構.

carton ['kɑːtn] *nc* cardboard container 紙板匣, 紙箱.

cartoon [kɑːˈtuːn] *nc* 1 drawing in a newspaper or magazine, dealing with topics in the news (esp. politics) (報紙、雜誌上針對新聞, 尤其政治新聞而作的) 漫畫. 2 film (usu. amusing) made by photographing a number of drawings, instead of photographing living actors 卡通片. (Also 亦作 **animated cartoon**).

cartridge [ˈkɑːtridʒ] *nc* **1** case made of metal or cardboard for holding gunpowder; bullet 彈藥筒; 子彈. **2** roll of camera film 一捲照相軟片, 膠捲.

carve [kɑːv] *vt / i* **1** cut (meat etc.) into slices 切(肉等)成碎片. **2** (with references to wood, stone etc.) cut into a shape, picture or pattern 雕刻(木石等). **carving** *nc* piece of stone, wood etc which has been carved. 雕刻品. 'carving knife large knife for cutting meat into slices 切肉刀.

cascade [kæsˈkeid] *nc* small waterfall 小瀑布. Also 亦作 *vi* fall in or like a cascade 匯成瀑布大量落下; 瀑布似地傾倒下來.

case[1] [keis] *nc* **1** example; condition; situation; event; happening 事例; 情況; 病例: *The headmaster had to deal with several cases of cheating* i.e. several of the pupils cheated. 校長必須處理幾椿考試作弊的事. *The doctor went to see a case of malaria* i.e. a person suffering from malaria. 醫生出診去看一個瘧疾病人. *He told me about the case of a girl who did not learn to speak until she was five* i.e. he told me the facts about this girl. 他告訴我有一個女孩子五歲才會講話的事例. *He said that he understood, but this was not the case* i.e. this was not true. 他說他懂得, 事實上並非如此. **2** a matter which a judge or other person in a court of law is asked to decide on 案件: *The lawyer put his case to the judge* i.e. the lawyer put forward his arguments. 律師就案情提出辯護. **3** (grammar) form of the noun / pronoun depending on the use of the noun / pronoun in the sentence (e.g. the difference between 'I' and 'me' is a difference of case). (語法) 名詞、代詞的格 (例如: 'I' 和 'me' 只是格上的不同). in **any case** whatever happens 無論如何. in **case** so as to be ready if something happens 萬一; 以防萬一: *You must take your umbrella in case it rains.* 你必須帶傘去, 以防萬一下雨. in **that case** if that is true (若是) 那樣的話: *The boy told me that he had lost his money and so, in that case, he could not buy a new football.* 那男孩子告訴我他把錢丟了. 那樣的話就沒辦法買個新足球了.

case[2] [keis] *nc* container or box for holding goods 盒子. **ciga'rette case** box (usu. of metal) used for carrying cigarettes 香烟盒(常用金屬製造). see also 參見 **suit**[1].

cash [kæʃ] *nu* money in notes and coins 現款, 現金. Also 亦作 *vt* change into cash: 兌現: *cash a cheque* 兌現一張支票. **cashier** [kæˈʃiə*] *nc* person in a shop or bank who deals with the cash 出納員.

cashmere [ˈkæʃmiə*] *nu* soft type of wool 開士米羊毛.

casino [kəˈsiːnou] *nc* building open to the public for gambling 賭場. *pl* 複數 **casinos.**

cask [kɑːsk] *nc* large or small container for liquid (usu. liquid for drinking) 裝液體的桶狀容器(通常用以裝飲料).

casket [ˈkɑːskit] *nc (US)* coffin (美) 棺材.

cassava [kəˈsɑːvə] *nu* type of plant grown in the tropics for its roots from which food (such as tapioca) is obtained 木薯. Also 亦作 **manioc.**

casserole [ˈkæsəroul] *nc* covered dish in which food can be cooked in an oven; food cooked in this way 焙盆(在烘箱內焙烤食物用的有蓋盆子, 上菜時連盆端到餐桌上); 砂鍋; 用焙盆, 砂鍋煮成的食品.

cassette [kæˈset] *nc* small flat box holding magnetic tape with recorded words or music 盒式錄音帶.

cast¹ [kɑːst] *vt / i* **1** throw 投, 拋, 撒: *cast a fishing line* 甩出釣竿上的線. *cast a shadow* 投下影子. *Note* 說明: apart from references to fishing or to shadows, *cast* in the sense of *throw* is rather *o.f.* use *throw*. 除指釣魚或影子以外, 作爲throw解釋的cast, 屬於舊式用法, 宜用throw. **2** let fall; lose; discard 脫落: *The horse cast a shoe.* 馬脫落了一隻蹄鐵. *The snake has cast its skin.* 蛇蛻了皮. **3** pour hot liquid metal into a mould or shape, in which it cools and becomes solid in the form of the mould 澆模, 鑄造. **4** give parts to actors in a play 分配劇中角色: *I cast John as Hamlet and Mary as Ophelia.* 我派約翰扮演哈姆萊特, 瑪麗扮演奧菲莉婭. *past* 過去式和過去分詞 **cast**.

cast² [kɑːst] *nc* (list of) actors in a play 劇中演員 (名單) **'castaway** person who has landed in a strange (and often uninhabited) country after being in a shipwreck 船隻遇難後, 流落異鄉 (常是無人烟地方) 的人. **'cast'iron** *nu* type of hard but brittle iron made by casting 鑄鐵. **'casting vote** vote given by a chairman of a meeting if the votes of the members are evenly divided 決定票 (指投票表決, 正反兩方票數相同須由會議主席加入投票, 以作決定的票).

castanet [kæstə'net] *nc* (usu. *pl*) instrument made of two pieces of wood, held in the hand and hit together to produce a sound (通常用複數) 響板, 雲板.

caste [kɑːst] *nc* one of a number of social and religious divisions in use among Hindus. A person is considered as being born into a particular

caste and cannot rise higher (印度的) 社會、宗教等級之一, 種姓 (按照此種區分, 每人生下來就屬於某一等級, 永遠不能改變).

castle ['kɑːsl] *nc* old type of building with thick walls, used for defence against enemies 城堡.

castor [kɑːstə*] *nc* small wheel put on a piece of furniture to make it easy to move 裝在傢具底部的小腳輪.

castor oil ['kɑːstərɔil] *nu* thick unpleasant-tasting oil used as a medicine 蓖麻油.

castor sugar ['kɑːstəʃugə*] *nu* type of very fine sugar 精製白糖.

castrate [kæs'treit] *vt* cut off part of the sexual organs of a male human or animal 閹割.

casual ['kæʒjuəl] *adj* **1** happening by chance or accident; not planned 偶然的, 碰巧的; 並非事先安排的: *a casual meeting* 巧遇, 偶遇. **2** careless and rather impolite in behaviour 漫不經心的, 隨便的: *He spoke in a rather casual way to the headmaster.* 他對校長講話的樣子, 稍爲太随便了一些. **3** (of clothes, shoes) informal, for wearing during leisure time (衣、鞋等)非正式場合穿的; 方便的. **casually** *adv*.

casualty ['kæʒjuəlti] *nc* person killed or injured in war or in an accident 傷亡人員.

cat [kæt] *nc* small domestic animal which can see in the dark and which catches and eats mice 貓. **catty** *adj* (usu. with reference to a woman or something she says) unkind; saying unkind things (通常用以形容婦女或其言論) 惡毒的, 挖苦的. **'cat call** *nc* (often *pl*) rough unpleasant noise made to express disapproval (常用複數) 表示不滿而發出的噓聲; 倒彩.

catalogue ['kætəlɔg] (*US* 美 **catalog**)

nc list of things. A library has a catalogue to help people find the books they want; some big stores issue catalogues of the things they have for sale 圖書總目; 商品目錄: Also 亦作 *vt* put into a catalogue 列入目錄: *The librarian catalogued the new books.* 圖書館管理員把新書登入目錄中.

catalyst ['kætəlist] *nc* something which helps a chemical change to take place without undergoing any change itself 催化劑.

catapult ['kætəpʌlt] *nc (Brit)* piece of wood or metal, shaped like a letter Y, with a piece of rubber attached, used for shooting small stones (英) 彈弓. (*US* 美 **slingshot**).

cataract ['kætərækt] *nc* 1 type of steep waterfall 直落而下的大瀑布. 2 disease of the eye, in which the centre of the eye becomes white and blind 白內障.

catarrh [kə'tɑ:*] *nu* disease of the nose and throat, causing the formation of a thick liquid; the thick liquid itself 卡他, 黏膜炎; 黏膜發炎時的分泌物.

catastrophe [kə'tæstrəfi] *nc* sudden and very bad accident or misfortune (e.g. a fire, earthquake, plane crash) 大災害, 嚴重不幸事件(例如: 火災, 地震, 飛機失事). **catastrophic** [kætəs'trɔfik] *adj*.

catch¹ [kætʃ] *vt / i* stop and hold; meet and stay with; capture 捕, 捉: *The policeman caught the thief.* 警察抓住小偷. *He caught a train to London.* 他趕上開往倫敦的火車. *He caught the ball in one hand* 他單手接球. *The beautiful picture caught my attention* i.e. I stopped and looked with interest at the picture. 美麗的圖畫引起我的注意. 即: 使我停步觀賞. *He caught influenza last year* i.e. he had this dis-

ease last year (with reference to infectious diseases only) (e.g. we can say *he caught a cold* but not *he caught cancer*) 他去年得了流感(這種用法只限於傳染病.例如: 他感冒英語可以說 he caught a cold,但他得了癌症,卻不能說he caught cancer). *past* 過去式和過去分詞 **caught** [kɔ:t]. **catching** *adj* (with reference to disease) infectious; easily caught (指疾病) 傳染性的, 易於傳染的. **catch someone up** 趕上某人: *John left five minutes ago, but if you hurry you will catch him up.* 約翰五分鐘以前走的, 不過你如果快些, 會趕上他. see **catch up with** (in sense 1). 見catch up with (義1). **catch up with someone / something** 1 go faster than somebody in front who is going in the same direction as oneself, so that one comes to where he is 趕上某人: *John left the house ten minutes before I did, but he walked so slowly that I was able to catch up with him.* 約翰比我早十分鐘離開. 可是他走得很慢, 因此我能趕上他. 2 do work which should have been done before 趕做早該做好的工作, 趕工: *I have been ill for two weeks, and so I must try to catch up with my work.* 我病了兩個星期, 因此我必須把工作補上. **catch fire** begin burning 着火; 火點着了.

catch² [kætʃ] *nc* 1 (esp. with reference to fish caught) something caught 捕獲物(尤指捕獲之魚). 2 something for fastening a door or window 門扣; 窗鈎. 3 trick; something which is intended to deceive somebody. (*informal* in sense 3) 圈套, 蹊蹺(義3爲非正式). **catchy** *adj* (with reference to music) easy to learn and pleasant (指音樂) 易學而動聽的: *a catchy tune* 動人的曲調. **'catchword / 'catch phrase** short statement or slogan which is easily learned (used for advertising or political purposes) (廣告或政治宣傳中使用的)引人注意而風行一時的口號, 短語.

catechism ['kætəkizəm] *nc* list of questions and answers (esp. such a list of religious teachings) to be learned by people wishing to become full members of the Christian churches 基督教教義問答集.

category ['kætəgəri] *nc* type; class; kind; division 種類, 類型; 範疇. **categorize** *vt* put into categories 分類. **categorical** [kætə'gorikl] *adj* (with reference to statements) definite; without any doubts (指陳述聲明)明確的; 斷言的.

cater ['keitə*] *vi* (usu. with for or to) provide or supply (esp. food) (通常與 for或to連用)供應(尤指食物): He catered for two hundred guests at the party i.e. he provided food for them 他為宴會兩百位客人提供了食物. The radio and television have to cater to many different types of interest and taste among the public. 無線電和電視必須滿足公衆多種不同的興趣和口味.

caterpillar ['katepilə*] *nc* worm-like animal which eats plants and which later turns into a moth or butterfly 蛾或蝶的幼蟲, 毛蟲.

cathedral [kə'θi:drl] *nc* church of a bishop or archbishop in some of the Christian churches (由主教或大主教主持的)大教堂.

cathode ['kæθoud] *nc* negative pole of electric current 陰極, 負極: cathode rays 陰極射線. (opp 反義詞 anode).

catholic ['kæθlik] *adj* 1 wide; with an interest in everything 廣泛的; 興趣多方面的. 2 of all the Christian churches taken together 基督教會的(此處基督教會指一切堂會). 3 (Catholic)

of the Roman Catholic Church (大寫)天主教的. Also 亦作 *nc* member of the Roman Catholic Church 天主教徒.

cattle ['kætl] *npl* cows, bulls and calves, taken all together 牛的總稱.

catty[1] ['kæti] *nc* (in China and Southeast Asia) weight equal to $\frac{1}{2}$ kilogram (在中國和東南亞國家的重量單位)斤.

catty[2] ['kæti] *adj* see 見 cat.

caught [ɔ:t] past of catch[1] catch[1]的過去式和過去分詞.

cauldron ['kɔ:ldrn] *nc* large pot used for cooking over a fire 大鍋.

cauliflower ['kɔliflauə*] *nc / u* type of vegetable like a cabbage but with a white flower-like head 菜花.

cause [kɔ:z] *nc* 1 thing which makes something happen 原因: What was the cause of your failure? i.e. why did you fail? 你失敗的原因是甚麼? You have no cause to worry i.e. there is nothing to worry about. 你沒有理由憂慮. 即: 不存在值得煩惱的事情. 2 purpose, movement or idea for which people work 目標, 事業, 主義: He was collecting money for a good cause i.e. he was collecting money for people or for something deserving the money. 他為了崇高的目標而募捐. The United Nations Organization has done a lot for the cause of world peace. 聯合國組織為了世界和平(事業)做了很多事. Also 亦作 *vt* make something happen; be the cause of something 引起; 成為某事的起因.

causeway ['kɔ:zwei] *nc* road built up above the surface of the land on either side (usu. across swampy land) (通常指穿過沼澤地帶的)堤道.

caustic ['kɔ:stik] *adj* (with reference to words) hurtful; cruel (指言詞) 刻薄的; 譏諷的.

caution ['kɔ:ʃən] *nu* action of being careful so as to avoid danger or mistakes 小心, 謹慎. Also 亦作 *vt* give a warning to somebody, before or after he has made a mistake or done something wrong 警告, 告誡. **cautious** *adj* **cautiously** *adv*.

cavalry ['kævəlri] *n sing or pl* 單數或複數 soldiers on horseback 騎兵.

cave [keiv] *nc* natural hole under the ground or in the side of a hill or cliff 山洞, 洞穴. **'caveman** person who lived in a cave in prehistoric times 史前時代的穴居人. **cave in** *vi* 1 (with reference to the walls or roof of a cave) fall down (指洞穴的頂部或牆壁) 坍塌. 2 agree to do what other people ask, because one is too weak to go on refusing. *(informal* in sense 2) 屈服, 順從(義 2 爲非正式).

cavern ['kævən] *nc* large cave 大洞穴. **cavernous** *adj*.

caviare, caviar ['kævia:*] *nu* the eggs of certain large fish, used as food 魚子醬.

cavity ['kæviti] *nc* hole (esp. in a tooth) 洞(尤指牙齒蛀洞).

cease [si:s] *vt / i* stop 停止. **ceaseless** *adj* without stopping; continuous; unending 不停的, 不絕的. **ceaselessly** *adv* **cease fire** *nc* an agreement in war to stop fighting (esp. for a short time) 停火(尤指短期停火).

cedar ['si:də*] 1 *nc* type of tree with wide, spreading branches and sweet-smelling wood 香柏樹, 西洋杉. 2 *nu* the wood of this tree 香柏木, 西洋杉木.

cede [si:d] *vt* make an agreement to give land or other property or rights to another person or country; give up 割讓(土地), 轉讓(財產); 放棄: *cede a point in an argument* 辯論中在某一點作出讓步.

ceiling ['si:liŋ] *nc* 1 the upper inner surface of a room 天花板. 2 upper limit (esp. the greatest height at which an aeroplane can fly) 上限, 最大高度(尤指飛機所能上昇的最大高度).

celebrate ['selibreit] *vt / i* 1 do something to show that one is happy about some event or day 慶祝: *The people celebrated the victory.* 人民慶祝勝利. *He celebrated his twenty-fifth birthday.* 他慶祝他的二十五歲生日. 2 perform a ceremony 舉行慶祝儀式. **celebration** [seli'breiʃən] *nc* act of celebrating 慶祝活動. **celebrated** ['selibreitid] *adj* wellknown; famous 著名的. **celebrity** [si'lebriti] *nc* famous person 著名人士.

celery ['seləri] *nu* type of vegetable with long crisp stems 芹菜.

celestial [si'lestjəl] *adj* of the sky; of heaven 天空的; 天的: *a celestial map* 天體圖; *The sun and the stars are celestial bodies.* 太陽和星星都是天體.

cell [sel] *nc* 1 small room in a prison in which prisoners are kept 牢房. 2 small piece of substance of which all plants and animals are formed 細胞. 3 apparatus for producing electricity by chemical action 電池. **cellular** ['seljulə*] *adj* 1 of cells; made of cells 細胞的, 細胞組成的. 2 (with reference to certain types of cotton cloth) loosely woven (指某些種棉布) 織得較鬆因而較多細孔的.

cellar ['selə*] *nc* room under a house, used for storing things (esp. fuel or wine) 地下室(尤指貯藏酒類, 燃料的地窖).

cello ['tʃelou] *nc* type of stringed musical instrument played with a bow 低音提琴. *pl* 複數 **cellos. cellist** *nc* person who plays the cello 低音提琴手. **Note** 說明: sometimes written with an apostrophe-'cello, 'cellist, because the word was originally *violoncello* 有時該兩詞前,加省字號,如'cello,'cellist,因爲cello原意爲violoncello.

Cellophane ['seləfein]* *nu* transparent type of paper used for wrapping goods for sale 玻璃紙(用於包裝商品出售).

cellulose ['seljulous] *nu* chief substance composing the cell walls or fibres of all plant tissue 細胞膜質; 纖維素.

Celsius ['selsiəs] *adj* referring to a system of measuring temperature, using 0 degrees for the temperature of melting ice, and 100 degrees for the temperature of boiling water 攝氏溫度制, 攝氏.

cement [si'ment] *nu* powdery substance which, when mixed with water, becomes very hard, used for building 水泥. Also 亦作 *vt* 1 join or fill with cement 用水泥黏接, 用水泥舖, 塗. 2 join or fasten firmly 加强, 鞏固: *cement relations between our two countries* 加强我們兩國間的關係.

cemetery ['semitri] *nc* piece of land where people are buried 公墓. *Note* 説明: a cemetery is not usu. joined to a church; the land around a church in which bodies are buried is called a *churchyard* 公墓通常不和教堂連在一起; 教堂週圍的墓地稱爲churchyard.

cenotaph ['senətɑ:f] *nc* monument to the memory of a person / people buried in another place (esp. a monument in memory of people killed in war) (爲葬於他處死者所立的, 尤指紀念陣亡者的)紀念碑

censor ['sensə*] *nc* person employed by the government or other official body to examine books, films, plays etc in order to decide whether they are suitable for the public. The censor may sometimes ask for certain things to be left out of a film, play etc for moral or political reasons.(新聞、書刊、劇本、電影等的) 審查員, 檢查員 Also 亦作 *vt* act as a censor 審查, 檢查: *censor a book* 審查一本書. **censorship** *nc* work of a censor; system of employing a censor to act in this way 審查工作; 審查制度.

censure ['senʃə*] *vt* blame; disapprove of 指責, 非難.

census ['sensəs] *nc* count made by the government or other official body to see how many people etc there are in a country, and to find out certain details about them 人口普查.

cent [sent] *nc* one hundredth of a dollar 百分之一元, 分. **per cent** for each hundred (written%) 每一百個當中(寫作 %): *five per cent* i.e. five out of each hundred 百分之五.

centenary [sen'ti:nəri] *nc* celebration 100 years after some event 一百週年紀念: *This year is the centenary of the birth of William Smith.* 今年是威廉·史密斯誕生一百週年紀念. Also 亦作 *adj*.

center ['sentə*] *nc* see 見 **centre.**

centigrade ['sentigreid] *adj* see 見 **Celsius.**

centimetre ['sentimi:tə*] (*US* 美 **centimeter**) *nc* one hundredth of a metre 一公分, 一公尺的百分之一.

centipede ['sentipi:d] *nc* type of small thin creature with many legs 蜈蚣.

centre ['sentə*] (*US* 美 **center**) *nc* 1 middle 中間: *He was standing in the centre of the room* i.e. he was not near any of the walls and he was equally far from the walls. 他站在房子中間. *He lives in the centre of the city* i.e. in the area to which the main railway lines and roads lead and in which the main shops and government buildings are. 他住在市中心。即: 鐵路公路幹線能到的地方，而且是大商店和政府機關所在地。 **2** building or organization for the use or benefit of people from many different areas 活動中心: *a social centre* 社交中心。

central *adj* **1** of a centre 中心的。 **2** most important 最重要的。 **centralize** *vt / i* **1** bring to the centre 集中。**2** put under the control of one central organization 實行中央集權。 **central heating** heating of a building through pipes 用管道供熱的中央供暖法，中央暖氣系統。 '**shopping centre** area of a town in which there are a number of shops 購物中心。

centrifuge ['sentrifju:dʒ] *nc* machine which, by rapid rotation, separates substances of different densities 離心機。

century ['sentjuri] *nc* period of one hundred years 世紀。

ceramic [si'ræmik] *adj* (esp. with reference to making or designing) of pottery; concerned with cups, plates etc. (尤指製造或設計)陶瓷的；陶(瓷)器的。

cereal ['siəriəl] *nc* any grain crop used as food (e.g. wheat, corn, rice) 穀類食物(例如小麥、玉米、大米)。

cerebral ['seribrl] *adj* of the brain 大腦的。

ceremony ['seriməni] *nc* special action or actions carried out at particular times and in particular places 儀式，典禮: *traditional ceremonies for crowning the king* 傳統的國王加冕典禮。 **ceremonial** [seri'mouniəl] *adj* of a ceremony 禮儀的，儀式的。 Also 亦作 *nc / u* actions performed at a ceremony 禮儀，儀式。

certain ['sə:tn] *adj* **1** sure; without doubt 有把握的，無疑的: *I think I'm*

right, but I'm not certain i.e. I may be wrong. 我想我是對的，不過我不能肯定。 *He risked certain death if he was caught* i.e. he would have been killed if he had been caught. 他冒着萬一被捕，必然被處死的危險。 **2** particular, but not named for some reason 某(一): *A certain person told me about the accident* i.e. somebody that I know, but do not wish to name. 有人告訴了我這件事故，即: 我認識的某一個人告訴我，可我不想說出名字來。 *It is very dangerous under certain conditions* i.e. I know what these conditions are, but it is unnecessary for me to mention them in detail. 某些情況下，這是很危險的。即: 我知道在哪些情況下很危險，但我不必要一一道出。 **certainly** *adv* without doubt; yes (in answer to a question) 無疑，必定；當然(可以)(後者用於回答問題時)。 **certainty** *nc / u* something certain; state of being certain. 必然的事，毫無疑問的事；肯定。 (*opp* 反義詞 **uncertainty**). **for certain** without doubt 肯定地。 **make certain** find out the truth 弄清楚，落實一下: *I think that I'm right, but you should ask somebody else to make certain.* 我想我是對的，不過你得另外請誰再落實一下。

certificate [sə'tifikət] *nc* official written statement of some fact 證書。 **certify** *vt* (esp. with reference to act of a doctor officially declaring somebody to be mad) officially declare to be true (usu. by giving a certificate) (尤指醫生正式宣佈某人為瘋子時) 正式加以證實(通常採取出具證明書辦法)。 *He had been behaving strangely for many years and at last he was certified.* 他舉止失常已經好多年了，終於醫生出具證明，正式加以證實。

chafe [tʃeif] *vt / i* make the skin sore by

rubbing 擦破, 擦痛.

chaffinch ['tʃæfintʃ] *nc* type of small European bird, the male of which has a blue-grey head and neck 蒼頭燕雀.

chain [tʃein] *nc* **1** number of metal rings joined together, used for fastening things / people 鐵鏈. **2** any series of things connected to each other 連鎖, 一連串: *a chain of events* 一連串的事件; *a mountain chain* i.e. a line of mountains 連綿群山; *a chain of ideas* 一系列的主意; *a chain of shops / restaurants* i.e. a number of shops or restaurants, all having the same appearance and all owned by the same person / persons 店東相同, 各店門面也一律的若干店舖/飯店: Also 亦作 *vt* (often with **up**) fasten with a chain (常與up連用) 用鏈子拴住. *The dog was chained up every night.* 每天晚上都把狗拴起來. '**chain re'action** (esp. in atomic physics with reference to a certain type of atomic explosion) process in which one thing causes a second thing to happen which in turn causes a third, and so on 連鎖反應(在原子物理學中尤指某種原子爆炸). '**chain smoker** person who starts a new cigarette as soon as he finishes one; person who smokes many cigarettes 一根接一根不停抽烟的人. '**chain store** one of a number of shops, all selling the same goods, and all owned by the same person / persons. 連鎖商店, 聯號.

chair [tʃeə*] *nc* **1** piece of furniture (usu. with four legs and a support for the back) on which one person can sit 椅子. **2** position of a professor in a university 大學教授的職位: *Dr Smith holds the chair of English* i.e. he is the professor of English. 史密斯博士是英語教授. **3** position of a person

in charge of a meeting 主席職務: *Mr Brown took the chair at the meeting* i.e. he was in charge of the meeting 白朗先生擔任會議主席. Also 亦作 *vt* be in charge of a meeting 主持(會議): *Will you chair the meeting or shall I?* 你主持會議呢, 還是要我來?

chairman person in charge of a meeting. (This word can be used to refer to a woman, but some people use the word **chairwoman**) 主席(婦女擔任主席, 也可以用chairman稱呼她, 但有的人用chairwoman).

chalet ['ʃælei] *nc* **1** small wooden house used by herdsmen in the Alps. 阿爾卑斯山牧人所住的小木屋. **2** house of this shape (often a holiday house) 牧人小屋式的房屋(常爲度假之用).

chalice ['tʃælis] *nc* metal wine cup, used for Communion in some of the Christian churches 某些基督教會所用的聖餐杯.

chalk ['tʃɔːk] *nu* **1** type of soft limestone 白堊. **2** substance like this used in schools etc for writing on blackboards 粉筆. Also 亦作 *vt* write with chalk 用粉筆書寫.

challenge ['tʃæləndʒ] *vt* **1** request somebody to fight, play a game or compete in some way 挑戰, 邀請比賽: *I challenged him to a game of chess.* 我請他賽一盤棋. *I challenged him to fight me.* 我要他和我對打. **2** say that one does not believe what somebody has said; ask for more proof of somebody's statement 表示懷疑; 要求更多的證明; 盤問. Also 亦作 *nc* **1** act of challenging 挑戰, 詰問, 質問. **2** the challenge itself (often a challenge in the sense of a task which provides excitement or interest) 挑戰(具有挑戰性的事物). **3** difficulty which makes one work harder than one would normally 困難足以激勵人, 使其格外努力. **chal-**

lenger *nc* **challenging** *adj* **1** containing a challenge 挑戰性的: *a challenging statement* 挑戰性的聲明. **2** difficult but interesting; 困難而有趣的: *challenging work* 有一定難度的有意思工作.

chamber ['tʃeimbə*] *nc* room (esp. a bedroom) *(o.f.)* 房間 (尤指卧室) (舊式). **chamber of commerce** group of businessmen who work together to improve business in a town or area 商會. '**chambermaid** woman who cleans and tidies bedrooms in a hotel (旅館中) 女服務員. '**chamber music** music written for a small group of musicians, suitable for playing in a room or small hall 室内樂.

chamois leather ['ʃæmi'leðə*] *nc / u* soft leather made from the skin of sheep and goats, used for cleaning glass 用以拭淨玻璃的羚羊皮片.

champagne ['ʃæm'pein] *nu* kind of French wine which bubbles when the bottle is opened 香檳酒.

champion ['tʃæmpiən] *nc* **1** person, team or animal winning first place in a competition or show, or doing better in some particular sport than any other player, team etc. 競賽中的優勝者, 冠軍. **2** person who fights or speaks to defend somebody else or to support some cause or movement 支持者, 擁護者: *Mr Smith is a champion of equal rights for women.* 史密斯先生是女權運動的支持者. **championship** *nc* competition to find a champion (in sense **1**) 冠軍争奪賽.

chance[1] [tʃɑːns] **1** *nc* opportunity 機會: *I had the chance of going to India last year, but I decided not to go* i.e. I was asked to go or it was made possible for me to go. 去年我本來有機會去印度, 但我決定不去. *I gave him another*

chance i.e. I allowed him to try again 我再給他一個機會. 即: 我讓他再試一下. **2** *nc* possibility or probability. 可能性: *Is there any chance that you will be able to find the money?* i.e. do you think that it is possible to find the money? 你可能找到那筆錢嗎? **3** *nu* the way in which things happen without any cause 偶然發生的事情, 機遇: *I didn't really mean to do that, it was just chance* i.e. it just happened, nobody planned it. 我並没有存心做這件事, 只是碰巧. *Leave it to chance* i.e. do not plan anything, just see what happens. 聽其自然. Also 亦作 *adj* accidental, not planned 意料不到的, 並非事先計劃的: *a chance meeting* 偶然的相遇, 不期而遇: *a chance discovery* 無意中的發現. **by chance** by accident; without planning 偶然地; 並非計劃中地: *It happened by chance.* 偶然發生. **take a chance** take a risk; do something although it is dangerous 冒險, 碰運氣; *He took a chance when he went near the enemy camp; he might have been shot.* 他走近敵營是很冒險的; 弄得不好可能被槍殺.

chance[2] [tʃɑːns] *vt / i* take a risk; do something although it may be dangerous or unpleasant 冒險: *chance it* i.e. take a risk *(informal)* 冒險一試 (非正式).

chancel ['tʃɑːnsl] *nc* area around and in front of the altar of a church, used by the priest and choir (教堂中牧師和唱詩班席位所在的) 聖壇.

chancellor ['tʃɑːnsələ*] *nc* an important official of various types (e.g. the head of government in some countries; the head of a university in England) 各種類型的重要行政人員 (例如: 某些國家的元首; 英格蘭的大學校長). **Chancellor of the Exchequer** chief finance minister in the British government 英國財政大臣.

chandelier [ˌʃændiˈliə*] *nc* branched holder for a number of lights, which hangs from the ceiling 枝形吊燈.

change¹ [tʃeindʒ] *vt / i* **1** become or make different 改變，變化: *He has changed the date of the meeting* i.e. he has announced that the meeting will be held on a date which is different from the date originally agreed on. 他已經改了會期. *He has changed his ideas since last year* i.e. he now has different ideas. 去年以來他已經改變了主意. *I want to change my seat* i.e. I want to sit in a different seat. 我要換個位子. *He went to the library to change his books* i.e. to get some different books. 他到圖書館換書去. **2** put on different clothes 換衣服; *I shan't be long; I'm just going to change.* 我用不了很多時間，只不過換一換衣服. **3** take money in one form and give it back in another form 換錢. *Can you change this £5 note for me?* i.e. can you give me five pound notes or the equivalent in exchange? 這張五英鎊鈔票請你換零錢給我好嗎? **change hands** pass from one person to another 易手，轉手: *This house has changed hands three times this year* i.e. three different people have bought it and sold it again. 今年這座房子已經換了三次房主人. **change one's mind** have a different opinion 改變主張: *I used to think he was clever, but I changed my mind* i.e. I now think he is not clever. 我以往總以爲他聰明，可是以後改變了看法. 即: 我現在認爲他不聰明.

change² [tʃeindʒ] **1** *nc* act of becoming or making different 更動，變化: *I'm going to make some changes in this*

room i.e. I'm going to put the furniture in different places, paint the room a different colour etc. 我打算在這個房間做一些變動. 即: 我打算把傢具放在不同地方，把房間漆成另一種顏色等. *There have been many changes in the world during the last 100 years.* 全世界在近百年來有許多變化. *He needs a change* (e.g. a holiday). 他要換換環境 (例如: 度假). **2** *nu* money given in return to a person who has given too much money for the goods being bought 找頭: *give someone change of a pound* 給某人一鎊的找頭; *I gave the shopkeeper a £1 note for a newspaper and I nearly forgot to take my change.* 我買報紙，給店老板一英鎊鈔票，卻幾乎忘了找頭. **3** *nu* small coins 輔幣，零錢. **changeable** [ˈtʃeindʒəbl] *adj* often changing 經常變化的: *The weather is very changeable today* i.e. it rains for a short time, and then the sun shines, and then it rains again, and so on. 今天天氣晴雨無定，變化很大.

channel [ˈtʃænl] *nc* **1** narrow stretch of water between two pieces of land 運河. **2** course along which a river or other body of water flows 河道. **3** means by which news or information is carried 消息傳播的途徑. **4** band of television frequencies on which a particular television service is broadcast (電視)頻道. **5** established procedure 既定程序: *apply through the usual channels* 按通常程序申請. Also 亦作 *vt* direct through a channel 引導，疏導.

chant [tʃɑ:nt] *nc* slow song or shout like a song, sung or shouted by many people 許多人同聲拉着腔吟唱的緩慢曲調; 多人發出的有節奏的喊聲. Also 亦作 *vt / i* sing or shout in this way 拉

着腔而有節奏地唱或呼喊，反覆單調地唱或呼喊：
The crowd in the street were chanting in support of their leader. 街上羣衆反覆呼口號，支持他們的領袖.

chaos ['keiɔs] *nu* condition in which there is no order or system 混亂：*After the revolution started, there was chaos in the country until the army took control of the government.* 革命開始以後，國家出現了混亂局面直到軍隊接管政府，這局面才結束.

chaotic [kei'ɔtik] *adj.*

chap¹ [tʃæp] *vt / i* (with reference to the action of the wind or cold on the skin) become or make sore and rough. (使)皮膚粗糙或裂開(指風或嚴寒對於皮膚的作用).

chap² [tʃæp] *nc* man or boy *(informal)* 傢伙，小伙子.(非正式).

chapel [tʃæp] *nc* **1** place in a building such as a school, college, prison etc used by Christians for prayer and hymn singing. 學校、監獄等附屬的小禮拜堂. **2** part of a church used for private prayers or prayers for a special purpose. 教堂内專供私人禱告或小型宗教儀式而設的處所. **3** (in England) church used by Christians who are not Roman Catholics or Anglicans (e.g. one used by Methodists). (英格蘭)爲天主教或聖公會以外的基督教教徒所使用的教堂(例如：美以美會教堂).

chaplain ['tʃæplin] *nc* priest etc who works in a prison, school, college etc, in the army, navy or air force, or in the household of an important or rich person. 顯貴富豪私邸中牧師；軍中牧師；監獄、學校等的小禮拜堂中牧師.

chapter ['tʃæptə*] *nc* one of the parts which a book is divided into. (書的)一章.

char¹ [tʃɑ:*] *vt / i* become or make black by burning 燒焦：*The book was charred when it fell into the fire.* 書掉進火裏，燒焦了.

char² [tʃɑ:*] *vi* work for several hours a day cleaning an office, school, house etc. 打雜工，幹雜活(每日幾個鐘頭在辦公室、學校、家庭等打掃、冲洗). **'charwoman** woman who works in this way. 女打掃工人，打雜女工.

character ['kæriktə*] **1** *nc* the way a person thinks and feels 性格：*He has a very cheerful character* i.e. he is usu. cheerful in his feelings and behaviour. 他有十分愉快的性格.即：他通常興高采烈. **2** *nu* (esp. with reference to qualities such as honesty, self-reliance, cheerfulness etc.) those parts of the way a person thinks and feels which are good 品德；(尤指諸如誠實、自立、樂觀等)好的性格：*He is a man of character* i.e. he shows these qualities. 他是個有品德的人.即：他具有種種美德. **3** *nc* person in a book or play 書中人物，劇中角色：*There are very many characters in the novels of Charles Dickens.* 狄更斯的小說中出現很多人物. **4** *nc* well-known person (esp. because he behaves in an unusual way) 寶貝，怪人：*Old Mr Jones is quite a character* i.e. he is well-known for his unusual behaviour. *(informal).* 老瓊斯先生是個怪人.即：他以舉止反常聞名.(非正式). **characteristic** [kæriktə'ristik] *adj* showing the character of; showing what is usual about a person, place etc. 典型的，特有的；表明(人、地方等)特點或性格的：*These small white houses are characteristic of the Greek islands* i.e. many Greek islands have small white houses. 這些白色小房子顯示了希臘島嶼的特色.即：許多希臘島嶼有白色小房子. *That behaviour is characteristic of him* i.e. he often behaves in that way.

那個舉動充分說明他的爲人. *(opp 反義詞 uncharacteristic)*. Also 亦作 *nc* usual or special quality of a person, place etc. 特徵, 特質: *I described to him the characteristics of Scottish people* i.e. I told him what Scottish people are like. 我向他們描述了蘇格蘭人民的特點. **characterize** *vt (often passive)* show the character of; be typical of (常用被動語態) 表示…的特徵: *The farms in this part of the country are characterized by small fields separated by stone walls.* 這一地區農場的特點是用石牆把田地隔成小塊. **out of character** not showing one's usual behaviour 不適合, 不相稱, 與其個性不符: *It's out of character for John to cheat* i.e. John does not usually cheat. 按照他的性格, 約翰不會作弊.

charade [ʃəˈrɑːd] *nc* game in which people have to guess a word or phrase after seeing other people act a number of short scenes, each containing or suggesting a syllable of the word or phrase (用不同動作, 表示的一個音節, 來影射單詞或短語的) 猜字遊戲.

charcoal [ˈtʃɑːkoul] *nu* black substance used as fuel or for drawing pictures, made by burning wood slowly in a tightly-closed oven 木炭.

charge[1] [tʃɑːdʒ] *nc* **1** attack made by going towards the enemy at great speed 衝鋒. **2** (not with reference to goods bought in a shop) the amount of money asked for services or certain goods 費用, 索價(但不指商店中購物價格): *The man made no charge for mending my watch* i.e. he did not ask for any money. 那個人替我修理錶, 卻沒向我收費. *The charges for electricity and gas will be increased next year.* 明年水電費要漲價了. **3**

statement that a person has done wrong (esp. such a statement in a court of law) 指責(尤指在法庭中的控告): *My friend denied the charge of dangerous driving* i.e. he said that he had not driven dangerously after somebody had accused him of this in a court of law. 對於危險開車的控告, 我的朋友加以否認. **4** the amount of gunpowder put into a gun 裝入砲中的炸藥量. **in charge** in control; responsible 負責, 主管: *You are in charge of the team, and everybody must do what you want.* 你負責這一組, 每一個人都要按照你的要求做. **take charge** be in control of; be responsible for 掌管, 負責: *I want you to take charge of the office until I come back.* 在我回來以前, 我要你掌管這個辦公室.

charge[2] [tʃɑːdʒ] *vt / i* **1** make an attack by going towards the enemy at great speed 衝鋒; 攻擊: *My soldiers charged the enemy.* 我們的士兵向敵人發起衝鋒. **2** ask a certain amount of money for goods or services 索費, 要價: *I charged him five pounds for repairing his car.* 我修理了他的車索費五鎊. **3** (with **with**) (esp in a police court) make a statement that a person has done wrong. (與 with 連用) 指責, 控告(尤指違警性質的控告): *He was charged with dangerous driving.* 他受到危險開車的控告. *The police charged him with dangerous driving.* 警察局指控他危險開車. **4** load or fill with electricity etc. 裝(料, 火藥); 充(電).

chariot [ˈtʃæriət] *nc* car with two wheels drawn by horses and used in ancient times for fighting, racing etc. 古代兩輪馬拉戰車; 賽車.

charisma [kəˈrizmə] *nu* quality which

makes people feel devotion, admiration and loyalty towards one (引起公衆愛戴效忠的) 魅力. **charismatic** [ˌkærizˈmætik] *adj* having this power 有魅力的.

charity [ˈtʃæriti] **1** *nu* act of giving money and other help to the poor 施捨. **2** *nc* society for helping the poor 慈善事業, 慈善團體. **charitable** *adj* showing love or kindness to the poor or to other people 慈善的, 仁慈的

charm¹ [tʃɑːm] **1** *nc / u* the nature of a person / thing which cause pleasure to other people 魅力, 吸引力, 可愛之處: *All the girls in that family have a lot of charm* i.e. they are pleasant and interesting girls. 那家的女孩子全都有其動人可愛之處. **2** *nc* object or words believed to work some magic or bring good luck 符咒; 護身符.

charm² [tʃɑːm] *vt / i* please very much; be very pleasant to 令 (人) 着迷, 給予快感: *The young girl charmed everyone she met* i.e. everybody liked her very much. 那個年輕女郎很動人, 所有見過她的人都被迷住了. **charming** *adj* showing charm; giving happiness and pleasure 迷人的, 可愛的: *She is a charming young lady.* 她是一個令人叫人着迷的年青姑娘. *This is a very charming village.* 這是一個極迷人的小鄉村.

chart [tʃɑːt] *nc* **1** map (esp. one of the sea) for use by sailors 地圖 (尤指海圖). **2** paper showing information in the form of graphs, tables and diagrams 圖表.

charter [ˈtʃɑːtə*] *nc* written statement by some authority, giving somebody the power to do something 特許狀. Also 亦作 *vt* hire a bus, plane, train etc for a special purpose 包汽車/飛機

/火車等: *The members of the club chartered a plane to take them on holiday to France.* 俱樂部會員包機到法國度假. **chartered** *adj* having a licence 有執照的: *a chartered accountant* i.e. a person who has an official licence to work as an accountant. 特許會計師. **'charter flight** journey by an aeroplane specially hired for this purpose, not part of a regular service 包機旅行.

chase [tʃeis] *vt* run after in order to catch or kill; drive away 追趕; 驅逐: *The policeman chased the thief.* 警察追趕小偷. *I chased the children out of my study.* 我把孩子們從書房裏趕出去. Also 亦作 *nc* act of chasing 追逐.

chasm [ˈkæzəm] *nc* deep opening in the earth 地殼的裂口.

chassis [ˈʃæsi] *nc* framework of a motorcar 汽車的底盤. *pl* 複數 **chassis** [ˈʃæsiz].

chaste [tʃeist] *adj* **1** pure; avoiding (immoral) sexual relationships 純潔的, 貞潔的. **2** not decorated; plain and simple in design 簡樸的; 樸素的. **chastity** [ˈtʃæstiti] *nu* purity; virginity; avoidance of (immoral) sexual relationships 純潔; 童貞; 貞潔.

chat [tʃæt] *vi* talk in a friendly way about unimportant topics 閑談: *We were chatting about the weather this morning.* 早上我們在閑聊天氣. *past* 過去式和過去分詞 **chatted**. Also 亦作 *nc* conversation of this kind 聊天. **chatty** *adj* fond of chatting (often in a way which is annoying or tiring for other people) 愛聊天的 (常指多話的, 喋喋不休的): *I don't like that woman very much; she's so chatty.* 我不太喜歡那個女人, 她太愛嘮叨了.

chatter [ˈtʃætə*] *vi* **1** talk about unimportant or foolish things 閒聊. **2** make a series of rapid sounds 咯咯作響; 吱吱作響: *His teeth were chattering with cold* i.e. his top teeth were striking his bottom teeth. 他冷得牙齒直打顫, 咯咯作響. *The monkeys were chattering.* 猴子嘰嘰連聲地啼着. Also 亦作 *nu* talk or noise of this type 喋喋不休, 嘰啾. **'chatterbox** person who chatters (esp. one who tires or annoys other people by chattering) *(informal)* 饒舌者, 嘮嘮叨叨的人. (非正式).

chauffeur [ˈʃəʊfə*] *nc* person whose job is to drive a motorcar for another person 汽車司機.

cheap [tʃiːp] *adj* **1** costing very little money 便宜的. **2** of poor quality 質量差的, 低劣的: *This is very cheap cloth; it will soon begin to look old.* 這布料質地很差. 很快就顯得舊了. **3** in poor taste, unkind 無聊的, 低級趣味的; 刻薄的: *a cheap joke about someone's thick glasses* 對於戴高度近視眼鏡的無聊笑話. **cheaply** *adv* **cheapen** *vt* cause to appear worthless or of low value 貶損價值, 使…顯得無價值.

cheat [tʃiːt] *vt / i* do something dishonest (to somebody) when one has been trusted to behave honestly (e.g. in a game, examination, buying and selling) 欺詐 (比賽、考試中) 作弊, (買賣中) 欺騙: *That boy tried to cheat in the examination* i.e. he tried to look at the answer written by somebody else or he took a book into the examination room 那個男孩子試圖在考試時作弊. *That shopkeeper cheats his customers* i.e. he does not give them the full amount of what they have bought or he does not give them enough money in change etc. 那個店老板對顧客不老實, 即: 短了斤兩或

是少給找頭等. *He cheated his brothers out of the land which their father had given to all of them* i.e. he got the land from his brothers by a trick. 他父親留下土地給他們幾個兄弟, 但他用欺詐手段把弟兄們應得的部份都騙走了. Also 亦作 *nc* person who cheats 騙子.

check¹ [tʃek] *vt / i* **1** look at in order to see whether something is correct 核對: *I'm not sure whether I've added up these numbers correctly; will you check them for me?* 我不敢肯定我把這些數字加對了沒有. 麻煩你核對一下, 好不好? **2** stop or hold back 制止, 控制, 制約: *The government scientists were working hard to check the spread of the disease.* 政府部門一些科學家正在努力控制疾病蔓延. **check in / out** report one's arrival / departure (at a hotel etc.) 到達 (旅館等) 辦理登記手續 / 離開 (旅館) 時, 付賬結算. **check up on something** look at or examine something so as to make sure that one understands it or knows what is necessary 核對, 檢查: *I'm not sure when my train leaves; I must go to the station to check up.* 我說不準我乘坐的火車什麼時候離站; 我得去火車站查清楚. *I am going to check up on the time of the train.* 我打算核對一下火車的時間.

check² [tʃek] *nc* **1** process of looking at something to see that it is correct 查對, 檢查: *You aren't very good at arithmetic; you ought to ask somebody to give your addition a check.* 你的算法不太高明. 你得請誰把你加出的數字核對一下. **2** something which stops or controls. 阻擋物; 抑制物: *The new drug acted as a check to the spread of the disease.* 新藥品對於疾病蔓延起了抑制作用. **3** (mainly *US*) piece of paper given to one in a restautant showing what food one has had and how much it costs (*Brit* usu **bill**) (主要用於美)餐後賬單. (英適常用 bill). **4** pattern formed of large squares 大方格子圖案. **5** *US* form of **cheque** cheque 的美語形式. 'check-'mate (chess) position in which one of the kings cannot escape capture. This wins the game for the other player (象棋)將軍; 取得勝局的局面. 'checkpoint place on a road etc where vehicles and travellers are inspected (過路車輛、行人)檢查站, 關卡. 'check-up *nc* inspection or examination to see that everything is correct (esp. a medical examination) 檢查(尤指體格檢查): *I'm going to the doctor for a check-up.* 我要去醫生那裏要檢查體格.

cheek¹ [tʃiːk] *nc* part of the face between the ear, nose and mouth 臉頰.

cheek² [tʃiːk] *nu* impolite words (esp. said by a child to an adult) 沒禮貌的話(尤其指小孩對成人所說的): *When I told those boys to stop breaking windows, they gave me a lot of cheek and ran away.* 我叫孩子們別再打破窗子了;他們卻說了許多沒大沒小的話跑了. **cheeky** *adj* impolite, but rather amusing 沒禮貌而又蠻有趣的. *He's a cheeky little boy, but he's very friendly.* 他是一個不懂禮貌而又蠻逗人的小孩子, 不過他很友善.

cheep [tʃiːp] *nc* the sound made by a small bird 小鳥的吱吱叫聲.

cheer¹ [tʃiə*] *vt / i* shout because of great happiness 歡呼: *The crowds cheered when they heard the news of the victory.* 聽到勝利喜訊, 羣眾高聲歡呼. **2** make somebody feel happy 使(某人)高興: *The old man was cheered by the visit of his grandsons.*

孫子們來看他, 老人很高興. **cheer up** become or make happy (使)感到高興: *Don't be so worried, try to cheer up.* 別發愁, 盡量開心些. *They went to visit the old man, in order to cheer him up.* 他們去探望老人, 好讓他高興.

cheer² [tʃiə*] *nc* shout of happiness 歡呼. **cheerful** *adj* full of happiness 愉快的, 高興的 **cheerfulness** *nu* **cheers** *interj* **1** expression of friendship, said before drinking an alcoholic drink 乾杯! (表示友好, 用於舉杯敬酒之時). **2** see 見 **cheerio.**

cheerio ['tʃiəri'ou] *interj* / *nc* (*Brit*) goodbye 再見. *pl* 複數 **cheerios.**

cheese [tʃiːz] *nu* type of solid food made from milk 奶酪.

chef [ʃef] *nc* male cook in a restaurant or hotel (esp. the chief cook) 旅館、飯店的廚師(尤指主廚).

chemistry ['kemistri] *nu* branch of science which deals with what various substances are made of and what happens when various substances are mixed together 化學. **chemical** ['kemikl] *adj* referring to chemistry 化學的, 化學上用的. Also 亦作 *nc* substance used in or made by chemical processes 化學變化中所用物質或其產物. **chemist** *nc* **1** person who studies chemistry 化學家. **2** person who sells drugs, medicine, soap, toothpaste etc in a shop 藥劑師 (其店中配方、賣藥之外, 也賣肥皂、牙膏等).

cheque [tʃek] *nc* (*Brit*) piece of paper asking one's bank to pay a specified sum of money to a certain person (英)支票. (*US* 美 **check**). 'cheque book number of printed cheques fastened together like a book, so that one can tear one out when it is needed 支票簿, 支票本. 'cheque card card which guarantees that a bank will pay a customer's cheque 支票保證卡, 銀行保證卡.

chequered, checkered ['tʃekəd] *adj* with many changes, varied (esp. in **a chequered career** a career or life story of somebody who has had many different jobs, travelled a lot etc.) 多變化的, 起伏無定的. (尤見於 in a chequered career即: 一種工作變動頻繁飄泊無定的生涯; 浮沉起伏的生涯).

cherish ['tʃeriʃ] *vt* (esp. with reference to keeping feelings or memories) keep or protect with great love 珍惜, 懷念 (尤指情感, 記憶): *He cherished the memory for many years.* 多少年來他一直珍惜這一段記憶. *I cherish the hope of meeting him one day.* 我熱切希望有一天會見到他.

cheroot [ʃəˈruːt] *nc* type of cigar (兩頭切平的) 方頭雪茄.

cherry ['tʃeri] *nc* type of small, yellow or red (usu. heart-shaped) fruit with a stone in the middle 櫻桃.

chess [tʃes] *nu* game played with various pieces on a board of 64 squares 國際象棋. **'chessboard** the board used in chess 棋盤. **'chessman** one of the pieces used in chess 棋子.

chest [tʃest] *nc* **1** large wooden box for storing things in 木箱. **2** upper part of the body at the front 胸部. **chest of drawers** piece of furniture for storing clothes 衣櫃.

chestnut ['tʃesnʌt] *nc* **1** type of large soft nut often eaten roasted 栗子. **2** the tree on which this nut grows 栗樹.

chew [tʃuː] *vt / i* move the teeth up and down in order to break up food etc. 咀嚼. **'chewing gum** type of soft sweet substance; which does not break up, and can be chewed as long as one wishes 口香糖.

chic [ʃiːk] *adj* (usu. with reference to women) smart and fashionable in appearance and behaviour (通常指婦女)時髦的, 漂亮的. Also 亦作 *nu* state of being chic. 時髦, 漂亮.

chick [tʃik] *nc* young bird (esp. a young chicken) 小鳥(尤指小鶏).

chicken ['tʃikin] *nc* **1** chick 小鳥; 小鶏. **2** type of large bird, kept for its eggs and meat, which are used as food 鶏. (Also 亦作 **hen**). **3** this bird used as meat 鶏肉. **'chickenpox** type of disease of young children, which causes red spots on the skin 水痘.

chicory ['tʃikəri] *nu* **1** type of plant used for food 菊苣屬植物. **2** the root of this plant, used for adding to coffee 菊苣根(研粉後滲入咖啡粉供食用).

chief [tʃiːf] *nc* **1** leader of a tribe 部落酋長. **2** leader of any group of people 首領. Also 亦作 *adj* most important 最重要的, 主要的. **chiefly** *adv*.

chieftain ['tʃiːftən] *nc* **1** chief of a clan or tribe 族長; 酋長 **2** leader or a band of robbers 強盜的頭目, 匪首.

chiffon ['ʃifɔn] *nu* type of very thin cloth (usu. silk) 雪紡綢, 薄綢.

chilblain ['tʃilblein] *nc* red sore or swelling on the hands or feet, caused by cold weather 凍瘡.

child [tʃaild] *nc* young human i.e. a baby, a young boy or a young girl 小孩, 嬰兒. *pl* 複數 **children** ['tʃildrn]. **childhood** *nu* time when one is a child 童年. **childish** *adj* of or like a child (e.g. weak or foolish) 幼稚的. *Note* 說明: compare *childlike* 比較 childlike. **'childbirth** process or act of giving birth to a child 分娩; *die in childbirth* 生產時死亡. **'childlike** *adj* like a child (e.g. innocent, always telling the truth, good and kind, trusting) 天真無邪的(例如: 純真不撒謊、善良、深

信不疑）. *Note* 説明: compare *childish* 比較 childish.

chill[tʃil] *nc* type of slight illness, often caused by cold, in which one sneezes and shivers 寒凍, 發抖, 感冒. Also 亦作 *vt* make cold 使變冷. **chilly** *adj* unpleasantly cold 寒冷的.

chime [tʃaim] *nc* musical sound of a bell (esp. a bell in a church or clock) 鐘聲（尤指教堂鐘聲或時鐘的鐘聲）. Also 亦作 *vt / i* make this noise. (使) 發出和諧的鐘聲: *The clock was chiming six when I came in.* 我走進來, 鐘正敲六下.

chimney [tʃimni] *nc* hollow structure in a house or other building for carrying smoke from a fire high into the air 烟囱.

chimpanzee [tʃimpən'zi:] *nc* type of very intelligent African ape 黑猩猩.

chin [tʃin] *nc* part of the face below the mouth 下巴頦.

china ['tʃainə] *nu* cups, plates, saucers etc., made of white clay which has been baked and glazed 瓷器.

chink [tʃiŋk] *nc* small hole (esp. in a wall or door) (尤指牆壁或門上的) 隙縫.

chip [tʃip] *nc* **1** small piece knocked or cut off wood, glass, stone, china etc. (木、玻璃、石、瓷器的) 碎片. **2** (*Brit*) (usu. *pl*) slice of potato fried in fat (英) (通常用複數) 油炸馬鈴薯條. (*US* 美 **French fried potato**). Also 亦作 *vt / i* make a chip (使) 有缺口. *This cup is chipped; bring me another one.* 這杯子缺了口, 另外拿一個來. *past* 過去式和過去分詞 **chipped**.

chiropody [ki'rɔpədi] *nu* science of the care of the feet and the treating of foot troubles (e.g. corns, painful toenails etc.) 修腳科 (治療雞眼、趾甲刺入肉等). **chiropodist** *nc*.

chirp [tʃə:p] *nc* noise made by small birds and some insects 吱吱的鳥叫聲; 唧唧的蟲聲. Also 亦作 *vt / i* make this noise (使) 發出吱吱/唧唧的聲音.

chisel ['tʃizl] *nc* tool with a long steel blade with a sharp edge at the end, for cutting wood or stone 鑿子.

chit [tʃit] *nc* piece of paper with a few words written on it, used to show that one has permission to get something or to do something (便條) (用以證明持條人可以取得某物或做某事).

chivalry ['ʃivəlri] *nu* **1** (in the Middle Ages) code of behaviour of knights. (中世紀的) 騎士精神. **2** polite and courageous behaviour of men (esp. towards women) (尤指男人對女人的) 彬彬有禮; 俠義. **chivalrous** *adj* polite and courageous 有騎士風度的, 俠義的. (*opp* 反義詞 **unchivalrous**).

chloride ['klɔ:raid] *nu* compound of chlorine with another element 氯化物: *sodium chloride* 氯化鈉, 食鹽; *chloride of lime* 漂白粉.

chlorine ['klɔ:ri:n] *nu* poisonous, greenish-yellow, gaseous chemical element, used in bleaching and disinfecting 氯, 氯氣.

chloroform ['klɔrəfɔ:m] *nu* thin, colourless liquid given, in the form of vapour, to make a person unconscious during a surgical operation 氯仿, 三氯甲烷 (俗稱歌羅芳).

chlorophyll ['klɔrəfil] *nu* green colouring matter of plants 葉綠素.

chloroplast ['klɔrəplæst] *nc* tiny body in the cells of green plants that contains chlorophyll 葉綠體.

chocolate['tʃɔklit] **1** *nu* sweet foodstuff made from the seeds of the cocoa tree 巧克力. **2** *nu* drink made from this substance 巧克力飲料. **3** *nc / u* hard piece of this substance, made to be eaten 巧克力糖.

choice [tʃɔis] *nc* **1** act of deciding which out of several things one likes best 選擇, 挑選: *Take your choice i. e.* take the one you like best. 你自己挑吧. **2** number of things from which one must make a choice 供選擇的東西: *If you go to a big shop you will have a better choice of dresses i. e.* the big shop will have more dresses (than a small shop). 你要是到大商店去, 會有更多連衣裙好挑. 即: 大商店比小商店有更多連衣裙. Also 亦作 *adj* carefully chosen (and therefore the best) 精選的. see 見 **choose**.

choir [ˈkwaiə*] *nc* group of singers (esp. a group which sings in church) 歌唱隊(尤指教堂中唱詩班).

choke¹ [tʃouk] *vt / i* **1** stop or almost stop breathing properly because of something in the throat 嗆: *He choked when he ate his food too quickly.* 他吃東西太快, 嗆住了. **2** prevent from breathing properly (esp. by pressing one's hands on somebody's throat) (使)窒息, 不讓呼吸通暢(尤指用手卡住某人喉嚨), **3** (often with **up**) fill up a pipe, passage, stream etc. (常與 up 連用)堵塞(管道、通道、溪流等): *The stream was choked (up) with weeds.* 溪流被雜草堵住.

choke² [tʃouk] *nc* part of a petrol engine for controlling the amount of petrol and air reaching the cylinders. 汽油機內控制油與空氣進入汽缸的活門.

cholera [ˈkɔlərə] *nu* type of disease in which the body keeps losing liquid 霍亂.

choose [tʃuːz] *vt / i* **1** say or decide which of several things one likes best 挑選, 選擇: *You can have one of these books; choose the one you want.* 這些

書中你可以有一本; 要哪一本, 自己挑吧. *He went to the shop to choose a present for his wife.* 他到店裏挑一件送他妻子的禮物. **2** decide; wish 決定, 願意: *He did not choose to help me i. e.* he decided not to help me. 他決定不幫助我. *past tense* 過去式 **chose** [tʃouz] *past past tense* 過去式 **chosen** [tʃouzn]. see 見 **choice**. **choosey** *adj* very careful to choose what one likes; not willing to accept just anything which is offered. *(informal)* 挑剔的(非正式).

chop¹ [tʃɔp] *vt* cut by hitting with a sharp tool such as an axe 砍, 劈: *He chopped a lot of wood for the fire.* 他劈許多柴生火用. *past* 過去式和過去分詞 **chopped**. **chop up** chop into small pieces 剁碎, 切成細塊, 敲碎: *She chopped up the meat and vegetables to make a stew.* 她剁碎肉和菜做燜菜. *He chopped up that old chair for firewood.* 他劈碎舊椅子當柴火燒.

chop² [tʃɔp] *nc* thick slice of meat (usu. containing a bone) 排骨. **choppy** *adj* (esp. with reference to the sea) covered with small rough waves (尤指大海)波浪起伏的.

chopsticks [tʃɔpstiks] *npl* sticks used in pairs by the Chinese for eating (instead of e. g. a spoon or fork) 筷子.

choral [ˈkɔːrl] *adj* with reference to a choir 合唱的, 合唱團的.

chord [kɔːd] *nc* several musical notes played together 和弦.

chore [tʃɔː*] *nc* small duty or job (esp. in a house) 零星工作(尤指家家常雜務).

choreography [kɔriˈɔɡrəfi] *nu* art of creating dances for the theatre 舞台舞蹈設計. **choreographer** *nc*.

chortle [ˈtʃɔːtl] *vi* laugh while snorting or making noises in the nose and throat 喉嚨裏喜咕咕作聲地大笑: *He* *chortled with glee.* 他開心地咯咯笑起來.

chorus ['kɔːrəs] *nc* **1** group of singers, actors or dancers (esp. a group which sings and dances in a theatre) 合唱團, 歌舞團 (尤指在戲院演出的). **2** song sung by such a group 合唱團合唱的歌曲. **3** part of a song which is repeated after each verse (usu. to be sung by a group of singers) 歌曲中的合唱部份. **4** words said or shouted by a number of people all together. 齊聲唸出的台詞; 異口同聲喊出來的話.

chose, chosen [tʃouz, 'tʃouzn] past tense and past part of **choose** choose 的過去式和過去分詞.

christen ['krisn] *vt* give a name to a child during the ceremony of baptism, by which the child is received into the Christian Church 洗禮時爲受洗兒童命名.

Christian ['kristiən] *adj* referring to Jesus Christ 耶穌基督教的, 基督徒的. Also 亦作 *nc* person who believes that Jesus Christ is the son of God 基督徒. **Christianity** [kristiˈæniti] *nu* the religion of Jesus Christ 基督教. **'Christian name** one of the names given to a child at birth by his parents (e.g. if somebody is named 'John Richard Smith' then 'John Richard' are his Christian names and 'Smith' is his family name or surname. If the person is not a Christian, the terms *first name* or *forename* are often used instead of Christian name) 教名 (嬰兒出生時父母所給名字. 例如: 全名爲約翰·理查·史密斯的人, 其教名即約翰和理查; 史密斯是他的姓, 非基督徒的名字常稱爲 first name 或 forename, 不稱爲 Christian name).

Christmas ['krisməs] *nc* time of celebration of the birth of Jesus Christ (in most Christian churches, 25th December) 聖誕節. **'Christmas tree** small tree of a special type, taken into a house at Christmas time and decorated with coloured paper and lights, and on which are hung presents for the family in the house. 聖誕樹. **Father 'Christmas** imaginary old man, who is said to bring presents to children at Christmas time 聖誕老人.

chromatography ['kroʊməˈtɔgrəfi] *nu* process of separating constituents of a mixture by running a solution of it through an adsorbent on which the substances are separated into bands 層析法.

chrome, chromium ['kroʊm(iəm)] *nu* type of shiny, silver metal which is one of the elements used e: g. to cover other metals (Cr) 鉻 (Cr).

chronic ['krɔnik] *adj* **1** (with reference to disease) going on for a long time, often without hope of cure. (指疾病) 慢性的: *a chronic invalid* 久病的人; *a chronic disease* 慢性病. **2** very unpleasant. (*informal* and usu. considered incorrect) 極不舒服 (非正式而且通常被認爲是不正確的用法).

chronological [krɔnəˈlɔdʒikl] *adj* usu. in **in chronological order** i. e. arranged in the order in which things happened 按事件發生前後排列的; 按年代次序排列的 (通常用於 in chronological order 短語中).

chrysanthemum [krisˈænθiməm] *nc* type of garden flower which usu. flowers in autumn 菊花.

chubby ['tʃʌbi] *adj* (usu. with reference to somebody / something that is young e.g. a baby or a puppy) fat 胖嘟嘟的 (通常指嬰兒, 小狗).

chuck [tʃʌk] *vt* throw (*informal*) 丟、扔.

（非正式）.

chuckle ['tʃʌkl] *vi* laugh quietly and happily 輕聲地笑,得意地閉口輕笑.

chum [tʃʌm] *nc* (esp. with reference to friendship among children) friend. 朋友(尤指兒童之間友情).

chunk [tʃʌŋk] *nc* thick piece (often *informal*) 厚厚的一塊(通常非正式).

church [tʃəːtʃ] *nc* **1** building in which Christians gather to pray and sing hymns 教堂. **2** group of Christians having the same beliefs 基督教會: *the Roman Catholic Church.* 天主教會; *the Methodist Church* 美以美教會. **'church 'service** occasion on which Christians meet together in a church to pray etc. 禮拜. **churchyard** land around the church (often used for burying dead people in) 教堂墓地(教堂週圍的空地常用以葬教友).

churlish ['tʃəːliʃ] *adj* very bad tempered and impolite 脾氣暴躁的,沒禮貌的.

churn [tʃəːn] *nc* large metal container for milk 奶桶(盛牛奶的大型金屬桶).

chute [ʃuːt] *nc* sloping tube or slide, used to allow things to fall down where they are wanted 斜槽,滑運道.

chutney ['tʃʌtni] *nu* substance made from fruit and spices and eaten with meat (由水果和香料調成和肉一道吃的)酸辣醬.

cicada [si'kɑːdə] *nc* large insect with transparent wings, the male makes a loud shrill sound 蟬.

cider ['saidə*] *nu* alcoholic drink made from apples. 蘋果酒.

cigar [si'gɑː*] *nc* roll of dried tobacco leaves, used for smoking 雪茄烟.

cigarette [sigə'ret] *nc* tube of paper containing tobacco and used for smoking. 香烟,紙烟.

cinch [sintʃ] *nc* something which is very easy or certain, *(informal)* 極容易做的事,必然發生的事.(非正式).

cinder ['sində*] *nc* piece of coal or wood which has been burned, but has not yet become ash 煤渣,未燒成灰燼的焦木塊.

cine- ['sini] *prefix* referring to moving pictures (e. g. **cine-camera** i. e. **camera for taking moving pictures**) 與電影有關的 (例如: cine-camera 即: 電影攝影機).

cinema ['sinəmə] *nc* building where films are shown 電影院. **the cinema** the art or science of making films 電影製作,電影藝術.

cinnabar ['sinəbɑː] *nu* **1** reddish mineral that is the chief source of mercury 硃砂,辰砂. **2** bright red 朱紅色.

cinnamon ['sinəmən] *nu* inner bark of an East Indian tree, used as a spice; its tree; yellowish brown 肉桂;肉桂樹;黃褐色.

cipher, cypher ['saifə*] *nc* system of writing in code, understood by certain people for whom the message is intended 密碼.

circle ['səːkl] *nc* **1** flat, perfectly round shape, like a coin 圓形. **2** group of things arranged in this shape 圓圈: *a circle of chairs* 圍成一圈的椅子. **3** group of people with interests in common 圈子,利益癖好相同的一羣人: *a large circle of friends* 廣泛的交遊. *people in business and political circles* i. e. businessmen and politicians 商界和政界. *the family circle* i. e. members of the family 一家人. **4** one of the upper parts of a cinema or theatre in which the seats are arranged in a curve. around the building 樓座(戲院或電影院中二樓座位). Also 亦作 *vt / i* move in a circle 環繞,環行: *The plane circled the airport*

several times before it landed. 飛機降
落前，在機場上空盤旋幾圈．

circuit ['sə:kit] *nc* **1** path along which
an electric current flows 電路． **2** a
going round 環行: *three circuits of a
racetrack* 環繞跑道三圈． **circuitous**
[sə:'kju:itəs] *adj* going a long way
round instead of taking the most
direct way 迂迴的; 繞彎子的．

circular ['sə:kjulə*] *adj* having the form
of a circle 圓的; 環形的． Also 亦作 *nc*
printed notice or advertisement, delivered or posted to a number of people 通函, 傳單, 廣告．

circulate ['sə:kjulit] *vt / i* move round
from place to place or from person to
person 傳播, 流通, 循環走動: *Traffic
circulates in the streets of a city.* 車馬
在城裏路上如梭來往． *The news was
circulated through the room* i. e. one
person told others. who in turn told
others, and so on. 消息在房間
裏傳播開. *Blood circulates around the
body.* 血液在身體內循環． **circulation**
[sə:kju'leiʃən] **1** *nu* movement around
循環． **2** *nc* number of copies of a
newspaper or magazine usu. sold 報
刊流通量． **3** *nc* movement of blood
around the body 血液循環．

circumcise ['sə:kəmsaiz] *vt* cut off the
loose skin at the end of a penis (for
religious or health reasons) 割除⋯包
皮(由於宗教或健康理由)．

circumference [sə'kʌmfərəns] *nc* **1**
outside edge of a circle 週圍． **2** distance round a circle 圓周．

circumscribe ['sə: kəmskraib] *vt* **1** draw
a line round in 週圍畫一條線．**2** con-
fine the scope of; restrict 限制⋯的範
圍; 劃界; 限制 ．**3** draw (a figure)
around another figure so as to touch
as many points as possible 使外切, 使
外接．

circumspect ['sə:kəmspekt] *adj* very
careful to avoid difficulty or danger
十分謹慎小心的．

circumstance ['sə:kəmstəns] *nc* (usu.
pl) fact, condition, event etc connected with something / somebody
(通常用複數) 情形, 情況: *Most countries would be willing to go to war
under certain circumstances* i. e. if the
reason for war was great enough. 在
一定情況下, 多數國家願意參戰. 即: 如
果作戰的理由充分的話．*I don't re-
member all the circumstances of the
quarrel* i. e. what exactly happened or
why it happened. 我記不清口角的全部
經過. 發生了甚麼事, 何以發生等,
我已記不清. *When I explained my circumstances to the old man , he decided to help me* i. e. when I explained why I needed help. 我把情況
對老人說明後, 他決定幫助我. 即: 我對
他說明過, 爲甚麼我需要幫助. **under
the circumstances** because this is
the case, when I think of these facts
etc. 既然這樣; 考慮到這些事實. *Under
the circumstances, you were lucky not
to be hurt* i. e. as it was very dangerous. 這種情況下, 你沒受傷, 實在萬幸.
*Under the circumstances, I cannot
help you* i. e. because of these facts.
既然這樣, 我沒辦法幫助你.

circus ['sə:kəs] *nc* **1** form of entertainment in which wild animals,
clowns, acrobats etc perform 馬戲．**2**
round place where a number of
streets meet 幾條街道匯集的圓形廣
場．

cistern ['sistən] *nc* metal or stone container for water (esp. in a lavatory) 貯
水箱(尤指廁所內所用)．

cite [sait] *vt* name something / somebody as an example or a proof of
something 引用, 引證, 舉例．

citizen ['sitizn] *nc* 1 person who lives in a town or city 城市居民, 市民. 2 any person who has full rights in a country i. e. a person who is not a foreigner 國民, 公民. **citizenship** *nu* (esp. with reference to the rights and duties of a person living in a particular country) state of being a citizen 公民身份(尤指其權利與義務).

citrus ['sitrəs] *adj* with reference to fruit or trees such as oranges, lemons, grapefruit (usu. in **citrus fruit**) 柑橘屬樹木或水果的 (通常用於 citrus fruit).

city ['siti] *nc* large and important town 城市. **the City** the oldest part of London, now an area of business and banking 倫敦商業區(倫敦最古老部份, 現為交易所及銀行集中的地方).

civic ['sivik] *adj* with reference to a city (esp. the administration of a city) 城市的(尤指市政的).

civil ['sivil] *adj* 1 with reference to citizens 公民的, 市民的. 2 with reference to people who are not soldiers, sailors or airmen 平民的(士兵、海員、飛行員以外人員的). *(opp* 反義詞 **military**). 3 polite 彬彬有禮的*(opp* 反義詞 **uncivil**).**civil engineering** *nu* building of roads, bridges, docks etc. 土木工程. **civil engineer** *nc* **civil law** law dealing with property, and the rights and duties of a citizen (not with crime) 民法. **civil rights** rights of a citizen (e. g. the rights of American Negroes to equality with white Americans) 公民權(例如: 美國黑人與白種美國人有平等權利). **civil service** *nu* all the departments of a government 政府中的文職機構. **civil servant** *nc* person who works for the government 公務員.**civil war** see 見 **war.**

civilian [si'vilian] *nc* person who is not a soldier, sailor or airman 平民, 老百姓(指非士兵, 海員或飛行員). Also 亦作 *adj.*

civilize ['sivilaiz] *vt* teach science and art, religion, government, reading and writing etc. to people who lack all or some of these branches of knowledge 教化, 開導: *The Romans civilized many of the tribes of northern Europe.* 羅馬人開化了北歐許多種族.**civilized** *adj* 1 polite; well-behaved 有禮貌的, 文明的: *behave in a civilized manner* 舉止文明. 2 cultured, not savage 有教養的, 非野蠻的: *a civilized community* 文明社會. **civilization** [sivilai'zeiʃen] 1 *nu* condition of being civilized 文明, 教化: *The Romans brought civilization to Britain.* 羅馬人把文明帶到英國. 2 *nu* all civilized people, towns and cities, the use of money, literacy, and science, religion etc. 文明: *Civilization may be destroyed if there is another world war.* 要是再來一次世界大戰, 文明就蕩然無存了. 3 *nc* one of the several large organized communities which have existed during the history of mankind 文化, 文明社會, 文明: *the Chinese civilization* 中國文明, 中國文化. *the Roman civilization.* 羅馬文明, 羅馬文化.

claim[1] [kleim] *vt / i* 1 say that one is taking, or wishes to take, something as one's own 聲稱屬於己有: *The United States claims certain islands in the Pacific at present held by New Zealand* i. e. the USA says that these islands belong to her. 美國聲稱目前由新西蘭管轄的某些太平洋島嶼是她的領土. *Nobody has come to claim this book which was found in the road* i. e. nobody has said that the book belongs to him 沒有人前來認領路上撿到

的這本書. **2** say that something is true (when other people may doubt this fact) 聲言, 自稱 (可是有人也許懷疑): *He claimed to be 100 years old.* 按他自己的說法, 他一百歲了. *He claimed to have read the book, but he couldn't answer any questions about it.* 他聲稱看過這本書, 可是關於這本書的問題, 卻一個也答不上.

claim²[kleim] *nc* **1** act of saying that something belongs to oneself 認領, 聲言爲己之物: *I made a claim for that book* 我認領那本書. **2** act of saying that something is true 聲稱, 聲明, 說法: *Nobody believed his claim to be 100 years old* 他自稱已有一百歲, 可沒有人相信他的說法. **3** right to something 對某事物的權利: *Children have the first claim on their parents* i. e. parents will help or protect their children before they will help or protect anyone else. 父母首先對其兒女應盡義務. 即: 父母在幫助或保護其他人以前應先幫助或保護其兒女. **claimant** *nc* person who makes a claim 申請者; 要求者.

clam [klæm] *nc* one of several types of shellfish often used as food 蛤; 蚌 **clam up** stop talking, refuse to give any more information. *(informal)*. 變爲沉默; 避而不談; 死不開口. *(非正式)*.

clamber ['klæmbə*] *vi* climb in an awkward way, using one's hands and feet. (吃力地) 攀登, 手足並用地爬.

clammy ['klæmi] *adj* cold and damp 冷而潮濕的: *clammy hands* 又冷又濕的雙手; *clammy walls* 濕冷的牆壁.

clamp [klæmp] *nc* instrument used for holding something tightly 夾鉗, 夾子. Also 亦作 *vt* hold or strengthen with a clamp 夾緊. **clamp down on someone / something** act in a very severe way in order to stop or forbid some-

thing 取締, 禁止, 打擊: *The policemen are clamping down on motorists who drive too fast* i. e. they are doing everything they can to prevent speeding. *(informal)* 警察採取嚴厲措施禁止超速駕駛. *(非正式)*.

clan [klæn] *nc* large group of families which are all related to each other 家族.

clang [klæŋ] *nu* loud ringing noise made by metal bling hit hard 敲擊金屬時叮叮噹噹的聲音. Also 亦作 *vt / i* make this noise (使) 發出叮叮噹噹的聲音.

clap¹ [klæp] *vt / i* strike the palms of the hands together (esp. to show that one likes something) 拍手 (尤指表示讚許, 滿意時), 鼓掌: *The audience clapped at the end of the play.* 劇終觀眾鼓掌. *He clapped his hands.* 他拍着雙掌. *past* 過去式和過去分詞 **clapped**.

clap² [klæp] *nc / u* noise made by striking the palms of the hands together. 鼓掌聲: *The audience gave him a clap.* 觀眾對他鼓掌. **Note** 說明: the plural is not often used; *clapping* is used to refer to a number of noises of this kind 此詞不常用複數; 如要表示紛紛鼓掌聲, 用clapping.

claret ['klærit] *nu* type of red wine 紅葡萄酒.

clarify ['klærifai] *vt / i* become or make clear; become or make more easy to understand 解釋, 澄清. **clarification** [klærifi'keiʃən] *nu*.

clarinet [klæri'net]. *nc* type of wind musical instrument played by blowing through it 單簧管.

clarity ['klæriti] *nu* clearness 清澈.

clash [klæʃ] *nc* **1** strong disagreement; short struggle or fight 衝突; 抵觸; 戰鬥: *There was a clash between the*

Prime Minister and the leader of the Opposition i. e. they had an argument. 首相和反對黨領袖之間發生一場爭論. *There was a clash between the two armies* i. e. there was a short battle. 雙方軍隊發生衝突. *There is a clash between these two colours* i. e. these two colours do not look right when they are put together. 這兩種顏色不調和. **2** loud noise made by metal being hit 金屬碰撞聲. Also 亦作 *vi* disagree strongly 抵觸,不調和.

clasp [klɑːsp] *nc* something which fastens two things together (e. g. the ends of a belt) 鈎子, 扣子 (例如: 皮帶兩端所用). Also 亦作 *vt* fasten or hold in this way 鈎住, 扣住.

class [klɑːs] *nc* **1** group of people or things of the same kind or treated in the same way for some purpose 等級, 種類: *They travelled first class on the ship* i. e. in the most comfortable and expensive way. 他們乘一等艙旅行. **2** group of pupils taught together 班級. **3** one of the divisions of society 社會等級, 階級: *the upper class* 上層社會, 富裕階層; *the middle class* 中產階級; *the working class* 工人階級. **4** (biology) group of plants or animals. (A class is divided into a number of orders) (生物) 綱 (下分爲若干科). Also 亦作 *vt* arrange in groups or classes 把…分類, 把…歸入某類. **classroom** room in which a class is taught in a school 教室.

classic¹ ['klæsik] *adj* **1** very good; agreed to be of very high quality (esp. in art or literature) 最優秀的, 經典的, 第一流的 (尤指藝術或文學). **2** having reference to ancient Greece and Rome 古希臘, 古羅馬的. **3** (with reference to art or literature) simple in style; without too much decoration

(指藝術、文學) 簡樸典雅, 不事雕琢的. **4** (with reference to certain horse-races, such as the Derby) very important and well-known (指某些賽馬如德貝馬地方的大賽馬) 極其重要, 家喻戶曉的.

classic² [klæsik] *nc* work of literature, or writer of the highest quality 經典著作; 文學名著; 大文豪: *'Hamlet' has become a classic.* 哈姆萊特已成經典. *Shakespeare is a classic.* 莎士比亞是文學巨匠. **the classics** *npl* the literature of ancient Greece and Rome. 古希臘, 羅馬文學.

classical ['klæsikl] *adj* **1** having reference to ancient Greece or Rome 古希臘的; 古羅馬的. **2** (with reference to art or literature) simple in style; without too much decoration (指藝術、文學) 簡樸典雅, 不事雕琢的. **3** (with reference to music) serious; not pop, jazz etc. (指音樂) 古典的 (嚴肅的, 與通俗曲調、爵士音樂等不同的).

classify ['klæsifai] *vt* arrange into classes or groups 把…分類. **classification** [,klæsifi'keiʃən] *nc/u.*

classmate ['klɑːsmeit] *nc* member of the same class in a school 同班同學.

clatter ['klætə*] *nu* type of noise like the noise made when plates or knives and forks knock together 盤碟刀叉等相撞擊時的聲音. Also 亦作 *vt/i* make this noise 發出盤碟刀叉相撞擊的聲音.

clause [klɔːz] *nc* **1** (grammar) sentence or part of a sentence, having a subject and a predicate. In 'He was eating when I arrived', 'He was eating' is a main clause, and 'when I arrived' is a subordinate clause (語法) 分句 (具備主語和謂語在 'He was eating when I arrived' 句中, 'He was eating' 是主句; 'when I arrived' 是從句). **2** (legal) one of the points in a legal statement (法律)條款.

claustrophobia [klɔːstrə'fəubiə] *nu* great fear of being shut in a small space 幽閉恐怖症.

claw [klɔː] *nc* one of the hard sharp points or nails on the feet of birds and some animals 脚爪. Also 亦作 *vt* scratch or pull with the claws or nails 用爪子或指甲抓、挖.

clay [klei] *nu* type of soft heavy earth, which is used for making plates, cups etc. 黏土.

clean [kliːn] *adj* 1 not dirty; washed; not used 乾淨的; 洗過的; 沒用過的. 2 pure 純潔的, 清白的. 3 regular; with no rough edges 整齊的; 邊綠光滑的: *a clean cut* 乾淨利落的切割. 4 well-shaped; smooth in shape 造型優美的, 流線型的: *The new ship has very clean lines.* 新船有非常勻稱的造型. Also 亦作 *vt* make clean 使潔淨.
cleanly *adj / adv* **cleanness** *nu.*
cleanliness ['klenlinis] *nu* habit of being clean 清潔的習慣. **cleaner** *nc* 1 person whose work is to clean rooms, buildings, roads, clothes etc. 清洗工人; 掃馬路工人; 洗衣店工人. 2 substance which cleans 清潔劑. **'clean-'shaven** *adj* with all the hair shaved off the face 鬍鬚刮光的. **clean out** remove dirt and rubbish from 清除垃圾加…, 把…打掃乾淨: *He cleans out his room once a week.* 他每週掃除房間一次. **clean up** make tidy or clean 打掃清潔, 收拾整齊.

cleanse [klenz] *vt* make clean; make free from dirt; make pure 弄乾淨, 清洗; 淨化, 使純潔. *Note* 說明: clean (verb) refers to the ordinary process of removing dirt; cleanse contains the idea of removing impurities so as to make pure. If in doubt, use clean

clean (vt) 指通常打掃、清除污物的過程; cleanse 含有除去雜質, 以達到純潔的意思, 在不能肯定時, 用clean.

clear¹ ['kliə*] *adj* 1 easily seen through; bright; not cloudy 明亮的; 清澈的; 透明的: *clear glass* i. e. glass which can be seen through 明亮的玻璃; *a clear sky* i. e. one without clouds 明朗的天空, 晴空; *a clear stream* i. e. one without any dirt in it 清澈的溪流. 2 easily heard 嘹亮的, 清晰可聞的: *the clear sound of a bell* 嘹亮的鐘聲. 3 easily understood 清楚的, 易懂的: *This paragraph is not clear to me, will you explain it please?* 這一段, 我還不明白, 請你解釋一下, 好嗎? 4 free from 不再和…有接觸的, 暢通的: *He drove slowly until he was clear of the town* i. e. until he left the town. 離開市區以前, 他一直車開得很慢. *The road in front was clear* i. e. there were no cars on it. 前途暢通無阻. 5 certain; obvious 明顯的: *It is quite clear that you do not understand.* 顯然, 你不明白. **clearly** *adv* **'clear-'cut** *adj* easily seen; having a definite shape; easily understood 清晰的, 輪廓分明的, 易懂的: *a clear-cut argument* 明確的論點. **all clear** safe 危險已經過去, 平安無事: *It's all clear, you need not hide any longer* i. e. the danger has gone away. 危險已經過去, 不必再躲著了. **stand clear** get out of the way; keep away 站開些; 躲開. **in the clear** free from suspicion 不受嫌疑.

clear² ['kliə*] *vt / i* 1 become or make clear (使) 變得清楚: *He cleared all the books and papers off his desk* i. e. he took them off his desk. 他把桌上所有的書和紙張都拿開. *He cleared all the stones from his garden.* 他清除園中石頭. *The sky has cleared* i. e. the clouds have gone and the sun is shining. 天空已經晴朗了. **2** get past or over (esp. without touching) 跳過(尤指沒有觸到): *The horse cleared the gate* i. e. it jumped over the gate. 馬越過籬笆門. **3** prove or decide that somebody is not guilty of doing something wrong 宣佈無罪, 證明某人無罪: *In the trial he was cleared of all the charges.* 審判時宣告他一切罪名都不成立. **clear something away** remove 清除: *He cleared away all the old boxes in his garage.* 他把汽車間裏的舊箱子全清除掉. **clear off** go away 走開: *I don't want you to help me, so clear off. (informal and impolite)* 我不要你幫我, 所以, 走開吧. (非正式且不禮貌) **clear something out 1** *vt* remove dirt or rubbish from 把…清一清: *He cleared out his desk.* 他清理書桌. **2** *vi* go away 走開: *You're causing a lot of trouble, so clear out. (impolite and informal)* 你惹出許多麻煩, 走開. (不禮貌且非正式). **clear something up** make tidy 收拾: *He cleared up his room before the visitors arrived.* 他在訪問者來到以前收拾房間. **2** explain something difficult to understand 解釋難以理解的問題, 消除疑團: *When the policeman arrived he soon cleared up the mystery of the broken window* i. e. he found out who had broken it. 警察來了, 很快就弄清玻璃是誰打破的.

clearance ['kliərəns] *nu* **1** act of making clear 清除, 清理. **2** space between two things which pass each other without touching 間隔, 距離. **3** official permission to do something. (作某事的) 官方許可, 正式批准.

clearing ['kliəriŋ] *nc* area of land, in a forest without any trees on it 林中空地.

cleave [kliːv] *vt / i* **1** cut open 劈開:

cleave an apple in two with a knife 用小刀將蘋果切成兩半. **2** go through; make by cutting 穿過; 劈通, 劈出: *The airplane cleaved the clouds.* 飛機穿入雲中. *They cleaved a path through the wilderness.* 他們在荒野中劈開一條路.

clef [klef] *nc* (music) sign used in music to show pitch (音樂)高、低音部譜號.

cleft [kleft] *nc* narrow opening (esp. in the ground or in a rock) 罅隙(尤指地面或岩石中).

clemency ['klemənsi] *nc* kindness (esp. to somebody who has done wrong) 仁慈, 寬厚(尤指對犯錯誤的人的寬大處理).

clench [klentʃ] *vt / i* (usu. with reference to the teeth or the fists) close tightly 合緊; 握緊.

clergy ['kləːdʒi] *npl* Christian priests or ministers 教士, 牧師. **clergyman** *nc* Christian priest or minister 教士, 牧師.

cleric ['klerik] *nc* Christian priest or minister 教士, 牧師. **clerical** *adj* **1** with reference to a cleric 教士的, 牧師的, 神職人員的. **2** with reference to the work of reading and writing 文書的, 書記的. see 見 **clerk.**

clerk [klɑːk, *US* 美 kləːk] *nc* **1** person who works in an office writing letters, keeping accounts etc. (辦公室的) 書記, 文員, 文書. **2** (*US*) person who sells goods in a shop (*Brit.* 英 **assistant** or 或 **shop assistant**) (美) 店員, 售貨員. **town 'clerk** person who arranges the official business of a town 鎮公所辦事員.

clever ['klevə*] *adj* **1** able to do things well; able to understand quickly; intelligent 聰明的: *a clever boy* 聰明的男孩子. **2** showing signs of skill or intelligence 熟練的; 機敏的; 精巧的: *a*

clever answer 機智的答案. *a clever piece of work* 一件精巧的工藝品.
cleverly *adv.*

cliche [ˈkliːʃei] *nc* expression or idea which has been used so often that it begins to lose its meaning 陳詞濫調.

clew [kluː] *nc US* form of **clue** clue的美式英語拼寫形式.

click [klik] *nc* sudden sharp sound like a light switch being turned on or off 卡嗒一聲. Also 亦作 *vt / i* **1** make this sound 發出卡嗒聲. **2** (of an idea etc.) be understood (suddenly) (*informal*) (主意等) (突然間) 得到了解 (非正式).

client [ˈklaiənt] *nc* **1** person for whom a lawyer or other professional person works 律師的當事人; 醫生的病人; 其他自由職業者的委託人. **2** person who buys from a shop (usu. **customer**) 顧客 (通常用 customer). **clientele** [kliːˈɑːntel] *n sing or pl* 單數或複數 number of clients or customers 當事人, 顧客.

cliff [klif] *nc* high rock edge, falling away steeply 懸崖.

climate [ˈklaimit] *nc* type of weather normally found in a particular area 氣候: *California has a very pleasant climate.* 加利福尼亞州氣候宜人.

climax [ˈklaimæks] *nc* the most interesting and exciting part of something (usu. the last part, and often of a book, film, play etc.) (書, 電影, 劇本等通常在末了部份的) 高潮.

climb [klaim] *vt / i* go up (攀) 登, 爬: *He climbed to the top of the tree.* 他爬上樹頂. *He climbed the hill.* 他爬山. Also 亦作 *nc* **1** act of climbing 攀登. **2** place where one climbs 陡坡. **climber** *nc* person who climbs (esp. one who climbs mountains for sport, using ropes and special equipment) 往上攀登的人 (尤指爬山的人, 登山運動員). **climbing** *nu* sport of climbing mountains using ropes etc. 登山運動. Also 亦作 *adj climbing plant* 爬藤植物. *climbing holiday* 爬山假日.

clinch [klintʃ] *vt* finally agree on 最終同意: *clinch a bargain* 做成買賣, 交易.

cling [kliŋ] *vi* hold tightly to 緊緊抓住: *He clung to the rope with both hands.* 他用雙手緊抓住繩子不放. *past* 過去式和過去分詞 **clung** [klʌŋ].

clingfilm [ˈkliŋfilm] *nu* thin, transparent polythene material which clings closely and is used for wrapping food 保鮮紙.

clinic [ˈklinik] *nc* place where people can go to receive medical advice and treatment 診所. **clinical** *adj* **1** with reference to that aspect of medical science which studies patients by observation 臨床的. **2** cold and scientific 冷靜的, 科學態度的.

clink [kliŋk] *nc* sharp sound like that made by drinking glasses knocking together (酒杯相碰時的) 叮噹聲. Also 亦作 *vt / i* make this sound (使) 發叮噹聲. *Note* 說明: the plural is not often used: *clinking* is used to refer to a number of noises of this kind. 不常用複數; 表示叮噹不已時, 用 clinking.

clip¹ [klip] *vt* (esp. with reference to hair, fur or plants) cut short (尤指毛髮, 皮或植物) 剪短. *past* 過去式和過去分詞 **clipped, clippers** *npl* instrument for cutting the hair, nails etc. 理髮刀, 指甲刀等. **clipping** *nc* piece cut off or out (esp. an article cut from a newspaper or magazine) 被剪掉或剪出的東西 (尤指剪報或雜誌剪摘文章).

clip² [klip] *nc* piece of metal for holding pieces of paper or a girl's hair 紙夾, 髮夾. Also 亦作 *vt* hold or keep in a clip 夾住. *past* 過去式和過去分詞 **clipped.**

clique [kli:k] *nc* group of people who keep together because of interests which they all have and who are unfriendly or unhelpful to other people 小集團，派系.

cloak [klouk] *nc* long outer garment without sleeves (usu. fastening at the neck) 斗篷. **'cloakroom 1** room where hats and coats can be left 衣帽間. **2** lavatory 衛生間，廁所.

clock [klɔk] *nc* instrument for measuring the time (not carried on the wrist or in the pocket like a watch) 鐘. **'clockwise** *adv* in the direction in which the hands of a clock move 順時針方向地. *(opp* 反義詞 **anticlockwise)** **'clock-work** machinery like that inside a watch or clock, using a spring 類似時鐘機構的裝置，發條裝置.

clog¹ [klɔg] *nc* wooden shoe 木底鞋，木屐.

clog² [klɔg] *vt / i* (often with **up**) fill up or become filled up so that it is difficult for anything to pass through (常與 up 連用) 塞滿: *The drains were clogged with dirt. and so the water could not flow away.* 陰溝裏塞堵滿了爛泥，水流不出去了. *past* 過去式和過去分詞 **clogged.**

cloister ['klɔistə*] *nc* (often *pl*) roofed area around the sides of a square (esp. in a monastery or college) (常用複數) (尤指修道院或大學建築物的)迴廊.

close¹ [klouz] *vt / i* **1** become or make shut 關閉: *The door has closed.* 門已經關了. *Close the door.* 關上門. **2** finish; come to an end 結束: *When do you think the meeting will close?* 你看會議甚麼時候會結束 **'closed 'shop** factory or other place of work, which employs only members of trade un-ions. 只雇用工會會員的工廠或商店等. **close something down** (often with reference to a factory, business, port etc.) shut completely 常指工廠、商號、港口等) 關閉，停歇 **.close in on / upon someone / something** come nearer to (often in a threatening or unpleasant way) 迫近(常有威脅性): *The soldiers closed in upon the town.* 士兵迫近市鎮. *The enemy were closing in.* 敵人正逐漸迫近.

close² [klous] *adj / adv* **1** near 近: *The bus drove very close to the car.* 公共汽車開到離汽車極近的地方. *He came quite close to where I was hiding, but he did not see me.* 他走到了離我藏身的地方，可是他沒看到我. *There were so many people in the room that we had to stand close together.* 房間裏人那麼多，我們必須緊挨着站在一起. *a close friend* i.e. a friend whom one likes very much 親密的朋友. **2** very careful; thorough 密切; 徹底的. *He gave very close attention to what I was saying.* 他對我所說的話，加以密切注意. **3** (with reference to the air) hot and wet, making it difficult to breathe easily or move freely (指空氣)悶熱的，窒息的. **4** (with reference to games and competitions) equal or almost equal (指競賽) 勢均力敵的，幾乎相等的: *It was a very close race* i.e. several runners nearly won. 賽跑成績極其接近. **closely** *adv.* **a close shave** see 見 **shave.** **'close-up** *nc* picture in a cinema film or photograph in which the camera is very near to what is being photographed 電影中的近距離特寫鏡頭.

close³ [klouz] *n sing* 單數 end 結束: *The national anthem was sung at the close of the meeting.* 會議結束時，齊唱國歌.

closet ['klɔzit] *nc* (mainly *US*) small room or cupboard (主要用於美) 小房間; 壁櫥.

closure ['klouʒə*] *nc* act of closing or stopping 關閉, 結束, 終止.

clot [klɔt] *nc* half-solid lump formed in the drying of certain liquids (esp. blood) 凝塊 (尤指血). Also 亦作 *vt/i* become or make solid in this way (使)凝結 *.past* 過去式和過去分詞 **clotted.**

cloth [klɔθ] **1** *nu* material made from wool, silk, cotton, nylon etc. 布; (羊毛、絲、棉、尼龍等)織物. **2** *nc* piece of cloth 作某特殊用途的一塊布. '**back-cloth** large printed cloth hung at the back of a stage in a theatre 背景幕布.

clothe [klouð] *vt* put clothes on (rather *o. f.* - use **dress**) 為…穿衣 (較舊式 ──宜用 dress).

clothes [klouðz] *npl* **1** coverings worn on the body, such as coats, trousers, dresses, hats 衣服(如上衣、褲、連衣裙、帽). *Note* 說明: this word is not used in the singular. To express the idea of one of these coverings for the body we can either name the thing (e. g. *a coat, a pair of trousers etc.)* or use the expression an article of clothing or the word garment. 此詞不用單數. 如要表達某一件蔽體物, 可以直指其名, 例如: 一件上衣, 一條褲子等或用短語 an article of clothing 或 garment 這個詞. **2** coverings for a bed i. e. sheets and blankets 床上舖蓋物, 即: 床單和毯. '**clothes line** line made of rope, nylon or plastic, from which clothes are hung to dry after they have been washed 晾衣繩. '**clothes peg** (*Brit* small wooden metal or plastic clip for fastening wet clothes to a clothes line (英)晾衣用衣夾. (*US* 美 **clothespin**).

clothing ['klouðiŋ] *nu* clothes (e. g. coats, trousers, dresses) 衣服.

cloud [klaud] *nc/u* **1** water vapour in the sky, which may fall as rain 雲. **2** anything like this (e. g. *a cloud of smoke; clouds of insects)* 空中一物(團、羣)遠看像雲的東西. 例如: a cloud of smoke (滾滾濃烟); clouds of insects (凌空而來的一大羣昆蟲). **cloudy** *adj* **1** covered with clouds. 多雲的. **2** (with reference to liquid) not clear, difficult to see through (指液體)混濁的. '**cloudburst** sudden and very heavy rain 大暴雨.

clout [klaut] *nc* blow with the hand (用手的)一擊. Also 亦作 *vt* hit with the hand (both *informal*) 用手猛擊 (均為非正式).

clove¹ [klouv] *nc* spice made from the dried flowerbuds of a tree growing in the tropics 丁香.

clove² [klouv] past tense of **cleave.** cleave 的過去式.

cloven ['klouvn] past part. of **cleave.** cleave 的過去分詞.

clover ['klouvə*] *nu* type of plant (usu. with three leaves) eaten by cattle. 苜蓿, 三葉草.

clown [klaun] *nc* person (usu. with a painted face and strange clothes) whose work is to do foolish things to amuse people (esp. in a circus) 小丑 (尤指馬戲團中小丑, 通常臉塗油彩, 奇裝異服). Also 亦作 *vi* do foolish things 扮小丑; 做出像小丑的舉動.

club [klʌb] *nc* **1** heavy piece of wood, with one end thicker than the other, used as a weapon 棍棒(一端較粗的木棒, 作武器用). **2** stick used in some games (e. g. golf)某些體育比賽(例如: 高爾夫球)中所用的球棒. **3** one of the four marks on playing cards, the mark itself 撲克牌中的梅花牌; 這種梅花標

誌. **4** group of people joined together for some purpose (usu. to play some sport or to enjoy their free time in some way); building used by these people 俱樂部; 俱樂部的會所. Also 亦作 *vt* hit with a club 用棍棒打. *past* 過去式 *and* 過去分詞 **clubbed. club together** *vi* join with other people in putting money together for some purpose (爲某種目的) 分攤 (費用), 湊錢: *The boys clubbed together to buy their teacher a present.* 男孩們湊錢給老師買禮物.

cluck [klʌk] *nc* sound made by a hen 母雞叫的咯咯聲. Also 亦作 *vi* make this sound 發出咯咯聲.

clue [klu:] *nc* (esp. with reference to a crime or a crossword puzzle) some information or sign which helps one to find the answer to a mystery or puzzle (尤指罪行或猜字謎的) 線索. **I haven't a clue** I don't know (often with the suggestjon that one is not interested). (*informal*)我不知道(常意味着對於眼下問題, 不感興趣). (非正式).

clump [klʌmp] *nc* number of things close together (usu. trees or plants) 一叢, 一簇 (常指樹木).

clumsy [ˈklʌmzi] *adj* not skilful or clever in movement; not wellshaped for a particular purpose 手腳不靈活的; 姿勢不雅觀的: *He is a clumsy boy; he is always breaking things.* 他是一個笨手笨腳的孩子; 老是打破東西.

clung [klʌŋ] past of **cling** cling 的過去式和過去分詞.

cluster [ˈklʌstə*] *nc* number of things gathered close together (密集的)一串/束/羣/簇. Also 亦作 *vi* (often with **round** or **around**) grow or be in a cluster (常與 round 或 around 連用) 叢生, 長成一簇.

clutch[ˈklʌtʃ] *vt / i* take hold of very tightly 緊緊抓住.

clutch² [klʌtʃ] *nc* **1** tight hold 緊握. **2** part of a car or similar machine which allows the power from the engine to be disconnected from the wheels; pedal which operates this part 離合器; 離合器踏板.

clutter [ˈklʌtə*] *vt* (often with **up**) make untidy (常與 up 連用)使亂糟糟地, 使雜亂: *These boxes have been cluttering up my garage for weeks.* 這些箱子亂七八糟地堆在汽車間裏已經好幾個星期了. Also 亦作 *n sing* 單數 untidy condition 凌亂. **cluttered** *adj.*

co- [kou] *prefix* giving the idea of 'with' (e. g. **co-owner** i. e. owner of something with somebody else) 共, 共同 (例如: co-owner, 即: 共有者).

coach [koutʃ] *nc* **1** large vehicle for passengers, pulled by horses 公共馬車. (Also 亦作 **stagecoach**) **2** bus which travels long distances (often from one town to another) 長途汽車 (常自一城到另一城). **3** (*Brit*) railway carriage. (*US* 美 **car**) (英) (鐵路上的)客車.

coach² [koutʃ] *nc* person who prepares athletes and teams to play games 教練. Also 亦作 *vt / i* prepare someone to play a game in this way 訓練, 指導.

coagulate [kouˈægjuleit] *vt / i* (with reference to liquids, esp. blood) become or make thick (指液體, 尤指血)凝結; 使凝結.

coal [koul] *nu* black substance found in the earth, which can be burned 煤. **'coalfield** area of a country where there is coal under the earth 煤田, 產煤區. **'coalmine, 'coalpit** *nc* place where coal is dug out of the earth 煤礦坑.

coalesce [kouəˈles] *vi* come together

and become one 聯合; 結合, 合併. **co-alescence** *nu*.

coalition [kouə'liʃən] *nc / u* joining of a number of groups (esp. the joining of a number of political parties in order to form a government) 若干團體的聯合 (尤指政黨聯合以組成政府).

coarse [kɔːs] *adj* **1** rough; not soft to the touch 粗糙的: *coarse cloth* 粗布. **2** having large pieces 顆粒粗大的: *coarse sugar* 粗砂糖; *coarse sand* 粗沙粒. **3** impolite; ignorant in language or behaviour 粗鄙的; 魯莽的.

coast [koust] *nc* land at the edge of the sea 海岸. **coastal** *adj* **coaster** *nc* ship which sails along the coast, never going far from land 靠海邊航行的船. '**coastguard** government official whose work is to watch the coast, in order to prevent smuggling and to help ships in difficulties 海岸緝私救護隊, 海岸巡邏隊 **coastline** outline or shape of a coast 海岸線.

coat [kout] *nc* **1** type of outer garment with sleeves buttoning down the front 大衣, 外套. **2** covering 表層: *a coat of paint* 一層漆; *a dog's coat* i. e. his hair 狗的毛皮. Also 亦作 *vt* put a covering on 蓋(塗)上一層: *The boy was coated with mud.* 那男孩子渾身是泥. **coating** *nc* something covering a surface 外層: *a coating of dirt.* 一層灰塵. **coat of arms** official sign of a country, city, family etc. 盾徽, 盾形紋章(國家、城市、家族等的標誌).

coax [kouks] *vt / i* make somebody do something by being gentle and using very friendly words 哄勸, 勸誘: *The boy coaxed his father into buying him a new bike.* 那男孩子對他爸爸說好話, 說動他爸買一架新腳踏車給他.

cob [kɔb] *nc* hard central part on which the grains of corn or maize grow 玉米

穗軸, 玉米棒子.

cobalt [kou'bɔːlt] *nu* hard, steel-grey, metallic chemical element 鈷.

cobble [kɔbl] *nc* large round stone, formerly used for making roads (以前用來鋪路的)大鵝卵石; (Also 亦作 **cobblestone**).

cobbler ['kɔblə*] *nc* man whose work is mending shoes 補鞋匠.

cobra ['kɔbrə] *nc* type of poisonous snake with a broad hood behind its head, found in Africa and Asia 眼鏡蛇.

cobweb ['kɔbweb] *nc* structure made by a spider to catch insects 蜘蛛網: *The old house was full of cobwebs.* 舊房子佈滿了蜘蛛絲網.

cocaine [kou'kein] *nu* drug used by doctors as a local anaesthetic (i. e. to deaden pain) 古柯鹼(用作局部麻醉劑), 可卡因.

cock[1] [kɔk] *nc* **1** male of the chicken 公雞. **2** male of other birds 雄鳥. **cock-pit** place in an aeroplane where the pilot sits 飛機駕駛座艙.

cock[2] [kɔk] *vt* **1** raise the hammer of a gun 扣扳機(扳起槍枝的擊鐵): *He cocked his gun.* 他扣動扳機準備射擊. **2** (often with **up**) raise or turn upwards in a lively way (常與 **up** 連用) 豎起: *He cocked his ears up* i. e. he suddenly began listening (usu. with reference to an animal). 他豎起耳朵. (通常指動物突然聽週圍有什麼聲音).

cockerel ['kɔkrl] *nc* young male of the chicken 小公雞.

cockle ['kɔkl] *nc* type of shellfish, used for food 烏蛤(可食用).

cockney ['kɔkni] *nc* person born in the East End of London 出生於倫敦東區的人.

cockroach ['kɔkroutʃ] *nc* large brown insect often found in kitchens and near water pipes 蟑螂.

cocktail ['kɔkteil] *nc* mixture of various alcoholic drinks (usu. drunk before meals) 鷄尾酒. '**cocktail bar** part of a hotel or restaurant where drinks are sold 旅館、飯店中供應酒類的部門, 酒吧.

cocoa ['koukou] *nu* **1** powder made from the seeds of the cacao tree 可可粉. **2** drink made from this powder 可可(飲料).

coconut ['koukənʌt] **1** *nc* large hard nut growing on a type of tropical tree 椰子. **2** *nu* sweet-tasting substance found inside the nut, used in cookery 椰肉(烹飪用).

cocoon [kə'ku:n] *nc* covering in which some insects live at the stage of their life cycle before changing into the fully-grown insect 繭.

cod [kɔd] *nc* type of large sea fish, eaten as food 鱈魚. *pl* 複數 **cod**.

code [koud] *nc* **1** system of secret writing, used so that messages can be read only by those who know the secret 密碼；代號, 代碼. **2** system of signals for sending messages (e. g. *the Morse code* i. e. used for sending messages by telegraph or by flashing lights) 電碼(例如莫爾斯電碼. 藉電報或閃光發出訊息). **3** set of ideas about the proper way to behave 禮法, (行爲)規範. **4** laws of a country, collected together and clearly set down 法典. Also 亦作 *vt* put into secret writing or into a system of signals 把…譯成密碼或電碼.

coeducation ['kouedju'keiʃən] *nu* system of educating boys and girls together, in the same school or in the same class 男女合校教育, 男女同校. **coeducational** *adj*.

coefficient [koui'fiʃənt] *nc* number or symbol put before and multiplying another 係數: *the coefficient of expansion of steel* 鋼的膨脹係數.

coerce [kou'ə:s] *vt* make somebody do what he does not with to do 强迫. **coercion** [kou'ə:ʃən] *nu*.

coexistence [kouig'zistns] *nu* condition of living together at the same time (and often in a peaceful way) 共存, 共處(常指和平共處).

coffee ['kɔfi] *nu* dark brown powder obtained from the seeds of a tropical bush used for making a drink; the drink itself 咖啡(粉末)；咖啡(飲料). '**coffee bar** bar where coffee and other refreshments are sold 咖啡館.

coffer ['kɔfə] *nc* chest or strongbox for keeping valuables 保險箱.

coffin ['kɔfin] *nc* box in which a dead person is put 棺木.

cog [kɔg] *nc* one of the teeth on the edge of a wheel in various machines (齒輪的)輪齒, 鈍齒.

cogent ['koudʒənt] *adj* (with reference to arguments, reasons, explanations etc.) strong; worth listening to; making one agree that something is true (指論點、理由、解釋等)强有力的, 令人信服的.

cognac ['kɔnjæk] *nu* type of strong alcoholic drink made in France 科納克酒(法國產的一種烈酒), 上等法國白蘭地酒.

coherent [kou'hiərnt] *adj* (esp. with reference to speeches, thoughts, ideas, explanations etc.) with various parts fitting together and therefore easy to understand (尤指言論、思想、主張、解釋等)前後呼應的, 條理分明的, 連貫的. (*opp* 反義詞 **incoherent**).

coil [kɔil] *nc* something arranged in a series of circles 圈形物. Also 亦作 *vt* arrange something in the form of a coil 把…捲成圈.

coin [kɔin] *nc / u* (piece of) metal used as money (一枚) 硬幣. **coinage** *nc* system of money used in a country 貨幣制度.

coincide [kouin'said] *vi* **1** (with reference to two or more things) take place at the same time (指兩個或兩個以上事物) 同時發生: *My holiday coincides with John's* i. e. John and I have our holidays at the same time. 我和約翰的假期在同一時間. *Our holidays coincide.* 我們假期時間相同. **2** (with reference to ideas, opinions etc.) agree (指主張, 意見等) 相符, 一致: *Our ideas on this matter coincide* i. e. we think the same. 對這件事, 我們意見一致. **coincidence** [kou'insidns] *nc / u* happening at the same time of two or more things (esp. a happening together which occurs by chance without any planning) (兩個或兩個以上的事情的) 同時發生(尤指巧合的). **coincidental** [kouinsi'dentl] *adj.*

coke [kouk] *nu* substance made by driving off the gas in coal and used as fuel to give a great heat 焦炭.

colander ['kʌləndə*] *nc* dish with many small holes in the bottom, used in cooking to drain water from vegetables etc. 濾鍋, 濾盆 (上有許多小孔, 烹飪時用以濾去蔬菜等中之水).

cold[1] [kould] *adj* **1** not hot 寒冷的: *Snow and ice are cold.* 冰和雪都是冷的. *The night is colder than the day.* 晚上比白天冷. *If you don't drink your tea it will get cold.* 你再不喝, 茶就要凉了. **2** unfriendly; showing no feelings of love or friendship 冷淡的. **coldly** *adv* **coldness** *nu* 'cold 'storage method of keeping food for a long time by putting it in a specially-built cold room 冷藏.

cold[2] [kould] **1** *nu* absence of heat 寒, 冷: *It is difficult to imagine the cold of the winter when one is enjoying a warm summer.* 人們在夏季暖和的時候, 很難想像像冬天的寒冷. **2** *nc* type of illness in which liquid runs from the nose 傷風. **catch cold** get the illness in which liquid runs from the nose 感冒, 着凉.

colic ['kɔlik] *nu* name given to various types of pain in the stomach (esp. in young children) 腹痛(常見於小孩).

collaborate [kə'læbəreit] *vi* work with somebody (esp. in writing a book) 合作(尤指在寫書方面): *John collaborated with his father in writing the book.* 約翰和他父親合寫這本書. *John and his father collaborated.* 約翰和他父親合作. **collaborator** *nc* **collaboration** [kəlæbə-'reiʃən] *nu.*

collapse [kə'læps] **1** *vi* fall down; break down 倒塌, 崩潰; 垮下: *The bridge collapsed three weeks after it was built.* 大橋建成後三星期就塌了. *My plans suddenly collapsed* i. e. it became impossible for me to carry out my plans. 我的計劃突然落空. *The woman collapsed when she was told of the death of her son.* i. e. she became unconscious. 那個女人聽說兒子死去後, 暈倒過去. **2** *vt / i* (with reference to things such as chairs, telescopes, tents etc which are intended to be folded or put flat when not in use) fold up. (指摺疊椅、遠望鏡、帳篷等) 摺疊: *He collapsed his tent and put it into his car.* 他摺起帳篷, 放進車裏. Also 亦作 *nc* falling down of this kind 倒塌、崩潰. **collapsible** *adj* able to be folded or put flat when not in use 可摺疊的.

collar ['kɔlə*] *nc* part of a coat, dress, shirt etc which fits around the neck

衣領. **'collarbone** bone joining the breastbone to the shoulder 鎖骨.

colleague ['kɔliːg] *nc* (with reference to work done in an office, school, college etc.) person with whom one works 同事.

collect [kə'lekt] *vt / i* get together come or bring to one place 聚集, 集合; 收集: *A crowd collected after the accident* i. e. people came together. 事故發生後, 週圍聚集了許多人. *He was collecting money to help the poor.* 他募款幫助窮人. *He collects stamps for a hobby.* 他有集郵的嗜好. **collector** *nc* **collected** *adj* **1** brought together 收集成的: *the collected poems of John Smith* 約翰·史密斯詩集. **2** calm; not losing control of one's feelings 鎮定沉着的. **collection** *nc / u* **1** things / people brought together 聚集一起的人; 搜集物: *a collection of people* 各種人物. *a stamp collection* 收集的郵票. **2** money given for some purpose by people at a meeting (esp. at a church) 捐款(尤指教堂奉獻). **3** act of collecting 收集. **collective noun** singular noun which refers to a group (e. g. flock, the staff) 集合名詞(單數形式而實指集體的名詞. 如flock, the staff).

college ['kɔlidʒ] *nc* name given to various types of places of learning (e. g. some schools are called colleges; some universities are made up of a number of separate colleges) and also the staff and students of these institutions, or the actual buildings 學院, 書院; 大學內的學院; (美國)大學; 學院, 書院的師生; 學院校舍.

collide [kə'laid] *vi* **1** come together with a hard knock 碰撞; 互撞: *My car collided with a lorry.* 我的汽車和貨車相撞. **2** have a strong disagreement

with 衝突, 抵觸, 反對. **collision** [kə'liʒən] *nc / u.*

collie ['kɔli] *nc* very intelligent type of dog, used for driving sheep 一種牧羊犬.

colliery ['kɔliəri] *nc* coalmine and the surrounding buildings and equipment 煤礦及其週圍建築物和設備.

collision [kə'liʒən] *nu / c* **1** act or an instance of colliding 碰撞; 互撞事件: *Six people were killed in the motorcar collision.* 六個人死於汽車互撞事件. **2** clash or conflict of opinions, interests etc. 抵觸; (利益、意見等的)衝突.

colloquial [kə'loukwiəl] *adj* (with reference to language) of the type of language used in everyday informal conversation 口語的. **colloquialism** *nc* word or expression used in informal conversation, but not usu. in formal speech or writing 口語; 口語體.

collusion [kə'luːʒən] *nc* secret agreement between two or more people to do something wrong 勾結, 串通.

colon ['koulɔn] *nc* the mark: 冒號, 即 ':'.

colonel ['kəːnl] *nc* (military) officer of high rank (軍)上校.

colonnade [kɔlə'neid] *nc* line of stone columns forming part of a building 柱廊; 一列柱子.

colony ['kɔləni] *nc* **1** country which is ruled by another country 殖民地: *Nigeria used to be a British colony but is now independent.* 尼日利亞過去是英國殖民地, 現已獨立. **2** group of people of one nationality or of one profession or occupation, living in another country or apart from others 一羣僑居外國的同國人; 聚居一起的同行、同業的人: *There is a large Italian colony in London* i. e. many Italians live in London. 倫敦有許多意大利僑民.

colonial [kə'lounɪəl] *adj* having reference to a colony 殖民地的; 關於殖民地的. Also 亦作 *nc* person living in a colony 殖民地居民. **colonialism** [kə'lounɪəlɪzəm] *nu* 1 policy by which one country tries to remain the owner and ruler of another country 殖民主義, 殖民政策 2 condition of being a colony 殖民地的地位(或特徵). **colonize** *vt* form a colony in a country, by going there or sending people there 開拓殖民地: *The English and the Spanish were among the first to colonize North America.* 首先在北美開拓殖民地的是英國人和西班牙人.

colossal [kə'lɔsl] *adj* very big 龐大的.

colour ['kʌlə*] (US 美 **color**) *nc / u* 1 sensation produced on the eye by light waves of different lengths 顏色. Green, blue and red are colours 綠、藍、紅都是顏色. 2 paint, dye or other substance used to change the colour of something 顏料; 染料. 3 redness of the face caused by heat, excitement, embarrassment etc. 臉紅. Also 亦作 *vt / i* put colour on 使…着色; 染色. **the colours** *npl* the flag of an army or section of an army 軍旗. **coloured** *adj* 1 having a colour 有色的. 2 (of people) having a skin which is not white 有色的(人種). **colourful** *adj* 1 having bright colours 艷麗的. 2 interesting and unusual, having many interesting details 生動的. **colouring** *nu* 1 substance used to colour something 顏料. 2 way in which something is coloured 着色法. **'colour bar** practice found in some societies in which people of one colour are treated worse than people of another colour 種族隔離; 種族歧視. **'colourblind** *adj* unable to see the difference between certain colours 色盲的. **'watercolour**

1 nu type of paint which is mixed with water, used for painting pictures 水彩顏料. *2 nc* painting painted in this way 水彩畫. **off colour** slightly ill 臉色不好的, 身體不舒服的.

colt [koult] *nc* young male horse 小雄馬.

column ['kɔləm] *nc* 1 tall round piece of stone or other material used as part of a building or as a monument 圓柱. 2 anything of this shape 柱狀物, 縱形物: *a column of soldiers* 一縱隊的士兵; *a column of dust* 灰塵柱 (灰塵在陽光投射下成柱狀). *The page of a newspaper is divided into columns* i. e. narrow sections stretching down the page. 報紙版面分成若干欄. 3 section of a newspaper (usu. written by a particular person or which is regularly devoted to a special subject) 報紙的專欄. **columnist** ['kɔləmnist] *nc* person who regularly writes a special section in a newspaper 專欄作家.

coma ['koumə] *nc* condition like a deep sleep, caused by injury, disease or poison 昏迷(由於外傷、疾病、或中毒而起).

comb¹ [koum] *nc* piece of metal, plastic, bone etc with teeth, used for making the hair tidy or for keeping it in place. 梳子.

comb² [koum] *vt* 1 use a comb to tidy the hair 梳(頭髮). 2 search very carefully in order to find something 徹底搜查; 查遍: *I combed the shops until I found a pair of shoes that I liked.* 我家家商店走遍, 終於找到我喜歡的一雙鞋子.

combat ['kɔmbæt] *nc* fight; battle 戰鬥. Also 亦作 *vt / i.* past 過去式和過去分詞 **combat(t)ed.** (US 美 **combated**).

combine¹ [kəm'bain] *vt / i* come or

bring together; mix 結合, 連結: *He was able to combine business with pleasure* i. e. he carried out some duty which was also a pleasure for him. 他能把公務和娛樂結合起來. *He combined his visit to England with a tour of Scotland* i. e. he visited both England and Scotland during the same journey or trip. 他趁去英國訪問的機會, 順便遊覽英格蘭和蘇格蘭. **combination** [ˌkɔmbiˈneiʃən] **1** *nu* act of coming or bringing together 聯合, 結合, 組合. **2** *nc* group of people or things joined together for some purpose 團體, 聯合體. **3** *nc* series of numbers or letters which is used to open a combination lock 數字(或字母)組合: *He had forgotten the combination of the safe.* 他已忘了保險箱的數碼. **combi'nation lock** type of lock with a dial on which there are numbers or letters. A particular arrangement of numbers or letters must be made before the lock can be opened 號碼(或字碼)鎖.

combine² [ˈkɔmbain] *nc* **1** group of people who have come together for a special purpose, often a political or business purpose 集團, 團體, 聯合體 (常因政治上和商業上原因而結合). **2** machine which cuts grain and takes out the seeds while driving along the field (Also 亦作 **combine harvester**) 聯合收割機.

combustion [kəmˈbʌstʃən] *nu* action of being burned; destruction by fire 燃, 燒. **combustible** [kəmˈbʌstibl] *adj* able to be burned 可燃的. (*opp* 反義詞 **incombustible**).

come [kʌm] *vi* **1** move towards or with another person, or move towards the place where somebody will be in the future 來: *John came to see me*

yesterday. 約翰昨天來看我. *Shall I come with you to the market?* 要我明天和你一起到市場去嗎? *I hope you will come to see me when I go to live in France next year.* 我希望我明年到法國定居時, 你會來看我. **2** arrive at; reach a place 到: *I've been waiting for an hour, but John hasn't come yet.* 我已經等他一個鐘頭, 可是約翰還沒到來. Also 亦作 *interj Come, come!* i.e. don't be worried; be cheerful; are you sure? etc. 來吧! 喂! 得啦! (其含意可能是「別擔心」,「振作起來」,「你能肯定?」等). *past tense* 過去式 **came**. *past part* 過去分詞 **come**. **come about** happen; occur by chance 發生. **come across some one / something** meet or find by chance 偶然碰到某人/某物: *I came across an old friend last week.* 上個星期我無意中碰到一個老朋友. **come apart** break into two or more pieces 破裂, 散開. **come back** return 回來. **'comeback** *nc* return to power or popularity 恢復原來的權力, 人望等; 捲土重來: *The old actor retired when he was 85, but he made a comeback two years later* i. e. he appeared on the stage again. 老演員八十五歲時候退休, 兩年後他東山再起. 即: 又登台演出了. (非正式). **come by something** get something 得到某物: *How did you come by that money?* 你怎麼弄到那筆錢的? **comedown** *nc* situation which is poor or unpleasant, after one has been used to something much better; loss of a good situation. (*informal*) (地位, 身份等之)降低, 沒落; 失去良好境遇. (非正式). **come forward** offer to do something or say something; volunteer 自告奮勇, 自願. **come from** be derived from 來自. **come in 1** enter 進來. **2** begin to be used 開始

流行. **come into 1** enter 進來. **2** get from somebody who has died; inherit 繼承: *He came into a large amount of money when his uncle died.* 他叔父死後，他繼承了一大筆財富. **come of something** have as a result 來自某事; 是某事的結果: *Nothing came of the meeting* i. e. we did not come to an agreement. 會議沒有結果. **come off 1** (with reference to special events) happen (指特殊事件) 發生，舉行: *The meeting will come off next week.* 會議將於下週舉行. **2** be in a certain condition at the end of a contest or fight. 比賽或戰鬥結束時處於…的狀況: *He came off worst* i. e. he lost the fight. 他輸了. **3** (with reference to an experiment or gamble) be successful (指實驗或賭博) 成功. **come off** it! i. e. don't say such silly things! 別胡說! **come on!** hurry up!; also used to encourage someone 快些! 也用於鼓勵對方的場合. **come out 1** be discovered as the truth 真相大白: *The whole story came out in the end* i. e. the truth was finally told. 全部真相終於大白. **2** (with reference to a book) be published; be offered for sale 出版: *His new book comes out next month.* 他的新書下個月出版. **come out with something** say, speak (忽然) 說出: *He came out with a long story to explain why he was late.* (informal) 他說了一大套話，來解釋爲甚麼來晚了. (非正式). **come round** return to consciousness 恢復知覺. **come to** return to consciousness 恢復知覺: *He was hit on the head by a brick, and did not come to for half an hour.* 他被一塊磚頭打中腦袋，半個鐘頭後才蘇醒過來. **come to something** amount to; total 等於，總計: *The food which I bought came to £3* i. e. it cost

£3. 我買的食物加起來一共三鎊. **come to do something** (usu. in questions) happen (經常用於問句中) 怎麼會…? *How did you come to break it?* 你怎麼會把它打破了呢? **come up to** come as far as; be as good as; equal 達到; 與…相等: *The water came up to the top of the steps.* 水漲到樓梯頂層. *The concert did not come up to expectations* i. e. was not as good as we thought it might be. 音樂會不如預期的好. 即: 不如我們想像的那樣好. **come up with** produce; present 提出, 提供: *come up with a useful suggestion* 提出一項有用的建議. **come / be of age** be recognized by law as an adult (in Britain, at age of 18) 成年 (依照英國法律十八歲就是成人). **come into effect / force** become law; take effect 成爲法律, 生效: *The new rules come into effect next year.* 新規定明年生效. **come true** happen, after having been an idea or hope (主張、希望) 實現. **to come** in the future 將來: *in years to come* 在未來的年月.

comedy [ˈkɔmədi] *nc* **1** type of play or film which is intended to make one laugh 喜劇. **2** any event which makes one laugh 喜劇性事件. **comedian** [kə-miːdiən] *nc* entertainer who tells funny stories and says and does funny things 喜劇演員.

comet [ˈkɔmit] *nc* star-like object in the sky with a long tail, moving around the sun 彗星.

comfort [ˈkʌmfət] **1** *nu* condition of being in pleasant circumstances, without any worries 安樂, 舒適; 無憂無慮: *He lived in comfort all his life* i. e. he always had nice food, good clothes and everything he wanted to make life happy. 他一輩子過着舒服的日子. **2** *nc* anything which makes life pleasanter for one, or which takes away pain or worry 使生活舒適的東西;減輕痛苦、憂慮的東西 *He liked the comforts of his home.* 他喜歡家中種種舒適. *He was a great comfort to his old mother* i. e. he helped her very much and made her life pleasant. 他給他老母親極大安慰. Also 亦作 *vt* do or say something to make somebody feel happier 安慰.

comfortable ['kʌmftəbl] *adj* making life pleasant and taking away pain or worry; without pain or worry 舒適的, 愜意的: *He has a very comfortable home.* 他有一個舒適的家. *This is a comfortable chair* i. e. it is pleasant to sit in it. 這張椅子坐起來很舒服. *The sick man had a comfortable night* i.e. he slept well and did not feel any pain. 病人很舒服地過了一晚. 即: 睡得好, 不感到痛苦. *(opp* 反義詞 **uncomfortable***)*.

comic¹ ['kɔmik] *adj* making one laugh; concerned with comedy 喜劇的. **comical** *adj* **comic strip** series of pictures in a newspaper, telling an amusing story (報刊上的) 連環漫畫.

comic² ['kɔmik] *nc* **1** comedian; person whose job is to say things to make people laugh. *(informal)* 喜劇演員(非正式). **2** type of magazine with pictures, written for children (sometimes, though not always, containing funny stories) 連環漫畫雜誌(對象爲兒童, 常登載滑稽故事).

comma ['kɔmə] *nc* the mark, 逗號, 即 ',' . **inverted commas** the marks " " 引號, 即 " ".

command¹ [kə'mɑːnd] **1** *nc* order 命令: *The soldiers obeyed the officer's command* i. e. they did what the officer told them to do. 士兵們服從軍官的命令. **2** *nu* ability to use, control 掌握;

運用能力: *He has a very good command of English.* 他精通英語. **in command** having the position of leader 統帥(地位): *General Smith was in command of the army.* 史密斯將軍統率全軍.

command² [kə'mɑːnd] *vt* **1** give orders to 命令: *He commanded the soldiers to attack.* 他命令士兵進攻. **2** be the leader of 統領: *General Smith commanded the army.* 史密斯將軍率領全軍. **3** be able to get if necessary 博得: *He was able to command the help of everybody in the country.* 他能取得全國人民的一致支持. *He can command more than a million pounds.* 他能籌款一百萬鎊以上. **commander** *nc* **1** one who gives orders or who is a leader 指揮官. **2** naval officer 海軍中校. **commanding** *adj* **1** having the position of a leader 處指揮地位的: *a commanding officer* 指揮官. **2** higher than; looking down on 高於; 俯瞰的: *a commanding view of the city* 從高處往下看的城市全景.

commandant [kɔmən'dænt] *nc* commanding officer, esp. of military academy 指揮官; 軍事學校校長.

commandment [kə'mɑːndmənt] *nc* **1** very important order or law (esp. one given by God) 命令; 戒律(尤指上帝所定戒律). **2** one of the ten laws given to the Israelites by God (The laws are known as **the Ten Commandments**) 上帝與以色列人訂定的十誡之一.

commando [kə'mɑːndou] *nc* soldier who is trained to enter enemy territory secretly and in small groups in order to destroy enemy property 突擊隊員. *pl.* 複數 **commandos**.

commemorate [kə'meməreit] *vt* do something or be a sign to remember some important person or event 紀

念: *The people built a new theatre to commemorate the birth of Shakespeare.* 人民建造新戲院來紀念莎士比亞的誕辰. *The new theatre commemorates the birth of Shakespeare.* 新戲院紀念莎士比亞的誕生. **commemoration** [kəmemə'reiʃən] *nc / u* **commemorative** [kə'memərətiv] *adj*.

commence [kə'mens] *vt / i* begin; start. *(formal)* 開始(正式).

commend [kə'mend] *vt* speak in praise of 推薦; 稱讚: *I can commend this book to you* i. e. I can tell you that this is a good book. 我可以向你推薦這本書. **commendable** *adj* deserving praise; of high quality 值得稱讚的. **commendation** [kɔmən'deiʃən] *nu* praise 稱讚, 讚揚.

commensurate [kə'mensjurit] *adj* of the same size or quantity as something else; of the right size or quantity for something (數量、大小上) 同樣大的, 相等的, 旗鼓相當的: *The danger of the journey was commensurate with its importance* i. e. the journey was as dangerous as it was important. 此行危險的程度, 正如其重要性.

comment ['kɔment] *vi* (often with **on** or **about**) say something; give an opinion (常與 on 或 about 連用) 評論: *He commented on the weather* i. e. he said something about the weather. 他聊了一會兒天氣. Also 亦作 *nc* something said or written to explain or criticize something 評論, 評語.

commentary ['kɔməntri] *nc* **1** description of some event (usu. a sporting event), made on the radio or television (usu. made while the event is actually taking place) 無線電或電視對事件的實況報導(常爲運動項目, 且常在比賽進行中直播). **2** number of writ-

ten or spoken notes which explain or criticize some-thing 評語, 評註. **commentator** ['kɔmənteitə*] *nc* person who makes a commentary 廣播評論員, 實況播報員.

commerce ['kɔmə:s] *nu* practice of buying and selling goods (esp. in large amounts) 貿易, 商業(尤指大量的). **commercial** [kə'mə:ʃl] *adj* Also 亦作 *nc* advertisement on radio or television 無線電或電視廣告. **commercialize** [kə'mə:ʃəlaiz] *vt* make something into an object to be bought and sold 使商業化. **commercial traveller** see 見 **travel.**

commiserate [kə'mizəreit] *vi* (usu. with **with**) show pity for or synpathy with someone (通常與 with 連用) 憐憫, 同情: *He commiserated with me on my failure in the examination.* 他對我考試失利表示同情.

commission [kə'miʃən] **1** *nc* group of people given special powers to carry out some particular task (處理專門事務的) 委員會: *The government appointed a commission to examine the country's educational system.* 政府任命一個委員會專門審查本國教育制度問題. **2** *nc* position of an officer in the army, navy, air force etc. 海、陸、空軍軍官的軍銜、職務. **3** *nc / u* amount of money given to somebody as payment for selling goods which belong to somebody else 佣金、酬勞金: *In some large shops the assistants get a commission on what they sell* i. e. they are paid for each item which they sell. 一些大商店的店員按所賣出商品得佣金. Also 亦作 *vt* give somebody an order to carry out some special piece of work; give somebody the power to do some piece of work 委任, 任命, 責成, 授權: *He was commis-*

sioned to write the music for that film.
責成他來為該影片譜寫音樂. **commis-
sioner** *nc* official of various types
(esp. a senior official in the police) 長
官; 高級專員; 官員 (尤指警方高級官
員).

commissionaire [kəmiʃə'nɛə*] *nc* man
wearing a uniform, whose job is to
stand outside the door of a cinema or
hotel and help people coming in and
out (電影院或酒店等處為進出顧客開
門的穿制服) 門警, 守門人.

commissioner [kə'miʃənə*] *nc* see 見
commission.

commit [kə'mit] *vi* do something (usu.
something wrong or foolish) 做 (壞事、
蠢事), 犯: *He committed a crime.* 他
犯罪. *past* 過去式和過去分詞 **committed. commitment** *nc* promise to
do something 承諾. **commit oneself**
promise or say that one will do something 承諾: *I have committed myself
to helping him.* 我答應過幫助他.

committee [kə'miti] *nc* group of people
given special powers (often by a larger group) to carry out some special
piece of work 委員會. *Note* 說明: the
word committee can be treated as
either *sing* or *pl* 此詞可視為單數或複
數.

commodity [kə'mɒditi] *nc* something
which is bought and sold 商品.

commodore ['kɒmədɔ:] *nc* naval officer
above captain and below rearadmiral;
senior captain of a shipping line 海軍
准將; 商船隊隊長.

common¹ ['kɒmən] *adj* **1** belonging to
several people and not to any individual 共有的: *In a block of flats, the
roof and the lift are often common
property* i. e. these things are owned
by all the people who own flats in
that block. 一棟公寓建築物中的屋頂和

電梯常常是公共財產. *Britain and
America share a common language* i.
e. English is spoken in both countries.
英美有共同的語言. 即: 兩國人都講英
語. **2** found in many places or over a
wide area 普通的: *This bird is common throughout Europe.* 全歐洲都有
這種鳥. **3** usual 通常的: *It is common
for a woman to leave her parents'
house when she gets married.* 婦女結
婚後通常離開父母的家. **4** showing little or no politeness; with no sense of
the proper way to behave 粗俗的, 不
懂禮貌的. (*opp* **uncommon** in senses
2 and **3**) (義2和義3的反義詞是 uncommon). **commonly** *adv* the
(**House of**) **Commons** (in Britain)
the assembly of elected members of
Parliament. (The other assembly, the
House of Lords, is not elected) (英國)
下議院. (議員由選舉產生, 而上議院非
經選舉產生). **the Common Market**
European Economic Community (*informal*) (歐洲) 共同市場 (即歐洲經濟
共同體) (非正式). **'commonplace** *adj*
ordinary; not interesting 平凡的, 陳腐
的. Also 亦作 *nc* remark or statement
which is ordinary and not interesting
or new 陳腐乏味的話, 老生常談.
'common room room for the use of
teachers, lecturers etc at a school,
college etc. (學校的) 教員公用室.
common'sense *nu* ordinary intelligence, which most people have 常識.
Also 亦作 *adj.* **the Commonwealth**
association of Britain with several of
the countries which were formerly
British colonies and protectorates 英
聯邦. **in common** with other people
共同: *They have a lot in common* i. e.
they are alike in many ways 他們有許
多共同之處.

common² [kɒmən] *nc* (mainly *Brit*)

open space covered with grass and trees, which is for the use of everybody (主要用於英) 公共林蔭地, 公用草地, 公園.

commotion [kəˈmouʃən] *nc* violent and noisy movement or excitement 騷動, 騷亂.

commune [ˈkɔmjuːn] *nc* large group of people living together in China and elsewhere; all land and property is owned by the group, and all the members work to produce goods and services for the group 公社. **communal** *adj* referring to a group of people living together; public. 社區的; 公共的: *He took no part in communal life* i. e. he did not share in activities organized by or for the people living around him. 他不參加社區生活. 即: 他不參加鄰里活動.

communicate [kəˈmjuːnikeit] *vt / i* 1 give information in speech or writing, or by signs 聯絡, 通訊息: *While he was in prison he was not allowed to communicate with his family.* 他坐牢期間, 不許和家人通訊或接觸. 2 pass disease to 傳染: *He communicated the disease to the rest of his family.* 他把疾病傳染給家裏其他人. 3 (with reference to rooms, houses etc.) be joined or connected (指房屋等) 相連. **communication** [kəˌmjuːniˈkeiʃən] *nc / u* 1 letter, speech, sign etc giving information 通訊; 訊息: *While he was in prison his family received no communication from him.* 他坐牢期間, 家裏得不到他的信件. 2 method of passing information over a wide area (e. g. telephones, roads, aeroplanes) 交通; 傳播手段. **communi'cation cord** cord which can be pulled by passengers to stop a train in an emergency (緊急情況時供乘客拉使火車急煞車的)

警報索.

communion [kəˈmjuːniən] 1 *nu* act of sharing ideas or property with other people 溝通. 2 *nc* group of people having the same religious ideas (有共同宗教信仰的) 教派, 教友. **Communion, Holy Communion** *nu* ceremony, carried out in many Christian churches, of giving bread or bread and wine to the people in memory of Christ 聖餐(儀式).

communique [kəˈmjuːnikei] *nc* official announcement (esp. one made by a government) 公報.

communism [ˈkɔmjunizəm] *nu* esp. with reference to the system of government in Russia, China and many countries of eastern Europe) social or political system in which property is owned by the government or the community, and not by individuals 共產主義. **communist** *nc* person who approves of this system (esp. one who is a member of the Communist Party) 共產主義者, 共產黨人. Also 亦作 *adj*.

community [kəˈmjuːniti] *nc* people living in one part of a town or country; any group of people living together 社區. **com'munity centre** building in a town or village, where people living in that place can go to meet each other and enjoy themselves 社區中心(該社區居民可以在該處晤面, 娛樂).

commutate [ˈkɔmjuːteit] *vt* reverse the direction (of a current or currents); convert (alternating current) into direct current 變換(電流的)方向; 把(交流電)轉爲直流電.

commute [kəˈmjuːt] *vi* travel every day by bus or train, between one's house and the place where one works (坐火車, 或公共汽車)每日往返住處與工作場

所之間. **commuter** nc.

compact¹ [kəm'pækt] adj fitting tightly together, using up very little space 緊湊的, 佔空間極小的.

compact² ['kɒmpækt] nc 1 agreement with somebody to do something 協定, 合同. 2 flat box for containing face powder, carried in a woman's handbag (婦女手提袋中携帶的)化妝小粉盒.

companion [kəm'pæniən] nc 1 person with whom one travels; person who is often or always with one 旅伴, 伴侶. 2 anything which goes with something else 成對(或成副)東西的一個. 3 person whose work is to live with another person 專責陪伴他人的人: *She was employed as a companion to an old lady.* 雇她來和老太太作伴.
companionship nu state of being a companion; friendly company 同伴之誼; 友誼.

company ['kʌmpəni] 1 nc number of people who have joined together for some purpose (爲某種目的而聚在一起的)一羣人. 2 nc business firm 公司. 3 nc small division of an army; small group of soldiers 連隊. 4 nu condition of being with other people 有伴: *He enjoys company* i. e. he likes to be with other people. 他喜歡有伴. **be good company** be a friendly and interesting person 是個有趣的夥伴: *He is very good company.* 他是一個十分有趣的夥伴. **have company** have visitors in the house 有客人. **keep somebody company** go with or be with somebody (usu. in a friendly way) 陪伴某人或陪某人一道去.

compare [kəm'pɛə*] vt 1 show or find out in what ways two or more things are like each other (or are different from each other) 比較: *He compared the two chairs before he decided which one to buy.* 他比較了那兩張椅子後, 才決定買哪一張. 2 (with to or with) say or show that something is like something else (和 to 或 with 連用)比作: *He compared the brave man to a lion.* 他把勇士比作獅子. **comparison** [kəm'pærisn] nc / u: make a comparison between two things 比較.

comparable ['kɒn: pərəbl] adj able to be compared 可比的: *This is comparable to / with that.* 這個可以和那個比. (opp **incomparable** - usu. with the meaning of very much better than) (反義詞爲 incomparable — 通常意爲好得許多, 無從比起). **comparative** [kəm'pærətiv] adj 1 making or showing a comparison (e. g. the study of comparative religion is the study of various religions to see in what ways they are alike and in what ways they differ) 比較的(例如: 比較宗教的研究就是要找出各種宗教的相似和不同). 2 (grammar) form of adjectives and adverbs which expresses the idea of 'more' (e. g. *easier, better, more beautiful, more quietly* are comparative adjectives and adverbs) (語法)比較級 (例如: easier, better, more beautiful, more quietly 是比較級形容詞和副詞). **comparatively** adv: *This is comparatively easy* i. e. it seems easy if we compare it with other things which are much more difficult. 這個比較容易. **by / in comparison (with)** when compared (with) (和)比較起來.

compartment [kəm'pɑ:tmənt] nc part of a container of some kind, separated in some way from the rest of the container (e. g. the compartments of a railway train; a purse or a wallet often has a number of compartments) 格

子,分隔空間(例如: 火車的小房間; 錢包的夾層).

compass ['kʌmpəs] *nc* **1** instrument containing a magnetic needle which points to the north, used for showing directions 指南針. **2** instrument for drawing circles (Sometimes **compasses** *pl* or **a pair of compasses**) 圓規 (有時複數用 compasses 或用 a pair of compasses).

compassion [kəm'pæʃən] *nu* very strong feeling of love and pity, caused by the unhappiness or suffering of somebody else 同情; 憐憫. **compassionate** [kəm'pæʃənit] *adj*.

compatible [kəm'pætibl] *adj* able or suitable to go together 和諧相處的; 相容: *Those two people are not compatible* i. e. they cannot be together in a friendly way. 這兩個人合不來. *His ideas are not compatible with mine.* 他的主張跟我的主張格格不入. (*opp* 反義詞 **incompatible**).

compel [kəm'pel] *vt* make somebody do something by using force or authority 強迫, 迫使: *I compelled him to come with me.* 我強迫他和我一道來. *past* 過去式和過去分詞 **compelled.** see 見 **compulsion.**

compensate ['kɔmpenseit] **1** *vt* give payment of some kind to somebody who has suffered a loss or injury 補償; 賠償: *The government compensated the families of the men who were killed in the accident.* 政府對在事故中死亡者的家屬給予賠償. **2** *vi* (often used for) be a payment of this kind (常與 for 連用) 補償, 賠償: *I hope that this present will compensate for the trouble I have caused you.* 我希望這個禮物可以補償我給你所添的麻煩. **compensation** [kɔmpen'seiʃən] *nc / u*.

compete [kəm'piːt] *vi* try to win or to gain something in a race. competiton, examination etc. 競賽: *Six runners competed in the last race.* 在上一個賽跑項目中, 六個人在競爭. *He was competing against / with his friends in the examination.* 他正和他的朋友們在考試中比個高低. **competition** [kɔmpi'tiʃən] **1** *nu* act of competing 競爭. **2** *nc* any occasion on which people compete 競賽. **competitive** [kəm'petitiv] *adj* showing competition; decided by competition 競爭性的. **competitor** [kəm'petitə*] *nc* person who competes 競爭者.

competent ['kɔmpitənt] *adj* having the ability or power to do something 能幹的, 能勝任的: *He is competent to do the work.* 他能勝任這個工作. (*opp* 反義詞 **incompetent**). **competence** *nu* ability or power to do something 權限; 能力. (*opp* 反義詞 **incompetence**).

compile [kəm'pail] *vt* (esp. with reference to collecting material when writing a book) collect together and arrange in order 搜集, 彙編(尤指爲寫書而搜集材料). **compiler** *nc*.

complacent [kəm'pleisnt] *adj* pleased or satisfied with oneself (usu. in a foolish or annoying way) 沾沾自喜的, 自鳴得意的, 妄自尊大的. **complacence, complacency** *nu*.

complain [kəm'plein] *vi* **1** say that something is wrong; say that one is not pleased with something 抱怨; 埋怨: *He complained about the food in the hotel.* 他嫌旅館伙食不好. **2** tell somebody that one is suffering from a disease or illness 告訴別人自己身體不好、有病: *He complained of pains in the stomach.* 他說他胃痛. **complaint** *nc* **1** statement that something is wrong 埋怨、申訴: *He made a complaint to the manager.* 他對經理提出申訴. **2** disease or illness 疾病.

complement ['kɔmplimənt] *nc* **1** anything which makes something complete 補足物. **2** full number of officers and men on a ship 船上的定員. **3** (grammar) noun or noun phrase following certain verbs, such as 'seem', 'be', 'become' (語法) 補語 (跟隨在某些動詞如'seem', 'be', 'become' 等後面的名詞或名詞短語). **complementary** [kɔmpli'mentəri] *adj.* Note 說明: do not confuse *complement* with *compliment* 不要將 complement 和 compliment 混淆.

complete [kəm'pliːt] *adj* **1** with nothing missing; finished; not needing anything more 完整的, 全部的: *The work is complete and so we can rest.* 工作已經完成, 我們可以休息了. **2** very great 十分: *a complete surprise* 十分意外, 全出意外. Also 亦作 *vt* finish; do everything which needs to be done 完成: *He completed the work.* 他完成了工作. **completion** *nu* **completely** *adv: completely different* 完全不同.

complex[1] ['kɔmpleks] *adj* made up of many different parts (and usu. difficult to understand) 複雜的. **complexity** [kəm'pleksiti] *nc / u.*

complex[2] ['kɔmpleks] *nc* **1** anything consisting of many different parts (e. g. an institution consisting of many different buildings) 綜合體 (例如: 包括許多不同建築物的機構). **2** condition of the mind, in which one has a large number of ideas and feelings which were caused by some event in the past, and which have a strong influence on one's behaviour 情結.

complexion [kəm'plekʃən] *nc* **1** appearance of the skin of one's face 臉部膚色. **2** general appearance or nature of some event 形勢, 局面.

complicate ['kɔmplikeit] *vt* make more difficult to do or understand, by adding something or by changing something; add another difficulty 使更費解; 使難處理; 使更難. **complication** [kɔmpli'keiʃən] *nc / u* **complicated** *adj* having many different parts and therefore difficult to do or understand 錯綜複雜的, 難以處理或理解的.

compliment ['kɔmplimənt] *nc* **1** friendly statement that somebody is good in some way 恭維話, 稱讚: *He paid Mary a compliment about her new hat* i. e. he said that he liked the hat. 他說她的新帽子好看. **2** (in *pl*) polite greeting (often a greeting sent to somebody who is not present) (用於複數) 問候, 致意 (常是對不在面前的人的問候、致意). Also 亦作 ['kɔmpliment] *vt: He complimented her on her new hat.* 他說她的新帽子好看. **complimentary** [kɔmpli'mentəri] *adj* saying pleasant things about somebody 恭維的, 表讚賞的. (*opp* 反義詞 **uncomplimentary**). **complimentary ticket** free ticket to a play, film or other entertainment 贈券, 免費入場券.

comply [kəm'plai] *vi* usu. **comply with someone's wishes** i. e. do what somebody wants one to do 通常出現於 comply with someone's wishes 遵從, 遵守; 應允.

component [kəm'pəunənt] *nc* one of the parts of which something is made up 組成成份, 組件: *This machine has 300 different components.* 這機器有三百個不同的組件.

compose [kəm'pəuz] *vt / i* **1** (often with reference to writing a book or poem, and esp. with reference to writing

music) arrange parts so as to make something new 創作(常指寫書、做詩，尤指作曲). **2** make calm 使平靜下來: *compose oneself* 讓自己鎮靜下來; *compose one's thoughts* 理出思路.
composer *nc* person who writes music 作曲家. **composed** *adj* calm; under control 鎮靜的，泰然自若的. **composed of** made up of 由…組成.
composition [kɔmpə'ziʃən] **1** *nc* piece of writing (esp. an essay written by somebody at school) 文章(尤指學生的作文). **2** *nc* piece of music 樂曲. **3** *nu* way in which something is made up of several parts; act of composing 組成的方式，結構，組成，構成.
compost ['kɔmpɔst] *nu* mixture of rotting vegetation, used in a garden to improve the soil 綠肥，混合肥料.
composure [kəm'pouʒə*] *nu* condition of being calm, having one's feelings and thoughts under control 鎮靜，沉著.
compound[1] ['kɔmpaund] *nc* **1** anything having several different parts (esp. a substance made up of several different substances) 混合物，合成品. **2** (chemistry) substance made by the combination of two or more elements (化)化合物. Also 亦作 *adj* '**compound 'interest** interest which is paid on both capital and interest earned formerly 複利.
compound[2] ['kɔmpaund] *nc* (usu. with reference to Asia and Africa only) enclosed land round a building belonging to one person or institution (通常只指亞洲或非洲)在私人或機關建築物四週用圍牆或籬笆圍起來的場地.
comprehend [kɔmpri'hend] *vt* **1** understand the meaning of 理解. **2** include or contain 包含，包括. **comprehension** *nu* act of understanding 領

悟. **comprehensive** *adj* including or containing a lot of everything 範圍廣泛的. **comprehensive school** type of secondary school to which all the children living in a particular area may go, whatever their level of ability. 凡在某一地區居住的兒童，不論其水平，均可入學的中等學校.
compress[1] [kəm'pres] *vt* make smaller by pressing or pushing together 壓縮，濃縮. **compression** *nu*.
compress[2] ['kɔmpres] *nc* piece of wet cloth which is tied tightly on a wound or injury to stop bleeding, reduce swelling or relieve pain (用以止血、消炎、止痛的)創口濕壓布，敷布.
comprise [kəm'praiz] *vt* be made up of 包括，由…組成: *The village comprises two hundred houses, three shops, a garage and a school.* 村莊有兩百幢房子、三個店舖、一個汽車修理站和一所學校.
compromise ['kɔmprəmaiz] **1** *vi* reach an agreement after a quarrel or disagreement, by each side agreeing to have less than it had first asked for 妥協，折衷. **2** *vt* make people think that somebody has done wrong 使受到嫌疑；使損名譽: *John compromised his friends by stealing the money* i. e. people thought that his friends had helped him to steal the money, although they had not. 約翰偷錢，連累他的朋友也受到嫌疑. Also 亦作 *nc* agreement reached by each side agreeing to have less than it had at first asked for 妥協.
compulsion [kəm'pʌlʃən] *nu* act of making somebody do something by force 強制. **compulsory** [kəm'pʌlsəri] *adj*: *Voting is compulsory in some countries* i. e. there is a law saying that people must vote. 有些國

家選舉是一種義務. 即: 法律規定人民必
須參加選舉. see 見 **compel**.

computer [kəm'pju:tə*] *nc* electronic
device which is capable of carrying
out very complex calculations on the
basis of the coded information which
is put into it 電腦, 電子計算機.

comrade ['kɔmrid] *nc* 1 person with
whom one is friendly, and with whom
one works 同事, 戰友. 2 title used instead of *Mr* or *Sir* (esp. in communist
countries) (尤用於共產主義國家)同
志 (用以代替 *Mr* 或 *Sir*).

concave ['kɔn'keiv] *adj* (esp. with reference to lenses) curving inwards; having the shape of the inside of a circle
or sphere (尤指透鏡)凹的. *(opp 反義
詞 **convex**).

conceal [kən'si:l] *vt* keep hidden or secret 隱藏, 掩蓋: *He could not conceal
the crime any longer.* 他不能再掩蓋這
個罪行了.

concede [kən'si:d] *vt* 1 agree that something is true (esp. something said by
a person with whom one is arguing or
disagreeing) 承認(某事是真的, 尤指爭
論或意見不同時). 2 give something to
one's opponent or enemy after disagreeing, fighting etc. 讓, 割讓: *After
the war the enemy had to concede
some territory.* 戰後敵人不得不割讓一
些領土. **concession** [kən'seʃən] 1 *nu*
act of conceding. 讓步. 2 *nc* something gained from somebody in this
way 讓與的東西.

conceit [kən'si:t] *nu* feeling of pleasure
because one thinks that one is very
good or very clever, when in fact one
is not as good or clever as one thinks
自負, 自滿. **conceited** *adj*.

conceive [kən'si:v] *vt* think or imagine;
have an idea of 想像, 構思: *He very
quickly conceived a new plan.* 他很快

想出一個新的計劃. **conceivable** *adj*
of what can be thought of or imagined 可以想像到的. *(opp 反義詞 **inconceivable**). **conception** [kən'sep-
ʃən] 1 *nc / u* idea or thought 概念, 觀
念. 2 *nu* process of becoming pregnant 懷孕.

concentrate ['kɔnsəntreit] *vt / i* 1 come
or bring together in a small area (使)
集中(於某處). 2 study carefully; give
careful attention to 集中注意; 全神貫
注: *He has concentrated on his work
this year.* 今年他集中精力在工作上.
You must try to concentrate. 你必須努
力集中注意力. **concentration**
[kɔnsən'treiʃən] 1 *nu* act of coming
or bringing together 集中. 2 *nc* something collected together 聚集起來的東
西. 3 *nu* careful study or attention 專
心. **concen'tration camp** (esp. with
reference to prisons in Germany during the rule of the Nazis) prison surrounded by barbed wire, where political prisoners are kept 集中營.

concentric [kɔn'sentrik] *adj* having the
same centre 同心的: concentric cir-
cles 同心圓.

concept ['kɔnsept] *nc* idea of something
觀念, 概念: *A small baby has no concept of right and wrong* i. e. these
ideas have no meaning for a small
baby 嬰兒沒有是非概念. **conceptual-
ize** [kɔn'sept-juəlaiz] *vt / i* form a concept 形成概念. **conception**
[kɔn'sepʃən] *nc / u* see 見 **conceive**.

concern¹ [kən'sə:n] *vt* have connection
with; be of importance to 關係到:
This matter concerns all of us. 這件事
和我們大家都有關係. **concerned** *adj*
1 having a connection with 有關的; 參
與的. *Are you concerned with this
matter.* 你對這事有關係嗎? 2 worried
or troubled 擔心的, 掛慮的: *Mrs Smith*

was very concerned when I was ill last year. 去年我生病的時候，史密斯太太很擔心。*Note* 說明: *concerned about / for* means worried or anxious; *concerned in / with* means having a connection with or taking part in. concerned about / for 意思是‘憂慮’、‘焦急’; concerned in / with 意思是與‘有關係’、或‘參與了’。 **concerning** *prep* having a connection with 關於: *questions concerning the future* 關係到未來的問題。

concern² [kən'sə:n] **1** *nu* what has connection with something or is of importance to something 利害攸關的事, 有重要性的事: *This matter is the concern of all of us.* 這事是我們大家都要關心的事; **2** *nu* feeling of worry or trouble 憂慮; 擔心: *Mrs Smith felt great concern when I was ill last year.* 我去年生病時候, 史密斯太太十分關切。 **3** *nc* business, shop, factory etc. 公司; 商店; 工廠等。

concert ['kɔnsət] *nc* entertainment at which a number of pieces of music are played or sung 音樂會。 **concerted** [kən'sə:tid] *adj* planned by those taking part; carried out together or at the same time (usu. **a concerted attack** or **concerted action**) 共同商定的, 一致行動的(通常出現於 a concerted attack 聯合攻擊 或 concerted action 一致行動)。 **in concert** together, at the same time 一致; 同時。

concerto [kən'tʃə:tou] *nc* piece of music written for a solo instrument or solo instruments and an orchestra 協奏曲。 *pl* 複數 **concertos**

concession [kən'seʃən] *nc / u* see 見 **concede.**

conciliate [kən'silieit] *vt* make somebody stop being angry by doing or saying something to please him 安慰;

安撫; 勸解。 **conciliation** [kənsili'eiʃən] *nu.*

conciliatory [kən'siliətri] *adj* intended to conciliate 意圖修好的; 撫慰性的: *a conciliatory letter* 願意修好的信; 爭取對方好感的信。

concise [kən'sais] *adj* saying a lot in few words 簡潔的。 *a concise letter / speaker* 一封簡要的信 / 一位言詞簡練的演說家。

conclave ['kɔnkleiv] *nc* (esp. with reference to a meeting of cardinals to elect a new pope) meeting to which the public is not admitted (尤指紅衣主教選舉新教皇的)秘密會議。

conclude [kən'klu:d] **1** *vt / i* finish; end 結束: *He concluded his speech with some words by Shakespeare.* 他用莎士比亞的話作爲演說詞的結束語。 *The meeting concluded after three hours.* 會議開了三個鐘頭後結束。 **2** *vt* make an agreement 締結; 訂定。 *conclude a treaty / an agreement.* 締結條約 / 訂立協定。 **3** *vi* come to a decision after thinking about a topic or after hearing what somebody says 作出結論, 斷定。 *He concluded that Jones had stolen the money.* 他斷定瓊斯偷了錢。 **conclusion** *nc* **1** end 結尾, 結束 **2** reaching an agreement 締結, 訂定。 **3** opinion reached after thought 推斷, 結論。 **conclusive** allowing one to decide 無可置疑的, 確定性的: *conclusive proof* 確鑿的證據。 *(opp* 反義詞 **inconclusive).* **conclusively** *adv* in **conclusion** to end with (often said near the end of a speech) 在結束時, 最後(在演說結尾常說的結束語)。

concoct [kən'kɔkt] *vt* **1** make food or drink by mixing toghther (usu. with reference to making a new food or drink in this way, and often with the suggestion that the food or drink is not very nice) 調製(食物、飲料)(通常 指試製新食品,且會暗示所調製食品不 很可口). **2** make up a story or excuse which is not true 捏造,編造(事實情 節、藉口等). **concoction** *nc / u*.

concord ['kɔŋkɔːd] *nu / c* **1** agreement; harmony 一致;和諧,協調. **2** treaty 協 定.

concordance [kən'kɔːdəns] *nu / c* **1** agreement; harmony 一致;和諧,協調. **2** alphabetical list of the words of a book with references to the passages in which they occur 詞彙索引.

concordant [kən'kɔː dənt] *adj* agreeing; harmonious 一致的;和諧的,協調的.

concordat [kɔn'kɔːdæt] *nc* agreement, esp. between the pope and a govern-ment 協定(尤指教會與政府間所訂者).

concourse ['kɔŋkɔːs] *nc* open space for the use of the public at a railway sta-tion or airport 火車、機場前群眾集散 的廣場.

concrete[1] ['kɔŋkriːt] *nu* hard substance made of sand and cement, used for building 混凝土.

concrete[2] ['kɔŋkriːt] *adj* real, not ex-isting merely as an idea or hope 具體 的. **concrete noun** (grammar) noun which refers to something which can be seen, felt, tasted, heard etc. (e. g. *house, fire, sugar, aeroplane*) (語法) 具體名詞(指可以通過視聽感官、味覺、 觸覺等感知之物體的名詞例如: house, fire, sugar, aeroplane). (*opp* 反義詞 **abstract noun**).

concurrent [kən'kʌrnt] *adj* happening at the same time 同時發生的. **con-currently** *adv.*

concussion [kɔn'kʌʃən] *nu* injury to the brain caused by a blow or fall 腦 震盪.

condemn [kən'dem] *vt* **1** (with refer-

ence to judges) say officially after a trial that somebody must be punished (法官)判罪: *The judge condemned him to five years in prison.* 法官判他 五年徒刑. **2** say that something is wrong 譴責: *Most people condemn war.* 大多數人譴責戰爭. **3** say offi-cially that something is not fit to use and must be destroyed 公開宣佈(某 物)不宜使用. **condemnation** [kɔn-dem'neiʃən] *nu.*

condense [kən'dens] *vt / i* **1** change from a gas into a liquid (使)凝結. **2** put into fewer words 縮寫,精簡: *He condensed his essay from 3000 to 1500 words.* 他將他的文章從三千字壓 縮到一千五百字. **condensation** [kɔndenseiʃən] *nu* **1** act of condens-ing 冷凝(作用);(文章的)壓縮. **2** drops of liquid formed when a gas condenses 冷凝而成的水珠狀液體. **condensed milk** very thick type of (often sweetened) milk, made by re-moving some of the water from the milk 煉乳.

condenser [kən'densə] *nc* **1** apparatus for converting gases or vapours to a liquid state 冷凝器. **2** lens for con-centrating light rays on an area 聚光 鏡. **3** apparatus which stores electric-ity 電容器.

condescend [kɔndi'send] *vi* act in a friendly way to somebody whom one considers inferior to oneself (often in a way which is unpleasant for the person who is considered inferior) 屈 尊,俯就. **condescending** *adj.*

condition[1] [kən'diʃən] **1** *nu* state which a person / thing is in 情況、狀態,狀況: *This car is in good condition* i. e. no-thing is broken or damaged. 這輛車狀 況良好. 即:毫無損壞. *The Prime Minister asked for a report on the* *condition of the national economy.* 首相要一份有關國民經濟情況的報告. **2** *nc* something which is necessary for something else to happen. 條件: *I shall lend you this money; my only condition is that you spend it carefully* i. e. I shall lend you the money if you promise to spend it carefully. 我可以把錢借給你，唯一條件是你得精打細算地用錢.

condition² [kən'diʃən] *vt* **1** put into a state of good health by exercise (通過鍛煉) 使處在健康狀態. **2** change or form the behaviour of a person or animal; train to act in a certain way 使 (人或動物) 產生條件反射. **3** (usu. *passive*) be a condition of (通常用於被動語態) 成爲…的條件; 制約: *The success of the government's school building programme is conditioned by the money available* i. e. the government can build schools only if it has enough money to do so. 政府的建造學校房屋計劃決定於手頭能有多少錢.

conditional *adj* depending on something 附有條件的: *He made a conditional promise to help me* i. e. he promised to help me if something else happened. 他答應有條件地幫助我. *The offer of the money was conditional on my accepting within three days* i. e. I could have the money if I took it within three days. 提供錢款的附帶條件是我必須在三天以內接受. (*opp* 反義詞 **unconditional**). **on condition that** if something else happens or is promised 如果; 在…條件下: *I shall lend you this money on condition that you give it back in one month.* 我可以把錢借給你，條件是一個月後就得還.

condolence [kən'doulns] *nc* (often *pl*) words or action showing that one is

sorry for somebody who has suffered a loss or misfortune (常用複數) 弔唁, 慰問: *She received many condolences when her father died.* 她父親死去, 她收到許多唁函, 唁電.

condone [kən'doun] *vt* forgive; allow some wrong action to go unpunished or be forgotten 寬恕, 寬容: *I cannot condone the damage you have caused.* 我不能寬恕你所造成的損害.

conducive [kən'djuːsiv] *adj* likely to result in or lead to 導致…的; 有助於…的: *This behaviour is not conducive to hard work* i. e. you or other people cannot work hard if you behave like that. 這種舉止行爲, 不可能認真勤奮地工作. *Exercise is conducive to good health.* 鍛煉有助於健康.

conduct¹ ['kɔndʌkt] *nu* **1** way of behaving 行爲: *The conduct of all the pupils was very good* i. e. they all behaved well. 所有這些小學生都很規矩. **2** way in which a business is organized 處理, 組織工作: *the conduct of a government department* 政府部門的組織工作.

conduct² [kən'dʌkt] *vt / i* **1** lead or guide 引導: *He conducted the members of the audience to their seats.* 他把觀衆帶到各自的座位上. **2** be in charge of; control and organize 掌管、處理: *The Minister of Education conducted the business of his department very successfully.* 教育部長對他本部門的工作處理得十分出色. **3** be the person in charge of an orchestra or choir at a concert 指揮演奏. **4** carry heat or electricity 傳導(熱量或電): *Copper wire conducts electricity.* 銅絲導電. **conductor** *nc* **1** person in charge of an orchestra or choir at a concert 樂隊(或歌詠團的)指揮. **2** person who sells tickets on a bus 售票員. (Also

conductress when a woman) (如係女
售票員, 亦作 conductress). **conduct
oneself** behave 表現: *She conducted
herself very badly.* 她表現極壞.

cone [koun] *nc* **1** solid object with a
circular base and pointed tip 圓錐體.
2 anything shaped like this (e. g. the
*cone of a volcano is the top of a vol-
cano; an ice cream cone is a kind of
biscuit, shaped like a cone, for holding ice cream)* 圓錐狀東西 (例如: the
cone of a volcano 是'火山頂'; an ice
cream cone 是'蛋捲冰淇淋'). **3** fruit
of certain trees (e. g. pine or fir).
冷杉毬果, 松子. **conical** ['kɔnikl]
adj.

confectionery [kənˈfekʃənəri] *nu* **1**
sweets and chocolates 糖果. **2** cakes.
糕餅. **confectioner** *nc* person who
makes or sells sweets and chocolates
or cakes 點心商, 糖果商.

confederation [kənfedəˈreiʃən] *nc*
group of nations, societies, business
firms etc which have joined together
because of some interest or purpose
which they share 同盟, 聯盟.

confer [kənˈfə:*] **1** *vi* talk together (esp.
on a matter of business, government
etc.) (尤指就商業, 政府等事務的)交換
意見. **2** *vt* give a medal, title or some
other offical reward 授予勳章、官衛、
學位等): *The king conferred a medal
on the soldier.* 國王授予該士兵一枚勳
章. *past* 過去式和過去分詞 **confer-
red. conference** ['kɔnfərns] *nc* meeting to discuss some matter of business, government etc. 會議.

confess [kənˈfes] *vt / i* **1** tell people that
one has done wrong; admit 承認, 供
認: *He confessed his crime to the
police.* 他向警方坦白罪行. *I must
confess that I was happy when she left.* 我
必須承認她離開時候, 我是很高興的. **2**

(in the Roman Catholic Church, and
some other churches) tell a priest
that one has done something wrong.
(天主教或某些教會向神父之)告解, 懺
悔. **confession** [kənˈfeʃən] *nc / u* act
of confessing 承認, 坦白; 懺悔, 告解.
confessor *nc* priest who hears con-
fessions 聽取告解的神父. **confes-
sional** [kənˈfeʃənl] *nc* place in a
church where a priest hears confes-
sions 神父聽取告解的隔絕室.

confetti [kənˈfeti] *nu* small pieces of
coloured paper, thrown about at weddings and other festivals (婚禮或其他
喜慶時所擲之)五彩碎紙.

confide [kənˈfaid] *vt / i* **1** give a duty or
piece of work to 委託: *I shall confide
this duty to you.* 我把這個任務交給你.
2 trust; have faith in 信任, 信賴: *You
can confide in the police* i. e. you can
be sure that the police will help you if
you need help. 你可以信任警方. **confidence** ['kɔnfidns] **1** *nc* secret; information confided to somebody 秘
密; 私房話. **2** *nu* trust or strong belief, lack of fear 信任; 信心: *I have
confidence in you* i. e. I am sure that
you will do right, succeed, win etc. 我
信任你. 即: 我相信你做得對/會成功/會
贏等. **confident** [kɔnfidnt] *adj sure*
(often of one's own abilities) 有信心
的 (常指自信有能力). **confidently**
adv **con-fidential** [kɔnfiˈdenʃl] *adj* **1**
secret; not to be told or shown to
other people 秘密的; 機密的: *This information is confidential.* 這情報是機
密的. **2** (with reference to a person)
given secrets as part of one's work
(指人) 參與機密的: *a confidential
secretary / agent* 機要秘書/密使. **confidence trick** (*Brit*) dishonest trick in
which a criminal gets money by persuading somebody to trust him (*US*

美 **confidence game**) (英)騙取財物
的騙局, 欺詐. **in confidence** as a
secret 私下, 秘密地: *I am telling you
this in confidence* i. e. you must not
tell other people. 我私下告訴你. 即: 你
千萬別告訴別人.

confine[1] [kən'fain] *vt* keep shut in, keep
within certain limits 監禁; 限制, 限於
…範圍: *The soldiers were confined to
the camp for three weeks* i. e. they
were not allowed to leave the camp.
士兵們被禁閉在兵營中三星期. **con-
finement** *nu* **1** act of keeping or
staying inside 禁閉, 足不出戶. **2** act
of giving birth to a baby 分娩. **confine oneself to** speak only about 講
話內容只限於: *I shall confine myself
to the subject of geography* i. e. I shall
not speak about other topic. 我將只談
地理這個題目.

confine[2] ['kɔnfain] *nc* (usu. *pl*) limit;
boundary; frontier 通常用複數)界限;
疆界, 邊界: *He passed his life within
the confines of his own country.* 他一
生都在自己國家內度過.

confirm [kən'fə:m] *vt* **1** say officially
that a story or rumour is true. 正式證
實: *The Prime Minister confirmed that
he would visit France next month.* 首
相證實他下個月將訪問法國. **2** make
stronger an opinion, idea, decision
etc. (使) 更堅定(意見、主張、決定等).
What you say confirms my opinion i.
e. you make me feel more certain that
I am right. 你所說的使我的意見更加堅
定. **3** admit to full membership of
some Christian churches 施以堅信禮,
使成爲基督教會正式教徒. **4** give official agreement to some arrangement
which already exists 正式批准. **con-
firmation** [kɔnfə'meiʃən] *nu*.

confiscate ['kɔnfiskeit] *vt* officially take
something away from somebody 沒

收. *The teacher confiscated the book
which the boy was reading in class.* 老
師沒收了男孩子在上課時候看的書.
confiscation [kɔnfis'keiʃən] *nu*.

conflict[1] ['kɔnflikt] *nc* fight; struggle;
disagreement 衝突; 爭執; 戰鬥.

conflict[2] [kən'flikt] *vi* (often **with with**)
disagree; fight. (常與 **with** 連用) 爭
執; 衝突; 戰鬥.

confluence ['kɔnfluəns] *nu / c* **1** flowing
together; place where two streams
meet 合流; 匯合處. **2** movement in
which people or things come together
聚集.

conform [kən'fɔ:m] *vt / i* behave, cause
to behave, in the same way as others.
(使) 符合, (使)順應: *He conformed to
the rules of the club* i. e. he did what
the rules said he must do. 他依照俱樂
部的規則行事. **conformist** *nc*.

confront [kən'frʌnt] *vt* **1** meet face to
face 面對: *He decided to confront his
enemies.* 他決定正面對付敵人. **2**
place before 放在…面前, 使…面對:
*He confronted them with the evidence
of the crime.* 他把罪證擺在他們面前.
confrontation [kɔnfrʌn'teiʃən] *nc / u.*

confuse [kən'fju: z] *vt* **1** make it difficult
for somebody to think clearly 把…弄
糊塗, 使發慌: *When I arrived in London, the crowds of people and the
traffic confused me.* 我到倫敦的時候,
人山人海、車水馬龍使我發慌, 不知所
措. **2** think that something is something else 弄錯, 混淆: *I confused you
with your brother* i.e. I thought that
you were your brother, or your
brother was you. 你們兄弟兩個, 我分
不清, 混起來了. *I confused the two
brothers.* 我把這兩兄弟, 彼此混起來.
confusion [kən'fju:ʒən] *nc / u.*

congeal [kən'dʒi:l] *vt / i* change from liquid to solid (esp. because of cold)

凝固; (尤指因冷而)從液體凝結爲固體.

congenial [kən'dʒiːniəl] *adj* 1 having the same interests and ideas, and therefore friendly 因興趣、主張相同而友好的, 志趣相同的: *a congenial companion* 一個志趣相投的朋友. 2 pleasant and suitable for oneself 愜意的; 宜人的: *congenial surroundings.* 令人心曠神怡的環境. (*opp* 反義詞 **uncongenial**).

congestion [kən'dʒestʃən] *nu:* traffic congestion i.e. too many cars etc on the roads 交通堵塞. **congested** *adj: The town is very congested on market days.* 每逢墟日, 市鎮十分擁擠.

conglomeration [kəŋɡlɒmə'reiʃən] *nc* anything made up of things put together without order 雜亂無章、堆聚一起的混合物; 密集體, 團, 塊.

congratulate [kən'ɡrætjuleit] *vt* tell somebody that one is pleased because he has been successful or fortunate in some way 祝賀: *I congratulated my friend on the birth of his new son.* 我對我朋友新添一男孩表示祝賀. **congratulation** [kəŋɡrætju'leiʃən] *nc* (usu. *pl*). (通常用複數).

congregate ['kɒŋɡrigeit] *vt / i* come or bring together 聚集: *The people congregated in the town square.* 人們聚集在市鎮廣場. **congregation** [kɒŋɡri'geiʃən] *nc* people present (or usu. present) at a church service (共同在教堂中做禮拜的)會衆.

congress ['kɒŋɡres] *nc* 1 special meeting of experts on some particular topic 某項問題專門會議, 專業人員代表會議. 2 (**Congress**) (*USA* and some other republics) lower legislative chamber of government 美國國會; (美國及某些共和國)衆議院. **congressional** [kən'ɡreʃənl] *adj* **Congressman** member or the American

Congress 美國衆議員, 美國國會議員.

congruent ['kɒŋɡruənt] *adj* (geometry) having exactly the same shape (幾何)全等的, 疊合的: *congruent triangles* 全等三角形. **congruence** *nu*.

conical ['kɒnikl] *adj* see 見 **cone**.

conifer ['kɒnifə*] *nc* type of tree which bears cones (e.g. fir or pine) 針葉樹 (例如: 杉或松). **coniferous** [kə'nifərəs] *adj.*

conjecture [kən'dʒektʃə*] *vt / i* guess; come to an opinion about some fact without having enough information 推測, 推想: Also 亦作 *nc* guess made in this way 推測, 猜想.

conjunction [kən'dʒʌŋkʃən] 1 *nc* (grammar) word like 'and', 'but', 'or' which joins clauses, phrases, words etc together. (語法)連(接)詞 2 *nc / u* act of joining things together 連接; 聯合. **in conjunction (with)** together (with) (和)共同: *I did the work in conjunction with three other people.* 這項工作是我和其他三個人合做的.

conjure ['kʌndʒə*] *vi* do tricks which seem to be magic, as a form of entertainment 變魔術, 變戲法. **conjurer, conjuror** *nc* person who provides entertainment by conjuring 魔術師. **conjuring** *nu* tricks which seem to be magic, done as entertainment 魔術、戲法. **conjure up** 1 make a ghost or spirit appear 用魔法召喚(鬼、魂): *He conjured up the ghost of his grandfather.* 他施幻術召來他祖父的鬼魂. 2 see, cause to see, very clearly in the imagination or memory (使)想像出: *This book conjures up a vivid picture of London.* 這本書使人腦際浮起倫敦的畫面, 栩栩如生.

connect [kə'nekt] *vt / i* 1 (often with **together** or **up**) join; fasten (常與 **together** 或 **up** 連用)連接: *The radio* *will not work unless you connect these two wires together.* 除非你把這兩根線接上, 收音機就不會響. *Connect this wire with / to that one.* 把這根線和那一根接起來. (*opp* 反義詞 **disconnect**). **2** think of together 聯想, 由…想到: *I always connect little girls with dolls and dolls' prams* i.e. these are the things which I think of when I think of little girls. 小女孩子總是使我想起洋娃娃和娃娃玩的嬰兒車. **3** (with **with**) (with reference to buses, trains, aeroplanes etc.) arrive at a place in time for one to catch another bus, train, aeroplane etc. (與 with 連用) (指長途汽車, 火車, 飛機等)銜接: *This train connects with one at Birmingham* i.e. this train will get to Birmingham in time for you to catch the other train. 這列火車和另一列車在伯明翰相銜接. **connection, connexion** *nc* **1** join; fastening 連接: *I can't see any connection between these two wires.* 我找不到這兩根線之間有甚麼結頭. **2** relation 關係: *Scientists have shown that there is a connection between cigarette smoking and certain diseases.* 科學家已經指出抽烟和某些疾病間的關係. **3** train, bus, aeroplane etc which meets another in time for one to change from one to the other (火車, 長途汽車, 飛機等的) 聯運. **4** person whom one knows in business etc and also might be of help to one 社會關係. **in connection with** with reference to, on the subject of 關於, 有關: *He asked me many questions in connection with life in Britain.* 他問我許多關於英國的生活的問題.

connoisseur [ˌkɔniˈsɑ:*] *nc* person with a great knowledge of some subject connected with art 鑑賞家: *a connoisseur of painting* 油畫鑑賞家.

conquer [ˈkɔŋkə*] *vt / i* **1** defeat by fighting; take land after fighting 征服: *Julius Caesar conquered the Gauls.* 凱撒征服了高盧. *The Mongols conquered India.* 蒙古人征服印度. **2** end by force or determination 克服, 抑制: *I conquered my dislike for mathematics* i. e. I made myself like mathematics. 我克制了自己對數學的厭惡. **conqueror** *nc* person who conquers a country 征服者. **conquest** [ˈkɔŋkwest] *nc / u* something conquered; act of conquering 征服地, 掠取物; 征服.

conscience [ˈkɔnʃəns] *nc / u* feeling within oneself which tells one the difference between right and wrong. 良心, 是非之心. **have something on one's conscience** have a feeling of unhappiness because one knows that one has done something wrong 內疚.

conscientious [ˌkɔnʃiˈenʃəs] *adj* taking care to do one's work or duty as well as possible 認真的; 憑良心做的. **conscientiously** *adv* **conscientious objector** person who refuses to serve in an army or fight in a war because he feels it is wrong to do so (為了避免良心譴責而)拒服兵役者.

conscious [ˈkɔnʃəs] *adj* **1** not asleep and knowing clearly what is happening around one 神志清醒的: *Although he had been hit on the head he was still conscious.* 雖然頭部受到打擊, 他還是清醒的. **2** taking note of what is happening 意識到的: *I wasn't conscious of being rude* i. e. although I may have been impolite, I did not know that I was being so. 我沒意識到自己太不禮貌了. (*opp* 反義詞 **unconscious**). **consciousness** *nu* self-'conscious *adj* shy, embarrassed; taking note of everything that one does, and so unable to act easily and happily 忸怩的, 不自然的, 不自在的, 矜持的. **the sub'conscious** *nu* part of the mind in which there are feelings and ideas which we do not know about 下意識, 潛意識 **subconscious** *adj*.

conscript ['konskript] *nc* person made to serve in the armed forces by law 應徵入伍之士兵. **conscription** [kən'skripʃən] *nu*.

consecrate ['konsikreit] *vt* 1 carry out a ceremony which marks someone or something as special for religious purposes (舉行儀式) 使某人或某事物神聖不可侵犯: *consecrate a bishop / a new church* 使就主教聖職/舉行新教堂成立聖典. 2 keep something for a special purpose 奉獻.

consecutive [kən'sekjutiv] *adj* following one after another 連續的: *three consecutive days* (e. g. Monday, Tuesday, Wednesday) 連續三天.

consensus [kən'sensəs] *nc* general agreement or feeling of a number of people 一致意見.

consent [kən'sent] *vi* (often with **to**) say that one will allow something to happen; agree (常與 to 連用)同意; 答應: *He has consented to the plan.* 他同意這個計劃. *He consented to go.* 他同意去. Also 亦作 *nc*.

consequence ['konsikwəns] *nc* what follows or is caused by something 後果, 結果: *Do you know what the consequences of your action will be?* i. e. what will happen if you do this. 你知道你的行為會帶來甚麼後果嗎? **consequently** *adv*.

conservancy [kən'sə:vənsi] *nu / c* 1 conservation of natural resources 自然資源的保護. 2 commission controlling a port, river etc. (港口, 河流等的)管理委員會.

conservation [,konsə'veiʃən] *nu* preservation; the official protection of rivers, forests, and other natural resources 保存; (河流, 森林及其它自然資源的)保護.

conservative [kən'sə:vətiv] *adj* 1 liking things as they are now; not liking change 保守的. 2 careful; not willing to take chances (esp. in business or politics) 謹慎的; 穩健的(尤指在商業或政治方面). **Conservative** *nc* member of the Conservative Party 保守黨人. Also 亦作 *adj*.

conservatory [kən'sə:vətri] *nc* room or building (usu. attached to a house) with glass walls, in which plants are kept 溫室.

conserve [kən'sə:v] *vt* save from loss or damage; keep to be used when needed 保存: *We must conserve the natural resources of the country* i. e. we must not waste things such as soil rivers, forests, coal, oil etc. 我們必須保護國家自然資源. **conservation** [,konsə'veiʃən] *nu*.

consider [kən'sidə*] *vt / i* 1 think about 考慮: *I have considered your request.* 我已經考慮過你的請求. 2 have an opinion 認爲: *I consider that you are wrong.* 我認爲你錯了. 3 think about what will be best or most helpful for other people 爲(他人)着想, 體諒: *You should consider other people before you behave like that.* 你在那樣做以前應該爲別人想一想. **considerable** *adj* very large; very great 極大的, 相當大的: *a considerable amount of money* 數目相當大的一筆款. **considerably** *adv*: *He has improved considerably.* 他有很大進步. **considerate** [kən'sidərit] *adj* thinking of what will be best or most helpful for other people 體貼的, 體諒的; 設想周到的: *a con-*

siderate person / action / suggestion 會
體貼別人的人/爲人着想的行動/設想周
到的建議. (*opp* 反義詞 **inconsider-
ate**). **consideration** [kənsidə'reiʃən]
1 *nu* act of considering 考慮. **2** *nc*
something which one should think a-
bout. 應考慮的事: *That is an important consideration* i. e. that is an important point to think about. 那是很重
要的(應當考慮的)事. **3** *nu* thought
for other people 體諒: *That boy
shows no consideration for other people.* 那個男孩子從不爲別人着想. **considering** *prep* if one thinks of or re-
members 就…而論, 照…來看, 考慮到:
*That child walks very well considering
that he is only fourteen months old.*
考慮到那孩子才十四個月, 他走路的樣
子就挺不錯了. *Considering the distance, he arrived very quickly.* 照路途
距離來看, 他來得十分快. **under consideration** being officially thought
about 在考慮中: *The plan is under
consideration by the Minister of
Education.* 這計劃教育部長正在考慮.
take into con-sideration think about
when making plans or arrangements
考慮到, 把…考慮進去. *If you are
planning a holiday in Britain, you
should take the weather into consideration.* 你必須把氣候因素考慮進去.

consign [kən'sain] *vt* send goods by
some means of transport 託運. **con-
signment** *nc* amount of goods sent or
to be sent; act of consigning 託運物;
託運.

consist [kən'sist] *vi* (with **of**) be made
up of (與 **of** 連用) 由…組成, 由…構
成: *This soup consists of tomatoes,
meat and peas.* 這湯裏有番茄、肉和豌
豆. **consistence, consistency** *nu* **1**
act of always behaving or thinking in

the same way 一貫, 前後一致, 言行一
致. **2** degree to which a liquid is firm
or solid (usu. 通常作**consistency**) (液
體)濃度, 堅度. **consistent** *adj* always
acting or thinking in the same way,
not easily changing 一貫的, 前後一致
的. (*opp* 反義詞 **inconsistent**).

console [kən'soul] *vt* try to make somebody more happy when he has suffered some loss or misfortune 安慰.
consolation [kɔnsə'leiʃən] *nc / u*
conso'lation prize given to
somebody who has not won a contest
or competition 安慰獎.

consolidate [kən'sɔlideit] *vt / i* become
or make stronger or more firm 鞏固:
*The army consolidated the position
which they had captured* i. e. they
made it more difficult for the enemy
to attack the position. 軍隊鞏固他們
佔領的陣地.

consonant ['kɔnsənənt] *nc* **1** sound
which is not a vowel; sound in which
the breath is stopped in the mouth or
throat in some way 輔音. **2** letter or
symbol which indicates this type of
sound (The letters b, d etc are con-
sonants) 輔音字母.

consort ['kɔnsɔːt] *nc* husband or wire of
a queen or king 國王或女王的配偶.

consortium [kən'sɔːtiəm] *nc* group of
people in business who have come
together for some special purpose 財
團. *pl* 複數 **consortiums** or **consor-
tia** [kən'sɔːtiə].

conspicuous [kən'spikjuəs] *adj* easily
seen 顯而易見的, 顯著的. (*opp* 反義
詞 **inconspicuous**.

conspire [kən'spaiə*] *vt* **1** make plans
with others (esp. to do something
wrong) 合謀 (尤指搞陰謀). **2** act
together to bring out some result 共
同促成 **conspiracy** [kən'spirəsi] *nc*

constable ['kʌnstəbl] *nc* policeman of the lowest rank 警察. **chief constable** head of a police force 警察局長.

constant ['kɔnstnt] *adj* not changing; not stopping 不變的; 不停的: *constant noise* 持續的噪音; *constant friend* 忠貞不渝的朋友. **constantly** *adv* **constancy** *nu.*

constellation [kɔnstə'leiʃən] *nc* group of stars having a name 星座; 星羣.

consternation [kɔnstə'neiʃən] *nu* great surprise and alarm or unhappiness 大吃一驚, 驚恐.

constipation [kɔnsti'peiʃən] *nu* difficulty in passing waste matter out of the body 便秘. **constipated** ['kɔnstipeitəd] *adj* having this difficulty 便秘的.

constituency [kən'stitjuənsi] *nc* area which is represented by a member of the House of Commons 下議院議員選區.

constituent¹ [kən'stitjuənt] *nc* 1 forming part of a whole thing 組成成份: *Oxygen and nitrogen are two important constituents of the air.* 氧氣和氮氣是空氣的兩個重要組成成份. 2 person having the right to vote in an election in a particular area 選民.

constituent² [kən'stitjuənt] *adj* 1 forming part of a whole thing 組成的. 2 having the power to make laws 有權制憲的: *a constituent assembly* 立憲會議.

constitute ['kɔnstitju:t] *vt* 1 be the same as 等於, 實質上是: *The behaviour of that country constitutes an act of aggression against her neighbours.* 該國所作所爲是對鄰邦的侵略行動. 2 make up; be the parts of 組成, 構成: *England, Wales, Scotland, Northern*

Ireland and some smaller islands constitute the United Kingdom. 英格蘭, 威爾士, 蘇格蘭, 北愛爾蘭和一些較小島嶼組成聯合王國.

constitution [kɔnsti'tju:ʃən] *nc* 1 laws and systems of government of a country, society etc; document containing these 憲法; 法規; 章程. 2 general health of somebody 體質, 健康狀況: *He has a very strong constitution.* 他體質強壯. **constitutional** *adj (opp* **unconstitutional** in sense 1) (義1的反義詞是 unconstitutional).

constrain [kən'strein] *vt* make somebody do something by force 強迫; 強制: *I constrained him to come.* (*formal*) 我迫使他來. (正式). **constraint** *nc / u.*

constrict [kən'strikt] *vt* fasten tightly so as to make smaller or prevent free movement 收縮; 束縛. *He felt constricted by the rules.* 他感到受規則的束縛. **constriction** *nc / u.*

construct [kən'strʌkt] *vt* make by building or putting parts together. 建築; 構造, 構成. **construction** 1 *nu* act of building 建築. 2 *nc* something built 建築物. 3 *nc* (grammar esp. with reference to Greek and Latin grammar) way of using words in a sentence (語法, 尤指希臘文、拉丁文文法) 句法結構. **constructive** *adj* (with reference to ideas, words, suggestions etc.) helpful (指主張、話語、建議等) 有益的. **under construction** being built 在建造中.

construe [kən'stru:] *vt* understand or explain words 理解或解釋(言詞).

consul ['kɔnsl] *nc* representative of a foreign government who lives in a town or city and one of whose duties is to help his fellow countrymen living or visiting there 領事. **consulate** ['kɔnsjulit] *nc* place where a consul works 領事館.

consult [kən'sʌlt] *vt* **1** ask somebody's advice about something 請教, 求教; *He consulted his lawyer.* 他請教自己的律師. **2** look into a book or other publication for a piece of information. 查閱／參考(書籍): *He consulted the dictionary.* 他查閱詞典. **consultation** [kɔnsəl'teiʃən] *nc/u* **consultant** *nc* **1** person to whom one goes for advice 顧問. **2** doctor with special knowledge and qualifications 高級醫生, 專家.

consume [kən'sju:m] *vt / i* use up; use completely (e.g. by eating, drinking, burning etc.) 徹底消耗, 消費. **consumer** *nc* person who buys and uses goods; person who is not a manufacturer of goods 消費者. Also 亦作 *adj*: consumer goods 消費品, 生活資料. **consumption** [kən'sʌmpʃən] *nu* act of using up food, drink, fuel etc. 消費.

contact ['kɔntækt] **1** *nu* act or state of touching something or being near something 接觸 **2** *nc/u* communication between people (by meeting, letter, speech etc.) 聯繫, 聯絡: *The prisoner was not allowed to have any contact with his family.* 不許這犯人和家屬有任何聯繫. **3** *nc* person whom one can meet for some purpose 熟人, 聯繫人: *The journalist has a contact in Paris.* 這個記者在巴黎有一個熟人. Also 亦作 *vt* arrange to meet somebody, write or telephone somebody etc. 接觸, 聯絡. **'contact 'lens** glass or plastic lens worn on the eyeball, under the eyelid, used instead of glasses (直接貼在眼球上的)隱形眼鏡.

contagious [kən'teidʒəs] *adj* **1** (esp. with reference to a disease) able to be spread by touch (尤指疾病)接觸傳染的. **2** (with reference to a person) spreading disease by touch (指人)有(接觸)傳染病的, 通過接觸擴散傳染病的.

contain [kən'tein] *vt* **1** have inside 裝有: *This box contains biscuits.* 這盒子裝有餅乾. **2** (with reference to feelings or to the enemy) hold back (指內心情感或對敵人)抑制, 遏制: *He contained his anger.* 他壓住怒火. *Our troops could not contain the enemy attack.* 我們部隊擋不住敵人的進攻. **container** *nc* **1** anything that can contain something (e.g. box, carton etc.) 容器 **2** very large sealed metal box used in shipping freight 集裝箱, 貨櫃. **contain oneself** keep one's feelings under control 自制.

contaminate [kən'tæmineit] *vt* make dirty, diseased or radioactive, and so unfit for use 污染. **contamination** [kəntæmi'neiʃən] *nu*.

contemplate ['kɔntəmpleit] *vt / i* think very deeply about something (esp. some religious subject) 沉思, 冥想(尤指宗教問題). **2** gaze at something 注視, 凝視. **3** think of as something which might happen 期望, 反覆打算: *I am contemplating buying some new furniture.* 我正打算買一些新傢具. **contemplation** [kɔntəm'pleiʃən] *nu*.

contemporary [kən'tempərəri] *adj* **1** living or existing at the same time as something or someone else 同時代的: *Shakespeare was contemporary with Queen Elizabeth I.* 莎士比亞和女王伊麗莎白一世是同時代人. **2** living or existing today and having modern ideas, a modern appearance etc. 當代的. Also 亦作 *nc* person living at the same time as someone else 同時代的人.

contempt [kən'tempt] *nu* feeling that something / somebody is very low in

value, very bad, very foolish etc. 蔑
視; 輕視: *We feel contempt for anyone
who steals from a child.* 我們蔑視偷小
孩子東西的人. **contemptible** *adj* deserving contempt 可鄙的: *a contemptible liar* 可鄙的撒謊的人. **contemptuous** [kən'temptjuəs] *adj* feeling contempt. 輕蔑的: *He was contemptuous
of the thief.* 他蔑視這個小偷.

contend [kən'tend] *vi* **1** (with **with**)
fight, struggle or argue with, in order
to get what one wants (與 with 連用)
競爭, 鬥爭, 爭論: *He had to contend
with many difficulties when he was a
young man.* 他年青的時候, 得和種種
困難作鬥爭. **2** (with **that**) argue; state
as a fact which one is quite sure of
while arguing with somebody. (與
that 連用)認爲, 堅決主張. **contender**
nc person fighting, struggling etc.
(esp. a boxer trying to win a championship title) 競爭者(尤指奪標中的
拳擊手). see 見 **contention.**

content[1] [kən'tent] *adj* pleased or happy with what one has; satisfied 滿足
的, 滿意的: *The cat was very content
after drinking the milk.* 貓兒在喝了牛
奶後, 十分滿足. *He was quite content
to do no work all day.* 他很願意整天
不做工作. Also 亦作 *vt* make pleased
or satisfied in this way 使滿足. **contented** *adj. (opp* 反義詞 **discontented***).*

content[2] ['kɔntent] *nc* **1** (usu. *pl*) what
is inside something (通常用複數) 内
容, 容納的東西. *the contents of the
box* 箱子裏的東西. *the contents of the
book* 書的內容. **2** the main ideas or
facts, as distinct from the way in
which the ideas or facts are expressed 要旨.

contention [kən'ten∫ən] **1** *nu* argument;
fight etc. 競爭, 爭論. **2** *nc* main idea

or point in an argument (爭論中的)論
點: *My contention was that America
was once a British colony, but James
said that this was not true.* 我的論點是
美國曾經是英國的殖民地, 但詹姆士說
這不符合事實. see 見 contend.

contest ['kɔntest] *nc* struggle, fight or
competition to gain some advantage.
競爭, 比賽. Also 亦作 [kən'test] *vt / i*
fight againt, fight to win something 競
爭, 比賽. **contestant** [kən'testənt] *nc*
person who takes part in a contest 參
加比賽者, 選手.

context ['kɔntekst] *nc* the words around
a particular word or phrase, helping
to give it meaning (文章的)上下文.

continent ['kɔntinənt] *nc* large land
mass (e. g. Europe, Asia, Africa) 大陸.
the Continent Europe not including
Britain or Ireland 歐洲大陸 (不包括英
國與愛爾蘭). **Continental** [kɔn-
ti'nentl] *adj* Also 亦作 *nc* person from
the continent of Europe 歐洲大陸人.

contingency [kən'tindʒənsi] *nc* the possibility that something will happen 可
能性. **contingent** *adj.*

contingent [kən'tindʒənt] *adj* see 見
contingency. Also 亦作 *nc* number of
soldiers sent to a particular place 特
遣隊.

continue [kən'tinju:] *vt / i* go on; go
further (without stopping or after
stopping) 繼續(可以是不中斷, 也可以
是中斷後再繼續): *John continued to
read / reading when I came into the
room* i. e. he did not stop reading. 我
進房時約翰仍舊在看書. 即: 他不曾中
斷過. *He continued his breakfast.* 他
繼續進早餐. *The cold weather continued for three weeks.* 寒冷天氣持續
了三個星期. *He stopped to buy some
bread and then continued his journey.*
他停下來買一些麵包, 然後繼續他的旅

程. *The president continued in office for another there years.* 院長又繼續擔任職務三年. **continuation** [kəntinju'eiʃən] *nc / u* **continual** *adj* **1** going on with short stops or pauses 頻繁的. **2** going on without stopping 不停的: *a continual noise* 不停的喧嚣. **continually** *adv* see Note following **continuous** 見 continuous 後 的 說明. **continuity** [kɔnti'njuiti] *nu* **1** condition of being continuous 連續(性). **2** condition of having no breaks or interruptions; the way in which one thing leads to something else (esp. in a story, book, film etc.) 不中斷; 連接, 銜接(尤指故事、書籍、電影等). *(opp* 反義詞 **discontinuity**). **continuous** *adj* going on without stopping until finished 連續不斷的: *five days of continuous rain* 五天不間斷的下雨. *(opp* 反義詞 **discontinuous**). **continuously** *adv*. **Note** 說明: continual and continuous very often have almost the same meaning. If however, one wishes to express the idea that something goes on for a long time, but with stops and starts, continual is the word to use; if one wishes to express the idea that something goes on for some time without stopping, continuous should be used. continual 和 continuous 常常有幾乎相同的意思, 但如要表示某事延續很長時間, 而其中時有間斷, 停而復始, 宜用 continual; 如要表示某事延續好一段時間, 毫無間斷, 則應用 continuous.

contort [kən'tɔ:t] *vt* bend something so that it loses its proper shape 扭曲. **contortion** *nc / u* **contortionist** *nc* person who contorts his body in order to entertain people 柔軟雜技演員.

contour ['kɔntuə*] *nc* line on a map along which all places have the same height above sea level 等高線. (Also 亦作 **contour line**).

contraband ['kɔntrəbænd] *nu* goods which have been brought into a country against the law (e. g. gems, gold, things on which tax must be paid) 違禁品, 走私品(例如: 珠寶、金、以及須納稅始能入境的物品).

contraception [kɔntrə'sepʃən] *nu* methods used to prevent the beginning of the growth of a baby inside a woman, until the woman wishes to have a child 避孕法. **contraceptive** *adj* Also 亦作 *nc* any device used for this purpose 避孕藥物; 避孕用具.

contract[1] ['kɔntrækt] *nc* formal agreement (esp. in business) 合同, 契約(尤用於商業).

contract[2] [kən'trækt] **1** *vt / i* make an agreement in business to do certain work or supply certain goods 立(約), 訂(合同): *contract to supply food to the school* 承包對學校供應食品. *contract an agreement* 立約, 訂合同. **2** *vt / i* become or make smaller 收縮, 縮寫. **contractor** [kən'træktə*] *nc* person who does work (esp. building houses) by making contracts 承包商 (尤指建築承包者).

contradict [kɔntrə'dikt] *vt / i* say or mean the opposite of 駁斥, 反駁, 否認, 相抵觸的話: *He contradicted me* i. e. he said that I was not telling the truth. 他反駁我. 即: 他說我沒講真話. *This book contradicts that one* i. e. this book says the opposite of what that one says. 這本書和那本書所說的恰相反. **contradiction** *nc / u*.

contralto [kən'træltou] **1** *nu* the lowest female voice 女低音. **2** *nc* woman who sings with this voice 女低音歌手. *pl* 複數 **contraltos**. Also 亦作

adj.

contraption [kən'træpʃən] *nc* machine or device with a strange or unusual appearance *(informal)* 形狀奇特的機械裝置(非正式).

contrary¹ ['kɒntrəri] *adj* **1** opposite to 相反的: *His opinion is contrary to mine.* 他的意見和我的相反. **2** (with reference to winds) unfavourable (指風) 逆向的. **on the contrary** the opposite is true 正相反地: *You think that he is a kind man, but on the contrary he is very unkind.* 你以爲他很和藹可親, 恰恰相反, 他很不近人情. **to the contrary** with the opposite meaning 意思相反的(地): *I shall meet him on Tuesday unless I hear anything to the contrary.* 除非有相反情況發生, 否則, 我會在星期二見他.

contrary² [kən'treəri] *adj* in the habit of doing or saying the opposite of other people 喜歡故意作對的.

contrast ['kɒntrɑːst] *nc* difference between one thing and another (對比之下顯出的)差別; 對照, 比較. Also 亦作 [kən'trɑːst] *vt / i* show or make a difference between one thing and another 形成對比; 顯出差別; 比較: *Black and white are contrasting colours.* 黑與白是對比色. *My hat contrasts with my coat.* 我的帽子和外衣形成對比. *He contrasted Britain and America.* 他就英美兩國作了比較.

contribute [kən'tribjuːt] *vt / i* **1** give as one's share 捐獻: *I contributed £5 to the party funds.* 我捐五鎊作爲開晚會的費用. **2** write for a newspaper or magazine 投稿: *He contributed an article to the Daily Post.* 他向《每日郵報》投稿. **3** help to cause; be one of the causes of 促成; 成爲原因之一:

The driver's carelessness contributed to the accident. 駕駛員的疏忽是事故原因之一. **contribution** [kɒntri'bjuːʃən] *nc / u* **contributor** *nc.*

contrite ['kɒntrait] *adj* very unhappy because one has done wrong, and wishing to do right in future 痛悔的, 悔恨的, 決心痛改前非的.

contrive [kən'traiv] *vt / i* cleverly manage to do something 巧妙地設法做; 發明; 設計: *He contrived to get an extra week's holiday.* 他巧妙地多爭取了一週的假期. **contrivance** *nc* machine or device which somebody has contrived 機械, 發明(物).

control [kən'troul] *vt* guide; rule; have under one's authority 指揮, 控制, 支配, 約束: *She cannot control her two brothers* i. e. they will not do what she tells them to. 她管不住兩個弟弟. *It was difficult to control the car on the mountain roads.* 山路上車子不容易控制. *past* 過去式和過去分詞 **controlled.** Also 亦作 *nu: She has no control over her two brothers.* 她管不住兩個弟弟. *He lost control of the car.* 他對車子失去操縱. **controller** *nc* **controls** *npl* the devices by which a machine is operated (esp. those used to fly an aeroplane) (尤指飛機) 操縱器: *The pilot was seated at the controls.* 駕駛員正坐在操縱器前面. **out of control** not under one's authority or guidance 失去控制: *The aeroplane got out of control and fell into the sea.* 飛機失去控制, 掉在海裏. **under (one's) control** under one's authority or guidance 被控制住: *The people began to break the windows, but the police soon had the situation under control.* 人們開始碰砸窗子, 不過警察立刻把局勢控制住. *The school library is under my control.* 學校圖

館在我管轄之下.

controversy [ˈkɔntrəvəːsi] *nc / u* argument about some matter of opinion (esp. one involving questions of right and wrong) (尤指是非曲直的)爭論. **controversial** [kɔntrəˈvəːʃl] *adj* causing controversies 引起爭論的.

convalescence [kɔnvəˈlesns] *nu* process of recovering health after a serious illness; period during which one becomes strong again after an illness 大病後逐漸痊愈; 病後康復期. **convalesce** [kɔnvəˈles] *vi* be regaining health and strength 康復, 痊愈. **convalescent** [kɔnvəˈlesnt] *nc* person who convalesces 康復期的病人. Also 亦作 *adj*.

convection [kənˈvekʃən] *nu* transmitting; the carrying of heat by currents of heated liquid or gas 傳送; 對流.

convenient [kənˈviːniənt] *adj* not causing difficulty 方便的: *I should like to talk to you, if it is convenient* i. e. if this will not cause you any difficulty. 如果你方便, 我想跟你談一些事. *This kitchen is a very convenient size for working in.* 這個廚房大小適中, 方便幹活. (*opp* 反義詞 **inconvenient**). **convenience 1** *nu* quality of being convenient 便利. **2** *nc something which is helpful or useful* (often in **modern conveniences** i. e. devices in a house such as a water supply, heating, refrigeration etc.) 方便的設施 (常見於 modern conveniences 即: 像供水、供熱、冷藏等現代化設備). **public convenience** (*Brit*) public lavatory (英) 公共廁所. **at one's (own) convenience** in a way or at a time which is convenient to one 以方便的方式; 在方便的時刻: *You may do this work at your own convenience.* 你可以在方便時做這項工作.

convent [ˈkɔnvənt] *nc* **1** group of nuns or women living together in a religious organization 女修道院的修女. **2** building where they live 女修道院.

convention [kənˈvenʃən] **1** *nc* large meeting called for some special purpose 爲特定目的而召開的大型會議. **2** *nc / u* any act which is done by nearly everybody and is accepted as the right thing to do 習俗: *In Britain it is not the convention to shake hands every time one meets a person.* 按照英國習俗, 不必每次見面都握手. **conventional** *adj* **1** happening by convention 傳統的, 習慣的. **2** not new or interesting 普通平凡的. **3** (of a person) acting according to conventions, unenterprising 保守的. (*opp* 反義詞 **unconventional**).

converge [kənˈvəːdʒ] *vi* move together (and meet) 會聚, 集中於一點: *These two lines converge.* 這兩條線集中在一點. *The crowd converged on the palace* i. e. everybody moved towards the palace. 人羣向宮殿集中.

conversant [kənˈvəːsnt] *adj* (with **with**) having some konwledge of (與 with 連用) 熟悉的; 精通的: *I am not conversant with the history of India.* (formal) 我不熟悉印度歷史. (正式).

conversation [kɔnvəˈseiʃən] *nc / u* friendly talk 談話; 聊天: *I had an interesting conversation with the old man.* 我跟這個老人有一次很有趣味的談話. *Conversation is one of the pleasures of life.* 聊天是人生樂趣之一. **conversational** *adj*.

converse [ˈkɔnvəːs] *nc* opposite 反面. *'Yes' is the converse of 'no'.* '是' 是 '否' 的反面. **conversely** *adv*.

convert [kənˈvəːt] *vt* **1** change from one thing into another 轉變: *Water is converted into steam if it is boiled.* 水沸

騰後變成蒸汽. **2** cause a person to change his religious beliefs 使改變信仰: *Many Africans were converted to Christianity.* 許多非洲人改信了基督教. Also 亦作 ['kɔnvə:t] *nc* person who has changed his religious belief 改變信仰者: *He is a Catholic convert.* 他改而信天主教. **conversion** *nc / u* **convertible** *nc* car with a top which can be folded back 有活動摺篷的汽車, 敞篷車.

convex ['kɔn'veks] *adj* (esp. with reference to lenses) curving outwards. having the shape of the outside of a circle or sphere (尤指透鏡) 凸狀的. see 見 **concave.**

convey [kən'vei] *vt* **1** (esp. of vehicles) carry something from one place to another (尤指車輛) 運載. **2** give information to somebody 傳達, 表達: *I conveyed the message to John.* 我把訊息傳遞給約翰. *It is difficult to convey what the Sahara desert is like to somebody who hasn't been there.* 對於沒有去過撒哈拉沙漠的人, 很難對他形容那沙漠是怎麼一個樣子. **conveyor** *nc* endless belt for moving things from one person to another in a factory 傳送帶. (Also 亦作 **conveyor belt.**)

convict [kən'vikt] *vt* (with reference to a judge, jury, lawyer etc.) say or prove that somebody is guilty of a crime (指法官、陪審團、律師等) 宣判⋯有罪; 裁決⋯有罪. 證明⋯有罪: *The judge convicted him of robbery.* 法官判決他犯搶劫罪. Also 亦作 ['kɔnvikt] *nc* person in prison after being found guilty of a crime 犯人. **conviction** *nc / u* **1** act of convicting 定罪; 裁決有罪; 證明有罪; **2** strong belief 深信, 堅信: *It's my conviction that you did not try hard enough.* 我深信你用功得不夠.

He said it with conviction. i. e. he sounded completely certain of it. 他深信不疑地說了這句話.

convince [kən'vins] *vt* make somebody believe that something is true, by using arguments or proofs 說服, 使信服: *He convinced me that he was right.* 他說服了我他是對的. *He convinced me of the difficulty of the work.* 他使我相信這項工作的困難性. **convincing** *adj* causing one to believe 有說服力的; 令人信服的: *a convincing argument* 有說服力的論點. (opp 反義詞 **unconvincing.**)

convivial [kən'viviəl] *adj* happy or causing happiness (usu. because of food and drink); sociable (通常指由於飲宴而) 感到歡樂或引起歡樂的; 愛交際的: *a convivial man / party.* 愛交際的人 / 興高采烈的宴會.

convoy ['kɔnvɔi] *nc* **1** in wartime, group of ships travelling together under protection (戰爭時期) 受到護航的船隊. **2** group of vehicles travelling together 車隊.

convulse [kən'vʌls] *vt* (usu. *passive*) shake with great force (通常用被動語態) 使劇烈搖動: *He was convulsed with laughter.* 他笑得前仰後合. **convulsion** *nc* (usu. *pl*) strong and uncontrollable movement of the body, caused by a disease or injury (通常用複數) 痙攣, 抽搐.

coo [ku:] *nc* soft noise (e. g. made by a pigeon or by a baby) (鴿子或嬰兒等發出的) 柔和的聲音. Also 亦作 *vi* make this noise 發出咕咕的聲音; 喁喁細語.

cook [kuk] **1** *vt / i* prepare food by using heat 燒(菜): *He cooked the dinner.* 他做飯(菜). **2** *vi* be prepared 在煮着: *The food is cooking.* 正在燒菜. Also 亦作 *nc* person who cooks (esp. as a servant or in a hotel or restaurant) (尤指旅館、餐館中的)廚師. **cooker** *nc* stove for cooking (usu. gas or electric) 爐(通常用煤氣或電加熱). '**cookery book,** '**cookbook** book which tells one how to prepare different types of food 烹飪書, 菜譜.

cookie, cooky ['kuki] *nc* (*US*) small, flat sweet cake. (美) 小甜餅乾. (*Brit* 英 **biscuit**).

cool¹ [ku:l] *adj* **1** between warm and cold 凉的, 凉快的: *The weather is rather cool today.* 今天天氣凉了一些. *Let your tea get cool before you drink it.* 你等茶凉了以後再喝. **2** not worried or excited by danger or difficulty. 冷靜的: *He remained cool when the enemy attacked.* 敵人進攻時候, 他仍然很沉着. **3** calm and unfriendly 冷淡的: *He gave me a very cool greeting.* 他十分冷淡地對我問候. **coolness** *nu.*

cool² [ku:l] *vt / i* (often with **down** or **off**) become or make cool. (常與 **down** 或**off** 連用) (使)變凉, (使)冷卻: *The tea has cooled down a little.* 茶已經凉一些了.

coop [ku:p] *nc* small cage or house for keeping chickens in 鷄籠. **coop up** (*often passive*) keep in a small space. (常用於被動態)限制在小範圍內: *The family were cooped up in two small rooms.* 這一家住在鷄籠子似的兩個小房間裏.

co-op ['kouɔp] *nc* cooperative store i. e. type of shop (*informal*) 合作社 (非正式).

cooperate [kou'ɔpəreit] *vi* work together for some purpose 合作: *All the people in the village cooperated to bring in the harvest.* 全村的人通力合作進行收割. **cooperation** [kouɔpə-'rei ʃən] *nu* **cooperative** [kou'ɔpə-rətiv] *adj* (*opp* 反義詞 **uncoopera-**

tive). **cooperative** *nc* business, shop, farm etc, which is owned by all the people who work in it 合作社.

coordinate [kou'ɔ:dineit] *vt* arrange in the right way or proper order; move together for some purpose 協調: *A baby cannot easily coordinate his movements* i. e. he cannot always move his arms and legs in the right way so as to get what he wants. 嬰孩不能協調自己的行動. **coordination** [kouɔ:di'nei ʃən] *nu.*

cop [kɔp] *nc* policeman (*informal*) 警察 (非正式).

cope [koup] *vi* (with **with** manage; control; organize (與 **with** 連用)應付; 克服. *She could not cope with all the work.* 她不能應付這一切工作. *He had a lot of work, but he was able to cope.* 他工作很多, 但他應付得開.

co-pilot ['kou'pailət] *nc* person who shares the work of the pilot of an aeroplane 飛機副駕駛員.

copper ['kɔpə*] **1** *nu* strong brown metal (Cu) 銅. **2** *nc* coin made of copper or bronze 銅幣. **3** *nc* (*Brit*) policeman (*informal*) (英) 警察(非正式).

copy¹ ['kɔpi] *vt / i* do or make something in the same way as something else 模倣, 抄襲: *The young boy copied his father's way of walking* i. e. he walked like his father. 小男孩子學他父親走路的樣子. **copy something out** write down a copy of 抄寫.

copy² ['kɔpi] *nc* **1** something made to look like something else 臨摹本, 副本: *This painting is a copy of one in the museum.* 這張畫是博物館一張油畫的臨摹本. **2** one book, newspaper or magazine (書本、雜誌的) 一本, (報紙的) 一份: *May I borrow your copy of 'David Copperfield'?* 我可以借你的那一本《大衛·科波菲爾》嗎? **copyright**

the right of an author, musician, film maker etc, to his own work, so that other people are forbidden by law to copy the work in any way without permission 版權.

copywriter ['kɔpiˌraitə] *nc* writer of copy, esp. for advertisements 撰稿員 (尤指寫廣告者).

coral ['kɔrəl] *nc / u* hard substance made by small tropical sea animals 珊瑚.

cord [kɔːd] *nc / u* type of thick string used for tying parcels etc. 索.

cordial¹ ['kɔːdiəl] *adj* very friendly 親切的; 熱誠的; 友善的; *a cordial greeting* 熱烈的歡迎.

cordial² ['kɔːdiəl] *nc / u* sweet drink made from concentrated fruit juice 濃縮果汁製成的甜酒.

cordon ['kɔːdn] *nc* group of people making a line or a circle to guard a person / thing 警戒線; 警戒圈. **cordon something off** put a cordon around or across 佈設警戒線, 圍住; *The police cordoned off the house.* 警察在房子週圍設了一道警戒線.

corduroy ['kɔːdərɔi] *nc* type of thick cotton cloth, with raised lines or ridges on it 燈芯絨.

core [kɔː*] *nc* 1 central part of some fruits (e. g. apples or pears) 水果(例如: 蘋果、梨)的芯. 2 central part of an idea, argument, etc. (主張論點等的)核心或主旨.

cork [kɔːk] 1 *nu* light substance which is the bark of the cork oak 軟木. 2 *nc* piece (usu. of this substance) used to put in the top of a bottle (通常爲軟木的)瓶塞. **'corkscrew** implement for pulling the cork out of a bottle (開瓶塞的)螺旋鑽子.

corn¹ [kɔːn] *nu* name given to several types of grain (in England **wheat** or any grain; in USA **maize**; in Scotland

oats) 穀物(在英國指小麥或任何穀物; 美國指玉米; 蘇格蘭指燕麥). **corncob** thick part of the maize plant, on which the seeds grow 玉米棒子的芯. **cornflour** flour made from maize 玉米. (*US* 美 **cornstarch**). **'cornflower** small blue flower 矢車菊.

corn² [kɔːn] *nc* type of painful swelling and hard growth (usu. on the foot) 雞眼(通常長在腳上).

cornea ['kɔːniə] *nc* transparent outer coat of the eyeball (眼球的)角膜.

corned [kɔːnd] *adj* in **corned 'beef** i. e. beef preserved in salt 出產於 corned beef: '醃牛肉'.

corner¹ ['kɔːnə*] *nc* 1 place where two lines or two sides meet 角, 角落: *A square has four corners.* 一個正方形有四個角. *He was standing on the corner of the street.* 他正站在街角轉彎的地方. 2 any distant, hidden or secret place. 遙遠、偏僻、隱藏的地方: *He has been in every corner of the world.* 天涯海角, 他隨便甚麼地方都去過. *I've lost my pen; I must have put it in some odd corner somewhere.* 我丟掉自來水筆; 肯定擱在甚麼意想不到的地方了. **'cornerstone** anything important on which other things depend. 基石: *Freedom of speech is the cornerstone of democracy.* 言論自由是民主政治的基礎.

corner² ['kɔːnə*] 1 *vi* drive a car round a corner 駕車轉彎: *He was cornering at 60 miles an hour.* 他以每小時六十英里的速度把車子拐彎. 2 *vt* drive or chase somebody into a corner or into a position from which he cannot escape 把…逼得走投無路: *The police finally cornered the thief.* 警察終於把小偷逼到無法逃脫的地方.

cornet ['kɔːnit] *nc* 1 brass musical instrument like a trumpet 喇叭. 2 piece of light biscuit for holding ice cream (盛冰淇淋用的)錐形脆薄餅.

corny ['kɔːni] *adj* old-fashioned. rather silly 陳舊的, 陳詞濫調的: *his corny jokes (informal)* 他那陳舊而無聊的笑話(非正式).

coronary ['kɔrənəri] *adj* referring to the arteries which supply blood to the heart (usu. in **coronary thrombosis** a disease in which one of these arteries is blocked by a clot of blood) 冠狀動脈的(通常用於 coronary thrombosis '冠狀動脈血栓形成'). Also 亦作 *nc: suffer a coronary* 冠狀動脈有毛病.

coronation [kɔrə'neiʃən] *nc* ceremony in which a king or queen is crowned 加冕典禮.

coroner ['kɔrənə*] *nc* official in charge of a court of law which enquiries into the cause of accidental and suspicious deaths 驗屍官.

corporal¹ ['kɔːprəl] *nc* rank in the army above a private and below a sergeant 下士.

corporal² ['kɔːprəl] *adj* with reference to the body 肉體的 **corporal punishment** punishment by beating 肉刑, 體罰.

corporation [kɔːpə'reiʃən] *nc* **1** group of people who govern a town or city (市鎮的)自治機關. **2** business firm which is treated by the law as though it were a single person 公司; 法人.

corps [kɔː*] *nc* **1** section of the army which does some special work (e. g. Signal Corps, Medical Corps) 特種兵團, 特種部隊(例如: 通訊部隊, 醫療隊). **2** any organized group of people doing a special job 從事特定工作的有組織的一羣人. *pl* 複數 **corps**.

corpse [kɔːps] *nc* dead body (usu. of a human being) (尤指人的)屍體.

corpus ['kɔːpəs] *nc* **1** body, esp. a dead one 身體(尤指屍體). **2** collection of writings or laws, esp. the whole collection of a particular period etc. (文獻, 法典的)全集. *the corpus of civil law* 民法全集. **3** substance of anything (任何事物的)主體. *pl* 複數 **corpora** ['kɔːpərə].

corpuscle ['kɔːpʌsl] *nc* one of the red or white cells which float in the blood to carry oxygen and destroy germs. (紅或白)血球.

correct¹ [kə'rekt] *adj* **1** true; right; without faults or mistakes 正確的: *What is the correct answer to question 7?* 第七題的正確答案是甚麼? **2** following what is thought to be the right thing to do 符合正當或正當做法的; 對的: *It is not considered correct for a man to wear a hat in church.* 男人在做禮拜時戴着帽子, 一般認為是不對的. *(opp* 反義詞 **incorrect)**. *correctly adv.*

correct² [kə'rekt] *vt* **1** change to what is correct 矯正, 改: *correct an essay* 改文章. **2** point out mistakes in 糾正: *correct someone's behaviour* 糾正某人的行爲. **3** punish in order to stop a child from behaving badly 責備, 懲罰: *The mother corrected the disobedient child.* 母親懲罰了不聽話的孩子. **4** repair mend; cure 改正, 修理: *I have corrected the fault in the radio.* 我已經把無線電的毛病修好了. *Note* 說明: in sense **4** the object of *correct* is generally a word like 'fault', 'trouble'. We do not usu. say *He corrected the radio.* we say *He repaired the radio.* 作義4 解的 correct, 其賓語一般是像 'fault', 'trouble' 這樣的字眼. 通常我們不講 He corrected the radio. 我們說 He repaired the radio. **correction 1** *nu* act of making correct and removing mistakes 校正, 改正, 勘誤. **2** *nc* what is written or said to replace a mistake 所修改的東西,修改處: *Look carefully at corrections which I have written down.* 注意看我修改過的地方.

correlate [ˈkɔrileit] *vt / i* (usu. in mathematics) be or make related in some way, show the relationship between (通常用於數學) (使) 相關聯; 顯示出相關關係. **correlation** [kɔriˈleiʃən] *nc / u*.

correspond [ˌkɔrisˈpɔnd] *vt* **1** (with **with**) exchange letters with (與 with 連用) 通信: *John and I have corresponded for many years.* 約翰和我通信了好幾年. *I have been corresponding with John.* 我一直和約翰通信. **2** (with **to** or **with**) be like; be similar to or equal to. (與 to 或 with 連用) 相似,對應; 符合: *Your story does not correspond with the facts* i. e. you are not telling the truth. 你所說的不符合事實. **correspondence** *nu* **corresponding** *adj* **correspondent** *nc* person who sends reports of news to a newspaper or radio station 通訊員,記者. **corres-'pondence course** series of lessons sent by post to a student, who writes essays or answers questions and sends them back to be corrected 函授課程.

corridor [ˈkɔridɔː] *nc* long passage in a building, with rooms and rooms on one side or both sides 走廊.

corroborate [kəˈrɔbəreit] *vt* give extra proof that a statement is true 證實: *I was able to corroborate John's story.* 我能證實約翰所說的話. **corroboration** [kərɔbəˈreiʃən] *nu*.

corrode [kəˈroud] *vt / i* wear away or damage by chemical change 腐蝕: *The metal was corroded by acid.* 金屬被酸腐蝕了. *Iron corrodes if it is not*

protected from the damp air. 鐵如不加保護,在潮濕空氣中會銹損. **corrosion** [kəˈrouʒən] *nu*.

corrugate [ˈkɔrəgeit] *vt / i* bend into a series of folds 弄皺,起波紋. **corru-gated iron / paper** iron sheets / paper, bent into a series of folds 波紋鐵 /波紋紙.

corrupt [kəˈrʌpt] *adj* **1** bad, wicked; evil 腐敗的. **2** taking bribes 貪污的. **3** rotten; decaying 腐爛的, Also 亦作 *vt* make corrupt 腐敗,收買. **corruption** *nc / u.*

corset [ˈkɔːsit] *nc* (often *pl*) stiff garment worn by a woman under a dress or skirt, in order to shape the body (常用複數)女緊身胸衣. *Note* 說明: the more modern version of this garment is called a *girdle, belt or roll-on* 更新式的稱 a girdle, belt 或 roll-on.

cortège [kɔːˈtɛːʒ] procession (esp. a funeral procession) (尤指喪禮的)行列.

cortex [ˈkɔːteks] *nc* bark or rind of a plant; outer layer of grey matter of an organ, esp. of the brain (植物的)皮層; (腦等的)皮質 .*pl* 複數 **cortices** [ˈkɔːtisiːz].

cortices [ˈkɔːtisiːz] *pl* of **cortex**. cortex 的複數.

cosh [kɔʃ] *nc* small weapon, made of wood, rubber, metal etc. used by criminals for hitting people on the head. (罪犯用以打人頭部的)木頭、橡膠或金屬短棒. Also 亦作 *vt* hit somebody with this 用短棒打(人).

cosine [ˈkousain] *nc* sine of the complement of a given angle or arc 餘弦.

cosmetic [kɔzˈmetik] *nc* (usu. *pl*) powder, cream etc used by women to make the face and various parts of the body more beautiful. (通常用複數)化妝品. Also 亦作 *adj.*

cosmopolitan [kɔzmə'pɔlitn] *adj* having people or ideas from many parts of the world 來自世界各地的. *London is a cosmopolitan city.* 倫敦是一個國際城市.

cosmos ['kɔzmɔs] *nc* the universe; the sun, planets and surrounding space 宇宙. **cosmic** ['kɔzmik] *adj* **cosmonaut** ['kɔzmənɔːt] *nc* person who travels in a spacecraft (esp. Russian – *US* **astronaut**) (尤指前蘇聯的)宇宙飛行員(美爲 astronaut).

cost [kɔst] *vt* **1** have a price 值得, 作價: *This book costs two pounds* i. e. we must pay two pounds in order to buy the book. 這本書賣兩鎊. *This chair cost me twenty pounds.* 這張椅子花了我二十鎊. **2** result in or cause the loss of 使失去: *One mistake may cost you your life / your job* i. e. may cause you to die / to lose your job. 只要有一個差錯, 你就得送命/你就得丟掉工作. *past* 過去式和過去分詞 **cost**. Also 亦作 *nc*: *What is the cost of this book?* 這本書多少錢? **costly** ['kɔstli] *adj* costing a lot of money 昂貴的. **cost of living** the average amount of money paid by a person or family for the necessary things of life (e. g. food, clothing, housing, travel) 生活費用(如衣, 食, 住, 旅行). **at all costs** whatever the difficulties or dangers may be 不惜任何代價, 無論如何: *I must finish the work by tomorrow at all costs.* 我必須不惜任何代價在明天以前完成工作.

costume ['kɔstjuːm] *nu* **1** type of clothes worn at one time or in one area (esp. clothes worn in a former time or in a particular place) 一時期、某一地區(尤其是從前或特定地區)的服裝式樣. **2** clothes worn by an actor in a play or film 戲裝.

cosy ['kouzi] *adj* warm and comfortable. 暖和舒適的.

cot [kɔt] *nc* **1** (*Brit*) bed for child, with bars up the sides to keep the child from falling out (英)四圍有柵的兒童床. (*US* 美 **crib**). **2** (*US*) narrow bed, often one made of canvas stretched on a frame (美)帆布床. (*Brit* 英 **campbed**).

cottage ['kɔtidʒ] *nc* small house (usu. in the country) where a farmer or farm worker lives or used to live 小農屋.

cotton ['kɔtn] *nu* **1** soft white substance obtained from a plant, used for making into cloth 棉花. **2** thread made from this substance, used for sewing 棉線. **3** cloth made from this substance 棉布. '**cotton 'wool** (mainly *Brit*) cotton in the natural state, cleaned and pressed into flat layers; used for cleaning wounds etc. (主要用於英)藥棉. (*US* 美 **absorbent cotton**).

couch [kautʃ] *nc* long chair looking like a bed 躺椅, 長沙發

cough [kɔf] *vi* push air from the lungs and out of the mouth in a sudden and noisy way (usu. because the throat is blocked because of an illness or some other reason) 咳嗽. Also 亦作 *nc* **1** action of this kind 咳嗽(指動作) . **2** illness of the throat which causes coughing 咳嗽(指病狀) .

could [kud] past of **can** can 的過去式和過去分詞.

council ['kaunsl] *nc* body of people to be consulted or to advise (esp. such a body governing a town or city) (尤指市鎮的)議會. **councillor** *nc* (*Brit*) member of a council. (英)地方議員. (*US* 美 **councilor**). see 見 **counsel.**

counsel ['kaunsl] *nu* 1 advice: suggestions *(formal)* 勸告、建議(正式). 2 lawyer or lawyers on one side in a law case 訴訟一方的律師. *past* 過去式和過去分詞 **counselled.** (*US* 美 **counseled**). **counsellor** (*US* 美 **counselor**) *nc* 1 person who counsels 顧問. 2 (*US*) lawyer (美)律師. *Note* 說明: do not confuse council and counsel. council 與 counsel 是不同的詞,不可混淆. **Queen's (King's) Counsel** lawyer who has the power to represent the British Government (有權代表政府的)英國王室律師.

count¹ [kaunt] *vt / i* 1 find out the number of 計算: *It is impossible to count the stars in the sky.* 天空中的星星數不清. 2 say numbers in order 數(到): *I shall count up to ten and then we can begin.* 我數到十,然後我們開始. 3 be important or consider as important 算數,有考慮的價值: *Don't think that winning a game is the only thing that counts* i. e. there are other important things about games, such as exercise, enjoyment, team spirit etc. 別以為贏才是重要的.比賽時還有其它重要東西,如鍛煉、娛樂,合作精神等. 4 be included or include in a total 算進去: *I've got five Russian postage stamps, or six if you count this torn one.* 我有五張俄國郵票,也可以說六張,如果把破的那一張也算進去的話. *That one doesn't count* i. e. is not to be included. 那一張不算. **count upon someone / something** rely on 依靠,指望,(某人/某事物): *I hope that we can count on your support in the election* i. e. I hope that you will vote for us. 我希望在選舉中能得到您的支持. **count something up** count to find the total of 加起來求總數: *I must count up how much money I've spent*

today. 我必須把今天所花的錢加起來算一下看總數有多少.

count² [kaunt] *nc* act of counting numbers or quantities 計數. **countless** *adj* very, very many, too many to count 數不清的. **countable noun** (grammar) noun such as *man, book, country, difference,* which can be made plural and which can have a in front 可數名詞.(前面可以有冠詞 a, 也存在複數形式的名詞, 如 man, book, country, difference 等). (*opp* **uncountable noun** i. e. a noun like 'rice', 'honesty') (反義詞 uncountable noun 不可數名詞, 即像'rice', 'honesty'這樣的名詞). **'countdown** (usu. with reference to the period during which a spacecraft is being inspected to see whether it is ready for flight) period before something starts, and during which somebody counts backwards, ending 5, 4, 3, 2, 1. (通常指發射宇宙飛船前進行檢查一切是否就緒的倒數計時階段. 即: 依序唸出五、四、三、二、一時立即開始的那段時間). **keep count** count,over a length of time, how many there are of something 在一段時間內連續計算,以得出正確數目: *I've been keeping count of the cars on this road.* 我一直在算路上有多少輛車子. **lose count** forget or stop counting how many there are of something 數了一段、沒再數下去;數了一段以後數亂: *I've lost count of the letters I've written to him about this.* 關於這件事,我給他究竟寫了幾封信,現在也記不清楚了.

count³ [kaunt] *nc* title of nobility in some countries on the continent of Europe (歐洲大陸某些國家的)伯爵. **countess** ['kauntis] *nc* 1 wife of a count 伯爵夫人. 2 (*Brit*) wife of an earl, or woman with the rank of an earl (英)伯爵夫人; 女伯爵.

counter¹ ['kauntə*] *adv* against; opposite to (與…)相反地: *His behaviour was counter to my wishes.* 他的行爲和我的願望正相反. Also 亦作 *vt / i* be opposite or against, oppose 反對: *He countered my plan with one of his own* i. e. he suggested his own plan instead of mine. 他以自己的計劃作爲代替我的計劃的反建議.

counter² ['kauntə*] *nc* **1** round flat piece of plastic, wood, metal etc used in playing certain games, or as an imitation coin 籌碼. **2** type of table in a shop, behind which the shopkeeper stands to serve the customers 櫃台.

counter-³ ['kauntə*] *prefix* opposite or against (e. g. **counter-attack**) 反, 逆 (例如: counter-attack 反攻, 反擊).

counteract [kauntə'rækt] *vt* have the opposite effect to; make harmless or of no effect 抵消; 中和; 消解: *This drug will counteract the poison* i. e. it will prevent the poison from doing harm. 這個藥可以解毒.

counter-attack ['kauntərətæk] *nc* attack made against somebody who attacked first 反攻, 反擊. Also 亦作 *vt / i.*

counter-espionage ['kauntər-'espiə-nɑ:ʒ] *nu* work of a spy who deceives or works against enemy spies 反間諜工作.

counterfeit ['kauntəfit] *nc* something false (esp. money) which is dishonestly made to look like the real thing 仿製品, 偽造物 (尤指貨幣): *This coin is a counterfeit* i. e. this is not a coin made by the government. 這個硬幣是偽造的. Also 亦作 *adj: a counterfeit coin* 一枚偽幣. Also 亦作 *vt* counterfeit money 偽造貨幣.

counterfoil ['kauntəfɔil] *nc* part of a cheque or receipt, which is kept as a record that the cheque etc has been given to somebody (支票或收據的)存根.

counter-offensive ['kauntərə-'fensiv] *nc* large attack made in war, after the enemy has attacked first 反攻, 反擊戰.

counterpart ['kauntəpɑ:t] *nc person / thing which is very similar to a person / thing in another business, situation etc.* 相對應的人或物.

counter-revolution ['kauntərevə'lu:ʃən] *nc* political movement which tries to get rid of a govern-ment set up by a revolution, and go back to the situation before the revolution 反革命. **counter-revolu-tionary** *adj.* Also 亦作 *nc.*

countess ['kauntis] *nc see* 見 **count³.**

country ['kʌntri] *nc* **1** state 國家: *France, Italy, Egypt, Japan are countries.* 法國、意大利、埃及、日本都是國家. **2** the people in a state 國民: *The whole country supported the Prime Minister.* 全國人民支持首相. **3** (only *sing*) land which is not a town or city (只用單數)鄉下, 農村: *He spends his holiday on a farm in the country.* 他在鄉下農場裏度假. Also 亦作 *adj* (before certain nouns) in the country; away from towns and cities. (在某些名詞前面)農村的: *He enjoys country life.* 他喜歡農村生活. **'country 'dance** *nc* type of dance (usu. with two rows of people facing each other) 英國土風舞. **country dancing** *nu.* **'countryman 1** person who lives in the country 鄉下人. **2** person from the same nation as oneself 同胞. (Often 常作 **fellow countryman**.) **'countryside** areas which are not towns or cities 農村, 鄉下.

county ['kaunti] *nc* **1** (*Brit, Ir*) one of

the divisions of the country （英、愛）
郡. **2** *(US)* one of the divisions of
each state （美）縣. **county 'town**
chief town of a county 郡 的 首府.
'Home 'Counties counties around
London 倫敦附近各郡.

coup [ku:] *nc* sudden and violent action
to end a government and set up
another one 政變. (Also 亦作 **coup-
d'état** [ku:deitɑ:]).

couple ['kʌpl] *nc* **1** two people or
things 一對, 一雙, 兩個. *a couple of
books.* *(informal)* 兩本書(非正式). **2**
man and woman who are married or
engaged to be married 夫婦, 未婚夫
婦. **3** man and woman dancing
together 跳舞中的一對男女. Also 亦
作 *vt* join two things together 連接.
coupling ['kʌpliŋ] *nc* device which is
used to join two things (esp. two railway carriages) 連接器(尤指兩節火車
車廂間的掛鈎).

coupon ['ku:pɔn] *nc* piece of paper
which gives the owner of it the right
to receive or do something 公債息券,
配給票, 贈品券: *Some manufacturers
give away coupons to people who buy
their goods; if one saves enough
coupons one is given a gift of some
kind.* 有些廠家對購買其貨品的人發出
贈品券, 積到一定的數量贈品券, 可以領
取贈品.

courage ['kʌridʒ] *nu* the ability to face
or accept pain, danger or difficulty
without fear, the power to continue
what one is doing, even though it
causes one pain, danger or difficulty
勇氣, 膽量, 勇敢. **courageous** [kə-
'reidʒəs] *adj.*

courier ['kuriə*] *nc* **1** person whose
work is to go with a group of
travellers and arrange their journey
for them 旅行團服務員. **2** person car-

rying a special message 信使.

course [kɔ:s] *nc* **1** (only *sing*) direction;
movement onwards or forwards (只用
單數)歷程, 過程: *During the course of
many years, the old man had seen
many surprising things* i. e. while
many years were passing. 在多年的經
歷中, 這位老人見過許多令人驚奇的事
物. **1** *I have studied the course of this
discussion* i. e. the way in which this
discussion has developed. 我研究過這
場討論的過程. **2** movement onwards;
path or direction 道路, 路線, 方向:
The ship continued on her course. 船
隻繼續它的航向. **3** action 行動, 作法:
*I have not decided what course to
take with those bad boys* i. e. what to
do to them. 我還沒決定對那些壞孩子
該怎麼辦. **4** series of lessons or lectures 課程. **5** series of treatments or
drugs for somebody who is ill 療程. **6**
one part of a meal put on the table at
one time 一道菜: *The first course was
soup or fruit juice.* 第一道菜是湯或果
汁. **7** ground for certain sports (e. g.
a golf course, a racecourse for horse-
racing) 某種運動的場地(例如: 高爾夫
球場, 跑馬場). **in the course of** during, as something goes on 在…的過程
中: *In the course of a term, both
pupils and teachers become tired.* 一
個學期當中, 學生老師都疲勞了. **in
due course** at the proper time; after
some time 在適當時候, 到(一定的)時
候: *I shall answer all your questions
in due course.* 到適當的時候, 我會回
答你的一切問題. **of course** certainly,
as one would expect; as everyone
knows 當然, 自然. **take a course 1**
(with *in*) study and attend lectures or
lessons (與 in 連用) 修讀課程: *I took
a course in geology last year.* 去年我
修了地理課. **2** (with *of*) use over a

period of time as a treatment for a disease (與 of 連用) 服用治療一定時間: *I took a course of drugs for my rheumatism.* 我吃了一療程的藥, 治療風濕病.

court¹ [kɔːt] *nc* **1** place where a judge or magistrate hears law cases 法院, 法庭. **2** officials in a court of law 法庭, 法院(指法官及其他承審人員). **3** place where a king or queen lives 宮廷. **4** king or queen with the officials who live at the court 朝廷(指國王、皇后及其侍臣). **5** small open space surrounded by buildings or walls 天井, 庭院. (Often 常作 **courtyard**). **6** room or open space with markings for certain games (運動) : *a tennis court* 網球場. **courtier** [ˈkɔːtiə*] *nc* person who attends or is present at the court of a king or queen 朝臣. **'courtmartial** *nc* court of law held under military law 軍事法庭; *pl* 複數 **courts-martial** *(formal)* (正式) or **court-martials** *(informal)* (非正式). Also 亦作 *vt* try somebody before a court-martial 對…進行軍事審判. **courtyard** see **court¹** (in sense 5) 見 court¹ (義5).

court² [kɔːt] *vt* be a companion of a woman whom one hopes to marry 追求, 求愛: *John has been courting Mary for three years.* 約翰追求瑪麗已經三年了. (非正式). **courteous** [ˈkɜːtiəs] *adj* very polite and kind 有禮貌的; 慇懃的. (*opp* 反義詞 **discourteous**). **courtesy** [ˈkɜːtisi] *nc / u* polite and kind behaviour or action 慇懃, 禮貌. (*opp* 反義詞 **discourtesy**). **by courtesy of** with the help or permission of 承蒙…支持或允許: *John Smith appears in this film by courtesy of XYZ Film Corporation* i. e. John Smith works as an actor for XYZ

Film Corporation, who have given permission for him to appear in a film made by another company. 承 XYZ 電影公司支持, 允許約翰·史密斯在本片中客串.

cousin [ˈkʌzn] *nc* son or daughter of a brother or sister of either of one's parents. 表兄弟姊妹.堂兄弟姊妹.

cove [kouv] *nc* small sheltered bay or inlet of the sea 小海灣.

cover¹ [ˈkʌvə*] *vt* **1** put something over, on or in front of 蓋某物在…上方, 表面或前面: *He covered the table with a cloth.* 他在桌上舖一塊桌布. *He covered the wall with green paint.* 他在牆上塗了綠色的油漆. **2** be over, on or in front of something 覆蓋在…上方(表面或前面). *Pieces of paper covered his desk.* 他的書桌上滿是紙片. *The blankets did not completely cover the bed.* 毯子蓋不滿床舖. *The streets were covered with ice and snow.* 街道都給冰雪蓋着. **3** (esp. with reference to war and fighting) protect. (尤指戰爭及戰鬥)保護, 掩護: *Our planes covered the tanks which were attacking the enemy* i. e. the planes prevented the enemy from attacking the tanks. 我們的飛機在空中掩護坦克進攻敵人. **4** (usu. with reference to war and fighting) be in a position to attack; be on guard near (通常指戰爭及戰鬥)控制住; 守住: *Two policemen covered the back door and two covered the front.* 兩個警察控制住後門, 兩個守着前門. **5** travel a certain distance 走過(路程): *He covered twelve miles a day when he was walking in the mountains.* 他在山裏走的時候, 一天走十二英里. **6** (with reference to books, lessons, lectures etc.) include. (指書籍、功課、講演等)包括: *This dictionary does not cover the whole of the Eng-*

lish vocabulary. 這詞典不包括全部英語詞彙. **7** (usu. with reference to money) be enough for (通常指錢)夠 (付…的錢): *Here is £5: that should cover all your expenses.* 這裏有五鎊, 夠你的一切開銷了. **8** act as a reporter for a newspaper or for radio or television 採訪; 報導: *The best reporters were sent to cover the war* i. e. send reports on the war. 派了最好的記者報導戰事消息. **9** buy an insurance policy against 給…保險: *I am covered against fire* i. e. if my house is damaged by fire, the insurance company will pay to repair the damage. 我保了火險.

cover² ['kʌvə*] **1** *nc* something made to be put over, on or in front of something 蓋子, 罩子: *I haven't got a cover to put on this box.* 我沒有蓋箱子的箱罩. **2** *nc* things behind which a person or animal can hide 掩蔽物: *The lion was able to find cover in the grass.* 獅子能夠在草中隱蔽起來. **3** *nu* insurance policy 保險: *I must get cover for my new car.* 我必須爲我的新車保險. **covering** *nc* something over, on or in front of something 覆蓋物/層: *There was a thick covering of snow on the street.* 街上厚厚一層的雪. **'cover charge** fixed charge in a restaurant etc for service etc. 飯館等所耗飲料、食品的附加費. **covering letter** letter which is sent with some other documents to explain something about the documents (郵送文件時, 爲作説明之) 附函. **from cover to cover** (with reference to reading a book etc.) completely (指閱讀書籍等)從頭到尾: *He read the book from cover to cover* i. e. he read every word. 他從頭到尾把書看完. **take cover** hide; get into a place which gives

protection 隱蔽、(利用掩護體)躲避: *Everybody took cover when the bombs began to fall on the town.* 炸彈落在巿裏時, 所有的人都隱蔽起來. **under cover (of something)** secretly, protected or hidden by something 秘密地; 藉…的掩護: *The army moved under the cover of darkness.* 軍隊趁着天黑移動.

coverage ['kʌvəridʒ] *nu* **1** amount, extent or area included or covered 所包含(或掩蓋)的數量(或程度、範圍等). **2** risks covered by an insurance 保險項目, 保險總額. **3** reporting of events etc for newspaper etc. 新聞報導.

covet ['kʌvit] *vt* want something very strongly (usu. something belonging to another person) (rather *o. f.*) 覬覦(稍舊式).

cow [kau] *nc* large, female domestic animal, kept to provide milk 母牛, 奶牛. **'cowboy** man whose work is to look after cattle in the western part of America 美國西部的牛仔, 牧童.

coward ['kauəd] *nc* person who is afraid of danger, person who runs away from danger or who will not fight because he is afraid 膽小鬼, 膽怯的人. **cowardly** *adj* **cowardice** ['kauədis] *nu*.

cower ['kauə*] *vi* bend down or move away because one is afraid 蜷伏, 畏縮.

cowrie ['kauri] *nc* small shell, at one time used as money in parts of Africa and Asia (古時在亞洲、非洲部份地區作爲貨幣用的) 小貝殼. (Also 亦作 **cowrie shell**).

cox [kɔks] *nc* short form of **coxswain** i. e. the person who steers a boat (esp. in a boat race) coxswain 的縮略形式即: 舵手(尤指賽艇艇長). Also 亦作 *vt / i* act as a cox 當舵手(艇長); 當(船)

的舵手或(賽艇)的艇長.

coy [kɔi] *adj* (usu. with reference to children or young women, and often with the suggestion that this fear is not completely real) afraid of strangers; unwilling to talk to strangers 怕羞的, 腼腆的, 忸怩的.

cozy ['kouzi] *adj* comfortable; snug 舒服的; 舒適的.

crab [kræb] *nc* 1 type of broad shellfish with big claws, which walks sideways 蟹.

crack¹ [kræk] *nc* 1 line where something is broken but has not separated into pieces 裂縫, 裂紋. 2 narrow opening 縫隙: *He hid the money in a crack in the wall.* 他把錢藏在牆縫裏. 3 sudden noise 爆裂聲: *a crack of thunder* 霹靂一聲; *the crack of a gun* 槍(砲)聲. 4 blow or knock on a part of somebody's body 重擊: *He got a crack on the head. (informal)* 他頭上重重挨了一下. (非正式). 5 joke. *(informal)* 笑話 (非正式). **cracker** *nc* 1 roll of paper containing a small present used at children's parties; when the cracker is pulled at both ends, it opens with a loud noise and the present falls out (內裝糖果等小禮品的)彩色爆竹. 2 thin hard biscuit, often eaten with cheese (常與奶酪同吃的)薄餅乾.

crack² [kræk] *vt / i* 1 break, cause to break, so that a line appears in the thing broken, but it does not separate into pieces (使)開了裂縫; 打破; 擊裂: *The cup cracked when I washed it, but you can still drink out of it.* 我洗杯子, 杯子裂了一道縫, 可是你還可以用這杯子喝水. *He cracked the cup.* 他把杯子碰裂了一道裂縫. 2 make a sudden noise 發出爆破聲: *The gun cracked.* 槍(砲)砰地一聲. 3 (with re-ference to a sound and esp. to a boy's voice when he is approaching man-hood) become harsh or shrill (指聲音, 尤指男孩子發音時的嗓音)變沙啞, 變嗓. 4 (with reference to a person) break down or be unable to continue because of difficulty (指人)精神崩潰, 垮了: *He cracked under the strain of work. (informal)* 工作太緊張, 他垮了. (非正式). **cracked** *adj* 1 broken but not separated into pieces 有裂縫的. 2 (with reference to a sound) harsh and shrill 沙啞的: *We heard the cracked note of the bell.* 我們聽到(破)鐘的沙啞聲. 3 mad; having strange ideas or opinions. *(informal in sense 3)* 瘋了的, 有怪念頭的(義3非正式). **crack down on somebody / something** act firmly to stop somebody / something 嚴厲取締; 禁止: *The police have de-cided to crack down on motorists who drive too fast.* 警察決定禁止超速駛的人開車. (非正式). **crack up** break; be unable to continue 崩潰; 不能繼續: *His health cracked up. (informal)* 他的身體垮了. (非正式). **crack a safe** break open a safe in order to steal what is inside. *(infor-mal)* 撬開保險箱(非正式).

crack³ [kræk] *adj* (usu. with reference to sportsmen) very good (通常指運動員)頂好的, 第一流的: *He is a crack shot.* i. e. he is very good at firing guns. 他是神槍手.

crackle ['krækl] *nu* number of small sharp sounds, such as the sound made by dry wood being burned 嗶嗶啪啪的響聲. Also 亦作 *vi* make this sound 嗶嗶啪啪地響. **crackling** *nu* 1 sound of something as it crackles 嗶啪的爆裂聲 2 hard skin of pork which has been roasted 烤豬的脆皮.

cradle ['kreidl] *nc* small bed for a baby,

often on curved pieces of wood which allow the cradle to be rocked backwards and forwards or from side to side 搖籃、小搖床.

craft [krɑːft] *nc* **1** job done with the hands, requiring skill and training 手藝: *the craft of the goldsmith / carpenter / painter etc.* 金(飾)工的手藝; 木工的工藝、(油)漆工的工藝等. **2** boat or ship. *pl* usu. **craft** in sense **2** 船. (在作此解時, 複數經常用 craft). **craftsman** *nc* **1** man who works with his hands at a job which needs skill and training 手藝人, 工匠. **2** somebody who does his work very well 精於一門手藝的人, 手藝精湛的人. **craftsmanship** *nu* skilled work done by a craftsman; skill in working (工匠的)技術; 工作的技巧, 技藝. **crafty** *adj* full of cunning 狡猾的.

crag [kræg] *nc* steep rocky cliff or hill 陡峭的山崖. **craggy** *adj.*

cram [kræm] *vt / i* **1** fill with too many things; push into something so that it becomes too full 硬塞, 塞滿. *He crammed the box with his papers.* 他在箱子裏塞滿論文. *He crammed the papers into the box.* 他把論文硬塞進箱子裏. **2** learn, cause to learn, by heart in order to prepare for an examination 死記硬背; 填鴨式地教(以應付考試): *The boys were cramming for the examination.* 男孩子們正在死記硬背應付考試. *past* 過去式和過去分詞 **crammed.** **'cram-'full** *adj / adv* very full 塞滿了的(地); *The box was cram-full of papers.* 箱子裏塞滿了論文.

cramp[1] [kræmp] *nc / u* sudden pain and tightening of the muscles, caused by cold or overuse of the muscles 抽筋, 痙攣.

cramp[2] [kræmp] *vt* (sometimes with up) prevent easy movement; keep in a small space (有時與 up 連用)阻礙; 束縛, 約束. **cramped** *adj* **1** with very little space in which to move 狹小的. **2** (with reference to handwriting) not spaced out (指筆跡)筆劃擠在一起的, 難以辨認的.

crane[1] [krein] *nc* **1** machine used for raising and lowering heavy things 起重機. **2** one of several birds with long legs, neck and beak which walk in water 鶴.

crane[2] [krein] *vt / i* stretch one's neck in order to see something 伸長脖子看: *He craned (his neck) to see over the heads of the crowd.* 他伸長脖子越過前面羣衆的頭張望.

crank[1] [kræŋk] *nc* handle of a machine 機器的曲柄. Also 亦作 *vt* (often with up) start a machine by using a crank (常與 up 連用)用曲柄開動(機器).

crank[2] [kræŋk] *nc* person with strong and unusual opinions 有強烈怪念頭的人, 古怪的人. **cranky** *adj.*

cranny ['kræni] *nc* small hole (esp. in a wall or in a rock) (尤指牆上或崖石上)小洞, 縫隙.

crash [kræʃ] *vt / i* **1** fall, break or hit something, making a loud noise 墮下; 打碎; 碰撞 (發出猛烈的聲音): *The aeroplane crashed into the houses.* 飛機撞毀了房子. *All the plates and cups crashed to the floor.* 所有杯盤都嘩啦啦地掉到地板上. *The driver crashed the bus.* 駕駛員把公共汽車撞壞了. **2** (with reference to a business firm, government or rich person) lose all one's money and be unable to meet one's debts (指商業公司、政府或有錢人)破產, 倒閉, 經濟崩潰. Also 亦作 *nc* **1** noise of something crashing 物體相撞時發出的巨響. **2** fall of an aeroplane to the ground, or accident to a vehicle while travelling 飛機墮毀; 車輛碰撞事故. **3** financial ruin of a business firm, government or rich person 破產, 倒閉, 經濟崩潰. **'crash course** course of lessons to do some work etc., which is carried out in the shortest possible time 速成課程. **'crash helmet** hard padded covering for the head worn by a motorcyclist etc. (摩托車駕駛人等戴的)安全頭盔. **'crash 'landing** *nc* forced landing made by an aeroplane when something goes wrong (飛機發生故障時的)迫降, 緊急着陸.

crate [kreit] *nc* large wooden box for carrying goods in 板條箱, 柳條箱.

crater ['kreitə*] *nc* **1** hole at the top of a volcano 火山口. **2** hole made by a bomb, large shell or an explosion (炸彈、砲彈落地爆炸後形成的)彈坑.

cravat [krə'væt] *nc* small scarf or piece of cloth, tied round the neck with the ends worn inside the shirt (兩端塞在襯衫內的)圍巾, 領巾.

craving ['kreiviŋ] *nc / u* strong wish or desire for something 渴望, 強烈的慾望.

crawl [krɔ:l] *vi* **1** move along on the hands and knees, as a baby does 爬, 爬行. **2** move along very slowly 極緩慢地移動, 徐行, 緩行. Also 亦作 *n sing* **1** movement on the hands and knees 爬行. **2** slow movement 緩慢的移動. **3** method of swimming 自由式游泳. **be crawling with** have present in large numbers things that are alive and unpleasant 爬滿了⋯, 到處是⋯在爬走動着: *This house was crawling with rats.* 房子裏跑來跑去都是老鼠.

crayon ['kreiən] *nc* stick of soft, coloured substance, used for drawing 顏色鉛筆(或蠟筆).

craze [kreiz] *nc* something in which

people have an interest, which is great but is not likely to last for a long time 狂熱, (一時的)着迷: *Everyone in the family had a craze for Chinese food. (informal)* 家裏每一個人都迷上中國菜.(非正式).

crazy ['kreizi] *adj* **1** mad *(informal)* 瘋狂的(非正式). **2** filled with strong interest 狂熱的, 着迷的: *He was crazy about old gramophone records last year. (informal)* 去年他對於舊唱片簡直入迷了.(非正式). **'crazy 'paving** *nu* path in a garden, made of pieces of stone of various sizes, put together, without any definite pattern 園中由大小不一的石頭隨意砌成的)碎石路.

creak [kri:k] *nc* noise like that made by a door which needs oiling 吱吱嘎嘎的聲音(如門久不上油所發出的聲音) Also 亦作 *vi* make this noise. 吱吱作聲. **creaky** *adj*.

cream [kri:m] *nu* **1** the thick substance in milk which rises to the top 奶油; 乳脂. **2** substance containing oil, to be put on the skin for various purposes 護膚霜, 雪花膏. Also 亦作 *vt* (cookery) make into a smooth substance like cream (烹飪)攪打成奶油狀: *She creamed the potatoes.* 她把奶油加進馬鈴薯裏打滑. Also 亦作 *adj* of a colour between white and yellow 奶油色的, 米色的. **creamy** *adj* **creamery** *nc* place where cream is made or sold 奶品廠; 奶品店. **'cream 'cheese** very soft, white kind of cheese 奶油乳酪, 軟乳酪. **the cream of something** the best part 精華: *the cream of society* i.e rich and influential people 社會精英.

crease [kri:s] *nc* line made in cloth or paper by folding (布或紙的)摺痕, 摺摺. Also 亦作 *vt / i This cloth does not crease.* 這塊布不起皺.

create [kri'eit] *vi* make something which is new 創造: *God created the world.* 上帝創造世界. *This news creates several difficulties for me.* 這條新聞給我造成許多麻煩. **creation** [kri'eiʃn] *nc* something created 創造物. **creative** *adj* having the ability to make new things 有創造力的: *He is a very creative writer.* 他是很有創造性的作家. **creator** *nc* person who creates 創造者: **The Creator** God 上帝.

creature ['kri:tʃə*] *nc* living thing (esp. an animal, bird, fish, insect, reptile etc-not usu. plants or human beings except in a pitying way-*poor creature*) 生物(尤指鳥、獸、蟲、魚、爬行動物等, 一般不指植物, 亦不指人, 除有表示憐憫意義外, 例如: poor creature: '可憐的人').

creche, crèche [kreʃ] *nc* place where babies and young children are taken care of during the daytime. 日托托兒所.

credentials [kri'denʃlz] *npl* letters or papers which show that somebody is the person that he says he is 證件; 國書.

credible ['kredibl] *adj* easily believed 可靠的, 可信的: *His story was quite credible.* 他說的那些十分可靠. *(opp* 反義詞 **incredible**). *Note* 說明: do not confuse *credible, credulous* and *creditable.* 不要將 credible, credulous 和 creditable 混淆起來.

credit¹ ['kredit] *nu* **1** money a person has in a bank etc. (銀行)存款: *I have a large credit with Brown's Bank.* 我在勃朗的銀行有大筆存款. **2** agreement by which one pays for goods some time after buying them 賒買貨物, 賒帳: *He buys all his food on credit* i.e. the shopkeeper allows him to take the goods and pay later. 他所有的食物都是用記帳辦法買來的. *This shopkeeper does not give credit* i.e. he does not allow people to buy goods in this way. 這個店東不肯賒帳. **3** honour; reputation; what other people think about one's behaviour 榮譽, 聲望, 信譽: *He gained a lot of credit from that journey* i.e. everybody thought that he was very good, very clever, very brave etc for making that journey. 他由於這次旅行聲望大增. **creditable** *adj* bringing praise or honour, making people think that one has done well 帶來聲譽的; 值得讚揚的: *a very creditable action* 非常值得稱讚的行動. *(opp* 反義詞 **discreditable**). *see Note on* **credible** 見 credible 條說明. **be a credit to someone / something** do something which brings honour to oneself or to someone / something else 爲某人 / 某物增光或帶來榮譽: *John is a credit to his old school* i.e. people think that John's old school is very good because John has done something very good. 約翰爲他的母校帶來榮譽.

credit² ['kredit] *vt* believe that something is true 相信: *I didn't credit his story.* 我不相信他編的那一套話. **creditor** *nc* person to whom one owes money 債主.

credulous ['kredjuləs] *adj* too ready to believe what one is told 輕信的: *He is a credulous fool; he thought that I was telling the truth when I said I could do magic.* 他是一個輕易受騙的人, 我告訴他我會巫術, 他竟信以爲真. *(opp* 反義詞 **incredulous**).

creed [kri:d] *nc* official statement of religious beliefs 教義, 信條.

creek [kri:k] *nc* **1** narrow arm of water off the main stretch of water (河、海延伸陸地的)細長小灣. **2** *(US)* small river (美)小河, 小溪.

creep [kri:p] *vi* **1** move along very slowly, quietly or secretly, often with the body close to the ground 徐緩輕聲或偷偷地匍匐前進. **2** (with reference to certain types of plant) spread out over a wide area (指某種植物)蔓延. *past* 過去式和過去分詞 **crept** [krept]. Also 亦作 *nc* unpleasant person. *(informal)* 馬屁精(非正式). **creeper** *nc* type of plant that spreads out over a wide area 攀藤植物. **creepy** *adj* causing fear or disgust 令人毛骨悚然的: *creepy ghost stories. (informal)* 令人毛骨悚然的鬼故事(非正式). **give one the creeps** give one a feeling of fear and disgust; give one a feeling of strong dislike and unhappiness. *(informal)* 令人毛骨悚然; 令人頂不舒服. (非正式).

cremate [kri'meit] *vt* burn a dead body (instead of burying it) 火化、火葬. **cremation** *nu* practice of burning dead bodies. 火葬. **crematorium** [kremə'tɔ:riəm] *nc* place where dead bodies are cremated 火葬場.

creosote ['kriəsout] *nu* thick oily liquid made from tar 木焦油; 木餾油; 雜酚油.

crepe, crêpe [kreip] *nu* name for various types of material which have small folds on the surface 縐綢(布、呢等). **'crepe 'paper** type of paper with many small folds on the surface, often brightly coloured and used for decoration etc. (裝飾等用的)縐紙.

crept [krept] past of **creep** creep 的過去式和過去分詞.

crescent [kresnt] *nc* anything shaped like the moon in its first or last quarter 新月狀物.

crest [krest] *nc* **1** top of a mountain ridge 山頂 **2** top of a wave 浪峯. **3** feathers which stick up on the top of a bird's head 鳥冠, 冠毛.**4** feathers or other decoration worn on the top of a knight's helmet or soldier's helmet 盔上的羽毛飾. **5** special mark or sign of a person, family, town, business firm, school etc. (often printed on writing paper used by these various people) 紋章, 紋飾; (市鎮、公司、學校等的)標誌 (常用於其專用信箋上). **'crestfallen** *adj* unhappy and disappointed because one has been unsuccessful 垂頭喪氣的: *He was crestfallen at his failure in the competition.* 他因競賽失敗而垂頭喪氣.

crevasse [kri'væs] *nc* deep crack in ice (in parts of the world where the ground is covered by thick ice) (冰川或厚冰上的) 裂縫.

crevice ['krevis] *nc* narrow opening (esp. in a wall or in rock) (尤指牆壁上或岩石上的)狹裂縫.

crew¹ [kru:] *nc* **1** all the men and officers sailing a ship or flying an aeroplane (船或飛機上的)全體乘務人員, **2** group of men doing certain jobs (e.g. a *train crew* drives a train). 幹某種工作的一羣人(例如 a train crew 駕駛火車的機組人員). **3** any group of people whom one dislikes or disapproves of *(informal in sense 3)* 一夥人, 一幫人(義3爲非正式). **'crewcut** type of haircut in which the hair is cut very short 平頭(指髮式).

crew² [kru:] past tense of **crow¹** crow¹ 的過去式.

crib¹ [krib] *nc* **1** (mainly *US*) small bed for a child (主要用於美) 嬰孩或兒童的小床. **2** model of the scene shortly after the birth of Jesus, showing the child, Mary, Joseph, the animals etc., found in churches and people's homes at Christmas time (聖誕節時教

堂及家庭中所佈置的)重現耶穌降生情
景的馬槽場面.

crib² [krib] *nc* **1** word-for-word translation of something originally written in
a foreign language, intended to help
students or pupils (供中、小學生學習
外語用的)逐字照譯的譯本. **2** set of
notes to help a student which gives
him the answer so that he does not
have to do the work himself (爲學生
捉刀的)問題解答. Also 亦作 *vt / i*
copy the work or idea of somebody
else in a dishonest way 抄襲: *He cribbed all the answers from the boy sitting next to him.* 他從鄰座男孩子那裏
抄襲答案. *past* 過去式和過去分詞.
cribbed. (all *informal*)均非正式.

crick [krik] *nc* stiffness and pain in a
part of the body (esp. the neck) 肌肉
痙攣(尤指頸部).

cricket¹ [krikit] *nu* game played by two
teams of eleven players each, using
bats and a ball 板球運動. **cricketer**
nc person who plays cricket 板球運動
員.

cricket² [krikit] *nc* type of insect which
makes a loud noise by rubbing its
wings together 蟋蟀.

cried [kraid] past of **cry¹** cry¹的過去式
和過去分詞.

cries [kraiz] pl of **cry²** (noun) cry²(名
詞)的複數形式; pres of **cry¹** (verb)
cry¹(動詞)的單數第三人稱現在式.

crime [kraim] **1** *nu* actions which are
against the law 罪行, 犯罪行爲(總
稱): *Part of the work of the police is
to fight against crime.* 和犯罪行爲作鬥
爭是警察部門工作的一部份.**2** *nc* action which is against the law (有具體
罪名的)罪行、犯罪行爲. *Murder and
robbery are crimes.* 殺人和搶劫是犯罪
行爲. **3** *nc* foolish or cruel action
which is not against the law 傻事, 醜

事, 罪惡: *It is a crime to throw away
all that good food. (informal in sense
3)* 把好的食物全部倒掉, 實在是罪過
(義3爲非正式). **criminal** [kriminl] *nc*
person who commits crimes. 罪犯.
Also 亦作 *adj: Murder is a criminal
act.*殺人是犯罪的行爲.

crimson [krimzn] *nu* very deep red colour 深紅色. Also 亦作 *adj.*

cringe [krindʒ] *vi* move the body away
or down in fear 退縮, 畏縮: *The dog
cringed before his cruel master.* 狗在
殘暴的主人面前畏縮後退.

crinkle [krinkl] *nc* small fold (esp. in
paper or cloth) (尤指紙或布上的)皺
紋. Also 亦作 *vt / i: He crinkled the
paper.* 他把紙弄皺了.

cripple [kripl] *nc* person who cannot
move his legs, arms or body properly
because of some disease or injury 肢
體受損不能活動自如的人, 殘廢人.Also
亦作 *vt* **1** make a cripple of 使殘廢. **2**
damage or weaken 使遭受重大損失,
挫敗, 削弱: *Our air force has crippled
the enemy.* 我們的空軍重創敵軍.

crisis [kraisis] *nc* time of great danger
or difficulty in some important matter
危機: *a crisis in the country's economy* 這個國家的經濟危機. *pl* 複數
crises [kraisiːz].

crisp¹ [krisp] *adj* **1** (esp. with reference
to food) hard and easily broken (尤
指食品)酥脆的, 易碎的. **2** (with reference to the weather) dry and cold (指
天氣)乾冷的.

crisp² [krisp] *nc* (*Brit*) thin slice of
potato, fried in oil until hard and
eaten cold (英)油炸馬鈴薯片. (*US* 美
potato chip).

criss-cross [kriskrɔs] *adj* made or
marked with lines that cross each
other 互相交叉的.

criterion [kraitiəriən] *nc* standard by

which one can judge something (判斷、評定的) 標準, 準繩: *There are several criteria of a good school* i.e. there are several things which tell one whether a school is good or not. 評定一所好學校有幾條標準. *pl* 複數 **criteria** [krai'tiəriə].

critic ['kritik] *nc* 1 person who says whether a book, film, play, piece of music etc is good or not, and gives reasons for his decision (usu. in a newspaper or magazine) (通常指在報紙、雜誌上對書籍、電影、戲劇、音樂發表評論的) 評論家, 批評家. 2 person who always notices the bad points and mistakes about anything 愛挑剔的人, 吹毛求疵的人. **criticize** ['kritisaiz] *vt / i* act, write, talk as a critic 批評, 評論. **criticism** ['kritisizəm] *nc / u* acts, writing, speech of a critic 批評, 評論. **critical** *adj* 1 having reference to critics or criticism 批評(家)的, 評論性的. 2 complaining and finding fault; disapproving 喜歡抱怨, 挑剔的, 苛求的: *He is too critical of his grandchildren.* 他對他的孫兒們過於苛求. 3 coming at a very important moment; of the right size or amount for something to happen 關鍵的, 臨界的: *He arrived at the critical moment* i.e. at the time when his arrival had a great effect. 在關鍵的時刻, 他(到)來了. 4 full of danger or difficulty in some important matter 危急的: *There is a critical weakness in the country's economy.* 這個國家經濟的脆弱已到危急關頭. see 見 **crisis**.

croak [krouk] *nc* deep harsh sound, like that made by a frog 深沉嘶啞的如青蛙叫的聲音, 嘎嘎聲. Also 亦作 *vt / i* make this sound 作蛙鳴聲, 發嘎嘎聲.

crochet ['krouʃei] *vt / i* make thread of cotton or wool into garments etc by

making a series of loops using a hook 用鈎針編織.

crockery ['krɔkəri] *nu* plates, cups, dishes etc. (usu. those made of baked clay or china) 陶器, 瓦器.

crocodile ['krɔkədail] *nc* large animal with a long nose and a lot of sharp teeth, which lives in rivers in the tropics and which looks like a floating log 鱷魚.

crocus ['kroukəs] *nc* small flower with white, yellow or purple blooms which grows in the early spring 藏紅花 *pl* 複數 **crocuses**.

crony ['krouni] *nc* very close friend. *(informal)* 知己, 好友 (非正式).

crook [kruk] *nc* 1 criminal; person who gets his living by robbery etc. *(informal)* 竊賊, 騙子 (非正式). 2 long stick with a hook on the end. used by shepherds (牧羊人用的) 彎柄杖. **crooked** ['krukid] *adj* 1 criminal; dishonest. *(informal).* 欺詐的, 不正當的. (非正式). 2 not straight; bent, curved or twisted 彎曲的.

croon [kru:n] *vt / i* sing in a low voice 低聲哼着唱: *The woman was crooning to her baby.* 婦人低聲對嬰兒哼着調子.

crop [krɔp] *nc* 1 farm produce grown in a particular area or at a particular-time 農作物, 莊稼: *Wheat is an important crop in many parts of the world.* 小麥在世界上許多地方是重要的作物. 2 quantity of farm produce collected at one time 收成: *I had a poor crop of apples this year* i.e. my trees did not produce many apples. 今年我的蘋果收成很不好. 3 large number of things which occur at one time (同時發生的)一大批: *There is a large crop of mistakes in your essay.* *(informal)* 你的文章中有大量錯誤. (非

正式). **crop up** occur unexpectedly or by chance 突然發生,不期而然地出現: *Various subjects cropped up in the conversation* i.e. we talked about various subjects, without our having decided earlier what we would talk about. 在談話過程中,各種問題不期而然地出現.

croquet ['kroukei] *nu* game in which wooden balls are knocked through hoops 草地槌球遊戲.

cross¹ [krɔs] *nc* **1** object shaped + on which Christ was killed, and which has become a symbol of the Christian religion 十字架,十字形的東西. **2** the mark shaped × or +, often used as a signature on a document by a person who cannot write; any similar shape or symbol 畫押. **3** mixture of races or breeds; person, animal, plant that has mixed origin 混血兒;雜種;雜交: *That dog is a cross between a sheepdog and a labrador.* 那條狗是牧羊犬和拉布拉多獵犬的混合種. **crossing** *nc* **1** journey by sea from one place to another 渡海,橫渡. **2** place in a road where people who are walking can go across the road 人行橫道,過街橫道. **3** place where a railway line goes across a road (Also *Brit* 英亦作 **level crossing,** *US* 美 **grade crossing**) (鐵路和公路) 平交道口. **'crossbreed** *nc* person, animal or plant of mixed origin 混血兒;雜種;雜交. **cross check** *vt / i* make completely sure that some information is correct by getting the same information from a different place to see whether there is any difference (從不同方面) 核對,查證. Also 亦作 *nc*. **'cross-'country** *adj / adv* across fields etc., not following roads or paths. (usu. in **cross-country race**) 越野的(通常見於 cross-country

race 短語中). **'cross-ex'amine** *vt / i* question very carefully to find out whether somebody is telling the truth (esp. in a court of law, when a lawyer questions a witness who has been giving evidence for the other side in the case) 盤問,詰問(尤指法庭審判時,律師對對方證人的反覆盤問). **'cross-'eyed** *adj* having a defect of the eyes, in which both eyes look towards the nose 鬥雞眼的,內斜視的. **'crossfire** firing of guns at a target from two or more points 交叉射擊;交叉火力. **'cross-'legged** *adj / adv* sitting with one leg over the other (坐着) 兩腿交叉的(地): *He was sitting cross-legged.* 他兩腿交叉地坐着. **'cross-'purposes** usu. in **at cross-purposes** i.e. failing to understand each other 雙方彼此誤解,話不投機(通常出現於 at cross-purposes 短語): *We were talking at cross-purposes.* 我們談不到一塊兒,我們話不投機. **'cross-'reference** words in a book which tell the reader to look in another part of the book 參照,對照. **'crossroads** *n sing* 單數 place where two or more roads cross each other 十字路口. **'cross 'section** *nc* **1** drawing showing what can be seen if something is cut open vertically 橫截面,橫斷面. **2** collection of different types of something 剖析;典型. *a cross section of society* i.e. a group of people coming from the various sections of society 社會各階層的剖析,社會的橫切面. **'crossword (puzzle)** puzzle in the form of a set of squares in some of which words have to be written 縱橫方格填字之謎.

cross² [krɔs] **1** *vt / i* go from one side to the other 穿過,越過: *He crossed the road.* 他穿越馬路. The road crosses the river there. 公路在那裏橫跨過

河流. **2.** *vt/i* meet and go past in opposite directions 迎面相對而過: *The two cars crossed on the road.* 這兩部車面對面地在路上相對駛過去. *Our letters crossed* i.e. I wrote to you before I received your letter, and you wrote to me before you received my letter. 我們雙方的信件在路上彼此錯過了. **3** *vt* put one thing across another. 交叉疊着: *He sat down and crossed his legs.* 他坐下來蹺着二郎腿. **4** *vt* mix one breed of animal or one type of plant with another in order to produce a new type of animal or plant. 使(動物或植物)雜交(以培育新品種).

cross something off draw a line through something written in order to show that one does not wish it to be written (e.g. with reference to names in a list, a list of jobs that one has to do etc.) 劃掉(名單上的名字或應完成的工作項目): *I crossed off the jobs as I finished each one.* 每項工作完成後, 我把它劃掉. *I crossed some names off the list.* 我把有些名字從名單上劃掉.

cross something out draw a line through somthing written in order to remove it or show that it is wrong 畫橫線穿過(以表示註銷或有錯誤); 刪去: *I have crossed out all the mistakes in your work.* 我把你的作業中的所有錯誤都用筆劃掉. *I have crossed that word out.* 我把那個詞用橫線刪掉.

cross a cheque draw two lines across a cheque, as a sign to one's bank that the money is to be paid into somebody's bank and not in cash. (The words '& Co.' are usu. written between the two lines) 在支票上劃線(凡劃線支票——支票上劃二平行線, 兩線間常有'& Co.'字樣. 該款只能存入某人帳戶, 不能直接現提取現金).

cross³ [krɔs] *adj* in a bad temper; angry 脾氣暴躁的, 生氣的.

crotch [krɔtʃ] *nc* place where a person's legs join; this place in a pair of trousers etc. 人體兩腿分叉處; 褲襠. (Also 亦作 **crutch**).

crotchet ['krɔtʃit] *nc* (Brit quarter note in music. (US 美 **quarter note**) 四分一音符. **crotchety** *adj* bad-tempered; angry. *(informal)* 脾氣暴躁的, 生氣的. (非正式).

crouch [krautʃ] *vi* bend the body downwards (e.g. in fear, or in preparation for attacking something) 彎下腰(例如: 出於畏懼或準備進攻).

crow¹ [krou] *nc* noise made by a cock 公鷄的叫聲. Also 亦作 *vi* make a noise like a cock 發出像公鷄叫的聲音. *past tense* 過去式 **crowed** or **crew** [kru:], *past part* 過去分詞 **crowed**. **crow over something** speak boastfully and unkindly to somebody whom one has defeated in a war, competition etc. *(informal)* 幸災樂禍地對失敗對手誇說(非正式).

crow² [krou] *nc* large black bird with a rough voice 烏鴉.

crowbar ['krouba:*] *nc* long piece of iron with a bent end, used for moving heavy objects, opening packing cases etc. 彎頭鐵棍, 鐵橇.

crowd [kraud] *nc* **1** large number of people who have corne together in one place 人羣. **2** number of people who work together, meet each other regularly or have some interest in common. *(ioformal)* (一起工作, 經常晤面或有共同興趣) 一羣人 (非正式). Also 亦作 *vt / i* come together or move as a crowd 擠滿, 聚集: *The people crowded round the Prime Minister.* 人們圍住首相. *The bus was crowded* i.e. full. 公共汽車裏擠滿了

人.

crown¹ [kraun] *nc* **1** band round the head, worn by a king or queen as a sign of authority (國王或女王的)王冠, 皇冠; **2** (with reference to power or authority, not to the king or queen as individuals) king or queen 王權, 君權: *The power of the crown is limited by parliament.* 君主權力受議會限制. **3** top part of a hat 帽頂. **4** top part of a tooth 牙冠. **5** top of the head 頭頂 **6** top or highest part of something 頂部 'crown 'prince (not usu. with reference to the British monarchy) eldest son of a king or queen, and the person who is likely to be the next king (通常不指英國王室) 皇太子, 皇儲.

crown² [kraun] *vt* put a crown on a king or queen in a special ceremony (called a **coronation**) 給…加冕(其典禮稱爲a coronation).

crucial ['kru:ʃl] *adj* very important, and coming at a time of great danger or difficulty 極重要的, 嚴重關頭的, 關鍵性的: *The Prime Minister has to make a crucial decision within the next few weeks.* 今後幾週內首相必須作出關鍵性的決定.

crucible ['kru:sibl] *nc* heat-resistant container for melting ores, metals, etc. 坩堝.

crucifix ['kru:sifiks] *nc* cross with a figure of Christ fastened to it 有耶穌受難像的十字架. **crucify** ['kru:sifai] *vt* kill by fastening to a cross 把…釘死在十字架上. **crucifixion** [kru:-si'fikʃən] *nc / u* the act of doing this 將人釘死在十字架上的刑罰.

crude [kru:d] *adj* **1** not polite; showing no signs of training in the right way to behave 粗魯的, 沒教養的: *a very crude person* 十分沒教養的人; *crude behaviour* 粗魯的行爲. **2** (with reference to certain materials) in the state in which something occurs naturally, before it has been treated (指某種原料)未加工的: *crude oil* 原油. **3** badly made or done 粗製濫造的: *a crude drawing* 粗劣的圖畫. **crudely** *adv* **crudeness** *nc* **crudity** *nc / u.*

cruel ['kruəl] *adj* **1** causing unnecessary pain and suffering to other people 殘酷的: *The king was very cruel to his pelple.* 國王對於他的人民極暴虐, 殘忍. **2** causing pain and suffering 造成痛苦的: *a cruel winter / war* 嚴寒的冬天／殘酷的戰爭. **cruelty** ['kruəlti] *nc / u.*

cruise [kru:z] *vi* **1** make a sea journey for pleasure 海上旅遊, 巡遊. **2** travel in a car or aeroplane at a comfortable speed (乘車或飛機)以舒適的速度旅行. Also 亦作 *nc* long journey by sea taken for pleasure 海上長途旅遊. **cruiser** *nc* light fast battleship 巡洋艦. 'cruising speed speed at which a car or aeroplane goes when the engine is being used in the most efficient way (車輛或飛機爲節省燃料而採取的)最佳行駛速度.

crumb [krʌm] *nc* **1** very small piece of bread or cake (麵包或糕餅的)碎屑. **2** small piece of something 些微, 少許: *a crumb of comfort* i.e. something which helps one a little or makes one feel a little happier 少許的安慰.

crumble ['krʌmbl] *vt / i* fall or break into crumbs or small pieces 弄碎; (使)碎成細片; 倒塌: *He crumbled his bread.* 他把麵包掰成碎片. *The walls of the houses were curmbling.* 屋子的牆壁都要倒塌了.

crumpet ['krʌmpit] *nc (Brit)* flat type of cake which is heated and eaten with butter (英)(塗上牛油熱吃的)扁烤餅.

crumple [ˈkrʌmpl] *vt / u* (often with up) fall or push into folds: break up under pressure or distress (常與up連用) 折皺,揉皺;壓碎,壓變了形: *He crumpled the piece of paper in his hand.* 他把那張紙片揉在手裏. *The car crumpled up when it hit the wall.* 車子撞到牆上,撞變了形.

crunch [krʌntʃ] *vt / i* 1 break something hard by biting noisily with the teeth 嘎吱嘎吱地咬嚼: *He crunched the apple.* 他嘎吱嘎吱地嚼蘋果. 2 make a sharp noise as somebody walks (某人走過時) 發出嘎吱嘎吱的聲音: *The hard snow crunched under his feet.* 他腳下堅實的雪嘎吱嘎吱響. **the crunch** the moment of crisis. (*informal*) 危急關頭(非正式).

crusade [kruːˈseɪd] *nc* 1 (Often **Crusade**) one of several wars during the Middle Ages, in which armies from Europe fought against the Turks, Arabs and Egyptians in order to win or hold Palestine. (常寫作Crusade)十字軍東征. 2 public campaign or movement in favour of or against something 支持或反對某事的鬥爭或運動.

crush¹ [krʌʃ] *vt / i* 1 press together with great force so as to break 擠碎,碾碎,榨: *Certain types of snake crush small animals to death before eating them.* 某些種類的蛇把小動物弄碎才吞下去. 2 develop or produce unwanted folds or creases in cloth 起皺: *This cloth will not crush* i.e. it always stays flat. 這布不會皺. 3 defeat and destroy 粉碎,鎮壓: *The Prime Minister said that he was determined to crush the enemies of the country.* 首相說他決心壓服國內敵人. **crushing** *adj* which defeats or destroys 壓倒的,毀滅性的: *a crushing blow* 毀滅性打擊.

crush² [krʌʃ] *nc* 1 large crowd of people very close to each other 擁擠的人羣. 2 drink made from juice of fruit 果汁. 3 strong liking felt by a girl or boy for another person (女孩或男孩的)迷戀: *Little girls sometimes have a crush on their teachers.* (*informal*) 小女孩有時會迷戀她們的老師. (非正式).

crust [krʌst] *nc* 1 the hard outside of bread or pies (麵包或餡餅的)硬皮. 2 hard outside covering of anything 外殼: *the crust of the earth* 地殼.

crutch [krʌtʃ] *nc* 1 stick with a support to go under the arm, used by people who cannot walk properly 丁字形拐杖. 2 see 見 **crotch**.

crux [krʌks] *nc* difficult part or most important part of a question or problem 癥結,關鍵: *the crux of the matter* 事情的癥結所在.

cry¹ [kraɪ] 1 *vi* allow tears to come from the eyes, shed tears, weep (*usu. because one is unhappy*) 哭: *She cried when she heard that her son was dead.* 當她聽說兒子死去時,她哭了. 2 *vi* shout loudly 大聲喊叫: *He cried for help when the thief attacked him.* 小偷對他行兇時,他大聲呼救. (Also 亦作 **cry out**). 3 *vt* shout in order to make something known 大聲宣告,叫賣: *past* 過去式和過去分詞 **cried** [kraɪd]. **cry off** say that one will not do something after promising or agreeing to do so 食言,毀約,打退堂鼓,打消原意: *John was going to help us, but he cried off.* (*informal*) 約翰原來說要幫我們,可後來又不幹了. (非正式).

cry² [kraɪ] *nc* 1 act of shedding tears 哭泣: *She had a cry about the sad news.* (*informal*) 對於這個傷心的消息,她哭了一場. (非正式). 2 loud shout 大喊: *We heard a cry for help.*

我們聽到求救的喊聲．**crying** *nu* (esp. with reference to a child) shedding of tears; noise made by somebody who is shedding tears (尤指兒童) 啼哭． Also 亦作 *adj* very bad; needing attention or change (usu. in **a crying shame**; **a crying need** etc.) *(informal in this sense)* 十分嚴重的；迫切需要注意的；急需改變的．(通常出現於 a crying shame, a crying need 等．) (本義非正式)．**a far cry from** very different from 十分不同的．

crypt [kript] *nc* room under the ground (esp. in a church) in which dead bodies were once buried. 一度埋葬屍體的地下室(尤指教堂地下墓穴)．

cryptic ['kriptik] *adj* having a hidden meaning 有隱藏意義的: *a cryptic remark / letter* 別有寓意的言論/信．

crystal ['kristl] **1** *nc* piece of a substance, having a regular shape 結晶體: *Salt and sugar occur as crystals.* 鹽與糖皆結晶體． **2** *nc* very good type of glass 水晶玻璃; **crystallize** ['kristəlaiz] **1** *vt / i* form into crystals (使)結晶: *The substance crystallized when it became cool.* 該物質冷却時結晶． **2** *vt / i* come to a definite form after being uncertain (使)具體化: *His plans have crystallized at last.* 他的計劃終於具體化．**'crystal ball** large glass ball, used by some people who claim to be able to say what will happen in the future 水晶球(算命的人自稱可以從中看出未來的吉凶禍福)．

cub [kʌb] *nc* young of certain animals (e.g. bear, fox, lion) 幼獸 (例如: 小熊, 小狐, 小獅)．

cubbyhole ['kʌbihoul] *nc* small hole, cupboard or room, in which things can be stored (可存放物品的)小壁橱或小房間．

cube [kju:b] **1** *nc* solid object having six square sides of equal size 立方體． **2** number obtained when a number is multiplied by itself twice (e.g. 3×3×3 =27; 27 is the cube of 3) (It can also be said that 3 is the cube root of 27) 立方 (例如: 27是3的立方 cube, 而 3 則稱爲 27 的立方根 cube root). **cubic** *adj: a cubic foot* i.e. volume of a cube whose sides are each one foot long 立方英尺．

cubicle ['kju:bikl] *nc* small room (esp. one for sleeping in e.g. in a hospital) 小室(尤指醫院中的小卧室)．

cubism ['kju:bizəm] *nc* style of painting practised in the early 20th century and using rectangles 立體畫派．

cuboid ['kju:bɔid] *adj* resembling a cube in form 立方形的; 骰子形的． Also 亦 作 *nc* rectangular parallelepiped; cuboid bone 長方體, 矩形體; 骰骨．

cuckoo ['kuku:] *nc* bird which makes a sound like this word and which lays its eggs in the nests of other birds 布穀鳥, 杜鵑. *pl* 複數 **cuckoos.**

cucumber ['kju:kʌmbə*] *nc / u* long thin vegetable with a green skin and firm flesh, eaten raw in salads 黃瓜．

cuddle ['kʌdl] *vt / i* hold tightly in the arms as a sign of love 擁抱． Also 亦作 *nc.*

cue¹ [kju:] *nc* **1** a few words said by an actor, which are the signal for another actor to begin speaking (舞台上的) 提示, 暗示． **2** signal or sign to somebody that he should begin to do something (行動的) 暗示．

cue² [kju:] *nc* long stick used' in the game of billiards 台球的球桿．

cuff¹ [kʌf] *nc* **1** end of the sleeve of a coat or shirt nearest the hand 袖口． **2** *(US)* fold at the bottom of a trouser leg (美) 褲脚的翻邊． *(Brit* 英 turnup) **'cufflink** type of fastening for the cuff of a shirt (襯衫的) 袖口扣.

cuff² [kʌf] *nc* light blow to the head given with the hand (用手對頭部的) 輕輕拍打. Also *vt* hit somebody in this way 輕輕拍打頭

cuisine [kwi'ziːn] *nc / u* cooking or style of cooking (esp. in a hotel or restaurant, or in a country as a whole) 烹飪 (尤指旅館, 酒店或某一國家的烹飪特色): *French cuisine is one of the best in the world.* 法國菜是是世界上最好的烹飪之一.

cul-de-sac ['kʌldəsæk] *nc* street with an opening at one end only 死胡同, 一頭閉塞只有另一頭可以通行的街巷.

culinary ['kʌlinəri] *adj* having reference to cooking 烹飪的.

culminate ['kʌlmineit] *vi* reach the end point in some process 達到頂點: *The long quarrel between Tom and his neighbour culminated in a fight.* 湯姆和他鄰居的口角最終發展到互相扭打.

culprit ['kʌlprit] *nc* person who has done something wrong (usu. something less serious than a crime) 犯有過失 (通常尚未構成罪行) 的人.

cult [kʌlt] *nc* **1** system of religious belief or behaviour (esp. one within a wider religion) 教派 (尤指某種宗教中一分支) 某種教派的信仰, 崇拜: *The cult of the Virgin Mary is an important part of Christianity.* 對童貞女瑪利亞的崇拜是基督教信仰的重要部份. **2** great interest in something (esp. an interest which is confined to a few people only) 狂熱的崇拜 (尤指只限於少數人中的).

cultivate ['kʌltiveit] *vt* **1** grow 栽培: *cultivate wheat* 種麥. **2** plant crops in 種植: *cultivate the land* 耕地. **3** try to improve or make better 培養, 提高, 修習: *cultivate one's knowledge of*

French 提高自己的法語知識. **cultivation** [kʌlti'vei∫ən] *nu* **cultivated** *adj* **1** (with reference to land) used for farming (指土地) 供耕作的. **2** (with reference to a person) having polite manners and a wide knowledge of art, music and literature (指人) 有教養的, 有文化素養的. (*opp* 反義詞 **uncultivated**).

culture ['kʌlt∫ə*] *nu* **1** knowledge of or training in art, music and literature 文化修養. **2** *nc / u* way of life of a particular group of people 文化: *Many ancient cultures can be found in Africa.* 在非洲可以發現許多古代文化. *African culture should be studied more carefully by Europeans.* 歐洲人應該更仔細地研究非洲文化. **cultural** *adj* **cultured** *adj* (with reference to a person) welleducated and polite (指人) 有教養的, 文雅的. (*opp* 反義詞 **uncultured**).

cumbersome ['kʌmbəsəm] *adj* large; heavy; difficult to use or move easily 笨重的.

cumulative ['kjuːmjulətiv] *adj* getting larger by being added to 累積的: *cumulative effect* 累積的效果.

cuneiform ['kjuːniifɔːm] *adj* wedge-shaped 楔形的. Also 亦作 *nu* cuneiform characters 楔形文字.

cunning ['kʌniŋ] *adj* clever and often dishonest 狡猾的: *a cunning thief* 狡猾的小偷; *a cunning trick* 詭計. Also 亦作 *nu*.

cup [kʌp] *nc* **1** vessel (usu. made of pottery or plastic and with a handle) used for drinking from 杯. **2** the amount that is contained in a cup 一杯 (的含量): *He drank a cup of water.* 他喝了一杯水. **3** large metal object (usu. shaped like a cup given to the winner of a game or competition (作

爲優勝獎品的)金杯,獎杯. Also 亦作 *vt* put in the shape of a cup (usu. in **cup one's hands**) 使成杯狀(通常用於 cup one's hands 短語中). *past* 過去式和過去分詞 **cupped.**

cupful ['kʌpful] *nc* as much as a cup will hold 一滿杯.

cupboard ['kʌbəd] *nc* (mainly *Brit*) piece of furniture, or place built into the wall and closed by a door, for storing things in (主要用於英)碗櫥, 衣櫥, 櫥櫃.

curate ['kju:rit] *nc* clergyman (esp. of the Church of England) who helps a vicar or rector (尤指英國教會的)副牧師, 助理牧師.

curator [kju'reitə*] *nc* person in charge of a museum or art gallery (博物館或美術館的)館長.

curb¹ [kə:b] *nc* **1** piece of leather or metal chain fastened under a horse's jaw and used to control the horse 馬勒, 馬銜索(勒馬的皮帶或鏈帶). **2** anything which acts as a control in this way 抑制物, 控制物. Also 亦作 *vt* use a curb on 抑制, 控制: *You must learn to curb your temper* i.e. you must not get so angry. 你要學會制怒.

curb² [kə:b] *nc* see 見 **kerb.**

curd [kə:d] *nc* (usu. *pl*) thick substance formed when milk becomes sour, and used in making cheese (通常用複數)凝乳(牛乳酸時, 所分離出的物體, 用以製造奶酪).

curdle ['kə:dl] *vt / i* (with reference to milk) form curds (指牛奶)(使)凝成凝乳.

cure [kjuə*] *vt* **1** make well by removing the cause of disease or illness 治愈: *The drug cured my fever.* 這藥治好我的發燒. **2** end something bad 矯正, 整治: *The government is trying to cure unemployment.* 政府試圖解決失業問題. **3** treat in some way in order to preserve (e.g. with reference to fish, meat, tobacco, furs, skins) 用曬燻, 醃製等辦法保存(魚, 肉, 烟草, 毛, 皮等). Also 亦作 *nc* something which cures 藥品; 對策. **curable** *adj* able to be cured 能治好的. (*opp* 反義詞 **incurable).**

curfew ['kə:fju:] *nc* time during which people are not allowed to leave their houses (e.g. during a time of rioting or revolution); the signal for this time to begin 戒嚴, 宵禁; 戒嚴開始的信號.

curio ['kjuəriou] *nc* unusual and interesting object 古玩, 古董, 珍品. *pl* 複數 **curios.**

curious ['kjuəriəs] *adj* **1** showing great interest in many things (esp. in matters which concern other people) 好奇的(尤指管閒事的). **2** strange and interesting 稀奇古怪的: *I heard a curious noise last night* i.e. a noise which I cannot explain. 昨天晚上我聽見一種古怪的聲音. **curiosity** [kjuə-ri'ɔsiti] **1** *nc* strong interest in many things 好奇心. **2** *nc* unusual and interesting thing 新奇有趣的東西.

curl [kə:l] *nc* piece of hair forming (part of) a circle 捲曲的頭髮. Also 亦作 *vt / i* form curls in hair 捲曲(頭髮). *Her hair curls naturally* i.e. they do not make the curls. 她的頭髮是天生捲曲的. *She curled her hair.* 她把頭髮捲起來. **curly** *adj* **curler** *nc* (usu. *pl*) object made of metal or plastic, used for putting a curl into a woman's hair (通常用複數)捲髮夾.

curlew ['kə:lju:] *nc* type of speckled bird with a very long curved beak and a shrill cry 麻鷸.

currant ['kʌrnt] *nc* **1** small dried grape used in cooking (烹飪用的)無核小葡萄乾. **2** name given to various types of small fruit (e.g. *red currant, black currant*) 茶藨子, 穗狀醋栗 (例如: red currant 紅茶藨子, black currant 茶藨子).

currency ['kʌrnsi] **1** *nc* money in use in a country 通貨, 貨幣: *Most countries have a decimal currency* i.e. a currency based on a unit divided into 100. 大多數國家採用十進制貨幣. **2** *nc* condition of being used at the present time 通行, 流通: *Many English words are in common currency throughout the world* i.e. have been taken into many different languages. 許多英語單詞在全世界各地流通. 即: 許多單詞被許多種語言採用. see **current¹**.

current¹ ['kʌrnt] *adj* in use at the present time 現時的, 現行的: *the current issue of a magazine* i.e. the most recent one 最近這期的雜誌; *current events* i.e. events which have occurred not long ago or which are occurring now 時事. **currently** *adv*.

current² ['kʌrnt] *nc* **1** movement of water, air or gas in one direction 水流; 氣流. **2** movement of electricity along a conductor 電流.

curriculum [kə'rikjuləm] *nc* course of study in a school or college 課程. pl 複數 **curricula** [kə'rikjulə] or **curriculums, cu'rriculum 'vitae** list of the main events of a person's life (e.g. schools, jobs etc.) 個人履歷.

curry ['kʌri] *nc / u* type of food made with spices which taste very hot 咖喱.

curse [kə:s] *vt / i* **1** use language asking for somebody / something to be punished or hurt (esp. asking God to do this) 詛咒 (尤指祈求上帝降禍於某人): *The old man cursed his enemies.* 那老人詛咒他的仇人. **2** use insulting language to 咒罵, 惡罵. Also 亦作 *nc* **1** language asking God to curse somebody / something 詛咒; 咒罵人的話: *The old man pronounced a curse on his enemies.* 老人詛咒他的仇人. **2** something which causes unhappiness and misfortune 災殃, 禍根.

cursory ['kə:səri] *adj* done in a hurry 粗略的, 草率的: *He took a cursory look at the title.* 他粗略地看了一下標題.

curt [kə:t] *adj* (with reference to speaking) short and impolite (指言詞) 簡單的, 草率的, 粗魯的: *He gave a very curt reply.* 他作出十分粗魯的答覆.

curtail [kə:'teil] *vt* make shorter or less 縮短, 削減: *I have had to curtail my spending* i.e. spend less money than I had wanted to. 我不得不節約開支.

curtain ['kə:tn] *nc* **1** large piece of cloth hung in front of a window inside a room 窗簾. **2** large piece of cloth which is used to hide the stage of a theatre from the audience (舞台上的) 幕. **3** anything which hides like a curtain 幕狀物: *a curtain of smoke* 烟幕; *a curtain of lies* 掩蓋真相的謊言. **'safety curtain** large sheet of asbestos or other fireproof material, which can be used in a theatre to prevent a fire from spreading from behind the stage to the rest of the building 安全幕 (石棉或其它防火材料製成, 舞台後台起火時, 可用以隔絕火路, 以免火勢蔓延).

curtsey, curtsy ['kə:tsi] *nc* bending of the knees made by a woman as a very formal sign of respect 婦女對於尊長表示尊敬的) 屈膝禮. Also 亦作 *vi* make this movement 行屈膝禮.

curve [kə:v] *nc* line with a rounded shape 曲線. Also 亦作 *vt / i* form a curve (使) 成曲線, 轉彎: *The road curved.* 道路轉彎了. *He curved the piece of wood.* 他把木頭弄彎.

cushion ['kuʃən] *nc* **1** small bag of cloth, filled with something soft and used in a chair to make one more comfortable 坐墊, 墊子. **2** anything which is soft like a cushion 軟墊, 緩衝的物體. Also 亦作 *vt* protect from a hard blow or shock 使減少震動; 緩和: *His hat helped to cushion the blow.* 他的帽子減輕了打擊的力量.

custard ['kʌstəd] *nc/u* sweet yellow substance made from milk and eggs and served with or as a pudding 牛奶蛋糊.

custody ['kʌstədi] *nu* duty or work of protecting something or keeping something safe 監護權; 保護; 監禁: *The police have the thief in custody* i.e. the thief is in prison or a police station. 警方把小偷拘留起來. *The father asked for the custody of his children when his wife left him.* 妻子離開他以後, 做父親的要求取得對孩子的管教及撫養權.

custom ['kʌstəm] **1** *nu* things which are usu. done by people 習慣, 風俗: *Custom has a strong influence on people's behaviour.* 風俗習慣對於人的行為有強烈的影響. **2** *nc* any action which is usu. done by people or by a person 習慣性的做法, 通常的做法: *It is not the custom in Britain to shake hands every time one meets a person.* 在英國, 通常的做法不須每一次見到人都握手. **3** *nu* practice of regularly buying goods from a certain shop 經常對某一商店的光顧: *The butcher lost a lot of custom by charging high prices* i.e. many people stopped buying from him. 肉店老闆索價太高, 失去許多生意. **customary** *adj* usually done 慣例的, 通常的. **customs** *npl* **1** taxes paid on goods brought into a country 關稅. **2** government department which

collects these taxes 海關. **3** see 見 **customs house. customer** *nc* person who buys goods from a shop 顧客. **'custom(s) house** building or office where taxes are collected on goods brought into a country 海關 (大樓). **'custom-'built** / **-'made** specially made for somebody 定製的, 定做的.

cut¹ [kʌt] **1** *vt / i* open or separate with something sharp 切; 割; 切開: *He cut his finger with a knife.* 他的指頭給刀割破了. *This knife doesn't cut very well.* 這把刀不好切. **2** *vi* allow cutting 容易切: *This piece of meat cuts very well* i.e. it is easy to cut the meat. 這塊肉很容易切. **3** *vt* make by cutting 挖成; 割出, 割成: *He cut a hole in the cloth.* 他在布上挖了一個洞. **4** *vt* make shorter by cutting 割短; 剪短: *Cut someone's hair* 把某人的頭髮剪短. **5** *vt* make smaller or less 縮小, 縮短: *A producer of a play sometimes cuts an actor's speeches* i.e. he tells the actor to speak only part of what is written down for him. 戲劇演出者有時要演員縮短台詞. *We must cut the cost of education* 我們必須削減教育經費. **6** *vt* not go to a lesson, lecture, meeting etc. *(informal)* 缺課, 缺席. (非正式). **7** *vt / i* divide a pack of playing cards into two or more lots (玩紙牌時發牌前) 切牌. **8** *vt* (esp. in geometry) cross (尤指幾何) 相交: *The line AB cuts the line DC at the point E.* AB線與DC線相交於E點. *pres part* 現在分詞 **cutting.** *past* 過去式和過去分詞 **cut out across something** go across, through or in front or in order to make a journey shorter 穿過: *We can get home quicker if we cut across the field, instead of keeping to the road.* 如果我們不順著路走, 而是穿過田野走, 我們會更早到家. *The car cut across* *my path* i.e. it moved right in front of where I was, so that I could not move forward easily. 車子在我前面攔着路. **cut something back** make smaller 削減, 剪短; 截短: *We must cut back our expenses.* 我們必須削減開支. *The gardener cut back all the bushes.* 花匠把所有的矮樹都修剪過. **cut something down** cause to fall by cutting 砍倒: *He cut down all the old trees.* 他砍倒所有的老樹. **cut down (on) something** make less 縮減, 刪減, 減少: *We must cut down on our expenses.* 我們必須縮減開支. *I have decided to cut down my smoking.* 我已下決心少抽煙. **cut in 1** go in front of somebody (esp. when driving a car) 搶在某人前面; (尤指)超車. **2** suddenly begin talking (often interrupting somebody else) 插嘴, 插話. **cut something off 1** remove by cutting 割掉, 剪掉: *He cut off some flowers from the bush.* 他從灌木中剪掉一些花. **2** stop suddenly 突然停止: *The government cut off the supply of oil to the enemy.* 政府中斷對敵人供應石油. **3** go between somebody and the place he is trying to get to 切斷. *Our troops cut off the enemy / the enemy's retreat.* 我們的部隊切斷了敵軍/敵人的退路. **cut something open** by cutting 割開: *He cut open the door of the safe.* 他把保險箱的門撬開. *The sharp stone cut his head open.* 尖利的石頭把他頭割開一個口. **cut out** (with reference to a machine etc) stop suddenly (指機器等)突然停止. *The radio cut out.* 無線電突然發聲音了. **cut something out 1** remove (esp. from inside) by cutting (尤指內部)切除, 割掉: *The surgeon cut out all the diseased tissue.* 外科醫生切除了一切有毛病的組織. **2** make by cutting 剪裁:

She cut out a new dress i.e. she cut the pieces in order to sew them into a dress. 她剪裁一件新連衣裙. **3** stop doing 停止: *Cut it out!* i.e. stop doing that. *(informal)* 住手! 不要做了! 住嘴! (非正式). **cut something short** (often with reference to talking) stop somebody who is doing something by beginning to do something oneself 打斷 (常指談話): *He began to explain his ideas to me, but I cut him short.* 他開始對我說明他的意見, 可我打斷了他的話. **cut something up** cut into pieces 切碎: *He always cuts up his food before he eats it.* 他總是把食物切碎才吃. **cut a corner 1** go across a corner instead of round it 抄近路, 不走彎路. **2** do something by a short, quick method 用簡捷的方法辦事, 走捷徑.

cut² [kʌt] *nc* **1** opening or separation made with something sharp 切口; 傷口: *He made a cut on this arm with a knife.* 他用刀在手臂上開了一個切口. **2** making shorter 縮短, 縮減: *The government is trying to make cuts in its spending this year* i.e. is trying to spend less money. 政府試圖削減今年的開支. **3** quick, sudden blow with a sword or whip, or with a bat in cricket and other games (鞭)抽, (劍的)擊, (板球等運動的)削球. **4** style in which clothes are made (衣服裁剪的)式樣: *Your new suit has a very good cut.* 你的新衣服式樣非常好. **5** share of money or property stolen or gained *(informal* in sense **5**) (盜竊或盈餘所得的)份額 (義 5 爲非正式). **cutting** *nc* **1** section cut out of a newspaper or magazine 剪報, 刊物剪輯下來的材料. **2** piece cut off a plant to be planted in another place 剪枝. **3** tunnel or way for a road or railway, cut through a hill 路塹. Also 亦作 *adj* **1** sharp 鋒利的. **2** (with reference to words) causing unhappiness to somebody (指言詞、字眼) 尖刻的: *a cutting remark* 尖刻的語言. **'cut-price** *adj* reduced in price 削價的. **cut-throat** *adj* very fierce 激烈的, 殘酷的: *cut-throat competition* 你死我活的競爭. **'short 'cut** way to a place which brings one there in less time than the main road 捷徑: *He took a short cut across the fields.* 他抄短路從田野裏橫穿過去.

cute [kju:t] *adj* **1** quick and clever 聰明的, 伶俐的. **2** (with reference to children or young women) pretty (指兒童或年輕女人) 嬌小可愛的. (both *informal*) (均爲非正式).

cuticle ['kju:tikl] *nc* the outside layer of skin (esp. the skin around the fingernails) 表皮(尤指指甲週圍的表皮).

cutlery ['kʌtləri] *nu* knives, forks and spoons used for eating food (西餐的)刀叉餐具.

cutlet [kʌtlit] *nc small piece of meat* 肉片.

cutter ['kʌtə] *nc* **1** person or thing that cuts 切割者; 切削工人; 切削器. **2** tailor who measures and cuts out the cloth (服裝的)裁剪師. **3** small sailing boat with one mast 單桅快艇.

cyanide ['saiənaid] *nu* very strong type of poison 氰化物.

cycle ['saikl] *nc* **1** bicycle 自行車. **2** series of events coming in a certain order 循環: *the cycle of the year* i.e. the seasons of the year 一年四季. Also 亦作 *vi* ride a bicycle 騎自行車.

cyclist *nc* person who rides a bicycle 騎自行車的人. **cycling** *nu* riding a bicycle 騎自行車.

cyclone ['saikloun] *nc* strong winds which move in a circle around a still centre 旋風.

cygnet ['signit] *nc* young swan 小天鵝.

cylinder ['silində*] *nc* **1** object with circular ends and straight sides (e.g. beer can, cigarette) 圓柱體(例如: 啤酒罐、香烟). **2** hollow part of a motor-car engine, shaped like a cylinder, in which air and petrol vapour are exploded 汽缸. **cylindrical** [si'lindrikl] *adj*.

cymbal ['simbl] *nc* large round flat piece of metal, used as a musical instrument. Two cymbals are usu. hit together 鐃; 鈸.

cynic ['sinik] *nc* person who thinks that people always have bad or selfish reasons for what they do, even if they seem to be acting in a good and kind way 憤世嫉俗者. **cynical** *adj* **cynicism** ['sinisizəm] *nu* beliefs of a cynic 憤世嫉俗.

cypher ['saifə*] *nc see* **cipher.**

cyst [sist] *nc* small growth like a bag, caused by certain diseases in people, plants and animals 包囊.

czar [za:*] *nc* title of the former emperors of Russia 沙皇. **czarina** [za:'ri:nə] *nc* wife of a czar 沙皇皇后. *Note* 說明: these words are also spelled with *ts-* or *tz-* instead of *cz-*. 這兩個詞的cz-也可拼寫作 ts-或tz-.

D,d

dad [dæd] *vt / i* touch very gently 輕觸；
輕拍；輕輕地塗抹：*She dabbed the
wound with a piece of cloth.* 她用一塊
布輕輕地擦傷口. Also 亦作 *nc* light
touch 輕觸；輕拍：*This wall
needs a dab of paint.* 這面牆需要薄薄
塗上一層油漆. *past* 過去式和過去分詞
dabbed.

dabble ['dæbl] *vt / i* put hands or feet
etc in and out of water 玩水：*He dab-
bled his fingers in the stream.* 他用指
頭在溪流中玩水. **dabble in some-
thing** study or take part in something
for amusement but not in any serious way 涉獵，淺嘗：*He used to dabble in politics.* 過去他也常涉獵政治.

dad [dæd], **daddy** ['dædi] *nc* informal
form of **father** father 的非正式形式.
'**daddy-'long-legs** type of insect with
long legs 長腳蜘蛛.

daffodil ['dæfədil] *nc* flower with a
trumpet-shaped centre surrounded by
circle of petals 水仙花.

daft [da:ft] *adj* mad, foolish. *(informal)*
愚蠢的；瘋狂的. (非正式).

dagger ['dægə*] *nc* short, pointed knife
used for stabbing 匕首, 短劍.

daily ['deili] *adj / adv* see 見 **day.**

dainty ['deinti] *adj* small and pretty 嬌
小的, 秀麗的；精緻的：*a very dainty
little girl* 十分秀麗的女孩子.

dairy ['dɛəri] *nc* place where milk is
kept, and where butter and cheese
are made or sold 牛奶場；製酪場.

dais ['deiis] *nc* raised platform in a
room for a speaker, lecturer or important person 講台.

daisy ['deizi] *nc* type of small, white

flower with a yellow centre 雛菊.

dam [dæm] *nc* wall or construction
which holds back water 堤壩. Also 亦
作 *vt* (often with **up**) keep back with
a dam (常與 up 連用) 築壩攔住：*They
dammed the river.* 他們築壩攔住河流.
past 過去式和過去分詞 **dammed.**

damage ['dæmidʒ] *vt* break or spoil
(but not destroy) 損壞, 損傷：*He
damaged my car with a stone.* 他用石
頭砸壞我的車子. Also 亦作 *nu*：*He did
a lot of damage to my car.* 他弄壞我
的車子, 毀損得很厲害. **damages** *npl*
money asked for or given in a law
case because somebody has damaged
the property, person or reputaion of
somebody else 損害賠償費.

dame [deim] *nc* **1** old word for a lady
(古 時) 貴婦. **2 (Dame)** title of a
woman equivalent to that of a knight
(Dame) 夫人 (婦女的銜頭, 相當於爵
士). *Note*說明：a woman with the title of Dame is addressed as 'Dame
Jane Smith' not as 'Dame Smith' 對有
Dame 銜頭的婦女, 應稱呼其爲"Dame
Jane Smith", 不可稱"Dame Smith"

damn [dæm] *vt* say that something is of
no value or use 詆毀：*He damned all
my suggestions.* 他把我的一切建議都
說得一無是處. Also 亦作 *interj* to express anger or dislike 表示憤怒或厭
惡：*Damn you* 你這個該死的! *Damn
this work!* 見鬼, 這種工作! **damned**
adj used to describe something/
someone which causes annoyance 糟
透的, 該死的：*that damned pen* 那壞
透的 筆. Also 亦作 *adv / intensifier*
very (加強口氣) 非常, 不得了：*a*

damned good book 了不起的好書.
(both *informal*) (均為非正式).

damp¹ [dæmp] *adj* slightly wet; moist
潮濕的: *The ground is still damp after
the rain.* 雨後地面仍舊潮濕. *The
damp climate does not suit her.* 她不
適應潮濕天氣. Also 亦作 *nu* slight
feeling of wetness 潮濕. *There's still
damp in these clothes.* 這些衣服沒全
乾, 還有一些潮濕.

damp² [dæmp] *vt* **1** make slightly wet
弄潮濕: *He damped his cloth before
cleaning the windows.* 他在揩窗子以
前先把布弄濕. **2** discourage 使沮喪,
給…潑冷水: *My failure last time has
not damped my interest.* 上次我雖然
失敗, 卻沒因此洩氣. **dampen** *vt* **1**
make damp 弄潮濕. **2** discourage 使
沮喪, 給…潑冷水. **damper** *nc* moveable plate in a stove, which can be
used to make the fire burn more or
less brightly 爐風調節閘. **put a damper on something** act or speak in a
way that causes other people to be
less interested in something 給某事潑
冷水, 煞某事的風景: *He put a damper
on our plans for a holiday, by telling
us how expensive it would be.* (*informal*) 他告訴我們度假是多麼花錢, 使我
們對原來的度假計劃興致大減. (非正
式).

damson ['dæmzn] *nc* **1** type of plum
with dark blue fruit 西洋李子, 布拉斯
李. **2** tree on which it grows 西洋李
子樹, 布拉斯李樹.

dance [dɑ:ns] *nc* rhythmical movement
of the body (usu. in time to music) 跳
舞. **2** party or social gathering held
for people to dance 舞會. Also 亦作
vt / i: *They were dancing.* 他們正在跳
舞. *He danced a few steps.* 他跳了幾
步舞步. **dancer** *nc* **dancing** *nu*
'dance hall building which people

pay to enter in order to dance (跳) 舞
廳, 舞場.

dandelion ['dændilaiən] *nc* small, yellow flower which grows wild, and
whose seeds fly in the air 蒲公英.

dandruff ['dændrʌf] *nu* small white
pieces of dead skin in the hair of the
head 頭皮屑.

dandy ['dændi] *nc* man who gives much
attention to dressing fashionably 花花
公子, 一味著重打扮的男人.

danger ['deindʒə*] *nu* **1** strong possibility of injury, death or harm of some
kind 危險: *The young child did not
realize the danger of playing on the
road.* 小孩子沒意識到在馬路上玩的
危險. **2** *nc* thing which causes danger
危險, 危害, 威脅: *Children who play
on the road are a danger to motorists.*
在馬路上玩要的兒童對於開汽車的人是
種威脅. **dangerous** ['deindʒrəs] *adj*
causing danger 招致危險的; 危險的:
He is a dangerous criminal. 他是一個
危險的罪犯. *It's dangerous to throw
stones.* 扔石頭是危險的. **dangerously**
adv **in danger** likely to be injured
or killed 易受殺傷, 在危險中: *Chil-
dren who play on the roads are in
danger.* 在馬路上玩耍的兒童是處在危
險之中.

dangle ['dæŋgl] *vt / i* hang loosely 垂着;
懸掛: *He dangled his arm over the
back of the chair.* 他的手臂垂在椅背
上.

dank [dæŋk] *adj* wet and cold 又濕, 又
冷的: *a dank cellar* 又濕又冷的地窖.

dare [dɛə*] *vt* **1** *aux* (used esp. in *negative* sentences, questions and after if)
be brave enough to (尤用於否定句, 疑
問句中或在if之後) 敢於: *I dare not tell
my father what has happened.* 我不敢
告訴父親發生了甚麼事. *How dare
you speak to me like that?* 你怎麼敢這

樣對我講話? He daren't go any higher. 他不敢再往上攀登. If you dare speak to me like that again, you will be sorry. 你要敢再這樣對我說話, 你會懊悔的. **2** vi be brave enough to 敢於: To our surprise, he dared to repeat his statements. 令我們驚奇的是他敢把自己的話重複一遍. He dares to behave like that in my house! 他好大膽子, 竟敢在我家裏這樣幹! The children don't dare (to) make a sound while their parents are sleeping. 孩子們在父母親睡覺時不敢出聲. Note 說明: **1** and **2** are different in structure, not in meaning. **1** is an auxiliary, does not take to, and has no s in the third person singular (he / she / it). **2** is a regular verb and normally takes to (e.g. dared to climb), but native speakers often miss out to as in the last example. 1和2結構不同, 但意思一樣. 1的dare是輔助動詞, 其後的不定式前不用to, 且在第三人稱單數的主語時不必在詞尾加s. 2是規則動詞, 通常後接to (例如: dared to climb), 但英美人常將to省略, 如最後一例句. **3** vt say that one thinks another person is not brave enough to do something challenge 說(對方)不敢做某件事; 挑激; I dared him to climb the wall. 我用挑戰性口吻, 問他敢不敢爬上牆. **daring** nu courage to do something dangerous 勇敢: That boy has a lot of daring. 那個男孩子很勇敢. Also 亦作 adj: a daring boy 一個膽子大的男孩子. '**daredevil** nc person who is so brave that his actions seem to be foolish 蠻幹的人, 膽大妄爲的人. Also 亦作 adj: a daredevil action 大膽而冒失的行爲. **I dare say** possibly; it may be right to say 可能; 大概是; 可以這麼說: I dare say (that) it will rain tomorrow. 看來明天會下雨.

dark [dɑːk] adj **1** without light or almost without light 黑暗的: The night is very dark. 夜裏, 天色十分黑. **2** not light in colour 深色的: He has dark eyes i.e. eyes which are brown or black. 他有一對深色的眼睛. 即: 棕色或黑色的眼睛. **3** (with reference to colours) containing an element of black (指顏色)帶有黑的成分的, 深色的: dark red 深紅的; dark blue etc. 深藍的等. Also 亦作 n sing absence of light 黑暗: Some animals can see in the dark. 有些動物在黑暗中能看得見. **darkness** nu **darken** vt / i become or make dark (使)變暗: Buildings often darken as they get older. 年代一長久, 建築物常常變得陰暗. '**dark 'horse** person who does something clever or successful when nobody expects him to do so. (informal) 爆冷門的優勝者. (非正式). **after / before dark** after / before the beginning of sunset 天黑以後 / 以前: There were not many people on the streets after dark. 天黑以後街上人不多.

darling ['dɑːliŋ] nc somebody whom one loves 親愛的, 心愛的人. Also 亦作 adj: my darling daughter 我心肝寶貝的女兒.

darn [dɑːn] vt / i mend a hole by weaving thread or wool 織補. Also 亦作 nc place where a hole or worn place has been darned 經過織補的地方.

dart [dɑːt] nc **1** small object made of wood, metal or plastic, with a point at one end, thrown at a board marked with numbers in a game (called **darts**) 鏢; 箭; 飛鏢(投鏢遊戲中所用). **2** sudden movement 急衝; 突進: He made a dart towards the door. 他飛也似地向門衝去. Also 亦作 vt / i make a sudden movement 急衝, 飛奔: He darted towards the door. 他飛也似地

向門衝去.

dash¹ [dæʃ] *nc* **1** sudden quick movement (esp. one made by running) 猛衝, 衝刺 (尤指跑步時): *He made a dash towards the house.* 他猛地向那房子衝去. **2** (often with reference to cooking) small amount of liquid etc. (常指烹飪) 少量的液體等: *You should add a dash of vinegar.* 你得加少量的醋. **3** the mark–used in writing 破折號.

dash² [dæʃ] **1** *vi* run; move quickly 猛衝, 衝刺: *He dashed towards the house.* 他猛地向那房子衝去. **2** *vt* throw in order to break 砸, 摔破: *He dashed the cup on the ground.* 他把杯子用力摔在地面上, 破了. **3** *vt* throw liquid 潑: *He dashed a glass of beer in my face.* 他把一杯啤酒潑在我臉上. **4** *vt* (often *passive*) disappoint (常用於被動語態) 使落空: *Our hopes were dashed by the news* i.e. the news told us that we would not get what we had hoped for. 消息傳來, 我們的希望破滅了. **dash!** exclamation showing annoyance 見鬼! 該死! (表示厭煩)

dashing *adj* smart and lively 精神抖擻的; 有朝氣的: *He looked very dashing in his new suit.* 他穿一套新衣服, 顯得朝氣蓬勃. **'dashboard** panel containing dials etc in front of the driver of a car, lorry etc. (汽車等的) 儀表板.

data ['deitə] *n sing* or *pl* 單數或複數 information which is known before one begins to solve a problem 資料. *Note* 說明: *data* is often treated as an uncountable noun. Originally it was a plural noun with a singular *datum*. It is sometimes used as a plural noun in formal and scientific writing. data常被看作不可數名詞, 原先它本是複數名詞, 其單數是datum. 有時在正式文章和科學文章中作爲複數名詞使用.

date¹ [deit] *nc* **1** time when something happened 日期, 年, 月, 日: *The date of the Norman Conquest of England is 1066.* 諾曼人征服英國的日期是1066年. *What is the date today?* i.e. what day of the month is it? 今天幾號? **2** arrangement to meet somebody (esp. an arrangement between a young man and a young woman) *(informal)* 約會 (尤指青年男女間的約會) (非正式). **out of date** old-fashioned; no longer used, or used by very few people 過時的; 陳舊的: *His clothes are rather out of date.* 他的衣服稍嫌式樣舊些. *These are very out-of-date ideas.* 這些是十分過時的思想. **up to date** modern and new 現代的; 時新的: *His ideas are up to date.* 他的思想趕得上時代.

date² [deit] *vt* **1** write a date on 寫上日期於: *He dated his letter 6 August 1967.* 他信上寫的日期是1967年8月6日. **2** decide the date of something 確定…的時期或年代: *The professor of Ancient History was asked to date the ruins which had been discovered.* 請了古代史教授來確定發現的古蹟遺址的年代. **3** arrange to meet a young man or young woman 和(年輕異性)約會: *John used to date Joan last year. (informal in sense 3)* 約翰去年經常和瓊約會(義3爲非正式). **dated** *adj* out of date; old and no longer used very much; unfashionable 過時的; 陳舊的: *His clothes are dated.* 他的衣服式樣過時.

date³ [deit] *nc* type of fruit which grows on trees (called **date palms**) in North Africa 棗(棗樹爲 date palms).

daub [dɔːb] *vt / i* **1** paint in an unskilled way 亂塗, 亂畫. **2** cover with something dirty or sticky 弄髒, (使)沾滿又

黐又黏的東西: *He daubed jam all over his face.* 他的臉上沾滿了果醬. *The people daub the walls of their huts with mud.* 這些人在他們茅屋的牆上塗滿了泥.

daughter ['dɔ:tə*] *nc* female child (of a parent) 女兒 '**daughter-in-law** *nc* wife of one's son 媳婦. *pl* 複數 **daughters-in-law.**

dawdle ['dɔ:dl] *vi* go slowly and lazily 閑蕩.

dawn [dɔ:n] *nc* beginning of the day 黎明. Also 亦作 *vi* begin to get light 破曉, 天亮: *The day was dawning.* 天剛破曉.

day [dei] *nc* **1** period of 24 hours 一天: *There are seven days in a week.* 一星期有七天. **2** period when it is light 白天: *In winter the day is shorter than the night in the northern hemisphere.* 在冬天, 北半球的白天比夜晚短. **3** (in *pl*) period of history (用於複數) 時代: *the days of the Romans* 羅馬(人)時代. **daily** *adj / adv* happening every day 每日的; 每日. Also 亦作 *nc* **1** daily newspaper 日報. **2** woman who does housework as a job (只在白天幫工, 而不住宿的) 女傭. '**daybreak / break of day** beginning of the day, when light first appears in the sky 破曉: *He goes to work at daybreak.* 他每天天一亮就去上班工作. '**daydream** *nc* thoughts about something pleasant and fanciful 白日夢, 幻想. Also 亦作 *vi* think in this way 做白日夢, 幻想: '**daylight** light of day 日光. '**daytime** period when it is light 白天. **day after day** for a long period of time (with the suggestion that the experience is very tiring or unpleasant) 日復一日, 天天如是: *I have to do this work day after day.* 我必須一天又一天重複這種工作. **day by day** every day 每一天. **one day** on a day in the past or future (過去或將來的)某一天, 有一天. **the other day** a few days ago 幾天前. **some day** at some time in the future 將來某一天.

daze [deiz] *vt* make confused or unable to think clearly 使眩暈, 使茫然. *He was dazed by a blow on the head.* 他頭部受到一記猛擊, 一時天旋地轉.

dazzle ['dæzl] *vt* make unable to see clearly 使眼花繚亂, 使目眩: *He was dazzled when he looked at the sun.* 他朝太陽看, 陽光照得他眼花.

dead [ded] *adj* **1** without life 死的, 無生命的: *The doctor arrived too late, for the old man was dead.* 醫生來得太晚, 因為老人已經死了. *These flowers are dead.* 這些花都死掉了. **2** without movement or activity or use 静止的, 不活動的, 沒作用的: *The volcano is dead* i.e. it no longer sends out fire and smoke. 這火山是座死火山. *The battery is dead* i.e. it no longer gives out an electric current. 這乾電池已經耗完了. *Latin is a dead language* i.e. nobody now speaks Latin as his mother tongue. 拉丁語是死的語言. 即: 現在已沒有人把拉丁語作爲母語. *That idea is completely dead* i.e. nobody considers that idea now. 那種思想已經完全過時了. Also 亦作 *adv* completely; straight 完全地; 直接地: *I'm dead tired.* 我累死了. **deaden** *vt* make less loud, less bright, less painful etc. 使不那麼大聲/不那麼光亮/不那麼痛苦等. **deadly** *adj* certain to cause death, dangerous 致命的, 危險的: *a deadly poison* 致命的毒藥. *deadly enemies* i.e. enemies who would like to kill each other 你不就沒有我的死對頭, 不共戴天的仇敵. **the dead** *npl* people who are dead 死去的人. '**dead 'end** *nc* **1** street with an opening at one end only 死胡同, 一頭不通的街道. **2** course, career, job etc which does not lead one to a higher position or to more money 沒有較好前途的路線、事業、工作等. **dead 'heat** *nc* result of a race in which two or more runners reach the winning post at the same time 不分勝負的賽跑. **'deadline** time by which one must do something 截止日期, 限期. **'deadlock** condition in which two sides in an argument or discussion are not able to agree 僵局, 相持不下: *After three hours of discussion the two governments reached deadlock.* 經過三個鐘頭的討論, 兩國政府相持不下, 形成僵局. **'deadpan** *adj* showing no expression on the face; not allowing one's feelings to show in one's face 無表情的; 不動聲色的.

deadweight ['dedweit] *nc / u* **1** weight of an inert person or thing 不動的人或物體的重量. **2** heavy or oppressive burden 重負, 重載. **3** dead load 靜負荷, 固定負載. **4** weight of a vehicle without a load 車輛的自重.

deaf [def] *adj* **1** unable to hear properly 耳聾的. **2** unwilling to listen 不願聽的: *He was deaf to my excuses.* 他不肯聽我的道歉. **deafness** *nu* **deafen** *vt* make deaf 使聽不見, 使聾. **deafening** *adj*: *deafening noise* i.e. a very loud one 震耳欲聾的嘈雜聲音. **'deaf-'mute** person who cannot hear or speak 又聾又啞的人.

deal¹ [di:l] *vt / i* (esp. with reference to giving out playing cards when playing a game) give out; share 分發 (尤指玩紙牌時發牌). *past* 過去式和過去分詞 **dealt** [delt]. **deal something out** share out 分給, 分發: *The teacher dealt out the books to the class.* 老師把書發給班上的學生. **deal with**

someone/something **1** be concerned with 管理; 處理: *This office deals with licences for motorcars.* 這個機構辦理機動車執照. **2** have business relations with; buy from or sell to 與…做買賣: *Manufacturers do not usually deal direct with members of the public* i.e. they sell their goods to shops and not to individual people. 廠商不常和公衆發生買賣關係. **3** take action about something 對付: *I don't know how to deal with these bad children* i.e. I don't know what to do with them. 對於這些壞孩子, 我真不知道怎麼辦才好.

deal² [di:l] business arrangement 交易協議. **dealer** *nc* **1** person who deals cards 發牌的人. **2** person who buys and sells goods 商人. **a good / great deal** very much 很多: *I spent a good deal of money last year.* 去年我花了很多錢.

dealt [delt] past of **deal¹**. **deal¹** 的過去式和過去分詞.

dear [diə*] *adj* **1** loved very much 親愛的: *His children were very dear to him.* 他非常愛他的孩子; **2** used to begin a letter (書信開頭的客套語) 親愛的: *Dear Sir;* 親愛的先生; *Dear Mr Smith* 親愛的史密斯先生. **3** costing a lot of money 昂貴的: *Sugar is very dear.* 糖非常貴. Also 亦作 *interj* used as a way of talking to a child or one's husband or wife etc. 對小孩子或丈夫、妻子講話時用的口頭語: *hullo dear!* 喂, 親愛的! Also 亦作 *adv* for a lot of money 高價地: *He sells his goods very dear.* 他的貨品賣得極貴. Also 亦作 *interj* to express surprise or sorrow 表示驚奇或悲傷: *Oh dear!; Dear me!* etc. 哎呀!

death [deθ] *nc* **1** end of life 死亡: *There have been 23 deaths from road acci-*

dents in the last week. 一週來由於公路上交通事故已經死了二十三人. **2** end or destruction of something 毀滅: *The fall of the Roman Empire did not mean the death of civilization in Europe.* 羅馬帝國的滅亡並不意味着歐洲文明的毀滅. **deathly** *adj* like death; causing death 死一樣的; 致命的: **'deathbed** bed on which somebody is dying or has died 瀕死者所躺卧的床; 死在其上的床.

debar [di'bɑ:] *vt* shut out; prevent; prohibit 關出; 排除; 阻擋; 阻止; 禁止: *debar someone from a place* 不讓某人進入某處; *People under eighteen are debarred from voting.* 十八歲以下的人沒有選舉權.

debate [di'beit] *nc* **1** meeting in which people argue for and against some idea 辯論會: *The Members of Parliament hold debates.* 議院議員舉行辯論會. **2** any discussion of reasons for and against something 辯論. Also 亦作 *vt / i: Parliament has been debating the financial situation.* 議院一直在辯論財政狀況. **debatable** *adj* not easily decided; allowing arguments for and against 不易決定的; 可辯論的, 值得爭辯的: *That's a debatable point; not everyone would agree with your opinion.* 那是一個會引起爭論的問題; 不見得每個人會同意你的意見.

debauchery [di'bɔ:tʃəri] *nc / u* too much enjoyment of the pleasures of the body 荒淫, 放蕩; 沉緬酒色.

debit ['debit] *nc* note of money owed or spent by a person, in a record of money received and spent (帳簿的) 借方. (*opp* 反義詞 **credit**). Also 亦作 *vt: The bank has debited the money against / to my account.* 銀行把一筆錢記在我帳户的借方.

debris, débris ['debri:] *nu* broken

pieces of something (esp. rock, brick etc.) caused by a bomb explosion (尤指岩石、磚塊等炸碎的) 碎片; 瓦礫堆.

debt [det] *nc* money or other commodity owed by somebody to somebody else 債務: *He lent me £5 last week and now he wants me to pay my debt* i.e. give back the £5. 上週他借給我5英鎊, 現在他要我還債. 即: 還5英鎊. **debtor** *nc* person who owes money 債務人, 借方. (*opp* 反義詞 **creditor**). **in debt** owing money 欠債, 負債: *I always try to avoid being in debt to anyone.* 我總儘量避免欠債.

debut, début ['deibju:] *nc* (esp. with reference to an actor or musician appearing for the first time in public) first appearance (尤指演員或音樂演奏者)初次公演, 初次登台.

decade ['dekeid] *nc* period of ten years 十年.

decadent ['dekədnt] *adj* having a lower standard of behaviour or excellence than in former times 頹廢的; 衰退的, 衰落的. **decadence** *nu.*

decant [di'kænt] *vt* pour liquid (often wine) from one container to another (usu. so as to leave any sediment or solid matter at the bottom of the first container) (把酒等從一個容器) 移注 (另一個容器, 通常為了留下沉澱物). **decanter** *nc* glass container for holding wine which has been decanted (用來盛裝經過移注的酒的) 玻璃器皿.

decapitate [di'kæpiteit] *vt* cut the head off 把…斬首, 砍…的頭.

decay [di'kei] *vt / i* become or make rotten (使) 腐爛, (使) 腐敗: *The fruit decayed in the damp weather.* 這種水果在潮濕的天氣裏腐爛了. Also 亦作 *nu* (esp. with reference to teeth) condition of being decayed; decaying substance (尤指牙齒) 蛀, 齲; 蛀牙, 齲齒.

decease [di'si:s] *nc* (usu. *sing*) death (*formal* and legal) (通常用單數)死亡(正式,法律). **the deceased** the dead person (*formal* and legal) 死者(正式、法律).

deceit [di'si:t] *nc / u* lying; hiding the truth; making somebody believe something which is not true 撒謊;隱瞞真相;欺騙. **deceitful** *adj* see 見 **deception. deceive** [di'si:v] *vt* make somebody believe something which is not true 欺騙: *The boy tried to deceive his father by saying that he did not know who broke the window.* 這個男孩欺騙他父親說,他不知道是誰打破了窗子.

decelerate [di:'seləreit] *vt / i* go, cause to go, more slowly (使)減速, (使)減緩.

December [di'sembə*] *n* last month of the year in the Western calendar 十二月.

decent ['di:snt] *adj* **1** suitable; proper; showing what is expected 合適的;恰當的;得體的: *He behaved in a decent manner.* 他舉止得體. (*opp* 反義詞 **indecent**). **2** good; satisfactory; kind 像樣的;令人滿意的;和善的: *That was a very decent meal.* 這餐飯很令人滿意. *He's quite a decent headmaster.* (*informal* in sense 2) 他是一位十分和氣的校長. (義2爲非正式) **decency** *nc / u.*

deception [di'sepʃən] *nc / u* words or behaviour intended to make somebody believe something which is not true 欺騙之言或行. **deceptive** [di'septiv] *adj* see 見 **deceit.**

decibel ['desibel] *nc* unit for the measurement of the loudness of sounds 分貝(測定音量的單位).

decide [di'said] **1** *vi* come to an opinion or decision after thought 決意;決定: *I*

have decided to help you. 我已決定幫助你. **2** *vt* cause a person to come to a decision 使下決心,使作出決定: *The news decided me.* 這消息使我作出決定. **3** *vt* end an argument or discussion by coming to a decision 解決: *John's information decided the argument.* 約翰提供的情況解決了這場爭論. see 見 **decision. decided** *adj* **1** clear; definite; easily noticed 清楚的;明確的;明顯的: *There was a decided improvement in my car after he repaired it.* 我的車子經他修理之後有了明顯的改善. **2** determined; having come to an opinion 決斷的;堅決的: *He was quite decided in his answer.* 他的答覆十分堅決.

deciduous [di'sidjuəs] *adj* (with reference to trees) losing leaves when the cold or dry weather approaches (指樹)季節性落葉的. (*opp* 反義詞 **evergreen**).

decimal ['desiml] *adj* based on counting in tens or tenths 十進制的. Also 亦作 *nc* number expressed as a decimal fraction (e.g. 0.7865) 小數(例如: 0.7865).

decimate ['desimeit] *vt* **1** kill one out of every ten 殺死…的1/10. **2** kill very many 大量殺死.

decipher [di'saifə*] *vt* **1** find the meaning of a message written in a code or cipher 譯解(密碼). **2** find the meaning of anything difficult to understand 解開(疑團).

decision [di'siʒən] **1** *nc* act of deciding; reaching an opinion after thought 決定;決斷: *The committee discussed the matter for three hours, but could not come to a decision.* 該委員會對這件事進行了三個小時的討論,但是未能作出決定. **2** *nu* ability to decide quickly 果斷: *He acted with decision as soon* *as he heard the news.* 他一聽到這消息就果斷地行動. see 見 **decide. decisive** [di'saisiv] *adj* **1** causing an argument, fight, disagreement, war etc to be settled (爭論, 戰鬥, 意見不一, 戰爭等)決定性的: *The allies won a decisive victory.* 盟國贏得了決定性的勝利. **2** showing the ability to decide quickly 果斷的. (*opp* 反義詞 **indecisive**).

deck¹ [dek] *nc* **1** floor in a ship 甲板, 艙面. **2** pack of playing cards 一副紙牌. **'deckchair** chair made of wood and canvas, which can be folded flat. It is used on beaches, ships and in other places (用於海濱, 船上等處的)折疊式木製帆布椅. **'deck hand** sailor of a low rank 甲板水手.

deck² [dek] *vt* cover with decorations or ornaments 裝飾, 點綴.

declaim [di'kleim] *vt / i* speak with great feeling (often in opposition to something) 譴責; 慷慨陳詞; 朗誦: *The newspapers declaimed against the new taxes.* 那家報紙譴責新稅法. *He declaimed a poem to the class.* 他向全班朗誦一首詩歌. **declamation** [deklə'meiʃən] *nc / u.*

declare [di'klɛə*] *vt* **1** make known publicly or strongly 宣佈, 宣告, 公告: *He declared the results of his experiments.* 他宣佈了自己的實驗結果. *He declared that he could not help us.* 他宣佈說他無法幫助我們. **2** say to a customs official what goods one is bringing into a country (向海關)申報, 報關: *I have nothing to declare* i.e. I am not bringing any taxable goods into the country. 我沒甚麼東西要報關的. 即: 我沒有帶進任何要納稅的物品. **declaration** *nc / u.*

decline [di'klain] **1** *vt / i* say that one does not want something which has

been offered 謝絕: *I declined his offer of help.* 他表示願意幫助我, 我謝絕了. **2** *vi* become weaker or less 衰弱, 衰落, 衰退. Also 亦作 *nc* (usu. only *sing*) process of becoming weaker or less (通常僅用單數)衰弱, 衰退: *There has been a decline in English cricket over the last ten years* i.e. England is not as good at cricket now as it was ten years ago. 過去的十年裏, 英國板球一直在走下坡路. 即: 如今英國的板球球技不如十年前了.

decode ['di:'koud] *vt* find the meaning of a message written in code 譯解(密碼).

decompose ['di:kəm'pouz] *vt / i* go, cause to go, bad or rotten and undergo chemical change (使)腐爛; (使)變質; (使)分解. **decomposition** [di:kɔmpə'ziʃən] *nu.*

decontaminate [di:kən'tæmineit] *vt* remove poison, gas, radioactivity or other harmful substances from a place or thing 使消毒; 消除(有害物質).

decor, décor ['deikɔ:*] *nc* (usu. only *sing*) decoration (e.g. of a house); scenery on a stage (通常只用單數)(房屋等的)裝飾; 舞台佈景.

decorate ['dekəreit] *vt / i* **1** add things to in order to make more beautiful (often as a sign of celebration) 裝飾, 裝潢, 點綴 (常做爲慶祝的標記): *She decorated her room with flowers in preparation for the party.* 她用花朵裝飾房間, 爲這次聚會做準備. **2** put new paint or wallpaper on a room or house 粉刷(房屋); 貼牆紙於(房屋): *I want to decorate my house this year.* 我想今年粉刷房子. **3** give somebody a medal 授予···勳章: *He was decorated in the war* i.e. he won a medal. 他在這場戰爭中獲得勳章. **decorative**

['dekərətiv] *adj* making more beautiful 裝飾(用)的, 裝潢(用)的. **decoration** [dekə'reiʃən] **1** *nu* act of decorating 裝飾, 裝潢. **2** *nc* something used in decorating 裝飾品, 裝潢材料. **3** *nc* medal 勳章. **decorator** *nc* person whose work is putting paint or wall-paper on rooms etc. 粉刷工人; 裝飾工人.

decorous ['dekərəs] *adj* proper or suit-able in behaviour; showing behaviour which people consider to be correct and polite 舉止得體的; 合乎禮節的, 合宜的 (*opp* 反義詞 **indecorous**). **decorum** [di'kɔːrəm] *nu*.

decoy ['diːkɔi] *nc* **1** artificial or real bird used to make other birds come near enough to be shot or caught 囮子, 人造囮子. **2** anything used in this way to lead a person into a certain posi-tion 圈套, 陷阱, 誘惑. Also 亦作 *vt* **1** shoot or catch a bird in this way 誘捕或誘殺 (鳥類). **2** lead a person into danger in this way 誘騙, 誘惑 (某人) 入圈套.

decrease [diː'kriːs] *vt / i* become or make smaller or less (使) 減少, (使) 減弱. Also 亦作 ['diːkriːs] *nu:* There has been a decrease in the number of uni-versity students in the last two years. 過去兩年裏大學生的數量減少了. (*opp* 反義詞 **increase**).

decree [di'kriː] *nc* official order or deci-sion (often one which is not made by the normal process of law-making) (常指不是通過正常立法程序制定的) 法令, 政令: The king decided to dismiss parliament and rule by decree i.e. rule by saying that people must do what he wanted them to do 該國王決定解散議會, 以發佈命令的方式進行統治. 即: 用指示人們必須按其意志行事的辦法進行統治. Also 亦作 *vt / i* make

decrees 頒佈(法令), 發佈(命令): The authorities decreed that nobody should walk on the grass. 當局發佈命令說, 任何人都不得在草地上行走.

decrepit [di'krepit] *adj* weak because of old age 老弱的, 衰老的; 破舊的.

dedicate ['dedikeit] *vt* **1** use something for a special purpose (often a reli-gious purpose) 供奉; 奉獻. Churches are dedicated to God. 教會供奉上帝. He dedicated his life to helping the poor. 他獻身於幫助窮人. **2** honour somebody by printing his name at the beginning of a book, poem, play etc which one has written (書, 詩歌, 戲劇等的) 題獻, 題贈: The author dedi-cated the book to his wife. 作者把這本書獻給妻子. **dedication** [dedi'keiʃən] **1** *nu* act of dedicating 奉獻; 供奉. **2** *nc* words which dedicate a book, poem etc to somebody 題獻詞. **3** *nu* great interest in and attention to one's work etc. 獻身; 專心致志.

deduce [di'djuːs] *vt* arrive at a conclu-sion by thinking about the evidence 推論, 推斷, 演繹: From the position of his body, the police deduced that the man had killed himself. 警方從他屍體的姿勢推斷他是自殺. see 見 **deduc-tion**.

deduct [di'dʌkt] *vt* take away a certain amount of 扣除, 減除: My employer deducted a pound from my wages this week to pay for the window which I broke. 老闆從我的工資裏扣除一英鎊, 以賠償我打破的窗子. **deduction 1** *nc* amount deducted 扣除額. **2** *nu* pro-cess of arriving at a conclusion by considering rules of logic 推論, 推斷. (*opp* 反義詞 **induction**). see 見 **deduce.**

deed [diːd] *nc* **1** something done. (rather *o.f.* or formal) 行爲(頗爲舊式

或正式). **2** legal document recording an agreement 法律文件, 契約, 證書.

deep [di:p] *adj* **1** going down a long way 深的: *The river is not deep; you can walk through it.* 這條河不深; 你可以涉水通過. *The river is only two feet deep.* 這條河只有二英尺深. **2** (usu. with reference to shelves) wide (通常指架子擱板) 寬的: *This shelf is not deep enough for these books.* 這個書架擱板不夠寬, 放不下這些書. **3** dark in colour 深色的: *a very deep blue coat* 一件偏深藍色的上衣. **4** low in sound (聲音) 低沉的: *He spoke in a deep voice.* 他說話聲音低沉. **5** showing great learning, knowledge, thought etc. 深奧的: *This book is too deep for me; I can't understand it.* 這本書對我來說太深了, 我看不懂. **6** showing strong feelings (感情) 深深的: *deep sorrow* 深深的悲傷. **deeply** *adv* **deepen** *vt / i* become or make deep (使) 加深. see 見 **depth**. **'deep-'freeze** container in which food can be stored for long periods at temperatures much lower than are found in an ordinary refrigerator (比普通雪櫃溫度低得多的) 冷藏櫃. **'deep'rooted / -seated / -set** *adj* firmly fixed, not easily removed 根深蒂固的: *a deep-rooted hatred for his enemies* 他對敵人的深仇大恨; *a deeprooted tradition* 根深蒂固的傳統.

deer [diə*] *nc* type of animal, the male of which usu. has wide spreading horns 鹿. *pl* 複數 **deer**.

deface [di'feis] *vt* damage or spoil‘ the appearance of 毀壞或損壞…的外觀: *He defaced the library book by writing in it.* 他亂塗亂寫污損了圖書館的圖書.

defame [di'feim] *vt* say bad things about a person to other people 誹謗,

中傷. **defamation** [defə'meiʃən] *nu*.

default [di'fɔːlt] *vi* fail to do something which is one's duty or which one has promised to do 不履行職責; 違約. **de-faulter** *nc* by default because of the failure of someone else and not because of one's own success 由於他人不出場或缺席(而非自己的成功): *John won the competition by default* i.e. because his opponent did not come to play against John. 由於對手沒來參賽, 因此約翰贏得了這場比賽.

defeat [di'fi:t] *vt* beat in the war, in a game etc. 戰勝, 擊敗: *Our troops defeated the enemy.* 我軍戰勝了敵軍. Also *nc / u* **defeatist** *nc* person who expects that he will be defeated in a war, game etc. 失敗主義者.

defect¹ ['di:fekt] *nc* fault; something which is wrong or which‘ does not work properly 缺點, 錯誤; 不正常: *There is a defect in the steering of this car* i.e. this car cannot be steered properly. 這部車子的駕駛部份有毛病. 即: 這部車子無法正常駕駛. **defective** [di'fektiv] *adj*.

defect² [di'fekt] *vi* (esp. with reference to people who leave their own country to join an enemy country) leave one's own group and join an enemy group 叛逃, 投敵; 變節: *The young soldier defected to the enemy.* 這個年青士兵投敵.

defence [di'fens] (*US* 美 **defense**) *nc / u* act of resisting an attack (in war, in a game, in politics etc.) 防禦, 防衛, 保衛: *Every country in the world keeps secret its plans for defence.* 世界各國對本國的防禦計劃總是保密的. **2** something used in fighting against an attack 防禦工事, 防禦物. **3** person answering a case or charge in a court of law, together with his lawyers 被告

及其辯護律師. **4** members of a team whose work is to guard the goal 防守隊員. see 見 **defend. defenceless** *adj* having no defence 無防守能力的, 無防禦力量的. **defensive** *adj* ready for defence; intended for defence 有防禦準備的; 用於防禦的, 防禦性的.

defend [di'fend] *vt* **1** fight against attack or guard against attack 保衛, 防禦: *The army was defending the town during the battle.* 部隊在這場戰役中保衛該鎮. **2** answer a case or charge in a court of law (在法庭上) 辯護, 答辯: *That lawyer is defending Mr Smith.* 那位律師正爲史密斯先生辯護. **3** guard a goal in a game (比賽中) 防守, 守衛. see 見 **defence. defendant** *nc* person against whom a case is brought in a court of law 被告.

defer [di'fə:*] *vt* wait until later before doing something 推遲, 使延期: *I have decided to defer the meeting until next week.* 我決定把會議延期到下週舉行. *past* 過去式和過去分詞 **deferred. deference** ['defərns] *nu* **deferential** [defə'ren ʃl] *adj.*

defiance [di'faiəns] *nu,* **defiant** [di'faiənt] *adj* see 見 **defy.**

deficient [di'fiʃənt] *adj* having something missing; not having enough of something 缺乏的; 不足的: *He is deficient in courage* i.e. he is a coward 他缺乏勇氣. 即: 他是懦夫. **deficiency** *nc / u.*

deficit ['defisit] *nc* amount of money which is wanting or which cannot be found 赤字; 虧空款額.

define [di'fain] *vt* **1** explain the exact meaning of a word or expression 給…下定義. **2** make clear and easy to see or understand 闡釋. **definite** ['definit] *adj* clear; well understood; not in any doubt 清楚的; 明瞭的; 明確的: *He*

made a definite promise to help us i.e. he promised that he would certainly help us. 他明確答應要幫助我們. (*opp* 反義詞 **indefinite**). **definitely** *adv*

definition [defi'niʃən] *nc* explanation of the meaning of a word or expression 詞或詞組的釋義, 定義. **definitive** [di'finitiv] *adj* final; conclusive 決定性的, 最終的; 確定的: *a definitive edition of a book* i.e. one which gives the final correct form so that there can be no further change 一本書的確定版本, 即: 具有正確校樣無需更改的最終版本. **definite article** (grammar) the word *'the'* and equivalent words in other languages (語法) 單詞 the 和其他語言中的等值詞, 定冠詞.

deflate [di'fleit] *vt* let air or gas escape from a balloon, tyre etc. 排出或放掉 (輪胎、氣球等的) 空氣或氣體, 洩氣.

deflect [di'flekt] *vt / i* turn, cause to turn, away from a direction (使) 轉向, (使) 偏離: *The ball hit the goalkeeper's boot and was deflected into the goal* i.e. the ball changed its direction when it hit the boot. 球碰到守門員的靴子, 折射進入球門. 即: 球碰到靴子時改變了方向.

deform [di'fɔ:m] *vt* (usu. with reference to parts of the body) cause something to have a bad shape; prevent something from growing 使畸形 (通常指身體的部位): *The boy had a serious illness when he was a baby and this deformed his arms and legs.* 該男孩在嬰兒時期過了重病, 結果他的雙臂和雙腿都畸形了. **deformity** *nc* **deformed** *adj.*

defraud [di'frɔ:d] *vt* fail to give somebody money or property which belongs to him 詐騙: *People who do not pay their taxes are defrauding the government.* 不繳納稅收的人是在詐騙

政府. *He defrauded me of the money.*
他詐騙我的錢.

defray [di'frei] *vt* pay (usu. in **defray the cost / expenses**) *(formal)* 支付 (通常用於 defray the cost / expenses 支付費用) (正式).

defrost ['di:'frɔst] *vt* remove ice from; unfreeze 使去冰, 使除霜, 使解凍.

deft [deft] *adj* light, quick and clever (esp. in using the hands in a job which needs skill) 熟練的, 敏捷的, 靈巧的(尤指在需要技術的工作中使用雙手的情況).

defunct [di'fʌŋkt] *adj* dead; no longer working or in use 已死的; 已失效的, 不再使用的.

defy [di'fai] *vt* **1** refuse to obey 拒不服從, 違抗: *Criminals defy the law.* 罪犯們違抗法令. **2** say that one is ready to fight somebody 向…挑戰: *He defied his enemies.* 他向敵人挑戰. **3** say that one thinks somebody cannot do something 激, 挑釁: *I defy you to find the answer to this problem.* 我看你找不到這個問題的答案. **4** be too strong or too difficult for somebody 使某所作爲, 使無能爲力: *This problem defies me* i.e. I cannot solve it. 這個問題難倒了我. 即: 我没法解決. *The city defied the enemy for three years* i.e. the enemy could not capture the city. 該城市抵禦敵軍達三年之久. 即: 敵軍無法攻陷該城. **defiant** *adj* **defiance** *nu.*

degenerate [di'dʒenəreit] *vi* become worse in appearance, behaviour or intelligence 退步, 退化; 墮落.

degrade [di'greid] *vt* make lower in reputation or honour 貶損, 貶低: *He degraded himself by his foolish behaviour.* 他愚蠢的行爲真丢臉. **degradation** [degrə'deiʃən] *nc / u* **degrading** *adj* causing one to be de-

graded 品質低劣的; 墮落的.

degree [di'gri:] *nc* **1** unit of measurement of temperature (溫度的單位)度: *degrees centigrade* 攝氏度數. **2** unit of measurement of angles, equal to sixty minutes (角的單位)度. **3** point on an imaginary scale for measuring people's qualities or behaviour (品質或行爲的)等級; 程度; 水平: *He has a very high degree of ability* i.e. he is very clever or able. 他的能力很强. 即: 他很聰明或能幹. **4** award or title given to a person who completes a course of study at a university 學位. **by degrees** gradually; a little at a time 逐漸地; 一步步地: *He did the work by degrees.* 他逐漸完成了工作.

dehydrate ['di:hai'dreit] *vt* remove water from, so as to make dry 使脱水, 使乾燥.

deign [dein] *vi* do something in order to be friendly to, or to take notice of people whom one considers very low or unimportant 屈尊, 垂顧: *The queen deigned to talk to the poor boy.* 女王屈尊同那個窮孩子談話.

deity ['di:iti] *nc* god or goddess 神或女神, 神祇.

dejected [di'dʒektid] *adj* quietly unhappy 沮喪的.

delay [di'lei] *vt / i* go, cause to go, slowly or be late (使)延緩, (使)延期, (使)耽擱: *He delayed for a long time before accepting my offer.* 他拖延了好久才接受我的建議. *They decided to delay the meeting* i.e. hold the meeting later than they had planned. 他們決定會議延期. 即: 在他們原來計劃的日期之後舉行會議. *You have delayed me for three hours* i.e. you have made me late. 你已經耽擱了我三小時. 即: 你使我遲到了. *He delayed answering the letter.* 他推遲覆信. Also 亦作 *nc / u:*

We must act without delay. 我們必須毫不遲疑地行動. *I hope we shall not have any more delays.* 我希望我們不會再有甚麼耽誤了. **delayed action** action which begins some time after the cause for the action (e.g. *a delayed-action bomb* is one which explodes some time after hitting the ground) 延遲動作 (例如 a delayed-action bomb 延時炸彈, 一種觸地一段時間後才爆炸的炸彈).

delegate ['deligət] *nc* somebody who has the duty of acting as the representative of a group of people (esp. such a person attending a meeting or conference) 代表(尤指參加會議者): *Each country sent three delegates to the meeting.* 每個國家派出三名代表參加會議. Also 亦作 ['deligeit] *vt* give somebody the duty of acting as a delegate 委派…為代表: *I have been delegated to attend the meeting.* 我被委派作為參加會議的代表. **delegation** [deli'gei∫ən] *nc* group of delegates 代表團: *Britain sent a large delegation to the meeting.* 英國派遣一個大型代表團參加會議.

delete [di'li:t] *vt* put a line through something written to show that it is wrong or that it is to be removed 刪去(文字等).

deliberate[1] [di'libərət] *adj* done with intention; not happening by accident 蓄意的; 故意的: *That was a deliberate act of cruelty* i.e. the person who did that wanted to be cruel. 那是一種蓄意的殘忍行為. 即: 這麼做的人想使別人痛苦. **2** slow and careful 審慎的: *He spoke in a very deliberate manner.* 他以一種很審慎的態度發言.

deliberate[2] [di'libəreit] *vi* think or talk about something very carefully 深思熟慮; 謹慎地談論: *The government is* *deliberating about what should be done to solve the problem.* 政府正謹慎考慮該怎麼解決這個問題. **deliberation** [dilibə'rei∫ən] *nc / u*.

delicate ['delikət] *adj* **1** soft; gentle; finely made 柔和的; 嬌嫩的; 精緻的; 精美的: *a delicate flower* 一朵嬌嫩的花; *delicate food* 精美的食品. **2** easily broken 脆弱的, 易損的: *A spider's web is very delicate.* 蜘蛛網很容易損壞. **3** needing careful attention 需要小心照料的: *That child is very delicate* i.e. he easily becomes ill. 那孩子需要十分小心照料. 即: 他很容易得病. *This is a delicate piece of work* i.e. great care and skill is needed to do this work. 這是一項細緻的工作. 即: 做這項工作需要非常的細心和技巧. *This is a delicate problem.* 這是個很微妙的問題. **4.** able to notice or record very small changes 靈敏的: *This is a very delicate piece of apparatus.* 這是一種非常靈敏的裝置. **delicacy** ['delikəsi] *nc* very pleasant-piece of food 精美好吃的食物: *He provided local delicacies for his guests' meal.* 就餐時, 他給客人們準備了當地的佳餚珍品.

delicatessen [delikə'tesn] *nc* shop which sells various special types of food (esp. foreign food) 出售各式特種食品(尤指外國食品)的商店.

delicious [di'li∫əs] *adj* very pleasant in taste or smell 美味可口的.

delight [di'lait] **1** *nu* great pleasure or happiness 欣喜; 快樂. **2** *nc* thing which causes great pleasure or happiness 令人極為愉快的事物. Also 亦作 *vt* cause great pleasure or happiness to 使喜悅, 使快樂: *The news delighted us all.* 這消息使我們大家都高興極了. **delightful** *adj* causing delight 令人極為愉快的. **delighted** *adj* feeling delight 感到愉快的.

delinquent [di'liŋkwənt] *nc* criminal; person who breaks the law (esp. a young person) 刑事犯; 犯人(尤指青少年). Also 亦作 *adj*: *delinquent behaviour* 青少年犯罪行爲. **delinquency** *nu*.

delirium [di'liriəm] *nu* condition of the mind like madness, lasting for a short time (often caused by physical illness) 譫妄, 精神錯亂(常由身體疾病引起). **delirious** *adj*.

deliver [di'livə*] *vt* 1 take something and give it to someone (e.g. with reference to a postman taking letters etc or a shopkeeper sending goods to people's houses) 交付, 遞送(例如郵遞員遞送信件等或店主送貨上門). 2 speak in public 公開演說, 發言: *He delivered a lecture to the students.* 他給學生們作了一次講座. **delivery** *nc / u* 1 act of taking something to somebody 交付, 遞送. 2 method of speaking in public 演說的方法.

delta ['deltə] *nc* area where the mouth of a river spreads out into several branches (河口數條支流形成的)三角洲.

delude [di'lu:d] *vt* make somebody believe something which is not true 欺騙, 哄騙: *The lawyer tried to delude us.* 該律師想哄騙我們. *Don't delude yourself* i.e. don't have a wrong belief. 別欺騙你自己. 不要有一種錯誤的信念. **delusion** [di'lu:ʒən] *nc / u*: *The belief that the world is flat is a delusion.* 認爲世界是扁平的是一種錯覺.

deluge ['delju:dʒ] *nc* 1 great flood of water; heavy rainstorm 大水; 大暴雨. 2 anything coming in great quantity like a flood of water 洪水般的大量湧來: *a deluge of questions* 大量的問題.

de luxe [di'lʌks] *adj* of very good quality 豪華的, 華麗的: *a de luxe hotel* 一

家豪華旅館.

demand¹ [di'ma:nd] *vt* 1 ask for very strongly and firmly, without trying to be polite 要求, 請求: *The boys stopped the old man in the street and demanded money.* 男孩子們在街上攔住那個老頭要錢. 2 need 需要: *This question demands my immediate attention* i.e. I must attend to this question at once. 這個問題需要我立刻注意. 即: 我必須馬上注意這個問題.

demand² [di'ma:nd] 1 *nc* something which one asks for very strongly; act of demanding 所要求之物; 要求: *I have several demands to make.* 我想提幾個要求. 2 *nc* need for something (對某事物的)需要: *There are many demands on my time at present* i.e. there are many things which I must do. 目前我的時間很緊. 即: 我必須做的事很多. 3 *nu* wish by people to buy something (購物之)需求: *Most newspaper shops in Britain do not sell foreign newspapers because there is no demand for them* i.e. not many people want to buy foreign newspapers. 英國的大部份報紙銷售店不賣外國報紙, 因爲沒有銷路. 即: 沒有多少人想買外國報紙. **in demand** wanted 需要: *He is always in demand when people are giving parties* i.e. people who are giving parties always want him to come. 人們舉行宴會時, 他總是人們要請的人. 即: 舉行宴會的人們總是想讓他來參加. **on demand** when asked for 一旦需要: *If you save money in the post office you can draw up to £20 on demand* i.e. you can take up to £20 of your savings out of the post office without having to wait. 如果在郵局存款的話, 一旦需要, 你可以提取20英鎊以內的款子. 即: 你可以在郵局請求即付20英鎊以內的款子.

demarcation [diːmɑːˈkeiʃən] *nu* marking or fixing of limits or boundaries (esp. with reference to an agreement fixing the type of work to be done by members of different trade unions working together) 劃界限; 定界限; 劃界線(尤指不同工會會員所做工作的分工): *The workers were on strike because of a dispute over demarcation.* 工人們罷工是因爲分工方面的爭執.

demean [diˈmiːn] *vt* (usu. **demean oneself**) make lower in dignity, reputation etc. (通常用於 demean oneself) 使降低身份, 使卑下, 貶低: *He demeaned himself by doing such dirty and badly-paid work.* 他做這種又髒報酬又低的工作真是自貶身份.

demeanour [diˈmiːnə*] *nu* way of behaving 舉止, 行爲: *His demeanour was very strange.* 他的舉止很奇怪.

demented [diˈmentid] *adj* mad; violent and strange in behaviour 瘋狂的; 行爲兇暴古怪的.

demobilize [ˈdiːˈmoubilaiz] *vt / i* allow soldiers to leave the army and return to normal life (使)復員; 遣散: *After the war many soldiers were demobilized.* 戰爭結束後, 許多士兵復員了. *The country did not demobilize immediately after the war.* 該國並沒有在戰爭一結束時就讓士兵復員. **demobilization** [ˈdiːmoubilaiˈzeiʃən] *nu.*

democracy [diˈmɔkrəsi] **1** *nu* form of government in which people choose their rulers by voting in elections 民主. **2** *nc* country having this form of government 民主國家. **3** *nc* country having free elections, freedom of speech, protection of the individual, government by an elected parliament etc. 具有自由選舉、言論自由、保護個人、由選舉的議會等統治的國家. **4** *nu*

practice of treating all people as one's equals 民主精神, 人人平等的做法.

democratic [deməˈkrætik] *adj* (*opp* 反義詞 **undemocratic**). **democrat** [ˈdeməkræt] *nc* person who is in favour of democracy 民主主義者.

demolish [diˈmɔliʃ] *vt* destroy; break completely 摧毀; 完全破壞: *The bomb demolished the house.* 炸彈炸毀了這座房子. **demolition** [deməˈliʃən] *nu.*

demon [ˈdiːmən] *nc* evil spirit 惡鬼, 惡魔.

demonstrate [ˈdemənstreit] **1** *vt / i* show clearly; make known 示範; 展示: *The teacher demonstrated the experiment to the class* i.e. he showed the class how to do the experiment. 教師向全班同學示範如何做這種實驗. **2** *vi* hold a political meeting (often in the open air) to protest against something or show support for something 示威: *Large crowds demonstrated outside the British Embassy.* 衆多的人羣在英國大使館外示威. **demonstration** [demənˈstreiʃən] *nc / u* **1** *He gave a demonstration of horse-riding.* 他示範了一下馬術. **2** *The workers held a demonstration against the government.* 工人們舉行反政府示威. **demonstrative** [diˈmɔnstrətiv] *adj* **1** clearly showing one's feelings or one's meaning 感情外露的, 熱情的; 明白表示的: *He greeted us in a demonstrative manner* i.e. he showed that he was glad to see us. 他熱情地歡迎我們. 即: 他表現出很高興見到我們. (*opp* 反義詞 **undemonstrative**). **2** (grammar) pointing out (語法)指示的: *'This' and 'that' are demonstrative pronouns.* "this" 和 "that" 是指示代詞. **demonstrator** *nc* **1** person who takes part in a political demonstration 參加政治示威者. **2** person in a school or college whose work is to show students how to do experiments in science (學校的)實驗示範員.

demoralize [di'mɔrəlaiz] *vt* take away somebody's courage, confidence, self-control etc. 使無鬥志, 使意氣消沉, 使洩氣: *After losing three important battles, the army had become demoralized.* 在三次重要戰役都敗北之後, 這個部隊士氣十分低落.

demote [di'mout] *vt* put into a lower rank or lower position 使降級, 使降職: *The soldier was demoted for failing to obey orders.* 這個士兵因不服從命令而被降級. (*opp* 反義詞 **promote**).

demure [di'mjuə*] *adj* (esp. with reference to young girls) quiet and rather afraid to talk to other people; prim (尤指少女)嫻靜的; 拘謹的; 矜持的.

den [den] *nc* **1** place where a wild animal such as a lion or tiger lives (獅, 虎等)獸穴. **2** place where a lion or tiger is kept at a zoo 動物園內獅、虎等獸籠. **3** room where one can be comfortable or work at one's hobbies. 私人工作室, 書房.

denary ['di:nəri] *adj* of the number ten; having ten as the basis of reckoning; decimal 十的; 以十作爲計算基礎的; 十倍的; 十進的.

denial [di'naiəl] *nc / u* 見 **deny**.

denim ['denim] *nu* strong type of cotton cloth 一種耐穿的斜紋粗棉布 **denims** *npl* trousers or overalls made of denim (藍色斜紋粗布做成的)工作服, 工裝褲.

denomination [dinɔmi'neiʃən] *nc* **1** any of the Christian churches (e.g. the Roman Catholic Church, the Church of England, the Methodist Church) (基督教)教派, 宗派(例如羅馬天主教, 英國國教, 美以美教會): *The service was*

attended by people of different denominations. 不同教派的人們參加了這個禮拜儀式. **2** type of unit of measurement, weight, money etc. (長度、重量、貨幣等的)單位: *Metres and centimetres are different denominations.* 米和厘米是不同的長度單位. **denominator** [di'nɔmineitə*] *nc* the number below the line in a vulgar fraction (e.g. in 2/3, 3 is the denominator) 分母(例如在 ⅔ 中, 3是分母).

denote [di'nout] *vt* be the sign for or name of something; mean 是…的符號, 爲…之名稱; 表示.

denounce [di'nauns] *vt* **1** speak against; show that one opposes 指責, 譴責; 抨擊: *The newspapers denounced the new taxes.* 報界紛紛譴責新稅收. **2** tell police etc about a crime committed by someone 告發; 揭發: *He denounced Mr Jones to the police* i.e. he told the police that Mr Jones had committed a crime 他向警方告發了瓊斯先生, 即: 他告訴警方說瓊斯先生犯有罪行.

dense [dens] *adj* **1** packed closely together 密集的, 稠密的: *dense crowds of people* 密集的人羣. **2** (with reference to gas etc) not easily seen through (指氣體等)不易看透的, 濃密的: *a dense fog* 濃霧. **3** (with reference to a person) stupid or unintelligent (指人)愚鈍的, 不開竅的. **density** *nc / u* **1** quality of being dense (in all senses) 稠密; 濃密; 愚鈍. **2** (physics) proportion of weight to volume (物理學)密度, 濃度.

dent [dent] *nc* place pushed in without breaking the surface 凹痕, 凹陷: *He made a dent in his car when he backed into the tree.* 他倒車時碰到樹上, 車子撞出一個凹痕. Also 亦作 *vt* make a dent 使凹陷, 使有凹痕.

dentine, dentin ['denti:n] *nu* hard bony material beneath the enamel, forming the main part of a tooth 牙質, 象牙質.

dentist ['dentist] *nc* doctor who treats the teeth 牙醫. **dentistry** *nu* work of a dentist 牙醫業. **dental** ['dentl] *adj* referring to the teeth or to dentists 牙齒的; 牙醫的. **denture** ['dentʃə*] *nc* artificial or false teeth 人造牙齒, 假牙.

denudation ['di:nju(:)'deiʃən] *nu* 1 action of denuding; denuding condition 剝光; 奪去; 光禿; 裸露. 2 (geology) laying bare of rock by erosion (地質) (由於侵蝕作用的) 岩石裸露.

denude [di'nju:d] *vt* 1 make bare; strip (something) of its clothing or covering 使赤裸; 使光禿; 剝光: *Most trees are denuded of their leaves in winter.* 多數樹木在冬季都掉光了葉子. 2 (geology) lay (a rock or land) bare by removing what lies above, especially by erosion (地質) 使岩石裸露; 使剝蝕: *land rapidly denuded by rain and river* 受雨水和河流迅速剝蝕的土地.

deny [di'nai] *vt* 1 say that something is not true 否認, 否定: *He denied that he had broken the window.* 他否認打破過窗子. *He denied the story.* 他否定這種說法. 2 say that one will not give 不肯給予: *He denied me any help while I was doing the work.* 我在做工作的時候, 他不肯給我任何幫助. 3 say that one has no connection with something 否認與…有關: *He denied all knowledge of the crime* i.e. he said that he did not know anything about the crime. 他否認對此罪行知情. 即: 他說他對這個罪行一無所知. see 見 **denial.**

deodorant [di:'oudərnt] *nc* something used to take away unpleasant smells from the body 除(體)臭劑.

depart [di'pɑ:t] *vi* go away; leave 離開: *The train will depart from Platform 2.* 火車將駛離2號月台. *We must not depart from this agreement* i.e. we must do what we have agreed to do. 我們不應該背離這項協議. 即: 我們應當按我們同意的那樣去做. **departure** *nc/u* 1 act of departing or starting 離開, 起身. 2 beginning of something new 起點, 開端: *Learning Russian is a new departure for him.* 學習俄語對他來說是個新的開端.

department [di'pɑ:tmənt] *nc* one of the sections of a large shop, government office, school, university etc. (大商店, 政府機構, 學校等的) 部門, 科系. **departmental** [di:pɑ:t'mentl] *adj* **department store** large shop selling many different kinds of goods 百貨公司.

depend [di'pend] *vi* (with **on** or **upon**) (與 on 或 upon 連用) 1 trust 信任, 信賴: *We can depend on him for help* i.e. we can be sure that he will help us. 我們可以指望他幫忙. 即: 我們可以肯定他會幫助我們. *You can depend on this newspaper* i.e. this newspaper always tells the truth 你可以相信這家報紙. 即: 這家報紙總是講真話. 2 get help or support from; get money or food and clothing from 依賴, 依靠: *He could not work and so he had to depend on his family.* 他不能工作, 因此得依賴家裏. 3 be influenced by 取決於: *The sort of job I get depends on my examination results* i.e. if I get good results I shall get a good job. 我得何種工作取決於我的考試成績. 即: 如果我成績好的話, 我會得到一份好工作. **dependable** *adj* able to be trusted 可信賴的: *This newspaper is dependable, it always tells the truth* 這家報紙可以信賴, 因爲它總是說真話.

dependant *nc* somebody who gets help, food, clothing etc from somebody else 依賴他人者; 靠人養活者; 眷屬: *A man's wife and children are his dependants.* 男人的妻子兒女是他的眷屬. **dependent** *adj*: *The children are dependent on their father.* (*opp* 反義詞 **independent**). **dependency** *nc* country controlled by another country 附庸國.

depict [di'pikt] *vt* show or make a picture of; describe very clearly so that one seems to see a picture when reading or hearing the description 描繪; 描寫.

deplete [di'pli:t] *vt* use so that little or none is left 用盡, 耗盡: *Our supplies of food have been much depleted.* 我們的食品供給已用完了大部份.

deplore [di'plɔ:ʳ] *vt* say or think that something is very bad 對…感到痛心, 惋惜: *He deplored the waste of time and money.* 他對浪費光陰和金錢感到痛心. **deplorable** *adj* very bad, and fit to be deplored 糟透的; 可悲的, 可嘆的.

deploy [di'plɔi] *vt* make soldiers move into a line ready for a battle 部署 (兵力).

depopulate [di:'pɔpjuleit] *vt* remove people from the place where they are living 使人口減少: *The north of Scotland has been greatly depopulated in the last 100 years* i.e. many people have left the north of Scotland. 在過去一百年裏, 蘇格蘭北部的人口大大減少了. 即: 許多人離開蘇格蘭北部. **depopulation** [di:pɔpju'leiʃən] *nu.*

deport [di'pɔ:t] *vt* make a foreigner leave the country 驅逐 (外國人) 出境. **deportation** [di:pɔ:'teiʃən] *nc/u.*

deportment [di'pɔ:tmənt] *nu* (esp. with reference to behaviour which is digni-fied and gentlemanly) way of behaving (尤指高貴優雅的) 舉止, 風度.

depose [di'pouz] *vt* make a king or other ruler leave his position 廢黜 (國王等統治者): *The army deposed the king and set up a republic.* 軍隊廢黜國王, 建立了共和國.

deposit [di'pɔzit] *nc* **1** amount of money left by somebody in a bank or other place 儲蓄, 存款. **2** amount of money paid as part payment for something 押金; 訂金. **3** amount of substance in or on the earth 礦藏; 沉澱物, 淤積物: *There was a thick deposit of mud at the bottom of the river.* 河底有一層厚厚的淤泥. *Several deposits of gold have been found in those hills.* 已發現這些丘陵中有好幾處金礦. Also 亦作 *vt* **1** make a deposit 使沉澱, 使淤積: *The sea has deposited a lot of stones on the beach.* 許多石頭被海水沖積在海灘上. **2** leave something in a safe place 把…存於安全之處: *He deposited his money in the bank.* 他把錢存到銀行裏.

depot ['depou] *nc* **1** building or place where goods are stored (esp. military supplies) 倉庫, 庫房 (尤指軍需庫). **2** *(US)* railway station (美) 火車站. **3** place where soldiers are trained when they first enter the army 新兵訓練中心, 補給站.

deprave [di'preiv] *vt* make bad or wicked in behaviour 使墮落.

depreciate [di'pri:ʃieit] *vt/i* become or make less in value or usefulness (使) 貶值; 跌價; (使) 作用減低: *Money usually depreciates in value over a period of years.* 貨幣通常在數年間發生貶值. **depreciation** [dipri:ʃi'eiʃən] *nu.*

depress [di'pres] *vt* **1** make very miserable or unhappy 使沮喪, 使消沉; 使灰

心; 使不快: *The bad news depressed us all.* 這個壞消息使我們全都灰心喪氣. **2** (with reference to a switch, key, button etc on an instrument or machine) press down (指儀器或機器上的開關、鍵、鈕等) 按, 壓, 撳. **depressing** *adj* causing one to be unhappy 令人沮喪的; 令人不快的. **depression 1** *nc / u* condition of being miserable or unhappy 沮喪, 消沉; 不快. **2** *nc* area of low atmospheric pressure 低氣壓地區. **3** *nc* hollow place on a surface 凹陷, 窪地: *a small depression in a field* 田野裏的窪地.

deprive [di'praiv] *vt* take something away from 奪: *deprive someone of his rights* 剝奪某人的權利. *I have been deprived of sleep for two nights.* 我已有兩個晚上沒睡覺了.

depth [depθ] **1** *nc* distance downwards 深度: *The depth of this river is three feet.* 這條河深三英尺. **2** *nc* distance across 寬度: *The depth of these shelves is six inches.* 這些書架子擱板寬度爲六英寸. **3** *nc / u* darkness in colour 深色. **4** *nc / u* lowness in pitch of sound (聲音)低沉. **5** *nc* (usu. *pl*) deepest or furthest part (通常用複數) 極深處: *Coal miners have to work in the depths of the earth.* 煤礦工人們得在地下深處幹活. see 見 **deep.**

depute [di'pju:t] *vt* give somebody one's permission and authority to do a certain part of one's own work 派⋯爲代理或代表: *I cannot go to the meeting, and so I am deputing you to go instead.* 我不能去開會, 因此委派你替我去. **deputy** ['depjuti] *nc* person who has been deputed (esp. **1** person given authority to work for a sheriff in America. **2** member of the lower house of parliament in France and other countries) 代理人, 代表(尤指1.

美國的代理縣級執法官. 2. 法國和其他國家的下院議員). **deputation** [depju'teiʃən] *nc* group of people having permission to speak for others (esp. to make a complaint) 代表團(尤指被授權代表他人提出控告者). **deputize** ['depjutaiz] *vi* act as a deputy 充當代理人, 代表: *I am deputizing for Mr Smith.* 我現在代表史密斯先生.

derail [di'reil] *vt* cause a train to leave the rails 使出軌. **derailment** *nc.*

derelict ['derilikt] *adj* left or abandoned as unwanted or useless 荒廢的, 被棄置的: *There were many derelict houses in the streets of the city.* 該市的街道上有許多荒廢的房屋.

deride [di'raid] *vt* laugh at as foolish 嘲笑: *He derided my plan* i.e. he thought my plan was foolish. 他嘲笑我的計劃. 即: 他認爲我的計劃很可笑. **derision** [di'riʒən] *nu* **derisory** [di'raisəri] *adj* causing derision 引人嘲笑的.

derive [di'raiv] *vt* get from 由⋯獲得: *He derives a lot of pleasure from reading.* 他從閱讀中得到許多樂趣. **2** *vi* (esp. with reference to words) come from; have as a beginning (尤指詞語) 來自; 起源於: *Many English words derive from French.* 許多英語詞語來自法語. **derivation** [deri'veiʃən] *nc / u* **derivative** [di'rivətiv] *nc* word or substance derived from another word or substance 派生詞; 衍生物.

derogatory [di'rɔɡətəri] *adj* showing that one has a bad opinion of somebody / something 貶低的, 毀謗的: *The boy made several derogatory remarks about his teacher.* 該男生說了好幾次貶低教師的話.

derrick ['derik] *nc* **1** tall machine for lifting and moving heavy weights 起重機. **2** tall metal framework over an oil well 油井架, 鑽井高塔.

descant ['deskænt] *nc* tune intended to be sung above another tune, making a harmony 高音部樂曲.

descend [di'send] *vt / i* go down 走下, 下, 下降: *He descended the hill.* 他下山. *The path descended steeply.* 這條路突然下降. **descendant** *nc* person having somebody as his ancestor 後代, 後裔: *He says that he is a descendant of Julius Caesar.* 他說他是朱利葉斯・凱撒的後裔. **descent** [di'sent] 1 *nc* movement down 下降, 降落: *He began the descent of the mountain.* 他開始下山. 2 *nu* ancestry 世系, 血統: *Many Americans are of English descent* i.e. their ancestors were English. 許多美國人係英國血統. 即: 他們的祖先是英國人. **descend on / upon someone / something** 1 make a sudden attack 突襲, 突擊: *The robbers descended on the lonely house.* 強盜們襲擊了這座孤寂零寥的住宅. 2 make a sudden visit 突訪: *They descended on us at lunchtime.* 午餐時分他們突然來訪問我們. **be descended from someone** have as one's ancestor 是…的後裔或後代: *Queen Elizabeth II is descended from Queen Victoria.* 伊麗莎白女王二世是維多利亞女王的後代.

describe [dis'kraib] *vt* say what somebody / something is like 描繪, 描述: *He described the town where he used to live.* 他描述了他以前居住過的城鎮. **description** [dis'krip∫ən] *nc / u* something written or said to describe a person / thing; act of describing 描寫或敘述的事物; 描繪, 描述. **descriptive** [dis'kriptiv] *adj* forming a description 描寫性的, 敘述性的: *descriptive writing* 描寫文. **of every description** of every type or kind 各種類型的, 各式各樣的: *There are shops*

of every description in this town. 這鎮中有各種各樣的商店.

desecrate ['desikreit] *vt* do something to spoil or damage something religious or beautiful 褻瀆; 玷污.

desegregate [di:'segrəgeit] *vt* allow mixing of races; end segregation 廢除種族隔離: *desegregate education* i.e. allow children of all races to attend the same schools 不分種族的教育. 即: 允許各種族的孩子到同一學校就學. **desegregation** ['di:segrə'gei∫ən] *nu*.

desert[1] ['dezət] *nc* large area covered by sand 沙漠. **desert island** island in the tropics on which nobody lives 熱帶荒島.

desert[2] [di'zə:t] *vt / i* go away without permission; leave in a cruel or unfriendly way 開小差, 擅離職守; 背棄, 拋棄: *The soldier deserted* i.e. he left the army without permission. 這個士兵開小差了. 即: 他未經許可就離開部隊. *He deserted his friends.* 他背棄了朋友. **desertion** *nu* **deserter** *nc* person who leaves military service without permission 逃兵.

deserve [di'zə:v] *vt* be worthy of 應得, 值得: *He deserves to have a holiday for his hard work* i.e. he ought to get a holiday because he has worked hard. 他工作很努力, 應當有個假期. *He deserves a reward.* 他應受獎賞.

desiccate ['desikeit] *vt / i* 1 dry thoroughly; dry; become dry 使完全乾燥, 使乾燥; 變乾燥: *The soil in a desert is desiccated by the dry air and sun.* 乾燥的空氣和陽光使沙漠中土壤的水份喪失殆盡. 2 preserve by drying thoroughly; dehydrate 用乾燥方法保存, 乾貯; 使脱水; *desiccated fruit* 水果乾; *desiccated milk* 奶粉.

desiccator ['desikeitə] *nc* 1 person or thing that desiccates (魚等的) 乾貨製

造者; 乾燥劑. **2** apparatus for drying fruit, milk, or other foodstuffs, or for absorbing moisture in a chemical (牛奶, 水果或其他食品的)乾燥器; 保乾器; 收濕器.

design¹ [di'zain] *vt / i* **1** make a plan of something before it is made 設計, 策劃: *The new building was designed by an American architect* 這座新建築物是一位美國建築師所設計的. **2** intend to do or use something in a certain way 企圖, 打算: *The road was not designed for heavy lorries* i.e. the road was not made for heavy lorries. 這條路並非爲重型貨車考慮的. 即: 這條路不是爲重型貨車而建的.

design² [di'zain] **1** *nc* plan or drawing of something before it is made 設計, 設計圖, 圖樣: *Here is a design of the house I want to build.* 這兒有一份我想建築的房屋設計圖樣. **2** *nu* art of planning things in this way 設計技巧: *He is studying furniture design.* 他正在研究傢具設計. **3** *nc* way something is planned 設計方式: *I like the design of your furniture.* 我喜歡你的傢具式樣. **4** *nc* pattern or picture on cloth, paper, pottery, glass etc. (布匹、紙張、陶器、玻璃等的)圖案, 花式. **designer** *nc* person who plans and draws something before it is made 設計者, 設計家, 打樣的人.

designate ['dezigneit] *vt* name somebody to take a certain position 指派, 任命: *The Prime Minister has designated three new members of his government* 首相已經任命了三名政府新成員. **designation** [dezig'neiʃən] *nc / u*.

desire [di'zaiə*] *vt* **1** want very much 極想, 渴望: *The only thing he desires is peace.* 他渴望的唯一事情就是和平. **2** ask for 要求: *He desires to speak to you. (formal)* 他要求和你談話. (正式).

Also 亦作 *nc / u* strong wish; request; something which is desired 強烈的願望; 要求; 渴望的事物. **desirable** *adj* **1** causing one to desire; pleasant 令人渴望的; 令人愉快的, 稱心合意的: *a very desirable house* 一座非常稱心合意的房子. **2** referring to the best course of action (指行動方針或步驟)最好的: *It is not desirable for us to go there.* 我們最好不要去那兒. (*opp* 反義詞 **undesirable**). **desirability** [dizaiərə'biliti] *nu.*

desk [desk] *nc* piece of furniture for writing at, and often with drawers or a space under the top for storing books etc. 書桌.

desolate ['desələt] *adj* **1** empty; bare; ruined; without many people 空蕩的; 荒涼的; 荒廢的; 人烟稀少的: *The farm was in a lonely desolate valley.* 該農莊位於一個孤寂荒涼的峽谷中. **2** unhappy and lonely 凄涼的: *After the death of their parents the children were desolate.* 父母雙亡之後, 孩子們孤苦伶仃. **desolation** [desə'leiʃən] *nu.*

despair [dis'pɛə*] *vi* lose hope 絕望, 失望: *After the failure of his plans he began to despair.* 他的計劃都失敗之後, 他開始感到絕望. *He despaired of finding the answer.* 他對找到答案喪失信心. Also 亦作 *nu* loss of hope 絕望: *be in despair* 處於絕望之中. see 見 **desperate**.

despatch [dis'pætʃ] *vt* see 見 **dispatch**.

desperate ['despərət] *adj* **1** having lost all hope 絕望的: *He was desperate after the failure of his plans.* 他的計劃失敗之後, 他感到絕望. **2** willing to do anything to get what is wanted 孤注一擲的, 極爲渴望而不顧一切的: *He was desperate for money and so he stole*

£5. 他極想有錢, 因此偷了五英鎊. **3** violent and dangerous 亡命的: *a desperate criminal* 一個亡命罪犯. **4** very difficult and dangerous 嚴峻的, 艱險的: *a desperate situation* 嚴峻的局勢.

desperately *adv* **desperation** [despə'reiʃən] *nu*: *He stole the money in desperation* i.e. because he had lost hope of getting what he wanted in any other way. 他於絕望之中偷了錢. 即: 因為他對以其他方式挣錢已經絕望了. see also **despair**.

despise [dis'paiz] *vt* think that someone / something is very low and of no use or value at all 藐視, 鄙視, 輕視: *He despised people who killed animals for pleasure.* 他藐視那些殺動物取樂的人. **despicable** [dis'pikəbl] *adj* deserving to be despised 可鄙的, 卑劣的: *a despicable act of cruelty.* 可鄙的殘酷行爲.

despite [dis'pait] *prep* in spite of 儘管, 不顧: *Despite the rain he went for a walk* i.e. although it was raining. 儘管下雨, 可他還是去散步了.

despond [dis'pɔnd] *vi* lose hope 失望, 沮喪: *You must not despond if your plans do not succeed.* 即便計劃沒有成功, 你也不該沮喪. **despondent** *adj*.

despot ['despɔt] *nc* king or other ruler who governs (often in a cruel way), without any consideration for the law 暴君; 獨裁者. **despotic** [dis'pɔtik] *adj*.

dessert [di'zə:t] *nc / u* sweet food eaten after the main part of a meal (主食結束後的) 甜食. **dessertspoon** spoon used for eating dessert 甜食用匙.

destination [desti'neiʃən] *nc* place to which one is going 目的地.

destine ['destin] *vt* (often *passive*) decide or plan to use something for a special purpose (常用被動態) 註定:

He seemed to be destined for great success i.e. it seemed as though nothing could stop him from being successful. 他好像註定要獲得巨大成功.

destiny 1 *nu* (Often **Destiny**) power in the universe which is thought of as planning what will happen in the future (常寫爲 Destiny) 天命, 神力. **2** *nc* things which will happen to one in the future 命運: *Nobody knows his own destiny.* 誰也不知道自己的命運如何.

destitute ['destitju:t] *adj* without (enough) food, clothing, housing etc. 窮困的, 貧困的, 匱乏的.

destroy [dis'trɔi] *vt / i* break down or break to pieces so as to make useless 毀壞, 破壞: *The house was destroyed by a bomb.* 這座房子爲一顆炸彈炸毀. **destruction** [dis'trʌkʃən] *nu* **destructive** [dis'trʌktiv] *adj* causing destruction; fond of destroying 毀滅性的; 破壞性的, 有害的. **destroyer** *nc* type of small, fast warship 驅逐艦.

detach [di'tætʃ] *vt* unfasten and take away 分開, 分離, 拿開: *She detached the baby's hand from her dress.* 她把嬰兒的手從她的衣服上拿開. **detachable** *adj* able to be detached 可分開的, 可分離的. **detached** *adj* **1** (with reference to a person) not showing strong feelings; not influenced by other people (指人) 超然的; 公平的: *He spoke in a detached way about the danger* i.e. he spoke as though he had no feelings about the danger 他用超然的態度談論這一危險. **2** (with reference to a house) not joined to another (指房屋) 獨立式的. see also 參見 **semidetached. detachment 1** *nc* group of soldiers etc sent somewhere for a special purpose (從事特殊任務的) 分遣部隊. **2** *nu* condition of not showing any feelings, or of not being influenced by other people 超然; 公平: *He spoke with complete detachment about the danger which threatened all of them.* 他以完全超然的態度談論那種威脅他們每個人的危險.

detail¹ ['di:teil] **1** *nc* small fact or small part of something 細節, 詳情: *He gave me all the details of his new job* i.e. he told me everything about it. 他把他的新工作的所有詳情都告訴了我. **2** *nu* small facts or small parts of something 瑣碎, 零碎事; 零部件: *There is a lot of detail in the sewing she is doing* i.e. she is sewing a design with many different colours or many small stitches. 她正在做的針線活中零碎事很多; 她正在縫一種顏色雜而且需要零繡碎補的圖案. *The detail in that film was good* i.e. the scenery, clothing etc were carefully chosen with attention to small details. 那部影片的細節不錯. 即: 風景、服裝等經過精心挑選, 連細節都注意到了. **in detail** giving full details 詳細地: *He told me in detail what I should do.* 他詳細地告訴我該做些甚麼.

detail² ['di:teil] *vt* **1** describe fully 詳述: *He detailed my new duties to me.* 他向我詳細講述了我的新職責. **2** send a group of soldiers etc to do some special duty 分遣, 派遣(士兵等): *He detailed six men to clean the windows.* 他派出六個人去打掃窗子.

detain [di'tein] *vt* keep back; prevent from leaving a place 扣留, 拘留, 扣押: *The policemen decided to detain the man until they had questioned him further.* 警察決定在進一步審問之前拘留這個男子. **detention** [di'tenʃən] *nu*: *The pupil was given two hours' detention for his bad behaviour.* 那個

學生因行爲不好而被罰留校二小時.

detect [di'tekt] *vt* find something hidden or secret 查明, 查覺, 查出: *He detected a fault in my car.* 他查出我車子上的故障. *I detect a strange smell.* 我嗅到一種奇怪的味道. **detector** *nc* person / thing that detects 察覺者; 探測器. **detective** *nc* person (often a policeman) whose job is to find criminals etc. 警探, 偵緝, 偵探.

deter [di'tə:*] *vt* prevent; discourage 阻止; 阻攔: *The bad weather deterred us from making the long journey* i.e. we did not make the journey or we were very unwilling to make the journey. 惡劣的氣候使我們無法長途旅行. *past* 過去式和過去分詞 **deterred. deterrent** [di'ternt] *nc* (esp. with reference to nuclear weapons, which deter one's enemies from starting a war) something which deters (尤指核武器, 可以震懾敵方使之不敢發動戰爭)威懾物, 制約力物. Also 亦作 *adj.*

detergent [di'tə:dʒənt] *nc* substance other than soap, used for cleaning clothes or plates, cups etc. 洗滌劑, 洗衣粉.

deteriorate [di'tiəriəreit] *vt / i* become or make worse (使) 惡化, (使) 變精: *His work has deteriorated.* 他的工作變精了. **deterioration** [ditiəriə'reiʃən] *nu.*

determine [di'tə:min] *vt / i* **1** make a firm decision to do something 決心, 下決心: *He determined to work harder.* 他決心更努力地工作. **2** cause something to be decided 決定: *The amount of money we have will determine the length of our holiday.* 我們擁有的那筆款子將決定我們假期的長短. **determination** [ditə:mi'neiʃən] *nu* **determined** *adj*: *He is determined to come* i.e. he has firmly decided on this. 他決心要求.

deterrent [di'ternt] *nc* see 見 **deter.**

detest [di'test] *vt* dislike very much 憎恨, 厭惡: *He detests watching television.* 他厭惡看電視. **detestable** *adj* very unpleasant 令人厭惡的.

dethrone ['di:'θroun] *vt* make a king or other ruler leave his position 廢黜(國王或其他統治者).

detonate ['detəneit] *vt / i* explode, cause to explode (使)爆炸; 引爆: *The soldiers detonated the bomb.* 士兵們引爆了那枚炸彈. **detonator** *nc* part of a bomb etc which starts the explosion 引信, 雷管.

detour ['di:tuə*] *nc* road which is used when the usual road cannot be used; journey made on such a road 彎路, 迂迴道; 繞道, 迂迴.

detract [di'trækt] *vi* (with **from**) take away part of the value or goodness of (與 from 連用)貶損, 貶低; 減損, 損壞: *I want nothing to detract from your enjoyment today.* 我不想讓任何事情影響你今天的歡樂.

detriment ['detriment] *nu* harm or damage 傷害, 損害: *The war caused great detriment to the nation's economy.* 這場戰爭給該國經濟造成巨大損害. **detrimental** [detri'mentl] *adj.*

devalue [di:'vælju:] *vt* officially declare that the money of one's country will in future be worth less than the equivalent money in foreign countries 正式宣佈(貨幣)貶值: *The British Government devalued the pound.* 英國政府宣佈英鎊貶值. **devaluation** [di:'vælju'ei∫ən] *nu.*

devastate ['devəsteit] *vt* destroy and make empty or ruined 摧毀; 破壞; 使荒廢: *The bomb devastated a large part of the city.* 這枚炸彈炸毀了該市大部份地區. **devastation** [devə's-

tei∫ən] *nu* **devastating** *adj* **1** causing destruction 破壞性的, 摧毀性的 **2** very effective *(informal* in sense **2**) 極好的; 非常有效的(義2爲非正式).

develop [di'veləp] *vt / i* **1** grow, cause to grow (使)生長, (使)成長; 發展: *The new town slowly developed until it became one of the largest towns in the country.* 這座新市鎮慢慢發展終於成爲該國最大的城鎮之一. *I have a few ideas, but I need more time to develop them properly* i.e. think about them fully. 我有一些想法, 但是我需要時間來恰當地拓展這些想法. **2** treat with chemicals to make the picture appear (使)顯影, 冲洗: *He developed the photographs which he had taken.* 他冲洗了他拍攝的照片. *He spent all day developing.* 他花一整天冲洗膠卷. **development 1** *nu* growth; developing or being developed 成長; 發展, 開發: *the development of mind and body* 身心之發展; *industrial development* 工業的發展. *The full development of the idea took many months.* 充分拓展這種想法需要好多個月的時間. **2** *nc* new event; result 新情況; 結果: *the latest developments in agriculture / medicine* 農業／醫學方面的最新成果. *The major development during the day* i.e. the most important piece of news 當日主要動態, 即: 最重要的新聞. **developing country** country without a fully-developed industrial system 發展中國家.

deviate ['di:vieit] *vi* turn away from the right course or from the way that one is on 越軌, 背離, 偏離(常軌): *He never deviated from complete honesty* i.e. he was always honest. 他從來沒有不誠實過. **deviation** [di:vi'ei∫ən] *nc / u.*

device [di'vais] *nc* **1** piece of apparatus used for a particular purpose (特定用

途的)裝置, 設備, 儀器: *He invented a device for sharpening old razor blades.* 他發明了一種可用於磨利舊剃鬚刀片的裝置. **2** trick or plan to solve some particular problem 詭計; 策略. see 見 **devise. leave somebody to his own devices** leave somebody alone, to do as he wishes, without giving him any help or advice 聽任某人自行其是, 讓某人自己去想辦法.

devil ['devl] *nc* **1** evil spirit 魔鬼. **2** (Often **the Devil**) chief evil spirit (常作 the Devil) 魔王. **3** cruel or wicked person 殘忍的人, 惡人. **devilish** *adj*.

devious ['di:viəs] *adj* **1** not straight, not direct, not the shortest 彎曲的, 迂迴的: *We travelled by a devious route.* 我們旅行走一條迂迴的路. **2** not completely honest 不太誠實的.

devise [di'vaiz] *vt* invent or think of a piece of apparatus, or a plan or trick 發明; 設計; 策劃. see 見 **device.**

devoid [di'void] *adj* (with **of**) without; lacking (與 of 連用) 無⋯的; 缺乏⋯的: *He is completely devoid of humour* i.e. he never makes jokes or laughs at jokes. 他根本沒有幽默感. 即: 他從來不開玩笑或者聽了笑話也不笑.

devote [di'vout] *vt* (with **to**) keep for a special purpose; apply oneself wholeheartedly (與 to 連用) 獻身於; 專注於: *This magazine is devoted to the study of African history.* 這本雜誌專門研究非洲歷史. *He devoted himself to helping the poor.* 他獻身於幫助窮人. **devotion** *nu* **devoted** *adj* showing great love and willingness to work or help 熱愛的; 忠誠的, 奉獻的: *He was a devoted servant.* 他是個忠實的僕人. **devotee** [devə'ti:] *nc* person devoted to something, or very interested in something 忠實者; 熱衷⋯

者; 獻身於⋯的人

devour [di'vauə*] *vt* **1** eat completely; eat with hunger 吞食, 吞噬; 狼吞虎嚥地吃. **2** burn completely 燒毀. **3** read with great interest 入迷地讀: *He devoured the book he had bought.* 他一口氣就把買來的書讀完了.

devout [di'vaut] *adj* careful to carry out all one's religious duties such as going to church and praying 虔誠的.

dew [dju:] *nu* moisture in the air, which forms in small drops during the night 露水, 露珠.

dexterity [deks'teriti] *nu* cleverness (esp. in using the hands) (尤指在使用雙手方面)靈巧, 敏捷.

diabetes [daiə'bi:ti:z] *nu* disease in which there is too much sugar in the blood 糖尿病. **diabetic** [daiə'betik] *nc* person suffering from diabetes 糖尿病患者. Also 亦作 *adj.*

diagnose [daiəg'nouz] *vt* find out what disease a person is suffering from by making an examination; similarly find out what is wrong in any situation 診斷(疾病); 判斷(情況). *The doctor diagnosed the disease.* 醫生診斷病情. **diagnosis** [daiəg'nousis] *nc* **1** process of diagnosing 診斷. **2** decision about what a disease is 診斷結果. *pl* 複數 **diagnoses** [daiəg'nousi:z].

diagonal [dai'ægənl] *nc* straight line going across from corner to corner 對角線. Also 亦作 *adj.*

diagram ['daiəgræm] *nc* drawing showing the important parts of something one is explaining 圖表, 圖解.

dial ['daiəl] *nc* surface marked with numbers or symbols and connected to various types of machinery (e.g. the dial of a clock tells one the time; the dial of a radio enables one to find the station one wants; the dial of a telephone enables one to call the person one wants to speak to; the dials in a car tell the driver how fast he is going, how much petrol he has etc.) 刻度盤, 儀表面, 號碼盤(如鐘表的刻度盤指示時間; 收音機的調諧刻度盤可以使人們找到想收聽的電台; 汽車撥號盤可以呼喚受話人; 汽車內的儀表盤指示駕駛速度和油耗等). Also 亦作 *vt* call on the telephone 撥(電話號盤), 打電話給…; *Dial the police.* 打電話給警方. Dial 999. 撥999. *past* 過去式和過去分詞 **dialled** (*US* 美 **dialed**). '**dialling tone** sound made by a telephone which means that it is possible to dial a number 撥號音.

dialect ['daiəlekt] *nc* spoken form of a language, found in a particular area of a country 方言, 土語, 地方語.

dialogue ['daiələɡ] *nc* conversation (esp. in a book or play) (尤指書或戲劇中的)對白, 對話.

diameter [dai'æmitə*] *nc* line passing from one side of a circle to the other through the centre 直徑. **diametrically** *adv*: *This is diametrically opposed to what I said* i.e. it is the exact opposite. 這同我所說的正好相反.

diamond ['daiəmənd] *nc* **1** very hard, bright, valuable stone found in the earth 金剛石, 鑽石. **2** four-sided shape on a playing card (紙牌)方塊.

diaper ['daiəpə*] *nc (US)* piece of cloth put between a baby's legs and fastened at his waist (美)尿布. (*Brit* 英 **nappy**).

diaphragm ['daiəfræm] *nc* area of muscle between the chest and the abdomen 橫膈膜, 膈(胸腹之間的肌肉).

diarrhoea [daiə'riə] (*US* 美 **diarrhea**) *nu* type of illness in which all waste matter is sent out of the body in liquid form (esp. when this happens

many times) 腹瀉(尤指多次發生者).

diary ['daiəri] *nc* book in which one writes down what happens each day; record of daily happenings 日記.

dice [dais] *nc* or *npl* small cube of wood, ivory, bone, plastic etc, marked with spots indicating numbers used in various games 骰子. *pl* 複數 **dice**. Also 亦作 *vt* cut vegetables etc into very small pieces 將(蔬菜等)切成小方塊. *Note* 說明: *dice was* originally the plural of a word *die*. However *die* is today *formal* and *o.f.*, and *dice* is used by many people as a singular word, which is unchanged in the plural. **dice** 原先是 die 的複數形式. 不過如今 die 是正式和舊式的用法, 而且許多人都把 dice 作爲單數詞使用. 單, 複數同形. **dicey** *adj* rather difficult and risky (*informal*) 艱險的; 冒險的.(非正式).

dictate[1] [dik'teit] *vt / i* say words for somebody to write down 口授: *He dictated a letter to his secretary.* 他向秘書口授一封信稿. **dictation** *nc / u.*

dictate[2] ['dikteit] *nc* (usu. *pl*) order which must or should be obeyed (通常用複數)命令, 驅使: *the dictates of common sense* i.e. what it is sensible to do 常識的驅使. **dictator** [dik'teitə*] *nc* person who rules a country by giving orders, without being himself under the control of the laws 獨裁者, 專制者. **dictatorship** [dik'teitəʃip] **1** *nu* position of a dictator; period during which a dictator rules 獨裁者的地位; 獨裁時期. **2** *nc* country ruled by a dictator 獨裁統治的國家.

diction ['dikʃən] *nu* way of speaking 措詞, 發音: *The actor spoke with a very clear diction* i.e. it was very easy to hear his words. 該演員吐字十分清楚.

即; 很容易聽清他的台詞

dictionary ['dikʃənəri] *nc* book containing a list of words, in alphabetical order, with their meanings 詞典, 字典.

did [did] past tense of **do.** do 的過去式.

die [dai] *vi* 1 stop living 死: *He became very ill and then he died.* 他病得很重, 接着就死了. 2 become weak; stop 變弱; 停止. *pres part* being in 分詞 **dying. die away** slowly become less strong 逐漸消失; 逐漸減弱: *The noise died away.* 吵鬧聲漸漸消失了. **die down** become less strong 減弱: *The fighting has died down.* 戰鬥漸漸平息. **die out** gradually come to an end and disappear 逐漸終止並消失; 滅絕, 絕跡, 過時. *Many of our traditions have died out.* 我們的許多習俗已經逐漸消失. **be dying for something / to do something** feel a strong wish to have / do something 渴望擁有／做某事物: *I'm dying to read John's new book.* (*informal*) 我渴望讀到約翰的新著. (非正式).

diesel ['di:zl] *nc* in **diesel engine** i.e. type of engine which burns diesel oil, often used for pulling trains. The train, or the engine, is often called a **diesel** 用於 diesel engine, 即: 柴油內燃機, 常用於帶動列車. 火車機車或上述這類機器通常稱爲 a diesel.

diet ['daiət] *nc* 1 food and drink which a person or animal usually has 飲食. 2 special food and drink which a person has for a special reason (often in order to lose weight) 爲了某種特別原因(常爲了減肥)的特種飲食: *be on a diet* 進規定的飲食, 節食. Also 亦作 *vi* have special food and drink for medical reasons (由於醫藥原因)進特種飲食; 節食: *She is dieting because*

she wants to lose weight. 她爲了減肥正在節食.

differ ['difə*] *vi* 1 be unlike 不同, 不一樣: *The climate in the north differs from the climate in the south.* 北方的氣候和南方的不同. 2 have a disagreement; quarrel 意見不同; 爭論: *John and his brother differ on the best way to cook fish* i.e. each has his own opinion. 約翰和他弟弟對怎樣把魚煮得最好吃, 意見不一. 即: 各執己見. **difference** *nc / u* 1 condition of being unlike 不同, 差異, 差別. *It is easy to see the difference between the two brothers* i.e. they do not have the same appearance. 很容易看出兩兄弟之間的差別. 即: 兩人外表不同. 2 quarrel or disagreement 爭論; 不同的意見: *John had a slight difference with his brother.* 約翰和他的弟弟意見署有不同. 3 amount by which one quantity is greater than another 差, 差距: *the difference between 90 and 60 is 30.* 90和60之差是30. **different** *adj* 1 not alike 不同的, 有差別的: *Winter in Britain is quite different from summer.* 在英國冬季與夏季大爲不同. 2 separate 分別的, 分離的, 各個的: *I have lived in four different houses in this city.* 我已在本市四所不同的房子裏住過. (*opp* 反義詞, 語 **similar** or the **same**). *Note* 說明: the expressions *different from* and *different to* are both widely used; however *different to* is said by some people to be incorrect 詞組 different from 和 different to 兩者都廣泛使用. 不過據某些人說 different to 是不正確的說法. **differential** [difə'renʃəl] *nc* (mathematics) very small difference between two values in a scale (數學)微分. **differentiate** [difə'renʃieit] *vt / i* make or see a difference between two or more things 分辨, 辨別, 區分: *It is difficult to differentiate between the two brothers* i.e. they look the same. 難以分辨這兩兄弟. 即: 他們長得一模一樣.

difficult ['difikəlt] *adj* **1** causing one to work hard 難的, 困難的: *Many people did not finish the work because it was so difficult.* 由於工作很難, 許多人都沒有完成. *That book is very difficult* i.e. not many people can understand it. 那本書很難. 即: 能讀懂的人並不多. *It was very difficult to repair my car.* 要修好我的車子很難. **2** (with reference to a person) unfriendly and quick to quarrel with others (指人) 不友好的, 難以相處的. **difficulty** *nc*.

diffident ['difidnt] *adj* not sure that one can do what one wants; lacking in confidence (esp. when meeting other people) 缺乏自信的; 羞怯的, 膽怯的: *He is so diffident that he is afraid to meet other people.* 他很怕羞, 不敢見其他人. (*opp* 反義詞 **confident**). **diffidence** *nu*.

dig¹ [dig] *vt / i* turn over earth with a spade, claws etc; make a hole in the ground 挖, 掘(洞): *The workmen dug a hole.* 工人們挖洞. *The dog began to dig.* 那隻狗開始刨土. *pres part* 現在分詞 **digging**. *past* 過去式和過去分詞 **dug**.

dig² [dig] *nc* sharp blow with something pointed 刺, 戳(尤指用手指頭). **digs** *npl* room or rooms in which a person lives and which are in a house belonging to somebody else 寄宿處: *live in digs.* (*informal* — **lodgings** is the more *formal* word) 居住在寄宿房內 (非正式— lodgings 是較爲正式的詞).

digest¹ [di'dʒest] *vt / i* **1** (with reference to food) change in the stomach so

that the body can make use of the substances in the food (指食物) 消化, 吸收: *He is digesting his dinner.* 他正在消化晚宴所吃的東西. *His food is still digesting.* 他吃下的食物仍在消化之中. **2** understand and think about information 領會, 領悟: *He is still digesting the sad news.* 他仍在領會這個令人傷心消息的意義. **digestible** *adj* easily digested 易消化的; 易領悟的. (*opp* 反義詞 **indigestible**). **digestion** *nu* **1** ability to digest 消化能力: *He has a good digestion.* 他消化能力很強. **2** process of digesting 消化; 領悟. see *ind* **indigestion.**

digest² ['daidʒest] *nc* summary or short ened form of a longer piece of speech or writing 概要, 摘要.

digit ['didʒit] *nc* **1** any of the numbers from 0 to 9 0-9中的任一數字. **2** a finger or a toe 手指頭或腳趾. **digital computer** type of electronic computer which uses numbers 數字電子計算機.

dignity ['digniti] *nu* feeling of calm or quiet importance and seriousness 尊嚴, 莊嚴: *That man has a lot of dignity* i.e. he feels important and serious. 那個男人舉止很莊嚴. 即: 他自己覺得高貴, 而且神情嚴肅. *He has no dignity; he is always behaving foolishly.* 他毫無尊嚴可言; 他的舉動總是傻乎乎的. **dignitary** ['dignitəri] *nc* person holding an important title / rank / position (often in a church) (常指教會中的)顯要, 顯貴, 名流. **dignify** ['dignifai] *vt* give dignity to 使尊嚴, 使高貴. **dignified** *adj* (*opp* 反義詞 **undignified**).

digress [dai'gres] *vi* turn aside from the subject which one is speaking or writing about, and deal with something else 離題, 岔開話題. **digression** *nc / u.*

dike, dyke [daik] *nc* **1** wall built to keep the sea or a river off the land (海或河的)堤，水壩. **2** ditch to carry away water 排水溝.

dilapidation [dilæpi'deiʃən] *nu* condition of being broken and old 破舊.
dilapidated *adj: a dilapidated fence* 破舊的籬笆.

dilate [dai'leit] *vt/i* (esp. with reference to parts of the body) become or make wider (尤指身體的某部份)(使)變大，(使)擴大: *His eyes dilated.* 他兩眼圓睜. *He dilated his nostrils.* 他張大鼻孔.

dilemma [dai'lemə] *nc* position in which one has to choose between two unpleasant things 進退兩難的困境，左右爲難: *The doctor was in a dilemma, should he tell his patient that he would probably not recover or should he tell a lie.* 大夫左右爲難，不知是該告訴病人說病大概治不好，還是不對病人說出真情.

diligence ['dilidʒəns] *nu* careful hard work 勤勉，勤奮，刻苦，用功. **diligent** *adj* showing diligence 勤勉刻苦的，勤奮的: *a diligent person* 一位勤勉刻苦的人; *diligent work* 工作勤奮.

dillydally ['dili'dæli] *vi* waste time (usu. by not coming to a decision) (*informal*) 磨磨蹭蹭(通常由於不做出決定)(非正式).

dilute [dai'lju:t] *vt* make a liquid weaker by adding another liquid (usu. water) (通常指用水)稀釋. Also 亦作 *adj* make weak in this way 稀釋的.

dim [dim] *adj* **1** not bright 暗的，暗淡的: *The lights are dim.* 燈光暗淡. **2** not intelligent. (*informal*) 糊塗的，傻的. (非正式) Also 亦作 *vt/i* become or make dim (使)變暗. *past* 過去式和過去分詞 **dimmed.**

dime [daim] *nc* (*US*) coin worth 10 cents. (*informal*) (美)十分幣，一角. (非正式).

dimension [dai'menʃən] *nc* **1** measurement of height / width / thickness 高度；寬度；厚度. **2** height, width, thickness 高；寬；厚.

diminish [di'miniʃ] *vt/i* become or make smaller 減少，縮小，減少.
diminutive [di'minjutiv] *adj* very small 小小的. Also 亦作 *nc* form of a word indicating something small (e.g. *piglet* meaning a baby pig) 表示小的詞(例如 piglet 意指小豬).

dimple ['dimpl] *nc* small hollow place on the body or face (often in the cheek, appearing when one smiles) (常指微笑時出現在兩頰的)酒渦，笑靨.

din [din] *nu* loud noise which goes on for some time 喧鬧聲，嘈雜聲.

dine [dain] *vi* eat dinner 用膳，進餐.
diner *nc* **1** person dining 用膳者，進餐者. **2** (mainly *US*) part of a train in which meals are served (主要用於美)餐車. **'dining car** part of a train in which meals are served 餐車. **'dining room** room specially used for meals 餐廳，飯廳.

dinghy ['diŋgi] *nc* small type of boat for rowing or sailing 小艇.

dingy ['dindʒi] *adj* dark and dirty 又黑又髒的: *a dingy room* 又黑又髒的房間.

dinner ['dinə*] *nc* **1** meal eaten at midday 午時正餐. **2** meal eaten in the evening 晚間正餐. **3** meal (usu. in the evening) held in honour of some important person or to celebrate some event (爲歡迎貴賓或慶祝某事而舉行的)晚宴.

dinosaur ['dainəsɔ:*] *nc* name given to several types of very large lizards which lived on earth thousands of years ago 恐龍.

diocese ['daiəsis] *nc* district under the control of a bishop 主教教區.

dioxide [dai'ɔksaid] *nu* chemical compound containing two atoms of oxygen to every one of another (stated) simple substance 二氧化物: *carbon dioxide* 二氧化碳.

dip¹ [dip] *vt / i* go, cause to go, down (使)下降, (使)下沉: *The road dips as it approaches the river.* 這條路在靠近河邊處傾斜. *He dipped his finger in the water.* 他手指頭在水裏浸了一下. *past* 過去式和過去分詞 **dipped.**

dip² [dip] *nc* 1 short swim 短暫的游泳, 洗浴, 浸, 泡. 2 movement downward 下降, 下傾. 3 place which is lower than the surrounding area 低窪處.

diphtheria [dip'θiəriə] *nu* disease of the throat (found esp. in children) 白喉 (尤見於兒童).

diphthong ['difθɔŋ] *nc* 1 sound made by two vowels running together as [ai] in *ice* 雙元音, 如 ice 的 [ai]. 2 two vowel letters representing one sound as *ea* in *meat* 表示一個音的兩個元音字母, 如 meat 的 ea.

diploma [di'ploumə] *nc* official piece of paper showing that a person has completed a certain course of study 文憑, 畢業證書; 及格證書.

diplomat ['dipləmæt] *nc* person whose work is to speak for his country in its relations with foreign countries 外交官. **diplomatist** [di'ploumətist] *nc* diplomat 外交官, 外交家. **diplomatic** [diplə'mætik] *adj* (*opp* 反義詞 **undiplomatic**). **diplomacy** [di'ploumosi] *nu*.

dire [daiə*] *adj* causing great fear 可怖的: *be in dire peril* i.e. in great danger 處於可怖的危險之中, 即: 處於極大的危險中.

direct¹ [dai'rekt] *adj* straight; not turning aside or stopping 直接的; 直率的; 直達的: *I want to travel by the most direct route* i.e. the way which goes straight to the place I am travelling to. 我想通過最爲直接的路線旅行. 即: 直達我將要旅行前往的地點. *He got a direct flight to Tangier* i.e. his plane did not stop anywhere before Tangier. 他乘直飛丹吉爾的航班. 即: 他所乘飛機在到丹吉爾前沒在任何地點着陸. *The bomb made a direct hit on the post office* i.e. the bomb fell straight down on to the post office. 炸彈直接命中郵局. *He gave me a direct answer to my question* i.e. he said exactly what I wanted to know, without trying to hide anything. 他對我的問題予以直截了當的回答. (*opp* 反義詞 **indirect**).

directly *adv* 1 at once; as soon as 立刻, 立即; 一⋯就: *He came directly I called.* 我一打電話他就來了. *Directly you feel any pains, you must go to the doctor.* 你一感到病痛, 就應該去看醫生. 2 straight 直接地: *He drove home directly.* 他駕車直接回家. *Note* 說明: in the following phrases, the stress is usually on the first syllable of *direct.* 在下列短語中, 重音通常落在 direct 的第一個音節上. **'direct 'object** (grammar) noun or noun phrase which completes the sense of a transitive verb in a statement (e.g. in *I saw John*, 'John' is the direct object) (語法) 直接賓語. (例如在 I saw John 中, "John" 是直接賓語). **'direct 'speech** method of reporting what a person has said, using the actual words spoken by that person 直接引語. (*opp* 反義詞 **indirect speech** or **reported speech**).

direct² [dai'rekt] *vt / i* 1 give orders; tell people what to do 命令; 指揮: *He directed the men to move the furni-*

ture 他命令人們搬傢具. **2** be in charge of the way something is done 主持; 指導; 導演: *I shall direct the work.* 我將主持這項工作. *Richard Smith directed that film.* 理查德·史密斯導演了那部影片. **3** tell a person the way to somewhere 指引, 指點: *Can you direct me to the post office?* 告訴我到郵局怎麼走好嗎? **4** turn towards 朝向, 轉向: *At a meeting, you must direct your remarks to the chairman* i.e. you must speak to the chairman and not to other people. 在會上, 你應該朝着主席說話. *He directed his attention to me* i.e. he turned to look at me or to deal with me. 他把注意力轉向我. *We directed our course towards Tangier* i.e. we turned and travelled towards Tangier. 我們把旅行路線轉向丹吉爾. **direction** [dai'rekʃən] **1** *nc* point to which one is travelling, or point where something is 方向: *London is in that direction* i.e. where I am pointing, where you are walking etc. 倫敦在那個方向. **2** *nu* control; guidance 控制; 指導: *work under somebody's direction* i.e. do what he tells one to do. 在某人指導下工作, 即: 按他所說的去做. **3** *nc* (often *pl*) orders or instructions (常用複數) 命令或指令: *I followed your directions* i.e. I did what you told me. 我遵從您的指令. 即: 我按您所說的做. **director** *nc* **1** one of the people in charge of a business firm 董事. **2** person in charge of some organization (esp. a person in charge of the production of a play or film) 某組織負責人 (尤指戲劇或電影的) 導演. **directory** *nc* book giving a list of people's names etc for various purposes 住址姓名簿, 人名錄.

dirge [də:dʒ] *nc* slow song sung at a

funeral 挽歌, 哀歌.

dirt [də:t] *nu* **1** mud, dust etc on the ground 地面的泥土, 塵埃: *He was sitting in the dirt.* 他坐在泥地裏. **2** mud, dust or other unclean substance 泥土, 泥巴; 塵埃; 污垢: *There is dirt on your face.* 你臉上有塵土. *She washed the dirt out of the clothes.* 她把衣服上的污垢洗掉了. **dirty** *adj* **1** not clean 骯髒的, 不乾淨的: *His hands were dirty after he had been working in the garden.* 他在花園裏幹活後, 雙手骯髒. **2** impure in word or thought (言語, 思想等) 下流的, 髒的, 黃色的. Also 亦作 *vt* make dirty 弄髒.

dis- [dis] *prefix* the opposite of something (e.g. **disagree, dislike, displease, dissatisfy**) 某事物的對立面 (例如 disagree, dislike, displease, dissatisfy).

disable [dis'eibl] *vt* **1** make somebody unable to use his arms or legs properly 使殘廢: *He was disabled in the accident.* 他在事故中受傷殘廢了. **2** make unfit in some way 使無能, 使無法勝任. **disability** [disə'biliti] *nc / u*

disadvantage [disəd'vɑ:ntidʒ] *nc / u* anything which makes one slower, weaker, poorer etc than other people 不利, 劣勢, 短處: *To have only one leg is a disadvantage.* 只有一條腿是種不利的. (*opp* 反義詞 **advantage**).

disagree [disə'gri:] *vi* **1** fail to agree 不同意; 不一致. *After a long discussion, the two sides still disagreed.* 長時間討論之後, 雙方仍未達成一致. **2** (with reference to food) cause one to be ill or to feel unwell (指食物) 有害健康, 不適合. *Some kinds of meat disagree with me.* 我不適合吃某些種類的肉. **disagreement** *nu* **disagreeable** *adj* badtempered; quick to quarrel with people; unpleasant 脾氣不好的; 易與

人爭吵的; 令人不快的: *a disagreeable task* 一件苦差事.

disallow [disə'lau] *vt* make an official decision to not to allow or accept something 正式拒絕接受, 不允許, 不承認: *The referee disallowed the goal.* 裁判裁決該球無效.

disappear [disə'piə*] *vi* go and be no longer seen 消失, 不見, 絕跡: *The snow on the roads disappeared when the sun shone.* 太陽出來時路上的積雪融化了. **disappearance** *nu*.

disappoint [disə'point] *vt* fail to do what one had promised, or what other people had hoped one would do 使失望: *I promised to buy my son a new bicycle but I had to disappoint him.* 我答應給我兒子買一輛新自行車, 可我只好讓他失望了. **disappointment** *nc / u* unhappy because one has not got what one hoped for 失望的. **disappointing** *adj* causing one to feel disappointed 令人失望的: *His examination results are disappointing* i.e. not as good as we hoped. 他的考試成績令人失望.

disapprove [disə'pru:v] *vi* have an unfavourable opinion of 不贊成: *I disapprove of children smoking cigarettes* i.e. I think they should not do this. 我不贊成兒童抽烟. 即: 我認為他們不該這麼做.

disarm [dis'a:m] **1** *vi* (with reference to a country) reduce the number of one's weapons, soldiers, aeroplanes etc. (指一國) 裁軍. **2** *vt* be friendly and so make somebody stop being angry 使息怒: *We were being angry but he disarmed us by his smile.* 我們很生氣, 但是他的微笑使我們的怒氣消了. **disarmament** [dis'a:məmənt] *nu* process of reducing the number of soldiers, weapons etc. 裁軍.

disarray [disə'rei] *nu* condition in which things are not arranged or organized properly 紊亂, 混亂: *Our army was in disarray after the battle.* 戰鬥過後我軍處於混亂狀態.

disaster [di'za:stə*] *nc / u* very great and terrible accident or misfortune 災禍; 災難: *Three hundred people were killed in the disaster.* 三百人死於這場災禍. **disastrous** [di'za:strəs] *adj*.

disband [dis'bænd] *vt / i* break up an organized group of people 解散 (團體): *The six criminals agreed to disband* i.e. leave each other and work separately. 六名罪犯同意散夥. 即: 分開後各自幹各的. *The government disbanded all political parties.* 政府解散了所有的政黨.

disbelieve [disbi'li:v] *vt* not believe 不相信; 不信任. **disbelief** [disbi'li:f] *nu*.

disc, disk [disk] *nc* **1** thin round flat object 圓盤. **2** gramophone record 唱片. '**disc jockey** person who introduces gramophone records on the radio or at a discotheque (電台或迪斯科舞廳的) 流行歌曲節目主持人, 唱片播放人.

discard [dis'ka:d] *vt* put aside or give away as useless or unwanted 摒棄, 廢棄: *He discarded all his old clothes.* 他把自己所有的舊衣服全扔掉了.

discern [di'sə:n] *vt* notice something (esp. something which is not easy to see, feel, smell etc.) 看出, 識別, 辨明 (尤指不易看到的, 感覺到, 嗅到等的東西). **discerning** *adj* able to understand well, and to decide what is good 有眼力的, 有洞察力的, 高明的.

discharge [dis'tʃa:dʒ] *vt* send out or send away 送出, 排出; 發射; 解雇; 送走; 釋放: *He discharged the gun* i.e. he fired it. 他開槍了. *He discharged his servant* i.e. he would not let his servant work for him any more. 他把傭人解雇了. *Some towns discharge rubbish into the sea.* 一些城鎮把垃圾傾倒入海裏. *The judge found him not guilty and discharged him* i.e. told him that he could go away. 法官認爲他無罪, 於是把他釋放了. Also 亦作 *nc*.

disciple [di'saipl] *nc* anyone who follows a religious leader (esp. the original twelve followers of Jesus) 信徒(尤指耶穌最初的十二個門徒).

discipline ['displin] **1** *nu* willingness to obey orders 紀律; 風紀: *Soldiers have to learn discipline.* 軍人得學會遵守紀律. **2** *nu* ability to make people obey orders 使人服從命令的能力: *The officer had no discipline over his men* i.e. he could not make them do what he ordered. 這個軍官指揮不動手下的人: 他無法讓他們服從命令. **3** *nc* any subject studied at a university etc. (大學等的)學科. Also 亦作 *vt* **1** make somebody willing to obey orders 管教, 訓練, 教導: *He disciplined the new soldiers.* 他訓練新兵. **2** punish 懲罰.

disclaim [dis'kleim] *vt* say that one has no connection with something 否認: *He disclaimed any interest in the plan* i.e. he said that he was not interested. 他否認對該計劃有任何興趣.

disclose [dis'klouz] *vt* **1** tell something which had been a secret 洩露, 透露: *He disclosed that he had made arrangements to buy a new car.* 他透露說, 他已經準備好要購買一輛新車. **2** show something hidden 揭露. **disclosure** *nc / u*.

disco ['diskou] *nc* short form of **discotheque**. *(informal)* discotheque 的縮略形式(非正式).

discolour [dis'kʌlə*] (*US* 美 **discolor**) *vt / i* spoil or damage the colour of

(使)變色; (使)褪色; 玷污: *Smoke and dirt had discoloured the walls.* 烟塵使得四壁污跡斑斑.

discomfort [dis'kʌmfət] *nu* lack of comfort; worry, distress 不舒適; 不安, 苦惱.

disconcert [diskən'sə:t] *vt* make a person feel puzzled and unhappy 使困窘; 使難堪: *We were rather disconcerted when he rudely refused our invitation.* 當他粗魯地拒絕我們的邀請時, 我們感到相當尷尬.

disconnect [diskə'nekt] *vt* (often with reference to some piece of machinery or some electric device) remove a connection from (常指機器的某一部份或某種電器裝置)使分離, 中斷連接.

disconnected *adj* (with reference to thought or speech) not well planned; with the parts having no connection with each other (指思想或話語)不連貫的; 無系統的.

discontent [diskən'tent] *nu* restless and rather angry feeling because one has not got what one wants 不滿. **discontented** *adj*.

discontinue [diskən'tinju:] *vt / i* stop; come or bring to an end (使)中斷; (使)終止.

discord ['diskɔ:d] *nc / u* **1** angry quarrelling 爭吵. **2** sounds (esp. in music) which do not go well together; unpleasant sounds (尤指音樂裏)不諧和音; 令人不快的聲音. **discordant** [dis-'kɔ:dnt] *adj*.

discotheque ['diskoutek] *nc* club for young people at which records of popular music are played 爲年青人開設的播放流行樂曲唱片的跳舞場所, 迪斯科舞廳.

discount ['diskaunt] *nu* amount of money which is taken from the price of goods for various reasons 折扣.

Some shops give a discount to students i.e. they sell their goods more cheaply to students than to other people. 一些商店給學生以折扣優待. 即: 售貨時他們對學生的售價低於對其他顧客的售價.

discourage [dis'kʌridʒ] *vt* make somebody less willing to do something 使洩氣, 使灰心; 阻攔; 妨礙: *I put new locks on my doors to discourage thieves* i.e. make it more difficult for thieves to come in. 我在門上加新鎖, 以阻止小偷進入. *I discouraged him from borrowing the money.* 我不讓他借錢.

discover [dis'kʌvə*] *vt* find something hidden or unknown 發現: *Columbus discovered America.* 哥倫布發現了美洲. **discovery** *nc / u.*

discredit [dis'kredit] *vt* cause one to think that somebody / something is dishonest or untrue 使成爲不可信: *Recent events have discredited your story* i.e. recent events have made me think that you did not tell the truth. 近來發生的事件已使我不相信你說的事. Also 亦作 *nc / u.*

discreet [dis'kri:t] *adj* careful in behaviour; not telling secrets to other people; not going beyond the limits of what is proper and sensible 舉止謹慎的; 言語審慎的; 考慮周到的. (*opp* 反義詞 **indiscreet**). **discreetly** *adv* **discretion** [dis'kreʃən] *nu* 1 quality of being discreet 謹慎. 2 ability to choose what to do 判斷力: *Use your own discretion* i.e. do what you think is best. 你自己看着辦吧. 即: 按你認爲最好的去做. (*opp* 反義詞 **indiscretion**).

discrepancy [dis'krepənsi] *nc* 1 (e.g. with reference to records of money) difference between what there should

be and what there actually is (例如指款項賬目)差額, 不符. 2 difference between several versions of the same story (說話)不一致, 不同: *There is a discrepancy between what you say and what John says.* 你說的和約翰說的不同.

discriminate [dis'krimineit] *vi* treat some people better than other people 偏愛: *A teacher must not discriminate between pupils.* i.e. he should not be more friendly to some pupils than to others 教師不該對學生有偏愛. **discrimination** [diskrimi'neiʃən] *nu* **discriminating** *adj* able to choose what is best 有辨別力的, 有識別力的.

discuss [dis'kʌs] *vt* talk about a topic from several points of view 討論. **discussion** [dis'kʌʃən] *nc / u.*

disdain [dis'dein] *vt* think of something as very low and dishonourable 輕視, 藐視: *He disdained to steal.* 他不屑去偷. Also 亦作 *nu* feeling in which one disdains something 輕視, 藐視. **disdainful** *adj.*

disease [di'zi:z] *nc / u* illness caused by germs or by incorrect growth of part of the body (e.g. smallpox or cancer are diseases, a broken leg or a bullet-wound are not diseases) 疾病, 病 **diseased** *adj.*

disembark [disim'bɑ:k] *vt / i* leave, cause to leave, a ship or aeroplane (使)離船上岸; (使)下機.

disentangle [disin'tæŋgl] *vt* 1 remove knots and tangles from string, rope etc. 解開 (繩, 結等). 2 find out the meaning or truth of something which is difficult to understand 弄清(奧秘, 真相等); 解決(疑難).

disfigure [dis'figə*] *vt* spoil or damage the appearance of 毀損…的外表: *He disfigured the picture by throwing ink* *at it.* 他把墨水濺到那幅畫上, 污損了畫面.

disgrace [dis'greis] *nu* **1** loss of honour or good name 恥辱, 丟臉: *He suffered the disgrace of being beaten by a boy much smaller than he was.* 他很丟臉, 因爲他被一個比他小得多的男孩打敗了. **2** somebody / something which brings disgrace 丟臉的人或事: *That boy is a disgrace to his family* i.e. he behaves very badly, and so makes his whole family seem bad. 那個男孩使他全家丟臉. 即: 他行爲十分惡劣, 因而使他全家在別人眼中似乎也很壞. Also 亦作 *vt* bring disgrace to 使丟臉. **disgraceful** *adj* **in disgrace** regarded with anger because of something wrong which one has done 受斥責: *That boy is in disgrace with the headmaster* i.e. the headmaster is angry with him. 那名男生受到校長的斥責. 即: 校長對他生氣了.

disgruntled [dis'grʌntld] *adj* angry and dissatisfied because one has not got what one wants (因未如願而) 不滿的.

disguise [dis'gaiz] *nc / u* anything changing one's appearance so that one is not recognized by other people 僞裝物, 假扮物: *He grew a moustache and wore dark glasses as a disguise because the police were looking for him.* 由於警方正在搜捕他, 因而他蓄鬚並且戴了一副墨鏡作爲僞裝. *He went to the house in disguise.* 他化了裝到那所房子去. Also 亦作 *vt* **1** change appearance 僞裝, 假扮. **2** conceal (feelings etc.) 隱藏 (感情等).

disgust [dis'gʌst] *nu* feeling that something is very unpleasant 厭惡, 憎: *The food tasted so unpleasant that I threw it away in disgust.* 這種食物味道十分糟糕, 於是我厭惡地把它扔了. Also 亦作 *vt* cause somebody to feel

disgust 使厭惡, 使作嘔: *The food disgusted me.* 這種食物令我作嘔. **disgusting** *adj* causing disgust 令人厭惡的, 令人作嘔的.

dish [diʃ] *nc* container in which food is brought to the table; the food itself 碟, 盤; 一道菜. **dishes** *npl* (often in **wash the dishes**) plates, cups, knives and forks etc used for a meal (常用於 wash the dishes) 餐具(包括盤、杯、刀叉等).

dishearten [dis'hɑ:tn] *vt* discourage; make less sure of success 使沮喪, 使洩氣; 使失去信心.

dishevelled [di'ʃevəld] (*US* 美 **disheveled**) *adj* (with reference to personal appearance) untidy; in disorder (指人的外表) 不整齊的; 凌亂的.

dishonest [dis'ɔnist] *adj* not honest 不誠實的, 欺詐的. **dishonesty** *nu*.

dishonour [dis'ɔnə*] (*US* 美 **dishonor**) *nu* loss of good name; something causing loss of good name 恥辱; 不名譽; 不名譽的事. **dishonourable** *adj*.

disillusion [disi'lu:ʒən] *vt* tell somebody the truth after he has been believing something untrue (usu. a truth which is less pleasant than the thing he believed) 使醒悟, 使幻想破滅, 曉以事實(尤指令人不快的): *He thought that he had won the prize, but I disillusioned him* i.e. told him that he had not won. 他以爲自己已獲獎, 但是我卻曉之以不愉快的事實. 即: 告訴他未獲獎這一事實.

disinfect [disin'fekt] *vt* remove germs from, so as to prevent disease 消毒, 淨化. **disinfectant** *nc / u* substance which disinfects 消毒劑. Also 亦作 *adj*.

disintegrate [dis'intigreit] *vt / i* break, cause to break, into small pieces (使)破碎: *The bomb disintegrated when it* *exploded.* 炸彈爆炸時變成碎片.

disinterested [dis'intərestid] *adj* **1** impartial; willing to listen to all sides of an argument; willing to judge what is right without any personal feelings 公正的; 不偏心的; 不偏倚的. **2** not interested; not wishing to know about something 不感興趣的; 漠不關心的. *Note* 說明: many people consider that this word should not be used in sense **2** for which there is another word *uninterested* 許多人認為此詞不應用於義 2. 義2可用另一個詞 uninterested 表示.

disjointed [dis'dʒɔintid] *adj* (with reference to speech or writing) not well planned; with the parts not well connected to each other (指說話或寫作) 不連貫的; 雜亂無章的.

disk [disk] *nc* see 見 **disc.**

dislike [dis'laik] *vt* not like 不喜歡, 討厭; *I dislike beer.* 我不喜歡喝啤酒. Also 亦作 *nc / u*: feel dislike for something 不喜歡, 討厭.

dislocate ['disləkeit] *vt* **1** put a bone in the body out of its proper position (e.g. in an accident) 使脫臼(例如在事故中); *He dislocated his arm in a fall.* 他摔倒時胳膊脫臼了. **2** disturb; disarrange; put out of order 擾亂; 使紊亂; 使混亂.

dislodge [dis'lɔdʒ] *vt* push something out of its place 逐出, 取出; 推開, 推離; *He dislodged a stone from the mountainside.* 他從山坡上推下一塊石頭.

disloyal [dis'lɔiəl] *adj* not loyal 不忠的, 背叛的.

dismal ['dizml] *adj* sad; unhappy; without brightness 憂愁的; 不快的; 陰暗的; *a dismal room / person* 陰暗的房間/憂愁的人.

dismantle [dis'mæntl] *vt / i* separate the parts which make up a whole 分解, 拆

開: *He dismantled his old car.* 他把自己的舊車拆開了. *These chairs dismantle for storage* i.e. they can be dismantled. 這些椅子可以拆開收藏.

dismay [dis'mei] *nu* feeling of alarm and loss of hope 驚懼; 沮喪. Also 亦作 *vt* fill with dismay 使驚懼, 使沮喪.

dismiss [dis'mis] *vt* send away 解散; 開除; 不理會: *After talking to the pupils, the headmaster dismissed them to their classrooms.* 在和這些學生談話之後, 校長把他們打發回教室去了. *He has been dismissed from his job with the railway.* 他被開除出鐵路部門. *I have dismissed the matter from my mind.* 我心裏已不再想這件事了. **dismissal** *nc / u.*

dismount [dis'maunt] *vt* get off a horse etc. 下(馬等).

disobey [disə'bei] *vt / i* refuse to obey 不服從: *disobey the headmaster* 不服從校長; *disobey an order* 不服從命令. **disobedient** [disə'bi:diənt] *adj.* **disobedience** [disə'bi:diəns] *nu.*

disorder [dis'ɔ:də*] **1** *nu* lack of order; untidiness 無秩序, 混亂; 凌亂; *His room was in disorder* i.e. the things in his room were not in their proper places. 他的房間凌亂不堪. **2** *nc / u* rioting or violence in public (usu. for political purposes) 騷亂, 騷動(通常爲了政治目的). **3** *nc* slight illness 小病. **disorderly** *adj* **1** untidy 混亂的; 凌亂的. **2** violent in public 騷亂的.

disown [dis'oun] *vt* say that something / someone does not belong to one, or that one has no connection with something / someone 否認…是自己的; 說與…有關係; 與…斷絕關係.

disparity [dis'pæriti] *nc / u* lack of equality, difference 不等, 差異, 不同: *There is a great disparity between the salaries of Mr Brown and Mr Smith.*

布朗先生和史密斯先生的工資收入差距很大.

dispassionate [dis'pæ∫ənət] *adj* calm and impartial; not considering one's personal feelings so able to decide what is right 冷静公正的; 超然的; 平心静氣的.

dispatch, despatch [dis'pæt∫] *vt* send away, send off 派遣; 發送: *He dispatched a telegram.* 他發了一封電報. Also 亦作 *nc* special message 急件; 電訊.

dispel [dis'pel] *vt* (esp. with reference to driving away doubts, fears, worries etc) drive away 驅散(尤指疑慮、恐懼、憂慮等). *past* 過去式和過去分詞 **dispelled.**

dispense [dis'pens] *vt / i* prepare and sell or give out medicine 配(藥)出售; 配(藥). **dispenser** *nc* **dispensary** [dis'pensəri] *nc* place where a dispenser works 藥房, 配藥室. **dispense with something** continue without something 免除; 省卻; 不需要, 沒有⋯也行: *I can dispense with these old clothes* i.e. I do not want them any more. 我可以不要這些舊衣服了.

disperse [dis'pəs] *vt / i* spread and go away; cause to do this (使) 散開; 驅散: *The crowd of people slowly dispersed.* 這羣人慢慢地四下散開了. *The police dispersed the crowd.* 警察驅散了這羣人. **dispersal** *nu.*

dispirited [dis'piritid] *adj* unhappy and without hope 沮喪的, 敗興的.

displace [dis'pleis] *vt* **1** put out of the right place 使脫離正當位置. **2** take the place of somebody / something 取代(某人 / 某事物); 擠掉, 趕走: *John has displaced Tom* i.e. John is now in the position where Tom used to be. 約翰已經取代湯姆. 即: 約翰如今處在湯姆過去的位置上.

display [dis'plei] *vt* show; allow people to see 陳列, 展覽; 顯示, 表現. Also 亦作 *nc / u* something displayed; act of displaying 陳列物, 展覽品; 陳列, 展覽; 顯示, 表現.

displease [dis'pli:z] *vt* opp of **please** 使不高興; 觸怒; 使煩惱.

disposal [dis'pouzəl] *nu* act of throwing away or giving away as useless or unwanted (廢物的) 處理, 清理. **at one's disposal** to be used as one wishes 任由某人支配; 任由某人使用: *He placed his house at my disposal* i.e. he allowed me to use his house as I wished. 他把自己的房子讓我自行支配. 即: 他允許我随意使用他的房子.

dispose [dis'pouz] *vi* **dispose of something** throw away or give away as useless or unwanted; finish or put an end to 處理, 處置; 除掉, 了結: *He disposed of his old car.* 他把舊車處理掉. *He disposed of all the difficulties.* 他把所有的困難都解決了.

disposition [dispə'zi∫ən] *nc / u* character; feelings and way of behaving 性格; 性情, 氣質: *He has a very friendly disposition* i.e. he is usually friendly. 他的性情十分和善.

disproportionate [,disprə'pɔ:∫ənət] *adj* not equal in size or amount; too great or too little (大小或數量) 不相稱的; 不均衡的; 不成比例的.

disprove [dis'pru:v] *vt* show that something is not true 證明⋯不成立; 反駁.

dispute [dis'pju:t] *vt / i* say that one thinks that something is untrue or dishonest 對⋯持異議, 懷疑, 反駁: *I disputed his story.* 我對他的說法持異議. Also 亦作 *nc* argument or quarrel 爭論; 爭吵.

disqualify [dis'kwɔlifai] *vt* take away permission to do something 使無資格, 使不能: *His age disqualifies him* *from entering the competition* i.e. he is too old or too young. 他因年齡關係無法參加比賽. 即: 他太老或太小. **disqualification** [diskwɔlifi'keiʃən] *nc / u.*

disregard ['disri'gɑ:d] *vt* take no notice of 無視, 不理: *He disregarded my advice* i.e. he did not do what I advised. 他不理睬我的勸告. 即: 他没按我的勸告去做. Also 亦作 *nu* act of disregarding 無視, 不理.

disreputable [dis'repjutəbl] *adj* well-known for bad behaviour, having the appearance of one who will behave badly 聲名狼藉的; 長相不體面的.

disrespect ['disri'spekt] *nu* lack of respect 不敬, 失禮, 無禮. **disrespectful** *adj.*

disrupt [dis'rʌpt] *vt* break up; prevent from continuing properly 使破裂; 擾亂; 破裂: *John disrupted our arrangements.* 約翰破壞了我們的安排. **disruption** *nc / u.*

dissatisfy [dis'sætisfai] *vt* fail to satisfy 使不滿. **dissatisfied** *adj* **dissatisfaction** [disætis'fækʃən] *nu.*

dissect [di'sekt] *vt* cut up a plant, animal or human body in order to study it 解剖(植物, 動物或人體以便研究).

dissent [di'sent] *vi* refuse to believe what other people believe 不同意, 持異議. **dissension** *nc / u* argument; quarrel; refusal to believe what others believe 爭論, 爭吵; 不同意.

dissertation [disə'teiʃən] *nc* long piece of writing, making a study of some subject 論文.

dissident ['disidnt] *adj* not agreeing with others; refusing to accept the beliefs or leadership of others 持異議的; 唱反調的; 持不同政見的. Also 亦作 *nc* person who is dissident 持不同政見者.

dissipate ['disipeit] *vt / i* **1** spend money etc in a useless way 揮霍, 浪費. **2** drive away 打消, 驅散: *He dissipated my fears.* 他消除了我的恐懼感. **dissipation** [disi'peiʃən] *nu.* **dissipated** *adj* unhealthy because of too much pleasure (e.g. drinking and gambling) 過度放蕩的(例如酗酒和賭博).

dissociate [di'souʃieit] *vt* separate into parts 使分離. **dissociate oneself from someone / something** stop being friendly with; say that one has no connection with or that one is not joining in 停止與某人友好; 否認與某事有關; 否認參與某事: *He dissociated himself from John and Tom.* 他不同約翰和湯姆交往了. *He dissociated himself from the committee's request.* 他否認與委員會的要求有關.

dissolute ['disəlu:t] *adj* living a wicked life of pleasure 過放蕩生活的.

dissolve [di'zɔlv] *vt / i* **1** change from solid into liquid form through the action of liquid (使)溶解: *Sugar dissolves in water.* 糖溶解於水. *He dissolved the sugar in his tea.* 他把糖溶在茶水中. **2** bring an arrangement to an end 解散; 結束: *They dissolved their partnership* i.e. they agreed not to work together any longer. 他們終止了夥伴關係. 即: 他們同意不再在一塊工作. *The Queen dissolved Parliament* i.e. she sent the Members of Parliament away in order to hold an election. 女王解散了議會. 即: 以便進行大選. *Parliament dissolved.* 議會解散了.

dissuade [di'sweid] *vt* persuade somebody not to do something; make somebody agree not to do something by talking to him 勸阻, 說服(某人)不做某事: *I dissuaded him from borrow-*

ing the money. 他勸他不要借錢.

distant ['dɪstnt] *adj* **1** far away; not near 遙遠的, 不近的: *The stars are distant from the earth.* 星星距離地球很遠. **2** unfriendly and not showing one's feelings 冷淡的, 疏遠的: *He greeted me in a very distant manner.* 他用很冷淡的態度跟我打招呼. **distance** *nc / u* the space between two things, places or times 距離: *The distance between the towns is only five miles.* 兩城相距只有五英里. **in the distance** a long way away 遠處.

distaste [dis'teist] *nu* dislike for something 討厭, 厭惡: *He looked at me with distaste.* 他厭惡地看着我. **distasteful** *adj* unpleasant; causing one to feel distaste 令人不快的; 令人厭惡的.

distemper [dis'tempə*] *nu* **1** type of paint (usu. used for walls) (通常用於漆牆的) 乳膠漆. **2** disease of dogs 犬瘟熱.

distend [dis'tend] *vt / i* (usu. with reference to the stomach) grow, cause to grow, bigger by pressure from within (通常指胃) (使) 膨脹, (使) 脹大.

distil [dis'til] *vt / i* **1** heat liquid until it becomes vapour; then collect pure liquid from the cooling vapour 蒸餾. **2** make spirits (e.g. whisky) in this way 以蒸餾法製造 (威士忌酒等). *past* 過去式和過去分詞 **distilled**. **distillery** *nc* place where spirits (e.g. whisky) are made 釀酒廠 (例如威士忌酒廠).

distinct [dis'tiŋkt] *adj* **1** clearly seen, heard etc. 清楚的, 清晰的: *The photograph is not distinct* i.e. what is on it cannot be seen clearly. 這張照片不清晰. (*opp* 反義詞 **indistinct**). **2** not the same 不同的. **distinctly** *adv* **distinction 1** *nc* difference 不同: *What is the distinction between a newspaper and a magazine?* i.e. in what ways are they different? 報紙和雜誌有何不同? **2** *nu* quality of being better than most 卓越: *He served with distinction in the army* i.e. he was a very good soldier. 他在服役期間表現卓越. *This is a car of great distinction* 這是一部非同凡響的小汽車. **3** *nc* reward or title given for being better than most 獎賞; 榮譽稱號: *He gained a distinction in the examination.* 他在這次考試中獲得獎賞. **distinctive** *adj* showing a difference 有特色的, 特別的: *This bird has several distinctive features* i.e. features which enable one to recognize the bird. 這種鳥具有幾種與別的鳥不同的特色.

distinguish [dis'tiŋgwiʃ] *vt* see in what way two or more things differ 辨別, 區分: *How do you distinguish between a star and a planet?* i.e. how do you know when you are seeing a star and when a planet? 你如何分辨恒星和行星? **distinguished** *adj* famous for doing something very well 著名的, 傑出的, 卓越的: *He is a distinguished soldier.* 他是個傑出的戰士. (*opp* 反義詞 **undistinguished**).

distort [dis'tɔːt] *vt* **1** change from the correct shape or appearance by force 使扭曲, 使變形: *The heat of the sun had distorted the railway lines.* 太陽的熱度使鐵路變形了. **2** change from the truth 歪曲, 曲解: *He distorted my story* i.e. he changed my story when he told it to others. 他歪曲了我的話. **distortion** *nc / u.*

distract [dis'trækt] *vt* cause somebody's attention to turn away from something 使分散注意力, 使分心, 擾亂: *The advertisements by the side of the road sometimes distract the attention of motorists.* 路旁的廣告有時會使駕駛

汽車的人分心. **distraction** *nc / u* something which distracts 分散注意力 的事物.

distraught [dis'trɔ:t] *adj* unable to think clearly because of worry or trouble 憂 心忡忡的, 心神不寧的.

distress [dis'tres] *nu* great unhappiness caused by worry or trouble; a cause of this unhappiness 憂傷, 悲痛; 引起憂 傷或悲痛的原因: *Her distress was very great when she read the letter.* 她讀了這封信感到十分悲傷. Also 亦 作 *vt* cause distress to 使憂傷, 使悲 痛. **distressing** *adj* causing distress 使人憂傷的, 令人悲痛的.

distribute [dis'tribju:t] *vt* give out or share out 分發; 分配: *Goods are taken from the factories by lorry and are distributed to the shops.* 貨物用卡 車從工廠運出, 然後分發給各商店. *The teacher distributed the books to the children.* 教師給孩子們分發書本. **distribution** [distri'bju:ʃən] *nu*.

district ['distrikt] *nc* part of a country, town or city (usu. a small part) (國 家、城鎮或城市的小部份) 區, 地區: **'district at'torney** local government law officer in America 美國地區法官.

distrust [dis'trʌst] *vt* think that some- body / something is not honest or true 不信任; 不相信: *I distrust that man.* 我不信任那個男人. Also 亦作 *nu*: *feel distrust for somebody* 對某人 不信任.

disturb [dis'tə:b] *vt* interrupt arrange- ments; break up peace or quiet 干擾; 擾亂: *You disturbed my sleep* i.e. you woke me up. 你干擾我的睡眠. 即: 你把 我弄醒了. *May I disturb you for a moment?* i.e. may I stop you from continuing what you are doing? 我能 不能打擾你一會兒? 即: 我可以打斷你正 在做的事兒嗎? *He disturbed our plans*

i.e. caused us to change our plans. 他 打亂了我們的計劃. **disturbing** *adj* **disturbance** *nc / u* act of disturbing (esp. in a violent way) 干擾; 擾亂(尤 指以暴力的方式): *political disturb- ances* i.e. riots and demonstrations 政 治動亂, 即: 騷動與示威.

ditch [ditʃ] *nc* long narrow place dug in the earth to allow water to flow away 水溝, 水渠.

ditto ['ditou] *nc* the mark meaning 'the same', used in making lists in order to avoid repeating words already written 表示"同上"的符號(用於表格中以免重 複已寫的文字). *pl* 複數 **dittos.**

divan [di'væn] *nc* low bed without back or sides (無靠背和扶手的)低沙發床.

dive[1] [daiv] *vi* **1** jump head first into water (usu. from a height) (從高處頭 朝下) 跳水. **2** (with reference to an aeroplane etc) move quickly forwards and downwards (指飛機等)俯衝. **3** move quickly into something. (*infor- mal* in sense **3**) 迅速鑽入, 伸入或插 入(義3為非正式). **diver** *nc.*

dive[2] [daiv] *nc* **1** act of jumping head first into water (usu. from a height) 跳水 **2** (with reference to an aero- plane etc) rapid movement forwards and downwards (飛機等的)俯衝.

diverge [dai'və:dʒ] *vi* go in different directions; be different from the nor- mal 分歧; 分開; 異常.

diverse [dai'və:s] *adj* different; not alike in any way 不同的; 無相似之處的: *John and his brother have diverse in- terests* i.e. they are not interested in the same things 約翰和他弟弟興趣各 異. **diversify** *vt* make diverse 使不 同; 使無相似之處. **diversity** *nu* differ- ence; number of different things 不同, 多樣化.

divert [dai'və:t] *vt* cause to go in

another direction 使轉向: *The police diverted the traffic.* 警察指揮交通.

divide [di'vaid] *vt / i* **1** separate 分開, 分: *Spain is divided from France by the Pyrenees.* 比利牛斯山脈把西班牙和法國隔開. *The road divides into two at the other side of the town.* 在該鎮的另一頭道路分岔爲兩條. *We divided into two teams.* 我們分成兩組. *He divided the money among his family* i.e. he gave each of his family some money. 他把錢分給全家人. 即: 他給每位家人一些錢. **2** (mathematics) find out how many times one number is contained in another (e.g. divide 10 into 190 = 19) (數學)除 (如用10除190得19). **dividend** ['dividend] *nc* **1** number to be divided (e.g. if we divide 10 into 190. 190 is the dividend) 被除數(例如我們用10除190, 190是被除數). see 見 **divisor**. **2** money paid out of profits by a business firm to people who have lent money to the firm 股息, 紅利. **dividers** *npl* instrument for measuring distances (on paper) or for dividing angles 兩腳規. **division** [di'viʒən] **1** *nu* process of separating into parts 分, 分開; 分割. **2** *nu* (mathematics) operation of dividing one number into another (數學)除 (法). **3** *nc* separate part 部份. **4** *nc* quarrel or disagreement 爭吵; 意見不合. **5** *nc* part of an army, consisting of about 15,000 men 師 (軍隊編制, 約15,000人). **divisor** [di'vaizə*] *nc* number which is divided into another number (e.g if we divide 10 into 190, 10 is the divisor) 除數(例如我們用10除190, 10是除數). see 見 **dividend.**

divine [di'vain] *adj* of or like God 神的; 像神的. **divinity** [di'viniti] **1** *nu* study of theology 神學. **2** *nc* god or god-

dess 神; 女神.

division [di'viʒən] *nc / u* **divisor** [di'vaizə*] *nc* see 見 **divide.**

divorce [di'vɔ:s] *nc / u* ending of a marriage by law 離婚. Also 亦作 *vt* end a marriage 與⋯離婚: *She divorced her husband.* 她與丈夫離婚.

divulge [dai'vʌldʒ] *vt* make known something secret 洩露(秘密).

dizzy ['dizi] *adj* having an uncomfortable feeling in the head, as though things were moving 頭暈目眩的, 頭暈眼花的: *I felt dizzy after travelling all day in the car.* 乘車旅行一整天, 我感到頭暈.

do [du:] **1** *aux* used to form negative sentences, questions, inverted sentences and emphatic forms of verbs, and to replace a verb that is not repeated 輔助動詞. 用於構成否定句, 問句, 倒裝句和動詞強調式, 並用來取代避免重複的動詞: *I like this book. Do you like it?* 我喜歡這本書, 你喜歡嗎? *I do not like it / I don't like it.* 我不喜歡. *Do you play football? Yes, I do* i.e. play football. 你踢足球嗎? 是的, 我踢足球. *Does he play the piano? No, he doesn't. Neither does John.* 他彈鋼琴嗎? 不, 他不彈. 約翰也不彈. *We arrived early, and so did they.* 我們到得早, 他們也到得早. *I do like music.* (emphatic) 我確實喜歡音樂. (強調式). *Do come to visit us.* (emphatic) 一定得來看我們. (強調式). **2** *vt* perform any action 做, 幹: *What is he doing?* 他在做甚麼? *You have done your work badly.* 你幹的活兒糟透了. **3** *vi* be suitable or satisfactory 合適, 行: *This will not do* i.e. this is not good enough. 這不行. 即: 這不夠好. **4** *vt* visit a place as a tourist. *(informal)* 遊覽, 參觀. (非正式) **5** *vi* have as one's work 從事; *What does your* *father do?* 你父親從事甚麼職業? **6** *vt* cook or prepare for eating or drinking 烹調, 煮: *He likes his steaks well done* i.e. cooked for a long time 他喜歡煎得老一點的牛排. **7** *vt* travel at a certain speed 以⋯速度行進: *This car does 110 miles an hour.* 這部車每小時行駛110英里. **8** *vt* cheat; get money from by a trick 欺騙; 詐騙(錢): *That shopkeeper did me.* 那家店主騙了我. (義8為非正式). *pres part* 現在分詞 doing ['duiŋ]. *past tense* 過去式 did [did]. *past part* 過去分詞 done [dʌn]. Also 亦作 *nc* meeting, party. *(informal)* 會議, 聚會. (非正式). **do something up** tie or fasten 綁, 繫, 包紮: *He did up his parcel.* 他包紮包裹. *He did up his shoelace.* 他繫鞋帶. **can / could do with something** have a wish or need for something 想要某事物, 需要某事物: *I could do with a drink* i.e. I want a drink. *(informal)* 我想喝一杯. (非正式). **do better** improve 改善, 提高: *Perhaps he will do better in his studies next year.* 也許明年他在學業方面會有所提高. **do someone / something good** make better, be helpful to; be useful to 有益於, 有助於某人／某事: *The medicine will do you good.* 這藥將對你有好處. *Complaining won't do you any good.* 抱怨對你沒有甚麼好處. **how do you do?** greeting (used when being introduced to another person. The other person also says *How do you do?*) 您好! (問候語, 被介紹給他人時用. 對方也以 How do you do? 作答). **do well** succeed 成功.

docile ['dousail] *adj* easily managed; willing to obey 溫順的; 聽話的.

dock¹ [dɔk] *nc* (often *pl*) place where ships can be loaded and unloaded (常用複數) 碼頭. Also 亦作 *vt / i* (with re-ference to ships) come or bring into dock (指船) (使) 駛入碼頭. **docker** *nc* person who loads and unloads ships 碼頭裝卸工人. **'dockyard** place where ships are built or repaired 造船廠; 修船廠.

dock² [dɔk] *nc* place where a prisoner stands in a court of law (法庭中的) 被告席.

doctor ['dɔktə*] *nc* **1** person trained and qualified in curing diseases and injuries 醫生, 大夫. **2** person who has received one of the highest degrees of a university 博士.

doctrine ['dɔktrin] *nc / u* official beliefs of a church or political party 教義, 教條; 主義.

document ['dɔkjumənt] *nc* anything in writing which gives information or proof 文件; 證件. **documentary** [dɔkju'mentəri] *adj* of documents 文件的; 證件的. Also 亦作 *nc* film which does not tell a story but illustrates some aspect of real life 紀錄影片.

dodge [dɔdʒ] *vt / i* **1** move quickly so as to avoid something 閃開, 躲開, 躲避. *He dodged the blow.* 他躲過了這一拳. **2** avoid a duty by a trick 搪塞, 逃避. Also 亦作 *nc* clever and dishon-est trick 詭計. **dodger** *nc* person who is clever and dishonest. *(informal)* 狡猾的逃避者. (非正式).

doe [dou] *nc* female of certain animals (e.g. rabbits, antelopes, deer) 某些雌性動物(如兔兒、雌羚羊、雌鹿).

dog [dɔg] *nc* type of domestic animal 狗. **'dog collar 1** collar for a dog 狗頸圈. **2** white collar, tied at the back of the neck, worn by clergymen 教士的白色硬領. **'dog-eared** *adj* (with re-ference to the pages of a book) with the corners bent over, like the ears of a dog (指書頁)摺角的.

dogged ['dɔgid] *adj* determined to continue even though there are difficulties and dangers 頑強的，堅忍不拔的。

dogma ['dɔgmə] *nc / u* official beliefs of a church 教條，教義。**dogmatic** [dɔg-'mætik] *adj* giving opinions without allowing discussion or without allowing other people to have different opinions 獨斷的。

dole [doul] *vt* (with **out**) give in small amounts (與 out 連用) 少量地發放：*He doled out the food to the children.* 他把少量的食品分發給孩子們。**the dole** *nu* money given every week by the government to people without work (政府每週分發的) 失業救濟金：*He's on the dole* i.e. receiving this money. *(informal)* 他靠救濟金生活。(非正式)。

doleful ['doulful] *adj* very miserable 非常可憐的，悲慘的。

doll [dɔl] *nc* child's toy in the form of a baby or adult person 玩偶，洋娃娃。

dollar ['dɔlə*] *nc* unit of money in America, Canada, Australia etc. 元(美國、加拿大、澳大利亞等國家的貨幣單位)。

dolphin ['dɔlfin] *nc* type of intelligent air-breathing sea creature with a beak-like mouth found in the Mediterranean and Atlantic 海豚。

domain [də'mein] *nc* **1** all the land ruled by a king or other ruler 版圖，疆土，領土。**2** land owned by a person (rather *o.f.*) 領地(頗爲舊式)。**3** area of study or knowledge (學習或知識的) 領域：*the domain of chemistry* 化學領域。

dome [doum] *nc* large rounded roof 大而圓的屋頂。

domestic [də'mestik] *adj* **1** concerning the home 家的，家庭的。**2** concerning one's own country 國內的。**3** (with

reference to animals) not wild; kept in the home or on farms (指動物) 馴服的；家養的。**domesticate** [də'mesti-keit] *vt* (with reference to animals) make able to live in a house or on a farm 馴養(動物)。

dominate ['dɔmineit] *vt / i* **1** have strong control over 支配，控制：*That big boy dominates the other boys in the class* i.e. they all do what he tells them to do. 那個大個子男生支配着班裏的其他男生。即：他們都按他吩咐的去做。**2** be most noticeable in 是…最顯而易見的；高聳：*That building dominates the town* i.e. it is much taller than the other buildings. 那座建築物在該鎮上最爲顯眼。即：它比其他建築物高得多。*Africa has dominated the news recently* i.e. most of the news in the newspapers has been about Africa. 近來非洲成爲新聞焦點。即：報紙上的絕大部份新聞都是有關非洲的。**dominant** ['dɔminənt] *adj* **domination** [dɔmi'neiʃən] *nu* **domineer** [dɔmi'niə*] *vi* (usu. with over) force other people to do what one wants them to do (通常與 over 連用) 霸道，專橫。**domineering** *adj* behaving in this way 霸道的，專橫的。

dominion [də'miniən] **1** *nu* condition of ruling or controlling 統治，管轄。**2** *nc* country ruled by a king or other ruler 版圖，領土。

domino ['dɔminou] *nc* small flat piece of wood or plastic with spots on one side, used in the game of **dominoes** 多米諾骨牌。*pl* 複數 **dominoes**.

don [dɔn] *nc* university lecturer (esp. at Oxford or Cambridge) 大學講師(尤指在牛津或劍橋大學者)。

donate [də'neit] *vt* give to a charity, political party etc. 捐贈。**donation** *nc* money etc donated 捐贈的錢或物。

done [dʌn] past part of **do**. do 的過去分詞.

donkey ['dɔŋki] nc **1** animal like a small horse, with long ears, used for carrying loads 驢. **2** foolish person (*informal*) 蠢人. (非正式) (Also 亦作 **ass**).

donor ['douna*] nc person who donates (esp. one who gives blood for use in hospitals) 捐贈者(尤指獻血者).

don't [dount] short form of **do not**. do not 的縮略形式.

doodle ['du:dl] vi make a drawing or pattern while thinking about something else 亂畫, 塗寫, 塗鴉: *People sometimes doodle while they are listening to a lecture*. 聽講座時人們有時會在筆記本上塗鴉.

doom [du:m] nc (usu. only sing) ruin, destruction or death (通常僅用單數) 毀滅; 死亡.

door [dɔ:*] nc **1** swinging or sliding piece of wood, glass, metal etc which is used to close a building, room, cupboard etc. (房屋、房間、碗櫥等的)門. **2** place where one enters a building or room (房屋、房間的)門口. '**doorman** person whose work is to open and close the doors of a hotel, restaurant, big shop etc. 看門人, 門房. '**doorstep** 1 step leading from a street up to the door of a house 門階. 2 area in front of the door of a house 門前地帶. '**doorway** place where one enters a building or room (房屋、房間的)門口. **in'doors** adv inside a house 在室内. '**next' door** adj / adv in the next house 隔壁的; 在隔壁: *The people who live next door*. 住在隔壁的人們. *next-door neighbours* 隔壁鄰居. **out of doors** in the open air 在户外.

dope [doup] nu drug (esp. one which makes one sleep) (*informal*) 麻醉藥; 安眠藥. (非正式) . Also 亦作 vt give drugs to 讓…吃麻醉藥或安眠藥.

dopey adj sleepy as though drugged (*informal*) 迷迷糊糊的, 似被麻醉的. (非正式).

dormant ['dɔ:mənt] adj (with reference to plants, volcanoes, animals, ideas, organizations etc not usu. of people) sleeping; not active but able to be active later on (指植物、火山、動物、想法、組織等, 通常不指人) 休眠的, 蟄伏的, 暫時靜止的, 暫停的.

dormitory ['dɔ:mitri] nc room where several people sleep (esp. in a school or college) (尤指學校裏的)宿舍.

dormouse ['dɔ:maus] nc type of small animal, which looks like a small squirrel, and which sleeps through the winter 睡鼠. pl 複數 **dormice** ['dɔ:mais].

dorsa ['dɔ:sə] pl of **dorsum**. dorsum 的複數

dorsal ['dɔ:səl] adj of, on or near the back, esp. of an animal (尤指動物的)背部的, 背面的; 近背部的: *the dorsal fin (e.g. of a shark)* (例如鯊魚的)脊鰭.

dorsum ['dɔ:səm] nc **1** back (of an animal) (動物的)背, 背部. **2** part corresponding to or like the back 背狀部份: *the dorsum of the hand* 手背.

dose [dous] nc amount of medicine to be taken at one time (藥的)一劑, 一服. Also 亦作 vt give medicine to 給…服一劑藥.

dossier ['dɔsiə*] nc collection of papers giving information about a person (esp. a criminal) or thing (尤指用作刑事犯的)卷宗, 檔案: *The police have a dossier on him*. 他被警方記錄在案.

dot [dɔt] nc small round mark 小圓點. Also 亦作 vt mark with a dot 打點於.

past 過去式和過去分詞 **dotted. on the dot** at the exact time 準時: *He arrived at one o'clock on the dot.* 他於一點鐘準時到達.

dote [dout] *vi* (with **on**) like very much in a foolish way (與 on 連用)嬌寵, 溺愛: *She dotes on her children.* 她溺愛自己的孩子.

double¹ ['dʌbl] *adj* having two of something; twice as much as; of or for two 雙的; 兩倍的; 雙人的: *a double bed* i.e. a bed for two people 雙人床. *He ate a double portion of food* i.e. the food for two people. 他吃了雙份飯. 即: 供兩人吃的飯. *This has a double purpose* i.e. it can be used for two purposes. 這有雙重目的. 即: 它可用於兩個目的. Also 亦作 *adv* twice as much 兩倍地. **doubly** *adv* twice over 加倍地. **'double 'bass** very large stringed musical instrument 低音大提琴. **'double-'breasted** *adj* (with reference to a coat, suit etc) made so that there is a double thickness of cloth on the chest when the coat is buttoned (指上衣、套裝等)前面襟相疊的, 雙排扣的. **'double 'chin** loose skin under the chin 雙下巴. **double-'cross somebody** cheat or betray somebody who trusts one 欺騙或出賣某人: *The leader of the gang double-crossed the other thieves. (informal)* 賊首出賣了其他的盜賊. (非正式). **'double-'decker** bus having two decks, one upstairs and one downstairs 雙層公共汽車, 雙層巴士.

double² ['dʌbl] *nc* person who looks exactly like another person 長得一模一樣的人. **doubles** *npl* tennis or badminton match for four players, two on each side (網球或羽毛球的)雙打. **at the double** running (usu. in the army etc). (通常用於軍隊等)跑步走.

double³ ['dʌbl] **1** *vt / i* become or make twice as much etc. (使)加倍: *The price has doubled since last year.* 自從去年以來, 價格增加了一倍. *I shall double your wages.* 我將給你加薪一倍. **2** *vt* fold or bend in two 折, 疊: *He doubled his blankets because it was a cold night.* 夜裏很冷, 他把毯子折疊起來蓋. **3** *vi* serve two purposes; take two parts at the same time 兼作; (演員)兼演兩角色.

doubt [daut] *vt / i* be uncertain about 懷疑: *I doubt whether we shall succeed* i.e. I think we may not succeed. 我懷疑我們是否會成功. 即: 我認爲我們可能不會成功. *I doubted his story* i.e. I thought that he might not be telling the truth. 我懷疑他的說法. 即: 我認爲他不太可能說實話. Also 亦作 *nc / u* feeling of uncertainty 懷疑. **doubtful** *adj* **1** feeling doubt 懷疑的. **2** causing doubt 令人懷疑的. **doubtless** *adv* without doubt; very probably 無疑地; 很可能地. **no doubt** probably 很可能: *No doubt he will help us if we ask him.* 如果我們要求他的話, 那麼他很可能會幫助我們. **without (a) doubt** certainly 無疑, 肯定: *Without (a) doubt you have been working very hard.* 毫無疑問, 你一直都很努力工作.

dough [dou] *nu* mixture of flour and water etc which becomes bread or pastry when baked 生麵團. **'doughnut** cake made from dough fried in fat 油炸餅.

dove [dʌv] *nc* type of pigeon, considered as a symbol of peace and tenderness 鴿子.

dowager ['dauədʒə] *nc* **1** widow with a title or property derived from her dead husband 擁有亡夫稱號或遺產的寡婦, 寡媚: *a queen dowager* 皇太后. **2** elderly woman of wealth and dignity 年長有錢的貴婦人.

dowdy ['daudi] *adj* (usu. with reference to clothes) old, untidy and unfashionable (通常指衣服)舊的; 不整潔的; 過時的.

down¹ [daun] *adv / prep* not up; in / to a lower position, size, quantity etc. 向下, 朝下: *He fell down* i.e. he fell to the floor. 他跌倒了. 即: 他倒在地板上. *He put his cup down* i.e. on the table etc. 他放下茶杯. 即: 放到桌上等. *He ran down the hill.* 他跑下了山. *His temperature has gone down* i.e. he now has a lower temperature. 他的體溫已經下降. 即: 他現在體溫比較低了. *Exports have gone down* i.e. fewer goods have been exported. 出口額已經下降. 即: 出口的貨物已經減少. *She isn't down yet* i.e. she is still upstairs. 她還沒下來. 即: 她還在樓上. *Write this down* i.e. write it. 把這寫下來. 亦作 *vt* knock down; hit so as to make someone fall 擊倒. **'downward** *adj*: *the downward climb* 向下爬, 向下攀行. **downwards** *adv* **'downcast** *adj* unhappy because of some disappointment 垂頭喪氣的. **'downfall 1** sudden and often violent ending of a government or ruler (政府或統治者的)垮台, 倒台. **2** thing which causes one to fail (in one's hopes) 使人希望破滅的事物. *Laziness was his downfall.* 懶惰是他沒落的原因. **'down'hearted** *adj* unhappy because of some disappointment 垂頭喪氣的. **'down'hill** *adj / adv* to / towards the bottom of a hill 下山的; 下山; *a downhill climb* 向山脚攀行; *run downhill* 跑下了山. *go downhill* i.e. become worse (e.g. in health, business) 走下坡路, 即: 變糟 (例如健康, 業務方面). **'downpour** heavy fall of rain 大雨, 豪雨. **'down-right** *adj / adv* **1** complete(ly) 徹底的

(地), 完全的(地): *a downright liar* 一個徹頭徹尾的騙子; *Downright foolish* 愚蠢至極. **2** honest; saying what one thinks 誠實的; 坦白的, 直爽的: *He spoke in a downright way.* 他說話很直爽. **'down'stairs¹** *adv* to a lower place by means of stairs 下樓, 到樓下: *He went downstairs.* 他下了樓. **'downstairs²** *adj* on a lower floor in the house 在(或往)樓下的: *the downstairs rooms* 樓下的房間. **'down'stream** *adv* in the direction in which a river is flowing 向下游地, 隨流而下: *He sailed downstream.* 他朝下游航行. **'down'town** *adj / adv* (mainly US) in / to the main part of the town (主要用於美)商業區的; 在(或往)商業區, 在(或往)市中心: *the downtown shops* 市中心商店. *He went off downtown.* 他離開了市中心. **down with somebody / something** exclamation showing that one is strongly opposed to somebody / something 打倒某人 / 某事物: *The crowd was shouting 'Down with the King!'* 羣眾在高呼: "打倒國王!"

down² [daun] *nu* soft feathers on a young bird; any soft hair or wool (幼鳥的)柔羽毛, 絨毛, 軟毛; (人的)汗毛; (男孩的)細軟短鬚; (植物的)茸毛; 軟羊毛.

dowry ['dauri] *nc* money and property which a woman brings to her husband at marriage 嫁妝.

doze [douz] *vi* have a light sleep 打盹, 打瞌睡: *He dozed in his chair after dinner.* 晚飯後他坐在椅子上打盹. Also 亦作 *nc* short sleep 小睡, 瞌睡.

dozen ['dʌzən] *nc* group of twelve 一打.

drab [dræb] *adj* dull; dark; uninteresting; without change 單調的; 陰鬱的; 乏味的; 無變化的.

draft [drɑːft] *nc* **1** first form of a piece of

of writing, which can be altered so as to make the final version 初稿, 草稿, 草案: *He made a draft of his essay.* 他寫了一份論文初稿. **2** (mainly *US*) group of men joining the army together (主要用於美)應徵入伍的一羣人. **3** piece of paper by which a person asks a bank to pay a certain sum of money 匯票. **4** see 見 **draught**. Also 亦作 *vt* make a plan of a piece of writing 起草, 草擬. **'draftsman** see 見 **draught.**

drag [dræg] **1** *vt / i* move or pull along slowly or roughly 拖, 拉, 曳: *He dragged the heavy table across the room* 他把笨重的桌子從房間的一邊拖到另一邊. **2** *vi* seem to take a long time and to be uninteresting 拖沓, 拖拖拉拉: *The last part of the play dragged a little* 該劇的最後一部份有點兒拖沓. **3** *vt* search the bottom of a lake or river by pulling nets or hooks across it 打撈, 拖撈. *past* 過去式和過去分詞 **dragged.** Also 亦作 *nc* a bore 令人討厭的人或事物: *This film is a drag.* 這部電影令人討厭.

dragon ['drægən] *nc* large imaginary creature with wings and a long tail (usu. breathing fire) 龍. **'dragonfly** large type of insect, with a long thin body and two pairs of very thin wings 蜻蜓.

drain [drein] *nc* **1** pipe or channel through which dirty water and other liquid can flow away 排水管道, 下水道. **2** anything which causes loss or waste of strength, property etc. 消耗, 耗費: *The cost of his children's education was a drain on his money.* 子女們的教育費用幾乎耗盡了他的錢. Also 亦作 *vt / i* **1** (with reference to liquids) flow, cause to flow away (指液體) (使) 排出, (使) 流掉: *The river*

drains into the sea. 該河流入海洋. *He drained his land.* 他給土地排水. *The water drained away.* 水流掉了. **2** become or make weak or poor by continual loss (使) 逐漸虛弱或缺乏: *The illness drained his strength.* 這場病使他體力逐漸虛弱. *His strength drained away.* 他的體力日漸虛弱. **drainage** *nu* system of drains (esp. for carrying water away from a house) (尤指房屋的)排水系統. **'drainpipe** pipe draining water from the roof of a building to the drains under the ground (連接屋頂和下水道的)排水管.

drake [dreik] *nc* male duck 公鴨.

dram [dræm] *nc* **1** ⅛ of an ounce of medicine or drugs 特拉姆(藥衡單位, 等於⅛盎司). **2** 1/16 of an ounce of other substances 特拉姆(常衡單位, 等於1/16盎司).

drama ['drɑːmə] **1** *nc* play (usu. serious) for the theatre, radio or television (通常爲嚴肅性的)戲劇. **2** *nu* art or study of such plays 戲劇藝術; 戲劇研究. **3** *nc* exciting event or series of events 令人激動的事件; 一系列戲劇性的事件. **dramatic** [drə'mætik] *adj* **1** of plays 戲劇的 (*opp* undramatic in sense 2) 激動人心的 (義2 反義詞為 undramatic). **dramatist** ['dræmətist] *nc* writer of plays 劇作家.

drank [dræŋk] past tense of **drink**. drink 的過去式.

drape [dreip] *vt* hang cloth loosely over something 把…披在某物上, 披: *He draped his coat over the back of his chair.* 他把上衣披在椅背上. Also 亦作 *nc* (usu. *pl*) piece of cloth draped over something (usu. at a window or on the stage of a theatre) (mainly *US* in this sense) (通常用複數)窗簾布; 幕布. (本義主要用於美). **draper** *nc*

(Brit) person who sells cloth (英) 布商.

drastic ['dræstik] *adj* having a strong effect 具有强烈效果的: *He took drastic action to cure the disease* 他采取猛烈的措施治该病. **drastically** *adv*.

draught [drɑːft] *nc* movement of air inside a room or in a fire 穿堂風; 爐裏的風. **draughty** *adj* having air moving inside a room 通風的: *a draughty room* 通風的房間. **draughts** *n sing* 單數 *(Brit)* game played with a board divided into 64 squares and 24 round pieces of wood or bone etc. (英) 跳棋. *(US* 美 **checkers).** **draughtsman** person who does technical drawings 繪圖員. **'draught 'beer** beer which is drawn from a barrel instead of being poured from a bottle 散裝啤酒.

draw[1] [drɔː] **1** *vt / i* make a picture by using a pencil, pen, crayon etc. 繪(圖), 畫(圖): *He is drawing.* 他正在繪畫. *He drew a house.* 他畫了一座房子. **2** *vt* pull 拉, 拖: *The engine drew the train from the station.* 機車拖着列車出了站. *He drew the curtains* i.e. opened or closed them. 他拉窗簾. 即: 拉攏或拉上窗簾. **3** *vt* take something from the place where it is kept 提取: *He drew some money from the bank.* 他從銀行提取了一些錢. **4** *vt* get or receive 得到; 收到: *What conclusions can we draw from this?* i.e. what opinions can we come to? 我們由此可以得到甚麼結論呢? **5** *vt* attract 吸引: *The play drew large audiences* i.e. many people came to see the play. 該戲劇吸引了大批的觀眾. **6** *vt / i* end a game with equal scores (使) 成為平局, (使) 不分勝負: *The two teams drew.* 兩個隊不分勝負. *They drew the game.* 他們比賽打成平局. **7** *vt / i* take playing cards from a pack to decide something 抽(牌)(以決定某事). **8** *vt / i* take out a gun or sword which one is carrying 抽(槍); 拔(劍): *He drew a gun.* 他抽出一把槍來. *He let the other man draw first.* 他讓對手先抽槍. *past tense* 過去式 **drew** [druː]. *past part* 過去分詞 **drawn.** **drawer** [drɔː*] *nc* container like a box which slides in and out of a table, desk or other piece of furniture 抽屜. **drawing 1** *nc* picture made with pencil, pen, crayon etc. 圖畫. **2** *nu* the art of making such pictures 繪畫藝術: *She teaches drawing.* 她教繪畫. **'drawbridge** type of bridge formerly used in castles etc made so that it can be raised up to prevent people entering the castle 吊橋. **'drawing pin** see 見 **pin**[1]. **'drawing room** room in a house where people can sit and talk 客廳. **'drawback** *nc* disadvantage 不利, 短處. *This is a good car; its only drawback is that it uses a lot of petrol.* 這是一輛好車; 其唯一不足是是耗油量大. **draw up** stop 停止: *The car drew up at the traffic lights.* 紅燈亮時汽車停住. **draw somthing up** make a formal document 起草, 擬訂(正式文件): *draw up a will / agreement / treaty etc.* 起草遺囑/協議/條約等.

draw[2] [drɔː] *nc* result of a game in which both sides have the same score 平局.

drawl [drɔːl] *vt / i* speak in a very slow and lazy way 拖腔拖調地說. Also 亦作 *nc* this way of speaking 用拖腔拖調說話.

dread [dred] *vt* feel great fear of 恐懼, 畏懼, 懼怕: *I dread the examination.* 我懼怕考試. Also 亦作 *nu* great fear 畏懼, 恐懼. **dreadful** *adj* **1** causing dread 恐怖的, 可怕的. **2** unpleasant; bad 令人不快的; 糟糕的: *The weather* *is dreadful.* 這種天氣真討厭. **dreadfully** *adv* 1 unpleasantly 討厭地. 2 very 很: *I'm dreadfully busy.* (*informal* in sense 2) 我很忙. (義2爲非正式).

dream [dri:m] *vt / i* 1 see and hear things while one is asleep 做夢, 夢見: *I dreamed that I was a king.* 我做夢我成了一個國王. 2 imagine; think possible 夢想, 想像; 認爲可能: *I never dreamt that I would be the winner of the competition.* 我做夢也沒想到自己會在這次比賽中獲勝. *past* 過去式和過去分詞 **dreamed** or **dreamt** [dremt]. Also 亦作 *nc* 1 something seen or heard while one is sleeping 夢. 2 something hoped for or imagined 理想; 夢想. **dreamy** *adj* of or like a dream 夢的; 夢幻般的: *a dream person* i.e. one who does not seem fully awake 精神恍惚的人. **dreamer** *nc* person who dreams; dreamy person 做夢者; 夢想者; 精神恍惚的人.

dreary ['driəri] *adj* dull; dark; uninteresting 單調的; 陰沉的; 乏味的: *a dreary room* 單調的房間; *dreary weather* 陰沉的天氣; *a dreary person* 乏味的人.

dredge [dredʒ] *vt / i* bring substance from the bottom of a river or lake or the sea 疏浚, 疏通, 撈取: *dredge the river* 疏通河流; *dredge mud from the river* 挖掉河裏的淤泥. Also 亦作 *nc* apparatus used for this 疏浚機, 挖泥機. **dredger** *nc* boat carrying a dredge 挖泥船.

dregs [dregz] *npl* small pieces of solid matter which sink to the bottom of liquid 沉澱物, 沉渣.

drench [drentʃ] *vt* make very wet 使浸濕, 使濕透: *We were drenched by the rain.* 我們被雨水淋透了.

dress¹ [dres] *nc* 1 garment worn by a woman or girl, covering the top and bottom parts of the body 女服; 連衣裙. 2 *nu* clothes of all kinds 服裝, 衣裳. **dresser** 1 *nc* person who helps an actor or actress to dress for a play 戲劇服裝師. 2 piece of furniture with shelves for holding plates, cups etc. 碗櫃. **dressing** *nc / u* 1 bandage etc put on a wound 包紮用品(如綳帶等). 2 oil, vinegar etc put on a salad (加於凉拌菜上的) 調味品. **'dress 'circle** part of a theatre, higher than the stage, where some of the audience sit 劇院的前排樓座. **'dressmaker** person who makes clothes for women 女裝裁縫. **'dress re'hearsal** last rehearsal of a play in which the actors wear the clothes which they will wear for the actual performance 彩排. **'dressing gown** (long) coat worn over a person's night clothes 晨衣. **'dressing table** table with mirrors and drawers, kept in a bedroom 梳妝台. **'evening dress** 1 *nc* long dress worn by a woman for formal occasions in the evening 女式晚禮服. 2 *nu* clothes worn by men and women for formal occasions in the evening 晚禮服.

dress² [dres] *vt / i* put on clothes 給…穿衣服; 穿衣服: *He dressed in his best suit.* 他穿上最好的衣服. *She dressed the children.* 她給孩子們穿衣服. **dress up** put on special clothes (esp. for a game, play, party etc.) 穿好, 裝扮, 着盛裝(尤指爲了參加比賽, 演出, 舞會等).

drew [dru:] past tense of **draw.** draw¹ 的過去式.

dribble ['dribl] 1 *vi* let saliva or liquid fall from the mouth 流口水. 2 *vt / i* (football) run forward while kicking the ball (足球)運(球), 盤(球), 帶(球). 3 *vi* (with reference to liquid) fall in small drops (指液體)滴, 淌.

dried [draid] past of **dry**. dry 的過去式
和過去分詞.

drier ['draiə*] nc see 見 **dryer**.

drift¹ ['drift] vt / i 1 move or be carried
along by water or air (使)漂流; (使)
飄蕩: The engine has broken down
and the boat is drifting. 機器抛錨了,
船在水面漂流. 2 (with reference to
snow) move or be moved into large
heaps (指雪)(使)堆積, 吹積. The
snow is drifting. 雪在堆積.

drift² [drift] 1 nu slow movement onwards by water or air 漂流; 飄蕩, 飄
浮. 2 nc large heap of snow or sand
brought together by the wind (沙, 雪
的)吹積堆, 堆積堆. '**driftwood** pieces
of wood carried onto land by the drift
of the sea 浮木.

drill¹ [dril] nc tool with a sharp end
which turns round, used for making
holes 鑽子, 鑽孔機, 鑽床. Also 亦作 vt
/ i make a hole with a drill 鑽(孔).

drill² [dril] nc / u 1 training of soldiers
in marching, using guns etc. 軍隊操
練. 2 any series of movements or any
exercise used in training soldiers or
teaching students 操練(軍隊); 訓練,
練習. Also 亦作 vt / i train or teach
people by drill 訓練, 操練.

drink [driŋk] vt / i 1 take liquid into the
body through the mouth 喝, 飲. 2 be
in the habit of taking alcoholic drinks
喝(酒); 酗酒. Also 亦作 vt / u 1 liquid
for drinking 飲料. 2 beer, wine, whisky etc. 啤酒, 葡萄酒, 威士忌等酒類.
past tense 過去式 **drank** [dræŋk]. past
part 過去分詞 **drunk** [drʌŋk]. **drink-
able** adj suitable for drinking 可飲用
的. (opp 反義詞 **undrinkable**).
drinker nc person who often drinks
alcoholic drinks 酗酒的人, 酒徒.

drip [drip] vt / i (with reference to li-

quids) fall, allow to fall, in small
drops (指液體)(使)滴, (使)淌: The
rain dripped from the trees. 雨珠從樹
上滴下來. past 過去式和過去分詞
dripped. Also 亦作 nc drop or small
particle of liquid 液滴, 液珠. **dripping** nu fat obtained from meat which
has been roasted (烤肉時産生的)油
汁, 油珠. '**drip-'dry** adj (with reference to cloth) able to become dry
and smooth if hung up immediately
after being washed (指布)快速晾乾免
熨的: a drip-dry shirt 快速晾乾免熨的
襯衣.

drive¹ [draiv] 1 vt / i cause a car or
other vehicle to move along 駕駛(車
輛): He drove the car. 他駕駛汽車.
Can you drive? i.e. do you know how
to drive a car? 你會開車嗎? I drove
my aunt to town i.e. I took her by car.
我開車送我姑媽進城. 2 vt cause
animals to go in a certain direction 驅
趕(動物): drive sheep 趕羊. 3 vt
cause a sharp object to enter something 刺, 釘: He drove a nail into the
door. 他把一枚釘子釘進門裏. He
drove a knife into his enemy. 他用刀
子戳敵人. 4 vt / i hit a ball hard in
certain games 用力擊(球). 5 vt / i go,
cause to go, with force (使)猛烈移動:
The wind drove against the windows.
風吹打着窗戶. The wind drove the
ship off its course. 這場風迫使該船偏
離航道. past tense 過去式 **drove**
[drouv]. past part 過去分詞 **driven**
['drivən].

drive² [draiv] 1 nc journey in a car etc.
駕駛汽車等旅行. 2 nc small road
leading to a house (通往私宅的)小車
道. 3 nc hitting of a ball in various
games 擊球. 4 nu energy; determination; ambition 精力, 勁勁; 決心; 抱負:
That man has plenty of drive i.e. he

has many plans and ideas, and is able to carry them out 那個男人充滿幹勁. 即: 他有許多計劃和想法並且有能力實行. **5** *nc* special attempt to do something 競賽, 發奮: *a drive to get new members for the club* 爭取俱樂部新會員的運動. **driver** *nc* person who causes a car etc to move (汽車等)駕駛人; 司機. **'driving licence** permission to drive a motor vehicle on public roads 駕駛執照. **'driving test** examination to decide whether someone should be allowed to drive a motor vehicle 駕駛執照考試. **drive-in cinema / store / church etc** cinema etc which people may attend while seated in their cars (人們坐在汽車裏即可觀看的)汽車電影院／(即可購物的)汽車商店／(可做禮拜的)汽車教堂.

drizzle ['drizl] *nu* rain which falls in very small drops 毛毛雨. Also 亦作 *vi* rain in this way 下毛毛雨.

droll [droul] *adj* funny; amusing (rather *o.f.*) 滑稽的; 有趣的 (相當舊式).

dromedary ['drɔmidəri] *nc* type of camel having one hump 單峰駱駝.

drone[1] [droun] *nc* male bee 雄蜂.

drone[2] [droun] *nc / u* low unchanging sound, like that made by a bee 嗡嗡的響聲.

droop [druːp] *vt / i* (often of plants) bend down through weakness or tiredness (常指植物)(使)低垂, (使)垂下.

drop[1] [drɔp] *nc* **1** small rounded ball of liquid 液滴, 液珠. **2** small amount of liquid 少量的液體. **3** distance or movement straight down 下降, 下跌; 下降或下跌的距離: *the drop from the top of the cliff* 從崖頂跌落; *a drop in the temperature* 溫度下降.

drop[2] [drɔp] **1** *vt / i* fall, allow to fall (使)落下: *The bomb dropped on the village.* 炸彈落到村莊裏. *He dropped his book on the floor.* 他把書掉在地上. **2** *vi* (with reference to temperature or wind) become lower or less strong (指溫度或風)降低, 減弱. **3** *vt* stop something 停止, 放棄: *I am trying to drop that bad habit.* 我打算改掉那個壞習慣. *I want to drop History* i.e. to stop studying History. 我想放棄歷史課. 即: 不學歷史課了. *He dropped his friends* i.e. stopped being friendly to them. (*informal*) 他與朋友們絕交. 即: 不再與他們交朋友. (非正式). *past* 過去式和過去分詞 **dropped. drop off** fall asleep (*informal*) 睡着了 (非正式). **drop out (of something)** stop taking part in something 不再參與(某事物). *A number of students drop out of university every year* i.e. leave the university. 每年都有一些學生從大學裏退學. **'dropout** *nc* person who leaves a college, university etc (too early) or leaves a conventional way of life 大學退學者; 不按傳統生活方式生活者. *There have been fewer dropouts this year.* (*informal*) 今年退學的學生比較少. (非正式).

drought [draut] *nc* period of dry weather, causing a shortage of water 乾旱.

drove[1] [drouv] past tense of **drive**[1]. drive[1] 的過去式.

drove[2] [drouv] *nc* number of sheep, cows etc moving together (走動的)畜羣.

drown [draun] **1** *vt / i* die, cause to die, under water through lack of air (使)溺斃, (使)淹死: *She drowned in the river.* 她淹死在這條河裏. *He drowned his wife.* 他淹死自己的妻子. **2** *vt* prevent a sound from being heard 淹沒(聲音): *The noise of the train* *drowned his voice.* 火車的嘈雜聲淹沒了他的聲音.

drowse [drauz] *vi* sleep lightly; be half asleep 打盹, 打瞌睡. **drowsy** *adj*.

drudgery ['drʌdʒəri] *nu* unpleasant and uninteresting work 苦差事, 苦工.

drug [drʌg] *nc* 1 any substance used in medicine 藥, 藥材. 2 substance which has a harmful effect on the mind or body 毒品. Also 亦作 *vt* add or give a drug to (usu. to make somebody fall asleep) 下(麻醉)藥於. *He drugged my drink.* 他在我的酒裏下了麻醉藥. *past* 過去式和過去分詞 **drugged. druggist** *nc* person who sells drugs (in sense 1) 藥商. **'drug addict** *nc* person who cannot stop using certain harmful drugs 某些毒品的癮君子. **drug addiction** *nu* **'drugstore** (mainly *US*) shop where drugs, and various kinds of food and drink are sold (主要用於美)(出售藥品、食物和飲料的)藥房.

drum [drʌm] *nc* 1 type of percussion instrument played using sticks 鼓. 2 large, round, hollow container for liquids (盛液體的大的)鼓狀容器. **drummer** *nc* person who plays a drum 鼓手.

drunk [drʌŋk] past part of **drink.** drink 的過去分詞. Also 亦作 *adj* unable to think or behave properly, through having had too much alcoholic drink 醉的, 喝醉的. Also 亦作 *nc* person who is drunk 醉酒者, 醉鬼.

dry [drai] *adj* 1 without liquid or moisture 乾的; 乾燥的. *The climate is dry.* 氣候乾燥. *The washing is dry.* 所洗的衣物乾了. *I feel dry* i.e. I want a drink. 我覺得口乾. 即: 我想喝水. 2 dull and uninteresting 枯燥無味的. *a dry book* 一本枯燥無味的書. 3 (with reference to wine) not containing

much sugar (指葡萄酒)不甜的. Also 亦作 *vt / i* become or make free from liquid or moisture (使)變乾; (使)乾燥; *The washing is drying.* 洗過的衣服快要乾了. *He dried the clothes.* 他烘乾了衣服. *past* 過去式和過去分詞 **dried. 'dry 'cleaning** *nu* method of cleaning clothes with chemicals without using water (衣服)乾洗. **'dry 'cleaner** *nc* person who cleans in this way 乾洗衣服者. **'dry-'clean** *vt* clean clothes in this way 乾洗(衣服). **'dry'rot** type of disease which destroys wood in buildings 木料乾腐病. **dry up** become completely dry; (of a river etc) stop flowing (河流等)乾涸.

dryer, drier ['draiə*] *nc* something used to dry something else 乾燥機: *a hair drier* 頭髮吹風機; *a clothes drier* 衣服乾燥機.

dual ['djuəl] *adj* of two; having two parts 雙的; 雙重的. **dual carriageway** road separated into two parts, with room for two or more lines of traffic on each side 雙行道.

dub [dʌb] *vt* put a new sound track on a film originally made in another language 為(譯製片)配音: *Many foreign films are dubbed when they are shown in England.* 許多外國影片在英國上演時都經過譯製配音. *past* 過去式和過去分詞 **dubbed.**

dubious ['djuːbiəs] *adj* 1 feeling doubt; uncertain 感到懷疑的, 沒有把握的: *I'm dubious about my chances of success* i.e. I don't think I shall succeed. 我對自己成功的機遇沒有把握. 即: 我不認爲自己會成功. 2 causing one to feel doubt (often doubt as to whether something is honest or sensible) 可疑的, 令人懷疑的(常指懷疑某事是否誠實或理智): *a dubious suggestion* i.e. a suggestion which might be dishonest

or foolish 令人疑慮的建議; 即: 可能不
誠實或愚蠢的建議.

duchess ['dʌtʃis] *nc* wife of a duke 公爵
夫人.

duck¹ [dʌk] *nc* one of various water
birds with webbed feet and flattened
beaks 鴨.

duck² [dʌk] **1** *vt / i* bend down quickly
to avoid something 急忙低頭閃避, 急
忙彎腰躲開: *He ducked.* 他急忙低頭
閃避. *He ducked his head.* 他急忙低
下頭. **2** *vt* push someone's head
under water 把(某人的頭)按入水中:
He ducked his friend. 他把朋友的頭按
入水中.

duckweed ['dʌkwiːd] *nu* any of a family
of very small flowering plants that
float on ponds and sluggish streams
and reproduce by a kind of budding;
so called because eaten by duck 浮
萍.

duct [dʌkt] *nc* tube for carrying liquid
輸送液體的管道.

dud [dʌd] *adj* of no use; not working 作
廢的, 沒用的; 不起作用的: *This is a
dud watch.* 這是一隻壞錶. Also 亦作
nc somebody / something that is dud.
(both *informal*) 廢物; 不中用的人; 不
值錢的東西. (均為非正式).

due [djuː] *adj* **1** owed; to be paid 欠的;
應付的: *Payment is now due.* 現在該
付款了. **2** expected 預期的: *He is due
to arrive today* 他定於今天到達. **3**
necessary or suitable 必要的; 適合的:
*Library books must be treated with
due care and attention.* (*opp* **undue**
in sense **3**) 必須小心認真地對待圖書
館裏的圖書. (義3的反義詞為 undue).
Also 亦作 *nc* **1** something owed;
something to be paid 所欠之物; 應付
之物. **2** (only *pl*) money paid by a
member to a club etc. (僅用複數) (俱
樂部等的) 會費. **duly** *adv* **due to**

caused by 因為, 由於: *The delay is
due to the bad weather.* 這次晚點是由
於天氣不好. *Due to bad weather, the
train was late.* 由於天氣不好, 火車晚
點了. *Note* 說明: some people consider the second of these examples
incorrect. They would use *due to* only
as an adjectival phrase; that is to say,
they would use the structure *something is due to something,* but not the
structure *due to something, another
thing happened.* People who follow
this rule would use *owing to* in the
second example above i.e. *Owing to
bad weather, the train was late.* 某些
人認為上述第二例不正確. 他們把 due
to 作為形容詞短語使用. 亦即他們使用
something is due to something 這種結
構, 而不用 due to something, another
thing happened 這種結構. 遵循這一規
則的人們在上述第二例中會使用 owing
to, 即 Owing to bad weather, the train
was late. 由於天氣不好, 火車晚點了.

duel ['djuəl] *nc* private fight following
certain rules between two people
(usu. with swords or pistols) (通常用
劍或手槍的) 決鬥.

duet [djuːˈet] *nc* song or piece of music
for two people 二重唱; 二重奏.

dug [dʌg] past of **dig**¹. dig¹ 的過去式和
過去分詞.

duke [djuːk] *nc* nobleman of high rank
公爵. (*fem* 陰 **duchess** ['dʌtʃis]).

dull [dʌl] *adj* **1** not bright 陰沉的, 陰暗
的: *a dull day* i.e. a day without sunshine 陰沉的一天, 即無陽光的一天. **2**
(with reference to sound) low in
sound and as if from far away (指聲
音) 低沉的: *a dull thud* 低沉的撞擊聲.
3 (with reference to pain) not felt
very sharply and lasting a long time
(指疼痛) 不劇烈的, 隱隱的. **4** boring;
uninteresting 無聊的; 乏味的: *a dull*

book 一本枯燥無味的書. **5** stupid; unintelligent 愚傻的; 笨的, 遲鈍的.

duly ['dju:li] *adv* 見 **due.**

dumb [dʌm] *adj* **1** unable to speak 不會説話的, 啞的. **2** unintelligent. *(informal* in sense 2) 傻的, 笨的. (義2為非正式)

dummy ['dʌmi] *nc* **1** something made to look like a person / thing 人體模型; 仿造物: *Shops which sell clothes often have dummies in the window* i.e. models which look like people, so as to show what the clothes look like when worn. 服裝店常常在櫥窗裏擺設人體模型作為衣服模特. **2** object made of rubber which is put in a baby's mouth for him to suck 橡膠奶頭. Also 亦作 *adj*.

dump¹ [dʌmp] *nc* **1** place where rubbish is left 垃圾場. **2** place where military stores are kept 軍需倉庫.

dump² [dʌmp] *vt / i* throw down or allow to fall down 傾卸, 傾倒.

dumpling ['dʌmpliŋ] *nc* **1** ball made of flour, fat and water, boiled with meat and vegetables (由麵粉, 油和水混合與肉、蔬菜共煮的) 麵糰. **2** ball made of flour and water containing fruit etc. (水果等作餡的) 麵糰.

dunce [dʌns] *nc* child who is not good at learning 笨孩子. **'dunce's 'cap** tall paper hat formerly worn by a dunce at school as a punishment (以前在學校裏作為懲罰給笨學生戴的) 高紙帽.

dune [dju:n] *nc* low hill of sand heaped up by the wind (風吹積成的) 沙丘.

dung [dʌŋ] *nu* waste matter sent out of the body of animals 動物的糞便.

dungarees [dʌŋgə'ri:z] *npl* garment consisting of coat or bib and trousers joined together, worn by people doing dirty work (衣褲連在一起的) 工作服.

dungeon ['dʌndʒən] *nc* room under ground, formerly used as a prison 地下室, 地牢.

dupe [dju:p] *vt* cheat; make somebody believe something which is not true, or get something from somebody by a trick 欺騙, 坑. Also 亦作 *nc* person who is tricked or cheated 受騙上當者.

duplicate ['dju:plikeit] *vt* do or make something exactly similar to something else 複製: *I duplicated his work* i.e. I did again the work which he had already done. 我複製他的作品. Also 亦作 ['dju:plikət] *adj: duplicate keys* 配的鑰匙.

durable ['djuərəbl] *adj* able to last a long time and not become damaged or broken 耐用的: *durable clothes / furniture etc.* 耐穿的衣服 / 耐用傢具等. **durability** [djuərə'biliti] *nu.*

duration [djuə'reiʃən] *nu* time during which something lasts 持續的期間: *for the duration of the holiday* i.e. for the whole period of the holiday 在整個假期期間.

during ['djuəriŋ] *prep* **1** for the whole of a certain period 在…期間 (指整段): *He worked during the day.* 他白天工作. **2** at one time or at different times in a period 在…的時候 (指一段時間中的某一時候或幾個時候): *Several important things happened during the year.* 這一年裏發生了幾件重要的事情.

dusk [dʌsk] *nu* time in the evening before it becomes completely dark 黃昏, 傍晚.

dust [dʌst] *nu* **1** very small pieces of dry earth, like powder 塵埃, 灰塵, 塵土. **2** substance like this (e.g. *chalk dust, gold dust*) 粉末(如粉筆粉末、金粉末). Also 亦作 **1** *vt / i* remove dust from 把…的塵埃揮掉, 揩, 抹, 擦拭.

She dusted the furniture. 她把傢具上的塵土撣掉. *She was dusting.* 她在撣掃灰塵. **2** *vt* cover with flour, sugar or other similar substance 撒粉狀物（麵粉、糖等）在…上. **dusty** *adj* dus-**ter** *nc* **1** cloth used to remove dust 抹布. **2** cloth used to clean chalk from a blackboard 黑板擦. **'dustbin** (*Brit*) container in which rubbish from a house is put to be taken away. (*US* 美 **garbage can**) （英） **'dustman** man whose job is to remove rubbish from houses 清潔工人. **'dustpan** metal or plastic object into which dust in a house can be brushed 畚箕, 畚斗.

duty ['dju:ti] **1** *nc / u* things which one must do, because one thinks it right to do them 職責, 責任, 本份: *It is your duty to fight for your country.* 為國而戰是你的本份. *The headmaster has many different duties.* 校長有許多不同的職責. **2** *nc* name given to various types of tax (esp. a tax on goods brought into a country) 稅（尤指關稅）. **dutiable** *adj* to be taxed if brought into a country 應徵關稅的. **dutiful** *adj* acting in a properly polite and obedient way to one's elders 順從的, 孝順的: *a dutiful daughter* 孝順的女兒. **dutifully** *adv* **'duty-'free** *adj* allowed to come into a country without being taxed 免稅的. **off duty** free from work 下班. see 見 **on duty**. **on duty** (e.g. with reference to soldiers, nurses etc) required to be ready to work (例如指士兵、護士等) 上崗, 值勤, 當班, 值班.

dwarf [dwɔ:f] *nc* **1** very small person 侏儒. **2** very small person in children's stories, often one having magical powers (童話中的) 小矮人.

dwell [dwel] *vi* live in a place 居住. *past* 過去式和過去分詞 **dwelt.** (*formal*) (正式). **dwelling** *nc* house (*formal*) 住處, 住所.(正式).

dwindle ['dwindl] *vi* (often with *away*) slowly become smaller (常與 away 連用)逐漸減少; 逐漸變小.

dye [dai] *nc / u* substance used for changing the colour of cloth; colour given to cloth in this way 染料; 染色. Also 亦作 *vt* change the colour of cloth using various substances 染: *She dyed her coat blue.* 她把上衣染成藍色. *pres part* 現在分詞 **dyeing.** *past* 過去式和過去分詞 **dyed.**

dying ['daiiŋ] *pres part of* **die²**. die² 的現在分詞.

dyke [daik] *nc* see 見 **dike.**

dynamic [dai'næmik] *adj* (with reference to a person) having a lot of energy; able to do things in a hurry and to make people do what one wants; having a strong and active character (指人) 精力旺盛的; 精幹的; 精悍的; 生氣勃勃的.

dynamite ['dainəmait] *nu* very powerful explosive 烈性炸藥.

dynamo ['dainəmou] *nc* any device which changes any force of energy into electricity (e.g. a device used on a bicycle for lighting the bicycle lamps) 小型發電機, 發電器 (例如自行車上用於使車燈發亮的裝置). *pl* 複數 **dynamos.**

dynasty ['dinəsti] *nc* series of kings etc belonging to the same family 王朝, 朝代.

dysentery ['disntri] *nu* disease of the bowels, causing diarrhoea 痢疾.

E,e

each [i:tʃ] *determiner / adv / pron* every one, taken separately 每一, 各自(地): *He spoke to each member of the team.* 他和該隊的每個隊員説話. *These books cost two pounds each.* 這些書每本價值二英鎊. *Each of the boys has a prize.* 這些男生每人都獲獎. *Each boy has a prize.* 每個男生都獲獎. *Mary and Peter saw each other last night* i.e. Mary saw Peter and Peter saw Mary. 瑪麗與彼得昨晚互相看望. 即: 瑪麗看望彼得, 彼得看望瑪麗. *Each and every one of them* i.e. all of them 他們每一個人, 即: 他們所有的人.

eager ['i:gə*] *adj* having a strong wish for something 渴望的, 熱切的: *He was eager to help us.* 他很想幫助我們. *He was eager for information.* 他渴望得到消息. **eagerly** *adv* **eagerness** *nu.*

eagle ['i:gl] *nc* type of large bird, with a hooked nose and very good eyesight, which eats small birds and animals 鷹.

ear [iə*] *nc* **1** part of the head by which animals, birds, humans etc hear 耳朵. **2** part of a cereal plant such as corn or wheat which contains the seeds (糧食作物的)穗. '**eardrum** part of the ear inside the head, which moves when sound waves strike it 耳鼓. '**earphone** device which is fastened over the ear, for receiving telephone or radio signals 耳機. **by ear** (with reference to playing music) from memory, without reading the notes (指演奏音樂時)憑記憶而不必視譜地.

earl [ə:l] *nc* British nobleman of high rank (英)伯爵.

early ['ə:li] *adj / adv* **1** near the beginning 早的, 早期的, 開初的: *in the early morning* 在清早; *in the early part of the book* 在該書的開頭部份. **2** before the usual or proper time 提早地: *We arrived too early.* 我們到得太早. **3** in ancient times 古代的: *early history* 古代歷史.

earn [ə:n] *vt* get by work 挣得: *He earns £20 a week.* 他一週挣20英鎊. *You have earned your holiday* i.e. you have worked hard and you should have a holiday 你已挣得了假期. 即: 你工作得很辛苦, 應當有個假期. **earnings** *npl* money which a person earns 工錢, 薪水.

earnest ['ə:nist] *adj* serious or too serious; unable to laugh or joke 鄭重其事的; 一本正經的. **in earnest** serious; not joking 鄭重地; 認真地: *I was in earnest when I told you that.* 我把那消息告訴你不是説着玩的.

earth [ə:θ] **1** *nu* soil; substance in which plants grow 泥土; 土壤 **2** *nu* land; whatever is not sea, river etc. 土地; 陸地. **3** *nu* (usu. **the earth**) the world (通常寫作 **the earth**)地球. **4** *nc* wire or other means of connection, which leads from an electrical device to the ground or completes an electrical circuit 地線. **5** *nc* hole where certain animals live (動物的)洞, 穴. Also 亦作 *vt* provide an electrical device with a connection to the ground 使接地線; 將(電器)…接到地上: *He earthed the radio.* 他把收音機接上地

線. **'earthenware** coarse plates, cups etc made of baked clay 陶器. **'earthquake** violent shaking of part of the earth 地震. **'earthworm** long thin creature which lives in soil and eats earth 蚯蚓.

earwig ['iəwig] *nc* type of small insect with pincers at the tail 蠼螋, 蚰蜒.

ease [i:z] *nu* 1 freedom from work or worry 安逸, 舒服; 悠閒, 無憂無慮. 2 ability to do something without trying hard or without difficulty 輕而易舉, 不費力: He did the work with ease. 他做這項工作很輕鬆. Also 亦作 *vt / i* (often with **off**) become or make less difficult, less strong, less tight etc. (常與 off 連用) (使) 困難減少; (使) 減弱; (使) 減鬆: The wind has eased off. 風勢減弱了. He eased the screw. 他旋鬆螺絲. **ease up** work less hard, be less severe 放鬆; 緩和: He worked hard at first, but he has eased up lately. 開始他工作很勤奮, 近來他鬆勁了. **at ease** free from worry or embarrassment 自由自在; 從容不迫: I never feel at ease when I talk to him. 我和他談話從未感到自在過. **ill at ease** worried; anxious, embarrassed 煩惱的; 焦慮的; 侷促不安的: The boy felt ill at ease when the headmaster spoke to him. 這個男生在校長和他談話時感到侷促不安.

easel ['i:zl] *nc* frame for holding a picture while it is being painted 畫架.

east [i:st] *adj / adv / nu* direction in which one first sees the rising sun 東的, 東方的; 在東方, 向東; 東, 東方: He travelled east. 他在東方旅行. An east wind was blowing i.e. a wind from the east 在吹東風. **eastern** *adj* **the east / East 1** Asia 亞洲. 2 the eastern part of any country or continent 任一國家 (或大陸) 之東部. **the Middle East**

countries around the eastern part of the Mediterranean (e.g. Egypt, Israel, Jordan etc.) 中東國家 (如埃及、以色列、約旦等). **the Far East** India, Pakistan, China, Japan etc. 遠東國家 (如印度、巴基斯坦、中國、日本等).

Easter ['i:stə*] *nc / u* period around the anniversary of the Crucifixion and Resurrection of Christ 復活節.

easy ['i:zi] *adj* 1 not causing difficulty 容易的; 不費力的: The work is easy. 這工作很容易. 2 free from pain or worry 舒服的, 輕鬆的: If you prepare your work well, you will be able to sit the examination with an easy mind. (opp **uneasy** in sense 2) 如果你準備充分, 考試的時候就會輕鬆自如. (義的反義詞為 uneasy). **easily** *adv*. **'easy chair** soft padded chair (usu. with arms) (通常帶扶手的) 安樂椅.

eat [i:t] *vt / i* take food in through the mouth 吃. 2 have a meal 吃飯. 3 (usu. with reference to destruction by acid or similar substance) destroy (通常指為酸類物質所) 侵蝕, 腐蝕. *past tense* 過去式 **ate** [et, eit]. *past part* 過去分詞 **eaten** ['i:tn]. *Note* 說明: in Britain ate is usu. pronounced [et]; some people use the pronunciation [eit]. In America the usual pronunciation is [eit], and [et] is considered incorrect 在英國 ate 通常發音為 [et]; 有些人則把它發成 [eit] 的音. 美國通常發音為 [eit], 而 [et] 則被認為是不正確的發音. **eatable** *adj* fit for eating 能吃的, 可食用的. (opp 反義詞 **uneatable**). **eat away something** (usu. with reference to acid or a similar substance) destroy (通常指酸類物質) 腐蝕 (某物), 侵蝕 (某物).

eau de cologne ['oudəkə'loun] *nc / u* type of perfume 科隆香水.

eaves [i:vz] *npl* part of a roof which

hangs out over a wall 屋檐. **'eaves-drop** *vi* (with on) listen secretly to a conversation between other people. (與on連用) 竊聽, 偷聽. *past* 過去式和過去分詞 **eavesdropped.**

ebb [eb] *nc* (usu. only *sing*) movement of the tide away from the land (通常僅用單數) 退潮. Also 亦作 *vi* move away from the land 退潮. *The tide was ebbing.* 潮水在退.

ebony ['ebəni] **1** *nu* very hard black wood 烏木, 黑檀木. **2** *nc* the tree from which this wood comes 烏木樹, 黑檀. Also 亦作 *adj* black in colour 烏木色的, 黑檀色的.

ebullient [i'buliənt] *adj* very lively by nature 生氣勃勃的, 活潑的: *He is an ebullient person.* 他是個非常活潑的人.

eccentric [ik'sentrik] *adj* (with reference to people) odd, unusual; rather strange (指人) 古怪的, 反常的; 怪異的. Also 亦作 *nc* eccentric person; person who behaves unusually 古怪的人; 有怪癖的人.

ecclesiastical [ikli:zi'æstikl] *adj* having reference to churches 教會的.

echo ['ekou] *nc* **1** bouncing of sound waves off a surface, so that any sound is heard again 回音, 回響. **2** any repetition of what has been said by somebody 附和. *pl* 複數 **echoes.** Also 亦作 *vt/i* **1** make an echo 發出回聲: *This room echoes* i.e. causes sound waves to bounce back. 這個房間可以回音. **2** be repeated in this way 共鳴, 回響: *The sound echoed through the room.* 這種聲音在房間裏回響. **3** repeat what has been said 附和: *He echoed my words.* 他附和我的話.

eclipse [i'klips] *nc* cutting off of light coming from a body (e.g. the sun) to

a second body (e.g. the earth) when a third body (e.g. the moon) moves in between (日或月)蝕: *a partial / complete eclipse* 偏 / 全蝕; *an eclipse of the sun* i.e. when the moon is between the sun and the earth 日蝕, 即: 月球處於太陽與地球之間; *an eclipse of the moon* i.e. when the earth is between the moon and the sun 月蝕, 即: 地球處於太陽與月球之間.

ecology [i:'kɔlədʒi] *nu* study of the relation of plants and animals to their environment 生態學. **ecologist** *nc* person who is interested in this 生態學家, 生態學者.

economy [i'kɔnəmi] **1** *nu* the condition of money, industry and employment in a country 國家的經濟狀況: *The economy of the country is in a bad condition.* 該國的經濟狀況很糟. **2** *nc* system of money, industry etc in a particular country 經濟體系. **3** *nc* something which enables one to spend less money 經濟, 節約措施: *Walking to work instead of driving one's car is an economy.* 步行而不是開車去上班是一種省錢的辦法. **economic** [i:kə'nɔmik] *adj* with reference to economy 經濟的. **economics** [i:kə'nɔmiks] *nu* study of the system of money, industry, employment etc used in various countries 經濟學. *Note* 說明: followed by a *sing* verb. 其後用單數動詞. **economical** [i:kə'nɔmikl] *adj* enabling one to spend less money; not wasteful 節約的, 經濟的. **economist** *nc* person who studies economics 經濟學者, 經濟學家. **economize** *vi* spend less money etc. 節約, 節省.

ecosystem [i:kə'sistəm] *nc* system made up of a group of animals, plants and bacteria and its physical and che-

mical environment, and the relationship between them 生態系(統).

ecstasy ['ekstəsi] *nc / u* very great
happiness so that one seems to be
changed in some way 狂喜, 心醉神怡.
ecstatic [ek'stætik] *adj.*

ecumenical [i:kju:'menikl] *adj* for or of
the whole Christian church 全球基督
教的; 為全球基督教的.

eczema ['eksimə] *nu* type of skin disease 濕疹.

edge [edʒ] *nc* **1** sharp side of a knife
etc. 刀刃, 刀口. **2** outer part of something; part not near the middle (某物
的)邊緣; 邊: *He stood at / on the edge
of the field* i.e. near the fence, road,
gate etc. 他站在田野的邊緣. 即: 靠近
圍籬, 公路, 大門等. **edging** *nu* border
or edge 邊緣, 邊; 邊飾: *put an edging
on a piece of cloth* 在一塊布上加邊
飾.

edible ['edibl] *adj* suitable for eating 可
食用的; edible food 食品. (*opp* 反義
詞 **inedible**).

edict ['i:dikt] *nc* official command by a
king or other ruler 法令; 敕令; 詔書.

edifice ['edifis] *nc* large building. *(formal)* 大廈(正式).

edit ['edit] *vt* prepare the writings of
somebody else for publication 編輯;
edit the works of Shakespeare 編輯莎
士比亞的著作. **editor** *nc* **edition**
[i'diʃən] *nc* number of books, newspapers etc printed at the same time
and all exactly the same (書籍, 報紙
等)一版所印的數目. **editorial** [edi't-
ɔ:riəl] *adj* of editing 編輯的; 編輯上
的. Also 亦作 *nc* article written in a
newspaper by the editor, in which he
discusses some item of news 社論.

educate ['edjukeit] *vt* teach (esp. at
school) (尤指學校裏)教育. **educa-
tion** [edju'keiʃən] *nu* process of

teaching; knowledge and learning possessed by a person 教學程序; 個人所
受的教育. **educational** [edju'keiʃənl]
adj **educated** *adj* (*opp* 反義詞 **uneducated**). *Note* 說明: *educate* refers
to teaching knowledge; for teaching
good manners etc in the home use
bring up. If a person has no manners,
he may have been *badly brought up.*
educate 指教授知識; 指在家庭所受的
禮貌等教育要用 bring up. 如果一個人
沒有禮貌, 他的教養可能很差.

eel [i:l] *nc* type of fish shaped like a
snake 鱔魚; 鰻魚.

eerie ['iəri] *adj* strange and making one
feel afraid 怪異可怕的: *an eerie story
about ghosts* 有關鬼的可怕故事.

efface [i'feis] *vt* rub out or remove a
stain or mark 擦掉; 抹去; 除掉.

effect [i'fekt] **1** *nc / u* result 影響; 效果,
結果: *What effects did the war have?*
這場戰爭產生了甚麼影響? *Punishment
does not have any effect on him.* 懲罰
對他毫無效果. *This drug has a strong
effect.* 這種藥具有強烈的效果. **2** *nc*
appearance of something 外觀, 外表:
*I like the effect of your red curtains
against your blue walls.* 我喜歡你屋裏
那些紅色窗簾配襯藍色牆壁的景象.
Also 亦作 *vt* cause something to happen 使發生: *He effected several important changes.* 他引起了幾個重要的
變化. *Note* 說明: see *affect.* 見 affect.
effects *npl* money and property owned by somebody 私人財產. **effective**
having a result 有效的. (*opp* 反義詞
ineffective).

effeminate [i'feminət] *adj* (with reference to a man) like a woman (指男
人)女人氣的.

effervescent [efə'vesnt] *adj* **1** giving off
bubbles of gas 冒氣泡的. **2** (with reference to a person) excitable and ac-

tive (指人) 興奮的, 興高采烈的.

efficient [i'fiʃənt] *adj* able to work well and give good results, without wasting time or effort 能勝任的, 效率高的. (*opp* 反義詞 **inefficient**). **efficiently** *adv* **efficiency** *nu*.

effigy ['efidʒi] *nc* object of wood, stone etc made to look like a person 模擬像.

effluent ['efluənt] *nc / u* stream flowing from a larger stream, or from a lake, sewage tank, etc. (從河、湖、陰溝等流出的) 水流; 支流, 污水. Also 亦作 *adj* flowing out or forth 流出的, 發出的.

effort ['efət] *nc / u* **1** attempt (esp. one needing some mental or physical work) 努力, 盡力: *I made an effort to read that book* i.e. I read or tried to read that book, although it was difficult 我盡力讀懂那本書. **2** hard work 苦幹, 勤奮: *He puts a lot of effort into his work* i.e. he works hard. 他工作很勤奮. **effortless** *adj* (usu. with reference to something that other people would find difficult) done easily (常指他人感到困難的事)容易做的, 不費力的.

effrontery [i'frʌntəri] *nu* boldness in doing wrong; ability to do wrong without feeling afraid of what people will say or think 厚顏; 無恥: *The student had the effrontery to accuse the professor of being stupid.* 這個學生竟恬不知恥地指責教授愚鈍.

egalitarian [igæli'teəriən] *adj* believing that all people should be equal 主張人人平等的.

egg [eg] *nc* **1** object produced by birds, insects, snakes, fish etc from which the young are born 蛋, 卵. **2** such an object produced by a hen, used as food 雞蛋. '**eggcup** small cup to hold a boiled egg (用來盛帶殼煮的蛋的)蛋

杯. '**eggshell** covering of a bird's egg 蛋殼.

ego ['i:gou] *nc* the self; a person considered as an individual 自我; 個人. *pl* 複數 **egos. egoist** ['egouist] *nc* person who thinks only of himself and not of others 自私自利者, 利己主義者. **egoism** ['egouizəm] *nu* **egotist** ['egətist] *nc* person who talks only about himself 自誇者, 自我中心者. **ego-tism** ['egətizəm] *nu.*

egret ['i:gret] *nc* kind of heron with beautiful long feathers in the tail and on the back; bunch of these feathers as an ornament 白鷺(尾部及背部生有美麗的長羽毛); 裝飾用的白鷺羽毛.

eiderdown ['aidədaun] *nc* cover for a bed, filled with the down of the eider duck; similar cover filled with feathers, cotton etc. 鴨絨被, 羽絨被; 棉被.

eight [eit] see appendix 見附錄.

either ['aiðə*] *determiner / pron / adv / conj* **1** one out of two 二者之一: *You can enter by either door.* 你可以從兩個門中的任何一個進屋. *Either of the two boys can do it.* 兩個男生中的任何一個都能做這事. *I can't come, and my wife can't come either.* 我不能來, 我太太也不能來. *I'm sure that either John or Peter has the book.* 我敢肯定不是約翰就是彼得有那本書. *Either you have made a mistake or we shall have to find more money.* 要麼你錯了, 要麼我們得多弄點錢. *Note* 說明: if *either ... or* joins two singular nouns, then a singular verb is used (e.g. *Either John or his uncle has the key*). 如果 either ... or 兩個單詞連用, 那麼就用單數動詞. (例如 Either John or his uncle has the key. 不是約翰有鑰匙, 就是他叔叔有鑰匙). **2** both (二者的)每一個: *There were trees on either side of the avenue.* 街兩邊都有

樹.

eject [i'dʒekt] *vt / i* throw out 投出；噴出；射出.

elaborate [i'læbərət] *adj* having many parts and many small details 複雜的；精緻的：*an elaborate story* 複雜的故事；*an elaborate decoration* 精緻的裝飾. Also 亦作 [i'læbəreit] *vt / i* add many small details (to)；describe in detail 詳盡地說明；詳細地描述.

elapse [i'læps] *vi* (with reference to time) pass (指時間) 消逝.

elastic [i'læstik] *adj* 1 made of or containing rubber；stretchable 橡皮的；有彈性的：*an elastic band* 橡皮帶. 2 able to bounce；able to regain the original shape after being pulled 有彈力的；有伸縮性的. Also 亦作 *nu* strips of rubber or cloth containing strips of rubber, used for fastening garments on the body etc. 橡皮筋；鬆緊帶.

elation [i'leiʃən] *nu* feeling of great happiness 得意揚揚，興高采烈.

elbow ['elbou] *nc* joint in the middle of the arm 肘.

elder[1] ['eldə*] *adj* (with reference to two people usu. in the same family) older；born earlier (通常指同一家的兩人中) 年長的：*my elder brother* 我哥哥. Also 亦作 *nc* senior person；old person 長輩；老一輩. **elderly** ['eldəli] *adj* **eldest** ['eldist] *adj* oldest 最年長的.

elder[2] ['eldə*] *nc* type of tree with white flowers and dark berries 接骨木.

elect [i'lekt] *vt* choose somebody by voting 選舉：*They elected Tom Jones as their Member of Parliament.* 他們選舉湯姆・瓊斯為他們的議會議員. **elector** *nc* person having the right to vote 合格選民，選舉人. **electorate** [i'lektərət] *nc* all the electors in a dis-

trict or a country (一個地區或國家的) 全體選民. **electoral** *adj* election *nc* process of choosing Members of Parliament or other representatives (議會議員或其他代表的) 選舉.

electricity [ilek'trisiti] *nu* form of energy which produces heat, light etc. 電，電力. **electrical** [i'lektrikl] *adj* **electric** [i'lektrik] *adj* worked by or producing electricity 電力產生的；發電的：*electric light* 電燈. **electrician** [elək'triʃən] *nc* person who installs and repairs electric devices 電工，電器技師，電器修理員. **electrify** [i'lektrifai] *vt* charge with electricity 使帶電. *past* 過去式和過去分詞 **electrified**. **electrification** [ilektrifi'keiʃən] *nu* **electrocute** [i'lektrəkju:t] *vt* kill by a charge of electricity 以電刑處決.

electronics [elək'trɔniks] *n sing* study and use of complex electrical devices such as those in radio and TV sets 電子學. **electronic** *adj* **electric blanket** covering for a bed, which can be heated electrically in order to warm the bed 電熱毯. **electric chair** chair in which a criminal sits to be killed by electricity (used in some states of America) 電椅 (美國某些州用以處決罪犯).

electroplate [i'lektroupleit] *vt* cover (silverware, printing plates, etc) with a coating of metal by means of electrolysis 電鍍 (銀器, 印鑄板等). Also 亦作 *n* 1 silverware or other metal covered in this way 鍍銀製品；鍍銀餐具；電鍍物品. 2 printing plate made by this process 電鑄板.

electrostatic [i'lektrou'stætik] *adj* 1 of or having to do with static electricity 靜電的. 2 of or having to do with electrostatics 靜電學的.

electrostatics [i'lektrou'stætiks] *npl*

(with singular verb) branch of physics that deals with static electricity and with objects charged with electricity (與單數動詞連用) 靜電學.

elegant [ˈeləgənt] *adj* **1** graceful, fashionable 高雅的, 優雅的. **2** beautiful in appearance and well-made 雅緻的, 精緻的. **elegance** *nu*.

element [ˈeləmənt] *nc* **1** (chemistry) substance from which other substances are made (化學) 元素: *Oxygen, hydrogen, copper etc are elements.* 氧, 氫, 銅等是元素. **2** anything which goes to make up something else 成份, 要素. **3** fire, earth, water or air (from which it was once thought everything was made) 火, 土, 水, 氣四元素(過去認爲一切皆產生於此四元素).

elementary [eləˈmentəri] *adj* **1** concerned with the early stages of learning 初級的, 基礎的: *an elementary school* i.e. one for young children 小學. **2** not developed; in a simple form 初級的; 未發展的; 簡單的. **3** easy to understand 易懂的, 淺顯的.

elephant [ˈelifənt] *nc* type of large animal with a thick skin, ivory tusks and a long trunk 象.

elevate [ˈeliveit] *vt* lift up high. *(formal)* 提高, 高舉. (非正式). **elevator** *nc* (US) machine for carrying goods and people up and down high buildings (美)電梯; 升降梯. *(Brit* 英 **lift**).

eleven [iˈlevən] see appendix 見附錄.

elf [elf] *nc* small magical creature shaped like a human being 形人小魔怪. *pl* 複數 **elves** [elvz].

elicit [iˈlisit] *vt* get information etc from somebody 獲悉, 探知: *elicit information / an answer / the truth* 探知消息 / 獲悉答覆 / 探明真相.

eligible [ˈelidʒibl] *adj* with the necessary qualifications; suitable 合格的, 有

資格的; 適合的: *Women are not eligible to be president of that club* i.e. the president must be a man. 女人不適合擔任該俱樂部的會長. 即: 會長必須是個男人. *(opp* 反義詞 **ineligible**).

eliminate [iˈlimineit] *vt* remove; get rid of 除去; 排除: *eliminate a difficulty* 排除困難. **elimination** [ilimiˈneiʃən] *nu*.

elite, élite [iˈliːt] *nc* select group of people, the richest, best educated, most powerful people in society 社會精英.

ellipse [iˈlips] *nc* regular oval 橢圓, 橢圓形.

ellipsis [iˈlipsis] *nc / u* **1** (grammar) omission of a word or words needed to complete the grammatical construction, but not the meaning, of a sentence (Ex *"if possible"* for *"if it is possible"*) (語法) 一句中字的省略; 省略法(例: *if possible* 代替 *if it is possible)* **2** marks (... or × × ×) used to show an omission in writing or printing 省略符號(…或×××).

elliptical [iˈliptikəl] *adj* **1** of, or having the form of, an ellipse 橢圓的; 橢圓形的. **2** of or showing ellipsis; having a word or words omitted 省略的; 表示省略的; 有字被省略的.

elm [elm] *nc* tall tree found in cool northern regions 榆樹; 榆木.

elocution [eləˈkjuːʃən] *nu* art of speaking well and clearly (esp. in public) 演講術.

elope [iˈloup] *vi* run away from one's parents in order to be married 私奔: *The young woman eloped with the man she loved.* 這位姑娘與所愛的男人私奔了. *They eloped.* 他們私奔了. **elopement** *nc / u.*

eloquent [ˈeləkwənt] *adj* able to speak well so as to persuade or influence other people 雄辯的, 善辯的. **eloquently** *adv* **eloquence** *nu.*

else [els] *adj / adv* other; otherwise; different(ly) 別的; 其他的, 否則; 不同的 (地): *somebody else* i.e. another person 別人, 他人; *Who else was there?* 還有誰在那兒? *What else did he say?* 他還說些甚麼? *You must work hard, or else you will fail your examination* i.e. if you don't work hard, you will fail. 你必須努力學習, 否則你考試會不及格的. **elsewhere** *adv* to / in another place 到別處; 在別的地方: *You had better try elsewhere.* 你最好到別處試試.

elucidate [i'lu:sideit] *vt / i* explain clearly something which is difficult to understand 闡明, 說明.

elude [i'lu:d] *vt* escape capture; escape from 逃脫; 規避. **elusive** [i'lu:siv] *adj* difficult to catch or remember 難懂的; 難記的.

elves [elvz] *pl* of **elf.** elf 的複數形式.

emaciated [i'meisieitid] *adj* thin because of illness or lack of food (因病或飢餓) 瘦弱的.

emanate ['emaneit] *vi* come from some source 來源於: *This story emanates from you* i.e. you started this story. 這個傳聞來源於你. 即: 你傳來了這個傳聞.

emancipate [i'mænsipeit] *vt* set free (esp. a slave) 解放, 使自由 (尤指奴隸). **emancipation** [imænsi'peiʃən] *nu* **emancipated** *adj* freed from former restraints; unconventional 擺脫束縛的; 不落俗套的.

embalm [em'bɑːm] *vt* treat a dead body with various substances to prevent it from decaying 對 (屍體) 進行防腐處理, 塗香料等於屍體以防腐.

embankment [em'bæŋkmənt] *nc* wall made of earth or stone to support a road which is higher than the surrounding land, or to prevent the land

beside a river being flooded 路基; 河堤.

embargo [em'bɑːgou] *nc* official order forbidding trade 禁止貿易 (令); 禁運令. *The government placed an embargo on trade with enemy countries.* 政府禁止與敵國進行貿易. *pl* 複數 **embargoes.**

embark [em'bɑːk] *vt / i* **1** go, cause to go, on a ship for a voyage (使) 搭船, 上船: *We embarked.* 我們搭船旅行. **2** start on a project (使) 開始, (使) 從事: *The officer embarked the soldiers* 軍官讓士兵們投入戰鬥. (*opp* 反義詞 **disembark**). **embarkation** [embɑː'keiʃən] *nu.*

embarrass [em'bærəs] *vt* make a person worried and uncertain what to do or say 使尷尬, 使困窘: *The small boy was embarrassed when he met the old lady.* 小男孩見到老太太時感到很難為情. **embarrassment** *nc / u.*

embassy ['embəsi] *nc* **1** place where an ambassador works (and usu. lives) in a foreign country; the ambassador himself and his staff 大使館; 大使; 大使館全體成員. **2** duty of an ambassador or other representative 大使或其他代表之職責.

embed, imbed [em'bed] *vt* fix into something very firmly 牢牢嵌入, 牢牢插於: *The foundations of the bridge are embedded in concrete.* 橋基牢牢地嵌入混凝土中. *past* 過去式和過去分詞 **embedded.**

embellish [em'beliʃ] *vt* make more beautiful 裝飾, 布置; 潤飾.

ember ['embə*] *nc* (usu. *pl*) small piece of coal or wood burning with a red glow (通常用複數) 餘燼.

embezzle [em'bezl] *vt* steal money belonging to other people which has been placed in one's care 貪污, 侵吞.

The bank manager embezzled the money. 銀行經理貪污了這筆款子.

embitter [im'bitə*] *vt* make a person have feelings of anger and hate 激怒; 使憤恨. *The failure of his plans embittered the old man.* 計劃的失敗使得這個老頭又氣又恨.

emblem ['embləm] *nc* drawing, sign or object which represents something. 象徵, 標誌: *A soldier has various emblems on his uniform to show the branch of the army he belongs to and his own rank and duties.* 一名軍人的軍服上有幾種標誌以表示所屬部隊及職務等級.

embody [em'bɔdi] *vt* 1 give form to an idea, plan, hope etc. 體現, 表現. 2 include 包括. **embodiment** *n/u.*

emboss [em'bɔs] *vt* to mark paper etc with raised letters or designs 加浮雕字母或花紋於(紙等)上.

embrace [em'breis] *vt / i* 1 put one's arms round somebody as a sign of love 擁抱, 摟抱: *He embraced her.* 他擁抱她. *They embraced.* 他們擁抱在一起. 2 include 包括: *His course of study embraces History, Geography and Economics.* 他的學習課程包括歷史、地理和經濟. Also 亦作 *nc* act of putting the arms round somebody as a sign of love 摟抱, 擁抱.

embroider [em'brɔidə*] *vt / i* sew a pattern or picture on to cloth 刺繡(於). **embroidery** *nc / u* art of sewing designs on cloth; cloth which has been embroidered 刺繡法; 刺繡品.

embryo ['embriou] *nc* animal, bird etc in the stage of development before it is born 胚胎. *pl* 複數 **embryos.**

emerald ['emərld] *nc / u* bright green precious stone; colour like this stone 祖母綠; 綠寶石; 翠綠色. Also 亦作 *adj.*

emerge [i'mə:dʒ] *vi* 1 come into view 露出, 出現: *He emerged from behind the tree.* 他從樹後面冒了出來. 2 become known 露出真相, 為人知曉; *The truth emerged at last* 最終真相大白.

emergent *adj* (usu. with reference to the development of countries) (通常指國家的發展)新興的. **emergence** *nu.*

emergency [i'mə:dʒənsi] *nc* unusual and dangerous situation in which one has to act quickly 緊急情況: *An outbreak of fire or an accident is an emergency.* 失火或發生事故都是緊急情況. **e'mergency 'exit** door in a bus, aeroplane, theatre etc which can be used if there is a fire, accident etc. 太平門.

emery ['eməri] *nu* in **emery paper** i.e. paper with a rough surface used for smoothing and polishing metal etc. 金剛砂紙.

emetic [i'metik] *nc* substance which causes one to throw out of the stomach whatever has been swallowed 催吐劑.

emigrate ['emigreit] *vi* go from one's own country to another country to live there (自本國)移居(他國). **emigrant** ['emigrnt] *nc* person who does this (移居外國的)移民. **emigration** [emi'greiʃən] *nu* act of emigrating 移居國外. *Note* 說明: an *emigrant* goes from his own country, an *immigrant* is a person who comes into a country. emigrant 是離開自己國家的移民; immigrant 則是進入一個國家的移民.

eminent ['eminənt] *adj* 1 (with reference to people) well-known and respected (指人)著名的, 傑出的: *an eminent lawyer / scientist / general etc.* 著名的律師／科學家／將軍等. 2 greater than usual 非常的, 非凡的; 卓越的

eminent honesty / intelligence / ability etc. 非常的誠實 / 非凡的智力 / 非凡的能力 等. **eminence** *nu* quality of being eminent 卓越, 傑出; 非凡.

emir [e'miə*] *nc* title of certain Muslim leaders 某些穆斯林領袖人的稱號.

emit [i'mit] *vt* send out 發出; 放射: *emit a sound / a smell / radiation / light etc.* 發出聲音 / 氣味; 放射出射線 / 光線等. *past* 過去式和過去分詞 **emitted**. **emission** [i'miʃən] *nc / u*.

emotion [i'mouʃən] *nc / u* feeling of the mind 情感, 感情: *Anger, happiness, hate, anxiety are emotions.* 憤怒、快樂、仇恨、焦慮都是情感. **emotional** *adj* of strong feelings; showing strong feelings 具有強烈情感的; 顯示出強烈情感的. (*opp* 反義詞 **unemotional**). **emotionally** *adv.*

emperor ['empərə*] *nc* ruler of an empire 皇帝.

emphasize ['emfəsaiz] *vt* call attention to something by making it especially noticeable in some way 強調, 着重; 使特別顯著: *He emphasized his instructions to us* i.e. he made us listen carefully to his instructions. 他強調他對我們的指示. 即: 他使我們認真聽他的指示. *He emphasized the word 'one'* i.e. he said this word slowly, loudly etc or he repeated it 他着重一這個詞. 即: 他緩慢地大聲地說這個詞或者重複這個詞. *She emphasized her eyes by painting her eyelids* i.e. she made her eyes seem bigger and brighter in this way. 她畫眼瞼來突出自己的眼睛. 即: 她以這種方法來使自己的眼睛顯得更大更明亮. **emphasis** ['emfəsis] *nu* process of emphasizing something 強調, 加強. **emphatic** [em'fætik] *adj* (*opp* 反義詞 **unemphatic**). **emphatically** *adv.*

empire ['empaiə*] *nc* 1 number of

countries ruled by one person or one government 帝國 (由一人或一個政府統治的幾個國家). 2 large country under one ruler (由一個人統治的)帝國.

empirical [em'pirikl] *adj* based on experiment or experience, not on theory 憑經驗的, 實證的.

employ [em'plɔi] *vt* 1 give work to 雇用: *He employs fifty men in his factory.* 他在他的工廠裏雇用了五十個人. 2 make use of 使用, 運用: *He employed statistical methods in his work.* 他在工作中使用統計方法. **employer** *nc* person who gives work to others 雇主. **employee** [emplɔi'i:] *nc* person who is employed 雇員. **employment** *nc* 1 process of employing or being employed 雇用; 就業. 2 work done by somebody 工作. **em'ployment agency** private business firm which finds jobs for people 職業介紹所. **em'ployment exchange** (*formal* - see labour exchange) (正式一非正式見 labour exchange).

empress ['empris] *nc* 1 wife of an emperor 皇后. 2 woman who rules an empire 女皇.

empty ['empti] *adj* 1 containing nothing 空的: *an empty box* 空盒子. 2 meaning nothing 無意義的, 空洞的: *an empty promise / threat* i.e. a promise or threat which will not be carried out 空洞的許諾 / 虛張聲勢的威脅. Also 亦作 *vt / i* become or make empty (使) 變空; (使) 用空: *The theatre emptied* i.e. the people left. 劇院裏空無一人. 即: 裏面的人都走了. *He emptied the box.* 他把箱子倒空了. *past* 過去式和過去分詞 **'emptied**. **emptiness** *nu* **empty-handed** *adj* not carrying anything, not having gained anything 空手的; 一無所獲的.

emu ['i:mju:] *nc* large bird which cannot fly, found in Australia 鶓鶓(產於澳大利亞的不會飛的大鳥).

emulate ['emjuleit] *vt* try to do something as well as or better than somebody else; try to do the same as somebody else 想趕上或超過(某人)、與(某人)競爭; 仿效(某人): *I tried to emulate his success.* 我想仿效他的成功之道.

emulsion [e'mʌlʃən] *nc / u* **1** (often with reference to a type of medicine) liquid with oil which has been broken into very small drops (常指一種藥)乳劑. **2** type of paint which is not shiny when it dries (乾後不亮的)乳狀漆. (Also 亦作 **emulsion paint**).

enable [i'neibl] *vt* make it possible for somebody to do something 使(某人)能够做(某事): *The money enabled me to take a holiday.* 這筆錢使我能够度假.

enact [i'nækt] *vt* **1** make into a law; decree; ordain 製定(法律); 頒佈; 規定: *Congress enacted a bill to restrict the sale of guns.* 國會通過限制銷售槍枝的法案. **2** perform in or as in a play 演出; 扮演: *He played the part of Hamlet.* 他扮演哈姆雷特的角色.

enactment [i'næktmənt] *nc / u* action of enacting; state of being enacted 制定; 頒佈; 規定; 演出; 扮演. **2** law or a single provision of a law 法律; 法令; 法規; 條例.

enamel [i'næml] *nu* **1** hard covering put on metal 搪瓷, 珐瑯. **2** type of hard paint which is shiny when it dries 漆, 光漆. (Also 亦作 **enamel paint**). **3** the hard covering of the teeth (牙齒表面的)珐瑯質.

enamoured [i'næməd] *adj* (with **of**) liking very much (與 **of** 連用)非常喜歡的: *I am not much enamoured of*

travelling. 我並不太喜歡旅行.

encampment [in'kæmpmənt] *nc* group of tents or other temporary dwellings (e.g. where soldiers or nomads are living for a short time) 宿營地, 營房 (例如士兵或遊牧部落短期居住之處).

encase [in'keis] *vt* surround by something 包裝, 包裹: *The machine was encased in plastic.* 這部機器包裝在塑料壳內.

enchant [in'tʃɑ:nt] *vt* **1** be very pleasant to somebody; be liked very much by somebody 使喜悅; 使迷戀: *She enchanted all her friends.* 她迷住了她所有的朋友. *The beautiful house enchanted everyone who saw it.* 這座美麗的房子使每個看見它的人都看了迷. **2** work a magic spell on 施魔法於: *The wizard enchanted the princess.* 巫士用魔法迷住了公主. **enchanting** *adj* very pleasant in this way 非常迷人的, 令人着魔的.

encircle [in'sə:kl] *vt* form a circle round; surround 環繞; 包圍: *The house is encircled by trees.* 這座房子四週樹木環繞.

enclose, inclose [in'klouz] *vt* **1** put a wall etc around (以牆等)圍繞: *The house was enclosed by a high wall.* 這座房子為一道高牆所圍繞. **2** put something in an envelope etc in addition to something else 隨寄, 隨函封入: *He enclosed a letter with the book which he sent to me.* 他隨書附寄一封信給我. **enclosure** [in'klouʒə*] *nc* **1** space surrounded by a wall etc. 圈地, 圈佔地. **2** something sent with a letter 隨信附寄物.

encore ['ɔŋkɔ:*] *nc* piece of music, song etc which is extra to the programme of a concert etc given because the audience has liked the concert very much (由於聽衆喜愛而)加唱的歌曲,

加演的節目. Also 亦作 *interj* call by the audience for an extra piece of music or song (聽衆用語)再來一個!

encounter [in'kauntə*] *vt* meet 遇到; *I encountered some difficulty in finishing the work.* 在完成這項工作中我遇到了某種困難. Also 亦作 *nc* **1** meeting 遇見. **2** battle or fight 遭遇戰.

encourage [in'kʌridʒ] *vt* give hope or confidence to 鼓勵, 激勵; 慫恿: *My success encouraged me to continue.* 成功激勵我繼續下去. *I encouraged him to buy the house* i.e. I told him that it would be a good idea for him to buy the house. 我慫恿他買房子. 即: 我告訴他買房子是個好主意. (*opp* 反義詞 **discourage**). **encouraging** *adj* giving hope or confidence 激勵的, 鼓勵的. **encouragement** *nc / u.*

encroach [in'krəutʃ] *vi* (with **on** or **upon**) go beyond the usual or proper limits (與 on 或 upon 連用)侵佔, 侵犯: *He encroached upon my land* i.e. he used my land without permission. 他侵佔了我的土地. 即: 他未經同意就使用了我的土地.

encumber [in'kʌmbə*] *vt* prevent free and easy movement 妨礙; 阻礙; 拖累: *His heavy clothes encumbered him.* 他那一身沉重的衣服妨礙了他的行動. **encumbrance** [in'kʌmbrns] *nc* something which encumbers 妨礙物.

encyclopaedia, encyclopedia [ensaik-lou'pi:diə] *nc* book or set of books containing information on all subjects or on one particular subject 百科全書; 專科全書.

end [end] *nc* **1** last part; furthest point 末端, 盡頭: *the end of the year* i.e. December 年終, 即十二月. *the end of the road* i.e. where the road stops 路的盡頭; *the two ends of a piece of string* 一條繩子的兩頭. **2** aim or object 目標. Also 亦作 *vt / i* have, cause to have an end (使) 終結, (使) 終止: *The road ends five miles from here.* 這條路的盡頭離此地五英里. *He ended his story.* 他講完了故事. **endless** *adj* without end 不盡的. **ending** *nc* **1** last part (esp. of a story) (尤指故事的) 最後部份, 結尾, 結局. *This novel has a happy ending.* 這本小說有個大團圓的結局. **2** letters added to a word to change its grammatical use (e.g. -s, -ed, -ing) 詞尾 (例如 -s, -ed, -ing). **'end 'product** thing which is produced by some industrial or scientific process 最後產品, 製成品. **end up** reach an end; finally come to somewhere 結束; 最終成爲; 最終到達: *He tried several different jobs, and he ended up as a lawyer.* 他試做過一些不同的工作, 最終成爲一名律師. *We walked through the forest for three hours and ended up where we had started.* 我們花了三小時穿過森林, 最終卻回到了原處. **in the end** finally 最終, 最後: *He bought the house in the end.* i.e. after having doubts about whether to buy it, or after having difficulties in doing so. 他最終買下了這所房子. 即: 對買與不買進行一番考慮之後或在買房子方面遇到困難之後. **at a loose end** not having anything to do; not knowing how to pass the time. *(informal)* 無事可做; 不知如何度過時光 (非正式). **on end 1** resting or standing on one end, instead of in the usual position 豎着: *He put the table on end* i.e. resting on two legs and the end of the top, instead of on its four legs. 他把桌子豎着放. 即: 把桌子豎着兩條桌腿和桌面的一邊豎着. **2** without stopping or without an interval 不停地; 連續地: *for six weeks on* *end* 連續六週; *for days on end* i.e. for many days 一連數日.

endanger [en'deindʒə*] *vt* put in danger, make it possible that harm or damage will be caused 使處於危險之中; 危害, 危及: *He endangered our lives by setting fire to the house.* 他放火燒房危害我們的性命. *He endangered his chances of success* i.e. he made it possible that he would not succeed 他損害了自己成功的機會. 即: 他已不可能成功.

endearing [in'diəriŋ] *adj* causing people to like one 惹人愛的, 可愛的.

endeavour [en'devə*] *vt* try very hard 竭力, 盡力: *He endeavoured to finish the work.* 他竭盡全力完成工作. Also *nc* act of trying 竭力, 盡力.

endorse, indorse [in'dɔ:s] *vt* 1 support 贊同: *I endorsed his plan* i.e. I said that I liked the plan. 我贊同他的計劃. 2 (with reference to a cheque or other document) write one's name on the back of a document, to show that one accepts the document as genuine 簽名於(支票或其他文件)背面(以示認可). **endorsement** *nc* / *u*.

endow [en'dau] *vt* give money to a college, school, library, museum etc. 捐款給(學校、圖書館、博物館等).

endure [en'djuə*] *vt* / *i* 1 suffer pain bravely 忍耐, 忍受: *He endured great pain in hospital.* 他住院治療時忍受了巨大的疼痛. 2 last, continue to exist 持續, 持久. **endurance** *nu*. **enduring** *adj* lasting a long time 持久的. **endurable** *adj* able to be endured (in sense 1) 可以忍受的, 可以忍耐的. (*opp* 反義詞 **unendurable**).

enemy ['enəmi] *nc* 1 person, country etc that one hates and which one fights against 敵人; 敵國; 敵方. 2 anything which is harmful or damaging 有害物. **the enemy** *n* *sing* or *pl* country which one is fighting against; the soldiers of that country (單數或複數)敵國; 敵軍.

energy ['enədʒi] *nu* 1 ability to work, play etc hard 幹勁, 精力; 能力: *He had no energy and he could not finish the work.* 他沒有幹勁, 所以完不成工作. 2 power from gas, coal, oil, electricity etc. (由氣體、煤、油、電等產生的)能. 3 (physics) capacity for doing work (物理學)能量. **energetic** [enə'dʒetik] *adj*.

enforce [en'fɔ:s] *vt* 1 cause a law to be carried out 實施(法律), 執行(法律): *The police enforce the law* 警察執法. 2 make somebody do something etc by force 強迫, 迫使: *enforce something on someone* 把某事強加給某人.

engage [en'geidʒ] 1 *vt* allow somebody to begin to work for one 雇用: *I engaged a new servant.* 我雇用了一個新僕人. 2 *vt* reserve something before one wishes to use it 預定, 訂房, 訂座: *I have engaged a room for the party next week.* 我已為下週的聚會預定了一個房間. 3 *vi* (with reference to moving parts of a machine) move and fit together (指機器的移動部份)嚙合, 啣接: *The two wheels engaged.* 這兩個輪子相互嚙合. 4 *vt* begin fighting 與⋯交戰: *We engaged the enemy.* 我們與敵軍交戰. **engaged** *adj* 1 having promised to marry somebody 已訂婚的: *John and Jill are engaged* 約翰與吉爾訂婚了. *the engaged couple* 這對已訂婚的男女. 2 talking to somebody as part of one's work 與人進行工作談話的: *The headmaster is engaged at the moment.* 校長眼下正忙着和人談話. 3 (with reference to a telephone) connected to another telephone (指電話)佔線的: *I phoned John last night* *but the number was engaged* i.e. he was already phoning somebody else. 昨晚我打電話給約翰, 但是他的電話佔線了. 即: 他當時正同別人電話交談. **4** (with reference to a toilet etc) being used (指厠所等)有人用的. **engagement** *nc* **1** promise (esp. a promise to marry) 許諾(尤指訂婚). **2** battle 交戰. **engaging** *adj* pleasant and attractive 美麗動人的: *a very engaging young woman* 一位非常美麗動人的少婦. **be engaged in something** be busy doing something 忙於做某事: *He was engaged in painting his house.* 他忙於粉刷自己的房子.

engender [en'dʒendə] *vt* cause or produce 導致, 產生: *The meeting engendered several quarrels.* 這次會議發生了幾次爭吵.

engine ['endʒin] *nc* machine for producing power (esp. one which works a motorcar or which pulls a train) 發動機; 機車. **engineer** [endʒi'niə*] *nc* **1** person who works with engines or on the building of bridges, ships, roads, machines etc. 工程師. **2** man in charge of the engines of a ship (船上的)輪機手. **3** (*US*) person who drives a train (美)火車司機. (*Brit* 英 **engine driver**). **engineering** [endʒi'niəriŋ] *nu* the making of bridges, ships, roads, machines etc. 工程.

engrave [en'greiv] *vt* cut words, a pattern or a drawing into metal or stone 雕刻, 刻: *He engraved my name on the silver plate.* 他在銀盤子上刻上我的名字. *He engraved the silver plate with my name.* 他把我的名字刻在銀盤子上. **engraving** **1** *nu* the art of engraving 雕刻術. **2** *nc* picture printed from an engraved piece of metal 金屬版畫.

engross [en'grous] *vt* (often *passive*)

occupy, hold somebody's attention or interest completely (常用被動語態)使全神貫注於, 使專注於: *He was engrossed in a book.* 他埋頭看一本書.

engulf [en'gʌlf] *vt* swallow up; cover completely and destroy 吞沒, 吞噬: *The little boat was engulfed by the waves.* 小船被波浪吞沒了.

enhance [en'hɑːns] *vt* add to the value or beauty of 增加…的價值; 增加…的美.

enigma [e'nigmə] *nc* **1** statement or question that is intended to be difficult to understand 謎, 有意使人費解的話或問題. **2** anything or anybody that is difficult to understand 難解的事物或人. **enigmatic** [enig'mætik] *adj.*

enjoy [en'dʒɔi] *vt* **1** be happy because of something 享受, 欣賞: *He enjoyed the film.* 他欣賞這部影片. **2** be fortunate in having something 享有, 享用: *He enjoys good health.* 他有一個健康的身體. **enjoyable** *adj* pleasant; making one happy 悅人的; 令人愉快的. **enjoyment** *nc/u* **enjoy oneself** be happy doing something (做某事)很開心, 很快活.

enlarge [en'lɑːdʒ] *vt/i* become or make larger or bigger 擴大, 擴展. **enlargement** *nc/u.*

enlighten [en'laitn] *vt* give more knowledge or help in understanding 教導, 開導. **enlightened** *adj* intelligent and not following untrue ideas 開明的, 有知識的; 有見識的. (*opp* 反義詞 **unenlightened**.)

enlist [en'list] **1** *vt/i* join, cause to join, the army, navy etc. (使)入伍, (使)參軍: *He enlisted in the army.* 他參軍了. *The government enlisted him* 政府徵募他入伍. **2** *vt* get help or support 獲得(幫助或支持).

enmity ['enmiti] *nu* feeling of hate or

enormity [i'nɔ:miti] **1** *nc* very great and wicked crime 暴行；大罪行. **2** *nu* great wickedness 極惡；兇惡.

enormous [i'nɔ:məs] *adj* very big 極大的，巨大的. **enormously** *adv*.

enough [e'nʌf] *determiner / adj / adv / pron* as much or as many as wanted 足夠的；足夠地；充分地；足夠: I haven't enough money to buy a new car i.e. I need more money. 我沒有足夠的錢買一輛新車. 即: 我需要更多的錢. Have you got enough time to finish it / time enough to finish it? 你有足夠的時間來完成這事嗎? He didn't work hard enough and so he failed the examination. 他學習不夠努力，因此考試不及格. Have you got enough or do you want some more? 你夠了嗎或者你想再多要一點嗎?

enquire [en'kwaiə*] *vt / i* see 見 **inquire.**

enrage [en'reidʒ] *vt* make very angry. 使暴怒.

enrich [en'ritʃ] *vt* **1** make richer 使更豐富，使更富裕. **2** make more valuable 使更有價值，改進.

enrol [en'roul] *vt / i* have one's name written on a list, or write somebody's name on a list (使) 註册，(使) 登記: I enrolled at the college i.e. I became a student at the college. 我在這所學院註册. 即: 我成了這所學院的學生. He enrolled me at the college. 他讓我在該學院註册入學. *past* 過去式 和過去分詞 **enrolled. enrolment** *nc / u*.

en route [ɑ:'ru:t] *adv* on the way 在途中: He was en route for Oxford 他正在前往牛津的途中.

ensign ['ensain] *nc* **1** flag (esp. on a ship) 旗幟 (尤指艦旗). **2** officer of the lowest rank in the US navy (美) 海軍少尉. **3** formerly, officer of the lowest rank in the British army (以前英國陸軍中的) 少尉.

enslave [en'sleiv] *vt* make a slave of 奴役，使成爲奴隸.

ensue [en'sju:] *vi* happen as a result 因而發生: What ensued from your conversation with John? 在你和約翰談話之後發生了甚麼事? **ensuing** *adj*.

ensure [in'ʃuə*] *vt* make sure or certain 確定；保證: I tried to ensure that everybody understood the instructions. 我想確保大家都明白這些指示.

entail [en'teil] *vt* make necessary as a result 因而需要: He bought a bigger house and this entailed buying more furniture. 他買了一座更大的房子，因此需要多買些像具.

entente [ɑ:n'tɑ:nt] *nc / u* **1** understanding or agreement as between nations (如國家之間的) 諒解；協議；協定；協約: Two powerful groups are ... to fix the basis for an entente. 兩大集團…將商定協議的基礎. **2** parties to an understanding; governments that have made an agreement 達成諒解的各方；有協定關係的各國政府: the Entente (countries) (第一次世界大戰時的) 協約國.

enter ['entə*] **1** *vt / i* come or go into 進入，走進: He entered the house. 他走進那座房子. **2** *vt* become or cause to take part in something 加入，使参加: He entered the school. 他入學了. The teacher entered the boy for the examination. 教師讓那個男生參加考試. **3** *vt* put down in written form in a book, list etc. 記錄，登記: He entered all his expenses in a notebook 他把自己的所有費用記在筆記本裏. see 見 **entrance[1], entrant** and **entry. enter into something 1** be part of something or join in something 成爲…的部

份; 參加(某事): *He entered into a discussion with us.* 他參加我們的討論. **2** talk about something 談論(某事): *He entered into an explanation.* 他進行解釋. **enter upon something** begin something 開始(某事).

enterprise ['entəpraiz] **1** *nu* ability to think of new plans and to carry them out 創業之能力. **2** *nc* (often business) new plan or arrangement (常指業務) 新計劃, 新安排. **enterprising** *adj* showing enterprise 顯示創業能力的.

entertain [entə'tein] **1** *vt* interest and amuse 使覺得有趣, 給…助興: *He entertained us by singing songs.* 他唱歌給我們助興. **2** *vt/i* act as a host; give food and drink to guests 作東; 款待, 招待, 請客: *We entertained him to dinner.* 我們以晚宴款待他. *We do not entertain very much* i.e. we do not invite people to eat with us. 我們不常請客. 即: 我們一般不邀他人與我們一道吃飯. **entertaining** *adj* interesting and amusing 有趣的. **entertainment** *nc/u.*

enthusiasm [in'θju:ziæzəm] *nu* feeling of strong interest and support 熱心, 熱情: *The Prime Minister's supporters were filled with enthusiasm.* 首相的支持者熱情滿腔. **enthusiastic** [inθju:-zi'æstik] *adj* (*opp* 反義詞 **unenthusiastic**) showing enthusiasm. **enthusiast** *nc* person who feels enthusiasm 熱心人, 熱衷者.

entice [in'tais] *vt* persuade to go to / from something or to do something bad 慫恿, 誘惑: *He enticed the dog into the house by offering it some meat.* 他用一些肉把狗引進屋裏. *He enticed her into breaking her promise.* 他慫恿她食言.

entire [en'taiə*] *adj* complete or whole 完全的, 全部的: *He spent the entire day in his room* i.e. he did not leave

his room during the day. 他在房間裏過了一整天. 即他當天沒有離開房間.

entirely *adv* **entirety** *nu* condition of being whole or entire 全部, 完整: *in its entirety* 作爲一個整體; 全面地.

entitle [en'taitl] *vt* **1** give somebody a right to something 使有…的權利: *Every child in Britain is entitled to free education at school.* 在英國每個孩子都有免費上學的權利. **2** give a title to a book or other piece of writing 給(書或其他作品)定名.

entity ['entiti] *nc* anything which exists 實在, 實體.

entourage [ɔntu'rɑ:ʒ] *nc* people who accompany some important person 隨從.

entrails ['entreilz] *npl* bowels and intestines; the contents of the lower part of the body 肚腸, 內臟.

entrance[1] ['entrns] **1** *nc / u* act of coming in 進入. **2** *nc* place where one comes in 入口. **3** *nc / u* act of becoming a member of something 加入. see 見 **enter**.

entrance[2] [en'trɑ:ns] *vt* fill with very great pleasure 使狂喜. **entrancing** *adj.*

entrant ['entrnt] *nc* person wishing to join the army, start a job, take part in an examination or a race etc. 想參軍者; 就業者; 想參加考試或競賽等的人. see 見 **enter**.

entrepôt ['ɔntrəpou] *nc* **1** place where goods are stored; warehouse 倉庫; 貨棧. **2** place where goods are sent for distribution; commercial centre 貨物集散地; 商業中心. *Antwerp ... had now become the principal entrepôt ... of Europe.* 安特衛普…現在已成爲歐洲的…主要貿易港口.

entrepreneur [ɔntrəprə'nə:] *nc* person who organizes a business undertaking, assuming the risk for the sake of profit 企業家; 創業者.

entrust [in'trʌst] *vt* give something to somebody to be cared for 委託, 託付: *I entrusted him with my money.* 我委託他代我管我的錢. *I entrusted my money to him.* 我把自己的錢託付給他.

entry ['entri] **1** *nc* act of coming in 進入: *He made an entry into the room.* 他進入房間. **2** *nc* place where one enters 入口. **3** *nu* act of becoming a member of something 加入: *He applied for entry to the university.* 他申請進大學學習. **4** *nc* something written down in a book, list etc. 記錄, 登記: *He made an entry in his notebook.* 他在筆記本裏作記錄. see 見 **enter.**

enunciate [i'nʌnsieit] *vt / i* speak clearly 清楚地說.

envelop [en'veləp] *vt* surround or cover completely 包圍, 籠罩; 包住: *Smoke from the burning house enveloped the whole street.* 燃燒着的房子冒出的濃烟籠罩了整條街.

envelope ['envəloup] *nc* paper cover for a letter 信封.

envious ['enviəs] *adj* see 見 **envy.**

environment [in'vaiərnmənt] *nc* surroundings, people, way of life, circumstances etc in which a person lives 週圍的狀況; (生活) 環境.

envisage [in'vizidʒ] *vt* see a picture of something in the mind; think possible 想像; 設想: *I can't envisage him doing such a terrible thing.* 我無法想像他會做出如此可怕的事來.

envoy ['envɔi] *nc* person representing his government in a foreign country 使節.

envy ['envi] *nu* feeling of unhappiness because somebody is luckier or better

than oneself 忌妒; 羨慕: Also 亦作 *vt* feel envy 忌妒: *I envy him.* 我忌妒他. **envious** *adj* feeling envy 妒忌的. **enviable** *adj* causing envy 令人忌妒的, 值得羨慕的.

enzyme ['enzaim] *nc* substance, produced by living cells, that affects the speed of chemical changes without itself permanently changing 酶: *digestive enzyme* 消化酶; *induced enzyme* 引導酶.

ephemeral [i'femərl] *adj* lasting a very short time 短暫的.

epic ['epik] *nc* long poem about the acts of heroes or gods (關於英雄或神的事蹟的) 長詩, 史詩. Also 亦作 *adj.*

epidemic [,epi'demik] *nc* disease which affects many people at one time 流行性傳染病, 時疫.

epidermal [,epi'dəːməl] **epidermic** [,epi'dəːmik] *adj* of or having to do with epidermis 表皮的, 外皮的.

epidermis [,epi'dəːmis] *nu* outer layer of the skin 外皮; 表皮 (層).

epigram ['epigræm] *nc* short, clever and usu. amusing statement or poem 警句; 諷刺短詩.

epilepsy ['epilepsi] *nu* disease in which a person sometimes loses consciousness and his body moves violently 癲癇症. **epileptic** [epi'leptik] *nc* person suffering from this disease 癲癇病人. Also 亦作 *adj.*

epilogue ['epilɔg] *nc* part of a poem, play, book etc added after the end (詩、戲劇、書本的) 結語, 尾聲, 收場白, 跋.

episode ['episoud] *nc* **1** one part of a story (esp. a story told over several weeks on radio or television) 故事的一段 (尤指電台或電視台數週連播的一段故事). **2** one event out of a series of events 一連串事件之一.

epistle ['ipisl] *nc* letter (*o.f.* esp. with reference to the letters written by the Apostles of Christ in the New Testament) 書信(舊式—尤指新約全書裏耶穌使徒們所寫的書信).

epitaph ['epitɑːf] *nc* words about a dead person (esp. words written on the stone above his grave) 墓誌銘.

epitome [i'pitəmi] *nc* example which is typical of a group or quality 縮影, 典型: *The epitome of laziness.* 懶惰的典型. **epitomize** [i'pitəmaiz] *vt* make or be an epitome of something 成為…的典型; 是…的縮影.

epoch ['iːpɔk] *nc* **1** an important period of history 重要歷史時期. **2** beginning of a period of history 新紀元, 轉折點.

equable ['ekwəbl] *adj* pleasant and not changing much 溫和的, 宜人的, 穩定的, 均勻的: *an equable person / climate* 性情温和的人／宜人的氣候.

equal ['iːkwl] *adj* the same 相同的, 相等的: *Two and two is equal to four.* 二加二等於四. *These two things are not equal* i.e. one is bigger than the other. 這兩個東西不相等. 即: 一個比另一個大. (*opp* 反義詞 **unequal**). Also 亦作 *vt* be equal to; be as good as 等於; 與…一樣: *Two and two equals four.* 二加二等於四. *past* 過去式和過去分詞 **equalled.** (*US* 美 **equaled**). Also 亦作 *nc* something which is equal to something else 相等物; 同等的人: *He is my equal* i.e. he is as strong, clever, rich etc as I am. 他和我同等, 即: 他和我一樣强壯、聰明、富有等. **equally** *adv* **equality** [i'kwɔliti] *nu* (*opp* 反義詞 **inequality**). **equalize** *vt* make equal 使相等.

equate [i'kweit] *vt* consider of the same importance or value 認為…具有同等重要性或價值; 使…相等: *She equates cruelty to animals with cruelty to peo-*

ple. 她把對動物的殘忍行為與對人的殘忍行為相提並論. **equation** [i'kweiʒən] *nc* (mathematics) an expression in which two quantities are said to be equal (數學)方程式, 等式.

equator [i'kweitə*] *nc* an imaginary line drawn round the earth, at an equal distance from north and south 赤道. **equatorial** [ekwətɔːriəl] *adj.*

equilibrium [iːkwi'libriəm] *nu* state of balance, mental or physical (身體或心理的)平衡.

equinox ['iːkwinɔks] *nc* one of the two times in the year when the sun seems to cross the equator and when all over the world night and day are each 12 hours long 晝夜平分時, 春分, 秋分.

equip [i'kwip] *vt* supply what is needed for some action (e.g. fighting, climbing etc.) 裝備. (例如為了戰鬥、登山等): *The government equipped the soldiers with new guns.* 政府用新槍裝備這些士兵. *past* 過去式和過去分詞 **equipped. equipment** *nu* things needed to do something 裝備, 設備: *His firm supplies kitchen equipment.* 他的公司供應廚房設備.

equity ['ekwiti] *nu* fairness; process of not treating somebody better than somebody else 公平; 公正. **equitable** *adj.*

equivalent [i'kwivələnt] *adj* having the same value or meaning 等值的; 等義的; 相等的; 同等的: *His behaviour was equivalent to treason.* 他的行為等於叛逆.

era ['iərə] *nc* period of time in history (usu. named by some happening or person) 時代 (通常以某個事件或人物命名): *the Victorian era* i.e. in the reign of Queen Victoria 維多利亞時代, 即: 在維多利亞女王統治時期.

eradicate [i'rædikeit] *vt* destroy, re

move completely; tear out by the roots 摧毀, 完全除去; 根除: *eradicate a bad habit* 根除壞習慣.

erase [i'reiz] *vt* rub out or remove 擦掉, 抹去: *Pencil marks can be erased with a piece of rubber.* 鉛筆筆跡可用橡皮擦掉. *He tried to erase the idea from his mind.* 他想從心裏抹去這種想法. **eraser** *nc* piece of rubber etc used to erase writing etc. 橡皮擦.

erect [i'rekt] *adj* standing up straight; not bending 直立的; 直的. Also 亦作 *vt* build; put up 建立; 竪起: *erect a building* 建一座大厦. **erection** *nc / u*.

erode [i'roud] *vt* wear away; destroy by taking away small pieces 侵蝕; 腐蝕: *The sea erodes the rocks.* 海水侵蝕岩石. **erosion** [i'rouʒən] *nu.*

err [ə:*] *vi* be wrong; do something wrong 犯錯誤; 做錯事.

errand ['ernd] *nc* journey to a shop to buy something 到商店買東西的短程差事, 跑腿. **'errand boy** employed by a shop to take goods to people's houses (商店裏的) 送貨僮僕.

erratic [i'rætik] *adj* not regular; not always behaving in the same way, and changing without good reason 反覆無常的, 怪癖的.

error ['erə*] *nc / u* mistake; something which is wrong 錯誤; 謬誤: *He made some errors in his essay.* 他的論文裏有幾處錯誤. **erroneous** [e'rouniəs] *adj* mistaken; wrong 錯誤的: *an erroneous belief* 錯誤的信念.

erudite ['erjudait] *adj* showing or having great learning 博學的, 飽學的: *an erudite professor* 博學的教授. **erudition** [erju'diʃən] *nu* great knowledge 淵博的知識.

erupt [i'rʌpt] *vi* burst out suddenly 迸發, 爆發: *The volcano erupted.* 火山爆發. **eruption** *nc / u.*

escalate ['eskəleit] *vt / i* grow bigger by stages; become or make more serious or more dangerous 升級; 擴大; (物價) 上漲; (使) 變得越發嚴重; (使) 變得越發危險: *The war has escalated.* 這場戰爭已經升級.

escalator ['eskəleitə*] *nc* staircase which moves up or down on an endless belt 自動梯.

escapade [eskə'peid] *nc* an exciting and rather foolish adventure (e.g. one carried out by young boys) 惡作劇.

escape [is'keip] *vt / i* get free from or remain free from 逃脫; 逃避; 漏出, 逸出: *The prisoners escaped.* 囚犯們逃走了. *He escaped capture.* 他沒被抓住. *He escaped from prison.* 他越獄逃走了. *The gas was escaping from the pipe.* 氣體正從管道中逸出. **2** be unknown or unnoticed 被忽略, 不爲…所知, 不爲…所注意: *He escaped notice* i.e. nobody saw him. 他沒有被人看到. *The word escapes me* i.e. **1** cannot remember the word. 我記不起這個詞. Also 亦作 *nc / u: He made an escape.* 他逃跑了. *Escape was difficult.* 逃跑是很困難的. *There was an escape of gas.* 有氣體逸出. **a narrow escape** an escape with little to spare 僥倖逃脫: *He had a narrow escape from being drowned* i.e. he was nearly drowned. 他差一點就淹死了.

escarp [is'ka:p] *vt* make into a steep slope; give a steep slope 把…築成陡坡, 使成陡坡. Also 亦作 *nc* see 見 **escarpment.**

escarpment [is'ka:pmənt] *nc* **1** deep slope; cliff 陡坡; 懸崖; 峭壁. **2** ground made into a steep slope as part of a fortification 城堡防禦土牆的陡坡.

escort [is'ko:t] *vt* go with somebody / something as a guard or protector 護送: *The soldiers escorted the old man*

to safety. 士兵們護送老人到安全地帶.
Also 亦作 ['eskɔːt] nc person / companion
(often in ships, cars, aeroplanes etc)
going with somebody / something as a
guard or companion 護送者, 護衛隊.

especial [es'peʃl] adj special; more
important than others 特別的; 出衆的.
especially adv most of all; particularly 尤其; 特別地: I like all of Dickens's
novels but especially 'Bleak House' i.e.
this is the one I like best. 我喜歡狄更
斯所有的小說, 但尤其喜歡他的《荒凉山
莊》. 即: 這本書是我最喜歡的.

espionage ['espiənaːʒ] nu process of
trying to find out the secrets of a
foreign country, in order to help one's
own country 間諜活動.

esplanade [esplə'neid] nc level open
space where people can walk (usu.
beside the sea or in front of a castle)
(通常指海濱或城堡前供人散步的)廣
場.

esquire [es'kwaiə*] title written after a
man's name in addressing letters etc,
written Esq. (e.g. J. L. Smith, Esq.) 寫
信時用在男人名字之後的稱呼, 寫作
Esq. (例如 J. L. Smith, Esq. J. L. 史密
斯先生). Note 說明: Esq. is rather
formal. It is not used in America, or
with any other title. Esq. 相當正式. 它
不在美國使用, 也不與其他稱呼連用.

essay ['esei] nc short piece of writing
on one subject 論文, 散文.

essence ['esns] nc 1 something
obtained from a substance by removing everything which is unnecessary
精華. 2 the central or most important
part of anything 本質, 精髓: Freedom
of speech is the essence of democracy.
言論自由是民主的精髓. **essential**
[i'senʃl] adj 1 very important and
necessary 重要的; 必不可少的: It is
essential to have enough money. 有足

夠的錢是萬分必要的. 2 of an essence
精華的, 精髓的: an essential oil 香精
油, 揮發油. Also 亦作 nc something
which is essential 必需品. **essential-
ly** adv.

establish [es'tæbliʃ] vt 1 organize; begin; set up 組織; 開始; 建立: He established a new shop. 他新開了一家商
店. He has established himself in his
new house i.e. he has arranged his
furniture and made everything comfortable. 他在新房子裏爲自己安排好了
一切. 即: 他已經安置好傢具並把一切
都安排得很舒適. 2 prove; show
something to be true 證明; 證實: The
police are trying to establish the facts.
警方想證實這些事實. **establishment**
1 nu process of establishing 創辦; 建
立; 設立; 確定: 2 nc anything established (esp. a house, shop, factory
etc.) 建立物(尤指房子, 商店, 工廠等).
the establishment group of important people who are believed to have
great influence on public life (esp. in
Britain) 當權派(尤用於英國).

estate [es'teit] nc 1 large area of land
belonging to a person 地産. 2 (legal)
a person's property (法律)個人財産.
estate agent person who arranges
the buying and selling of houses and
land 房地産經紀人, 房地産掮客. 'real
estate (in a legal sense) land and the
buildings etc on it (法律用語)房地
産.

esteem [es'tiːm] nu feeling that somebody is very good and deserves to be
praised 尊敬, 尊重: They hold him in
high esteem. 他們十分尊重他.

esthetic [is'θetik] adj see 見 **aesthetic.**

estimate ['estimeit] vt / i judge a size,
amount, quantity etc without measuring or weighing 估計, 評定. Also 亦作
['estimit] nc 1 judgment or guess

made in this way 估計, 評定. **2** statement of how much some work or service will probably cost, made by the person who will do the work. (The actual cost may be more or less than the estimate) 費用估算, 預算. **estimation** [estiˈmeiʃən] **1** *nc* estimate 估計; 估算. **2** *nu* feeling that somebody is very good 尊敬, 尊重: *a high estimation for him.* 對他十分尊敬. **3** *nu* judgment or opinion 判斷; 意見: *In my estimation, we shall not be successful* i.e. I do not think we shall be successful. 據我看, 我們不會成功.

estuary [ˈestjuəri] *nc* part of a river reached by tides 河口.

et cetera [itˈsetrə] (usu. written *etc.*) and other things (通常寫作 etc.) 等等.

eternal [iˈtəːnl] *adj* lasting for ever; having no beginning and no end 永恆的; 無窮的. **eternally** *adv* **eternity** [iˈtəː-niti] *nc / u*.

ethane [ˈeθein] *nu* odourless, colourless hydrocarbon, found in natural gas etc and used as a fuel 乙烷(存在於天然氣等中, 用作燃料): *ethane acid* 醋(乙)酸.

ethanol [ˈeθənɔl] *nu* colourless liquid that vaporizes readily, is the intoxicating agent in beer, wine, etc and is also used as a solvent-called also alcohol, ethyl alcohol 乙醇.

ether [ˈiːθə*] *nu* liquid which causes one to become unconscious when its vapour is breathed in 醚(麻醉劑).

ethics [ˈeθiks] *n sing* or *pl* 單數或複數 study or knowledge of what is right and wrong; ideas and beliefs about the right or good way to behave 倫理學; 倫理, 道德規範. **ethical** *adj* good, correct in thought or behaviour (思想或行為) 符合倫理的, 道德的. (*opp* 反義詞 **unethical**).

ethnic [ˈeθnik] *adj* with reference to a race or nation 種族的, 民族的: *There are many ethnic groups in New York* i.e. there are Italians, Poles, Irishmen, Swedes etc. 在紐約有許多種族集團. 即: 有意大利人、波蘭人、愛爾蘭人、瑞典人等.

ethyl [ˈeθil, ˈiːθail] *nu* univalent radical present in many organic chemical compounds; ordinary alcohol contains ethyl 乙基, 乙烷基.

ethylene [ˈeθiliːn] *nu* flammable; gaseous hydrocarbon used as a fuel, anaesthetic, etc. 乙烯; 乙撑; 次乙基(用作燃料, 麻醉劑等).

etiquette [ˈetiket] *nu* ideas about what is polite; polite behaviour 禮節; 禮儀; 禮貌的舉止.

Eucharist [ˈjuːkərist] *nc / u* ceremony of taking bread and wine in memory of the death of Christ; the bread and wine itself 聖餐儀式; 聖餐時食用的麵包和酒.

eulogy [ˈjuːlədʒi] *nc* speech or piece of writing in praise of somebody / something 頌詞, 頌文. *pl* 複數 **eulogies.**

euphemism [ˈjuːfəmizəm] *nc / u* practice of using a more pleasant word or expression for an unpleasant idea (e.g. *pass away* is a euphemism for *die*) 婉言, 委婉的說法(如 pass away 是 die 的委婉語).

euphoria [juːˈfɔːriə] *nu* state of feeling great happiness 幸福感, 非常快樂. **euphoric** [juːˈfɔrik] *adj*.

European [juərəˈpiːən] *nc* native of Europe 歐洲人. Also 亦作 *adj* of Europe 歐洲的. **European Economic Community** economic union of various European countries including France, Italy, Germany, Britain etc. 歐洲經濟共同體.

evacuate [iˈvækjueit] *vt* send away or

send out; leave, withdraw from 疏散；
撤離: *During the war, many people
were evacuated from the city* i.e. sent
to live out of the city 戰爭期間，許多
人被疏散撤離該市. 即: 被送到該市之外
的地方居住. **evacuation** [iˌvækjuˈei-
ʃən] *nc / u.*

evade [iˈveid] *vt* escape; get away from
or keep away from 逃避；避開；避躲:
*The thief evaded the policeman who
was chasing him.* 小偷避開追捕他的警
察. *He tried to evade his duties.* 他想
逃避責任. **evasion** [iˈveiʒən] *nc / u*
evasive [iˈveisiv] *adj* trying to evade
something 逃避的，迴避的: *He gave
an evasive answer* i.e. he tried to
avoid telling the truth. 他的答覆含糊
其詞. 即: 他不想說實話.

evaluate [iˈvæljueit] *vt* decide the value
of something 評價，估計.

evangelist [iˈvændʒəlist] *nc* **1** one of
the writers of the Gospels in the Bible
i.e. Matthew, Mark, Luke, John 四福音
書(馬太, 馬可, 路加, 約翰)的作者之一.
2 person who teaches a type of Protestant Christianity in which the most
important belief is faith 福音傳教士.
evangelical [iˌvænˈdʒelikl] *adj.*

evaporate [iˈvæpəreit] *vt / i* (with reference to a liquid) change, cause to
change, into vapour (使) 蒸發. **evaporation** [iˌvæpəˈreiʃən] *nu* **evapo-
rated milk** type of milk from which
some of the water has been removed
煉乳.

evasion [iˈveiʒən] *nc / u* see **evade**.

eve [iːv] *nc* day before (usu. in **Christmas Eve, New Year's Eve**) 前夕 (常
用於 Christmas Eve 聖誕前夕, New
Year's Eve 新年前夕, 除夕).

even[1] [ˈiːvən] *intensifier / adv* to an extreme degree 甚至, 連: *Even now
some people still believe that the*

earth is flat. 甚至現在還有人認爲地球
是平的. *He didn't even try* i.e. one
would have thought that he would try.
but he did not. 他連試都沒試一下. 即:
原以爲他會試試, 可他沒有這麼做. *It
was even more unpleasant than I had
thought it would be* i.e. I had expected
it to be unpleasant, but it was more
unpleasant than I had expected. 這要
比我原來所想的更加令人不快. **even
though** in spite of the fact that 即使
…也: *Even if he comes I shall not see
him.* 即使他來, 我也不會見他. *Even
though you say so, I do not believe it.*
即使你這麼說, 我也不相信.

even[2] [ˈiːvən] *adj* **1** smooth or regular;
having the same quality all over or all
through 平的, 平坦的; 勻稱的; 穩定的:
an even surface i.e. one with no
points higher or lower than the rest
光滑的表面. **2** equal 相等的: *The two
boxers were even in strength and skill*
i.e. one was not stronger or more skilful than the other. 這兩個拳擊手在力
量和技巧方面不分高低. 即: 其中一個並
不比另一個更有力或技巧更高. (*opp*
uneven in senses 1 and 2) (義 1 和
義 2 的反義詞爲 uneven). **3** (with reference to numbers) able to be divided by two (e.g. **2, 4, 6, 8, 10** are
even numbers) (指數字)偶數 (例如2,
4, 6, 8, 10等). (*opp* 反義詞爲 **odd**). Also
亦作 *vt* (often with **up**) make even
(常與 up 連用)使平坦, 使相等. **even-
ly** *adv* **get even with somebody** hurt
or harm somebody who has hurt or
harmed oneself. (*informal*) 跟某人算
賬, 向某人報復. (非正式).

evening [ˈiːvniŋ] *nc / u* time after the
day and before one goes to bed (上床
睡覺前這一段) 夜晚. **'evening dress**
see 見 **dress**[1].

evensong [ˈiːvənsɔŋ] church service

held in the evening in the Church of England 英國國教之晚禱.

event [i'vent] *nc* **1** something which happens (usu. something important or exciting) 事件 (通常是重要或激動人心的事件). **2** race or other item in an athletics contest 比賽項目. **eventful** *adj* full of important or exciting events 充滿重大或激動人心的事件的; *an eventful life* 波瀾起伏的一生. **at all events** whatever happens 無論如何. **in any event** whatever happens 無論如何. *I shall come with you in any event.* 無論如何我都將和你一起來. **in the event of something** if something happens 如果發生了 (某事); *Here is what you must do in the event of my death.* 如果我死了, 那麼這就是你必須做的事.

eventual [i'ventʃuəl] *adj* happening at the end as a result of something 結果的, 最後的. **eventually** *adv: It was a long journey, but we eventually arrived.* 雖然旅途遙遠, 但是我們終於到達了.

ever ['evə'] *adv* **1** at any time 曾, 曾經: *Have you ever been to France?* 你曾去過法國嗎? *Don't you ever take any exercise?* 你不曾進行鍛煉嗎? *He hasn't ever spoken to me.* 他不曾同我說過話. **2** always 總是, 永遠: *He is ever hopeful.* (rather *o.f.* in sense **2**) 他老懷有希望. (義 2 為相當舊式).

'evergreen *nc* tree which does not lose its leaves in winter 常青樹. Also 亦作 *adj.* **ever'lasting** *adj* never dying or never coming to an end 永恆的; *the Everlasting God* 永恆的上帝. **ever after** always after some event 從此以後: *They got married and lived happily ever after.* 他們結了婚, 從此以後幸福地生活着. **hardly ever** not often 不常. **ever since (something)**

always after some event 自從…以來: *I have been worried ever since I lost my money.* 自從我丟了錢以來我一直都在發愁. *I lost my money and I have been worried ever since.* 我丟了錢以後一直都在發愁. **ever so** very 非常: *I am ever so grateful. (informal)* 我非常感激. (非正式).

every ['evri] *determiner* each one 每個: *He talked to every person in the room* 他和房間裏的每個人談話. *I used to see him every day.* 以前我每天都見到他. *Every pupil was present this morning.* 今天早上每個學生都出席. *Take one of these pills every four hours* i.e. there should be four hours between each pill. 每四小時吃一個藥丸. **'everybody** *n sing* each person; all the people 每個人; 大家; 所有人. **every other** alternate (e.g. the first, the third, the fifth etc, or the second, the fourth, the sixth etc.) 每隔一 (例如第一, 第三, 第五等或者第二, 第四, 第六等). **'everyone** *n sing* everybody 每個人, 大家. **'everything** *n sing* each thing; all things 每件事物; 一切事物. **'everywhere** *adv* to / in all places 往／在各處, 到處.

evict [i'vikt] *vt* make a person leave a house or land by means of the law 依法驅逐: *The owner of the house evicted the people who did not pay their rent.* 房東把不付房租的人趕出去. **eviction** *nc / u.*

evidence ['evidns] *nu* facts brought forward to show that something is or is not true (e.g. in a court of law or in a scientific experiment) 證據 (例如出庭或進行科學實驗時提出的).

evident ['evidnt] *adj* easy to see or understand 顯然的, 明顯的, 明白的: *It was evident that he was telling the truth.* 顯然, 他說的是實話. **evidently**

adv.

evil ['i:vil] *adj* very bad in thought or behaviour 邪惡的, 惡毒的. Also 亦作 I *nu* wickedness; condition of being very bad 邪惡; 不幸. **2** *nc* anything very bad. 邪惡的事或物: *War is an evil.* 戰爭是一種邪惡.

evoke [i'vouk] *vt* produce; cause to appear 產生; 引起: *The photograph evoked happy memories* i.e. when we looked at the photograph we remembered the time when we were happy. 這張照片引起了幸福的回憶. 即: 每當我們看到這張照片, 我們就會想起那幸福的時光. *His stories evoked laughter from all of us.* 他講的故事使我們所有的人哈哈大笑. **evocative** [i'vɔkətiv] *adj* causing one to remember something 使人回憶起…的, 激發或喚起…的回憶的.

evolution [i:vəˈlu:ʃən] *nu* (esp. with reference to the development of plants, animals etc from very simple forms of life) process of change and development (尤指動, 植物等的) 進化. see 見 **evolve**.

evolve [i'vɔlv] *vt / i* develop, cause to develop (使) 發展, 形成: *The plan gradually evolved.* 該計劃逐步形成. *They evolved a new plan.* 他們設計了一項新計劃. see 見 **evolution**.

ewe [ju:] *nc* female sheep 母羊.

ex- [eks] *prefix* former (e.g. **ex-president** i.e. a man who used to be president) 先前的 (例如 ex-president 前總統等).

exact[1] [eg'zækt] *adj* without mistakes; correct 準確的; 正確的: *The exact weight is 25.68 kilograms* 準確的重量是25.68公斤. *He did some very exact work* i.e. very careful and correct work. 他幹了些活細緻又準確. (*opp* 反義詞 **inexact**). **exactly** *adv: I gave*

him exactly what he asked for i.e. not more and not less. 我給他的正是他所要的. 即: 不多也不少. *Exactly!* i.e. that's correct. 對! 一點不錯! **exactness** *nu.*

exact[2] [eg'zækt] *vt* I get by use of force 勒索, 強求: *exact money from people* 向人們勒索錢財. **2** need or require 需要; 要求. **exacting** *adj* difficult to please; making great demands 苛求的; 要求嚴格的: *exacting work* i.e. work which needs great care and attention 極費心血的工作.

exaggerate [eg'zædʒəreit] *vt / i* say more than is true (e.g. if one saw thirty cows and one says one saw hundreds of cows. one is exaggerating) 誇大, 誇張. **exaggeration** [egzædʒə-'reiʃən] *nc / u.*

exalt [eg'zɔ:lt] *vt* give a high rank or position to 提拔, 提升: *someone in an exalted position* 已獲提升的某人.

exam [eg'zæm] *nc* examination (in sense 2) *(informal)* 考試(非正式).

examine [eg'zæmin] *vt* I put questions to a student or pupil, in order to test knowledge or give awards 考, 對…進行考試. **2** look at very closely; inspect 審視; 檢查. **examination** [egzæmi'neiʃən] **1** *nu* process of examining 檢查. **2** *nc* formal test of the knowledge of a student or pupil 考試. **examiner** *nc* person who sets the questions in an examination of students or pupils 主考人.

example [ig'zɑ:mpl] *nc* **1** thing which is taken to show what other things of the same kind are like 例證, 範例: *Cows and horses are examples of domestic animals* i.e. we can learn something of the nature of domestic animals if we consider cows and horses. 牛和馬是家畜的例證. 即: 如果

我們對牛和馬加以留意的話，就可以了解到家畜特性的某些方面．**2** person whom one should copy because he has done well 模範，榜樣；**3** problem in arithmetic. 算術題．**for example** to name one or more out of many 例如：*There are many big cities in Europe, for example, London, Paris and Rome.* 歐洲有許多大城市，例如倫敦、巴黎、和羅馬．

exasperate [eg'za:spəreit] *vt* make very angry and impatient 激怒．**exasperation** [egzɑ:spə'reiʃən] *nu* feeling of anger and impatience 惱怒．

excavate ['ekskəveit] *vt / i* dig; make by digging; uncover by digging 挖；挖掘；發掘：*The archaeologists excavated an ancient city.* 考古學家發掘出一座古城．**excavation** [ekskə'veiʃən] **1** *nu* process of digging 挖掘．**2** *nc* hole; place uncovered by digging 洞，窟；發掘地．**excavator** *nc* machine used for digging 挖掘機，挖土機．

exceed [ek'si:d] *vt* be greater or do more than 超過，超出：*Cars must not exceed thirty miles an hour in certain areas* i.e. must not travel faster than this. 在某些地區車速不應超過每小時三十英里．*The result exceeded my expectation* i.e. was greater than I had expected. 結果出乎我的意料．**exceedingly** *adv* very much 非常，極爲．

excel [ek'sel] *vt / i* do something better than other people 優於（他人）；勝過（他人）：*He excels at football.* 他擅長踢足球．*past* 過去式和過去分詞 **excelled. excellent** ['eksəlnt] *adj* very good; of high quality 優秀的；傑出的：*excellent work* 極佳的工作；*an excellent dinner* 豐盛的晚宴．**excellence** *nu* **excellency** ['eksəlnsi] *nc* title of an ambassador, president, governor etc. (usu. addressed as **Your Excel-**lency)* 閣下 (用以稱呼大使、總統、州長等，通常說 Your Excellency）．

except [ek'sept] *prep* not including 除…之外：*I invited everyone except James.* 除詹姆士以外，我每個人都邀請了．**excepting** *prep* not including 除…之外．**exception** *nc* something which is not included 例外．**exceptional** *adj* **1** unusual 異常的．**2** very much better or worse than usual or than others 特別好（或糟）的．(*opp* 反義詞 **unexceptional**). **exceptionally** *adv.*

excerpt ['eksə:pt] *nc* piece of writing, speech or music taken from a longer passage, book. poem, lecture etc. (段落、著作、詩、演講等的）摘錄，摘要，選錄．

excess [ek'ses] *nc* something which is greater in amount than what is normal or proper 過多之物，過量之物：*He has an excess of fluid in his body* i.e. he has too much fluid in his body. 他體液過多．**excessive** *adj* too great in quantity or amount 過多的，多餘的．**excessively** *adv* '**excess 'baggage** baggage or luggage which weighs more than one is allowed to take with one (esp. in an aeroplane), unless one pays extra (尤指乘飛機時的）超重行李．

exchange¹ [eks'tʃeindʒ] *vt / i* give one thing to get another 交換：*John and James exchanged hats* i.e. John took James's hat and James took John's. 約翰和詹姆士互相交換帽子．*James exchanged his hat for John's.* 詹姆士拿自己的帽子換約翰的帽子．**exchange words / blows** quarrel; fight 爭吵；打架．

exchange² [eks'tʃeindʒ] **1** *nc / u* process of exchanging 交換．**2** *nc* central building or office for various special

purposes e.g.: '**labour exchange**
(Brit) former name of the **Employment Services Agency,** a government office where people can go to find work 供多種專門目的的中心大樓或辦公處．例如: labour exchange (英) 原名為 Employment Services Agency, 政府所屬勞工介紹所． **rate of exchange** value of one country's money in the money of another country 國際貨幣兌換率． '**stock exchange** see 見 **stock.** '**telephone exchange** see 見 **telephone.**

exchequer [eks'tʃekə*] *nc* government department having control over money 財政部．

excise¹ ['eksaiz] *nu* tax paid on certain goods manufactured in a country (國產)貨物稅．

excise² [ek'saiz] *vt* (esp. with reference to cutting out a part of the body or a part of something written) cut out or remove 切除(尤指身體某一部份)；割除(尤指文章某一部份)．

excite [ek'sait] *vt* **1** cause strong feelings of interest 使興奮, 使激動: The football match excited all the boys. 這場足球賽使所有的男生都很激動． **2** cause certain other feelings 激起, 激發: excite anger / envy / interest 激怒/引起嫉妒/引起興趣: He was excited by all new ideas. 他爲一切新思想所激勵． **excitement** *nc / u* **excitable** *adj* easily made excited 容易激動的． **excited** *adj* having strong feelings of interest etc. 興奮的, 激動的． **exciting** *adj* causing excitement 令人興奮的, 令人激動的: exciting film / story 激動人心的電影/故事．

exclaim [eks'kleim] *vt / i* say something suddenly and loudly 驚叫, 驚呼． **exclamation** [eksklə'meiʃən] *nc / u* **exclamation mark** the mark! 驚嘆

號"!".

exclude [iks'klu:d] *vt* keep out; prevent from entering 排除; 排斥; 拒絕: I excluded John from the invitation i.e. I did not invite John. 我把拒絕邀請約翰即: 我不邀請約翰． (*opp* 反義詞 **include**).

exclusion [iks'klu:ʒən] *nu* **exclusive** [iks'klu:siv] *adj* **1** welcoming or being friendly to only a few people 不公開的, 不面向大衆的: an exclusive club / school / person 只對少數人公開的俱樂部/不面向社會大衆招生的專設學校/孤僻的人． **2** for one person alone; not shared with others 獨自的; 專用的: the exclusive possession of something 獨自擁有某物． **exclusively** *adv.*

excommunicate [ekskə'mju:nikeit] *vt* (esp. with reference to the Roman Catholic Church) punish somebody by not allowing him to continue as a member of his church (尤指羅馬天主教會)把…逐出教會．

excrete [eks'kri:t] *vt* discharge (waste matter) from the body 排泄; 分泌: The skin excretes sweat. 皮膚出汗．

excretion [eks'kri:ʃən] *nc / u* **1** discharging of waste matter from the body 排泄; 分泌: the excretion of sweat 出汗; the excretion of urine 排尿． **2** waste matter that is discharged 排泄物: Sweat is an excretion. 汗是一種排泄物．

excretory [eks'kri:təri] *adj* excreting; having the function of excreting; of or having to do with excretion or excretions 排泄的; 分泌的; 有排泄功能的; 排泄物的: The kidneys are excretory organ. 腎是排泄器官． No animal can live long with an impairment of its excretory function. 動物如其排泄功能受到損害便不能活長久． Also 亦作 excretory organ or duct 排泄器官; 排

洩導管.

excruciating [eks'kru:ʃieitiŋ] *adj* very painful; causing great suffering 非常痛苦的, 非常難受的: *excruciating pain / torture* 難以忍受的痛苦/折磨.

excursion [eks'kə:ʃən] *nc* journey made for pleasure (esp. one made by several people) (尤指多人結伴的)旅遊.

excuse¹ [eks'kju:s] *nc* reason given for doing something which might be considered bad 借口, 藉口: *He made an excuse for arriving late* i.e. he explained why he was late. 他為遲到找藉口. 即: 他解釋為甚麼遲到.

excuse² [eks'kju:z] *vt* 1 forgive somebody for doing a small wrong 原諒(某人的小錯): *I excused him for coming late* i.e. I did not punish or blame him. 我原諒他的遲到. 即: 我沒有罰他或責備他. 2 allow somebody to be absent from something 允許(某人)缺席: *Will you excuse me from the meeting?* i.e. will you allow me to stay away? 你能否同意我不來開會? **excuse oneself** 1 offer an excuse 請求原諒: *He excused himself for being late.* 因為遲到, 他請求原諒. 2 ask to be allowed to be absent 請求允許缺席: *He excused himself from the meeting* 他請求允許他不來開會. **excuse me** polite expression, used especially when first speaking to a stranger to attract his attention. (客套話, 尤用於首次同陌生人講話以引起其注意)對不起.

execute ['eksikju:t] *vt* 1 punish somebody by killing him after a trial in a court of law 處決, 處死. 2 carry out; do what is necessary 實行; 執行: *execute an order* 執行命令. 3 play a piece of music, make a picture or statue etc. 演奏(音樂); 畫(圖畫); 雕塑等.

execution [eksi'kju:ʃən] 1 *nc / u* legal punishment by killing 依法處決. 2 *nu* carrying out an order etc. 執行命令等. 3 *nu* way in which a piece of music is played 演奏(音樂)的技巧.

executioner [eksi'kju:ʃənə*] *nc* person whose job is to punish criminals by killing them 死刑執行人, 劊子手.

executor [eg'zekjutə*] *nc* person who is named in a will to carry out the wishes of the dead person (遺囑中指定的)遺囑執行人. (*fem* 陰 **executrix** [eg'zekjutriks]). **executive** [eg'zekju-tiv] *nc* person whose work is to organize business firms 經理. Also 亦作 *adj*. **the executive** the part of the government of a country which organizes whatever is required by the laws 行政部門.

exemplary [ig'zempləri] *adj* suitable to be an example 值得模仿的: *John's exemplary behaviour* i.e. John's very good behaviour which ought to be followed by other people 約翰的值得傚效的行為. **exemplify** [ig'zemplifai] *vt* be or make an example 舉例說明, 成為…的例子: *This exemplifies what I mean* i.e. this is an example of what I mean. 這正好作為我所說的一個實例.

exempt [ig'zempt] *adj* not required to do something 不必(做某事)的: *He is exempt from the examination* i.e. he does not have to take the examination and he is considered to have passed it. 他不必參加考試. 即: 他被認為已經通過考試了. Also 亦作 *vt* make somebody exempt 使不必做某事. **exemption** [ig'zempʃən] *nc / u*.

exercise¹ ['eksəsaiz] 1 *nc / u* movements of the body, games etc done for the sake of health 鍛煉, 運動: *Exercise makes one strong.* 鍛煉使人強壯. *He was doing his exercises.* 他正

在鍛煉. **2** *nc* special series of actions and movements done by soldiers etc, to practise fighting in war 演習: *The soldiers were sent into the mountains for three weeks on an exercise.* 士兵們被派遣進山進行為時三週的演習. **3** *nc* series of questions to be answered by pupils or students in order to practise something they have learned 練習, 習題.

exercise² ['eksəsaiz] **1** *vt / i* carry out, cause to carry out, bodily movements for the sake of health (使)鍛煉, (使)運動: *He exercises every morning.* 他每天早晨鍛煉. *He was exercising his dog* i.e. going for a walk with his dog. 他讓狗進行運動. 即: 和狗一道去散步. **2** *vt* use the mind or some quality in some way 運用: *He exercised his intelligence to solve the problem.* 他用智慧解決了這個難題.

exert [ig'zə:t] *vt* use some quality 運用: *exert one's strength* 用力; *exert pressure* 施加壓力. **exertion** *nc / u* use of strength; hard work 用力, 努力: *He was tired after his exertions.* 經過數次努力之後, 他累了. **exert oneself** try hard to do something 努力做某事: *He never exerts himself* i.e. he never works hard. 他從不努力工作.

exeunt ['eksiʌnt] *vi* they go out (written in a play to indicate that several people leave the stage) (舞台指示) (衆人)下場.

exhale [eks'heil] *vt / i* (with reference to a gas) breathe out, come out, cause to come out. (指氣體)呼出; 放出; (使)散發.

exhaust¹ [ig'zɔ:st] *vt* **1** make weak 使衰弱: *The game of football has exhausted me.* 這場足球賽使我精疲力盡. **2** finish completely; use up 耗盡; 用光: *The government has exhausted*

all its money. 政府已經把錢用光了. *We have exhausted the subject of politics* i.e. we have talked about politics so much that we have said everything that can be said. 我們已對政治問題作了詳盡無遺的論述. **exhaustion** *nu* weakness; tiredness 虛弱; 疲憊. **exhaustive** *adj* saying everything that can be said 詳盡論述的: *an exhaustive discussion* 一次詳盡的討論.

exhaust² [ig'zɔ:st] *nc* **1** place for steam, gas, vapour etc to escape from a machine (esp. the pipe at the back of a motorcar) (尤指汽車的)排氣管. **2** steam, gas, vapour etc escaping in this way (排氣管排出之)廢氣.

exhibit [ig'zibit] **1** *vt / i* show publicly in a museum, art gallery etc. 展出, 展覽: *He exhibited his paintings.* 他展出自己的畫. *He often exhibits.* 他常常舉辦展覽會. **2** *vt* show signs of 顯示: *He exhibited fear.* 他露出恐懼的神色. Also 亦作 *nc* something exhibited (esp. in a museum) (尤指博物館中的)展品.

exhibition [eksi'biʃən] *nc* **1** act of exhibiting 展出, 展覽; 顯示. **2** number of objects shown publicly 展覽會; 展覽品. **exhibitor** *nc* person who shows things in a museum etc. 展出者. **exhibitionist** [eksi'biʃənist] *nc* person who behaves in an unusual way in order to make people take notice of him 風頭主義者, 愛出風頭的人.

exhilarate [ig'ziləreit] *vt* fill with a strong feeling of happiness and excitement 使興奮, 使激動. **exhilaration** [igzilə'reiʃən] *nu* **exhilarating** *adj* causing exhilaration 令人興奮的, 令人激動的.

exhort [eg'zɔ:t] *vt* speak to somebody using strong feelings, in order to persuade him to do something 勉勵, 鼓勵: *The general exhorted his soldiers* *to fight bravely.* 將軍勉勵士兵們勇敢戰鬥.

exile ['eksail] *vt* force somebody to leave his own country (often as a punishment) 流放, 放逐. Also 亦作 **1** *nu* condition of being exiled 流放, 放逐: *He was living in exile.* 他過着流放生活. **2** *nc* person who has been exiled 被流放者, 被放逐者.

exist [eg'zist] *vi* be; occur 存在, 生存; 出現: *Wild elephants no longer exist in Europe.* 歐洲不再有野象生存了. **existence** *nu*.

exit ['eksit] *nc* **1** action of leaving (esp. a room or the stage during a play) (尤指在一場戲當中) 退場; 下場: *He made his exit through the window.* 他從窗子出去了. **2** door in a cinema, theatre etc by which one may leave the building (電影院, 劇院等的) 出口. Also 亦作 *vi* he goes out (written in a play to indicate to an actor to leave the stage) (舞台指示) (單人) 下場.

ex officio [ˌeksə'fiʃiou] *adj / adv* (Latin) because of one's office or position (拉丁) 依據官職的 (地); 由於職位, 職位上: *an ex officio member of the committee* 委員會的當然委員; *present at the meeting ex officio* 依據職權出席該會議.

exorbitant [eg'zɔːbitnt] *adj* much dearer than is reasonable 過份的, 過多的, 苛求的: *an exorbitant price* 過高的價格.

exotic [ig'zɔtik] *adj* coming from a foreign country (usu. a distant one) 來自外國的 (通常指遠處的外國).

expand [iks'pænd] *vt / i* become or make large 擴大; (使) 變大; *His business has expanded.* 他的業務擴大了. *He expanded his lungs.* i.e. filled his lungs with air. 他進行深呼吸. 即: 使肺

部充滿了空氣. **expansion** *nu* **expanse** [eks'pæns] *nc* large surface area 廣闊的表面區域.

expatriate [eks'pætriət] *nc* person living in a country which is not his own 居住或流亡國外者. Also 亦作 *adj*.

expect [iks'pekt] *vt* **1** think that something will happen 預期, 預料: *I expect he will come soon.* 我預料他很快就會來. **2** wait for somebody who is coming 期待: *I am expecting the postman; he usually comes at this time.* 我正等着郵遞員; 他通常這個時候來. *She is expecting a baby* i.e. she is pregnant; she is carrying a child inside her body. 她懷孕了. **3** think something to be true or 以為, 認為: *I expect you've forgotten my name.* 我認為你已經忘了我的名字. **expectation** [ekspek-'teiʃən] *nc / u* **expectant** *adj* waiting or expecting 期待的; 預期的: *an expectant mother* 孕婦, 未來的母親.

expedient [eks'piːdiənt] *nc* plan or idea which helps to overcome a difficulty 權宜之計. Also 亦作 *adj* useful to oneself but perhaps not correct or moral 有 (私) 利的, 對己有用的 (但也許不對或不道德): *It would be expedient to help someone with such political influence.* 幫助具有這種政治影響的人物可能是有利的. (*opp* 反義詞 **inexpedient**). **expedience** *nu* **expediency** *nc / u*.

expedite ['ekspidait] *vt* make a plan or arrangement proceed more quickly 使 (計劃或安排) 加速: *He expedited the arrangements.* 他加速進行安排.

expedition [ekspi'diʃən] *nc* **1** journey done for a purpose (有目的之) 遠征, 探險. **2** the people who make such a journey 遠征隊; 探險隊.

expel [eks'pel] *vt* **1** send away from a place (e.g. a school) as a punishment

開除 (出學校等). **2** send out with force 用力推出. *past* 過去式和過去分詞 **expelled. expulsion** [eks'pʌlʃən] *nc / u.*

expend [eks'pend] *vt* use up 用光, 耗盡: *expend time / money / energy* 耗盡時間／金錢／精力. **expendable** *adj* not needed, and so suitable for using up or wasting 可耗盡的; 可花費的. **expenditure** *nu* money which is spent 支出, 費用.

expense [eks'pens] *nu* money which is needed for some purpose 花費, 費用: *the expense of buying a new car* 購買一部新車的費用. **expensive** *adj* costing a lot of money 昂貴的. (*opp* 反義詞 **inexpensive**). **expenses** *npl* money paid to someone who has to travel or spend money in some way while he is working 費用. **at the expense of something** by losing or damaging something 以…爲代價; 犧牲: *They rushed through the work at the expense of the results* 他們不顧後果倉促完成了工作.

experience [eks'piəriəns] **1** *nu* process of seeing things, doing things etc. 經驗: *He learned by experience* i.e. he learned by doing it, not by reading or by being told by other people. 他通過經驗學習. 即: 他通過做事來學習, 而不是通過讀書或聽別人講. *He has a lot of experience as an engineer* i.e. he has worked as an engineer for many years. 他有作爲一名工程師的豐富經驗. 即: 他當工程師已經多年了. **2** *nc* something which happens 發生的某事, 經驗: *I had a strange experience last night.* 昨夜我遇到一件奇怪的事. Also 亦作 *vt* have experience of 經歷, 體驗: *experience life in prison* 經歷監獄生活; *experience a pain* 感受痛苦. **experienced** *adj* having knowledge of

some work etc gained by experience 有經驗的. (*opp* 反義詞 **inexperienced**).

experiment [eks'perimənt] *nc / u* **1** scientific test carried out with various types of apparatus, to find out what happens and what the result is 實驗. **2** anything tried out to see what will happen 試驗. Also 亦作 *vi* carry out an experiment 進行實驗(或試驗). **experimental** [eksperi'mentl] *adj.*

expert ['ekspə:t] *nc* person having special knowledge 專家. Also 亦作 *adj.*

expertise [ekspə:'ti:z] *nu.*

expire [eks'paiə*] *vi* **1** die 去世. **2** send out breath from the lungs 呼氣. **3** (with reference to a period of time) come to an end (指一段時間) 終止, 期滿. **expiration** [ekspi'reiʃən] *nu,* **expiry** *nu* end of a period of time 期滿, 終止.

explain [eks'plein] *vt / i* **1** give a meaning; make clear 解釋, 說明: *Can you explain this (word) to me?* 你能給我解釋一下這個(詞)嗎? *I don't know what you mean; please explain* 我不懂你的意思, 請解釋一下. **2** give a reason 說明: *Can you explain why you were late?* 你能說明爲甚麼遲到嗎? **explanation** [eksplə'neiʃən] *nc / u* **explanatory** [eks'plænətəri] *adj.*

explicit [eks'plisit] *adj* clearly saying what is meant 明確的: *I gave him explicit instructions.* 我給他明確的指示. (*opp* 反義詞 **inexplicit**). **explicitly** *adv.*

explode [eks'ploud] **1** *vt / i* blow up, cause to blow up (使) 爆炸: *The bomb exploded.* 炸彈爆炸了. *He exploded a bomb.* 他引爆了一枚炸彈. **2** *vi* suddenly show some strong feeling 感情突發: *He exploded with / in laughter / anger.* 他突然哈哈大笑了起

來／他 勃然大怒. **explosion** [eks'-plouʒən] *nc* **explosive** [eks'plousiv] *adj* intended to blow up; likely to blow up 爆炸的；易爆炸的. Also 亦作 *nc / u* something intended to explode (e.g. a bomb) 爆炸品(例如火彈).

exploit¹ ['eksplɔit] *nc* brave and exciting action 英勇的事跡,功勞,功績.

exploit² [eks'plɔit] *vt* make use of to get profit 開發；剝削: *exploit a gold mine* i.e. get gold from it 開發金礦; *exploit a person* i.e. get a profit by using somebody without paying him properly 剝削人. **exploitation** [eksplɔi'teiʃən] *nu*.

explore [eks'plɔː] *vt / i* **1** travel in an unknown country in order to find out what is there 勘探；在 … 探險: *Many Europeans explored the continent of Africa in the 19th century.* 十九世紀許多歐洲人在非洲大陸探險. **2** look carefully at something or consider something carefully, in order to find out what is there 探測,探索,探討. **exploration** [eksplə'reiʃən] *nc / u* **explorer** *nc* person who travels in an unknown country 探險者；勘探者. **exploratory** [eks'plɔrətəri] *adj* done in order to find out what is there 探測的,探索的: *an exploratory meeting* 探討會.

explosion [eks'plouʒən] *nc* see 見 **explode.**

exponent [eks'pounənt] *nc* person who explains an idea or theory (某種觀點或理論的)解釋者,闡述者. see 見 **expound.**

export ['ekspɔːt] *nc* goods sold to another country or sent to another country for sale there 外銷商品,出口品. (*opp* 反義詞 **import**). Also 亦作 [eks'pɔːt] *vt / i* send goods abroad in this way 外銷,出口.

expose [eks'pouz] *vt* **1** leave uncovered, leave open 使暴露: *The general exposed his men to danger* i.e. sent them into a dangerous position. 這個將軍使他的士兵面臨危險. 即: 把他們派到一個危險的陣地. *His house is exposed to the weather* i.e. it is not protected by trees or surrounding houses. 他的房子受風吹日曬. 即: 他的房子沒有樹木或週圍房屋的遮蔽. *This film has been exposed* i.e. it has been used in a camera (to take photographs). 這膠捲已經曝光了. 即: 它已經於照相機中照過相了. **2** make known 揭露,揭發: *The detective exposed the criminal* i.e. showed who had committed the crime. 偵探揭露了罪犯. *He exposed the plan to the newspapers* i.e. he wrote to the newspapers to tell them about a secret plan. 他向報界揭發了這個計劃. 即: 他寫信給報界把一個秘密計劃告訴了他們. **exposure** [eks'pouʒə*] **1** *nu* condition of being without protection from bad weather 暴露 (於惡劣天氣之中): *He died of exposure.* 他凍死了. **2** *nu* telling of something hidden 揭露,揭發. **3** *nc* section of a reel of photographic film 底片: *This film has 36 exposures* i.e. one can take 36 photographs with it. 這膠捲有36張底片. 即: 可用來照36張相.

exposé [eks'pouzei] *nc* making public of something dishonest or unpleasant (esp. in the newspapers) (對卑劣事情的)公開揭發(尤指在報紙上).

expound [eks'paund] *vt* explain an idea 解釋,闡述: *expound an idea / a theory / a philosophy etc.* 闡述一種觀點／理論／哲理等. see 見 **exponent.**

express¹ [eks'pres] *vt* say what one means; make plain; show 表達；表明；表示: *express one's ideas, gratitude* *etc*. 表明想法, 表示感謝等. **express oneself** speak, write, paint, act etc in a way which shows other people what one is feeling and thinking (說話、寫文章、繪畫等) 表達自己的思想和感情.

express² [eks'pres] *adj* **1** travelling fast 快速的: *an express train* 快車; *express delivery* 快遞郵件. **2** clearly understood; definite (usu. in **express wish/purpose**) 明瞭的; 明確的 (通常用於 express wish/purpose 明確的願望/目的). Also 亦作 *nc* fast train, which does not make many stops 快車. **expressly** *adv* clearly 清楚地, 明白地: *I expressly told you to wait for me*. 我明白地告訴過你要等我.

expression [eks'preʃən] **1** *nc* appearance of the face, showing one's feelings 表情: *an angry expression* 憤怒的表情. **2** *nu* process of showing feelings in some way 感情的表露: *He played the music with a lot of expression*. 他以豐富的情感演奏音樂. **3** *nc* word or group of words: part of a sentence 措辭; 詞語. **expressive** [eks'presiv] *adj* clearly showing the feelings 富有表情的, 顯露感情的. (opp 反義詞 **unexpressive**).

expropriate [eks'prouprieit] *vt* take somebody's private property for the use of the public 徵用: *The government has expropriated his land*. 政府徵用了他的土地.

expulsion [eks'pʌlʃən] *nc / u* see 見 **expel**.

exquisite [eks'kwizit] *adj* beautiful; finely made 美麗的; 精緻的.

extend [eks'tend] *vt / i* **1** stretch (使) 延伸, (使) 延長: *The land extends for three miles in that direction*. 這片土地朝那個方向延伸三英里. *The headmaster has extended the term for three weeks* i.e. he has added three

weeks to the term. 校長把這個學期延長三週. **2** offer 給與, 提供: *extend an invitation / welcome / congratulations* (*formal* in sense **2**) 提出邀請/給與歡迎/給與祝賀 (義 2 為正式). **extension** [eks'tenʃən] **1** *nu* process of extending 延伸, 延長: *The pupils disliked the extension of the term*. 學生們不喜歡延長學期. **2** *nc* something added 增加之物: *They are building an extension to the school* i.e. some more buildings. 他們正擴建這所學校. 即: 增建一些房子. **3** *nc* extra telephone added to an existing telephone system (esp. in a big building) 電話分機. **extensive** *adj* **1** stretching a long way 廣闊的: *His land is very extensive*. 他有大片的土地. **2** large in amount 大量的: *The bomb did extensive damage to the house*. 這枚炸彈炸壞了這座房屋的大部份. **extent** [eks'tent] *nu: the extent of his land* 他擁有的土地的範圍; *the extent of the damage* 損壞的範圍 (或程度).

extenuate [eks'tenjueit] *vt* find a reason which makes a fault, mistake or crime seem less bad 找理由使 (過錯或罪行) 減輕. **extenuating circumstances** circumstances which make the crime etc seem less bad 可使罪行等減輕的藉口, 情有可原的情況.

exterior [eks'tiəriə*] *nc* outer surface 外表, 外面. Also 亦作 *adj*. (opp **interior** in both senses) (兩義的反義詞均為 interior).

exterminate [eks'təmineit] *vt* completely destroy or kill a large number or large quantity 滅絕, 大量殺死: *He exterminated the rats on his farm*. 他在自己的農莊裏滅鼠. **extermination** [ekstəːmiˈneiʃən] *nu*.

external [eks'təːnl] *adj* on or for the outside 外面的, 外用的. (opp 反義詞

internal). **externally** *adv.*

extinct [eks'tiŋkt] *adj* **1** (with reference to types of animals, plants etc.) no longer in existence (指動物, 植物等的種類) 絕種的. **2** (with reference to a volcano) no longer active (指火山) 不再活動的. **3** (with reference to feelings or ideas) no longer felt strongly or thought about (指感情或想法) 冷淡的, 破滅的. **extinction** *nu.*

extinguish [eks'tiŋgwiʃ] *vt* put out a light or fire 熄滅 (燈或火). **'fire extinguisher** apparatus filled with chemicals or water for putting out small fires 滅火器.

extol [eks'toul] *vt* give high praise to 讚美. *past* 過去式和過去分詞 **extolled**.

extort [eks'tɔ:t] *vt* get by force or the threat of force 強取, 豪奪; 敲詐, 勒索: *He extorted money from the poor.* 他向窮人敲詐錢財. *He extorted a promise from me.* 他逼我許諾. **extortion** *nu* **extortionate** [eks'tɔ:ʃənit] *adj* asking for too much 要求過多的, 要求過份的.

extra¹ ['ekstrə] *adj* more than is usual 額外的: *an extra holiday* 額外的假期; *extra money* 額外的金錢.

extra² ['ekstrə] *nc* **1** something which is extra, or more than what is usual 額外之物. **2** person who acts small parts in films and who is paid each day for the work he does (拍電影時以工作日計酬的) 臨時跑龍套演員.

extract¹ [eks'trækt] *vt* get from; take out 得到; 取出: *The police extracted information from the thief* i.e. they made the thief give some information. 警方從這個小偷嘴裏取得口供. *A miner extracts gold from the earth.* 礦工從地裏淘金. *The dentist extracted one of my teeth.* 牙醫拔掉我的一顆牙齒.

extraction *nu* **1** process of extracting

獲得, 取出. **2** origin of one's ancestors 血統, 祖籍: *He is of Russian extraction* i.e. his parents or grandparents came from Russia. 他有俄國血統. 即: 他的雙親或祖父母是俄國人.

extract² ['ekstrækt] **1** *nu* substance in concentrated form 濃縮物: *Beef extract is sometimes used for making soup.* 牛肉汁有時用來做湯. **2** *nc* piece of writing or speech taken from a longer piece 摘錄; 選粹: *an extract from a book* 一本書的摘錄.

extracurricular [ˌekstrəkə'rikjulə] **extracurriculum** [ˌekstrəkə'rikjuləm] *adj* (esp. of activities such as sports, music, acting) outside the regular course of study 課程以外的 (尤指運動、音樂、表演等活動): *Football, dramatics and debating are extracurricular activities in our high school.* 足球, 戲劇和辯論是我們中學裏的課外活動.

extradite ['ekstrədait] *vt* hand over to the police of his own country a foreigner wanted by them 引渡 (外國的罪犯): *The British Government extradited the man wanted by the French police.* 英國政府把法國警方通緝的那個男子引渡回法國.

extraneous [eks'treiniəs] *adj* not belonging to something; having no connection with something 無關的; 沒有聯繫的: *He tries to bring in extraneous questions when I have a discussion with him* i.e. he mentions topics which we are not discussing. 我和他討論時, 他提了一些無關的問題.

extraordinary [eks'trɔ:dnri] *adj* very strange; very unusual 奇特的; 非常的.

extravagant [eks'trævəgənt] *adj* **1** spending a lot of money in a foolish way 揮霍的, 浪費的, 奢侈的. **2** beyond the limits of what is sensible or reasonable 無節制的, 不合理理的, 過份的: *extravagant ideas* 過份的想法. **extravagance** *nu*.

extreme [eks'triːm] *adj* **1** at the furthest point 位於極點的, 位於末端的: *He lives in the extreme north of the country.* 他居住於該國的最北部. **2** of the highest degree; very great or very much 極端的; 非常的: *extreme cold* i.e. very great cold 極冷, 即: 非常冷. **3** with reference to ideas which are very far from those of most people (指觀點等) 過激的; 極端的. Also 亦作 *nc* something which is the opposite of something else 相反的事. **extremely** *adv* very much 非常地, 極端地: *extremely tired* 累極了. **extremist** *nc* person who has extreme views in politics (often violent or revolutionary ones) (政治上的) 極端主義者; 過激分子. **extremity** [eks'tremiti] *nc* **1** furthest point 端點, 極端. **2** great misfortune or danger 極端不幸; 極為危險. **the extremities** hands and feet of a person 手足, 四肢.

extricate ['ekstrikeit] *vt* free someone from something which prevents him from moving 使擺脫, 使解脫: *He extricated his friend from the chains.* 他幫朋友掙脫了鎖鏈. *He extricated himself from debt.* 他擺脫了債務.

extrovert ['ekstrəvəːt] *nc* person interested mainly in things and people, and not in his own thoughts 性格外向者, 不喜歡用腦者. Also 亦作 *adj* (*opp* 反義詞 **introvert**).

extrude [eks'truːd] *vt / i* **1** push out; force out; expel 擠出; 壓出; 逐出; 趕走: *He extruded toothpaste from the tube.* 他從牙膏管裏擠出牙膏來. **2** shape (metal, plastics, etc) by forcing through dies (將金屬, 塑料等) 擠壓成: *Plastics material is extruded through* *very small holes to form fibres.* 塑料從細孔中擠壓出來形成纖維. **3** stick out; protrude 伸出; 突出.

extrusion [eks'truːʒən] *nc / u* **1** act or process of extruding; form or product produced by this process 擠壓; 擠壓過程; 擠壓法; 擠壓成形; 壓出品: *extrusion moulding* 擠壓模塑法; *an extrusion press* 擠壓機. **2** expulsion 逐出. **3** flowing out of lava onto the earth's surface; mass of rock formed by extrusion (熔岩的) 噴出; 熔岩噴出形成的大塊岩石.

exuberant [ig'zjuːbərnt] *adj* full of life; strong; growing strongly 充滿活力的; 強壯的; 茂盛的. **exuberance** *nu*.

exude [ig'zjuːd] *vt / i* come out, allow to come out, in small drops of liquid (使) 滲出: *Blood exuded through the bandage.* 血從繃帶中滲出來. *His wound exuded blood.* 他的傷口滲出血來.

exult [eg'zʌlt] *vi* be filled with great happiness (usu. at something important) (通常指為某重要事情而) 歡騰, 喜悅: *The people exulted when they heard the news of the great victory.* 人們聽到這個偉大勝利的消息時都歡呼雀躍. **exultation** [egzʌl'teiʃən] *nu* feeling of great happiness 歡欣, 狂喜.

eye [ai] *nc* **1** part of the body with which people and animals see 眼睛. **2** something shaped like an eye (e.g. the hole at the top of a needle through which the thread goes, a small mark in a potato) 眼狀物 (如針眼, 馬鈴薯上的斑眼). Also 亦作 *vt* look at someone carefully, or with-longing 細看, 打量; 盯着看: *He eyed me carefully.* 他仔細地打量着我. *He eyed her up and down.* 他眼睛自勾勾地在她身上掃來掃去. **'eyeball** that part of the eye which is white and which has a coloured portion at its centre 眼球. **'eyebrow** line of hair on the face above the eye 眉毛. **'eyelash** small hair growing from the eyelids 睫毛. **'eyelid** one of the pieces of skin which can be moved to close the eyes 眼瞼, 眼皮. **'eyeopener** *nc* something which causes great surprise 使人大開眼界之事物, 新奇事物: *His story of how it really happened was an eyeopener for me.* 他對這事發生的真實過程的叙述使我大開眼界. **'eyeshadow** coloured substance put on the eyelids 眼瞼膏, 眼影. **'eyesight** ability to see 視力: *He has good eyesight.* 他的視力很好. **'eyesore** something which looks very unpleasant 刺眼的東西, 難看的東西: *That new statue which has been put up in the main street is an eyesore.* 在大街上的那座新塑像真難看. **'eyewitness** person who sees something happening (often one who sees a crime) (常指罪行) 見證人, 目睹者. **keep an eye on someone / something** watch someone / something carefully. (*informal*) 密切注意某人/某事(非正式).

F,f

fable ['feibl] *nc* story (esp. about animals) intended to teach a lesson about behaviour 寓言故事.

fabric ['fæbrik] *nu* cloth 織物, 布.

fabricate ['fæbrikeit] *vt* 1 make, construct etc; manufacture 裝配, 建造; 製造: *All of the furniture is fabricated on the premises.* 所有那些像具都是在屋內裝配. 2 make up (a story, lie, etc.) 編造(故事, 謊言等): *The story was fabricated.* 這故事是虛構的. **fabrication** [fæbri'keiʃən] *nc*.

fabulous ['fæbjuləs] *adj* 1 very good; very big. *(informal)* 很好的; 很大的. (非正式). 2 strange; unusual and interesting; amazing 奇怪的; 怪異的; 驚人的.

facade, façade [fə'sɑːd] *nc* 1 front of a building 建築物的正面. 2 surface appearance of anything 外表: *Under a facade of respectability he was in fact the leader of a gang of criminals* i.e. he appeared to be respectable or honest. 他看起來體面高尚, 實際上是一夥罪犯的頭子.

face[1] [feis] *nc* 1 front part of the head containing the eyes, mouth, nose etc. 臉, 面部. 2 front of something 某物的正面: *the face of a clock / of a building* 時鐘的數字面/建築物的正面. **facing** *prep* opposite 正對, 面對: *I live in the house facing the church.* 我住在面對教堂的那座房子裏. **'face 'value 1** value marked on a banknote, cheque etc. (鈔票, 支票等的)面值. 2 value or usefulness which something appears to have 表面價值; 表面意義; 表面作用: *take something at its face value* 根據表面價值而採用某事物. **face to face** coming together so as to be able to talk 面對面: *The two leaders at last met face to face.* 兩位領導人終於當面相會. **in the face of something** on meeting something 在某事物面前, 面對某事物: *He became afraid in the face of danger.* 在困難面前, 他變得害怕起來. **on the face of it** as something appears before further enquiry 就表面看, 乍看起來: *On the face of it, you are responsible (although in fact you may not be).* 從表面上看, 你負責任. 即; 看來你很負責(儘管事實上你不一定如此).

face[2] [feis] *vt* 1 turn towards 朝向; 面對: *He faced his enemies.* 他面對敵人. 2 be placed in a certain position 處於某種位置: *Our house faces north.* 我們的房子朝北. **face up to something** accept some unpleasant fact or situation 正視或面對(不快的事實或形勢): *He tried to face up to his difficulties.* 他不想迴避自己面臨的困難. **let's face it** we should admit some fact (usu. an unpleasant fact) 面對現實吧 (常指令人不快的事實). *Let's face it, we are getting old. (informal)* 面對現實吧, 我們畢竟一天天老了. (非正式).

facet ['fæsit] *nc* 1 one of the sides of a precious stone which is cut into shape 寶石的刻面. 2 part of something (某事物的)方面. *There are many facets to his character.* 他具有多面性的性格.

facetious [fə'siːʃəs] *adj* (with reference to jokes, often jokes which are not very funny) not serious (指開玩笑) 不正經的, 輕浮的. **facetiously** adv.

facile ['fæsail] adj easily done; not requiring much effort or skill (and often of a poor quality) 容易做的; 不費力的; 膚淺的: *He made a facile speech.* 他的演說內容膚淺.

facilitate [fə'siliteit] vt make easier 使更爲容易, 促進: *I decided to employ a secretary in order to facilitate the work.* 爲便於工作, 我決定雇用一名秘書.

facility [fə'siliti] **1** nu ability to do things easily 靈巧, 熟練. **2** nc (often pl) something which makes life or work easier, more pleasant etc. (常用複數) 設施; 設備.

facsimile [fæk'simili] nc (usu. of something written) an exact copy (通常指文字材料) 複製本.

fact [fækt] nc / u something known or thought to be true 事實: *The police tried to find out the facts* i.e. what had actually happened. 警方想弄清事實.
　factual ['fæktjuəl] adj in fact really; to tell the truth 事實上; 說實在地. **as a matter of fact** really; actually 事實上; 實際上. **in point of fact** actually; to tell the truth 實際上; 說實在地.

faction ['fækʃən] nc group of people within a political party (esp. a group opposed to the official leaders of the party) 政黨內的派系 (尤指反對該黨正式領導人的派系).

factor ['fæktə*] nc **1** fact; one of a number of facts 實際情況; 因素: *He tried to consider all the factors in the situation.* 他想考慮一下這種局勢的各方面因素. **2** (mathematics) one of the several numbers which form a total when multiplied together (e.g. the factors of 10 are 2 and 5) (數學)因數, 因子 (例如 2 和 5 都是10的因子).

factory ['fæktəri] nc place where goods are made (usu. with machinery) 工廠.

faculty ['fækəlti] nc **1** power or ability of the mind or brain (心智的) 天賦, 才能, 能力. **2** department in a university (大學裏的)系. **3** (US) teaching staff of a university (美)一所大學的全體教員.

fade [feid] vt / i become or make pale, less loud, less strong etc. (使) 褪色, (使) 減弱; (使) 衰弱: *The sun faded the cloth.* 陽光使這布褪色了. *The sound has faded.* 聲音減弱了. **fade away** slowly fade and disappear 逐漸消失: *The sound faded away.* 聲音逐漸消失了.

faeces ['fi:si:z] npl waste matter expelled from the bowels; excrement 糞便; 排泄物.

fag [fæg] nc (Brit) cigarette. (informal) (英)香烟(非正式).

Fahrenheit ['færənhait] temperature scale used in Britain and America, in which freezing point is 32 degrees and boiling point is 212 degrees 華氏溫度計 (使用於英國和美國, 其中水的冰點是32度, 沸點是212度).

fail [feil] **1** vi be unsuccessful 失敗: *His plans failed* i.e. he was not able to do what he had planned. 他的計劃失敗了. 即: 他未能按原計劃的那樣去做. *I fail to understand* i.e. I cannot understand. 我不明白. **2** vi become weak 衰退, 衰弱: *The radio is failing* i.e. becoming less loud. 收音機的聲音越來越小了. **3** vt decide that someone has been unsuccessful in a test or examination 評定(某人)不及格: *The examiner failed 25 of the candidates.* 主考人評定25位考生不及格. **failing**[1] nc weakness of character (品行的) 弱點, 錯誤, 不足: *He has one failing; he tells lies.* 他有一個缺點; 他總說謊.

failing² *prep* without; unless 如果沒有: *Failing that, we must think of another plan* i.e. if that does not happen, we must think of another plan. 如果那事不發生的話,我們必須考慮另一項計劃. **failure** ['feiljə*] **1** *nc/u* lack of success; not doing 失敗; 沒做: *a terrible failure* 極度的失敗; *failure to do something* 未做某事. **2** *nc* person who fails 失敗者. **fail an examination / test** etc be unsuccessful in an examination etc. 未通過考試/測驗等. **without fail** certainly; without forgetting; always 肯定地; 不會忘記地; 總是: *He came to visit me every Thursday without fail.* 他總是在每星期四來看我.

faint¹ [feint] *vi* lose consciousness 昏倒, 昏厥: *She fainted when she heard the news.* 聽到這個消息, 她昏倒了. Also 亦作 *nc* loss of consciousness 昏倒, 昏厥.

faint² [feint] *adj* **1** weak 虛弱的: *He felt faint through lack of food.* 他因為飢餓而感到眩暈. **2** not clearly seen or heard 模糊的, 微弱的: *He heard a faint sound.* 他聽到一種微弱的聲音. **faintly** *adv* **faintness** *nu* **'faint-'hearted** *adj* lacking in courage; afraid of danger 缺乏勇氣的, 懦弱的; 膽小的, 不敢冒險的.

fair¹ [feə*] *adj* **1** just; giving each person what he ought to have 公正的; 公平的: *He didn't think that the arrangement was fair* i.e. he thought that he ought to get more. 他認為這種安排不公平. 即: 他認為他應當多得一點兒. (*opp* 反義詞 **unfair**). **2** according to the rules 按照規則的, 公平的: *The result of the game was not fair.* 比賽結果是不公平的. **3** (with reference to people, esp. people having yellow or golden hair) light in colour (尤指黃髮

或金髮的人) 髮色淡的. **4** (with reference to the weather) without rain (指天氣) 晴朗的. **5** (often with reference to work by a pupil or student or to the probability of something) neither very good nor very bad (常指學生的作業或指某種可能性) 還可以的, 相當的: *a fair chance* 中等的機會. **6** beautiful (*o.f.* in sense **6**) 美麗的 (義 6 為舊式). Also 亦作 *adv* according to the rules 按照規則: *play fair* 按規則行事. **fairness** *nu* **fairly** *adv/intensifier* **1** justly 公正地: *He acted very fairly to us.* 他對待我們很公正. **2** according to the rules 按照規則: *He played fairly.* 他按規則辦事; 他辦事公正. **3** neither very much nor very little 相當地: *This book is fairly interesting.* 這本書相當有趣.

fair² [feə*] *nc* **1** travelling entertainment, having various mechanical things to ride on, games of chance and skill etc. 巡迴遊樂場. (also 亦作 **fun fair**). **2** market held at certain times of the year 集市. **3** international or national exhibition of manufactured goods (工業品) 展覽會.

fair-haired ['feə*'heəd] *adj* having blond hair 金髮的.

fairy ['feəri] *nc* small imaginary creature with magic powers 小精靈, 小妖精. **'fairy story / tale** story about fairies etc for children 童話, 神話故事.

faith [feiθ] **1** *nu* strong belief 信仰, 信心: *have faith in God* i.e. believe that God will help one 信仰上帝, 即: 相信上帝會幫助. *have faith in someone* i.e. believe that someone will succeed 對某人有信心, 即: 認為某人會成功. **2** *nc* religious belief 宗教信仰: *people of different faiths* 具有不同宗教信仰的人們. **faithful** *adj* **1** following one's duty; doing what one has promised 忠實的; 可靠的: *faithful to one's country* 忠於自己國家的. (*opp* 反義詞 **unfaithful**). **faithfully** *adv* **in good faith** believing something to be true 真誠地, 有信心地: *I made the agreement in good faith* i.e. believing that the agreement would be kept. 我滿懷信心地簽訂了這個協定. 即: 相信這協定會得到遵守. **Yours faithfully** used at the end of a letter to somebody whom one does not know as a friend or colleague (給不熟悉者書信的結尾客套語) 您忠實的; 拜上; 謹啟.

fake [feik] *adj* false, but made to look real 僞造的: *a fake accident* 僞造的事故. Also 亦作 *nc* something which is fake 僞造物, 贋品. Also 亦作 *vt* make a fake. (all *informal*) 僞造(均爲非正式)

falcon ['fɔ:lkən] *nc* type of bird which eats small birds and animals and is sometimes trained to catch them for men 獵鷹.

fall¹ [fɔ:l] *nc* **1** act of falling 落下; 跌落; 跌倒: *He had a fall and broke his leg.* 他跌了一跤, 把腿摔斷了. **2** (*US*) autumn (美) 秋天. **3** decrease 下降: *a fall in prices* 價格下降. **4** capture 陷落, 淪陷: *the fall of Constantinople* 康斯坦坦丁堡的陷落. **5** defeat (esp. the defeat of a government or a powerful man) (尤指政府或有勢力者的) 失敗, 垮台.

fall² [fɔ:l] *vi* **1** come down 落下; 跌落: *He was climbing a tree when he fell to the ground* 他在爬樹時跌落在地. *The snow was falling* 雪正在下著. **2** become less or lower 減少; 降低: *The price of flour has fallen.* 麵粉的價格已下跌. **3** be defeated 垮台, 失敗: *The government has fallen.* 該政府已經垮台. *past tense* 過去式 **fell** [fel]. *past part* 過去

分詞 **fallen** ['fɔ:lən] **fall behind 1** go more slowly than others 落後; 落後於別人. **2** fail to continue something 未能繼續, 拖欠: *He fell behind with his rent* i.e. he could not make the payment at the right time. 他拖欠租金. 即: 他未能準時付租金. **fall down** fall to the ground 跌倒. **fall for something** be deceived by something 爲…所騙. 對…信以爲真: *He fell for the trick.* (*informal*) 他對這一詭計信以爲真. (非正式). '**fallout** *nu* radioactive substance released in the atmosphere by the explosion of a nuclear bomb (核彈爆炸後飄落大氣層的) 輻射塵. **fall out (with someone)** quarrel. (*informal*) (與某人) 爭吵 (非正式). **fall through** fail 失敗: *The plan / scheme / arrangements fell through.* (*informal*) 該計劃/設計/安排失敗了. (非正式). **fall flat** fail completely 完全失敗: *His plans fell flat.* (*informal*) 他的計劃完全失敗了. (非正式). **fall in love (with someone)** begin to love someone 愛上 (某人): *He fell in love with her.* 他愛上了她. *They fell in love.* 他們相愛了. **fall short of** be less than was expected 未能達到: *The amount I have been given falls short of my requirements.* 人家給我的數目未能達到我的要求.

fallacy ['fæləsi] *nc* **1** belief which is untrue 錯誤的信念. **2** argument which is false 謬論.

fallible ['fæləbl] *adj* likely to make a mistake 易犯錯誤的. (*opp* 反義詞 **infallible**).

fallow ['fæləu] *adj* (with reference to land on a farm) not planted with seed (指農場的土地) 休閑的.

false [fɔ:ls] *adj* untrue; not real 假的; 不真實的: *a false statement* 不真實的聲明; *a false name* i.e. a name which is

not the real name of the person 化名,
假名. **falsely** *adv.*

falter ['fɔːltə*] *vi* move or behave in an
uncertain or unsteady way 蹣跚; 躊
躇: *The old man faltered as he
climbed the hill.* 老人搖搖晃晃地爬山.

fame [feim] *nu* condition of being well-
known by a large number of people
名聲, 名望. **famous** *adj* well-known
in this way 聞名的, 著名的.

familiar [fə'miliə*] *adj* **1** well-known to
one 熟悉的: *a familiar face* 一張熟悉
的臉. (*opp* 反義詞 **unfamiliar**). **2** too
friendly; acting as though a friend 過
份親熱的; 親密的; 隨便的: *He spoke to
her in a very familiar way.* 他對她說
話的樣子過份親熱. **familiarity** [fəmi-
li'æriti] *nc / u* **familiarize** *vt* make
familiar 使熟悉; 使親密. **familiar
with something** having a good knowledge of something 熟悉某事物的.

family ['fæmili] *nc* **1** mother, father and
children (父母和子女組成的) 家庭. **2**
children of a man or his wife 子女. **3**
people related to one by blood or
marriage (e.g. uncles, aunts, cousins,
nephews, nieces etc.) 家族, 族人. '**family'tree 1** diagram showing all one's
ancestors 族譜, 家譜. **2** the ancestors
themselves 先輩.

famine ['fæmin] *nc / u* lack of food over
a large area, causing death or disease
饑荒.

famished ['fæmiʃt] *adj* **1** starving 令人
饑餓的. **2** hungry. (*informal* in sense
2) 饑餓的(義2爲非正式).

famous ['feiməs] *adj* see 見 **fame.**

fan[1] [fæn] *nc* object used to create a
movement of air (usu. in order to
make one feel less hot) 扇子; 風扇.
Also 亦作 *vt* use a fan or something
like a fan 搧: *She fanned herself.* 她用
扇子搧自己. *He fanned the fire* i.e. to

make it burn better. 他搧火. 即: 使火
燒得旺些. *past* 過去式和過去分詞
fanned.

fan[2] [fæn] *nc* person who takes a great
interest in a sport or in some public
entertainer. (*informal*) 對運動或某位
知名演藝人員極感興趣的人, 迷. (非正
式). '**fanmail** letters sent by fans to
singers, actors, sportsmen etc. 崇拜者
給歌星、影星、體育明星等的信件.

fanatic [fə'nætik] *nc* person having a
strong religious or political belief,
which makes him likely to act violently (宗教或政治的) 狂熱者. **fanatical**
adj.

fancy[1] ['fænsi] *vt* **1** think something to
be true 以爲, 幻想: *I fancied I had
met him before.* 我以爲以前見過他. **2**
like or want 喜愛; 想要: *I fancy a cup
of coffee and a piece of cake.* 我喜歡
喝一杯咖啡再加上一塊蛋糕. *I don't
fancy walking in the rain.* (*informal* in
sense 2) 我可不想冒雨步行. (義2爲
非正式). (**just**) **fancy** exclamation
meaning 'how surprising!' (*informal*)
真怪! 想想看! (非正式).

fancy[2] ['fænsi] **1** *nu* ability to imagine
things 想像力. **2** *nc* something imagined but untrue 想像之物, 幻想, 幻覺.
fanciful *adj* imagined but unreal 想像
的; 不真實的.

fancy[3] ['fænsi] *adj* brightly coloured;
made to look pleasing. (*informal*) 色
彩鮮艷悅目的(非正式). '**fancy 'dress**
unusual and interesting dress, worn
to a party or dance 爲參加聚會或舞會
而穿的奇裝異服.

fanfare ['fænfeə*] *nc* blowing of trumpets etc. 吹奏喇叭聲, 喇叭等的吹奏
聲.

fang [fæŋ] *nc* sharp tooth of an animal
動物的尖牙.

fantastic [fæn'tæstik] *adj* **1** strange, unusual and difficult to believe 奇異的、怪誕的. **2** very good; very big. (*informal* in sense **2**) 很好的; 很大的 (義 2 爲非正式).

fantasy ['fæntəsi] *nc* very strange idea or dream 怪異的念頭; 幻想.

far [fɑː*] *adv* **1** a long way; distant 遠途地; 遠地: *He didn't walk far.* 他沒走遠. *The next village is not very far.* 下一個村莊不很遠. *How far is it to London?* 到倫敦有多遠? **2** very much 很、極: *This book is far more interesting than that one.* 這本書要比那本書有趣得多. *I would far sooner go with John than James* i.e. I would prefer to go with John. 我寧願和約翰而不是詹姆士一起走. Also 亦作 *adj* distant 遠的: *the far side of the moon* i.e. the side most distant from the earth 月球的遠地側. *comparative* 比較級 **farther** ['fɑːðə*] or **further** ['fɜːðə*]. *superlative* 最高級 **farthest** ['fɑːðist] or **furthest** ['fɜːðist]. *Note* 說明: some people make a distinction between *farther / farthest* and *further / furthest*, using the first two to refer to distance, and the second two to refer to time, quantity etc. (e.g. *three miles farther, but to go further in an investigation*). Not all speakers of English make this distinction, and *further / furthest* is probably commoner. 有些人對 farther / farthest 和 further / furthest 加以區分. 用前兩個詞指距離, 用後兩個詞指時間、數量等 (例如 three miles farther 再三英里遠, 但是 to go further in an investigation 作進一步調查). 不是所有操英語的人都這樣區分, 因而 further / furthest 可能較爲通用.

'faraway *adj* **1** distant 遙遠的: *a faraway place* 遙遠的地方. **2** thinking of things very distant (usu. **in a faraway look**) 心在遠處的, 神情恍惚的 (通常用於 a faraway look). 恍惚的眼神).

'far'fetched *adj* difficult to believe; very improbable 牽強的; 極不可能的: *a far-fetched story* 牽強附會的故事.

'far'reaching *adj* having effects on many distant things 影響深遠的: *far-reaching changes in government policy* 在政府政策方面影響深遠的變化.

as far as to the degree that 盡⋯, 就⋯ *As far as I know, he has not been here* i.e. although he may have been here without my knowledge. 就我所知, 他沒有來過這兒. 即: 雖然他可能來過這兒, 而我不知道. **by far** by a large amount 大大地, 最: *This is by far the best.* 這是最好的.

farce [fɑːs] *nc* **1** stage play or film having many foolish and improbable incidents, intended to make people laugh 鬧劇. **2** anything in real life which is like a farce (現實生活中)鬧劇性事情. **farcical** ['fɑːsikl] *adj.*

fare [fɛə*] *nc* money paid to travel on a bus, train, aeroplane etc. (公共汽車、火車、飛機等的)票費. **bill of fare** list of food which can be bought in a restaurant 菜單.

farewell [fɛə'wel] *interj / nc* goodbye. (rather *o.f.*) 再會 (相當舊式).

farm [fɑːm] *nc* **1** large area of land for growing crops and raising animals 農場. **2** house where the farmer lives 農舍. Also 亦作 *vt / i: He farms in Scotland* i.e. he has a farm there. 他在蘇格蘭務農. 即: 他在那兒有一個農場. **farmer** *nc* owner or manager of a farm 農場主, 農場經理人. **'farmyard** open space around a farmhouse 農家庭院.

farther, farthest ['fɑːðə*, 'fɑːðist] see 見 **far.**

fascinate ['fæsineit] *vt* be very interesting to; claim all the attention of 對⋯

有魅力; 迷住: *Old houses fascinate me.* 古老的房屋使我入迷. **fascination** [ˌfæsiˈneiʃən] *nc / u* **fascinating** *adj*: *a fascinating story* 一個迷人的故事.

fascism [ˈfæʃizəm] *nu* political belief taking various forms (but usu. favouring dictatorship, the use of force, belief that some members of the community are inferior, and a liking for parades, uniforms, badges etc.) 法西斯主義(通常贊成獨裁、使用武力, 認為社會的某些成員是低劣的, 而且喜愛遊行、制服、徽章等). **fascist** [ˈfæʃist] *nc* follower of this political belief or movement 法西斯主義分子.

fashion [ˈfæʃən] **1** *nc / u* changes in what is thought to be very modern in clothes, music, art etc. (衣著、音樂、藝術等方面的)時髦, 風尚: *Fashion has more influence on women than on men.* 時裝對婦女比對男人更具影響力. *She always reads the newspapers to find out the new fashions in dress.* 她經常看報以便弄清服裝的時新款式. **2** *nc* (usu. only *sing*) way or manner (通常僅用單數)方式, 姿態. Also 亦作 *vt* make (usu. using the hands and simple tools) (通常用手或簡易工具)製作: *He fashioned a walking stick for his father.* 他為他父親製作了一根手杖. **fashionable** *adj* following fashion; of the upper classes 時髦的; 上流社會的: *a fashionable person* 時髦的人; *a fashionable part of the town* i.e. one where fashionable people live. 該城的上流社會區. 即: 上流社會的人居住的地方. (*opp* 反義詞 **unfashionable**) **in fashion** considered to be the best at the moment 時髦的, 流行的: *Short skirts are in fashion* i.e. women who wish to be fashionable wear short skirts. 短裙很流行. 即: 想穿

著入時的婦女都要穿短裙. (*opp* 反義語 **out of fashion**).

fast¹ [fɑːst] *adj* **1** quick; not slow 快的: *a fast train* 快車. *This clock is fast* i.e. ahead of time. 這鐘走得快. **2** firmly fixed in or on something 緊的, 牢的: *fast colours* i.e. colours which will not come out of cloth when it is washed 不易褪掉的顏色; 洗滌時布的顏色不易褪掉. Also 亦作 *adv* quickly 快: *He ran very fast.* 他跑得很快. **ˈfast aˈsleep** in a deep sleep; not easily woken 沉睡的; 熟睡的. **make something fast** tie something securely 綁緊(某物): *He made fast the rope.* 他綁緊繩索.

fast² [fɑːst] *vi* go without food (for religious or medical purposes) 齋戒; 停食. Also 亦作 *nc* period of going without food 齋戒期.

fasten [ˈfɑːsn] *vt / i* become or make tight or fixed in place 縛緊, 繫牢; 繫住: *This dress fastens at the back* i.e. the buttons etc are at the back. 這件衣服從背後扣緊. 即: 扣子等在背後. *She fastened her dress.* 她把衣服扣緊. (*opp* 反義詞 **unfasten**). **fastener** *nc* something used for fastening 用以扣緊之物.

fastidious [fæsˈtidiəs] *adj* having the habit of disliking many things 難以取悅的, 苛求的, 講究的.

fat¹ [fæt] *nu* **1** white or yellow substance found in animal and human bodies 脂肪. **2** similar substance obtained from plants and used for cooking in the same way as animal fat (用於烹飪的)植物油. **fatty** *adj*: *fatty tissue* 多脂組織.

fat² [fæt] *adj* **1** having much fat in the body 肥胖的: *a fat man* 肥胖的男子. **2** thick, as though having fat 厚的: *a fat book* 一本厚厚的書. *comparative*

比較級 **fatter.** superlative 最高級 **fattest. fatten** vt make fat 使肥胖, 養肥.

fatal ['feitl] adj causing death or destruction 致命的; 毀滅性的: *a fatal illness* 致命的疾病. **fatally** adv **fatality** [fə'tæliti] nc / u accident, misfortune that causes death 致命的災禍或不幸.

fate [feit] **1** nu power which is thought of as deciding what will happen 命運. **2** nc what is decided by fate 命中註定之事: *I opened the letter in order to learn my fate* i.e. learn what was going to happen to me. 我打開信以便知道自己的命運. 即: 瞭解自己將會發生甚麼事. **fateful** adj decided by fate (and often causing death or destruction) 命中註定的 (常是致命或毀滅性的).

father ['fɑ:ðə*] nc **1** male parent 父親. **2** person who invents, founds or begins something 發明者; 創建者; 開創者. **3 (Father)** Roman Catholic priest (羅馬天主教教士) 神父. **fatherly** adj like a father 父親般的. **(the) Father** God 上帝. **'father-in-law** nc father of one's wife or husband 岳父; 公公 (丈夫之父). pl 複數 **fathers-in-law.**

fathom ['fæðəm] nc unit of measurement of the depth of water (= 1.8 metres) 噚 (= 1.8公尺). Also 亦作 vt find out the meaning of 瞭解.

fatigue [fə'ti:g] nu condition of being very tired 疲乏. Also 亦作 vt make tired 使疲乏.

fatuous ['fætjuəs] adj foolish, but thinking oneself clever 愚蠢卻自以爲聰明的.

faucet ['fɔ:sit] nc (US) tap for controlling the flow of liquid (美)水龍頭, 旋塞. (Brit 英 **tap**).

fault [fɔ:lt] nc **1** mistake or error; something wrong 錯誤, 缺陷; 錯事: *There is a serious fault in his character.* 他的性格有嚴重缺陷. *The driver of the lorry admitted that the accident was his fault* i.e. that he had caused the accident. 貨車司機承認這個事故是他的錯. **2** (geology) crack along which rock has moved up or down (地質學) 斷層. **faulty** adj having faults 有缺點的, 有毛病的. **faultless** adj without faults 無缺陷的, 完美的. **faultlessly** adv **at fault** causing something wrong; in the wrong 導致不正常的; 錯誤的: *The driver of the lorry was at fault when the accident happened.* 該貨車司機出了差錯, 此時事故發生了.

fauna ['fɔ:nə] nu animals of a particular area or a particular time 動物區系.

favour ['feivə*] (US 美 **favor**) **1** nc / u friendly help and support 友好的幫助或支持: *I did him a favour* i.e. I did something to help him. 我幫了他一個忙. **2** nu help and support which is too great, too much and which is unfair to others 偏袒, 偏愛. (opp 反義詞 **disfavour**). Also 亦作 vt **1** give help or support to 幫助; 贊同: *I favour your suggestion.* 我贊成你的建議. **2** give too much help or support to 偏愛: *The teacher must not favour some children more than others.* 老師不應該對某些孩子有偏愛. **favourable** adj giving help or support 給予幫助的; 贊同的: *a favourable reply* 滿意的答覆. **favourably** adv (opp 反義詞 **unfavourable**; **unfavourably**). **favourite** ['feivərit] adj most liked 最喜愛的. Also 亦作 nc **1** person / thing most liked 最喜愛的人/物. **2** person who receives an unfair amount of help or support (esp. a child receiving help from a teacher) 受寵的人, 被偏愛的人 (尤指得到老師寵愛、偏愛的學生). **3** person, horse, team etc thought most likely to win a race or game 最

有希望贏得比賽的人、馬、隊等.
favouritism ['feivəritizəm] *nu* practice of giving too much help and support to somebody (esp. a teacher helping a pupil) (尤指老師對學生的) 偏愛, 偏心. **in favour of someone / something** supporting or approving of someone / something 支持或贊同某人 / 某事: *I am in favour of making John the captain of the team.* 我贊成讓約翰擔任隊長.

fawn [fɔːn] **1** *nc* young deer 小鹿. **2** *nu* yellow-brown colour 黃褐色. Also 亦作 *adj* (in sense 2) 黃褐色的.

fear [fiə*] *vt / i* be afraid 害怕, 怕: *He always feared the dentist.* 他老是害怕牙醫. *They feared for his life* i.e. they were afraid he was going to die. 他們為他的生命繁憂. 即: 他們擔心他會死. Also 亦作 *nc / u* condition of being afraid 害怕. **fearful** *adj* **1** causing fear; causing death and destruction 可怕的; 恐怖的. **2** very bad or very great. (informal) 很糟糕的; 極大的. (非正式). **fearless** *adj* without fear 無畏的; 不怕的. **fearlessly** *adv.*

feasible ['fiːzəbl] *adj* possible; able to be done or carried out 可能的; 可行的: *a feasible idea* 可行的想法. **feasibility** [fiːzə'biliti] *nu.*

feast [fiːst] *nc* large meal eaten for some special purpose (usu. to celebrate a happy occasion) (通常指喜慶) 盛宴, 宴會.

feat [fiːt] *nc* some action which requires great strength or skill 壯舉; 偉業; 功績.

feather ['feðə*] *nc* one of the soft, light things covering a bird's body 羽毛.

feature ['fiːtʃə*] **1** important part of something 特色; 特色. **2** part of the face 面貌的一部份: *beautiful features* 美麗的容貌. *Her eyes are her best fea-*

ture. 她的雙眼長得最好看. **3** important article in a newspaper etc. (報紙等的)特寫; 特別報導. Also 亦作 *vt* be or have a feature 是…的特色; 有…的特色: *The economy featured very largely in the Prime Minister's speech* i.e. this was one of the main topics of his speech. 首相的講話的特色是以經濟爲主. 即: 經濟是他的一個主要話題. *This film features John Smith* i.e. he is the main actor. 這部電影由約翰·史密斯主演. 即: 他是主要演員. **featureless** *adj* having no main features 無特色的.

February ['februəri] *n* second month of the year 二月.

fed [fed] past of **feed**[1] feed[1]的過去式和過去分詞. **fed up** *adj* unhappy and dissatisfied. (informal) 厭煩的; 不滿的. (非正式).

federation [fedə'reiʃən] **1** *nc* group of states, countries, societies etc which have joined together to act as one for some or all purposes 聯邦政府; 同盟國; 聯合會. **2** *nu* process of coming together in this way 聯合, 同盟. **federal** ['fedərəl] *adj.*

fee [fiː] *nc* money paid by people for certain services (e.g. money paid to doctors, lawyers, schools, universities etc.)費用(如診費、訴訟費、學費等).

feeble ['fiːbl] *adj* very weak 虛弱的, 衰弱的. **'feeble-'minded** *adj* having very low intelligence 智能很低的.

feed[1] [fiːd] **1** *vt* give food to 餵: *She was feeding the baby.* 她正在給嬰兒餵奶. **2** *vi* (with reference to animals or babies) eat (指動物或嬰兒)吃. **3** *vt* supply material to 提供(材料)給: *feed a machine* 向機器送料; *feed information to a government department* 向政府部門提供情報. *past* 過去式和過去分詞 **fed** [fed].

feed² [fiːd] **1** *nc* milk or food taken by a baby (嬰兒的) 一餐, 飲食: *The baby has four feeds a day.* 這嬰兒一日餵四餐. **2** *nu* food given to animals (動物的) 飼料. **'feedback** information about the result of some process, passed back to the person or machine in charge of the process 反饋.

feel [fiːl] *vt / i* **1** touch with the hand or other part of the body 觸, 摸: *I felt the water to see whether it was hot.* 我摸摸水看熱不熱. **2** give an impression when touched 觸(或摸)時有⋯的感覺: *The water felt cold.* 這水摸起來挺涼的. **3** have some sensation 感覺: *I feel tired / hungry / bored / angry etc.* 我感到累/餓/煩/生氣等. **4** have an opinion (which may be wrong) 覺得, 認為: *I feel that your idea is the best one.* 我覺得你的主意最好. *past* 過去式和過去分詞 **felt** [felt]. Also 亦作 *nu* impression given by feeling 感覺, 觸覺: *the feel of a piece of cloth* 布料的手感. *I haven't got the feel of this car yet* i.e. I'm not used to it. 我還不習慣這輛新車. **feeler** *nc* part of the body with which an insect feels (昆蟲的) 觸鬚. **feeling** *nc / u* **1** ability to feel 知覺. **2** something felt in the mind; emotion of any type 感覺. **3** idea or opinion (which might be wrong) 感覺, 看法. **feel like something 1** have an impression of being something 覺得像: *I felt like a fool.* 我覺得像個傻瓜. **2** wish to have something 想要: *I feel like a cup of coffee.* 我想喝一杯咖啡.

feet [fiːt] *pl* of **foot.** foot 的複數形式.

feign [fein] *vt / i* pretend; try to appear what one is not 假裝; 偽裝: *He feigned illness* i.e. he was not really ill. 他裝病. 即: 他不是真病.

feint [feint] *nc* action or appearance which is feigned 假裝; 假象.

fell¹ [fel] past tense of **fall¹**. fall¹的過去式.

fell² [fel] *vt* knock down or cut down 打倒; 砍倒: *fell a tree* 砍倒一棵樹.

fellow ['felou] *nc* **1** man. *(informal)* 人 (非正式). **2** person with whom one is associated in some way 同伴, 同事: *my fellow prisoners / passengers / students* 我的囚友/旅伴/同學. **3** member of certain societies of scholars and scientists (學會) 會員. **fellowship 1** *nu* friendly feeling 友情. **2** *nc* group of people having similar interests 團體, 會.

felony ['feləni] *nc / u* serious crime 重罪.

felt¹ [felt] past of **feel.** feel 的過去式和過去分詞.

felt² [felt] *nu* type of hard cloth made from wool 毛氈.

female ['fiːmeil] *adj* **1** of woman 女性的. **2** of what corresponds to women in animals, birds, plants etc. 雌性的 (動植物). Also 亦作 *nc*.

feminine ['feminin] *adj* **1** of, or like women 女人的, 女性的; 女人用的; 像女人的: *feminine charm* 女性的魅力. **2** (grammar) belonging to a certain class of nouns in Latin, French and other languages, or referred to by the pronoun 'she' in English (語法) 陰性的. **feminism** ['feminizəm] *nu* movement which tries to get more rights and opportunities for women 女權運動. **feminist** *nc* supporter of this movement 女權運動支持者.

fence¹ [fens] *nc* something made of wood or metal dividing two pieces of land 籬笆, 圍牆. Also 亦作 *vt* (often with **off**) surround or separate with a fence (常與 off 連用)用籬笆或圍牆隔開.

fence² [fens] *vi* fight with swords (usu. for sport) (通常爲了體育運動) 擊劍. **fencing** *nu* the sport of fighting with swords 擊劍.

fend [fend] *vi* (with **off**) act to avoid (與 off 連用) 避開: He fended off the blow. 他避開了這一拳. **fend for oneself 1** provide oneself with everything that one needs 自己照料自己, 獨自謀生. **2** fight back if attacked 還擊.

fender ['fendə*] *nc* **1** metal object like a small wall put in front of a fireplace 壁爐前的金屬圍欄. **2** (US) piece of metal over the wheel of a car etc. (美)擋泥板. (*Brit* 英 **mudguard**).

ferment¹ ['fə:ment] *nu* excitement and change (esp. political) (尤指政治方面的) 騷動.

ferment² [fə'ment] *vi* undergo chemical change, giving off a gas 發酵. **fermentation** [fə:men'teiʃən] *nu*.

fern [fə:n] *nc* type of green plant, with leaves that look like big feathers 羊齒植物.

ferocious [fə'rouʃəs] *adj* very angry and violent 暴怒的, 兇猛的. **ferocity** [fə'rɔsiti] *nu*.

ferry ['feri] *nc* **1** boat which sails backwards and forwards across a narrow piece of water, carrying goods and passengers 渡船. **2** place where such a boat travels 渡口. Also 亦作 *vt / i* go or take in a ferry (使)乘船渡過.

fertile ['fə:tail] *adj* able to produce (crops, children etc.) 肥沃的, 多產的; 能生育的: fertile land 肥沃的土地; a fertile mind i.e. one having many ideas 有才智的頭腦. **fertility** [fə'tiliti] *nu* condition of being fertile 肥沃; 多產; 繁殖, 生育. **fertilize** ['fə:tilaiz] *vt* make fertile 使多產; 使能生育. **fertilization** [fə:tilai'zeiʃən] *nu* process of fertilizing 施肥; 受精. **fer-**

tilizer ['fə:tilaizə*] *nc* substance used for making land fertile 肥料.

fervent ['fə:vənt] *adj* having or showing strong feelings 熱情的, 熱烈的: He is a fervent supporter of the local football team. 他是當地足球隊的一名狂熱支持者.

festival ['festivl] *nc* **1** occasion of public celebration, enjoyment etc. 節日, 喜慶日. **2** several performances of plays, films, music etc. at the same time in one place (戲劇、電影、音樂等)節: the Edinburgh festival 愛丁堡藝術節.

festivity [fes'tiviti] *nc* (often *pl*) festival (常用複數)節日, 喜慶日. **festive** ['festiv] *adj*.

festoon [fes'tu:n] *vt* hang flowers ribbons etc. on as a decoration 以鮮花、綵帶等裝飾.

fetch [fetʃ] *vt* **1** go and get 取來: He went to fetch some meat from the market. 他到市場上去買點肉. **2** be sold at 以…價出售: This fruit fetches fifteen pence a pound. (informal in sense 2) 這種水果一磅賣十五便士. (義2爲非正式).

fete, féte [feit] *nc* festival (often to collect money for a special purpose) (常爲某一目的而籌款的)節日, 喜慶日.

fetter ['fetə*] *nc* (usu. *pl*) chain for holding a prisoner (通常用複數)鐐銬.

feud [fju:d] *nc* quarrel between two people, two families etc lasting a long time (兩人、兩家等的)世仇, 宿怨. Also 亦作 *vi* quarrel in this way 世代結仇, 長期不和.

feudalism ['fju:dəlizəm] *nu* **1** economic and political system of Western Europe, from about the 9th to the 15th centuries, by which people held land in return for services given to the owner of the land (大約從九到十五世紀西歐的) 封建制度. **2** similar

system found in other parts of the world (世界其他地區的) 封建制度.
feudal *adj*.

fever ['fiːvə*] *nc / u* one of various types of illness, in which the temperature rises very high 高燒, 高熱; 熱病.
feverish *adj* **feverishly** *adv*.

few [fjuː] *determiner / pron* not many; a small number 不多; 很少: *I have met a few of these people before.* 以前我遇到過一些這樣的人. *Few of them are my friends.* 他們差不多都不是我的朋友. *If you want something to read, there are a few magazines on the table.* 如果你想讀點甚麼, 桌上有幾本雜誌. *There are hundreds of books in the school library, but few of them are really interesting.* 學校圖書館裏有數百本書, 但是沒有幾本是真正有趣的. *Note* 說明: *few* gives the idea of 'not many' or 'not enough'. *Few of my friends were willing to help me.* *a few*, however, gives the idea of 'some' without the suggestion that the number was too small. few 意爲 "不多" 或 "不足". *Few of my friends were willing to help me.* 我的朋友差不多都不願意幫助我. a few 則意爲 "一些", 並無很少的意思. **a good few, quite a few** several; quite a lot; more than a small number of 一些; 相當多; 不少多: *He has quite a few / a good few friends here.* 他在此地有不少朋友.

fiancé [fi'ɔnsei] *nc* man whom a woman has promised to marry 未婚夫. (*fem* 陰 **fiancée**).

fiasco [fi'æskou] *nc* complete failure of a plan or arrangement (計劃或安排的) 完全失敗. *pl* 複數 **fiascos.**

fib [fib] *nc* small and not very important lie 小謊, 無關緊要的謊言. Also 亦作 *vi* tell a fib. 撒小謊. *past* 過去式和過去分詞 **fibbed.** (*informal*) (非正式).

fibre ['faibə*] (*US* 美 **fiber**) *nc* thin thread (e.g. of wool, muscle tissue. coconut etc.) (羊毛, 肌肉組織、椰子等的) 纖維. '**fibre-glass** very strong material made from thin threads of glass 玻璃纖維.

fiction ['fikʃən] **1** *nu* novels and stories which tell about things which did not actually happen 小說 (總稱). **2** *nc* a story of this type; any untrue story (一篇) 小說; 虛構的故事. **fictitious** [fik'tiʃəs] *adj*.

fiddle ['fidl] *nc* **1** violin 小提琴. **2** dishonest arrangement 弄虛作假, 欺詐. Also 亦作 **1** *vi* play the violin 演奏小提琴. **2** *vt / i* make a dishonest arrangement; cheat somebody 弄虛作假; 欺騙. **3** *vi* continually touch or move something in a nervous and restless way 緊張不安地擺弄或撥弄: *He was fiddling with his pen while he was talking to me.* 他邊和我談話邊擺弄手中的鋼筆. (all *informal*) (均爲非正式). **fiddler** *nc* violinist. (*informal*) 小提琴手(非正式).

fidelity [fi'deliti] *nu* **1** faithfulness; willingness to give support and help to somebody whatever the danger or difficulties 忠實; 忠誠. **2** accuracy; ability to produce the same sound, shape, colour etc as an original 精確; 逼真.

fidget ['fidʒit] *vt / i* continually move in a restless and nervous way (使) 坐立不安. Also 亦作 *nc* person who fidgets 坐立不安的人. **fidgety** *adv*.

field [fiːld] *nc* **1** area of land (usu. enclosed by a fence or wall) used for growing crops or grazing animals 田地, 田野. **2** piece of land of various types (各式) 場地: *a football field* 足球場; *a coalfield* i.e. land with coalmines on it 煤田; *an airfield* 飛機場;

a battlefield 戰場. **3** branch of knowledge (知識)領域; *the field of nuclear physics* 核物理領域. '**field day 1** day on which an athletics contest etc is held (esp. a school or college) (尤指學校的)體育比賽日. **2** any day on which there is unusual and enjoyable action 有愉快的重要活動的日子. '**field 'marshal** officer of highest rank in an army 陸軍元帥.

fiend [fiːnd] *nc* **1** devil or evil spirit 惡魔, 魔鬼. **2** wicked person 兇惡的人. **fiendish** *adj*.

fierce [fiəs] *adj* angry and dangerous 兇猛的: *a fierce lion* 兇猛的獅子; *a fierce fire* 烈火. **fiercely** *adv* **fierceness** *nu*.

fiery ['faiəri] *adj* **1** like or of fire, very hot 如火的; 火的; 火熱的. **2** easily made angry 易怒的, 暴躁的.

fiesta [fi'estə] *nc* religious holiday with public celebrations (usu. in the Mediterranean countries or in South America) (通常指地中海沿岸諸國或南美的)宗教節日, 狂歡節.

fifth [fifθ] see appendix 見附錄.

fig [fig] *nc* type of small, soft, fleshy fruit grown in warm regions 無花果.

fight¹ [fait] *nc* struggle or contest (esp. one in which people try to hurt each other, or try to overcome some difficulty) 作戰, 戰鬥; 打架; 鬥爭: *The two boys had a fight.* 這兩個男生打了一架. *The police are continuing the fight against crime.* 警方正繼續與犯罪作鬥爭. **fighter** *nc* **1** person who fights (esp. a boxer) 戰士, 戰鬥者; 打鬥者, (尤指)拳擊手. **2** type of fast plane used for attacking enemy planes 戰鬥機.

fight² [fait] *vt / i* have a fight 參加戰鬥; 作戰; 與…打架; 打架; 與…鬥爭, 鬥爭: *The two boys fought.* 這兩個男生打架

. *John fought (with / against) James.* 約翰和詹姆士打架. *The police fought against crime.* 警方與犯罪作鬥爭. *past* 過去式和過去分詞 **fought** [fɔːt]. **fight somebody / something off** fight to keep somebody / something away 擊退某人/極力擺脫某事物: *He fought off his attacker.* 他打退了進攻者.

figment ['figmənt] *nc* usu. only in **a figment of the imagination** i.e. something imagined but untrue (通常僅用於 a figment of the imagination) 虛構的東西.

figure¹ ['figə*] *nc* **1** shape or outline of the human body 人的體形; 人影: *I saw a figure in the darkness.* 我看到黑暗中有個人影. **2** important person 重要人物. **3** diagram or drawing made to explain something 圖表, 插圖. **4** form drawn in geometry (e.g. a square or circle) 幾何圖形(如方形或圓形). **5** amount of money 價錢. **6** one of the numbers from 0 to 9 (0—9中的一個)數字. **figurative** ['figjurətiv] *adj* using figures of speech; using words which have a meaning other than the normal one (e.g. saying that a brave man is a lion) 用辭手段的, 借喻的, 比喻的(如說一個勇敢的人是一頭獅子). **figuratively** *adv* '**figurehead 1** wooden carving formerly carried on the front of ships 船首木雕像. **2** person in an important position who has no real power 有名無實的首領, 傀儡. **figure of speech** expression which is not really true, but which is used to give an idea of the meaning (e.g. if we say that a brave man fought like a lion, we are using a figure of speech) 修辭手段, 比喻, 借喻(例如, 我們使用修辭手段說勇士像獅子一般戰鬥).

figure² ['figə*] *vt* **1** take an important

part 佔重要部份; 起重要作用: *The economy figured very largely in the Prime Minister's speech* i.e. this was one of the main topics in his speech. 經濟問題在首相的講話中佔十分重要的部份. 即: 是他講話的一個主題. **2** (mainly *US*) think; arrive at an opinion after thought (主要用於美)想; 認爲: *I figured that I could help you.* (*informal* in sense **2**) 我想我可以幫助你.(義 2 爲非正式). **figure someone / something out** understand someone / something after careful thought 領會, 理解, 弄清楚: *I tried to figure out what he meant.* (*informal*) 我想弄清楚他的意思.(非正式).

filament ['filəmənt] *nc* wire in an electric light bulb 電燈絲.

file[1] [fail] *nc* metal tool with a rough surface used for smoothing hard materials 銼子. Also 亦作 *vt* smooth or cut with a file 銼平; 銼. **filings** *npl* small pieces of metal removed by a file 銼屑.

file[2] [fail] *nc* **1** something for holding papers, letters etc. 文件夾; 文件櫃. **2** collection of papers giving information about somebody or something 檔案: *The police have a file on him* i.e. information about him has been written down and is kept by the police. 警方已把他記錄在案. 即: 有關他的情況已被警方記下並且保存起來. Also 亦作 *vt* put in a file 把…歸檔, 把…存檔.

file[3] [fail] *nc* line of people one behind the other 行列; (軍隊)縱隊: *in single file* 成單行, 成一路縱隊. Also 亦作 *vi* move in a file 成單行或縱隊行進: *They filed past the coffin.* 他們排成縱隊走過靈柩. *They filed out of the room.* 他們一個接一個走出房間. **the rank and file** ordinary members of some society, movement or commu-

nity; all those who are not the leaders 羣衆; 老百姓.

fill [fil] *vt / i* become or make full 裝滿; 使滿: *The room filled with people* i.e. many people came into the room. 房間裏擠滿了人. 即: 許多人進了房間. *He filled the box with books* i.e. he put many books in the box. 他在箱子裏裝滿了書. **filling** *nc / u* substance which fills something (esp. substance used by a dentist to fill holes in teeth) 填料(尤指牙醫所用以補牙者). **'filling station** (*Brit*) place where a motorist can get petrol, oil etc for his car (英)加油站. **fill something in 1** write what is necessary on an official piece of paper 填寫: *fill in an application* 填寫申請表格; *fill in one's name* 填寫姓名. **2** put something into a hole so as to fill it completely 填滿: *He filled in the hole.* 他把這洞填上了. **fill something up 1** fill completely 裝滿: *He filled up my cup.* 他爲我倒滿杯. *I filled the room up with furniture.* 我在房裏擺滿了傢具. **2** write what is necessary on an official paper 填寫: *fill up a form* 填表.

fillet ['filit] *nc* **1** thick piece of meat or fish from which the bones have been removed (去骨的)魚片或肉片. Also 亦作 *vt* remove bones from meat or fish 給(魚或肉)去骨.

film [film] **1** *nc* cinema picture 電影. **2** *nu* substance on which photographs and cinema pictures are made 膠捲, 膠片. **3** *nc* thin covering 薄膜, 薄覆蓋物: *a film of oil / dust* 一層油膜/灰塵. Also 亦作 *vt / i* make a cinema film (of something) 把…拍成電影; 攝製電影.

filter ['filtə*] *nc* any device or substance for allowing liquid to pass through it while not allowing anything solid to pass through 過濾器. Also 亦

作 **1** *vt* pass through a filter 過濾: *He filtered the liquid.* 他過濾這種液體. **2** *vi* (usu. with **down** or **through**) move slowly to reach many people (通常與 down 或 through 連用) 漸爲人知: *The new ideas filtered down to the majority of people.* 這種新觀念漸爲大多數人所知. *People filtered across the border* i.e. came in small groups. 小股小股的人穿越邊境.

filth [filθ] *nu* very unpleasant dirt 骯髒, 污物. **filthy** *adj* very dirty 污穢的, 很髒的.

filtrate ['filtreit] *vt* filter 過濾. **filtration** [fil'treiʃən] *nu* act or process of filtering 過濾.

fin [fin] *nc* **1** one of the parts of its body which a fish uses for swimming 鰭. **2** something shaped like a fin (e.g. on a bomb or rocket) 鰭狀物(例如炸彈或火箭的安定翼).

final ['fainl] *adj* last; coming at the end 最後的; 終極的: *He was completing the final stages of the work.* 他正在完成這工作的最後幾個階段. *What was the final score of the football match?* 足球賽的最後得分是多少? *The headmaster's decision is final* i.e. his decision cannot be questioned or changed. 校長的決定不可更改. **finally** *adv* the **finals** *npl* **1** last contest in a series of contests 決賽. **2** last set of examinations in a course of study at a college or university 期末考試. **finalist** ['fainəlist] *nc* person competing in the last of a series of contests or examinations 決賽選手. **finale** [fi'nɑːli] *nc* last part of a piece of music 終曲, 樂曲的最後部分. **finalize** *vt* finish making plans or arrangements 完成 (計劃或安排).

finance ['fainæns] **1** *nu* management of public money 財政. **2** *nc* (often *pl*)

(public) money (常用複數) 公款. Also 亦作 *vt* supply money for something 提供資助給: *The government have financed a new factory.* 政府提供資金給一家新建工廠. **financial** [fai'nænʃl] *adj* **financially** *adv* **financier** [fai'nænsiə*] *nc* person whose work is concerned with finance 財政家, 金融業者.

find¹ [faind] *vt* get somebody / something that was lost, hidden or unknown 發現; 找到; 得知; 發覺: *I found some money in this old coat.* 我在這件舊上衣裏找到一些錢. *Large deposits of oil and gas have been found under the sea.* 已經在海底找到了大量埋藏的石油和煤氣. *In the morning we found that the car would not start* i.e. we had not known this before. 早晨我們發現汽車不能起動. 即: 我們以前不知道這種情況. *I find that I am unable to help you* i.e. I thought earlier that I could help you. 我發覺我不能幫你. 即: 我原以爲我能够幫你. *past* 過去式和過去分詞 **found** [faund]. **findings** *npl* decision made by a judge, jury, committee of enquiry etc. 裁決, 判決. (陪審團、調查委員會等的)裁决, 判決. **find out** find by searching, asking etc. 查出: *I tried to find out the answer in the library.* 我想在圖書館裏查出答案. *I don't know when he is arriving but I will try to find out.* 我不知他何時到達, 不過我會想辦法查出的. **find someone out** discover that someone is dishonest 發現某人不誠實: *He used to cheat in the examinations until the teacher found him out.* 在老師發現之前, 他考試一直都作弊. **find somebody guilty / not guilty** decide after a trial in a court of law that somebody is guilty or not guilty 判定某人有罪／無罪. **be found** exist 存在:

Kangaroos are found in Australia. 袋鼠生長在澳大利亞.

find² [faind] *nc* something valuable or pleasant which has been found 已被發現的有價值的或令人愉快的東西.

fine¹ [fain] *adj* **1** very delicate; small and made with skill 精緻的; 精巧的, 精細的: *A watchmaker does very fine work.* 鐘錶匠幹的是精細活. **2** very small or thin 細小的: *very fine rain* 毛毛細雨; *a fine point to a pencil* 鉛筆的細筆尖; *fine cotton* 細棉. **3** pure 純粹的: *fine gold* 純金. **4** good or pleasant 良好的; 令人愉快的: *a fine house* 一座舒適的房子; *a fine meal* 一頓美味的飯菜. **5** without rain and pleasant 晴朗的: *fine weather* 晴朗的天氣; *a fine day* 晴朗的一天. **finery** ['fainəri] *nu* very good clothes; clothes worn for a special occasion 華麗的衣服; 禮服. **'fine'arts** painting, music, sculpture etc. 美術(繪畫, 音樂, 雕刻等).

fine² [fain] *nc* sum of money taken from somebody as a punishment 罰金. Also 亦作 *vt* make somebody pay a fine 對(某人) 罰款.

finesse [fi'nes] *nu* ability to deal with difficult situations in a skilful way 手段, 權術.

finger ['fiŋgə*] *nc* one of the five parts at the end of each hand 手指頭. Also 亦作 *vt* touch with the fingers 以指觸摸. *Note* 說明: the thumb is sometimes not included as one of the fingers. thumb (拇指)有時不算作 fingers 之一. **'fingernail** hard substance at the end of a finger 指甲. **'fingerprint** *nc* mark made by the end of a finger 指紋. **'fingertip** end of a finger 指尖. **have something at one's fingertips** know some subject very well 精通或熟知(某事).

finicky ['finiki] *adj* disliking many things (esp. types of food) 苛求的, 過份講究的(尤指對食物).

finish¹ ['finiʃ] *vt / i* end 完成, 結束: *I've nearly finished; wait another ten minutes.* 我差不多要做完了, 請再等十分鐘. *I've finished the work.* 我已結束工作. **finished** *adj* ended 結束的. (opp 反義詞 **unfinished**). **'finishing school** private school which teaches girls how to behave in society (e.g. how to dance, choose clothes, make conversation etc.) 教導少女如何社交(如: 如何跳舞, 如何挑選衣服, 如何交談等)的私立學校, 儀表進修學校. **finish something off / up** finish completely 全部完成; 全部吃光: *I hurried to finish off the work.* 我匆匆完成全部工作. *I finished up all the food in the house* i.e. I ate it. 我吃光了屋裏所有的食品.

finish² ['finiʃ] *n sing* **1** last part; end 最後部份; 終點. **2** (often with reference to the polish or paint put on something) way in which some work is completed (常指塗於某物之上的光亮劑或油漆) 修整, 潤飾.

finite ['fainait] *adj* having an end or limit 有終端的; 有限的. (opp 反義詞 **infinite** ['infinit]).

fiord, fjord [fjɔːd] *nc* narrow inlet of the sea (esp. in Norway) (尤指挪威的)峽灣.

fir [fə:*] *nc* type of evergreen tree which has thin leaves shaped like needles 樅樹.

fire¹ ['faiə*] **1** *nc / u* burning 火: *Animals are afraid of fire.* 動物怕火. *There was a fire in the town yesterday.* 城裏昨天起火. **2** *nc* something burning 某種火: *He lit a fire because the room was cold.* 他生火因為房間很冷. **3** *nc* gas or electric apparatus for warming a room (usu. showing the part which gives out heat) 暖氣爐; 電暖爐. **4** *nu* shooting of guns 開砲, 砲火: *We heard the enemy's fire* 我們聽到敵軍的砲火聲.

fire² ['faiə] **1** *vt / i* shoot a gun 開(槍), 射擊: *He fired at me.* 他向我射擊. *He fired a gun.* 他開槍了. *The gun fired.* 這門砲開火了. **2** *vt* cause to burn. (**set fire to** is more common) 使燃燒 (set fire to 更爲常見). **3** *vt* excite, arouse strong feelings 激起; 使充滿熱情: *The speaker fired the audience with enthusiasm.* 演說者激起了群衆的熱情. **4** *vt* dismiss a person from a job. (*informal*) 解雇 (非正式). '**fire alarm** warning of a fire in a building etc; apparatus for giving this warning 火警; 報警器. '**firearm** gun which can be held in the hands 槍, 輕武器. '**fire brigade** people whose job is to stop fires in buildings etc. 消防隊. '**fire engine** vehicle carrying hosepipes and other apparatus used in stopping fires 消防車. '**fire escape** stairs (usu. on the outside of a building) which can be used if there is a fire in the building 太平梯, 防火梯. '**fire extinguisher** see 見 **extinguish**. '**firefly** type of insect which gives out a light 螢火蟲. '**fireguard** object like a fence, for putting in front of a fire in a room 爐欄. '**fireman** man whose work is to stop fires in buildings etc. 消防隊員. '**fireplace** place where a fire is lit to warm a room 壁爐. '**fireproof** *adj* made so as not to burn 耐火的, 防火的: *fireproof curtains* 防火簾. '**fireside** area around a fire in a room 爐邊. '**firewood** pieces of wood intended for burning 柴火. '**firework** something containing gunpowder and other substances, making a loud noise and a bright light when lit, used for celebrations after dark 烟花, 焰火. **on fire** burning 燃燒着, 起火. **set fire to something, set something on fire** cause something to burn 使(某物)燃燒. **under fire 1** being fired at by guns 遭受砲火攻擊. **2** being attacked in words 遭受抨擊.

firecracker ['faiə,krækə] *nc* roll of paper containing an explosive, set off at celebrations, etc. 鞭砲, 爆竹.

firm¹ [fəm] *nc* business company 公司.

firm² [fəm] *adj* solid; fixed; not easily moved 結實的, 堅硬的; 堅定的; 堅牢的: *The leg of that chair is not very firm* i.e. it is loosely fixed to the chair. 那椅子腿兒不太牢固. *He spoke in a firm voice* i.e. in a strong and determined way, showing that he would not change his opinion. 他說話聲音很堅決. 即: 他以強硬地堅決的方式說話, 表示他不會改變自己的意見. **firmly** *adv* **firmness** *nu*.

first [fəst] *adj / adv* coming before all others 第一的(地), 最先的(地): *He lives in the first house in that street* i.e. the house you come to first as you walk along the street. 他住在那條街上的第一座房子裏. 即: 你沿街走時遇到的第一座房子. *He came first in the race* i.e. he won the race. 他在賽跑中獲第一名. **firstly** *adv* first 首先地, 第一地. '**first aid** help which can be given to a person who has been injured, before a doctor arrives 急救. '**first-class** *adj* **1** very good; excellent 非常好的, 優秀的. **2** (of ways of travelling etc) the most expensive (指旅行方式等) 頭等的, 最昂貴的. '**first night** evening on which a play is performed for the first time; the performance of the play itself 首演之夜; 頭場戲. '**first-rate** *adj* very good; excellent. (*informal*) 非常好的, 優秀的. (非正式)

. **at first** in the beginning 起初, 最初.

fiscal ['fiskl] *adj* having reference to government money 政府財政的.

fish [fiʃ] **1** *nc* type of creature which lives in water and does not need to come to the surface to breathe air 魚類. **2** *nu* fish used as food 食用魚肉: *He eats a lot of fish.* 他吃了不少魚肉. *pl* 複數 **fish** or **fishes**. Also 亦作 *vt/i* catch, try to catch, fish 捕魚, 釣魚. **fishing** *nu* act of catching fish, as work or as a sport 捕魚, 釣魚. **fishy** *adj* causing suspicion. *(informal)* 可疑的 (非正式). '**fishmonger** man who sells fish in a shop 魚販, 魚商. '**fisherman** man who catches fish, either as his work or for sport 漁夫, 釣魚者. '**fishing rod** long piece of wood, to which is attached a strong thread with a hook at the end, used for catching fish as a sport 釣竿.

fishery ['fiʃəri] **1** *nc/u* place where fish are caught or bred 漁場, 養魚場: *deep-sea fisheries* 遠洋漁場. **2** *nc* business of catching fish 漁業.

fission ['fiʃən] *nu* (usu. with reference to the breaking up of an atom in a nuclear explosion) process of dividing into several parts (原子) 核裂變.

fist [fist] *nc* hand with the fingers bent to touch the palm 拳頭.

fit¹ [fit] *adj* **1** strong and healthy 強健的: *He felt fit after his holiday.* 度假之後, 他感到身強體壯. **2** suitable 適合的: *The house was not fit to live in* i.e. it was a very bad house. 這座房子不適合居住. 即: 它是一座很糟的房子. *He is not a fit person to decide what should be done* i.e. he has not the authority or ability to decide. 他不是一個合適的決策者. 即: 他沒有決策的權力或能力. *(opp* 反義詞 **unfit**).

fit² [fit] **1** *vt/i* be the right size for

合: *I could not find a pair of shoes which fitted me.* 我找不到一雙適合我穿的鞋. **2** *vt* put some piece of apparatus or furnishing in place 安裝; 配備 (傢具): *The electrician fitted my new cooker.* 電工爲我安裝新炊具. *I have been fitting a carpet in this room.* 我一直在這個房間裏舖地毯. **3** *vt* make suitable 使適合: *His long experience fits him for the job.* 他有長期的經驗適合做這項工作. *past* 過去式和過去分詞 **fitted**. **fitter** *nc* person who fits apparatus in place (esp. one who has a knowledge of mechanical or electrical engineering). 裝配工 (尤指機械或電氣裝配工). **fitting** *adj* suitable 適合的; *a fitting punishment* 適當的懲罰. Also 亦作 *nc* **1** something fitted in a building etc (e.g. a light, fire, water pipe etc.) 樓房配備裝置 (如電燈, 爐具, 水管等) **2** occasion when one tries on a garment being made for one to see whether it fits 試穿衣服看是否合身. **fit in** be suitable 適合: *We invited him to join our club but he didn't fit in* i.e. he did not have the same interests as the other members. 我們邀請他加入我們的俱樂部, 可是他覺得不適合. 即: 他與俱樂部的其他會員的興趣不同. **fit someone / something out** provide what is necessary 供以 (必需物): *fit out a boy for school* i.e. buy his uniform and his books 爲上學的孩子提供必需品, 即: 爲他買制服和書籍. **a good / bad fit** the right / wrong size for 很合穿/不合穿: *This pair of shoes is a good fit for me.* 這雙鞋正合我的腳.

fit³ [fit] *nc* **1** sudden illness in which one loses consciousness and makes movements which one cannot control 失去知覺並且發生痙攣的突發病. **2** something similar to this happening suddenly 一陣突發疾病: *a fit of coughing* 一陣猛咳; *in fits of laughter* 陣陣笑聲. **fitful** *adj* often stopping and starting 斷斷續續的: *a fitful sleep* 時睡時醒. **by fits and starts** often stopping and starting 斷斷續續地: *He worked by fits and starts. (informal)* 他斷斷續續地工作. (非正式).

five [faiv] see appendix 見附錄.

fix¹ [fiks] *vt* 1 fasten 固定: *He fixed the cupboard to the wall with nails* 他用釘子把碗櫥固定在牆上. 2 arrange; agree on 安排;商定: *fix a date / price* 定日期/價格; *fix up a meeting* 商定開一次會議. 3 mend 修理: *fix a watch* 修手錶. 4 prepare; make ready 準備;備好: *fix a drink. (informal* in sense 4) 調製飲料 (義 4 為非正式). **fixed** *adj* 1 placed in position and not moving 固定的. 2 arranged or agreed on 安排好的;商定的. **fixture** *nc* 1 something which is fixed in a building (e.g. a light, a water pipe etc.) 固定裝置, 設備 (如燈、水管等). 2 game or sports contest which takes place on a date arranged before 事先安排好的比賽項目.

fix² [fiks] *nc* (usu. only sing) difficult position (通常只用單數) 困境, 窘境: *He's in a fix. (informal)* 他正處於困境. (非正式).

fizz [fiz] *vi* make a sound like that of bubbles of gas coming out of a liquid 嘶嘶地響. Also 亦作 *nc* **fizzy** *adj*: *a fizzy drink* 汽水 (或汽酒等起泡沫的飲料).

fizzle ['fizl] *vi* in **fizzle out** i.e. end in a weak and disappointing way 用於 fizzle out 即: 虎頭蛇尾般地結束; 終於失敗: *His plans fizzled out.* 他的計劃結果失敗了.

fjord [fjɔːd] *nc* see 見 **fiord**.

flabbergast ['flæbəgɑːst] *vt* surprise

very greatly 使大吃一驚,使目瞪口呆. **flabbergasted** *adj* (both *informal*) (均為非正式).

flabby ['flæbi] *adj* fat and soft 肥胖鬆弛的.

flag¹ [flæg] *nc* 1 piece of cloth etc with a design which represents a country, town, person, club etc. 旗, 旗幟. 2 small piece of paper, like a flag, sold in the streets for charity (售賣募捐用的) 小紙旗. **'flagpole** long pole or piece of wood on which a flag is flown 旗竿. **'flagstone** large flat piece of stone used for making paths etc. (舖路用的) 石板.

flag² [flæg] *vi* become weak 衰退, 減退, 變弱: *The runners were flagging.* 賽跑的人漸漸跑不動了. *past* 過去式和過去分詞 **flagged.**

flagrant ['fleigrənt] *adj* (with reference to something dishonest or bad) not hidden 罪惡昭彰的; 明目張膽的; 公然的: *flagrant disobedience* 公然違抗.

flair [flɛə*] *nc* (usu. only *sing*) natural ability to do something (通常只用單數) 天賦, 才華: *He has a flair for mathematics.* 他在數學方面有天賦.

flake [fleik] *nc* small light piece of something 薄片: *flakes of snow* 雪花. **flaky** *adj* consisting of flakes 薄片狀的: *flaky pastry* 酥餅. **flake (off)** come off in flakes 剝落: *The paint is flaking off.* 油漆正在剝落.

flamboyant [flæm'bɔiənt] *adj* brightly coloured; easily noticed because of bright colours; showy 艷麗的; 顯眼的; 炫耀的.

flame [fleim] *nc* one of the red or yellow tongues of burning gas seen where there is a fire 火焰, 火舌.

flamingo [flə'miŋgou] *nc* type of bird with long legs and neck and pinkish feathers 火烈鳥, 火鶴, 紅鶴. *pl* 複數

flamingos or **flamingoes**.

flammable ['flæməbl] *adj* easily set on fire 易燃的. *Note* 說明: the opposite sense is expressed by *not flammable*. The word *inflammable* also means easily set on fire. 其反義用 not flammable 表示. inflammable 的意思也是 "易燃的".

flan [flæn] *nc* shallow open tart 果醬餅, 果餡餅.

flank [flæŋk] *nc* **1** side of an animal (and sometimes of a human being) (動物, 有時指人的)脇, 腰窩. **2** side of an army (軍隊的)側翼. Also 亦作 *vt* be at the side of 位於…的側面.

flannel ['flænl] **1** *nu* type of cloth made from wool 法蘭絨. **2** *nc* piece of cloth used for washing oneself (洗澡用的) 法蘭絨巾. **flannels** *npl* trousers made of flannel (used esp. for sport) 法蘭絨長褲(尤指運動褲).

flap¹ [flæp] *nc* **1** anything which hangs down from / over something else (e.g. on a pocket, envelope etc.) 垂下物; 蓋 (如口袋蓋, 信封口蓋等). **2** noise of a large surface moving; the movement itself 拍打聲; 拍打, 拍動: *The flap of a large bird's wing*. 大鳥的鼓翼. Also 亦作 *vt / i* move a large surface 拍打: *The bird flapped its wings*. 那鳥拍動翅膀. *past* 過去式和過去分詞 **flapped**.

flap² [flæp] *vi* (*Brit*) become excited and worried (英)激動; 焦慮. Also 亦作 *nc* (*Brit*) state of excitement and worry (英)激動; 焦慮狀態: *be in a flap*. (both *informal*) 惴惴不安(均為非正式).

flare [flɛə*] *vi* burn for a short time with a bright light (火焰)閃耀. Also 亦作 *nc* **1** (often with reference to one used as a signal) bright light burning for a short time 閃耀(常指閃光信號).

2 widening of a skirt etc towards the lower edge (as in **flared skirt**) 裙子等下部的展開 (如用於 flared skirt). **flare up 1** burn with a flare 驟然燃燒起來. **2** suddenly start; suddenly get angry 爆發, 突然發作; 突然發怒: *A quarrel flared up.* 突然爆發了一場爭吵.

flash¹ [flæʃ] *nc* **1** sudden bright light 閃光: *a flash of lightning* 閃電的一閃. **2** short piece of news received or sent by radio or telegraph 簡短的新聞電訊.

flash² [flæʃ] **1** *vt / i* make a flash (使)閃光: *The lightning flashed in the sky*. 閃電閃過天空. *He flashed his torch for a few seconds*. 他把手電筒閃亮了幾秒鐘. **2** *vi* move very quickly 飛馳; 閃過: *The cars were flashing past*. 一輛輛汽車飛馳而過. *An idea flashed into his mind*. 他腦子裏閃過一個念頭. **3** *vt* send a message by radio or telegraph 發出(電訊): *He flashed the news to us*. 他把這消息電告我們. **flashy** *adj* bright but of poor quality or value 俗麗的: *flashy clothes* 俗麗的衣服. '**flashback** sequence in a cinema film which goes back to show events which happened before the main part of the story (電影的)倒叙, 閃回. '**flashlight** piece of apparatus used by a photographer for making a sudden bright light (攝影)閃光燈. (Also 亦作 **flash**). **in a flash** suddenly; very quickly. 轉瞬間; 即刻.

flask [flɑːsk] *nc* **1** type of bottle used in laboratories (實驗室用的)燒瓶. **2** flat bottle for carrying in the pocket or fastened to one's belt etc. used in (便於放進口袋或掛在皮帶上携帶) 扁瓶; 扁酒瓶. **3** vacuum flask i.e. container made in such a way that a liquid put into it remains at the same temperature for a long time 保溫瓶; 冷藏瓶; 熱水瓶.

flat¹ [flæt] *nc* **1** (*Brit*) number of rooms on one floor of a building. (US = **apartment**) (英)(同一層樓的)一套房間. **2** flat part of anything 任何東西的平坦部份. **3** flat tyre 沒氣的輪胎. **4** musical note which is lowered by one semitone; e.g. B flat is one semitone below B natural; (音)降半音音音符(如降B比B低半音).

flat² [flæt] *adj* **1** level; smooth; without bumps or hills 平的; 平滑的; 平坦的; *a flat surface* 平面. **2** uninteresting 乏味的, 單調的. **3** (with reference to beer or other such drinks containing gas) old and with the gas gone (啤酒等飲料) 走了氣的. **4** (music) below the true pitch (音樂)降音的; 降半音的. **5** (with reference to a tyre) punctured; without air (輪胎)被刺破的, 沒氣的. **6** definite; without further discussion 斷然的, 明確的; 不容再議的; *a flat refusal* 斷然拒絕. **flatness** *nu* **flatly** *adv* in a definite way 斷然, 直截了當地; *He flatly refused to help me.* 他斷然拒絕幫助我. **flatten** *vt* make flat 把…弄平. **flat 'rate** charge made for goods or services, to which no extra charges will be added 統一收費率. **go flat out** go at full speed. (*informal*) 全速前進(非正式).

flatter ['flætə*] *vt* tell somebody that he is very good, very clever etc when in fact he is not 諂媚; 奉承; 恭維. **flattery** *nc* / *u* process of flattering 奉承; 諂媚; 恭維. **flatterer** *nc* person who flatters 奉承者, 拍馬屁的人.

flatulent ['flætjulənt] *adj* having too much gas in the stomach 胃裏氣脹的. **flatulence** *nu*.

flaunt [flɔ:nt] *vt* / *i* behave in a bad or foolish way to make people take

notice of one 炫耀, 誇耀, 誇示; *She was flaunting her new clothes.* 她正在炫耀她的新衣服.

flavour ['fleivə*] (*US* 美 **flavor**) *nc* / *u* **1** taste; quality which can be experienced by the mouth 味; 味道; *This food has a strong flavour.* 這種食品味道很濃. **2** special quality of anything, or a suggestion of it 風味; 特色; *This book has a romantic flavour.* 這本書有浪漫色彩. Also 亦作 *vt* increase the flavour of, give flavour to 給…調味, 加味於. **flavouring** *nc* something used to give flavour to food 調味品, 香料.

flaw [flɔ:] *nc* **1** crack in a glass or pottery (玻璃或陶器的) 裂痕. **2** mistake or fault 缺點, 瑕疵; *a flaw in an argument* 論點裏的一個漏洞. **flawless** *adj* without a flaw; perfect 無懈可擊的; 完美的.

flax [flæks] *nu* type of plant, used for making a kind of cloth (called **linen**) 亞麻(可織亞麻布). **flaxen** *adj* (usu. with reference to the colour of hair) light yellow (頭髮)亞麻色的, 淺黃色的.

flea [fli:] *nc* small insect which lives on the blood of animals, birds, human beings etc. 跳蚤.

fleck [flek] *nc* small mark or spot 斑點, 小點. Also 亦作 *vt* mark with flecks 使有斑點, 飾以斑點.

fled [fled] past of **flee**. flee 的過去式和過去分詞.

fledged [fledʒd] *adj* usu. in **'fully-'fledged** properly qualified 通常用於 fully-fledged (有充份資格的): *a fully-fledged member of the club (informal)* 俱樂部的正式成員 (非正式). **fledgling** *nc* young bird just learning to fly 剛學飛的小鳥.

flee [fli:] *vt* / *i* run away 逃, 逃走; *The robbers fled.* 強盜逃跑了. *He fled his* *enemy.* 他從敵人那裏逃脫. *past* 過去式和過去分詞 **fled** [fled].

fleece [fli:s] *nc* wool of a sheep 羊毛.

fleet[1] [fli:t] *nc* **1** number of ships or boats sailing together or under one command 艦隊; 船隊. **2** number of buses etc owned by one person or one company 車隊.

fleet[2] [fli:t] *adj* fast *(o.f.)* 快速的, 敏捷的 (舊式). **fleeting** *adj* moving fast 疾馳的, 飛逝的: *a fleeting glance* 短暫的一瞥.

flesh [fleʃ] *nu* **1** soft part of the body over the bones 肉, 肌肉. **2** the body (as opposed to the soul) 肉體 (與靈魂相對). **'flesh-coloured** *adj* of the colour of Europeans; pinkish (具有)白人膚色的; 帶粉紅色的. **'flesh wound** small wound which is not very deep 輕傷, 皮肉之傷. **in the flesh** in real life, and not as a picture etc. 活生生的; 本人(而非照片). **one's own flesh and blood** one's own family (e.g. one's parents, children, brothers, sisters etc.) 親骨肉, 親屬(如父母、子女、兄弟、姊妹等).

flew [flu:] past tense of **fly**[2]. fly 的過去式.

flex[1] [fleks] *nc / u* thin insulated wire for carrying electricity 花線, 皮線.

flex[2] [fleks] *vt* bend 屈曲, 彎曲: *He flexed his muscles.* 他活動自己的肌肉.

flexible ['fleksibl] *adj* **1** easily bent into different shapes 易彎曲的. **2** willing to change one's opinions, plans etc. 可變通的. (*opp* 反義詞 **inflexible**). **flexibility** [fleksi'biliti] *nu*.

flick [flik] *vt* hit quickly and lightly 輕打; 輕彈. Also 亦作 *nc* quick light blow 輕打. **'flick knife** type of knife in which the blade can be pushed into the handle and released by a

spring 彈簧摺刀.

flicker ['flikə] *vt / i* (usu. with reference to a light) move quickly and unsteadily (通常指燈光)閃爍, 搖曳. Also 亦作 *nc* quick and unsteady movement of a light (燈光的)閃爍, 搖曳.

flight [flait] **1** *nu* act of flying 飛翔, 飛行. **2** *nc* journey in an aeroplane 乘飛機旅行. **3** *nc* act of running away 逃亡, 逃走: *the flight of the enemy* 敵人的潰逃. **4** *nc* set of stairs between two level places 一段樓梯, 一段階梯. **flighty** *adj* not serious; always looking for amusement 不嚴肅的; 輕浮的, 尋歡作樂的: *a flighty young woman* 輕浮的年輕女人. **'flight deck** part of an aircraft used by the pilot etc. (飛機的)駕駛艙. **in flight** while flying 飛行中的. **take flight** run away 逃走.

flimsy ['flimzi] *adj* not strongly made; easily torn; of poor material 輕而薄的, 不結實的; 易撕破的, 易損壞的; 質地差的.

flinch [flintʃ] *vi* move back a little because of danger or pain (因危險或痛苦)退縮, 畏縮.

flinders ['flindəz] *npl* small fragments or splinters 碎片, 破片: *to break something in flinders* 打碎某物; *to fly in flinders* 破碎.

fling [fliŋ] *vt / i* throw with force (用力地)扔, 擲, 抛, 丟: *The boy was flinging stones.* 那男孩正在扔石頭. *past* 過去式和過去分詞 **flung** [flʌŋ].

flint [flint] *nc / u* **1** very hard type of stone 燧石. **2** stone in a cigarette lighter etc which produces a spark when hit with a piece of steel (打火機等的)打火石.

flip [flip] *vt* hit quickly and lightly 輕彈, 輕擊. *past* 過去式和過去分詞 **flipped**.

flippant ['flipənt] *adj* not serious; making jokes about things which other people treat seriously 不嚴肅的；無禮的，輕率的. **flippancy** nu.

flipper ['flipə*] nc **1** limb of certain sea creatures (e.g. the seal) which helps it to swim (海豹等的) 鰭狀肢. **2** long piece of rubber attached to the foot to help people to swim (游泳用的) 橡皮脚掌.

flirt [flə:t] vi play at love etc for amusement 調情；打情罵俏；不嚴肅對待: *She was flirting with him.* 她正在跟他打情罵俏. *He flirted with the idea* i.e. he was not seriously interested in it. 他並沒有認真考慮這個主意. Also 亦作 nc person who does this 調情者. **flirtation** [flə:'teiʃən] nc/u.

flit [flit] vi move quickly and lightly from place to place 輕快地掠過: *The birds were flitting about in the trees.* 鳥兒在樹木間輕快地飛來飛去. past 過去式和過去分詞 **flitted.**

float¹ [flout] vt/i rest, cause to rest, on the top of liquid (使) 漂浮: *The boy was floating his boat.* 那男孩讓他的小船在水上漂起. **2** vi be held up by air, gas etc. 浮動，飄動: *The boat was floating on the water.* 船在水面漂浮着. *Dust floats in the air.* 灰塵飄浮在空中. **float the pound** let the pound find its own value as international currency 使英鎊浮動.

float² [flout] nc **1** piece of cork, plastic etc, on a fishing line, which floats on the water and shows the fisherman where the line is (釣魚用的) 浮子. **2** vehicle carrying something to be shown in a procession (遊行時用的) 彩車, 載着展品遊行的車輛.

flock [flɔk] nc number of sheep, goats or birds together 羊羣；鳥羣. Also 亦作 vi move together in a large group 成羣移動: *The people were flocking*

to the theatre. 人們成羣地走向戲院.

flog [flɔg] vt **1** hit many times very hard with a stick or whip 多次重打；抽打；鞭打. **2** sell (informal in sense **2**) 出售(義 2 爲非正式). past 過去式和過去分詞 **flogged. flogging** nc severe beating 重打，鞭打.

flood [flʌd] nc **1** flow of water over land which is usually dry 洪水；水災. **2** something like a flood, large amount 大量, 大批: *a flood of ideas / requests / tears / light* 許多想法／許多請求／泉水般湧出的眼淚／一片强光. Also 亦作 vt / i: *The river has flooded.* 河水泛濫. *He was flooded with applications for tickets.* 他收到了大量要求得到票的申請. **'floodlight** nc strong light, often used to show the outside of buildings at night 泛光燈. Also 亦作 vt light with a floodlight 用泛光燈照明. past 過去式和過去分詞 **floodlit** ['flʌdlit].

floor¹ [flɔ:*] nc **1** part of a room on which one walks (室内的)地面, 地板. **2** all the rooms in a building at the same height from the ground 樓層: *This building has two floors* i.e. there are rooms at ground level, and more rooms upstairs. 這座房子有兩層. 即: 樓上樓下都有房間. Note 說明: (Brit) the floor at the bottom of a building is called the *ground floor* and the floor above is called the *first floor.* (US) the floor at the bottom is called the *first floor* and the one above is called the *second floor* (英) 樓房的底層叫 ground floor, 二樓叫 first floor. (美) 樓房的底層叫 first floor, 二樓叫 second floor. **'floor show** entertainment presented in a restaurant etc. 餐廳等的文娛表演.

floor² [flɔ:*] vt **1** hit somebody so that he falls to the floor (informal) 把某人

打倒在地(非正式). **2** be too difficult for somebody to understand (*informal*) 把某人難倒(非正式).

flop¹ [flɔp] *vi* fall heavily and without much control over one's movements 沉重地, 不由自主地倒下: *He flopped into a chair.* 他撲通一下坐在椅子上. *past* 過去式和過去分詞 **flopped.** **floppy** *adj* hanging loosely 鬆散下垂的. **floppiness** *nu.*

flop² [flɔp] *nc* failure 失敗: *The new play was a flop* i.e. very few people came to see it. 新戲是個大失敗. 新戲幾乎沒有甚麼人來看這齣戲. Also 亦作 *vi* fail 失敗. *past* 過去式和過去分詞 **flopped.** (both *informal*) (均為非正式).

flora [ˈflɔːrə] *nc / u* all the plant life in a particular area or at a particular period of time (某地區或某時期的)植物羣.

floral [ˈflɔːrəl] *adj* with reference to flowers 花的.

florid [ˈflɔrid] *adj* **1** (with reference to the face) red in colour (臉色)紅潤的. **2** with too much decoration 裝飾過多的; 華麗的.

florist [ˈflɔrist] *nc* person who sells flowers 花商.

floss [flɔs] *nu* **1** rough silk threads on the outside of a silkworm's cocoon (蠶繭外層的)粗絲. **2** soft, silky fluff or fibre 絨毛; 絲線; 細絨線.

flotilla [fləˈtilə] *nc* small number of warships 小艦隊.

flotsam [ˈflɔtsəm] *nu* objects from a wrecked ship floating in the sea (飄浮在海上的)遇難船隻的殘骸或物品.

flotsam and jetsam useless things of various types (Properly *flotsam* refers to things floating in the sea, and *jetsam* to things washed on to land by the sea.) 各種廢物 (嚴格地說來, flot-

sam 指飄浮在海上的廢物, jetsam 指被海浪冲到岸邊的廢物).

flounce [flauns] *vi* move angrily and noisily 暴跳; 怒衝衝地走動: *She flounced out of the room.* 她怒氣衝衝地跑出房間.

flounder [ˈflaundə*] *vi* (often with reference to movement in water) move with great difficulty, making violent efforts (常指在水中)挣扎.

flour [ˈflauə*] *nu* powder made from wheat, corn etc, used for making bread etc. 麵粉. **floury** *adj.*

flourish¹ [ˈflʌriʃ] **1** grow well 茂盛. **2** *vi* be most active at a certain time 繁榮; 興隆; 處於旺盛時期: *The British Empire flourished in the 19th century.* 英帝國在十九世紀處於全盛時期. **3** *vt* make large movements in the air 揮舞; *He was flourishing a sword.* 他正在舞劍.

flourish² [ˈflʌriʃ] *nc* movement of something in the air 揮舞, 揮動: *He was making flourishes with his sword.* 他正持劍揮舞. **2** short piece of loud music 高昂的樂段, 花腔.

flout [flaut] *vt* treat as though foolish and unimportant 輕蔑, 輕視: *He tried to flour the headmaster's authority* i.e. he showed no respect for the headmaster. 他試圖對校長的權威嗤之以鼻: 他不尊敬校長.

flow [flou] *vi* (usu. with reference to liquids) move along (通常指液體)流動. Also 亦作 *nc* (usu. only *sing*) (通常只用單數) movement of liquid 流, 流動. **flowing** *adj* moving or curving smoothly; hanging gracefully 流動的; (輪廓等)圓滑的; 下垂的, 飄拂的.

flower [ˈflauə*] *nc* **1** blossom; part of a plant from which seeds are produced 花. **2** any small plant which is grown for the sake of its flowers 花, 花卉

Also 亦作 *vi* produce flowers 開花:
The trees are flowering. 那些樹木正在
開花. **flowery** *adj* 1 of flowers 花的.
2 using too many poetical words 詞藻
華麗的: *a flowery speech* 詞藻華麗的
演説. **flowerbed** part of a garden
where flowers are grown 花壇.

flown [floun] past part of **fly²**. fly² 的過
去分詞.

flu [flu:] *nu* short form of **influenza** 流
行性感冒 (influenza 的縮略形式).

fluctuate ['flʌktjueit] *vi* frequently
change from higher to lower; vary in
level (e.g. with reference to temperature, price, amount etc.) 波動, 漲落,
起伏 (如指温度, 物價, 數量等). **fluc-
tuation** [flʌktju'eiʃən] *nc / u.*

fluent ['flu:ənt] *adj* able to speak easily
説話流利的: *He is a fluent speaker.* 他
説話流利. *He made a fluent speech.*
他作了一次流利的演講. **fluently** *adv*
fluency *nu.*

fluff [flʌf] *nu* small pieces which have
come off cloth (esp. wool) (織物上掉下的
毛織品上掉下的) 絨毛. **fluffy** *adj* like
fluff 絨毛狀的, 毛茸茸的.

fluid ['flu:id] *nc* 1 liquid 液體: *Water,
oil, blood, milk are fluids.* 水、油、血、
牛奶等是液體. 2 liquid or gas 流體,
液體或氣體. Also 亦作 *adj* 1 of or like
a fluid 流體的; 液體的. 2 (with reference to plans, arrangements etc) not
fixed; able to be changed if necessary
(指計劃、安排等) 不固定的; 可改變的.

fluke [flu:k] *nc* success which happens
by chance. *(informal)* 僥倖成功 (非正
式).

flung [flʌŋ] past of **fling**. fling 的過去式
和過去分詞.

flunk [flʌŋk] *vt / i* fail, cause to fail, a
test or examination at school or college. *(informal)* (使) 考試不及格 (非正
式).

fluorescent [fluə'resnt] *adj* giving off
light when exposed to electricity 熒光
的, 發熒光的.

fluoride ['fluəraid] *nu* compound of
fluorine and another substance 氟化
物.

fluorine ['fluəri:n] *nu* corrosive, poisonous, greenish-yellow, gaseous chemic-
al element (F)氟.

flurry ['flʌri] *nc* sudden movement of
wind, snow etc. 疾風; 驟雨; 驟然
降下的一陣雪等.

flush¹ [flʌʃ] 1 *vi* become red in the
face because of excitement, embarrassment, exercises, food and drink
etc. (因激動、窘迫、體育鍛煉、飲食等)
臉紅, 漲紅臉. 2 *vt* make clean by a
strong flow of water 冲洗: *flush a
lavatory* 冲洗廁所.

flush² [flʌʃ] *nc* redness of the face,
caused by excitement, exercise, drink
etc. (因激動、體育鍛煉、飲酒等引起的)
臉紅, 紅暈.

flush³ [flʌʃ] *adj* meeting exactly at the
edges 邊緣齊平的: *The window is not
flush with the wall* i.e. there is an
open space between the window and
the wall. 窗與牆不貼合. 即: 窗與牆之
間有空縫.

fluster ['flʌstə*] *vt* make somebody too
excited or worried to be able to do
something properly 使(某人因激動或
焦慮)驚慌失措, 使困惑. Also 亦作 *nu*
condition of being flustered 困惑; 驚
慌失措: *He is in a fluster.* 他驚慌失
措.

flute [flu:t] *nc* type of musical instrument consisting of a tube of metal or
wood with holes in it which are covered by the fingers or by keys 長笛
(一種樂器).

flutter ['flʌtə*] *vt / i* (usu. with reference
to the wings of birds) move quickly

backwards and forwards （鳥）振翼. Also 亦作 *nc* movement of this kind 振翼.

flux [flʌks] *n sing* usu. in **in a state of flux** i.e. always changing 通常用於 in a state of flux, 即：處於不斷的變化中, 動蕩不定.

fly¹ [flai] *nc* **1** type of small winged insect 蒼蠅. **2** (usu. *pl* in Britain) front of a pair of trousers fastened by buttons or a zip （英通常用複數）（遮住長褲紐扣或拉鍊的）遮布, 遮紐蓋.

fly² [flai] **1** *vt / i* move, cause to move, in the air （使）飛行：*The aeroplane was flying.* 飛機正在飛行. *He flew the aeroplane.* 他駕駛飛機. **2** *vi* hurry; go very quickly 趕緊, 匆忙; 飛跑, 飛奔：*She flew down the stairs to greet him.* （*informal* in sense 2）她飛奔下樓去迎接他.（義 2 為非正式）. *pres part* 現在分詞 **flying**. *past tense* 過去式 **flew** [flu:]. *past part* 過去分詞 **flown** [floun]. **'flyover** road built to pass over another road 立交橋. **'flypast** (*Brit*) flight of aeroplanes over a city etc as a celebration of something (*US* 美 **flyover**)（英）飛越（飛機飛越城市等以示慶祝）. **'flying 'saucer** one of various objects which people claim to have seen flying at great speed and thought to be from another planet （據稱是來自其他行星的）飛碟. **'flying squad** police with very fast cars 快速特警隊, 警察機動隊. **'flying 'visit** visit during which one stays for a very short time 短暫的訪問. **with flying colours** with great success (usu. in **pass an examination with flying colours**) 大獲全勝 (通常用於 pass an examination with flying colours).

foal [foul] *nc* young horse 駒.

foam [foum] *nu* very small bubbles 泡沫. Also 亦作 *vi* form small bubbles

起泡沫. **'foam 'rubber** type of rubber, like foam in appearance, used for making cushions etc. 泡沫橡皮, 海綿橡皮.

fob [fɔb] *vt* in **fob somebody off** i.e. deceive somebody; make somebody accept something which is false or worthless 用於 fob somebody off, 即：欺騙某人, 用偽、劣賣矇騙某人：*He fobbed me off with an excuse.* 他找了一個藉口矇騙我. *past* 過去式和過去分詞 **fobbed**. (*informal*)（非正式）.

focal ['foukəl] *adj* see 見 **focus**.

fo'c's'le ['fouksl] *nc* see 見 **forecastle**.

focus ['foukəs] *nc* **1** point where rays of light meet 焦點. **2** part where there is most activity or interest (活動或興趣的)中心, 集中點：*the focus of the trouble* 糾紛的焦點; *a focus of interest* 眾人感興趣的中心. *pl* 複數 **focuses** or **foci** ['fouki:]. Also 亦作 *vt* **1** adjust a telescope, camera etc so that the rays of light meet and make a clear image 調節 (望遠鏡、照相機等的) 焦距, 對焦. **2** give careful attention to something 集中精神於：*focus one's mind on something* 把注意力集中在某事. *past* 過去式和過去分詞 **focussed**. (*US* 美 **focused**). **focal** *adj* out of focus not clear or sharp; indistinct 焦距沒有對準的, 不清楚的, 模糊的：*This photograph is out of focus.* 這張照片的焦距沒有對準. (*opp* 反義語 **in focus**).

fodder ['fɔdə*] *nu* food for cows, horses, sheep etc which have been stored 草料, 飼料.

fog [fɔg] *nc / u* thick vapour or cloud which comes down to the level of the ground and which makes it difficult for one to see properly 霧. **foggy** *adj* **'foghorn** thing which makes a loud noise, used to warn ships during fog (起霧時警告船隻的)霧號, 霧角.

foible ['fɔibl] *nc* unimportant and unusual idea or way of behaving, which one thinks important (自鳴得意的)怪念頭;(自己頗欣賞的)怪癖, 小缺點.

foil¹ [fɔil] **1** *nu* metal hammered into a thin sheet like paper 箔. **2** *nc* person / thing which makes another person / thing seem better, more beautiful, more clever etc in contrast 陪襯的角色, 襯托物.

foil² [fɔil] *vt* prevent somebody from doing something (esp. something wrong) 阻止某人做某事(尤指錯事); I *foiled the thief*. 我阻止那小偷作案. I *foiled his attempt to steal the money*. 我使他要偷錢的企圖不能得逞.

fold¹ [fould] *vt / i* **1** (often with **up**) bend, cause to bend (常與 **up** 連用) (把…)折疊起來; *She folded her dress up and put it in a drawer*. 她疊好衣服放進抽屜. *He folded up the letter and put it in the envelope*. 他把信摺好裝進信封. **2** (with reference to businesses etc) fail (*informal* in sense 2) (指商業等)失敗. (義 2 爲非正式). Also 亦作 *nc* mark made by folding 褶痕. **folder** *nc* piece of stiff cardboard, folded for holding loose papers 文件夾.

fold² [fould] *nc* small space surrounded by a fence or wall, for keeping sheep in; the sheep themselves 羊欄; 羊羣.

foliage ['fouliidʒ] *nu* leaves on a tree or bush (樹上的所有)葉子.

folk [fouk] *npl* people (rather *o.f.*) 人們 (頗爲舊式). **folks** *npl* one's parents. (*informal*) 父母 (非正式). **'folklore** study and collection of old stories, songs and beliefs of a tribe, community etc 民間傳說、民歌、民間信仰等的搜集和研究; 民俗學. **'folksong 1** *nc* old song sung by ordinary people 民歌. **2** *nu* songs in general 一般歌曲.

folksinger *nc*.

follow ['fɔlou] *vt / i* **1** go or come after 跟隨, 接着; *The hunters were following a lion*. 當時獵人們正在追獵一頭獅子. *Famine and disease followed the war*. 饑饉和疾病隨着戰爭而來. *vt / i* understand 領會, 明白: *I don't follow you*. 我沒有聽懂你的話. **3** *vt* act in accordance with 聽從, 遵循: *follow somebody's advice / example* 聽從某人的勸告/效法某人的榜樣. **4** take an interest in 密切注意, 感興趣: *He follows football*. 他對足球感興趣. **follower** *nc* person who supports or follows a leader 門徒, 信徒, 追隨者. **following** *n sing* people supporting somebody 追隨者: *The Prime Minister has a large following* i.e. many people support him. 首相的追隨者很多. 即: 許多人擁護他. Also 亦作 *adj* coming after 其次的: *I met him on the following day*. 我第二天碰到了他. **follow something up** go further in doing something 繼續做某事; 進一步努力做某事: *I want to follow up this subject* i.e. learn more about it. 我要繼續研究這個專題. 即: 要學習與此有關的更多東西. *They followed up their victory* i.e. they continued to drive away the enemy. 他們乘勝追擊. 即: 他們繼續趕走敵人. **it follows** it is seen to be true because of something else 由此得出結論, 因而斷定: *If today is Monday 15 March, it follows that tomorrow is Tuesday 16*. 要是今天是三月十五日星期一, 明天就是十六日星期二.

folly ['fɔli] *nc / u* foolish words or behaviour 傻話; 蠢事; 荒唐事.

fond [fɔnd] *adj* **1** loving or liking (often loving too much) 喜愛的 (常指溺愛的): *a fond father* i.e. one who allows his children too much freedom 溺愛(孩子)的父親, 即: 太依從孩子的父親.

2 foolish 愚蠢的: *a fond hope* 不大可能實現的希望. **fondness** *nu* **fondly** *adv* **1** with love 親愛地. **2** foolishly 愚蠢地. **be fond of someone / something** like someone / something 喜歡某人／愛好某物: *He is fond of his grandmother.* 他喜歡他奶奶. *He is fond of potatoes.* 他愛吃馬鈴薯.

fondle ['fɒndl] *vt* touch in a loving way 愛撫.

food [fu:d] *nu* what is eaten by people and animals or taken in by plants 食物；養料. **'foodstuff** (with reference to trade, shipping, laws etc) anything which can be eaten (指貿易、航運、法律等)食物, 糧食, 食品.

fool [fu:l] *nc* person who does and says stupid things (which show that he does not think very much) 傻瓜, 笨人. Also 亦作 **1** *vt* trick somebody, so that he seems foolish 愚弄. **2** *vi* (often with **about** or **around**) behave like a fool (常與 about 或 around 連用)幹蠢事, 遊手好閒, 鬼混: *The boys were fooling around instead of doing their work.* 男孩們遊手好閒不幹活. **foolish** *adj* **foolishly** *adv* **foolishness** *nu* **'foolhardy** *adj* brave but foolish 魯莽的, 有勇無謀的. **'foolproof** *adj* very easy to do (so that not even a fool can do it wrong); that cannot go wrong 極其簡單的; 錯不了的: *a foolproof method* 萬無一失的方法. **play the fool** behave in a foolish way 幹傻事; 裝傻.

foot [fut] *nc* **1** end of a leg, on which one stands 腳. **2** (only sing) bottom of something (只用單數)底部, 基部: *the foot of a mountain / a bed / a page / the stairs* 山腳／床腳／一頁的下端／樓梯的下端. **3** measure of length of 12 inches 英尺. *pl* 複數 **feet** [fi:t].

footing *n sing* **1** position of the feet

立足點, 立足處: *He lost his footing* i.e. he fell down. 他沒有站穩. 即: 他跌倒了. **2** place; foundation 地位; 基礎: *He placed the business on a firm footing* i.e. he made sure that the business was carried on properly and that there was enough money etc. 他使公司有穩固的基礎. 即: 他使公司生意興隆, 資金雄厚. **'football 1** *nu* one of several games played by two teams with a leather ball 足球(運動); 橄欖球(運動). **2** *nc* the ball itself 足球; 橄欖球. *Note* 說明: *(Brit)* 'football' usu. refers to *Association Football*, played by two teams of 11 men each, of whom only the goalkeepers are allowed to touch the ball with the hands; the word is, however, also used by some people to refer to the game of *rugby*. *(US)* the word refers to a different kind of game played mainly in the *USA*. (英) football 通常指 Association Football. 由兩支球隊比賽, 每隊十一人. 只有守門員才可以用手觸球. 也有人用 football 來指 rugby. (美) football 指主要在美國玩的另一種球類運動. **'footbridge** bridge for people who are walking (not for vehicles) (只供人行, 不准車輛通過的)小橋, 行人橋. **'foothill** low hill at the bottom of high mountains 山麓小丘. **'foothold** place where one can put one's foot (e.g. in climbing a mountain) 立足點 (如在登山中). **'footlights** see light[1]. **foot-and-mouth disease** disease of cows and other animals (牛等牲口的)口蹄疫. **'footnote** note at the bottom of a page in a book etc. 腳註. **'footpath** path through a field, mountains etc for people who are walking (越過田野、山等的)小徑, 人行小路. **'footprint** mark made by a shoe or foot 腳印. **'footsore** *adj* having sore feet, caused by walking 脚痛的, 走痛了脚的. **'footstep** *nc* (usu. *pl*) noise or mark made by somebody walking (通常用複數) 脚步聲; 足跡. **follow / tread in somebody's foot-steps** do what somebody did earlier 步某人的後塵; 效法某人. **'footwear** boots and shoes鞋類. **on foot** walking 步行. **underfoot** on the ground 在地面, 在地上: *It is very wet underfoot* i.e. the ground is wet. 地上很濕. **foot the bill** pay for something (usu. something bought by somebody else). (*informal*) 付賬(通常指爲別人買的東西付賬) (非正式). **put one's foot in it** do or say something which causes trouble and difficulty although one did not intend to cause trouble. (*informal*) (並非有意地)說錯話, 做錯事 (非正式).

for [fɔː*] *prep* **1** in exchange 作爲交換, 以…的代價: *sell a book for a pound* 以一英鎊的價格出售一本書. **2** in support of 支持: *I am for the plan* i.e. I think the plan should be carried out. 我支持這項計劃. 即: 我主張實行這項計劃. **3** in place of 代替: *I'll do your work for you if you want to leave early.* 要是你想早些走, 我來替你做事. **4** with the purpose of 爲了: *He went for a walk.* 他去散步. **5** in order to reach 以…爲目的地; 開往; 向…: *He left for London.* 他動身去倫敦. *He ran for shelter.* 他跑去躲避. **6** over a distance or time (表示時間或距離)延續; 計: *walk for a mile / an hour* 走一英里 / 一小時. **7** with an intended use 爲; 適合於: *a box for keeping papers in* 裝文件的盒子; *a party for children* 爲兒童舉辦的聚會. **8** feeling towards 對…的感情: *love for somebody* 對某人的愛. **9** in contrast to 與…對比, 與…比起來: *for every one*

who voted 'yes', fifty voted 'no' 每有一個人投贊成票, 就有五十個人投反對票. **10** considering that 就…而論; 考慮到: *It is warm for January* i.e. January is usually colder than it is this year. 就一月說來, 今年是很暖和的. 即: 往年的一月要比今年冷. *He is rather tall for his age* i.e. children of his age are usually smaller. 就他的年齡說來, 他稍微高了一些. 即: 他這個年齡的孩子通常沒有這麼高. **11** because of 因爲: *He was sent to prison for stealing the money.* 他因偷竊而入獄. Also 亦作 *conj* because (*formal* in this sense) 因爲(此義爲正式). **for ever** always 永遠. **for all** despite 儘管: *For all your cleverness, you could not win* i.e. although you are clever 儘管你很聰明, 你不可能取勝. **but for** if there had not been; without 倘沒有, 要不是: *I would have won the competition but for bad luck* i.e. I lost because of bad luck. 我要不是運氣不好, 本來是會贏得這場比賽的. 即: 我因爲運氣不好才輸掉.

forbade [fəˈbæd] past tense of **forbid**. forbid 的過去式.

forbear, forebear [ˈfɔːˌbɛə*] *nc* (usu. *pl*) ancestor (*o.f.*) (通常用複數)祖宗, 祖先(舊式).

forbid [fəˈbid] *vt* say that something must not happen 不准; 禁止: *I forbade him to go to the party.* 我不准他去參加那個聚會. *The government decided to forbid the meeting.* 政府決定禁止召開這次會議. past tense 過去式 **forbade** [fəˈbæd]. past part 過去分詞 **forbidden**. **forbidding** *adj* unpleasant and dangerous in appearance (容貌)令人厭惡的; 險惡的. **God forbid!** I hope that does not happen. (*informal*) 但願不發生這樣的事情! (非正式).

force¹ [fɔːs] **1** *nu* strength 力,力量: *the force of the wind / the blow / the explosion* 風力/一擊之力/爆炸力. **2** *nc* organized group of men 部隊;隊伍: *police force; air force; armed forces etc.* 警察;空軍;軍隊等. **3** *nc* anything having an effect 有影響的事物: *The United Nations Organization is a force for good* i.e. it produces good effects. 聯合國有好的影響力. 即:它產生好影響. **forcible** ['fɔːsəbl] *adj* using force 強行的;強迫的;用暴力的. **forcibly** *adv*.

force² [fɔːs] *vt* **1** use force on 強制;強迫;強使: *We forced him to come* i.e. he did not want to come. 我們強迫他來. 即:他本來不打算來. *He forced the door* i.e. opened it by using force. 他用力撞開門. 即:用暴力把門打開. **2** (usu. with reference to plants) cause to grow more quickly than usual by giving extra warmth and food etc. (通常指植物)(用提高溫度和增加養份的辦法)使迅速生長,促成生長. **forceful** *adj* showing determination and strength of character 堅決的;性格堅強的. **in force 1** legally required; effective 法律所要求的;有效的: *These rules are still in force* i.e. they must still be obeyed. 這些規定仍然有效. 即:仍應遵守這些規定. **2** (usu. with reference to soldiers etc.) in a large group (通常指士兵等)大批的,大羣的: *an attack in force* 大規模的進攻.

forceps ['fɔːseps] *npl* instrument used by doctors for holding things tightly (醫療用品)鉗子,鑷子.

ford [fɔːd] *vt* go through a river at a shallow place 涉水: *ford a river* 涉水過河. Also 亦作 *nc* place in a river one can do this (河流的)淺灘;水淺可涉處.

fore¹ [fɔː*] *adj* (usu. with reference to a

ship) of the front part (通常指船)前面的,船頭的.

fore-² [fɔː*] *prefix* front; before (e.g. **forearm; foreshore**) 前面的;在…之前(如 forearm; foreshore).

forearm ['fɔːrɑːm] *nc* lower part of the arm 前臂.

forebear ['fɔːbɛə*] *nc* see 見 **forbear.**

foreboding [fɔːˈbouding] *nc* feeling that danger or difficulty is coming 對危險或困難的預感: *have a foreboding about something* 預感會發生不幸的事.

forecast ['fɔːkɑːst] *nc* (esp. with reference to the weather) statement about what will happen in the future (尤指天氣)預報. Also 亦作 *vt* make a forecast 預報: *forecast rain* 預報有雨. *past* 過去式和過去分詞 **forecast.**

forecastle, fo'c's'le ['fouksl] *nc* front part of a ship, where sailors live (船前面的)水手艙.

forefather ['fɔːfɑːðə*] *nc* ancestor 祖先,祖宗.

forefinger ['fɔːfiŋɡə*] *nc* finger next to the thumb 食指.

forefront ['fɔːfrʌnt] *n sing* front part where there is the most activity 最前面,活動最多的地方: *There is an idea in the forefront of my mind that…* i.e. I have been thinking a lot about this idea. 有一個主意佔據了我腦海裏最重要的位置…即:關於這個主意我一直想得很多.

forego [fɔːˈgou] *vt* see 見 **forgo.**

foregoing ['fɔːˈgouiŋ] *adj* previous; mentioned earlier. *(formal)* 以前的,前述的. (正式).

foregone [fɔːˈgɔn] *adj* usu. in **foregone conclusion** i.e. result which everybody knew would happen (通常用於 foregone conclusion, 即:預料中必然的結局.

foreground ['fɔːɡraund] *nu* part of a

picture or scene near the person looking at it (圖畫、景色的) 前景.

forehead ['fɔrid] *nc* part of the face above the eyes 前額.

foreign ['fɔrin] *adj* **1** of another country 外國的: *a foreign language* i.e. a language spoken in another country 外國語; *foreign trade* i.e. trade with other countries 對外貿易. **2** not naturally part of 無關的, 不相干的: *This is foreign to our experience* i.e. we have never experienced this. 我們從來沒有經歷過這樣的事. **foreigner** *nc* person from another country 外國人. **foreign body** something not naturally belonging (esp. something which has got into part of the body) 異物 (尤指體內異物).

foreman ['fɔːmən] *nc* **1** man in charge of a group of workers 工頭, 領班. **2** chief member of a jury 陪審團團長.

foremost ['fɔːmoust] *adj* most important 最重要的: *our foremost duty* 我們最重要的責任. **first and foremost** *adv* first and most importantly 首要地, 重要地.

forensic [fə'rensik] *adj* having reference to law and detection 法庭的; 法律的; 偵查的.

forerunner ['fɔːrʌnə*] *nc* person / thing coming before another (and usu. more important) person / thing 前鋒, 先驅: *This invention was the forerunner of many important developments in space travel.* 這項發明是星際航行方面許多重要發展的先驅.

foresee [fɔː'siː] *vt* know or see that something will happen before it does 預知, 預見: *I made careful preparations because I foresaw that we would be very busy this year.* 我仔細地作了準備, 因為我預料今年我們會很忙. *pres part* 現在分詞 **foreseeing.** *past*

tense 過去式 **foresaw** [fɔː'sɔː]. *past part* 過去分詞 **foreseen.**

foreshadow [fɔː'ʃædou] *vt* be a sign that something dangerous or unpleasant is coming 預兆, 預示(會發生危險或不快的事).

foreshore ['fɔːʃɔː*] *nc* land by the side of the sea 海灘, 海邊土地, 前灘.

foresight ['fɔːsait] *nu* ability to know or guess what will happen in the future 先見之明, 遠見.

forest ['fɔrist] *nc / u* large area of trees 森林. **forestry** *nu* work of protecting and developing forests 林業.

forestall [fɔː'stɔːl] *vt* do something with the aim of preventing another person from doing it (預先採取行動以)阻止; 先發制人: *forestall somebody* 先某人一着.

foretaste ['fɔːteist] *nc* small experience of something which one will have in larger quantities later on 預先的體驗.

foretell [fɔː'tel] *vt* tell about something before it happens 預言, 預示, 預測: *foretell disaster* 預言災難. *past tense* 過去式 和過去分詞 **foretold** [fɔː'tould].

forever [fə'revə*] *adv* always 永遠地.

forewarn [fɔː'wɔːn] *vt* tell somebody of some danger etc which is coming 預先警告.

foreword ['fɔːwəd] *nc* short section of a book which introduces the book to the reader 序言, 前言.

forfeit ['fɔːfit] *vt* lose something as a punishment or as a result of one's actions (因受罰或因過失而)喪失. Also 亦作 *nc* something lost in this way 喪失的東西; 沒收物.

forgave [fə'geiv] past tense of **forgive.** forgive 的過去式.

forge¹ [fɔːdʒ] *vt / i* make money or copy a document, painting etc in order to deceive 偽造(錢、文件、名畫等). **forger** *nc* person who does this 偽造者. **forgery** *nc / u* the crime of copying money, documents etc; something forged 偽造罪; 偽造物, 贗品.

forge ahead move forward and in front of others (e.g. in a race) 向前推進; 超過別人(如在賽跑中).

forge² [fɔːdʒ] *nc* place where a blacksmith makes horseshoes and other iron objects 鐵匠舖, 鐵匠工場.

forget [fə'get] *vt / i* fail to keep in the mind or in the memory 忘記: *I forgot to buy the book.* 我忘了買書. *I forget where you live.* 我忘了你住的地方. *pres part* 現在分詞 **forgetting.** *past tense* 過去式 **forgot** [fə'gɔt]. *past part* 過去分詞 **forgotten** [fə'gɔtn]. **forgetful** *adj* often forgetting 健忘的. **forgetfulness** *nu.*

forgive [fə'giv] *vt / i* decide that one is not angry with somebody who has done wrong, and that one does not wish to punish him 原諒, 饒恕, 寬恕: *I forgave him for losing my book.* 他丟了我的書, 我原諒了他. *I forgave his behaviour.* 我寬恕了他的行爲. *pres part* 現在分詞 **forgiving.** *past tense* 過去式 **forgave** [fə'geiv]. *past part* 過去分詞 **forgiven** [fə'givən]. **forgiveness** *nu* process of forgiving 饒恕, 寬恕.

forgo, forego [fɔː'gou] *vt* be willing not to have something (usu. something pleasant) 放棄(通常指某種樂趣): *He decided to forgo sugar in his tea.* 他決定喝茶不加糖. *past tense* 過去式 **forwent** [fɔː'went]. *past part* 過去分詞 **forgone** [fɔː'gɔn]. see also 參見 **foregone.**

forgot, forgotten [fə'gɔtn] past tense and past part of **forget.** forget 的過去式和過去分詞.

fork [fɔːk] *nc* **1** instrument with several sharp points, used for carrying food to the mouth 餐叉. **2** large instrument shaped like this, used for digging earth or working on a farm 耙, 草叉(農具). **3** place where a road divides into two or more roads, or where a tree trunk puts out a branch (路、樹木等的)分岔處. Also 亦作 *vi* divide into two 分叉: *The road forked.* 路分岔了. **forked** *adj* divided into two 叉狀的, 分叉的: *a forked tongue* i.e. a tongue like a snake 叉狀舌, 即: 像蛇舌一樣分叉的舌頭. **fork out** pay money 支付, 交付: *fork out four pounds (informal)* 付出四英鎊·(非正式).

forlorn [fə'lɔːn] *adj* left alone and unhappy 孤獨的; 淒涼的. **forlorn hope** plan or attempt which is not likely to succeed 渺茫的希望.

form¹ [fɔːm] **1** *nc / u* shape; outline; appearance 形狀; 輪廓; 外貌: *She made a cake in the form of a letter 'S'.* 她做了一塊S形的蛋糕. *The word 'sheep' has the same form in the singular and the plural.* sheep 這詞單複數同形. *Form is as important as colour in the art of painting.* 在繪畫藝術方面, 形象和色彩同樣重要. **2** *nc* type or sort 類型; 種類: *There are many different forms of food throughout the world.* 世界上有多種多樣不同的食物. **3** *nc* official paper with spaces for one to write information in 表格. **4** *nc* (Brit) class in a school. (US 美 **grade**) (英)班, 年級. **5** *nu* usual ability of a racehorse, athlete etc. (比賽用的馬、運動員等的)通常技能: *This horse is off form* i.e. not running as fast as it normally does. 這匹馬的競技狀態不佳. 即: 跑得不如平常快. **6** *nc* long wooden seat on which several people can sit 長板櫈.

form² [fɔːm] *vt / i* **1** come or make into a shape 形成, 構成: *Ice was forming on the river.* 河面上正在結冰. *He formed a ball of earth in his hands.* 他用雙手搓出一個泥球. **2** come into existence or make 生出, 產生: *An idea was forming in his mind.* 他腦子裏開始想出一個主意. *He formed a football club.* 他成立了一個足球俱樂部.

formal [ˈfɔːml] *adj* done or made according to certain rules; following generally accepted ideas of what is the correct way of doing something; not conversational 合乎規定的; 合乎慣例的; 正式的. (*opp* 反義詞 **informal**). **formally** *adv* **formality** [fəˈmæliti] *nc / u* behaviour which is necessary in order to follow the rules etc but which does not mean very much 形式上的手續. (*opp* 反義詞 **informality**).

format [ˈfɔːmæt] *nc* shape and size of a book, magazine etc. (書刊的) 版式, 開本.

formation [fəˈmeiʃən] *nc / u* way in which something is shaped or arranged in order 組成的方式; 結構; 隊形: *The planes were flying in formation* i.e. keeping the same distance from each other and forming a particular shape. 飛機正在編隊飛行. 即: 飛機間保持等距離並組成特殊隊形.

formative [ˈfɔːmətiv] *adj* causing somebody / something to have a certain type of nature 形成個性的: *the formative years* i.e. the years of childhood, when a person's character and intelligence are being formed 個性形成的, 即: 孩童性格及智力形成的時期.

former¹ [ˈfɔːmə*] *adj* **1** the first one mentioned of two things or people 前者. (*opp* 反義詞 **latter**). **2** earlier in time; of the past 以前的; 從前的: *in former times* 往昔, 從前. **formerly** *adv* at an earlier time 以前, 從前.

former² [ˈfɔːmə*] *nc* in **first / second etc former** i.e. member of a particular class in a school 用於 first / second etc former 即: 一/二…年級學生.

Formica [fɔːˈmaikə] " *nu* laminated, heat-resistant plastic used for table tops etc. 福米卡 (做桌面等的抗熱塑料薄板).

formidable [ˈfɔːmidəbl] *adj* fearful; difficult to deal with 可怕的; 難以對付的: *a formidable enemy* 勢力強大的敵人; *a formidable task* 艱巨的任務.

formula [ˈfɔːmjulə] *nc* **1** set of scientific or mathematical symbols (e.g. H_2O, πr^2) 式, 公式 (如 H_2O, πr^2). **2** set of words which does not have much meaning (e.g. good morning, how do you do) 慣用語句, 客套話 (如 good morning, how do yo do). **3** (*US*) baby's milk feed (美)用牛奶等配製成的嬰兒食品. *pl* 複數 **formulas** or **formulae** [ˈfɔːmjuliː]. **formulate** [ˈfɔːmjuleit] *vt* express an idea etc clearly and precisely 清楚準確地表達: *formulate his theories* 提出了他的理論.

forsake [fəˈseik] *vt* (usu. with reference to leaving one's friends or family, or something which is dear to one) leave 遺棄 (通常指朋友, 家人或心愛的物品); 放棄. *pres part* 現在分詞 **forsaking.** *past tense* 過去式 **forsook** [fəˈsuk]. *past part* 過去分詞 **forsaken.**

fort [fɔːt] *nc* building which is made so that it can be defended against attack by enemies 堡壘; 要塞.

forte [ˈfɔːti] *n sing* something that somebody does well 長處; 擅長: *Driv-*

ing is his forte i.e. driving is the thing he does best 駕駛汽車是他的特長.

forth [fɔ:θ] *adv* forward; out; away far 前; 向外; 離: *He went forth to attack the enemy* (o.f.) 他衝上去進攻敵人. (舊式). **and so forth** etc; and so on; and the rest 等等.

forthcoming [fɔ:θ'kʌmiŋ] *adj* **1** to appear soon 即將出現的: *a forthcoming book* i.e. one which will be published soon. 即將出版的書: *It was not forthcoming* i.e. it did not appear when needed or expected. 它不是預期的. 即: 在需要它時不能隨要隨有. **2** friendly, ready to give information etc. 友善的, 樂於提供消息的.

forthright ['fɔ:θrait] *adj* saying what one thinks, without trying to hide anything 率直的, 直截了當的.

fortify ['fɔ:tifai] *vt* **1** build walls and other things to defend a place against attack 設防. **2** (esp. of food and drink) make stronger 強化 (尤指在食品中加維生素, 在酒中加酒精等). **fortification** [fɔ:tifi'keiʃən] *nc* / *u* something built to defend a place 防禦工事.

fortitude ['fɔ:titju:d] *nu* bravery; ability to face danger or pain etc. 勇敢; 堅忍不拔的精神.

fortnight ['fɔ:tnait] *nc* two weeks 兩週, 兩星期. **fortnightly** *adj* / *adv*.

fortress ['fɔ:tris] *nc* place which can be defended against attacks by enemies 堡壘; 要塞.

fortuitous [fɔ:'tjuitəs] *adj* happening by chance or accident 偶然的, 意外的.

fortune ['fɔ:ʃən] *nc* / *u* **1** chance; luck; whatever happens to one 機會, 運氣, 好運; 偶然碰上的事: *He had good fortune* i.e. something pleasant happened to him. 他交了好運. 即: 好事落到了他頭上. (*opp* 反義詞 **misfortune**). **2**

large amount of money 財富, (大量的) 財產: *He made his fortune by selling cars.* 他靠銷售汽車發了財. **fortunate** ['fɔ:tʃənət] *adj* having or causing good luck 幸運的. (*opp* 反義詞 **unfortunate**). **fortunately** *adv* **tell fortunes / tell someone's fortune** say what will happen to someone in the future by using various methods such as looking at playing cards or the hands of the person (用撲克牌或看手相等辦法) 算命/替某人算命. **'fortuneteller** *nc*.

forty ['fɔ:ti] see appendix 見附錄.

forum ['fɔ:rəm] *nc* any place where people can have discussions 討論的場所; 論壇.

forward¹ ['fɔ:wəd] *adv* to the front 向前: *He ran forward.* 他向前跑.

forward² ['fɔ:wəd] *adj* **1** in the front 在前面的. **2** (with reference to children) more like an adult than other children of the same age (and often rather impolite to adults) (指兒童) 早熟的 (如指成人, 常頗爲不禮貌). **forwardness** *nu.*

forward³ ['fɔ:wəd] *nc* player in the front line of certain games (e.g. football) 球賽 (如足球) 的前鋒.

forward⁴ ['fɔ:wəd] *vt* (esp. with reference to sending letters etc to a new address after a person has left his former address) send forward (尤指在收信人遷址後把信件或轉送新址) 轉遞, 轉交.

fossil ['fɔsl] *nc* what remains of a very old plant, animal etc, which has been kept from destruction in hard rock 化石.

foster ['fɔstə*] *vt* **1** help the growth and development of 培養, 助長, 促進: *foster a political movement* 促進一場政治運動. **2** take a child which is not one's own into one's family 收養, 領養: *foster a child* 收養一個孩子. **'foster mother / brother / child etc** mother, brother, child etc related to one not by blood, but by the act of fostering 養母/奶兄弟/養子, 養女等. **'foster home 1** home into which a foster child is taken 收養了孩子的家庭; 養父家, 養母家. **2** institution in which children without proper homes are brought up 孤兒院.

fought [fɔ:t] past of **fight²**. fight² 的過去式和過去分詞.

foul¹ [faul] *adj* bad or dirty and unpleasant 惡劣的, 污穢的, 難受的: *foul air* 污濁的空氣; *a foul taste* 令人噁心的味道; *foul language* 下流話. **foul play 1** murder 謀殺. **2** behaviour which is against the rules of a game 犯規.

foul² [faul] *nc* action which is not allowed by the rules of a game (e.g. kicking in a boxing match) 犯規(如在拳擊比賽中用腳踢).

foul³ [faul] **1** *vt* make dirty and unpleasant 污染; 使不愉快: *The smoke fouled the air.* 烟霧污染了空氣. **2** *vt / i* do something which is not allowed by the rules of a game (對⋯)犯規: *The footballer tried to foul.* 該足球隊員試圖犯規. *He fouled his opponent.* 他對他的對手犯了規. **3** *vt* (with reference to a boat or ship etc) become tangled with; run into (指船隻)與⋯纏住; 碰撞: *The ship fouled its anchor* i.e. could not pull up its anchor. 該船的錨被纏住了. 即: 該船難以起錨.

found¹ [faund] past of **find¹**. find¹ 的過去式和過去分詞.

found² [faund] *vt* begin something 建立, 創立, 締造: *found a city / school / club* etc. 興建一座城市/創辦一所學校/創立一個俱樂部等. **founder¹** *nc*

foundation [faun'deiʃən] **1** *nu* act of founding 建立, 創辦. **2** *nc* (usu. *pl*) the part of a building which is below the ground, on which the building rests (通常用複數)地基, 房基. **3** *nc / u* something like the foundation of a building 基礎; 根據: *the foundations of democracy* i.e. the ideas on which democracy is based 民主的基礎, 即: 作爲民主根據的思想. *This theory has no foundation in fact.* 這種理論沒有事實根據.

founder² ['faundə*] *vt / i* (with reference to ships) fill with water and sink (使船隻)進水沉没.

foundry ['faundri] *nc* place where things are made from molten metal 鑄造廠.

fountain ['fauntin] *nc* place where water rises up (esp. where it is made to rise into the air as an ornament in a street or garden) 噴泉, 噴水池(尤指街道, 公園等處的). **'fountain pen** type of pen in which the ink is sucked inside the pen 自來水筆, 鋼筆.

four [fɔ:*] see appendix 見附錄. **'foursome** group of four people (esp. a group playing a game) 四人的一組(尤指有四人參加的比賽). **on all fours** see 見 **all.**

fowl [faul] *nc* chicken, goose, turkey or other domestic bird (鷄、鵝、火鷄等)家禽.

fox [fɔks] *nc* type of wild animal like a dog with red fur and a bushy tail 狐狸. **'foxtrot** *nc / u* type of dance 狐步舞.

foyer ['fɔiei] *nc* large public room at the entrance of a hotel, cinema or large building (旅館、電影院等大型建築的)門廳.

fracas ['frækɑ:] *nc* noisy quarrel 吵鬧. *pl* 複數 **fracas** ['frækɑ:z].

fraction ['frækʃən] *nc* **1** small part 小部份. **2** quantity less than one (e.g. ½, ¼, ⅛) 分數(如$\frac{1}{2}$, $\frac{1}{4}$, $\frac{1}{8}$). *Note* 說明: in ordinary use, expressions of the type ½, ¼, ⅛ are called *fractions*, and expressions of the type 0.5, 0.25, 0.125 are called *decimals;* in mathematics, however, both types of expression are regarded as fractions 在日常使用中, $\frac{1}{2}$, $\frac{1}{4}$, $\frac{1}{8}$ 等稱爲 fractions, 而 0.5, 0.25, 0.125 等稱爲 decimals. 但在數學上, 上述兩種都看作是 fractions.

fracture ['fræktʃə*] *nc* breaking of a bone 骨折. Also 亦作 *vt / i* break, cause to break (使)破裂; (使)斷裂.

fragile ['frædʒail] *adj* **1** easily broken 易碎的, 易損壞的. **2** (of health etc) weak (體質等)弱的. **fragility** [frə'dʒiliti] *nu*.

fragment ['frægmənt] *nc* small piece broken off from a larger whole 碎片. **fragmentary** *adj*.

fragrant ['freigrənt] *adj* smelling very sweet, like a flower 香的, 芬芳的. **fragrance** *nu*.

frail [freil] *adj* weak (and often old) 虛弱的; (年老)體衰的.

frame[1] [freim] *nc* **1** the border of wood, metal etc around a picture or around the glass of a window 框架; 畫框; 窗框. **2** body of a human being or animal (人或動物的)身軀, 身體. **3** (esp. with reference to a house, ship, plane) structure supporting the other parts of something (房子、船、飛機等的)骨架, 構架. **frame of mind** state of mind 心情, 心境: *I'm not in the right frame of mind for a party.* 我沒有好心情去參加聚會.

frame[2] [freim] *vt* **1** put a frame around 給…裝框: *frame a picture* 給一張照片裝上框架. **2** put into words 用言詞表達: *frame a sentence / a law* 說出一句話/制定好一項法律. **3** make an innocent person seem to be guilty of a crime. (*informal* in sense **3**) 誣陷(義3爲非正式). **'frame-up** *nc* arrangement to make an innocent person seem to be guilty of a crime. *(informal)* 誣害, 陰謀 (非正式). **'framework** 1 structure which supports the other parts (e.g. of a house, ship, plane) (房子、船、飛機等的) 骨架, 構架. **2** main ideas or parts 主導思想; 主體部份: *the framework of society / of the economy* 社會結構/經濟體制.

franchise ['fræntʃaiz] *n sing* right to vote in elections 選舉權.

frank [fræŋk] *adj* saying what one thinks without trying to hide anything 坦率的: *a frank answer* 坦率的回答. **frankly** *adv* **frankness** *nu*.

frankincense ['fræŋkinsens] *nu* sweet-smelling substance obtained from certain trees 乳香(從某些樹木得到的香料).

frantic ['fræntik] *adj* very worried or excited, so that one cannot think or behave properly 瘋狂的, 狂亂的. **frantically** *adv*.

fraternal [frə'tə:nl] *adj* of a brother 兄弟般的. **fraternity 1** *nc* society or group of men who work together or help each other in some way 兄弟會; 互助會. **2** *nc (US)* such a group at a school or college (美)學生聯誼會. **3** *nu* friendly feeling between brothers 手足之情. **fraternize** ['frætənaiz] *vi* (esp. with reference to people who were recently enemies) be friendly (尤指與不久前的敵人)友好交往.

fraud [frɔ:d] **1** *nu* crime of making somebody believe something which is not true, in order to get something from him 欺騙, 騙局. **2** *nc* person / thing that makes people believe what is not true 騙子; 假貨. **fraudulent** ['frɔːdjulənt] *adj*.

fraught [frɔːt] *adj* filled 充滿…的. (usu. in 通常用於 **fraught with some- thing**: *fraught with horror / terror / risk / danger etc.* 充滿恐怖/驚駭/風險 /危險).

fray¹ [frei] *nc* fight or struggle. (rather *o.f.*) 吵架, 打架, 衝突 (頗爲舊式).

fray² [frei] *vt / i* (with reference to cloth, rope etc) become or make worn so that there are loose threads (指布, 繩索等) 磨損, 磨破, 擦散.

freak [friːk] *nc* plant, animal, person etc which is unusual and unnatural in form 畸形, 怪物; 有怪癖的人. Also 亦作 *adj*: *a freak storm* i.e. a storm which is unusual and unexpected 反常的暴風雨. 即: 不尋常的和意料不到的暴風雨.

freckle ['frekl] *nc* one of the several light brown marks found on the face and arms of people who have very fair skin 雀斑; 斑點.

free [friː] *adj* **1** not costing any money 免費的: *Education is free in Britain* i.e. people can send their children to school without paying any money. 教育在英國是免費的. 即: 人們送孩子上學不用花錢. **2** not under the control of anybody or anything 不受控制的; 自由的: *The thief is still free* i.e. he is not in prison. 小偷仍逍遙法外. 即: 他尚未入獄. *Nobody is free to do what he likes* i.e. everybody must obey some rules. 沒有人可以不受約束地爲所欲爲. 即: 人人都要服從某些法規. *In 1940 India was not yet free* i.e. it was still ruled by Britain. 1940年印度尚未獲得自由; 當時印度仍爲英國所統治. **3** not following any rules 隨意的; 不守規

則的. **4** generous 慷慨的. **5** without duties 空閑的; 沒有任務的: *I'm free this afternoon.* 今天下午我有空. *com- parative* 比較級 **freer** ['friə*]. *superla- tive* 最高級 **freest** ['friːist]. Also 亦作 *vi* make free 使自由: *free the prison- ers* 釋放囚犯. **freely** *adv* **freedom** *nu*. **'freelance** *nc* writer, artist etc who lives by selling his work to anyone who wants it, instead of working for one employer (自由出售作品而並非受雇於某人的) 自由投稿作家, 自由職業家. Also 亦作 *adj / vi* **'freemason, Freemason** *nc* member of an interna- tional secret society 共濟會會員. **free trade** trade in which goods can be taken into and out of a country without taxes (免徵進出口關稅的) 自由貿易. **free will** ability to decide for oneself what one wishes to do 自由意志, 自願. **free and easy** *adj* friendly and not following strict rules of politeness and correct behaviour. (in- formal) 友好的, 不拘禮儀的 (非正式). **'free-for-all'** fight or struggle in which anyone can join. (informal) 任何人都可以自由參加的競賽, 爭論, 或打群架(非正式).

freeway ['friːwei] *nc* divided highway for fast travelling on which usually no tolls are charged; expressway 快車道; 高速公路.

freeze [friːz] **1** *vt / i* become ice or make ice (使) 結冰: *The river froze last night.* 昨晚河水結了冰. *He froze the water in his refrigerator.* 他把水放在冰箱裏結冰. *It's freezing* i.e. the temperature is below freezing point. 天氣極冷. 即: 溫度低於冰點. **2** *vt / i* become or make very cold (使) 變得很冷: *My feet are freezing.* 我的雙腳凍僵了. **3** *vi* suddenly become very still and quiet 獃住, 愣住, 僵住: *The* *hunter froze when he saw the lion.* 當獵人看到獅子時，他愣住了. **4** *vt* (with reference to prices, wages etc) prevent from rising higher or prevent any more from being paid (指物價、工資等)穩定，凍結: *The government decided to freeze prices for six months.* 政府決定穩定物價六個月. *pres part* 現在分詞 **freezing.** *past tense* 過去式 **froze** [frouz]. *past part* 過去分詞 **frozen** ['frouzn]. Also 亦作 *n sing* **1** period of very cold weather 嚴寒期. **2** official action to prevent prices, wages etc from rising higher (官方對物價、工資等的)穩定，凍結. **freezer** *nc* see 見 **deep-freeze. freezing point** temperature at which a liquid becomes solid 冰點，凝固點.

freight [freit] *nu* **1** movement of goods by some means of transport 貨運. **2** the goods themselves (被運的)貨物. **freighter** *nc* boat which carries goods 貨船.

french [frentʃ] *adj* in **french window** door made of glass like a window, opening on to a garden etc. 用於 **french window** (向花園等開的落地玻璃窗).

frenzy ['frenzi] *nu* state of great excitement or fear, so that one cannot think or act properly (激動或恐懼引起的)狂亂. **frenzied** *adj.*

frequent[1] ['fri:kwənt] *adj* happening very often 時常發生的: *He made frequent visits to the hospital.* 他常去醫院. (*opp* 反義詞 **infrequent**). **frequently** *adv* **frequency 1** *nu* state of being frequent 屢次，頻繁. **2** *nc* (esp. with reference to the number of cycles per second of alternating current broadcast by a radio station) rate at which something happens 頻率.

frequent[2] [fri'kwent] *vt* go to very often

常到，常去，時常出入: *frequent cinemas* 常去電影院.

fresco ['freskou] *nc* picture painted on (wet) plaster on a wall 壁畫.

fresh [freʃ] *adj* **1** new; recent; not stale 新的；新近的；新鮮的: *fresh news* i.e. news received not long ago 新消息. *a fresh arrival* i.e. somebody who has arrived a short while ago 新來的人. *fresh fruit* i.e. fruit which is not in a tin or packet 新鮮水果. **2** (with reference to the colour of somebody's face) healthy and bright (指面容)健康的；氣色好的. **3** (with reference to streams, rivers, lakes etc.) without salt (指水質)淡的. **4** (with reference to wind) strong (指風力)強勁的. **5** cheeky (*informal* in sense **5**) 厚顏無恥的(義 5 為非正式). **freshly** *adv* **freshness** *nu* **freshen** *vt / i* become or make fresh (使)顯得新鮮；使有精神；(風)變強. **'freshman, fresher** student in his first year at a university 大學一年級學生.

fret [fret] *vt / i* (often with reference to children) become or make worried and bad-tempered (常指孩子)(使)煩惱，(使)煩躁: *The baby was fretting because he was hungry.* 嬰兒因為餓了而顯得煩躁不安. *past* 過去式和過去分詞 **fretted.**

friar ['fraiə*] *nc* member of certain religious organizations in the Roman Catholic Church (羅馬天主教的)修道士.

friction ['frikʃən] *nu* **1** rubbing of one thing against another 摩擦. **2** continual arguments and disagreements 衝突，不和.

Friday ['fraidi] *n* day after Thursday 星期五. **Good Friday** day on which the crucifixion of Christ is remembered 耶穌受難日.

fridge [fridʒ] *nc* (Brit) short informal form of **refrigerator** (英) 冰箱 (refrigerator 的非正式縮略形式).

friend [frend] *nc* person whom one knows well and likes 朋友. **friendly** *adv* (*opp* 反義詞 **unfriendly**). **friendliness** *nu* **friendship** *nc / u.*

frieze [fri:z] *nc* long narrow band of decoration near the top of the walls of a room or building 中楣; (靠近牆頂部裝飾用的) 橫條.

frigate [ˈfrigit] *nc* fast type of ship 快艇.

fright [frait] *nc / u* 1 great fear 驚嚇: *He got a fright when he found a snake in his bath.* 他看到澡盆裏有一條蛇, 嚇得要死. 2 person who looks unusual (often because of the way he is dressed) (*informal*). (常因奇裝異服而顯得) 奇形怪狀的人 (非正式). **frighten** *vt / i* make somebody afraid (使) 驚恐, (使) 吃驚: *The snake frightened him.* 那條蛇使他嚇得要命. *The cat frightened the mice away* i.e. made them run away. 貓把老鼠嚇跑了. *He doesn't frighten easily* i.e. is not easily made afraid. 他不是輕易就害怕的. **frightening** *adj* causing fear 嚇人的.

frightful *adj* causing fear; terrible; very unpleasant 嚇人的; 可怕的; 討厭的, 不愉快的. **frightfully** *adv* 1 in a frightening way 嚇人地; 可怕地. 2 very 十分, 非常: *I'm frightfully sorry.* (*informal*) 我非常抱歉. (非正式).

frigid [ˈfridʒid] *adj* 1 very cold 寒冷的. 2 very unfriendly; showing no emotions 冷淡的; 冷漠的.

frill [fril] *nc* 1 piece of cloth used as a decoration on a dress etc. (服裝的) 飾邊. 2 anything unnecessary and used only as a decoration 不必要的裝飾品, 虛飾物.

fringe [frindʒ] *nc* 1 hair covering the forehead 額前垂髮, 劉海兒. 2 decoration of loose threads (usu. tied in small bunches) on the edge of a dress, carpet, scarf etc. (女服、地毯、圍巾等的) 鬚邊, 繸. 3 edge or outside (e.g. of a forest, political party, group of people, city etc.) (森林、政黨、人羣、城市等的) 邊緣, 外圍: *on the fringe of a group* 在人羣的外圍.

frisk [frisk] *vt* search somebody to see whether he is carrying a weapon. (*informal*) 搜身, 搜查武器 (非正式). **frisky** *adj* in the habit of jumping and running 活潑的, 喜歡蹦蹦跳跳的.

fritter[1] [ˈfritə*] *vi* in **fritter away something** i.e. waste or use something foolishly in small bits 用於 fritter away something. 即: 一點一點地浪費或亂用某物: *He frittered away his money.* 他把錢浪費掉了.

fritter[2] [ˈfritə*] *nc* piece of fruit, meat or vegetable fried in batter (果、肉、菜等做餡的) 油炸餡餅.

frivolous [ˈfrivələs] *adj* not serious; making jokes about things which other people treat seriously 不嚴肅的, 輕浮的; 輕薄的. **frivolity** [friˈvɔliti] *nc / u.*

frizzy [ˈfrizi] *adj* (with reference to the hair) having small tight curls (指頭髮) 鬈曲的.

fro [frou] *adv* used in **to and fro** i.e. backwards and forwards 僅用於 to and fro. 即: 來來回回.

frock [frɔk] *nc* dress worn by a woman or a girl 女裝.

frog [frɔg] *nc* small animal which lives sometimes in water and sometimes on land, and which can jump well 蛙. **frogman** man who does various types of work under water, wearing a special suit and carrying a supply of air 蛙人, 穿潛水服帶空氣罐在水下進行各種作業的潛水員.

frolic ['frɔlik] *nc* any noisy and happy action 嬉戲，作樂. Also 亦作 *vi* behave noisily and happily 嬉戲，鬧着玩.

from [frɔm] *prep* **1** out of; away 從，由，自；離開: *He travelled by train from London.* 他乘火車離開倫敦. *He comes from Germany* i.e. he is a German. 他是德國人. *I waited here from ten o'clock* i.e. I started waiting at that time. 我從十點鐘開始在此等候. *He took a book from the shelf.* 他從書架上拿了一本書. *She made soup from meat and carrots.* 她用肉和胡蘿蔔煮湯. *I've searched the house from top to bottom* i.e. I've searched all of it. 我在房子裏上上下下地搜尋. 即: 我把整個房子都找遍了. **2** because of 由於，出於: *He acted from fear.* 他出於恐懼而採取行動. *He was suffering from measles.* 他患麻疹.

front [frʌnt] *nc* **1** (usu. only *sing*) the part which one comes to first (通常只用單數) 前面，正面，前部: *the front of a house* i.e. the part one sees from the road 房子的正面，即: 房子朝路的一面. **2** part of a town which is by the sea or a lake (城鎮) 臨海或靠湖的部份. **3** area where there is fighting during a war 前方，前線. **4** number of different political parties which have joined together for some purpose 陣線，聯合陣線. **5** organization etc used to hide something 掩護用的組織等, 出面的組織等: *The club was a front for a drug racket.* 俱樂部只是門面，實際上是做毒品生意. Also 亦作 *adj*: *the front seat of a car* i.e. the seat where the driver or the person next to him sits 汽車的前座, 即: 司機座或與之緊靠的座位. Also 亦作 *vt / i* (often with **onto**) be opposite to (常與 onto 連用) 面對，朝向: *His house fronts onto a*

field i.e. there is a field in front of his house. 他的房子朝着一片田地. 即: 他房子的前面有一片田地. **frontage** ['frʌntidʒ] *nc* part of a land or a building which can be seen from the road (土地或建築物的) 正面，臨街的一面.

in front (of something) before (something) in position 在 (某物的) 前面: *He parked his car in front of the house.* 他把車停在房子前面.

frontier ['frʌntiə*] *nc* that part of a country which is near another country; place where two countries meet 邊境；邊界.

frost [frɔst] **1** *nc / u* weather in which the temperature is below freezing point 溫度在冰點以下的天氣；嚴寒: *We have had several frosts this winter.* 今年冬天我們已經有過幾次嚴寒. **2** *nu* this white covering of frozen water on windows, trees, the ground etc. 霜. **frosty** *adj* very cold in weather or manner 寒冷的；冷若冰霜的: *She greeted me with a frosty smile.* 她對我冷淡地笑了笑，作爲打招呼. **'frostbite** *nu* damage to a part of the body caused by cold or frost 凍瘡；凍餒. **'frostbitten** *adj* damaged by frostbite 凍傷的. **'frosted 'glass** glass with a rough surface which lets light through but prevents one seeing through it 毛玻璃.

froth [frɔθ] *nu* small bubbles on the top of liquid (e.g. on a glass of beer) 泡沫 (如啤酒的泡沫). **frothy** *adj* having froth or being like froth 有泡沫的；泡沫狀的.

frown [fraun] *vi* cause the eyebrows to move downwards and together, as a sign of anger or puzzlement 皺眉頭 (表示憤怒或困惑). Also 亦作 *nc* appearance of the face caused by this 皺着眉頭的樣子. **frown (up)on**

something disapprove of something; think or say that something is bad 不贊同某事, 不喜歡某物; 認爲某物不好.

froze [frouz], **frozen** ['frouzn] past tense and past part of **freeze.** freeze 的過去式和過去分詞.

frugal ['fru:gəl] *adj* spending or costing very little money 節儉的, 節約的: *a frugal housewife* 節儉的主婦; *a frugal meal* 一餐節約飯.

fruit [fru:t] **1** *nu* part of certain trees and bushes which is eaten (e.g. apples, bananas, oranges, grapes, figs, peaches) 水果(如蘋果、香蕉、橘子、葡萄、無花果、桃子等). *Note* 說明: *fruit* with this meaning is nearly always uncountable. *He bought some fruit in the market.* fruit 意爲"水果"時幾乎總是不可數的. *He bought some fruit in the market.* 他在市場上買了一些水果. **2** *nc / u* part of any plant which contains the seeds 果實. **3** *nc* (often *pl*) anything which is the result of hard work and development (常用複數)成果, 結果; 產物: *the fruits of the earth* i.e. all crops 大地的產物即: 所有作物; *the fruits of your hard work* i.e. what you gain by hard work 你辛勤勞動的成果. Also 亦作 *vi* produce fruit 結果實. **fruiterer** ['fru:tərə*] *nc* person who sells fruit 水果商. **fruitful** *adj* **1** producing much fruit 果實結得多的. **2** producing many good results 富有成效的. (*opp* 反義詞 **unfruitful**). **fruition** [fru'iʃən] *nu* condition in which there are the good results which were wanted 實現, 完成: *bring one's work / hopes / plans to fruition* 完成自己的工作/實現自己的希望/完成自己的計劃.

frustrate [frʌs'treit] *vt* prevent somebody from doing what he wants to do (and often make him angry and unhappy) 挫敗, 阻撓: *He frustrated us.* 他使我們遭到失敗. *He frustrated our plans.* 他使我們的計劃落了空. **frustration** *nc / u*.

fry[1] [frai] *vt / i* cook in hot oil or fat (使)油炸, (使)油煎: *The fish was frying.* 魚正在炸. *He fried the bacon.* 他用油煎火腿. *past* 過去式和過去分詞 **fried. 'frying pan** container used for frying 煎鍋, 長柄平鍋.

fry[2] [frai] *npl* small fishes recently come out of their eggs 魚苗. **'small fry** *npl* unimportant people (often young children) (*informal*) 小人物(常指小孩)(非正式).

fudge [fʌdʒ] *nu* soft sweet substance made from sugar, butter, milk etc. (用糖、黃油、牛奶等做的)軟糖.

fuel [fjuəl] *nc / u* any substance which is burned in order to supply heat or power (e.g. coal, oil, gas, wood) 燃料 (如: 煤、油、煤氣、木柴等).

fugitive ['fju:dʒitiv] *nc* person who runs away 逃犯, 逃亡者. Also 亦作 *adj*.

fulcrum ['fʌlkrəm] *nc* support on which a lever turns in raising something 支點, 支軸: *Use this stone as a fulcrum to lever out the tree-stump.* 以這石塊作支點, 用槓桿把樹樁撬起來. *pl* 複數 **fulcrums** or **fulcra** ['fʌlkrə].

fulfil [ful'fil] *vt* do something completely or satisfactorily 履行, 實現, 完成: *fulfil one's duty* i.e. do what one must do 履行自己的職責; *fulfil a promise* i.e. do what one has promised 履行諾言. *past* 過去式和過去分詞 **fulfilled. fulfilment** *nc / u.*

full [ful] *adj* **1** containing as much or as many as possible 滿的: *a full glass of beer* i.e. one could not put any more beer in the glass 滿滿的一杯啤酒. **2** containing very much or very many (裝得)很多的; (含量)豐富的: *The* *room was full of people* i.e. there were many people in the room. 房間裏擠滿了人. *He has a very full face* i.e. a fat face. 他的臉很豐滿. 即: 又圓又胖. *He drove at full speed* i.e. as fast as possible. 他駕車以全速前進. 即: 開得盡量快. *She was wearing a very full coat* i.e. a coat which was very loose on her. 她穿着一件非常寬大的外衣. 即: 外衣穿在她身上很寬鬆. **fully** *adv* **fullness** *nu* **'fullback** player in football etc whose position is near his own goal (足球等的) 後衛. **'fully-'fledged** see 見 **fledged. full-moon** the moon seen as a complete circle or disc 滿月, 圓月. **in full** completely 充分地, 十足地; 完全地: *He told me the story in full.* 他把事情的經過全部告訴我. **at full blast** (usu. with reference to a machine) as fast, loud etc as possible. *(informal)* (通常指機器) 以最高速度; 非常響亮地(非正式).

fumble ['fʌmbl] *vt / i* use the hands without skill 亂摸, 摸索; 笨手笨腳地做: *He fumbled in his pocket* i.e. he moved his hand around in his pocket trying to find something. 他的手在口袋裏摸索. 即: 他用手在口袋裏摸來摸去找東西. *He fumbled the catch* i.e. he dropped a ball which he should have caught. 他沒有接住球. 即: 他把應當接住的球掉了.

fume¹ [fju:m] *nc* (usu. *pl*) strongsmelling and unpleasant gas or vapour (通常用複數) 濃烟, 難聞的烟; 汽.

fume² [fju:m] **1** *vi* give off fumes 冒烟; 冒汽. **2** *vi* be very angry (因某事不如意) 發怒: (usu. because one does not get what one wants) (常因沒有得到某物) 發怒.

fumigate ['fju:migeit] *vt* destroy germs, infection, insects etc by the action of smoke or fumes (爲消滅細菌、防止傳

染、殺蟲等) 烟燻: *fumigate a room* 烟燻房間消毒.

fun [fʌn] *nu* happiness and amusement 愉快; 娛樂, 樂趣: *He had fun playing football.* 他踢足球踢得很開心. *The journey home was really great fun* i.e. we enjoyed it very much. 回家的路上非常有趣. 即: 我們在回家的路上很開心. *It's not much fun being lost in the rain* i.e. it's miserable. 在雨中迷路可不是好玩的事. 即: 這糟透了. *Have fun!* i.e. enjoy yourself! 盡情地玩吧! **fun fair** see 見 **fair²** (in sense 1) (義 1). **for / in fun** as a joke; not seriously 開玩笑地; 不認真地: *I said that in fun.* 我講這話是開玩笑的. **he's (great) fun** he is amusing to be with. *(informal)* 他是個有趣的人(非正式). **make fun of, poke fun at** mock, tease 嘲弄; 取笑: *make fun of someone's bad accent* 取笑某人口音不準.

function ['fʌŋkʃən] *nc* **1** usual work done by somebody / something 職責; 功能; 功用: *the functions of a magistrate* 地方行政官的職責. *the function of a part of a machine* 機器某一部份的功能. **2** public gathering for a special purpose (e.g. a wedding, christening, party etc.) 典禮, 集會 (如婚禮、洗禮儀式、聚會等). Also 亦作 *vi* serve; work 盡職責, 起作用; 工作, 運行: *The school dining room functions as a meeting place for teachers and students.* 學校的膳廳用作師生集會的會場. *My car is not functioning properly* i.e. there is something wrong with it. 我的汽車運轉不太正常. 即: 這車有點毛病. **functional** *adj* **1** of a function 官能的, 機能的; 職務上的. **2** intended for use and not for decoration 實用的; furniture of very functional design 設計得非常實用的傢具.

fund [fʌnd] *nc* **1** (often *pl*) money intended to be used for a certain purpose (常用複數) 資金, 基金, 專款: *The club is holding a dance in order to raise funds for new equipment.* 該俱樂部正在舉辦舞會以便為購買新設備籌集資金. **2** amount or supply of something 數量; 儲備: *a fund of information* 大量的信息.

fundamental [ˌfʌndə'mentl] *adj* of great importance; forming the necessary part of anything; basic 重要的; 必要的; 基礎的, 根本的: *fundamental changes* 根本的變化. Also 亦作 *nc* (often *pl*) fundamental part of anything (常用複數) 重要部份, 根本部份.

funeral ['fju:nərl] *nc* burial or cremation of a dead person, together with any ceremonies 喪禮, 葬禮.

fungus ['fʌŋgəs] *nc / u* type of plant which grows on other plants and on decaying matter 真菌, 蕈類. *pl* 複數 **funguses** or **fungi** ['fʌŋgai].

funicular [fju:'nikjulə*] *adj* of a rope or cable 繩索的; 纜索的. **funicular railway** type of railway going up the side of a mountain. The cars do not always travel on the ground but are sometimes pulled through the air on steel cables 纜索鐵道, 纜車道.

funnel ['fʌnl] *nc* **1** type of tube with a wide mouth and a narrow bottom, used for pouring liquid etc into a container 漏斗. **2** part of a steamship or steam engine where smoke comes out (輪船或蒸汽機的) 烟囱.

funny ['fʌni] *adj* **1** causing one to laugh 有趣的, 可笑的. **2** unusual and difficult to understand. (*informal* in sense 2) 不尋常的, 難以理解的 (義 2 爲非正式). **funnily** *adv* '**funny bone** part of the elbow which feels a sharp pain if it is hit 肘部尺骨端(此處受敲擊會酸痛). **funnily enough** although it is

strange or unusual 奇怪得很.

fur [fə:*] **1** *nu* hair covering an animal 獸類的軟毛. **2** *nc* skin of an animal, with fur on it, often used to make clothing 毛皮. **furry** *adj* of or like an animal's fur 毛皮的, 像毛皮的.

furious ['fjuəriəs] *adj* very angry and violent 狂怒的; 猛烈的; 狂暴的: *a furious man / wind / struggle* 大發雷霆的人/狂風/猛烈的鬥爭. **furiously** *adv* see 見 **fury.**

furlong ['fə:lɔŋ] *nc* distance of approximately 200 metres 浪(英國長度單位, 約爲200公尺).

furlough ['fə:ləu] *nc / u* (esp. with reference to a soldier) period during which one is permitted to be absent from one's work or duty (尤指軍人的) 休假, 休假期: *have a furlough* 獲准休假; *go / be on furlough* 去休假/在休假中.

furnace ['fə:nis] *nc* large structure containing a very hot fire, used for heating a building etc or for various manufacturing processes; the fire itself 火爐; 爐火; 熔爐.

furnish ['fə:niʃ] *vt* **1** provide with tables, chairs etc. (用傢具) 佈置, 裝備: *furnish a room* 用傢具佈置房間. **2** provide what is needed 供應, 提供: *furnish proof / help / materials etc.* 提供證據/幫助/原料 等. **furnishings** *npl* tables, chairs, curtains, carpets etc. (esp. in a shop which sells these things) (傢具, 室內陳設品(如桌、椅、窗簾、地毯等, 尤指這些東西陳列在商店時).

furniture ['fə:nitʃə*] *nu* tables, chairs, beds etc. 傢具. **Note** 說明: for one article use *piece of furniture* 一件傢具要說 *piece of furniture.*

furrow ['fʌrou] *nc* mark made in the ground by a plough (田地犁過後的) 犁

溝.

furry ['fəːri] *adj* 見 **fur**.

further[1] ['fəːðəˣ] *adv* 1 to or at a greater distance 更 遠 地: *He travelled
further than I did.* 他旅行得比我遠. **2**
to a greater degree 進一步地, 深一層
地: *He studied the subject further than
I did.* 他研究這課題要比我深入. see
Note on **farther** 見 farther 的說明.

further[2] ['fəːðəˣ] *adj / determiner* **1**
more distant 更遠的. **2** additional; extra 更多的; 附加的: *I don't want to
cause any further trouble* i.e. there
has already been some trouble. 我不
想引起更多的麻煩. 即: 已經有一些麻煩
事了. **3** see 見 **furthermore**. **further
education** (usu. with reference to
study done by people who are also
working at a job) education continued
after one has left school 成人教育, 延
續教育. **'further'more** *adv* also; in
addition 而且; 此外, 另外: *Furthermore, I must tell you...* i.e. I have
already told you something. 此外, 我
還得告訴你…即: 我已經告訴你一些事
了. **furthest** *adj* most distant 最遠的.

further[3] ['fəːðəˣ] *vt* cause to develop 促
進, 推動: *further a plan / development
/ growth etc.* 促成一項計劃/促進發展/
促使生長.

furtive ['fəːtiv] *adj* secret; not wishing
to be seen by other people (and usu.
dishonest) 偷偷摸摸的, 鬼鬼祟祟的: *a
furtive person / action / look* 鬼鬼祟
祟的傢伙/詭秘的行動/偷眼一瞧. **fur-
tively** *adv.*

fury ['fjuəri] *nc / u* great anger (often
violent anger) 盛怒, 狂怒. see 見 **furious**.

fuse[1] [fjuːz] *nc* part of an electric circuit which is intended to melt or
break if the current becomes too
strong and this protects the circuit

from damage 保險絲, 熔絲. Also 亦作
vt / i melt, cause to melt, in this way
(使) 保險絲熔斷: *The light has fused.*
因保險絲熔斷, 那盞電燈不亮了. *He
fused the lights.* 他把保險絲弄得熔斷,
燈都不亮了.

fuse[2] [fjuːz] *nc* length of cord etc which
is lit to carry fire to an explosive 導火
線.

fuse[3] [fjuːz] *vt / i* (often with **together**)
become or make one by the action of
great heat (常與 together 連用) (使)
熔合: *The two pieces of metal had
fused together.* 兩片金屬熔合了.

fuselage ['fjuːzilɑːʒ] *nc* body of an aeroplane, without the wings and tail 飛機
機身, 機艙.

fusion ['fjuːʒən] *nc / u* process of mixing or joining 混合; 結合, 聯合: *a fu-
sion of various races / languages /
ideas etc.* 不同種族/語言/思想等的混
合(結合).

fuss [fʌs] *nu* unnecessary worry or excitement about small things 大驚小
怪, 小題大作: *She made a fuss when
the boy kicked a football into her garden.* 男孩把足球踢進她的花園時, 她就
小題大作聞個不停. Also 亦作 *vt / i*
make a fuss (over) (爲某事) 大驚小
怪, 小題大作. **fussy** *adj* **1** often disliking many things; unhappy if everything is not exactly as one wishes 挑
別的; 稍不稱心就不高興的. **2** giving
great attention to small details 過份注
意細節的.

futile ['fjuːtail] *adj* producing no good
results 無益的, 無效的: *They made a
futile search* i.e. they did not find anything. 他們白白搜尋了一番; 即: 他們一
無所獲. **futility** [fjuˈtiliti] *nu.*

future ['fjuːtʃəˣ] *nc* time which has not
yet happened (e.g. the year 2500 AD)
將來, 未來, 今後(如公元2500年). Also

亦作 *adj* of the future 將來的, 未來的:
future happiness 未來的幸福; *future
years* 未來的歲月. **future tense**
(grammar) form of the verb which re-fers to the future (語法) 將來式.

fuzzy ['fʌzi] *adj* **1** covered with very
short hair 有絨毛的. **2** not clear 模糊
的: *a fuzzy picture* 模糊的照片.

G,g

gabble ['gæbl] *vt / i* speak quickly and without meaning 急促不清地説話: *They sometimes gabble when they are excited.* 他們在激動時有時説話又快又不清楚. *In his haste to finish, he gabbled the speech he had to make.* 他急着要早些講完, 就把他不得不作的講話講得很快.

gable ['geibl] *nc* upper part of the outside wall of a house (usu. triangular in shape) between two sloping roofs i.e. a house with a flat roof has no gables (人字屋頂之間的) 山牆, 三角牆 (平頂房屋是没有山牆的).

gadget ['gædʒit] *nc* a piece of machinery (usu. small and laboursaving) 小機械裝置 (通常小巧玲瓏, 又可節省勞力): *Her kitchen is very modern and full of gadgets.* 她的廚房非常現代化, 擺滿了小機械裝置.

gag [gæg] *nc* something put over or into the mouth to stop someone speaking or making a noise (使人不能講話或叫喊的) 塞口物. Also 亦作 *vt* prevent someone speaking or making a noise by using a gag; prevent speech or expression 使不能講話; 壓制言論自由: *The thieves gagged him before they took his money.* 盜賊先塞住他的嘴, 然後搶走他的錢. *The government has no right to try to gag this newspaper.* 政府無權限制這家報紙的報導. *past* 過去式和過去分詞 **gagged.**

gaggle ['gægl] *nc* flock of geese 鵝羣 full.

gaiety ['geiiti] *nu* **gaily** ['geili] *adv* see 見 **gay.**

gain [gein] *nc* profit; advantage; in-

crease in something which is wanted 利益; 利潤; 增進: *The gains are balanced by the losses.* 得失相抵消. *We all work for gain.* 我們都爲得利而工作. *A gain in health / strength / knowledge etc is a good thing.* 健康 / 力量 / 知識等的增進是件好事. Also 亦作 *vt / i* **1** obtain something wanted 獲得, 贏得: *He gained full marks in the examination.* 他考試得了滿分. *He went abroad to gain more experience.* 他出國以便獲得更多的經驗. *Nothing is gained by being lazy.* 懶惰就一無所獲. **2** (usu. with **on** or **upon**) go further ahead; make better progress; improve (通常與 on 或 upon 連用) 超過; 進步; 改善, 增進: *In the race he gained on the other runners quite easily.* 在比賽中他很輕易地超過了其他選手. *Oil is steadily gaining on coal in the world market.* 在世界市場上石油正在穩步地超過煤. *His work is sure to gain if he uses these new methods.* 要是他採用這些新方法, 他的工作必定有進步.

gait [geit] *nc* manner of walking 步法, 步態: *He walked with a shuffling gait.* 他拖着脚步走.

gala ['gɑ:lə] *nc* festival; special show or event 節日; 慶祝活動. '**swimming gala** organized competition in swimming 游泳比賽.

galaxy ['gæləksi] *nc* **1** huge mass of millions of stars 星系: *Our universe is made up of many galaxies.* 我們的宇宙是由許多星系組成的. **2** (usu. **Galaxy**) that part of the galaxy to which the Earth belongs and which is seen at night as a faint band of light across the sky (Often **the Milky Way**) (通常用 Galaxy)銀河系(常用 the Milky Way).

gale [geil] *nc* strong wind 大風: *The tree was blown down in / by the gale.* 樹被狂風吹倒了. *Gales are common in winter.* 冬季常颳大風. '**gale force** force or speed of a gale 風力; 風速: *The wind reached gale force last night.* 昨晚風力達到大風級.

gall [gɔːl] *nu* bitter liquid that is made in the body by the liver 膽汁. '**gall bladder** vessel of the body containing gall 膽囊. '**gallstone** solid mass that sometimes forms in the gall bladder 膽石.

gallant ['gælnt] *adj* 1 brave 勇敢的. 2 polite, attentive (esp. to women) 彬彬有禮的; 獻慇懃的 (尤指對女人): *You were very gallant at the party last night.* 你在昨晚的聚會上大獻慇懃. **gallantry** *nu*.

galleon ['gæliən] *nc* (in former times) Spanish sailing ship (舊時的)西班牙大帆船.

gallery ['gæləri] *nc* 1 long, narrow passage or room sometimes open on one side 長廊; 陽台. 2 number of such rooms used for showing works of art 畫廊, 美術品陳列室: *The National Gallery contains many valuable pictures.* 英國國家美術館裏藏有許多珍貴的名畫. *The art galleries of Florence are very famous.* 佛羅倫薩的一些美術館非常有名. 3 upper floor with seats, built at one end of a large hall, to allow more people to watch and listen 樓座: *The visitors' gallery in the House of Commons was full when the Prime Minister began speaking.* 首相開始演講時,下院大廳的樓座上賓席擠滿了人. 4 top floor or balcony in a

theatre where the seats are cheapest 劇院頂樓的廉價樓座.

galley ['gæli] *nc* 1 single-decked ship or warship of the past, moved mainly by a large number of oars but sometimes also by sail. (The rowing was usu. done by slaves or criminals) (古代用奴隸或囚犯划的)單層甲板大帆船或戰船. 2 ship's kitchen 船上的廚房.

gallon ['gæln] *nc* liquid measure of 8 pints 加侖(液量單位, 等於 8 品脫).

gallop ['gæləp] *vi* 1 (usu. of a horse) run at its fastest speed (通常指馬)飛奔, 疾馳: *The horses galloped across the field.* 羣馬飛奔穿過田野. 2 (usu. with **through**) hurry; do in haste (通常與 through 連用)趕緊; 匆忙: *The boy galloped through his dinner.* 男孩匆忙地吃完飯. Also 亦作 *n sing* a horse's fastest speed (馬的)飛奔, 疾馳: *The other horse passed mine at a gallop.* 那另一匹馬飛奔著超過了我的馬.

gallows ['gælouz] *nc* strong wooden frame like high goalposts, used for putting people to death by hanging 絞刑架. *Note* 說明: *gallows* is *sing.* gallows 爲單數. *Long ago the gallows was on this hill.* 很久以前絞刑架樹立在這座小山上.

galvanize ['gælvənaiz] *vt* suddenly awaken or stimulate by electricity or shock (用電)刺激; 突然喚醒: *The alarm bell galvanized them into action* i.e. the alarm bell made them suddenly active as if they had received an electric shock. 警鈴聲喚醒他們採取行動. 即; 警鈴聲使他們像受到電流刺激一樣突然活躍起來.

galvanometer [ˌgælvəˈnɔmitə] *nc* instrument for detecting and measuring a small electric current 電流計.

gamble ['gæmbl] *vi* play a game of chance or skill for money; take risks in the hope of gaining money or advantage 賭博, 打賭; 冒險: *He made a lot of money gambling at cards;* 他賭牌贏了不少錢; *gamble in cotton / steel / soap etc* i.e. in buying and selling shares in them 搞棉花/鋼/肥皂等投機, 即: 買賣棉花/鋼/肥皂股票. *I gambled on his not seeing me* i.e. I took the risk that he would not see me. 我冒了他不肯見我的危險. *He gambled away all the money his father left him* i.e. he lost it by gambling. 他把他父親遺留給他的所有錢財都賭光了. 即: 因為賭博把錢輸光了. Also 亦作 *nc* risk; uncertainty 冒險, 風險; 難以確定的事情: *The attack was a gamble which did not succeed.* 這次進攻是一種冒險, 最後並沒有成功.

gambler *nc* **gambling** *nu* act or practice of playing for money 賭博: *Gambling is forbidden in some countries.* 有些國家禁止賭博.

gambol ['gæmbl] *vi* jump or dance playfully like young animals or children (像小動物或小孩一樣) 蹦蹦跳跳, 嬉戲. *past* 過去式和過去分詞 **gambolled.**

game [geim] **1** *nc* play; sport; contest with rules (e.g. football, tennis, chess, bridge) 遊戲, 運動, 比賽 (如足球、網球、棋類、橋牌等): *Football is a game played everywhere.* 足球是到處都有的運動. *We hope to have a game of football next Saturday* i.e. we hope to play a game of football. 我們希望在下星期六踢一場足球. **2** *nc* (only *pl*) meeting at which several games or contests (esp. athletic contests) take place (僅用複數) 運動會: *The Olympic Games are held every four years.* 奧林匹克運動會每四年舉行一次. *He* won the mile (race) in the school games. 他在學校運動會的一英里賽跑中獲勝. **3** *nu* animals or birds (e.g. deer, pheasants etc) hunted for sport (usu. protected for this purpose by special laws) 獵物 (通常指根據狩獵法准予捕獵的鳥獸, 如鹿、雉鸡等). Also 亦作 *adj* brave; willing; ready 勇敢的; 願意的; 樂意的: *He was game to the last* i.e. he went on fighting until the end. 他勇敢地戰鬥到底. *I'm game for anything* i.e. ready to do anything. 我甚麼事都樂意幹. **'gamekeeper** man employed to look after and breed game on a country estate 獵場看守人. **'game park / reserve** large area in which big game is protected 禁獵區. **'game ranger / warden** man employed to protect big game (保護大獵物的) 獵場看守人. **big game** *npl / nu* large animals when being hunted for sport 大獵物: *He went big-game hunting in Africa.* 他去非洲捕獵大動物.

gammon ['gæmən] *nu* smoked ham 燻腿.

gamut ['gæmət] *n sing* complete range of anything (esp. feelings and emotions) 全範圍, 全部 (如各種感情、情緒等): *The actor can express a whole gamut of emotions.* 這演員能表演出人的全部感情.

gander ['gændə*] *nc* male goose 雄鵝.

gang [gæŋ] *nc* group of people (usu. criminals, workmen or friends) 一羣, 一幫 (通常指罪犯、工匠或 (非正式) 朋友等): *The bank robbery was the work of a gang* i.e. a group of criminals. 銀行搶劫案是一羣罪犯幹的. *Our gang used to meet in this cafe* i.e. group of friends. 我們這幫朋友以前常在這家咖啡館碰頭.

gangster ['gæŋstə*] *nc* member of a gang of dangerous criminals 盜匪, 歹

徒, 暴徒.

gangrene ['gæŋgriːn] *nu* decay of part of a living body 壞疽.

gangway ['gæŋwei] *nc* **1** movable bridge from ship to shore to allow people to board and leave a ship 舷梯, (乘客上下船的)跳板: *The ship's captain stood at the gangway to welcome the passengers aboard.* 船長站在舷梯旁歡迎旅客上船. **2** passage between rows of seats (e.g. in a theatre or cinema) (劇場或電影院裏)座位間的過道: *Please do not block the gangway.* 請不要堵塞過道.

gaol, jail [dʒeil] *nc* public prison 監獄. Also 亦作 *vt* send to prison 監禁, 把…關進監獄: *He was gaoled / jailed for six months.* 他被囚禁了六個月.
gaoler, jailer, jailor *nc* person in charge of those sent to gaol / jail (*o.f.* -use **prison officer**) 監獄看守(舊式—現在用 prison officer). *Note* 說明: *gaol* is the official term in Britain but *jail* is the most used. Like *prison*, neither is used with an article except when meaning the actual building: *in jail; sent to jail; escape from jail* but *The jail is on a hill above the town.* 在英國, gaol 是正式用語, 但 jail 最常用. 這兩個詞和 prison 一樣, 不跟冠詞連用. 但在指具體建築物時有冠詞: *in jail* 在押, 關在監獄中; *sent to jail* 送入監獄; *escape from jail* 越獄. 但 *The jail is on a hill above the town.* 監獄建在俯瞰市鎮的小山上.

gap [gæp] *nc* opening; space between (which should be filled); way through 裂縫; (應當填補的) 缺口; 通路: *He escaped through a gap in the wall.* He 從牆上的缺口逃跑. *There are gaps in our knowledge of the moon* i.e. we do not know everything; there is more to learn. 我們對月球還不够瞭解. 即: 我們

不瞭解全部情况, 要知道的還很多: *There is a great gap between his ideas and mine.* 他的想法和我的想法差距很大. *The main road goes through a mountain gap.* 大路穿過山間隘口.

gape [geip] *vi* look at; stare with the mouth open in surprise; yawn. 看; 目瞪口獃地凝視; 打呵欠: *Why are you gaping at these pictures?* 你爲什麼目瞪口獃地凝視着這些圖片? **gaping** *adj* wide open; large 張開的; 很大的: *There is a gaping hole in the roof.* 屋頂有一個大洞.

garage ['gærɑːʒ] *nc* building where a motorcar is kept or repaired or where petrol is sold 汽車庫; 汽車修理站; 加油站. Also 亦作 *vt* put a motorcar in a garage 把(汽車)送入車庫(或修車站, 加油站).

garbage ['gɑːbidʒ] *nu* rubbish (usu. scraps of food from a kitchen) 廢料, 垃圾(通常指廚房清出的殘渣剩飯).

garble ['gɑːbl] *vt* give the facts of a report, speech etc in a mixed-up, confused way or wrongly (對報告、講演等)混淆, 曲解, 篡改: *The newspaper account of the minister's speech was completely garbled.* 報紙對部長講演的報導完全是歪曲.

garden ['gɑːdn] *nc* **1** place for growing fruit, vegetables and flowers 果園; 菜圃; 花園. **2** (only *pl*) public park or open space (僅用複數) 公園; 露天場所: *zoological gardens* 動物園; *botanical gardens* 植物園; *Kew gardens* 倫敦西郊國立植物園. **gardener** *nc* person who works in a garden 園丁, 花匠, 園林工人. **gardening** *nu* working in a garden 園藝: *Gardening is very popular in summer.* 園藝在夏天很流行. **'garden party** party (usu. large) held out of doors in a garden (通常是

大型的)遊園會. **'kitchen garden** see
見 **kitchen. 'market 'garden** *(Brit)*
(英) see 見 **market.**

gargle ['gɑːgl] *vi* wash inside of the
mouth or throat with liquid by throwing back the head and using breath to
prevent liquid going down throat 漱
口, 漱喉, 含漱: *I gargle every morning*
when I have a cold. 我感冒時每天清
晨漱口. Also 亦作 *nc* act of gargling;
liquid used for gargling 漱口; 含漱劑:
Hot water with salt makes a good
gargle. 熱水加鹽就是一種很好的含漱
劑.

gargoyle ['gɑːgɔil] *nc* small stone or
metal figure at the edge of the roof of
a building (usu. a church) to carry off
rainwater. The figure is usu. of an
ugly man or animal, and the rainwater
is passed through its mouth (屋頂邊
緣的)承霤口, 滴水嘴.

garish ['geəriʃ] *adj* bright and showy;
too brightly coloured 華麗而俗氣的;
過份鮮艷的: *The room is spoilt by the*
garish wallpaper. 這房間因為貼了花花
綠綠的牆紙而變得俗不可耐.

garland ['gɑːlnd] *nc* circle of leaves or
flowers (usu. placed on the head as
an ornament or sign of victory or
celebration) 花環, 花冠(通常用作裝飾
或表示慶祝).

garlic ['gɑːlik] *nu* small plant with a
root like an onion, used in cooking,
and having a strong taste and smell
蒜.

garment ['gɑːmənt] *nc* **1** (in *sing*) piece
of clothing *(o.f.)*. (用於單數) 衣服(舊
式). **2** (in *pl*) clothing (用於複數)服
裝, 衣著: *This shop sells garments of*
all kinds. (formal) 本店發售各式衣著.
(正式). **'undergarment** piece of clothing (e.g. vest, pants) worn under
outer clothes 内衣(如背心、短褲等).

Note 說明: the words *garments* and
esp. *undergarment(s)* continue to be
used because they are thought polite
by some people. Also *undergarment* is
the most useful word for one article
of *underclothes* which has no *sing.* 有
些人認為 garments, 尤其是 undergar-
ments 是禮貌的用語, 因此這些詞仍繼
續使用. undergarment 是表示"一件
underclothes"的最常用的詞. underclothes 沒有單數.

garnish ['gɑːniʃ] *vt* (usu. with reference
to a dish of food) decorate with small
things (通常指一盤食物)加配菜於:
The cook garnished the beef with on-
ions. 廚子用洋蔥配飾牛肉. Also 亦作
nu something used to decorate a dish
of food (e.g. parsley, mint etc.) 配菜
(如芫荽、薄荷等). *Note* 說明: *garnish,*
garnishing are sometimes used of unnecessary decorations or additions to
things other than food. *What I want is*
a plain statement without any gar-
nishing. garnish 和 garnishing 除了指
"配菜"外, 有時也指對其他事物的不必
要的裝飾或添加. What I want is a
plain statement without any garnishing. 我只要清楚明白的陳述, 不要
添油加醋.

garret ['gærit] *nc* very small room just
under the roof of a house 閣樓, 頂樓
的小室.

garrison ['gærisn] *nc* troops put in a
town or fort to defend it 駐軍, 衛戍部
隊. Also 亦作 *vt* occupy town or fort
as a garrison; put troops in town or
fort as a garrison 屯兵; 駐守: *The Ro-*
mans garrisoned all the forts near the
border. 羅馬人派兵駐守靠近邊界的所
有要塞. *The general garrisoned the*
town with his own troops after the vic-
tory. 勝利之後將軍命令他自己的部隊
駐守市鎮.

garrulous ['gærjuləs] *adj* talking a lot about uninteresting things 喋喋不休的.

garter ['gɑ:tə*] *nc* band worn round the leg to keep a stocking in place 襪帶.

gas [gæs] **1** *nc* matter like air in density and form (The other two forms that matter can take are liquid and solid) 氣體(物質的另外兩種形式是液體和固體): *Oxygen is a gas.* 氧是氣體. *Air is a mixture of nitrogen, oxygen and other gases.* 空氣是氮、氧和其他氣體的混合物. **2** *nu* gas commonly used for heating and working, supplied to factories and houses through pipes. These are either **coalgas**, made by burning coal, or **natural gas**, found deep below the ground. 煤氣(包括燒煤製成的煤氣和天然氣). **3** *nu* (*US*) informal short form of **gasoline.** (*Brit* 英 **petrol**) (美) 汽油 (gasoline 的非正式縮畧形式). **4** *nu* anaesthetic (*informal* in sense 4) 麻醉劑 (義 4 爲非正式). Also 亦作 *vt* harm or kill with poisonous gas 用毒氣傷害或殺死. *past* 過去式和過去分詞 **gassed.**

gassy ['gæsi] *adj* of, like gas 氣體的, 像氣體的: *There's a gassy smell down here.* 這裏有某種氣體的味道. **'gas 'cooker** cooker which uses lighted gas 煤氣爐. **'gas 'fire** fire which uses lighted gas 煤氣取暖器. **'gas meter** instrument for measuring how much gas is used 煤氣表, 氣量計.

gash [gæʃ] *nc* long, deep cut (usu. in flesh) (深長的)切口, 傷口 (通常指肌肉的切口). Also 亦作 *vt* make a gash (在…上) 割深長切口, 割傷: *His cheek was gashed by a knife.* 他的面頰被又深又長地割了一刀.

gasket ['gæskit] *nc* ring or strip of soft material placed tightly between two parts of a joint in a pipe etc to pre-

vent gas, steam etc from escaping 墊片, 墊圈, 接合墊.

gasoline ['gæsəli:n] *nu* (*US*) petrol (美) 汽油.

gasp [gɑ:sp] *vi* take short, quick breaths; fight for breath with mouth open 短促地呼吸; 張着口喘氣: *After the race he stood gasping for air.* 他參加賽跑之後站着喘氣. *His bad behaviour left me gasping* i.e. open-mouthed and speechless with surprise or anger. 他的惡劣行爲使我瞠不過氣. 即: 因吃驚或憤怒而張口結舌. Also 亦作 *nc* short, quick breath (of pain, surprise, anger etc) (因痛苦、驚奇、憤怒 等)喘息: *His jokes caused a few gasps among the audience.* 他的笑話好幾次使聽衆笑得喘不過氣來. *We shall fight to the last gasp* i.e. to the end; until we die. 我們將戰鬥到底. 即: 戰鬥到最後, 直到我們戰死. *That dog is at its last gasp* i.e. it is completely exhausted or is about to die. 那狗已經奄奄一息. 即: 那狗已經筋疲力盡, 即將死去.

gassy ['gæsi] *adj* see 見 **gas.**

gastric ['gæstrik] *adj* of the stomach 胃的. *Note* 說明: *gastr-, gastro-* are prefixes used in many medical terms about the stomach. gastr- 和 gastro- 是前綴, 用在許多有關胃的醫學術語中.

gate [geit] *nc* opening into a place (e.g. a field, garden, sports ground) which can be closed; kind of door used to close this opening 大門(如場地、花園、運動場的大門): *He walked through the gate into the garden.* 他通過大門走進花園. *Please shut the gate when you leave the field.* 你離開場地時請把大門關好. *The gate is too high to climb.* 門太高了, 爬不上去. **'gatecrash** *vt* enter place without paying or being invited 無票入場, 不

請自來: *He tried to gatecrash the party.* 他企圖擅自闖入那次聚會. **'gate-way** actual entrance, way in, at a gate 門口, 入口: *He stood in the gateway to stop her going in* i.e. in the middle of the opening. 他堵住門口不讓她進去.

gateau ['gætou] *nc* cake, often with cream, chocolate etc. 奶油巧克力蛋糕. *pl* 複數 **gateaux** ['gætouz].

gather ['gæðə*] **1** *vt / i* come together, bring together; pick up, collect (使)聚集; 集合; 採集; 收集: *The people gathered in the street.* 人羣在街上聚集. *She gathered her children round her.* 她把孩子聚攏在她週圍. *Gather your books together and follow me.* 把你的書收拾在一起跟我來. *He is busy gathering information about birds.* 他正忙於搜集關於鳥類的資料. **2** *vi* understand; find out; 瞭解; 打聽到, 弄清楚: *I gather you live here.* 我猜想你住在這裏. *From what he said I gathered that he was not pleased.* 從他的話我斷定他不太高興. **3** *vt* pull cloth together into folds with a thread (用線將布片)打皺褶: *The child's dress is neatly gathered at the neck.* 孩子的衣服在領口處打着整齊的皺褶.

gathering *nc* meeting of people 集會, 聚會: *sports gathering* i.e. meeting for sport 運動會.

gaudy ['gɔːdi] *adj* bright and showy 華麗而俗氣的: *That's a gaudy tie you are wearing* i.e. I don't like it because it is too bright. 你的領帶太俗氣了. 即: 我不喜歡你的領帶, 我嫌它太鮮豔.

gauge¹ [geidʒ] *vt* measure size, contents, power etc of things; estimate; (usu. of feelings, thoughts etc) guess 測量, 測定 (體積, 容積, 功率等); 估計, 估量; 猜測 (通常指感情, 想法等): *With a long stick you can gauge the*

amount of water in this well. 用一根長竿便可以測量這口井的水量. *It is not easy to gauge his thoughts about your plan.* 很難揣度他對於你的計劃有些甚麼看法.

gauge² [geidʒ] *nc* **1** measure of thickness, contents etc. (e.g. wire, nails, pieces of metal, barrels); measure of distance between pairs of rails (線材, 釘子, 金屬板, 桶等的粗細, 厚度, 容積等的)標準規格; (鐵路的)軌距: *This wire is sold in several gauges* i.e. several thicknesses. 這種線材按幾種相同規格出售. *The standard gauge for British railways is 4 feet 8½ inches* i.e. the distance between pairs of rails. 英國鐵路的標準軌距是四英尺八又二分之一英寸. **2** instrument for measuring 量規, 量器, 量計.

gaunt [gɔːnt] *adj* thin, looking ill, from hunger or pain (因飢餓或痛楚)瘦削的, 氣色不好的.

gauntlet ['gɔːntlit] *nc* strong glove to protect the hands and wrists (e.g. in fighting, fencing) (搏鬥或擊劍時保護手及腕部的)手套, 防護手套.

gauze [gɔːz] *nu* type of thin cloth which one can see through; fine netting (e.g. of wire) 薄紗, 羅; 金屬網紗: *The windows are covered with wire gauze* i.e. fine netting made of wire to keep out insects etc. 窗子上裝了金屬絲網. 即: 防蟲等的細金屬絲網.

gave [geiv] past tense of **give.** give 的過去式.

gay [gei] *adj* **1** happy and lively; without worries or cares; (of colours) bright and cheerful 快樂的; 無憂無慮的; (色彩)鮮豔的: *The dinner party was certainly a gay one.* 宴會無疑是令人愉快的. *When we were young and gay* i.e. happy and without any cares. 當我們年輕快樂時, 即: 當我們高高興興無憂無

慮時. *The room was gay with flowers*
i.e. flowers made the room look bright
and cheerful. 鮮花使房間顯得明亮令
人心情舒暢. **2** homosexual (*informal*
in sense 2) 同性戀的(義 2 爲非正式).
gaily *adv* **gaiety** ['geiiti] *nu*.

gaze [geiz] *vi* look at for a long time
(usu. in wonder or admiration) 凝視,
注視(通常指驚奇地或羨慕地): *The*
children gazed round the shop. 孩子
們在商店裏環顧四週. *He stood gazing*
at the view. 他站着注視眼前的景色.
Also 亦作 *nc* long look 凝視, 注視.

gazelle [gə'zel] *nc* type of small graceful animal (usu. reddish with a white
stomach) which is rather like a deer
瞪羚 (一種顏像鹿的小動物).

gazette [gə'zet] **1** *nc* newspaper 報紙. **2**
official publication containing announcements (政府) 公報: *an official*
gazette 正式公報.

gazetteer [gæzə'tiə*] *nc* geographical
dictionary giving lists of place names
in alphabetical order 地名詞典, 地名
索引.

gear [giə*] *nc* **1** any equipment or
mechanism which controls or guides
a machine 控制或操縱機器的裝置:
The lifting gear of a crane. 起重機的
升降裝置. **2** wheels with teeth which
fit into each other to change the
speed or power given by an engine 齒
輪; 排檔: *This car has three forward*
gears. 這種汽車有三個前進檔. **3**
apparatus in general 一般的設備, 一般
的裝置; 工具: *Put your fishing gear in*
the bag i.e. rod, hooks, boots etc used
when fishing. 把你的漁具放進袋子.
即: 釣魚時用的漁竿、漁鈎、長統靴
等. **'gearbox** box in a machine or car
which contains the gears 齒輪箱, 變速
箱. **'gear lever** (in a motorcar or on
an engine) short bar which is moved

to change gears 變速桿.

geese [giːs] *pl* of **goose**. goose 的複數.

gelatin, gelatine ['dʒelətiːn] *nu* substance used in cooking (usu. obtained
by boiling animal bones and tissues)
which melts in hot water and becomes a jelly when cold 骨膠, 動物
膠, 明膠.

gelignite ['dʒelignait] *nu* type of explosive 葛里炸藥, 炸膠.

gem [dʒem] *nc* valuable stone (usu.
when cut and polished for wearing)
寶石, 美玉.

gender ['dʒendə*] *nc* (grammar) one of
the three classes into which words
can be put according to the sex given
them i.e. masculine, feminine and
neuter genders (語法)性(陽性, 陰性和
中性): *The gender of the word 'boy'*
is masculine, of the word 'girl' femi-
nine, and of the word 'house' neuter.
'boy' 這個詞陽性, 'girl' 陰性, 'house'
中性.

general¹ ['dʒenərl] *adj* **1** for, by everybody or almost everybody; common;
not special 全體的; 普通的; 一般的:
Watching television has become
general i.e. most people watch television. 看電視已經很普遍了. 即: 有許多
人看電視. **2** not exact; not in detail
大體的; 籠統的: *The general idea is to*
wait and see. 大致的想法是要採取觀
望態度. *We had a general talk about*
books i.e. not about any particular
book. 我們籠統地談了一些書籍的問
題: 即: 沒有具體談某一本書. **general-**
ly *adv* **1** usually, commonly 一般地,
通常地: *I am generally at home after*
7 o'clock. 我通常七點之後在家. **2**
without giving details; by everybody
or almost everybody 大體上; 普通地,
廣泛地: *I can only speak generally.*
我只能在大體上談一下. *Your promise*

is generally believed. 大多數人相信你的許諾. **generalize** *vi* make a general statement about something 概括, 歸納, 作出一般性結論: *One cannot generalize from a few examples.* 不能從少數幾個例子來歸納出一般性的結論. **generalization** [dʒenərəlai'zeiʃən] *nc / u* general statement 一概而論, 籠統的說法: *It is a generalization to say that men are stronger than women.* 說男人比女人強壯是一種籠統的說法. **general election** election held all over the country (for Parliament) 全國大選, (對議會議員的) 普選. **general knowledge** what is known about many things; what is known by many people 一般知識, 常識: *This examination will test your general knowledge.* 本次考試將測驗你們的一般知識. *It is general knowledge that he will come tomorrow.* 大家都知道他明天會來. **general post office** post office for a large area, as compared with a local one 郵政總局. **general practitioner** doctor who treats many kinds of illness, not one special kind of illness 普通醫生, 通科醫生 (通看各科的開業醫生). see 見 **specialist**. **in general** without details; as a whole 一般地, 大體上; 總的說來: *Women in general like fashionable clothes.* 女人一般都喜歡時髦的衣服. *In general I agree with you.* 我大體上同意你的主張.

general² ['dʒenərl] *nc* army officer of very high rank 將軍, 上將.

generalissimo [dʒenərə'lisimou] *nc* commander in chief of all the armed forces, or of several armies in the field 總司令, 最高統帥, 大元帥.

generate ['dʒenəreit] *vt* cause; make; make to happen 引起; 使產生; 使發生: *A fire generates heat.* 火發出熱. *The*

machine generates electricity / gas / steam etc. 這機器用來發電/生產煤氣/供應蒸氣等. *His kind smile soon generated friendliness.* 他那和藹的笑容很快帶來了友誼. **generator** *nc* machine which generates electricity / gas / steam etc. 發電機/煤氣發生器/蒸氣發生器. **generation** [dʒenə'reiʃən] 1 *nu* generating 產生, 發生: *the generation of electricity by atomic power* i.e. making electricity 用原子能發電. 2 *nc* people who belong by age to the same period of time 代, 一代人: *Grandfathers, fathers and sons belong to three different generations* 祖父、父親和兒子分別屬於不同的三代人; *the younger / rising generation* i.e. all young people not yet grown up 青年一代, 即: 所有未成年的人.

generous ['dʒenərəs] *adj* ready to give or spend; kind and helpful 慷慨的; 大方的: *They are generous with their advice / money / time.* 他們樂於提出忠告/提供幫助/花錢/花時間. *Be generous to him; he has been ill.* 對他寬宏大量一些, 他一直在生病. **generously** *adv* **generosity** [dʒenə'rɔsiti] *nc / u*.

genetics [dʒi'netiks] *nu* science which studies how heredity works 遺傳學.

genial ['dʒi:niəl] *adj* cheerful and cheering; kindly; pleasant 高興的; 友善的; 令人愉快的: *in genial company* 跟愉快的朋友在一起; *genial neighbours* 友善的鄰居; *genial climate / weather* 宜人的氣候/天氣.

genie ['dʒi:ni:], **jinn** [dʒin] *nc* spirit or fairy found in Eastern stories (東方神話中的) 神怪, 妖怪. *pl* 複數 **genies** or **genie**.

genital ['dʒenitl] *adj* sexual 關於兩性的; *genital organ* 生殖器, 外陰部. **genitals, genitalia** [dʒeni'teiliə] *npl* genital organs 生殖器, 外陰部.

genius ['dʒiːniəs] **1** *nu* very great intelligence or ability 天賦, 天資, 天才: *a writer of genius* 天才作家. *Genius is needed to solve this problem.* 解答這個問題需要天才. **2** *nc* someone having very great intelligence or ability 天才人物. *Shakespeare was a genius.* 莎士比亞是一個天才. *Only a genius can solve this.* 只有天才人物才能解答這類問題.

gent [dʒent] *nc* short informal form of **gentleman** 男士, 紳士 (gentleman 的非正式縮略形式). **Gents** *npl* public lavatory for men, *(informal)* 公共男廁 (非正式).

genteel [dʒen'tiːl] *adj* too polite or well-mannered in a false way; pretending to be what one is not 假裝彬彬有禮的; 假裝的.

gentile ['dʒentaɪl] *nc* someone who is not Jewish 非猶太人. Also 亦作 *adj*.

gentle ['dʒentl] *adj* kind; soft; not rough or strong and tender 和善的; 柔和的; 不粗魯的, 不猛烈的: *a gentle smile* 輕盈的一笑; *a gentle knock on the door* 在門上的輕輕一敲; *a gentle manner* 文雅的儀態; *gentle rain* 細雨; *a gentle slope* i.e. one which is not steep 不很陡的斜坡. **gently** *adv* **gentleness** *nu*.

gentleman ['dʒentlmən] *nc* **1** man of good family, of upper classes (in the past, one just below the nobility); man of wealth and leisure 出身高貴的人, (舊時僅次於貴族的) 上流社會人士; 有錢有閒階級人士, 紳士: *Since he became rich he lives like a gentleman.* 他致富之後過着紳士一樣的生活. **2** man who behaves as a gentleman should i.e. has good manners and can be trusted 有紳士風度的人, 即: 有可以信任的人: *He is no gentleman* i.e. he is bad-mannered or not to be trusted.

他決不是紳士. 即: 他不值得信任. **3** polite word for **man** 對男子的尊稱: *There is a gentleman to see you.* 有一位先生想見您. *Please sit down, gentlemen.* 先生們, 請坐. *pl* 複數 **gentlemen** ['dʒentlmən]. *Note* 說明: the *fem* form *gentlewoman* is *o.f.;* therefore the polite way to address mixed company is *ladies and gentlemen. Gentlemen* is the form used in the *pl.* For *sing* use *Sir. Please sit down, gentlemen* but *Please sit down, Sir. Gentleman* used in the third person (e.g. *There is a gentleman to see you.*) is slightly *o.f.* but it is more usual when the gentleman is within hearing. Otherwise use *man. He is a very rich man not He is a very rich gentleman.* 陰性形式 gentlewoman 是舊式的. 因此, 聽眾中有男女時有禮貌的稱呼應當是 ladies and gentlemen. Gentlemen 是用於複數的形式, 單數應當用 Sir. 如 Please sit down, gentlemen. (先生們, 請坐.) 但是要說 Please sit down, Sir. (先生, 請坐.) 用於第三人稱的 gentleman (如 There is a gentleman to see you. 有一位先生想見您.) 稍微有些舊式, 但是如果那位先生聽得見這句話, 這樣說也很平常. 不然的話用 man 就可以了. 如 He is a very rich man (他很有錢). 用不着說 He is a very rich gentleman.

gentry ['dʒentri] *npl* those of the upper class 紳士們, 上流社會人士: *All the gentry in this part of the country like fishing.* 該國這一地區的所有上流社會人士都喜愛釣魚.

genuine ['dʒenjuin] *adj* real; true; not a copy but the real thing 真實的; 真實的; 非倣製品的: *a genuine gold ring* i.e. made of real gold 真金戒指, 純金戒指. *His illness is genuine* i.e. he is not pretending to be ill. 他的病是真的. 即: 他不是裝病. *A* genuine old Roman coin i.e. not a copy of one 一枚真正的古羅馬錢幣，即：非仿製品. **genuinely** adv.

geography [dʒi'ɔgrəfi] nu science of the earth's lands, seas, climates, peoples, products etc. 地理，地理學.

geographic, geographical [dʒiəgræfik(l)] adj **geographer** nc someone who is expert in geography 地理學家.

geology [dʒi'ɔlədʒi] nc science of the earth's rocks and how they were formed 地質學. **geologist** nc someone expert in geology 地質學家. **geological** [dʒiə'lɔdʒikl] adj.

geometry [dʒi'ɔmətri] nu mathematical study of lines, angles, surfaces and shapes 幾何學. **geometric, geometrical** [dʒiə'metrik(l)] adj **geometrically** adv.

germ [dʒə:m] nc **1** very small living part of a plant or animal which causes it to grow 幼芽；胚：*germ of wheat* 麥芽. **2** something very small which causes anything to grow, bigger 萌芽, 起源：*I have the germ of an idea* i.e. I have the beginning of an idea which may grow into something more definite. 我有一種初步的想法. 即：我的想法只是開頭，以後可能會發展得具體一些. **3** very small living thing (microbe or bug) which is harmful 微生物；病菌, 細菌：*Colds are spread by germs.* 感冒是由病菌傳染的.

germicide ['dʒə:misaid] nc / u substance that destroys the germs which cause disease 殺菌劑. **germicidal** [dʒə:mi'saidl] adj.

germinate ['dʒə:mineit] vt / i (usu. of seeds) begin or make to grow (通常指種子) (使) 發芽. **germination** [dʒə:mi'neiʃən] nu.

gestate ['dʒesteit] vt carry in the uterus during pregnancy 妊娠, 懷孕, 孕育.

gestation [dʒes'teiʃən] n.

gesticulate [dʒes'tikjuleit] vi make gestures while, or instead of, speaking 做手勢示意. **gesticulation** [dʒestikju'leiʃən] nc act of gesticulating 做手勢；示意的動作(或姿勢).

gesture ['dʒestʃə*] nc **1** movement of the body (esp. of hands, arm or head) to show what one feels or thinks 手勢, (手, 臂或頭的) 姿勢：*He made a rude gesture with his fingers.* 他用手指比了一個下流的手勢. *He shook his fist in a gesture of anger.* 他揮動拳頭以表示憤怒. **2** any movement to show what one feels or thinks 姿態, 表示：*His quick reply to your letter is an encouraging gesture.* 他迅速答覆你的信就是一種令人鼓舞的表示. Also 亦作 vi make a gesture 打手勢, 用姿勢示意. *Note* 說明：gesture (verb) has the same meaning as gesticulate, but the latter also describes movements which are violent and not controlled. *He always gesticulates when he is excited.* 動詞 gesture 和 gesticulate 同樣意爲"打手勢". 但 gesticulate 還可以表示猛烈的和失去控制的動作. 如 He always gesticulates when he is excited. 他一激動起來總是搖胸頓足.

get [get] vt / i **1** obtain, earn, buy 獲得；贏得, 掙得；買：*He got his degree by working hard.* 他靠努力得到學位. *I am getting £2,500 a year.* 我歲入 2,500英鎊. *She has gone to get some bread.* 她去買麵包. *Go and get your breakfast* i.e. obtain and eat. 去吃早飯吧. **2** (with reference to food) prepare (指食物) 準備：*Get some food for the visitors.* 替客人們準備食物. *She is getting lunch.* 她正在準備午餐. **3** receive 收到, 受到：*I got your letter this morning.* 今天上午我收到了你的信. *This country gets very little rain.* 這個

國家雨量很少. *John got a kick on the leg.* 約翰的腿上被人踢了一腳. So, with reference to illnesses 指疾病: *get a cold / a fever / malaria etc.* 患感冒 / 發燒 / 患瘧疾等. *Note* 說明: *get cold* i.e. become cold; get a cold i.e. catch the infection; get cold, 即: 變冷; get a cold, 即: 患感冒. **4** become 變得, 成爲: *He soon got tired.* 他很快就累了. *In summer it gets very hot here.* 夏天這裏很熱. **5** put oneself in a certain state 使自己處在某種狀態: *Get ready / shaved / washed / dressed etc.* 準備好 / 刮好臉 / 洗乾淨 / 穿好衣服等. *They got to know.* 他們逐漸有所瞭解. *I'll never get to understand him.* 我永遠不會理解他的. **6** go, come, arrive, travel (sometimes with difficulty or effort) (有時指克服困難或經過努力後) 去; 來; 到達; 旅行: *We'll get there somehow.* 我們將會設法到達那裏. *How do we get across the river?* 我們要怎樣渡河呢? *He got back last week.* 他上星期回來了. *I hope they get home soon.* 我希望他們很快就到家. **7** cause someone / something to go, come, arrive etc; cause to happen; put someone / something in a certain state (often with difficulty or effort) (常指克服困難或經過努力後) 使去, 使來, 使到達; 使發生; 把…弄得, 使處於某種狀態: *We'll get you there somehow.* 我們將設法把你送到那裏. *How do we get a car across the river?* 我們要怎樣把汽車弄到河對岸去呢? *He got his son back to school.* 他使他兒子回學校去. *Get me home at once.* 馬上送我回家. *Has she got the baby dressed yet?* 她已經給嬰兒穿好衣服了嗎? *He is getting his clothes packed.* 他正在把衣服裝進箱子. *I cannot get him to agree.* 我無法使他表示同意. *past* 過去式和過去分詞 **got** [gɔt]. (*US past part*

is **gotten** ['gɔtn] in the sense of obtained or become) (在美國英語中 get 意爲"獲得"或"成爲"時過去分詞爲 gotten). **have got** have 有: *I've got two pairs of shoes.* 我有兩雙鞋. *Note¹* 說明¹: *have got is probably more usual than have* (esp. in speech). 尤其在講話時, have got 可能比 have 更爲常用. *Note²* 說明²: being one of the most common verbs in the English language (esp. in speech), *get* is used with many *preps* and *advs* and in many phrases, mostly as informal variants of other verbs. A list of them, by no means complete, is given below: get 是英語(特別是英語口語)裏最常用的動詞之一, 它和許多介詞和副詞連用; 並且用在許多短語中, 主要是作爲其他動詞的非正式變體. 以下列舉了部份帶 get 的短語: **get about** go about; travel 走動; 旅行: *He can't get about on his leg after breaking it.* 他的腿骨折斷了, 無法走動. **get across** go, come across; cause to do so (使) 過去; (使) 過來; (使) 通過. **get along 1** succeed; make progress 成功; 有進步, 有起色: *Is he getting along all right in his new job?* 他擔任新的工作有成績嗎? **2** agree, cooperate with 相處融洽: *He is so kind that he gets along with everyone.* 他很和藹, 跟大家相處得很好. **3** nonsense, go away! 去你的! 胡說! **Get along with you!** (*informal* in sense 3) 滾蛋吧! (義 3 爲非正式). see also 參見 **get on. get at 1** reach 拿到, 夠着: *The little boy cannot get at the books on the top shelf.* 小男孩夠不着書架頂層上的書. **2** find out 理解, 查明: *It is difficult to get at the real cause of this.* 很難搞清這件事的真實原因. **3** mean, hint 意指: *What exactly are you getting at?* i.e. what do you mean? 你究竟指甚麼? 即: 你到底是

甚麼意思? **get away** escape, depart from; cause to do so (使) 逃脫; (使) 離開: *The prisoner got away from his guards*. 囚犯從看守那裏逃脫. *I cannot get away from the office before six o'clock*. 六點之前我無法離開辦公室. **'getaway** *nc* quick escape (esp. from a crime) 迅速的逃走, 逃脫(尤指逃脫罪責). **get away with something** succeed without being harmed or punished 僥倖成功, 做了錯事而不被發覺或不受處罰: *He thinks he can always get away with telling lies*. 他以為他可以老是撒謊而不受處罰. **get back** return; cause to do so (使) 回來: *We got back before nightfall*. 我們在天黑前回來. **get by** pass; cause to do so (使) 通過: *How can I get by while you stand in the way?* 你擋住了路, 我怎麼過得去? *Get him by the policeman and he will be safe*. 幫他躲過警察, 他就安全了. **get one down** depress; discourage; make one feel unhappy 使沮喪; 使氣餒; 使不高興: *His bad manners get me down*. 他的不禮貌行為使我很不愉快. *Don't let the other team get you down*. (*informal*) 別叫另一個隊把你搞得垂頭喪氣的. (非正式). **get home 1** arrive, return home; cause to do so 到家, 回家; 把…送到家. **2** hit the target or mark 擊中目標; 說得中肯: *Two of the shots got home*. 有兩槍命中. *How can I get this home to him?* i.e. make him understand it. 我怎樣才能使他理解這點呢? **get in / into 1** go in / into; arrive; cause to do so (使) 進入; (使) 到達: *Get into bed and stay there*. 快上床, 別下來. *We got in late last night*. 我們昨晚很遲才到家. *They will get into London this afternoon*. 他們今天下午會到倫敦. *Get the washing in before it rains*. 在下雨之前把晾着的衣物收進來. *The*

bus got me into the village at two o'clock*. 兩點鐘時公共汽車把我送進村子裏. **2** have something (usu. unpleasant) happen to one 使某人陷入, 使某人遭遇(不愉快的事): *He got into a rage / temper*. 他勃然大怒. *I am afraid I'll get into trouble*. 恐怕我會遇到麻煩. *They got into debt*. 他們負債了. *This mistake may get him into difficulties*. 這一錯誤將使他陷入困境. **get (someone / something) off 1** go, come off; leave; cause to do so (使) 下來, (使) 離開: *She got off the bus*. 她下了公共汽車. *Get off the floor at once*. 立即從舞台席上下來. *At what time do you get off (work / from work)?* 你甚麼時候下班? *We must get the car off this busy road*. 我們得使汽車離開這條繁忙的公路. *The boy is getting off his wet clothes*. 這男孩正在脫掉濕衣服. **2** send away 送走: *He got the report off to his teacher last week*. 他上星期已經託人把報告送給老師了. *We cannot get our guests off to London before Monday*. 星期一之前我們無法讓客人去倫敦. **3** begin 開始: *They at last got off to sleep*. 他們終於睡着了. *The concert got off to a good start* i.e. it began well. 音樂會開始得很好. **4** avoid damage, danger, punishment; cause to do so (使) 免受損失, (使) 免遭危險: *You won't get off next time you do it*. 下次你再這麼幹, 你可跑不了. *Blaming the other driver did not get him off*. 責怪另一個司機並不能替他自己開脫責任. *They could not get them off until the storm ended* i.e. from some place of danger. 在暴風雨停止之前他們無法躲開危險. 即: 無法脫離危險地區. **get on 1** succeed, make progress 成功; 取得進步: *How are you getting on at school?* 你在學校裏過得怎麼樣? *That* *man is sure to get on.* 那人必定大有出息. **2** (usu. of time) pass, move (通常指時間) 流逝; 推移: *Time is getting on* i.e. it is late. 時候已晚了. *He is getting on in years* i.e. he is becoming old. 他漸漸有了年紀了. *He is getting on for sixty* i.e. he is almost sixty years old. 他年近六十. *I have to get on my way* i.e. move, begin going 我得上路了. 我得走了. **get on something** mount, climb on, cause to do so (使)登上; (使)騎上: *Get on a horse / bicycle / roof / wall etc.* 上馬/騎上自行車/爬上屋頂/爬上牆. *Get on one's feet.* i.e. stand. 站起來. *They got him on his bicycle.* 他們扶他上自行車. **get on with someone** agree, cooperate with; be friendly with 相處融洽; 與⋯友好: *I get on well with my mother-in-law.* 我跟岳母關係不錯. **get out** go, come out; escape; cause to do so (使)出去, (使)出來; (使)逃走: *He got out the door / window.* 他走到門外/他跳到窗外. *Our dog has got out.* 我們的狗出去了. *We got the box out the door / window.* 我們把盒子扔到門/窗外. **get out of something 1** see 見 **get out**. *When did you get out of bed?* 你甚麼時候起床? *The prisoner got out of the cell by breaking down the door.* 囚犯破門逃離囚室. *Please get me out of here.* 請幫助我離開這裏. *Note* 說明: it is only with doors, windows and other openings that either *get out* or *get out of* is used, *get out* having the special meaning here of going out through these openings. With all other words *get out of* is used. 跟門、窗等通道有關時既可以用 *get out* 也可以用 *get out of*. 這裏 *get out* 有從這些通道出去的特殊意義. 跟所有其他的詞有關時要用 *get out of*. **2** avoid; cause to do so (使)避免;

You cannot get out of paying your debts. 你免不了得還債. *My illness got me out of having to see him* i.e. as I was ill I didn't have to see him. 我的病使我不用見他. **3** obtain; benefit from 得到; 從⋯獲益: *All I got out of him was twenty pence.* 我從他那裏得到的全部東西只有二十便士. **get over (something)** climb over, cause to do so; put over (使)爬過, 越過; 傳遞過: *The boy is getting over the fence / gate / wall etc.* 這男孩正在爬過籬笆/大門/牆等. *It was difficult to get the pole over the hedge.* 要把這根竿子傳遞過樹籬很困難. **get over something** recover from something unpleasant, succeed in overcoming 從不愉快的事中恢復過來; 克服: *The parents will never get over the death of their son.* 這對父母將永遠不能從喪子的悲痛中恢復過來. *How can a person get over being blind?* 一個人怎麼能夠忍受雙目失明的痛苦呢? **get round (something)** go, come round; cause to do so. (使)繞過一圈; (使)繞過去: *You can get round the park in half an hour.* 繞這個公園一圈只要半個小時. *We got the car round the corner without being seen.* 我們駕車拐過了街角, 沒有讓人看到. **get round something** avoid a difficulty 避開困難: *They have got round the difficulty by writing to the headmaster.* 他們向校長寫信, 渡過了難關. **get round someone** persuade; win over 說服; 把⋯爭取過來: *He got round the others by pretending to help them.* 他用假裝幫助他們的辦法說服了其他人. *When shall we get him round to helping us?* 我們甚麼時候才能說服他來幫助我們? **get (something) through 1** go or come, pass through; cause to do so (使)穿過; (使)通過: *I was able to get* *through the forest by myself.* 我能够獨自穿過這道森林. *He tried to get the box through the window.* 他試圖從窗戶把箱子弄過去. **2** (usu. of a message, telephone call, radio) reach; cause to do so (通常指消息,電話,無線電等)到達;與…聯繫上: *He could not get through to his mother last night* i.e. by telephone. 昨晚他無法和他媽媽聯繫上. 即: 電話沒有打通. *Letters did not get through until after the floods.* 直到水災之後才恢復通郵. *I want you to get this message through to headquarters.* 我要你把這條消息向司令部報告. **3** make oneself understood 使 (別人)瞭解自己: *I can't get through to her.* 我無法使她明白我的意思. **get through something 1** finish 完成; 花光,用光,吃光: *They got through the meal without speaking.* 他們一言不發地吃完了飯. *You must get through this book before Monday.* 你得在星期一之前看完這本書. *She got through her husband's money in a year* i.e. spent it all 她在一年之內把她丈夫的錢花光. **2** (of examinations, courses) succeed in, pass; cause to do so (使)考試及格: *Did you get through your driving test?* 你通過了駕駛考試了嗎? *His job as a tutor is to get me through this examination.* 他當家庭教師的職責就是幫助我通過這次考試. **get together** come together; meet; cause to do so (usu. for a purpose) (使)聚集;(使)集合(通常爲了某一目的). **get up 1** rise from bed in the morning; stand; cause to do so (使)起床;(使)站起來: *I got up very early* i.e. from bed. 我起得很早. 即: 很早起床. *The pupils get up when their teacher comes into the classroom* i.e. stand. 教師走進教室時學生起立. *The teacher got the boys up when the headmaster came into the classroom.* 校長走進教室時教師要男孩們起立. **2** climb; cause to do so (使)登上,(使)爬上: *We got up the ladder to the roof.* 我們用梯子登上房頂. **get up to 1** arrive close to; reach 靠近到;到達: *The enemy got up to the wall of the town before they attacked.* 敵人靠近城牆之後才開始進攻. *Yesterday I got up to page 100.* 昨天我讀到第100頁. **2** (usu. of children) plan or being something naughty (常指小孩)搞…,胡鬧: *What are these children getting up to now?* 這些孩子現在在搞甚麼鬼?

geyser ['giːzə*] *nc* **1** spring which spouts hot water into the air from time to time 間歇熱水噴泉. **2** small, domestic, gas water heater 小型家用煤氣熱水器.

ghastly ['gɑːstli] *adj* **1** shocking, terrible 駭人聽聞的,可怕的: *It was a ghastly murder.* 這是駭人聽聞的謀殺. **2** pale and miserable, like a dead person 蒼白的,悲慘的;形同死人的.

ghetto ['getou] *nc* **1** part of a town where Jews once had to live (以前的)猶太人區. **2** part of a town where any separate group of people (usu. poor and of a different race from the majority) live 窮人或少數民族聚居區. *pl* 複數 **ghettos.**

ghost [goust] *nc* spirit of a dead person which is said to be seen or heard etc by a living person 鬼,鬼魂,幽靈: *He told me the ghost of his father appeared at his bedside.* 他告訴我他先父的幽靈曾在他的床邊出現. **ghostly** *adj.*

giant ['dʒaiənt] *nc* someone / something much larger than usual 巨人,巨物. Also 亦作 *adj: a giant box of chocolates* 一大盒巧克力; *a giant animal* 巨型動物.

gibberish [ˈdʒibəriʃ] *nu* meaningless talk, nonsense 無意義的話, 胡言亂語.

gibbon [ˈgibən] *nc* small, slender, long-armed ape 長臂猿.

gibe, jibe [dʒaib] *nc* blame mixed with contempt 嘲弄, 譏笑: *He could not bear the gibes of the other boys.* 他忍受不了其他男孩的譏笑.

giddy [ˈgidi] *adj* 1 seeing things as if they were going round so that one feels one is about to fall down; dizzy 眩致的; 頭暈的: *High buildings make me giddy.* 高層建築使我暈眩. 2 pleasure-loving; thoughtless 輕浮的; 愛玩樂的; 沒頭腦的: *just a giddy young girl* 不過是一個輕佻的年青姑娘. **giddiness** *nu*.

gift [gift] *nc* 1 something given, a present 贈品, 禮物: *a wedding / birthday gift* 結婚／生日禮物. *Officials are not allowed to receive gifts from the public.* 官員不得接受公衆饋贈的禮品. 2 special natural ability 天賦, 天資: *I have no gift for foreign languages.* 我沒有學習外語的天份. 3 something very easy 輕而易舉的事: *In the examination paper Question 2 was a gift.* (*informal* in sense 3) 考卷上的第二題太容易了. (義 3 爲非正式).

gifted *adj* having special natural ability 有天賦的, 有才華的: *a gifted speaker* 才華橫溢的演說者.

gigantic [dʒaiˈgæntik] *adj* of giant size, unusually big 巨大的, 龐大的: *He says he caught a gigantic fish.* 他說他釣到一條特別大的魚.

giggle [ˈgigl] *vi* laugh in a silly way 傻笑: *Tell those girls to stop giggling.* 告訴那些姑娘不要傻笑. Also 亦作 *nc* silly laugh 傻笑.

gild [gild] *vt* cover thinly with gold or gold paint 鍍金, 塗以金色.

gill¹ [gil] *nc* (usu. *pl*) parts of the head of a fish through which it breathes (通常用複數的) 鰓.

gill² [dʒil] *nc* quarter of a pint 及耳 (等於十品脫).

gilt [gilt] *nu* thin covering of gold or gold paint 鍍金的薄層; 金色塗層. Also 亦作 *adj*: *a gilt brooch* 鍍金的胸針.

gimmick [ˈgimik] *nc* (esp. with reference to actors and those who advertise and sell things) trick to get attention or increase popularity (尤指演員或做廣告推銷商品的人) 騙人的花招, 花招, 噱頭: *Changing the colour of the packet and not its contents is just a gimmick.* (*informal*) 更換包裝的顏色而不換內容不過是一種騙人的玩意. (非正式).

gin [dʒin] *nc / u* kind of strong colourless alcoholic drink 杜松子酒.

ginger [ˈdʒindʒə*] *nu* plant root with a hot, spicy taste used for flavouring food and drinks 薑. **gingerly** *adv* carefully, cautiously 謹慎地, 小心地: *He lifted the baby very gingerly* 他小心翼翼地抱起嬰兒. **'ginger 'beer / 'ale** drink made from or flavoured with ginger 薑汁汽水, 薑啤. **'gingerbread** cake flavoured with ginger 薑餅.

gipsy, gypsy [ˈdʒipsi] *nc* person belonging to a wandering tribe of people found in Europe and Asia 吉普賽人.

giraffe [dʒiˈrɑːf] *nc* large African animal with a very long neck and big dark spots 長頸鹿.

girder [ˈgəːdə*] *nc* long, strong piece of steel used in the framework of buildings and bridges (鋼)大樑, 桁.

girdle [ˈgəːdl] *nc* 1 woman's undergarment worn round the hips (女子的)緊身褡, 束腹. 2 belt tied round the waist 腰帶.

girl [gəːl] *nc* 1 female child 女孩: *All*

their children are girls. 他們的孩子全是女的. **2** daughter 女兒: *My girl left school last year.* 我的女兒去年離開學校. **3** young unmarried woman 姑娘, 未婚年輕女子: *The town is full of lovely girls* 市鎮裏有許多漂亮姑娘. **4** man's female friend. (Often **girlfriend**) 女朋友, 情人 (常作 girlfriend): *John and his girlfriend were married yesterday.* 約翰和他的女友昨天結婚.

girlish *adj* foolish; like a young girl 愚蠢的; 少女似的. **Girl Friday** female employee in an office, usually performing secretarial duties 女秘書.

Giro ['dʒairou] *nu* banking system operated by post offices and banks (英國郵局和銀行的) 郵政轉賬服務.

girth [ɡə:θ] *nc* **1** belt round a horse to keep the saddle on its back (馬的) 肚帶, 腹帶. **2** measurement round something (e.g. pillar, tree, waist); circumference (柱子、樹幹、腰部等的) 周長, 圍長: *He is a man of great girth* i.e. big round the waist. 他的腰圍很大. 即: 腰身很粗.

gist [dʒist] *nu* (always with **the**) (usu. with reference to what has been said or written) most important points of something (總是與 the 連用) (說話或文章的) 要點: *He gave me the gist of the headmaster's report.* 他把校長報告的要點告訴了我.

give [ɡiv] *vt / i* this verb has the general meaning of causing somebody / something to have, but not necessarily to keep for ever 本動詞一般指使某人/某物佔有, 但不一定永久保留. **1** cause to have, hand over 交給: *They gave him a good breakfast.* 他們讓他吃了一頓豐盛的早餐. *She will give it a wash.* 她將把它洗一下. *She gives me her cat to look after while she is away.* 她把貓交給我, 讓我在她不在時照看牠. *He*

gave the letter to the boy to post. 他把信交給男孩去寄. *I gave her my coat and hat* i.e. to put away, hang up etc not keep. 我把外套和帽子交給她. 即: 讓她把它們放在一邊或掛起來, 並不是送給她. **2** cause to have and keep as a gift 贈送: *At Christmas my father gave me £5.* 聖誕節時我父親給了我五英鎊. *He gave all his books to the school library.* 他把所有的圖書都贈送給學校圖書館. *Give me some of your ink.* 把你的墨水勻給我一點. **3** cause to have, hand over something (in exchange or return) for something else, to buy, pay, sell. 交換, 買賣, 付給: *I'll give you five pounds for these stamps.* 我將付給你五英鎊買這些郵票. *The shopkeeper gave us two packets of soap for the price of one.* 店主以一塊肥皂的價格賣給我們兩塊肥皂. *They would give anything to be with us now* i.e. they want very much to be with us. 他們爲了能跟我們在一起, 願意付出任何代價. 即: 他們很想跟我們在一起. **4** supply; produce 供給; 生產: *Hens give us eggs.* 母雞給我們下蛋. *The lamp gave very little light.* 這燈發出很微弱的光. *His letter gave the latest news.* 他的來信提供了最新消息. *He forgot to give us the date.* 他忘了把日期告訴我們. *This book gives few details.* 這本書所提供的細節很少. **5** (often with reference to time) allow to have (常指時間) 使有, 允許: *Please give them another chance.* 請再給他們一次機會. *I must be given more time to finish it.* 得多給我一些時間來做完這件事. *We gave him five minutes to decide.* 我們給他五分鐘時來作出決定. *They should give themselves two hours to get here.* 他們得有兩個小時才能到達那裏. *He is honest, I give him that* i.e. I agree he is honest. 他是

誠實的, 我相信這一點. 即: 我同意他是誠實的. **6** cause to have some emotion or feeling 造成或引起某種情緒或感情: *Give them our best wishes / love / regards / thanks etc.* 請代我向他們致意/問好/致以問候/表示感謝等. *Did the child give you any trouble?* 孩子給你惹麻煩了嗎? *The sudden noise gave her a shock.* 突如其來的聲音使她大吃一驚. *This tooth is giving me pain.* 我的這顆牙齒痛. *It gives me great pleasure to open this school.* 我非常高興地開辦這所學校. *Please give me your attention.* 請注意聽我說. **7** (with special reference to bodily action) cause to have (指身體)做一個動作: *Give someone / something a thump / kick / knock / look / pull / punch / push / sign / smile / tap etc.* 對某人/某物重重地捶一下/踢一腳/狠狠敲一下/看一眼/拉一把/打一拳/推一下/打一個手勢/笑一下/輕輕拍一下等. **8** express feelings by bodily action 用身體動作表達某種感情: *Give a cry / groan / jump / shout / shrug / sign.* 發出一聲叫喊/發出一聲呻吟/跳一下/發出一聲叫喊/聳一聲肩/打一個手勢. **9** bend, become weak 彎下, 變弱: *The roof began to give because of the great weight on it.* 屋頂開始往下陷, 因爲上面太重了. *His knees gave / He gave at the knees* i.e. they bent because he was weak or very tired. 他的膝關節支撐不住了. 即: 因爲他身體羸弱或疲勞, 他的雙膝往下彎. *past tense* 過去式 **gave** [geiv]. *past part* 過去分詞 **given. give something away 1** (usu. with reference to several people) cause to have and keep as a gift 分贈; 分發: *He gave away all his pictures* i.e. for nothing to several people. 他分贈了所有的圖畫. 即: 不取分文地把圖畫分送給幾個人. *After the*

sports he gave away the prizes i.e. presented them to all the winners. 運動會後他頒發獎品. 即: 他給所有的優勝者發獎. **2** make known something secret 洩露秘密: *He gave away the plan of attack to the enemy.* 他向敵人洩露了進攻計劃. **give someone away 1** hand over the bride to the bridegroom at a wedding 在婚禮上把新娘交給新郎: *she was given away by her uncle.* 她的伯父將她交給新郎. **2** betray; tell a secret 背叛某人, 出賣某人; 洩露某人的秘密: *Please don't give me away* i.e. don't make known what I have done or plan to do. 請不要洩露我的秘密. 即: 不要讓人知道我做過的事或者計劃要做的事. **give (something) back** return 歸還: *He won't give me back my pen.* 他不肯把筆還給我. **give (something) in 1** yield, surrender 讓步, 屈服, 投降: *After much fighting the enemy gave in.* 激烈的戰鬥之後敵人投降了. *He is always giving in to other people* i.e. following their wishes. 他總是向人讓步. 即: 順從別人的意願. **2** hand in something to someone in authority 交上, 呈交: *You should give in your names to the headmaster.* 你們應當把姓名報給校長. *I gave in my driving licence* i.e. to the office dealing with driving licences. 我把駕駛執照交了上去. 即: 交給辦執照的辦公室. **give off (something)** send out 發散, 放出: *This flower gives off a pleasant smell.* 這種花發出宜人的芳香. *The engine gives off smoke and steam.* 發動機放出烟和蒸氣. **give out** hand round; distribute 分發: *Open the cupboard and give out the books.* 打開櫥櫃分發書本. **give (something) up 1** surrender 放棄; 自首: *I had to give up my place in the queue.* 我只得放棄排隊的

位置. *He gave himself up to the police.* 他向警方自首. **2** leave, stop doing 離開, 中輟: *Why are you giving up your job?* 你爲甚麼要辭去工作? *He has given up playing football.* 他不踢足球了. **3** stop trying to help someone 不再幫助某人: *The teacher gave him up because he was so lazy.* 因爲他懶惰, 老師已經對他失去信心. *They gave him up for lost* i.e. stopped trying to help, or do anything, because they believed he was lost. 他們認爲他已經遇難, 便放棄了救援. **4** lose heart; despair 喪失勇氣或信心; 失望: *Don't give up, you may still win.* 不要灰心, 你仍然有可能獲勝. **give way 1** allow to pass first 讓路: *At the roundabout give way to traffic from the right.* 在環形交叉路口要給從右邊來的車輛讓路. **2** yield to; yield to one's own feelings 讓步; 無法控制自己的感情: *They had to give way to the writers' complaints.* 他們不得不對作家的抱怨作出讓步. *Give way to grief / sorrow / despair* etc. 過度悲傷/悲痛/失望等. **3** break, collapse under strain 坍陷, 倒塌: *The rope gave way.* 繩子斷了. *The bridge / floor / roof suddenly gave way.* 橋/地板/屋頂突然塌下去了.

glacier ['glæsiə*] *nc* mass of ice formed from snow, which moves very slowly down a mountain 冰河, 冰川.

glad [glæd] *adj* happy, pleased; making happy 高興的, 歡喜的; 令人高興的: *They are very glad about their new house.* 他們因爲有了新居而十分高興. *I would be glad of your help.* 對於你的幫助我將感到到高興. *He looks / feels glad.* 他看起來/顯得很高興. *I am glad to see you.* 見到你很高興. *comparative* 比較級 **gladder.** *superlative* 最高級 **gladdest. gladly** *adv* glad-

den *vt* make glad 使高興.

glamour ['glæmə*] (*US* 美 also 亦作 **glamor**) *nu* attractiveness; that which causes one to be very interested 吸引力; 魔力, 魅力: *the glamour of the stage* 舞台的魅力. *There is no glamour in office work.* 辦公室的工作引不起人們的興趣. **glamorous** *adj*.

glance [glɑːns] *vi* **1** take a quick look (at, into, over, round, through) 匆匆一瞥, 粗略地看一眼: *I glanced at the newspaper.* 我瀏覽了一下報紙. *We glanced through the book.* 我們瀏覽了一下那本書. *The teacher glanced round the classroom.* 老師環視了一下教室. **2** hit and then slide off 擦過: *The bullet glanced off the wall.* 子彈擦過牆壁. Also 亦作 *nc* quick look 一瞥, 瞥視: *I took a glance at the newspaper;* 我粗略地看了一下報紙; *see at a glance* i.e. see quickly 一眼就看出, 即: 很快看出. **glancing** *adj: a glancing blow* 斜擊的一拳.

gland [glænd] *nc* small organ which controls certain functions of the body 腺: *sweat gland* 汗腺. **glandular** ['glændjulə*] *adj*.

glare [gleə*] *vi* **1** (usu. with reference to the sun) shine too brightly (通常指太陽) 發強光; 發眩目光. **2** look fiercely 瞪眼, 怒目注視: *The angry father glared at his son.* 怒氣衝衝的父親對兒子瞪着眼. Also 亦作 *nc / u* **1** fierce bright light 刺目的強光: *I have to wear sunglasses because of the glare of the sun.* 因爲陽光刺眼, 我得戴上墨鏡. *He stood in the glare of the car's headlights.* 他站在汽車前燈的刺目強光中. **2** fierce look 瞪眼, 兇狠的目光. **glaring** *adj* **1** too bright 耀眼的, 刺目的: *glaring light* 刺目的光線; *glaring colours* 耀眼的色彩. **2** fierce and shining 怒目而視的: *glaring eyes* 怒目

而視的目光. **3** so bad as to be easily seen 顯眼的, 明顯的: *glaring mistake* 明顯的錯誤; *glaring injustice* 明顯的不公正現象.

glass [glɑːs] **1** *nu* hard, easily broken material through which light can pass, used for making windows and other things 玻璃: *He broke the glass of the front window.* 他打破了前窗的玻璃. *This jar is made of thick glass* 這罐子是厚玻璃做的. **2** *nc* thing made of glass 玻璃製品: *drinking glasses* 飲酒杯. *The glass fell out of my watch* i.e. the piece of glass covering its face. 我的錶面玻璃脫落了. *She looked at herself in the glass* i.e. mirror (rather o.f.) 她照鏡子. (頗爲舊式). *The glass is rising* i.e. the barometer. 氣壓計的水銀柱正在上升. *The sailor watched the distant ship through his glass* i.e. telescope; 水手用望遠鏡觀察遠方船隻; *a magnifying glass* 放大鏡. **3** *nc* contents of a drinking glass 玻璃杯裏裝的東西: *drink a glass of beer / milk / water etc.* 喝一玻璃杯啤酒/牛奶/水等. *Thank you, I'll have a glass* 謝謝, 我喝一杯; *a glass(ful) of wine* 一杯酒. **glassy** *adj* like glass. smooth; dull and lifeless 像玻璃的; 平滑的; 獃傻的, 沒有神采的: *a glassy sea* 平靜如鏡的海面. *He had a glassy look in his eyes* 他目光獃滯. **glasses** *npl* spectacles 眼鏡: *I must put on my glasses to read this.* 看這東西我得戴上眼鏡. **glasshouse** see 見 **greenhouse.** **'glassware** articles made of glass 玻璃器皿. see 見 **glaze.**

glaze [gleiz] *vt* **1** fit with glass 配玻璃, 裝玻璃. **2** *vt* cover with a thin coat of glass (e.g. in making china); make smooth, polish 上釉, 上光; 使表面光滑. Also 亦作 *nu* thin covering of glass 釉. **glazed** *adj* having a glaze

上了釉的. **glazier** ['gleiziə*] *nc* person who glazes windows etc. 裝玻璃工人.

gleam [gliːm] *nc* weak beam of light that does not usu. last long 微光, 閃光: *I saw the gleam of his lamp in the wood.* 我看到樹林中他那微弱的燈光. Also 亦作 *vi* send out gleams; shine 發微光; 閃爍: *The newly-polished car stood gleaming in the sunshine.* 新擦過的汽車在陽光下閃閃發亮. *His eyes gleamed with pleasure.* 他的眼睛流露出愉快的神情.

glee [gliː] *nu* happiness, amusement, because of success or satisfaction (因成功或滿足而)歡喜, 高興: *His defeat caused great glee among his enemies.* 他的失敗使他的敵人拍手稱快.

glen [glen] *nc* (esp. in Scotland) narrow valley (尤指蘇格蘭的)峽谷, 幽谷.

glib [glib] *adj* of smooth, easy talk which is not to be trusted 隨便的, 圓滑的, 油腔滑調的: *This salesman is a glib speaker.* 這推銷員是個油嘴滑舌的人. *I don't believe his story; it is too glib.* 我不信他的說法; 他說得太油腔滑調了.

glide [glaid] *vi* move smoothly and quietly 滑動, 滑行: *The bird glided to the ground.* 鳥滑翔到地上. *The dancers glided over the floor of the room.* 跳舞的人們在室內地板上輕快地滑動. Also 亦作 *nc* gliding movement 滑動, 滑行. **glider** *nc* type of aircraft which has no engine 滑翔機. **gliding** *nu* sport of flying in gliders 滑翔運動.

glimmer ['glimə*] *n sing* very small sign or show of anything 微小的信號; 少說, 微量: *a glimmer of light* 一線微光; *a glimmer of hope* 一線希望.

glimpse [glimps] *nc* quick but not complete look 一瞥: *I caught / got a glimpse of his face as he ran past.* 他

跑過去的時候, 我看了一眼他的臉.
Also 亦作 *vt / i: We glimpsed the
field through the trees.* 我們透過樹叢瞥見
田野.

glint [glint] *vi* send out a short sharp
beam of light 閃爍, 閃光: *The sun is
glinting through the clouds.* 太陽透過
雲層發出光芒. *His eyes glinted with
anger.* 他的眼睛閃耀着憤怒的目光.
Also 亦作 *nc: a glint of light* 一次閃
光: *He had an evil glint in his eyes.*
他的眼睛裏有一種邪惡的光芒.

glisten ['glisn] *vi* (usu. of something wet
or polished) shine (通常指濕的或磨光
擦亮的東西) 閃耀, 閃亮: *glisten with
sweat* 汗水閃光: *Her eyes glistened
with tears.* 她的眼睛裏有淚珠閃耀.

glitter ['glitə*] *vi* shine with a sharp,
bright, changing light 閃爍, 閃耀, 閃閃
發亮: *The diamond ring glittered on
her finger.* 鑽石戒指在她的手指上閃閃
發光. Also 亦作 *nu: the glitter of ice
on the road* 路面上冰的閃光. **glittering** *adj* shining in this way 閃閃發光
的: *glittering jewels* 閃閃發光的寶石.

gloat [glout] *vi* look at with too great
pleasure, satisfaction 高興地注視; 心
滿意足地注視: *He gloats over / on his
money.* 他得意揚揚地看着他的錢.
They gloated over / on my failure. 他
們對我的失敗幸災樂禍.

globe [gloub] *nc* **1** something round
like a ball 球, 球狀物. **2** the world
shown on a globe 地球儀: *If you look
at this globe you will see where the
equator is.* 你看着地球儀就會看見赤道
在哪裏. **global** *adj* world-wide 全球
性的, 全世界的: *The war became
global.* 這場戰爭變成全球性的了.

gloom [glu:m] *nc* **1** almost complete
darkness (幾乎是完全的) 黑暗: *He
walked through the gloom of the thick
forest.* 他走過陰暗的密林. **2** feeling of

sadness, despair 憂鬱, 絕望: *His illness has caused great gloom among
his friends.* 他的病使他的朋友們鬱鬱
不樂. **gloomy** *adj: a gloomy room* i.e.
dark, badly lit 陰暗的房間, 即: 黑暗的,
光照不足的: *The bad weather has
made everyone gloomy* i.e. sad, de-
spairing. 壞天氣使大家沮喪. **gloomi-
ly** *adv* **gloominess** *nu.*

glorify ['glɔːrifai] *vt* worship, praise,
honour 崇拜; 讚美; 尊敬: *All men
should glorify God.* 人人應當讚美上
帝. *The history book glorifies the
country's heroes.* 這本歷史書表彰了該
國的英雄. **glorification** [glɔːri-
fi'keiʃən] *nu.*

glory ['glɔːri] *nc* something beautiful or
deserving praise 壯麗, 美麗的事物, 值
得讚頌的事物: *the glory of flowers in
the spring* 春天百花齊放之壯麗景色.
the glories of our past history. 我們過
去的光榮史跡. Also 亦作 *vi* (with **in**)
be very proud of; get great pleasure
from (與 in 連用)因⋯而自豪; 因⋯而
得意: *He glories in his skill at football.* 他爲自己踢足球的技巧而感到自
豪. *They gloried in showing me my
mistakes.* 他們因爲指出了我的缺點而
得意揚揚. **glorious** *adj: It was a glorious victory.* 這是輝煌的勝利. (*opp*
反義詞 **inglorious**).

gloss [glɔs] *nc / u* smooth, shining surface 平滑, 有光澤的表面: *This paint
has a fine gloss.* 這種油漆有很好的光
澤. **glossy** *adj* smooth, shiny 光滑的,
有光澤的: *glossy magazines* i.e. expensive magazines full of glossy pictures 紙面有光澤的雜誌, 即: 印着許多
光彩照人的照片的高檔雜誌. **gloss
over** cover up faults 掩蓋, 掩飾: *He
tried to gloss over his past mistakes.*
他企圖掩蓋他過去的錯誤.

glossary ['glɔsəri] *nc* list of glosses; list

of words needing special explanation 詞彙表, 難詞彙編: *All the technical terms are shown in the glossary at the back of the book.* 所有術語都列入書後的詞彙表.

glove [glʌv] *nc* covering for the hand and wrist (usu. with a separate place for each finger) 手套 (通常指分指手套).

glow [glou] *vi* **1** send out light and heat without flame 無焰地燃燒; 發紅光: *Red-hot iron glows.* 赤熱的鐵放出紅光. **2** look, feel brighter or warmer 顯得更加明亮或溫暖: *These red curtains certainly glow in this dull room.* 這些紅色的窗簾確實使這單調的房間顯得亮堂. *His cheeks glowed after the race.* 他在賽跑之後兩頰通紅. *Their faces were glowing with joy.* 他們高興得容光煥發. Also 亦作 *nc* (only *sing*) (僅用單數): *the glow of the fire* 火光; *a glow of pleasure* 愉快的表情.

glower ['glauə*] *vi* look angrily at 怒目而視, 兇狠狠地瞪視.

glucose ['glu:kous] *nu* type of sugar 葡萄糖.

glue [glu:] *nc / u* sticky substance used for fastening things (esp. wood) together 膠, 膠水. Also 亦作 *vt* stick with glue 膠合, 黏牢: *Glue the boards together.* 把木板黏在一起. *He glued it to the desk.* 他把它跟書桌黏在一起.

glum [glʌm] *adj* sad-looking; sullen 陰鬱的; 悶悶不樂的.

glut [glʌt] *vt* supply too much 供應過多, 使充斥: *At present coffee is glutting the world market* i.e. more is being grown than can be sold. 目前咖啡充斥着世界市場. 即: 咖啡種得太多了賣不出去. *past* 過去式和過去分詞 **glutted.** Also 亦作 *nc*: *There is a glut of coffee.* 咖啡供過於求.

glutton ['glʌtn] *nc* person who eats too much 貪吃者. **gluttonous** *adj.*

glycerine ['glisəri:n] *nu* thick, sweet, colourless liquid, used in medicine and for making explosives 甘油, 丙三醇.

glycerol ['glisərɔl] *nu* colourless, syrupy liquid made from fats and oils, used in explosives, skin lotion, etc, and in explosives. 甘油, 丙三醇.

glycogen ['glikoudʒen] *nu* starch like substance produced in animal tissues and changed into sugar as the body needs it 糖原, 動物澱粉.

gnarled [nɑ:ld] *adj* knotted and twisted 多瘤的, 多節的; 扭曲的.

gnash [næʃ] *vt* in gnash one's teeth i.e. bring one's teeth together in anger or pain 用於 gnash one's teeth, 即: 咬牙切齒.

gnat [næt] *nc* type of very small stinging insect 蚊; 蚋; 叮人的小昆蟲.

gnaw [nɔ:] *vt / i* keep biting or chewing something hard 咬, 啃: *The dog gnawed (at) the bone.* 狗啃骨頭.

gnome [noum] *nc* small fairy said to live underground (據說住在地下的) 小神, 地精.

gnu [nu:] *nc* large deer-like animal found in Africa 角馬, 牛羚 (產於非洲, 體形像鹿的一種大羚羊). (Also 亦作 **wildebeest**).

go [gou] *vi* **1** move from one place to another; travel 行走, 移動; 旅行: *The train goes from London to Glasgow.* 火車從倫敦開往格拉斯哥. *He went by boat / car / steamer etc.* 他坐船/汽車/輪船等去. *This aeroplane can go at 600 miles per hour.* 這種飛機每小時能飛六百英里. **2** move about in a certain state 處於某種狀態: *All the men here go armed.* 這裏所有的男人都武裝起來了. *The children must not go hungry.* 不能讓孩子們挨餓. **3** (with

-ing form of another verb) move to another place to do something (與另一動詞的 -ing 形式連用) 去做某事: *go swimming / shopping / looking for etc.* 去游泳／購物／尋找等. **4** leave; pass; disappear 離開; 推移, 流逝 消失: *We must go now.* 我們得走了. *The time went quickly.* 時間過得很快. **5** become 變成: *He is going blind.* 他快瞎了. *Her hair has gone grey.* 他的頭髮變得灰白了. *The old man went crazy.* 那個老人瘋了. **6** reach, stretch from one place to another 到達, 通, 延伸, 伸展: *How far does this railway go?* 這條鐵路通到多遠的地方? *The path goes to the village.* 小路通向村莊. *Her skirt went to her knees.* 她的裙子長到膝蓋. **7** do its work; perform. 運轉; 行動, 進行: *Our new plans are going well.* 我們的新計劃進展順利. *The meeting went badly.* 會開得很糟糕. *The engine goes smoothly.* 發動機運轉平穩. **8** intend to do; be about to do or happen. 打算; 將要: *I am going to study harder next term.* 下學期我要更加努力學習. *It is going to be hot today.* 今天天氣會很熱. **9** break, fail 開; 失敗, 停止作用: *He felt the branch go beneath him.* 他感到身下的樹枝斷了. *His eyesight is going* 他的視力正在衰退. *The brakes of the car went.* 汽車的制動器失靈了. *past tense* 過去式 **went** [went]. *past part* 過去分詞 **gone** [ɡɒn]. Also 亦作 *nc / u (informal)* in such phrases as (非正式) 用於下列短語中: **have a go (at)** try 試做, 嘗試. **at one go** at one attempt 一舉, 一下子, 試一下. *pl* 複數 **goes. going** *adj* usu. only in a **going business / concern** i.e. successful 通常僅用於 a going business / concern, 即: 成功的. **go about** move from one place to another (usu. several places) 四處走

動: *He always goes about with his children.* 他總是帶着孩子到處走. *The story is going about that you are leaving.* 紛紛傳說你要走了. **go after someone / something** follow to get; try to obtain 追逐; 追求: *Go after him! He is running away.* 追上他, 他要逃走了. *They are going after the first prize.* 他們的目標是獲得一等獎. **go against something** move in the opposite direction to; be contrary to. 向相反的方向移動, 轉向; 與…相反: *The boat is going against the tide.* 船在逆潮流前進. *This goes against their belief.* 這違背他們的信念. *The game was going against us* i.e. we were losing 我們在比賽中甚不順利. 即: 我們快要輸了. **go ahead with** start; do quickly, actively 開始; 迅速、積極地做: *They are going ahead with the plan.* 他們在積極執行這項計劃. '**go-ahead** *adj* active; progressive 積極的; 有進取心的: *We have a very go-ahead committee. (informal)* 我們有一個進取心很強的委員會. (非正式). **go along 1** move, travel along 前進; 步行. **2** continue 繼續, 進行: *You will learn as you go along.* 你可以一面做一面學. **go along with someone 1** accompany 陪同前往: *I went along with them to London.* 我跟他們一起去倫敦. **2** agree; cooperate 贊同, 附和; 合作, 配合: *We are ready to go along with you in this plan. (informal* in sense **2**) 我們樂於跟你們合作實現這項計劃. (義 2 爲非正式). **go at someone / something** attack; deal busily with 攻擊, 衝向; 忙於, 努力做: *He went at them with a knife.* 他持刀向他們衝去. **go back 1** return 回去. **2** date from 追溯到: *The quarrel goes back to the New Year.* 爭執可以追溯到新年的時候. **go back on something** fail to carry out 食言, 違背諾言: *He went back on his promise.* 他沒有遵守諾言. '**go-between** *nc* person who goes from one person or group to another to settle their differences 中間人, 從中斡旋的人: *The two governments used him as their go-between when discussing peace.* 兩國政府利用他從中斡旋討論和平問題. **go down** 1 sink, fall 沉下; 落下: *The ship / moon / sun went down.* 船沉了/月亮落下/太陽落下. *The wind / sea is going down* i.e. becoming quieter. 風勢減弱/大海變得平靜. *Prices here never go down.* 這裏的物價從來不曾下降. 2 be accepted, approved. 被接受; 受歡迎, 得到贊同: *His story went down (well) with his friends.* 他的故事受到朋友們的歡迎. 3 be recorded 被記錄在案: *Everything you say will go down in writing.* 你說的每一句話都將被記錄下來. 4 be defeated 被打敗, 被征服: *France went down to Germany.* 法國被德國打敗. **go for someone / something** 1 move to have; obtain 爲…去; 去請, 去拿, 去找: *go for a walk / holiday etc.* 去散步/去度假等. *She has gone for a newspaper.* 她去找一份報紙. 2 attack 攻擊, 襲擊: *The wounded lion went for the hunter.* 受了傷的獅子向獵人撲去. see 見 **go at.** 3 be sold for 以…出售, 賣(多少錢): *Shoes are going for four pounds a pair.* 鞋賣四英鎊一雙. 4 apply to 適用於: *These remarks go for all of you.* 這些話對你們都適用. 5 like something; try to get something. (*informal* in sense 5) 喜歡, 想得到. (義5 爲非正式) **go in for something** 1 enter for 參加: *Are you going in for the mile (race)?* 你報名參加一英里賽跑嗎? 2 take up; become interested in 愛好, 對…感興趣: *He went in for*

teaching. 他喜歡當教師. *Many boys go in for stamp collecting.* 許多男孩愛好集郵. **go into something** 1 (arithmetic) be an exact part of (算術) 用(小數) 除 (大數): *Two goes into six three times.* 用 2 除 6 得 3. 2 begin doing, take up (usu. a job); begin feeling. 從事(某一行業); 進入(某種情緒): *He has gone into teaching.* 他已開始當教師. *He went into a rage.* 他大發雷霆. 3 look at, examine. 調查, 研究: *You should go into its cost before buying it.* 你應當先問它的價錢再買. **go off** 1 leave 離開. 2 make a sudden noise; be fired 突然響起; 被發射: *The gun went off.* 槍打響了. 3 become worse 退步, 變壞: *His work has gone off recently.* 最近他的工作大不如前. *The milk / meat is going off* i.e. becoming sour / bad. 牛奶/肉變質了. 即: 發酸了/變壞了. 4 proceed; take its course 進行; 自然地發展: *The lessons went off well.* 課上得很順利. 5 fall asleep; lose consciousness 睡着; 失去知覺: *The child soon went off into a deep sleep.* 孩子很快就熟睡了. *He went into a trance.* 他進入昏睡狀態. **go on** 1 continue 繼續: *I am going on to the next town.* 我將到下一個城鎮去. *The concert went on for hours.* 音樂會進行了好幾個小時. *Don't go on about it* i.e. don't continue talking about it. 不要繼續下去了. 即: 不要繼續談這件事了. 2 do something next. 接着做某事: *He went on to show us how to do it.* 他接着向我們示範怎樣做. 3 rely, depend upon 以…爲根據: *We have only his word to go on.* 我們只能以他的話爲根據. 4 happen 發生, 進行: *There is always a lot going on here.* 總是有很多事情在這裏發生. '**goings-'on** *npl* happenings (usu. ones not approved of) 發生的事

情 (通常指不良行為): *The goings-on in that house are shocking.* (*informal*) 那座房子裏發生的事情是駭人聽聞的. (非正式) **go out 1** leave (esp. home) 離開 (尤指離開家): *They do not go out much these days.* 他們最近很少出門. *I am going out to Africa.* 我將要出國去非洲. **2** stop, finish 終止; 結束: *The fire went out* i.e. stopped burning. 火熄了. *Long skirts have gone out* i.e. out of fashion. 長裙子過時了. 即: 不再時興了. **go over (something) 1** look at, examine 檢查, 審閱: *They went over the plans which they had made.* 他們檢查了他們訂好的計劃. *Let us go over your answer again.* 我們來把你的答案再看一遍. **2** change sides: join 投到對方去; 參加, 加入: *Most of the army went over to the enemy.* 軍隊中的大部份人投向敵人一邊. **go round (something) 1** reach round 延伸在…週圍: *This belt does not go round my waist.* 這條帶子不夠繞我的腰部一圈. **2** visit somebody / something nearby 順便訪問某人/順便去某地: *Let us go round and ask him.* 我們順便過去問他吧. **3** be enough for everyone 足夠分配: *Twenty books will not go round this class.* 二十本書不夠在這個班級裏分發. **go through (something) 1** look at; examine carefully 察看; 仔細檢查: *We shall go through these papers together.* 我們將一起認真閱讀這些文件. *They went through our luggage at the customs.* 在海關他們檢查了我們的行李. **2** spend 用光, 花完 (錢): *He went through all the money his father gave him.* 他把他父親給的錢全用光了. **go up 1** rise, increase 上升, 增加: *Fees will go up next year.* 明年費用會增加. **2** rise suddenly into the air because of an explosion; be destroyed 被炸毀; 被摧毀: *The whole village went up when it was bombed.* 整個村莊在遭到轟炸時被徹底破壞. *The hut went up in flames.* 小屋被燒毀了. **go with (something) 1** be suited to, mix well with 適合於; 與…相配, 與…協調: *The green hat does not go with your blue coat.* 綠帽子跟你的藍色外套不相配. *Potatoes don't go with ice cream* i.e. don't taste good together. 馬鈴薯跟冰淇淋配不到一起. 即: 它們一起吃味道不好. **go without** be or manage without 在缺少…的情況下勉強對付: *They had no food so they went without.* 他們沒有食物, 所以只得甚麼都不吃. **go far 1** move, reach a great distance. 走得遠. **2** last a long time; be of much use 很耐用, 能維持很久; 很有用: *A pound doesn't go far these days* 如今一英鎊沒有多大用處. *A pound doesn't go far these days.* **3** be successful 成功: *This young man should go far.* 這個年輕人定會大有出息. **go slow** work more slowly in protest against something (e.g. poor wages) 怠工, 磨洋工 (如因抗議工資太低): *The dockers agreed to go slow.* 碼頭工人同意怠工. **'go-'slow** *nc* act of working in this way 怠工. **'go-'kart** *nc* small, motorized vehicle for one person, used in racing 微型競賽汽車.

goad [gəud] *nc* **1** sharp stick for driving cattle (趕牛用的) 刺棒. **2** anything driving someone to do something 刺激物. Also 亦作 *vt*: *Their laughter goaded him to try it again.* 他們的笑聲激得他再試一次. *The teacher was goaded into fury by their stupid mistakes.* 他們愚蠢的錯誤使教師發怒.

goal [gəul] *nc* **1** (in games like football and hockey) in the space between two posts through which the ball must pass to gain a point (足球和曲棍球等的) 球門: *He kicked the ball towards* the other team's goal. 他把球踢向另一隊的球門. **2** point gained by the ball passing through the goal (球入門而) 得分: We scored a goal in the first minute of the game. 我們在開賽後的頭一分鐘就得了一分. **3** any end or aim 目的, 目標: His goal is to be a doctor. 他的目標是當一名醫生. **'goalkeeper** nc player who keeps goal 守門員.

goat [gout] nc type of long-haired animal with horns, kept as a domestic animal 山羊.

gobble ['gɔbl] vt / i **1** eat in lumps, quickly and noisily 狼吞虎嚥: Because they were late they gobbled (down) their food. 因爲已經遲了, 他們把食物猛吞下去. **2** make a bubbling noise like a turkey 發出火鷄般的咯咯叫聲.

goblet ['gɔblit] nc drinking cup with a stem and no handle (無柄)高腳酒杯.

goblin ['gɔblin] nc ugly, evil fairy or spirit 惡鬼, 小妖精.

god [gɔd] nc **1 (God)** Supreme Being; Creator, used in many phrases calling on God 神, 上帝; 造物主(用於許多祈求上帝保佑的短語中): God forbid! 蒼天難容! 絕對不行! God (only) knows! i.e. I don't know. 天曉得! 即: 我不知道. God help us! 願上帝幫助我們! **2** any divine being worshipped by man 神, 偶像: These people pray to many gods; 這些人向許多偶像祈禱; the god of war 戰神. **goddess** ['gɔdis] nc female god 女神. **'godparent** person, not the real parent, who promises at the child's baptism to bring the child up as a Christian 教父或 教母. **'godfather / 'godmother** man / woman who promises in this way 教父 / 母. **'godchild / 'godson / 'goddaughter** child / son / daughter about whom such a promise is made

教子或教女/教子/教女.

goggle ['gɔgl] vi roll the eyes; stare (眼睛) 轉動; 盯, 凝視: Stop goggling at the visitors. 別把眼睛死盯着客人. His eyes goggled with surprise. 他吃驚地瞪着眼睛.

goggles ['gɔglz] npl large spectacles to keep out dust, water etc. 護目鏡; 風鏡; 潛水鏡.

gold [gould] nu soft, heavy, yellow metal of great value 黃金. Also 亦作 adj made of gold 金製的, 含金的: gold coin / ring / watch 金幣/金戒指/金錶. **golden** adj **1** made of gold 金製的, 含金的. **2** like gold; gold in colour; valuable; ripe 像黃金的, 金色的; 貴重的; 成熟的: golden grain 金燦燦的穀物; the golden rays of the sun 金燦燦的陽光. **3** best of its kind 最好的: a golden opportunity 絕好機會; golden rule 金科玉律; golden age 黃金時代; the golden age of English literature i.e. when English literature was at its best 英國文學的黃金時代, 即: 英國文學最爲鼎盛的時期. **'goldfish** nc / u type of yellow or red fish, kept as pets 金魚. **'gold mine** mine from which gold is dug 金礦, 金山.

golf [gɔlf] nu outdoor game of hitting a small ball into holes with a long stick 高爾夫球. **golfer** nc **'golf club 1** stick for hitting a golf ball 高爾夫球棍. **2** group of persons who associate to play golf 高爾夫球俱樂部: I belong to the local golf club. 我參加了本地的高爾夫球俱樂部. **'golf course** piece of land on which golf is played 高爾夫球場.

gone [gɔn] past part of **go.** go的過去分詞.

gong [gɔŋ] nc round piece of metal which makes a deep, ringing noise when struck 鑼.

good¹ [gud] *adj* **1** virtuous, behaving properly 品德高尚的; 規規矩矩的: *The priest is a good man.* 這位牧師是個好人. *Try to be a good boy.* 做個乖孩子. **2** superior; above the ordinary 優良的; 好的: *a good family* 好家庭; *good clothes* 好衣服. *They live in a good neighbourhood.* 他們住在一個和睦的區域裏. **3** right; proper kind for its purpose 恰當的; 合用的: *a good book about flowers* 一本關於花卉的好書; *a good cooking pot* 一隻合用的鍋. *This medicine is good for a cold.* 這種藥治感冒有效. **4** improving; beneficial 在變好的; 有益的: *Eat this food; it is good for you* 請吃這種食物, 它對你有好處. *Games are good for the health.* 做遊戲有益於健康. **5** efficient 效率高的, 能勝任的: *a good cook / farmer / football player* 一個好廚師 / 農民 / 足球隊員; *good housekeeping* 良好的家務管理. *She is very good with young children.* 她很會照看小孩. *She is good at games.* 她善於玩遊戲. **6** pleasant, enjoyable, successful 令人愉快的; 有趣的; 成功的: *Did you have a good holiday?* 假期愉快嗎? *It's good to see you again.* 很高興再次見到你. *That is a good story.* 那是一個有趣的故事; *a good hard game* 一種有趣而困難的遊戲; *a good long sleep* 長時間的熟睡. **7** kind; helpful 好心的, 慈善的; 樂於助人的: *It is good of him to come.* 他能夠來真是好心. *He is good to his servants.* 他對僕人很慈善. *Will you be good enough to hold my bag?* 請您幫個忙替我拿一下袋子好嗎? **8** complete; satisfactory 十足的, 充分的; 令人滿意的: *Have a good breakfast / a good rest.* 好好吃一頓早飯 / 休息一下吧. *He has a good excuse / reason.* 他的藉口 / 理由很充分. *Take a good look at it.*

它. *It needs a good wash.* 得把它好好洗一洗. **9** of a lot of anything 許多的: *a good deal of arguing* 無休止的爭論; *a good number of people* 許多人; *a good few examples* i.e. quite a number 不少例子, 即: 相當多的例子. *comparative* 比較級 **better** ['betə*]. *superlative* 最高級 **best** [best]. (*opp* 反義詞 **bad**). **well** [wel] *adv* **goodness** *nu* **1** quality of being good: best part of something 善良, 良好, 優良; 養份, 精華: *If you cook it too long you lose the goodness.* 要是你把它煮得太久, 它的養份都損失了. *Would you have the goodness to stop that noise?* 請不要再發出那種吵鬧聲好嗎? **2** exclamation instead of God (代替 God) 表示驚訝: *Goodness knows!* 天曉得! *For Goodness sake!* 看在老天爺份上! *Thank Goodness!* 謝天謝地! **'good-for-nothing** *adj* useless 沒有用處的, 無價值的人. Also 亦作 *nc* useless person 無用的人, 飯桶. **'good-natured** *adj* kind; friendly 脾氣好的, 溫厚的, 和善的. **'good-tempered** *adj* not easily annoyed 脾氣好的, 和氣的. **good humour** cheerful state of mind 心情好, 脾氣好, 愉快的. **goodhumoured** *adj* **good looks** personal beauty 美貌. **have a good mind** to feel very much like doing; be very inclined to 很想(做某事): *I have a good mind to punish you.* (*informal*) 我真想好好懲罰你. (非正式). **good morning / afternoon / evening / day / night** form of greeting and farewell i.e. may you have a good morning etc. 問候或告別語, 即: 早安, 早上好 / 下午好 / 晚上好 / (白天的問候語)您好 / (夜晚道別用語)晚安, 明天見. *Note* 說明: all except *good night* can be used both when meeting and leaving someone, although it is more common to use them only when meeting, and to use *goodbye* when leaving. But *good night* is used only when leaving someone in the evening. *Good evening, Mr Jones; I am glad to see you. Good night, Mr Jones; I'll see you tomorrow.* 除 good night 外, 上述各種問候語可用於會見某人或跟某人告別. 而更常見的用法是只在會見時用上述問候語, 告別時用 goodbye. good night 只用於夜晚跟某人道別. *Good evening, Mr Jones; I am glad to see you.* 晚上好, 瓊斯先生; 很高興見到您. *Good night, Mr Jones; I'll see you tomorrow.* 晚安, 瓊斯先生, 明天見. **goodwill** kind feeling; sympathy 親善, 善意; 同情.

good² [gud] **1** *nu* something that is good 好事; 好處: *The new rules are for the good of the school* i.e. for the benefit of. 新規章對學校有好處. 即: 對學校有利. *You should do it for your own good.* 爲你自己着想, 你應當這樣做. *A rest will do you good.* 休息一下對你有好處. *see* also **good¹**. **2** *nu* use 用處: *What is the good of staying here?* 呆在這裏有甚麼用? **3** *nc* (only *pl*) things bought, sold or owned (僅用複數) 商品, 貨物; 動產, 財物: *This shop has foreign goods for sale.* 這家商店出售進口貨. *During the war they lost all their goods.* 戰爭期間他們的財物損失殆盡. **for good** for ever; permanently 永久地; 永遠地: *He has gone for good.* 他已經一去不復返了.

goodbye [gud'bai] *interj* said when people leave (告別用語) 再見: *Goodbye, my dear!* 再見, 親愛的! *They said goodbye and left.* 他們道了再見就分手了. Also 亦作 *nc: There were many sad goodbyes.* 有許多令人傷心的別離.

goods [gudz] *npl* **1** merchandise; object etc for sale 商品: *to bring goods into

market* 將商品投放市場. **2** articles sent by rail (由鐵路運輸的) 貨物: *Please send the goods off today.* 請於今天把貨物發出.

goose [gu:s] *nc* large water bird like a duck, but bigger and usu. with a longer neck 鵝. *pl* 複數 **geese** [gi:s]. **'gooseflesh, 'goosepimples** roughness of skin caused by cold or fear (因寒冷或恐懼而起的) 雞皮疙瘩: *This silent house gives me gooseflesh.* 這靜悄悄的房子使我起麻皮疙瘩.

gooseberry ['guzbəri] *nc* type of berry used as food 醋栗.

gore [gɔ:*] *vt* wound with horns 以角牴傷: *The bull gored the farmer.* 公牛用角牴傷了農民.

gorge [gɔ:dʒ] *nc* narrow pass between hills 山峽, 峽谷: *The river flows through a gorge.* 河水穿過峽谷. Also 亦作 *vt / i* fill oneself by eating greedily and too much 塞飽, 大吃, 貪婪地吃: *The lions were gorged with meat.* 獅子吃飽了肉. *The children gorged themselves with cakes.* 孩子們狼吞虎嚥地吃蛋糕.

gorgeous ['gɔ:dʒəs] *adj* splendid, very attractive 華麗的, 動人的: *a gorgeous view of the mountain* 這座山的壯觀景色; *a gorgeous blonde* 美麗的金髮女郎. *We had a gorgeous time.* 我們玩得真痛快. **gorgeously** *adv.*

gorilla [gə'rilə] *nc* largest type of ape 大猩猩.

gorse [gɔ:s] *nu* type of prickly bush with small, yellow flowers 荊豆.

gory ['gɔ:ri] *adj* bloody 血淋淋的, 駭人聽聞的.

gosh [gɔʃ] *interj* exclamation of surprise (表示驚訝) 哎呀!

Gospel ['gɔspl] *nc* story of Christ's life in one of the first four books of the New Testament in the Bible 福音; 福

音書 (新約聖經的頭四卷之一): *He went to Africa to preach the Gospel* i.e. spread Christianity. 他去非洲佈講福音. 即: 傳基督教.

gossamer ['gɔsəmə*] *nu* **1** very thin thread(s) of a spider's web 蛛絲. **2** type of very thin cloth 薄紗.

gossip ['gɔsip] **1** *nu* talk when one is not busy (usu. about other people and often unkind) 閒談, 說別人的閒話, 關於旁人的流言蜚語: *At lunch I heard all the gossip about Jones.* 吃午飯時我聽到了關於瓊斯的一切流言蜚語. *Have you heard the latest gossip?* 你聽到最新的傳聞了嗎? **2** *nc* person fond of gossip 愛說別人閒話的人: *All the people in the village are gossips.* 這個村子裏所有的人都愛談論東家長西家短. Also 亦作 *vi* talk or write gossip 閒聊, 傳播閒言碎語: *Our wives sat gossiping in the garden.* 我們的老婆們正坐在園子裏說長道短.

got [gɔt] past of **get.** get 的過去式和過去分詞.

gotten ['gɔtn] *US* form of **got.** (美) got 的過去分詞. see 見 **get.**

gourd [guəd] *nc* **1** large fruit of a climbing or spreading type of plant 葫蘆. **2** dry, hard skin of this fruit as a container 葫蘆瓢.

gout [gaut] *nu* disease causing painful swelling (esp. of the big toe or thumb) 痛風.

govern ['gʌvən] *vt* rule, control, direct 統治; 操縱; 控制; 指導: *For many years Great Britain governed India.* 英國曾統治印度多年. *These laws govern the sale of beer and wine.* 這些法則控制啤酒和酒類的銷售. **governing** *adj*: *the governing body of the school* 學校的董事會. **governess** ['gʌvənis] *nc* woman employed to teach children at their home 家庭女教師. **government**

1 *nu* act of governing 統治, 管轄, 管理: *In the past the government of the country was in the hands of the king.* 過去由國王掌管對這個國家的統轄治理. **2** *nc* kind of government 政府(的種類): *We voted for a Labour government.* 我們投票贊成工黨政府. *This country now has self-government.* 這個國家現已自治. **3** *nu* (usu. **Government**) persons who govern (通常作 Government) 政府, 政府成員: *The Government have (has) increased taxes.* 政府增加了稅收. *The President is forming a new Government* i.e. is choosing Ministers to help him to govern. 總統正在組織新政府. 即: 正在選定部長們以治理國家. **governor** *nc* **1** person appointed to govern a colony, province or state 總督; 省長; 州長. **2** person appointed to any governing body (e.g. of a college, school, hospital) 主管人員, (學校、醫院等的) 董事長: *Our school has its own board of governors.* 我校有自己的校董會. '**governor-'general** *nc* person appointed to represent the Queen in a dominion of the British Commonwealth (英聯邦領地的) 總督. *pl* 複數 **governorsgeneral** (*formal*) (正式) or **governorgenerals** (*informal*) (非正式). see 見 **dominion.**

gown [gaun] *nc* **1** woman's dress 女服. **2** long, loose coat worn over ordinary clothes by judges, university staff, students, schoolteachers etc. 法官服; 大學教職員制服; 大學生校服; 中、小學教師制服.

grab¹ [græb] *vt / i* **1** seize quickly with the hands 攫取; 抓住: *He grabbed my jacket.* 他抓住了我的外套. *I'll grab him as he comes out.* 等他出來時我會抓住他. **2** seize greedily 貪婪地奪取. *past* 過去式和過去分詞 **grabbed.**

grab² [græb] *nc* **1** seizing quickly (急速的)攫取: *He made a grab at my jacket.* 他向我的外套抓去. **2** device for seizing and lifting something 抓揚機, 挖掘機: *The crane has a grab* (for lifting earth etc.). 起重機有個(挖泥沙土等用的)抓斗.

grace [greis] **1** *nu* something pleasing (esp. movement or manners), correct behaviour, charm (動作)優美(態度)文雅(舉止)端莊; 魅力: *We admired the grace with which she walked across the room.* 我們讚賞她穿過房間時的風度. *He agreed with (a) good / bad grace* i.e. willingly / unwillingly. 他爽快地/勉強地同意了. 即: 他情願地/不情願地表示同意. *Knowing he was not wanted, he had the grace to refuse the invitation.* 他知道人們並不歡迎他, 便知趣地沒有接受邀請. **2** *nc / u* kindness, favour 仁慈; 恩惠: *By the grace of God I was not killed.* 蒙上帝恩典我得以倖存. *Give me a month's grace and I will pay you* i.e. allow me one more month. 給我一個月的寬限, 我會給你錢. 即: 讓我再拖欠一個月. *He fell from grace* i.e. out of favour. 他失寵了. **3** *nc / u* short prayer made at the beginning and / or end of a meal thanking God for his kindness 飯前和 / 或飯後的感恩禱告. *Also* 亦作 *vt* favour, add charm to (by being present) 偏愛; (以出席)使…增光: *It is good to see so many important people gracing our meeting.* 看到這麼多重要人物光臨本次會議, 不勝榮幸之至. **graceful** *adj* **gracefully** *adv* **gracious** [ˈgreiʃəs] *adj* charming, kind 優雅的; 仁慈的: *She has a gracious smile.* 她慈祥地微微一笑. *Also* 亦作 *interj*: *Goodness gracious!* 啊呀! 天哪!

gradation [grəˈdeiʃən] *nc / u* (esp. in colour and music) successive stages of development, passing slowly from one thing to another (尤指色彩和音樂)等級; 階段; 層次: *The gradations of public opinion ran from sympathy to anger;* 各種程度的公眾輿論從同情到憤怒都有; *the pleasant gradation of sounds in this music* 這支樂曲中樂音的愉快交替.

grade¹ [greid] *nc* **1** order, level of rank, quality 等級; 級別: *Only the highest grade of goods is sold here;* 此處只銷售高檔貨物; *a poor grade of steel* 劣質鋼; *low grades of oil* 低級油. **2** year into which a school's work is divided (學校的)年級: *The youngest pupils are in the first grade, the oldest pupils in the sixth grade.* 年齡最小的學生在一年級, 年齡最大的學生在六年級. *Note* 說明: mainly *US* in sense **2**; *class or form* are common in the UK and the Commonwealth. 義 **2** 主要用於美; 在英國和英聯邦國家中比較常用 *class* 或 *form*. **3** mark or position given for work done at school or college (學校的)評分等級: *make the grade* i.e. reach the required standard, be successful 及格, 即: 達到標準, 成功. **4** *(US)* degree of slope. *(Brit* 英 **gradient)** (美)坡度.

grade² [greid] *vt* put in order of size, quality etc. 分類, 分等, 評分: *He graded the students according to ability.* 他按學生的能力給他們打分.

gradient [ˈgreidiənt] *nc* degree of slope 坡度: *On that hill the road has a gradient of 1 in 6.* 那座山上公路的坡度是每六米升高一米.

gradual [ˈgrædjuəl] *adj* happening slowly, step by step 逐漸的; 逐步的: *There was a gradual change in the weather;* 天氣逐漸變化; *a gradual slope* i.e. one that rises slowly 緩坡, 即: 坡度不大的坡. **gradually** *adv*.

graduate¹ ['grædʒueit] *vt* divide, mark in units of measurement 標上刻度: *The container is graduated in pints, quarts and gallons for measuring liquids.* 該容器標上了計液量用的品脫、夸脫和加侖等刻度.

graduate² ['grædʒueit] *vi* 1 take a university degree 獲得大學的學位: *At what university did you graduate?* 你是在哪一所大學獲得學位的? 2 *(US)* finish a course of any school or college (美) 畢業: *He graduated from high school.* 他中學畢業了. Also 亦作 ['grædʒuət] *nc* 1 person who has taken a degree 已經獲得學位的人. 2 *(US)* person who has finished a course (美) 畢業生. **graduation** [grædʒu'eiʃən] *nu* taking a degree; ceremony at which degrees are given 獲得的儀式; 授與學位的儀式.

graft [grɑ:ft] *vt* transfer part of one living thing to another (e.g. buds or branches from one tree to another; skin or bones from one part of the body to another or from one person to another) 嫁接; 移植: *He grafted the branch onto the apple tree.* 他把枝條嫁接到蘋果樹上. *His hands were so badly burned that the doctors had to graft new skin onto them.* 他的雙手燒傷如此嚴重, 醫生只得爲他植上新皮. Also 亦作 *nc / u* thing grafted; act of grafting 接穗, 移植物; 嫁接, 移植手術.

grain [grein] 1 *nc / u* seed of corn, rice or other food plants 穀物: *a store full of grain* 裝滿穀物的倉庫. *The hen ate the grains of corn on the ground.* 母雞啄食地上的穀粒. 2 *nc* any small piece of anything 細粒, 一點點: *a grain of powder / salt / sand / sugar etc.* 一粒粉末/一粒鹽/一粒沙/一粒糖等. *a grain of honesty / truth etc.* 一點點的誠實/些微的真理等. *There is not a grain of*

truth in what he says i.e. it is completely untrue. 他的話中沒有一點實情. 即: 完全是假話. 3 *nc / u* natural marking on marble, stone, wood etc. (大理石, 石材或木材等的) 紋理: *This kind of wood has a very fine / coarse grain.* 這種木頭的紋理很細/粗.

gram, *gramme [græm] *nc* metric unit of weight, equal to the weight of one cubic centimetre of water 克 (公制重量單位, 相當於 1 立方厘米水的重量).

grammar ['græmə*] 1 *nu* rules for speaking or writing a language correctly 語法: *good / bad grammar* i.e. correct / incorrect use of grammar 通順/不通順的文理. 即; 語法的正確/不正確使用. 2 *nc* book that teaches grammar 語法書: *Take out your English grammars.* 把英語語法書拿出來. **grammatical** [grə'mætikl] *adj* following the rules of grammar; having good grammar 符合語法規則的, 語法通順的. (*opp* 反義詞 **ungrammatical**). **'grammar school** secondary school in which Latin grammar was once the most important subject; now one giving an academic education (以前以拉丁語爲主課的) 中等學校; (現在的) 普通中學.

gramophone ['græməfoun] *nc* (*Brit*) machine which produces sounds of music and speech from records (Also 亦作 **record player**) (*US* 美 **phonograph**) (英) 留聲機.

granary ['grænəri] *nc* store for grain 穀倉, 糧倉.

grand¹ [grænd] *adj* 1 noble, splendid 高貴的, 壯麗的: *He lives in a grand house;* 他住在豪華的宅第裏; *a grand fellow* 達官貴人; *in a grand manner* 富麗堂皇地. 2 more important, superior, complete 重要的; 最高的; 完整的: *grand finale* i.e. impressive ending of a concert etc. 高潮性結尾, 即: 音樂會等動人的終場演奏. *grand piano* i.e. a big type of piano 大鋼琴, 三角鋼琴; *grand total* i.e. including everything 總計. **grandeur** ['grændjə*] *nu* being grand, magnificence 宏偉, 壯麗. '**grandstand** place with a roof from which to watch games etc, usu. with expensive seats (運動場等的)正面看台, 大看台.

grand-² ['grænd] *prefix* used to express certain family relationships **grandfather** i.e. the father of one's mother or father; **grandmother; grandparent; grandson** i.e. child of one's son or daughter; **granddaughter**) 用來表示家庭成員間的某種關係(如 grandfather 祖父, 外祖父; grandmother; grandparent; grandson 孫子, 外孫; granddaughter 孫女).

grandiose ['grændiouz] *adj* planned on a large scale; meant to impress 舖張, 誇大的; 浮誇的; 存心要嘩衆取寵的.

granite ['grænit] *nu* type of hard rock 花崗岩.

grant [grɑ:nt] *vt/i* 1 allow to have; give 准予; 授予, etc. *The headmaster granted us an extra holiday.* 校長准許我們多一天假期. *I cannot grant your request.* 我不能同意你的請求. 2 agree 同意. *I grant that what you say is correct.* 就算你沒有說錯. Also 亦作 *nc* gift, allowance of money 授與之物, 補助金. *The council made a grant of land to the people.* (市)議會授與人民一些土地. *Students in this country receive a grant from the government.* 這個國家的學生從政府領取助學金. **take for granted** believe to be certain 認爲是當然的. *Do not take his help for granted.* 別以爲他一定會幫忙.

grape [greip] *nc* type of fruit, used for making wine 葡萄. '**grapefruit** type

of fruit like a big, yellow orange 葡萄柚.

graph [grɑ:f] *nc* diagram showing by a line or lines the relation between two quantities 座標圖, 圖表: *A graph showing the increase in trade by years from 1900 to 1940.* 表明1900年至1940年貿易增長情況的曲線圖.

graphic ['græfik] *adj* 1 of writing or drawing 書寫的, 圖示的. 2 clear, vivid 鮮明的, 生動的: *He gave a graphic account of his adventures.* 他生動地叙述了他的奇遇.

graphite ['græfait] *nu* kind of carbon used as 'lead' in pencils 石墨.

grapple ['græpl] *vt/i* seize (and usu. struggle with) 抓住; 與 … 格鬥: *He grappled with the thief.* 他跟小偷扭打起來. *They are grappling with the problem.* 他們正在盡力解決這個問題.

grasp [grɑ:sp] *vt/i* seize firmly; understand 緊緊抓住; 掌握, 領會: *I had to grasp the rope to stop falling.* 我得抓緊繩子才不致跌倒. *It is difficult to grasp his meaning.* 很難領會他的意思. Also 亦作 *nu*: *He held my hand in a friendly grasp.* 他友好地握住我的手. *You seem to have a good grasp of English history.* 看來你對英國歷史瞭解得很透徹. **grasping** *adj* seizing, greedy 攫取的, 貪婪的.

grass [grɑ:s] 1 *nu* type of green plant with very narrow leaves which can cover large areas 草, 青草: *Cattle eat grass.* 牛吃草. *Let us sit on the grass.* 我們坐在草地上吧. 2 *nc* particular types of this plant 特定種類的青草: *Not all the grasses found in this country can be eaten by animals.* 這個國家的各種青草不是都能餵牲口. **grassy** *adj* of grass, covered with grass 長滿草的. '**grassland** large area of land covered with grass 草地, 草原: *the* grasslands of North America 北美大草原. '**grass snake** kind of harmless snake, with a yellow mark on the head, which lives near water 青草蛇 (沼澤地帶的無毒小蛇).

grasshopper ['grɑːsˌhɔpə] nc plant-eating insect with two pairs of wings and powerful hind legs for jumping 蚱蜢; 蝗蟲.

grate¹ [greit] vt / i 1 rub into small pieces with something rough (usu. for cooking) 磨碎, 擦碎 (通常用於烹飪): She grated the cheese into a bowl. 她把乳酪磨碎裝進碗裏. 2 make a rough, unpleasant sound through rubbing; annoy 使發刺耳的磨擦聲; 激怒: The sharp stone grated on the window. 鋒利的石塊跟窗子摩擦, 發出刺耳的聲音. His boasting grates on everyone. 他的自吹自擂使大家感到惱火. **grating** adj: a grating voice 刺耳的聲音. **grater** nc instrument with a rough surface for grating food etc. 擦菜板, (擦碎食物等的廚房用具) 擦子.

grate² [greit] nc small metal framework in a room for bolding a fire 爐架, 爐柵.

grateful ['greitful] adj thankful; expressing thanks 感激的, 感謝的: I am grateful (to you) for your help. 我感謝你的幫助. They sent us a very grateful letter. 他們給我們送來了一封千恩萬謝的信. (opp 反義詞 **ungrateful**). **gratefully** adv **gratefulness**, **gratitude** ['grætitjuːd] nu (opp 反義詞 **ingratitude**).

gratify ['grætifai] vt satisfy, please 使滿足; 使高興: He was gratified to learn you could come. 他得知你能來非常高興. **gratifying** adj: It was gratifying for him to learn this. 令人高興的是他已經知道了這件事. **gratification** [ˌgrætifiˈkeiʃən] nu feeling of being

gratified 滿足; 滿意; 喜悅: I had the gratification of seeing him win. 看到他贏了, 我很高興.

grating ['greitiŋ] nc frame made of bars to cover an opening 栅欄.

gratitude ['grætitjuːd] nu being grateful for, thankfulness 感激; 感謝; 感恩: He gave them a lovely bookcase in gratitude for their kindness. 他送給他們一個精緻的書櫥以答謝他們的好意. see 見 **grateful**.

gratuitous [grəˈtjuːitəs] adj given or done for nothing or for no reason, without charge (usu. with added meaning of not being wanted) 無償的; 無緣無故的, 不必要的: I was given plenty of gratuitous advice / help / information etc. 我得到了許多不必要的勸告 / 幫助 / 信息等; a gratuitous remark i.e. unnecessary one made without reason 不必要的評論, 即: 沒有必要、沒有理由的評論.

gratuity [grəˈtjuːiti] nc 1 payment of money in addition to his salary made to someone at the end of his period of employment 退職金. 2 amount of money given to someone for a service he has done; tip 賞金; 小費.

grave¹ [greiv] nc hole in the ground in which a dead person is buried; place where a dead person is buried 墳穴; 墳墓: He visited his father's grave. 他探視了他先父的墓地. '**gravestone** stone marking a grave 墓碑. '**graveyard** place where there are graves; cemetery 墓地; 墳場.

grave² [greiv] adj very serious, solemn 嚴重的; 莊嚴的: The situation is grave. 局勢很嚴重. His face is always grave. 他總是陰沉着臉. **gravely** adv.

gravel ['grævl] nu small stones, coarse sand 礫石; 砂礫: The bottom of the river is covered with gravel. 河底佈滿

砂礫.

gravitate ['græviteit] *vi* be attracted towards and move towards 受吸引; 向…移動: *Everyone gravitated to / towards the bright lights.* 所有的人都向明亮的燈光走來.

gravity ['græviti] *nu* 1 force of attraction between bodies as shown e.g. by objects tending to fall towards the centre of the earth 引力; 地心引力, 重力. 2 state of being grave, seriousness 莊重, 嚴肅: *You do not seem to understand the gravity of your mistake.* 看來你還沒有認識到你的錯誤的嚴重性.

gravy ['greivi] *nu* juice from meat when it is being cooked; sauce made from the juice 肉汁; 肉滷.

gray [grei] *nc / u, adj* see 見 **grey**.

graze¹ [greiz] *vt / i* 1 eat grass 吃草: *The cows are grazing in the field.* 牛羣正在田野吃草. 2 feed on grass, put out to graze 餵草; 放牧: *The farmers graze their sheep here.* 農民們在這裏牧羊.

graze² [greiz] *vt / i* 1 touch, rub in passing 擦過: *The car grazed (against) the wall.* 汽車擦着了牆. 2 damage skin by grazing against 擦傷 (皮膚); 抓破: *I grazed my hand on the wall.* 我的手在牆上擦破了皮. Also 亦作 *nc*: *a graze on the knee* 膝部的擦傷.

grease [gri:s] *nu* soft animal fat; very thick oil 動物脂; 油膏. Also 亦作 *vt*: *I must grease the wheels.* 我得給輪子上點潤滑油. **greasy** *adj* of grease, covered with grease; slippery 油膩的; 塗了油的; 潤滑的: *a greasy road* 滑溜溜的路.

great¹ [greit] *adj* 1 big 大的: *a great building* 巨大的建築物. *We reached a great city.* 我們來到了一座大城市. 2 bigger, more than average 重要的; 超乎尋常的: *He's a great friend of ours.* 他是我們的好朋友. *That man is a great rogue* 那人是個大流氓. *a great eater / reader / talker etc.* 飯量很大的人/酷愛讀書的人/健談的人等. *Take great care of her.* 好好照顧她. 3 outstanding, famous 傑出的; 著名的: *Shakespeare was a great writer.* 莎士比亞是偉大的作家. *This is a great book.* 這是一部偉大的作品. 4 a lot of anything 很多的: *a great deal of trouble* 一大堆麻煩; *a great many people* 許多人; *a great number of questions* 許多問題. 5 with some *adjs* of size to emphasize them 強調某些表示大小長短的形容詞: *a great big cake* 很大的蛋糕; *a great fat sheep* 一隻很肥的綿羊; *a great long stick. (informal)* 一根很長的棍子 (非正式). 6 splendid, enjoyable 了不起的; 極有趣的: *It would be great if we could meet again. (informal)* 要是我們能再見面, 那真是好極了. (非正式). **greatly** *adv* **greatness** *nu*.

great² [greit] *prefix* to grandfather etc. 用在 grandfather 等詞前. **great-'grandfather** grandfather of one's father or mother 曾祖父, 外曾祖父. **great-'granddaughter** granddaughter of one's son or daughter etc. 曾孫女, 外曾孫女.

greed [gri:d] *nu* desire for too much 貪心, 貪婪: *Their greed for power / praise / wealth etc.* 他們對權力/讚譽/財富等的貪慾. **greedy** *adj* (usu. for food) (通常指對食物): *a greedy child* 貪吃的孩子. **greedily** *adv* **greediness** *nu*.

Greek [gri:k] 1 *nc* native of Greece 希臘人. 2 *nu* the Greek language 希臘語. Also 亦作 *adj* of Greece, its people or language 希臘的; 希臘人的; 希臘語的.

green [gri:n] 1 *nc / u* colour of growing

grass 綠色: *the green of the trees* 樹木的綠色. *I like the greens in that picture.* 我喜歡那幅圖畫裏的綠顏色. **2** *nc* piece of land covered with grass (e.g. *bowling green* i.e. for playing bowls) 草地(如保齡球的場地). **3** *nc* (in *pl*) green vegetables (用於複數)綠色蔬菜. Also 亦作 *adj* **1** *green fields and trees* 綠色的田野和樹木. **2** not ripe 未成熟的: *green corn / dates / berries etc.* 嫩玉米/未熟的棗/未熟的草莓等; *green wood* i.e. just cut and so not dry 未乾的木材, 即: 剛砍下的木材. **3** without experience, training 無經驗的; 未受訓練的: *The team is still very green.* 這個隊沒有受過訓練. **4** looking sick, pale 有病容的; 臉色蒼白的: *The rough sea made him turn green.* 波濤洶湧的大海使他面色蒼白. *I am green with envy.* 我十分妒忌. **greenish** *adj* rather green 帶綠色的. **'greengrocer** *nc* shopkeeper who sells fruit and vegetables 蔬菜水果商. **'greenhouse** *nc* building made of glass to protect growing plants 玻璃暖房, 溫室. (Also 亦作 **glasshouse**).

greenery ['griːnəri] *nu* (leaves of) green plants 綠葉; 草木: *Add some greenery to that vase of flowers.* 給那瓶花加上些綠葉.

greet [griːt] *vt* **1** express welcome, express pleasure at meeting someone (in words) 歡迎, 致問候: *They greeted me at the door by saying 'Good morning'.* 他們在門口向我道‘早安’問候. **2** receive or meet, not necessarily in a friendly way 受到, 遇到(不一定指遇到好事): *They were greeted with loud laughter.* 他們聽到高聲說笑. *The rain greeted us as soon as we went out.* 我們一出門就遇上下雨. *Shouts of anger greeted our ears.* 我們聽到憤怒的喊

聲. **greeting** *nc*: *When you meet somebody in the evening the correct greeting is 'Good evening', not 'Good night'.* 晚上遇到人時, 問候語應當是 Good evening, 而不是 Good night. *Give our greetings to your mother* i.e. good wishes. 請代我們向你媽媽致意.

gregarious [grə'gɛəriəs] *adj* living in groups; fond of company 羣居的; 愛交際的: *Man is very gregarious.* 人類喜愛羣居.

grenade [grə'neid] *nc* small bomb thrown by hand or shot from a rifle 手榴彈; 槍榴彈.

grew [gruː] past tense of **grow.** grow 的過去式.

grey, gray [grei] *nc / u* colour between black and white, like ashes 灰色: *the grey of the sky on a rainy day* 雨天天空的灰色. Also 亦作 *adj*: *grey skies* 灰濛濛的天空. **greyish** *adj* rather grey 淺灰色的. **'grey-'haired** *adj* with grey hairs, old 頭髮灰白的; 年老的.

greyhound ['greihaund] *nc* type of swift dog used for hunting and racing 靈提 (一種獵犬及比賽用犬).

grid [grid] *nc* **1** frame with bars; grating 格子; 格柵. **2** numbered squares printed on a map to give exact positions 地圖上的座標方格. **3** network of main power lines for distributing electricity 輸電網.

grief [griːf] *nu* great sorrow 悲痛, 憂傷: *I was filled with grief when I heard of his death.* 得知他的死訊我感到非常悲傷.

grieve [griːv] *vt / i* feel, cause grief (使)傷心: *Nothing grieves me more.* 沒有甚麼使我更傷心的了. **grievance** *nc* something to grieve or complain about 抱怨, 抱怨的原因: *He won't listen to our grievances.* 他不肯聽我們陳情.

grill [gril] *nc* device on a cooker for providing heat, under which to cook meat, toast bread etc. (烤肉、麵包等用的)烤架. Also 亦作 *vt/i* **1** cook or be cooked on a grill 在烤架上炙烤. **2** torture by questioning closely for a long time 拷問; 長時間嚴加盤問: *He was grilled by the police after his arrest.* (*informal* in sense **2**) 他被捕後受到警方的嚴厲盤問. (義 **2** 爲非正式).

grim [grim] *adj* severe, stern, fierce 嚴厲的; 嚴格的; 殘忍的: *He had a grim look on his face.* 他表情冷酷. *We had a grim struggle before we won;* 我們經過嚴酷的鬥爭才取得勝利; *a grim sense of humour* i.e. a bitter, cruel one 冷酷無情的幽默感. **grimly** *adv*.

grimace [gri'meis] *nc* ugly twist of the face to show contempt, dislike etc. (表輕視、厭惡等)面部扭曲, 鬼臉. Also 亦作 *vi* make a grimace 扮怪相, 做鬼臉.

grime [graim] *nu* layer of dirt, difficult to remove 塵垢, 污垢: *Miners at work soon get covered with grime.* 礦工工作時身上很快積滿了塵垢. **grimy** *adj*.

grin [grin] *vt/i* smile showing the teeth; show the teeth in contempt; show the teeth in pain 露齒而笑; 因輕視或痛苦而露齒而咧嘴: *Everyone in the classroom grinned when he dropped his book.* 他的書掉下時教室裏的人都咧嘴而笑. *past* 過去式和過去分詞 **grinned**. Also 亦作 *nc*: *Take that grin off your face!* 不許你咧嘴傻笑.

grind [graind] *vt/i* **1** crush into very small pieces 磨碎: *grind corn into flour* 把玉米磨成粉. *I ground my cigarette into the ashtray.* 我把香烟在烟灰缸裏碾碎了. **2** polish, make sharp by rubbing with something rough 磨光; 磨快: *Grind these knives, they are blunt.* 這些刀鈍了, 把它們磨快. **3** rub, strike together 磨擦; 碾磨:

He was grinding his teeth with rage 他氣得咬牙切齒. *past* 過去式和過去分詞 **ground** [graund]. **'grindstone** stone for sharpening knives etc. 磨刀石.

grip [grip] *vt/i* seize and hold firmly 緊握, 抓牢: *Grip this stick and don't let go.* 抓緊這根棍子, 不要放手. *Worn tyres do not grip (on) wet roads.* 磨損了的輪胎在濕漉漉的路面上容易打滑. *The book gripped my attention.* 這本書引起了我的注意. *past* 過去式和過去分詞 **gripped**. Also 亦作 *nc* **1** *He had a stick in his grip.* 他手中緊握着一根棍子. **2** travelling bag 旅行手提包, 旅行袋. **gripping** *adj*: *a gripping story* 扣人心弦的故事.

grisly ['grizli] *adj* horrible, terrible 恐怖的, 可怕的.

gristle ['grisl] *nu* rough substance like white elastic, found in meat 軟骨.

grit [grit] *nu* small piece of stone, sand etc. 砂礫, 砂粒: *I have a piece of grit in my eye.* 我眼睛裏有一粒砂子. Also 亦作 *vt*: *grit one's teeth* 咬牙. *past* 過去式和過去分詞 **gritted**.

groan [groun] *vt/i* make a deep sound because of pain or sorrow; (of things) make a deep sound because of strain 呻吟; 因重力拉壓而嘎吱作響: *He groaned when he broke his arm.* 他因手臂跌斷而呻吟. *The floorboards groan when you walk on them.* 人在上面走時活動地板嘎吱作響. Also 亦作 *nc*: *He gave a groan.* 他發出一聲呻吟. *The bad news was received with loud groans.* 人們聽到這壞消息時發出了很大的抱怨聲.

grocer ['grousə*] *nc* person who sells many kinds of things needed in a house (e.g. tea, coffee, sugar, salt, tinned foods, soap etc.) 食品雜貨商. **groceries** *npl* articles sold by a grocer 食品雜貨.

groggy [ˈgrɔgi] *adj* unsteady on the feet, weak 脚步跟蹌的; 體弱的: *The blow on the head made him groggy.* 當頭的一擊使他站立不穩.

groin [grɔin] *nc / u* line between the belly and the top of the leg where they meet 腹股溝, 鼠蹊.

groom [gru:m] *nc* **1** servant who looks after horses 馬伕. **2** see 見 **bridegroom**. Also 亦作 *vt* **1** look after a horse by feeding and esp. brushing it 照料(馬匹), 餵養和洗刷(馬匹). **2** prepare someone for a special purpose 培訓: *He is being groomed for the job of manager.* 他正接受訓練, 準備當經理.

groove [gru:v] *nc* long, hollow line cut in something (esp. to guide something else that moves) 凹槽: *The door slides along the groove in the floor.* 門是沿地板上的凹槽滑動的. *A gramophone needle moves round in a groove.* 唱針在唱片的紋路裏滑動.

grope [group] *vt / i* feel about with one's hands blindly to find something 摸索, 搜尋: *I groped for the door.* 我摸索着找門. *We groped our way through the dark forest.* 我們在黑暗的森林裏摸索前進.

gross¹ [grous] *nc* 144, twelve dozen 羅, 12打.

gross² [grous] *adj* **1** unpleasantly fat 肥胖的, 臃腫的: *Since he stopped taking exercise. he has become gross.* 他停止鍛煉之後, 變得肥胖. **2** (of manner) coarse, rough, rude (舉止) 粗俗的, 粗野的, 粗魯的: *His language and behaviour are gross.* 他言行粗俗. **3** obvious, flagrant 明顯的; 明目張膽的: *a gross mistake* 嚴重的錯誤; *gross impertinence* 十足的傲慢無禮; *gross indecency* 十足的下流無恥. **4** total 總共的, 全部的: *the gross amount* 總數;

100 tons gross 毛重100噸. (*opp* 反義詞 **net**). **grossly** *adv.*

grotesque [grəˈtesk] *adj* strangely formed, unusual, absurd 奇形怪狀的; 怪誕的; 荒唐的: *These designs are grotesque.* 這些設計構思奇特. *His face has a grotesque appearance.* 他的面部表情特別怪.

grotto [ˈgrɔtou] *nc* cave (usu. an imitation one in a park or garden) 洞穴(通常指公園或花園裏的倣製洞穴). *pl* 複數 **grottoes** or **grottos**.

ground¹ [graund] *nu* soil, earth 土壤, 土地: *The ground here is fertile.* 這裏土壤肥沃. **2** *nc / u* surface (esp. of the earth) 地面(尤指地球表面): *above / below ground* 在地上(或在世)/在地下(或死了). *I fell to the ground.* 我倒在地上. *They are lying on the ground.* 他們躺在地上. **3** *nc* piece of land for a special purpose 場地: *a cricket / football / hockey ground* 板球場/足球場/曲棍球場. **4** (in *pl*) piece of land round a house (用於複數) 房屋四週的空地, 庭園: *The castle stands in lovely grounds.* 城堡四週有宜人的庭園. **5** *nc / u* (usu. *pl*) reason, excuse (通常用複數) 理由, 藉口: *You have no ground(s) for believing that.* 你沒有理由相信那種説法. *He has good ground(s) for doing it.* 他完全有理由那樣做. *He was excused on the ground(s) of his illness* i.e. because of illness. 他因病而受到原諒. '**ground 'floor** see 見 **floor**. '**groundnut** kind of nut that grows under the ground 落花生. (Also 亦作 **peanut**). '**groundwork** work done before the main work or event 準備工作: *Producing a play needs a lot of groundwork.* 上演一個劇本要做大量的準備工作.

ground² [graund] *vt / i* **1** touch the ground 擱淺, 登灘; 登陸: *The boat* *grounded on the rocks*. 船觸礁了. **2** place, keep on the ground 把…放在地上; 使…停在地面: *The boat was grounded in the storm*. 船在暴風雨中被擱到灘上. *They grounded the aircraft because it had engine trouble*. 他們不讓這架飛機起飛, 因爲它的發動機出了毛病. **3** teach thoroughly (esp. the first stages of a subject) 給…以全面的基礎訓練: *Primary school teachers must ground their pupils in correct English*. 小學教師要給學生進行正確英語的全面基礎訓練. **grounding** *nu* (in sense 3): *a good grounding in English* (義 3): 良好的英語基礎訓練.

ground³ [graund] past of **grind**. grind 的過去式和過去分詞.

group [gruːp] *nc* persons / things which are together 羣; 批; 組: *a group of people / buildings / trees* 一羣人/一組建築物/樹叢. *They stood in groups*. 他們三五成羣地站着. Also 亦作 *vt / i*: *He grouped the children according to ability*. 他按能力給孩子們分組.

grove [grouv] *nc* group of trees (smaller than a wood) 樹叢, 小樹林.

grovel ['grɔvl] *vi* lie or crawl face downwards because of fear, or to show respect; show shame or fear 匍匐; 趴; 五體投地; 卑躬屈節: *The slaves grovelled before their master*. 奴隸們匍匐在主人面前.

grow [grou] *vt / i* **1** increase in size, develop 生長, 長大; 發育: *Very little grows in the desert*. 沙漠裏幾乎寸草不生. *He has grown very tall*. 他已長得很高了. *The seed grew into a tree*. 種子長成了樹木. *The farmers here grow corn*. 這裏的農民種植玉米. **2** become something slowly 漸漸變得: *It is growing cold*. 天氣逐漸轉冷. *The light grew fainter*. 燈光慢慢暗淡. *I am* *growing to hate him*. 我逐漸恨起他來了. *past tense* 過去式 **grew** [gruː]. *past part* 過去分詞 **grown. grower** *nc* person who grows things 種植者: *fruit grower* 種植果樹的人. **grow up** develop in full become an adult 成熟, 長成; 成年: *When you grow up you will earn your own living*. 你長大後將獨力謀生. **'grown-'up** *adj*: *a grown-up daughter* 成年的女兒. Also 亦作 *nc*: *This meeting is for grown-ups only*. 這次會議只請成人參加.

growl [graul] *vt / i* make a low, angry-sound 嗥叫, 咆哮: *The dog growled at the stranger*. 狗向生人吠叫. *He growled a reply*. 他咆哮着回答.

grown [groun] past part of **grow**. grow 的過去分詞.

growth [grouθ] **1** *nu* growing, development, increase 成長; 發展; 增加: *He has not yet reached full growth*. 他還沒有充分發育成熟. *the growth of democracy* 民主的發展. **2** *nc* something which has already grown 生長物: *a growth of hair / bushes / trees etc*. 長出來的毛/灌木叢, 矮樹叢/樹叢等. **3** *nc* something which has grown in the body because of disease (e.g. cancer) 瘤; 癌: *He has a growth in the stomach*. 他胃裏長了腫瘤.

grub¹ [grʌb] *nc* larva of an insect 蠐螬, 蛆.

grub² [grʌb] *nu* food (*informal*) 食物 (非正式).

grubby ['grʌbi] *adj* dirty 骯髒的: *grubby hands* 髒手.

grudge [grʌdʒ] *vt* be unwilling to give or allow 吝惜, 不願給: *I do not grudge him anything*. i.e. I am willing to give him anything. 對他我並不吝惜. 即: 我甚麼都願意給他. *He grudges paying his taxes*. 他不願意納稅. Also 亦作 *nc* feeling of dislike. 怨恨, 憎惡.

He bears me a grudge / He bears a grudge against me. 他對我懷恨在心.
grudging *adj.*

gruelling ['gruəliŋ] *adj* strenuous; severe 緊張的; 激烈的; 使極度疲勞的: *a gruelling walk* 讓人走得精疲力竭的一段路.

gruesome ['gru:səm] *adj* disgusting to see, horrible 可憎的; 可怕的: *The injured man, with blood all over his face, was a gruesome sight.* 受傷的人滿臉是血, 看來十分可怕.

gruff [grʌf] *adj* rough in manner or voice 粗暴的, 生硬的; 聲音粗啞的.

grumble ['grʌmbl] *vi* complain (usu. in a low, unhappy voice) 低聲抱怨; 嘟囔着發牢騷: *These lazy workmen grumble at / about / over everything* 這些懶惰的工人對甚麼事情都要抱怨. Also 亦作 *nc* **grumbler** *nc.*

grumpy ['grʌmpi] *adj* bad-tempered, sulky 脾氣壞的; 生氣的. **grumpily** *adv* (both *informal*) (均爲非正式).

grunt [grʌnt] *vi* make a short, deep noise like a pig (豬等) 發出咕嚕聲. Also 亦作 *nc.*

guarantee¹ [gærən'ti:] *nc* **1** formal promise (often in writing) that something will be done (正式的、常指書面的) 保證: *I give my guarantee that he will be here tomorrow.* 我向你保證他明天一定會來這裏. *I offer my house as a guarantee* i.e. I lose my house if something is not done. 我以房產作抵押擔保. 即: 要是某事沒有辦好, 我就輸了房子. **2** statement (often in writing) that something is genuine or will work properly etc. 保證書; 合格證: *The radio has / carries a twelve months' guarantee.* i.e. if it does not work properly during that time it will be repaired or replaced without cost. 這台收音機有十二個月的保用期. 即:

在此期間內損壞可免費修理或更換.

guarantee² [gærən'ti:] *vt* give a guarantee 保證, 擔保: *I guarantee that he will pay the money.* 我保證他會付這筆錢. *We guarantee to be here tomorrow.* 我們保證明天來這裏. *The radio is guaranteed for twelve months.* 這台收音機保用十二個月. *Nobody can guarantee good weather.* 誰也不敢擔保會有好天氣.

guard¹ [gɑ:d] *vt / i* take care of, watch over, protect 照顧; 看守, 守衛; 保護: *A mother always guards her children.* 母親總是照顧着她的孩子們. *They guarded the bridge.* 他們守衛着這座橋. **guarded** *adj* careful, cautious 小心的; 謹慎的: *a guarded statement* 措詞謹慎的聲明. *He was very guarded in his answers.* 他回答得非常小心.

guard² [gɑ:d] **1** watchfulness; readiness to meet danger, attack etc. 警惕, 警戒; 防範; 守衛: *The soldiers keep guard / are on guard round the President's house.* 士兵們在總統住宅的周圍警戒. **2** *nc* person(s) who guard(s) 衛兵, 哨兵: *The officer inspected the guard.* 軍官視察衛隊. *The guards stopped me at the gate.* 衛兵在門口擋住了我. **3** *nc* (*Brit*) person in charge of a train (*US* 美 **conductor**) (英) 列車員. **fireguard** see 見 **fire².** '**mudguard** see 見 **mud. be on one's guard** be ready to meet an attack, danger etc. 守衛; 防範; 警惕. (*opp* 反義語 **off one's guard**).

guardian ['gɑ:diən] *nc* person with the duty of looking after someone who cannot look after himself (e.g. young children) (年幼兒童等的) 保護人, 監護人: *When your father died, I became their guardian.* 他們的父親去世後, 我成爲他們的監護人.

guerilla, guerrilla [gə'rilə] *nc* fighter

who wages war in small groups which do not belong to the regular army 游擊隊員. Also 亦作 *adj: guerilla war* i.e. kind of war waged by guerillas 游擊戰, 即: 游擊隊員們進行的戰爭.

guess¹ [ges] *vt / i* **1** estimate, judge, state something without being sure 臆測, 猜度: *Not knowing which way to go, I had to guess.* 我不知道該走哪條路, 只得猜測. *Can you guess its weight / how much it weighs?* 你猜得出它的重量/它有多重嗎? **2** (mainly US) suppose (主要用於美) 推想, 猜想, 認爲: *I guess he's right.* 我想他是對的.

guess² [ges] *nc* opinion one cannot be sure about, rough estimate 猜測, 推測; 粗略的估計: *I'll have to make a guess.* 我得猜猜看. *At a guess there are a hundred people here.* 估計有一百人在這裏. **'guesswork** result from guessing 猜測, 推測, 臆測: *Their answer is just guesswork.* 他們的回答只是猜測而已.

guest [gest] *nc* **1** person who visits or is invited to one's house 客人: *We usually have guests at the weekend.* 週末我們通常有客. **2** person who stays at a boarding house or hotel 旅客; 房客: *This hotel has rooms for fifty guests.* 這家旅店的客房可接待五十名客人. **'guest-house** boarding house; house where guests pay for their rooms and food (供膳的) 寄宿處; 賓館.

guffaw [gʌˈfɔː] *nc* loud laugh 哄笑, 大笑. Also 亦作 *vi.*

guide [gaid] *nc* **1** person who shows the way and / or place of interest 嚮導, 導遊: *You will need a guide if you wish to climb that mountain.* 你要爬那座山得有一位嚮導. *The guide showed them round the church.* 導遊員領他們參觀了教堂. **2** thing that shows the way, give instructions or information 指南, 指導: *a good guide to British flowers* i.e. a book giving information about them. 英國花卉指南, 即: 一本提供關於英國花卉信息的書; *a short guide to sailing* 航海簡覽. **3** member of the (Girl) Guides. see below 見下文. Also 亦作 *vt* act as guide, lead 導遊; 引導: *He will guide you to the top of the mountain.* 他將帶你登上山頂. *They will be guided by what you say.* 他們將以你說的話作爲指導方針.

guidance *nu* guiding or being guided 指引; 指導; 引導: *He wrote the report under the guidance of the manager.* 他在經理的指導下寫出報告. **the Girl Guides** organization for girls similar to the Boy Scouts 女童子軍. **'guide-book** book telling tourists about travelling and places of interest 旅行指南. **guided missile** military rocket which can be controlled from the ground or from a ship or aircraft 導彈.

guild [gild] *nc* group of persons (e.g. tradesmen) with same interests or work who join together to help one another 行會; 同業公會: *There were many guilds in London during the Middle Ages.* 中世紀時倫敦有不少行會.

guile [gail] *nu* cunning, trickery 狡詐; 詭計. **guileless** *adj* honest, innocent 正直的; 坦率無邪的.

guillotine [ˈgiləti:n] *nc* machine for beheading a person by a heavy knife which slides down grooves from above 斷頭台. Also 亦作 *vt.*

guilt [gilt] *nu* state of having done wrong; being responsible for having done wrong 有罪; 對罪行有責任. **guilty** *adj* **1** having done wrong 有罪

的: *I am not guilty of this crime.* 我没有犯这罪罪. *Do you plead guilty to stealing the bicycle?* 你對於被指控偷了這輛自行車服罪嗎? **2** showing, feeling guilt 内疚的, 愧疚的: *a guilty conscience* 良心的不安, 問心有愧. *comparative* 比較級 **guiltier.** *superlative* 最高級 **guiltiest.**

guinea-pig ['ginipig] *nc* **1** kind of small rodent with no tail, often used in experiments 豚鼠; 天竺鼠. **2** person who is used in this way 供作實驗用的人: *We are the guinea-pigs for his new ideas about teaching science.* 我們是他的關於教學科學新想法的試驗品.

guise [gaiz] *nc / u* appearance (esp. an assumed one) 外貌, 偽裝: *They got into the school in the guise of inspectors.* 他們假裝成視察員進了學校.

guitar [gi'ta:*] *nc* type of musical instrument with six strings played by running the fingers over the strings 吉他, 六弦琴.

gulf [gʌlf] *nc* **1** large bay going far inland 海灣. **2** deep, wide hole in the ground 深淵, 深坑.

gull [gʌl] *nc* see 見 **seagull.**

gullet ['gʌlit] *nc* tube by which food passes the mouth to the stomach 食道; 嚥喉: *The dog had something stuck in its gullet.* 那隻狗的咽喉被甚麼東西梗住了.

gullible ['gʌlibl] *adj* easily cheated 易受騙的.

gully ['gʌli] *nc* **1** small, narrow valley 溪谷. **2** deep, narrow ditch caused by rainwater running down a slope (雨水沖鑿而成的)溝渠.

gulp [gʌlp] *vt / i* **1** swallow quickly 狼吞虎嚥: *They gulped (down) their food.* 他們把食物猛吞下去. **2** choke 喘不過氣來, 哽塞: *He was gulping with ex-*

citement. 他因激動而哽塞. Also 亦作 *nc*: *He drank the glass of water in one gulp / at a gulp.* 他把那杯水一飲而盡.

gum¹ [gʌm] *nc* (usu. *pl*) flesh in which the teeth are set (通常用複數)齒齦. **'gumboil** abscess of the gums 齒齦膿腫.

gum² [gʌm] **1** *nu* thick liquid from certain trees 樹膠; 樹脂. **2** *nu* similar substance, used for sticking papers etc together 黏膠, 膠水. **3** *nc* sweets which are like gum 橡皮糖, 口香糖: *chewing gum* 口香糖. **4** *nc* kind of tree, eucalyptus 桉樹. (Also 亦作 **gum tree**). **5** *nu* rubber 橡膠; *gumboots* i.e. rubber boots reaching to the knees 高統膠靴, 即: 齊膝高的膠靴. Also 亦作 *vt* stick together with gum 用樹膠黏合.

gun [gʌn] *nc* weapon with a metal tube from which objects such as bullets are thrown by the force of an explosion (e.g. revolver, pistol, rifle, machine gun, cannon) 砲, 槍(如左輪手槍、手槍、步槍、機槍、大砲等). **gunner** *nc* **1** (in the army) private in an artillery regiment or *(informal)* person of any rank in an artillery regiment (英國陸軍的)砲手或(非正式)砲兵部隊成員. **2** (in the navy) warrant officer in charge of guns (英國海軍的)砲長. **'gunman** criminal with a gun 持槍歹徒, 槍手. **'gunpowder** explosive powder 黑色火藥, 有烟火藥. **'gunshot** range of a gun 槍砲的射程: *Keep out of / within gunshot.* 使在槍砲射程之外/内.

gurgle ['gə:gl] *nc* bubbling noise (流水的)潺潺聲, 汩汩聲. Also 亦作 *vi*.

gush [gʌʃ] *vi* **1** flow out suddenly and in great quantity 湧出, 噴出: *The water gushed from the broken pot.* 水從破鍋中流出. **2** talk very enthusiastically about 滔滔不絕地說: *They were gushing over the new play.* 他們滔滔不絕地談論着新劇本. Also 亦作 *nc.*

gusset ['gʌsit] *nc* piece of cloth put in a coat, dress etc to make it wider or stronger. (加固或撐大衣物用的)三角形布片.

gust [gʌst] *nc* **1** sudden, short increase of wind, rain, smoke etc. 陣風; 陣雨; 一股濃烟: *We were walking along peacefully when a gust of wind blew our hats off.* 我們正在悠閒地散步, 突然一陣大風吹走了我們的帽子. **2** sudden increase of feeling (感情的)迸發.

gusto ['gʌstou] *nu* enjoyment, zest 興味; 熱忱.

gut[1] [gʌt] **1** *nc* (in *pl*) bowels (用於複數)腸子: *I have a pain in my guts. (informal)* 我肚子痛. (非正式). **2** *nc* (in *pl*) courage (用於複數)勇氣: *You haven't the guts to do it. (informal)* 你沒有做這事的膽量. (非正式).

gut[2] [gʌt] *vt* **1** remove the inside organs of a fish 取出魚的內臟. **2** destroy the contents of a building 損毀房屋的內部設備: *The factory was gutted by fire.* 工廠被大火焚燒後徒剩四壁. *past* 過去式和過去分詞 **gutted.**

gutter ['gʌtə*] *nc* **1** channel on the roof of a building or at the side of a road to carry away rainwater (屋簷下的)簷槽; (路邊的)排水溝. **2** dirtiest part of a street 貧民窟.

guy[1] [gai] *nc* rope to keep something in place (e.g. a tent) (帳篷等的)牽索. (Also 亦作 **guy-rope**).

guy[2] [gai] *nc* **1** dummy of Guy Fawkes burned on 5 November. 十一月五日焚燒的蓋伊·福克斯模擬像. **2** *(mainly US)* man. *(informal* in sense **2)** (主要用於美)像伙, 人(義 2 爲非正式).

guzzle ['gʌzl] *vt / i* eat or drink greedily 貪婪地吃喝, 大吃大喝.

gym [dʒim] *nc / u* informal short form of **gymnasium, gymnastics** 體育館, 體操(gymnasium, gymnastics 的非正式縮寫形式).

gymnasium [dʒim'neiziəm] *nc* building or large room equipped for physical exercise 體育館, 健身房. **gymnast** ['dʒimnæst] *nc* expert in gymnastics 體操家, 體育家. **gymnastic** [dʒim'næstik] *adj* **gymnastics** [dʒim'næstiks] *npl* physical exercises (usu. difficult ones) 體操; 健身操.

gypsy ['dʒipsi] *nc* see 見 **gipsy.**

gyrate [dʒai'reit] *vi* move in a circle or spiral 旋轉, 迴旋.

H,h

haberdasher ['hæbədæʃə*] *nc* **1** (*Brit*) person who sells buttons, ribbons, thread etc for clothes and hats (英)縫紉用品商. **2** (*US*) dealer in men's shirts, ties etc. (美)男子服飾用品商. **haberdashery** [hæbə'dæʃəri] **1** *nc* haberdasher's shop (now often a department in a store) 男子服飾用品店(或櫃台); 縫紉用品店(或櫃台). **2** *nu* the articles which he sells 男子服飾用品; 縫紉用品.

habit ['hæbit] *nc* **1** something that is done so often that it becomes a fixed practice 習慣: *It is a good habit to eat slowly* 慢慢進食是一種好習慣. *He has a habit of arriving early.* 他有早到的習慣. **2** woman's dress with skirt worn by nuns (修女所穿的)法服. **3** woman's dress for riding sidesaddle on a horse 婦女的騎裝.

habitable ['hæbitəbl] *adj* able to be lived in for people: *Although the house is very old, it is quite habitable.* 這屋子雖然很舊, 還可以住人. (*opp* 反義詞 **uninhabitable**).

habitat ['hæbitæt] *nc* natural home or surroundings of animals and plants (動物的)棲息地; (植物的)産地: *The natural habitat of the tiger is Asia, not Africa.* 老虎的自然棲息地在亞洲, 而不是在非洲.

habitation [hæbi'teiʃən] **1** *nu* act of living in a place 居住: *The North Pole is not suitable for human habitation.* 北極不適於人類居住. **2** *nc* house; home (*o.f.* in sense **2**) 住宅; 家 (義 2 爲舊式).

habitual [hə'bitjuəl] *adj* caused by

habit; usual 習慣的; 慣常的: *They are habitual visitors to our house.* 他們是我家的常客. **habitually** *adv*.

hack [hæk] *vt / i* cut roughly or carelessly 亂劈, 亂砍: *He hacked the branch off the tree.* 他從樹上把樹枝砍下來. *They are hacking the meat to pieces* 他們在把肉剁碎. *Don't hack at it.* 別砍它. **'hacksaw** saw for cutting metal 鋼鋸.

hackneyed ['hæknid] *adj* used too often (*usu.* what is said or written) 陳詞濫調的: *The essay is spoilt by having too many hackneyed phrases.* 陳腐的語句太多, 把這篇文章搞糟了.

had [hæd] past of **have.** have 的過去式和過去分詞.

haddock ['hædək] *nc* type of sea fish, found in the North Atlantic and used for food 黑線鱈(産於北大西洋的食用魚). *pl* 複數 **haddock** or **haddocks**.

haemo- ['hi:mou] *prefix* 見 **hemo-**.

haemoglobin [,hi:mou'gloubin] (US 美 hemoglobin) *nu* oxygencarrying substance in red blood cells 血紅蛋白.

haggard ['hægəd] *adj* looking tired or worried 顯得疲倦的; 焦慮的: *His face was haggard from lack of sleep.* 因爲沒有睡好, 他面容憔悴.

haggle ['hægl] *vi* argue about the price of something 討價還價: *In many countries you have to haggle before you buy anything.* 在許多國家裏買東西之前都得討價還價.

hail¹ [heil] *nc / u* rain frozen into small, hard drops 冰雹. **'hailstone** small, hard piece of hail 冰雹. **'hailstorm** storm during which hail falls 雹暴.

hail² [heil] *vt / i* shout to welcome or to call attention 表示歡迎或引人注意的喊聲: *They hailed him (as) a hero.* 他們向他歡呼, 稱他是英雄. *We hailed a passing boat.* 我們向一艘駛過的船打 (信號) 招呼.

hair [hɛə*] 1 *nu* threadlike growth on the skin of animals and humans (with humans usu. the growth on the head) 頭髮; 毛; 獸毛: *The bodies of most animals are covered with hair;* 大多數動物都長着一身毛; *brush / comb / cut one's hair* i.e. the hair on one's head 刷 / 梳 / 剪頭髮. 2 *nc* separate thread of hair (一根) 毛; (一根) 頭髮; *not a hair out of place* i.e. very neatly brushed 頭髮紋絲不亂, 即: 梳得整齊: *There are hairs on your jacket.* 你的短上衣上有幾根頭髮. **hairy** *adj* covered with hair 長毛的, 多毛的. **'hairbreadth, hair's breadth** *nu* thickness of one's hair 一髮之差, 極微小的距離: *The car missed me by a hair's breadth.* 那輛汽車險些兒沒撞上我. Also 亦作 *adj. Note* 說明: the *pl* form of *hairs* is only used to describe a very small number of separate threads of hair. The *sing* form *hair* is always used to describe the whole growth of hair on the human head (e.g. *What lovely hair you have. Your hair has grown very long*) 複數形式 hairs 指少數幾根毛; 單數形式 hair 總是指全部頭髮 (例如: What lovely hair you have. 您的頭髮多好看. Your hair has grown very long. 你的頭髮很長了.) **'hairbrush** brush for the hair 髮刷. **'haircut** cutting of the hair 剪髮, 理髮: *I must get a haircut.* 我得理髮了. **'hairdresser** person who cuts and attends to hair (尤指女) 理髮師. **'hairpin** 1 pin used by a woman to keep up her hair 髮夾, 髮卡; 簪. 2

bend in a road so sharp that the road turns almost in the opposite direction (道路的) 急轉彎. (Also 亦作 **hairpin bend**).

half [hɑːf] 1 *nc / adj* exactly one of two equal parts into which something can be divided 半, 一半; 一半的: *(The) half of ten is five.* 十的一半是五. *The money was divided into two halves;* 錢已被分成兩半; *three and a half hours or three hours and a half* 三個半小時; *half a minute / mile / dozen / pound etc.* 半分鐘 / 半英里 / 半打 / 半磅等; *a half-minute / -mile / -dozen / -pound etc.* 半分鐘 / 半英里 / 半打 / 半磅等. 2 *nc / determiner* approximately one of two parts 約一半: *half (of) my time* 我的一半時間; *half (of) my friends* 我的半數朋友. Also 亦作 *adv* partly; incompletely 部份地; 不完全地; *half-cooked meat* 半生不熟的肉; *half asleep* 半睡半醒; *half open* 半開. *pl* 複數 **halves** [hɑːvz]. **halve** [hɑːv] *vt* 1 divide into two equal parts 二等分, 平分. 2 make less by half 減半: *The cost of food has been halved.* 食物的費用已減少一半. **'half-back** (football, hockey etc.) player between forwards and backs (足球, 曲棍球等的) 中衛: *centre-half; right-half, left-half* i.e. half-back who plays in the centre; on the right; on the left 中堅; 右衛; 左衛. **'half-breed** person whose father and mother are of different races. (rather *impolite*) 混血兒 (頗爲不禮貌). **'half-hearted** *adj* without interest or effort 不感興趣的; 不作努力的; 半心半意的: *a half-hearted cheer* 不熱心的喝彩. at **half-'price** at half of the price 以半價: *Students can get in (at) half-price.* 學生可半價入場. **'half-'time** 1 half of the usual working time 通常工作時間的一半: *Some of the workers are on*

half-time because business is bad. 由
於生意清淡,有些工人只得做半工支半
薪. **2** resting time between two parts
of a game 半場(球賽上下半場間的休
息 時間): *The football players
changed round at half-time.* 足球隊員
們在半場時交換場地. '**half 'way** *adj /
adv* **1** equally distant from two places
半路的(地); 中途的(地): *The town is
halfway between the hill and the river.* 該鎮在小山和河流之間的中點. *We
met halfway.* 我們在半途相遇. **2** incomplete 不徹底的(地); 部份的(地):
This solution is only a halfway one.
這種解決方案只是折衷辦法.

halibut ['hælɪbət] *nc* large type of flat
fish found in the Atlantic and used as
food 大比目魚(產於大西洋的食用魚).
pl 複數 **halibut.**

hall [hɔːl] *nc* **1** large room 大廳: *assembly hall* 會議廳; *dining hall* 膳廳; *lecture hall* 演講廳. **2** large building for
meetings, business, amusement etc;
residential building at a university 會
議,營業,遊樂等大樓; 大學裏的宿舍大
樓: *town hall* 鎮公所,市政廳; *dance
hall* 舞廳; *concert hall* 音樂廳. **3**
room at the entrance to a house from
which one enters other rooms 門廳,
走廊. '**hallmark** set of marks put on
gold or silver to guarantee the standard of purity of the metal (金銀的純
度)檢驗印記,質量證明.

hallelujah [hælɪ'luːjə] *interj* loud praise
to God 哈利路亞(讚美上帝語). Also
亦作 *nc.*

hallo [hʌ'lou] *nu / interj* see 見 **hello.**

hallucination [həluːsɪ'neɪʃən] *nc* something which is imagined, which is not
really there 幻覺: *Drugs can cause
hallucinations.* 毒品可引起幻覺.

halo ['heɪlou] *nc* ring of light round
something (e.g. the sun or moon, or

the circle or ray painted in pictures
round the heads of holy persons) (日
月之)暈輪;(畫像上聖人頭部週圍之)光
環. *pl* 複數 **halos** or **haloes.**

halt [hɔːlt] *vt / i* stop, cause to stop, for
a time (使)停止;(使)暫停: *The train
halted at the station.* 火車在車站停了
下來. *He halted the children at the
street corner.* 他讓孩子們在街角停了
下來. Also 亦作 *nc* **1** act of halting 立
定,停止行進. *The soldiers came to a
halt* i.e. they halted. 兵士們停止前進.
2 place to halt at 暫停處.

halter ['hɔːltə*] *nc* rope or strap put
round the head of a horse, camel etc
to hold or lead it (馬,駱駝等的)籠頭,
繮繩.

halve [hɑːv] *vt* see 見 **half.**

ham [hæm] *nu* salted and smoked or
dried meat made from the upper part
of a pig's leg 火腿: *I like ham and
eggs for breakfast.* 我喜歡吃火腿和鷄
蛋當早餐.

hamburger ['hæmbəːɡə*] *nc* **1** small,
round piece of hot minced meat 牛肉
餅. **2** sandwich made with meat like
this 漢堡包.

hamlet ['hæmlət] *nc* small village 小村.

hammer ['hæmə*] *nc* tool with a handle
and a heavy end for hitting things
(e.g. nails) 錘;鐵錘. Also 亦作 *vt / i*
hit with a hammer 錘打: *He hammered the nails into the wall.* 他把釘
子釘進牆壁. *He hammered in the
nails.* 他釘釘子.

hammock ['hæmək] *nc* bed made of
cloth and ropes and hung between
two posts 吊床.

hamper¹ ['hæmpə*] *vt* hinder; prevent
easy movement 阻礙; 妨礙: *The
army's advance was hampered by
bad weather.* 惡劣的天氣使軍隊的前
進受到阻礙.

hamper² ['hæmpə*] *nc* large basket with a lid, used for carrying food, wine, laundry etc. (攜帶食物、酒、要洗的衣物等的)有蓋提籃.

hand¹ [hænd] *nc* **1** the end of arm below the wrist 手: *Each hand has five fingers.* 一隻手有五個指頭. **2** pointer on the face of clock or other instrument (鐘錶等的)指針: *the hour / minute hand* 時針/分針. *The two hands on my watch are broken.* 我的手錶的兩根指針都斷了. **3** worker; sailor 工人；水手: *This factory employs a thousand hands;* 這工廠雇用一千名工人；*all hands on deck* i.e. order to sailors to come on deck; any order to start work 全體水手甲板集合；各就各位, 開始幹活. **4** something done by using one's hands; skill 手藝；技巧: *He writes a good hand* i.e. clearly. 他寫得一手好字. 即: 字跡清楚. *He is a good hand at painting* i.e. he is skilled in painting. 他是繪畫能手. *I am an old hand at teaching* i.e. I have long experience. *(informal)* 我是教書老手. 即: 我有長期的經驗. (非正式). **5** (usu. *pl*) possession; responsibility (通常用複數)掌握；責任: *The stolen car is now in the hands of the police.* 被盜的汽車現在在警方手中. *The book changed hands many times.* 這本書曾經多次易手. *Your success is in your own hands* i.e. you are responsible for your own success. 你的成功在你自己的掌握之中. 即: 你對你自己的成功負有責任. **6** applause 鼓掌: *Let's give him a big hand* i.e. clap hands loudly. *(informal in sense 6)* 讓我們為他熱烈鼓掌. (義 6 爲非正式). **'handbag** small bag carried by a woman 女用手提包. **handball** team ball game played with the hands 手球 (遊戲). **'handbook** book of information 手册, 便覽, 指南.

'handcuff *nc* one of the rings joined by a short chain to secure the hands of a prisoner 手銬. Also 亦作 *vt* put handcuffs on 給…上手銬: *The policeman handcuffed the thief.* 警察給小偷上了手銬. **'handful 1** amount that can be held in one hand 一把: *a handful of rice* 一把米. **2** small number 少數: *a handful of men* 少數人. **3** somebody / something difficult to manage 難控制的人/事: *This class of boys is quite a handful.* *(informal in sense 3)* 這個班的男孩真難管教. (義 3 爲非正式). **'handshake** act of shaking hands 握手. **'handstand** balancing on one's hands with one's feet above one's head 倒立；竪蜻蜓: *It is difficult to read his handwriting.* 他的筆跡難認. **at hand** near 在附近；即將到來: *Christmas is at hand.* 聖誕節快到了. *The post office is close at hand.* 郵局離這裏不遠. **by hand 1** not made by machine 用手；手工製做的: *My shoes were made by hand;* 我的鞋是手工做的；*handmade shoes* 手工做的鞋. **2** personally 親自地: *The letter came to me by hand* i.e. it was brought by somebody, not sent through the post. 這信是由專人送來給我的. 即: 由人送來, 不由郵寄. **hand-in-hand** holding hands 手牽手的(地): *The boy and girl arrived hand-in-hand.* 那男孩和女孩手牽手地來到. **hand-to-'hand** *adv* closely; near to one another (usu. when fighting) 逼近地；互相接近地(通常指打仗時): *They threw down their rifles and fought hand-to-hand with knives.* 他們丟掉了步槍, 進行白刃戰. Also 亦作 *adj*: *hand-to-hand fighting* 肉搏戰；白刃戰. **hands off** *interj* do not touch or take 請勿動手. **hands up** *interj* raise the hands above head as a sign of surrender 舉起手來(表示投降). **in hand 1** being dealt with (工作等)在進行中: *The building of the new bridge is now in hand.* 建新橋的工作正在進行. **2** under control 掌握住; 控制住: *The students should be taken in hand* i.e. should be brought under control. 應當把學生管好. 即: 應當把學生控制住. **out of hand** not under control 無法控制: *The angry crowd got out of hand* 人羣怒不可遏. **'second'hand** *adj* **1** indirect, through somebody else 間接的; 第二手的: *His news is secondhand* i.e. he heard it from somebody else. 他的消息是間接知到的. 即: 是從別人那裏聽來的. **2** already used by somebody 別人用過的: *secondhand books* 舊書; *secondhand clothes* 舊衣服.

hand² [hænd] *vt* pass to somebody 傳遞給某人: *I handed him his hat / I handed his hat to him.* 我把帽子遞給他. **hand something down 1** pass to somebody from above (從高處)把東西往下遞給某人: *Please hand me down my books from the top shelf.* 請把我的書從最上面一層書架遞給我. **2** pass to succeeding generations 傳給後代: *Our fathers handed down these customs to us.* 祖先把這些風俗習慣傳給我們. **hand something on** pass to somebody, often to several persons one after the other 依次傳遞某物: *They will hand on the photograph to those who have not seen it.* 他們會把這張照片傳給還沒有見到它的人. **hand something out** distribute 分發: *Please hand out the history books.* 請分發這些歷史書.

handicap² [ˈhændikæp] *nc* **1** something

that hinders or weakens 障礙; 使變弱的東西: *Bad health is a great handicap.* 身體不好是一大障礙. **2** (sport) something which reduces the advantage of a good competitor so that the competition is more equal for all competitors (運動)爲平衡得勝機會而加給強者的障礙或不利條件: *Your handicap in the mile race is ten yards.* 你在一英里賽跑中要多跑十碼. *What is your handicap in golf?* 打高爾夫球時你要讓掉多少分?Also 亦作 *vt* hinder or weaken 妨礙; 削弱: *His lack of English handicaps him.* 他因不懂英語而十分不便. *past* 過去式和過去分詞 **handicapped**. Also 亦作 *adj*: *handicapped children* i.e. children with some mental or physical disability 殘廢兒童. 即: 智力不足或身體有缺陷的兒童.

handicraft [ˈhændikrɑːft] *nc* **1** product of the skill of the hands 手工藝品. **2** skill of producing these 手工藝, 手工: *The chief handicrafts of this country are pottery and wood carving.* 該國的主要手工藝品是陶器和木雕.

handkerchief [ˈhæŋkətʃif] *nc* square piece of cloth, carried in the pocket or a handbag, for wiping the face or nose 手帕.

handle¹ [ˈhændl] *nc* part of something by which it is held 柄, 把手: *the handle of a cup / door / jug / knife etc.* 杯子把兒/門把手/水罐把兒/刀柄等; also 亦作 *cup handle, door handle etc.* 杯子把手, 門把手等. **'handlebars** bar on the front of a bicycle for steering it 自行車的車把.

handle² [ˈhændl] *vt* **1** touch; hold in the hands 觸; 摸; 拿; 弄: *You should not handle broken glass.* 不要去玩弄碎玻璃. **2** deal with; control 對付; 控制, 統轄: *I'll handle this matter.* 我來處理這件事. *The manager knows how to* *handle his staff.* 經理知道怎樣指揮職員.

handsome ['hænsəm] *adj* **1** good-looking 漂亮的; 俊俏的, 清秀的. **2** generous 慷慨的, 大方的: *handsome gifts* 大方的禮物.

handy ['hændi] *adj* **1** skilful with the hands 手巧的: *He is handy at tying knots.* 他善於繫繩結. **2** nearby; ready for use 手邊的; 近便的: *Is there a postbox handy?* 附近有郵筒嗎? *Have you a hammer handy?* 你手頭有鐵錘嗎? *This house is handy for the shops.* 這座房子離商店不遠. **'handyman** man skilful with his hands at many kinds of work 手巧能幹雜活的人.

hang [hæŋ] *vt / i* **1** be held or suspended from above (usu. with the bottom end down 通常底朝下): *Her hair hangs down.* 她的頭髮披散着. *His coat is hanging (on a nail) behind the door.* 他的外套掛在門後的(釘子上). *Your shirt is hanging out* i.e. outside your trousers. 你的襯衫下擺露在外邊. 即: 沒有塞進褲子裏頭. **2** put up or suspend something with the bottom end down (底朝下) 懸掛: *They hung (up) their coats.* 他們把外套掛好. *My mother is hanging out the washing* i.e. hanging it outside. 我媽媽正在晾衣服. 即: 把洗好的衣服晾在外邊. **3** put somebody to death by dropping him from above with a rope round his neck 絞死, 吊死; *hang a murderer* 絞死殺人犯. past 過去式和過去分詞 **hung** [hʌŋ] (in senses 1 and 2) (用於義 1 和 2). past 過去式和過去分詞 **hanged** (in sense 3) 用於(義 3). **hanger** *nc* something on which things are hung 掛鈎: *clothes hanger* 衣架; *coat hanger* (掛外套的) 衣架. **'hang gliding** gliding through the air while being suspended from a type of large kite. 鳶式滑翔, 懸吊滑翔. **hanging** *nc / u* death by being hanged 絞死, 絞刑: *There are no more hangings in this country.* 該國已廢除絞刑. **'hangman** person who hangs people 執行絞刑者, 劊子手. **'hangover** feeling of illness after drinking too much alcohol the evening before 宿醉(酒醉翌日的不適感). **hang about / around** stay near without doing anything 在附近逗留, 在附近閒蕩: *Don't hang about my office.* (informal) 別在我的辦公室附近閒呆着. (非正式). **hang on 1** keep a firm hold of something; refuse to let go 緊緊握住; 拒不放棄: *Although the branch was breaking, he hung on.* 儘管樹枝快斷了, 他還是抓住不放. **2** not lose hope; wait 堅持; 等待: *Although we are beaten, we must hang on.* 儘管我們失敗了, 我們得堅持下去. *Hang on! I'll call him.* (informal) 別掛斷! 我去叫他. (非正式). **3** listen eagerly to something; 專注地聽地聽: *They hung on every word he said.* 他們全神貫注地聽他講的每一句話. **'hanger-'on** *nc* person who attaches himself to somebody in the hope of gaining some advantage 食客, 奉承者: *Every famous man has his hangers-on.* 任何名人都有為其捧場的人. **hang up** end a telephone call i.e. by hanging up or replacing the receiver. 掛斷電話. 即: 掛上或放回話筒.

hangar ['hæŋə*] *nc* large shed for aircraft 飛機庫.

hank [hæŋk] *nc* bunch of thread or wool 一束, 一捲(紗線或毛線).

hanker ['hæŋkə*] *vi* (with **after**) want very much (與 after 連用) 渴望: *hanker after success* 渴望成功.

hanky ['hæŋki] *nc* short informal form of **handkerchief** 手帕 (handkerchief 的非正式縮畧形式).

haphazard [hæp'hæzəd] *adj / adv* by chance; without design 隨意的(地); 偶然的(地): *a haphazard choice* 隨意的選擇.

happen ['hæpən] *vi* 1 take place 發生: *It happened very suddenly.* 這事發生得很突然. *What happened to you?* 您怎麼啦? 2 be by chance able to, or in the position to 碰巧能够: *I happen to know where he is.* 我恰好知道他在哪裏. *They happened to meet in town.* 他們在城裏巧遇. *As it happens, they are here* i.e. by chance they are here. 碰巧他們在這裏. 即: 他們偶然在這裏. **happening** *nc*.

happy ['hæpi] *adj* 1 glad; pleased; joyful 幸福的; 愉快的; 快樂的: *Everyone was happy at the good news.* 聽到這個好消息, 每個人都很高興. *I shall be happy to come.* 我將樂於前來. 2 lucky 幸運的: *By a happy coincidence we were there at the same time.* 碰巧我們同時到達那裏. *(opp* 反義詞 **unhappy**). **happily** *adv* **happiness** *nu*.

harass ['hærəs] *vt* (usu. *passive*) worry (通常用被動語態) 使煩惱: *You look very harassed.* 你看上去愁容滿面. *They were harassed by debt.* 他們苦於負債.

harbour ['hɑːbəʳ] *(US* 美 **harbor**) *nc* safe place for ships 港口; 港灣: *During the gale the ships stayed in (the) harbour.* 風大時船隻在港內避風. Also 亦作 *vt* give shelter to; protect 庇護; 保護: *It is an offence to harbour escaped prisoners.* 窩藏在逃的犯人是犯法的.

hard¹ [hɑːd] *adj* 1 firm; solid 堅固的; 結實的: *Iron is hard.* 鐵是硬的. *The dry ground was very hard.* 乾旱的土地是硬梆梆的. *(opp* 反義詞 **soft**). 2 difficult to do or understand 難做的; 難懂的: *They find arithmetic hard.* 他們感

到算術很難. *This book is too hard for children.* 這本書對孩子們來說太難了. *He is hard to please.* 他是難以討好的. *He is a hard man to please.* 他是難以討好的人. *(opp* 反義詞 **easy**). 3 unkind; strict 冷酷的; 嚴格的, 嚴厲的: *He is a hard father.* 他是一個嚴厲的父親. *Don't be hard on them.* 不要對他們過份嚴厲. *(opp* 反義詞 **soft**). 4 strenuous; uncomfortable 費勁的; 艱難的: *It was a hard game.* 這場比賽進行得很艱難. *We had a hard winter.* 我們度過了一個嚴寒的冬天. *Life is hard.* 生活是艱難的. *(opp* 反義詞 **easy**). **'hardback** book with hard covers 硬封面的書, 精裝本. *(opp* 反義詞 **paperback**). **hard of hearing** *adj* rather deaf 耳朵有點聾. **'hard-'hearted** *adj* stern; cruel 嚴厲的; 無情的. **hard labour** having to work hard as a punishment 苦役; 苦工: *He was sentenced to two years' hard labour.* 他被判處服兩年苦役. **hard luck, hard lines** bad luck. *(informal)* 不幸 (非正式). **'hardware** metal goods used in the home (e.g. pots, pans, nails) 家用金屬器具 (如平底鍋, 鐵鍋, 釘子等).

hard² [hɑːd] *adv* 1 with force or effort 努力地; 使勁地: *Hit it hard!* 使勁地打! *It is raining hard.* 正下着大雨. *play / try / work hard* (指球員) 賣力地打球/ 拚命試試看/ 努力工作. 2 so that something becomes hard i.e. solid or firm 堅硬地; 堅固地: *The ground was baked hard by the sun.* 地面被太陽曬得堅硬; *boil an egg hard* 把鷄蛋煮老. **'hard'boiled** *adj*: *a hard-boiled egg* 一個煮得太老的鷄蛋. **'hard'working** *adj* working with great energy 努力工作的.

harden ['hɑːdn] *vt / i* become or make hard (使)變硬: *Clay hardens when it* *becomes dry*. 黏土乾後變硬. *They harden clay by putting it in a fire.* 他們用火燒黏土使之變硬.

hardly ['hɑːdli] *adv* scarcely; only just 幾乎不, 簡直不; 才, 僅: *hardly any / anyone / anything / anywhere* 幾乎沒有/簡直沒有甚麼人/簡直沒有甚麼東西/簡直沒有甚麼地方: *He can hardly spell the easiest words.* 他連最容易的詞都幾乎不會拼. *We hardly ever meet.* 我們很少見面. *It is hardly true to say that it was his fault.* 說這是他的過錯大概不對.

hardship ['hɑːdʃip] *nc / u* suffering; discomfort 苦難; 困苦: *the hardships of poverty* 貧困之苦.

hardy ['hɑːdi] *adj* **1** able to bear discomfort; not easily killed 能吃苦耐勞的; 生命力強的; *hardy plants* i.e. plants which can endure all kinds of weather 耐暑耐寒的植物. 即: 能忍受各種氣候的植物. **2** bold 勇敢的.

hare [heə*] *nc* small animal like a rabbit but slightly larger and with stronger legs 野兔.

harem [hɑːriːm] *nc* women's part of a Muslim house; women who live in it (伊斯蘭教國家的)閨房; 伊斯蘭教家庭中的女眷.

hark [hɑːk] (usu. *imperative*) listen (to) (通常用祈使語氣)聽.

harm [hɑːm] *nu* injury; damage 傷害; 損害: *The storm did a lot of harm.* 暴風雨造成了很大的損害. *It will do them no harm to try.* 試一試對他們不會有甚麼害處. *There is no harm in trying* i.e. you might as well. 試一試沒有害處; 你不妨一試. Also 亦作 *vt* cause injury or damage 傷害; 損害: *Doctors say smoking harms our health.* 醫生說吸烟危害健康. **harmful** *adj (opp* 反義詞 **harmless**).

harmonica [huːmɔnikə] *nc* small

musical instrument which is played by sliding it along the lips and blowing 口琴.

harmonize ['hɑːmənaiz] *vt / i* be in harmony (使) 協調: *These colours harmonize beautifully.* 這些色彩調和得很好看. see 見 **harmony.**

harmony ['hɑːməni] **1** *nc* pleasing arrangement of musical sounds, colours, shapes etc. (樂聲、色彩、形狀等的) 調和, 和諧, 協調: *The choir sang in perfect harmony.* 唱詩班唱得非常協調. **2** *nu* agreement, peace 融洽, 一致; 平靜: *There can be no harmony between two selfish people.* 兩個自私的人不可能融洽相處. *They lived in harmony.* 他們和睦相處.

harness ['hɑːnis] *nu* fittings such as a collar and reins to tie a horse to what it pulls or to keep a baby safe 馬具, 挽具; 捆在小孩身上使不跌倒的繩帶. Also 亦作 *vt* put a harness on (a horse) 給(馬)套上馬具; 套車.

harp [hɑːp] *nc* musical instrument with many strings played with the fingers 豎琴. Also 亦作 *vi* play the harp 彈豎琴.

harpoon [hɑːpuːn] *nc* spear to which a long rope is tied (usu. fired from a gun to which whales) (通常指捕鯨的)魚叉; 捕鯨砲.

harrow ['hærou] *nc* heavy metal frame pulled over ploughed ground to break it up more and make it more even 耙. Also 亦作 *vt* break up with a harrow 用耙耙(地). **harrowing** *adj* painful, distressing 悲痛的; 傷心的: *a harrowing experience* 慘痛的經驗.

harry ['hæri] *vt* **1** raid and ravage or rob; attack frequently 蹂躪; 劫掠; 不斷侵襲: *The soldiers harried the enemy out of their country.* 士兵們不斷進行襲擊, 把敵人趕出他們的國境. **2** torment or worry (somebody) frequently 折磨(某人)，騷擾(某人)：*He never pays his debts unless you harry him.* 除非你纏着他，否則他絕不會還債的．

harsh [hɑːʃ] *adj* **1** rough and unpleasant 粗糙的；刺目的，刺耳的：*a harsh voice* 刺耳的嗓音． **2** severe 嚴厲的：*harsh treatment* 苛刻的待遇；*a harsh parent* 嚴厲的父親或母親．
harshly *adv* **harshness** *nu.*

harvest ['hɑːvist] *nc* time when food crops are cut and gathered; food crop gathered 收穫季節；收成，產量：*It rained during the harvest.* 收穫季節下雨． *The harvest this year is a good one.* 今年收成不錯． Also 亦作 *vt* cut and gather food crops 收割，收穫．
harvester *nc* **1** person who harvests 收穫者． **2** machine which harvests 收割機．

hashish ['hæʃiːʃ] *nu* type of intoxicating drug 海吸希(一種麻醉品)．

haste [heist] *nu* hurry 急忙，忽忙．

hasten ['heisn] *vt / i* move, cause to move or act quickly 趕緊，趕快；催促，促進：*They hastened to deny it* i.e. lost no time in denying it. 他們趕忙否認．即：不失時機地否認． *He hastened my departure.* 他催我快離開．

hasty ['heisti] *adj* **1** done or made in a hurry 急速的，倉促的：*a hasty visit* 倉促的訪問；*a hasty breakfast* 忽忙的早餐． **2** easily made angry 急躁的，易怒的：*He is too hasty with people he does not like.* 他對於他不喜歡的人過份急躁． **hastily** *adv.*

hat [hæt] *nc* something worn on the head 帽子．

hatch[1] [hætʃ] *vt / i* **1** come out, cause to come out, of an egg (使)孵出；(蛋)孵化：*Seven chickens hatched this morning.* 今天上午孵出了七隻小鷄． *The hen hatched all the eggs.* 母鷄孵

出了所有的蛋． **2** prepare in secret 圖謀；秘密策劃：*They are hatching a plan to escape.* 他們正密謀逃跑．

hatch[2] [hætʃ] *nc* **1** cover over an opening, or the opening itself, in the deck of a ship through which cargo is put 艙蓋；艙口：*Hatches are closed when a ship is at sea.* 船隻出海時艙口是蓋着的． **2** openings in a wall between two rooms, through which things can be passed 兩個房間之間的傳物窗．

hatchet ['hætʃit] *nc* small axe with a short handle 短柄小斧．

hatching ['hætʃiŋ] *nu* shading by fine parallel lines (製圖)影線；影線法．

hate [heit] *vt* dislike greatly 憎恨；厭惡：*I hate liars.* 我痛恨撒謊的人．*I hate to say it.* 我真不喜歡說這件事． *They hated being laughed at.* 他們討厭受人嘲笑． Also 亦作 *nc / u: his hate of / for injustice* 他對不公正現象的憎恨．
hatred ['heitrid] *nu* **hateful** *adj* causing great dislike 可恨的；討厭的．

haughty ['hɔːti] *adj* thinking greatly of oneself but not of other people; proud 目中無人的；傲慢的：*He is very haughty towards people poorer than himself.* 他非常瞧不起比他窮的人．
haughtily *adv.*

haul [hɔːl] *vt* pull with effort or force 拖曳；用力拉：*They hauled him out of the river.* 他們把他從河裏拉上來． Also 亦作 *nc* amount of something obtained by effort or force 辛苦得來的東西；一次得量：*The thieves made a good haul* 這些小偷一次偷了很多值錢的東西；*a haul of fish* 一大網魚．
haulage *nu* carrying of heavy goods 搬運：*road haulage* i.e. carrying heavy goods by road 公路貨運． '**haulage contractor** person who does haulage by contract (貨物)承運人．(Also 亦作 **haulier**).

haunch [hɔːntʃ] *nc* part of the body between the ribs and thighs; hip (肋骨與大腿之間的)腿臀部; (動物的)腰腿.

haunt [hɔːnt] *vt* **1** (usu. said of ghosts or spirits, which cause fear) visit often (通常指嚇人的鬼魂)常出沒於, 常去: *The spirit of his dead father haunted the village;* 他先父的幽靈常在村裏出現; *a haunted castle* 鬧鬼的古堡. **2** keep coming back to the mind (usu. to cause fear or sadness) 縈繞心頭(常引起恐懼或憂愁): *The years of the war still haunt me;* 那些戰爭的歲月仍然縈繞在我的心頭; *a haunting tune* i.e. one which keeps coming back to the mind 老是縈繞心頭的調子. 即: 難以忘懷的調子. Also 亦作 *nc* place often visited 常去的地方: *This cafe is one of his haunts.* 這咖啡館是他常到的地方.

have [hæv] *vt* **1** *aux* to form the perfect tense 構成完成時: *I have seen him.* 我見到他了. **2** *had* before the subject means *if.* had 在主語之前意為 if: *Had he been here, he would have spoken* i.e. if he had been here ... 要是他在這裏, 他會講話的. **3** own; possess; contain 有; 擁有; 含有: *I have a bicycle.* 我有一輛自行車. *He has no children.* 他沒有孩子. *She has a nice smile.* 她有一種令人愉快的笑容. *This house has many rooms.* 這屋子有許多房間. *Each day has 24 hours.* 一天有二十四小時. Also 亦作 **have got.** *I have / I've got a bicycle etc.* 我有一輛自行車, 等. (For shortened forms *I've etc* see *Note[1]*) (縮略形式 I've 等見說明[1]). **4** take; receive 進行, 從事; 享有: *have breakfast* 用早餐; *have visitors* 有客, 接待客人. Also in this sense with many nouns instead of their verbs 在本義中 have 還可以和許多名詞連用, 以代替其相應的動詞: *He had a walk*

i.e. he walked. 他散了一次步. 即: 他散步了. *Shall we have a look?* i.e. shall we look? 我們看一看好嗎? 即: 我們可以看看嗎? *have a dance / drink / fight / rest / smoke / swim / wash etc.* 跳一個舞/喝一杯/打一次架/休息一下/抽一口煙/游一會兒/洗一洗, 等. **5** experience; suffer from 經歷; 遭受: *We are having a good time.* 我們過得很愉快. *They had some difficulty in doing this.* 他們做這件事時遇到了困難. *I had my money stolen.* 我的錢被偷了. **6** cause to happen or be done 要; 叫; 使: *You must have this work finished by Monday.* 星期一之前你得讓人把這件事做完. *They are having their house painted.* 他們請了人正在粉刷房子. *I would have you know that I am ill.* i.e. I want you to know. 我讓你知道我病了. *They will have it that they are right* i.e. they insist. 他們堅持認爲他們沒有錯. Also in this sense with the meaning of get 在本義中 have 還有 get 的含義: *have the best / worst of something / somebody* 勝過/敗給某事/某人; *have one's own way* 爲所欲爲. **7** be obliged to; must 不得不; 必須: *They had to do it.* 他們必須做這件事. *I have to go now.* 現在我得走了. (For questions and negatives see *Note[2]*) (have 在疑問句和否定句中的用法見說明[2]). Also 亦作 *I have got to go now.* 現在我得走了. **8** cheat 欺騙, 哄騙: *I've been had* i.e. I have been cheated. (*informal* in sense **8**) 我受騙啦. (義 8 爲非正式). *Note[1]* 說明[1]: the shortened forms of *have, has* and *had* are usu. used in conversation. They are 've, 's and 'd. *I've got two pounds. You've finished. He's read it. I'd no idea. It'd fallen.* In questions there is no shortening. *Have I two pounds? Have you finished? etc.* In the same way the negative *not* is shortened to *n't* in conversation and is joined to *have*. *I haven't (got) a penny. You haven't finished. He isn't read it. I hadn't any idea.* have, has 和 had 的縮寫形式 've、's 和 'd 通常用於對話. *I've got two pounds.* (我有兩英鎊.) *You've finished.* (你完成了.) *He's read it.* (他看過了.) *I'd no idea.* (我不知道.) *It'd fallen.* (它掉下來了.) 疑問句中不用縮寫形式. *Have I two pounds?* (我有兩英鎊嗎?) *Have you finished?* (你完成了嗎?) 等. 同樣, 否定詞 not 在對話中縮寫爲 n't 并且和 have 連寫. *I haven't (got) a penny.* (我連一個辨士都沒有.) *You haven't read it.* (他還沒看見.) *I hadn't any idea.* (我絲毫不知.) *Note[2]* 說明[2]: questions and negatives of have (in sense **7**) can be shown in three ways: (a) *Do you have to go to school?* (b) *Have you to go to school?* (c) *Have you got to go to school?* (a) usu. gives the sense of something that is done often i.e. going to school is something done all the time, as a habit. (b) and (c) usu. give the sense of a particular time i.e. *have you to go or have you got to go early / now / today? etc.* This difference between (a), (b) and (c) is not, however, always followed. In the same way (a) *You don't have to go to school* i.e. you need not ever go. (b) *You haven't to go to school* and (c) *You haven't got to go to school.* i.e. to-day, during the holidays etc have (用於義 **7**) 的疑問句和否定句可用三種形式表示: (a) Do you have to go to school? (你得上學嗎?) (b) Have you to go to school? (你得上學嗎?) (c) Have you got to go to school? (你得上學嗎?) (a) 通常表示某事經常發生,

即: 一直在上學, 或上學是一種習慣. (b) 和 (c) 通常表示某事發生在某一特定時間, 即: Have you to go 或 Have you got to go early / now / today? (你很早 / 現在 / 今天就得去嗎?) 等. 但是 (a) 句和 (b)、(c) 兩句之間的差別並不總是那麼嚴格遵行的. 同樣, (a) You don't have to go to school. 指: 你用不着去上學. 而 (b) You haven't to go to school. 和 (c) You haven't got to go to school. 指: 你今天或你在假期中不用去上學.

have something on wear 穿著: *She had a coat on.* 她穿著外套.

haven ['heɪvn] *nc* harbour; place of safety 港口; 避難所.

haversack ['hævəsæk] *nc* cloth bag for holding food etc. (usu. carried on the back) 帆布背包; 乾糧袋.

havoc ['hævək] *nu* damage; ruin 大破壞; 浩劫: *Wars cause great havoc.* 戰爭造成了嚴重的破壞.

hawk [hɔːk] *nc* general name for any bird (except the eagle), which catches small animals for food during the day, including falcons, kestrels etc. 隼; 茶隼; (除鷹之外的) 食肉鳥.

hawker ['hɔːkə] *nc* **1** person who hunts with hawks 携鷹打獵者. **2** person who travels from place to place selling goods 叫賣小販: *She never buys anything from hawkers.* 她從來不買小販的東西.

hay [heɪ] *nu* grass cut and dried by the sun and used as food for animals (作牲口飼料用的) 乾草. '**hay fever** running nose etc caused by dust from hay and other plants 枯草熱, 花粉熱. '**hayrick, haystack** hay put in a large heap to store it for use 乾草堆. '**haywire** *pred adj* wrong; crazy 混亂的, 亂七八糟的; 瘋狂的: *All our plans went haywire. (informal)* 我們所有的計劃都亂作一團了. (非正式).

hazard ['hæzəd] *nc* risk; danger 危險: *A soldier's life is full of hazards.* 士兵的生活充滿了危險. Also 亦作 *vt* risk; run the risk of 冒險: *They hazarded all they had to win.* 他們爲了得勝, 不惜孤注一擲. **hazardous** *adj*.

haze [heiz] *nu* light mist; air that is not clear 靄; 薄霧: *The sun shone through the haze;* 陽光透過薄霧照耀; *a haze of smoke* 一片輕烟. **hazy** *adj*.

hazel ['heizl] *nc* type of small tree found in cool, northern regions, which has a small, round nut which can be eaten 榛樹. Also 亦作 *adj* (usu. used to describe the colour of eyes) having a brown colour like the nut of a hazel (通常指眼睛的顏色)淡褐色.

he [hi:; hi] *pron* male person or animal that has been mentioned before (指曾經提及的單個男人或單個雄性動物)他: *I spoke to your father just before he went out.* 在你父親出門之前, 我跟他談過. *He is coming / He's coming.* 他來了. see 見 **him, his.**

head [hed] *nc* **1** the part of the body above the neck 頭部: *He has no hair on his head.* 他沒有頭髮. **2** top or upper part of something 頂端, 上部: *the head of a nail / page / valley* 釘帽/書頁的天頭/山谷的頂端; *the head of a bed* i.e. the part where one puts one's head 床頭; *the head on a glass of beer* i.e. the foaming part above the beer itself 一杯啤酒上的泡沫. **3** mental ability 智力: *He has a good head for figures.* 他有數字頭腦. *He found the answer out of his own head* i.e. using his own ability. 他獨力找到了答案. *Use your head!* i.e. think hard. (*informal*) 用你的腦袋想想吧! 好好想想. (非正式). **4** most important person of a group or organization 首腦, 首長: *the head of state* (e.g. king, president) 國家元首(如國王, 總統等); *heads of departments* 系主任. **5** the side of a coin on which the head of a country's president etc is stamped (硬幣印有頭像的)正面. (*opp* 反義詞 **tail**). *Heads or tails?* (said when throwing a coin into the air to decide something according to whether the coin falls with the head or tail upwards) 你要正面還是反面?(擲硬幣決定某事情時說). **6** (no *pl*) one unit of a herd or group (不用複數)動物的頭數; 小組的人數: *a hundred head of cattle* i.e. a hundred cows 一百頭牛. *The cost of the journey is fifty pence a / per head* i.e. each. 旅費是每人五十辨士. Also 亦作 *vt* **1** hit a football with one's head 用頭頂(足球): *He headed the ball.* 他頂了個頭球. **2** be at the top or in a leading position 站在…的前頭; 率領: *head the list* 是名單上的第一名. **heady** *adj* affecting one's mind; exciting 易使人醉的; 令人興奮的: *This is a heady drink;* 這種酒容易醉人; heady news 令人激動的消息. **'headache** pain in the head 頭痛. **'headdress** ornamental covering of the head 頭巾; 頭飾. **'headlamp, 'headlight** lamp fixed on front of a car, bicycle or train to show the way (汽車、自行車或火車的)前燈. **'headland** piece of land which projects into the sea or a lake; cape 岬. **'headline** short summary in large print at the top of a newspaper to attract attention (報紙的)大字標題: *I only had time to read the headlines.* 我只有唸一下標題的時間. **'head'master, 'head'mistress** man, woman in charge of a school 校長; 女校長. **'head-'on** *adj / adv* hitting each other with the front parts (usu. cars etc.) 迎頭的(地), 正面的(地)(通常指汽車等)

a head-on collision 正面相撞. *The two buses crashed head-on.* 兩輛公共汽車正面相撞. **'headphones** radio or telephone receivers held on the ears by a band of metal over the head 頭戴受話器; 耳機. (Also 亦作 **earphones, headset**). **'head'quarters** centre from which an organization is controlled 指揮部, 總部. **'headstone** stone put at the head of a grave 墓石. **'headway** progress; advance 前進; 進展: *We could make no headway in the huge crowd.* 我們在一大羣人當中被擠得寸步難行. **headwind** wind blowing in the opposite direction to the way one is going 逆風. **head for someone / something** go towards 朝某人/某物而去; *head for the hills* 朝山上走去. **head someone / something off** get in front of so as to turn back or aside 攔截某人/某物: *He tried to head off the angry mob.* 他企圖攔阻憤怒的暴徒. **at the head of 1** in front of; leading 在⋯的最前面; 領導的: *The band was at the head of the parade.* 樂隊走在遊行隊伍的最前面. **2** in the most important place 在最重要的位置: *at the head of the table* 居首席. **head first** *adv* with the head in front (as in a dive) 頭向前地(如在跳水時). **head over heels** turning over; upside down 顛倒地; 頭朝下地: *He went head over heels into the water.* 他一個倒栽葱跌進水裏.

header ['hedə*] *nc* **1** jump or fall head first 倒栽, 頭朝下的一跳/跌落. **2** hitting of a football with one's head 頭頂球.

heading ['hedɪŋ] *nc* word(s) at the top of something written or printed, showing what it is about 標題, 題目.

'headlong ['hedlɔŋ] *adj / adv* hurried; head first 匆忙的(地); 頭向前的(地).

headlong flight 倉皇逃跑. *He fell headlong.* 他頭先着地摔了一跤.

headstrong ['hedstrɔŋ] *adj* determined to have one's own way 任性的, 倔强的.

heady ['hedi] *adj* see 見 **head**.

heal [hi:l] *vi* (usu. of injuries and wounds) become well (通常指傷口)癒合: *The cut on my leg has healed.* 我腿上的傷口已經癒瘉. **heal up** (with reference to a wound etc.) become cured (指傷口等)治瘉, 痊癒.

health [helθ] *nu* general condition of the body 身體的一般狀况: *good health* 健康; *bad / poor health* 不健康. Also 亦作 general condition of being well 健康: *Health comes before wealth* i.e. good health 健康比財富重要. **healthy** *adj* with good health; causing good health 健康的, 有益於健康的: *a healthy baby* 健康的嬰兒. *a healthy place to live in* 有益於健康的住處; *a healthy respect for the law* i.e. it is good to have this respect 對法律應有的尊重. 即: 這種尊重是有益的. (*opp* 反義詞 **unhealthy**).

heap [hi:p] *nc* **1** number of things lying on top of one another 堆: *The fallen leaves lay in heaps.* 落葉成堆; *a heap of stones* 一堆石頭. **2** plenty of something 許多; 許多: *We have heaps of time.* 我們有充裕的時間. *They have heaps of money.* (*informal* in sense 2) 他們有很多錢. (義2為非正式). Also 亦作 *vt* They are heaping wood on the fire. 他們正把木柴架在火上. **heaped** *adj*: *a heaped plate of rice* 裝得很滿的一盤米飯.

hear [hiə*] *vt* **1** receive sounds in the ears 聽, 聽見: *I heard the drums.* 我聽到鼓聲. **2** be informed; receive news 聽說; 得知: *I hear you are leaving.* 我聽說你們要離開. *Have you heard* *from home?* 你收到家信了嗎? **3** listen to; attend to 注意聽, 聽取; 處理: *The judge heard the case this morning.* 今天上午法官審理了此案. *I will hear your story before I give an answer.* 我得聽你說完之後才作回答. *past* 過去式和過去分詞 **heard** [hɑːd]. **Hear! Hear!** *interj* showing agreement with what has been said 聽啊! 聽啊! (或: 說得對! 說得對!) **hear somebody out** listen to somebody until he has finished speaking 聽某人把話講完.

hearing ['hiəriŋ] **1** *nu* receiving of sounds in the ears 聽力: *He is hard of hearing / He has poor hearing* i.e. he cannot hear well. 他耳朵有點聾. 即: 他聽力不佳. **2** *nc* opportunity to give one's views etc. 申訴的機會: *They gave him a hearing.* 他們聽他申訴.

hearsay ['hiəsei] *nu* secondhand information; rumour 風聞; 傳聞, 流言.

hearse [həs] *nc* carriage or car for carrying a coffin 柩車, 靈車.

heart [hɑːt] *nc* **1** organ which pumps blood round the body 心臟: *He has a weak heart.* 他的心臟很弱. **2** centre which controls one's feelings 心, 心眼, 心地, 心腸: *She has a kind heart.* 她心眼兒好. *They took the bad news to heart* i.e. they were very upset by it. 他們對這個壞消息耿耿於懷. 即: 他們對此想不開. *I did not have the heart to tell him* i.e. I did not have the courage. 我不忍心告訴他們. 即: 我沒有這個勇氣. **3** centre; inner part 中心; 内部: *the heart of the city* 城市的中心, *the heart of the matter* 事情的中心, *the heart of a lettuce* 萵苣的菜心. **4** something in the shape of a heart (esp. on playing cards) 心形物 (尤指紙牌的紅桃): *ace / king / queen of hearts* 紅桃A / K / Q. **hearty** *adj* **1**

cheerful; healthy 愉快的; 強健的: *a hearty laugh* 放聲的歡笑. **2** large and enjoyable 豐盛的: *a hearty breakfast* 豐盛的早餐. **heartily** *adv* **heartless** *adj* without feeling; cruel 無情的; 殘忍的. **'heart attack** illness in which the heart suddenly stops working properly (often causing death) 心力衰竭; 心臟病發作. **'heartbeat** pumping motion of the heart 心跳, 心搏: *The doctor listened to my heartbeat.* 大夫聽了我的心跳. **'heartbreaking** *adj* causing great sorrow 使心碎的. **'heartbroken** *adj* suffering from great sorrow 悲痛欲絕的, 極度傷心的. **'heartburn** *nu* pain in the chest caused by indigestion 胃灼熱, 心口灼熱, 胃痛. **'heartfelt** *adj* deeply felt; sincere 深深感覺到的; 衷心的: *my heartfelt thanks* 我的衷心感謝. **'heartrending** *adj* causing great sorrow 悲慘的; 使傷心的, 使斷腸的. **by heart** correctly from the memory 熟記; 記住: *know / learn / repeat something by heart* 筆記憶; 記住, 背誦: *He knows the multiplication tables by heart* i.e. he can remember them correctly without the help of a book of multiplication tables 他會背乘法表. **take heart** be encouraged 鼓起勇氣. (*opp* 反義語 **lose heart**).

hearth [hɑːθ] *nc* large, flat stone under and in front of a fireplace 爐底石; 爐邊.

heat¹ [hiːt] *nu* **1** hotness 熱, 熱度: *the heat of a fire* 火的熱力. (*opp* 反義詞 **cold**). **2** strong feelings; anger 激動, 激烈; 激怒: *They argued with great heat.* 他們爭論得很激烈. **3** division of a sports competition to decide who will take part in the final competitions (體育比賽) 預賽: *Because he won his heat he will run in the finals.* 他在預賽中獲勝, 因此將參加賽跑決賽.

'**heatspot** spot on the skin which becomes red and feels hot 痱子. '**heatstroke** illness caused by heat (e.g. of the sun) 中暑. '**heatwave** unusually hot weather 熱浪; 特別熱的天氣. **dead heat** race in which two or more competitors finish in first place 不分勝負的賽跑.

heat² [hi:t] *vt* make hot 把…加熱: *The sun heats the earth*. 太陽曬熱大地.
heated *adj* made hot; angry 加熱了的; 生氣的: *a heated room* 有供暖的房間; *a very heated meeting* 爭論激烈的會議. **heater** *nc* apparatus for giving heat or making something hot 加熱器; 暖氣設備. **heating** *nu* system for giving heat 暖氣系統. **heat something up** make hot (often for a second time) 把…熱一下: *Let me heat up some soup for you.* 我替你把湯熱一熱.

heath [hi:θ] *nc* piece of unused open land 荒地.

heathen ['hi:ðən] *nc* person who believes in a god or gods different from one's own (esp. one who is not a Christian, Jew or Muslim) 異教徒 (尤指不信基督教, 猶太教或伊斯蘭教者). Also 亦作 *adj*: *a heathen country* 異教國家.

heather ['heðə*] *nu* type of short plant with small flowers found on rough, unused land and mountains 石南屬植物.

heave [hi:v] **1** *vt* lift, move or throw something heavy 舉起、移動或拋開(重物): *They heaved their luggage into the car.* 他們把行李抬進汽車. **2** *vi* pull hard (usu. a rope) 用力拉(繩子): *Heave! / Heave away!* telling someone to pull hard 用力拉啊! **3** *vi* move up and down or in and out 起伏; 進出: *The sea was heaving.* 海浪洶湧. *His*

chest heaved. 他的胸脯起伏着. Also 亦作 *nc*: *He pulled it out with one heave*. 他猛地一拉就拔出來了. *past* 過去式和過去分詞 **heaved** or **hove** [houv]. *Note* 說明: *hove is less usual and is generally only used of ships heaving to*. hove 較不常用, 一般只用於船隻的停駛. **heave a sigh** give a sigh, moving the chest to do so 長嘆一聲.

heaven ['hevən] *nc* **1** place above the earth where God is believed to be 天國. **2** (usu. **Heaven**) God himself (通常用 Heaven)上帝: *It is Heaven's will*. 那是天意. *Thank Heaven!* 謝天謝地! **3** (usu. *pl*) the sky (rather *o.f.*) (通常用複數)天空(頗爲舊式). **4** condition of being very happy 極樂: *It's heaven to be here. (informal* in sense 4) 能在這裏是一大樂事. (義 4 爲非正式). **heavenly** *adj* of heaven; causing great happiness; delightful 天空的; 極樂的; 愉快的.

heavy ['hevi] *adj* **1** having great weight 重的: *The box is too heavy to carry*. 這箱子太重, 搬不動. **2** slow; dull 緩慢的; 遲鈍的: *heavy with sleep* 睏極. **3** greater than usual 大的; 多的: *heavy crops* 大豐收; *heavy rain* 大雨; *heavy seas* 波濤洶湧的海面; *heavy work* 繁重的工作. **heavily** *adv*: *heavily-laden* i.e. with a heavy load 負擔沉重地. *comparative* 比較級 **heavier**. *superlative* 最高級 **heaviest**.

Hebrew ['hi:bru:] **1** *nc* jew 希伯來人, 猶太人. **2** *nu* language of the Jews 希伯來語. Also 亦作 *adj* of the Jews or their language 希伯來人的, 猶太人的; 希伯來語的.

heckle ['hekl] *vt* interrupt a public speaker with questions and remarks 詰問, 詰難.

hectare ['hektɑ:*] *nc* measure of area in

the metric system equal to 2.47 acres 公頃(等於 2.47 英畝).

hectic ['hektik] *adj* very busy or exciting 忙碌的; 興奮的: *We had a hectic holiday.* 我們度過了一個緊張興奮的假日.

hedge¹ [hedʒ] *nc* line of bushes used as a wall round a field or garden 樹籬.

hedge² [hedʒ] *vi* be reluctant to make a decision or give an opinion 躲閃, 規避, 推諉: *Stop hedging and say what you think.* 不要再支吾其詞了, 你怎麼想就怎麼說吧.

hedgehog ['hedʒhɔg] *nc* small animal covered with long, sharp points (刺) 猬.

heed [hi:d] *vt* pay attention to 注意, 留意. Also 亦作 *nu*: *They give / pay no heed to what I say.* 他們把我的話完全當作耳旁風. *You should take heed of what I say.* 你應當留意我的話. **heedful** *adj*: *They are more heedful of what I say.* 他們比較注意我的話. **heedless** *adj* careless; inattentive 不注意的; 掉以輕心的.

heel [hi:l] *nc* **1** back part of the foot 腳後跟, 踵. **2** part of a sock or stocking which covers the heel 襪子的後跟: *There is a hole in the heel of your sock.* 你的短襪後跟上有一個洞. **3** part of a boot or shoe below the heels 鞋後跟: *high heels* 高跟; *flat heels* 平跟.

hefty ['hefti] *adj* big and strong; heavy 大的; 強壯的; 重的: *hefty football player* 健壯的足球隊員; *hefty piece of cheese* i.e. a big one. *(informal)* 一大塊乳酪(非正式).

height [hait] *nu* distance from bottom to top 高, 高度: *What is the height of that building?* 那幢建築有多高? *He is six feet in height.* 他身高六英尺.

heighten *vt / i* make or become higher

or greater 提高; 增大; 加強: *The news heightened our fears.* 這消息使我們更加害怕. *The tension heightened.* 緊張狀態更加嚴重了.

heir [ɛə*] *nc* person entitled to receive the money, property or rank of another person when that person dies 後嗣, 繼承人: *I am my uncle's heir.* 我是我伯父的繼承人. *He was heir to the throne.* 他是王位的繼承人. *(fem* 陰 **heiress** ['ɛəris]).

heirloom ['ɛəlu:m] *nc* a personal article which has been in the possession of a family for generations 傳家寶.

held [held] *past of* **hold¹**. hold' 的過去式和過去分詞.

helicopter ['helikɔptiə*] *nc* type of aircraft which has horizontal revolving blades on top, enabling it to take off and land vertically and remain in the air without having to move forward 直升飛機.

helium ['hi:ljəm] *nu* very light nonflammable colour less adourless element that is an inert gas: used for inflating balloons, etc. 氦.

hell [hel] *nu* **1** place of punishment for the wicked after death 地獄. **2** any place or condition of suffering and misery 極苦之地; 苦境; 極大的痛苦.

hello, hallo [hʌ'lou] *interj* shout to greet or to call attention 喂, 哈囉(招呼用語).

helm [helm] *nu* tiller i.e. a long handle, or wheel, for turning the rudder of a ship 舵, 舵柄, 舵輪. **'helmsman** man holding the helm 舵手.

helmet ['helmit] *nc* hard covering to protect the head 頭盔: *Soldiers wear steel helmets in battle.* 士兵在打仗時戴鋼盔.

help¹ [help] *vt* **1** do something for somebody; do part of somebody's work 幫助, 幫忙; *The rich should help the poor.* 富人應當幫助窮人. *I help my father in the garden.* 我在園子裏幫父親幹活. *He helped me (to) cook the food.* 他幫我燒飯菜. **2** give food or drink to 使…進食; 款待: *May I help you to some pudding?* 我給你一些布丁好嗎? *Help yourself to a beer!* 請喝一杯啤酒! **3** (with **can** or **could**) avoid; stop (與 can 或 could 連用) 避免; 阻止: *I can't help laughing* 我禁不住笑了. *They talked too much; they couldn't help themselves.* 他們說得太多, 已經控制不住自己了. **helper** *nc* person who helps 幫手, 助手. see also 參見 **help**². **helping** *nc* amount of food given or taken 一份食物, 一客食物: *He had two helpings of pudding.* 他吃了兩份布丁.

help² [help] **1** *nu* act of helping; assistance 幫助; 協助: *I am grateful for your help.* 我感謝你的幫助. *We need all the help we can get.* 我們需要一切能夠得到的幫助. *He gave us no help.* 他沒有給我們任何幫助. **2** *nc* servant who works in a house 僕人, 傭人: *a daily help* 朝來夜去的女傭. **helpful** *adj* giving help; willing to help 有幫助的; 樂意幫助的. (*opp* 反義詞 **unhelpful**). **helpless** *adj* **1** without help 無助的, 未受到幫助的. **2** unable to help oneself 不能自助的, 孤弱的, 無依無靠的.

helter-skelter [ˈheltəˈskeltə*] *nc* tower with a spiral chute down which people slide (公園或遊樂場所的) 從高塔上螺旋下降的滑梯.

hem [hem] *nc* edge of a piece of cloth folded over and sewn (衣服等的) 摺邊: *the hem of a dress / handerkerchief* 衣服/手帕的摺邊. Also 亦作 *vt* **1** put a hem on 給…縫邊, 給…鑲邊. **2** surround; enclose on all sides 包圍;

The garden is hemmed in / round with trees. 園子的周圍種着樹木. *past* 過去式和過去分詞 **hemmed.**

hemisphere [ˈhemisfiə*] *nc* half of a sphere; half of the earth 半球; 地球的半面: *the Northern / Southern hemisphere* i.e. the north / south of the equator 北半球/南半球, 即: 赤道的北/南面; *the Eastern / Western hemisphere* i.e. the half east / west of a line going through Great Britain (called the **Greenwich meridian**) 東半球/西半球, 即: 以通過英國格林尼治的本初子午線爲界的地球東/西半面.

hemo-, haemo- [ˈhiːmou,ˈhemou] *prefix* blood (e.g. **hemorrhage**) 血 (例如: hemorrhage).

hemorrhage [ˈheməridʒ] *nu* bleeding 出血.

hemorrhoids [ˈhemərɔidz] *npl* painful swollen veins round the anus; piles 痔.

hemp [hemp] *nu* type of plant used to make ropes and rough cloth 大麻.

hen [hen] *nc* female bird (esp. a chicken) 雌禽 (尤指母雞). (*masc* 陽 **cock**). **'henpecked** *adj* (with reference to a husband) ruled by his wife. (*informal*) (指丈夫) 怕老婆的, 懼內的. (非正式).

hence [hens] *adv* **1** from now 從此以後, 今後: *a year hence* (*o.f.* – *use a* **year from now** or **in a year's time**) 一年以後 (舊式—現在用 a year from now 或 in a year's time). **2** for this reason 因此.

henchman [ˈhentʃmən] *nc* loyal follower of an important or powerful person 親信, 心腹. *pl* 複數 **henchmen** [ˈhentʃmən].

her [həː*] *pron* form which **she** takes when it is the subject of a verb or preposition (she 的賓格)她: *You saw her there.* 你看到她在那邊. *Give it to* *her*. 把這給她. Also 亦作 *determiner* form which **she** takes to show possession (she 的所有格的): *It's her book / problem etc.* 這是她的書/問題等. **herself 1** emphatic form of **her** (her 的強調形式)她親自, 她本人: *She went to choose it herself.* 她親自去選中了它. **2** reflexive form of **her** (反身代詞)她自己: *She can now feed herself without help.* 現在她已能自己進食, **by herself** without help; alone 獨立地; 獨自地.

herald [herəld] *nc* person who in the past used to carry and make known important messges from his chief or king (舊時的)傳令官. **heraldry** *nu* science which deals with the history and the coats of arms of noble families 紋章學.

herb [həːb] *nc* type of plant used as medicine or to flavour food 藥草; 香草. **herbivorous** [həːˈbivərəs] *adj* feeding on plants, not meat 食草的. see 見 **carnivorous**.

herbivore [ˈhəːbivɔː] *nc* animal that feeds on grass and other plants 食草動物.

herd [həːd] *nc* group of certain types of animals 獸羣; 牧羣: *a herd of buffaloes / cattle / deer / elephants* 一羣水牛/牛/鹿/象. Also 亦作 *vt* look after a herd 放牧: *The little boy is herding his father's cattle.* 小男孩在放牧父親的牛羣.

herder [ˈhəːdə] *nc* person who cares for or drives herds of cattle or flocks of sheep, esp. on an open range 牧人.

herdsman [ˈhəːdzmən] *nc* person who keeps or tends a herd 牧人; 牧主. *pl* 複數 **herdsmen**.

here [hiə*] *adv* **1** at / in / to this place 在這裏; 向這邊: *I am sitting here.* 我在這裏坐. *He works here.* 他在這裏工作. *Come here!* 到這裏來! Note 說明: *here* is often used at the beginning of a sentence expressing an exclamation. When it is, the subject of the verb comes before the verb if it is a personal pronoun, and after the verb if it is a noun. *Here they are! Here are the books! Here he comes! Here comes my friend!* here 常用來引起表感嘆的句子.這類句子的主語如果是人稱代詞, 主語要用在動詞之前; 如果主語是名詞, 則用在動詞之後.Here they are! 它們在這裏! Here are the books! 那些書在這裏! Here he comes! 他來了! Here comes my friend! 我的朋友來了! **2** this place 這裏: *I live near here.* 我住在附近. *Come over here* i.e. to the place where I am 到這邊來.即:到我這裏來. *Behind here is a garden* 這後面有一個花園. **3** at a particular point in an action 在這點, 到這裏: *Let us stop here* (e.g. in reading) *and find out what is meant.* 我們先讀到這裏, 看看它是甚麼意思. *Here I cannot agree with you.* 這一點我不敢苟同. **here and there** in several places 各處, 到處.

hereafter [ˌhiərˈɑːftə] *adv* from now on, in the future 今後, 將來: *She should have died hereafter.* 此後她應不在人世.

hereby [ˌhiəˈbai] *adv* by this means 以此, 特此: *I hereby declare that I will not be responsible for any of her debts.* 我特此聲明, 我將不負責她所欠的任何債務.

heredity [hiˈrediti] *nu* the passing of certain qualities from one generation to another; the qualities passed in this way 遺傳; 遺傳的特徵: *The colour of our skin is due to heredity.* 我們的膚色是由於遺傳. **hereditary** [hiˈreditəri] *adj* passed from one generation to another 遺傳的: *hereditary diseases* 遺傳病; also of rank or position 世襲的: *a hereditary chief* i.e. one who became chief when his father died 世襲的首領, 即: 接替其先父而成爲首領.

herein ['hiər'in] *adv* (*formal*) in or into this place, thing, document, etc. (正式)此中, 於此(地, 物, 文件等)中: *Herein lies the ansers.* 這裏包含着答案.

heresy ['herisi] *nc* religious belief which is not considered to be correct; any belief not considered to be correct 異教; 異端邪説. **heretic** ['heritik] *nc* person who supports a heresy 異教徒; 信奉異端邪説的人. **heretical** ['hi'retikl] *adj*.

heritage ['heritidʒ] *nc* something which is, or can be, inherited 遺産: *English poetry is one of our great heritages.* 英國詩歌是我們的一項重要遺産.

hermit ['həmit] *nc* person who lives alone (often in order to lead a religious life) 隱士; 修道者.

hernia ['həniə] *nc* condition of the body caused e.g. by part of the bowel projecting through the muscles of the abdomen; rupture 疝, 疝氣, 脱腸.

hero ['hiərou] *nc* 1 man famous for his great qualities (e.g. his courage) 英雄; 勇士. 2 principal man in a play, poem or storybook 男主角, 男主人公. *pl* 複數 **heroes**. (*fem* 陰 **heroine** ['herouin]). **heroism** ['herouizəm] *nu* **heroic** [hi'rouik] *adj* of or like a hero 英雄式的; 英勇的.

heroin ['herouin] *nu* habit-forming drug, used medically to relieve pain 海洛因.

heron ['hern] *nc* type of bird with long legs, neck and beak, which walks in the water 蒼鷺.

herring ['heriŋ] *nc* type of small sea fish

used as food 鯡魚. *pl* 複數 **herrings** or **herring**.

hers [həːz] *pron* what belongs to her 她的(東西): *We'll have to separate hers from yours.* 我們得把她的東西和你的東西分開. Also 亦作 *pred adj* belonging to her 她的: *This dress is hers.* 這件衣服是她的.

hesitate ['heziteit] *vi* stop or pause (usu. because one is not certain) 躊躇; 猶豫: *He hesitated before choosing a book.* 他在選書之前猶豫了一下. *These men hesitate at nothing.* 這些人做甚麼事都毫不遲疑. *I hesitate to say so.* 我本不想開口, 但實在不得已. **hesitation** [hezi'teiʃən] *nu* **hesitant** ['hezitnt] *adj*.

hew [hju:] *vt* cut with heavy blows (e.g. using an axe, hatchet or sword) (用斧、刀等)砍; 劈: *He hewed the trunk of the tree into logs.* 他把樹幹砍成圓木段. *They hewed a path through the thick forest* i.e. they made a path by cutting down the branches åt the side. 他們在茂密的森林中砍伐出一條路來. 即: 他們把旁邊的樹枝砍掉, 開出一條路來. *past tense* 過去式 **hewed**. *past part* 過去分詞 **hewed** or **hewn** [hju:n].

hexagon ['heksəgən] *nc* (geometry) figure with six sides (幾何)六角形, 六邊形.

hey [hei] *interj* expressing surprise or attracting somebody's attention 嗨(表示驚奇或招呼人注意).

heyday ['heidei] *nu* time of greatest power or prosperity 全盛時期: *The country was then in its heyday;* 當時這個國家正在其全盛時期; *in the heyday of its power* 在其權力鼎盛時期.

hibernate ['haibəneit] *vi* sleep through the winter (as many animals e.g. bears do) 冬眠. **hibernation** [hai-bə'neiʃən] *nu.*

hibiscus ['hi'biskəs] *nu* cultivated plant or shrub with brightly coloured flowers 芙蓉.

hiccup, hiccough ['hikʌp] *nc* short, sudden and noisy interruption of the breath (often caused by eating or drinking too quickly) 打嗝, 打呃. Also 亦作 *vi.*

hid [hid], **hidden** ['hidn] past tense and past part of **hide**[1]. hide[1] 的過去式和過去分詞.

hide[1] [haid] *vt / i* keep or put out of sight; keep secret 隱藏; 隱瞞: *They are hiding in the wood.* 他們躲藏在樹林裏. *We hid (ourselves) in the wood.* 我們躲藏在樹林裏. *He tried to hide his anger.* 他企圖掩蓋他的憤怒. past tense 過去式 **hid** [hid]. *past part* 過去分詞 **hidden** or **hid** ['hid(n)]. Also 亦作 *nc* place to hide (esp. in order to watch wild animals) (尤指觀察野獸活動的)躲藏處. **hideaway, 'hideout** place to hide (esp. to escape the law) (尤指躲避法律的)躲藏處. **'hide-and-seek** children's game in which some hide and the others try to find them 捉迷藏. **'hiding place** place to hide 躲藏處. **be in hiding** be hidden 躲藏者. (Also 亦作 **go into / come out of hiding).**

hide[2] [haid] *nc* skin of an animal (esp. when removed from the animal and prepared for sale) 獸皮, 皮革. **hiding** *nc* beating 痛打, 鞭打: *He gave him a good hiding.* (*informal*) 他狠狠揍了他一頓. (非正式)

hideous ['hidiəs] *adj* horrible to look at; frightful 醜陋的, 可憎的, 可怕的: *a hideous face* 醜陋的面孔; *a hideous mistake* 嚴重的錯誤. **hideously** *adv.*

hierarchy ['haiərɑːki] *nc* organization strictly according to grade or rank 階層, 等級制度.

hieroglyph ['haiərəglif] *nc* picture or symbol representing a word, syllable, or sound, used by the ancient Egyptians and others 象形文字.

hi-fi [,hai'fai] *nu* (stort form of **high fidelity**) reproduction of sound using electronic equipment that gives faithful reproduction with little or no distortion 高保真度.

high [hai] *adj* **1** raised up; measuring from bottom to top 高的: *high mountains* 高山; *a high wall* 高牆. *The tree is fifty feet high.* 這樹有五十英尺高. *Note* 說明: in this sense use *tall* for persons and most animals. 說人的身高和多數動物的高度要用 tall. **2** important; above others in position 重要的; 地位較高的, 職務較高的: *the high priest* 主教; 大祭司; *high society* 上流社會; *high school* i.e. one above a primary school 中學. **3** great 高度的; 強烈的; 大的; 非常的: *high prices* 高價; *high speed* 高速度. *high winds* 強風, 疾風. *in high regard* 十分尊敬. **4** good; admirable 良好的; 令人欽佩的: *a man of high principles / high character* 操守高潔的人/品格高尚的人; *high ideals* 崇高的理想. **5** near the top of the scale in music; sharp 高音調的; 尖聲的: *a high note* 高音符; *high voices* 尖嗓門. Also 亦作 *adv*: *high-placed officials* 高級官員; *play high* i.e. play a high card in a card game 大賭; 出大牌. *They climbed high.* 他們爬得高. *They held their heads high.* 他們趾高氣揚. **'highbrow** *adj* having more knowledge or better tastes than others 有高度文化修養的. Also 亦作 *nc* person who has, or thinks he has, more knowledge or better tastes. (*informal*) (自以為)有高度文化修養的人, 自命不凡的人. (非正

式）. **High Commissioner** *nc* representative of one of the British Commonwealth countries in another Commonwealth country 高級專員(英聯邦成員國之間互派的使節). **High Commission** *nc* office of a High Commissioner 高級專員公署. **'high-handed** *adj* using one's authority without any thought for others 專橫的; 霸道的: *the government's high-handed policies* 政府的高壓政策. **'highlands** *npl* mountainous country 高地, 高原. **'high-level** *adj* attended by important people; important 高階層的; 重要的: *a high-level meeting* 高階層的會議. **'highlight** 1 most important, most enjoyable part of something 最重要的部份; 最精彩之處: *Your performance was the highlight of the show.* 你的表演是這場演出中最精彩的部份. 2 part of a photograph, painting etc on which there is the greatest effect of light 照片或圖畫上光線最強的部份. **'high-pitched** *adj* having a sharp, high sound 音調高的; 尖聲的: *a high-pitched voice* 尖嗓門. **'high 'spirits** *npl* great and excited happiness 高興, 快樂. **high-spirited** *adj* **'high(ly) strung** *adj* very easily excited; nervous 易激動的; 神經質的. **'highway** *nc* road (esp. a main road) 公路(尤指幹線).

highly ['haili] *adv* very 很, 非常: *a highly dangerous job* 極其危險的工作. *He is highly pleased.* 他非常高興. *He spoke highly of you* i.e. he praised you. 他稱讚你. *Note* 說明: the difference between *highly* and *high* as an *adv* is small. In many phrases either can be used *high / highly strung; high / highly paid.* But one can only say *climb / play high,* and speak highly of; *highly pleased* etc. 副詞 highly 和作副

詞用的 high 差別不大. 在很多短語中兩詞可以通用. high / highly strung 易激動的; high / highly paid 領高薪的. 但是只能說 climb high 爬得高; play high 大賭, 出大牌; 以及 speak highly of 稱讚; highly pleased 非常高興等.

highness ['hainis] *nc* title of persons belonging to a royal family 對王室成員的尊稱: *His (Royal) Highness* 殿下(間接提及時用). *Your Highness* 殿下(直接稱呼時用). *Their (Royal) Highnesses* 諸位殿下(間接提及且不止一位殿下時用).

hijack ['haidʒæk] *vt* (esp. with reference to an aeroplane, van etc or its cargo) take or steal by force 劫持(飛機、貨車等); 搶劫(飛機、貨車裏的貨物). **hijacker** *nc* **hijacking** *nc / u.*

hike [haik] *nc* long walk for pleasure (usu. in the country) (通常指去鄉間的)遠足, 長途徒步旅行. Also 亦作 *vi* **hiker** *nc.*

hilarious [hi'lɛəriəs] *adj* 1 loud and happy 歡鬧的; 狂歡的. 2 causing one to be very amused 有趣的: *a hilarious film* 有趣的電影. **hilarity** [hi'læriti] *nu.*

hill [hil] *nc* 1 piece of raised ground; small mountain 小山, 丘陵. 2 slope, steep part of a road 斜坡, 坡路: *The bus got stuck on the hill.* 公共汽車在坡上被堵住了. **hilly** *adj* having many hills 多小山的, 丘陵起伏的. *comparative* 比較級 **hillier.** *superlative* 最高級 **hilliest.** **'hillside** side of a hill (小山的)山腰, 山坡.

hilt [hilt] *nc* handle of a sword or dagger (劍、匕首等的)柄.

him [him] *pron* form which **he** takes when it is the object of a verb or preposition (he 的賓格)他: *You saw him there.* 你看到他在那邊. *Give it to him.* 把這個給他吧. *Note* 說明: *It's him.* 是

他. **himself 1** emphatic form of **him** (him 的強調形式) 他親自, 他本人: *He had to do it himself.* 他要親自做這件事. **2** reflexive form of him (反身代詞) 他自己: *The boy has hurt himself.* 這男孩弄傷了自己. **by himself** without help; alone 獨自地, 獨力地.

hind¹ [haind] *nc* female deer 雌鹿.

hind² [haind] *adj* at the back (usu. of the back legs of animals)後面的 (通常指動物的後腿): *The dog has hurt its hind leg.* 這狗的一隻後腿受了傷.

hinder ['hində*] *vt* stop, try to stop, somebody from doing something; delay 阻止; 阻礙; 耽擱, 延誤: *The crowd hindered him from leaving.* 人羣使他無法離開. *I was hindered by the heavy traffic.* 擁擠的交通使我耽擱了.

hindrance ['hindrns] *nc* somebody / something that hinders 障礙, 妨礙的人 / 物: *Children are a hindrance when you wish to work quietly.* 在你想安靜工作的時候, 孩子總是妨礙.

Hindu ['hin'du:] *nc* follower of Hinduism 印度教的教徒. Also 亦作 *adj* **Hinduism** ['hindu:izəm] *nu* religion of most of the people of India 印度教.

hinge [hindʒ] *nc* piece of metal which joins two things so that they can open and shut (e.g. on a door, gate or box with a lid) 鉸鏈: *The door opens easily because the hinges are oiled.* 鉸鏈上了油, 因此門很容易開. Also 亦作 *vi* depend 依賴, 隨…而定: *The result hinges on / upon his reply.* 結果如何, 要看他如何答覆而定.

hint [hint] *vt / i* say something in an indirect, roundabout way; suggest 暗示; 提示; 建議: *He hinted that I should go.* 他暗示我該走了. *They hinted at his bad behaviour.* 他們暗示他的行為不軌. Also 亦作 *nc: They gave no hint of their plans.* 對於他們的計劃, 他們沒

有作甚麼暗示. *I took the hint and left at once* i.e. I was able to see, without being told, that I should leave, and did so. 我領會了暗示, 立即離開了. *This book is full of good hints* i.e. good suggestions. 這本書裏有許多好建議.

hip¹ [hip] *nc* top of the leg where it joins the side of the body 臀部.

hip² [hip] *interj* (only in **hip, hip, hurrah!**) (僅用於 hip, hip, hurrah!) see 見 **hurrah.**

hippopotamus [hipə'pɒtəməs] *nc* very large African animal found in rivers and lakes 河馬. *pl* 複數 **hippopotamuses** or **hippopotami** [hipə'pɒtəmai].

hire ['haiə*] *vt* give or get the use of something for an agreed price 租; 雇: *They hire (out) boats to people on holiday.* 每逢假日他們出租船隻. *I hired a boat so that I could go fishing.* 我租了一條小船可以去釣魚. Also 亦作 *nu:* boats on / for hire 供出租的船隻. *Note* 說明: hire is for a short period and a definite purpose. *They want to hire a hall for the concert.* Rent is usu. for a long(er) period and for general purposes. *He rented a house for the summer.* 爲了某種特定的用途短期租用某物用 hire. They want to hire a hall for the concert. 他們要租一個大廳開音樂會. 爲了一般用途較長期地租用某物用 rent. He rented a house for the summer. 他租了一座房子夏天住. **'hire 'purchase** method of paying for goods by which one can use the goods while making payments towards the total amount 分期付款購買法.

his [hiz] *pron* what belongs to him 他的 (東西): *We'll have to separate his from yours.* 我們得把他的東西跟你的

東西分開. Also 亦作 *determiner* form which **he** takes to show possession (he 的所有格) 他的: *It's his book / problem* etc. 這是他的書/問題等. Also 亦作 *pred adj* belonging to him 他的: *The suit is his.* 這套衣服是他的.

hiss [his] *vt / i* make a sound like the letter s' 發出"嘶嘶"聲: *Snakes hiss when angry.* 蛇在憤怒時發嘶嘶聲. *The crowd hissed (at) him as he passed* i.e. rnade this sound to show they did not like him. 他走過時人羣向他發出噓聲. 即: 發噓聲表示不喜歡他. Also 亦作 nc: *the hisses of the crowd* 人羣的噓噓聲.

histogram ['histəgræm] *nc* (statistics) graph of a frequency distribution in which vertical rectangles or columns are constructed with the width of each rectangle being a class interval and height a distance corresponding to the frequency in that class interval (統計學) 直方圖.

historian [his'tɔːriən] *nc* person who writes or studies history, esp. one who is an authority on it 歷史學家.

history ['histəri] *nc* the study or record of the past 歷史: *History is his main subject at college.* 歷史是他在大學的主修課. *They are writing a new history of Africa.* 他們正在編寫一部新的非洲史. **historic** [his'tɔrik] *adj* famous or important in history 歷史上有名的, 有歷史意義的: *a historic battle* 一次歷史上有名的戰役. **historical** [his'tɔrikl] *adj* actually happening in history; dealing with history 歷史上發生過的, 史實的; 有關歷史的: *a historical novel* i.e. one describing actual events and people in history, rather then imaginary ones 歷史小說, 即: 根據史實而非虛構的小說; *from a historical point of view* i.e. from the point of view of history 從歷史觀點.

hit[1] [hit] *vt* **1** strike; give a blow to; reach something aimed at; collide with; bring something against something else with force 打, 打擊; 擊中; (使) 碰撞: *He hit me on the chest.* 他打我的胸部. *I am hitting the nail with a hammer.* 我正在用鐵鎚釘釘子. *The bullet hit the target.* 子彈擊中了目標. *The car hit the wall.* 汽車撞上了牆. *He hit his hand on / against the door.* 他的手碰在門上. **2** (usu. with **hard**) cause to suffer (通常與 hard 連用) 使遭受, 使受打擊: *The death of his father hit him hard.* 他父親去世使他十分傷心. *The farmers were hit by the drought.* 農民們受到旱災的沉重打擊. *pres part* 現在分詞 **hitting.** *past* 過去式和過去分詞 **hit.**

hit[2] [hit] *nc* **1** blow or stroke 一擊, 擊中. **2** great success 巨大的成功: *This song is one of the hits of the year.* 這首歌是今年最流行的歌曲之一.

hitch[1] [hitʃ] *vt* **1** raise with a quick movement 急拉, 猛拉: *He hitched up his trousers.* 他很快繫上長褲. **2** fasten by a rope (usu. quickly and easily) (很快很容易地用繩子) 拴住, 套住: *They hitched the horses to the wagon.* 他們把馬套上車.

hitch[2] [hitʃ] *nc* **1** sudden pull or push 急拉; 急推. **2** type of knot made in a rope 索結, 繩結. **3** something that causes a delay 障礙, 阻礙: *There has been a hitch in the discussions.* 討論中存在着障礙.

hitchhike ['hitʃhaik] *vi* travel by getting free lifts in cars or lorries 搭便車旅行. **hitchhiker** *nc* **hitherto** [,hiðə'tuː] *adv* until this time; to now 迄今; 至今: *Hitherto, she had been living in France.* 直到目前爲止, 她一直住在法國.

hive [haiv] *nc* place where bees live; type of box made for them to live in; the bees themselves in the hive 蜂巢; 蜂箱; (蜂巢裏的)蜂羣.

hoard [hɔːd] *nc* secret store of something (esp. money or food) 秘密的貯藏 (尤指錢財或食物). Also 亦作 *vt* **hoarder** *nc*.

hoarding [ˈhɔːdiŋ] *nc* **1** temporary wooden fence round a house or piece of land 臨時圍籬, 臨時圍板. **2** very large board on which advertisements are stuck 招貼板, 廣告牌.

hoarse [hɔːs] *adj* **1** rough and harsh sounding (聲音)粗糙刺耳的: *a hoarse cry* 嘶啞的叫喊聲. **2** having a hoarse voice 嗓門嘶啞的: *I am hoarse because I have a bad cold.* 我得了重感冒, 因此嗓音嘶啞.

hoax [houks] *vt* trick or deceive somebody as a joke 欺騙, 戲弄: *The people were hoaxed by his false story.* 人民被他編造的說法所欺騙. Also 亦作 *nc*: *The report that a bomb had been put in the room was a hoax.* 房間裏安着炸彈的報告是一個騙局.

hob [hob] *nc* top of a cooker, on which saucepans are heated (爐上的)鍋架.

hobble [ˈhɔbl] *vi* walk as when one leg is injured; limp 跛行.

hobby [ˈhɔbi] *nc* activity which one likes doing in one's spare time 癖好, 業餘愛好: *Gardening is the hobby of many businessmen.* 園藝是許多商人的癖好.

hobo [ˈhoubou] *nc (US)* person without work who wanders from place to place (美)流浪漢; 無業遊民. *pl* 複數 **hoboes** or **hobos.** *(informal)* (非正式)

hockey [ˈhɔki] *nu* **1** *(Brit)* team game played on a field with a ball and curved sticks. *(US* 美 **field hockey)**

(英) 曲棍球. **2** *(US)* similar game played on ice. *(Brit* 英 **ice hockey)** (美)冰球.

hoe [hou] *nc* tool for digging the soil and clearing weeds 鋤頭.

hog [hɔg] *nc* (esp. *US*) a pig; a castrated male pig (尤指美)豬; 閹過的公豬.

hoist [hɔist] *vt* lift; raise up (usu. by pulling a rope) 升起; 絞起: *hoist a flag / sail* 升旗/揚帆. Also 亦作 *nc* apparatus used for hoisting 起重機.

hold¹ [hould] *vt/i* **1** keep with or in the hands (用手) 拿住, 握住: *They held me so that I could not move.* 他們抓住我, 使我無法動彈. *Please hold my bag for me.* 請替我拿一下手提袋. **2** keep with a part of the body (用身體的某一部份) 抓住, 夾住: *She was holding the baby in both arms.* 她用雙臂抱着嬰兒. *He held the rope in / with his teeth.* 他用牙齒咬住繩子. **3** keep back or under control 抑制, 止住; 約束: *Hold your tongue!* i.e. be quiet 住嘴! *We held our breath.* 我們屏住氣. *There is no holding him when he is angry.* 他生氣時誰也管不住他. **4** keep in a certain position or condition 保持(某種姿勢); 維持 (某種狀況): *I held my hands at my side.* 我雙手又攏. *They held their heads high.* 他們高昂着頭. *They are holding themselves ready.* 他們準備好了. *The speech held our attention.* 講演把我們吸引住了. **5** contain; be able to contain 容納, 裝得下: *How much does this bag hold?* 這隻袋子能裝多少? *past* 過去式 和過去分詞 **held** [held]. **holding** *nc* something possessed or occupied 佔有物; 擁有的財產: *I have holdings in the business* i.e. shares 我有這家商行的股份. *He has a small holding near here* i.e. he possesses or occupies a small farm. 他在離這裏不遠的地方有一個小農場. **hold back** be unwilling to do something 躊躇, 退縮不前; 不願做某事. **hold somebody back** keep somebody from going forward or doing something 阻止, 阻擋某人. **hold something back** keep something secret 隱瞞某事: *He is holding back important information.* 他隱瞞了重要的消息. **hold on** wait 等一等; 稍候(打電話時用語): *Hold on a minute!* (informal) 慢著, 別掛上! (非正式). **hold on to something** keep (firmly) in one's hands or possession 抓住某物不放: *He held on to the rope.* 他牢牢抓住繩子. *You should hold on to your lovely house.* 你不應當不要這座漂亮房子. **hold out** refuse to give up; endure; last 堅持, 不退讓; 忍耐; 持續: *The troops held out for a week.* 軍隊堅持了一星期. *The water won't hold out much longer.* 水維持不了多久了. **hold something out** offer; promise 提供; 允諾: *I can hold out no hope for you.* 我不能給你甚麼希望. **hold up 1** delay 延遲, 拖延: *The storm held us up.* 暴雨使我們耽擱了. **2** stop in order to rob 攔路搶劫: *The thieves held up the van and took everything in it.* 盜賊們攔截了貨車, 將其洗劫一空. **3** raise or show so that others see 舉起…展示: *Hold up your exercise books!* 出示你們的練習本! *They held him up to ridicule* i.e. they caused other people to laugh at him by showing his weaknesses etc. 他們舉出他的弱點當衆加以嘲笑. **'holdup** *nc* **1** delay 延遲, 拖延. **2** robbery with violence 攔劫, 搶劫.

hold² [həuld] **1** *nu* act of holding 抓; 掌握, 控制: *catch / lay / seize / take hold of somebody / something* 抓住某人/某物. (opp 反義語 **let go / lose (one's**

hold) **2** *nc* something which can be held on to 可抓攀的東西; 可踐踏的地方; 支撐點: *There were no holds for the hands on the wall.* 牆上沒有可用手抓住的東西. *He found a foothold* i.e. a place to support his foot while climbing 他找到了立足點. 即: 攀登時踩腳的地方.

hold³ [həuld] *nc* place below the deck of a ship where the cargo is put (船的)貨艙, 底艙.

hole [həul] *nc* **1** opening or space in something 洞: *There is a hole in the roof, which lets in rain.* 屋頂有個洞, 雨水從洞裏漏進來. *They dug a big hole in the ground.* 他們在地上挖了一個大洞. *Golf courses have either nine or eighteen holes.* 高爾夫球場有九洞或十八個洞. **Also** 亦作 *vt* **1** cause to have a hole 鑽洞, 穿孔. **2** (golf) put in a hole 把(高爾夫球)打入洞中: *He holed the ball from a distance of twenty feet.* 他從二十英尺遠的地方擊球入洞.

holiday ['hɔlidei] *nc* **1** day free from work 假日: *The headmaster has made Friday a holiday.* 校長決定星期五放假. **2** (often *pl*) any period of time free from work (常用複數)假期: *The school is closed for Christmas / summer holidays.* 聖誕節假期中/暑假中學校不上課. *They went on holiday last week.* 上星期他們去度假了. **'holidaymaker** person on holiday 度假者.

holiness ['həulinis] *nu* condition of being holy 神聖.

hollow¹ ['hɔləu] *adj / adv* **1** not solid; empty inside 空心的(地); 中空的(地); *Pipes are hollow.* 管子是空心的. **2** giving a sound like that made by something hollow (聲音)空洞的(地): *He has a hollow voice.* 他的聲音給人一種空洞的感覺. **3** false; not to be relied upon 虚假的; 不可靠的(地): *These are hollow words.* 這些全是空話. *It was a hollow victory.* 這是虚假的勝利. Also 亦作 *adv* completely 完全地: *They beat us hollow. (informal)* 他們完全勝過了我們. (非正式).

hollow² ['hɔlou] *nc* wide, shallow hole; ground which is lower than the surrounding area (大而淺的)洞, 坑; 低地, 窪地: *The cottage is in the hollow.* 小屋建在低窪的地方. Also 亦作 *adj* like a hollow 凹的, 凹陷的: *hollow eyes / cheeks* i.e. sunken 深陷的眼睛/雙頰. Also 亦作 *vt* make a hollow in 把…挖空. **hollow something out** form by making a hollow in something 把…挖空(以製造…).

holly ['hɔli] *nu* type of evergreen tree with sharp pointed leaves and red or yellow berries, used as decoration at Christmas 冬青樹(可作聖誕節裝飾用).

holster ['houlstə*] *nc* case in which a pistol or revolver is carried (usu. over the hip) 手槍皮套.

holy ['houli] *adj* of God or a religion; good and pure 神的, 宗教的; 神聖的, 聖潔的: *the Holy Bible* 聖經; *the Holy Koran* 可蘭經; *a holy man* 虔誠的信徒; *a holy life* 聖潔的生活. (*opp* 反義詞 **unholy**). **holiness** *nu.*

homage ['hɔmidʒ] *nu* act of respect to somebody famous (and usu. dead) (對名人,通常是死者的)崇敬: *We all paid homage to the great man.* 我們都崇敬這位偉人.

home [houm] **1** *nc / u* house or place where one was born 出生之處, 家鄉. **2** *nc* house or place where one lives 家; 住宅: *He has a pleasant home near the river.* 他在河邊有一座舒適的住宅. *England was his home.* 他的家在英國. *The home of the lion is afri-*

ca. 獅子原產於非洲. **3** *nc* special building for persons needing help or attention 收容所: *a home for the aged* 養老院, 敬老院; *a children's home* 孤兒院; *a nursing home* 療養院. Also 亦作 *adj* of the home or one's own country or the place one belongs to 家庭的; 本國的; 本地的: *the home team* 主隊; 本國隊; 本地隊; *a home game* 在本地舉行的比賽; *home cooking* 家常菜; *home trade* 國內貿易. Also 亦作 *adv* at or to one's home or one's own country 在家, 在家鄉, 在本國; 回家; 到家: *They went home.* 他們回家了. *He's home.* 他在家; 他到家了. **homeless** *adj* without a home 無家可歸的. **'homecoming** coming to one's own home 回到家裏, 回到家鄉; 回到本國. **'home'grown** *adj* grown in one's own country i.e. not abroad 本國產的, 土產的. **'home'made** *adj* made at home, not in a factory 家裏自製的. **'homesick** *adj* longing to be at home 想家的, 懷鄉的. **'home 'truth** truth that someone tells one about another person or about oneself (often an unpleasant truth) 使人難堪的事實; 逆耳忠言. **'homework** work done at home (usu. by a school pupil in the evening) 家庭作業. **at home 1** in one's own house 在家: *I keep my tools at home.* 我把工具放在家裏. **2** at the place one belongs to (usu. a sports team) (運動指球隊)在本地: *Our football team plays at home next Saturday.* 我們的足球隊下星期六在本地比賽. (*opp* **away** in sense **2**) (義**2**的反義詞為 **away**).

homely ['houmli] *adj* plain and simple 家常的; 簡樸的: *homely speech* 簡單樸實的一番話; *homely food* 家常便飯. *Note* 說明: *(US) homely* used of people has the sense of *ugly*: *a home-*

ly face i.e. a face that is plain, not good-looking 在美國英語中, homely 指人時意爲"不漂亮的". a homely face 即: 並不好看的容貌.

homeostasis [,houmiou'steisis] *nu* tendency of an organism to maintain internal equilibrium, as of temperature and fluid content, by the regulation of its bodily processes (生物的) 體內平衡. **homeostatic** *adj* of or having to do with homeostasis 體內平衡的.

homestead ['houmsted] *nc* place, esp. a farm, where a family makes its home, including the land, house, and outbuildings 家宅(包括田地, 房屋和庫房、畜棚等).

homicide ['hɔmisaid] *nu* killing of another person 殺人.

homogeneous [hɔmə'dʒi:niəs] *adj* of the same kind throughout 同種的; 同類的: *The people of this country are homogeneous* i.e. they are all of one kind. 該國居民屬於同一種族.

homogenize [hɔ'mɔdʒinaiz] *vt* treat (milk) so that fat droplets are emulsified and cream does not separate; make (a mixture) become evenly spread 使(牛奶的)油脂粒均勻分佈; 使 (混合物)均勻: *homogenized milk* 均質牛乳.

homonym ['hɔmənim] *nc* word which has the same sound and / or spelling as another word but has a different meaning (e.g. *bear* and *bare*) 同音異義詞; 同形異義詞; 同音同形異義詞(如 bear 和 bare).

homosexual [,hɔmou'seksjuəl] *adj* loving somebody of the same sex (e.g. a man loving a man instead of a woman) 同性戀的(如男人戀男人而不戀女人). Also 亦作 *nc* a person (usu. a man) who loves in this way 同性戀

者(通常指男同性戀者). *Note* 說明: the usual word for a homosexual woman is *lesbian*. 女同性戀者通常稱爲 lesbian.

honest ['ɔnist] *adj* true; fair; not cheating 忠實的; 公正的; 不欺詐的: *He is honest in all he does.* 他的一切行爲誠實正派. *They gave me an honest answer.* 他們向我作了誠實的回答. *an honest face* i.e. the *face* of an honest person 誠實的面孔. (*opp* 反義詞 **dishonest**). **honestly** *adv* 1 in an honest way 誠實地: *He got the money honestly.* 他的錢是正當得來的. 2 truly; in fact 真正地, 確實地; 事實上: *Honestly, I don't know.* 我實在不知道. **honesty** *nu.*

honey ['hʌni] *nu* the sweet, thick liquid made by bees 蜂蜜. **honeycomb** *nc* thing consisting of very small six-sided cells in which bees store honey and eggs 蜂房, 蜂巢.

honeymoon ['hʌnimu:n] *nc* the holiday taken by a husband and wife immediately after their marriage 蜜月.

honk [hɔŋk] *nc* noise made by a goose; any noise like this (esp. the noise made by the born of a motorcar) 雁鳴聲; 汽車喇叭聲. Also 亦作 *vi* make a honk 發出雁鳴聲; 按汽車喇叭.

honorary ['ɔnərəri] *adj* 1 working without pay 義務的: *the honorary secretary of our club* (usu. written *hon. secretary*) 本俱樂部的義務秘書(通常寫作 hon. secretary). 2 given as an honour 榮譽的: *an honorary degree of the university* 大學的榮譽學位; *honorary membership of the students' society* 學生社團的名譽會員.

honour¹ ['ɔnə*] *adj* 1 *nu* (*US* 美 **honor**) 1 *nu* great respect; high regard 尊敬; 敬意: *There will be a special meeting in honour of the President.* 將特別召開會

議歡迎這位總統。 **2** *nu* good character or reputation 名譽; 好名聲; 聲望: *He is a man of honour.* 他是一個講信譽的人。 *They fight for the honour of their country.* 他們為國家的榮譽而戰。 *I promise on my honour that it will be done.* 我以名譽擔保這件事一定會做好。 **3** *nu* person / thing which brings honour 被引以為榮的人/事: *You are an honour to your school.* 你爲你的學校增光。 **4** *nc* title of respect (usu. to a judge) (通常用於對法官的尊稱)閣下, 先生: *His Honour the Judge* 法官先生(間接提及時用); *I am not guilty, Your Honour.* 我沒有犯罪, 法官先生(直接稱呼時用)。 **5** *nc* (usu. *pl*) act or title that gives honour or respect to somebody (通常用複數)給某人以榮譽或向某人表示敬意的儀式或稱號: *The general was buried with military honours* i.e. with special acts of respect (e.g. the playing of military music, the firing of guns etc.); 將軍以軍葬禮下葬。(如奏軍樂、鳴砲等); *birthday honours* i.e. the list of honours (in sense 5) given by the King or Queen of Great Britain on his or her birthday 英國國王或女王誕辰時所授與的爵位及勳章: *He took honours at this university* i.e. a type of degree which is better than an ordinary one; 他獲得了該大學的優等學位; *an honours degree* 優等學位。

honour² [ˈɒnə*] (*US* 美 **honor**) *vt* **1** respect greatly; give or feel honour 尊敬; 授與榮譽; 感到榮幸: *Children should honour their father and mother.* 子女應當尊敬父母。 *The king honoured him with a knighthood.* 國王授與他騎士稱號。 *I am honoured to be asked to speak.* 我應邀發言, 不勝榮幸。 **2** pay a bill / cheque etc when one has promised to 兌現, 支付(賬單、

支票等): *He has not enough money to honour his cheques.* 他的錢不够付支票。 (*opp* 反義詞 **dishonour**).

honourable [ˈɒnərəbl] (*US* 美 honorable) *adj* deserving or satisfying honour 榮譽的, 光榮的; 體面的: *He has done honourable work.* 他做了體面的工作。 *We must have an honourable peace.* 我們必須得到體面的和平。 (*opp* 反義詞 **dishonourable**).

hood [hud] *nc* **1** cloth covering for the head and neck, often part of a cloak or gown 兜帽, 頭巾。 **2** type of covering with other uses (e.g. the soft, folding cover on top of a carriage or motorcar, the covering over a chimney) 其他遮蓋物(例如: 車篷, 烟囱帽等)。 **3** (*US*) cover over the engine in the front of a car. (*Brit* 英 **bonnet**) (美)(汽車的)發動機罩。

hoodwink [ˈhudwiŋk] *vt* cheat; deceive 欺騙; 欺騙。

hoof [hu:f] *nc* the hard part of the foot of a horse, cow, sheep etc. 蹄。 *pl* 複數 **hooves** [hu:vz]

hook¹ [huk] *nc* bent piece of metal etc shaped like a J used to catch something or hang something up 鈎: *a fish hook* 釣魚鈎; *a boat hook* 帶鈎的撐篙。

hook² [huk] *vt* / *i* **1** fasten, hang or catch with a hook or hooks 用鈎鈎住; 掛在鈎上; 用鈎鈎(魚): *This dress hooks down the side.* 這件女服在一側裝掛鈎。 *He hooked up his coat.* 他把外套掛在鈎子上。 *I have hooked a fish.* 我釣到了一條魚。 **2** put in the shape of a hook. 彎成鈎狀: *He hooked his fingers over the branch.* 他用手指鈎住樹枝。 **hooked** *adj* **1** having hooks; shaped like a hook 有鈎的; 鈎狀的。 **2** addicted 上癮的: *hooked on drugs* 吸毒成癮。

hooligan [ˈhu:ligən] *nc* rough, noisy

person who fights or causes trouble in the streets 流氓, 歹徒, 不良分子.

hoop [hu:p] *nc* thin ring of metal, wood, plastic etc. 箍: *Wooden barrels are fitted with iron hoops.* 木桶上裝着鐵箍.

hoot [hu:t] *nc* **1** noise made by an owl 貓頭鷹的叫聲. **2** sound showing anger, disapproval, amusement etc. 表示憤怒, 不贊成或逗樂的喊叫聲. **3** noise made by the horn of a motorcar, factory whistle or siren 汽車喇叭聲; 工廠汽笛聲. Also *vcr vt / i* I heard an owl hooting. 我聽見了貓頭鷹在叫. *He hooted with laughter.* 他狂笑. *They hooted him down* i.e. shouted in anger so that he could not be heard. 他們給他喝倒彩. *At the corner I hooted my horn.* 在拐彎處我按了喇叭. **hooter** *nc* factory whistle or siren (esp. used to signal when work begins and stops) 工廠的汽笛 (尤指上下班時拉響的汽笛).

Hoover [ˈhuːvə] ℞ *nc* type of vacuum cleaner 一種真空吸塵器. **hoover** *vt* clean a floor etc with a vacuum cleaner 用真空吸塵器清潔地板.

hooves [huːvz] *pl* of **hoof.** hoof 的複數.

hop[1] [hɔp] *nc* type of climbing plant or its fruit (used to flavour beer) 蛇麻草, 蛇麻草籽 (用以使啤酒帶苦味).

hop[2] [hɔp] *vt / i* (of persons) jump on one foot; (of birds and animals) jump on both or all feet (人) 單足跳; (鳥, 獸) 齊足跳.

hop[3] [hɔp] *nc* short jump 跳, 跳躍.

hope[1] [houp] *vt / i* wish or expect that something will happen 希望, 盼望: *I hope (that) you will come.* 我希望你會來. *We hope to see you again.* 我們希望能再和你見面. *Will he come? I hope so.* 他會來嗎? 我希望他會來. *Will they be angry? We hope not.* 他們

會生氣嗎? 我們希望不至於如此. *They hoped for victory.* 他們希望能够獲勝.

hope[2] [houp] *nc / u* wish or feeling that something good will happen 希望: *We have some hope of success.* 我們有幾分成功的希望. *There is little hope that he will come.* 他來的希望不大. *I have great hopes of victory.* 我獲勝的希望很大. **hopeful** *adj* having or giving hope 懷有希望的; 有希望的: *They continue to be hopeful.* 他們繼續抱有希望. *This is hopeful news.* 這是有希望的消息. *He is one of our most hopeful scientists* i.e. one who is likely to be very successful. 他是我們最有希望的科學家之一. 即: 他可能大有成就. **hopefully** *adv* having no hope 沒有希望的, 絕望的; **hopeless** *adj* having no hope 沒有希望的, 絕望的: *The situation is hopeless.* 局勢已經毫無希望. *You are completely hopeless* i.e. you are so bad, weak etc that there is no hope for you. 你已經毫無指望了. 即: 壞得或衰弱得無可救藥了.

horde [hɔːd] *nc* large number of people or animals (usu. not under control) (通常指亂紛紛的) 人羣, 動物羣: *Hordes of people tried to get into the hall.* 亂紛紛的人羣試圖湧入大廳.

horizon [həˈraizn] *nc* line where the sky seems to meet the earth or sea 地平線: *We saw a ship far away on the horizon.* 我們看見遠處地平線上有一艘船.

horizontal [hɔriˈzɔntl] *adj* parallel to the horizon; level 水平的; 橫的. *(opp* **vertical).** 反義詞 **vertical.**

hormone [ˈhɔːmoun] *nc* type of chemical substance made by certain glands of the body 荷爾蒙; 激素.

horn [hɔːn] **1** *nc* hard, pointed growth projecting from the head of certain animals (e.g. cattle) 角: *A bull has two horns.* 公牛有兩隻角. **2** *nu* the substance which forms a horn 角質物: *The dagger has a handle of horn.* 這匕首有角製的柄. **3** *nc* type of musical instrument, played by blowing into it (now usu. made of metal, not horn) 號角，喇叭 (現在通常用金屬而不用角製成): *a hunting horn* 獵號. **4** *nc* type of instrument for making a warning noise 警報器: *a motor horn* 汽車喇叭; *a foghorn* 霧角 (濃霧信號).

hornet ['hɔːnit] *nc* type of large wasp, which can sting severely 大黃蜂.

horoscope ['hɔrəskoup] *nc* plan of the positions of the stars (esp. at the time of a person's birth) from which it is believed his future can be told 占星術.

horrible ['hɔribl] *adj* **1** causing horror; dreadful 恐怖的; 可怕的: *horrible injuries* 可怕的傷害. **2** very unpleasant 令人極不愉快的: *This food is horrible.* 這食物難吃極了.

horrid ['hɔrid] *adj* very unpleasant; disgusting 令人極不愉快的; 討厭透頂的: *Why are you so horrid to him?* 爲甚麼你這麼討厭他?

horrify ['hɔrifai] *vt* cause, or fill with, horror 使恐怖，嚇.

horror ['hɔrə*] *nc* feeling of great fear etc. 恐怖; 戰慄: *She has a horror of small insects.* 她很怕小蟲子. *Rock climbing has no horrors for me.* 攀登山岩並不會給我帶來恐怖感. *To their horror the roof of their house caught fire.* 使他們感到恐怖的是他們的房頂着火了. *They ran in horror from the room.* 他們驚恐萬分地從那房間跑出來.

horsd'oeuvre [ɔːˈdəːvr] *nc* light savoury dish eaten before the main part of a meal 正餐前的開胃小菜.

horse [hɔːs] *nc* type of animal used for riding, carrying loads and pulling

vehicles 馬. **horsy** *adj* **1** like a horse 馬的，似馬的. **2** fond of horses and horseracing 愛馬的; 愛賽馬的. **'horseback** only in **on horseback** i.e. on the back of a horse 騎馬於 on horseback, 即: 在馬背上. **'horse 'chestnut** *nc* **1** type of tree with large leaves 歐洲七葉樹. **2** inedible nut of this tree 歐洲七葉樹的果實. **'horseman** *nc* man on horseback; man skilled in riding a horse 騎馬者; 騎手，騎師. **'horsepower** a measure of the power of an engine i.e. the power needed to lift 550 pounds to a height of one foot in one second (usu. shortened to *h.p*) (發動機動力單位) 馬力 (1 馬力 = 550 英尺磅/秒, 通常縮寫爲 h. p.). **'horse-race** race between horses with riders 賽馬. **'horseshoe** iron shoe shaped like a U which is nailed to the hoof of a horse 馬蹄鐵.

horticulture ['hɔːtikʌlt[ə*]* *nu* gardening; the growing of flowers, fruit and vegetables 園藝.

hose [houz] *nc* long soft pipe through which running water is passed (e.g. to put out a fire or water plants) (救火或澆花用的) 軟管. **'hosepipe** type of large hose; part of a hose 一種較粗的軟管; 一段軟管: *a short length of hosepipe* 一段不長的軟管.

hospitable [hɔsˈpitəbl] *adj* friendly and kind to guests 好客的; 慇懃的. *(opp* 反義詞 **inhospitable**).

hospital ['hɔspitl] *nc* building(s) in which sick and injured people are attended to and cared for 醫院. *Note* 說明: *hospital without the* usu. has the sense of the attention and care given. *He is in hospital* i.e. he is staying there to be attended to. *He is in the hospital* i.e. he is there as a visitor or for some other reason, not to be attended to. *The driver left hospital* i.e. because he was now well he was able to go home. *The driver left the hospital* i.e. he did not go there to be attended to, but for some other reason, and left afterwards. hospital 一詞前沒有 the 時通常表示在醫院受到的治療和護理。He is in hospital. 他住院了。即: 他作爲病人正在醫院裏接受治療。He is in the hospital. 他在醫院裏。即: 他去醫院辦別的事, 而不是去看病。The driver left hospital. 司機病癒出院。The driver left the hospital. 司機離開了醫院。即: 司機不是去醫院看病的, 他辦完事走了。

hospitality [hɔspi'tæliti] *nu* friendliness and kindness to guests 好客; 慇懃, 款待。see 見 **hospitable**.

host¹ [houst] *nc* large number 一大羣: *We met hosts of students.* 我們遇到了成羣的學生。

host² [houst] *nc* person who receives and looks after guests (款待客人的) 主人: *Last night we were hosts to a few friends.* 昨晚我們招待了幾位朋友。

hostage ['hɔstidʒ] *nc* person handed over or kept as a prisoner until what has been promised or demanded is done 人質: *The enemy took hostages from the village after they captured it* i.e. to make sure the people of the village remained quiet; 敵人佔領村子後, 扣留了一些村民作爲人質。即: 防備村民反對他們。*take someone hostage* 扣留某人作爲人質。

hostel ['hɔstl] *nc* house in which students and young people etc live when they are away from home 招待所; 寄宿舍; (在校外的)學生宿舍。

hostess ['houstes] *nc* woman who receives and looks after guests; wife of a host (款待客人的)女主人; (款待客人的)男主人之妻。

hostile ['hɔstail] *adj* of an enemy; unfriendly; opposed 敵方的, 敵對的; 反對的: *Bombing the town was a hostile act.* 轟炸該城是敵意的行動。*The crowd outside is hostile.* 外面的人羣懷有敵意。*The people are hostile to any change.* 人民反對任何變革。**hostility** · [hɔs'tiliti] **1** *nu* unfriendliness; opposition 敵意, 敵視; 敵對狀態; 反對。**2** *nc* (in *pl*) war; acts of war (用複數)戰爭; 戰事: *Hostilities ended when the treaty was signed.* 條約簽訂後戰爭即告結束。

hot [hɔt] *adj* **1** having great heat; very warm 熱的; 炎熱的: *The climate of that country is hot.* 該國氣候炎熱。*Hot water is better than cold water for washing clothes.* 用熱水洗衣服比用冷水好。*I feel hot.* 我覺得很熱。*Pepper is hot* i.e. it has a hot taste. 胡椒很辣。**2** violent; very active; keen 激烈的; 活躍的; 敏銳的: *He has a hot temper.* 他脾氣急躁。*The argument became hot.* 爭論變得激烈。*comparative* 比較級 **hotter**. *superlative* 最高級 **hottest**. **hotly** *adv*: *They argued hotly.* 他們爭論得很激烈。'**hot-blooded** *adj* quick-tempered; passionate 性情急躁的; 易怒的; 熱情的; 充滿激情的。**hot-bloodedly** *adv* ·**hot dog** sandwich with a hot sausage inside 熱狗(夾香腸麵包)。'**red-hot** very hot 赤熱的, 熾熱的。

hotel [hou'tel] *nc* building which provides meals and rooms for travellers (usu. bigger than an inn) 酒店, 旅館 (通常比 inn 大)。*Note* 說明: either *a hotel* or *an hotel*. 可以說 a hotel 也可以說an hotel.

hotline ['hɔtlain] *nc* telephone line for direct, instant communication in an emergency, esp. between heads of state 熱線, (尤指國家首腦)直接聯繫的

電話線.

hound [haund] *nc* type of dog used in hunting (esp. hunting by its sense of smell) 獵狗(尤指事其嗅覺打獵的獵狗). Also 亦作 *vt* chase a person as if with hounds 追逐: *They hounded him out of the country.* 他們把他從這個國家追趕出來.

hour ['auə*] *nc* **1** twenty-fourth part of a day; sixty minutes 小時; 六十分鐘: *The journey took three hours.* 旅程花了三個小時. *The meeting lasted hours.* 會議開了幾個小時. *I'll see you in an hour's time.* 我過一個小時跟你見面. **2** indefinite period of time 時光,一段時間: *These were the most interesting hours of my life.* 這是我一生中最有趣的時光. *They arrived at all hours.* 他們一天到晚任何時間來到的都有. **3** definite period in time 特定的時間: *I heard the clock strike the hour.* 我聽到鐘敲響報時. *He arrived on the hour.* 他準時到達. **4** (in *pl*) fixed times (用於複數)固定的時間: *Visiting hours at the hospital* 醫院允許探望病人的時間; *office hours* 辦公時間. **5** distance which takes an hour to travel 一小時內所完成的行程: *My house is two hours from the town;* 我家離城兩小時的路程; *a two hours' journey* 兩小時的路程. **hourly** *adv* **1** once every hour 每小時一次: *The clock strikes hourly.* 鐘每小時敲響. **2** at any hour 隨時: *His arrival is expected hourly.* 他隨時都可能來到. Also 亦作 *adj: an hourly train to London* 每小時一班開往倫敦的火車. **'hourhand** the smaller hand or pointer on a clock or watch which shows the hours (鐘錶的)時針.

house¹ [haus] *nc* **1** building in which people live; building in which animals or goods are kept 住宅, 房子; 棚; 庫:

Our house has three bedrooms; 我們的住宅裏有三間卧室; *a henhouse* 鶏棚; *a storehouse* 倉庫; *a warehouse* 貨棧, 倉庫. **2** building where people meet for a certain purpose 聚會場所: *a picture house* 電影院; *a gambling house* 賭場; *a roadhouse* 小客棧; *(Brit) the House of Commons* (英)下院, 下議院; *(US) the House of Representatives* (美)衆議院. **3** those in a house where people meet 觀衆, 聽衆, 參加會議者: *a full house* 滿座; 戲院 theatre full of people (大廳)滿座; (戲院)客滿. *The Prime Minister addressed the House (of Commons).* 首相在(下)議院致辭. *pl* 複數 **houses** ['hauziz]. **houseful** *nu* enough to fill a house 滿屋,一屋子: *a houseful of guests* 一屋子客人. **'houseboat** flat-bottomed boat for living in rather than sailing 船屋, 水上住家. **'housebreaker** *nc* person who breaks into a house to steal 侵入住宅行竊者. **housebreaking** *nu* **household** *nu* all the people who live in one house 全家人, 家屬. Also 亦作 *adj.* **'householder** person living in a house who either owns it or has rented it 住户. **'housekeeper** *nc* woman who is employed to look after a house 女管家. **'housekeeping** *nu* **1** management of a house 家務管理, 家政: *Good housekeeping saves money.* 家務管得好, 開支可減少. **2** money for the management of a house 家用開支. **'houseproud** *adj* proud and concerned about the appearance of one's house 關心家事的; 講究家庭擺設的. **'housetrained** *adj* trained to behave properly in a house (e.g. of a dog or cat) (貓、狗) 訓練成不在室內大小便的. **'house warming (party)** party given to welcome friends to one's new

home 遷入新居的慶宴, 喬遷之喜宴.
'**housewife** married woman responsible for the house where she lives 家庭主婦. '**housework** work done in a house i.e. cleaning and cooking etc. 家務勞動 (如打掃、烹調等).

house² [hauz] *vt* **1** put or take into a house; store 把…帶進房子; 給地方儲藏: *They housed the visitors in the next village.* 他們讓客人在鄰村住下了. **2** supply with houses 提供住房. **housing** *nu*: *The government has a serious housing problem.* 政府面臨嚴重的房荒問題. Also 亦作 *adj*. '**housing estate** area in which a large number of new houses are built (usu. by a local authority) (通常由地方當局建造大批新房的) 住宅區.

housefly ['hausflai] *nc* two-winged fly found in and around houses, it feeds on rubbish, manure, and food 蒼蠅. *pl* 複數 **houseflies.**

hovel ['hɔvl] *nc* small, dirty and miserable house 簡陋的小屋.

hover ['hɔvə*] *vi* **1** stay almost still in the air 翱翔, 盤旋: *The bird hovered over its nest.* 鳥在其鳥巢上空盤旋. **2** stay near; wait 逗留在附近, 徘徊; 等待: *The children hovered at the door.* 孩子們在門口等待. '**hovercraft** type of vehicle which travels just above the water or the ground, being held up by strong jets of air 氣墊船.

how [hau] *adv* **1** in what way 怎樣, 怎麼, 如何, 以甚麼方式: *How did you do it?* 你怎樣做這件事? **2** to what degree 多少, 多麼, 到甚麼程度: *How big is it?* 它有多大? *How many are there?* 有多少? **3** in what condition 怎樣, 情況如何: *How are you?* 你身體怎樣? 您好! *How do you do?* 您好! **4** for what reason 怎麼, 爲甚麼: *How is it that they are not here?* 他們怎麼沒有來? **5**

what is your opinion? (你以爲)…怎麼樣? *How about a cup of tea?* i.e. do you think we should have one? 喝杯茶好嗎? *How do you find your new school?* i.e. what do you think of it? 你以爲你們的新學校怎樣? 即: 你是怎麼想的? **6** as an exclamation (用於感嘆句) 多麼: *How kind of you!* 您好客氣! *How tall he is!* 他真高! Also 亦作 *conj: Tell me how you are.* 告訴我您的情況如何. **how ever** *adv* in whatever way; to whatever degree 無論如何, 不管怎樣. *However loudly you shout, you won't be heard.* 不管你喊得多響, 沒有人能聽得見. Also 亦作 *conj* nevertheless 儘管如此, 然而.

howl [haul] *vt / i* give a long, loud cry; cry out loudly in anger, pain, laughter etc. 號叫; 怒吼; 痛哭大喊; 狂笑: *I could hear the wolves howling in the forest.* 我能聽見狼在樹林中嗥叫. *We howled with laughter.* 我們高聲狂笑. *The boy howled when he was hit.* 男孩被砸痛了之後大聲哭叫. *They howled him down* i.e. shouted angrily so that he could not be heard. 他們叫喊得使人們聽不到他的講話. Also 亦作 *nc.* **howler** *nc* stupid but amusing mistake (esp. one by a student or pupil) (*informal*) 愚蠢可笑的錯誤 (尤指學生的錯誤) (非正式).

hub [hʌb] *nc* **1** central part of a wheel (輪) 轂. **2** central and important part of anything 中心, 最重要的部份: *This office is the hub of the whole company.* 這個辦公室是全公司的中心.

hubbub ['hʌbʌb] *nu* uproar; confused noise 吵鬧聲; 喧嘩聲: *I could not hear myself speak above the hubbub.* 在一片喧鬧聲中我聽不見自己的講話聲.

huddle ['hʌdl] *vt / i* crowd together (把…) 擠作一團: *We all huddled round* *the fire.* 我們都圍着火擠成一圖. *They huddled the poor children into a corner.* 他們把可憐的孩子們擠到角落. Also 亦作 *nc* confused crowd or heap 亂紛紛的一羣人; 亂糟糟的一堆東西.

hue¹ [hju:] *nc* colour 顏色, 色彩: *the hues of the woods in autumn.* 林中秋色.

hue² [hju:] *nu* shout (only in **hue and cry** i.e. a cry of warning when a criminal is being chased or a cry of protest against an injustice) 叫喊聲 (僅用於 hue and cry, 即: 追揖犯人時的警告聲和對不公正現象的抗議聲).

huff [hʌf] *nu* fit of bad temper 發怒: *He walked away in a huff. (informal)* 他怒氣冲冲地走了. (非正式)

hug [hʌg] *vt* **1** hold tightly in the arms (esp. to show love or pleasure) 摟抱: *She hugged her sister when she met her.* 她一見她妹妹就緊緊地摟抱她. **2** keep close to 緊靠: *The boat is hugging the coast.* 船正靠着海岸前進. *We hugged the wall to avoid being seen.* 我們把身體貼着牆以防被人看見. Also 亦作 *nc*: *Give me a hug.* 摟抱我吧. *pres part* 現在分詞 **hugging.** *past* 過去分詞 **hugged.**

huge [hju:dʒ] *adj* very great 巨大的.

hulk [hʌlk] *nc* **1** ship that is too old to be used at sea 廢舊大船. **2** big clumsy person 巨大笨重的人. **hulking** *adj* clumsy; unwieldy 笨重的; 龐大的.

hull [hʌl] *nc* frame or body of a ship 船身, 船殼.

hullo [hʌˈlou] *interj* used to greet, call attention, show surprise and answer telephone calls 喂; 哈囉. *pl* 複數 **hullos.** (Also 亦作 **hallo, hello**).

hum [hʌm] *vt / i* **1** sing with the mouth shut; make a sound like the letter *m* for a long time 哼 (歌曲); 發拖長的 m 音: *He hummed the tune to me.* 他把

調子哼給我聽. *I hear the insects humming.* 我聽見蟲在嗡嗡叫. **2** be busy, full of activity 忙碌; 活躍, 充滿活力: *The office is humming with activity* i.e. it is filled with the sounds of busy people 辦公室裏一片忙碌聲. Also 亦作 *nc* humming noise 嗡嗡聲: *There was a hum of approval* 人羣中有一片低語聲表示贊同.

human ['hju:mən] *adj* of man; having the qualities of man 人的; 有人性的: *There is no human life on Mars.* 火星上沒有人. *To starve a child is not human.* 讓孩子挨餓是不通人情的. **humanity** [hjuˈmæniti] *nu* **1** the human race; human nature 人類; 人性. **2** behaviour expected of man; kindness 仁愛; 仁慈: *They treated the prisoners with humanity.* 他們以仁慈對待犯人. **humanities** *npl* studies of the Arts i.e. of history, literature, philosophy etc. 人文學科. 即: 歷史, 文學, 哲學等. **humane** [hjuˈmein] *adj* gentle; kindhearted 文雅的, 溫柔的; 仁慈的: *the humane treatment of prisoners* 對囚犯的仁慈待遇. *(opp* 反義詞 **inhumane).**

humanism ['hju:mənizəm] *nc / u* belief or attitude emphasizing common human needs and seeking solely rational ways of solving human problems; cultural movement of the Renaissance, based on classical studies 人道主義; 人文主義. **humanist** *nc.*

humble ['hʌmbl] *adj* **1** having no pride in oneself; modest 謙遜的; 謙恭的: *Why were you so humble in the manager's office?* 你在經理的辦公室裏爲甚麼如此畢恭畢敬? **2** of low rank; poor 地位低下的, 卑賤的, 貧窮的: *He is of humble birth.* 他出身寒微. *They live in a humble street.* 他們住在一條簡陋的街上.

humdrum ['hʌmdrʌm] *adj* dull, unexciting 單調的; 索然寡味的: *Life in a small village can be very humdrum.* 小村子裏的生活可能是平淡無趣的.

humid ['hju:mid] *adj* (usu. of the air or climate) damp (通常指空氣或氣候)濕潤的. **humidity** [hju:'miditi] *nu.*

humiliate [hju:'milieit] *vt* make ashamed; hurt the pride of 羞辱; 傷…的自尊: *They humiliated us by laughing at everything we said.* 他們對我們的每一句話都加以嘲笑, 使我們出醜. **humiliating** *adj* **humiliation** [hju:mili'eiʃən] *nc / u* **humility** [hju:'militi] *nu* being humble or without pride 謙遜.

humour ['hju:mə*] (*US* 美 **humor**) *nu* **1** ability to see or describe what is amusing 幽默感: *They have a good / keen / no sense of humour.* 他們很有 / 有很強的 / 缺乏幽默感. *His reports are famous for their humour.* 他的報告以幽默著稱. **2** temper, mood 脾性; 情緒, 心情: *He was in a good / bad humour.* 他興致勃勃/興致索然. Also 亦作 *vt* amuse; make somebody happy by doing what he wants 逗…高興; 遷就…; 使高興: *They humoured him by agreeing they were wrong.* 他們承認自己不對的辦法來哄着他. **humorous** *adj* amusing; funny 幽默的; 有趣的. **humorist** *nc* humorous talker or writer 談吐幽默風趣的人; 幽默作家.

hump [hʌmp] *nc* round lump caused by a bend in the back (駝)峯: *Camels have humps.* 駱駝有駝峯.

humph [hʌmf] *interj* showing doubt or dissatisfaction 哼! (表示懷疑或不滿).

humus ['hju:məs] *nu* brown or black-organic part of the soil, resulting from the partial decay of plant and animal matter 腐殖質, 腐殖土壤.

hunch [hʌntʃ] *nc* **1** round lump caused by a bend in the back; hump 背部的隆肉; 肉峯, 駝背. **2** idea or belief not based on evidence; suspicion 直覺, 預感; 疑心: *The detective had a hunch about the crime* i.e. he thought he knew who committed the crime. 偵探對罪行有一種直覺. 即: 他認爲他知道罪犯是誰. Also 亦作 *vt* bend into the shape of a hunch 使彎成弓狀: *He sat hunched up on a chair.* 他弓着背坐在椅子上. **'hunchback** person having a bent spine, causing a lump on the back 駝背的人.

hundred ['hʌndrid] see appendix 百 (見附錄).

hundredweight ['hʌndridweit] *nc* weight of 112 pounds 英擔 (等於112磅).

hung [hʌŋ] past of **hang**[1]. hang[1]的過去式和過去分詞.

hunger ['hʌŋgə*] *nu* **1** desire for food; lack of food 飢餓; 飢荒: *We satisfied our hunger.* 我們吃東西充飢. *These children often suffer from hunger.* 這些孩子常常挨餓. **2** any strong desire 渴望: *their hunger for news from home* 他們對來自家鄉消息的渴望. **hungry** ['hʌŋgri] *adj* feeling or causing hunger 飢餓的, 引起飢餓的. **hungrily** *adv.*

hunt [hʌnt] *vt* **1** go after wild animals to catch or kill them either for food or for sport 打獵: *Lions hunt zebra.* 獅子獵食斑馬. *I have never hunted big game.* 我從未打過大獵物. **2** look for something that is lost 搜尋: *We hunted everywhere for the money.* 我們到處尋找這筆錢. Also 亦作 *nc* act of hunting; search 打獵; 搜索: *We helped in the hunt for the money* 我們幫忙尋找這筆錢. **hunter** *nc* **1** person who hunts 獵人. **2** horse used for hunting 獵馬. **hunting** *nu* actions of a person who hunts 打獵: *Hunting in these hills is dangerous;* 在這些山上打獵很危險; *a hunting knife* 獵刀. **hunt something down** go after something until one catches or finds it 追尋…直至捕獲; 搜尋…直至發現. **hunt something out** look for and find something (usu. something hidden) 搜尋出(通常指搜尋出隱藏的東西): *I hunted out my old notes.* 我找出了我的舊筆記.

hurdle ['hə:dl] *nc* **1** frame used to jump over in a race (賽跑用的)欄: *He won the 120 yards hurdle-race / hurdles.* 他在120碼跳欄比賽中獲勝. **2** problem or difficulty 障礙, 困難: *We soon got over that particular hurdle.* 我們很快就克服了那獨特的困難.

hurl [hə:l] *vt* throw with great force 用力投擲: *He hurled himself at the door.* 他向門猛撲過去.

hurrah [hu'ra:], **hurray** [hu'rei] *interj* used as a shout of joy or applause 好哇! (歡呼聲): *Hip, hip, hurray!* 嗨! 嗨! 萬歲!

hurricane ['hʌrikən] *nc* very strong wind 颶風.

hurry ['hʌri] *vt / i* move or do something quickly or in haste (使)匆忙; 趕快: *We hurried to school.* 我們匆匆忙忙地趕到學校. *Why are you hurrying them?* 你爲甚麼催促他們? *What made him hurry away / off?* 他爲甚麼匆匆離去? *Hurry along, please!* 請趕快走! *Hurry up! I'm waiting.* 快一些, 我在等你. Also 亦作 *nu*: *What's (the reason for) your hurry?* 你爲甚麼這樣急? *There's no hurry.* 沒有必要這麼匆忙. **hurried** *adj* done quickly or in haste 匆促的, 慌忙的: *We just had time for a hurried talk before he left.* 我們剛來得及匆忙談了幾句他就走了. **hurriedly**

adv.

hurt [hə:t] *vt / i* injure; cause pain to 傷害; 使疼痛; (使)傷心, 使痛苦: *He hurt his arm when he fell.* 他摔倒時傷了手臂. *My feet hurt (me).* 我的兩腳痛. *They were very hurt by your rude remarks* i.e. their feelings were hurt. 你的粗魯言詞傷了他們的感情. *I was hurt at not being asked.* 因爲沒有受邀請, 我很難過. *It won't hurt them to wait.* 讓他們等一等沒有關係. *past* 過去式和過去分詞 **hurt**. Also 亦作 *nc / u.* **hurtful** *adj* causing injury 造成傷痛的; 有害的: *Smoking is hurtful to our health.* 吸烟危害健康.

hurtle ['hə:tl] *vi* rush or fly with great speed 猛衝; 急駛: *The spears hurtled through the air.* 長矛在空中颼颼飛過.

husband ['hʌzbənd] *nc* man to whom a woman is married 丈夫.

hush [hʌʃ] *vt / i* become or make silent (使)安靜下來: *Hush!* i.e. be silent. 噓即: 安靜! *They hushed the crying children.* 他們把孩子哄得不哭了. Also 亦作 *nu.*

husk [hʌsk] *nc* dry outer covering of certain seeds (種子的)外殼, 皮.

husky[1] ['hʌski] *adj* (esp. of the voice) dry rough (尤指聲音)沙啞的: *His voice is husky because he has a cold.* 他感冒了, 聲音有些沙啞.

husky[2] ['hʌski] *nc* type of dog used for pulling sledges over snow 拉雪橇的狗.

husky[3] ['hʌski] *adj* big and strong 高大強壯的: *a fine, husky fellow* 一個很壯實的人.

hustle ['hʌsl] *vt / i* act or move quickly; push (使)趕快做, (使)快速移動; 推: *They hustled him into a car and drove off.* 他們把他推進汽車並把車開走. Also 亦作 *nu.*

hut [hʌt] *nc* small, simply-made build

ing 小屋, 棚屋.

hutch [hʌtʃ] *nc* small wooden cage for keeping small animals (esp. rabbits) 養小動物的箱(尤指兔箱).

hyacinth ['haiəsinθ] *nc* type of sweet-smelling spring flower 風信子.

hyaena [hai'i:nə] *nc* see 見 **hyena.**

hybrid ['haibrid] *nc* mixture of two different species of animals or plants 雜種: *A mule is a hybrid* i.e. its parents are a horse and a donkey. 騾子是雜種. 即: 騾子是馬和驢雜交而生的.

hydrant ['haidrnt] *nc* water pipe to which a hose can be attached (usu. found in streets and beside large buildings, such as factories and schools, so that fires can be put out quickly) 消防龍頭; 消防栓.

hydraulic [hai'drɔ:lik] *adj* operated by water or other liquid 水力的; 液壓的: *a hydraulic press* 水壓機.

hydroelectric ['haidroui'lektrik] *adj* producing electricity by using the force of falling water 水力發電的: *This hydroelectric scheme uses the waters of the River Nile.* 這項水力發電計劃要使用尼羅河的水.

hydrofoil ['haidroufɔil] *nc* boat equipped with device for raising hull out of water to enable rapid motion 水翼船.

hydrogen ['haidrədʒən] *nu* type of very light gas which forms water (when mixed with oxygen) (H) 氫.

hydroplane ['haidrəplein] *nc* type of motorboat which travels very quickly on the surface of the water 水面快艇, 水上滑行艇.

hydroxide [hai'drɔksaid] *nc* any compound containing an-OH group 氫氧化物.

hyena, hyaena [hai'i:nə] *nc* type of flesh-eating wild animal like a dog, which comes out at night, found in Africa and Asia 鬣狗.

hygiene ['haidʒi:n] *nu* science of keeping people in good health 衛生學; 保健術. **hygienic** [hai'dʒi:nik] *adj* (opp 反義詞 **unhygienic).**

hymn [him] *nc* song of praise or thanks to God 讚美詩. Also 亦作 *vt* praise or thank with hymns 唱讚美詩.

hyphen ['haifən] *nc* the mark used to divide one word into syllables (e.g. Mon-day) or join two words (e.g. self-help) 連字號(即-).

hypnotize ['hipnətaiz] *vt* put a person into a type of deep sleep during which he can be made to do things without his own knowledge 催眠, 使進入催眠狀態. **hypnotic** [hip'nɔtik] *adj* **hypnotism** ['hipnətizəm] *nu* **hypnotist** ['hipnətist] *nc* person who can hypnotize 催眠師. **hypnosis** [hip'nousis] *nu* state of being in this type of sleep 催眠狀態: *Doctors can sometimes cure a patient under hypnosis.* 有時醫生能用催眠療法治愈病人.

hypochondriac [haipə'kɔndriæk] *adj.* Also 亦作 *nc* a person who worries unnecessarily about his health. 憂鬱症患者; 疑病狂患者.

hypocrisy [hi'pɔkrisi] *nc / u* pretending to be morally better than one really is 偽善, 矯飾, 虛偽. **hypocrite** ['hipəkrit] *nc* person who pretends in this way 偽君子, 虛偽的人. **hypocritical** [hipə'kritikl] *adj.*

hypotenuse [hai'pɔtinju:z] *nu* side in a right-angled triangle that is opposite the right angle (直角三角形的)斜邊; 弦.

hypothesis [hai'pɔθisis] *nc* something which is assumed in order to argue or explain 假設, 假說: *His theory is based on the hypothesis that all men are born equal.* 他的理論是基於人皆

生來平等的假設之上的. *pl* 複數 **hypotheses** [haipəˈθisiːz]. **hypothetical** [haipəˈθetikl] *adj* assumed; not certain 假設的; 不肯定的.

hysteria [hisˈtiəriə] *nu* nervous excitement causing feelings and behaviour that cannot be controlled 歇斯底里,

癔病: *mass hysteria* i.e. hysteria suffered by a large number of people at the same time 羣體歇斯底里, 人羣的過度興奮, 即: 許多人同時患此症. **hysterical** [hisˈterikl] *adj*. **hysterics** [hisˈteriks] *n sing or pl* 單數或複數 an attack of hysteria 歇斯底里症發作.

I,i

I [ai] *pron* used by a person, who is speaking, to refer to himself 我: *I am / I'm leaving now.* 我這就走. *Note* 說明: there are two question forms in general use. am I not (formal) and aren't I ['a:ntai] (less formal. normal expression when speaking). *I am quite tall, am I not / aren't I?* 普通使用的問句形式有兩種. 正式的用法是 am I not; 口語中正常使用的, 較不正式的用法是 aren't I ['a:ntai]. I am quite tall, am I not / aren't I? 我相當高, 不是嗎?

ice[1] [ais] *nu* water which has been turned solid by cold 冰: *In winter the lake is covered with ice.* 冬天裏湖面結了冰. **icy** *adj* like ice; very cold; covered with ice 冰的; 極冷的; 冰覆蓋的: *icy winds* 寒風; *an icy welcome* 冷淡的歡迎; *icy streets* 覆蓋着冰的街道. **'ice age** time long ago when the world was much colder and thick ice covered large areas 冰河時代. **'iceberg** a mountain of ice which has broken off from a glacier and floats in the sea 冰山, 浮冰. **'icebox** *(US)* refrigerator (美)冰箱. **'ice'cream** *nc / u* sweetened cream or substance like cream which has been made as cold as ice 冰淇淋. **'ice hockey** *(Brit)* type of hockey played on ice. *(US* (美) **hockey)** (英)冰上曲棍球, 冰球. **'ice rink** open space covered with ice used for skating or other sports 溜冰場.

ice[2] [ais] *vt / i* **1** (usu. with **over** or **up**) cover, become covered, with ice (通常與over或up連用)(使)結冰, 用冰覆蓋: *The river has iced over.* 河給冰封

住了. **2** cover with icing 撒上糖霜: *His mother iced his birthday cake.* 他媽媽給他的生日蛋糕撒上糖霜. **icing** *nu* mixture of fine sugar and the white of eggs etc used for covering cakes etc. (糕餅表面的) 糖衣, 糖霜.

icicle ['aisikl] *nc* long, pointed piece of ice made from slowly dropping water (e.g. from a roof) (從屋簷等處垂下的) 冰柱.

idea [ai'diə] *nc* **1** plan; aim; suggestion 計劃; 目標; 建議, 意見: *Their idea is to sell their big house and buy a smaller one.* 他們打算賣掉大房子, 買一座小的. *Have you any idea how we should do it?* 你對於我們該怎樣做這件事有甚麼建議嗎? **2** feeling that something will happen 預感; 猜想: *·I had no idea you would go away.* 我沒有想到你會走開. *Where did you get the idea that I could not come?* 你怎麼會認爲我不能來? **3** mental picture; thought 概念; 想法: *They have no idea of life in a hot country.* 他們不知道在氣候炎熱的國家裏人們如何生活. *My idea of happiness is not the same as yours.* 我的幸福觀和你的不一樣.

ideal [ai'diəl] *adj* the best one can think of; existing only in the mind; not real 理想的; 概念的; 虛構的: *This is the ideal place to spend a holiday;* 這是理想的度假場所; *an ideal society in which nobody is rich and nobody poor* 沒有貧富之分的理想社會. Also 亦作 *nu* best example; highest aim 完美的典型; 最高的目標: *He is not my ideal of a good teacher.* 他不是我心目中的理想老師. *Their ideals are peace* *and prosperity.* 他們理想的目標是和平和繁榮. **ideally** *adv* **idealism** *nu* **1** aiming at what is most perfect 理想主義: *Young people in their idealism think war is impossible.* 信奉理想主義的年青人認爲戰爭是絕不可能的. **2** belief that only ideas are real and can be known 唯心主義. *(opp* 反義詞 **materialism). 3** imaginative treatment in art with little thought for what is real 注重想像脫離現實的文藝手法. *(opp* 反義詞 **realism). idealist** *nc* person who believes in idealism 唯心主義者; 理想主義者.

identical [ai'dentikl] *adj* the very same; exactly alike 完全相同的; 十分相像的: *My hat is identical to / with yours.* 我的帽子和你的一模一樣. *Your hat and mine are identical.* 你的帽子和我的一模一樣. **identical twins** twins born from one ovum of their mother and so exactly alike 同卵雙胞胎.

identify [ai'dentifai] *vt* **1** recognize; tell or show who or what somebody / something is 辨認; 認出: *I cannot identify this signature* i.e. I cannot tell whose it is. 我認不出這簽名. 即: 我不知道這是誰的簽名. **2** consider to be the same 使等同於; 認爲 … 一致: *Wealth cannot be identified with happiness.* 財富不等於幸福. **identification** [aidentifi'keiʃən] *nu* identifying somebody / something; being identified 認出, 識別; 確認: *the identification of criminals by their fingerprints* 根據指紋鑒定罪犯.

Identikit [ai'dentikit]" *nc* picture drawn from descriptions of persons wanted by the police 識別罪犯用的面部拼圖部件.

identity [ai'dentiti] **1** *nu* being exactly the same or alike 同一 (性); 一致. **2** *nc / u* who or what somebody / some-

thing is 身份, 特性: *The police are trying to find out the identity of the man killed in the accident.* 警方正在設法查明事故中死亡者的身份.

ideogram ['idiougræm], **ideograph** ['idiougra:f] *nc* graphic symbol representing an object or idea without expressing the sounds that from its name 表意文字.

ideology [aidi'ɔlədʒi] *nc* set of ideas in which a person or group of persons firmly believe (esp. philosophical and political ideas) (尤指哲學及政治方面的)思想體系, 意識形態, 思想意識: *our democratic ideology* 我們的民主意識; *the ideology of a dictator* 獨裁者的思想.

idiocy ['idiəsi] *nc / u* see 見 **idiot.**

idiom ['idiəm] *nc* the way a person naturally speaks or writes his own language where the meaning is given by words together not separately (e.g. in English *What do you take me for?* i.e. What sort of person do you think I am?) 習語, 成語; 語言習慣用法(如 What do you take me for? 即: 你把我當作甚麼人來看?).

idiosyncrasy [idiou'siŋkrəsi] *nc* what makes a person different from anyone else (e.g. odd ways of behaving, thinking, speaking etc.) (人的)特質; 特性, 癖性 (如行爲、思想、講話的特殊方式等).

idiot ['idiət] *nc* person with a very weak mind; a fool 白癡; 傻子. **idiotic** [idi-'ɔtik] *adj* **idiocy** ['idiəsi] **1** *nu* being an idiot 白癡, 極端愚蠢. **2** *nc* a very stupid act 極端愚蠢的行爲.

idle ['aidl] *adj* **1** not doing any work; not in use 空閑的; 閑着的: *Many workmen were made idle when the factory was closed.* 工廠關閉時, 許多工人閑着無事. *It is a pity that all this* *equipment is left idle.* 遺憾的是所有這些設備都閒置着. **2** lazy; not willing to work 懶惰的; 不願工作的: *He is too idle to do anything.* 他懶得甚麼事都不做. **3** of no use or effect 無用的; 無效的: *idle gossip / talk* 無聊的閑話/談話. Also 亦作 *vt / i* **1** (with **about** or **away**) be idle; waste (與about或away連用) 虛度, 無所事事; 空費: *He is always idling about street corners.* 他老是在街道拐角處閑逛. *They idled away two hours doing nothing.* 他們浪費了兩個小時, 甚麼事也沒做. **2** (with reference to an engine not in gear) run slowly (指發動機)空轉, 慢轉: *The car engine is very quiet when it is idling.* 這輛汽車的發動機空轉時聲音很小. **idleness** *nu* **idler** *nc*.

idol ['aidl] *nc* **1** object made to look like a human or animal and worshipped as a god 偶像. **2** somebody / something which is greatly admired 崇拜的對像, 寵物: *This football player is the idol of the crowd.* 這位足球運動員是羣衆的偶像. **idolize** *vt* make an idol of 把…當偶像崇拜.

idyll ['idil] *nc* **1** type of poem usu. about happy country life 田園詩, 牧歌. **2** any scene or description of happiness 美妙的景色, 美景的描寫. **idyllic** [i'di-lik] *adj*.

if [if] *conj* **1** supposing that, on condition that 如果, 假如: *If he comes he will tell you.* 如果他來, 他會告訴你. *If he had come, he would have told you.* 如果他來過, 他早就會告訴你. *If he were to come (or If he came) he would tell you etc.* 如果他來的話, 他就會告訴你. **2** (with future tense) please (與將來式連用)請: *If you will hold my bag, I'll open the door.* 請拿着我的袋子, 我來開門.

3 when; whenever 當; 無論何時: *If they are tired, they have a short rest.* 當他們累時, 他們便稍稍休息一下. **4** whether 是否: *Can you tell me if he is coming?* 你能告訴我他是否來? **5** (with negative in *interj*) giving the sense of surprise (在感嘆句中與否定式連用)表示驚奇: *Well, if it isn't our old friend Smith!* 啊, 那就是我們的老朋友史密斯!. **6** although 雖然: *He is a very good man if rather dull* i.e. although he is dull, he is good. 雖然有點笨, 他是一個很好的人. **as if** 彷彿; 好像: *He talks as if he knows everything* i.e. he talks in a way that makes people believe he knows everything. 他談起話來好像他樣樣都知道. *As if I cared!* i.e. I do not care. 好像我會在乎! 即: 我不在乎. *It isn't as if he is coming* i.e. he is not coming. 他不像要來. 即: 他不來. **even if** although 雖然, 即使: *Even if you did do it, I forgive you.* 即使你真的幹了這種事, 我也寬恕你. *He will come even if he is ill.* 即使他生病, 他也會來. *I want to go even if you don't.* 即使你不去, 我也要去. **if only** in *interj* giving the sense of a wish 在感嘆句中表示願望: *If only I had more money!* i.e. I wish I had more money. 要是我有更多的錢該好了! 即: 我希望我有更多的錢. *If only he had seen me!* 要是他見到我該多好啊!

igloo ['iglu:] *nc* round house with the roof and walls made of blocks of ice or hard snow, in which Eskimos live 愛斯基摩人所居住的用冰塊或硬雪塊做屋頂和牆的圓頂小屋; 冰屋.

ignite [ig'nait] *vt / i* catch fire; set on fire 着火; 點燃: *Dry grass ignites easily.* 乾草容易着火. **ignition** [ig'niʃən] *nu* apparatus which ignites the gas in an engine (e.g. to start a car) (汽油引擎的)發火裝置(例如: 發動汽車).

ignoramus [ignə'reiməs] *nc* person who does not know much (but often pretends he does) 不學無術的人; 冒充博學的愚人.

ignorant ['ignərənt] *adj* not knowing anything; not educated 無知識的; 未受教育的: *They are ignorant of / about what happened.* 他們對發生的事情一無所知. *He is so ignorant that he cannot write his own name.* 他目不識丁連自己的名字都不會寫. **ignorance** *nu*: *There is no excuse for their ignorance of English.* 他們不懂英語不能作為藉口.

ignore [ig'nɔ:*] *vt* take no notice of; pretend not to see or hear somebody / something 忽視; 不理睬; 裝着沒看見或沒聽見某人 / 某物: *His letters to the editor were ignored.* 他給編輯的幾封信都無人過問. *Because he does not like me, he ignores me when we meet.* 因為他不喜歡我, 當我們相遇時他假裝沒看見我.

ill [il] **1** *pred adj* in bad health; sick 有病的; 生病的: *He was ill for two days.* 他病了兩天. **2** *adj* bad: harmful 壞的; 惡劣的; 有害的; *ill health* 不健康; *ill repute* 聲名狼藉; *ill will* i.e. hatred 敵意, 即: 憎恨. Also 亦作 *adv* badly 惡劣地: *You should not speak ill of your friends.* 你不應該說你朋友的壞話. *I can ill afford the money* i.e. not easily. 我無力負擔這筆錢. Also 亦作 *nc* misery; pain 苦難; 痛苦: *Man's life is full of ills.* 人生充滿着苦難. **illness 1** *nu* bad health 不健康, 疾病: *There has been no illness at school this term.* 本學期學校裏沒有發現疾病. **2** *nc* particular type or time of illness 某種疾病: *As a child he had several illnesses.* 他小時候患了幾種疾病. *Your illness is not serious.* 你的病不嚴重. '**ill-ad'vised** *adj* badly advised; not wise

魯莽的; 不明智的. '**ill-at-'ease** *adj* not comfortable; embarrassed 不舒服的; 侷促不安的. '**ill-'bred** *adj* badly brought up; rude 無教養的; 粗魯的. '**ill-'fated** *adj* unlucky; causing misfortune 不幸的, 不吉祥的; 招致不幸的. '**ill 'feeling** unfriendliness 敵意; 仇視. '**ill-'mannered** *adj* badly mannered; rude 無禮貌的; 粗野的. '**ill-'natured** *adj* bad-tempered; rude 脾氣壞的; 性情暴躁的. '**ill-'timed** *adj* badly timed; done at the wrong time 不合時宜的; 失時機的. '**ill-'treat** *vt* treat cruelly 虐待. '**ill 'will** unfriendliness; hate 敵意; 憎恨. **fall ill, be taken ill** become sick 得病, 生病.

illegal [i'li:gl] *adj* forbidden by law; unlawful 違法的; 不合法的.

illegible [i'ledʒibl] *adj* not able to be read 難讀的, 難以辨認的: *Your writing is illegible.* 你的字跡不易辨認.

illegitimate [ili'dʒitimət] *adj* (esp. with reference to a child whose parents are not married to each other) unlawful; against the law; against rules (尤指私生子) 不合法的; 違法的; 違例的; 私生的.

illicit [i'lisit] *adj* forbidden by law; not allowed 違禁的, 違法的, 不正當的.

illiterate [i'litərət] *adj* not able to read or write 目不識丁的, 文盲的. Also 亦作 *nc* person who is not able to do so 目不識丁者, 文盲. **illiteracy** *nu*.

illogical [i'lɔdʒikl] *adj* not according to the rules of logic; unsound 不合邏輯的; 不合常理的.

illuminate [i'lu:mineit] *vt* **1** give light to; light up 使明亮; 照亮. **2** make attractive with coloured lights and decorations (esp. shops and streets because of a happy event) 用彩燈裝飾 (商店和街道以示慶祝): *All the streets are illuminated at Christmas.* 聖誕節所有

的街道燈火輝煌. **illumination** [ilu:-
mi'neiʃən] **1** *nu* act of illuminating;
state of being illuminated 照明;亮光.
2 *nc* (in *pl*) coloured lights and decorations (用於複數) 燈飾: *We are
going to town to see the illuminations.*
我們進城去看燈飾.

illusion [i'lu:ʒən] *nc* something which
is thought to exist but does not;
something which is not what it is
thought to be; a false belief 幻覺;錯
覺;錯誤的觀念: *Perfect happiness is
an illusion.* 完美無缺的幸福是一種幻
想. *This picture gives the illusion that
the flowers in it are real.* 這張畫給人
一種錯覺,以為畫中的花是真的. *He
has no illusions about his children* i.e.
he does not believe they are better
than they really are. 他對他的孩子不
存幻想. **illusive** [i'lu:siv] *adj* **illusory**
[i'lu:səri] *adj* caused by an illusion;
deceptive 由錯覺產生的;欺騙的.
optical illusion illusion caused by a
mistake made by the eye (e.g. that on
a windy night the moon rushes
through the clouds; it is really the
clouds which are driven by the wind
in front of the moon) 視錯覺(例如:颳
大風的夜晚,月亮衝破雲團;實際上是月
亮前面的風驅趕雲團).

illustrate ['iləstreit] *vt* explain by
means of pictures; diagrams or examples; put or use pictures, diagrams etc
in a book, lesson or lecture (用圖表或
例子)說明; (在書,課文或演講中)加插
圖: *He illustrated his lesson about
France with photographs of the people
who live there.* 他用法國人民的照片來
講解有關法國的課文. **illustration**
[ilə'streiʃən] *nc / u* **1** something illus-
trating; something being illustrated;
example 說明;例證;實例: *As an illustration of his poor work just look at*

this essay. 只要看看這篇文章就足以說
明他的著作質量很差. **2** picture, diagram etc. 插圖,圖解等: *I like magazines full of illustrations.* 我喜歡有很
多插圖的雜誌. **illustrative** ['ilə-
strətiv] *adj*.

illustrious [i'lʌstriəs] *adj* having great
honour or dignity. *(formal use* **celebrated** *or* **distinguished**) 傑出的. (正
式一非正式用 celebrated 或 distinguished).

image ['imidʒ] *nc* **1** mental picture of
somebody / something 心象,圖像,肖
像. **2** statue or model of somebody /
something (usu. made to be worshipped) 塑像;偶像: *In the temple there
are the images of many gods.* 這座寺
院裏有很多神像. **3** exact likeness 相
像的人(物): *That boy is the image of
his father.* 這男孩活像他的父親. **4**
way an object is seen in the lens of a
camera or in a mirror 影象;映象. **imagery** ['imidʒəri] *nu* images, references in a poem etc to things and
feelings 形象;比喻: *This poem is full
of imagery.* 這首詩充滿了比喻.

imagine [i'mædʒin] *vt* **1** form an idea of
something in the mind 想像: *I cannot
imagine what life on the moon would
be like.* 我無法想像月球上的生活情景.
*We tried to imagine ourselves as old
men.* 我們極力想像我們自己是老人. **2**
suppose; believe 設想;以為: *Do you
imagine they will help?* 你認為他們會
幫忙嗎? *Don't imagine that you are
the only person in trouble.* 別以為只
有你一人處境困難. **imaginable** *adj*
that can be imagined 可想像的. *(opp*
反義詞 **unimaginable**). **imaginary**
[i'mædʒinəri] *adj* not real; existing
only in the mind 不真實的;想像中的;
虛構的: *an imaginary person* i.e. one
who does not exist 一個虛構的人,即:

一個不存在的人. **imagination** [im-ædʒineiʃən] *nu* ability to imagine clearly; ability to invent 想像力；創造力: *You must have imagination to write a good play.* 創作一個好劇本得有想像力. **imaginative** *adj* having or using imagination 富於想像力的；想像的: *an imaginative person* i.e. one with a lot of imagination 富於想像力的人. *(opp* 反義詞 **unimaginative**).

imbecile ['imbəsail] *adj* mentally weak; stupid 低能的；愚笨的. Also 亦作 *nc* person who is mentally weak or stupid 低能者；笨人.

imbed [im'bed] *vt* see 見 **embed**.

imbue [im'bju:] *vt* (usu. with reference to feelings) fill (通常指感情)使充滿，灌輸: *The speech imbued us with a desire to help.* 這次演說給我們灌輸樂於助人的思想.

imitate ['imiteit] *vt* behave in the same way as somebody else; copy 模倣；倣效: *Children like to imitate adults.* 小孩子喜歡模倣成年人. *He can imitate a lion's roar.* 他會模倣獅子的吼叫聲.

imitator *nc* person who imitates 模倣者. **imitation** [imi'teiʃən] 1 *nu* act of imitating 模倣；倣效: *Children learn by imitation.* 小孩子靠模倣學習. 2 *nc* something copied 倣製品；模擬之物: *He gives a good imitation of a lion's roar.* 他模倣獅子的吼叫聲很像. *These drawings are poor imitations of the original ones.* 這些圖畫是粗劣的倣製品. Also 亦作 *adj*: *imitation gold* i.e. made to look like gold 人造金.

immaculate [i'mækjulət] *adj* without a spot or stain, pure 無斑點的；純潔的；潔淨的: *The tablecloth was immaculate.* 這塊桌布清潔乾淨.

immaterial [imə'tiəriəl] *adj* (with **to**) not important; not relevant. (與 to 連用)不重要的；無關的: *What you say is*

immaterial to the discussion. 你說的話與本討論無關.

immature [imə'tjuə*] *adj* not yet fully grown or developed 發育未完全的；未成熟的.

immediate [i'mi:diət] *adj* 1 at once; without delay 立即的；即刻的: *I asked for an immediate reply to my letter.* 我要求對我的信立即作出答覆. 2 very near; close; direct 鄰近的；直接的: *There is a hotel in the immediate neighbourhood.* 在鄰近地區有一家旅館. *These are my plans for the immediate future.* 這些是我最近期的計劃. **immediately** *adv* at once; closely; directly 馬上，立即；緊密地；直接地.

immense [i'mens] *adj* very large 極大的；巨大的. **immensely** *adv* very much 非常；極大地: *He has grown immensely.* 他長得很高大. *I enjoyed myself immensely.* 我玩得很開心.

immerse [i'mə:s] *vt* 1 put below water or another liquid 浸入 (水或別的液體)；使沉浸: *He immersed the knife in boiling water.* 他把小刀浸沒在沸水中. 2 cause to become very interested (so that one does not pay attention to anything else) 沉浸於；專心於: *He immersed himself in work.* 他專心工作. *The pupil was immersed in a book.* 這個小學生被一本書迷住了. **im'mersion heater** electric apparatus which is immersed in water and heats it 浸入式電熱水器.

immigrate ['imigreit] *vi* enter a country and live there. (A tourist or visitor stays only for a short time) 移居入境 (旅遊者或參觀者只作短暫停留). **immigration** [imi'greiʃən] *nc / u* **immigrant** ['imigrnt] *nc* person who immigrates (自外國移入的)移民.

imminent ['iminənt] *adj* (usu. with reference to something unpleasant) probably about to happen soon (通常指不愉快的事) 即將發生的; 逼近的: *War seems imminent.* 戰爭迫在眉睫.

immobile [i'moubail] *adj* not able to move or be moved 不能移動的; 不動的. **immobility** [imə'biliti] *nu* **immobilize** [i'moubilaiz] *vt* make immobile 使不動; 使固定: *Heavy snow immobilized all traffic.* 大雪使得全部交通停頓.

immoderate [i'mɔdərət] *adj* beyond what is proper, too much 不適中的; 過多的, 無節制的: *He is immoderate in his drinking* i.e. he drinks too much. 他暴飲. 即: 他喝得太多了.

immodest [i'mɔdist] *adj* not decent; rude 不正經的; 不莊重的; 無禮的, 粗魯的: *Her skirt is so short that it is immodest.* 她的裙子短得有失體統.

immoral [i'mɔrəl] *adj* (often with reference to sexual behaviour) wrong; evil (常指性行為) 不道德的; 邪惡的; 猥褻的, 淫蕩的: *the immoral earnings of a prostitute* 娼妓賺得的骯髒錢. **immorality** [imə'ræliti] *nc / u* immoral act or state 不道德的行為; 不道德.

immortal [i'mɔːtl] *adj* living or famous for ever 不朽的; 流芳百世的: *Gods are immortal* 神是不朽的; *the immortal poetry of Shakespeare* 莎士比亞不朽的詩篇. Also 亦作 *nc: Shakespeare is one of the immortals.* 莎士比亞是不朽的人物之一. **immortality** [imɔː'tæliti] *nu* **immortalize** *vt* make famous for ever 使不朽; 使不滅.

immune [i'mjuːn] *adj* free or safe (usu. from the attacks of something e.g. a disease) 免除的; 安全的(通常指免受某事物的襲擊, 例如: 疾病): *This medicine will make you immune to / from malaria.* 這種藥會使你免受瘧疾的傳染. **immunity** *nu* **immunize** ['imjunaiz] *vt* make immune 使免除; 使免

疫: *I have been immunized against typhoid.* 我對傷寒有免疫力. **immunization** [imjunai'zeiʃən] *nc / u.*

imp [imp] *nc* little devil; naughty child 小鬼; 頑童.

impact ['impækt] *nc* **1** force of two things hitting each other; collision 衝擊(力); 碰撞: *When the car hit the wall, the impact broke the windscreen.* 當汽車撞到牆時, 衝擊力把汽車的擋風玻璃震破. **2** influence; impression 影響; 效果: *This book had / made a great impact on its readers.* 這本書對讀者有很大的影響.

impair [im'pɛə*] *vt* make less in value; strength or goodness; weaken; damage 減少; 削弱; 損害: *You need spectacles if your eyesight is impaired.* 要是你的視力減弱了, 你需要配眼鏡.

impale [im'peil] *vt* fix somebody / something on a sharp point (e.g. a spear, sword or stake); put somebody to death in this way. 把...釘在尖椿上; (用矛、劍、尖椿等) 刺穿; 對...施以刺刑.

impart [im'paːt] *vt* give; grant; hand on 給與; 授予; 傳遞: *A teacher's aim is to impart knowledge.* 教師的目的就是傳授知識.

impartial [im'paːʃəl] *adj* just; fair to both sides 公平的; 不偏袒的: *A judge must be completely impartial.* 法官必須絕對公平無私. **impartiality** [impaː-ʃi'æliti] *nu.*

impassable [im'paːsəbl] *adj* not possible to travel on or go over or through 不能通行的; 不可逾越的: *This road is impassable during the rains* 下雨期間這條路不能通行; *impassable mountains* 不可逾越的山脈; *an impassable forest* 無路可通的森林地帶.

impassioned [im'pæʃənd] *adj* full of passion or strong feelings 熱情洋溢的; 激動的: *an impassioned request* for help 懇切請求幫助.

impatient [im'peiʃənt]*adj* not patient; restless; unwilling to wait 不耐煩的; 煩躁的; 忍耐不住的: *They are impatient to go.* 他們急着要去. *He is impatient of anything stupid* i.e. he does not tolerate anything stupid. 他不能忍受任何無聊的事. **impatiently** *adv* **impatience** *nu.*

impeach [im'pi:tʃ] *vt* charge with a crime against the State 控告 (某人叛國).

impeccable [im'pekəbl] *adj* without error or fault; perfect 沒有錯誤的; 無瑕疵的; 完善的.

impede [im'pi:d] *vt* stop the progress of; hinder; hold back 阻礙; 妨礙; 阻止…前進: *Bad weather impeded us during our journey.* 天氣不好妨礙了我們的旅行. **impediment** [im'pedimənt] *nc* something that impedes (esp. something that impedes talking e.g. a stammer) 障礙物; 障礙 (尤指說話的障礙, 如: 口吃): *The little boy has an impediment in his speech.* 這個小男孩講話口吃.

impend [im'pend] *vi* (usu. in *pres part*) be about to happen (通常用現在分詞) 即將發生: *our impending return to school* 我們即將返校.

impenetrable [im'penitrəbl] *adj* not able to be passed through 不能通過的; 不能穿過的.

imperative [im'perətiv] *adj* **1** very necessary 必要的; 必須的: *It is imperative for him to be taken to hospital at once / It is imperative that he should be taken to hospital at once.* 必須立即把他送進醫院. **2** mood of the verb which expresses commands (e.g. Stop!) 祈使語氣的; 命令式的 (例如: 停止!). Also 亦作 *nc* (in sense **2**) (用於義2).

imperceptible [impə'septibl] *adj* difficult or impossible to see, feel, hear etc. 難以察覺的; 察覺不到的: *He gave an almost imperceptible nod* i.e. one that could hardly be seen. 他極輕微地點了點頭. 即: 他的點頭幾乎沒人覺察到.

imperfect [im'pə:fikt] *adj* **1** not perfect; not complete; faulty 不完善的, 不完全的; 有缺點的. **2** tense of the verb expressing an action not yet completed (e.g. *I was walking along the street.*) (動詞時態) 未完成體的(例如: 我正沿着街道走). Also 亦作 *nc* (in sense **2**) (用於義 2). **imperfection** [impə'fekʃən] *nc / u.*

imperial [im'piəriəl] *adj* of an empire or an emperor 帝國的; 皇帝的: *imperial Rome* 古羅馬帝國. **imperialism** *nu* desire to have or belief in, an empire; system of government of an empire 帝國主義; 帝制. **imperial system** system of weights and measures (formerly the official one in Britain) (英國昔時法定的) 度量衡制.

impermeable [im'pə:mjəbl] *adj* not permeable; not permitting passage, esp. of fluids 不可滲透的; (尤指液體) 通不過的: *Clay is impermeable by water.* 黏土不透水.

impersonal [im'pə:sənl] *adj* **1** with reference to no particular person; without personal feelings 非特指某人的; 非個人的; 無個人感情的: *an impersonal manner* 客觀的態度. **2** with reference to verbs used with *it* (指與 it 連用的動詞) 非人稱的; 無人稱的: *It is going to rain* i.e. *it*, the subject, is not a person and does not refer to any particular thing. 快要下雨. 即: it (主語) 不是人也不指任何特指的事物.

impersonate [im'pə:səneit] *vt* pretend to be or act the part of somebody else; imitate 假扮; 扮演; 模做: *The prisoner escaped by impersonating a policeman.* 這個囚犯假扮成警察逃跑了. **impersonation** [ɪmpɜ:sə'neɪʃən] *nc/u.*

impertinent [ɪm'pɜ:tɪnənt] *adj* rude; impudent (esp. to older persons) 粗魯的; 無禮的 (尤指對年長者): *The pupils were impertinent to their teacher.* 這些學生對他們的教師無禮.

imperturbable [ɪmpə'tɜ:bəbl] *adj* not able to be made angry or excited 沉着的; 冷靜的.

impervious [ɪm'pɜ:vɪəs] *adj* 1 impermeable 不可滲透的, 穿不過的: *a fabric impervious to moisture* 防潮的織品. 2 (with **to**) not affected by (與 to 連用) 不受影響的: *impervious to threats* 不爲威脅所動.

impetuous [ɪm'petjʊəs] *adj* 1 acting hastily and without thought 衝動的; 魯莽的: *There was no reason for his impetuous refusal to come.* 他輕率地拒絕來是沒有理由的. 2 moving with great force 猛烈的; 迅疾的.

impetus ['ɪmpɪtəs] *nc* force with which something moves or which makes something move 動力; 原動力; 衝力: *The impetus of the falling rock caused it to make a deep hole in the ground.* 落下岩石的衝力在地上砸了個深坑. *His success gave a great impetus to the others.* 他的成功極大地激勵了其他人. *pl* 複數 **impetuses**.

impinge [ɪm'pɪndʒ] *vt* (with **on** or **upon**) touch; strike against; interrupt (與 on 或 upon 連用) 接觸; 影響到; 衝擊; 打斷: *This work is impinging on my spare time.* 這項工作影響到 (或佔用) 我的業餘時間.

implacable [ɪm'plækəbl] *adj* (with reference to anger, hate, hostility etc.) not able to be changed or made less

(指憤怒、仇恨、敵意等) 難以和解的; 難平息的: *an implacable enemy* 不共戴天的敵人, 宿敵.

implant [ɪm'plɑ:nt] *vt* (usu. with reference to feelings or ideas) put deeply into (通常指感情或思想) 灌輸; 注入: *His visit to the country implanted in him a love for its people.* 他對這個國家的訪問使他熱愛它的人民.

implement[1] ['ɪmplɪmənt] *nc* tool or instrument 工具; 器具: *A spade is an implement for digging.* 鏟子是一種挖掘工具.

implement[2] ['ɪmplɪment] *vt* fulfil a promise or undertaking 履行; 實現; 完成: *The government is implementing its policy of helping the unemployed.* 政府在執行救濟失業人員政策.

implicate ['ɪmplɪkeɪt] *vt* make a connection with; show that somebody is connected with something (usu. something that is wrong or unpleasant) 牽連; 顯示 (某人) 與 (某事, 通常指謀事或不愉快的事) 有牽連; 涉及: *This evidence implicates them in the robbery.* 這一證據顯示他們與這起搶劫案有牽連. *I don't want to be implicated in your plans.* 我不想被捲入你們的計劃. **implication** [ɪmplɪ'keɪʃən] 1 *nu* implicating or being implicated 牽連. 2 *nc* something which is only suggested and not said openly 暗示; 含意; 含蓄: *The implication of your statement is that I was wrong.* 你的話的暗示是我錯了. see also 參見 **imply.**

implicit [ɪm'plɪsɪt] *adj* 1 not said openly but suggested or implied 暗示的; 含蓄的: *It is implicit in your statement that I was wrong.* 你話中的含意是我錯了. (*opp* 反義詞 **explicit**). 2 without questioning; complete 無疑的; 全然的, 絕對的: *He has an implicit belief in democracy.* 他絕對信仰民主政治.

implore [im'plɔ:*] *vt* ask earnestly for; beg 哀求; 乞求; 懇求: *I implore you to help me.* 我懇求你幫助我.

imply [im'plai] *vt* not say openly but only suggest; show in an indirect way 含有…的意思; 暗示; 暗指: *Your statement implies that I am wrong.* 你的話的意思是說我錯了. *The bad behaviour of a child sometimes implies that he is unhappy.* 一個孩子的行爲不良有時表明他並不幸福.

impolite [impə'lait] *adj* rude; having bad manners; not polite 粗魯的; 失禮的; 不禮貌的.

impolitic [im'pɔlitik] *adj* illadvised; not in one's own interests 不高明的; 失策的; 不利的: *It would be impolitic to ask him now, because he is very angry.* 現在去問他是失策的, 因爲他正在生氣.

imponderable [im'pɔndərəbl] *adj* not able to be measured or estimated 無法衡量的; 無法估計的.

import[1] [im'pɔ:t] *vt* bring into a country from abroad 輸入, 進口. (*opp* 反義詞 **export**). **importation** [impɔ:'teiʃən] *nc / u* something imported; act of importing 輸入品, 進口貨; 輸入, 進口. **importer** *nc* person who imports (usu. goods) 輸入者; 進口商.

import[2] ['impɔ:t] *nc* (usu. *pl*) goods that are imported (通常用複數) 輸入品, 進口貨.

important [im'pɔ:tnt] **1** *adj* having great value or effect 重要的; 重大的: *The battle was the most important one in the war.* 這個戰役是這次戰爭中最重要的戰役. **2** (with reference to persons) having power, worth paying attention to (指人) 有權力的; 顯要的: *The Prime Minister is the most important person in the government.* 首相是政府中最有權力的人. **importance** *nu*.

impose [im'pouz] *vt* **1** force or place something on somebody (e.g. a punishment, tax or duty) 強加; 強迫; 加 (懲罰、稅或義務) 於 (某人): *The judge imposed a fine of ten pounds on him.* 法官判處他罰款拾鎊. *A new tax has been imposed on cigarettes.* 香烟已被課以新稅. **2** force oneself into the company of other people 硬纏着 (某人): *They are always imposing themselves on their relatives.* 他們老是硬纏着他們的親戚. **3** take advantage of 利用: *May I impose upon your kindness?* 我可以得到你的幫助嗎? **imposing** *adj* looking important; having a grand appearance; impressive 莊嚴的; (儀表) 堂皇的; 給人深刻印象的: *The castle is an imposing building* 這座城堡是一座宏偉的建築; *an imposing headmaster* 一位神情嚴肅的校長.

imposition [impə'ziʃən] *nc* something forced on somebody 強加於某人之事物: *the imposition of a fine of ten pounds* 罰款拾鎊的懲罰.

impossible [im'pɔsibl] *adj* **1** not able to exist or be done 不可能的; 做不到的: *It is impossible to be in two places at once.* 同時在兩個地方是不可能的. *It's impossible for me to be there before 7 o'clock.* 七點之前我不可能到達那裏. **2** not able to be endured 無法忍受的: *This is an impossible state of affairs.* 這是無法忍受的情況. *She's impossible!* 她真是令人難以忍受! Also 亦作 *interj* of course not; absurd 當然不; 荒唐. **impossibility** [impɔsə'biliti] *nc/u* something impossible; state of being impossible 不可能的事; 不可能.

impostor [im'pɔstə*] *nc* person who pretends to be somebody else; person who deceives others; a cheat 冒名頂替者; 騙子.

impotent ['impətnt] *adj* (often with reference to the sexual power of a male) weak; without power (常指男子)陽萎的; 虛弱的; 無力的.

impound [im'paund] *vt* enclose or keep (until legal action is taken) 扣留; 扣押: *Cattle found wandering on a road can be impounded* i.e. until their owner pays a fine. 發現牛在公路上走來走去可以把牠們關起來. 即: 直到牠們的主人付了罰款才放. *The judge ordered the documents to be impounded.* 法官下令扣留這些文件.

impoverish [im'pɔvəriʃ] *vt* make poor; make wores 使窮困; 使更差, 使更壞: *They are impoverished by heavy taxes.* 他們因付重稅而變窮. *Bad farming impoverishes good soil.* 粗糙的耕作使得肥沃的土壤變貧瘠.

impracticable [im'præktikəbl] *adj* not able to be carried out; (with reference to roads or paths) not passable 不能實行的; (指道路)不能通行的.

impregnable [im'pregnəbl] *adj* not able to be taken by force; not able to be moved or changed 不能攻破的, 堅不可摧的; 堅定不移的; 毫不動搖的: *an impregnable castle* 攻不破的城堡; *an impregnable belief.* 堅定不移的信念.

impregnate ['impregneit] *vt* 1 make fertile or pregnant 使受精; 使懷孕. 2 fill; soak 使充滿; 灌注; 使浸透: *The wood is impregnated with a chemical which prevents decay.* 這塊木頭用防腐化學藥品浸泡.

impresario [imprə'sɑːriəu] *nc* person who organizes public entertainments (esp. concerts and operas) 文藝演出的主持人; (樂園、歌劇的)經理. *pl* 複數 **impresarios.**

impress [im'pres] *vt* 1 mark by pressing something on something else 蓋印; 壓印. 2 cause to remember; influence greatly 使銘記; 給予強烈影響: *He im-*

pressed on me the importance of the work. 他使我牢記這項工作的重要性. *He impressed me with the importance of the work.* 他使我牢記這項工作的重要性. *I was impressed by all he said.* 他的話給我留下深刻的印象. **impressive** *adj* causing one to be impressed (in sense 2) 給人深刻印象的; 感人的: *an impressive book* 一本感人的書. *(opp* 反義詞 **unimpressive)** **impression** *nc* 1 mark made by pressing something on something else 印; 印痕: *the impression of his thumb on the clay* 他在黏土上的拇指印. 2 something printed (esp. the amount printed at one time) 印刷品(尤指印刷一次之總數); 一版: *The first impression of this book was sold very quickly, so two more impressions were ordered.* 此書第一版很快就售完, 因此又安排了另外兩次印刷. 3 influence on the mind; idea of something (often an uncertain or wrong one) 印象; 觀念(常指不確定的或錯誤的): *The news made a great impression on those who heard it.* 這則消息給那些聽到的人留下很深的印象. *He is under the impression that I did it* i.e. he thinks wrongly that I did it. 他以為我幹了這事. 即: 他錯誤地認爲我幹了這事. *These are only my impressions, I don't really know.* 這些只是我的印象, 我並不真的知道. **impressionable** *adj* easily influenced 易受影響的: *an impressionable young man* 一個易受影響的青年男子. **impressionism** *nu* type of art; writing or music which aims at showing the general impressions made on the senses rather than giving detailed descriptions (寫作或音樂的)印象主義; 印象派.

imprint [im'print] *vt* put firmly in the mind 銘刻; 牢記: *The terrible accident* *is still imprinted on my memory.* 那起可怕的事故至今仍深深地留在我的記憶中.

imprison [im'prizn] *vt* put or keep in prison 下獄; 監禁. **imprisonment** *nu*.

improbable [im'prɔbəbl] *adj* not likely to happen or to be true 不大可能發生的; 未必確實的.

impromptu [im'prɔmptju:] *adj / adv* without being previously prepared 無準備的(地); 即席的(地); 臨時的(地); *an impromptu lesson* 無準備的課; *play a tune impromptu* 即興演奏一曲.

improper [im'prɔpə*] *adj* 1 not suiable 不合適的(地); 不適當的; 臨時的(地); *Short trousers are improper at a dance.* 在舞會上穿短褲是不合適的. **2** not decent; not fit for polite company 不正派的; 下流的; 不雅的; *improper jokes* 下流的玩笑.

improve [im'pru:v] *vt / i* become or make better 改善; 改進; *Your English has improved.* 你的英語有進步. *He is trying to improve his English.* 他在努力提高他的英語水平. **improvement** *nc / u* something which improves; improving or being improved 改進的事物; 改進; 改善; *The improvements to the school buildings cost a lot of money.* 學校建築物的修繕花了許多錢. *There is some improvement in your work this term.* 這學期你的工作有所改進.

improvise ['imprəvaiz] *vt / i* do or make quickly without being prepared or having all that is needed 即席而作; 臨時製作; 臨時湊成; *He improvised a song about the football team's victory.* 他即席創作一首足球隊勝利之歌. *We left the tent poles behind, so we had to improvise* i.e. by finding other sticks or pieces of wood and using them as poles. 我們忘記帳篷的支柱, 因此我們不得不臨時拼湊. 即: 找別

的木棒或木頭中它們作爲支柱. **improvisation** [imprəvai'zeiʃən] *nc / u.*

imprudent [im'pru:dnt] *adj* careless; rash, unwise 不謹慎的; 輕率的; 不明智的: *It was imprudent of you to lend money to a stranger.* 你借錢給一個陌生人是欠考慮的.

impudent [impjudnt] *adj* rude; insolent; disrespectful 粗野的; 無禮的; 冒失的; *That impudent boy put his tongue out at me.* 那個粗野的男孩子對我伸舌頭. **impudence** *nu.*

impulse ['impʌls] **1** *nc* movement or activity caused by something else 推動; 鼓舞; 刺激: *The nerves carry impulses to the brain.* 神經傳送刺激到大腦. **2** *nc / u* sudden desire to do something 衝動: *I bought it on impulse* i.e. suddenly without stopping to think. 我一時心血來潮就把它買下了.即: 沒有停下來進行思考突然就把它買下了. *I had an impulse to hit him.* 我一時衝動打了他. **impulsive** [im'pʌlsiv] *adj.*

impunity [im'pju:niti] *nu* state of not being liable to be punished or harmed for what one does 免受懲罰; 不受損害.

impure [im'pjuə*] *adj* not pure; dirty; evil 不純的; 髒的; 邪惡的; *impure food* 不乾淨的食物; *an impure mind* 壞念頭; *impure intentions* 惡意. **impurity** *nc / u* something impure; state of being impure 雜質; 混雜物; 不純.

in [in] *adv* **1** (with verbs of motion) entering or causing to enter (與表示動作的動詞連用)進入; 使進入: *come / get / go / jump / walk in* 進來/進入/進去/跳入/走進; *get / move / push / put / throw the box in* 把箱子放/移/推/放/扔進去. **2** (with certain verbs) causing to enter (與某些其他動詞連用)使進入: *call / have / let / see / show* *him in* 叫/請/讓/帶/領他進來. **3** having arrived; ready; obtainable 到達; 預先準備好; 可買到: *Our train is in* i.e. it has arrived or is waiting. 我們的火車到站了. *Fresh apples are now in* i.e. are obtainable. 新鮮的蘋果上市了. **4** not-allowing to get out 不讓出去: *keep / lock / shut in* 留/鎖/關在裏面. **5** (with the verbs **be, find** etc.) at home, work or where one is expected to be (與動詞be,find等連用) 在家; 在辦公室等: *Is your father in?* i.e. is he at home? 你父親在家嗎? *The manager is not in yet* i.e. at his office or place of work.經理還沒回家. 即: 在他的辦公室或工作場所. *Our team is in* i.e. batting, not fielding during a game of baseball or cricket. 我隊在擊球. 即: 在棒球或板球賽中擊球而不是接球. **6** a great number of special senses 許多特殊的意義: *The fire was in* i.e. was burning. 火在燃燒. *The Labour Party is in* i.e. has been elected, holds power. 工黨獲選在執政. *Short skirts are in* i.e. are fashionable. 短裙在時興. Also with many other verbs 也與許多其他動詞連用; *fill in* i.e. complete 填滿; *give in* i.e. yield 屈服; *run in (an engine)* i.e. make it ready by running it 試轉(發動機); *take in* i.e. cheat etc. 欺騙等. Also 亦作 *prep* **1** place where or towards 場所或方向: *in the room* 在房間裏; *in the village* 在村莊; *in London* 在倫敦; *in Europe* 在歐洲; *in the dark* 在黑暗中; *in the rain* 在雨中. *Throw it in the fire.* 把它丟到火裏. *Go in that direction.* 往那個方向去. *Note* 說明: *I in* and *into* with the sense of motion are almost the same. We can say either *Throw it in the fire* or *Throw it into the fire. Into* has more definitely the sense of entering or causing to enter from the outside,

so we usu. say *He went into the room. He looked in the room* could have the sense of looking for something,while in the room but *He looked into the room* has only the sense of looking from the outside. Generally it is safer to use *into* when motion is expressed. 具有動作意義的 in 和 into 幾乎是一樣的. 我們可以說 Throw it in the fire 或 Throw it into the fire. 把它丟到火中. Into 具有較確切的進入或從外面進入的意思, 因此通常我們說 He went into the room. 他走進房間. He looked in the room. 可能有在房間找東西的意思, 但是 He looked into the room 只有從外面往房間裏看的意思.總之, 當表達動作時, 使用 into 較穩妥. **2** *in* with reference to place without motion refers to an area rather than one point. If we think of a small place as an area we can use *in* (e.g. *He lives in a little village called XY*). But if we think of it as being a point we can say *He lives at a little village called XY*). We normally think of large places as being areas rather than points, and so generally say *He lives in London. His house is in New York etc.* But if we think of the large place as a point, for instance a point X in a journey, we can say *The plane didn't stop at New York*. We would, however, use *in* not *at* with names of places bigger than a city (e.g. *The plane didn't stop in Italy on its way to Africa*). in 指場所不表示動作時指一個地區而不是一點. 如果我們把一個小地方看作一個地區, 我們可以用 in (例如: He lives in a little village called XY. 但是如果我們把它看作一點, 我們就說 He lives at a little village called XY). 我們通常把大地方看作是地區而不是點, 所以一般說 He lives in London. His house is in New

York 等. 但是如果我們把大地方看作一個點, 如在一次旅程中的X點, 我們可以說 The plane didn't stop at New York. 可是, 在與比城市大的地名連用時, 我們要用 in 而 不 是 at (例如: The plane didn't stop in Italy on its way to Africa). **2** place or type of work. 工作場所; 工作類型: *I am in insurance.* 我從事保險業. *He's in the Navy.* 他在海軍服役. *They are in research.* 他們從事研究工作. **3** wearing 穿 戴; the *woman in the red hat* 戴紅帽子的女人. **4** time when, during, within 在…之時; 在…期間; 在…之内: *in the 19th century* 在19世紀; *in the morning* 在早晨; *in winter* 在冬天; *in old age* 在晚年; *in the future* 在 將來; *in their absence* 他們不在時. *I'll be back in a week* i.e. within the period of one week. 我會在一星期内回來. *Note* 說明: *in* has the sense of a period of time, *at* of a point in time. *He got up in the morning* but *He got up at 7.30 in the morning*; *in winter* but *at Christmas*; *in the future* but *at a future date etc.* 在有一段時間的意思, 在指時間的一點. He got up in the morning. 他早上起床, 但是 He got up at 7.30 in the morning: 他早上七點三十分起床; in winter 在冬天, 但是 at Christmas 在聖誕節; in the future 在將來; 但是 at a future date 日後等. **5** part of something. 某物的部份: *one in a hundred* 一百分之一; *12 inches in a foot* 一英尺有十二英寸; *the best in the class* 班裏最好的. **6** condition or circurnstances 狀態或情況: *in anger* 發怒; *in doubt* 懷疑地; *in a hurry* 匆忙地; *in poor health* 健康不佳; *in secret* 秘密地; *in trouble* 處 於 困境 中. **7** by means of; using 藉由: *He wrote in pencil.* 他 用 鉛 筆 寫 字. *I spoke in French.* 我用法語講話. *He paid me in*

dollars. 他付我美元. *He shouted in a loud voice.* 他大聲叫喊. *The room is painted in bright colours.* 這房間用鮮明的顔料漆過. **8** with reference to; referring to 關於; 有關: *He is lame in one leg* 他瘸一條腿; *weak in character* 性格懦弱; *rich in gold* 黄金儲藏豐富; *greater in size* 體積更大; *forty miles in length* 長度爲四十英里. *In him we have an excellent headmaster.* 我們有他這位優秀的校長. **in any case** whatever happens 無論如何. **be in for** 1 likely to suffer something unpleasant 可能遭到 (不愉快的事): *You're in for toruble.* 你會遭遇到麻煩事. **2** entered for a competition 參加 (競爭): *I'm in for the mile race.* 我要參加一英里賽跑.

inability [inəˈbiliti] *nu* state of not being able 無能; 無才能.

inaccessible [inækˈsesibl] *adj* not able to be reached 達不到的.

inaccurate [inˈækjurit] *adj* not right or correct 錯誤的; 不正確的. **inaccuracy** *nc / u* something inaccurate; state of being inaccurate 不正確的事物; 錯誤; 不準確.

inaction [inˈækʃən] *nu* not doing anything 不做事; 不活動. **inactivity** [inækˈtiviti] *nu*.

inadequate [inˈædikwit] *adj* not enough; not suitable 不充足的; 不適當的: *inadequate amount* 數量不足. *He's inadequate for the job.* 他不能勝任這項工作. **inadequacy** *nc / u*.

inadvertent [inədˈvəːtnt] *adj* resulting from inattention; careless; not on purpose 不注意的; 疏忽的; 非故意, 出於無心的: *an inadvertent mistake* 過失. **inadvertently** *adv.*

inadvisable [inədˈvaizəbl] *adj* unwise; not safe, suitable etc. 不明智的; 不妥當的.

inane [i'nein] *adj* silly; stupid 傻的; 愚蠢的.

inanimate [in'ænimit] *adj* not alive; not lively 無生命的; 無生氣的: *Wood is inanimate.* 木頭是無生命的.

inapplicable [inə'plikəbl] *adj* (esp. with reference to rules and laws) not suitable to be used (尤指規則和規律) 不適用的.

inappropriate [inə'proupriət] *adj* not proper; not suitable; not correct for a particular purpose 不適當的; 不相宜的.

inapt [in'æpt] *adj* not suitable or fitting 不適當的; 不合適的. **inaptitude** [in'æptitju:d] *nc / u.*

inarticulate [inɑː'tikjulət] *adj* (with reference to a person) not able to speak well and clearly; not able to express one's ideas in speech (指人) 説話不清楚的; 不善於表達自己思想的: *Uneducated people are usually inarticulate.* 未受過教育的人通常是詞不達意.

inattention [inə'tenʃən] *nu* not noticing; not listening carefully etc. 不注意; 漫不經心. **inattentive** [inə'tentiv] *adj.*

inaudible [in'ɔːdibl] *adj* not loud enough to be heard 聽不見的.

inaugurate [i'nɔːgjureit] *vt* introduce somebody or begin something in a formal manner 爲⋯舉行就職典禮; 爲⋯舉行開幕式: *He was inaugurated as professor.* 他開始擔任教授職務. *The Queen inaugurated the exhibition* i.e. she opened it formally. 女王主持展覽會的開幕式. **inaugural** [i'nɔːgjurl] *adj* **inauguration** [inɔːgju'reiʃən] *nc / u.*

inborn ['in'bɔːn] *adj* possessed when born; natural 天生的; 天賦的: *Intelligence is said to be inborn* i.e. persons are born with it. 才智據説是天賦的.

inbred ['in'bred] *adj* **1** possessed when born 天生的: *inbred courage* 天生的勇氣. **2** having ancestors who were too closely related to each other 近親繁殖的.

incalculable [in'kælkjuləbl] *adj* too great to be measured or counted 不可勝數的; 數不清的.

incandescent [inkæn'desnt] *adj* white hot and giving out light 白熾的; 遇熱發光的.

incantation [inkæn'teiʃən] *nc* set of words used to produce a magical effect 咒語.

incapable [in'keipəbl] *adj* not able; not having the power or nature to do something 不能的; 無能力的; 不會⋯的: *He is incapable of being unkind to people.* 他不會刻薄待人.

incapacitate [inkə'pæsiteit] *vt* (with or from) make incapable; disqualify (與for或from連用) 使無能力; 使無資格: *The accident has incapacitated him from working* i.e. made him unable to work. 這次事故使他不能工作. **incapacity** *nu* state of being incapable 無能力: *their incapacity to learn / for learning* 他們無能力學習.

incarcerate [in'kɑːsəreit] *vt* put in prison. *(formal)* 監禁; 禁閉. (正式).

incarnation [inkɑː'neiʃən] *nu* taking human form (esp. by Christ) (尤指基督) 化身爲人.

incendiary [in'sendiəri] *nc* **1** person who unlawfully sets fire to houses, buildings etc. 縱火犯. **2** type of bomb which causes fire 燃燒彈. Also 亦作 *adj: an incendiary speech* i.e. one urging people to behave violently 煽動性演説.

incense¹ [in'sens] *vt* make angry 激怒.

incense² ['insens] *nu* substance which gives off a sweet-smelling smoke when burnt (usu. used for religious purposes) 香 (通常爲宗教目的而使用).

incentive [in'sentiv] *nc* anything which makes somebody do something (esp. work harder) 刺激; 動機: *The best incentive in business is the chance of making more money.* 商業上最好的刺激就是有機會賺更多的錢.

incessant [in'sesnt] *adj* continuing without stopping 持續不斷的; 不停的; 連續的. **incessantly** *adv*.

incest ['insest] *nu* unlawful sexual intercourse between persons belonging to the same family (e.g. between brother and sister, father and daughter) 亂倫 (例如: 兄妹, 父女間通姦).

inch [intʃ] *nc* measure of length equal to one twelfth of a foot (2.54 centimetres) 英寸; 吋 (= 1/12 英尺或2.54公分). Also 亦作 *vt/i* move very slowly (使) 緩慢地移動: *He inched (his way) across the high roof.* 他慢慢挪動, 爬過高高的屋頂. **inch by inch** slowly; little by little 漸漸地; 一點一點地. **within an inch of** almost 幾乎; 差點兒: *He was/came within an inch of death* i.e. he almost died. 他幾乎送了命.

incidence ['insidns] *nu* number of times which, or the way in which, something has an effect on other persons/things 發生率: *the incidence of malaria in Africa* i.e. the number, or kind, of people who get malaria 非洲瘧疾的發病率.

incident ['insidnt] *nc* happening; event (usu. one that is not very important) 事件 (通常指不很重要的事件): *The meeting passed without incident* i.e. without anything unusual or unpleasant happening. 會議開過了, 沒發生甚麼事. *There were several incidents on the frontier* i.e. several small raids or fights. 在邊界發生了幾起事件. 即, 幾次小襲擊或戰鬥.

incidental [insi'dentl] *adj* happening or likely to happen at the same time as 附帶的; 伴隨的; 可能同時發生的: *the pleasures incidental to teaching young children* 教育小孩得到的樂趣 — *incidental expenses* i.e. expenses caused while doing something else 額外開支.

incidentally *adv* by the way 順便一提; 附帶地: *Incidentally, I should like to raise another point...* 順便提一句, 我想提出另一個論點....

incinerator [in'sinəreitə*] *nc* container or furnace in which rubbish is burnt (垃圾等的) 焚化爐.

incipient [in'sipiənt] *adj* just beginning 剛開始的; 初發的; 初期的: *an incipient disease* 初期的病.

incise [in'saiz] *vt* (often with reference to surgical operations) cut into (常指外科手術) 切入; 切割. **incision** [in'siʒən] *nc*: *The doctor made an incision in the patient's arm.* 醫生在病人的胳臂上開了一個切口.

incisive [in'saisiv] *adj* (with reference to thoughts and words) sharp; acute (指思想, 言語) 敏銳的; 鋒利的; 尖刻的: *He refused the request in a few incisive words.* 他用幾句尖刻的話拒絕了這種要求.

incisor [in'saizə] *nc* one of the four front cutting teeth in the upper or lower jaw 門牙.

incite [in'sait] *vt* urge somebody to do something (usu. something wrong) 激勵; 鼓動; 煽動: *He is inciting them to go on strike.* 他在煽動他們舉行罷工.

inclement [in'klemənt] *adj* (usu. with reference to the weather) not mild; severe (通常指天氣) 寒冷的; 狂風暴雨的; 嚴酷的.

incline¹ [in'klain] *vt/i* **1** bend, slope 彎; (使) 傾斜: *The road inclines to the* left. 這條路向左傾斜. **2** cause somebody to wish or be ready to do something; (in *passive*) be ready or have a tendency to do something 使傾向; (用於被動態) 有意做某事; 經常做某事: *The argument inclines me to agree.* 這個論點使我傾向同意. *They are inclined to be late* i.e. they are often late. 他們常常遲到. **inclined** *adj* (*opp* 反義詞 **disinclined**). **inclination** [ɪnkliˈneiʃən] *nc*: *an inclination of the head* 點頭; *My inclination is to agree.* 我點頭就是同意.

incline² [ˈinklain] *nc* slope 斜坡: *The road has a steep incline.* 這條路有陡坡.

inclose [inˈklouz] *vt* **inclosure** [inˈklouʒə*] *nc* see 見 **enclose**.

include [inˈkluːd] *vt* contain; have as part of or as belonging to 包含; 把…包括在內: *The book includes two chapters on grammar.* 這本書包括兩章語法部份. *Please include me in your group.* 請把我算在你的小組內. **inclusive** [inˈkluːsiv] *adj* including 包含的; 包括的: *from Tuesday to Friday inclusive* i.e. including Tuesday and Friday as well as Wednesday and Thursday 從星期二到星期五, 首尾兩天也包括在內; *the inclusive cost* i.e. including everything 一切包括在內的費用. **inclusion** *nc* / *u*.

incognito [inkɒgˈniːtou] *adj* / *adv* in disguise; under another name 化裝的 (地); 微行的 (地); 化名的 (地): *To avoid the crowds the film star travels incognito.* 爲避開人羣, 這位電影明星微裝出遊.

incoherent [inkouˈhiərnt] *adj* (esp. with reference to speeches, thoughts; ideas; explanations) not fitting together, not easy to understand (尤指言語、思想等) 不連貫的; 無條理的; 語

無倫次的; 難理解的.

income [ˈinkʌm] *nc* money which is regularly received for work done, from trade etc. 收入; 收益; 所得: *He has an income of £3,000 a year.* 他一年收入三千鎊. **income tax** tax put on a person's income 所得稅.

incomparable [inˈkɔmpərəbl] *adj* not able to be compared; better than any other 不能比較的; 無法比擬的; 無比的; 無以匹敵的: *incomparable skill* 無與倫比的高超技能.

incompatible [inkəmˈpætibl] *adj* not able or suitable to go together 不相容的; 不能和諧共存的: *Those two people are incompatible* i.e. they cannot be together in a friendly way. 這兩人合不來. 即: 他們無法友好相處.

incompetent [inˈkɔmpitnt] *adj* not having the ability or power to do something 無能力的; 不適合的: *He is incompetent at working with his hands.* 他不適合用雙手幹活. **incompetence** *nu*.

incomplete [inkəmˈpliːt] *adj* not having all that is needed; not finished; needing something more 不完全的; 未完成的; 不完善的.

incomprehensible [inkɔmprihenˈsibl] *adj* not able to be understood 不能理解的; 不可思議的.

inconceivable [inkənˈsiːvəbl] *adj* not able to be thought of or imagined 不可思議的; 無法想象的.

inconclusive [inkənˈkluːsiv] *adj* not allowing one to decide; without a definite result 非決定性的; 不充分的; 無確定結果的: *inconclusive evidence* 不能使人信服的證據.

incongruous [inˈkɔŋgruəs] *adj* not having anything in common; not in agreement with 不能使人信服的; 不調和的; 不相稱的; 不一致的: *They are an in-*

congruous couple i.e. they are very different in many ways 他們是不相稱的一對. 即: 他們在很多方面有很大的差異; *an incongruous remark* 自相矛盾的話. **incongruity** [inkɔŋˈgruːiti] *nc/u* something incongruous; state of being incongruous 不協調之物; 不相稱之物; 不調和; 不相稱; 不一致.

inconsequential [inkɔnsiˈkwenʃl] *adj* 1 not following what happened before 不連貫的; 前後不一的. **2** not important 不重要的.

inconsiderate [inkənˈsidərət] *adj* not thinking of what will be best for or most helpful to other people 不替別人着想的; 不體諒別人的; 輕率的; *inconsiderate behaviour* 輕率的行爲.

inconsistent [inkənˈsistnt] *adj* not acting or thinking in the same way; changing easily 不一致的; 矛盾的; 易變的; 反覆無常的. **inconsistency** *nc/u* inconsistent act; state of being inconsistent 不一致或矛盾的行爲; 不一致; 矛盾; 易變; 反覆無常. **inconsistent with** not suitable for; not in agreement with 不適合 …; 與 … 不一致: *What you say is inconsistent with what you do* i.e. you say one thing and do something else. 你的言行不一致. 即: 你說的是一套, 做的是另一套.

inconspicuous [inkənˈspikjuəs] *adj* not easily seen; not wellknown 難以覺察的; 不顯眼的; 不引人注意的.

inconstant [inˈkɔnstnt] *adj* (esp. with reference to feelings) changing easily (尤指感情) 多變的; 反覆無常的; 輕浮的. **inconstancy** *nu*.

incontestable [inkənˈtestibl] *adj* not able to be disputed or denied 無可爭辯的; 無可否認的.

incontinent [inˈkɔntinənt] *adj* not having control over one's feelings and behaviour (esp. control over feelings

of sexual desire or control over urine etc.) 無節制的; 縱慾的; (小便等) 失禁的. **incontinence** *nu*.

inconvenient [inkənˈviːniənt] *adj* causing difficulty or trouble (引起) 不方便的; 麻煩的: *Saturday is an inconvenient day to see him*. 星期六去看他有所不便. **inconvenience** *nc/u*: *Your visit caused him great inconvenience* 你的來訪給他帶來很多麻煩. *the inconvenience of having to travel a long way to work* 上班路遠的不便之處 (或困難). Also 亦作 *vt*: *I hope my visit will not inconvenience you.* 我希望我的來訪不會打擾你.

incorporate [inˈkɔːpəreit] *vt/i* join into a whole; put something into something else to make a whole (使) 合併; 結合; 併入; 編入: *May I incorporate what you have written in my book?* 我可以把你寫的文章編入我的書嗎? **incorporated** *adj (US)* formed into a public company or corporation (usu. in the name of business firms and usu. written **Inc**. e.g. *Todd Stores Inc.) (Brit **Ltd** for limited)* (美) 組成公司的 (通常在公司名稱後寫 Inc. 例如: 托德斯托里斯公司) (英 Ltd代表Limited).

incorrect [inkəˈrekt] *adj* not true; wrong 不正確的; 錯誤的.

incorrigible [inˈkɔridʒibl] *adj* (with reference to persons) not able to be corrected or reformed (指人) 難以糾正的; 難改的; 不可救藥的: *an incorrigible thief* 屢教不改的小偷.

incorruptible [inkəˈrʌptibl] *adj* not able to be bribed 不貪污受賄的; 收買不了的; 廉潔的.

increase [inˈkriːs] *vt/i* become or make greater 增加; 增大; 增多. Also 亦作 [ˈinkriːs] *nc/u* **increasingly** *adv* more and more 漸增地; 逐漸地.

incredible [inˈkredibl] *adj* not to be believed; difficult to believe 不可相信的; 難以置信的. **incredibly** *adv*.

incredulous [in'kredjuləs] *adj* not believing 不相信的; 懷疑的: *When they heard his story they were at first incredulous.* 他們聽到他的身世時, 起初他們不相信. *He gave me an incredulous look* i.e. his look showed he did not believe what he saw or heard. 他用懷疑的眼光看我. **incredulity** [inkri'dju:liti] *nu*.

increment ['inkrimənt] *nc* increase (esp. of a salary each year) (尤指每年薪水的) 增加: *You will get your next increment on 1 July.* 你下次增加薪水是在7月1日.

incriminate [in'krimineit] *vt* cause somebody to be thought guilty of a crime 控告; 連累; 牽連.

incubate ['inkjubeit] *vt / i* sit on eggs to hatch them; hatch eggs 孵(卵). **incubation** [inkju'beiʃən] *nu* **incubator** *nc* apparatus which gives out the warmth necessary to hatch eggs or to protect babies born too soon 孵卵器; 育嬰箱.

incur [in'kə:*] *vt* become responsible for; bring upon oneself 對…有責任; 招致; 蒙受: *He has incurred many debts.* 他負債纍纍. *You will incur your father's disapproval.* 你會因到你父親的反對. *past* 過去式和過去分詞 **incurred.**

incurable [in'kjuərəbl] *adj* not able to be cured 不能治療的; 無可救藥的.

incursion [in'kə:ʃən] *nc* sudden attack; raid 侵襲; 襲擊.

indebted [in'detid] *adj* **1** being in debt 負債的. **2** grateful 感激的: *We are greatly indebted to them for their kind welcome.* 我們很感激他們的熱情歡迎.

indecent [in'di:snt] *adj* (esp. with reference to talk and behaviour connected

with sex) shameful; disgusting (尤指言談、行爲等)下流的; 猥褻的; 粗鄙的. **indecency** *nc / u* indecent act; state of being indecent 粗野、非禮; 下流; 猥褻; 粗鄙.

indecision [indi'siʒən] *nu* not being able to decide 躊躇; 優柔寡斷; 猶豫不決. **indecisive** [indi'saisiv] *adj* **1** not settling an argument / fight / disagreement / war etc. (辯論/戰鬥/爭論/戰爭等) 非決定性的: *The result of the game was indecisive and another will have to be played.* 這場比賽的結果不是決定性的, 還得進行另一場比賽. **2** unable to decide quickly 優柔寡斷的; 猶豫不決的: *He is a very indecisive man.* 他是個十分優柔寡斷的人.

indeed [in'di:d] *adv* in fact; certainly 事實上; 確實; 的確: *He is indeed the man we want.* 他確實是我們需要的人! *·Are you coming with us? Yes, indeed.* 你和我們一道去嗎?是的, 真的要去. *He is very fat indeed.* 他實在很胖.

indefinable [indi'fainəbl] *adj* not possible or easy to explain; vague 難下定義的; 模糊不清的.

indefinite [in'definit] *adj* doubtful; not clear or exact 模糊的; 不明確的; 不確定的. **indefinitely** *adv* **1** not clearly or exactly 模糊地; 不確定地. **2** for an unknown period of time 無限期地: *He is staying here indefinitely.* 他打算無限期地呆在這裏. **indefinite article** *a* or *an* 不定冠詞 a 或 an.

indelible [in'deləbl] *adj* not able to be rubbed out 擦不掉的; 不可磨滅的: *an indelible pencil* i.e. one which makes marks that cannot be rubbed out 筆跡擦不掉的鉛筆.

indelicate [in'delikət] *adj* (with reference to speech or behaviour) rude; coarse (指言、行)粗鄙的; 不雅的; 粗魯

的.

indemnify [in'demnifai] *vt* pay for loss or damage; protect against future loss or damage 賠償，補償；保障，保護：*The company indemnifies you against any injuries you may suffer while at work.* 該公司保障你免受工作中可能遭到的傷害.

indent[1] [in'dent] *vt / i* **1** make jagged in outline 把…刻成鋸齒狀. **2** make an order on (a source or supply) or for (something) 訂貨. **3** place (printed matter) in from the margin, as at the beginning of a paragraph 縮排. Also 亦作 *nc* **1** notch or cut in an edge 凹口，鋸齒形. **2** an order form, esp. one used in foreign trade (尤指外貿) 訂單. **3** any contract or sealed agreement between two or more parties 合同，契約. **4** leaving of space or the amount of space left between a margin and the start of an indented line 空格，(印刷的) 縮進.

indent[2] [in'dent] *vt* **1** make a dent or depression in 在…上壓凹痕. **2** press (a mark, etc.) in 在…上壓印(記號等).

independent [indi'pendnt] *adj* not under the control of somebody else; not having to rely on somebody / something 獨立的；自主的；自食其力的：*It is an independent country, not a colony* 那是一個獨立的國家，不是殖民地；*an independent worker* i.e. one who works by himself and does not rely on others 獨立工作的工人. **independence** *nu*

indescribable [indis'kraibəbl] *adj* not able to be described 難以描述的，難以形容的.

index ['indeks] *nc* **1** list of names, subjects etc arranged in alphabetical order (e.g. at the end of a book) (書等後面的) 索引. **2** something which

points out or shows 指示物；標誌：*The number of servants he has is an index of his wealth* 他擁有僕人的數目是他富有的標誌；*the index finger* i.e. the finger next to the thumb, used for pointing 食指. *pl* 複數 **indexes** or **indices** ['indisi:z].

indicate ['indikeit] *vt* point out; be a sign of; show by a sign 指出；象徵；表明；暗示：*He indicated my seat at the table.* 他指出我在餐桌上的座位. *They indicated that they were very tired.* 他們暗示他們很累. **indication** [indi'keiʃən] *nc / u*: *This map gives no indication of the heights of the hills.* 這幅地圖沒有標出山的高度. *Are there any indications of an improvement?* i.e. signs. 有任何改進的跡象嗎? **indicative** [in'dikətiv] *adj* (grammar) *the indicative mood of a verb* i.e. the one that states something as a fact not as a wish etc. (語法)陳述的；直陳的.Also 亦作 *nc* **indicator** *nc* person / thing that points out or gives information (e.g. about a machine). 指示者；指示物；指示器：*The indicator on his car showed that he was going to turn left.* 他車上的方向指示燈顯示他要向左轉了.

indict [in'dait] *vt* charge with a crime 控告；對…起訴：*He was indicted for murder / as a murderer / on a charge of murder.* 他被控告謀殺/為兇手/犯謀殺罪. **indictable** *adj* for which one should be indicted 可提出控告的；可起訴的：*an indictable offence* i.e. one serious enough to require a trial by a jury in a court of law 刑事罪. **indictment** *nc / u* act of indicting; state of indicting or being indicted 控告；起訴.

indifferent [in'difərənt] *adj* **1** not interested in; not caring for, not concerned about 不感興趣的; 不重視的; 冷淡的; 漠不關心的: *He was indifferent to all our appeals for help.* 他對我們所有求援的呼籲漠不關心。 **2** neither very good nor very bad; of poor quality 不好不壞的; 平常的; 質量不高的: *indifferent health* 身體一般; *indifferent pupil* 水平不高的學生; *indifferent work* 平凡的工作。 **indifference** *nu*.

indigenous [in'didʒinəs] *adj* born in or belonging to a country; native 本土的; 土生土長的: *the indigenous peoples of South America* 南美洲的土著人。

indigestible [indi'dʒestibl] *adj* not easily digested 不易消化的。 **indigestion** [indi'dʒestʃən] *nu* inability to digest; pain or discomfort caused by not being able to digest 不消化; 消化不良症。

indignant [in'dignənt] *adj* (esp. with reference to what is thought to be wrong or unjust) angry 憤怒的; 憤慨的: *They are indignant about the increased prices.* 他們對物價上漲憤慨不平。 **indignation** [indig'neiʃən] *nu*.

indignity [in'digniti] *nc / u* rude treatment causing somebody to lose dignity and feel ashamed 輕蔑; 侮辱; 有損自尊, 受屈辱: *He suffered the indignity of being kept waiting for three hours.* 讓他等三小時, 他覺得是不給他面子。

indigo ['indigou] *nu* **1** deep blue colour 靛青。 **2** dye of this colour 靛青染料。 Also 亦作 *adj*.

indirect [indi'rekt] *adj* not straight; round about; not to the point 間接的; 迂迴的; 不直截了當的: *I travelled to London by an indirect route* i.e. I did not travel straight there. 我經由迂迴的路線旅行到倫敦。 *He gave only an indirect answer to my question* i.e. his

answer was neither a clear 'yes' nor a clear 'no'. 他只是兜着圈子回答我的問題。即他的回答既不是明確的 '是' 也不是明確的 '不是'。 **indirectly** *adv* **in-direct object** (grammar) noun or noun phrase which completes or tells more about the action of a transitive verb (e.g. He threw the ball. ('the ball' is the direct object). He threw him the ball / He threw the ball to him ('him' is the indirect object)) (語法) 間接賓語(例如: He threw the ball. 他拋球。 ('the ball' 是直接賓語)。 He threw the ball to him; 他把球拋給他。 ('him' 是間接賓語))。 **in-direct speech** (grammar) method of writig or speaking about what a person has said, not by using his actual words but by giving the sense of them or reporting them (e.g. He said 'I will do it' (direct speech). He said that he would do it (indirect speech)) (語法) 間接引語(例如: He said 'I will do it'! 他說 '我會做這件事' (直接引語)。 He said that he would do it. 他說他會做這件事(間接引語))。 (Also 亦作 **reported speech**).

indiscreet [indis'kri:t] *adj* careless in behaviour; telling secrets to other people; going beyond the limits of what is proper or sensible 不慎的; 洩漏秘密的; 輕率的; 不得體的。 **indiscretion** [indis'kreʃən] *nc / u* indiscreet act; state of being indiscreet 輕率的舉動; 欠慎重的行為; 不慎重; 輕率。

indiscriminate [indis'kriminət] *adj* without taking the trouble to choose or to find out 不加選擇的; 不加區別的; 不分青紅皂白的: *indiscriminate punishment* i.e. punishing without taking the trouble to find out who was really to blame or how serious the offence was 不分青紅皂白的懲罰; 亂

罰.

indispensable [indis'pensibl] *adj* without which something cannot be done; necessary 不可缺少的; 必需的: *Books are indispensable to a scholar.* 對一個學者來說, 書是必不可少的.

indisposed [indis'pouzd] *adj* slightly ill 有病的; 不舒服的: *I stayed at home because I was indisposed.* 我呆在家裏, 因爲我身體不舒服.

indisputable [indis'pju:təbl] *adj* certain: not able to be argued about 不容置疑的, 無可爭辯的.

indistinct [indis'tiŋkt] *adj* not clearly seen / heard etc. 不清楚的; 模糊的; 不清晰的: *Your voice is indistinct.* 你的聲音模糊不清.

individual [indi'vidjuəl] *adj* special to, belonging to, one particular person / thing 獨特的; 個別的; 單獨的: *Everyone has an individual way of signing his name.* 每個人都有其獨特的簽名方式. Also 亦作 *nc* a person who regarded as a single, separate being 個人; 個體: *The purpose of the law is to protect the rights of the individual.* 法律的目的是保護個人的權利. **individually** *adv* **individuality** [individju'æliti] *nu* **individualism** *nu* acting only for oneself without considering others or what they do 個人主義. **individualist** *nc* person who believes in or practises individualism 個人主義者.

indoctrinate [in'dɔktrineit] *vt* teach particular ideas and beliefs in a way that prevents the learner from thinking for himself 灌輸 (某種思想或信仰). **indoctrination** [indɔktri'neiʃən] *nu.*

indolent ['indələnt] *adj* lazy 懶惰的.

indoor ['indɔ:*] *adj* in a building; not outside 户内的; 室内的: *indoor games* 室内遊戲. **indoors** *adv into a building;* 在户内; 在室内; 入户内: *to play indoors* 在室内遊戲. *They went indoors.* 他們進入室内.

indorse [in'dɔ:s] *vt* see 見 **endorse.**

indubitable [in'dju:bitəbl] *adj* not able to be doubted 不容置疑的; 無疑的.

induce [in'dju:s] *vt* persuade; cause 誘導, 勸誘; 引起, 招致: *They induced me to go away with them.* 他們勸我和他們一起離開. *The doctor induced the birth of the child* i.e. caused the birth to take place, perhaps because it was overdue. 醫生以藥物催生嬰兒. **inducement** *nc*: *They added £10 to his salary as an inducement to stay.* 他們給他加薪拾鎊以此促使他留下.

induct [in'dʌkt] *vt* (esp. with reference to introducing a clergyman formally to his work) bring in; introduce (尤指牧師) 使正式就職; 引入; 介紹.

indulge [in'dʌldʒ] *vt / i* allow oneself to enjoy something; allow somebody to have his own way 盡情享受; 使 (自己) 沉迷; 縱容; 遷就: *We indulged in an expensive supper after the concert.* 音樂會後, 我們盡情享受豐盛的晚餐. **indulgent** *adj* **indulgence** *nc / u*: *One of my few indulgences is having breakfast in bed on Sunday morning.* 我的幾個嗜好之一是星期天早上在床上吃早飯. *Indulgence in drink can harm your health.* 酗酒會傷害你的健康. **'self-in'dulgence** indulging oneself (usu. too much) (通常過份) 放縱自己.

industry ['indəstri] *nc/u* 1 ability and willingness to work hard 勤勉; 勤奮: *A country's greatest wealth is the industry of its people.* 一個國家的最大財富是這個國家的人民勤奮. 2 making large quantities of goods by using machines; a particular branch of this process or branch of trade generally

工業；產業；行業；*That country is mainly agricultural and has few industries* 那個國家主要是農業，幾乎沒有甚麼工業；*the iron and steel industry* 鋼鐵業；*the shipping industry* 航運業. **industrial** [in'dʌstriəl] *adj* (in sense **2**）(用於義2)：*the industrial part of the city* i.e. where the factories are 城市的工業區. **industrious** [in'dʌstriəs] *adj* (in sense **1**）(用於義1)：*an industrious pupil* 勤奮的學生. **industrialize** [in'dʌstriəlaiz] *vt* build up industries 使工業化；*industrialize a country* 使國家工業化. **industrialist** [in'dʌstriəlist] *nc* owner or manager of a large industry 工業家；實業家.

inebriate [in'i:brieit] *vt* cause to be drunk. (*formal* or rather *o.f.*) 使醉(正式或較舊式).

inedible [in'edibl] *adj* not suitable for eating 不可食的；不宜食用的.

ineffective [ini'fektiv] *adj* not having any result; not successful 無效的；無用的；無能的：*He is an ineffective salesman.* 他是個無能的推銷員.

ineffectual [ini'fektjuəl] *adj* not having a result; unsuccessful 無效的；不成功的；無能的.

inefficient [ini'fiʃənt] *adj* not able to work well and produce good results 效率低的；無效的. **inefficiency** *nu.*

inelegant [in'eligənt] *adj* **1** not having very good manners 不雅的；粗俗的. **2** not beautiful in appearance or well-made 不精緻的；粗糙的.

ineligible [in'elidʒibl] *adj* not fit to be chosen (for some reason) 無資格的；不適當的.

inept [i'nept] *adj* **1** not suitable 不適當的；不合時宜的：*an inept remark* 不恰當的話. **2** slow at learning 愚笨的；遲鈍的：*an inept pupil* 理解力差的學生.

ineptitude *nc / u*

inequality [ini'kwɔliti] *nu* state of not being equal 不平等；不平均；不相同.

ineradicable [ini'rædikəbl] *adj* not able to be dug out or removed 不能除的；根深蒂固的：*ineradicable error* 無法根除的錯誤.

inert [i'nə:t] *adj* **1** not able to move, be active or change 無自動力的；無活動力的；不起變化的：*an inert gas* i.e. one that does not change if heated or treated in any way 惰性氣體, 即: 加熱或其它處理時不起化學變化的氣體. **2** without moving; slow 不動的；不活潑的；遲鈍的：*He lay inert on the ground.* 他在地上一動不動地躺着. **inertia** [i'nə:ʃə] *nu* **1** state of being inert 不活動；遲鈍. **2** (science force which makes it difficult for a body to begin moving. and when it is moving makes it difficult for it to stop (科學)惰性；慣性.

inescapable [inis'keipəbl] *adj* not able to be escaped from: inevitable 逃避不了的；不可避免的.

inestimable [in'estiməbl] *adj* not able to be estimated; very large, valuable etc. 無法估計的；極大的；貴重的：*inestimable wealth* 實貴的財富.

inevitable [in'evitəbl] *adj* not able to be avoided; certain to happen or appear 不可避免的；一定發生的；必定出現的：*Defeat was inevitable.* 失敗是不可避免的. *She gave us her inevitable smile* i.e. one we knew would appear. 他跟往常一樣向我們微笑.

inexact [inig'zækt] *adj* not correct in every way; having mistakes 不精確的；不正確的.

inexcusable [iniks'kju:zəbl] *adj* not able to be excused 不可原諒的；不可寬恕的；無法辯解的.

inexhaustible [inig'zɔ:stəbl] *adj* not

able to be exhausted 無窮無盡的，用不完的.

inexorable [in'eksərəbl] *adj* not able to be prevented even when one begs or prays that it should be; without mercy 不爲所動的；無情的: *The spread of the disease was inexorable.* 疾病的蔓延是無情的.

inexpensive [iniks'pensiv] *adj* not expensive; cheap 不貴的；價廉的.

inexperience [iniks'piəriəns] *nu* lack of experience 缺乏經驗；無經驗. **inexperienced** *adj*

inexplicable [iniks'plikəbl] *adj* not able to be explained 無法解釋的；費解的.

inexpressible [iniks'presəbl] *adj* not able to be described or expressed in words 無法形容的；言語無法表達的.

inextricable [iniks'trikəbl] *adj* not able to be solved or made simple 不能解決的；解不開的；不能擺脫的: *He was in inextricable difficulties.* 他處於無法擺脫的困境.

infallible [in'fæləbl] *adj* 1 not able to do wrong or be wrong 不會做錯事的；不會錯的: *He is so proud that he thinks himself infallible.* 他太驕傲了，認爲他不會做錯事. 2 sure; certain 可靠的；確實的: *This is an infallible way to get good results.* 這是獲得好成績的可靠方法.

infamous ['infəməs] *adj* known for being wicked 聲名狼藉的；不名譽的. **infamy** *nu* public disgrace; evil 不名譽；邪惡.

infant ['infənt] *nc* very young child 嬰兒；幼兒. Also 亦作 *adj* of or for infants 嬰兒的；幼兒的；爲嬰（或幼）兒設置的: *infant years* 幼年; *infant school* 幼兒園. **infantile** ['infəntail] *adj* like an infant; common among infants 似嬰兒的；幼稚的；嬰兒的: *He is a grown man but his jokes are infantile* 他是成

年人，但他開玩笑的話卻是幼稚的; *infantile diseases* 小兒病. **infancy** *nu* 1 state of being an infant 嬰兒期；幼年（期）. 2 first stage of anything 初期；搖籃階段: *Modern science was then in its infancy.* 現代科學當時處於萌芽階段.

infantry ['infəntri] *nu* (company of) foot soldiers 步兵（連）. 'infantryman foot soldier 步兵: *120 infantrymen in one company of infantry.* 一步兵連的120名步兵.

infatuate [in'fætjueit] *vt* (usu. *passive*) make foolish because of too much admiration for somebody / something (通常用被動式)使迷戀: *He is infatuated with her* i.e. he loves her so much that he cannot see her as she really is. 他迷戀她. 即他太愛她，以致看不清她的真面目. **infatuation** [infætju'eiʃən] *nc / u.*

infect [in'fekt] *vt* cause to get a disease; cause to have a certain feeling 傳染；感染: *If you do not keep away from the children, you will infect them with your cold.* 如果你不避開孩子，你會把感冒傳染給他們. *This meat is infected* i.e. it contains the germs of a disease 這塊肉引受到感染. 即: 肉含有病菌. *His sadness infected us all.* 他的悲傷感染了我們所有的人. **infection 1** *nu* (esp. with reference to spreading disease through the air or water) act of spreading a disease or feeling (尤指通過空氣或水的)傳染；感染. see 見 **contagious.** 2 *nc* disease or feeling spread in this way 傳染病；影響，感染. **infectious** [in'fekʃəs] *adj: an infectious disease* 傳染病; *infectious laughter* 有感染力的笑聲.

infer [in'fə:*] *vt* decide or conclude after considering the evidence or facts 推斷；推論: *We infer from his letters* *that he is very unhappy.* 我們從他的信中推斷他很不幸. *past* 過去式和過去分詞 **inferred. inference** ['infərəns] **1** *nu* act of inferring 推斷; 推論. **2** *nc* something that is inferred 推斷的結果; 結論: *We can draw / make other inferences from his letters.* 我們從他的信中可以作出其他的論斷.

inferior [in'fiəriə*] *adj* lower in position, quality, value etc. 下級的; 下等的; 劣等的; 差的; 較低的: *An assistant manager is inferior in position to a manager.* 助理經理的地位比經理低. *This cloth is inferior to that one.* 這種布的質量比那種布差. Also 亦作 *nc*: *The manager is not friendly with his inferiors.* 這位經理對他的下屬人員不友善. **inferiority** [infiəri'ɔriti] *nu* **inferiority complex** state of feeling inferior which often causes a person to behave in the opposite way by pretending to be brave, confident and successful 自卑情結; 自卑感.

infernal [in'fə:nl] *adj* **1** belonging to help devilish 地獄的; 魔鬼似的. **2** nasty; annoying 令人厭惡的; 討厭的: *an infernal noise. informal* in sense 2) 可惡的吵鬧聲(義 2 爲非正式).

inferno [in'fə:nou] *nc* hell; any place which fire makes as hot and as horrible as hell 地獄; 地獄般的場所: *The fire turned the forest into an inferno.* 大火把森林變成一片火海. *pl* 複數 **infernos.**

infertile [in'fə:tail] *adj* not fertile; barren 不肥沃的; 不毛的: *infertile ground* 不毛之地.

infest [in'fest] *vt* (esp. with reference to somebody / something unpleasant) enter in very great numbers (尤指不愉快的人或物) 大批進入; 成羣加入: *The food store was infested with rats.* 食品倉庫裏老鼠成災.

infidel ['infidl] *nc* person who does not believe in what is considered to be the true religion 不信奉正統宗教者; 不信仰宗教者; 異教徒: *To Muslims all Christians are infidels.* 對於伊斯蘭教徒來說, 所有的基督徒都是異教徒.

infidelity [infi'deliti] *nc / u* act or state of being unfaithful (esp. to one's husband or wife) (尤指夫妻間的) 不忠實行爲; 不貞; 不忠實.

infiltrate ['infiltreit] *vt / i* enter, cause to enter, quietly, gradually, or one by one (使) 滲透; 透入: *During the war the enemy tried to infiltrate spies into our country.* 戰爭期間敵人試圖派遣間諜潛入我國.

infinite ['infinit] *adj* without limit or end; not able to be counted or measured 無限的; 無止境的; 無法計量的: *the infinite space of the universe* 宇宙的無限空間. *The storm caused infinite damage.* 這場暴風雨造成極大的損失.

infinitude [in'finitju:d] **1** *nu* state of being infinite 無限; 無窮. **2** *nc* infinite number or quantity 無窮數; 無限量.

infinity [in'finiti] *nc / u* infinitude 無限; 無窮; 無窮數; 無限量.

infinitive [in'finitiv] *adj* (grammar) form of the verb used without reference to person, number or time (語法) 不定式的(例如: to be. to go etc.) (語法) 不定式的(例如: to be, to go 等). Also 亦作 *nc*.

infirm [in'fə:m] *adj* (esp. with reference to old persons) weak; not in good health (尤指老人) 虛弱的; 體弱的. **infirmity 1** *nu* state of being infirm 虛弱; 體弱. **2** *nc* something which causes one to be infirm 疾病.

inflame [in'fleim] *vt* make red or angry 使紅 (腫), 使發炎; 使憤怒: *The dust inflamed my eyes.* 灰塵弄得我雙眼紅腫. *The people were inflamed by the news.* 人民被這則消息激怒了. **in-**

flammation [inflə'meiʃən] *nu* state of being inflamed 發炎: *inflammation of the eyes* 眼睛發炎.

inflammable [in'flæməbl] *adj* (mainly Brit) easily set on fire (主要用於英) 易燃的. (US 美 **flammable**) (opp 反義詞 **uninflammable** or **not inflammable**).

inflate [in'fleit] *vt* 1 cause to swell with air or gas (用空氣或氣體) 使膨脹: *I had to inflate the tyre.* 我得給輪胎灌氣. 2 cause prices to increase by increasing the amount of money in use 使通貨膨脹. **inflation** [in'fleiʃən] *nu*.

inflexible [in'fleksibl] *adj* not easily changed, moved or bent 不易改變的; 堅定的; 不屈的; 不易彎曲的: *He is inflexible on this matter.* 他在這個問題上是堅定的.

inflict [in'flikt] *vt* cause something unpleasant to happen to somebody 使遭受 (不快的事): *They inflicted defeat on / upon their enemies.* 他們使敵人遭到失敗. **infliction** *nc* something that is inflicted or suffered 所受的痛苦.

influence ['influəns] 1 *nc* effect on one's mind or actions; the cause of this effect 影響; 感化; 影響力; 感化力: *Religion has a great influence on man's behaviour.* 宗教對人的行為有很大的影響. *He is one of the good influences in the school.* 他是學校裏有好影響的人物之一. 2 *nu* power to cause this effect (usu. because of social position or wealth) 勢力; 權力: *People with influence get the best jobs here.* 在這裏有權勢的人找到最好的工作. Also 亦作 *vt: influence somebody's decision* 影響某人的決定. **influential** [influ'enʃl] *adj*.

influenza [influ'enzə] *nu* type of disease which causes a feverish cold (informally shortened to **flu**) 流行性感冒

(非正式縮寫爲 flu).

influx ['inflʌks] *nc* flowing in; arrival of many persons / things 流入; 注入; 湧進; (人或事物的) 彙集. *pl* 複數 **influxes**.

inform [in'fɔːm] *vt* make known to 告訴; 通知: *He will inform us where to go.* 他會告訴我們要去的地方. *He informed him of their arrival.* 他們通知他他們已到達. **information** [infə'meiʃən] *nu* **informative** *adj* giving information 提供消息(知識)的.

informal [in'fɔːml] *adj* 1 done without ceremony 不拘禮儀的; 非正式的: *an informal meeting of heads of state* 非正式的國家首腦會議; *an informal dinner* 便宴; *informal clothes* i.e. ordinary clothes, not specially put on for the occasion 便服. 2 used in ordinary speech or writing 通俗的; 俗用的; 口語的: *an informal expression* 俗語. **informality** [infɔ'mæliti] *nc / u.*

infrared ['infrə'red] *adj* having the type of rays of light which are below the colour red in the spectrum and are thus invisible 紅外線的.

infrequent [in'friːkwənt] *adj* not often 不常的; 少有的; 罕見的.

infringe [in'frindʒ] *vt* 1 break a law or rule 違反 (法規): *People who drive without a licence infringe the law.* 無駕駛執照開車的人違反法規. 2 use, or interfere with, something without having the right to do so 侵犯; 侵害: *You must not infringe the copyright of this article.* 你決不可侵犯這篇文章的版權. *He has infringed our privacy.* 他侵犯了我們的私生活. **infringement** *nc / u.*

infuriate [in'fjuərieit] *vt* make furious 使發怒; 激怒.

ingenious [in'dʒiːniəs] *adj* (with reference to persons) clever at inventing or discovering new ideas (指人) 有獨

創性的; 機靈的. **ingenuity** [indʒi-'njuːiti] nu.

ingot ['iŋgət] nc (esp. of gold or silver) short bar of metal (尤指金、銀的)條或塊; 錠.

ingrained [in'greind] adj (esp. with reference to habits, beliefs etc.) firmly fixed (尤指習慣、信仰等)根深蒂固的; 習染極深的.

ingratiate [in'greiʃieit] vt make (oneself) liked by, or popular with, somebody (usu. for selfish reasons) 討好; 逢迎; 巴結: He ingratiated himself with the new master. 他討好新主人.

ingratitude [in'grætitjuːd] nu absence of thankfulness or gratitude 忘恩負義.

ingredient [in'griːdiənt] nc one of the parts of a mixture (混合物中的)成份; 配料: a cake made from flour, sugar and various other ingredients 由麵粉、糖和各種其他配料製成的糕餅.

inhabit [in'hæbit] vt live in 居住於. **inhabitant** nc person who lives in a place 居住者; 居民.

inhale [in'heil] vt / i breathe in; draw in with the breath into the lungs 吸氣; 吸入(肺部): They say it is dangerous to inhale cigarette smoke. 據說吸香烟是危險的.

inhere [inhiə*]vi (with reference to qualities) naturally belong to or exist in (o.f.) 原有, 生來即存在於(舊式). **inherent** adj: Love of their children is inherent in all parents. 愛孩子是所有父母親的天性.

inherit [in'herit] vt **1** receive money, property or position on the death of someone (usu. a relative) 繼承: He inherited his uncle's farm i.e. he got the farm on the death of his uncle. 他繼承他叔父的農場. 即: 他叔父死後, 他得到這農場. **2** receive a quality of somebody from whom one is de-

scended 由遺傳而得(特性等): He has inherited his grandfather's skill in making money. 他繼承了他祖父賺錢的本領. **inheritance** nc / u.

inhibit [in'hibit] vt cause, be likely to cause, somebody not to do something; make it difficult for somebody to do something 禁止; 抑制; 阻塞: His bad English inhibits him from speaking freely / He is inhibited from speaking freely by his bad English. 由於他的英語不好, 他不能自由地進行交談. (opp 反義詞 uninhibited). **inhibition** [inhi'biʃən] nc / u feeling or state of being inhibited 心理障礙; 受抑制; 禁止: He has no inhibitions about speaking French. 他沒有講法語的心理障礙.

inhospitable [inhɔs'pitəbl] adj not hospitable; not friendly or ready to welcome 不慇懃的; 冷淡的; 不好客的.

inhuman [in'hjuːmən] adj not human; cruel 無人性的; 不人道的; 殘忍的.

inimitable [i'nimitəbl] adj not able to be imitated; better than or different from any other 無法模倣的; 無雙的; 無與倫比的: his inimitable way of making his students interested in their work 他使學生對工作感興趣的獨特方法.

iniquitous [i'nikwitəs] adj very wicked or unfair 極邪惡的; 極不公正的. **iniquity** [i'nikwiti] nc / u act or state of being iniquitous 極邪惡或不公正的行為; 極邪惡; 極不公正.

initial [i'niʃl] adj first 開始的; 最初的. Also 亦作 nc first letter of a person's name or of a word (e.g. J.S. are the initials of John Smith; U.N.O. of the United Nations Organization) 姓名或單詞的首字母(例如: J.S. 是 John Smith 的首字母; U.N.O.是the United Nations Organization 的首字母). Also 亦作 vt sign by using only one's initials 簽姓名首字母於. *past* 過去式和過去分詞 **initialled** (*US* 美 **initialed**). **initially** *adv* at first 起初；開始.

initiate [i'niʃieit] *vt* **1** begin. cause something to begin 開始；發起；着手： *He has initiated talks about opening new schools.* 他開始談論開辦新學校的事. **2** make known for the first time; introduce 引進；介紹： *The lecture initiated us into the problems of living abroad.* 這篇講演向我們介紹了在國外生活的問題. *We were initiated into the sports club by one of the members.* 運動俱樂部的一位會員介紹我們加入該俱樂部. **initiation** [iniʃieiʃən] *nu* act of initiating or being initiated 開始；着手；指引；正式加入. **initiative** [i'niʃətiv] *nu* ability to do, or begin, something without the help or suggestions of others 主動精神；主動；首創力： *He went to see the headmaster on his own initiative* i.e. it was his own idea to see him. 他主動去見校長. 即：去見校長是他自己的主意. *He's got no initiative.* 他沒有創始精神. *He took the initiative by speaking first at the meeting.* 他在會上首先發言採取主動.

inject [in'dʒekt] *vt* throw in; (esp. with reference to putting a fluid below the skin by means of a hollow needle) force in 插進；注射；注入： *The doctor injected the drug into my arm.* 醫生往我的胳臂上注射藥. **injection** *nc* / *u*: *I have been given an injection by the doctor.* 醫生給我打了一針.

injure ['indʒə*] *vt* do harm or damge (usu. to living creatures) 傷害；損害 (通常指生物). **injured** *adj* **1** harmed or damaged 被傷害的；受損害的. **2** hurt; offended; complaining 感情受到傷害的；被觸怒的；受委屈的： *She*

spoke in an injured voice. 她用受委屈的聲音講話. Also 亦作 people who have been injured in an accident etc. (在事故等中)受傷者. **injury** *nc* harm; damage; wound 傷害；損害；(負)傷： *Because of his many injuries he was taken to hospital.* 由於多處負傷, 他被送進醫院.

injustice [in'dʒʌstis] **1** *nu* being without justice 不公正；不公平；非正義. **2** *nc* unjust act 不公正的行為： *They did me a great injustice by calling me a liar.* 他們說我撒謊, 太冤枉我了.

ink [iŋk] *nc* type of black or coloured liquid used for writing, printing and drawing 墨水；油墨. **inky** *adj* **1** covered or marked with ink 染有墨水 (或油墨)的. **2** as black as ink 漆黑的： *inky darkness* 漆黑.

inkling ['inkliŋ] *nc* very small hint, a little knowledge 細微的暗示；署知： *They have an inkling of his plans.* 他們對他的計劃署有所知.

inland ['inlənd] *adj* far away from the sea; inside a country 內地的；內陸的；國內的： *Birmingham is an inland city* 伯明翰是一個內陸城市； *inland postal services* i.e. those carried on inside a country 國內郵政. Also 亦作 ['in-lænd] *adv* away from the sea 在內地；向內地： *They travelled inland from the coast.* 他們從沿海地區往內地旅行. *The city lies inland.* 這座城市在內地. '**inland** '**revenue** money obtained from taxes (e.g. income tax) raised inside a country 國內稅收 (例如：所得稅).

in-laws ['inlɔːz] *npl* short informal form of **mother-in-law, father-in-law** etc. mother-in-law,father-in-law等的非正式縮署式. *He has gone to see his in-laws.* 他已去看他的岳父、岳母.

inlet ['inlet] *nc* narrow area of water;

small bay 水灣; 小灣.

inmate ['inmeit] *nc* person who lives with others in a building (usu. a hospital or prison) 同屋居住者(通常指在同醫院或同監獄).

inn [in] *nc* building which supplies travellers with food, drink and a place to sleep (usu. found in the country, not towns) 小旅館, 客棧(通常指在鄉村的). **'innkeeper** person in charge of an inn 小旅館(或客棧)老闆.

innate [i'neit] *adj* born in a person; natural 生來的; 固有的; 天生的: *man's innate desire for happiness* 人的天生渴求幸福的願望.

inner ['inə*] *adj* further in; inside something else 內在的; 內部的: *the inner circle* i.e. the one inside another circle 內圈; 裏面的小圈.

innocent ['inəsnt] *adj* 1 doing no wrong; not guilty 清白的; 無罪的: *I am innocent of the crime.* 我是清白無罪的. 2 knowing no wrong; simple; easily deceived 天真無邪的; 單純的; 頭腦簡單的; 無知的; 易受騙的: *He is innocent about night life in a big city.* 他天真無邪地看待大城市的夜生活. *They were innocent enough to believe him.* 他們太單純了, 竟然相信他. **innocence** *nu.*

innocuous [i'nɔkjuəs] *adj* harmless 無害的.

innovate ['inəveit] *vi* change by bringing in something new 創新; 革新: *The young teachers wish to innovate.* 青年教師希望革新. **innovation** [inə'veiʃən] *nc / u: the young teachers' innovations in classroom work* 這位青年教師在課堂工作方面的革新.

innuendo [inju'endou] *nc / u* indirect hint or statement made about somebody (usu. attacking his behaviour or character) 暗諷; 影射(通常指攻擊人的

行為或人格). *pl* 複數 **innuen does.**

innumerable [i'nju:mərəbl] *adj* too many to be counted 無數的; 數不清的.

inoculate [i'nɔkjuleit] *vt* protect somebody against a disease by giving him a little of the disease so that his body makes itself able to meet a severe attack 給…預防注射; 給…接種疫苗: *The doctor inoculated the children against influenza* 醫生給孩子打針預防流行性感冒. **inoculation** [inɔkju'leiʃən] *nc / u.*

inopportune [in'ɔpətju:n] *adj* happening at the wrong time; not convenient 不合時宜的; 不方便的.

inordinate [i'nɔ:dinət] *adj* not under control; too great 無節制的; 過度的: *inordinate pride* 過份驕傲.

inorganic [inɔ:'gænik] *adj* not belonging to, or having the structure of, animals or plants (e.g. metals or rocks) 無機的(例如: 金屬或岩石).

in-patient ['inpeiʃənt] *nc* person who lives in a hospital while being attended to 住院病人. *(opp 反義詞 out-patient).*

input ['input] *nc* what is put into something (e.g. the electric power put into a battery; the money and labour put into a business) 輸入物; 投入物(例如: 輸入電池的電力; 投入商行的資金和勞力) *(opp 反義詞 output).*

inquest ['inkwest] *nc* public inquiry made under the law into any matter (esp. into the cause of somebody's death) 審訊; 調查(尤指調查某人的死因); 驗屍.

inquire, enquire [in'kwaiə*] *vt / i* ask questions about; try to find out 詢問; 打聽, 調查, 查問: *I inquired about his daughter.* 我問起他女兒的情況. *They inquired where to go.* 他們打聽要去的

地方. *The police are inquiring into the murder.* 警察正在調查這宗謀殺案.
inquiring *adj* always trying to find out 愛打聽的; 好問的; 好奇的; *an inquiring mind* 好奇的心理; 好奇的精神.
inquiry *nc*: *I have to make inquiries about his name and address.* 我得查問他的名字和住址. **inquire after** ask for news about somebody 問候.

inquisitive [in'kwizitiv] *adj* wishing to know about other people's business; too ready to ask questions 好管閒事的; 好問的; 好奇的: *Our neighbours are very inquisitive about our friends.* 我們的鄰居很喜歡打聽有關我們朋友的事.

inroad ['inroud] *nc* **1** sudden invasion or raid 突然侵犯, 突然襲擊. **2** (usu. *pl*) any injurious encroachment (通常用複數) 損害: *to make inroads on somebody's health* 使某人的健康受到損害.

insane [in'sein] *adj* mad; mentally diseased 瘋狂的; 患精神病的. **insanity** [in'sæniti] *nu.*

insanitary [in'sænitəri] *adj* (esp. with reference to the absence of proper sanitation) dirty and unhealthy (尤指沒有適當的衛生設備) 不衛生的; 有害健康的.

insatiable [in'sei∫əbl] *adj* not able to be satisfied; always wanting more 無法滿足的; 不知足的; 貪得無厭的.

inscribe [in'skraib] *vt* (often with reference to writing cut on something hard like wood or stone) write in or on 題寫; 銘刻: *He inscribed his name in the book.* 他在這本書中題名. *Their names are inscribed on the stone above their grave.* 在他們的墓碑上刻上他們的名字. **inscription** [in'skrip∫ən] *nc/u.*

inscrutable [in'skru:təbl] *adj* not able

to be discovered or understood 高深莫測的; 不可理解的; 不可思議的: *His face was inscrutable* i.e. nobody could discover his feelings by looking at it. 他的臉部表情令人費解. 即: 看他的臉, 沒有人能看出他的感情.

insect ['insekt] *nc* type of very small animal with six legs (e.g. a fly, a bee or an ant) 昆蟲(例如: 蒼蠅、蜜蜂或螞蟻). **insecticide** [in'sektisaid] *nc* chemical substance used for killing insects 殺蟲劑.

insecure [insi'kjuə*] *adj* not properly fastened; not safe 不牢靠的; 不穩固的; 不安全的; 有危險的: *These boxes are insecure.* 這些箱子不牢固. *I feel insecure in this lonely house.* 在這偏僻的房子裏我感到不安全. **insecurity** *nu.*

insensible [in'sensibl] *adj* **1** without bodily feeling; unconscious 無感覺(力)的; 麻木的; 失去知覺的; 不省人事的: *He is still insensible after the blow on his head.* 他在頭部被打之後至今仍昏迷不醒. **2** too small or slow to be noticed 太小或太慢而無法注意到的; 難以察覺的: *the insensible growth of a tree* 樹的成長不易察覺.

insensitive [in'sensitiv] *adj* not sensitive; not quick to feel; not easily hurt 不敏感的; 感覺遲鈍的; 不易受傷害的: *insensitive to pain* 對疼痛無感覺的.

inseparable [in'sepərəbl] *adj* not able to be separated 不能分離的; 分不開的.

insert [in'sə:t] *vt* put in; place among others 插入; 嵌入; 刊入: *The book would be improved by inserting another chapter.* 這本書再插進一章會更好. Also 亦作 ['insə:t] *nc* something inserted 插入物; 嵌入物. **insertion** *nc /u* act of inserting; something inserted (often with reference to an advertise-

ment put in a newspaper) 插入；嵌入；
插入廣告 (常指報紙中插入的廣告) .

inshore ['in'ʃɔ:*] *adj / adv* near, toward
the shore 近海岸的 (地)；向海岸的
(地) .

inside ['in'said] **1** *adj* within the sides of
內部的；靠內面的: *the inside pages of
a book* 書的裏頁 . **2** *adv: Let's go inside.* 讓我們到裏面去 . *There is a boy
inside.* 有個男孩在裏面 . **3** *prep: Let's
go inside the house.* 讓我們到屋裏去 .
There is a toy inside the box. 盒子裏
有個玩具 . Also 亦作 *nc: I want to see
the inside of the house.* 我要看房子的
內部 . *He has a pain in his inside* i.e.
in his stomach, *(informal)* 他肚子痛 .
(非正式) . **inside out 1** with the inside on the outside 裏朝外地；內部向
外翻地: *He is wearing his coat inside
out.* 他的上衣穿反了 . **2** completely 徹
底地: *They know this town inside out.*
他們對這城城市瞭如指掌 .

insidious [in'sidiəs] *adj* causing harm
or damage without being seen or felt
暗中爲害的，陰險的；詭詐的 .

insight ['insait] *nc / u* ability to see the
real meaning of something; clear and
quick understanding of a problem 洞
察 (力)；見識；頓悟: *He has a great insight into modern science.* 他對現代科
學很有見識 . *His speech gave us a
valuable insight into the problems of
education.* 他的講話給我們提供了對教
育問題的寶貴見解 .

insignia [in'signiə] *npl* signs or badges
showing rank or authority (表明地位、
等級或權威的) 標幟；徽章；動章 .

insignificant [insig'nifikənt] *adj* not important; of little use or value 不重要
的；無足輕重的；無用的；無價值的 .

insincere [insin'siə*] *adj* not sincere;
false 不誠實的；虛假的 . **insincerity**
[insin'seriti] *nu.*

insinuate [in'sinjueit] *vt* **1** (usu. with
oneself) move slowly and cunningly
into (通常與oneself連用) 使逐漸而巧
妙地進入；使潛入: *He insinuated himself into all our discussions.* 他巧妙地
加入我們所有的討論 . **2** say something unpleasant in an indirect way 暗
諷；暗示: *They have insinuated to me
that you drink too much.* 他們已向我
暗示你喝得太多了 . **insinuation** [in-
sinju'eiʃən] *nc / u.*

insipid [in'sipid] *adj* **1** without taste 没
有味道的；淡而無味的: *insipid food* 淡
而無味的食物 . **2** not interesting; not
lively 無趣的；枯燥無味的；無生氣的:
an insipid meeting 死氣沉沉的會議 .

insist [in'sist] *vt / i* state or urge strongly (esp. against those who state or
urge differently) 堅決主張；堅持: *I insist on your being here.* 我堅持要你呆
在這裏 . *I insist that you be here /
shall be here.* 我堅持要你呆在這裏 .
He insists on the need to work hard.
他堅持需要努力工作 . **insistent** *adj*
insistence *nu.*

insolent ['insələnt] *adj* very rude (esp. to
somebody who is older or more im-
portant) (尤指對較年長或較重要的人)
無禮的；粗野的: *He was insolent to his
teacher.* 他對老師無禮 . **insolence** *nu.*

insoluble [in'sɔljubl] *adj* **1** not able to
be dissolved 不能溶解的 . **2** not able
to be solved or explained 不能解決
的；不能解釋的: *an insoluble problem*
不能解決的問題 .

insolvent [in'sɔlvənt] *adj* not able to
pay one's debts 無力償付債務的 .

insomnia [in'sɔmniə] *nu* state of not
being able to sleep 失眠 .

inspect [in'spekt] *vt* (esp. with reference
to an official seeing that something is
done) look carefully at 檢查；視察: *A
man came to inspect our school*

yesterday i.e. to see that it was doing well. 昨天有個人來視察我們學校. **inspection** [in'spekʃən] *nu* inspecting or being inspected 檢查; 視察: *On inspection the meat was found to be bad.* 經過檢查發現肉壞了. **2** *nc* act of inspecting 檢查或視察的行爲. **inspector** *nc* **1** person who inspects (esp. tickets on trains and buses) 檢查員, 視察員; (尤指火車和公共汽車上的) 查票員. **2** police officer above a sergeant in rank (警察的) 巡官.

inspire [in'spaiə*] *vt* cause somebody to have better thoughts or feelings 鼓舞, 激勵: *The good news inspired us with hope.* 好消息激起我們的希望. *His speech inspired us to try again.* 他的講話激勵我們再試一次. **inspired** *adj* having great thoughts and powers 有靈感的; 有感召力的: *an inspired artist* 有靈感的藝術家. **inspiring** *adj*: *an inspiring speech* 鼓舞人心的講話. (*opp* 反義詞 **uninspiring**). **inspiration** [inspə'reiʃən] *nu* act of inspiring; impulse towards creative work; guidance from God 鼓舞; 激勵, 靈感; 好主意; 神的啓示.

instability [instə'biliti] *nu* (usu. with reference to behaviour or character) state of not having stability; lack of firmness or determination (通常指行爲或性格) 不穩定; 不堅決, 動搖; 三心兩意.

install [in'stɔːl] *vt* **1** put somebody in his new position (usu. at a ceremony and often with reference to a church or university) 使就職 (通常在儀式上, 常指教堂或大學): *The new Vice-Chancellor of the university has been installed.* 這所大學新的副校長已就職. **2** put something in its position ready for use 裝設; 安裝: *install an electric light / a bathroom / a fireplace etc.* 安

裝電燈 / 浴室 / 壁爐等. **installation** [instə'leiʃən] **1** *nu* act of installing or being installed 就職; 裝設; 安裝. **2** *nc* something which has been installed (e.g. a piece of machinery or equipment) 裝置物 (例如: 機器或設備).

instalment [in'stɔːlmənt] *nc* **1** regular payment in small fixed amounts of money for something which one has already been allowed to own 分期付款: *We are paying for our car by / in monthly instalments of £10.* 我們按月付拾鎊購買汽車. **2** regular supply of something in parts 分批定期提供之物: *I am looking forward to the next instalment of his book in the Sunday newspaper.* 我盼望着看到在星期天報紙上刊登他的書的下一部份.

instance ['instns] *nc* example; occasion 例子; 情況; 場合: *This is the first instance of fever in the village.* 這是這個村子的第一個熱病病例. **for instance** for example 例如.

instant[1] ['instnt] *adj* **1** quick; urgent; without delay 迅速的; 立即的; 緊迫的; 刻不容緩的: *an instant reply* 即刻答覆. *The sick boy needs instant attention.* 這個生病的男孩需要立即治療. **2** prepared by a manufacturer and ready for use 即可用的; 速食的: *instant coffee* 速溶咖啡. **instantly** *adv*.

instant[2] ['instnt] *nc* moment of time; very short time 即刻, 即時; 刹那, 瞬間: *He came the instant I called his name* i.e. immediately after I called his name. 我一叫他的名字, 他立刻就來. *Go away this instant!* i.e. now; at once. 馬上走開! *He finished the work in an instant* i.e. in a very short time. 他一會兒就做完了這件工作.

instead [in'sted] *adv* taking the place of, or as a change from, somebody / something 代替; 更換: *He didn't give*

John the money, but he gave it to me instead. 他沒有把錢給約翰，但是他把錢給了我. *Last night I stayed at home. Tonight I'm going out instead.* 昨天晚上我呆在家裏，而今天晚上我要出去. **instead of** *prep* in place of 代替: *Instead of giving him the money he gave it to me.* 他不給他錢而把錢給了我. *I'll go instead of you.* 我會代你去. *He studies in the evening instead of during the day.* 他在晚上而不在白天學習.

instigate ['instigeit] *vt* urge somebody to do something; cause something to happen by urging (usu. something bad) 唆使某人做某事; 教唆; 煽動: *They instigated the crime.* 他們教唆犯罪.

instinct ['instiŋkt] *nc / u* inclination, readiness, to behave in certain fixed ways which one already has when born and does not learn afterwards 本能; 天性: *Ants build ant-hills by instinct.* 螞蟻築蟻塚是出於本能. *Man is controlled by his instincts as well as by reason.* 人既受理智的支配又受本能的支配. **instinctive** [in'stiŋktiv] *adj* caused by instinct 本能的; 天性的.

institute ['institju:t] *nc* group of people organized for a particular purpose (usu. to increase their knowledge); the building in which they work (通常指爲增長知識而設的) 協會, 學會; 學院; 研究所: *Many universities have institutes of education.* 許多綜合性大學設有教育學院. **institution** [insti'tju:ʃən] *nc* 1 organization to meet a public need; its buildings 公共機構; 社會團體; 學校, 醫院等: *A hospital is an institution to cure the sick.* 醫院是醫治病人的公共機構. 2 well-established custom, habit, law or person in a society 風俗; 慣例; 制度; 眾所週知的

人: *Slavery was one of the institutions of ancient Greece.* 奴隸制是古希臘的一種制度. *That old man has lived here so long that he is an institution.* 那位老人在這裏住了很久, 成爲一位眾所週知的人物.

instruct [in'strʌkt] *vt* 1 teach 教: *He instructs his pupils in mathematics.* 他教學生數學. 2 give orders to 下令; 命令; 指示: *He instructed them to listen.* 他命令他們聽. **instructor** *nc* (fem 陰 **instructress** [in'strʌktris]. **instruction** 1 *nu* act of instructing or being instructed (in sense 1) 教授; 教導; *instruction in mathematics* 教授數學. 2 *nc* (usu. *pl*) orders; explanation of how to use something etc. (通常用複數) 命令; 指示: **instructive** *adj* giving useful instruction or information 有教益的; 給與有用知識的.

instrument ['instrumənt] *nc* 1 tool or apparatus (esp. for scientific purposes) 器具; 器械; 儀器 (尤指爲科學上的目的). 2 something made to give a musical sound (e.g. a drum, violin, trumpet) 樂器 (例如: 鼓、小提琴、小號); 3 person / thing used by somebody to get what he wants 被利用的人, 傀儡; 工具; 手段: *He made the army his instrument to gain power.* 他使軍隊成爲他奪權的工具. **instrumental** [instrə'mentl] *adj* 1 used or acting as an instrument (in sense 3) 作爲手段 (或工具) 的; 有幫助的; 有作用的: *They were instrumental in getting him home safely.* 他們有助於使他安全回家. 2 of musical instruments 樂器的.

insubordinate [insəbɔːdinit] *adj* disobedient; refusing to obey orders 不服從的; 反抗的. **insubordination** [insəbɔːdi'neiʃən] *nu*.

insufferable [in'sʌfərəbl] *adj* not able

to be endured; unbearable 不可容忍
的; 難以忍受的: *insufferable conduct*
令人難以忍受的行為.

insufficient [insə'fiʃənt] *adj* not
enough 不夠的, 不足的. **insufficient-**
ly *adv*.

insular ['insjulə*] *adj* narrowminded;
prejudiced 心胸狹窄的; 有偏見的: *an*
insular outlook 眼光短淺的觀點. **in-**
sularity [insju'læriti] *nu*.

insulate ['insjuleit] *vt* (with reference to
electricity, heat, damp, noise etc) cover with a special substance so that it
is protected or kept separate 使 (電、
熱、濕氣、噪聲等)與外界絕緣或隔離:
Rubber is used to insulate electric
wires. 橡膠被用作電線的絕緣體. *The*
room is insulated against noise. 這房
間能隔音. **insulating** *adj* causing in-
sulation 絕緣的; 隔離的: *insulating*
tape. 絕緣包帶.

insulin ['insjulin] *nu* **1** chemical produced inside the body which controls
the amount of sugar in the blood 胰島
素. **2** artificial substance containing
this chemical, used for treating the
disease of diabetes (用於治療糖尿病
的) 人造胰島素.

insult [in'sʌlt] *vt* be rude to 對…無禮;
侮辱. Also 亦作['insʌlt] *nc*. **insulting**
adj.

insuperable [in'su:pərəbl] *adj* not able
to be overcome 不能克服的: *insuper-*
able difficulties 不能克服的困難.

insure [in'ʃuə*] *vt* arrange to pay regularly sums of money so that one
large sum is received if one dies or
suffers injury or loss 保險; 投保: *He*
has insured himself for £6,000 i.e. if
he dies, £6,000 will be paid to his
family. 他給自己保人壽險六千鎊. 即:
如果他死了, 要付給他的家屬六千鎊.
My house is insured against fire and

theft. 我的房子投保了火險和偷盜險.

insurance *nu* money paid to insure
somebody / something; money paid to
a person who is insured 保險費; 保險
(賠償)金額: *I pay my insurance every*
January. 我每年一月付保險費. *When*
his car was damaged he got £100 in-
surance. 他的汽車損壞後, 他得到一百
鎊的保險賠償費. **in'surance policy**
agreement by which one is insured 保
險單: *He took out an insurance policy*
against accidents in the home i.e. he
obtained one from an insurance company. 他取得一份家中事故保險的保險
單.

insurmountable [insə'mauntəbl] *adj*
not able to be overcome 不能克服的.

insurrection [insə'rekʃən] *nc* act of rising against lawful authority 造反; 叛
亂.

intact [in'tækt] *adj* not having been
touched; not damaged; complete 未動
過的; 未受損的; 完整的: *The parcels I*
sent by post arrived intact. 我郵寄的
包裹完整無損地到達了.

intake ['inteik] *nc* somebody / something taken in 納入; 吸入: *This college*
has an intake of 200 students each
year i.e. it takes in 200 students. 這所
學院每年招收200名學生.

intangible [in'tændʒibl] *adj* not able to
be touched; not able to be clearly
understood 觸摸不到的; 無形的; 難以
理解的; 不可捉摸的、模糊的: *an in-*
tangible sensation of fear 一種莫明其
妙的恐懼感.

integer ['intidʒə*] *nc* (mathematics)
whole number (e.g. 2,4,7 etc), not a
fraction 整數 (例如: 2, 4, 7等).

integral ['intigrl] *adj* necessary to make
something whole or complete 構成整
體所必需的: *Your help is an integral*
part of our plan. 你的幫助是我們計劃

中的不可缺少的一份.

integrate ['intigreit] *vt* make something complete from a number of parts; bring somebody into a group from outside it 使成一整體; 使結合; 使併入: *We must integrate people who come to live here into the community.* 我們必須把來這裏居住的人納入社區. **integration** [inti'greiʃən] *nu.*

integrity [in'tegriti] *nu* complete honesty and goodness 誠實; 正直: *His integrity prevents him (from) doing anything wrong.* 他為人正直, 不會幹壞事.

intellect ['intəlekt] *nu* power to reason and think 智力; 思維力, 推理能力. **intellectual** [intə'lektjuəl] *adj* 1 of the intellect 智力的: *intellectual interests* 智力愛好. 2 having great intellect 有智力的; 聰明的: *an intellectual teacher* 聰明的教師. Also 亦作 *nc* person who is intellectual (esp. one who judges everything by his intellect and is thus ahead of ordinary people or does not think as they do) 知識分子.

intelligence [in'telidʒəns] *nu* 1 ability to learn and understand 智力; 聰明才智: *His intelligence is poor.* 他的智力差. *They had the intelligence to answer the question correctly.* 他們聰明, 能正確回答問題. 2 news; information collected for a specific purpose 消息; 情報: *an intelligence agent* i.e. a person who gets information about an enemy secretly; a spy 情報員; 間諜. **intelligent** *adj* having great intelligence 有智力的; 聰明的; 有才智的. (*opp* 反義詞 **unintelligent**). **intelligently** *adv.*

intelligible [in'telidʒibl] *adj* able to be understood 可理解的; 明白的: *speak intelligible English* 講清晰的英語. (*opp* 反義詞 **unintelligible**).

intemperate [in'tempərət] *adj* not controlled; excessive: 無節制的; 過度的: *an intemperate rage* 狂怒; *intemperate drinking* 暴飲.

intend [in'tend] *vt* have in mind; be one's purpose 想要; 打算: *I intend to come back soon / I intend coming back soon.* 我打算很快就回來. *I intend you to come with me.* 我打算讓你和我一道去. *You are intended to come with me.* 本來就打算讓你和我一道去. *I intend that we shall arrive tomorrow.* 我想我們將在明天到達. see 見 **intention**.

intense [in'tens] *adj* (with reference to qualities and feelings) great and powerful (指性質和感情)強烈的; 非常的; 劇烈的: *intense cold / heat* 嚴寒/酷熱; *intense anger / suffering* 極度的憤怒/痛苦; *an intense young man* i.e. one who has intense feelings 熱情的青年人. **intensely** *adv* **intensity** *nu* **intensive** *adj* thorough; (with reference to one particular part) concentrated 透徹的; 深入細緻的; (特指某一部份) 密集的; 集中的: *He made intensive inquiries* i.e. inquiries which were thorough with reference to one particular problem 他進行了深入細緻的調查; *intensive farming* i.e. using improved methods on a small area of land so as to get better crops from it 密集農業, 密集耕作. **intensively** *adv.*

intent¹ [in'tent] *adj* attending to or examining with great care 專注的; 專心的: *He was intent on / upon winning the race.* 他一心一意要在這場比賽中獲勝. *He gave me an intent look.* 他目不轉睛地注視著我. **intently** *adv.*

intent² [in'tent] *nu* intention; (usu. in legal phrases) purpose 意圖; (通常用於法律短語)目的: *He entered the house with intent to steal.* 他進入這座

房子, 有意進行偷竊. **to all intents and purposes** for all practical purposes 實質上; 實際上.

intention [in'tenʃən] *nc / u* plan; aim; purpose 計劃; 目標; 目的; 意圖: *We do not know their intentions.* 我們不知道他們的意圖. *It is their intention to return as soon as possible.* 他們的意圖是儘快返回. *I have no intention of meeting them.* 我不打算見他們. **intentional** *adj* done on purpose 有意的; 故意的: *an intentional insult* 有意的侮辱. (*opp* 反義詞 **unintentional**). **intentionally** *adv* see 見 **intend**.

inter- ['intə*] *prefix* between; among (e.g. **interchange**) 在⋯之間; 在⋯之中 (例如: **interchange** 交換).

inter² [in'tə:*] *vt* bury in the ground or in a tomb 埋葬. *past* 過去式和過去分詞 **interred**.

interact [intə'rækt] *vi* act on each other 互相作用. **interaction** *nc / u.*

intercede [intə'si:d] *vt* try to settle an affair; ask a favour for somebody 從中調停; 代爲求情; 代爲懇求: *He interceded in the argument* i.e. he tried to settle it by getting those who were arguing to agree. 他在這場爭論中進行調解工作. *I interceded with the headmaster for / on behalf of the boys who were to be punished* i.e. I asked him not to punish them. 我替那些要受處罰的男生向校長求情. 即: 我請求校長不要處罰他們.

intercept [intə'sept] *vt* seize or stop somebody / something while he or it is moving from one place to another 中途攔截; 截取: *They intercepted him before he crossed the road.* 在他越過公路之前, 他們就把他截住了.

interchange [intə'tʃeindʒ] *vt* change the places of two things 互換 (位置); 交換: *You should interchange the*

tyres on your car i.e. each tyre should be changed around onto a different wheel. 你應當把汽車的輪胎互換位置. Also 亦作 ['intə'tʃeindʒ] *nc* place in a motorway system, where two or more roads meet (高速公路的) 立體交叉道. **interchangeable** [intə'tʃeindʒibl] *adj* able to be interchanged 可互換的; 可交換的; 可交替的: *The front wheels are interchangeable with the back ones.* 前輪可跟後輪互換.

intercom ['intəkɔm] *nu* radio system used by a group of people in a building, plane etc for talking to each other (樓內、機上等工作人員的) 内部通話裝置; 對講裝置; 對講機.

intercourse ['intəkɔ:s] *nu* movement of goods, ideas, messages etc between persons or countries (人或國家之間的) 交流; 交往; 交際: *Trade is the main form of intercourse between Europe and the Far East.* 貿易是歐洲和遠東之間的主要交往形式. **sexual intercourse** sexual act between two people or two animals (人或動物的) 性交.

interest ['intrist] **1** *nu* attention given to somebody / something 關心; 興趣: *He takes (a) great interest in sport.* 他對運動很有興趣. *Have you lost interest?* 你已失去興趣了嗎; *news of little interest* 人們不感興趣的消息. **2** *nc* something to which one gives attention; something which causes pleasurable attention 感興趣的事; 愛好: *My only interests are books and the theatre.* 我唯一的愛好是書和戲劇. **3** *nc* advantage; personal profit 利益; 私利: *It is in your (own) interests to be honest.* 誠實對你有好處. **4** *nu* profit made from lending money extra money paid for borrowing money 利息: *This bank charges 12 per cent in-*

terest on all money borrowed from it. 向這家銀行借款要付12%的利息. **5** *nc* claim; share 所有權; 股份: *They have interests in gold mining* i.e. have shares in a company which mines gold. 他們在金礦開採公司中有股份. Also 亦作 *vt* cause somebody to have or take, interest in 使(某人)發生興趣: *He interested me in football.* 他使我對足球感興趣. *His story interested me.* 他的身世引起了我的興趣. **interested** *adj* **1** having interest (in sense 1) 關切的; 感興趣的: *interested studenst* 感興趣的學生. *I am interested in him.* 我喜歡他. **2** having shares or claims (in sense 5) 有股份的; 有利害關係的: *the two interested people in this dispute* i.e. the two people who will gain or lose in it. 這場辯論中的兩個參與者. **interesting** *adj* causing interest (in sense 2) 有趣味的; 引起興趣的: *a very interesting story* 十分有趣的故事. (*opp* 反義詞 **uninteresting**).

interfere [intə'fiə*] *vi* **1** concern oneself with somebody / something without being asked (esp. with the affairs of others) 干涉; 干預 (尤指別人的事): *You should not interfere in other people's arguments.* 你不要干預別人的爭論. *Who interfered with my camera?* i.e. who damaged it? 誰亂弄我的照相機? 即: 誰弄壞了照相機? **2** get in the way of; hinder 妨礙; 阻礙: *The noise interfered with my studies.* 嘈雜聲妨礙了我的學習. **interference** *nu* (often with reference to one wavelength interfering with another on radio or television) act of interfering (常指聲波光波或電波的)干擾.

interior [in'tiəriə*] *adj* inner; inside 內部的; 裏面的: *the interior walls of a house* 房子裏邊的牆壁. Also 亦作 *nc* **1** the inside 內部: *The interior of the*

house is very pleasant. 這房子的內部是很舒適的. **2** inside part of a country 內地: *He was lost in the interior of Africa for many years.* 他在非洲內地失蹤多年.

interjection [intə'dʒekʃən] *nc* (grammar) word used to indicate a sudden emotion (e.g. Oh!, Ah!, Gosh!). (語法) 感嘆詞 (例如: Oh! 哦! Ah! 啊 Gosh! 天哪!).

interlock [intə'lɔk] *vt / i* lock or join firmly together (使)連鎖; (使)連結: *The different parts of this puzzle should interlock.* 這拼圖板的不同部份應拼合在一起.

interloper ['intəloupə*] *nc* person who enters where he has no right to (usu. to do something wrong) 闖入者 (通常爲了做壞事).

interlude ['intəlu:d] *nc* period of time between two events during which something else happens or is done (e.g. between two acts of a play) (兩事件的)間歇; 穿插事件; (戲劇的)幕間, 幕間插入的戲.

intermarry [intə'mæri] *vi* become related to a different group of people by marrying somebody belonging to it 通婚: *For many years these people have intermarried with foreigners.* 多年來這些人和外國人通婚. **intermarriage** [intə'mæridʒ] *nu*.

intermediary [intə'mi:diəri] *nc* person who maintains contact between people; a go-between 中間人; 調解人; 媒人.

intermediate [intə'mi:diət] *adj* being between; in the middle 居間的; 中間的: *an intermediate examination* i.e. one in the middle of a course 期中考試.

interminable [in'tə:minəbl] *adj* never ending; too long to be enjoyed 漫無止

境的; 沒完沒了的; 冗長的: *an inter-minable speech* 冗長的演說.

intermission [intə'miʃən] *nc / u* pause; rest 暫停, 中斷; 休息: *They worked all night without intermission.* 他們通宵達旦不停地工作.

intermittent [intə'mitnt] *adj* stopping and starting again; not happening all the time 間歇的; 斷斷續續的: *He sends only intermittent news.* 他發來的只是斷斷續續的消息.

intern[1] [in'tə:n] *vt* (esp. with reference to people of another country during a war) put together in a certain place; imprison 拘留(尤指戰時的外國人); 監禁: *During the last war all Germans living in Great Britain were interned.* 在上次戰爭期間住在英國的所有德國人都被拘留. **internment** *nu*

intern[2] [in'tə:n] *nc* (esp. with reference to a doctor living in the hospital where he works) person who lives where he works (尤指住在醫院的)實習醫生; 住在工作單位的人.

internal [in'tə:nl] *adj* of the inside 內部的: *internal pains* (e.g. inside the stomach) 內痛 (例如: 胃內部); *a country's internal problems* i.e. problems about what is happening inside, not outside it 一國的國內問題. **internally** *adv*.

international [intə'næʃənl] *adj* between nations 國際的: *international trade* 國際貿易; *international understanding* 國際諒解. Also 亦作 *nc* **1** (football etc.) match between nations (足球等)國際比賽. **2** player in one of these matches 參加國際比賽的運動員.

interplanetary [intə'plænitəri] *adj* between planets 行星間的; 星際間的.

interplay ['intəplei] *nu* the effect or influence of two persons / things on

each other 相互作用; 相互影響: *The interplay of the two main characters in the play is interesting.* 劇中兩個主要人物的相互影響很有趣.

interpret [in'tə:prit] *vt* (esp. with reference to explaining in one language what has been said in another) explain the meaning 口譯; 解釋; 說明: *They interpreted his arrival as showing that he wished to be their friend.* 他們認爲他的到來表明他希望和他們做朋友. *He quickly interpreted to me what the Russian was saying.* 他把俄國人講的話很快地翻譯給我聽. **interpretation** [intə:pri'teiʃən] **1** *nu* act of interpreting 翻譯; 解釋; 說明. **2** *nc* something which has been interpreted 含意: *His arrival can be given more than one interpretation.* 他的到來可以有不只一種的含意. **interpreter** *nc*

interrelate [intəri'leit] *vt / i* connect with each other (使)相互關連: *These matters are interrelated.* 這些問題是相互關連的.

interrogate [in'terəgeit] *vt* question; examine by questioning 訊問; 審問; 質問: *The police interrogated him for two hours.* 警察當局審問他兩小時. **interrogator** *nc* **interrogation** [interə'geiʃən] *nc* questioning 訊問; 審問. **interrogative** [intə'rɔgətiv] *adj* **1** asking a question 疑問的: *in an interrogative tone of voice* 用疑問的聲調. **2** (grammar) used in asking questions (e.g. 'Why' is an interrogative adverb) (語法)用於表示疑問的(例如: 'Why' 是疑問副詞). Also 亦作 *nc* an interrogative word 疑問詞.

interrupt [intə'rʌpt] *vt / i* **1** break in on someone who is speaking; stop something being done for a time 打斷(講話); 打岔; 打擾. **2** get in the way of; stop moving 妨礙; 阻斷: *The storm* *has interrupted all travel by sea.* 暴風雨使所有海上旅行中斷了. **interruption 1** *nu* state of interrupting or being interrupted 打斷, 打岔; 中斷. **2** *nc* something which interrupts 障礙物; 使中斷之事物: *He could not say all he wished because of the interruptions.* 由於有人多次打岔, 他無法把他想說的話都說出來.

intersect [intə'sekt] *vt / i* cross one another; divide into parts 相交; 交叉; 橫斷: *The two lines intersect at point X.* 這兩條線相交於X點. *This line intersects the other at point X.* 這條線與另一條線於X點相交. *The village is intersected by two main roads.* 這座村子位於兩條大道的交叉處. **intersection** *nc* crossroads 交叉路口; 十字路口.

intersperse [intə'spə:s] *vt* scatter among; give variety by putting in something here and there 散置; 散佈; 點綴: *The trees are interspersed with grass.* 樹林裏長着青草.

interval ['intəvl] *nc* **1** time or distance between two events or places (時間或距離的) 間隔; 間歇: *At school there is an interval between the third and fourth periods.* 在學校裏第三和第四節課之間有一段休息時間. *There will be a short interval after the second act of the play.* 在戲劇的第二幕之後有短時間的幕間休息. **2** (music) difference in pitch between two notes (音樂) 音程. **at intervals 1** with short periods of time between 不時; 常常: *She brought us coffee at intervals.* 她不時給我們送來咖啡. **2** with a short distance between 相隔不遠; 相隔一定的距離: *There are houses at intervals along the road.* 沿着這條路相隔不遠就有房子.

intervene [intə'vi:n] *vi* come between

either in time or place 插入; 介入; 介於 (時間或地點): *Three years intervened before I heard from him again.* 時隔三年我再度收到他的信. *The government had to intervene in the strike* i.e. in order to try to settle it. 政府不得不干預這次罷工. **intervention** [intə'venʃən] *nc / u*.

interview ['intəvju:] *nc* meeting to find out, by questions and answers, about somebody or about his views 採訪; 會談; 會見; 接見: *The parents had an interview with the headmaster about school fees.* 家長和校長會談學費問題. *Before he left, the Prime Minister gave an interview to the newspaper reporters.* 首相離開前, 接見了新聞記者. Also 亦作 *vt* have an interview with 訪問; 會見; 接見. **interviewer** *nc* person who interviews others (esp. on radio or television) 訪問者; 會見者; 接見者, 被採訪者(尤指在無線電廣播或電視中).

intestate [in'testeit] *adj* not having made a will 未留遺囑的: *He died intestate.* 他沒有立遺囑就死了.

intestine [in'testin] *nc* (often *pl*) part of the body through which waste matter from the stomach passes out of the body (常用複數)腸. **intestinal** *adj*.

intimate[1] ['intimət] *adj* **1** very friendly indeed 親密的, 密切的: *They are intimate friends.* 他們是親密的朋友. **2** private; secret 私人的, 個人的; 秘密的: *I cannot tell them my intimate thoughts.* 我不能把我內心的想法告訴他們. **intimately** *adv* **intimacy** *nu* state of being intimate 親密; 密切.

intimate[2] ['intimeit] *vt* make known (often in an indirect way) 通知; 暗示: *He intimated to them that he did not agree.* 他向他們暗示說他不同意.

intimidate [in'timideit] *vt* make somebody do, or not do something by frightening him 威脅; 恐嚇: *The thieves intimidated the boy into not telling the police.* 小偷威脅這孩子不要報警察. **intimidation** [intimi'deiʃən] *nu.*

into ['intə, 'intu] *prep* **1** showing motion to the inside of 進入…之內; 到…裏: *He walked into the room.* 他走進房間. **2** showing change from one state to another 變成…之狀況; 成爲: *When it is boiled, water changes into steam.* 水煮沸時, 就變成蒸氣. *He broke the stick into pieces.* 他把木棒劈成碎片.

intolerable [in'tɔlərəbl] *adj* not able to be endured 無法忍受的.

intolerant [in'tɔlərnt] *adj* not tolerant; not able to tolerate 不容忍的, 不寬容的; 不能忍受的; 不能寬恕的: *He is intolerant of fools.* 他不寬容愚人. **intolerance** *nu.*

intonation [intə'neiʃən] *nu* movement up or down in the pitch of the voice; accent 語調; 音調.

intoxicate [in'tɔksikeit] *vt* make drunk; make very excited, as if one were drunk 使醉; 使陶醉; 使極度興奮: *They were intoxicated by their victory.* 他們被勝利所冲昏了頭腦. **intoxication** [intɔksi'keiʃən] *nu.*

intransitive [in'trænsitiv] *adj* (grammar) with reference to verbs which do not have a direct object (e.g. the verb *come*) (語法) (指動詞) 不及物的 (例如: 動詞 come).

intrepid [in'trepid] *adj* without fear 無畏的.

intricate ['intrikət] *adj* made up of many parts; difficult to understand 複雜的; 難懂的: *the intricate works of a clock* 鐘的複雜的機件; *an intricate argument* 費解的論點. **intricacy** *nu* state of being intricate 複雜; 難懂.

intrigue [in'tri:g] *vt / i* make interested or curious (使) 感興趣; (使) 好奇: *Their sudden arrival intrigues me.* 他們突然到達使我感到好奇. Also 亦作 *nc* secret plan 秘密計劃; 陰謀. **intriguing** *adj* very interesting 很有趣的; 迷人的.

intrinsic [in'trinsik] *adj* (with reference to qualities) being inside; real; natural (指性質) 内在的; 真正的; 固有的: *the intrinsic value of his work* i.e. the real value of the work itself and not what people may think about it 他的工作的真正價值, 即: 工作本身的真正價值而不是人們對它的評價.

introduce [intrə'dju:s] *vt* **1** bring in, make known, for the first time 傳入; 引進; 創導: *The Romans introduced roads into Britain.* 羅馬人把公路引進英國. *My father introduced me to the game of football.* 我父親引導我第一次參加足球比賽. **2** bring people together and make them known to one another by name 介紹相識: *He introduced me to his mother and father.* 他把我介紹給他的母親和父親. *Have you been introduced?* 你被介紹過了嗎? **introduction** [intrə'dakʃən] **1** *nu* act of bringing in for the first time 引進; 傳入: *the introduction of roads into Britain* 公路引進英國. **2** *nc* introducing people 介紹: *Before the meeting began I made the necessary introductions.* 會議開始前, 我作了必要的介紹. **3** *nc* first part of a letter, speech or book etc. (with reference to a book usu. to explain what the book is about) 引言; 序言; 開場白; 序論. **introductory** [intrə'daktəri] *adj* giving an introduction 介紹的; 導言的.

introspect [intrə'spekt] *vi* look into or be concerned with one's own thoughts and feelings 内省; 反省. **in-**

trospection *nc / u* **introspective** *adj* caused by, having the habit of, introspection 內省的; 好反省的; *He is a very introspective person.* 他是一個很會自我反省的人.

introvert ['intrəvɜ:t] *.nc* person who keeps his thoughts and feelings to himself and does not express them openly in any way 內向性格的人.(*opp* 反義詞 **extrovert**).

intrude [in'tru:d] *vt / i* enter without being invited; push in where one is not welcome 未請自入; 侵入; 闖入; 打擾; *I hope I am not intruding (upon you).* 我希望我沒有打擾(你). **intruder** *nc* (often of someone who has intruded to steal) someone / something which intrudes 侵入者; 闖入者(常指闖入行竊者). **intrusion** [in'tru:ʒən] *nc / u: Please excuse my intrusion.* 請原諒, 打擾你了. **intrusive** [in'tru:siv] *adj.*

intuition [intju:'iʃən] **I** *nu* ability to understand something quickly without having to think about it carefully 直覺; 直覺之能力: *They say women have more intuition than men.* 據說女人比男人更有直覺. **2** *nc* knowledge gained by this ability 直覺知識. **intuitive** [in'tju:itiv] *adj* having intuition; understood by intuition 直覺的; 直觀的; 由直覺判斷的; *an intuitive guess* 直觀猜測.

inundate ['inʌndeit] *vt* cause trouble by arriving in great numbers 使不勝其擾: *We were inundated with visitors.* 我們被絡至杳來的來訪者弄得頭昏腦脹.

invade [in'veid] *vt* **1** enter a country with an army to attack it 侵略(一國); 侵入: *The Germans invaded France in 1940.* 德國人在1940年入侵法國. **2** enter any place in great numbers or in

order to cause a disturbance 蜂擁而入; 侵犯; 侵擾: *People from the town invade the country at the weekend.* 週末城裏的人大量來到鄉間. *I object to our privacy being invaded.* 我反對侵犯我們的私人生活. **invasion** [in'veiʒən] *nc / u* **invader** *nc* person who invades 侵略者; 侵入者; 侵犯者.

invalid[1] ['invəlid] *adj* in poor health; disabled 有病的; 傷殘的; *The invalid boy cannot play games.* 這個傷殘的男孩不能做遊戲. Also 亦作 *nc* person who is invalid 病人; 傷殘人.

invalid[2] [in'vælid] *adj* not valid; no longer in use; useless 無效的; 作廢的; 無用的; *This law is now invalid.* 這項法令現在無效. *The cheque is invalid unless you sign it.* 你不簽字, 這張支票無效. **invalidate** [in'vælideit] *vt* make invalid 使無效; 使作廢.

invaluable [in'væljuəbl] *adj* too great to be able to be valued 無法估價的; 無價的; 極寶貴的; *Thank you for your invaluable help.* 感謝你的極寶貴的協助.

invariable [in'veəriəbl] *adj* never changing; always the same 永不變的; 恒定的. **invariably** *adv.*

invasion [in'veiʒən] *nc / u* see 見 **invective.**

invective [in'vektiv] *nc / u* blaming or criticizing in very strong language; cursing 猛烈抨擊; 痛罵.

invent [in'vent] *vt* **1** make something which did not exist before 發明; 創造: *We do not know who invented the wheel.* 我們不知道誰發明了車輪. **2** make up something; invent 虛構; 杜撰. *He invented a story to explain why he was late* i.e. the story was not true. 他編造一個故事來解釋他為甚麼遲到. 即: 這故事是不真實的. **inventor** *nc* **invention** *nc* something which is invented. 發明

物; 虛構的事物. **inventive** *adj* able to invent 有發明才能的; 有創造力的.

inventory ['invəntri] *nc* (usu. with reference to the contents of a house, shop, store etc.) complete list (通常指房子、商店、倉庫等裏面的東西的) 完整的清單; 財產目錄; 存貨清單: *take an inventory* i.e. make or check an inventory 編製財產目錄或開清單.

inverse ['in'və:s] *adj* opposite in order, position etc to something else 倒轉的; 相反的.

invert [in'və:t] *vt* put the other way round; put upside down 使反向; 倒轉; 顛倒. **inverted commas** see 見 **comma.**

invertebrate [in'və:tibrət] *adj* not having a backbone (e.g. like a worm or insect) 無脊椎的 (例如: 像蠕蟲, 昆蟲). Also 亦作 *nc* invertebrate animal 無脊椎動物.

invest [in'vest] *vt / i* **1** put money in something so as to get a profit 投資: *I have invested all my money in cotton* i.e. in a business which deals in cotton. 我已把我所有的錢都投資在棉花方面. *Have you invested in anything?* 你在哪方面投資了? **2** give rank or authority to 授予 (軍銜、權力等): *The government invested him with special powers to deal with the situation.* 政府授予他特權處理這一事態.

investor *nc* person who invests money 投資者. **investment** *nc / u* act of investing money; money which is invested 投資; 投資額; 投入的資本.

investiture [in'vestitʃə*] *nc* special occasion when people are invested with rank or authority 授銜、授權等之儀式.

investigate [in'vestigeit] *vt* inquire into; examine carefully 審查; 調查: *The police are investigating the murder* i.e.

to find out who did it. 警察正在調查這起謀殺案. **investigator** *nc* **investigation** [investi'geiʃən] *nc / u*: *The police are carrying out investigations.* 警察正在進行調查.

investiture [in'vestitʃə*] *nc* see 見 **invest.**

investment [in'vestmənt] *nc / u* see 見 **invest.**

inveterate [in'vetərət] *adj* firmly fixed by habit; established for a long time 積習很深的; 長期形成的; 根深蒂固的: *He is an inveterate liar.* 他是個撒謊老手. *They are inveterate enemies.* 他們是不共戴天的仇敵.

invigilate [in'vidʒileit] *vi* watch and control a written examination so that those taking it obey the rules 監考. **invigilation** [invidʒi'leiʃən] *nc / u* **invigilator** *nc.*

invigorate [in'vigəreit] *vt* give vigour to; make stronger 使精力充沛, 使有活力; 使健壯: *The walk in the fresh air invigorated us.* 在新鮮的空氣中散步使我們精力充沛.

invincible [in'vinsibl] *adj* not able to be defeated 不可征服的; 不可戰勝的.

inviolate [in'vaiələt] *adj* not violated; secure; pure 未被破壞的; 未受侵犯的; 無損的; 純潔的.

invisible [in'vizibl] *adj* not able to be seen 看不見的; 無形的.

invite [in'vait] *vt* ask somebody to do something or come somewhere 邀請: *At the meeting they invited me to speak.* 在會上他們請我講話. *He invited us to his wedding.* 他邀請我們參加他的婚禮. **inviting** *adj* attractive 吸引人的; 誘人的: *This food looks inviting.* 這種食物誘人垂涎. (*opp* 反義詞 **uninviting**). **invitation** [invi'teiʃən] **1** *nu* act of inviting or being invited 邀請; 被邀請: *You can see the school* *only by invitation.* 只有受到邀請你才能參觀這所學校. **2** *nc* request which invites 請柬; 請帖: *She sent out many invitations to her wedding.* 她發出許多邀請參加她婚禮的請帖.

invoice ['invɔis] *nc* list of goods with prices given to the person who has bought them 發票.

invoke [in'vouk] *vt* ask by prayer for the help of God or of something powerful 祈求神等的幫助; 求助於; 祈求: *They invoked the power of the law when they were accused.* 他們被指控時, 他們求助於法律的力量.

involuntary [in'vɔləntəri] *adj* not controlled by the will; done without one's intending to do it 非意志控制的; 本能的; 非本意的: *When I touched his arm he gave an involuntary jump.* 我碰到他胳臂時, 他本能地跳了起來. **involuntarily** *adv.*

involve [in'vɔlv] *vt* **1** cause to be included in or troubled by something 使捲入; 使陷入; 拖累: *They always involve me in their quarrels.* 他們爭吵時老把我牽扯進去. *Don't get yourself involved with these people.* 別和這些人糾纏. **2** make necessary a particular result 必然導致: *Being a sailor involves long periods away from home.* 作為水手必然要長期離家. **involved** *adj* difficult to understand because everything in it is mixed up 複雜的; 難理解的; 含混不清的: *He told me an involved story about his family.* 他給我講他家庭的複雜經歷. **involvement** *nc / u* state of being included in 捲入; 牽連; 包含.

invulnerable [in'vʌlnərəbl] *adj* not able to be wounded or harmed 不能傷害的, 無懈可擊的.

inward ['inwəd] *adj* (esp. with reference to one's own thoughts and feelings) inside (尤指一個人自己的思想和感情)

內在的; 內心的; 內部的. **inwardly** *adv*

inwards *adv* towards the inside 向內.

iodide ['aiədaid] *nu* compound of iodine with another element or with a radical 碘化物.

iodine ['aiədi:n] *nu* type of chemical found in sea water used for cleaning wounds and in photography 碘.

ionic [ai'ɔnik] *adj* of, relating to, occurring in the form of ions 離子的.

ionize ['aiənaiz] *vt / i* change or become changed into ions (使)電離; (使)電離成離子.

irascible [i'ræsibl] *adj* easily made angry 易怒的; 性情暴躁的.

irate [ai'reit] *adj* angry 發怒的; 憤怒的.

iris ['airis] *nc* **1** coloured part of the eye (眼球的)虹膜. **2** type of plant with sword-shaped leaves and large flowers 鳶尾屬植物.

Irish ['airiʃ] *adj* of Ireland 愛爾蘭的. Also 亦作 *npl* Irish people 愛爾蘭人. **Irishman** *nc* **Irishwoman** *nc.*

iron[1] ['aiən] **1** *nu* the most common and useful metal 鐵. **2** *nc* implement heated by electricity used for making clothes. smooth 熨斗. **irons** *npl* chains used to tie somebody 鐐銬: *The thief was put in irons.* 那小偷被戴上鐐銬. **iron 'curtain** formerly frontiers between the countries of western Europe and the USSR and her allies in eastern Europe 鐵幕(指以前西歐國家和蘇聯及其東歐盟國之間的界線): *the iron-curtain countries* i.e. the USSR and her allies 鐵幕國家, 即: 蘇聯和她的盟國. **'ironmonger** ['aiən-mʌŋgə*] *nc* (*Brit*) person who sells hard goods like those made of iron (英)鐵器商; 五金商. (*US* 美 **hardware dealer**). **'ironworks** *n sing* or *pl* factory where iron is smelted or iron goods are made 鋼鐵廠; 鐵工廠.

iron² ['aiən] *vt* make smooth and flat with a hot iron (用熨斗) 熨平. **ironing** *nu*: *My mother is doing her ironing.* 我的母親正在熨衣服. **'ironing board** board on which clothes etc are ironed 熨衣板. **iron something out 1** make smooth something that is rough 熨平. **2** remove a difficulty 消除 (困難): *The bank manager has ironed out all my worries about money.* 銀行經理消除了我對錢款的各種憂慮.

irony ['airəni] *nu* using words in a way which gives a meaning opposite to the words themselves (e.g. *Aren't we clever!* when we have done something which is not clever) 反語, 反話 (例如: 我們幹了傻事時說 Aren't we clever! 我們真聰明!) **ironic(al)** [ai'rɔnik(l)] *adj* **ironically** *adv.* *Note.* 說明: the difference between *irony* and *sarcasm* is that irony is often amusing; sarcasm is used to hurt a person's feelings. irony 和 sarcasm 的差別是 irony 常常是有趣, 適人笑的; sarcasm 則用於傷人的感情.

irrational [iræʃənl] *adj* not controlled by reason 無理性的: *irrational behaviour* 無理性的行爲. **irrationally** *adv.*

irreconcilable [irekən'sailəbl] *adj* not able to be made to agree 不能和解的; 不能調和的.

irrefutable [iri'fju:təbl] *adj* not able to be proved false 不能反駁的; 駁不倒的.

irregular [i'regjulə*] *adj* **1** not having any order in time, size, shape, place etc.; not regular 不定時的; (大小、形狀、地方等) 不規則的; 不整齊的; 無規律的; *The trains from here are irregular* i.e. they do not leave at fixed times.

從這裏開出的火車是不定期的. *The fields are irregular in shape* i.e. they have different shapes. 這些田地的形狀不規則. 即: 它們大小不一. **2** not following normal rules 不合常規的: *To go away without telling your father is most irregular* 沒有告訴你父親就離開是很不正常的; *an irregular verb* i.e. one which changes its form in a way different from others (e.g. *go, went, gone*) 不規則動詞 (例如: go, went, gone). **irregularity** [iregju'læriti] *nc / u.*

irrelevant [i'reləvənt] *adj* having nothing to do with the subject 不相關的; 離題的: *Your answer to my question is irrelevant.* 你對我的問題的回答是不切題的. **irrelevance** *nu* state of being irrelevant 不相關; 離題.

irreligious [iri'lidʒəs] *adj* against, or not interested in, religion 反宗教的; 對宗教無興趣的; 無宗教信仰的.

irreparable [i'repərəbl] *adj* not able to be repaired or put right 不可彌補的; 無法挽回的: *He has suffered irreparable losses.* 他蒙受了無法挽回的損失.

irrepressible [iri'presəbl] *adj* not able to be controlled 不能抑制的; 控制不住的: *irrepressible delight at hearing the good news* 聽到好消息欣喜若狂.

irreproachable [iri'prəutʃəbl] *adj* without fault or blame 無過失的; 無可非議的.

irresistible [iri'zistəbl] *adj* not able to be resisted; too strong 不能抵抗的; 不能壓制的; 強烈的: *I had an irresistible desire to run away.* 我有強烈的離家出走的願望.

irresolute [i'rezəlu:t] *adj* not decided; hesitating 無決斷的; 猶豫不決的; 優柔寡斷的.

irrespective [iri'spektiv] *adj* without regard for; without paying attention to

不考慮…的; 不顧…的: He is going to
buy it irrespective of what you say. 不
管你說甚麼, 他還是要把它買下.

irresponsible [iri'spɔnsəbl] *adj* **1** (of
persons) not able to be made responsible for their actions (指人) (對
其行爲) 不須負責任的: By law babies
are irresponsible. 根據法律嬰兒是不須
負責任的. **2** not having a proper
sense of responsibility 無責任感的; 不
負責任的: Your irresponsible refusal
to help your friends surprised me. 你
不負責任地拒絕幫助你的朋友使我感到
驚奇. **irresponsibility** [irispɔnsəbili-
ti] *nu*.

irrevocable [i'revəkəbl] *adj* not able to
be revoked or changed; final 不能撤回
的; 不可改變的; 最後的: an irrevocable decision 最後的決定.

irrigate ['irigeit] *vt* take water to land
by leading it from a river, well etc
through pipes or channels 灌溉: They
irrigate their crops with water from
this river. 他們用這條河的水灌漑作物.
irrigation [iri'geiʃən] *nu*.

irritate ['iriteit] *vt* **1** make angry or
annoyed 激怒; 使煩躁: Your poor
work irritated him. 你的工作不好使他
很惱火. **2** cause pain to, or make
sore, a part of the body 使疼痛; 使不
舒服; Thick clothes irritate my skin. 粗
的衣服使我的皮膚怪難受的. **irrita-
tion** [iri'teiʃən] *nu* act of irritating;
state of being irritated 激怒; 煩躁.
irritable ['iritəbl] *adj* easily made
angry or annoyed 易怒的; 煩躁的.
irritability [iritə'biliti] *nu* **irritant**
['iritnt] *nc* something which irritates
刺激物; 刺激劑: Dust in the eyes is an
irritant. 眼裏的灰塵是種刺激物.

Islam ['izla:m] *nu* religion of the
Prophet Mohammed; all those who
believe in this religion i.e. all Muslims

伊斯蘭教, 回教; (總稱)伊斯蘭教徒, 穆
斯林, 回教徒. **Islamic** [iz'læmik] *adj*.

island ['ailnd] *nc* piece of land with water all round it; something that looks
like an island (e.g. a traffic / street island i.e. a place in the middle of a
busy street where persons crossing it
can stop) 島, 島嶼; 島狀物 (例如): a
traffic / street island 街道上的安全
島). **islander** *nc* person who lives on
an island 島民, 島上居民.

isle [ail] *nc* island (usu. used in poetry
except sometimes in the names of
places e.g. the British Isles) 島(除有時
用於地名——例如the British Isles
不列顛諸島——通常用於詩中).

isobar ['aisouba:] *nc* line on a map connecting points having equal atmospheric pressure (地圖上的)等壓線.

isohyet [,aisou'haiət] *nc* line on a map
connecting places having equal rainfall (地圖上的)等雨量線.

isolate ['aisəleit] *vt* keep or place apart
or alone 使隔離; 使孤立; 使隔絕: The
village was isolated for a week by the
floods i.e. nobody could go in or
come out. 這個村莊因洪水與外界隔絕
了一星期. **isolation** [aisə'leiʃən] *nu*:
During the flood they lived in isolation. 在洪水泛濫期間他們過着與外界
隔絕的生活.

isosceles [ai'sɔsili:z] *adj* (of a triangle)
having two sides of equal length (三
角形) 等腰的: isosceles triangle 等腰
三角形.

isotherm ['aisouθə:m] *nc* line on a map
linking places of equal temperature
(地圖上的)等溫線.

issue ['iʃu:] *vt* send out; supply 發出; 發
行; 配給; 發給: He issued orders to his
men. 他向士兵發佈命令. This maga-
zine is issued weekly. 這種雜誌每週出
版一次. They have issued food to the

hungry people / the hungry people with food. 他們向饑民分發食物. *This office issues driving licences*. 本辦公室發放駕駛執照. Also 亦作 **1** *nu* act of sending out, supplying 發出, 發行; 分發: **2** *nc* something that is sent out or supplied 發行物: *issues of this magazine* 本雜誌的發行本. **3** *nc* question; problem which is much discussed 問題; 爭端: *The great issue today is whether there will be war or peace.* 當今的大問題是會爆發戰爭還是保持和平. **at issue** in dispute; being argued about; not decided 在爭論中; 待解決的: *The matter / point at issue is whether you go or stay.* 爭論的問題／爭論的焦點是你走還是留下.

isthmus ['isməs] *nc* narrow strip of land connecting two relatively large land areas 地峽. *pl* 複數 **isthmuses** or **isthmi** ['ismai].

it [it] *pron* **1** used with reference to things without life, animals and sometimes young children 它(用以指無生命的東西, 動物, 有時也指幼兒): *Where is it? It's here.* 我的書在哪裏? 在這裏. *The dog is tired. It is also hungry.* 那狗累了, 也餓了. *The baby is asleep. It will wake up soon.* 嬰孩睡着了; 很快就會醒來. **2** used in answering or giving information about somebody / something already mentioned (用於回答或提供已經提到的某人或某事物的消息)這, 那, 它: *Who is that? It's my father.* 那是誰? 那是我的父親. *What is this? It's a flower.* 這是甚麼? 這是一朵花. *It was they who did it.* 那 是 他們 幹 的. **3** used as the general subject of many verbs which do not need a definite one 用於許多不需要有明確主語的動詞作主語: *It was raining.* 下雨了. *It's ten o'clock.* 十點鐘了. *It is four miles from here to*

the shop. 從這裏到商店有四英里. *It's no use crying.* 哭是沒用的. *It seems a silly thing to do.* 看來要幹件蠢事. **4** used when referring to something that is going to be mentioned later in the sentence 用於指句中即將提到的事物: *It is obvious that he is very tired.* 很明顯, 他很累. **Its** *determiner* of it; belonging to it (it 的所有格)它的. *The book has lost its cover.* 這本書的封面掉了. *The baby opened its eyes.* 嬰孩睜開眼睛. *Note* 說明. do not confuse with it's meaning *it is* or *it has*. 不要和it's (意思是 it is 或 it has)混同. **itself 1** emphatic form of it (it 的強調形式)自身; 本身: *The dog found the food itself.* 狗自己找到食物. **2** reflexive form of it (it 的反身形式)它自己; 它本身: *The dog has hurt itself.* 狗跌傷了. **by itself** without help; alone. 自行; 單獨地: *The tree stands by itself in the garden.* 這棵樹孤零零地長在花園裏.

italic [i'tælik] *adj* (with reference to printed letters) sloping; *printed like this* (指印刷字母)斜體的; 斜體印刷的. Also 亦作 *npl*: *Parts of this dictionary are printed in italics.* 這本辭典有些部份是用斜體字印刷的.

itch [itʃ] *nu* **1** feeling on the skin which makes one want to scratch 癢: *I have an itch on my left hand.* 我的左手覺得很癢. **2** strong desire 強烈的慾望, 渴望: *They have an itch to travel abroad.* 他們渴望到國外旅行. Also 亦作 *vi*: *My left foot itches / is itching.* 我的左腳癢. *They are itching to travel abroad.* 他們渴望着到國外旅行. **itchy** *adj*.

item ['aitəm] *nc* one of a list of things; one of many 項(目); 條(款); 一條, 一則: *Please check the items in this bill.* 請核對賬單裏的項目. *There are no* *items of interest in today's newspaper.* 今天報上沒甚麼有趣的新聞.

itinerant [ai'tinərnt] *adj* travelling from place to place 巡迴的.

itinerary [ai'tinərəri] *nc* details or record of a journey made or of the route to be taken 旅行日誌; 行程表; 旅行路線.

its, itself [its, it'self] *determiner / pron*

see 見 **it**.

ivory ['aivəri] *nu* hard, white substance of which the tusks of elephants are made 象牙(質). Also 亦作 *adj* made of ivory; the colour of ivory 象牙製的; 象牙色的.

ivy ['aivi] *nu* type of dark green climbing plant 常春藤.

J,j

jab [dʒæb] *vt* push something sharp (e.g. a stick or finger) into somebody / something; give a sharp blow to 刺; 戳; 猛擊: *He jabbed his stick into me / He jabbed me with his stick.* 他用手杖戳我. *past* 過去式和過去分詞 **jabbed**. Also 亦作 *nc* **1** *He gave me a jab.* 他猛擊我一拳. **2** injection (*informal in sense* 2)注射(義 2 為非正式)

jabber ['dʒæbə*] *vt / i* talk quickly and in a way not easy to understand 快而含糊地說: *He is always jabbering.* 他總是含含糊糊地說話. *He jabbered something to me.* 他嘰哩咕嚕地對我說了些話.

jack [dʒæk] *nc* **1** (**Jack**) informal form of the name **John** John (約翰) 的俗稱. **2** apparatus for lifting heavy objects from underneath (e.g. for raising the wheel of a car above the ground) 起重器; 千斤頂(例如: 支起車輪離開地面). **3** playing card below the queen in importance (紙牌中低於王后的) 傑克. Also 亦作 *vt* (in sense 2). *We must jack* (up) *the car to change the wheel.* 我們必須用千斤頂把汽車頂起來換車輪. **jackdaw** type of bird like a crow 穴鳥; 寒鴉. **jack-of-'all-trades** *nc* (usu. *sing*) person who is able to do many different kinds of work (通常只用單數) 萬事通. **'jack-in-the-box** type of toy consisting of a small box out of which a small figure suddenly jumps when the lid is opened 玩偶盒(一種玩具, 盒蓋啓開時, 有一小假人跳出). **'jackknife** type of folding knife 摺合小刀. **'jackpot** large amount of money won by gambling

(賭博中贏得的)大賭注.

jacket ['dʒækit] *nc* **1** short coat 短上衣; 茄克衫, 夾克. **2** covering round something 護套: *book jacket* i.e. paper cover on a book 書的封面套紙; (書的)護封. **3** skin of a (cooked) potato (煮過的)馬鈴薯皮.

jade [dʒeid] *nu* type of hard green stone used to make ornaments etc. 翡翠; 玉.

jaded ['dʒeidid] *adj* tired and unhappy 疲憊不堪的; 厭倦的.

jag [dʒæg] *vt* cut or tear roughly 不均勻地割或撕開, 把…撕(割)成鋸齒狀: *I jagged my finger on a rusty nail.* 我的手指被生銹的鐵釘割破. *past* 過去式和過去分詞 **jagged** [dʒægd]. Also 亦作 *nc* something rough and sharp which jags; cut caused by this 尖銳的突出物; 鋸齒狀的缺口. **jagged** ['dʒægid] *adj* rough and sharp 粗糙而尖銳的, 鋸齒狀的: *the jagged pieces of a broken bottle* 破瓶子的參差不齊的碎片.

jaguar ['dʒægjuə*] *nc* type of large, spotted wild animal of the cat family, found in South America (南美產的)美洲虎.

jail [dʒeil] *nc* see 見 **gaol**.

jam[1] [dʒæm] *vt / i* **1** press tightly; push into a small space 壓緊; 塞進: *We were jammed together in the large crowd.* 我們被擠在人羣中. *I jammed my books into the bag.* 我把書塞進袋裏. *He jammed on the brakes of the car* i.e. made them tight on the wheels by pressing the brake pedal hard. 他利住了車. **2** stop something moving because it is pressed tightly or hindered in some way (使)塞住不動; (使)發生故障: *The door has jammed.* 門卡住了. *past* 過去式和過去分詞 **jammed.** Also 亦作 *nc* **1** *There was such a jam of people that we could not get in.* 人羣擁擠我們無法進入. **2** difficulty; trouble 困難; 困境: *Because I lost my money I was in a jam.* (*informal* in sense **2**) 因爲我丟了錢, 所以我的處境困難. (義 2 爲非正式). '**traffic jam** crowding together of traffic so that none of it can move 交通阻塞.

jam² [dʒæm] *nu* mixture of fruit and sugar boiled together and used cold on bread, in cakes etc. 果醬.

jamboree [dʒæmbəˈri:] *nc* large, friendly meeting (esp. of Boy Scouts from many nations) (尤指來自許多國家的)童子軍大會.

jangle [ˈdʒæŋgl] *vt / i* make, cause to make, an unpleasant noise like pieces of metal striking one another (使)發出如金屬撞擊般刺耳的聲音.

janitor [ˈdʒænitə*] *nc* doorkeeper, *(Scot, US)* person who looks after a building 看門人, 管門人; (蘇格蘭, 美國)建築物之管理員.

January [ˈdʒænjuəri] *n* first month of the year in the Western calendar 一月.

jar¹ [dʒɑ:*] *nc* type of container made of glass or china etc with a wide opening at the top 廣口瓶, 罐子.

jar² [dʒɑ:*] *vt / i* **1** make an unpleasant sound (使)發出刺耳之聲. **2** have an unpleasant effect; cause a shock 産生不愉快的結果; (使)震動: *Their loud voices jar on my nerves / ears.* 他們大聲嚷嚷刺激我的神經/耳朵. *I fell from the tree and jarred my back.* 我從樹上跌下來, 背部震傷. *past* 過去式和過去分詞 **jarred. jarring** *adj*.

jargon [ˈdʒɑ:gən] *nu* (esp. with reference to the special and technical words used by experts) language which is difficult for ordinary people to understand (尤指專家使用的)專門術語; 行話: *When engineers talk about their work, they use a lot of jargon.* 工程師們在談論工作時使用很多專門術語.

jaundice [ˈdʒɔ:ndis] *nu* type of disease which makes the skin and the whites of the eyes yellow 黃疸病.. Also 亦作 *vt* (usu. *passive*) make bitter and suspicious (通常用被動式)使妒忌, 怨恨和猜忌; 使有偏見: *He has a very jaundiced opinnion of their work.* 他對他們的工作很有偏見.

jaunt [dʒɔ:nt] *vi* make a short journey for pleasure 作短程旅遊. Also 亦作 *nc: They went for a jaunt in their car.* 他們乘自己的車去旅遊.

jaunty [ˈdʒɔ:nti] *adj* lively; carefree 活潑的; 愉快的; 無憂無慮的.

javelin [ˈdʒævəlin] *nc* type of spear for throwing (esp. in sport) (尤指運動用的)標槍.

jaw [dʒɔ:] *nc* **1** one of the two bones which contain the teeth 顎. **2** (in *pl*) part of a tool or machine which holds or crushes like jaws (通常複數)工具或機器的鉗夾部份: *the jaws of a vice* 老虎鉗之鉗口.

jay [dʒei] *nc* type of noisy bird with bright feathers 樫鳥. '**jaywalker** person who crosses busy roads without paying attention to the traffic 不遵守交通規則而穿越馬路者.

jazz [dʒæz] *nu* type of lively music (usu. with a regular rhythm) begun by Negroes in the USA 爵士樂. **jazzy** *adj* bright; lively; having many colours 歡快的; 活潑的; 花哨的: *wearing a jazzy tie* 繫一條花哨的領帶.

jealous ['dʒeləs] *adj* **1** having a feeling of envy because somebody has something, or has gained something, which one does not have having 嫉妒的; 妒忌的: *He is jealous of me because I won and he did not.* 他妒忌我, 因爲我贏了而他沒贏. *They are jealous of his wealth.* 他們妒忌他的財富. **2** having a feeling of fear that one may lose somebody / something 生怕會失去某人或某物的: *He is very jealous if his girl talks to another man.* 如果他的女朋友跟另一個男人談話, 他就很擔心會失去她. **3** guarding very carefully 留心防衛的; 珍惜的: *The people here are jealous of their freedom.* 這裏的人民珍惜他們的自由. **jealously** *adv* **jealousy** *nu* jealous feeling 嫉妒; 妒忌: *his jealousy of me because I won* 他因爲我贏了對我妒忌.

jean [dʒi:n] **1** *nu* type of strong, cotton cloth 斜紋布. **2** *nc* (in *pl*) trousers made from this cloth (用於複數) (斜紋布做的) 工裝褲; 牛仔褲.

jeep [dʒi:p] *nc* small, powerful vehicle, able to travel over rough ground 吉普車.

jeer [dʒiə*] *vt / i* laugh rudely at; make fun of in an unkind way 嘲笑; 嘲弄: *When the player fell, the crowd jeered.* 比賽者跌倒時, 人羣發出嘲笑聲. *They jeered at him.* 他們嘲弄他. Also *nc*: *the jeers of the crowd* 人羣的嘲笑聲.

jelly ['dʒeli] *nc / u* **1** clear, almost solid substance made from gelatin or from boiling fruit juice and sugar together; cold food made from gelatin mixed with fruit juice 凍子; 果子凍: *My mother is making apple jelly.* 我的母親在做蘋果凍. *Children like jelly and ice cream.* 孩子們喜歡果子凍和冰淇淋. **2** any almost solid substance like

this 似凍子之物; 膠狀物. **'jellyfish** type of sea creature which looks like a piece of jelly 水母; 海蜇.

jemmy ['dʒemi] *nc* type of iron bar used by thieves to open doors and windows (盜賊用來撬門窗的) 鐵棒.

jeopardize ['dʒepədaiz] *vt* put in danger 使受危險; 危害. **jeopardy** ['dʒepədi] *nu* usu. only in **be in jeopardy** i.e. be in danger 通常只用於 be in jeopardy, 即: 處於危險中.

jerk [dʒə:k] *vt* pull, push or twist suddenly 猛地一拉 (或一推、一扭): *He jerked the letter out of my hand.* 他猛地一抽, 抽出我手中的信. *The boy jerked out an answer* i.e. he gave an answer suddenly and with difficulty. 這男孩突然斷斷續續地說出答案. Also 亦作 *nc* sudden movement 急動: *When I touched his arm, he gave a jerk.* 當我碰到他的胳臂時, 他猛然一動. *The car started with a jerk.* 車子猛然一震便開動了. **jerky** *adj.*

jerkin ['dʒə:kin] *nc* short coat with or without sleeves (usu. made of leather and worn by men) (通常爲皮製, 男子穿的) 短上衣.

jersey ['dʒə:zi] *nc* tight-fitting garment with sleeves and few or no buttons in front (usu. made from wool or cotton) (前面很少或沒有鈕扣的) 緊身上衣 (通常爲毛製或布製); 運動衫: *In cold weather he wears a jersey under his jacket.* 在寒冷的天氣他外穿一件短上衣, 裏面穿一件運動衫.

jest [dʒest] *nc* something said or done to amuse; joke 笑話; 俏皮話; 滑稽事; 玩笑: *Their jests make everyone laugh.* 他們講的笑話使大家都笑了. Also 亦作 *vi* **jester** *nc* (in ancient times) person employed by a king or lord to entertain by jesting (古代的) 弄臣.

jet¹ [dʒet] *nc* **1** strong flow of gas, liquid or flame from a pipe or small hole (氣體、液體或火焰的)噴射; 射流: *The jet of water from the hosepipe soon put out the fire.* 水龍軟管噴出的水流很快就把火撲滅了. **2** pipe or small hole which causes a jet (e.g. the jet in the carburettor of a car engine) 噴射口; 噴嘴(例如: 汽車發動機汽化器裏的噴嘴). **3** type of aircraft which is pushed through the air by jets of hot gas 噴氣式飛機: *Four enemy jets flew over the town.* 四架噴氣式敵機飛過城市的上空. **'jetpro'pelled** *adj* pushed through the air by jets 噴氣式推進的. **jet propulsion** *nu.*

jet² [dʒet] *nu* type of hard, black mineral which is polished and used for ornaments 黑玉. **'jet-'black** *adj* as black and shiny as jet 烏黑發亮的: *Her hair is jet-black.* 她的頭髮烏黑發亮.

jetsam ['dʒetsəm] *nu* **1** goods thrown from a ship in order to make the ship lighter and safer. (爲使船減輕重量比較安全而從船上)投棄的貨物. **2** goods of this kind which are washed onto the shore 冲至岸上的投棄貨物. 參見 **flotsam**.

jettison ['dʒetisn] *vt* throw from a ship or aircraft in order to make it lighter and safer; abandon (爲使船或飛機減輕重量比較安全而從船上或飛機上)拋棄; 放棄.

jetty ['dʒeti] *nc* long, narrow structure built into the sea for getting into or out of a boat, or to protect a harbour 碼頭; 防波堤.

jewel [dʒuəl] *nc* precious stone; ornament with precious stone(s) in it 寶石; 鑲寶石的飾物; 珠寶: *The ladies were wearing their jewels.* 女士們佩戴珠寶. **jeweller** *nc* person who buys

and sells jewels 珠寶商; 寶石商. **jewellery, jewelry** *nu* jewels, or ornaments with jewels in them 珠寶; 珠寶飾物, 珠寶首飾.

jib¹ [dʒib] *nc* small front sail 船首小帆.

jib² [dʒib] *vt / i* (esp. with reference to horses) stop and refuse to go further (尤指馬)停下來不肯往前走, 退縮. *past* 過去式和過去分詞 **jibbed**.

jibe [dʒaid] *vi* see 見 **gibe.**

jiffy ['dʒifi] *nu* moment of time 瞬間; 片刻: *I'll be ready in a jiffy. (informal)* 我馬上就好了. (非正式).

jig [dʒig] *nc* lively dance; the music for it 基格舞(曲); 快步舞(曲).

jigsaw ['dʒigsɔ:] *nc* **1** type of narrow saw driven by a machine 線鋸; 鋸曲線機. **2** puzzle made by cutting up a picture on wood or card into pieces which have to be put together again 益智板, 拼圖玩具. (Also 亦作 **jigsaw puzzle**).

jilt [dʒilt] *vt* refuse to marry somebody after having promised to do so; end a relationship with a lover (女子)拋棄 (情人): *She jilted him the day before they were to be married.* 在他們就要結婚的前一天她拋棄了他.

jingle ['dʒiŋgl] *vt / i* make, cause to make, sharp sounds of small pieces of metal striking together (使)叮噹響: *As he ran, the pennies and keys in his pocket jingled.* 他跑的時候, 口袋裏的硬幣和鑰匙叮叮噹噹響. Also 亦作 *nc.*

jinks [dʒiŋks] *npl* only in **high jinks** i.e. noisy fun 只用於 high jinks, 即: 大嚷大鬧; 狂歡作樂: *The boys are having high jinks in the playground.* 男孩子在操場上大嚷大鬧的玩耍.

jinn [dʒin] *nc* see 見 **genie.**

jinx [dʒiŋks] *nc* something which is said to cause bad luck 不吉祥的事物, 倒霉的事: *There is a jinx on this plan* i.e. there has been a lot of bad luck in the carrying out of the plan. 這計劃不吉利.即: 在執行計劃的過程中出現了不少倒霉的事情.

jitters ['dʒitəz] *npl* (with **the**) great nervousness (與 the 連用) 極度緊張不安: *I have got the jitters about the examination next week.* 我對下星期的考試極爲緊張不安. **jittery** *adj* (both *informal*) (兩者均爲非正式).

job [dʒɔb] *nc* **1** piece of work done (一件) 完成的工作; 成品; 成果: *The new building was a big job.* 這座新大樓真大. *The builders have done a good job of it / made a good job of it.* 建築工人幹得很好. **2** employment; work 職業; 工作: *I have a job in a shop.* 我在一家商店找到一份工作. *Jobs are not easy to get.* 工作不容易找到. **3** something difficult 困難的事; 費力的事情: *It was a job to get him to agree.* (*informal* in sense **3**) 要說服他同意不是件容易的事. (義 3 爲非正式). **a good job** a lucky happening or state of affairs 幸運之事: *It was a good job that you had a friend with you to help.* (*informal*) 真幸運, 你有個朋友友在一起幫忙. (非正式). **odd jobs** unimportant work of many different kinds 零碎工作; 雜務: *He likes doing odd jobs in his garden.* 他喜歡在花園裏幹雜活.

jockey ['dʒɔki] *nc* person who is paid to ride horses in horse-races 賽馬的職業騎師. **'disc jockey** person employed on a radio programme to introduce records 無線電唱片音樂節目主持人.

jocular ['dʒɔkjulə*] *adj* fond of jesting; amusing 喜愛開玩笑的; 詼諧的; 打趣的.

jodhpurs ['dʒɔdpəz] *npl* long trousers worn for horse riding, fitting closely to the leg from knee to ankle 馬褲 (膝至踝部份爲緊身的長褲).

jog [dʒɔg] *vt / i* **1** move slowly and steadily (usu. with the sense of being shaken up and down at the same time) 緩慢平穩地移動 (通常同時含有上下顛簸之意): *They jogged along the narrow road on their horses.* 他們騎馬沿着狹窄的道路緩步行進. *John jogs along at school* i.e. although he does nothing special, he is doing quite well. 約翰平平穩穩地學習. 那輛雖然他的成績並非特別突出, 但是他學習得不錯. **2** shake up and down; push slightly 上下搖動; 輕推; 輕撞: *The old bus jogged us on the rough road.* 那輛舊公共汽車在崎嶇不平的路上行駛, 使我們上下顛簸不已. *He jogged my elbow, making me spill my drink.* 他撞到我的胳臂肘, 我的酒都撒了. *past* 過去式和過去分詞 **jogged**. Also 亦作 *nc* **jog someone's memory** cause somebody to begin remembering 喚起某人的記憶; 提醒某人. **jogging** *nu* slow jolting run used in keeping fit 小跑步, 緩跑.

joggle ['dʒɔgl] *vt* shake often but slightly 輕搖. Also 亦作 *nc*.

join [dʒɔin] *vt / i* **1** come together or meet 交會; 會合: *The three roads join near the bridge.* 這三條路在近橋的地方相會合. **2** (usu. with reference to two persons / things) bring or put together (通常指兩人/事物) 使連接; 使結合: *He joined the two pieces of wood (together) with nails.* 他用釘子把兩塊木頭連接起來. *The priest joined the man and woman in marriage* i.e. he married them. 牧師使這一男一女結成夫婦. 即: 他爲他們證婚 (或主持婚禮). **3** enter the company of; become one of a group 與⋯共在一起; 加入; 成爲⋯的一員: *Please join us for dinner.* 請和我們一起吃飯. *They* joined him in a visit to London. 他們和他一起遊覽倫敦. *I have joined the football club.* 我已加入足球俱樂部. Also 亦作 *nc* place where two things are joined and held firmly together 連接處. **join in (something)** take part in 參加: *join in the singing* 參加唱歌; *be asked to join in* 被邀請參加. **join up** join the army, navy etc. *(informal)* 參軍; 入伍. (非正式). **join battle** begin fighting 開戰; 交戰: *join battle with the enemy* 與敵人交戰. **join forces** come together, unite, for a purpose 合作; 聯合起來: *We joined forces with them to finish the work.* 我們與他們合作完成這項工作.

joiner ['dʒɔinə*] *nc* person whose work is to make the wooden parts inside a building (not usu. the furniture) 細木工匠. **joinery** *nu* work of a joiner 細木工; 細木作.

joint¹ ['dʒɔint] *nc* **1** (esp. with reference to the bones of the body) place where, or thing by which, two things are joined (尤指人體骨頭的)關節; 連接處; 連接物: *He has hurt the joints of his fingers.* 他的手指關節受傷了. **2** large piece of meat cut for cooking 大塊肉: *We had a joint of beef for dinner.* 我們晚餐吃一大塊牛肉. **3** *(US)* cheap, rough place used for drinking and gambling (*informal* in sense **3**) (美)下流場所(指低級酒館或賭窟) (義 **3** 爲非正式).

joint² ['dʒɔint] *adj* shared by, belonging to, two or more persons 共同的; 共有的: *They made a joint request to the manager.* 他們向經理提出共同的請求. *They are the joint owners of the hotel.* 他們是這家旅館的共有者. *I was made joint heir with my brother.* 我和我的兄弟被指定爲共同繼承人. **jointly** *adv.*

joist [dʒɔist] *nc* beam to which the boards of a floor or the laths of a ceiling are fixed at right angles (地板)托樑; 擱柵; 小樑.

joke [dʒouk] *nc* something said or done to make one laugh 笑話; 玩笑: *They made jokes about my old hat.* 他們拿我的舊帽子開玩笑. Also 亦作 *vi* make jokes (about). 開玩笑: *They are always joking.* 他們老愛開玩笑. **jokingly** *adv* **joker** *nc* **1** person who makes jokes 喜歡開玩笑的人. **2** extra card in a pack of playing cards (紙牌中的)鬼牌; 百搭.

jolly ['dʒɔli] *adj* merry; happy 歡樂的; 快樂的. Also 亦作 *adv* very 很; 非常: *He played a jolly good game.* (*informal* in this sense) 他手法很高明. (此義爲非正式). **jollity** *nu.*

jolt [dʒoult] *vt / i* shake while moving; shake suddenly; give a shock to 顛簸而行; 震搖; (使)震驚: *The car jolted along the rough road.* 汽車沿着崎嶇不平的路顛簸行駛. *The train jolted us from our seats by stopping suddenly.* 火車突然停車把我們震離座位. Also 亦作 *nc: The bad news gave us a jolt.* 這壞消息使我們大吃一驚.

joss [dʒɔs] *nc* figure of a Chinese god (中國的)神像; 菩薩.

jostle ['dʒɔsl] *vt / i* push roughly against (usu. where there is little room e.g. in a crowd) 推撞; 擠(通常指幾乎沒有空間的地方, 例如: 在擁擠的人羣中): *We had to jostle through the crowd to reach the gate.* 我們不得不擠過人羣到達大門. *The crowd jostled against us.* 人羣推撞我們. Also 亦作 *nc.*

jot¹ [dʒɔt] *nc* (usu. *sing and with negative*) something very small and of no importance (通常用單數與否定結構連用)一點兒; 少許: *I won't change my story (by) one jot.* 我一點也不改動我說的事情.

jot² [dʒɔt] *vt* write quickly; make a quick note of something 匆匆寫下; 匆匆記下: *I jotted down the name of the book which he was talking about.* 我把他正在談論的書名草草記下. *past* 過去式 和 過去 分詞 **jotted. jotter** *nc* notebook 筆記本. **jottings** *npl* quick-ly-written notes 簡略的筆記.

journal ['dʒə:nl] *nc* **1** daily record of news, events etc.; diary 日誌; 日記: *Do you keep a journal of the amount of work you do?* 你把你做的工作記在日記上了嗎? **2** daily newspaper; paper or magazine published frequently 日報; 定期刊物; 雜誌. **journalism** *nu* work of writing for or publishing jour-nals, magazines, newspapers etc. 新聞業; 新聞工作; 新聞寫作; 新聞出版. **journalist** *nc* person who does jour-nalism 從事新聞業者; 新聞記者; 報紙 (雜誌) 撰稿人.

journey ['dʒə:ni] *nc* travel from one place to another (usu. to a distant place and by land, by sea use **voyage**); distance travelled in a par-ticular time 旅行 (通常指遠距離陸地旅行, 水上旅行用 voyage); 旅程: *We made the journey from Paris to Berlin by car.* 我們乘汽車從巴黎旅行到柏林. *From Paris to Berlin is a journey of one day / one day's journey by car.* 從巴黎到柏林乘汽車是一天的行程.

journeyman ['dʒə:nimən] *nc* **1** worker who has learned his trade 熟練工人. **2** experienced craftsman of average ability 工匠.

jovial ['dʒouviəl] *adj* happy and friendly 快活的; 友善的.

joy [dʒɔi] **1** *nu* great delight; great happiness 高興; 歡樂: *They received the good news with joy.* 他們收到好消息感到很高興. *To our great joy he agreed to help us.* 使我們感到非常高

興的是他同意幫助我們. *The children jumped with joy when they saw the new toys.* 孩子們看見新的玩具高興得跳起來. **2** *nc* something which causes joy 樂事; 樂趣: *One of the joys of liv-ing here is the friendliness of the peo-ple.* 住在這裏的樂趣之一是人們的友情. **joyful** *adj* causing or filled with joy 令人高興的; 充滿歡樂的. **joyfully** *adv* **joyfulness** *nu* **joyous** *adj* filled with joy 充滿歡樂的. **joyousness** *nu* **'joy ride** short ride for pleasure (esp. a ride in a stolen motorcar) *(infor-mal)* 乘汽車兜風 (尤指乘偷來的汽車兜風) (非正式).

jubilant ['dʒu:bilnt] *adj* expressing joy; rejoicing 歡呼的; 喜悅的: *They gave him a jubilant welcome after his vic-tory.* 他獲勝後, 他們興高采烈地歡迎他. **jubilation** [dʒu:bi'leiʃən] *nc / u.*

jubilee ['dʒu:bili:] *nc* fiftieth year or anniversary after a great event 五十週年紀念.

judge [dʒʌdʒ] *nc* **1** person appointed to hear important cases in a court of law and to decide what the punish-ment, if any, should be 審判官; 法官. **2** person who decides the result of a competition, an argument etc. 裁判員; 評判員: *He was one of the judges at the boxing match.* 他是拳擊比賽的裁判員之一. **3** person whose opinion about somthing is valuable because of his knowledge and experience 鑑賞家; 鑑定人: *He is a good judge of modern art.* 他是現代藝術的好鑑賞家. *Because I do not know him well, I am no judge of his character.* 因為我不熟悉他, 所以對他的性格我無法評價. Also 亦作 *vt / i* **1** act or decide as a judge (in senses **1** and **2**) 審判; 裁判; 評判. **2** have, give, an opinion about somebody / something 判斷; 斷定; 評

論: *We judged him to be a stranger.*
我們斷定他是個陌生人. *He judges it*
safer to go away than to stay. 他認爲
走比留下來更安全. **judgment, judge-**
ment 1 *nu* act of judging or being
judged 審判; 被審判. **2** *nc* decision
made by a judge 判決: *The judgments*
of the court are reported in all news-
papers. 法院的判決各報都予以報導. **3**
nc / u opinion 意見: *In their judgment*
he is stupid. 他們認爲他是愚蠢的. **4**
nu ability to decide correctly 判斷力:
Our doctor is a man of judgment. 我
們的醫生是個判斷力强的人.

judicial [dʒu:'dʃl] *adj* of a judge or
court of law 法官的; 法院的; 司法的.

judicious [dʒu:'diʃəs] *adj* having good
judgment; wise 明斷的; 有見識的; 明智
的.

judo ['dʒu:dou] *nu* type of Japanese
wrestling (日本的) 柔道.

jug [dʒʌg] *nc* container with a handle
for holding and pouring liquids (帶柄
盛液體的) 壺, 罐. **jugful** *nc* amount
contained by a jug 一壺 (之量); 一罐
(之量).

juggle ['dʒʌgl] *vt / i* do tricks with the
hands (esp. by throwing things in the
air and catching them quickly) 變 (戲
法); 要 (把戲) (尤指把東西拋入空中又
很快接住). **juggler** *nc*.

juice [dʒu:s] *nc* liquid found in meat,
fruit, vegetables etc. (肉、水果、蔬菜等
的) 汁, 液: *I like a glass of tomato*
juice at breakfast. 吃早飯時我喜歡喝
一杯番茄汁. **juicy** *adj* **1** full of juice
多汁液的: *a juicy piece of meat* 一塊
多汁的肉. **2** interesting and shocking
有趣 (但不正當) ; 刺激性的: *There*
are some juicy reports about him. (*in-*
formal in sense 2). 有一些關於他的有
趣報導. (義 2 爲非正式). **juiciness**
nu.

jukebox ['dʒu:kbɔks] *nc* type of record
player which plays when coins are
put in it (投入硬幣卽放唱片的) 自動電
唱機.

July [dʒu'lai] *n* seventh month of the
year 七月.

jumble ['dʒʌmbl] *vt / i* be mixed, mix,
in an untidy way 混雜; 混合; 亂堆: *His*
books and mine were jumbled
together. 他的書和我的書混雜在一起.
Also 亦作 *nc*: *a jumble of books* 一堆
書. **'jumble sale** sale of many kinds
of old goods (esp. to get money to
help the poor, the sick or any good
cause) 舊雜貨拍賣 (尤指義賣).

jumbo ['dʒʌmbou] *adj* unusually big
(*informal*) 特大的; 巨大的. (非正式).
jumbo 'jet large jet aeroplane able to
carry several hundred passengers 大
型噴氣式客機.

jump [dʒʌmp] *vt / i* **1** go up into the air
by pushing off the ground with the
feet 跳; 躍: *Can you jump over this*
wall? 你能跳過這堵牆嗎? *I jumped*
into the water. 我跳入水中. **2** move
quickly 猛跳; 跳動: *My heart was*
jumping with fear. 我怕得心直跳. *He*
jumped out of his car. 他從汽車裏跳
出來. *The boys jumped to their feet*
when the teacher came into the room
i.e. they stood up quickly. 當老師進到
屋裏時, 男孩子都一躍而起. 卽: 他們很
快站起來. **3** cross, pass over, by
jumping 越過; 跳過: *You jumped the*
wall easily. 你輕易地跳過了這堵牆. **4**
rise or increase suddenly 突升; 猛增:
Last week the price of food jumped.
上星期ण食品價格暴漲. *The number of*
students in universities has jumped. 大
學生的總數猛增了. Also 亦作 *nc* **1** *He*
won the high / long jump. 他在跳高/
遠中獲勝. **2** *My heart gave a jump.*
我的心猛跳了一下. **3** *There has been*

a jump in the price of food. 食品價格
突然上漲了. **jumpy** *adj* nervous 神經
緊張的. **jumpiness** *nu* **jumper¹** *nc*
person or animal that jumps 跳躍者;
跳蟲(如蚤等). **jump a queue** get to
the front unfairly by not standing in a
queue with other people 不按次序排
隊; 插隊. **'queue-jumper** *nc*

jumper² ['dʒʌmpə*] *nc* woollen garment put over the head and reaching
just below the waist 套頭毛衣.

junction ['dʒʌŋkʃən] *nc* place of joining or meeting 接合點; 會合處: *We
stopped at the road juncuon* i.e. where
two or more roads meet. 我們在道路
的交叉處停下來.

juncture ['dʒʌŋktʃə] *nc* particular moment in a situation 時機; 關頭: *The
people began to throw stones. At this
juncture the police arrived.* 人們開始
扔石頭. 就在這時候警察來了.

June [dʒuːn] *n* sixth month of the year
六月.

jungle ['dʒʌŋgl] *nc* (usu. with **the**)
land in the tropics covered with thick
forest and undergrowth (通常與 **the**
連用)(熱帶)叢林.

junior ['dʒuːniə] *adj* younger; of lower
rank 較年幼的; 等級(或地位)較低的:
My other brother is junior to me. 我的
另一個兄弟年齡比我小. *In the army a
captain is junior to a major* 在陸軍裏,
上尉的軍階低於少校. Also 亦作 *nc*
person who is younger or of lower
rank 較幼者, 年少者; 等級(或地位)較
低者: *My other brother is my junior*
我的另一個兄弟年齡比我小.*A captain
is a major's junior* 上尉是少校的下級.
Junior 1 (mainly *US*) son having the
same first name as his father (主要用
於美)父子同名時對兒子的稱呼: *John
Smith, Junior* 小約翰·史密斯. **2** younger of two brothers at school 學校裏

兩兄弟中之年幼者: *Williamson Senior
and Williamson Junior* 大威廉森和小
威廉森.

junk¹ [dʒʌŋk] *nc* type of Chinese sailing
ship 中國帆船; 舢板.

junk² [dʒʌŋk] *nu* things thrown away
as useless; rubbish. *(informal)* 廢棄的
舊物; 垃圾. (非正式).

jurisdiction [dʒuərisdikʃən] *nu* administration of justice; right or power to
administer justice 司法(權); 裁判權;
審判的權限: *This crime is not within
the jurisdiction of this court* i.e. this
court does not have the right or power to deal with it. 這類罪行不在本法庭
管轄權限之內. 即: 本法庭無權受理.

jurisprudence [dʒuərispruːdns] *nu* science of law; study of the principles of
law 法律學; 法理學.

jury ['dʒuəri] *nc* **1** group of persons
(usu. twelve in number) chosen to listen to the evidence of a case in a
court of law and to decide on it. (The
jury does not decide what the punishment should be) 陪審團(通常由十二
人組成). (陪審團不判刑): *The jury
found him guilty of murder.* 陪審團裁
定他共謀殺罪. **2** group of persons to
give evidence in a competition etc.
(比賽等之)評判委員會.

juror ['dʒuərə*] *nc* person in a jury 陪
審員; 評判員. (Also 亦作 **juryman;
jurywoman**).

just¹ [dʒʌst] *adj* fair; true; right 公平的;
正直的; 公正的: *This is a just deci-
sion.* 這是公正的決定. (opp 反義詞
unjust).

just² [dʒʌst] *adv / intensifier* **1** exactly
正好; *Tell me just what happened.* 告

訴我究竟發生了甚麼事. *This coat is just the right size.* 這件上衣大小正好. **2** a short time ago 剛才: *They have just gone.* 他們剛剛走. *I am just out of hospital.* 我剛剛出院. *They went just before we did.* 他們剛剛在我們走之前走了. **3** almost at once; very soon 即刻; 很快: *They are just going.* 他們就要走. *I am just about to write him a letter.* 我正要給他寫信. *They went just after we did.* 他們在我們走後不久就走了. **4** only; merely 僅僅; 只是: *He just stood there looking at us.* 他只是站在那裏看看我們. *He is just a child.* 他只是個孩子. *I need just two more days to finish it.* 我只需要再有兩天就完成了. *Just a minute!* i.e. wait a minute! 等一下! **5** (often with *only*) scarcely; almost not (常與 *only* 連用) 剛好; 幾乎不: *The bullet (only) just missed him.* 子彈差點兒就打中了他. *We had (only) just enough money to pay the bill.* 我們的錢僅夠付賬. **6** certainly; without a doubt 當然; 無疑地: *The food is just wonderful.* 這種食品簡直太好了. *I just can't wait to see them.* 我當然急着要見他們. **just about** has the sense of not being sure or of almost 大約; 幾乎: *I left my hat just about here.* 我大概把帽子忘在這兒附近. *This box is just about big enough for my books.* 這個箱子幾乎可以裝下我的書. *I am just about finished.* 我快要完成了. **just as 1** exactly as 正像; 正當…的時候: *I did just as you told me.* 我正是照你的吩咐做的. *Leave it just as it is.* 保持原狀, 別動它. **2** equally; quite 同樣地; 相當地: *I am just as brave as you are.* 我和你一樣勇敢. *It would be just as well if he left.* 如果他離開, 那也好. **just now 1** a very short time ago 剛才: *They gave it to me just now.* 他們剛才把它

給了我. **2** at this very time 這時, 此刻: *Just now they are asleep.* 這會兒他們睡着了. **just so** exactly; certainly 正是如此; 一點不錯.

justice ['dʒʌstis] *nu* **1** being just; fairness 正義; 公平; 合理: *Children expect justice from their parents.* 孩子們期望得到父母親的公平對待. **2** the purpose of the law i.e. to be just; punishment according to the law 公正; 法律制裁; 審判: *It is the duty of the police to bring those who break the law to justice* i.e. bring them to court to be punished. 把違法者送交法院審判是警察的義務.

justify ['dʒʌstifai] *vt* be or give a good reason for something; explain satisfactorily 作爲…的正當理由; 爲…辯護, 辯明, 說明…是正確的: *His illness does not justify his long absence.* 他的病不能作爲他長期缺席的正當理由. *You will have to justify your work to the others.* 你只好向別人說明你的工作是對的. **justifiable** *adj* able to be justified 可證明爲正當的; 有理由的; 無可非議的. (*opp* 反義詞 **unjustifiable**). **justifiably** *adv* **justification** [dʒʌstifi'keiʃən] *nc / u* something which justifies; state of being justified 理由; 辯護; 辯明: *His justification for being absent is his illness.* 他缺席的理由是他病了.

jut [dʒʌt] *vi* (with *out*) stick out; project (與 *out* 連用) 突出; 伸出: *The rocks jut out above the trees.* 岩石在樹林的上方突出來. *past* 過去式和過去分詞 **jutted**.

juvenile ['dʒuːvənail] *nc* young person 少年. Also 亦作 *adj*: *juvenile books* 少年讀物; *juvenile court* i.e. a court of law which deals with young persons 少年法庭; *juvenile employment* i.e. employment of young persons 雇用童工.

K, k

kaleidoscope [kə'laidəskoup] *nc* apparatus fitted with mirrors and pieces of coloured glass etc which shows many coloured patterns 萬花筒.

kangaroo [kæŋgəru:] *nc* type of animal found in Australia, with strong back legs on which it stands and leaps forward 袋鼠.

kapok ['keipɔk] *nu* substance like cotton wool obtained from a tropical tree and used for filling pillows etc. 木棉.

karate [kə'rɑ:ti] *nu* method of fighting etc using the edge of the hand 空手道.

kayak ['kaiæk] *nc* type of covered canoe used by the people who live in the Arctic; any canoe of this shape（住在北極區的人使用的）獨木舟; 小划子.

keel [ki:l] *nc* long piece of wood or steel along the bottom of a ship to which the sides of the ship are fixed（船的）龍骨. **keel over** turn over; fall over 翻身; 傾覆: *The ship keeled over in the storm.* 這隻船在暴風雨中傾覆了.

keen [ki:n] *adj* 1 (with reference to persons) eager; very interested（指人）渴望的; 熱心的: *He is a keen football player.* 他是個熱心的足球運動員. *He is always keen to play.* 他是想去玩. 2 (with reference to the mind, senses and feelings) sharp; quick; deep（指心智、感官和感情）尖銳的; 敏捷的; 深切的: *He has a keen brain.* 他有敏捷的頭腦. *They have keen sight / are keen-sighted* i.e. they have good eyesight, they can see well. 他們有敏銳的視力. 即: 他們視力很好, 能看得很清楚. *My hearing is not as keen as it used to be.* 我的聽力不如從前那樣敏銳了. *He takes a keen interest in his work.* 他對他的工作深感興趣. **keenly** *adv* **keenness** *nu* **be keen on** be very fond of; be eager to 喜愛; 渴望: *He is keen on that girl.* 他很喜歡那姑娘. *I am keen on fishing.* 我很喜歡釣魚. *They are keen on buying a new house. (informal)* 他們渴望買一座新房子. (非正式).

keep¹ [ki:p] *vt / i* 1 have or hold, either for a time or always 保持; 保存; 保留: *You may keep my book for a fortnight.* 你可留着我的書兩星期. *Please keep the picture. I don't want it.* 請留下這張圖片, 我不要了. 2 look after; take care of; be responsible for 照料; 照顧; 對 … 負責: *He is keeping my coat and hat for me until I return.* 他在替我保管我的上衣和帽子, 直到我回來為止. *She keeps house for her brother.* 她為她兄弟管家. *He keeps goal in our football team.* 他是我們足球隊的守門員. *I am keeping the cake for tea tomorrow.* 我在保留明天喝茶時吃的這塊糕. 即: 在明天喝茶前不要把它吃掉. 3 own, manage 經營; 管理: *My father keeps a grocer's shop.* 我父親經營一家雜貨店. *The farmers here keep cattle.* 這裏的農夫養牛. 4 pay for; support 負擔 … 的費用; 贍養: *I have a wife and three children to keep.* 我要養活妻子和三個孩子. *They get enough money to keep themselves in food and clothing.* 他們掙足夠的錢

給他們自己購買食品和添置衣服。**5** hold back; cause to stay; prevent 阻止; 使停留; 防止: *What kept you?* i.e. what held you back / delayed you? 甚麼事把你耽擱了? *The doctors are keeping him in hospital for another week.* 醫生們在勸說他再住院一星期。*I kept him from running away.* 我不讓他逃跑。**6** continue, cause to continue, to be in a particular state or place (使)繼續處於某種狀態或地點; 保持: *Although they have many difficulties, they keep happy.* 雖然他們有許多困難, 但他們一直很愉快。*Good food keeps you healthy.* 好的食物使你身體健康。*You must keep inside the house during the cold weather.* 在寒冷的天氣, 你必須呆在屋裏。*Will this fish keep?* i.e. will it continue to be fresh and fit to eat? 這魚能放久嗎?即: 它能保持新鮮可食嗎? **7** continue, cause to continue, to do something (使)繼續做(某事): *He keeps coming back for more.* 他不斷地回來要更多東西。*I kept them working all day.* 他要他們整天工作。**8** follow; obey; observe 遵循; 執行; 遵守: *They keep early hours* i.e. they always go to bed early. 他們養成早睡習慣。*Everyone must keep the law.* 每一個人都必須遵守法律。*He always keeps his promise.* 他總是履行諾言。*Most people keep Christmas at home.* 多數人在家裏過聖誕節。*past* 過去式和過去分詞 **kept** [kept]. **keeper** *nc* person who looks after, is responsible for, something 管理人; 負責人。(Used with many other words e.g. *gamekeeper; goalkeeper; housekeeper; innkeeper; shopkeeper*) (與許多其它詞連用, 例如: 獵物看守人, 守門員, 女管家, 客棧老闆, 店主)。**keeping** *nu* **1** care 保管; 管理: *Your books are in good keeping if he is looking after*

them. 你的書, 如果他在看管, 會保管得很好。**2** being suited to; being in agreement with 適合; 一致: *The speech was in keeping with the happy event.* 這篇講話與這件喜事很協調。*What he says now is out of keeping with what he said before.* 他現在說的話同他從前說的話不一致。**keepsake** gift made to somebody who, by keeping it, can remember the person who gave it 紀念品。**keep (someone) back** stay, cause to stay, back (使)留在後面: *They all ran forward but I kept back.* 他們都向前跑, 我卻留在後面。*I also kept my friend back.* 我也讓我的朋友留在後面。**keep something back** refuse to tell everything 拒絕透露; 隱瞞: *He may be telling the truth but he is keeping something back.* 他可能在說實話, 但他仍有所隱瞞。**keep something from someone** hide; not allow to see or know 瞞着某人; 不讓某人知道: *They kept the truth from him* i.e. they did not tell him the truth. 他們不讓他知道真實的情況。即: 他們沒把真實情況告訴他。**keep in with someone** continue to be friendly with for one's own benefit 討好某人: *He keeps in with his manager.* 他討好經理。**keep off** stay, cause to stay, away from (使)離開, (使)不接近: *Keep off the grass.* 勿踏草地。*Keep your dog off the grass.* 別讓狗進入草地。*The rain keeps off* i.e. it does not come near or begin. 雨不下了。**keep on** continue, cause to continue, to do something (使)繼續(做某事): *They kept on working after dark.* 天黑後, 他們仍繼續工作。*He didn't stop running. He just kept on.* 他沒有停下來, 仍在繼續跑着。**keep something on** continue to wear 繼續戴(或穿)着不脫: *He kept his hat on even when* he went into the house. 即使他進到屋裏, 他仍戴着帽子. **keep out of something** stay, cause to stay, outside or out of (使)置身於…之外, (使)不參與, (使)不介入: *I keep out of his troubles.* 我不介入他的麻煩事. **keep (someone / someting) up 1** stay, cause to stay, high, cheerful or good (使)保持高昂、高興或良好的狀態: *Their spirits are keeping up although they have many troubles.* 雖然他們遇到不少困難, 他們仍然情緒高昂. *The good news keeps our spirits up.* 好消息使我們精神振奮. *I hope the weather keeps up.* 我希望天氣繼續晴朗. **2** continue, cause to continue (使)繼續: *They keep up the habit of visiting old friends.* 他們保持看望老朋友的習慣. *Keep it up!* i.e. don't stop! 堅持下去! 別停下! **3** not allow to go to bed 不讓…睡覺; 使熬夜: *They kept me up for three hours talking about their work.* 他們談自己的工作談了三小時不讓我睡覺. **keep up with someone / something 1** go as quickly as; do as well as 與…並肩前進; 和…並駕齊驅; 跟上: *They could not keep up with us when we climbed the mountain.* 我們爬山時, 他們跟不上我們. *He can't keep up with his rich friends* i.e. spend as much as they do. 他無法和他的有錢朋友們比排場. 即: 他無法像他們那樣花錢. **2** continue to be informed or about 對…很瞭解; 熟悉: *keep up with the news* 消息靈通. **keep one's head** remain calm 保持鎮靜: *He survived the accident because he kept his head* i.e. he did not panic. 他在這次事故中幸免於死, 因爲他保持鎮靜. 即: 他沒有驚慌失措. (*opp* 反義詞 **lose one's head**). **keep (oneself) to oneself** stay by oneself, not mix with others 不交際; 不與他人來

往: *At the party he kept to himself.* 在宴會上, 他獨來獨往, 不與他人交往. **keep something to oneself** not tell anyone 不告訴別人; 保守秘密: *He keeps his thoughts to himself.* 他不把自己的想法告訴別人.

keep² [kiːp] **1** *nc* the inner and strongest part of a castle 城堡的最堅實部份. **2** *nu* board and lodging given to somebody 膳食費; 生活費: *Everybody living here pays for his keep.* 住在這裏的每一個人都要付生活費.

kennel ['kenl] *nc* small hut in which a dog is kept 狗窩.

kept [kept] past of **keep.** keep 的過去式和過去分詞.

kerb [kɜːb] (*US* 美 **curb**) *nc* edge of a pavement 人行道的石邊: *Please park your car close to the kerb.* 請把車子停在靠近人行道石邊的地方. **'kerbstone** stone which is part of a kerb 街道的邊石.

kernel ['kɜːnl] *nc* **1** inner part of a seed or nut 穀粒; (堅果的) 仁; 核. **2** inner or most important part of anything 要點; 中心; 核心: *The kernel of his problem is lack of money.* 他的問題的中心是缺錢.

kerosene ['kerəsiːn] *nu* paraffin oil 煤油; 火油.

kestrel ['kestrl] *nc* type of small bird of prey 茶隼.

ketchup ['ketʃəp] *nu* type of sauce (usu. made from tomatoes) 番茄醬, 番茄沙司.

kettle ['ketl] *nc* metal container with a handle and spout used for boiling liquids 壺. **'kettledrum** type of drum with a curved bottom 銅鼓; 定音鼓.

key [kiː] *nc* **1** instrument to open and shut a lock 鑰匙: *Have you got the key of this door?* 你有這門的鑰匙嗎? **2** set of musical notes which have a definite relation to one another and form a scale (音樂的)調. **3** lever in a musical instrument or typewriter which is pressed down by the fingers (樂器或打字機的)鍵: *A piano has a row of black and white keys.* 鋼琴有一排黑色鍵和白色鍵. *Typewriters have a key for each letter of the alphabet.* 打字機有字母表裏每個字母的鍵. **4** something which explains, solves or answers 題解; 解答; 答案: *The key to this problem is better planning.* 解決這個問題的關鍵是要有更好的計劃. *I need a key when I am reading Latin* i.e. a book which gives a translation. 我在讀拉丁文時需要一本逐字對譯本. **5** (usu. used as an *adj*) something which is very important (通常用作形容詞)非常重要的; 關鍵的; 基本的: *He has the key post in this factory* i.e. the most important post. 他在這家工廠裏佔有舉足輕重的職位. 即: 最重要的職位. *He is the key man.* 他是關鍵人物. *The enemy hold all the key positions.* 敵人佔據了全部主要陣地. **'keyboard** row of keys on a piano, typewriter etc. (鋼琴, 打字機等的)鍵盤. **'keyhole** hole in a lock into which one puts the key to open and shut it 鑰匙孔; 鎖眼. **keynote** principal idea; theme 要旨; 主旨: *The keynote of all his writings is the need for peace.* 他所有作品的主旨是要和平. **key something up 1** put in tune 校準音調. **2** make excited 使激動; 使緊張: *They were keyed up for the examination.* 考試使得他們很緊張.

khaki ['kɑːki] *nu* the colour of yellowish dust 土黃色. **2** cloth of this colour (used in making soldiers' uniforms) 黃卡其布(用於製做士兵的制服). Also 亦作 *adj*.

kibbutz [ki'buːts] *nc* collective farm in Israel 以色列的集體農場. *pl* 複數 **kibbutzim** [ki'buːtsiːm].

kick [kik] **1** *vt* hit with the foot 踢: *He kicked the ball.* 他踢球. **2** *vi* move the feet violently in order to hit somebody / something 踢跳: *He kicked and shouted when the police caught him.* 當警察捉住他時, 他亂踢亂叫. Also 亦作 *nc* **1** *He gave the ball a kick.* 他踢球. **2** powerful effect; pleasure 刺激; 樂趣: *The drink he gave me had a kick in it.* 他給我的酒勁够勁. *He did it for kicks.* (*informal* in sense **2**) 他是爲追求刺激而幹的. (義 2 爲非正式).

kick off begin a game of football or begin the second half of a game, by kicking a ball (足球比賽)開球. **'kick-off** *nc* (usu. only *sing*) beginning of a game of football; beginning of any activity (通常只用單數)(足球比賽開始時的)開球; 開始. **kick out** push out violently (not necessarily by using one's foot) 驅逐; 逐出: *He has been kicked out of his job.* (*informal*) 他被解雇了. (非正式). **kick up a fuss / row** cause a fuss / row by protesting violently (由強烈抗議而)引起騷動; 大吵大鬧.

kid¹ [kid] *nc* **1** young goat 小山羊. **2** leather made from the skin of a young goat 小山羊皮. **3** child (*informal* in sense **3**)小孩(義 3 爲非正式).

kid² [kid] *vt* deceive; pretend 欺騙; 假裝: *Don't listen! He's kidding you.* 別聽他的, 他在騙你. *I was only kidding* i.e. joking. 我只不過是開玩笑罷了. *past* 過去式和過去分詞 **kidded.** (*informal*) 非正式.

kidnap ['kidnæp] *vt* carry somebody off by force (esp. a child in order to be paid money if the child is returned to its parents) 綁架(尤指綁架小孩). *past* 過去式和過去分詞 **kidnapped. kid-**

napper *nc* **kidnapping** *nc / u.*

kidney ['kidni] *nc* either of two organs of the body which take urine from the blood 腎.

kill [kil] *vt* **1** put to death; cause the death of 殺死; 使死亡: *He killed him with a spear.* 他用矛刺死他. *Malaria killed them.* 瘧疾奪走了他們的生命. **2** destroy; bring to an end 破壞, 毀掉; 使終止: *He has killed our chances of success.* 他毀掉了我們成功的機會. Also 亦作 *n sing* (esp. with reference to animals killed in hunting) act of killing; thing killed (尤指) 獵獲之動物; 殺死; 擊毀之物. *We saw the lion sitting beside its kill.* 我們看見獅子坐在它的獵獲物旁邊. **killer** *nc* person / thing that kills 殺人者; 致死的事物; 吃人的野獸. **killjoy** person who stops, tries to stop, the happiness of others 掃興的人. **kill something off** kill so that none is left 殺光; 消滅: *Hunters have killed off all the large animals in this country.* 獵人消滅了這個國家所有的大動物. **kill time** do something in order to fill up time 消磨時間; 消遣: *The train was very late, so we killed time by playing cards.* 這趟火車很晚, 因此我們玩紙牌消磨時間.

kiln [kiln] *nc* large oven in which substances (e.g. clay, bricks, lime) are dried, made hard or burnt (烘乾陶器、磚、石灰等的) 窰.

kilo(gram), kilo(gramme) ['ki:lou(græm)] *nc* unit of weight equal to one thousand grams 千克; 公斤.

kilometre ['kiləmi:tə*] (*US* 美 **kilometer**) *nc* unit of length equal to one thousand metres 千米; 公里.

kilt [kilt] *nc* type of short skirt traditionally worn by Scotsmen (蘇格蘭男子穿的) 短裙.

kimono [ki'mounou] *nc* type of loose

coat with a broad belt worn by the Japanese; dressing gown of this type (日本人穿的) 和服; 和服式女晨衣. *pl* 複數 **kimonos**.

kin [kin] *npl* family relations; people related by family ties 親戚; 家族. **next of kin** closest relations, family of a person 至親; 家屬.

kind¹ [kaind] *nc* type; sort; class 種; 類; 屬: *Rice is a kind of grain.* 大米是一種穀類. *I don't like this kind of school* 我不喜歡這種學校; *many kinds of people / people of many kinds* 許多種人. *He is the kind (of person) who always arrives late.* 他是那種老是來遲的人. **a kind of** often used when something is not fully known or is difficult to describe 常用於對某事不甚瞭解或難以描述時: *It was a kind of animal with long ears and a short tail.* 那是一種有長耳朵和短尾巴的動物. *We have a kind of feeling that we are being followed.* 我們有一種被人跟蹤的感覺. **nothing of the kind** certainly not 決不; 一點也不; 沒那回事: *You're drunk! I'm nothing of the kind!* 你醉了! 我一點也不醉! **of a kind** not very good; not as good as one would expect 蹩脚的; 徒有其名的: *He is a football player of a kind.* 他是個蹩脚的足球運動員. *They gave us a welcome of a kind.* 他們給予我們低規格的歡迎.

kind² [kaind] *adj* gentle; friendly; helpful and kind; 親切的; 有助的: *I have a kind father and mother.* 我有慈祥的父親和母親. *They are very kind to children.* 他們對孩子和藹可親. *It was kind of them to ask us to the concert.* 感謝他們邀請我們出席音樂會.(*opp* 反義詞 **unkind**). **kindly** *adv*: *They kindly asked us to the concert.* 他們盛情邀請我們出席音樂會. *Would you kindly* *lend me your pen?* i.e. would you please? 請你把筆借給我好嗎? *I do not take kindly to the cold weather* i.e. I do not like it. 我不喜歡寒冷的天氣.

kindness *nc / u* act or state of being kind 和藹; 親切; 好意; 友好的行為; 好事: *Thank you for your many kindnesses.* 感謝你幫了我許多忙. **out of kindness** because of being kind 出於好意: *He did not know me, but out of kindness he helped me.* 他不認識我, 但出於好意он幫助了我.

kindergarten ['kɪndəgɑːtn] *nc* school for very young children 幼兒園, 幼稚園.

kindle ['kɪndl] *vt / i* **1** catch fire, set on fire (使) 着火; 點燃, (使) 燃燒: *Damp wood does not kindle.* 濕木頭點不着. *He kindled the wood with a match.* 他用小火柴點着了這塊木頭. **2** have, cause to have, a particular feeling 引起, 激起(某種感情): *The story kindled our desire for adventure.* 這個故事激起我們進行冒險的願望.

kindly[1] ['kaɪndlɪ] *adv* see 見 **kind**[2]

kindly[2] ['kaɪndlɪ] *adj* pleasant; friendly 爽快的; 宜人的; 友善的; 親切的: *He has a kindly manner.* 他的態度和藹可親. **kindliness** *nu.*

kindred ['kɪndrɪd] *adj* related 有關連的; 有親戚關係的: *They belong to kindred tribes and speak kindred languages.* 他們屬於同族部落且講同源語言.

kinetic [kɪ'netɪk] *adj* connected with, or caused by, motion 運動的; 由運動引起的: *kinetic energy* 動能.

king [kɪŋ] *nc* **1** male ruler of a country (esp. by descent) 國王, 君主(尤指世襲的). **2** most important piece in the game of chess (象棋中的)王. **3** most important playing card after the ace (紙牌中小於A的)老K. '**kingfisher**

type of brightly coloured bird which catches fish 魚狗(一種食魚鳥); 翠鳥. '**kingpin** **1** pin which keeps a wheel in place 中心立軸. **2** important person on whom everything depends 中心人物; 重要的人: *The kingpin of this company is not the manager but his assistant.* 這家公司的中心人物不是經理而是他的助理.

kingdom ['kɪŋdəm] *nc* **1** country ruled by a king or queen 王國. **2** one of the three main divisions of nature i.e. *the animal kingdom; the vegetable kingdom; the mineral kingdom* 自然三界之一, 即: 動物界; 植物界; 礦物界.

kink [kɪŋk] *nc* **1** twist or bend (made by accident) in a rope, wire, hose or long piece of something (繩、金屬絲、軟管等的)紐結; 絞纏: *If you pull the rope tight, the kinks in it will disappear.* 你把繩子拉緊, 繩子上的紐結就消失了. **2** mental twist; strange way of thinking 奇想; 怪念頭: *He had a kink about religion.* 他對宗教有種怪念頭. **kinky** *adj* odd or unusual in appearance or behaviour (esp. in a fashionable way) (表現或行為)古怪的; 乖僻的.

kinsman ['kɪnzmən] *nc* male relative 男親屬.

kiosk ['kiːɒsk] *nc* small hut used for selling newspapers, tobacco etc, or for a public telephone (For a public telephone, also **callbox**) (賣報紙、烟等的)小亭; 公用電話亭(公用電話亭亦作 **callbox**).

kipper ['kɪpə*] *nc* herring i.e. type of sea fish, split open, salted and dried in smoke until it is brown in colour (醃或燻的)鮭魚乾; 鯡魚乾. Also 亦作 *vt* prepare herring in this way 醃或燻製(鮭魚等).

kiss [kɪs] *vt / i* place the lips against somebody's mouth, cheek, hand etc, or against something to show love or respect, or as a greeting 吻; 親吻: *When the two sisters met they kissed.* 兩姐妹見面時親吻。 *He kissed his mother goodbye.* 他向母親吻別。Also 亦作 *nc* **kiss of life** method of getting someone breathing normally again (e.g. if he has just been rescued from drowning) 口對口人工呼吸(例如一方剛從溺水中被救起來)。

kit [kit] *nc* **1** all the equipment and clothes of a soldier, airman or sailor (士兵、飛行員或海員的)裝備。 **2** set of tools, materials, clothes or equipment for a particular purpose 成套工具(或用具、物件、衣服、器材等): *carpenter's kit* 一套木工用具，木工工具箱。 *first-aid kit* 一套急救器材; *football kit* 一套足球用具。 **kitbag** large canvas bag used by soldiers, airmen or sailors to carry kit (士兵、飛行員或海員的)帆布行囊。

kitchen ['kitʃin] *nc* room used for cooking 廚房。 **'kitchen 'garden** garden or part of a garden where vegetables are grown 菜圃;菜園。

kite [kait] *nc* light frame covered with paper or cloth which rises high in the air and is tied to a very long piece of string, held by somebody on the ground 風箏。

kitten ['kitn] *nc* young cat 小貓。

kitty ['kiti] *nc* **1** money which is gambled for in various games 賭注。 **2** kitten (*informal* in sense **2**) 小貓(義2爲非正式)。

kleptomania [kleptou'meiniə] *nu* strong urge to steal caused by mental illness 偷竊狂;盜癖。 **kleptomaniac** [kleptou'meiniæk] *nc* person who has kleptomania 有偷竊狂的人。

knack [næk] *nu* skill in doing something (usu. gained by long practice) 竅門;

技巧(通常指通過長期練習而獲得的): *There is a knack in tying ropes together.* 把繩子綁在一起有點技巧。 *He has the knack of disappearing when he is needed.* 需要他時，他有脫身的本事。

knapsack ['næpsæk] *nc* small bag with straps, carried on the back (esp. by soldiers and travellers) (尤指士兵和旅行者用的)背包。

knave [neiv] *nc* **1** person who is not honest and cannot be trusted (*o.f.*) 騙子(舊式)。 **2** playing card below the queen in importance (紙牌中的) J, 傑克。 (Also 亦作 **jack**). *The knave of hearts.* 紅心J。

knead [ni:d] *vt* mix together by pressing and squeezing with the hands (e.g. flour and water to make bread, or soft clay to make pots) 揉;捏;捏製(例如: 揉麵粉和水做麵包,或捏陶土製陶器)。

knee [ni:] *nc* joint in the middle of the leg where it bends; part of one's clothing which covers the knees 膝;膝蓋;衣物的膝蓋部份: *You have to bend your knees to sit down.* 你得屈膝才能坐下。 *My mother mended the holes in the knees of my trousers.* 我母親把我褲子膝部的破洞補了。 **'kneecap** bone on the front of the knee 膝蓋骨。 **knee-'deep (in something)** *adj / adv* deep enough to reach the knees 深及膝的(地): *He stood knee-deep in the river.* 他站在河中,水深及膝。 **knee-'high** *adj / adv* high enough to reach the knees 高及膝的(地): *The corn is not yet knee-high.* 穀類作物還不到膝蓋高。

kneel [ni:l] *vi* go down on the knees 跪下;跪着: *Every evening they kneel (down) to pray / in prayer.* 每天晚上他們跪下祈禱。 *past* 過去式和過去分詞 **knelt** [nelt]

knew [nju:] past tense of **know**. know 的過去式.

knickers ['nikəz] *npl* pants, undergarment worn by women and girls, covering the bottom part of the body 女用短內褲.

knife [naif] *nc* tool or weapon with a sharp blade of steel fixed to a handle, used for cutting food etc. (有柄的)小刀(用於切食品等). *pl* **knives** [naivz]. Also 亦作 *vt* stab with a knife 用小刀刺.

knight [nait] *nc* **1** (in the Middle Ages) man who was given the right to carry arms by his king or ruler (中古時代的)武士; 騎士. **2** (in modern times in Britain and some other countries) man who is given as an honour or reward a special rank above ordinary people with the title of *Sir* instead of *Mr* (現代在英國和其他一些國家的)爵士(其稱號爲Sir 而非Mr). **3** piece in the game of chess, shaped like a horse's head (國際象棋中)馬, 有馬頭的棋子. Also 亦作 *vt* make somebody a knight (in sense **2**) 封…爲爵士: *Mr John Smith was knighted by the Queen and became Sir John Smith.* 約翰·史密斯先生被女王封爲爵士, 成了約翰·史密斯爵士. *Note* 説明: one can say *Sir John Smith* or *Sir John*, but not *Sir Smith.* 人們可説約翰·史密斯爵士或約翰爵士, 但不可説史密斯爵士. **knighthood** rank of knight; all knights with the title of Sir (或爵士)的地位(或身份); 所有的騎士(或爵士): *He has been given a knighthood* i.e. he has been knighted. 他已被授予爵士勳位. 即: 他已被封爲爵士.

knit [nit] *vt/i* **1** make material or something to wear etc by using needles to link together threads of wool etc. 編結; 編織(毛、線等): *She is knitting a pair of socks.* 她在編織一雙襪子. *She likes to knit in the evening.* 她喜歡在晚上編織毛線. **2** join firmly 接合; (使)緊密結合: *Danger knits people together.* 危險使人們緊密結合在一起. *The two broken bones in his arm have knitted well.* 他胳臂上的兩塊斷骨接合得很好. *past* 過去式和過去分詞 **knitted** *or* **knit. knitting** *nu* **1** act of knitting 編織; 編結. **2** something that is being made by knitting 編織物: *Mother can't find her knitting.* 母親找不到她編織的東西. **'knitting needle** long needle made of steel, wood etc used for knitting 編織用的長針, 織針, 毛衣針. **knit one's brows** bring the brows together; frown 蹙額; 皺眉頭: *He knits his brows when he is thinking hard.* 他在苦思時皺着眉頭.

knives [naivz] *pl* of **knife.** knife 的複數形式.

knob [nɔb] *nc* **1** round lump on the surface or at the end of something 球狀物; 節; 圓頭: *He carries a stick with a big knob on it.* 他携帶一根有大圓頭的手杖. **2** handle or lever shaped like a knob 圓形把手; 旋鈕: *He opened the door by turning the knob.* 他轉動圓形把手把門打開. *A television set has a number of knobs which control vision and sound.* 一部電視機有若干控制影像和聲音的旋鈕. **3** small round lump 小圓塊: *a knob of butter* 一塊球形黃油.

knock [nɔk] *vt/i* **1** strike; beat (usu. making a noise while doing so) 擊; 撞; 敲; 打(通常發出聲響): *He knocked his head against the wall.* 他的頭撞在牆上. *I knocked at his door before going in.* 進屋前, 我先敲他的門. **2** speak unfavourably about 抨擊; 攻擊: *He is always knocking his country's foreign policy.* (*informal* in sense **2**)

他老是攻擊國家的外交政策. (義2爲非
正式). Also 亦作 nc: *There is a knock
at the door.* 有敲門聲. **knocker** *nc*
handle on a hinge for knocking at a
door (instead of using one's hand) 門
環. '**knock-'kneed** *adj* having legs
bent in together at the knees 膝內翻
的; 兩腿向內彎曲的. **knock someone
/ something about** push here and
there by striking 粗暴對待 (某人 / 某
物): *They say he knocks his children
about. (informal)* 人們說他虐待他的孩
子. (非正式). **knock someone /
something down** knock to the
ground 擊倒; 打倒: *He knocked him
down with one blow of his fist.* 他一拳
把他打倒在地. **knock (something)
off 1** take away from; deduct 減去; 除
去: *They knocked five pounds off the
price.* 他們減價五鎊. **2** stop working
停止工作: *We knock off every day at
5 p.m. (both informal)* 我們每天下午
五點鐘下班. (義1和義2均爲非正式).
knock someone out (esp. in boxing)
hit somebody so hard that he loses
consciousness (尤指拳擊) 擊昏; 打倒.
'**knockout** *nc*: *He won the boxing
match by a knockout.* 他一拳將對方打
倒贏了這場拳賽.

knot [nɒt] *nc* **1** fastening made with a
piece of thread, string or rope by
twisting and turning the ends (線繩索
等的) 結: *He tied the two ropes
together with / in a knot.* 他將兩條繩
子打個結接在一條. **2** hard, round
piece of wood in a wooden board (木
板上的) 節; 木節. **3** measure of the
speed of ships in one nautical mile
(1852 metres) per hour (測船速的單
位) 節, 即: 海里 (約1852米) / 小時; 海里,
浬: *The ship was sailing at 15 knots.*
這船以時速15浬航行. Also 亦作 *vt / i*
have or take knots; tie with knots 打

結; 捆紮: *This rope does not knot as
well as that.* 這種繩子不如那種繩子好
打結. *He knotted the pieces of string
together.* 他把線連接在一起. *past* 過
去式和過去分詞 **knotted. knotty** *adj*
1 full of knots (in senses **1** and **2**) 多
結的; 多節的. **2** difficult 困難的: *a
knotty problem* 難題.

know [nəʊ] *vt / i* **1** have information a-
bout somebody / something; under-
stand; be aware of 知道; 瞭解; 懂得: *I
know (that) he lives here.* 我知道他住
在這裏. *He knows three languages.* 他
懂得三種語言. *We did not know
whether we were right or wrong.* 我們
不知道我們是對還是錯. *I'm your
friend. Yes, I know.* 我是你的朋友. 對,
我知道. *Do you know how to use this
machine?* 你知道怎樣使用這種機器嗎?
2 recognize somebody; be acquainted
with somebody 認出; 認識; 熟悉: *I
know your brother but not your sister.*
我認識你的兄弟但不認識你的姐姐:
They have known me for many years.
他們認識我好多年了. **3** be able to
judge the value of, or to tell the difference between, things 識別; 分辨:
*They know good food when they taste
it.* 他們只要試一下味道就能分辨出食
品的好壞. *He doesn't know a lion
from a tiger.* 他分辨不出獅子和老虎.
past tense 過去式 **knew** [njuː] *past
part* 過去分詞 **known. known** *adj*
(*opp* 反義詞 **unknown**). **knowing** *adj*
showing that one knows; clever; sly
知情的, 會意的; 聰穎的; 狡猾的): *He
gave me a knowing look.* 他心照不宣
地看了我一眼. **knowingly** *adv* **1** *He
looked at me knowingly.* 他心照不宣
地看我. **2** on purpose 故意地; 有意
地: *We did not knowingly leave you
behind.* 我們不是故意把你丟在後面.
'**know-all** person who thinks he

knows everything. *(informal)* 自以爲無所不知的人(非正式). **'know-how** knowing how to do something because of experience (esp. something practical) *(informal)* 實際知識, 技能 (非正式). **be known as 1** be regarded or considered as 被認爲是…: *He is known as the best engineer in the country.* 他被認爲是這個國家最優秀的工程師. **2** known by the name of 以…知名; 叫做: *the man known as Smith* 這人名叫史密斯. **know about something** be aware of; have information about 知道; 聽說關於…的事情: *He knew about my father's arrival before I did.* 他比我先知道我父親到了. see also 參見 **know of. know better than** have enough sense or information not to do something 知道不該(做某事); 知道(某事)是不對的: *I know better than to lend him any money.* 我知道不該把錢借給他. *He ran away from school. He ought to have known better.* 他從學校逃跑, 他本來就應該知道那是不對的. **know of** be aware of; have information about 知道; 聽說關於…的事情: *Has he gone? Not that we know of.* 他走了嗎? 據我們所知他沒有走. **make oneself known to somebody** introduce oneself 向…自我介紹: *When I saw the new teacher I made myself known to him.* 我看見這位新來的教師時, 我向他做了一番自我介紹. **there is no knowing** it is impossible to know 不可能知道: *There is no knowing what he'll do next. (informal)* 不可能知道他下一步會做甚麼. (非正式).

knowledge ['nɒlidʒ] *nu* **1** understanding; learning 理解; 瞭解; 知識; 學問: *I have no knowledge of mathematics.* 我不懂數學. *He has a good knowl-*

edge of English. 他通曉英語. **2** information about; experience of 消息, 見聞; 經驗: *Our knowledge of our neighbours is not very great.* 我們對鄰居的認識并不深. *He has no knowledge of life in a small village.* 他對小鄉村的生活一無所知. **knowledgeable** ['nɒlidʒəbl] *adj* having much knowledge 有知識的: *He is very knowledgeable about cars.* 他對汽車很內行. **to the best of one's knowledge** as far as one is aware 據某人所知: *To the best of my knowledge he still lives in London.* 據我所知, 他仍住在倫敦. **without the knowledge of somebody** without somebody knowing or being informed 沒讓某人知道: *He went out of the classroom without the knowledge of his teacher.* 他沒讓老師知道就走出教室.

knuckle ['nʌkl] *nc* (with reference to persons) bone where a finger is joined to the hand or in a finger where it has a joint (指人)指關節. **knuckle under** yield; cause no more trouble 屈服; 不再鬧事: *After being punished the pupils knuckled under.* 學生被處罰後不再鬧事了.

kosher ['kouʃə*] *adj* (with reference to food etc.) in accordance with Orthodox Jewish Law (指食品等)合乎正統猶太戒律的, 猶太人可食用的.

kraal [krɑːl] *nc* in South Africa, village protected by a fence; a pen for animals protected by a fence (南非有柵欄防護的)村莊; (有柵欄防護的)家畜欄.

kudos ['kjuːdɒs] *nu* honour; credit 光榮; 榮譽; 稱譽: *We did the work but we didn't get much kudos for it.* 我們做了這項工作, 但我們並沒有爲此而贏得很多稱讚.

L, l

lab [læb] *nc* short form of **laboratory**. laboratory 的縮畧式.

label ['leibl] *nc* piece of paper or other material fixed to something to show what it is, who it belongs to or where it is to be sent 標籤; 籤條: *When you are travelling you should put labels on your luggage.* 你旅行時, 應在行李上貼上標籤. Also 亦作 *vt* attach a label to 貼標籤於; 用籤條標明: *He labelled the parcel before posting it.* 郵寄包裹前, 他在包裹上貼上標籤. *past* 過去式和過去分詞 **labelled**. (*US* 美 **labeled**).

labia ['leibiə] *pl* of **labium**. labium 的複數.

labium ['leibiəm] *nc* **1** lip or liplike organ liplike fold of the vulva 唇; 唇狀器官; 陰唇. **2** lower lip of a labiate corolla (唇狀花冠的) 下唇瓣.

labor ['leibə*] *US* form of **labour**. Labour 的美國拼寫形式.

laboratory [lə'bɔrətəri] *nc* building or room in which scientific work, teaching and tests are carried out 實驗室.

laborious [lə'bɔ:riəs] *adj* (with reference to things) requiring hard work; not easy 勤勞的; 困難的; 費力的: *They had the laborious task of cutting down the huge tree.* 他們接受砍大樹的艱苦工作. **laboriously** *adv*.

labour[1] ['leibə*] (*US* 美 **labor**) **1** *nc/u* hard work 勞動: *They have succeeded by their own labours.* 他們靠自己的勞動成功了. **2** *nu* persons who work with their hands and are not employers or owners of a business;

the working class 勞工; 工人階級: *This country has not enough skilled labour.* 這個國家沒有足夠的熟練工人. *The factory has had trouble with its labour.* 廠方跟勞工鬧糾紛. **'labour exchange** see 見 **exchange**. **'Labour Party** the British socialist party (英國)的工黨. **'laboursaving** *adj* made to reduce hard work 減輕勞動的; 節省勞力的; 省力的: *They have a modern house which is full of labour-saving devices.* 他們有一幢省力裝置完備的現代化房子.

labour[2] ['leibə*] (*US* 美 **labor**) *vt / i* **1** work hard 努力工作; 勞動: *I laboured at the English course for two years.* 兩年來我努力學習英語課程. **2** move with difficulty 艱難地移動; 費力地前進: *They laboured through the thick forest and up the steep hill.* 他們艱難地通過森林爬上陡峭的小山. **labourer** *nc* person who does hard unskilled work without machinery 勞工; (做艱苦無需技能工作的) 工人; 苦力.

labrum ['leibrəm] *nc* **1** lip or liplike part 唇; 唇狀部份. **2** upper lip of insects and certain other arthropods (昆蟲或其他某些節肢動物的)上唇. *pl* 複數 **labra** ['leibrə].

laburnum [lə'bə:nəm] *nc / u* type of small tree with yellow flowers 金鏈花.

labyrinth ['læbirinθ] *nc* number of paths which cross one another in so many different ways that one easily becomes lost in them 迷宮.

lace [leis] **1** *nu* material like a net, made of cotton, linen, silk etc, with the threads making patterns 花邊; 飾邊: *The tablecloth has lace round the edges.* 這塊桌布的邊上飾有花邊. **2** *nc* string put through holes and pulled tight to fasten the two edges of something together (e.g. *shoelaces*) 帶; 繫帶 (例如鞋帶). Also 亦作 *vt / i* fasten with a lace 用帶繫牢: *He laced (up) his shoes.* 他繫好鞋帶. **lacy** *adj* of or like lace 花邊的; 似花邊的; 帶狀的.

lacerate ['læsəreit] *vt* wound by tearing the flesh 撕裂; 劃破.

lack [læk] *vt / i* not have something which is needed 缺乏; 短少; 沒有: *They lack the courage to do it.* 他們缺乏勇氣幹這種事. Also 亦作 *nu*: *I cannot buy it because of my lack of money.* 因爲沒錢, 我不能買; *They are ill for lack of good food.* 他們因缺乏好的食物生病了.

lackadaisical [ˌlækə'deizikl] *adj* appearing or pretending to be without energy or interest (裝作)無精打采的; (裝作)懶洋洋的: *He has a very lackadaisical attitude towards his work.* 他的工作態度是懶洋洋的.

laconic [lə'kɔnik] *adj* saying something in the fewest possible words; brief 說話簡短的; 簡潔的; 簡明的: *He gave laconic answers to all our questions.* 他對我們提出的所有問題作了簡短的答覆.

lacquer ['lækə*] *nu* **1** type of paint which when it dries gives a hard, bright surface (used for painting metal and wooden articles) 漆. **2** liquids sprayed on hair to keep it in place (固定髮型的)髮蠟, 定型劑. Also 亦作 *vt* cover with lacquer 塗漆於.

lactic ['læktik] *adj* of or obtained from milk 乳的; 乳汁的: *lactic acid* 乳酸.

lacy ['leisi] *adj* see 見 **lace**.

lad [læd] *nc* boy; young man. (*informal*) 男孩; 少年; 青年男子; 小伙子. (非正式).

ladder ['lædə*] *nc* **1** apparatus made of two long pieces of wood, metal or rope, joined together by short pieces (called **rungs**) up which one climbs 梯子. **2** (*Brit*) tear in a woman's stocking which has the shape of a ladder (英)(女長襪上因抽絲形成的)梯形裂縫. (*US* 美 **run**). Also 亦作 *vt / i* have, cause to have, a ladder in one's stocking (使)襪子抽絲: *She has laddered her best stockings.* 她最好的長襪子抽絲了.

laden ['leidn] *adj* carrying something heavy; loaded 負重的; 載滿的: *The bushes were laden with fruit.* 灌木叢裏果實纍纍. *They arrived laden with luggage.* 他們滿載行李到達了.

ladle ['leidl] *nc* large, deep spoon with a long handle used for serving liquids 長柄杓.

lady ['leidi] *nc* **1** polite word for a **woman** (對婦女的文雅稱呼)女士: *There is a lady to see you.* 有一位女士要見你. *This shop sells ladies' hats.* 這家商店賣女帽. **2** woman of good family, of the upper classes (formerly, one just below the nobility); woman of wealth and leisure 貴婦人; 淑女: *Because she has a rich husband she lives like a lady.* 因爲她有一個有錢的丈夫, 所以她過着像貴婦人一樣的生活. **3** (**Lady**) (*Brit*) the title of the wife of a nobleman (below the rank of duke) or of a knight (e.g. *Sir Winston and Lady Churchill*) (英)…夫人(對公爵以下貴族或爵士的妻子的尊稱) (例如: 溫斯頓爵士和邱吉爾夫人). Also 亦作 with a first name as the title of a daughter of a nobleman (e.g. *Lady Jane*) (與名字連用, 對貴族女兒的尊

稱)…小姐(例如; 簡小姐). *Note* 說明:
the *masc* form is gentleman (先生),
therefore the polite way to address mixed company is *ladies and gentlemen*, *ladies*
is the usual form of address in the *pl*;
in the *sing* use *madam. Please come
in, ladies* but *Please come in, madam*
(although in *US* lady is also used.
Come this way, lady). *Woman* as a
form of address is rude. *Shut up,
woman!* But the uses of *lady* and
woman in other ways are not so
clear. *Woman* is generally less polite.
*She pays a woman to clean her house
twice a week. The woman who lives
next door is a nuisance.* On the other
hand, *woman doctor, woman lawyer
etc* are now used, not *lady doctor,
lady lawyer etc* which are rather *o.f.*
男性的稱呼是 gentleman (先生),因此
對男女混合的人羣的尊稱是 Ladies
and gentlemen (女士們, 先生們).
Ladies (女士們) 是複數的通常的稱呼,
單數用 madam (女士). 請進來, 女士們
(ladies),但請進來, 女士(madam). 儘管
在美國也用 Lady, 這兒走, 女士(lady).
woman 作稱呼是不禮貌的. Shut up,
woman! (住嘴, 女人!). lady 和
woman 在其他方面的用法並不如此明
顯. Woman 一般說是不大禮貌. 她雇一
個婦女打掃房子,一星期兩次. 住在隔壁
的女人是個討厭的人. 另一方面, 現在用
woman doctor (女醫生), woman
lawyer (女律師) 等, 不用 lady doctor
(女醫生), lady lawyer (女律師) 等, 這
些已頗爲舊式. **Ladies** *npl* public
lavatory for women 公共女廁所; 女盥
洗室. **'ladylike** *adj* like a lady; behaving as a lady should 貴婦人似的; 舉止
高貴的. (*opp* 反義詞 **unladylike**).
ladyship *nc* rank of a Lady 貴婦人的
身份. Also 亦作 sometimes used
when addressing or speaking about

one (有時用於稱呼或提到) 夫人(或小
姐): *Yes, Your Ladyship.* 是, 夫人.
Her Ladyship will see you now. 夫人
現在要見你. **'ladybird** type of small
insect 瓢蟲.

lag¹ [læg] *vi* move more slowly than
others 落後; *Some of the runners in
the race began to lag.* 在賽跑比賽中有
些人開始跟不上了. *The little boy lagged behind the older ones.* 這個小男
孩落在比他大一點的人的後面. *past* 過
去式和過去分詞 **lagged. 'time lag** delay in time between two happenings
遲延的時間; 時滯: *There was a time
lag between making the plan and carrying it out.* 在制訂計劃和執行計劃之
間有一段相隔時間.

lag² [læg] *vt* put material round a water
pipe, boiler etc to prevent freezing or
loss of heat 給水管, 鍋爐等加上護套
(以防結冰或散熱). *past* 過去式和過去
分詞 **lagged. lagging** *nu* material
used in this way (覆蓋水管, 鍋爐的)
護套; 防護套.

lager ['lɑːgə*] *nu* type of light beer 淡啤
酒.

lagoon [lə'guːn] *nc* lake (esp. a saltwa-
ter one) joined by a narrow channel
to the sea 鹹水湖.

laid [leid] past of **lay¹**. lay¹ 的過去式和
過去分詞.

lair [lɛə*] *nc* place where a wild animal
lives 獸窩; 獸穴.

laity ['leiəti] *n sing* (with **the**) persons
who are not clergy (單數) (與 the 連
用) 俗人; (未受神職訓練的) 信徒. see
also 參見 **lay³**.

lake [leik] *nc* large area of water with
land all round it 湖.

lam¹ [læm] *vt / i* beat; thrash; flog. (*informal*) 打; 鞭打; 抽打. (非正式): *lam
into somebody* i.e. thrash him 鞭打某
人 (非正式). *past* 過去式和過去分詞

lammed.

lam² [læm] *nc* (US 美) sudden flight or escape (esp. to avoid arrest). (*imformal*) 突然潛逃, 逃走. (非正式) . **on the lam** making an escape 在潛逃中 . **take it on the lam** escape or flee, esp. from the police (尤指從警察手裏)潛逃. Also 亦作 *vi* escape or flee 逃走, 潛逃 . *past* 過去式和過去分詞 **lammed.**

lamb [læm] **1** *nc* young sheep 小羊; 羔羊. **2** *nu* its flesh used as food 羔羊肉. **'lambswool** fine wool cut from lambs 細羊毛.

lame [leim] *adj* **1** not able to walk properly (usu. because a leg has been injured or is weak) 跛的: *The lame man needs a stick when he walks.* 那跛子走路時需帶一根手杖. **2** (with reference to an argument, excuse, reason etc.) weak; not satisfactory (指論據、辯解、理由等) 不充分的; 不能令人滿意的: *He gave a lame excuse for being late.* 他提出了不充分的理由爲遲到辯解.

lament [lə'ment] *vt / i* show great sorrow (usu. by crying); feel great sorrow 哀悼; 痛哭; 悲傷: *The children lament the death of their mother.* 孩子們哀悼母親的去世 . *They lament for her.* 他們哀悼她 . *We lamented over our bad luck.* 我們爲自己的不幸而悲傷. Also 亦作 *nc* cry or song of great sorrow 慟哭; 哀歌; 挽歌: **lamentable** ['læməntəbl] *adj* sad; causing regret 可悲的; 令人惋惜的: *His examination results were lamentable* i.e. were very poor, disappointing. 他的考試成績很差 (或令人失望). **lamentation** [læmən'teiʃən] *nc / u* act of lamenting; loud expression of sorrow 哀悼; 悲傷; 慟哭.

laminate ['læmineit] *vt / i* (with reference to wood, metal etc.) split, cause to split, into thin sheets or layers, make by putting these thin sheets together (指木材, 金屬等)分成薄片; 把…分成薄片; 用疊合薄片做成: *laminated wood* i.e. wood made by fixing several thin sheets of wood together, one above the other, cover with a thin layer of something (e.g. plastic) 膠合板, 層積木, 即: 幾塊薄木片一層疊一層覆以塑膠等薄層固定成的木材.

lamp [læmp] *nc* apparatus for giving light by using electricity, gas, oil etc. 燈. **'lamppost** long, metal post in a street which has a lamp on top 街燈柱, 路燈柱 . **'lampshade** covering of glass, paper or cloth etc put over a lamp 燈罩.

lance¹ [lɑːns] *nc* type of spear with a very long handle once used in war by soldiers on horses (從前騎兵用的)長矛 . **'lance corporal** soldier having the rank just above an ordinary soldier and just below a corporal 上等兵, 一等兵.

lance² [lɑːns] *vt* cut with a lancet 用柳葉刀切開: *The doctor lanced the boil on his hand.* 醫生用柳葉刀切開他手上的水泡 . **lancet** ['lɑːnsit] *nc* small knife used by doctors for surgery 醫生外科手術用的小刀; 柳葉刀; 刺血針.

land¹ [lænd] **1** *nu* firm part of the earth's surface which is not covered by sea 陸地: *After sailing for two days we reached land.* 我們航行兩天後到達陸地 . *They travelled by / by land and sea.* 他們曾在陸上和海上旅行. **2** *nc* particular part of the earth i.e. a country, which is the usual word (*land* is more literary) 國家(文學用語, country 是普通用語): *the land where I was born* 我出生的國家; *land of the free* 自由人民的國家. *He has* *lived in many lands.* 他在許多國家住過. **3** *nc/u* area of land which is owned 地產; 田地: *This farmer has a lot of land.* 這個農夫有很多田地. *All these lands belong to the church.* 所有這些田地屬於教堂. **4** *nu* soil; ground 土壤; 土地: *The land here is very fertile.* 這裏的土地很肥沃. *He does not get good crops because the land is poor.* 他沒有得到好收成, 因爲土地貧瘠. **landed** *adj* owning land; having land 擁有土地的; 有地的: *landed gentry* 擁有土地的紳士. **landlady 1** woman who owns land or a house which she allows somebody else to occupy as a tenant paying rent 女地主; 女房東. **2** woman who lives in a house, part of which she allows to be occupied by others for payment, (Meals are also often provided) 旅舍, 寄宿舍等的女主人(常常也提供膳食). **'landlocked** *adj* surrounded, or almost surrounded by land 被陸地包圍或幾乎包圍的: *a landlocked harbour* 一個幾乎被陸地包圍的港口. **'landlord 1** person who owns land or a house which he allows somebody else to occupy as a tenant paying rent 地主; 房東. **2** person who manages a pub, inn or lodgings 酒店, 旅舍或寄宿舍的主人. *Note* 說明: *landlord* can be used with reference to both a man and a woman; *landlady* is usu. used in sense 2 landlord 可指男的和女的; landlady 通常用於義 2. **'landlubber** (sailor's) word for somebody who is not a sailor (水手稱非水手的用語) 旱鴨子, 未下過海的. **'landmark 1** anything which can be clearly seen from a distance and so makes it easier to know where one is 遠處顯而易見的標誌; 陸標: *The large rock on top of the hill is a landmark to all the people who live nearby.* 山頂上的大岩石是住在附近所有人的一個陸標. **2** any great event which is remembered because of its important results (歷史上的) 重大事件: *The discovery of the cause of malaria was a landmark in the history of medicine.* 發現瘧疾的病因是醫學史上重大的事情. **'landowner** person who owns land 土地所有者; 地主. **'landscape** view or picture of an area of land; scenery 風景; 景色: *From the hill he looked down on the peaceful landscape.* 他從山上俯瞰寧靜的景色. **'landslide 1** fall of a great amount of rock and earth from the side of a hill 山崩. **2** sudden change of public opinion (esp. in politics when one party gets far more votes than is expected) (尤指一政黨意外地獲得) 壓倒多數票, 大勝利.

land² [lænd] *vt/i* **1** come, go, bring to land 登陸; (使)着陸; 卸下. *We landed in London last night* i.e. after travelling by air or sea. 昨晚我們在倫敦着陸(或登陸). 即: 乘飛機旅行後着陸或乘船旅行後登陸: *He landed the boat on the beach.* 他將小船攔在海灘上. *The fishermen landed many fish.* i.e. caught and brought to land. 漁民們卸下許多魚. 即: 捕到許多魚並帶上岸. **2** fall, cause to fall, into (使)陷入; (使)處於: *His laziness has landed him in trouble.* 由於懶惰他已陷入困境. *I landed myself in an argument with them.* 我跟他們發生爭論.

landing ['lændiŋ] *nc* **1** coming, or bringing, to the ground of an aeroplane; coming, or bringing, ashore from a ship (飛機)着陸; (從船上)上岸, 登陸: *The aeroplane made a safe landing.* 飛機安全着陸. **2** level part between two sets of stairs 樓梯平台. **'landing craft** type of flat-bottomed ship which can be run ashore so that the people in it can land easily 登陸艇. **'landing field** place where an aircraft can land 飛機着陸場. (Also 亦作 **landing strip). 'landing stage** place (often a floating one) where people and goods are landed from a ship 棧橋(常浮於水上,供人,貨登陸); 浮動碼頭. **'landing strip** see 見 **landing field.**

lane [lein] *nc* **1** narrow road in the country; narrow street 鄉村小道; 巷. **2** section of road (usu. marked by lines) allowing traffic going in the same direction to move side by side (路上劃線的)單向行車道: *The motorway has four lanes of traffic.* 高速公路有四條單向行車道. *Heavy vehicles should keep to the left-hand lane.* 重型車輛應靠左邊車道行駛.

language ['læŋgwidʒ] **1** *nu* expression of ideas and feelings by words or writing 語言. **2** *nc* particular type of such expression used by a race, nation or group 一個種族、國家或羣體使用的語言: *There are many African languages* 有許多種非洲語言; *the Russian language* 俄語; *legal / scientific / technical language* 法律/科學/專門術語. **3** *nc* any expression of meaning by signs or symbols 用言語表達意思的方法: *Deaf and dumb people use a finger language.* 聾啞人使用手語.

languid ['læŋgwid] *adj* weak; feeble; without much energy 弱的; 無力的; 沒精打采的.

languish ['læŋgwiʃ] *vi* become languid (usu. because one is without something) (通常因缺乏某物)變得衰弱無力; 無生氣, 不高興: *They languished in prison for many years* i.e. without freedom, news from home etc. 他們在獄中受苦多年. 即: 無自由、無家中的消息等. *Orphans languish in ... / for a*

mother's love i.e. they need it badly. 孤兒渴望母愛而苦惱. 即: 他們非常需要母愛.

lank [læŋk] *adj* (with reference to hair) long and straight; lifeless (指頭髮)長且直的; 無生氣的. **lanky** *adj* (with reference to persons) tall, thin and rather clumsy (指人)瘦長而難看的: *a lanky youth* 一個瘦長難看的年輕人.

lantern ['læntn] *nc* case with glass sides for protecting a candle or oil flame (usu. with a handle for carrying)燈籠; 提燈.

lap¹ [læp] *nc* front part of the body between the waist and the knees of somebody who is sitting. 人坐着時大腿膝上部份(腰與膝之間): *She sat by the fire with a book in / on her lap.* 她坐在爐火旁, 腿上放着一本書.

lap² [læp] *nc* once round a race or running track (跑道的)一圈: *The race was over two laps of the track.* 這次賽跑超過跑道的四圈. *He began to pass the other runners on the last lap.* 他在跑最後一圈時, 開始超過別的運動員.

lap³ [læp] *vt / i* **1** take food or drink into the mouth by using the tongue, as some animals do 舐: *The dog lapped (up) the water.* 那狗把水舐光了. **2** make a sound like an animal lapping its food 輕拍, 拍打: *The sea was lapping on / against the rocks.* 海浪拍打着岩石. *past* 過去式和過去分詞 **lapped.**

lapel [lə'pel] *nc* front part of coat, dress or jacket, below the collar, which is folded back 大衣, 連衣裙、上衣等的翻領: *He wore a badge in / on the lapel of his jacket.* 他在夾克衫的翻領上佩戴一枚徽章.

lapse [læps] *nc* **1** small mistake (e.g. in speaking, writing or behaviour) (說一個短暫的

話、書寫或行爲等的) 小錯誤: *a lapse of memory* 記錯. **2** failure to do what is right 失誤, 過失: *a lapse from his usual high standards of honesty* 他的道德上的過失. *a lapse into crime* 誤入法網. **3** period 一段時間: *after a long lapse of time* 一段長時間之後.

larceny ['lɑ:sənɪ] *nc / u* theft; stealing 偷竊; 偷竊行爲.

lard [lɑːd] *nu* pig's fat used for cooking 豬油.

larder ['lɑːdə*] *nc* room or cupboard where food is kept 食物貯藏室, 食櫥. see also 參見 **pantry.**

large [lɑːdʒ] *adj* of great size; big 巨大的; 大的: *He has a large farm and a large herd of cattle.* 他有一個大農場和一大羣牛. *They have a large area of responsibility.* 他們承擔廣大地區的職責. **largely** *adv* mainly 主要地; 大部份: *The people in the town are largely strangers to me.* 我對這城裏的人大部份都不認識. **'large'scale** *adj* on a large scale; big and important 大規模的, 大比例的; 大型的: *a large-scale map* 大比例尺繪製的地圖; *large-scale changes in our lives* 我們生活大幅度的變化. **at large 1** free; escaped from prison 自由的; 逃脫監獄的: *Two prisoners are at large in the city.* 兩個囚犯在城裏逍遙法外. **2** generally 一般地; 普遍地: *the world at large* 整個世界.

lark[1] [lɑːk] *nc* one of several kinds of small brown birds that often sing while flying 雲雀; 百靈鳥.

lark[2] [lɑːk] *nc* fun; amusing play 歡樂; 嬉要: *He did it for a lark* i.e. in fun. 他是爲了好玩而做的. Also 亦作 *vi* (often with **about**): *The children were larking about in the garden.* (both *informal*) (常與 **about** 連用) 孩子們在花園裏嬉鬧. (均爲非正式).

larva ['lɑːvə] *nc* insect in the caterpillar or grub stage of its life i.e. after coming out of its egg 昆蟲的幼蟲. *pl* **larvae** ['lɑːviː].

laryngitis [ˌlærɪn'dʒaɪtɪs] *nu* inflammation of the larynx 喉炎.

larynx ['lærɪŋks] *nc* the part of the throat, above the windpipe, which contains the vocal chords 喉.

lash[1] [læʃ] *nc* **1** long strip of leather or piece of cord used for striking animals or persons 鞭子. **2** blow given with a lash 鞭打, 抽打: *He gave the prisoner ten lashes.* 他打了這囚犯十鞭.

lash[2] [læʃ] *vt* **1** strike with a lash or whip 鞭打: *The rider lashed his horse to make it go faster.* 這騎馬的人鞭打馬讓馬跑得更快些. **2** strike, or move, violently or suddenly 猛擊; (海浪等) 沖擊: *The waves lashed (against) the sides of the ship.* 海浪沖擊着船舷. *He lashed out at them with his fists* i.e. he attacked them violently with his fists. 他用拳猛擊他們. *He lashed out at us* i.e. he criticized us severely, attacked us with bitter words. 他抨擊我們. 即: 他嚴厲地批評我們; 用激烈的言語攻擊我們. **3** tie tightly with string or rope 用線或繩綁緊: *They lashed their prisoner to a tree so that he would not run away.* 他們把囚犯綁在樹上, 這樣他就無法逃跑.

lass [læs] *nc* young woman. (informal and sometimes *o.f.*) 女孩; 少女 (非正式, 有時爲舊式).

laser ['leɪzə] *nc* (device that produces) a narrow and very intense beam of light 激光器; 激光 (俗稱鐳射): *They were cutting sheet metal with a laser.* 他們正在用激光切割金屬板.

lasso [læ'suː] *nc* rope which is thrown to catch horses and cattle 套索 (用以

捕捉馬、牛等). *pl* lassos or lassoes.
Also 亦作 *vt* throw a rope over in this
way 投套索捕捉.

last¹ [lɑːst] *adj* **1** following all the
others 最後的, 末尾的: *He was the
last person to leave.* 他是最後離開的
人. *December is the last month of the
year.* 十二月是一年的最後一個月.
(opp 反義詞 **first**). **2** just before the
present 就在現在之前的, 剛過去的:
*We met last night / week / month /
year.* 我們在昨晚／上週／上月／去年見
面. *The last few days have been cold.*
近幾天來一直是冷的; *last Saturday /
on Saturday last* 剛過去的星期六; *last
June* 剛過去的六月. (opp 反義詞
next). **3** most unlikely 最不可能的:
He is the last person to tell a lie. 他決
不會撒謊. **4** only remaining 唯一剩下
的: *This is your last chance to do it.*
這是你做這種事的最後一次機會. *We
spent the last days of our holiday at
home.* 我們在家度過假日的最後幾天.
Also 亦作 *adv*: *He laft last.* 他最後離
開. (opp 反義詞 **first**). *We last met
two years ago.* 我們上次見面是在兩年
前. (opp 反義詞 **next**). Also 亦作 *nu*:
He was the last of the visitors to leave.
他是參觀者中最後離開的人. *He has
spent the last of his money.* 他把唯一
剩下的錢都花光了. *He hasn't heard
the last of it* i.e. he will hear more later (usu. of something unpleasant). 他
還沒聽到事情的完結. (通常指不愉快的事). '**last-
'minute** *adj* done with little time left
最後一分鐘作出的, 緊急作出的: *The
headmaster had to make some 'last-
minute changes in the timetable.* 校長
不得不對時間表作出某些緊急的更動.

at (long) last finally; in the end (after waiting, trying etc for a time) 最
後; 終於: *At last he has passed the examination.* 最後他考試及格了. *My son
is home at last.* 我的兒子終於回家了.

last² [lɑːst] *vi* continue; be enough, be
good enough, for a particular period
of time 持續; (使) 足够; 維持; 耐久:
The war lasted five years. 這次戰爭持
續了五年. *Our money will not last until the end of the month.* 我們的錢無法
維持到月底. *This watch has lasted me
since I was a child.* 這塊錶我從小時候
用到現在. **lasting** *adj* continuing, for
a long time; permanent; strong 持久
的; 永久的; 耐久的.

latch [lætʃ] *nc* **1** small piece of wood or
iron used to fasten a door 門閂. **2**
type of simple door lock opened by a
latch key 門鎖, 彈簧鎖.

late [leit] *adj* **1** after the usual or proper time 遲的; 晚的: *He was late for
school.* 他上學遲到. **2** near the end of
a period of time 晚期的; 末期的: *He
came here in late June.* 他六月底來到
這裏. *He is a man in his late forties*
i.e. his age is between 45 and 50. 他是
個近五十歲的人. 即: 他的年齡在四十五
歲至五十歲之間. **3** just before the
present; recent 不久前的; 新近的: *the
late agreement between the two countries* 不久前兩國間的協議. *This newspaper has the latest news.* 這張報紙登
有最新消息. **4** dead 已故的: *the
funeral of the late President* 已故總統
的葬禮. Also 亦作 *adv*: *He always arrives late.* 他老是遲到. *He goes to bed
late and gets up late.* 他遲睡覺, 遲起
床. *Note* 說明: *latest* has only the
sense of the most recent. *last* has two
senses (a) most recent, (b) final; with
no others to follow. *Have you read
his last book?* i.e. either his most recent one or the one he wrote just before he died or before he stopped
writing etc. *latest* 只有最近的意義.

Last 有兩種意義(a)最近的,(b)最後的;
最末的. Have you read his last book?
即: 或是他最近的一本或是他臨死前寫
的那本或他停止寫作前的那本等. **late-
ly** *adv* recently 最近; 近來: *Have you
seen him lately?* 你最近見到過他嗎?
Note 說明: lately is usu. used in questions, in the *negative*, with *only*, or in
the phrase *as lately as* (e.g. *I haven't
been here lately. I came to this town
only lately. He came as lately as last
week).* Otherwise use *recently. I have
been here recently.* lately 通常用於問
題, 否定, 與 only 連用, 或用於 as lately as 短語 (例如: 我最近不在這兒. 我最
近才來此鎮. 他上週才來.) 在其他情況
用 recently. *I have been here recently.*
我最近在這兒. **at the latest** no later
than; not after 最遲; 至遲: *You must
finish your work by / on Friday at the
latest.* 你最遲星期五必須完成工作. **la-
ter on** afterwards; at a later time 以
後; 後來: *Can we talk about it later
on?* 我們可以以後談此事嗎? **sooner
or later** at some time or other 遲早;
總有一天.

latent ['leitnt] *adj* hidden; not active but
ready to be so 隱藏的; 潛伏的, 潛在
的: *Young children have many latent
abilities.* 少年兒童有許多潛在能力.

lateral ['lætərəl] *adj* of, at, to or from
the side; sideways 側面的; 旁邊的; 橫
的: *lateral buds* 側芽; *lateral position*
側翼位置.

lath [lɑ:θ] *nc* one of several thin narrow
strips of wood used to provide a support framework for plaster, tiles, etc.
(用以作灰泥、屋瓦等的支架的)板條.

lathe [leið] *nc* apparatus which makes a
piece of wood or metal turn round
quickly while it is cut and shaped 車
床, 鏇床.

lather ['lɑ:ðə*] *nu* foam made from

soap or detergent and water, or from
sweat 肥皂泡沫; 汗沫: *To shave properly you need a good lather on your
face.* 要把臉刮得乾淨, 你需要在臉上塗
上足量的肥皂泡沫. *After the race the
horse was in a lather* i.e. of sweat. 比
賽後該馬滿身汗水. Also 亦作 *vt / i*:
This soap does not lather easily. 這肥
皂不易起泡沫. *You must lather your
face before shaving.* 在刮臉之前, 你必
須在臉上塗肥皂沫.

Latin ['lætin] *nu* language of ancient
Rome 拉丁語. Also 亦作 *adj* of this
language; of peoples who speak modern languages descended from Latin
(e.g. French, Italian, Spanish) 拉丁語
的; 拉丁語系民族的(例如: 法國人的, 意
大利人的, 西班牙人的).

latitude ['lætitju:d] *nu* distance in degrees north or south of the equator
緯度; 緯線. see 見. **longitude.**

latrine [lə'tri:n] *nc* hole dug in the
ground for the waste matter from the
human body 廁所, 茅坑.

latter ['lætə*] *adj* **1** the second of two
just mentioned. (The first is the former.) (剛提及之兩者中的) 後者(前者
是 former): *John and James are
brothers. The former is a teacher; the
latter,* i.e. James, *is an engineer.* 約翰
和詹姆斯是兄弟. 前者是教師; 後者, 即
詹姆斯, 是工程師. **2** more recent 更近
的: *During the latter part of the lesson
we read our notes.* 後半堂課我們看筆
記. **latterly** *adv* more recently 最近,
近來.

laudable ['lɔ:dəbl] *adj* worthy of praise
值得稱讚的: *a laudable attempt to do
better* 值得稱讚的試圖幹得更好的努
力.

laugh[1] [lɑ:f] *vt /i* make sounds which
show amusement or pleasure 笑; 發
笑: *They laughed loudly when I told*

them the story. 我把這件事告訴他們時，他們都大笑起来. **laughable** *adj* causing amusement; ridiculous 有趣的; 可笑的: *a really laughable attempt* 一個實在可笑的嘗試. **laughing** *adj* showing amusement or pleasure 帶笑的; 高興的: *They all had laughing faces.* 他們都笑容滿面. **'laughing stock** someone / something people laugh at, make fun of 笑柄; 被人嘲笑的人或事物: *Because of his stupid mistakes he became the laughing stock of the whole school.* 由於他的愚蠢的錯誤, 他成了全校的笑柄. **laugh at someone / something 1** be made to laugh by something 因…而發笑: *They laughed at my story.* 他們聽了我的叙述都笑了. **2** show contempt for, make fun of 漠視, 一笑置之; 嘲笑: *They laughed at their own failure.* 他們對自己的失敗一笑置之. *He laughs at us when we try to help.* 我們試圖幫助時, 他嘲笑我們.

laugh² [lɑːf] *nc* sound showing amusement or pleasure; act of laughing 笑聲; 笑: *They gave a loud laugh when I told them the story.* 我把這件事告訴他們聽時, 他們都大笑. *He's a laugh* i.e. he's an amusing character. (*informal* in the example) 他是個逗人笑的人. (此例爲非正式).

laughter [ˈlɑːftə*] *nu* act or sound of laughing 笑; 笑聲: *The laughter of the crowd could be heard everywhere.* 到處可聽到人羣的笑聲.

launch [lɔːntʃ] *vt* **1** (with reference to a ship) put into the water for the first time 使 (新船) 下水. **2** begin; get started 着手; 開始: *The government has at last launched a new plan to build more houses.* 政府終於着手進行一項增建房的新計劃. *They're holding a big party to launch the new film* i.e.

to introduce it to the public. 他們舉行大規模聚會首次放映這部新影片. 即: 把它介紹給公衆. **3** send 發射; 發出: *The Americans and Russians have launched many rockets into space.* 美國人和俄國人已把許多火箭發射至太空. *The enemy launched an attack against us at dawn.* 敵人於拂曉時對我們發動進攻. Also 亦作 *nc* **1** motorboat used for travelling short distances 遊艇. **2** launching of a ship or rocket (船的) 下水; (火箭的) 發射. **launching** *nc* act of launching 下水; 開辦; 發射. **'launching pad** place from which a rocket or missile is launched into space 火箭或導彈發射台.

launder [ˈlɔːndə*] *vt / i* wash and iron clothes 洗燙衣服 **launderette** [ˈlɔːndˈret] *nc* laundry where coins are used to operate automatic machines which wash clothes etc. 自動洗衣店. **laundry** [ˈlɔːndri] **1** *nc* place where clothes are washed and ironed 洗衣房; 洗衣店. **2** *nu* clothes sent to this place; clothes which need to be laundered 送洗衣店去洗的衣物; 待洗的衣物: *She is helping her mother with the laundry.* 她幫助她母親洗衣服.

laurel [ˈlɔrl] *nc* type of small tree with evergreen leaves used in ancient times as a sign of honour or victory; bay tree 月桂樹(古代用作榮譽或勝利的象徵).

lava [ˈlɑːvə] *nu* melted rock coming out of a volcano and becoming hard when cool 熔岩.

lavatory [ˈlævətəri] *nc* room for getting rid of waste matter from the body; water closet 衛生間; 厠所.

lavender [ˈlævəndə*] *nu* **1** type of plant with small, blue, sweetsmelling flowers which can be dried and used as a scent 歐薄荷；薰衣草. **2** colour of lavender flowers 淡紫色. Also 亦作 *adj*.

lavish ['lævɪʃ] *adj* generous; extravagant 慷慨的, 大方的; 浪費的: *He gave his friends lavish gifts.* 他送給他的朋友豐富的禮物. *He was lavish in his help to others.* 他慷慨助人. Also 亦作 *vt* give generously or extravagantly. 慷慨地給予; 過多地贈送: *They lavished their attention on us.* 他們過於注意我們.

law [lɔː] **1** *nc* rule made by the government or other authority 法規、法令；規則: *The laws of the country are made by Parliament.* 這個國家的各項法規是由議會制定的. *There is no law in this country against living where you want to.* 在這個國家沒有法規禁止自由遷居. *The laws of football do not allow the players to fight.* 足球的規則不允許運動員打架. **2** *nc* scientific rule or principle which has been discovered 定律；規律；法則: *the law of gravity* 地心引力定律; *an important law in chemistry* 重要的化學定律; *the laws of nature* 自然法則. **3** *nu* (with the) laws as a whole (esp. those of a country) (與 the 連用) 法律: *All citizens should obey the law.* 所有的公民都應守法. *If you break the law you will be punished.* 如果你犯法, 你將受到懲罰. **4** *nu* (without **a** or **the**) science or principles of laws or particular types of laws (不用 a 或 the) 法學；法律學；特殊法規: *My brother is studying law.* 我的弟弟在攻讀法律. *He is an expert in company / criminal / international law.* 他是公司法/刑法/國際法的專家. **lawful** *adj* according to, allowed by, the law 合法的; 法定的; 法律許可的. (*opp* 反義詞 **unlawful**). **lawfully** *adv* **lawyer** ['lɔːjə*] *nc* person who is skill-

ed in law and practises it 律師. '**law-abiding** *adj* obeying the law 守法的. '**law court** court where it is considered whether or not persons have broken the law and where punishment is decided upon 法庭. '**lawsuit** request made to a law court in order to get back something lost or to be paid for a damage suffered 訴訟: *They brought a lawsuit against them for refusing to pay back the money he lent them.* 由於他們拒還欠款. 他對他們提出訴訟.

lawn [lɔːn] *nc* area of grass which is cut very short and is well cared for (e.g. in the garden of a house) (經過修剪, 精心管理的) 草地, 草坪 (例如: 房子花園中者) '**lawnmower** machine for cutting grass very short 割草機. '**lawn 'tennis** game played by two or four players who hit a ball across a low net between them 草地網球. *Note* 說明: it is usu. called *tennis*. Although its full name is *lawn tennis*, the game is not only played on a lawn, but on hard surfaces as well. 雖然它的全稱是草地網球, 但是這種運動不只是在草地上進行, 也在堅硬的地面上進行.

lawyer ['lɔːjə*] *nc* see 見 **law**.

lax [læks] *adj* careless; not severe 疏忽的; 馬虎的, 不嚴格的: *lax behaviour* 散漫的行爲; *lax discipline* 鬆懈的紀律.

laxative ['læksətɪv] *adj* causing the contents of the bowels to move easily 通便的. Also 亦作 *nc* medicine which does this 通便劑; 輕瀉劑.

lay¹ [leɪ] *vt / i* **1** put down; place 放下; 安置; 擱: *Lay the sticks on the ground.* 把柴放在地上. *He laid the book on the table.* 他把書放在桌上. **2** (with reference to eggs) produce 下 (蛋), 產

(卵): *Birds lay eggs.* 鳥下蛋. *My hens are laying well.* 我的母鷄很會下蛋. **3** make ready 準備; 安排: *lay the table* i.e. make it ready for a meal 擺設餐具, 即: 準備吃飯; *lay a floor with carpets* 把地毯鋪在地板上; *lay a fire* i.e. make it ready for lighting 準備生火; *lay a trap* 設置陷阱; *lay breakfast / lunch / dinner / supper* make a table ready for these meals 準備開早飯/午飯/正餐/晚飯. **4** put down money as a bet 下賭注; 打賭: *Don't lay money on that horse. It won't win.* 別在那匹馬上下賭注; 它不會贏. *I'll lay you a pound that the horse will win* i.e. I shall make a bet of a pound with you. 我和你打賭一鎊, 這馬會贏. *past* 過去式 and past participle 過去分詞 **laid** [leid] '**layabout** *nc* lazy person. *(informal)* 懶漢(非正式). **lay / put / keep something aside / by 1** put down; stop using 放下, 把…擱置一旁; 停止使用. **2** save for the future 貯存(以備將來之用); 儲蓄: *I have laid aside enough money for our holidays.* 我已儲蓄了足夠的錢以備我們度假用. '**lay-by** *nc* place where a special road has been made so that traffic can stop and drivers can have a rest 路旁停車處. **lay something down 1** put down 放下; *Lay down the sticks.* 把柴放下. **2** give up; surrender 放棄; 交出: *He laid down his life for his country.* 他爲國家獻出自己的生命. *The soldiers laid down their arms* i.e. handed over or surrendered their weapons. 士兵們交出他們的武器. **3** (with reference to rules, principles etc.) make 制定(規則、原則等): *The headmaster has laid down new rules about work in the evening.* 校長已制定了晚間作業的新規則. **lay someone off** cause to stop working (often temporarily) 使停止工作, 解雇(常指暫時

地): *The factory laid off 100 men last week* i.e. stopped employing them. 這家工廠上週解雇了一百工人. **lay something on** arrange; supply 安排; 提供: *The pupils are laying on a big concert for the visitors. (informal)* 學生們正在爲來賓安排一場大型音樂會. (非正式). **lay something out 1** arrange something so as to be ready 佈置; 準備: *His wife has laid out all the clothes he will need for the journey.* 他妻子已爲他準備好旅行所需的所有衣服. *They laid out the body / corpse* i.e. made it ready for burial. 他們準備埋葬屍體. **2** plan; arrange according to a plan 設計; 佈置: *The new town is laid out to keep factories and houses as far apart as possible.* 這座新城是以工廠盡量遠離住房的原則設計的. '**layout** *nc* plan; arrangement 設計; 安排, 佈局: *the layout of the new town* 新城的佈局. **lay one's hands on 1** seize; catch 抓住; 捉住, 逮住: *The police are waiting to lay (their) hands on him.* 警察等着抓他. **2** find. 找到: *I can't lay my hands on the letter he sent me.* 我找不到他寄給我的信.

lay¹ [lei] past tense of *lie²*. Lie 的過去式.

lay² [lei] *adj* of or by persons who are not clergy or who do not belong to a profession (esp. that of law or medicine) 普通人的; 凡俗的(對牧師而言), 非屬於專門職業的; 外行的(尤指對法律和醫學而言): *the lay mind* i.e. the mind or opinion of persons who are not experts 外行的意見, 即: 非專家的意見. see also 參見 **laity.** '**layman** person who is not an expert 門外漢, 外行.

layer ['leiə*] *nc* something that lies or is spread on top of or between something else; horizontal division in thickness 層: *The cake has a layer of jam inside.* 這蛋糕裏有一層果醬. *The earth's surface is made up of many layers of rock.* 地球的表面是由許多層岩石構成的.

laze [leiz] *vt / i* be lazy; pass the time without doing anything 懶散; 懶散地混(時光), 混日子: *We lazed (away) the whole week.* 我們懶散地混過一整週. **lazy** *adj* unwilling to work or to be active in any way 懶惰的; 懶散的, 慢吞吞的: *He comes to school by bus because he is too lazy to walk.* 他乘公共汽車來上學, 因爲他太懶了不願走路; *a lazy morning* i.e. a morning when one does nothing or very little 令人懶洋洋的上午, 即: 一上午甚麼事也沒做, 或做得非常少. **lazily** *adv* **laziness** *nu* **'lazybones** person who is lazy 懶漢, 懶骨頭. *pl* 複數 **lazybones.** *(informal)* (非正式).

lea¹ [li:] *nc* meadow, grassy field, or pasture; grassland 草地; 牧場; 草原.

lea² [li:] *nc* unit for measuring lengths of yarn, usu. taken as 80 yards for wool, 120 yards for cotton and silk, and 300 yards for linen 縷, 小絞 (通常指毛紗長80碼; 棉紗長120碼; 麻紗長300碼).

lead¹ [led] *nu* **1** soft, heavy metal, grey in colour, used on roofs and for making pipes, etc because it does not rust (Pb) 鉛. **2** graphite used in pencils (鉛筆中的)鉛心: *lead pencils* 鉛筆. *He is sharpening his pencil because the lead is broken.* 他在削鉛筆, 因爲筆心斷了.

lead¹ [li:d] *vt / i* **1** show by going first; guide 帶領; 引導: *He led us through the forest to the river.* 他帶領我們穿過森林來到河邊. *I led the blind man across the road.* 我領着盲人橫過馬路. **2** be in first place; be in front of 居首位; 領先: *He is leading in the race / competition.* 他在賽跑/比賽中領先. *Our football team leads theirs by two goals.* 我們的足球隊比他們隊領先兩分. **3** be in charge of; direct 領導, 率領; 指揮: *He will lead the party of scientists going to London.* 他將率領這批科學家去倫敦. *He led the expedition to Africa.* 他率領探險隊去非洲. **4** go 通, 達: *This road leads to our house.* 這條路通往我們的住宅. *One path leads down to the river. The other leads up the hill.* 一條小路通往河流, 另一條通向山上. **5** pass; spend 過; 使過: *They lead a quiet life.* 他們過着安靜的生活. *past* 過去式和過去分詞 **led** [led]. **leader** *nc* **1** person who leads 領導者, 領袖. **2** article in a newspaper in which the editor gives his opinions about the most important news. (報紙的)社論. (Also 亦作 **leading article**). **leading** *adj* most important 最重要的: *the leading newspapers* 主要的報紙; *the leading members of the committee* 委員會的主要成員. **leadership** *nu* state or powers of being a leader 領導; 領導權. **'leading lady** actress with the most important part in a play 女主角. **lead the way** show the way by going in front 引路, 帶路.

lead² [li:d] **1** *n sing* (with **a** or **the**) example; help, guidancc (單數) (與 a 或 the 連用)榜樣; 幫助; 引導: *We could not get the correct answer until the teacher gave us a lead.* 直到老師給我們提示, 我們才找到正確的答案. *They follow the lead of the older men.* 他們效法老人. **2** *n sing* (with **the**) first or most important place (單數) (與 the 連用)首位; 最重要的地位. *He is in the lead in this race.* 他在這次賽跑中居首

位. *He took the lead at the beginning.* 開始時他領先. *He has / plays the lead in the school play* i.e. the most important part to be acted. 他在學校演戲擔任主角. **3** *n sing* amount by which somebody / something is in front or ahead (單數) 領先的量. *Our football team has a lead of two goals.* 我們的足球隊領先兩分. **4** *nc* something which leads to, or joins, something else 引線; 導線: *The leads on the battery are dirty* i.e. the wires joining it to a motor, radio etc. 電池的引線很髒. 即: 連接電池至馬達、無線電設備等的電線很髒. **5** *nc* chain, rope or strap for leding an animal (esp. a dog) 牽動物 (尤指狗) 的鍊、繩或皮帶: *He had kept his dog on a lead in the public park.* 在國家公園裏他牽着狗.

leaf [li:f] *nc* **1** one of the many small, flat parts that grow on a plant or tree (usu. green when growing and brown or yellow when they fall off or are about to fall off) 葉: *The leaves of the trees gave us good shade.* 樹葉給我們提供很好的樹蔭. **2** one of the parts of the top of a table which can be raised on a hinge or put in to make the top larger (撑起來或插入即可增大桌面的) 活動桌板. *pl* 複數 **leaves** [li:vz]. **leafy** *adj* having many leaves 多葉的. **leaflet** ['li:flit] *nc* printed sheet of paper containing an advertisement, a notice of a meeting etc. 傳單; 散頁印刷品.

league¹ [li:g] *nc* measure of distance equal to about 3 miles or 5 kilometres 里格(長度名, 約等於三英里或五公里).

league² [li:g] *nc* **1** group of persons or nations who agree to help one another; the agreement made by this group 聯盟, 同盟; 盟約: *The League of Nations was formed after the First World War to try to keep peace.* 國際

聯盟是在第一次世界大戰後爲努力維護和平而成立的. **2** group of sports teams who play matches against each other 運動競賽聯合會: *This football team is at the top of the league* i.e. it has won the most matches in its group of teams. 這個足球隊在聯合會裏名列前茅. 即: 它在聯合會的比賽中贏的場數最多. **in league with** joined together with (usu. for a dishonest purpose). 與…聯合; 與…勾結.

leak [li:k] *nc* **1** crack or hole which allows a liquid or gas to flow in or out when it should not 漏; 漏洞: *We have no water because of a leak in the water pipe* i.e. a hole allowing water to run out. 由於水管漏, 我們沒有水. *There is a leak in the boat* i.e. a hole allowing water to come in. 小船有個漏洞. 即: 水從洞灌進來. **2** liquid or gas which flows in or out in this way 漏進或漏出的液體或氣體. Also 亦作 *vt / i* **1** flow, allow to flow, in or out through a leak 漏; 使滲漏: *The water leaked from the pipe.* 水從管裏漏出來. *The boat is leaking.* 這隻船漏了. **2** (with reference to information and news) become, allow to become, known when it should not be known (指情報和消息) 洩漏; 使洩漏: *News of the changes in government has leaked out.* 政府變動的消息已洩漏出去. **leaky** *adj* having a leak 有漏隙的; 漏的: *a leaky roof* 漏的屋頂.

lean¹ [li:n] *adj* (with reference to persons and animals) not having much fat; thin (指人和動物) 少脂肪的; 瘦的: *lean meat* i.e. meat which has very little fat 瘦肉. 即: 很少脂肪的肉.

lean² [li:n] *vt / i* **1** slope; bend; rest at an angle 傾斜; 傾身, 彎; 斜靠, 倚: *The trees lean in the strong wind.* 在大風中樹垂風吹斜了. *He was leaning over* *his desk.* 他俯身在書桌上. *The ladder is leaning against the wall.* 這梯子靠在牆上. **2** cause to slope, bend or rest at an angle; put 使傾斜; 使傾身; 使斜靠; 放: *He leaned his arms on his desk.* 他兩肘靠在書桌上. *I leaned the stick against the wall.* 我將手杖靠在牆上. **3** (with **on** or **upon**) need (與 on 或 upon 連用)需要: *They always lean on / upon us when they are in trouble.* 他們有困難時, 總是依賴我們. *past* 過去式和過去分詞 **leaned** or **leant** [lent]. **leaning** *nc* (with **towards**) interest in; tendency (與 towards 連用)嗜好; 傾向: *Their leanings are towards education for everybody.* 他們傾向於全民教育. **'lean-to** *nc* small building with a sloping roof built against the wall of a larger building 披屋(單斜面屋頂之屋, 其屋頂的一邊緊靠在另一大屋的牆壁上).

leap [li:p] *vt / i* jump; go, cause to go, over, by jumping 跳; (使)跳: *He leapt into the river.* 他跳進河裏. *past* 過去式和過去分詞 **leapt** [lept]. Also 亦作 *nc* **'leapfrog** game in which children jump over each other's backs 跳蛙遊戲, 跳背遊戲. **'leap year** year which has 366 days instead of the usual 365. (In a leap year, February has 29 days instead of 28. It comes every fourth year.) 閏年(在閏年, 二月份有29天而不是28天, 每隔四年一次).

learn [lə:n] *vt / i* **1** gain knowledge or skill 學習; 學會: *We go to school to learn.* 我們上學學習. *I am learning (to speak) English.* 我在學(講)英語. *He is learning (how) to play football.* 他在學(如何)踢足球. **2** be told 聽到; 獲悉: *We learnt / learned the news this morning.* 我們今天早上聽到這消息. *I learnt / learned of his arrival or I learnt / learned that he had arrived.*

我獲悉他已到達. *past* 過去式和過去分詞 **learned** or **learnt. learner** *nc* person who is learning 學習者. **learning** *nu* act of knowledge (esp. gained by study) 學問; 知識: *Our teacher is a man of learning.* 我們的老師是個有學問的人. *We admire his great learning.* 我們欽佩他學識淵博. **learned** ['lə:nid] *adj* having a lot of knowledge (esp. by study) 有學問的; 博學的: *Our teacher is a learned man* 我們的老師是一個有學問的人; *a learned book* i.e. one that needs much knowledge to understand or one which has been written by a learned man 一本學術著作, 即: 一本需要豐富的知識才能理解的書或一本有學問的人寫的書.

lease [li:s] *nc* agreement by which somebody allows somebody else to use a house or land for a certain time on payment of rent i.e. agreed sums of money paid from time to time 租約: *We have (taken) this house on a ten years' lease / on a lease of ten years.* 我們租了這幢房子, 租期十年. *After ten years the lease expires* i.e. comes to an end, is finished. 十年後租約滿期. Also 亦作 *vt* allow to use, or get the use of, a house or land in this way 租出; 租用(房子或土地): *He has leased the house to us for ten years.* 他把這房子租給我們爲期十年.

leash [li:ʃ] *nc* string or strip of leather for holding a dog (usu. fastened to a collar) 拴狗的皮帶, 皮條(通常拴在狗頸上的項圈上): *Dogs must be kept on the leash in this public park.* 在這個公園裏, 狗必須用皮帶拴住.

least [li:st] *adj / adv / nu* smallest; the smallest amount 最小的; 最少的; 最少; 最小: *He has least money of all of us.* 我們當中他的錢最少. *He works*

least. 他工作最少．*He has the least.*
他最少．*Note* 說明：*least* is the superlative of *little.* The comparative is
less. least 是 little 的最高級, 比較級是
less. **at least** not less than 至少：
There were at least 100 people i.e.
there were certainly 100 people, probably more. 至少有一百人, 肯定有一
百人, 或許更多．*Even if you tell nobody else you should at least tell me.*
即使你不告訴別人, 至少你要告訴我．
not in the least not at all, 一點也不：
'Are you tired?' 'Not in the least.' '你
累嗎?' '一點也不．' *They don't like
this teacher in the least.* 他們一點也不
喜歡這位老師．

leather ['leðə*] *nu* skin of an animal as
used for making shoes, bags etc. 皮
革. Also 亦作 *adj* made of leather 皮
革製的：*a leather coat* 皮上衣.

leave¹ [li:v] *vt / i* **1** go away from, either
for a long time or for ever 離開 (長時
期或永遠)：*He leaves for work every
morning at 8 a.m.* 他每天早上八點鐘
去上班．*My brother left school last
year.* 我弟弟去年離開學校．*His wife
has left him.* 他的妻子已離開他. **2**
allow or cause, to remain 把 ... 留在,
留下：*Did he leave a message for me?*
他有話留給我嗎? *Please leave your
books on the desk.* 請把你的書留在書
桌上．**3** allow or cause to remain in a
certain condition 聽任；使 ... 處於(某種
狀態)：*Leave him alone!* i.e. leave
him in peace! stay away from him! 別
打擾他! *She has left the door open.*
她讓門開着．**4** forget to take or bring
忘記：*I left my pen at home.* 我把筆忘
在家裏了．*He left his watch in the
hotel.* 他把錶忘在旅館裏了．**5** allow
or cause to remain over after doing
something 剩下, 剩餘：*If you take 2
from 6, 4 is left.* 從六減去二, 還剩四．

2 *from 6 leaves 4.* 六減二剩四．*If I
pay the bill, I shall be left with only
five pence.* 要是我付了賬, 我就只剩下
五個便士了．*Is there any coffee left?*
i.e. after others have had some. 有咖
啡剩下嗎?即：在其他人喝了一些之後.
6 trust; rely on; hand over 委託；信賴,
交給：*We are leaving him to do it.* 我
們委託他辦此事. *I'll buy the food but
I'll leave the cooking to you.* 我去買食
品但我要把煮飯的事交給你．**7** hand
over, give after one's death (死後) 遺
留：*My father died last month and left
all his money to my mother and me.*
我父親上月去世, 他將所有的錢都留給
我母親和我．Also with reference to
those in a family still alive after
somebody's death 也指某人死後家庭
裏還活着的人．*He left a widow and
one son.* 他死後遺下一妻一子. *past* 過
去式 and *past* 過去分詞 *left* [left]. **leave
something behind** forget to take or
bring 忘記携帶；遺忘：*I've left my coat
behind in the bus.* 我把上衣遺忘在公
共汽車上了. **leave someone / something out** not put in; forget to put in
遺漏；忽略：*He has been left out of the
football team* i.e. they have forgotten
or decided not to put him in. 他沒被
選爲足球隊員. 即: 他們忘了或決定不
選他. *You've left some figures out in
your calculations.* 你在計算中遺漏了
一些數字. **'left-overs** *npl* something
remaining or not finished 剩餘物：*After dinner the children ate the left-
overs* i.e. the food which had not been
eaten. 宴會後孩子們吃剩菜殘羹. 即: 沒
吃完的食物．

leave² [li:v] **1** *nu* permission to do
something (esp. to be absent from
one's work or duty) 許可, 准許；准假；
休假：*The headmaster gave us leave
to go to the concert.* 校長准許我們去

聽音樂會. **2** *nc* period of time during which one is allowed to be absent from work or duty (esp. in the army or civil service) 假期(尤指軍隊或文職機關中): *The soldiers are given two leaves each year.* 士兵每年有兩次假. *We are on leave until December.* 我們休假到十二月. *They were given six weeks' leave.* 他們獲准六星期的假. **3** *nu* (usu. with **take**) formal goodbye (通常與 take 連用) 告別; 離去: *I stayed for an hour and then took my leave* i.e. said goodbye to those who were there. 我逗留了一個小時, 然後告辭. 即: 向在那裏的人告別. *I took leave of my friends.* 我向朋友告別. **'sick leave** absence from work or duty because one is ill. 病假.

leaves [li:vz] pl of **leaf.** leaf 的複數.

lecherous ['letʃərəs] *adj* lustful, full of sexual desire 好色的, 淫蕩的; 色情的.

lecture [lektʃə*] *nc* **1** long talk giving information (esp. to students in a university) 演講; 講課(尤指對大學生). **2** long spoken warning or scolding 訓誡; 責罵, 譴責: *My father gave me an angry lecture for smoking* i.e. he was angry and told me not to smoke. 我父親責罵我抽烟. 即: 他很生氣, 要我別抽烟. Also 亦作 *vt/i: The professor lectures to his students twice a week.* 這位教授一星期給學生講課兩次. *My father lectured me for smoking.* 我父親責罵我抽烟. **lecturer** *nc* person who gives lectures (at a university, a junior member of the staff) 演講者; (大學的)講師.

led [led] past of **lead.** lead 的過去式和過去分詞.

ledge [ledʒ] *nc* narrow level place on a cliff, wall or anything which is very steep (懸崖、牆壁或任何直立物的)突出的狹長部份: *a window ledge* 窗台.

ledger ['ledʒə*] *nc* book in which accounts of money are written 帳簿, 總帳.

lee [li:] *nu* place on the side away from the wind, which gives shelter 背風處: *The ship stayed in the lee of the island during the storm.* 暴風雨期間這船停泊在島後避風處. **'leeway** **1** movement of a ship to the side away from the wind 風壓 (船隻受風影響向下風處偏離航線); **2** freedom to adapt or change a fixed plan 餘地.

leech [li:tʃ] *nc* type of worm which fastens itself to the skin and sucks blood 水蛭, 螞蟥.

leek [li:k] *nc* type of vegetable with green leaves and a white stem, smelling and tasting like an onion 韭.

leer [liə*] *vi* look in a cunning or evil way (狡猾地或不懷好意地)睨視, 斜眼瞧: *The old man leered at the girl.* 這老頭色迷迷地睨視這姑娘. Also 亦作 *nc*.

leeward ['li:wəd] *adj* in the direction towards which the wind blows 順風的; 在下風方向的. Also 亦作 *nu* side or direction towards which the wind blows 下風, 下風方向. Also *adv*.

left¹ [left] past of **leave.** leave 的過去式和過去分詞.

left² [left] *adj / adv / nu* of or on the side of a person's body where the heart is 左的; 在左邊; 左邊. (opp 反義詞 **right**). *Most people write with their right hand, not their left one.* 多數人用右手寫字, 而不用左手. *Turn left at the next corner.* 在下一個拐角處向左轉. *In Britain road traffic keeps to the left.* 在英國, 道路交通靠左邊走. **'left-hand** *adj* on the left side 左邊的. **'left-'handed** *adj* (with reference to a person) using the left hand rather than the right one (指人)慣用左手的,

左撇子. **the Left, the left wing** *n* sing or *pl* (politics) those who want great changes in government in favour of the working classes (e.g. socialists and communists). (單數或複數) (政治) 左翼 (例如: 社會黨人和共產黨人).

left-overs [ˈleftouvəz] *npl* see 見 **leave.**

leg [leg] *nc* **1** one of the two parts of the body used for standing and wlking 腿. **2** part of one's clothing which covers the legs (衣物遮蓋腿部的部分) 褲腿, 襪統, 靴統: *the legs of his trousers* 褲腳管. **3** part of a bed, chair, table etc on which it stands (床、椅、桌等的) 腿: *Most chairs have four legs.* 多數椅子有四條腿. **-legged** [ˈle-g(i)d] *adj*: *three-legged* i.e. having three legs 三條腿的. *bare-legged* i.e. having bare legs 光着腿的. **leggings** *npl* coverings for the legs made of strong cloth or leather 護脛, 護腿. **'legroom** space for one's legs when sitting (e.g. in a motorcar) (在汽車等裏面)供乘坐者伸腿的空間.

legacy [ˈlegəsi] *nc* **1** money or property left by somebody on his death to somebody else 遺產. **2** anything left from the past 遺留物; 傳代物: *One of the legacies of the war was famine.* 戰爭的後遺症之一是饑荒.

legal [ˈliːgl] *adj* of the law; according to the law 法律(上)的; 合法的. *I leave all legal matters to my lawyer.* 我把所有法律上的問題都委託我的律師處理. *Is it legal to marry one's cousin?* 和表兄(或表妹)結婚合法嗎? (*opp* 反義詞 **illegal**). **legally** *adv* legally. **le'galize** [ˈliːgəlaiz] *vt* make legal 使合法化: *The government has legalized gambling.* 政府已使賭博合法化.

legation [liˈgeiʃən] *nc* **1** all those below the rank of ambassador working for

their government in a foreign country 公使館全體人員. **2** their houses and offices there 公使館.

legend [ˈledʒənd] *nc* story from ancient times (not usu. a true one) 傳說; 傳奇: *the legends of Greece and Rome* i.e. stories about gods and goddesses in the early history of Greece and Rome 希臘和羅馬的傳說, 即: 古希臘和羅馬關於神的故事. **legendary** [ˈledʒəndri] *adj* found in legends; famous 傳奇中的; 著名的.

leggings [ˈlegiŋz] *npl* see 見 **leg.**

legible [ˈledʒibl] *adj* (with reference to handwriting, print etc.) able to be read (指筆跡, 印刷字體等) 易讀的; 清楚的: *In an examination your handwriting must be legible.* 在考試中, 你的字跡必須清楚易讀. (*opp* 反義詞 **illegible**). **legibly** *adv* **legibility** [ledʒiˈbiliti] *nu.*

legion [ˈliːdʒən] *nc* division of an ancient Roman army (about 5,000 men) 古羅馬軍團(約五千人).

legislate [ˈledʒisleit] *vi* make laws 制定法律, 立法. **legislative** [ˈledʒislətiv] *adj* **legislation** [ledʒisˈleiʃən] *nu* act of making laws; laws made 立法; 法律. **legislature** [ˈledʒislətʃə*] *nc* body of persons with power to make laws (e.g. a parliament or national assembly) 立法機關(例如: 議會或國民議會).

legitimate [liˈdʒitimət] *adj* **1** lawful 合法的. **2** reasonable; genuine 合理的; 真實的: *He has a legitimate excuse for being absent from school.* 他缺課有正當的理由. **3** born of parents who are married to each other 婚生的, 嫡出的: *a legitimate child* 嫡出子. (*opp* 反義詞 **illegitimate**).

leisure [ˈleʒə*] *nu* time when one is free from work; spare time 空閑; 閑暇: *He spends his leisure reading* *newspapers and magazines.* 他以讀報和看雜誌消遣他的閒暇. Also 亦作 adj: *I have little leisure time.* 我幾乎沒有空閒時間. **leisurely** adj without hurry; slowly 從容的; 緩慢的. **at one's leisure** without any rush 不急, 無須匆忙; *Finish the job at your leisure.* 你有空時完成這項工作.

lemon ['lemən] nc type of yellow, bitter-tasting fruit 檸檬. Also 亦作 adj **1** made from lemons 檸檬製的. **2** having the yellow colour of a lemon 檸檬黃的, 淡黃的. **lemonade** [lemə'neid] nu drink made from the juice of lemons, sugar and water 檸檬汽水, 檸檬汁.

lend [lend] vt allow somebody to have something only for a time 把…借給, 借出: *Will you lend me ten pounds?* i.e. give me ten pounds which I shall return to you later. 你借給我十鎊好嗎?即: 給我十鎊, 以後我將還給你十鎊. *He lent me his pen / He lent his pen to me.* 他把筆借給我. *past* 過去式和過去分詞 **lent** [lent]. **lend oneself / itself** allow oneself to be used to help something 參與; 有助於: *I refuse to lend myself to such a stupid plan.* 我拒絕參與此種愚蠢的計劃. *This music doesn't lend itself to dancing.* 這種音樂不適合跳舞. **lend a hand** help 幫助: *He lent me a hand with the heavy boxes. (informal)* 他幫我提沉重的箱子. (非正式).

length [leŋθ] nc measurement of something from one end to the other, period of time 長度; 一段時間, 期間: *The length of the stick is 2 metres / The stick is 2 metres in length* 這根棍子長 2 米; *a classroom 10 metres in length and 5 metres in breadth* 長10米寬5米的教室. *The length of time we were there was 2 hours.* 我們在那裏呆

了兩小時. **lengthen** vt / i become or make longer 變長; 使長; 加長. **lengthy** adj going on for a long time; very long 冗長的; 很長的: *a lengthy argument* 冗長的辯論. **lengthways, 'lengthwise** adj / adv along the length of something 縱長的(地): *He put the sticks lengthwise on the table* i.e. not across it. 他把棍子縱放在桌上. **at length 1** at last 終於. **2** for a long time; thoroughly; completely 長時間地; 徹底地; 完全地: *He explained the difficulty at great length.* 他詳細地講解難題.

lenient ['liːniənt] adj forgiving; not severe; merciful (esp. to somebody who has done wrong) 寬大的, 不嚴厲的; 仁慈的 (尤指對做錯事的人): *The headmaster is never lenient to / towards boys who tell lies.* 校長對說謊的學生從不寬恕. **leniently** adv **leniency** nu.

lens [lenz] nc piece of glass or substance like glass, with one or both sides curved (used in binoculars, cameras, glasses or spectacles, telescopes etc.) 透鏡 (用於雙筒望遠鏡, 照相機, 眼鏡, 望遠鏡等): *He has broken one of the lenses in his glasses.* 他打破了他眼鏡的一個鏡片. **'contact lens** see 見 **contact.**

lent [lent] past of **lend.** lend 的過去式和過去分詞.

Lent [lent] nu period of 40 days before Easter during which some Christians eat simple food, stop smoking etc. 四旬齋 (復活節前的四十天, 在此期間一些基督徒吃簡單的食物, 停止抽煙等).

lentil ['lentl] nc **1** type of plant with a small bean called 扁豆(植物). **2** the bean itself 扁豆.

leopard ['lepəd] nc large animal of the cat family which has a dark yellow coat with many black spots on it 豹.

leper ['lepə*] *nc* person who has the disease of leprosy 麻瘋病患者.

leprosy ['leprəsi] *nu* type of disease which slowly destroys the skin, the flesh underneath and the nerves 麻瘋病.

lesbian ['lezbiən] *nc* woman who sexually prefers other women to men 搞同性戀的女子.

less [les] *adj / determiner* smaller in amount, size, number 較少量的; 較小的; 較少數的. *They now do less work than they did before.* 他們現在做的工作比以前少. *He has less money.* 他的錢較少. *You should take less with you.* 你應身應少帶些(錢). (*opp* 反義詞 *more*). *Note* 說明: *less* is usu. used with a *nu* or a word in its *nu* sense. With a *nc* fewer should be used *They work on fewer days. You should take fewer boxes with you.* Less 通常與不可數名詞或意義上不可數的詞連用. 與可數名詞連用時應當用 fewer. *They work on fewer days.* 他們幹活的天數較少. *You should take fewer boxes with you.* 你應隨少帶些箱子. Also 亦作 *adv* to a smaller extent; not so much 更少(或更小)地; 較少(或較小)地: *Talk less and work more.* 少談話, 多工作. *You look less sad today.* 你今天不那麼愁容滿面了. *They are running less quickly.* 他們跑得不那麼快. (*opp* 反義詞 *more*). *Note* 說明: with *not*, *so* should be used instead of *less.* *You don't look so sad today. They are not running so quickly.* 與 not 連用, 應用 so 而不用 less. *You don't look so sad today*, 你今天不那麼愁容滿面了. *They are not running so quickly.* 他們跑得不那麼快. Also 亦作 *nu* smaller amount, size, time 較少量; 較小; 較少的時間. *He ate less of the food.* 他較少吃這種食物. *I bought it*

for less than ten pence. 我用不到十便士買了這個. (*opp* 反義詞 *more*). Also 亦作 *prep* minus 減去. *6 less 4 is 2.* 六減四餘二. **less and less** to an increasingly smaller extent as time passes 越來越小(或少)地. *As I spoke to him he became less and less angry.* 我和他講話時, 他的怒氣逐漸消失. (*opp* 反義詞 *more and more*). **more or less** see 見 **more.**

lessen ['lesn] *vt / i* become or make less 變少; 減少; 減輕.

lesson ['lesn] *nc* something which is to be learnt or taught; time spent in learning or teaching (usu. in a class) 課程; 功課; 一節課: *Afternoon lessons begin at 2 p.m.* 下午的課程在下午兩點鐘開始.

lest [lest] *conj* **1** in order that ...not; for fear that ... 以免; 惟恐: *We hid the money lest it should be stolen.* 我們把錢藏起來以免被偷. **2** (with **be afraid,** *fear*) that (與 be afraid, fear 連用) that (起連接從句作用, 無實際意思): *We were afraid lest it should be stolen.* 我們擔心它會被偷走.

let¹ [let] *vt* **1** (with *infinitive* but not *to*) allow (與無 to 的不定詞連用) 允許; 讓: *The headmaster lets them play football every Saturday.* 校長允許他們每星期六踢足球. *They want to play football on other days but he won't let them.* 他們想在其他日子踢足球但是他不允許. **2** (with **me, us, it** or **them**) as an *imperative* to express a wish, request, suggestion etc. (與 me, us, it 或 them 連用) 作爲祈使句表示希望, 請求, 建議等: *Let us / Let's go for a walk.* 我們散散步去. *Let me try.* 讓我試試. *Let him do it.* 讓他做. *Note* 說明: in the following examples of *let* with other words it should be noted that the position of these words can sometimes change the sense. *He let the boy go* has the sense of either he allowed the boy to go away or he stopped holding him. But *He let go the boy* has only the sense of he stopped holding him. Also *let him alone* has the sense of leave him alone; do not bother him, but *let alone him* has the sense of without him; not to mention him. 在下列 let 與其他詞連用的例子裏應注意到這些詞的位置有時會改變意思. He Let the boy go 有他 允許這男孩走開或他放開他之意. 但是 He Let go the boy 只有放開他的意思. 同樣, Let him alone 的意思是: 別打擾他. 但 Let alone him 的意思是: 沒有他; 別提他. **let somebody down** fail in a promise made to somebody; harm 對…失約; 損害: *He let his friends down by arriving late.* 他遲到了對他的朋友失約. **'let-down** nc disappointment *(informal)* 失望, 掃興. (非正式). **let something down** allow to fall; lower 放下; 放低: *He let down the rope to us / He let the rope down to us.* 他把繩子放下來給我們. **let someone / something in** allow to enter 讓…進來, 放進: *The roof lets in the rain.* 這屋頂漏雨. **let oneself in** get into a house or building by opening the door 開門進去 (房子裏): *Please don't wait until I return. I have a key and can let myself in.* 在我回來以前請不要等, 我有鑰匙能開門自己進來. **let somebody off** forgive; allow to escape severe punishment 從輕處理: *I'll let you off if you promise never to do it again.* 如果你答應決不再幹這種事, 我就饒了你. *The headmaster let me off with a warning* i.e. he could have punished me more severely but didn't. 校長寬恕我, 只給我警告了事. 即: 他原可嚴厲懲罰我但他沒有這樣做.

let something off 1 allow to come out 放掉: *This engine lets off steam.* 這部機車放掉蒸汽. **2** (with reference to guns etc.) fire (指槍等)射擊: *He let his revolver off at the crowd.* 他把左輪手槍對準人羣射擊. **let somebody out** allow somebody to go or come out 讓某人出來. **let something out 1** allow something to go or come out 讓…出來; 放出: *He let the air out of my tyres.* 他把我輪胎裏的氣放掉. **2** (with reference to clothes which are tight) make larger (指緊的衣服)放寬, 加長: *He has grown so much that he has had to let out his jacket.* 他長得這麼大, 只好把那長衣衫放寬, 加長. **let go** see *Note* above 見上面說明.

let² [let] *vt* allow somebody to use a house or land for a certain time on payment of rent i.e. agreed sums of money paid from time to time 出租 (房屋, 土地): *I have let my house to him while I am abroad.* 我在國外時我已將我的房子租給他了. *There are plenty of houses to let here.* 這裏有許多房子招租.

lethal ['li:θl] *adj* causing, able to cause, death 致命的; 可致命的.

lethargy ['leθədʒi] *nu* lack of energy; feeling of not wanting to do anything 無生氣; 嗜睡, 懶洋洋. **lethargic** [le'θɑːdʒik] *adj.*

letter ['letə*] *nc* **1** mark used in writing to represent a sound 字母: *A, B and C are letters (of the alphabet).* A, B 和 C 是 (字母表的) 字母. **2** message or account which is written or sent to somebody 書信, 函件: *Letters are usually sent by post.* 信件通常是郵遞的. **3** (in *pl*) (esp. with reference to literature) learning (用於複數)(尤指文學)學問: *a man of letters* 文人; 文學家. **lettering** *nu* style used in writing letters (in sense **1**) 字體: *The lettering on the front of the newspaper is large and clear.* 這報紙頭版的字體大且清楚. **'letterbox** box for receiving letters (in sense **2**) either inside a house or in a street or post office 信箱.

lettuce ['letis] *nc* type of vegetable with green leaves(usu. eaten uncooked) 萵苣(通常生吃).

leukaemia, leukemia [luːˈkiːmiə] *nu* disease of the blood 白血病.

levee ['levi] **1** embankment alongside a river constructed to prevent flooding 防洪堤: *the levees along the Mississippi* 密西西比河大堤. **2** quay 碼頭.

level¹ ['levl] *adj* **1** horizontal; flat; without hills 水平的; 平的, 平坦的; 無山的: *Football should be played on level ground.* 應在平地上踢足球. **2** making the same progress; equal 同等的; 相等的: *These two boys are about level in mathematics.* 這兩個男孩的數學成績不相上下. **'level 'crossing** *(Brit)* place where a road and railway cross on the same level (not passing over or under each other by means of a bridge or tunnel) (英)(公路與鐵路的)平交道. *(US* 美 **grade crossing).** **'level-'headed** *adj* (with reference to persons) steady; not easily upset (指人)穩健的; 頭腦冷靜的. **level off / out 1** make flat or even 使平; 使平坦: *level off a piece of wood* 削平一塊木頭. **2** come into a horizontal position 進入水平位置: *The pilot levelled off at 10,000 feet.* 這位飛行員在一萬英尺的高空作水平飛行.

level² ['levl] *nc / u* (esp. with reference to height) anything flat and horizontal (尤指高度)平面, 水平面: *The town is 5,000 feet above sea level* i.e. the level

of the sea. 這城高出海平面五千英尺. *Because of the heavy rain the level of the lake has risen 6 inches.* 由於大雨湖面已上升六英寸.

level³ ['levl] *vt / i* become or make level 變平; 使平: *They levelled the house to the ground* i.e. destroyed it so that nothing above the level of the ground was left. 他們把這房子夷爲平地. *past* 過去式和過去分詞 **levelled.** *(US* 美 **leveled)**

lever ['liːvə*] *nc* long bar or rod which pivots at one point so that when one part of it is pressed something attached to another part is moved (e.g. *gear lever* in a car) 槓桿 (例如: 汽車裏的變速槓). Also 亦作 *vt* move with a lever 用槓桿移動; 撬動. **leverage** *nu* power of a lever 槓桿所產生之力; 槓桿作用. **'gear lever** see 見 **gear.**

levity ['leviti] *nc / u* treating serious or important matters lightly or without respect 輕浮, 輕率.

levy ['levi] *vt* make somebody pay or give 徵 收: *The government levies taxes on motorists.* 政府向駕駛汽車者徵稅. Also 亦作 *nc* act of levying 徵收.

lewd [luːd] *adj* lustful; sexually improper 好色的; 淫蕩的.

liable ['laiəbl] *adj* **1** obliged by law to pay for 有(法律)責任的; 應付的: *He is liable for all the damage done by his workmen.* 他有責任賠償他的工人所造成的全部損失. **2** likely to do or suffer from 易於…的; 易患…的: *They are liable to run away if you speak to them.* 如果你對他們説話, 他們可能跑掉. *In winter I am liable to (get) bad colds.* 在冬天, 我常患重傷風. **liability** [laiəˈbiliti] **1** *nu* state of being liable 責任, 義務; (易於…的)傾向: *his liability for all the damage done* 他的賠償

造成所有損失的責任；*my liability to (get) bad colds* 我易患重傷風. **2** *nc (in pl)* debts（用於複數）債務.（*opp* 反義詞 **assets**）. **3** *nu* someone / something which causes trouble 引起麻煩的人（或事）：*He is a liability to us.* 他是我們討厭的人.

liaison [li:'eizɔn] *nu* cooperation; process of keeping the different parts of a large organization (esp. an army or armies) in touch with each other 合作；(尤指軍隊或軍隊間的）聯絡：*Victory depended on close liaison between the American and British armies.* 勝利取決於美、英軍隊間的密切合作.

liar ['laiə*] *nc* see 見 **lie.**

libel ['laibl] *nc / u* something printed or written which accuses somebody wrongly and so harms him; anything that harms somebody wrongly 誹謗人的圖片或文章；誹謗；中傷：*Editors of newspapers must be very careful that they do not publish libels.* 報紙的編輯必須非常謹慎，不發表誹謗人的文章. *Your silly letter is a libel on an honest man.* 你的無聊的信對誠實人是一種侮辱. Also 亦作 *vt* publish a libel about somebody（發表文章等）誹謗. *past* 過去式和過去分詞 **libelled.**（*US* 美 **libeled**）. **libellous** *adj.* Note 說明：*libel* strictly has the sense of something printed or written, not spoken, although it is often used informally about anything harmful. The correct word for something spoken in this way is slander. libel 雖然常常被非正式地用於指任何有害的事物，但嚴格地說它指印刷或書寫（不指口頭）的事物. 口頭的誹謗、中傷，其正確用詞是 slander.

liberal ['libərl] *adj* **1** generous; ready to give 大方的；慷慨的：*My father gives*

me a liberal amount of money each week i.e. more than enough for my needs. 我父親每星期給我大量的錢. 即：比我需要的錢還要多. *They were liberal in their help.* 他們慷慨地給予幫助. **2** able to understand others and sympathize with their ideas; broadminded 寬厚的；寬宏大量的；開明的：*Our headmaster has liberal views about what his pupils should wear.* 我們的校長對學生的穿著持開明的見解.（*opp* 反義詞 **illiberal**）. **3 (Liberal)** of the British political party interested in social reform 英國自由黨的. Also 亦作 *nc* **1 (Liberal)** member of the Liberal Party 自由黨黨員. **2** broad-minded person 寬宏大量的人；開明的人. **liberally** *adv.*

liberate ['libəreit] *vt* give freedom to 解放；釋放. **liberation** [libə'reiʃən] *nu* act of giving, or being given, freedom 解放；釋放；被釋放.

liberty ['libəti] **1** *nc / u* state of being free; of being able to do and behave as one wishes 自由；隨意. **2** *nc* (usu. with **take**) behaviour which may not be approved（通常與 take 連用）冒昧；失禮：*I took the liberty of using my friend's pen* i.e. I am not sure if he will approve. 我冒昧地使用我朋友的筆.即：我不能確定是否他會贊成. *You are taking too many liberties with the English language* i.e. you are using it too freely and in a way that cannot be approved. 你在濫用英語.即 at liberty free 自由的，隨意的：*You are at liberty to say what you like.* 你可隨意說你喜歡說的話. *The escaped prisoner is still at liberty.* 那逃犯仍逍遙法外.

library ['laibrəri] *nc* **1** room or building for keeping books 圖書室；圖書館. **2** the books kept there 藏書. **librarian** [lai'breəriən] *nc* person in charge of a library 圖書館館長; 圖書館管理員.

lice [lais] *pl* of **louse**. Louse 的複數.

licence ['laisns] (*US* 美 **license**) *nc* (usu. with a) right or permission given to do something; this right as it is written or printed (通常與 a 連用) 許可(證); 特許(證); 執照: *In Britain you must have a licence if you want to sell beer.* 在英國, 如果你要賣啤酒, 你必須持有執照. *Have you a driving licence?* 你有駕駛執照嗎? *This office deals with driving licences* i.e. the cards showing one has a licence to drive. 本辦公室辦理駕駛執照.

license ['laisns] *vt* give a licence to 發許可證給…; 許可; 特許: *This shop is licensed to sell tobacco.* 本店被特許賣烟.

lichen ['laikən] *nu* type of very short plant which grows on stones and trees 地衣; 青苔.

lick [lik] *vt* **1** pass the tongue over 舔: *He licked the stamp and stuck it on the letter.* 他用舌頭舔濕郵票把它貼在信上. **2** touch in the way a tongue does 像舌頭一樣伸吐; 捲過: *The flames of the fire licked the coal.* 火焰捲燒煤塊. Also 亦作 *nc* act of licking 舔: *He gave the stamp a lick.* 他用舌頭舔濕郵票. **licking** *nc* beating; defeat heavily; 擊敗: *Our team gave theirs a licking.* (informal) 我們的隊擊敗他們的隊. (非正式)

licorice ['likəris] *nc* / *u* see 見 **liquorice**.

lid [lid] *nc* cover on top of something which can be raised or taken off 蓋子: *the lid of a pot / box* 鍋/箱蓋.

lido ['laidou] *nc* place built for swimming and sunbathing 游泳池; 浴場. *pl* 複數 **lidos**.

lie¹ [lai] *vi* say something which one knows is not true 說謊: *He lied to me when he said he didn't do it.* 他對我說謊, 說他沒幹那件事. *pres part* 現在分詞 **lying** *past* 過去式和過去分詞 **lied.** Also 亦作 *nc*: *He told a lie.* 他撒了個謊. **liar** ['laiə*] *nc* person who lies or has lied 說謊的人: *You're a liar!* i.e. I do not believe what you have said. (*impolite*) 你撒謊! 即: 我不相信你說的話. (不禮貌)

lie² [lai] *vi* **1** be, remain, or rest, flat 平放; 平躺: *He was lying on the ground.* 他躺在地上. *I lay in bed all day.* 我整天臥床. *The papers are lying on the desk.* 報紙平放在書桌上. **2** be situated; be placed 位於; 處在: *Uganda lies far from the coast.* 烏干達遠離海岸. *The difficulty lies in their great poverty* i.e. is caused by their great poverty. 困難在於他們極爲貧窮. *What we do next lies with him* i.e. he must decide. 下一步我們怎麼辦取決於他. 即: 他必須決定. **3** remain in a particular state 保持在特定的狀態: *He lay dead on the floor.* 他倒斃在地板上. *The machine lay idle all week* i.e. was not used. 這機器整星期被擱着不用. *The road to the sea lay open before us.* 通向大海的路在我們面前展開. *pres part* 現在分詞 **lying.** *past tense* 過去式. **lay** [lei]. *Note* 說明: the *past part* is lain [lein] which is rather *o.f..* Therefore instead of *have lain* use *have been lying* (e.g. *The papers have been lying on your desk since yesterday*). 過去分詞是 lain, 頗爲舊式. 因此現在用 have been lying 而不用 have lain (例如 The papers have been lying on your desk since yesterday. 這些報紙從昨天起一直放在你的書桌上). **lie back** rest one's back on 躺; 背靠: *He lay back on the pillow.* 他靠枕頭躺着. **lie down** put oneself in a flat, resting position 躺下: *He told* his dog to lie down. 他叫狗躺下. *Why don't you go and lie down?* i.e. go to your bed and rest on it. 爲甚麽你不去躺下休息?即:上床去休息. **lie in** stay in bed in the morning longer than usual 睡懶覺;懶床. **lie low** keep out of sight (until trouble has passed) 藏匿;躲藏起來. **lie in wait** hide while waiting to attack or catch 埋伏以待;伏擊: *The police lay in wait for the thieves.* 警察埋伏着等待捉拿小偷.

liege [li:dʒ] *adj* **1** entitled to the service and allegiance of his vassals 君主的. **2** (of a vassal or observant) owing feudal allegiance 臣民的; **liege subjects** 臣下. Also 亦作 *nc* **1** liege lord 君主. **2** liegeman or true subject 臣民.

Lieutenant [lef'tenənt. *US* 美 lu:'tenənt] *nc* **1** junior officer in the army or navy 陸軍或海軍中的低級軍官;尉級軍官. (英) 陸軍中尉;海軍上尉. **2** officer having the next lower rank (usu. used with the word for that rank) 比與其連用的詞所示的官階低一級的官員.

life [laif] **1** *nu* condition of humans, animals and plants which makes them different from sticks, stones or anything dead 生命: *Life depends on air, food and water.* 生命依靠空氣、食物和水. **2** *nu* living things in general 生物: *There seems to be no life on the moon.* 月球上似乎没有生物. *We should protect wildlife* i.e. animals living in their natural existence 我們應該保護野生動物. **3** *nc* a person as a living creature (活的)人; 生命: *Thousands of lives were lost during the war.* 成千上萬的人在戰爭期間喪生. **4** *nc* period of time between birth and death; between birth and the present; between the present and death 一生;一輩子;終身: *He spent his*

whole life in one country. 他在一個國家度過了他的一生. *I have lived here all my life.* 我在這裏住了一輩子. *He intends to spend the rest of his life abroad.* 他打算在國外度過他的餘生. **5** *nc* written story of somebody's life 傳記: *He is reading the life of Napoleon.* 他在讀拿破崙的傳記. **6** *nc/u* general state of society; way of spending time 生活;生活方式: *How do you find life in a big city?* 你對大城市的生活覺得怎樣? *They have very busy lives.* 他們過着忙忙碌碌的生活. **7** *nu* energy 活力: *The children are full of life.* 孩子們精力充沛. *pl* 複數 **lives** [laivz]. **lifeless** *adj* **1** not having life; dead 無生命的;死的. **2** not lively; dull 無生氣的,不活躍的;沉悶的: *a lifeless expression* 死氣沉沉的表情. **lifelike** *adj* like something living; very like the person himself 生動的;逼真的;栩栩如生的. *This is a lifelike drawing of my father.* 這是一幅我父親惟妙惟肖的素描. **'lifebelt** belt which saves a person's life by keeping him afloat in water 救生帶,浮帶. **'lifeboat** special type of boat used to save lives at sea (e.g. when a ship sinks) 救生艇. **'lifebuoy** floating ring which is thrown to a person who is in danger of drowning 救生圈. **'lifeguard** person trained to save the lives of those in danger of drowning at the seaside 救生員. **'life jacket** jacket that is inflated to keep a person afloat (used like a lifebelt) 救生衣. **'lifeline 1** rope which saves lives (e.g. one thrown to a sinking ship or fastened to a lifebuoy) 救生索(例如:抛到正在下沉的船或繫於救生圈的索). **2** any means of safety 任何安全的方法,救生索,生命線: *During winter the telephone is our lifeline.* 在冬季電話是我們唯一聯絡的

方法. 'lifelong *adj* lasting all one's life 畢生的; 終身的; *a lifelong friendship* 終身的友誼. 'life-size(d) *adj* (esp. with reference to pictures and photographs) having the same size as the person whose picture or photograph it is (尤指畫和照片)與真人一般大小的. 'lifetime whole period of one's life 一生, 終身: *the chance of a lifetime* i.e. a chance which one is likely to have only once during one's life 一生中唯一難得的機會. **come to life** become alive; become well or conscious again 使活; 恢復知覺, 蘇醒過來: *She fainted but came to life when we threw cold water over her.* 她昏倒了, 但我們對她潑冷水她又蘇醒過來. **take one's own life** kill oneself 自殺. **take somebody's life** kill somebody 殺死某人.

lift¹ [lift] **1** *vt* raise 提起, 舉起: *I can't lift it. It is too heavy.* 我無法把它提起來, 太重了. *Lift it up on the table.* 把它提到桌上. **2** *vi* (esp. with reference to cloud, fog and mist) rise; go away (尤指雲, 霧, 靄)上升; 消散: *We saw the mountain when the clouds lifted.* 雲散了, 我們看見山. 'lift-off *nc* (with reference to a rocket or spaceship) act of leaving the ground (指火箭或宇宙飛船)升空; 發射: *We have lift-off* i.e. the rocket has successfully got into the air. 我們升空了. 即: 火箭成功地進入空中. see also **shop**.

lift² [lift] *nc* **1** act of lifting 提起, 舉起. **2** help on a journey by taking a person in one's car etc. 讓人搭乘自己的車, 搭便車: *I gave him a lift to the railway station.* 我讓他搭我的車到火車站. **3** (*Brit*)machine for carrying goods and people up and down high buildings (英)電梯. (*US* 美 **elevator**.

ligament [ˈligəmənt] *nc* strong sub-stance joining the bones of the body 韌帶.

light¹ [lait] **1** *nu* that which makes one able to see 光: *the light of the sun* 陽光. *We read by the light of a candle / by candlelight.* 我們在燭光下讀書. **2** *nc* something which gives light 發光體: *traffic lights* 交通燈. *Turn off all the lights.* 把所有的燈關掉. **3** *nu* something which starts a fire 引火物: *He put a light to the old papers* i.e. he set them on fire (e.g. with a match). 他點燃舊報紙(例如: 用一根火柴). *Can you give me a light?* (e.g. for my cigarette) 能借個火嗎? (例如: 點香煙) **4** *nc* information; point of view 見解; 觀點: *His speech throws a different light on what happened.* 他的演說使人們對發生的事有不同的看法. *He does not see this matter in the same light as we do* i.e. he has not the same point of view. 他對這個問題的看法和我們不一致. 即: 他有不同的觀點. 'lighthouse tall tower with a strong light built on land to guide ships or warn them of danger 燈塔. 'lightship ship which does the same work as a lighthouse 燈塔船; 信號船. 'light year the distance travelled by light in the period of one year. (Light travels at the speed of 186,000 miles per second used to measure the distance between stars and the earth) 光年(光每秒走186,000英里走一年的速度——用於度量星球和地球之間的距離). 'daylight **1** light during the day 日光. **2** dawn 黎明, 破曉: *Let us wait until daylight.* 讓我們等到天亮吧. 'footlights row of lights at the front of the stage in a theatre 舞台上的腳燈. 'moonlight light given by the moon 月光. 'skylight window in the roof of a building to let in light 天窗. 'sun-

light direct light from the sun 陽光, 日光.

light² [lait] *vt / i* **1** set fire to; give light to 點火; 使明亮: *Shall I light a fire?* 我要把火點着嗎? *The lamp lights the room quite well.* 燈照得房間亮堂堂的. *The lamp lights up the room.* 燈照亮了房間. *The whole town is lit up.* 全城燈火輝煌. **2** (esp. with reference to the eyes and face) show happiness. (尤指眼睛和臉)露出愉快的表情: *The children's faces lit up when they saw the food.* 孩子們看見食物,臉上露出笑容. *past* 過去式和過去分詞 **lit** [lit] (more usual) (較常用), or **lighted.** **'lighting-'up time** time when, by law, lamps (esp. on vehicles) should be lit (法令規定的)行車點燈時間.

light³ [lait] *adj* **1** allowing one to see well; not dark 明亮的;亮的: *His room is light and airy.* 他的房間明亮又通風. **2** pale in colour 蒼白的;淺色的: *light red* 淺紅的; *light coloured* 淺色的.

light⁴ [lait] *adj* **1** having little weight 輕的: *Your bag is very light.* 你的提袋很輕. (*opp* 反義詞 **heavy**). **2** used with many words to give the sense of lack of power or strength of being gentle or easy 與許多詞連用表示缺乏力量的,輕度的或容易的意思: *light beer* i.e. not strong 淡啤酒,即:不烈; *a light illness* i.e. not a severe one 輕病,即:不嚴重的病; *a light meal* i.e. a small, easily-eaten one 清淡的飯菜或便餐,即:少量的,容易吃完的飯菜; *a light touch* i.e. a gentle one 輕觸; *light reading* i.e. something easily read and often amusing 輕鬆的讀物,即:易讀且有趣的讀物; *light work* i.e. done easily 輕活兒,即:容易做的工作. **3** having no cares or any sense of responsibility 輕鬆愉快的: *We went away with a*

light heart. 我們帶着輕鬆愉快的心情離開了. *The drink gave me a light head.* 喝酒使我有點頭暈. Also 亦作 *adv: We always travel light* i.e. without heavy luggage. 我們總是輕裝旅行.即:不帶笨重的行李. **lightness** *nu.*

lightly *adv: He slept lightly.* 他稍微睡了一下. *Note* 說明: *adv* **light** and **lightly** have the same sense but **light** cannot always be used; **lightly** is and is therefore safer to use (e.g. one can *travel* either **light** or **lightly**, but one can only *touch* a person **lightly**). 副詞的 **light** 和 **lightly** 有相同的意思,但不能無例外地使用 **light**; **lightly** 則可以用而且使用起來較保險(例如:輕裝旅行可用 travel light 或 lightly,但輕輕地碰一個人只能用 touch lightly).

'light-'headed *adj* not in full control of oneself; dizzy 昏頭昏腦的;頭暈目眩的. **'light-'hearted** *adj* without any cares; cheerful 無憂無慮的;愉快的. **lightweight** *adj* not heavy; below the usual weight 輕量的;不到平常重量的.

lighten¹ ['laitn] *vt / i* become or make light 變亮;使亮: *The sky lightened at dawn.* 黎明時天空變亮了. see 見 **light¹**.

lighten² ['laitn] *vt / i* become or make lighter 變輕;減輕: *He lightened his bag by taking out some books.* 他拿出幾本書以減輕提袋的重量. see 見 **light⁴**.

lighter¹ ['laitə*] *nc* type of boat used to take goods to or from a ship to the shore where there is no harbour 駁船.

lighter² ['laitə*] *nc* (usu. with other words) person / thing that lights (usu. **cigarette lighter**). (通常與其他詞連用)點火的人;照明物,點火物(通常指 cigarette lighter). see 見 **light²**.

ciga'rette lighter small machine for

lighting cigarettes 打火機.

lightning ['laitniŋ] *nu* flash of light made by electricity passing between two clouds or between a cloud and the ground. (The sound made is called **thunder**). 閃電. (發出的聲音叫 thunder 雷). '**lightning conductor** piece of metal fixed to a high building and joined by a thick wire to the ground to take the electricity of lightning to the ground and so prevent damage to the building by lightning 避雷針.

like¹ [laik] *vt / i* **1** be fond of; be pleased with 喜歡; 中意: *I like good food.* 我喜歡對健康有益的食品 *.Do you like my new hat?* 你喜歡我的新帽子嗎? *I like our teacher.* 我喜歡我們的老師. **2** wish; prefer 希望; 寧願: *I should like to see him again.* 我想再見他. *Would you like a cup of tea?* i.e. do you want one? 你想喝杯茶嗎? (*opp* 反義詞 **dislike**). **liking** *nu* **1** fondness 愛好; 喜歡: *I have a liking for good food.* 我喜歡對健康有益的食品. *They took a liking to me* i.e. they became fond of me. 他們對我產生了好感; 他們變得喜歡我了. **2** wish; satisfaction 願望; 滿意: *The journey was not to my liking* i.e. was not as I wanted it to be. 這次旅行不合我的心意. 即: 不是像我希望的那樣.

like² [laik] *adj / prep* **1** the same or not different 同樣的; 相似的: *Have you a book like this?* 你有一本像這樣的書嗎? **2** in the same way as 像…一樣, 如同: *You are talking like a fool.* 你像個傻瓜似的在談話. *It tastes like salt.* 這東西吃起來像鹽. **3** what is to be expected from 正像…: *It was (just) like them to leave the work to us.* 把工作留給我們, 這正像他們的為人. *Isn't it (just) like a woman to want*

new clothes? 那不正像女人喜歡新衣服嗎? **4** (with **feel** and **look**) as if ready for, as if about to (與 feel 和 look 連用) 想要; 好像要, 似乎: *I feel like going for a walk / I feel like a walk* i.e. I want or would enjoy a walk. 我想去散散步. *He looks like winning the race.* 他看來好像要在賽跑中獲勝. Also 亦作 *nc: I have never seen the like of it* i.e. anything like it. 我從未見過這樣的事. *We have met the likes of you before* i.e. persons like you. 以前我們曾遇見過像你這樣的人. *Note* 說明: *like* is also used as a *conj* (e.g. *He doesn't speak English like I speak it*). This use is informal and thought by many to be wrong. it is more correct to use *as* or *in the same way as*. like 也被用作連接詞 (例如: *He doesn't speak English like I speak it.* 他不會像我一樣講英語). 這種用法是非正式的且許多人認為是錯的. 使用 as 或 in the same way as 更正確. **likeness** *nc: This photograph is not a good likeness of you.* 這張照片不大像你. '**likewise** *adv* in the same way or a not very different way 同樣地; 照樣地: *This is how I do it. I want you to do likewise.* 我是這樣做的. 我要你照樣做. Also 亦作 *conj* also 也.

likely ['laikli] *adj / adv* probable; probably; (as) expected 可能的; 可能地; 如預期的: *This is a likely place for him to stay.* 這是他可能停留的地方. *He is likely to do very well / It is likely that he will do very well.* 他可能會幹得很好. *They very likely won't come.* 他們很可能不會來. (*opp* 反義詞 **unlikely**). **likelihood** *nu* probability 可能性: *There is no likelihood that he will come / of his coming.* 他不可能來. *In all likelihood I shall be at home* i.e. very probably. 我很可能會在家裏.

liken ['laikən] *vt* show or say that something is like something else; compare 把…比做; 比喻為.

lilac ['lailək] *nc / u* **1** type of bush with white or purple flowers 紫丁香. **2** the flower itself 紫丁香花. Also 亦作 *adj* light purple colour like lilac 淡紫色的.

lilt [lilt] *nc* pleasant tune, way of speaking etc, with a strong but simple rhythm 輕快的旋律或節拍. Also 亦作 *vt / i* sing or speak in this way 輕快、有節拍地唱或說. **lilting** *adj*.

lily ['lili] *nc* various types of flower, often bell-shaped 百合花; 百合.

limb [lim] *nc* arm, leg 肢(手或足).

limber up ['limbər ʌp] *vi* loosen stiff muscles by doing exercises 做體操使肌肉柔軟; 做柔軟運動; 做準備活動; 熱身. *The runners limbered up before the race.* 賽跑者在賽跑前做準備動作.

limbo ['limbou] *nc / u* place to put people or things which are not wanted; neglect 安置被遺棄的人或物的地方; 被遺棄: *be in limbo* 處於困境.

lime[1] [laim] *nu* white substance obtained from limestone, sea shells etc by burning them (used e.g. when mixed with sand to join bricks together) 石灰. '**limestone** type of rock from which lime is obtained 石灰石. **in the limelight** receiving great attention from the public 爲衆人所注視, 引人注目: *Famous athletes are always in the limelight.* 著名的運動員總是引人注目的.

lime[2] [laim] *nc* **1** type of tree with a bitter green fruit (like a lemon) 酸橙樹. **2** the fruit itself 酸橙.

lime[3] [laim] *nc* linden tree 菩提樹.

limerick ['limərik] *nc* amusing poem of five lines and having a special rhythm 五行打油詩.

limit ['limit] *nc* **1** farthest point to which something reaches; point beyond which one cannot go 界限; 邊界: *There is a limit to the amount of money we can spend* 我們花得起的錢要有個限度. *He sees no limits to man's progress.* 他明白人類的進步是無止境的. **2** somebody / something that cannot be endured or tolerated 無法忍受的人 / 事物: *That man's the limit.* (*informal* in sense **2**) 那個人真叫人受不了. (義 2 爲非正式). Also 亦作 *vt* put a limit to; keep within limit 限制; 限定: *We must limit the amount of money we spend.* 我們必須限制花錢的數量. **limited** *adj* small; narrow; confined 少的; 狹窄的; 有限的: *The amount of money we have is limited.* 我們有的錢額有限. *I have only a limited knowledge of the language.* 我的語言知識很狹窄. (*opp* 反義詞 **unlimited**). **limited company** (*Brit*) one in which the members of the company are limited to paying debts equal to the amount of money they have put in the company (英)有限公司.

limousine ['liməzi:n] *nc* large, expensive motorcar (usu. with a separate compartment for the driver) 大型貴重轎車(通常帶有司機隔間).

limp[1] [limp] *adj* not stiff; soft; weak 柔軟的; 軟弱的: *The book has a limp cover* 這書有軟封面; *a limp hand* 軟弱的手. **limply** *adv*.

limp[2] [limp] *vi* walk unevenly because of lameness 跛行: *After being kicked on the ankle, the player limped off the field.* 腳踝被踢傷後, 這位運動員一瘸一拐地離開場地. Also 亦作 *nu* (usu. with a) (通常與a連用): *He walks with a limp.* 他走起路來一瘸一拐.

limpet ['limpit] *nc* type of small shellfish which sticks firmly to rocks 蠑(一種小貝類,附生岩石上).

limpid ['limpid] *adj* (esp. with reference to liquids and the eyes) clear (尤指液體和眼睛)清澈的.

linden ['lindn] *nc* type of tree with yellowish-white flowers, grown for ornament or shade 菩提樹. Also 亦作 **lime³**.

line¹ [lain] *nc* **1** cord string, thread or wire 索,細繩;線;金屬線: *throw a line to a ship.* i.e a rope 把一條繩子拋到船上; *a fishing line* 釣魚線; *a clothes line* i.e. a rope to hang and dry clothes on 晾衣繩; 用來掛晾衣服的繩子; *telephone lines* i.e. wires 電話線. **2** thin mark on something 線條: *the finishing line in a race* i.e. mark on the ground to show when a race ends 賽跑的終線; *He drew the picture in bold lines.* 他用粗線條畫圖畫. *The lines on his face showed that he was worried* i.e. wrinkles. 他臉上的皺紋表明他很煩惱. **3** row of persons / things (人或物的)排,列: *a line of soldiers* 一排士兵; *The people stood in a line at the bus stop* 在公共汽車站人們排成一列; *a long line of trees* 一長排樹; *a single line of traffic* 單向交通; *a few lines of verse* 幾行詩. *There are forty lines of print on each page of the book.* 這本書的每一頁上印有四十行. **4** edge; boundary; limit 邊緣;邊界;界限: *The top of the mountain is above the snow line.* 這山頂在雪線之上. *Ships sailing from South Africa to Europe have to cross the line* i.e. the equator 船從南非駛往歐洲必須通過赤道; *contour lines on a map* 地圖上的等高線. **5** track on which a railway train runs 鐵軌: *the main line between Edinburgh and London* 愛丁堡和倫敦之間的鐵路幹線; *the line is cov-*

ered with snow. 鐵軌被雪覆蓋. **6** direction; course 方向; 路線: *The army's line of retreat was through the wood.* 該軍隊的退卻路線是穿過樹林. *We tried a different line of approach.* 我們試了不同的接近路線. **7** method of doing something; business (行事)方法;行業: *We·must take a firm / strong line with these people* i.e. act firmly in dealing with them. 我們必須採取強硬的措施對付這些人. *You cannot win the games on these lines* i.e. in this way. 靠這些方法你無法在比賽中獲勝. *His line is bookselling* i.e. his business. *(informal)* 他的職業是賣書. (非正式). *That's not in my line* i.e. I am not interested; it is not my business. 那不是我所擅長的. 即: 我不感興趣; 那不是我的職業. **liner** *nc* large passenger ship 大客輪; 班輪. **linesman** *nc* (in football, tennis etc.) person who decides whether or not the ball has crossed a line (in sense **2**) (足球,網球等的)邊線裁判員; 司線員. **toe the line** obey; do what others agree to do. *(informal)* 服從命令; 遵守規則(非正式).

line² [lain] *vt* border; form a line along 加邊線於; 沿…排列, 排成行列: *Tall trees line the road.* 道路旁邊高樹成行. *The crew lined the sides of the ship.* 全體船員排列在船的兩側. **line up** put in a line; get into a line 使排成行列; 排隊: *The teacher lined up the boys in front of his desk.* 老師叫學生在講台前排成一行. *We lined up to buy tickets.* 我們排隊買票. **'line-up** *nc* line of players ready to begin playing (e.g. football) (比賽開始時)球員的排列(例如:足球).

line³ [lain] *vt* cover the inside of something 加襯裏於: *He lined the box with clean paper.* 他用清潔的紙做箱子的襯

裏. *Her coat is lined with silk.* 他的上衣是用綢做襯裏的. **lining** *nc* inside covering; material used as an inside covering 襯裏; 襯料: *I tore the lining of my jacket.* 我把茄克衫的襯裏撕掉.

linear ['liniə] *adj* **1** of or relating to a line or lines 線的, 直線的: *linear design* 線構成的圖案. **2** of length 長度的: *linear measure* 長度, 長度單位. **3** made of or using lines 線條的, 線形的.

linen ['linin] *nu* **1** type of cloth made from flax 亞麻布. **2** tablecloths, shirts, sheets, handkerchiefs etc made from linen or some other cloth (亞麻布或其他布的) 桌布, 襯衫, 被單, 手帕等: *We must change the linen on the bed* i.e. take off the dirty sheets and put on clean ones. 我們得換床單了. 即: 把髒的床單拿掉, 舖上乾淨的床單. Also 亦作 *adj*: *a linen tablecloth* 亞麻桌布.

liner ['lainə*] *nc* see 見 **line**[1].

linesman ['lainzmən] *nc* see 見 **line**[2].

linger ['liŋgə*] *vi* stay a long time; be unwilling to go away 逗留; 徘徊: *We lingered in the garden until it was dark.* 我們在花園裏逗留到天黑. *Why is he lingering about the school?* 爲甚麼他在學校週圍徘徊? **lingering** *adj* lasting a long time 拖久的: *a lingering look* 戀戀不捨的表情.

lingerie ['lænʒəri] *nu* women's underwear 女內衣.

linguist ['liŋgwist] *nc* person skilled at speaking more than one language 通曉數種語言的人. **linguistics** [liŋ'gwistiks] *n sing* scientific study of language (單數) 語言學.

liniment ['linimənt] *nc / u* type of oil or ointment rubbed on the body (esp. to remove stiffness) 塗擦劑(尤指消除僵硬者).

lining ['lainiŋ] *nc* see 見 **line**[3].

link [liŋk] *nc* **1** one ring of a chain 鏈環. **2** somebody / something that joins two things together 連接的人或物: *The road was our only link with the village.* 這條道路是我們惟一連接這個鄉村的路. Also 亦作 *vt* join, be joined by, a link 連接; 環接. **link up** be or become joined together 連接起來; 結合. **'link-up** *nc*.

lino ['lainou] *nu* short form of **linoleum** 的缩畧形式.

linoleum [li'nouliəm] *nu* covering for a floor made of canvas, cork and oil 油地氈.

linseed ['linsi:d] *nu* seed of flax 亞麻子. **linseed oil** yellow oil extracted from seeds of the flax plant 亞麻子油.

lint [lint] *nu* linen with one side made soft like wool, used for covering cuts and wounds 裹傷用的亞麻布; 軟麻布.

lion ['laiən] *nc* large animal of the cat family, found in Africa and Asia. (The male has a big mane of hair on its head and neck) 獅子. (*fem* 陰 **lioness** ['laiənis]).

lip [lip] *nc* **1** one of the two outer edges of the mouth 唇: *the lower / upper lip* 下/上唇. *He kissed her on the lips.* 他吻她的唇. **2** edge of anything (esp. if shaped like a lip) (尤指唇狀物的)邊緣: *the lip of a cup* 杯邊. **'lip-reading** way of understanding what somebody says by watching his lips moving (used by those who are deaf) (耳聾者使用的)唇讀法(通過觀察嘴唇的動作以瞭解說話內容的方法). **'lip service** saying that one agrees or will do something etc but not meaning it 口惠; 口頭上說得好聽的話: *They pay lip service to my ideas but they do not really believe them.* 他們對我提出的

辦法口頭上贊成但他們並不真正相信這些辦法. **lipstick** stick of coloured material used by women to put on their lips 口紅; 唇膏.

lipstick ['lipstik] *nc / u* small stick of cosmetic paste, set in a case, for colouring the lip 口紅, 唇膏: *She was wearing red lipstick.* 她塗着紅色唇膏.

liquefy ['likwifai] *vt / i* become or make liquid (使)液化.

liqueur [li'kjuə*] *nc* type of strong, sweet, alcoholic drink often flavoured with fruit (usu. taken in a very small glass after a meal) 甜露酒(通常飯後飲一小杯).

liquid ['likwid] *nc / u* matter like water or oil in density and form (The other two forms matter can take are gas and solid) 液體(物質的另外兩種形狀是氣體和固體). Also 亦作 *adj* like liquid 液態的.

liquidate ['likwideit] *vt* settle the affairs of a bankrupt business company by selling its property to pay its debts; (with reference to the business) be settled in this way 清盤, 清理, 清算(破產的公司); 了結(債務); 結束(業務). **liquidation** [likwi'deiʃən] *nu: go into liquidation* i.e. become bankrupt 破產.

liquor ['likə*] *nc / u* alcoholic drink (esp. *US* strong, alcoholic drink or spirits) 酒; 酒類(尤指美烈性酒).

liquorice, licorice ['likəris] *nc / u* **1** type of plant from which is obtained a substance used to make sweets and medicines (用於藥品和糖果中的)甘草. **2** the substance itself 甘草.

lisp [lisp] *vt / i* speak incorrectly (esp. by saying 'th' instead of 's' e.g. *'thip'* instead of *'sip'*) 口齒不清地說話(尤指將's'說成'th'例如: 將'sip'說成'thip').Also 亦作 *nc* habit of lisping 口齒不清:

The boy speaks with a lisp / has a lisp. 那男孩說話口齒不清.

list[1] [list] *nc* number of things written down or printed for a particular purpose 表; 清單, 目錄: *wine list* i.e. names of kinds of wine printed on paper so that one can choose the kind one wants 酒單, 即: 各種酒名印在紙上以便人們挑選; *shopping list* 購物單. *He made a list of the friends he knew.* 他把認識的朋友列一表. Also 亦作 *vt* make a list; put on a list 把…編列成表; 把…編入目錄. **on the short list** on the final list of applicants who are to be considered for a post etc. 在有可能被錄用等的申請人的最後名單上.

list[2] [list] *vi* (esp. with reference to a ship) lean to one side (尤指船) 傾斜. Also 亦作 *nc: a ship with a list* 側傾的船.

listen ['lisn] *vt / i* **1** pay attention to (esp. so that one can hear) 聽, 留神聽: *I often listen to music.* 我常常聽音樂. *Although we were listening, we did not hear him coming.* 雖然我們在聽, 但沒聽到他來的聲音. **2** follow the advice of 聽從: *Children should listen to their parents.* 小孩應聽從父母親的話. **listener** *nc* person who listens 聽者.

listless ['listlis] *adj* not having enough energy or interest to do something 沒精打采的; 漠不關心的. **listlessness** *nu.*

lit [lit] past of **light.** Light 的過去式和過去分詞.

liter ['li:tə*] *US* form of **litre.** litre 的美國拼法形式

literacy ['litərəsi] *nu* see **literate.**

literal ['litərl] *adj* word for word; following the exact meaning 逐字的; 原原本本的: *This is a literal translation in French of an English proverb.* 這是

一英語諺語的法語直譯. *In its literal sense 'anti' means 'against'.* 'Anti' 的字面意思是 '反對'. **literally** *adv* **1** word for word 逐字地. **2** really; in fact 真的; 實際上.

literary ['litərəri] *adj* of literature; (with reference to a person) interested in literature 文學的; (指人) 對文學感興趣的.

literate ['litərət] *adj* able to read and write 能讀能寫的. (*opp* 反義詞 **illiterate**). **literacy** ['litərəsi] *nu.* (*opp* 反義詞 **illiteracy**).

literature ['litəritʃə*] *nu* books (esp. those by good writers) 文學作品 (尤指優秀作家的).

litigate ['litigeit] *vt / i* go to law 訴訟, 提出訴訟.

litmus ['litməs] *nu* type of blue substance which is made red by an acid and then blue again by an alkali, and so used to indicate the presence of these substances 石蕊. '**litmus paper** paper covered with litmus 石蕊試紙.

litre ['li:tə*] (*US* 美 **liter**) *nc* unit of liquid measure equal to approximately 1¾ pints 公升 (約合1¾品脫).

litter ['litə*] **1** *nu* useless material which is thrown down and left (e.g. old newspapers, empty bottles, cigarette ends); rubbish 四下亂丟的廢物 (例如: 舊報紙、空瓶子、烟蒂); 垃圾: *Many public parks are spoilt by litter.* 許多公園的景緻被亂丟的廢物破壞了. **2** *nc* family of young animals born at the same time 一胎生下的小動物: *a litter of kittens* 一窩小貓. Also 亦作 *vt* cover or make untidy with litter (用廢物) 丟滿; 使雜亂.

little ['litl] **1** *adj* (*comparative* **less** or **lesser.** *superlative* **least**) small in size (比較級 less 或 lesser, 最高級 least) 小的: *a little box* 小盒子. **2** *adj*

/ *determiner* small in amount; short in time 少量的; (時間) 短的: *May I have a little sugar?* 給我點糖, 好嗎? *He spent a little time talking to us.* 他跟我們談了一會兒. **3** *adj* young 年輕的: *We met Mrs Smith with her two little ones* i.e. with her two young children. 我們遇見史密斯太太和她的兩個小孩. *All the little children are in Class I.* 所有這些小孩都在第一班. *Note* 說明: **1** *little* without *a* or *the* has the sense of 'not enough' , 'hardly any' (e.g. *They have little money for extra food* i.e. they have hardly any money set aside for extra food and will probably not buy it). *There is little hope of seeing him again.* **2** Although *little* very often has the same sense as *small*, there are some differences (e.g. *Would you like a little pudding?* i.e. a small amount, or small helping of a fairly big pudding. *Would you like a small pudding?* i.e. one separate pudding which is small in size). Also *little* is often used with another *adj* to show that one likes, or is pleased with, something, not to show that it is small. *He made a nice little profit in the market* i.e. a good profit. One cannot say *a nice small profit;* small profits are never nice. *She's a pretty little girl* i.e. she is pretty and I like her. *She's a pretty small girl* i.e. she is a rather small girl and may not be pretty at all. **1** Little 前無 a 或 the 有 '不足' , '幾乎沒有' 的意思 (例如: They have little money for extra food i.e. they have hardly any money set aside for extra food and will probably not buy it 他們沒甚麼錢用來買特別的滋養品之用且可能不會買). There is little hope of seeing him again. 沒有甚麼希望再見到他. **2** 雖然 little 經常與

small 的意思相同，但有些差別(例如:
Would you like a little pudding? i.e. a
small amount, or small helping of a
fairly big pudding. 你想要吃點布丁嗎?
即: 少量或一小份頗大的布丁。Would
you like a small pudding? i.e. one
separate pudding which is small in
size. 你想要一個小布丁嗎? 即: 一個單
獨的小布丁)。Little 也常和另一個形容
詞連用表示人們喜歡某物或對某物表示
滿意，不表示是小的。He made a
nice little profit in the market i.e. a
good profit. 他在市場上獲得厚利。人們
不可說 a nice small profit; 小額利潤決
不令人愉快。She's a pretty little girl
i.e. she is pretty and I like her. 她是個
漂亮可愛的姑娘。即: 她漂亮且我喜歡她
。She's a pretty small girl. i.e. she is a
rather small girl and may not be pretty at all. 她是個頗小的姑娘，可能一點
也不漂亮。see also 參看
pretty. Also 亦作 *nu* a small amount,
size etc. 少量: *I drank a little of the
wine.* 我喝了一點這種葡萄酒。*I am
not surprised at the little he does. I am*
對他盡到的僅有的一點力量並不感到意
外。Also 亦作 *adv* not by much; hardly at all 很少; 幾乎一點也不: *They
will come back a little latter.* 他們會稍
遲些回來。*They live very little in this
country.* 他們很少住在這個國家。Note
說明: *little* as an *adv* is often used
before the verb with the sense of
something happening which is not expected. *He little thought that his life
was in danger* i.e. it *was* in danger.
*We little believed that he would harm
us* i.e. we were wrong; he *did* harm
us. Little 作爲副詞常常用於表示意外
發生的事的動詞之前。*He little
thought that his life was in danger i.e.
it was in danger.* 他幾乎沒想到他的生
命處於危險之中。*We little believed*

that he would harm us i.e. we were
wrong; he did harm us. 我們幾乎不相
信他會傷害我們。即: 我們錯了; 他確實
傷害了我們。**little by little** gradually;
step by step 逐漸地; 一步一步地。

live¹ [liv] *vt / i* **1** have life; not be dead
(**be alive** is more usual) 生活; 活着
(**be alive** 較 live 更常用)。**2** continue
to be alive 繼續活着: *Not many people live to a hundred* i.e. until they
are a hundred years old. 很少人活到
一百歲。*She is so badly injured that
she is not likely to live.* 她傷得很重，看
來她不大可能活下去。**3** have one's
home 居住: *Where do you live?* 你住
在哪裏? *We live in London.* 我們住在
倫敦。**4** (usu. with *adv*) spend one's
time in a particular way (通常與副詞
連用)(以某種方式)生活，過活: *They
live quietly in the country.* 他們在鄉村
過寧靜的生活。*When I was rich I lived
very well.* 我在富裕時，生活得很好。
5 (with reference to things) continue;
be remembered (指事物)繼續存在; 被
記住，留存在人們的記憶中: *His poetry
will live forever.* 他的詩將永世流傳。
live something down make others
forget something wrong which one
has done, by behaving well afterwards
(悔過自新)使別人忘卻(以往的過錯):
*He will not easily live down his very
rude behaviour at the party.* 他很難使
別人忘記他在宴會上十分粗魯的行爲。
live in (e.g. with reference to servants) live in the place where one is
employed (僕人等)住在主人家; 住在
工作的地方。(*opp* 反義詞 **live out**)。
live off take money, food etc from 靠
…供養; 靠…生活: *He doesn't work,
he just lives off his friends.* 他不工作,
只是靠他的朋友生活。**live on** continue to live 繼續活着: *After her
mother's death she lived on in the*

house by herself. 母親死後, 她自己一人住在這房子裏. **live on something** keep alive by earning or eating 靠…生活; 以吃…維持生命: *He and his family live on £20 a week.* 他和他的家人靠一星期二十鎊生活. *These people live on meat and milk.* 這些人以肉和牛奶爲主食. **live out** (e.g. with reference to servants) not live in the place where one is employed (僕人等)不住在主人家; 不住在工作的地方. (*opp* 反義詞 **live in**). **live up to something** (esp. with reference to behaviour, standards etc.) be as good as (尤指行爲, 標準等)和…一樣好; 與…相當: *I try to live up to the high standards of the school.* 我設法無愧於學校的高標準.

live² [laiv] *adj* 1 having life 有生命的, 活的: *a live mouse* i.e. one which is not dead 活老鼠; *a live broadcast* i.e. a programme on radio or television sent out while it is happening 實況廣播. *Note* 說明: *live* in the sense of 'not dead' cannot be a *pred adj-use alive* or *living* (e.g. *the live mouse* but *The mouse is alive / living*). Live 表示 '活的' 意思時不能用作表語形容詞; 這語形容詞要用 alive 或 living (例如: the live mouse, The mouse is alive / living). 2 having power, energy etc. 有力量, 電力, 活力, 能量等的: *Be careful, this wire is live* i.e. it has an electric current 當心, 這條電線有電. 即: 這條電線有電流通過; *a live bomb* i.e. one which is ready to be exploded 有爆炸力的炸彈, 真炸彈, 即: 隨時可爆炸的炸彈.

livelihood ['laivlihud] *nc* way in which one earns money to live 生計; 營生方式: *For many years teaching was his livelihood.* 多年來教書是他的謀生之道.

lively ['laivli] *adj* 1 full of life; quick; active 充滿生氣的; 活潑的; 活躍的: *Young children are usually lively.* 小孩通常是活潑有生氣的. *He has a lively mind.* 他有靈活的頭腦. *Because of all the arguments the meeting was a lively one.* 由於提出各種各樣的論點, 這次會議是一次活躍的會議. 2 true to life; vivid 真實的; 生動的: *He told a very lively story about his life in Africa.* 他講了關於他在非洲生活的一個非常生動的故事. **liveliness** *nu*.

liven ['laivən] *vt / i* (often with **up**) become or make lively (常與 **up** 連用) (使)活潑起來; (使)活躍起來: *He livened up the class by telling an interesting story.* 他講個有趣的故事使班級活躍起來.

liver ['livə*] 1 *nc* large organ of the body which cleans the blood 肝臟. 2 *nu* this organ taken from an animal and used as food (供食用的動物的)肝.

livery ['livəri] *nc* special dress worn by the servants of an important person (昔日要人的僕人穿的)特殊制服.

lives [laivz] *pl of* **life**. Life 的複數.

livestock ['laivstɔk] *nu* animals kept by man for his own use (e.g. cattle, sheep, goats etc *-not* dogs or cats or other pets) 家畜, 牲畜(例如: 牛, 綿羊, 山羊等*-不*指狗或貓或其他寵物).

livid ['livid] *adj* having the colour of lead i.e. grey 鉛色的; 灰色的: *He is livid with anger* i.e. so angry that his face is grey. 他氣得臉發青.

living¹ ['liviŋ] *adj* existing now; alive 現存的; 活的: *English is a living language.* 英語是現行的語言. *He is a living example of courage.* 他是活生生的無畏的榜樣.

living² ['liviŋ] *nu* way in which one

lives; way in which one gets what is needed to live 生活; 生計: *The standard of living in poor countries is very low.* 貧困國家的生活水準很低. *Rich men like good living* i.e. great comfort, good food etc. 富人喜歡優裕的生活. *He earns / makes his living by growing rice.* 他靠種水稻謀生. '**living room** room in a house where the people of the house spend most of their time when they are at home and awake 起居室; 客廳.

lizard ['lizəd] *nc* type of small animal with a long tail and dry scaly skin 蜥蜴; 石龍子.

load¹ [loud] *vt/i* **1** put something (usu. something heavy) in or on something else (e.g. on a lorry, on a ship etc.) to be carried away; give somebody something heavy to carry 裝, 裝載; 加重擔於(某人); 使…負擔: *They are loading the bags of rice on to the lorry.* 他們正在把一袋一袋的大米裝到卡車上. *He loaded me with books.* 他讓我揹很多書. **2** (with reference to a gun, rifle etc) put in a shell or cartridge 給(槍、砲等)裝彈藥; 裝上彈藥: *Be careful! That gun is loaded.* 當心! 那槍上了子彈. **3** (with reference to a camera) put in a film 把膠捲裝入(照相機); 裝上膠捲: *I forgot to load my camera.* 我忘記把膠捲裝入照相機. (*opp* 反義詞 **unload**)

load² [loud] *nc* **1** something which is loaded in or on something else 負荷物; 載荷物: *He has stopped the lorry for a load of wood.* 他開了卡車來裝木頭. **2** amount which something can carry (often with another word) 裝載量(常與另一詞連用): *three lorryloads of wood* 三卡車木頭; *a shipload of cotton* 一船棉花. **3** anything which is heavy or causes trouble 重擔; 負擔:

The good news has taken a load off my mind i.e. has stopped me worrying. 好消息消除了我的思想負擔. 即: 使我不再煩惱了. *He carries a heavy load of responsibility.* 他擔負重擔.

loaf [louf] *nc* lump of bread (usu. before it is cut into slices) 一條麵包(通常指被切成片之前的麵包): *I bought a brown loaf and a white one* i.e. a loaf of brown bread and one of white bread. 我買了一條黑麵包和一條白麵包. *pl* 複數 **loaves** [louvz]. Also 亦作 *vi* waste time; go around in a lazy manner 浪費時間, 虛度光陰; 遊蕩, 遊手好閑: *Tell these boys to stop loafing (about).* (*informal*) 叫這些男孩不要閑逛了. (非正式).

loam [loum] *nu* type of fertile soil 肥土, 沃土.

loan [loun] *nc* (esp. with reference to money for interest) something which is lent; act of lending or being lent (尤指貸款)借出物; 貸款; 借出: *The government needs a big loan to build more schools.* 政府需要一大筆貸款用來增建學校. *I gave him the loan of my pen* i.e. I lent my pen to him. 我把筆借給他. *We have the car on loan from a friend.* 我們向朋友借來這部汽車. Also 亦作 *vt* lend (which is more usual) 借出(lend 一詞較常用).

loathe [louð] *vt* hate; be disgusted by 憎恨; 厭惡: *She loathes watching television.* 她不喜歡看電視. **loathing** *nu*.

loaves [louvz] *pl* of **loaf**. loaf 的複數.

lobe [loub] *nc* soft part of the bottom of the ear. 耳垂.

lobster ['lɔbstə*] *nc* type of shellfish with eight legs and two large claws and a tail 龍蝦.

local ['loukl] *adj* of a particular place or area 地方的; 當地的; 本地的: *We went to the local shop* i.e. one which serves the small area we were in 我們去本地商店; *local news* i.e. news about the small district round about 地方新聞; *local injury* i.e. one of only a particular part of the body 局部受傷, 即: 只有身體的某一部份受傷。也 *nc* **1** person who lives in a particular place 本地居民: *We stopped in the village and asked one of the locals the way to the post office.* 我們在村裏停下來, 問一位當地人去郵局的路。**2** public house in a particular place 本地酒店: *He's always in the local in the evening. (informal)* 晚上他總是在本地的酒店裏。(非正式)。**locally** *adv* **locality** [lou'kæliti] *nc* place; area 地方; 地區: *There are no hotels in this locality.* 在這個地區沒有旅館。

locate [lou'keit] *vt* **1** find the position of 找到…的位置: *Can you locate your seat in the cinema?* 你能在電影院裏找到你的座位嗎? **2** put in a particular position 把…設置; 設於: *The company wishes to locate its new factory beside the river.* 那家公司想把它的新工廠設在河邊。**location** *nc/u* **1** position 位置。**2** place outside in the open air where a film is made (電影的) 外景; 外景拍攝地: *The film actors are on location in Jamaica.* 這些電影演員在牙買加拍外景。

loch [lɔx] *nc (Scot)* lake or narrow stretch of water open at one end to the sea (蘇) 湖; 狹長的海灣。

loci ['lousai] *pl of* **locus**. locus 的複數。

lock[1] [lɔx] *nc* **1** device for fastening a door, lid of a box etc. 鎖。**2** part of a river or canal which has a gate at each end. By opening or shutting these gates the level of the water can be raised or lowered to allow boats to pass through 有水閘的河道。

lock[2] [lɔk] *vt/i* **1** fasten with a lock 鎖, 鎖上: *He locked the door and put the key in his pocket.* 他把門鎖上, 把鑰匙放在口袋裏。**2** be able to be fastened in this way 鎖得上: *This door doesn't lock.* 這門鎖不上。**3** be unable, cause to be unable, to move (使) 固定; 卡住: *His car hit the wall because the front wheels locked.* 他的汽車撞在牆上, 因爲前輪卡住了。*He locked my arm in a firm grip.* 他緊緊地抓住我的手臂, 一動也不動。**lock oneself out** lock from the outside the door of a building, room etc (usu. accidentally) so that one cannot get in again (通常爲偶然地) 把自己鎖在外面(無法進門)。**lock someone out** lock from the inside the door of a building, room etc to stop someone getting in 把(某人)鎖在外面(不讓進入): *Because I was very late in returning home my father locked me out.* 因爲我很遲回家, 我的父親把我關在門外。**lock someone up** put someone in a place where he will be safe or can do no harm and then lock the door (e.g. in a prison) 把(某人)鎖起來; 把(某人)關押起來(例如: 關在監獄裏)。**lock something up 1** put something in a safe place which can be locked 把…鎖藏起來: *I always lock up my money in a strong box.* 我總是把錢鎖藏在一個牢固的箱子裏。**2** (with reference to buildings etc.) lock all doors and windows so that nobody can get in 把(建築物等的) 門窗鎖好: *We locked up our house when we went away on holiday.* 我們離家度假時, 我們把房子的門窗都鎖好。

lock[3] [lɔk] *nc* number of hairs which hang together 一綹頭髮: *He had a lock of hair over his left eye.* 他在左眼上方有一綹頭髮。

locker ['lɔkə'] *nc* box with a lid which can be locked (usu. fixed to a wall and used in places where there are many people each of whom can have his own for his clothes, books etc.) 有鎖的小櫥櫃(通常固定在牆上在公共場所供個人存放衣服, 書籍等用): *In this school pupils keep their books in lockers.* 在這所學校裏, 學生把書存放在有鎖的小櫥櫃裏.

locket ['lɔkit] *nc* small flat box (usu. made of gold or silver and hung round the neck on a thin chain) in which there is a picture or some of the hair of a person one loves (裝有心愛的人的相片或頭髮的)小平盒(通常是金或銀質的細鏈項下).

locomotive [loukə'moutiv] *nc* railway engine 火車頭; 機車.

locus ['loukəs] *nc* 1 position or point 位置; 地點. 2 (*mathematics*) set of points or lines whose location satisfies or is determined by one or more specified conditions (數學)軌跡.

locust ['loukəst] *nc* type of winged insect found in Africa and Asia, which moves in very large numbers and destroys crops 蝗蟲.

lodge[^1] [lɔdʒ] *nc* 1 small house or room at the entrance to the grounds of a large house or at the entrance to a large building (e.g. a school or college) (大宅入口處的)小屋. (學校或學院的)門房, 傳達室. 2 house used by people when they are away from home shooting or hunting (供離家狩獵者用的)小屋: *a shooting / hunting lodge* 狩獵者用的小屋.

lodge[^2] [lɔdʒ] *vt / i* 1 (with **at, in** or **with**) live in somebody's house for payment (與 at, in 或 with 連用)寄宿: *When I was at college I lodged at No. 12 Smith Street.* 我在大學時, 寄宿在史密斯街12號. *I lodged with one of the staff.* 我寄寓在一位職員家中. 2

put or receive somebody in a place where he can live for a time 供(某人)以臨時住所: *They lodged the soldiers in the town until the army camp was ready.* 他們在城裏爲士兵提供臨時住所直到軍營準備好爲止. 3 be held firmly; be fixed 卡住; 被固定: *The stick was lodged between two big stones.* 這樹枝被卡在兩塊大石頭之間.

lodger *nc* person who pays for a room to live in 房客; 寄宿人. **lodgings** *npl* room or rooms where one can lodge 寄宿的房間; 出租的房間.

lodge a complaint make an official complaint to the person who can deal with it 提出指控; 投訴: *Some parents have lodged a complaint with the headmaster against one of the teachers.* 一些家長已向校長指控一位教師.

loess ['louis] *nu* light-coloured fine-grained accumulation of clay and silt particles that have been deposited by the wind (被風吹積起來的)黃土.

loft [lɔft] *nc* room at the top of a building just under the roof 閣樓; 頂樓.

lofty ['lɔfti] *adj* 1 (with reference to things, not persons) very high (指事物, 不指人) 很高的: *the lofty tops of the mountains* 高高的山頂. 2 (with reference to a person's feelings) noble; to be admired (指人的感情)高尚的; 令人欽佩的, 崇高的: *He has lofty ideals about life.* 他對生活有崇高的理想. 3 (with reference to a person's behaviour) proud; haughty (指人的行爲)驕傲的; 傲慢的: *He spoke to me in a lofty manner.* 他態度傲慢地對我講話.

log[^1] [lɔg] *nc* rough piece of wood cut from a tree (樹上砍下的)木頭; 原木. **'log 'cabin** small house built with logs, not smooth planks 小木屋.

log² [lɔg] *nc* daily written record of a ship's speed, distance it sails each day, its position etc 航海日誌. **'log-book** book used as a log 航海日誌.

logarithm ['lɔgəriðəm] *nc* number put in a form which makes calculating easier by using addition and subtraction instead of multiplication and division 對數. (Also 亦作 **log**).

loggerheads ['lɔgəhedz] *npl* only in **be at loggerheads with someone** i.e. argue or quarrel with 僅用於 be at loggerheads with someone, 即: 與(某人)爭論; 與(某人)不和.

logic ['lɔdʒik] *nu* science of reasoning correctly; ability to reason correctly 邏輯, 論理學; 正確推理的能力. **logical** *adj*: *He gave a logical answer to the question.* 他對這個問題作了合乎邏輯的回答. (*opp* 反義詞 **illogical**). **logically** *adv*.

loin [lɔin] *n* (*usu pl*) **1** lower part of the back between the hipbones and the ribs (通常用複數)腰. **2** front part of the hindquarters of beef, lamb, veal, etc. (牛、羊、小牛等的)腰肉.

loiter ['lɔitə*] *vi* go slowly and lazily from one place to another; stand about idly 閑逛; 閑蕩: *They loitered all the way to school.* 他們上學一路上邊走邊玩. *Why are these boys loitering in the playground?* 爲甚麼這些學生在操場上閑蕩?

loll [lɔl] *vi* stand, sit or lie lazily 懶洋洋地站, 坐或躺着: *He was lolling in a chair with his hands in his pockets.* 他兩手插在口袋裏懶洋洋地靠在椅子上.

lollipop ['lɔlipɔp] *nc* type of sweet at the end of a stick 棒糖: *The child was licking a lollipop.* 那孩子在舔吃棒糖.

lone [loun] *adj* by oneself; by itself; without others near; alone 獨自的; 孤獨的. **lonesome** *adj* feeling lonely; wanting the company of others 感到寂寞的; 渴望伴侶的, 孤單的. *Note* 說明: *alone* and *lonely* are more usual than *lone* alone 和 lonely 比 lone 較常用.

lonely ['lounli] *adj* by oneself; by itself; without others near 獨自的; 孤獨的: *He was lonely because there were no other boys to play with.* 他感到孤獨, 因爲沒有其他男孩和他玩. *He lives in a lonely house far away from the village.* 他住在遠離村子的一棟孤立的房子裏. **loneliness** *nu*.

long¹ [lɔŋ] *adj* **1** extending; measuring more than the usual distance 延長的; 長的: *He has long legs.* 他的腿很長. *I have been here a long time.* 我已在這裏很久了. (*opp* 反義詞 **short**). **2** (after a noun showing what the measurement is) measured from one end to the other (在表示量度的名詞後)有若干長度的: *The stick is 1 metre long.* 這根木棒有一米長. *A year is 12 months long.* 一年有十二個月之久. *How long is the new stretch of motorway?* 這條新的高速公路有多長? Also 亦作 *nu* (with reference to time 指時間). *Was he here for long?* 他在這裏很久嗎? *We shall finish before long.* 我們不久就結束. *Note* 說明: there is a great difference in meaning between *before long* i.e. soon and *long before* i.e. a long time ago. before long (不久) 和 long before (很久以前) 兩者之間在意義上有很大的差別. see 見 **long²**. **'long wave** (radio) sound wave measuring from 1,053-2,000 metres (in Britain) (無線電)長波(在英國, 聲波從 1,053 到 2,000 米). see also 參看 **short wave**, **medium wave**. **'long-'winded** *adj* talking too much; boring. (*informal*) 冗長的; 令人厭煩的. (非正式). **have long sight**

be able to see things at a great distance 能遠視. **long-sighted** adj.

long² [lɔŋ] adv **1** for a great period of time 長期地；長久地: He did not sleep for long. 他沒睡多久. He waited as long as he could. 他盡可能地等. **2** (with **all**) for a whole period of time (與 all 連用) 經過一整段時間: They worked all night long. 他們整夜工作. **3** (with a prep) at a much earlier or later time (與介詞連用) 遠在更早或更遲的時間: He went home long ago. I came long before he did. 他很久以前回家；我在他來之前老早就來了. They finished long after the others. 他們在別人之後很久才完成. Note 說明: see Note under **long¹** on difference between long before and before long. 見 long¹ 條下關於 long before 和 before long 之間差別的說明. **longer** (with **any, no, much** etc.) beyond a certain time (與 any, no, much 等連用) 晚於 (或超過) 某時: I could not wait any much longer. 我不能再等了. How much longer must he stay here? 他還得在這裏停留多久? **long-'standing** adj having existed for a long time 存在已久的，長期存在的. **long-'suffering** adj suffering or enduring patiently 忍受長期苦難的；善忍耐的，堅忍的.

long [lɔŋ] vi want very much 渴望: The people longed for peace. 人民渴望和平. He is longing to meet you. 他渴望見到你. **longing** nc / u: their longing for peace 他們對和平的渴望. Also 亦作 adj: He had a longing look on his face. 他臉上顯出渴望的神色.

longitude ['lɔŋgitju:d] nu distance in degrees east or west of a line drawn over the surface of the earth between the north and south poles 經度. see 見 **latitude**.

loo [lu:] nc lavatory (informal) 廁所 (非正式).

loofah ['lu:fə] nc dried inside of a plant used to rub the skin when having a bath 絲瓜絡 (用於洗澡時擦皮膚).

look [luk] vt / i **1** turn one's eyes towards; try to see 望，視；看: I want you to look at this map. 我要你看這張地圖. He looked everywhere but could not find it. 他四處看但沒找到. If you look carefully, you will see a small mark on the paper. 如果你仔細看，你會看到紙上有一個小標記. **2** appear to be 看來像是，顯得: They looked very happy. 他們看來好像很高興. The box looks heavy. 那箱子看上去很重. The school looks closed. 那學校看上去關着. Also with **like** and **as if** 也與 like 和 as if 連用: He looks like a soldier. 他看起來像個士兵. It looks like rain / It looks as if it will rain. 看來要下雨. **3** (with reference to things) face, be turned, in a particular direction (指事物) 面向；朝向: Our house looks south. 我們的房子朝南. **4** be careful; pay attention to 留神；注意: Look where you are going! 當心走路! Look what he's done! 瞧他幹的事! Also 亦作 nc **1** act of looking 望；視；看: He had / took a look at the picture. 他看了一下這張圖畫. **2** appearance; what one's face shows 外表；臉色；神情: He gave me a thankful look. 他向我表露了感激的神情. **3** (in pl) appearance of the face (用於複數) 面貌，容貌. The cut above his eye has spoilt his looks. 他眼睛上方的傷口損壞了他的容貌. **look after someone** take care of him: Who is looking after the children? 誰在照顧這些孩子? **look at someone / something 1** turn the eyes towards 朝…看，看 **2** examine; consider 檢查；考慮: The doctor looked at his in-

jured hand. 醫生檢查他受傷的手. *They refuse to look at my suggestion.* 他們拒絕考慮我的建議. **look back** turn the eyes to what is behind 回頭看: *He stopped at the door and looked back.* 他在門口停下, 回頭看了看. **look down on someone / something** think oneself better than; despise 瞧不起; 輕視: *The rich look down on the poor.* 富人瞧不起窮人. **look for something 1** try to find 尋找. **2** expect 期待: *Don't look for any help from him.* 別指望他的幫助. **look forward to** expect / wait for with pleasure (以愉快的心情)期待; 盼望: *I am looking forward to seeing my parents again.* 我在盼望着再次見到我的父母親. **look into something 1** turn the eyes towards the inside of 朝…裏面看: *He looked into the hole.* 他朝洞裏看. **2** examine; consider 檢查, 調查; 思考: *The police are looking into the complaint.* 警察正在調查這起投訴. **look on 1** watch without taking part 旁觀: *When they began fighting he just looked on.* 他們開始打架時, 他只是旁觀. **2** read a book together with somebody (與某人)合讀, 合看: *Because I lost my history book I looked on with him.* 因為我把歷史書丟了, 所以我和他合看. 即: 我和他兩人一起看他的書. **look out 1** turn the eyes towards what is outside 朝外看: *The boy looked out (of) the window.* 那男孩從窗口向外望. **2** (with reference to things) face towards; have a view of (指物) 面朝; 有…的景色: *His house looks out to sea.* 他的房子面對大海. *The garden looks out over the mountains.* 那花園朝着山. **3** be careful 小心: *Look out!* 當心! **'look-out 1** *nc* person who keeps watch 守望者, 瞭望

員. **2** *nc* place where someone keeps watch 瞭望台. **3** *nu* state of being ready or careful 謹防; 留意: *You must keep a good look-out for snakes.* 你必須小心提防蛇. **look up** raise the eyes 向上看, 仰視. **look something up** find and study in a book etc. (在書等裏)查找: *You should look up all new words in your dictionary.* 你應當在詞典中查找所有的生詞.

loom¹ [lu:m] *nc* machine for weaving cloth 織布機.

loom² [lu:m] *vi* be seen, but not clearly and so appear to be larger and more frightening 隱約出現(因此顯得更大、更害怕): *The trees loomed through the mist.* 樹在霧中隱約出現.

loop [lu:p] *nc* shape made by a line drawn on paper, a piece of rope, wire etc when it is curved back over itself 圈; 環. Also 亦作 *vt / i* make, tie with, a loop (使)成圈或環; 把…打成環. *He looped the rope round the post.* 用繩子環繞柱子打圈繫住. *The road loops through the forest.* 這條路迂迴曲折穿過森林.

loophole ['lu:phoul] *nc* way out of a difficulty, restriction etc. 漏洞: *Wealthy people often look for loopholes in the tax laws.* 富人常常尋找稅法中的漏洞.

loose [lu:s] *adj* **1** not tight; not fixed 不緊的, 寬的, 鬆的, 不固定的, 不牢的: *loose knot* 未繫牢的結; *loose screw* 鬆動的螺釘; *loose tooth* 鬆動的牙齒; *loose coat* 寬鬆的上衣; *a box full of loose stones* 裝滿鬆散石頭的箱子. **2** free; not under control 自由的; 無約束的: *The horses are running loose in the field.* 這些馬在田野裏亂跑. *Our dog got loose last night.* 我們家的狗昨晚跑了. **3** (with reference to behaviour) too free; immoral (指行爲)過份隨便的, 放蕩的; 不道德

的; *a loose woman* 放蕩的女人. *He leads a loose life.* 他過着放蕩的生活. **4** (with reference to the body) able to move freely (指身體) 不結實的, 鬆弛的: *He has loose limbs.* 他的四肢鬆弛難看. Also 亦作 *vt* make loose (*o.f.* use **loosen**) 解開; 放鬆; 使自由(舊式 —— 用在用 **loosen**). **loosely** *adv* **break loose** become free by breaking a door, the rope by which something was tied etc. 挣脱; (破門、斷繩) 逃脱: *During the storm the boxes on the ship broke loose.* 暴風雨期間船上的箱子被水冲走.

loosen ['lu:sn] *vt / i* become or make loose 變鬆; 放鬆; 放寬; 解開; 釋放.

loot [lu:t] *nu* property which is stolen or taken illegally by force 臟物; 掠奪物: *The thieves were caught with their loot by the police.* 警察抓住小偷並繳獲臟物. Also 亦作 *vt / i* take loot from 掠奪; 強奪: *The angry mob looted the shops.* 憤怒的人羣洗劫了商店.

lop [lɔp] *vt* (with **off** or **away**) cut easily (esp. the end or top of something) (與 **off** 或 **away** 連用) 砍去 (尤指某物的末端或頂部): *He lopped off the small branches of the tree.* 他砍掉樹的小樹枝. *past* 過去式和過去分詞 **lopped.** **'lop-'sided** *adj* hanging down more on one side than the other 傾側的; 不平衡的.

lord [lɔ:d] *nc* **1** master; ruler; king 主人; 統治者; 國王. **2** (**Lord**) God; Christ 上帝; 基督: *the Lord's Day* i.e. Sunday 主日, 即: 星期日. **3** (*Brit*) nobleman; peer (英) 貴族: *The House of Lords* i.e. the upper house of Parliament in Britain, the members of which are lords 上議院, 即: 英國議會的上議院, 其成員都是貴族. **4** (*Brit* (**Lord**) title given to persons in certain important positions (英) 對某些要人的尊稱:

Lord Chancellor 大法官; **Lord Mayor** 市長. **lordly** *adj* like a lord; proud 似貴族的; 高傲的. **lordliness** *nu* **lordship** *nc* (with **His, Your, Their**) formal way of speaking to or about a lord (與 His, Your, Their 連用) 閣下 (對貴族說話或提到貴族時的正式稱呼): *I am very pleased Your Lordship could come.* 閣下的到來我非常高興.

lore [lɔ:*] *nu* knowledge (esp. that passed by the older people to the younger) (尤指老人傳給年輕人的) 學問或知識: *In the past every young man learnt the lore of his tribe.* 過去每個青年人都學習本部落先輩傳下的知識.

lorry ['lɔri] *nc* (*Brit*) long vehicle used for carrying heavy loads (英) 載貨卡車. (*US* 美 **truck**).

lose [lu:z] *vt / i* **1** have, cause to have, no longer 失去; 使失去: *If you are not careful, you will lose your money.* 如果你不小心, 你會把錢丢了. *He has lost his father* i.e. by death. 他失去了父親. 即: 父親死亡. *Laziness lost him his job.* 由於懶惰他失業了. **2** be unable to find 找不到; 遺失: *You will lose your way if you go alone.* 如果你一個人去, 你會迷路. *I have lost my cigarettes.* 我的香烟丢了. **3** be too late for 未能趕上: *Hurry up! You may lose your train.* 快點! 你或許趕不上火車. **4** be, become slower in time (時間) 慢了: *This clock loses five minutes each day.* 這鐘每天慢五分鐘. **5** be unable to win; be defeated 未能獲勝; 輸, 失敗: *Our team lost the game* 我們隊比賽輸了. (*opp* 反義詞 **win**). **6** (in *passive*) die 陣亡 (用於被動語態) 死: *Thousands of soldiers were lost in the battle.* 成千上萬的士兵戰死. *His brother was lost an sea.* 他的兄弟在海上喪生. *past* 過去式和過去分詞 **lost** [lɔst]. **'loser** *nc* person who loses 輸

者: *bad loser* i.e. person who does not like losing and shows his feelings about it 輸不起的人; *good loser* i.e. person who loses cheerfully and does not complain about losing 輸得起的人.

loss [lɒs] **1** *nu* act or state of losing or having lost 損失; 喪失; 失敗: *The loss of his job worries him.* 他爲失去工作而憂愁. *The accident caused a great loss of time.* 這次事故造成時間的重大損失. *The loss of the last game by our team surprised us.* 我們隊上次比賽失敗使我們大爲驚愕. **2** *nc* somebody / something lost 傷亡者; 損失物; 喪失物: *The enemy retreated after heavy losses* i.e. after losing many men. 敵人在遭受重大傷亡後退却了. *The profits are greater than the losses.* 盈利大於虧損. **be at a loss** not know what to say or do 不知道(該說甚麼或做甚麼): *I was at a loss as to / about what to tell him.* 我不知道該告訴他甚麼.*They were at a loss for words* i.e. they did not know what to say. 他們不知道說甚麼好.

lost [lɒst] past of **lose.** lose 的過去式和過去分詞.

lot [lɒt] *nc* **1** one of a number of objects used to decide something by chance (e.g. a piece of paper with a number or one's name) 籤, 鬮(例如: 寫有數字或名字的一張紙). **2** number of articles sold together at an auction sale (拍賣中一起出售的)一組物件. **3** number of articles of the same kind 若干相同的物件, 一批物件: *The class has been given & new lot of reading books* 班上得到新的一批讀本. **a lot of, lots of** a great amount or number of 許多; 很多: *He has a lot / lots of money.* 他有很多錢. *A lot / lots of people came.* 許多人來. *We see a lot of him these days* i.e. we see him often. 現在我們常常看到他. Also 亦作 *adv: He is a lot / lots fatter.* 他胖了好多. *Note* 說明: *lots* is usu. *informal; a lot* is normal. lots 通常爲非正式; a lot 爲正常說法.

lotion ['ləʊʃən] *nc* type of liquid rubbed on the skin or hair to cure a disease or improve one's appearance. (擦於皮膚上或頭髮上, 用於治病或改善外觀的)洗液, 洗劑; 護膚液; 護髮劑: *Women use many kinds of skin lotion.* 婦女使用多種的護膚液.

lottery ['lɒtəri] *nc* method of giving prizes to a few persons out of the many who have bought numbered tickets. The winning tickets are chosen by chance 抽彩給獎法(得獎純屬偶然).

lotus ['ləʊtəs] *nc* any of several water lilies of tropical Africa and Asia (熱帶非洲和亞洲的)蓮, 荷花.

loud [laʊd] *adj* **1** making a great sound; easy to hear 大聲的; 吵鬧的; 響亮的; 宏亮的: *The loud noise of the guns could be heard for miles.* 大砲的巨響數英里外都聽得見. *He spoke in a loud voice.* 他大聲說話. **2** (with reference to colours or behaviour) too bright or too noisy (指顏色和行爲)過份艷麗的, 過份炫耀的: *He was wearing a loud tie.* 他繫着過份花哨的領帶. **loud, loudly** *adv: He should not speak so loud / loudly.* 他不應該這樣大聲說話. *He was very loudly dressed.* 他穿得很不可耐. **loudness** *nu* **'loud'speaker 1** device which produces the sound in a radio or television set etc. (收音機, 電視機等的)喇叭. **2** apparatus which increases the sound of a voice sent by wire from a central point (e.g. in a large railway station or factory) (大火車站、工廠裏

的)揚聲器, 擴音器.

lounge [laundʒ] *vi* sit or stand lazily; spend time idly 懶洋洋地坐着或站着; 閑蕩, 虛度光陰: *The pupils were lounging about the playground.* 學生在操場上到處閑逛. Also 亦作 *nc* 1 place where one can sit or rest (e.g. in a hotel, an airport etc.) (旅館, 機場等處的)休息室, 休息處. 2 sitting room in a house 起居室; 客廳. '**lounge suit** (mainly *Brit*) man's suit of jacket and trousers, with or without a waistcoat, for everyday use (主要用於英)男子日常所穿的西裝(包括上衣, 褲子, 背心, 或不包括背心).

louse [laus] *nc* type of small insect which lives on the skin and in the hair of animals and humans 蝨子. *pl* 複數 **lice** [lais]. **lousy** ['lauzi] *adj* 1 having lice 生蝨子的; 多蝨子的. 2 bad 糟糕的, 壞的: *He made a lousy speech.* (*informal* in sense 2) 他發言很糟糕. (義2爲非正式).

lout [laut] *nc* tough, ill-mannered man 舉止粗野的男人.

love [lʌv] *nu* fondness; affection; very great liking 喜愛; 愛; 鍾愛; 熱愛: *He always had a love of / for sport.* 他始終愛好運動. *It is easy to understand their love for their parents.* 不難理解他們對父母親的愛. 2 *nu* fondness between a man and a woman; sexual desire. 男女之間的愛; 性愛; 性慾: *They are in love with each other.* 他們在相愛. 3 *nc* somebody / something which causes fondness 討人喜歡的人 / 物: *She was his one and only love.* 她是他唯一所愛的人. *Hunting is their great love.* 狩獵是他們的最大嗜好. 4 *nu* (sport esp. tennis) no score; nil. (運動尤指網球)零分; 零: *The score is now 40-love* i.e. 40 points to nil 比分現在是四十比零; *love all* i.e. no score

by either side 零比零. Also 亦作 *vt*: *He loves his parents.* 他愛他的父母親. *He loves football.* 他喜愛足球. *They love each other.* 他們彼此相愛. **lover** *nc* (usu. with reference to a man if sense is **love** 2) person who loves (通常指男性)情人, 情夫. '**love affair** (usu. with reference to sexual relations between those who are not married to each other) period when a man and woman are very much in love with each other (通常指非夫妻男女之間的性關係)短暫戀愛, 風流韻事. '**love letter** letter about love sent to somebody with whom one is in love 情書. **make love to somebody** engage in acts of love (in sense 2) with somebody 與某人發生性關係.

lovely ['lʌvli] *adj* beautiful; delightful 美麗的; 可愛的; 令人愉快的: *She is a lovely woman.* 她是個美人兒. *We are having lovely weather just now.* 現在的天氣真好.

loving ['lʌviŋ] *adj* feeling love 愛的; 親愛的; 鍾情的. **lovingly** *adv*.

low [lou] *adj* 1 near the ground; not high 靠近地面的; 不高的: *A low shelf ran round the room.* 房間的四週擺放着低的架子. *Behind there was a row of low houses.* 那裏後面是一排低矮的屋子. 2 (with reference to sound, light, pressure, temperature etc.) not great (指聲音, 光, 壓力, 溫度等)不大的; 不高的; 低的: *He spoke in a low voice.* 他低聲說話. *The lamp was low.* 燈光微弱. *In winter temperatures are low.* 冬天溫度低. 3 below, or less than, usual 低於通常的; 少於通常的: *It was a very low tide.* 潮水很低. *We bought it at a low price.* 我們以低價買下. 4 (with reference to persons) poor; without social position; not important (指人)貧窮的; 沒有社會地位

的; 卑賤的; 不重要的: *He has a low
position in the factory.* 他在工廠裏的
地位很低. **5** rough; coarse 粗魯的; 粗
俗的; 粗魯的: *He enjoys low company.* 他喜歡結交下層社會的朋友.
*They have low manners and a low
sense of humour.* 他們態度粗魯, 幽默
感低級. *comparative* 比較級 **lower**.
superlative 最高級 **lowest**. Also 亦作
adv: *You must speak low.* 你必須小聲
說話. *comparative* 比較級 **lower**. *superlative* 最高級 **lowest**. '**lowlands**
npl country which is low and flat
compared with the hills round it 低
地. **lie low 1** lie down close to the
ground 伏於; 平臥. **2** keep hidden or
out of the way 隱匿; 躲藏; 潛伏; *The
thieves are lying low until they can
leave the country.* 盜賊躲藏起來一直
到能逃出這個國家才出來. **run low**
become scarce; be almost finished 短
缺; 減少; 幾乎耗盡: *Before the end of
the holiday my money was running
very low.* 假期還沒有結束我的錢已花
得所剩無幾.

lower ['ləuə*] *vi / i* **1** become, cause to
become, less high; come or bring
down 降低; 減低; 降下; 落下; 放下:
They lowered the flag at sunset. 他們
在日落時將旗降下. *This shop has lowered its prices.* 這家商店已降低了價
格. **2** make less or weaker 減少; 使減
弱; 削弱: *You must lower your voice.*
你必須把聲音放低. *I lowered the
pressure in the tyre.* 我把輪胎的壓力
放低.

lowly ['ləuli] *adj* low in social position;
not proud; simple 社會地位低的; 謙遜
的; 平凡的; 簡單的.

loyal ['lɔiəl] *adj* faithful 忠實的; 忠誠的:
He is a loyal friend. 他是一個忠實的
朋友. *We should be loyal to our
country.* 我們必須忠於國家. (opp 反

義詞 **disloyal**). **loyally** *adv* **loyalty** *nc
/ u.*

lozenge ['lɔzindʒ] *nc* **1** four-sided figure
in the shape of a diamond 菱形. **2**
small tablet containing medicine
which is sucked (usu. to cure a sore
throat) 供吮食的小藥片 (通常用於治療
咽喉炎).

lubricate ['lu:brikeit] *vt* make an apparatus or machine work more smooth-
ly by putting oil or grease on it. 加油
潤滑; 使潤滑: *You should lubricate
the wheels of your bicycle once a
month.* 你應當給你的自行車的車輪每
月潤滑一次. **lubrication** [lub-
ri'keiʃən] *nu.*

lucid ['lu:sid] *adj* **1** clear; easily understood 清楚的; 易懂的: *He gave a lucid
description of what happened.* 他對所
發生的事情作了清晰的描述. *He has a
lucid brain* i.e. one that thinks clearly.
他有一個清楚的頭腦. 即: 思考條理清
楚. *adj* **2** sane; fully conscious (usu.
between periods of insanity or unconsciousness) 神志正常的; 完全清醒的
(通常指神經錯亂或昏迷之間的清醒時
間); *in his lucid moments* 在他神志清
醒的時候. *He was lucid for a few minutes before he lost his senses again.*
他清醒了幾分鐘又昏迷了過去. **lucid-
ly** *adv* **lucidity** [lu:'siditi] *nu.*

luck [lʌk] *nu* chance, either good or
bad; something which happens by
chance to somebody (好或壞的) 運氣;
機遇: *It was luck that saved his life.*
是運氣救了他的性命. *Our luck made
us lose.* 運氣使我們遭受損失. *They
have good / bad luck in their lives.*
他們無論做甚麼都走運/不走運. **lucky**
adj bringing, having good luck 幸運
的; 好運的; 僥倖的: *You are a lucky
man.* 你是一個幸運的人. (opp 反義詞
unlucky). **luckily** *adv*: *Luckily I was*

able to help him. 幸虧我能幫助他. **be in luck** have good luck. *(informal)* 運氣好; 走運. (非正式). **be out of luck** have bad luck 運氣不好; 不走運: *When at last we reached the railway station we were out of luck. The train had gone.* *(informal)* 我們真不走運, 當我們終於到達火車站時, 火車已經開走了. (非正式).

lucrative ['lu:krətiv] *adj* profitable 有利 (可圖)的, 賺錢的.

ludicrous ['lu:dikrəs] *adj* causing laughter; very foolish 可笑的; 十分愚蠢的. **ludicrously** *adv* **ludicrousness** *nu*.

lug [lʌg] *vt* pull with force; drag roughly or with effort 用力拉; 使勁急拖: *They lugged the boxes across the field.* 他們吃力地把箱子拖過易地. *past* 過去式和過去分詞 **lugged**.

luggage ['lʌgidʒ] *nu* a traveller's bags, boxes etc. 行李 (esp. *US* 尤美 **baggage**).

lugubrious [lu'gu:briəs] *adj* sadlooking; gloomy 悲哀的, 愁容滿面的; 憂鬱的, 陰鬱的.

lukewarm ['lu:k'wɔ:m] *adj* **1** (with reference to liquids) slightly warm (指液體)微溫的. **2** (with reference to feelings, behaviour etc) indifferent; weak (指感情, 行爲等)冷淡的; 軟弱無力的: *They have only a lukewarm interest in the plan.* 他們對這個計劃不怎麼感興趣.

lull [lʌl] *vt / i* become, cause to become, quiet slowly (使)慢慢安靜下來, (使) 緩和: *During the night the wind lulled.* 風在夜間逐漸停了下來. *She lulled the baby to sleep.* 她哄嬰孩入睡. Also 亦作 *nc* period of quiet, in a storm or when there is noise and activity 間歇, 喧囂, 活動的) 停歇時期, 間歇, 暫停: *There was a lull in the storm.* 風暴已暫停了. *During the holi-*

days there was a lull in business. 假日期間生意暫時停歇.

lullaby ['lʌləbai] *nc* song sung to a child to lull it to sleep 搖籃曲, 催眠曲.

lumbago [lʌm'beigou] *nu* illness which causes pain in the muscles of the lower back above the hips 腰痛, 腰肌痛, 腰部風濕痛.

lumber ['lʌmbə*] *nu* things which are not in use and are not needed but are kept until they are 存放起來的不用物品. Also 亦作 *vt* give someone something unpleasant 塞給(某人不合意的事物): *I was lumbered with this job.* 我肩負着這項困難的工作. **lumberjack** man who cuts down trees 伐木工人.

luminous ['lu:minəs] *adj* giving light; shining; clear 發光的, 發亮的; 照耀着的; 清楚的: *The clock has a luminous face* i.e. the numbers and hands shine in the dark. 這時鐘有夜光鐘面. 即: 數字和指針會在黑暗中發亮.

lump [lʌmp] *nc* **1** small piece of matter without a definite shape (一小) 塊, 團: *a lump of bread* 一塊麵包; *a few lumps of coal* 幾塊煤. **2** swelling on the body (身上的) 腫塊, 隆起: *There is a lump on his head where it hit the wall.* 他的頭在碰到牆的部位腫起了一塊. Also 亦作 *vt* (usu. with **together**) put together (in a lump); consider as being the same as (通常與 together 連用) 把…放在一起(形成一塊); 堆成一堆; 認爲相同: *We lumped all our money together to buy our teacher a present.* 我們把所有的錢合在一起給老師買一件禮物. *We can't lump all these different things together.* 我們不能把這些不同的東西歸併在一起. Also 亦作 *vt* put up with 忍受, 容忍: *If you don't like it you can lump it. (infor-*

mal) 你不喜歡也得忍着點. (非正式).

lumpy *adj* '**lump** '**sum** payment in one single amount, not in instalments 一次性付清的款項.

lunacy ['lu:nəsi] *nu* see 見 **lunatic**.

lunar ['lu:nə*] *adj* of the moon 月亮的, 太陰的.

lunatic ['lu:nətik] *adj* mad 瘋的, 瘋狂的. Also 亦作 *nc* person who is mad 瘋子; 狂人. **lunacy** ['lu:nəsi] *nu* madness 瘋狂; 精神錯亂, 瘋狂的行爲.

lunch [lʌntʃ] *nc / u* meal taken in the middle of the day 午餐; 午飯: *He will be back from lunch soon.* 他很快就會吃完午飯回來. Also 亦作 *vt / i* have, give, lunch 吃午餐; 供給午飯, 請吃午餐: *We usually lunch at home.* 我們通常在家裏吃午飯. *They lunched us at the hotel.* 他們在旅館裏請我們吃午餐.

luncheon ['lʌnʃən] *nc / u* lunch (*rather formal*) 午餐 (較爲正式). '**luncheon voucher** voucher given to an employee to confirm that he can have lunch in a restaurant at his employer's expense (雇主發給員工在餐館用午膳, 費用由雇主負擔的) 就餐憑證.

lung [lʌŋ] *nc* one of the two organs of breathing in animals and humans (指人或動物兩肺中之一) 肺.

lunge [lʌndʒ] *nc* quick, forward movement of the arm and body (esp. with a sword or other weapon) (身體和胳臂一起的) 向前猛衝; (尤指用劍或其他武器的) 刺, 戳. Also 亦作 *vt / i: He lunged at me with his stick.* 他用手杖向我猛戳過來.

lurch [lə:tʃ] *nc* sudden movement to one side 突向一邊的傾斜, 傾側: *The ship gave a lurch.* 船突然傾斜了一下. Also 亦作 *vi* move with a lurch; stagger 突然傾斜; 蹣跚: *The ship lurched through the rough sea.* 船在波濤洶湧

的海上東倒西歪地行駛. *The beaten boxer lurched into his corner after the fight.* 拳擊後被擊敗的拳擊手搖搖晃晃地回到自己的角落.

lure [luə*] *nc* **1** something bright used to attract wild birds and animals (引誘野禽、野獸的) 鮮艷誘餌. **2** anything which attracts 誘惑物, 吸引力: *The lure of gold caused them to explore the country.* 黃金的誘惑促使他們去勘探那個國家. *He left home because of the lures of life in the city.* 由於城市生活的誘惑他離家出走了. Also 亦作 *vt* attract 吸引, 引誘, 誘惑: *Life in the city lured him from home.* 城市生活誘使他離開家庭.

lurid ['luərid] *adj* **1** brightly coloured (esp. light yellow like a flame) 顏色鮮明的 (尤指似火焰的淡黃色). **2** shocking and unpleasant 驚人的; 可怖的; 令人不愉快的: *He told us many lurid stories about the war.* 他告訴我們許多有關戰爭的恐怖故事.

lurk [lə:k] *vi* stay hidden (usu. in order to attack) 潛伏, 埋伏 (通常指伺機出擊): *There is a lion lurking somewhere in the long grass.* 在長草叢裏潛伏着一隻獅子.

luscious ['lʌʃəs] *adj* very sweet and pleasant to eat 極爲甜美的, 美味的, 可口的. *luscious fruit* 甜美的水果.

lush [lʌʃ] *adj* **1** (with reference to plants and grass) fresh and growing thickly (指植物、草) 蒼翠的, 茂盛的. **2** showing an abundance of anything; rich 繁茂的; 豐富的: *lush surroundings (informal in sense* 2) 豪華的環境 (義2爲非正式).

lust [lʌst] *nc / u* sexual desire; any strong desire for something 性慾, 淫慾; 強烈的慾望: *He is filled with a lust for power.* 他熱衷於追求權力. Also 亦作 *vi* have lust 貪求, 渴望: *He lusts*

for / after power. 他渴求權力. **lustful**
adj.

lustre ['lʌstə*] (*US* 美 **luster**) *nu* brightness (e.g. of polished metal, smooth cloth etc.) (拋光的金屬, 平滑的布料等的) 光澤, 光亮.

lusty ['lʌsti] *adj* strong; vigorous 強壯的; 精力充沛的.

luxuriant [lʌg'zjuəriənt] *adj* growing thickly; in great quantity 茂盛的; 大量的: *After the rains the grass is luxuriant* 雨後草地長勢繁茂.

luxury ['lʌkʃəri] **1** *nu* enjoyment of pleasures and possessions which only great wealth can obtain 奢侈, 奢華(的享受): *The king lived in luxury.* 國王過着奢華的生活. **2** *nc* something expensive and enjoyable but not necessary 奢侈品: *In some places white bread is a luxury.* 在一些地方白麵包是奢侈的東西. Also 亦作 *adj*: *a luxury hotel* i.e. a very comfortable but expensive one 豪華的旅館, 即: 非常舒適但費用高昂的旅館. **luxurious** [lʌg'zjuəriəs] *adj* having luxuries; very comfortable or pleasing, but expensive. 奢侈享受的; 豪華的: *He leads a luxurious life.* 他過着奢侈的生活. *The carpets in the house are luxurious.* 屋子裏的地毯是很豪華的.

lying ['laiiŋ] *pres part of* **lie.** lie 的現在分詞.

lymph [limf] *nu* almost colourless fluid, containing chiefly white blood cells, that is collected from the tissues of the body 淋巴; 淋巴液.

lynch [lintʃ] *vt* kill without bringing to a court of law 私刑處死: *The angry mob lynched the criminal.* 憤怒的暴民把歹徒犯處死.

lyre [laiə] *nc* small stringed instrument played by the ancient Greeks (古希臘的)豎琴.

lyrics ['liriks] *npl* words of a song (usu. a pop song) (通常指現代流行歌曲的)歌詞. **lyrical** *adj* full of emotion 充滿感情的: *When he speaks about his own country he becomes lyrical.* 當談到自己的國家時, 他就感情激動起來.

M,m

ma [mɑː] *nc* child's name for **mother.** *(informal)* (兒語) 媽 (非正式).

ma'am [mæm] *n* short form of **madam.** madam 的縮畧形式.

mac [mæk] *nc* short form of **mackintosh.** mackintosh 的縮畧形式.

macabre [məˈkɑːbr] *adj* filling one with fear or horror 駭人的; 令人毛骨悚然的: *The film I saw last night frightened me; it had some very macabre scenes.* 昨晚看的電影把我嚇壞了; 影片中有一些非常駭人的鏡頭. *He has a macabre sense of humour* i.e. he gets amusement from frightening or horrifying subjects. 他有恐怖幽默感, 即: 他從駭人的問題中得到樂趣.

macaroni [ˌmækəˈrouni] *nu* mixture of wheat flour made into long tubes and cooked for eating (originally an Italian dish) 通心粉 (原係意大利食品).

mace [meis] *nc* kind of rod carried in the presence of a high official (e.g. the mayor of a town) to show the importance of his position (持於高級官員面前, 作爲職位標誌的) 權杖.

machine [məˈʃiːn] *nc* something which has been made with moving parts to do a certain job (e.g. a *printing machine, a sewing machine*) and which usu. works by electricity or steam 機器, 機械 (通常用電力或蒸汽驅動, 例如 printing machine 印刷機, sewing machine 縫紉機). **machinery** [məˈʃiːnəri] *nu* **1** machines in general 機器的總稱. **2** parts of a machine 機器的機件, 部件. **3** way a thing is run 辦事方式或方法; 管理制度或機構: *In*

this lesson we are going to study the machinery of government. 這一課我們將研究政府的組織機構. **machinist** *nc* person who works a machine 機器的操作工人, 機工. **ma'chine gun** gun which fires without stopping while the trigger is pressed 機關槍, 機槍.

mackerel [ˈmækrl] *nc* small fish found in the Atlantic and used as food 青花魚, 鯖魚 (生存於大西洋可供食用的小魚). *pl* **mackerel** or **mackerels.**

mackintosh [ˈmækintɔʃ] *nc* coat made to keep out rain 雨衣.

mad [mæd] *adj* **1** not having the power to think normally 癲的, 發癲的, 精神錯亂的: *When he heard of his son's death, the poor old man went mad.* 那可憐的老人聽到他兒子死亡便發癲了. **2** very stupid or wild 極爲愚蠢的; 瘋狂的; 狂妄的: *It was a mad idea to climb the mountain in this bad weather.* 想在這樣的壞天氣裏去爬山是愚蠢透頂的主意. **3** very angry or upset 非常生氣的, 惱火的: *He is mad at losing all his money.* (informal in sense 3) 他丟了所有的錢, 心中十分惱火. (義3爲非正式). **madly** *adv* **madness** *nu* **madden** *vt* make somebody angry 使生氣: *Your insolent attitude maddened him.* 你那傲慢的態度使他很生氣. **maddening** *adj* **'madman** person who is mad 瘋子, 狂人. **drive someone mad** make someone mad 使得某人發瘋, 氣得某人發狂. **go mad** become mad (in sense 1). 發瘋, 發狂.

madam [ˈmædəm] *n* respectful way of speaking to a woman (esp. if you do not know her name) It is therefore very often used by shop assistants etc. 夫人, 太太, 女士, 小姐 (對婦女的尊稱, 尤用於稱呼不知其姓名的婦女, 因此常被店員等用以稱呼顧客). **Dear Madam** expression often used as a way of beginning a formal letter, whether you know the person's name or not 親愛的女士 (正式書信開頭的尊稱語; 不管寫信人是否認識對方均用此稱呼).

made [meid] past of **make**. make 的過去式和過去分詞.

Madonna [mə'dɒnə] *nc* Mary, the Mother of Jesus Christ 聖母瑪利亞 (耶穌的母親).

magazine [mægə'zi:n] *nc* printed collection of short stories, articles, photographs etc appearing regularly (usu. every week or month) 雜誌: *He made some money from writing short stories for magazines.* 他爲雜誌寫短篇小說掙些錢.

magenta [mə'dʒentə] *nu* purplish red 紫紅色.

maggot ['mægət] *nc* fly or insect in its early stages, often found in bad meat 蛆 (蒼蠅或昆蟲的幼蟲, 常存在於腐敗的肉中).

magic ['mædʒik] *nu* **1** ability which people are sometimes supposed to have to make things happen through charms, spirits etc. 魔法; 法術; 妖術; 巫術: *The villagers thought that the young man had been killed by magic.* 村民認爲那年青人是被妖術害死的. **2** use of stage tricks to make things happen that seem impossible 魔術; 戲法: *In a display of magic. the performer pulled a rabbit out of a hat.* 在表演魔術時, 表演者從帽子裏拉出一隻兔子. **3** special charm or influence 魔力; 魅力: *the magic of his words* 他說話的魅力. **magical** *adj* **magician**

[mə'dʒiʃən] *nc* person who uses magic 魔術師; 術士.

magistrate ['mædʒistreit] *nc* person appointed to act as a judge in the lower courts. Justice of the Peace (J.P.) 地方法官; 治安官 (J.P.).

magma ['mægmə] *nu* hot melted rock found below the solid surface of the earth; crude pasty mixture of mineral or organic matter 岩漿; (礦物或有機物的) 稀糊狀混合物.

magmata ['mægmətə] *pl* of **magma**. magma 的複數.

magnanimous [mæg'næniməs] *adj* generous and noble 寬宏大量的, 慷慨的; 高尚的: *After winning the war. the magnanimous victor set all his prisoners free.* 在贏得戰爭勝利以後, 寬宏大量的勝利者釋放了所有的俘虜. **magnanimity** [mægnə'nimiti] *nu* generosity 慷慨, 寬宏大量.

magnate ['mægneit] *nc* somebody who is rich or important (esp. in business) 闊人; 權貴; (尤指工商界的) 巨頭, 大亨: *He started off poor but he eventually became an oil magnate.* 他開始時很窮, 但是最後成爲石油大王.

magnesium [mæg'ni:zjəm] *nu* light, silver-white, metallic chemical element 鎂.

magnet ['mægnit] *nc* piece of metal (usu. iron or steel and often shaped like a horseshoe) which is able to attract another piece of metal 磁鐵 (通常用鐵或鋼做成, 形狀常爲馬蹄形). **magnetic** [mæg'netik] *adj* **1** acting like, produced by, a magnet 磁的, 有磁性的; 磁化的; 由磁性產生的; *magnetic field* 磁場; *magnetic needle* i.e. one which points north in a compass 磁針即: 羅盤的指北針. **2** attractive. 有吸引力的: *He has a magnetic personality.* 他的個性很有魅力.

magnetism *nu.*

magnificent [mæg'nifisnt] *adj* **1** wonderful, excellent 驚人的; 非凡的; 卓越的; 傑出的: *He is a magnificent athlete.* 他是一個了不起的運動員. **2** of splendid appearance 壯觀的; 壯麗的; 華麗的: *In their full uniforms the soldiers looked magnificent.* 士兵們穿着全套軍禮服看起來很神氣. **magnificently** *adv.* **magnificence** *nu* splendid appearance 壯麗; 華麗, 堂皇, 莊嚴: *We had to admire the magnificence of the court.* 我們不得不讚嘆宮廷的宏偉莊嚴.

magnify ['mægnifai] *vt* make something appear bigger (with a special lens) (用特殊透鏡) 放大, 擴大: *The microscope magnified the object one hundred times.* 這台顯微鏡把物像放大100倍. **magnifying glass** curved piece of glass used to magnify something 放大鏡.

magnitude ['mægnitju:d] *nc / u* largeness or amount 巨大; 廣大; 重大: *It is a problem of some magnitude* i.e. a large problem. 這是一個重大的問題.

magpie ['mægpai] *nc* noisy black and white bird of the crow family, which sometimes steals small bright objects 鵲.

maharajah [ma:hə'ra:dʒə] *nc* Indian prince 印度大君, 印度土邦主.

mahogany [mə'hɔgəni] **1** *nc* tropical tree found esp. in America 桃花心木樹, 紅木樹(尤指產於美洲的桃花心木樹). **2** *nu* hard wood from this tree, often used for furniture 桃花心木, 紅木(常用於製作傢具). **3** *nu* colour of this wood, dark reddish-brown 桃花心木的顏色, 暗紅褐色. Also 亦作 *adj.*

maid [meid] *nc* **1** woman servant 女僕人; 女傭人; 婢女. **2** girl (*o.f.* in sense 2) 少女(義 2 爲舊式). **old maid 1**

elderly lady who has not married and is unlikely to marry 老處女, 年老未婚的女子. **2** fussy person who becomes annoyed about unimportant things. (*informal*) 爲瑣事煩惱的人, 挑剔的人. (非正式).

maiden ['meidn] *nc* girl, unmarried woman; virgin 少女, 未婚女子; 處女. Also 亦作 *adj.* (both *o.f.*) (兩者均爲舊式) **maiden name** woman's surname before her marriage 女子未婚時的娘家姓. **maiden speech** first speach (e.g. in Parliament) 處女演說, 初次演說(如在議會的首次發言). **maiden voyage** first voyage of a ship (船舶的) 處女航, 首次航行.

mail [meil] *nu* **1** anything sent by post (e.g. letters and parcels) 郵件(例如信和包裹): *The mail is sorted into bags.* 用郵袋分揀郵件. **2** delivery of mail. 郵件的投遞: *Has the morning mail arrived yet?* 早班的郵件到來了嗎? **3** postal service 郵政; 郵遞業務: *Send it by mail* 由郵寄出(信件). Also 亦作 *vt*: *Please mail these letters for me.* 請將這些信件郵寄給我. **mailbox** (*US*) box to which letters are delivered by the post office (美) 郵政信箱, 信箱. **mailman** (*US*) person who delivers mail (美) 郵差, 郵遞員. (*Brit* 英 **postman**) **mail-order** method of buying goods by post instead of visiting a shop 郵購(以郵寄方式購物). **mailing list** list of people to whom letters etc are to be sent regularly (e.g. by a business) (如工商企業定期寄出信件等的) 收郵件人名單, 郵寄名單. **airmail** letters etc delivered by plane 航空郵件; 航空信件.

maim [meim] *vt* injure in such a way that a part of the body becomes useless or partly useless; disable, cripple 使身體受傷致殘; 使傷殘, 使殘廢: *The* *accident maimed him and he was un-able to work.* 這次事故使他受傷致殘，因而無法做工.

main¹ [mein] *adj* most important. 最重要的, 主要的: *With him, pleasure is the main thing in life!* 對他來說, 享樂是生活中最重要的事! *Traffic is busiest on the main road.* 主要道路上的交通是最繁忙的. **mainly** *adv* chiefly, mostly 主要地; 大部份, 大體上. **mainland** 1 a continent or country without its islands (e.g. *the mainland of Scotland*) 大陸; 本土 (不計附近島嶼, 例如蘇格蘭本土). 2 the largest area of land near an island 靠近島嶼的最大陸地: *The ship left the island and headed for the mainland.* 那船離別小島朝附近的最大陸地駛去. **in the main** mostly 大部份, 大體上.

main² [mein] *nc* large pipe for carrying gas, water etc (e.g. *gas main*) (輸送煤氣, 水等的) 總管道 (例如煤氣總管道).

mainstay ['meinstei] *nc* chief support 主要的依靠.

maintain [mein'tein] *vt* 1 keep in good condition; repair 使保持良好狀態; 保養, 維修: *The Town Council maintains the roads* 鎮議會維修道路. 2 continue with, keep unchanged 繼續; 維持; 保持: *The two countries maintained friendly relations in spite of their differences* i.e. they remained friendly. 這兩個國家儘管有分歧仍然保持友好的關係. 3 look after, feed etc. 照顧, 照料; 贍養, 供養: *He has to maintain a wife and five children.* 他必須贍養妻子和五個孩子. 4 keep an opinion, belief etc in spite of contradiction 主張; 堅持(意見信仰等): *I still maintain that I am right and you are wrong.* 我仍然堅持我是對的, 你是錯的. **maintenance** ['meintənəns] *nu* keeping something (esp. a machine etc) in

good condition 維修, 保養(尤指機器等的維修).

maize [meiz] *nu* kind of grain plant 玉米, 玉蜀黍.

majesty ['mædʒisti] *nu* quality of causing one to feel humble or impressed, as in the appearance of a king or queen or the height of mountains etc (帝王等的) 威儀, 威嚴, 尊嚴; (高山等的) 雄偉, 壯麗, 莊嚴: *We could not help being impressed by the majesty of the mountains, as they rose high above us.* 雄偉的高山聳立在我們的上頭不能不給我們留下深刻的印象. **majestic** [mə'dʒestik] *adj* **His (Her, Your) Majesty** respectful way of referring to or speaking to a king or queen (對國王或王后的稱呼) 陛下.

major ['meidʒə*] *adj* great, important 大的; 重要的: *Road accidents are a major problem these days.* 目前道路交通事故是個大問題. *He is having a major operation* i.e. a serious operation. 他在接受一次大手術, 即: 嚴重的手術. *This dispute will be settled by the major powers* i.e. the larger, more powerful countries. 這個爭端要由大國來解決. 即: 由強國解決. (opp 反義詞 **minor**). Also 亦作 *nc* (military) officer of middle rank (軍隊) 少校. **majority** [mə'dʒɔriti] *nc* 1 greater number, more than half 大部分; 大多數; 半數以上: *The majority of households in Britain now have television.* 大多數英國家庭現在都有電視機. (opp 反義詞 **minority**). 2 difference between the number of votes given to the winning party or candidate in an election and the next party or candidate (選舉中得勝政黨或候選人與另一政黨或候選人在所得選票上的) 票數差距, 多得的票數, 超過的票數: *The party I support has won by a majority of 264 votes.* 我所

支持的政黨以超過對方264票獲勝. **3** age after which one can vote etc (in Britain 18) (可以投票等的)法定年齡; 成年(英國爲十八歲): *reach one's majority* 達到法定年齡; 成年.

make [meik] *vt* **1** cause to exist (either out of nothing or by putting things together or changing them in some way) 創造; 做; 生產; 製造; 建造: *God made the world.* 上帝創造世界. *This factory makes cars.* 這家工廠製造汽車. *You can make bread from flour* i.e. flour is one of the things used in making bread. 你可以用麵粉做麵包, 即: 麵粉是做麵包的原料之一. *That house is made of stone* i.e. stone is one of the raw materials. 那棟房子是用石頭建造的. 石頭是原料之一. **2** cause to be 使; 致使; 使成爲: *Your answer made him angry* i.e. he is angry because of what you have said. 你的答覆使他生氣. *The stones at the bottom of the bag made it heavy.* 袋子底部放的石頭使袋子很沉重. **3** force somebody / something to do something 迫使某人/某物做某事: *The robbers made me give them all my money.* 強盜迫使我交出所有的錢. *They made the naughty boy go to bed early.* 他們强使那淘氣的男孩早上床睡覺. *Note* 說明: **1** in this kind of sentence, it is wrong to use *to* with the verb that comes after *make. He made me stand up.* **2** if the sentence is passive, *to* is used in this way: *I was made to stand up.* 1. 在這種句子裏, make 的後面使用帶 to 的動詞是錯誤的. He made me stand up. 2. 如果句子爲被動語態, to 的用法是這樣: I was made to stand up. **4** earn, get 賺得; 掙得; 獲得; 賺取; of money. 他賺很多錢. *He makes £20 a week.* 他一星期賺20英鎊. **5** be the

same as, equal 和…相同, 等於: *One hundred centimetres make one metre.* 一百厘米等於一米. *past* 過去式和過去分詞 **made** [meid]. *Make out a person / thing that makes something.* **maker** *nc* person / thing that makes something. (Often in compounds e.g. *shoemaker*) 製造者; 能進行製造的機器或工具(通常用於複合詞中, 例如: shoemaker). **make for something** go towards 走向…; 朝…前進: *The ship is making for the nearest port.* 這船正朝向最近的港口駛去. **make off** go away; escape 走開; 離開; 逃走: *The boys made off when we shouted at them.* 男孩們在我們向他們大聲叫喊時拔腳就跑. *The thief made off with our money.* 竊賊偷走了我們的錢. **make something out** write out 寫出; 開出: *Make out a cheque for what you owe me.* 開一張你欠我款項的支票. **make someone / something out** be able to see or understand 辨認出; 理解, 懂得: *Can you make out what that object is on the other side of the valley?* 你能看出山谷另一邊的那個物體是甚麼東西嗎? *Can you make out what he is saying?* 你能聽清楚他在說甚麼嗎? **make something up 1** invent; think up; create 捏造, 虛構; 想出; 創作: *The teacher asked the children to make up a story about a trip to the moon.* 老師叫孩子們虛構一個到月球旅行的故事. *It's not true; he made it up.* 這不是真實的, 是他捏造的. **2** stop a quarrel 停止爭吵; 和解; 和好: *They made it up.* 他們言歸於好. **make up (one's face etc)** put liquid, powder etc on the face in order to improve one's appearance 化裝, 扮扮, 化妝(臉部等): *These days many girls make up when they are still quite young.* 現在許多女孩子年紀輕輕的就開始化妝. *She made up her face.* 她在臉上塗脂抹粉.

make-up *nu*. **make up for** compensate for 補償; 賠償; 彌補: *This payment should make up for the time you have wasted.* 這筆付款應該會補償你所花費的時間. **make amends** show that one is sorry for a misdeed etc by doing something to improve things 賠罪; 贖罪; 賠償. **make / pull a face at someone** twist one's face into a strange or amusing shape 向某人裝鬼臉; 向某人做怪相. **make a fool of somebody** cause somebody to seem silly 愚弄某人; 使某人當傻瓜; 使某人出醜: *It is very cruel of these boys to make a fool of that old man.* 這些男孩子作弄那個老人真是殘忍極了. **make it 1** (usu. with reference to time, distance etc) judge or estimate, either by guessing or using some means of measurement (通常指時間、距離等)(用推測, 測量方法進行) 推斷, 判斷, 估計: *What time do you make it?* i.e. what time is it on your watch? 你看現在幾點鐘? 即: 你的錶幾點了? *I make it one o'clock.* 我估計一點鐘了. *How far do you make it to the beach?* 你估計到海灘有多遠? **2** reach; manage to arrive (esp. where there is some difficulty involved); be successful 到達; 設法到達(尤指涉及困難); 成功: *Do you think the ship will make it to the shore?* 你認爲這船能到岸嗎? *We're too late; I don't think we'll make it.* 我們太遲了, 我認爲我們到達不了. *After years as an unsuccessful businessman he's finally made it.* (informal) 在幾年生意不起色之後, 他終於獲得了成功. (非正式). **make a living** earn enough to pay for what one needs 謀生, 營生: *He makes his living from mending shoes.* 他以補鞋爲生. **make use of** use 利用. **make one's way** go (usu. slowly or in spite of some difficulty) (通常指緩慢地或不顧困難地) 走, 行進; 前進: *I made my way carefully down the narrow staircase.* 我小心翼翼地從狹窄的樓梯走下去.

make² [meik] *nc* type of manufacture, style, brand (製造品的)牌號; 樣式; 商標.

make-believe ['meikbili:v] *nu* things which are imaginary 假想的東西; 虛構的東西: *That's nothing but make-believe.* 那只不過是虛構的東西(或想象中的東西).

makeshift ['meikʃift] *adj* used as a substitute for the real thing 權宜之計的; 臨時湊合代用的: *They used the boxes as makeshift chairs.* 他們臨時用木箱當椅子坐.

maladjusted [mælə'dʒʌstid] *adj* mentally or emotionally handicapped in a way that prevents one behaving normally (因精神或情感的不順應使人)舉止行動不正常的, 不適應環境的; 適應不良的: *school for maladjusted children.* 爲不適應環境的兒童設立的學校.

malaria [mə'lɛəriə] *nu* disease caused by the bite of a certain kind of mosquito 瘧疾.

male [meil] *adj* of the sex that does not give birth to young 雄性的, 男性的: *A bull is a male animal, a cow is not.* Bull 是雄性動物, 而 cow 不是 (opp 反義詞 **female**). Also 亦作 *nc* male person, animal etc 男人, 雄性動物等.

malevolent [mə'levəlnt] *adj* wanting to do harm to other people 懷有惡意的, 惡毒的: *He gave me a malevolent look* i.e. by the way he looked at me, I knew he wanted to do me harm. 他惡狠狠地看我一眼, 即: 從他的眼裏, 我看出他想傷害我. **malevolence** *nu*.

malice ['mælis] *nu* unfriendly feelings 惡意; 敵意. **malicious** [mə'liʃəs] *adj*

maliciously *adv*.

malign [mə'lain] *vt*. purposely say untrue and bad things about somebody 誹謗；中傷；譭軆：*They maligned her character as much as they could.* 他們竭力詆毀她的人格．**malignant** [mə'lignənt] *adj* (with reference to diseases) able to cause death (指疾病) 能致命的；惡性的：*a malignant growth on the body* 長在身體上的惡性腫瘤．

mallet ['mælit] *nc* hammer with a wooden head 木槌．

malnutrition [mælnju'triʃən] *nu* poor state of health caused by the lack of enough food or the right kind of food 營養不良：*The poeple in this area suffer from malnutrition.* 這個地區的人患營養不良．

malpractice ['mæl'præktis] *nc/u* (legal) not doing one's duty, or doing one's job dishonestly for personal gain (法律) 玩忽職守，瀆職；為謀取私利的不法行爲，營私舞弊：*The doctor who had neglected his patient was found guilty of malpractice.* 這個醫生因對病人疏忽大意被裁定犯有治療錯誤罪．

malt [mɔːlt] *nu* grain (e.g. barley, oats) specially treated in making beer or spirits 麥芽 (係經過特殊處理的穀物如大麥,燕麥,用於釀造啤酒或酒精)．

maltreat [mæl'triːt] *vt* behave cruelly towards someone 虐待：*This man is accused of maltreating his children.* 這個人被指控虐待他的孩子．

mammal ['mæml] *nc* animal of the kind whose young take milk from the mother's breast 哺乳類動物：*Dogs and cats are mammals.* 狗和貓是哺乳類動物．

mammoth ['mæməθ] *adj* very large 巨大的,龐大的：*a mammoth parade* 盛大的遊行．

mammy ['mæmi] *nc* (child's word for)

mother (兒語) 媽媽．

man [mæn] **1** *nc* male person who has grown up i.e. not a woman, girl or boy 成年男子；男人：*Save the women and children first and let the men out afterwards.* 先救出婦女和兒童,然後再讓男人出來．**2** *n sing* (Often **Man**) the human race (常用 **Man**) 人類：*What wonderful things Man has achieved!* 人類的成就多麼驚人啊！*Note* 說明：in this sense use the word in the *sing* with no article. 此義僅用單數,不帶冠詞．*pl* 複數 **men** [men]. Also 亦作 *vt* put men (esp. soldiers or sailors) where they are needed 給 (需要的地方) 配備人員 (尤指士兵,水手)：*An order was given to man the boats.* 已下命令給各小船配備船員．*past* 過去式和過去分詞 **manned. manly** *adj* brave, strong etc, having the qualities a man is supposed to have 勇敢的；剛強的；雄赳赳的；男子氣概的．(*opp* 反義詞 **unmanly**). **manliness** *nu* **manfully** *adv* bravely; with determination 勇敢地；果斷地,決心地：*The drowning boy struggled manfully against the waves.* 溺水的男孩勇敢地同波浪進行搏鬥．**'man'kind** all human beings 人類：*The scientist's discoveries are of great help to mankind.* 科學家的發現對人類有極大的幫助．**'manpower** men needed to do a certain job (e.g. workers) 人力 (例如：工人)：*There is a shortage of manpower in many of our industries.* 我們許多工業部門人力不足．**manservant** *nc man who is paid to work in a house, or to attend on someone (o.f.* -use **servant**) 男僕,男傭人 (舊式—現在用 **servant**). *pl* 複數 **menservants. 'manslaughter** crime of killing a person, but without meaning to 過失殺人罪；非預謀殺人罪；誤殺：*The driver of the car which killed* the child was accused of manslaughter. 輾死小孩的汽車司機被指控犯有過失殺人罪.

manage ['mænidʒ] *vt / i* **1** be in charge of 負責; 管理; 處理; 經營: *He manages a large business for his mother* i.e. his mother owns the business, but he runs it. 他替他的母親管理一家大商店, 即他的母親擁有該商店但他負責經營. **2** succeed; be able to do something 完成; 有能力做某事: *I'll manage somehow.* 我會設法應付過去. *How does he manage to get such high marks?* 他是怎樣設法獲得這樣高的分數? **manageable** ['mænidʒibl] *adj* able to be controlled. 可控制的; 可駕馭的; 可管理的. (*opp* 反義詞 **unmanageable**). **management 1** *nu* way something is run or organized 管理; 處理; 經營; 安排: *I'll leave the management of my affairs to you.* 我要把我的事務交給你處理. **2** *nc / u* people who run a business etc. 管理階層; 資方: *She is going to report the whole thing to the management.* 她要將全部情況向資方(或管理階層)彙報. *The management and the workers disagree.* 資方和工人意見不同. **manager** *nc* person who is in charge of a firm or department etc. 經理. (*fem* 陰 **manageress** [mænidʒə'res]).

mandarin ['mændərin] *nc* **1** (in former times) important Chinese official (昔日的)中國重要官員. **2** small kind of orange 橘子.

mandate ['mændeit] *nc* **1** instruction or permission (esp. from a superior official) (尤指上級下達的)命令; 指令; 訓令; 許可: *The magistrate was given a mandate on how to deal with the case.* 地方法官接到如何處理這一案件的命令. **2** permission to do things for another person (爲他人做事的)授權,

權限: *The country gave the Prime Minister a mandate to carry out new policies.* 國家授權首相執行新的政策. **mandatory** ['mændətəri] *adj* compulsory 強迫的; 強制的; 義務的: *mandatory power* i.e. power which must be obeyed 受託管理國; 委任統治國, 即統治託管地的國家.

mane [mein] *nc* long hair on the back of the neck of some animals (e.g. horse, lion) (馬, 獅子等動物頸部上的)鬃毛.

maneuver [mə'nu:və*] see 見 **manoeuvre**.

manganess ['mæŋgəni:z] *nu* hard, brittle, light-grey metal used in making steel, glass etc. 錳.

manger ['meindʒə*] *nc* long open box that cattle and horses feed from (牛, 馬的)飼料槽.

mangle ['mæŋgl] *vt* crush; damage badly. (*informal*) 壓碎; 嚴重地毀壞. (非正式).

mango ['mæŋgou] *nc* **1** tropical fruit which has yellow skin when ripe 芒果. **2** tree bearing this fruit 芒果樹. *pl* 複數 **mangoes**.

mangrove ['mæŋgrouv] *nc* tropical tree which grows thickly on soft wet land (esp. near the sea) (茂密生長於沼澤地尤指靠近海的)熱帶紅樹.

manhandle ['mænhændl] *vt* move (something heavy or awkward) by using the strength of men, not machines; treat roughly 以人力搬動(笨重物體); 粗暴地對待.

manhole ['mænhoul] *nc* hole, with a cover, through which a man can climb to look at or repair pipes. sewers etc under the ground. 人孔(檢查或修理地下管道, 排水管, 下水道等的出入口).

mania ['meiniə] *nc* **1** madness 瘋狂, 躁

狂. **2** great interest in something 狂熱，癖好: *He has a mania for collecting stamps.* 他有集郵的癖好. **maniac** ['meiniæk] *nc* madman 瘋子，狂人.

manicure ['mænikjuə*] *nc* treatment of the hands and fingernails to improve their appearance 修指甲. Also 亦作 *vt.*

manifest ['mænifest] *adj* able to be seen easily; obvious 顯而易見的; 顯然的: *He is a manifest liar.* 他是一個明顯的說謊者. Also 亦作 *vt* show clearly 表明，顯示: *The prisoner's guilt soon manifested itself* i.e. it was soon clear that he was guilty. 很快證明犯人有罪. 即: 很快弄清楚他是有罪的. **manifestation** [ˌmænifes'teiʃən] *nc* any way in which people's feelings, thoughts etc are shown (思想、感情等的) 表明，表現: *The boy's bad behaviour is a manifestation of his unhappiness.* 那男孩舉動不規矩表明他不高興. **manifesto** [ˌmæni'festou] *nc* public declaration by a party, group etc of what they believe in or intend to do (政黨, 組織等的) 宣言, 聲明. *pl* 複數 **manifestos.**

manifold ['mænifould] *adj* **1** having many forms, parts etc. 多樣的, 多形式的; 許多部份的. **2** of many sorts 多種的.

manioc ['mæniɔk] see 見 **cassava.**

manipulate [mə'nipjuleit] *vt* use skilfully; control 熟練地使用, 操作; 控制, 操縱: *He manipulated the controls of the plane so well that it did not crash.* 他非常靈巧地操縱飛機的控制器使飛機不至於墮毀.

manner ['mænə*] *nc* **1** way in which a thing is done or happens 方法; 方式: *You must use your knife in this manner* i.e. in this way. 你應該這樣使用刀子. **2** way in which a person behaves 態度; 舉止: *a strange manner* i.e. a

strange way of behaviour 奇怪的態度. 即: 舉動態怪. **manners** *npl* social behaviour 禮節, 禮貌: *good manners* 良好的禮貌, 有禮貌; *bad manners* 不良的禮貌, 沒禮貌. *He has no manners* i.e. he behaves badly. 他沒有禮貌. **mannerism** *nc* way of behaving which is typical of a person 癖性, 習氣: *That woman has many annoying mannerisms.* 那個女人有許多討厭的癖性.

manoeuvre [mə'nuːvə*] (*US* **maneuver**) *nc* **1** planned movement of soldiers, armies, ships etc. (軍隊, 軍艦等的) 調動, 演習. **2** clever plan 策略; 巧計; 花招. Also 亦作 *vt / i* **1** make, cause others to make, manoeuvres (使) 調動, (使) 演習. **2** force somebody into doing something 強使, 迫使: *He was manoeuvred into selling his land.* 他被迫出賣土地. *The enemy were manoeuvred out of their strong position.* 敵人被迫撤出堅固的陣地. **3** move something skilfully 靈巧地移動 (某物): *He manoeuvred his car into the garage.* 他設法把車開進了車庫.

manor ['mænə*] *nc* **1** (in former times) area of land owned by a person of high birth (昔日的) 采地, 采邑. **2** large, old house 古老的大宅第, 宅邸. (Also 亦作 **manor house**).

mansion ['mænʃən] *nc* large house (usu. belonging to a rich man) 公館, 宅邸, 大廈 (通常爲富人所有).

mantelpiece ['mæntlpiːs] *nc* shelf above a fire on which things can be put 壁爐台.

mantle ['mæntl] *nc* **1** loose, sleeveless cloak 無袖外套, 斗篷. **2** anything that covers like a mantle 覆蓋物: *The ground was covered with a mantle of snow.* 地上覆蓋着一層雪.

manual ['mænjuəl] *adj* done with the

hands 用手做的, 手工做的: *manual work* 手工, 體力勞動. Also 亦作 *nc* textbook (often intended to be a useful guide to some difficult subject) 手冊.

manufacture ['mænju'fækt∫ə*] *vt* make things in large numbers (often by machinery) (通常用機器) 大量製造. Also 亦作 *nc*. **manufacturer** *nc. Note* 說明: the place where manufactured goods are made is called a *factory*. 製造貨物的地方叫做 factory (工廠).

manure [mə'njuə*] *nc / u* animal waste used to make crops grow 動物的糞肥.

manuscript ['mænjuskript] *nc* book etc written by hand 手稿; 原稿; 手抄本: *Some ancient manuscripts were found.* 發現了幾本古代手稿.

many ['meni] *determiner / pron* (used with countable nouns) a large number (與可數名詞連用) 許多的, 多的; 許多人, 許多: *Do you have many visitors?* 訪問你的人很多嗎? *No, not many.* 不, 不多. *I haven't got many books.* 我沒有多少書. *Many people came here to stay.* 許多人留下不走了. *You have made too many mistakes.* 你的錯誤太多了. (*opp* 反義詞 **few**). *Note* 說明: 1 comparative **more**. superlative **most**. 2 in affirmative sentences it is often more natural to say a *large number of* or *a lot of*. Therefore say *The baby has a lot of toys* rather than *The baby has many toys*. 1.比較級 more. 最高級 most. 2. 在肯定句中, 通常更爲自然的說法是 a large number of 或者 a lot of. 所以人們說 The baby has a lot of toys 而不說 The baby has many toys.

map [mæp] *nc* plan showing where different places are 地圖; (位置的) 示意圖: *map of Africa* 非洲地圖; *map of the heavens* i.e. showing the posi-

tions of stars as they appear in the sky 天體圖.即: 星辰位置圖. Also 亦作 *vt* make such a plan 繪製地圖. *past* 過去式和過去分詞 **mapped.**

maple ['meipl] *nc / u* 1 trees with five-pointed leaves grown for wood or shade 楓樹. 2 wood of this tree 楓木.

mar [mɑ:*] *vt* damage; spoil 破壞; 損壞: *His essay was marred by careless mistakes.* 粗心大意的錯誤損害了他的文章. *past* 過去式和過去分詞 **marred.**

marathon ['mærəθən] *nc* 1 (in athletics) foot race of 26 miles (體育) 馬拉松賽跑(全程26英里). 2 any long race, journey or activity 長距離的比賽, 旅行或活動. 3 any event going on for a long time 長時間進行的比賽項目.

maraud [mə'rɔ:d] *vt / i* attack places and steal things from them 搶劫, 掠奪. **marauder** *nc*.

marble ['mɑ:bl] 1 *nu* kind of hard stone which can be polished and used for buildings, statues etc. 大理石: *The temple had a marble floor.* 這寺院舖有大理石地板. 2 *nc* small glass or plastic ball used by children for playing a game (兒童玩的玻璃或塑料)彈子, 彈珠: *play marbles* 玩彈子遊戲.

march [mɑ:t∫] *vi* walk in the steady even way that soldiers do (士兵的)齊步前進, 整步行進. Also 亦作 *nc* 1 walk of this kind 行進; 行軍: *a long march* 長途行軍, 長征. 2 tune for marching to 進行曲: *The band played a military march.* 樂隊奏起軍隊進行曲. **march-past** occasion when soldiers march by in front of an important person (e.g. an officer) 分列式.

March [mɑ:t∫] *n* third month of the year 三月.

mare [meə*] *nc* female horse 母馬.

margarine [mɑ:dʒə'ri:n] *nu* fat from plants or animals (specially treated so that it resembles butter) (用植物或動物油脂製成的類似天然黃油的)人造黃油.

margin ['mɑːdʒin] *nc* **1** white space at the top, bottom and sides of a page 頁邊的空白處: *While reading, he would write some words in the margin.* 他總是一面閱讀,一面在書頁旁邊的空白處寫點東西. **2** amount more than what is needed 餘裕,餘額,餘地: *Our plans allowed a wide margin for error* i.e. they will work even if there are many mistakes. 我們的計劃對差錯留有充裕的餘地. 即: 即使有許多錯誤,計劃仍行得通. **marginal** *adj* small 小的;少量的: *a marginal increase / success* 小增加/成功.

marigold ['mærigould] *nc* type of yellow flower 金盞花,萬壽菊.

marijuana, marihuana [mæri'wɑːnə] *nu* type of intoxicating drug made from dried hemp 大麻,大麻烟.

marine [mə'riːn] *adj* **1** connected with the sea 與海的,近海的,海生的: *marine plants* 海生植物. **2** connected with ships 船的,船運的: *marine insurance* 海上保險,海險. Also 亦作 *nc* soldier serving on a ship. 海軍陸戰隊士兵. **mariner** ['mærinə*] *nc* sailor *(o.f.)* 水手,海員,船員(舊式).

marionette [mæriə'net] *nc* small wooden figure which can be moved by strings 提線木偶.

marital ['mærit] *adj* having to do with marriage 婚姻的,與婚姻有關的: *marital vows* i.e. promises made when people get married 婚誓. 即: 結婚時新郎新娘所作的誓言.

maritime ['mæritaim] *adj* having to do with the sea 與海有關的: 海的;近海的;船的. *maritime law* i.e. the law affecting ships etc. 海商法. 即: 有關船舶等的法律. *maritime countries* i.e. countries near the sea, or having many ships 沿海國家. 即: 靠近海洋的或擁有許多船舶的國家.

mark [mɑːk] *nc* **1** something (e.g. a stain) which alters the appearance of something else 斑點;疤痕: *There are dirty marks on the wall.* 牆上有污點. **2** sign; indication 記號, 標記; 跡象: *Grey hairs are a mark of old age.* 頭髮灰白是年老的象徵. **3** score (in examinations etc.) (考試等的)分數,評分,點數: *good marks* 優良的成績; *a good mark* 好的評分. **4** sign written by someone who cannot write his own name (不會寫名字的人的)花押: *He put his mark at the bottom of the page.* 他在那頁的下端畫花押. Also 亦作 *vt* **1** spoil the appearance of 弄污,留下痕跡於: *The hot water has marked the table.* 熱水在桌子上留下印痕. **2** indicate; show 指出; 表明: *Mark where you have stopped in your reading.* 標出你停止閱讀的地方. **3** give points in an examination etc. 打分數,記分: *mark an essay* 給文章打分數. **4** (sport) follow the movements of a player of the other team (運動)盯(人). **marked** *adj* easily seen 易見的,顯著的: *a marked improvement* 明顯的改進. **mark time 1** march on the same spot 原地踏步. **2** not advance or go forward 停滯不前,沒有進展: *Our business is marking time* i.e. it is not progressing. 我們的業務停頓不前. 即: 沒有取得進展.

market ['mɑːkit] *nc* **1** place where goods are bought and sold 市場,集市: *the village market* 鄉村集市. *She took the cattle to (the) market.* 她把牲畜帶到集市去. **2** areas where people are willing to buy goods 有銷路的地區. *Traders are looking for new markets.* 商人在尋找新市場. **3** demand for goods 銷路: *a good market for meat* i.e. meat will be easily sold. 肉類銷路好, 即: 容易賣出. '**market day** day set aside for buying and selling goods. 集市日. '**market 'garden** (Brit) garden where vegetables etc are grown for sale (US 美 **truck garden**) (英)(以應產市場爲目的的)商品. 菜園. '**market place** place where goods are bought and sold 市場, 集市場所. '**black 'market** *nc* means by which people can illegally buy things which are scarce 黑市: *He bought it on the black market.* 他在黑市買的. *blackmarket prices* i.e. prices that are very high 黑市價. 即: 非常高的價格.

marksman ['mɑːksmən] *nc* man skilled in shooting guns well 射手; 神槍手; 狙擊手.

marmalade ['mɑːməleid] *nu* kind of jam made from oranges (or other citrus fruits) cooked and sweetened 橘子醬.

maroon[1] [mə'ruːn] *nu* reddish brown colour 栗色, 褐紅色, 紫醬色, 茶色. Also 亦作 *adj*.

maroon[2] [mə'ruːn] *vt* leave somebody on a desert island or in any uncomfortable and lonely place (e.g. as a punishment) 把…放逐到荒島或無人烟的地方.

marquee [mɑː'kiː] *nc* large tent 大帳篷.

marquis, marquess ['mɑːkwis] *nc* title of nobility 侯爵. (*fem* 陰 **marchioness** ['mɑːʃənis]).

marrow ['mærou] **1** *nu* the soft fat inside bones 骨髓. **2** *nc* type of large, oval, green and yellow vegetable 葫蘆.

marry ['mæri] **1** *vt / i* take someone as one's husband or wife 和…結婚; 娶; 嫁. *Philip has married Jane.* 菲利普已和珍妮結了婚. **2** *vt* join two people together as man and wife 爲…主持婚禮, 爲…證婚: *What is the name of the priest who married you?* 爲你們主持婚禮的牧師名叫甚麼? **marriage** ['mærid3] *nc / u* **married** *adj.* (*opp* 反義 **unmarried**).

marsh [mɑːʃ] *nc* area of lowlying, wet land 沼澤地, 濕地. **marshy** *adj.*

marshal ['mɑːʃl] *nc* (US) official, not in the police force, in charge of seeing that the law is enforced in a certain area (美)執法官. Also 亦作 *vt* arrange things or people in a certain order 整理; 排列; 列隊; 安排: *to marshal one's thoughts* 整理思想. *past* 過去式和過去分詞 **marshalled** (US 美 **marshaled**).

martial ['mɑːʃl] *adj* having to do with war 戰爭的; 軍事的: *martial music* i.e. warlike music 軍樂; *martial law* i.e. rule by soldiers instead of by civilians 軍事管制法, 戒嚴令.

martyr ['mɑːtə*] *nc* person who will suffer death rather than change what he believes in 烈士; 殉難者; 殉道者. **martyrdom** *nc / u.*

marvel ['mɑːvl] *nc* something wonderful and astonishing 奇妙的事物; 令人驚奇的事物: *It is a marvel how he works so hard.* 他如此勤奮工作真是了不起. Also 亦作 *vt / i* wonder, be astonished 驚奇; 感驚訝: *I marvel at his tremendous achievements.* 我對他的巨大成就深感驚訝. *They marvelled that he could do so much* 他會做那麼多, 他們感到奇怪. *past* 過去式和過去分詞 **marvelled.** (US 美 **marveled**). **marvellous** *adj* wonderful; surprising; very good 奇妙的; 驚人的; 極好的, 了不起的: *It's been a marvellous day.* 那是一個不平常的日子. **marvellously** *adv.*

marzipan ['mɑːzipæn] *nu* sweet substance made from nuts, eggs etc, put on cakes 杏仁糖漿(用杏仁、蛋等做成, 置於糕餅上).

mascara [mæsˈkɑːrə] *nu* preparation used to make the eyelashes darker 睫毛膏; 睫毛油.

mascot [ˈmæskət] *nc* something / somebody that is supposed to bring good luck (被認爲會帶來好運的)吉祥人; 吉祥物.

masculine [ˈmæskjulin] *adj* 1 male; having to do with men 男性的; 與男子有關的; 男子氣概的; *a masculine sport* 男性的運動或遊戲. 2 (grammar) kind of gender i.e. not feminine or neuter (語法)陽性的. 即:非陰性或中性; *'Bull' is masculine, but 'cow' is feminine.* "Bull"是陽性的, 而"cow" 是陰性的.

mash [mæʃ] *nc/u* any kind of soft mixture (任何搗成糊狀的)混合物; 泥; 漿. Also 亦作 *vt*: *mashed potatoes* 馬鈴薯泥.

mask [mɑːsk] *nc* covering for the face or part of the face 面罩; 假面具: *The robbers were wearing masks.* 強盜戴着面具. Also 亦作 *vt* cover or conceal something 掩飾; 隱藏; 遮蔽; 僞裝: *They masked their true intentions.* 他們把真正的意圖掩蓋起來.

masochism [ˈmæzəkizəm] *nu* unnatural pleasure in being hurt (性)受虐狂. **masochist** *nc*. **masochistic** [mæzəˈkistik] *adj*.

mason [ˈmeisn] *nc* person who works with stone etc. (esp. for building) 石匠, 磚石工(尤指修建房屋). **masonry** *nu* stonework 石屋, 房屋中的石造部份: *crumbling masonry* 崩塌中的石屋.

masquerade [mɑːskəˈreid] *vi* pretend to be, somebody / something else (esp. by dressing up) 假裝; 僞裝(尤指用化裝方法).

mass [mæs] 1 *nc* large numbers collected together (聚在一起的)大量, 衆多, 許多: *There is a mass of stones in the yard.* 院子裏滿是石頭. *There are masses of people in the hall.* 大廳裏擠滿了人. 2 *nc* large lump of some material. 塊; 團; 堆: *The workmen left a huge mass of concrete behind.* 工人們留下一大堆混凝土. 3 *nu* (science) amount of matter in a body, measured by its resistance to a change of motion. (科學)質量. Also 亦作 *vt/i* collect together 聚集; 集合: *The enemy are massing their forces for an attack.* 敵人在集結兵力準備進攻. **'mass 'meeting** meeting of large numbers of people (usu. to protest about something) (通常爲抗議某事而舉行的)羣衆大會. **'mass 'media** see 見 **medium**. **'mass-pro'duce** *vt* make things cheaply in large numbers 成批生產(廉價物品). **mass-produced** *adj* **mass production** *nu*.

Mass [mæs] *nc* religious ceremony (esp. Roman Catholic) to commemorate Christ's Last Supper 彌撒(尤指羅馬天主教的領聖餐): *hear Mass* 望彌撒; *say Mass* 作彌撒.

massacre [ˈmæsəkə*] *nc* killing of a large number of (usu. defenceless) people 大屠殺(通常指屠殺手無寸鐵的人羣) Also 亦作 *vt* kill in this way 大屠殺: *When the soldiers captured the town, they massacred all the inhabitants.* 士兵攻佔該城鎮時屠殺了全鎮居民.

massage [ˈmæsɑːʒ] *vt* take away stiffness or pain by rubbing and pressing parts of the body 按摩. Also 亦作 *nc/u* **masseur** [mæˈsə:*] *nc* man skilled in doing this 按摩師. (*fem* 陰 **masseuse** [mæˈsə:z]).

massive [ˈmæsiv] *adj* large and heavy

巨大的; 粗重的: *massive doors* 大而重
的門.

mast [mɑːst] *nc* high pole on a ship to
which sails are attached 船桅, 檣.

master ['mɑːstə*] *nc* **1** person who
owns or controls something 主人; 控
制者; 擁有者; *a dog's master* 狗的主
人; *master of the house* 家長. **2** person who gives orders to others 發號
施令的人, 主人; *servants and their
master* 僕人和主人. **3** male teacher
男教師. **4** skilled worker who does
not work for someone else 師傅, 熟練
工人; *a master builder* 建築師傅. **5**
title used before a boy's name (用在
男孩名字前面的稱呼) 少爺: *Master
John Brown* 約翰·布朗少爺. Also 亦
作 *vt* gain control of something 控制
住; 掌握: *master a new language* 掌握
一種新語言. **masterly** *adj* very clever
很靈巧的, 很聰明的; *in a masterly
fashion* 用巧妙的方式. **mastery** *nu*
control; command 控制; 掌握. **'mas-
termind** *nc* very clever person (esp.
in crime) 很聰明的人, 很有智謀的人
(尤指在犯罪方面). Also 亦作 *vt*: *mas-
termind a plan* i.e. direct it cleverly
策劃一個方案. **'masterpiece** great or
greatest achievement 傑作; 名作; 傑出
的成就.

masturbate ['mæstəbeit] *vi* indulge in
sexual behaviour with oneself 手淫.
masturbation [mæstə'beiʃən] *nu.*

mat¹ [mæt] *nc* covering for protecting a
surface against dirt, heat etc. (防污,
防熱等的) 席; 墊: *doormat* i.e. for wiping one's shoes on before entering a
room (門前的) 擦鞋墊; *tablemat*
i.e. for placing under plates etc. (用以
墊盤子等的) 小墊. **matted** *adj* twisted
together; tangled 纏繞在一起的, 纏結
的: *matted hair* 亂成一團的頭髮.

mat², **matt** [mæt] *adj* smooth but not

shiny 平而無光澤的: *a mat surface* 不
反光的表面; *mat paintwork* 無光澤的
油漆面.

match¹ [mætʃ] *nc* very small piece of
wood with material at one end which
lights easily (used for lighting fires,
cigarettes etc.) 火柴.

match² [mætʃ] *nc* **1** game between two
sides 比賽: *a football match* 足球比
賽. **2** person who is just as clever,
strong etc as another person 對手, 敵
手; *He met his match.* 他遇到了對手.
3 thing that goes with or fits into
another 相配的東西: *This chair is a
match for that one.* 這隻椅子和那隻椅
子很相配. **4** marriage 婚姻: *She
made a good match* i.e. found a good
or wealthy husband. 她的婚姻很美滿,
即: 找到一個好的或有錢的丈夫. Also
亦作 *vt* / *i* **1** find something that goes
with something else 找到相配的東西
使相配: *She matched the carpet with
some very nice curtains.* 她給地毯配上
幾個好看的窗簾. **2** put into a contest
together 使比賽, 使較量: *He matched
his brother against / with the champion.* 他讓他的兄弟和冠軍比賽.
matching *adj* going together; suitable
to be together 相配的; 相稱的: *match-
ing chairs* 相匹配的椅子. **matchless**
adj not able to be equalled 無比的, 無
雙的, 無可匹敵的.

mate [meit] *nc* **1** fellow worker 夥伴, 工
友. **2** companion. *(informal)* 同伴, 同
事. (非正式). **3** (usu. with reference
to animals) male living with a female
or female living with a male (通常指
動物的) 配偶: *a lion and his mate* 獅
子和它的配偶. **4** officer below a captain in a ship 船長的副手: *first mate*
大副. Also 亦作 *vt* / *i* come, bring
together so as to have young 交配:
The animals were mated last spring.

動物在去春交配.

material [məˈtiəriəl] *nc / u* **1** something that something else can be made from 材料；原料；物資. **2** cloth 織物，布料：*dress material* 衣料；*clothes made from beautiful material* 用美麗衣料做成的衣服. Also 亦作 *adj* **1** having to do with matter. not the spirit 物質的；非精神的. (*opp* 反義詞 **spirtual**). **2** (usu. legal) important; necessary (通常指法律上)重要的；必要的：*material evidence* 重要的證據；實質性的證據. (*opp* 反義詞 **immaterial**). **materially** *adv* **materialize** *vi* become real, true 成為事實，實現：*Their hopes did not materialize* i.e. what they had hoped for did not happen. 他們的希望沒有實現.

maternal [məˈtəːnl] *adj* of or like a mother or one's mother's side 母親的；似母親的；母方的，母系的：*maternal care* i.e. loving care 母親的關懷，母親般的操心；*maternal grandfather* i.e. father of a person's mother 外祖父. (*masc* 陽 **paternal**). **maternity** *nu* condition of being a mother 母性，母道. Also 亦作 *adj*：*maternity hospital* 產科醫院；*maternity clothes* 孕婦服裝.

mathematics [mæθəˈmætiks] *nu* science of space and numbers 數學：*Mathematics is a subject studied in nearly every school.* 數學是幾乎每個學校都開設的科目. *Note* 說明：followed by a *sing* verb. 後面接單數動詞. **mathematical** [mæθəˈmætikl] *adj* **mathematician** [mæθəməˈtiʃən] *nc* expert in mathematics 數學家. **maths** (*US* 美 **math**) *nu* short informal form of **mathematics** mathematics 的非正式縮寫形式.

matinée [ˈmætinei] *nc* theatre show taking place in the morning or afternoon

上午或午後的演出，日戲，日場.

matins [ˈmætinz] *npl* **1** (Church of England) morning service (聖公會的)晨禱. **2** (Roman Catholic Church) prayers said at dawn (羅馬天主教的)早課.

matriculate [məˈtrikjuleit] *vt / i* (allow to) enter a college or university as a student, usu. after passing an examination; be matriculated (准許) 進入大學(通常指考試及格之後)，錄取；被錄取.

matriculation [mətrikjuˈleiʃən] *nu* **1** act of matriculating 錄取入學. **2** examination held by colleges or universities which must be passed before a student can be admitted (學院或大學的)入學考試.

matron [ˈmeitrn] *nc* **1** woman in charge of nurses in a hospital 護士長. **2** woman in charge of the feeding, medical care etc in a school (學校的)女總管，女舍監. **matronly** *adj* dignified; having to do with a matron 尊嚴的，高貴的，莊重的；適合女總管身份的，與女總管有關的：*matronly appearance* 莊重的儀表；*matronly duties* 女總管的責任.

matted [ˈmætid] *adj* see 見 **mat**.

matter [ˈmætə*] **1** *nu* stuff out of which all things are made 物質，物料，物體：*the matter of the universe* 宇宙的物質. **2** *nc* subject; topic 事情，問題；主題，論題：*a very difficult matter* 很困難的問題(或事情)；*another matter* 另外一回事；另一題目. **3** *nu* poisonous yellow substance in a wound etc. 膿. **4** *nu* content; what is being written, spoken about 要意，要旨；內容：*The matter of his speech was good.* 他講話的內容是好的. Also 亦作 *vi* be important 有重要性，有關系，要緊. *It doesn't matter* i.e. it is not important. 沒有甚

麼關係. 即: 不重要. **be the matter with someone** be wrong 有毛病, 發生問題: *What's the matter with you?* i.e. what's wrong with you? *(informal)* 你怎麼啦? 你出了甚麼事? (非正式). **a matter of fact** something true 事實, 確實的事: *as a matter of fact* i.e. to speak truthfully 事實上, 實際上. 即如實地說.

matting ['mætiŋ] *nu* rough material used for covering floors etc. 地席.

mattress ['mætris] *nc* long, flat bag filled with hair, feathers or some other soft material, and used for sleeping on 褥墊, 床墊.

mature [mə'tjuə*] *adj* **1** completely developed; completely grown-up 充分發展的, 完善的; 長成的, 成人的: *mature person* i.e. someone who is completely adult and sensible 成年人. **2** ripe 成熟的. (*opp* 反義詞 **immature**). Also 亦作 *vt / i* become or make completely developed; become or make ready (使) 成熟, (使) 充分發展; (使) 做好準備. **maturity** *nu*.

maul [mɔːl] *vt* treat or injure in a rough manner 虐待, 粗暴傷害: *be mauled by a lion* 被獅子撕傷得傷無完膚.

mausoleum [mɔːzə'liəm] *nc* large tomb 陵墓.

mauve [mouv] *nc / u* pale bluish purple colour 淡紫色. Also 亦作 *adj*.

maxi- ['mæksi] *prefix* large, long (e.g. **maxiskirt** i.e. long skirt) 長的; 大的 (例如 maxiskirt, 即長及腳踝的長裙).

maxim ['mæksim] *nc* statement of what most people would agree to be true 格言, 箴言: *The book contained many wise maxims.* 這本書裏面有許多名言.

maximum ['mæksiməm] *nc* greatest amount of something that is possible, or has actually been recorded 最大量; 最大值: *My salary is at its max-*

imum i.e. I shall not earn more per year. 我的薪水已達到最高的極限: 我每年挣的薪水不會比這更多. Also 亦作 *adj* greatest possible or recorded 最大值的; 最大量的: *His maximum speed was 80 miles per hour.* 他的最高速度是每小時80英里. (*opp* 反義詞 **minimum**).

may [mei] *aux.* *Note* 說明: past tense is *might* and there is no other tense form. Negative is *may not, might not* or *mayn't.* 過去式爲 might, 沒有其他時態. 否定詞爲 may not, might not 或 mayn't. **1** expressing possibility (表示可能性) 可能, 也許: *Our team may win tomorrow.* 明天我們的隊也許會贏. *You may see him if you hurry.* 如果你趕緊去, 可能見到他. *He might be there, but I don't think so.* 他也許在那裏, 但我想不會. *I am afraid that your son may have been injured.* 我恐怕你兒子也許受了傷. *Note* 說明: *might* indicates that something is less likely than when one uses *may.* Study these sentences and notice also how tense is indicated: (a) *They may arrive now / tomorrow* i.e. it is possible. (b) *They might arrive now / tomorrow* i.e. it is less likely. (c) *They may have arrived yesterday* i.e. it is possible. (d) *They might have arrived yesterday* i.e. it is less likely. (e) *They might have arrived yesterday, but their plane could not land* i.e. it was possible once, but not any longer. 用 might 表示某事的可能性比用 may 小. 仔細閱讀這些句子並注意所示的時態: (a) They may arrive now / tomorrow. 表示有可能. (b) They might arrive now / tomorrow. 表示可能性較小. (c) They may have arrived yesterday. 表示有可能. (d) They might have arrived yesterday. 表示可能性較小. (e)They might have arrived yesterday, but their plane could not land. 表示一度可能, 但不再可能. **2** asking or giving permission (請求或表示許可) 可以: *May I leave now?* 現在我可以走了嗎? *Might I ask what you paid for it? Yes, of course.* 我可以問一問這個東西你花多少錢買的?當然可以. *May we go to the cinema tomorrow?* 明天我們可以去看電影嗎? *Note* 說明: in these questions, might indicates greater hesitation or reluctance. 在這些句子裏, might 表示更爲猶豫或勉强的意思. **3** request or very polite command (表示請求或很有禮貌的命令) 請; 應該: *You might post these letters on your way home.* 請您在回家路上把這些信寄出去. *You might try to get that finished for tomorrow.* 你應該爭取明天完成那件工作. **4** expressing a wish 祝, 願; 但願: *May they both be very happy!* (o.f. -say **I hope you'll both be very happy!**) 祝你們倆非常幸福! (舊式一現在說 I hope you'll both be very happy!) **5** with the meaning of although 雖然, 儘管: *He may not study much, but he gets good marks* i.e. he... 雖然他學習不多, 但他卻得到好的分數(或成績). **maybe** ['meibi:] *adv* perhaps 也許, 大概: *Maybe he will come tomorrow.* (informal) 他明天也許會來. (非正式). **may / might as well** (used when one thing is preferable to another) would be wiser to (用於一事比另一事更可取時)還是…爲好: *It's very cold so we might as well take the car.* 天氣非常冷, 我們還是乘車好.

May [mei] *n* fifth month of the year 五月.

mayonnaise [meiə'neiz] *nu* thick yellow cream used for flavouring salads i.e. cold vegetable dishes, sandwiches etc.

蛋黃醬(用作色拉即: 冷盤、三明治等的調味品).

mayor [mɛə*] *nc* chief elected official in a town or city 市長; 鎮長. **mayoress** ['mɛəres] *nc* mayor's wife 市長夫人; 鎮長夫人.

maypole ['meipoul] *nc* pole round which people used to dance (人們圍繞着跳舞的)五月柱.

maze [meiz] *nc* paths which cross one another in so many different ways that the traveller easily becomes lost 迷宮, 迷津.

me [mi:] *pron* form which I takes when it is the object of a verb or preposition (I 的賓格, 作爲動詞或介詞的賓語)我: *You saw me there.* 你看見我在那裏. *Give it to me.* 把它拿給我. *Note* 說明: it is more usual to say It is me than It is I in reply to questions like Who is there? 在回答諸如 Who is there? 的問題時, 更常用的說法是 It is me 而不是 It is I.

meadow ['medou] *nc* piece of grassy land; piece of land where hay is grown 草地; 牧草場.

meagre ['mi:gə*] (*US* **meager**) *adj* not enough 貧乏的, 不足的: *meagre wages* 微薄的工資; *a meagre supply* 不足的供應.

meal[1] [mi:l] *nc* **1** occasion when food is regularly taken (e.g. breakfast, dinner etc.) 進餐時刻(例如早餐、正餐等): *We get three meals a day at the hotel.* 我們在旅館一天吃三頓飯. **2** food taken at a meal 一餐飯菜, 膳食: *I feel like a meal* i.e. I feel hungry. 我想吃一頓飯. 即: 我餓了.

meal[2] [mi:l] *nu* coarsely ground grain (未碾細的)穀類粗粉.

mean[1] [mi:n] *vt / i* **1** intend; have a certain purpose 意欲, 打算; 計劃; 意指: *They mean to leave by the midnight* *train.* 他們打算乘午夜火車離開. *He meant to go home early, but he didn't.* 他打算早回家, 但是並沒有這樣做. *The young couple were meant for each other.* 這對青年男女是天生的一對. *What do you mean by saying that?* i.e. why did you say that? 你說那樣的話是甚麼意思?即: 你為甚麼說那樣的話? **2** have the sense of 有…的意義或含意: *What does this word mean?* 這個詞是甚麼意思? **3** cause 引起, 造成: *Failing one paper means failing the whole examination.* 一份考卷不及格會使整個考試不及格. *I'm afraid that this means war* i.e. war will come. 我恐怕這意味着(或會導致)戰爭. 即: 戰爭會來臨. *past* 過去式和過去分詞 **meant** [ment]. **meaning** *nc / u* sense; intention 意義, 意思; 意圖: *What is the meaning of this word?* 這個詞的含意是甚麼? *We've been trying to discover the meaning of his actions.* 我們一直在設法弄清他行動的意圖. Also 亦作 *adj* having some special significance 有特殊意義的, 意味深長的: *She gave him a meaning look* i.e. she wanted him to understand something by it. 她意味深長地看了他一眼, 即: 她要他從中理解某事: **meaningful** *adj* important, significant 重要的; 富有意義的. **meaningless** *adj* without meaning; useless 無意義的; 無用的.

mean² [mi:n] *adj* **1** unwilling to spend or give money 小氣的, 吝嗇的: *a man who is greedy and mean* 一個貪婪, 吝嗇的人. **2** old and neglected 年久失修的, 粗陋的; 破爛不堪的: *a mean street* 簡陋的街道 **3** contemptible; unworthy of a person 卑鄙的; 下賤的: *a mean act* 卑鄙的行為. **4** vicious in behaviour 行為惡劣的, 行為兇惡的: *Watch him; he can be really mean*

(informal in sense 4) 要提防他: 他有時會真兇惡的.義4為非正式).

mean³ [mi:n] *nc* **1** something that is halfway between two extreme quantities or qualities 中間; 中庸: *We must find a mean between hope and despair* 我們必須在希望和絕望之間找到一種折衷的東西; *a mean between heat and cold* 熱和冷的中間狀態. **2** average of a list of numbers 平均數: *The mean of 68, 77 and 83 is 76.* (68 + 77 + 83 = 228; 228 ÷ 3 = 76). 68, 77, 83的平均數是76.

meander [mi'ændə*] *vi* (with reference to a stream, river etc.) change direction very often (指溪流, 河流等)蜿蜒而流.

means [mi:nz] *n sing or pl* **1** way of doing something; method 方式; 辦法; 方法: *He forced the snake to come out from where it was hiding by means of a long pole.* 他用長竿迫使蛇從藏匿的地方出來. *I don't know what means they used.* 我不知道他們使用甚麼方法. *Keep working in the meantime.* 與此同時繼續工作. **2** money; wealth 金錢; 財產; 財富: *They say that he is a man of means* i.e. quite rich. 據說他是一個有錢人. **by all means** certainly; of course 一定; 當然; 當然可以: *May I leave now? By all means.* 我現在可以離開嗎?當然可以.

meantime ['mi:ntaim], **meanwhile** ['mi:nwail] *n sing* in the time between; during the time something else is happening 其間; 其間; 此時; (與此)同時: *You will be allowed to rest shortly; in the meantime you must keep working.* 即將讓你休息; 此時你必須繼續工作. *Keep working in the meantime.* 與此同時繼續工作. 在此期間繼續工作. Also 亦作 *conj*: *You pack the cases; meanwhile I'll get the car ready.* 你裝箱子, 我去把車子準備好.

measles ['miːzlz] *nu* illness, which can be caught from another person, causing fever with red spots appearing on the skin 麻疹. *Note* 說明: followed by a *sing* verb 後接單數動詞.

measly ['miːzli] *adj* not enough, in the opinion of the speaker (說話人認爲) 不足夠的: *He paid us a measly fifty pence. (informal)* 他只付給我們區區50便士. (非正式).

measure ['meʒə*] 1 *nc* object used to find out the length of something 長度量度器, 尺. 2 *nu* system of methods for finding out the length, height, weight etc of things 量度; 度量衡制; 計量制度. 3 *nc* action 辦法; 措施: *I shall have to take stern measures* i.e. strict actions. 我將不得不採取嚴厲的辦法. 即: 嚴厲的行動. 4 *nc* something which the government will or may make into a law. 法案; 議案: *Parliament is considering new measures against crime.* 議會正在考慮反對犯罪行爲的新法案. Also 亦作 *vt* 1 find out the length, height, weight etc of something 量; 量度; 測量; 計量: *They measured the room.* 他們量房間(的大小). 2 be of a certain size 有…的大小: *The board measured 90 centimetres by 120 centimetres.* 這木板長寬90厘米長120厘米. **measurement** *nc / u* act of measuring 測量, 計量. **measurements** *npl* size of something (esp. when measuring a person for clothes) 尺寸, 大小(尤指做衣服時量的尺寸): *The tailor took my measurements* i.e. measured me. 那裁縫給我量尺寸. **measured** *adj* slow and even 緩慢而均勻的: *He walked with measured steps.* 他用緩慢而平穩的步伐行走. **made to measure** *adj* (with reference to clothes) made for a certain person after his measurements have been taken (指衣服)依照量得的尺寸縫製的.

meat [miːt] *nu* flesh of animals eaten as food 供食用的(動物的)肉.

mechanic [mi'kænik] *nc* person who repairs machines 機修工; 技工; 機械工.

mechanical *adj* 1 having to do with machines; worked by machines. 機械的; 用機械工作的: *mechanical toys* 機械(開動)的玩具. 2 done as if by a machine i.e. without thinking 機械般的, 沒有經過思考的: *a mechanical reply* 機械般的回答, 歟板的回答. **mechanics** *nu* science of how machines work 機械學. *Note* 說明: followed by a *sing* verb. 後接單數動詞. **mechanism** ['mekənizəm] *nc* 1 how a machine is made 機械的構造或結構, 機械裝置. 2 how anything complicated works 機理, 機制, 機能; 機構, 結構: *the mechanism of government* 政府的機構. **mechanize** ['mekənaiz] *vt* use machines for 使機械化, 用機器於: *mechanized agriculture* 機械化的農業. **mechanization** [mekənai'zeiʃən] *nu.*

medal ['medl] *nc* small piece of metal (usu. like a coin with some design or words on it) given as a reward for something (e.g. bravery) or so that some event may be remembered 獎章; 獎章; 紀念章. **medallion** [mi'dæliən] *nc* object like a medal (often worn or used as an ornament) (通常作佩戴或裝飾用的)獎章; 紀念章; 動章. **medallist** ['medəlist] (*US* **medalist**) *nc* someone who has been awarded a medal 動章或獎章的獲得者: *gold-medallist.* 金獎獲得者.

meddle ['medl] *vi* interfere (in what does not concern one) 干涉, 干預(他人事務): *I hope he doesn't try to meddle in my affairs.* 我希望他不來干

預我的事情.

media ['miːdiə] *pl* of **medium.** medium 的複數形式.

mediaeval [medi'iːvl] *adj* see 見 **medieval.**

mediate ['miːdieit] *vi* bring peace or an understanding (usu. between people who are not on friendly terms) 調停, 調解; 斡旋: *She mediated between the two enemy forces.* 她在兩支敵對軍隊之間進行調停. **mediation** [miː-di'eiʃən] *nu* **mediator** *nc.*

medicine ['medsin] **1** *nu* art and science of preventing and curing disease. 醫學; 醫術; 内科學. **2** *nc / u* something taken (e.g. a liquid) to prevent or cure a disease 藥, 藥劑. **medical** ['medikl] *adj* having to do with medicine. 醫學的; 醫術的; 内科的, 醫藥的: *medical instruments* 醫療器械; *medical students* 醫科學生; *medical school* i.e. part of a university where doctors are trained (大學的) 醫學院. **medically** *adv.* **medicated** ['medikeitid] *adj* having medicine in it 加入藥物的, 含藥的: *medicated cotton wool* 藥棉, 藥用脫脂棉. **medicinal** [me'disinl] *adj* used to prevent or cure illness 藥用的; 用於治療的, 用於防病的: *He kept a little brandy for medicinal purposes.* 爲了醫療上的目的, 他保持喝少量白蘭地酒.

medieval, mediaeval [medi'iːvl] *adj* in European history, having to do with the Middle Ages (roughly from 1100 A.D. to 1500 A.D.) (歐洲歷史的) 中世紀的, 中古的 (約指從公元1100年至1500年的時期).

mediocre [miːdi'oukə*] *adj* not very good and not very bad 中等的, 普通的.

meditate ['mediteit] *vt / i* think seriously about something 考慮; 沉思; 深思:

meditate suicide i.e. consider committing suicide 考慮自殺; *meditate on / upon what one has done* 沉思或反省自己已做的事. **meditation** [medi'teiʃən] *nc / u.*

medium ['miːdiəm] *nc* **1** means by which something is done 方法, 手段; 工具: *Money is a medium for buying and selling.* 貨幣是買賣的媒介. **2** means of communication with large numbers of people 傳播媒介, 宣傳工具: *Television is a very efficient medium for spreading information.* 電視是一種非常有效的傳播消息的媒介 (或工具). **3** middle point; middle way 中間點, 中間位置; 中間: *happy medium* i.e. not too much or too little 中庸之道. *pl* 複數 **media** ['miːdiə]. Also 亦作 *adj* not going to one extreme or the other; average 中間的; 適中的; 普通的, 平常的: *of medium height* 中等身材的: **'medium wave** (radio) sound wave measuring from 187-571 metres (in Britain) 無線電中波 (在英國爲187-571 米). **'mass 'media** *npl* means of communication with large numbers of people (e.g. radio, television, newspapers etc.) 大衆傳播媒介 (如無線電廣播, 電視, 報紙等).

medley ['medli] *nc* mixture of different things (esp. tunes, articles and stories etc.) 混雜, 混合, 雜燴 (尤指不同的曲調, 文章, 故事等的混雜在一起).

meek [miːk] *adj* mild and gentle; uncomplaining 溫順的; 馴服的. **meekly** *adv.*

meet [miːt] *vt / i* **1** come together from different places or directions 遇見, 相見: *I met him in the street last night.* 昨天晚上我在街上遇見了他. *We met (up) in Paris last year.* 去年我們在巴黎相遇. **2** be introduced to 被引見, 被

介紹相識: *Would you like to meet my brother?* 你願意會見我的兄弟嗎? *Pleased to meet you* i.e. I am glad that we have met, a phrase sometimes used instead of *How do you do?* 見到您很高興. (有時用此語代替 How do you do?). **3** wait for the arrival of 迎接: *meet someone at the station* 到車站去接某人. **4** answer satisfactorily; deal with 滿足答覆; 對付, 應付: *meet a complaint.* 答覆抱怨. **5** pay 償付, 付還: *meet a bill* 如期償付到期的票據. *past* 過去式和過去分詞 **met** [met]. **meeting** *nc* coming together of people (usu. for some definite purpose) 會合, 聚會, (通常指) 集會, 會議: *sports meeting* 運動會; *political meeting* 政治會議.

megaphone ['megəfoun] *nc* metal horn for speaking through to make the voice sound louder. 傳聲筒, 喇叭筒, 擴音器.

melancholy ['melənkəli] *nu* feeling of sadness 憂鬱; 悲哀. Also 亦作 *adj*.

mellow [melou] *adj* **1** (with reference to sounds, taste, colours etc.) soft and ripe (指聲音, 味道, 顏色等) 圓潤的, 柔和的; 甘美的, 甜熟的, 芳醇的; 柔美的. **2** (with reference to people) kind and gentle (指人) 和藹的, 溫和的, 寬厚的, 文雅的: *One is mellower as one gets older.* 人上了年紀就會和善起來. Also 亦作 *vt / i*.

melodrama ['meloudrɑːmə] *nc* exciting and crudely emotional play 情節劇. **melodramatic** [meloudrə'mætik] *adj* behaving in a very emotional and excited way; intended to arouse emotions 非常激動人的; 激起感情的; *a melodramatic speech* 激起 (聽眾) 情感的演說.

melody ['melədi] *nc* pleasant tune. 悅耳的曲調, 美妙的音樂. **melodious**

[mi'loudiəs] *adj* tuneful 曲調悅耳的, 音調優美的.

melon ['melən] *nc / u* type of large fruit which is very juicy inside 瓜, 甜瓜.

melt [melt] *vt / i* **1** make or become liquid with heat 使熔化; 使融化; 熔化, 融化: *melting snow* 融化的雪. **2** soften, become soft 使軟化; 變軟: *Her tears melted my anger.* 她的眼淚打消了我的怒氣. *past* 過去式和過去分詞 **melted. molten** ['moultn] *adj* (with reference to metals) melted (指金屬) 熔化的. **melt away** go away; disappear 走開, 散去; 消失: *His followers melted away at the first sign of danger.* 他的追隨者一發現有危險便紛紛散去. **melt something down** use heat to turn articles into ordinary metal. 熔化某物 (熔化物件成爲普通金屬): *They melted down the silver cups.* 他們熔毀銀杯子.

member ['membə*] *nc* person belonging to a group, society, club etc. 團體的一員; 成員; 會員: *Member of Parliament.* 下院議員; *club member* 俱樂部會員. **membership** *nu* **1** state of belonging to a society etc. 會員的身份, 地位, 資格: *renew one's membership* 恢復會員資格. **2** number of people in a society etc. 成員人數, 會員人數: *a very large membership* 會員人數很多, 很多的會員.

membrane ['menibrein] *nc* thin covering or connection inside an animal or plant (動物或植物體內的) 薄膜, 隔膜, 膜.

memento [mə'mentou] *nc* something which one keeps to remember a person / thing 紀念品; 令人回憶的東西. *pl* 複數 **mementos** or **mementoes**.

memo ['memou] *nc* short form of **memorandum** memorandum 的縮寫形式. *pl* 複數 **memos**.

memoir ['memwɑ:*] *nc* (often *pl*) written account of someone's life (esp. one's own life) (常用複數)傳記;傳略,回憶錄(尤指自傳).

memorandum [memə'rændəm] *nc* type of informal business letter 非正式商業書信,便函,便箋. *pl* 複數 **memorandums** or **memoranda** [memə'rændə].

memory ['meməri] **1** *nu* power of remembering 記憶力: *He has a very good / bad memory* i.e. he can remember many / few things. 他的記憶力非常好/差. *I have a good memory for faces* i.e. I can remember people's faces easily. 我對面孔的記憶力很好. 即: 我很容易記住人們的面貌. *His memory is going* i.e. he is finding it more difficult to remember. 他的記憶力在衰退. **2** *nc* something that can be remembered 可回憶起的事物;回憶: *I have very pleasant memories of my travels abroad.* 我對在國外的旅行有着極愉快的回憶. **memorable** *adj* worth remembering 值得紀念的;值得記憶的. **memorial** [mi'mɔ:riəl] *nc* something intended to make sure that something is remembered 紀念物;紀念碑: *war memorial* i.e. statue etc in memory of people who died in war. 戰爭紀念碑. Also 亦作 *adj* **memorize** *vt* learn something so well that one can remember it exactly 記住;熟記: *memorize a poem* 熟記一首詩. **in memory of someone** to the honour of someone; so that someone may not be forgotten 紀念某人;對某人永誌不忘.

men [men] *pl* of **man.** man 的複數形式.

menace ['menəs] *nc / u* **1** danger; threat 危險; 威脅: *The arms race is a menace to world peace.* 軍備競賽是對世界和平的威脅. **2** promise to injure or harm 恐嚇. **3** person / thing causing annoyance. (*informal* in sense 3) 引起困擾的人/事(義3爲非正式). Also 亦作 *vt / i* promise to injure or harm, threaten 恐嚇;威脅;恫嚇. **menacing** *adj* dangerous 危險的. **menacingly** *adv.*

menagerie [mi'nædʒəri] *nc* collection of wild animals for show (one that is taken from place to place) 供展出的獸群,野獸展覽(尤指至各地展出者).

mend [mend] *vt* repair something that has been broken, torn etc. 修補; 修理; 縫補: *mend a broken chair* 修理破椅子; *mend a stocking with a hole in it* 補有一破洞的襪子. **on the mend** getting better (esp. in health) (*informal*) 在好轉中(尤指健康狀況)(非正式).

menial ['mi:niəl] *adj* low or degrading 粗俗的,卑下的;卑劣的: *a menial task* 卑賤的工作,傭人的工作.

menstruation [menstru'eiʃən] *nu* woman's monthly discharge of blood from the womb 月經;行經. **menstrual** ['menstruəl] *adj* **menstruate** ['menstrueit] *vi.*

mental ['mentl] *adj* having to do with the mind 心智的;精神的: *mental illness* 精神病; *mental hospital* i.e. hospital for those who are mentally ill 精神病院; *mental arithmetic* i.e. arithmetic problems done in the mind without the help of pencil and paper 心算,即不用紙筆做算術題. **mentally** *adv* **mentality** [men'tæliti] *nc / u* person's way of thinking 思想方法,思考方式.

mention ['menʃən] *vt* speak or write about something briefly 簡短地提及;說到;寫到: *I must just mention that everyone has been very kind to us here.* 我得提一提大家對我們實在太好. Also 亦作 *nc* brief reference to somebody / something 簡短的提及(某人/某事).

menu ['menjuː] *nc* list of different kinds of food that can be obtained in a hotel, restaurant etc. (旅館、餐館等的)菜單. *pl* 複數 **menus.**

mercenary ['məːsinəri] *adj* doing something only for money 雇傭的, 爲錢的, 唯利是圖的: *mercenary person* 爲錢工作的人, 貪財的人, 唯利是圖的人; *mercenary motives* i.e. reasons of greed only 出自圖利的動機. Also 亦作 *nc* soldier fighting for a foreign country for money only (not for love of the country) 雇傭兵.

merchandise ['məːtʃəndaiz] *nu* goods bought and sold (esp. manufactured goods) 商品, 貨物(尤指製造品).

merchant ['məːtʃənt] *nc* 1 person who buys and sells things on a large scale (做大批生意的)商人. 2 person who has a special interest in a certain kind of goods (對某種商品特別感興趣的)商人: *wine merchant* 酒商; *coal merchant* 煤炭商. '**merchant 'navy** ships and sailors connected with trade 商船; 商船船員.

mercury ['məːkjuri] *nu* heavy silver-white metal liquid at ordinary temperatures, used in thermometers etc. 水銀, 汞.

mercy ['məːsi] *nu* kindness shown to someone that one has in one's power 憐憫; 寬恕; 仁慈; 慈悲: *He showed mercy to the defeated enemy.* 他對失敗的敵人表示寬大. *The judge gave the convicted man no mercy.* 法官決不寬恕有罪的人. *They had no mercy on their prisoners.* 他們對俘虜毫無憐憫之心. **merciful** *adj* showing mercy 寬大的, 寬容的; 仁慈的. (*opp* 反義詞 **unmerciful**). **merciless** *adj* without mercy 無情的, 殘忍的. **at the mercy**

of in the power of 受…的支配, 任憑…的擺佈, 在…的掌握中: *The ship was at the mercy of the wind and waves.* 那隻船任憑風浪的擺佈毫無辦法.

mere [miə*] *adj* no more than; no better than; only 僅僅, 不過; 幾乎就是; 只: *a mere child* 僅僅是個小孩子. **merely** *adv* only 僅, 只.

merge [məːdʒ] *vt / i* become part, cause to become part, of something else 使併合; 使併入; 合併; 混入, 併入: *It was decided that the two businesses should be merged.* 已經決定兩個商店要合併在一起. **merger** *nc* union of two business companies (兩個公司的)合併.

meridian [mə'ridiən] *nc* 1 circle of the earth passing through the geographical poles and any given point on the earth's surface 子午圈, 子午線: *All places on the same meridian have the same longitude.* 在同一子午線上的地方都有相同的經度. 2 the highest point; the highest point of power, success etc. 頂點; (權力, 成就等的)全盛時期: *He is now at the meridian of his intellectual power.* 他現在正處智力的全盛期. Also 亦作 *adj.*

meringue [mə'ræŋ] *nc / u* cake made from a mixture of sugar and the whites of eggs (糖和蛋白混合製成的)蛋白甜餅.

merit ['merit] *nc / u* quality deserving praise 長處, 優點; 功績: *There is a great deal of merit in what he has achieved.* 他取得的成就非常有價值. *His greatest merit is his courage.* 他的最大優點是勇敢. Also 亦作 *vt* deserve 值得, 應得: *This book merits our close attention.* 這本書理應受到我們的密切注意. **merited** *adj* (*opp* 反義詞 **unmerited**).

mermaid ['məːmeid] *nc* imaginary creature supposed to live in the sea, with a woman's body but a fish's tail instead of legs (傳説中的)美人魚.

merry ['meri] *adj* **1** gay; happy 歡樂的; 愉快的; 高興的: *having a merry time* 過得愉快的, 玩得快活的. **2** rather drunk (*informal* in sense **2**) 微醉的. (義2爲非正式). **merrily** *adv* **merriment** *nu* '**merry-go-round** amusement for children consisting of a revolving platform with wooden horses etc on which children may sit (供兒童玩樂乘坐的) 旋轉木馬. Merry Christmas! conventional greeting said on Christmas Day or around that time. 聖誕快樂! (聖誕節的祝賀詞): *wish someone a* **Merry Christmas.** 祝某人聖誕快樂.

mesh [meʃ] *nc* space between the lines in a net 網孔, 網眼; 篩孔, 篩眼: *this net has a fine mesh* i.e. the holes are small. 這張網的網眼很小.

mesmerize ['mezməraiz] *vt* hypnotize 對…施催眠術; 使人迷.

mess¹ [mes] *nu* dirty or confused state 骯髒; 混亂; 雜亂: *Tom is very untidy; he always leaves his room in a mess.* 湯姆很不整潔, 他總是讓房間又髒又亂. *That's another mess I'll have to clean up.* 那又是一堆雜亂的東西我得去收拾乾淨. *What a mess!* 多麼髒亂啊! **messy** *adj* dirty 骯髒的: *Working underneath the car is always a messy job* i.e. one gets dirty easily. 在汽車底下工作始終是件髒活. 即: 容易把人弄髒. **mess about** waste time; spend time doing unimportant things. (*informal*) 浪費時間; 瞎忙; 無所事事 (非正式). **mess something up** spoil; disorganize 破壞; 打亂; 瓦解; 弄糟: *You've messed up all our arrangements. (informal)* 你已打亂了我們的全部安排. (非正式). **make a mess of something 1** make something untidy or dirty 把某事物弄亂或弄髒. **2** fail to do something properly. (*informal* in sense 2) 沒有把某事做好, 把某事弄糟. (義2爲非正式).

mess² [mes] *nc* **1** group of people (e.g. soldiers etc.) who eat together 集體用膳的人羣 (例如士兵等). **2** meals taken together by such a group (集體用膳人羣的) 伙食. **3** place where these meals are taken 食堂: *officers' mess* 軍官食堂; *sergeants' mess* 軍士食堂.

message ['mesidʒ] *nc* information sent from one person to another 消息; 音信, 信息: *We received our first message from him after six months.* 六個月後我們第一次收到他的音信. **messenger** ['mesindʒə*] *nc* person who carries a message 送信人, 信差.

met [met] past of **meet.** meet 的過去式和過去分詞.

metabolism [me'tæbəlizəm] *nc / u* all the processes of change which go on in the body 新陳代謝.

metal ['metl] *nc / u* mineral substance like iron, silver, lead etc. 金屬: *The spears were made of metal.* 矛是用金屬製成的. **metallic** [me'tælik] *adj* like, connected with metal 金屬似的; 與金屬有關的: *metallic sound* i.e. sound like that made by striking metal 金屬聲音. 即: 撞擊金屬時發出的鏗鏘聲音.

metamorphosis [metə'mɔ:fəsis] *nc* a profound change of appearance or nature 變形; 變質; 變狀; 變態: *metamorphosis of a caterpillar into a butterfly / a criminal into a saint* 毛蟲蛻變成蝴蝶 / 罪犯脱胎換骨變成聖人. *pl* 複數 **metamorphoses** [metə'mɔ:fəsi:z]

metaphor ['metəfɔ:*] *nc / u* (example of) way of using words so that one thing is given the name of another because of something they have in common (e.g. *You are the rock on which we depend* i.e. a rock is strong and immovable and so are you) 隱喻, 暗喻 (例如: '你是我們依靠的磐石' 中的 rock, 即 rock 是堅固不動的, 你也一樣). **metaphorical** [metə'fɔrikl] *adj* like a metaphor; containing many metaphors 隱喻般的; 含有許多隱喻的. *Note* 說明: a metaphor is like a simile, which also compares things, but a simile will use *like* or *as* (e.g. *You are as firm as a rock or You are like a rock).* metaphor 跟 simile (明喻) 一樣, 不過 simile 對事物作比喻時要用 like 或 as (例如 You are as firm as a rock 或 You are like a rock).

metaphysics [metə'fiziks] *nu* part of philosophy which deals with being and knowledge i.e. what we really are and how we know things 形而上學; 玄學. *Note*: 說明: followed by a *sing* verb. 後接單數動詞.

meteor ['mi:tiə*] *nc* mass of matter travelling through space which glows with heat when it enters the earth's atmosphere. (Often **shooting star** or **falling star**) 流星. (常用 shooting star 或 falling star). **meteoric** [mi:ti'ɔrik] *adj* very quick 極快的, 快速的: *a meteoric rise to fame* 曇花一現似的成名. **meteorite** ['mi:tiərait] *nc* meteor that has landed on earth 隕石.

meteorology [mi:tiə'rɔlədʒi] *nu* science of the conditions in the earth's atmosphere (esp. with regard to forecasting future weather) 氣象學 (尤指有關天氣預報). **meteorological** [mi:tiərə'lɔdʒikl] *adj* having to do with meteorology 與氣象學有關的, 氣象的: *the meteorological office* (Often colloquially abbreviated to **met** [met]; *the

met office*) 氣象局, (口語上通常被縮略成 met; the met office).

meter¹ ['mi:tə*] *nc* instrument used for measuring (esp. gas, electricity, water etc.) 計量器; 儀表; 計; 表 (尤用於計量煤氣, 電, 水等): *gas meter* 煤氣表, 氣量計; *electric meter* 電表, 電度表; *water meter etc.* 水表等. **'parking meter** .machine placed near a space where a car may be left for a certain length of time. Some money is placed in the machine, which then shows if the car is left there too long 停車計時表.

meter² ['mi:tə*] *nc/u* see 見 **metre**.

methane ['mi:θein] *nu* colourless, odourless, flammable gas 甲烷, 沼氣.

method ['meθəd] **1** *nc* way of doing something 方法, 辦法: *new methods of teaching English* 新英語教學法. **2** *nu* system; planning 條理; 秩序; 規劃: *There is not much method in the way he does things.* 他做事没有甚麼章法. *There is method in his madness* i.e. there seems to be no system in what he does, but in fact there is. 他貌似瘋狂, 卻實有深意. 即: 他做事看似胡來, 其實是有條有理. **methodical** [mi'θɔdikl] *adj* **1** planned; systematic 有規劃的; 有秩序的; 有條理的. **2** fond of planning things out. 喜歡規劃的, 喜歡有條不紊的: *He is very methodical.* 他是一個很有條理的人.

Methodist ['meθədist] *nc* member of a Christian sect following the teachings of John Wesley 衛理公會派教徒, 美以美教會教徒. Also 亦作 *adj.*

methylated ['meθileitid] *adj* usu. in **methylated spirits** i.e. kind of alcohol used for giving heat and light 甲基化了的, 加入甲醇的 (通常用於 methylated spirits 甲基化酒精, 一種用於發熱、發光的燃料)

methylene ['meθili:n] *nu* hydrocarbon radical (CH₂) 次甲基 (CH₂).

meticulous [me'tikjuləs] *adj* very careful about small details; showing that such care has been taken 極爲細心的; 注意細節的: *meticulous work* 極爲細緻的工作; *a meticulous worker* 細心的工人.

metre¹ ['mi:tə*] (*US* 美 **meter**) *nc* unit of measurement (39.35 inches) 米, 公尺 (39.35英寸). **metric** ['metrik] *adj* having to do with the metre or the metric system 米的; 米制的, 公制的. **'metric system** international system of measurement based on the *metre* as the unit of length, and the *gram* as the unit of mass or weight. 公制 (以米和公斤爲度量單位的國際度量制).

metre² ['mi:tə*] (*US* 美 **meter**) *nc / u* arrangement of words in a poem so that certain words are stressed or emphasized in a regular way (詩的)節拍, 音步. **metrical** ['metrikl] *adj*.

metropolis [me'trɔpəlis] *nc* chief city in a country (not necessarily the capital) 一國的主要城市 (不一定是首都). *Note* 說明: the *capital* of a country is where the government is but it may not be large, or important in other ways. 首都是一國政府所在地, 但也許不大, 或者在其他方面也許不很重要.

miaow [mjau] *nc* sound made by a cat 咪, 喵(猫叫聲). Also 亦作 *vi* make this sound 咪, 喵, 做猫叫聲.

mica ['maikə] *nu* mineral that can be easily divided into thin partly transparent layers, used as electrical insulator 雲母.

mice [mais] *pl* of **mouse**. mouse的複數形式.

micro- ['maikrou] *prefix* small 小的.

microbe ['maikroub] *nc* living creature, which is so small that it cannot be seen with the naked eye, frequently the cause of disease. 微生物; 細菌.

microphone ['maikrəfoun] *nc* instrument which can change sound waves into electric waves, and can therefore be used in recording people's voices etc. 話筒, 麥克風, 傳聲器.

microprocessor [maikrou'prousesə*] *nc* small electronic device containing a silicon chip and used in calculators, computers etc. 微信息處理機.

microscope ['maikrəskoup] *nc* instrument with lenses which makes very small things appear to be bigger so that they can be examined more easily 顯微鏡. **microscopic** [maikrəs'kɔpik] *adj* very small 極小的.

mid [mid] *adj / prefix* in the middle of (used to form many compounds) 在…的 中間(用於構成許多複合詞). **'midday** (in the) middle of the day; noon 日中, 中午, 正午: *at midday* 在正午. **'midnight** *nc* **1** 12.00 p.m. 晚上12時, 午夜. **2** the middle of the night 半夜, 午夜: *at midnight* 在半夜, 在午夜; *a midnight swim* 夜半游泳. **'midsummer** (in the) middle of the summer 仲夏: *midsummer days* 仲夏日子. **'midway** *adv* halfway 中途地, 中間地: *midway between Moscow and New York* 在莫斯科和紐約中間.

middle ['midl] *nc* point, area etc coming between and equally distant from two or more other points, areas etc. 中部, 中間, 中央: *the middle of the room* 房間中央; *in the middle of the lake* 在湖中央. Also 亦作 *adj* central; equally distant from certain limits 中央的, 中間的, 中部的: *the middle book* 中間那一本書. *the middle finger* 中指. **'middle-aged** *adj* not young and not old, often applied to people between 40 and 60 years of age 中年的

(常用以指40歲至60歲之間的人). **the Middle 'Ages** period roughly between 1100 A.D. and 1500 A.D. (Also sometimes applied to the period between 500 A.D. and 1500 A.D.) 中世紀(約指公元1100年至1500年之間的時期; 有時亦指公元500年至1500年之間的時期). **'middle 'classes** *npl* section of society which is not of noble birth, but not working-class either (e.g. lawyers, doctors, teachers etc.) 中產階級(非出身貴族但亦非工人, 例如律師, 醫生, 教師等). **'middle-class** *adj* **'middle-man** person who sells goods which he has not produced himself (e.g. a greengrocer who does not grow his own vegetables etc.) 經紀人, 中間人(經賣的貨物非自己所生產; 例如蔬菜水果商). **'middle 'name** name coming between first name and surname (e.g. Winston *Spencer* Churchill) 中間名(在首名與姓之間的名字, 例如 Winston Spencer Churchill). **Middle 'East** general area between Egypt and Iran 中東(一般指埃及至伊朗之間的地區).

midge [midʒ] *nc* type of small winged insect that bites (叮人的)小飛蟲; 蠓, 蚊.

midget ['midʒit] *nc* very small person 矮人, 侏儒. Also *adj* very small 極小的, 極小型的: *midget submarine* 小型潛艇.

midriff ['midrif] *nc* part of the body between the chest and the abdomen (esp. with reference to this part of the body if left uncovered when one is clothed) (胸與腹之間的)中腰部(尤指穿裸露上衣時, 身體露出的部分).

midst [midst] *n* middle (*o.f.*) 中央, 中間, 中部(舊式). **in the midst of** among; in the middle of 在…中間; 在…當中; 在…之中: *I saw him in the midst of the crowd.* 我看見他在人羣之中.

midwife ['midwaif] *nc* woman whose job is to assist at the birth of babies 助產士; 接生婆.

might[1] [mait] past tense of **may**. may 的過去式.

might[2] [mait] *nu* power, strength 權力; 力量: *He fought with all his might.* 他竭力奮戰. **mighty** *adj* powerful; strong; huge 有力的; 強大的; 巨大的: *a mighty king* 威力顯赫的國王; *a mighty tree* 巨大的樹. Also *adv* very 非常: *I'm mighty glad.* (*informal* in this sense) 我非常高興. (此義爲非正式).

migraine ['mi:grein] *nc / u* very painful type of headache (usu. on one side of the head only) 偏頭痛.

migrate [mai'greit] *vi* (with reference to birds and fish) go from one region to another according to the time of year (指鳥和魚)隨季節定期從一地移居至另一地, (鳥)定期移棲, (魚)迴游: *Swallows migrate in the winter.* 燕子在冬季移棲. **migration** *nu* act of migrating 移居; 移棲; 迴游: *He studies the migration of birds.* 他研究鳥類的定期移棲. **migrant** ['maigrənt] *nc* person, animal etc that migrates 移居的人或動物等; 移民; 候鳥. Also *adj*.

mike [maik] *nc* short informal form of **microphone** microphone 的非正式縮畧形式.

milage ['mailidʒ] *nc* see **mile**.

mild [maild] *adj* **1** gentle; soft 和善的; 溫和的; 溫柔的: *a mild person* 和善的人; *a mild way of speaking* 溫和的說話方式; *mild weather* i.e. not too hot or too cold 溫和的天氣. **2** not very bitter or strong 不很苦的; 不強烈的; 淡的; 不濃的: *a mild flavour* 不濃的味道, 淡的味道. **mildly** *adv* **1** gently; softly 和善地; 溫和地, 溫柔地. **2**

rather; not very 有點兒; 不很: *They seem mildly interested* 看來他們有些興趣; *mildly amused* 覺得有點好笑的. **mildness** *nu.*

mildew ['mildju:] *nu* **1** kind of plant disease in which plants are covered with a whitish growth (患病植物上面所長的白色)黴菌. **2** growth which comes on materials (e.g. cloth, leather etc.) when they are damp for a long time (長期潮濕的布、皮革等所生的)黴.

mile [mail] *nc* measure of length equal to 1,760 yards (1.61 kilometres) 英里, 哩 (等於 1, 760 碼或 1.61 公里). **mileage, milage** ['mailidʒ] *nc* number of miles travelled in a certain time 英里數; 哩程. **milestone 1** stone at the roadside which indicates the distance in miles to or from somewhere 里程碑. **2** important point in a person's life; important event 人生的重要時刻; 重大事件: *a milestone in the history of medicine* 醫學史上的劃時代大事; 醫學史上的里程碑.

milieu ['mi:ljə:] *nc* (usu only *sing*) surroundings; background 環境; 背景(通常只用單數). *living in an artistic milieu* 生活在藝術環境中.

militant ['militnt] *adj* in a mood for fighting; warlike; actively engaged in fighting what one regards as evil 戰鬥性的; 富有戰鬥精神的; 好戰的; 積極從事反邪惡戰鬥的: *a militant socialist* 戰鬥的社會主義者; 富有戰鬥精神的社會主義者.

military ['militəri] *adj* having to do with the army or war 軍事的; 軍隊的; 軍人的; 陸軍的; 戰爭的: *military uniform* 軍服, 軍裝; *military life* 軍隊生活; *military police* 憲兵; *military service* i.e. period of time to be spent in the army 服兵役期. **the military** armed forces 武裝部隊, 軍隊. **militate**

against something act against 妨礙某事, 不利於某事; 違反某事: *He won't rest, and that militates against his early recovery.* 他不願休息, 那就不利於他早日康復.

militia [mi'liʃə] *nc* trained group of men who do not serve full-time in the army, but can be called upon to defend their country when necessary 民兵; 民兵組織. *Note* 說明: *sing* form can be treated as *pl* 單數與複數同一形式.

milk [milk] *nu* **1** whitish liquid on which mammals feed their young 奶; 乳. **2** this liquid taken from cows and used by human beings as a drink and for making butter cheese etc. 牛奶. Also 亦作 *vt* take milk from 擠…的奶: *milk a cow* 擠牛奶. *Note* 說明: the word *milk* nearly always means cow's milk. milk 一詞幾乎總是作牛奶解釋. **milky** *adj* of milk; like milk (esp. in colour) 乳的; 牛奶的; 似牛奶的, 乳狀的 (尤指乳白色的). **'milkman** man who delivers milk to people's houses 送牛奶的人, 賣牛奶的人. **'milk 'shake** drink made from cold milk and ice cream 冷牛奶和冰淇淋製成的飲料, 奶昔. **Milky Way** very large group of stars appearing as a broad whitish band of stars stretching across the sky 銀河, 天河.

mill[1] [mil] *nc* **1** building containing machinery for making something 工廠, 製造廠: *paper mill* 造紙廠; *steel mill* 鋼鐵廠, 鐵工廠. **2** building containing machinery for grinding (e.g. wheat) into flour. (穀物)磨坊, 碾磨廠, 麵粉廠. **3** machine or device for grinding any substance finer 磨粉機, 碾磨機: *coffee mill* 咖啡碾磨機 (或器). **miller** *nc* person who owns or uses machinery for making grain into flour 磨坊主人; 麵粉廠主; 磨坊工人.

windmill flour mill in which the driving power of the machinery is supplied by the wind blowing outside, caught by sails 風車磨坊.

mill² [mil] **1** *vt* put through a mill or grinding machine (用磨粉機) 碾磨, 碾碎: *mill coffee, flour etc.* 磨咖啡, 麵粉等. **2** *vi* move round in an aimless or confused manner 無目的地繞來繞去; 胡亂兜圈子: *The crowds milled around outside the hall.* 人羣在禮堂外面轉來轉去.

millennium [mi'leniəm] *nc* period of 1,000 years 一千年. *pl* 複數 **millenniums** or **millennia** [mi'leniə].

millet ['milit] *nu* plant bearing grain in the form of very small seeds 粟, 黍, 小米.

milligram, milligramme ['miligræm] *nc* one thousandth part of a gram in the metric system 毫克(千分之一克).

millimetre ['milimi:tə*] (*US* **millimeter**) *nc* one thousandth part of a metre in the metric system 毫米(千分之一米).

milliner ['milinə*] *nc* person who makes, designs or sells women's hats 女帽商(指製造, 設計或銷售女帽的人). **millinery** *nu* **1** women's hats and other items of dress made by milliners 女帽及其他服飾物. **2** business of making or selling women's hats etc. 女帽製造業; 女帽銷售業.

million ['miljən] *nc* one thousand thousand i.e. 1,000,000 一百萬. **millionaire** [miljə'nɛə*] *nc* **1** person who has a million pounds or dollars 百萬富翁. **2** extremely rich man 大財主, 有錢人.

mime [maim] *nc* / *u* actions done without words, often as an entertainment (通常作爲娛樂的)啞劇表演. Also 亦作 *vt* / *i* do actions of this kind 作啞劇表演.

mimic ['mimik] *vt* copy other people's ways of speaking or behaving 模倣, 摹擬. *past* 過去式和過去分詞 **mimicked.** Also 亦作 *nc* person who is clever at copying the way others speak or behave 善於模倣他人言行的人; 效顰者. **mimicry** *nu.*

mince [mins] *vt* / *i* **1** cut meat or other food up into very small pieces 將(肉或其他食物)切碎, 剁碎. **2** walk with short steps in a manner that is meant to be elegant but only looks foolish 扭扭捏捏地小步走(意欲優雅, 實則可笑). Also 亦作 *nu* meat which has been cut up into very small pieces 剁碎的肉, 碎肉. Also 亦作 **minced meat**). **'mincemeat** mixture of minced apples or other fruit, currants, sugar etc. (用切碎的蘋果或其他水果, 葡萄乾, 糖等物混合製成的)百果餡.

mind¹ [maind] **1** *nc* / *u* part of a person which thinks and reasons; power to reason 心, 頭腦, 腦筋; 智力, 見解力, 思考力: *have a quick mind* i.e. be quick-thinking 頭腦靈活, 即思想敏捷; *be out of one's mind* i.e. be insane 精神錯亂, 神志不清, 發狂: *He is not in his right mind* i.e. he is insane. 他精神不正常. 即: 他發瘋了. **2** *nu* memory 記憶: *bear / keep something in mind* i.e. not forget something 記住某事, 不忘某事. **3** *nc* opinions; what one believes or intends 見解, 意見; 志向; 意圖: *change one's mind* i.e. change one's intention or belief 改變主意. **mindful** *adj* being careful about; remembering 留心的, 注意的; 記住的, 不忘的: *mindful of the danger involved* 留意其中所包含的危險. (*opp* 反義詞 **unmindful**). **mindless** *adj* careless; stupid 不注意的; 愚蠢的. **make up one's mind** decide 決意, 決定, 下決心: *He's made up his mind to go* *home.* 他決定回家.

mind² [maind] *vt / i* **1** attend to 專心, 留心: *Mind what you're doing:* 專心做你在做的事. **2** be careful 注意, 小心: *Mind the step* i.e. don't trip over the step. 當心台階, 即: 不要被它絆倒. *Mind you don't say anything to offend them.* 注意不要說任何冒犯他們的事. **3** look after; take care of 照顧, 照料, 關心: *I'm staying home to mind the children.* 我呆在家裏照顧小孩. **4** object; dislike 反對; 介意; 厭惡: *Do you mind if I smoke / open the window?* 我抽煙 / 把窗子打開你反對嗎? *Would you mind coming over here?* 請您過來一下好嗎? **never mind** don't worry 別擔心, 別難過, 沒關係: *I'm afraid he's just gone, but never mind-he'll be back in a few minutes.* (informal) 不湊巧他剛剛出去, 但不用焦急, 他幾分鐘後就回來. (非正式). *Note* 說明: *mind* is very commonly used in commands, warnings etc. mind 很常用於命令告誡等.

mine¹ [main] *pron* what belongs to me 我的 (東西): *We'll have to separate mine from yours.* 我們將不得不把我的和你的分開. Also 亦作 *pred adj* belonging to me. (屬於) 我的: *This shirt is mine.* 這件襯衫是我的.

mine² [main] *nc* **1** deep tunnel in the earth made so that valuable ores or stones, coal etc can be taken out 礦, 礦井. **2** any source which gives something valuable in large amounts 豐富的資源, 寶藏; 寶庫: *That man is a mine of information about history.* 那個人是歷史資訊的活寶庫. **3** container of high explosives placed near the surface of the sea, or on land, which will explode when it touches something 地雷; 水雷: *a landmine* 地雷. Also 亦作 *vt / i* **1** dig up ores, precious

stones, coal etc from the earth 開採礦物; 掘礦井; 開礦. **2** place containers of high explosives in a certain area 佈雷; 敷設地雷或水雷: *mine an area* 在某地區佈雷. *They mined the entrance to the harbour.* 他們在港口佈設了水雷. **3** destroy by using mines (in sense 3) 用地雷或水雷炸毀: *The ship was mined early this morning.* 那隻船今天清晨被水雷炸毀. **miner** *nc* someone who takes coal, precious stones etc from the earth 礦工. **minefield** stretch of land or sea where mines (in sense 3) have been laid 佈雷區; 佈地雷的區域; 佈水雷的水域. '**minesweeper** ship specially used to remove mines (in sense 3) which may be dangerous to other ships 掃雷艇.

mineral ['minərl] *nc* any material obtained from the earth (e.g. gold, coal, oil) 礦物 (例如黃金, 煤炭, 石油). Also 亦作 *adj*: *mineral wealth* 礦物資源, 礦藏; *mineral rights* i.e. right to mine in a certain area 開礦權. '**mineral water** *nc / u* **1** water containing salts or gases, taken for health 礦泉水. **2** type of drink with bubbles of gas in it 蘇打水; 汽水.

mingle ['miŋgl] *vt / i* mix; be or put in the company of 使混合; 混合; 使混在一起; 混在一起: *They mingled with the other people at the party.* 他們與聚會上其他的人混在一起.

mini- ['mini] *prefix* specially made smaller than usual (e.g. minibus i.e. type of vehicle like a small bus; miniskirt i.e. very short skirt) (特別做得比平常) 小的 (例如 minibus 小型公共汽車; miniskirt 超短裙).

miniature ['minitʃə*] *attrib adj* copied on a small scale 小型的: *miniature railway* 小型鐵路. Also 亦作 *nc* **1**

very small picture of someone 小畫像，袖珍畫．**2** any very small thing 極小之物，微型物．

minimize ['minimaiz] *vt* reduce to the smallest amount 使減至最少；使縮到最小：*minimize the risk of an accident* 把事故的危險減至最小程度．

minimum ['miniməm] *nc* smallest amount of something that is possible or has actually been recorded 最小量，最少數：*That is the very minimum that I shall accept.* 那就是我會接受的最低數額．Also 亦作 *adj* smallest possible or recorded 最小的；最少的；最低的：*minimum rainfall* 最低降雨量．(*opp* 反義詞 **maximum**). **minimal** *adj*.

minister ['ministə*] *nc* **1** person in charge of a department in a government 部長；大臣：*Minister of Social Security* 社會保障部部長．**2** clergyman 牧師：*Presbyterian minister* 長老會牧師．**ministerial** [minis'tiəriəl] *adj*

ministry ['ministri] *nc* **1** department in a government; building containing a certain government department (政府的) 部；部的辦公大樓：*Ministry of Defence* 國防部；*refer something to the Ministry* 把某事提交給部．**2** period during which someone is a minister 部長的任期：*His ministry lasted from 1925 to 1930.* 他的部長任期從1925年延續到1930年．'prime 'minister chief minister in a government 總理；首相．

mink [miŋk] **1** *nc* type of small animal 水貂．**2** *nu* expensive fur from this animal (名貴毛皮) 貂皮．Also 亦作 *adj*: *mink coat* 貂皮外衣．

minor ['mainə*] *adj* small; unimportant 小的；不重要的：*a minor operation* i.e. not a dangerous one 小手術，即無性命危險的手術．*They discussed the future of the club and other minor problems*

他們討論了俱樂部的前途及其他次要的問題．Also 亦作 *nc* (in a legal sense) person under 18 (法律上用語) 十八歲以下的人 (未到法定年齡的人).

minority [mi'nɔriti] *nc* lesser number; less than half 較少數；未到半數：*supported by only a minority of the voters* 只得到少數投票人的支持．

minstrel ['minstrl] *nc* (in former times) person who wandered from place to place entertaining people with songs etc. (昔日的) 吟遊詩人；遊藝人．

mint¹ [mint] **1** *nu* plant used to flavour food etc. 薄荷．**2** *nc* sweet flavoured with mint 薄荷糖．

mint² [mint] *nc* place (usu. official) where coins are made from metal (通常為官方的) 造幣廠．Also 亦作 *adj* brand-new 嶄新的；新造的：*in mint condition* 完整如新的；完美的．

minuet [minju'et] *nc* old, slow, graceful dance 小步舞．

minus ['mainəs] *prep* **1** less (shown in mathematics by the sign-) 減 (去) (數學上用"－"符號表示)：*Five minus two equals three (5−2=3).* 5減去2等於3．**2** without; having lost 無，沒有；失去：*He returned from the war minus an arm.* (*informal* in sense 2) 他從軍回來losing了一隻手臂．(義2爲非正式). Also 亦作 *nc* the minus sign 減號；負號．

minute¹ ['minit] *nc* 1／60 of an hour 分鐘：*five minutes past six* 六點五分；*in twenty minutes' time* 在20分鐘的時間．**minutes** *npl* record of what is said and decided at a meeting 會議記錄．

minute² [mai'nju:t] *adj* very small; giving all the details 非常小的；詳細的；細緻的：*a minute amount* 極小量；*a minute account of something one has seen* 對所見某事的詳細描述．**minutely** *adv*.

miracle ['mirəkl] *nc* **1** happening which cannot be explained naturally and is due to a god or other supernatural power 奇跡: *be able to work miracles* i.e. perform miracles 能創造奇跡. **2** any strange or wonderful happening or achievement 奇特的事件; 非凡的成就: *miracles of modern science.* 現代科學的非凡成就 (或奇跡). *It's a miracle you arrived so early.* 你這麼早就到達真令人驚奇. **miraculous** [mi'rækjuləs] *adj* strange or wonderful; due to supernatural causes 奇妙的; 非凡的; 神奇的; 不可思議的. **miraculously** *adv.*

mirage ['mira:ʒ] *nc* illusion caused by air conditions in hot areas (esp. deserts) by which things which are actually far away seem to be near, or in which one seems to see something which is not actually there 海市蜃樓, 幻景 (尤見於沙漠地區).

mirror ['mirə*] *nc* shiny surface (usu. of glass) in which things are reflected 鏡子: *She was looking at herself in the mirror.* 她在照鏡子. Also 亦作 *vt* give an exact copy or reflection of 反映, 映出: *The mountains were mirrored in the lake.* 高山倒映在湖裏.

mirth [mə:θ] *nu* laughter; merriment 歡笑; 歡樂.

misanthropist [mi'zænθrəpist] *nc* person who hates or does not trust mankind, or who avoids meeting people 憤世嫉俗者.

misapprehension [misæpri'henʃən] *nc / u* misunderstanding 誤解; 誤會: *be under a misapprehension* i.e. have a false or mistaken idea about something. 處於誤解的情況中. 即: 對某事物的看法或見解有錯誤.

misappropriate [misə'prouprieit] *vt* take something and use it for a wrong purpose; use what belongs to another for one's own purposes 濫用; 盜用; 挪用; 私吞: *The treasurer misappropriated the society's funds.* 司庫挪用會社的公款. **misappropriation** [misəproupri'eiʃən] *nu.*

misbehave [misbi'heiv] *vi* (usu. with reference to children) behave badly (通常指小孩) 行爲不當, 舉止不端. **misbehaviour** [misbi'heivjə*] (*US* 美 **misbehavior**) *nu* act of misbehaving 不良的行爲; 不規矩的舉動.

miscarriage ['miskæridʒ] *nc* **1** mistake; failure 錯誤, 差錯; 失敗: *miscarriage of justice* i.e. a wrong verdict 判決不公; 誤判. **2** accidental birth of a baby before the proper time with the result that it dies 小産, 流産.

miscellaneous [misi'leiniəs] *adj* consisting of different and varied parts; mixed 含有各種各樣的; 混合的; 混雜的: *a miscellaneous collection of books* 一批各種各樣的書籍; *a miscellaneous crowd of people* 一羣各色各樣的人; *miscellaneous objects* 雜七雜八的東西.

mischance [mis'tʃɑ:ns] *nc* misfortune; piece of bad luck 不幸; 災禍; 不幸事件: *by some mischance* 由於某種不幸事故.

mischief ['mistʃif] *nu* (esp. with reference to children) trouble caused by foolish or naughty behaviour (尤指小孩) 惡作劇; 搗蛋: *always up to mischief* 總是搗鬼; *often getting into mischief* 常愛胡鬧. **mischievous** ['mistʃivəs] *adj* **1** annoying or troublesome (but usu. not in a serious way) 討厭的; 惱人的; 令人煩惱的 (通常並不嚴重): *a mischievous child* 惹煩惱的小孩, 淘氣的孩子. **2** teasing; sly 戲弄的; 取笑的; 淘氣的; 頑皮的: *a mischievous glance* 調皮的眼色. **mischievously**

adv.

misconception [miskən'sepʃən] *nc* failure to understand, wrong idea 誤解, 錯誤的看法, 錯誤的觀念.

misconduct [mis'kɔndəkt] *nu* 1 bad or wrong behaviour (esp. adultery) 行爲不端(尤指通姦). 2 wrong behaviour of someone in a responsible position (e.g. acceptance of a bribe by an official etc.) (擔任要職人員的)胡作非爲, 瀆職(例如官員等的接受賄賂).

misconstrue [miskən'stru:] *vt* take the wrong meaning from 曲解, 誤解: *misconstrue someone's actions / words* etc. 曲解某人的行動/話等.

misdeed ['mis'di:d] *nc* crime; evil act 罪行; 惡行; 不良的行爲: *He will pay for his misdeeds.* 他必將因惡行而受到懲罰.

misdemeanour [misdi'mi:nə*] *nc* wrong or unlawful act which is not very serious (不嚴重的)不正當行爲, 犯法行爲: *guilty of a misdemeanour* 犯了輕罪.

miser ['maizə*] *nc* person who loves money for its own sake and spends or gives away as little of it as he can 守財奴; 吝嗇鬼; 小氣鬼. **miserly** *adj* mean 吝嗇的, 小氣的.

miserable ['mizərəbl] *adj* 1 unhappy 不愉快的; 愁苦的: *feeling very miserable* 感到十分痛苦. 2 poor; wretched 貧困的; 可憐的; 悲慘的: *living in miserable circumstances* 過着悲慘的生活(或貧苦的生活). **miserably** *adv* **misery** ['mizəri] *nc / u* 1 unhappiness 痛苦; 悲慘. 2 poverty; wretchedness 貧困; 可憐; 悲慘.

misfire ['mis'faiə*] *vi* 1 (with reference to a gun etc.) fail to fire properly (指槍等)射不出. 2 generally fail in some way 不奏效; 失敗: *The engine misfired.* 發動機發動不起來. *His*

plans misfired. 他的計劃失敗了.

misfit ['misfit] *nc* someone who is unsuitable for a position or for his surroundings 不適合其職位的人; 不適應環境的人: *a misfit in the post he holds* 一個不稱職的人.

misfortune [mis'fɔ:tʃən] *nu* bad luck 不幸; 災禍.

misgiving [mis'giviŋ] *nc / u* (often *pl*) fear; doubt; distrust (常用複數)害怕; 疑慮; 不信任: *I had some misgivings about lending him the money.* 借給他錢, 我有些擔心.

misguided [mis'gaidid] *adj* foolish; mistaken (esp. as a result of others' advice) 愚蠢的; 錯誤的(尤指因聽從他人的指導所致): *a misguided attitude* 錯誤或愚蠢的態度.

mishap ['mishæp] *nc* unfortunate accident or event (usu. not serious) (通常指不嚴重的)不幸事件: *a slight mishap* 小小的不幸.

misinterpret [misin'tə:prit] *vt* explain wrongly, not understand correctly 錯譯; 誤解; 曲解; 解釋錯: *I think you misinterpreted my meaning.* 我想你誤解了我的意思. **misinterpretation** [misintə:pri'teiʃən] *nc / u.*

mislay [mis'lei] *vt* put a thing somewhere and be unable to find it later (將某物隨便置放, 後來尋找不到)誤置; 擱忘; 丟失. *past* 過去式和過去分詞 **mislaid.**

mislead [mis'li:d] *vt* cause someone to have the wrong ideas, opinions etc. 使有錯誤想法或意見; 使誤解: *I'm sorry I misled you into thinking I would be at home.* 很抱歉我使你誤認爲我會在家. *past* 過去式和過去分詞 **misled** ['mis'led].

misnomer [mis'noumə*] *nc* wrong name for someone / something 錯誤的名稱; 不正當的名稱: *The name 'Curly'* *for someone who is bald would seem to be a misnomer.* 把禿頭的人稱作'鬈髮'看來是張冠李戴.

misplace [mis'pleis] *vt* put in the wrong place or a place afterwards forgotten 把…放錯地方, 誤置; 把…放置一處隨後忘記.

misprint ['misprint] *nc* mistake in printing 印刷錯誤.

misrepresent [misrepri'zent] *vt* give a wrong idea of 曲解; 歪曲; 理解錯; 誤釋: *You are misrepresenting my views on this matter.* 你是在歪曲我對此事的看法.

miss[1] [mis] *vt/i* **1** not succeed in doing something one wants or tries to do 未完成; 未成功; 未達到: *fire at a target and miss* 向目標射擊但沒有打中; *miss a train one wants to get* 沒趕上要坐的火車; *miss the point of something one wants to understand* 沒能領會要弄懂的要點. **2** feel lonely after; regret the absence of 懷念, 思念, 惋惜失掉: *I miss John now that he is abroad.* 我想念在國外的約翰. *She misses having her breakfast in bed.* 她懷念在床上吃早餐(的享受). **missing** *adj* not to be found; absent 找不到的; 失蹤的; 失去的; 不在的: *missing in action* i.e. of a soldier in battle (士兵)在戰鬥中失蹤的; *a couple of words missing* 掉了兩個詞. **a near miss** explosion or shot (e.g. in bombing) which is not quite on the target 靠近彈, 近失彈(例如轟炸等, 雖未命中, 但距目標很近).

miss[2] [mis] *n* title of an unmarried woman or girl (未婚女子或少女的稱呼)小姐: *Miss Brown* 布朗小姐.

misshapen [mis'ʃeipən] *adj* deformed 畸形的: *a misshapen body* 畸形的身體.

missile ['misail, *US* 'misl] *nc* **1** object thrown or otherwise sent through the air so as to injure or cause damage (e.g. stone, arrow etc.) 投擲物, 發射物 (如 石塊, 箭 等): *The angry crowd threw stones, rocks and other missiles.* 憤怒的羣衆投擲石頭, 大石塊和其他東西. **2** large explosive rocket for use in war 導彈.

mission ['miʃən] *nc* **1** journey (usu. abroad) made for a special purpose (not pleasure) (通常指到國外)執行艱巨的特殊任務的旅行: *a mission to China* 赴華執行使命. **2** group of people travelling somewhere and entrusted with some special duty 代表團, 特使團: *a trade mission* 貿易代表團, 貿易考察團; *a diplomatic mission* 外交使團. **3** group of people living in a foreign country for religious reasons; also, the buildings etc which they put up 傳敎團, 佈道團; 傳敎機構, 傳道地區: *a Christian mission* 基督敎傳敎團; *the mission near the village* 村莊附近的傳敎機構(或傳道會). **missionary** ['miʃənri] *nc* someone who goes to work in a foreign country for religious reasons (usu. to convert people there to his own beliefs) (在國外工作的)傳敎士.

misspent ['mis'spent] *adj* wasted; used foolishly 浪費掉的; 亂用的: *a misspent youth* i.e. the time when a person was young was wasted on foolish things 虛度年華的青年人.

mist [mist] *nc/u* water vapour which reduces the distance one can see; thin fog 使視界朦朧的水蒸氣; 薄霧; 靄: *The hills were covered in mist.* 小山被薄霧籠罩着. **misty** *adj* **1** covered in mist; having a lot of mist 被薄霧籠罩着的; 多薄霧的: *the misty plains below us* 位於我們下方的霧中平原; *a misty evening* 多霧的夜晚. **2** not clear; not definite 朦朧不清的; 模糊

的; *misty idea* 模糊的觀點; *misty notions* 模糊的想法; 模糊的概念. **mist over** become covered in mist 被罩上薄霧: *The windows have misted over.* 窗子已被罩上薄霧.

mistake [mis'teik] *nc* error; wrong idea or act 錯誤; 差錯; 想錯; 弄錯: *There are five mistakes in this composition.* 這篇作文裏有五個錯誤. *Lending him the money was a mistake.* 借錢給他是錯誤的. Also 亦作 *vt* not understand; have the wrong idea about 不理解; 誤解; 誤會. *I mistook his purpose completely* i.e. I had the wrong idea about why he did that. 我完全誤解了他的意圖. 即; 誤解了他爲甚麼那樣做. *past tense* 過去式 *mistook* [mis'tuk]. *past part* 過去分詞 **mistaken. mistaken** *adj* wrong; in error 錯誤的; 弄錯的; 不正確的: *be quite mistaken* i.e. be completely wrong 完全弄錯了: *a mistaken act* 錯誤的行動. **mistake somebody / something for** imagine that somebody / something is somebody / something else 誤認某人 / 某物爲…, 誤把某人 / 某物當作…: *I mistook him for his brother* i.e. I thought he was his brother. 我錯把他當作他的兄弟.

mister ['mistə*] *n* see 見 **Mr.**

mistletoe ['misltou] *nu* plant with small, white fruit, which grows on other plants, and is used for decoration at Christmas 檞寄生(一種果實小而白, 寄生於他樹的植物; 作聖誕節裝飾用).

mistook [mis'tuk] past tense of **mistake.** mistake 的過去式.

mistress ['mistris] *nc* **1** woman who has control of something 支配某事物的女人; 女主人: *mistress of the household* i.e. in charge of a home 家庭的女主人, 主婦; *mistress of the situation* i.e. in control of what is happening 能控制局面的女人. **2** (Brit) woman

teacher (英) 女教師: *the English mistress* i.e. the woman who teaches English. 女英語教師.

mistrust [mis'trʌst] *vt / i* feel suspicious or doubtful about 懷疑; 不相信; 不信任: *mistrust someone* 不信任某人. Also 亦作 *nu.*

misunderstand [misʌndə'stænd] *vt* not get the right meaning from someone's words / actions etc. 誤解, 誤會; *misunderstand what someone said* 誤解某人說的話. *past* 過去式和過去分詞 **misunderstood** [misʌndə'stud]. **misunderstanding** *nc / u* failure on the part of different people to understand things in the same way (esp. when this leads to a quarrel) 誤解, 誤會(尤指導致爭吵): *slight misunderstanding* 輕微的誤解.

misuse [mis'ju:z] *vt* **1** use for a wrong purpose 誤用, 錯用, 濫用; *He damaged his tools by misusing them.* 他因使用不當損壞了工具. **2** treat badly 虐待, 處理不當. Also 亦作 [mis'ju:s] *nc / u.*

mite [mait] *nc* small insect, often found in decayed food etc. 小蟲, 螨(常見於腐爛的食物等之中).

mitigate ['mitigeit] *vt* make something less severe or serious 減輕; 使較不嚴重, 使較不厲害; *mitigate pain* 減輕疼痛; *mitigate a punishment* 減輕懲罰.

mitre ['maitə*] (*US* 美 **miter**) *nc* **1** headdress worn by bishops 主教冠. **2** method of fitting together two pieces of wood so that they form an angle (usu. 90°) (used e.g. to fit the sides of a picture frame together) (通常爲90度的)斜角接, 斜角縫, 斜接, 斜榫(例如用於連接畫框的角).

mitten ['mitn] *nc* glove in which four of the fingers fit into one part and the thumb into another (拇指分開, 其餘四

指連在一起的)連指手套, 無指套.

mix [miks] **1** *vt* put things together so that they are united in some way 使混合, 使混在一起: *mix the ingredients for a cake* 拌和配料做糕餅; *mix people together* 與人混雜在一起. *One should never mix business with pleasure* i.e. they should be done separately. 永遠不要把工作和娛樂混在一起. 即: 應該分開進行. **2** *vt* make something from certain ingredients 調製, 配製: *mix mortar* 調配灰漿. **3** *vi* come together to form a unit; be united 相混合; 融合在一起: *Oil and water won't mix.* 油和水不能融合在一起. **4** *vi* come together in company or society 交往, 相處; *mix with people at a party* 與宴會上的人交往; *races mixing together* 相處在一起的各色人種. Also 亦作 *nc* **1** mixture; what results from mixing 混合; 混合物: *cement mix* 水泥混合物. **2** food preparation sold in shops requiring only the addition of water etc. (商店出售, 只需加水等的)調製食品; 速煮食品; *cake-mix* 糕餅粉, 蛋糕粉. **mixed** *adj* including or made up of different kinds of things 混合的, 混雜的: *mixed marriage* i.e. marriage between people of different races or religions 異族通婚; 不同宗教信仰男女之間的通婚; *mixed bathing* i.e. men and women bathing together 男女混合浴. **mixture 1** *nu* act of being mixed; being 被混合的動作; 混合. **2** *nc* something formed by mixing things together 混合物: *tea mixture* 混合茶, *tobacco mixture* 混合烟草. *mixture of good and bad qualities* 優劣不分的混合物 **mix something up** confuse; put together or arrange badly or mistakenly 混淆; 混同; 搞亂; 弄錯. **'mixed 'up** *adj* confused 混亂的; 迷惑的; 弄不

清的: *I'm all mixed up about this* i.e. I do not understand it. 這事完全把我弄糊塗了. 即: 我不懂這事.

moan [moun] *nc* low sound as from someone who is in pain or suffering 呻吟聲; 嗚咽聲, 悲嘆聲: *a moan of pain* 疼痛的呻吟聲. Also 亦作 *vi*: *moan with pain* 痛苦地呻吟.

moat [mout] *nc* deep ditch (usu. round a castle) filled with water, and intended to make a place easier to defend (通常指城堡的)護城河, 壕溝.

mob [mɔb] *nc* confused and disorderly crowd 混亂無法紀的人羣; 暴民: *a mob of people* 混亂的民衆; 一羣暴民; *an uncontrollable mob* 控制不了的暴民. Also 亦作 *vt* crowd found in order to show hostility or enthusiasm 成羣圍聚 (表示敵意或熱情): *The crowd mobbed the popular film star.* 人羣團團圍住受人歡迎的電影明星. *past* 過去式和過去分詞 **mobbed**.

mobile ['moubail] *adj* able to move or be moved easily 能移動的; 易移動的: *He has not been so mobile since his accident.* 他自從遭受意外事故以後, 就沒有這樣活動過. **mobility** [mou'biliti] *nu*.

moccasin ['mɔkəsin] *nc* type of shoe completely made from soft leather (e.g. deerskin) 用軟皮(例如鹿皮)做的鞋.

mock [mɔk] *vt / i* make fun of (esp. by imitating) 嘲笑, 嘲弄(尤指通過模仿進行): *The children mocked his way of speaking.* 孩子們模仿他説話的樣子來嘲笑他. Also 亦作 *adj* not real; imitation 非真的; 模擬的: *a mock battle* 模擬戰, 假想戰. **mockery** ['mɔkəri] **1** *nu* act of mocking 嘲笑, 嘲弄: *the mockery of the crowd* 人羣的嘲笑. **2** *nc* somebody / something that is made fun of 被嘲笑的對象, 笑柄, 笑料: *They made a mockery of him.* 他們把他作爲笑料. '**mock-up** *nc* model of something (e.g. an aeroplane) to show what it will look like when it is finished 實物模型(例如飛機; 顯示實物完成後的樣子).

model ['mɔdl] *nc* **1** copy of something on a smaller scale 模型: *model of an aeroplane* 飛機模型. **2** something which has to be, or ought to be, copied 模範, 典範; 典型: *A perfect model for a student* 學生的完美典範. **3** something / somebody to be drawn, painted etc by an artist (畫家作畫的)模特兒, 模型: *The girl worked as an artist's model.* 那少女當畫家的模特兒. **4** girl who shows something for sale (usu. clothes) 女性服裝模特兒: *a fashion model* 時裝模特兒. **5** small copy made as a toy (作玩具)模型: *a model car* 玩具汽車, 模型汽車. Also 亦作 *adj* excellent; worthy of imitation 優秀的; 值得模倣的: *a model husband* 模範丈夫. Also 亦作 *vt* **1** make or shape from some soft material (e.g. clay) 用軟材料(如黏土)做成. **2** show clothes to customers by wearing them 做模特兒展示服裝: *model gowns* 當模特兒穿長袍示樣. *past* 過去式和過去分詞 **modelled.** (*US* 美 **modeled**).

moderate[1] ['mɔdərit] *adj* **1** not going too far; not extreme 不過火的, 不過分的; 不走極端的: *moderate opinions* 溫和的意見, 不偏激的意見. **2** not too little, not too much; medium 不多不少的; 中等的; 適度的: *a moderate amount* 不多不少的量; 適中的量; *a moderate income* 中等收入. (*opp* 反義詞 **immoderate**). Also 亦作 *nc* person who does not hold extreme views (esp. in politics) 溫和主義者(尤指在政治方面). **moderately** *adv*.

moderate[2] ['mɔdəreit] *vt / i* become or make less violent or extreme (使)緩和; (使)減輕; 節制: *moderate one's anger* 節制自己的憤怒; 壓低自己的怒火. **moderation** [mɔdə'reiʃən] *nu* quality of being moderate 溫和; 緩和; 減輕; 中等; 適度.

modern ['mɔdn] *adj* **1** having to do with present or recent times; not ancient 現代的, 近代的; 非古代的: *modern ideas* 現代思想, 新思想; *modern history* 近代史. **2** up-to-date 時新的, 新式的: *modern furniture* 新式傢具. **modernize** *vt* bring up to date; make modern 使符合時代的方式; 使現代化: *modernize business methods* 使營業方法現代化. **modernization** [mɔdənai'zeiʃən] *nc / u.*

modest ['mɔdist] *adj* **1** not thinking too highly of one's own powers; not proud 謙虛的; 謙遜的; 不驕傲的: *a modest person* 謙遜的人. **2** not very large, grand etc. 不很大的, 不很堂皇的: *a modest crowd* 不大的人羣. **modestly** *adv* **modesty** *nu.*

modify ['mɔdifai] *vt* **1** change slightly (輕微的)改變, 變更, 修改: *modify the original plan* 修改原計劃. **2** make less 減輕, 緩和: *modify one's demands* 降低要求. **modification** [mɔdifi'keiʃən] *nc / u* change 變更, 改變, 修改.

mohair ['mouhɛə] *nu* type of very soft wool 馬海毛(一種很柔軟的羊毛). Also 亦作 *adj: a mohair scarf* 馬海毛圍巾.

Mohammedan [mə'hæmidn] *nc* follower of Mohammed 伊斯蘭教徒, 穆斯林. Also 亦作 *adj* connected with Mohammed or his religious system 穆罕默德的; 伊斯蘭教的. **Mohammedanism** *nu.* Note 說明: *Muslim* is preferred instead of Mohammedan, and *Islam* instead of Mohammedanism 最好用 Muslim 代替 Mohammedan 與 Islam 代 Mohammedanism.

moist [mɔist] *adj* slightly wet; damp 微濕的; 潮濕的. **moisten** ['mɔisn] *vt / i* become or make damp 使潮濕; 變潮濕. **moisture** ['mɔistʃə*] *nu* 1 wetness 濕, 濕氣, 潮濕. 2 condensed liquid (usu. water) on the surface of something in the form of small drops 凝結在表面上的水珠: *moisture on the window* 凝結在窗子上的水珠.

molar¹ ['moulə] *nc* grinding tooth 臼齒. Also 亦作 *adj* pertaining to a grinding tooth 臼齒的.

molar² ['moulə] *adj* 1 pertaining to a body of matter as a whole 質量(上)的. 2 pertaining to a solution containing one mole of solute per litre 克分子的, 容模的.

mold [mould] *nu* see 見 **mould.**

mole¹ [moul] *nc* small, furcovered animal that eats insects and lives in tunnels which it makes under the ground 鼹鼠, 田鼠.

mole² [moul] *nc* dark spot on the skin, often present from birth 黑痣.

molecule ['mɔlikjuːl] *nc* smallest division of a substance possible without changing its chemical nature 分子. **molecular** [mɔ'lekjulə*] *adj* connected with molecules 與分子有關的, 分子的.

molest [mə'lest] *vt* deliberately give trouble to someone; interfere with 騷擾; 干擾: *The crowd molested the policeman who was trying to do his duty.* 人羣干擾在設法執行任務的警察.

molt [moult] *vt / i* see 見 **moult.**

molten ['moultn] *adj* see 見 **melt.**

moment ['moumənt] 1 *nc* point in time; very short period of time 片刻; 瞬間;

刹那: *For a moment I thought you were going to refuse.* 我一時認爲你會拒絕. *The feeling only lasted a moment.* 這種感覺僅僅持續了一會兒. *He's probably thinking of you at this moment.* 他很可能正在想你. 2 *nu* importance 重要, 重大: *of great moment* 很重要的. **momentary** ['moumǝntri] *adj* lasting only for a very short time 頃刻的, 短暫的, 刹那間的, 瞬間的: *a momentary sensation* 一時的轟動, 短暫的轟動. **momentarily** *adv* **momentous** [mou'mentǝs] *adj* extremely important 極重要的: *a momentous decision* 極爲重要的決定.

momentum [mou'mentǝm] *nu* force or speed of a moving body 動量: *The truck gained momentum as it rolled down the steep road.* 卡車駛下陡峭的路時, 速度愈來愈快.

monarch ['mɔnǝk] *nc* king or emperor 國王, 皇帝. **monarchist** *nc* person who is in favour of rule by a monarch 支持君主政治的人, 擁護君主制度者, 君主主義者.

monastery ['mɔnǝstǝri] *nc* building where monks live together 男修道院; 僧院, 寺院. **monastic** [mǝ'næstik] *adj* connected with a monastery, or with monks or their way of life 修道院的; 寺院的; 修道士的; 僧侶的; 修道生活的; 禁慾生活的: *monastic vows* 修道誓願 (貧窮, 童貞, 服從三條); *monastic existence* 僧侶的生活; 禁慾生活.

Monday ['mʌndi] *n* second day of the week, following Sunday 星期一.

monetary ['mʌnitǝri] *adj* see 見 **money.**

money ['mʌni] *nu* metal (e.g. gold or silver) stamped in special way (coins), or paper printed in a special way (notes), which can be used to buy goods or services 錢; 貨幣(硬幣

和紙幣). **monetary** ['mʌnitri] *adj* having to do with money 貨幣的; 金錢的: *the monetary system* 貨幣制度. 'moneybox small box with a narrow opening at the top through which coins may be dropped, used when making collections 儲蓄箱, 錢錢箱, 撲滿. 'moneylender person who lends money and charges a certain amount (called **interest**) for this service 收取利息的放債者; 貸主. 'money order order of a certain value which can be bought at a post office by one person and sent to someone else who will get the value of it at another post office 郵政匯票.

mongrel ['mʌŋgrəl] *nc* **1** dog of mixed breed 雜種狗. **2** any animal or plant of mixed breed or origin 雜種動物; 雜交植物. Also 亦作 *adj* of mixed origin (esp. where the origins do not seem fitting for one another) 雜種的, 混血的 (尤指種源或血統似乎互不適合).

monitor ['mɔnitə*] *nc* schoolboy appointed to help in the running of a school (e.g. in keeping discipline or in performing some task) 被任命協助管理學校(如維持秩序等工作)的學生; 班長; 級長: *a class monitor* 班長. Also 亦作 *vt* listen to radio broadcasts (esp. from a foreign country in order to get information) 監聽(尤指對外國廣播的監聽).

monk [mʌŋk] *nc* one of a group of men who devote their lives to God and live together in a religious community (called a **monastery**) 修道士; 僧侶 (*fem* 陰 **nun**) [nʌn].

monkey ['mʌŋki] *nc* **1** one of the group of animals which is most closely related to Man and nearly all of which have tails 猴子; 猿. **2** mischievous child (*informal* in sense 2) 淘氣的小

孩, 頑童. (義2爲非正式). 'monkey nut groundnut 落花生.

mono- ['mɔnou] *prefix* one (e.g. **monosyllable**). 單一(例如 monosyllable).

monocle ['mɔnəkl] *nc* eyeglass held in one eye 單片眼鏡.

monogram ['mɔnəgræm] *nc* two or more letters (usu. someone's initials) written together to form one sign 花押字(用兩個或兩個以上的字母, 通常爲姓名的第一字母, 組合寫成).

monolith ['mɔnəliθ] *nc* large single block of stone, as used for a pillar, column etc. (用作柱子等的)獨塊巨石; 獨石柱(或碑等). **monolithic** [mɔnə-'liθik] *adj*.

monologue ['mɔnəlɔg] *nc* long talk or speech by one person 一個人的長篇大論, 滔滔不絕的獨白.

monopoly [mə'nɔpəli] *nc* **1** state which results in business if only one person or company can supply a certain type of goods 壟斷, 獨佔, 專利: *a monopoly in sugar* 對糖的壟斷, 壟斷糖的銷售. **2** something the supply of which is controlled by one person or company 壟斷商品: *Tea was a monopoly.* 茶葉是獨佔經營商品. **monopolize** *vt* keep all of something for one's own use or profit 壟斷; 獨佔; 專營: *He monopolized the conversation* i.e. no one else got a chance to speak. 他壟斷了談話. 即; 別人沒有機會插嘴說話.

monosyllable ['mɔnəsiləbl] *nc* word made up of only one syllable (e.g. *yes*, *no*) 單音節詞(例如 yes, no). **monosyllabic** [mɔnəsi'læbik] *adj*.

monotone ['mɔnətoun] *nc* level way of speaking or singing, without raising or lowering one's voice (語調或歌調)單調, 無變化: *speak in a monotone* 以平淡無變化的語調說話. **monotonous**

[mə'nɔtənəs] *adj* unchanging and therefore dull; uninteresting 單調的; 無變化的; 枯燥乏味的; 無趣味的: a *monotonous journey* 單調乏味的旅程.

monotony [mə'nɔtəni] *nc / u*: the *monotony of a long train journey* 乘火車長途旅行的單調乏味.

monsoon [mɔn'su:n] *nc* 1 seasonal wind (mainly in South-East Asia) blowing from the south-west for part of the year and from the north-east for another part 季風(主要在東南亞, 一年中部份時間吹西南風, 部份時間吹東北風). 2 rainy season caused by the south-west monsoon (西南季風帶來的)雨季.

monster ['mɔnstə*] *nc* 1 animal etc which is huge, or frightening in some other way 巨獸; 怪獸; 怪物; 巨大或可怕的東西. 2 person who is unnaturally cruel or wicked 兇惡的人; 殘忍的人; 窮兇極惡的人. **monstrous** ['mɔnstrəs] *adj* 1 very wicked. 極兇惡的; 極令人厭惡的: *It's monstrous to treat a child like that.* 那樣對待小孩太兇了. 2 huge and frightening 巨大的; 恐怖的: a *monstrous animal* 巨大而又可怖的動物. **monstrosity** [mɔn-'strɔsiti] *nc / u* something frightening or very ugly 恐怖的東西; 醜陋的東西.

month [mʌnθ] *nc* 1 one of the twelve divisions of the year (e.g. January, February) 月份(例如: 一月, 二月): *I'll see you at the end of the month.* 我要在月底見你. (Also 亦作 **calendar month**). 2 period from the date in one month to the same date in the next (e.g. from 10th February to 10th March) 一個月的時間(例如: 二月十日至三月十日): *in a couple of months* 在三兩個月內; *in a month's time* 在一個月時間內. **monthly** *adj / adv* (happening) once a month 每月一次的

(地), 每月的(地): a *monthly meeting* 月會. Also 亦作 *nc* magazine etc which appears once a month 月刊.

monument ['mɔnjumənt] *nc* 1 pillar, statue etc built to keep alive the memory of some person or event 紀念碑; 紀念塑像; 紀念建造物. 2 something which is a proof of outstanding quality 顯著的, 突出的證據: a *monument to someone's ability* 某人能力的有力例證. **monumental** ['mɔnju'mentl] *adj* 1 (with reference to buildings etc.) very large (指建築物等)很大的. 2 having very great qualities of size, cleverness etc. (尺寸, 聰明等)高度的: a *monumental achievement* 巨大的成就.

mood [mu:d] *nc / u* state of feeling at a particular time 心境, 心情, 情緒: *in a cheerful mood* 心情愉快; *in a good / bad mood* i.e. feeling, pleased / angry 心情好 / 不好, 即: 高興 / 生氣; *in the mood for something* 想做某事. **moody** *adj* changing quickly from one kind of mood to another; sullen 心情易變的, 喜怒無常的; 悶悶不樂的; 憂鬱的, 陰沉的: a *moody person* 心情變化不定的人. **moodily** *adv*.

moon [mu:n] *nc* smaller body going round the earth and seen at night as it reflects the light of the sun 月, 月亮, 月球. '**moonlight** *nu* light from the moon 月光. Also 亦作 *adj*: a *moonlight walk* 月光下散步, 月夜散步. '**moonlit** *adj* made bright by the moon 給月光照亮的: *moonlit gardens* 月色下的花園; a *moonlit night* 月明之夜.

moor[1] [muə*] *nc / u* area of open land not used for growing crops and often overgrown with heather (常長滿石南屬植物的)荒野, 曠野地. '**moorland**

wasteland (usu. covered with heather) 荒地(通常長滿石南屬植物).

moor² [muə*] *vt / i* make a ship secure, so that it will not drift away, by attaching it to something with rope or chains, an anchor etc. 使(船)停泊; 繫泊(船隻); 下錨, 繫住(船): *The ship was moored just inside the harbour.* 那條船就停泊在港內. **moorings** *npl* ropes or chains etc used to keep a ship in the same place 繫船用的繩索, 鐵鍊等物.

moot [mu:t] *adj* usu. in **a moot point** i.e. something which is doubtful; something which can be discussed 通常用於 **a moot point** 未確定的, 未決的; 可以討論的, 尚在爭論的: *Whether or not the entrance fee should be raised is a moot point.* 入場費是否提高尚未確定. Also 亦作 *vt* put up for discussion 提出…供討論: *moot a question* 提出問題供討論.

mop [mɔp] *nc* **1** bundle of strings, pieces of cloth etc tied together, or piece of sponge at the end of a small pole (usu. used for cleaning floors) 拖把. **2** thick hair 蓬亂的頭髮: *a mop of red hair* 一頭亂蓬蓬的紅頭髮. Also 亦作 *vt* clean by using a mop 用拖把清掃. *past* 過去式和過去分詞 **mopped.**

mope [moup] *vi* feel sad; be unable to take an interest in anything 憂愁; 鬱鬱不樂; 對甚麼都不感興趣: *He's been moping all day.* 他整天悶悶不樂. **moping** *nu.*

moral ['mɔrl] *adj* **1** connected with the choice between right and wrong 道德上的; 倫理的, 道義上的: *a moral problem* 道德問題. **2** pure, not evil 純潔的; 有道德的; 非邪惡的: *a moral book* 道德教育書籍; *moral behaviour* 合乎道德的行爲, 正派的行爲.

(*opp* **immoral** in sense 2) (義2的反義詞爲 immoral). Also 亦作 *nc* lesson; moral teaching 教訓; 道德上的教誨: *the moral of the story* 這故事的教訓.

morality [mə'ræliti] *nu* ideas of what is good or evil; goodness, purity 道德, 美德, 德行; 純潔; 完美. **morally** *adv* **1** in a good or pure way 品行端正地; 純潔地; 有道德地. **2** from the point of view of what is good 從道德觀點看; 道德上; 道義上: *feel morally obliged to help someone* 道義上覺得有義務幫助某人. **morals** *npl* **1** rules of what is good or evil 道德律, 倫理學; *a student of morals* 倫理學的學生或研究者. **2** good or pure behaviour 端正或純潔的行爲. *person with no morals* 不講道德的人, 品行不佳的人.

morale [mɔ'rɑːl] *nu* attitude towards difficulties etc. 對待困難的態度; 士氣; 信念; 精神力量: *The morale of the troops is high* i.e. they are feeling cheerful, ready to fight etc. 軍隊的士氣很高. 即: 士兵心情愉快, 樂於作戰.

morass [mə'ræs] *nc* low-lying area of soft, wet ground; marshy area 潮濕低窪的地區, 沼澤地.

morbid ['mɔːbid] *adj* (with reference to a state of mind etc.) unhealthy, not normal (指心境等) 不健康的, 病態的, 不正常的: *a morbid attitude to death* 對於死亡的不正常態度.

more [mɔː*] **1** determiner in a greater quantity; to a greater degree 更多的, 較多的; 更甚的: *more people than yesterday* 人比昨天多; *more money than ever before* 錢比以往任何時候都多; *more heat than usual* 比平常熱. **2** determiner in addition 另外的, 附加的: *Do you want more money?* 你要錢嗎? *Is there any more food?* 還有食物嗎? **3** *n* additional amount or number 額外的數量: *Here are some* *cakes. Will you need any more?* 這裏有些糕餅，你還要嗎？ *He asked for some more.* 他再要一些. *More than one can count* i.e. very many. 比人能計算的還多，即；非常多. **4** *adv / intensifier* in a greater degree (used to form the comparative of all *adjs* and *advs* with more than two syllables, and some with only two syllables) 更 (用於與兩個以上音節的形容詞及副詞構成比較級；亦和一些只有兩個音節的形容詞及副詞構成比較級)；*more dangerous (than)* (比) 更危險；*more delicious (than)* (比) 更可口；*more careless (than)* (比) 更粗心；*more cleverly (than)* (比) 更巧妙地. *Note* 說明：*more* is the *comparative* form of *much* or *many; most* is the *superlative* more 是 much 或 many 的比較級；most 是最高級. **more·over** *adv* also 而且；此外；再者：*He is stupid and inattentive and, moreover, he is lazy.* 他很笨，注意力不集中，而且還懶惰. **any more** any longer 再：*I don't go there any more.* 我不再到那裏去了. **more or less** almost 幾乎，差不多：*The work is more or less finished.* 這工作差不多快完成了.

morgue [mɔːg] *nc* place where the bodies of people who have died (esp. as a result of violence or an accident) are kept until they can be identified and buried (待人辨認屍體的) 陳屍所 (尤指死於暴力或意外故者).

moribund [ˈmɔrɪbʌnd] *adj* dying 快要死的，垂死的，臨終的；行將完結的：*a moribund person* 將死的人，垂死的人.

morning [ˈmɔːnɪŋ] *nc* early part of the day until about noon 早晨，上午：*early in the morning* 一大早，清晨，絕早；*tomorrow morning* 明天早上；*Sunday morning* 星期日上午；*one morning last November* 剛過去的十一月的某一

上午；*on the morning of 20 December* 十二月二十日上午. Also 亦作 *attrib adj* connected with the morning 早上的：*the morning papers* 早報，晨報；*a morning walk* 早晨的散步. **'morning dress** dress worn by men in western countries at formal occasions (e.g. weddings) 常禮服 (西方男人在正式場合例如婚禮穿的衣服). **Good morning!** greeting used in the early part of the day. 早上好! 你好! *He wished me good morning.* 他祝我早上好.

moron [ˈmɔːrɔn] *nc* person of very low intelligence 低能兒；愚蠢的人. **moronic** [mɔˈrɔnɪk] *adj.*

morose [məˈrous] *adj* silent and bad-tempered 抑鬱的，悶氣的，壞脾氣的：*in a morose mood* 心情鬱鬱不樂.

morphine [ˈmɔːfiːn] *nu* white powder used for lessening pain and helping people to sleep 嗎啡.

Morse [mɔːs] usu. in **Morse code** i.e. system of using long and short sounds or long and short flashes of light in order to send messages 通常用於 Morse code 莫爾斯電碼 (利用聲音或閃光的長短發送訊息的系統).

morsel [ˈmɔːsl] *nc* small piece of food; bite 一小塊食物；一口食物，小量食物：*not a morsel left* 一點兒食物也沒剩下.

mortal [ˈmɔːtl] *adj* **1** certain to die 終有一死的，不免一死的：*a mortal being* 凡人，世人，塵世之人. (*opp* 反義詞 **immortal**) **2** causing death 致命的：*a mortal wound* 致命傷. **3** extreme; very great 極端的；非常大的：*in mortal fear* 極為恐懼的 (地). **4** deadly; unforgiving 不共載天的，無可寬恕的：*a mortal enemy* 不共戴天的敵人；*mortal sin* 不可饒恕的大罪，該入地獄的罪. Also 亦作 *nc* human being 人.

mortally *adv* **mortality** [mɔːˈtæliti]

nu **1** state of being mortal 必死的狀況，不免一死，必死性. **2** number of deaths (e.g. in a special area) 死亡人數 (例如: 在一特定地區): *a high rate of mortality* 死亡率高.

mortar¹ ['mɔ:tə*] *nu* mixture of lime or cement or both with sand and water, used in building to hold bricks, stones etc in place 灰泥，泥，灰漿 (石灰或水泥或兩者和水、沙的混合物，用以黏合磚頭，石塊等).

mortar² ['mɔ:tə*] *nc* short gun which fires shells high into the air 臼砲，迫擊砲.

mortgage ['mɔ:gidʒ] *vt* give someone a claim on one's house land etc as security for a loan i.e. if the loan is not repaid then one must give up one's house, land etc. 抵押(房子、土地等): *He mortgaged his house for £3,000.* 他把房子作抵押借款三千英鎊. Also 亦作 *nc* legal agreement to mortgage something 抵押單據，抵押證書: *a mortgage of £3,000* 借款三千英鎊的抵押單據.

mortify ['mɔ:tifai] *vt / i* hurt the feelings of; make someone feel ashamed or embarrassed 傷害…感情; 使感到羞恥; 使感到難爲情: *We were mortified by his silly behaviour.* 我們因他的愚蠢行爲而感到羞恥.

mortuary ['mɔ:tjuəri] *nc* building or room where dead bodies of people are kept before being buried 停屍室; 太平間.

mosaic [mou'zeiik] *nc* picture, design etc made up of small pieces of coloured material (usu. stone or glass) 鑲嵌細工, 鑲嵌圖案; 馬賽克畫.

Moslem ['mɔzləm] see 見 **Muslim**.

mosque [mɔsk] *nc* building where Muslims worship 伊斯蘭教寺院, 清真寺.

mosquito [mɔs'ki:tou] *nc* small flying insect which sucks blood and sometimes spreads diseases (esp. malaria) 蚊子. *pl* 複數 **mosquitoes. mosquito net** screen which keeps out mosquitoes 蚊帳.

moss [mɔs] *nc / u* small plant which grows thickly on rocks, trees etc and wet surfaces 苔蘚, 苔; 地衣. **mossy** *adj*.

most [moust] **1** *adj* in the greater quantity; to the greatest degree 多數的,多半的, 最大的, 最高程度的: *I like tennis and cricket but I get most pleasure from football.* 我喜愛網球和板球但從足球得到最大的樂趣. *Most people go there.* 大多數人都到那裏去. **2** *n* greatest amount number etc. 最大量; 最多數: *Most of the audience had left.* 大多數聽衆都已經離開. *He lost most of his money.* 他丟失了大部份的錢. *Most sports are exciting to watch.* 大多數運動使觀衆看得激動起來. **3** *n* greatest possible number or amount 最大可能的數或量: *The most you can hope for is £5.* 五英鎊是你可以希望得到的最大數目. **4** *adv / intensifier* in the greatest degree (used to form the *superlative* of all *adjs* and *advs* with more than two syllables, and some with only two syllables) 最 (與兩個音節以上的形容詞及副詞構成最高級; 亦或若干僅有兩個音節的形容詞及副詞組成最高級): *most dangerous* 最危險的; *most delicious* 最可口的; *most careless* 最粗心的; *most cleverly* 最巧妙地. **mostly** *adv*. Note 說明: *most* is the *superlative* form of *much* or *many*; *more* is the *comparative* form 最高級; *more* 是其比較級. **make the most of** take full advantage of 盡量利用: *make the most of an opportunity* 盡量利用機會.

motel [mou'tel] *nc* hotel which makes special arrangements for customers who have cars (附有旅客停車場場所的) 汽車旅館.

moth [mɔθ] *nc* winged insect which flies mostly at night, is attracted by bright lights and (in some species) eats clothes, carpets etc. 蛾; 蠹蟲, 蛀蟲. **'mothball** *nc* (often *pl*) small white ball with a very strong smell which keeps moths away from cloth (常用複數) 樟腦丸. **'moth-eaten** *adj* eaten by moths 被蛀蟲咬的; 蛀壞了的.

mother ['mʌðə*] *nc* female parent 母親. Also 亦作 *vt* care for something / somebody as a mother would care for her child (母親般地) 照顧, 愛護. **motherly** *adj* **'mother-in-law** *nc* mother of one's wife or husband 岳母; 婆婆. *pl* 複數 **mothers-in-law.**

motherland ['mʌðəlænd] *nc* one's own or one's ancestors' native country 祖國.

motif [mou'ti:f] *nc* main or most frequent feature or pattern in music, art etc. (音樂、藝術等的) 主題.

motion ['mouʃən] **1** *nu* movement 移動; 運動: *perpetual motion* i.e. movement which never stops 永恒運動, 即: 永不靜止的運動. **2** *nc* way of moving or acting 移動的方式, 動作的方式: *strange motions of his hand* 他的奇怪手勢. **3** *nc* suggestion put forward for discussion at a meeting 提議; 動議: *a motion to declare the meeting closed* 宣佈會議結束的提議. Also 亦作 *vt* direct by some sign (e.g. with the hand) 以示意動作指引(例如用手); 示意: *I motioned him to come forward.* 我示意他站出來. **motionless** not moving 不動的; 靜止的. **'motion 'picture** film shown in a cinema 電影.

motive ['moutiv] *nc* reason for acting 動機; 目的: *He gave you help from the purest motives.* 他出於純潔的動機幫助你. **motivate** ['moutiveit] *vt* give someone a reason for acting 激發; 促動; 給予動機: *motivated by greed* 被貪婪所驅使. **motivation** [mouti'veiʃən] *nc / u.*

motley ['mɔtli] *adj* made up of different elements; varied 成份混雜的; 雜亂的; 各種各樣的: *a motley crowd of people* 混雜的人羣.

motor ['moutə*] *nc* **1** engine which supplies power (esp. to something that moves e.g. car, aircraft). 發動機, 馬達 (尤指驅動汽車, 飛機的發動機). **2** car; vehicle 汽車; 機動車. Also 亦作 *adj* driven by an engine 由馬達驅動的: *motorboat* 汽船, 汽艇; *motorcar* 汽車. Also 亦作 *vi* travel in a car 乘汽車旅行; 開汽車旅行: *motor to Italy* 開汽車去意大利旅行. **motorist** *nc* person who drives a car 駕駛汽車的人. **'motorbike, 'motorcycle** vehicle with two wheels like a bicycle but driven by an engine 機動脚踏車; 摩托車; 機車. **'motorway** (*Brit*) road which is built for fast driving (英) 高速公路. (*US* 美 expressway).

mottled ['mɔtld] *adj* marked with spots of different sizes and colours 雜色的, 斑點的, 斑駁的: *mottled leaves* 斑駁的葉子.

motto ['mɔtou] *nc* short sentence or phrase (usu. giving a rule of behaviour) 箴言; 座右銘; 格言: *Our school motto is 'Work hard'* 我們學校的校訓是"勤奮". *pl* 複數 **mottos or mottoes.**

mould[1] [mould] (*US* 美 **mold**) *nc* hollow container which gives shape to what is poured into it 模子; 鑄模; 鑄型: *The molten (liquid) metal was* *poured into a mould.* 將熔化的金屬倒進鑄模. Also 亦作 *vt* make into a required shape; change to a particular form 澆鑄, 鑄造; 塑造, 形成; *mould a statue* 鑄造塑像. *mould someone's character* 塑造某人的性格.

mould² [mould] (*US* 美 **mold**) *nu* growth on decaying substance (e.g. old cheese, bread etc.) 黴菌; 黴; 霉. **mouldy** *adj* affected by mould 長霉的, 發霉的: *mouldy bread* 發霉的麵包.

moult [moult] (*US* 美 **molt**) *vt / i* (with reference to birds, animals) lose feathers, hair etc which will be replaced in time (指鳥, 動物) 換羽毛; 換毛; 脱毛: *moulting season* 換羽毛季節, 換毛或脱毛季節.

mound [maund] *nc* **1** artificial pile of earth (人造的) 土堆, 土墩. **2** large pile of anything (東西的) 堆, 垛: *a mound of letters* 一堆信件.

mount [maunt] *vt* place a photograph etc on a card 裱貼或裱褙 (照片等). **mount (a horse etc.)** get on to (a horse etc.) 騎上 (馬等): *They mounted their horses and rode off.* 他們騎上馬奔馳而去. (*opp* 反義詞 **dismount**).

mountain ['mauntin] *nc* **1** very high hill 高山, 山岳: *a chain of mountains* 山脈, 山系. **2** anything very large; very large amount 巨大, 極大量: *a mountain of books* 一大堆書. Also 亦作 *adj*: *mountain scenery* 山地景色, 山景. **mountaineer** [maunti'niə*] *nc* person who climbs mountains 爬山家, 登山運動員. **mountaineering** *nu* **mountainous** *adj* containing mountains 多山的; 山地的: *a mountainous region* 山區. **'mountain 'range** line of connected mountains 山脈. **'mountainside** slope of a mountain 山坡.

mourn [mɔːn] *vt / i* feel or show sadness (usu. for someone's death) (通常因某人之死) 哀悼, 哀傷, 悲痛; 對⋯表示哀悼: *She mourned the death of her two sons.* 她爲兩個兒子的死亡而悲傷. **mourner** *nc* **mournful** *adj* showing sadness 悲傷的, 哀痛的: *a mournful face* 悲傷的面容. **go into mourning** show one's grief in some way (e.g. by wearing black clothes) 舉哀, 居喪, 戴孝, 服喪 (例如: 穿黑色衣服).

mouse [maus] *nc* small animal with a long tail 鼠, 耗子. *pl* 複數 **mice** [mais].

moustache [məs'tɑːʃ] (*US* 美 **mustache**) *nc* hair grown on the upper lip (蓄在上唇的) 髭, 小鬍子.

mouth¹ [mauθ] *nc* **1** opening through which a human or animal takes some food, 嘴: *The child put the sweet into its mouth.* 這小孩把糖果放進嘴裏. **2** open part of something 口狀物; 出入口: *mouth of a cave* 洞口; *mouth of a bottle* 瓶口; *mouth of a river* 河口. **mouthful** *nc* amount taken into the mouth at one time 一口的量; 滿口: *I took only a mouthful of food and then left.* 我只吃了一口食物便離去. **'mouth organ** small musical instrument which is played by sliding it along the lips while breathing in and out 口琴. **'mouthpiece 1** part of something (e.g. pipe, musical instrument) that goes into or onto the mouth 東西含在口中的部份 (例如烟斗嘴; 樂器的吹口). **2** person, newspaper etc that gives the opinions of others 代言人, 發言人; 喉舌: *The newspaper was only a mouthpiece of certain rich people.* 這家報紙僅僅是某些有錢人的喉舌.

mouth² [mauð] *vt* **1** say words in an unnaturally careful way 裝腔作勢地仔

細 說 (話): *He tried to impress by mouthing all his words.* 他裝腔作勢一字一板地說完所有的話，試圖打動人心. **2** speak without making any sound 不出聲地說.

move¹ [mu:v] *vi* **1** go from one place or position to another 移動；從一處移至另一處：*Will you move so that I can pass?* 你移動一下讓我過去好嗎? *Cars were slowly moving down the road.* 數輛汽車正沿道路緩慢行駛. *The birds were silent and nothing moved.* 鳥兒寂靜無語，一切都靜止不動. *The people who live across the road are moving* i.e. going to another house. 住在馬路對面的人正在搬家. **2** *vt* cause to go from one place to another 搬動；移動；使從一處移到另一處. *Move those boxes over here.* 把那些箱子搬到這裏來. **3** *vt* cause to feel sorry, sad etc. 感動，打動，使傷心：*deeply moved by someone's sufferings* 被某人的苦難深深打動. **4** *vt* cause to do something 使做某事；推動；促使：*What moved him to say that?* 甚麼東西使他說那樣的話?

move² [mu:v] *nc* **1** something done to gain a certain end (爲達到一定目的所採取的) 行動，步驟：*a move in the right direction* i.e. the correct thing to do 朝着正確方向的步驟，即：應該採取的行動. *a good move* i.e. a correct action or decision 漂亮的一着，即：正確的行動或決定. **2** change of place or position 移動；遷移：*I asked him to leave but he didn't make the slightest move.* 我請他離開，但是他一動也不動. **3** (in certain board games) the opportunity to change the position of a piece (棋類) 走一步棋；一着：*It's your move now* i.e. your turn to move. 現在輪到你下了. **movable, moveable** ['mouvibl] *adj* able to be

taken from one place to another 可移動的，活動的. (*opp* 反義詞 **immovable**). **movement** **1** *nc / u* changing of place or position 移動；動作；遷移：*a movement of the hand* 手的擺動，揮動手，手勢. *We suspected that the lion was hiding in the grass, but there was no sign of movement.* 我們懷疑那獅子藏在草叢裏，但是沒有半點動靜. **2** *nc* group of people who have come together to achieve a certain aim, or the actions of such a group (爲達到某一目的而進行的) 運動；(參加此運動的)羣眾的) 行動：*movement for the abolition of slavery* 廢除奴隸制度的運動. **3** *nc* separate part of a long piece of music 樂章. **movie** *nc* ['mu:vi] (mainly *US*) film shown in a cinema. (*Brit* 英 film) (主要用於美)電影，影片. **the movies** (mainly *US*) a cinema show (主要用於美)電影：*going to the movies.* (*Brit* 英 **the pictures**) 去看電影. **move along / down / up etc** go, make someone go, in a certain direction (使)朝某一方向移動：*The policeman told us to move along.* 警察叫我們往前走. *He moved us along.* 他要我們往前走. **move in** take one's furniture, belongings etc into the house one is going to live in 搬入，遷入. **move (someone) on** go, make someone go, from one place to another (使)繼續前進，(使)朝前走：*They just keep moving on from one place to another.* 他們就繼續不停地從一個地方到另一個地方. **move out** leave one's home for good 搬出，搬走，遷出去：*We're moving out of our old house next week.* 下星期我們要搬出老家. **move house** take one's furniture etc from one house to another 搬家：*I see that our neighbours are moving house.* 我知道我們的鄰居要搬

家. **get a move on** hurry up. (*informal*) 趕快, 趕緊 (非正式).

movie ['mu:vi] *nc* **1** (mainly *US*) cinema picture (主要用於美) 電影. **2** cinema theatre 電影院.

mow [mou] *vt / i* cut grass etc with a scythe or a machine (以鐮刀或機器) 割草等; 收割: *This is the time to mow grass.* 現在是割草的時候了. *past tense* 過去式 **mowed**. *past part* 過去分詞 **mowed** or **mown** [moun].

Mr ['mistə*] *n* title of a man 先生 (男人的稱呼): *Mr Smith* 史密斯先生.

Mrs ['misiz] *n* title put before the surname of a married woman. (Thus if a girl called Jane Smith marries a man called John Brown, her title will be *Mrs Brown*) (置於已婚婦女姓氏前面的稱呼) 太太, 夫人 (如果叫 Jane Smith 的姑娘嫁給叫 John Brown 的人, 則她的稱呼爲 Mrs Brown). *Note* 說明: the words *Mr, Mrs,* and *Ms* should always be used with the person's surname and not alone. Mr, Mrs, Ms 等詞必須與人的姓連用, 不可單獨使用.

Ms [miz] *n* title used for both married and unmarried women 女士(對已婚或未婚女子的稱呼).

much [mʌtʃ] **1** *adj / n* in great quantity, degree etc.; great quantity, degree etc of 許多的, 大多的, 大量的; 許多; 大量: *He has given much thought to the problem.* 他對這個問題已花費了不少心思. *Much of what you say is true.* 你說的話大部分是正確的. *He hasn't got much land.* 他沒有多少土地. *Note* 說明: **1** *much* is used with *sing* uncountable nouns, but *not* with *pl* countable nouns. So we can say *much salt, much time etc* but *many books, many things etc.* **2** in *affirmative* sentences (i.e. not questions or *negatives*) it is usu. better to say *a lot* (*of*); plenty (*of*) etc. So we say *He has a lot of money* or *He has plenty of money* not *He has much money. Much* is more often found in questions or *negatives: How much land has he? He hasn't much time.* **1.** much 與單數不可數名詞連用, 不與複數可數名詞連用. 因此說 much salt, much time 等; many books, many things 等. **2.** 在肯定句 (即非疑問句或否定句) 中, 最好使用 a lot (of); plenty (of) 等. 因此說 He has a lot of money 或 He has plenty of money. 他有很多錢, 不說 He has much money. much 較常用於疑問句或否定句中: How much land has he? 他有多少土地? He hasn't much time. 他沒有多少時間. **2** *adv* to a great extent or degree; greatly 多, 更, 非常: *This is much better than the others.* 這個比其餘的好多了. *It's much longer than I thought.* 這比我想像中的長多了. *Note* 說明: *comparative* 比較級 **more.** *superlative* 最高級 **most.**

muck [mʌk] *nu* **1** rubbish; dirt 垃圾; 污物, 髒物: *You'll have to clear all the muck out of that cupboard.* (*informal*) 你必須把食櫥上的髒物清洗乾淨. (非正式). **2** farmyard manure 糞肥, 農家肥.

mucous ['mju:kəs] *adj* usu. in mucous membrane i.e. soft moist lining or skin (e.g. on the inside of the nose or mouth) 通常用於 mucous membrane 黏膜 (例如: 鼻子或口腔內部的黏膜).

mucus ['mju:kəs] *nu* liquid produced by the mucous membrane (黏膜分泌的) 黏液.

mucus ['mju:kəs] *nu* slippery liquid produced in certain parts of the body 黏液.

mud [mʌd] *nu* soft, wet earth 軟泥, 泥; 泥濘: *After the rain, the roads were covered in mud.* 雨後路面上滿是泥. *You find mud at the bottom of a*

pond. 池塘底有軟泥. **muddy** *adj*
'**mudguard** (*Brit*) cover placed over
the wheel of a bicycle, motorcycle etc
so as to protect people from the mud
thrown up by the wheel. (*US* 美 **fender**) (英) (自行車, 摩托車等車輪的)擋
泥板.

muddle ['mʌdl] *vt* mix things up;
confuse 搞亂, 把…弄糟; 使混亂, 使糊塗,
使慌亂: *He's muddled all the arrangements.* 他把全部安排搞亂了. *I'm feeling a bit muddled* i.e. confused. 我覺
得有點迷糊了. Also 亦作 *nc* confused
state 混亂, 迷糊: *in a muddle* i.e. confused 在混亂中, 迷糊的. **muddle
through** be successful in something
without proper work or planning 應付
過去; 混過去: *Somehow he managed
to muddle through university.* 不知怎
麼的他居然胡亂地讀完了大學.

muff [mʌf] *nc* piece of warm cloth or
fur like a tube with open ends into
which women or children put their
hands to keep them warm (婦女, 兒童
禦寒用的)暖手筒, 皮手筒.

muffle ['mʌfl] *vt* 1 wrap up in order to
keep warm (爲防寒而)包裹, 裹住, 圍
住: *The children were well muffled up*
i.e. they were wearing coats, scarves
etc. 孩子們都包裹得嚴嚴實實的.即: 他
們都穿上外衣, 圍上圍巾等. 2 make
the sound of something less by wrapping it in cloth etc. (用布等將某物蒙
住以壓低(聲音), 壓抑(聲音); 包紮, 包
住: *We muffled the oars so that people on the riverbank could not hear
us.* 我們把槳包紮起來使河岸上的人聽
不到我們划船的聲音.

mug [mʌg] *nc* 1 large drinking glass or
cup with a handle 有柄的大杯子. 2
person who is easily deceived. (*informal*) 容易上當受騙的人; 笨蛋. (非正
式).Also 亦作 *vt* attack and rob

someone. (*informal*) 對…行兇搶劫(非
正式).

muggy ['mʌgi] *adj* (with reference to
weather) unpleasantly warm and
damp (指天氣)悶熱而潮濕的.

mulatto [mju'lætəu] *nc* person who has
one white parent and one black parent 黑白混血兒. *pl* 複數 **mulattoes.**

mulberry ['mʌlbəri] *nc* 1 tree whose
leaves are used for feeding silkworms
桑樹. 2 its fruit 桑椹. 3 purplish red
紫紅色.

mule [mju:l] *nc* offspring of an ass and
a horse (esp. of a male ass and a
female horse) 騾(尤指由公驢和母馬所
生的).

mull [mʌl] *vi* (with **over**) think carefully about something (與 over 連用)仔
細考慮, 深思熟慮: *I'll give you time to
mull it over.* 我會給你時間好好考慮.

multi- ['mʌlti] *prefix* many 多的.

multilateral [mʌlti'lætərəl] *adj* 1 having many sides 多邊的: *a multilateral
figure* 多邊形. 2 involving many
groups, countries etc. 涉及多方面的,
多國參加的: *multilateral aid* 多方援
助.

multiple ['mʌltipl] *adj* having many
parts 複合的; 多樣的; 多重的; 多倍的.
Also 亦作 *nc* number which contains
another number a certain number of
times exactly (e.g. 30 is a multiple of
10) 倍數(例如: 30是10的倍數).

multiply ['mʌltiplai] *vt* / *i* 1 find the
sum of a number added to itself a
certain number of times 乘; 使相乘; 做
乘法: *Five multiplied by six equals
thirty* (5×6=30). 五乘以六等於三十 (5
×6 = 30). 2 increase in number 增
多, 增加: *Mistakes have been multiplying rapidly.* 錯誤已迅速增多. **multiplication** [mʌltipli'keiʃən] *nu* act of
multiplying or being multiplied 乘法,

乘法運算; 增多, 增加.

multitude ['mʌltitjuːd] *nc* large number; crowd (*o.f.* - usu. in **a multitude of sins**) 多數, 大數目; 人羣, 羣衆 (舊式—通常用於 a multitude of sins).

mum[1] [mʌm] *adj* silent 沉默的, 緘默的, 不作聲的.

mum[2] [mʌm] informal form of **mother** 母親的非正式形式.

mumble ['mʌmbl] *vt / i* speak in a low indistinct way so that the words are difficult to understand 喃喃地說; 咕噥; 咕嚕: *Stop mumbling and speak clearly!* 別再咕嚕, 清清楚楚地說! Also 亦作 *nu*.

mummy[1] ['mʌmi] *nc* dead body treated in a special way so that it does not decay i.e. embalmed (esp. as done by the Ancient Egyptians) 木乃伊(尤指古埃及所做的木乃伊).

mummy[2] ['mʌmi] *nc* informal form of **mother** 母親的非正式形式.

mumps [mʌmps] *nu* infectious disease which causes painful swelling in the neck 腮腺炎. *Note* 說明: followed by a *sing* verb. 後接單數動詞.

munch [mʌntʃ] *vt / i* eat noisily with a lot of movement of the jaws 用力咀嚼; 大聲咀嚼用力或大聲地吃: *The children were all munching apples.* 孩子們都在大聲地咀嚼蘋果.

mundane [mʌn'dein] *adj* **1** worldly, not spiritual 世俗的, 塵世的, 非精神的. **2** of everyday importance 平常的, 日常的, 普通的.

municipal [mju:'nisipl] *adj* having to do with a town or city; run or owned by the ruling body of a town 市的; 市政的; 市辦的; 市立的: *municipal transport* 城市運輸, 城市交通.

munitions [mju:'niʃənz] *npl* things used for fighting (esp. guns and shells) 軍需品, 軍火 (尤指槍砲, 彈藥): *muni-tions factory* i.e. where guns, shells etc are made 軍火工廠.

mural ['mjuərl] *nc* painting done on a wall 壁畫.

murder ['məːdə*] *vt* illegally kill a person on purpose: 謀殺; 兇殺; 殺害: *murder someone for his money* 謀財害命. Also 亦作 *nc / u*: *commit murder* 犯謀殺罪; *accused of murder* 被控犯謀殺罪的. **murderer** *nc (fem* 陰 **murderess** ['məːdəris]). **murderous** *adj* threatening; dangerous 恐嚇的; 兇殘的; 危險的: *a murderous look.* 兇惡的表情; 兇相.

murky ['məːki] *adj* dark; badly lit. 黑暗的; 幽暗的; 朦朧不亮的: *a murky street* 黑暗的街道、燈光昏暗的街道.

murmur ['məːmə*] *vt / i* **1** make a low, unclear sound going on for some time 發低沉不清的連續聲音: *murmuring of bees / a stream / a crowd* 蜜蜂的嗡嗡叫/溪水的潺潺作響/人羣的嘁嘁喳喳說話. **2** say something in a low voice 低聲說: *murmur a few words* 低聲說幾句話. Also 亦作 *nc*: *There was a murmur of voices in the room.* 房間裏有輕輕的說話聲. *He left without a murmur.* i.e. without saying anything, without complaining. 他毫無怨言地離開.

muscle [mʌsl] *nc / u* fibres within the body which produce movement when tightened or loosened 肌肉: *He developed the muscles in his legs by running.* 他跑步來鍛煉腿的肌肉. **muscular** ['mʌskjulə*] *adj* **1** of the muscles 肌肉的: *muscular pain* 肌肉的疼痛. **2** having strong muscles 肌肉發達的, 健壯的: *a muscular man* 強壯的人.

museum [mju:'ziəm] *nc* building containing and displaying interesting or beautiful things (esp. things con-

nected with art, science etc.) 博物館,
博物院.

mush [mʌʃ] *nu* fine grain, boiled in water, or any such soft, wet mixture (煮
成的) 糊狀物, 粥狀物: *mush for the
cattle* 牲口的糊狀飼料. **mushy** *adj*.

mushroom ['mʌʃrum] *nc* type of quickly growing fungus that can be eaten
蘑菇, 食用菌類. Also 亦作 *vi* grow
quickly 迅速生長: *The town
mushroomed into a city.* 這個小鎮已
迅速發展成爲城市.

music ['mjuːzik] *nu* 1 art of making
pleasant sounds using special instruments or the human voice 音樂藝術:
study music 學音樂. 2 sounds made
in this way 音樂: *listen to beautiful
music* 傾聽優美的音樂. 3 printed or
written signs representing musical
sounds 樂譜: *read music* i.e. be able
to sing or play an instrument from
this system 看懂樂譜, 即: 能够唱或演
奏譜中樂曲. **musical** *adj* 1 connected with music; skilled in, fond of,
music 有關音樂的, 音樂的; 擅長音樂
的; 喜愛音樂的: *musical instruments*
樂器; *a musical family* 愛好音樂的家
庭. 2 pleasant to listen to 悅耳的, 好
聽的: *a musical voice* 悅耳的嗓音.
Also 亦作 *nc* motion picture or play
in which music, singing etc plays an
important part 音樂片; 音樂喜劇.
musically *adv* **musician** [mjuːˈzɪʃən]
nc person who is skilful in playing a
musical instrument or in composing
music 音樂家; 演奏家; 樂師; 作曲家.

Muslim ['mʌzlim], **Moslem** ['mɔzləm]
nc follower of the religion (called
Islam) taught by Mohammed 穆斯林,
伊斯蘭教徒. Also 亦作 *adj*.

mussel ['mʌsl] *nc* kind of small blue or
black shellfish, used as food 貽貝, 淡
菜, 殼菜.

must [mʌst] *aux* 1 be obliged to; have
to 不得不; 必須: *You must leave immediately.* 你必須馬上離開. *I must
leave now, otherwise I shall be late.*
現在我得走了, 否則要遲到了. *All stu-
dents must keep quiet in the library.*
所有學生在圖書館裏都必須保持安靜.
Visitors must not walk on the grass. 遊
客不得在草地上行走. *Note* 說明: ab-
sence of obligation is expressed by
needn't or *don't have to* (e.g. *You
needn't leave* i.e. you can leave or
stay as you please; but *You mustn't
leave* i.e. you must stay here. needn't
或 don't have to 表示不必要, 不需要.
例如: You needn't leave. 你不必離開.
即你可以隨你的意離開或留下; 但是
you mustn't leave. 你不得離開. 即: 你
必須留在這裏. 2 (used when something seems very likely) be bound to
(用於表示某事似乎非常可能) 必定; 一
定; 理應, 諒必: *It must have stopped
raining by now.* 這會兒雨該已停了吧.
*This must be the place we are looking
for.* 這一定就是我們尋找的地方. *You
must have heard of Columbus.* 你一定
聽人說過哥倫布. *Note* 說明: must has
only one form for past, present, future
etc; *must not*, which expresses a pro-
hibition, may be shortened to *mustn't*.
must 的過去式, 現在式, 將來式等均爲
同一形式; must not 表示禁止的意思,
可以縮惡爲mustn't. **a must** something
necessary; something that must be
seen, heard etc. 必需的事物; 必須看,
聽等的事物: *Don't miss his latest play;
it's a must.* (informal) 不要錯過他新近
上演的戲劇; 這是非看不可的. (非正
式)

mustache [məsˈtɑːʃ] *nc* see 見 **moustache.**

mustard ['mʌstəd] 1 *nc* kind of plant
芥. 2 *nu* yellow powder made from

the crushed seeds of this plant mixed with water, and used for flavouring 芥末, 芥子醬.

muster¹ ['mʌstə] *vt / i* assemble (troops etc.); collect; summon 集合 (部隊等); 集中; 召集; 鼓起 (勇氣): *Muster up your courage. The difficulty will soon be overcome.* 鼓起勇氣來, 困難很快就可以克服的.

muster² ['mʌstə] *nc* **1** assembling as of troops for inspection (部隊的) 集合 (檢閱). **2** persons or things assembled 聚集的人 (或物). **pass muster** measure up to the required standards 達到要求的標準, 合格. **3** commercial sample 樣品.

musty ['mʌsti] *adj* (of smell or taste) unpleasant, stale (usu. in places or things that are old or damp or have not been used for some time) (指氣味, 味道) 霉臭的; 霉味的; 發霉的; 走了味的; 陳腐的. (用於地方或東西陳舊、潮濕或已久不使用).

mute [mju:t] *adj* **1** silent; not speaking 沉默的; 不說話的. **2** unable to speak 說不出話的: *mute with astonishment* 驚愕得說不出話來. Also 亦作 *nc* person who cannot speak 啞吧.

mutilate ['mju:tileit] *vt* **1** cut off a part of the body 使 (肢體) 殘缺不全; 殘害. **2** severely damage 嚴重毀壞: *The book had been mutilated through someone tearing out the pages.* 這本書因被人撕去數頁受到了嚴重的損壞. **mutilation** [mju:ti'leiʃən] *nc*.

mutiny ['mju:tini] *nc / u* open rising against authority (esp. of soldiers or sailors against their officers) 叛變, 抗命 (尤指士兵、水手的嘩變或兵變). Also 亦作 *vi* rise against authority; rebel 叛變; 反抗, 反叛. **mutinous** *adj* guilty of mutiny; about or ready to mutiny; rebellious 犯有叛變罪的; 即將

或打算叛變的; 叛變的, 反叛的; 反抗的.

mutter ['mʌtə*] *vt / i* say something (usu. a threat or complaint) in a low indistinct voice 低聲說出, 喃喃說出, 咕噥 (通常用於威脅或抱怨): *He was quite annoyed, and went off muttering threats under his breath.* 他很是生氣, 邊走開邊壓低嗓門咕噥著威脅的話. Also 亦作 *nc: He heard a mutter from the audience.* 他聽見觀衆中的喃喃抱怨聲.

mutton ['mʌtn] *nu* meat from a sheep 羊肉.

mutual ['mju:tjuəl] *adj* shared by two or more people with respect to each other 相互的; 彼此的; 共同的: *mutual respect* 互相尊重. *They were mutual enemies* i.e. each hated the other. 他們是對敵 (或對頭). 即: 互相仇恨. **mutually** *adv*.

muzzle ['mʌzl] *nc* **1** mouth and nose of an animal (e.g. dog, horse) 動物 (如狗、馬) 的口和鼻. **2** something (e.g. straps or wires) put over an animal's mouth to prevent it from biting (動物的) 口套, 口絡, 鼻籠. **3** mouth of a gun etc. 槍等的口. Also 亦作 *vt* **1** put a muzzle (in sense 2) on an animal 給 (動物) 戴上口絡. **2** prevent a person, newspaper etc from saying what he or it thinks (使人、報紙等) 保持緘默, 封住…的嘴: *There was a lot of discontent, but the press was muzzled.* 存在着很大的不滿, 但報紙被迫保持緘默.

my [mai] *determiner* **1** belonging to me 我的: *my books* 我的書; *my pen* 我的筆. **2** used in exclamations to express surprise, admiration etc. (用於感嘆句中表示驚訝, 讚美等) 哎呀: *My, you're very clever!* 哎唷, 你太聰明! *My dear fellow!* 親愛的朋友! 老朋友! 老兄! *My goodness!* 天啊! **myself** emphatic form of **I** or **me** I 或 me 的

强调形式: *I did it myself.* 我親自做的.
2 reflexive form of **I** or **me** 我 或 me 的反身形式: *I was only fooling myself.* 我只不過是自己在愚弄自己. **by myself** without help; alone 無人幫助; 單獨地; 獨自.

myopic [mai'ɔpik] *adj* unable to see clearly things which are far away; short-sighted 近視的; 缺乏遠見的.

myriad ['miriəd] *nc* very great number 極大數量. Also 亦作 *adj* countless 無數的.

myrrh [mə:*] *nu* sweet-smelling substance 沒藥(有香味的物質).

myself [mai'self] see 見 **my.**

mystery ['mistəri] *nc / u* **1** something which is puzzling, difficult or has not been explained 神秘的事物; 迷惑不解的事物; 不可思議的事物; 難以理解的事物: *This whole affair is a mystery to me.* 這整個事情對我來說是個謎. **2** condition of being puzzling or strange 不可思議; 神秘: *an air of mystery* 神秘的氣氛. *wrapped in mystery.* 被籠罩在神秘之中; 神秘莫測; 真相未明. **mysterious** [mis'tiəriəs] *adj* puzzling; strange 神秘的; 難懂的; 不可思議的; *a mysterious event* 神秘事件. **mysteriously** *adv.*

mystic [mistik] *adj* supernatural; strange; mysterious 超自然的; 不可思議的; 神秘的; *mystic ceremonies* 神秘的儀式或作法; *mystic experience* 神秘的經歷或體驗. Also 亦作 *nc* person who tries to get direct experience of God through prayer, contemplation etc and not through the senses 試圖用祈禱, 默想等方法直接感受上帝靈性

的人; 玄想者; 通靈者; 神秘主義者. **mystical** *adj* mystic 神秘的; 不可思議的. **mysticism** ['mistisizəm] *nu* experiences or way of thought typical of a mystic 玄想; 通靈; 神秘主義. **mystify** ['mistifai] *vt* cause people to be puzzled 使迷惑; 使困惑: *His speech mystified everyone* 他的發言使大家感到困惑.

mystique [mis'ti:k] *nu* atmosphere of mystery or secrecy which surrounds any activity (often encouraged by those who understand the activity in order to puzzle outsiders) 神秘氣氛, 秘密氣氛 (常被熟知內幕的人用來迷惑局外人): *The medical profession has a mystique which impresses most people.* 醫生職業有一種給多數人留下深刻印象的神秘氣氛.

myth [miθ] **1** *nc / u* story or belief handed down from ancient times (usu. explaining some fact of nature); collection of such stories or beliefs 神話故事; 神話: *an early myth explaining the seasons* 一個解釋季節的古代神話. **2** *nc* something untrue; false belief 假的事物, 虛構的事物; 謬誤的信念: *They say his great cleverness is just a myth.* 據說他的聰明過人只是一個騙人的鬼話. **mythical** *adj* connected with myths; untrue; unreal 與神話故事有關的; 假的, 不真實的; 想像的, 虛構的. **mythology** [miˈθɔlədʒi] **1** *nc* collection of myths 神話; 神話集: *mythology of Greece and Rome* 希臘和羅馬的神話. **2** *nu* study of myths 神話學. **mythological** [miˈθəˈlɔdʒikəl] *adj.*

N, n

nab [næb] *vt* seize; catch hold of. *past* 過去式和過去分詞 **nabbed.** *(informal)* 逮住; 捉住; 抓住. (非正式).

nag [næg] *vt / i* continually find fault with someone 不停地找…的岔子; 不斷地挑剔; 嘮叨: *She is always nagging (at) her husband.* 她總是不斷地找她丈夫的岔子. *past* 過去式和過去分詞 **nagged. nagging** *adj* continuing; never giving someone rest 繼續的, 持續的; 令人煩惱不已的: *nagging pain* 令人不得安寧的病痛.

nail [neil] *nc* **1** horny substance growing at the end of a finger or toe 指甲; 手指甲; 腳趾甲. **2** thin piece of metal, with a point at one end and a head at the other, used to fasten things together or in place 釘. Also 亦作 *vt* fix or secure things with a nail 把…釘住, 把…釘牢. **'nail polish, 'nail varnish** substance used by women to polish or colour the nails (in sense 1) 指甲油. **nail somebody down** make a person keep a promise or say exactly what he means 使某人遵守諾言; 使某人確切地說出本意; 使某人明確表態: *We've been trying to nail him down to a precise agreement. (informal)* 我們一直設法使他對一嚴格的協議表明看法. (非正式).

naive, naïve [nai'i:v] *adj* simple and innocent in what one says and does, through lack of experience or ability 天真的; 幼稚的; 無知的; 缺乏經驗的: *naive behaviour* 幼稚的行爲. **naively** *adv*.

naked ['neikid] *adj* without clothes; uncovered; bare 赤裸的, 裸體的; 無遮蓋的; 不掩飾的; 直率的. **nakedness** *nu*.

name¹ [neim] *nc* **1** word or words by which somebody / something is known 姓名; 姓; 名字; 名稱: *His name is Brown.* 他姓布朗. *Do you know the name of that tree?* 你知道那棵樹的名稱嗎? *The headmaster knows all his pupils by name.* 這位校長知道所有學生的名字. **2** reputation 名譽, 名聲: *He has a good name for honesty.* 他以誠實出名. **nameless** *adj* without a name; unknown 沒有名字的; 無名的; 不知名的. **namely** *adv* that is 即; 也就是: *I am pleased with only one boy, namely George* 我只對一個小孩即喬治感到滿意. **'namesake** person with the same name as another 同姓名的人.

name² [neim] *vt* **1** give a name to (a child, pet etc.) 給 (小孩, 愛畜等) 取名, 命名: *They named him Paul.* 他們給他起名保羅. **2** state the name of 提名; 指名; 道出…的名字: *the witnesses have been named* 已說出目擊者的名字. **3** state; say 規定, 說: *Name your price* i.e. say how much you want. 你開出價格. 即: 說出你要多少錢.

nanny ['næni] *nc* nurse who looks after children 褓姆.

nap¹ [næp] *nc* short sleep 小睡, 打盹: *have a nap in the afternoon* 在下午小睡, 睡午覺. Also 亦作 *vi past* 過去式和過去分詞 **napped.**

nap² [næp] *nu* soft, hairy surface of some kinds of cloth (esp. wool) (某種織物尤指羊毛織物上面的) 絨毛.

nape [neip] *nc* back of the neck 頸背.

napkin ['næpkin] *nc* **1** square piece of

cloth or paper, used when eating to protect clothes and to clean fingers and lips. 餐巾. **2** (*Brit*) soft cloth or paper worn as pants by a baby. (*US* 美 **diaper**) (英)尿布.

nappy ['næpi] *nc* napkin (in sense **2**) 尿布.

narcotic [nɑː'kɔtik] *nc* **1** drug which causes sleep and makes pain less severe 催眠藥;麻醉劑. **2** type of dangerous drug which is bought and sold unlawfully. (一種非法經營的)麻醉毒品.

narrate [nə'reit] *vt* tell a story 說(故事);講述 **narrator** *nc* **narrative** ['nærətiv] *nc* story; storytelling 故事;講述故事. Also 亦作 *adj*. **narration** *nc/u*.

narrow ['nærou] *adj* **1** small, measured across when compared with length; not wide 狹窄的, 狹的;不寬的; *a narrow piece of wood* 一塊狹窄的木頭. **2** small, limited 小的, 有限的; *a narrow range of interests* i.e. with few interests 興趣範圍狹小. 興趣狹小. Also 亦作 *vi* get smaller, narrower (e.g. a road) (如道路)變小, 變狹窄. **narrowly** *adv* only just; closely 幾乎不, 勉强地; 嚴密地, 仔細地: *He narrowly escaped death.* 他差一點死掉. **'narrow-'minded** *adj* not prepared to understand other people's beliefs or points of view 氣量狹窄的, 有偏見的.

nasal ['neizl] *adj* connected with the nose 與鼻有關的; *a nasal voice* i.e. one that seems to come through the nose 帶鼻音的聲音. 即: 聲音似乎從鼻子發出.

nasty ['nɑːsti] *adj* **1** unpleasant; disgusting 令人不愉快的; 討厭的; 令人作嘔的; *a nasty little boy* 討厭的小男孩. **2** dangerous 危險的; *There is a nasty bend in the road.* 道路上有一處容易發生意外的拐彎. **nastily** *adv* **nastiness** *nu.*

nation ['neiʃən] *nc* group of people of common descent or with a common language or culture; group of people ruled by one government 民族; 國家. **national** ['næʃənl] *adj* connected with a nation 與國家或民族有關的. Also 亦作 *nc* person belonging to a certain nation (某一國家的)國民; *a French national.* 法國國民;法國僑民. **nationally** *adv* **nationalism** ['næʃənəlizəm] *nu* **1** love of one's country; patriotism 愛國心;愛國主義;愛國精神. **2** movement for self-government 自治運動;民族主義;國家主義. **nationalist** ['næʃənəlist] *nc* **nationality** [næʃə'næliti] *nc/u* state of belonging to a nation 國籍; *of British nationality* 英國國籍的. **nationalize** ['næʃənəlaiz] *vt* take over private property for the state 使國有化, 把⋯收歸國有: *nationalize the mines* 將礦山收歸國有. **nationalization** [næʃənəlai'zeiʃən] *nu* **national anthem** official song of a country 國歌.

native ['neitiv] *adj* **1** connected with where one was born: 出生地的; *my native land* 我的祖國. **2** possessed from birth 與生俱來的; 天生的; 天賦的; *his native intelligence* 他的天賦才智. **3** not introduced into a country, not taken from outside 本國的, 本地的; 土產的; 非外來的: *Tobacco is a plant native to America.* 烟草是原産於美洲的植物. **4** connected with the original inhabitants (in countries settled by people of a different race) (有不同種族居住的國家内)與原住民有關的, 土著的, 土人的, 當地土人的: *the native quarter* 當地人居住區, 土著居住區. Also 亦作 *nc* **1** person born in a place 生於某一地方的人; *a native of France* 出生於法國的人. **2** original inhabitant of a country that has been settled by outsiders (有外來人居住的國家内) 原住民; 土人, 土著; 當地人.

nativity [nə'tiviti] *nc* birth (esp. of Christ) 出生; 誕生(尤指基督的誕生).

natural ['nætʃərəl] *adj* 1 connected with or produced by nature 有關自然的; 自然的; 天然產生的, 天然的: *natural sciences* 自然科學. 2 possessing qualities born with one; not acquired from outside 與生俱來的, 天生的, 生來的; 非獲得的: *a natural writer* 天生的作家; *his natural abilities* 他的天生的才能. 3 happening in the normal course of events, ordinary 順乎自然進程的, 自然的; 普通, 平常的: *die a natural death* i.e. not be killed etc. 壽終正寢, 得終天年, 因年老等而自然死亡(非橫死). *It is not natural to hate one's children.* 憎恨自己的孩子是反常的(或不近人情的). 4 not false, not put on to impress 不虛假的; 不矯揉造作的: *a natural way of behaving* 舉止自然的. (opp 反義詞 **unnatural**). **naturally** *adv* 1 normally; in the usual way 正常地; 以平常方式: *speak naturally* 照平常樣子說話. 2 of course; as one might expect 當然; 必然地: *Naturally, he denied that he had committed the crime.* 他當然否認犯了那罪行. **naturalist** *nc* student of natural history 博物學家. see below 見下面. **naturalize** *vt* 1 make someone a citizen of a country he was not born in 使歸化; 使入國籍. 2 adopt a word from another language 採納, 吸收(外來語詞). **natural history** study of the earth and what it produces (esp. botany, zoology and geology) 博物學.

nature ['neitʃə*] *nc / u* 1 power which is in control of the world 控制世界的力量, 自然力: *the forces of nature* 大自然力量. 2 the world (esp. as untouched by man) i.e. plants, animals etc. 自然界(尤指未經人類觸動過)即動, 植物等: *the beauties of nature* 自然界的美. 3 sort; type 種類; 類型: *things of this nature* 這類事物. 4 qualities in someone / something which make it the way it is 特徵; 特性; 本性; 天性: *It is not in his nature to be cruel.* 殘忍不是他的本性. *He has a kind / cruel nature.* 他秉性善良/殘忍.

naught [nɔ:t] *n* nothing (o.f.) 無(舊式).

naughty ['nɔ:ti] *adj* (with reference to children) bad; mischievous (指小孩)壞的; 不聽話的, 淘氣的, 頑皮的: *a naughty child* 頑皮的小孩. **naughtily** *adv* **naughtiness** *nu*.

nausea ['nɔ:siə] *nu* feeling of sickness or of disgust 作嘔; 噁心; 厭惡, 憎惡. **nauseate** ['nɔ:sieit] *vt* make one feel sick or disgusted 使作嘔; 使想吐; 使厭惡, 使憎惡. **nauseating** *adj*.

nautical ['nɔ:tikl] *adj* connected with ships or sailors 與船舶或水手有關的; 船舶的; 海員的.

naval ['neivl] *adj* connected with a navy 海軍的; 軍艦的: *naval officers* 海軍軍官.

nave [neiv] *nc* main, central part of a church, from the main entrance to the choir 教堂的中殿(從主要入口處至唱詩班席位之間).

navel ['neivl] *nc* the hollow in the surface of the stomach 肚臍, 臍.

navigate ['nævigeit] *vt* guide (a ship, aeroplane etc.) on its course; find one's way along (e.g. a river). 駕駛, 導航(船舶, 飛機等); 航行於(例如河流). **navigator** *nc* **navigable** ['nævigəbl] *adj* able to be sailed along (e.g. a river); 可通航的: *a navigable river* 可通航的河流. **navigation** [nævi'geiʃən] *nu* science of navigating 航海術; 航空術, 導航學; 航行學.

navvy ['nævi] *nc* unskilled workman

doing work such as digging roads etc.
(做挖掘道路等的) 不熟練工人; 做粗活
的工人, 壯工.

navy ['neivi] *nc* all the warships of a
country and their officers and men 海
軍. **'navy 'blue** *adj* dark blue 深藍色
的.

near¹ [niə*] **1** *adv* close; not far away
接近, 近; 不遠: *come nearer* 走近些;
stand near to the door 站在門的附近.
2 *prep* close to 靠近, 接近: *near the
house* 靠近房子; *near fainting* i.e. a-
bout to faint 快要暈倒; 幾乎昏過去.
comparative 比較級 **nearer.** *superlative* 最高級 **nearest.**

near² [niə*] *adj* **1** not far away in place
or time (時間, 空間) 近的, 不遠的:
The holidays are near i.e. we shall be
having our holidays soon. 假期快到
了. 即; 我們不久將休假. **2** close in
kinship or affection 近親的; 親密的: *a
near relative* 近親. **3** (with reference
to cars etc.) *(Brit)* on the left-hand
side, on the right-hand side elsewhere
(指汽車等)(英) 在左手邊的 (別處爲在
右手邊的): *on the near side* 在左側,
在左邊; *the front nearside wheel* 左前
輪. *(opp* 義3的反義
詞爲 off). **nearness** *nu* **nearly** *adv*
almost 幾乎: *nearly dead* 將近死亡.
'nearby *adv* not far away 在附近; 附
近地: *There is a house nearby* 附近有
一幢房子. **'nearby** *adj*: *a nearby
house* 附近的房子. **a near miss** see
見 **miss¹.**

near³ [niə*] *vt / i* come close (to);
approach 走近; 接近, 臨近: *We were
nearing the harbour.* 我們快要到碼頭
了.

neat [ni:t] *adj* **1** tidy; well-arranged 整潔
的, 整齊的: *a neat desk* 整潔的書桌
(辦公桌). **2** fond of having things
tidy or well-arranged 愛整潔的; 愛整

齊的: *a neat person* 喜愛整潔的人. **3**
(with reference to drinks) not mixed
with water (指酒類) 不摻水的; 純淨的:
He drinks his whisky neat. 他喝純威士
忌. **neatly** *adv* **neatness** *nu.*

nebulous ['nebjuləs] *adj* vague; not
clear. 含糊的; 模糊不清的: *a nebulous
shape / idea* 模糊不清的形狀 / 觀念.

necessary ['nesəsəri] *adj* which is required; needed; which must be done
必需的; 必須的; 必要的; 必須做的:
Food is necessary for health. 食物是健
康所必需的. *(opp* 反義詞 **unneces-
sary).* **necessaries** *npl* things which
are needed 必需品. **necessarily** *adv*
as something required 必須地, 必要
地, 必然地: *You don't necessarily
have to leave now* i.e. you may stay if
you wish. 你現在並不一定非走不可.
即; 如果你想留下也可以. **necessitate**
[ni'sesiteit] *vt* make necessary 使被需
要; 使成爲必要. **necessity** [ni'sesiti] **1**
nu great need 急需; 必需; 必要: *The
tablets are to be taken only in case of
necessity.* 藥片只在急需時服用. **2** *nc*
something that one has to have, or
that has to be 必需品, 必然的事:
Sleep is a necessity. 睡覺是不可缺少的
事.

neck [nek] *nc* **1** part of the body which
connects the head to the shoulders
頸, 脖子. **2** anything which connects
the top of something to its main part;
anything which resembles a neck (in
sense 1) 連接頂部與主體的部位; 頸狀
部: *the neck of a bottle* 瓶頸. **'neck-
lace** ['nekləs] *nc* chain or string of
beads, precious stones etc worn
round the neck 項鍊. **'necktie** *nc*
(mainly *US*) piece of cloth tied round
the neck (主要用於美) 領帶. *(Brit* 英
tie). **neck and neck** side by side 肩並
肩地, 並駕齊驅: *finish neck and neck*

in a race 在賽跑中一起到達終點.

nectar ['nektə] *nu* **1** (in Greek Myth) drink of the gods (希臘神話) 衆神飲的酒. **2** any delicious beverage 甘美的飲料. **3** sweet liquid of plants, from which bees get honey 花蜜. **nectarous** ['nektərəs] *adj*.

née [nei] *adj* (with reference to married women) whose unmarried name was ... (e.g. *Mrs Smith née Brown*) (指已婚婦女) 婚前原名爲...; 本姓爲...; 娘家姓爲...(例如: 婚前原姓布朗的史密斯太太).

need¹ [ni:d] *nu* state in which something is required or necessary 需要; 必要: *be in need of money* 需要錢; *no need to hurry* 不必匆匆忙忙; *great need for more doctors* 急需更多的醫生, 還很需要醫生. **needs** *npl* things which are necessary for life 生活必需品: *earn enough for ones needs* 賺得的錢足够生活上的需求. **needless** *adj* unnecessary 不必要的; 不需要的; *needless suffering* 不必要的受苦. **needlessly** *adv* **needy** *adj* poor; without money 貧困的; 貧窮的; 沒有錢財的.

need² [ni:d] *vt* **1** require; want; have need of 需要: *To buy a car you need a lot of money* 你要買車需要很多錢; *need help* 需要幫助. *That child needs to be disciplined* i.e. he should be disciplined. 那個小孩需要處罰. **2** be necessary 必需, 必要: *You don't need to go immediately* i.e. it is not necessary for you to go now. 你不必要立即走. *Note* 說明: this is a regular verb and must not be confused with *need³*. 這是規則動詞, 不得將其與 need³ 相混淆.

need³ [ni:d] *aux* (usu. *negative or interrogative*) be necessary; be forced or obliged to (通常用於否定句或疑問句)

必要; 必須; 不得不: *He needn't come if he doesn't want to.* 他如果不想來就不必來. *Need we come? No, you needn't* (or *Yes, you must*). 我們一定要來嗎?不, 你們不必來 (或: 是, 你們必須來).

needle ['ni:dl] *nc* **1** long thin pointed piece of metal with a hole (called an **eye**) at one end, used for sewing 針; 縫針. **2** similar instrument used for injecting a drug into the body 注射針. **3** pointer on a dial 指針: *needle of a compass* 羅盤上的指針. **4** long, thin leaf of fir and pine trees (冷杉和松樹的) 針葉. **'needlework** sewing 縫紉.

negative¹ ['negətiv] *adj* **1** expressing denial; indicating 'no' or 'not': 否定的; 否認的: *a negative answer* i.e. 'no' 否定的回答. 即 "不". **2** unhelpful; not contributing anything 無用的; 無助益的; 不起任何作用的; 消極的: *a negative attitude* 消極的態度. *Note* 說明: in sense **1** the opposite is *affirmative*; in sense **2** the opposite is *positive*. (義1的反義詞爲 affirmative; 義2的反義詞爲 positive. **negation** [ni'geiʃən] *nu* act of denial or of saying 'no' 否認; 否定.

negative² ['negətiv] *nc* (photography) plate or film in which light things seem dark and dark things seem light (攝影術) 底片.

neglect [ni'glekt] *vt* **1** not take care of; pay no attention to 疏忽; 忽略; 忽視: *neglect one's children* 沒有好好照管自己的小孩. **2** fail to do 漏做; 忘記做; 遺忘: *He neglected to return the book.* 他忘了還書. Also 亦作 *nu* **1** failure to attend to something 疏忽; 忽略; 忽視: *neglect of one's family* 忽視家庭; 沒有照顧好家庭. **2** condition of not being cared for or attended to 被疏忽或忽

略的狀況: *The room was in a state of neglect.* 這房間沒有人管理.

negligent ['neglidʒənt] *adj* not careful enough 疏忽的; 忽略的; 粗心的: *a negligent worker* 粗心大意的工人. **negligently** *adv* **negligence** *nu* **negligible** ['neglidʒəbl] *adj* very small 很小的; 微不足道的: *a negligible amount* 很小的量; 微量; 可忽略不計的量.

negligée ['negliʒei] *nc* long, loose gown. worn by a woman when she is going to bed or when she has just got up 長而寬鬆的女睡衣.

negotiate [ni'gouʃieit] *vt / i* **1** discuss something to try to come to an agreement 商談; 談判; 協商: *The two countries are negotiating for a peaceful settlement.* 這兩個國家正在就和平解決問題進行談判. **2** get or give money for 兑現: *negotiate a cheque* 兑現支票. **3** get through or over (some obstacle) 通過, 越過, 克服 (障礙等): *negotiate a difficult part of the river* 通過這條河流難以航行的部份. **negotiation** [nigouʃi'eiʃən] *nc / u* **negotiator** *nc* **negotiable** [ni'gouʃəbl] *adj* (with reference to a cheque etc.) able to be exchanged for cash (指支票等) 可兑現的.

Negro ['ni:grou] *nc* **1** member of the African races south of the Sahara (非洲撒哈拉沙漠以南的) 黑人. **2** descendant of these races living outside Africa (非洲以外的) 黑人後裔: *an American Negro* 美洲黑人; 美國黑人. *pl* 複數 **Negroes**. (*fem* 陰 **Negress** ['ni:gres]). Also 亦作 *adj*.

neigh [nei] *nc* long loud cry that a horse makes 馬嘶聲. Also 亦作 *vi* make such a sound (馬) 嘶叫.

neighbour ['neibə*] (*US* 美 **neighbor**) *nc* **1** person who lives next to or

close to another person 鄰居, 鄰人. **2** person, country etc that is next to another 鄰近的人; 鄰國; 鄰近的東西.

neighbourhood *nc* **1** place where people live near one another; the people living there 鄰里; 四鄰; 街坊; 街道: *a friendly neighbourhood* 和睦的鄰里. **2** area near a certain place 附近地區: *in the neighbourhood of the town hall* 在市政廳附近的地區).

neighbouring *adj* near each other 相鄰的, 鄰近的, 附近的; 接壤的: *neighbouring towns* 鄰近的城鎮. **neighbourly** *adj* friendly 和睦的, 友善的, 親近的.

neither ['naiðə*, 'ni:ðə*] **1** *adj / pron* not one, nor the other (of two) (兩者) 都不: *Neither man was guilty.* 兩個人都沒有罪. *Neither of them told the truth.* 兩個人都不說真話. **2** *adv / conj* not: nor 不; 也不: *I can neither admit it nor deny it.* 我既不能承認也不能否認. *He can't do it, and neither can I.* 他不會做, 我也不會.

neo- ['ni:ou] *prefix* new 新的.

neolithic [,niou'liθik] *adj* of the later Stone Age 新石器時代的.

neon ['ni:ɔn] *nu* gas used in making bright electric street signs or lamps 氖 (用於做街道的電氣招牌或燈): *a neon sign* 氖虹燈廣告牌.

nephew ['nefju:] *nc* son of one's brother or sister 姪兒; 外甥. (*fem* 陰 **niece** [ni:s]).

nepotism ['nepətizəm] *nu* giving of special favours (esp. employment) by an important person to his relatives 裙帶關係, 裙帶風; 重用親戚; 任人唯親.

nerve [nə:v] **1** *nc* part of the body which carries impulses or messages between the brain and other parts of the body 神經. **2** *nu* courage; boldness 勇氣; 大膽; 魯莽; 厚顏: *have the* *nerve to do something. (informal* in sense 2) 居然有臉做某事, 竟然敢做某事.(義2爲非正式). **nervous** *adj* **1** connected with nerves in the body 與神經有關的: *the nervous system* 神經系統. **2** worried; easily excited 焦慮的; 煩惱的; 易激動的; 易緊張不安的: *a nervous young man* 易緊張的青年人. **nervously** *adv* **nervousness** *nu* '**nerve-racking** *adj* overexciting; dangerous 令人過度緊張的; 傷腦筋的; 危險的: *a nerve-racking experience* 令人緊張的經歷. **nervous breakdown** mental illness caused by overwork, too much worry etc. 精神崩潰(由過度工作、憂慮等引起).

nest [nest] *nc* place built or chosen by a bird in which to lay its eggs; place where certain types of insects etc keep their young 巢; 鳥窩; 某些昆蟲的窩: *a wasp's nest* 黄蜂窩.

nestle ['nesl] *vt / i* lie or press comfortably against something 舒適地卧在; (使)偎依在; 使緊貼, 摟抱; 懷抱. *nestle into one's bed* 舒適地躺在床上; *nestle against one's mother* 偎依在母親身旁.

net[1] [net] *nc* lengths of cord, string etc tied together to form squares 網, 網狀物: *a fishing net* 魚網; *a mosquito net* 蚊帳. **netting** *nu* material in the form of a net 網狀編織物. *wire netting* 金屬網, 鐵絲網. '**netball** game in which a ball is thrown into a net hanging from a pole 無板籃球. '**network 1** system of things which cross one another 網狀系統; 網狀組織: *a network of roads.* 公路網, 道路網. **2** system of things which are connected in some way 相關連的系統: *a network of radio stations* 無線電台廣播網.

net[2] **nett** [net] *adj* remaining when nothing more is to be added or taken away 純的, 淨的, 實在的: *net price of an article* i.e. real price, lowest price 一件商品的實價即最低的價格; *net profit* i.e. the profit that is left after all expenses have been paid 純利, 淨利; *net weight of an article* i.e. the weight of the article itself, excluding the wrappers, container etc. 一件物品的淨重.

nettle ['netl] *nc* common plant which causes pain when it is touched (會刺痛人的)蕁麻科植物.

neurosis [njuə'rousis] *nc* nervous or mental illness 神經機能病; 精神病. *pl* 複數 **neuroses** [njuə'rousi:z]. **neurotic** [njuə'rɔtik] *adj* suffering from a nervous illness 患神經機能病的; 神經病的; 神經過敏的. Also 亦作 *nc.*

neuter ['nju:tə*] *adj* **1** neither male nor female 無雌雄之别的; 無性的. **2** (with reference to words) neither masculine nor feminine (e.g. *boy* is masculine, but *stone* is neuter) (指字、詞)中性的(例如: boy 是陽性, 而 stone 是中性).

neutral ['nju:trl] *adj* **1** not supporting either side in a war or quarrel (在戰爭或爭吵中)中立的; 不支持任何一方的: *neutral territory* i.e. land which does not belong to either country (e.g. in a war etc.) 中立國地區, 即不屬於交戰雙方的領土. **2** (with reference to colour, sound etc.) having no definite quality; not bold or distinct (指顏色、聲音等)無確定性質的; 不鮮明的; 不清晰的. **neutrality** [nju'træliti] *nu* state of being neutral (e.g. in war) 中性; 中立(例如戰爭中的中立). **in neutral** (with reference to a car) not in any of the gears which makes the engine drive the wheels (指汽車)位於空檔.

never ['nevə*] *adv* **1** at no time 永不, 决不; 從未, 未曾: *I have never seen him before.* 我從來沒有見過他. *They shall* *never leave this house.* 他們永遠不得離開這房子. **2** not (emphatic form) 不; 不要 (強調形式): *This will never do!* 這決不行! **neverthe'less** *adv* in spite of that 雖然如此; 不過; 仍然; 然而.

new [nju:] *adj* **1** never having existed before; appearing for the first time; unused 新的; 從未有過的; 初次出現的; 未曾用過的: *Where are the new books?* 新書在哪裏? *This is a new design.* 這是一種新的設計 (或新式樣). *I'll show you my new suit.* 我會給你看我的新衣服. *After he cleaned the car, it was just like new.* 他把車子清洗乾淨後, 車子就像是新的. *They are building new houses everywhere.* 到處都在蓋新房屋. **2** existing before but only recently seen, discovered, bought etc; extra; additional 新近爲人見到的; 新發現的; 新買到的; 另外的; 附加的: *learn a new language* 學習新語言; *discover a new planet* 發現新行星. Also 亦作 *adv* recently 新近; 最近: *newborn baby* 新生嬰兒; *new-laid eggs* 新下的蛋, 剛下的蛋. **newness** *nu* **newly** *adv* **1** recently 新近, 最近: *a newly-married couple* 新婚夫婦. **2** in a different way 以不同的方式: *a newly-designed system* 重新設計的系統.

'newcomer someone who has recently arrived in a town etc. 新來的人: *I'm a newcomer to these ideas* i.e. they are new to me. 這些意見我現在才知道. **new moon** thin crescent showing at the time when the moon is beginning to get bigger 新月. **New Year's day** lst, January 元旦, 一月一日. **new to** not accustomed to; recently arrived in 不習慣的; 剛來到的: *I'm new to this job.* 我對這工作不熟悉.

news [nju:z] *nu* report or account of things which have recently happened 新聞; 消息; 新聞報導: *I have some news for you.* 我有些消息告訴你. *Have you heard the news?* 你聽到這消息嗎? *I heard all about it on the news* i.e. on radio or television. 這事我從新聞報導 (即從收音機或電視機) 中全部聽到了. *I heard several items / pieces of news.* 我聽到幾則新聞. **'newsagent** shopkeeper who sells newspapers 報刊經售人. **'newspaper** paper printed regularly containing news 報紙.

next [nekst] **1** *adj / n* nearest; immediately following 最貼近(的); 最接近(的); 緊接着來到的; 下一個(的); 下次(的): *Go up to the next street after this one.* 去這條街下面的一條街. *You will have to be the next (person) to go.* 你應是下一個走的人. *Not that book, but the next one.* 不是那本書, 是下一本. *We are leaving for Europe next Sunday / summer / year.* 我們下星期日/明年夏天/明年動身去歐洲. *Note* 說明: presence of *the* means that some other time has been previously mentioned. *They stayed here for one week and left the next week.* He was here last Friday and promised to come back the next day. 有 the 表示前面已提過其他的時間. *They stayed here for one week and left the next week.* 他們在這裏停留了一星期, 第二星期離開. *He was here last Friday and promised to come back the next day.* 他上星期五在這兒, 並且答應次日來訪. **2** *adv* after this (that) 在這 (那) 以後; 之後; 其次; 下一步; 然後; 接着: *What happened next?* 以後怎麼樣了? *When I next saw him, he was a wealthy man.* 當我下一次見到他時, 他已是個有錢人. *What will you be up to next?* (expressing surprise) 你下一步又要做甚麼? (表示驚訝) **3** *prep* be-

side, next to 在…旁邊, 靠近, 貼近:
The desk is next to the wall. 那張辦公
桌緊靠着牆. **next door** in the next
house 隔壁: *The people who live next
door* 居住在隔壁的人; *next-door
neighbours* 隔壁鄰居.

nib [nib] *nc* metal point of certain kinds
of pen (not of ballpoint pens) 鋼筆尖.

nibble ['nibl] *vt* take tiny bites of 一點
一點地咬; 啃; 細咬: *The fish were nib-
bling at the bait.* 魚在一點一點地咬
餌.

nice [nais] *adj* **1** pleasant; good 令人愉
快的; 宜人的; 好的, 友善的: *a nice
person* 和藹的人. **2** difficult to judge;
requiring care 難以判斷的; 須要小心
謹慎的: *a nice point of law* 法律上難
以判定之點. **nicely** *adv.*

niche [nitʃ] *nc* **1** hollow place in a wall
for a statute, bust, vase etc. 壁龕. **2**
suitable position 合適的職務 (或地
位).

nick [nik] *nc* small V-shaped cut made
in wood etc. (often as a record) (木頭
等上的) V 形小刻痕 (常作爲記錄).

nickel ['nikl] **1** *nu* type of hard, white
metal 鎳. **2** *nc* American coin worth 5
cents 美國的五分鎳幣. Also 亦作 *adj.*

nickname ['nikneim] *nc* name used instead of one's real name 綽號; 渾名.
Also 亦作 *vt: nickname someone Jock*
給某人取綽號叫 Jock.

nicotine ['nikəti:n] *nu* poison found in
tobacco (烟草中含的有毒物質) 烟鹼;
尼古丁.

niece [ni:s] *nc* daughter of one's brother
or sister 姪女; 甥女. (*masc* 陽
nephew ['nefju:]).

night [nait] *nc / u* period of darkness
from sunset to sunrise 夜晚, 黑夜 (指
從日落至日出); *last night* 昨晚; *three
nights ago* 三個夜晚以前; *on Sunday
night* 在星期天晚上; *nine o'clock at

night* i.e. 9 p.m. 晚上九點. Also 亦作
adj **nightly** *adv* occurring at night or
every night 晚上的, 夜間的; 每晚的.
'**nightcap** drink taken before going to
bed 睡前喝的酒. '**night club** place of
entertainment which is open late at
night 夜總會. '**nightdress** long dress
worn by women and children in bed
婦女和小孩穿的長睡衣. '**nightfall** beginning of the night 傍晚, 黄昏, 日暮.
'**nightmare** *nc* **1** horrible dream 惡
夢, 夢魘. **2** any horrible experience
恐怖的經歷. '**night school** school or
place of study for those who cannot
attend classes during the day 夜校.
'**night-time** period of darkness at
night 夜間. '**night 'watchman** person
employed to guard buildings etc during the night (大廈等雇用的) 守夜人
by night during the night 在夜間.

nightingale ['naitiŋgeil] *nc* small bird
famous for its beautiful singing, heard
mostly at night 夜鶯.

nil [nil] *n* nothing (often used in giving
scores) 無, 零 (通用於記分分): *win
by two goals to nil* 以二比零的得分獲
勝.

nimble ['nimbl] *adj* **1** quick in movement (動作) 敏捷的, 靈敏的; 迅速的: *a
nimble climber* 敏捷的爬山者. **2** clever; quick to understand 聰明的; 敏銳
的; 理解快的: *a nimble mind* 才思敏
捷, 聰慧.

nine [nain] see appendix 見附錄.

nip¹ [nip] *vt* take flesh between two fingers and press it, causing pain; take a
small bite of (用兩手指) 捏, 挾; 咬: *be
nipped in the leg* 腿被捏了一下; *be
nipped by a dog* 被狗咬. *past* 過去式
和過去分詞 **nipped.** Also 亦作 *nc*
nippy *adj* quick. (*informal*) 敏捷的, 迅
速的. (非正式).

nip² [nip] *nc* small amount of spirits 少

量的烈酒: *a nip of whisky* 一小口威士忌酒.

nipple ['nipl] *nc* point of the breast through which milk comes 乳頭.

nitrate ['naitreit] *nc* **1** salt or ester of nitric acid 硝酸鹽. **2** potassium nitrate or sodium nitrate, used as a fertilizer 硝酸鉀或硝酸鈉(用作肥料).

nitric ['naitrik] *adj* of or containing nitrogen 氮的, 含氮的: *nitric acid* 硝酸.

nitrogen ['naitrədʒən] *nu* gas without colour, taste or smell, forming about four-fifths of common air 氮.

no [nou] **1** *adv* opposite of yes 不, 不是 (yes 的反義詞): *Did you say anything? No, I didn't.* 你有沒有說甚麼?沒有, 我甚麼也沒說. *You didn't see him? No I didn't.* 你沒看見他?不, 我沒有看見. **2** *intensifier* (with *comparatives*) not any 加強詞(與比較級連用)毫不, 一點也不, 並不: *I shall go no further* i.e. I shall stay here. 我不再往前走了. 即: 我要停留在這裏. *We have no more time to waste here.* 我們再也沒有時間浪費在這兒. **3** *adv* (before numerals and 'other') with the idea 'There does not exist...' (置於數字和 'other' 前面) 不存在⋯, 沒有⋯: *No two fingerprints are the same.* 沒有兩個指紋印是一樣的. *No other person would have done it.* 沒有別的人會做那件事. **4** *determiner* not any; not one 無, 沒有: *I have no money.* 我沒有錢. *She has no sense.* 她沒有見識(不通情達理). *They have no books.* 他們沒有書. *We have no house.* 我們沒有房子. **5** *determiner* (meaning the opposite of the word which follows) 並非, 決非, 根本不是: *He is no friend of mine* i.e. he is my enemy. 他決不是我的朋友. 即: 他是我的敵人. *He is no lover of animals.* 他根本不是愛護動物的人. **'no-man's land** area

between two enemy armies in a battlefield 戰場上敵對軍隊之間的地區, 真空地帶, 無人地帶. **by no means** not at all 一點也不, 根本不. *He is by no means poor.* 他根本不窮. **no-one** nobody 沒有人, 沒一人. **in no time** in a very short time. 很快, 馬上, 立刻.

noble ['noubl] *adj* **1** to be admired; very fine 崇高的, 高尚的; 堂皇的, 卓越的; 極好的: *a noble person* 高尚的人. *a noble gesture* 美好的姿勢. (*opp* 反義詞 **ignoble**). **2** high in rank; of high birth 高貴的; 貴族的: *a noble family* 貴族家庭. Also 亦作 *nc* person of high birth 貴族. **nobly** *adv* **nobility** [nou'biliti] *nu* nobles as a group or class 貴族(階層). **'nobleman** noble 貴族.

nobody ['noubədi] *pron* no person; no-one. 沒有人; 無人; 沒一人: *We saw nobody in the kitchen.* 我們看見廚房裏空無一人. *There was nobody in the whole house.* 整個屋子裏一個人也沒有. *I hope nobody has missed the bus.* 我希望沒有人趕不上公共汽車. *Note* 說明: it is also common to say e.g. *I hope nobody has missed their bus* (esp. if both men and women are being referred to) although this form is considered a mistake by some people. *I hope nobody has missed their bus* 的說法也很普通(尤其是同時提到男人和女人時), 但有些人認為這種說法是錯誤的. Also 亦作 *nc* person of no importance 無名小卒; 小人物; 無足輕重的人: *a nobody* 一個無名小卒.

nod [nɔd] *vi* **1** make a quick, downward movement of the head (usu. a sign of greeting, agreement or to give a command) 點頭(通常用於打招呼, 表示同意或發出命令). **2** let the head fall forward with tiredness 打盹, 打瞌睡. *past* 過去式和過去分詞 **nodded.** Also

亦作 nc.

node [noud] nc knot; knob; point of intersection 結; 節; 瘤; 交叉點.

noise [nɔiz] nc / u sound (esp. a loud or unpleasant one) 響聲(尤指喧鬧聲, 嘈雜聲); 噪聲. **noisy** adj loud; making a lot of noise 喧鬧的, 嘈雜的, 多雜聲的. **noisily** adv.

nomad ['noumæd] nc member of a tribe which wanders from one place to another seeking food, pasture etc. 遊牧部落的人. **nomadic** [nou'mædik] adj.

nominal ['nɔminl] adj 1 in name only, not in reality 名義上的, 有名無實的: the nominal ruler of a country i.e. a person who has the name of ruling a country which is in fact ruled by somebody else 一個國家名義上的統治者; 即: 實際上是他人在統治國家. 2 very low in value 價值極微小的, 微不足道的, 極小的: a nominal amount 極小的數量. **nominally** adv.

nominate ['nɔmineit] vt put forward, suggest someone as being a suitable person for some position 提名; 任命; 指派: nominate someone as secretary 任命某人爲秘書. **nomination** [nɔmi'neiʃən] nc / u act or power of nominating someone 提名; 任命; 提名權; 任命權. **nominee** [nɔmi'ni:] nc person nominated 被提名者; 被任命者.

non- [nɔn] prefix not (e.g. **nonfiction**) 非; 無; 不(例如: non-fiction 非小說類文學作品).

nonchalant ['nɔnʃələnt] adj not being, or pretending not to be, interested or excited 冷淡的; 不激動的, 無動於衷的; 假裝冷淡的; 假裝不激動的.

non-committal ['nɔnkə'mitl] adj not giving any clear decision on a matter 不作出明確決定的; 態度不明朗的.

nonconformist ['nɔnkən'fɔ:mist] nc 1 one who does not act or believe as others do 不隨人行動或信仰的人. 2 (**Nonconformist**) (in England) Protestant who is not a member of the Church of England (在英格蘭) 不信奉英國國教的基督徒. Also 亦作 adj.

nondescript ['nɔndiskript] adj of very ordinary appearance; not easy to describe 極爲平凡的; 難以描述的.

none [nʌn] adv / pron 1 not any; not one 毫無; 無一; 一個也沒有: I looked for some pencils but there were none there. 我找些鉛筆, 但那裏一枝也沒有. Have you any money left? No, none at all. 你還有錢嗎? 沒有, 一點也沒有. None of them came. 他們一個也沒有來. None of that! i.e. Stop that! (command) 不要這樣! 別再這樣! (命令). None of your cheek! i.e. be cheeky! (i.e. impudent). 別那麼不要臉! 2 in no way; not at all 決不, 一點也不; 毫不: I'm afraid he is none too clever i.e. not at all clever. 恐怕他一點也不聰明. He is none the worse for his terrible hardships i.e. they have done him no harm. 他並沒有受到可怕苦難的傷害. '**nonethe'less** adv / conj nevertheless 然而; 不過; 雖然如此.

nonentity [nɔ'nentiti] nc person of no importance 不重要的人; 無足輕重的人.

nonetheless [ˌnʌnðə'les] adv nevertheless 仍然, 不過.

non-fiction ['nɔn'fikʃən] nu writing which is not in a novel or short story 非小說類文學作品: Poetry, biography and travel will all be found among the non-fiction in the library. 詩, 傳記, 遊記都全部存放在圖書館中非小說類文學作品中. Also 亦作 adj.

nonplus ['nɔn'plʌs] vt surprise or puzzle a person so much that he does

not know what to say or do 使驚訝得
不知所措; 使窘困; 使狼狽不堪: *completely nonplussed* 完全不知所措.
past 過去式和過去分詞 **nonplussed.**

nonsense ['nɔnsns] *nu* words which do
not mean anything; anything foolish
or silly 胡說; 胡扯; 廢話; 毫無意義的
話; 愚蠢的事.

non-stick ['nɔn'stik] *adj* coated with a
substance that stops food adhering
(塗有某種物質而)不黏食物的: *a nonstick saucepan* 不黏食物的平底鍋.

noodles ['nu:dlz] *npl* long strips made
from flour and eggs, used in soups
etc. 麵條.

noon [nu:n] *n* 12 o'clock midday 中午,
正午; 中午12點.

no-one ['nouvʌn] *pron* **nobody.**

noose [nu:s] *nc* loop of rope with a running knot so that the rope becomes
tighter as it is pulled 套索; 活繩結.
hangman's noose i.e. rope used for
hanging people 執行絞刑者的套索.
即: 絞索.

nor [nɔ:*] *conj* (used after **neither** or
not) and not (用於 neither 或 not 之
後) 也不, 亦不: *Neither he nor his
friends came back.* 他和他朋友都沒有
回來. *He has neither the time nor the
ability to do it properly.* 他沒有時間也
沒有能力把這事做好. *I don't think it
will rain. Nor do I.* 我想不會下雨. 我想
也不會.

norm [nɔ:m] *nc* **1** rule; standard; most
common thing 準則; 標準; 規範; 典範.
2 amount or number of things that
has to be produced in a factory etc.
定額; 工作量: *Our norm is forty
machines per day.* 我們的定額是每日
40台機器.

normal ['nɔ:ml] *adj* ordinary; usual; regular 普通的; 正常的, 平常的, 常態的;
正規的: *a normal day* 平常的日子; *a*

normal person 正常的人. (*opp* 反義詞
abnormal). **normally** *adv.*

north [nɔ:θ] *adv* roughly in the direction to the right of someone facing
the setting sun 向北方; 在北方:
travelling north 往北方旅行. **the
north** area of a country etc lying to
the north; one of the points of the
compass (一國等的)北部; 北, 北方.
(*opp* 反義詞 **the south**). **northern**
adj in or of the north 在北部的; 北部
的. **'northwards** *adv* towards the
north 向北, 向北方.

nose [nouz] *nc* **1** part of the face above
the mouth used for smelling and
breathing 鼻子. **2** power of smelling;
ability to find out things 嗅覺; 發現的
能力: *a nose for scandal* i.e. ability to
find out secrets etc. 嗅出醜聞的能力.
即偵查出內情等的能力. **nosey** *adj*
curious, inquisitive (esp. about other
people's affairs) (*informal*) 好奇的, 愛
打聽的(尤指愛打聽別人的事情). (非正
式). **'nosedive** *nc* sudden headlong
descent by an aircraft 飛機垂直俯衝.
Also 亦作 *vt/i.*

nostalgia [nɔs'tældʒiə] *nu* **1** great desire to be back at home when one is
far away or to be at any place that
one is a long way from 懷鄉病; 思念舊
地; 思念故土. **2** longing for times
gone by 留戀過去; 懷舊. **nostalgic**
[nɔs'tældʒik] *adj.*

nostril ['nɔstril] *nc* one of the two
openings in the nose 鼻孔.

not [nɔt] *adv* **1** used to express the
negative of a verb with a subject (finite verb) 用於使帶主語的動詞成爲否定:
*This desk is tidy but
that one is not.* 這張書桌很整潔, 而那
張(書桌)不整潔. *Some people work
but there are others who do not work.*
有些人工作但有一些人不工作. *Note*

說明: *not before a finite verb must be used with certain verbs (e.g. does, can etc.), and is often shortened to n't: he can't go; they aren't ready; isn't he clever?* 限定動詞前面的 not 必須與某些動詞(例如: does, can 等)連用, 並且常被縮略爲 n't: he can't go; 他不能去; they aren't ready; 他們還沒有準備好; isn't he clever? 他不聰明嗎? **2** used to express the negative of participles and infinitives 用於使分詞和不定式成爲否定: *Not being an expert, I cannot tell you.* 我不是專家不可能告訴你. *They were ordered not to leave.* 他們被命令不得離開. **3** used to express the negative of some previous statement 用於否定某一先前的陳述: *Do you think it will rain? I hope not* i.e. I hope it does not rain. 你想會下雨嗎?我希望不會. *I suppose he won't come. No, I suppose not* i.e. I too think he will not come. 我想他不會來.是的,我想不會. 即:我也認爲他不會來. **4** used to express the opposite of *adjs* or *advs* 用於使形容詞或副詞成爲相反的意義: *not seldom* i.e. often 常常,經常.

notable ['noutəbl] *adj* worth noticing; deserving to be remembered 值得注意的; 值得記住的: *a notable event* 值得注意的事件, 重要的事件. **notably** *adv* especially 特別地, 尤其.

notch [nɔtʃ] *nc* V-shaped mark in a piece of wood etc. (木頭等上面的)V字形刻痕, 凹口.

note [nout] **1** *nc* musical sound; sign standing for a musical sound; black or white key on a piano etc, which produces a musical sound 樂音, 音調; 音符; (鋼琴等的)琴鍵: *strike a note on the piano* 在鋼琴上彈一樂音(或一琴鍵). **2** *nu* attention 注意; *worthy of note* i.e. deserving attention 值得注意

的. **3** *nc* something written to help one's memory 筆記; 記錄; 備忘錄: *take notes* i.e. write them down 記錄, 做筆記; *make notes for one's speech* 寫發言稿, 便條. **5** *nc* paper money; promise to pay money 紙幣; 票據; 借據: *a bank-note* 鈔票. **6** *nc* comment on or explanation of a word or passage in a book etc. 按語; 評論; 註釋; 註解. **7** *nu* fame; importance 名聲, 名望; 重要: *a man of note* i.e. a famous man 名人, 著名人士. Also 亦作 *vt* pay attention to 注意: *note the beautiful colours in this picture* 注意這畫的美麗色彩.

noted *adj* famous; well-known 有名的; 著名的: *a man who is noted for his generosity* 以慷慨出名的人. **'notebook** book for keeping a record of things 筆記簿. **'notepaper** paper for writing letters 信箋, 信紙.

nothing ['nʌθiŋ] *adv / n* **1** not anything 無事; 沒有東西; 沒有甚麼: *He had nothing to say.* 他沒有話要說. *Nothing he says will change my mind.* 他說甚麼也不會使我改變主意. *I looked in the room, but there was nothing there.* 我朝房裏一看, 裏面甚麼也沒有. **2** not at all 毫不, 一點也不: *It was nothing like what I had imagined.* 這一點也不像我所想像的. **for nothing** free 免費的. *I got this book for nothing.* 我免費得到這本書.

notice ['noutis] **1** *nu* attention 注意: *bring something to someone's notice* 使某事爲某人所注意. *take no notice of* i.e. pay no attention to 不注意, 不理睬. **2** *nc* written or printed information about something that has happened or is going to happen 通告; 佈告; 告示; 啓事: *put up a notice* 張貼佈告. **3** *nu* warning (esp. about the end of a contract etc.) 警告, 通知(尤指關

於合同等的到期): *He gave his secretary a month's notice* i.e. warned her a month beforehand that she was to be dismissed 他通知他的秘書一個月後離職; *at short notice* i.e. without much warning 一接通知馬上就; 立即; 迅速. Also 亦作 *vt / i* take note of; see 注意到; 看到. **noticeable** ['noutisəbl] *adj* easily noticed 顯而易見的; 顯著的. (*opp* 反義詞 **unnoticeable**) **notice board** (*Brit*) board on which notices can be put (英)佈告欄. (*US* 美 **bulletin board**)

notify ['noutifai] *vt* make something known to someone; report 通知; 報告: *notify someone's death to the police / notify the police of someone's death* 向警方報告某人死亡. **notification** [noutifi'keiʃən] *nc / u.*

notion ['nouʃən] *nc* idea; opinion (esp. one for which there is not much proof) 觀念, 概念; 意見, 看法, 想法(尤指沒有甚麼證據): *have some strange notions* 有一些奇怪的念頭或想法; *no notion of* 沒有…的想法; 不明白; 不懂.

notorious [nə'tɔ:riəs] *adj* well-known for something bad 臭名昭彰的; 聲名狼藉的: *a notorious criminal* 臭名昭彰的罪犯. **notoriously** *adv* **notoriety** [noutə'raiəti] *nu.*

notwithstanding [notwið'stændiŋ] *adv / prep* **1** in spite of 儘管. **2** although 雖然; 然而.

nougat ['nu:gɑ:] *nu* type of sweet with nuts inside it 果仁糖(一種內含堅果仁的糖果).

nought [nɔ:t] *n* nothing; 0 無物; 無; 零.

noun [naun] *nc* name of person, thing, quality etc. (e.g. in the sentence *The frightened people ran to their houses, people* and *houses* are nouns) 名詞(例如: 在 The frightened people ran to their houses 句中, people 和

houses 爲名詞).

nourish ['nʌriʃ] *vt* give food to 給與食物, 養育: *nourish one's children* 養育小孩. **nourishing** *adj* **nourishment** *nu* food 食物, 營養品.

nova ['nouvə] *nc* new star 新星.

novel[1] ['nɔvl] *adj* new; strange; different 新的; 奇妙的; 不同的: *a novel idea* 新奇的想法. **novelty 1** *nu* strangeness; newness 奇妙; 新奇. **2** *nc* something not heard or seen before 未聞未見的事物; 新奇的事物.

novel[2] ['nɔvl] *nc* book telling a story about people made up by the writer or sometimes based on historical events and characters 小説. **novelist** *nc* person who writes novels 小説家.

November [nə'vembə*] *n* eleventh month of the year 十一月.

novice ['nɔvis] *nc* beginner; someone who is not experienced 新手; 生手; 初學者: *a mere novice* 十足的生手.

now [nau] *adv / conj* **1** at the present time; as things are 現在; 目前; 照目前情況, 在目前形勢下: *He is working in London now.* 他現在在倫敦工作. *He will be home by now* i.e. by this time. 他這時將到家了. *He has been found guilty of theft; who will trust him now?* i.e. in these circumstances. 他被裁決犯有偷竊罪; 這樣誰會信任他? **2** used often in speech with no reference to present time (esp. in commands or in telling a story) 未指現在, 常用於説話中(尤用於命令或講故事): *Now there were three bears in the forest.* 且説森林裏有三隻熊. *Now, stop talking!* 好了, 別説話! **nowadays** ['nauədeiz] *adv* in these times; in these days (esp. when compared with former times) 現今; 時下; 當今: 現在(尤用於與過去比較): *Children are not so well-behaved nowadays as they used to be.* 現在小

孩子不像過去那樣規矩了. **now and again, now and then** sometimes 不時, 有時: *He still visits me now and then.* 他仍不時來看望我.

nowhere ['nouweə*] *adv* in no place; not anywhere 到處都沒有; 無處: *The child is nowhere to be found.* 那小孩到處都找不到. *My watch was nowhere to be seen.* 我的手錶到處都看不到.

nozzle ['nɔzl] *nc* metal end of a tube or hose from which water etc. comes (管子或軟管末端放出水等的)噴嘴, 噴頭, 管嘴.

nuance ['njuːɔns] *nc* slight feeling or shade of meaning, which is not easily recognized (難以辨認的)細微感情; 細微意義.

nucleus ['njuːkliəs] *nc* central part round which something may grow etc. 核心, 中心: *the nucleus of a new society* 新社會的核心. *pl* 複數 **nuclei** ['njuːkliai]. **nuclear** ['njuːkliə*] *adj* connected with a nucleus (esp. that of an atom) 與核心有關的, 核的(尤指原子核的): *nuclear energy* i.e. power obtained from the splitting of atom nuclei 原子核能; *nuclear physics* i.e. study of the nuclei of atoms (原子)核物理學, 即: 研究原子核的學科.

nude [njuːd] *adj* uncovered; without clothes on 無覆蓋物的; 赤裸的, 裸體的. Also 亦作 *nc* unclothed human figure (in a painting; a statue etc.) (繪畫, 塑像等的)裸體人像. **nudity** *nu*

nudist *nc* person who believes that it is good and healthy not to wear clothes 裸體主義者(認爲裸體有益健康的人).

nudge [nʌdʒ] *vt* touch with the elbow, so as to attract attention 用肘觸碰(以促人注意).

nugget ['nʌgit] *nc* lump of metal esp.

gold, as found in the earth (天然的)塊金; 礦塊.

nuisance ['njuːsns] *nc* thing / person that is annoying or causes trouble. 討厭的東西; 討厭的人.

null [nʌl] *adj* having no force 無效力的, 無約束力的. **nullify** *vt* cause or declare to have no effect 使無效; 宣無無效. **null and void** (legal) having no legal force (法律)無法律效力的, 無效的: *Their marriage was declared null and void.* 他們的結婚被宣佈爲無效.

numb [nʌm] *adj* not able to feel or move 麻木的, 無感覺的, 不能動彈的: *fingers numb with cold* 凍僵了的手指; *numb with fear* 嚇得手足不能動彈. Also 亦作 *vt* make numb 使麻木; 使失去感覺, 使不能動彈. **numbness** *nu.*

number[1] ['nʌmbə*] *nc* 1 word or sign used for counting 數; 數字, 數碼: *5 and 7 are numbers;* 5和7是數字; *six and ten are numbers.* 六和十是數字. 2 amount 數量: *a large number of people* 很多人. 3 copy of a newspaper, magazine etc. (報紙, 雜誌等的)期, 册, 本: *Have you seen the current number of 'Time'?* 你看過最近一期的 "時代"週刊嗎? 4 song or other part of a programme in a theatre etc. (戲院等節目單上的)歌曲或其他節目. Also 亦作 *adj* (in sense 1), *number 33.* 33號; *room No. 5* i.e. number 5. 5號房間.

number[2] ['nʌmbə*] *vt / i* 1 give a number to 給…編號. *We numbered them 1 to 10.* 我將他們從1到10編號. 2 amount to 合計, 總計, 計有: *They numbered 15 in all* i.e. altogether. 他們總共有15人.

numeral ['njuːmərl] *nc* figure or mark which stands for a number 數字: *roman numerals* i.e. I, II, V etc. 羅馬

數字, 即: I, II, V 等; *arabic numerals* i.e. 1, 2, 5 etc. 阿拉伯數字, 即: 1、2、5 等. **numerical** [nju:'merikl] *adj* connected with numbers 與數字有關的; 數字的; *in numerical order* i.e. first number one, second number two etc. 按數字次序, 按號數, 即: 第1一號, 第2二號, 等. **numerous** ['nju:mərəs] *adj* very many 極多的, 非常多的.

numerate ['nju:mərit] *adj* able to count 能計算的: *All children should be numerate by the time they leave school.* 所有小孩離開學校時都應會計算. (*opp* 反義詞 **innumerate**).

numerator ['nju:məreitə] *nc* **1** number above the line in a vulgar fraction (分數的) 分子: *The numerator of the fraction 2/3 is 2.* 分數2/3的分子是2. **2** person or thing that numbers 計算者; 計算器.

nun [nʌn] *nc* one of a group of women who have taken special vows devoting their lives to God 修女; 尼姑. (*masc* 陽 **monk** [mʌŋk]).

nurse[1] [nə:s] *nc* **1** person who looks after sick people (esp. one who has been trained in this) 護士, 看護 (尤指受過護理訓練的): *a registered nurse* i.e. a nurse whose qualifications have been approved 註冊護士. 即經過官方考試合格的護士. **2** woman or girl who looks after young children 褓姆.

nurse[2] [nə:s] *vt* **1** look after a sick person 看護, 護理 (病人). **2** hold or carry a young child carefully 小心抱 (幼兒), 愛撫. **3** keep careful watch over; pay special attention to in 細心照管; 特別關心: *He nursed the garden carefully at*

the beginning. 他從開始就細心管理這花園. **nursery** ['nə:səri] *nc* **1** place, room which children can use for play etc. 託兒所, 保育室, 嬰兒室. **2** piece of ground where plants, trees etc are grown (usu. for sale) 苗圃 (通常供出售). **'nursery rhyme** verse, poem for young children 童謠; 兒歌. **'nursing home** private hospital 私人醫院.

nut [nʌt] *nc* **1** eatable seed with a hard shell (可食用的) 堅果仁: *a walnut* 核桃, 胡桃; *a hazelnut* 榛子. **2** small piece of metal for screwing onto a bolt in order to hold machinery together 螺帽, 螺母. **'nutcrackers** instrument for breaking the shell of nuts 軋碎堅果的鉗子; 胡桃鉗; 堅果鉗. **in a nutshell** as briefly as possible. (*informal*) 極簡短地, 簡而言之. (非正式).

nutmeg ['nʌtmeg] *nc* seed of an East Indian fruit, often made into a powder and used for flavouring food 豆蔻, 肉豆蔻; 豆蔻粉 (用作香料).

nutrient ['nju:triənt] *nu* nourishing food 營養物, 營養品; 養份. **nutrition** [nju:'triʃən] *nu* science of how nourishing different kinds of food are 營養學. **nutritious** [nju:'triʃəs] *adj* good as food; nourishing 有營養的; 滋養的: *These vegetables are very nutritious.* 這些蔬菜很有營養.

nylon ['nailən] *nu* very strong material used for making stockings, shirts etc. 尼龍 (強韌物質可用以製造長襪, 襯衣等). Also 亦作 *adj*: *a nylon shirt* 尼龍襯衣.

O,o

O¹ [ou] symbol for **nought** 零的符號.

O², **oh** [ou] *interj* cry expressing fear, surprise, doubt etc. (表示恐懼, 驚訝, 疑慮等) 啊; 哦; 唉; 哎呀. *Note* 說明: the commoner form is *oh*. oh 是更普通的形式.

oaf [ouf] *nc* stupid, clumsy fellow 蠢人; 獃子; 笨漢. *Careful, you great oaf!* 小心, 你這十足的蠢貨!

oak [ouk] **1** *nc* type of large tree found in cool northern areas (生長於北方寒冷地區的) 橡樹. **2** *nu* hard wood from this tree 橡木.

oar [ɔ:*] *nc* pole with a flat blade at one end, used in rowing a boat 槳; 櫓.

oasis [ou'eisis] *nc* area in a desert which is fertile because there is water there (沙漠中的) 綠洲. *pl* 複數 **oases** [ou'eisi:z].

oat [out] *n* (usu. *pl*) grain used for food (通常用複數) 燕麥.

oath [ouθ] *nc* **1** promise made in God's name that one is going to do something, or that one is telling the truth 誓言; 誓約: *swear / take an oath* 宣誓; 立誓; 發誓; *on (one's) oath* i.e. having taken an oath 發過誓. **2** disrespectful use of the name of God, or of some other holy person / thing 詛咒; 咒罵: *a terrible oath* 可怕的咒罵. *pl* 複數 **oaths** [ouðz].

oats [outs] *npl* type of grain used as food 燕麥.

obedient [ə'bi:diənt] *adj* willing to do what one is told to do 服從的; 順從的. 聽話的, 恭順的: *an obedient child* 聽話的小孩; *a very well-trained and obedient dog* 一隻受過嚴格訓練、絕對

服從 (命令) 的狗. (*opp* 反義詞 **disobedient**) **obedience** *nu*: *obedience to someone's commands* 服從某人的命令.

obese [ou'bi:s] *adj* very fat 極為肥胖的: *an obese old man* 非常肥胖的老人. **obesity** *nu*.

obey [ə'bei] *vt / i* do what one is told to do 服從; 順從; 遵從; 聽從: *obey a command* 服從命令.

obituary [ə'bitjuəri] *nc* announcement of somebody's death. often in a newspaper and often with an account of his life (登於報刊並常附死者傳略的) 訃告; 訃聞.

object¹ ['ɔbdʒekt] *nc* **1** thing that can be seen or touched (可見, 可摸的) 物體, 物件: *an unusual object* 奇特的物體. **2** purpose; aim 目的; 目標: *What is his object in doing that?* 他做那件事的目的是甚麼?

object² [əb'dʒekt] *vi* say that one does not agree to something; not be in favour (of) 反對; 不贊同 (舊式): *I object to people working for such low wages.* 我反對人們爲這樣的低工資工作 *They wanted to close down the railway line, but hundreds of people objected.* 他們想關閉這條鐵路線, 但數以百計的人反對. **objection** *nc* act of objecting; reason or argument against something 反對, 異議; 反對的理由, 反對的論據: *Do you have any objections to this?* 你對這有異議嗎? **objectionable** *adj* unpleasant 令人不愉快的; 討厭的. **objector** *nc* person who objects 反對者.

object³ ['ɔbdʒekt] *nc* (grammar) part of

a sentence which completes the sense of a transitive verb (e.g. in *The boy threw the ball, 'the ball'* is the object). In sentences like *The boy gave him the ball* or *The boy gave the ball to him, 'the ball'* is called the **direct object** and *'him'* (to him) is called the **indirect object.** (語法) 賓語; 受詞(例如: 在 The boy threw the ball 男孩子投球一句中, 'the ball' 是賓語)。 在 The boy gave him the ball 或 The boy gave the ball to him (那男孩子給他球) 句中, 'the ball' 叫做直接賓語, 'him' (to him) 叫做間接賓語。

objective [əb'dʒektiv] *adv* not influenced by one's own feelings; fair 客觀的, 公正的: *an objective account of the quarrel* i.e. not sympathizing with either side 關於爭吵的客觀報導。即: 不同情任何一方。(*opp* 反義詞 **subjective**). Also 亦作 *nc* what is aimed at; what is to be achieved or captured (esp. in a battle etc.) 目的, 目標; 出擊目標(尤指戰役等): *important military objectives* 重要軍事目標。 **objectivity** [ɔbdʒek'tiviti] *nu*: *a judge famous for his objectivity* 以客觀公正著名的法官。

obligation [ɔbli'geiʃən] *nc* 1 duty; what ought to be done 責任; 義務; 職責: *the obligations of children towards their parents* 孩子對父母親的責任。 2 duty of being thankful to someone who has been kind to one 感恩; 恩惠; 人情債: *be under an obligation to someone* 受某人的恩惠; 欠某人的情。 **obligatory** [ə'bligətəri] *adj* necessary; required 必須的; 必要的; 要求的; 應盡的: *Attendance at lectures is obligatory for all students.* 所有學生均須到堂聽講。

oblige [ə'blaidʒ] *vt* 1 require to do something 要求做某事: *He felt obliged to answer his father's letter* i.e.

he felt he ought to answer it 他覺得應該回他父親的信。 2 do something for someone 爲某人做某事; 施惠: *Could you oblige me by posting this letter?* 勞您駕替我寄這封信好嗎? **obliging** *adj* helpful to others 樂於助人的。

oblique [ə'bli:k] *adj* sloping; slanting: 歪的; 斜的; 傾斜的; 偏斜的: *an oblique line* 斜線; *an oblique stroke* i.e. the mark / 斜 / 筆) 劃, 即: / 記號。

obliterate [ə'blitəreit] *vt* rub out; destroy completely 擦掉; 徹底毀滅: *obliterate every sign of the damage* 去掉損壞的痕跡; *obliterate a whole village* 毀滅整個村莊。

oblivion [ə'bliviən] *nu* state of being forgotten 被忘卻的狀態; 湮沒: *This village, once famous, has sunk into oblivion.* 這個曾經一度出名的村莊現在已湮沒無聞。**oblivious** [ə'bliviəs] *adj* not noticing 不以爲意的, 不在意的。 *The girl was quite oblivious of the sensation she was creating.* 這女孩對她引起的轟動頗不在意。

oblong ['ɔblɔŋ] *nc* (geometry) shape having four sides like a square, with angles of 90°, but longer than it is broad 長方形。Also 亦作 *adj* shaped like an oblong 長方形的。

obnoxious [ɔb'nɔkʃəs] *adj* giving offence; unpleasant; nasty 令人生厭的; 令人不愉快的; 可憎的; 討厭的: *an obnoxious smell* 臭味, 難聞的氣味; *an obnoxious play* 討厭的遊戲。

oboe ['oubou] *nc* type of wooden wind instrument 雙簧管。

obscene [ɔb'si:n] *adj* indecent; disgusting 猥褻的; 淫穢的; 令人厭惡的: *an obscene book* 淫穢書籍。**obscenity** [ɔb'seniti] *nc / u* state of being obscene; anything obscene (esp. obscene language) 猥褻; 淫褻; 任何猥褻淫穢的事物(尤指淫穢的語言)。

obscure [əb'skjuə*] *adj* **1** dark; not easy to understand 暗的; 模糊的; 難解的: *an obscure remark* 費解的話. **2** not famous 不著名的: *an obscure little village* 一個不出名的小村莊. Also 亦作 *vt* make obscure 使黑暗; 掩蔽; 使理解. **obscurity** *nu*.

obsequious [əb'si:kwiəs] *adj* too eager to obey or serve 逢迎的; 諂媚的: *an obsequious servant* 諂媚的僕人.

observation [ɔbzə'veiʃən] *nc / u* **1** act of watching 觀察; 監視; 注視: *keep someone under observation* i.e. watch carefully everything that someone does 監視某人. 即注意某人所作所為; *come under observation* i.e. be carefully watched 被監視. **2** remark; what someone says 評論; 意見: *a chance observation* i.e. what someone just happens to say 偶然發表的意見. **3** report, statement on what one has observed 觀察報告, 根據觀察所作的陳述: *his observations on his travels* 他的旅行觀察報告. **4** ability to notice things 觀察事物的能力: *powers of observation* 觀察力. **escape observation** not be seen or noticed 未被覺察; 未被注意.

observe [əb'zə:v] *vt / i* **1** watch carefully; look at with attention; notice 監視; 觀察; 注意到: *observe someone's behaviour* 觀察或監視某人的行為; *observe that someone is looking pale* 注意到某人面色蒼白. **2** keep (laws etc.) 遵守; (對儀式的) 慶祝或奉行: observe (a feast day etc.) 遵守 (法律等); 慶祝 (節日等). **3** make a remark; say 評論; 說: *He observed that it was unusually hot for the time of year.* 他說就季節而言, 這樣的天氣算是反常的熱. **observable** *adj* able to be observed; having to be observed 觀察得到的; 應遵守的; 應慶祝的. **observance** *nu* keeping of a law; celebration of a ceremony (對法律的) 遵守; (對儀式的) 慶祝或奉行. **observant** *adj* quick to notice things 善於觀察的; 機警的: *an observant mind* 觀察力敏銳的頭腦. (*opp* 反義詞 **unobservant**). **observatory** [əb-'zə:vətri] *nc* building from which the sun, stars etc are observed 天文臺; 氣象臺. **observer** *nc* person who observes (in sense 1) (第一義) 觀察者; (esp. someone sent to attend meetings etc without taking part in them) 觀察者 (尤指出席會議等的觀察員): *act as an observer* 當觀察員.

obsess [əb'ses] *vt* occupy one's thoughts all the time 時刻困擾; 纏住: *obsessed by hatred* 被憎恨思想所困擾的. **obsession** *nc / u* something that occupies one's mind continually 縈繞於心的擺脫不了的事物: *With him, gambling is an obsession.* 對於他來說, 賭博是無法擺脫的. **obsessive** *adj*.

obsolete ['ɔbsəli:t] *adj* not now in use; out-of-date 已不用的, 已廢棄的; 過時的: *obsolete weapons* 舊式武器.

obstacle ['ɔbstəkl] *nc* something that stands in the way or hinders 障礙; 妨礙物; 阻礙: *Ignorance is an obstacle to progress.* 無知是進步的障礙. '**obstacle race** race in which the competitors have to overcome obstacles (e.g. going through a sack etc.) 障礙賽跑.

obstetrics [ɔb'stetriks] *n sing* branch of medicine concerned with childbirth 產科學; 助產術.

obstinate ['ɔbstinət] *adj* **1** not easily changed from one's opinion; refusing to obey 固執的; 頑固的; 倔強的, 不服從的: *an obstinate child* 倔強的小孩. **obstinately** *adv* **obstinacy** *nu*

obstreperous [əb'strepərəs] *adj* noisy and making unnecessary difficulties for others 吵鬧的; 頑固對抗的; 難管束的

的.

obstruct [əb'strʌkt] *vt* get in the way of something; block; try to prevent something 阻礙, 妨礙; 阻塞; 阻撓; 阻撓: *obstruct traffic* 阻塞交通; *obstruct the passing of a government act* 阻撓政府法令的通過. **obstruction** *nc / u* something that obstructs; act of obstructing 障礙物, 阻礙物; 阻礙; 阻撓; 阻塞. **obstructive** *adj* deliberately causing obstruction 故意阻礙的.

obtain [əb'tein] *vt* get 獲得; 得到: *obtain high marks* 獲得高分數. **obtainable** *adj* that can be obtained 可獲得的; 可得到的. (*opp* 反義詞 **unobtainable**).

obtrusive [əb'tru:siv] *adj* 1 sticking out very much 大爲伸出的, 非常突出的. 2 fond of pushing oneself, one's ideas etc forward 愛突出自己的; 愛出風頭的; 愛强迫人接受己見的; 炫耀(自己想法等)的. (*opp* 反義詞 **unobtrusive**).

obtuse [əb'tju:s] *adj* stupid; dull 愚笨的; 遲鈍的.

obvious ['ɔbviəs] *adj* easy to see or understand; clear 顯而易見的; 明顯的; 清楚的. **obviously** *adv*.

occasion [ə'keiʒən] *nc / u* 1 time when something is happening 時刻; 時節; 場合: *on the occasion of the queen's visit* 在女王(或王后)訪問的時候; *some other occasion* 另外時節, 其他場合; *a wedding is not an occasion for sorrow* i.e. a propes time for. 婚慶不是悲傷的時候. 2 need; reason 需要; 理由: *He had no occasion to buy a car.* 他沒有必要買一輛汽車. Also 亦作 *vt* be the reason for; be the occasion of 是…的原因; 引起: *The boy's return occasioned great rejoicing.* 那男孩的回來使人欣欣鼓舞. **occasional** *adj* happening from time to time 偶而的; 非經常的: *an occasional meeting.*

偶而舉行的會議. **occasionally** *adv* not often; now and then 偶爾; 非經常地; 不時.

occlude [ə'klu:d] *vt* close or block (a passage) 使閉塞; 封鎖.

occlusion [ə'kluʒən] *nu* state of being occluded 閉塞.

occult [ɔ'kʌlt] *adj* having to do with magic or the supernatural 玄妙的; 巫術的; 超自然的: *occult ceremonies* 神秘儀式. **the occult** magic practices and ceremonies 神鬼之事, 神秘之事, 秘術.

occupy ['ɔkjupai] *vt* 1 take and keep possession of 佔有; 佔領; 佔據: *occupy another country after a war* 戰爭之後佔領另一國家. 2 live in; use 居住; 使用; 佔用: *This room / house is occupied* i.e. there is someone in it. 這房間 / 房屋已有人住. 3 take up; fill 佔去; 佔滿; 盤據: *occupy one's time* 佔時間; *occupy one's mind* 盤據在心上. **occupant, occupier** '*nc* person who occupies (a house etc.) (房屋等)的居住者, 佔有人. **occupation** [ɔkju'peiʃən] *nc / u* 1 act of taking or having in one's possession 佔領; 佔有; 佔用: *the occupation of a house / a country* 佔有一房屋 / 佔領一國家. 2 job; employment 工作; 職業: *What is his occupation?* 他從事甚麼職業? **occupational** [ɔkju'peiʃənl] *adj* having to do with work, or one's own particular work 職業的; 與特定職業有關的: *an occupational disease* 職業病.

occur [ə'kə:*] *vi* 1 happen; take place 發生; 出現: *an accident occurred.* 發生事故. 2 be found; exist 見到; 存在. *That sound does not occur in my language.* 我說的語言裏沒有那個音. 3 come into one's mind 被想到; 被想起: *it occurred to me that ...* 我想起….

occurrence [əˈkʌrns] *nc / u* happening; event 發生; 事件; 事變: *a strange occurrence* 奇怪的事件.

ocean [ˈouʃən] *nc* 1 large area of salt water that extends over a great part of the earth 海洋. 2 one of the sections into which this area is divided 洋: *the Atlantic Ocean* 大西洋; *the Indian Ocean* 印度洋.

ochre [ˈoukə*] *nu* yellowish-brown colour 赭色; 黃褐色. Also 亦作 *adj*.

o'clock [əˈklɔk] *adv* according to the clock 根據時鐘; …點鐘.

oct-, octa-, octo- [ˈɔkt(ə)] *prefix* eight (e.g. **octagon**) 八(例如 octagon).

octagon [ˈɔktəgən] *nc* (geometry) plane figure with eight sides and eight angles (幾何學) 八角形, 八角形. **octagonal** [ɔkˈtægnl] *adj* eight-sided 八邊形的.

octane [ˈɔktein] *nu* substance in petrol which improves its quality 辛烷(改善汽油質量的物質); 辛烷值: *a car which uses high-octane fuel* 使用高辛烷值燃料的汽車.

octave [ˈɔktiv] *nc* (music) interval (difference in pitch) of twelve semitones in a musical scale; note that is six whole tones above or below any given note; a note and its octave played together (音樂) 八度音, 八音度階; 高八度音, 低八度音; 八度和音.

October [ɔkˈtoubə*] *n* tenth month of the year 十月.

octopus [ˈɔktəpəs] *nc* sea creature with eight arms 章魚.

odd [ɔd] *adj* 1 strange; unusual 奇異的; 不平常的. *an odd thing to do* 古怪人才做的怪事 *a very odd person* 十分古怪的人. 2 (with reference to numbers) not even (指數目)奇數的, 單數的: *1, 3, 5 and 7 are odd numbers* 1、3、5、7是奇數. 3 not complete in some

way (e.g. one of a pair, part of a set etc.) 單隻的, 不成對的(例如一雙中的一隻); 單個的; 零散的(例如一組中的單個): *an odd sock* 單隻的短襪; *an odd piece of carpet* 單件地毯, 零件地毯. 4 with a few or a little more (used to indicate numbers roughly) 有零頭的(用於表示大約數目). *I found £5 odd.* 我得出五鎊多. **oddity** *nc* 1 strangeness 奇特, 古怪. 2 strange person, thing etc. 怪人; 怪事, 怪異的事物. **oddments** *npl* things left behind or remaining 殘餘的東西; 零頭: *oddments of clothing.* 零星衣服. **odds** *npl* chances for or against (the probability of) a thing happening (某事會發生的)機會, 可能性: *The odds are he won't come back* i.e. he probably won't come back. 他可能不會回來. **be at odds with someone** disagree with someone 與某人意見不和, 與某人有爭執. **odds and ends** small articles which have little value (沒有甚麼價值的)零碎物, 零星的東西.

ode [oud] *nc* kind of poem 頌; 賦; 歌.

odious [ˈoudiəs] *adj* hateful; unpleasant 可憎的; 討厭的; 令人作嘔的.

odour [ˈoudə*] (*US* 美 **odor**) *nc / u* smell 氣味.

oesophagus [iːˈsɔfəgəs] *nc* food canal which leads from the mouth to the stomach 食道.

of [ɔv, əv] *prep* 1 (used to indicate distance from or separation from) (表示距離或分離): *within two miles of the church* 離教堂兩英里以內; *east of Suez* 蘇伊士以東; *robbed of every penny he possessed* 搶走他所有的錢. 2 (used to indicate source, origin) (表示出處; 作者; 來源; 出身): *the works of Shakespeare* 莎士比亞的著作; *a girl of good family* 出身名門的女子; *a man of the people* i.e. from the ordinary people 平民出身的人. **3** (used to indicate cause or reason) (表示原因，理由)：*die of hunger* 飢餓而死. **4** (used to make a noun have the force of an adjective) (使名詞具有形容詞的意義)：*that idiot of a boy* i.e. that idiotic boy 那個白癡的男孩子；*that fool of a manager* i.e. that foolish manager 那個笨經理. **5** (used to indicate what something is made of or contains) (表示製造的材料或包含的東西)：*a dress of silk* 綢衣服. *a sack of potatoes* 一袋馬鈴薯；*an area of hills and rivers.* 丘陵河流交錯的地區. **6** (used to indicate ownership or connection) (表示所有權，連接關係)：*the president of the society* 會社的會長，社長；*the owner of this watch* 這隻錶的所有人. **7** (used to indicate part of a larger group) (表示大組中的一部份)：*two members of the team* 兩名隊員；*much of the time* 大部份時間. **8** (used to indicate measure) (表示分量)：*a pint of milk* 一品脫牛奶；*two pounds of butter* 兩磅黃油. **9** (used with a possessive noun or pronoun to indicate one from the number of) (與所有格名詞或物主代詞連用表示其中之一)：*a friend of mine* i.e. one of my friends 我的一個朋友，即我的朋友中的一個；*a saying of John's* 約翰的一句名言. **10** (used with **this** or **that** and a possessive noun or pronoun) (與 this 或 that 及一所有格名詞或物主代詞連用)：*That son of mine is in trouble* 我那個兒子處於困境之中；*this new book of Jane's* 簡的這本新書. **11** (used to indicate an object function) (表示賓語的功能)：*tired of waiting* 厭倦等候；*love of animals* i.e. the love that people have for animals. see sense 12 愛動物，即：人對動物的愛(見義12). **12** (used to indicate a subject function) (表示主語的功能)：*the love of animals* i.e. the love that animals can show for people. see sense **11** 動物的愛，即：動物對人顯示的愛(見義11)；*the despair of Man* i.e. Man's despair 令人類感到絕望的事物. **13** on the part of 出自…，由…作出的：*It was good of you to remember me.* 感謝你沒有忘記我. *It was silly of her to say that.* 她說那樣的話真是愚蠢. **14** (*US:* used to indicate time before a certain hour) (美：表示某一小時之前的時刻)：*ten minutes of seven* 六點五十分，差十分七點. (*Brit* 英 **ten minutes to seven**). **15** (used to indicate the qualities etc that go with a person / thing) (表示人／物帶有的特性等)：*a man of great learning* 學問淵博的人；*a child of five (years)* 5歲的小孩；*a town of great beauty* 非常美麗的城鎮.

off¹ [ɔf] *adv* **1** (used to give general idea of distance or separation) (表示距離或分離)：*He lives two miles off* i.e. two miles away. 他住在兩英里外. *He went off rather quickly.* 他相當迅速地走掉. *They're off!* i.e. they are going away; they have started (often used at the beginning of a race). 他們要出發啦! 他們出發了! (常用於比賽的開始). *The handle is about to come off.* 把手快要掉啦. *The ship cast off* i.e. started to leave the harbour. 那隻船已解纜. 即：開始離開港口. *He took off his jacket.* 他脫下上衣. *Keep off!* i.e. don't come near. 讓開! 即：不要走近. **2** completely; thoroughly 完全地；徹底地：*kill off all the wild animals* 殺盡所有的野獸. *finish off one's work* 完成工作. **3** free from work 閑着，不工作：*have Sunday off* 星期日不上班. **be well off** be wealthy 富裕，富有：*They are quite well off.* 他們相當富有. **be well- / badly-off for friends /**

money etc. have plenty of / few friends / much / little money etc. 有很多/沒有甚麼朋友/錢等. **be better / worse off** be in a better / worse state 處境更好/更壞. **on and off / off and on** occasionally 斷斷續續地,不定時地;不時地; *I still see him off and on.* 我仍不時看到他. **straight off** immediately. *(informal)* 立刻,馬上. (非正式).

off² [ɔf] *prep* not on; from 不在…;從…離開;從: *Keep off the grass.* 勿踐草地. *The rider fell off his horse.* 騎馬人從馬背上跌下來. *He took ten pence off the price.* 他減價十便士. *We are off duty* i.e. not working. 我們下了班. *There's a petrol station just off the main road* i.e. not far from. 汽油加油站就在離大路不遠的地方. **'off-'colour** *adj* not in normal good health 氣色不好,身體不舒服; *I'm a bit off-colour this morning. (informal)* 我今天早上有點不舒服. (非正式). **'off 'hand** *adj* casual; careless 隨便的,漫不經心的;草率的,粗心的; *a rather off-hand manner* 相當隨便的方式. Also 亦作 *adv* without time to consider 未經思考地;立即: *It is difficult to give an opinion offhand.* 很難立即發表意見. **'off 'shore** *adj* 1 not far out to sea 在近海處的; *offshore islands* (靠近大陸的) 濱海島嶼, 外圍島嶼. 2 from the land; seawards 從陸地來的,向海洋的; *an offshore breeze* 吹向海洋的微風. **'off 'side** *adj / adv* (in hockey or football) in a position (usu. near one's opponent's goal) where one cannot receive the ball without breaking the rules (在曲棍球或足球中的) 越位.

off³ [ɔf] *adj* 1 (with reference to cars etc.) *Brit* on the right-hand side; on the left-hand side elsewhere (指汽車等) [英] 在右手邊的,在右側的; (別處

爲) 在左手邊的: *the front offside wheel* 右前輪 (opp 反義詞 *near*). 2 not fresh 不新鮮的: *This cheese is a bit off. (informal)* 這乳酪有點變味了. (非正式). 3 free from work 不工作的,下了班的: *my day off* 我的休息日; *the off season* i.e. the times when hotels etc are not busy 淡季. 即;旅館等不繁忙的時節. 4 cancelled 取消了的: *The game is off.* 比賽取消了. **'off-licence** permission for a shop to sell bottles of beer, wine etc which must be taken away from the shop before they can be opened and drunk; the shop licensed 只許向外出售酒類,不許在店內飲用的執照;持有此種執照的商店.

offal ['ɔfl] *nu* parts of an animal which are not considered as good as the flesh for food (e.g. heart, intestines etc.) (動物身上被認爲不好吃的心、腸子等部份) 內臟,下水.

offence [ə'fens] (*US* 美 **offense**) *nc / u* 1 crime; sin; breaking of a rule 罪行;罪過;犯法: *an offence against God* 觸犯神的罪過; *a major offence.* 嚴重的罪行或犯罪. 2 anything that makes people annoyed or angry 令人煩惱的事物;令人生氣的事物: *an offence against good taste* 有失風雅的事;有失體面的事.

offend [ə'fend] *vt / i* 1 do wrong; commit an offence 做錯事;犯法;犯罪. 2 anger; annoy 發怒;觸怒;使煩惱;煩擾. **offender** *nc* someone who offends by breaking the law 罪犯: *a young offender* 青少年犯. **offensive** [ə'fensiv] *adj* 1 unpleasant; causing annoyance or anger 令人不快的;令人煩惱的;討厭的;令人發怒的: *an offensive smell* 難聞的氣味. (opp 反義詞 **inoffensive**). 2 connected with attack 與攻擊有關的: *offensive weapons* i.e.

weapons used for attacking 進攻性武器. (*opp* 反義詞 **defensive**). Also 亦作 *nc* attack 攻擊; 進攻; 攻勢: *take the offensive* i.e. start to attack 開始進攻; 發動攻勢.

offer ['ɔfə*] *vt / i* put forward something so that it can be accepted or rejected 提出, 提供(某物以以供接受或拒絕): *offer a suggestion* 提出建議; *offer someone £5 for his watch* 出五英鎊向某人買他的手錶. Also 亦作 *nc* something offered 提供或提出之物. **offering** *nc* something offered (esp. to God) 提供或提出之物(尤指奉獻給上帝).

office ['ɔfis] *nc* 1 place where business is carried on; part of a business where clerical work and administration (running of the business) is done 營業處; 事務所; 辦事處; 辦公室. 2 government department 政府的部, 局, 司, 處: *the Foreign Office* 外交部. 3 post; official position 職位; 官職; 公職: *resign one's office* 辭職; *out of office* i.e. no longer in power 在野; 下野; 不執政. A politician who is out of office 在野的政治家. **'office boy** employed as a messenger and who does small jobs 辦公室的勤雜工.

officer ['ɔfisə*] *nc* 1 person who is of higher rank than others in the armed forces, police force etc. 軍官; 警官: *a naval officer* 海軍軍官. 2 person who holds some position of authority 高級職員: *the officers of the club* 俱樂部的高級職員.

official [ə'fiʃl] *adj* 1 supported by some kind of authority (often government authority) 官方的; 正式的; 法定的: *an official statement* 正式聲明. (*opp* 反義詞 **unofficial**). 2 having to do with an office or business; not personal 官職的; 公務的; 非私人的: *official corres-*

pondence 公務往來書信, 公函. Also 亦作 *nc* someone employed by the government 官員; 公務員. **officially** *adv* by or according to authority 憑權力; 根據職權; 官方地; 正式地.

officious [ə'fiʃəs] *adj* too anxious to help; interfering; too eager to show one's authority 過分慇懃的; 多管閑事的; 愛顯示權力的.

offing ['ɔfiŋ] *n* usu. in **in the offing** (with reference to an event) about to happen 通常用於 **in the offing**(指事件)即將發生: *Is there anything exciting in the offing?* 有甚麼激動人心的事即將發生嗎?

offset ['ɔfset] *vt* make up for: balance 補償; 抵銷: *The high price of food there was offset by the money we saved on bus fares.* 那裏的食物價格很高, 但我們用節省公共汽車費的錢抵銷了. *past* 過去式和過去分詞 **offset**.

offspring ['ɔfspriŋ] *n* child; young of animals 兒女, 子孫; 後裔; 動物的幼仔, 崽. *pl* 複數 **offspring**.

often ['ɔfn] *adv* many times 常常; 經常: *We go there often.* 我們經常去那裏. *He often sees us.* 他常常同我們見面. *Very often he comes in late.* 他經常來得很遲. *How often?* i.e. how many times? 多少時候一次?多少次?

ogle ['ougl] *vt / i* look at in a way that shows one loves or desires (向…)做媚眼, 送秋波.

ogre ['ougə*] *nc* imaginary, maneating giant (described in children's stories etc.) (童話中的)吃人巨妖. (*fem* 陰 **ogress** ['ougris]).

oh [ou] *interj* see 見 **O²**.

oil [ɔil] *nc / u* greasy liquid of different kinds, obtained from the fat of animals, plants or from under the ground and used for lighting, cooking, machinery etc. 油. Also 亦作 *vt* put oil on or into (a machine etc.) 加油於(機器等); 給…加潤滑油. **oily** *adj* covered with oil. 塗有油的; 油膩的. **'oil-can** can used for oiling machinery 油壺; 油罐; 加油器(用於給機器加油潤滑). **'oilfield** area where oil (petroleum) can be got from under the ground or under the sea (陸上或海上)油田. **'oil painting 1** *nc* picture painted using oil colours 油畫. **2** *nu* art of painting such pictures 油畫藝術. **'oilskin** type of coat etc which is waterproof 油布衣; 防水衣. **'oil tanker** large ship or vehicle for carrying oil in large quantities 油輪; 運油車. **'oil well** well from which oil is obtained 油井.

ointment ['ɔintmənt] *nc / u* medicine containing oil or fat to be rubbed on the skin 油膏; 軟膏; 藥膏: *antiseptic ointment* i.e. ointment which prevents a cut from becoming poisoned 防腐軟膏, 抗菌軟膏, 即; 防止傷口感染發炎.

O.K., okay ['ou'kei] *interj* good; I agree; fine 好; 不錯; 我同意; 可以; 行; 很好. Also 亦作 *nc*: *give someone the O.K.* i.e. give someone permission to do something. 同意某人做某事. Also 亦作 *vt* agree to, approve of, (all *informal*) 同意; 認可; 批准. (全部乃非正式).

old [ould] *adj* **1** having lived a long time; not young 年老的; 上年紀的; 老的: *an old man* 老人; *in old age* 年老了, 在晚年; *suitable for an old person* 適合老年人的. **2** having existed, been in use for a long time 年代久的; 古老的; 用舊的: *put on an old shirt* 穿上一件舊襯衣; *a very old custom* 非常古老的風俗. **3** of age 年歲的: *a baby two years old* 兩歲的嬰兒. *How old is your son?* i.e. what age is he? 你的兒子幾歲了? **4** familiar; known for a long time 親近的; 熟悉的; 認識許久的: *an old friend of mine* i.e. long-known, but not necessarily old in years 我的一個老朋友; 即: 認識很久, 未必年老. **5** used to express affection or contempt 用於表示親切或輕蔑: *Good old John!* 老約翰! *I don't want that old thing.* (*informal* in sense 5) 我不要那個東西. (義5乃非正式). *Note* 說明: the more usual forms of the *comparative* and *superlative* are **older** and **oldest**; **elder** and **eldest** also exist but mostly refer to comparing age in a family: *my elder brother; your eldest son.* 比較級和最高級的形式較常為 older 和 oldest; elder 和 eldest 也同時存在, 但大都指家庭中歲數的比較: my elder brother 我的哥哥; your eldest son 你的長子. **old age** later part of life 晚年; 暮年. **old boy 1** former pupil of a school 校友; 老同學. **2** form of address used between men. (*informal* in sense 2) (男人之間的招呼用語)老朋友, 老弟*(義2乃非正式). **'old-'fashioned** *adj* out-of-date; keeping to old ways, clothes etc. 過時的; 舊式的; 老式的; 守舊的: *old-fashioned ideas* 守舊的想法; *an old-fashioned inn* 老式的客棧. **old maid** see 見 **maid.**

olive ['ɔliv] *nc* **1** tree grown for its fruit, mostly in Mediterranean countries 橄欖樹. **2** small fruit of this tree 橄欖. Also 亦作 *adj* brownish green in colour 橄欖色的; 橄欖綠的; 茶青色的. **'olive'oil** oil made from olives 橄欖油.

ombudsman ['ɔmbʌdzmən] *nc* official whose work is to investigate complaints made by private citizens against the government 民情調查官 (專門調查公民對政府的投訴的官員).

omelette ['ɔmlət] *nc* eggs beaten up and fried (sometimes with cheese, ham etc added) 煎蛋捲 (有時放上乳酪, 火腿等作餡): *a ham omelette* 火腿蛋捲.

omen ['oumən] *nc* sign that something good or bad is going to happen 預兆; 兆頭; 徵兆: *A rainbow in the sky is sometimes regarded as a good omen.* 天上的彩虹有時被認爲是好兆頭.

ominous ['ɔminəs] *adj* threatening; suggesting that evil is to come 不祥的; 不吉的; 凶兆的.

omit [ə'mit] *vt* leave out; miss out 省略; 遺漏: *Omit pages 20 to 24* i.e. do not read those pages. 畧去第20至第24頁. 即: 不必閱讀那幾頁. *You have omitted a word in this sentence.* 你在這個句子裏漏掉了一個字. *past* 過去式和過去分詞 **omitted. omission** 1 *nc* something omitted 省畧或遺漏的事物. 2 *nc/u* act of omitting something 省畧; 遺漏: *sin of omission* i.e. fault of not doing something 未做某事的罪責, 疏忽罪.

omni- ['ɔmni] *prefix* all (e.g. **omnipotent** [ɔm'nipətnt] all-powerful) 全部, 總, 遍 (例如 omnipotent 全能的, 萬能的).

omnivorous [ɔm'nivərəs] *adj* eating any sort of food; feeding on all kinds of food 甚麼食物都吃的; 雜食的: *an omnivorous animal* 雜食動物.

on¹ [ɔn] *prep* 1 in contact with the surface of something 在…之上: *on the floor* 在地板上; *on the table* 在桌子上; *on the wall* 在牆上; *on the window* 在窗子上; *on the grass* 在草地上; *a ring on one's finger* 戴在手指上的一隻戒指; *a flag on a pole* 懸掛在旗杆上的旗. 2 (used to indicate some kind of support, base etc.) (表示某種支撐, 基礎等): *a painting on canvas* 畫在畫布上的油畫; *wheels on a car* 裝在汽車上的車輪. 3 (used to indi-

cate position in space or time) (表示空間或時間的位置): *the sign on the main road* 大路上的標誌; *on the 8th of October* 在十月八日; *on Sunday of last week* 在上星期日(上星期的星期日); *on the day we were married* 在我們結婚的那一天. 4 (used to indicate nearness) (表示靠近, 接近): *a house on the river* 臨河的房子; *an island on the lake* 湖邊的別墅. 5 in the direction of 朝…方向, 向着: *on my right* 在我右邊; *advance on one's enemies* 向敵人進攻. 6 by means of 藉着; 依靠; *a car runs on petrol* 汽車靠汽油行駛; *on the authority of the king* 根據國王所授的權力; *hear something on the radio* 從收音機聽到某事. 7 about; on the subject of 關於: *a book on politics* 一本關於政治的書; *keen on football* 愛好足球. 8 (used to indicate a state or condition) (表示情況或狀況): *on strike* 在罷工中. 9 (used to indicate the basis, reason for something) (表示某事物的根據或理由): *on his solemn promise* 依照他的莊嚴諾言; *live on a pension* 靠養老金過活; *retire on medical advice* 按照醫生的忠告而退休.

on² [ɔn] *adj* 1 in action; in use 在活動中; 在運轉中; 在使用中: *The handbrake is on.* 手煞車已煞住. *Is the light on or off?* 燈是開着還是關着? *The tap is on* i.e. water is running from it. 水龍頭開着. 2 taking place; occurring 發生中的; 進行中的: *There is a show on just now.* 戲此刻正上演. *The dance is on, after all* i.e. it will take place. 舞會畢竟將舉行. *What's on tonight?* i.e. what (entertainment) is taking place tonight? 今天晚上有甚麼節目? *Have you anything on tonight?* i.e. are you doing anything tonight? 今晚你有事嗎? 3 (in a theatre, studio etc.) performing (在戲院, 演播室等) 表演中: *You're on!* i.e. it is your turn to perform. 輪到你上台表演了! 輪到你出場了. **4** available; able to be used 可得到的; 能用的; 可用的. *Because of a fire, the water won't be on until midnight.* 由於火災, 午夜以前沒有自來水.

on³ [ɔn] *adv* **1** (used to indicate something going forward or continuing) (表示某事物在進展中或繼續活動中): *They went on walking.* 他們不停地走下去. *Carry on with your work* i.e. continue. 繼續做你的工作. *The soldiers marched on.* 士兵們往前行進. **2** (used to indicate contact or support) (表示接觸或支撐): *He had his hat on.* 他戴上了帽子. *The child had nothing on* i.e. it was naked. 那孩子沒穿衣服. 即: 一絲不掛. *Hold on tight.* 緊緊抓住. **3** with an indicated part forward (以所指的部份) 向前: *I tackled him head on* i.e. with my head forward. 我迎面 (或一頭) 攔住他. **and so on** other similar things 等等: *paper and pencils and so on* 紙和鉛筆等等. **later on** sometime afterwards 後來, 以後: *I'll attend to you later on.* 我以後會照應你.

once [wʌns] *adv* **1** one time, on one occasion 一次, 一回: *We go to the theatre once a month.* 我們每月去看一次戲. *He only did it once.* 他只做過一次. *He never once lost his temper* i.e. never at any time. 他從不發脾氣. **2** at one time; sometime in the past 曾經; 一度; 從前: *He was once a policeman, but he resigned from the force.* 他從前是個警察, 但他已辭去警察職務. *That kind of music was once very popular.* 那種音樂曾經一度很受人歡迎. **Also** 亦作 *conj* as soon as; if 一旦…(就…); 如果. *Once he said that, I knew he was lying.* 他一說那件

事我就知道他在撒謊. *Once you have learned Spanish you will find Italian easy.* 如果你學會了西班牙語, 你就會感到意大利語容易. **at once 1** immediately 馬上; 立即: *Leave at once!* 立即離開! **2** at the same time 同時: *Don't all shout at once!* 不要同時呼喊! **once more** again. 再來一次, 再一次: *Do it once more.* 再做一次. **once upon a time** at one time in the past (way of beginning children's stories) (兒童故事的開頭) 從前, 過去.

one¹ [wʌn] *nc* **1** lowest whole number 一 (最少的整數): *One plus two equals three.* 一加二等於三. **2** sign for this number i.e. 1. *Write down the number one.* 寫下數目字1. **3** (used to form compound nouns) (用於組成複合名詞): *twenty-one* 二十一; *thirty-one* 三十一. **one by one** one at a time 一個一個地, 一個接一個地; 依次地. **one or two** a few 一兩個, 一些, 幾個: *There are one or two books left.* 還剩下幾本書.

one² [wʌn] *determiner* **1** a single 單一的; 唯一的; 一個的: *one man* 一個人; *one chair* 一把椅子. *You cannot take any one apple* i.e. you must not take any more (otherwise use *a* or *an* e.g. *Please take an apple or two*). 你可以拿一個蘋果. 即: 你不得多拿. (否則用 *a* 或 *an*. 例如: *Please take an apple or two.* 請拿一個或兩個蘋果.) *He had one good coat and two others that were dirty.* 他有一件好外衣和另外兩件髒的外衣. **Note** 說明: (in measurements) *one and a half years; one pound of sugar; one and a half million people* etc are rather formal; it is more common to say *a year and a half; a pound of sugar; a million and a half people.* (在量度大小方面) *one and a half year; one pound of sugar;*

one and a half million people 等說法均相當正式; 較常的說法是 a year and a half; a pound of sugar; a million and a half people. **2** a certain 有一, 有一個: *I first saw him one day last summer.* 去年夏季有一天我第一次看到他. *One evening we all arrived late.* 有一天晚上我們都來得很晚. *Note* 說明: after *on* use *a* or *an* (e.g. *I first saw him on an evening in July / on a July evening*). 在 *on* 後面使用 *a* 或 *an* (例如: I first saw him on an evening in July / on a July evening. 七月裏的一個晚上我第一次看到他). **3** some (indefinite) 某一 (不明確的): *One day I shall be rich.* 總有一天我會富起來. **4** the same 同一的; 同樣的: *They are all of one opinion.* 他們都意見相同. **5** united; joined together 團結的, 聯合起來的: *some day all our people will be one.* 總有一天我們的人民會團結起來. **6** (used to form compound *adjs*) (用於組成複合形容詞): *twenty-one years of age* 二十一歲. **'one-way 'street** in which cars are allowed to move in one direction only 單行道.

one³ [wʌn] *pron* **1** some person / thing 某人 / 物. *pl* 複數 **some:** *one of his friends* 他的一個朋友 (即他的朋友之一); *one of those flowers* 那些花中的一朵. (*pl* 複數 **some of those flowers**) *He is one of my best friends.* 他是我最好的朋友之一. *I haven't a notebook; can you lend me one?* i.e. any notebook. 我沒有筆記簿; 你能借我一本嗎? 即: 任何一本筆記簿. *Note* 說明: compare the last sentence with *I see you have a notebook there; can I borrow it?* i.e. that particular notebook 將最後句子與下述句子進行比較, I see you have a notebook there; can I borrow it? 我看到你那裏有一本筆記簿; 我能借嗎? 即: 借看到的那一本筆記

簿. **2** (used after an *adj*, *pl* **ones**) (用於形容詞之後, 複數亦作 ones): *That garden is beautiful; I don't think I've seen a nicer one.* 那座花園很美麗; 我想我沒有見過更美麗的花園. *You should see Philip's photographs; he's taken some very good ones.* 你應該看一看菲力普的照片; 他拍了一些非常好的照片. **3** that 那, 那個. *pl* 複數 **ones.** *This house is much bigger than the one you used to have.* 這棟房子比你過去擁有的那一棟大多了. *The children are playing with some toys—the ones your aunt gave them* i.e. the toys that your aunt gave them. 孩子們在玩一些玩具—你姑母給他們的那些玩具. **4** the sort of person 這樣的人; 那種人: *Charles is not one to be frightened easily* i.e. he is not the sort of person who is easily frightened. 查爾斯不是那種輕易就被嚇倒的人. **5** any person; every person 任何人; 每一個人: *One must keep quiet in the library.* 在圖書館裏每一個人都必須保持安靜. *One must try to keep one's temper even when one is being annoyed.* 人即使在厭煩時也應盡力忍着性子. **6** used instead of 'I' to avoid committing oneself 用於代替 '我', 以避免自己發表意見: *One would think he ought to retire next year.* 看來 (人家認為) 他明年應該退休. *Note* 說明: in *USA* you can say *One must try to keep his temper even when he is being annoyed.* In British English this is thought to be wrong by some people, which results in longer sentences sounding formal and rather clumsy. It is often better to use 'you', 'everyone', 'we' etc. (e.g. *You must try to keep your temper etc. Everyone must keep quiet in the library*). 在美國, 可以講 One must try to keep his temper even when he is being annoyed. 但在英國英語中有些人認爲這種說法是錯誤的, 這種說法容易句子較長, 聽起來非正式但相當彆扭. 通常比較好的辦法是使用'you', 'everyone', 'we' 等 (例如: You must try to keep your temper etc. Everyone must keep quiet in the library). **oneself** *pron* one's own self 自己; 自身: cut oneself 割傷自己; wash oneself 洗澡 (洗自己). **one another** each other 互相; 彼此: They hit one another i.e. each one hit the other. 他們打架. They went to one another's house i.e. each went to the other's house / the others' houses. 他們去彼此的家裏. 即: 每一個人都去對方的家 / 其餘的人的家.

onerous ['ɒnərəs] *adj* heavy; requiring great effort 繁重的; 艱巨的; 需要很大力氣的: an onerous task 繁重的任務.

onion ['ʌnjən] *nc* round vegetable with a strong smell and taste, used in cooking 洋蔥, 洋蔥頭.

onlooker ['ɒnlʊkə*] *nc* person who watches something that is happening; spectator 旁觀者.

only ['ounli] *determiner / adv / conj* **1** sole; by itself or themselves; with no others 唯一的; 獨一的; 僅有的: You are the only survivor. 你是唯一的倖存者. He is an only son. 他是個獨子. Those are the only houses left on the street. 街上剩下來的房子僅有那一些. **2** best 最好的: He is the only man for the post. 他是擔任這個職位的最佳人選. **3** and nothing more; and no one else 只有; 僅僅: Only three of them were there. 只有他們當中的三個人在那裏. There are only two copies left. 只剩下兩本. I was only trying to help. 我只是想盡力幫點忙. He will only repeat what he hears the others say. 他只會把聽到別人說的話重複一遍而已. This compartment is for ladies only.

這個隔間專供婦女使用. If you would only tell me where it is, I would get it myself. 只要你告訴我在甚麼地方, 我就會自己去取. **4** but 但是; 不過: The room is cheap enough, only it's rather small. 這房間是够便宜的, 不過小一點. He would have enough money for his family, only he gambles most of his wages away. 他本來是有够的錢膽養活一家庭, 可是他把大部份工資都給賭光了.

onset ['ɒnset] *nc* beginning 開始: the onset of some disease 某種疾病的初起 (或發作).

onshore ['ɒn'ʃɔ:] *adj* moving towards the shore; on the land 向着海岸的; 陸上的. Also 亦作 *adv*.

onslaught ['ɒnslɔ:t] *nc* fierce, strong attack 猛攻; 猛襲.

onto ['ɒntu:] *prep* on to; upon 到…上, 在…上: He jumped up onto the table. 他跳到桌子上. Please step onto the scales. 請跨到磅秤上.

onus ['ounəs] *n sing* 單數 burden; responsibility for 義務, 擔子; 責任: The onus of the proof is on us i.e. we must try to prove it. 提出證據的責任落在我們身上. 即: 我們必須盡力提出證據.

onward ['ɒnwəd] *adj / adv* forward; on from here 向前的 (地); 前進的 (地): move onward 向前走動; 向前移動; 向前進; from now onward i.e. from now on 從現在起.

ooze [u:z] *vi* pass slowly through a small opening 緩慢地流出; 滲出; 分泌出: Blood oozed from his wounds. 他的傷口在流血.

opaque [ou'peik] *adj* not allowing light to pass through; impossible to see through 不透光的, 不透明的; 晦暗的: opaque sheet of glass 不透明的玻璃板.

open¹ ['oupən] *adj* **1** not shut or closed; allowing things, persons etc to go in or out 開 (着) 的; 可自由進出的: *an open gate* 開着的大門. *The window was open.* 窗户是開着的. *The shop is not yet open.* 商店還没有開門. **2** not having its door, lid etc shut (門, 蓋子等) 開着的; 敞開的: *an open room* 門、窗敞開的房間, 開着的房間; *an open box* 蓋子開着的箱子. **3** not covered 無蓋的; 未遮蓋的: *an open carriage* 敞篷車; *an open drain* 明溝. **4** spread out 展開的; 擺開的; 鋪開的: *an open book* i.e. with its pages spread out 翻開着的書. **5** willing to receive new ideas 樂於接受新思想的; 開明的: *an open mind* 虚心; 豁達的心胸, 無成見的胸懷. **6** not filled 空缺着的: *a post that is still open* 仍空缺着的職位. **7** that anyone can enter 任何人可以参加的: *an open competition* 公開比賽; *the open day of a school* i.e. when parents and outsiders are invited to the school 學校的開放日, 即邀請學生家長和外人到校的日子. **8** without barriers (e.g. walls, fences etc.) 開闊的; 空曠的: *the open country* 空曠的土地, 曠野; 開闊地; *the open air* 野外; 户外. **9** not forbidden 不受禁止的; 開放的: *the open season for game* i.e. when game can legally be hunted 狩獵開放期. 即: 可以合法狩獵的時期. **10** not hidden 無隱瞞的; 公開的: *have open contempt for someone* 公然蔑視某人; *an open quarrel* 公開的争吵. **11** generous 慷慨的; 大方的. **12** honest; not concealing anything 誠實的; 坦率的, 坦白的: *I want to be open with you.* 我要對你坦誠相見. **openly** *adv* without secrecy; not concealing anything 公開地, 公然地; 坦白地; 坦率地. **'open-'minded** willing to consider new ideas or suggestions; not prejudiced 願接受新思想或意見的; 虚心的; 無成見的. **the open air** the coun-

tryside, away from cities, outside houses etc. 鄉下; 野外; 户外; be fond of the open air 喜愛野外. **'open-'air** *attrib adj* taking place outside, in the open air, fond of the open air 户外舉行的; 露天的, 喜愛野外的: *an open-air meeting* 露天會議.

open² ['oupən] *vt / i* **1** make something open; cause to be open; unlock 開; 打開; 使張開; 開啓; 開…的鎖: *He opened the door.* 他開門. **2** become open 開; 張開: *The door opened.* 門開了. *The shop opens at five o'clock.* 這家商店在五點開門. **3** spread out; become spread out 使展開; 展開; 張開: *He opened the book at page five.* 他翻開書第五頁. *Their ranks opened when we fired.* 我們開火時他們的隊伍便散開. **4** make; clear 開出; 開闢: *open a path through the forest* 從森林中開出一條路來; *open a way through the crowd* 從人羣中穿過去. **5** begin; start (使) 開始: *open with a prayer* 以禱告開始; *open a debate* 開始辯論. **6** officially declare that something may be used, may start its business etc. 正式宣佈可以使用或可以進行; 開通; 開張: *open a new road* 正式開通一條新路; *open Parliament* 宣佈議會開會. **opener** *nc* something used to open something else 開啓的工具: *a bottle-opener* 開瓶器; *a tin opener* 開罐頭刀 **open something up 1** make or become open 打開; 張開; 展開: *open up a wound* 打開傷口. **2** develop 發展; 開發: *open up a new territory* 開發新地區. **3** start 開始: *open up a new business* 開設一家新商店. **open fire at or on something/someone** start shooting 向某物／某人開火: *The soldiers opened fire on the rioters.* 士兵向暴徒開火.

opening ['oupniŋ] *nc* **1** clear space or

gap 空地; 洞; 孔; 穴; 空隙: *They got it through an opening in the wall.* 他們使那個東西穿過牆上的一個洞. **2** opportunity; position in a firm that is to be filled 機會; (廠商中職位的) 空缺: *new openings in industry* 工業的新空缺. **3** start; beginning 開始; 開端: *the opening of your speech* 你演說的開始部份. Also 亦作 *adj* beginning 開始的; 開頭的: *his opening words* 他的開場白.

opera ['ɔperə] *nc* play with music in which most or all of the words are sung 歌劇. **operatic** [ɔpə'rætik] *adj* connected with operas 與歌劇有關的.

operate ['ɔpəreit] *vt/i* **1** work; cause to work; keep at work (使) 操作; 工作; 開動; (使) 運轉; (使) 起作用: *The machinery operates continuously.* 機器不停地運轉. *Who operates that machine?* 誰操作那部機器? **2** cut the body with special instruments in order to remove a diseased part 開刀; 施行手術: *It may be necessary to operate.* 也許需要開刀. *The doctor operated on several patients that night.* 那天晚上這位醫生給幾個病人動手術. **operation** [ɔpə'reiʃən] *nc/u* **1** working; the way a thing works 工作; 操作; 運轉; 運轉或工作的方式: *not in operation* i.e. not in use 不在運轉中, 不在實施中; *the operation of this machine* 這台機器的操作. **2** action; task 行動; 作用; 任務: *a difficult operation* 困難的行動; 艱巨的任務. **3** act of operating (in sense 2) 手術: *perform an operation on someone* i.e. operate on someone 給某人做手術; *undergo an operation* i.e. be operated on 經受手術. **operative** ['ɔpərətiv] *adj* effective; in force 生效的; 有效的; 實施中的: *rules that are operative now* 現在還有效的規則. (*opp* 反義詞

inoperative). Also 亦作 *nc* worker 工人. **operator** *nc* person who is skilled in making something work 操作人員; *wireless operator* 無線電員, 無線電報務員; *telephone operator* i.e. person who connects telephone calls 電話接線員.

opinion [ə'pinjən] *nc* **1** belief; what one thinks is true 信念; 意見; 看法; 主張: *respect other people's opinions* 尊重別人的意見; *in my opinion* i.e. it seems probable to me 按照我的看法, 依我看. **2** advice from an expert (of a lawyer, doctor etc.) (律師、醫生等) 專家的意見或忠告. *get an opinion* 徵求專家的意見; *get a second opinion* i.e. find out what another doctor etc. thinks on some tricky problem 聽取另一位專家的意見. 即: 聽取另一位醫生等對某些複雜問題的意見.

opium ['oupiəm] *nu* drug made from poppies which makes pain less and helps one to sleep, and can also be used like alcohol to intoxicate 鴉片.

opponent [ə'pounənt] *nc* person who is against one in a game, argument, fight 對手; 敵手; 反對者.

opportune ['ɔpətjuːn] *adj* fortunate; suitable; happening at the right time 幸運的; 恰好的; 合適的; 及時的; 適時的: *your opportune arrival* 你的及時到達. (*opp* 反義詞 **inopportune**). **opportunist** *nc* person who will seize any chance to gain his own ends, not caring whether his actions are fair or right 機會主義者. **opportunity** [ɔpə't-juːniti] *nc/u* good chance; favourable time 機會; 時機: *an opportunity for promotion* 提升的機會; *an opportunity for getting a bargain* 買到便宜東西的機會. *an opportunity to buy something cheaply* 廉價購買某物的機會.

oppose [ə'pouz] *vt* **1** fight against a person / thing 反對; 反抗: *oppose the practice of slavery* 反對實行奴隸制度. **2** set one thing against another as a contrast 使相對; 使對立; 使對抗: *oppose love to hatred* 用愛對付憎恨.

opposite ['ɔpəzit] *adj* **1** facing 對面的; 相對的: *the man opposite me* 我對面的那個人. **2** completely different; reverse 完全不同的; 相反的: *The opposite direction to north is south* 與北相反的方向是南; *opposite number* i.e. person holding an equivalent rank in a different organization etc. (在不同機構等)居相等職位的人; 對等的人; 職務相等的人. **opposition** [ɔpə'ziʃən] *nu* action against; resistance 反對; 對抗: *The prison was built there in spite of great opposition from the local people.* 不顧當地居民的強烈反對在那裏建造了一座監獄. **the Opposition** (members of) the political party which is against the Government 反對黨(黨員).

oppress [ə'pres] *vt* **1** rule unjustly or harshly 壓迫; 壓制: *oppress the poor* 壓迫窮人. **2** cause to feel ill, sad or depressed 壓抑; 使感鬱抑; 使難忍; 使感沮喪: *oppressed by the unpleasant climate* 因氣候不好而感抑鬱. **oppression** *nu* **oppressive** *adj* **1** unjust; cruel 不公平的; 殘酷的: *an oppressive government* 暴虐的政府. **2** difficult to bear 難以忍受的: *this oppressive climate* 這種難以忍受的氣候. **oppressively** *adv*.

opt [ɔpt] *vi* make a choice 選擇; 抉擇. **opt for something** choose 選擇, 挑選 (某事物): *Choosing between a high salary and a secure but lowly-paid job, he opted for the high salary.* 當他在高薪水和可靠但工資低的職位之間作出選擇時, 他選擇了高薪水. **opt out of something** withdraw from some-

thing (esp. a difficult or tiresome situation) 選擇撤出或退出某事(尤指困難或令人厭倦的處境).

optical ['ɔptikl] *adj* having to do with the eyes 有關眼睛的; 視力的: *optical instruments* i.e. microscopes etc. 光學儀器即顯微鏡等幫助視力的工具; *an optical illusion* i.e. something which deceives the eyesight 視錯覺即視力上的幻覺; 視覺幻象. **optician** [ɔp'tiʃən] *nc* person who makes or sells (eye) glasses and other optical instruments. 眼鏡和光學儀器製造者; 眼鏡和光學儀器商人.

optimism ['ɔptimizəm] *nu* habit of seeing the hopeful side of things; belief that everything will turn out well 樂觀; 樂觀主義. (*opp* 反義詞 **pessimism**). **optimist** *nc* person who always sees the hopeful side 樂觀者; 樂觀主義者. **optimistic** [ɔpti'mistik] *adj*.

optimum ['ɔptiməm] *adj* best; most profitable 最有益的; 最有利的: *What would you say was the optimum age for retirement?* 你認爲最佳的退休年齡是多少大年紀?

option ['ɔpʃən] *nc / u* right of choosing; freedom to choose; thing that may be chosen 選擇權; 選擇的自由; 可選擇的事物: *You have no option* i.e. you have no choice. 你沒有選擇的自由. **optional** *adj* which may or may not be chosen, as one wishes 可任意選擇的: *an optional question in an examination* 考試中的自由選擇題或任意選擇題.

opulent ['ɔpjulnt] *adj* rich; luxurious 富裕的; 繁盛的; 豐富的. **opulence** *nu*.

opus ['oupəs] *nc* composition (esp. musical) 作品(尤指樂曲). *pl* 複數 **opera** ['ɔpərə]. **magnum opus** chief work of a writer, musician etc. (作家、

音樂家等的)主要作品, 傑作.

or [ɔː] *conj* **1** (used to indicate a choice) (指明選擇): *You can go or stay.* 你可以走也可以留下. *You can take a pen or a pencil.* 你可以取一枝鋼筆或者一枝鉛筆. *They can come on Friday, (or) Saturday or Sunday.* 他們可以在星期五, (或)星期六或者星期天來. **2** otherwise; if not 否則; 不然: *You must study now or you'll fail.* 你現在必須學習, 否則你會考不及格. **3** that is; which means 那就是; 即指; 或者說: *He believed in astrology, or telling the future from the stars.* 他相信占星術, 也就是說相信根據星辰占卜未來. **either ... or** see *Note* on **either** 見 **either** 的說明. **or else 1** otherwise; if not 否則; 不然: *We must leave immediately, or else we'll be late.* 我們必須馬上走, 否則會遲到. **2** suggesting the idea of a threat 表示威脅: *Do it again or else!* i.e. if not you will be punished. *(informal)* 再做一次, 否則有你的好看! 即: 否則你要受懲罰. (非正式). **or so** roughly; about 粗畧地; 大約: *Give me twenty or so.* 給我二十個左右. **whether ... or, if ... or.** 是…還是…; 不論…或…: *I don't care whether you agree or disagree.* 我不在乎你同意還是不同意.

oracle [ˈɔrəkl] *nc* answer of a god to a question; prophecy 神諭; 預言.

oral [ˈɔrl] *adj* spoken, not written 口頭的; 口述的: *an oral examination* 口試.

orange [ˈɔrindʒ] **1** *nc* juicy, round fruit with a thick, reddish-yellow skin 橙; 柑; 橘. **2** *nc* tree on which this fruit grows 橙樹; 柑樹; *orange tree* 柑樹; 橙樹; 橘樹. **3.** *nc/u* colour of this fruit 橙黃色的; 橘色的. Also 亦作 *adj* reddish-yellow in colour 橙黃色的; 橘黃色的; 赤黃色的: *an orange*

dress 橙黃色的衣服.

oration [əˈreiʃən] *nc* formal public speech 正式的演說; 演講: *a funeral oration* 悼詞. **orator** [ˈɔrətə*] *nc* person who is good at making speeches 演說家, 以雄辯著稱的演說家.

orbit [ˈɔːbit] *nc* curved path of one star or planet or man-made satellite round another (恒星、行星或人造衛星圍繞另一天體運行的)軌道: *the orbit of the earth around the sun* 地球繞太陽運行的軌道.

orchard [ˈɔːtʃəd] *nc* piece of ground where fruit trees are grown 果園: *an apple orchard* 蘋果園.

orchestra [ˈɔːkistrə] *nc* **1** group of people playing musical instruments (esp. at a concert, opera or play) 管弦樂隊 (尤指在音樂會, 歌劇或戲劇上演奏的). **2** part of a theatre where the orchestra plays (劇院中的)樂隊席. *Note* 說明: an *orchestra* is different from a *band*, in that it generally plays more serious music or has a different and usu. wider range of instruments. 管弦樂隊與樂隊不同, 管弦樂隊一般演奏較爲嚴肅的音樂, 或者擁有各種各樣的通常種類較爲齊全的樂器. **orchestral** [ɔːˈkestrl] *adj*: *an orchestral concert* 管弦樂音樂會.

orchid [ˈɔːkid] *nc* type of plant with flowers, many of which have bright colours and strange but beautiful shapes 蘭科植物, 蘭花.

ordain [ɔːˈdein] *vt* **1** (with reference to God, the law or some other high authority) order; decide (指上帝, 法律或其他高層當局) 命令; 決定: *The law ordains that anyone who commits a crime must be punished.* 法律規定任何人犯罪必須受懲罰. **2** make someone a priest or minister 任命(某人爲神父, 教士或牧師).

ordeal [ɔ:'di:l] *nc* severe test; unpleasant experience 嚴峻的考驗；不愉快的經驗；折磨: *the ordeal of being shipwrecked* 遭受船難的痛苦經驗，船難的折磨．

order¹ ['ɔ:də*] *nc / u* 1 way in which things are arranged 順序；次序: *in order of size* 按大小的次序; *names in alphabetical order* i.e. names beginning with A coming before names beginning with B etc. 按字母順序排列的名字，即以B開頭的名字排在以A開頭的名字的後面，以此類推．2 state in which everything is properly arranged or in place 整齊；井然有序: *put the room in order* 把房間整理或收拾好．3 way in which something works. 工作方式，工作狀況: *My car is in good order.* 我的汽車運行情況正常．4 condition in which rules or laws are obeyed 秩序；安定: *keep order in a classroom* 維持課堂的秩序．5 command 命令: *give an order* 下令，發出命令; *under doctor's orders* i.e. ill and therefore having to obey a doctor 聽從醫生的吩咐．6 paper saying that money etc is to be handed over 匯票；匯單；授權證明書: *a postal order for 50p* 50便士的郵政匯票．7 body of rules for conducting a public meeting 會議規則或程序；議事規則: *a point of order* 有關議事規程問題．8 request for goods from a shop etc.; goods supplied 定單；定貨；定購的定貨: *deliver an order* 交付定貨．

orderly *adj* 1 wellarranged; in order 有秩序的；整齊的；有條不紊的．2 wellbehaved; peaceful 守秩序的；守紀律的；安靜的: *an orderly crowd* 守紀律的人羣．Also 亦作 *nc* 1 (military) soldier who attends on an officer to carry messages etc. 勤務兵；傳令兵；通訊員．2 hospital attendant who keeps

things clean and in order (醫院的)護理員，勤雜工．**in order that** so that 爲了⋯，以⋯爲目的: *He died in order that the others could be saved.* 爲了讓別人能得救他死了．**in order to** so as to; as a means to 以便，爲了；作爲達到⋯的手段: *You must buy a ticket in order to be allowed in.* 你必須買票方能入場．

order² ['ɔ:də*] *vt* 1 arrange; put in order 安排；把⋯整理好: *order things well* 把事情安排好．2 give a command 命令；指令: *I ordered him to leave immediately.* 我命令他馬上離開．*The doctor ordered that we should all stay in bed.* 醫生囑咐我們都必須呆在床上．3 ask to be supplied with (at a shop etc.) 要求供應；定購；定做: *I should like to order two copies of that book.* 那本書我想定購兩本．

ordinal ['ɔ:dinl] *adj* showing position in a series 順序的，依次的: *First, second and third are ordinal numbers.* 第一，第二和第三是序數．

ordinary ['ɔ:dnri] *adj* 1 usual; average; common 普通的；通常的；平常的: *just an ordinary person* 只是一個普通人．2 (US) below average; rather poor (美)在一般水平之下的；相當劣等的: *His speech was just ordinary.* 他的演講真是太差勁了．**ordinarily** *adv*.

ordination [ɔ:di'neiʃən] *nc / u* ceremony when someone is ordained i.e. made a priest or minister 任命教士或牧師的儀式．

ordnance ['ɔ:dnəns] *nu* heavy guns; military weapons, ammunition etc. 大砲；兵器；軍火；軍械．**ordnance survey maps** maps of the British Isles prepared by a British government department (英國政府陸地測量部測繪的)不列顛諸島地圖．

ore [ɔː*] *nc / u* rock, earth etc containing metal 礦; 礦砂; 礦石: *a piece of iron ore* 一塊鐵礦石; *an area containing different ores* 蘊藏各種礦石的地區.

organ [ˈɔːgən] *nc* 1 part of a plant or animal which performs some special function (e.g. the eye, nose, lungs, heart are organs of the body) (動、植物的)器官: *the organs of speech* 發音器官; 語言器官. 2 musical instrument consisting of pipes of different lengths through which air is forced, and played by using keys and pedals 風琴: *a church organ* 教堂風琴. 3 any of certain other instruments using air to produce music 類似風琴的樂器: *a mouth organ* 口琴. **organist** *nc* person who plays the **organ** (in sense 2) 風琴演奏者; 風琴手. **organic** [ɔːˈgænik] *adj* connected in some way with plants or animals 以某種方式與動植物有關的; 有機體的; 有機物的; 有機的: *an organic compound* 有機化合物; *organic chemistry* i.e. study of the nature of materials found in plants and animals (carbon compounds) 有機化學. (*opp* 反義詞 **inorganic**). **organism** *nc* 1 animal or plant; extremely small animal or plant 動物; 植物; 極微小的動物或植物. 2 living thing made up of parts that work together 生物; 有機體.

organize [ˈɔːgənaiz] *vt* put into working order; arrange in some system; make preparations for 組織; 組合; 編組; 編制; 籌辦做⋯的準備: *organize an expedition* 組織探險隊或考察隊; *organize a birthday party* 籌辦生日宴會. **organizer** *nc* **organization** [ɔːgənaiˈzeiʃən] 1 *nc* group of people who meet or work together for some special purpose 組織; 團體; 機構; 社

團; *a Church organization* 教會組織. 2 *nu* act of organizing 組織的行動; 組織; *requiring a lot of organization* 需要許多組織工作. 3 *nu* way in which different parts of a thing work together 組織; 機構; 結構; 體制: *efficient organization* 效率高的組織.

orgy [ˈɔːdʒi] *nc* wild celebration 狂歡活動: *a drunken orgy* 縱酒狂歡宴.

Orient [ˈɔːriənt] *n* the East; Asia 東方; 亞洲. **oriental** [ɔːriˈentl] *adj* eastern; from or connected with Asia 東方的; 來自亞洲的; 有關亞洲的.

orienteering [ɔːrienˈtiəriŋ] *nu* sport in which competitors use a map and a compass to find their way over rough country (參賽者自帶地圖和羅盤的)越野識途賽.

origin [ˈɔːridʒin] *nc* thing from which anything or anyone comes; birth; family 起源; 由來; 血統; 出身門第: *the origin of life on earth* 地球生命的起源; *a man of humble origins* 出身低賤的人. **originate** [əˈridʒineit] *vt / i* 1 begin; come into being 開始; 發起; 發生; 形成. 2 bring something into being; start; invent 使產生; 引起; 創始; 發明; 創作.

original [əˈridʒinl] *adj* 1 first; earliest 原先的; 原始的; 最早的; 最初的: *the original inhabitants of a country* 一個國家的最早居民; 一地區的原住民. 2 new; not taken from somebody else 新的; 新穎的; 非抄襲的: *an original idea* 新奇的思想; 獨到的見解. 3 able to think of new things or ideas 能思考新事物的; 有創造性思想的: *an original mind* 有創見的人. (*opp* **unoriginal** in senses **2** and **3**) (義2和義3的反義詞爲 unoriginal). Also 亦作 *nc / u* 1 thing from which something was taken or copied 原物; 原作品; 原版: *This painting is a copy; the original is* *in Paris.* 這幅畫是複製品；原作存於巴黎. **2** language in which a book etc was first written 原著的語言；原文: *He reads Tolstoy in the original* i.e. he reads Tolstoy's works in Russian. 他讀托爾斯泰的原著. 即: 讀俄文本. **originally** *adv* **originality** [əridʒiˈnæliti] *nu* ability to think up new things, ideas etc. 創造能力；獨創性；創見: *an inventor of great originality* 很有創造能力的發明家.

ornament [ˈɔːnəmənt] *nc* something that decorates; something intended or used to add beauty 裝飾品；裝飾物. **ornamental** [ɔːnəˈmentl] *adj* of or for ornament 裝飾的；作裝飾用的.

ornate [ɔːˈneit] *adj* very much ornamented; decorated 過份裝飾的；裝飾美麗的.

ornithology [ɔːniˈθɔlədʒi] *nu* scientific study of birds 鳥類學.

orphan [ˈɔːfən] *nc* child whose parents are dead; child whose father or mother is dead 孤兒(指父母雙亡或父母親當中一人去世). Also 亦作 *vt* cause to be an orphan 使成爲孤兒: *orphaned when his home was burnt down* 在他的家被燒毀以後成爲孤兒. **orphanage** *nc* home for orphans 孤兒院.

orthodox [ˈɔːθədɔks] *adj* generally accepted or approved; holding ideas that are generally accepted (esp. in religion) 正統的；公認的；傳統的；持正統思想的(尤指在宗教上): *orthodox behaviour* 拘於習俗的行爲; *an orthodox believer* 正統的信徒. (opp 反義詞 **unorthodox**)

orthopaedic, orthopedic [ɔːθəˈpiːdik] *adj* having to do with the study or care of deformed bones and joints (esp. in children) 矯形術的，矯形學的，整形外科的(尤用於小孩).

oscilloscope [əˈsiləˌskoup] *nc* instrument that visually displays an oscillating electrical ware on a fluorescent screen, as of a cathoderay tube 示波器.

ostensible [ɔsˈtensibl] *adj* pretended; intended to conceal something 假裝的；存心掩蓋的；表面的；外表的: *His ostensible reason for borrowing the money was that he had some debts to pay, but I knew he intended to spend it on gambling.* 他借錢的表面理由是用於還債，但是我知道他打算用於賭博. **ostensibly** *adv*.

ostentation [ɔstenˈteiʃən] *nu* showing-off; display of wealth etc, intended to make other people admiring or envious 炫耀；誇示，賣弄(財富等以使人羨慕或嫉妒). **ostentatious** *adj* fond of display; intended to make other people envious 好誇耀的；誇示的，炫耀的，賣弄的: *an ostentatious dinner party* 炫耀闊氣的宴會.

ostracize [ˈɔstrəsaiz] *vt* refuse to meet or talk to someone as a kind of punishment 拒絕與⋯見面或交談；排斥；擯棄: *After behaving so disgracefully he was completely ostracized by his neighbours.* 在他做出十分可恥的舉動之後，鄰居便完全不與他往來.

ostrich [ˈɔstritʃ] *nc* largest living bird, found in Africa and Arabia. It has long legs and a long neck, runs fast but cannot fly. (It is supposed to hide its head in the sand when in danger) 鴕鳥(據說鴕鳥遇到危險時把頭埋在沙裏).

other [ˈʌðə*] *determiner* **1** what remains of two or more things or people mentioned 其餘的；其他的；別的: *I don't want this one; I want the other one.* 我不要這一個；我要另一個. *Jones* *is here, but where are the other boys?* 瓊斯在這裏, 但是其他男孩在哪裏? *All the other papers carry the same news.* 其餘的報紙全都刊登同樣的消息. **2** extra; additional 額外的; 另外的; *Every member must bring one other person.* 每一個會員都必須再帶一個人來. *Have you any other books besides these?* 除了這些書之外, 你還有沒有別的甚麼書? **3** different; not the same 不同的; 不一樣的; *Please come back some other time, as I'm busy now.* 我現在忙着呢, 請你在別的時間來. *I would not want him other than the way he is* i.e. to be different from what he is now. 我不希望他同現在不一樣. Also 亦作 *pron* **1** other one; remaining one of the people / things being talked about 另一個; 剩餘的人 / 物: *Each of them praises the other.* 他們兩人互相吹捧. *When will the others be coming?* 其餘的人甚麼時候來? **2** different person / thing 不同的人 / 事物: *We should not think only of our own children: there are others to be cared for also.* 我們不應該只想到自己的孩子。還要關心其他人的孩子. Also 亦作 *adv* in a different way 以不同的方式: *He cannot be other than clever when his parents are so intelligent* i.e. almost certainly he is clever. 既然他的父母是那樣聰明, 他也只能是聰明的. **each other** see 見 **each. every other 1** all the others 所有其他: *Our car arrived safely, but every other car broke down.* 我們的車子平安到達, 但其他的車子都拋錨了. **2** every second; alternate 每隔一個的; 輪流的: *He comes every other week* i.e. every second week. 他每隔一星期來. **one another** see 見 **one**[3]. **the other day / week** recently 新近; 最近, 不久之前: *He must still be in town, because I just*

saw him the other day. 他一定還在城裏, 因爲我不久前剛看到他.

otherwise ['ʌðəwaiz] *adv* **1** in other ways 在其他方面: *He is rather quiet but very pleasant way.* 他相當沉靜, 但在其他方面卻非常討人喜歡. **2** in another way 以其他的方法: *I was otherwise engaged* i.e. I was busy with something else. 我在忙着别的事情. Also 亦作 *conj* or else; if not 否則; 不然: *Get dressed otherwise you will be late.* 穿上衣服否則你會遲到.

otter ['ɔtə*] *nc* small, fish-eating animal with brown fur and webbed feet 獺, 水獺.

ouch [autʃ] *interj* exclamation of pain 哎唷! 痛呀!

ought [ɔ:t] *aux* **1** have a duty to (負有責任) 應該: *You ought to help your father.* 你應該幫助你的父親. *Everyone ought to work harder.* 每個人都應該努力工作. **2** should probably; should, if things go as one expects (如果情況一如所料) 應該; 必定, 大概, 總該: *They ought to be there when we arrive.* 我們到的時候他們總該在那裏了. *We ought to have the money we need saved by Christmas.* 到聖誕時, 我們總該儲蓄够我們所需要的錢. **3** be right; be suitable 正確; 合適: *That old house ought to be pulled down.* 那棟舊房子應當拆掉. **4** (used when giving advice) be wise (用於勸告時) 明智: *It is really a very useful thing; you ought to buy it.* 這東西實在是非常有用; 你應該買下. **5** (used in speech when describing something very beautiful, dramatic, funny etc.) (用於談話中描述某些很美麗, 有趣, 戲劇性等的東西): *You ought to have seen his face when I told him I was leaving!* i.e. it is a pity that you did not see… 當我告訴他我要走時他那張

臉的表情要是你能看到就好了! 即: 很可惜你沒有看到… *Note* 說明: **1** this verb has no other form except *ought.* The question form is *ought I? ought he? etc.* The negative is *ought not* (in speech *oughtn't*) (e.g. *You ought not to go* i.e. you should not go). The opposite is *need not* (in speech *needn't*) (e.g. the answer to *Ought I to go?* is either *You ought* or *No, you needn't*). **2** it is followed by to (e.g. *ought to go; ought to do etc.*). **3** *ought* is used for both present and future. *You ought to see him now / tomorrow.* Past tense is *ought* + *have* (e.g. *You ought to have seen him yesterday*). 1. 此動詞除 ought 外並無其他形式. 問句是 ought I? ought he? 等. 否定句是 ought not (說話中用 oughtn't) (例如: You ought not to go. 即 you should not go 你不該去). 反義詞爲 need not (說話中用 needn't) (例如: Ought I to go? 我該去嗎? 回答是 You ought 你該去. 或者是 No, you needn't. 你不必去). 2. ought 後面接 to (例如: ought to go; ought to do 等). 3. ought 用於現在式和將來式兩種時態. You ought to see him now / tomorrow. 你現在/明天應該同他見面. 過去式是 ought + have (例如: You ought to have seen him yesterday. 你昨天本應同他見面).

ounce [auns] *nc* unit of weight, one sixteenth of a pound avoirdupois i.e. 28.35 grams or one twelfth of a pound troy i.e. 31.1 grams 盎司, 英兩, 唡 (常衡爲1/16磅即28.35克; 金衡爲1/12磅即31.1克).

our ['auə*] *determiner* of us; belonging to us etc. 我們的; 屬於我們的: *our house* 我們的房子; *our country* 我們的國家; *Our Lady* i.e. the Virgin Mary 聖母瑪利亞; *Our Lord* i.e. Jesus Christ 耶穌基督. **ours** *pron / pred adj* belonging to us; the one or ones belonging to us 我們的; 我們的東西: *That land over there is ours.* 那一邊的那塊土地是我們的. *This house became ours when our father died.* 我們的父親去世時這所房子便成爲我們的. **ourselves** [auə'selvz] *pron* **1** emphatic form of **we** and **us** (we 和 us 的强調形式) 我們自己, 我們親自: *We shall have to do it ourselves.* 我們將必須自己做. **2** reflexive form of **us** (us 的反身形式) *First we have to wash ourselves.* 首先我們必須洗澡.

oust [aust] *vt* drive or push somebody out (e.g. from a position, job etc.) 驅逐; 攆走; 把…逐出 (例如: 從職位, 工作等攆走某人): *ousted from his post.* (他) 被撤職.

out[1] [aut] *adj* **1** not present; away 不在的; 缺席的; 離去的; 在外的: *He has been out all evening.* 他整個晚上不在家. *The book you are looking for is out* i.e. has been borrowed. 你在找的那本書借出去了. **2** not in control; not in power 不在執政的; 下台的: *Labour are in, and the Conservatives are out.* 工黨執政, 保守黨下台. **3** far away; distant 遠離的; 遠隔的: *My friend has been out in Australia for years.* 我的朋友遠在澳大利亞好多年了. **4** not in use; not in action 不在使用的; 不在活動的: *The light is out.* 燈已熄滅了. *The fire is out.* 火已滅了. **5** exposed; so that it can be plainly seen etc. 暴露的; 顯現的, 清晰可見的: *The truth is out at last.* 真相終於大白了. *The sun is out today.* 今天太陽出來了. *His new book is just out* i.e. just published. 他的新書剛剛出版. **6** used to indicate mistake or loss 指出錯誤或損失: *I am 50p out in my calculations.* 我的計算有50便士的差錯. *I am five pounds out because of that party.* 由

於那次聚會我虧了五鎊. *You are not far out in your guess.* 你幾乎猜對了.

out² [aut] *adv* **1** (used to give the idea of movement away, either towards somebody else or to the outside, in the open air) (表示向別人, 向外面, 向戶外移動而去的概念)離去; 出; 出去; 在外: *give out (leaflets)* 分發, 散發 (傳單); *hand out (tickets)* 免費分發 (入場券); *go out (into the street)* 出去 (到街上); *rush out* 奔出去, 衝出去; *put somebody out (of his house)* 把某人趕出 (屋去); *lock somebody out* 把某人鎖在外面. **2** to the end 到底, 結束: *completely tired out* 完全精疲力竭; *fight it out* 鬥争到底; 決一雌雄; *a fire burning itself out* 燒滅了的火. **3** loudly; clearly 大聲地; 清楚地: *speak out* 大聲說; 明白了當地說; *call out* 大聲叫; *say something out loud* 大聲地說出某事. **4** so that something can be seen 明顯可見; 顯露出來: *His intelligence stands out.* 他的智力很突出. *It brings out the best in him.* 這事充分顯示出他身上的最優秀品質. *His pockets were turned out.* 他的口袋翻了出來. **5** (used to give idea of taking something from a bigger mass or group) (表示從一大堆或一大羣中取到): *find out facts* 查明事實; *pick someone out from a crowd of people* 從人羣中認出某人. Also 亦作 *vi* become known 成爲衆所週知: *Truth will out* i.e. it cannot be hidden. 真相終將大白. 'out-of-'date unfashionable; not now used etc. 不時髦的; 舊式的; 過時的: *out-of-date clothes / ideas etc.* 不時髦的衣服 / 過時的觀念等. 'out-of-'doors in the open air 在野外, 在戶外. **out for** interested only in 只關心; 只愛好; 一心爲: *He is out for as much money as he can get.* 他一心撲在盡量掙錢上面. **out of 1** because of 因爲, 由於: *do*

something out of hate / spite / kindness etc. 出於憎恨 / 惡意 / 好意等才做某事. **2** without 沒有: *out of money* 沒有錢; *out of work* 沒有, 沒有工作. **3** away from 離開: *He is out of town.* 他不在城裏. *The ship was seven miles out of Portsmouth harbour.* 這隻船駛離樸次茅斯港七英里. *They ran out of the house.* 他們從屋裏奔跑出來. **4** from among 從…當中: *in nine cases out of ten* 十次有九次. *I chose the best pictures out of his whole collection.* 我從他的全部藏畫中挑選出最好的畫. **5** from 從; 用 (製成): *made out of wool* 用羊毛製成的; *drink out of a cup* 用杯子喝; *like a scene out of a play* 像戲裏的一場景. **out of order** not working 不在運轉; 壞了; 發生故障: *This machine is out of order.* 這台機器出了故障. **out of sight** not seen 看不見, 在視線外: *Keep out of sight.* (使)處於視線之外; 躲起來. **out to** anxious to: keen to 渴望; 急要: *out to better oneself* 急於要改善自己的地位 (或經濟狀況); *out to improve things* 急於改善情況或境遇. 'out-of-the-'way difficult to reach or get at remote 偏僻的: *a rather out-of-the-way little village* 一個相當偏僻的小村莊.

outback ['autbæk] *adj* of the back country 內陸的. Also 亦作 *adv* to the back country 向內地. Also 亦作 *n* the back country 內地.

outboard ['autbɔːd] *adj* usu. in **outboard motor** i.e. engine which can be attached to the outside of a boat 通常用於 outboard motor, 即: 裝於小船外側的馬達; 艇外推進機. Also 亦作 *nc.*

outbreak ['autbreik] *nc* beginning; start 開始; 開端; 爆發: *the outbreak of war* 戰争的爆發.

outbuilding ['autbildiŋ] *nc* small building (e.g. a shed) near a larger building 大樓旁的小建築物(例如:棚,車庫).

outburst ['autbəːst] *nc* sudden happening; explosion (of a feeling) 突發,進發;(情感的)爆發: *outburst of violence* 突然爆發暴力行為,暴動; *outburst of laughter* 爆發笑聲.

outcast ['autkɑːst] *nc* person without a home or friends 無家可歸又無親友的人;被遺棄的人;流浪者. Also 亦作 *adj*.

outclass ['aut'klɑːs] *vt* be much better than 遠遠勝過或超過;遠優於: *He outclasses everyone else at running.* 在賽跑上他遠遠領先於別人.

outcome ['autkʌm] *nc* result of something 結果;結局;後果;成果: *the outcome of what happened yesterday* 昨天所發生的事情的後果.

outcry ['autkrai] *nc / u* 1 loud shouting or crying out 大聲喊叫;吶喊. 2 public show of anger 公開顯示的憤怒: *a great outcry all over the country against the government's actions* 反對政府行動的強烈怒火燒過全國.

outdated ['aut'deitid] *adj* old-fashioned; not modern. 老式的;過時的.

outdo [aut'duː] *vt* do better than 勝過;優於. *past tense* 過去式 **outdid** [aut'did]. *past part* 過去分詞 **outdone** [aut'dʌn].

outdoor [aut'dɔː*] *adj* done, used etc in the open air, not inside a house 做於露天的,用於野外的;野外的;戶外的;室外的: *the outdoor life* 戶外生活; *outdoor games* 戶外遊戲,室外遊戲. **outdoors** *adv* in the open air 在戶外,在野外.

outer ['autə*] *adj* on the outside; farther from the centre 外面的,外部的,外邊的,遠離中心的: *outer garments* 外衣; *flights to outer space* i.e. to the more distant planets and stars 飛往外層空間,星際航行.

outfall ['autfɔːl] *nc* 1 outlet of a river, drain etc.; river mouth (河流溝渠等的)出口;河口. 2 sortie 出擊.

outfit ['autfit] *nc* all the clothes or tools etc that are needed for a certain job or occasion (某一工作或場合所需的)全部服裝;全套工具,整套裝備: *an outfit for school* 上學的用品; *a camping outfit* i.e. tent, pegs etc. 露營的裝備即:帳篷,帳篷樁等. **outfitter** *nc* person who sells clothing, sports equipment etc. 出售衣服,運動器械等的商人.

outgo [,aut'gou] *vt* go beyond or faster than; excel 走得比…遠或快;優於. Also 亦作 *nc* money paid out; expenditure 支出;開支.

outgrow [aut'grou] *vt* 1 grow too big for clothes etc. 長得太大而不適於(原有衣服等): *outgrow one's clothes* 因長大穿不下衣服. 2 become too old or wise for childish things 長大或變得懂事不再愛(幼稚的事物): *He has outgrown his interest in toys.* 他已長大對玩具已沒有興趣.

outing ['autiŋ] *nc* short pleasure trip 遠足,郊遊: *go on / have an outing* 去遠足,去郊遊.

outlandish [aut'lændiʃ] *adj* strange; looking as if it comes from a foreign country; distant, remote 奇怪的;似異國的;遙遠的,偏僻的: *an outlandish costume* 奇裝異服; *an outlandish place* 偏僻的地方.

outlaw ['autlɔː] *nc* criminal; person who lives outside the law 罪犯;不法之徒;亡命之徒. Also 亦作 *vt* make it public that someone is a criminal, or that some activity is now illegal 宣佈(某人)爲罪犯;宣佈(某種活動)爲非法: *outlaw a person* 宣佈一個人爲罪犯; *outlaw the sale of drink* 宣佈賣酒爲非法.

outlay ['autlei] *nc / u* spending; amount of money spent on something 花費, 費用: *Our total outlay on repairing the house was eighty pounds.* 我們修理房子的全部費用是八十鎊.

outlet ['autlet] *nc* **1** way through which something goes out 出口, 排洩口: *the outlet of a river* 河流的出口. **2** way of using or releasing something 利用或發洩(某事)的方法: *an outlet for one's energy / anger etc.* 發洩精力 / 憤怒等的途徑或機會.

outline ['autlain] *nc* **1** line that shows the shape of something 輪廓; 外形: *an outline map of Europe* 歐洲略圖. **2** rough plan; list of main points (of a speech etc.) 草案; 大綱; 概要; (談話等的) 要點, 提綱: *I have prepared my speech in outline.* 我已準備了發言提綱. Also 亦作 *vt* **1** draw the general shape of something 畫(某物)的輪廓. **2** make a rough plan of 概括; 署述; 作…的大綱.

outlive [aut'liv] *vt* live longer than; live (on) until something is forgotten 比…活得長久; 活到(某事)被忘掉: *outlive one's disgrace.* 活久而淡忘自己所受恥辱.

outlook ['autluk] *nc* **1** what seems likely to happen 前景; 前途; 展望: *The outlook for world peace is not bright* i.e. not good. 世界和平的前景暗淡無光. **2** way of looking at things or at life (對事物和人生的) 看法; 觀點: *He seems to have a very gloomy outlook.* 他似乎持非常悲觀的看法.

outlying ['aut'laiiŋ] *adj* far from the centre (of a town etc.); distant 遠離(城鎮等的)中心的邊遠的: *several outlying farms* 幾個邊遠的農場.

outmoded [aut'moudid] *adj* old-fashioned; not modern 老式的; 過時的.

outnumber [aut'nʌmbə*] *vt* be more than 比…多: *They outnumbered us three to one* i.e. there were three times as many of them. 他們在人數上以三比一勝過我們. 即: 他們的人數是我們的三倍.

outpatient ['autpeiʃ(ə)nt] *nc* person who gets treatment at a hospital but does not live there during treatment 門診病人: *the outpatients' department* 門診部.

outpost ['autpoust] *nc* any lonely or dangerous place 邊遠的荒涼地區; 前哨; 前哨基地. *outpost of civilization* 文明的邊遠地區; 文明的前哨站.

output ['autput] *nu* amount of goods etc produced or work done 產量; 產品: *The factory must increase its output.* 工廠必須提高產量.

outrage ['autreidʒ] *nc* something very wrong or cruel which shocks and angers people (令人震驚和憤怒的)暴行; 殘暴; 凌辱: *a terrible outrage* 可怕的暴行. Also 亦作 *vt* do something which shocks people; act cruelly towards someone 引起…的義憤; 虐待.
outrageous [aut'reidʒəs] *adj* shocking; very bad 令人震驚的; 極不道德的: *an outrageous crime* 駭人聽聞的罪行.

outright ['autrait] *adv* **1** completely; not gradually 完全地; 徹底地; 直率地; 坦白地: *buy something outright* i.e. pay for it all at once 一次買下某物, 即: 即刻付清款項. **2** plainly; holding nothing back 坦率地; 無保留地: *I told him outright what I thought of him* 我坦白地告訴他我對他的看法. **3** immediately 立刻, 馬上: *be killed outright* 立即被殺死. Also 亦作 *adj* complete 完全的; 徹底的: *an outright denial / loss* 徹底的否認 / 損失.

outset ['autset] *nc* beginning 開始, 開

端; *at the outset of the journey* 在旅程的開頭.

outside ['aut'said] *nc* outer side or surface; outer part; open air 外邊; 外面; 外部; 露天: *the outside of a house* i.e. the outer walls etc. 房子的外部, 即: 外牆等. Also 亦作 *adj* 1 on the outside; near the outside 在外部的; 外頭的: *an outside broadcast* i.e. not given from a studio 實況轉播, 即: 不在播音室内進行的播音. 2 greatest possible; largest 可能性最大的; 最大的: *an outside estimate of how much something will cost* 對某事物費用的最高估計. 3 from the outside (of a house, organization etc.) 來自 (房子、組織等的) 外部的: *outside help* 外部或外界的幫助. 4 unlikely 不大可能的, 未必可能的: *only an outside chance of winning* 只不過是一次不大可能獲勝的機會. Also 亦作 *adv* on or to the outside 在外面; 向外面: *I think there is someone waiting outside.* 我想有人在外面等着. *Go outside and see what you can find.* 到外面去, 看你能找到些甚麼. Also 亦作 *prep* 1 at or on the outer side of 在…外面; 在…外邊: *outside the house* 在房子的外面. 2 beyond the limits of 超出…範圍: *outside the city* 在市外 **outsider** *nc* 1 person who is not allowed into a group, society etc or who does not wish to belong to it 外人; 非會員; 局外人. 2 horse etc which is not expected to win a race 被認爲不能贏得比賽的馬等.

outsize ['autsaiz] *attrib adj* larger than the usual size 特大號的: *outsize skirt* 特大號的裙子.

outskirts ['autskə:ts] *npl* outer parts of a town etc. (城鎮等的) 郊區; 市郊.

outspoken [aut'spoukən] *adj* saying openly what one thinks 直言不諱的;

坦率的: *outspoken criticism* 坦率的批評.

outstanding [aut'stændiŋ] *adj* 1 excellent; very much better than others 優秀的; 傑出的: *outstanding work* 卓越的工作. 2 still to be done or paid 未完成的; 未付款的: *have some work outstanding* 有一些未完成的工作; *an outstanding debt* 未償還的債務. 3 easily noticed; easily remembered; important 顯著的; 不易忘卻的; 重要的: *outstanding event in history* 歷史上的重要事件.

outstay [aut'stei] *vt* stay or remain longer than 比…停留得久; 逗留得較…長久: *outstay one's welcome* i.e. remain too long in a place 逗留過久而令主人生厭.

outstretched ['autstretʃt] *adj* stretched out; extended 伸開的; 伸展的: *welcome someone with arms outstretched* 伸開雙臂歡迎某人.

outward ['autwəd] *adj* 1 going out; going away to the outside 外出的; 向外的; 往外去的: *the outward voyage* 海外航行. 2 outer; on the outside 外在的; 外面的: *To all outward appearances, he is a rich man.* 外表上他是一個富翁. **outwardly** *adj* on the surface; as regards outward appearances 在表面上; 外表上: *Outwardly he seemed calm, but he was really very nervous.* 他外表上顯得很沉着, 其實是很緊張的.

outweigh [aut'wei] *vt* be more in weight, value, importance etc than 在重量 (價值、重要性等) 上超過…: *Honour should outweigh one's own safety.* 名譽應比個人的安全更重要.

outwit [aut'wit] *vt* deceive, defeat by being more clever than 以智騙過; 以智勝過. *past* 過去式和過去分詞 **outwitted**.

oval ['ouvl] *adj* egg-shaped 卵形的; 椭圆形的.

ovary ['ouvəri] *nc* **1** one of the pair of organs in a female in which eggs are produced 卵巢. **2** part of a plant enclosing the young seeds (植物的) 子房.

ovation [ou'veiʃən] *nc* joyful welcome (e.g. of someone who is admired); outburst of applause 熱烈的歡迎 (例如: 對所欽佩的人的歡迎); 熱烈的鼓掌; 突發的歡呼: *an ovation for a hero* 對英雄的熱烈歡迎; *a thunderous ovation at the end of a speech* 演説結束時掌聲雷動.

oven ['ʌvn] *nc* closed-in space in a cooker etc which is heated to cook food 烤爐; 烤箱.

over¹ ['ouvə*] *adv* **1** downwards; to the side 往下, 向下; 到旁邊: *be knocked over by a car* 被汽車撞倒. *He was working at the edge of the roof when he fell over.* 他正在屋頂邊沿工作時, 跌了下來. **2** upwards, then to the side or down 滿出; 溢出: *spill over* 溢出; 外流; *boil over* 煮沸溢了出來. **3** so that another side etc can be seen 翻轉過來: *turn a page over / turn over a page* 翻過一頁. **4** right through; completely 透徹地; 完全地: *read something over* 仔細通讀某事; *look over some papers* 把某些文件全部看過. **5** again; in repetition 再; 重複: *ten times over* 重複十次. **6** across i.e. idea of distance being covered 越過: *Ask your friends over to see us.* 請你的朋友過來看我們. *He is over in Germany for a week.* 他已在德國一星期. **7** remaining 剩餘; 餘下來: *have money over* 有剩餘的錢. **8** upwards; in excess 以上; 超過: *The school is open to children of five and over.* 學校招收五歲及五歲以上的兒童. *I have all I need and a bit over.* 我已擁有稍微超過我所需要的全部東西. **9** from one person, place, group etc to another 從一個人、地方、團體等轉到另一個. *He betrayed us by going over to our enemies.* 他投向我們的敵人, 出賣了我們. *Hand over that gun.* 把武器交出來. **10** everywhere; in every part 處處; 到處: *travel all over* 遊遍各地. Also 到處 *adj* finished 結束的, 完了的. *The war is over.* 戰爭結束了.

over² ['ouvə*] *prep* **1** placed above, higher than something 被置於…上方: *There was a table with an electric light over it.* 擺有一張桌子, 其上方有一盞電燈. *The ceiling over us was about three metres high.* 我們頭頂上的天花板約三米高. **2** lying on; covering or partly covering 平放在…上面; 覆蓋或部份覆蓋: *They had put a cloth over his wound.* 他們已給他的傷口蓋上一塊布. *He put some paper over the desk to keep it clean.* 他在書桌上舖上一些紙張以保持乾淨. **3** across 越過: *jump over a wall* 跳過牆; *leap over a gate* 躍過籬笆門. **4** across and down 越過…而落下: *throw oneself over a balcony* 從陽台上摔了下來; *fall over a cliff* 從懸崖掉下來. **5** all through; to many or all parts of 遍經, 遍及, 遍至: *travel all over Europe* 遊遍歐洲. *The stain spread over the carpet.* 地毯上到處都有污點. **6** in command of; in a higher position than 控制…; 職位高於…. *Who is over you in your new job?* 誰是你新職務的頂頭上司? *A captain is over a sergeant.* 上尉高於軍士. **7** during 在…期間: *I got to know him well over the years.* 經過這幾年我已逐漸對他有了很好的瞭解. **8** by means of 通過; 依靠; 用: *talk over the telephone* 通電話; *hear something over the radio* 從無線電廣

播中聽到某事. **9** in connection with 與…有關係; 關於: *quarrel over a dispute* 爲一爭執而吵架. *talk over a matter* 討論一個問題; *fall asleep over one's work* i.e. while doing it 工作時睡着了, 邊工作邊睡覺.

over-³ ['ouvə*] *prefix* too; too much 太; 太多; 過份: (before *adjs*) (置於形容詞前面) *over-excited* i.e. too excited so as to become too excited i.e. too much confidence 過於自信 *overpayment* i.e. too much payment etc. 付款過多; 報酬過高; (before *verbs*) (置於動詞前面) *overeat* i.e. eat too much (使) 吃得過多; *overpraise* i.e. praise too much etc. 過份稱讚.

overact ['ouvər'ækt] *vt / i* act a part in a play in an unnatural, exaggerated fashion 表演一角色過火, 演技過火.

overall ['ouvərɔ:l] *nc* (often *pl*) loose garment worn over normal clothes to keep them clean while working 常用複數) 寬大的罩衫(用於工作時保持衣服乾淨).

overawe [ouvər'ɔ:] *vt* control someone by filling him with fear or respect 威壓; 使敬畏: *The children were overawed by the presence of the headmaster.* 孩子們被校長的出現嚇住了.

overbalance [ouvər'bæləns] *vt / i* fall over; cause something to fall over 跌倒, 翻倒; 使(某物)倒下或翻倒.

overbearing [ouvər'bɛəriŋ] *adj* expecting other people to fall in with what one wishes 專橫的; 跋扈的: *No one liked her overbearing attitude.* 誰都不喜歡她那盛氣凌人的態度.

overboard [ouvə'bɔ:d] *adv* from a ship into the water 從船上落入水中: *fall overboard* 從船上落入水中; *man overboard!* i.e. someone has fallen off

the ship! 有人落水!

overcast ['ouvə'ka:st] *adj* cloudy; dark 多雲的, 陰暗的: *an overcast sky* 陰雲密佈的天空; 陰暗的天空.

overcharge [ouvə'tʃɑ:dʒ] *vt / i* charge too much 對…索償太高; 要價太高: *I was overcharged for my ticket.* 我買的入場券買貴了.

overcoat ['ouvəkout] *nc* long, heavy coat 大衣, 長大衣.

overcome [ouvə'kʌm] *vt* conquer; get the better of 戰勝, 克服; *overcome poverty and disease* 戰勝貧困和疾病. *past tense* 過去式 **overcame** [ouvə'keim]. *past part* 過去分詞 **overcome.**

overdo [ouvə'du:] *vt* do too much; cook (meat etc.) too much 做過頭; 表演過火; 煮(肉類等)過久或過熟: *The meat was overdone.* 肉煮得過久了. *past tense* 過去式 **overdid** [ouvə'did]. *past part* 過去分詞 **overdone** [ouvə'dʌn].

overdose ['ouvədous] *nc* too big a dose, amount of medicine etc. (藥物等)劑量過大; 過量用藥: *an overdose of sleeping pills* 過量的安眠藥.

overdraw [ouvə'drɔ:] *vt / i* get from a bank (e.g. by signing a cheque) more than one is entitled to 透支(銀行存款, 例如開支票透支). *past tense* 過去式 **overdrew** [ouvə'dru:]. *past part* 過去分詞 **overdrawn.**

overdraft ['ouvədra:ft] *nc* amount by which a bank account is overdrawn 透支額: *have a large overdraft* 透支額大得很.

overdrive [ouvə'draiv] *nu* type of high gear in a car, in addition to the ordinary gears, which allows it to cruise at a fast speed 超速轉動裝置; 超速檔.

overdue [ouvə'dju:] *adj* later than the arranged time (for payment, arrival etc.) (付款, 到達等)晚於規定時間的; 過期未付的: *This bill is overdue.* 這賬單已過期尚未付清.

overflow [ouvə'flou] *vt / i* **1** flow over the top 漫出; 溢出: *The milk is overflowing.* 牛奶正在溢出來. **2** have contents which flow over the top (東西) 漲滿, 滿得溢出: *His cup is overflowing.* 他的杯子滿得溢出來了. Also 亦作 ['ouvəflou] *nu* **1** what has flowed over 溢出物; 超出額. **2** pipe etc where liquid can overflow 溢流管; 排水管; 溢流口; 溢洪道.

overgrown [ouvə'groun] *adj* covered; grown over thickly: 長滿的: *garden overgrown with weeds* 長滿了雜草的花園.

overhaul [ouvə'hɔːl] *vt* examine or repair something thoroughly (e.g. the engine of a motorcar) 徹底檢查或修理 (例如: 汽車的發動機). Also 亦作 ['ouvəhɔːl] *nc* thorough examination for repairs etc. 徹底的檢修; 大修.

overhead [ouvə'hed] *adv* above one's head; in the sky; above 在頭頂上; 在天空; 在上面: *the sky overhead* 頭頂上的天. Also 亦作 *adj* passing overhead; not touching the ground 越過頭頂上的; 架空的: *overhead wires* 架空電線. **overheads** ['ouvəhedz] *npl* expenses involved in running a business (e.g. heating, lighting, rent etc.) which are not directly connected with the purpose of the business (與營業無直接關係的) 企業一般管理費 (例如: 取暖, 照明, 房租等).

overhear [ouvə'hiə*] *vt* hear what one is not intended to hear; hear by chance 無意中聽到; 偶然聽到: *I overheard him saying that he was closing down his shop.* 我無意中聽他說他要關閉他的店舖. *past* 過去式和過去分詞 **overheard** [ouvə'hɜːd].

overjoyed [ouvə'dʒɔid] *adj* very glad; delighted 非常高興的; 極爲快樂的: *overjoyed at the news* 聽到消息非常高興.

overland ['ouvəlænd] *adj* going by land 經由陸路的: *an overland route / journey etc.* 陸上路線 / 旅程等. Also 亦作 [ouvə'lænd] *adv: travel overland* 作陸上旅行.

overlap [ouvə'læp] *vt / i* partly cover something and extend beyond it 部份重疊; 搭接: *a roof made of overlapping tiles* 用相互搭接的瓦片舖成的屋頂. *Our holidays overlap* i.e. part of mine is the same as part of yours. 我們的假期有部份時間重疊. 即: 有幾天是我的假期也是你的假期. *past* 過去式和過去分詞 **overlapped.** Also 亦作 [ouvə'læp] *nc / u.*

overload [ouvə'loud] *vt* put too much in or on 使超載; 使裝載過重: *overload a truck* 使卡車超載.

overlook [ouvə'luk] *vt* **1** have a view from above 俯瞰; 俯視; 眺望: *This window overlooks the garden.* 這個窗子俯瞰着花園. **2** fail to notice 忽察; 沒注意到: *I overlooked this problem and shall have to tackle it now.* 我忽署了這個問題, 現在必須着手處理. **3** deliberately take no notice of; excuse 故意不注意; 寬恕; 原諒: *I shall overlook your disobedience this time.* 我原諒你這一次不服從.

overnight [ouvə'nait] *adv* during the night; for the night 在夜間, 在晚上; 一夜間: *stay overnight* 停留過夜. Also 亦作 ['ouvənait] *adj* during or for the night 在夜間的; 夜裏的; 一夜的: *an overnight journey* 夜間旅程, 一夜旅程.

overpower [ouvə'pauə*] *vt* be too strong for 壓服; 制服: *overpower an opponent* 壓倒對手. **overpowering** *adj* very strong 非常強的; 太強烈的: *an overpowering feeling of hatred* 非常強烈的憎恨感.

overrate [ouvə'reit] *vt* value something / someone too highly 過高估計 (某事 / 某人), 對⋯評價過高: *His work is greatly overrated.* 他的工作受到太過高的評價.

overrule [ouvə'ru:l] *vt* decide against 駁回; 否決; 不准: *The judge overruled the lawyer's objections.* 法官宣佈律師的反對意見無效. *Our suggestions were overruled by the committee.* 我們的建議被委員會否決掉.

overseas ['ouvə'si:z] *adj* to, from, situated in places across the sea 向海外的; 來自海外的; 在海外的, 在國外的: *overseas countries* 海外國家; *overseas trade* 海外貿易; 對外貿易. Also 亦作 *adv*: *come from overseas* 從海外來, 從國外來.

oversee ['ouvə'si:] *vt* direct (e.g. work or workers); supervise 指導, 指揮 (工作或工人); 監督. **overseer** ['ouvəsiə*] *nc*.

overshadow [ouvə'fædou] *vt* be more important than 比⋯較爲重要; 使黯然失色: *My success over-shadowed his.* 我的成功遠遠超過他的成功.

oversight ['ouvəsait] *nc* failure to notice something or think of something 忽累; 疏忽; 失察: *Your essay was not marked through an oversight on my part.* 由於我的疏忽沒有給你的文章打分數.

oversleep [ouvə'sli:p] *vi* sleep longer than intended 睡過頭; 睡太久. *past* 過去式和過去分詞 **overslept** [ouvə'slept].

overspill ['ouvəspil] *nc / u* (esp. with reference to the movement of people away from crowded cities so as to house them elsewhere) what spills over (尤指把人口遷出擁擠城市, 移居他處的) 過剩人口; 溢出物.

overstate [ouvə'steit] *vt* say too much

or speak too strongly about 把⋯說過頭, 把⋯講過火; 誇大: *overstate one's case* i.e. put one's arguments too strongly 誇大自己的論點; 對自己的論點言過其實. **overstatement** *nc*.

overt [ou'və:t] *adj* open; not hidden 公開的; 公然的, 不隱藏的: *Not standing up when he was told to was an overt act of disobedience.* 叫他起立而他沒站起來是一種公然不服從的行爲.

overtake [ouvə'teik] *vt* catch up with and pass (e.g. in a vehicle) 追上; 趕上; 追過 (例如乘坐車輛): *Only one car overtook us.* 只有一輛車追 (上並超) 過我們. *past tense* 過去式 **overtook** [ouvə'tuk]. *past part* 過去分詞 **overtaken** [ouvə'teikən].

overthrow [ouvə'θrou] *vt* defeat; destroy; take away the power of 打倒; 摧毀; 推翻; 顛覆: *overthrow the king* 推翻國王. Also 亦作 ['ouvə'θrou] *nc*.

overtime ['ouvətaim] *nu* time beyond the usual working hours, for which extra money is paid 超出正常工作的時間; 加班的時間: *work overtime* 加班工作.

overtone ['ouvətoun] *nc* suggestion; hint 聯想; 含意; suggestion: *The ceremony had overtones of sadness* 儀式帶有悲哀的氣氛.

overture ['ouvətjuə*] *nc* piece of music played at the beginning of an opera, concert etc. (歌劇, 音樂會等的) 前奏曲, 序曲, 序樂.

overturn [ouvə'tə:n] *vt / i* turn over; cause something to turn over 打翻; 翻倒; (使) 傾覆; 推翻: *The car over-turned and the driver was killed.* 汽車翻倒, 司機死亡.

overweight [ouvə'weit] *adj* weighing too much; too fat 過重的; 超重的; 過胖的, 太胖的: *You are overweight and so you must eat less.* 你太胖了, 所以必

須少吃.

overwhelm [ouvə'welm] *vt* overcome completely 徹底制服, 壓倒: *overwhelmed by superior forces* 被優勢兵力所擊敗. *overwhelmed by someone's kindness* 對某人的好意不勝感激. **overwhelming** *adj*.

overwrought [ouvə'rɔːt] *adj* tired out by too much work, excitement etc.; very nervous (因過度工作、興奮等而)過份勞累的; 過度緊張的: *She is not to be disturbed in her present over-wrought condition.* 她目前正精疲力盡, 不能受到打擾.

ovum ['ouvəm] *nc* (biology) unfertilized egg (生物) (未受精的)卵, 卵子, 卵細胞.

owe [ou] *vt / i* have to pay; be in debt 應該償付; 欠負(債): *I owe John five pounds for those chairs he sold me.* 我欠約翰買椅子的錢五鎊. *How much do I owe you?* 我欠你多少錢? He owes a lot of money to his father. 他欠他的父親很多錢. *He owes his success to hard work.* 他把他的成功歸功於辛勤工作. **owing** *adj* not yet paid 欠着的; 未付的: *There is ten pounds owing* 尚欠十鎊. **owing to** because of 由於: *Owing to the storm, the ship stayed in the harbour.* 由於暴風雨, 船隻停留在港口.

owl [aul] *nc* bird with large eyes which hunts mice and small birds (usu. at night) 貓頭鷹, 梟, 鴟鵂.

own[1] [oun] *adj* **1** belonging to or connected with oneself personally; not concerning other people 屬於自己的, 與自己有關的; 與別人無關的: *That is his own house / That house is his own.* 那棟屋子是他自己的. *I mind my own business* i.e. I do not meddle in other people's affairs. 我不干涉別人的事. *For reasons of my own, I am having*

to do with it i.e. reasons which I do not wish to discuss with others. 由於我自己私下的原因, 我和那件事有關係. **2** by oneself; without the help of other people 單獨的, 獨自的; 沒有別人幫助的: *Do you cook your own meals?* 你自己煮飯嗎? *She makes all her own clothes.* 她所有的衣服都是自己做的. **hold one's own** not be defeated; be doing as well as one's rival 不被打敗; 堅持住; 能與對手相匹敵; *As an athlete he is still holding his own against younger men.* 作為運動員, 他仍能與年輕人相匹衡. **of one's own** belonging to oneself 屬於自己的: *a house of one's own* 自己的房子. **on one's own** not with other people 單獨地; 獨自地: *He likes to be on his own.* 他喜歡單獨一人生活. *He did it on his own.* 他獨自一人做.

own[2] [oun] *vt / i* have; possess 有; 擁有: *Do you own that house?* 你擁有那棟房子嗎? **owner** *nc* person who possesses something 物主, 所有人. **ownership** *nu*. **own up to something** admit to something 承認某事: *He owned up to the theft* 他承認偷竊. *A book has been stolen, but no-one will own up.* 一本書被偷了, 但沒有人願意承認.

ox [ɔks] *nc* fully-grown castrated bull, used for pulling carts etc, or for beef (供拉車或食用的)閹公牛. *pl* 複數 **oxen** ['ɔksn].

oxide ['ɔksaid] *nc / u* (chemistry) compound of oxygen with another element (化學)氧化物.

oxygen ['ɔksidʒən] *nu* gas without colour, taste or smell, which must be present for animals and plants to live and for fire to burn (O) 氧; 氧氣 (O).

oyster ['ɔistə*] *nc* kind of shellfish taken as food, and inside which a pearl (a kind of jewel) is sometimes found 蠔, 牡蠣(可供食用, 有時能產珍珠).

P,p

pa [pɑ:] *n* child's word for **father** (*informal*) (兒語) 爸爸, 父親(非正式).

pace [peis] *nc* **1** single step in walking or running (走或跑的) 一步: *take a pace forward* 向前走一步. **2** length of a single step in walking i.e. about 2½ feet 一步的長度, 步度(約2½英尺): *several paces away* 離幾步遠. **3** speed 速度: *at a fast pace* 以飛快的速度, 快速地. *He made the pace* i.e. set the speed. 他領頭跑. 即: 他定步速. Also 亦作 *vt / i* **1** walk or walk over with even steps 以均勻的步伐走; 踱步: *pace the room* (often a sign of nervousness etc.) 在房間裏踱步(常用表明緊張不安等). **2** measure something by taking paces 用步子測量, 步測: *pace out a length of about seven metres* 用步子測出約七米長. **keep pace with** keep up with 跟上⋯, 與⋯齊步前進: *I could scarcely keep pace with the new discoveries in biology* i.e. there are so many new discoveries in biology that I cannot easily learn about all of them. 我簡直跟不上生物學上的新發現. 即: 新發現太多我無法都學到.

pacification [pæsifiˈkeiʃən] *nu* process of making peace 和解的過程. **pacifism** *nu* belief that all wars are wrong 和平主義. **pacifist** *nc* person with this belief, who refuses to take part in war 和平主義者. **pacify** *vt* make quiet or peaceful 使安静; 使平静. *pacify a crying child* 使哭泣的小孩安静下來; *pacify a country in turmoil* 使處於混亂中的國家恢復平静.

pack¹ [pæk] *nc* **1** number of things tied

up or wrapped together so that they can be carried (可以揹負的) 包裹; 捆: *packhorse* i.e. horse used for carrying packs 馱馬. **2** (often used to express contempt) number of persons / things (常用於表示輕蔑) 一夥; 一幫; 一大堆. *a pack of lies* 連篇的謊話; *a pack of thieves* 一夥竊賊. **3** number of dogs kept for hunting or of wild animals that hunt together (獵犬、野獸的) 一羣: *a pack of hounds / wolves* 一羣獵狗 / 狼. **4** complete set of playing cards (usu. 52) (紙牌的) 一副(通常爲52張). *a pack of cards* 一副紙牌.

pack² [pæk]*vt / i* **1** put things together in a box, bale etc.; fill with things 捆紮; 包紮; 裝(箱等); 把⋯打包; 裝滿(東西): *Pack your clothes.* 把你的衣服包紮好(或裝好). *Pack that case* i.e. put clothes etc into it. 裝那隻箱子. 即: 把衣服等裝進去. *Have you packed?* 你打包好了沒有? **2** crowd closely together 擁擠; 擠進; 擠滿: *Thousands of people packed into the stadium.* 數以千計的人擠進體育場. *The roads are packed with people.* 道路擠滿了人. **3** put soft material (e.g. straw) round something to keep it from breaking when it is being transported 包紮; 包裝(以防運輸中破損): *packed in straw* 用稻草包裝. **packing** *nu* **1** soft material used to prevent articles being broken while they are being transported 包裝材料; 填塞材料. **2** act of packing a suitcase etc. 包裝; 打包; 打行李: *do one's packing* i.e. pack one's suitcase 收拾行李; 打行李. **'packing case** large wooden box used for packing things in. 裝運東西的大木箱;裝貨箱.

package ['pækidʒ] *nc* thing or bundle of things packed or wrapped together (smaller than a pack) 包裹;包;捆(比 pack 小).

packet ['pækit] *nc* small bundle, box containing a number of things (e.g. cigarettes, envelopes etc.) (裝香烟,信封等的)小包,小盒.

pact [pækt] *nc* agreement 協定;公約;條約;盟約: *trade pact* 貿易協定; *suicide pact* i.e. agreement between two or more people to commit suicide. 自殺盟約. 即:兩人以上之間約定自殺.

pad [pæd] *nc* **1** something soft like a cushion, filled with or made of soft material and intended to give protection, to make more comfortable or to improve the appearance (of e.g. a dress, coat etc.) (用於提供保護,舒適或改進衣服等外形的)墊子,襯墊,護墊. **2** number of sheets of notepaper fastened together along one edge 拍紙簿,便箋簿: *writing pad* 拍紙簿,信紙簿. Also 亦作 *vt / i* **1** fill something out with soft material (用軟材料)裝填,襯填,填塞. **2** walk softly 輕步走. *past* 過去式和過去分詞 **padded. padding** *nu* **1** material (e.g. hair etc.) used to make pads (in sense 1) (墊子的)裝填物,填塞物(如毛髮等). **2** unnecessary words used to make a speech etc longer (拉長演講等的)拼湊話.

paddle ['pædl] *nc* short oar with a broad blade at one end or both ends (短而闊的)槳. Also 亦作 *vt / i* **1** use a paddle or paddles to move a boat, canoe etc through the water 用槳划(小船,獨木舟等);蕩槳. **2** walk in the water 在水中行走,涉水.

paddock ['pædək] *nc* small grass field used for grazing cattle or keeping horses in (放牧牛馬的)小草場.

paddy field ['pædifi:ld] *nc* field of rice growing in water (水)稻田.

padlock ['pædlɔk] *nc* detachable lock with a hoop to go through a ring 掛鎖;扣鎖.

paediatrician [pi:diə'triʃən] *nc* see 見 **pediatrician.**

pagan ['peigən] *nc* **1** person who does not believe in one of the great world religions 非世界大宗教之一的信徒;異教徒. **2** person who does not believe in any religion 沒有宗教信仰的人. Also 亦作 *adj*: *pagan beliefs* 異教信仰. *pagan practice* 異教習俗,異教做法.

page¹ [peidʒ] *nc* one side of a sheet of paper 頁,一面.

page² [peidʒ] *nc* boy servant (in a hotel etc.) (旅館等處的)僮僕,男侍應,小聽差.

pageant ['pædʒənt] *nc* form of public entertainment held in the open air in which people dress up in special costumes, show scenes from history etc. 古裝歷史事件的露天表演. **pageantry** *nu* splendid and colourful display 華麗的表演;絢麗多彩的展示.

pagoda [pə'goudə] *nc* oriental tower with many stories, shaped like a tall pyramid; ornamental building in imitation of this 塔;塔式建築物.

paid [peid] past of **pay**. pay 的過去式和過去分詞

pail [peil] *nc* open container with handle for carrying water etc.; bucket 桶;提桶;水桶.

pain [pein] *nc / u* **1** suffering of the body or mind (肉體或精神的)痛苦: *suffer a lot of pain* 受很多苦;遭受很大苦痛; *Do you suffer much pain?* 你覺得非常痛嗎? **2** suffering in a particular place (某一部位的) 痛, 疼痛: *a pain in one's head* 頭疼; *stomach pains* 胃痛. **painful** *adj* causing pain 使痛苦的; 使疼痛的; **painless** *adj* without pain 無痛苦的. **pains** *npl* trouble, effort 辛苦, 辛勞; 努力: *He was at great pains to comfort me.* 他十分苦心地安慰我. *The artist took great pains with the painting.* 那畫家十分用心地繪畫. **'painkiller** drug used to make pain less severe 止痛藥. **'painstaking** *adj* taking great care while doing something; requiring great care and trouble (做事時) 小心的, 細心的; 辛勤的, 苦心的; 苦幹的.

paint [peint] *nc / u* liquid colouring substance which can be put on something to make it a certain colour 油漆; 塗料; 顏料: *a pot of red paint* 一罐紅漆. Also 亦作 *vt / i* **1** make something a certain colour by putting paint on it 油漆, 漆: *paint the doors white* 把門漆成白色. **2** make a picture by using paints (用顏料) 畫, 繪畫: *The artist was painting a field and some trees* i.e. making a picture of them. 畫家在畫田野和樹木. **painter** *nc* **1** person who puts paint on something (e.g. a building, doors etc.) 油漆工. **2** person who paints pictures 畫家. **painting 1** *nc* painted picture 油畫; 水彩畫. **2** *nu* art of painting pictures 繪畫藝術.

pair [peə*] *nc* **1** two things of the same kind which are always used together 一雙: *a pair of stockings* 一雙長襪. *a pair of gloves* 一副或一對手套. **2** single thing made of two parts that cannot be used separately (由兩部分做成不能分開使用的東西) 一把, 一條, 一副: *a pair of scissors* 一把剪刀; *a pair of trousers* 一條褲子. **3** two people or things which are the same or similar (相同或相似的兩個人或物品) 一對: *a pair of scoundrels* 一對惡棍.

pajamas [pi'dʒɑːməz] *npl* see 見 **pyjamas.**

pal [pæl] *nc* friend *(informal)* 朋友, 夥伴. (非正式)

palace ['pæləs] *nc* large house for a ruler (e.g. a king) or a bishop (統治者例如國王住的) 宮殿; (主教住的) 邸宅. **palatial** [pə'leiʃl] *adj* like a palace; very grand 宮殿似的; 宏偉的; 堂皇的.

palate ['pælit] *nc* **1** roof of the mouth 上顎. **2** sense of taste 味覺. **palatable** *adj* pleasing to the taste or mind 可口的, 美味的; 愜意的, 宜人的: *a palatable dish* 一盤美味可口的菜. *To some the truth is not palatable.* 對某些人來說, 這真相是不合他們口味的. (*opp* 反義詞 **unpalatable**).

palatial [pə'leiʃl] *adj* see 見 **palace.**

palaver [pə'lɑːvə*] *nc / u* unnecessary complication (esp. one involving talk or discussion). *(informal)* (尤指談話或討論的) 空談 (非正式).

pale [peil] *adj* **1** not having much colour; bloodless 蒼白的; 沒有血色的: *Her face went pale and she fainted.* 她面色變得蒼白昏了過去. **2** not dark and not bright 暗淡的; 淡的, 淺的: *pale blue colour* 淡藍色, 淺藍色.

palette ['pælit] *nc* thin board with a hole for the thumb at one end, on which an artist mixes his colours (畫家用的) 調色板.

palisade [pæli'seid] *nc* fence of strong wooden stakes pointed at the top, used as a means of defence 欄柵, 木柵(用頂部削尖的粗木樁做成, 作防禦之用).

pall¹ [pɔːl] *nc* **1** heavy cloth which is put over a coffin, tomb etc. 柩衣; 棺罩; 墓布. **2** any kind of dark, heavy covering 暗色而厚重的遮蓋物; 帷幕: *a* *pall of smoke* 一片烟幕.

pall² [pɔ:l] *vi* become uninteresting because there is too much of it (因過多而) 厭倦, 生厭, 感到乏味: *His stories palled on me after a while.* 他的故事不久便使我感到生厭.

pallid ['pælid] *adj* (with reference to the skin) bloodless; very pale; ill-looking (指皮膚) 沒有血色的; 非常蒼白的; 病狀的.

palm¹ [pɑ:m] *nc* inner part of the hand between the wrist and the fingers 手掌; 手心. **palmistry** ['pɑ:mistri] *nu* art of telling the future by examining the lines and marks on the palm of someone's hand 手相術. **palmist** *nc*.

palm² [pɑ:m] *nc* name of various types of trees growing in the tropics, with no branches but broad leaves growing at the top 棕櫚(樹): *coconut palm* 椰子樹; *date palm* 棗椰樹.

palpable ['pælpəbl] *adj* 1 easily seen; obvious 顯而易見的; 明顯的: *a palpable mistake* 明顯的錯誤. 2 that can be felt or touched 可觸知的; 摸得出的: *something palpable* 摸得出的東西. (*opp* 反義詞 **impalpable**).

palpitate ['pælpiteit] *vi* 1 beat very quickly 急速地跳動: *His heart was palpitating.* 他的心臟直撲騰. 2 tremble 發抖; 顫動: *palpitating with fear* 嚇得直發抖. **palpitation** [pælpi'teiʃən] *nc / u* violent beating of the heart 心臟急速跳動; 心悸.

paltry ['pɔ:ltri] *adj* almost worthless; of no importance 幾乎無價值的; 微不足道的; 不重要的: *be offered a paltry sum of money* 得到一筆微不足道的錢.

pamper ['pæmpə*] *vt* be too kind to; indulge too much 嬌養; 溺愛; 縱容: *pamper a child* 溺愛小孩.

pamphlet ['pæmflət] *nc* small paper-covered book (esp. on some subject of topical interest) 小冊子(尤指有關時事問題的小冊子).

pan [pæn] *nc* metal dish, often shallow, used for cooking and other household purposes 平底鍋; 盤; 盆: *frying pan* 煎鍋, 長柄平鍋; *saucepan* 長柄有蓋的深平底鍋. **'pancake** thin, flat cake made from batter fried in a pan 薄煎餅.

panacea [pænə'siə] *nc* something which is supposed to cure all diseases or solve all difficulties 萬應藥, 治百病的靈藥; 解決一切弊病的方法: *There is no panacea for all our problems.* 根本沒有解決我們所有問題的方法.

pancreas ['pæŋkriəs] *nc* gland near the stomach, discharging a juice which helps digestion 胰; 胰腺.

panda ['pændə] *nc* large black and white animal living at high altitudes in China 熊猫.

pandemonium [pændi'mouniəm] *nu* uproar and confusion 喧嚣; 騷動; 混亂: *There was pandemonium in the hall* 禮堂裏一片混亂.

pander ['pændə*] *vi* (with to) give help and encouragement (to something that is bad in people) (與 to 連用)幫助; 鼓勵; 慫恿, 迎合: *Films sometimes pander to the public by showing violence and immorality* 電影有時以映出暴力和傷風敗俗的行爲來迎合觀衆.

pane [pein] *nc* single sheet of glass in a window, section of a window, door etc. 窗上的單塊玻璃片; 窗格玻璃片.

panel ['pænl] *nc* 1 separate area of a door, wall, panel etc which is different in some way from the surface around it (usu. by being higher or lower than it) (門、牆、衣服等上的)鑲嵌物, 方格, 鑲板, 嵌板; (縫在衣服上的)不同質料的布塊. 2 group of people who have to answer questions 回答問題小組;

panel game i.e. a game played on radio or television where a group of people take part in some kind of competition (無線電, 電視中舉行的)問答小組競賽. **panelling** (US 美 **paneling**) *nu* panels 鑲板: *the panelling on a door* 門上的鑲板.

pang [pæŋ] *nc* sharp, sudden pain or feeling 突發的劇痛; 突發的悲痛: *the pangs of hunger* 飢餓的疼痛; 餓得發痛. *a pang of anxiety* 憂慮的折磨.

panic ['pænik] *nc / u* mad fear (esp. one spreading quickly through a crowd) 恐慌; 驚慌: *The fire caused a panic in the cinema.* 火災在電影院裏引起了一陣驚慌. Also 亦作 *vi* feel fear in this way 驚慌, 受驚. *past* 過去式和過去分詞 **panicked. panicky** *adj*.

pannier ['pæniə*] *nc* one of a pair of baskets for carrying things in, slung across the back of a horse, donkey etc. (掛於馱馬、馱驢等兩側的)駄籃.

panorama [pænə'rɑːmə] *nc* wide uninterrupted view of the surrounding area (四週環境的)全景: *a fine panorama* 優美風景的全貌. **panoramic** [pænə'ræmik] *adj*.

pansy ['pænzi] *nc* short, colourful flower with flat petals 三色紫羅蘭; 三色堇.

pant [pænt] *vt / i* **1** breathe quickly 喘氣, 喘息: *pant after running* 跑後氣喘吁吁. **2** speak while breathing quickly 喘着氣說: *pant out a few words* 氣喘吁吁地說出幾句話. Also 亦作 *nc* short, quick breath 喘氣; 喘息.

pantheon [pænˈθiːən] *nc / u* **1** temple dedicated to all the gods; all the gods of a people 萬神殿; (一個民族信奉的)衆神. **2** (often *P*) building in which the famous dead of a nation are buried or given honour (常大寫首字母)偉人祠.

panther ['pænθə*] *nc* leopard (esp. a black one); (*US*) cougar (both wild animals of the cat family) 豹(尤指黑豹); (美)美洲獅(兩者均屬貓科動物).

panties ['pæntiz] *npl* item of underclothing worn by women, covering the lower part of the body above the legs 婦女穿的緊身短內褲.

pantomime ['pæntəmaim] *nc / u* (*Brit*) play for children based on a fairy tale, with music and dancing (英)(根據神話組成, 伴有音樂、舞蹈的)童話劇, 兒童劇.

pantry ['pæntri] *nc* small room in which food, dishes etc are kept 食品室; 餐具室.

pants [pænts] *npl* **1** trousers (usu. for men) (*informal*) 褲子(通常爲男人的褲子)(非正式). **2** item of underclothing fastened at the waist and extending to about the top of the leg 緊身短內褲.

papa [pə'pɑː] *n* child's word for **father.** (*informal* and *o.f.*) (兒語) 爸爸(非正式, 舊式).

papal ['peipl] *adj* connected with the Pope or the Roman Catholic Church. 羅馬教皇的; 羅馬天主教會的.

papaya [pə'paiə; pə'pɑːjə] *nc* palmlike tree of tropical America, or its fruit 木瓜樹; 木瓜.

paper ['peipə*] *nc / u* **1** material made into thin sheets from wood, rags etc which is used for making books and newspapers, putting on walls, covering parcels etc. 紙: *a bale of paper* i.e. for covering parcels 一捆紙, 即: 用於包東西. **2** piece or sheet of paper 一張紙: *The floor was covered with papers.* 地板用紙蓋着. **3** newspaper 報紙: *buy a morning paper* 買一張晨報. **4** piece of paper with writing or printing on it 文件: *I left all my papers in my case.* 我把我的所有文件都放

在我的箱子裏了. **5** set of examination questions 考卷: *a difficult paper* 一份難做的考卷. **6** something written about a matter of interest, to be read at a meeting of a society etc. 論文: *He is preparing a paper on World Population for our next meeting.* 他正在為我們下次會議準備一篇有關世界人口問題的論文. Also 亦作 *vt* cover walls etc with paper 用紙糊牆. **papers** *npl* documents which tell who or what one is 證件: *You will have to show your papers at the gate.* 你在門口要出示你的證件. '**paperback** book with paper covers 平裝書. '**paperweight** heavy object placed on loose papers to prevent them from being blown away 紙壓, 文鎮, 鎮紙.

papier-mâché ['pæpiei'maeʃei] *nu* paper which is made into a soft mass, so that it can then be made into any desired shape. (When it dries it becomes hard and keeps the shape) 混凝紙, 型製紙. Also 亦作 *adj* made from papier-mâché 用混凝紙做的: *The children are making a papier-mâché doll.* 孩子們正在做一個混凝紙的娃娃.

papyrus [pə'pairəs] *nc / u* **1** tall water plant from which the Ancient Egyptians and others made a kind of paper to write on 紙草(古埃及人等用以製紙的一種長長的水草). **2** paper made from this plant 水草製成的紙. *pl* 複數 **papyri** [pə'pairai] or **papyruses**.

par [pɑ:*] *nu* **1** average or normal amount or condition 一般標準, 同等程度, 常態: *feel below par* i.e. not feel as well as one usually does 覺得不舒服, 即: 覺得不像平常那麼好. **2** value of a bond, share etc, that is printed on it 債券或票證的面值: *Your shares are above / at / below par* i.e. they are

above / at / below the printed value. 你的股份高於/等於/低於票面價值. **3** (golf) score which is considered as a standard for a particular golf course (高爾夫球賽中) 標準桿數. **be on a par with someone / something** be equal with someone / something 跟某人/某物相等: *I don't think his ability is on a par with yours.* 我認爲他的能力跟你不同.

parable ['pærəbl] *nc* story used to teach a moral lesson 寓言, 比喻: *talk in parables* 以比喻講道.

parachute ['pærəʃu:t] *nc* apparatus which allows a man to be dropped from an aeroplane without being hurt, or goods to be dropped without being damaged 降落傘. Also 亦作 *vi*: *parachute to the ground* 跳傘落地.

parade [pə'reid] *nc* march for a display 遊行; 檢閱: *parade of troops* 閱兵; *circus parade* 馬戲團的遊行. Also 亦作 *vt* come together for a display: march in procession 列隊行進; 遊行: *The troops paraded by.* 這些軍隊列隊走過去.

paradise ['pærədais] *nc* **1** place or state of great happiness or beauty 樂園, 樂境; 極美麗的地方: *an island paradise* 極樂島. **2** heaven 天堂, 天國. **3** Garden of Eden 伊甸樂園.

paradox ['pærədɔks] *nc* saying which at first may seem to be nonsense but may actually contain some truth (e.g. *More haste, less speed* is a paradox, because sometimes you can get things done more quickly if you do them without rushing) 似非而是的雋語. (例如: More haste, less speed. "欲速則不達"是似非而是的雋語, 因爲如果你不匆匆忙忙去做, 有時你會把事情做得更快).

paraffin ['pærəfin] *nu* type of oil used

as a fuel for lamps, heating, cooking stoves etc. 石蠟油.

paragon ['pærəgɒn] *nc* example of goodness which should be imitated; someone / something which seems to have no faults 模範, 典型; 完美的人/物: *a paragon of virtue* 美德的典型.

paragraph ['pærəgrɑːf] *nc* division in a piece of writing which begins with a new line (and usu. consists of a group of sentences which deals with one main idea) (文章等的)段, 段落.

parallel ['pærəlel] *adj* **1** forming lines which are the same distance apart for the whole of their length 平行的: *two parallel lines* 兩條平行線. *one line parallel to another* 一條線跟另一條線平行. **2** similar; corresponding 相似的, 相應的: *parallel developments in both countries* 兩個國家相似的發展. Also *亦作 nc* comparison which shows how things resemble one another 比較.

parallelogram [,pærə'leləgræm] *nc* four-sided figure whose opposite sides are parallel 平行四邊形.

paralysis [pə'rælisis] *nu* loss of the power to feel or move in any part or all parts of the body 麻痹; 癱瘓; 中風.

paralyze ['pærəlaiz] *vt* **1** affect with paralysis 使麻痹, 使癱瘓: *paralyzed in both legs* 雙腿癱瘓. **2** make powerless or helpless 使失去能力, 使無法活動: *paralyze industry by a general strike* 一場總罷工使工業癱瘓.

paramecia [,pærə'miːsiə] *nc* pl of **paramecium**. paramecium 的複數.

paramecium [,pærə'miːsiəm] *nc* slipper-shaped insect 草履蟲.

paramount ['pærəmaunt] *adj* most important: most powerful 最重要的; 最高權力的, 至上的: *of paramount importance* 最重要的; *the paramount chief*

最高首領.

paranoia [,pærə'nɔiə] *nu* type of mental illness in which the person suffers from severe delusions (e.g. of persecution) (精神科疾病)妄想狂.

parapet ['pærəpit] *nc* low wall at the edge of a bridge, flat roof etc. (平屋頂,橋樑等邊緣的)低牆, 欄杆.

paraphernalia [,pærəfi'neiliə] *npl* various small things belonging to a person (個人的)隨身用品.

paraphrase ['pærəfreiz] *vt* state the meaning of something (e.g. a written passage etc) in other words 釋義, 意譯.

parasite ['pærəsait] *nc* **1** animal or plant which lives in or on another and gets its food from it 寄生蟲; 寄生植物. **2** person who lives on others without giving anything in return 白白靠他人為生的人.

parasol ['pærəsɒl] *nc* umbrella which gives protection from the rays of the sun 陽傘.

paratrooper ['pærətruːpə*] *nc* soldier who is trained to drop by parachute 傘兵部隊, 空降部隊. *pl* 複數 **paratroops.**

parcel ['pɑːsl] *nc* thing or bundle of things wrapped up and tied together (e.g. to be sent through the post); package 包裹; 包. Also 亦作 *vt* make into a parcel or parcels 將…打成一包或包裹. *past* 過去式和過去分詞 **parcelled** (*US* 美 **parceled**).

parch [pɑːtʃ] *vt* **1** make hot and dry 使焦乾: *parched by the sun* 被陽光弄得又乾又熱; *parched with thirst* 極渴. **2** make dry by heating 烘; 烤: *parched corn* 烘乾的玉米.

parchment [pɑːtʃmənt] *nc / u* writing material made from the skin of a shees, goat etc. 羊皮紙.

pardon [pɑːdn] *vt* 1 forgive, excuse 原諒, 寬恕: *Pardon my interruption*. 原諒我插話. 2 set free from prison 赦免 (罪犯): *The king pardoned all the prisoners*. 國王赦免所有的犯人. Also 亦作 *nc* forgiveness 饒恕. **Pardon?** what did you say? 請再說一遍吧?你說甚麼? **I beg your pardon** please excuse me. 對不起, 請原諒.

parent [peərnt] *nc* father or mother 父; 母. **parental** [pəˈrentl] *adj* of a parent 父的;母的.

parenthesis [pəˈrenθisis] *nc* one of the two brackets ( ) [ ] etc used to separate part of a sentence from the rest 圓括號或方括號之一邊. **parentheses** [pəˈrenθisiːz].

parish [ˈpærɪʃ] *nc* 1 area with its own church and priest or minister 教區. 2 people in this area 教區內的居民.

parity [ˈpærɪti] *nu* being equal; being at par 平等;同等: *struggle for parity of treatment* 為同等的待遇而鬥爭.

park [pɑːk] *nc* 1 place laid out for pleasure with gardens and grassy areas 公園: *public park* 公園. 2 area of grassland with trees around a large house 花園. Also 亦作 *vt / i* leave one's car etc in a certain place for a time 停車: *look for somewhere to park*. 找個地方停車. **'car park** place laid out so that cars can be left in it for a time 停車場. **'parking meter** see 見 **meter**[1].

parliament [ˈpɑːləmənt] *nc* highest lawmaking body in a country 國會, 議會. **parliamentary** [pɑːləˈmentəri] *adj* connected with parliament 國會的, 議會的. **Parliament / Houses of Parliament** (in Britain) highest lawmaking body, made up of the House of Commons and the House of Lords 英國議會(由上院和下院組成).

parlour [pɑːlə*] (*US* 美 **parlor**) *nc* sit-

ting room in a house (*o.f.*) 客廳, 會客室(舊式).

parochial [pəˈroukiəl] *adj* 1 connected with a parish 教區的: *a parochial hall* 教區的會堂. 2 narrow; limited 狹隘的;有限的: *a parochial outlook* 狹隘的觀點.

parody [ˈpærədi] *nc* 1 piece of writing written in the manner or style of someone else so as to amuse people 遊戲詩文. 2 poor imitation 拙劣的模倣.

parole [pəˈroul] *nu* 1 solemn promise on the part of a prisoner not to misuse his privileges 犯人的宣誓. 2 release from prison, under certain conditions, before one's full sentence (term of imprisonment) is complete (在刑期屆滿前)假釋出獄: *He was on six months' parole*. 他獲得了六個月的假釋.

parquet [ˈpɑːkei] *nu* floor made of pieces of wood fitted together to form a design 木條鑲花地板. Also 亦作 *adj*: *a parquet floor* 蓆紋地板.

parrot [ˈpærət] *nc* bird (usu. brightly coloured) with a hooked bill which can often be taught to repeat sounds and words or phrases 鸚鵡.

parry [ˈpæri] *vt* turn aside (e.g. a blow, a weapon, a question etc.) 擋開, 閃避.

parsley [ˈpɑːsli] *nu* garden plant whose curly leaves are used for flavouring food or decorating food when it is served 香菜, 芫荽.

parsnip [ˈpɑːsnip] *nc / u* kind of sweet, white, root vegetable related to the carrot 根可食用的防風草.

parson [ˈpɑːsn] *nc* minister or priest in charge of a parish 教區牧師. any minister or priest (*o.f.*) 牧師(舊式). **parsonage** *nc* house provided for a minister or priest 教區牧師的住宅.

part¹ [pɑːt] *nc* **1** something which is smaller than the whole 部份: *This part of the road is rough, but the rest is good.* 這部份的道路崎嶇不平, 但其他部份是好的. *A small part of the garden is covered with grass.* 這花園的一小部份給草覆蓋了. **2** piece into which something is divided 片段, 劃分的部份: *The story is told in three parts.* 這故事分三個部份來說. *A centimetre is a hundredth part of a metre.* 一厘米是一米的百分之一. **3** what someone in a play says and does 劇中人物, 角色: *learn one's part* i.e. what one has to say etc. 學習某個角色, 即: 學習自己的台詞等. *get a part in a play* i.e. be chosen to act in a play 在劇中演個角色, 即: 給戲上參加演出. **4** share 本份: *do one's part* i.e. do what one has to do 盡一個人的本份即: 做一個人應該做的事. **partly** *adv* to some extent 部份地: *be partly responsible for something* 對某件事部份地負責任. **'part'time** *adj / adv* for only part of the working week 部份時間的(地), 兼任的(地): *take a part-time job* 幹兼職的工作. *work part-time* 兼職. **for the most part** usually; mostly 通常地; 主要地; 大部份地. **in part** to some extent; in some ways 在某種程度上; 有幾分.

part² [pɑːt] *vt / i* separate; divide 使分開; 散開: *We had to part the two men who were fighting.* 我們必須把正在打架的兩個人分開. *The crowd parted to make way for the doctor.* 羣衆散開給醫生讓路. **parting** *nc / u* **1** line on each side of which the hair is combed in opposite ways 頭髮分梳線. **2** time or occasion when people part from each other 分手. **part with something** give up or away 放棄, 割愛(某物): *I don't want to part with my col-* lection of books 我不想放棄我的藏書.

partial ['pɑːʃl] *adj* **1** not complete 部份的, 局部的: *a partial loss* 部份的損失. **2** favouring one side more than the other 偏袒的, 不公平的, 偏向一方的: *a partial judgment* (opp **impartial** in sense **2**) 不公平的判決(義 2 反義詞爲 impartial). **partially** *adv* not completely 部份地. **be partial to** be rather fond of 偏愛: *be partial to sweet food* 偏愛甜食.

participate [pɑːˈtisipeit] *vi* have a share; take part in something 分享; 參加. **participation** [pɑːtisiˈpeiʃən] *nu.*

participle ['pɑːtisipl] *nc* name given to various forms of the verb (e.g. **gone; going; walked; walking**) 分詞(如 gone; going; walked; walking).

particle ['pɑːtikl] *nc* **1** very small piece 微粒: *particle of dust* 灰塵微粒. **2** (grammar) article i.e. **a, an, the**; adverb or preposition (e.g. **up, on** etc); conjunction (e.g. **and, but** etc); prefix or suffix (e.g. **in-, inter-, -ly** etc) (語法) 虛詞: 包括冠詞(如: a, an, the), 副詞或介詞(如: up, on 等), 連接詞(如: and, but 等), 前轍或後轍(如: in-, inter-, -ly 等).

particular [pəˈtikjulə*] *adj* **1** considered separately from others 獨特的, 某種的: *That particular house is very nice, although the rest of them are not.* 那座房子很好, 雖然其他房子不太好. **2** special; great 特別的; 不尋常的: *He is a particular friend of mine.* 他是我的一個不尋常的朋友. *Pay particular attention now.* 現在要特別注意. **3** difficult to please; careful 難以取悅的, 挑剔的; 講究的: *be very particular about what one eats* 對食物非常挑剔. Also 亦作 *nc* detail; single point 細節; 一點: *correct in every particular* 每一點都正確. **particularly** *adv* especially

特別地.

partisan [pɑ:ti'zæn] *nc* strong supporter of a person, a group or an idea; person who will not listen to different arguments 某人、某黨派或某種觀點的強硬支持者; 聽不得相反意見的人.

partition [pɑ:'tiʃən] *nc / u* 1 division into parts 分割, 瓜分: *the partition of a country after war* 戰後一個國家的瓜分. 2 thin wall between rooms (房間之間的)隔牆.

partner ['pɑ:tnə*] *nc* 1 person who takes part with another person / other people in some activity 合作者; 夥伴, 合夥人. 2 person who partly owns a business 股東. 3 one of two people who play cards together, dance together etc. (打牌等的)搭檔; 舞伴. Also 亦作 *vt* be a partner to 與…合作或合夥 **partnership** *nc / u* 1 state of being a partner or being partners 合夥; 合股. 2 business company where two or more people share the risks and the profits 合營公司.

party ['pɑ:ti] *nc* 1 group of people having the same political ideas 政黨. 2 group of people doing some activity together 團體; 一夥人; *party of tourists* 旅遊團. 3 meeting of a group of people who have been invited to a house for some kind of celebration 聚會; 宴會; *birthday party* 生日宴會. 4 person who takes part in an action or knows about it 同謀; 當事人; 參與者: *He was (a) party to our scheme.* 他是我們的計謀的參與者. 5 one of the people or groups of people concerned in a legal matter (e.g. a contract etc.) (合同或訴訟中的)一方.

pass[1] [pɑ:s] *vt / i* 1 go by; go on; move past or over 走過; 前進; 超過; *pass an interesting building* 走過一座有趣的樓房; *pass another car* 超過另一部車子;

pass from one place to another 從一個地方走到另一個地方. 2 hand around; transfer 傳遞; 給與: *My documents were passed from one official to another.* 我的文件從一個官員傳到另一個官員. 3 put; make go 穿過, 通過: *The rope was passed through an iron ring.* 繩子穿過鐵圈. 4 change; go from one state to another 改變; 變成: *Water passes from a liquid to a solid when it freezes.* 水結冰時由液體變成固體. 5 happen 發生: *What passed between you?* 你們之間發生了甚麼事? 6 go by, end 消失; 終止, 結束: *The time for talking has passed.* 談話的時間結束了. 7 go from one person to another 轉讓, 傳給: *His property passed to his eldest son.* 他的財產傳給他的大兒子. 8 (sport) send a ball to another player by kicking, throwing etc. (運動) 傳遞, 傳: *The ball was passed to the centre forward.* 球被傳給中鋒. 9 inspect something (e.g. accounts) and say that it is good or satisfactory (帳目)檢查後認可或滿意. 10 say that someone is successful in something 使及格, 認為某人…是成功的: *The examiners passed all the candidates.* 主考人使所有投考人都及格了. 11 be successful in something (e.g. an examination, test etc.) 通過 (考試, 測驗等), 合格. 12 spend (time) 度過, 消磨: *We passed the evenings playing cards.* 我們玩牌消磨了幾個晚上. 13 go beyond 超出, 令人無法…: *That passes my comprehension* i.e. I cannot understand it. 那使我無法理解, 即: 我不明白. **passable** *adj* 1 fairly good but not very good 還好的, 不差的, 可及格的: *He has a passable knowledge of French.* 他的法文知識還好. 2 that can be used or gone over 可通過的: *passable 'river / road etc.*

可通過的河/路等. (*opp* **impassable** in sense 2 (義 2 的反義詞爲 impassable). **passably** *adv* '**password** secret word by which sentries, guards etc know that one is not an enemy 口令. **pass away** come to an end; die 結束, 終止; 死, 去世. '**passer'by** one who happens to be going by 過路人: *The injured man was helped by a passer-by.* 那個受傷的男人得到一個過路人的幫助. *pl* 複數 **passers-by**. **pass for someone / something** be accepted as someone / something 被當做某人/某物. **pass something / someone / oneself off as** pretend that something etc is something else 以某物/某人冒充; 自己冒充: *He passed himself off as a doctor, but he was found out in the end.* 他自己冒充醫生, 但最後被查出來了. **pass out** become faint; become unconscious. (*informal*) 昏迷; 失去知覺. (非正式).

pass² [pɑːs] *nc* **1** success in an examination; grade in an examination; grade in an examination which is not a fail, but below a merit, distinction, honours etc. 考試及格; 及格; 及格分數. **2** path through mountains 山路. **3** permission to enter some place; free ticket (to a theatre etc.) (戲院等的) 免費票, 招待券, 入場券. **4** (sport) act of sending the ball to another person (運動) 傳球動作.

passage ['pæsɪdʒ] *nc / u* **1** way through a building etc, corridor 通道. **2** voyage; journey by sea 海上旅行; 航行: *book one's passage* 預定船票. **3** part of a speech or piece of writing (講話, 文章的) 一節, 一段: *an interesting passage* 有趣的一段.

passenger ['pæsɪndʒə*] *nc* person travelling in a train, bus, plane, etc, or in a car in addition to the driver 旅客, 乘客.

passion ['pæʃən] *nc / u* very strong feeling 熱情, 激情, 強烈的感情: *Hate and anger are passions.* 仇恨和憤怒是強烈的感情. **passionate** ['pæʃənɪt] *adj* having strong feelings; caused by strong feelings 熱情的, 熱烈的; 激昂的: *a passionate character* 一個熱情洋溢的人. *a passionate speech* 熱情洋溢的講話. **passionately** *adv* have a **passion for** like very much 愛好, 癖好: *have a passion for paintings* 愛好繪畫.

passive ['pæsɪv] *adj* **1** being acted on without doing anything in return; suffering without resistance; not fighting back 被動的, 消極的; 受苦而不反抗的, 不反擊的: *a passive mind* 消極的心理; *passive obedience* 唯命是從; *passive resistance*, i.e. refusing to do something, without using force and without defending oneself against force 消極的抵抗, 即: 反對採取行動, 不使用武力自衛, 反對武力. **2** (grammar) form of the verb as in *a stone was thrown through the window*. (語法) 被動語態的. 如: a stone was thrown through the window 中的動詞形式. (*opp* 反義詞 **active**). **in the passive** having the passive form of the verb 被動語態.

Passover ['pɑːsəʊvə*] *n* Jewish feast 猶太人的逾越節.

passport ['pɑːspɔːt] *nc* document to be carried when visiting foreign countries, with details concerning oneself and showing that one has the protection of one's government 護照.

past [pɑːst] *adj* **1** gone by; ended 過去的; 結束的: *We've had terrible weather in the past week.* 過去的一週裏, 我們碰上了很壞的天氣. *Our difficulties are past.* 我們的困難過去了. **2** having been in office 以前的, 卸任的: *a past president* 以前的會長; 卸任的總統. Also 亦作 *nu* **1** time gone by 過去: *talk about the past* 談論過去. **2** person's previous experience (esp. if they are unknown or not to his credit) (個人的) 過去的經歷(尤指不爲人知的或不體面的): *know about someone's past* 瞭解某人的過去. Also 亦作 *prep* **1** up to and beyond 經過, 超過: *walk past someone* 走過某人前面. **2** after (in time) 以後(時間): *past midnight* 午夜以後. **3** beyond 超出: *His stupidity is past belief.* 他的愚蠢令人難以相信. Also 亦作 *adv* up to something and beyond 走到, 超過: *We watched the people hurry past.* 我們看到人們匆匆走過.

paste [peist] *nu* **1** substance used for sticking things together (e.g. wallpaper to a wall) 漿糊. **2** hard material used to make imitations of precious stones 製造假寶石的材料: *a paste diamond* 假寶石. Also 亦作 *vt stick things with paste (in sense 1)* 用漿糊黏貼.

pastel ['pæstl] *adj* soft and light in colour (色彩) 輕淡的: *pastel shades / colours* 輕淡而柔和的色彩/顏色.

pastille, pastil ['pæstl] *nc* small sweet (usu. containing medicine for the throat) 潤喉片.

pastime ['pɑːstaim] *nc* any pleasant way of passing time; game or recreation 消遣; 娛樂.

pastor ['pɑːstə*] *nc* minister in charge of a church 牧師.

pastoral ['pɑːstərl] *adj* **1** connected with a clergyman 牧師的: *pastoral letter* i.e. letter from a bishop to the people in his diocese 牧師寫給他教區人民的公開信. **2** (literature, music, painting) having to do with shepherds

and country life 田園詩的; 牧歌式的 (文學、音樂、繪畫).

pastry ['peistri] **1** *nu* paste of flour, fat etc which is baked in an oven (often with fruit, meat etc.) 用麵粉和油等烤成的糕點 (常加上水果和肉等). **2** *nc / u* pie, tart etc which is made in this way 用此法做成的帶餡的糕點.

pasture ['pɑːstjuə*] *nc / u* grassland on which cattle, horses etc can feed 牧場, 草地.

pasty[1] ['peisti] *adj* pale and unhealthy 蒼白的; 不健康的: *a pasty complexion* 蒼白的臉色.

pasty[2] ['pæsti] *nc* pastry baked with meat in it 肉餡餅.

pat [pæt] *vt* hit gently with the open hand as a sign of sympathy, encouragement etc. 輕拍(表示同情、鼓勵等): *pat someone on the back* 拍拍某人的背(表示恭維或讚美). *past* 過去式和過去分詞 **patted.** Also 亦作 *nc* act of gently hitting with the open hand or with something flat 輕拍.

patch [pætʃ] *nc* **1** piece of material fixed onto another material in order to mend or protect it 補丁: *patch on a torn shirt* 破襯衫上的補丁; *eyepatch* i.e. protection over an injured eye 眼罩, 即: 用以保護受傷的眼睛. **2** part of a surface which is a different colour from the rest of it 斑點, 斑紋: *a black dog with a white patch on its back* 一隻背上有白斑點的黑狗. Also 亦作 *vt* protect or mend by using patches 補綴. **patchy** *adj* good in some parts but not in others 不協調的; 斑駁的. 'patchwork' pieces of cloth of various sizes, shapes and colours sewn together 雜色布片湊成的縫綴物.

patent ['peitnt] *nc* **1** authority from the government to manufacture something and also to prevent it from

being imitated 專利, 專利權: *get a patent for a new kind of car.* 獲得一種新型汽車的專利. **2** something that is protected by a patent. Also 亦作 *vt* get a patent for 獲得…的專利: *He patented his invention* 他獲得了他的發明專利. Also 亦作 *adj* **1** plain; easily seen 明白的; 顯而易見的: *It is patent that a country must educate its people to make progress.* 顯而易見, 一個國家必須教育它的人民求進步. **2** protected by a patent 有專利的: *patent medicines* 專利藥品. **patently** *adv: He is patently a fool* i.e. everyone can see that he is a fool. 他顯然是個笨蛋.
'patent 'leather leather with a very glossy smooth surface 漆皮.

paternal [pə'tə:nl] *adj* of or like a father; on one's father's side 父親的, 像父親的; 父系的, 父方的: *paternal care* 慈父般的關懷, 父愛; *paternal aunt* 姑母.

path [pɑ:θ] *nc* **1** way made across fields, through woods etc by people or animals walking 小路, 小徑: *mountain path* 山路. **2** line along which someone / something moves 路線, 通道: *the path of a ship across the ocean* 橫渡大洋的船隻航綫. *pl* 複數 **paths** [pɑ:ðz]. 'pathway path 小路, 小徑.

pathetic [pə'θetik] *adj* making one feel full of pity; sad 引起憐憫的; 悲傷的. **pathetically** *adv* see 見 **pathos**.

pathogen ['pæθədʒin] *nc* any microorganism or virus that can cause disease 病菌; 病原體.

pathogenesis [‚pæθə'dʒenisis] *nc* mode of production or development of disease 致病; 發病.

pathogenic [‚pæθə'dʒenik] *adj* producing disease 致病的, 發病的.

pathology [pə'θɔlədʒi] *nu* study of diseases 病理學. **pathologist** *nc* expert in pathology 病理學家.

pathos ['peiθɔs] *nu* quality in something which makes one feel sad, full of pity 悲愴, 哀楚. see 見 **pathetic**.

patience ['peiʃəns] *nu* **1** willingness to put up with delay, pain and other discomforts; ability to keep waiting or trying for something until one is successful 容忍; 忍耐, 耐性. **2** card game (usu. for one person) 紙牌 (通常指單人玩的) **patient** *adj* having or showing patience 忍耐的. (*opp* 反義詞 **impatient**). Also 亦作 *nc* person being treated by a doctor 病人, 患者.

patio ['pætiou] *nc* open courtyard within a house; open part outside a house (usu. paved and used for dining etc.) 房子中的內院; 房子外的涼台 (常用作就餐等的地方). *pl* 複數 **patios**.

patriarch ['peitriɑ:k] *nc* **1** father and ruler of a family or tribe 家長; 族長. **2** man of great age and dignity; founder 元老; 創始人. **3** (in Eastern Churches) bishop of highest honour (東正教中的)大主教.

patriot ['pætriət] *nc* person who loves and defends his country 愛國者. **patriotic** [‚pætri'ɔtik] *adj* **patriotism** *nu* love of one's country 愛國主義; 愛國心.

patrol [pə'troul] *vt / i* go round a town, camp etc to guard and protect it 巡邏, 巡查. *past* 過去式和過去分詞 **patrolled.** Also 亦作 *nc* **1** act of patrolling 巡邏, 巡查: *on patrol* 巡邏中. **2** group of men, ships, planes etc sent out to find out something about the enemy (人、艇和飛機等的)巡邏隊. **3** group of men who patrol 巡邏組, 巡邏兵.

patron ['peitrn] *nc* **1** person who gives help to another person, to a society, cause etc. 資助人, 贊助人. **2** saint or god who takes special care of a certain person or group of people, a church, a town etc. 守護神: *the parton siant of the town* 這小城的守護神.

patronage *nu* act of being a patron; act of patronizing 資助, 贊助, 光顧, 惠臨.

patronize ['pætrənaiz] *vt* **1** buy regularly at a shop 光顧: *I always patronize this shop.* 我常常光顧這家商店. **2** treat somebody in a friendly way while showing one thinks he is lower than oneself 屈尊俯就: *The rich man patronized his poor friends* 這富人對他的窮朋友屈尊俯就.

patter[1]['pætə*] *nu* sound of a series of quick, light blows or steps 急速的輕拍聲: *the patter of rain on a rooftop* 屋頂上淅瀝的雨聲. Also 亦作 *vi* make this sound 啪嗒啪嗒地響.

patter[2] ['pætə*] *nu* (usu. with reference to a person selling something or to a person who tells stories or does tricks to entertain others) quick and clever way of talking 順口溜.

pattern ['pætn] *nc* **1** decorative arrangement of colours and shapes on wallpaper, clothes etc 圖案, 花樣: *a beautiful pattern* 美麗的圖案. **2** model or guide for something to be made 式樣, 樣樣: *a dress pattern* 一件服裝式樣, 紙樣. **3** model which should be imitated 模範, 模型: *a pattern of good conduct* 好行爲的模範.

paunch [pɔ:ntʃ] *nc* fat stomach (胖子的)大肚子.

pauper ['pɔ:pə*] *nc* very poor person (esp. one who receives charity) 貧民 (尤指接受救濟的人).

pause [pɔ:z] *vi* stop for a while; wait 停頓, 暫停, 延緩: *He paused before speaking again* 他停頓了一下, 再說下

去. Also 亦作 *nc* short break in doing something 暫停.

pave [peiv] *vt* cover (a street, path etc) with flat stone, bricks, concrete etc. 鋪. **pavement** *nc* (Brit) paved way at the side of a street for people to walk on (英)人行道. (US 美 **sidewalk**).

pavilion [pə'viliən] *nc* **1** building at the side of a sports ground for the use of players and spectators 看台. **2** decorated building for concerts, dancing etc. 舞會, 音樂會等的彩樓.

paw [pɔ:] *nc* foot of an animal having claws or nails 腳爪: *the paws of a cat* 貓爪. Also 亦作 *vt* scratch, touch with the paws (with reference to a horse, bull etc.) 用腳爪抓或扒(指牛,馬等). strike the ground with a hoof 用蹄扒地.

pawn[1] [pɔ:n] *nc* (chess) one of the pieces which are least important 無足輕重的人或物; 卒(國際象棋中最不重要的棋子).

pawn[2] [pɔ:n] *vt* get money by leaving something of value (e.g. jewellery, clothes) which will be returned to one only when the money is paid back 典當, 抵押. **'pawnbroker** person who lends money at interest to those who pawn goods with him 典當商, 開當舖者. **'pawnshop** pawnbroker's shop 當舖.

pay [pei] *vt / i* **1** give a person money for his goods, the work he has done etc. 付款, 報酬: *pay good wages* 付給高工資. **2** be useful or profitable 有利於, 合算, 值得: *It pays to be pleasant to other people.* 對別人客氣不吃虧. **3** suffer; undergo pain or suffering 受懲罰; 報應: *pay the penalty* 遭到罰款. *past* 過去式和過去分詞 **paid.** Also 亦作 *nu* money given for work done 工資, 報酬: *bring home good pay* 拿到

好報酬. **payable** *adj* which must or may be paid 應付的. **payment** *nc / u* 1 paying or being paid 支付. 2 amount paid 付款額, 報酬. **pay (someone) back** 1 give back money which has been borrowed 償還. 2 punish someone for a wrong he has done to one 報復. **pay for something** 1 give money for 支付. 2 suffer as a result of one's crimes 受到懲罰.

pea [pi:] *nc* 1 plant with small, green seeds inside a pod 豌豆類. 2 small green seeds of this plant, commonly used as a food 豌豆. '**peanut** seed with a hard shell which grows under the ground 花生. (Also 亦作 **groundnut**).

peace [pi:s] *nu* 1 freedom from war or fighting 和平, 太平: *peace between nations* 國與國之間的和平: *be at peace* 和睦, 安息. 2 calm; quietness 安寧; 平靜: *peace of mind* 心地的平靜; *hold one's peace* i.e. not say anything 保持沉默, 即: 不說甚麼. **peaceful** *adj* loving peace 愛好和平的; *peaceful person* 愛好和平的人. 2 calm; quiet 安靜的; *peaceful scene* 寧靜的景象. '**peace offering** something which shows that one wants peace 和解的禮物.

peach [pi:tʃ] *nc* slightly furry, juicy fruit containing a large, rough stone 桃子.

peacock ['pi:kɔk] *nc / u* male bird famous for its beautiful tail feathers 雄孔雀. (*fem* 陰 **peahen**).

peak [pi:k] *nc* 1 pointed top of a mountain 山尖, 山頂, 山峯. 2 mountain that stands alone 孤山 3 pointed top or front of anything 尖頭, 尖端: *peak of a cap* 帽舌. 4 highest point or amount 頂點, 頂峯: *Traffic accidents reach their peak at weekends.* 週末交通事故最多.

peal [pi:l] *nc* 1 loud and continuous sound 響亮而持久的聲音: *peals of laughter / thunder etc.* 一陣哄笑, 雷聲隆隆等. 2 ringing of bells 鈴聲, 鐘聲. Also 亦作 *vt / i* sound, cause to sound, loudly; ring 使響; 使鳴/響; 鳴.

peanut ['pi:nʌt] *nc* 1 groundnut 花生. 2 (pl.) trifling sum (複數) 小數目.

pear [peə*] *nc* sweet, juicy fruit shaped like a falling drop of water 梨.

pearl [pə:l] *nc* small white, or almost white, gem which sometimes forms inside oysters 珍珠.

peasant ['peznt] *nc* person who works on a farm or owns a very small farm 農夫, 農民, 小農場主. *Note* 說明: the word *peasant* is not usu. used with reference to modern Britain 此詞通常不指現代的英國.

pebble ['pebl] *nc* small stone (usu. worn and made round by the action of water) 小卵石, 石子: (通常指被流水沖洗過所形成的卵石.) *some pebbles on a beach* 沙灘上的卵石.

peck [pek] *vt / i* 1 strike at, hit with the beak 以啄啄: *The bird pecked the cat.* 這隻鳥以啄啄貓. 2 pick up food with a quick striking movement 啄食: *The hens were pecking the grain.* 母雞啄食穀粒. 3 make a hole in something with the beak 啄穿: *The bird had pecked a hole in the tree.* 鳥把樹啄了一個洞. Also 亦作 *nc* 1 stroke made by a bird with its beak 啄. 2 quick striking kiss 匆匆一吻: *a peck on the cheek (informal in sense 2)* 在臉上的匆匆一吻(義2為非正式).

peculiar [pi'kju:liə*] *adj* 1 strange; unusual 奇怪的, 不尋常的. 2 special to someone 特殊的; 特殊的: *something of peculiar value* 有特殊價值的東西. **peculiarly** *adv*. **peculiarity** [pikju:li'æriti] *nc / u* 1 strangeness 奇異, 怪僻. 2 something strange 不平常的東西. **3** (of a person) something typical 特性, 特色, 特點. **peculiar to** used by, belonging to, one person / thing and not another 僅由…所使用的, 屬於(某人某物)所特有的: *plants peculiar to the Antarctic* 南極洲所特有的植物.

pecuniary [pɪ'kjuːnɪərɪ] *adj* of money 金錢上的, 金錢的: *a pecuniary reward* 獎金.

pedal ['pedl] *nc* part of a machine or instrument which is pressed by the foot 踏板: *the pedal of a bicycle / piano / sewing machine etc.* 腳踏車／鋼琴／縫紉機上的踏板. Also 亦作 *vt / i* work the pedal or pedals of something (esp. a bicycle) 踩…踏板(尤指腳踏車): *He pedalled uphill.* 他踏上了小山. *past* 過去式和過去分詞 **pedalled**. (*US* 美 **pedaled**).

peddle ['pedl] *vt / i* go from house to house selling things (usu. of small value) 挨戶販賣(通常指小貨物). **pedlar** ['pedlə*] *nc* person who does this 小商販.

pedestal ['pedəstl] *nc* base (raised piece of stone etc) on which a column or statue stands; base of a lamp, tall vase etc. 基座, 燈座; 大花瓶底座.

pedestrian [pə'destrɪən] *nc* person who goes on foot along roads or streets used also by vehicles; walker 步行者; 行人. Also 亦作 *adj* **1** connected with walking; for pedestrians 徒步的, 步行的. **2** dull; without imagination; uninspired 乏味的; 缺乏想像力的; 沒趣的: *a pedestrian novel* 一部枯燥無味的長篇小說. **pe'destrian 'crossing** place marked on a road where pedestrians may cross the road 人行橫道.

pediatrician, paediatrician [piːdɪə'trɪʃən] *nc* doctor who specializes in the diseases etc of children 小兒科醫

生. **pediatrics** [piːdɪ'ætrɪks] *nu* study of the diseases of children 小兒科; 兒科學.

pedigree ['pedɪɡriː] *nc* line of ancestors; line of descent 家譜, 家系: *pedigree dog* i.e. dog whose ancestors are known and recorded 純種的狗, 即: 血統可考的狗.

pedlar ['pedlə*] *nc* see 見 **peddle**.

peek [piːk] *vi* look at quickly (and sometimes secretly) 匆忙看過, 偷看: *peek at something;* *(informal)* 偷看某物(非正式).

peel [piːl] *vt / i* **1** take off the skin or outer covering of 剝皮: *peel an orange* 剝個橘子. **2** (esp. of human skin, wallpaper, bark of a tree etc) come off in bits 蛻皮, 脫落: *Because it is sunburnt my skin is peeling.* 由於太陽曝曬, 我脫皮了. *The wallpaper on the damp wall is peeling.* 濕牆上的牆紙正在脫落. Also 亦作 *nu* skin of fruit, potatoes etc. 果皮, 樹皮, 馬鈴薯皮等. **peelings** *npl* pieces peeled off (esp. from potatoes) 剝下的皮. (尤指馬鈴薯剝下的皮).

peep [piːp] *vi* **1** look through a hole, crack or other small opening (從洞縫中)看. **2** look quickly and secretly at something 偷看. Also 亦作 *nc* **1** look through a hole, crack etc. 窺視. **2** quick, secret look 一瞥, 偷看.

peer¹ [pɪə*] *vi* look at something long and closely, as a person who cannot see well does 細看, 凝視, 盯著: *peer at a badly written letter* 細看一封字跡不清的信; *peer into a dark room* 向黑乎乎的房間裏盯著看.

peer² [pɪə*] *nc* **1** person who has the same rank, ability etc as another 匹敵, 同輩, 同等的人: *be judged by one's peers* 由某人的同輩人來判定; person who has a noble title (e.g. a duke, earl, count etc.); person of high birth 貴族 (如公爵, 伯爵等). **peerless** *adj* without equal 無匹敵的, 最優秀的: *of peerless quality* 具有最優秀的品質.

peeve [piːv] *vt* annoy *(informal)* (使)惱怒(非正式).

peevish ['piːviʃ] *adj* easily annoyed; always complaining 易怒的; 愛抱怨的. **peevishness** *nu*.

peg [peg] *nc* small piece of wood, metal, plastic etc used to fasten things, to hang things on etc. 木釘, 釘子, 掛釘等: *hat peg* 掛帽釘: *tent peg* i.e. peg attached to a tent rope and hit into the ground 繫帳篷的椿, 即: 把帳篷的繩子釘在地上的椿子: *clothes peg* i.e. peg used to keep washed clothes on a rope so that they can dry 晾衣夾, 即: 用於將衣服夾在繩子上晾乾用的夾子. Also 亦作 *vt* fasten with pegs 用釘釘緊: *peg down a tent* 將一個帳篷釘於地上. *past* 過去式和過去分詞 **pegged.**

pekinese [piːkiˈniːz] *nc* type of small dog with long hair and a flat face 哈吧狗, 小獅子狗.

pelican ['pelikən] *nc* fish-eating water bird with a large bill and a pouch in the throat for storing food 塘鵝, 鵜鶘.

pellet ['pelit] *nc* **1** little ball made from something soft (e.g. mud or bread) 軟物做成的小丸, 小球. (例如: 泥球, 麵包球). **2** little ball of lead to be fired from a gun 小彈丸.

pelmet ['pelmit] *nc* type of framework covering the top of a curtain (窗簾上的)狹長木條.

pelt¹ [pelt] *vt / i* **1** attack by throwing things at 投擲, 投擊: *The crowd pelted him with stones.* 人羣向他擲石頭. **2** (with reference to rain, hail etc.) come down heavily (雨, 冰雹等)

猛降: *The rain is pelting down.* 雨得很大. *It is pelting with rain.* 猛降大雨啦.

pelt² [pelt] *nc* skin of an animal with the fur still on it 毛皮.

pelvis ['pelvis] *nc* hollow formed by the hipbone and the lower part of the backbone 骨盆.

pen¹ [pen] *nc* instrument used for writing in ink 鋼筆. **'penfriend** person in another country whom one has got to know through letter-writing 筆友. **'penknife** small folding knife (sometimes **pocket knife**) 小刀, 削鉛筆刀 (有時作 pocket knife). **'pen name** name used by a writer instead of his real one 筆名.

pen² [pen] *nc* small enclosed area for sheep, cattle, goats etc (家畜的)圈欄.

penal ['piːnl] *adj* having to do with punishment 刑事的, 刑罰的: *a penal offence* i.e. one for which a person can be punished by law 刑事罪, 即: 一個人會受到法律懲罰的罪; *penal servitude* i.e. imprisonment with hard labour 苦役監禁, 即: 監禁後從事艱苦的勞動. **penalize** *vt* **1** declare that an action can be punished by law or in the rules of a game 處罰, 宣佈犯規: *All fouls in football should be penalized.* 足球比賽中的犯規動作要受到處罰. **2** punish in some way 受罰, 懲罰: *Our team was penalized for turning up late.* 我們隊因遲到受罰. **penalty** ['penlti] *nc* **1** punishment 懲罰, 刑罰: *The penalty for spitting is £5.* 隨地吐痰罰款五個英鎊. **2** (sport etc.) some kind of disadvantage given against a team because it has broken a rule (運動等)犯規受罰.

penance ['penəns] *nu* punishment which one gives to oneself (often on the advice of a priest) because of

some wrong that one has done 自我
懲罰, 苦行: *do penance for one's sins*
對罪過的自我懲罰.

pence [pens] *npl* see 見 **penny.**

pencil ['pensl] *nc* narrow, pointed instrument (often made of wood and
graphite) used for writing and drawing 鉛筆.

pendant ['pendnt] *nc* hanging ornament
(e.g. something hanging from a neck-
lace etc) 垂環, 垂飾.

pending ['pendiŋ] *adj* waiting to be decided or settled 未決定的, 待裁決的:
Your case is still pending. 你的事仍未
決定. Also 亦作 *prep* while waiting
for until 在……之中; 直到; 在…之前:
pending the judge's decision 在法官決
定之前.

pendulum ['pendjuləm] *nc* weight
swinging freely from side to side:
the pendulum of a clock 鐘擺.

penetrate ['penitreit] *vt / i* **1** go into or
through 穿入, 透入: *The knife had
penetrated his body.* 刀刺入他的身體.
2 see through 看穿, 洞察, 瞭解: *Our
eyes could not penetrate the mist.* 我
們的眼睛不能看透大霧. **3** spread
through 滲透, 瀰漫: *A smell penetrated the whole house.* 一種氣味瀰漫
了全屋. **penetration** [peni'treiʃən] *nu*
penetrating *adj* **1** loud and clear 銳
利的, 尖銳的, 響亮的: *a penetrating
cry* 尖銳的喊聲. **2** piercing 敏銳的, 有
見識的: *a penetrating glance* 敏銳的
觀察.

penguin ['peŋgwin] *nc* bird found in the
Antarctic which has small wings (called flippers) used for swimming 企鵝.

penicillin [peni'silin] *nu* drug which
prevents the growth of some types of
bacteria 青黴素, 盤尼西林.

penicillium [ˌpeni'siliəm] *nc* any fungus
of the genus penicillium, certain spe-

cies of which are used in cheesemak-
ing and as the source of penicillin 青
黴菌.

peninsula [pe'ninsjulə] *nc* area of land
almost surrounded by water or stretching far out into the water 半島.

penis ['pi:nis] *nc* the male sex organ 陰
莖, 雄性動物的生殖器.

penitence ['penitns] *nu* sorrow for having done wrong 悔罪, 懺悔. **penitent**
adj feeling or showing regret 悔罪的,
後悔的. (*opp* 反義詞 **impenitent**).

penitentiary [peni'tenʃəri] *nc* (mainly
US) prison (主要用於美) 監獄.

pennant, pennon ['penən(t)] *nc* long,
narrow flag (usu. like a triangle in
shape) 信號旗, 小旗(常呈三角形).

penny ['peni] *nc* copper coin of low
value 便士. (in Britain formerly 12
pennies＝1 shilling, now 100 pennies
＝1 pound, in the USA and Canada a
penny is another name for a cent, and
100 cents＝1 dollar). (在英國, 以前12
便士等於一先令, 現在一百便士等於一
鎊, 在美國和加拿大也叫做分, 一百分等
於一元). *pl* 複數 **pennies** (for a number of coins) and **pence** [pens] *npl*
for value (e.g. *a pencil costing five
pence*). pennies 指許多銅幣或硬幣,
pence 指價值(例如: 一枝價值五便士的
鉛筆). **penniless** *adj* without any
money 身無分文的; 貧困的.

pension ['penʃən] *nc* regular payment
which is not in exchange for work
(e.g. money given by the State to old
people or injured soldiers, or by an
employer to someone who used to
work for him) 養老金, 退休金, 撫恤金.
(例如: 政府給老人或傷殘退伍士兵, 老
闆給以前的雇員的錢). **pensioner** *nc*
person who receives a pension 領養
老金或退休金者.

pensive ['pensiv] *adj* deep in thought

沉思的，焦慮的：*look rather pensive*
顯得比較焦慮．

pent-up ['pent'ʌp] *adj* shut-in; not
released 關閉的；壓鬱的：*pent-up emotions* 壓抑的情緒．

pentagon ['pentəgən] *nc* figure with five
sides and five angles 五角形．

penthouse ['penthaus] *nc* 1 (mainly *US*)
apartment or house on the top of a
building (主要用於美) 閣樓：*luxury
penthouse* 豪華的閣樓．2 kind of hut
built against a wall with its roof sloping down from the wall 遮簷，披屋．

people ['piːpl] *n* 1 men, women and
children 人：*The room was full of
people.* 屋裏都是人．*He knows a lot
of people.* 他認得許多人．2 persons
in a state, as a group 人民；民眾：
*Government should be for the benefit
of the people.* 政府應該維護人民的利
益．3 working classes those without
the benefit of wealth, position 工人階
級；平民：*He rose from the people to
be a cabinet minister.* 他從平民擢升爲
內閣部長．4 race; nation 民族；家族：
a very brave people 一個很勇敢的民
族；*the different peoples of the world*
世界上不同的民族．Also 亦作 *vt* fill
with people; put people in a country
使住滿，居住．*Note* 說明：in senses 1,
2, 3 *people* is *sing* in form but should
be treated as a *pl* noun in every other
way (e.g. taking a *pl* verb *Many people were there* and *pl adj* where
needed *many people*, not much people) 用於義 1, 2, 3的 people 形式上是
單數，但應作複數處理（例如：用複數動
詞，和形容詞用 many，不用 much）．In
sense 4 *people* is a countable noun
like *race* or *nation* 用於義 4 的 people
和 race, nation 一樣，都是可數名詞．

pep [pep] *nu* energy; liveliness 精力，活
力，精神：*pep pills* i.e. pills to give

energy (*informal*) 提神丸，即：可提神
活力的藥丸(非正式)．

pepper ['pepə*] 1 *nu* hot-tasting powder made from crushed seeds of certain plants, and used for flavouring
food 胡椒粉．2 *nc* one of different
kinds of green or red vegetables used
as food 一種可食用的紅或綠的蔬菜．
Also 亦作 *vt* put pepper on food 撒胡
椒粉於(食物)．**peppermint 1** *nu*
plant grown for its oil, which is used
in medicine and for flavouring sweets
薄荷．2 *nc* type of sweet flavoured
with peppermint 薄荷糖．

peptic ['peptik] *adj* 1 digestive; promoting digestion 消化的；助消化的．2 of
or pertaining to pepsin 胃液的．Also
亦作 *nc* substance promoting digestion 消化劑．

per [pɜː*] *prep* for each; in each 每：*a
salary of £2,000 per annum* i.e. for
each year 每年兩千英鎊的工資；*fifty
per cent* i.e. 50 in every hundred 百分
之五十，即：每一百個中佔五十個；*cost-
ing 5 pence per ounce* 每盎司價格爲
五便士．

perceive [pə'siːv] *vt* become aware of
through any of the senses; see; understand 察覺；發覺；理解：*I perceive that
you are tired* 我看出你累了．**per-
ceptible** [pə'septibl] *adj* that can be
perceived 可覺察的，可理解的：*a per-
ceptible change in temperature* 可覺察
的溫度變化 (*opp* 反義詞 **impercepti-
ble**)．**perception** [pə'sepʃən] *nc / u*
act or power of perceiving 洞察力，理
解力．**perceptive** *adj* connected with
perception; having perception 感覺敏
銳的；有洞察力的：*a very perceptive
person* i.e. one who understands
things well 一個很有洞察力的人，即：
一個善於理解事物的人．

percentage [pə'sentidʒ] *nc* amount

given as if it is part of a whole which is a hundred 百分率, 百分比.

perch¹ [pə:tʃ] *nc* branch, rod or anything else on which a bird rests 棲枝, 棲木. Also 亦作 *vt / i* **1** come to rest on 棲息: *The bird perched on my shoulder.* 這隻鳥棲息在我的肩上. **2** set or be situated in a high place 坐, 座落 (於高處): *perched on a high stool* 坐在高櫈子上; *a building perched on top of a hill* 座落在山頂上的樓房.

perch² [pə:tʃ] *nc* type of freshwater fish 鱸魚.

percolator ['pə:kəleitə*] *nc* kind of coffee pot in which boiling water is made to pass through ground coffee 煮咖啡壺.

percussion [pə'kʌʃən] *nu* striking of two (usu. hard) things against one another 撞擊. **per'cussion instrument** musical instrument which is played by striking it (e.g. drums) 打擊樂器. (例如: 鼓).

peremptory [pə'remptəri] *adj* **1** fond of giving commands; insisting that commands must be obeyed 專橫的; 強制的; *person with a peremptory manner* 態度專橫的人. **2** not allowing any question or refusal 不容反抗的, 絕對的; *a peremptory command* 絕對的命令.

perennial [pə'reniəl] *adj* **1** lasting for a very long time 永久的, 不斷的, 長久的; *a perennial source of pleasure* 永久的快樂的源泉. **2** (with reference to flowers etc) lasting more than two years (指花等)四季不斷的, 終年的. Also 亦作 *nc* perennial plant 多年生植物.

perfect ['pə:fekt] *adj* **1** without any fault; excellent 完美的, 無瑕的; 優越的; *in perfect condition* 條件優越, 完

好無損. (*opp* 反義詞 **imperfect**). **2** complete; with all its parts 全部的; 完整的. **3** complete; utter 完全的; 絕對的; 不折不扣的. *a perfect stranger* 完全陌生的人. Also 亦作 [pə'fekt] *vt* make perfect 使完美無瑕. **perfectly** *adv* completely; very well 正確地; 非常好地. **perfection** [pə'fekʃən] *nc / u* state of making perfect or being perfect 完全, 完美, 圓滿. **perfectionist** [pə'fekʃənist] *nc* person who is very careful about small details and is not satisfied unless something is perfect 至善論者, 力求完美者.

perforate ['pə:fəreit] *vt / i* make a hole or holes through (esp. through a piece of paper so that it can easily be torn off) 打洞, 穿孔. (尤指在紙上打洞, 便於撕開). **perforation** [pə:fə'reiʃən] **1** *nc* hole made in something 穿孔, 打洞. **2** *nu* line of holes made on paper (e.g. on a sheet of stamps so that each stamp can be easily torn off) 排孔, 接縫孔. (例如: 郵票上的接縫孔, 便於撕開).

perform [pə'fo:m] *vt / i* **1** do; carry out 做; 實行, 執行: *The doctor performed a difficult operation.* 醫生做了一個困難的手術. *They performed their tasks.* 他們執行了他們的任務. **2** do something for an audience (e.g. sing, act etc.) 表演, 演, 奏(例如: 唱歌, 演戲等): *perform in a play / concert etc.* 演戲, 音樂會上演出等. **performance** *nc / u* **1** something performed 完成的事; *the performance of one's duties* 某人任務的完成. **2** something done before an audience (e.g. a play, concert etc) 演出, 表演(例如: 演戲, 音樂會等): *Did you enjoy the performance last night?* 你喜歡昨晚的演出嗎? **performer** *nc* person who performs (esp. before an audience) 表演者. (尤指上台演出).

perfoming animals animals which have been trained to do tricks before an audience 會表演的動物.

perfume ['pə:fju:m] *nc / u* **1** sweet, pleasant smell 芳香, 香味: *the perfume of a flower* 花香. **2** liquid that has a sweet, pleasant smell 香水.

perfunctory [pə'lʌŋktəri] *adj* **1** done carelessly and without interest 草率的, 敷衍的: *give something only a perfunctory glance* 對某事不屑一顧. **2** acting in a careless, uninterested manner 行爲草率的, 不關心的.

perhaps [pə'hæps] *adv* it may be; possibly 也許; 可能: *Perhaps he will be there tonight.* 也許他今晚會到那裏去.

peril ['peril] *nc / u* great danger 危險: *in peril* 在危險中: *at your peril* i.e. at your own risk 冒危險, 即: 你自己承擔風險. **perilous** *adj* dangerous 危險的.

perimeter [pə'rimitə*] *nc* **1** outside boundary of a surface or figure 週界, 週圍, 周. **2** length of such a boundary 周長.

period ['piəriəd] *nc* **1** certain length of time 時期, 時代: *the period of the French Revolution* 法國大革命時期. *a period of war and confusion* 戰爭混亂時期: *a period of five minutes* 五分鐘時間. **2** one of the parts into which a school day is divided 一節, 一堂: *the mathematics period* 數學課. **3** mark which indicates the end of a sentence in writing 句點. (Also 亦作 **full-stop**). **4** same as **menstruation** 月經期; 同 menstruation. Also 亦作 *adj* typical of a certain time in the past 有某時代特徵的: *period furniture* 具有某時代特徵的傢具. **periodic** [piəri'ɔdik] *adj* happening from time to time 不時發生的, 週期的. **periodical** [piəri'ɔdikl] *adj* periodic 週期的. Also 亦作 *nc*

magazine, journal or newspaper 定期刊物, 雜誌. **periodically** *adv*.

periphery [pə'rifəri] *nc* line or area around something 外圍, 四週, 週界. **peripheral** *adj*.

periscope ['periskoup] *nc* long tube with mirrors placed in it so that people who are lower down (e.g. in a submarine) can see what is happening above them (潛水艇的)潛望鏡.

perish ['periʃ] *vt / i* **1** die in a fire, accident etc (在災禍中)死掉: *Five people perished in the fire* 五人死于大火. **2** (with reference to certain substances) decay or become useless; make useless; destroy (指某些物質)毀壞, 腐爛: *The rubber has perished.* 橡膠已損壞了. **perishable** *adj* (esp. of food) liable to go bad (尤指食品)易壞的. (*opp* 反義詞 **imperishable**). **perished with cold** feeling very cold 感到很冷.

perjury ['pə:dʒəri] *nc / u* act of swearing on an oath (usu. in a court of law) that something is true when it is not (通常用于法院)僞證, 假誓, 僞證罪.

perk¹ [pə:k] *vi* (always with **up**) **1** become lively and gay (after being depressed or ill etc.)(常與 up 連用)快活起來, 振作起來. (病後或沮喪之後等): *The child soon perked up when he saw his mother.* 孩子看到他母親時精神馬上振作起來. **2** raise quickly 竪起: *The dog perked up its ears.* (*informal*) 狗竪起牠的耳朵. (非正式). **perky** *adj* smart; lively. (*informal*) 活潑的; 伶俐的. (非正式).

perk² [pə:k] *nc* informal short form of **perquisite.** perquisite 非正式縮畧形式.

perm [pə:m] *nc* informal short form of **permanent wave** and of **permutation.** permanent wave 和 permutation

非正式縮畧形式.

permanent [ˈpəːmənənt] *adj* continuing for a long time; intended to last 永久的; 耐久的: *a permanent arrangement* 長期的安排: *a permanent building* 永久性的樓房. (*opp* 反義詞 **temporary**). **permanently** *adv* **permanence** *nu* **permanent wave** way of treating hair so that it is shaped with waves or curls which are supposed to stay in place for some months (informally shortened to **perm**) 電燙髮(非正式地縮寫爲 perm).

permeate [ˈpəːmieit] *vt / i* spread through; soak through 擴散;深透;滲入: *Water had permeated (through) the sand.* 水滲入沙中. *The new ideas had permeated (through) the whole country.* 新思想擴散到全國. **permeable** [ˈpəːmiəbl] *adj* able to be permeated by liquids 可滲透的, 可透過的: *a permeable layer of soil* 一層可滲透的泥土. (*opp* 反義詞 **impermeable**).

permit [pəˈmit] *vt / i* allow 允許, 容許, 讓: *Permit me to explain.* 請讓我來解釋. *Smoking is not permitted.* 不准吸烟. *past* 過去式和過去分詞 **permitted**. Also 亦作 [ˈpəːmit] *nc* written order which permits one to do something, go somewhere etc 許可證: *a special permit to visit a military area* 訪問軍事區的特別許可證. **permissible** [pəˈmisibl] *adj* that may be allowed 可容許的, 可承認的. **permission** [pəˈmiʃən] *nu* act of permitting 允許, 准許: *His parents gave him permission to go to the scout camp.* 他的父母允許他去露營. *Ask your teacher's permission.* 請求你的老師的准許. **permissive** [pəˈmisiv] *adj* allowing too many things 縱容的: *permissive parents* 縱容子女的父母.

permutation [ˌpəːmjuˈteiʃən] *nc*

(mathematics) order or change of the order in which a certain number of things are arranged (informally shortened to **perm**) (數學)排列變化. (非正式地縮寫爲 perm).

perpendicular [ˌpəːpənˈdikjulə*] *adj* **1** standing straight up; upright 垂直的. **2** at right angles to another line or surface 成直角的.

perpetrate [ˈpəːpitreit] *vt* do or commit something bad (e.g. a crime or mistake) 做(壞事), 犯(過失) (例如: 犯罪, 犯錯誤等).

perpetual [pəˈpetjuəl] *adj* **1** lasting forever; lasting for a long time 永久的; 終身的: *He is on a perpetual search for truth.* 他在尋找永恒的真理. **2** continual; happening often 不斷的; 常發生的: *That dog is a perpetual nuisance.* 那隻狗是經常惹人討厭的東西. **perpetually** *adv* **perpetuate** [pəˈpetjueit] *vt* preserve; keep from being forgotten 使永存;使人永記不忘: *perpetuate someone's memory* 使某人名垂不朽. **perpetuity** [ˌpəːpiˈtjuːti] *nu* state of being perpetual 永恒, 永存: *in perpetuity* i.e. forever 久傳, 永遠, 即: 永遠地.

perplex [pəˈpleks] *vt* puzzle; confuse 使迷惑;使混亂: *This problem perplexes me* 這個問題使我迷惑不解. **perplexed** *adj* **perplexity** *nc / u* being confused or puzzled 混亂, 困惑.

perquisite [ˈpəːkwizit] *nc* anything one gets regularly and legally from one's work apart from pay 額外補貼, 工資以外的收入, 臨時津貼, 獎金: *One of the perquisites of the post is a free car* (informally shortened to **perk**) 職務的一個補貼是一輛供自己使用的轎車. (非正式縮寫爲 perk).

persecute [ˈpəːsikjuːt] *vt* treat cruelly (尤指宗教或政治信仰的)迫害. (esp.

because of religious or political beliefs). **persecution** [pə:si'kju:ʃən] *nc / u* persecuting or being persecuted 迫害或受迫害.

persevere [pə:si'viə*] *vi* keep on doing something which is unpleasant or difficult 堅忍, 堅持: *persevere at / in / with one's studies* 堅持學習 (孜孜不倦). **perseverance** *nu*.

persist [pə'sist] *vi* last; continue to exist 持久; 堅持, 持續: *The smell persisted even after we had cleaned the room.* 我們打掃房間以後, 臭味還有. **persistent** *adj* continuing; not stopping 持續的; 不斷的: *a persistent headache* 持續不斷的頭痛. **persistently** *adv* **persistence** *nu*.

person ['pə:sn] *nc* **1** man, woman or child 人: *There is the person I was talking about.* 有個我正談起的人. **2** body of a human being 身體, 外貌: *attacks against the person* 對某人的攻擊; *carrying a knife on his person* i.e. in his pocket etc 他身上藏刀. 即: 他口袋裏有刀. **3** (grammar) class of pronoun or verb according to whether it relates to the person speaking (*first person*), the person spoken to (*second person*) or the person / thing spoken about (*third person*) (語法) 人稱. *Note* 說明: the word *people* is normally used for the *pl* of sense **1**. people 一詞用作義 1 的複數. **personable** *adj* good-looking; attractive 英俊的, 風度好的: *a personable young man* 英俊的男青年. **personify** [pə'sɔnifai] *vt* be an example of (some quality) 成…典型, 為…的化身: *When I was a child, my father personified for me everything that was good.* 當我小的時候, 我的父親對我來說成了一切好事的典型. **personification** [pəsɔnifi'keiʃən] *nc / u* **personnel** [pə:sə'nel] *nu* people

working in any job, service etc. 人員: *army personnel* 軍事人員, 陸軍人員. **in person** oneself, not someone else 親自: *The president came to the school in person* i.e. he came himself, instead of sending someone else to represent him 總統親自到學校來. 即: 他自己來, 而不是派別人代表他來.

personal ['pə:snl] *adj* **1** having to do with oneself and not others 私人的, 個人的: *personal property* 私人的財產; *a personal letter* i.e. a private letter 私人的信件; *a personal opinion* 個人的意見. **2** done directly by a person himself 親自的, 本人的: *a personal interview / appearance etc.* 親自會見/露面等. **3** connected with the body 容貌的, 身體的: *personal cleanliness* 個人衛生. **4** about or against a person 個人的; 攻擊個人的: *personal abuse* 人身攻擊: *Don't be personal* i.e. don't make remarks about, or ask questions about, a person 不要涉及私事. 即: 不要評論或提起私人的問題. **personally** *adv* **1** in person, not through others 親自地: *The owner of the hotel welcomed us personally.* 這旅館的主人親自歡迎我們. **2** speaking for oneself 就個人而言: *Personally, I think he is a very good man, but you may not agree.* 就個人而言, 我認為他是個很好的人, 但你也許不同意. **3** as a person 就人而論: *I like him personally, but I hate what he believes in.* 我喜歡他這個人, 但我討厭他所信仰的東西.

personality [pə:sə'næliti] *nc / u* **1** what makes one person different from another; what makes a person stand out 個性; 特性: *a man with / of great personality* 一個很有個性的男子漢. **2** important or well-known person 名人, 要人: *a stage personality* i.e. a well-known actor or actress 舞台名

人，即：著名的男女演員．

perspective [pə'spektiv] *nc / u* **1** art of drawing or painting things so that some look farther away than others, as they do in real life 透視畫法．**2** way of seeing things 觀察事物的方法：*see things in the right perspective* i.e. see a matter properly, what is important and what is not etc. 正確地觀察事物，即：準確地判斷事物甚麼是重要的，甚麼是不重要的等．

Perspex ['pə:speks] * *nu* transparent type of plastic used as a substitute for glass 透明塑料．

perspire [pə'spaiə*] *vi* (used more of human beings than animals) sweat (多用於指人) 流汗．**perspiration** [pə:spi'reiʃən] *nu*.

persuade [pə'sweid] *vt* **1** get someone to do what one wants by pleading or arguing 說服，勸誘：*I persuaded my friends to stay* 我勸說我的朋友住了下來．**2** make a person believe something 使相信：*We persuaded him of our good intentions.* 我們使他相信我們的好意．*I persuaded the teacher that what I said was true.* 我使老師相信我所說的話是真的．**persuasion** [pə'sweiʒən] **1** *nu* persuading 勸說，說服：*He decided to leave only after much persuasion.* 經過多方勸說，他才決定離開．**2** *nc* belief 信仰：*people of different persuasions* (宗教) 信仰不同的人．**persuasive** [pə'sweisiv] *adj* able to persuade 能說服的；善於遊說的：*persuasive arguments* 能說服人的辯論．

pert [pə:t] *adj* bold; not showing respect 魯莽的；淘氣的，無禮的：*a pert child* 淘氣的孩子．

pertain [pə'tein] *vi* (always with **to**) (常與 to 連用) 關於，有關：have to do with. *The inspector was interested in*

everything pertaining to the school. 視察員對有關學校的一切都感興趣．

pertinent ['pə:tinənt] *adj* having to do directly with what is being discussed etc; very suitable 有關的；中肯的，恰當的：*a pertinent question* 有關的問題．

perturb [pə'tə:b] *vt* disturb; make anxious 煩擾；使不安：*some very perturbing news* 非常令人不安的消息．

pervade [pə'veid] *vt* spread through; get into every part of 遍及；瀰漫：*An unpleasant smell pervades the house.* 一種難聞的氣味瀰漫了全屋．

perverse [pə'və:s] *adj* **1** refusing to do what is right or what one is told 任性的，固執的：*a perverse child* 任性的孩子．**2** deliberately wrong; unnatural 錯誤的，荒謬的；反常的：*perverse behaviour* 反常的行為：*perverse beliefs* 荒謬的信仰．**perversely** *adv*.

pervert [pə'və:t] *vt* **1** turn someone / something away from what is right and normal 使墮落，引人邪路，使變壞：*He was perverted by his evil companions.* 他被他的壞夥伴引入邪路．**2** something for a bad purpose 濫用：*He was accused of perverting justice.* 他被控告濫用法律．Also *nc* 亦作 ['pə:və:t] *nc* perverted person (esp. one with a sexual perversion) 行為反常的人 (尤指性變態者)．**perversion** *nc / u* perverting or being perverted; perverted behaviour 墮落，變態行為．

pessimism ['pesimizəm] *nu* tendency to look on the unhappy side of things, to believe that the worst is going to happen 悲觀主義．(*opp* 反義詞 **optimism**). **pessimist** *nc* person who tends to look on the unhappy side of things 悲觀主義者．**pessimistic** [pesi'mistik] *adj*.

pest [pest] *nc* someone / something that causes trouble or harm 有害的人或

物，令人討厭的人或物: *That disobe-
dient boy is a pest.* 那不聽話的男孩令
人討厭. *The flowers were attacked by
garden pests* i.e. insects. 這些花遭到植
物寄生蟲(即:害蟲)的侵蝕. **pesticide**
['pestisaid] *nc / u* substance for killing
insects 殺蟲劑.

pester ['pestə*] *vt* annoy; trouble 使煩
惱, 糾纏: *pestered by people asking
for money* 被乞錢的人所糾纏.

pestle ['pesl] *nc* instrument for pounding or grinding something to a fine
powder (搗研用的)杵, 碾槌. Also 亦作
vt / i pound or grind with a pestle
(用杵)搗研;碾碎.

pet [pet] *nc* 1 animal that is kept out of
affection 供賞玩的動物: *Dogs make
good pets.* 狗是好玩的動物. 2 someone who is loved and made much of;
favourite 受寵愛的人;寵物. Also 亦作
adj 1 treated as a pet 受寵愛的: *a pet
dog* 受寵愛的狗. 2 showing affection
寵愛的, 得意的: *a pet name* i.e. a special name for someone who is loved
暱稱, 即:對某人特別的愛稱. Also 亦
作 *vt* 1 treat as a pet; make much of
把⋯當作寵兒;奉承. 2 pat or stroke
in an affectionate way 愛撫. *past* 過去
式和過去分詞 **petted.**

petal ['petl] *nc* coloured leaf-like part of
a flower 花瓣: *the red petals of a rose*
玫瑰花的紅花瓣.

peter ['pi:tə*] *vi* (always with **out**) become gradually smaller in amount of
size and finally end (常與 out 連用)漸
減少最後消失, 逐漸枯竭; 終止: *Our
supply of food petered out.* (informal)
我們的食物供應已經終止. (非正式)

petition [pə'tiʃən] *nc* formal letter
(signed by many people) to someone
in authority, asking for something (許
多簽名的)向當權者提出某些要求的)請
願書: *Everyone signed the petition to*

the County Council for a new school
in our village. 大家在致縣委會的請願
書上簽了名, 要求在我們村裏辦一所新
學校.

petrify ['petrifai] *vt / i* make unable to
think, move etc through fear, surprise
etc. 嚇獃, 使麻木: *The poor child was
petrified with fear.* 這窮孩子給嚇呆了.
petrifying *adj* very frightening (*informal*) 非常害怕(非正式).

petrol ['petrl] *nu* (Brit) form of oil used
esp. to drive engines of motorcars
etc. (英)汽油. (US 美 **gasoline**). **petroleum** [pi'trouliəm] *nu* oil from
which petrol, paraffin etc are obtained
石油.

petticoat ['petikout] *nc* same as **slip** (in
sense 3) 同 slip (義3).

petty ['peti] *adj* 1 unimportant 不重要
的: *petty details* 不重要的細節. 2
mean; narrow-minded 卑賤的;小器的:
a petty remark 小器的話. **pettiness**
nu. '**petty 'cash** amount of money
that is kept ready for making small
payments 零用錢, 零星收支. '**petty
'officer** (navy) non-commissioned
officer (海軍)士官,軍士,下級官佐.

petulant ['petjulnt] *adj* easily made
angry over small things; bad-
tempered 愛發脾氣的;暴躁的.

pew [pju:] *nc* bench with a back to it,
for people to sit on in church 教堂的
條棍式座位.

pewter ['pju:tə*] *nu* metal made from
mixing tin and lead 錫鉛合金, 白鑞.

phantom ['fæntəm] *nc* ghost; supposed
appearance of someone who is dead
鬼怪;幽靈.

pharmacy ['fa:məsi] 1 *nu* preparing
drugs and medicine 製藥, 配藥, 製藥
學: *student of pharmacy* 藥學學生. 2
nc place where drugs and medicines
are sold; chemist's shop 藥房;藥店.

pharmacist *nc* person who prepares medicine 藥劑師.

pharynx ['færiŋks] *nc* cavity leading from the mouth and nasal passages to the larynx and oesophagus 咽. *pl* 複數 **pharynxes or pharynges.**

phase [feiz] *nc* **1** one of the changing states or stages of development that people / things go through 階段, 時期: *There was not much fighting in the first phase of the war.* 在戰爭的第一階段, 沒有多少仗打. *My son is going through a difficult phase at the moment.* 現在, 我的兒子正經歷着一個困難時期. **2** appearance of the moon or planet at a given time (月等的)變相, 盈虧: *the phases of the moon* 月亮的盈虧.

phenomenon [fə'nɔminən] *nc* **1** any natural event that can be observed 現象: *A rainbow is an interesting phenomenon.* 虹是個有趣的現象. **2** very unusual person / thing 特殊的人或物. *pl* 複數 **phenomena** [fə'nɔminə]. **phenomenal** *adj* very unusual; extraordinary; extremely good 異常的; 非凡的, 極好的: *He is a phenomenal runner.* 他是個非凡的賽跑選手.

philanthropy [fi'lænθrəpi] *nu* **1** love of mankind 慈善心. **2** help given to people (esp. those who are unfortunate in some way) 樂善好施. **philanthropist** *nc* person who loves and helps others 慈善家.

philately [fi'lætəli] *nu* collecting of postage stamps as a hobby 集郵. **philatelist** *nc* stamp collector 集郵者.

philosophy [fi'lɔsəfi] **1** *nu* search for truth and knowledge of the most general kind 哲學. **2** *nc* particular explanation for the universe; system of thought 哲學體系; 哲理, 原理: *He is looking for a philosophy he can believe in.* 他正在尋找一種他能相信的哲理. **philosopher** *nc* person who studies philosophy 哲學家. **philosophical** [filə'sɔfikl] *adj* **1** connected with philosophy 哲學上的. **2** calm; accepting disappointment, danger etc without protesting 冷靜的; 明達的.

phlegm [flem] *nu* thick liquid coming from the nose and throat (esp. when one has a cold) 痰. **phlegmatic** [fleg'mætik] *adj* slow; not easily interested or excited 冷靜的; 不衝動的.

phobia ['foubiə] *nc* unnatural fear or dislike of something 恐懼, 厭惡: *She has a phobia about animals.* 她很怕動物.

phoenix ['fi:niks] *nc* (Egyptian myth) bird said to live 500 or 600 years, to burn itself on a funeral pile, and rise again from the ashes, fresh and beautiful, for another long life (埃及神話)不死鳥(相傳此鳥活五、六百年之後, 自焚為灰, 然後由灰中復生, 活潑而美麗); 鳳凰.

phone [foun] *nc* short form of **telephone.** telephone 的縮略式. Also 亦作 *vt / i: Phone me up.* (both *informal*) 打電話給我. (均爲非正式).

phonetics [fə'netiks] *nu* study of the sounds of speech and how they are produced 語音學. *Note* 說明: followed by a *sing* verb 後面用單數動詞.

phoney ['founi] *adj* false; untrue; insincere 假的; 僞造的; 不誠懇的. Also 亦作 *nc* false or insincere person 冒充者, 虛僞的人: *This man is a phoney* i.e. not what he claims to be. (both *informal*) 這男人是個騙子. 即: 並非他自稱的那種人. (均爲非正式).

phonograph ['founəgra:f] *nc* (US) instrument for reproducing sounds which have been recorded on flat wax

discs (called **records**) (美) 留聲機 .
(*Brit* 英 **gramophone**).

phosphate ['fɔsfeit] *nu* salt containing phosphorus (esp. used as a fertilizer) 磷酸鹽(尤指用於作肥料).

phosphorus ['fɔsfərəs] *nu* one of the elements (P) 磷.

photo ['foutou] *nc* short informal form of **photograph** 相片 (photograph 非正式縮畧形式). *pl* 複數 **photos**.

photocopy ['foutoukɔpi] *nc* photographic copy of written or printed material 影印本. Also 亦作 *vt* make a photocopy of 影印.

photogenic [foutou'dʒenik] *adj* having an appearance that would make a good photograph 上鏡頭的, 適於拍照的: *a very photogenic face* 一個適於拍照的面孔.

photograph ['foutəgra:f] *nc* picture made by light passing through a curved piece of glass (called a **lens**) onto a specially prepared surface (called a **film**) 照片. Also 亦作 *vt* take a photograph of 照相, 拍照: *He photographed the castle.* 他拍了這城堡的照片. **photographer** [fə'tɔgrəfə*] *nc* 攝影師. **photography** *nu* taking of photographs 攝影術: *an expert in photography* 攝影專家. **photographic** [foutə'græfik] *adj*.

photosynthesis ['foutou'sinθəsis] *nu* formation in green plants of organic substances, chiefly sugars, from carbon dioxide and water in the presence of light and chlorophyll 光合作用.

phrase [freiz] *nc* small group of words (usu. without a finite verb) making part of a sentence (e.g. *in the house, too slowly, by working hard etc.*) 組詞, 短語, 成語. (例如: in the house, too slowly, by working hard 等). Also

亦作 *vt* say or write something in a certain way 措辭: *I phrased my request very carefully.* 我仔細地寫明我的要求.

physical ['fizikl] *adj* **1** of the body 身體的: *physical exercise* 體操, 運動; *physical beauty* 身體的健美. **2** material (as contrasted with moral and spiritual) 物質的 (與思想和精神相對的): *physical things* 物質的東西. **3** according to the law of nature 按照自然法則的: *It is a physical impossibility for a person to be in two places at the same time.* 一個人同時身處兩地按照自然法則是不可能的. **physically** *adv*.

physician [fi'ziʃən] *nc* doctor of medicine 醫生.

physics ['fiziks] *npl* science that deals with aspects of matter and energy (e.g. heat, light, sound, electricity etc) but not usu. including chemistry or biology 物理學. *Note* 說明: followed by a *sing* verb 後面跟單數動詞. **physicist** ['fizisist] *nc* expert in physics 物理學家.

physiology [fizi'ɔlədʒi] *nu* study of the way in which the body of a living thing works under normal conditions 生理學.

physiotherapy [fiziou'θerəpi] *nu* treatment of disease by physical exercises, heat etc. 物理療法.

physique [fi'zi:k] *nu* way in which the body is formed or developed 體格: *person of strong physique* i.e. one who does not easily become ill 體格強壯的人, 即: 不容易生病的人.

piano [pi'ænou] *nc* large musical instrument played by pressing keys with the fingers 鋼琴. *pl* 複數 **pianos.** **pianist** ['piːənist] *nc* person who plays the piano 鋼琴家.

piccolo ['pikəlou] *nc* small flute 短笛 .

pl 複數 **piccolos.**

pick¹ [pik] *nc* heavy tool with two sharp points used for breaking up roads, rock etc 尖鎬鋤, 鑿子. (Also 亦作 **pickaxe**)

pick² [pik] *vt / i* **1** choose from a selection 選擇: *Just pick the book you would like.* 就選你喜歡的書. *He picked the best room.* 他選了最好的房間. **2** take with the fingers; gather 採摘; 收集: *pick fruit from the trees* 摘樹上的果實. **3** use something (usu. pointed) to take things from something else 挑, 拈, 剔: *pick one's teeth* 剔牙; *pick a bone* 剔骨頭. **4** make by picking 挖成, 鑿成: *pick a hole in something* 在某物上挖個洞. **pick on someone** choose someone in connection with something unpleasant (e.g. for punishment, for an unpleasant task etc) 找麻煩, 抱怨, 指責: *Why does he always pick on me?* (informal) 他爲甚麼經常我找麻煩呢? (非正式). **pick out 1** choose from a selection 選擇, 選出: *Pick out which toy you would like to have.* 選擇你想要的玩具吧! **2** make out, distinguish from other people, objects etc. 區分, 辨認: *Can you pick out your friend in that group?* 你能在那羣人中認出你的朋友嗎? **pick up 1** lift up and hold 拾起, 舉起, 拿起: *He picked up his hat and went out.* 他拿起他的帽子走出去. **2** get; gain 偶得; 求得, 加速: *The car picked up speed* i.e. went faster 車子增加了速度. 即: 走得更快了. **3** get up after falling etc 跌倒再站起來: *He slipped, but soon picked himself up.* 他滑倒了, 但很快就再站起來. **4** regain; get something back (esp. health) 重獲, 恢復 (尤指健康): *He's not feeling very well at the moment, but he'll soon pick up.* 他現在在感到不舒服, 但很

快會恢復健康. **5** learn without being taught 學會, 無師自通: *He picked up French while he was staying in Paris.* 他在巴黎逗留期間, 學會了法語. **6** manage to see or hear something by using some kind of apparatus 找到: *We picked up the radio signals on our receiver.* 我們在接收機上找到了無線電信號. **7** take someone with one (in a car) 携帶, 搭載: *I picked up some young people who were hitch-hiking to London.* 我搭載了幾個沿途乘別人便車去倫敦旅行的年輕人. **'pickup** **1** part of a record player which carries the needle or stylus onto the record 電唱機唱頭. **2** small van or truck 小型輕便貨車. **pick someone's pocket** steal something from someone's pocket 扒竊. **'pickpocket** *nc* person who steals from people's pockets 扒手. **pick a quarrel with someone** deliberately cause a quarrel with someone 故意招惹, 向某人找事端吵架.

pickaback ['pikəbæk] *adv* (with reference to the way a child is carried) on someone's back or shoulders (指揹小孩) 在背上. (Also 亦作 **piggy-back**).

picket ['pikit] *nc* person who is posted near a factory during a strike to prevent other workers from going in 罷工糾察員. Also 亦作 *vt* **1** put pickets near a place 監視: *picket a factory* 派糾察員監視工廠以阻止上工. **2** act as a picket 當糾察員.

pickle ['pikl] *vt* put meat, vegetables etc in salt water or vinegar etc so that they can be kept fresh 醃汁, 泡菜等: *pickled meat* 醃肉. Also 亦作 *nu* vegetables which have been pickled 醃菜. (Also 亦作 **pickles**).

picnic ['piknik] *nc* pleasure trip in which food is taken to be eaten in the open air 野餐. Also 亦作 *vi* go on a picnic 去郊遊野餐. *past* 過去式和過去分詞 **picknicked. picknicker** *nc*.

pictorial [pik'tɔ:riəl] *adj* in pictures; having pictures 以圖畫表示的; 有圖畫的: *a pictorial record of the sports meeting* 運動會畫刊.

picture ['piktʃə*] *nc* 1 painting, drawing or photograph 圖畫, 照片: *He showed us some pictures he took while on holiday.* 他給我們看了一些他在假日拍的照片. *The artist had painted a very fine picture.* 這藝術家畫了一幅很優美的畫. 2 example 範例, 模範, 化身: *She was the picture of happiness* i.e. a perfect example of happiness 她是幸福的化身, 即: 幸福的完美範例. 3 cinema film 影片; *motion picture* 電影. Also 亦作 *vt* imagine 想像, 描述: *You can picture the scene.* 你能想像那個情景.

picturesque [piktʃə'resk] *adj* 1 pretty or interesting enough to be made into a picture 美麗的, 有趣的, 風景如畫的: *a picturesque old village* 一個風景如畫的老村子. 2 vivid; lively 生動的, 活潑的: *a picturesque way of speaking* 生動的講法. **the pictures** performance of a cinema film 電影: *I'm going to the pictures tonight* i.e. I am going to a cinema. 今晚我將去看電影. 即: 我將到電影院去.

pidgin ['pidʒin] *adj* of a mixed language which uses the words of two or more languages and a simplified grammar of one of them 大雜燴的語言, 不純正的語言: *pidgin English* i.e. language based on English used by uneducated people in some African and Asian countries 混雜不純的英語, 即: 一些亞非國家裏平民所使用的英語.

pie [pai] *nc* fruit or meat covered in pastry and baked 餡餅: *a fruit pie* 水果餡餅: *a meat pie* 肉餡餅.

piebald ['paibɔ:ld] *adj* (with reference to a horse) with large black and white patches (指馬)黑白斑紋的.

piece [pi:s] *nc* 1 bit; part of a thing that has been divided or broken 塊, 片: *a piece of land* 一片土地; *a piece of soap* 一塊肥皂. *He dropped the cup and now it is in pieces.* 他把杯子掉下來, 杯子摔成碎片. 2 small amount 小量, 一點兒, 一段: *a piece of advice / news etc.* 一點兒建議/消息等. 3 single one in a set 全部物件中的單個: *We bought this tea set last year and two of the pieces are broken already.* 去年我們買了這套茶具, 已經打破了兩個. 4 coin 硬幣: *a ten pence piece* 十便士的硬幣. 5 one of a set of coloured disks, figures etc used in playing chess and other board games 棋子: *lose an important piece* 丟了重要的一隻棋子. Also 亦作 *vt* put parts together 修補, 黏合, 編結, 彙總: *We pieced the broken cup together again.* 我們把打破的杯子又黏好了. *The police pieced together all they had found out about the wanted man.* 警察將所發現的有關這個通輯犯的材料彙總在一起.

pier [piə*] *nc* structure of wood or stone etc built out into the sea and used as a landing place for boats or as a place to walk 水上平台, 碼頭.

pierce [piəs] *vt* 1 (with reference to something sharp or pointed), go into; make a hole in (指鋒利的東西) 刺入, 戳入; 穿過: *The needle pierced his skin.* 針刺入他的皮膚. *A nail pierced the ball.* 一顆釘子戳入皮球. 2 (with reference to cold, pain etc) force its way into; affect deeply (指寒冷, 痛苦等) 穿入; 深深地影響: *The freezing wind pierced us to the bone.* 寒風使我們刺骨. 3 sound sharp and clear 響

徵: *A cry of pain pierced the night air.* 痛苦的叫聲響徹夜空. **piercing** *adj* **1** very cold 刺骨的, 凜冽的. **2** very sharp and clear in sound (聲音) 尖銳的.

piety ['paiiti] *nu* quality of being pious i.e. religious, respecting God 虔誠. (*opp* 反義詞 **impiety**). see 參見 **pious**.

pig [pig] *nc* **1** animal which is usu. fat and eats a lot, raised for its meat (called **pork**). **2** dirty, greedy or unpleasant person, (*informal and impolite*) 骯髒的人, 貪心的人, 討厭的人 (非正式, 不禮貌). **'piggy-back** *adv* see 參見 **pickaback**. **'pig'headed** *adj* stubborn; obstinate 頑固的, 固執的: *I've given him advice but he's too pigheaded to accept it.* 我給他提了建議, 但他太固執了, 不能接受. **'pigskin** *nc* pig's skin leather made from pig's skin 豬皮, 豬皮革. Also 亦作 *adj.* **'pigsty 1** small place where pigs are kept 豬欄. **2** dirty place 髒地方: *This kitchen is an absolute pigsty.* 這廚房是個極髒的地方. (*informal* in sense 2) (義 2 爲非正式). **'pigtail** *nc* length of hairs twisted together and hanging down at the back of, or one at each side of, the head 辮子.

pigeon ['pidʒən] *nc* bird of the dove family (esp. a fairly large bluish-grey bird which lives in towns) 鴿子. **'pigeonhole** *nc* one of a set of box-like openings for putting documents etc into 文件格, 分類架. Also 亦作 *vt* **1** put something in a pigeonhole 把…插入分類架上. **2** put something where one can refer to it again 分類記存.

pigiron ['paiaiən] *nu* crude iron, as it comes from the blast furnace 生鐵.

pigment ['pigmənt] *nc / u* **1** colouring matter which is used to make paints,

dyes etc (粉狀) 顏料. **2** substance which gives the hair, skin of animals and the leaves of plants their colour 天然色素. **pigmentation** [pigmən'teiʃən] *nu.*

pigmy ['pigmi] *nc* see 見 **pygmy.**

pike¹ [paik] *nc* long spear formerly used by soldiers (昔日士兵用的) 矛.

pike² [paik] *nc* large, thin freshwater fish which eats other fish, frogs etc. 梭魚, 狗魚. *pl* 複數 **pike.**

pile¹ [pail] *nc* **1** heap of things lying one on top of the other 堆: *a pile of books* 一堆書. **2** large amount of something heaped up 一大堆: *a pile of earth* 一大堆土. **pile up** grow larger in amount 越來越多, 積聚: *His debts began to pile up.* 他所欠的債越來越多. **'pileup** *nc* **1** piling up of anything 堆積. **2** road accident involving several vehicles 連環車禍.

pile² [pail] *nc* very large, heavy piece of wood, steel or concrete driven into the earth, often under water, and used to support a bridge etc. 橋樁.

pile³ [pail] *nc / u* soft, thick surface of threads or hairs found on velvet, some carpets etc. 軟毛, 細毛, 絨毯或地毯上的絨毛.

piles [pailz] *nu* illness in which there is a painful swelling around the anus 痔瘡.

pilfer ['pilfə*] *vt / i* steal (a small amount or things of small value) 偷 (小東西): *He was fined for pilfering some fruit.* 他因偷了水果被罰款.

pilgrim ['pilgrim] *nc* person who travels to a sacred or holy place 朝聖者, 香客: *a pilgrim to Mecca* 去麥加的朝聖者. **pilgrimage** *nc* journey made by a pilgrim 朝聖.

pill [pil] *nc* small ball or disk of medicine, to be swallowed whole 藥丸.

the Pill pill taken regularly by women to prevent the conception of a child 口服避孕丸: *on the pill* i.e. taking pills for this purpose 開始服用避孕丸, 即: 爲了避孕而服此丸.

pillage ['pilidʒ] *vt / i* plunder; steal things, with violence, from a place that has been captured in war 掠奪; 搶劫.

pillar ['pilə*] *nc* thin, upright post, used in a building etc either to support it or as an ornament 柱子. '**pillar box** box, placed in the street, in which letters can be posted 郵筒.

pillion ['piliən] *nc* on a motorcycle, the pad or seat behind the driver's on which a passenger can sit 摩托車的後座. *ride pillion* i.e. sit in this position 騎在後座, 即: 坐在後座的位置上.

pillory ['piləri] *nc* (in former times) bar of wood to which the head and hands of wrongdoers could be secured as a punishment 頸手枷(古時的一種刑具). Also 亦作 *vt* make someone's faults or crimes public 使受衆辱, 揭露.

pillow ['pilou] *nc* bag filled with soft material on which the head can rest 枕頭. '**pillowcase**, '**pillowslip** cover for a pillow (made of cotton, linen etc.) 枕套.

pilot ['pailət] *nc* **1** person who guides a ship in and out of a harbour, or any place that requires special knowledge 領航員: *We got a pilot who guided us through the dangerous reefs.* 我們找到一個領航員, 他帶我們穿過危險的暗礁. **2** person who flies an aeroplane 飛行員. Also 亦作 *vt* guide (a ship etc); fly (an aeroplane) 領航(輪船); 駕駛(飛機). '**pilot** '**survey / project / experiment etc** survey etc which is carried out in order to see whether the idea behind it will work, and is a

preparation for a much larger survey etc. 試驗性的, 示範性的調查/計劃/實驗等.

pimp [pimp] *nc* man who finds customers for prostitutes 男淫媒, 拉皮條的人.

pimple ['pimpl] *nc* small, inflamed spot on the skin 丘疹, 粉刺.

pin¹ [pin] *nc* small, thin piece of metal with a head, sharp at one end, put through things to keep them together (e.g. pieces of paper, cloth etc.) 別針. '**pincushion** small cushion or pad into which pins are stuck until they are needed 針墊. '**pinpoint** *nc* something very small 細小, 針尖, 一點點: *a pinpoint of light* 一點點的光. Also 亦作 *vt* describe or reveal exactly 準確描述, 揭示: *The teacher pinpointed the reasons why I had done badly in the last examination.* 老師準確地說明了我在期終考失利的原因. '**pinup** picture of a beautiful woman, taken from a newspaper or magazine and fastened on a wall etc. *(informal)* 從報刊上剪下來貼在牆上的美女照片(非正式). **drawing pin** *(Brit)* pin with a flat head (英)圖釘. *(US* 美 **thumbtack**). **pins and needles** prickling feeling one gets in the skin when blood has not been circulating properly in a certain part of the body and then comes back again (四肢的)刺麻, 發麻.

pin² [pin] *vt* **1** keep things together by using a pin 別住, 釘住: *pin some papers together* 把紙別在一起: *pin a flower onto one's coat* 將花別在某人的上裝上: *pin a notice on the wall* 將通知釘在牆上. **2** keep in one position 使不能動, 使固定: *The fallen tree had pinned his leg to the ground.* 掉下來的樹把他的腿壓在地上不能動. *past* 過

去式和過去分詞 **pinned**.

pinafore ['pɪnəfɔ:*] *nc* loose covering worn over a child's or woman's clothes to keep them clean 圍裙.

pincers ['pɪnsəz] *npl* tool for gripping things and holding them tight (used e.g. to take nails out of wood etc) 鉗子.

pinch [pɪntʃ] *vt / i* 1 press between two hard surfaces, press between thumb and forefinger 揑, 掐, 夾住: *My finger was pinched in the doorway*. 我的手指頭在門口給夾住了. *He pinched the child's cheek*. 他掐這孩子的臉. 2 give pain by squeezing tightly 夾痛: *These shoes must be too small because they pinch*. 這些鞋一定太小了, 因爲它們夾脚. 3 steal *(informal)* 偷 (非正式). Also 亦作 *nc* 1 act of pinching or squeezing 揑, 掐: *a pinch on the cheek* 臉上一掐. 2 amount that can be taken up between the thumb and forefinger 一撮: *a pinch of salt* 一撮鹽.

pine¹ [paɪn] 1 *nc* kind of evergreen tree with needle-shaped leaves, and bearing cones 松樹. 2 *nu* the wood of this tree 松木.

pine² [paɪn] *vi* 1 long (for) eagerly; want something very much 渴望; 苦思: *pine for one's home* 思家. 2 become thin and weak through hunger, illness, pain etc. 消瘦, 憔悴: *The poor child was just pining away* 這可憐的孩子正在消瘦.

pineapple ['paɪnæpl] *nc / u* large, juicy, yellow tropical fruit with hard uneven skin 菠蘿.

ping [pɪŋ] *nc* high-pitched ringing noise as of a drinking glass knocked by something hard 乒聲.

ping-pong ['pɪŋpɒŋ] *nu* table tennis 乒乓球.

pink [pɪŋk] *nc / u* 1 pale red colour 粉紅色, 淡紅色. 2 kind of flower 石竹. Also 亦作 *adj* pale red 粉紅的.

pinnacle ['pɪnəkl] *nc* 1 pointed rock or high peak 尖岩石, 尖峯. 2 highest point (e.g. of someone's career, achievements etc) 頂點, 極點 (例如: 某人的事業、成就等).

pint [paɪnt] *nc* unit for measuring liquids, equal to 0.57 litres 品脫 (量液體的單位, 等于0.57升): *a pint of milk* 一品脫牛奶: *a pint of beer* 一品脫啤酒.

pioneer [paɪə'nɪə*] *nc* person who does something first and so prepares the way for others; explorer; early settler in a new country or undeveloped area 先鋒, 拓荒者, 先驅者, 開拓者: *the pioneers of the American west* 美國西部的拓荒者: *a pioneer of aviation* 航空先驅者.

pious ['paɪəs] *adj* having or showing deep love of God; religious 虔誠的; 宗教的: *pious works* 宗教作品; *a pious person* 虔誠的人. (*opp* 反義詞 **impious**). **piety** ['paɪɪti] *nu*.

pip [pɪp] *nc* 1 small seed in an apple, orange etc. (蘋果、橘子等的)小粒種子. 2 note of the time signal on the telephone or radio (電話機或收音機的)尖音信號.

pipe¹ [paɪp] *nc* 1 tube through which gas or liquid flows 管: *gaspipe* 煤氣管; *water pipe* 水管; *drainpipe* i.e. one which takes water etc away through 管, 即: 將水排掉的管. 2 tube with a bowl at the end of it, used for smoking tobacco 烟斗. 3 musical instrument with a hollow tube blown by the player; hollow tube forming part of an organ 笛; 風琴上的金屬管. **pipes** *npl* 1 bagpipes 風笛. 2 set of musical pipes 管樂器. '**pipeline** long line of connected pipes (used e.g. to send petroleum long distances) 管道, 渠道。 **in the pipeline** being produced at the moment, but not yet complete or ready 在進行中, 在完成中。

pipe² [paip] *vt / i* bring gas or liquid by means of a pipe 用管輸送: *pipe water into a village* 用管把水輸送到村裏。 **piper** *nc* person playing a pipe; person playing bagpipes 吹風笛者; 吹笛人。 **piping** *nu* **1** pipes length of pipes 管道的總長: *one hundred feet of piping* 一百英尺的管道。 **2** playing of a pipe; music produced by playing a pipe 吹笛; 笛聲。 Also 亦作 *adj* high shrill 尖聲的: *a piping voice* 很尖的噪音。 **piping hot** very hot 滾熱的: *The food here is always served piping hot.* 這裏的食品老是供應滾熱的。

piquant ['pi:kənt] *adj* **1** clever; interesting; stimulating to the mind 聰明的; 有趣的; 令人痛快的: *a piquant idea* 有趣的主意。 **2** having a pleasant, sharp taste 開胃的, 辛辣的: *a piquant sauce* 辣醬油。

pique [pi:k] *nu* feeling of anger when one's pride is hurt (指自尊心受損傷的)不高興, 不平之氣: *a fit of pique* 不高興。

pirate ['paiərət] *nc* person who attacks ships and steals from them 海盜。 **piracy** *nu* **pirate 'radio station** radio transmitter operating without a licence 非法廣播電台。

pirouette [piru'et] *nc* (dancing) turn round very quickly while balanced on one foot or on the toes (舞蹈)以足尖或足趾急速旋轉。 Also 亦作 *vi* make a pirouette; make one pirouette after another 用趾尖旋轉。

pistol ['pistl] *nc* small, short gun fired with one hand 手槍。

piston ['pistn] *nc* piece of metal (usu.

cylindrical) which moves to and fro inside a hollow tube (called a **cylinder**) as part of the mechanism of engines, pumps etc. 活塞(常用於汽缸内)。

pit [pit] *nc* **1** deep hole in the ground (esp. one which has been dug out for some reason) 礦井, 坑: *a coalpit* 煤礦。 **2** part at the back of the ground floor of a theatre 戲院的後座。 Also 亦作 *vt* **1** mark with small scars 使有傷痕或痘瘢; 使成麻口: *His face had been pitted with smallpox.* 他的臉因患天花留下麻子。 **2** match someone / something against another in a fight, contest etc. 使相鬥, 使抗衡: *He had pitted himself against a much stronger man.* 他自己跟一個比他强壯得多的人相鬥。 *past* 過去式和過去分詞 **pitted**. **'pitfall** hidden or unexpected danger 隱蔽的危險, 没料到的危險。

pitch¹ [pitʃ] *vt / i* **1** throw 投, 抛, 擲: *He pitched the ball to the other end of the field.* 他把球抛到球場的另一端。 **2** fall, cause to fall, forward 使向前跌: *He pitched forward onto the road.* 他向前跌在路上。 *They were pitched from the car.* 他們從車上跌下來。 **3** set up; put in position 紮; 釘牢; 竪起: *pitch a tent* 紮帳篷。 **4** move up and down with the movement of a ship's bow i.e. front part of a ship (船)上下顛簸: *The ship was pitching badly in the storm.* 船在暴風雨中上下顛簸很厲害。 **'pitchfork** tool with a long handle and two metal prongs, used for lifting and moving hay 乾草叉, 草耙。

pitch² [pitʃ] **1** *nc* act of throwing; distance something is thrown 投; 擲。 **2** *nc* length of grass in a cricket ground between wickets 板球場草地高度。 **3** *nc / u* highness or lowness of a sound (聲音的高低度)音調。 **4** *nu* degree; point

程度；度：*at a tremendous pitch of excitement* 極為興奮． **5** *nc* ground where football, hockey etc are played（足球，曲棍球等的）球場．

pitch³ [pitʃ] *nu* dark-coloured, sticky substance found as asphalt or turpentine etc, used to fill in cracks or spaces, in building boats, making roads etc. 柏油，瀝青．**'pitch-'black, 'pitch-'dark** *adj* very black, difficult to see in 很黑的，漆黑的．

pitcher ['pitʃə*] *nc* large jug for liquids 水罐．

piteous ['pitiəs] *adj* making one feel pity, deserving pity 令人憐憫的；值得同情的．

pith [piθ] *nu* **1** soft substance inside the stem etc of some plants（植物莖內的）木髓．**2** most necessary, essential part of a speech etc. 要點，精髓．**pithy** *adj* short and to the point; forceful and direct 簡練的；有力的；中肯的：*a pithy speech* 簡練的講話．

pittance ['pitns] *nc* very small payment or allowance of money 微薄的薪俸或津貼：*work for a (mere) pittance* 幹活拿點津貼．

pity ['piti] *nu* **1** sorrow for the suffering or misfortunes of others 憐憫：*We helped him out of pity* i.e. because we felt sorry for him 我們因憐憫而幫助他．即：因為我們可憐他．**2** something that causes one to feel sorrow 不幸的事，令人遺憾的事：*It's a pity that you missed the train.* 你沒趕上火車，真遺憾！*Note* 說明：in this sense can be used with an a, but hardly ever used in the *pl* 作此義時可加個 a. 但複數很少用．*Also* 亦作 *vt* feel sorry for 表示同情：*pity someone* 同情某人．**pitiable** *adj* deserving pity 令人同情的；*in a pitiable condition* 處於令人同情的境地．**pitiful** *adj* **1** deserving pity

值得同情的．**2** deserving contempt 可鄙的．**pitifully** *adv* **pitiless** *adj* without pity; without mercy 無情的；冷酷的：*a pitiless enemy* 冷酷的敵人．

pivot ['pivət] *nc* bar, point etc on which something balances 樞軸：*The wheel turned on a pivot in the centre.* 輪子在中間的樞軸上旋轉．Also 亦作 *vt/i* turn on a pivot 在樞軸上旋轉．

pixie, pixy ['piksi] *nc* type of fairy 小仙子，小妖精．

placard ['plækɑːd] *nc* public notice put up where it can be easily seen 廣告，佈告，招貼．

placate [plə'keit] *vt* take away someone's anger; make peaceful 安撫，撫慰；使和解：*We tried to placate them with gifts.* 我們盡量用禮物來撫慰他們．

place¹ [pleis] *nc* **1** special or particular space occupied by someone / something 地方：*His house is in a quiet place near the river.* 他的房子在靠河邊一個安靜的地方．**2** area, building etc used for some special purpose（某種專用的）場所：*a market place* 市場；*a place of worship*（教堂）做禮拜的場所．**3** city, town, district etc. 市，鎮，區：*The people had come from different places.* 人們來自不同的地區．**4** particular area on the surface of something 表面上某部份：*There is one place on the ceiling where the water has come through.* 天花板上有個地方漏水了．**5** division of an argument, speech, discussion etc. 步驟，層次：*I would not advise you to read that book, because, in the first place, it is very difficult and, in the second place, it is rather dull.* 我不願意勸你讀那本書，因為首先它很難讀，其次它比較沉悶．**6** proper position 座位，正當的位置：*Nobody in the class may leave his place without permission.* 班

上任何人都不能未經許可離開座位. **7** part of a book, reading passage etc. (書中的) 部分, 段, 頁: *I've lost my place* i.e. I can't find the part of the book I was last reading. 我不知道讀到哪一頁. 即: 我找不到上次讀到的段落. **8** position of a figure in a number 一個數的位: *give a number to two places of decimals (e.g. 4.55).* 算到小數點第二位(例如: 4.55). **9** position in a race (比賽的) 名次: *come in second place* 獲得第二名. **10** rank; position in life 身份; 職位; 生活方式: *one's place in society* 個人的社會地位; *keep someone in his place* i.e. treat someone in a way which shows he is not so important as oneself 貶低某人的身份; 使某人安份守己. **11** duty; what one has to do 任務; 責任; 職責: *It is your place to greet the guests as they arrive.* 你的責任是客人來時向他們致意. **12** house; where one lives 住宅; 住地: *John invited us over to his place.* 約翰請我們到他的住宅去. **13** name of some streets or squares in a town 城內街道或廣場的名稱: *St. James's Place* 聖詹姆士廣場. **'place mat** to put under a plate on a table 餐具的墊布. **in place** in the proper position 在適當的位置: *I hope you left all the books in the library in place.* 我希望你把所有的書放在圖書館適當的位置. **in place of** instead of 代替 *Jones will play for the team in place of Brown.* 瓊斯將代替布朗爲此隊踢球. **out of place 1** not in the proper position 錯位的, 不在適當的位置. **2** not suitable. ill-mannered 不適當的, 不得體的: *It was out of place for you to cheer when the headmaster said he was leaving.* 校長說他要走的時候, 你爲他喝彩是不適當的.

place² [pleis] *vt* **1** put in a certain posi-

tion, condition etc. 放置, 排列: *He placed the book on the desk.* 他把書放在書桌上. *He placed sentries round the camp.* 他在營房四週派了哨兵. **2** remember someone fully; identify 詳細記得, 認出: *I've heard his name but I can't place him.* 我聽說過他的名字, 但我認不出他. **3** give (an order etc); put 發出(訂單); 訂(貨); 把…寄托於: *place an order with a shopkeeper* 跟一個店主訂貨; *place confidence in a friend.* 信賴朋友. **4** give someone a certain position; get someone a post 任命; 安置. **be placed** be first, second or third in a race (比賽中) 位列 (第一, 第二或第三): *My horse wasn't even placed.* 我的馬竟未列入前三名.

placid ['plæsid] *adj* peaceful; not easily made angry 平和的, 寧靜的; 不易生氣的: *a placid scene* 寧靜的景色; *someone having a placid nature* 生性平和的人; **placidity** [plə'siditi] *nu.*

plague [pleig] *nc* **1** very dangerous disease which spreads quickly 瘟疫. **2** anything that annoys or troubles 惹人煩惱的東西; 討厭的東西: *a plague of wasps* i.e. very large number of wasps causing harm and annoyance 黃蜂之災, 即: 大量黃蜂造成的災害. Also 亦作 *vt* (esp. of a large number of something) annoy or trouble 困擾, 使煩惱: *be plagued by a child's questions* 困擾; *be plagued by requests for money* 被錢的要求所困擾.

plaice [pleis] *nc* kind of flat sea fish 鰈. *pl* 複數 **plaice.**

plaid [plæd] *nc* long piece of woollen cloth with many colours, worn over the shoulders in former times by Scotsmen 以前蘇格蘭人所披的彩色呢絨披肩.

plain¹ [plein] *adj* **1** easy to see, hear or

understand 明白的, 清楚的: *You have made your meaning plain.* 你已經把你的意思講明白了. *His voice was quite plain over the telephone.* 他的聲音在電話上非常清楚. **2** simple; ordinary; without ornament 簡單的; 普通的; 樸素的: *plain food* 普通的食物; *a plain man* 普通人; *a plain dress* 樸素的衣服. **3** not pretty or handsome 難看的, 不漂亮的: *a rather plain girl* 相當難看的姑娘. **4** honest; frank 誠實的; 坦白的: *I must be plain with you.* 我必須對你說實話. Also 亦作 *adv* clearly 清楚地; *speak plain* 說得很明白. **plainly** *adv* **plainness** *nu* in **plain clothes** (usu. with reference to policemen) in ordinary clothes, not in uniform (常指警察) 穿便服 (不穿制服).

plain² [plein] *nc* flat stretch of land 大平原.

plaintiff ['pleintif] *nc* person who brings an action to a court of law 原告.

plaintive ['pleintiv] *adj* sad, asking for pity 悲哀的, 哭訴的: *a plaintive voice* 哭訴的聲音.

plait [plæt] *vt* join three or more lengths of hair, straw etc by twisting each one under or over the others so as to make one length 髮辮, 辮繩. Also 亦作 *nc* something made in this way 辮子: *a girl wearing her hair in plaits* 留着髮辮的少女.

plan [plæn] *nc* **1** way of making or doing something that has been thought out in advance 計劃; 安排, 打算: *What plans do you have for the holidays?* 你對假日有甚麼打算? **2** drawing or diagram showing the different parts of a house or garden etc. (usu. as if seen from above) 平面圖, 圖樣: *Here is a plan of the ground floor.* 這兒是底層的平面圖. *If you*

look at this plan of the school grounds you will see where the football field is. 假如你看看這張學校場地的平面圖, 你就會知道足球場在哪裏. **3** drawing or diagram to show the different parts of a machine (機器各部份的) 說明圖. **4** government scheme for making a country richer etc. 發展計劃: *a five-year plan* 一個五年計劃. Also 亦作 *vt* **1** think out in advance how something is to be made or done 計劃; 安排: *plan a surprise for someone* 爲某人安排意想不到的事. *I am planning to go to London next week.* 我準備下週到倫敦去. **2** make a drawing or diagram of something 設計, 作…的圖樣. *past* 過去式和過去分詞 **planned.** **plan out** think something out, arrange something in advance 籌劃, 籌備: *I'm planning out the school debate.* 我正在籌備學校的辯論會. **according to plan** in the way that was arranged 按計劃: *Everything went according to plan.* 一切按計劃進行.

plane¹ [plein] *nc* **1** flat or level surface 平面. **2** level 水準, 程度: *The discussion was on too high a plane for me* i.e. it was too difficult for me to understand 對我來說, 這次討論的水準太高了. 即: 這太難了, 我聽不懂. **3** aeroplane; aircraft 飛機; 飛行器. **4** tool with a blade, used to smooth down wood so that it has a level surface 刨子. Also 亦作 *vt / i* make flat or smooth with a plane (in sense 4) 用刨子將…刨平. Also 亦作 *adj* flat; lying along a level surface 平面的: *a plane figure* 平面圖形.

plane² [plein] *nc* kind of tree with large leaves often planted in towns 法國梧桐.

planet ['plænit] *nc* one of the worlds

which go round the sun (e.g. Venus, the Earth) 行星. (例如: 金星, 地球).

plank [plæŋk] *nc* long, flat piece of wood; large board 板條; 厚板.

plankton [ˈplæŋktən] *nu* mass of small plants and animals drifting on or near the surface of seas or lakes 浮游生物.

plant [plɑːnt] **1** *nc* living thing that is not an animal (e.g. tree, flower etc.) 植物(例如: 樹, 花等). **2** *nu* machinery and buildings used for some special purpose 工廠: *plant for making aircraft* 飛機工廠. Also 亦作 *vt* **1** put plants, seeds etc in the ground to grow 種植. **2** set or place firmly 牢牢地安置, 穩牢: *She planted herself in my path.* 她狠狠地擋住我的去路.

plantation [plænˈteiʃən] *nc* **1** large farm producing tea, cotton, sugar etc. (esp. one in a tropical country) 大種植園, 大農場. **2** large area where trees have been planted 林場.

plantain [ˈplæntin] *nc* **1** kind of large banana 大蕉. **2** tree it grows on 大蕉樹. **3** type of wild plant 野生植物.

plaque [plæk] *nc* flat piece of metal etc used as an ornament or in remembrance of something 匾, 飾板.

plasma [ˈplæzmə] *nu* liquid part of blood 血漿.

plaster [ˈplɑːstə*] *nu* **1** mixture made up of lime, sand, water etc which becomes hard when it is dry, and is used for giving walls, ceilings etc a smooth surface 灰泥. **2** plaster of Paris (see below) used to keep broken limbs straight 石膏粉. Also 亦作 *vt* **1** put plaster (in sense 1) on walls etc. 塗以灰泥. **2** cover thickly 塗上厚厚的東西: *His hair was plastered with oil.* 他的頭髮塗上厚厚的一層油. **plaster of Paris** mixture like plaster (in sense 1) used in making fi-

gures, statues, moulds etc. 燒石膏, 石膏粉. **'sticking plaster** medical covering which sticks to the skin, used to cover cuts, boils etc. 藥膏.

plastic [ˈplæstik] *adj* **1** easily made into different shapes 可塑的, 易塑的: *Clay is a plastic material.* 黏土是易塑的物質. **2** easily changed; easily influenced *(o.f.)* 易變化的; 易受影響的(舊式). **3** concerned with changing the shape of something 造型的: *the plastic art of sculpture* 雕塑的造型藝術; *plastic surgery* i.e. part of medicine concerned with changing a person's appearance 整形外科, 即: 改變一個人面容的外科手術. **4** made of plastic 塑料的: *plastic cups* 塑料杯; *plastic raincoats* 塑料雨衣. Also 亦作 *nu* man-made material which can be made into many different shapes when soft and which keeps its shape when it becomes hard 人造的可塑性材料, 塑料.

Plasticine [ˈplæstisiːn] * *nu* substance like clay, which can be formed into various shapes in the hands, used by children for playing with 塑像, 黏土.

plate [pleit] **1** *nc* round and almost flat dish, mostly used for serving food 盤, 碟: *dinner plate* 餐盤; *tea plate* 茶盤. **2** *nc* food etc on such a dish 一盤食物: *a plate of soup* 一盤湯. **3** *nu* dishes and other articles made of silver or gold, or having a surface of silver or gold 金銀器具, 鍍金或鍍銀器具: *cupboard full of gold plate* 擺滿金質器具的碗櫥. **4** *nc* thin, flat sheet of metal, glass etc. 薄板: *steel plates* 薄鋼板.

plateful *nc* amount that a plate holds 一盤(或碟)之量: *plateful of rice* 一盤飯. **'plate 'glass** thick, polished and very expensive glass, used for shop windows etc. 厚玻璃板.

plateau ['plætou] *nc* large, flat area of land high above sea level 高原. *pl* 複數 **plateaus** or **plateaux** ['plætouz].

platform ['plætfɔːm] *nc* raised, level surface 平台, 講台, 站台: *He spoke to us from a platform in the school hall.* 他在學校大廳裏的講台上給我們演講. *He was coming by train, so I waited on the platform* i.e. the raised part for passengers beside the railway lines 他坐火車來, 所以我在站台上接他. 即: 在鐵路線旁邊旅客等候上車的平台上.

platinum ['plætinəm] *nu* soft, white, valuable metal (Pt) 鉑, 白金.

platitude ['plætitjuːd] *nc* statement of something obvious or of something which has often been said before, but now used by a speaker as if it were something new 陳詞濫調: *His speech was full of platitudes.* 他的講話充滿了陳詞濫調.

platoon [plə'tuːn] *nc* small number of soldiers organized as a single unit (軍隊的)排.

platter ['plætə*] *nc* (US) large dish for serving food (esp. meat and fish) (美) (尤指盛魚肉的)大淺盤.

plausible ['plɔːzibl] *adj* **1** appearing to be true or reasonable 似合理的, 似真實的, 好像有理的: *a plausible excuse* 好像有理的藉口. **2** good at making up plausible excuses etc. 花言巧語的, 嘴巧的: *a plausible liar* 花言巧語的騙子. (*opp* 反義詞 **implausible**). **plausibly** *adv* **plausibility** [plɔːzi'biliti] *nu*.

play¹ [plei] *vt / i* **1** amuse oneself; do something for pleasure, not as work 玩耍; 娛樂: *The children are playing outside.* 孩子們正在外面玩耍. **2** take part in a game 參加體育運動或遊戲: *We play football / at football every Saturday.* 我們每星期六踢足球. *Do*

you play chess? 你下象棋嗎? **3** take part in a game against someone 跟…比賽: *Our school is playing another team at hockey on Friday.* 星期五, 我們學校將跟另一隊進行曲棍球比賽. **4** put someone in a team 使成爲(某隊)一員, 起用: *They are playing some of their best men in this game.* 在這場比賽中, 他們將起用一些他們最好的隊員. **5** reveal a card in a card game when one's turn comes 出牌: *He played the king of hearts.* 他出了紅心K的牌. **6** perform; carry out 做; 實行: *play a joke / trick on someone* 開某人的玩笑. **7** make music from 演奏, 彈: *play the piano* 彈鋼琴; *play a tune* 演奏樂曲. **8** act the part of someone in a play etc. 扮演: *play (the part of) Hamlet* 扮演哈姆萊特的角色. **9** move about quickly 閃着: *The sunlight played upon the water.* 陽光在水面上閃着. *A smile played on his lips* i.e. he seemed to want to smile but did not actually do so 他嘴角上閃過一絲微笑. 即: 他似笑非笑. **play-off** *nc* match, game etc, played again, so that a decision can be made about which team is winner 加賽(以決勝負).

play² [plei] **1** *nu* amusement; fun 玩耍; 遊戲; 娛樂: *The children are at play.* 孩子們在玩耍. *Life should not be all work and no play* i.e. every person who works should also have some amusement 生活不能全是工作, 而沒有娛樂. 即: 每個人既要工作, 也要娛樂. **2** *nu* action in a game 運動, 表演: *There was some exciting play near the end of the game.* 比賽快結束時, 有些精彩的表演. **3** *nc* drama; story written to be performed in a theatre 戲劇; 演出的戲: *the plays of Shakespeare* 莎士比亞的劇本; *see an amusing play* 看一場令人發笑的戲. **4**

nu freedom of movement or action 鬆動: *Give the rope more play* i.e. do not keep it so tight 給繩子鬆動一下. 即: 不要綁得太緊. **5** *nu* quickly changing movement 閃動: *the play of sunlight on water* 陽光在水面上閃動. **6** *nu* activity, use; working 活動, 使用; 利用: *bring all one's skill into play* i.e. use all one's skill 使出某人全部本領, 即: 利用某人的一切技術. **'playfellow, 'playmate** child with whom another child plays 遊伴. **'playground** area where children can play 遊樂場, 運動場. **'playpen** small enclosure used to keep a child in one place 圍欄. **'plaything** something that a child plays with; toy 玩物. **'playtime** *nc / u* length of time set aside for play 遊戲時間. **'playwright** person who writes plays; dramatist 劇作家. **'fair 'play** justice; the same opportunities for everyone 公正; 公平比賽; 機會均等: *see that there is fair play* 要保証公平競賽.

plea [pli:] *nc* **1** request; prayer 懇求, 祈求: *pleas for help* 求助. **2** statement made in reply to a charge in court 辯解, 答辯, 申辯: *a plea of guilty* 爲犯罪申辯.

plead [pli:d] *vt / i* **1** beg for something 懇求, 祈求: *plead for mercy* 懇求憐憫; *She pleaded with him to show some pity.* 她求他給予憐憫. **2** answer a charge in court; argue a case in court 在法庭上爲犯罪辯護; 爲案件申辯: *The prisoner pleaded guilty.* 犯人服罪. *He got a good lawyer to plead his case.* 他找到一個好律師爲他的案件辯護. **3** offer as an excuse 找藉口, 託稱: *The man we found stealing money from the house pleaded poverty.* 我們抓到的那個從屋裏偷錢的男人託稱沒錢用.

pleasant ['pleznt] *adj* **1** giving pleasure; agreeable 愉快的; 可喜的: *a pleasant occupation* 愉快的職業. **2** friendly; likeable 友好的; 可愛的: *a pleasant young man* 可愛的男青年. (*opp* 反義詞 **unpleasant**). **pleasantly** *adv* **pleasantness** *nu*.

please [pli:z] *vt / i* **1** (used in asking for something politely) 請(常用於禮貌地懇求): *Please come in.* 請進來! *Could I please have your attention?* 我可以請你注意聽嗎? *A cup of tea, please.* 請來一杯茶. *Would you like a biscuit? yes, please.* 你喜歡吃餅乾嗎?是的, 請給一點. **2** give pleasure or enjoyment to 使高興, 使欣喜, 使愉快: *I was very pleased to see my son's school report.* 我很高興看我兒子的學習成績單. *I think the arrangements pleased her very much.* 我認爲這些安排使她非常高興. *She was pleased with the arrangements.* 她對這些安排很滿意. (*opp* **displease** in sense **2**)(義2的反義詞爲 displease). **3** wish; choose 希望; 選擇: *Come whenever you please.* 你甚麼時候想來就來. **pleased** *adj* satisfied 滿意. (*opp* 反義詞 **displeased**). **pleasing** *adj* giving pleasure; enjoyable 令人喜歡的, 愉快的. (*opp* 反義詞 **displeasing** or **unpleasing**).

pleasure ['pleʒə*] **1** *nu* feeling of being happy or pleased 快樂, 愉快: *It gives me much pleasure to be here.* 到這裏來使我很愉快. *He takes pleasure in listening to music.* 他很樂意聽音樂. *I shall do it with pleasure* i.e. I shall be happy to do it. 我將樂於去做那件事. 即: 我將愉快地去做那件事. **2** *nc* something which makes one happy or pleased 樂趣: *Reading is my chief pleasure in life.* 讀書是我生活中的主要樂趣.

pleat [pli:t] *nc* flat, narrow fold in a garment (衣服上的) 褶. Also 亦作 *vt* arrange in pleats 打褶. *a pleated skirt* 褶裙.

plebeian [pli'bian] *nc* one of the lower classes 平民. Also 亦作 *adj* of the lower classes; vulgar, common 平民的; 庶民的. **pleb** [pleb] *nc* (often *pl*) (常用複數) one of the masses; a worker (often *impolite*) 百姓; 下層平民(常爲不禮貌用語).

plebiscite ['plebisit] *nc* vote by the people in an area or country on some important matter 公民投票: *The question of whether drinking alcohol should be legal was decided by a plebiscite.* 喝酒是否合法由公民投票決定.

pledge [pledʒ] *nc* promise 誓言, 誓約, 保證: *a pledge of secrecy* 發誓保密. Also 亦作 *vt* make a solemn promise 保證, 發誓: *He pledged never to return / that he would never return.* 他保證決不回來.

plenty ['plenti] *n* all that one needs; more than one needs 許多, 充分, 足夠: *Don't hurry, there's plenty of time.* 不要急, 我們有充分的時間. *If you need more chairs, there are plenty upstairs.* 如果你需要多幾張椅子, 樓上有很多. *I think two more bottles of milk will be plenty.* 我想再來兩瓶牛奶就足夠了. **plentiful** *adj* more than enough; large quantity 足夠的; 大量的: *a plentiful supply of water* 水的大量供應.

pleurisy ['pluərisi] *nu* serious disease of the outer covering of the lungs 胸膜炎, 肋膜炎.

pliable ['plaiəbl] *adj* easily bent 易曲的, 柔軟的: *pliable piece of metal* 易曲的金屬片. **pliability** [plaiəbiliti] *nu*.

pliers ['plaiəz] *npl* tool for holding things tightly or for bending or twist-

ing them. (often **pair of pliers**) 鉗子 (常用 pair of pliers)

plight [plait] *nc* bad or sorrowful condition (惡劣的或悲傷的) 處境, 情況, 情勢: *The homeless family was in a terrible plight.* 這無家可歸的一家人處境很悲慘.

plimsoll ['plimsəl] *nc* type of shoe made of canvas, with a rubber sole 膠底帆布鞋.

plod [plɔd] *vi* 1 walk slowly and heavily 慢步或重步走: *You could see he was tired by the way he plodded along the road.* 從他沿途拖着沉重的步子走, 你可看出他太累了. 2 work slowly but without resting 孜孜從事, 辛苦工作: *plod away at a task* 孜孜不息地工作. *past* 過去式和過去分詞 **plodded.**

plop [plɔp] *nc* noise made by e.g. a stone falling into water (石頭落入水中的) 撲通聲. Also 亦作 *vi*: *The stone plopped into the water.* 石頭撲通一聲落入水中. *past* 過去式和過去分詞 **plopped.**

plot [plɔt] *nc* 1 secret plan 陰謀: *a plot against the government* 反政府的陰謀. 2 outline of the story of a play, novel etc. (戲劇、小說等的) 情節: *an unusual and interesting plot* 異常有趣的情節. 3 small piece of ground 一小塊地: *a garden plot* 一小塊做花圃的地. Also 亦作 *vt* 1 make secret plans with others 共同密謀, 策劃: *plot to overthrow the government* 共同策劃推翻政府; *plot against the president* 密謀反對總統. 2 mark the position of something on a chart, map etc. 在圖上標出. *past* 過去式和過去分詞 **plotted. plotter** *nc*.

plough [plau] (*US* 美 **plow**) *nc* heavy instrument for cutting into the soil and turning it over 犁. Also 亦作 *vt / i* 1 break up land with a plough; use a plough 以犁耕地: *plough a field* 犁田. **2** (esp. of a ship through water) force a way through something 奮力前進(尤指船破浪前進). **3** fail (an examination) (*informal* in sense **3**) (考試)不及格(義 3 爲非正式).

plow [plau] *nc US* form of **plough** (美) plough 的形式.

ploy [plɔi] *nc* idea or action which is often used to gain some advantage 手法, 花招: *His favourite ploy is to pretend to be stupid and then people try to help him.* 他愛用的花招是裝傻, 使人盡力幫助他.

pluck [plʌk] *vt / i* **1** pull off, pick (flowers, fruit) 摘, 採: *pluck flowers from a field* 到地裏摘花. **2** pull on (the strings of a musical instrument) 拉(弦樂器). Also 亦作 *nu* courage 勇氣: *someone with a lot of pluck* 很有勇氣的人. **plucky** *adj* brave 勇敢的, 果斷的. **pluck up one's courage** be brave; overcome one's fears 鼓起勇氣; 别害怕.

plug [plʌg] *nc* **1** piece of wood, rubber etc used to stop up a hole 塞子, 栓: *A plug was put in the hole to prevent the water from escaping.* 用塞子堵住洞, 阻止水流掉. **2** device to make an electrical connection 電插頭: *plug for a lamp* 電燈的插頭. Also 亦作 *vt / i* stop up a hole by using a piece of wood etc. 堵, 塞住. *past* 過去式和過去分詞 **plugged. plug something in** make an electrical connection using a plug (in sense **2**) 接上插頭通電: *plug in the lamp* 接上燈的插頭.

plum [plʌm] *nc* round, juicy fruit with a stone in it which grows in cool dry areas 梅. **'plum 'pudding** boiled pudding containing currants, raisins etc mostly eaten at Christmas 聖誕節吃的葡萄乾布丁.

plumage ['plu:midʒ] *nu* bird's feathers (鳥的)羽毛: *a bird with bright plumage* 羽毛鮮艷的鳥.

plumb [plʌm] *nc* small heavy object at the end of a line, used to find out how deep water is, or how straight a wall etc is (用以測量水深或牆壁是否垂直的)鉛錘: *The wall was out of plumb* i.e. not vertical 這堵牆不垂直. 即: 不成直角. Also 亦作 *adv* exactly 準確地: *His shot was plumb on the target.* 他的射擊準確地打中目標. **'plumbline** line with a plumb at the end of it 錘線, 鉛錘線, 測深線.

plumber ['plʌmə*] *nc* person who puts in and repairs pipes for water, gas etc in buildings 管子工, 修水管工人. **plumbing** *nu* **1** work of a plumber 修理水管的工作. **2** pipes and tanks having to do with water and gas supply in a building 建築物中供氣供水的管道和蓄水裝置: *a house with very poor plumbing* 一座管道很糟的房子.

plume [plu:m] *nc* feather or bunch of feathers (usu. as an ornament) 羽毛 (常作飾物用): *She wore an ostrich plume in her hat.* 她戴了一頂插着鴕鳥羽毛的帽子.

plump¹ [plʌmp] *adj* fat in an attractive way 豐滿的: *a plump little baby* 豐滿的嬰兒; *plump cheeks* 豐滿的兩腮.

plump² [plʌmp] *vt / i* drop, allow to drop, suddenly or heavily 突然落下, 重落, 癱倒: *Tired out, he plumped himself down on the chair.* 他累極了, 突然癱倒在椅子上. *I just plumped the heavy load on the ground.* 我剛把重物扔在地上. **plump for someone / something** choose someone / something without hesitation 大力贊成, 毫不猶豫地選出: *They all plumped for the same candidate.* (*informal*) 他們都毫不猶豫地選了同一個候選人. (非正

式).

plunder ['plʌndə*] *vt / i* take things from places or people by force (usu. in a war, riot etc.) 搶劫, 掠奪 (常指在戰爭或暴風中等): *The bandits plundered every village.* 匪徒們搶劫了每個村莊. Also 亦作.*nu* **1** things taken by force 劫奪品: *The robbers escaped with their plunder.* 強盜們帶着他們的劫奪品逃走了. **2** act of plundering 搶劫.

plunge [plʌndʒ] *vt / i* **1** jump into; throw oneself into 跳入; 使陷入; *plunge into the river* 跳入河中; *plunge oneself into debt* 負債累累. **2** put something violently or suddenly into a certain state 使陷入 (某種狀態): *plunge a country into war* 使國家陷入戰爭. *plunge a room into darkness* 房間陷入黑暗中.

plural ['pluərl] *adj* containing or referring to more than one 複數的. Also 亦作 *nc* form of a word which shows that it refers to more than one (e.g. the plural of *chair* is *chairs,* the plural of *I* is *we*) 一個詞的複數形式 (例如: chair—chairs, I—we).

plus [plʌs] *prep* (used mainly in mathematics) and; with the addition of (主要用於數學) 加; 和: *Three plus two equals five* (3+2=5). 3 加 2 等於 5.

plush [plʌʃ] *nu* thick, soft cloth material 長毛絨. Also 亦作 *adj* very expensive 豪華的: *a very plush house in London (informal)* 倫敦一幢很豪華的房子 (非正式).

ply¹ [plai] *nc* **1** thin layer of wood (夾板) 層: *three-ply wood* i.e. piece of wood made up of three different layers stuck together 三層夾板, 即: 由三層不同的板壓製成的木板. **2** strand of rope etc. (線, 繩等) 股: *three-ply*

rope i.e. rope made of three strands twisted together 三股繩, 即: 三股搓成的繩子.

ply² [plai] *vt / i* **1** work at 從事: *someone who plies a trade* 從事貿易的人. **2** go regularly between 經常來往於: *a ship that plies between London and New York* 一條經常來往於倫敦和紐約之間的船. **3** ask often 常問: *ply someone with questions / requests* etc. 常問某人問題/要求等. *pres part* 現在分詞 **plying**. *past* 過去式和過去分詞 **plied** [plaid].

plywood ['plaiwud] *nu* material made of thin layers of wood glued and pressed together 膠合板, 夾板.

pneumatic [nju:'mætik] *adj* **1** filled with air 充氣的: *pneumatic tyre* 氣胎. **2** worked by air 由氣壓推動的, 氣動的: *pneumatic drill* 風鑽, 氣壓鑽孔機.

pneumonia [nju:'mouniə] *nu* serious illness of the lungs 肺炎.

poach¹ [poutʃ] *vt / i* hunt or steal birds or animals on someone else's land 偷獵. **poacher** *nc.*

poach² [poutʃ] *vt* cook an egg (without its shell) or fish in water which is almost at boiling point 用沸水煮 (無殼的) 蛋或魚.

pock [pɔk] *nc* mark on the skin caused by smallpox 痘點, 痘疤. **'pockmarked** *adj* with pocks on the skin 有麻子的; 表面有凹痕的.

pocket ['pɔkit] *nc* **1** small bag sewn into an article of clothing 衣袋: *He put the money in his coat pocket.* 他把錢放在他的大衣口袋裏. **2** hole in the earth containing some ore (e.g. gold) 礦穴 (例如: 金礦穴). **3** small area of something 一圍, 一簇: *a pocket of resistance* 一股阻力. Also 亦作 *vt* **1** place in one's pocket 放到某人袋裏. **2** take something (esp. when one is not entitled to it) 揩油, 竊取. **pocketful** *nc* amount that a pocket holds 一袋, 滿袋. **'pocketbook 1** *(US)* woman's purse. **2** small notebook 小筆記本. **3** small leather case for carrying paper money (usu. **wallet**) 小皮包, 皮夾子 (通常用 wallet). **'pocket knife** small knife with one or more blades which fold into the handle (可摺合的) 小刀. **'pocket money** small amount of money given to children, usu. every week (通常指每週) 給小孩的零用錢. **in / out of pocket** having gained / lost money 挣錢, 有錢 / 丟錢, 花錢: *As a result of having entertained his friends, he was three pounds out of pocket.* 由於招待朋友他花了三個英鎊.

pod [pɔd] *nc* long seed vessel containing the seeds e.g. peas or beans 豆莢.

podgy ['pɔdʒi] *adj* short and fat 矮胖的.

poem ['pouim] *nc* arrangement of words to produce a beautiful effect (often with lines that rhyme and are usu. of regular length and rhythm) 詩. **poetry** ['pouitri] *nu* **1** poems 詩 (總稱): *book of poetry* 詩冊. **2** art of writing poems 寫詩的藝術, 作詩法. **poet** ['pouit] *nc* person who writes poems 詩人. **poetic, poetical** [pou'etik(l)] *adj* **1** having to do with poems or poets 詩的, 詩人的. **2** written in verse 以詩的方式寫成的: *poetic drama* 詩劇.

poignant ['pɔinjənt] *adj* very painful; very moving 傷心的; 極動人的: *a poignant scene* 動人的一幕.

point¹ [pɔint] *nc* **1** sharp end of something 尖: *the point of a pin* 針尖. **2** small, round mark 點: *decimal point* i.e. mark used in the decimal system

(e.g. 3.7 *(three point seven)*) 小數點, 即: 用於作爲小數的標記 (例如: 三點七寫作 3.7). **3** (geometry) something having position but no size (幾何學上只有位置而沒有大小的) 點: *a point on the line AB* AB 線上的一點. **4** spot, position in space or time (時間或空間的) 點, 位: *From that point onwards they were always good friends.* 從那時以來, 他們一直是好朋友. **5** position on a scale 在刻度尺上的位置: *The water had reached boiling point.* 水已達到沸點. **6** one of the 32 points of the compass (e.g. *NW, NNE* etc.) 羅盤上的方位點. (例如: NW, NNE 等). **7** (games) unit of scoring (體育比賽的) 分數: *win by five points* 以五分取勝; *win on points* i.e. in boxing, win without knocking out one's opponent 得分, 即: 拳擊中未擊倒對手而獲勝. **8** use; purpose 用處; 目的: *What is the point of wasting time?* 浪費時間有甚麼用處呢? *There is no point in staying.* 待着沒有用. **9** detail; single item 細節; 單項: *I answered him point by point.* 我仔細地回答了他. **10** main idea; most important thing 要點; 含意: *He missed the whole point of my speech* i.e. he did not understand what it was really about 他沒抓住我講話的全部要點. 即: 他不明白我究竟講了甚麼. **11** something that makes a person different or outstanding 特點, 特質: *his main point as a writer* 他作爲作家的主要特點; *her strong point* i.e. something she is really good at 她的優點. 即: 她真正擅長的事情. **points** *npl* rails which can be moved so that a train can move from one track to another 轉軌器. **pointless** *adj* useless; having no purpose 無用的; 沒意義的; 沒目的的: *We were given many pointless things to do.* 我們被安排幹了

許多沒意義的事. **pointlessly** adv
'point-'blank adj 1 very close to the
target 近距離直接瞄準的, 直射的:
take point-blank aim 近距離直接瞄準
目標. 2 complete and direct 直率的:
point-blank refusal 直率的拒絕. Also
亦作 adv: *He fired at his victim point-
blank.* 他向他的犧牲品直接瞄準開火.
He refused point-blank. 他直率地拒絕
了. **'point duty** work of directing traffic (esp. at crossroads) 站崗, 值勤(尤
指在交叉路口指揮交通). **at the point
of** very near to 即將, 瀕於: *at the
point of death* 瀕臨死亡. **make a
point of doing something** make the
effort to do something which one
considers necessary 強調, 認為有必
要: *He always made a point of knowing the students by name.* 他常常強調
要熟悉學生的名字. **on the point of**
just about to 正要: *When he was on
the point of winning he stumbled and
fell.* 他正要獲勝時竟摔倒了. **to the
point** having to do with what is being
discussed 中肯. **point of view** way in
which one sees something or thinks
about something 觀點: *From your
point of view this may be important;
but from mine it is not.* 從你的觀點來
看, 這也許是重要的, 但從我的觀點來看
卻不重要.

point² [pɔint] vt / i 1 show the position
or direction of something (e.g. by using a finger) 指向. (例如: 用手指頭
指): *He pointed to the house I was
looking for.* 他指着我正在找的房子. 2
aim or direct a finger, gun etc at
someone 瞄準: *He pointed the gun at
me.* 他把槍對着我瞄準. **pointed** adj
1 coming to a point 尖尖的: *pointed
roof* 尖屋頂. 2 aimed at someone,
often to hurt or reprove them 針對某
人的: *pointed remark* 針對某人的話.

pointedly adv **pointer** nc long stick
used to point things out on a blackboard, map etc. 指物棒. **point something out to somebody** call someone's attention to something (對某人)
指出, 警告, 提醒: *He pointed out that
the road was not safe in winter.* 他警
告說冬天裏這條路不安全.

poise [pɔiz] vt / i 1 place something in
a certain way so that it remains
steady; balance 使平衡; 保持平衡: *He
poised the pencil upright on the table.*
他使這枝鉛筆在桌上豎起, 保持平衡. 2
hold raised in a certain way 懸着. 3
hover, prepare for action 躍躍欲試:
The lion was poised to spring. 獅子躍
躍欲跳. Also 亦作 nu way of holding
the head and body (身體. 頭部等的)
姿態, 體態.

poison ['pɔizn] nc / u substance which
causes sickness or death if it comes
in contact with, or is consumed by,
living things 毒物. Also 亦作 vt 1 kill
by using poison 毒殺. 2 put poison in
or on 放毒, 下毒. **poisonous** adj.

poke [pouk] vt / i 1 push something /
someone with the finger, a stick etc.
戳; 撥動: *poke someone in the ribs* 戲
謔地觸某人肋骨; *poke a fire* i.e. stir
up the coals 撥火, 即: 攪動煤火. 2
push a stick etc in or through something; make (a hole) in this way 戳穿,
刺: *He poked a hole in the wall with
a stick.* 他用棍子在牆上戳了個洞.

poker¹ nc long, metal rod for stirring
up the coals, wood etc in a fire 撥火
棒. **'poker-faced** adj not showing
what one is thinking or feeling 面無表
情的.

poker² ['poukə*] nu card game which is
usu. played for money 撲克牌遊戲.

poky ['pouki] adj (with reference to a
room, house etc) too small to be

comfortable or pleasant (指房間、屋子等)太狹小而不舒適.

Polaroid ['pəulərɔid] *nu* type of plastic that eliminates glare and which is used in sunglasses etc. (用於太陽鏡等的)偏光片. **2** camera that develops and prints photographs instantly 即拍即現的照相機.

pole¹ [pəul] *nc* long, thin rod of wood or metal used for holding something up 桿, 竿: *telegraph pole* i.e. one to support telephone wires 電綫桿; 即: 拉電綫的桿子; *tent pole* 帳篷竿; *flag-pole* 旗竿. **'pole vault** jump made with the help of a long pole 撑竿跳高.

pole² [pəul] *nc* **1** one of the two ends of the axis of the earth or another planet i.e. the line around which the earth etc turns (地球或其他星球)南北兩極之一: *the North Pole and the South Pole* 北極和南極. **2** either of the two ends of a magnet or battery 磁極或電池的一端: *the positive pole and the negative pole* 正極和負極. **polar** *adj* connected with, or near, the North or South Pole 北極的或南極的; 近北極的或近南極的: *polar bear* i.e. large. white bear living near the North Pole 北極熊; 即: 生活在北極附近的大白熊.

police [pə'li:s] *n* (always followed by a *pl* verb) (常跟複數動詞). **1** body of men whose duty it is to keep order and arrest those who break the laws of a country 警察: *The police are going to question everyone in the house.* 警察將審問屋裏的每個人. **2** department of the government concerned with keeping order and arresting wrongdoers 警察局, 公安局. Also 亦作 *vt* control; keep order in 控制; 管治; 監視: *police the streets* 派警察管治

各條街. **po'liceman** member of the police force 警察. (*fem* 陰 **police-woman**). **po'lice station** police office 警察分局, 派出所.

policy¹ ['pɔlisi] *nc / u* plan of conduct; statement of what is going to be done (esp. by the government, a business company etc.) 政策; 方針(尤指政府的或商業公司的): *It is a good policy to save some money when you can.* 你們能省錢就省錢, 這是個好方針. *Have you read about the new government policy to deal with unemployment?* 你看過政府對付失業的新政策嗎?

policy² ['pɔlisi] *nc* written agreement that an amount of money will be paid to someone if a certain thing happens 保險單: *He took out a fire insurance policy for his house* i.e. if his house was burnt down he would be paid some money 他申請了他的房屋火險保險單. 即: 假如他的房屋被火燒了, 他會得到一筆賠償款.

polio ['pəuliəu] *nu* type of disease which causes paralysis (Short for **poliomyelitis** ['pəuliəumaiə'laitis] 小兒麻痺症(poliomyelitis 的縮略式).

polish ['pɔliʃ] *vt* make smooth and shiny by rubbing 擦亮: *polish one's shoes* 擦亮某人的鞋. Also 亦作 *nu* **1** substance used to make something smooth and shiny 上光粉, 擦亮劑: *shoe polish* 鞋油. **2** smooth and shiny surface 光滑, 光澤: *the polish on a table* 桌子的光澤. **polished** *adj* made smooth and shiny 擦亮的, 磨光的; 洗練的, 優美的. **polish something up** **1** make something better in some small way 潤飾: *polish up an essay* 潤飾一篇雜文. **2** refresh one's memory 溫習, 複習: *I'm going to Paris, so I must polish up my French.* (*informal*) 我將到巴黎去, 所以我得把法語熟悉一

下．(非正式).

polite [pə'lait] *adj* having or showing good manners; wellbehaved 有禮貌的: *polite children* 有禮貌的小孩. (*opp* 反義詞 **impolite**). **politely** *adv* **politeness** *nu*.

politic ['pɔlitik] *adj* wise, prudent 精明的, 有智慧的, 有策略的: *a politic action / scheme etc.* 有策略的行動/計謀等. (*opp* 反義詞 **impolitic**).

political [pə'litikl] *adj* of or concerned with the government of a country 政治的: *a political party* 政黨; *political science* i.e. the study of politics 政治科學, 即: 對政治的研究. **politically** *adv* **politician** [pɔli'tiʃən] *nc* person concerned with government 政治家, 政界人士, 政客.

politics ['pɔlitiks] *nu* matters concerning the running of a country, city etc. 政治學; 政治; 政策; 政見: *be interested in politics* 對政治感興趣.

poll [poul] *nc* 1 collection of votes i.e. papers which show who has been chosen for some purpose, often to form a government 投票: *A poll was organized in every village.* 各村組織選舉投票. 2 number of votes given 投票數目: *a heavy poll* i.e. many people voted 踴躍投票, 即: 許多人投了票. 3 list of people (esp. those who can vote) 選舉人名冊: *have one's name on the poll* 選舉人名冊上有某人的名字. 4 investigation into what people think on a certain subject 民意測驗. Also 亦作 *vt / i* 1 receive a certain number of votes 獲選票: *He polled 80 votes.* 他獲得80張選票. 2 vote in an election 投票: **the polls** *npl* polling booths 投票處. **'polling booth** place where people go to vote 選民去投票的地方.

pollen ['pɔln] *nu* fine dust (usu. yellow) which is found on flowers and which makes other flowers fertile when it is brought to them (e.g. by the wind, bees etc.) 花粉.

pollute [pə'lu:t] *vt* make unhealthy 污染: *The river has been polluted with oil.* 這條河已經給油污染了. **pollution** *nu*.

polo ['poulou] *nu* game played by men on horseback, in which a ball is hit with long sticks with wooden heads (called **mallets**) 馬球.

poly- ['pɔli] *prefix* many (e.g. **polygamy**) 多(例如: polygamy).

polyester [ˌpɔli'estə] *nu* synthetic resin used in making plastics, fibres etc. 聚酯.

polygamy [pə'ligəmi] *nu* act or custom of having more than one wife 一夫多妻制.

polygon ['pɔligən] *nc* plane figure having more than four angles and four sides 多角形; 多邊形.

polytechnic [pɔli'teknik] *nc* institution (usu. for adults) where many different subjects are taught (esp. practical subjects) 理工學院(尤指應用學科).

polythene ['pɔliθi:n] *nu* kind of strong plastic material which is used as wrapping and for making many different articles 聚乙烯.

pomegranate ['pɔmigrænit] *nc / u* tough-skinned fruit, about the size of an apple, containing many seeds 石榴樹.

pommel ['pʌml] *vt* beat with the fists 拳打. *past* 過去式和過去分詞 **pommelled.** (*US* 美 **pommeled**). (Also 亦作 **pummel**).

pomp [pɔmp] *nu* solemn, magnificent display 盛況, 大場面: *The queen was greeted at the town hall with much pomp and ceremony.* 女王在市政廳受

受到儀式盛況空前的歡迎. **pompous**
adj too dignified; trying to seem very
important 傲慢的; 自大的: *a pompous
official* 傲慢的官僚. **pompously** *adv.*

pond [pɔnd] *nc* area of still water,
smaller than a lake 池塘: *Some cattle
were drinking at the pond.* 有牲畜正
在池塘喝水.

ponder ['pɔndə*] *vt / i* think about
something carefully 細想, 考慮: *ponder (over) a problem* 考慮問題.

ponderous ['pɔndərəs] *adj* **1** very
heavy 沉重的, 笨重的: *a ponderous
weight* 沉重的物品. **2** slow and clumsy 粗笨的; 笨拙的: *ponderous movements* 粗笨的動作. **3** (with reference
to a person) dull and slow (指人) 獃
板的, 沉悶的.

pontificate [pɔn'tifikeit] *vi* give opinions, decisions etc in a very pompous
way as though one were much more
important than one really is 發表武斷
的意見, 口出狂言, 自以為是地說 (或
寫).

pontoon [pɔn'tuːn] **1** *nc* flat boat or
similar floating thing used to hold up
a bridge 平底船, 浮筒: *pontoon bridge*
浮橋. **2** *nu* type of card game 一種紙
牌遊戲.

pony ['pouni] *nc* kind of small horse 小
馬.

poodle ['puːdl] *nc* type of dog kept as a
pet 獅子狗.

pool¹ [puːl] *nc* **1** small area of still water 水坑. **2** small amount of water
lying on a road, the floor etc. 成堆的
水: *There were pools of water all
over the house after the pipe burst.*
水管破裂以後, 屋裏全是一堆堆的水. **3**
part of a river that is still and deep
潭: *fish in a pool* 潭中的魚. **4** place
specially made for people to swim in
游泳池. (Also 亦作 **swimming pool**).

pool² [puːl] *nc* **1** amount of money to
be won in a gambling game (made up
of what the different players have paid
in) 賭金. **2** arrangement by different business firms to work together
and share the money they make (不
同公司, 商號的) 聯營. **3** anything that
is shared among many people 共享
的, 共同使用的東西: *a pool of experience* 共同的經驗. **4** (*US*) game played
on a special table with six pockets.
The aim is to drive balls into the
pockets with long wooden sticks (美)
(有 6 個小網袋的) 撞球遊戲. (目的是用
長木棒將球擊進袋中). (called **cues**).
Also 亦作 *vt* put money etc together
for the benefit of all who have put
some in 集中 (錢等) 共同使用: *We
pooled all our money so as to buy a
car.* 我們把錢全部集中起來, 以便買一
輛汽車. '**football pools** form of
gambling in which money can be won
by saying correctly what the results
of football matches will be 足球賽賭
彩.

poor [puə*] *adj* **1** having little or no
money 貧窮的, 沒錢的: *The failure of
his business left him a poor man.* 他的
生意的失敗使他變成窮人. **2** unlucky;
unfortunate 不幸的; 可憐的: *That
poor woman has lost her son.* 那可憐
的女人失去了她的兒子. **3** bad 劣質
的, 壞的, 低於標準的, 差的: *These
clothes are of poor quality.* 這些衣服
質量低劣. *He is a poor speaker.* 他演
講很差. *There was a poor attendance
at the meeting.* 到會的人很少. **the
poor** poor people 窮人: *care for the
poor* 關心窮人. **poorly** **1** *adv* badly
拙劣地, 差, 糟: *He did poorly in the
examination.* 他考得很糟. **2** *pred adj*
in bad health 不舒適, 不健康: *She has
been keeping poorly* i.e. she has not

been well 她一直感到不舒服. 即: 她身體不好. (*informal* in sense **2**) (義 2 為非正式).

pop¹ [pɔp] *vt / i* **1** make a short, sharp sound (e.g. when a cork is taken out of a bottle) 砰地響, 嚓啪地響. **2** move, go, come quickly or unexpectedly 快速或出其不意地來去: *I popped the book into my bag.* 我很快地把書放進袋裏. *I've just popped in to say hello.* 我剛進來表示問候. *She keeps popping in and out* i.e. entering and leaving the house often 她總是進進出出. 即: 常常進出房子. *past* 過去式和過去分詞 **popped**. Also 亦作 *nc* short, sharp sound as when a cork is taken out of a bottle 砰然一聲, 嚓啪的響聲. **'popcorn** maize puffed out and sweetened 爆玉米花, 爆穀.

pop² [pɔp] *nu* type of modern music which appeals mainly to young people 流行音樂. Also 亦作 *adj*: *a pop record* 流行音樂唱片. *Note* 說明: short for *popular* (music), but now used as a full word. popular 的縮畧式, 但現在可當為一個完整的詞使用.

pope [poup] *nc* head of the Roman Catholic Church 羅馬天主教教皇.

poplar ['pɔplə*] *nc* tall, thin tree that grows very quickly 白楊樹.

poppy ['pɔpi] *nc* **1** plant with large red, white or yellow flowers 罌粟. **2** flower of this plant 罌粟花.

popular ['pɔpjulə*] *adj* **1** liked by many people 受歡迎的, 流行的: *be very popular with one's fellow students* 受到同學的歡迎. (*opp* 反義詞 **unpopular**). **2** of or for the people 大衆的: *a popular government* 大衆的政府. **popularly** *adv* **popularity** [pɔpju'læriti] *nu* condition of being liked by many people 普遍, 流行, 受歡迎. **popularize** *vt* make popular (in sense

1) 使受歡迎.

populate ['pɔpjuleit] *vt* fill with people 移民於, 殖民於: *America was populated mostly by Europeans.* 美洲大部份給歐洲人所殖民. *Japan is a densely populated country.* 日本是個人口稠密的國家. **population** [pɔpju'leiʃən] *nc / u* **1** people living in a country, city etc; number of these people 人口; 人口總數: *the population of London* 倫敦的人口. **2** special section of the people living in a country etc. 族, 羣體, 種羣: *the Negro population of the United States* 美國的黑人種族.

porcelain ['pɔːslin] *nu* **1** fine china i.e. baked white clay used for making cups, saucers etc. 瓷. **2** articles (cups etc) made from fine china 瓷器.

porch [pɔːtʃ] *nc* area at the entrance to a house, church etc that is covered over 門廊.

porcupine ['pɔːkjupain] *nc* small animal like a rat covered with quills i.e. sharp, stiff hairs 豪豬, 箭豬.

pore¹ [pɔː*] *vi* (usu. with **over**) look at or study something carefully for a long time (通常與 over 連用) 用心閱讀, 仔細研究: *He is always poring over his books.* 他總是用心讀書.

pore² [pɔː*] *nc* very small opening in the skin 毛孔: *Human beings sweat through their pores.* 人從毛孔出汗.

pork [pɔːk] *nu* meat of a pig 豬肉. see also 亦見 **bacon, ham.**

pornography [pɔː'nɔgrəfi] *nu* writing or pictures intended to arouse sexual feelings 春宮, 春畫; 色情照片, 色情文字, 色情書刊. **pornographic** [pɔːnə'græfik] *adj.*

porous ['pɔːrəs] *adj* allowing liquid to pass through 可滲透的: *porous soil* 可滲透的土壤.

porpoise ['pɔːpəs] *nc* type of air-breathing sea animal about four to eight feet long with a blunt nose 海豚.

porridge ['pɔridʒ] *nu* food made of grain (e.g. oatmeal) boiled in water or milk 麥片粥, 粥.

port¹ [pɔːt] *nc* 1 place for sheltering ships; harbour 港; 港口. 2 town with a harbour, where ships can be loaded and unloaded 港市.

port² [pɔːt] *nu* left side of ship when one faces forward 左舷. **'porthole** small round window on the side of a ship 舷窗.

port³ [pɔːt] *nu* type of sweet wine (usu. red) 紅葡萄酒.

portable ['pɔːtəbl] *adj* able to be carried 手提式的, 輕便的: *a portable typewriter* 手提式打字機.

portcullis [pɔːt'kʌlis] *nc* strong, iron gate which can be slid up and down, used in former times to protect castles which were being attacked 古代城堡的吊閘, 吊門.

portend [pɔː'tend] *vt* be a sign or warning that something is going to happen 預兆, 預示. **portent** ['pɔːtent] *nc* sign or warning 凶兆, 前兆.

porter ['pɔːtə*] *nc* 1 person employed to carry cases, bags etc. 搬運工, 挑伕: *railway porter* 火車站行李工. 2 doorkeeper 看門人. 3 (*US*) sleeping-car attendant on a train [美] 卧車的服務員.

portfolio [ˌpɔːt'fouljou] *nc* 1 flat, portable case for loose papers etc. 公事包, 文件夾, 紙夾. 2 office of a minister of state or a member of a cabinet 部長職, 閣員職. *pl* 複數 portfolios.

portion ['pɔːʃən] *nc* 1 part; share of something 一份; 部份: *The money was divided into seven portions.* 這些錢被分成七份. 2 amount 一些, 一客:

a small portion of cheese 少量的乳酪.

portly ['pɔːtli] *adj* fat 肥胖的: *a portly old gentleman* 肥胖的老紳士.

portrait ['pɔːtrit] *nc* picture of a person 人像, 肖像. **portray** [pɔː'trei] *vt* 1 describe; picture in words 描寫, 描繪. 2 act the part of someone on the stage 扮演, 飾演. **portrayal** [pɔː'treiəl] *nc* 1 act of portraying 扮演, 描繪. 2 description 描寫.

pose [pouz] *vt / i* 1 hold a certain position while one is being photographed, painted etc. 擺姿勢: *pose for a picture* 擺姿勢照個相. 2 state something to be answered or discussed 提出, 陳述: *pose a question / problem etc.* 提出問題等. 3 pretend to be what one is not 假裝, 偽裝: *He posed as a rich man.* 他假裝成富人. Also 亦作 *nc* 1 position of the body when being photographed etc. 姿勢, 姿態. 2 way of behaving which is intended to impress others 擺樣子, 造作. **poser** *nc* difficult problem 難題.

posh [pɔʃ] *adj* rich and fashionable, belonging to the upper classes (*informal*) 時髦的, 高級的, 豪華的; 上流社會的. (非正式).

position [pə'ziʃən] *nc* 1 place where a person / thing is 位置, 方位: *The table used to be in this position.* 這張桌子常擺在這個位置. 2 way in which a person / thing is placed 職位, 位置: *find a more comfortable position* 找個比較舒適的位置. 3 job; employment 職業; 工作: *apply for a certain position* 申請某職業. 4 rank 地位, 身份: *someone in a high position* i.e. of high rank 地位高的人, 即: 高層人士. 5 attitude; point of view 態度; 觀點, 看法: *What is your position on this matter?* 你對這件事的看法怎樣? 6 state or condition 情況, 狀態: *I'm not in a position to* *help you* i.e. I cannot help you 我不能夠幫你的忙. 即: 我不能幫助你. Also 亦作 *vt* put into a position 放置; 把…放在某位置.

positive ['pɒzitiv] *adj* 1 sure; definite; certain 肯定的; 確定的; 沒疑問的: *receive positive instructions* 得到明確的指示; *be positive about something* 確定某事. 2 helpful; constructive 有益的; 建設性的: *Positive suggestions will be welcomed.* 歡迎有益的建議. 3 (mathematics) greater than 0; + (數學) 正的: *a positive number* 正數. **positively** *adv* definitely; without doubt 肯定地; 無疑地.

posse ['pɒsi] *nc* group of people gathered together in order to chase a criminal 治安隊, 民團隊.

possess [pə'zes] *vt* own; have 擁有; 具有; 佔有: *He possesses a lot of property.* 他擁有許多財產. **possessor** *nc* **possession** 1 *nu* condition of owning or having 有, 擁有: *be in possession of something* 擁有某物; *take possession of something* 獲得某物. 2 *nc* (often *pl*) thing owned (常用複數) 所有物, 財產: *I lost most of my possessions during the war.* 戰爭期間, 我喪失了我的大部份財產. **possessive** *adj* 1 too anxious to have or keep 佔有的, 認爲自己獨有的; 有佔有慾的: *That child is very possessive about / with his toys, he won't let other children play with them.* 那孩子認爲他的玩具是他所獨有的, 他不讓別的孩子玩它們. 2 (grammar) showing possession (e.g. **my, your, man's** are possessive forms) (語法) 所有格的 (例如: my, your, man's 是所有格的形式).

possible ['pɒsibl] *adj* 1 that can be done; that can happen 可能的; 可能發生的: *Anything is possible.* 一切都是可能的. *Is it possible to do this*

another way? 做這件事可能有別的辦法嗎? 2 that may be accepted; reasonable 可接受的, 適當的, 合理的: *a possible solution* 合理的解決辦法; *a possible candidate* 適當的候選人. (*opp* **impossible**). **possibly** *adv* 1 by any possibility; by any means 可能地; 無論如何: *Can you possibly come?* 你可能來嗎? 2 perhaps 也許: *He may possibly be there.* 他也許在那裏. **possibility** [pɒsi'biliti] *nc / u* 1 state of being possible 可能, 可能性: *There is some possibility (that) he may be late.* 他也許會遲到, 這是有可能的. 2 something that is possible; a job with great possibilities i.e. opportunities 可能的事: *It's only a possibility* i.e. it's not certain. 這僅僅是個可能的事. 即: 這不能肯定.

post¹ [pəust] *nc / u* 1 (Brit) system of sending and delivering letters, parcels etc. (英) 郵政: *send something by post* 郵寄東西. (*US* 美 **mail**). 2 letters etc delivered or collected at one time 一次收送的郵件: *This letter arrived with the morning post.* 這封信是跟早上的郵件來的. *The last post is at 7.15 p.m.* 最後一次收送郵件是下午七點一刻. Also 亦作 *vt*. 1 send something by post 郵寄. 2 take a letter etc to a post office or pillar box 投寄: *Please post these letters for me.* 請幫我寄這些信. **postage** *nu* amount to be paid for sending letters etc by post 郵資, 郵費. **postal** *adj* connected with the post (in sense 1). 郵政的; 郵寄的 (義 1): *postal services* 郵政業務. **postal order** i.e. kind of receipt for a small amount of money which can be bought at a post office, posted and then cashed at any post office by the person who receives it 郵政匯票. 即: 小額款項的匯票從郵局寄出, 收款人可

從其他郵局領取現款. **'postcard** card which can be posted (usu. without being placed in an envelope) (通常不用放在信封内) 明信片 . **'postman** (*Brit*) man who delivers letters (*US* 美 **mailman**) (英) 郵差, 郵遞員 . *pl* 複數 **postmen**. **'postmark** mark put on letters etc over the stamp to cancel it, and also to show when and where the letter was posted 郵戳 . Also 亦作 *vt*. **'postmaster, 'postmistress** man, woman in charge of a post office 郵政局長, 女郵政局長 . **'post office 1** government department which runs the postal services 郵政部 . **2** shop or office for postal services (e.g. buying stamps, posting letters etc) 郵政局 . **'postage stamp** stamp stuck on letters etc to show that postage has been paid 郵票.

post² [poust] *nc* **1** place where a soldier, policeman etc is on duty 哨所, 崗位, 站: *No-one may leave his post without permission.* 任何人不得擅自離開崗位. **2** job 工作, 職位: *apply for a post as a teacher* 謀求當教師的工作.

post³ [poust] *nc* piece of wood, metal etc placed upright (usu. to support or mark something) 標柱, 標桿, 柱. (通常用於做某種標記): *a bedpost* 床桿; *the winning post* i.e. in a race 起跑點標桿, 終點標桿, 即: 用於賽跑中; *a doorpost* 門柱 . Also 亦作 *vt* (usu. with **up**) put something up on a notice board to be seen by many people (常與 up 連用) 貼出公告, 公佈, 宣佈: *The list of those who were chosen was posted up.* 中選者的名單已公佈出來 . **poster** *nc* public notice (esp. used for advertising) 海報, 招貼 (尤指用於廣告的).

post-⁴ [poust] *prefix* later than; after (e.g. **postgraduate**) 後; 次 (例如:

postgraduate).

posterity [pɔs'teriti] *nu* **1** person's descendants 子孫. **2** people who will be living at some future time 後代: *discoveries which will be of great benefit to posterity* 對後代極有益的發現.

postgraduate ['poust'grædjuət] *adj* done after taking a degree 獲得學位後繼續研究的: *postgraduate studies* 研究生學習. Also 亦作 *nc* someone who continues his studies after he has got a degree 研究生.

posthumous ['pɔstjuməs] *adj* after the death of someone 死後的: *a posthumous child* i.e. one born after the death of its father 遺腹子, 即: 其父去世後出生的孩子; *a posthumous book* i.e. one published after the death of its author 遺著, 即: 作者死後出版的書.

post mortem ['poust'mɔːtəm] *nc* examination of a corpse to discover the cause of death 驗屍.

postpone [pəs'poun] *vt* put off, delay until a later time 延期, 擱置, 推遲: *His visit was postponed because of illness.* 由於生病, 他的訪問延期了. **postponement** *nc/u*.

postscript ['poustskript] *nc* something added at the end of a letter, after the signature (usu. introduced by the letters P.S.) 附言, 又及, 再者 (通常用 P.S. 表示).

postulate ['pɔstjuleit] *vt* take something as true without proof in order to reason from it 假定, 假設.

posture ['pɔstʃə*] *nc* position of the body; way of holding the body 姿勢; 體態: *lie in a lazy posture* 以懶惰的姿勢躺着; *have good posture* 具有良好的體態.

posy ['pouzi] *nc* bunch of flowers 小花束, 束花: *The little girl was holding a posy.* 小姑娘正拿着一束花.

pot [pɔt] **1** *nc* round container made of earthenware, metal etc used to hold liquids and other things 罐, 鍋, 盆, 瓶, 壺: *a cooking pot* 燒飯鍋; *a flowerpot* 花盆; *a teapot* 茶壺. **2** *nc* amount held in such a container 一罐, 鍋, 壺之量: *make a pot of tea* 泡一壺茶. **3** *nu* marijuana i.e. type of intoxicating drug (*informal* in sense 3) 大麻 (義 3 爲非正式). Also 亦作 *vt* **1** put something into a pot (usu. to make it stay fresh longer) 放入 … (鍋, 盆 等): *potted ham* 罐裝火腿. **2** put a plant into a pot of earth 把 … 栽在花盆裏. **pottery 1** *nu* pots etc made from clay and hardened by heat 陶器. **2** *nu* art of making pots in this way 陶器製造術. **3** *nc* place where pots are made 陶器作坊或工廠. **potter** *nc* person who makes pots etc from clay 陶工. **'pothole** *nc* **1** hole in a road 小坑, 坑窪. **2** very deep hole underground 地下洞穴. **'potholing** *nu* sport of exploring potholes (in sense 2) 洞穴探險運動 (義 2) **take 'pot'luck** accept what is available without knowing much about it (*informal*) 糊塗地接受 (非正式).

potassium [pəˈtæsjəm] *nu* soft, silver-white, metallic chemical element 鉀.

potato [pəˈteitou] *nc / u* roundish root plant with white flesh commonly used as a vegetable 馬鈴薯. *pl* 複數 **potatoes**.

potent [ˈpoutnt] *adj* powerful; strong 有力的; 強烈的; 有效的: *a potent argument* 有力的論據. *a potent remedy for disease* 治病的良藥. **potency** *nu* **potentate** [ˈpoutnteit] *nc* powerful ruler 當權者, 統治者.

potential [pəˈtenʃl] *adj* which may come into effect or existence 潛在的, 可能的: *Although this area is very poor just now, its potential wealth is great* i.e. the basis for this wealth is there 雖然這個地區目前很貧困, 但它的潛在的財富是巨大的. 即: 這些財富的基礎就在那裏. Also 亦作 *nu* possibilities 可能性, 潛力: *an area of great potential* 具有巨大的潛力的地區. **potentially** *adv*.

potion [ˈpouʃən] *nc* drink of medicine, or poison 一服藥水, 一劑藥.

potter¹, pottery [ˈpɔtə(ri)] *nc, nu* see 見 **pot**.

potter² [ˈpɔtə•] *vi* (with *about*) go from one little job to another (常與 *about* 連用) 走來走去做些瑣碎的事情: *He likes pottering about in the garden.* (*informal*) 他喜歡在花園裏各處做些瑣碎的事情(非正式).

potty [ˈpɔti] *adj* mad; crazy 發狂的; 着迷的. Also 亦作 *nc* child's pot, used to urinate in (both *informal*) (小孩用的)尿壺(均爲非正式).

pouch [pautʃ] *nc* **1** small bag 小袋子: *tobacco pouch* 煙袋. **2** part of the body coming out to form a bag 肚袋, (動物藏食物的)頰袋: *kangaroo's pouch* 袋鼠的肚袋.

poultry [ˈpoultri] **1** *npl* (followed by *pl* verb) chickens, hens, ducks, geese etc. (用複數動詞)家禽. **2** *nu* flesh of these birds as meat 家禽肉.

pounce [pauns] *vi* come down suddenly on; jump on 猛撲; 突襲: *The lion pounced on its prey.* 獅子向它的獵物猛撲過去. Also 亦作 *nc* sudden jump or swoop 猛撲, 下攫.

pound¹ [paund] *nc* **1** measure of weight 1 pound (avoirdupois) = 16 ounces; 1 pound (troy) = 12 ounces (常衡時等於十六盎司, 金衡時等於十二盎司): *The sugar weighed five pounds.* 這糖重五磅. **2** unit of money in Great Britain etc 1 pound formerly = 20 shillings; now 1 pound=100 new pence 英鎊 (以前一英鎊等於二十先令, 現在一英鎊等於一百便士.): *This coat cost ten pounds.* 這件大衣值十英鎊. *Note* 説明: the difference between *five pounds* and *a five-pound note.* five pounds (五英鎊) 和 a five-pound note (一張五英鎊的鈔票) 不同.

pound² [paund] *vt / i* **1** hit hard again and again 連續猛擊, 狠敲: *pound at / on the door with one's fists* 用拳頭猛敲門. **2** crush into a powder 搗碎, 舂爛: *pound ears of corn into grain* 將穀穗搗成穀粒. **3** beat violently 劇烈地跳動, 重擊: *When I stopped running, my heart was pounding.* 我跑步停下來時, 我的心劇烈地跳動着.

pound³ [paund] *nc* closed-in place where animals (usu. lost animals) can be kept 獸欄, 圈欄 (收留迷失的動物).

pour [pɔ:*] *vt / i* **1** cause liquids to flow 流, 倒出, 澆入: *I poured some milk from the bottle into the jug.* 我把瓶裏的牛奶倒入大壺中. **2** move in large numbers 蜂擁: *People were pouring out of the burning building.* 人們從起火的樓裏蜂擁而出. **3** rain heavily 傾盆大雨: *It's pouring outside.* 屋外大雨傾盆. *He stood in the pouring rain.* 他站在傾盆大雨中.

pout [paut] *vt / i* push out the lips, as an angry child does 噘嘴. Also 亦作 *nc*.

poverty ['pɔvəti] *nu* state of being poor 貧困: *live in poverty* 生活貧困. **'poverty-stricken** *adj* very poor 極度貧困: *poverty-stricken area* 極貧困的地區.

powder ['paudə*] *nc / u* **1** anything that has been made into dust 粉. **2** special kind of powder (e.g. *face powder; gunpowder*) 特種粉 (例如: 撲面粉, 火藥). Also 亦作 *vt / i* **1** put powder on

塗粉: *She powdered her face.* 她在臉上塗粉. **2** make into powder 搗成粉: *powdered milk* 奶粉. **powdery** *adj* like powder 粉狀的: *powdery snow* 粉狀的雪. **'powder puff** small pad of cloth etc for putting on face powder 粉撲.

power ['pauə*] **1** *nu* strength 力量: *a display of military power* 軍事力量的顯示. **2** *nu* ability; what one can do 能力; 能幹: *I shall do everything in my power for him.* 我將盡我的能力爲他做一切事. **3** *nc* control; authority 控制; 權力: *Does he have the power to arrest anyone?* 他有權抓人嗎? *I have him in my power.* 我控制了他. **4** *nc* special kind of ability 智能: *He is losing his powers of reasoning.* 他正在失去理智. **5** *nc* person, department, country etc having authority 有勢力者, 強國: *the great world powers* 世界強國. **6** *nu* energy force 力; 力量: *a mill driven by water power* 水力推動的磨房. Also 亦作 *vt* provide energy or force for 提供動力: *powered by a new type of engine* 以新型的發動機提供動力. **powerful** *adj* having great power or strength 強大的, 有力的: *a powerful country* 一個強大的國家. **powerless** *adj* without strength; unable to do something 沒能力的; 辦不到的: *I am powerless to help you.* 我沒能力幫助你. **'power cut** occasion when electric power is cut off (e.g. by a strike) 停電 (例如: 由於罷工而停電). **'power station** place where electrical power is produced 發電廠.

pox [pɔks] *nc* any disease that covers the body or parts of the body with sores 痘; 疹; 膿疱.

practice ['præktis] **1** *nu* doing something many times so as to be able to do it well 練習: *In order to play the* *piano well, one must have plenty of practice.* 一個人為了彈好鋼琴, 必須進行大量練習. **2** *nu* action of doing something 實行, 實施: *How do you think this scheme will work out in practice?* i.e. when it is tried 你認為這個計劃實際上怎麼進行? 即: 付諸實行時. **3** *nu* something done regularly as a habit 習慣: *It is my practice always to rise early.* 總是早起是我的習慣. **4** *nc* business of a doctor or lawyer (醫生或律師的) 業務, 生意: *Dr Jones has a very good practice.* 瓊斯醫生的生意很好. **practicable** ['præktikəbl] *adj* that can be done 可行的: *a practicable scheme* 可行的計劃, 即: 可以實行的計劃. (*opp* 反義詞 **impracticable**). **practical** ['præktikl] *adj* **1** concerned with actually doing a thing 實際的: *It sounds like a good idea, but there are some practical difficulties.* 它聽起來像個好主意, 但有些實際的困難. **2** useful 有用的, 實用的: *practical suggestion* 有用的建議. **3** good at doing or making things 有實際經驗的: *a practical person* 有實際經驗的人. (*opp* **unpractical** in sense 3) (義 3 的反義詞為 unpractical). **practically** *adv* almost; nearly 幾乎地; 差不多地: *He was practically penniless.* 他幾乎身無分文. **in practice** in effect; when actually done 實際上, 事實上. **be out of practice** not be able to do something because one has not been doing it many times recently 生疏, 荒廢.

practise ['præktis] (*US* 美 **practice**) *vt / i* **1** do something many times so as to be able to do it well 練習, 實習: *If you keep practising, your playing will improve.* 如果你堅持練習, 你的演奏就會進步. **2** do something regularly as a habit 常做, 慣做. **3** work as a doc-

tor / lawyer 執業, 從事: *practise medicine / law* 行醫/從事律師職業. **practitioner** [præk'tiʃənə*] *nc* person who practises medicine or law 開業者: *a medical practitioner* 行醫者, 開業醫生.

prairie ['preəri] *nc* (esp. in North America) large area of flat land with grass but no trees (尤指北美洲)大草原.

praise [preiz] *vt* **1** say that someone / something is good 讚美, 稱讚: *I praised her cooking.* 我稱讚她的烹調技術. **2** give honour to God 崇拜, 讚頌(神). Also 亦作 *nu* words praising someone / something 頌詞, 讚美的話. '**praise-worthy** *adj* deserving praise 值得讚揚的: *a praise-worthy cause* 值得讚揚的事業.

pram [præm] *nc* (*Brit*) carriage for a baby, pushed by hand (英) 嬰兒車. (*US* 美 **baby carriage**).

prance [prɑːns] *vi* **1** jump about on the hind legs 騰躍: *a prancing horse* 騰躍的馬. **2** move in a lively way 歡躍, 神氣地走: *The children pranced about.* 孩子們在歡蹦亂跳.

prank [præŋk] *nc* playful, harmless trick 玩笑, 惡作劇: *a child's prank* 孩子的惡作劇: *play a prank on someone* 作弄某人.

prattle ['prætl] *vt / i* talk as a child does; talk without thinking 小孩般的談話; 空談; 閒聊.

prawn [prɔːn] *nc* type of shellfish with thin legs which can be eaten 大蝦, 明蝦.

pray [prei] *vi* speak to God; direct one's thoughts to God 祈禱; 乞求: *pray to God for peace* 向上帝祈求安寧. **prayer** [preə*] **1** *nu* act of praying 祈禱: *a life devoted to prayer* 專心祈禱的一生. **2** *nc* words used in praying 祈禱文: *a child who knows his* *prayers* 知道他的祈禱文的孩子.

pre- [pri:] *prefix before (e.g.* precede; prefix; prejudge) 前, 先 (例如: precede; prefix; prejudge).

preach [pri:tʃ] *vt / i* **1** give a sermon in church 講道; 佈道. **2** give advice to others on religious matters; earnestly advise people to do something 傳教; 宣揚, 鼓吹. **preacher** *nc.*

precarious [pri'keəriəs] *adj* dangerous; uncertain 危險的; 不肯定的: *a precarious existence* i.e. living in such a way that nothing is certain 危險的生活, 即: 生活在一切都捉摸不定的氣氛中. **precariously** *adv.*

precaution [pri'kɔ:ʃən] *nc / u* care taken to prevent something unpleasant happening 預防措施: *take precautions against fire* 謹防火災. **precautionary** [pri'kɔ:ʃənri] *adj.*

precede [pri'si:d] *vt / i* come or go before 在…前, 先行: *The king was preceded by his nobles.* 貴族們走在國王前面. *The Greek civilization preceded the Roman one.* 希臘文明先於羅馬文明. **precedence** ['presidns] *nu* greater importance 更重要: *This problem should be discussed first, as it takes precedence over all the others.* 這個問題應該先討論, 因爲它比其他一切問題更重要. **precedent** [presidnt] *nc* something which has been done before, which can now be taken as an example or rule 先例, 前例: *If he is allowed to do this, it will be a precedent for others.* 如果他獲准做此事, 它將爲別人開了先例.

precinct ['pri:siŋkt] *nc* **1** land around an official or religious building, or enclosed shopping area 區域, 界限, 範圍: *the precincts of the school* 校區, 學校的範圍; *shopping precinct* 購物區. **2** *(US)* official area within a

boundary (美) 行政管區: *a police precinct* 警區, 管區.

precious ['preʃəs] *adj* **1** of great value 貴重的, 珍貴的: *Gold is a precious metal.* 金是貴重金屬. **2** very dear to one; much loved 珍愛的; 可愛的.

precipice ['presipis] *nc* very steep cliff or face of a rock, mountain etc. 懸崖: *The climber fell over a precipice.* 那個登山者跌下懸崖.

precipitate [pri'sipiteit] *vt* make something happen at once, or more quickly than it might have done 加速, 突然引起: *The killing of the prime minister precipitated a war.* 殺害總理突然引起一場戰爭. Also 亦作 [pri'sipitət] *adj* done very quickly; done without thinking carefully 匆忙的; 魯莽的; 突然的; *a precipitate departure / decision etc.* 匆忙的離開/決定等.

precipitous [pri'sipitəs] *adj* very steep 陡峭的.

precise [pri'sais] *adj* **1** exact; without mistakes 正確的; 準確的: *He gave a precise description of the thief.* 他對那個賊作了準確的描述. **2** careful about details 考究的, 嚴格的: *a very precise worker* 一個很嚴格的工人. (*opp* 反義詞 **imprecise**). **precisely** *adv* (often used when agreeing with someone) just so; exactly (常用於同意某人的看法時) 正是如此; 對的. **precision** [pri'siʒən] *nu* exactness 正確, 精確.

preclude [pri'klu:d] *vt* make impossible; prevent 使不可能; 阻止: *The condition of the roads precludes us from driving anywhere tonight.* 由於道路的情況我們今晚不可能到別處去.

precocious [pri'kouʃəs] *adj* having grown up or developed earlier than usual: 早熟的: *a precocious child* i.e. one that is more advanced than most children of the same age 早熟的孩子,

即: 比大部份同齡的孩子長大得快.

preconceive ['priːkən'siːv] *vt* form an idea or opinion before one has actually seen a thing / person 預思, 預想. 先入之見: *Before he went to America, he had all sorts of preconceived ideas about it.* 他去美國以前, 他對它就有各種各樣的成見.

precursor [priːˈkəːsə*] *nc* someone / something which comes before something else, as a sign of it; forerunner 先驅, 先兆, 前輩.

predatory ['predətəri] *adj* living by killing other animals 食肉的: *a predatory bird* 食肉鳥.

predecessor ['priːdisesə*] *nc* person who had a job or position before another person 前任.

predestine [priːˈdestin] *vt* (usu. with reference to fate or God) decide in advance (通常指命運或上帝) 預定, 註定: *He believed that the time of his death was predestined* i.e. that he could do nothing to avoid dying at a certain time 他相信他死亡的時間是命中註定的. 即: 他無法避免到某時死去. **predestination** [priːdesti'neiʃən] *nu*.

predetermine [priːdiˈtəːmin] *vt* decide before an event occurs 預定, 先定.

predicament [pri'dikəmənt] *nc* awkward situation that is difficult to get out of 困境, 窘境.

predicate ['predikət] *nc* part of a sentence which says something about the subject (e.g. in the sentence *The man is busy today*, the predicate is *is busy today*) 謂語, 述語. (例如: 在 The man is busy today 中 is busy today 是謂語).

predict [pri'dikt] *vt* say that something will happen 預測, 預言: *He predicted a war in the next few years / He predicted that war would break out in the*

next few years. 他預測未來幾年內會有一場戰爭/他預測未來幾年會發生戰爭.

prediction *nc / u* 1 act of predicting 預測. 2 something that has been predicted 預言.

predominant [pri'dɔminənt] *adj* bigger, stronger, more noticeable etc than others 有勢力的, 主要的, 較顯著的: *the predominant number* 佔優勢的多數; *the predominant feature* 主要的特徵. **predominantly** *adv* **predominance** *nu* **predominate** *vi* be predominant 支配, 佔優勢: *John predominated in the discussion.* 約翰在討論中佔了優勢.

pre-eminent [priːˈeminənt] *adj* most outstanding; best 卓越的, 傑出的; 最優秀的.

pre-empt [priːˈemt] *vt* act first and so prevent one's opponent or some other person from taking further action 搶先取得, 預先佔有.

preen [priːn] *vt* 1 smooth and arrange feathers with the beak. (鳥用嘴) 整理: *The bird was preening itself / its feathers.* 這鳥正在以喙整理牠自己/牠的羽毛. 2 show that one is proud of one's dress etc. (對自己的衣服等) 感到驕傲: *She was preening herself in front of the mirror.* 她在鏡子前面對自己的服裝感到驕傲.

prefabricate ['priːˈfæbrikeit] *vt* (with reference to buildings) manufacture parts in a factory, ready to put together at the building site (指房屋) 預製.

preface ['prefəs] *nc* note by an author at the beginning of a book 序言.

prefect ['priːfekt] *nc* pupil who is put in authority over other pupils 級長.

prefer [pri'fəː*] *vt* like better 較喜歡, 寧願: *I prefer the country to the town.* 鄉村和城鎮, 我比較喜歡鄉村. *I prefer*

to resign rather than obey his orders
我寧願辭職，而不願服從他的命令．
past 過去式和過去分詞 **preferred.**
preferable ['prefərəbl] *adj* better; to
be preferred 較好的；更合適的．**pref-
erably** *adv* by choice 較適合地，更可
取地；*You can phone me any time,
but preferably in the morning.* 你隨時
都可以打電話給我，但早上較適合．
preference ['prefərns] 1 *nc / u* act of
preferring 偏愛，寧要: *have a preference for meat rather than fish* 偏愛肉，
而不愛魚．2 *nc* something that is
liked better, given better treatment
etc. 偏愛物，嗜好物: *state one's preference* 說明某人的嗜好物．**preferen-
tial** [prefə'renʃl] *adj* giving or receiving preference 優先的: *preferential
treatment* 優待．

prefix ['priːfiks] *nc* group of letters
which, when put in front of a word,
can change or add to its meaning
(e.g. the prefix **mis-**, found in words
like **misbehave, misinform** etc.) 前
綴，字首(如: misbehave, misinform 等
詞中的 mis-)．

pregnant ['pregnənt] *adj* 1 (of woman)
having a child in the womb 懷孕的．2
full of meaning 深意的，豐富的: *a pregnant remark* 意味深長的話．**pregnancy** *nc / u.*

prehistoric ['priːhis'tɔrik] *adj* belonging
to the time before recorded history
i.e. before events were written down
史前的: *prehistoric man* 史前時期的
人．

prejudice ['predʒudis] *nc / u* opinion
formed before looking at the facts 偏
見，成見: *Some people have a prejudice against all foreigners.* 有些人對
外國人抱有偏見．**prejudiced** *adj*
(*opp* 反義詞 **unprejudiced**).

preliminary [pri'liminəri] *adj* coming

before something; preparing for something 初步的，預備的: *preliminary examination* 初試．Also 亦作 *nc* preliminary action, event etc. 初步，開端．

prelude ['preljuːd] *nc* event, action,
piece of music etc which comes before another and introduces it 序幕．

premature ['premətjuə*] *adj* too soon;
done or happening before the proper
time 早熟的，過早的: *a premature decision* 過早的決定．**prematurely** *adv.*

premeditate [priː'mediteit] *vt* plan or
think over something before doing it
預謀: *a premeditated murder* 謀殺．
premeditation [priːmedi'teiʃən] *nu.*

premier ['premiə*] *adj* first; chief 第一
的；首要的．*of premier importance* 非
常重要，最重要．Also 亦作 *nc* prime
minister; head of government 首相；總
理．

première [premi'eə*] *nc* first performance of a play, film etc. (戲劇、影片等
的) 首次公演．

premise ['premis] *nc* statement which
is taken to be true and from which
certain conclusions are drawn 前提．
premises *npl* house or building, including the land etc belonging to it 房
屋連四週土地．

premium ['priːmiəm] *nc* amount paid in
or for insurance 保險費: *I have insured my house for £5,000, at a premium of only £10 per year.* 我把我的
房子去保險五千英鎊，每年的保險費僅
十英鎊．

premonition [premə'niʃən] *nc* feeling
that something (usu. something unpleasant) is going to happen (通常指
不祥的) 預感，前兆: *a premonition of
danger* 危險的前兆．

preoccupy [priː'ɔkjupai] *vt* take up so
much of someone's attention that he
does not notice what is going on

around him 使全神貫注於, 使出神:
look preoccupied 看起來心不在焉;
preoccupied by / with family troubles
由於家庭的麻煩而心事重重. **preoc-
cupation** [priˈɔkjuˈpeiʃən] *nc* something that takes up all one's attention
全神貫注, 出神.

prep [prep] *nu* preparation for school
lessons; homework. *(informal)* 預習;
家庭作業(非正式).

prepare [priˈpeə*] *vt / i* get ready, make
ready 預備; 準備: *prepare a meal* 準
備飯菜; *prepare to leave* 準備動身;
prepare for someone's visit 爲某人的
訪問做準備; *be prepared to* i.e. be
willing to prepare, i.e. 願意去…. **preparation** [prepəˈreiʃən] *nu* preparing. 準
備: *The meeting will require a lot of
preparation.* 會議需要大量準備工作.
preparations *npl* things done to prepare for something 準備, 安排: *They
are making tremendous preparations
for the president's visit.* 他們正在爲總
統的訪問進行大規模的準備.

preposition [prepəˈziʃən] *nc* word used
to show how one word is related to
another (e.g. *to, by, with, from* etc
can be used as prepositions) 介詞(例
如: to, by, with, from 等).

preposterous [priˈpɔstərəs] *adj* foolish;
completely against reason 可笑的; 荒
謬的; 愚蠢的: *a preposterous idea* 荒
謬的想法.

prerequisite [priˈrekwizit] *nc* thing required before one can have or do
something else 必備的, 先決條件: *A
good pass in the school certificate is a
prerequisite for (the) university.* 以優
良的成績獲得中學畢業證書是進入大
學的先決條件.

prerogative [priˈrɔgətiv] *nc* special
power or right which no-one else has
特權: *It was the prerogative of the

king to pardon criminals.* 寬赦犯人是
國王的特權.

prescribe [priˈskraib] *vt / i* **1** order the
use of 開處方, 指定: *prescribe medi-
cine for an illness* 開治病的藥方; *pre-
scribed books* i.e. books which must
be read by students 指定的書, 即: 學
生必讀的書. **2** order with authority 規
定, 命令: *The government prescribes
laws to be obeyed by its citizens.* 政府
命令它的市民必須遵守法律. **pre-
scription** [priˈskripʃən] *nc* written
note of a doctor's instructions for
making up a medicine; the medicine
itself 藥方; 藥方上所開的藥.

present¹ [ˈpreznt] *adj* **1** in the place
being spoken of 出席的, 到會的: *Was
James present?* 詹姆士出席了嗎? *He is
not in the present company* i.e. not
among those present 他沒有到會. 即:
他沒有到會. **2** at this time 現
在的: *She cannot save on her present
wages.* 以她現在的工資她不能存錢.
presently *adv* **1** soon 立刻, 馬上: *He
will be here presently.* 他馬上就到這
裏來. **2** (mainly *US*) now (主要用於
美)現在: *He is presently living in New
York.* 他現在正住在紐約. **presence**
nu fact or state of being present 在
場: *Don't mention this in John's presence* i.e. while John is present 約翰在
場時, 別提這件事. **at present** now 現
在: *He is with Jones at present.* 現在
他跟瓊斯在一起. **for the present** in
the meantime 同時, 目前; 暫時: *We
shall not need any more for the present.* 我們暫時不再需要甚麼. **pre-
sence of mind** ability to think quickly
and sensibly in dangerous or unexpected circumstances 鎮定: *Thanks
to his presence of mind, the children
were saved.* 由於他的鎮定, 孩子們得
救了.

present² [pri'zent] *vt* **1** give to someone
送給, 贈予: *We presented him with a
cheque / We presented a cheque to
him.* 我們送給他一張支票. **2** bring before someone 提交, 呈遞, 演出: *They
presented their petition to the Governor.* 他們把他們的請願書直接呈交市
長. *The school is presenting a play*
i.e. giving a public performance 這學
校將演個戲. 即: 進行一次公演. **3** introduce to someone (esp. someone of
high rank) 介紹, 引見: *He was presented to the Queen.* 他被引見給女王.
Also 亦作 ['preznt] *nc* something
given 禮物: *birthday present* 生日禮
物. **presentable** *adj* suitable to be
seen 好看的, 漂亮的, 像樣的: *look
presentable* 看起來是漂亮的. (*opp* 反
義詞 **unpresentable**). **presentation**
[prezn'teiʃən] *nc / u* **1** giving of something to someone (esp. at a public
ceremony) 贈送. **2** presenting or
being presented (in senses 2 and 3 義
2 和義 3) 演出, 介紹.

preserve [pri'zə:v] *vt* **1** keep safe,
healthy, free from danger etc. 保護, 維
護: *preserve one's life* 保護生命. **2**
keep from going bad 保藏, 保存: *preserve food* 保藏食物. **3** protect fish,
animals etc from being unlawfully
hunted or killed 保護. Also 亦作 *nc*
cooked fruit which is sweetened and
sealed jam 水果罐頭; 果醬 **preservation** [prezə'veiʃən] *nu* **1** state of
being preserved 保護, 維持: *the preservation of peace / one's health etc.*
維持和平／健康等. **2** condition of
something which is being preserved
保存: *The old house was in q good
state of preservation.* 這舊房子保存得
很好. **preservative** [pri'zə:vətiv] *nc*
something which prevents things from
going bad or decaying 防腐劑: *Most*

tins of meat contain preservatives. 大
部份罐頭肉含有防腐劑.

preside [pri'zaid] *vi* control; have
charge of 負責, 主持; 指揮: *preside at
a meeting* 主持會議; *preside over a
large business* 負責大批業務. **presi-
dent** ['prezidnt] *nc* **1** head of a state
(esp. a republic) (共和國的) 總統. **2**
head of a business, college, department etc. 會長, 大學校長, 院長, 部長
等. *Note* 說明: *President (in sense* **1**)
(用於義 1). can be used as a title instead of *Mr* (e.g. *President Kennedy*)
President 可作爲稱呼代替Mr (例如: 肯
尼迪總統). **presidency** *nc* **1** office of
president 總統職位: *a candidate for
the presidency* 總統職位的候選人. **2**
time during which someone is president 總統的任期. **presidential** [prezi-
'denʃl] *adj* connected with the presidency 總統的: *a presidential election*
總統選舉.

press¹ [pres] *vt / i* **1** push something
against something else 按, 按動: *He
pressed the bell* i.e. with his finger 他
按了鈴. 即: 他用手指頭按動了鈴. *He
pressed his hand against the door.* 他
把他的手放在門上. *These two pieces
of paper will stick if you press them
together.* 這兩張紙將黏貼著, 如果你把
它們放在一起. **2** put weight on top of
something 壓; 熨平: *He gets the juice
from the grapes by pressing them.* 他
把葡萄壓出汁來. *He was pressing his
jacket* i.e. making it smooth by using
an iron 他熨平他的夾克衫. 即: 用燙斗
把它熨平. **3** push against something
擠, 擠壓: *The people were pressing so
hard against the President's car that
they almost overturned it.* 人們這麼緊
緊地擠壓着總統的轎車, 幾乎把它擠翻
了. **4** hold tightly 緊握, 緊抱: *He
pressed my hand warmly as he said*

goodbye. 當他說再見時, 他熱烈地緊握
我的手. *When he at last found his
daughter, he pressed her to him.* 當他
最後找到他的女兒時, 他把她緊抱在懷
裏. *He is pressing me for an answer.*
他正堅持要我給個回答. *He pressed
the money on me* i.e. forced me to
accept it 他堅持要給我錢. 即: 逼我接
受它. **pressing** *adj* demanding attention or an answer now 急迫的: *This
matter is very pressing* i.e. urgent 這件
事是很急的. 即: 緊急的. **be press-
ed for** be short of 不夠, 缺少: *I'm
rather pressed for time.* 我的時間比較
不夠.

press² [pres] *nc* **1** act of pressing 燙熨:
give one's clothes a quick press i.e.
with an iron 快速熨平某人的衣服, 即:
用燙斗熨平. **2** machine for pressing
壓榨機: *He put the grapes into the
wine press.* 他把葡萄放入榨酒機. **3**
machine for printing 印刷機. **4** business firm which prints books etc. 出
版社. **5** (mainly *US*) cupboard with
shelves for keeping books, clothes
etc. (主要用於美) 壁櫥. **the press**
newspapers or journalists 新聞, 報刊:
defend the freedom of the press 保衛
新聞自由. **'press conference** meeting which has been arranged between
someone of importance and newspaper reporters 記者招待會. **'press cutting** something cut out of a newspaper and kept 剪報.

pressure ['preʃə*] *nu* **1** force or weight
of one thing pushing against another
壓力: *The pressure of my finger
against the lid was enough to open it.*
我的手指頭對蓋子的壓力足以把蓋子打

開. *What is the pressure of air in your
tyres?* 你的輪胎裏的氣壓如何? **2** trouble or strain of something 困擾, 困苦:
*He could not come to the party be-
cause of pressure of work* i.e. he was
too busy. 由於工作的困擾, 他不能來參
加酒會. 即: 他太忙了. **pressurized**
adj made so that the pressure of the
air inside can be controlled 使保持正
常的氣壓: *an aeroplane with a pressurized cabin* 具有氣壓正常的機艙的
飛機. **'pressure group** group of people using political pressure to further
their own interests (爲謀私利而施加
政治壓力的)壓力集團.

prestige [pres'tiːʒ] *nu* power; respect
admiration 威望; 聲望; 讚賞: *Winning
the first prize in the sports meeting
brought him a lot of prestige.* 在運動
會獲得一等獎使他很有聲望.

presume [pri'zjuːm] *vt / i* **1** take something for granted without proof; take
it that something is true or that
something is allowed 假定; 假設: *A
man should be presumed innocent until it is proved that he is guilty.* 一個人
應該被當作無罪, 直到事實證明他犯了
罪. **2** dare; be bold enough to 敢於;
大胆: *I would not presume to question him.* 我不敢擅自審問他. **presumption** [pri'zʌmpʃən] *nc* something taken to be true 假定, 推定: *The
police are searching the area, on the
presumption that the thief is still there.*
警察正在搜查這地區, 假定賊還在那
裏. **2** *nu* boldness of behaviour 大胆
的行動, 冒昧: *It was sheer presumption for him to come when he was not
invited.* 他沒被邀請就來, 這對他來說,
完全是大胆的行動. **presumptuous**
[pri'zʌmpʃəs] *adj* too bold; ill-
mannered 放肆的; 胆大妄爲的.

pretend [pri'tend] *vt / i* **1** make oneself

appear to be something or to be doing something 偽裝: *pretend to be surprised* 他偽裝吃驚. **2** say or claim falsely 偽稱, 假託: *He pretends to like you, but he doesn't really.* 他偽稱喜歡你, 但事實上他並不喜歡你. **3** claim that one has something (usu. to avoid difficulty or danger) 聲口, 假裝. (通常爲了避免困難或危險): *pretend sickness* 裝病. **pretence** (*US* 美 **pretense**) **1** *nu* make-believe; pretending 偽裝; 掩飾: *under the pretence of friendship* 在友誼的掩飾下. **2** *nc* excuse; false claim 藉口; 託詞. **pretension** [pri'tenʃən] **1** *nc* claim 自命, 要求: *I have no pretensions to being an athlete.* 我不敢自命爲運動員. **2** *nu* state of being pretentious 自負, 自命不凡. **pretentious** [pri'tenʃəs] *adj* pretending to be, or showing that one pretends to be, clever or important etc. 自命不凡的, 虛飾的: *a pretentious speech* 一篇誇誇其談的演講 (*opp* 反義詞 **unpretentious**).

pretext ['pri:tekst] *nc* false reason given for doing something 藉口: *He was absent from school on the pretext that he was ill.* 他藉口生病, 不到學校裏來.

pretty ['priti] *adj* pleasing; attractive (but not extremely beautiful or grand) 漂亮的; 迷人的 (但不是極美的): *pretty dress* 漂亮的衣服; *pretty girl* 漂亮的姑娘. Also 亦作 *intensifier* rather 十分, 頗, 很. *He's pretty good at sports.* (*informal* in this sense) 他在運動方面是很好的. (此義頗非正式). **prettily** *adv*.

prevail [pri'veil] *vi* **1** win; be successful 戰勝, 佔優勢: *He prevailed over / against his enemies.* 他戰勝了他的敵人. **2** be common or usual 普遍, 盛行: *This custom prevails over the whole area.* 這種風俗在整個地區都很普遍. **3** persuade 勸說, 敦促: *I pre-*

vailed upon him to join us i.e. I persuaded him to join us 我勸說他和我們一起. 即: 我說服他和我們爲伴. **prevailing** *adj*: *prevailing winds* 常吹的風. **prevalent** ['prevələnt] *adj* generally used; generally found 通用的; 流行的: *a prevalent idea / fashion etc.* 流行的思想/款式等.

prevaricate [pri'værikeit] *vi* try to hide the truth by not answering questions truthfully or clearly 支吾, 搪塞. **prevarication** [priværi'keiʃən] *nc / u*.

prevent [pri'vent] *vt* **1** stop something from happening 防止, 預防: *prevent an accident* 防止意外事故. **2** stop someone from doing something 阻止: *I prevented him from hitting the child.* 我阻止他打小孩. **prevention** *nu* **preventable** *adj* that can be avoided 可避免的: *preventable accidents* 可避免的事故. **preventive** *adj* that prevents 預防的: *preventive medicine* i.e. to prevent illness 預防的藥物, 即: 可預防疾病.

preview ['pri:vju:] *nu* private performance of a film or play, before it is shown to the public (影片或戲劇正式公演前的)預演. Also 亦作 *vt*.

previous ['pri:viəs] *adj* earlier; coming before 早先的; 以前的: *a previous meeting* 以前的見面. **previously** *adv* **previous to** *prep* before 以前. *Previous to coming here, I worked in London.* 來這裏以前, 我在倫敦工作.

prey [prei] *nu* animal or bird hunted or killed by another one 獵物, 被捕食的動物: *The lion was hunting for its prey.* 這獅子正在尋捕它的獵物. Small animals are sometimes the prey of eagles. 小動物有時是鷹捕食的對象. *An eagle is a bird of prey* i.e. it lives by killing other birds or animals. 鷹是一種食肉的鳥. 即: 它靠捕食別的鳥或動

物爲生. **prey up-on something** 1 hunt other animals etc as prey 捕食. 2 trouble; injure 使苦惱; 損害.

price [prais] *nc* 1 money for which a thing can be bought or sold 價格: *the price of a book* 一本書的價格. 2 reward offered for capturing someone 懸賞: *a price on his head* 懸賞緝捕他. 3 what must be done or suffered for something 代價: *the price of freedom* 自由的代價. Also 亦作 *vt* put a price on something; ask the price of something 定價, 標價, 詢價. **priceless** *adj* of great value 無價的, 極貴重的.

prick [prik] *vt/i* 1 make a small hole in something 刺: *prick something with a needle* 用針刺某物; *prick one's finger* 刺破手指. 2 cause sharp pain 刺痛. Also 亦作 *nc* 1 small hole made by a sharp point 小洞. 2 sharp pain 刺痛. **prick up** (of the ears) lift up 竪起: *The dog pricked up its ears when its master called it.* 當它的主人叫它時, 這條狗就竪起它的耳朵.

prickle ['prikl] *nc* (esp. of a plant, animal etc) sharp point 棘, 刺: *the prickles on a thorn* 荊棘上的刺. **prickly** *adj* 1 having prickles 長刺的, 多刺的. 2 sharp; stinging 尖利的; 刺痛的.

pride [praid] *nu* 1 feeling of pleasure and satisfaction one has in the things / people connected with him 自豪, 榮耀: *He takes great pride in his children's success at school.* 他對他的子女在學業上的好成績感到自豪. *He looked at his garden with pride.* 他自豪地看着他的花園. 2 high opinion of oneself 自尊: *His pride would not allow him to beg for money.* 他的自尊心使他不能去乞錢. 3 too high an opinion of oneself 驕傲, 自負: *He was hated because of his pride.* 由於他的

驕傲, 大家都討厭他. 4 something one is proud of 引以自豪的、值得誇耀的物或人: *That child is his mother's pride and joy.* 那孩子是他的母親引以自豪和高興的人. see 見 **proud. pride oneself upon / on** take pride in; be pleased with 感到自豪, 覺得高興: *She prided herself on the cleanliness of her house.* 她對她的房子的清潔感到自豪.

priest [pri:st] *nc* person specially chosen to lead prayers and other religious services 牧師, 神父. (*fem* 陰 **priestess** ['pri:stis]).

prig [prig] *nc* person who is too pleased with himself, and anxious to show how bad others are 自命不凡者, 沾沾自喜者.

prim [prim] *adj* very correct and stiff in one's manner or behaviour 一本正經的, 規矩的: *a prim old lady* 一本正經的老太太.

primary ['praiməri] *adj* 1 first in time 最初的: *primary school* 小學. 2 great in importance 首要的, 主要的: *a primary consideration* 主要的考慮; *of primary importance* 最重要的. **primarily** *adv* firstly; mostly 首先地; 主要地. **the primary colours** red, yellow and blue (from which it is believed all other colours can be obtained by mixing in different ways) 原色(紅、黃、藍三色).

primate¹ ['praimit] *nc* archbishop 大主教.

primate² ['praimeit] *nc* one of the highest classes of animals, containing men, apes, monkeys etc. 靈長類(動物包括人類, 猩猩, 猴子等).

prime [praim] *adj* 1 first in importance; chief 首要的; 主要的; 第一的: *the Prime Minister* 首相, 總理. *of prime importance* 最重要的. 2 very good 最

佳的: *in prime condition* 處於最佳的
狀態. Also 亦作 *nu* best time; best
part 全盛期; 最佳部份: *in the prime of
life* i.e. when one is fully grown, but
not yet old 壯年, 即: 已完全長大成人,
但還沒老.

primer ['praimə*] *nc* first book in a
subject used by a child at school 初學
讀物, 入門書.

primeval [prai'mi:vl] *adj* belonging to
the earliest times; very, very old 原始
的; 太古的: *primeval forests* 原始森
林.

primitive ['primitiv] *adj* 1 of the earliest
times 原始的: *In primitive times, peo-
ple lived in caves.* 在原始的時代, 人們
住在山洞裏. 2 very simple or crude
簡單的, 粗陋的: *a primitive kind of
tool* 一種簡陋的工具.

primrose ['primrouz] *nc* small pale yellow flower which blooms in early
spring in cool northern areas 櫻草.

prince [prins] *nc* 1 son of a king or
emperor 王子. 2 person who rules a
small state (小國的)君主. **princess**
[prin'ses] *nc* 1 daughter of a king or
emperor 公主. 2 wife of a prince 王
妃.

principal ['prinsipl] *adj* most important;
chief 最重要的; 主要的: *Manchester is
one of the principal towns in England.*
曼徹斯特是英國最重要的城市之一.
Also 亦作 *nc* 1 head of a college or
school 校長, 院長. 2 amount of
money put into a business, bank etc
on which more money (called interest) is earned 本金. **principally**
adv chiefly 主要地.

principality [prinsi'pæliti] *nc* small
country, ruled by a prince 公國, 封邑.

principle ['prinsipl] *nc* 1 important
truth or law on which other things
depend 原理, 原則: *the principles of*

science 科學的原理; *principle of free
speech* 言論自由的原則. 2 something
that one believes in or follows as a
rule 準則: *Stealing is against my principles.* 偷竊違背我的行動準則.

print¹ [print] *vt* 1 press marks on paper
or on cloth using ink or dye 印刷:
*This page in the newspaper has been
badly printed.* 報紙上這一頁印刷得很
不好. 2 make books etc in this way
出版: *They printed a hundred copies
of the book.* 那本書他們印了一百冊. 3
make words or letters so that they
look like print instead of handwriting
把…寫成印刷體字: *Please print your
names so that they can be read clearly.* 請把你的名字寫成印刷體字, 以便別
人能看清楚. 4 make a photograph
from a negative film 曬印(相片).

print² [print] *nu* 1 words or letters
made by printing (印刷)字體: *Can
you read the small print at the bottom
of the page?* 你能讀這一頁下面的小字
體嗎? 2 *nc* picture or design made by
printing 印成的圖片或花樣: *This is a
beautiful print which I bought yesterday.* 這是我昨天買的一張美麗的印刷
圖片. 3 *nc* photograph made from a
negative (洗出的)相片. 4 *nc* (often
used to make compound nouns) mark
made by pressing on a surface 痕跡
(常用於複合名詞): *You can see the
children's footprints in the sand.* 你可
以看到孩子們在沙子上的腳印. 5 *nc /
u* cloth with a design printed on it 印
花布. **printer** *nc* person who works
at printing books etc. 印刷者, 印刷工.

prior¹ ['praiə*] *adj* earlier 預先的, 較早
的: *I cannot come as I have a prior
engagement.* 我不能來, 因為我早有約
會. **prior to** before 在前的: *What did
you do prior to coming here?* 你在來
這裏以前做甚麼?

prior² ['praɪə*] *nc* head of a religious house 小修道院院長. **priory** *nc* religious house run by a prior 小修道院.

priority [praɪ'ɒrɪti] **1** *nc / u* right or need to receive attention before other people / things 優先權, 優先考慮: *You must give this matter priority* i.e. you must deal with this matter before anything else 你必須先於別的事處理這件事. 即: 你必須先於別的事處理這件事. **2** *nc* person / thing given priority 優先處理的人或事.

prise [praɪz] *vt* open something by force (usu. with a lever of some kind) 撬開: *I prised open / up / off the lid of the box.* 我撬開／撑起這個箱子的蓋子.

prism ['prɪzm] *nc* **1** solid figure with similar, equal, and parallel ends and with sides which are parallelograms 稜柱, 柱體. **2** transparent solid, often of glass, having the shape of a prism, usu. with three sided ends, which will separate white light passing through it into the colours of the rainbow 稜鏡, 三稜鏡. **3** loosely, prismatic colours or spectrum 光譜的七色; 光譜.

prison ['prɪzn] *nc* **1** building where people who have broken the law are kept 監獄. **2** place where someone is kept against his will 拘留所, 禁閉室. **prisoner** *nc* **1** person kept in prison 囚犯, 犯人. **2** soldier who is captured in a war 俘虜: *be taken prisoner* 被俘虜.

private ['praɪvɪt] *adj* **1** for or of one person, or a few people, not people in general 個人的, 私人的: *a private room* 私人的房間: *a private letter* i.e. one which is about personal matters, not business 私人的信件, 即: 關於私事而非公事的信件. **2** secret; kept hidden 秘密的; 不公開的: *private information* 秘密的情報. Also 亦作 *nc*

private soldier 列兵. **privately** *adv* **privacy** ['praɪvəsi] *nu* in **private** not in front of other people 私下地: *talk to someone in private* 私下跟某人談話.

privilege ['prɪvɪlɪdʒ] *nc / u* special right or advantage belonging only to a certain person or group of people 特權. **privileged** *adj* having, or having been given, a privilege or privileges 有榮幸的, 有特權的.

privy ['prɪvi] *adj* secret; private 秘密的; 私下的. **'privy 'council** group of people appointed to advise a king or queen 樞密院.

prize [praɪz] *nc* **1** something given to a person because he has shown that he is better than others 獎品: *win first prize in a race / examination etc.* 在賽跑／考試中獲得第一名. **2** something that is worth working for 值得競爭的事物. Also 亦作 *adj* given a prize; given as a prize 得獎的; 作爲獎品的: *prize cattle* i.e. cattle which have won prizes at an agricultural exhibition 獲獎的牲口, 即: 在農業展覽會上得獎的牲畜; *prize money* 獎金. Also 亦作 *vt* value something highly 珍視. **'prize fight** *nc* boxing match between two men which people pay money to see 職業拳擊賽. **prize fighter** *nc* 職業拳擊手.

pro¹ [prou] *nc* short informal form of **professional** (usu. in sport). professional 非正式縮略式. (通常用於運動): *He played amateur tennis, and then turned pro.* 他是個業餘網球手, 後來當了職業運動員.

pro-² [prou] *prefix* on the side of (e.g. **pro-British**) 親, 贊成. (例如: 親英的) **pros and cons** reasons for and against 贊成與反對的理由: *Before we decide, we must weigh up the pros* and cons i.e. consider the reasons for and against 在决定以前, 必须權衡贊成與反對的理由. 即: 考慮贊成與反對雙方的理由.

probable ['prɔbəbl] *adj* likely to happen; likely to be true 很可能的, 大概是真的: *Colder weather is probable.* 天氣變冷是可能的. (*opp* 反義詞 **improbable**). **probably** *adv* **probability** [prɔbə'biliti] **1** *nu* condition of being likely to happen or likely to be true 可能, 可能性: *There is not much probability that he will come.* 他不大可能來. **2** *nc* something likely to happen or to be true 可能發生的事: *The probability is that he is ill.* 他可能是病了.

probation [prou'beiʃən] *nu* (in a legal sense) system by which a person who has committed only one crime is not sent to prison as long as he does not break the law again (法律) 緩刑: *be on probation* 被判緩刑. **probationary** *adj* **probationer** *nc* person on probation 緩刑中的犯人. **pro'bation officer** person who reports on the behaviour of people (esp. young people) on probation 緩刑犯 (尤指青少年犯) 的監護員.

probe [proub] *nc* **1** thin piece of metal, blunt at one end, used by doctors to find the depth and direction of a wound etc. 探針, 探傷器. **2** (often with reference to investigation by a spacecraft) investigation; close examination 調查; 細察. Also 亦作 *vt* **1** examine closely, inquire closely 探查, 盤問: *probe into someone's secrets* 探查某人的秘密. **2** examine with a probe (in sense **1**) 用探針細查.

probity ['proubiti] *nu* honesty 正直, 廉潔, 老實; *an official of the highest probity* 最廉潔的官員.

problem ['prɔbləm] *nc* difficult decision; difficult question 問題; 難題: *This situation presents us with many problems.* 這種情況給我們出了許多難題. *That's no problem.* 那是沒問題的. **problematic** [prɔblə'mætik] *adj* doubtful; uncertain; difficult 有疑問的; 未決的; 難辦的: *How this matter will end is problematic.* 這件事怎麼了結是很難辦的.

procedure [prə'si:dʒə*] *nc / u* **1** way of doing something 手續, 程序: *a new procedure* 新程序. **2** way something has to be done 程序: *legal procedure* 訴訟程序. **procedural** *adj*.

proceed [prə'si:d] *vi* **1** go forward (to a place) 前進, 前進: *The crowd proceeded to the church.* 人羣行進到教堂. **2** go on, after having stopped (停止後) 繼續進行: *Please proceed with what you were doing.* 請把你原來做的事繼續做下去. **3** begin to do something 開始進行: *The crowd proceeded to attack the building.* 人羣開始攻擊那座房子. **proceeds** ['prousi:dz] *npl* money got from selling something 賣貨所得的錢. **proceedings** *npl* **1** legal action in a court 訴訟程序: *start / take proceedings against someone* 控訴某人. **2** record of things said and decided at a meeting 會議記錄.

process ['prouses] *nc* **1** number of actions or changes involved when something happens 過程, 進程: *the process of getting old* i.e. the changes that take place over a time 衰老的過程, 即: 某時發生的變化. **2** way of manufacturing something 製法, 方法: *a new process for making steel* 煉鋼新方法. Also 亦作 *vt* treat or prepare food etc in some special way 調製, 加工: *processed cheese* 特製的乳酪. **in (the) process of** going forward 在…

進行中: *A new building is in process of being constructed.* 一座新樓正在建設中.

procession [prə'seʃən] *nc* line of people, cars etc moving slowly forward in an ordered way 行列: *a funeral procession* 送葬行列.

proclaim [prou'kleim] *vt* make something known publicly and officially 正式宣佈, 宣告: *proclaim a public holiday* 正式宣佈一個公假日. *The young prince was later proclaimed king.* 年輕的王子後來宣佈當國王. **proclamation** [prɔklə'meiʃən] *nc / u* something proclaimed; act of proclaiming 文告, 宣言; 宣告, 公佈.

procure [prə'kjuə°] *vt* get, obtain (usu. with difficulty) 取得, 謀獲: *This kind of book is difficult to procure.* 這種書是難於取得的.

prod [prɔd] *vt / i* push with something pointed 刺, 戳: *prod an animal with a stick* 用棍子戳動物. *past* 過去式和過去分詞 **prodded**. Also 亦作 *nc* act of prodding 刺, 刺激.

prodigal ['prɔdigl] *adj* spending too much; wasteful 揮霍的; 浪費的: *be prodigal of one's money / time etc.* 浪費金錢/時間等.

prodigious [prə'didʒəs] *adj* **1** very great 很大的: *a prodigious amount* 很大的數額. **2** unusual; wonderful 非凡的, 驚人的: *a prodigious event* 驚人的事件.

prodigy ['prɔdidʒi] *nc* someone who is unusually clever, able etc. 不凡的人: *a child prodigy* 神童.

produce [prə'dju:s] *vt* **1** make 製造, 出產: *a factory that produces cars* 一家製造汽車的工廠. **2** cause to appear; yield 提出; 生產; 引起: *A hen produces eggs.* 母雞生蛋. *Some fields produce maize.* 有些土地生產玉米.

He was not able to produce sufficient evidence. 他不能提出充分的證據. *Hard work produces success.* 努力工作會帶來成功. **3** bring a play etc before the public 公演, 演出. Also 亦作 ['prɔdju:s] *nu* things that are produced (esp. from a farm e.g. crops, eggs etc.) 產品, 農產品. **producer** *nc* **1** someone who makes goods 生產者, 製造者. **2** someone who is responsible for bringing a play etc before the public (電影) 製片人; 舞台監督. **product** ['prɔdʌkt] *nc* something that is produced 產品: *factory products* 工廠產品; *farm products* 農產品. **productive** [prə'dʌktiv] *adj* **production** [prə'dʌkʃən] **1** *nu* act of producing 生產. **2** *nc* play etc shown before the public 上演的作品. **productivity** [prɔdʌk'tiviti] *nu* efficiency with which work is done; amount of work done in a certain time 生產力: *increase the productivity of a factory* 提高工廠的生產力.

profane [prə'fein] *adj* showing disrespect to God or religion 褻瀆神明的: *profane language* 褻瀆神的語言.

profess [prə'fes] *vt* **1** claim (to be someone, or to be able to do something) 聲稱, 自稱: *I don't profess to be an expert.* 我不想自稱專家. **2** declare, say (that one has something) 宣稱, 明言, 說: *I asked him, but he professed ignorance* i.e. said he did not know 我詢問他, 但他說一無所知. 即: 他不知道. **3** state openly (one's beliefs etc.) 公開宣佈, 表示: *profess one's loyalty to the state* 某人公開宣佈忠於國家. **profession** *nc* **1** occupation that requires special learning (e.g. law, medicine, teaching etc.) 職業 (例如: 律師, 醫生, 教師等). **2** statement of what one believes, feels etc. 宣佈, 表白: *a profes-*

sion of friendship 友誼的表白.

professional [prəˈfeʃənl] *adj* 1 connected with a profession 職業的，專業的: *Doctors and teachers are professional men.* 醫生和教師是專業人員. 2 doing something (esp, sport) for money 以…爲職業的: *a professional footballer* 職業足球隊員. 3 expert; done or made in an expert way 專家的; 內行的: *a professional piece of work* 一部專業著作. Also 亦作 *nc* person who makes a living from an occupation (e.g. sport, music) which others do for pleasure 專業人員，行家. (*opp* 反義詞 **amateur**).

professor [prəˈfesə*] *nc* teacher of the highest rank in a university 教授. *Note* 說明: *Professor can be used as a title.* (e.g. *Professor Jones*) 此詞可用作稱呼. (例如: Professor Jones).

proficient [prəˈfiʃənt] *adj* skilled; clever 精通的; 熟練的: *proficient in / at speaking English* 英語口語熟練. **proficiency** *nu*.

profile [ˈproufail] *nc* 1 side view (e.g. of someone's face) 側面 (例如: 某人的臉). 2 edge or outline of something seen against a background 輪廓，外形. 3 summary of a person's character and career in a newspaper or on television (報紙或電視上的) 人物簡介.

profit [ˈprɔfit] 1 *nu* what is gained or obtained from some situation or experience 利益. 2 *nc* money gained from business 利潤: *a company that earns huge profits.* 一家賺大錢的公司. Also 亦作 *vt / i* 1 make a gain 獲利: *profit from a deal* 從一筆交易中獲利. 2 be helped by 得益: *profit by one's mistakes* i.e. learn from one's mistakes 從某人的失誤中得益，即: 從某人的失誤中學習. **profitable** *adj* bringing profit

有利可圖的，可賺錢的: 有益的: *a profitable business* 有利可圖的生意. (*opp* 反義詞 **unprofitable**). **profitably** *adv*

profiteer [prɔfiˈtiə*] *nc* person who makes very large profits by taking advantage of others (e.g. during a war) 投機獲暴利者，奸商 (例如: 發戰爭橫財者). Also 亦作 *vi* make large profits in this way 牟取暴利.

profound [prəˈfaund] *adj* 1 deep 極深的: *profound sleep* 酣睡. 2 showing great knowledge; not easily understood 深奧的; 淵博的: *a profound thinker / book / mystery etc.* 深奧的思想家 / 書 / 秘密等. **profoundly** *adv* deeply 深奧地，深深地，深刻地: *be profoundly grateful* 深深地感謝.

profuse [prəˈfjuːs] *adj* very many; abundant 很多的; 豐富的: *Please accept my profuse apologies.* 請接受我無限的歉意. **profusely** *adv* **profusion** [prəˈfjuːʒən] *nu* great quantity; plenty 大量; 豐富: *Wild flowers were in profusion everywhere.* 到處有大量野花.

programme [ˈprougræm] (*US and computers* 美和計算機程序 **program**) *nc* 1 list of items or events for a concert, play etc. 節目表. 2 plan of what is to be done 計劃: *a programme of instruction* 指導計劃. Also 亦作 *vt* give a set of instructions to a computer 給計算機輸入指令性的程序: *program(me) a computer* 按程序操作計算機.

progress [ˈprougres] *nu* 1 advance; going forward 前進; 進步: *the progress of civilization* 文明的進步. *work in progress* 工作在前進. 2 improvement 進展，改進: *show some progress* 表明有些進展. Also 亦作 [prəˈgres] *vi* make progress 有進步. **progression** [prəˈgreʃən] *nu* moving onward 進展，進步: *different methods of progression*

進展的不同方法. **progressive**
[prə'gresiv] *adj* **1** going on to new
things; advancing 進步的; 前進的: *a
progressive country* 進步的國家:
progressive ideas 進步的思想. **2** moving forward 向前的, 前進的: *a progressive movement* 進步的運動. **3** increasing by regular amounts 日益增長
的: *a progressive scale of taxation*
累進稅的幅度.

prohibit [prə'hibit] *vt* forbid; stop
someone from doing something or
something from being done 不准; 禁
止: *Smoking prohibited* 禁止吸煙.
prohibitive *adj* costing so much that
one cannot pay 很貴的, 高昂的: *prohibitive prices* 高昂的價格. **prohibi-
tion** [prouhi'biʃən] *nc / u* **1** act of forbidding 禁止. **2** law against the making or selling of liquor 禁酒.

project ['prɔdʒekt] *nc* plan; scheme 計
劃; 設計: *a project for making the desert fertile* 使沙漠變良田的計劃. Also
亦作 [prə'dʒekt] *vt / i* **1** make plans
for 制定計劃: *project a new housing
scheme* 制定新的住房計劃. **2** stick
out from the surrounding surface 使
突出, 冒出來: *a nail projecting from
the wall* 一個釘子從牆上冒出來. **3**
make pictures etc show on a surface
投影, 放映: *project films onto a screen*
使電影映在銀幕上. **projection**
[prə'dʒekʃən] **1** *nu* act of projecting
發射, 投出. **2** *nc* something which
sticks out 突出物. **projectile**
[prə'dʒektail] *nc* something to be shot
forward (e.g. a stone or bullet) 拋射
物, 發射物 (例如: 石頭或子彈). **pro-
jector** [prou'dʒektə*] *nc* machine for
projecting films onto a screen 放映
機, 投影機.

proletariat [prouli'tɛəriət] *nu* all the
working people 無產階級, 勞動階級.

proletarian *nc* member of the proletariat 無產者. Also 亦作 *adj*.

prolific [prə'lifik] *adj* producing much
or many 多產的: *a prolific author* i.e.
one who writes many books 多產的作
家, 即: 寫了許多書的作家.

prologue ['proulɔg] *nc* speech said at
the beginning of a play 開場白, 序幕.

prolong [prə'lɔŋ] *vt* make longer 延長.
prolonged *adj* very long 很長的: *a
prolonged speech* 長篇的演講.

promenade [prɔmə'nɑːd] *nc* wide road
that is used for walking up and down
(esp. by the sea) 供散步的大道 (尤指
海濱).

prominent ['prɔminənt] *adj* **1** well-
known; important 出名的; 重要的:
prominent politician 重要的政客. **2**
easily seen; standing out 顯著的; 突出
的: *prominent hill* 突起的小山. **prominence 1** *nu* fame; importance
著名; 重要; 卓越: *give prominence to
something* 使某物出名. **2** *nc* some
place or thing that stands out 突出的
地方, 突出的東西.

promiscuous [prə'miskjuəs] *adj* having
love affairs with many different people (性方面) 濫交的: *a promiscuous
person* 一個濫交的人. **promiscuity**
[prɔmis'kjuːiti] *nu*.

promise ['prɔmis] *vt / i* **1** say that one
will do something, give something etc.
答應, 允諾: *We promised them that
we would come.* 我們答應他們, 我們會
來. *You must promise not to mention
it.* 你必須答應不提起它. *I promised
him a book.* 我答應給他一本書. **2**
cause one to hope (that something
will happen) 預示, 可望: *It promises
to be fine tomorrow* 可望明天是晴天.
Also 亦作 **1** *nc* act of promising something, either in speech or in writing 諾
言: *make / keep / break a promise* 許

下/信守/違背諾言. **2** *nu* something that causes one to have hopes of excellence 有希望的事物; 成功的希望: *His work shows much promise.* 他的工作表明很有成功的希望. **promising** *adj* likely to do well or to turn out well 有希望的, 有前途的: *a promising pupil* 有希望的小學生.

promontory ['prɔməntri] *nc* high point of land standing out into the sea 海角, 岬.

promote [prə'məut] *vt* **1** raise to a higher position 提陞, 提拔: *promote someone from clerk to manager* 把某人從職員提陞爲經理. **2** help something develop or increase 促進, 增進: *promote peace/education etc.* 促進和平/教育等. **3** start something (esp. a business) 創辦, 開辦(尤指某種商業). **promoter** *nc* person who helps to start a business 創辦人, 資助者, 發起人. **promotion** *nc/u.*

prompt[1] [prɔmpt] *adj* quick; without delay 迅速的; 及時的; 快捷的; 立刻的: *prompt service* 快捷服務. *prompt to obey commands* 立刻服從命令. **promptly** *adv* **promptness** *nu.*

prompt[2] [prɔmpt] *vt* **1** cause a person to do something 促使, 激起: *What prompted you to ask that question?* 甚麼促使你問那個問題? *His actions were prompted by fear.* 他的行動是由於害怕引起的. **2** remind an actor of the words he has to say 提示. **prompter** *nc* person who prompts actors 提示者, 提臺員.

prone [prəun] *adj* **1** lying face down 俯臥的: *He was lying prone on the ground.* 他正俯臥在地上. **2** inclined 易於⋯的: *be prone to anger* i.e. easily angered 易於生氣, 即: 容易發怒.

prong [prɔŋ] *nc* thin, pointed end of something (e.g. a fork) 尖頭(例如: 叉子).

pronoun ['prəunaun] *nc* word used in place of a noun (e.g. *I, he, which, this* etc.) 代詞. (例如: I, he, which, this 等).

pronounce [prə'nauns] *vt/i* **1** make the sound of a word etc. 發音: *Try to pronounce your words clearly.* 吐詞要盡量清楚. **2** make an official announcement 宣稱, 宣判: *The judge pronounced sentence on the prisoner.* 法官對犯人宣判. **3** give an opinion 發表意見: *I don't know enough to pronounce on this matter.* 我懂得不多, 沒法對這件事發表意見. **pronounced** *adj* strongly marked; easily noticed; clear 強硬的; 明顯的, 明確的: *a pronounced dislike of dogs* 明顯的不喜歡狗. **pronouncement** *nc* official statement 聲明, 宣告. **pronunciation** [prənʌnsi'eiʃən] *nc/u* **1** someone's way of pronouncing; way in which a language is pronounced 發音; 發音法: *improve one's pronunciation* 改進某人的發音; *the pronunciation of English* 英語發音. **2** way of pronouncing a word 讀音, 讀法: *a word with two pronunciations* 有兩種讀法的一個詞.

proof pru:f] *nc/u* **1** way of showing that something is true 證明: *Have you any proof that he is a thief?* 你有任何證據證明他是賊嗎? **2** way of finding out if something is true 驗證: *The scientist put his theories to the proof.* 這位科學家對他的理論進行驗證. **3** first printing of a book etc, which can be corrected before other copies are made 校樣, 清樣. Also *adj* able to give safety against; able to withstand 防⋯的; 耐⋯的, 抵抗的: *proof against temptation* 抗誘惑的. *rainproof coat* 防雨大衣. *foolproof scheme* i.e. so good that even a foolish or careless person could follow it 極簡單明瞭的計劃, 即: 連愚蠢的和粗心的人也能明白. see 見 **prove.**

prop¹ [prɔp] *nc* support used to hold something up 支撐物, 支架: *pit props* i.e. pieces of wood or metal which keep up the roof of a mine 坑道支架, 即: 支撐礦頂的金屬或木頭架子. Also 亦作 *vt* help; keep in position 支持, 支撐: *The house was propped up with planks of wood.* 這房子是用木板支撐着的. *past* 過去式和過去分詞 **propped.**

prop² [prɔp] *nc* (often *pl*) thing used on the stage when a play is being performed (but not including the scenery) (short form of **property**) (常用複數) 舞台道具 (property 的縮畧式).

propaganda [ˌprɔpəˈgændə] *nu* **1** organized attempts (e.g. by a government) to spread certain beliefs 宣傳. **2** beliefs that are spread in this way 宣傳的信仰或言論.

propagate [ˈprɔpəgeit] *vt* **1** increase the number of plants or animals by reproduction 繁殖. **2** spread news, opinions etc. 傳播, 傳送: *propagate scientific ideas* 傳播科學的思想. **propagation** [ˌprɔpəˈgeiʃən] *nu* propagating 傳播; *the propagation of new ideas* 新思想的傳播.

propel [prəˈpel] *vt* push forward or onward 推進. *past* 過去式和過去分詞 **propelled.** see 見 **propulsion. propeller** *nc* set of rotating blades used for driving a plane or ship 螺旋槳, 推進器.

proper [ˈprɔpə*] *adj* **1** correct; right; suitable 正確的; 適當的; 正當的: *You must learn the proper way to behave.* 你必須學會舉止得體. *A classroom is not the proper place for a football match.* 教室不是足球比賽適當的地方.

(*opp* 反義詞 **improper**). **2** in the strict sense of the word 本身的, 嚴格意義上的: *Spiders are not insects proper* i.e. they should not be called insects 蜘蛛本身並不是昆蟲. 即: 它們不該被稱爲昆蟲. **properly** *adv* **1** correctly 適當地, 正確地: *do something properly* 好好地做點事. **2** strictly 嚴格地: *properly speaking* i.e. to be exact 嚴格地說, 即: 準確地說. **proper noun** noun that is always written with a capital letter (e.g. *Mary; London*) 專有名詞 (例如: Mary; London).

property [ˈprɔpəti] *nc / u* **1** things which are owned (esp. land and buildings) 財產, 所有物, (尤指房地產): *That pen is my property.* 那枝鋼筆是我的東西. *The price of property has risen greatly* i.e. the price of land or buildings 房地產的價格大漲了. 即: 房屋和土地的價格. **2** special quality that a thing has 性質, 屬性: *Steel is a metal with the property of great strength.* 鋼是具有巨大張力屬性的金屬. **3** see 見 **prop.**

prophecy [ˈprɔfisi] *nc / u* **1** power of telling what is going to happen; statement about the future 預見; 預言. **prophesy** [ˈprɔfisai] *vt* say what is going to happen 預言, 預示: *He prophesied that there would be a great famine within seven years.* 他預言七年內會發生大饑荒. **prophet** [ˈprɔfit] *nc* **1** person who teaches what he says has been directly revealed to him by God 預言者, 先知. **2** person who can foretell the future 預言家. (*fem* 陰 **prophetess** [ˈprɔfitis]) **prophetic** [prəˈfetik] *adj* connected with prophecy or a prophet 預言的, 預言家的.

proportion [prəˈpɔːʃən] **1** *nu* relation of one thing to another in number, amount, size etc. 相稱，均衡: *The amount of money you get will be in proportion to the work you do* i.e. the more you work, the more money you will get. 你所得到的款數將和你所做的工作相稱．即: 你做得越多，你得的錢就越多. **2** *nc* part 部份: *A large proportion of my time is spent in studying.* 我的時間大部份花在學習上. Also 亦作 *vt* fit or arrange things together 使相稱，勻稱，使均衡: *The different parts of the house are well proportioned.* 這房子的不同部份是很勻稱的. **proportions** *npl* size; measurements 大小; 容積; 比例: *a room of large proportions* 一個大房間. *The building had pleasing proportions* i.e. the different parts of it were the correct size for one another 這座樓的造型令人喜愛. 即: 它的不同部份的相互比例是是適當的. **proportional** *adj* in proper proportions; corresponding 成比例的; 相稱的: *The cost of the party will be proportional to the number of people invited.* 這個聚會的開支將和所邀請的人數成適當的比例. **proportionate** [prə'pɔ:ʃənət] *adj* proportional 成正比例的. (*opp* 反義詞 **disproportionate**).

propose [prə'pouz] *vt / i* **1** suggest; put forward for consideration 建議; 提議: *I propose that we leave now.* 我建議我們現在就離開. *He proposed another meeting.* 他建議另開個會. **2** intend 打算，企圖: *I propose to go home next week.* 我打算下星期回家. **3** make an offer of marriage 求婚: *John has proposed to Mary.* 約翰向瑪麗求婚. **4** put forward someone's name for office, membership 提名; 推薦: *He proposed Mr Jones for secretary.* 他提名瓊斯先生當秘書. **proposal** *nc* **1** plan, suggestion 計劃; 建議. **2**

offer of marriage 求婚. **proposition** [prɔpə'ziʃən] *nc* **1** something to be considered; proposal 主張; 提議: *a business proposition* 商務上的主張. **2** (*esp.* of mathematical problem) statement (尤指數學問題) 命題.

propound [prə'paund] *vt* put forward an idea, problem etc for consideration 提出(主意、問題等)供考慮.

proprietary [prə'praiətri] *adj* owned by a private person or company 專賣的，私有的，專利的: *proprietary medicine* i.e. medicine made by a firm of manufacturers and sold with their name on it 專賣藥品, 即: 廠家製造的藥品以它們的名稱銷售.

proprietor [prə'praiətə*] *nc* owner (*esp.* of land or a shop) 所有人, 業主 (尤指土地和商店). (*fem* 陰 **proprietress** [prə'praiətris]).

propulsion [prə'pʌlʃən] *nu* driving force 推進力: *jet propulsion* i.e. movement by means of jet engines 噴射推力, 即: 靠噴射發動機驅動. see 見 **propel**.

prosaic [prou'zeiik] *adj* dull, not exciting 單調的, 平淡無趣的.

prose [prouz] *nu* ordinary way of speaking and writing, not verse 散文: *This writer is good at writing both prose and poetry.* 這位作家善於寫散文和詩.

prosecute ['prɔsikju:t] *vt* take legal action against 告發, 起訴: *Anyone who drives carelessly will be prosecuted.* 不負責任開車的任何人都將被起訴. **prosecution** [prɔsi'kju:ʃən] **1** *nc / u* taking of legal action 起訴, 訴訟: *threaten someone with prosecution* 威脅要起訴某人. **2** *nu* people (often the state) who take legal action against another 原告: *the case for the prosecution* 對原告有利的判決.

prospect ['prɔspekt] **1** *nc* something that one expects or looks forward to 展望, 前景: *The prospects for a young man in this job are excellent.* 對青年人來說, 本職業的前景是很好的. **2** *nu* hope; possibility 希望; 可能性: *Is there any prospect of your returning soon?* 你有可能很快回來嗎? Also 亦作 [prə'spekt] *vt / i* search; look for 尋找; 勘探: *prospecting for gold* 勘探金礦.

prospective [prə'spektiv] *adj* expected; looked forward to; 預期的; 有希望的, 未來的: *a prospective customer* 未來的顧客. **prospector** [prə'spektə*] *nc* person who explores an area for gold etc. 探礦者.

prospectus [prə'spektəs] *nc* printed document which advertises a school, business etc by giving details of how it is run etc. 章程, 簡介.

prosper ['prɔspə*] *vi* succeed; do well in business 成功; 繁榮; 發達. **prosperity** [prɔs'periti] *nu* state of being successful or rich 繁榮, 興旺. **prosperous** *adj* successful; rich; fortunate 成功的; 富強的; 興隆的: *have a prosperous business* 繁榮的商業; *a prosperous country* 富強的國家.

prostitute ['prɔstitjuːt] *nc* woman who offers sexual intercourse for money 妓女, 娼妓.

prostrate ['prɔstreit] *adj* lying flat (usu. face down) 全身俯卧的; 拜倒在地下的: *lie prostrate from exhaustion / out of respect to someone etc.* 趴在地上, 五體投地(表示對某人的尊敬等). Also 亦作 [prə'streit] *vt* throw down; make flat 使平卧; 平放, 俯伏; 匍匐: *They prostrated themselves before the emperor.* 他們拜倒在帝王的面前.

protagonist [prə'tægənist] *nc* main person in a story or play; leader (in a contest etc) (戲劇或小說中的)主人公; 主角; (比賽中的)主將: *The struggle between the two protagonists lasted one hour.* 兩個主將之間的爭鬥持續了一小時.

protect [prə'tekt] *vt* keep safe; defend 保護, 保衛: *protect someone from his enemies / from danger / against the cold* 保護某人免受他的敵人的攻擊/脫離危險/不受凉. **protection 1** *nu* act of protecting or being protected 保護: *ask the police for protection* 要求警察保護. **2** *nc* something that protects 保護物: *This coat will be a protection against the cold.* 這件大衣將是禦寒的好東西. **protective** *adj* protecting; preventing injury 保護的; 防護的: *protective clothing* 防護服. **protector** *nc* someone / something that protects 保護者, 保護物.

protégé ['prɔteʒei] *nc* person who is being helped or protected by someone else 受提拔者, 被保護者.

protein ['proutiːn] *nc / u* type of body-building substance which is necessary to good health, and found in such foods as meat and eggs 蛋白質.

protest [prə'test] *vt / i* object to; speak against 反對; 抗議: *protest against an injustice* 抗議(社會的)不公正. **2** state very seriously; declare 鄭重聲明; 斷言: *He protested that the charges against him were untrue.* 他鄭重聲明對他的控告是不真實的. Also 亦作 ['proutest] *nc / u* objection; statement against something 反對; 抗議: *We must make some kind of protest against this.* 我們必須對此提出某種抗議. *They left without protest.* 他們冷靜地離開了. *He accepted our decision under protest* i.e. unwillingly 他在抗議之下接受了我們的決定. 即: 不願意地.

Protestant ['prɔtistənt] *nc* Christian who is not Roman Catholic or Greek

Orthodox 新教徒. Also 亦作 *adj*.

protocol ['proutəkɔl] *nc / u* rules of behaviour (esp. between officials of different governments) 外交禮節, 官方禮節: *Everything was arranged according to protocol.* 一切都按外交禮節安排.

proton ['prouton] *nc* tiny particle carrying one unit of positive electricity 質子.

protoplasm ['proutəplæzəm] *nu* semifluid, jelly-like substance that is the living matter of all animal and plant cells 原生質; 細胞質.

prototype ['proutətaip] *nc* first or trial model of something (e.g. a machine etc) which is later to be made in larger numbers 原型, 典型; 試製型式, 樣機.

protract [prə'trækt] *vt* make longer 延長, 拖長: *a protracted argument* i.e. one which lasts for a long time 長期的爭論, 即: 持續了長時間的爭論.

protractor *nc* instrument for measuring angles on a flat surface 量角器, 分度規.

protrude [prə'tru:d] *vi* stick out; stand out 突出; 伸出: *stone protruding from the wall* 從牆上伸出的石頭.

protuberance [prə'tju:bərəns] *nc* something that bulges out 突出物.

proud [praud] *adj* having a high opinion of oneself, or of something or someone connected with oneself 驕傲的, 自負的, 自豪的: *a proud man* 驕傲的男人; *a proud father* i.e. one who has a high opinion of his children 自豪的父親, 即: 對他的子女感到自豪的父親; *a proud day for someone* i.e. a day on which something happens to make someone pleased with himself 某人最光榮的一天, 即: 有喜事而使某人極愉快的一天; *be proud of one's son*

對兒子感到自豪. *proudly adv*. see 見 **pride.**

prove [pru:v] *vt / i* **1** show that something is true 證明, 證實: *You must prove his guilt.* 你必須證明他有罪. *Vasco da Gama proved that the world was round.* 伽馬證實地球是圓的. **2** put to the test; try out 試驗; 試探: *prove someone's ability* 試探某人的才能. **3** turn out to be 表明, 顯示: *The extra room proved very useful when we had visitors.* 我們有客人來的時候, 這多餘的房間顯得很有用. see 見 **proof.**

proverb ['prɔvə:b] *nc* short, wise saying which has been used by people for a long time 格言, 諺語.

provide [prə'vaid] *vt / i* **1** give; supply 給予; 供應: *We provided him with food / We provided food for him.* 我們供應他食物. **2** give what is needed; support 供給; 支持; 贍養; 撫養: *A father must provide for his children.* 父親必須撫養他的子女. **3** take care; make arrangements 準備; 防備; 安排: *We must provide for the future / against danger.* 我們必須爲將來做準備 / 防備危險. *The rules do not provide for any exceptions* i.e. do not allow 這些規定不包有任何例外, 即: 不允許. see 見 **provision. provided (that)** *conj* on (the) condition that 假如, 倘若: *She may come with us provided (that) she arrives in time.* 假如她準時到達, 她可以跟我們一起來. **providing** *conj* on (the) condition that 假如: *You may go out providing you do your homework first.* 假如你先做你的作業, 你可以出去.

Providence ['prɔvidns] *nu* God; God's care for human beings 上帝; 保佑; 天意: *leave something to Providence* 讓上帝保佑.

province ['prɔvins] *nc* **1** main division of a country 省: *the provinces of Canada* 加拿大各省. **2** division of knowledge, work etc. (學問等方面的)範圍,部門: *the province of science* 科學的範圍; *outside one's province* i.e. outside what one has studied, done etc. 在某人的知識範圍之外, 即: 不是某人所學習、工作等的範圍. **the provinces** area in a country outside the capital 首都以外各地.

provincial [prə'vinʃl] *adj* **1** connected with a province 省的. **2** narrow in interests and outlook 心胸狹窄的. 狹隘的: *a rather provincial attitude* 很狹隘的態度.

provision [prə'viʒən] *nc / u* **1** arrangement; care taken for what may happen 安排; 準備; 預備: *There is no provision for any change in the plans.* 對計劃中的任何改變沒有安排. **2** (in a legal sense) condition in a will etc. (法律上)遺囑等中的規定, 條款. see **provide. provisions** *npl* food 食物, 糧食. **make provision for** provide for (in sense 3) 準備, 預備(用於義3): *make provision for the possibility that someone may arrive late* 做好準備有人可能會遲到.

provisional [prə'viʒənl] *adj* for the present time only; temporary 暫時的; 臨時的: *a provisional arrangement* 臨時安排. **provisionally** *adv*.

proviso [prə'vaizou] *nc* condition in an arrangement (esp. a legal arrangement) 附文, 附帶條款: *with the proviso that* i.e. on condition that 以… 爲條件. *pl* 複數 **provisos** or **provisoes**.

provoke [prə'vouk] *vt* **1** make angry 激怒: *If you provoke him, he will beat you* 如果你惹他生氣, 他會打你. **2** cause 引起: *His foolish behaviour*

provoked laughter. 他的愚蠢行爲引起大笑. **3** deliberately cause someone to do something 招惹, 激起: *She provoked him into beating her.* 她惹得他打她. **provoking** *adj* annoying 惱人的. **provocation** [prɔvə'keiʃən] **1** *nu* provoking or being provoked 激怒, 刺激: *do something under provocation* i.e. when provoked 在被激怒下做了的事. *on / at the slightest provocation* i.e. at the slightest excuse 爲了一點小事就…, 即: 找了一點小藉口就…. **2** *nc* something that annoys one 惹人惱火的事. **provocative** [prə'vɔkətiv] *adj* arousing one's emotions, anger, interest etc. 煽動性的, 刺激性的, 挑釁的: *a provocative statement* 煽動性的聲明.

prow [prau] *nc* pointed front part of a ship or boat 船首.

prowess ['praues] *nu* **1** daring; brave actions 勇敢; 勇猛. **2** skill; ability 技術; 本領: *his prowess on the football field* 他在足球方面非凡的技術.

prowl [praul] *vi* move about quietly searching for something to eat or steal 潛行覓食或偷盜: *animals prowling round a camp* 在營寨四週潛行覓食的動物; *a thief prowling round a house* 一個在房子四週潛行的賊. **prowler** *nc* **on the prowl** prowling about 徘徊, 潛行.

proximity [prɔk'simiti] *nu* nearness 接近, 附近: *in the proximity of something* i.e. near something 在某物附近, 即: 靠近某物.

proxy ['prɔksi] *nc / u* **1** right to act for another person (esp. in voting) 代表權; 代理權(尤指投票): *vote by proxy* 委託代表投票. **2** person who acts for someone else in this way 代理人, 代表.

prude [pru:d] *nc* person who is too correct or modest 過份拘謹的人. **prud-ish** *adj*.

prudent ['pru:dnt] *adj* sensible; careful 敏感的; 慎重的; 謹慎的: *You should be prudent with your money.* 你應該慎重花錢. (*opp* 反義詞 **imprudent**). **prudently** *adv* **prudence** *nu*.

prune[1] [pru:n] *nc* dried plum 梅乾, 李脯.

prune[2] [pru:n] *vt* cut off unwanted branches etc from a tree, bush etc, so as to improve it 修剪(樹枝).

pry [prai] *vi* (with **into**) look into; investigate (esp. other people's affairs) 打聽; 偵查. (尤指別人的私事): *pry into things which do not concern one* 打聽跟某人無關的事.

psalm [sɑ:m] *nc* **1** song or poem to God 讚美歌, 讚美詩, 聖詩. **2** song or poem from the Book of Psalms in the Old Testament《聖經·舊約》中的《詩篇》.

pseudo- ['sju:dou] *prefix* not real; pretending to be 假的, 偽的, 冒充的.

pseudonym ['sju:dənim] *nc* name used by a writer instead of his real name (作家的) 假名, 筆名: *write under a pseudonym* 用筆名寫作.

psychiatry [sai'kaiətri] *nu* science of treating mental disease 精神病學. **psychiatric** [saiki'ætrik] *adj* **psychiatrist** *nc*.

psychic ['saikik] *adj* connected with the soul or mind 精神的, 心靈的; 靈魂的.

psychoanalysis [saikouə'nælisis] *nu* (art of) careful examination of someone's mental condition so that the reasons for his mental or nervous illness can be discovered 精神分析 (學). **psychoanalyst** [saikou'ænəlist] *nc* person trained to carry out psychoanalysis 精神分析學家. **psychoanalyse** [saikou'ænəlaiz] *vt*.

psychology [sai'kɔlədʒi] *nu* scientific study of the mind and how it works 心理學. **psychologist** *nc* expert in psychology 心理學家. **psychological** [saikə'lɔdʒikl] *adj*.

psychosomatic ['saikousə'mætik] *adj* referring to an illness of the body which is caused by nervous or mental illness 由精神或身體不適引起的, 身心的: *psychosomatic illness* 身心病.

pub [pʌb] *nc* short informal form of **public house** public house 非正式縮略式.

puberty ['pju:bəti] *nu* age at which a person is physically able to become a parent 青春期, 發情期.

public ['pʌblik] *adj* **1** general; concerning everyone 公衆的; 公家的: *public affairs* 公衆事務; *a matter of public concern* 一件公衆關心的事. **2** provided for everyone; open to everyone 公用的; 公共的: *public relief* 公衆的救濟; *public parks / libraries etc.* 公園, 公共圖書館等. **3** run by or employed by the government 政府辦的, 公辦的: *public works* 公共建設; 公共工程; *public official* 政府官員. **4** known to everyone 公開的: *The matter became public.* 這件事公開了. (*opp* 反義詞 **private**). **publicly** *adv* **the public** the people in general 民衆, 大衆, 衆人: *a matter of little interest to the public* 公衆興趣不大的事情. **public house** place where alcoholic drink can be bought and drunk 酒吧, 小酒店. (Also 亦作 **pub**). **public relations** *nu* relations between a government department or firm etc and the public 公共關係. **public school 1** (Brit) boarding school mostly run by private fees (英) 寄宿中學, 私立學校. **2** (US) government school (美) 公立學校. **'public-'spirited** *adj* willing to do things for the good of the public 熱心公益

的, 願爲公衆服務的. **in public** openly; not in private 公然; 公開地.

publican ['pʌblikən] *nc* owner of a public house 酒吧老闆.

publication [pʌbli'keiʃən] **1** *nc* anything that is published (e.g. book,
paper, magazine) 出版物(例如: 書籍和
雜誌). **2** *nu* act of publishing something 出版, 刊行.

publicize ['pʌblisaiz] *vt* make publicly
known; advertise 廣爲宣傳; 公佈; 做廣
告. **publicity** [pʌb'lisiti] *nu* process
of advertising 宣傳, 推廣, 廣告.

publish ['pʌbliʃ] *vt* **1** produce in
printed form, as a book, magazine,
newspaper etc. 出版. **2** make publicly
known 公佈, 公開. **publisher** *nc* person who produces books etc in
printed form 出版人, 出版社. **publishing** *nu* work of a publisher 出版
業.

pucker ['pʌkə*] *vt* (esp. with reference
to the face) twist; pull together (尤指
臉部)起皺; 縮攏: *The child puckered
up his face and began to cry.* 孩子臉
上起皺就開始哭了.

pudding ['pudiŋ] *nc / u* **1** food of various types (usu. consisting of pastry,
custard, fruit etc) served after the
main part of a meal 布丁. **2** any
sweet food served after the main part
of a meal 甜點心(飯後吃的). **3** food
(usu. consisting of pastry / suet and
meat) served with the main part of a
meal 肉布丁(跟主食同時吃).

puddle ['pʌdl] *nc* small area of water
(esp. one made by rain) 水坑, 窪. (尤
指下雨所造成的).

puerile ['pjuərail] *adj* childish; foolish
稚氣的; 孩子氣的; 傻的.

puff [pʌf] *nc* slight movement of air,
smoke etc. 一陣, 一股, 吹, 噴: *a puff
of wind* 一陣風; *a puff of smoke* 一縷

煙. Also 亦作 *vt / i* breathe jerkily 抽
噴: *puff a pipe* 抽烟斗. **puffy** *adj*
(with reference to part of the body
which is injured or diseased) swollen
腫脹的. '**powder puff** see 見
powder.

puffin ['pʌfin] *nc* type of Arctic sea bird
with a large beak 海鸚.

pull [pul] *vt / i* cause to come towards
one or in the same direction as one
拉, 拖: *The engine pulled the train up
the hill.* 火車頭把火車拉上小山. *He
pulled as hard as he could.* 他盡力拉.
Also 亦作 *nc* (usu. only *sing*) act of
pulling (僅用單數)拉, 拖. Also 亦作
nu unfair influence; ability to get
some advantage because one knows
someone in an official position. (*informal*) 影響力, 門路. (非正式). **pull
something down** (with reference to
a building) destroy, often in order to
build something else 拆毀, 推倒(指某
建築物): *pull down an old house* 拆
毀舊房子. **pull in** (with reference to
a car) stop near or at something (指
汽車)停靠: *Pull in at the next garage.*
在第二個停車場停靠. **pull through**
recover from a dangerous illness 恢復
健康. **pull up** (usu. with reference to
a car etc) stop; stop suddenly (通常
指汽車)停下; 突然停住. **make / pull a
face at someone** see 見 **make¹. pull
oneself together** become calm again
after having been excited, worried etc.
恢復鎮定, 振作起來. **pull one's
weight** do one's full share of work; do
as much as others who are working
with one 竭盡全力; 盡應盡之力.

pulley ['puli] *nc* apparatus for lifting
things, consisting of a wheel over
which a rope can be moved
滑輪, 滑車.

pullover ['puləuvə*] *nc* garment for the

upper part of the body, pulled on over the head 套頭衫.

pulp [pʌlp] *nu* **1** soft part of a fruit or vegetable 果肉, 蔬果的肉質部份. **2** soft, wet mass of wood or cloth, used for making paper (用於造紙的) 紙漿.

pulpit ['pulpit] *nc* structure in a church reached by steps, and from which the priest, minister etc speaks 教堂的講壇.

pulse [pʌls] *nc* **1** regular movement of the blood pumped by the heart 脈搏. **2** any regular beat or movement like this 拍子, 節奏, 律動. **pulsate** [pʌl'seit] *vi* move regularly in this way 有節奏的振動, 跳動.

pummel ['pʌml] *vt* hit many times with the fists 用拳頭接連地打. *past* 過去式和過去分詞 **pummelled**. (*US* 美 **pummeled**). (Also 亦作 **pommel**).

pump¹ [pʌmp] *nc* apparatus for forcing gas or liquid into or out of something 抽水機, 水泵, 氣筒. Also 亦作 *vt / i* **1** move by a pump 打氣: *pump air into a tyre* 往輪胎裏打氣. **2** work a pump 使用唧筒: *He pumped for half an hour.* 他用氣筒打了半小時. **pump something up** fill by pumping 給…打滿.

pump² [pʌmp] *nc* light dancing shoe 輕便舞鞋.

pumpkin ['pʌmpkin] *nc* large, round, orange-coloured fruit, eaten as a food (esp. in the USA) 南瓜(尤指在美國).

pun [pʌn] *nc* type of joke in which words have more than one meaning, or in which two expressions sound the same 雙關語. Also 亦作 *vi* make such a joke 用雙關語開玩笑. *past* 過去式和過去分詞 **punned**.

punch¹ [pʌntʃ] *vt* hit with the closed fist 用拳猛擊. Also 亦作 *nc* blow given in this way 拳打, 一拳.

punch² [pʌntʃ] *nc* device for making holes 打孔機, 打洞器. Also 亦作 *vt* make a hole with a punch 打洞, 鑽孔: *punch a hole* 打個洞; *punch a ticket* i.e. on a bus etc. 剪票, 即: 在公共汽車上剪票等.

punch³ [pʌntʃ] *nu* type of hot drink made from wine, rum etc. 混合熱飲料.

punctual ['pʌŋktjuəl] *adj* coming at the right time 準時的, 按時的. **punctually** *adv* **punctuality** [pʌŋktju'æliti] *nc*.

punctuate ['pʌŋktjueit] *vt / i* use full stops, commas etc in writing 加標點: *punctuate a sentence* 給句子加標點. **punctuation** [pʌŋktju'eiʃən] *nu*: *punctuation marks* i.e. full stops, commas etc. 標點符號, 即: 句號, 逗號等.

puncture ['pʌŋktʃə*] *nc* hole made by a sharp object (esp. a hole in a tyre) 刺孔, 穿孔(尤指車胎上的洞). Also 亦作 *vt* make a hole in 刺破, 刺穿.

pundit ['pʌndit] *nc* learned man; expert 學者; 專家.

pungent ['pʌndʒənt] *adj* sharp to the taste or sense of smell 刺鼻的, 刺激的, 辣的: *a pungent smell* 刺鼻的臭味.

punish ['pʌniʃ] *vt* cause pain, loss or discomfort to in return for some wrong 處罰, 懲罰: *The teacher punished the boy who had broken the window.* 老師處罰了打破窗子的男孩. **punishment** *nc / u* **punishable** *adj* likely to be punished; deserving punishment 該處罰的; 可處罰的: *a punishable offence* 該處罰的過錯.

punitive ['pju:nitiv] *adj* concerned with punishment; done in order to punish 懲罰的; 刑罰的.

punt [pʌnt] *nc* type of flat-bottomed boat, moved by pushing a pole against the bottom of a river 方頭平

底船.

punter ['pʌntə*] *nc* person who makes bets on horse-races, football matches etc. (賽馬, 足球賽時)下賭注者.

puny ['pju:ni] *adj* small and weak 弱小的.

pup [pʌp] *nc* puppy 小狗.

pupil¹ ['pju:pil] *nc* young person being taught in a school or by a teacher 小學生.

pupil² ['pju:pil] *nc* dark area in the centre of the eye (眼睛的)瞳孔, 瞳仁.

puppet ['pʌpit] *nc* **1** small doll, which can be made to move by wires, strings, the fingers etc. 木偶, 布偶. **2** person or government completely controlled by someone else 傀儡.

puppy ['pʌpi] *nc* young dog 小狗.

purchase ['pə:tʃis] *vt* buy 購買. Also 亦作 *n* **1** something bought 所購物, 買到的東西. **2** (usu. only *sing*) tight hold on something to prevent it or oneself from falling etc. (通常僅用單數)支點: *get a purchase on a rope* 在繩子上搞個支點. **purchaser** *nc*.

pure [pjuə*] *adj* **1** not mixed with other things 純的, 純粹的. **2** having no unclean or immoral thoughts; acting in a moral way 純潔的; 無邪的: *pure thoughts* 純潔的思想. (*opp* **impure** in senses 1 and 2) (義1和義2的反義詞爲 **impure**). **3** mere; nothing more than 僅僅的; 完全的; 十足的: *pure chance* i.e. only chance, without intention 十足的運氣, 即: 只憑運氣, 沒有意圖: *pure luck* 十足的幸運. **4** (with reference to science and mathematics) concerned with theory, and not with practical application (指科學和數學)理論的, 抽象的: *pure science* 純科學, 理論科學. **purely** *adv* **purity** *nu* condition of being pure 純潔, 純淨. **purify** *vt* make pure 使純潔, 洗

滌. **purification** [pjurifi'keiʃən] *nu*

purist *nc* person who is always careful to use language which he considers correct 力求語言純正的人.

puree, purée ['pjuərei] *nc / u* **1** type of thick soup 濃湯. **2** food like thick soup 像濃湯的食物.

purge [pə:dʒ] *vt* make pure and clean 清洗, 洗滌. Also 亦作 *nc* act of purging 清洗.

puritan ['pjuəritn] *nc* person who is very strict in morals and religion (宗教道德上)極拘謹的人. **puritanical** [pjuəri'tænikl] *adj* very strict, or too strict, in morals and behaviour 極嚴格的; 太拘謹的.

purple ['pə:pl] *nc / u* colour obtained by mixing red and blue together 紫色. Also 亦作 *adj*.

purpose ['pə:pəs] *nc* **1** what one intends to do; plan 目的; 意圖; 打算: *What is your purpose in doing this?* 你做這件事的目的是甚麼? **2** what a thing is used, made for etc. 用途, 效果, 結果: *This machine has been made for a certain purpose.* 這機器是爲某種用途而製造的. **purposeful** *adj* showing that one has a definite purpose 有目的的, 故意的: *walk in a purposeful manner* 以故意的姿態步行. **purposely** *adv* intentionally; deliberately 故意地; 特意地: *He arrived late purposely so as to annoy me.* 他故意遲到, 氣我. **on purpose** deliberately 故意: *do something on purpose* 故意做某事.

purr [pə:*] *nc / u* soft sound like that made by a cat when it is pleased (貓高興時發出的)嗚嗚聲. Also 亦作 *vi* make this sound 發出嗚嗚聲.

purse [pə:s] *nc* **1** small bag for carrying money in 小錢包. **2** (*US*) woman's handbag (美)女人的手提袋. Also 亦作

vt draw the lips together into the shape of a small circle (often to show displeasure) 噘起嘴唇(常表示不高興).

purser ['pə:sə*] *nc* officer on a ship who is in charge of stores and money (船上的)事務長.

pursue [pə'sju:] *vt* **1** follow in order to catch or kill 追捕, 追殺: *pursue a wild animal* 追捕野生動物. **2** carry on with; continue to work at 從事; 繼續: *pursue one's study of English* 繼續英語學習. **pursuit** [pə'sju:t] **1** *nu* act of pursuing 追捕, 追趕, 追求: *He was captured without much pursuit* 他沒經多少追趕就被捕了. *in pursuit of pleasure* 快樂的追求. **2** *nc* something in which one is interested or spends time on 研究, 嗜好, 愛好: *literary pursuits* i. e. writing books etc. 文學的愛好, 即: 寫書等.

pus [pʌs] *nu* thick, yellow liquid which comes out of a poisoned area of the body (e.g. a wound, boil etc.) 膿(例如: 傷口的化膿, 癤子等).

push¹ [puʃ] *vt / i* **1** make someone / something go farther away by using force against him / it; press against 推; 擠: *The little boy pushed his sister away from him.* 小男孩把他姐姐從他身邊推開. *If the door does not open at first, push it harder.* 假如這個門起先不能開, 就多用點力推開它. *If you don't stop pushing, someone may get hurt.* 假如你不停止亂擠, 有人可能會受傷. *Push the table against the wall.* 把桌子推到牆邊. *If you push this button, a bell rings.* 假如你按動這個開關, 鈴就響了. **2** try to make people have a favourable idea of oneself, something one is selling etc. 促進, 推銷, 推動: *push oneself forward* 極力表現自己; *push one's ideas* 推行自己的主意; *push something through* i. e. to persuade others to agree to it 努力促成某事, 即: 說服別人同意. **3** sell drugs illegally. 販賣(毒品). *(informal* in sense **3)** (義3爲非正式). **pusher** *nc* **1** person who pushes (in sense **2)** 推者, 推動者, 推銷者(用於義2). **2** person who pushes drugs *(informal)* 販毒者(非正式). **pushing, pushy** *adj* inclined to draw attention to oneself too much 好出風頭的.

push² [puʃ] *nc* act of pushing 推, 推進, 推的動作: *The door was stuck, but it opened with a push / when I gave it a push.* 門給塞住, 但推一下就開了/但我推一下時就開了.

puss, pussy [pus(i)] *nc* child's informal name for a **cat** 貓咪(小孩給貓取的非正式的名字).

put [put] *vt / i* **1** place; cause to be in a certain position 放, 置於, 處於: *He put his book on the table.* 他把他的書放在桌上. *I put my hand in my pocket.* 我把手放在我的口袋裏. *You have put me in a difficult situation* i. e. a situation which annoys or embarrasses me. 你把我置於困難的境地. 即: 使我處於難堪和苦惱的境地. *It is time to put the children to bed.* 是讓孩子們上床的時候了. **2** say; state 說; 表白; 提出: *Can I put a suggestion to you?* 我可以向你提個建議嗎? **3** write; mark 寫, 標上: *Put the prices on these cards.* 把價格寫在這些牌子上. *Put your name here* i. e. sign your name 將你的名字寫在這裏. 即: 簽上你的名字. *pres part* 現在分詞 **putting.** *past* 過去式和過去分詞 **put. put about** change direction 改變航向: *The ship put about.* 這船改變了航向. **put something across** make someone understand 使人理解: *It's a pity he cannot put his ideas across. (informal)* 很遺憾, 他不能使他

的觀點讓人理解. (非正式). **put something by** save 儲蓄, 備用: *He used to put some money by / put by some money every week.* 他經常每週儲蓄一點錢. **put something down 1** place down 放下: *Put the books down on the floor* 把這些書放在地板上. **2** stop by strong action 鎮壓, 平定, 制止: *put down a rebellion* 鎮壓叛亂; *put down gambling* 制止賭博. **put something forward** ask for something to be considered 提出, 建議: *put forward a new idea* 提出新的觀點; *put oneself forward for election* 提名自己爲候選人. **put someone / something off 1** delay until later 延期: *We shall have to put off the party until next week.* 我們將不得不把聚會延期到下禮拜. **2** discourage someone; make someone dislike something 使不喜歡; 反感: *The bad service we got last time put us off going back to that hotel.* (informal) 上次我們受到不好的接待, 我們不喜歡回到那家旅店去. (非正式). **put something on 1** clothe with 穿上: *put on one's coat* 穿上 (某人的) 大衣. **2** increase 增加: *put on speed* 增加速度; *put on weight* i. e. get fatter 增加體重, 即: 長胖些. **3** cause to work or happen 使運行, 加開: *put on extra buses* 增開額外的公共汽車; *put on the radio* 開收音機; *put on a play* i. e. cause a play to be shown on the stage 上演一個戲劇, 即: 使一個戲演出. **put someone / something out 1** cause to be outside 逐出, 趕出: *If you talk in the library, you will be put out.* 假如你在圖書館裏講話, 你將被趕出去. **2** cause something to stop burning or being lit 撲滅, 熄: *put out a fire / the light etc.* 熄火 / 燈 等. **3** hold out 伸出: *put out one's hand / one's tongue etc.* 伸出手 /

舌頭 等. **4** trouble (oneself) 麻煩: *Please don't put yourself out for us* i. e. we would not like to cause you any trouble. 請別爲我們麻煩了你自己. 即: 我們不想給你找麻煩. (informal in sense 4) (義 4 爲非正式). **put someone through** connect by telephone 接通 (電話): *I asked the operator to put me through to the hospital.* 我請電話員接醫院. **put someone / something up 1** raise 舉起, 提高: *put up one's hand* i. e. raise it above one's head 高高舉起某人的手, 即: 把手舉過某人的頭. **put up prices** 提高價格. **2** put in a place where it can be seen 張貼: *put up a notice* 張貼佈告. **3** give a place to sleep for a short time (sometimes with food) 暫供膳宿, 找個落腳的地方: *Can you put us up for the night?* 晚上你能給我們找個落腳的地方嗎? (informal in sense 3) (義 3 爲非正式). **put up to** tell someone to do something bad or show him how to do it 唆使, 鼓動: *I don't know who has put him up to this mischief.* (informal) 我不知道誰唆使他做出這個惡作劇? (非正式) **put up with something** suffer, bear without complaining 忍受, 忍耐: *The food is not very good, but we shall just have to put up with it.* (informal) 食物是不很好, 但我們只好將就吃下去了. (非正式).

putrid ['pju:trid] *adj* having gone rotten; decayed 已腐爛的; 腐臭的: *putrid fish* 臭魚.

putt [pʌt] *vt / i* (in golf) hit the ball gently so that it rolls towards / into the hole on the green (高爾夫球) 短打, 輕打使球滑向或滾進洞. Also 亦作 nc.

putty ['pʌti] *nu* soft mixture of white powder and oil (used e. g. for fixing panel of glass in windows) 油灰 (例

如: 用於固定窗框上的玻璃).

puzzle ['pʌzl] *nc* **1** something that is difficult to understand 難題. **2** problem which tests a person's knowledge, intelligence etc, and is done as an amusement 謎. Also 亦作 *vt / i* think or cause someone to think hard (使) 苦思, 使迷惑: *I have been puzzling about this question for weeks now.* 現在, 我爲這個問題一直苦思了幾個禮拜. *His strange behaviour puzzles me* i. e. I do not understand it. 他的古怪的行爲使我迷惑不解. 即: 我不明白. **puzzling** *adj* difficult to understand 難以理解的, 困惑的. **puzzle something out** find an answer, or reason, for something by thinking hard about it 苦思後找出答案. **puzzle over something** think hard about something 思索.

pygmy, pigmy ['pigmi] *nc* member of a race of small people that lives in Africa 居住在非洲的矮小黑人, 俾格米人.

pyjamas [pi'dʒɑːməz] (*US* 美 **pajamas)** *npl* loose-fitting jacket and trousers for wearing in bed (usu. made of a light cloth) 寬鬆的睡衣褲.

pylon ['pailn] *nc* high sort of tower made of steel, used for carrying electric wires 架高壓電纜的鐵塔.

pyramid ['pirəmid] *nc* solid object usu. square at the bottom and coming to a point 錐體.

python ['paiθən] *nc* type of large snake which kills the animals it wants to eat by winding itself very tightly round them 蟒蛇.

Q, q

quack¹ [kwæk] *nc* sound a duck makes 鴨叫聲. Also 亦作 *vi* make this sound (鴨) 嘎嘎地叫.

quack² [kwæk] *nc* person who pretends to have knowledge (esp. of medicine) which he does not really possess 江湖醫生; 庸醫; 騙子; 假充内行的人.

quadrangle ['kwɔdræŋgl] *nc* four-sided area surrounded by buildings (e. g. in a college) (建築物圍着的) 四方院子. (例如: 大學裏的方院). (Also 亦作 **quad**).

quadratic [kwɔ'drætik] *adj* (mathematics) involving a quantity or quantities that are squared but none that are raised to a higher power (數學) 二次的. Also 亦作 *nc* quadratic equation 二次方程式.

quadrilateral [kwɔdri'lætrl] *nc* flat, four-sided figure 四邊形.

quadruped ['kwɔdruped] *nc* animal that has four feet 四足動物.

quadruple [kwɔ'drupl] *adj* made up of four parts, including four people 由四部份 (包括四人或四方) 組成的: *a quadruple agreement* 四方協議. Also 亦作 *vt / i* make or become four times greater 使成四倍或變成四倍.

quad(s) [kwɔd(z)], **quadruplet(s)** [kwɔ'dru:plit(s)] *n* (usu. *pl*) (one of) four babies born to the same mother at the same time (通常用複數) 四胞胎孩子中的一個.

quagmire ['kwɔgmaiə*] *nc* area of very soft, muddy ground 泥沼, 沼澤地.

quaint [kweint] *adj* interesting or pleasing because it is unusual or old 離奇有趣的; 古色古香的: *quaint old village church* 古色古香的鄉村教堂. **quaintly** *adv* **quaintness** *nc / u*.

quake [kweik] *vi* shake; tremble 震動; 發抖: *quake with fear* 怕得發抖: *The earth quaked under our feet.* 大地在我們的脚下震動. Also 亦作 *nc* short form of **earthquake**. earthquake 的縮畧形式.

qualify ['kwɔlifai] **1** *vt* train; make a person good enough 訓練; 使合格, 使勝任: *His ability qualified him for the job.* 他的能力使他能勝任這工作. **2** *vi* be trained; be good or skilled enough 被訓練, 合格, 適合: *qualified to teach* 勝任教書: *qualified as a doctor / lawyer etc.* 有資格當醫生/律師等; *a qualified teacher* 一個合格的教師; *be qualified for a certain post* 有擔任某職位的資格. **3** *vt* make a remark less general in meaning 限定, 修飾, 使較不籠統. **qualified** *adj* 合格的, 够格的. (*opp* 反義詞 **unqualified**). **qualification** [kwɔlifi'keiʃən] *nc* **1** training or examination which makes a person fit to do something (通過訓練或考試而獲得的) 資格: *a doctor with good medical qualifications* 很有資格行醫的醫生. **2** something that changes, makes weaker or less general etc. 限定, 限制條件: *I can say, without any qualification, that he is an excellent worker* i. e. without any doubt etc. 我可以毫無保留地説, 他是個優秀工人. 即: 毫無疑問地説.

quality ['kwɔliti] **1** *nc* something that a person / thing has which makes him / it different from others 特性, 特質: *One quality of wood is that it can*

burn. 木材的一個特性是它可以燃燒.
2 *nu* standard of excellence that a thing / person has 品質: *cloth of good / poor quality* 優／劣質布; *a shop famous for its quality* i. e. the goodness of what it sells 以優質聞名的商店, 即: 它賣的商品質量好. Also 亦作 *adj.*

qualm [kwɑːm] *nc* (often *pl*) feeling of anxiety or guilt about whether one has done right (常用複數)不安, 疑懼: *have no qualms about doing something* 做某事並沒有感到不安.

quandary ['kwɔndri] *nc* state of doubt; feeling of difficulty 困惑; 進退兩難: *be in a quandary about what to do* 不知道該做甚麼.

quantity ['kwɔntiti] **1** *nc / u* amount 量, 數量: *add a small quantity of water* 加少量的水. *He used equal quantities of milk and water.* 他用了同樣數量的牛奶和水. **2** *nu* large amount 大量: *buy things in quantity* 購買大量物品.

quarantine ['kwɔrəntiːn] *nu* separation from others so that disease is not spread 隔離(以防止疾病傳染), 檢疫: *People coming from an infected area must be kept in quarantine.* 來自傳染病流行區的人們必須進行隔離.

quarrel ['kwɔrl] *nc* **1** angry disagreement 爭吵, 爭辯: *have a quarrel with someone about / over something* 爲某事跟某人發生爭吵. **2** reason for disagreement 爭論的原因.Also 亦作 *vi* to have a quarrel 爭吵, 爭辯: *I quarrelled with him last night.* 我昨晚跟他爭吵. *These two people are always quarrelling.* 這兩個人常常爭吵. 過去式和過去分詞 quarrelled. (US 美 quarreled). quarrelsome *adj* fond of quarrelling 愛爭吵的.

quarry¹ [kwɔri] *nc* place at ground level from which stone, slate, marble

etc are obtained (usu. by blasting) 採石場.

quarry² ['kwɔri] *nc* animal etc chased or hunted 獵物.

quart [kwɔːt] *nc* measure for liquid equal to two pints 夸脫(液體計量單位, 等於二品脫).

quarter¹ ['kwɔːtə*] *nc / u* **1** fourth part of something 某物的四分之一: *Give a quarter of the cake to each of the four children.* 給四個孩子每人分四分之一的餅. **2** fourth part of an hour i. e. 15 minutes 一刻鐘, 即: 十五分鐘: *It's (a) quarter past three* i. e. 3.15. 是三點一刻; 3:15. *It's (a) quarter to three* i. e. 2.45. 是二點三刻, 即: 2:45. **3** fourth part of a year i. e. 3 months 季, 即: 三個月: *We pay our fuel bills every quarter.* 我們每三個月付一次燃料費. **4** fourth part of a *US* dollar i. e. 25 cents 一美元的四分之一, 即: 25分. **5** direction; place 方向, 方位. *People came running from every quarter.* 人們從四面八方跑來. **6** part of a town 區, 住地: *the Chinese quarter* i. e. where the Chinese live 華人區, 即華人居住的地方. **7** one of the four phases of the moon, each lasting about 7 days 弦(月球週期的四分之一, 每弦七天): *The moon was in its first quarter.* 月亮是上弦. see also 亦見 **phase**.

quarterly *adv* every three months 每季的, 每年四次的. **quarters** *npl* place to live or stay 住宅, 寓所. '**quartermaster** soldier or sailor in charge of supplies etc. 軍需官, 負責後勤的水手等.

quarter² ['kwɔːtə*] *vt* **1** divide into four parts 分爲四份. **2** find rooms for soldiers to stay in (爲士兵)提供住地, 駐紮: *The soldiers were quartered in the village.* 士兵們駐紮在這鄉村裏.

quartet, quartette [kwɔːˈtet] *nc* **1** group

of four singers or instrument players 四重奏(樂團); 四重唱(樂團). **2** piece of music for such a group 四重奏曲, 四重唱曲.

quartz [kwɔːts] *nu* type of hard rock (often colourless and semitransparent) used in the electrical industry 石英.

quash [kwɔʃ] *vt* end by an offical or legal decision 取消, 廢除, 撤銷: *quash a conviction* i. e. decide by law that somebody is not guilty after he has been found guilty by another court 撤銷判決, 即: 駁回另一個法院的判決.

quasi- [ˈkweizai] *prefix* seemingly, not really 類似的, 假的. (e. g. **quasi-official; quasi-historical**) (例如: quasi-official; quasi-historical).

quaver [ˈkweivə*] *vt / i* shake; tremble 震顫; 發抖. Also 亦作 *nc* **1** trembling sound 顫音. **2** type of musical note 八分音符.

quay [kiː] *nc* place (often built of stone) where ships are loaded or unloaded 碼頭.

queasy [ˈkwiːzi] *adj* **1** having a feeling of sickness 令人作嘔的, 不舒服的: *feel rather queasy* 感到很不舒服. **2** easily made sick 易嘔的: *a queasy stomach* 易作嘔的胃.

queen [kwiːn] *nc* **1** wife of a king 王后, 皇后. **2** woman ruler of a country 女王. **3** female in group of bees, ants etc who lays eggs 雌蜂, 雌蟻 (如: *a queen bee* 雌蜂, 蜂后. **4** playing card next in importance to king (撲克牌中的)女王. **5** important piece in the game of chess 棋中的后.

queer [kwiə*] *adj* **1** strange; odd 奇怪的; 古怪的: *have queer ideas, act in a queer way* 有奇怪的想法, 行爲古怪. **2** sick; unwell 不舒服的; 頭暈眼花的: *feel queer* 感到不舒服. **3** homosexual

同性戀的. (*informal in senses* **2** and **3**) (義 2 和義 3 爲非正式). Also 亦作 *nc* homosexual man (*informal*) 男同性戀者(非正式).

quell [kwel] *vt* **1** put down 鎮壓, 制止: *quell a rebellion / riot etc.* 鎮壓叛亂/暴動等. **2** stop; put an end to 消除: *quell someone's fears* 消除某人的恐懼.

quench [kwentʃ] *vt* put out; put an end to 消滅; 停止, 結束: *quench one's thirst* i. e. by drinking water 解渴, 即: 喝水以解渴. *quench a fire* 滅火.

query [ˈkwiəri] *nc* **1** question 問題, 詢問; *raise a query* 提問. **2** the mark ? put after a question or beside something to show doubt 問號. Also 亦作 *vt / i* ask about 詢問, 質問. **2** express doubt about 質疑, 表示懷疑: *query something* 對某事表示懷疑. *query if / whether something is true* 懷疑某事是否真實.

question [ˈkwestʃən] *nc* **1** something asked; request for knowledge 問題; 疑問: *Children are always asking questions.* 孩子們常常提問題. *Answer my question.* 回答我的問題. **2** something to be discussed; problem 討論的事; 論題: *the question of world poverty* 世界貧困的問題. *It's a question of money.* 這是個錢的問題. Also 亦作 *vt / i* **1** ask questions of 詢問, 質問: *be questioned for hours* 被問了數小時. **2** doubt 懷疑: *I question his honesty* i. e. I am not sure that he is honest. 我懷疑他的誠實. 即: 我不能肯定他是誠實的. **questionable** *adj* doubtful; not certain 有問題的, 不確定的: *questionable statements* 有問題的聲明. (*opp* 反義詞 **unquestionable). questionnaire** [kwestʃəˈneə*] *nc* (printed) list of questions to find out what people think about a certain subject (爲專題

調查而印的)一組問題, 問卷. **'question mark** the mark ? put after a question or beside something to show doubt 問號. **out of the question** impossible 不可能. **without / beyond question** without (a) doubt; certainly 無疑問地; 肯定地.

queue [kju:] *nc* line of waiting people, cars etc. (人或車輛等的)長隊, 行列: *a queue outside a cinema* 電影院外面的長隊; *form a queue* 排成一行; *stand in a queue* 站成一行. Also 亦作 *vi* form or stand in a queue 排隊: *We had to queue for hours.* 我們不得不排了幾小時的隊.

quibble ['kwibl] *vt* find fault by concentrating on trifling details 吹毛求疵; 在小問題上爭持.

quick [kwik] *adj* **1** fast; sudden; done in a short time 快的; 快速的; 迅速完成的; *go for a quick walk* 去快速的散步; *have a quick meal* 吃了一頓快餐; *be a quick runner* 做個快跑選手. **2** clever 敏捷的, 伶俐的: *a quick child* 聰明伶俐的孩子; *quick to understand* 敏於理解. Also 亦作 *nu* **1** tender flesh under the fingernails and toenails (手指甲下的) 嫩肉, 肉根. **2** one's feelings 感情: *be cut to the quick* i. e. be deeply offended 被傷害感情, 即: 被深深地冒犯了. Also 亦作 *adv* quickly (*informal* in this sense) 快速地(此義爲非正式). **quickly** *adv* **quickness** *nu* **quicken** *vt / i* **1** move more quickly 加快, 加速: *quicken one's pace* 加快步伐. **2** make or become lively, more lively 使(變得)生氣勃勃; 使更活躍, 激發: *The old sailor's story quickened the boy's imagination.* 老水手的故事激發了男孩的想像力. **'quicksand** area of very wet sand into which men, ships etc can sink 流沙.

quid [kwid] *nc* one pound or one hundred pence 一鎊, 一百便士. *pl* quid. (*informal*) (非正式).

quiet ['kwaiət] *adj* **1** making little or no movement or sound 安靜的, 靜止的: *Tell the children to be quiet.* 叫孩子們保持安靜. **2** peaceful; not causing disturbance 平靜的; 和睦的: *quiet neighbours* 和睦的鄰居. **quietly** *adv* **quietness** *nu* **quieten** *vt*.

quill [kwil] *nc* (in former times) hollow stem of a large stiff feather used as a pen (從前)用作筆的硬而大的羽毛, 翎筆.

quilt [kwilt] *nc* bed covering made of two pieces of cloth with some kind of soft material between them 被, 棉被. **quilted** *adj*.

quinine [kwi'ni:n] *nu* bitter medicine made from the bark of a tree and used as a remedy for fevers (e. g. malaria) 奎寧(用以治發熱病, 如瘧疾).

quintet, quintette [kwin'tet] *nc* **1** group of five singers or instrument players 五重唱演出組; 五重奏樂團. **2** piece of music for such a group 五部曲, 五重奏曲.

quin(s) [kwin(z)], **quintuplet(s)** [kwin-'tju:plit(s)] *n* (*usu. pl*) (one of) five babies born to the same mother at the same time (通常用複數)五胞胎孩子中的一個.

quip [kwip] *nc* clever saying; witty remark 妙語; 俏皮話. Also 亦作 *vi* make a quip 說俏皮話. past 過去式和過去分詞 **quipped**.

quirk [kwə:k] *nc* peculiar or odd event, saying or action 奇行, 怪癖, 巧事.

quit [kwit] *vt / i* **1** stop 停止, 放棄: *quit gambling* 停止賭博. **2** leave; leave suddenly 離開; 離去: *He quit the room angrily.* 他生氣地離開房間. *pres part* 現在分詞 **quitting**. *past* 過去式和過去分詞 **quit** or **quitted**. **be quits**

be on even terms with someone (by paying back a debt or by having one's revenge etc.) 清帳, 了結: *Give me back the money and then we'll be quits. (informal)* 把錢還給我, 那麼我們就算了結了. (非正式).

quite [kwait] *intensifier* **1** completely 完全, 十分: *quite useless* 完全沒有用; *quite different* 完全不同; *Is that right? No, not quite.* 那是對的嗎?不, 不完全對. **2** rather to some extent 頗, 相當: *quite clever* 相當聰明. *Note* 說明: when *quite* means 'rather' it often comes before a as in *quite a nice party, quite a pretty dress.* quite用於義 2 時常出現在 a 前, 如: quite a nice party (相當好的聚會), quite a pretty dress (相當漂亮的衣服). **quite, quite so I agree** 好的; 不錯; 對的.

quiver[1] [ˈkwivə*] *vt/i* shake, tremble 顫抖, 發抖: *quivering with cold / fear etc.* 冷/怕得發抖等.

quiver[2] [ˈkwivə*] *nc* case for holding arrows 箭筒, 箭囊.

quiz [kwiz] *vt* find out what someone knows by asking questions 考問. *past* 過去式及過去分詞 **quizzed.** Also 亦作 *nc* game in which people try to answer questions 問答遊戲. *pl* **quizzes. quizzical** [ˈkwizikl] *adj* **1** strange, amusing 奇特的, 有趣的. **2** teasing; making fun of someone 戲弄的; 揶揄的: *a quizzical smile* 揶揄的一笑.

quoit [kɔit] *nc* ring made of metal, rubber etc which is used in certain games (often played on board ships) (在甲板上玩擲環套樁遊戲用的)繩圈, 金屬環, 橡皮圈. **quoits** *npl* one such game, played by throwing a quoit at a small pole 擲環套樁遊戲.

quorum [ˈkwɔ:rəm] *nc* number of people that must be at a meeting, according to the rules of a society, before anything can be decided 法定人數: *If we don't have (enough for) a quorum, we shall have to meet again.* 如果我們沒有足夠的法定人數, 我們將要再開會.

quota [ˈkwoutə] *nc* amount of something that one must give or receive 定量, 配額, 限額: *exceed one's quota* i.e. give or receive more than one has to 超過限額, 即: 多於該得或該給的數額.

quote [kwout] *vt* **1** repeat or write the exact words of another 引用: *quote Shakespeare* 引用莎士比亞的話. **2** give something as an example of what one means 舉例說明, 引證. **3** give the price of, in arranging a commercial agreement 報價, 定價: *quote a price for something* 報某商品的價. Also 亦作 *nc* quotation mark 引號. see below 見下條 **quotation** [kwouˈteiʃən] *nc/u* quoting; something quoted 引用; 引文; 行市; 行情, 估價: *quotations from Shakespeare* 莎士比亞作品的引文. *a quotation of a price* 報價 **quoˈtation marks** marks " " or ' ' used to show the beginning and end of what is quoted (e. g. "Come here," he said) 引號, 即: " "或' '.

quotient [ˈkwouʃənt] *nc* number of times one number can be divided by another (e. g. if you divide 21 by 3, the quotient is 7) 商數(例如: 21÷3＝7, 7 是商數). **inˈtelligence quotient** number describing a person's intelligence, based on certain tests 智力商數, 智商.

R, r

rabbi ['ræbai] *nc* teacher of the Jewish religion and law; Jewish priest 猶太教教士和猶太法學教師，先生；拉比． *Note* 說明：it can also be used as a title 此詞也可用作頭銜或稱謂．

rabbit ['ræbit] *nc* small animal with long ears which lives in holes in the ground 兔．

rabble ['ræbl] *nc* mob; rough, disorganized crowd 暴民；烏合之衆．

rabid ['ræbid] *adj* 1 very angry and violent 狂怒的，過激的． 2 (of dogs etc) affected by rabies 患狂犬病的，瘋的．

rabies ['reibiːz] *nu* disease which causes madness (esp. in dogs) 狂犬病． *Note* 說明：followed by a *sing* verb 跟單數動詞．

race[1] [reis] *nc* contest to see if one person / thing can move faster than another 賽跑；*a horse-race* 賽馬；*a five-mile race* 五英里賽跑．Also 亦作 *vi* move quickly 快走，全速行進；*race for the door* 向門口快走． **racing** *nu* running of horses, greyhounds, camels etc in races 賽馬，賽狗，賽駱駝等． **the races** *npl* occasion when horses etc race against one another 賽馬大會． **'racecourse** place where horses race against one another 賽馬場，賽馬跑道． **'racehorse** horse specially intended to run in races 賽馬專用的馬．

race[2] [reis] *nc* 1 group of people descended, or believed to be descended, from the same ancestors; section of mankind different from others in colour etc. 種族；*people of different races* 不同種族的人． 2 section of living things 種屬，族類；*the human race* 人類． **racial** ['reiʃl] *adj* connected with race 人種的，種族的；*racial discrimination* i. e. giving privileges to one race which are not given to another 種族歧視，即：一個種族有特權，另一個種族卻沒有． **racialism** ['reiʃəlizəm] *nu* political or social beliefs based on differences in race; belief that one race is superior to others or that races should be kept apart 種族主義，種族偏見；種族優劣論． **racialist** ['reiʃəlist] 種族主義者． *nc / adj* **racism** *nu* **racist** *nc / adj*.

rack [ræk] *nc* frame on which things are kept (e. g. *plate rack, tool rack*, (in trains) *luggage rack* etc.) 放物品的架子(例如：盤子架，工具架，行李架等.) **rack one's brains** think very hard 絞盡腦汁，冥思苦思．

racket[1] ['rækit] *nc* 1 loud noise 喧嘩，吵鬧． 2 not strictly honest way of making money 詐騙，勒索．

racket[2], **racquet** ['rækit] *nc* light kind of stringed bat used in playing tennis etc. (網球等的)球拍．

radar ['reidɑ:*] *nu* method or detecting the presence of planes, ships etc by electronic means instead of by sight, also used for navigation 雷達． **radar trap** device used by police to detect motorists who are travelling too fast (警察用的)雷達跟踪器(用以檢測汽車駕駛員是否超速)．

radiant ['reidiənt] *adj* 1 bright and happy 明亮的，喜悅的；*a radiant smile* 喜悅的微笑． 2 sending out rays of light or heat 輻射的，放熱的． **radiance** *nu*.

radiate ['reidieit] *vt / i* **1** send out light or heat 放散, 放射(光或熱): *The sun radiates both light and heat.* 太陽發出光和熱. **2** spread out from a centre 輻射: *From the town square, roads radiate in every direction.* 道路從市中廣場通向四面八方. **radiation** [reidi'eiʃən] *nu* **1** sending out rays of heat, light, sound etc. 放射, 輻射. **2** radioactivity 放射性. **radiator** *nc* **1** instrument for heating houses etc by means of pipes through which hot water or steam is passed 暖氣管. **2** part of a motor car for cooling the engine (汽車引擎的)冷卻器.

radical ['rædikl] *adj* **1** changing something completely 完全的, 徹底的: *a radical reform of the law* i. e. a big change in the law 法律上的大改變, 即: 法律上的大改革. **2** wanting big changes (esp. in politics) 激進的, 偏激的(尤指政治上). Also 亦作 *nc* person who wants big changes in the way a country is run 激進份子.

radio ['reidiou] **1** *nu* way of sending out speech, music etc through the air without using a connecting wire 無線電通訊. **2** *nc* device for receiving speech, music etc sent out in this way 收音機, 無線電收訊裝置. *pl* 複數 **radios.** **'radio'active** *adj* giving out energy in the form of rays, which can have a harmful effect on living things 放射性的, 有輻射能的. **'radioac'tivity** *nu* see 見 **radiation. radiographer** [reidi'ɔgrəfə*] *nc* person whose work is to take X-ray photographs 放射線照相師, X光照相師.

radish ['rædiʃ] *nc* red or white root used in salads 小蘿蔔.

radium ['reidiəm] *nu* radioactive metal used in treating people for certain diseases 鐳.

radius ['reidiəs] *nc* **1** line going straight from the centre of a circle to the edge of the circle 半徑. **2** area as measured from a centre point 半徑範圍: *There is no other house within a radius of a mile.* 在一英里半徑範圍內, 沒有別的房子.

raffia ['ræfiə] *nu* fibre from a type of palm tree, used for making baskets, mats etc. (一種棕櫚樹的)樹葉纖維(可用於做籃子和蓆子等).

raffle ['ræfl] *nc* game of chance in which people buy numbered tickets to have a chance of winning an article 抽彩售貨.

raft [rɑ:ft] *nc* flat boat made from large pieces of wood bound together 木筏.

rafter ['rɑ:ftə*] *nc* one of the sloping beams which helps to support a roof 椽.

rag¹ [ræg] *nc* torn piece of cloth 破布: *clean the floor with an old rag* 用舊破布擦地板. **rags** *npl* old and torn clothes 破爛的衣服: *be dressed in rags* 穿著破破爛爛的衣服. **ragged** ['rægid] *adj* **1** old and torn 破舊的, 襤褸的: *ragged clothes* 破爛的衣服. **2** dressed in rags 衣衫襤褸的, 穿著破爛的. **3** not straight; having sharp points 不直的; 參差不齊的: *a ragged edge* 凹凸不平的一邊.

rag² [ræg] *vt / i* make fun of; play jokes (on) 戲弄; 開玩笑. *past* 過去式和過去分詞 **ragged.** Also 亦作 *nc: a student rag* i. e. procession etc organized by students to raise money for charities 學生的募捐遊行, 即: 學生們爲慈善事業捐款而組織的遊行.

rage [reidʒ] *nc* **1** wild anger 盛怒, 狂怒: *be in a rage* 勃然大怒. **2** great desire for something 熱衷; 熱望. Also 亦作 *vi* **1** be very angry 極怒. **2** be very violent 狂暴, 兇猛: *A storm was raging.*

暴風雨颳得兇猛.

raid [reid] *nc* sudden attack 突然襲擊: *an air raid* 空襲. Also 亦作 *vt / i* attack suddenly 突 襲. **raider** *nc* someone / something making an attack 發動突然襲擊的人或物, 侵入者.

rail [reil] *nc* **1** long, narrow piece of wood or metal, or a number of pieces like this, used in making fences or at the side of stairs to keep people from falling etc. 欄杆. **2** one of the two metal bars in a railway track 鐵軌. **3** railway 鐵路: *go by rail* 乘火車去. **railing** *nc* (sometimes used in *pl*) fence made from rails (有時用複數)欄杆, 圍欄. **'railroad** *(US)* railway (美) 鐵路. **'railway** *nc* **1** tracks on which trains travel 鐵路: *a railway from London to Glasgow* 從倫敦到格拉斯哥的鐵路. **2** everything used in carrying people or goods by train (including trains, stations etc.) 鐵路系統.

rain [rein] *nu* water coming down from the clouds 雨. Also 亦作 *vt / i* come down in drops of water 下雨. **rainy** *adj* having much rain 多雨的: *a rainy day* 多雨的一天; *a rainy climate* 多雨的天氣. **the rains** *npl* season in tropical countries when there are frequent heavy falls of rain (熱帶地區的)雨季. **'rainbow** ['reinbou] arch or bow of different colours sometimes seen in the sky (esp. after rain) 虹. **'raincoat** coat which is worn to protect one from the rain 雨衣. **'raindrop** single drop of rain 雨滴, 雨點: *There were raindrops on the window.* 窗戶上有雨滴. **'rainfall** amount of rain, hail, snow that has fallen in a certain time in a certain area 降雨量.

raise [reiz] *vt* **1** lift up; put at a higher level 舉起, 揀起: *raise one's hand* 舉手; *raise something that has fallen down* 揀起掉下去的東西. **2** put in a higher position 提升, 提拔. **3** cause to grow or increase in number 種植, 飼養: *raise wheat / sheep etc.* 種小麥, 養羊等. **4** increase in amount 提高, 增加: *raise the rent / temperature etc.* 提高房租/溫度等. **5** cause something to rise 使揚起, 昇起: *raise a cloud of dust* 揚起一片灰塵. **6** bring up for discussion 提出: *raise several points* 提出幾個論點. **7** manage to get or bring together 招募, 集結, 召集: *raise an army* 招募一支軍隊; *raise money* 籌款. **8** bring up; rear 供養; 撫養: *raise a family* 供養一家人. Also 亦作 *nc (US)* increase of wages price etc. (美)增加工資, 提高價格等. (*Brit* 英 **rise**) *Note* 說明: raise is the verb which is used when someone / something is placed in a higher position by some other person / thing. *The injured boy was raised onto the bed.* Compare this with *The boy rose* i. e. he did the action himself. raise 作動詞時表示某人/某物被別人/物扶起或抬起來. 例如: The injured boy was raised onto the bed. (受傷的男孩被扶上床) 試以此句和The boy rose. (男孩站起來了. 即: 他自己站了起來)對比. see 參見 **rise**.

raisin ['reizn] *nc* dried grape (sometimes put into bread, cakes etc) 葡萄乾.

rake [reik] *nc* tool with teeth and a long handle, used mainly for gathering together loose leaves, stones etc. 耙子. Also 亦作 *vt / i* move with a rake 耙平: *rake the soil* i. e. make smooth and free of stones 耙地, 即: 把地搞平整, 除掉石頭; *rake the leaves together and burn them* 將樹葉耙在一起燒掉.

rakish ['reikiʃ] *adj* smart; giving an impression of self-confidence 漂亮的; 俏

皮的; 自信的: *have one's hat at a rakish angle* i. e. a steep angle which shows that one is confident 戴了角度很俏皮的帽子, 即: 角度斜斜的, 顯得很自信.

rally ['ræli] *vt / i* **1** bring people together again (esp. after a defeat) 重整 (尤指失敗後): *rally troops* 重整軍隊. **2** gain strength; give strength to 康復; 復原: *rally during an illness* 病中康復. Also 亦作 *nc* **1** large meeting 大會, 羣衆集會: *a political rally* 政治集會. **2** act of recovering 康復.

ram [ræm] *nc* **1** male sheep 公羊. **2** instrument used for pushing something or giving heavy blows 撞擊機, 衝壓機. Also 亦作 *vt* push or strike with a ram; run into something with great force 撞入, 擠入, 猛壓, 重擊, 塞進: *ram a ship* 撞上一隻船. *past* 過去式和過去分詞 **rammed.**

ramble ['ræmbl] *vi* **1** go for a long walk for enjoyment 漫步, 散步. **2** talk or write without stating clearly what one means 漫談; 寫隨筆. *ramble on for hours* 漫談數小時. Also 亦作 *nc* long walk taken for pleasure (esp. in the country) 漫步, 散步 (尤指在鄉間). **rambling** *adj* with one bit added onto another, as if it had not been planned 雜亂的, 沒計劃的: *a rambling town / house / speech etc.* 雜亂的小城 / 房子 / 談話等.

ramification [ˌræmifiˈkeiʃən] *nc* part of something (esp. an idea, argument, set of rules etc) that is very complicated 分支, 細節, 門類: *I have never got to know all the ramifications of his business.* 我從來沒弄清楚他的業務的全部細節.

ramp [ræmp] *nc* slope that connects two places at different levels 斜坡, 坡道: *drag stones up a ramp to build*

something 把石頭拉上斜坡去造個甚麼.

rampage [ræmˈpeidʒ] *vi* rush about wildly or angrily 狂暴地亂衝. **be on the rampage** behave in an excited or angry way 暴怒, 狂跳.

rampant ['ræmpənt] *adj* **1** growing without being controlled 蔓延的, 失去控制的, 猖獗的: *Crime is rampant.* 犯罪是失去控制了. **2** standing up on the hind legs (as animals are sometimes shown on coats of arms) (臂章上所畫的動物的) 後足直立.

rampart ['ræmpɑːt] *nc* wide bank of earth, sometimes with a wall on top of it, built around a fort, castle etc to defend it 土壘, 壁壘, 城牆.

ramshackle ['ræmˌʃækl] *adj* almost falling down 快倒塌的, 搖搖欲倒的: *a ramshackle house* 搖搖欲倒的房子.

ran [ræn] past tense of **run¹**. run¹ 的過去式.

ranch [rɑːntʃ] *nc* **1** (US) very large cattle farm (美) 大牧場. **2** (US) any kind of farm (美) 農場: *a chicken ranch* 養雞場. **rancher** *nc*.

rancid ['rænsid] *adj* bad; stale 敗壞的, 陳腐的, 不新鮮的: *rancid butter / fat etc.* 壞掉的黃油 / 脂肪等.

rancour ['ræŋkə*] (US 美 **rancor**) *nu* bitter feelings lasting for a long time 怨恨, 深仇.

random ['rændəm] *adj* by chance; unplanned 任意的, 隨便的: *ask random questions* 隨便問些問題. **at random** by chance; without any plan 隨便地; 無計劃地: *speak to people at random* 隨便跟人們說話.

rang [ræŋ] past tense of **ring²**. ring² 的過去式.

range¹ [reindʒ] *nc* **1** line of things, one beside the other 行, 列, 排: *a range of mountains* 一列山脈. **2** way things change between limits 範圍，界限: *a wide range of prices* i. e. many different prices from high to low 很大的價格範圍，即: 從高到低有許多不同的價格: *a wide range of materials to choose from* 可選擇的物品的很大範圍. **3** how far a gun can fire 射程: *a range of five miles* 五英里的射程. **4** place where people can practise with guns 打靶場，射擊場: *a firing range* 一個射擊場. **5** large old-fashioned type of stove 舊式的大火爐: *a kitchen range* 廚房爐竈.

range² [reindʒ] *vt / i* **1** move or occur between certain limits 在某範圍之內浮動: *prices ranging from 50 pence to 75 pence* 價格從五十便士至七十五便士不等. **2** put in a line or in lines 排列，使成行: *He ranged the boys in order of size.* 他按高低的順序把男孩排成一行. **3** move freely over; go all over 漫遊; 徘徊: *animals that ranged the plains* 在平原上漫遊的動物. **4** stretch; run in a line 伸展; 延及: *ranging east and west* i. e. running on a line going from east to west 東西綿延，即: 由東到西相連. **ranger** *nc* person whose work is looking after a forest or other type of countryside 護林員或鄉村巡邏隊員.

rank¹ [ræŋk] **1** *nc* line of something (esp. soldiers) 一列 (尤 指 士 兵); *drawn up in ranks* i. e. standing in lines 排成隊列，即: *a taxi rank* i. e. a place where taxis wait to be hired 出租汽車(的士)車隊，即: 的士排成一列等候客人. **2** *nc / u* level; position (esp. in the army) 官階，地位 (尤指軍隊中): *the rank of captain* 上尉官銜; *an actor of the first rank* i. e. one of the best 第一流的演員，即: 最佳演員之一; *a man of rank* i. e. high position 有地位的人，即: 社會地位高的人.Also

亦作 *vt / i* come or put in a certain class 列於，居第幾位: *London ranks as one of the world's largest cities.* 倫敦被列爲世界上最大的城市之一.

rank² [ræŋk] *adj* **1** bad to taste or smell 惡臭的，臭味的: *rank tobacco* 臭味的烟草. **2** very bad; completely bad 很壞的; 極壞的: *rank dishonesty* 極不老實.

rankle ['ræŋkl] *vi* continue to cause anger or bitterness 令人憤怒或痛心: *an insult that rankles* 令人痛心的侮辱.

ransack ['rænsæk] *vt* **1** search thoroughly (often causing great untidiness or disorder) 徹底搜查: *ransack a room for something* 爲找某物把房間搜遍. **2** steal everything from 洗劫，搶光: *Thieves ransacked the house.* 小偷們把屋裏洗劫一空.

ransom ['rænsəm] *nc / u* amount of money that has to be paid before someone is set free 贖金. **hold someone to ransom** keep someone a prisoner until money is paid for his release 綁票; 抓了某人勒取贖金.

rant [rænt] *vt / i* speak wildly or violently 大聲叫喊: *a ranting speaker* 大聲叫喊的演講者.

rap [ræp] *nc* sharp, light blow 輕敲: *a rap at / on the door* 輕輕的敲門聲. Also 亦作 *vt / i* give a rap 敲擊: *rap loudly* 大聲敲擊. past 過去式和過去分詞 **rapped**.

rape [reip] *vt* use force to commit a sexual crime against a woman 強姦. Also 亦作 *nu*.

rapid ['ræpid] *adj* quick-moving; fast 迅速的; 快的: *a rapid worker* 幹得快的工人; *a rapid increase in the number of cars* 小汽車數量的迅速增加. **rapidly** *adv* **rapidity** [rə'piditi] *nu* **rapids** *npl* part of a river where the water is shallow and moves very quickly over rocks 急流, 湍流.

rapt [ræpt] *adj* thinking about something so deeply that one is not aware of what is going on around one 全神貫注的, 專注的: *rapt in thought* 專心思索.

rapture ['ræptʃə*] *nu* great joy 狂喜, 大喜; *happy: listen with rapture* 極其高興地聽着. **rapturous** *adj*.

rare [reə*] *adj* not common; not often seen or found 不平常的; 罕見的, 稀有的: *Gold is a rare metal.* 金是稀有金屬. **rarely** *adv* not very often 罕見地, 極少有的. **rarefied** ['rɛərifaid] *adj* thin; made thinnner 稀薄的; 稀薄了的: *the rarefied air on high mountains* 高山上稀薄的空氣. **rarity 1** *nc* rare (and usu. valuable) thing 珍品. **2** *nu* state of being rare 稀罕, 少有.

rascal ['rɑːskl] *nc* **1** bad, dishonest person 壞蛋, 惡棍, 流氓. **2** (used in fun) mischievous child (用於開玩笑) 小淘氣, 惡作劇的孩子: *a little rascal* 小傢伙. **rascally** *adv*.

rash[1] [ræʃ] *adj* careless; done or said without proper thought 粗心的, 魯莽的; 未作適當考慮的: *a rash decision / statement etc.* 輕率的決定 / 聲明等. **rashly** *adv* **rashness** *nu*.

rash[2] [ræʃ] *nc* breaking out of small red spots on the skin caused by certain illnesses 疹, 皮疹.

rasher ['ræʃə*] *nc* thin slice of bacon 火腿薄片.

rasp [rɑːsp] *vi* **1** make a harsh unpleasant sound 發出刺耳的聲音: *a rasping voice* 刺耳的聲音. **2** annoy, irritate 激怒; 惱人: *His voice rasped on my nerves.* 他的聲音刺激了我的神經.

raspberry ['rɑːzbəri] *nc* kind of small, red fruit growing on a bush 蕊莓, 木莓.

rat [ræt] *nc* **1** animal like a mouse, but larger 大老鼠. **2** nasty person 叛徒, 卑鄙的人. '**rat race** situation among professional workers in which a person competes with his colleagues to obtain a better position etc for himself *(informal)* 職業工人為自己謀職而與同伴競爭的境况; 激烈競爭.(非正式).

ratchet ['rætʃit] *nc* toothed wheel with a catch which allows the wheel to move in one direction only 棘齒, 棘爪.

rate [reit] *nc* **1** speed 速率, 速度, 進度: *at the rate of ten miles in two hours* 以兩小時十英里的速率. **2** amount one pays or is paid 工資數額: *pay workers at a rate of a pound an hour* 付給工人一小時一英鎊的工資. **3** amount of anything as measured against another thing 比率; 率: *the birthrate* i.e. the number of births measured against the number of people living in a place 出生率, 即: 一個地方生數與人口數的比較. **4** local tax paid in a town or local area for some purpose 地方稅: *the water rate* 自來水費. Also 亦作 *vt / i* consider; measure the quality of 認為; 估計: *How do you rate our team's chances of winning?* 你認為我們隊獲勝的機會如何? **at any rate 1** in any case; whatever happens 無論如何; 不管怎樣. **2** at least 至少. **at this / that rate** in these / those circumstances 如照這種/那種情形. **first-rate** very good 一等的, 第一流的, 很好的.

rather ['rɑːðə*] *adv / intensifier* **1** more willingly 寧願, 寧可: *He would rather go than stay* i. e. he would prefer to go 他寧願去而不願呆下來. 即: 他喜歡去. **2** somewhat; to a certain extent 有幾分; 頗, 稍微: *rather good* 頗好; *rather too difficult for me* 對我來說, 有

點太難了. **3** more truly; more accurately 更確實地; 更正確地說: *I met him very late on Friday night, or rather, early on Saturday morning.* 我在星期五晚上深夜見到他, 更確實地說, 是在星期六凌晨.

ratify ['rætifai] *vt* confirm; approve 確認; 批准: *The agreement between the two countries has been ratified.* 這兩國間的協議已被批准. **ratification** [rætifi'keiʃən] *nu.*

rating ['reitiŋ] *nc* class to which something (e. g. a ship) belongs (船的) 等級.

ratio ['reiʃiou] *nc* way that numbers or quantities are related to one another 比例, 比率: *The ratio of pupils to teachers was 30 to 1* i. e. there were 30 pupils for every 1 teacher 小學生與教師的比例是三十比一. 即: 每個教師教三十個小學生. *pl* 複數 **ratios**.

ration ['ræʃən] *nc* amount of something (e. g. food) given out to each person 口糧, 定量, 配量. Also 亦作 *vt* allow only a certain amount 配給, 定量: *Food was rationed during the war.* 戰爭期間, 食品是定量配給的.

rational ['ræʃənl] *adj* reasonable; able to reason; based on reason or common sense 合理的; 明理的; 有理性的: *a rational explanation* 合理的解釋. (*opp* 反義詞 **irrational**). **rationally** *adv.*

rationale [ræʃə'nɑːl] *nc* logical reasons for a course of action 基本原理, 理論基礎.

rattan [ræ'tæn] *nc / u* **1** climbing palm with long, slender, tough stems 藤. **2** these stems, used in making wicker work, etc. 藤條.

rattle ['rætl] *vt / i* make a number of short, sharp sounds 嘎嘎地響; 咔嗒咔嗒地響. *rattle a box with some coins*

in it. 匣子裏的錢幣搖得嘎嘎響. Also 亦作 *nc / u* **1** rattling noise 嘎嘎響聲. **2** child's toy which makes a rattling noise 嘎嘎作響的兒童玩具. **'rattle-snake** poisonous American snake which makes a noise with its tail 響尾蛇.

raucous ['rɔːkəs] *adj* sounding harsh; rough 沙啞的; 粗糙的: *a raucous voice* 沙啞的聲音; *raucous shouts* 沙啞的呼喊.

ravage ['rævidʒ] *vt / i* destroy; damage badly 破壞; 毀壞: *a city ravaged by high winds* 遭暴風毀壞的城市. **ravages** *npl* destruction or damage caused by something (毀壞的) 殘跡, 災害, 創傷: *the ravages of time* 時間的侵蝕.

rave [reiv] *vi* talk wildly; talk in a mad or foolish way 說胡話; 亂講: *While she had the fever, she raved for hours.* 當她發燒時, 她說胡話好幾小時.

raven ['reivən] *nc* large black crow with a black beak and a deep voice 大烏鴉.

ravenous ['rævənəs] *adj* very hungry 極餓的.

ravine [rə'viːn] *nc* long, deep, narrow valley 峽谷, 深谷.

raw [rɔː] *adj* **1** not cooked 生的, 未煮熟的: *raw meat* 生肉. **2** in the natural state; not treated or prepared 天然的; 未處理的: *raw materials* 原料; *raw hides* i. e. not yet made into leather 生皮, 即: 還未製成皮革的皮. **3** not trained or experienced 未訓練過的, 沒經驗的: *a raw recruit* i. e. someone who has just joined 新兵, 新手, 即: 剛入伍的, 剛來的人.

ray [rei] *nc* line or beam of light, heat etc. 光線或光束等.

rayon ['reiɔn] *nu* man-made material

which can be made to look like silk, wool or cotton 人造絲: *a rayon shirt* 人造絲襯衫.

raze [reiz] *vt* destroy houses, towns etc by levelling them to the ground (把房子, 城鎮等) 夷爲平地: *The village was completely razed during the battle.* 這鄉村在交戰中被完全夷爲平地.

razor ['reizə*] *nc* instrument with a sharp blade used for shaving 剃刀, 刮鬍刀.

re- [ri:] *prefix* again (e. g. **rearm** 再, 又, 重新(例如: rearm 重新武裝等).

reach [ri:tʃ] *vt / i* **1** get to; arrive at 到; 到達, 抵達: *reach the top of a mountain* 到達山頂. **2** stretch out for with the hand 伸手: *reach for a book* 伸手去拿書. **3** stretch; extend 伸展; 延伸: *a wall that reaches to the end of the road* 延伸到這條路的盡頭的一堵牆. **4** hand something to someone 伸手遞給: *Reach me that book, please.* 請把那本書遞給我. Also 亦作 *nc / u* **1** distance that one can reach 手伸得到的距離: *beyond my reach* 在我的手伸得到的距離之外. **2** straight part of a river 筆直的河段: *the upper reaches of the Amazon* 亞馬遜河的上流.

react [ri'ækt] *vi* behave in a certain way because of something that has been done to one 反應: *When I punished him, he reacted by bursting into tears.* 我處罰他時, 他的反應是突然大哭.

reactor *nc* apparatus for producing power from nuclear reactions 核反應堆. (Also 亦作 **nuclear reactor**).

reaction [ri'ækʃən] *nc / u* **1** movement of feeling away from someone / something; movement back to a former condition 恢復原狀: *This made him popular for a time, but then a reaction set in* i. e. he became unpopular again 這使他一度很受歡迎, 但後來又

恢復了原狀. 即: 他又不受歡迎. **2** feelings and thoughts about 感覺, 看法: *What was your reaction to him?* 你對他的感覺是甚麼? **3** process of change when certain substances are brought together 反應: *chemical reaction* 化學反應; *nuclear reaction* 核反應. **reactionary** *adj* against progress or change (esp. in politics) 反動的 (尤指政治上).

read [ri:d] *vt / i* **1** look at printed or written letters and be able to understand them 閱讀, 看懂: *read a book* 讀一本書; *be able to read* 能讀. **2** say aloud what is written or printed 唸, 朗讀: *The teacher read a story to the class.* 老師給全班唸了一個故事. **3** study a subject at university (在大學) 修讀: *read history* 讀歷史. *past* 過去式和過去分詞 **read** [red]. **reader** *nc* **1** person who reads (esp. someone whose job it is to decide whether a story etc ought to be published) 讀者 (尤指出版物的審稿人). **2** schoolbook used for reading 讀物, 課本. **reading 1** *nu* act of looking at and understanding print 讀書: *interrupt someone's reading* 打擾某人讀書. **2** *nc* saying aloud of what is written or printed 朗誦: *a reading from Shakespeare* 莎士比亞作品朗誦.

ready ['redi] *adj* **1** prepared 準備好的: *The dinner is ready.* 飯菜準備好了. *Tom is ready for school now.* 湯姆現在準備上學去. **2** willing 願意: *Are you ready to serve your country?* 你願意爲你的國家服務嗎? **3** quick 敏捷的, 迅速的: *have a ready answer* 敏捷的回答. **4** available; within reach 可得到的; 伸手可及的: *He always kept a gun ready.* 他常常身邊帶着一枝槍. **readily** *adv* **1** willingly 願意地, 欣然, *I would readily help you.* 我願意幫助

你. 2 without difficulty 沒困難地, 容易地; *readily available* 容易得到的.

readiness *nu* **'ready-'made** *adj* able to be used immediately 現成的, 做好的: *ready-made clothes* i. e. ready to be worn, not made to measure 成衣, 即; 馬上可穿的衣服, 而不是定做的. **'ready 'reckoner** book of tables which makes calculations easier 計算表.

real [riəl] *adj* true; actual; not made up 真的, 真正的; 實在的; 真實的; *the real reason for doing something* i. e. not a false one 做某事的真正的原因, 即: 不是假的; *a real hero* 真正的英雄. *Is it a real diamond or is it a fake?* 是一塊真的鑽石或是假的? **realism** *nu* 1 (in stories, paintings etc) showing of life as it really is, not trying to hide its bad aspects 現實主義(小說, 繪畫等如實地反映生活, 不掩蓋它的陰暗面). 2 act of seeing life as it really is, with no false ideas about it 面對現實. **realist** *nc* someone who practises realism 現實主義者. **realistic** [riəˈlistik] *adj* 1 true to life 忠於生活的, 現實主義的. 2 practical; not having false ideas 真實的; 實際的. *(opp* 反義詞 **unrealistic). realistically** *adv* **reality** [riˈæliti] 1 *nu* state of being real or true; fact 實在; 真實; 事實; *believe in the reality of God* i. e. that God in fact exists 相信上帝確實有, 即; 上帝真的存在. 2 *nc* something that is real or true 現實, 真實的事物, 實事. **really** 1 *adv* truly 真; 真實地, 真正地. 2 *Do you really mean that?* 你真的是哪個意思嗎? 2 *intensifier* very 很, 非常. *The show was really good.* 這個演出很好. 3 *interj* expression which can show interest, doubt, anger etc, according to the way it is said 真的呀! (用以表示興趣、懷疑、憤怒等). (Also 亦作

Really! and **Not really!**). **'real estate** see 見 **estate. in reality** in fact 事實上.

realize [ˈriəlaiz] *vt* 1 understand 認識到, 瞭解, 認清; *Does he realize what he has done?* 他認識到他做了些甚麼嗎? 2 make something actually happen 實現: *realize one's hopes* 實現願望. **realization** [riəlaiˈzeiʃən] *nu*.

realm [relm] *nc* 1 kingdom *(o. f.)* (舊式)王國. 2 area 領域, 範疇: *the realm of science* 科學的領域; *the realms of the imagination* 想像的範疇.

reap [riːp] *v* / *i* cut grain (e. g. wheat etc) 收割(小麥等). 2 get 獲得: *reap large profits* 獲得巨大的利潤. **reaper** *nc* machine that reaps 收割機.

reappear [riːəˈpiə*] *vt* appear again 再現. **reappearance** *nu*.

reappraisal [riːəˈpreizl] *nc / u* process of examining a situation again in order to decide whether to change any previous decisions 重新考慮, 再作評估.

rear¹ [riə*] *n sing* back part 後部, 背後: *at the rear of the house* 在房子後面. Also 亦作 *attrib adj* back 後面的: *the rear wheels of a car* 汽車的後輪.

rear² [riə*] *vt* / *i* make grow; help to grow 飼養; 撫養: *rear poultry* i. e. hens etc. 飼養家禽, 如; 母雞等. 2 rise up on the hind legs 用後腿站立: *the horse reared* 馬用後腿站立.

rearm [riːˈɑːm] *vt* / *i* provide (oneself) with weapons again 重新武裝, 重整軍備. **rearmament** *nu*.

reason¹ [ˈriːzn] 1 *nc / u* cause; purpose in doing something 原因, 理由: *Is there any reason why he should be rude to you?* 有甚麼原因使他對你粗暴嗎? 2 *nu* ability to think 理智: *lose one's reason* i. e. go mad 喪失理智, 即; 發瘋. 3 *nu* good sense; common sense 道理; 常識: *try to make some-one listen to reason* 盡力使人聽從道理.

reason² ['ri:zn] *vt / i* **1** use powers of thinking; think 推理; 思考: *Do you think some animals can reason?* 你認爲有的動物會思考嗎? **2** use reasons or arguments to prove something 論證, 推斷. **reasonable** *adj* **1** sensible; willing to listen to others' views 合情合理的; 講道理的: *a reasonable person* 講道理的人. **2** according to reason 合乎道理的, 有道理的: *a reasonable argument* 有道理的論點. **3** fair; just; which one could accept 公道的; 合理的; 可接受的: *a reasonable price / excuse etc.* 合理的價格/藉口等. (*opp* 反義詞 **unreasonable**). **reasonably** *adv*.

reassure [ri:ə'ʃuə*] *vt* make someone confident again 使恢復信心. **reassuring** *adj* **reassurance** *nc / u*.

rebate ['ri:beit] *nc* return of part of the money one has paid 折扣, 回扣: *a rebate of one's income tax* 所得稅的回扣部份.

rebel [ri'bel] *vi* **1** use violence to fight against the government 造反, 反叛: *The people rebelled.* 人民造反了. **2** fight against or resist anything 反抗, 鬥爭, 反對: *The boy rebelled against having to come home so early.* 這男孩反對必須這麼早回家. *past* 過去式和過去分詞 **rebelled.** Also 亦作 ['rebl] *nc* person who rebels 造反者, 反叛者. **rebellion** [ri'beliən] *nc / u* act of rebelling 造反, 叛亂: *The government put down the rebellion.* 政府平息了叛亂. **rebellious** [ri'beliəs] *adj* resisting the government or any other authority; difficult to control 反叛的, 造反的; 難控制的.

rebound [ri'baund] *vi* spring back; hit something and come back 彈回; 跳回: *The ball rebounded from the wall.* 球從牆上彈回. Also 亦作 ['ri:baund] *nc* act of rebounding 彈回, 跳回: *catch a ball on the rebound* 接住反彈回來的球.

rebuff [ri'bʌf] *nc* unkind action towards someone who is trying to be friendly 駁斥, 拒絕.

rebuke [ri'bju:k] *vt* find fault with someone 指責, 嚴斥: *The teacher rebuked the boy for his laziness.* 老師指責這男孩懶惰. Also 亦作 *nc*: *give a rebuke to someone* 指責某人.

recalcitrant [ri'kælsitrənt] *adj* disobedient 不服從的, 頑抗的. 不聽話的: *a recalcitrant child* 不聽話的孩子.

recall [ri'kɔ:l] *vt* **1** remember 記得, 記起: *I can't recall his name.* 我記不得他的名字. **2** tell to come back; order back 叫回; 召回: *The government has recalled its ambassador from Paris.* 政府召回了它駐巴黎的大使. **3** take back 收回: *The car factory recalled all the cars which were supposed to be faulty.* 汽車廠收回了全部可能有毛病的汽車.

recant [ri'kænt] *vt / i* say that one no longer believes in something one used to believe in 宣佈改變或放棄(信仰).

recapitulate [ri:kə'pitjuleit] *vt / i* repeat the main ideas of something that has already been said 扼要重述. **recapitulation** [ri:kəpitju'leiʃən] *nc / u*.

recede [ri'si:d] *vi* move, appear to move, backwards 向後移動, 後退: *As the train went faster, the railway station receded from view.* 火車加速跑時, 火車站從視野中退去.

receipt [ri'si:t] *nc* piece of paper which shows that something has been paid for 收據, 收條: *get a receipt for every-*

thing one buys 買每件物品都要收據.
receipts *npl* money received from
some kind of business 進款, 收益, 收
入.

receive [ri'si:v] *vt / i* **1** get; be given 收
到; 得到: *receive presents / letters
from home etc.* 收到家裏寄來的禮品/
信件等. **2** accept something that has
been sent or given 接受, 領受. **receiver** *nc* part of a telephone that is
held to the ear (電話的)耳機, 聽筒.

recent ['ri:snt] *adj* made or having happened a short time ago; modern 最近
的; 近來的; 近代的: *a recent event* 最
近的事件; *recent history* 近代史. **recently** *adv*: *I haven't seen him recently.* 我最近沒見過他.

receptacle [ri'septikl] *nc* container of
any kind 容器.

reception [ri'sepʃən] **1** *nc* way of receiving or being received 接待, 歡迎:
*The winning team got a wonderful re-
ception in their home town.* 這獲勝的
球隊在他們的家鄉受到熱烈的歡迎. **2**
nc party or gathering to entertain visitors 招待會, 歡迎會: *a wedding reception* 婚宴. **3** *nu* people in a hotel
whose job is to receive guests etc; the
place where such people work (旅館
的)接待部門; 接待處. **recep-
tionist** *nc* someone (usu. a woman)
whose job it is to receive people visiting a hotel, a doctor etc. 接待人員, 招
待員. **receptive** [ri'septiv] *adj* quick
to understand new ideas; willing to
accept new ideas (對新思想)易於接受
的; 願於接受的. *(opp* 反義詞 **unre-
ceptive).**

recess [ri'ses] *nc* **1** period of time during which work stops 休息時間; 休假
期; 休會期. *a recess of thirty minutes*
三十分鐘的休息時間. **2** space in a
wall for a bed, cupboard etc. 壁凹. **3**

inner part of something; remote place
深處; 隱蔽處: *the dark recesses of a
cave* 一個洞的烏黑的深處.

recipe ['resipi] *nc* instructions on how
to prepare a certain kind of food 製
法, 烹飪法: *a recipe for a cake* 蛋糕的
製法.

recipient [ri'sipiənt] *nc* person who receives something 接受者, 收受者.

reciprocal [ri'siprəkl] *adj* given or received in return 相互的, 互惠的: *reciprocal liking* i. e. each liking the
other 互相喜歡, 即: 彼此都喜歡對方.

reciprocate [ri'siprəkeit] *vt / i* give etc
in return 答謝, 酬答: *He did not reciprocate my friendship* i. e. I was
friendly with him, but he was not
friendly with me 他不答謝我的友情.
即: 我對他友好, 但他對我不友好.

recite [ri'sait] *vt / i* **1** say something
aloud from memory 背誦: *recite a
poem* 背誦一首詩. **2** give a list of
something 詳述, 一一說出: *recite
one's complaints* 把抱怨一一說出. **re-
cital** *nc* performance of music or
poetry by one person or a few people
音樂會或詩明誦會. **recitation** [re-
si'teiʃən] *nc / u* reciting 背誦: *a recitation from Shakespeare* 背誦莎士比
亞的作品.

reckless ['rekləs] *adj* not caring about
danger; very careless 不顧危險的; 魯
莽的, 輕率的: *a reckless driver* 魯莽的
駕駛員. **recklessly** *adv* **recklessness**
nu.

reckon ['rekən] *vt / i* **1** arrive at a number without counting exactly 估計, 猜
想: *Have you reckoned the number of
cattle you have?* 你估計了你的牲畜數
目嗎? **2** consider; think 考慮; 認爲:
*He is reckoned to be a very good
teacher.* 他被認爲是個很好的教師.
reckoning *nc / u* way of counting;

reclaim [ri'kleim] *vt* bring back into use 回收, 開墾: *reclaim land from the sea* 填 海 造 田. **reclamation** [reklə'meiʃən] *nu*.

recline [ri'klain] *vt / i* **1** lie down 橫臥: *recline on a couch* 橫臥在長沙發上. **2** lay down; put in a resting position 斜倚; 倚靠: *recline one's head* 斜倚着頭.

recluse [ri'kluːs] *nc* person who lives alone, and tries to avoid meeting other people 隱居者; 遁世者.

recognize ['rekəgnaiz] *vt* **1** remember, know the name of; identify as something seen before 記得; 認得; 認出: *I could hardly recognize my friend.* 我認不出我的朋友. **2** admit; consider; realize that something is true 承認; 考慮; 認清: *He has to recognize the danger of what he is doing.* 他不得不承認他所作所爲的危險. **3** agree to have diplomatic relations with 正式承認 (同意建立外交關係): *recognize a foreign government* 正式承認一個外國政府. **4** give official approval to 讚許, 讚揚; 表彰: *His sacrifices for his country have at last been recognized.* 他爲國犧牲, 終於受到表彰. **recognition** [rekəg'niʃən] *nu*.

recoil [ri'kɔil] *vi* **1** draw back in fear, disgust etc. 畏縮, 退卻等: *recoil from the sight of a snake* 看到蛇就退縮. **2** spring back 反彈, 彈回: *The rifle recoiled when it was fired.* 步槍射擊時就彈回了. Also 亦作 *nc / u* act of recoiling 退縮, 彈回.

recollect [rekə'lekt] *vt / i* remember 記起, 想起: *I can't recollect his name.* 我記不起他的名字. **recollection 1** *nc* something remembered 回憶, 回想: *recollections of his childhood* 他的童年的回憶. **2** *nu* power of remember-ing 記憶力: *to the best of my recollection* i. e. as far as I can remember 如果我沒有記錯, 即: 憑我所能記憶的.

recommend [rekə'mend] *vt* **1** speak in favour; say that someone / something is good for a certain purpose 介紹, 推薦, 讚許: *I recommend these pills for your cough.* 我介紹這些藥丸給你治咳嗽. *He recommended me for the post of headmaster.* 他推薦我去當校長. **2** advise 勸告, 建議: *I recommend you to follow your doctor's advice.* 我勸你按照你的醫生的建議去做. **recommendation** [rekəmen'deiʃən] *nc / u* **1** act of recommending 勸告, 推薦, 讚許. **2** letter etc which says that someone is suitable for a particular job etc. 推薦信.

recompense ['rekəmpens] *vt* give money to someone for some loss, injury etc that he has suffered 賠償, 酬答. Also 亦作 *nc / u* reward; payment 報酬; 酬金: *work hard without recompense* 不計報酬地辛勤工作.

reconcile ['rekənsail] *vt* **1** make people friendly again after they have quarrelled 和解, 講和. **2** make things agree 使一致, 協調: *It is sometimes difficult to reconcile people's statements with their actions* i. e. they say one thing and do another 有時候, 要使人們言行一致是困難的. **reconciliation** [rekənsili'eiʃən] *nc / u* act of reconciling; act of being reconciled (重新)和好, 復交; 調和, 調停: *bring about a reconciliation between people who have quarrelled* 促使爭吵的雙方和好.

reconnoitre [rekə'nɔitə*] (*US* 美 **reconnoiter**) *vt / i* go near to where enemy soldiers are in order to find their exact position, numbers etc. 偵察敵情. **reconnaissance** [ri'kɔnisns] *nc / u* act of reconnoitring 偵察, 探查.

reconstruct [ˈriːkənˈstrʌkt] *vt* build up again after destruction or damage 重建, 再建. **reconstruction** *nc / u.*

record¹ [riˈkɔːd] *vt* **1** put down in writing for future use 記錄: *record what was said at the meeting* 記錄會上的發言. **2** keep something in any form that people can refer to again 記載: *a book that records the events of the Second World War* 一本記載第二次世界大戰的事件的書. **3** put onto a gramophone disc 錄音: *That singer has recorded some popular songs.* 那位歌手已錄了幾首流行歌曲.

record² [ˈrekɔːd] *nc* **1** written account 記錄: *keep a record of what was said* 留下發言的記錄. **2** disc to be played on a gramophone 唱片: *a hit record* i. e. one which has sold many copies 一張受歡迎的唱片, 即: 已賣了許多的唱片. **3** facts about the past of someone / something 履歷, 行爲記錄: *have a good record at school* 在學校有良好的行爲記錄. **4** limit or point which has been reached; (sport) the best yet done 最高記錄; (運動的) 最好成績: *a new record for the high jump* 跳高的新記錄. Also 亦作 *attrib adj*: *a record attendance* i. e. more people than have ever attended before 創記錄的聽眾, 即: 前從來沒有那麼多人來. **'record player** gramophone; machine that plays gramophone records 唱機.

recount [riˈkaunt] *vt* tell 描述: *recount everything that happened* 描述所發生的每件事.

re-count [ˈriːkaunt] *nc* second count 再數, 重新計算. Also 亦作 [ˈriːkaunt] *vt* count again 重新計算, 再數.

recoup [riˈkuːp] *vt* win again what one has lost 重獲, 彌補, 補償: *recoup one's losses* 彌補損失.

recourse [riˈkɔːs] *nc / u* person / thing that is turned to for help etc. 求助的人 / 物: *have recourse to someone / something* 求助於某人 / 某事.

recover [riˈkʌvə*] *vt / i* **1** get back what has been lost, taken away etc. 取回, 收回: *recover stolen goods* 取回被偷的物品. **2** get well again 痊愈, 恢復: *recover from an illness* 病後康復. **recovery** *nu.*

recreation [rekriˈeiʃən] *nc / u* game; way of occupying free time pleasantly 娛樂; 消遣: *Reading books is one kind of recreation.* 讀書是一種消遣. **recreational** *adj.*

recrimination [rikrimiˈneiʃən] *nc* accusation made in reply to an accusation 反控告, 反責.

recruit [riˈkruːt] *nc* **1** soldier who is still being trained (仍在受訓的) 新兵. **2** person who has just joined something 新成員, 新手. Also 亦作 *vt / i* get recruits; get someone as a recruit 招募新兵; 招收新成員.

rectangle [ˈrektæŋgl] *nc* foursided figure with the opposite sides equal and four right angles 長方形, 矩形. **rectangular** [rekˈtæŋgjulə*] *adj.*

rectify [ˈrektifai] *vt* put right: 改正, 修正: *rectify a mistake* 改正錯誤.

recuperate [riˈkuːpəreit] *vi* get well again after being ill 康復, 復原.

recur [riˈkə*] *vi* come back; happen again 重現, 再發生. *past* 過去式和過去分詞 **recurred. recurrent** [riˈkʌrnt] *adj* **recurrence** [riˈkʌrns] *nc / u.*

recycle [riːˈsaikl] *vt* treat (waste material) so that it can be used again (廢物處理後) 反覆使用.

red [red] **1** *nc / u* the colour of blood flowing from a vein 紅色. **2** *nc* Communist 共產黨人. *(informal* in sense 2) (義 2 爲非正式). Also 亦作 *adj.* **redden** *vt / i* **1** make red 使變成紅色.

2 become red; blush (with etc) 紅了臉; 羞紅. **Red Cross** international organization which gives help to the injured or wounded victims of war etc. 紅十字會 (救死扶傷的國際組織). **'red 'herring** something which is brought up to take people's attention from something else (e. g. in an argument); subject which has nothing to do with what is being discussed (*informal*) (在辯論中) 用於分散人們注意力的與議題無關的東西 (非正式). **'red-'hot** see 見 **hot**. **'red-'letter** day day which will be remembered because something very pleasant happened on it 值得紀念的大喜日子. **red tape** see 見 **tape**. **in the red** in debt 赤字, 欠債, 賠本: *be five pounds in the red* (*informal*) 虧本五英鎊 (非正式). **catch red-'handed** find in the act of doing something wrong 正在幹壞事的當兒被捕; 當場被抓.

redeem [ri'di:m] *vt* 1 buy back; get back in some way 買回; 贖回: *redeem a pawned article* 贖回典押品. 2 set free; save 救贖; 拯救: *redeem from sin* 贖罪.

redouble [ri:'dʌbl] *vt / i* increase greatly 激增, 加倍: *redouble one's efforts* 加倍努力.

reduce [ri'dju:s] *vt / i* 1 make smaller; make less 減少; 減低: *reduce speed* 減低速度; *reduce one's weight* 減輕體重. 2 bring to a certain state 使人處於某種狀況: *reduce a person to tears / silence etc* 使某人流淚/沉默等. **reduced** *adj* **reduction** [ri'dʌkʃən] *nc / u* 1 act of reducing or being reduced 減少, 縮減, 減低: *a reduction in prices* 減價. 2 amount by which something is reduced 減少或減低的數量: *a small reduction* 少量減低.

redundant [ri'dʌndnt] *adj* not needed

多餘的, 過剩的, 不需要的: *Several hundred workers have been declared redundant* i. e. dismissed because their services are no longer needed 幾百名工人被宣佈是過剩的. 即: 他們被解雇了, 因爲他們沒工作可做. **redundancy** *nc / u*.

reed [ri:d] *nc* tall grass-like plant which grows in wet places 蘆葦.

reef [ri:f] *nc* narrow line of rocks etc just above or below the surface of the sea 暗礁: *be wrecked on a reef* 觸礁沉沒.

reek [ri:k] *vi* smell strongly 發出強烈的氣味或惡臭: *reeking of drink* 一股酒的惡臭味.

reel[1] [ri:l] *nc* roller on which thread, film etc can be kept 綫軸, 捲綫筒, 磁帶盤, 影片盤. Also 亦作 *vt* wind something onto a reel 將某物繞到軸上.

reel[2] [ri:l] *vi* 1 sway after a blow, shock etc. 站立不穩, 搖搖: *He reeled when he heard the terrible news* 當他聽到可怕的消息時, 他站立不穩. 2 stagger 蹣跚地走: *The drunk man reeled home.* 那醉漢蹣跚地走回家.

refectory [ri'fektəri] *nc* large room in which meals are taken (e. g. in a school, monastery etc.) (學校、寺廟等的) 大食堂.

refer [rifə*] *vt / i* 1 hand over; send to be decided 交給; 提交: *The dispute between the two countries was referred to the United Nations.* 這兩個國家間提交聯合國解決. 2 go to for information or help 查閱, 探詢: *refer to a dictionary for the spelling of a word* 查閱詞典, 找一個詞的拼寫. 3 mention; speak about 提到, 說起: *refer to someone* i. e. speak about him 提到某人, 即: 說起他. *past* 過去式和過去分詞 **referred**. **referee** [refə'ri:] *nc* 1 judge in a game (e. g. boxing, football etc.) (拳擊、足球比賽等的)裁判員. **2** person asked to give to an employer information about the character and ability of a person seeking a job, scholarship etc. 鑑定人, 推薦人. Also 亦作 *vt / i* act as a referee (for) 裁判. **reference** ['refərns] **1** *nc/u* act of referring 參考, 查閱: *This book is for reference only* i. e. you can only refer to it, not take it away 此書僅供查閱. 即: 你只能參考, 不能帶走. **2** *nc* person who can give information about someone's character, ability, work etc. 介紹人, 證明人. **3** *nc* written information about someone's character 介紹信, 證明書: *You should bring your references to the interview.* 你要把介紹信帶來面試. **4** *nc* statement, part of book etc to which one is referred 參考材料: *This reference can be found at the end of the book.* 這段參考材料可在本書後面找到. **referendum** [refə'rendəm] *nc* act of asking all the people in a country to vote on some problem 全民投票: *The government is going to hold a referendum on whether gambling should be forbidden.* 政府將就要不要禁止賭博進行全民投票.

refine [ri'fain] *vt / i* **1** make something (e. g. sugar, oil etc) pure by taking out dirt and waste matter etc. 使純, 精煉, 精製: *refined sugar* 精製糖. **2** make someone / something more polite, more educated etc; make free from coarseness 使(人)有教養, 文雅; 使(物)精緻 *a refined voice* 文雅的聲音. **refinement** *nu* **1** goodness of feeling, politeness etc 文雅, 高尚, 精美等: *a person of refinement* 文雅的人. **2** improved form of something that works better 改良, 精製: *a refinement of earlier methods* 早期方法的改良.

refinery *nc* building where sugar, metal etc is refined 精煉廠: *sugar refinery* 煉糖廠.

reflect [ri'flekt] *vt / i* **1** throw back light, heat, sound etc. 反射, 映射: *The smooth surface of the lake reflected the lights of the houses.* 光滑的湖面映射着房屋的燈光. **2** send back an image or likeness 照出, 映出: *The mirror reflected her face.* 鏡子照出她的臉. **reflection, reflexion** *nc* something that is reflected 映像, 影像: *the reflection of light on the water* 燈光在水上的倒影. **2** *nc / u* careful thinking; idea 考慮, 沉思; 看法. *On reflection, I have decided not to go.* 考慮以後, 我決定不去.

reflex ['ri:fleks] *adj* done without willing 不自主的, 反射的: *a reflex action* i. e. an action that is not done on purpose and cannot be prevented (e. g. shivering when one is cold) 反射作用, 即: 非個人意志所能控制的. (例如: 冷得發抖). Also 亦作 *reflexion* *nc / u* reflex action 反射作用 **reflexion** *nc / u* see 見 **reflection.**

reform [ri'fɔ:m] *vt / i* improve; make or become better by changing 改良, 改進, 改革: *reform someone's character* 改造某人的性格. Also 亦作 *nc / u* improvement; example of an improvement 改革, 改善, 革新; 改革的範例: *Our society needs reform* 我們的社會需要改革. *introduce several reforms* 採用幾項改革. **reformation** [refə'meiʃən] *nc / u* change or improvement 改革, 改善, 革新, 改進. **reformer** *nc* person who is in favour of reforms or who brings them about 改革家, 革新者.

refrain [ri'frein] *vi* hold oneself back from something, or from doing something 抑制, 克制: *refrain from smok-*

ing 戒烟.

refresh [ri'freʃ] *vt* make new again; give more strength to 恢復精神; 給予新力量, 使更新: *refresh one's memory* i. e. make something easier to remember by referring to notes etc. 喚起記憶, 即: 靠筆記使一些事容易記住; *refresh oneself with a drink of water* 喝一些水提神. **refreshing** *adj* pleasant; new; making one feel better 令人身心爽快的; 使人精神振作的; 提神的: *a refreshing sleep* 令人恢復精神的睡眠.

refreshment *nu* (often *pl*) food and drink (常用複數) 茶點, 點心和飲料.

refrigerator [rifridʒəreitə*] *nc* container designed to keep things (usu. food, drink) cold 電冰箱. (usu. **fridge**) (通常作 fridge). **refrigeration** [rifridʒə'reiʃən] *nu.*

refuel ['ri:'fjuəl] *vt / i* (esp. with reference to an aeroplane) get or provide with more fuel (尤指飛機)加油, 加燃料. *past* 過去式和過去分詞 **refuelled.**

refuge ['refju:dʒ] *nc / u* shelter or protection from danger etc. 避難處, 庇護所. **refugee** [refju'dʒi:] *nc* person who has escaped from danger (e. g. war, persecution, famine etc) 難民.

refund [ri'fʌnd] *vt / i* pay back money 退款, 退還, 償付.Also 亦作 ['ri:fʌnd] *nc / u* paying back of money; money paid back 退款; 退回之款: *When the concert was cancelled, many people demanded a refund.* 音樂會被取消時, 許多人要求退款.

refuse¹ [ri'fju:z] *vt / i* **1** not do what one is asked or told to do 拒絕, 謝絕: *She refused to go home.* 她拒絕回家. **2** not accept something 不願接受(某物), 拒收: *I refused his offer of money.* 我不願接受他的錢. **refusal** *nc / u* act of refusing 拒絕.

refuse² ['refju:s] *nu* things which have been used and thrown away; waste matter 廢物, 垃圾.

refute [ri'fju:t] *vt* prove that someone / something is wrong 證明某人/某事不對, 駁斥, 反駁: *refute someone's arguments* 駁斥某人的論點.

regain [ri'gein] *vt* **1** get back again 收回, 復得: *The army has regained the town.* 軍隊收回了這城鎮. **2** reach again; get back to 再到; 重回: *regain the shore* 重回岸邊.

regal ['ri:gl] *adj* belonging to or suitable for a king or queen 帝王的, 女王的; 莊嚴的, 堂皇的. **regalia** [ri'geiliə] *npl* symbols of royalty used at a coronation (e. g. a crown etc) 王室的標誌(例如: 用於加冕中的王冠等): *in full regalia* i. e. dressed in the official costume for an occasion 穿著全套官服, 即: 節日時身穿官服.

regard¹ [ri'gɑ:d] *vt* **1** consider; think something / someone to be 認爲; 看作: *Most people regard stealing as wrong.* 大多數人認爲偷盜是不正當的. **2** look at 看, 瞧: *He regarded me thoughtfully.* 他若有所思地望着我. **regarding** *prep* about or 關於; 有關: *I must speak to you regarding this matter.* 關於這件事, 我必須對你說一說.

regard² [ri'gɑ:d] *nu* **1** thought; attention 考慮; 關心: *have no regard for the feelings of others* i. e. not think about how others feel 不考慮別人的感情, 即: 不考慮別人怎麼想. **2** good opinion; respect 好感, 尊敬; 敬重: *hold someone in high / low regard* 極/不尊敬某人. **regards** *npl* good wishes 問候: *Give him my kind / best regards.* 代向他致以親切的/最好的問候. **regardless of** not worrying about 不管, 不顧: *He bought her what she wanted, regardless of the expense.* 不

管花多少錢, 她要甚麼, 他就給她買甚麼. **with regard to** concerning; about. Used to introduce a topic, often one which has already been referred to previously 關於; 有關(常用以引導前面已提到的話題): *With regard to the problem which I mentioned last week, I suggest...* 關於我上星期提到的這個問題, 我建議......

regatta [ri'gætə] *nc* meeting in which boats race against one another 賽船會.

regent ['ri:dʒənt] *nc* person who acts for a ruler who is too young, old, ill etc to perform his duties 攝政者. **regency** *nc*.

régime [rei'ʒi:m] *nc* method of ruling; government 政權, 政制; 政府: *the old régime* i. e. government that ruled before a revolution or reform took place 舊政權, 即: 革命或改革前的政府.

regiment ['redʒimənt] *nc* part of an army, larger than a battalion and smaller than a brigade, and usu. commanded by a colonel (軍隊的)團. **regimental** [redʒi'mentl] *adj* **regimentation** [redʒimən'teiʃən] *nu* very strict control of people (對人民)極嚴格的控制或管理.

region ['ri:dʒən] *nc* area of land 地區, 區域: *different regions of England* 英國的不同地區. **regional** *adj*.

register[1] ['redʒistə*] *nc* **1** list; record 名單; 記錄; 註冊: *a register of births, marriages and deaths* 出生, 婚姻和死亡的記錄. **2** book containing lists or records 登記簿, 註冊簿: *a school attendance register* 學生註冊簿. **registrar** ['redʒistrɑ:*] *nc* official who makes up lists or keeps records (e. g. of births, marriages and deaths) 記錄員, 登記員. **'registry office** place where people can be married without

a religious ceremony 結婚公證處.

register[2] ['redʒistə*] *vt / i* **1** write in a list or record 記錄, 註冊. **2** have one's name written in a list or record 列入名冊, 登記: *register as a voter* 選民登記. **3** pay extra money when sending a letter or parcel by post so that more care may be taken of it 寄掛號: *register a parcel* 包裹寄掛號; *a registered letter* 掛號信. **registration** [redʒis'treiʃən] *nc / u* **regis'tration number** licence number of a car, displayed on the number plates (汽車)登記證號碼.

regret [ri'gret] *nu* feeling of sorrow at not having done something, or having done something unpleasant or wrong 抱歉, 遺憾: *I left my home with some regret.* 我遺憾地離開了我的家. Also 亦作 *vt* be sorry about something 抱歉, 惋惜: *I regret that I shall not be able to come.* 我很抱歉, 我不能夠來. *past* 過去式和過去分詞 **regretted.** **regretfully** *adv* **regrettable** *adj* that one ought to feel sorry about 令人遺憾的, 不幸的, 可惜的: *regrettable behaviour* 令人遺憾的行為.

regular ['regjulə*] *adj* **1** normal; usual 正常的; 通常的: *This is his regular day for visiting us.* 這是他通常訪問我們的日子. **2** coming often 常來的: *be a regular visitor* 作爲一個常客. **3** evenly shaped; attractive 端正的, 整齊的, 勻稱的; 引人注目的: *regular features* 五官端正的. **4** orderly or normal 規則的, 有規律的: *a person of regular habits* i. e. who always does things at the same time or in the same way, or acts in a normal way 生活有規律的人, 即: 按時照章辦事的人. Also 亦作 *nc* regular customer at a pub or shop *(informal)* 老主顧(非正式). **regularly** *adv* **regularity** [regju-

'læriti] *nu*.

regulate ['regjuleit] *vt* 1 control by rules 管理, 控制: *regulate a country's imports* 管理國家的進口. 2 make a machine work properly 調整, 調節, 校準: *regulate one's watch* i. e. to keep the right time 校準手錶, 即: 使手錶走得準. **regulation** [regju'leiʃən] 1 *nc* rule to be obeyed 規章, 規則, 條例: *There are too many regulations nowadays.* 如今, 規章太多了. 2 *nu* control by rules 管理, 節制, 控制: *the regulation of the hours a young person may work* 年輕人工作時間的規定.

rehabilitate [ri:hə'biliteit] *vt* 1 put back into good condition; make able to work again 恢復; 修復, 使恢復正常工作; 使能重新工作: *rehabilitate an injured soldier* i. e. train him to carry out a new job and help find work for him 使傷兵恢復就業資格, 即: 訓練他從事新職業並幫助他找工作. 2 put back into a former position, rank etc. 復職, 復位: *He was rehabilitated as secretary.* 他恢復了作秘書的職務. **rehabilitation** ['ri:həbili'teiʃən] *nu*.

rehearse [ri'hə:s] *vt / i* practise a play or music etc for public performance 排練, 排演, 預演: *rehearse a part* 排練 (戲中的) 角色: *Don't interrupt while we are rehearsing.* 我們排練時, 不要打擾. *He rehearsed the actors* i. e. he made them practise 他使演員們排練. 即: 他讓他們試演. **rehearsal** *nc*.

reign [rein] *nc* period of a king's rule 統治時期, 王朝: *during the reign of George III* 在喬治第三的統治時期. Also 亦作 *vi* 1 rule as a king 統治, 稱王: *reign over a country for many years* 統治一個國家好多年. 2 be found everywhere 支配, 盛行, 佔優勢: *Peace reigned throughout the region.* 全區都

平靜了.

reimburse [ri:im'bə:s] *vt* pay back 償還, 退款, 補償: *reimburse someone* 補償某人; *reimburse somebody for the money he has spent* 償還某人他已花的錢.

rein [rein] *nc* (usu. *pl*) long, narrow strap used for controlling a horse or child (通常用複數) 繮繩.

reindeer ['reindiə*] *nc* kind of large deer with horns, found in Arctic regions (e. g. Lapland) 馴鹿. *pl* 複數 **reindeer**.

reinforce [ri:in'fɔ:s] *vt* make stronger by adding more men, materials etc. 增援, 增強, 加強: *reinforce an army / bridge etc.* 增援軍隊 / 加固橋樑等. **reinforcement** *nc* (often *pl*) (常用複數). **reinforcements** *npl* men etc sent to reinforce 援兵: *wait for reinforcements before attacking* 進攻前等待援兵.

reinstate [ri:in'steit] *vt* put back into a former position or condition 使復原位, 恢復原職, 恢復原狀: *The manager was dismissed, but he was reinstated later.* 經理被解職, 但不久他恢復了原職.

reiterate [ri:'itəreit] *vt* say or do something several times 重申, 重做, 反覆說, 反覆做: *reiterate a statement* 重新聲明.

reject [ri'dʒekt] *vt* refuse to accept 拒絕, 不接受: *reject someone's help* 拒絕某人的幫助. Also 亦作 ['ri:dʒekt] *nc* someone / something that has been rejected 遭拒絕的某人/某事.

rejoice [ri'dʒɔis] *vt / i* be glad 高興, 快樂: *rejoice at some good news* 爲好消息而高興.

rejoin [ri'dʒɔin] *vt / i* answer; reply 回答; 答覆.

relapse [ri'læps] *nc* falling back (esp.

into illness) (疾病) 復發, 惡化; *He seemed to recover for a short time, but then he had a relapse.* 他好像短時間恢復了, 但後來又復發.

relate [ri'leit] *vt / i* **1** tell a story etc. 叙述, 說: *relate one's adventures* 叙述自己的奇遇. **2** connect; be connected with 聯繫; 與…有關係; *How is this fact related to that one?* 這個事實怎麼跟那個事實聯繫起來? **related** *adj* **1** connected 有聯繫的, 有關的. *(opp* 反義詞 **unrelated).** **2** belonging to the same family 親屬的, 有親戚關係的: *Are you related to him?* 你跟他有親戚關係嗎? **relation 1** *nu* way in which people / things are connected 關係: *They discussed the relation between poverty and crime.* 他們討論了貧窮與犯罪的關係. **2** *nc* member of one's family; relative 親屬; 親戚: *She brought all her relations with her.* 她把她所有的親戚都帶來了. **relationship** *nc* connection 關係. **relative** ['relətiv] *adj* compared with each other compared with something else 相互的; 比較的, 相應的: *Let us examine the relative amounts of work done by the students.* 讓我們檢查學生們所做的相應的工作量. *He is living in relative poverty* i. e. compared to other people 他的生活是比較貧苦的. 即: 跟別人相比. Also 亦作 *nc* member of one's family 親屬, 親戚: *live with an elderly relative* i. e. an old person who is related 跟一個年長的親戚住在一起, 即: 一個老人親戚. **relatively** *adv* when compared with something / someone else 比較地, 相對地: *relatively rich* 比較富的. **relative pronoun** word like *who, which, that* etc as in the sentence. *The pen that I bought yesterday is broken.* 關係代詞(如 *who, which, that* 等). 例如:

The pen that I bought yesterday is broken. (我昨天所買的鋼筆斷了.) 中的 *that*.

relax [ri'læks] *vt / i* **1** make or become less stiff or less strict 放鬆, 鬆弛, 放寬: *His body relaxed* 他的身體鬆弛了. *They relaxed the regulations.* 他們放寬了規定. **2** become free of care 使輕鬆: *take a week's holiday and relax* 度一週假放鬆一下. **relaxation** [ri:læk'sei∫ən] *nc / u* act of relaxing; enjoyment and amusement 鬆弛; 娛樂和消遣.

relay ['ri:lei] *nc* fresh supply of men or horses to replace tired ones 替補人員或馬匹, 輪班: *The people of the village worked in relays to put out the fire.* 村民們輪班地工作把火滅了. Also 亦作 [ri'lei] *vt* receive and pass further on 轉播, 接轉: *relay a message / broadcast etc.* 接轉信息 / 廣播等.

release [ri'li:s] *vt* set free; allow to go 釋放; 放出: *release prisoners* 釋放犯人. Also 亦作 *nc / u* act of releasing or being released 釋放, 赦免: *The prisoner was questioned before his release.* 那犯人在釋放前被查問過了.

relegate ['reləgeit] *vt* put into a lower position, rank etc. 使降級, 使降位: *The football team was relegated to the lowest division.* 這支足球隊被降到最低級的隊.

relent [ri'lent] *vi* become less cruel or less firm 變溫和, 變寬厚, 憐憫. **relentless** *adj* without pity 無情的.

relevant ['reləvənt] *adj* connected with what is being discussed 有關的: *a relevant question* 有關的問題. *(opp* 反義詞 **irrelevant). relevance** *nu.*

reliable [ri'laiəbl] *adj* that can be trusted or relied on 可靠的, 可信賴的. *(opp* 反義詞 **unreliable). reliably** *adv* **reliance** [ri'laiəns] *nu* act of depending on or trusting in 信任, 信賴, 依靠.

relic ['relik] *nc* **1** something belonging to a saint and kept after his death as a mark of respect (聖人死後被保存的) 聖物; 聖骨. **2** something which still exists to remind us of the past 遺物; 遺跡; 遺蹟: *relics of an ancient civilization* 古代文明的遺跡.

relief [ri'li:f] *nu* **1** lessening of pain or suffering (痛苦, 苦難的) 減輕: *a medicine which gives relief from pain* 止痛藥. **2** something given to lessen suffering; food, clothes etc given to the poor 救濟品; (賑濟貧民的) 食物、衣服等: *send relief* 送救濟品. **3** change that gives pleasure or adds interest 消遣; 解悶的調劑: *enjoy some light relief while on duty* 值班時, 喜歡來點輕鬆消遣. **4** change in duty; person who comes to take over a duty 換班; 接班者: *be waiting for one's relief* 在等待換班. **5** design, drawing etc which is raised above the surface it is on 浮雕; 形象鮮明突出的繪畫等: *in relief* 浮雕的; 鮮明的. **re'lief map** map which uses colours or shading to show the height of the land 立體地圖 (用顏色或明暗表示地勢的高度).

relieve [ri'li:v] *vt* **1** make pain or trouble less 減輕 (痛苦、苦難): *a medicine that will relieve a headache* 一種止痛的藥. **2** give pleasure or interest by change (用調劑) 使解悶; 使消遣: *relieve the monotony of something* 解去某事的單調乏味. **3** take over a duty from someone for a time 換 (某人的) 班. **4** take something from someone 從某人手中接取某事物: *I relieved John of some of the work* i. e. I did some of the work in order to help John. 我替約翰做了一些工作. 即: 我爲了幫助約翰而做了一些工作.

religion [ri'lidʒən] **1** *nu* belief in God or any other kind of supernatural power 信仰. **2** *nc* system of belief in God or any other kind of supernatural power 宗教: *people of different religions* 不同宗教信仰的人. **religious** *adj* **1** connected with religion 宗教的: *a religious service* 宗教儀式. **2** observing the rules of a religion carefully 信奉宗教的; 虔誠的: *a religious person* 虔誠的教徒. (*opp* **irreligious** in sense 2) (義 2 的反義詞爲 irreligious).

relinquish [ri'liŋkwiʃ] *vt* give up; yield 放棄; 讓與: *The prince relinquished his claim to the throne.* 那王子放棄繼承王位的權利要求.

relish ['reliʃ] *nc* something which gives an extra taste to food 調味品; 作料: *olives, sardines and other relishes* 橄欖、沙丁魚和其他調味品.Also 亦作 *vt* enjoy 享受; 喜愛: *relish a good story* 津津有味地聽一個有趣的故事.

reluctant [ri'lʌktnt] *adj* unwilling; slow to do something because one is unwilling 不情願的; 勉强的. **reluctantly** *adv* **reluctance** *nu*.

rely [ri'lai] *vi* usu. in **rely on/upon** i. e. depend on; trust 通常用於 rely on / upon, 即: 依靠; 信任. *I can rely on you.* 我可以信任你. see 見 **reliable**.

remain [ri'mein] *vi* **1** be left after something has been removed 留下; 剩下: *He kept all that remained of his father's money.* 他父親留下的錢由他全部掌管. **2** stay in the same place 逗留 (在同一地方): *He remained there for five years.* 他在那裏逗留了五年. **remainder** [ri'meində*] *nu* what is left 剩餘物: *You can keep the remainder of the money.* 剩餘的錢你就拿着吧. **remains** *npl* **1** what is left 剩餘物: *the remains of a meal* 殘羹剩飯. **2** dead body 遺體. **3** ancient ruins of buildings etc. 遺址.

remand [ri'ma:nd] *vt* send back to prison until a trial is held 還押 (候審). Also 亦作 *nu.*

remark [ri'ma:k] *vt / i* say or write something; speak or write about something; 說; 寫; 陳述: *He remarked on the neatness of the pupils' work.* 他談了學生作業的整潔問題. *He remarked that he would be leaving soon.* 他說他不久就要走. Also 亦作 *nc / u* something said or written in few words (言語; 評論) 三言兩語: *a clever remark* 珠璣妙語. **remarkable** *adj* unusual; worth noticing 不同尋常的; 值得注意的. **remarkably** *adv.*

remedy ['remədi] *nc / u* 1 way of relieving sickness, pain etc. (病痛等的) 治療法: *a remedy for headaches* 一種頭痛治療法. 2 way of setting right any bad thing or situation 補救方法; 糾正方法. Also 亦作 *vt* **remedial** [ri'mi:diəl] *adj* able to cure or help 可治療的; 可補救的.

remember [ri'membə*] *vt / i* 1 keep in mind; not forget 記住; 不忘記: *remember one's schooldays* 回憶學生時代; *remember to do something* 別忘記去做某事. 2 bear greetings 問候; 致意: *Remember me to your father when you see him.* i. e. give him my greetings. (*informal* in sense 2) 見到你的父親時, 請代我向他致意. 即: 向他表達我的問候. (義 2 爲非正式.) **remembrance** [ri'membrns] *nu* act of remembering 回憶, 紀念: *A monument was built in remembrance of those who had died.* 建了一座緬懷死者的紀念碑. *Note* 說明: the difference between e. g. *I remembered to open the door* i. e. I had to open the door and I did so; and *I remember opening the door* i. e. I opened the door, and I

know that I did it 注意例句 I remembered to open the door (我記得去開門. 即: 我得去開門, 而且我這樣做了) 和 I remember opening the door (我記得開門. 即: 我開了門, 而且我知道我做了) 之間的差別.

remind [ri'maind] *vt* cause one to remember; make one think of someone / something 提醒; 使記起; 使想起: *Remind him to close the door when he leaves.* 提醒他離開時別忘關門. *That house reminds me of the one I was born in.* 此幢房子使我想起我在裏面出生的那幢房子. **reminder** *nc* something that helps one to remember 提醒物; 催詢單: *If he doesn't pay his bill, send him a reminder.* 如果他沒付清帳, 送張催詢單提醒他.

reminisce [remi'nis] *vi* remember past events in a pleasant way 緬懷 (追憶) 往事. **reminiscences** *npl* memories (esp. written down to make a book) (尤指成書的) 回憶錄: *publish one's reminiscences* 出版回憶錄. **reminiscent** *adj* reminding one of 使人想起的: *scenes reminiscent of one's childhood* 令人想起童年時代的景象.

remission [ri'miʃən] 1 *nc / u* freeing from a debt, a punishment etc. (債務, 處罰等的) 免除; 赦免: *the remission of school fees* i. e. some or all of the school fees do not have to be paid 減免學費, 即: 不用繳交部份或全部學費; *remission of a prison sentence* 坐牢開釋. 2 *nu* forgiveness of sin (罪過的) 寬恕.

remit [ri'mit] *vt / i* send money 匯 (錢): *remit some money to one's parents* 給父母親匯一些錢. *past* 過去式和過去分詞 **remitted. remittance** *nc / u* sending of money; amount of money sent 匯款; 匯款額: *send a weekly remittance* 送每週匯款.

remnant ['remnənt] *nc* **1** small part that is left 殘餘；剩餘：*the remnants of a defeated army* 潰軍的殘餘. **2** small piece of cloth left over and often sold at a cheaper price 零頭布(常減價出售)：*a remnant sale* 零頭布拍賣.

remonstrate ['remənstreit] *vi* protest against something; argue with someone 抗議(某事)；規諫，規諫(某人)：*I remonstrated against the chairman's decision.* 我對主席的決定表示異議. *I remonstrated with the chairman about his decision.* 我就其決定規諫主席. **remonstrance** [ri'mɔnstrns] *nc / u.*

remorse [ri'mɔːs] *nu* deep sorrow for having done wrong (對做錯事) 後悔，悔恨：*be filled with remorse* 十分後悔. **remorseful** *adj* full of remorse 後悔的；悔恨的. **remorseless** *adj* without remorse; without pity 不知懊悔的；殘忍的. **remorselessly** *adv.*

remote [ri'mout] *adj* far away; distant in place or time (空間，時間上) 遙遠的；很久的：*a remote country* 遙遠的國家；*a remote time in the past* 很久很久以前.

remove [ri'muːv] *vt* take away; take off 拿走；脫掉：*remove one's hat* 脫帽；*be removed to a hospital* 給送去醫院. **removal** *nc / u* act of removing 搬遷；撤除：*A van came for the removal of our furniture.* 搬運卡車開來爲我們搬傢具.

remuneration [rimjuːnə'reiʃən] *nu* payment; reward 報酬；酬勞. **remunerative** [ri'mjuːnərətiv] *adj* which pays well 報酬高的：*a very remunerative job* 報酬很高的工作.

renal ['riːnl] *adj* of the kidneys 腎的.

render ['rendə*] *vt* **1** make; cause to be 致使；使成：*be rendered helpless with laughter* 因哄堂大笑而弄得不知所措. **2** translate 翻譯. **rendering** *nc / u.*

rendez-vous ['rɔndeivuː] *nc* **1** agreement to meet at a certain time 約會：*make a rendez-vous with someone* 與某人約會. **2** place where one is going to have an arranged meeting with someone 約會地點.

renew [ri'njuː] *vt* **1** make again; begin again; get again 重做；重新開始：*renew an attack* 再度進攻；*renew a promise* 重申諾言. *renew a contract* 續訂合同. **2** make something as it was when it was new or fresh (使) 更新；恢復：*start working with renewed vigour* i. e. as at the beginning 又精神抖擻地開始工作，即：跟最初那樣. **3** replace with something of the same sort 更換：*I must renew my radio licence* i. e. get one for this year. 我得更換我的無綫電執照，即：領取今年的執照. **renewal** *nc / u* act of renewing or being renewed 重做；更新；更換.

renounce [ri'nauns] *vt* **1** give up entirely 放棄，拋棄：*renounce one's privileges / claims etc.* 放棄特權/要求等. **2** say that one will have no more connection with 宣佈與···斷絕關係：*renounce one's own family* 宣佈與家庭斷絕關係. **renunciation** [rinʌnsi'eiʃən] *nu.*

renovate ['renəveit] *vt* make like new again 翻新；修理：*renovate an old building* 修繕舊樓. **renovation** [renə'veiʃən] *nc / u.*

renown [ri'naun] *nu* fame 名望；聲譽. **renowned** *adj* famous 著名的.

rent [rent] *nc / u* money paid regularly for the use of a room, house etc which belongs to someone else 房租；租金. Also 亦作 *vt* **1** pay for the use of something 租用：*rent a room from someone* 向某人租一間房. **2** allow someone to use one's house etc in return for payment 出租：*rent a room* *to someone* 把一間房租給某人.

rental ['rentl] *nc* amount of money received or paid as rent; income from rents 租金額; 租金收入. Also 亦作 *adj* pertaining to rent 出租的; 租用的.

renunciation [rinʌnsi'eiʃən] *nu* see 見 **renounce**.

repair [ri'peə*] *vt* **1** put something damaged or worn into good condition; mend 修理; 修補: *repair a damaged bridge* 修繕一座壞橋; *repair worn shoes* 修補破鞋. **2** put right; make up for 改正; 補償: *How can I repair the damage I have caused?* 我怎樣才能彌補我所造成的損失呢?Also 亦作 *nc / u* act of repairing or being repaired 修理; 修補: *a road that is under repair* 一條在維修的路. *Repairs are being carried out on the damaged building.* 這幢壞樓正在修繕.

repartee [repɑː'tiː] *nu* witty, clever answers in conversation 巧妙的回答: *be good at repartee* 能言善辯.

repay [ri'pei] *vt* pay back; return 付還; 回報: *repay money that was borrowed* 付還借款; *repay the kindness someone has done* 報答某人所給的好意. **repayment** *nc / u.*

repeal [ri'piːl] *vt* end, cancel a law 廢除; 撤銷(法令): *The unjust law was finally repealed.* 這不公正的法令最後被廢除了. Also 亦作 *nc* (usu. only sing) act of repealing (通常只用單數) 廢除; 取消.

repeat [ri'piːt] *vt* **1** say or do again 再說; 再做: *repeat a statement* 重申聲明; *repeat a mistake* 重犯錯誤; *repeat oneself* i. e. say the same thing again 再說一遍, 即: 重複說同樣的事. **2** say what one has learned 複述: *repeat a poem* 背誦詩歌. **3** tell to someone else 把…告訴他人: *Don't repeat what you have seen today.* 別把

你今天看到的事告訴別人. **repeatedly** *adv* very often 再三地; 反覆地. **repetition** [repi'tiʃən] **1** *nu* act of repeating 重說; 複述; 背誦; 重複; 反覆: *after much repetition* 經過許多反覆以後. **2** *nc* something repeated 重演: *I hope there is not a repetition of this.* 我希望沒有這種事的重演. **repetitive** [ri'petitiv] *adj.*

repel [ri'pel] *vt* **1** force back; push away 擊退; 驅開: *repel an enemy* 擊退敵人. **2** cause a feeling of dislike in someone 使反感; 使厭惡: *His dirty appearance repelled the girl.* 他蓬頭垢面的樣子令姑娘反感. *past* 過去式和過去分詞 **repelled. repellent** *adj* unattractive; causing a feeling of dislike 不中看的; 令人反感的: *something that is repellent to a person* 令人反感的東西. Also 亦作 *nc* something which is intended to repel 驅開物: *an insect repellent* 驅蟲劑.

repent [ri'pent] *vt / i* feel sorry for having done something wrong (使) 後悔; 悔恨(做錯事): *repent (of) one's sins* 懺悔自己的罪過. *repent having done wrong* 後悔做錯了事. **repentance** *nu* sorrow for having done wrong 悔恨; 後悔.

repercussion [riːpəkʌʃən] *nc / u* (often *pl*) something which is caused by something else in an indirect way (常用複數) 反應; 影響: *If this law is passed, it will have repercussions throughout the world* i. e. it will not only affect this country but also, indirectly, affect others 如果通過這項法令, 這將會在全世界引起反響, 即: 這不僅影響這個國家, 而且也間接影響別國.

repertoire ['repətwɑː*] *nc* set of plays which a company can perform; set of songs etc which a group or a person can perform (劇團, 演員的) 常備劇目;

演唱節目.

repertory ['repətəri] *nu* system by which a group of actors presents a number of different plays during the course of a short period of time (劇團 多套的) 常備劇目; 保留節目: *act in repertory* 上演保留節目.

repetition [repi'tiʃən] *nc / u* see 見 **repeat**.

replace [ri'pleis] *vt* 1 take the place of 取代: *In many areas, cars have replaced horses as a means of transport.* 在許多地區, 汽車已經取代馬匹作爲交通工具. 2 get something to take the place of 置換: *I must replace the cup that was broken.* 我必須置換這隻破杯. 3 put back in the proper place 把…放回原處: *replace a book on a shelf.* 把書放回架上. **replacement** *nc / u* act of replacing; thing / person that replaces 取代; 置換; 放回; 替換人 / 物.

replay ['ri:plei] *nc* match played again 重賽.

replenish [ri'pleniʃ] *vt* fill up again 再裝滿: *replenish the cupboard with food.* 給食櫥再裝滿食物.

replete [ri'pli:t] *adj* completely filled; well-supplied 塞滿的; 供應充足的.

replica ['replikə] *nc* (esp. of a painting etc) exact copy (尤指原畫等的) 複製品.

reply [ri'plai] *vi* answer; give in return 回答; 答覆: *reply to a question* 回答問題; *reply to enemy gunfire* 回擊敵人的砲火. Also 亦作 *nc* answer 回答.

report[1] [ri'pɔ:t] *nc* 1 description of what one has seen, done, heard etc. 報告; 報導: *write a report on what has been decided* 就已決定的事寫個報告. 2 sound of a shot or explosion 槍聲; 爆炸聲: *a loud report* 一聲轟隆巨響. **school re'port** list of marks or grades of a pupil at school, together with teachers' comments etc, sent by a school to a pupil's parents 學生成績報告單(上有學生成績、教師評語等通知照家長的事項).

report[2] [ri'pɔ:t] *vt / i* 1 describe; tell about 報導; 報告: *She reported what she had seen to the police.* 她向警察報告所目睹的事. 2 go to some place or person, and say why one has come or ask instructions etc. 報到: *Report for duty here at six o'clock.* 六點在這裏報到值勤. 3 make a complaint about someone to his superior 告發: *I shall report that insolent child to the headmaster.* 我要向校長告發那個無禮的孩子. **reporter** *nc* someone who gets news for a newspaper (採訪) 記者. **reported speech** see 見 **indirect**.

reprehensible [repri'hensibl] *adj* deserving blame 應受譴責的; 應加非難的.

represent [repri'zent] *vt* 1 stand for; be a sign of 表示; 象徵: *On this map, the black dots represent cities and the blue part represents the sea.* 這幅地圖上的黑點表示城市, 藍色部份表示海洋. 2 show 呈現: *This painting represents a country scene.* 這是一幅田野風景畫. 3 speak on behalf of 代表: *represent a certain district in Parliament* 代表某一地區的議會議員. **representation** [reprizen'teiʃən] *nc / u* act of representing; something represented 表示(物); 呈現(物); 代表(物); 圖像: *make representations* i. e. protest officially 請願, 即: (溫和的) 正式抗議. **representative** [repri'zentətiv] *nc* someone who is appointed to speak or act for others 代表; 代理人: *the representative of a company* 公司代表.

repress [ri'pres] *vt* 1 bring under control 抑制: *I repressed a desire to hit* *him* 我抑制住要揍他一頓的念頭. **2** put down 鎮壓: *repress a rebellion* 鎮壓叛亂. **repressive** *adj* **repression** *nu.*

reprieve [ri'pri:v] *vt* say that the execution of someone condemned to death will take place later or not take place at all 暫緩處刑; 緩期處死: *The President reprieved the condemned man.* 總統下令暫緩處決此犯人. Also 亦作 *nc* order stopping an execution; stopping of an execution 緩處死刑(命令): *The condemned murderer was granted a reprieve.* 此殺人犯獲准暫緩處決.

reprimand ['reprimɑ:nd] *vt* blame severely 申斥: *reprimand a naughty child* 訓誡一個頑童. Also 亦作 *nc* statement blaming or scolding 申斥; 叱責: *give someone a reprimand* 狠狠教訓某人一頓.

reprisal [ri'praizl] *nc / u* (often *pl*) wrong which is done in revenge for another wrong (常用複數) 報復: *When our village was attacked by the enemy, we attacked one of theirs in reprisal.* 我們的村莊遭到敵人的攻擊時, 我們就攻擊他們的一個村莊作爲報復.

reproach [ri'prout∫] *vt* blame someone sadly rather than angrily (傷心地) 責備: *reproach a child for being rude* 責備孩子粗野無禮; *reproach oneself* i. e. blame oneself 自我責備. Also 亦作 *nc / u* **1** disgrace; something that brings shame 恥辱; 丟臉的東西: *without reproach* 沒受污辱. **2** act of reproaching 責備. **reproachful** *adj* full of, or showing, reproach 責備的; 可叱的: *a reproachful look* 責備的眼光.

reproduce [ri:prə'dju:s] *vt* cause something to be seen or heard again 複製; 再版; 播放: *reproduce sound by using*

a record player 用唱機播出聲音. **reproduction** [ri:prə'dʌkʃən] *nc / u* **1** copy 複製品, 拷貝. **2** act of reproducing 複製; 播放.

reproof [ri'pru:f] *nc / u* blame; words of blame 責備; 訓斥; 斥責的話. **reprove** [ri'pru:v] *vt* blame; find fault with; rebuke 責備; 指責; 責罵: *reprove a child for coming to school late* 指責孩子上學遲到.

reptile ['reptail] *nc* type of cold-blooded animal that creeps or crawls (e. g. a lizard, snake or crocodile) 爬行動物; 冷血動物(例如: 蜥蜴、蛇或鱷魚).

republic [ri'pʌblik] *nc* country ruled by a president and representatives chosen by the people 共和國; 共和政體. **republican** [ri'pʌblikən] *adj* of a republic 共和國的; 共和政體的. Also 亦作 *nc* person who favours a republic as a means of government 共和論者; 共和主義者; 擁護共和政體者.

repudiate [ri'pju:dieit] *vt* i *refuse to accept* 拒絕接受; 駁斥: *repudiate a belief* 駁斥某種信念; *repudiate a gift* 拒收禮物.

repugnant [ri'pʌgnənt] *adj* causing a feeling of great dislike 令人厭惡的. **repugnance** *nu* strong dislike for something 厭惡; 反感.

repulse [ri'pʌls] *vt* **1** drive back by force 擊退: *repulse an enemy attack* 擊退敵人的進攻. **2** refuse to accept; treat with coldness 拒絕接受; 冷淡對待: *repulse someone's friendship* 拒絕某人的友誼. **repulsion** *nu* feeling of strong dislike 厭惡. **repulsive** *adj* causing strong dislike 令人厭惡的.

reputation [repju'teiʃən] *nc / u* what people think about someone / something 名譽; 名望: *have a good / high reputation* i. e. be well thought of 很有名望, 即: 享有盛名. **reputable**

['repjutəbl] *adj* having a good reputation 名譽好的: *a reputable firm* 有信譽的公司. **repute** [ri'pju:t] *nu* reputation (usu. good reputation) (通常爲好的)名譽: *a man of repute (o. f.)* 名人 (舊式). **reputed** [ri'pju:tid] *adj* thought by most people 被多數人認爲: *someone who is reputed to be very generous* 某個據說是十分慷慨大方的人.

request [ri'kwest] **1** *nu* act of asking for 要求: *I came at his request* i. e. because he asked me 我應他的請求而來. 即: 因爲他請求我. **2** *nc* something asked for 請求的事物: *make a special request* 提出特別請求的事.Also 亦作 *vt* ask; ask for 要求; 請求: *request something* 要東西; *request someone to do something* 求某人做某事; *request that something should be done* 請求辦某事.

requiem ['rekwiəm] *nc* **1** religious services for the dead 安魂彌撒. **2** music for such a service 安魂曲; 挽歌.

require [ri'kwaiə*] *vt* **1** need 需要. *Do you require help?* 你需要幫助嗎? **2** oblige; order 要求; 命令: *You are required to stay here until tomorrow.* 要求你待在這裏一直到明天. **requirement** *nc / u* act of requiring; something required 需要; 要求(物). **requisite** ['rekwizit] *nc* something needed 必需品: *food and other requisites* 食物和其他必需品.Also 亦作 *adj*.

rescind [ri'sind] *vt* cancel; put an end to 廢除; 取消: *rescind a law* 廢除一項法令.

rescue ['reskju:] *vt* save from danger 營救; 拯救: *rescue someone from drowning / from his enemies etc.* 拯救某人免於溺斃/免落敵手等.Also 亦作 *nc / u* act of rescuing or being rescued 營救; 拯救: *go to someone's rescue* 前往營救某人. **rescuer** *nc*.

research [ri'sə:tʃ] *nu* careful examination of some subject to find out new facts 研究; 探討: *do research on a new scientific theory* 研究一種新興科學理論; *do research in chemistry* 從事化學研究.Also 亦作 *vt / i*.

resemble [ri'zembl] *vt* look like; be like 像; 相似: *He resembles his brother.* 他像他的兄弟. **resemblance** *nc / u* likeness 相似.

resent [ri'zent] *vt* feel angry at 對…感到憤怒: *resent being treated rudely* 對粗魯的接待感到氣憤. **resentful** *adj* resentment *nu*.

reserve [ri'zə:v] *vt* keep for the use of a particular person 保留; 預訂: *reserve a seat in the theatre* 預定一戲院座位. Also 亦作 *nc* **1** something kept to be used later; keeping something like this 儲備物; 儲備: *a reserve of food* 儲備糧. **2** area of land kept apart for a special purpose 保護區: *a game reserve* i. e. place where wild animals can live freely 獵物保護區. 即: 野生動物能自由生息的地方. **3** (with reference to football etc) person whose job is to take the place of any member of a team who is injured or unable to play (指足球球隊等)候補隊員. **reservation** [rezə'veiʃən] **1** *nc / u* arrangement to keep something for the use of a particular person 保留; 預訂: *make a plane reservation* i. e. arrange for a seat to be kept for one on a plane 預定飛機票, 即: 預定飛機的座位. **2** *nc / u* limit; condition 限制; 保留條件: *accept something without reservation* 無保留地接受某事物. **3** *nc* area of land set aside for a special reason (e. g. one of the areas set aside for the use of the Red Indians in

America) 保留地(例如: 美國印第安人保留地). **reserved** *adj* **1** kept for a particular use or person 預定的; 保留的: *a reserved seat in a theatre* 劇院的保留座位. **2** not saying much; not showing much emotion 話語不多的; 不苟言笑的: *a reserved person* 一個沉默寡言的人.

reservoir ['rezəvwɑ:*] *nc* place, often a man-made lake, where water is stored (e. g. to provide a water supply for a city) 水庫(如常爲城市提供用水的人工湖).

reside [ri'zaid] *vi* live in 居住: *reside at / in a certain town* 住在某一城鎮. **residence** ['rezidns] **1** *nc* house; home. *(formal)* 住宅; 家(正式). **2** *nu* act of residing 居住: *be in residence* 住於任所的; 住校的. **resident** ['rezidnt] *nc* someone who lives in a place, not a visitor 居民. **residential** [rezi'denʃl] *adj* for living in, not working in 居住的; 住宅的: *a residential area* i. e. where there are no factories etc. 住宅區, 即: 沒有工廠或企業的地區.

residue ['rezidju:] *nc* what is left of anything after some of it has been taken away 剩餘; 餘渣; 餘財產.

resign [ri'zain] *vt / i* give up a job or position 辭職: *resign one's post* 辭去職務; *resign from a committee* 辭去委員會的職位. **resigned** *adj* accepting what happens without complaining 順從的; 聽任的: *He is resigned to losing the competition.* 競爭失敗, 他處之泰然. **resignation** [rezig'neiʃən] **1** *nc* act of resigning 辭職. **2** *nc* written statement that one intends to resign 辭職書: *hand in one's resignation* 遞交辭呈. **3** *nu* state of being resigned 順從; 聽任.

resilience [ri'ziliəns] *nu* quality of being able to return to a former

shape or position after being bent, crushed, pulled etc. 彈性; 彈力; 恢復力. **resilient** *adj*.

resin ['rezin] *nc / u* sticky material that comes out of certain trees and is often used in medicine or for making varnish 樹脂; 松香(可用來配藥或製凡立水).

resist [ri'zist] *vt* **1** act against; fight against 抵抗; 反抗; 抗拒; 抵擋: *resist the spread of disease* 防止疾病蔓延; *resist the enemy* 抵抗敵人. **2** (usu. with negative) keep from (通常與否定式連用) 忍住; 抑制: *She can't resist sweet things.* 她一看見甜食就忍不住要吃. **resistance** *nu* act of resisting 抵抗; 反抗: *The defenders of the city put up a tremendous resistance.* 城市守軍奮力抵抗.

resolute ['rezəlu:t] *adj* firm; not changing one's decision 堅決的; 剛毅的. *(opp* 反義詞 **irresolute**). **resolution** [rezə'lu:ʃən] **1** *nu* firmness; quality of being resolute 決心; 毅力; 果斷. **2** *nc* something decided on; decision (esp. one made at a meeting) 決定(尤指會議通過的)決議: *make a resolution* i. e. a decision 作出決定; *pass a resolution* 通過一項決議.

resolve [ri'zɔlv] *vt / i* **1** decide; make up one's mind 決定; 下決心: *He resolved to work harder / that he would work harder.* 他決心要更加發奮工作. **2** put an end to; explain 解決; 解釋: *This book will resolve all your difficulties.* 這部書會解決你所有的困難.

resonant ['rezənənt] *adj* continuing to sound; filling with sound; tending to make sounds louder or longer 洪亮的; 共鳴的; 回響的: *a resonant voice* 洪亮的嗓音; *resonant walls* 迴音壁.

resort [ri'zɔ:t] *vi* use (esp. when other means fail); turn to for help (尤在其

他方法失效時)利用; 求助; 訴諸: *You should never resort to violence.* 你們應該永遠不訴諸暴力. *He was so poor that he resorted to stealing.* 他窮到只得靠偷竊爲生. Also 亦作 *nc* 1 place people go to 勝地: *a seaside resort* 海濱勝地. 2 person / thing gone to for help 所求助的人 / 物. **as a / in the last resort** if all other means fail (其他都失效後)作爲最後的手段: *borrow money as a last resort* 萬不得已才借錢.

resound [ri'zaund] *vt / i* give back sound; be filled with sound 反響; 迴蕩; 充滿聲響: *The hall resounded with the shouts of the people.* 大廳裏人聲鼎沸. **resounding** *adj*.

resource [ri'sɔːs] *nu* ability to think of ways of getting help 智謀; 策略; 應變能力: *a man of resource* 足智多謀的人. **resources** *npl* 1 wealth which a country has (國家的)資源; 財力. 2 wealth, or means of getting money, that a person has (個人的)財富; 手段. **resourceful** *adj* able to get things done or to overcome difficulties 足智多謀的. **natural resources** things in a country which its people can use (e. g. minerals, soil, water supplies etc.) 天然資源(例如: 礦物、土壤、供水量等).

respect [ris'pekt] 1 *nu* honour; admiration 尊敬; 尊重: *show respect to one's parents* 尊敬父母; *have great respect for someone* 對某人十分尊重. 2 *nu* consideration; care 重視; 關心: *to show respect for other people's wishes* 對他人的願望表示重視. 3 *nu* reference 關於; 涉及: *with respect to* 關於; 涉及. 4 *nc* (often *pl*) detail; point (常用複數)方面; 地方; 點: *a good plan in many / some respects* 在許多 / 有些方面是個好計劃. Also 亦作 *vt* 1 give

honour to 尊敬: *respect one's parents* 尊敬父母. 2 show consideration for; care for 重視; 關心: *respect the feelings of others* 珍重他人的感情. **respects** *npl* greetings 敬意: *Please accept this gift with our respects.* 請接受這份表達我們敬意的禮物. **respectable** *adj* 1 well-behaved; of good character 正派的; 文雅的; 高尚的: *respectable citizens* 高尚的公民. 2 fit to be seen 體面的: *respectable clothes* 體面的衣著. **respectful** *adj* well-mannered; showing respect 有禮貌的; 恭敬的: *be respectful to one's teacher* 尊敬老師. (*opp* 反義詞 **disrespectful**). **respective** *adj* of each 各自的; 各個的: *The two boys were told to return to their respective homes* i. e. each boy was to return to his own home. 有人告訴兩個男孩回到各自的家. 即: 每個男孩得回自己家. **respectively** *adv* each in turn; in the order given 分別地; 各自地: *The first, second and third prizes went to John, James and Tom respectively* i. e. the first prize went to John, and so on. 頭獎、二獎和三獎分別歸約翰、詹姆士和湯姆所得. 即: 頭獎歸約翰所得, 等等.

respiration [respi'reiʃən] *nu* breathing 呼吸.

respite ['respait] *nc / u* period of rest or relief from work, pain etc. 休息, 暫停工作、緩痛等的期間: *work without (a) respite* 不停地工作.

resplendent [ri'splendnt] *adj* very bright; shining; splendid 燦爛的; 輝煌的; 華麗的.

respond [ris'pɔnd] *vi* 1 answer; reply 回答; 答覆: *respond to a letter* 回信. 2 be affected by something in a positive way 有反應; 有效果: *respond to kindness* 感恩; *respond to treatment* i. e. begin to recover from an illness 治療

後有起色，即：開始從病中康復．**response** [ris'pɒns] *nc / u* **1** answer 回答．**2** act of responding 反應：*Our appeal for help met with no response.* 我們求援的呼籲沒有得到任何的反應．

responsible [ris'pɒnsibl] *adj* **1** in charge of 有責任的；負責的：*You will be responsible for keeping your room tidy.* 你要負責保持你房間的整潔．**2** to be blamed or praised for 歸咎於；歸於：*The storm was responsible for most of the damage.* 這次損失的大部份都要歸咎於這場暴風雨．**3** reliable; able to be trusted 可靠的；可信賴的：*a job for some responsible person* 需認真負責的人去做的工作．(*opp* 反義詞 **irresponsible**). **4** important; requiring a reliable person 責任重大的；需要可靠的人的：*a responsible position* 要職．**responsibly** *adv* **responsibility** [rispɒnsi'biliti] **1** *nu* state of being responsible 責任；負責：*Some young people have no sense of responsibility* i. e. they are not reliable. 有些年青人毫無責任感．即：他們是不可靠的．**2** *nc* something one is responsible for 職責：*Keeping the room tidy is your responsibility, not mine.* 保持這個房間的整潔是你的職責，而不是我的．

rest¹ [rest] **1** *nc / u* freedom from anything that is tiring; sleep 休息；睡眠：*an hour's rest* 一小時休息；*work without rest* 不停地工作；*lie down for a rest* 躺下休息．**2** *nc* something that supports 支架；支托：*Use this pillow as a rest for your arm* 用這個枕頭當你的扶手．Also 亦作 *vt / i* **1** be free from anything that is tiring; sleep 休息；睡眠：*rest after working* 工後休息；*rest for an hour* 休息一小時．**2** give a rest to 使休息：*rest one's eyes after reading* 閱讀後休息一下眼睛．**3** stop moving; be no longer active 停止；靜

止：*The ball rested at the foot of the hill.* 球停在山腳下．*Let the matter rest there* i. e. discuss it no further. 此事就到此爲止吧．即：不再討論下去了．**4** be supported; cause to be supported (使) 倚靠：*rest one's head on a pillow* 頭擱在枕頭上．**restful** *adj* quiet; peaceful 平靜的；寧靜的．**restive** *adj* unable or unwilling to stay still; disobedient 煩躁不安的；難駕馭的；不聽話的：*The horses are getting restive because of the storm.* 馬羣越來越不受覊束，因爲狂風暴雨大作．**restless** *adj* unable to rest; moving about; without rest 坐卧不寧的；不停活動的；不休息的：*I feel too restless to sit down and read;* 我心煩意亂得很，無法坐下讀書；*spend a restless night* 度過一個不眠之夜．**restlessly** *adv* **restlessness** *nu.*

rest² [rest] *n* only in **the rest** i. e. what is left 只用於 **the rest**，即：其餘的：*Take the good apples and throw away the rest.* 揀好的蘋果拿去，其餘的丟掉．

restaurant ['restərɒn] *nc* place where meals can be bought and eaten 飯店；餐廳．

restitution [resti'tju:ʃən] *nu* making up for something that has been lost, stolen etc either by giving back the thing itself or by making a payment 歸還；賠償．

restore [ri'stɔ:*] *vt* **1** bring back 恢復：*restore old customs* 恢復古老風俗；*restore someone to his old position* 恢復某人原職．**2** give back 歸還：*restore stolen property* 歸還被偷的財物．**3** make something as it was when new 修復：*restore old buildings / furniture etc.* 修繕舊樓／修理傢具等．**restoration** [restə'reiʃən] *nc / u* act of restoring or being restored 恢復；歸還；修復．

restrain [ris'trein] *vt* prevent someone

from doing something; control 防止;
遏制; 控制: *restrain someone from
doing something* 制止某人做某事; *restrain one's curiosity* 抑制自己的好奇
心. **restraint 1** *nu* restraining or
being restrained 制止; 抑制. **2** *nc*
something that restrains 束縛; 拘束
(物) **restrained** *adj (opp* 反義詞 **un-
restrained).**

restrict [ri'strikt] *vt* keep within limits
限制: *restrict wages and prices* 限制工
資和物價. **restriction 1** *nu* restricting
or being restricted 限制; 拘束: *move
about without restricion* 無拘束地四處
行動. **2** *nc* something that restricts;
law or rule 管制; 限定; 法律, 規章.

result [ri'zʌlt] *nc* **1** what happens because of something 結果; 效果. *This
cold I have is the result of going out
without a coat yesterday.* 我這次感冒
是我昨天外出沒穿大衣的後果. **2**
score in a match or competition 比賽
或競賽的得分: *listen to the football
results* 聽廣這場足球賽的比分. Also 亦
作 *vi* follow as a result 起因於: *His
failure resulted from not working hard
enough.* 他所以失敗是因爲他工作不夠
努力. **resultant** *adj.*

resume [ri'zju:m] *vt* begin again 重新開
始, 繼續: *resume one's studies* 繼續學
習. **resumption** [ri'zʌmpʃən] *nu.*

resurgence [ri'sə:dʒəns] *nu* appearance
again with new strength 復蘇: *a resurgence of interest in the Middle Ages*
i. e. there is again a strong interest in
the Middle Ages, after a period when
people were not interested in this
time 對中世紀的興趣的復蘇; 人們
對中世紀曾有過一段時間不感興趣, 在
此以後又有強烈的興趣了.

resurrection [rezər'ekʃən] *nu* coming
back to life 復活. **the Resurrection 1**
rising again of Christ after being

buried 耶穌復活. **2** rising again on
the last day of all those who have
died 最後審判日所有死者的復活.

resuscitate [ri'sʌsiteit] *vt / i* bring
someone back to consciousness (使)
蘇醒: *resuscitate someone who has
almost drowned* 使奄奄一息的溺水者
蘇醒. **resuscitation** [risʌsi'teiʃən] *nu.*

retail [ri'teil] *nu* sale of goods in small
amounts to the ordinary public, not
to shopkeepers 零售, 零賣. *(opp* 反義
詞 **wholesale).** Also 亦作 *adj.* Also
亦作 *vt* sell or be sold by retail 零售,
零賣: *retail groceries* 零售雜貨;
*goods which retail at / for fifty pence
each* 五十便士一件的零售貨物. **re-
tailer** *nc* shopkeeper who sells goods
by retail 零售商.

retain [ri'tein] *vt* keep; continue to hold
保留; 保持: *You must retain your tick-
ets.* 你們的票一定要保留. *The dull
speaker could not retain the interest
of his audience.* 枯燥無味的演說者無
法保持聽衆的興趣.

retaliate [ri'tælieit] *vi* pay back one
wrong or injury with another 報復; 反
擊: *If you strike me, I shall retaliate.*
你若打我, 我就還手打你. **retaliation**
[ritæli'eiʃən] *nc / u.*

retarded [ri'tɑ:did] *adj* (usu. with reference to the mental and educational
development of children) developing
more slowly than is normal (通常指孩
子的智育發展) 遲鈍的.

reticent ['retisnt] *adj* not saying much
沉默寡言的; *be reticent about one's
past* 對往事諱莫如深. **reticence** *nu.*

retinue ['retinju:] *nc* group of servants
and followers going with a person
(esp. one of high rank) (尤指高級人士
的) 隨員, 侍從.

retire [ri'taiə*] *vt / i* **1** give up one's job,
or be required to do so (usu. because

one is getting old) (使) 退休 (通常因年老緣故): *Most teachers retire at 65.* 多數教師在65歲時退休. **2** go away to where it is quiet 隱居: *retire from society* 遁世隱居. **3** go to bed (*o. f.* in sense **3**) 就寢 (義 **3** 爲舊義). **retired** *adj* no longer doing a job (usu. because of one's age) 退休的 (通常因年齡緣故): *a retired civil servant* 一個退休的公務員. **retirement** *nu* state of being retired 退休; 隱居. **retiring** *adj* not anxious to meet other people 不愛交際的: *be of a retiring nature* 生性不愛交際.

retort [ri'tɔːt] *vt* / *i* reply quickly and sharply (e. g. to an accusation) (例如: 對非難) 反駁. Also 亦作 *nc* reply 回嘴, 反唇相譏.

retrace [ri'treis] *vt* go back over 折回; 回顧; 追想: *retrace one's steps from where one started* 順開始的原路返回; *retrace past events in one's memory* 回顧記憶中的往事.

retract [ri'trækt] *vt* / *i* **1** take back; deny; withdraw 收回; 否認; 撤銷: *retract a statement / an offer etc.* 撤回聲明 / 提議等. **2** draw back or in 縮回; 縮進. *A cat can retract its claws.* 貓能縮回它的爪子. **retractable** *adj* able to be retracted 可收回的; 可縮回的.

retreat [ri'triːt] *vi* go back; withdraw 撤退; 退卻: *The army was defeated and had to retreat.* 部隊潰敗, 不得不退卻. Also 亦作 *nc* / *u* **1** act of retreating 撤退. **2** place where one goes to rest 休息處所, 隱退處所.

retribution [retri'bjuːʃən] *nu* punishment that is deserved 應得的懲罰; 報應: *retribution for evil deeds* 作惡多端得到報應.

retrieve [ri'triːv] *vt* **1** get back something which has been lost 尋回; 找回. **2** put something back to the way it was before 恢復; 挽回: *retrieve one's fortunes* i. e. end a period of bad luck 又走好運, 即: 結束壞時運. **retriever** *nc* dog trained to bring back shot birds to its master (經訓練) 可啣回獵物的獵犬.

retrograde ['retrougreid] *adj* making worse 使惡化的: *a retrograde action* i. e. something which will make matters worse 使情況惡化的行動, 即: 使事態變壞的行動.

retrospect ['retrəspekt] *nu* act of looking at past events 回顧. **retrospective** [retrou'spektiv] *adj* having an effect on something already done 有追溯效力的: *retrospective legislation* i. e. laws which make illegal something which has already been done 追溯法, 即: 對業已做了的某些事可判定爲非法的法律. **in retrospect** when looking back at past events 回顧.

return [ri'tɜːn] *vt* / *i* **1** go back; come back 歸去; 回來: *return to one's village* 回鄉. **2** give back 歸還: *return a book to the library* 把書還給圖書館. **3** make an official announcement 正式宣佈: *The jury returned a verdict of guilty* 陪審團裁決有罪. **4** elect someone to Parliament 選出某人爲議會議員. Also 亦作 *nc* / *u* **1** going or coming back 歸去; 回來: *On my return, I found the house empty.* 我回來時, 發現房子空空的. **2** official statement 正式報告: *the election returns* i. e. statement of who has been elected 選舉結果公報, 即: 關於誰當選的報告. **3** (often *pl*) amount received; profit (常用複數) 贏利; 利潤: *a business which gives good returns* 一間很有賺頭的企業. Also 亦作 *adj* having to do with returning 回來的; 歸去的: *the return journey* i. e. the journey back 回程, 即: 返回的旅程; (*Brit* 英) *a return*

ticket i. e. a ticket which allows one to get to a place and then come back again 來回票, 即: 來回路程都有效的票. (*US* 美 **round-trip ticket**). **returnable** *adj* that can, or must, be returned 可送回的; 應送回的.

reunion [riːˈjuːnɪən] *nc* **1** act of joining together again 再結合. **2** meeting of friends or colleagues who have been separated for a long time (久別的親友、同事的)聚會. **reunite** [riːjuːˈnait] *vt/i*

rev [rev] *nc* revolution of an engine in a car etc. (汽車等發動機的)旋轉. Also 亦作 *vi* (with **up**) cause an engine to move faster (與 up 連用)使發動機加速. *rev up a motorbike* 使摩托車加速. *past* 過去式和過去分詞 **revved**. (both *informal*). (均爲非正式).

reveal [riˈviːl] *vt* **1** make known 洩露; 透露. *reveal a secret* 洩露秘密. allow to be seen 顯露; 顯示. *a remark that reveals one's ignorance of something* 一語顯露出某人對某事的無知. **revelation** [revəˈleiʃən] **1** *nu* act of revealing 洩露; 透露; 顯示, 啓示. **2** *nc* something which is revealed (esp. something surprising or important) 洩露或透露出來的事物(尤指令人吃驚或重大的事件).

reveille [riˈvæli] *nc/u* signal for soldiers to get up in the morning (軍人)起床號; *sound (the) reveille* 吹起床號.

revel [ˈrevl] *vi* make merry; pass the time by drinking, dancing etc. 行樂; 縱酒狂歡. *past* 過去式和過去分詞 **revelled.** (*US* 美 **reveled**). **reveller** *nc* (*US* 美 **reveler**). **revelry** *nu* wild and noisy merrymaking 狂歡作樂. **revel in something** enjoy very much 酷愛; *He revels in hard work.* 他酷愛艱苦工作.

revelation [revəˈleiʃən] *nc/u* see 見 **reveal**.

revenge [riˈvendʒ] *vt* punish a person in return for some wrong that he has done to oneself 報仇; 報復. Also 亦作 *nu* punishment given because of some wrong that has been received 報仇; 報復; *kill someone in revenge* 殺死某人以報仇雪恨; *take revenge on someone* 向某人報仇; *get one's revenge* i. e. punish somebody in this way 盡雪前恥, 即: 爲報復而懲罰某人. see *Note* on **avenge** 見 avenge 的說明. **revengeful** *adj* feeling or showing a wish for revenge 一心要報仇的; 不共戴天的.

revenue [ˈrevənjuː] *nc/u* money coming in (esp. to the government from taxes etc.) 收入(尤指政府的稅收等).

reverberate [riˈvəːbəreit] *vt/i* throw back sound; be thrown back; be filled with sound (使)反響; 回響; *The sound of his voice reverberated from wall to wall.* 他的聲音從一堵堵牆上回響開來. **reverberation** [rivəːbəˈreiʃən] *nc/u.*

revere [riˈviə*] *vt* respect deeply 崇敬; *The temple was revered as a sacred place.* 這座廟宇被推崇爲聖地. **reverence** [ˈrevərns] *nu* feeling of great respect 崇敬之情; *hold someone / something in reverence* i. e. respect deeply 崇敬某人/某物, 即: 十分敬重. **the Reverend** title for clergymen 對牧師的尊稱; *the Reverend James Brown / the Reverend Mr Brown* 詹姆士·布朗牧師/布朗牧師先生. *Note* 說明: it is usu. considered incorrect to say *the Reverend Brown* or *Reverend Brown* 通常認爲, the Reverend Brown 或 Reverend Brown 的說法是不正確的. **reverent** [ˈrevərnt] *adj* feeling or showing reverence 恭敬的; 虔誠的.

(*opp* 反義詞 **irreverent**).

reverie ['rɛvəri] *nc / u* daydream; state of thinking pleasant thoughts 白日夢; 美好幻想: *lost in reverie* 想入非非.

reverse [ri'vɜːs] *adj* opposite 相反的: *on the reverse side* 在反面.Also 亦作 *nc / u* **1** opposite 相反: *The result was the reverse of what I expected.* 結果與我所期望的相反. **2** back; opposite side 背面; 反面: *Turn the coin over and see what is on the reverse.* 翻轉這枚硬幣, 看看背面上是甚麼. **3** defeat 失敗: *suffer an unexpected reverse* 遭到意外的失敗. **4** gear which causes a car to go backwards 汽車的倒檔: *put a car into reverse* 把車倒開.Also 亦作 *vt* **1** cancel 取消: *reverse a decision* 取消決定. **2** cause to go in the opposite direction (使)倒退: *reverse a car* 開倒車. **3** put in the opposite position 顛倒: *reverse arms* i.e. point a rifle downwards 倒槍, 即: 槍口朝下. **reversal** *nc* act of reversing or being reversed 取消; 倒退; 顛倒. **reversible** *adj* **1** that can be reversed 可取消的; 可倒退的; 可顛倒的. **2** able to be used on either side 正反兩用的: *reversible cloth* 正反面兩用的布.

revert [ri'vɜːt] *vi* go back; return 恢復; 復歸: *When the ground was not cultivated, it reverted to jungle.* 這塊地不耕種時, 又恢復成叢林.

review [ri'vjuː] *vt / i* **1** examine again; go over again 再檢查; 回顧: *review the situation* 審時度勢; *review the events of the day* 回顧一天來的事件. **2** write a report on what one has read 評論: *review books for a Sunday newspaper* 爲一家星期日報刊寫書評. **3** inspect soldiers etc in a special ceremony 檢閱(軍隊等).Also 亦作 *nc / u* **1** act of reviewing 再檢查; 回顧; 評論; 檢閱: *The government policy is under re-view.* 政府的方針政策正經受審查. **2** article written about books etc. 書評; 評論文章: *His book got good reviews.* 他的書獲得好評. **3** special ceremony of inspection of soldiers etc.: 檢閱(軍隊等): *a naval review* 海軍檢閱. **4** regularly appearing paper or magazine which gives an account of new books, recent events etc. 評論性報刊、雜誌. **reviewer** *nc* person who writes reviews for a newspaper etc. 評論家.

revise [ri'vaiz] *vt* **1** read through something carefully (esp. in order to correct or improve) (尤指爲改正或改進而)校閱; 校訂. **2** change one's opinion of something 修正, 改變(對某事的看法): *revise one's opinion* 改變意見. **revision** [ri'viʒən] *nc / u* act of revising; something revised 校閱; 校訂; 修正, 修改; 校訂本, 修訂版.

revive [ri'vaiv] *vt / i* **1** come or bring back to health or consciousness (使)康復; (使)蘇醒: *After a few minutes the rescued man began to revive.* 幾分鐘後, 被救的人開始蘇醒. **2** make or become fresh and lively again (使)復活; (使)重振精神: *revive someone's spirits* 使某人重振精神. **3** bring back into use 復用; 復興: *revive an old play / custom etc.* 重演一齣老戲/復興舊風俗等. **revival 1** *nc / u* act of reviving or being revived 復活; 復用. **2** *nc* attempt to cause greater interest in religion by holding special sermons, religious services etc. (試圖提高信教興趣的)信仰復興運動.

revoke [ri'vouk] *vt* cancel 取消: *revoke an order* 撤銷一道命令.

revolt [ri'voult] *vt* **1** rise against a leader or the government 反叛; 造反: *the troops revolted* 軍隊嘩變. **2** cause to be disgusted (使)嫌惡. *Their cruel behaviour revolted him.* 他們的暴行令

他厭惡. Also 亦作 *nc / u* rebellion 造反; 叛亂; *be in a state of revolt* 處在叛亂狀態. **revolting** *adj* disgusting; extremely unpleasant 令人噁心的; 令人反感的.

revolution [revəˈluːʃən] **1** *nc* armed rising against the government 革命. **2** *nc / u* great change 巨大的變革. *The invention of the motorcar has brought about a revolution in transport* 發明汽車使交通發生巨大的變革. **3** *nc* movement of something in a circle 環繞; 旋轉; *the revolution of the earth round the sun* 地球繞着太陽的公轉. **4** *nc* one complete movement in a circle 旋轉一週; *fifty revolutions per minute* 每分鐘旋轉五十次. see 見 **revolve**. **revolutionary** *adj* **1** connected with a revolution 革命的; 革命性的; 旋轉的. **2** suggesting or causing great changes (暗示或引起)改革性的, 大變革的; *revolutionary ideas* 大變革的思想. Also 亦作 *nc* someone who wants great political changes (usu. by violent means)(通常想用暴力實施政治大變革的)革命家, 革命者. **revolutionize** *vt* cause great changes in 徹底變革.

revolve [riˈvɔlv] *vt / i* move round in a circle 繞轉: *The earth revolves round the sun* 地球繞着太陽公轉. see 見 **revolution**.

revolver [riˈvɔlvə*] *nc* type of pistol 左輪手槍.

revulsion [riˈvʌlʃən] *nu* (often with **a**) sudden and complete change of feeling from liking to hate or disgust (常與 **a** 連用)感情突變; 嫌惡; 反感.

reward [riˈwɔːd] *nc* **1** something given in return for a service 報答; 報酬. **2** money given for the return of something that has been lost or stolen, or for information given to the police 酬金; 獎賞. Also 亦作 *vt* give a reward

報答; 獎賞: *reward someone for his services* 獎賞某人作出的貢獻; *reward someone's bravery* 嘉獎某人的英勇行爲. **rewarding** *adj* bringing great benefits or rewards 很有益的; 有價值的: *a rewarding experience* 很有價值的經驗.

rhapsody [ˈræpsədi] *nc* something said or written which shows that one is wildly delighted (顯示狂喜心情的) 狂話, 狂文, 狂詩. *go into rhapsodies* i.e. say how delighted one is 熱情讚嘆, 即: 大談多麼高興的話.

rhetoric [ˈretərik] *nu* art of using words to persuade 修辭學. **rhetorical** [riˈtɔrikl] *adj* **1** concerned with rhetoric 修辭上的. **2** intended to arouse the emotions 誇張的; 矯飾的, 華麗的.

rheumatism [ˈruːmətizəm] *nu* disease causing painful swelling of the joints 風濕病. **rheumatic** [ruːˈmætik] *adj* **1** connected with rheumatism 風濕病的. **2** having, or liable to have, rheumatism (易)患風濕病的.

rhinoceros [raiˈnɔsərəs] *nc* type of large, thickskinned animal with a horn on its nose, found in Africa and Asia 犀牛(產於非洲、亞洲, 皮厚、鼻上長一角的大動物).

rhododendron [roudəˈdendrn] *nc* kind of shrub with oval leaves and large flowers 杜鵑花(屬).

rhombi [ˈrɔmbai] *pl* of **rhombus**. rhombus 的複數.

rhombus [ˈrɔmbəs] *nc* four-sided figure with equal sides, and angles which are not right angles 菱形, 斜方形.

rhubarb [ˈruːbɑːb] *nu* plant with thick juicy stalks which can be cooked, sweetened and eaten as food 大黃(莖粗大多汁, 可加糖煮食).

rhyme, rime [raim] **1** *nu* sameness of sound in the last part of words (e.g.

between *chair* and *dare* or *repeat* and *defeat*) 韻; 韻腳 (詞的尾音相同, 例如: chair 和 dare 同韻, repeat 和 defeat 同韻) . **2** *nc* verse or verses with words that rhyme 詩; 押韻文.Also 亦作 *vi* sound the same in the last part 押韻: *What words rhyme with 'school'?* 哪些詞跟'school'押韻呢?

rhythm [ˈriðəm] *nc / u* regular beat of music, dancing, poetry etc. 節奏; 節拍; 韻律. **rhythmic, rhythmical** [ˈriðmik(l)] *adj.*

rib [rib] *nc* any one of the curved bones stretching from the backbone round to the chest 肋骨. **ribbed** *adj* having narrow parts raised a bit above the surface 表面有稜線的: ribbed silk 羅紋綢.

ribald [ˈribəld] *adj* causing offence by indecent talk or behaviour 講下流話的; 粗野下流的: *a ribald person* 言行下流的人; *a ribald song* 下流歌曲.

ribbon [ˈribən] *nc / u* **1** long, narrow band of silk or other material 絲帶; 狹長帶子: *tied with a silk ribbon* 用一條絲帶紮上 . **2** anything like this in shape 狹長的東西: *typewriter ribbon* 打字帶.

rice [rais] *nu* white grain from a plant grown widely in India, China and other places, which is cooked and eaten as food 稻米; 大米.

rich [ritʃ] *adj* **1** having a lot of money and possessions 富有的; 有錢的: *a rich man* 富人. **2** producing much 肥沃的; 富饒的: *rich soil* 沃土. **3** showing signs of wealth 昂貴的; 華麗的: *rich clothes and jewels* 昂貴的衣服和珠寶. **4** (with reference to food) containing a lot of sugar, cream, butter, eggs, flavouring etc. (指食物) 含大量糖、奶油、牛油蛋、調味品的; 豐盛的: *rich food* 豐盛的食物. **5** deep; strong

深沉的; 醇厚的: *rich colours / sounds etc.* 鮮麗的顏色 / 洪亮的聲音等.

riches *npl* a lot of money and possessions 財富; 財寶. **the rich** *npl* wealthy people 富人.

rick [rik] *nc* stack of hay, straw etc. 一堆乾草 (或稻草等).

rickets [ˈrikits] *nc* disease of children, characterised by softness of the bones caused by deficiency of vitamin D 軟骨病 (小兒因缺乏維他命D所致).

rickety [ˈrikiti] *adj* likely to break or fall down 搖搖欲墜的: *a rickety old chair* 一張搖搖欲墜的舊椅子.

rickshaw [ˈrikʃɔ:] *nc* small, two-wheeled carriage pulled by a man 人力車, 黃包車.

ricochet [ˈrikəʃei] *nc / u* jumping movement of a bullet or stone etc when it hits against something (子彈或石片擊中某物後的)彈, 跳飛; 漂掠.Also 亦作 *vt / i* move, cause to move, in this way 跳飛; 漂掠: *A bullet can ricochet off a wall* 子彈打在牆壁上可能會跳飛出來. *pres part* 現在分詞 **ricocheting** [ˈrikəʃeiiŋ]. *past* 過去式和過去分詞 **ricocheted** [ˈrikəʃeid].

rid [rid] *vt* make free from 擺脫; 除去: *rid a house of rats* 消除屋內的老鼠. *past* 過去式和過去分詞 **rid. get rid of 1** make oneself free from 擺脫; 除去: *try to get rid of unwelcome visitors* 設法擺脫不受歡迎的客人. **2** do away with 去掉; 廢除.

ridden [ˈridn] past part of **ride.** ride 的過去分詞.

riddle¹ [ˈridl] *nc* puzzling question, situation, person etc. 謎 (難理解的問題、情況、人等): *Can you answer this riddle?* 你能解答這個謎嗎? *That man is a riddle to me* i.e. I cannot understand him. 此人對我來說是個謎.即: 我無法理解他.

riddle² [ridl] *vt* put many holes in (在…上面)打許多洞: *The door was riddled with bullets.* 門被子彈打得盡是窟窿.

ride [raid] *vt / i* **1** sit on something and be taken along by it 騎;乘: *ride (on) a horse* 騎馬. **2** be carried along in something 乘;搭: *ride in a bus* 乘公共汽車. Also 亦作 *nc* journey on the back of a horse, in a car etc. (騎馬、乘車等)旅行: *go for a ride in the park* 到公園去騎一會馬. *past tense* 過去式 **rode** [roud]. *past part* 過去分詞 **ridden** [ridn]. **rider** *nc* **1** someone who rides 騎馬的人, 騎師. **2** statement added on to the end of a document, official statement, verdict of a jury etc. (公文、正式聲明、陪審團裁決書等後的)附文, 附件.

ridge [ridʒ] *nc* **1** edge where two upward sloping surfaces meet 脊: *the ridge of a roof* 屋脊. **2** long, narrow stretch of raised land or hills 狹長高地;山脊. **3** any long, narrow object raised above the surrounding surface 隆起的脊狀物.

ridicule ['ridikju:l] *vt* make fun of 嘲笑. Also 亦作 *nu* words or actions that make fun of someone / something 嘲笑;嘲弄;奚落, 挖苦. **ridiculous** [ri'dikjuləs] *adj* foolish; deserving ridicule 愚蠢的, 可笑的, 荒謬的.

rife [raif] *pred adj* common; found everywhere 普遍的;流行的: *Crime is rife in this city.* 犯罪在這個城市十分猖獗.

riff-raff ['rifræf] *nu* worthless people of the lowest class 賤民;地痞;渣滓.

rifle¹ ['raifl] *nc* gun with a very long barrel (usu. fired from the shoulder) 步槍;來復槍.

rifle² ['raifl] *vt* search through and steal everything of value 搜劫;搶劫: *All the drawers had been rifled.* 所有的抽屜都被洗劫一空.

rift [rift] *nc* split; crack; break 裂縫;隙縫;裂口: *cause a rift between two friends* 使兩個朋友離乾不和.

rig [rig] *vt* (with reference to an election etc.) bring about the result that one wants by dishonest means (指選舉等)操縱;舞弊. *past* 過去式和過去分詞 **rigged. rigging** *nu* ropes etc used to support the masts and sails of a ship (支撐船桅和帆的)索具等. **'oil rig** type of installation, used for drilling for oil under the sea 海上鑽油台. **rig something up** put something together quickly, using whatever materials are available (用一切可用的材料)趕忙拼湊: *rig up a shelter* 匆匆搭起一個遮蔽所.

right¹ [rait] *adj* **1** good; just 對的;正當的: *do what is right* 凡是對的,就做. **2** correct 正確的: *give the right answer.* 作出正確的回答. **3** best; proper 最好的;適當的: *The stain doesn't show on the right side* i.e. the side that is meant to be seen 污點沒顯露在讓人看得見的一面上. **4** healthy 健康的: *in his right mind* i.e. sane 他神智健全. (*opp* **wrong** in senses 1 and 2 義 1 和義 2 的反義詞爲 wrong). Also 亦作 *adv / intensifier* **1** properly; correctly 適當地;正確地: *You did it right the first time.* 你第一次做對了. *I hope it turns out right* i.e. succeeds 我希望事情順利. 即:成功. **2** exactly 正好;就: *Stop right there.* 就停在那裏. **3** directly; not going to one side or the other 直接地;一直地: *Go right on to the end of the road.* 一直走到路的盡頭. **4** completely 完全地: *He fell right off the chair.* 他從椅子上完全跌下來. Also 亦作 **1** *nu* what is good and just 正當: *know the difference between right and wrong* 明辨是非. **2** *nc / u* just claim; something to which one is entitled 正當權利; 有權要求的東西; *She has no right to be so rude.* 她無權這樣無禮. *I have a right / the right to say what I think.* 我有權說我想說的話. Also 亦作 *vt* correct; put something the way it should be 改正; 糾正; *right an injustice* 洗雪冤屈. **righteous** ['raitʃəs] *adj* virtuous; just 正直的; 正義的: *the righteous and the wicked* 正直的人和邪惡的人; *righteous anger* 義憤. (opp 反義詞 **unrighteous**). **rightful** *adj* lawful; according to justice 合法的; 合理的: *the rightful owner* 合法所有人. **rightfully** *adv* **all right** see 見 **all**. '**right angle** angle of 90° 直角. **right now** (mainly *US*) immediately (主要用於美) 立刻. **be in the right** be correct; have justice on one's side 對的; 有理的.

right² [rait] *adj / adv / nu* (of or on) the side of a person's body that is farther away from the heart 右邊的 (遠離心臟的一則): *my right hand* 我的右手. *In Europe road traffic mostly keeps to the right* 在歐洲, 街上車輛行人多靠右行. *Turn right when you reach the square.* 你到了廣場, 就向右轉. (opp 反義詞 **left**). '**right-hand** *adj* on the right side 右手的; 右邊的. '**right-handed** *adj* using the right hand rather than the left 用右手的: *a righthanded person* 慣用右手的人. **the right, the right wing** *nu* (politics) those who are conservative, or against socialism or communism 右派; 右翼 (指政界中持保守觀點或反對社會主義、共產主義的人); *a right-wing politician* 一名右翼政客.

rigid ['ridʒid] *adj* 1 stiff 堅硬的. 2 strict 嚴格的: *rigid rules* 嚴格的規則. **rigidly** *adv* **rigidity** [ri'dʒiditi] *nu.*

rigmarole ['rigmaroul] *nu* long story without much meaning; foolish talk 冗長無聊的廢話; 胡言亂語.

rigour ['rigə⁎] *(US* 美 **rigor**) 1 *nu* strictness; lack of mercy 嚴格; 嚴厲. 2 *nc* (often *pl*) hardship (常用複數) 艱苦. *the rigours of winter* 寒冬的嚴酷. **rigorous** *adj* 1 strict 嚴格的: *rigorous discipline* 嚴格的紀律. 2 exact 嚴密的: *a rigorous search* 嚴密搜查. **rigorously** *adv.*

rile [rail] *vt* annoy; make angry 惹怒; 激怒.

rim [rim] *nc* (usu. of something round) edge (通常指圓形物體的) 邊; 緣: *the rim of a cup / wheel etc.* 杯緣/輪緣等.

rind [raind] *nc / u* hard outer surface of cheese, bacon etc. 奶酪皮; 醃肉皮; 外皮.

ring¹ [riŋ] *nc* 1 circle 圓圈; 圓環: *stand in a ring round something* 繞某物站成一圈. 2 round band of metal or other material 金屬環; 環狀物: *a gold wedding ring* 結婚金戒指. 3 any kind of closed-in space where things can be shown 陳列場; 表演場地: *a cattle ring* 家畜展覽場; *a boxing ring* i.e. a square area where two men can fight using their fists 拳擊場, 即: 兩個人可進行拳擊的方形場. 4 group of people working together for their own purposes (usu. unfair or dishonest purposes) (通常指從事不法勾當的) 幫派; 集團. **ringlet** *nc* long hanging curl of hair 鬈髮. '**ringleader** someone who leads others in doing wrong 首領; 黨魁. '**ring road** road built round a town to relieve traffic in the centre 環城公路.

ring² [riŋ] *vt / i* 1 give sound like a bell 發出鈴似的響聲; 鳴: *The telephone is ringing.* 電話在響. 2 cause to give this sound 使響; 使鳴: *ring a bell* 按

鈴. **3** telephone 打電話: *I'll ring you later.* 我以後會打電話給你. **4** have a loud, hollow sound 回響: *The room rang with his laughter.* 房間回響着他的笑聲. *The sound of his voice rang in my ears.* 他的聲音還回響在我的耳朵裏. *past tense* 過去式 **rang** [ræŋ]. *past part* 過去分詞 **rung** [rʌŋ]. Also 亦作 *nc* noise of a bell 鈴聲: *a ring at the door* 門鈴響了. **ring off** end a telephone conversation 掛斷電話. **ring someone up** phone 打電話給 (某人): *I'll ring you up later.* 我以後會給你打電話.

rink [riŋk] *nc* area of ice or other smooth surface used for skating on 溜冰場: *an ice rink* 滑冰場.

rinse [rins] *vt* wash with clean water (usu. to remove soap) 漂清; 漂洗: *rinse (out) a shirt* 漂洗一件襯衫; *rinse soap out of one's hair* 冲洗頭髮上的肥皂沫. Also 亦作 *nc* act of rinsing 漂清; 漂洗: *give clothes a rinse before drying them* 先把衣服漂洗乾淨, 然後才弄乾.

riot ['raiət] *nc* **1** wild and unlawful behaviour by a group of people 暴動; 騷亂: *The police came to put down the riots.* 警察前來鎮壓騷亂. **2** wild behaviour 放蕩; 鬧事. **3** bright display 鮮艷奪目: *a riot of colour* 彩色繽紛. Also 亦作 *vi* take part in a riot 參與鬧事(暴動): *riot in the streets* 街上在鬧事. **rioter** *nc* **riotous** *adj* disorderly; wild 混亂的; 放蕩的: *riotous behaviour* 放蕩不羈的行為.

rip [rip] *vt / i* **1** pull or tear violently 用力撕開; 扯開: *rip a piece of cloth into small pieces* 把一塊布撕成碎片. **2** be torn 撕裂; 扯裂: *His coat ripped when it was caught in the door.* 他的大衣被門夾住時, 撕破了. *past* 過去式和過去分詞 **ripped**. Also 亦作 *nc: a rip in his* *coat* 他大衣上的一個裂口.

ripe [raip] *adj* fully grown and ready to be taken 成熟的: *ripe fruit* 成熟的水果; *ripe crops* 成熟的莊稼. **ripen** *vt / i* become or make ripe (使)成熟.

ripple ['ripl] *nc* **1** very small wave 微波; 漣漪: *the ripples in a stream* 溪流上的漣漪. **2** sound of a very small wave; sound like this 潺潺聲; 起伏聲: *the ripple of a stream* 溪流的潺潺聲; *a ripple of laughter* 一陣嘻嘻哈哈的笑聲. Also 亦作 *vt / i* **1** flow with ripples 起漣漪. **2** cause to have ripples 使起漣漪: *A wind rippled the surface of the lake.* 一陣風吹來, 使湖面泛起漣漪.

rise [raiz] *vi* **1** get up 起床: *rise from bed* 起床. **2** go higher 上升: *The level of the river is rising.* 河的水面在漲高. **3** start, begin 發生, 起源: *A quarrel rose between them.* 他們之間發生了爭吵. **4** rebel 造反: *The people rose against their rulers.* 人們起來反抗他們的統治者. *past tense* 過去式 **rose** [rouz]. *past part* 過去分詞 **risen** ['rizn]. Also 亦作 *nc* **1** (Brit) increase (英)增加: *a rise in wages* 增加工資. (US 美 **raise**). **2** small slope upwards 隆起的小斜坡: *a rise in the ground* 一個高地. see 見 **raise**.

risk [risk] *nc / u* danger; chance of meeting danger or harm 危險; 風險; 冒險: *If you go out in this weather, there is a risk of catching cold.* 你如果在這種天氣出門, 就有着涼危險. Also 亦作 *vt* **1** be or put in danger (使)冒…危險; 拚: *risk one's life* 拚着性命. **2** take a chance of meeting some harm 冒…風險: *risk being injured* 冒受傷的風險. **risky** *adj* dangerous 危險的.

rite [rait] *nc* ceremony (esp. a religious ceremony) (尤指宗教的)儀式; 典禮: *the marriage rites* 婚禮. **ritual** ['ritjuəl] *nc/u* system of rites 儀式；典禮：*the ritual of a church* 教堂的禮拜儀式．Also 亦作 *adj* connected with rites 宗教儀式的：*a ritual dance* 祭神舞蹈．

rival ['raivl] *nc* person who tries to get the same thing as another; person who tries to do better than another 競爭者；對手；敵手．Also 亦作 *vt* try to be the same as or better than 與…競爭；與…對抗．與…比高低．*past* 過去式和過去分詞 **rivalled**. (*US* 美 **rivaled**). Also 亦作 *adj* **rivalry** *nc/u* state of being rivals; competition 競爭；對抗；比賽．

river ['rivə*] *nc* wide stream of water flowing to the sea or into a lake or another river 河；江．

rivet ['rivit] *nc* metal bolt like a nail, used for fastening sheets of metal together 鉚釘．Also 亦作 *vt* 1 fasten with rivets 鉚接，鉚牢．2 fix firmly 固定：*He riveted his eyes on me.* 他的眼睛死死地盯著我．3 attract strongly 吸引：*The scene riveted our attention.* 那風景吸引我們的注意．

roach¹ [routʃ] *nc* cockroach 蟑螂．

roach² [routʃ] *nc* European freshwater fish related to the carp 石斑魚(歐洲産的一種鯉科淡水魚)．

road [roud] *nc* 1 way specially prepared for people, cars etc to travel on 道路；公路：*the roads out of London* 倫敦城外公路．*travel by road* 乘車旅行．2 way; means 途徑；手段；方法：*the road to success* 走向成功的途徑．'**road-block** barrier put across a road by police etc for some purpose 路障．'**roadway** middle part of a road which cars etc use i.e. not the footpath, which pedestrians use 車行道，即：不是人行道．'**roadworthy** *adj* (of a car etc.) in a suitable or safe condition to be driven on the roads (汽車等)適

於在路上行駛的．

roam [roum] *vi* wander 漫遊；閑逛：*roam about the country* 漫遊全國．*He likes to roam.* 他喜歡去閑逛．

roar [rɔ:*] *nc* loud, deep sound 吼；咆哮；吼嘯：*the roar of a lion* 獅子的怒吼．Also 亦作 *vt/i* 1 make a sound like this 吼；咆哮；呼嘯：*The crowd roared.* 羣衆怒吼．2 say loudly 大聲說：*roar a command* 大聲發出命令．3 move making a loud, deep sound 轟鳴移動：*The plane roared past us.* 飛機轟鳴地掠過我們．

roast [roust] *vt/i* cook or heat by using dry heat i.e. over a fire, or in an oven (在火上或烤箱中)烤；烘：*roast meat* 烤肉．Also 亦作 *nc/u* meat that has been roasted 烤肉．

rob [rɔb] *vt* take away by using force 搶奪；搶劫：*Thieves robbed him of all his money.* 竊賊搶走他所有的錢．*past* 過去式和過去分詞 **robbed**. **robber** *nc* **robbery** *nc/u* act of robbing 搶奪；搶劫．

robe [roub] *nc* 1 long, loose outer garment 長袍．2 garment of this kind worn by some officials 官服；袍 *a judge's robes* 法官的袍．

robin ['rɔbin] *nc* type of small, piump, brown bird with a red breast 知更鳥；紅襟鳥．

robot ['roubɔt] *nc* machine that can work like a man 機器人．

robust [rou'bʌst] *adj* strong; healthy 强壯的：*a robust man* 壯漢．

rock¹ [rɔk] *nc/u* 1 large mass of stone 岩石：*cut a road through solid rock* 鑿穿硬岩築路．2 piece of stone 石塊：*Rocks fell down the hillside.* 一塊塊石頭滾下山坡．3 sweet in the form of a stick 硬條棒棒糖．**rocky** full of rocks; like a rock 多石的；硬如石的：*rocky soil* 多石的土壤．'**rock-bottom** *adj* very lowest; most inferior 最低的; 最賤的: *rockbottom prices (informal)* 最低價格(非正式). **rockery, 'rock garden** garden, or part of a garden, with plants growing between rocks (種植岩生植物的)岩石庭園. **on the rocks 1** (with reference to a ship) wrecked, destroyed on the rocks in the sea (指船)觸礁的. **2** (of whisky etc.) with ice (*informal* in sense **2**) (指威士忌酒等)加冰的(義 2 爲非正式).

rock² [rɔk] *vt / i* **1** move backwards and forwards or from side to side (前後或左右)搖動: *rock oneself to sleep* 搖動到使自己睡着. **2** move violently 搖撼: *The building rocked during the earthquake.* 大樓在這次地震中搖拽. **'rocking chair** chair made so that it can move backwards and forwards 搖椅. **'rocking horse** child's toy in the form of a horse which can move backwards and forwards 搖木馬.

rocket ['rɔkit] *nc* **1** large tube which goes high into the air by sending out jets of burning fuel and which can be used as a weapon or to carry men into space etc. (軍事、航天用的)火箭; 火箭彈; 運載火箭. **2** small object which goes up into the air and explodes into designs of different colours 烟花, 燄火: *The people fired rockets to celebrate their victory.* 人們放烟花慶祝勝利.

rod [rɔd] *nc* long piece of metal, wood or plastic (金屬、木或塑膠製的)竿; 桿: *a fishing rod* 釣魚竿.

rode [roud] past tense of **ride.** ride 的過去式.

rodent ['roudnt] *nc* small animal of the kind that has special teeth for gnawing things (e.g. rats, mice, rabbits etc.) 齧齒動物(如鼠、兔等).

rodeo ['roudiou] *nc* (*US*) show of shill

in which untamed horses are ridden etc. (美)騎烈馬等的騎術表演.

roe¹ [rou] *nu* mass of eggs in a fish 魚卵塊.

roe² [rou] *nc* kind of small deer found in the woods of Europe and Western Asia (產自歐洲和西亞森林的)小鹿. *pl* 複數 **roes** or **roe.**

rogue [roug] *nc* **1** dishonest person 騙子; 歹徒; 無賴. **2** mischievous person 淘氣鬼, 愛捉弄別人的人. **roguish** *adj* playful; mischievous 惡作劇的; 淘氣的.

role [roul] *nc* **1** part for an actor in a play (演員扮演的)角色: *an interesting role* 一個有趣的角色. **2** part a person plays in real life (現實生活中的)作用, 責任: *The headmaster plays an important role in the good running of a school.* 校長在辦好一所學校中起重要的作用.

roll [roul] *vt / i* **1** move along by turning over and over 滾動: *The ball rolled into the net.* 球滾進網裏. **2** make into the shape of a ball 把⋯弄圓, 把⋯圈成球狀: *roll paper into a ball* 把紙圈成球. **3** make something by putting it into the shape of a tube 捲: *roll a cigarette* 捲紙烟. **4** move from side to side 搖晃: *a ship rolling in the storm* 一艘在暴風雨中搖晃的船. **5** rise and fall in gentle slopes 徐緩起伏: *We admired the rolling countryside.* 我們欣賞這起伏有致的鄉村景色. **6** make a long, deep sound 發出隆隆聲: *Thunder rolled in the distance.* 遠處雷聲隆隆. *Drums rolled.* 鼓聲隆隆. Also 亦作 *nc* **1** something rolled up; something looking like a tube 一捲; 捲狀物: *a roll of carpet* 一捲地毯. **2** small loaf of bread 麵包捲: *breakfast rolls* 早餐吃的麵包捲. **3** long, deep sound 隆隆聲: *the roll of drums / thunder* 隆隆的

鼓聲/雷聲. **4** movement from side to side 搖動: *the roll of a ship* 船的搖動: **5** list 點名簿. *call the roll* i.e. read out the names on a list 點名, 即: 出聲讀點名簿上的名字. '**roller** *nc* heavy, tube-shaped piece of metal etc (used e.g. for smoothing grass or making a road even) (金屬製的)輥子(如輾草坪機、壓路機). '**roll call** reading out of names on a list (e.g. at a school or prison) 點名(如在學校或監獄). '**rolled** '**gold** thin covering of gold on another metal 金箔. '**roller skate** skate with small wheels, for moving on a smooth surface 輪式溜冰鞋. '**rolling pin** piece of wood or other material shaped like a tube and used for making dough flat 擀麵杖.

rollicking ['rɔlikiŋ] *adj* noisy and merry 嬉戲歡鬧的.

Roman ['roumən] *adj* connected with Rome 羅馬的: *Roman Empire* 羅馬帝國. Also 亦作 *nc* someone from Rome 羅馬人. **Roman Catholic** *nc* member of the Church of Rome 羅馬天主教徒. **roman numerals** numbers like LXXX, XL, MDCLV etc in which I＝1, V＝5, X ＝10, L＝50, C＝100, D＝500 and M＝ 1,000 羅馬數字, 如在 LXXX, MDCLV 等數中 I＝1, V＝5, X＝10, L＝ 50, C＝100, D＝500, M＝1,000.

romance [rə'mæns] **1** *nc* love story 愛情故事. **2** *nc* story or poem which tells of the adventures of kings, knights etc. 國王、騎士等的傳奇故事或詩篇. **3** *nu* love and adventure 愛情和冒險的浪漫生活: *in search of romance* 追求愛情和冒險的浪漫生活.

romantic [rə'mæntik] *adj* **1** dealing with love or adventure in a fanciful way; concerned with this 浪漫的; 風流的; 傳奇的; 想入非非的: *a romantic story* 一件風流韻事; *a romantic per-*

son 一個想入非非的人. **2** appealing to the feelings rather than reason 浪漫派的; 浪漫主義的(重感情勝過理性的): *romantic poetry* 浪漫派詩歌.

romp [rɔmp] *vi* run, jump and play about in a noisy way 頑皮嬉鬧: *The children like to romp in the garden.* 孩子們都喜歡在花園裏頑皮嬉鬧. Also 亦作 *nc* rough, lively kind of play 頑皮嬉鬧. **rompers** *npl* loose, outer clothes worn by young children when playing (小孩玩時穿的)寬鬆連褲外衣.

roof [ru:f] *nc* **1** top covering of a building 屋頂. **2** top covering of anything 頂部: *the roof of a car* 車頂; *the roof of the mouth* 上顎. Also 亦作 *vt* cover with a roof, act as a roof for 給…蓋上屋頂; 充當…的頂.

rook[1] [ruk] *nc* large, black bird which flies about in flocks (習慣羣飛的)白嘴鴉.

rook[2] [ruk] *nc* one of the pieces in a game of chess (國際象棋)車.

room [ru:m] **1** *nc* part of a house divided by walls from another part 房間; 室. **2** *nu* space for someone / something 空間; 空位: *Is there room in your car for one more person?* 你的車還可多載一個人嗎? **rooms** *npl* lodgings; rented house 出租的房間; 公寓: *living in rooms* 租房住. **roomy** *adj* having plenty of space 寬敞的; 寬闊的.

roost [ru:st] *nc* bar, pole on which birds rest 棲架; 雞舍: *a hen on a roost* 棲架上的一隻母雞. Also 亦作 *vi* sleep or rest on a roost 棲息. **rooster** *nc (US* 美)cock, male chicken 公雞.

root [ru:t] *nc* **1** part of a plant that is usu. under the ground 根: *the roots of a flower / tree etc.* 花根/樹根等. **2** cause; that which brings about something 根源; 原因: *the root of a prob-*

lem 問題的原因. *Money is the root of all evil.* 金錢是萬惡的根源.

rope [roup] *nc* thick, strong line or cord, made by twisting thinner cords together 粗繩; 纜.

rosary ['rouzəri] *nc* string of beads used in the Roman Catholic Church to count the number of prayers one has said (羅馬天主教徒祈禱用的)唸珠.

rose¹ [rouz] past tense of **rise.** rise 的過去式.

rose² [rouz] *nc* sweet-smelling flower which grows on a thorny stem, and can be red, white, pink or yellow. 薔薇花; 玫瑰花. **rosy** *adj* **1** pink 粉紅的: *rosy cheeks* 紅潤的面頰. **2** hopeful; bright 充滿希望的; 光明的: *a rosy future* 光明的未來. **rosette** [rou'zet] *nc* decoration made in the shape of a rose 薔薇花飾; 玫瑰花結.

roster ['rɔstə*] *nc* list of people showing what jobs they must do and when they must do them 勤務簿; 值勤表.

rostrum ['rɔstrəm] *nc* raised platform from which someone can speak 講壇.

rot [rɔt] *vt / i* **1** decay, go bad 腐爛; 變質: *The fruit was left to rot.* 水果放着爛掉. **2** cause to go bad 使變質: *wood rotted by the damp* 受潮濕腐爛的木頭. *past* 過去式和過去分詞 **rotted.** Also 亦作 *nu* **1** decay 腐爛: *wood affected by rot* 已經腐爛的木料. **2** nonsense 廢話; 胡說: *Don't talk rot! (informal* in sense 2) 別胡說! (義2為非正式) **rotten** *adj* **1** decayed; bad 腐爛的; 變壞的: *rotten eggs* 臭蛋. **2** bad; unpleasant thing 不愉快的: *a rotten film (informal* in sense 2) 一部壞電影 (義2為非正式).

rota ['routə] *nc* list of things to be done; list of persons to do certain things in a certain order 勤務簿; 值勤人員表.

rotary ['routəri] *adj* turning round, as a

wheel does 旋轉的; 轉動的: *a rotary movement* 旋轉運動. **rotate** [rou'teit] *vt / i* **1** move round a centre 旋轉: *The earth rotates on its axis.* 地球繞着地軸自轉. **2** change round in a regular manner (使)輪流: *rotate crops* 輪種作物. **rotation** [rou'teiʃən] *nc / u* **1** movement round a centre 旋轉. **2** regular change 輪流: *in rotation* i.e. one after the other in a regular way 輪流; 輪換.

rotund [rou'tʌnd] *adj* round and fat 圓胖胖的: *a rotund face* 圓胖面孔.

rough [rʌf] *adj* **1** not smooth; not level 粗糙的; 不平的: *a rough road* 崎嶇不平的道路. **2** uncomfortable 不舒服的: *a rough journey* 艱苦的旅程. **3** not polite; harsh 無禮的; 刺耳的: *a rough voice* 刺耳的聲音. **4** ill-mannered; ill-behaved 粗魯的; 粗野的: *rough companions* 粗野的夥伴. **5** not finished; not complete 未完成的; 不完全的: *a rough sketch* 草圖; *a rough idea* 不成熟的想法. **6** stormy 暴風雨的: *rough seas* 波濤洶湧的大海. Also 亦作 *nc* ill-mannered and violent person 粗暴的人. **roughness** *nu* **roughen** *vt / i* make or become rough (使)變粗糙. **roughly** *adv* **1** in a rough manner 粗糙地; 粗魯地. **2** about; approximately 大約; 約莫地: *There were roughly twenty people there.* 那裏大約有二十人.

roughage ['rʌfidʒ] *nu* **1** coarse fodder 素材; 粗飼料. **2** coarse food that promotes intestinal movement 粗糙食物.

roulette [ru:'let] *nu* gambling game played with a ball which moves on a revolving wheel 輪盤賭.

round [raund] *adj* **1** shaped like a circle or ball 圓形的; 球形的: *a round ball* 圓球. **2** full; complete 完整的; 完全

的: *a round dozen* 整整一打.Also 亦作 *nc / u* **1** stage in a game or competition (比賽) 回合; 局; 場: *a boxing match lasting ten rounds* 打了十個回合的拳擊比賽. *be defeated in the third round of a competition* 在比賽的第三輪中被打敗. **2** number of things one after the other; number of duties (一連串的)事情; 任務: *a policeman's round* 警察的巡邏任務. *the daily round* 日常工作. **3** bullet 子彈: *a round of ammunition* 一發子彈.Also 亦作 *adv* **1** in a circle or part of a circle 旋轉地; 圍繞地: *turn round* 轉過來; *wheels that go round* 旋轉的輪子; *gather round* i.e. be on all sides 聚集一起,即: 圍在一起. **2** by a longer way 迂迴地; 繞道地: *We went round by the post office, instead of coming straight here.* 我們不是直接來這裏,而是繞道經郵局走來. **3** for everyone 給每個人: *There are not enough cups to go round.* 沒有足夠的杯子供每人一個. **4** here and there; in different places nearby 到處; 四面八方: *I'm looking round to see if I can find my book.* 我正到處找,看是否能找到我的書.Also 亦作 *prep* **1** on all sides of 在…週圍: *build a fence round a field* 在一塊田地週圍築一道籬笆. **2** in a circle about 環繞: *walk round a tree* 繞着一棵樹散步. **3** so as to get to the other side of 繞過: *walk round a corner* 步行繞過拐彎地方.Also 亦作 *vt* go to the other side of 繞行: *round a bend in the road* 繞過路上的一道彎口. **rounders** *nu* game played by children with a ball (兒童玩的)軟球粗棒球. **'roundabout** *adj* not direct 間接的: *I heard it in a roundabout way* i.e. not in the direct, usual way. 這事我間接聽到的,即:非以直接、通常方法聽到的.Also 亦作 *nc* **1** part of a road

where cars cannot go directly on, but must go round in a circle 環行交叉路; 繞行道. **2** mechanical device used as entertainment for children on which they can go round in a circle, sitting on wooden horses etc. 旋轉木馬. **'roundsman** grocer, milkman or other tradesman who goes round to people's houses to accept orders or deliver goods (挨戶)推銷員; 送貨員. **'round 'trip 1** trip that comes back by a different route 週遊. **2** journey to a place and back to the starting point 來回旅程. **'round-'trip ticket** *(US)* return ticket (美)來回票. **round something off** finish completely 圓滿完成. **round someone / something up** get and bring together 把…趕攏; 使…集結; 圍捕: *round up cattle* 把牛趕在一起; *round up a gang of criminals* 把一夥罪犯一網打盡. **'roundup** *nc* act of rounding up 趕攏; 集結; 圍捕.

rouse [rauz] *vt / i* wake up; interest; excite 喚醒; 鼓勵; 激發: *rouse someone from sleep* 叫醒某人; *roused to anger* 激起怒火. **rousing** *adj*.

rout [raut] *vt* defeat completely; put to flight 徹底打敗; 打跑: *rout an army* 擊潰一支軍隊.Also 亦作 *nc* complete defeat; flight from danger 潰敗; 逃命.

route [ru:t] *nc* way one intends to go; road 路線; 航線: *What route are you taking?* 你要走哪條路線?

routine [ru:'ti:n] *nc* regular way of doing things 例行公事; 日常工作; 常規: *his usual routine* 他通常的例行公事.Also 亦作 *adj* ordinary; regular; usual 日常的; 例行的; 常規的: *a routine job* 日常工作.

rove¹ [rouv] *vi / t* wander 漫遊; 流浪. **2** (of the eyes) look in changing directions (眼睛)轉來轉去.Also 亦作 *nu* wandering 漫遊；流浪.

rove² [rouv] *vt* form (slivers of wool, cotton etc.) into slightly twisted strands in preparation for spinning 紡成粗紗. Also 亦作 *nc* roved sliver 粗紗.

row¹ [rou] *nc* **1** line of people or things 行；列；排: *children standing in a row* 站成一行的孩子. **2** line of seats in a theatre 劇場的一排座位.

row² [rou] *vt / i* **1** make a boat go forward by using oars (用槳) 划 (船): *row across a river* 划到河對岸. **2** take someone / something from one place to another by using a rowing boat 划船載運: *row someone across the river* 划船送某人渡河. **'rowing boat, 'row-boat** boat that is made to move by using oars 划艇.

row³ [rau] *nc* **1** quarrel 吵架: *have a row with someone* 跟某人爭吵. **2** loud noise 吵鬧: *make a row* 起哄. **3** trouble 麻煩: *get a row for not doing something properly (informal)* 因沒妥善辦某事而惹出麻煩 (非正式). **rowdy** ['raudi] *adj* rough and quarrelsome 粗暴吵鬧的. Also 亦作 *nc* rowdy person 粗暴的人；吵鬧的人. **rowdiness** *nu*.

royal ['rɔiəl] *adj* belonging to, or connected in some way with, a king or queen 王的；女王的；王室的；皇家的: *royal palace* 王宮；王宮. *the royal household* 王室. **royalist** *nc* person who supports a king, or government by a king 保皇黨員. **royalty** *nc / u* **1** royal persons 皇族: *be in the presence of royalty* i.e. in the company of a king or queen etc. 在御前，即: 在國王或女王等跟前. **2** payment made to a writer every time a copy of one of his books is sold, or to a musician whenever one of his records is played publicly etc.; payment made to some-

one who owns land which is being used for profit by someone else 版稅；上演稅；土地使用費: *He became rich on the royalties the oil company paid him.* 他靠石油公司付給他的礦區使用費變成富翁.

rub [rʌb] *vt / i* move one thing against another 擦；摩擦 *rub one's hands to warm them* 搓手取暖: *rub away / out a stain* i.e. remove it by rubbing 擦去污點，即：用擦的方法去除去. *past* 過去式和過去分詞 **rubbed.** Also 亦作 *nc* act of rubbing 摩擦: *give something a quick rub* 把某物快擦一下.

rubber ['rʌbə*] **1** *nu* substance obtained from a certain kind of tree, and used for making balls, tyres, shoes etc. 橡膠. **2** *nc* (Brit) piece of rubber used for removing pencil or pen marks (英) 橡皮擦. (US 美 **eraser). rubbery** *adj* like rubber 似橡膠的.

rubbish ['rʌbiʃ] *nu* **1** material that has been thrown away; useless stuff 廢物；垃圾. **2** nonsense 廢話: *talk rubbish* 胡說八道.

rubble ['rʌbl] *nu* broken stones or bricks 碎石；破磚: *After the earthquake, the village was just a pile of rubble* 地震後，村子只剩下一堆碎磚破瓦.

ruby ['ru:bi] *nc* red, precious stone 紅寶石；紅玉. Also 亦作 *adj* dark red in colour 深紅色的.

rucksack ['rʌksæk] *nc* bag carried on the back, used when walking long distances etc. (遠足用的)背包.

rudder ['rʌdə*] *nc* movable flat piece of wood or metal at the end of a boat, used to guide or steer it (船)舵.

ruddy ['rʌdi] *adj* red and healthy looking 紅潤的；氣色好的: *ruddy cheeks* 紅潤的面頰.

rude [ru:d] *adj* **1** not polite; illmannered 無禮的; 粗魯的: *a rude remark* 無禮的話; *a very rude person* 十分粗魯的人. **2** not done or made in an exact way; roughly made 簡陋的; 粗製的: *rude tools* 簡陋工具. **3** violent; harsh 猛烈的; 嚴厲的: *a rude shock* 猛烈衝擊. **rudely** *adv* **rudeness** *nu*.

rudiment ['ru:dimənt] *nc* (usu. *pl*) first things to be learnt in a subject (通常用複數) 初階; 基礎; 入門: *the rudiments of chemistry* 化學入門.

rudimentary [,ru:di'mentəri] *adj* elementary; to be learnt when beginning a subject 初步的; 簡單的; 基本的: *a few rudimentary facts* 一些基本事實.

ruffian ['rʌfiən] *nc* rough and cruel man 暴徒; 惡棍.

ruffle ['rʌfl] *vt / i* make or become uneven (使)變皺; 弄亂: *The wind ruffled the smooth surface of the lake* 風吹皺平靜的湖面. **2** make feathers stand up 竪起(羽毛): *The bird ruffled its feathers.* 這隻鳥竪起羽毛.

rug [rʌg] *nc* **1** covering for a floor (usu. made of wool or animal skin) (通常爲毛織或獸皮製的)地毯. **2** thick, warm piece of material which can be put over the legs when travelling etc. (旅行等蓋膝用的)圍毯.

rugby ['rʌgbi] *nu* kind of football in which the ball, which is ovalshaped, can be touched by the hands as well as the feet 橄欖球(橄欖形足球,可手足並用). (Also 亦作 **rugby football**).

rugged ['rʌgid] *adj* **1** rough and uneven 崎嶇不平的: *rugged countryside* 崎嶇不平的鄉間田野. **2** having many wrinkles; not regular or even in form 多皺紋的; 粗獷的: *a rugged brow* 滿是皺紋的額頭; *rugged features* 粗獷的容貌.

rugger ['rʌgə*] *nu* rugby football (*informal*) 橄欖球(非正式).

ruin ['ru:in] **1** *nu* complete loss or destruction 毀滅; 毀壞: *All his plans came to ruin.* 他所有的計劃全落空了. **2** *nc* building which has been partly destroyed 廢墟: *an interesting old ruin* 一個使人感興趣的古老廢墟. Also 亦作 *vt / i* destroy; be destroyed 毀滅: *His life was ruined by drink.* 酗酒毀掉他的一生. *Bad weather ruined our holiday.* 壞天氣毀了我們的假日. **ruins** *npl* what remains of a building which has been destroyed or has decayed 廢墟. **ruinous** *adj* bringing ruin; enough to cause ruin 毀滅性的; 足以使人破產的: *ruinous debts* 足以使人破產的債務.

rule [ru:l] **1** *nc* law; statement of what must be done 法規; 規則: *If you want to play this game, you must obey the rules.* 如果你要參加這場比賽, 你就必須遵守規則. **2** *nu* government; power 支配; 統治: *achieve freedom from foreign rule* 擺脫外國的統治. **3** *nc* habit; what is usu. done or what usu. happens 習慣; 慣例: *It is my rule to get up early.* 早起是我的習慣. *It never rains here, as a rule* i.e. normally. 通常(即: 在正常情況下), 這裏從不下雨. **4** *nc* straight piece of wood or metal etc used for measuring 尺: *a foot rule* i.e. one which measures 12 inches 一英尺長的尺, 即: 12英寸長的尺. Also 亦作 *vt / i* **1** be in control of; govern 控制; 統治: *rule a country* 統治一個國家. **2** decide; command 裁定, 裁決; 命令: *The judge ruled that the new evidence should be considered.* 法官裁決新的證據應予考慮. **3** mark lines on (用尺)在…劃綫. **ruler** *nc* **1** person who rules (e.g. a king) 統治者 (如國王) **2** straight piece of wood or metal etc used for measuring 尺. **ruling** *nc* decision made by someone in authority (e.g. a judge) 裁定,裁決;(法官的)判決.Also 亦作 *adj* that rules 統治的;裁決的;劃線用的. **work to rule** slow down work of a factory etc by keeping exactly to rules, in order to gain some object (e.g. higher wages) 怠工 (死扣規章而降低生產效率,以求達到提高工資等目的).

rum [rʌm] *nu* strong drink made from sugar cane 朗姆酒;甘蔗酒.

rumble ['rʌmbl] *vi* **1** make a deep, heavy sound going on for some time 發出隆隆聲: *Thunder rumbled in the distance*. 遠方雷聲隆隆. **2** move with this sound 隆隆地移動: *A heavy cart rumbled along the street*. 一架重載馬車轆轆地駛過街道.Also 亦作 *nc* this kind of sound 隆隆聲.

rummage ['rʌmidʒ] *vi* turn things over and over in the search for something 翻查: *rummage through some old clothes* 把一些舊衣服都搜遍了; *rummage about in a drawer* 在抽屜裏到處翻找.

rumour ['ruːmə*] (*US* 美 **rumor**) *nc/u* what people are saying; story which people are repeating, which may or may not be true 謠言;傳聞: *Rumour has it that the president is coming to visit our school*. 據傳聞,總統要來訪問我們的學校. *I have heard some rumours about your leaving that you are going to leave*. 我聽到一些謠傳,說你要走/你打算離開.Also 亦作 *vt* (usu. passive) (通常用被動式): *It is rumoured that you are going to leave*. 聽說,你打算離開!

rump [rʌmp] *nc* tail end of an animal (獸的)臀部;尾部.

rumple ['rʌmpl] *vt* cause to have creases or wrinkles 弄皺;弄亂: *rumple a dress* 弄皺一件衣服.

rumpus ['rʌmpəs] *nc* disturbance; noise. (*informal*) 騷動;喧嚷.(非正式).

run¹ [rʌn] *vt / i* **1** go along by moving the legs quickly 跑;奔: *run somewhere instead of walking* 不是走去而是跑去某處. *run as fast as one can* 盡快跑. **2** move quickly; rush 迅速移動;趕緊: *We ran to his help*. 我們趕緊跑去幫他. *Run for your lives!* i.e. save yourselves. 你們快逃命吧! 即:你們要保全性命. *A thought ran through my mind* i.e. I suddenly thought of something. 有個念頭掠過我的腦海.即:我突然想起某事. **3** cause to move quickly 使迅速移動: *run one's eyes over a page* 匆匆瀏覽一頁. **4** move from one place to another; go 行駛;走: *There is a bus that runs every hour*. 每個鐘頭有一班公共汽車行駛. *This river runs into the sea* i.e. flows. 這條河流入大海. **5** cause to go; drive; push (使)去;刺;撞: *run a knife into someone* 用刀刺某人; *run a car into a tree* 開車撞到樹上. **6** work; operate 運轉: *an engine that runs on petrol* 用汽油開動的發動機. *leave a car engine running* i.e. switched on 讓汽車發動機繼續運轉,即:不熄火. **7** stretch; extend; continue 伸展;擴展;繼續: *a pipe running all the way to the top of the wall* 一條管道直通牆頭. *a play that runs for several months* 一齣連演幾個月的戲; *several days running* i.e. without a break 連續幾天,即:沒有中斷的. **8** spread 擴散: *If you wash this dress in hot water, the colours will run*. 如果你用熱水洗這件衣服,顏色會褪掉的. **9** enter for a race, competition or election 參加賽跑,競賽,競選: *run a horse in a race* 使馬參加賽跑; *run in the hundred metres* 參加百米賽

跑; *run for President* 競選總統. **10**
become 變: *run short of food* 食物短
缺. *During the election, feelings ran
high* i.e. became strong. 選舉期間,羣
情激昂. **11** have under one's control;
be in charge of 掌管;經營: *run a car*
i.e. pay all the expenses connected
with running a car 掌有一輛汽車,即:
支付一切有關掌有一輛汽車的費用.
past tense 過去式 **ran** [ræn]. *past part*
過去分詞 **run. run away** leave;
escape from home; 離開;逃跑: *He ran
away from home at the age of fifteen.* 他十
五歲就離家出走. **run someone
down 1** knock down while driving 開
車撞倒: *He ran down an old man
who was crossing the street.* 他駕車撞
倒一個橫過街道的老人. **2** say bad
things about 誹謗: *She is always running down her neighbours.* 她總是講
她鄰居的壞話. '**run**'**down** *adj* unfit;
not in good health 不適的; 身體不好
的: *I think I should take a holiday,
because I'm feeling rather run-down.*
我感到身體相當不好,我想我該去度假.
run into someone I meet by chance
偶然遇見: *I ran into an old friend of
mine yesterday.* 我昨天碰到我的一個
老朋友. **2** hit 撞上: *run into a wall* 撞
到牆上. **run out of something** use
up one's supply of something 用盡:
We ran out of petrol yesterday. 昨天
我們用光了汽油. *We have run out of
time, and so we must end the meeting.* 我們已經沒時間了,因此我們必須
結束會議. **run over someone /
something 1** go over while driving.
開車撞倒; 輾過: *A crowd gathered
round the child that had been run
over.* 一羣人聚攏在被車輾過的孩子週
圍. **2** revise; mention again 把…看一
遍;複述: *At the end of each lesson he
ran over the main points.* 每聽完一

課,他都把要點複習一遍. **run
through something** read, go over
something quickly 瀏覽; 匆匆處理:
*Could you just run through this article
and tell me what you think of it? (informal).* 請你把這篇文章過過目,並把
你的看法告訴我好嗎?(非正式). **run
something up 1** cause oneself to be
in debt 積欠(債、帳): *run up bills* 積
欠許多帳單; *run up debts* 債台高築.
2 sew quickly 匆忙縫製: *She ran up a
dress. (informal* in sense **2).** 她趕縫了
一件衣服.(義2爲非正式).

run² [rʌn] *nc* **1** act of moving quickly
on the legs 跑: *set off at a run* 跑步出
發. **2** trip; journey 旅遊,旅行: *go for
a run in the car* 坐車去兜兜風. **3**
journey made regularly 行程;航程:
The bus had finished its last run. 這輛
公共汽車駛完了最後的行程. **4** num-
ber or performances 連演: *the play
had a run of two years* 這齣戲已連演
了兩年. **5** number of things happening one after the other 一連串事情: *a
run of bad luck* 接連不幸. **6** number
of demands 連續需要: *a run on the
banks* i.e. by people demanding their
money back 各間銀行發生擠兌,即:儲
戶紛紛要求提款. **7** freedom to use 使
用的自由: *have the run of someone's
house* 有使用某人房子的自由. **8** number of small holes in cloth where a
thread has broken 脫線的裂口: *a run
in a stocking* 襪子上一個脫線的裂口.
9 unit of scoring in cricket or baseball (板球、棒球的)得分,一分: *make
a lot of runs* 得了許多分. **10** closed-in
space for animals 養牧場: *a chicken /
sheep run* 養雞場／牧羊場. **in the
long run** in the end; eventually 最終;
終究: *Studying may be difficult just
now, but you will benefit in the long
run.* 眼下學習也許困難,但是你會最終

受益的. **on the run** running away 逃走: *The enemy army was on the run.* 敵軍逃之夭夭. *The escaped convict was on the run for two weeks* i.e. hiding from the police. 該逃犯逃脫(即: 躲避警察)達兩個星期之久.

runaway [ˈrʌnəwei] *nc* person, horse etc that runs away 逃跑者; 逃馬等. Also 亦作 *adj*.

rung¹ [rʌŋ] past part of **ring²**. ring² 的過去分詞.

rung² [rʌŋ] *nc* wooden or metal bar (e.g. used to make a step in a ladder, or to strengthen the legs of a chair) 橫檔(例如: 梯子的梯級; 椅腿間的橫撐).

runner [ˈrʌnə*] *nc* **1** someone / something that runs 跑的人/物: *There are twelve runners in that race.* 那次賽跑有十二名選手. **2** part on which something slides or moves 滑行裝置; 滑橇. **'runner-'up** *nc* person or team that is second in a competition 亞軍.

running [ˈrʌniŋ] *nu* act of someone / something that runs 跑; 奔跑. Also 亦作 *adj* **1** done while running 邊跑邊做的: *a running jump* 急行跳. **2** without a break; continuous 連續的; 不斷的: *give a running commentary* (e.g. on a race) 連續評說(例如: 賽跑實況); *for three nights running* 連續三夜. **3** flowing 流動的: *hot and cold running water* i.e. hot and cold water flowing through taps 冷、熱自來水, 即: 水龍頭有冷熱水流.

runway [ˈrʌnwei] *nc* area of hard surface in an airfield on which planes land and take off (機場)跑道.

rupture [ˈrʌptʃə*] *nc / u* **1** break; act of breaking 破裂; 決裂: *the rupture of a blood vessel / a friendship etc.* 血管/友誼破裂等. **2** pushing of an organ through another part of the body that

should keep it in (usu. in the abdomen). sometimes caused by lifting heavy weights (舉重物有時引起)器官破裂(通常爲腸腸, 疝).

rural [ˈruərl] *adj* connected with the country 農村的; 鄉村的: *a rural area* 農村地區. (*opp* 反義詞 **urban**).

ruse [ruːz] *nc* trick 詭計: *be deceived by a clever ruse* 中了錦囊妙計.

rush¹ [rʌʃ] *vt / i* **1** move quickly or violently 趕快; 猛衝: *We rushed to where the noise came from.* 我們衝到傳來鬧聲的地方. **2** cause to move quickly or violently 使趕快; 使猛衝: *He rushed more police to the riot.* 他趕派更多警察去平息鬧事. **3** attack quickly or violently 突襲: *The crowd rushed the palace gates.* 人羣突然襲擊王宮大門. **4** decide quickly without thinking 貿然決定: *Don't rush into anything.* 別貿然行事. Also 亦作 *nc / u* act of rushing 急忙; 衝鋒; 襲擊: *a sudden rush of water* 一股急瀉的奔流. **the 'rush hour** busy time in a city when many people are going to work or coming from it (城市上下班的)高峯時間; 交通擁擠時刻.

rush² [rʌʃ] *nc* tall plant that grows in wet areas 燈芯草.

rusk [rʌsk] *nc* piece of bread baked hard or type of biscuit (usu. given to young children) (通常分給小孩的)乾麵包片; 脆餅乾.

rust [rʌst] *nu* reddish-brown coating that forms on iron when it is left damp or open to the air 銹. Also 亦作 *vt / i* become covered, cause to become covered, with rust 使)生銹. **rusty** *adj* covered with rust 生銹的: *a rusty old gun* 一門生銹的舊砲.

rustic [ˈrʌstik] *adj* belonging to, or suitable for, the country 鄉村的; 適合鄉村的: *The house has a rustic charm.* 這

幢房子頗有鄉村風味.

rustle ['rʌsl] *nc* soft sound, like the sound leaves make in the wind (似風吹動葉子的)沙沙響聲: *the rustle of leaves* 樹葉的颯颯聲; *the rustle of a skirt* 裙子的窸窣聲. Also 亦作 *vt / i* **1** make this sound 發出沙沙聲. **2** cause something to make this sound 使發出沙沙聲: *rustle papers* 把文件弄得沙沙作響. **3** (*US*) steal cattle (美)偷牛.

rut [rʌt] *nc* track made in soft ground by a wheel 車轍; 車印. **get into a rut** get into a fixed and uninteresting kind of life that is difficult to change 因循守舊: *If you stay in the same place too long, you can get into a rut.* (*informal*) 如果你老呆在一個地方, 那你可能會因循守舊. (非正式).

ruthless ['ruːθləs] *adj* merciless; cruel 無情的; 殘忍的: *a ruthless enemy* 兇殘的敵人.

rye [rai] *nu* **1** type of cereal plant that grows in cold regions 裸麥; 黑麥. **2** grain from this plant used in making flour 裸麥粒.

S, s

Sabbath ['sæbəθ] *n* (with **the**) (與 the 連用) **1** the seventh day of the week in the Jewish religion, on which people are supposed to do no work 猶太教的安息日(星期六). **2** Sunday, considered as equivalent to the Sabbath by some Christians who believe that God has set this day aside as a day of rest for man. 一些基督徒的安息日(星期天).

sabotage ['sæbətɑːʒ] *nu* damage to machinery, roads, bridges etc which has been deliberately done to interfere with work, transport and movement in war 陰謀破壞(有意破壞機器、道路、橋樑等來干擾工作、交通和軍事行動).Also 亦作 *vt: The workmen sabotaged their machines because they were not given higher wages.* 工人破壞他們的機器,因爲沒有提高工資. **saboteur** [sæbə'tɜ:*] *nc.*

sac [sæk] *nc* bag-like cavity in an animal or plant, esp. filled with liquid 囊;液囊.

saccharin ['sækərin] *nu* very sweet substance, used instead of sugar 糖精.

sachet ['sæʃei] *nc* small bag containing sweet-smelling powder, shampoo etc. 小香粉袋、小包洗髮劑.

sack[1] [sæk] *nc* large bag made of coarse cloth 大粗布袋;麻袋: *a sack of potatoes* 一大袋馬鈴薯. **sacking** *nu* strong cloth for making sacks 袋布;粗麻布.

sack[2] [sæk] *vt* steal from and destroy a town that has been captured 劫掠(被佔領的城鎮).

sack[3] [sæk] *vt* dismiss someone from

work *(informal)* 解雇(非正式). **get the sack** be dismissed from one's work *(informal)* 被解雇(非正式). **give someone the sack** dismiss someone from work *(informal)* 解雇某人(非正式).

sacrament ['sækrəmənt] *nc* important religious ceremony of the Christian Church (基督教重大的)聖禮.

sacred ['seikrid] *adj* holy; connected with God or religion 神聖的;上帝的;宗教的: *a sacred building* 宗教建築; *sacred music* 聖樂.

sacrifice ['sækrifais] *nc / u* **1** act of offering something to God; thing offered 祭祀;祭品. **2** something given up for some good purpose; act of giving something up 犧牲品;犧牲: *the sacrifice of one's life to save a friend* 爲救一位朋友而犧牲自己的生命.Also 亦作 *vt / i* give up something; do without 犧牲;獻出: *sacrifice one's life* 獻出自己的生命; *sacrifice everything for one's children* 爲了孩子而犧牲一切.

sacrilege ['sækrilidʒ] *nu* act of being disrespectful to a holy person / thing 褻瀆神聖: *guilty of sacrilege* 犯褻瀆神聖罪的.

sacrosanct ['sækrousæŋkt] *adj* that is, or should be, protected from harm because it is sacred or holy 神聖不可侵犯的.

sad [sæd] *adj* not happy; feeling or causing sorrow 悲哀的;傷心的;令人難過的. **sadly** *adv* **sadness** *nu*.

saddle ['sædl] *nc* seat for the rider of a horse or a bicycle 鞍;馬鞍;自行車車座.Also 亦作 *vt* **1** put a saddle on 加

鞍；上鞍：*saddle one's horse* 給馬套鞍. **2** put a burden of any kind on someone 使負擔：*saddle a heavy responsibility on someone* 使某人擔負重任；*be saddled with debts* 揹了一身債.

sadism ['seidizəm] *nu* love of cruelty; cruelty done for pleasure 虐待狂；殘忍癖；殘暴色情狂. **sadist** *nc* person who gets pleasure from cruelty and from being cruel 虐待狂者；殘忍癖者；性虐待狂者. **sadistic** [sə'distik] *adj*.

safari [sə'fɑːri] *nc* journey in Africa, often for the purpose of hunting (非洲的) 旅行；狩獵旅行.

safe [seif] *adj* **1** free from danger 安全的：*a safe place* 安全場所. **2** not harmed 無恙的：*He arrived home safe and sound.* 他平安無恙地回到家. **3** not able to be harmed; not in danger 保險的；不會有危險的：*be safe from one's enemies* 不會遭到仇人的傷害. **4** careful 謹慎的：*a safe driver* 謹慎的司機. **5** reliable; dependable: 可靠的；可信賴的：*a safe guide* 可靠的嚮導. Also 亦作 *nc* strong, metal box in which valuables may be kept 保險箱 (櫃). **safely** *adv* **safety** *nu* state of being safe 安全；謹慎. **'safeguard** *vt* keep safe, protect 保護；防衛. Also 亦作 *nc* protection 防衛. **'safety belt** belt which can keep the person wearing it safe if an accident happens 安全帶：*have safety belts fitted in one's car* 車上安裝了安全帶. **'safety pin** pin which has a cover for its sharp point when it is closed 安全別針.

sag [sæg] *vt* **1** hang down in the centre 下陷：*a sagging ceiling* 下陷的天花板. **2** hang down unevenly 鬆垂：*a sagging curtain* 鬆垂的簾子.

saga ['sɑːgə] *nc* **1** story of brave deeds (esp. those done long ago by men from Iceland, Norway, Sweden and Denmark) (尤指冰島、挪威、瑞典和丹麥等古代人的) 英雄傳說，冒險故事. **2** any long story about a family or group (家族、團體的) 長篇故事.

sagacious [sə'geiʃəs] *adj* keenly perceptive, farsighted etc. 精明的；敏銳的；富有洞察力的；有遠見的. **sagaciously** *adv* **sagacity** [sə'gæsiti] *nu*.

sage [seidʒ] *nc* very wise man 哲人，賢人，智者. Also 亦作 *adj* wise; having or showing wisdom or good judgement 睿智的；賢明的；精明的. **sagely** *adv* **sageness** ['seidʒnis] *nu*.

sago ['seigou] *nu* white, starchy food used in making pudding etc. 西米 (做布丁等用的白色澱粉質食品).

said [sed] past of **say.** say的過去式和過去分詞.

sail [seil] *nc* **1** sheet of canvas or other strong material, stretched out so as to catch the wind and drive a boat or ship forward 帆：*The ship was under sail* i.e. with its sails stretched out. 這隻船在揚帆航行. 即：張帆航行. **2** short journey in a boat 短途航行：*a sail down the river* 一次沿江而下的短途航行. Also 亦作 *vt / i* **1** travel in a boat or ship 坐船航行：*sail across the sea* 乘船越過海. **2** control a boat or ship 駕駛 (船)：*We are learning to sail.* 我們在學駛船. **3** travel on water by using a sail or sails 揚帆航行. **4** begin a voyage on water 開航：*sail at dawn* 黎明啓航. **5** move smoothly 平穩地移動：*The ball sailed into the net.* 球平穩進網. **sailor** *nc* person who works on a ship; member of a crew 水手；船員；海員. **'sailing boat** (Brit) boat which uses sails (英) 帆船. (US 美 **sailboat**).

saint [seint] *nc* holy or very good person 聖人；十分好的人：*He is widely* *regarded as a saint.* 他廣被認爲是個十分好的人.

sake [seik] *nu* usu. in **for the sake of** i.e. because of; in order to help 通常用於 for the sake of, 即: 因爲; 爲了幫助: *He was willing to die for the sake of his country.* 他爲了國家願意出生入死. **for my sake / your sake etc** because of, in order to help me / you etc. 因爲或爲了幫助我/你等: *Please do this for my sake.* 爲了我, 請做這事吧.

salad ['sæləd] *nc / u* **1** uncooked or cold vegetables served as food (often with oil, vinegar etc. and sometimes also with eggs, meat, fish etc.) 色拉; 涼拌生菜(常用油, 醋等調拌; 有時還加魚, 肉, 蛋等): *tomato salad* 番茄色拉. **2** any green vegetables which can be eaten uncooked (e.g. lettuce) 可生吃的綠葉蔬菜(如萵苣). **'fruit 'salad** mixture of fruits, cut up and eaten cold 什錦水果, 水果沙拉.

salami [sə'lɑ:mi] *nu* type of sausage (意大利式)臘腸.

salary ['sæləri] *nc* fixed amount of money to be paid for work done, and usu. stated as so much per annum 薪水(通常稱爲年薪若干): *He earns a salary of £4,000 per annum* i.e. £4,000 a year. 他年薪四千英鎊, 即: 每年薪水四千英鎊. *Note* 說明: money paid to lower-paid workers is usu. called *wages* (or *wage*) and stated as so much per week: *get a wage of £10 a week. Salaries* are usu. paid monthly, *wages* weekly. 支付給低收入工人的錢通常叫工資 wages (或 wage), 稱爲每週工資若干, 如每週工資十英鎊. Salaries 通常按月付給, wages 按週付給.

sale [seil] *nc / u* **1** act of selling 賣; 出售: *look at goods on sale* i.e. which can be bought 瞧出售的商品, 即: 可買到的商品. *make a sale* i.e. sell something 成交一筆買賣, 即: 賣出某物. **2** occasion when things are sold more cheaply than usual 大減價: *go to the winter sales* 去逛冬令大減價商場; *buy something cheap at a sale* 大減價時買便宜東西. **'salesman, 'saleswoman** man, woman who sells goods in a shop (女)店員; (女)售貨員.

salient ['seiliənt] *adj* easily seen or noticed; most important 顯著的; 惹人注目的; 最重要的: *the salient points of a speech* 一篇演說的要點.

saliva [sə'laivə] *nu* liquid that comes into the mouth to help chewing etc. 唾液.

sallow ['sælou] *adj* (of complexion) pale yellowish colour (膚色)灰黃的.

sally ['sæli] *nc* **1** sudden rushing forth, as if troops to attack besiegers (軍隊對圍攻者發起的)突圍; 出擊: *make a successful sally* 成功地發動一次突圍. **2** quick witticism; quip 俏皮話; 妙語. **3** excursion 遠足; 遊覽. Also 亦作 *vi* **1** make a sally 突圍; 出擊: *sally out against the besiegers* 向圍困者出擊. **2** (with **forth** or **out**) set out on a trip (與 forth 或 out 連用)出發, 外出旅行.

salmon ['sæmən] *nc / u* large fish valued as food, which lives in the sea but swims up freshwater rivers to lay eggs 鮭魚; 大馬哈魚(生活在大海, 但溯河產卵). *pl* 複數 **salmon.**

salon ['sælɔ] *nc* place where paintings and other works of art are put on show 沙龍; 油畫和其他藝術品展覽場所.

saloon [sə'lu:n] *nc* **1** large room where people can be together 大廳; 交誼廳: *the dining saloon of a ship* 輪船的餐廳. **2** closed-in car for four people or more (可坐四人以上的)大轎車. **3** (*US*) place where strong drink is

bought and drunk (美)酒店; 酒吧間.
(Brit 英 **public house**).

salt [sɔlt] *nu* 1 white substance found in sea water and certain rocks, used to flavour food 鹽; 食鹽. 2 (chemistry) compound of an acid and a metal (化學)鹽類; 酸和金屬合成的化合物. Also 亦作 *vt* put salt in or on food, either to flavour it or to prevent it from going bad 加鹽調味; 用鹽醃(食物). **salt, salty** *adj* containing salt; tasting of salt 有鹽的; 有鹹味的.

salutary ['sæljutəri] *adj* having a good effect 有益的: *salutary advice / exercise etc* 有益的忠告/練習等.

salute [sə'lu:t] *vt / i* welcome someone, or show respect to someone, in a special way (e.g. by raising the hand to the forehead as a soldier does, by firing guns or by lowering and raising a flag) 歡迎; 致敬; 敬禮(例如; 軍人的舉手禮; 放禮砲; 降、升旗禮): *The soldier saluted the officer.* 士兵向軍官敬禮. Also 亦作 *nc* act of saluting 敬禮; 致敬: *a twenty-one gun salute* 二十一響禮砲.

salvage ['sælvidʒ] *nu* 1 act of saving a ship from some kind of serious damage 船舶救助. 2 act of saving goods, buildings etc from being damaged in a fire etc. (大火等災中的)財產搶救等. 3 ship, goods etc saved from damage 被救的船舶; 被救的財產等. Also 亦作 *vt* save from fire, shipwreck etc. (從火災、船難中)搶救.

salvation [sæl'veiʃən] *nu* act of saving from sin or disaster; state of being saved from sin 超度; 救助; 拯救; 得救.

salvo ['sælvou] *nc* firing of many guns at the same time (禮砲、排砲)齊鳴.

same [seim] *adj* not different; alike 同一個的; 相同的: *My brother and I went to the same school.* 弟弟跟我都上同一

所學校. *They all said the very same thing.* 他們大家都說到那同一件事. *That same man married her twenty years later* i.e. the man already referred to. 二十年後, 還是那個男子娶她, 即: 以前已提到過的男子. **the same** the same thing; the same way 同一事物; 同一方式: *Your sister behaves well, and you must do the same.* 你姐姐守規矩, 你也應該這樣. *I feel the same as you (do)* i.e. I agree with you. 我跟你都有同感. 即: 我同意你的看法. **all / just the same** see 見 **all**.

sample ['sɑ:mpl] *nc* example; part of a thing (or one of a number of things) which shows what the rest is like 樣品; 貨樣: *give away free samples of something one wants to sell* 免費分送推銷貨物的樣品. Also 亦作 *vt* take a sample or samples of 抽樣; 抽檢: *The cook sampled the food to make sure it tasted right.* 廚師試嘗一點食物, 以確定味道合適.

sanatorium [sænə'tɔ:riəm], (US 美) **sanitarium** [sæni'tɛəriəm] *nc* kind of hospital (esp. one in a school, or one for people suffering from tuberculosis) 療養院(尤指學校的隔離病房; 結核病醫院).

sanctify ['sæŋktifai] *vt* make holy; set apart as being holy 使神聖; 使神聖不可侵犯.

sanctimonious [sæŋkti'mouniəs] *adj* pretending to be holy 偽裝神聖的; 偽善的.

sanction ['sæŋkʃən] *nc / u* 1 permission of someone in authority; general approval 批准; 贊同: *do something with official sanction / with the sanction of society* 獲得正式批准做某事/得到社會贊同做某事. 2 punishment (esp. that given by other nations to a nation which is held guilty of break-

ing international law) 制裁(尤指縱國
對一個違反國際法的國家所實施的).

sanctity ['sæŋktiti] *nu* holiness 神聖; 聖
潔: *His life was famous for its sanctity.* 他的一生以聖潔聞名.

sanctuary ['sæŋktjuəri] **1** *nc* holy place.
聖所. **2** *nu* protection given to someone who needs it 庇護: *give sanctuary to refugees* 庇護難民. **3** *nc*
place where someone / something is
protected 庇護所;保護區: *a sanctuary
for those who have broken the law* 爲
犯法的人提供的庇護所; *a bird sanctuary* 鳥類禁獵保護區.

sand [sænd] *nu* very small grains of
worndown rocks or shells, found by
the sea and in deserts etc. 沙. **sandy**
adj **1** covered with sand; containing
sand 多沙的;沙質的. **2** yellowish red
in colour 沙色的; 黃褐色的: *sandy
hair* 黃褐色頭髮. **the sands** area covered with sand 沙地. **'sandpaper**
strong paper with sand stuck to it,
used to rub wood smooth 砂紙.

sandal ['sændl] *nc* kind of shoe, made
up of a sole kept on by straps above
平底涼鞋.

sandwich ['sændwitʃ] *nc* two slices of
bread with meat or cheese etc between them 三明治;夾心麵包. Also
亦作 *vt* put a thing / person between
two others, although there is not
much room 把…夾(擠)在(兩者)之間:
*The child was sandwiched in between
his parents.* 這個孩子被擠在他父母之
間.

sane [sein] *adj* **1** having a healthy mind;
not mad 心智健全的; 神志清楚的. **2**
showing good sense; sensible 穩健的,
明智的: *follow a sane policy* 奉行明智
的政策. *(opp* 反義詞 **insane)**. **sanity**
['sæniti] *nu* state of being sane 明智;
穩健;神志清楚. *(opp* 反義詞 **in-**

sanity).

sang [sæŋ] past tense of **sing**. sing的過
去式.

sanguine ['sæŋgwin] *adj* hopeful; cheerful 充滿希望的; 樂觀的: *have a sanguine nature* 有樂觀開朗的性格.

sanitarium [sæni'tɛəriəm] *nc* see 見
sanatorium.

sanitary ['sænitəri] *adj* **1** connected
with health; preventing disease 保健
的;衛生的: *sanitary regulations* 衛生
規則. **2** free from dirt and therefore
free from disease 清潔的; 衛生的:
sanitary conditions 衛生條件. *(opp*反
義詞 **insanitary)**. **sanitation** [sæni-
'teiʃən] *nu* arrangements for preventing dirt and disease 環境衛生; 公共衛
生. **'sanitary towel** *(Brit)* pad used to
absorb flow of blood during menstruation (英)月經帶;衛生巾. *(US* 美
sanitary napkin.

sank [sæŋk] past tense of **sink**. sink的
過去式.

sap[1] [sæp] *nu* liquid in a plant or tree
which carries nourishment to its various parts 樹液(在植物體內輸送養料
到各部份).

sap[2] [sæp] *vt / i* make weak; use up 使
衰弱; 耗竭: *The long illness sapped
his strength.* 長期患病使他體力衰竭.

sapling ['sæpliŋ] *nc* young tree 樹苗.

sapphire ['sæfaiə*] *nc* clear, blue, precious stone 藍寶石.

sarcasm ['sɑːkæzəm] *nc / u* **1** bitter remarks often intended to hurt someone's feelings 諷刺話;挖苦話. **2** act of
making this kind of remark 諷刺; 挖
苦. **sarcastic** [sɑː'kæstik] *adj* using
sarcasm; containing sarcasm 用諷刺
話的; 諷刺的;挖苦的.

sardine [sɑː'diːn] *nc* type of small sea
fish (often preserved in oil in a tin
and eaten as food) 沙丁魚(常是罐裝

油浸食品).

sardonic [saːˈdɔnik] *adj* scornful; mocking 嘲笑的; 冷笑的: *a sardonic smile* 冷笑.

sari [ˈsɑːri] *nc* type of Indian dress (印度女人的)莎麗服.

sash [sæʃ] *nc* broad strip of cloth worn over the shoulder or round the waist 肩帶; 腰帶.

sat [sæt] past of **sit**. sit的過去式和過去分詞.

Satan [ˈseitn] *n* the Devil; the chief of evil spirits 撒但; 魔鬼, 惡魔; 魔王. **satanic** [səˈtænik] *adj* connected with Satan; evil 魔鬼的, 惡魔的; 邪惡的.

satchel [ˈsætʃl] *nc* small bag 小包; 書包: *carry one's school books in a satchel* 用書包裝帶課本.

satellite [ˈsætəlait] *nc* planet which goes round another planet; anything in space which goes round the earth 衛星; 人造衛星: *The moon is a satellite of the earth.* 月亮是地球的衛星. *An earth satellite has been launched.* 已經發射了一顆人造衛星.

satin [ˈsætin] *nu* kind of cloth which is very smooth and shiny on one side 緞. Also 亦作 *adj* made of satin; like satin 緞的; 光滑如緞的.

satire [ˈsætaiə*] **1** *nu* way of attacking a person, idea, custom etc by making him or it seem foolish 諷刺. **2** *nc* poem, book, place etc which uses this way of attacking a person / thing 諷刺詩; 諷刺作品; 諷刺場所等. **satirical** [səˈtirikl] *adj* **satirist** [ˈsætirist] *nc* person who writes satires 諷刺作家. **satirize** [ˈsætiraiz] *vt* attack with satire 諷刺.

satisfy [ˈsætisfai] *vt* **1** give enough to; be enough for 滿足; 符合: *satisfy one's appetite with a large meal* 飽餐一頓來滿足食慾. *Will this information*

satisfy your curiosity? 這消息會滿足你的好奇心嗎? **2** make happy 使滿足: *I feel quite satisfied now.* 我現在深感滿意. **3** make someone free from doubt. 使消除疑念; 使深信: *I must satisfy myself that he is innocent.* 我必須使自己深信他是無辜的. **satisfied** *adj* contented 滿足的, 滿意的. (opp 反義詞 **dissatisfied**). **satisfaction** [ˌsætisˈfækʃən] *nc / u* condition of being satisfied 滿意; 滿足. (opp 反義詞 **dissatisfaction**). **satisfactory** [ˌsætisˈfæktəri] *adj* **1** giving pleasure 稱心如意的. **2** good enough for some purpose (but usu. not very good) 令人滿意的(但通常不是很好的). (opp 反義詞 **unsatisfactory**). **satisfactorily** *adv*.

saturate [ˈsætʃəreit] *vt* make very wet or as wet as possible 浸; 浸透; 浸濕. **saturation** [ˌsætʃəˈreiʃən] *nu*.

Saturday [ˈsætədi] *n* seventh day of the week, coming after Friday 星期六, 禮拜六.

sauce [sɔːs] *nc / u* **1** pleasant tasting liquid (often thick) made from cooked fruit, vegetables etc and added to food to make it taste nicer 調味汁; 醬油: *tomato sauce* 番茄醬; *apple sauce* 蘋果醬. **2** impolite behaviour or words by children to adults. (informal in sense **2**) (小孩對成人的)無禮言行; 頂撞(義2爲非正式). **saucy** *adj* (in sense **2**)(用於義2). **saucily** *adv* (both informal) (均爲非正式).

saucepan [ˈsɔːspən] *nc* metal cooking pot with a handle and usually a lid (有柄並常帶蓋的)平底鍋.

saucer [ˈsɔːsə*] *nc* small, curved plate on which a cup is placed 茶杯托; 茶碟.

sauna [ˈsɔːnə] *nc* type of steam bath 桑拿; 蒸氣浴.

saunter [ˈsɔːntə*] *vi* walk along in a

slow, carefree way 閑逛; 漫步: *saunter through the park* 漫步穿過公園. Also 亦作 *nc* slow, carefree walk or way of walking. 閑逛; 漫步.

sausage ['sɔsidʒ] *nc* meat which is cut up into very small pieces, flavoured and put into a tube-like skin 香腸; 臘腸.

savage ['sævidʒ] *adj* 1 wild, uncivilized 野蠻的; 未開化的. 2 cruel 殘忍的; 粗野的: *He has a savage temper.* 他脾氣粗暴. Also 亦作*nc* 1 savage person 殘暴的人. 2 member of a primitive tribe 野蠻人, 未開化部落的人. Also 亦作 *vt* (with reference to a horse or dog) attack and bite (指馬或狗)亂咬; 亂踏; 猛襲: *The dog savaged his master.* 那條狗猛襲他的主人. **savagery** *nu.*

savanna, savannah [sə'vænə] *nc* treeless plain in or near the tropics (熱帶或靠近熱帶的)無樹木大平原, 熱帶大草原.

save [seiv] *vt / i* 1 take out of danger 救出; 保全: *save someone who is drowning* 搶救某溺水者. 2 not spend; keep for later use 儲蓄; 儲存: *save most of one's wages* 儲蓄大部份工資. 3 not use up 節省: *save one's strength* 節省體力. 4 make less 省去: *save trouble by doing something in a different way* 用一種不同的方法做某事, 省去麻煩. 5 (in the Christian religion) set free from sin (基督教)赦罪; 拯救. Also 亦作 *prep* except (rather *o.f.*) 除了(相當舊式). Also 亦作 *conj* unless (*o.f.*) 除非(舊式). **saving** *nc* way of saving money, time etc.; amount saved 節約; 節儉. **savings** *npl* money saved 儲蓄金; 存款. **'savings bank** bank which accepts small savings and pays interest on them 儲蓄銀行.

saviour ['seiviə*] (*US* 美 **savior**) *nc* 1 one who saves someone from danger, injury etc. 拯救者; 救助者. 2 (**Saviour**) Jesus Christ (救世主)耶穌基督.

savour ['seivə*] (*US* 美 **savor**) *nc* pleasant taste or smell 可口味道; 香氣. Also 亦作 *vt* enjoy the taste or smell of something 品嘗; 欣賞. **savoury** *adj* having a pleasant taste or smell that is not sweet 美味可口的(但不是甜的). Also 亦作 *nc* piece of savoury food 美味小盤菜餚.

saw¹ [sɔ:] past tense of **see¹**. see¹的過去式.

saw² [sɔ:] *nc* type of tool with toothed edge, used for cutting wood, metal etc. 鋸; 鋸機. Also 亦作 *vt / i* use a saw to cut something 鋸: *saw wood* 鋸木. *past tense* 過去式 **sawed.** *past part* 過去分詞 **sawn.** **'sawdust** very small pieces of wood which fall when wood is being sawn 鋸屑, 鋸末.

saxophone ['sæksəfoun] *nc* metal musical instrument, played by blowing through a reed and pressing finger keys 薩克斯管.

say [sei] *vt / i* 1 speak 說; 講: *I want to say something to you in private.* 我想私下跟你說些事. 2 put into speech 表達; 聲明: *say what one thinks* 說出自己的想法. 3 give an opinion 拿定主意; 斷定: *Don't ask me what I think of him because I can't really say* i.e. I haven't decided. 別問我對他有甚麼看法, 因爲我確實還說不準. 即: 我還沒有拿定主意. 4 let us suppose 比如說; 大約: *There are, say, fifty million people in Britain.* 英國大約有五千萬人口. *past* 過去式 and *past part* 過去分詞 **said** [sed]. *Note* 說明: the form *says* in *he / she etc says...* is pronounced [sez]. 在 he / she等says...句子中, says 一詞發音爲 [sez]. **saying** *nc* something commonly said; proverb 諺語; 格言.

scab [skæb] *nc* **1** crust that forms over a wound while it is healing 痂; 瘡疤. **2** person who works when other workers are on strike *(informal* in sense **2**) 照常上班不參加罷工的工人 (義2爲非正式). **scabby** *adj* covered with scabs 結痂的.

scaffold ['skæfould] *nc* high platform on which criminals are put to death 斷頭台; 絞架. **scaffolding** *nu* structure made up of poles put up at the side of a building which is being built, repaired, knocked down etc so that workmen can reach the different parts of the building easily (建築用的)脚手架.

scalar ['skeilə] *adj* **1** in, on or of a scale 梯狀的; 分等級的. **2** (mathematics) designating or of a quantity that has magnitude but no direction in space (數學)純量的; 數量的; 標量的; 無向量的; 無矢量的. Also 亦作 *nc* scalar quantity 無向量; 無矢量; 標量; 純量.

scald [skɔːld] *vt* **1** burn with hot liquid or steam 燙傷: *scald one's hand with boiling water* 被滾水燙傷了手. **2** clean by using boiling water or steam 用開水或蒸氣燙洗消毒: *scald dishes* 燙洗碟子. Also 亦作 *nc* burn caused by hot liquid or steam 燙傷.

scale¹ [skeil] *nc* **1** line of marks one after the other which is used for measuring 刻度; 分度; 尺度: *A thermometer has a scale.* 溫度計上有刻度. **2** something which has marks on it used for measuring 有刻度的度量器; 尺; 秤. **3** system of steps or differences 等級; 級別: *a new wages scale* 新的工資級別. **4** size of a map, plan etc compared to the thing it stands for; this information on a map, plan etc. 比例; 比例尺; 縮尺: *a map drawn*

to a scale of one inch for each ten miles 按一英寸代表十英里的比例繪成的一張地圖. *refer to the scale on a map* 查閱地圖上的比例尺. **5** extent; amount 規模; 大小: *entertain on a large scale* i.e. do a large amount of entertaining 大規模地款待, 即: 給予盛大的款待. **6** set of musical notes going up or down in a particular manner (e.g. major scale, minor scale) 音階(例如: 大音階; 小音階). Also 亦作 *vt* climb; climb over 攀登; 爬越: *scale the walls of a castle.* 爬越城堡的道道城牆. **scales, pair of scales** instrument used for measuring weight 天平; 秤.

scale² [skeil] *nc* one of the thin, flat, hard plates on the skin of snakes, fish, lizards etc. 鱗; 鱗片.

scalene ['skeiliːn] *adj* (of a triangle) having unequal sides and angles (指三角形)不等邊的.

scallop ['skɔləp] *nc* **1** kind of sea animal with two deeply grooved, curved shells; shell of such a sea animal (一種其兩個彎曲貝殼上面有深槽的)扇貝; 扇貝殼. **2** large muscle of this mollusc, used as food (供食用的)扇貝肉. **3** any of a series of curves, etc forming an ornamental edge (形成裝飾邊的)扇形花樣. Also 亦作 *vt* **1** cut the border of in scallops 把邊緣剪成扇貝花樣. **2** bake with sauce and bread crumbs in a dish 加醬汁和麵包屑在盤中烘烤.

scalp [skælp] *nc* skin and hair on the top of the head 頭皮. Also 亦作 *vt* cut off the scalp of an enemy as a sign of victory (formerly a custom among some American Indian tribes) 剝去(敵人的)頭皮作爲戰利品(昔時一些北美印第安人的習俗).

scalpel ['skælpl] *nc* small knife used by

a doctor 解剖刀.

scamper ['skæmpə*] *vi* run about quickly, as children and small animals do (孩子，小動物) 蹦蹦跳跳地跑，奔跑: *The children scampered home.* 孩子們蹦蹦跳跳地跑回家. *The mouse scampered away when it saw the cat.* 老鼠看見貓就奔逃了.

scan [skæn] *vt / i* **1** look carefully at every part of 細看; 審視: *After the storm the people on the shore anxiously scanned the lake for any sign of the boat.* 暴風雨過後，岸邊的人們焦慮地細察湖面，渴望能看到那隻船的踪影. **2** look quickly through 瀏覽; 掃視: *scan a newspaper quickly* 匆匆瀏覽一下報紙. *past* 過去式和過去分詞 **scanned.**

scandal ['skændl] *nc / u* **1** unkind talk about someone 誹謗; 中傷; 詆毀: *You shouldn't spread scandal.* 你不應該散佈流言蜚語. *I heard a bit of scandal about your friend.* 我聽到一些關於詆毀你朋友的話. **2** something disgraceful; something which causes public anger 可恥的事; 引起公憤的醜事: *I think that the way that child is treated is a scandal.* 我認爲這樣對待孩子是可恥的事. *There was a tremendous scandal when it was revealed that some policemen had been accepting bribes.* 一些警察已在接受賄賂的消息曝光出來時，激起極大的公憤. **scandalous** *adj* disgraceful; very bad 可恥的; 惡劣的. **scandalize** *vt* shock; make angry by doing something wrong 震驚; 使反感; 使感到憤慨.

scant [skænt] *adj* not enough 不足的: *pay scant attention* 不够注意. **scanty** *adj* very small 很少的; *a scanty amount* 一點點; 少量. **scantily** *adv.*

scapegoat ['skeipgout] *nc* person who is blamed for wrong things done by other people 代人受過的人; 替罪羊.

scar [skɑː*] *nc* mark left on the skin by a wound, sore etc which has healed 傷痕; 傷疤. Also 亦作 *vt* mark with a scar or scars 使留傷痕; 使留疤痕: *a scarred leg* 有疤痕的腿. *past* 過去式和過去分詞 **scarred.**

scarce [skeəs] *adj* **1** difficult to get; few in number or little in amount 難得的; 不足的; 缺乏的: *Some kinds of fruit are scarce here in winter.* 冬天這裏一些水果缺貨. **2** rare 稀有的; 珍貴的: *a very scarce coin* 一枚十分稀有的硬幣. **scarcity** *nc / u* **scarcely** *adv* **1** almost not; only with difficulty 幾乎不; 勉強: *be so tired one can scarcely walk* 累得幾乎走不動. **2** surely not 一定不: *He would scarcely have made such a rude remark.* 他不至於會說出這樣無禮的話.

scare [skeə*] *vt* frighten 使驚恐: *The noise scared the children.* 吵鬧聲把孩子都嚇住了. Also 亦作 *nc* **1** fright 驚嚇: *give someone a scare* 使某人嚇了一跳. **2** state of being frightened 恐慌: *There was a scare that war had broken out.* 人們有種戰爭已經爆發的恐慌. **'scarecrow** figure in the shape of a man, with old clothes on it, put in a field to frighten birds away 稻草人(竪在田裏驅鳥的假人). **'scaremonger** someone who spreads frightening news 散佈恐怖消息的人.

scarf [skɑːf] *nc* piece of cloth worn round the neck or on the head (usu. for warmth) 圍巾; 頭巾(通常爲保暖用). *pl* 複數 **scarves** [skɑːvz].

scarlet ['skɑːlit] *nu* bright red colour 猩紅; 緋紅. Also 亦作 *adj* **scarlet 'fever** disease which can be easily spread from one person to another, in which red marks appear on the skin and there is pain in the throat 猩紅熱

(病).

scarp [skɑːp] *nc* **1** steep slop 陡坡. **2** inner slop on side of a ditch surrounding a fortification; escarp 城堡防禦壕溝的內斜面; 壕溝內岸.

scathing [ˈskeiðiŋ] *adj* very bitter and attacking 尖刻的; 嚴厲的: *a scathing speech* 尖刻的發言; *a scathing article in a newspaper* 報上的一篇抨擊文章.

scatter [ˈskætə*] *vt / i* **1** throw here and there 散播; 撒: *scatter sand on an icy road* 把沙子撒在結冰的路面上. **2** send, drive in different directions 使分散; 驅散: *scatter a crowd of children* 驅散一羣孩子. **3** go in different directions 分散; 四散: *The mob scattered.* 那羣暴民四處散開. **scattering** *nc* small quantity of something widely spread 稀疏的少量: *a scattering of farms on the hillside* 疏疏落落地散佈在山坡上的農莊.

scavenge [ˈskævindʒ] *vt / i* **1** pick over (discarded objects) for things to use or sell (從廢物中)挑揀可用或可賣的東西; 揀破爛. **2** remove dirt and rubbish from (a street, surface of a river, etc) 清除(街道、河面上等的)污物和垃圾. **3** feed on (carrion or refuse) 食腐肉, 以垃圾爲食物. **4** look for food 尋找食物. **scavenger** *nc* **1** person who scavenges 清道夫; 清掃工; 拾垃圾的人; 揀破爛的人. **2** bird or animal that eats refuse and decaying organic matter 食腐鳥類; 食腐野獸; 食腐動物.

scene [siːn] *nc* **1** view; something seen 風景; 景色: *The sun setting behind the trees made a beautiful scene.* 樹後的落日構成一幅美景. **2** place where something happens, either in real life or in a book (事情的)發生地點; 場景: *the scene of one's childhood* 童年時代成長的地方. **3** part of an act in a play (戲劇的)一場: *Act 1, scene 2 of 'Mac-*

beth' 《麥克白斯》的第一幕第二場. **4** show of anger or other strong feeling 吵鬧; 發脾氣: *He made a scene when I told him to get out of my house.* 當我叫他滾出我的房子時, 他大吵大鬧.

scenery *nu* **1** theatre scene 佈景: *The scenery for the play must have been very expensive* 爲這齣戲造的佈景諒必花費很大. **2** general appearance of the countryside 自然景色; 風景: *mountain scenery* 山景. **scenic** [ˈsiːnik] *adj* connected with scenery 佈景的; 自然景色的; 風景優美的.

scent [sent] **1** *nc / u* pleasant smell 香味: *the scent of roses* 玫瑰花香; *scents from different flowers* 百花飄香. **2** *nu* sense of smell in dogs (狗的)嗅覺: *Hunting dogs have a very keen scent.* 獵狗都有十分靈敏的嗅覺. **3** *nc* smell left by an animal or person (動物的)遺臭; 臭跡; (人的)踪跡: *The dogs were able to follow the scent of the fox.* 這些狗都能跟踪那隻狐狸的臭跡. **4** *nu* liquid which has a pleasant smell; perfume 香水: *Most ladies use a little scent.* 大多女士都噴灑一點香水. Also *vt* **1** smell; detect 嗅; 聞: *The dogs have scented a fox.* 這些狗嗅出一隻狐狸. **2** fill with a pleasant smell 使充滿香味: *The newly-cut flowers scented the room.* 新採的鮮花使房間溢滿花香.

sceptic [ˈskeptik] (*US* 美 **skeptic**) *nc* person who doubts the truth of something (esp. religion). **sceptical** *adj* **scepticism** [ˈskeptisizəm] *nu* state of being in doubt (尤指宗教的)懷疑者; 懷疑論者; 懷疑(態度); 懷疑主義.

sceptre [ˈseptə*] (*US* 美 **scepter**) *nc* rod or staff carried by a ruler to show his authority 權杖; 王節: *a king's sceptre* 王杖.

schedule [ˈʃedjuːl, *US* 美 ˈskedjuːl] *nc*

scheme 790 *science*

list of details; timetable 一覽表; 時間表: *Everything is going according to schedule* i.e. as planned. 事事都按照時間表進行, 即: 按預定計劃進行. Also 亦作 *vt* plan; arrange 計劃; 安排.

scheme [ski:m] *nc* **1** plan 計劃; 方案: *a scheme for developing a poor area* 發展一個貧困地區的方案. **2** dishonest plan 詭計; 陰謀: *scheme to cheat people out of their money* 騙人錢財的詭計. **3** arrangement of things in an orderly way 系統; 配合: *colour scheme for a room* i.e. so that the colours will suit one another 房間的色彩配合, 即: 使各種色彩彼此調和. Also 亦作 *vi* make plans (esp. of a secret kind) 策劃(尤指密事): *He is scheming to become President.* 他圖謀當總統. **scheming** *adj* making dishonest plans 詭計多端的.

schism ['skizəm] *nc* division of a church etc into two or more groups, caused by differences of opinion among its members (教會的)分派; 宗派.

schist [ʃist] *nu* kinds of crystallic rock which splits easily into thin plates 片岩, 頁岩, 結晶片岩.

schizophrenia [skitsə'fri:niə] *nu* type of madness 精神分裂症. **schizophrenic** [skitsə'frenik] *adj*.

schnorkel ['ʃnɔ:kl], **snorkel** ['snɔ:kl] *nc* tube through which a swimmer can breathe under water (潛水者用的)通氣管.

scholar ['skɔlə*] *nc* **1** person having much knowledge (esp. of a certain subject) 學者(尤指某一學科的). **2** student who is given money to continue his studies (usu. after doing well in an examination in which he has to compete with other students) (因成績優異而)享有獎學金的學生. **scholarly**

adj showing great learning 學識淵博的: *a scholarly book / teacher etc* 內容淵博的書/學識淵博的教師等. **scholarship** **1** *nu* knowledge gained by studying 學問; 學識. **2** *nc* money given to a student to continue his studies 獎學金. **scholastic** [skə'læstik] *adj* connected with schools or education 學校的; 教育的.

school[1] [sku:l] **1** *nc* place where young people are taught 學校: *They are building a new school here.* 他們正在這裏建一所新學校. **2** *nu* (without a or the) lessons (不與a或the連用)課業: *There will be no school tomorrow.* 明天不上課. **3** *nu* (without a or the) state of being taught at a school (不與a或the連用)上學; *be at school* 在上學; *leave school* 放學回家; 退學(畢業)離校; *go to school* 上學去. **4** *nc* (with a or the) children in a school (與a或the連用)全校學生: *give a talk to a school* 給全校學生講一次話. *talk to the whole school* 對全校學生講話. **5** *nc* group of painters, writers, philosophers etc who use the same methods 學派; 流派. **6** *nc* department in a university (大學的)學院; 系: *School of Medicine* 醫學院. Also 亦作 *vt* train; teach 訓練; 教導: *schooled by experience* 從經驗中得到訓練. **schooling** *nu* education at school 學校教育. **'schoolmaster**, **'schoolmistress** man, woman teaching in a school 男(女)教師.

school[2] [sku:l] *nc* large number of fish or water animals swimming together. (魚、水族)羣.

schooner ['sku:nə*] *nc* kind of sailing ship with two or more masts (有兩個或兩個以上桅杆的)縱帆船.

science ['saiəns] **1** *nu* knowledge of facts concerning the physical aspects of the universe (usu. got by observation, experiments etc.) 科學: *be interested in science* 對科學有興趣. **2** *nc* knowledge of such facts about some special subject 某門科學; 學科: *the science of chemistry* 化學. **scientific** [saiən'tifik] *adj* of or connected with science 科學的; 有關科學的: *a scientific instrument* 科學儀器; *scientific discovery* 科學發現. **scientist** ['saiəntist] *nc* person who has studied science 科學家. **'science 'fiction** stories based on scientific ideas (esp. those dealing with space travel and the future) 科幻小說.

scintillate ['sintileit] *vi* sparkle, shine 發出火花; 閃爍; *frost scintillating in the sun* 在陽光下閃爍的霜. *a scintillating conversation* i.e. very witty and intelligent 一次閃爍火花的談話, 即: 才智橫溢的談話.

scissors ['sizəz] *npl* instrument with two blades, used for cutting cloth, paper etc. (Often **a pair of scissors**) 剪刀 (常用 a pair of scissors 一把剪刀).

scoff[1] [skɔf] *vi* **1** make fun of something one does not believe in 嘲笑: *scoff at an idea* 嘲笑一種想法. **2** make fun of someone 嘲弄.

scoff[2] [skɔf] *vt* eat greedily *(informal)* 狼吞虎嚥地吃 (非正式).

scold [skould] *vt / i* blame angrily; speak angrily to 責罵; 叱責: *She scolded the child for being rude to the guests.* 她責罵孩子對客人粗魯無禮.

scone [skɔn] *nc* kind of flat, plain cake (usu. round and made from flour) 烤餅, 茶點小蛋糕.

scoop [sku:p] *nc* **1** tool like a shovel, used for lifting and moving things 杓子; 圓匙; 簸; 鏟斗: *a large scoop for moving earth* 運土大鏟斗; *a kitchen*

scoop for lifting sugar etc. 舀糖等用的廚房圓匙. **2** good story which is printed in one newspaper before the other newspapers *(informal* in sense **2**) 搶先刊登的獨家新聞 (義2爲非正式). Also 亦作 *vt* **1** lift up and move as a scoop does 舀: *scoop up sugar* 舀糖. **2** make a hole by using a scoop or something similar 挖; 掘: *scoop out a hole* 挖出一個洞.

scooter [sku:tə*] *nc* **1** type of children's toy on wheels, which can be moved along by using one foot 踏板車 (可用一腳觸地推動的小孩玩車). **2** type of small motorcycle 小型摩托車.

scope [skoup] *nu* **1** opportunity 機會: *give someone scope to show his ability* 提供某人舒展個人才能的機會. **2** limits of what someone / something can do 範圍: *a task that is beyond one's scope* 超越某人能力範圍的任務. *The scope of this new theory is quite enormous.* 這門新理論所涉及的範圍十分廣闊.

scorch [skɔ:tʃ] *vt* burn something slightly; mark something with heat 燒焦; 烤焦: *scorch a shirt while ironing it* 熨衣時把一件襯衫燙焦了. Also 亦作 *nc* mark made by scorching 焦痕.

score [skɔ:*] *nc* **1** number of points, goals etc won in a game 得分; 比分: *The score was 2-0 for the home team.* 比分二比零, 本地隊獲勝. *What's the score?* 比分多少? **2** printed sheet of music which shows the notes for the different instruments that have to play, and voices that have to sing 樂譜 (標明每一樂器該演奏的, 每一聲部該演唱的音符). **3** twenty 二十: *There must have been a score or more there* i.e. at least twenty. 那裏諒必有二十多. 即: 至少有二十. Also 亦作 *vt / i* **1** make a point, goal etc in a game 比賽

中得(分), 進(球): *score a goal* 進一
球: *Our team has just scored.* 我們的
隊剛得分. **2** keep a record of the
number of points, goals etc won in a
game (比賽中)記分. **scorer** *nc* **1** person who scores a goal etc. 得分的運
動員. **2** person who keeps a record of
the score in a game (比賽)記分員.

scorn [skɔːn] *nu* feeling that someone /
something is not worth any respect
鄙視: *be full of scorn for someone* 對
某人嗤之以鼻. Also 亦作 *vt* look
down on; feel no respect for others
鄙視: *scorn a cowardly act* 瞧不起懦
夫的行為. **scornful** *adj* showing or
feeling scorn 鄙視的.

scorpion [ˈskɔːpiən] *nc* small creature
with a sting in its tail, which is a
member of the spider family 蝎.

Scot [skɔt] *nc* person from Scotland 蘇
格蘭人. **Scots / Scottish** *adj*

Scotch [skɔtʃ] *nc / u* whisky 威士忌酒.
Also 亦作 *adj* from Scotland (usu. of
food and drink) 蘇格蘭的(通常指食物
和酒). *Note* 說明: for people, customs etc *Scotch* is *o.f.* and *Scots* or
Scottish should be used 指人, 指風俗
等, 用 Scotch 是舊式, 應用 Scots 或
Scottish.

scoundrel [ˈskaundrl] *nc* evil person 惡
棍; 無賴.

scour¹ [ˈskauə*] *vt* clean a dirty surface
by rubbing with something rough 擦
淨: *scour some pots and pans* 擦淨一
些鍋盤.

scour² [ˈskauə*] *vt* look everywhere for
搜尋: *scour the countryside for a lost
child* 在那鄉間到處找尋一個走失的孩
子.

scourge [skə:dʒ] *nc* anything which
causes pain and suffering 禍患; 禍害:
*Disease is one of the scourges of man-
kind.* 疾病是人類的禍害之一.

scout [skaut] *nc* **1** person, aeroplane,
ship etc which is sent ahead to get information about the enemy's movements etc. 偵察員; 偵察艦; 偵察機等.
2 member of the Boy Scouts 童子軍.
see below 見下. Also 亦作 *vi* go
ahead as a scout 偵察. **the Boy
Scouts** organization for boys, which
teaches them how to look after themselves and how to be useful to others
童子軍(訓練兒童如何自理和有助他人
的兒童組織).

scowl [skaul] *nc* angry look made by
lowering the brows 皺眉的怒視. Also
亦作 *vi* have such a look 皺眉; 怒視:
scowl at someone 瞪眼怒視某人.
scowl angrily 滿臉怒容.

scraggy [ˈskrægi] *adj* thin and bony 瘦
而多骨的: *a scraggy piece of meat* 一
塊帶骨的瘦肉.

scram [skræm] *vi* go away quickly 急速
離開; 滾. *past* 過去式和過去分詞
scrammed. (*informal*) (非正式).

scramble [ˈskræmbl] *vi* **1** go forward
using the hands and knees 爬; 攀登:
scramble over rocks 爬越岩壁. *scramble up a steep hill* 攀登陡山. **2** struggle with others for something 爭奪; 搶
奪: *scramble for a ball during a game*
比賽時, 爭先恐後去搶球. Also 亦作 *vt*
1 walk or climb over hilly ground 攀
登; 爬越. **2** act of struggling for something. 爭奪: *As soon as the performance ended, there was a scramble for
the door* i.e. to get out. 演出一結束, 大
家都爭先恐後地奪門而出. **'scrambled
'eggs** *nu* eggs cooked by beating
them up and then cooking them in a
saucepan 炒蛋.

scrap¹ [skræp] **1** *nc* small piece; part
left over 小塊; 碎屑: *a scrap of paper*
一小塊碎紙. **2** *nu* articles that are no
longer of use 廢物: *collect scrap* 收集

破爛; *sell one's car for scrap* i.e. just for the value of the materials it is made of 把汽車當作廢物出售，即：僅僅收回製車材料的費用; *scrap iron* i.e. things made of iron which are to be melted down so that the iron can be used again 廢鐵(回爐鑄鐵再用). Also 亦作 *vt* give up; abandon something as being useless: 放棄; 廢棄: *scrap an idea* 拋棄一種想法; *scrap some work one has done* 放棄一些已做過的工作. *past* 過去式或 過去分詞 **scrapped.**

scrappy *adj* made up of bits and pieces; not properly connected and arranged 拼湊的; 散亂的; 組織不周密的: *a scrappy essay* 一篇雜亂無章的文章. **'scrapbook** book with blank pages on which one can put photographs, pieces cut from newspapers etc. 相片簿; 剪貼簿. **'scrap heap** pile of things that are no longer wanted 廢物堆; 垃圾堆: *throw something on the scrap heap* i.e. throw away as being useless 把某物扔進廢物堆，即: 作爲無用廢物丟掉.

scrap² [skræp] *vi* fight 打架. *past* 過去式或過去分詞 **scrapped.** Also 亦作 *nc* (both *informal*) (均爲非正式).

scrape [skreip] *vt / i* **1** rub with something sharp or rough in order to make level, smooth or clean 刮; 削平; 擦淨: *He cleaned the wire by scraping it with a knife.* 他用一把小刀把那條電線刮乾淨. **2** take paint off by rubbing in this way 刮掉油漆: *scrape a door before painting it again* 把門上舊漆刮掉，然後重新上漆. **3** accidentally rub against something that is sharp or rough 擦傷: *scrape one's knee* 擦傷膝蓋; *scrape one's car* 擦傷汽車. **4** get past or through something by a very narrow amount 勉強通過; 勉強應付: *scrape through an examination* 勉強

通過一門考試. **5** rub with an unpleasant sound 發出使人不愉快的刮擦聲: *a pen that scrapes on the paper* 筆尖刮紙發出沙沙聲的筆. Also 亦作 *nc* **1** act of scraping 刮; 削; 擦. **2** sound made by scraping 刮擦聲. **3** awkward situation; difficulty 困境; 困難: *always be getting into scrapes* 總是陷入困境.

scratch [skrætʃ] *vt / i* **1** cut, make a line in, with something sharp or rough 劃; 劃花: *My knife slipped and scratched the table.* 我的小刀一滑就劃花了桌面. **2** rub part of one's body with the fingernails, either because one has an itch or as a matter of habit etc. 搔; 抓癢: *scratch one's head when one is puzzled* 茫然不知所措時, 搔搔頭. **3** cut with the nails 抓傷; 扒傷: *be badly scratched by an animal* 被一隻動物嚴重抓傷. Also 亦作 *nc* **1** mark made by scratching 抓痕; 劃痕: *The new table has a scratch on it already.* 新桌子已有一道劃痕在桌面上. **2** cut on the skin that is not serious 微傷: *just a scratch* 只是抓破了點皮而已. Also 亦作 *adj* collected or prepared in a hurry 臨時湊成的; 倉促準備的: *a scratch team* 臨時湊成的球隊.

scrawl [skrɔ:l] *vt / i* write or draw carelessly or in a hurry 潦草地寫或畫. Also 亦作 *nc* something scrawled 潦草的書寫; 瞎畫.

scream [skri:m] *vt / i* **1** make a loud, sharp cry 尖聲叫喊: *scream with pain / fear / anger etc.* 因痛苦/恐懼/憤怒等而尖聲喊叫. **2** say in a loud, high voice 高聲說出: *scream a command* 大聲發出命令. Also 亦作 *nc* loud, sharp cry or noise 尖叫聲.

scree [skri:] *nu* steep mass of broken and fallen rocks on the side of a mountain 山腳碎石堆.

screech [skri:tʃ] *vt / i* make a loud, high noise 尖叫: *screech with pain* 痛得尖叫. Also 亦作 *nc* loud high noise 尖叫聲: *the screech of brakes when a car stops suddenly* 汽車突然停住時的尖銳刺耳的煞車聲.

screen [skri:n] *nc* 1 covered frame used to protect or hide someone / something 屏風; 遮簾: *In hospitals they sometimes put a screen round your bed if the doctor is examining you.* 在醫院, 醫生若要給你檢查, 有時會在你病床週圍拉上一道屏風. 2 cover made of pieces of wire with holes in between, like a net 紗罩: *There were screens on the windows to prevent insects from getting in.* 窗户裝有紗窗以防昆蟲亂飛. 3 surface on which film is shown 銀幕. 4 part of a television set on which the picture appears 屏幕; 熒光幕. Also 亦作 *vt* 1 protect or hide with a screen, or as if with a screen 庇護; 藏匿: *screen oneself from public view* 把自己遮住, 不讓公眾看見. *He screened his old friend from the police.* 他掩護他的老朋友躲開警察. 2 project a film onto a screen; show a film (在銀幕上) 放映 (電影).

screw [skru:] *nc* 1 kind of nail which is driven into wood and other materials by being turned round and round 螺旋; 螺絲釘: *The handle of this door is kept in place by two screws.* 這門的把手用兩顆螺絲釘固定. 2 propellor at the back of a ship which helps to drive it forward (船尾的) 螺旋槳. Also 亦作 *vt / i* 1 join together or tighten by using a screw or screws (用螺絲釘) 擰緊: *screw together two pieces of wood* 用螺絲釘把兩塊木板擰緊在一起. 2 twist; turn round 擰轉; 旋轉: *screw the lid off a jar* 擰開瓶蓋. 3

force someone to do, tell or give up something 強迫; 勒索; 榨取: *screw the truth / more money out of someone* 強迫某人說出事實真相 / 榨取某人更多的錢財.

'screwdriver tool used for putting in or taking out screws by turning them 螺絲刀; 螺絲起子.

scribble [ˈskribl] *vt / i* write quickly and carelessly 潦草書寫, 胡亂塗鴉: *scribble a note to someone* 潦草地寫了張便條給某人. Also 亦作 *nc / u* something scribbled 潦草的字跡.

scribe [skraib] *nc* person whose profession is to write 抄寫員.

script [skript] 1 *nu* writing done by hand; print that looks like handwriting 手寫文件; 書寫體印刷品. 2 *nc* written version of a play, talk etc. (usu. for radio, television or the stage) 手稿, 腳本 (電台廣播稿; 電視演講稿; 舞台戲劇腳本等): *The actor was studying his script.* 這個男演員正在研讀他的戲劇腳本.

Scripture [ˈskriptʃə*] *nc* also 亦作 the **Scriptures** the Bible 《聖經》.

scroll [skroul] *nc* long piece of paper or skin which can be rolled up, used in ancient times for writing on (古代用於書寫的) 紙、羊皮紙等卷軸.

scrounge [skraundʒ] *vt / i* get things by taking or borrowing from other people, instead of by buying them. (both *informal*) 擅取; 乞取 (均為非正式).

scrub¹ [skrʌb] *vt / i* clean by rubbing (usu. by using a hard brush) 擦洗, 擦淨 (通常用硬毛刷): *scrub the floor* 擦洗地板.

scrub² [skrʌb] *nu* low trees and bushes; land covered with low trees and bushes 矮樹叢; 叢林地: *travel through miles of scrub* 跋涉穿過連綿數英里的叢林地.

scruff [skrʌf] *nc* back of the neck (usu.

in **by the scruff of the neck**) 頸背
(通常用在 by the scruff of the neck).

scruffy ['skrʌfi] *adj* rather dirty and untidy in appearance 不整潔的; 襤褸的;
邋遢的.

scruple ['skru:pl] *nc* feeling of doubt as
to whether one is doing right 顧忌; 遲
疑; 猶豫; *I shall have no scruples a-
bout forcing him to give me the
money.* 我會毫無顧忌強逼他把那筆錢
給我. **scrupulous** ['skru:pjuləs] *adj*
very careful not to do wrong 謹慎小
心的; 謹小慎微的. *(opp* 反義詞 **unscrupulous) scrupulously** *adv.*

scrutiny ['skru:tini] *nc / u* careful examination in detail 細察; 審查: *Every-
thing you do will be subject to close
scrutiny.* 你所做的一切都須經嚴格的審
查. **scrutinize** *vt* examine carefully
仔細檢查.

scuffle ['skʌfl] *nc* fight; confused struggle 扭打; 混戰.

sculpture ['skʌlptʃə*] **1** *nu* art of making figures out of stone clay, wood
etc. 雕刻(術); 雕塑(術). **2** *nc* figure
made in this way 雕刻品; 雕塑品: *a
beautiful sculpture* 一件美麗的雕刻品.
sculptor ['skʌlptə*] *nc* artist who
makes sculptures 雕刻家; 雕塑家.

scum [skʌm] *nu* **1** layer of dirt at the
top of a liquid 浮渣; 浮垢: *The pond
was covered with scum.* 那個池塘水面
被浮渣覆蓋. **2** bad, useless people 壞
人; 無用的人: *the scum of the earth* 人
類的渣滓.

scurrilous ['skʌriləs] *adj* using words
which are coarse and rude (語言) 下
流的; 講粗話的; 謾罵的: *a scurrilous
attack* 謾罵攻擊.

scurry ['skʌri] *vi* run or move quickly
急跑; 疾行: *scurry for cover* 急忙找地
方隱蔽. *Also* 亦作 *nu.*

scurvy ['skə:vi] *nu* disease resulting

from a deficiency of vitamin C in the
body 壞血病. *Also* 亦作 *adj* mean;
contemptible 卑鄙的; 下流的.

scuttle ['skʌtl] *vi* run; move quickly 急
忙跑; 疾行: *The two thieves scuttled
away when they saw the policeman.*
那兩個小偷看見警察就急忙逃跑.

scythe [saið] *nc* tool with a long, curved
blade, used for cutting grass, wheat
etc. 長柄大鐮刀.

sea [si:] **1** *nu* the part of the earth's surface covered by water 海; 海洋: *go to
sea* i.e. become a sailor 當海員; 做水
手: *The ship put out to sea* i.e. left the
harbour etc. 船啟航出海, 即: 離開港口
等. **2** *nc* large area of water, smaller
than an ocean 內海: *the Mediterranean Sea* 地中海. **3** *nc* large amount
or number 大量; 衆多: *a sea of faces
looking at us* 瞧着我們的無數張臉.
'seaboard *nc / u* land near the sea 沿
海地區; 海濱; 海岸: *on the Western
seaboard* 西部沿海地區. **'seafarer** *nc*
sailor 海員; 水手. **'seafaring** *adj*
travelling or working on the sea 航海
的; 海上工作的. **'seagull** type of bird,
usu. white or grey, found near the sea
海鷗. **'sealevel** height of sea when
halfway between high and low tide 海
平面(高低潮間的平均海平): *a hill 708
feet above sea level* 一座海拔708英尺
高的山. **'seaman** sailor 海員; 水手, 船
員. **'seaport** town on a sea coast or
connected to the sea, with harbour,
docks etc. 海港; 港埠, 港口都市.
'seashore *nc / u* land beside the sea
海岸; 海濱: *go down to the seashore
to play* 到海濱去玩. **'seasick** *adj* ill
because of the movement of a boat or
ship 暈船的. **seasickness** *nu* the
'seaside place near the sea 海邊; 海
濱. **'seaweed** plants growing in the
sea 海草; 海藻. **'seaworthy** *adj* good

enough for sailing on the sea 適於航海的: *seaworthy boat* 適於航海的船. *(opp* 反義詞 **unseaworthy**).

seal¹ [si:l] *nc* **1** design which is put on a piece of wax, lead etc to show the authority of the person who put it there (封蠟片、封鉛片等上表明負責人的)印記或圖記; 封印: *the seal at the bottom of a certificate* 蓋在證書下方的印記; *the seal on the back of an envelope* 信封後面的封印. **2** something which can put such a design onto wax, lead etc. 印章; 圖章: *He pressed his seal into the hot wax.* 他把自己的印章按到那熱封蠟紙上. **3** something that closes or fastens a thing tightly 封蠟; 封鉛; 封緊用的東西. Also 亦作 *vt* **1** mark with a seal 蓋印; 蓋章: *seal a document* 在文件上蓋章. **2** close or fasten 封; 密封: *seal a letter* 封信. **'sealing wax** kind of wax which is used to seal letters etc. 封蠟; 火漆.

seal² [si:l] *nc* animal, which can live in the sea or on land, which makes a barking sound and is often hunted for its skin 海豹.

seam [si:m] *nc* **1** line where two pieces of cloth etc are joined together 縫; 接縫. **2** layer of coal, metal etc in the earth, with rock etc on either side of it 煤層; 礦層. **seamstress** ['si:mstris] *nc* woman whose work is sewing 女縫工; 女裁縫. **seamy** *adj* unpleasant 不愉快的: *the seamy side of life* (e.g. poverty, crime etc.) 生活的陰暗面(例如: 貧窮; 犯罪等).

search [sə:tʃ] *vt/i* examine carefully in order to find something 搜查; 搜尋: *search a room* 搜查房間. Also 亦作 *nc* act of examining in order to find something; act of looking for something 搜查; 探索. **searching** *adj* examining carefully 仔細檢查的; 銳利的:

a searching glance 銳利的眼光. **'searchlight** electric lamp with a very bright beam (e.g. one used to show an enemy aeroplane during darkness) 探照燈(如夜間用來照射敵機). **search for something** look for 尋找: *search for a book that has been lost* 尋找一部已經丟失的書.

season ['si:zn] *nc* **1** part of the year that is different from other parts because of the weather usual at that time 季: *Some parts of the world have four seasons, others have only two.* 世界上有些地區一年分四季, 有些地區只分二季. **2** part of the year that is suitable for something, or when something occurs 季節; 旺季; 活躍季節: *the Christmas season* 聖誕節前後的歡樂季節; *the holiday season* 休假旅遊季節. **3** period of time 一段時間; 一時: *a play that is running for a season* 連續上演一段時間的一齣戲. Also 亦作 *vt* improve the taste of food by adding something 給…調味: *meat seasoned with salt* 加鹽調味的肉. **seasonal** *adj* connected with the seasons; depending on the time of year 季節性的; 隨季節變化的: *seasonal trade* 季節性貿易. **seasoning** *nc / u* something that improves the taste of food (e.g. salt)調味, 佐料(如鹽). **'season ticket 1** *(Brit)* ticket that gives a person the right to travel between two places for a certain time (英) 乘車月票; 季票. *(US.* 美 **commutation ticket).** **2** ticket that allows a person to visit a theatre, cinema etc as often as he likes for a certain time (看戲、看電影等)定期入場券; 長期票.

seat [si:t] *nc* **1** piece of furniture on which one sits (e.g. a chair) 座位(例如: 一張椅子). **2** part of a chair etc on which one sits (椅子等的)座部. **3**

part of the body on which one sits i.e. the buttocks, or the clothing covering it 臀部, 褲襠. Also 亦作 *vt* **1** have seats for 有…座位; 可坐…: *a hall that seats one hundred people* 有一百人座位的大廳. **2** place someone on a seat or chair 使…坐下, 使…就座. '**seat belt** strap or belt fastening one to one's seat in a car or plane 安全帶.

secede [si'si:d] *vi* (with reference to a group of people) leave an organization or state (指一羣人) 退出; 脱離: *secede and form one's own organization* 脱離關係, 並成立自己的組織.

secluded [si'klu:did] *adj* quiet; undisturbed 僻静的; 不受干擾的, 隔絶的: *a secluded area* 幽静的地區. **seclusion** [si'klu:ʒən] *nu* act of secluding or being secluded; secluded place 隱退; 與外界隔絶的所在: *live in seclusion* 隱居.

second[1] ['sekənd] *adj* **1** coming after the first 第二的: *Go down the second street on the right.* 沿右邊第二條街走. **2** another; other 另一的; 又一的: *give someone a second chance* 給某人另一次機會. Also 亦作 *adv* come after the first 名列第二: *come second in a race* 獲得賽跑第二名. Also 亦作 *nc* person / thing coming one after the first 第二. Also 亦作 *vt* support (esp. something that has been suggested for discussion) 支持; 贊成(尤指已提出的動議); 附議: *second a motion* 附議一項動議. **seconds** *npl* articles which are not of the best quality or which have something wrong with them 二等貨; 次品. '**second-best** *adj* not the best or finest 次好的; 第二好的: *my second-best suit* 我的第二件好衣服. '**second-'class** *adj* not of the best class 非頭等的; 第二等的: *a second-class carriage* 二等車廂. **second floor** floor above

the first. *(Brit* two floors above ground level; *US* one floor above ground level)* (英) 三樓; (美) 二樓. '**second'hand** see 見 **hand**[1]. **second nature** what one does without thinking about it 第二天性; 習性: *Driving a car is second nature to him.* 開車是他的習性. '**second-'rate** *adj* not the best; next to best 次等的; 次等書的: *a second-rate book* 次等書. **second thoughts** different decision taken after thinking about something 重新考慮; 重想: *On second thoughts, I will come with you.* 經重新考慮後, 我願意陪你來.

second[2] ['sekənd] *nc* **1** (time) 1 / 60 part of a minute 秒(一分鐘的六十分之一): *run a mile in four minutes and ten seconds* 跑一英里用四分十秒時間. **2** very short time 片刻; 很快: *I'll be with you in a second.* (informal in sense 2) 我很快就來陪你(義 2 爲非正式).

secondary ['sekəndəri] *adj* **1** of less importance; coming after what is first 次要的; 從屬的; 第二的. **2** coming after primary school and before university 中等教育的: *secondary school / education etc.* 中學/中等教育等.

seconder ['sekəndə] *nc* person who expresses support of a proposal at a meeting 會議中贊成某項動議的人, 附議者.

secret ['si:krit] *adj* not to be made known to others; known to only a few people; hidden 秘密的; 機密的; 隱秘的: *a secret meeting / passage / place etc.* 秘密會議/通道/地點等. Also 亦作 *nc* **1** something secret 秘密. **2** hidden reason for something 秘訣; 訣竅: *What is the secret of your success?* 你成功的秘訣是甚麼? **secretly** *adv* **secrecy** *nu* state of being secret 秘密(狀態); 隱秘(狀態): *in great secrecy*

極其秘密地. **secretive** *adj* having the habit of not allowing other people to know things 守口如瓶的; 秘而不宣的: *He is very secretive about his past.* 他對個人的往事守口如瓶.

secretariat [͵sekrə'tɛərɪət] *nc* **1** office or position of secretary or secretary-general 秘書或秘書長的職位; 書記或書記長的職位. **2** department, including staff, buildings, etc., controlled by a secretary or secretary-general 秘書處; 書記處; 秘書處或書記處的全體人員: *The United Nations secretariat* 聯合國秘書長處.

secretary ['sekrətəri] *nc* **1** person who writes letters, keeps a record of meetings etc for an employer or a club or other organization 秘書; 書記. **2** (esp. US) person in charge of a department of the government (尤美)部長; 大臣; 相: *the Foreign Secretary (Brit)* 外務大臣 (英), *the Secretary of State (US)* i.e. in charge of foreign affairs 國務卿 (美), 即: 外交部長. **secretarial** [͵sekrɪ'tɛərɪəl] *adj* connected with a secretary or his work 秘書(工作)的; 文書(工作)的.

sect [sekt] *nc* group of people who hold certain ideas in common (esp. a group who have broken away from a bigger religious group) 宗派; 教派 (尤指分裂出來的小教派). **sectarian** [sek'tɛərɪən] *adj* connected with sects or with a particular sect 宗派的; 教派的; 派系的.

section ['sekʃən] *nc* **1** part separated by cutting, splitting, breaking etc. 切片; 斷 (截、剖) 面; 部份 等: *divide something into sections* 把某物分成幾部份. **2** part of something that can be fitted into another part (可組合的) 段; 零件; 部件: *fit together sections of a pipe* 把管子的各段拼接起來. **sectional** *adj* **1**

connected with a particular part of a town, country, group etc. 地方的; 區域的; 派系的; 局部的 等; *sectional interests* 局部利益. **2** made of sections 由各部份組成的; 組合式的: *a sectional bookcase* 一個組合書架.

sector ['sektə*] *nc* part of an organization etc. 部門; 界 等: *the public sector* i.e. part of industry which is owned by the government 公營部門, 即: 政府工業部門.

secular ['sekjulə*] *adj* concerned with this world, material things, not with religious or spiritual matters 現世的; 世俗的; 物質的; 非宗教的; 非精神的: *secular matters* 世俗問題.

secure [sɪ'kjuə*] *adj* **1** safe from danger, loss etc. 安全的; 平安的: *Are your valuables secure?* 你的貴重物品都安全無事嗎? **2** well-fastened; not likely to break or give way 關牢的; 穩固的; 可靠的. (*opp* 反義詞 **insecure**). Also 亦作 *vt* **1** fasten well 關緊; 弄牢: *secure a rope* 繫牢繩. **2** get; obtain 弄到; 獲得: *secure a ticket for someone* 爲某人弄到一張票. **securely** *adv*.

security [sɪ'kjuərɪtɪ] **1** *nu* freedom or protection from danger, loss etc. 安全; 平安; 安穩: *in the security of one's own home* 在自己家裏安穩自在. (*opp* 反義詞 **insecurity**). **2** *nc / u* something valuable given to a person who lends one money, which one can get back only if one returns the money 抵押品; 擔保品: *give someone a gold watch as security for a loan* 交給某人一隻金錶作爲一筆貸款的抵押品.

sedan [sɪ'dæn] *nc* **1** type of closed automobile having a front and a rear seat and seating four or more persons 轎車. **2** (also 亦作 **sedan chair**) covered chair for one person, carried on poles by two men 轎子.

sedate [si'deit] *adj* quiet; serious 安靜的; 莊重的: *a sedate little girl* 嫻靜的少女; *behave in a sedate manner* 舉止莊重.

sedation [si'deiʃən] *nu* condition of quietness brought about by drugs (服用鎮靜劑後的)鎮靜狀態.

sedative ['seditiv] *nc / u* medicine which makes people calm 鎮靜劑; 安定片: *take a sedative before going to bed* 睡前服鎮靜劑.

sedentary ['sedntri] *adj* done sitting down 坐着做的: *a sedentary occupation* 一種坐着做的工作.

sediment ['sedimənt] *nu* matter that sinks to the bottom of a liquid; e.g. mud at the bottom of a river) 沉澱物 (如河床淤泥).

sedition [si'diʃən] *nu* speech or action causing discontent or rebellion against the government; incitement to discontent or rebellion 煽動性的言論或行動; 煽動不滿或叛亂.

seduce [si'dju:s] *vt* 1 persuade a person to have sexual intercourse with one 誘姦. 2 persuade someone to do wrong 誘使··· 幹壞事. **seduction** [si'dʌkʃən] *nc* 1 act of seducing or being seduced 誘姦; 引誘; 誘惑. 2 something attractive (but not necessarily wrong) 魅力; 吸引力(但不一定是壞的): *the seductions of modern life* 現代生活的魅力. **seductive** [si'dʌktiv] *adj* very attractive 吸引人的 誘惑人的.

see [si:] *vt / i* 1 be able to use one's eyes; observe with one's eyes 看見; 觀察: *The blind cannot see.* 盲人不能看. *Do you see that house?* 你看見那幢房子嗎? 2 understand 領會; 理解: *I see what you mean* 我領會你的意思. 3 visit; meet 訪問; 會見: *see a doctor because one is ill* 因爲生病, 去看醫生.

past tense 過去式 **saw** [sɔ:]. *past part* 過去分詞 **seen** [si:n]. **see about something** attend to something 注意或過問某事: *I must see about booking a seat.* 我必須留意定個座位. **see someone off** go to a railway station, airport etc with someone who is travelling 給某人送行. **see someone out** go to the outside door of a house with someone 送某人到大門口: *Don't bother, I'll see myself out* i.e. do not trouble to come to the door with me. 別麻煩, 我自己會走出去. 即: 不必麻煩陪我到門邊. **see something through** continue with something difficult until it is done properly or completely 辦好某事; 將某事做到底. **see through someone** understand the true feelings of someone who is trying to deceive one 識破或看穿某人. **see to something** get something done 設法做某事; 保證做某事: *I'll see to it that you are well looked after* 我保證使你得到很好的照顧. **I'll / we'll etc see** I / we etc shall decide later 我(我們等)以後會決定. **let me see** give me time to think or remember 讓我想想; 讓我考慮考慮.

seed [si:d] *nc* fertile part of a plant or animal 種子; (動物的)精液: *plant seeds in one's garden* 在花園裏播種. *pl* 複數 **seeds** or **seed**. **seedy** ill; neglected. *(informal)* 有病的; 破舊的. (非正式的). **seedling** *nc* young plant; small tree 幼苗; 樹苗.

seek [si:k] *vt* 1 try to get; look for 追求; 尋求: *seek advice / help etc.* 尋求意見/幫助等. 2 look for 尋找: *seek something one has lost* 尋找失物. *past* 過去式和過去分詞 **sought** [sɔ:t].

seem [si:m] *vi* 1 appear to be 看似是; 彷彿; 好像: *The judge's sentence seemed (to be) rather harsh* 法官所作

的判決似乎相當嚴厲. *He may seem poor, but he is really very wealthy.* 他也許看起來窮, 但是他確實很有錢. **2** be reported to be 據說; 好像: *It seems (that) he is very clever* i.e. this is what I have heard. 據說, 他十分聰明. 即: 我聽人說是這樣的. *So it seems* i.e. what you are saying appears to be true. 好像如此, 即: 你所說的似乎是對的.

seemingly *adv* **1** perhaps only in appearance 表面上; 外觀上: *a seemingly nice person* 表面上不壞的人. **2** from report 據說: *Seemingly he is very clever.* 據說, 他十分聰明.

seemly ['si:mli] *adj* proper; correct 適宜的; 合乎禮儀的: *seemly behaviour* 合乎禮儀的舉止. (*opp* 反義詞 **unseemly**).

seen [si:n] past part of **see¹**. see¹ 的過去分詞.

seep [si:p] *vi* (with reference to a liquid) pass slowly through (指液體) 滲; 漏: *Water is seeping through the ceiling.* 水從天花板上滲進來.

seesaw ['si:sɔ:] **1** *nu* children's game played with a board so that one child goes up as the other comes down 蹺蹺板 (遊戲). **2** *nc* board on which this game is played 蹺蹺板.

seethe [si:ð] *vi* feel something very strongly 激昂; 沸騰: *seething with anger / excitement etc.* 大發雷霆/大爲激動等; *a place seething with people* i.e. full of excited people 人羣沸騰的地方, 即: 擠滿激動人羣的地方.

segment ['segmənt] *nc* part cut off; part into which something can be divided 片段; 片; (可分成的) 部份: *a segment of an orange* 一瓣橘子.

segregate ['segrigeit] *vt* keep separate from others 隔離; 分開: *segregate people of different races* 對不同種族實行隔離. **segregation** [segri'geiʃən]

nu.

seismic ['saizmik] *adj* connected with an earthquake or earthquakes 地震的: *a seismic disturbance* 一次地震.

seismograph ['saizməgrɑ:f] *nc* instrument for recording the direction, intensity, and duration of earthquakes or other movements of the earth's crust 地震儀.

seize [si:z] *vt / i* **1** take hold of suddenly and violently 抓住; 攫取: *seize someone by the throat* 一把揢住某人的喉嚨; *seize a weapon* 攫取武器. **2** take legally 依法沒收: *seize goods that have been stolen* 把偷來的臟物充公. **3** stop suddenly 驟停: *The engine seized (up).* 發動機驟然停轉. **seizure** ['si:ʒə*] *nc* sudden attack of a disease (esp. of the heart) (疾病, 尤指心臟病) 驟發; 發作.

seldom ['seldəm] *adv* not often 不常; 很少: *He seldom comes late.* 他很少遲到.

select [si'lekt] *vt* choose 選擇; 挑選: *He showed me five pens and I selected the red one.* 他拿五枝筆給我看, 我挑了這枝紅的. Also 亦作 *adj* chosen carefully (經過) 精選的: *A select group of people were used for this experiment.* 使用一班經過精心挑選的人來做這次實驗. **selection** **1** *nu* act of selecting 選擇; 挑選. **2** *nc* thing or group of things, chosen by someone, or from which one can choose 精選品; 供選擇的東西: *a large selection of books* 大量的精選書籍. **selective** *adj* **1** having the power to select 有選擇力的. **2** choosing only the best 選拔的: *a selective examination* 一次選拔考試. **selector** *nc* person who selects, or helps to select, the members of a team (esp. for an international competition) 挑選者 (尤指挑選運動員參加

國際比賽的選拔人）.

self¹ [self] **1** *nu* one's own interests, wishes etc. 私利; 私心; 私慾: *act with no thought of self* i.e. only for other people 毫不爲己的行動, 即: 只考慮他人利益的行動. **2** *nc* one's personality or character 自己; 自我; 本性: *be changed from one's former self* 跟從前的有所改變; *one's better self* i.e. the better side of one's character 本性中良好的一面. *pl* 複數 **selves** [selvz]. *Note* 說明: *self / selves* can be added onto a *pron* like *my, him* etc and so give *myself, yourself, himself, herself, itself, ourselves, yourselves, themselves, oneself.* These are used to emphasize (*I'll do it myself*), or after a verb (*Have you hurt yourself?*). self / selves 可與 my, him 等中一個代詞結合組成 myself, yourself, himself, herself, itself, ourselves, themselves, oneself. 這些組合代詞可用來表示強調 (I'll do it myself 我會自己做), 或用在動詞的後面(Have you hurt yourself? 你弄傷自己了嗎?).

self-² [self] *prefix* **1** concerning oneself 有關自己的. **2** caused by oneself, itself etc. 自己造成的. **3** working by oneself, itself etc. 自動的. **'self-a'ssured** *adj* sure of one's own abilities 自信的. **'self-'centred** (*US* 美 **self-centered**) *adj* thinking only of one's own wishes 自我中心的; 自私自利的. **'self-'confidence** *nu* belief in one's own ability and worth 自信; 有把握. **self-confident** *adj* **'self-'conscious** *adj* see 見 **conscious.** **'self-con'tained** *adj* containing everything that is necessary 設施齊全的; 獨立的: *a self-contained flat* 獨立公寓套間. **'self-con'trol** *nu* control of one's feelings, actions etc. 克己; 自制 (力). **'self-de'fence** (*US* 美 **self-defense**)

act of defending oneself against attack of any kind 自衛. **'self-'discipline** control of one's actions 自律; 自我約束. **'self-em'ployed** *adj* working in one's own business etc. 自行經營的. **'self-'evident** *adj* obvious 自明的; 不言而喻的: *a self-evident truth* 不言而喻的真理. **'self-ex'planatory** *adj* containing all the information needed for an explanation 不解自明的: *This letter is self-explanatory* i.e. if you read the letter you will understand what it is about. 這封信的含義不解自明, 即: 這封信你讀了, 你就會明白它說些甚麽. **'self-'government** *nu* control of a nation by its own people, or of any group by its own members 自治; 自治政府; 自治團體. **'self-in'dulgent** *adj* not being strict enough with oneself 自我放縱的; 任性的. **'self-'interest** thinking of one's own needs rather than of others' needs 自身利益; 自私自利. **'self-'made** *adj* having become successful through one's own efforts 自力成功的; 白手起家的: *a self-made man* 自力成功的人. **'self-'pity** act of feeling sorry for oneself (顧影) 自憐. **'self-re'liant** *adj* not depending on others 自力更生的; 不靠他人的. **'self-re'spect** *nu* feeling that one need not be ashamed of oneself 自尊 (心); 自重. **'self-re'specting** *adj* **'self-'righteous** *adj* believing that one is more virtuous than others 自以爲是的; 自命清高的. **'self-'satisfied** *adj* too pleased with one's own abilities or achievements 自滿的; 自鳴得意的. **'self-'service** act or system of serving oneself in a restaurant, shop etc. 自助 (的); 自動售貨 (的): *a self-service store* 自動售貨商店. **'self-suf'ficient** *adj* not requiring help from others 自給自足的.

selfish ['selfiʃ] *adj* thinking only of one's own interests; intended to help only oneself at the expense of others 自私自利的; 損人利己的行動: *a selfish action* 自私自利的行動. *(opp* 反義詞 **unselfish). selfishness** *nu*.

selfless ['selflis] *adj* not selfish 無私的; 忘我的.

sell [sel] *vt / i* **1** give something for money 賣; 售: *sell a bicycle cheaply* 廉價出賣一輛自行車; *a shop that sells fruit* 賣水果的商店. **2** be given for money 售出; 有銷路: *These goods are selling well* i.e. many people are buying them. 這些貨物正大有銷路. 即: 許多顧客正興趣採購. *past* 過去式 *and* 過去分詞 **sold** [sould]. **seller** *nc* person who sells 賣主; 賣方: *a bookseller* 書商. **a 'best'seller** something (usu. a book) which is bought by many people 暢銷品 (通常指暢銷書). **be sold out of something** have sold all that one had of a particular kind of thing 賣完; 全部脫銷: *We are sold out of bread.* 我們的麵包都賣光了.

Sellotape ['seləteip]* *nu* type of adhesive tape 透明膠帶. Also 亦作 *vt* stick or seal using adhesive tape 用透明膠帶貼上 (或封緊).

semantics [si'mæntiks] *nu* study of meaning and development of meaning in words 語意學.

semaphore ['seməfɔ:*] *nu* system of sending messages (usu. by holding flags in certain positions, each position standing for a letter of the alphabet) 信號, 旗語 (通常指旗語, 以旗在特定位置代表特定字母的方式傳送訊息).

semi- ['semi] *prefix* **1** half (e.g. **semicircle**) 半 (例如: semicircle 半圓). **2** partly; not completely (e.g. **semiconscious**) 部份; 沒完全 (例如: semiconscious 神智部份清醒的). **3** occurring twice in some unit of time (e.g. **semiannual**) (一段時期出現) 兩次的 (例如: semi-annual 一年兩次的). **'semicircle** *nc* half of a circle 半圓; 半圓形. **'semi'circular** *adj* **'semi'colon** the mark; 分號; **'semi'conscious** *adj* partly conscious 神智部份清醒的. **semide'tached** *adj* having one wall in common with one other house (房屋) 一間與他屋相接的; 半獨立式的: *a semidetached house* 一幢半獨立式的房子. **'semi'final** round, match etc before the final one in a competition 半決賽. **'semi'skilled** *adj* having or needing only a limited degree of skill (usu. in **semiskilled work(er)**) 半熟練的; (只需) 技能有限的 (通常用在 semiskilled work(er) 技能有限的工作/工人).

seminar ['seminɑ:*] *nc* group of university students etc who meet together with a teacher to study by means of a discussion 研討班, 研討小組 (與一個教師相聚一起研討問題的大學生等班組).

semolina [semə'li:nə] *nu* type of food made from wheat 粗粒小麥粉; 以粗粒小麥粉做的布丁.

senate ['senit] *nc* one of two lawmaking groups in many governments (e.g. in the United States) (美國等的) 參議院; 上議院: *The bill was passed by the lower house, but rejected by the senate.* 這議案在下議院獲得通過, 但遭到上議院的否決. **senator** *nc* member of the senate in a government 參議員; 上 (議) 院議員.

send [send] *vt* **1** cause someone / something to go or come 派; 送; 打發: *send a letter* 送信; *send someone away from school* 勒令某人退學. **2** cause someone to do something 促使; 使做:

The fire sent everyone running out of the building. 火災促使人人都跑離此幢大樓. *past* 過去式和過去分詞 **sent** [sent]. **send for someone / something** ask for someone / something to come; ask for something to be sent 派人去叫; 派人去拿: *send for a doctor* 派人去請醫生; *send for supplies* 派人去拿供應品. **'send-off** *nc* meeting of well-wishers to send someone off on a journey 歡送會; 送別. **send something off** send something by post, rail etc. 寄出; 發出: *send off a parcel* 寄出一個包裹.

senile ['si:nail] *adj* showing old age; caused by old age 年老的; 年老所致的: *senile decay* 年老體衰. **senility** [si'niliti] *nu* weakness of body or mind, caused by old age 衰老; 老糊塗; 老化.

senior ['si:niə*] *adj* **1** higher in position; with longer service 地位較高的; 資深的: *Jones is senior to Smith.* 瓊斯是史密斯的上級. **2** the older 年長的; *James Jones Senior* i.e. the father, not the son who has the same name 老詹姆士·瓊斯, 即: 父親, 非同名的兒子. (*opp* 反義詞 **junior**). Also 亦作 *nc* senior person 年長者; 資深者; 上級; 高班生. **seniority** [si:ni'oriti] *nu* state of being senior 年長; 資深; 上級.

sensation [sen'sei∫ən] *nc / u* **1** feeling 感覺; 知覺: *a sensation of weakness* 虛弱的感覺; *Seeing him again after so many years was a strange sensation.* 那麼多年以後又見到他, 是一種不可思議的感覺. **2** feeling of great excitement 激動; 轟動: *His unexpected success caused a sensation.* 他出人意料的成功引起轟動. **sensational** *adj* **1** causing strong feeling 激起強烈感情的: *a sensational crime* 駭人聽聞的罪行. **2** trying to cause strong feelings

聳人聽聞的: *a sensational article in a newspaper* 報上一篇聳人聽聞的文章.

sense [sens] **1** *nc* power by which a person is aware of things outside himself 感官; 官能: *the sense of hearing / touch / sight etc.* 聽覺/觸覺/視覺等. **2** *nc* feeling one has by using these powers 知覺; 感覺: *look at a garden with a sense of pleasure* 心曠神怡地觀賞花園. **3** *nc* knowledge of what a certain thing is or how to use it 意識; 觀念; …感; …心: *have a sense of humour* i.e. be able to laugh at funny things 有幽默感, 即: 能覺察有趣事而發笑. **4** *nu* ability to think and act wisely 理智; 見識; 判斷力: *a man of sense* 有理智的人; *use one's common sense* i.e. the ordinary ability to think and act wisely which most people have 運用常識, 即: 多數人都有的普通見識. **5** *nc / u* meaning 意義; 意思: *use a word in a different sense* 使用一個多義詞. Also 亦作 *vt* feel 感覺到: *I sensed that I was not welcome.* 我覺得我是不受歡迎的. **senseless** *adj* **1** unconscious 無知覺的; 不省人事的: *fall senseless* 暈倒. **2** foolish 愚蠢的: *a senseless action* 愚蠢的行動. **make sense** seem reasonable; be able to be understood 似有道理; 可以理解: *This message doesn't make sense.* 這則消息令人不知所云.

sensibility [sensi'biliti] *nc / u* possession of delicate feelings 敏銳的感受力; 敏感: *a man of sensibility* i.e. a man who feels pity or some emotion, where another person might not 感覺敏銳的人, 即: 可感受到他人未必可感受到的憐憫等一類情感的人.

sensible ['sensibl] *adj* having or showing good judgment 明智的; 有判斷力的; 有見識的; 有鑑賞力的: *a sensible person / action etc.* 明智的人/行動等.

sensibly *adv.*

sensitive ['sensitiv] *adj* easily affected by something 敏感的; 易受影響的; *the eye is sensitive to light* 眼睛對光敏感; *be sensitive to blame* 容易因責備而引起情緒波動; *a sensitive child* i.e. one whose feelings are easily hurt 神經過敏的孩子, 即: 感情易受傷害的孩子. *(opp* 反義詞 **insensitive). sensitivity** [sensi'tiviti] *nu* state of being sensitive; extent to which one is sensitive 敏感; 敏感度. *(opp* 反義詞 **insensitivity).**

sensory ['sensəri] *adj* of the senses or sensation 感覺的, 知覺的; *sensory organs / nerves* 感覺器官/神經.

sensual ['sensjuəl] *adj* connected with the feelings of the body rather than of the mind or spirit 肉體感覺上的; *sensual pleasures* 肉體上的快感. **sensuous** *adj* affecting, or caused by, the feelings of the body 影響肉體感覺的; 肉體感覺所致的. *Note* 說明: *sensual and sensuous* have very similar meanings, but *sensual* usu. carries the idea of blame, while *sensuous* does not. sensual 和 sensuous 意思十分相似, 但 sensual 通常帶有貶義, sensuous 則沒有.

sent [sent] past of **send.** send 的過去式和過去分詞.

sentence ['sentns] *nc* **1** group of words forming the largest grammatical unit in a language 句(子). **2** punishment given by a judge (法官的)判决; 宣判; *a sentence of six months imprisonment* 監禁六個月的判決. Also 亦作 *vt* give a punishment to someone for doing wrong 宣判; 判决: *The judge sentenced the murderer to death* 法官宣判殺人犯死刑.

sentiment ['sentimənt] *nc* feeling; mixture of feelings and ideas 感情; 情緒;

情操: *full of lofty sentiments* i.e. high feelings and ideas 充滿高尚的情操, 即: 高尚的感情和思想. **sentimental** [senti'mentl] *adj* **1** having or showing too much feeling (often feeling which is not deeply felt) 傷感的; 多愁善感的: *a sentimental novel / girl etc.* 傷感的小說/多愁善感的少女等. **2** acting from, connected with, what one feels 感情用事的; 寓有情感的: *a sentimental person* 感情用事的人; *of sentimental value* i.e. not really valuable, but connected with something / someone one feels strongly about 寓有情感價值的, 即: 並非真有價值的, 但跟寓有深情的物品/人有關. **sentimentality** [sentimen'tæliti] *nu.*

sentry ['sentri] *nc* soldier who has to keep watch 哨兵; 步哨.

separate ['seprit] *adj* apart; not joined; not connected 分開的; 單獨的; 各別的: *two separate houses / ideas / people etc.* 兩幢獨立的房子/兩種不同的思想/兩個不相干的人等. *We were kept separate from our friends.* 我們跟我們的朋友一直被隔開. Also 亦作 ['sepəreit] *vt / i* **1** keep apart (使) 分開; *separate two children who are fighting* 把兩個打架的孩子分開. **2** go apart; break a connection 分手; 解散: *We once worked together, but now we have separated.* 我們曾一起工作過, 但是我們現在已分手了. *The crowd separated* i.e. people went in different directions. 人羣解散了, 即: 各人走各人的路. **separation** [sepə'reiʃən] *nu.*

September [sep'tembə*] *n* ninth month of the year 九月.

septic ['septik] *adj* infected, poisoned by germs 受感染的; 膿毒性的: *a septic wound* 受到感染的傷口.

sequel ['si:kwl] *nc* **1** something that follows, as a result of or after, something else 結局; 結果; 後果. **2** book, film etc which carries on the story of a previous one 續集; 續篇.

sequence ['siːkwəns] *nc / u* number of things following one another 一連串; 順序: *a sequence of disasters* 一連串 災難. *in sequence* i.e. one following the other 按順序, 即: 一個接一個.

sequin ['siːkwin] *nc* very small, metal ornament, sewn on clothing (裝飾衣服用的) 小金屬片.

serene [si'riːn] *adj* peaceful; calm 寧靜的; 安詳的: *a serene smile* 安詳的微笑. **serenely** *adv* **serenity** [si'reniti] *nu*.

serf [səːf] *nc* person who is not allowed to leave the land on which he works; slave 農奴 (終生被困在土地上做工的人); 奴隸.

sergeant ['sɑːdʒənt] *nc* **1** (military) noncommissioned officer 軍士. **2** rank in the police force, above an ordinary policeman but below an inspector 警官; 警長.

serial ['siəriəl] *nc* story appearing in parts once weekly, monthly etc. 連載小說; 電視連續劇等: *A new serial is starting on television tonight.* 今晚電視開播一部新的電視連續劇. **serialize** *vt* put in form of a serial 分期刊載; 連載; 連續廣播.

series ['siəriːz] *nc* number of things coming one after the other 連串; 連續; 系列: *a series of disappointments / stormy days / good harvests etc.* 一連串的失望/連續幾天的風暴/連年豐收等. *pl* 複數 **series**.

serious ['siəriəs] *adj* **1** in earnest; not joking or playful 認真的; 非開玩笑的; 非玩世不恭的: *Try to be serious for a moment.* 請正經一下. **2** thoughtful; not interested in pleasure 深思的, 嚴肅的; 不耽於玩樂的; 莊重的: *a serious*

kind of person 一個嚴肅莊重的人. **3** important and perhaps dangerous 重大的; 嚴重的; 危險的: *a serious problem* 一個嚴重問題. **seriously** *adv* **seriousness** *nu*.

sermon ['səːmən] *nc* talk given by a priest or minister in church 佈道; 講道; 說教.

serpent ['səːpənt] *nc* snake 蛇.

serrated [si'reitid] *adj* shaped like the teeth of a saw 鋸齒形的: *a serrated edge* 有鋸齒的刀口.

serum ['siərəm] *nc / u* watery liquid taken from the blood of an animal which has had a certain disease, and put into the blood of a person to prevent him from having that disease (防疫) 血清.

servant ['səːvənt] *nc* person paid to do housework 僕人; 傭人; 雇工. *Note* 說明: the word *servant* is often avoided in the USA and Britain, and the term *help* or *domestic help* is used instead. servant 一詞在英美兩國常避免使用, 而用 help 或 domestic help 取代.

serve [səːv] *vt* **1** work for; do something for 爲…服務; 爲…盡力: *serve an employer* 爲雇主工作; *serve one's country well* 爲國盡力. **2** bring food or drink 端上(飯菜); 斟(酒): *serve dinner* 上菜開飯. **3** give something that is required (esp. to a customer in a shop) 侍候; 接待(尤指商店顧客): *The assistant will serve you.* 這店員會接待你. **4** (tennis etc.) put the ball into play (網球等) 發(球). **serve someone right** be what he deserves 給某人應得的報應; 活該: *If he loses his job, it will serve him right. (informal)* 要是他失去工作, 那他活該. (非正式).

service ['səːvis] **1** *nc* something done by one person for another 服務; 幫助; 貢獻: *thank a doctor for his services* 感

謝醫生的幫助. **2** *nu* state of being a servant (in sense **1**) 侍候; 幫傭: *be in service* 當傭人. **3** *nc* department of the government; people employed in a government department 政府部門 (人員); *the civil service* 文職部門 (人員); *the services* i.e. the Army, Navy and Air Force 陸海空三軍. **4** *nc* supply or amount of something 供應設施數量; 業務: *a good train service* i.e. plenty of trains 火車客運業務良好, 即: 有許多列車運行. **5** *nc* religious ceremony (宗教) 儀式: *the Sunday service* 星期日禮拜; *the marriage service* 婚禮. **6** *nu* way in which one is served 服務(態度、水平): *The service in this hotel is good.* 這家旅館的服務水平良好. **7** *nc* set of dishes 全套餐具: *a tea service* 一套茶具. **8** *nc* act of checking up on something mechanical or electrical to make sure that it works properly 檢修; 維修: *a car that needs a service* 一部需要維修的汽車. **9** *nc / u* (tennis etc.) putting the ball into play (網球等) 發球.Also 亦作 *vt* check up on something mechanical or electrical 維修; 檢修: *have one's car serviced* 把汽車送去檢修. **serviceable** ['sə:visəbl] *adj* **1** useful 有用的. **2** useful for a long time 耐用的. *(opp* 反 義 詞 **unserviceable).** '**service charge** amount that is added to a hotel or restaurant bill, to take the place of leaving a tip for the waiter etc. 服務費. '**service station** place which provides oil, petrol etc for motorists 加油站.

serviceman ['sə:vismən] *nc* **1** member of the armed forces 軍人. **2** person whose work is serving or repairing something 維修人員; *an automobile serviceman* 汽車修理工.

serviette [sə:vi'et] *nc* small cloth to be

put over the knees while one is eating, to prevent clothes being stained etc. 餐巾.

servile ['sə:vail] *adj* showing too much respect, as a slave would 阿諛的; 奴性的: *servile flattery* 阿諛奉承; *a servile attitude* 一副奴才相.

session ['seʃən] *nc* **1** meeting (esp. of a law court, Parliament etc.) (尤指法庭、議會等) 開庭; 開會. **2** number of such meetings 開庭期; 開會期; 會議的一屆: *the summer session* 夏季會期.

set¹ [set] *vt / i* **1** place; put 放; 擺: *set a cup on the table* 把杯子放在桌上; *set a meal before someone* 在某人面前擺上飯菜; *set pen to paper* i.e. write 在紙上揮筆寫字. *set a match to something* i.e. light it with a match 擦火柴點燃某物; *set a hen on her eggs / set eggs under a hen* i.e. so that they will be hatched 使雞孵蛋/使蛋受殼孵化. **2** fix 規定; 撥準: *set a price* 規定價格; *set a time* i.e. agree on a time 確定時間, 即: 同意一個時間; *set one's watch to the correct time* 把錶撥準; *set an alarm clock* i.e. so that it will sound at a certain time 撥好鬧鐘, 即: 使在預定時間鳴響. **3** give something to be done 指派; 指定; 提出: *set an examination* 出考試題目; *set someone a difficult task* 指派某人承擔一項困難的任務. **4** become hard or more firm 變硬; 凝固: *The cement / jelly has set.* 水泥/果子凍凝固了. **5** cause someone / something to be in a certain condition 使處於某種狀態: *set someone free* 放了某人; *set a house alight* 放火燒房子. **6** (with reference to the sun) go below the horizon (指太陽)下落: *The sun was setting.* 太陽冉冉下沉. *pres part* 現在分詞 **setting.** *past* 過去式和過去分詞 **set.** Also 亦作 *adj* arranged 約定的: *at a set time* 在約定

的時間. **2** fixed; unchanging 固定的; 不變的: *a set smile on one's face* i.e. when one is not really amused 強作笑顏, 即: 在並非真正高興時; *a set phrase* 成語; 固定詞組. **setting** *nc* **1** scenery of a play 劇景; 佈景: *beautiful settings* 美麗的佈景. **2** music which is written to go with certain words 配曲; 譜曲: *compose a setting for a poem* 爲一首詩譜曲. **set about something** begin something 開始某事; 着手某事: *set about a task* 着手一項任務. **set about someone** attack someone 攻擊某人. **set someone / something back 1** hinder 阻礙: *set back someone's plans* 妨礙某人的計劃. **2** cost 花費: *His daughter's wedding set him back hundreds of pounds.* (informal in sense **2**) 他女兒的婚禮花了他數百英鎊. (義 **2** 爲非正式) **setback** *nc* difficulty which hinders progress 挫折. **set off** begin a journey 出發; 動身: *set off on a long hike* 出發作一次遠足旅行. **set something off 1** cause to explode 引爆; 燃放: *set off a rocket / firework etc.* 發射火箭／燃放烟花等. **2** make a pleasant contrast with 襯托出; 使更爲美觀: *The green carpet is set off by the yellow curtains.* 綠地毯在黃窗簾的襯托下顯得格外美觀. **set out** begin a journey 出發; 動身: *set out for Paris* 動身去巴黎. **set something out 1** make known 陳述; 闡明: *set out one's ideas* 表明意見. **2** arrange 安排; 佈置: *Your composition is not very well set out.* 你的文章佈局並非太好. **set someone / something up 1** start someone in business 使開業營…; 使經營: *set oneself / one's son up as a grocer* 使自己／兒子開業當雜貨商人. **2** build; place in position 建立; 豎立: *set up an altar* 豎立祭壇. **3** begin 開始: *set up a busi-*

ness 開了一家商店; *set up house* i.e. start living in one's own house 開始住在自己的房子裏. **'setup** *nc* situation; arrangement 位置; 佈置: *a strange setup (informal)* 一個奇怪的佈置(非正式).

set² [set] *nc* **1** group of things / people that go together 組; 套; 副; 羣: *a set of golf clubs* 一套高爾夫球球棒; *a set of false teeth* 一副假牙; *a tea set* i.e. dishes used for serving tea 一套茶具, 即: 沏茶的全套用具; *the smart set* i.e. group of people who think of themselves as being the leaders in fashion, social matters etc. 時髦人士, 即: 自認爲領導社會新潮流的一羣人. **2** radio or television receiver 收音機; 電視機: *a transistor set* 晶體管(或半導體)收音機. **3** scenery of a play, film etc. 佈景; 場景: *They had built a very impressive set.* 他們設置的佈景給人印象很深. **4** group of games in tennis (網球賽的)一盤, 一局. **'set square** piece of wood or other material in the shape of a triangle with an angle of 90° 三角板.

settee [se'ti:] *nc* long seat with a back and arms 長靠椅.

settle ['setl] *vt / i* **1** decide 決定; 了結: *settle on a time / place etc.* 決定時間／地點等; *settle a dispute* 結束爭論. **2** arrange 安排; 交代: *settle one's affairs* i.e. make sure that there will be nothing to be disputed or left unfinished on one's death 把自己的後事安排妥當, 即: 作個交代, 以免去世時留下爭議未決的事. **3** go to live in; send people to live in (使)定居: *settle in London* 定居倫敦; *settle overseas* 定居國外; *settle refugees in a new country* 遣送難民到一個新國家定居. **4** make comfortable 使舒適: *settle oneself in a chair* 使自己舒服地坐在椅上. **5** make calm or peaceful 使平靜; 使安寧: *medicine to settle one's nerves.* 安神藥. **6** pay 付; 結算: *settle a bill* 結賬. *If you leave the bill with me, I'll settle up.* 如果你把帳單留給我, 我會付清. **settlement 1** *nc / u* act of deciding or arranging something; agreement 解決; 和解; 協議: *the settlement of a dispute* 爭論的解決; *reach a settlement* 達成協議. **2** *nc* group of people who have settled in a country 移民. **3** *nc* the place where they have settled 移居地; 新住宅區. **4** *nc / u* payment 結算; 清償: *give money in settlement of a debt* 付錢還清一筆債. **settler** *nc* person who settles in a new country 移民; 僑民. **settle down 1** stay in one place 安居下來: *After years of travelling, he decided to settle down.* 旅行奔波多年以後, 他決定安居下來. **2** get used to something new 習慣: *How are you settling down in your new job / house?* 你如何在你的新工作/新房子中習慣下來? **3** become calm, peaceful 安靜下來; 定下心來.

seven ['sevn] see appendix 見附錄. **at sixes and sevens** see見 **six.**

sever ['sevə*] *vt* cut; break off 切斷; 斷絕: *sever relations with someone* 與某人斷絕關係. **severance** *nu*.

several ['sevərl] *adj / determiner* three or more but not many 幾個的; 三個或數個的: *on several occasions* 數次. Also 亦作 *pron* more than two or three but not many 幾個的; 二、三個或數個: *I've got some cups, but I think I'll need several more.* 我已有一些杯子, 但我想我還需要幾個.

severe [si'viə*] *adj* **1** strict; stern; harsh 嚴厲的; 嚴格的; 苛刻的: *a severe warning* 嚴厲的警告; *a severe punishment* 嚴厲的懲罰. **2** difficult 困難的: *a severe examination* 困難的考試. **3**

very plain; without ornament 樸素的; 簡樸的: *a severe style of dress* 樸素的衣著. **4** dangerous 危險的: *a severe illness* 重病. **severely** *adv* **severity** [si'veriti] *nu* state of being severe 嚴格; 困難; 樸素; 危險.

sew [sou] *vt / i* **1** use a needle and thread to join two or more things 縫; 縫合: *sew a button on a jacket* 在外套上縫上一個鈕扣. **2** make clothes by using a needle and thread 縫製 (衣服). *past tense* 過去式 **sewed.** *past part* 過去分詞 **sewed** or **sewn** [soun]. **sewing** *nu* work done with a needle and thread 縫紉; 針綫活. **'sewing machine** machine for sewing 縫紉機.

sewer ['su:ə*] *nc* underground pipe or tunnel that carries off waste matter from houses in a town 陰溝; 污水管; 下水道. **sewage** *nu* waste matter carried off by sewers (陰溝中的)污水; 污物.

sewn [soun] past part of **sew.** sew的過去分詞.

sex [seks] **1** *nu* condition of being male or female 性; (男女的)性別: *People should have equal opportunities, regardless of race or sex.* 不分種族, 不分性別, 人人都應機會均等. **2** *nc* division of humans into either male or female 男性; 女性: *the male sex* 男性; 男人; *the fair / gentle / weaker sex* i.e. women 女性, 即: 女人. **sexism** *nu* discrimination on the basis of sex 性別歧視. **sexist** *adj / nc* **sexual** ['sek-sjuəl] *adj* connected with sex or the sexes 性的; 兩性的. **sexy** *adj* sexually attractive *(informal)* 性感的; 有性的吸引力的. (非正式).

shabby ['ʃæbi] *adj* **1** having been worn a lot 襤褸的; 破舊的: *a shabby old coat* 一件破舊大衣. **2** dressed in old and worn clothes 衣衫襤褸的: *a* *shabby beggar* 一個衣衫襤褸的乞丐. **3** mean; low 卑鄙的; 下流的: *a shabby action* 一個卑鄙的行動. **shabbily** *adv* **shabbiness** *nu*.

shack [ʃæk] *nc* roughly-built shed 窩棚; 簡陋的小屋.

shackle ['ʃækl] *nc* (often *pl*) iron ring round the wrist or leg of a prisoner, slave etc which is fastened to something to prevent him from escaping (常用複數)手銬; 腳鐐; 鐐銬.

shade [ʃeid] **1** *nu* area of darkness and coolness, out of the sunshine 蔭; 蔭涼處: *There is not much shade here.* 這裏不太陰涼. *Let us sit in the shade of that tree.* 我們坐在那棵樹的樹蔭下吧. **2** *nc* something that keeps an amount of light out or makes it less bright 遮光物: *an eyeshade* 眼罩; *a shade for a lamp* 燈罩. **3** *nc* lighter or darker kinds of colour (顏色的)深淺, 濃淡: *I would like something in a darker shade of blue* 我要藍色深一點的. **4** *nc* small difference; a small amount 細微差別; 些許: *a word with different shades of meaning* 一個有多層微妙含義的詞; *a jacket that is a shade too long* 一件稍爲長了一點的外套. Also 亦作 *vt / i* protect from the full light or heat of the sun 遮陰; 擋熱: *This seat is shaded by a tree.* 這個座位有樹遮蔭. **shady** *adj* **1** giving protection from the light of the sun 遮蔭的: *a shady tree* 一棵遮蔭的樹. **2** probably not honest (*informal* in sense 2) 靠不住的; 可疑的(義2爲非正式).

shadow ['ʃædou] *nc* area of darkness caused by a person / thing with the light coming from another side of him or it (陰)影; 影子: *They were standing in the square and, as the sun was setting, their shadows were getting longer.* 他們站在廣場裏, 隨着日落, 他們的影子變得越來越長. Also 亦作 *vt* follow someone without the person knowing 尾隨; 盯梢: *The police have been shadowing him for months.* 警察已經尾隨他幾個月了. **shadowy** *adj* containing a lot of shadows 多陰影的. '**shadow** '**cabinet** (*Brit*) group of men chosen by the leader of the opposition party to represent its official views in Parliament (英)影子內閣(反對黨領袖挑選的班子, 以在議會上陳述該黨的正式觀點).

shaft [ʃɑːft] *nc* **1** long (usu. wooden) stem of an arrow or spear 箭桿; 矛柄 (通常是木製的): *hold a spear by the shaft* 抓住矛柄. **2** bar which turns part of a machine (機)軸. **3** long, narrow space running down the inside of a building, or extending underneath the ground to a mine etc below ground level 烟囱; 通風管道; 昇降機井; 礦山堅坑. **4** long, narrow beam of light 光線.

shaggy ['ʃægi] *adj* **1** covered in rough hair 粗毛髮的: *a shaggy dog* 粗毛狗. **2** long and rough 又長又粗的: *shaggy eyebrows* 濃眉.

shake [ʃeik] *vt / i* **1** move violently or quickly in one direction and then in another 搖動: *trees shaking in the wind* 樹木隨風搖曳; *shake one's fist at someone* i.e. to show that one is angry 對某人揮拳, 即: 表示氣憤. *shake a box to see if it contains anything* 搖動盒子, 看看裏面是否有東西. **2** tremble 發抖; *shake with fear* 嚇得發抖; *in a shaking voice* 聲音顫抖地說. **3** affect badly 使煩亂; *be shaken by the news of a disaster* 被災難的消息弄得心情煩亂. **4** make less firm 動搖: *Your actions have shaken my faith in your ability.* 你的行動已經動搖了我對你的能力的信心. *pres part* 現在分詞

shaking. *past tense* 過去式 **shook** [ʃuk]. *past part* 過去分詞 **shaken**. Also 亦作 *nc* **1** act of shaking 搖動; 顫抖: *He refused my request with a shake of his head.* 他搖了一下頭, 拒絕了我的請求. **2** drink made by shaking various things together 加料攪合飲料: *milk shake* 泡沫奶, 奶昔, 牛奶冰淇淋攪合飲料. **shaky** *adj* **1** not steady; not secure 不穩的; 不牢固的: *a shaky platform* 不牢固的講台; *in a shaky position* 處在不穩的地位. **2** trembling 發抖的: *a shaky voice* 顫抖的聲音. **shakily** *adv* **shakiness** *nu* **shake someone up** rouse, make active. (*informal*) 激勵; 喚起; 使振作. (非正式).

'shake-up *nc* act of rousing people, making them active 激勵; 振作: *Nobody is working properly in this office; we need a good shake-up.* (*informal*) 這辦公室的人沒有一個是在好好工作的, 我們得好好鞭策一下. (非正式).

shake hands / by the hand greet someone by holding his hand (usu. the right one) 握手問候 (通常用右手).

shake one's head move one's head from side to side to mean 'no' or to show doubt etc. 搖頭表示"不"或懷疑等.

shale [ʃeil] *nu* fine-grained rock, formed from hardened clay or mud, which splits easily into thin layers, and from which oil is sometime obtained 頁岩. **shale-oil** oil obtained from bituminous shale 頁岩油.

shall [ʃæl] *aux* **1** often, but not always, used with *I* and *we* to express that something is going to happen (常 (但非總) 跟 I 和 we 連用); 將; 會: *We shall be leaving in five minutes.* 五分鐘後, 我們將離開. *I shall see you next week.* 下星期我會見你. **2** used to express that something must be done 必

須; 得; 該; 要: *You shall not leave this room.* 你不要離開這個房間. *All pupils shall be present.* 所有的學生都得出席. **3** used with *I* and *we* making a suggestion (跟 I 和 we 連用) …嗎? …好嗎? *Shall I do that for you?* 我幫你做那事好嗎? *past* 過去式和過去分詞 **should** [ʃud].

shallow ['ʃælou] *adj* not deep 淺的: *shallow river* 淺河; *shallow person* i.e. one who does not think seriously about things 膚淺的人, 即: 思考事情不認真的人.

sham [ʃæm] something meant to deceive other people 假貨; 虛偽: *His pious behaviour is just a sham.* 他的虔誠舉動純是假裝. Also 亦作 *adj* pretended; false 假裝的; 假的: *sham diamond* 假鑽石.

shamble ['ʃæmbl] *vi* walk in an unsteady way 蹣跚; 跟蹌: *The tired old beggar was just shambling along the street.* 那疲倦的老乞丐正沿着街道跟蹌而行.

shambles ['ʃæmblz] *n sing or pl* 單數或複數 (with **a**) any scene of violence; state of disorder (與 a 連用) 任何暴力場所; 混亂: *The room was in a shambles after the explosion.* 發生爆炸後, 房內一片混亂.

shame [ʃeim] *nu* **1** painful feeling that one has acted wrongly or foolishly 羞愧; 羞恥: *blush with shame* 羞得臉紅; *feel shame for having told a lie* 因說了謊話而感到羞愧. **2** disgrace 恥辱: *bring shame on one's family* 使家庭受恥辱. Also 亦作 *vt* cause to feel shame 使羞愧; 使丟臉: *shame one's family by one's conduct* 自己的行爲令家人感到丟臉. **shameful** *adj* disgraceful 可恥的: *To steal money from a blind person is a shameful act.* 偷盲人的錢是可恥的行爲. **shameless** *adj* without shame; immodest 無恥的; 不要臉的. **'shame'faced** *adj* feeling shame 羞愧的; 羞怯的. **it's a shame that** it is unfair or a pity that …是不公平的; …是可惜的事: *It's a shame that he is so poor.* 他竟窮得那樣, 太不公平了. **What a shame!** What a pity! How terrible! 真可惜! 太不像話了!

shampoo [ʃæm'puː] **1** *nc / u* special soap, liquid etc for washing the hair 洗髮劑; 洗髮粉. **2** *nc* act of washing the hair by using this (用洗髮劑等)洗頭髮. Also 亦作 *vt* wash the hair in this way (用洗髮劑等)洗(頭髮). **shampoo and set** washing and setting the hair (usu. by a hairdresser) 洗頭做髮(通常靠理髮師).

shamrock [ʃæmrɔk] *nc* small, green plant with small leaves in sets of three; the national emblem of Ireland 白花酢漿草(愛爾蘭國花).

shan't [ʃɑːnt] *vi* short form of **shall not.** shall not 的縮畧形式. see 見 **be.**

shape [ʃeip] *nc / u* **1** form; appearance 形狀; 方式; 外形: *piece of wood in the shape of a square* 方形木塊; *round in shape* 圓形的; *give help in the shape of money* ie. give money 用錢資助, 即: 給錢. Also 亦作 *vt* give a certain shape or form to 使具有…形狀; 影響; 決定: *shape a pot out of clay* 用泥土製作瓦罐; *shape one's future* i.e. affect in a certain way 決定自己的前程, 即: 對自己的前程有所影響. **shapeless** *adj* without a definite shape 無定形的. **shapely** *adj* (often of women) well-formed (常指女人)樣子好看的; 勻稱的. **take shape** have a clearer form 形成; 具體化: *My ideas are taking shape* i.e. taking on a clearer pattern. 我的想法開始有頭緒了. 即: 變得具體起來了.

share [ʃɛə*] **1** *nc / u* part of something

份; 一份: *We shall all have a share of the profits.* 收益我們大家都將有份. *We'll do our share of the work if they'll do their share.* 我們會做我們的工作份額, 如果他們會做他們的工作份額的話. **2** *nc* one of the parts into which the ownership of a business company is divided 股; 股份: *buy 100 shares in a company* 購買一公司的股票一百股. Also 亦作 *vt / i* **1** use or do with others 共用; 同做: *share a room with someone* 與某人同住一間房; *shared pleasures* 同享樂趣. **2** give part of something to others; divide into parts which are given to others 分給; 分配; 均分: *share one's wealth* 分財產. **3** take part in 參與; 分擔: *share (in) the expenses* 分擔費用. **'shareholder** someone who owns shares in a business company 股東.

shark [ʃɑːk] *nc* kind of large fish with a large fin on its back, which eats other fish and can be dangerous to man 鯊魚.

sharp [ʃɑːp] *adj* **1** having a fine edge 鋒利的: *sharp knife* 快刀. **2** coming to a fine point 尖銳的: *sharp pin* 尖針. **3** sudden; violent 急劇的; 猛烈的: *sharp bend in the road* 路上的一處急轉彎; *make a sharp turn* 急轉; *sharp struggle* 激烈的鬥爭; *in sharp contrast* i.e. complete 形成鮮明的對照; *sharp pain* 劇痛. **4** severe 嚴厲的; 尖刻的: *speak sharp words to someone* 對某人嚴詞申責; *sharp wind* i.e. cold and biting 凜冽的風, 即: 刺骨寒風. **5** quick to notice or understand 敏銳的; 聰明的: *have sharp eyes* 有敏銳的眼睛; *sharp intelligence* 聰慧; *keep a sharp lookout* 嚴密監視. **6** quick to take an advantage for oneself 精明的: *a sharp businessman* 一個精明的商人. **7** high; piercing 高聲的; 刺耳的: *a sharp cry*

一聲尖叫. Also 亦作 *adv* **1** exactly; promptly 準; 整: *Be there at 9 (o'clock) sharp* 準九點(鐘)到達那裏. **2** abruptly; at a sudden angle 突然地; 急劇地: *Turn sharp right at the next corner.* 在下一個街口向右急轉. **sharply** *adv* **sharpness** *nu* **sharpen** *vt / i* make or become sharp (使)變鋒利, 激化. **sharpener** *nc* instrument which makes something sharp 削具; 磨具: *pencil sharpener* 鉛筆刀; 轉筆刀.

shatter ['ʃætə*] *vt / i* **1** break suddenly into small pieces (使)粉碎; (使)破碎: *The cup was shattered on the floor.* 杯子摔到地板上, 破成碎片. **2** destroy; (使)震驚; 毀滅: *shatter one's hopes / nerves* 使自己的希望破滅/神經崩潰.

shave [ʃeiv] *vt / i* **1** take hair from the face etc by using a razor 剃(鬍鬚); 刮(臉): *I shave every day.* 我每天刮鬍子. **2** cut thin slices off something 把…切成薄片; 刨; 削. **3** come very close to someone / something without touching him or it 擦過; 掠過: *The car just shaved past the pedestrian.* 汽車從那行人身邊擦過. Also 亦作 *nc* act of shaving the face 刮臉; 剃鬍子: *have a shave* 刮一下臉. **shavings** *npl* small pieces which come off wood when it is being made smooth 木頭刨花. **'shaving brush** brush for putting soap on the face before shaving 修面刷, 剃鬍子的刷毛皂刷 **'clean-'shaven** having been well-shaved 剃光鬍子的: *clean-shaven youth* 剃光鬍子的年青人. **a close shave** a narrow escape from danger (*informal*) 九死一生; 倖免於難. (非正式).

shawl [ʃɔ:l] *nc* piece of cloth (usu. square in shape) worn by women over the shoulders or on the head, or

sometimes used for wrapping a baby in (女人通常用的方形)披肩, 圍巾; (嬰兒用的)兜巾.

she [ʃi:, ʃi] *pron* female person or animal that has been mentioned before. It also refers to a few things which are thought of as being feminine (e.g. a ship) 她(指提到過的女人, 雌性動物, 乃至被認為屬陰性的少數東西, 如船等): *If you are looking for your mother, she is in the kitchen.* 如果你是在找你的媽媽, 她在廚房裏. *She is coming / She's coming.* 她來啦. see 見 **her**.

sheaf [ʃi:f] *nc* number of things gathered together or bound together 束; 捆; 疊: *sheaf of corn* i.e. a number of corn stalks tied together 一捆小麥稈 (英); 一捆玉米稈 (美). *sheaf of papers* 一疊文件; *sheaf of arrows* 一束箭. *pl* 複數 **sheaves** [ʃi:vz].

shear [ʃiə*] *vt* cut wool from sheep by using shears 剪(羊)的毛. *past tense* 過去式 **sheared**. *past part* 過去分詞 **sheared** or **shorn** [ʃɔ:n]. **shears** *npl* large pair of scissors i.e. two sharp blades joined together, used for cutting wool, thin branches etc. 大剪刀 (剪羊毛, 剪樹枝等用).

sheath [ʃi:θ] *nc* cover for a sharp weapon or instrument (劍)鞘; (器具)套. **sheathe** [ʃi:ð] *vt* put a weapon etc in its sheath 插…入鞘(套).

shed¹ [ʃed] *nc* building used for keeping things in 棚; 房: *toolshed* 工具房; *cattle shed* 牛棚.

shed² [ʃed] *vt* **1** cause to fall 使落下; 流出: *shed tears* 流淚; *trees that shed their leaves* 散葉的樹. **2** throw out 散發; 放射: *a fire shedding light and warmth* 散發光和熱的火. *pres part* 現在分詞 **shedding**. *past* 過去式和過去分詞 **shed**.

sheen [ʃi:n] *nu* gleaming brightness; lustre 光輝, 光彩, 光澤: *the sheen of silk* 絲綢的光澤.

sheep [ʃi:p] *nc* animal raised for its wool and its meat 羊; 綿羊. *pl* 複數 **sheep. sheepish** *adj* foolish and self-conscious 愚蠢的; 腼腆的: *look sheepish* 看來侷促不安. **'sheepdog** dog trained to help a shepherd to control sheep 牧羊犬.

sheer [ʃiə*] *adj* 1 so thin that it can easily be seen through 質薄透明的; *sheer silk* 透明絲綢. 2 complete 完全的; *sheer nonsense* 完全瞎扯. 3 straight up and down 垂直的; 陡峭的: *a sheer drop of a hundred feet* 一百英尺的垂直降落. Also 亦作 *adv* straight up and down 垂直地; 陡峭地: *cliffs rising sheer from the sea* 兀立在海上的懸崖.

sheet [ʃi:t] *nc* 1 piece of cloth (cotton, linen, nylon etc.) used on a bed 被單; 褥單. 2 flat, thin piece of paper, glass, iron etc. 張; 片; 塊; 層.

sheik, sheikh [ʃeik] *nc* 1 head of an Arab family, village or tribe (阿拉伯的)家長; 村長; 族長. 2 title of an Arab ruler (阿拉伯的統治者尊稱)酋長.

shelf [ʃelf] *nc* thin, flat piece of wood, glass, stone etc attached to the wall or the side of a cupboard so that things (e.g. books) can be left on it 擱架; 擱板: *a bookshelf* 書架. *pl* 複數 **shelves** [ʃelvz]. **shelve** [ʃelv] *vt* put aside to be dealt with later 擱置: *shelve a problem* 擱置一個問題.

shell [ʃel] *nc* 1 hard outer covering of an egg, seed etc., or of certain water animals (called **shellfish**) and of some land animals (e.g. tortoise) (卵、種子、貝、烏龜等的)殼. 2 frame (e.g. of a building) (建築物的)框架; 骨架: *Only the shell of the building has been put up so far.* 迄今, 才建好屋架. 3 metal container filled with explosives, for firing from a gun (usu. a large gun) 砲彈; 子彈. Also 亦作 *vt* 1 take the shell from 去…的殼; 剝…的殼, 剝; *shell peas* 剝豌豆. 2 fire shells at, from a gun 砲轟; *shell a town* 砲轟城鎮. **'shellfish** *nc / u* type of water animal that has a hard shell 甲殼類動物. *pl* 複數 **shellfish.**

shelter ['ʃeltə*] 1 *nc* something that covers or protects one 隱蔽處; 庇護所: *bus shelter* i.e. building which gives protection from the weather to people who are waiting for a bus 公共汽車候車室. 2 *nu* protection; cover 庇護; 遮蔽: *look for shelter* 找地方遮蔽; *run for shelter from the rain* 跑去避雨. Also 亦作 *vt / i* give protection or cover to 保護; 掩蔽: *shelter refugees* 收容難民. 2 find cover or protection 躲避; 避難: *shelter in a farmhouse* 躲在一間農舍裏; *shelter from a storm* 躲避暴風雨.

shelve,shelves [ʃelv(z)] *vt, npl* see 見 **shelf.**

shepherd ['ʃepəd] *nc* man who takes care of sheep 牧羊人. *(fem* 陰 **shepherdess** ['ʃepədis]). Also 亦作 *vt* direct or guide 引領; 指導: *be shepherded into a room* 被引進一間房裏去.

sheriff ['ʃerif] *nc* (now mainly *US* and *Scot*) important legal officer in a country (現主要用在美國和蘇格蘭)縣(郡)行政司法長官.

sherry ['ʃeri] *nu* type of yellow or brown wine 雪利酒; 葡萄酒.

shield [ʃi:ld] *nc* 1 (in former times) piece of metal, leather etc carried to protect the body from injury while fighting (古時打仗時用於護身的)盾. 2 something that protects 防護物; 護罩.

Also 亦作 *vt* protect (esp. from punishment) 保護; 庇護(尤指免受處罰); *shield a wrongdoer* 包庇一個做壞事的人.

shift [ʃift] *vt / i* change from one position, person etc to another, move (使) 變動; 移動: *shift one's position slightly* 稍微移動一下位置; *shift a person from one job to another* 調動某人的工作; *try to shift the blame for something onto someone else* 企圖諉過他人. Also 亦作 *nc* **1** change of workers; group of workers working in turn with another group or other groups (職工) 輪班: *We can keep the factory going all the time because we have two shifts–a dayshift and a nightshift.* 我們可使工廠一直生產,因為我們分兩班——日班和夜班——輪流工作. **2** change in position 變動. **shifty** *adj* not to be trusted; deceitful 不可靠的; 詭詐的: *shifty behaviour* 居心叵測的行爲.

shilling [ˈʃiliŋ] *nc* formerly, British coin worth twelve old pence (5 pence) 先令(英國舊硬幣,面值十二舊便士,等於現在五便士).

shimmer [ˈʃimə] *vi* shine with an unsteady light 微微發光; 閃爍: *a lake shimmering in the moonlight* 在月光下粼粼發光的湖水. Also 亦作 *nu*.

shin [ʃin] *nc* front part of the leg, from the knee to the ankle 小腿外脛.

shine [ʃain] *vt / i* **1** give out light; be bright 照耀; 發亮: *the moon shining on the sea* 月亮照亮了海面; *a face shining with excitement* 一張興高彩烈的臉. **2** cause to give out light 使發亮; 使照耀: *shine a torch* 亮手電筒. **3** polish 擦亮: *shine one's shoes* 擦皮鞋. *past* 過去式和過去分詞 **shone** [ʃɔn]. Also 亦作 *nu* brightness; polish 光輝; 擦亮: *put a shine on one's shoes*

把皮鞋擦亮. **shiny** *adj* shining; bright 閃光的; 發亮的: *a shiny new coin* 一枚鋥亮的新硬幣.

shingle [ˈʃiŋgl] *nu* small, rounded stones on the seashore 圓卵石; (海灘)砂石: *Do you prefer sand or shingle on a beach?* 你喜歡海灘上的沙還是圓卵石?

shingles [ˈʃiŋglz] *nu* type of nerve infection which affects the skin 帶狀匍行疹; 纏腰龍.

ship [ʃip] *nc* large seagoing vessel; large boat 船; 海船; 艦. Also 亦作 *vt* send goods in a ship 用船運: *ship a cargo of wheat to New York* 用船把小麥貨物運往紐約. **2** take in water (e.g. during a storm) (遇風雨時船) 灌進(海水): *ship water* (船) 灌進海水. *pres part* 現在分詞 **shipping**. *past* 過去式和過去分詞 **shipped**. **shipping** *nu* all the ships of a country, city or business company (某國、某市、某船運公司的) 全部船舶; 船舶總噸數. **shipment 1** *nu* act of sending goods by ship 船運. **2** *nc* amount of goods sent 裝載貨量: *a large shipment of grain* 裝載大宗的穀物貨物. **shipbuilding** *nu*. **'shipshape** *adj* properly arranged; tidy 井然有序的; 整潔的: *Everything in his room is shipshape.* 他房內的一切東西都井然有序. **'shipwreck 1** *nu* destruction of a ship at sea (e.g. in a storm) (如在風暴中)船隻失事; 海難: *a man who has suffered shipwreck three times* 一個遭遇過三次船隻失事的男人. **2** *nc* ship that has been destroyed in this way 失事船. **'shipyard** place where ships are built or repaired 船塢; 造船廠; 修船廠.

shire [ˈʃaiə] *nc* one of the areas into which Britain is divided (英)郡. *Note* 說明: this word is *o.f.* except in compounds (where it is pronounced [ʃə*]) e.g. *Oxfordshire* – otherwise use *county* e.g. *the counties of England.* 這詞爲舊式，除非用在複合詞中 (此處發音爲 [ʃə*])，如：*Oxfordshire——* 否則用 county，例如：*the counties of England* (英格蘭各郡).

shirk [ʃəːk] *vt / i* avoid doing something one finds unpleasant 逃避；規避：*shirk one's duty / responsibilities etc.* 逃避義務／責任等.

shirt [ʃəːt] *nc* garment for the upper part of a man's body (usu. of thin cloth) (男式) 襯衫. **in one's shirt sleeves** not wearing a jacket 沒有穿外衣，只穿襯衫.

shiver [ˈʃivə*] *vi* shake with cold or fear (因冷或恐懼) 發抖. Also 亦作 *nc* act of shivering 發抖.

shoal [ʃoul] *nc* large group of fish (魚) 羣：*see a shoal of fish swimming by* 看見一大羣魚游過.

shock [ʃɔk] **1** *nc* sudden and violent blow or shaking 衝擊；震動：*shock caused by an earthquake* 地震引起的震動. **2** *nc* sudden and violent disturbance caused to the mind by great pain, hearing bad news etc. 震驚；打擊：*The news of his father's death was a terrible shock to him.* 他父親去世的消息對他是最嚴重的打擊. **3** *nu* condition of the body or mind caused by the disturbance of suffering great pain, hearing bad news etc. 休克：*be suffering from shock* 發生休克；*in a state of shock* 處在休克狀態. **4** *nc* feeling caused when a current of electricity passes through the body 電擊；電震 (感覺)：*electric shock* 電擊. Also 亦作 *vt* cause to feel sorrow, surprise, disgust, horror etc. 使噁心、震驚、厭惡、恐懼等：*be shocked by someone's behaviour* 對某人的行爲感到震驚.

shocking *adj* **1** causing surprise and pain 令人震驚的；令人痛苦的：*shocking news* 駭人聽聞的消息. **2** causing disgust or anger 令人厭惡的；令人憤慨的：*shocking behaviour* 令人髮指的行爲. **3** very bad 很壞的：*shocking handwriting* 糟透的筆跡.

shod [ʃɔd] past of **shoe.** shoe 的過去式和過去分詞.

shoddy [ˈʃɔdi] *adj* poorly made or done 劣質的：*a shoddy piece of work* 一件劣貨.

shoe [ʃu:] *nc* covering for the foot (usu. not going above the ankle) 鞋 (通常鞋幫不過踝骨). see 見 **boot.** Also 亦作 *vt* put shoes on 給…穿鞋；給 (馬) 釘蹄鐵：*shoe a horse* 給馬釘上蹄鐵；*well- / badly-shod* i.e. wearing good / poor shoes 穿好鞋／壞鞋. *past* 過去式和過去分詞 **shod** [ʃɔd]. 'shoelace string, long piece of leather etc used for tying up a shoe 鞋帶. **on a shoestring** very cheaply 非常便宜地：*When he was away from home, he managed to live on a shoestring. (informal)* 他離家外出時，日子總設法過得十分節儉. (非正式).

shone [ʃɔn] past of **shine.** shine 的過去式和過去分詞.

shook [ʃuk] past tense of **shake.** shake 的過去式.

shoot [ʃu:t] *vt / i* **1** fire a bullet from a gun or an arrow from a bow; injure or kill someone in this way 發射；射中；射傷；射死：*shoot someone in the shoulder* 射中某人的肩膀. *He was shot in the street.* 他在街上中彈. *Tell them to stop shooting.* 告訴他們停止射擊. **2** move very quickly 迅速移動：*A pain shot up my leg.* 我的腿一陣劇痛. *He shot out of the room.* 他衝出房間. *He shot out his hand.* 他突然伸出手. **3** photograph 拍照；拍攝：*shoot a scene for a film* 爲一部電影拍攝一個

場景. *past* 過去式和過去分詞 **shot** [ʃɔt]. Also 亦作 *nc* young growth on a plant; young branch on a tree 芽; 苗; 嫩枝. **shooting** *nc / u* act of shooting 發射; 射中; 射殺; 迅速移動; 拍攝; *Did you hear about the shooting?* 你有聽到射擊聲嗎? **shooting star** small, quickly-moving body in the sky which burns brightly as it passes through the earth's atmosphere 流星; 隕星.

shop [ʃɔp] *nc* 1 building, or part of a building, where things are sold; place where some service is given for money 商店; 店舖; 服務部; *chemist's shop* 藥房; *barber's shop* 理髮店. 2 workshop i.e. place where things are made or repaired by machinery 工廠; 修理廠; 車間; *engineering shop* 機械車間. Also 亦作 *vt / i* go into shops to buy things 買東西(去), 購物(去); 到(商店)買東西; *spend a morning shopping* 花了一個上午上街買東西; *go shopping for clothes* 去買衣服. *past* 過去式和過去分詞 **shopped**. **shopper** *nc* person who shops 顧客; 買東西的人. **shopping** *nu* action of going to shops to buy things 買東西, 購物. **'shop assistant** person who serves customers in a shop 店員. **'shopkeeper** person who owns a shop 店主, 零售商人. **'shoplifter** *nc* person who steals things from a shop 店舖扒手. **shoplifting** *nu* **'shop-soiled** *adj* not completely clean or new because it has been handled in a shop 商店已擺舊的, (在店舖中陳列過或被人觸摸過多的)殘舊了的. **'shop 'steward** official of a trade union working in a factory etc. (一個工廠等)工會代表. **'shopping centre** area where many shops are grouped together 購物中心. **talk shop** see 見 **talk**.

shore [ʃɔ:*] *nc* land at the edge of the sea or a lake (海、湖)岸; 濱; *the shores of Britain* 英國海岸; *jump onto the shore from a boat* 從船跳上岸. **shore something up** support something by placing long pieces of wood etc against it (用支柱等)支撐某物.

shorn [ʃɔ:n] past part of **shear**. shear 的過去分詞.

short [ʃɔ:t] *adj* 1 not long; measuring little from one end to the other; lasting a little time 不長的; 短的; 短暫的; *short stick* 短棍; *short rest* 短暫的休息; *short memory* 善忘, 記性差. (*opp* 反義詞 **long**). 2 not tall; less than the usual height 矮的; 低的; *short grass* 矮草; *short man* 矮人 (*opp* 反義詞 **tall**). 3 less than the correct amount 不足的; 短缺的; *Our group is two people short.* 我們組缺了兩人. *He gave me short change* i.e. less than the correct amount of money. 他少找給我錢, 即: 錢找不夠. 4 saying so little that one is impolite; very brief and therefore impolite 簡慢的; 無禮的; *short with someone* 對某人冷淡; *give someone a short answer* 給某人一個簡慢無禮的回答. Also 亦作 *adv* suddenly 突然地; *He stopped short when he saw the strange sight.* 他看到那奇異的景象時突然停住. **shortage** *nc / u* lack of something; amount by which something is lacking or needed 短缺; 不足額; *large shortage / not much shortage of food* 食物大量短缺/短缺不多. **shorten** *vt / i* make or become shorter (使)變短; *shorten one's stay in a place* 縮短在某地的逗留時間. **shortly** *adv* soon 立刻; 不久; *He will be arriving shortly.* 他不久就會到達. **shortness** *nu* **shorts** *npl* type of short trousers worn while playing sports or sometimes on other occasions in hot countries (運動)短褲;

'shortbread type of sweet biscuit 脆甜的酥餅. **'short-'circuit** *nc* condition in which an electrical current escapes, instead of going through a circuit (電流)短路. Also 亦作 *wi: The kettle has short-circuited.* 電水壺發生短路. **'shortcoming** *nc* (usu. *pl*) fault; weakness (通常用複數) 缺點; 短處: *Like everyone else, he has his short-comings.* 跟大家一樣, 他也有自己的缺點. **'short cut** see 見 *cut².* **'short-hand** quick way of writing down speech by using special signs 速記: *shorthand typist* i.e. someone who can type and also knows shorthand 速記打字員. **'short-'lived** *adj* not lasting a long time 短命的; 曇花一現的: *His interest in camping as a hobby was short-lived.* 他把野營生活當作愛好的興趣是短暫的. **'short-'sighted** *adj* 1 having poor eyesight (for distant objects) 近視的. 2 not looking far enough into the future 眼光短淺的: *a short-sighted plan* 缺乏遠見的計劃. **'short-'tempered** *adj* easily made angry 暴躁的; 易怒的. **'short wave** (radio) sound wave measuring from 11-75 metres (in Britain) 短波在英國波長在11—75公尺之間的無線電波).

cut something short see 見 *cut¹.*
fall short of see 見 *fall².*

shot¹ [ʃɔt] past of *shoot.* shoot的過去式和過去分詞.

shot² [ʃɔt] *nc* 1 firing of a gun etc. 射擊; 發射: *fire several shots* 開了幾槍. 2 sound made by a gun firing 槍聲; 砲聲: *hear a shot* 聽到一下槍聲. 3 attempt; try 試圖; 嘗試: *make / have a shot at (doing) something* 嘗試做某事. 4 person who shoots 射手; 槍手: *be a good shot* i.e. skilful in using a gun 是優秀的射手, 即: 打槍老練. 5 injection 注射; 打針: *The doctor gave*

him a shot of morphine to ease the pain. (*informal* in sense 5) 醫生給他打了一針嗎啡鎮痛(義5爲非正式). **'shotgun** gun used for firing very small balls of lead 散彈槍; 獵槍. **like a shot** very quickly 立刻; 馬上; *accept something like a shot* (*informal*) 馬上接受某事物(非正式).

should [ʃud] past of *shall.* shall的過去式. *Note* 說明: as well as being the past tense of *shall,* should has also other meanings. should不僅是shall的過去式, 而且還有其他意思. 1 duty to i.e. showing duty (表示責任) 應該: *You should go back and say you're sorry.* 你應該回去說聲你真抱歉. 2 to show that the speaker is not certain (表示不肯定) 據; 按: *I should say that about thirty people were there.* 據我看, 那裏約有三十人. 3 to show that something is likely (表示可能性) 該; 大概: *Your brother should be home by now.* 你的兄弟現在該到家了. 4 used with who, what etc to show surprise (與 who, what 等連用, 表示驚訝) 竟會…: *Who should be there but Charles, whom I hadn't seen for ten years.* 想不到那邊竟會是查理, 我已有十年沒見到他了.

shoulder ['ʃouldə*] *nc* part of the body between the top of the arm and the neck; part of an animal or bird that joins the leg or wing to the body 肩; 肩膀; 肩胛. Also 亦作 *vt* 1 put on the shoulder 擔; 掮: *shoulder a sack* 掮起一袋. 2 accept; bear 接受; 承擔: *shoulder a responsibility* 承擔責任. **shoulders** *npl* upper part of the back, including the two shoulders 肩背; 雙肩.

shout [ʃaut] *vt / i* 1 give a loud cry 呼, 喊, 叫: *shout with joy / excitement / pain* 高興得/興奮得/痛得大喊大叫. 2

say something loudly 大聲講: *shout a warning to someone* 對某人大聲發出警告; *'Stand still!' he shouted.* "站住!"他喊道. Also 亦作 *nc* loud cry 呼喊: *give a shout* 大喊一聲. **shouting** *nu.*

shove [ʃʌv] *vt/i* push 推; 推動. Also 亦作 *nc* (both informal) (均爲非正式). **shove off** *vt/i* **1** go away (informal) 離開; 走掉. (非正式). **2** push (a boat) from the shore etc. (撑岸等)使(船)離開.

shovel [ˈʃʌvl] *nc* tool with a handle and broad blade used for moving materials like coal, snow, sand etc. 鏟; 鍬. Also 亦作 *vt* move something with a shovel 鏟起; 鏟動: *shovel coal* 鏟煤. *past* 過去式和過去分詞 **shovelled.** (US 美 **shoveled**).

show[1] [ʃou] *vt/i* **1** cause something to be seen; let something be seen 給看; 顯示; 出示: *He showed me his new car.* 他給我看他的新車. *He showed that he was very proud of his son.* 他顯示出他爲自己的兒子感到自豪. **2** make something clear 說明; 告訴: *He showed me where I had gone wrong.* 他向我說明我錯在甚麼地方. **3** guide or direct someone 帶領; 引導: *show someone the way* i.e. indicate where he has to go 給某人引路, 即; 指出得往哪裏走; *show someone to the door* i.e. go with him so that he finds the way out easily 帶某人到門口, 即; 送走, 使他容易找到出口. **4** give 給與; 施與: *show mercy on someone* 憐憫某人; *show kindness to someone* 親切對待某人. **5** appear 呈現: *Anger showed on her face.* 她臉露慍色. *past tense* 過去式 **showed.** *past part* 過去分詞 **shown** [ʃoun]. **showmanship** *nu* behaviour which attracts attention to oneself 引人注目的舉動. **'show-**

down *nc* occasion when someone has to state truthfully what his thoughts and feelings are 攤牌(攤出真實的想法與感情的時刻): *If it comes to a showdown, I'll certainly tell him what I think of him.* (informal) 到了攤牌的時候, 我肯定會告訴他我對他的看法(非正式). **show off** try to impress others by showing one's wealth, importance or anything one is proud of 賣弄; 炫耀: *a man who is always showing off* 總愛賣弄自己的人. **'show-off** person who behaves in this way (informal) 喜歡賣弄的人; 愛炫耀的人. (非正式). **show up 1** cause the truth about someone / something to be known 揭穿; 揭露: *My questions showed him up as a cheat.* 我提出的問題揭穿他是個騙子. **2** cause to be seen more easily 使醒眼; 使易見: *The bright light showed up the dirtiness of the room.* 亮光照得房間裏的骯髒東西格外顯目.

show[2] [ʃou] *nc* **1** act of showing 的; 顯示: *vote by a show of hands* i.e. approve by putting up one's hand 舉手表決, 即; 舉手表示贊成. **2** *nc* exhibition of something; public display 展覽(會), 展示: *horse show* 馬展; *flower show* 花展. **3** *nc* play, film or other entertainment (戲、電影等)娛樂, 演出; 節目: *Did you enjoy the show?* 你喜歡這節目嗎? **4** *nu* appearance; false appearance 外觀; 假象: *show of honesty* 表面誠實. **'show business** entertainment industry (e.g. cinema, the theatre etc.) 娛樂性行業(例如: 電影院、戲院等).

shower [ˈʃauəʳ] *nc* **1** short fall of rain 陣雨: *Don't bother about your coat – it's only a shower.* 別爲你的大衣操心——只是一場陣雨而已. **2** number of things coming at the same time 同時大量湧到的東西: *shower of arrows /*

letters etc. 一陣箭雨/信件雪片似地飛來等. **3** pipe with a device which sprays water on one like rain; act of washing oneself in this way 淋浴設備; 淋浴: *go for a shower* 去淋浴. Also 亦作 *vt / i* come or send all at once 陣雨般湧來; 傾注. **showery** *adj* with showers falling frequently 多陣雨的: *showery weather* 多陣雨的天氣.

shrank [ʃræŋk] past tense of **shrink**. shrink的過去式.

shred [ʃred] *nc* small piece torn or cut off 裂片; 碎片: *shirt torn to shreds* 撕成碎片的襯衫. Also 亦作 *vt / i* tear into small pieces; become small pieces 撕碎; 破碎. *past* 過去式和過去分詞 **shredded.**

shrew [ʃru:] *nc* small animal like a mouse but with a pointed nose 鼩鼱 (一種似鼠尖鼻的小動物).

shrewd [ʃru:d] *adj* **1** having a keen mind; having good judgment in business matters etc. 敏銳的; 有眼光的: *a shrewd businessman* 精明的商人. **2** well-informed; clever 見聞廣博的; 聰明的: *make a shrewd guess* 作出聰明的推斷. **shrewdness** *nu.*

shriek [ʃri:k] *nc* loud, sharp cry 尖叫: *a shriek of fright* 一下驚恐的尖叫. Also 亦作 *vt / i* make a loud, sharp cry; say something in a loud, sharp way 尖聲喊叫; 尖聲講話.

shrill [ʃril] *adj* high and sharp in sound 尖厲的; 刺耳的: *a shrill cry* 一聲刺耳的喊叫.

shrimp [ʃrimp] *nc* type of small shellfish, with ten legs, taken as food 小蝦.

shrine [ʃrain] *nc* **1** box which contains a holy object 神龕. **2** building which is connected with some holy person / thing 聖祠; 神殿.

shrink [ʃriŋk] *vt / i* become or make

smaller (使)收縮: *a shirt that will not shrink when it is washed* 一件洗不縮水的襯衫. *past tense* 過去式 **shrank** [ʃræŋk]. *past part* 過去分詞 **shrunk** [ʃrʌŋk]. **shrinkage** *nu* **1** act of shrinking 收縮; 皺縮. **2** amount of shrinking 收縮量.

shrivel [ˈʃrivl] *vt / i* make or become twisted and dried up (使)捲縮; (使)枯萎; *plant shrivelled with heat* 遇熱捲縮的植物; *person shrivelled with age* 年老萎縮的人. *past* 過去式和過去分詞 **shrivelled.** (*US* 美 **shriveled**).

shroud [ʃraud] *nc* cloth that is wrapped round a dead body 屍布; 壽衣. Also 亦作 *vt* make something difficult to see or understand 遮蔽; 使費解: *a crime shrouded in mystery* 一樁神秘莫測的犯罪案件.

shrub [ʃrʌb] *nc* bush; type of plant like a tree, with branches and leaves, but much smaller 灌木. **shrubbery** *nc* place where many bushes are planted 灌木叢; 灌木叢生的地方.

shrug [ʃrʌg] *vt / i* raise one's shoulders to show that one is not interested or does not know or does not care 聳(肩)(表示不感興趣、不知道、不在乎): *I asked him for his advice, but he just shrugged.* 我向他徵求意見, 但他只聳聳肩膀. *past* 過去式和過去分詞 **shrugged.** Also 亦作 *nc* this kind of movement 聳肩.

shrunk [ʃrʌŋk] past part of **shrunk**. shrink的過去分詞.

shudder [ˈʃʌdə*] *vi* shake suddenly with horror, fear, cold etc. (因恐懼、害怕、寒冷等而)發抖; 戰慄. Also 亦作 *nc* this kind of movement: 發抖; 戰慄: *give a shudder* 不禁哆嗦.

shuffle [ˈʃʌfl] *vt / i* **1** walk without lifting one's feet 拖着腳走: *The feeble old man was shuffling along the* *street*. 這個屠弱的老人正挨着脚步沿街走着. **2** mix up the order of playing cards (usu. before starting a game) 洗(紙牌)(通常在發牌前): *shuffle the cards* 洗牌. Also 亦作 *nc: give the cards another shuffle* 把這副牌再洗一遍.

shun [ʃʌn] *vt* keep away from; avoid meeting 躲開; 避免: *shun bad company* 避免與壞人交往. *pres part* 現在分詞 **shunning**. *past* 過去式和過去分詞 **shunned**.

shut [ʃʌt] *vt / i* **1** close 關; 閉: *shut a door / window etc.* 關門/窗等. **2** be closed 關上: *This window won't shut.* 這扇窗關不上. **3** stop something from entering or leaving by closing a door etc or putting up some kind of barrier 把…關在門外; 把…關住; 禁閉: *shut someone out* 把某人關在門外; *shut in all day* 整天閉整天. *pres part* 現在分詞 **shutting**. *past* 過去式和過去分詞 **shut**. **shut something down** close something so that no work is done in it; stop working 關閉; 停工; 停業: *shut down a factory* 關閉一間工廠. *The factory has shut down.* 工廠已經停工. **shut something off** stop; 阻斷; 停止: *shut off the water supply* 停止供水. **shut up** stop talking 閉嘴; 不講話: *Tell him to shut up.* 叫他閉嘴 (非正式).

shutter [ʃʌtə*] *nc* movable cover made of wood, metal etc which can be put over a window to keep out sunlight, cold, thieves etc. 百葉窗 (遮光、禦寒、防賊等用).

shuttle [ʃʌtl] *vt / i* move quickly from one place to another and back again 往返移動; (使) 穿梭般活動. '**shuttlecock** piece of cork with small feathers stuck into one side, used in playing certain net games 羽毛球. '**shuttle**

service quick regular service of buses, trains etc between two places that are usu. not very far from one another (兩地間的) 往返快車等.

shy [ʃai] *adj* **1** uncomfortable, not at ease, in the company of other people (esp. strangers) (尤指在陌生人前) 難為情的; 不自在的; 羞怯的. **2** easily frightened; timid 易受驚的; 膽小的: *The wild animals here are rather shy because they are not used to people.* 這裏的野生動物相當膽小, 因爲不習慣人來. Also 亦作 *vi* (with reference to horses) move suddenly to one side (指馬) 急速跳開或躲開: *The horse shied when it saw the snake.* 那匹馬看見蛇趕忙跳開. *pres part* 現在分詞 **shying**. *past* 過去式和過去分詞 **shied** [ʃaid]. **shyly** *adv* **shyness** *nu*.

sick [sik] *adj* **1** ill; unwell 患病的; 不適的. *Note* 說明: (Brit) the normal word is *ill* (e.g. *He has been ill for six months*). (US) *sick* is commonly used in the sense of *ill* 在英國ill爲正常用詞 (例如: *He has been ill for six months* 他已病了六個月). 在美國通常用 sick 來表達ill 的含意. **2** (Brit) faint and giddy; vomiting i.e. throwing up food from the stomach (英) 頭暈的; 使人作嘔的: *The baby was sick twice in the car.* 那個嬰孩量車兩次. *I think I'm going to be sick.* 我想我要嘔吐. **3** mentally unhealthy 病態的; 不健康的: *a sick mind* 病態心理; *a sick joke* 下流的玩笑. **sicken** *vt / i* **1** become ill (o.f.) 生病 (舊式). **2** make ill; disgust 使生病; 使厭惡: *The sight of so much cruelty sickened him.* 看到這樣多的暴行令他感到噁心. **sickening** *adj* disgusting 令人厭惡的: *sickening cruelty* 令人厭惡的暴行. **sickly** *adj* **1** ill; unwell 患病的; 不適的. **2** often ill 多病的: *a sickly child* 多病的孩子. **3** caus-

ing sickness or disgust 疾病流行的；使
人厭惡的：*sickly smell* 令人噁心的氣
味. **sickness 1** *nu* bad health 健康不
佳：*several absences due to sickness*
有幾個因健康不佳缺席．*2* *c/u* ill-
ness; disease 病；疾病：*seasickness* 暈
船．**'sickbed** bed of a sick person 病
床．

sickle ['sɪkl] *nc* tool with a short,
curved blade on a short handle, used
for cutting grass, reaping grain, and
the like 鐮刀．

side [saɪd] *nc* **1** one of the surfaces of
an object 面；邊：*He painted all four
sides of the box.* 他把箱子四面都塗上
漆．**2** one of the surfaces of an object
but not the top or bottom, front or
back 旁邊；側面：*go in by the side of
the building* 從房屋的旁邊進去．**3** one
of the two surfaces of paper, cloth
etc. (紙、布等的)面：*write on one side
of the paper* 寫在那張紙的一面上．**4**
one of the inside or outside surfaces
of something 裏邊；外邊：*the side of
the room* 房邊．**5** area thought of in
connection with a central point or
line (與想像的中心點、綫有關的)地帶：
left-hand side of the room 房間的左手
邊；*east side of the city* 城市的東邊．**6**
group playing against, or in disagreement, with another group (比賽、對峙
的)一方；邊：*get both sides in an
argument to agree* 使爭吵雙方言和；
be on someone's side i.e. agree or
sympathize with him 站在某人一邊，
即：同意或同情他．**7** either the left-
hand or right-hand part of a human
being, animal etc. (人或動物軀體的)
側邊；脅：*be wounded in the side* i.e.
on the side of the body somewhere
between the waist and the shoulder
脅部受傷，即：肩部與腰之間的部位受
傷．**8** aspect; way of looking at a

question or problem 方面；方法：*a
problem with many sides to it* 一個涉
及多方面的問題；*look on the bright
side of life* 看生活的光明面．Also 亦作
adj at the side of something 旁的；側
的：*enter by a side door* 從旁門進．
siding *nc* short railway track beside
the main one, where trains can stay
without holding up the main line (鐵
路的)側綫；岔道．**'sideboard** *(Brit* 英*)*
1 piece of furniture with drawers and
shelves, used in the dining room or
living room to hold dishes etc. 餐具
櫃．**2** (usu. *pl*) hair growing down the
cheek of a man (通常用複數)(蓄於兩
頰的)絡腮鬍子．*(US* 美 **sideburn**).
'sideline 1 line at the side of a football pitch etc. (足球場等的)邊綫；界
綫．**2** something else from which one
earns money in addition to one's
main job 兼職；副業：*do photography
as a sideline* 兼職攝影．**'sidelong** *adj*
to or from the side 橫的；斜的；側向
的：*a sidelong glance* i.e. made without turning one's head. 睨視；沒有轉
頭斜眼看人．**'sidetrack** *vt* turn someone from what he was originally intending to do 使改變初衷．**'sidewalk**
(US) place to walk on at the side of a
street (美)人行道．*(Brit* 英 **pave-
ment)**. **'sideways** *adv* **1** from, towards one side 從一邊；斜着：*look
sideways at someone* 睨視某人．**2**
with the side first 一邊向前地；側着：
*bring something sideways through a
narrow door* 側着携物穿過一道窄門．
side with someone / something
support; feel sympathy with 支持；同
情．

sidle ['saɪdl] *vi* approach or leave a person as if not wishing to draw too
much attention to oneself 側身挨近；
側身而行：*sidle up to someone* 側身挨

近某人.

siege [siːdʒ] *nc* act of surrounding a town in order to capture it (usu. by cutting off its supplies) 圍城 (通常切斷供應線).

sierra [ˈsiərə] *nc* range of mountains with a saw-toothed appearance 鋸齒山脊, 峰巒起伏的山嶺.

sieve [siv] *nc* frame with wire or plastic netting used to separate liquids from solids and large pieces of something (e.g. flour etc.) from smaller pieces 篩; 濾器. Also 亦作 *vt* separate large pieces of something from small ones in this way 篩; 濾. see 見 **sift**.

sift [sift] *vt / i* **1** put or come through a sieve 篩; 過濾: *sift flour / grain etc.* 篩麵粉/穀等. **2** examine very carefully 細查: *sift the evidence* 甄別證據.

sigh [sai] *vt / i* let out a deep breath, as when one is tired, sad, no longer anxious etc. 嘆息; 嘆氣 (例如, 在疲倦、悲傷、不再憂慮時): *sigh with relief* 放心地鬆了口氣. Also 亦作 *nc* act of sighing; sound of a sigh 嘆氣; 嘆息聲: *heave a sigh* 發出一聲嘆息.

sight [sait] **1** *nu* power of seeing 視力: *lose one's sight* 喪失視力. **2** *nc* thing seen (esp. something worth seeing in a particular area) 景象; 風景 (尤指名勝): *see the sights of the city* 看看城市的風光; *beautiful / terrible sight* 美麗的/可怕的景象. **3** *nu* act of seeing or being seen 看; 瞥見: *be overjoyed by the sight of a loved one* 看到所愛的人而大為高興; *at first sight* i.e. on seeing someone / something for te first time 初次看見時, 乍看起來. **4** *nc* (always with a) something that looks strange (總與 a 連用) 看來奇怪的事: *What a sight she looks in those clothes!* (*informal* in sense 4) 她穿上那些衣服, 樣子多麼古怪可笑呀! (義4爲

非正式). Also 亦作 *vt* see 看見; 發現: *At last the explorers sighted land.* 探險家們終於看見了陸地. '**sightseer** *nc* person looking at interesting buildings etc. 觀光者; 遊客. **sightseeing** *nu* **in / within sight** able to be seen 能看得見; 在望: *There was not a soul in sight* i.e. nobody to be seen 連個人影都沒見到, 即, 沒有看見人.

sign [sain] *nc* **1** mark which stands for something or points out something 記號; 符號; 招牌; 標誌: *mathematical signs* i.e. signs like +, ÷ and so on; 數學符號, 即, 類似+、÷等符號: *traffic sign* 交通標誌. **2** movement which stands for a word or idea (示意) 動作; 手勢: *use signs to communicate with a person who speaks only a foreign language* 用手勢跟一個只會說一種外語的人通話. **3** indication; something which reveals a fact to the person that observes it 跡象; 痕跡: *White hair is often a sign of old age.* 白髮常是年老的跡象. *We searched for the ring, but there was no sign of it anywhere.* 我們尋找那隻戒指, 但到處都毫無蹤影. **4** something which shows what is going to happen 徵兆; 預兆: *A cloudy sky is often a sign of rain.* 天空多雲常是下雨的徵兆. Also 亦作 *vt / i* write one's name on something 簽名 (於…); 簽字 (於…): *sign a letter / cheque etc.* 在信上/支票等上簽名. *Please sign here.* 請在這裏簽名. '**signpost** post for the guidance of travellers, placed on a road or at a crossroads, with the names of places attached to it 路標.

signal [ˈsignl] *nc* any kind of mark, light, sound, movement etc which gives an idea to someone, or controls his actions in some way 信號; 暗號: *traffic signals* i.e. coloured lights controlling traffic 交通信號, 即: 交通燈; *give a signal that one wishes to stop* 發出某人願意停止的暗號; *A red light is a signal of danger.* 紅燈是危險的信號. Also 亦作 *vt / i* make a signal or signals 發信號. *past* 過去式和過去分詞 **signalled.** (*US* 美 **signaled**).

signature ['signətʃə*] *nc* person's name written by himself 簽名; 簽字: *recognize someone's signature* 認出某人的簽字.

signify ['signifai] *vt / i* 1 mean; be a sign of 意味; 象徵: *What does that remark signify?* 那句話是甚麼意思? 2 show by some sign (以動作) 表示: *signify approval by nodding one's head* 點頭表示贊同. **significance** [sig'nifikəns] *nu* meaning; importance 意義; 重要(性): *something of great significance* 意義重大的事. **significant** [sig'nifikənt] *adj* 1 important 重要的; 重大的: *significant victory* 重大的勝利. (*opp* 反義詞 **insignificant**). 2 having a special meaning 有特殊意義的: *give a significant look* 意味深長地看了一眼.

silence ['sailns] 1 *nc / u* quietness; absence of sound 寂靜; 無聲: *the silence of a deserted street* 行人絕跡的街道闐然無聲. 2 *nu* state of not speaking 緘默; 無言: *listen in silence* 默不作聲地聽. Also 亦作 *vt* make silent 使沉默; 使安靜. **silencer** *nc* device that makes something quieter 消音器; 減音器: *silencer of a car / gun etc.* 汽車/砲等的消音器. **silent** ['sailnt] *adj* 1 quiet; without a sound 寂靜的; 無聲的: *The forest was silent.* 森林一片寂靜. 2 not speaking; not in the habit of saying much 無言的; 寡言的: *tell someone to be silent* 叫某人別說話; *silent person* 沉默寡言的人. **silently** *adv.*

silhouette [silu:'et] *nc / u* anything seen against a light background as a solid black shape 側面影像; 剪影; 輪廓. Also 亦作 *vt* show dark against a lighter background 使現出輪廓: *trees silhouetted against the setting sun* 落日映出樹木的輪廓.

silicon ['silikən] *nu* non-metallic chemical element (非金屬元素) 硅. **silicon chip** small electronic device which is used as a circuit in microprocessors etc. (用作微機電路等的) 硅片.

silk [silk] *nc* fine thread spun by a special type of insect (called a silkworm) and made into a fine cloth (蠶) 絲; 絲綢: *clothes made of silk* 絲綢做的衣服. Also 亦作 *adj: a silk dress* 一件絲織女服. **silky** *adj* smooth, soft and shiny, like silk 絲一樣的; 光滑的; 柔軟的.

sill [sil] *nc* flat piece of wood or stone across the bottom of a window 窗台.

silly ['sili] *adj* foolish 愚蠢的: *a silly thing to do* 做蠢事. **silliness** *nu.*

silt [silt] *nu* fine earth and sand which is left by a river 淤泥; 淤沙.

silver ['silvə*] *nu* 1 shining, white, precious metal used for making ornaments, spoons etc. 銀. 2 coins, knives spoons, bowls etc made of silver 銀幣; 銀餐具; 銀器. Also 亦作 *adj* made of silver; like silver in colour 銀製的; 銀白色的. **silvery** *adj* like silver 似銀的; 銀白色的.

similar ['similə*] *adj* like; not different from 相似的; 類似的: *two similar houses* 兩幢相似的房屋; *a car that is similar to another one* 類似的一輛汽車. (*opp* 反義詞 **dissimilar**). **similarly** *adv* **similarity** [simi'læriti] 1 *nu* state of being similar 相似; 類似: *There is not much similar-*

ity between the two brothers. 這兩個兄弟之間沒有多少相似之處. **2** *nc* point of resemblance 相似點: *Have you noticed any similarities between them?* 你有沒有注意到他們之間有任何相似之處嗎?

simile ['simili] *nc / u* (example of) way of using words so that one thing is compared to another because of something they have in common (e.g. *He fought like a wild animal. He is as rich as a king*) 直喻, 明喻(例如: 他像野獸一樣搏鬥; 他跟國王一樣有錢). see 見 **metaphor.**

simmer ['simə*] *vt / i* boil gently 慢慢燒滾; 溫火煮, 燉, 煨.

simple ['simpl] *adj* **1** easy; not difficult 容易的; 簡易的: *a simple problem* 簡單的問題; *explain something in simple language* 用淺顯易懂的話來解釋某事物. **2** with only a few parts; not complicated 簡單的; 不複雜的: *a simple machine* 簡單的機器. **3** plain; bare; with nothing added 樸實的; 樸素的; 無裝飾的: *the simple truth* 樸實的真理; *lead a simple life* 過簡樸的生活; *simple clothes* 樸素的衣服. **4** weak in the mind; stupid 頭腦簡單的; 愚蠢的. **simplicity** [sim'plisiti] *nu* state of being simple 簡單; 樸實; 天真. **simplify** ['simplifai] *vt* make simpler or easier 簡化; 使簡易. **simplification** [simplifi'keiʃən] **1** *nu* act of simplifying 簡化; 簡易. **2** *nc* something simplified 簡化物; 簡易物. **simply** *adv* **1** in a simple way 樸素地; 簡單地: *live simply* 簡樸地生活. **2** only 僅; 只不過: *We want a boy who is not simply intelligent but also hardworking.* 我們想要個男孩, 他不僅要聰明, 還要勤奮.

simulate ['simjuleit] *vt* pretend to be or to have 假裝; 冒充; 模仿: *simulate en-*

thusiasm 假裝熱情. **simulation** [simju'leiʃən] *nu.*

simultaneous [siməl'teiniəs] *adj* happening or done at the same time 同時(發生、做出)的. **simultaneously** *adv.*

sin [sin] *nc / u* act of breaking the laws of God (違反上帝法旨的)罪; 罪惡; 過失: *commit sin* 犯罪; *guilty of many sins* 罪惡纍纍. Also 亦作 *vi* break the laws of God 犯罪; 違反教規. *past* 過去式和過去分詞 **sinned. sinful** *adj* wrong; wicked 有過的; 邪惡的: *sinful deed* 過失; *sinful man* 罪孽深重的人. **sinner** *nc* person who commits sin 罪人.

since [sins] *prep* **1** from a past time until the present without a break 從⋯以來: *I have been waiting here since nine o'clock.* 我從九點鐘一直在這裏等着. **2** between some time in the past and now 自⋯以後: *I haven't heard from him since he left England.* 自他離開英國以後, 我再也沒有聽到他的音訊. Also 亦作 *adv: He left this morning and hasn't been home since.* 他早上出門, 到現在還沒有回家. *He left his native village twenty years ago and has since returned only twice.* 他二十年前離開家鄉, 此後才回鄉兩趟. Also 亦作 *conj* **1** from the time when 從⋯以來; 自⋯以後: *Tell me what sort of work you have done since you left school.* 告訴我, 你離開學校以後, 做過哪種工作. **2** because 因為; 既然: *Since you are so very tired, I'll drive you home.* 既然你這樣疲倦, 我開車送你回家. *Note* 說明: in all the above meanings of *since* connected with a length of time i.e. all the meanings except the last one, note the use of *since* with the perfect tense (e.g. *have been waiting, haven't heard etc.*) 在上述所有有關since與時間長短的意思

中，即: 在除了最後一個意思的所有意思中，要注意since跟完成時的連用(例如:
have been waiting, haven't heard等).

sincere [sin'siə*] *adj* 1 real; not pretended 真誠的; 不虛偽的: *a sincere speech* 真誠的講話. 2 meaning what one says; not deceitful 真摯的; 不騙人的: *a sincere friend* 真摯的朋友. (*opp* 反義詞 **insincere**). **sincerely** *adv* **sincerity** [sin'seriti] *nu*.

sine [sain] *n* (trigonometry) ratio between the side opposite a given acute angle in a rightangled triangle and the hypotenuse (三角學) 正弦.

sing [siŋ] *vt / i* 1 make a musical sound with the voice (usu. with words) 唱; 歌唱: *sing a song* 唱歌. 2 make pleasant sounds 發出悅耳聲音: *The birds were singing*. 眾鳥在婉轉鳴叫. *past tense* 過去式 **sang** [sæŋ]. *past part* 過去分詞 **sung** [sʌŋ]. **singer** *nc* **singing** *nu* sound of singing; act of singing; skill in singing 歌聲; 唱歌(技巧): *hear singing* 聽唱歌; *teach singing* 教唱歌.

singe [sindʒ] *vi* burn slightly 微微燒焦: *singe a shirt while ironing it* 熨衫時, 把一件襯衫燒焦了.

single [siŋgl] *adj* 1 one and not more 唯一的; 單一的: *not a single person there* i.e. no-one there at all 那裏一個人都沒有的; 根本沒有人在那裏. 2 for one only 單人的: *single room / bed etc.* 單人房/床等. 3 not married 未婚的; 單身的: *remain single* 尚未結婚. Also 亦作 *nc* 1 ticket for a journey in one direction only i.e. not a return ticket 單程票. see見 **single ticket**. 2 (often *pl*) (tennis etc.) match in which only one person plays on each side (常用複數) (網球等)單打. **singly** *adv* one by one; separately 一個個地; 各自地. **single file** *nc / u* one after

the other 單行; 一路縱隊: *walk in single file* 成單行走; 一路縱隊行走.
'single-'handed *adj / adv* done by one person by himself 單獨(的); 獨力(的). **'single-'minded** *adj* giving all one's attention to one thing only 一心一意的; 專心致志的. **'single ticket** (*Brit*) ticket on bus, train etc which is for one journey in one direction only (英)單程票. (*US* 美 **one-way ticket**). **single someone / something out** choose one person / thing from others 揀出; 選取.

singly [siŋgli] *adv* 1 one by one 逐一地; 一個一個地; 依次地: *deal with the questions singly* 一個一個地處理問題. 2 alone 單獨地; 獨自地: *live singly* 過單身生活. 3 unaided 獨力地; 單槍匹馬地: *He singly and successfully defended the position*. 他獨自一人成功地守住了陣地.

singular [siŋgjulə*] *adj* 1 unusual; extraordinary 不尋常的; 非凡的: *man of singular courage* 膽略超羣的人; *singular event* 不尋常的事件. 2 (grammar) form used in referring to one person / thing (e.g. *boy* is singular, but *boys* is plural) (語法)單數(例如: boy是單數, 但boys是複數). **singularly** *adv*.

sinister [sinistə*] *adj* promising evil; threatening 不祥的; 陰險的; 兇惡的: *sinister look* 兇惡的表情. *There was a sinister air about the old house*. 那幢老屋到處有種陰森森的氣氛.

sink [siŋk] *vt / i* 1 go downwards (下)沉: *The ship struck a rock, and sank*. 那隻船觸礁沉沒. *The boat sank to the bottom of the river*. 小艇沉到河底. *The sun was sinking in the west*. 日落西沉. *The injured man sank to his knees*. 那受傷的男子屈膝跪下. 2 make a ship etc go under water 使沉

没: *The enemy air force has sunk all our ships.* 敵人的空軍把我們的船隻全擊沉了. *past tense* 過去式 **sank** [sæŋk]. *past part* 過去分詞 **sunk** [sʌŋk]. see also 參見 **sunken.** Also 亦作 *nc* fixed basin for washing dishes etc, with a pipe to take away the dirty water (廚房的)洗滌槽.

Sino- ['saɪnəʊ] *prefix* Chinese (e.g. **Sino-Japanese trade**) 中國(的)(例如: Sino-Japanese trade 中日貿易).

sinuous ['sɪnjʊəs] *adj* not straight; twisting and curving 不直的; 蜿蜒的, 彎曲的.

sip [sɪp] *vt / i* drink by taking a small amount at a time 一點一點地喝, 啜飲; *The child sipped the cup of tea* 孩子從杯中呷茶. *past* 過去式和過去分詞 **sipped.** Also 亦作 *nc* small amount taken in sipping 一啜之量: *sip of medicine* 啜一點藥.

siphon, syphon ['saɪfən] *nc* bottle filled with soda water, which can be pushed out of a tube by the force of the gas that is in the bottle 蘇打水瓶.

sir [sɜː*] *n* **1** respectful way of talking to an older man, someone in authority etc. 先生, 閣下(對年齡比自己大的男子、權威人士等的尊稱). **2** (**Sir**) title of a knight 爵士; *Sir Walter Scott* 沃爾特·司各特爵士.

sire ['saɪə] *nc* **1** male parent of an animal (動物的)雄親, 父親. **2** title of respect used in addressing a king or emperor 陛下(對國王或皇帝的尊稱). **3** (poetic) father or forefather (詩)父親, 祖先. Also 亦作 *vt* beget, be the father of, said esp. of animals (尤指動物)生殖, 為…的雄親.

siren ['saɪərən] *nc* instrument which produces a loud noise to give warning of something 汽笛; 警報器; *Ships use their sirens in thick fog.* 船舶在濃霧中

鳴放汽笛.

sissy ['sɪsɪ] *nc* boy who is rather like a girl in his behaviour (*informal*) 女孩氣的男孩(非正式).

sister [sɪstə*] *nc* **1** daughter of one or both of one's parents 姊; 妹; 姊妹: *Mary and Jane Brown are sisters.* 瑪莉·布朗和珍妮·布朗是姊妹. **2** (**Sister**) member of a religious order; nun 修女; 尼姑; *Sisters of Charity* 仁愛修女會. **3** nurse who is in charge of a ward in a hospital 護士長; 護士. '**sister-in-law** *nc* sister of one's wife or husband; wife of one's brother; wife of the brother of one's wife or husband (配偶的姊妹)姑, 姨; 嫂; 弟媳; 姻兄、姻弟之妻. *pl* 複數 **sisters-in-law.**

sit [sɪt] *vt / i* **1** let the weight of the body rest on the buttocks 坐: *sit on a chair / the floor etc.* 坐在椅上/地板上等. **2** (with reference to a court, committee etc.) hold meetings; be in action (指法庭、委員會等)開會; 開庭: *Is the court sitting today?* 法院今天開庭嗎? *pres part* 現在分詞 **sitting.** *past* 過去式和過去分詞 **sat** [sæt]. **sitting** *nc* meeting of a court, committee etc. 開庭; 開會: *the next sitting of Parliament* 議會的下一次開會. '**sitting room** room in a house, used for relaxing in etc. 起居室, 客廳. **sit (for) an examination** take an examination 參加考試. '**sit-in** *nc* form of strike, in which workers refuse to leave their place of work 靜坐示威. **sit up 1** take up the sitting position after lying down, leaning etc. 坐起; 端坐: *The injured man is now able to sit up in bed.* 受了傷的人現在已能在床上坐起來了. **2** not go to bed 熬夜: *We sat up with the sick child night after night.* 他天天熬夜, 照顧生病的孩子.

site [saɪt] *nc* place where something has

happened or will happen 遺址; 場所; 用地: *site of a new building* 一幢新樓工地.

situate ['sitjueit] *vt* place 使位於: *a town situated near the coast* 瀕臨海濱之城. **situation** [sitju'eiʃən] *nc* **1** place 地方; 位置: *a good situation for building a house* 建屋的好地點. **2** circumstances; condition 形勢; 狀況; 事態: *The situation after the storm was very bad.* 暴風雨過後的情況很糟. **3** job 工作; 職業: *situations vacant* 事求人(報紙上的招聘廣告標題).

six [siks] see appendix 見附錄. **at sixes and sevens** in confusion *(informal)* 亂七八糟(非正式).

size [saiz] **1** *nu* largeness or smallness of something 大小; 規模: *size of a room, a town etc.* 房間的大小/城鎮的規模等. **2** *nc* measurement of how large clothes etc are (usu. expressed by a number) (服裝等的)尺碼; 號: *What size does he take in shoes? / What size shoes does he take?* 他穿鞋要穿幾號?/他穿幾號鞋? *He takes size 7.* 他量尺碼. **sizable** *adj* fairly large 相當大的; 頗爲可觀的. **.size someone / something up** understand someone / something very well *(informal)* 十分瞭解某人/某事物(非正式).

sizzle ['sizl] *vi* make a hissing sound, as when something is being fried in fat 發噝噝聲(油炸食物時).

skate [skeit] *nc* sharp blade which can be attached to a boot, for moving quickly over ice (刀式)溜冰鞋. see 見 **roller skate.** Also 亦作 *vi* move on skates 溜冰. **skater** *nc* **'skating rink** place where people skate as a form of entertainment 溜冰場.

skeleton ['skelitn] *nc* **1** framework of bones inside the body of a human being or animal (人或動物的)骨骼. **2** framework of bones of a human being or animal, without the flesh (人或動物的)骨架; 骸骨. **3** outline of the main parts of a building, idea, plan etc. (建築物、思想、計劃等)的骨架; 輪廓; 綱要.

skeptic ['skeptik] *adj* see 見 **sceptic.**

sketch [sketʃ] *nc* **1** quickly-made drawing, painting etc. 草圖; 素描; 概要. **2** short play (usu. humorous) (通常詼諧的) 短劇. Also 亦作 *vt / i* **1** draw a sketch of something (給…)繪草圖; (給…)作速寫. **2** make sketches 草擬; 畧述.

skewer ['skju:ə*] *nc* long kind of pin made of wood or metal, used for keeping meat together while it is being cooked 烤肉叉; 串肉扦.

ski [ski:] *nc* one of a pair of long, narrow pieces of wood etc attached to a person's boots, so that he can move easily over snow 滑雪板. Also 亦作 *vi* move over snow by using skis 滑雪. *past* 過去式和過去分詞 **skied** [ski:d]. **skiing** *nu* sport of moving over snow using skis 滑雪運動. **'water-ski** *nc* type of ski used for moving over water 滑水橇. **water-skiing** *nu.*

skid [skid] *vi* slide sideways 滑向一側; 打滑: *The car skidded on the icy road.* 汽車在結冰的路上打滑. *past* 過去式和過去分詞 **skidded.** Also 亦作 *nc* act of sliding sideways 打滑: *The car went into a skid.* 汽車打滑.

skill [skil] *nc / u* ability to do something well by training or practice 技能; 技藝; 技巧: *What skills has he got?* 他有甚麼技能? *He does not have very much skill in writing* 他寫作並非很有技巧. **skilled** *adj* trained in some special ability 熟練的; 有技能的: *skilled workman* 熟練工人. *(opp* 反義詞 **unskilled).** **skilful** *(US* 美 **skillful)**

adj having skill 熟練的; 有技巧的; 老練的: *a skilful surgeon* 技術熟練的外科醫生. (*opp* 反義詞 **unskilful**).

skim [skim] *vt / i* **1** remove something from the top of a liquid 撇去 (液面的東西): *skim milk* i.e. remove the cream 撇去牛奶上的奶油. **2** move quickly over a surface, touching it very lightly; move quickly a small way above 掠過; 滑過; 掠過: *The low-flying plane seemed to skim the rooftops* 那架低飛的飛機看似從屋頂飛掠而過. **3** read through something very quickly 快讀; 瀏覽. *past* 過去式和過去分詞 **skimmed**.

skimp [skimp] *vt / i* not supply enough of something; not use enough of something 剋扣; 吝嗇; 節儉: *skimp one's food in order to save money* 節儉飲食, 爲了省錢. **skimpy** *adj* too small 太小的: *a skimpy dress* 一件太小的衣服.

skin [skin] **1** *nu* outer covering of the body 皮; 皮膚. **2** *nc* outer covering of an animal, with or without the fur 獸皮; 毛皮; 皮革. **3** *nc* outer covering of fruit (果) 皮; 殼: *banana skin* 香蕉皮. *Note* 說明: with certain fruits use peel (e.g. *apple peel*) 某些水果要與peel連用 (例如: *apple peel*). Also 亦作 *vt / i* take the skin off 剝 (皮); 去 (皮): *skin an animal* 剝獸皮. *past* 過去式和過去分詞 **skinned**. **skinny** *adj* very thin 很瘦的; 皮包骨的: *skinny person (informal)* 瘦骨嶙峋的人 (非正式). '**skin diving** *nu* sport of diving under the sea, wearing special breathing apparatus (只帶面罩不穿潛水衣的) 徒手潛水 (運動).

skip [skip] *vt / i* **1** jump with a short, light step 跳; 蹦. **2** jump over a rope swung to pass under the feet 跳繩. **3** miss out something; miss out a part

of a book that one is reading 略過; 跳讀: *skip a few pages* 略過幾頁不讀. *past* 過去式和過去分詞 **skipped**. Also 亦作 *nc* act of skipping 蹦跳; 跳讀; 略過. '**skipping rope** piece of rope used for skipping (in sense **2**) 跳繩用的繩子.

skipper ['skipə*] *nc* captain of a ship 船長.

skirmish ['skəːmiʃ] *nc* fight, often not planned, between small groups of soldiers etc. 小戰鬥; 小衝突.

skirt [skəːt] *nc* woman's garment that hangs from the waist 女裙. Also 亦作 *vt* be, lie, go along the edge of 位於, 沿着或繞着…的邊緣: *road that skirts the city* 環城公路.

skittle ['skitl] *nc* one of the nine bottle-shaped pieces of wood which are knocked down with a ball in the game of skittles 九柱戲用的瓶狀木柱. **skittles** *nu* the game 九柱戲.

skulk [skʌlk] *vi* move about trying to avoid being seen, in order to avoid danger or work, or for some bad purpose 躲躲閃閃地移動; 潛行.

skull [skʌl] *nc* bony part of the head 頭蓋骨; 腦殼.

skunk [skʌŋk] *nc* small black and white animal which gives off an unpleasant smell if it is frightened or attacked 臭鼬(黑白毛相間的小動物, 受驚或遇敵時放出惡臭).

sky [skai] *nc / u* space above the earth where we see clouds, the sun, moon, stars etc. 天; 天空: *The sky is cloudy today.* 今天天空多雲. *There are millions of stars in the sky.* 天上繁星數以百萬計. *There should be a clear sky tonight.* 今晚天空將是晴朗的. *There is a difference between cold northern climates and the blue skies of the tropics.* 寒冷的北方氣候跟熱帶的藍天有

分別. *Note* 說明: this word is usu. *sing.* and used with *the (the sky)*, except when there is an *adj* in front of sky when *a / an* is used (*a clear sky*); it can also be used in the *pl* (*the skies; the blue skies*). 此詞通常是單數, 並跟 the 連用(the sky), 除非 sky 前面有一形容詞時, 則使用 a / an (a clear sky); 此詞也可用複數形式 (the skies; the blue skies). '**skylight** window in a roof (usu. level with the roof) 天窗. '**skyscraper** very high building 摩天樓.

slab [slæb] *nc* large, flat piece of stone etc. 石板/板.

slack [slæk] *adj* 1 not tight or stretched 鬆的; 沒拉緊的: *slack rope* 鬆弛的繩子. 2 not busy; not active 蕭條的; 清淡的: *slack time of the year for business* 一年中生意蕭條的時期. 3 not working hard; lazy; careless 鬆懈的; 懶惰的: 馬馬虎虎的; *a slack employee* 做事馬虎的雇員. Also 亦作 *vi* be lazy or careless 偷懶; 疏忽: *You must stop slacking.* 你別偷懶了. **slackness** *nu* **slacker** *nc* person who tries to avoid hard work 逃避艱苦工作的人; 懶鬼.

slacken *vt / i* 1 make or become slower (使)放慢; slacken one's pace i.e. walk, run etc more slowly 放慢速度, 即: 走慢點; 跑慢點等. 2 make or become looser (使)放鬆: *slacken a rope* 放鬆繩索. **slacks** *npl* 1 kind of trousers worn on informal occasions (平時穿的)褲子. 2 kind of trousers worn by women 女褲.

slag [slæg] *nu* fused refuse separated from a metal in smelting 礦渣; 熔渣; 爐渣; 燦岩渣. **slag heap** large pile of waste matter from coal-mining or metal-smelting 礦渣堆; 熔渣堆; 爐渣堆. Also 亦作 *vt / i* form into slag (使)成渣.

slam [slæm] *vt / i* 1 close or shut with a loud sound 砰地關上: *He angrily slammed the door behind him.* 他氣憤地隨後把門砰地關上. *The window slammed shut.* 窗砰地一聲關上. 2 throw or hit something using great force 猛摔; 猛擊: *He slammed the book down on the table.* 他使勁把書摔在桌上. *past* 過去式和過去分詞 **slammed.** Also 亦作 *nc* loud noise made by something being closed, hit etc with force 使勁關門聲; 猛擊聲.

slander [ˈslɑːndə*] *nc* untrue statement made to harm someone's reputation. 誹謗; 詆毀; 中傷. Also 亦作 *vt* make untrue statements about someone in order to harm him 誹謗; 詆毀; 中傷: *slander someone* 誹謗某人. **slanderous** *adj.*

slang [slæŋ] *nu* words and phrases often heard in everyday speech, but not suitable for formal or serious occasions (esp. words and phrases used only by a certain group of people) 俚語(尤指某一階層人的慣用語): *schoolboy slang* 學生俚語; *army slang* 軍隊俚語.

slant [slɑːnt] *vt / i* slope (使)傾斜. Also 亦作 *nc.*

slap [slæp] *nc* blow with the open hand or with something flat 掌擊; 摑; 拍. Also 亦作 *vt* hit with the open hand or something flat 掌擊; 拍打; 摑: *slap someone on the back* 拍拍某人背. *past* 過去式和過去分詞 **slapped.** '**slapdash** *adj* careless; untidy. (*informal*) 草率的; 潦亂的. (非正式). '**slapstick** *nu* film, play etc containing much foolish and violent comedy 低級滑稽電影(戲等); 鬧劇.

slash [slæʃ] *vt / i* 1 cut with a long, sweeping stroke 揮砍; 揮擊: *slash grass* 砍草. 2 cut down, reduce severely 削減；大幅度減少：*slash expenditure* i.e. reduce what is spent 大幅度削減開支． Also 亦作 *nc* cut or wound made by slashing 砍痕；砍傷．

slate [sleit] **1** *nu* bluish-grey rock which breaks easily into thin sheets 板石；板岩． **2** *nc* thin piece of this rock used for covering the roofs of houses, or for writing on 石板瓦；石板． Also 亦作 *vt* say that someone / something is very bad 責罵；抨擊：*The critics slated his latest play.* 這些批評家抨擊他最近的劇本．

slaughter ['slɔːtə*] *nu* **1** killing of animals 屠宰(動物)． **2** killing of many people at the same time 屠殺；殘殺． Also 亦作 *vt*.

slave [sleiv] *nc* person who is owned by another and has to work for him for nothing 奴隸． Also 亦作 *vi* work very hard 辛苦工作，苦幹：*slave at one's work* 努力從事本職工作；*slave for one's living* 爲了生存而拼命工作． **slavery** *nu* **1** condition of being a slave 奴隸身份：*be sold into slavery* 被賣爲奴． **2** system of having slaves 奴隸制度：*abolition of slavery* 廢除奴隸制度． **3** hard work that is badly paid 苦役；低酬工作．

slay [slei] *vt* kill with violence; murder 殘殺；謀殺． *past tense* 過去式 **slew** [sluː]．*past part* 過去分詞 **slain** [slein].

sled, sledge [sled(ʒ)] *nc* carriage which moves on two long, smooth pieces of metal or wood, instead of wheels, for use on ice or snow etc. 雪橇(不用輪子而用兩將金屬板或木板爲履,滑行於冰雪上的交通工具)．

sleek [sliːk] *adj* **1** smooth and shiny 光滑的：*sleek hair / fur etc.* 光滑的頭髮／毛皮等． **2** having smooth and shiny hair or fur 有光滑頭髮或毛皮的：*a sleek cat* 毛皮光滑的貓．

sleep [sliːp] *vt / i* be unconscious or in a state of complete rest with the eyes closed, as people are in bed at night 睡；睡着；睡覺：*Did you sleep well?* 你睡得好嗎? *I sleep in this room.* 我睡在這間房． *past* 過去式和過去分詞 **slept** [slept]． Also 亦作 **1** *nu* act of resting completely with the eyes closed, as people do in bed at night 睡眠． **2** *nc / u* (usu. with a or an) period of resting like this (通常與a或an連用) 睡眠時間：*have a good sleep* 睡個好覺；*a good night's sleep* 一夜安睡．**sleeper** *nc* railway carriage with beds in it (火車)卧車． (Also 亦作 **sleeping car**). **sleepless** *adj* without sleep; not able to get sleep 不眠的；睡不着的；失眠的：*sleepless night* 不眠之夜． **sleeplessness** *nu* **sleepy** *adj* **1** ready to sleep 欲睡的；想睡的：*sleepy child* 昏昏欲睡的孩子． **2** very quiet 寂靜的：*sleepy little village* 寂靜的小村．**sleepily** *adv* **sleepiness** *nu* **'sleepwalker** *nc* person who gets out of bed and walks about while he is still asleep 夢遊者，患夢遊症者． **sleeping bag** bag specially made to keep a person sleeping in it warm and dry (usu. while sleeping outdoors) (通常户外用的)睡袋． **'sleeping car** railway carriage with beds in it (鐵路的)卧車． **'sleeping pill** pill to make a person sleep 安眠藥片． **sleep in** stay asleep or in bed after the time at which one normally gets up 睡過頭；睡懶覺．

sleet [sliːt] *nu* rain which is frozen or partly frozen 凍雨；雨夾雪；霙；雨淞． Also 亦作 *vi*.

sleeve [sliːv] *nc* **1** part of a garment which covers the arm 袖子；衣袖：*sleeve of a coat / shirt etc.* 外套／襯衫等的袖子． **2** cover of a gramophone record 唱片的封套．

sleigh [slei] *nc* carriage which is pulled by horses across ice or snow, and has two long smooth pieces of metal or wood instead of wheels 雪橇；雪車(行於雪地的馬拉車，以兩片金屬板或木條板爲履，不用輪子).

sleight [slait] *nc* only in **sleight of hand** i.e. quickness in using the hand to perform tricks etc. 只用於 sleight of hand 手法；花招.

slender ['slendə*] *adj* 1 thin and graceful 苗條的；纖細的: *slender girl* 苗條的少女; *slender waist* 細腰. 2 slight; not enough 微少的；不足的: *slender income* 微薄的收入; *slender hope of success* 成功的希望渺茫.

slept [slept] past of **sleep**. sleep的過去式和過去分詞.

slice [slais] *nc* thin, flat piece cut from something 薄片；切片；片: *slice of bread / meat etc.* 麵包片/肉片等. Also 亦作 *vt* cut into slices 把…切成薄片: *slice bread* 把麵包切成片; *slice off a piece of meat* 切下一塊肉.

slick [slik] *adj* smooth; clever (perhaps too clever) 圓滑的；聰明的；滑頭的: *slick move.* (*informal*) 滑頭的行動(非正式). Also 亦作 *nc* amount of oil etc on the surface of the sea 海面上的浮油. (Also 亦作 **oilslick**). *Many birds are being killed by the oilslicks near our beaches.* 許多鳥正被我們海灘附近的浮油毒死.

slide [slaid] *vt / i* 1 move smoothly over 滑(動): *slide on ice* 滑冰. 2 pass into a condition by small steps 逐漸陷入: *slide into bad habits* 漸漸染上壞習慣. 3 pass without being noticed 不知不覺地流逝: *The days slip by.* 時光飛逝. *pres part* **sliding**. *past* 過去式和過去分詞 **slid** [slid]. Also 亦作 *nc* 1 smooth surface (e.g. ice) for sliding on (冰等的)滑面. 2 device for

sliding down, used by children (兒童) 滑梯. 3 coloured pictures for showing on a screen 彩色幻燈片. '**slide rule** instrument which looks like a ruler, used for making quick calculations 計算尺.

slight [slait] *adj* 1 not important; small 不重要的；微小的: *slight decay* 有點變壞. 2 of small build; slender 瘦小的；苗條的: *slight man* 身材瘦小的男子. Also 亦作 *vt* treat someone as if he were unimportant; rudely ignore 藐視；怠慢: *feel slighted* 感到被怠慢. Also 亦作 *vi* rude behaviour; lack of proper attention 怠慢；藐視. **slightly** *adv* a little bit 稍微: *slightly better* 畧好轉.

slim [slim] *adj* thin; slender 纖細的；苗條的: *She eats very little in order to keep slim.* 爲了保持身姿苗條，她吃得很少. Also 亦作 *vi* become slim by eating less and / or taking exercise (由於節食或鍛煉而)變苗條；減肥. *past* 過去式和過去分詞 **slimmed.**

slime [slaim] *nu* soft, sticky matter (e.g. mud) 軟而黏滑的東西(例如: 稀泥). **slimy** *adj* like slime; covered with slime 黏糊糊的；泥濘的.

sling [sliŋ] *nc* piece of cloth etc which is fastened round the neck in order to keep an injured arm in position (懸在脖子上用來固定傷臂的)吊帶, 三角巾. Also 亦作 *vt / i* throw, using the hand (*informal*) 抛, 扔. (非正式). *past* 過去式和過去分詞 **slung** [slʌŋ].

slink [sliŋk] *vi* move quickly so as not to be seen 潛行；溜走: *He was slinking away from the scene of his crime.* 他正從他的犯罪現場溜離. *past* 過去式和過去分詞 **slunk** [slʌŋk].

slip [slip] *vt / i* 1 slide without wanting to; slide and fall 滑(倒)；跌跤: *slip on a patch of ice* 滑倒在一塊冰地上. 2

move quickly or quietly 溜走；悄悄行動；塞：*He slipped out of the room, while the others were talking.* 大家談興正濃時，他溜出房間．*I slipped him a note* i.e. gave it to him this way. 我悄悄塞給他一張紙條．*He slipped off his jacket.* 他急忙脫掉他的夾克衫．**3** make a small mistake 疏忽；弄錯．*past* 過去式和過去分詞 **slipped.** Also 亦作 *nc* **1** act of slipping 滑倒；溜走．**2** small mistake 過失，失誤：*slip of the tongue* i.e. mistake of saying something one did not intend 失言，即：無意說錯話．**3** light, sleeveless garment worn by a woman under her dress （女人）內衣；襯裙．**4** small piece of paper 小紙片．**slipper** *nc* type of loose, comfortable shoe (usu. worn indoors) （通常是户內穿的）拖鞋；便鞋．**slippery** *adj* smooth enough to cause one to slip 滑的；使人滑致的：*The roads are slippery with ice.* 路結冰而光滑難行．**slips** *npl* sloping area beside the water where ships are built or repaired, so that they can easily slide into the sea when they are finished (修造船隻的)滑台；船台；斜滑道．(Also 亦作 **slipway).** **'slipshod** *adj* careless (esp. in the way one dresses or behaves) 隨便的；馬虎的 (尤指衣著或儀容)．**'slipway** see **slips** above 見上述 **slips**．**'slip-up** *nc* mistake *(informal)* 失誤；過失．(非正式)．

slit [slit] *nc* long, narrow cut or hole 狹長切口；狹縫．Also 亦作 *vt / i* make a long narrow cut in; tear in a straight line 切開；撕開；扯裂：*slit someone's throat* 切開某人的喉嚨；*slit open an envelope* 拆開信封．*pres part* 現在分詞 **slitting.** *past* 過去式和過去分詞 **slit.**

slither ['sliðə*] *vi* **1** slide unsteadily 不穩地滑動：*He was slithering about on*

the icy surface. 他搖搖提提在滑冰．**2** slide like a snake 蜿蜒地滑行．

slog [slɔg] *vi* work hard 拼命工作；苦幹．*past* 過去式和過去分詞 **slogged.** **slogger** *nc*.

slogan ['slougən] *nc* easily remembered word or phrase used by a political group, business firm etc to represent its policy, what it is selling etc. 標語；口號；商業施政，商業推銷商品的淺顯易記的詞句)：*The party's new slogan was 'Higher wages for everyone'.* 此黨的新口號是"人人都長工資".

slop [slɔp] *vt / i* (of liquids) flow, let flow, over the edge of a container; spill 溢出；濺出；潑出：*The tea slopped out of the cup.* 茶溢出杯子．*She slopped the coffee onto the saucer.* 她把咖啡潑灑到茶托上．*past* 過去式和過去分詞 **slopped. sloppy** *adj* careless 草率的：*The schoolboy was warned about presenting sloppy work.* 這個男生因作業草率而被警告．

slope [sloup] **1** *nc* surface, line etc which is at an angle i.e. neither straight up and down nor flat (斜)坡；斜面；傾斜：*slope of a hill* 山坡．**2** *nu* amount of steepness of such a surface 斜度；坡度；傾斜度．Also 亦作 *vt / i* be at, cause to be at, an angle (使)成斜度；(使)傾斜：*The land sloped down to the sea.* 陸地向海傾斜．*The sergeant ordered the soldiers to slope arms* i.e. rest their rifles on their shoulders. 軍士命令戰士扛槍. 即：把槍放在肩上．

slot [slɔt] *nc* small, narrow hole for putting or fitting something into 狹孔；槽；投幣孔．**'slot machine** machine which will deliver something (e.g. cigarettes) if a coin is put into a slot (投幣)自動售貨機．

slouch [slaut∫] *vi* stand, sit or move in a lazy, ungraceful way 懶散地 (很不雅觀地) 站、坐或移動: *be slouched over a table* 很不雅觀地探身到桌子上.

slovenly ['slʌvənli] *adj* dirty; careless 邋遢的; 馬虎的: *slovenly dress / appearance / work etc.* 邋遢的衣服/外表;馬虎的工作等.

slow¹ [slou] *adj* 1 not fast; taking more time than should be necessary (緩)慢的;費時的: *slow journey* 緩慢的旅程; *slow train* i.e. one that has many stops 慢車, 即:有許多站要停的火車. 2 not clever 遲鈍的;笨的: *slow pupil* 遲鈍的學生. 3 (with reference to a clock etc.) show an earlier time than it should (指時鐘等)慢於…的;晚於…的;慢了的: *My watch is slow.* 我的錶慢了. *It is five minutes slow.* 慢五分鐘. Also 亦作 *vt / i* (often with **down** or **up**) go, cause to go, at a slower speed (常與down或up連用)(使)慢;(使)減速: *Slow down when you come to the main road.* 你到了那條主幹路時, 要減速. **slowly** *adv* **slowness** *nu* **in slow motion** at less than its usual speed 慢動作: *a film in slow motion* 電影的慢鏡頭.

slow² [slou] *adv* slowly 緩慢地: *Try to go slow here.* 試試慢慢走過來. *Note* 說明: *slow* is not used so commonly as *slowly*, and can only be used in certain positions or phrases. slow 不如slowly那樣通用, 只能用在某些部位或詞組中. **go slow** see見 **go.**

sludge [slʌdʒ] *nu* thick mud 爛泥; 泥漿.

slug [slʌg] *nc* slow-moving creature like a snail, but without a shell 蛞蝓(鼻涕蟲). **sluggish** ['slʌgi∫] *adj* slow-moving; lazy 行動緩慢的; 偷懶的, 懶惰的.

sluice [slu:s] *nc* kind of gate which can be closed to hold back the water of a canal, river etc or opened to let it through 水閘, 水閘.

slum [slʌm] *nc* street or building in a crowded, dirty part of a town 貧民窟, 貧民區. **the slums** *npl* crowded, dirty part of a town 貧民區.

slump [slʌmp] *vi* 1 fall heavily 沉重地倒下;崩塌: *The injured man slumped to the floor.* 那受傷的人沉重地倒在地板上. 2 fall steeply and suddenly 暴跌: *Business slumped after the war, and so did prices.* 戰後生意一落千丈, 物價也暴跌. Also 亦作 *nc* period when business or employment decreases (生意或就業的)不景氣; 蕭條.

slung [slʌŋ] past of **sling.** sling 的過去式和過去分詞.

slur [slə:*] *vt / i* say something in an unclear way 含糊不清地説: *The drunk man slurred his words.* 那醉漢含糊不清地説話. *past* 過去式和過去分詞 **slurred.** Also 亦作 *nc* 1 something said against someone; insult 誹謗;中傷;侮辱: *a slur on his character* 對他人格的一個侮辱. 2 act of slurring 含糊不清的説話.

slush [slʌ∫] *nc* snow that has partly melted 半融的雪;雪水.

sly [slai] *adj* acting in a clever, untruthful way 狡黠的;詭詐的. **slyly** *adv* **slyness** *nu.*

smack [smæk] *nc* blow given with the flat of the hand 掌摑. Also 亦作 *vt* hit with the flat of the hand 用巴掌打;摑: *smack a child* 用巴掌打孩子. **smack / lick one's lips** show one is enjoying something or is looking forward to enjoying something 咂咂嘴唇, 舔嘴唇(表示滿意某物或垂涎某物): *The hungry man smacked his lips when he saw the food.* 餓漢看到那食物時, 就咂嘴唇舔唇.

small [smɔ:l] *adj* not large; little 小的;

少的; *small town* 小鎮; *small amount of money* 少量錢; *small boy* 小男孩. **smallness** *nu* 'small hours early hours of the morning (between, say, 1 a.m. and 4 a.m.) 凌晨(夜半後一點至四點的時間): *talk into the small hours* 談話一直談到凌晨. 'smallpox type of disease, which is easily spread, and which often leaves marks on the skin which do not go away 天花. 'small talk see 見 talk.

smart¹ [smɑ:t] *adj* 1 neat; well-dressed 整潔的; 衣冠楚楚的: *She looks smart in her new dress.* 她穿那套新衣服看來整潔漂亮. 2 clever 聰明的; 伶俐的: *smart child* 聰明的孩子. 3 fashionable 時髦的: *smart hotels* 時髦的旅館. 4 quick 輕快的; 敏捷的: *at a smart pace* 以輕快的步伐. **smartly** *adv* **smartness** *nu* **smarten something up make neater** 使更爲整潔: *smarten up one's appearance* 整裝打扮儀表.

smart² [smɑ:t] *vi* feel stinging pain 感到刺痛: *My eyes were smarting from the smoke.* 我的眼睛因煙燻得發痛.

smash [smæʃ] *vt/i* 1 break into pieces 打破; 打碎: *smash a pane of glass* 打碎一塊玻璃. 2 be broken into small pieces 破碎; 撞毀: *The cup smashed on the floor.* 杯子摔到地板上碎了. 3 completely defeat 擊潰: *smash an attack* 擊潰一次進攻. Also 亦作 *nc* act of smashing 打碎; 撞毀; 擊敗: *car smash* 汽車撞毀. **smash-and-grab raid** raid by thieves smashing or breaking a shop window and grabbing the goods inside (砸碎商店櫥窗搶走陳列商品的)砸搶行劫.

smattering ['smætərɪŋ] *nc* (usu.with a) slight knowledge (通常與 a 連用)一知半解; 膚淺的知識: *have a smattering of Greek* 懂得一點希臘語.

smear [smɪə] *vt* mark by spreading with something oily or dirty 塗; 抹; 弄髒: *He smeared the window with his dirty hands.* 他那雙髒手把窗子弄髒了. *You must smear this ointment over the wound.* 你必須在傷口上敷上這種藥膏. Also 亦作 *nc* mark left by smearing 污點; 油漬; 塗抹痕跡.

smell [smel] *vt/i* 1 become aware of by using one's nose 聞到; 嗅出; 嗅: *I smell something cooking.* 我聞到燒菜煮飯的香味. 2 put the nose near in order to receive a sensation 嗅; 聞: *I can't smell these flowers.* 我聞這些花聞不出. 3 give out a smell 發出氣味: *This food smells nice.* 這食物很香. 4 give out a bad smell 發出臭味: *The food that has been lying there is smelling.* 一直擱在那裏的食物在發臭. *past* 過去式和過去分詞 smelt. Also 亦作 1 *nu* power of smelling 嗅覺: *Sight, smell and touch are three of the five senses.* 視覺、嗅覺和觸覺是五種官能中的三種. 2 *nc/u* what is noticed by the sense of smell 氣味: *nice smell* 芬芳氣味; *smell of cheese* 乾酪的氣味. 3 *nc* what is noticed by the sense of smell as unpleasant 難聞的氣味: *There is a smell in the kitchen.* 廚房裏有一股難聞的氣味. **smelly** *adj* with an unpleasant smell 難聞的; 發臭的.

smile [smaɪl] *vi* look pleased or amused by curving the mouth upwards 微笑; 露出笑容: *smile happily* 幸福地微笑. Also 亦作 *nc* act of smiling 微笑; 笑容.

smirk [smɜ:k] *vi* smile in a silly or self-satisfied way 傻笑; 自得其樂地笑. Also 亦作 *nc* this type of smile 傻笑; 得意的笑.

smith [smiθ] *nc* person who works with metal 金屬工匠; 鍛工: *goldsmith* 金匠; *silversmith* 銀匠. see 見 black. **smithy** ['smiði] *nc* place where a blacksmith works 鐵匠舖.

smock [smɔk] *nc* loose outer garment 罩衫.

smog [smɔg] *nu* mixture of smoke and fog in the air 烟雾.

smoke [smouk] **1** *nu* cloud of gases etc which rises when anything burns 烟: *smoke from a wood fire* 柴火冒出的烟. **2** *nc* act of smoking tobacco 抽烟: *have a smoke* 抽一口烟. Also 亦作 *vt/i* **1** give out smoke 冒烟: *an oil lamp that is smoking* 一盏冒烟的油灯: *a fire that is smoking* i.e. the smoke from the fire is going into the room instead of up the chimney 烟燻燻的炉火, 即: 烟燻入室内, 没从烟囱逸出. **2** draw in smoke from a cigarette, cigar, pipe etc through the mouth, then blow it out again 抽烟. **3** use cigarettes etc regularly 有抽烟习惯: *Do you smoke?* 你抽烟吗? **4** dry fish or meat so as to preserve it and give it a special flavour 燻製(鱼、肉). **smoker** *nc* person who smokes tobacco 吸烟者. **smoky** *adj* **1** giving off smoke; full of smoke 冒烟的; 烟雾瀰漫的. **2** like smoke 似烟的, 烟状的. **smokeless** *adj* **1** burning without smoke (燃烧)無烟的: *smokeless fuel* 無烟燃料. **2** free from smoke 無烟的: *smokeless zone* i.e. area where fuels giving out smoke must not be used 無烟區, 即: 禁用冒烟燃料的地區.

smooth [smu:ð] *adj* **1** with an even surface, like glass 平滑的; 光滑的: *as smooth as silk* 跟丝一样光滑. **2** not rough 平稳的, 顺利的: *smooth sail* 一帆风顺. **3** friendly and polite, but perhaps not sincere 友好礼貌的; 圆滑的: *smooth talker* 圆滑的谈话人. Also 亦作 *vt* make smooth 使平滑(平稳、平和): *smooth matters down* 使事态平稳下来; *smooth a dress that has been crushed* 烫平被弄皱的衣服. **smoothly**

adv in a smooth manner 平滑地; 顺利地; 圆滑地: *The meeting went very smoothly* i.e. there was no trouble. 会议进展十分顺利. 即: 没有遇到甚麽麻烦. **smoothness** *nu*.

smother ['smʌðə*] *vt / i* kill by keeping air from (使)窒息; (使)闷死.

smoulder ['smouldə*] (*US* 美 **smolder**) *vi* burn slowly, give off smoke but no flame 慢燃, 燻烧.

smudge [smʌdʒ] *nc* **1** dirty mark 污點; 污迹. **2** mark left by ink that has been rubbed while wet 墨渍痕. Also 亦作 *vt / i*.

smug [smʌg] *adj* too pleased with oneself; self-satisfied 沾沾自喜的; 自鸣得意的. **smugly** *adv* **smugness** *nu*.

smuggle ['smʌgl] *vt / i* **1** get something into another country secretly and illegally 走私; 私运: *smuggle stolen goods into the country* 把偷来的赃物私运到这个国家; *smuggle something through the customs* 走私某物通过海关. **2** get something / someone into or out of a place secretly 偷偷带进; 偷带出. **smuggling** *nu* **smuggler** *nc* person who gets money from smuggling goods 走私者.

snack [snæk] *nc* light, quickly-taken meal 快餐; 小吃; 點心. '**snack bar** place where such meals can be taken 快餐馆; 小吃店; 小吃摊.

snag [snæg] *nc* unexpected difficulty 意外的困难; 潜在的困难.

snail [sneil] *nc* small creature with a shell on its back, which moves very slowly 蜗牛.

snake [sneik] *nc* long, thin, crawling reptile with no legs and sometimes with a poisonous bite 蛇.

snap [snæp] *vt / i* **1** make a short, sharp sound, like a thin piece of wood breaking 使发嘶啪声. **2** break suddenly into two pieces 突然折斷: *The rope snapped* 繩索突然斷了. **3** say something quickly and harshly 厲聲說: *snap a command* 厲聲下達命令. **4** quickly take a photograph of someone 急速拍攝. *past* 過去式和過去分詞 **snapped.** Also 亦作 *nc* **1** short, sharp sound 噼啪聲: *the snap of a branch breaking* 樹枝折斷的噼啪聲. **2** act of snapping 折攝; 厲聲. **3** snapshot. see below (*informal* in sense 3) 見下述 (義 3 爲非正式). Also 亦作 *adj* done quickly 倉促的; 倉就的: *make a snap judgment* 作出倉促的決定. **snappy** *adj* smart; lively. (*informal*) 時髦的; 聰明的; 活潑的. (非正式). '**snapshot** quickly-taken photograph 快照; 快相.

snare [sneə*] *nc* device with a loop for catching small animals and birds 羅網; 陷阱; 圈套. Also 亦作 *vt*.

snarl [snɑ:l] *vt / i* **1** growl and show the teeth 吠; 噥: *The dog snarled at the stranger.* 狗對着陌生人猛猛吠叫. **2** say in a very angry manner 咆哮着說; 怒罵: *snarl a command* 咆哮着下命令. Also 亦作 *nc* act or sound of snarling 吠(聲); 咆哮(聲).

snatch [snætʃ] *vt* take quickly and violently 攫取; 強奪: *The thief snatched the handbag and ran away.* 小偷搶走手提包逃跑了. Also 亦作 *nc* **1** act of snatching 攫取; 強奪. **2** short period or amount 一陣; 片段: *hear a snatch of song* 聽到一陣歌聲.

sneak [sni:k] *vt / i* move in a quiet and secret manner 鬼鬼祟祟行動; 偷偷移動: *sneak past a sentry* 躡手躡腳地躲過了哨兵. Also 亦作 *nc* cowardly, un-trust-worthy person 怯懦不可靠的人.

sneer [sniə*] *vi* show contempt by one's expression or by what one says 嘲笑; 譏諷: *sneer at someone / something* 對某人/某事嗤之以鼻. Also 亦作 *nc*

expression or words which show one's contempt 嘲笑; 譏諷. **sneering** *adj*.

sneeze [sni:z] *nc* sudden expelling of air through the mouth and nose which one cannot control 噴嚏. Also 亦作 *vi* give a sneeze 打噴嚏.

sniff [snif] *vt / i* **1** breathe in air through the nose in a way that can be heard (often done as a sign of contempt) 帶聲地吸氣; 嗤之以鼻 (常表示輕視). **2** smell in this way 吸氣聞; 嗅: *The dog sniffed (at) the lamppost.* 狗嗅着嗅路燈柱; *sniff the sea air* 深吸海上的空氣. Also 亦作 *nc* act or sound of sniffing 吸氣(聲).

snigger ['snigə*] *nc* type of quiet laugh, often showing disrespect 竊笑; 暗笑. Also 亦作 *vi* laugh in this way 竊笑; 暗笑.

snip [snip] *vt / i* cut with scissors with short cuts 剪; 剪斷: *snip off a piece of cloth* 剪下一塊布. Also 亦作 *nc* act of snipping 剪.

snipe [snaip] *vt / i* shoot (an enemy) from a place where one cannot be seen 狙擊. **sniping** *nu* **sniper** *nc* someone who shoots in this way 狙擊手; 狙擊兵.

snippet ['snipit] *nc* **1** small piece cut off 小片 (斷): *snippet of cloth* 布碎片. **2** (often *pl*) small piece of writing, news, information etc. (常用複數) (作品, 新聞, 消息等的) 片斷; 摘錄.

snivel ['snivl] *vi* complain while crying 哭訴; 啜泣. *past* 過去式和過去分詞 **snivelled.** (*US* 美 **sniveled**).

snob [snɔb] *nc* person who cares only for people who are rich or of high birth 勢利小人; 趨炎附勢的人. **snob-bery, snobbishness** *nu* **snobbish** *adj*.

snooker ['snu:kə] *nu* (*Brit*) game played

with coloured balls which have to be knocked into pockets at the side of a table (英) 撞球落袋遊戲. (US 美 **pool**).

snoop [snu:p] *vi* spy on other people 探聽; 窺探: *Someone came snooping round the house today.* (*informal*) 今天有人到房屋四週窺探.(非正式).

snooze [snu:z] *nc* short period of sleep 打瞌睡; 打盹. Also 亦作 *vi* have a snooze (both *informal*) 打瞌睡; 打盹 (均爲非正式).

snore [snɔ:] *vi* breathe with a loud noise while sleeping 打鼾; 打呼嚕. Also 亦作 *nc* sound made in this way 鼾聲; 呼嚕聲. **snoring** *nu*.

snorkel ['snɔ:kl] *nc* see 見 **schnorkel**.

snort [snɔ:t] *vt / i* force air violently through the nose 噴鼻息; 哼鼻: *The horse snorted.* 那匹馬哼鼻噴鼻. Also 亦作 *nc* sound made when snorting 哼鼻聲; 鼻息聲.

snout [snaut] *nc* nose of an animal (動物)的鼻子: *pig's snout* 豬鼻.

snow [snəu] *nu* **1** water in the air which becomes frozen and falls to the ground in little, soft, white pieces 雪. **2** mass of these white pieces lying on the ground 積雪: *street covered in snow* 積雪覆蓋的街道. Also 亦作 *vi It has been snowing all day.* 整天一直在下雪. **'snowball** *nc* ball made of snow pressed together for throwing in play 雪球(用於投擲嬉戲). **'snowdrift** heap of snow piled up by the wind (風吹成的) 雪堆. **'snowdrop** type of plant with small, white flowers, which often blooms before the last of the snow has disappeared 雪花(常在殘雪融化前綻開小白花的植物). **'snowflake** small piece of falling snow 雪片. **snowman** figure which looks like a man made of snow 雪人. **'snowplough** (US 美

snow plow) machine for clearing snow away from roads, railway lines etc. 雪犁; 掃雪機.

snub¹ [snʌb] *vt* refuse to notice 不理睬; 冷落; 怠慢. *past* 過去式和過去分詞 **snubbed.** Also 亦作 *nc* act of treating someone / something in this way 不理睬; 冷落; 怠慢.

snub² [snʌb] *adj* only in snub nose i.e. nose which is short and turned up at the tip 只用於 snub nose 獅子鼻, 即: 短而鼻尖上翻的鼻.

snuff [snʌf] *nu* powdered tobacco, drawn up the nose 鼻烟: *take snuff* 吸鼻烟.

snug [snʌg] *adj* warm and comfortable 溫暖而舒適的.

snuggle ['snʌgl] *vi* (usu. with **up**) come close to someone / something for warmth and comfort (通常與 up 連用)偎倚; 溫暖而舒適地蜷伏: *The child snuggled up to its mother.* 那孩子偎倚在母親身旁.

so¹ [səu] *adv / intensifier* **1** in this way; in that way 這樣; 那樣: *You must stand so.* 你必須這樣站. **2** also 也; 同樣地: *I like football and so does he.* 我喜歡足球, 他也喜歡. *Jane was there and so was John.* 珍妮在那裏, 約翰也在那裏. (*opp* 反義詞 **neither**: *Jane wasn't there and neither was John* 珍妮不在那裏, 約翰也不在那裏). **3** to such an extent (表示程度)那麼; 像…那樣; 得…使: *Don't talk so much.* 別說那麼多. *He shouldn't drive so fast.* 他未不該開那麼快. *Jane is not so clever as John is.* 珍妮不如約翰聰明. *He is not so ill as I thought.* 他不像我所想的那樣病重. *He was so angry that he hit her.* 他氣得把她揍一頓. *He ran so fast that we couldn't catch up with him.* 他跑得那麼快, 使我們追不上他. **4** very; very much 非常; 極; 很: *You are so* *kind.* 你太好了. *That is so true* i.e. to show that one completely agrees. *(informal)* 千真萬確, 即: 表示完全同感. (非正式) . **5** it is true (agreeing with what someone has said) 對(同意某人說的話): *He is very kind. So he is.* 他爲人很好. 對, 很好. *John was there too. So he was.* 約翰也在那裏.是的, 他也在. *I suppose so.* 我想是這樣. *So I hear.* 不錯, 我聽說. **6** approximately; about 左右; 大約: *He walked for a mile or so.* 他步行了一英里左右. *Note* 說明: apart from the informal uses in sense **4** *so* cannot normally be used to mean *very*. It is therefore better to say *He is very intelligent* or *They say he is not very well*, rather than use *so* in these sentences 除了義 **4** 的非正式用法之外, 通常不可用 so 來表示 very, 因此最好還是說 He is very intelligent (他很聰明) 或 They say he is not very well (他們說他身體不太好), 不要在這些句子裏用 so.

so² [sou] *conj* **1** and for that reason; and therefore 所以; 因此: *I had lost my pencil so I had to buy a new one.* 我丟掉我的鉛筆, 所以我得買枝新的. *We walked quickly so the journey did not take us long.* 我們走得快, 因此這次旅程沒花我們多久時間. **2** as an exclamation (表示驚嘆) 好; 啊: *So you've come back!* 啊, 你已回來啦! *So you think you're clever!* 行啊, 你認爲自己聰明!

soak [souk] *vt / i* **1** make very wet or wet through 浸; 使濕透: *I was caught in the rain and my clothes were soaked.* 我淋了雨, 我的衣服濕透了. *If you want to take out the stain, soak the cloth in cold water.* 如果你想除掉這污漬, 就把布泡在冷水裏. **2** become very wet or wet through 浸濕; 濕透: *Let the clothes soak in water*

overnight. 把衣服泡水泡過夜. **3** make wet by going through or into 滲透; 浸入: *The rainwater has soaked through the roof.* 雨水已經滲透屋頂. **soaking** *adj* very wet 濕透的.

soap [soup] *nu* material used with water to wash oneself, clothes etc. 肥皂. **soapy** *adj* covered with soap 沾滿肥皂的.

soar [sɔː*] *vi* go or fly up very high 高飛; 翱翔: *a bird soaring into the sky* 一隻騰空高飛的鳥.

sob [sɔb] *vi* draw in the breath while crying 嗚咽; 啜泣; 抽噎: *sob with grief* 悲傷而泣. *past* 過去式和過去分詞 **sobbed.** Also 亦作 *nc* act or sound of sobbing 嗚咽(聲); 啜泣(聲); 抽噎(聲).

sober ['soubə*] *adj* **1** not drunk 沒有醉的; 清醒的: *avoid drink and stay sober* 避免喝酒, 要保持清醒. **2** calm; sensible; serious 沉着的; 明智的; 嚴肅的: *sober life* 嚴肅的生活; *sober expression* 沉着的表情; *sober opinion* 明智的意見.

soccer ['sɔkə*] *nu* type of football in which the ball may not normally be touched by the hands, except by the goalkeeper (英式)足球 . (Also 亦作 **Association Football**)

sociable ['souʃəbl] *adj* friendly; fond of meeting other people 友善的; 好交際的. (*opp* 反義詞 **unsociable**)

social ['souʃl] *adj* **1** living together in groups 羣居的: *Bees are social insects.* 蜂是羣居昆蟲. *Man could be called a social animal.* 可說是種羣居動物. **2** having to do with people living in groups, or with people as part of society 社會的; 有關社會的: *social problems such as crime and poverty* 犯罪和貧困這一類的社會問題. **3** having to do with being in the company of other people 社交的; 交際的:

social evening 社交晚會; *social club* i.e. one where people can meet new friends 聯誼會, 即: 可結交新友的會所.

socially *adv* **'social worker** *nc* person whose work is concerned with trying to improve people's social conditions 社會工作者(關心改善人民社會條件的人). **social work** *nu*.

socialism ['souʃəlizəm] *nu* belief that the main sources of a country's wealth (e.g. mines, large industries etc.) should be owned by the government for the good of the people 社會主義(主張政府擁有國家的主要財富資源, 如礦山、大型工礦企業等, 以之為人民謀福利的學說). **socialist** *nc* person who believes in socialism 社會主義者.

society [sə'saiəti] **1** *nc* group of people who have joined together because of some interest they have in common 會; 社; 團體; 協會: *debating society* 辯論社. **2** *nc* group of people living together who have certain beliefs, customs etc in common 社會: *Western society* 西方社會; *African society* 非洲社會. **3** *nu* way that people live together having certain rules and customs 群體生活; 社會體制: *work for the good of society* 為社會福利工作. **4** *nu* people who are wealthy or of high birth 上流社會; 社交界.

sociology [sousi'ɔlədʒi] *nu* study of society (in sense **2**) and its development 社會學(研究社會及其發展). **sociological** [sousiə'lɔdʒikl] *adj* **sociologist** *nc*.

sock [sɔk] *nc* short covering for the foot and part of the leg; short stocking 短襪: *pair of socks* 一雙短襪. *Note* 說明: men usu. wear socks; women usu. wear *stockings*. 男人通常穿 socks (短襪); 女人通常穿 stockings (長襪).

socket ['sɔkit] *nc* hollow in which

something fits or turns (承物或轉物的)窩; 腔; 插座; 凹槽: *lamp socket* 燈座; *socket of the eye* 眼窩.

sod [sɔd] *nc* piece of earth with grass on it (一塊)草皮; 草地.

soda ['soudə] **1** *nu* name given to various types of chemical material used for washing, baking and many other things 蘇打; 碳酸鈉: *washing soda* 洗用蘇打; *baking soda* 烹調蘇打; 小蘇打. **2** *nc / u* soda water; drink of soda water 蘇打水; 汽水. **'soda water 1** *nu* water filled with a gas to make it bubble 蘇打水; **2** *nc* drink of this 汽水.

sodden ['sɔdn] *adj* very wet; wet through (很濕的; 濕透的): *sodden clothes* 濕透的衣服.

sodium ['soudjəm] *nu* silver-white, alkaline metallic chemical element (Na) 鈉(化學符號為 Na). **sodium chloride** common salt 氯化鈉, 食鹽.

sofa ['soufə] *nc* long, comfortable seat with cushions, and a back and arms沙發.

soft [sɔft] *adj* **1** giving way when one touches; not hard 軟的; 柔軟的: *soft bed* 軟床; *soft ground* 軟地. **2** smooth 柔滑的: *soft skin* 柔滑的皮膚; *as soft as silk* 絲一樣的柔滑. (*opp* 反義詞 **rough**). **3** not loud or noisy 輕柔的: *soft voice* 細聲; *soft music* 輕柔的音樂. **4** not sharp 不明顯的: *soft outlines* 模糊的輪廓. **5** not harsh or glaring 柔和的; 不刺目的: *soft, restful light* 柔和舒適的燈光. **6** gentle; kind 溫和的; 仁慈的: *having a soft heart* 有一副軟心腸. **7** weak; not manly 軟弱的; 不強健的: *Muscles become soft without exercise.* 沒運動, 肌肉就變軟. **8** silly; weak in the mind 愚蠢的; 懦弱的: *soft in the head (informal)* 笨頭笨腦的(非正式). **softly** *adv* **softness** *nu* **soften** ['sɔfn] *vt / i* make or become soft 使

軟; 變軟; 使柔和; 變柔和; 使溫和; 變溫
和; 使軟弱; 變軟弱. '**soft** '**drink** cold
drink which does not contain alcohol
軟飲料 (不含酒精的冷飲). '**soft-
hearted** *adj* gentle; (too) kind 心腸軟
的; (太) 仁慈的.

soggy ['sɔgi] *adj* 1 very wet; wet
through 濕潤的; 濕透的: *soggy ground*
潮濕地面. 2 heavy and damp 又重又
濕的: *soggy bread* 未烤完的麵包.

soil¹ [sɔil] *nu* earth (esp. in connection
with growing things) 土 (壤); 土地:
rich soil 沃土; *sandy soil* 沙質土.

soil² [sɔil] *vt / i* make or become dirty
弄髒; 變髒: *soil a clean shirt* 弄髒一件
乾淨襯衫.

solar ['soulə*] *adj* of, connected with,
the sun 太陽; 與太陽有關的: *solar
energy* 太陽能.

sold [sould] past of **sell**. sell 的過去式
和過去分詞.

solder ['souldə*] *nu* easily melted metal
used for joining other pieces of metal
together 焊料 (用於熔接其他金屬板). Al-
so 亦作 *vt* join together with solder
焊 (接).

soldier ['souldʒə*] *nc* man who serves
in an army 軍人; 士兵.

sole¹ [soul] *adj* one; only 單獨的; 唯一
的: *He was the sole survivor.* 他是唯
一的倖存者. **solely** *adv* only; alone 唯
一; 單獨地. *If anything goes wrong,
you will be held solely responsible* 如
果出了差錯, 你將要獨自承擔責任.

sole² [soul] *nc* bottom part of a foot,
shoe, boot etc 腳底; 鞋底; 靴底等.

sole³ [soul] *nc* type of flat sea fish 鰈魚
(一種扁平海水魚). *pl* 複數 **sole**.

solemn ['sɔləm] *adj* 1 serious; unsmil-
ing 嚴肅的; 不苟言笑的: *look solemn*
表情嚴肅. 2 done in a serious way 肅
穆的; 隆重的: *solemn procession of
mourners* 肅穆的送葬行列; *solemn*

ceremony 隆重的儀式.

solicitor [sə'lisitə*] *nc* in Britain, a
lawyer who advises on the making of
wills etc and who prepares cases for
another kind of lawyer (called a **barrister**) who conducts the cases in
court (英) 初級律師 (爲立遺囑提供諮
詢, 並爲辯護律師 barrister 出庭準備訴
訟案件). *Note* 說明: in some countries there is no distinction between
solicitors and *barristers*. 在一些國家沒
有 solicitors 和 barristers 之分.

solid ['sɔlid] *adj* 1 not liquid or gas 固
體的: *use solid fuel for heating* i.e.
not oil, gas etc. 用固體燃料加熱, 即:
不用油, 可燃氣等. 2 of the same material throughout 全部同質的; 純粹的:
ring made of solid gold 純金造的戒指.
3 not hollow 實心的: *The walls are
solid.* 這些牆都是實心的. 4 dependable; reliable 可靠的; 可依賴的: *solid
business* 穩固的企業; *solid citizen* 忠
實的公民. Also 亦作 *nc* 1 not liquid
(or gas) 固體: *She cannot eat solids.*
她不能吃固體食物. 2 (mathematics)
figure which has height, breadth and
length (數學) 立體圖形. **solidly** *adv*

solidarity [sɔli'dæriti] *nu* oneness of
feelings, interests, aims etc. 團結; 一致
(指情感, 利益, 目標等): *working-class
solidarity* 工人階級團結一致. **solidify**
[sə'lidifai] *vt / i* make or become solid
or hard (使) 變硬; 固化; (使) 團結.
solidity [sə'liditi] *nu* quality of being
solid 固體; 堅實; 牢實; 團結.

solitary ['sɔlitəri] *adj* 1 without other
people, away from other people 孤獨
的; 獨居的: *solitary walk* 獨自散步;
solitary life 獨居的生活. 2 not often
visited; lonely 人跡罕到的; 寂寞的:
solitary place 偏僻的地方. **solitude**
['sɔlitjuːd] *nu* state of being away
from other people 孤獨; 隱居; 寂寞.

solitude of a hermit's life 隱士生活的寂寞.

solo ['soulou] *nc* **1** piece of music to be played or sung by one person 獨奏(曲); 獨唱(曲). **2** performance by one person 單獨表演; 獨奏; 獨唱. *pl* 複數 **solos. soloist** *nc* person who performs a solo 獨奏者; 獨唱者.

solstice ['sɔlstis] *nc* either of the two times each year when day and night are equally long 至, 至日, 至點: *summer solstice* (about June 22) 夏至 (約在六月二十二日); *winter solstice* (about December 22) 冬至 (約在十二月二十二日).

soluble ['sɔljubl] *adj* able to be dissolved in a liquid 可溶的: *Salt is soluble in water.* 鹽可溶於水. *(opp* 反義詞 **insoluble).**

solution [sə'lu:ʃən] *nc* **1** answer to a problem; way of explaining something 解答; 解決; 解法: *solution of / to a mystery* (對) 奧秘的解答. **2** mixture made by dissolving a solid or a gas in a liquid 溶解; 溶液.

solve [sɔlv] *vt* find the answer to; explain 解答; 解決; 解釋: *solve a mystery* 解釋奧秘.

solvent ['sɔlvənt] *adj* able to pay what one owes 有償付能力的. *(opp* 反義詞 **insolvent).**

sombre ['sɔmbə*] *(US* 美 **somber)** *adj* **1** dark 昏暗的: *sombre colours* 暗淡的顏色. **2** sad 憂鬱的: *sombre expression* 憂鬱的表情.

some [sʌm] *determiner* **1** certain amount or number of 一些(的); 有些(的); 若干(的): *Give me some water.* 給我點兒水. *Some friends of yours are here.* 你有些朋友在這裏. *You may have to wait for some time.* 可能你得等一會. *Note* 說明: in questions and negatives it is necessary to use *any.*

Have you any water? There aren't any apples left. But note that if the speaker expects the answer 'Yes', he may use *some* in a question, in this sense. *Haven't you some water?* The same thing happens when the question is really an invitation or request. *Would you like some bread?* 在問句和否定句中, 需用 any. Have you any water? (你有水嗎?) There aren't any apples left. (沒有剩下蘋果.) 但要注意, 如果說話人期待肯定的回答, 他可在這樣的問句中用 some. Haven't you some water? (你不是有水嗎?) 當問題實際上是邀請或請求時, 亦可用 some. Would you like some bread? (你吃點麵包好嗎?) **2** about 大約: *There were some thirty people there.* 那裏大約有三十人. **3** quite a large number or amount of 相當多的; 不少的: *He has been waiting for some time* i.e. quite a long time 他已等了一些時候.即: 相當長的時間. **4** very great; very good 很了不起的; 極好的: *That was some party!* i.e. a very enjoyable party *(informal)* 那是極好的聚會!即: 令人盡興的聚會 (非正式). **5** not known; not requiring to be named 某一; 有一: *I read it in some book or other.* 這是我在某一本書上看到的. Also 亦作 *pron* a certain amount; a certain number 一些; 有些: *Some of the boys were late.* 有些男孩遲到了. *Note* 說明: the same rules apply as are mentioned in the *Note* above on *some determiner.* 上述說明提及限定詞 some 的規則,同樣適用.

somebody ['sʌmbədi] *pron* person who is not known or who does not have to be named; someone 有人; 某人: *Somebody is knocking at the door.* 有人在敲門. *Note* 說明: in questions and negative sentences, use *anybody. I don't know anybody of that name.* 在

問句和否定句中, 用 anybody. I don't know anybody of that name. (我不認識那個名字的人.) Also 亦作 *nc* important person 重要人物: *He is somebody in his own town but just a nobody here.* (informal) 在他住的城裏他是個大人物, 但在這裏他是個小人物. (非正式)

somehow ['sʌmhau] *adv* in one way or another 設法: *They will try to keep us out, but we shall get in somehow.* 他們會想法把我們關在門外, 但我們會設法進去. *I've never liked him, somehow* i.e. I don't know the exact reason. 反正, 我從未喜歡過他. 即: 我不曉得甚麼緣故.

someone ['sʌmwʌn] *pron* somebody 有人; 某人.

somersault ['sʌməsɔ:lt] *nc* act of jumping, so that one turns over completely, head over heels 觔斗, 滾翻: *make / turn / do a somersault* 翻觔斗, 滾翻. Also 亦作 *vi*.

something ['sʌmθiŋ] *pron* thing which is not known or does not have to be named 某事; 某物: *There is something inside this box.* 這盒子裏有東西. *There is something in what you say* i.e. there is some truth. 你說的話有些道理. *Note* 說明: in questions and negative sentences, use *anything*. *There isn't anything in the cupboard.* 在問句和否定句中, 用 anything. There isn't anything in the cupboard. (碗櫥裏沒有東西.)

sometime ['sʌmtaim] *adv* at some time in the future; at some time in the past 未來某個時間; 過去某個時候: *We'll meet again sometime next week.* 我們在下星期找個時間再見面. *I met him sometime last year.* 我在去年某個時候遇上他. *Note* 說明: do not confuse this word *sometime* with the two

words *some time,* which mean 'a fairly long time'. *I spent some time in India when I was young.* 別把 sometime 這詞與 some time 這兩個詞混淆了, some time 意為 "相當長的一段時間". I spent some time in India when I was young. (我年青時, 曾在印度度過一段時間.) see also 參見 *sometimes.*

sometimes ['sʌmtaimz] *adv* from time to time 有時; 不時; 間或: *I usually go on foot, but sometimes I take the bus.* 我通常步行, 但有時我坐公共汽車.

somewhat ['sʌmhwɔt] *adv* to some extent, degree, etc. 在某種程度上; 稍微; 有幾分: *I was somewhat surprised.* 我有點驚訝. *He was somewhat encouraged by your words.* 他聽了你的話受到了一些鼓勵. **somewhat of** rather 稍; *I found it somewhat of a difficulty.* 我感到這事有些困難.

somewhere ['sʌmweə*] *adv* in or to some place unknown (在)某處; 到某處: *He is living somewhere in England.* 他住在英國某地. *Note* 說明: in questions and negative sentences, use *anywhere.* *I can't find it anywhere.* 在問句和否定句中, 用 anywhere. I can't find it anywhere. (我甚麼地方都無法找到它.)

son [sʌn] *nc* male child (of a parent) 兒子. '**son-in-law** *nc* husband of one's daughter 女婿. *pl* 複數 **sons-in-law.**

sonata [sə'nɑːtə] *nc* piece of music usually in three or four movements, and usually written for one instrument (e.g. the piano) 奏鳴曲 (通常有三個或四個樂章, 供一種樂器 (如鋼琴) 演奏的樂曲).

song [sɔŋ] *nc* type of short poem that is sung; words and music for the voice 詩歌; 歌曲: *popular song* 流行歌曲.

sonic ['sɔnik] *adj* concerned with sound

or the study of sound 有關聲音的; 有關聲學的. **sonic boom** noise of an aeroplane flying faster than sound 聲震; 音爆(以超音速飛行的飛機所發的響聲).

sonnet ['sɔnit] *nc* poem of 14 lines which rhyme with one another in a special way 十四行詩; 商籟詩.

soon [su:n] *adv* 1 in a short time 即刻; 不久. *I shall be back soon*. 我很快就回來. *He died soon after the accident*. 這次事故以後不久, 他就去世了. 2 early 早; 快: *We did not expect you so soon*. 我們沒想到你這麼早. *How soon can you come?* 你最快在甚麼時候能來? **as / as soon as** at the moment when 一…就: *As soon as he heard the news, he phoned the police*. 他一聽到消息就打電話給警察. *They did not come as / as soon as they had promised*. 他們沒有像他們所答應的那麼早來. *Note* 說明: with negative sentences, *so* is often used instead of *as*, as in the last example. 在否定句中, 如在最後的例句中, 常用 *so*, 不用 *as*.

soot [sut] *nu* black powder which is left by smoke 黑煙灰: *The walls of houses in industrial cities are often dirtied with soot*. 工業城市的房屋牆壁常被黑煙灰弄得髒髒的.

soothe [su:ð] *vt* 1 calm; quieten 安慰; 使鎮定: *soothe someone who is nervous and excited* 安慰神經緊張、情感激動的某人. 2 make less painful 減輕(痛苦), 鎮痛: *ointment that soothes wounds* 減輕傷痛的藥膏. **soothing** *adj*.

sopping ['sɔpiŋ] *adj* very wet; wet through 很濕的; 濕透的.

sophism ['sɔfizəm] *nc / u* clever and plausible but fallacious argument or form of reasoning, whether or not in-

tended to deceive 詭辯; 似是而非的論點.

sophist ['sɔfist] *nc* 1 person practising clever, specious reasoning 詭辯者; 詭辯家. 2 (often Sophist) in ancient Greece, any of a group of teachers of rhetoric, philosophy, etc. (常用大寫) 古希臘修辭學、哲學的教師; 詭辯學者.

sophisticated [sə'fistikeitid] *adj* 1 wise in the ways of the world; cultured; elegant 世故的; 老練的; 有教養的; 優雅的: *sophisticated person* 老於世故的人. 2 advanced 高級的; 尖端的: *sophisticated techniques* i.e. advanced ways of doing things 先進技術, 即: 高級技術. (*opp* 反義詞 **unsophisticated**). **sophistication** [səfisti'keiʃən] *nu*.

sophomore ['sɔfəmɔ:*] *nc (US)* student in his second year of high school or college (美國高中或大學)二年級學生.

soporific [sɔpə'rifik] *adj* causing sleep 催眠的: *soporific drug* 催眠藥.

soprano [sə'prɑ:nou] 1 *nu* highest singing voice in boys or women 男童聲最高音(部); 女最高音(部). 2 *nc* singer who has a voice like this (男童或女)最高音歌手; 女高音歌唱家. *pl* 複數 **sopranos**.

sorcerer ['sɔ:sərə*] *nc* man who can do things by magic with the help of evil spirits 男巫; 術士; 魔法師. (*fem* 陰 **sorceress** ['sɔ:səris]). **sorcery** *nu* magic performed with the help of evil spirits 巫術; 妖術; 魔法.

sordid ['sɔ:did] *adj* 1 dirty, wretched 骯髒的; 破爛的: *live in sordid circumstances* 生活在骯髒的環境裏. 2 mean; showing lack of good feelings 卑鄙的; 惡意的: *sordid act* 卑鄙的行動.

sore [sɔ:*] *adj* 1 painful 疼痛的: *sore knee / throat / ankle etc.* 膝痛/喉痛/腳脖子痛 等. 2 causing anger or

annoyance 惹人惱怒的; 使人煩惱的:
That matter is a sore point with him
i.e. it causes him annoyance when he
thinks about it. 那事是他的痛處. 即: 他
一想起那事就感到煩惱. **3** annoyed;
angry 煩惱的; 惱火的: *He got rather*
sore with me. (informal) 他對我相當
惱火. (非正式). Also 亦作 *nc* painful
place on the body (身上的)痛處: *You*
should cover that sore on your hand.
你應遮住你手上的痛處. **soreness** *nu*
sorely *adv* greatly 非常; 很.

sorghum ['sɔ:gəm] *nu* tropical cereal
grass grown for grain, syrup, fodder,
etc. 蜀黍; 高粱.

sorrow ['sɔrou] *nu* sadness; grief 悲痛;
悲哀: *His heart was full of sorrow.* 他
的心情十分悲痛. **sorrowful** *adj* **sor-**
rowfully *adv.*

sorry ['sɔri] *adj* **1** feeling sadness, regret etc. 感到悲傷, 遺憾等: *I'm sorry*
(that) I'm late. 真對不起, 我遲到了. *I*
feel rather sorry for him i.e. pity
him. 我頗爲他惋惜. 即: 我可憐他. *We*
are sorry to be such a nuisance. 我們
這麼討厭, 心裏十分難過. **2** poor: pitiful 貧窮的; 可憐的: *sorry sight* 貧困的
景象; *in a sorry state* 處在可憐的境
地. Also 亦作 *adv* expressing regret
(usu. over small things) 抱歉; 對不起
(通常對小事表示歉意): *Can you*
direct me to the station? Sorry, I can't.
請問到車站怎麼走? 抱歉, 我不知道.

sort [sɔ:t] *nc* class; kind; type 類; 種; 型:
books, papers and that sort of thing
書籍, 紙張和這一類的東西; *things of a*
different sort 與之不同類型的東西;
new sort of car 新型汽車. Also 亦作
vt put things into different classes,
grades etc. 分類; 整理: *sort letters* i.e.
separate them according to the
addresses on them 把信件分類, 即: 按
地址分開.

sought [sɔ:t] past of *seek.* seek的過去
式和過去分詞.

soul [soul] *nc* **1** spiritual part of a person; part that is supposed to live for
ever 精神; 靈魂: *A man's body dies,*
but his soul lives on. 人的軀體死了, 但
他的靈魂依然活着. **2** human being
人: *I didn't see a soul.* 我没看見一個
人. *Poor soul, she has suffered a lot.*
(informal) 可憐的人呀, 她已吃了許多
的苦. (非正式). **soulful** *adj* full of
feeling; showing great feeling 充滿感
情的; 表達深情的: *large soulful eyes*
又大又充滿深情的眼睛. **soulless** *adj*
without noble feeling 没有高尚情感
的; 卑鄙的: *soulless task* i.e. a task
which does not allow one to have noble feelings 卑鄙的工作, 即: 不容人有
高尚情感的工作.

sound¹ [saund] *nc / u* what can be
heard by the ears 音響; 聲音: *sound*
of trains passing 火車開過的聲音;
sound of a rifle going off 步槍開槍的
聲音; *loud sound* 大聲; *speed of*
sound 音速. *Sound travels in waves.*
聲音以波的形式傳播. **'soundproof**
adj not letting sound pass through 隔
音的: *soundproof walls* 隔音牆. Also
亦作 *vt* make soundproof 使隔音.
'sound track record of words and
music made along the edge of a cinema film 聲帶; 音帶(影片邊上的錄音部
份).

sound² [saund] *vt / i* **1** give out sound
發出聲音; 響: *The trumpet sounded.*
喇叭吹響了. **2** give the signal for 發出
… 的信號: *sound the retreat, alarm*
etc. 發出撤退信號、警報等. **3** seem 似
乎; 聽起來: *That sounds very reason-*
able. 那聽起來似乎很有道理.

sound³ [saund] *adj* **1** healthy; free from
injury or decay 健全的; 無恙的; 没有
腐爛的: *sound in mind and body* 身心

健康. **2** strong; safe 有力的; 安全的:
sound decision 有力的決定; *sound
company / firm* 財力充實的公司/商行.
sound investment 穩妥的投資. (opp
反義詞 **unsound**). **3** complete; thorough 完全的; 徹底的: *a sound beating*
痛打一頓. **4** deep; undisturbed 深的;
沒受騷擾的: *sound sleep* 酣睡.
soundly adv **soundness** nu.

sound⁴ [saund] nc narrow piece of water (usu. joining two larger pieces of
water) 海峽; 水峽.

soup [suːp] nu liquid food made by
boiling meat, vegetables etc in water
湯; 羹: *chicken soup* 鷄湯.

sour ['sauə*] adj **1** having a bitter taste
酸的; 酸味的. **2** having gone bad;
spoiled 變質的; 酸腐的: *sour milk* 發
酸的奶. **3** unkind; showing anger, disappointment etc. 乖戾的; 慍怒的; 掃興
的: *sour remark* 尖酸刻薄的話. **sour-
ness** nu.

source [sɔːs] nc **1** place where a river,
stream etc starts 水源; 源頭; 源泉:
source of the River Amazon 亞馬遜河
的發源地. **2** beginning or first cause
of anything 根源; 原因: *We must look
for the source of the trouble.* 我們必須
找出毛病的原因. **3** book etc from
which information is obtained 原始資
料.

south [sauθ] adv roughly in the direction to the left of someone facing the
setting sun 向南; 在南方: *travelling
south* 往南旅行. Also 亦作 adj from
this direction 來自南方的. (opp
north in both senses) (兩義兼有的反
義為 **north**). **southerly** ['sʌðəli] nc
wind coming from the south 南風.
Also 亦作 adj from this direction 來自
南方的. **southern** ['sʌðən] adj in or
of the south 在南方的; 南方的. **south-
wards** adv towards the south 向南.

the south area of a country etc lying
to the south 南部地區.

souvenir [suːvə'niə*] nc something that
reminds one of a person or place 紀
念物(品): *Tourists often buy souve-
nirs to remind them of the places they
have visited.* 遊客常買紀念品, 紀念他
們所遊覽過的地方.

sou'wester [sau'westə*] nc **1** waterproof
hat worn by sailors, which has a long
flap at the back to protect the neck
(海員用的)護頸防水帽. **2** strong wind
from the south-west 西南大風.

sovereign ['sɔvrin] nc king or queen;
chief ruler 君主; 元首. Also 亦作 adj
not ruled by another (country etc.) 主
權的; 獨立自主的: *sovereign state* 主
權國家. **sovereignty** nu supreme
power; sovereign power 至高無上的權
力; 主權.

Soviet ['souviət] adj Russian 蘇聯的; 俄
國的.

sow¹ [sou] vt / i scatter or plant seeds
播; 種: *sow wheat* 播種小麥; *sow a
field with barley* 在田裏播種大麥.

sow² [sau] nc female pig 母豬.

soya bean ['sɔiəbiːn] (US 美 **soybean**)
nc leafy plant related to the pea,
grown for its seeds (from which oil is
made) and as a food crop 大豆; 黃豆.

spa [spɑː] nc **1** spring, the water of
which can be used as a medicine 礦
泉; 溫泉(有療效作用的泉水). **2** place
where there is a spring like this 礦泉
或溫泉療養地.

space [speis] **1** nu area without boundaries or limits outside the earth 空間;
太空: *It will soon be common for men
to travel through space.* 人們穿越太空
旅行將很快成爲尋常的事情. **2** nc / u
limited area between objects, boundaries etc. 間隔; 距離; 空位: *space
measuring five feet by four.* 面積五英

尺乘四英尺的場地. *Is there any space between the table and the wall?* 桌子和牆壁之間有間隔嗎? *There is space for one more person.* 還有一個人的空位. **3** *nc* length of time (一段) 時間: *within the space of ten minutes* 在十分鐘時間內. Also 亦作 *vt* place objects with a certain distance between them 把…分隔開: *Space the chairs out a little more.* 把椅子的間隔再分開點.

spacious ['speiʃəs] *adj* with plenty of room; large 寬敞的; 大的: *spacious house* 大房子. **'spacecraft, 'spaceship** *nc* type of vehicle for travelling through space to other planets etc. 宇宙飛行器; 宇宙飛船. *pl* 複數 **spacecraft. outer space** space beyond the earth's atmosphere or beyond the solar system 外層空間; 星際(宇宙)空間.

spade [speid] *nc* **1** tool used for digging 鏟; 鍬. **2** one of the four marks on playing cards; the mark itself (紙牌中的)黑桃; 黑桃牌.

spaghetti [spə'geti] *nu* mixture of wheat flour, water etc made into long tubes and cooked for eating 通心粉, 空心麵條.

span¹ [spæn] past tense of **spin¹**. spin¹ 的過去式和過去分詞.

span² [spæn] *nc* **1** distance between supports: 兩支柱間的距離; 墩距; 跨度: *span of a bridge* 橋的跨度. **2** stretch of time 持續的一段時間: *span of someone's memory* 某人的記憶廣度; *short span of time* 短暫的時間. Also 亦作 *vt* extend from one side to another 跨越; 架設: *A bridge spans the river.* 有座橋跨越那條河. *past* 過去式和過去分詞 **spanned.**

spaniel ['spænjəl] *nc* one of different types of dogs with long hair and long ears 長毛垂耳狗.

spank [spæŋk] *vt* punish a child by hitting it several times with the flat of the hand 用巴掌打罰孩子.

spanner ['spænə*] *nc* tool for loosening and tightening nuts or screws and bolts 扳鉗; 扳頭; 扳手.

spar¹ [spa:] *nu* kinds of shiny, crystalline mineral that cleaves easily into flakes 晶石. **Sparry** *adj*.

spar² [spa:] *nc* **1** strong pole, as a mast, or boom for supporting the sails on a ship 圓材(船上撐帆的桅杆, 檣, 帆桁). **2** lengthwise support for the ribs of an aircraft wing (飛機的)翼樑.

spar³ [spa:] *vi* **1** box with jabbing or feinting movements, landing few heavy blows, as in practice matches (在練習賽中)佯攻性地拳擊. **2** dispute; argue 爭論; 爭吵; 辯論.

spare¹ [speə*] *vt* **1** protect; save (usu. because of kindness or pity). 保護; 赦免(通常出於仁慈或憐憫): *The king spared the lives of the women and children* i.e. he did not kill them because he pitied them. 國王饒了婦女孩童的命. 即: 他因爲憐惜他們而沒有殺害他們. *They never spare themselves* i.e. they make every effort. 他們從來就不遺餘力. 即: 他們竭盡全力. **2** have available or left over 提供; 剩下: *Have you a minute to spare so that we can talk about him?* 你可抽出一分鐘時間讓我們能談談他的事好嗎? *Can you spare me a minute?* 我能欨擱你一分鐘嗎? *Because he is very rich, he has money to spare.* 因爲他十分富有, 他還有錢剩下. **sparing** *adj* (with of or with) careful; giving unwillingly (與of和with連用) 謹慎的; 捨不得給的: *He is very sparing with his money.* 他用錢十分節儉. **sparingly** *adv*.

spare² [speə*] *adj* extra; more than is needed 額外的; 剩下的: *Every lorry* *should carry a spare wheel.* 每輛載貨卡車都應有一個備用輪胎. *He is so busy that he has no spare time.* 他忙得沒有空暇. Also 亦作 *nc* extra part (usu. to take the place of a damaged part of a machine) 備件 (通常用來替換損壞的機件): *If you are going to travel a great distance in your car, you should take plenty of spares with you.* 如果你打算駕車長途跋涉旅行, 那你得隨身帶許多備件. **spare part** see 見 **spare²** (noun).

spark [spɑːk] *nc* tiny piece of bright burning matter which rises from a fire, or is made when metal or stone strike together; short electric flash 火花; 火星; 電花: *The sparks from the forest fire rose high in the air.* 森林大火揚起的火花衝天. *There was a spark when the two electric wires touched each other.* 這兩條電綫一接觸就會爆出火花. **'sparking plug, 'spark plug** device which makes a spark to explode the mixture of petrol and air in the engine of a motorcar (汽車發動機的) 火花塞.

sparkle [spɑːkl] *vi* send out quick, changing gleams of light 閃閃發光; 閃耀: *Most jewels sparkle.* 多數寶石都會閃爍發光. *His eyes were sparkling with happiness.* 他的眼睛閃露喜悅的神色.

sparrow ['spærou] *nc* small, brown bird which eats insects 麻雀.

sparse [spɑːs] *adj* spread widely and in small numbers 稀少的; 稀疏的: *The trees on the hill were sparse.* 山上的樹木稀疏落落的. **sparsely** *adv.*

spasm ['spæzəm] *nc* short and sudden movement of the muscles; any short and sudden movement or feeling 痙攣; 抽筋; 一陣突發動作或情感: *A spasm of coughing stopped him*

speaking. 一陣咳嗽使他說不下去.

spasmodic [spæz'mɔdik] *adj* happening suddenly at any time 陣發性的: *He is a spasmodic worker* i.e. he works for a little, then stops suddenly, then starts again. 他是個做事忽冷忽熱的人. 即: 他工作一會兒突然停, 然後又開始幹.

spastic ['spæstik] *nc* person who cannot control his limbs because his brain is not controlling his body properly 患大腦性麻痺者.

spat [spæt] past of **spit¹**. spit¹ 的過去式和過去分詞.

spate [speit] *nu* **1** high level of a river caused by heavy rain 洪水; 猛漲: *After the storm the river was in spate.* 暴風雨過後, 河水猛漲. **2** large, sudden flow of anything 大量; 大批湧到: *They could not deal with the spate of work.* 他們無法招架這次蜂湧而至的大量工作.

spatter ['spætə*] *vt / i* **1** throw drops of water, mud etc over 濺; 潑; 灑: *The lorry spattered me with mud.* 那輛載貨卡車濺了我一身泥. *The ink bottle broke and spattered ink on us.* 這個墨水瓶摔破, 墨汁濺到我們身上. **2** fall in drops 滴落: *The rain was spattering on the window.* 雨正淅淅瀝瀝地落在窗上. Also 亦作 *nc:* spatter of mud / rain 污泥飛濺/陣雨.

spatula ['spætjulə] *nc* broad, flat knife used to mix and spread paints and other substances 抹刀; 刮鏟.

spawn [spɔːn] *nu* eggs of fish, frogs etc. (魚, 蛙等的) 卵. Also 亦作 *vt / i* produce spawn 產卵.

speak [spiːk] *vt / i* **1** say in words; talk 說 (話); 講; 談: *I am speaking the truth.* 我在說事情的真相. *He always speaks in a quiet voice.* 他說話總是輕聲細語的. *A dumb person cannot* *speak*. 啞巴不能說話. *Will you speak to him about his work?* 你跟他談談他的工作好嗎? **2** be able to use a language 能使用某種語言: *They speak English as well as French.* 他們的英語說得和法語一樣好. **3** make a speech 演說; 演講: *The chairman spoke for ten minutes at the beginning of the meeting.* 主席在會議開始時發表了十分鐘演說. *past tense* 過去式 **spoke** [spouk]. *past part* 過去分詞 **spoken** ['spoukən]. **speaker** *nc* **1** person who speaks 說話人; 演說者; 發言人. **2** short form of loudspeaker. loudspeaker 的縮寫形式. **speak up** speak more loudly 說大聲點: *Please speak up; we can't hear you.* 請說大聲點, 我們聽不見. **not be on speaking terms with somebody** not speak to somebody because one either does not know him or has quarrelled with him 和某人不交談(因爲不相識或吵過架).

spear [spiə*] *nc* weapon made of a sharp metal point fixed to a long stick, used for fighting, hunting and fishing 矛; 標槍; 叉. Also 亦作 *vt* push a spear into (用矛)刺; 戳.

special ['speʃl] *adj* not usual; of a particular type; for a particular purpose 特別的; 特殊的; 特設的: *You should give special attention to this matter.* 你應該特別注意這事. *A special tool is needed to cut iron.* 切鐵要用專門工具. *They are getting a special bus to take us to the football match.* 他們正要一輛專車送我去看足球比賽. Also 亦作 *nc*: *He will travel by the special to the football match* i.e. special bus or train. 他將乘坐專車去看這場足球比賽. 即: 專用的公共汽車或火車. **specially** *adv* **specialist** *nc* person who is very skilled in, or has great knowledge of, a particular type of work or

study; an expert 專家; 行家: *He is a heart specialist* i.e. a doctor who is an expert on diseases of the heart 他是個心臟病專家. 即: 是個治療心臟病的專家. **speciality** [speʃi'æliti], **specialty** ['speʃlti] *nc* particular type of work, study, activity etc in which one is very skilled or interested 專業; 專門研究; 專長: *His speciality / specialty is heart surgery.* 他的專業是心臟手術. *My mother's speciality / specialty is making jam.* 我母親的專長是製做果醬. *Note* 說明: *speciality* is more usual in British English, *specialty* in American English. speciality 通常用於英國英語, specialty 通常用於美國英語. **specialize** *vt / i* (with **in**) study specially a particular type of skill or learning; become a specialist (與 in 連用)專攻; 專門研究; 變爲專家: *During his last two years at school he specialized in biology.* 他在學校的後二年中, 專攻生物學. *This doctor has a specialized knowledge of the heart.* 這位醫生對心臟有一套專研知識.

species ['spi:ʃi:z] *nc* (biology) smallest group into which animals and plants are normally divided (生物)(物)種.

specify ['spesifai] *vt* give the name or details of a particular person / thing 指明; 詳細說明: *The book of instructions specifies one-inch nails for making a desk.* 這本說明書指明做桌子要用一英寸長的釘子. **specific** [spə'sifik] *adj* given by name or in detail; exact; particular 明確的; 詳盡的; 精確的; 特殊的: *The book gives specific instructions on how to make a desk.* 本書對如何做桌子作了詳細說明. *I know he came here for a specific reason.* 我知道他來這裏別有緣故. **specifically** *adv* **specification** [spesifi'keiʃən] *nc / u* (usu. *pl*) exact measurements or details of something to be done (通常用複數)規格; 詳細說明: *The specifications for the new classroom to be built next year are now ready.* 明年建造的那間新教室的詳細說明現在準備好了.

specimen ['spesimən] *nc* something used as an example to be studied or tested 樣品; 標本: *The teacher showed us some specimens of wild flowers.* 老師給我們看了一些野花標本. *The doctor took a specimen of my blood to see if I had malaria.* 醫生為驗了我的血液取樣, 看我是不是患了瘧疾.

specious ['spi:ʃəs] *adj* not good or correct, although appearing to be so 貌似有理的; 似是而非的; 華而不實的: *He gave a specious reason for being late.* 他說了一個似是而非的遲到理由. **speciously** *adv* **speciousness** *nu*.

speck [spek] *nc* very small piece of something; very small mark 微粒; 斑點: *There is a speck of dust on your nose.* 你鼻尖上有點灰塵. *From a great distance the boys looked like specks on the field.* 從老遠的地方望去, 男孩們成了田野上的斑斑點點.

speckle ['spekl] *nc* very small mark (usu. one of many) 斑點 (通常是許多中的一點). **speckled** *adj* marked with speckles 有斑點的: *The snake has a speckled skin.* 這條蛇有花斑的皮.

specs [speks] *npl* see **spectacle** (in sense 2) 見 spectacle (義2).

spectacle ['spektakl] *nc* **1** something unusual or impressive which makes people look at it 奇觀; 壯觀; 景象: *The marching soldiers made a fine spectacle.* 齊步前進的軍人隊伍, 蔚爲壯觀. *The burning house was a terrible spectacle.* 這幅正燒着的房屋呈現

一幅可怕的慘狀. *By arguing loudly with the policeman, he made a spectacle of himself.* 他跟警察大聲爭辯, 使他丟人現眼. **2** (in *pl*) pair of lenses worn over the eyes so that one can see better (用於複數)眼鏡. (Also 亦作 **glasses; specs**). **spectacular** [spek'tækjulə*] *adj* causing people to look or pay attention; making a spectacle 壯觀的; 引人注意的; 驚人的: *He made a spectacular jump from the burning building.* 他從熊熊烈火的大樓上驚人地跳出來.

spectator [spek'teitə*] *nc* person who watches (a game or show etc.) (比賽或展覽等的)觀衆.

spectre ['spektə*] (*US* 美 **specter**) *nc* spirit of a dead person appearing to a person who is alive; ghost 鬼魂; 幽靈.

spectrum ['spektrəm] *nc* range of colours (from infrared to ultraviolet) into which light can be divided when passed through a glass block. (A rainbow shows part of this range) 光譜(光線通過一種鏡片依紅外線至紫外線的次序排列出的彩色光帶). (彩虹顯示這光帶中的部份顏色). *pl* 複數 **spectra** ['spektrə].

speculate ['spekjuleit] *vi* **1** think in a general way without really knowing; guess 設想; 推測: *We can only speculate about life on other planets.* 對其他星球上的生命我們只能推測. **2** buy and sell goods and shares in the hope of making a profit quickly 做投機買賣: *It is dangerous to speculate unless you study the market.* 除非你對市場有所研究, 否則做投機買賣是危險的. **speculative** ['spekjulətiv] *adj* **speculation** [spekju'leiʃən] *nc / u*: *our speculations about life on other planets* 我們對其他星球上的生命所作的推測; *goods bought on speculation* i.e. on trial (informally shortened to

on spec) 投機買進的貨物, 即: 試買(非正式地縮寫為on spec).

sped [sped] past of **speed²**. speed²的過去式和過去分詞.

speech [spiːtʃ] **1** *nu* ability to speak; way of speaking 言語; 説話; 談話; 能力; 講話方式: *Babies have to learn speech.* 嬰孩得學習講話. *His speech showed that he was drunk.* 他說話的樣子表明他醉了. **2** *nc* long talk made in public 演説; 講話: *The headmaster gave / made a speech about / on good manners to the whole school.* 校長向全校作關於禮貌的報告. **speechless** *adj* not able to speak (usu. because of anger, surprise etc) 説不出話來的, 啞口無言的 (通常因氣憤, 驚訝等): *He was speechless with rage.* 他氣得說不出話來. *Their bad manners left us speechless.* 他們不禮貌的舉止使我們目瞪口呆.

speed¹ [spiːd] *nc / u* **1** quick movement; swiftness 迅速; 快: *The speed of the attack surprised them.* 這場進攻發動之快使他們吃驚. **2** movement as measured 速度; 速率: *at a low / high speed* i.e. slowly / quickly 低速/高速, 即: 緩慢地/迅速地. *A man's normal walking speed is 4 miles per hour.* 人的正常步行速度是每小時四英里. *The motorcar turned the corner at full / top speed.* 摩托車全速轉彎. **speedy** *adj* quick 快的; 迅速的. **speedily** *adv* **'speedboat** type of motorboat which moves very quickly 高速快艇. **'speed limit** speed above which one should not go 速度最高限制: *The speed limit in the town is 30 miles per hour for all traffic.* 此城的速度極限是每小時三十英里, 適用於一切行人車輛. *The police stopped him for exceeding the speed limit.* 警察攔住他, 因為他超速行駛. **speedometer** [spiˈdɒmitə*] in-

strument inside a motorcar, lorry etc which shows the speed at which it is going 速度計. **'speedway** track on which cars and motorcycles race (汽車、摩托車的)賽車跑道.

speed² [spiːd] *vi* go quickly 急行: *It is dangerous to speed in a car when it is dark.* 天黑駕車急行是危險的. *The lorry sped through the village.* 這輛載貨卡車疾駛駛過村莊. *past* 過去式和過去分詞 **sped** [sped]. **speeding** *nu* going too quickly (esp. in a motorcar, lorry etc) (尤指)超速行駛: *Speeding in a busy street is against the law.* 在繁忙街道超速行駛是違法的. **speed up** go, cause to go, more quickly (使)加快速度: *The lorry speeded up when it left the town.* 這輛載貨卡車離城時加速行駛. *Please try to speed up your work* i.e. work more quickly 請努力加緊工作, 即: 加快工作. *past* 過去式和過去分詞 **speeded up.**

spell¹ [spel] *vt / i* **1** say or write the letters of a word in their correct order 拼(寫): *He spelt the word wrongly.* 他把字拼錯了. **2** (with reference to letters) make a word (用字母)拼成: *B-O-O-K spells book.* B-O-O-K拼成book. **3** mean 意味着: *This news spells disaster.* 這條消息意味着災難. *past* 過去式和過去分詞 **spelt** [spelt] or 或 **spelled** [speld]. **spelling** *nc / u* way in which a word is spelt 拼(寫)法: *'Labour' is the British spelling, 'labor' the American spelling.* 'Labour'是英國的拼法, 'labor'是美國的拼法.

spell² [spel] *nc* short period of time 一段短時間: *spell of duty* 值班時間; *spell of good weather* 連日好天氣.

spell³ [spel] *nc* **1** words which are believed to produce a magic effect 符咒; 咒語. **2** fascination, charm, attraction of something unusual and beauti-

ful 誘惑力; 魅力; 吸引力. **'spellbound**
adj strongly attracted or fascinated by
something 着了迷的; 被迷住的; *The
boy stood spellbound, listening to the
old man's story.* 那男孩站住聽老人講故
事聽着迷了.

spelt [spelt] past of **spell**[1]. spell[1]的過去
式和過去分詞.

spend [spend] *vt / i* **1** pay out money in
order to get something 用 (錢); 花
(錢); *His wife never stops spending.*
他的老婆老是不停地花錢. *He spent
all his money on new books* i.e. to
buy new books 他把他所有的錢都用在
新書上. 即: 購買新書. **2** pass time; finish 度過 (時間); 用盡; *They spent
their holidays at home.* 他們在家度
假. *I spent an hour looking for you.*
我花了一個鐘頭找你. *He has spent all
his strength trying to help them.* 他已
竭盡全力去幫助他們. past 過去式和過
去分詞 **spent** [spent]. **spent** *adj* exhausted; worn out 筋疲力盡的; 用壞了
的; *The soldiers looked spent after
their long march.* 長途行軍後, 士兵們
都顯得疲憊不堪.

sperm [spəːm] *nu* fluid of male animals
which fertilizes female animals (動物
的)精液.

sphere [sfiə*] *nc* **1** body shaped like a
ball (e.g. the earth; a planet) 球形; 球
體 (例如: 地球, 行星). **2** range of
knowledge or interests 知識領域; 興趣
範圍; *Biology is not (in) my sphere.*
生物非我所長. *He has done good
work in many spheres of science* i.e.
many branches of science 他在許多科
學領域中都卓有建樹. 即: 在許多科學學
科中. **spherical** ['sferikl] *adj* shaped
like a sphere 球形的.

sphinx [sfiŋks] *nc* **1** ancient Egytian statue having a lion's body and a human
head (古埃及) 獅身人面像. **2** person

who is hard to understand 難以理解
的人; 謎樣的人.

spice [spais] *nc / u* vegetable matter,
often in the form of a powder, used to
flavour food (e.g. ginger, cinnamon,
curry powder) 香料; 調味品 (例如: 薑,
肉桂、咖喱粉). **spicy** *adj* flavoured
with spice 加有香料的. **spiciness** *nu*.

spick [spik] *adj* only in **spick and span**
i.e. clean and tidy 只用在 spick and
span 中, 即: 整潔的.

spider ['spaidə*] *nc* type of small creature with eight legs which makes a
web to catch insects for food 蜘蛛.
spidery *adj* (esp. with reference to
handwriting) thin like the thread of a
spider's web (尤指筆跡) 細如蜘蛛絲
的.

spied [spaid] past of **spy**. spy的過去式
和過去分詞.

spike [spaik] *nc* something with a sharp
point (e.g. on a fence, top of a wall,
the soles of running shoes, the tops of
flowers or grain) 尖狀物 (例如: 籬笆、
牆頭、跑鞋上的尖釘; 花穗; 穀穗);
*There is a row of spikes on top of the
prison wall to prevent the prisoners
escaping.* 監獄牆頭上裝有一排尖釘, 以
防犯人逃跑. **spiky** *adj* having spikes
有尖端的; 有尖釘的.

spill [spil] *vt / i* fall, cause to fall, out of
something (使) 溢出; (使) 灑出; *The
milk has spilt over the table* i.e. it has
fallen out of its bottle, jug etc. 牛奶灑
到桌上了. 即: 溢出瓶、罐等容器了.
Who spilt ink on my books? 誰把墨水
潑到我的書上? *The lorry hit a tree
and spilt the driver and his friend into
the bushes.* 載貨卡車撞上一棵樹, 把司
機和他的朋友都拋到灌木叢裏. past 過
去式和過去分詞 **spilt** [spilt] or 或
spilled [spild].

spin[1] [spin] *vt / i* **1** twist cotton, silk,

wool etc into threads. (The threads can then be woven-see **weave** -to make cloth) 紡紗. (然後用紗織布, 見 weave). **2** make from threads 以絲或 線做成: *I saw the spider spinning its web.* 我看見那隻蜘蛛在吐絲結網. **3** go, cause to go, round quickly (使)快 速旋轉: *The dancer spun on her toes.* 舞蹈演員踮着腳尖飛快旋轉. *The box fell spinning from the high window.* 箱 子從高處的窗上飛旋而下. *pres part* 現在分詞 **spinning**. *past tense* 過去式 **span** [spæn] or 或 **spun** [spʌn]. *past part* 過去分詞 **spun**. **'spinning wheel** simple machine with a large wheel used to spin cotton, silk, wool etc into threads 紡車. **spin out** make to last a long time 使維持一段長時間, 延 長使用: *We were able to spin our money out until the end of our holi-days. (informal)* 我們有法子使我們的 錢一直用到我們的假期結束. (非正式).

spin² [spin] *nc/u* turning movement 旋 轉: *He gave the wheel a spin.* 他把輪 子旋轉了一下. *In cricket, bowlers try to give spin to the ball.* 打板球時, 投球 手都設法投出旋轉球. *The aeroplane went into a spin.* 飛機開始盤旋下降. **'spin-'drier** machine which removes water from clothes by spinning them in a container (洗衣機的)旋轉式脱水 機.

spinach ['spinitʃ] *nu* type of green vegetable 菠菜.

spindle ['spindl] *nc* thin rod round which something (e.g. a wheel) turns 紡錘; 紗錠; (機器之)軸. **spindly** *adj* long and thin 細長的.

spine [spain] *nc* **1** backbone 脊椎骨. **2** sharp thorn of some types of plant or sharp point on the skin of some types of animals (植物或動物皮上的)刺; 針; 棘刺. **3** outside part of a book where

the pages join and which is seen when it stands in a row with other books 書背; 書脊.

spinster ['spinstə*] *nc* woman who is not married 未婚女人; 老處女.

spiral ['spairl] *adj* going round and up like a screw 螺旋形的: *spiral stair* 螺 旋形樓梯. Also 亦作 *nc*: *The smoke was rising in spirals.* 烟在盤旋上升. Also 亦作 *vi*: *The smoke was spiral-ling into the air.* 烟盤旋着升空. *past* 過去式和過去分詞 **spiralled.** (*US* 美 **spiraled).**

spire ['spaiə*] *nc* pointed roof, rising high in the air on top of a building (esp. a church) (尤指教堂的)塔尖; 尖 頂.

spirit ['spirit] *nc/u* **1** soul; part of man which is not body 心靈; 精神: *The spirit is willing but the flesh is weak.* 力不從心; 心有餘而力不足. **2** being which has no body; ghost 靈魂; 鬼魂: *The spirit of his dead father stood by his bed.* 他父親的鬼魂站在他的床邊. *They are afraid of evil spirits.* 他們害 怕惡魔. **3** energy; courage; person as an example of energy, courage etc. 精 力; 勇氣; 精力, 勇氣等當榜樣的人: *He fought with spirit.* 他勇敢戰鬥. *They have no spirit for the dangerous journey.* 他們沒有勇氣作這次危險的旅 行. *He was one of the greatest spirits of his age.* 他是他那個時代最偉大的人 物之一. **4** (*in pl*) state of mind; mood (用於複數)心境; 心情: *He was in high spirits* i.e. cheerful 我們心情愉 好. 即; 興高彩烈; *in low / poor spirits* i.e. sad; depressed. 情緒低落/意氣消 沉, 即; 憂愁的; 沮喪的. **5** (usu. *pl*) alcohol; strong alcoholic drink (e.g. brandy, gin, whisky etc) (通常用複數) 酒; 烈酒(例如: 白蘭地、杜松子酒、威士 忌等). **spirited** *adj* full of energy;

brave 精力充沛的; 勇敢的: *spirited fight* 勇猛的戰鬥: *spirited reply* 鏗鏘有力的回答. **'spirit level** instrument which shows that a surface is level by the position of a bubble of air 酒精水準器. **'high-'spirited** *adj* cheerful 興高彩烈的. **Holy Spirit** God (as a part of the Trinity in Christian religion) 聖靈 (基督教).

spiritual ['spiritjuəl] *adj* of the soul; of a being which has no body 精神的; 靈魂的: *Priests are concerned with man's spiritual problems.* 教士們關心人的靈魂問題. *The people waited for a spiritual sign* i.e. from a being which has no body (e.g. the spirit of a dead person). 那些人正等候一個幽靈的顯現. 即: 沒有軀體的靈魂 (例如: 某死者的鬼魂). Also 亦作 *nc* religious song (esp. one sung by American Negroes) (尤指美國黑人唱的) 聖歌. **spiritualism** *nu* belief that the spirit of a dead person can be made to appear to living persons or send them messages 招魂論; 唯靈論.

spit[1] [spit] *vi* 1 push out the liquid in the mouth (often to show anger or contempt) 吐口水 (常表示憤怒或蔑視): *People who spit can spread disease.* 隨地吐痰的人會傳播疾病. *When he met his enemy, he spat at him.* 他遇到他的仇人時, 便對他吐口水. 2 make a noise like somebody spitting 發出吐唾沫聲. 3 (with reference to rain or snow) fall in rain, scattered drops (指雨、雪) 霏霏下降: *It was spitting when I went outside.* 我出門時, 正細雨霏霏. *pres part* 現在分詞 **spitting.** *past* 過去式和過去分詞 **spat** [spæt]. Also 亦作 *nu* liquid which is spat from the mouth. 口水; 唾液: *Wipe the spit off your chin.* 擦掉你下巴上的口水. (Also 亦作 **spittle**). spit-

ting image exact likeness 一模一樣; 極其相像.

spit[2] [spit] *nc* pointed bar put through meat so that the meat is cooked on all sides as the bar is turned slowly 烤肉叉.

spite[1] [spait] *nu* hatred; ill will 怨恨; 惡意: *Spite made him tell the teacher I had lost my book.* 惡意驅使他告訴老師說我丟掉課本. *He told the teacher out of spite.* 他出於惡意告訴老師. *He had a spite against me.* 他對我懷恨在心. Also 亦作 *vt* harm because of spite 惡意傷害: *He told the teacher just to spite me.* 他告訴老師, 僅爲了向我洩憤. **spiteful** *adj* having spite 懷恨的; 惡意的.

spite[2] [spait] only in **in spite of** i.e. with no concern for; without troubling about 只用於 **in spite of**, 即: 不顧; 不管: *In spite of the danger they climbed the mountain.* 他們不顧危險攀登此山.

spitfire ['spit,faiə] *nc* person, esp woman or girl, who is easily aroused to violent outbursts of temper 脾氣暴躁的人, 烈性子的人 (尤指女人).

spittle ['spitl] *nu* liquid in the mouth; saliva 口水; 唾沫. see also 參見 **spit**[1] *nu.*

splash [splæʃ] *vt / i* 1 (with reference to liquids) fall, cause to fall, in large drops (usu. with a noise) (指液體)(使)濺落, 飛濺 (通常有聲): *The water splashed into the deep hole.* 水飛濺到深穴裏. *He splashed ink over his desk / He splashed his desk with ink.* 他把墨水濺到他的桌上/他使他的桌子濺上墨水. *The big waves splashed against the side of the boat.* 大浪撞擊船舷, 濺起水花. 2 move or do something so that a liquid splashes 涉水; 濺水 (行動): *I can hear him splashing in the* *bath.* 我能聽見他在浴缸中濺水. *We splashed through the mud.* 我們濺着泥漿而行. Also 亦作 *nc* noise or mark caused by splashing 飛濺聲; 濺污的斑點: *The stone rolled into the river with a splash.* 石頭噗通一聲濺進河裏. *He had splashes of ink on his hands.* 他雙手都濺有斑斑墨跡.

splendid ['splendid] *adj* magnificent; causing admiration 華麗的; 輝煌的; 壯觀的; 堂皇的: *He lives in a splendid house.* 他住在一幢富麗堂皇的房子裏. **splendidly** *adv.*

splendour ['splendə*] *nc* brightness, magnificence; glory 光輝; 壯麗; 榮耀: *splendour of a sunset in the tropics* 熱帶夕陽的絢麗多彩. *He told us about the splendours of ancient India.* 他告訴我們有關古代印度的種種榮耀.

splice [splais] *vt* join two ends of rope by weaving the strands together; join two pieces of wood or metal by placing one over the other and tying them 編接 (繩頭); 疊接 (木板); 接合 (金屬板).

splint [splint] *nc* piece of hard material for keeping a broken bone in the right position (固定骨折的) 夾板: *The doctor put my broken arm / leg in splints.* 醫生用夾板夾住我的折臂／斷腿.

splinter ['splintə*] *nc* sharp piece of wood, metal etc which has been broken off, or projects from, a larger piece 尖片; 碎片; 裂片; 刺: *When I picked up the broken box I got a splinter in my finger.* 我撿起破箱時, 我的指頭給扎了一根刺. Also 亦作 *vt / i* break into splinters 裂成碎片; 碎裂.

split[1] [split] *vt / i* **1** break or cut into parts (esp. lengthwise) (尤指縱長地) 劈開; 切開: *This wood splits easily.* 這木頭容易劈開. *He split the wood with an axe.* 他用斧子劈開木頭. **2** tear,

burst open, suddenly 撕開; 裂開: *His coat, which was very light, split from top to bottom.* 他那件輕飄飄的大衣從衣肩一直裂到衣脚. *pres part* 現在分詞 **splitting.** *past* 過去式和過去分詞 **split.** Also 亦作 *adj* **splitting** *adj* painful 劇痛的: *I have a splitting headache.* 我的頭痛得厲害. **split something up** divide into parts 分開: *He split up the class into three groups.* 他把班分成三組. *After the meeting we split up and went home* i.e. divided into groups. 開會後, 我們便分開回家.

split[2] [split] *nc* tear; narrow crack 裂口; 裂縫: *There is a long split in his coat.* 他的大衣上有條長裂縫.

splutter ['splʌtə*] *vt / i* **1** talk quickly in an excited manner (usu. with liquid thrown from the mouth) 急促而激動地說 (通常口沫橫飛). **2** make a hissing or spitting sound 發噼嚦聲; 作嚦啪聲; 發爆烈聲: *The rain caused the lamp to splutter.* 雨水打得油燈噼啪響.

spoil[1] [spɔil] *vt / i* **1** (with reference to things) damage; make worse (指事物) 損壞; 弄糟: *He has spoilt his work by being careless.* 他做事馬虎, 把工作弄糟了. *The rain will spoil her new hat.* 下雨會毀壞她的新帽子. **2** (with reference to persons esp. children) harm behaviour and character by being too kind and gentle (指人, 尤對孩子) 寵壞; 溺愛: *She has only one son and she spoils him.* 她只有一個兒子, 她溺愛他. *Nobody likes spoilt children.* 沒有人喜歡嬌生慣養的孩子. *past* 過去式和過去分詞 **spoilt** or 或 **spoiled.** **spoilt, spoiled** *adj* (*opp* 反義詞 **unspoilt, unspoiled**). '**spoilsport** person who stops others enjoying themselves *(informal)* 掃興的人; 妨礙他人歡娛的人. (非正式).

spoil² [spɔil] *nc* (usu. *pl*) plunder; stolen goods (通常用複數) 掠奪物; 贓物: *spoil / spoils taken away by the thieves* 竊賊偷取的贓物.

spoke¹ [spouk] past tense of **speak.** speak 的過去式.

spoke² [spouk] *nc* one of the thin rods connecting the centre of a wheel to its outside edge (車輪的) 輻條.

spoken [ˈspoukən] past part of **speak.** speak 的過去分詞.

spokesman [ˈspouksmən] *nc* person who speaks for others 發言人; 代言人: *a Labour Party spokesman* 工黨發言人; *a spokesman for the government* 政府發言人.

sponge [spʌndʒ] *nc* **1** type of sea animal with a body full of holes to allow water to enter (When dried it is used for cleaning and wiping.) 海綿. (乾時用於清潔擦拭.) **2** substance full of holes used for cleaning and wiping 海綿狀的東西(用於清潔擦拭): *rubber sponge* 橡皮海綿. **3** type of very soft, light cake 鬆軟蛋糕. (Also 亦作 **sponge cake**). Also 亦作 *vt* clean or wipe with a sponge 用海綿揩拭、擦拭: *She sponged the cut on my head.* 她用海綿揩拭我頭上的傷口. **spongy** *adj* soft and full of holes like a sponge 像海綿的; 柔軟多孔的.

sponsor [ˈspɔnsə*] *nc* **1** person who promises to be responsible for another person 主辦人; 發起人; 保證人. **2** person or business company which gives financial support to a radio or television programme, a concert, exhibition etc (usu. in return for publicity and the right to advertise goods) 廣播、電視節目、音樂會、展覽會等的贊助人或商行(通常爲了揚名和有權爲商品做廣告). Also 亦作 *vt* sponsor for 主辦; 發起; 贊助: *I spon-*

sored the first proposal. 我領銜提出第一個建議. *The tobacco company sponsors several television programmes.* 這家烟草公司資助上演幾套電視節目.

spontaneous [spɔnˈteiniəs] *adj* at one's own wish; not forced; natural. 自動的; 自發的; 自然的: *They made a spontaneous decision to work for an extra halfhour* i.e. nobody told them to work more; they decided themselves 他們自發作出決定, 加班半小時. 即: 沒有人叫他們加班; 是他們自己決定的. **spontaneously** *adv* **spontaneity** [spɔntəˈneiiti] *nu.*

spool [spu:l] *nc* small cylinder made of wood or metal on which thread, wire, the film of a camera etc is wound. (繞線、鐵絲、照相軟片等的)管、筒、捲軸、捲盤.

spoon [spu:n] *nc* instrument with a small bowl at the end of a handle used for mixing, taking food to the mouth etc (used with many other words to show what the spoon is used for e.g. *eggspoon, soupspoon, teaspoon*) 匙; 調羹(通常與許多其他的詞連用, 以表明用途, 例如: eggspoon 蛋匙、soupspoon 湯匙、teaspoon 茶匙). **spoonful** *nc* amount that can be taken in a spoon 一匙的量: *He put two spoonfuls of sugar in his tea.* 他在茶裏加了兩匙糖. **'spoon-feed** *vt* **1** feed with a spoon (e.g. a baby or sick person who cannot feed himself) 用匙餵(嬰兒、無法自理的病人等). **2** do too much for somebody so that he does not look after himself 過份伺候而使不用自理.

sporadic [spɔˈrædik] *adj* happening one by one or here and there 個別發生的; 散發的: *There has been sporadic fighting in the capital during the last* *few days.* 近日來，首都已出現零星的戰鬥.

spore [spɔ:;spɔə] *nc* small reproductive body produced by bacteria, mosses, ferns, etc and capable of giving rise to new individual (細菌、苔蘚、蕨類植物的)孢子.

sport [spɔ:t] *nc* 1 game played or exercise taken for enjoyment (esp. in the open air e.g. football and baseball; hunting and swimming) 運動；遊戲(尤指戶外進行的活動，例如：足球和棒球；打獵和游泳). 2 (in *pl*) meeting for athletics i.e. running, jumping, throwing etc (用於複數) 運動會(例如：跑、跳、擲等): *Are you going to run in the school sports?* 你要參加校運會賽跑嗎? 3 person who is not angry when he loses; person who is willing to join in a game etc. 失敗而不氣餒的人；有運動精神的人: *John is a (good) sport. He is ready to try anything.* (*informal* in sense 3) 約翰是條(好)漢子, 他甚麼事都準備試試身手. (義3爲非正式). **'sports car** motorcar made for speed. 賽車；高速跑車. **'sports coat / jacket** man's jacket, worn on informal occasions, and not part of a suit 運動衣. **'sportsman** 1 man who is fond of, or good at, sport 愛好運動的人；運動員；運動家. 2 man who is willing to take a chance 甘冒風險的人. **'sportsmanship** *nu* behaviour expected from a sportsman 運動員精神；運動家風格. **'sportswoman** woman who is fond of, or good at, sport 女運動愛好者；女運動員；女運動家.

spot¹ [spɔt] *nc* 1 small mark or stain 點；污點: *He was wearing a blue tie with white spots.* 他繫着有白色斑點的藍色領帶. *There were spots of ink on his white collar.* 他的白色衣領上沾有墨水漬. 2 small, red mark on the skin; pimple (皮膚上的) 紅瘡；面皰, 粉刺: *His face was covered with spots.* 他臉上長滿粉刺. 3 small amount 少量，一點點: *I'll have a spot of whisky.* 我要喝點威士忌酒; *a few spots of rain* (*informal* in sense 3) 幾滴雨 (義 3 爲非正式). 4 particular place 地點, 場所: *This is the spot where he stood.* 這是他站過的地方. *He lives in a quiet spot far away from the town.* 他住在遠離城鎮的寧靜地方. **spotted** *adj* marked with spots 有斑點的；有污點的: *spotted tie* 有斑點的領帶; *leopard's spotted coat* 豹斑外衣. **spotless** *adj* very clean 無瑕疵的；純潔的，一塵不染的. **spotlessly** *adv*:*His clothes were spotlessly clean.* 他的衣服極爲乾淨. **spotty** *adj* covered with spots (esp. in sense 2) 多紅痣的；長滿粉刺的；多斑點的；盡是污點的: *The boy has a spotty face.* 這個男孩有一張長滿粉刺的臉. **spottiness** *nu* 'spotlight *nc* apparatus for shining a strong light on a particular place or person (e. g. on the stage of a theatre); the light itself 聚光燈(例如在舞台上)；聚光燈的照明圈. **on the spot** immediately; just there 立即；在現場: *He paid me on the spot.* 他立即付給我錢. *He was killed on the spot.* 他當場被殺.

spot² [spɔt] *vt / i* 1 mark, become marked, with spots (使) 沾上斑點；(使)變污: *His collar was spotted with ink.* 他的領帶沾有墨跡. 2 recognize among many; choose correctly 認出；認準: *I spotted my father in the crowd.* 我在人羣中找見我的父親. *Do you think you can spot the winner of the next race?* 你想你能認準下場比賽中的獲勝者嗎? *past* 過去式和過去分詞 **spotted.**

spouse [spaus] *nc* husband or wife.

(rather *o. f.*). 夫; 妻; 配偶(頗爲舊式).

spout [spaut]*vt / i* (with reference to liquids) pour out, push out, violently (指液體)噴出; 湧出: *Blood was spouting from the deep cut in his arm.* 血從他胳膊上深深的傷口裏湧出來. *The broken pipe spouted water all over the room.* 破水管噴了一屋子的水. Also 亦作 *nc* pipe or channel from which a liquid is poured 管口; 噴口: *spout of a teapot / kettle.* 茶壺嘴/壺嘴. *Rain from the roof goes down a long spout.* 房頂上的雨水從一條長落水管中流下來.

sprain [sprein] *vt* twist violently the muscles of a joint (e. g. the ankle or wrist). 扭傷(關節) (例如踝或腕): *I sprained my ankle playing football.* 我踢足球時扭傷了腳脖子. Also 亦作 *nc*: *I have a sprain in my ankle.* 我扭傷腳脖子.

sprang [spræŋ] past tense of **spring¹**. spring¹ 的過去式.

sprawl [sprɔ:l] *vi* lie or sit with the arms and legs stretched out; fall and lie this way 攤開四肢躺或坐; 攤開四肢躺倒: *They were sprawling on the grass.* 他們四肢伸開躺在草地上. *The blow from the heavy stick sent him sprawling.* 一擊重棍把他打倒在地.

spray¹ [sprei] *vt* spread a liquid in very small drops over 噴灑; 噴液體於…: *They spray their cattle with a chemical which kills insects.* 他們將化學殺蟲藥水噴到牛身上. Also 亦作 *nc / u* **1** very small drops of water (e. g. water blown from the sea by the wind) (海水被風吹起的)水沫; 水霧; 浪花: *During the storm the boat was covered with spray.* 在暴風雨中, 船上濺滿了浪花. **2** type of liquid which is sprayed 噴液: *I bought some spray for my cattle.* 我買了些噴牛用的(殺蟲)噴射液. *My wife uses a hair spray.* 我妻子使用噴髮液. **3** apparatus for spraying 噴霧器. (Also 亦作 **sprayer**).

spray² [sprei] *nc* small branch with leaves and flowers, used as an ornament; any ornament like a spray. (有葉有花作飾物用的)小枝; 枝狀花飾.

spread [spred] *vt / i* **1** stretch out; extend in space or time. 伸展; (空間)擴展或(時間)延長: *The forest spreads from here to the river.* 這片森林從這裏延伸到河邊. *The trees spread their branches over the house.* 這些樹的樹枝蓋過房子. *He stood up and spread his arms.* 他站起來伸開雙臂. *Our visits to England were spread over a period of six months.* 我們在英國的遊覽爲時六個月. **2** cover the surface of 舖蓋; 塗敷: *He spread the bed with a blanket / He spread a blanket on the bed.* 他把毯子舖在牀上. *Did you spread the bread with butter? / Did you spread butter on the bread?* 你在麵包上塗了黃油嗎? **3** extend to cover a larger area; pass, cause to pass, to more people 散佈; 傳播: *The patch of oil spread slowly over the floor.* 油斑在地板上漸漸滲開. *The disease spread over the whole country.* 疾病蔓延到全國. *Who spread the news that he was ill?* 誰傳播他生病的消息? past 過去式和過去分詞 **spread.** Also 亦作 **1** *nu* extent 伸展: *the spread of his arms* 他的雙臂的伸開. **2** *nc* plenty of food and drink on a table 酒席; 宴會: *At Christmas we had a good spread. (informal in sense 2)* 聖誕節我們吃了一桌豐盛的酒席. (義 2 爲非正式).

spree [spri:] *nc* gay time; celebration 縱情狂歡; 作樂; 慶祝: *After winning the game they had a spree.* 比賽獲勝後,

他們縱情歡樂了一番. *He went out on a spree i. e. he went out drinking and enjoying himself. (informal)* 他們出去飲酒作樂. (非正式).

sprig [sprig] *nc* small shoot of a plant or tree with leaves and flowers (有葉有花的) 嫩枝; 小枝.

sprightly ['spraitli] *adj* lively; merry 活潑的, 愉快的.

spring¹ [spriŋ] *vt / i* **1** jump or move suddenly 跳; 跳躍; 躍起: *The lion sprang from the long grass.* 獅子突然躍出草叢. *He sprang out of bed when he heard the bell.* 聽到鈴聲他從床上一躍而起. **2** (usu. with **up**) appear or grow suddenly (通常與 **up** 連用) 出現; 迅速長出: *A storm sprang up.* 暴風雨來了. *After the rain, grass sprang up everywhere.* 雨過之後, 雜草到處叢生. *past tense* 過去式 **sprang** [spræŋ]. *past part* 過去分詞 **sprung** [sprʌŋ].

spring² [spriŋ] **1** *nc* act of jumping or moving suddenly 跳; 跳躍: *The lion made a spring at the hunter.* 獅子向獵人撲去. *With a spring he reached the top of the wall.* 他一跳到了牆頭. **2** *nc* place where water appears at the surface of the ground 泉; 水源; 源頭: *We stopped near a spring.* 我們在泉水附近停了下來. **3** *nc* something which springs back or returns to where it was before being pulled or pushed 彈簧; 發條; 彈板: *Motorcars have springs above the wheels.* 汽車輪子的上方有彈板. *The spring of my watch is broken.* 我的手錶發條斷了. **4** *nu* power to spring back 彈力; 彈性. **springy** *adj* having spring (in sense **4**); elastic; light 有彈力的; 有彈性的; 輕快的: *The branches of the tree are springy.* 樹枝有彈性. *He walks with a springy step.* 他邁着輕快的步伐. **springiness**

nu '**springboard** springy board which helps those who jump or dive into water from it (跳水或跳躍用的) 跳板; 彈板.

spring³ [spriŋ] *nc* season of the year when plants begin to grow i. e. March, April and May in Britain 春季; 春天 (在英國爲三月、四月、五月). *In spring the weather gets warmer.* 春天天氣變暖. Also 亦作 *adj: spring weather* 春季的天氣; *spring term at school* i. e. between the Christmas and Easter holidays (學校的) 春季學期, 即在聖誕節和復活節之間. '**spring-'cleaning** thorough cleaning of a house, room etc. (esp. in the spring) (尤指在春季) 對房屋、房間等進行的大掃除, '**spring-time** season of spring 春季.

sprinkle ['spriŋkl] *vt* throw sand, drops of water etc over something 撒; 灑: *They sprinkled sand on the floor.* 他們把沙撒到地面上. *They sprinkled the floor with sand.* 他們把沙撒到地面上. *I sprinkled my face with some water.* 我在臉上灑了一些水.

sprint [sprint] *vi* run a short distance at full speed 短距離疾跑. Also 亦作 *nc: He won the hundred yard sprint.* 他在百碼短跑中獲勝. **sprinter** *nc.*

sprout¹ [spraut] *vt / i* (with reference to plants) begin to, cause to begin to, grow (指植物) (使) 開始生長; (使) 發芽: *The beans we planted are sprouting.* 我們種的豆子在發芽. *The damp corn is sprouting shoots.* 潮濕的穀子開始發芽了.

sprout² [spraut] *nc* (usu. *pl*) type of cabbage with very small round cabbages growing on the stem. (Sometimes **Brussels sprout**) 球芽甘藍 (有時作 Brussels sprout).

spruce¹ [spruːs] *adj* neat in dress; smart 衣著整潔的; 漂亮的.

spruce² [spru:s] *nc* type of tall, cone-shaped, evergreen tree with pointed leaves on every side of the twig 針樅; 雲杉.

sprung [sprʌŋ] past part of **spring**¹. spring¹ 的過去分詞.

spry [sprai] *adj* active; lively 活躍的; 活潑的: *Although he is old, he is still spry.* 他雖然老了，但還很矯健.

spun [spʌn] past part of **spin**¹. spin¹ 的過去分詞.

spur [spə:*] *nc* **1** instrument with a small, pointed wheel or a point worn on the heel of a rider's boot and pushed against the side of a horse to make it go faster 馬刺; 馬扎子. **2** something which makes somebody try harder, be more active etc. 激勵物; 刺激物; 驅策力: *The hope of freedom was their spur.* 希望自由是他們的驅策力. Also 亦作 *vt / i* (often with **on**) (常與 on 連用) **1** make a horse go faster by using spurs 以馬刺驅策 (馬): *He spurred (on) his horse so that he would pass the others.* 他驅策坐騎以便超過其他人. **2** make more active 使再接再勵; 激勵: *They were spurred(on) by the hope of freedom.* 希望自由激勵了他們. past 過去式和過去分詞 **spurred. on the spur of the moment** suddenly, without thinking 突然地; 不加思索地: *On the spur of the moment I gave him my coat.* 我一時衝動將我的外衣給了他.

spurious ['spjuəriəs] *adj* false but made to appear real 偽造的; 假的; 假託的; 欺騙性的: *His claim is spurious* i. e. he has no genuine reason to make a claim. 他要求的所有權是偽造的. 即: 他沒有真正的理由要求承認其所有權.

spurn [spə:n] *vt* kick or drive away; refuse to accept 一腳踢開; 拒絕接受: *They spurn all our offers of help.* 他們

拒絕接受我們提出的一切援助.

spurt [spə:t] *vt / i* (with reference to liquids, fire etc) come out, cause to come out, suddenly (指液體, 火燄等) 噴出, (使) 湧出 (使) 進出: *Water spurted from the broken pipe.* 水從破裂的水管中噴出. *Their guns spurted fire.* 他們的槍瞄射出火燄. Also 亦作 *nc* **1** sudden flow from an opening 噴出; 湧出; 進出: *spurts of water from the broken pipe* 水從破裂的水管中噴出. **2** short, sudden effort or activity 短暫而突然的活動或努力; 突然奮起: *He made a sudden spurt.* 他突然奮起.

spy [spai] *nc* person who acts in secret to get information about another country; secret agent; person who watches others secretly 間諜; 密探; 偵探; 秘密監視者. Also 亦作 *vt / i* (with **on, upon** or **into**) (與 on, upon 或 into 連用). **1** act as a spy; watch secretly 作偵探; 偵察; 窺探: *Our government knows that the enemy is spying on / upon our army.* 我國政府知道敵人正在偵察我們的軍隊. *The woman in the next house likes spying on her neighbours.* 隔壁的女人喜歡暗中監視她的鄰居. *Why do they spy into our affairs?* 他們爲甚麼窺探我們的事情? **2** see; notice 看見; 察覺: *I spied him trying to hide behind the tree.* 我察覺他想藏在樹後. past 過去式和過去分詞 **spied** [spaid].

squabble ['skwɔbl] *vi* argue or quarrel noisily about something which is not important (爲小事而) 爭論; 吵嘴: *The boys were squabbling about who was the best runner.* 這些男孩子在爭論誰跑得最快. Also 亦作 *nc: family squabbles* i. e. noisy quarrels, about unimportant matters, between members of a family 家庭爭吵, 即: 家庭成員之間因小事而大聲爭吵.

squad [skwɔd] *nc* small group (e. g. of soldiers) working together. 小組, 小隊, 班(例如士兵) '**firing squad** group of soldiers etc chosen to execute somebody by shooting him (挑選來執行槍決的)行刑隊。

squadron ['skwɔdrn] *nc* **1** group of 120 to 200 men forming part of a cavalry regiment (120至200人的)騎兵隊。**2** group of warships or aircraft 艦隊; 空軍中隊。

squalid ['skwɔlid] *adj* dirty and unpleasant (esp. because of neglect) (尤指因被忽視而)污穢的, 不潔的; 邋遢的: *They live in a squalid hut in the poorest part of the village.* 他們居住在村裏最窮困地帶的污穢小屋中。**squalor** ['skwɔlɔ*] *nu* state of being squalid 污穢; 骯髒; 邋遢: *They live in squalor.* 他們居住在骯髒的環境中。

squall [skwɔːl] *nc* sudden strong wind or storm (常夾帶雨或雪的)狂風, 風暴。**squally** *adj* having spualls 有狂風的; 有暴風雨的: *squally weather* 狂風大作的天氣。

squander ['skwɔndə*] *vt* (with reference to money, possessions etc) waste; spend carelessly (指錢, 財產等)浪費; 亂花: *He squanders all the money which his father gives him.* 他揮霍了他父親給他的全部錢財。*A country which squanders the skill of its people cannot grow rich.* 浪費人才的國家不可能富裕起來。

square[1] [skwɛə*] *nc* **1** figure with four equal sides and four right angles; anything with this shape. 正方形; 正方形物: *Graph paper is divided into squares.* 坐標圖紙分成若干正方形。**2** open space of this shape in a town and the buildings round it (城市中四周有房屋的)廣場; 方場: *We sat in the square watching the people passing.*

我們坐在廣場中看着人們來來往往。*I live in George Square.* 我住在喬治廣場。**3** instrument shaped like L used for drawing or testing right angles; one shaped like T (called a **T-square**) used in this way 直角規; 丁字尺。**4** (mathematics) product of a number multiplied by itself (數學)平方; 自乘: *The square of 3 is 9.* 3 的平方是 9。**5** person who does not understand or enjoy the music, clothes, ideas etc of young people. (*informal* in sense **5**) 古板守舊的人(義 5 爲非正式)。

square[2] [skwɛə*] *adj* **1** having the shape of a square 四方形的; 有四方形的: *square room* 四方形的房間。**2** of a number multiplied by itself 平方的; *square inch* i. e. an area each side of which equals one inch 平方英寸, 即: 各邊均爲 1 英寸。*3 square miles* 3 平方英里。*Note* 說明: in this sense the position of square is important (e. g. *3 square miles* is not the same as *3 miles square*, which equals 9 square miles i. e. the *square* of 3 square miles) 本義中 square 的位置很重要 (例如: 3 square miles 與 3 miles square 不同, 後者爲3英里見方, 等于 9 平方英里, 即 3 平方英里的平方)。**squarely** *adv* **1** firmly; straight 堅定地; 挺直地: *He sat squarely in his chair.* 他端正地坐在椅子上。*He looked (at) me squarely in the eye* i. e. not from the side but directly 他直瞪瞪地望着我; 朝: 不是斜視而是直視。**2** honestly 正直地: *He deals squarely with everybody.* 他待人正直。**a square meal** a good and satisfying meal 豐盛的一餐。**square root** (mathematics) 平方根(數學): *The square root of 9 is 3.* 9 的平方根是 3。

squash [skwɔʃ] *vt / i* **1** become or make flat by pressing; crush (使)壓

扁; (使) 壓碎: *This hat squashes easi-ly.* 這頂帽子很容易壓扁. *He squashed the insect with his finger.* 他用手指把小蟲壓扁了. **2** (often with **in** or **into**) press together in a small space (常與 in 或 into 連用) 擠壓; 擠進: *He squashed his clothes into a box.* 他把衣服塞進箱子. *The people in the bus were so squashed that they could not move.* 公共汽車裏十分擁擠, 人們無法轉身. Also 亦作 **1** *n sing* group of people pressed together 擁擠的人羣: *There was an awful squash in the train* 火車裏人羣擁擠. **2** *nc / u* drink made from squashed fruit 果汁飲料: *lemon / orange squash* 檸檬/橘子汁. **3** *nu* usual form of **squash rackets.** squash rackets 的通常形式. **squash rackets** game played with a small soft ball and rackets in a court with walls all round. 軟式網球 (在有圍牆的球場內用球拍和打軟球的一種球戲).

squat [skwɒt] *vi* **1** sit on one's heels; (with reference to animals) have the body close to the ground. 蹲; 蹲坐; (指動物) 伏下, 蜷伏: *We squatted round the camp-fire.* 我們圍蹲在營火旁. **2** settle on land or in a house which is not occupied, without proper rights or permission 非法擅自佔住空地或空房子. *past* 過去式 和 *past part* 過去分詞 **squatted.** Also 亦作 *adj* short and thick 粗矮的. **squatter** *nc* person who squats (in sense 2) 非法擅自佔住空地或空房的人: *The farmers here are angry about the squatters who live on their land.* 這裏的農夫對擅自佔住在他們土地上的人們很氣憤.

squawk [skwɔ:k] *nc* (esp. with reference to a bird when frightened) short, harsh cry (尤指鳥受驚時) 粗厲的叫聲: *The hen gave a squawk when it saw the cat.* 母雞見到貓時咯咯叫了起來.

Also 亦作 *vi* give a short, harsh cry. 發出粗厲的叫聲; 咯咯地叫: *The hen squawked.* 母雞咯咯地叫.

squeak [skwi:k] *nc* short, sharp, high-pitched cry or noise 短促的尖叫聲; *squeak of a mouse* 老鼠吱吱的叫聲; *squeaks made by his old shoes* 他的舊鞋發出的嘎吱聲. Also 亦作 *vt / i*: *This little boy squeaked (out) his answer* i. e. in a voice like a squeak 這個小男孩尖聲回答. **squeaky** *adj* making squeaks 發短促尖聲的: *squeaky shoes* 嘎吱嘎吱作響的鞋; *a squeaky voice* 嘎吱叫的聲音.

squeal [skwi:l] *nc* long, high-pitched cry or noise 長而尖銳的叫聲: *The children gave a squeal of fright.* 孩子們發出驚嚇的尖叫聲. *He stopped his car suddenly with a squeal of his brakes.* 他突然停車, 制動器吱吱叫. Also 亦作 *vt / i* give or make a squeal 長聲尖叫; 用長而尖銳的聲音說: *The children squealed with fright.* 孩子們因驚駭而尖叫. *The brakes of the car squealed.* 汽車的煞車發出吱吱聲. *She squealed (out) to us that we were in great danger* i. e. shouted to us in a voice like a squeal. 她尖聲對我們叫喊, 我們處境十分危險.

squeamish [ˈskwi:miʃ] *adj* feeling sick; easily made sick; too easily disgusted 要嘔吐的; 易於嘔吐的, 易感厭惡的: *The rough sea made me squeamish.* 大海波濤洶湧我很要嘔吐了. *He was squeamish about changing the baby's nappies.* 他厭惡給嬰孩換尿布. **squeamishness** *nu.*

squeeze [skwi:z] *vt / i* press (usu. into a different shape or a smaller space) 擠壓 (通常指壓成不同的形狀或壓小); 壓榨: *I squeezed the tube of toothpaste.* 我擠牙膏. *He squeezed her hand.* 他

緊握她的手. *She is squeezing an orange* i. e. to get its juice 她在挤压橘子. 即: 榨橘汁. Also 亦作 **1** act of squeezing 压榨; 挤: *He gave her hand a squeeze.* 他紧握一下她的手. **2** amount got by squeezing 榨出量; 挤出量. *She put a squeeze of orange in my drink.* 她把少许橘子汁加入我的饮料中. **3** small space because of squeezing 拥挤: *It was a tight squeeze in the crowded bus.* 挤满了人的公共汽车里非常拥挤. **4** (esp. with reference to money) force; extortion; difficulty (尤指钱) 榨取; 勒索; 强取; 困境; 紧迫: *We cannot borrow money during the present credit squeeze* i. e. when it is difficult to get credit 在当前紧缩贷款, 我们借不到钱. 即: 很难得到贷款之时.

squib [skwib] *nc* small firework in the shape of a short tube (短管) 小鞭炮; 小烟火.

squid [skwid] *nc* type of sea creature with ten arms, which sends out a black substance when attacked 鸟贼; 墨鱼.

squint [skwint] *vi* look in a different direction with each eye because of a defect 斜视: *The doctor says that the child squints.* 医生说这个小孩斜视. Also 亦作 *nc*: *Her child has a squint.* 她的孩子患斜视眼.

squire ['skwaiə*] *nc* (in England) land-owner; country gentleman (用於英) 地主; 乡绅.

squirm [skwəm] *vi* move like a snake; twist the body like one (often through embarrassment etc) 蠕动; 扭曲身体 (常因困窘等); 侷促不安: *The little boy squirmed with shame.* 这个小男孩因羞愧而侷促不安.

squirrel ['skwirl] *nc* type of small ani-mal with a bushy tail which lives in trees and which stores up food for

the winter 松鼠.

squirt [skwə:t] *vt / i* (with reference to liquids or powder) push out or be pushed out with force through a small hole (指液体或粉末) 喷咽; 喷射: *She squirted water from the hose onto the flowers.* 她通过软管将水喷洒到花上. *The oil from the engine squirted into my face.* 发动机里的机油喷了我一脸.

stab [stæb] *vt* wound deeply with a pointed instrument (e. g. a knife). 刺伤; 戳伤: *He stabbed him in the back* 他刺伤他的背部. Also 亦作 *nc: a stab in the chest* 胸部刺痛.

stable[1] [steibl] *adj* firmly fixed; not easily moved or upset 坚固的, 稳定的; 不动摇的: *We need a stable gov-ernment.* 我们需要一个稳定的政府. *He is a very stable person.* 他是一位很坚定的人. (opp 反义词 **unstable**). **stability** [stə'biliti] *nu* (opp 反义词 **instability**). **stabilize** ['steibilaiz] *vt* make stable 使坚固; 使稳定. **stabili-zation** [steibilai'zeiʃən] *nu* **stabili-zer** ['steibilaizə*] *nc* somebody / some-thing which stabilizes (esp. the device which keeps a ship or aircraft from moving too much from side to side at sea or in the air). 使稳定之人或物(尤指使船舶或飞机稳定的装置); 稳定器; 平衡器.

stable[2] ['steibl] *nc* building in which horses are kept 马厩; 马房.

staccato [stə'ka:tou] *adj* (with reference to music) played in a short and sharp manner (指音乐) 断奏的; (奏成) 断音的, 不连贯的.

stack [stæk] *nc* **1** large heap or pile made neatly and carefully 整齐的堆: *stack of wood* 木材堆; *stacks of hay in the field* 田裡的乾草堆; *stack of books on the teacher's desk* 教师桌上的书堆. **2** number of chimneys standing together. (Usu. **chimney stack**) 林立的烟囱羣 (通常用chimney stack). Also 亦作 *vt* put in a pile neatly and carefully 使成堆；堆放；堆起.

stadium ['steidiəm] *nc* large sports ground (esp. one having many rows of seats round it) 大運動場 (尤指週圍有多層看台的). *pl* 複數 **stadia** ['steidiə] or **stadiums**.

staff [stɑːf] *nc* **1** stick used when walking or climbing, or as a weapon (走路或攀爬用的, 或作爲武器的) 棍；杖；棒. **2** group of persons working together under a manager or head (輔佐經理等的) 全體職員；全體工作人員：*The manager here has a staff of fifty.* 這裏的經理有五十名工作人員. *The headmaster and his staff met to discuss the new timetable* i. e. the headmaster and the teachers. 校長及教師們開會討論新的課程表. Also 亦作 *vt* supply with staff (in sense 2) 爲…配備職員；提供工作人員. *We have not enough money to staff all our schools.* 我們沒有足够的錢爲所有的學校配備教師.

stag [stæg] *nc* male deer 雄鹿.

stage [steidʒ] *nc* **1** platform in a hall, theatre etc which is above the floor so that the persons on it can be seen better 講台；舞台：*The actors left the stage at the end of the play.* 劇終時演員們離開舞台. **2** part of a journey 一段行程；站：*We travelled to London by stages* i. e. having rests or stops on the way 我們分段旅行去倫敦. 即：沿途停停歇歇；*What is the bus fare to the next stage along?* 到下一站的公共汽車票價是多少？ **3** particular point in progress or change (發展或變化的) 特定階段或時期：*Our baby is at the walking stage* i. e. he is beginning to be able to walk. 我們的小孩正在學走路的階段. 即：他開始能走路了. Second-

ary education is the next stage after primary education. 初等教育之後的下一階段教育是中等教育. Also 亦作 *vt* put on the stage of the theatre etc; show to the public 把…搬上舞台等；表演；上演：*Our school stages a play every year.* 我們學校每年都上演一個劇. **the stage** work and life of a theatre 戲劇生涯；戲劇業：*He writes books about the stage.* 他寫有關戲劇生涯方面的書. *He went on the stage when he was a boy* i. e. became an actor 當他還是孩子的時候就走上了舞台. 即：做了演員. **'stagecoach** (in former times) vehicle pulled by horses, which carried persons from one place to another (昔時之) 驛站馬車. **'stage 'whisper** loud whisper which is meant to be heard 舞台上演員對台下觀衆的大聲私語 (假裝不爲其他演員聽見)；有意使人聽見的低語.

stagger ['stægə*] *vt / i* **1** walk or stand, cause to walk or stand, unsteadily (使) 蹣跚；搖提：*The drunk man staggered across the road.* 醉漢蹣跚地穿過道路. *The blow on the head staggered me.* 我頭上挨了一拳搖擺欲倒. **2** surprise greatly; shock 使驚愕；使震驚：*The bad news staggered me.* 這壞消息使我驚愕. **3** cause to happen at different times 使發生在不同一時間；錯開時間：*The manager staggers the holidays of those working in the factory so that everybody is not away at one time.* 經理把工廠工休日錯開，以便在同一時間内不至於大家都休假. Also 亦作 *nc* act of staggering (in sense **1**) 蹣跚；搖提.

stagnant ['stægnənt] *adj* **1** (with reference to water) not moving, therefore dirty. (指水) 不流動的；停滯的；污濁的：*The old pot was full of stagnant rainwater.* 這舊罐裏積滿了污濁的雨

水. **2** (with reference to business, work etc) not busy or changing (指生意, 工作等) 不景氣的; 蕭條的; 呆滯的; 不發展的: *Trade with other countries was stagnant.* 沒有發展和其他國家的貿易往來. **stagnate** [stæg'neit] *vi* become stagnant 變得不景氣; 變蕭條; 不流動; 不發展. **stagnation** [stæg-'nei∫ən] *nu.*

staid [steid] *adj* (with reference to persons) too quiet and well behaved (指人) 過於沉靜而有禮貌的; 嚴肅呆板的.

stain [stein] *vt* change the colour of something; mark something with a different colour; make something dirty 使⋯改變顏色; 沾染; 沾污: *She has stained the floorboards dark brown* i. e. changed their colour to dark brown 她將地板染成深棕色. *His hands were stained with ink.* 他的手沾上了墨水. *bloodstained cloth* 沾有血跡的布. Also 亦作 *nc* **1** substance used for staining 染料. **2** mark made by staining 污點: *ink stains on his hands* 他手上的墨水漬. **stainless** *adj* (esp. with reference to metals) not able to be stained or become rusty (尤指金屬製品) 不銹的: *The knife is made of stainless steel.* 這把小刀是用不銹鋼製造的.

stair [steə*] *nc* **1** (usu. *pl*) number of steps one above the other on which one can go up or down in a building (通常用複數) 階梯: *I went up the stairs to my room.* 我上樓去我的房間. **2** one of these steps 樓梯(階梯)之一級: *He was standing on the top stair.* 他站在樓梯的最上面一級上. **'staircase, 'stairway** flight(s) of stairs (usu. with banisters) inside or outside a building 室內或室外樓梯(常有扶欄).

stake [steik] *nc* **1** length of wood with a

point which can be driven into the ground 椿; 柱. **2** money used in a game of chance or in guessing the result of an event (e. g. a horserace); any great interest in something (esp. if money is involved) (賽馬等的) 賭注, 賭金; 利益; (尤指錢財的) 利害關係: *I want you to hold the stakes until the race is finished.* 我要你保管賭金, 直到比賽結束. *He has a big stake in the cotton industry.* 他與棉花工業有着很大的利害關係. Also 亦作 ready as a stake (in sense 2); risk 下賭注; 賭: *I staked ten pence on a horse. and it won.* 我在一匹馬上下了十便士的賭注, 結果贏了. **stake something off / out** mark or separate by driving in stakes. 立椿標出或劃分: *They have staked out a claim to all this land.* 他們已立界標以表明這片土地全屬他們所有. **at stake** risked; in danger 瀕於危險; 在危險中: *If we fail, our lives will be at stake.* 如果我們失敗, 我們的生命將瀕於危險.

stalactite ['stæləktait] *nc* deposit of carbonate of lime formed by the evaporation of water dripping from the roof of a limestone cave, and hanging down in many different shapes and sizes 鐘乳石.

stalagmite ['stæləgmait] *nc* object just like a stalactite but rising from the floor of a limestone cave 石筍.

stale [steil] *adj* not fresh; kept too long; used too much 不新鮮的; 陳舊的: *The bread is stale.* 這麵包不新鮮.

stalemate ['steilmeit] *nc / u* (chess) state in which neither player can win or lose because no other moves can be made (棋) 和, (棋) 僵局; 相持不下的狀態.

stalk[1] [stɔ:k] *nc* part of a plant between its flowers or leaves and the ground;

part of a plant which joins its fruit or leaves to the main and thicker part; stem (草本植物的)柄; 梗; 莖; 幹.

stalk² [stɔːk] *vt / i* **1** hunt a wild animal by moving towards it quietly and without being seen 潛近獵捕(野獸): *We stalked the elephant all day but never got near enough to shoot it.* 我們一整天潛獵大象, 但始終未能靠近向牠開槍. **2** walk in a slow, serious manner as when one is angry, proud etc. (由於生氣或高傲而)高視闊步; 大踏步走: *The teacher stalked out of the classroom.* 老師大踏步走出教室.

stall¹ [stɔːl] *nc* **1** compartment of a stable etc in which a horse, cow etc is kept (畜舍內的)分隔欄; 厩: *Each horse has its own stall.* 每匹馬都有自己的馬棚. **2** type of small shop, or a table from which goods are sold 攤; 售貨台: *I bought fruit from a stall in the market.* 我從市場中的一個小攤上買了水果. *There is a bookstall at the railway station.* 火車站有一個書攤. **3** (Brit) seat in a theatre or cinema on the ground floor (and usu. in front) (英)劇院或影院正廳(並且通常指前排)的座位: *front stalls* 正廳前排座位; *back stalls* 正廳後排座位. (US 美 **parquet**)

stall² [stɔːl] *vi* **1** (with reference to an engine) stop running because it has not enough power to do its work (指發動機)因功率不足而停止轉動: *Because our car was carrying five people it stalled on the steep hill.* 我們的小汽車因載了五個人, 在陡坡上拋錨了. *The aeroplane was going so slowly that it stalled.* 這架飛機飛得很慢而失速. **2** avoid giving a definite answer or making a definite decision 支吾其詞; 敷衍: *When I asked him what he was going to do, he stalled. (informal*

in sense **2**) 我問他打算做甚麼, 他支支吾吾. (義 2 爲非正式)

stallion ['stæliən] *nc* male horse (esp. one used for breeding) 公馬(尤指種馬).

stalwart ['stɔːlwət] *adj* strong, brave and loyal 健壯的; 勇敢的; 忠實的. Also 亦作 *nc* person who is stalwart 堅定忠實的人; 高大健壯的人.

stamen ['steimən] *nc* male part of a flower, bearing pollen 雄蕊(生産花粉的部份).

stamina ['stæminə] *nu* strength which makes a person or animal able to work hard and endure pain or illness (人或動物的)體力; 精力; 毅力: *A man who can run twenty miles has great stamina.* 能够跑二十英里的人有充沛的體力.

stammer ['stæmə*] *vt / i* **1** speak with difficulty, saying the same sounds again and again (e. g. P - p - please, m - m - may I g - g - go?) 口吃; 結結巴巴地説話. **2** say something in this way 口吃地説; 結巴地説: *He stammered (out) his answer.* 他結結巴巴地説出他的回答. Also 亦作 *nc: He speaks with a stammer.* 他説話口吃.

stamp¹ [stæmp] *vt / i* **1** push one's foot down heavily 踩脚; 頓足: *He was stamping with rage.* 他氣憤憤地頓足. *They stamped into the room.* 他們嘖嘖嘖地走進房間. *We stamped the ground to keep our feet warm.* 我們在地面上踩踏, 使雙脚暖暖. **2** make a mark on something by pressing on it a design, word etc which has already been prepared 蓋戳; 蓋圖章; 壓印: *He stamped 'urgent' on the letter.* 他在信上蓋上"急件". *I stamp my name on all my books.* 我在我所有的書上蓋上有我名字的圖章. **3** stick a postage stamp or other kind of paper stamp

on a letter, parcel, card etc. 貼郵票或
印花於(信,包裹,明信片等): *You must
stamp these letters before you post
them.* 寄這些信之前你必須貼上郵票.

stamp² [stæmp] *nc* **1** act of stamping 踩
腳; 頓足. **2** something with a design,
words etc cut on it so that they can
be stamped on something else. 印章;
圖章: *He put 'urgent' on the letter
with a rubber stamp.* 他用一枚橡皮圖
章在信上蓋上"急件". **3** piece of coloured paper put on a letter, parcel,
card etc to show that postage etc has
been paid 郵票; 印花: *postage stamp*
郵票; *insurance stamp* 保險印花.
'stamp album book in which a person who collects postage stamps
keeps them 集郵簿; 郵票簿. **'stamp
collector** person who collects postage stamps 集郵者; 集郵家.

stampede [stæm'piːd] *nc* rush of animals or people caused by fear (受驚
的動物或人)驚逃; 奔竄. Also 亦作 *vt /
i* rush, cause to rush, in this way (使)
驚逃; (使)奔竄.

stance [stæns] *nc* position of the feet in
certain games etc. (e. g. the place before
the player hits the ball) (某些球賽例
如高爾夫球選手擊球前的)站立姿勢.

stand¹ [stænd] *vt / i* **1** remain upright
on the feet without moving; cause to
be upright 站立; 站住; 起立(使)豎起;
(使)直立: *Who is the man standing
near the door?* 站在門邊的那個男人是
誰? *Never stand if you can sit.* 能坐就
不要站着. *Every man in the team
stands over six feet* i. e. is over six
feet in height 這個隊裏每人的身高都
超過六英尺. *He stood his stick in the
corner.* 他把他的手杖豎在牆角裏. *The
mother stood her child on a chair.* 母
親扶着她的小孩站在椅子上. **2** be in,
or have, a particular place 在某處;

The school stands between two roads.
學校坐落在兩條馬路之間. *These
books stand on that desk* i. e. their
usual place is on that desk. 這些書在
那張書桌上.即: 它們通常的位置就在那
張書桌上. **3** remain without change;
be in a particular state 維持原狀; 處於
某種狀態: *My decision to go abroad
stands.* 我去國外的決定不變. *Their
profits stand at £50.* 他們的贏利爲50
英鎊. *As things now stand, we shall
win.* 按照現狀看來, 我們將獲勝. **4** endure; be patient with 忍耐; 忍受: *I
can't stand his silly talk.* 我不能忍受他
的蠢話. *Our teacher stands no nonsense* i. e. refuses to have any nonsense from anybody 我們的老師不允
許任何人胡說八道. *past* 過去式和過去
分詞 **stood** [stud]. **stand by** be ready
作好準備; 準備行動: *The police are
standing by to control the crowd, if it
is necessary.* 警察準備必要時控制人
羣. **'stand-by** *nc* **1** something which
is ready to replace something else if
necessary 備用品. **2** system by which
one is allowed to travel in an aeroplane without having previously
booked a seat, if there is room on the
aeroplane (如有座位出缺, 允許未預定
機票的乘客臨時買票乘機的)候補機票
制: *be on stand-by* i. e. travel in this
way 買候補機票旅行. Also 亦作 *adj*:
stand-by passenger 買候補機票的乘
客; *stand-by flight* 買候補機票的航行.
stand by someone give support to
someone 支持某人; 援助某人: *He
stood by me through all my troubles.*
他一直幫助我渡過了層層難關. **stand
down** leave a post or position (often
so that somebody else can take it) 退
出職位或位置(常指以便別人能夠取得
職位): *The chairman is standing
down so that a younger man can take*

his place. 主席辭職, 以便較年青的人能上任. **stand for something 1** mean; represent 意 指; 代表; 表示: *USA stands for the United States of America.* USA 代表美利堅合眾國. *We like our school and all it stands for.* 我們喜歡我們的學校和它所代表的一切. **2** endure; be patient with 忍受; 忍耐: *I am not standing for any bad behaviour. (informal in sense 2)* 我受不了任何惡劣的行爲. (義 2 爲非正式). **stand in** take the place of 代替: *He is standing in for the player who is ill.* 他在代替生病的演員. **'stand-in** *nc* person who takes the place of somebody (often an actor taking the place of another actor) 替身 (常指代替演員). **'stand-offish** *adj* not friendly 不親切的; 冷漠的; 疏遠的. **stand out** be easily seen among others 顯著的; 傑出的: *A very tall man stands out in a crowd.* 一個很高的男人在人羣中很突出. **stand up** get on one's feet; rise and stand 站立; 站起; 起立: *The boys stood up when the teacher came into the classroom.* 老師進入教室時, 男孩子們起立. **stand up for someone / something** be ready to help; support. 樂於幫助; 支持: *All my friends will stand up for me.* 我所有的朋友將支持我. **'standstill** *nu*: *Everything is at a standstill* i. e. nothing is being done 事事都處於停頓狀態. 即: 甚麼事也沒做.

stand² [stænd] *nc / u* **1** particular place or structure for something 置物處或放東西的架子: *At the door there is a hatstand* i. e. piece of furniture to hang one's hat on 門邊有一個帽架. 即: 供人掛帽的傢具. **2** place (usu. with a roof) from which to watch games etc. (通常帶有頂蓋的) 看台: *grandstand* i. e. best place of this kind

with the most expensive seats 正面看台; 大看台. 即: 設有豪華座位的最好看台. **3** *(US)* place in court where a witness stands or site (美) (法庭中的) 證人席: *The witness took the stand.* 證人就位作證. **'standpoint** point of view; opinion 立場; 觀點: *From the stand point of the parents, the school is doing well.* 根據學生家長的看法, 這所學校辦得很好. **make a stand against** stop retreating and fight 停止撤退以抵抗: *The army made a stand against the advancing enemy* 軍隊抵擊向前推進的敵人.

standard ['stændəd] *nc* **1** flag, or pole with a flag on it 旗; (掛旗) 旗竿. **2** weight, measure, quality etc to which other weight, measures, qualities should be equal or try to be equal 標準; 基準: *The standard of length in that country is the metre, not the yard.* 那個國家的長度標準是米, 不是碼. *This food is below standard* i. e. its quality is not as good as it should be. 這種食物低於標準. 即: 達不到質量要求. *The houses are up to standard.* 這些房屋達到標準. *Our teacher sets very high standards of work in his class.* 我們的老師對班裏的工作提出很高的標準. Also 亦作 *adj* (in sense **2**) (用於義 2). *The standard length is the metre.* 標準長度是米. **standardize** *vt* cause to be the same in weight, size, quality etc. 使合標準; 使標準化: *Most tobacco companies have standardized the length of cigarettes.* 大多數烟草公司都使香烟的長度標準化. **standardization** [stændədaɪ'zeɪʃən] *nu* **'standard lamp** lamp fixed to a long pole and not to the wall 落地燈. **standard of living** wealth; possessions and comfort 生活水準: *The people of the USA have a high stand-*

ard of living. 美國人民的生活水準高. *Many countries have a low standard of living.* 許多國家的生活水準低.

standing ['stændiŋ] *adj* without change; permanent 不變的; 永久的: *His long beard is a standing joke* i. e. it has been a joke for a long time. 他的長鬍鬚是個老笑話. *She has a standing order for ten pounds of sugar at the shop* i. e. she has asked for and regularly gets ten pounds of sugar; *standing army* i. e. a permanent one 她在這家商店裏有十磅糖的長期定單. 即: 她要求定期得到十磅糖; 常備軍. Also 亦作 *nc / u* **1** period of time 期間: *He is an engineer of long standing* i. e. he has been an engineer for a long time. 他長期以來是一名工程師. **2** position in society; rank 社會地位; 身份: *Doctors have a high standing in our country.* 在我們國家醫生享有很高的地位.

stank [stæŋk] past tense of **stink.** stink 的過去式.

staple[1] ['steipl] *nc* chief product of a country or part of a country (一個國家或地區的) 主要產品: *Coffee is the staple of this district.* 咖啡是這一地區的主要產品. Also 亦作 *adj: Coffee is the staple product of this district.* 咖啡是這一地區的主要產品. *Corn is our staple food.* 小麥是我們的主食.

staple[2] ['steipl] *nc* **1** U-shaped piece of metal with pointed ends, which is driven into wood or a wall etc to keep something in position U 形釘: *The long wire is fastened to the posts by staples.* 長電線用 U 形釘固定到木柱上. **2** bent piece of metal which fastens sheets of paper together 釘書釘. Also 亦作 *vt* fasten with a staple 用釘書釘或 U 形釘釘牢. **stapler** *nc* device for fastening sheets of paper together 釘書機.

star [stɑ:*] *nc* **1** one of the bodies shining in the sky at night, seen as a small point of light (not the sun, moon or a planet) 星(不指太陽,月亮或行星). **2** something which looks like a star (e. g. *): 星狀物; 星形符號(例如 *): *There are five stars on their national flag.* 他們的國旗上有五顆星. **3** famous actor, actress or singer 著名演員或歌唱家; 明星: *The film is a good one with many stars in it.* 這是一部好影片,裏面有許多明星. Also 亦作 *vt / i* be, or have as, the leading actor, actress or singer 擔任主角; 主演,主唱; 由…主演(或主唱): *She starred in two films.* 她在兩部電影中擔任主角. *The new play stars three of Britain's best actors.* 這個新劇由英國三個最好的演員主演. *past* 過去式和過去分詞 **starred. starry** *adj* of a star; shining like a star; covered with stars 星的; 星一樣閃亮的; 佈滿星星的: *starry light in the distance* 遠處的星光; *girl with starry eyes* 眼睛明亮的女孩; *starry sky* 佈滿星星的天空. **'starfish** type of sea creature shaped like a star 海星; 海盤車(星狀的海生動物): **'starlight** *nu* light from the stars 星光. **'starlit** *adj* lit by the stars 星光照耀的: *starlit sky* 星光燦爛的天空. **'starry-'eyed** *adj* having great but not very practical ideas 幻想的; 不切實際的: *starry-eyed young people who think they can do everything* 自以為甚麼事都能做的不切實際的年青人.

starboard ['stɑːbəd] *nu* righthand side of a ship as one faces the front end 船之右舷: *The ship turned to starboard.* 船轉向右舷航行. (opp 反義詞 **port**)

starch [stɑːtʃ] *nu* **1** white substance which is the main type of food found in bread, grain, potatoes etc. 澱粉.

Poor people usually eat too much starch and too little meat. 窮人通常吃澱粉太多, 吃肉太少. **2** this substance mixed with water and used to make clothes stiff (和水混合用於漿硬衣服的)漿粉. **starchy** *adj*.

stare [steə*] *vt / i* look for a long time with wide-open eyes 凝視; 瞪視; 張大眼睛看: *He stared at the strange animal.* 他瞪大眼睛注視這奇怪的動物. *Cows like to stand and stare.* 母牛喜歡站立和瞪視. *Who is the man with the staring eyes?* 在凝視的那個男人是誰? Also 亦作 *nc: They looked at him with a stare of surprise.* 他們驚奇地睜大眼睛看着他.

stark [stɑːk] *adj* stiff; bleak 僵硬的; 荒涼的, 不毛的; 裸露的. Also 亦作 *adv: stark naked* 一絲不掛的; 赤裸裸的.

starling ['stɑːliŋ] *nc* type of bird with black speckled feathers which quarrels a lot 歐椋鳥; 燕八哥.

start¹ [stɑːt] *vi / i* **1** begin 開始: *We start lessons at 9 a. m.* 我們每天九點鐘開始上課. *It has started raining.* 天已開始下雨了. *He started to say something and then changed his mind.* 他剛要說甚麼又改變了主意. **2** begin a journey 出發; 啟程; 動身: *They started early for the village.* 他們一早就出發前往那個村莊. **3** cause to begin 使開始: *My father started me playing football.* 父親使我開始踢足球. *He started (the engine of) the car so as to be ready to drive away* i. e. he set the engine going. 他發動汽車(發動機)準備開走. **4** move suddenly (usu. because of fear, surprise, pain etc.) (通常因恐懼, 驚愕, 痛苦等)驚起; 跳起: *He started from his bed when he heard the gun.* 他聽到槍聲從床上驚跳起來. *I started at the sound of the bell.* 我聽到鈴聲嚇了一跳. **starter** *nc*

1 person who causes a race to begin by giving a signal (e. g. by firing a gun) 賽跑開始的發令員. **2** device for setting an engine going 起動裝置. **'starting point** place from which something starts 起點; 出發點. **start up** move suddenly (usu. because of fear, surprise, pain etc.) (通常因恐懼, 驚愕, 痛苦等)驚起: *I started up from my chair when I heard the noise.* 我聽到吵鬧聲從椅子上驚跳起來. **start something up** begin, cause to begin or move 開始或發動: *A fight started up.* 戰鬥開始了. *He started up his car.* 他開動了汽車.

start² [stɑːt] *nc* **1** sudden movement (usu. because of fear, surprise, pain etc.) (通常因恐懼, 驚愕, 痛苦等)驚起; 跳起: *I woke with a start.* 我驚醒了. **2** beginning of a journey; beginning of anything 啓程; 動身; 着手; 開端: *We make a start for school at 8.30 a. m.* 我們在早上八點半鐘動身去學校. *Rain delayed the start of the game.* 下雨把比賽開始的時間推遲了. **3** amount by which somebody is in front 領先: *I gave him a start of half a mile before I began following him.* 我在跑之前, 讓他先跑半英里. *He had a good start.* 他有了好開頭.

startle ['stɑːtl] *vt* give a fright or surprise to; cause to move suddenly (because of fear or surprise) 使大吃一驚; 使驚起(因恐懼或驚奇): *The loud noise startled me.* 大聲的喧嘩使我嚇了一跳. **startling** *adj* frightening; surprising 令人吃驚的, 驚人的: *startling news* 驚人的消息.

starve [stɑːv] *vt / i* die or suffer, cause to die or suffer, from hunger (使)餓死; (使)挨餓: *Because there is no food, the people are starving.* 因爲沒有食物, 人們正在挨餓. *The enemy is* *trying to starve us to death.* 敵人在試圖將我們餓死. **starvation** [stɑ:'veiʃən] *nu: They are dying of starvation.* 他們死於飢餓.

stasis ['steisis] *nc* stoppage of the flow of a bodily fluid, as of blood 壅滯, 停滯, 鬱積 (例如血液): *intestinal stasis* 腸道壅滯; 便秘; *venous stasis* 静脈鬱滯. *pl* 複數 **stases** ['steisi:z]

state¹ [steit] *nc / u* **1** condition of somebody / something (人或物的) 狀態; 情形: *He is in a poor state of health.* 他的健康狀況不佳. *His business is in a good state.* 他的生意興隆. *Their clothes were in a terrible state.* 他們的衣服很不整潔. **2** (often **State**) government; country or large political division of a country (常作 State) 政府; 國家; 州; 邦: *We must pay taxes to the State.* 我們必須向國家納稅. *Education is provided by the State.* 國家提供教育. *The United States of America has fifty states.* 美國有五十個州. **3** position; rank; dignity 地位; 身份; 階層; 威嚴; 高貴: *The king travelled in great state* i. e. with many followers and great ceremony 國王旅行十分威嚴. 即: 有許多隨從和隆重的儀式. Also 亦作 *adj* (in senses 2 和 3) (用於義 2 和 3): *The president will make a state visit to our country* i. e. a formal, official visit suitable to his position as president 總統將對我們國家進行國事訪問. 即: 以總統身份進行正式, 官方的訪問; *state control* i. e. control by the state 國家控制; 受國家的控制; *state secrets* 國家機密. **stately** *adj* having dignity; grand 莊嚴的; 高貴的; 雄偉的; 堂皇的. **stateliness** *nu* **'statesman** person who is skilled in government and holds a high position in it. 政治家.

state² [steit] *vt* express clearly in words or writing (口頭或書面) 說明; 叙述; 陳述; 闡明: *Please state exactly what you did.* 請如實說明你所做的事. *It states in the newspaper that there will be a meeting tomorrow.* 據報紙報導明天將召開一個會議. **stated** *adj* already decided or made known 已決定了的; 預定的; 作過說明的: *He arrived at the stated time / the time stated.* 他在預定的時間到達. **statement** *nc / u* act of stating; information 陳述; 聲明; 報告: *The government has made a statement explaining what happened.* 政府發表聲明解釋發生的事情. *I have just seen my bank statement* i. e. paper showing how much money I have in the bank 我剛看了我的銀行報告. 即: 表示我在銀行還有多少錢的單據.

static ['stætik] *adj* not moving 静止的; 静態的. Also 亦作 *nu* noises heard on a radio because of electrical disturbances in the air 静電干擾. **static electricity** electricity present in particles that are not moving 静電.

station ['steiʃən] *nc* **1** place where railway trains start and stop; place where buses start and finish their journeys 火車站; 汽車站: *This train stops at every station.* 這列火車每站都停. **2** position or place where something is done (e. g. work or duty) 崗位; 位置; 場所; 局; 署; (廣播電) 台: *The soldiers took up their stations along the road.* 士兵沿路站崗. *We went to the police station* i. e. the building where the police have their offices 我們去了警察局. *broadcasting station* 廣播電台; *fire station* 消防局. Also 亦作 *vt* put in a place for a certain purpose 駐紮; 設置: *The soldiers stationed themselves along the road.* 士兵沿路駐紮. *I was stationed at district headquarters* i. e. was put there by my employers to live and work 我被分派在地區總部.即:我的雇主把我安排在那裏生活和工作. **stationary** ['steiʃənri] *adj* not moving; fixed 不動的,固定的: *He remained stationary so as not to be seen.* 他一動也不動以便不被發現. **'station master** man in charge of a railway station 火車站站長. **'station wagon** type of motorcar with a special body for carrying goods as well as people 客貨兩用車. (Also 亦作 *Brit* 英 **estate car**).

stationer ['steiʃənə*] *nc* person who sells writing materials 文具商. **stationery** ['steiʃənri] *nu* writing materials 文具.

statistics [stə'tistiks] **1** *npl* facts given in the form of numbers 統計;統計數字: *Statistics show that there are more boys than girls at school.* 統計數字表明,學校裏的男生比女生多. **2** *n sing* science of facts in the form of numbers 統計學. **statistical** *adj.*

statue ['stætjuː] *nc* figure of a person, animal etc made of stone, metal etc. (以石頭,金屬等製成的)雕像;塑像. **statuette** [stætju:'et] *nc* small statue 小雕像;小塑像.

stature ['stætʃə*] *nu* (with reference to a person)(指人) **1** height, size 身高;身材. **2** importance 重要性;重要意義.

status ['steitəs] *nu* (with reference to a person) social position or rank in relation to others (指人)身份;地位: *Doctors have great / high status in most countries.* 醫生在大多數國家裏都享有很高的地位. **'status symbol** something which is a sign, or is considered to be a sign, of great status 表示地位高的東西;社會地位的表徵: *Having a sports car is the status symbol among the students of this college.*

在這所學院的學生中擁有一輛跑車,表示該生有社會地位.

status quo ['steitəs'kwou] *nu* condition or state of affairs at one particular time 現狀.

statute ['stætjuːt] *nc* law passed by the law-making assembly of a country (由立法機關通過的)法令;法規. **statutory** ['stætjutəri] *adj* as laid down by statute 法定的;依照法令的.

staunch [stɔːntʃ] *adj* (with reference to a person) firm; loyal. (指人)堅定的;忠誠的.

stay¹ [stei] **1** *vt / i* remain in the same place, same condition etc; not leave 停留;停止;待下來;留下;不離開: *I stayed at home last night.* 昨天晚上我待在家裏. *They are staying to see the football match.* 他們留下來看足球賽. *She stays in every evening* i.e. does not leave the place where she lives 每天晚上她都不離家外出. **2** be able to finish 能夠完成: *I do not think the runner will stay the distance* i.e. be able to run the whole distance of the race 我認為這位賽跑運動員不能夠跑到終點.即:不能夠堅持跑完全程. **stay away** remain away; not go near 不在,外出;別走近: *He stayed away from school when he was ill.* 他生病時沒去上學. *You must stay away from these rough boys.* 你必須離這些舉止粗野的孩子遠點. **stay out** remain outside (esp. later than usual) 待在戶外(尤指比平時晚): *Her mother does not allow her to stay out in the evening.* 她媽媽不允許她晚上待在外面. **stay up** not go to bed 不睡覺: *We stayed up until midnight talking about our work.* 我們談論工作直到半夜才睡.

stay² [stei] *nc* period of remaining in the same place 停留期間: *He has come to us for a short stay.* 他已來我

們這裏作短暫之逗留.

steadfast ['stedfɑ:st] *adj* firm; loyal 堅定的, 忠誠的.

steady ['stedi] *adj* **1** firmly fixed; not shaking; not likely to move or change 堅固的; 不動搖的; 穩定的; 不變的: *You must hold the gun steady when shooting.* 射擊時你必須把槍握緊. *He filled my glass with a steady hand.* 他穩穩當當地給我斟滿酒. **2** regular; not stopping 有規律的; 不停的: *He is making steady progress.* 他在不斷地進步. *The wind was steady.* 風向穩定. **3** reliable; regular in habits 可靠的; (習慣)有規律的: *He is a steady man who is never late.* 他是一位堅持從不遲到的人. *(opp* 反義詞 **unsteady**. Also 亦作 *vt / i* become or make steady 使堅固; 使穩定; 變堅固; 變穩定: *The wind is steadying.* 風在穩定下來. *He steadied himself with his hand on the table.* 他的手摁在桌子上使自己站穩; *past* 過去式和過去分詞 **steadied. steadily** *adv* **steadiness** *nu*.

steak [steik] *nc* thick piece of meat or fish 肉塊; 魚塊.

steal [sti:l] *vt / i* **1** unlawfully take away something which belongs to somebody else 偷; 竊取 (他人之物): *It is a crime to steal.* 偷竊是犯罪行爲. *He stole my book.* 他偷了我的書. **2** come or go quietly 悄悄地來或去; 潛行: *They have stolen into the house.* 他們已潛入屋內. *A smile stole across her face.* 她的臉上掠過一絲笑意. *past tense* 過去式 **stole** [stoul]. *past part* 過去分詞 **stolen** ['stouln].

stealth [stelθ] *nu* in **by stealth** i.e. quietly or secretly 用於 by stealth, 即: 偷偷地; 秘密地. **stealthy** *adj* **stealthily** *adv*: *The thieves stealthily entered the building.* 賊偷偷地進入這

座房屋.

steam [sti:m] *nu* water in the form of a gas; mist or vapour which rises from boiling water 蒸汽; 水氣: *Many engines are driven by steam.* 許多發動機由蒸汽推動. *The steam from the kettle showed that the water was boiling.* 壺中冒出來的蒸汽表示水開了. Also 亦作 *vt / i* **1** send out steam 蒸發; 冒蒸汽. *The kettle was steaming.* 壺在冒汽. **2** move by the force of steam 由蒸汽推動; 行駛: *The ship steamed up the river.* 這艘船逆江而上. **3** cook by steam 蒸煮: *She is steaming fish for supper.* 她正蒸魚準備晚飯. **steamer** *nc* ship driven by steam 汽船; 輪船. **steamy** *adj* of steam; full of, covered with, steam 蒸汽的; 多蒸汽的; 水氣濛濛的: *steamy kitchen* 充滿水氣的廚房; *steamy windows* 水氣濛濛的窗戶. **'steam engine** engine driven by steam; moving railway engine driven by steam 蒸汽機. **'steamroller** heavy machine driven by steam for pressing down stones and levelling the surface when making roads, or a similar modern machine driven by a diesel engine (this modern machine is also called a **road roller**) 蒸汽壓路機或由柴油機驅動的類似機器 (這種現代機器又叫 road roller)

steel [sti:l] *nu* hard metal made from iron mixed with carbon or other substances 鋼. (Most knives, machinery and tools are made of steel) (多數刀、機器、工具由鋼製成). Also 亦作 *adj*: *steel knife* 鋼刀. Also 亦作 *vt* (esp. with reference to the feelings) make as hard as steel; get rid of one's feelings of kindness, fear etc. (尤指感情) 使像鋼般堅硬; 使冷酷; 使堅強等: *They steeled themselves against the attack.* 他們決心抵抗襲擊. *I steeled myself to*

try again. 我硬着頭皮再試一試.
'**steelworks** *n sing or pl* 單數或複數 factory where steel is made 鋼廠. *Note* 說明: often followed by a *sing* verb 常與單數動詞連用.

steep¹ [stiːp] *adj* **1** having a sharp slope; more vertical than horizontal 陡峭的; 險峻的: *steep path up the mountain* 往山上的陡峭小徑. **2** excessive 過份的: *That's a bit steep. The prices in this shop are steep. (informal* in sense **2** *)* 這家商店裏的價格太高. (義 2 爲非正式).
steeply *adv* **steepness** *nu*.

steep² [stiːp] *vt / i* become or make completely wet; soak in a liquid (使) 浸透, (在水中) 浸泡: *I left my dirty clothes to steep.* 我將髒衣服浸在水中. *She steeped the vegetables before cooking them.* 煮菜前她將蔬菜先浸泡在水中.

steeple ['stiːpl] *nc* tower of a church with a tall, pointed spire (教堂的) 尖塔. '**steeplechase** *nc* race on foot or on a horse during which ditches, fences, hedges etc have to be jumped. 障礙賽跑; 障礙賽馬. '**steeplejack** *nc* man skilled in climbing steeples, high chimneys etc to repair them. 尖塔, 高烟囱等的修理工; 高空作業工人.

steer [stiə*] *vt / i* guide the course of a ship, motorcar etc by means of a rudder, wheel etc. 掌舵; 駕駛: *He steered the boat between the islands.* 他行船於兩島之間. *Steer your car slowly into the garage.* 慢慢將你的汽車駛進汽車間. *This car steers easily* i.e. it is easy to steer. 這輛汽車容易駕駛. '**steering wheel** wheel by which a car or ship is steered (車之) 駕駛盤, 方向盤; (船之) 舵輪.

stem [stem] *nc* thin upright part of a plant between the ground and its leaves or flowers; thin part of a plant which joins a leaf or fruit to a thicker part 莖; 幹; 葉柄; 花梗; 花梗: *Tall flowers have long stems.* 高花有長花梗. Also 亦作 *vt* (with **from**) come or begin (與 from 連用) 起源於, 來自: *This result stems from what was done before.* 這結果源於以前所做的事情. *past* 過去式和過去分詞 **stemmed**.

stench [stentʃ] *nc* very unpleasant smell 惡臭; 臭氣.

stencil ['stensil] *nc* device for printing copies of letters or designs by rubbing ink or paint on a thin sheet of metal, plastic, card, paper etc, on which the letters or designs have been cut or stamped (用於印刷或複印的) 金屬模板, 塑料板, 紙型板, 蠟紙等. Also 亦作 *vt* mark or print in this way 用模板印刷; 用蠟紙印: *His name is stencilled on all his boxes.* 他的名字印在他所有的箱子上. *past* 過去式和過去分詞 **stencilled**. (*US* 美 **stenciled**).

stenograph ['stenəgrɑːf] *nc* **1** writing in shorthand 用速記寫成的文章; 速記文字. **2** kinds of various keyboard machines, somewhat resembling a typewriter, used for writing in shorthand 速記機.

step¹ [step] *vt / i* move and then put down the foot 舉步; 行走; 跨步: *Be careful when you step off the bus.* 下車時請當心. *He stepped over the dog at the door.* 他跨過門邊的狗. *past* 過去式和過去分詞 **stepped**. '**stepping stone** stone for stepping on when crossing a river or muddy place (供跨越淺河或泥濘地的) 踏腳石. **step something up** increase 增加; 促進: *This factory has stepped up its output of cars.* 這家工廠已增加了汽車產量.

step² [step] *nc* **1** act of moving and then putting down one foot (腳) 步; 步

幅: *The soldier took one step forward.* 這個士兵向前走了一步. *She walks with quick, short steps.* 她短步快走. **2** noise made in this way 腳步聲: *I heard the steps of my mother at the door.* 我聽到了門口媽媽的腳步聲. (Also 亦作 **footstep**). **3** place where one puts one's feet when going up or down something (e. g. a ladder or stair) 梯級; 台階: *He was standing on the top step of the stairs.* 他正站在樓梯頂層的階梯上. *She fell down the steps in front of the house.* 她跌倒在房前的台階上. **4** something done in order to cause something else to happen later 步驟; 措施: *They took steps to close the school.* 他們採取措施關閉學校. *My next step is to tell my father.* 我下一步是要告訴我父親. **'stepladder** ladder with flat steps instead of rungs 活梯; 摺梯 (Also 亦作 **steps** *npl*) **step by step** slowly; gradually 慢慢地; 逐漸地.

step-³ [step] *prefix* related by later marriage 再婚關係的; 後; 繼. **'stepchild** child of one's husband or wife by his or her earlier marriage 前夫或前妻的子女; 繼子或繼女. (Also 亦作 **stepson; stepdaughter**). **'stepfather** husband of one's mother by her later marriage to him 繼父. (Also 亦作 **stepmother**). **'stepbrother**, **'stepsister** child of one's stepfather or stepmother by a former marriage 異父或異母之兄弟; 異父或異母之姐妹.

steppe [step] *nc* **1** vast, level, treeless plain in southeastern Europe and in Asia, especially found in Siberia (東南歐和亞洲, 尤指西伯利亞的) 大草原. **2** vast, treeless plain 無樹木的大草原; 大草原.

stereo (phonic) ['steriou] ('fɔnik]) *adj* (with reference to gramophone re-

cords etc.) having sound which, by using two loudspeakers, is more natural because the sound seems to come from various directions; of the device which records sound of this kind (指唱片等) 立體音響的; (指儀器) 錄製立體音響的. **stereo** ['steriou] *nu* use of sound in this way 使用立體音響: *This record is on stereo* i.e. it is intended for playing on a gramophone having two loudspeakers. 這唱片用於裝有兩個擴音器的留聲機播放. Also 亦作 *adj*.

stereotype ['sterioutaip] *nc / u* typical example; true copy 典型; 樣板; *He is the stereotype of an army officer.* 他是典型的軍官.

sterile ['sterail] *adj* not able to produce children, seeds or crops etc; barren 不能生育的; 不結果實的; 不長五穀的; 貧瘠的: *sterile woman* i.e. one who is unable to have children 不能生育的婦女. *This land is sterile.* 這是一片不毛之地. **sterility** [ste'riliti] *nu* **sterilize** ['sterilaiz] *vt* make sterile 使不能生育; 使不能結實; 把⋯消毒: *In some countries women are sterilized to reduce the birth rate.* 在一些國家裏使婦女絕育以降低出生率. *The doctor sterilized his instruments.* 醫生把他的器具消毒. **sterilization** [sterilai'zeiʃən] *nu* **sterilized** *adj* (opp 反義詞 **unsterilized**).

sterling ['stə:liŋ] *adj* **1** (with reference to gold and silver) of fixed value and purity (指金和銀) 標準成份的: *These spoons are made of sterling silver.* 這些調羹是用標準成份的銀製成的. *£1 sterling* i. e. one British pound. 一英鎊. **2** reliable; of good quality 可靠的; 質量好的. Also 亦作 *nu* British money 英國貨幣: *They wish to be paid in sterling, not dollars.* 他們希望對方用英鎊而非用美元支付. **the**

'**sterling area** countries which have currencies linked to the British pound 英鎊地區(用英鎊作貨幣的國家).

stern¹ [stə:n] *adj* severe; strict 嚴厲的; 嚴格的; 嚴肅的: *He has a stern face.* 他面孔嚴肅. *We have a very stern headmaster.* 我們有一位很嚴厲的校長. **sternly** *adv* **sternness** *nu*.

stern² [stə:n] *nc* back end of a ship 船尾.

stethoscope ['steθəskoup] *nc* instrument used by doctors to listen to the sounds made by the lungs or the heart 聽診器.

stevedore ['sti:vədɔ:*] *nc* man who loads and unloads ships 裝卸船貨的工人, 碼頭工人.

stew [stju:] *vt / i* cook, be cooked, slowly in a closed dish or saucepan with a little water 用文火煮; 燜; 燉. Also 亦作 *nc / u* food cooked in this way 燜過的食物: *beef stew* 燜牛肉.

steward ['stjuəd] *nc* **1** man who looks after the passengers on a ship or aircraft. (客船或客機上的)服務員; 侍者. **2** man who manages, helps to manage, meetings (e. g. sports or race meeting, public meeting, dance etc) 聚會(例如運動員, 賽馬會, 集會, 舞會等的)籌備人. **stewardess** [stjuə'des] *nc* woman steward (in sense 1) (客輪或客機上的)女服務員; 女侍者, 空中小姐. '**shop** '**steward** member of a trade union in a factory who is chosen by the other workers to look after their interests 工廠的工會代表.

stick¹ [stik] *vt / i* **1** fasten, become fastened, with glue or any substance like it 黏貼; 張貼: *He stuck the stamp on the letter.* 他把郵票貼在信上. *Glue sticks to one's fingers.* 膠黏在手指上. *The pages of the book are stuck together.* 書頁黏在一起了. **2** fix something pointed in something else 將尖物插入(某物); 刺入; 戳: *He stuck his knife into the table.* 他將小刀插到桌子上. *The post has been stuck into the ground.* 杆已插在地上. **3** not be able to move 不能動彈; 卡住: *The window is stuck* i.e. it cannot be opened or shut. 窗戶卡住了. 即: 窗戶不能開關. *Our car was stuck in the mud for two hours.* 我們的汽車陷在泥裏兩小時了. *I'm stuck with this problem.* 我被這個問題難住了. *past* 過去式和過去分詞 **stuck** [stʌk]. **sticker** *nc* piece of paper etc which can be stuck on something 貼紙. **sticky** *adj* likely to stick to something 黏的; 黏性的: *The glue has made my fingers sticky.* 膠使我的手指黏黏的. **stick (something) out** project, cause to project. (使)突出; (使)伸出: *The papers were sticking out of his pocket.* 證件從他的衣袋裏露出來. *Don't stick your head out.* 不要將頭伸出去. *He stuck out his tongue at me.* 他向我伸舌頭. **stick (something) up** project, cause to project, upwards (使)豎立: *He saw the flag sticking up above the trees.* 他看見旗子掛在樹梢上. **stick up for someone** support strongly; defend 支持; 維護, 替…辯護: *Whatever happens, I'll stick up for you.* (informal) 無論發生甚麼事, 我都會支持你. (非正式). **stuckup** *adj* very proud, conceited. (informal) 傲慢的; 自大的. (非正式).

stick² [stik] *nc* **1** small branch from a tree 小樹枝: *We made a branch from the sticks which were lying about.* 我們用週圍的樹枝生火. **2** branch of a tree or piece of wood made into something 棍, 棒, 杖: *walking stick* 手杖; *hockey stick* 曲棍球棒. **3** anything long and thin like a stick 棒狀物; 條狀物: *stick of chalk* 粉筆.

stickler ['stiklə*] *nc* (with **for**) person who pays great attention to something so that it is done properly (與 for 連用) 堅持要求一絲不苟者: *My father is a stickler for neatness and honesty.* 我父親是個堅持整潔和誠實的人.

stiff [stif] *adj* **1** difficult to bend or move 不易彎曲的; 難以移動的: *I have a stiff leg.* 我的一條腿彎曲不便. *This book has a stiff cover.* 這本書有一個硬封面. *They made a stiff mixture of flour and water.* 他們用水把面粉調得稠稠的. **2** difficult to do 難做的; 棘手的: *We sat a very stiff examination.* 我們參加了一次很難的考試. *It was a stiff climb to the top of the hill.* 爬到山頂很艱難. **3** strong 濃烈的; 強烈的; 猛烈的: *The boat was sailing in a stiff breeze.* 船在強風中航行. *What he needs is a stiff drink.* 他所需要的是喝烈酒. **4** (with reference to behaviour etc) formal; unfriendly (指行爲等) 拘謹的, 冷淡的: *He is very stiff with strangers.* 他跟陌生人在一起時顯得很拘謹. **5** very much 極點: *bore someone stiff* i.e. frighten / bore very much (*informal*) 使某人嚇得要死 (非正式). **stiffly** *adv* **stiffness** *nu* **stiffen** *vt* / *i* become or make stiff 使硬; 使難做; 變得費勁; 使猛烈; 使猛烈; 使拘謹; 變得拘謹; 使冷淡; 變得冷淡.

stifle ['staifl] *vt* / *i* **1** stop the breath; make breathing difficult 悶死; (使) 窒息: *The heat of the sun at midday was stifling.* 中午的太陽熱氣悶人. *The children were stifled by the smoke.* 孩子們被烟嗆得透不過氣來. **2** stop; keep from being heard 遏止; 壓制; 使聽不到: *The government soon stifled these complaints.* 政府不久便將這些抱怨壓了下去. *We had to stifle our*

laughter. 我們不得不忍住笑.

stigma ['stigmə] *nc* mark of disgrace; mark on the skin 恥辱的標誌, 污名; 皮膚斑點: *stigma of failure* 失敗的恥辱. *pl* 複數 **stigmata** [stig'mɑːtə] or **stigmas.**

stile [stail] *nc* steps for climbing a fence or wall (攀越柵欄或圍牆用的) 階梯; 梯磴.

still¹ [stil] *adj* / *adv* **1** not moving; silent 不動的; 靜止的; 寂靜的, 無聲的: *The water in the pool was very still.* 池中的水很平靜. *The child kept still while his mother dressed him.* 當媽媽給小孩穿衣服的時候, 這個小孩一動也不動. **2** (with reference to wine or other drinks) not bubbling with gas (指酒或其他飲料) 不含氣泡的. **stillness** *nu* **'stillborn** *adj* dead when born 死胎的; 死産的; 生下來即已死亡的. **'still 'life** painting etc of things without life (e. g. fruit, flowers) 靜物畫等(例如: 水果, 花).

still² [stil] *adv* / *intensifier* **1** up to this or that moment; even now; even then 還; 仍然; 尚: *He still comes to see us.* 他仍然來看我們. *They were still asleep when I left.* 我離開時他們還在睡覺. *Note* 說明: *still* has the sense of something continuing; *yet* of something which is about to happen. *Is your baby still talking?* i.e. it has already at some time begun to talk; *Is your baby talking yet?* i.e. it has not, as far as the questioner knows, begun to talk. still 則指某事仍在延續的意思; yet 則指某事即將發生. *Is your baby still talking?* 你的小孩仍在說話嗎?即: 小孩已在前些時候開始說話. *Is your baby talking yet?* 你的小孩已說話了嗎?即: 據提問者所知, 還未開始說話. **2** yet; (with *comparative*) to a greater extent (與比較級連用) 更; 愈: *He is* fat, but his brother is still fatter / fatter still. 他胖，但是他的兄弟更胖．**3** however 但是，還，然而: *You did wrong. Still, I am ready to forgive you.* 你做錯了，然而，我還是願意原諒你．

stilt [stilt] *nc* one of two long poles, each with a footrest so that one can walk high above the ground when using them 高蹺．

stilted ['stiltid] *adj* (with reference to behaviour, writing etc) stiff; artificial; not natural (指行爲，寫作等) 生硬的；獃板的；做作的，不自然的；浮誇的．

stimulate ['stimjuleit] *vt* increase energy; excite 增强；刺激；激發: *Better wages have stimulated them to work harder.* 較高的工資激發了他們更加努力工作．**stimulating** *adj*: *stimulating book* 振奮人心的書; *stimulating weather* 撩人的天氣．**stimulation** [stimju'leiʃən] *nc / u* **stimulant** ['stimjulnt] *nc* drink or drug which stimulates 刺激物；興奮劑: *Athletes are forbidden to take stimulants before a race.* 賽跑比賽前禁止運動員服用興奮劑．**stimulus** ['stimjuləs] *nc* something which stimulates 刺激物；刺激；激勵: *The good news was a stimulus to all who heard it.* 這個好消息對所有聽到的人來說是一種激勵．**stimuli** ['stimjulai:]．

sting¹ [stiŋ] *nc* **1** small, pointed part of some insects, used as a weapon (某些昆蟲用作武器的)刺；螫針: *Bees have stings.* 蜜蜂有螫針．**2** pain, or mark on the skin, caused by a sting 表皮的刺痛或螫傷痕跡: *There was a big sting on his neck.* 他的頸部有一塊很大的螫痕．

sting² [stiŋ] *vt / i* push in a sting 刺；螫；叮: *The bee stung him on the neck.* 蜜蜂螫了他的脖子．*Most flies do not* sting. 大多數蒼蠅都不會叮人．*past* 過去式和過去分詞 **stung** [stʌŋ]．

stingy ['stindʒi] *adj* unwilling to spend money or to give anything; miserly; mean 吝嗇的；小氣的；自私的．**stingily** *adv* **stinginess** *nu* (all *informal*) (均爲非正式)．

stink [stiŋk] *vt / i* give out a very unpleasant smell 發臭；有惡臭味: *The meat is not fresh. It stinks.* 這肉不新鮮，發臭了．*Their clothes stank of sweat.* 他們的衣服有汗臭味．*past tense* 過去式 **stank** [stæŋk] or **stunk** [stʌŋk]．*past part* 過去分詞 **stunk**. Also 亦作 *nc*: *the stink of rotting fruit.* 爛水果的臭味．(all *informal*) (均爲非正式)．

stint [stint] *vt* cause to be left with nothing or very little; not have or give enough of 節省；限制；吝惜: *He stints himself in food and clothes so as to be able to pay for his education.* 他節衣縮食以便能够支付教育費用．Also 亦作 *nc* fixed amount of work 定額工作． *I have done my stint for the day.* 我已做完我一天的工作量．

stipulate ['stipjuleit] *vt* make something part of an agreement; make certain conditions 要求以…作爲協議的條件；訂定，規定: *They say they will repair the door but they stipulate that they must be paid as soon as they have finished.* 他們說他們願意修理這扇門，不過要求一修理完，就得馬上給他們錢．**stipulation** [stipju'leiʃən] *nc / u* something which is stipulated 規定；約定；條款: *I agreed to help on the stipulation that others would also help.* 我同意幫助，但條件是其他人也要幫助．

stir [stə:*] *vt / i* **1** move; begin to move 動；移動；活動；開始移動: *The animals were stirring in the forest.* 動物在森林

裏活動. *Has the child stirred yet?* i. e.
woken up 小孩已經醒了嗎? **2** move
an instrument (e. g. a stick) round in
a liquid etc to mix it 攪和; 攪拌: *I put
milk in my tea and stirred it.* 我把牛奶
倒進茶裏並且攪拌. pres part 現在分
詞 **stirring.** past 過去式和過去分詞
stirred. **stirring** *adj* exciting 令人興
奮的; 鼓舞人心的: *a stirring book* 激
動人心的書. **stir something up**
cause; arouse 引起; 惹起; 激起: *They
are always stirring up trouble.* 他們總
惹麻煩.

stirrup ['stirəp] *nc* loop of iron, leather
or rope. hanging from a saddle in
which one puts one's foot when riding
a horse (從馬鞍上垂下的)馬鐙.

stitch [stitʃ] *vt / i* **1** join by using a needle and thread; decorate in this way;
make a complete movement of the
needle in knitting etc. 縫合; 縫飾; 縫;
補綴: *She stitched the buttons on the
coat.* 她把鈕扣縫在外衣上. *I am
stitching flowers on the table-cloth.* 我
正在枱布上繡花. **2** close a wound
with needle and thread 縫合傷口:
*The doctor stitched the big cut above
my eye.* 醫生縫合我眼睛上方的大切
口. Also 亦作 *nc* **1** amount of thread
which has been put through cloth by
a needle to join or decorate 縫線; 針
腳: *She mended the coat with a few
stitches.* 她幾針就將外衣縫補好了. **2**
thread keeping a wound closed 傷口
縫線: *I had three stitches put in my
head.* 我的頭部縫了三針. **3** sharp
pain in the side often felt when running (跑步時常感覺到的)脇部劇痛:
get a / the stitch 脇部劇痛.

stock [stɔk] **1** *nc / u* goods kept ready
for use or sale; store of things or
material which is ready to be used 存
貨; 現貨; 庫存品; 庫存原料(或材料):

*This shop has a good stock of boys'
shoes.* 這家商店有充足的男童鞋存貨.
We have blue ink in stock i. e. we
have a ready supply of blue ink. 我們
有藍墨水的現貨. 即: 我們現可供應藍墨
水. *Red ink is out of stock* i. e. we
have no red ink. 紅墨水無存貨. 即: 我
們沒有紅墨水. *He has collected a
stock of facts about motorcars.* 他已收
集到有關各式汽車的豐富資料. **2** *nu*
juice from boiled bones, meat etc,
ready for making soup, gravy etc. (用
骨、肉等煮成的)原汁; 湯料. **3** *nu*
animals kept on a farm 家畜: *Farmers
need plenty of grass to feed their
stock.* 農民們需要充足的草料餵養他們
的家畜. (Also 亦作 **livestock**). **4** *nc /
u* money shares in a business; money
lent to a government. 股票; 公債: *I
have put all my money in government
stock.* 我已將我所有的錢全部購買了公
債. Also 亦作 *vt* get or keep a stock of
something 儲備; 備有: *Does this
shop stock English books?* 這家商店備
有英語書嗎? **laughing stock** see 見
laugh[1]. **'stockbroker** person who
buys and sells stocks (in sense **4**) and
shares 證券經紀人. **'stock exchange**
place where stocks (in sense **4**) and
shares are bought and sold 證券交易
所. **'stockpile** *vt* buy large amounts
of materials which may become dearer or less easy to get later (e. g. a
government buying materials which it
may need for war) 大量購買; 囤積(將
來可能會漲價或短缺的物資。例如: 政府購買戰爭可
能需要的物資). Also *nc.* **'stocktaking**
nc / u work of counting stock 清點存
貨; 盤點: *The shop is closed for its
annual stocktaking.* 商店關門進行每年
一度的盤點. **take stock of** find out
what the position is, what has to be
done etc. 估量; 審度: *The general*

took stock of the enemy and decided to attack at once. 將軍估量了敵人的情況，決定立刻進攻.

stockade [stɔ'keid] *nc* fence made of upright poles (usu. put round a building to defend it) 柵欄；圍欄 (通常圍住建築物，作防禦用): *stockaded building* i. e. one with a stockade round it 用柵欄圍起來的建築物.

stocking ['stɔkiŋ] *nc* covering of wool, cotton, silk, nylon etc which fits the leg and foot tightly and reaches to the knee or to the top of the leg 長襪.

stocky ['stɔki] *adj* (with reference to persons, animals and plants) short and strong (指人, 動植物) 粗短而結實的；矮而壯的.

stodgy ['stɔdʒi] *adj* (with reference to food) thick and tasteless (指食物) 濃膩的.

stoic ['stouik] *nc* person who suffers without complaint and who is not affected by either pleasure or pain 忍受痛苦而不抱怨的人；不以苦樂爲意的人, 對苦樂淡泊的人. **stoical** *adj* **stoicism** ['stouisizəm] *nu* endurance of pain, hardship etc without complaint 堅忍克制.

stoke [stouk] *vt / i* (often with **up**) put coal or other fuel on a fire (esp. a large fire giving heat for an engine i. e. a furnace) (常與 up 連用) 給 (爐子尤指給發動機供熱之大火爐) 添煤或其他燃料: *The furnace must be stoked up every two hours.* 每隔兩小時就得給爐子加煤.

stole [stoul] past tense of **steal**. steal 的過去式.

stolen ['stouln] past part of **steal**. steal 的過去分詞.

stolid ['stɔlid] *adj* difficult to arouse or excite; dull 不易激動的；感覺遲鈍的.

stoma ['stoumə] *nc* **1** opening or pore

in a plant; breathing pore (植物的) 氣孔. **2** small mouthlike opening in an animal, especially in a lower animal (尤指低等動物的) 氣門, 呼吸孔.

stomach ['stʌmək] *nc* organ inside the body, like a bag, into which food goes when it is swallowed, and in which the food is then digested 胃；肚子: *Nobody can work well on an empty stomach* i.e. if his stomach is empty 沒有人空着肚子能工作得好. *It is difficult to run quickly on a full stomach.* 飽着肚子難以跑得快. Also 亦作 *vt* (usu. *negative*): *I can't stomach such behaviour* i.e. I dislike such behaviour very much. (通常用於否定句) 我不能容忍這種行爲. 即: 我非常不喜歡這種行爲.

stomata ['stoumətə] *pl* of **stoma**. stoma 的複數.

stone [stoun] *nc / u* **1** hard substance of which rock is made; piece of rock 石；石頭；石塊: *The building is made of stone.* 這座建築物是用石頭建成的. *The soil is full of stones.* 這土壤裏滿是石塊. Often used with other words to show types of rock (e.g. *limestone; sandstone*) or the uses of stone (e.g. *gravestone; millstone; stepping stone*) 常與其他詞連用以表示岩石的類型 (例如: limestone 石灰石；sandstone 砂岩) 或石的用途 (例如: gravestone 墓石；millstone 磨石；stepping stone 踏脚石). Also 亦作 *adj* made of stone 石製的: *stone house* 石屋；*stone walls* 石牆；*stone floor* 石地面. **2** jewel 寶石: *precious stones* 寶石. **3** hard seed inside some types of fruit (一些果子的) 核: *There are large stones inside dates and plums.* 棗和李子有大核. **4** weight of 14 pounds 呎 (重量單位, 十四磅): *My weight is 12 stone.* 我的體重是一百六十八磅. *pl* 複數 **stone**

(not used in USA) (不用於美國).

stony *adj* like stone; full of stones 似石的; 多石的: *stony soil* 多石的土壤.

'Stone Age period in man's history, before metal was discovered, when tools and weapons were made of stone 石器時代. **'stone-** *adj* completely (e.g. **stone-cold; stone-dead; stone-deaf**) 完全地; 徹底地 (例如: stone-cold 冷透的; stone-dead 死得硬梆梆的; stone-deaf 全聾的).

stood [stud] *past of* **stand¹**. stand¹ 的過去式和過去分詞.

stool [stu:l] *nc* small chair without a back 凳子.

stoop [stu:p] *vt / i* bend the upper part of the body forward and downward 屈身; 俯身; 彎腰: *She stooped to talk to the little child.* 她彎下身來對那小孩説話.

stop¹ [stɔp] *vt / i* **1** come to the end of a movement or activity; bring a movement or activity to an end 停止, 中止 (動作或活動): *The train does not stop here.* 火車不在這裏停. *The noise stopped.* 嘈雜聲停了. *He stopped his car at the corner.* 他把車停在角落上. *Rain stopped the game.* 因為下雨, 比賽停了. **2** prevent; hinder 阻止; 妨礙: *What stopped him (from) coming?* 甚麼事情使他不能來? *He can read what he likes. I won't stop him.* 他喜歡讀甚麼就讀, 我不會阻止. **3** cease; leave off 停止; 中止: *He has stopped smoking.* 他已停止抽烟. *past* 過去式和過去分詞 **stopped.** **stopper** *nc* something which fills up an opening 阻塞物; 塞子: *Have you the stopper of this bottle?* 你有這個瓶子的塞子嗎? **stoppage** *nc* state of being stopped; something which obstructs 阻塞; 堵塞; 阻礙; 阻塞物: *There have been several stoppages (of work) at the factory.* 工廠裏

已發生了好幾次停工. *I must remove the stoppage from the water pipes.* 我必須排除水管中的阻塞物. **stop over** stop for a time during a journey (在旅途中)停留; 中途停留: *We shall stop over at a hotel for one night before going on to London.* 我們將在旅館住一晚, 然後前往倫敦. **'stopover** *nc* place where one stops in this way (often during a journey by air); act of stopping in this way (常指乘飛機旅行) 中途停留地; 中途停留. **stop something up** fill up an opening 填塞; 阻塞(口子): *I am stopping up the hole in the wall.* 我在填塞牆上的洞.

stop² [stɔp] *nc* **1** act or state of stopping or being stopped 停止; 中止: *The train came to a stop a mile from the station.* 火車在離車站一英里處停了下來. *He put a stop to the noise.* 他制止了吵鬧. **2** place where buses etc usually stop during their journeys (公共汽車等途中的)停車站; 車站: *We get off at the next stop.* 我們在下一站下車. *He was standing at the bus stop.* 他在公共汽車站站着. **3** punctuation mark shown by i.e. a full stop 句點(標點符號). **'stop-'press** (mainly *Brit*) latest news put in a newspaper (usu. in a space left empty for it) after printing has begun (主要用於英)(報紙開印後, 通常在空欄裏加上的)最新消息. **'stopwatch** type of watch with hands which can be started and stopped by pressing a knob (used to find out the exact time taken to do something. e. g. run a race) (賽跑等用的)跑錶, 計秒錶.

stopcock ['stɔpkɔk] *nc* device for turning the flow of a liquid or gas on or off; valve; tap 管門; 柱塞; 活栓; 旋塞閥; 龍頭.

store [stɔː*] *nc* **1** supply of something kept ready for use when needed 貯藏; 儲備: *We have a good store of grain until the next harvest.* 在下次收穫到來之前我們儲備有大量糧食. Used in *pl* when it refers to many different kinds of things 指多種不同物品時用複數: *He is in charge of the stores at the hospital.* 他在醫院負責管理物品. **2** place where goods are kept 倉庫; 貨棧: *The boys are getting pens and pencils from the school store.* 這些男孩正從學校倉庫裏領取鋼筆和鉛筆. **3** shop 商店: *drugstore* 藥店; *liquor store* 酒店; *department store* i.e. large shop selling many different kinds of goods 百貨店. *Note* 說明: *store* in the sense of a shop is more common in the USA than in Britain. store 用作商店在美國較英國常見. store 亦作 *vt* **1** keep something ready for use 儲備; 貯藏: *After harvest we store the grain.* 收穫之後, 我們貯藏糧食. **2** put in a safe place 存入倉庫; 放入庫裏: *They have stored their furniture until they return from abroad.* 他們已將傢具存入倉庫直到他們從國外回來. **storage** *nu* **1** act of storing 儲藏; 貯存. **2** place where goods are stored 儲藏所; 倉庫: *They have put their furniture in storage.* 他們已將傢具存入的儲藏庫. **'storeroom** room in a house etc where goods which are not in use are kept 儲藏室; 庫房. **store something up** collect and keep ready for use when needed 貯藏; 儲備: *They are storing up all the food they can buy.* 他們正在儲備能夠買到的所有食物.

storey, story ['stɔːri] *nc* rooms on one floor of a building; floor or level of a building 一層的房間; (建築物的) 層; 樓: *My bedroom is on the second*

storey i.e. two levels up 我的卧室在三樓. *pl* 複數 **storeys** or **stories**. *Note* 說明: the use of *storey* or *floor* can be confusing. (*US*) one level up is called the *second floor* or *storey*; (*Brit*) one level up is called the *first floor* or *storey*. *storey* or *floor* 的使用可能混淆. (美) 二樓爲 the second floor 或 storey. (英) 二樓爲 the first floor 或 storey. **-storeyed,-storied** *adj* having storeys, stories 有 (若干) 層樓的: *six-storeyed / storied building* 六層樓的建築物.

storm [stɔːm] *nc* **1** bad weather (usu. with strong winds) 風暴; 暴風雨: *The storm last night blew down the tree.* 昨夜的風暴將樹吹倒了. (Often used with another word to show what kind of storm. 常與其他詞連用表示風暴的類型): *dust storm* 塵暴; *sandstorm* 沙暴; *snowstorm* 暴風雪; *thunderstorm* 雷雨). **2** expression of strong feelings 強烈感情的爆發: *The speech caused a storm among those who heard it.* 演說使聽衆羣情激昂. Also 亦作 *vt* / *i* **1** express strong feelings 暴怒: *He stormed out of the room* i. e. he left the room shouting angrily. 他怒氣衝衝地走出房間. **2** attack strongly and capture quickly 猛攻; 襲取: *Our soldiers stormed the town.* 我軍攻佔了這座城鎮. **stormy** *adj* of a storm; having a storm 暴風雨的; 有暴風雨的: *stormy sea* 咆哮的大海; *stormy weather* 暴風雨的天氣. **take by storm** attack strongly and capture quickly 猛攻; 襲取.

story[1] ['stɔːri] *nc* account of what has happened, either true or imaginary 故事; 軼事; 小說; 傳奇; 事情經過: *He told us the story of his life.* 他告訴我們他的生平. *Children like stories about fairies.* 孩子們喜歡神話故事. *He is* *reading a storybook.* 他正在看一本故事書. *Don't believe all the stories he tells you.* 別相信他告訴你的所有的事情. **'storyteller** person who tells or writes stories 講或寫故事的人.

story² ['stɔːri] *nc* see 見 **storey.**

stout [staut] *adj* **1** strong; tough 強壯的; 堅韌的: *He had a stout stick in his hand.* 他手裏拿了一根結實的手杖. *He has a stout heart* i.e. he is brave. 他有勇氣. 即: 他勇敢. **2** (with reference to persons only) rather fat (僅指人) 相當胖的: *He is too stout to run quickly.* 他太胖了, 跑不快. Also 亦作 *nu* type of strong, dark beer 一種烈性的黑啤酒. **stoutness** *nu.*

stove [stouv] *nc* apparatus with a fire enclosed inside, used for heating a room and / or for cooking; cooker heated by gas or electricity 火爐; 暖爐; 煤氣爐; 電爐.

stow [stou] *vt* put or load carefully and tightly 裝載; 裝填: *He stowed his books in the box.* 他將書裝了箱. *They are stowing the heavy goods in the hold of the ship.* 他們正將重貨物裝在船艙裏. **'stowaway** *nc* person who hides himself on a ship or aircraft to avoid paying the fare 藏匿於輪船或飛機中的揩油乘客; 偷乘者.

straddle ['strædl] *vt / i* stand or walk with the legs wide apart; stand, sit or walk across something with one leg on each side of it 叉開腿跨立或走動; 跨坐, 跨立, 跨騎: *He straddled the log of wood.* 他跨騎在圓木上.

straggle ['strægl] *vi* fall behind the others while going somewhere 落後; 落伍: *The young children straggled behind the older ones.* 年幼的小孩落在大一點的小孩後面. **straggler** *nc* person who falls behind 落後者; 落伍者.

straight¹ [streit] *adj* **1** not curved or bent; going directly from one point to another 直的; 直進的; 直線的: *Draw a straight line between A and B.* 在A、B之間劃一直綫. *The road from here to the village is straight.* 從這兒到村裏去的路是筆直的. **2** honest; true 誠實的; 正直的: *You will find him very straight.* 你會發現他很誠實. *I want a straight answer to my question.* 對我的問題我想得到一個坦率的回答. Also 亦作 *pred adj* tidy; in order 整齊的; 井井有條的: *I am putting my room straight before he comes.* 在他來之前, 我正把我的房間收拾整齊. Also 亦作 *nc* (usu. *sing* with **the**). *He came round the bend into the straight ten yards in front of the other runners* i.e. into the straight part of the running track between the two bends. (通常單數與 the 連用). 他轉彎進入直綫跑道比其他賽跑的人領先十碼. **straighten** *vt / i* become or make straight 使直; 使平直; 變直; 變平直: *The road has been straightened.* 這條路已經修直了. *He is trying to straighten (out) the matter* i.e. put it right 他正盡力使問題得到解決.

straight² [streit] *adv* **1** not in a curve; without turning 一直地; 無轉彎地: *Go straight on until you reach the church.* 一直向前走, 直到你走到教堂. *He drove straight into the tree.* 他筆直開車, 撞到樹上. **2** without any delay; by the quickest route 立即地; 由直路; 直接地: *As soon as he arrived he went straight into the meeting.* 他一到就立即去開會了. *My mother wants me to go straight home.* 我媽媽要我直接回家. **3** honestly; directly 誠實地; 正直地; 逕直地: *Tell me straight! Is he dead?* 坦率告訴我, 他死了嗎? *He looked me straight in the eyes.* 他直瞪

瞪地看着我. **straight away** at once 立刻; 馬上.

straightforward [streit'fɔ:wəd] *adj* simple; without difficulties 簡單的; 易懂的: *The first question he asked me was quite straightforward*. 他向我提出的第一個問題很簡單.

strain¹ [strein] *vt / i* **1** pull very tight 拉緊; 扯緊; 張緊: *They strained the wire between the two posts*. 他們拉緊兩柱之間的電線. **2** use to the utmost 盡力使用: *We strained our ears to hear what he was saying*. 我們聚精會神地聽他說話. **3** damage by using too much (因過份使用而)損壞; 損傷: *He strained his heart by running too far*. 他跑得太遠而損傷了心臟. *If you read in a bad light you will strain your eyes*. 如果你在昏暗的燈光下看書, 會損壞視力. **4** pass a substance through a sieve or filter (e.g. through a cloth or wire mesh) to separate the liquid from the solids in it 濾: *She boiled the potatoes and then strained them* i.e. separated the potatoes from the water in which they had been boiled. 她煮馬鈴薯, 然後濾去水. **strained** *adj* not natural; unhappy 不自然的; 不愉快的: *He had a strained smile on his face*. 他面帶勉強的笑容. *The mistake has caused strained relations between the manager and his staff*. 這次誤解使經理和他的工作人員之間的關係緊張. **strainer** *nc* device for separating liquids from solids 濾器; 濾網: *vegetable strainer* 濾菜器; *tea strainer* 濾茶器.

strain² [strein] *nc / u* **1** something which is so great that it causes damage of discomfort 過勞; 緊張: *We suffered the strain of having to wait a week for the news*. 我們不得不等了一星期才知道消息, 感到十分疲勞. *Ex-aminations cause mental strain*. 考試使得精神緊張. **2** inherited nature or tendency 遺傳氣質或傾向: *There is a criminal strain in the whole family*. 那一家族的人都有犯罪傾向. *He owns a good strain of cattle* i. e. a good breed 他擁有良種牛. **3** (in *pl*) music; tune (用於複數)音樂; 曲調: *We marched to the strains of the school band*. 我們和着學校樂隊的樂曲行進. (rather *o. f.* in sense **3**) (義 3 頗爲舊式).

strait [streit] *nc* narrow stretch of water open at both ends 海峽: *The ship passed through the strait between the two islands*. 船通過兩島之間的海峽. (Often *pl* with proper names 與專有名詞連用時常用複數: *the Straits of Dover* 多佛海峽). **'strait jacket** type of coat put on somebody who is mad, to stop him being violent (拘束瘋人的) 緊身衣. **'strait-laced** *adj* narrow in thought and manners (在觀念和習俗方面)狹隘的: *They are too strait-laced to approve of dancing*. 他們觀念過於狹隘不贊成跳舞.

strand¹ [strænd] *nc* one of the strings or wires from which a rope is made; a single thread of anything (繩、線等的)股; 縷; 根: *There were strands of hair on his coat*. 他的外衣上有幾根頭髮.

strand² [strænd] *vt / i* **1** go, cause to go, on the shore or on the rocks etc. (使)擱淺或觸礁: *Their boat was stranded on the rock*. 他們的船觸礁了. **2** be in difficulty, alone, without money, food etc. (因無錢, 無食物等)處於困境; 孤立無援: *We were stranded in the big town because we missed the train*. 沒趕上火車, 我們在這大城鎮裏一籌莫展.

strange [streindʒ] *adj* **1** not known, met or seen before, therefore odd; queer 奇異的; 奇特的; 奇怪的: *Who is* *that strange man over there?* 那邊那個陌生人是誰? *He says some very strange things.* 他說了些很奇怪的事情. **2** not accustomed to 不習慣的; 陌生的: *The new boys are strange to the school.* 新來的男孩們對學校感到生疏. **strangely** *adv* **strangeness** *nu*

stranger *nc* **1** person not known, met or seen before 陌生人: *Don't talk to strangers.* 不要跟陌生人談話. **2** person who is not accustomed to something 不習慣於某事物的人; 外行; 生手: *He is a stranger in / to the big city.* 他對大城市感到陌生. *I am a stranger to politics.* 我對政治很外行.

strangle ['stræŋgl] *vt* kill by holding the throat tightly 扼殺; 勒死; 掐死. **strangulation** [stræŋgju'leiʃən] *nu* act of strangling or being strangled 扼殺; 勒死; 扼死: *death by strangulation* 勒死. **'stranglehold** act of holding in order to strangle; power to stop completely 束縛; 壓制; 箝制: *They have a stranglehold on our trade.* 他們壓制我們的貿易.

strap [stræp] *nc* long, narrow piece of leather, cloth or metal 皮帶; 布帶; 金屬帶: *He has broken the strap of his wrist watch.* 他把他的手錶帶弄斷了. *Some teachers still use a strap* i.e. a long, narrow piece of leather to punish children 一些老師仍然使用皮帶. 即: 懲罰孩子們的細長皮帶. Also 亦作 *vt* **1** fasten with a strap 用帶繫牢; 用帶捆紮: *He strapped his books to his bicycle.* 他將書捆在自行車上. **2** beat with a strap 用皮帶抽打: *past* 過去式和過去分詞 **strapped. strapping** *adj* big and strong 高大健壯的; 魁偉的: *He is a strapping young man.* (*informal*) 他是一個身材魁梧的年青人. (非正式).

strata ['strɑːtə] *pl* of **stratum.** stratum

的複數.

stratagem ['strætədʒəm] *nc / u* scheme or trick to deceive an enemy during a war; any scheme or trick to deceive somebody (戰時誘騙敵人的) 戰畧; 策畧; (欺騙某人的) 詭計; 計謀.

strategy ['strætədʒi] *nc / u* **1** (esp. with reference to moving and using large military forces) art of waging war (尤指以最佳方案調遣和使用軍事力量的) 戰畧 (學). **2** general plan of action 策畧; 計謀. *Note* 說明: **tactics** *npl* is the art of moving and using smaller military forces during a battle. tactics npl 指一次戰役中調遣和使用較小的軍事力量的藝術; 戰術. **strategic** [strə'tiːdʒik] *adj* of strategy; required by strategy 戰畧 (上) 的; 戰畧所要求的: *The strategic defence of the country depends on a powerful air force.* 這個國家的戰畧防禦依靠強大的空軍力量; *strategic materials* i.e. materials required to wage war 戰畧物資, 即: 進行戰爭所需要的物資. **strategist** *nc* person skilled in strategy 戰畧家; 謀畧家; 兵法家.

strati ['streitai] *pl* of **stratus.** Stratus 的複數.

stratum ['strɑːtəm] *nc* layer of rock or earth 岩層; 地層. *pl* 複數 **strata** ['strɑːtə].

stratus ['streitəs] *nc* low, uniform, horizontal layer of grey cloud that spreads over a large area, occurring at heights under 6,500 feet 層雲.

straw [strɔː] **1** *nc / u* dry stalk of corn etc after the grain has been taken out 稻草; 麥稭: *The hut has a roof of straw.* 這間小屋有一個稻草蓋起來的屋頂. *The cattle were lying on the straw.* 牛躺在稻草上. **2** *nc* tube used for drinking liquids (喝飲料用的) 吸管: *The children were sucking their* milk through straws. 孩子們正用吸管吸牛奶. **the last straw** something unpleasant which, by being added, makes a situation unbearable 使情況終於變得難以忍受的不愉快之事: *I lost all my money. Losing my coat as well was the last straw. (informal)* 我丟掉了所有的錢.我的外衣又丟了,實在使人受不了.(非正式).

strawberry ['strɔːbəri] *nc* **1** type of plant with red fruit which grows near the ground 草莓樹. **2** the fruit of this plant 草莓.

stray [strei] *vi* wander from the proper place or path; get lost 走離;偏離;迷路,走失: *The cattle strayed from the field.* 牛在田野裏走失了. *The teacher strayed from the subject of his lesson.* 老師講課離題了. Also 亦作 *nc / adj*: *The farmer is looking for strays* i.e. cattle etc which have wandered or got lost 農民正在尋找走失的牲畜. *Where are the parents of these stray children?* 這些迷路的孩子的父母親在哪裏?

streak [striːk] *nc* **1** line or layer of a different colour (不同顏色的)線條;條紋;層: *He has streaks of grey in his dark hair.* 他的黑髮中有幾絲白髮. **2** anything which is different from what is around it or from what is expected. 與周圍不同或異於所期待的事物: *He is a very kind man but he has a streak of cruelty.* 他人很厚道,但有點殘忍. *I usually do well but last night I had a streak of bad luck.* 我通常都很順手,但昨夜卻有點運氣不佳. Also 亦作 *vt* mark with streaks 在…加線條或條紋; *His face was streaked with paint.* 他的臉上有幾道顏料. **streaky** *adj* having streaks 有線條的;有條紋的: *streaky bacon* i.e. with layers of fat in it like streaks 五花醃肉(肥瘦相間的醃肉).

stream [striːm] *nc* **1** small river; flow of a river 小河,溪;水流: *We crossed the stream by the bridge.* 我們從橋上過小河. *The boat sailed upstream / downstream* i.e. up / down the river 船逆流而上/順流而下. **2** flow of anything 流出;流: *Streams of sweat were running down his face.* 汗水從他的臉上不停地往下流. *A stream of people came out of the building.* 人羣從大樓裏湧出來. *He annoyed us with a stream of insults.* 他一連串的辱罵使我們很生氣. **3** division of pupils of the same age into classes in a school 學校按同齡學生分成的班: *This is a very large secondary school with four streams in each form* i.e. each form is divided into four classes 這是一所很大的中學,每一年級都有四個班. Also 亦作 *vi* flow; wave 流出;流出;飄揚;招展. *Tears streamed from her eyes.* 淚水從她眼睛裏奪眶而出. *The flags streamed in the wind.* 旗幟迎風招展. **streamer** *nc* narrow flag; long, narrow piece of paper used for decoration 旗幟;(作裝飾用的)彩帶. '**streamline** shape which passes most easily through air or water 流線型. '**streamlined** *adj*: *streamlined racing car* 流線型賽車.

street [striːt] *nc* road in a town (usu. with buildings at the sides) 街;街道. '**streetcar** *(US)* 美 tramcar.

strength [streŋθ] *nu* quality of being strong 力;力量;力氣;強度: *He hasn't the strength to lift it.* 他沒有舉起它的力氣. *They built a wall of great strength.* 他們建了一堵很堅固的牆. *The strength of whisky is greater than that of beer.* 威士忌酒的強度比啤酒大. **strengthen** *vt / i* become, or make, strong or stronger 增強;加強;變強. see 見 **strong.**

strenuous ['strenjuəs] *adj* full of, or requiring, great effort 渾身是勁的; 費勁的; *He played a strenuous game of football.* 他打了一場很緊張的足球賽. *Digging is strenuous work.* 挖掘是很費勁的工作. **strenuously** *adv.*

stress [stres] *nc / u* **1** pressure; force; violence 緊迫; 壓力; 猛烈: *He does not like the stress of life in a big city.* 他不喜歡大城市生活的緊迫感. *He agreed to do it under great stress.* 在強大的壓力之下他同意做那事. **2** weight; importance; emphasis 重要(性); 強調; 重音: *My parents lay great stress on honesty.* 我父母親很強調誠實. *Stress is shown in this dictionary by the sign'.* 重音在這本字典裏用"'"符號來表示. Also 亦作 *vt* give weight or emphasis to 着重; 強調; 重讀: *I stressed the importance of coming early.* 我強調了早來的重要性. *The word 'happy' is stressed on the first syllable.* "happy" 一詞的第一音節重讀.

stretch [stretʃ] *vt / i* **1** make longer or wider by pulling 拉長; 拉寬: *They stretched the rope between the two posts.* 他們拉緊兩柱之間的繩子. *He stood up and stretched himself.* 他站了起來, 伸伸懶腰. **2** lie spread out 伸展: *The plain stretches for many miles.* 曠野綿延許多英里. Also 亦作 *nc: The stretch of sea between England and France is called the English Channel.* 英國和法國之間那一片海洋叫做英吉利海峽. **stretcher** *nc* frame (usu. covered with canvas) for carrying somebody who is sick or injured 擔架. **stretch (something) out** **1** stretch to full length 伸長; 伸直: *I stretched out my hand for the money.* 我伸手取錢. *John was stretched out on the beach* i.e. was lying at full length 約翰伸直身子躺在海灘上. **2** (with reference to land etc) lie spread

out (指陸地等)伸展; 延伸: *From the top of the hill they could see the forest stretched out before them.* 從山頂上他們能夠看見森林在他們面前延伸.

stricken ['strikən] *pred adj (past part of* **strike**[1]. **strike**[1] 的過去分詞) struck by; affected by 侵襲的: *They were stricken with terror (o. f.* 舊式) */ They were terror-stricken.* 他們受恐怖的折磨.

strict [strikt] *adj* **1** severe; stern; to be obeyed 嚴厲的; 嚴格的; 須服從的: *He has strict parents.* 他的父母嚴厲. *Discipline at school is very strict.* 學校裏的紀律十分嚴格. **2** exact; accurate; limited 精確的; 準確的; 限定的: *This work requires strict measurement.* 這項工作要求精確的測量. *Tell me the strict truth.* 告訴我千真萬確的實情. *He told me in strict confidence that he was going abroad.* 他極其秘密地告訴我他要去國外了. **strictly** *adv* **strictness** *nu* **strictly speaking** to tell the complete truth 嚴格說來.

stride [straid] *nc* long step; length of a long step 大步; 闊步; 步幅: *He crossed the road in a few strides.* 他幾大步就過了馬路. *I was standing three strides from the gate.* 我站在離大門三步遠的地方. Also 亦作 *vt / i: We watched him striding across the road.* 我們看着他大步穿過馬路. *They strode away / off without saying anything.* 他們大步走開了, 甚麼也沒說. *past* 過去式和過去分詞 **strode** [stroud].

strident ['straidnt] *adj* loud and unpleasant 刺耳的: *He has a strident voice.* 他的嗓音刺耳.

strife [straif] *nu* fighting; quarrelling 爭鬥; 衝突; 爭吵.

strike[1] [straik] *vt / i* **1** hit; give a blow to 打; 擊; 敲: *A stone struck me on the head.* 一塊石頭打在我的頭上. *He* *struck the nail with a hammer.* 他用鐵鎚敲敲釘子. *He struck me (a blow) on the face.* 他(一拳)打中我的臉部. **2** (with reference to clocks) show by making a sound (指時鐘) 敲響: *The town clock has just struck six* i.e. shown it is six o'clock by sounding six times 鎮上的鐘剛剛敲過六下. 即: 敲響六次來表示六點鐘. *We waited for the clock to strike.* 我們等待時鐘敲響. **3** come to, cause to come to, the mind suddenly or strongly (使)突然, 或強烈想起: *A new idea struck me.* 我突然想到一個新主意. *It strikes us that you are wrong.* 我們看來你是錯的. *John strikes me as (being) honest.* 我覺得約翰很誠實. **4** (with **for**) refuse to continue work (usu. in order to get better pay conditions) (與 for 連用) (通常為要求提高工資待遇而)罷工: *I am sure the bus drivers will strike.* 我確信公共汽車司機們將舉行罷工. *They are striking for higher pay.* 他們正為爭取提高工資而罷工. **5** find suddenly 突然發現: *At last we struck the main road.* 最後我們找到大路了. *They hope to strike oil here* i.e. find it by boring a hole 他們希望在這裏找到油田. 即: 鑽孔找到油田. *past* 過去式 和過去分詞 **struck** [strʌk]. *past part* 過去分詞 also 亦作 **stricken** ['strikən] (*o. f.* 舊式). **striker** *nc* **1** person who strikes (esp. in sense **4**) 罷工者; 打擊者. **2** (football) forward (足球) 前鋒. **striking** *adj* remarkable 顯著的; 引人注目的: *She was wearing a striking hat.* 她戴了一頂引人注目的帽子. **strikingly** *adv*: *strikingly dressed* 穿著引人注目的. **strike someone down** cause to fall down or kill by striking; cause to be very ill 擊倒; 擊斃; 使病倒: *He struck down the animal with his spear.* 他用矛擊倒動物. *Malaria has struck him down.* 瘧疾使他病倒了. **strike up (something)** begin to play music 開始演奏(歌曲): *The band struck up when the president arrived.* 總統到達時樂隊開始奏樂. *The band struck up a tune.* 樂隊開始演奏一歌曲.

strike² [straik] **1** *nc / u* refusal to continue work 罷工: *The bus drivers are on strike.* 公共汽車司機們舉行罷工. **2** *nc* (esp. with reference to metals and minerals) sudden discovery (尤指金屬和礦藏的)突然發現: *There was a gold strike here many years ago.* 許多年以前, 這裏突然發現金礦. **3** *nc* attack (usu. by aircraft) (通常用飛機)攻擊: *They made an air strike on the enemy's position.* 他們對敵軍陣地進行空襲. **'strikebreaker** person who refuses to join a strike (in sense **1**) or who tries to stop it 破壞罷工者. **come / go out on strike** begin a strike (in sense **1**) 開始罷工.

string [striŋ] *nc / u* **1** thick thread (generally used for tying things) 粗綫繩(一般用於繫東西): *The parcel is tied with string.* 包裹用繩子捆着. *Have you a piece of string?* 你有一根繩子嗎? **2** thread on which things are arranged in a line; line of anything 串繩; 一行; 一串; 一列: *She was wearing a string of beads.* 她戴着一串小珠子. *A string of people stood outside.* 一行人站在外面. **3** stretched cord or wire of a musical instrument (樂器的)弦: *I need a new string for my guitar.* 我的吉他需要一根新弦. **4** (in *pl*) stringed instruments in an orchestra (e. g. violins) (用於複數)管弦樂隊的弦樂器(例如小提琴). **'string 'bean** type of bean, the outside covering of which is eaten. (Usu. **French bean**) 菜豆(通常爲 French bean).

stringent ['strindʒənt] *adj* requiring strict obedience; severe 要求嚴格遵守的; 嚴厲的: *There is a stringent rule against talking during an examination.* 有一條嚴禁在考試中説話的規定.
stringency *nc* / *u*.

strip [strip] *vt* / *i* **1** take one's clothes off 脱去衣服: *The doctor told me to strip.* 醫生叫我脱去衣服. **2** take off a covering; take away 脱去; 除去 (遮蓋物); 拿走: *I stripped off my shirt.* 我脱去襯衫. *They are stripping the paint from / off the wall.* 他們正除掉牆上的油漆. *The thieves stripped me of all my money.* 賊偷去了我全部的錢. *past 過去式和過去分詞* **stripped.** Also 亦作 *nc* long, narrow piece of something 條; 帶; 細長片: *strip of land* 狭長的一片土地; *strip of cloth* 布條. '**strip car'toon** set of drawings which tell a story 連環圖畫; 連環漫畫. '**strip'tease** type of entertainment in which a woman removes her clothes one article at a time (usu. to music) 脱衣舞 (通常有配樂). **strip something down** (with reference to an engine, apparatus etc) take off all the movable parts (e. g. to repair or clean it) (指發動機, 裝置等) 拆卸 (以進行修理或清洗等).

stripe [straip] *nc* long narrow band or mark (usu. of a different colour) 狭長的條紋或標誌 (通常爲不同顏色): *He was wearing a white tie with black stripes.* 他繫着一條有黑條紋的白領帶.
striped *adj* having stripes 有條紋的: *striped tie* 斜條領帶.

strive [straiv] *vt* / *i* try hard; struggle 努力; 奮力; 奮斗: *They are striving to win.* 他們努力争取勝利. *Most people strive for wealth.* 多數人奮力求財富. *A doctor is always striving against disease.* 醫生總是在跟疾病作鬥爭. *pres*

part 現在分詞 **striving.** *past tense 過去式* **strove** [strouv]. *past part 過去分詞* **striven** ['strivən].

stroboscope ['stroubəskoup] *nc* instrument for studying the successive phases of the periodic motion of a body by means of periodically interrupted light 頻閃觀測器; 閃光測頻儀; 頻閃儀.

strode [stroud] *past tense of* **stride**. stride 的過去式.

stroke¹ [strouk] *nc* **1** act of striking 打擊, 一擊: *He cut the log in half with one stroke of his axe.* 他一斧把木頭劈成兩半. *The golfer reached the hole in four strokes* i.e. by striking the ball with a golf club four times 這位高爾夫球選手四桿擊球進洞, 即: 用球棒擊球四次. **2** sudden illness which damages the brain and therefore the power of the body 中風: *He has not been able to walk or speak since he had a stroke.* 他中風後不能走路或説話. **3** something which needs effort or is caused suddenly by effort or accident 費力的事; 努力的結果; 意外的事: *He did not do a stroke (of work) last week.* 他上星期甚麼事也沒做. *It was a stroke of luck that we met here.* 我們在此會面真幸運.

stroke² [strouk] *vt* move the hand gently and often over something 撫摸: *His mother stroked his hair.* 她媽媽撫摸他的頭髮. *Cats like being stroked.* 貓喜歡被撫摸. Also 亦作 *nc* movement of this kind (esp. one made by a brush, pen or pencil); mark made in this way 輕觸 (尤指用筆一劃); 筆劃: *With one stroke of his pen he changed the number.* 他用筆一劃改了數字. *He painted the picture in a few strokes.* 他幾筆就畫好了那張畫.

stroll [stroul] *vi* walk slowly (usu. for

pleasure) 散步, 漫步, 閑逛. Also 亦作
nc: We went for a stroll. 我們去散步.
We took a stroll. 我們去散步.

strong [strɔŋ] *adj* **1** (with reference to
persons) powerful in body or mind
(指人) 強壯的; 堅強的: He has very
strong arms. 他的雙臂粗壯有力. She
hasn't a very strong will. 她的意志不
很堅強. **2** (with reference to things)
firm; solid; not easily broken or damaged (指物) 結實的; 堅固的; 不易破損
的: I need a strong box for my books.
我 要 有 一 個 結 實 的 箱 子 裝 書. The
walls of the castle are strong. 城堡的
牆壁堅固. **3** having a powerful effect
on the senses or feelings 強烈的, 猛烈
的: There was a strong smell of gas
in the room. 房 間 裏 煤 氣 味 很
濃. The strong light of the sun made
him shut his eyes. 陽光太強, 他只得閉
上眼睛. He has a strong desire to
meet you. 他很想見你. **4** (with reference to liquids) not weakened by having too much of something else in it
(指液體) 濃烈的: This drink is rather
strong. May I have some more water
in it? 這種飲料相當濃, 我可以多攙點水
嗎? strong tea 濃茶; strong coffee 濃
咖啡. **5** (with reference to persons)
healthy; well (指人) 健康的, 身體好的:
He is not a strong boy. 這男孩身體不
怎麼健壯. I hope to be strong again
after I have had a holiday. 我希望假
期 之 後 能 健 壯 如 初. (opp 反義詞
weak). **strongly** *adv* **strength**
[streŋθ] *nu* '**stronghold** fort 要塞, 堡
壘. '**strong-room** room built for
keeping money and other things of
value (存放貴重物品的) 保險庫: Most
banks have a strongroom. 大多數銀行
都有保險庫.

strove [strouv] past tense of **strive**.
strive 的過去式.

struck [strʌk] past tense and past participle of **strike**[1]. strike[1] 的過去式和過
去分詞.

structure [ˈstrʌktʃə*] **1** *nc* building
(esp. a large one) 建築物(尤指大型建
築物): They are studying the structure of the
atom. 他們在研究原子的結構.
structural *adj*.

struggle [ˈstrʌgl] *vi* fight violently; use
force or effort 搏鬥; 扎扎; 奮鬥; 同⋯鬥
爭: The two boys struggled on the
ground. 這兩個男孩在地上搏鬥. We
had to struggle against / with poverty
and disease. 我們得跟窮困和疾病作鬥
爭. Also 亦作 nc: their struggle for
freedom 他們爲爭取自由而作的鬥爭.

strum [strʌm] *vt / i* run the fingers over
the strings of a stringed musical instrument, often without skill 亂彈; 不
熟練地彈奏弦樂器: He was strumming
(on) his guitar. 他正在亂彈吉他. He
was strumming a popular tune on his
guitar. 他正用吉他亂彈着一支流行曲
調. *past* 過去式和過去分詞
strummed.

strut [strʌt] *vi* walk in a stiff, proud
manner 趾高氣揚地走; 高視闊步: He
struts about as if he owned the place.
他神氣活現地踱來踱去, 儼然是這裏的
主人. *past* 過去式和過去分詞
strutted.

stub [stʌb] *nc* short part of anything remaining after use 殘餘部份, 殘端: He
threw away the stub of his cigarette.
他扔掉了烟蒂. He was writing with
the stub of a pencil. 他在用鉛筆頭寫
字. stub of a cheque book i.e. smaller
piece remaining in the book after a
cheque has been torn out; counterfoil
支票簿存根. **stubby** *adj* short and
thick 粗短的.

stubble ['stʌbl] *nu* **1** short ends of the stalks of grain left standing after the grain has been harvested (莊稼收割後的) 殘茬. **2** short growth of hair on a man's face 短鬚, 鬍子茬: *He should shave the stubble off his face.* 他該把臉上的鬍子茬刮掉.

stubborn ['stʌbən] *adj* fixed in opinion; hard to move; refusing to yield 頑固的, 執拗的; 不易移動的; 倔強的: *He is a very stubborn man.* 他非常頑執. *The nuts and bolts on the wheel were stubborn.* 輪子上的螺母和螺栓不容易撐開; *stubborn fight* 頑強的搏鬥. **stubbornly** *adv* **stubbornness** *nu.*

stuck [stʌk] *past of* **stick**¹. stick¹ 的過去式和過去分詞.

stud¹ [stʌd] *nc* **1** type of movable button to fasten a collar to a shirt or to fasten the front of a shirt (用以固定硬領或襯衫前胸的) 活動扣. **2** nail with a large head 大頭釘: *Football boots have studs in the soles* i.e. to prevent the players slipping 足球鞋鞋底釘有大頭鞋釘. 即: 防滑. *The gate is covered with iron studs* i.e. to make it stronger 大門上佈滿了鐵的大頭釘. 即: 以使其更爲堅固. Also *v tr*: *Get your football boots studded.* 找人給你的足球鞋釘上鞋釘. *The sky was studded with stars* i.e. stars all over the sky like studs 天空佈滿了星星. 即: 繁星似到點綴着天空.

stud² [stʌd] *nc* number of horses kept for racing or breeding 爲賽馬或繁殖而飼養的馬羣. '**stud farm** place where horses are bred 種馬場.

student ['stjuːdnt] *nc* person who studies (esp. at a university or a college) 學生(尤指大學生) .Note 說明: *(Brit)* a person who studies at a school is called a *pupil.* *(US)* student is used with reference to schools as well as universities and colleges, and *pupil* is not often used. 在英國, 中、小學生叫 pupil; 而在美國, 中、小學生和大、專院校學生都叫 student, 不常用 pupil 一詞.

studio ['stjuːdiou] *nc* **1** room where an artist, sculptor or photographer works 畫室; 攝影室; 雕塑家的工作室. **2** room where films are made 電影攝影棚, 製片場. **3** room equipped for broadcasting radio and television programmes; room where gramophone records are made 廣播或電視節目演播室; 錄音室. *pl* 複數 **studios.**

studious ['stjuːdiəs] *adj* **1** fond of, having the habit of, studying 好學的, 用功的. **2** deliberate 故意的. **studiously** *adv.*

study¹ ['stʌdi] *nc / u* **1** work done, effort made, in order to learn (esp. from books) 讀書; 學習; 研究: *He is making a study of ancient history.* 他在研究古代史. *I shall not end my studies when I leave school.* 我離校後不會停止研究. **2** branch of learning 學科: *Biology is the study of living things.* 生物學是研究有生命的東西的學科. **3** room used for study 書房: *In this college each student has a study.* 這所大學裏每個學生都有一個書房.

study² ['stʌdi] *vt / i* **1** work, make an effort, to learn 讀書; 研究; 學習: *I am studying English.* 我在學英語. **2** give careful attention to 細看, 詳察: *He studied my face before he answered.* 他仔細看了看我的臉, 然後才回答. *This school studies the needs of all the children in it.* 這所學校認真考慮所有學童的需要. *past* 過去式和過去分詞 **studied. studied** *adj* on purpose; deliberate 故意的; 深思熟慮的: *studied bad manners* 故意沒有禮貌的舉止.

stuff¹ [stʌf] *nc / u* **1** substance 物質; 實

料: *Her coat is made of silk and other expensive stuffs.* 她的上衣是用絲綢和其他貴重料子做的. *Whisky is strong stuff.* 威士忌是烈性飲料. **2** something which is not well-known or cannot be named 不著名的東西; 說不出名稱的東西: *What stuff have you (got) in your bag?* 你的袋子裏有甚麼東西? *He brought me some stuff to read.* (*informal* in sense **2**) 他買來一些東西讓我看. (義 **2** 爲非正式)

stuff² [stʌf] *vt* **1** push tightly into; fill tightly 把…塞進; 把…裝滿: *He stuffed his clothes into the bag.* 他把衣服塞進袋子. *I stuffed the box with books.* 我在盒子裏裝滿了書. *I have a stuffed-up nose* (when someone has a cold in the nose and cannot breathe properly). 我患感冒, 鼻子塞住了. **2** fill the inside of birds, roasts of meat etc, before cooking them, with a special mixture of (usu. spicy) food 填餡, 往…裏塞佐料. **stuffing** *nu* material used for stuffing 餡, 填料; 填充物: *The stuffing came out of the torn pillow.* 枕頭破了, 裏面的東西散落出來. *We had stuffing with our turkey at Christmas.* 聖誕節時我們吃了餡的火鷄.

stuffy ['stʌfi] *adj* **1** (with reference to a room etc.) hot and without enough air (指房間等) 悶熱的, 窒悶的. **2** (with reference to a person) with no sense of humour (*informal* in sense **2**) (指人) 鬱悶的, 古板的; 一本正經的; 缺乏幽默感的 (義 **2** 爲非正式). **stuffiness** *nu*.

stumble ['stʌmbl] *vi* put one's foot down wrongly and almost fall 沒有踩穩, 幾乎絆倒, 絆跌: *I stumbled over the stone on the road.* 我被路上的石頭絆倒了. *The man stumbled and fell.* 那人絆了一跤跌倒了. **'stumbling block** something causing delay or dif-

ficulty 絆脚石; 障礙.

stump [stʌmp] *nc* **1** short part of a tree left above ground after the tree has fallen or been cut down 樹椿. **2** any short remaining part of something 殘餘部份: *The stump of a pencil* (用剩的) 鉛筆頭. *He has no arms, only stumps.* 他失去了雙臂, 只留下殘肢. Also 亦作 *vt* be too difficult for; defeat 難倒; 使不成功, 挫敗: *This problem stumped us.* (*informal*) 這個問題把我們難倒了. (非正式)

stun [stʌn] *vt* **1** make unconscious by a blow on the head (打在頭上) 把…打暈, 使昏迷. **2** shock; surprise greatly 使震驚; 使極爲驚奇: *The bad news stunned me.* 那壞消息使我目瞪口獃. *past* 過去式和過去分詞 **stunned.** **stunning** *adj* very surprising or attractive 極爲驚人的; 極富魅力的: *stunning news* 驚人的消息. *stunning blonde* 迷人的金髮女郎.

stung [stʌŋ] *past* of **sting²**. sting² 的過去式和過去分詞.

stunk [stʌŋk] *past* of **stink**. stink 的過去式和過去分詞.

stunt¹ [stʌnt] *vt* stop the growth 阻礙…的發育 (或成長): *The children have been stunted by disease.* 孩子們因病發育不良.

stunt² [stʌnt] *nc* something done deliberately to get attention or publicity 故意引人注目的行動, 花招, 噱頭.

stupefy ['stju:pifai] *vt* make foolish or unable to think properly 使茫然; 使發獃; 使恍惚: *The sudden loss of all our money stupefied us.* 我們的錢突然丢失, 這使我們驚獃了.

stupendous [stju:'pendəs] *adj* causing great admiration or surprise 了不起的; (大得) 驚人的: *The amount of work he did was stupendous.* 他做的工作多得使人吃驚.

stupid ['stju:pid] *adj* foolish; not intelligent 愚蠢的; 笨的: *Don't make stupid mistakes.* 別犯傻錯誤. *He is a stupid man who finds it difficult to understand the problem.* 他是個連這問題都難理解的傻瓜. **stupidly** *adv* **stupidity** [stju:'piditi] *nc / u.*

stupor ['stju:pə*] *nc / u* state of being almost unconscious because of illness, drugs or shock (因病、藥物或因震驚) 昏迷, 不省人事: *The drunk man was lying on the ground in a stupor.* 醉漢躺在地上不省人事.

sturdy ['stə:di] *adj* strong and well-built; determined; powerful 強健的; 堅定的; 有力的: *He is a sturdy boy.* 他是一個強健的男孩. *They put up a sturdy defence against a better team.* 他們堅定有力地防守強隊的進攻. **sturdily** *adv* **sturdiness** *nu.*

stutter ['stʌtə*] *vt / i* speak with difficulty, saying the same sounds again and again (e. g. P-p-pleasem-m-may I g-g-go) 口吃地說, 結結巴巴地說. Also 亦作*nc*: *He speaks with a stutter.* 他說話口吃.

sty[1] [stai] *nc* small building or enclosure in which pigs are kept (Often **pigsty**) 豬圈 (常作 pigsty). *pl* 複數 **sties.**

sty[2], **stye** [stai] *nc* red swelling on the part of the eyelid where the eyelashes are 瞼腺炎, 麥粒腫. *pl* 複數 **sties** or **styes.**

style [stail] *nc / u* **1** way of expressing thoughts or feelings etc in writing, speaking, painting etc. (esp. with reference to the way a particular writer, artist or period in history does so) (文章、談話、繪畫等的) 風格 (尤指某作家、畫家或某歷史時期的): *He has a style (of writing) like that of Dickens.* 他的文章與狄更斯的相似. *The*

house is built in the Victorian style. 這房子是依照維多利亞式建造的. **2** particular kind of appearance, behaviour etc; particular way of doing something 風度; 作風; 工作方式: *I like the style of your new coat.* 我喜歡你的新外衣的式樣. *They lived in Japan in Japanese style.* 他們住在日本, 過着日本式的生活. *He does things in style* i.e. in a grand, expensive way 他辦事體面堂皇. 即: 辦得豪華奢侈. **stylish** *adj* having style 時髦的, 式樣新穎的: *stylish clothes* i.e. smart, fashionable clothes 時新衣著, 即: 漂亮時髦的衣著. **stylishly** *adv.*

stylus ['stailəs] *nc* needle used for playing gramophone records (唱機的) 唱針.

suave [swɑ:v] *adj* pleasant and agreeable; with smooth manners 令人愉快的; 態度溫和的.

sub- [sʌb] *prefix* under; less than; almost (e. g. **subnormal; subtropical**) 在…之下, 低於; 少於; 幾乎 (如 subnormal 低於正常的; subtropical 亞熱帶的).

subconscious ['sʌb'kɔnʃəs] *adj, nu* see 見 **conscious.**

subdivide ['sʌbdi'vaid] *vt / i* divide again into more parts (把…) 再分. (把…) 細分: *The country is divided into provinces and the provinces are subdivided into districts.* 國分爲省, 省又細分爲地區. **subdivision** ['sʌbdiviʒən] *nc / u* result of being subdivided; act or state of subdividing 由再分分成的部份; 再分, 細分: *A district is the subdivision of a province.* 地區是由省分而成的.

subdue [səb'dju:] *vt* conquer; bring under control 征服; 使屈從; 壓制: *The country was subdued by the enemy.* 該國已被敵人征服. **subdued** *adj* less strong, bright etc. 緩和的, 溫和的; 柔和的: *They spoke in subdued voices.* 他們柔聲細語. *The colours of the dress are subdued.* 這件衣服顏色柔和.

subject¹ [sʌbdʒikt] *adj* under the control of somebody else 從屬的, 受支配的: *the subject people of the colonies.* 殖民地裏受統治的人民. **subject to** *adj / adv* likely to get; according to; conditional on 易受…的, 常患…的; 依據, 按照; 以…爲條件的, 視…而定的: *He is subject to headaches.* 他常患頭痛. *We are all subject to the rules of the school.* 我們都應應遵守學校的規則. *He will do it subject to his father's consent.* 他須經他父親同意才能那樣做.

subject² [ˈsʌbdʒikt] *nc* 1 member of a country 國民, 臣民: *They are British subjects.* 他們是英國國民. 2 something which is spoken or written about, or studied 主題, 題目; 話題; 科目. *The subject of their conversation was the war.* 他們談話的話題是戰爭. *He has written about / on many subjects in his books.* 他在他的著作裏寫到了許多問題. *In a primary school the main subjects are reading, writing and arithmetic.* 小學的主要科目是閱讀、寫字和算術. 3 somebody / something which is used for an experiment, operation or research 用於實驗、手術或研究的人/物: *The new drug was given to hundreds of subjects before it was finally approved.* 這種新藥在最後得到批准之前曾分發給幾百名病人試用. 4 somebody / something which is the cause of a feeling or action (感情或行動的) 原因, 理由: *I won't be the subject of their jokes.* 我不願意成爲他們的笑料. *Human suffering is always a subject for pity.* 人

間疾苦總是一件值得憐憫的事. 5 (grammar) word or words in a sentence about which the verb tells something (e. g. in the sentence *John gave me a book, John* is the subject, *me* and *a book* are objects) (語法) 主語 (如在 John gave me a book 一句中, John 是主語, me 和 a book 是賓語).

subject³ [səbˈdʒekt] *vt* 1 put under control; conquer 統治, 支配; 征服; 使隸屬: *This country was once subjected to foreign rule.* 這個國家一度被外國統治. 2 cause to happen to 使受到, 使遭遇: *He subjected us to a very difficult test.* 他讓我們經受一次十分困難的考試. *They will subject themselves to criticism if they make any more mistakes.* 要是他們再犯錯誤, 他們將受到批評. **subjection** *nu* act or state of subjecting or being subjected to 統治, 支配; 征服; 服從; 隸屬: *Their aim was the subjection of all their enemies.* 他們旨在征服一切敵人. *This country was held / kept in subjection until it gained independence.* 該國獨立前處於被統治地位.

subjective [səbˈdʒektiv] *adv* giving the thoughts or feelings of one particular person 主觀的: *The writer of the book has a very subjective view of modern life* i.e. it is a personal view which may not agree with the facts. 該書作者對現代生活持非常主觀的觀點. 即: 這種個人觀點可能跟事實不符. *(opp* 反義詞 **objective**). **subjectively** *adv.*

subjunctive [sʌbˈdʒʌŋktiv] *adj* of the subjunctive mood which expresses a condition or wish 虛擬語氣的. Also 亦作 *nc* subjunctive mood (e.g. in the sentence *If you were a king, you would live in a palace, were* and *would* are subjunctives or are in the subjunctive mood) 虛擬語氣(如在 If you were a king, you would live in a palace 一句中, were 和 would 是虛擬語氣).

sublet ['sʌb'let] *vt / i* let to somebody property which one has oneself rented from a landlord 轉租, 分租(房屋或土地). *past* 過去式和過去分詞 **subletted** or **sublet.**

sublime [sə'blaim] *adj* **1** very noble; causing great admiration 崇高的; 高貴的; 絕妙的; 壯美的; 雄偉的: *The view from the mountain was sublime.* 登山俯瞰, 景色壯美. **2** astonishing 驚人的: *He has a sublime confidence in himself.* 他有着令人驚訝的自信心. **sublimely** *adv: He is sublimely confident.* 他驚人地自信.

submarine [sʌbmə'ri:n] *nc* type of ship which can travel below the surface of the sea 潛水艇.

submerge [səb'mə:dʒ] *vt / i* go under, or put under, water or other liquid (使)沉沒; 浸沒, 淹沒; 潛入水中: *The crocodile submerged when it saw the boat.* 鱷魚見到船就潛入水中. *He submerged his hands in warm water.* 他把雙手浸在溫水中.

submit [səb'mit] *vt / i* **1** yield; give in (使)服從; (使)屈服; 投降: *After being defeated they submitted to the enemy.* 他們被打敗後向敵人投降. *The enemy made them submit.* 敵人迫使他們投降. **2** ask to be considered; bring to somebody's attention so that it may be considered, approved etc. 提交, 提出; 認爲; 主張: *You must submit your request to the committee.* 你必須向該委員會提出請求. *He submits that he is not to blame.* 他認爲這不是他的過錯. *pres part* 現在分詞 **submitting.** *past* 過去式和過去分詞 **submitted. sub-**

mission *nc / u* **1** act of yielding 屈服, 降服, 歸順: *The enemy forced them into submission.* 敵人迫使他們屈服. **2** argument for somebody to consider 意見, 看法, 建議: *It is his submission that he is not to blame.* 他的看法是, 這不是他的過錯. **submissive** *adj* ready to yield; obedient 服從的; 順從的.

subnormal ['sʌb'nɔ:ml] *adj* below normal 低於正常的; 遜常的; 低能的: *subnormal intelligence* 智力低能.

subordinate [sə'bɔ:dinət] *adj* lower in rank or importance 下級的; 次要的: *In the army a captain is subordinate to a major.* 在陸軍裏上尉低於少校. *This is our main aim; all the other aims are subordinate to it.* 這是我們的主要目標, 與之相比其他目標都是次要的. Also 亦作 *nc* person who is lower in rank 部屬, 部下; 下級職員. Also 亦作 [sə'bɔ:dineit] *vt.*

subpoena [sə'pi:nə] *nc* order made to someone to appear before a judge as a witness (法律)傳票. Also 亦作 *vt* make such an order (用傳票)傳喚, 傳訊.

subscribe [səb'skraib] *vt / i* **1** give, promise to give, with other persons, money for a special purpose 捐款; 捐助, 認捐(款項): *We have subscribed £10 to the fund for poor children.* 我們向救濟貧困兒童基金捐款10英鎊. **2** order and pay regularly for a newspaper, magazine etc for a period of time 預訂, 訂閱(報紙、雜誌等): *I subscribe to one daily newspaper and one weekly magazine.* 我訂閱一種日報和一種週刊. **3** agree with; support 同意, 贊成; 贊助: *I cannot subscribe to the belief that the government is always wrong.* 我不能贊同認爲政府一貫錯誤的想法. **subscriber** *nc* **1** person

who subscribes 捐款者, 贊助者; 訂户.
2 person who rents a telephone from
a telephone company 電話用户. **sub-
scription** [səb'skrip∫ən] *nc / u* **1**
money which is subscribed 認捐額; 贊
助的款項, 訂閱費: *Have they paid
their subscriptions to the fund for poor
children?* 他們向救濟貧困兒童基金認
捐的款項付款了没有? **2** act of sub-
scribing or being subscribed 認捐; 贊
助; 訂閱: *They hope to get the rest of
the money for the new library by sub-
scription.* 他們希望通過認捐募集建築
新圖書館所需的其餘資金.

subsequent ['sʌbsikwənt] *adj* happening later 隨後的, 後來的: *subsequent
events* 後來發生的事件. **subsequent-
ly** *adv*.

subside [səb'said] *vi* **1** fall or sink lower 沉降; 下陷, 凹陷; 消退: *The river
subsided when the rain stopped.* 雨停
後河水消退. **2** become quieter; grow
less 平靜, 平息; 減退: *The wind has
subsided.* 風平息了. *His anger soon
subsided.* 他的憤怒很快就平息了.
subsidence ['sʌbsidns] *nc / u* act or
state of subsiding 沉降; 塌陷; 消退; 平
息.

subsidiary [sʌb'sidiəri] *adj* giving help
or support to somebody / something
more important; secondary 輔助的; 補
助的; 次要的; 副的; 附屬的: *My work
as an assistant is subsidiary to the
work of the senior staff.* 作爲助手, 我
的工作是輔助高級職員. *study French
with German as a subsidiary subject*
學法語而把德語作爲次要課程. Also
亦作 *nc* person / thing which is subsidiary 輔助者; 輔助物; 附屬機構.

subsidy ['sʌbsidi] *nc* money paid (esp.
by a government) to help an industry
or another country to keep prices up
or down etc. (尤指政府向企業或別國

提供以調節物價等的) 補助金, 津貼; 資
助: *In Britain and the USA, farmers
receive subsidies from the government
to grow certain crops.* 在英國和美國,
農民種植某些作物得到政府的補助金.
subsidize ['sʌbsidaiz] *vt* give a subsidy to 發補助金或津貼給…; 資助.

subsistence [səb'sistns] *nu* way of
staying alive 生存; 生計.

subsonic [sʌb'sɔnik] *adj* of a speed
less than the speed of sound i. e. less
than 750 miles per hour 亞音速的, 即:
每小時少於750英里的. *(opp* 反義詞
supersonic)

substance ['sʌbstns] *nc / u* **1** particular
type of matter; what something is
made of 物質: *Carbon is a substance
found in many forms* (e. g. diamonds,
coal and soot). 碳是一種以多種形式存
在的物質 (如金剛石, 煤和煤烟). **2**
most important matter or point of a
book, speech, discussion etc. 本旨, 主
旨; 要義; 真義: *The substance of his
speech was that the country was in
danger.* 他講話的要旨是該國處境危
險. **3** wealth 財富, 資産: *He is a man
of substance.* 他資産雄厚. **4** strength;
importance 力量; 重要性: *There is not
much substance in what he says* i. e.
what he says is not true or not important 他説的話無足輕重. 即: 他説的話
不真實或不重要. **substantial** [səb-
'stæ∫l] *adj* made of good material;
solid; strong; large 質地好的; 結實的;
堅固的; 大的: *a substantial meal* i.e.
good food and plenty of it 豐盛的一
餐; 即: 食物又好又多. *(opp* 反義詞 **in-
substantial**). **substantially** *adv*.

substandard ['sʌb'stændəd] *adj* less
good than usual or than the average
標準以下的; 不合格的; 不够平均水準
的.

substantiate [səb'stæn∫ieit] *vt* bring

evidence to show that something is true 證實, 確證: *He had with him a letter from his doctor to substantiate his statement that he had been ill.* 他有醫生的信件證明如他所說他確實病了.

substitute ['sʌbstitjuːt] *nc* somebody / something which takes the place of somebody / something else 代替者; 代用品: *Because he is ill, I am playing as his substitute in the football match.* 因爲他病了, 我作爲替補他的隊員參加足球比賽. Also 亦作 *vt / i* become or make a substitute 作代替者; 用…代替: *I am substituting for him in the football match.* 我頂替他參加足球比賽. *Let us substitute x for y in the equation.* 在該方程式中, 設以 x 代替 y. **substitution** [sʌbsti'tjuːʃən] *nc / u*.

substrata [sʌb'strɑːtə, sʌb'streitə] *pl* of **substratum**. substratum 的複數.

substratum [sʌb'strɑːtəm, sʌb-'streitəm] *nc* **1** level lying below another 下面一層, 底層: *Beneath the sandy soil there was a substratum of clay ten feet thick.* 在沙質土下面有一層十英尺厚的粘土. **2** basis; foundation 根據; 基礎: *The story has a substratum of truth.* 這故事有事實根據.

subtend [səb'tend] *vt* be opposite to 對着; 對向: *The side AC subtends the angle ABC.* 斜邊 AC 對着角 ∠ABC.

subtense [səb'tens] *nc* (geometry) the chord of an arc or any other subtending line (幾何) 弦; 角的對邊.

subterfuge ['sʌbtəfjuːdʒ] *nc / u* something done to avoid difficulty or trouble; false excuse; trick 遁詞, 託詞; 欺騙; 詭計: *He says he is ill, but it is really a subterfuge to stay in bed instead of going to school.* 他的稱病實際上是一種臥床逃學的藉口.

subterranean [sʌbtə'reiniən] *adj* under

the ground 地下的.

subtitle ['sʌbtaitl] *nc* **1** extra title of a book (usu. one which explains more) (書籍的) 副標題. **2** writing shown on a film to explain the story or to translate the dialogue (電影的) 字幕: *We saw a French film with English subtitles.* 我們看了一部有英文字幕的法國電影.

subtle ['sʌtl] *adj* **1** difficult to explain or understand 微妙的, 難以捉摸的: *There is a subtle difference between the two words.* 這兩個詞有細微的差別. **2** clever and cunning 敏銳的; 狡猾的: *They are using subtle methods to get what they want.* 他們使用詭計以求得到他們所要的東西. **subtly** *adv* **subtlety** *nc / u*.

subtract [səb'trækt] *vt* take one number from another to find the difference 減去, 扣除: *If you subtract 4 from 6 you get 2.* 6 減 4 得 2. **subtraction** *nc / u* act of subtracting 減去, 扣除; 減法: *The difference is found by subtraction.* 用減法得出差額.

subtropical ['sʌb'trɔpikl] *adj* near the tropics; almost tropical 亞熱帶的.

suburb ['sʌbəːb] *nc* (often *pl*) part of a city which is outside its centre (usu. the part where people live) (常用複數) 郊區, 市郊 (通常指市郊住宅區). **suburban** [sə'bəːbən] *adj* of or in a suburb 郊區的, 市郊的. **suburbia** [sə'bəːbiə] *nu* **1** suburban areas 郊區. **2** way people live in a suburb (often supposed to be lacking in good taste and culture) 郊區居民的習俗 (常被認爲粗俗, 土氣, 缺乏教養等): *He hates suburbia and all it stands for.* 他痛恨市郊習俗及其所代表的一切.

subvert [səb'vəːt] *vt* overthrow something (e. g. a government or set of beliefs) by destroying people's faith or confidence in it 顛覆(政府)；破壞(信念). **subversive** [səb'vəsiv] *adj* likely to subvert 顛覆性的，起破壞作用的: *He was arrested for making a subversive speech to the soldiers.* 他因向士兵作策反演說而遭拘捕. **subversion** [səb'və:ʃən] *nu.*

subway ['sʌbwei] *nc* **1** underground passage (usu. so that people can pass from one side of a very busy street to the other) (過街)地道，行人隧道. **2** (mainly US) underground railway (*Brit* 英 **underground**) (主要用於美)地下鐵道.

succeed [sək'si:d] *vt / i* **1** do what one has wished to do; achieve an aim 成功，達到目的: *The plan has succeeded.* 這個計劃成功了. *He succeeded in (passing) the examination.* 他考試及格. **2** come immediately after and take the place of 接替，繼任: *Mr Jones will succeed Mr Brown as headmaster.* 瓊斯先生將接替布朗先生出任校長. *The Queen succeeded her father to the throne.* 女王繼承其父王的王位.

success [sək'ses] *nc / u* getting what one has wished 成功: *We are very pleased with your success in the examination.* 我們對於你考試及格感到很高興. *I tried to meet him but without success.* 我想跟他見面但是沒見到. *The school had several successes in the games* i.e. several of its pupils won 該校在運動會上有幾項獲勝. 即: 該校有幾名學生獲勝. **successful** *adj* (*opp* 反義詞 **unsuccessful**). **successfully** *adv.*

succession [sək'seʃən] *nc / u* **1** act of following one after the other; number of persons / things following one after the other 連續，接連; 接二連三的人或事: *Last week we had a succession of*

visitors. 上星期我們家的客人絡繹不絕. **2** right to take the place of somebody and get his title, rank, property etc. 繼承權: *The eldest son has succession to his father's property.* 長子有繼承其父親財產的權利. **successive** *adj* coming one after the other 連續的，接連的: *on successive days* 連續幾天.

successor [sək'sesə*] *nc* somebody / something which comes immediately after and takes the place of somebody / something else 繼承人；繼任者；後繼的人或事: *Mr Jones is the headmaster's successor.* 瓊斯先生是繼任校長.

succinct [sək'siŋkt] *adj* expressed clearly in few words 簡明的，簡潔的.

succulent ['sʌkjulnt] *adj* full of juice 多汁的.

succumb [sə'kʌm] *vt / i* yield; die 屈服，屈從；死: *At last he succumbed to our desire to go.* 最後他依照我們的要求去了. *The man succumbed to the injuries he received in the accident.* 那個人因在事故中受傷而死去.

such [sʌtʃ] *adj / determiner / pron* **1** (with **as**) of the same kind, degree or quality (與 **as** 連用)這樣的，這種的；如此的. *Note* 說明: in the examples which follow the position of *such* is before *a* but after *all, many, no* and *some.* 在下列例子中 *such* 的位置在 *a* 之前, 在 all, many, no 和 some 之後. *Such books (as these) are useful.* 這一類書很有用. *Such a book is useful.* 這樣的一本書很有用. *All such books are useful.* 這一類書都很有用. *I have read many such books.* 我唸過不少這樣的書. *No such books are useful.* 這類書都無用處. *He bought a dictionary or some such book.* 他買了一本詞典或類似的書. *Boys such as John and James are very friendly.* 像約翰和詹姆

士這樣的男孩是很友善的. *Such boys as John and James are very friendly.* 像約翰和詹姆士這樣的男孩是很友善的. **2** so much; so great; so good etc. 如此的 (多, 大, 好等): *He is such a kind man.* 他如此和藹可親. *We have never seen such a big town.* 我們從未見過這麼大的城鎮. **3** of the kind already mentioned; this or that; these or those 上述這一類的; 這或那; 這些或那些: *Such is my wish.* 這就是我的希望. *Such was the way he spoke to us.* 他就是用這種方式對我們說話的. **4** somebody / something already mentioned; this or that; these or those 上述的人/事物; 這或那; 這些或那些; *I haven't much money but you can use such as I have.* 我沒有多少錢, 但是只要是我的錢, 你都可以用. *He is my father and as such can tell me what to do.* 他是我父親, 以父親的身份, 他可以告訴我應該做甚麼. **suchlike** *adj* of that kind 那類的: *He admires football players and suchlike people. (informal)* 他羨慕足球選手和那類的人. (非正式). **such-and-such** *adj* this or that; not definite 這種那種的; 某某: *If he arranges to come on such-and-such a day we shall see him. (informal)* 要是他安排在某一天來, 我們將和他見面. (非正式).

suck [sʌk] *vt / i* **1** draw liquid into the mouth by using the lips and tongue; draw liquid from 吮吸; 吸: *He sucked the juice from the orange.* 他吮吸橘子的汁. *I sucked the blood from my finger.* 我吸掉手指上的血. *The baby was sucking its bottle.* 嬰兒在吸奶瓶. **2** hold and move about in the mouth 吮食; 舔食: *You must not suck sweets in class.* 你不能在上課時吃糖果.

sucker [ˈsʌkə*] *nc* **1** organ by which some animals can stick to something

(動物的) 吸盤. **2** device made of rubber, leather etc which sticks to something by suction (橡膠、皮革等做的) 吸板. **3** person who is easily cheated *(informal in sense 3)* 容易受騙的人 (義 3 爲非正式).

suction [ˈsʌkʃən] *nu* **1** act of sucking or drawing in (caused by taking air or liquid out of a container so that another gas or liquid comes in to replace it) 吸引, 吸入; 空吸 (抽掉某容器內的空氣或液體以使另一氣體或液體流入): *Many pumps work by suction.* 許多泵靠空吸工作. **2** force which makes one thing stick to another when the air between is taken away (抽去兩物之間的空氣後所產生的) 吸力.

sudden [ˈsʌdn] *adj* happening without warning; done quickly 突然的, 驟然的 迅速的; 即刻的: *His sudden death shocked everybody.* 他的突然死亡使大家震驚. *She gave a sudden smile.* 她驟然一笑. **suddenly** *adv* **suddenness** *nu* **all of a sudden** see 見 **all.**

suds [sʌdz] *npl* masses of bubbles caused by a mixture of soap, air and water 肥皂泡沫.

sue [su:] *vt / i* bring a claim or case against somebody in a court of law 控告, 控訴, 告狀: *If you don't pay me the money, I'll sue you.* 要是你不給我錢, 我要告你.

suede [sweid] *nu* type of soft leather with a dull surface 表面不光亮的軟皮革. Also 亦作 *adj: He was wearing suede shoes.* 他穿着麂皮皮鞋.

suffer [ˈsʌfə*] *vt / i* **1** feel pain; meet trouble or loss 受痛苦; 蒙受苦難或損失: *We could see that the injured man was suffering.* 我們可以看到受傷的人十分痛苦. *If you are lazy, only you yourself will suffer.* 你要是懶惰, 受苦的只能是你自己. **2** bear or endure something unpleasant. 經受(不愉快的事情): *The army suffered great losses in the battle.* 這次戰門中，軍隊傷亡慘重. *They have suffered hunger and thirst.* 他們忍受飢渴之苦. **3** be patient with; tolerate 對…有耐心; 忍受, 容忍: *Their parents refused to suffer their bad manners.* 他們的父母親不能容忍他們的無禮. **suffering** *nc / u* pain or distress 痛苦; 苦難: *the sufferings of the wounded men* 傷員們所受的痛苦; *relieve pain and suffering* 減輕痛苦. **sufferer** *nc* person who suffers 受難者, 受苦者.

suffice [sə'fais] *vt / i* be enough; satisfy 足夠; 滿足: *If the weather is cold, your thin coat will not suffice. (formal)* 要是天氣冷, 你的衣服單薄, 不足保暖. (正式). **sufficient** [sə'fiʃənt] *adj* enough 足夠的, 充分的: *Is £5 sufficient?* 五英鎊夠了嗎? *He has sufficient knowledge for the work.* 他有做這工作的足夠知識. *(opp* 反義詞 **insufficient**). **sufficiently** *adv.*

suffix ['sʌfiks] *nc* letter or group of letters added to the end of a word (e. g. in the word *playful*, *ful* is a suffix) 後綴, 詞尾(如 *playful* 一詞的 *ful* 是後綴). *pl* 複數 **suffixes** . *(opp* 反義詞 **prefix***).*

suffocate ['sʌfəkeit] *vt / i* kill or die through lack of air (使)窒息, (把…)悶死: *He suffocated the sleeping man with a pillow.* 他用枕頭把正睡着的那個人悶死. *Three children suffocated when the house caught fire.* 房子着火時有三名兒童窒息致死. **suffocation** [sʌfə'keiʃən] *nu.*

sugar ['ʃugə*] *nu* sweet substance used in food and drink 食糖: *Do you take sugar in your tea?* 您的茶裏要放糖嗎? Also 亦作 *vt* make sweet with sugar 加糖使甜. **sugary** *adj* of sugar; very

sweet 含糖的; 甜的. **sugar beet** type of root vegetable from which sugar is obtained 甜菜. '**sugar cane** type of tall plant from which sugar is obtained 甘蔗.

suggest [sə'dʒest] *vt* **1** put forward an idea or plan (for somebody to consider) 建議, 提出(意見或計劃): *I suggest that we tell him.* 我建議我們告訴他. *He suggested London for their meeting.* 他建議他們在倫敦相聚. **2** cause somebody to believe or think something 使人認爲; 使人想起: *His large house suggests wealth* i.e. it makes people think he is wealthy. 他的寬敞住宅使人們認爲他很富有. *Another way to find out has suggested itself to me* i.e. has come into my mind and made me think. 我想到了另一種查明真相的辦法. **suggestion** *nc / u* **1** act of suggesting; what is suggested 建議; 意見: *Any suggestions for the concert?* 對於音樂會有甚麼建議? *We did it on / at his suggestion.* 我們是根據他的建議而做的. **2** small sign; hint 細微的跡象; 暗示: *There was a suggestion of anger in his voice.* 他説話的聲音裏透露怒意. **suggestive** *adj* **1** causing somebody to think or believe something 引起聯想的; 提示性的: *Your idea is a very suggestive one.* 你的想法很有啓發性. *Their clothes were suggestive of poverty* i.e. their clothes made people think that they were poor. 他們的衣着使人們認爲他們很窮. **2** causing somebody to think about something indecent 猥褻的, 挑逗色情的: *He made suggestive remarks to the ladies.* 他用挑逗性的話語調戲女士們.

suicide ['su:isaid] **1** *nc* person who kills himself intentionally 自殺者. **2** *nc / u* act of doing so 自殺: *In some coun* *tries suicide is a crime.* 在有些國家裏自殺是一種犯罪行爲. *The number of suicides has increased.* 自殺數字有所增加. *He committed suicide when he was quite young.* 他很年青時就自殺身亡. **3** *nu* act which causes disaster to oneself 自毀行爲; 自取滅亡: *If he does this it will be professional suicide* i.e. he will ruin his professional career. 要是他這樣做, 等於在事業上自毀前途. 即: 他將在事業上自毀前途. **suicidal** [su:i'saidl] *adj.*

suit¹ [su:t] *nc* **1** set of clothes made of the same material 一套衣服: *man's suit* i.e. jacket and trousers, with or without a waistcoat 男裝, 即: 上衣和褲子, 有時包括背心; *woman's suit* i.e. jacket and skirt 女裝, 即: 上衣和裙子. **2** claim made in a court of law; legal case 起訴, 訴訟; 訟案: *They brought a suit against him for not paying the money.* 他們控告他不付錢. **3** one of the four sets of playing cards. 同花色的一組紙牌: *In a pack of cards there are four suits: clubs, diamonds, hearts and spades.* 一副紙牌有四種花色: 梅花、方塊、紅桃和黑桃. **suitor** *nc* man who asks to marry a woman (f.) 向女子求婚的男子(舊式). **'suitcase** type of flat container with handle for holding clothes when travelling 手提箱, 衣箱. **follow suit** do the same as has been done already 效法, 照着做: *We thanked the chairman. The others followed suit* i.e. they also thanked him after we did. 我們向主席表示感謝, 其他人也照着做. 即: 其他人隨後也感謝主席.

suit² [su:t] *vt / i* **1** be satisfactory; please; be fitted to 滿足; 合⋯之意; 適合: *Will it suit you if we go early?* 要是我們早些動身, 對你合適嗎? *The changes did not suit his plans.* 這些變

動不合他的計劃. **2** improve the appearance; look well 使顯得好看; 相稱, 相配: *Long hair does not suit him.* 他留長頭髮不好看. *You shouldn't wear red because it doesn't suit you.* 你不該穿大紅的衣服, 你穿紅色不好看.
suitable *adj* well fitted for the purpose 合適的, 適宜的: *Have you a suitable book for a young child?* 你有適合幼童讀的書嗎? *Eleven o'clock will be suitable (for us).* 十一點鐘(對我們)很適合. (*opp* 反義詞 **unsuitable**). **suitably** *adv* **suitability** [su:tə'biliti] *nu*

suite [swi:t] *nc* **1** number of things used together 套; 組: *suite of furniture* i.e. set of furniture for one room 一套傢具, 即: 一個房間裏的成套傢具; *bedroom suite* i.e. set of furniture for a bedroom 一套臥室用的傢具. *suite of rooms* i.e. set of rooms for one or two persons 一套房間, 即: 一、兩人居住的套房. *hotel suite* i.e. set of rooms in a hotel with a private sitting room and bathroom etc as well as a bedroom 旅館套房, 即: 包括臥室、獨用起居室和盥洗室的一套旅館房間. **2** number of musical compositions joined together (音樂)組曲.

suitor ['su:tə*] *nc* see 見 **suit¹**.

sulk [sʌlk] *vi* (usu. with reference to children) show one's bad temper by looking angry and refusing to speak (通常指兒童)生悶氣, 慍怒. **sulky** *adj.*

sullen ['sʌlən] *adj* **1** (with reference to persons) bad-tempered and saying nothing (指人)悶悶不樂的, 愁眉不展的. **2** (with reference to things) gloomy; dark (指事物)陰沉的; 陰暗的: *sullen weather* 陰沉的天氣.

sulphate ['sʌlfeit] (US 美 sulfate) *nc / u* salt of sulphuric acid 硫酸鹽; 硫酸酯: *ammonium sulphate* 硫酸銨; *calcium*

sulphate 硫酸鈣.

sulphide ['sʌlfaid] (US 美 sulfide) *nc* / *u* compound of sulphur and another element 硫化物; 硫醚: *hydrogen sulphide* 硫化氫.

sulphur ['sʌlfə*] *nu* yellow substance which burns with a blue flame and has a strong smell (S) 硫, 硫磺. **sulphuric acid** [sʌl'fjuərik'æsid] type of very strong acid 硫酸.

sultan ['sʌltn] *nc* Muslim prince or ruler 蘇丹(伊斯蘭國家的君主或統治者).

sultana [sʌl'tɑːnə] *nc* 1 wife of a sultan 蘇丹之妻. 2 type of small dried fruit used in cooking 無核小葡萄乾.

sultry ['sʌltri] *adj* (with reference to the weather) hot, damp and uncomfortable (指天氣)悶熱的, 酷熱的.

sum [sʌm] *nc* 1 full amount obtained by adding 總數, 總和. 2 amount of money 金額: *He paid a large sum for his house.* 他花了一大筆錢買房子. 3 work of adding, subtracting etc; problem in arithmetic 計算, 運算, 做算術; 算術題: *My sums were not correct.* 我算得不對. *We do sums first period every morning.* 每天上午第一節課我們做算術. Also 亦作 *vt* / *i* (with up) give the main points (與 up 連用) 總結, 概述, 舉出要點: *At the end of the meeting the chairman summed up (the opinions of the members).* 會議結束前主席(就大家的意見)作了總結. *past* 過去式和過去分詞 **summed.** '**sum** '**total** full total or amount 全部, 總共. **summing-'up** *nc* act of giving the main points (esp. in a court of law) (尤指在法庭裏)總結, 概述: *In his summing-up, the judge explained what the evidence had shown.* 法官在概述中闡述了已經出示的證據. *pl* 複數 **summings-up.**

summary ['sʌməri] *adj* short; done quickly 概括的; 即刻的: *He gave a summary description of the country.* 他對這個國家作了概要的描繪. *Our headmaster believes in summary punishment* i.e. punishment given quickly, without delay 我們的校長主張即刻處分. 即: 毫不拖延地進行處分. Also 亦作 *nc* short statement giving the main points of something longer 摘要, 概要: *We had to write a summary of the chapter.* 我們得寫出這一章的概要. **summarize** *vt* give a summary of the 概述, 總結.

summer ['sʌmə*] *nc* hottest season of the year in countries in the tropics 夏季, 夏天: *We go on holiday in (the) summer.* 我們夏天去度假. Also 亦作 *adj*: *summer holidays* 暑假. **summery** *adj* like summer; suitable for summer 如夏天的; 適合夏天的. **summerhouse** small hut in a garden used for sitting in during the summer (花園裏的)涼亭.

summit ['sʌmit] *nc* 1 highest point (esp. of a mountain) 頂點, 絕頂, 巔峯 (尤指山頂). 2 (usu. as *adj*) highest level of government (通常用作 adj) 政府首腦級(的), 最高級(的): *There will be a summit conference in London next week.* 下星期將在倫敦舉行最高級會議.

summon ['sʌmən] *vt* order to be present; send for 傳喚; 召喚, 召集: *I have been summoned to give evidence in court* i.e. in a court of law. 我被傳喚出庭作證. *The headmaster summoned them to his office.* 校長召集他們到他的辦公室. **summon something up** find by oneself without any help 鼓起, 喚起, 振作起: *I hope he will summon up enough courage to ask her.* 我希望他能鼓起勇氣去邀請她.

summons ['sʌmənz] *nc* order to be present in a court of law 傳票; 傳喚: *He has received a summons for careless driving.* 他因駕車不慎受到傳喚. *pl* 複數 **summonses.** Also 亦作 *vt* send a summons to 傳…到法庭; 發傳票給; 傳喚: *He was summoned for careless driving.* 他因駕車不慎被傳喚.

sump [sʌmp] *nc* lowest part of an engine where the oil collects (發動機底部的)油盤, 貯油槽.

sumptuous [ˈsʌmptjuəs] *adj* costing a large amount of money; very splendid 奢侈的; 豪華的: *He lives in a sumptuous house.* 他住在豪華的住宅裏.

sun [sʌn] *nc* **1** (with *the*) the one bright body in the sky which gives heat and light to the earth, and round which the earth travels (與 *the* 連用)太陽. **2** (with *the*) heat and light from the sun (與 *the* 連用)日光, 陽光: *They were lying in the sun.* 他們在躺着曬太陽. *You should take your child out of the sun.* 不要讓陽光曬到你的孩子. **sunny** *adj* **1** warm and bright because of the sun 向陽的, 陽光充足的: *This is a sunny place to have a rest.* 這地方向陽, 可以在此休息一下. **2** cheerful 歡樂的; 愉快的: *He has a sunny nature.* 他生性開朗. **'sunbathe** *vi* expose one's body to the sun 作日光浴. **sunbathing** *nu* **'sunbeam** ray of light from the sun (一道)日光, 陽光. **'sunburn** *nu* red, painful skin caused by too much sun 曬焦; 曬斑. **sunburned, sunburnt** *adj.* **'sundial** device which shows the time of day from the shadow made by the sun 日晷. **'sundown** (mainly *US*) time when the sun sets (主要用於美)日落時分. **'sunflower** type of plant with a large flower 向日葵. **'sunglasses** spectacles with dark glass etc to protect the eyes from the bright light of the sun

太陽眼鏡, 墨鏡. **'sunlight** light of the sun 日光, 陽光. **'sunrise** rising of the sun; time when the sun rises 日出; 黎明, 拂曉: *It was a beautiful sunrise.* 這是美麗的日出景色. *We left home at sunrise.* 我們黎明時動身. **'sunset** setting of the sun; time when the sun sets 日落; 黃昏. **'sunshine** light of the sun 日光, 陽光. **'sunstroke** type of illness caused by being too much in the sun 中暑, 日射病. **'suntan** darkening of the skin seen in people with white skin, caused by exposure to the sun 曬黑的膚色: *get a good suntan* 皮膚曬得黑黑的.

sundae [ˈsʌndei] *nc* ice cream with fruit or nuts on top 新地, 聖代(加水果或果仁的冰淇淋). *pl* 複數 **sundaes.**

Sunday [ˈsʌndi] *n* first day of the week in the Christian calendar 星期日, 禮拜日.

sundries [ˈsʌndriz] *npl* sundry items; miscellaneous thing 雜項; 雜事; 雜物, 雜貨.

sundry [ˈsʌndri] *adj* separate; several 各別的; 各種的: *sundry things* i.e. small things which are not worth mentioning separately 零星雜物, 即: 沒有必要一一列舉的小件東西. *pl* 複數 **sundries. all and sundry** all different types; everybody 各種各樣的人; 所有的人: *All and sundry agree.* 所有的人都同意.

sung [sʌŋ] past part of **sing.** sing 的過去分詞.

sunk [sʌŋk] past part of **sink.** sink 的過去分詞.

sunken [ˈsʌŋkən] *adj* **1** below the surface of water; under the sea etc. 水面下的; 沉沒的: *sunken treasure* 沉在水底的財寶. **2** below the level of something else 低於另一平面的; 凹陷的: *sunken garden* 低地公園. see 見

sink.

sunny ['sʌni] *adj* see 見 **sun.**

sup¹ [sʌp] *vt / i* eat the evening meal; take supper; give a supper to or for 吃晚飯; 給與晚飯; 供應…晚餐: *sup on noodles / bread* 吃麵條 / 麵包當晚餐.

sup² [sʌp] *vt / i* drink (liquid) in small mouthfuls; drink a small mouthful; 喝一小口, *supping his beer* 啜飲啤酒. Also 亦作 *nc* small mouthful (of liquid) 一啜; 一小口; 少量: *have a sup of soup* 喝一小口湯.

super¹ ['supə*] *adj* very good; splendid. (informal) 極好的; 頂呱呱的. (非正式).

super-² ['supə*] *prefix* above; beyond; greater than usual (e.g. **superhuman**; **supersonic**) 在…之上; 超; 超過 (如 **superhuman** 超人的; **supersonic** 超音速的).

superannuate [supə'rænjueit] *vt* consider somebody as no longer able to work because of age or illness; give somebody a pension for this reason (因年老或有病) 使退職; 給養老金使退休. **superannuation** [su:pərænju'eiʃən] *nc / u* pension of somebody who has been superannuated; amount of money paid regularly by somebody so that he can have a pension 退休金, 養老金; 爲日後領取退休金而定期繳納.

superb [su:pə:b] *adj* grand; splendid 華麗的; 壯麗的.

supercilious [su:pə:'siliəs] *adj* proud and full of disdain 傲慢的, 目空一切的.

superficial [su:pə'fiʃl] *adj* 1 on the surface; not deep 表面的; 淺的: *He had a superficial cut on his face.* 他臉上的傷口不深. 2 understanding only what is obvious; not thorough 膚淺的; 皮毛的; 淺薄的: *They have a superficial knowledge of the matter.* 他們對此事

瞭解得很膚淺. **superficially** *adv.*

superfluous [su'pə:fluəs] *adj* more than is needed or wanted; not needed 多餘的; 累贅的; 不必要的.

superhuman ['supə'hju:mən] *adj* more than human in power, size etc. 超人的.

superimpose [su:pərim'pouz] *vt* put something on top of something else 把…放在另一物的上面: *He superimposed the photograph on the page of the magazine.* 他把照片放在雜誌頁面的上面.

superintendent [su:pərin'tendnt] *nc* (in the British police force) police officer above an inspector (英國警察部隊裏) 高於巡官的警官, 警察局長.

superior [su:'piəriə*] *adj* 1 higher, better or greater 較高的; 較好的; 較大的: *He is my superior officer* i.e. his rank is higher than mine. 他是我的上級軍官. 即: 他的軍階比我高. *This car is superior to that one.* 這輛汽車比那輛汽車好. *They are superior in numbers to us.* 他們人數比我們多. (opp 反義詞 **inferior**). 2 showing that one thinks oneself better than others 傲慢的: *We were angry at his superior behaviour to the visitors.* 他們客客高傲無禮, 我們對此感到憤慨. Also 亦作 *nc* person with a higher rank of somebody 上級; 長官: *He is my superior in rank.* 他是我的上司. **superiority** [su:piəri'oriti] *nu* state of being superior 優越.

superlative [su:'pə:lətiv] *adj* better than all others 最好的, 最佳的; 最高級的. Also 亦作 *nc*: 'Biggest' is the superlative of 'big'. 'Biggest' 是 'big' 的最高級形式. 'Most quickly' is the superlative of 'quickly'. 'Most quickly' 是 'quickly' 的最高級形式.

supermarket ['su:pəma:kit] *nc* large shop in which the customers themselves collect what they wish to buy and pay on the way out 超級市場.

supernatural [su:pə'næt∫əl] *adj* not controlled by the laws of nature; spiritual 超自然的; 神奇的: *They believe that holy men have supernatural powers.* 他們相信聖人有超自然的力量. **the supernatural** *nu* forces or powers not controlled by the laws of nature 超自然力, 超自然現象.

superpower ['su:pəpauə*] *nc* country which has much stronger military power than other countries 超級大國.

supersede [su:pə'si:d] *vt* replace; make old-fashioned 取代; 淘汰: *Motorcars have superseded horses on the road.* 在公路上, 汽車取代了馬匹.

supersonic [su:pə'sɔnik] *adj* of a speed greater than the speed of sound i.e. more than 750 miles per hour 超音速的, 即: 每小時750英里以上的速度. (*opp* 反義詞 **subsonic**).

superstition [su:pə'sti∫ən] *nc / u* belief in, or fear of, magic and what is unknown 迷信: *Many people have the superstition that 13 is an unlucky number.* 許多人迷信十三爲不吉利的數目. **superstitious** *adj.*

supertanker ['su:pətænkə*] *nc* very large, fast tanker 超級油船, 大型快速油船.

supervise ['su:pəvaiz] *vt / i* watch to make sure that something is done; direct someone's work 監督; 指導: *The teacher is supervising games in the playground.* 老師照管着運動場上的比賽. *Tomorrow he will supervise all the pupils taking the English examination.* 明天他將爲所有參加英語考試的學生監考. **supervisor** *nc* **supervision** [su:pə'viʒən] *nu: They will study for the English examination under his supervision.* 他們將在他的指

導下學習, 準備英語考試. **supervisory** ['su:pəvaizəri] *adj* supervising 監督的; 指導的.

supper ['sʌpə*] *nc* last meal of the day 晚飯, 晚餐.

supple ['sʌpl] *adj* easy to bend or move 柔軟的, 易彎曲的; 靈活的: *A dancer has a supple body.* 舞蹈演員身體柔軟. **suppleness** *nu.*

supplement ['sʌplimənt] *nc* something added to complete something else or give more information 增補; 增刊; 附錄; 補編: *At the end of the dictionary there is a supplement of verb tables.* 該詞典卷末有動詞表附錄. *This magazine has a supplement about new motorcars.* 該雜誌附送介紹新汽車的增刊. Also 亦作 ['sʌpli'ment] *vt* add as a supplement 增補, 補充. **supplementary** ['sʌpli'mentəri] *adj* added; extra 增補的; 附加的.

supply [sə'plai] *vt* give what is needed or asked for 供給, 供應, 提供: *This shop supplies us with all we need / This shop supplies all our needs.* 這家商店供應了我們需要的一切東西. Also 亦作 *nc / u* act of supplying; something; which is supplied or can be supplied 供應(物); 提供(物): *This shop has a good supply of all kinds of food.* 這家商店大量供應各種食品. *He looks after the school's supplies of books and writing materials.* 他負責學校的書籍和書寫材料的供應. **supplier** *nc* person who supplies 供應者, 供應商; 提供者. **in short supply** not easily obtainable; scarce 供應不足; 短缺.

support [sə'pɔ:t] *vt* **1** keep from falling; hold up 支撐; 支承: *The floors of the building are supported by wooden beams.* 這座建築的樓板靠木樑支承. **2** help by agreeing with; help to continue 贊助; 支持: *Will you support my* *request for more money? / Will you support me in my request for more money?* 我要求多借點錢,你支持我嗎? *Our school is supported by the government.* 本校由政府資助. **3** give what is needed to live 供養: *I can't support my wife and children on such a small salary.* 我養俸如此微薄,無法養活妻子. Also 亦作 *nc / u* **1** something which supports; act of supporting or being supported 支撐物; 支撐; 贊助; 支持; 供養: *The supports of the floors are very strong.* 樓板的支柱非常結實. *Will you give me your support if I ask for more money?* 要是我要求多借點錢,你會支持我嗎? *He spoke in support of the plan.* 他發言支持這項計劃. **2** person who supports. 贊助者; 支持者; 供養者; 賺錢養家的人: *I am the only support of my family.* 我是全家唯一賺錢養家的人. **supporter** *nc* person / thing that supports 贊助者; 支持者; 供養者; 支撐物: *Are you a supporter of the local football team?* i.e. do you support it by going regularly to see it play? 你支持本地足球隊嗎?即:你經常到場觀看比賽助威嗎?

suppose [sə'pouz] *vt* **1** think to be true 假定; 以爲: *They suppose (that) all rich men are wicked.* 他們以爲凡是有錢的人都很壞. **2** think 料想, 認爲: *What do you suppose they are doing?* 你認爲他們在幹甚麼? *Is he right? Yes, I suppose so.* 他說對了嗎?是,我想是這樣. *Was he ever wrong? No, I suppose not.* 他搞錯過嗎?不,我想他從來不會搞錯. *I don't suppose you can give me five pounds* i.e. would you please give me five pounds (but I shall not be surprised if you cannot). 說不定你能給我五英鎊吧. 即:請給我五英鎊(但是如果你不肯,我也不會大吃一驚). **supposed** *adj* accepted as true but

actually not true 假定的, 被信以爲真的: *His supposed illness was found to be just laziness.* 大家都以爲他病了,結果發現他不過是懶惰. **supposedly** [sə'pouzidli] *adv* **supposing** *conj* if 要是, 如果: *Supposing he does not come, shall we go without him?* 要是他不來,我們將撇開他出發嗎? **supposition** [sʌpə'ziʃən] *nc / u* act of supposing; something supposed 假定; 料想; 猜想; 想法: *We shall make our plans on the supposition that they will help us.* 我們假定他們會幫助我們而制訂計劃. *I want facts not suppositions* i. e. guesses. 我要的是事實而不是猜想. **be supposed to** be assumed or expected to 被期望; 得, 應該: *Every pupil is supposed to be in his classroom at 9 a. m.* 上午九點鐘時每個學生都應當在教室裏. *You are not supposed to talk to strangers* i. e. you should not. 你們不該和陌生人談話.

suppress [sə'pres] *vt* **1** stop; bring to an end 禁止; 制止: *The police are trying to suppress the sale of dangerous drugs.* 警方試圖查禁危險藥物的銷售. **2** prevent being known 隱瞞: *You cannot suppress the truth for long.* 你不能長期隱瞞真相. **suppression** *nc / u.*

supra- ['su:prə] *prefix* above; beyond (e. g. **supranational** i.e. beyond the national level) 上; 超, 越過 (如 supranational 超國家的).

supreme [su'pri:m] *adj* **1** highest in authority 具有最高權力的: *supreme commander of the allied forces* 盟軍最高統帥; *Supreme Court of the USA* 美國的聯邦最高法院. **2** best or greatest possible 最好的; 最大的: *By a supreme effort, he won the race.* 他盡了最大的努力在賽跑中獲勝. **supremely** *adv* **supremacy** [su'premə-si] *nu.*

surcharge [ˈsəːtʃɑːdʒ] *nc* an extra charge 附加費.

sure [ʃuə*] 1 *pred adj* believing fully 確信的; 肯定的: *Are you sure (that) he is honest?* 你確信他是誠實的嗎? *I am sure of his honesty.* 我對於他的誠實確信無疑. *Some people are not sure about him or about his honesty.* 有的人不相信他或者不相信他的誠實. (*opp* 反義詞 **unsure**). 2 *pred adj* certain 確實的; 一定的: *We are sure to win* i. e. there is no doubt that we will win. 我們必勝. 即: 我們無疑會勝利. 3 *adj* reliable 可靠的: *Dark clouds are a sure sign of rain.* 烏雲是下雨的可靠征兆. **sure-'footed** *adj* not likely to put one's foot in the wrong place; not likely to fall 腳步穩的; 不會摔倒的: *People who climb mountains must be sure-footed.* 爬山的人腳步要穩. **sure enough** *adv* certainly; without a doubt 確實地; 無疑地: *He promised to come and sure enough he did.* 他答應要來並且果然來了. **make sure that / of** make certain that something is correct, available etc. 安排妥當; 查對無誤; 核實; 保證: *He made sure that he had enough food for the journey.* 他有足夠的食物供旅途中食用. *Let's make sure of this house before we buy it.* 在我們購買這座房子之前先要把房子的情況弄清楚.

surely [ˈʃuəli] *adv* 1 as expected 不出所料; 一定: *They will surely win.* 他們一定能贏. 2 giving the sense of hope or belief that something will happen 想必, 諒必: *Surely you don't expect me to go.* 你不至於在盼着我走開吧. *Surely we cannot buy it so cheaply.* 我們諒不能這麼便宜地買到它吧. 3 (*US* in answer to a question) of course; certainly (美)(用於回答問題)當然; 沒有

問題: *Will you come? Surely.* 你會來嗎?當然啦. (*Brit* 英 **certainly**). *Note* 說明: in sense 1 *surely,* which is put next to the verb, is less usual than *certainly;* in sense 2 *surely* is put before or after the subject, or at the end of the sentence. surely 在義 1 中的位置緊接動詞, 但不如 certainly 常用; surely 在義 2 中可以位於主語前後, 也可以位於句末.

surf [səːf] *nu* waves of the sea as they break when they reach land 拍岸浪; 拍岸浪花. **surfing** *nu* sport of riding on the top of a big wave while standing or lying on a narrow board 沖浪運動. **'surfboard** type of board used in this sport 沖浪板.

surface [ˈsəːfis] *nc* 1 outside of anything 面, 表面: *Paper has a flat surface.* 紙的表面是平的. *Only the surface of the wood was burnt.* 只是木頭的表面燒焦了. 2 top of liquid (esp. a stretch of water) 液體的表面(尤指一片水面): *He dived below the surface.* 他潛入水底. 3 that which can be easily seen or understood; outward appearance 皮毛; 外觀: *On the surface he was calm, but he was really very angry.* 他看起來鎮定自若, 其實非常憤怒. Also 亦作 *vt / i* come to the surface. 顯露; 露出水面, 浮出水面: *He swam underwater and then surfaced.* 他潛游後浮出水面. **'surface mail** mail sent by sea or land, not by air 平郵, 非航空郵件: *send a letter by surface mail* 以平郵寄信.

surfeit [ˈsəːfit] *nu* (with **a**) (esp. with reference to food and drink) too much of something (與 a 連用)(尤指飲食)過量, 過多: *a surfeit of cakes* 過多的蛋糕.

surge [səːdʒ] *nc* forward movement of a wave; any strong movement like that of a wave 波濤洶湧; 洶湧; 澎湃: *I felt a surge of pity for them.* 我心中湧起一陣憐憫他們之情. Also 亦作 *vi* move in this way 洶湧; 澎湃.

surgeon ['sə:dʒən] *nc* doctor who does surgery 外科醫師. **dental surgeon** dentist who can do surgery 牙科醫師; 口腔外科醫師.

surgery ['sə:dʒəri] *nc / u* 1 branch of medicine which deals with disease and injuries by operating i.e. by cutting, tying, fitting parts of the body, not by using only drugs and medicines 外科. 2 (*Brit*) room where a doctor sees his patients. (*US* 美 **office**) (英) 診所. 3 (*Brit*) time when a doctor sees his patients (英) 看病時間: *Dr Brown holds a surgery every morning.* 布朗醫生每天上午看病. **surgical** ['sə:dʒikl] *adj*.

surly ['sə:li] *adj* rude and bad-tempered 粗野無禮的, 脾氣暴躁的.

surmise [sə:'maiz] *vt / i* suppose; think without reason 猜測; 臆測.

surmount [sə'maunt] *vt / i* climb over; overcome 越過; 克服: *I think that I can surmount these difficulties.* 我想我能克服這些困難.

surname ['sə:neim] *nc* family name 姓: *My surname is Smith; my first / Christian name is John.* 我姓史密斯; 名/教名叫約翰.

surpass [sə'pɑ:s] *vt* be or do better than 比⋯好; 勝過: *The result surpassed their hopes.* 結果比他們的預期要好.

surplus ['sə:pləs] *nc* amount left over when all that is needed is taken; amount by which income is greater than expenditure 剩餘, 剩餘額; 盈餘: *This country keeps the corn it needs and sells the surplus abroad.* 該國留足國內自需的穀物後, 將剩餘部分銷往國外. Also 亦作 *adj*: *This country sells its surplus corn abroad.* 該國將其剩餘的穀物銷往國外.

surprise [sə'praiz] *vt* 1 astonish by not being expected 使驚奇, 使感到意外: *His success surprised us all.* 他的成功使我們都感到驚奇. *We were surprised by his success.* 我們因他的成功而感到驚奇. 2 attack or come upon when not expected 突然襲擊; 撞見, 意外地遇見: *The enemy surprised us at dawn.* 敵人在拂曉時對我們進行突然襲擊. *They surprised him having a quiet drink.* 他們撞見他正在悄悄喝酒. Also 亦作 *nc / u*: *His success was a great surprise.* 他的成功非常令人驚奇. *To our surprise he succeeded.* 出乎我們的意料, 他成功了. Also 亦作 *adj* not expected 出人意外的: *The enemy made a surprise attack at dawn.* 敵人在拂曉時進行奇襲. **surprised** *adj* feeling surprise 感到意外的. **surprising** *adj* causing surprise 驚人的. **surprisingly** *adv*.

surrender [sə'rendə*] *vt / i* yield; hand over to the power of somebody 放棄; 屈服; 投降: *The defeated soldiers soon surrendered.* 敗兵很快就投降了. *You must surrender your guns to the police.* 你們得把槍枝交給警方. Also 亦作 *nc*.

surreptitious [ˌsʌrəp'tiʃəs] *adj* done secretly 鬼鬼祟祟的, 偷偷摸摸的; 秘密的. **surreptitiously** *adv*.

surround [sə'raund] *vt* be on all sides of; encircle 圍繞, 環繞; 包圍: *A high wall surrounds the field.* 場地的四週圍著高牆. *I was surrounded by a crowd of happy children.* 我被一羣快樂的孩子包圍著. **surrounding** *adj*: *The town's water comes from the surrounding hills* i.e. the hills round the town. 小鎮所用的水來自四週的羣山.

即: 來自環繞小鎮的羣山. **surround-ings** *npl* everything that is round about; neighbourhood 週圍的事物; 環境.

surveillance [sə'veilns] *nu* careful watch; supervision 監視; 監督.

survey [sə'vei] *vt* 1 look over 俯瞰: *We were able to survey the city from the top of the high building.* 我們可以從高樓頂部俯瞰全城. 2 consider as a whole; deal with generally 全面考慮; 概述: *The chairman, in his talk, surveyed the work done at the previous meetings.* 主席在發言中概述了之前幾次會議所做的工作. 3 measure land carefully and make a map of it 勘測, 測量(土地). 4 examine; inspect 檢查; 視察: *He is surveying the empty factory to see if it is suitable.* 他正在視察空着的工廠看看是否合用. Also 亦作 ['sə:vei] *nc* 1 general view 概觀, 全面的評述: *chairman's survey of work done* 主席對已做工作的概述. 2 measurement of land 勘測, 測量: *They are doing a survey of the land through which the new road will pass.* 他們正在查勘新公路要經過的地段. 3 detailed examination of a building, house etc. 對房屋等的詳細檢查. **surveying** *nu* work of measuring land carefully and making a map of it 勘測, 測量. **surveyor** *nc* person who surveys land or inspects buildings etc. 勘測員; (房屋等)檢查員.

survive [sə'vaiv] *vt / i* remain alive; live longer than 倖存; 比…活得久: *Only a few soldiers survived the battle.* 那次戰鬥之後只有少數士兵倖存. *My father has survived all his brothers and sisters.* 我父親所有的兄弟姐妹都先他去世. **survival** *nc / u* act of surviving; something left over from a former time 倖存; 殘存物. **survivor** *nc* per-

son who has survived 倖存者.

susceptible [sə'septibl] *adj* easily impressed; sensitive 易受感動的; 敏感的; *Children are more susceptible than adults.* 兒童要比大人更容易受外界影響. *I am susceptible to colds.* 我易患感冒. **susceptibility** [səsepti'biliti] *nc / u* (often *pl*) weakness or sensitive spot in a person's body or mind (常用複數) (身、心的)弱點或敏感點.

suspect [səs'pekt] *vt* 1 think that something is possible without knowing definitely 猜想, 猜疑: *We suspected that it was a trick to get our money.* 我們猜疑那是騙取我們錢財的詭計. 2 (with *of*) think that somebody may be guilty (與 *of* 連用) 懷疑(某人有罪); 認為 (某人有嫌疑): *I suspect them of stealing my books.* 我懷疑他們偷了我的書. 3 be doubtful or not sure about 懷疑: *Everybody suspects his story about what he did during the war.* 關於戰爭期間他幹了些甚麼, 人人對他的敍述抱有懷疑. Also 亦作 ['sʌspekt] *nc / pred adj* person who is suspected of doing something wrong; doubtful 嫌疑犯; 可疑的: *The police are looking for all suspects.* 警方正在查找所有的嫌疑犯. *His reason for being absent is suspect.* 他缺席的理由令人起疑.

suspend [səs'pend] *vt* 1 cause to hang from 吊, 懸掛: *They suspended the box from a branch of the tree.* 他們把盒子吊在樹枝上. 2 hold back; stop for a time 抑制; 中止, 暫停: *They have suspended work until next week.* 他們已暫停工作, 一直到下個星期. 3 stop somebody from working or having a certain position for a time 使暫時停工或停職; *The committee suspended two members of the football team.* 委員會決定兩名足球隊員停賽. **suspender** *nc* 1 device to keep up a stocking or sock when worn 吊襪帶. **2** (in *pl*) (US) straps worn over the shoulders to keep up trousers. (Brit 英 **braces**) (用於複數)(美)吊褲帶.

suspense [səs'pens] *nu* state of uncertainty and worry 懸而不決; 掛慮: *We were kept in suspense for an hour before we were told the results.* 在被告知結果之前, 我們擔心了一個小時.

suspension [səs'penʃən] **1** *nc* act of suspending 懸掛; 抑制; 中止, 暫停: *We were told about the suspension of the two players.* 我們被告知兩名隊員停賽的事. **2** *nu* state of being suspended 暫停工作; 暫停比賽; 暫時停職. **3** *nc / u* part of the equipment of a car etc which is used to give a smooth ride (汽車)的防震懸架. **sus'pension bridge** type of bridge which is suspended on strong wire ropes stretched between two towers 吊橋.

suspicion [səs'piʃən] *nc / u* feeling of doubt or that something is wrong without knowing definitely; act of suspecting 懷疑; 猜疑: *We have suspicions about his story.* 我們對他的說法有懷疑. *The police arrested him on suspicion* i.e. because they suspected him 警察因他涉嫌而逮捕了他. 即: 因爲警察懷疑他. **suspicious** *adj* having or causing suspicion 有疑心的; 可疑的: *I feel suspicious about / of him.* 我覺得他可疑. *There is a suspicious man standing outside the bank* i.e. one who causes suspicion about why he is there. 銀行門口站着一個可疑的人; 他爲甚麼在那裹令人懷疑. **suspiciously** *adv*.

sustain [sə'stein] *vt* **1** keep from falling; hold up 支撐; 承受: *These two posts sustain the whole roof.* 這兩根柱子支撐整個屋頂. **2** (in a legal sense) support; agree with (法律用語)確認, 認

可; 准許: *The judge sustained my request for more time to pay the money.* 法官准許我延期付款的要求. **3** cause to continue; keep strong 使繼續; 維持 …的體力: *How much longer can you sustain the argument that you never make a mistake?* 你認爲你從來不犯錯誤的論點能維持多久? *This food will sustain you.* 這些食物足以維持你的體力. **4** suffer; endure 蒙受; 遭受; 忍受: *I sustained a broken arm in the accident.* 我在這次事故中斷了一隻胳臂.

sustenance ['sʌstənəns] *nu* (esp. with reference to food and drink which keeps one strong and healthy) something which sustains 支撐物; 維持物 (尤指維持體力的飲食).

swab [swɔb] *nc* piece of cotton wool or gauze used by a doctor for cleaning or to obtain specimens (e. g. from the mouth) 藥棉或紗布拭子, 棉簽(在口腔等處清洗或取樣用).

swagger ['swægə*] *vi* walk in a proud way; behave in this way 昂首闊步, 大摇大擺地走; 狂妄自大. Also 亦作 *nu*.

swallow¹ ['swɔlou] *vt / i* put down the throat into the stomach 吞下, 嚥下: *He swallowed the pill.* 他吞服了藥丸. Also 亦作 *nc* act of swallowing; amount swallowed 吞, 嚥, 吞嚥之量. **swallow something up** use completely; cause to disappear 耗盡, 用盡, 吞沒, 淹沒: *Taxes have swallowed up all my money.* 稅收耗盡了我的所有錢財. *The crowd swallowed them up* i.e. they went into the crowd and could no longer be seen. 人羣把他們淹沒了. 即: 他們走進人羣後就不見了.

swallow² ['swɔlou] *nc* type of small bird, with a thin body and thin pointed wings, which eats insects 燕子.

swam [swæm] past tense of **swim.**

swim 的過去式.

swamp [swɔmp] *nc / u* land which is soft and covered with shallow water 沼澤. Also 亦作 *vt* (with **with**) receive too much of something (與 with 連用) 使應接不暇, 使難以應付: *I have been swamped with offers of help.* 不斷有人表示願意幫忙, 這使我應接不暇. **swampy** *adj.*

swan [swɔn] *nc* type of large (usu. white) water bird with a long neck. 天鵝.

swap [swɔp] *vt / i* see 見 **swop.**

swarm [swɔːm] *nc* 1 large number of insects or small animals (esp. when they are moving) (移動中的昆蟲或小動物)羣: *swarm of bees* 蜂羣. 2 large moving crowd of people (移動中的)人羣: *swarms of visitors at the seaside* 海邊成羣的遊客. Also 亦作 *vi* move or be present in large crowds 蜂擁; 羣集: *The boys swarmed into the classroom.* 男孩們蜂擁進入教室. *The classroom was swarming with boys.* 教室裏擠滿了男孩.

swarthy ['swɔːði] *adj* having a dark skin (膚色)黝黑的.

swat [swɔt] *vt* (esp. with reference to insects) hit quickly and kill 拍打(尤指昆蟲). *past* 過去式和過去分詞 **swatted.**

sway [swei] *vt / i* 1 move, cause to move, from side to side 搖擺; (使)擺動: *The dancers swayed to the music.* 舞蹈家們隨着音樂婆娑起舞. 2 have influence or control over 影響; 左右; 操縱: *He is a good speaker and can sway all those who listen to him.* 他能言善辯, 足以影響所有聽衆.

swear [sweə*] *vt / i* 1 say or promise positively or in God's name; cause somebody to promise in this way (使)宣誓; (使)發誓: *I swear that my* story is true. 我發誓我說的是實話. *He swore to tell the truth.* 他宣誓要講真話. 2 use bad language 咒罵: *The angry driver swore at us.* 司機生了氣咒罵我們. *They were all swearing about their bad luck.* 他們都在咒罵自己的壞運氣. *You should not swear in front of the children.* 你不應該在孩子面前咒罵. *past tense* 過去式 **swore** [swɔː*]. *past part* 過去分詞 **sworn** [swɔːn]. **'swearing** *nu* bad language 詛咒, 罵人的話. **'swearword** bad word which should not be used in polite talk 詛咒, 罵人的話.

sweat [swet] *nu* 1 liquid which comes from the body through the skin (esp. when one is very hot or frightened) (尤指因炎熱或受驚嚇而出的)汗. 2 something which causes sweat; hard work; worry 吃力的工作; 苦差使; 焦慮, 煩惱: *Learning a new language is an awful sweat.* (*informal* in sense 2) 學習一種陌生的語言是可怕的苦差使. (義 2 爲非正式). Also 亦作 *vi* 1 produce, cause to produce, liquid through the skin 出汗; 使出汗: *We sweated in the hot sun.* 我們在烈日下流汗. 2 work hard (*informal* in sense 2) 努力工作(義 2 爲非正式). **sweaty** *adj* making one sweat; wet with sweat 使人流汗的; 汗濕透的.

sweater ['swetə*] *nc* woollen jersey or jacket 羊毛衣, 厚運動衫.

Swede [swiːd] *n* native of Sweden 瑞典人.

Swedish ['swiːdiʃ] *nu* language of Sweden 瑞典語. Also 亦作 *adj* of Sweden, its people or its language 瑞典的; 瑞典人的; 瑞典語的.

sweep¹ [swiːp] *vt / i* 1 remove loose dirt, dust etc with a brush or broom; clean in this way 打掃, 掃除; 清掃: *They are sweeping the rubbish out of* *the classroom.* 他們在把垃圾掃出教室. *My mother sweeps the kitchen every day.* 我媽媽每天打掃廚房. **2** move, cause to move, quickly (使)掃過; (使)急速移動: *The crowd swept into the field.* 人羣湧進球場. *The river swept the boat away.* 河水把小船沖走了. **3** extend over a large area in a curve (成曲線)連綿, 延伸: *The hills sweep into the distance.* 羣山連綿不斷, 伸向遠方. *The new road sweeps round the city.* 新公路環繞該城市. *past* 過去式和過去分詞 **swept** [swept]. **sweeping** *adj* **1** moving quickly; having great effect 急速移動的; 大大的, 徹底的: *There have been many sweeping changes in the country.* 該國發生了許多巨大的變化. *They won a sweeping victory.* 他們大獲全勝. **2** with no attention to details; general 籠統的; 一般的: *You should not make sweeping statements about such important matters.* 對於這樣重要的事情不該泛泛而論.

sweep² [swi:p] *nc* **1** act of sweeping 打掃: *My mother gave the kitchen a sweep.* 我媽媽把廚房打掃了一番. **2** quick movement 快速移動: *With one sweep of his hand he cleared the books from his desk* 他用手一揮, 把書桌上的書都掃掉了. **3** person who cleans chimneys 掃烟囱的人. (Also 亦作 **chimney sweep**). **'sweepstake** type of gambling (usu. on the result of a horserace) in which all the money paid by those who take part is given to those who draw the tickets of the winning horses (通常指賽馬)賭金獨得. (Also 亦作 **sweep**).

sweet [swi:t] *adj* **1** tasting like sugar; containing sugar 甜的; 含糖的: *I like sweet cakes.* 我喜歡吃甜糕點. *This coffee tastes sweet* i.e. has a sweet

taste 這咖啡是甜的. **2** fresh; pleasant; attractive 新鮮的; 可愛的; 動人的: *These flowers have a sweet smell.* 這些花有香味. *She has a sweet face.* 她容貌美麗. Also 亦作 *nc* **1** (*Brit*) something very sweet to eat (usu. made from sugar) (*US* 美 **candy**) (英) 糖果. **2** dish of sweet food (e. g. pudding) (usu. eaten at the end of a meal) (通常指餐後的)甜點(如布丁). **sweetly** *adv* **sweetness** *nu* **sweeten** *vt / i* become or make sweet (使)變甜. **sweetened** *adj* (*opp* 反義詞 **unsweetened**). **'sweetheart** lover; person loved 愛人; 被愛的人, 心上人. **'sweet 'pea** type of plant with sweet-smelling flowers 香豌豆.

swell [swel] *vt / i* become, cause to become, larger in volume (使)膨脹; (使)腫脹: *The heat made my feet swell.* 酷暑使我的雙腳腫脹. *The heavy rain swelled the river.* 暴雨使河水上漲. *His face was swollen with insect bites.* 他的臉因蟲咬而腫起. *past tense* 過去式 **swelled**. *past part* 過去分詞 **swollen** ['swouln]. Also 亦作 *nc* (*in sing*) large but slow rise and fall of the sea (用於單數)大浪, 巨浪: *The ship rolled in the heavy swell.* 船隻在滔天巨浪中顛簸. Also 亦作 *adj* rich; smart; very good. (*informal and mainly US*) 有錢的; 漂亮的; 了不起的(非正式, 主要用於美). **swelling** *nc* state of being swollen; lump 膨脹; 腫脹, 腫塊: *There is a swelling on top of his head where he was hit by a stone.* 他頭頂被石塊擊中的地方有一個腫塊.

swelter ['sweltə*] *vt / i* feel, or cause to feel, very warm and uncomfortable (使)感到熱得難受; (使)中暑: *in sweltering heat* 在酷熱中.

swept [swept] past of **sweep¹**. sweep¹ 的過去式和過去分詞.

swerve [swə:v] *vt / i* move cause to move, suddenly to one side (使) 突然轉向: *The motorcar swerved to avoid a hole in the road.* 汽車突然轉向以避開公路上的坑。 Also 亦作 *nc*.

swift¹ [swift] *adj* quick; fast 快的, 迅速的。 **swiftly** *adv* **swiftness** *nu*.

swift² [swift] *nc* type of bird, which can fly very fast and eats insects it catches when flying 褐雨燕。

swig [swig] *vt / i* drink quickly 一口氣喝下去; 大口地喝。 *past* 過去式和過去分詞 **swigged**. Also 亦作 *nc*: *He took a swig at his glass of beer.* (both informal) 他拿着整杯啤酒喝一大口(均爲非正式)。

swill [swil] *vt / i* (usu. with **out**) pour liquid over or through in order to clean (通常與 out 連用) 冲洗, 灌洗: *They are swilling out the empty buckets.* 他們正在冲洗空桶。 Also 亦作 *nu* waste food and liquid (usu. used as food for pigs) 泔水; 殘湯剩飯; 豬食。

swim [swim] *vt / i* **1** move through the water by moving the limbs, fins, tail etc; cross a stretch of water in this way (魚) 游; (人) 游泳; 游過一段距離: *All fish swim.* 魚都會游泳。 *I learnt to swim when I was a boy.* 我還是小孩時就學會了游泳。 *He swam a mile yesterday.* 昨天他游了一英里。 **2** be full of; be covered with (esp. with a liquid) 滿足, 充滿; 浸, 泡 (在液體裏): *Her eyes swam with tears.* 她眼淚汪汪。 *The room was swimming in / with water from the burst pipe.* 水管破了, 房間裏都是水。 **3** appear to go round; feel dizzy 搖搖, 似乎在旋轉; 眩暈: *My head was swimming from the blow.* 我因爲頭部被擊中而感到天旋地轉。 *pres part* 現在分詞 **swimming.** *past tense* 過去式 **swam** [swæm]. *past part* 過去分詞 **swum** [swʌm]. Also 亦作 *nc* act

of swimming 游; 游泳: *I am going for a swim.* 我去游泳。 **swimsuit** dress / costume for swimming in 游泳衣。 **'swimming bath** *nc* (often *pl*) place for swimming (usu. indoors) (常用複數) (通常指室內的) 游泳池。

swindle ['swindl] *vt / i* cheat; get by cheating 詐騙; 騙取: *The company made a lot of money by swindling the public.* 該公司用詐騙公衆的手段賺了不少錢。 *He swindled me out of £1 i.e. he got £1 from me by cheating me.* 他騙了我一英鎊。 即: 他用欺詐手段從我這裏拿去一英鎊。 Also 亦作 *nc* act of swindling; something by which one is swindled 欺詐, 騙局; 騙人的東西。 **swindler** *nc*.

swine [swain] *nc* **1** pig (*o. f.*) 豬 (舊式)。 **2** unpleasant person. (*impolite*) 豬玀; 令人討厭的人 (不禮貌) *pl* 複數 **swine.**

swing [swiŋ] *vt / i* **1** move, cause to move, from side to side or backwards and forwards (esp. when hanging down or with one end fixed) (使) 左右搖擺; (使) 來回擺動 (尤指懸掛着或一端固定時): *The door was swinging on its hinges.* 門靠鉸鏈搖擺。 *The soldiers swung their arms as they marched.* 士兵行軍時擺動手臂。 **2** turn, cause to turn quickly. (使) 迅速轉向, (使) 迅速轉身: *The car swung towards the side of the road.* 汽車猛地轉向路邊。 *I swung round to see who was following me.* 我猛一轉身, 看看是誰在跟踪我。 *past* 過去式和過去分詞 **swung** [swʌŋ]. Also 亦作 *nc* **1** act of swinging 搖擺; 擺動。 **2** seat fixed to ropes on which one can swing backwards and forwards 鞦韆。 **'swing bridge** type of bridge which can be swung to the side (usu. over a river or canal to allow ships to pass) (平) 旋橋, 平轉

橋. **in full swing** going well; working fully 正起勁; 正在全力進行: *When we arrived the meeting was already in full swing.* (*informal*) 我們到達時, 會議正開得熱烈. (非正式).

swipe [swaip] *vt* **1** hit with a wide, sweeping blow 猛揮, 重擊: *He swiped me on the shoulders with his stick.* 他用手杖猛擊我的肩膀. **2** steal 偷. Also 亦作 *nc*: *He took a swipe at the fly on the wall.* (all *informal*) 他猛拍牆上的蒼蠅. (均爲非正式).

swirl [swə:l] *vt / i* (with reference to air or liquid) move, cause to move, round quickly and in a confined way (指氣體或液體) (使) 打漩; 旋轉; 捲走: *The flooded river swirled round the rocks.* 上漲了的河水繞着岩石打漩. *The branches of the tree were swirled away by the flood.* 樹枝被洪水捲走. Also 亦作 *nc*: *The wind blew swirls of dust across the field.* 大風捲起滾滾塵埃吹過田野.

swish [swiʃ] *nc* sound made by a stick or something thin moving very quickly through the air; sound made by cloth moving over a surface (棍子等揮動的)嗖嗖聲; (衣服摩擦的)瑟瑟聲: *swish of a whip* 鞭子揮動的嗖嗖聲; *swish of their long robes over the floor* 他們的長袍拖過地板時發出的瑟瑟聲. Also 亦作 *vt / i* move and make a sound like this 嗖地揮動, 嗖嗖作響; 發瑟瑟聲: *The animal swished its tail.* 那頭牲口嗖嗖地揮動尾巴.

Swiss [swis] *n* native of Switzerland 瑞士人. *pl* 複數 **Swiss.** Also 亦作 *adj* of Switzerland or its people 瑞士的; 瑞士人的.

switch [switʃ] *nc* **1** device for turning electric current on or off (電器) 開關. **2** sudden change of opinion, direction etc. (意見, 方向等的) 突然改變. Also

亦作 *vt / i* **1** turn electric current on or off 接通或切斷…的電流: *Please switch off the lights when you leave the room.* 你離開房間時請把燈關掉. *He switched on the radio.* 他打開了收音機. **2** change 改變: *He is always switching jobs.* 他老是在變動工作.

switchback type of railway which goes up and down steeply (usu. built for amusement) 遊樂園中上下陡坡的小鐵路. Also 亦作 *adj*: *switchback railway* 來回上下陡坡的遊樂園小鐵路. *switchback road* 之字形登山公路.

'switchboard board for connecting telephone lines as required (e.g. on a telephone exchange) 電話交換台, 電話總機.

swivel ['swivl] *vt / i* turn, cause to turn, round on, or as if on, a swivel (使) 在旋轉接頭上旋轉; (使) 旋轉: *He swivelled round his chair.* 他把轉椅轉了過來. *past* 過去式和過去分詞 **swivelled.** (*US* 美 **swiveled**).

swollen ['swəuln] past part of **swell.** swell 的過去分詞.

swoop [swu:p] *vt / i* (with *down on*) attack suddenly from above; attack suddenly (與 *down on* 連用) 俯衝攻擊; 猛撲, 突然襲擊: *The hawk swooped down on the chickens.* 鷹猛地撲向小鸡. Also 亦作 *nc* act of swooping 撲擊; 襲擊.

swop, swap [swɔp] *vt / i* exchange 交換: *We swopped jerseys.* 我們交換運動衫. *I'll swop places with you.* 我來跟你換個位置. *past* 過去式和過去分詞 **swopped.** Also 亦作 *nc* (both informal) (均爲非正式).

sword [sɔ:d] *nc* type of weapon with a long steel blade and a handle (or hilt) 劍; 刀. **swordfish** type of fish with a long, stiff upper jaw shaped like a sword 箭魚, 旗魚.

swore [swɔ:*] past tense of **swear.** swear 的過去式.

sworn [swɔ:n] past part of **swear.** swear 的過去分詞.

swot [swɔt] *vt / i* study hard 用功學習. *past* **swotted.** 過去式. Also 亦作 *nc* **1** hard study 用功的學習. **2** person who studies hard. (all *informal*) 用功的人 (均爲非正式).

swum [swʌm] past part of **swim.** swim 的過去分詞

sycamore ['sikəmɔ:*] **1** *nc* one of several types of tree (歐洲) 楓樹; (美洲) 梧桐; (中東) 無花果樹. **2** *nu* the wood from this tree 上述樹木之硬木材.

syllable ['siləbl] *nc* sound made by one action of the voice and usually containing one vowel 音節: *The word monumental has four syllables.* monumental 一詞有四個音節.

syllabus ['siləbəs] *nc* outline of a course of lessons or studies 課程提綱; 教學大綱: *All our schools follow the same English syllabus.* 我們所有的學校都實行英國的同一種教學大綱. *pl* 複數 **syllabuses** or **syllabi** ['siləbai].

symbol ['simbl] *nc* something which represents something; sign; mark 象徵, 代表物; 記號; 符號: + *is the mathematical symbol for addition.* "+"是數學的加號. *H₂O is the chemical symbol for water.* H_2O 是水的化學符號. *The crescent moon is the symbol of Islam.* 新月是伊斯蘭教的標誌. **symbolic** [sim'bɔlik] *adj* **symbolical** [sim'bɔlikl] *adj* **symbolically** *adv* **symbolism** *nu* use of symbols to represent ideas (e.g. in art) (如藝術上的) 象徵主義; 象徵手法. **symbolize** *vt* be the symbol of 象徵, 代表.

symmetry ['simətri] *nu* balance between the different parts of something; exact agreement of opposite

sides of a figure to each other; harmony 勻稱, 平衡; 對稱; 協調: *A well-designed building has symmetry.* 設計優良的建築有對稱美. **symmetrical** [si'metrikl] *adj*: *A triangle with all sides equal is symmetrical.* 各邊相等的三角形是對稱的. (*opp* 反義詞 **asymmetrical**).

sympathy ['simpəθi] *nc / u* feeling which is the same as what somebody else feels; feeling by which one shares the pain or troubles of somebody else 同感; 同情 (心); 惻隱之心; 慰問: *When his father died, he had my sympathy.* 他父親去世時, 我們向他表示慰問. *We felt sympathy for him.* 我們同情他. *Please give him my sympathies.* 請代我向他表示慰問. **sympathetic** [simpə'θetik] *adj* having sympathy; showing that one feels pity for someone; caused by sympathy 有同感的, 有同情心的; 表同情的; 出于同情的: *He wrote me a very sympathetic letter.* 他給我寫了一封信表示非常同情. *I don't like Peter, but I must say he was very sympathetic when my father died.* 我不喜歡彼得, 但我要說當我父親去世時, 他對我是很同情的. **sympathetically** *adv* **sympathize** ['simpəθaiz] *vi* feel or show sympathy 同情; 表示同情: *I sympathize with all those who are poor.* 我同情所有的窮人. **sympathizer** ['simpəθaizə*] *nc*.

symphony ['simfəni] *nc* musical composition (usu. in four parts) for a full orchestra (供大型交響樂團演奏的) 交響樂, 交響曲 (通常分爲四個樂章). **symphonic** [sim'fɔnik] *adj*.

symposium [sim'pouziəm] *nc* meeting of several persons to discuss and exchange ideas; number of essays by several persons about one subject 專題討論會; 專題論文集. *pl* 複數 **sym-**

posiums or **symposia** [sim'pouziə].

symptom ['simptəm] *nc* **1** change in the body, or outward sign on the body, which shows it has a disease 症狀, 徵候: *A high temperature is a symptom of malaria*. 高燒是瘧疾的一種症狀. **2** sign showing that something exists 徵兆: *Bad behaviour is often a symptom of unhappiness*. 態度不好常常是心裏不痛快的一種表現. **symptomatic** [simptə'mætik] *adj* (with *of*) *A high temperature is symptomatic of malaria*. (與 of 連用) 高燒是瘧疾的一種症狀.

syn- [sin] *prefix* together; with; at the same time as (e.g. **synchronize**; **synthesis**) 共, 同; 與; 同時 (如 synchronize 同步; synthesis 綜合).

synagogue ['sinəgɔg] *nc* place where Jews worship; meeting of Jews to worship 猶太教的會堂; 猶太教的集會.

synchronize ['siŋkrənaiz] *vt* / *i* agree, cause to agree, in time; happen, cause to happen, at the same time (使) 同步; (使)同時發生; 對準 (鐘錶): *Before the attack, the army officers synchronized their watches* i.e. put their watches to exactly the same time 進攻開始之前, 軍官們對準了錶. 即: 使他們的錶走時一致.

syndicate ['sindikət] *nc* number of business firms which group together for a certain purpose 聯合企業, 辛迪加.

syndrome ['sindroum] *nc* number of symptoms of an illness occurring together 綜合癥, 徵候羣.

synonym ['sinənim] *nc* word which has the same meaning as another word in the same language 同義詞: *'big' and 'large' are synonyms*. 'big' 和 'large' 是同義詞. (*opp* 反義詞 **antonym**). **synonymous** [si'nɔniməs] *adj*.

synopsis [si'nɔpsis] *nc* summary (usu.

of something which has been written or printed) (通常指書面文字的) 摘要, 概要; 梗概, 大意. *pl* 複數 **synopses** [si'nɔpsiːz].

syntax ['sintæks] *nu* part of grammar which deals with making sentences and putting words in their correct order 句法.

synthesis ['sinθəsis] *nc* putting together several parts into a whole; result of doing this 綜合; 綜合物: *This method of teaching is a synthesis of many methods which have been used elsewhere*. 這種教學法是在別處用過的多種方法的綜合物. *pl* 複數 **syntheses** ['sinθəsiːz]. **synthetic** [sin'θetik] *adj* artificial 合成的; 人造的: *Synthetic fibres are often used instead of wool or cotton to make clothes*. 合成纖維常用來代替羊毛或棉花製作衣服.

syphilis ['sifilis] *nu* type of venereal disease 梅毒.

syphon ['saifən] *nc* see 見 **siphon**.

syringe [si'rindʒ] *nc* device made of a tube with a piston for drawing in a liquid and pushing it out again through a very small hole 注射器; 注水器; 注油器; 洗滌器; (醫用) 灌腸器.

syrup ['sirəp] *nu* **1** liquid obtained when sugar cane is boiled 糖漿. **2** thick mixture of sugar and water. 濃糖水. **syrupy** *adj* thick and very sweet 糖漿狀的; 極甜的.

system ['sistəm] *nc* / *u* **1** number of things arranged to make one complete working whole 系統, 體系: *the solar system* i.e. the sun, planets etc. 太陽系; 即: 太陽和行星等; *the nervous system* i.e. the nerves in the human body 神經系統; 即: 人體的神經. **2** the way things are arranged to work; method 制度, 體制; 方法, 方式: *public transport system* 公共交通網; *different* *systems of government* 不同的政體. *There is no system in his work.* 他工作缺乏條理. **systematic** [sistə'mætik] *adj* following a system; well-organized; orderly 有系統的, 成體系的; 組織得很好的, 有條不紊的, 有條理的; 秩序井然的: *a systematic approach to the problem* 研究這個問題的系統方法. *(opp* 反義詞 **unsystematic). systematically** *adv.*

T, t

.ta [tɑ:] *interj* informal word for **Thank you.** Thank you 的非正式詞.

tab [tæb] *nc* **1** small piece of cloth etc sewn to something larger to show whose it is or who made it 標籤. **2** small strip of cloth sewn to the top of a coat, dress etc so that it can be hung up (縫在外衣等衣領內緣以便懸掛的) 小布環.

tabby ['tæbi] *nc* cat (usu. female) with striped fur 斑貓 (通常指雌性的). (Also 亦作 **tabby cat**).

table ['teibl] *nc* **1** flat surface made of wood, metal etc standing on legs and used as a piece of furniture for working at or eating meals etc 桌子: *card table* i.e. one used for playing cards 牌桌, 即: 打牌用的桌子; *dining table* 餐桌; *coffee table* 咖啡桌. *sitting at the table* 坐在桌子旁. **2** short, clear arrangement or list of facts or figures (項目) 表, 表格: *multiplication tables* 乘法表; *timetable* 時間表; *table showing the important events in English history* 英國歷史大事記表. Also 亦作 *vt* bring a proposal to the attention of a meeting 提議; 建議; 將…列入會議議程. **tablecloth** cloth put on a table (usu. at mealtimes) 桌布. **'table lamp** small lamp which is put on a table 枱燈. **'tablespoon** type of large spoon used at meals (usu. for serving) (通常指就餐時分食物用的) 大湯匙. **'table tennis** game like tennis played on a long table with a small, light ball and small bats 乒乓球.

tablet ['tæblit] *nc* **1** small block of something hard 小塊, 小片: *tablet of*

soap 一塊肥皂; *aspirin tablet* 阿司匹林藥片. **2** piece of flat stone or metal (usu. fixed to a wall) telling about somebody / something 碑, 牌, 圖 (通常嵌在牆上).

taboo [tə'bu:] *nc* something which is forbidden by religious belief or custom (宗教或習俗的) 禁忌, 忌諱, 避諱: *This tribe has many taboos about the kinds of food women may eat.* 這個部落對於婦女的食物有多種禁忌. *The top of that sacred hill is under a taboo* i.e. it is forbidden to go there. 那座聖山的山頂屬禁忌之列. 即: 禁止任何人登上山頂. Also 亦作 *pred adj*: *Eating eggs is taboo in this tribe.* 這個部落忌諱吃蛋. *Arguments about politics are taboo in many countries.* 在許多國家裏避諱辯論政治.

tabulate ['tæbjuleit] *vt* arrange facts or figures shortly and clearly in a list 將 (事實或數字) 列表.

tachograph ['tækəgrɑ:f] *nc* instrument fitted to a vehicle to record its speed and the distance travelled etc. (車輛的) 速度計, 里程計.

tacit ['tæsit] *adj* accepted or understood without anything being said 默認的, 心照不宣的: *By sitting quietly at the meeting, he gave his tacit approval to the plan.* 開會時他靜靜地坐着, 表示對這項計劃已默認. **tacitly** *adv*.

taciturn ['tæsitə:n] *adj* (with reference to a person) saying little; silent by habit (指人)說話不多的; 沉默寡言的.

tack¹ [tæk] *nc* **1** type of small, sharp nail with a flat head 圖釘, 平頭釘. **2**

type of stitch made quickly with needle and thread to fasten pieces of cloth together until closer and more permanent stitches are made (固定布片用的)粗縫, 假縫. Also 亦作 *vt* fasten with tacks (用平頭釘)釘住; 粗縫: *We tacked the map on the board.* 我們把地圖釘在板上. *She tacked up the hem of her dress.* 她用線粗縫衣服的摺邊.

tack² [tæk] *nc* **1** course of a sailing ship in relation to the wind (跟風向相關的)帆船航向: *The yacht left the harbour on the starboard tack* i.e. with the wind blowing from the starboard or righthand side 遊艇離港時作右舷順風行駛. 即: 風從右舷吹來. **2** any course of action 行動步驟, 方針: *These scientists are on the right / wrong tack.* 這些科學家的方針是正確/錯誤的.

tackle ['tækl] **1** *nu* set of ropes and pulleys for lifting heavy weights or moving a ship's sails 滑車; 帆船的滑車索具. **2** *nu* equipment needed for a game or for work (運動、遊戲或工作的)用具, 裝備; 運動器材: *fishing tackle* i.e. rod, line. bait etc needed to fish 釣魚用具, 即: 釣魚需用的魚竿、綫、餌等. **3** *nc* (in football etc) move by a player to stop an opponent who has the ball (美式足球賽等)阻擋(指抱住帶球跑的對方球員). Also 亦作 *vt / i* seize and stop an opponent who has the ball; try to stop somebody 抱住並擋住(帶球跑的對方球員); 試圖擋住(某人): *The policeman tackled the thief as he tried to escape.* 小偷打算逃跑時警察擋住了他. **2** begin doing something with determination 着手處理(某事): *We must tackle the problem of poverty as soon as possible.* 我們要盡快着手解決貧困問題.

tacky ['tæki] *adj* (with reference to glue, paint etc.) sticky; not quite dry (指膠水、顏料、油漆等)黏的, 未乾的.

tact [tækt] *nu* understanding of, and sympathy for, the feelings of others so that one knows what is the right thing to do or say in any difficult situation 老練, 機智; 圓滑, 世故: *Our teacher showed great tact in dealing with the angry parents.* 我們的老師在對付生氣的學生家長時顯得機智練達. **tactful** *adj* (opp 反義詞 **tactless**).

tactics ['tæktiks] *npl* science of putting armed forces in the right place before or during a battle; any plans made to get something done 戰術; 策畧, 謀畧; 手法. **tactical** *adj*.

tadpole ['tædpoul] *nc* young frog after it has left its egg and before it is fully grown 蝌蚪.

tael [teil] *nc* **1** any of various units of weight of East Asia; esp. Liang (old Chinese unit of weight) (亞洲東部的衡量單位; 尤指中國的舊衡量單位)兩. **2** former Chinese unit of money originally a tael, in weight, of silver (中國從前的貨幣單位)銀兩: *100 taels of silver* 一百兩銀子.

tag [tæg] *nc* **1** small card which is fastened to something; label (附在某物上的)小卡片; 標簽: *Have you put tags on your luggage?* 你的行李貼上標簽沒有?; *price tag* i.e. label showing the price of something 價格標簽. **2** children's game in which one child chases and tries to touch another 捉迷藏, 兒童捉人遊戲. Also 亦作 *vt* (with **after** or **behind**) follow behind (與 after 或 behind 連用)跟在……後面, 尾隨: *The little boy tagged after his older sister wherever she went.* 不管他姐姐走到哪裏, 這小男孩都跟在他姐姐後面. *past* 過去式和過去分詞 **tagged**.

tail [teil] *nc* **1** movable part at the back end of an animal, bird or fish (動物、鳥、魚等的) 尾巴: *Cows use their tails to keep away flies.* 牛用尾巴趕蒼蠅. **2** something like a tail (usu. at the end of something else) 尾狀物 (通常在某物的末端): *tail of a long line of people* 一長隊人的末尾; *tail of an aircraft* 飛機的尾部; *tail of a letter* i.e. the upward or downward stroke made when one finishes writing a letter of the alphabet 字母的尾巴, 即: 寫字母時最後筆鋒上翹或下撇部份. **3** reverse side of a coin 錢幣的背面, 反面. (*opp* 反義詞 **head**). *Heads or tails?* (said when throwing a coin into the air to decide something according to whether the coin falls with the head or tail upwards?) 你猜正面還是反面? (用擲錢幣的辦法來決定某事時的用語). Also 亦作 *vt* follow behind 尾隨, 跟蹤: *The detective tailed the thief through the crowd* i.e. followed him secretly 偵探在人羣中跟蹤小偷. 即: 秘密地跟着他. **'tail coat** man's evening dress coat with a short front and a long back divided at the bottom 燕尾服. **'tail 'end (with the)** last part (與...連用) 最後部份: *We were so late that we only saw the tail end of the play.* (*informal*) 我們去得遲, 只看到這齣戲的末尾. (非正式).

tailor ['teilə*] *nc* person who makes outer clothes (e.g. men's suits) (裁製外衣, 例如男裝的) 裁縫. **'tailor-'made** *adj* **1** (*Brit*) made by a tailor to fit a particular person. (*US* 美 **custom-made**) (英)定製的. **2** specially made to suit some particular purpose (爲某一目的) 特製的.

taint [teint] *vt / i* become, cause to become, decayed or infected (使) 腐敗; (使) 感染: *This food is tainted be-*

cause it is not fresh. 這食物不新鮮, 已經腐壞了.

take [teik] *vt / i* **1** seize and hold 抓住; 拿着: *I took my father's hand* i.e. I held his hand in mine. 我抓住我父親的手: *She took the baby in her arms.* 她抱着嬰兒. *The dog took the stick between its teeth.* 狗用牙咬住棍子. **2** get; have 得到; 享有: *I shall take a small house in the village.* 我將在村子裏買一座小房子. *We are taking the bus to London.* 我們正要搭公共汽車去倫敦. *He is taking a bath.* 他正在洗澡. *They took a walk round the garden.* 他們在花園裏各處散步. *Please take a seat and wait.* 請坐下等一會兒. **3** capture; win; gain 奪得; 贏得; 獲得, 博得: *The enemy has taken the castle.* 敵人攻克了城堡. *Our team took the first game and lost the second.* 我隊贏了第一場, 輸了第二場. *Her strange dress took everybody's attention.* 她的奇裝異服引起了每個人的注意. **4** receive; accept; earn 收到; 接受; 賺到: *He took the blow on the chin.* 他下巴上挨了一拳. *This hotel does not take children.* 這家旅社不收兒童房客. *Will you take me as your partner?* 你要我當你的合夥人嗎? *I take your word for it* i.e. I believe you. 我相信你的話. *The shop took about £20 during the morning.* 這家商店上午賺了約20英鎊. **5** remove without permission; steal 未經許可拿走; 偷: *Somebody has taken my coat.* 有人拿走了我的外套. *The thieves took all they could carry.* 小偷們把能帶走的東西都偷走了. **6** carry; move; cause to go 把...帶(到); 使移動; 使...去: *He has taken his shoes (to the shop) to be repaired.* 他把鞋子帶(到店鋪)去修理. *I took my books to school.* 我把書帶到學校去. *They will take us with* *them to the cinema.* 他們會帶我們去看電影. *The road took them over the hill.* 他們順著這條路翻越過了小山. **7** be necessary; need 必須; 需要: *This work will take a long time.* 這工作得花不少時間. *How long did you take to come here?* 你來這裏要多少時間? *It took three men to lift the box.* 要抬起這箱子得有三個人. **8** make a record of 記錄: *The policeman took the number of my car* i.e. he wrote it down. 警察記下了我的汽車號碼. *Do you take notes of the lectures?* 你作了聽課筆記嗎? *He wants to take our photograph.* 他要給我們拍照. **9** think; suppose 認爲; 以爲; 假定: *They took us for strangers.* 他們把我們當成陌生人. *May I take it that you agree?* 我是否可以認爲你已經同意了? **10** act or deal with something in a certain way (以某種方式) 處理, 對待: *Take care that you do not fall.* 當心別跌倒. *We took pity on him* i.e. we felt sorry for him. 我們可憐他. *The horse took fright* i.e. became frightened. 馬驚了. *He takes life quietly.* 他寧靜處世. *They took the news badly* i.e. they were very upset by it. 這消息使他們心煩意亂. *He takes his work seriously.* 他認真對待他的工作. *past* 過去式 **took** [tuk]. *past part* 過去分詞 **taken** ['teikən].

takings *npl* receipts; money earned 收入; 進項: *The takings for the concert were over £50.* 音樂會的收入超過50英鎊. **take after** someone behave or look like 舉動像某人; 長得像某人: *The boy takes after his father.* 這男孩長得像他父親. **take one back** cause one to remember 使回憶起: *This picture takes me back to the war. (informal)* 這張照片使我回憶起戰爭年代. (非正式). **take something back 1** return 歸還: *Take this book back to*

the library. 把這本書還給圖書館. **2** agree to have returned; accept back 同意退還; 收回: *The trousers which you sold me are too big. Will you take them back?* 你賣給我的褲子太大了. 你同意我把褲子退回嗎? **3** admit that what one has said is wrong and apologize. 承認說錯…並道歉: *He took back the story he told about me.* 他承認所說的關於我的話說錯了並向我道歉. **take something down** write down 記下, 寫下: *The pupils took down what the teacher had told them.* 學生們記下了老師告訴他們的話. **take someone / something in 1** receive; accept (usu. for payment) 接受 (某人) / 承接 (某事) (通常爲了收錢): *His mother takes in lodgers* i.e. she earns money by having lodgers in her house. 他媽媽接收房客等, 即; 她把房子出租給寄宿者以收取房租. **2** understand; see; listen 理解, 領會; 看見; 聽見: *The lesson was too difficult for the class to take in.* 這課太難, 這個班級的學生聽不懂. *He does not seem to be listening but he is in fact taking everything in.* 看上去他不像在聽, 但實際上他甚麼都聽見了. **3** deceive 欺騙: *Don't be taken in by his promises.* 不要輕信他的諾言. **take (someone / something) off 1** remove; put in another place 脫掉; 移開; 把…帶往(別處): *He took off his coat and hung it up.* 他脫掉外套, 把它掛好. *Please take your elbows off the table.* 請雙肘別放在桌子上. *The police took him off to prison.* 警察將他送進監獄. **2** leave the ground 起飛: *Our plane takes off at 4 p.m.* 我們的飛機下午四時起飛. **'takeoff** *nc*: *What time is the takeoff?* 飛機甚麼時候起飛? **take someone off** imitate somebody (usu. to make others laugh) 模倣某人的舉動(通常以

博一笑): *He is good at taking off the headmaster.* 他學校長的樣子維妙維肖. **'takeoff²** *nc*: *His takeoff of the headmaster was very amusing.* (*informal*) 他學校長的樣子好笑極了. (非正式) **take on 1** receive; accept 接納;接受; 招收: *The college is taking on more staff* i. e. employing more staff 該學院正在增聘教職員. *I cannot take on this work.* 我不能承擔這項工作. *The bus took on more passengers.* 公共汽車接納了更多乘客. **2** play a game against 與…比賽; 與…較量: *He took me on at tennis.* 他要跟我在網球場上一見高低. **3** change in appearance; assume 改變(面貌); 呈現(新面貌): *His face took on an angry look.* 他面有慍色. **take out 1** cause to accompany one to an entertainment etc at one's own expense (出錢)帶…出去(消遣等): *He took us out to lunch.* 他帶我們出去吃午飯. **2** get for oneself (usu. a document) 領取(文件, 執照等): *I must take out an insurance policy for my car.* 我得給我的汽車投保. **take something over** become responsible for; take control of 開始對…負責; 掌管, 接管: *He is taking over my job while I am on holiday.* 我去度假時由他接替我的工作. *This large company has taken over many small ones.* 這家大公司吞併了許多家小公司. **'takeover** *nc*: *This company is planning another takeover.* 這家公司正計劃接管另一家公司. **take to someone / something** begin to like 開始喜歡: *I took to him as soon as I saw him.* 我一見到他就喜歡上他了. **take someone / something up 1** lift; pick up 提起, 舉起; 拾起, 撿起: *We took up our luggage and followed him.* 我們拿起行李就跟他走了. **2** begin doing, become interested in 從事於; 專注於:

take up gardening 開始對園藝感興趣. **3** (with reference to time and space) use; fill 佔用; 佔去(時間或空間): *The meeting took up the whole morning.* 這次會議佔用了整個上午. *The large desk takes up most of the office.* 這張大辦公桌佔去了辦公室的大部份地方. **be taken aback** be surprised 大吃一驚. **take into account** remember while considering something 考慮, 重視: *When deciding what to do we must take into account all the difficulties.* 在決定應做事項時, 我們必須考慮到所有的困難. **be taken by** be attracted by; be pleased with 被吸引; 對…感到滿意: *We were greatly taken by the children's good behaviour.* 孩子們的好品行使我們非常喜歡. **be taken ill** become ill 得病. **take one's mind off** prevent someone from worrying about 不考慮(某事), 不想(某事): *He took his mind off the problem by playing a game of tennis.* 他打了一場網球, 不去想那問題. **take part in** join in 參加: *We all took part in the discussion.* 我們都參加了討論. **take place** happen 發生; 舉行: *The concert takes place next Friday.* 音樂會下星期五舉行. **take the place of** occupy a place or position instead of 代替: *He will take my place in the football team because I shall be absent.* 我會暫時不在, 由他頂替我在足球隊裏的位置.

talc [tælk] *nu* **1** type of mineral that can be made into a fine powder 滑石. **2** powder made from talc, used on the skin (usu. scented) 爽身粉(通常有香味). (Also 亦作 **talcum (powder)**).

tale [teil] *nc* story; account (often a false one) 故事; 傳說(常是假的). **tell tales** (often with reference to children) make known what should be kept secret; spread bad reports (about somebody) (常指孩子) 講出內情; 講 (某人的) 壞話: *She is always telling tales about her classmates.* 她老是在講同班同學的壞話. **'telltale** *adj* revealing; making something known 揭示的, 暴露的; 顯露實情的, 洩露底細的: *There are telltale marks on the floor which showed that an intruder had been in the house.* 地板上的痕跡, 表明這屋子裏有外人來過. Also 亦作 *nc* person who tells tales 講出內情的人; 講別人壞話的人.

talent ['tælnt] *nc* special ability; natural power 天資, 天賦; 天才: *You have a talent for making friends.* 你有交朋友的才能. *He is a man with many talents.* 他多才多藝. **talented** *adj* having talent 有才氣的: *a talented speaker* 有才華的演說家.

talk [tɔːk] *vt / i* speak; discuss; converse; gossip 講話; 討論; 交談; 閑聊: *He talks to everybody he meets.* 他跟他碰到的每一個人都聊上幾句. *Today our teacher talked about Africa.* 今天我們的老師講到非洲的情況. *Animals cannot talk.* 動物不會說話. Also 亦作 **1** *nc* speech; lecture; discussion 談話; 演講; 討論: *Did you hear the president's talk last night?* 你聽了總統昨天晚上的演說嗎? *The two countries are having talks about trade.* 兩國正在進行貿易談判. **2** *nu* rumour 謠言; 傳說: *There is some talk of the president resigning* i.e. some people say he may resign. 有人傳說總統可能辭職. **talker** *nc* person who talks 談話者, 講話者: *He is a good / poor / slow / quick talker.* 他是一個善於交談 / 不善交談 / 講話很慢 / 講話很快的人. **talkative** ['tɔːkətɪv] *adj* fond of talking 健談的; 多嘴的. **'talking point** something to be discussed or worthy of discussion

(用來討論的或值得討論的)話題, 論題. **'small talk** talk about matters which are not important (e.g. the weather) 閑談, 關於瑣事(如天氣)的交談. **talk back** answer rudely; argue 頂嘴; 反駁, 爭辯: *Don't talk back to your father like that!* 別那樣頂撞你爸爸! **talk down to somebody** talk to someone in a proud, superior manner 用高人一等的口氣對某人說話. **talk someone into something** persuade by talking 說服某人做某事. **talk someone round** persuade someone who is unwilling 說服某人. **'talking-to** *nc* scolding 責備, 斥責: *My father gave me a good talking-to. (informal)* 我父親狠狠訓斥了我一通. (非正式) **talk shop** talk about one's own business or interests *(informal)* 說行話, 三句不離本行. (非正式)

tall [tɔːl] *adj* **1** (with reference to persons) high; of greater height than usual (指人身材) 高的; 個子高於常人的: *I am the tallest boy in the class.* 我是全班個子最高的男孩. *He is tall for his age.* 按他的年齡來說, 他長得很高. *Note* 說明: *tall* is also used with reference to things which are high but not wide and can thus be compared with persons *(e.g. tall pole; tall tree; tall building)*. For this reason one cannot usually say: *tall hill; tall desks* etc. tall 也可指高但不寬, 可以和人相比的東西(如 tall pole 高竿; tall tree 高樹; tall building 高樓等). 因此, 通常不說 tall hill; tall desk 等. **2** difficult; unreasonable 困難的; 不合理的: *This is a tall order* i.e. a job or request which is difficult to carry out. 這是件難辦的差使. 即: 這要求太苛刻或這件事太難做到. *He tells tall stories* i.e. stories which are difficult to believe. *(informal in sense 2)* 他常講令人難以置信

信的故事.(義2爲非正式). **tallness** *nu*.

tally ['tæli] *vi* agree; be the same 符合; 吻合, 一致: *Your story does not tally with mine.* 他所說的跟我所說的不一樣. *The expenditure and the receipts should tally.* 支出與收入應當相符.

talon ['tæln] *nc* long hooked claw of certain types of birds (e.g. the hawk) 猛禽(如鷹等)的鈎形長爪.

tambourine [tæmbə'ri:n] *nc* type of small, round drum, with pieces of metal at the sides, which is beaten with the hand and shaken 鈴鼓, 手鼓.

tame [teim] *adj* **1** (with reference to animals) accustomed to human beings; not wild or fierce (指動物) 馴服的, 溫順的, 不兇猛的: *He keeps a tame lion.* 他飼養一隻馴服的獅子. **2** (with reference to persons / things) obedient; dull (指人或事物) 順從的; 平淡乏味的: *He is so tame that he agrees with everybody.* 他萬事隨和, 每一個人的話他都同意. *I think cricket is a tame sport.* 我認爲板球是一種平淡無味的運動. Also 亦作 *vt* cause to be tame 馴服, 制服; 使順從; 使變得平淡乏味. **tameness** *nu* **tamer** *nc* (usu. with another word) person who tames (通常與另一詞連用) 馴服或制服…的人; *liontamer* 馴獅人.

tamper ['tæmpə*] *vi* interfere; change; damage 干擾; 竄改; 損害: *Somebody has tampered with the lock on the door.* 有人撬過門上的鎖. *He was accused of tampering with the examination papers.* 他被指責竄改考卷.

tan [tæn] *nc / u* light brown colour 棕褐色, 黃褐色: *The sun has given your skin a tan.* 太陽把你的皮膚曬得黑黑的. Also 亦作 *adj*: *She was wearing tan shoes and carrying a tan bag.* 她

穿着黃褐色的鞋子, 拿着黃褐色的手提包. Also 亦作 *vt / i* make light brown in colour (使)曬黑, (使)成黃褐色: *His face was tanned by the sun and wind.* 經過日曬風吹, 他的臉色變得黝黑.

tandem ['tændəm] *nc* type of bicycle with two seats, one behind the other, and two sets of pedals (前前後座位並有兩套踏板的)雙人自行車.

tang [tæŋ] *nc* strong, distinctive smell or taste 強烈的氣味; 與衆不同的味道: *tang of wood smoke* 木頭冒烟的氣味. *fruit with a pleasant tang* 氣味芳香的水果. **tangy** *adj*.

tangent ['tændʒənt] *nc* straight line which touches a curve at one point only 切線; 正切線.

tangerine [tændʒə'ri:n] *nc* type of small, slightly flat orange with loose skin 紅橘; 柑橘.

tangible ['tændʒibl] *adj* able to be touched; real 可觸摸的; 真實的: *The plan has produced tangible results.* 這項計劃確有成效. (opp 反義詞 **intangible**).

tangle ['tæŋgl] *nc* **1** (with reference to thread, string, hair) mixed-up and untidy mass (指綫, 繩子, 頭髮等) 纏結: *Her hair was full of tangles.* 她的頭髮纏結成團. *All the ropes were in a tangle.* 所有的繩子都纏結. **2** confusion; disorder 混亂; 雜亂: *His affairs are in a tangle.* 他的事務一片混亂. Also 亦作 *vt / i* become, cause to become, confused or disordered (使)糾纏; (使)混亂; 弄亂. (opp 反義詞 **untangle**).

tank [tæŋk] *nc* **1** large container for liquid or gas (裝液體或氣體的)大容器: *water tank* 水箱 *petrol tank* 汽油箱. **2** heavily armoured vehicle with a gun, used in war 坦克. **tanker** *nc* **1** ship with large tanks for carrying oil.

油船. **2** heavy lorry with a large tank for carrying oil or other liquids 油槽汽車.

tankard ['tæŋkəd] *nc* large drinking pot, often with a lid (通常連蓋的)大酒杯.

tanner ['tænə] *nc* person whose work is tanning hides 製革工人, 鞣皮工人.

tantalize ['tæntəlaiz] *vt* cause to hope or wish for something that is not possible, or not easily obtained (以不可能實現或很難實現的希望)逗引, 逗弄: *They tantalized the poor prisoner with promises of freedom.* 他們以允諾給予自由來逗弄那可憐的囚犯. **tantalizing** *adj*: *tantalizing promises of freedom* 給予自由的誘人許諾.

tantamount ['tæntəmaunt] *adj* (with **to**) equal in meaning to; the same as (與 to 連用)意義相等的, 相同的: *His silence was tantamount to saying he disagreed.* 他的沉默等於說他不同意.

tantrum ['tæntrəm] *nc* sudden fit of bad temper (usu. about something which is not important) (通常指爲小事)脾氣發作: *This child is always having tantrums.* 這孩子老是在生氣. *The old man went away in a tantrum.* 老人氣呼呼地走開了.

tap¹ [tæp] *nc* (Brit) device for allowing liquid or gas to come out of a pipe or container (英) (水或氣的)旋塞, 龍頭: *She turned on the tap and filled the pot with water.* (US 美 **faucet**) 她捜開龍頭, 把罐子罐滿水. Also 亦作 *vt* **1** put a tap, make a cut, in something to take out the liquid inside 在…裝置龍頭或旋塞使液體流出: 在…割一切口使液體流出: *He is tapping the barrel of beer.* 他正在開啤酒桶的旋塞取酒. *The workers tap the rubber trees every morning* i.e. make a cut in them to get the liquid rubber from them 工人每天清晨割橡膠. 即: 在橡膠樹上割一

條切口以使膠汁流出. **2** (of a telephone) fasten a wire secretly to it so that another person can listen to what is said (在電話線上)搭線竊聽: *Our telephone has been tapped.* 我們的電話被竊聽了. *past* 過去式和過去分詞 **tapped.**

tap² [tæp] *nc* light blow 輕拍, 輕敲: *I felt a tap on my shoulder.* 我感到有人拍我的肩膀. Also 亦作 *vt* give a light blow to 輕拍, 輕敲: *He tapped me on the shoulder.* 他拍拍我的肩膀. *Somebody is tapping at / on the door.* 有人在輕輕敲門. *past* 過去式和過去分詞 **tapped.** **'tapdance** *nc* type of dance in which the feet are tapped on the floor in time with the music 踢躂舞.

tape [teip] *nc* **1** narrow piece of cloth or other material for tying or fastening (捆綁用的)帶子, 布帶. **2** narrow piece of cloth or other material with other uses (作其他用途的)帶子. Also 亦作 *vt* record on a magnetic tape 用磁帶錄音: *He taped my speech on his tape recorder.* 他用磁帶錄音機錄下了我的講話. **'tape measure, 'measuring tape** tape marked in feet or metres etc for measuring things 捲尺, 軟尺. **'tape recorder** *nc* apparatus which records sounds and music on a magnetized tape 磁帶錄音機. **magnetic tape** type of magnetized tape used on a tape recorder to record sounds and music 錄音磁帶. **red tape** unnecessary rules made by an organization (e.g. by a government or a large company) 官樣文章, 繁文縟節(如由政府或大公司制訂的不必要規章等): *The plan to build a new school has been delayed by red tape.* (informal) 建新校的計劃被繁難的公事程序所耽擱了. (非正式).

taper¹ ['teipə*] *vt / i* become, cause to

become, thinner at one end (使)一端 逐漸變細: *The pencil tapers to a sharp point.* 鉛筆的一端細成筆尖. *He tapered the stick with a knife.* 他用小刀把棍子的一端削尖. **tapering** *adj.*

taper² ['teipə*] *nc* type of thin candle 極細的蠟燭.

tapestry ['tæpistri] *nc / u* 1 woven hanging (usu. wool) with pictures or designs (通常是羊毛織的)掛毯. 2 fabric made by sewing pictures or designs in coloured wools or silks, used for hangings, chair coverings etc. 繡帷; 織錦(作窗帷、椅套等用).

tapioca [tæpi'oukə] *nu* type of starchy food obtained from the cassava or manioc plant 木薯澱粉.

tar [ta:*] *nu* type of thick, black, sticky liquid obtained from coal or wood and used for making roads, preserving wood and as an antiseptic 焦油, 瀝青, 柏油. **'tarma'cadam, 'tarmac** *nu* mixture of tar and small stones used to make the surface of a road, airport runway etc. 柏油碎石(用於舖公路、機場跑道等). Also 亦作 *adj*: *We travelled all the way on a good tarmac road.* 我們的整個旅程都走在一條非常好的柏油碎石公路上.

target ['ta:git] *nc* 1 something aimed at (e.g. when practising or competing in shooting) 靶子, 目標(如射擊練習或比賽時所用的靶子): *He hit the target with every shot he fired.* 他開的每一槍都打中靶子. 2 somebody / something attacked or criticized 攻擊或批評的對象: *The minister is the target of many complaints.* 部長受到許多人抱怨. 3 aim or total which it is desired to reach 指標, 爭取實現的目標, 爭取達到的總數: *The target of the new plan is primary education for all children.* 新計劃的目標是使所有兒童都受到初等教

育.

tariff ['tærif] *nc* 1 tax charged on goods brought into a country; list of goods taxed in this way 關稅; 關稅表; 貨物課稅表. *Will the USA lower / raise the tariff on foreign motorcars?* 美國會降低/提高進口汽車的關稅稅率嗎? 2 list of charges made (e.g. in a hotel or restaurant) (旅館或飯店等的)收費表, 價目表.

tarmac ['ta:mæk] *nu* see 見 **tar**.

tarnish ['ta:niʃ] *vt / i* 1 (usu. with reference to metal) become, cause to become, dull or less bright (通常指金屬)(使) 失去光澤: *Brass tarnishes quickly in wet weather.* 天氣潮濕時黃銅會很快失去光澤. 2 spoil 玷污, 敗壞: *His bad behaviour has tarnished the good name of the school.* 他行爲不軌, 敗壞了學校的聲譽.

tarpaulin [ta:'pɔ:lin] *nc* canvas sheet made waterproof by being treated with tar 防水帆布, 油布.

tarry¹ ['tæri] *vi* 1 delay; linger; lodge 停留, 逗留; 住: *He tarried a few days at an inn.* 他在客棧住(或逗留)了幾天. 2 stay for a time, esp. longer than intended; be tardy 耽擱; 遲延: *Why do you tarry so long?* 你爲甚麼耽擱這麼久? 3 wait 等候: *tarry for a person* 等候一個人.

tarry² ['ta:ri] *adj* 1 of or like tar 柏油的; 像柏油的. 2 covered or smeared with tar 塗有柏油的; 給柏油弄髒.

tart¹ [ta:t] *adj* 1 having a sour taste 酸的. 2 sharp; severe 尖刻的; 嚴厲的: *He gave a tart reply.* 他作了尖刻的回答.

tart² [ta:t] *nc* type of pie containing fruit or jam 果餡餅.

tart³ [ta:t] immoral woman; prostitute. *(informal)* 輕佻的女人; 妓女. (非正式).

tartan ['tɑ:tn] *nu* type of woollen cloth with a pattern of coloured squares 格子花呢. Also 亦作 *adj tartan jacket* 格子花呢外套.

tartar ['tɑ:tə*] *nu* hard deposit on the teeth 牙垢, 牙石.

task [tɑ:sk] *nc* piece of work which has to be done 任務, 工作. *I was given the task of cleaning the room.* 給了我打掃房間的任務. **'task force** part of any army or navy sent to carry out a special operation; any group having similar special duties 特遣部隊; 艦工; 執行特別任務的小組. **'taskmaster** man, woman who gives somebody tasks to do and keeps him busy 工頭, 監工: *Our teacher is a hard taskmaster.* 我們的老師要求很嚴格. **take somebody to task** scold; question closely 申斥; 盤問: *My father took me to task about my dirty hands.* 我父親因我手髒而責備我.

tassel ['tæsl] *nc* number of threads fastened together at one end and used as an ornament, e.g. on cushions 纓, 流蘇(如座墊、靠墊上的流蘇).

taste¹ [teist] *vt / i* 1 have a particular flavour in the mouth有某種味道; *The tea tasted sweet.* 這茶有甜味. *Some oranges taste bitter.* 有些橘子吃起來是苦的. *This soup tastes too much of salt.* 這湯太鹹了. 2 feel or try the flavour of something in the mouth嘗, 品嘗: *Can you taste the sugar in your coffee?* 你能嘗出咖啡的甜味嗎? *She tasted the pudding to see if it was sweet enough.* 她嘗了嘗布丁, 看看夠不夠甜. 3 have experience of; meet 體驗, 領嘗; 遇到, 經歷: *They tasted defeat for the first time.* 他們初次嘗到失敗的滋味.

taste² [teist] *nc / u* 1 (*sing* with **a** or **the**) sense or feeling given by something in the mouth (單數與 a 或 the 連用) 味覺; 味道: *Children like the taste of sugar.* 孩子們喜歡糖的味道. *Some oranges have a bitter taste.* 有些橘子有苦味. *Food which is cooked too much has no taste.* 煮得太久的食物吃起來沒有味道. 2 (*sing* with a) small quantity for sample (單數與a連用) 一口, 一點, 少量: *May I have a taste of your pudding?* i.e. to see what it is like 我可以嘗一嘗你的布丁嗎? 即: 看看味道如何. *He gave us a taste of his bad temper* i.e. enough to show us how bad-tempered he could be 他讓我們領教了一下他的壞脾氣. 即: 足以讓我們知道他的脾氣能有多壞. 3 liking for 愛好: *She has a taste for expensive hats.* 她愛戴昂貴的帽子. *His tastes in music are not the same as mine.* 他在音樂方面的愛好跟我的愛好不同. 4 choice; judgment; appreciation 品味; 判斷力; 鑑賞力: *Their house is furnished in very good taste* i.e. the furniture is well-chosen and suitable 他們的房子佈置得雅緻大方. 即: 像具選擇得當. *His reply to their question was in bad taste* i.e. was made with poor judgment and caused offence 對於他們的問題, 他的回答不得體. 即: 判斷不當, 令人反感. *We all admire your taste in art* i.e. your good judgment and choice 我們都欽佩你的藝術鑑賞力. **tasteful** *adj* having, showing good taste 雅緻的; 有鑑賞力的: *The furniture is very tasteful.* 他們家的傢具非常雅緻. **tastefully** *adv* **tasteless** *adj* 1 without taste in the mouth 無味的, 不好吃的: *The food is tasteless.* 這種食物吃起來毫無味道. 2 having, showing bad taste 庸俗的: *A tasteless colour scheme* 庸俗的配色. **tasty** *adj* having a pleasant taste in the mouth 美味的,

可口的: *a tasty cake* 一塊美味的蛋糕.
tastily *adv.*

tatters ['tætəz] *npl* torn pieces of cloth, paper etc. 破布條, 碎紙片等: *His coat was in tatters* i. e. badly torn 他衣衫襤褸.即:破碎不堪. **tattered** *adj*: *He was wearing a tattered coat.* 他穿着一件破爛的外套.

tattoo[1] [tə'tu:] *nc* coloured design or picture put on the skin by making holes in it with a needle and rubbing in the colours 紋身. *pl* 複數 **tattoos.** Also 亦作 *vt* mark the skin in this way 刺花, 紋刺.

tattoo[2] [tə'tu:] *nc* 1 public show (usu. given at night) by a large number of soldiers 軍隊夜間表演操. 2 quick beating or tapping 連續的敲擊: *His fingers beat a tattoo on the desk as he listened.* 他一面聽, 一面用手指敲擊書桌.

tatty ['tæti] *adj* shabby; untidy. (*informal*) 襤褸的, 邋遢的.(非正式).

taught [tɔ:t] past of **teach.** teach 的過去式和過去分詞.

taunt [tɔ:nt] *vt* say cruel or insulting words to somebody 嘲諷, 嘲弄: *He taunted me for / with being weak.* 他嘲諷我的軟弱. *He taunted me with weakness.* 他嘲諷我的弱點. Also 亦作 *nc*: *his taunts about my weakness* 他對我的弱點的嘲諷.

taut [tɔ:t] *adj* tight; fully stretched 緊的; 繃緊的: *The skin of the drum is taut.* 鼓皮繃得很緊.

tavern ['tævən] *nc* inn; place where beer, liquor etc are sold and drunk (*o. f.*) 小旅館, 客棧; 酒館(舊式).

tawdry ['tɔ:dri] *adj* bright and showy but of poor quality 花哨低級; 俗麗的: *She was wearing a tawdry hat.* 她戴着一頂花哨低級的帽子.

tawny ['tɔ:ni] *adj* yellow-brown in col-

our 黃褐色的.

tax [tæks] *nc / u* money which has to be paid to the government of a country by those who live in it 稅: *The government has increased the tax on motorcars.* 政府已提高了汽車稅. *People who refuse to pay tax can be put in prison.* 拒絕納稅者會被送進監獄. Also 亦作 *vt* 1 put a tax on; make somebody pay a tax 對…徵稅; 使納稅: *He wants all liquor to be heavily taxed.* 他想讓所有酒類都被課以重稅. *Governments do not usually tax children.* 政府通常不向孩子們收稅. 2 test severely 嚴峻地考驗: *The war taxed the soldiers' courage.* 戰爭考驗士兵的勇氣. **taxation** [tæk'seiʃən] *nu* money taken by taxes; act of taxing 稅收; 課稅: *The new government has increased taxation.* 新政府已提高了稅收. **'tax-free** *adj* not taxed 免稅的. **'taxpayer** person who pays tax 納稅人.

taxi ['tæksi] *nc* motorcar for hire (usu. fitted with a device which measures the distance travelled and shows the cost of the journey) 出租車, 計程車, 的士. *pl* 複數 **taxis.** Note 說明: the full title is *taxicab;* short forms are *(Brit)* taxi and *(US)* cab 全稱是 taxicab; 縮略式是: (英) taxi; (美) cab. Also 亦作 *vi* (with reference to aircraft) move along the ground (指飛機) 沿地面滑行. **'taxi driver** person who drives a taxi 出租車駕駛員, 的士司機. **'taxi rank** place where taxis wait to be hired 出租車停車處.

taxidermy ['tæksidəmi] *nu* art of preparing and filling the skins of dead animals so that they look alive 動物標本剝製術. **taxidermist** *nc* person skilled in taxidermy 動物標本剝製專家.

tea [ti:] **1** *nu* type of plant, the dried leaves of which are used to make a drink by pouring boiling water over them 茶樹; 茶葉. **2** *nu* drink made in this way 茶: *He is having a cup of tea.* 他正喝杯茶. *Mother is making (the) tea* i. e. making the drink by pouring boiling water over the dried leaves 母親正在泡茶. **3** *nu* time when tea is drunk (usu. about **4** p. m.) 下午茶時間 (通常指下午 4 點鐘左右). *I won't be home until after tea.* 我要到午後茶過後才會回家. **4** *nc / u* light meal taken with tea 茶點: *This hotel serves teas.* 這家旅館提供茶點服務. **'tea bag** small bag containing tea used for making tea. (It is placed in a cup or pot and hot water is added.) 袋裝茶, 茶包. **'tea caddy** small box or tin in which tea is kept ready for use 茶罐; 茶筒. **'teacake** type of flat cake (usu. served hot with butter) 一種扁平狀糕點 (通常塗黃油熱吃). **'teacloth** small cloth for drying cups, saucers etc after they have been washed 擦拭杯盤用的布. **'tea cosy** thick cover put over a teapot keep it hot 茶壺保暖罩. **'teacup** cup used for drinking tea 茶杯. **'tea leaf** *nc* (usu. *pl*) leaf left in a teapot or cup after tea has been made and drunk (通常用複數) 泡飲過的茶葉. **'teapot** pot in which tea is made 茶壺. **'tearoom** restaurant which provides light meals and tea 茶館. **'tea service, 'tea set** cups, saucers, plates, teapot etc used at tea 茶具. **'teaspoon** small spoon used for stirring tea 茶匙. **'teaspoonful** amount that can be contained in a teaspoon 一茶匙之量. **'high 'tea** large cooked meal with tea, taken in the evening (usu. by those who do not have dinner later) 具有豐盛熟食的傍晚茶點 (通常取代晚間正餐).

teach [ti:tʃ] *vt / i* instruct; give lessons; educate 教; 教導; 教書; 教育: *My sister teaches* i. e. her work is teaching. 我姐姐教書. *She likes teaching children.* 她喜歡教小孩. *He is teaching me (how) to ride a bicycle.* 他正在教我騎自行車. *I taught English to all my friends.* 我向我所有的朋友傳授英語. *I taught all my friends English.* 我教我所有的朋友學習英語. *past* 過去式和過去分詞 **taught** [tɔ:t]. **teacher** *nc* **teaching** *nu* work of a teacher 教學工作.

teak [ti:k] **1** *nc* type of tall tree with hard wood 柚木樹. **2** *nu* the wood of this tree used in shipbuilding etc. 柚木 (可用於造船等).

team [ti:m] *nc* **1** group of persons, working or playing together (運動比賽的) 隊; (工作) 組; (作業) 班: *The discovery was made by a team of scientists.* 這是一組科學家發現的. *He plays for the second football team.* 他爲第二足球隊踢球. **2** two or more dogs, horses, oxen etc which pull a sledge, cart etc together (同拉一部雪橇、車子等的) 一隊牲口, 兩隻或兩隻以上的狗、馬、牛等. **'team 'spirit** feeling of cooperation among those in a team (隊或組內的) 合作精神. **'teamwork** work done by a team; cooperation 集體的合作; 配合. **team up with someone** begin to work together or cooperate with someone (*informal*) 與某人一同工作或配合 (非正式).

tear[1] [tiə*] *nc* drop of water from the eye 眼淚: *The tears ran down her cheeks as she cried.* 她哭泣時眼淚順着兩頰流了下來. *The little boy burst into tears* i. e. tears came from his eyes 小男孩哭了起來. **tearful** *adj* having tears; crying 含淚的; 哭泣的.

'teargas type of gas which causes tears (used by the police to control angry crowds) 催淚彈.

tear² [tɛə*] *vt / i* **1** break or damage by pulling apart 撕; 撕破; 扯裂: *She tore her stockings while putting them on.* 她穿襪子時把襪子扯壞了. *I tore the newspaper in half / to bits / to pieces.* 我把報紙撕成兩半/碎塊/碎片. **2** become broken or damaged 破; 損壞: *Paper tears easily.* 紙張易破. *This type of cloth does not tear.* 這種布耐穿. **3** move quickly 飛奔: *He tore through the town in his car.* 他坐車飛速穿過該鎮. *Because he was late he tore out of the house.* 由於遲了, 因此他飛奔出屋. *past tense* 過去式 **tore** [tɔ:*]. *past part* 過去分詞 **torn** [tɔ:n]. Also 亦作 *nc* place which has been torn 撕破處; 扯壞處: *There is a tear in your jacket.* 你的茄克衫有個破口.

be torn between be unable to decide which of two things to do 無法抉擇: *He was torn between staying at home and going abroad.* 他進退維谷, 不知該留在國內還是該出國.

tease [ti:z] *vt* laugh at or make fun of someone to annoy him or for amusement 取笑; 戲弄: *The other boys tease him because he is fat.* 由於他很胖, 所以其他男生取笑他. *We teased her about her new hat.* 她戴了頂新帽子我們爲此而戲弄她. Also 亦作 *nc* person who likes teasing others 喜歡取笑或戲弄他人者. **teasing** *nu*.

teat [ti:t] *nc* **1** point of the breast through which milk comes; nipple 乳頭, 奶頭. **2** rubber mouthpiece of child's feeding bottle 奶瓶嘴.

technical ['teknikl] *adj* of some special type or art or skill 技術性的; 工藝的: *Engineers must have great technical knowledge.* 工程師必須具備許多技術

知識; *technical education* i.e. education in practical skills and in the uses of modern machinery etc. 技術教育, 即: 實用技術方面和現代機械使用方面等的教育. **technically** *adv* **technicality** [tekni'kæliti] *nc* **1** word which is special to a particular art or skill; special way of dealing with something 專門處理方法; 術語: *He was not allowed to buy the land on a / because of a technicality.* 根據規定, 他不得購買這塊土地.

technician [tek'niʃən] *nc* person who is trained in a particular art or skill (esp. a practical one connected with machines etc); skilled workman 技術員; 技師; 技工.

technique [tek'ni:k] *nc / u* skilled way of doing something 技術; 技能; (藝術上的) 技巧: *He is learning the technique of painting.* 他正在學習繪畫技巧. *Writing poetry requires great technique.* 寫詩需要了不起的技巧.

technology [tek'nɔlədʒi] *nu* science or study of the practical uses of scientific discoveries (e.g. in industry and in making machines etc) 工業技術; 工藝; 應用科學; 製造學; 工藝學: *Modern civilization depends greatly on technology.* 現代文明大多取決於工業技術. **technological** [teknə'lɔdʒikl] *adj* **technologist** *nc* person who is skilled in technology 工業技術人員; 工程技術專家. *Note* 說明: *a technologist is more highly qualified than a technician* (e.g. the person who designs a new type of engine is a *technologist*; the person who helps to make, maintain or repair it is a *technician*). technologist 比 technician 具有較高資格

(例如設計一種新型機器者是 technologist, 而幫助製造、維修這種機器者則是 technician).

tedious ['ti:diəs] *adj* long and uninteresting; dull and wearying 冗長乏味的; 令人厭煩的: *Travelling by a slow train is very tedious.* 乘慢車旅行令人煩悶. **tediously** *adv* **tedium** ['ti:diəm] *nu*.

tee [ti:] *nc* small heap of sand or peg on which a golfball is placed so that the player can hit it better with a golf club; place where a golfball is put in this way i.e. only at the beginning of each hole of a golf course (高爾夫球) 球座(發球時擱球的沙堆等); 發球區.

teem [ti:m] *vi* (with **with**) have in great numbers (與 with 連用) 充滿, 到處都是, 有很多; *The forest teemed with wild animals.* 森林裏到處都是野生動物. *His mind is teeming with ideas.* 他腦子裏充滿了各種想法.

teens [ti:nz] *npl* numbers ending with **teen** i.e. 13-19 以 teen 結尾的數字, 即: 13-19. *His son is in his teens* i.e. is in age over 12 and under 20 他的兒子十多歲. 即: 超過12歲, 但不足20歲. **teenage** ['ti:neidʒ] *adj* of young person over 12 and under 20 years of age 13-19歲的, 少年的: *He is too old now for teenage parties.* 他年齡太大了, 不適於參加少年聚會. **teenager** *nc* young person in his or her teens (13-19歲的)少年, 少女.

tee shirt ['ti:ʃə:t] *nc* type of light shirt with short sleeves 短袖圓領汗衫.

teeth [ti:θ] *pl* of **tooth**. tooth 的複數形式.

teethe [ti:ð] *vi* (with reference to a baby) begin to have teeth (指嬰兒)開始長牙: *Our baby is teething.* 我們的嬰兒正在長牙. **'teething troubles** troubles which often come at the be-

ginning of something but soon disappear 某事開初遇到的暫時困難: *The new plan is having its teething troubles. (informal)* 新的計劃正遭遇暫時困難. (非正式).

teetotal [ti:'toutl] *adj* refusing to drink, not allowing alcoholic liquor 戒酒的; 禁酒的: *His father is teetotal.* 他父親是個滴酒不沾的人. *It will be a teetotal party.* 這將是個不喝酒的宴會. **teetotaller** (*US* 美 **teetotaler**) *nc* person who refuses to drink alcoholic liquor 戒酒者, 滴酒不沾者.

tele- ['teli] *prefix* far; over a distance (e.g. **telephone; telescope**) 遠的; 長距離的(例如 telephone 電話; telescope 望遠鏡).

telecommunications ['telikəmju:ni-'keiʃənz] *npl* communications over a distance by using electricity (e.g. by radio, telephone etc.) 電信(如使用無線電, 電話等的通訊).

telegram ['teligræm] *nc* / *u* message sent by telegraph 電報; 電文.

telegraph ['teligra:f] *nc* / *u* instrument for sending messages (called **telegrams**) by electricity along a wire or by radio 電報機. **telegraphic** [teli-'græfik] *adj* **'telegraph pole, 'telegraph post** long pole which carries telegraph wires high above the ground 電線桿. **'telegraph wire** wire along which messages are sent by telegraph 電報電纜.

telepathy [tə'lepəθi] *nu* passing of thoughts and feelings from one person to another without using the normal senses of sight, sound, touch or smell 心靈感應, 精神感應. **telepathic** [teli'pæθik] *adj*.

telephone ['telifoun] *nc* instrument for sending and receiving the sound of the voice by electricity along a wire or on radio 電話機: *He has three tele-phones on his desk.* 他的桌上有三部電話機. *I told him the news by tele-phone.* 我打電話告訴他這個消息. Also 亦作 *vt / i* send a message by telephone; speak to somebody by telephone 打電話(給). *She has tele-phoned for the doctor* i.e. asked by telephone for him to come 她已經打了電話請醫生; *Don't telephone me when I am busy.* 在我忙的時候不要打電話給我. *Note* 說明: often phone for noun and verb 經常把 phone 作爲名詞和動詞使用. **telephonist** [tə-'lefənist] *nc* person who sends and receives messages by telephone (esp. one in charge of a telephone ex-change or telephone switch-board) 電話接線員. **'telephone box** box in which a person can stand to make a telephone call 電話亭. **'telephone exchange** place where telephone connections are made 電話交換台; 電話局.

telephoto ['teli'foutou] *adj* short form of **telephotographic.** telephotographic 的縮寫式.

telephotography ['telifə'tɔgrəfi] *nu* photography of distant objects by us-ing a special lens 遠距離攝影. **tele-photographic** ['telifoutə'græfik] *adj* (Usu. **telephoto** e.g. *a telephoto lens*) (通常寫作 telephoto. 例如 a telephoto lens 長焦距鏡頭).

teleprinter ['teliprintə*] *nc* electrical machine which automatically sends and receives typed messages by tele-graph 電傳打字機.

telerecording [teliri'kɔ:diŋ] *nc* pro-gramme recorded for television (e.g. in video tape) 電視錄像(例如錄製於錄像帶上的節目).

telescope ['teliskoup] *nc* instrument

through which distant objects appear larger and nearer 望遠鏡. Also 亦作 *vt / i* push one part inside the other (as is done when closing a telescope) (使)套疊在一起; (使)凹陷; 嵌進: *When the car hit the wall, the front was telescoped.* 車子撞牆時, 車子前部被撞得凹了進去. **telescopic** [teli-'skɔpik] *adj* 1 of or having a telescope 望遠鏡的; 具有望遠鏡的. 2 made like a telescope and so able to be made shorter or longer in the same way 套疊式的, 伸縮式的: *telescopic umbrella* 摺疊傘.

television ['teliviʒən] *nu* sending and receiving of pictures by radio. (Often informally **TV** or **telly**) 電視(非正式常作 TV 或 telly): *We watched the game on television / TV / telly.* 我們看電視播出的比賽. **televise** ['telivaiz] *vt* send by television 由電視播送: *Important football games are televised.* 重要的足球賽都由電視播出.

telex ['teleks] *nc / u* method of sending messages by telegraph 電傳. Also 亦作 *vt / i.*

tell [tel] *vt / i* 1 inform; explain; speak. 告訴; 解釋; 講: *Please tell us who you are.* 請告訴我們你是誰. *They told me (that) they were tired.* 他們告訴我他們累了. *The teacher told his pupils how to do it.* 教師告訴學生怎麼做. *I told him all about it.* 我把與此有關的一切都告訴他. *He is telling the truth.* 他在講真話. 2 (usu. with **can** or **be able**) know; judge; recognize (通常與 can 或 be able 連用) 懂; 判斷; 分辨: *The little boy can't tell the time yet* i.e. read the time on a clock or watch 這個小男孩看不懂鐘錶指示的時間. *They were able to tell the difference be-tween the two books.* 他們能夠區別這兩本書之間的差異. *I couldn't tell him* *from his brother* i.e. the difference between him and his brother. 我無法分辨他和他弟弟. *It is difficult to tell his weight just by looking at him.* 僅看着他是難以判斷他的體重的. **3** order; instruct 命令;指示: *He told me to come.* 他叫我來. *You must do as you are told.* 你必須按你得到的指示去做. **4** make known a secret 洩露秘密: *I'll show you where it is, if you promise not to tell.* 如果你保證不說出去,我就告訴你它在甚麼地方. **5** have an effect 產生效果,發生影響: *When you are old, every year tells.* 你老的時候會一年不如一年. *past* 過去式和過去分詞 **told** [tould]. **teller** *nc* person who counts money in a bank as he receives it or pays it out (銀行)出納員. **telling** *adj* having great effect 非常有效的: *He made a very telling speech about their mistakes.* 他就他們的錯誤作了有力的發言. **'telltale** see 見 **tale.** **tell someone off** rebuke; scold 責備;訓斥: *We were told off for being late.* (informal) 我們因遲到而受責備. (非正式). **tell on someone 1** make known a secret about somebody 告發某人: *He told on his friends.* (informal) 他告發朋友. (非正式). **2** have an effect on (對某人)產生影響. *His age is beginning to tell on him.* 他的年齡開始對他產生影響. **all told** including all; altogether 總共,合計: *Fifty people came all told.* 總共來了五十個人.

telly [ˈteli] *nc / u* short informal form of **television.** television 的非正式縮畧式.

temerity [təˈmeriti] *nu* boldness; impudence 魯莽;無禮: *He had the temerity to argue with the manager.* 他竟敢與經理爭論.

temp [temp] *nc* temporary employee (usu. a secretary) (informal) 臨時雇員 (通常指代用秘書)(非正式).

temper [ˈtempə*] *nc / u* state of the mind or feelings 脾氣;心情;情緒: *He was in a good temper* i.e. happy and pleasant 他情緒很好. *He was in a (bad) temper* i.e. angry and unpleasant 他情緒很壞. Also 亦作 *vt / i* **1** make a metal hard and strong by heating and cooling it (使)淬硬,(使)回火. **2** soften; make more pleasant 冲淡;緩和: *He tempered his refusal with a smile.* 他以微笑來緩和由於他拒絕而產生的緊張氣氛. **-tempered** *adj* having a temper of a particular kind 具有…性情的: *He is a good- / bad- / hot- / short-tempered man.* 他是個好/壞/急/暴躁性子的人. **lose one's temper** become angry (often suddenly and against one's will) 生氣,發怒 (常指突然而且不由自主地).

temperament [ˈtemprəmənt] *nc / u* somebody's character as shown by his behaviour and feelings 性格;性情,氣質: *He has a happy temperament.* 他性格開朗. *James hasn't the temperament for work in an office.* 詹姆士的性格不適合在辦公室工作. *She and I have similar temperaments.* 她與我具有類似的氣質. **temperamental** [temprəˈmentl] *adj* easily excited; moody 易激動的;喜怒無常的: *Many great artists are temperamental.* 許多偉大的藝術家多易激動的.

temperance [ˈtempərns] *nu* control over oneself in behaving, eating etc (and esp. in drinking) 在行爲,飲食等方面(尤指喝酒)的節制,克制. *temperance society* i.e. one which is opposed to alcoholic drinks 禁酒會.

temperate [ˈtempərət] *adj* **1** not eating or drinking too much; controlling one's behaviour 飲食有節制的;克己的: *He is temperate in his habits.* 他能

够节制自己的习惯. (opp 反义词 **in-temperate**). **2** (with reference to parts of the world) not too hot and not too cold (气候) 温和的: *Great Britain has a temperate climate.* 英国气候温和.

temperature ['temprətʃə*] *nc / u* **1** amount of heat or cold 温度: *In summer the temperature is high and in winter it is low.* 夏天温度高, 冬天温度低. **2** too much heat in the body 发烧: *When he was ill, he had / ran a temperature* i.e. the temperature of his body was higher than usual. 他生病时发烧. 即: 他的体温高於平时. **take somebody's temperature** measure the temperature of somebody's body (with a thermometer) (以温度计) 测量某人的体温.

tempest ['tempist] *nc* violent wind 暴风雨. **tempestuous** [tem'pestjuəs] *adj* stormy; violent 有暴风雨的; 猛烈的: *tempestuous sea* 波涛汹涌的海洋; *tempestuous argument* 激烈的争论.

template ['templit] *nc* thin, flat piece of wood or metal etc of a particular shape or pattern, used when cutting out or checking other shapes and patterns (切木, 金属等用的) 样板, 木模板, 金属模片.

temple¹ ['templ] *nc* building where a god is worshipped 寺院, 庙宇. *Note* 说明: the building for Christian worship is usu. called a *church* or *chapel* 供基督教徒礼拜的建筑物通常叫 church 和 chapel.

temple² ['templ] *nc* part of the head between the eye and the ear 太阳穴.

tempo ['tempou] *nc / u* speed at which music is played (音乐节奏进行的) 速度: *The tune has a fast / slow tempo.* 该曲调节奏快慢. *pl* 复数 **tempos**.

temporal ['tempərl] *adj* **1** of time 时间

的. **2** of this world; not spiritual 此世的; 现世的; 世俗的: *A king has temporal powers, a bishop spiritual ones.* 国王有世俗权力, 主教有宗教权力.

temporary ['tempərəri] *adj* lasting or intended to be used for a short time 暂时的, 短暂的: *temporary absence* 暂时缺席; *temporary buildings* 临时建筑物. (opp 反义词 **permanent**). **temporarily** *adv*.

tempt [tempt] *vt* **1** make, try to make, somebody do something he should not do 引诱或怂恿(某人)干不正当之事; *His friend tempted him to steal / into stealing the money.* 他的朋友引诱他偷钱. **2** cause to want or wish for 使思想: *Can I tempt you to (have) another cup of tea?* 我能让你再喝一杯茶吗? **temptation** [temp'teiʃən] *nc / u*: *There are many temptations to steal in a large shop.* 在大商店里诱人偷窃的东西很多. *I resisted the temptation to tell him.* 我克制住自己, 没有告诉他. **tempting** *adj* attractive 吸引人的, 诱人的.

ten [ten] see appendix 见附录.

tenable ['tenəbl] *adj* **1** able to be held or occupied 可保有的: *The position as chairman is tenable for three years.* 主席职位任期 3 年. **2** able to be defended or justified 无懈可击的; 站得住脚的: *Do you think his argument is tenable?* 你认为他的论点站得住脚吗? (opp 反义词 **untenable**).

tenacious [tə'neiʃəs] *adj* holding firmly; giving nothing away; strong 坚持的; 坚韧不拔的, 顽强的; 记忆力强的; 坚强的. *tenacious defence against the enemy* 顽强地抵御敌军; *a tenacious memory* i.e. one which does not forget much 很强的记忆力. **tenacity** [tə'næsiti] *nu*.

tenant ['tenənt] *nc* person who pays the owner for the use of a house, room or land 房客; 佃戶; 承租人. **tenancy** *nu* occupation as a tenant 租賃.

tend¹ [tend] *vi* be inclined to; be likely to 傾向於; 很可能: *He tends to speak too quickly.* 他講話往往太快. **tendency** *nc: He has a tendency to speak too quickly.* 他講話往往太快. *All children have a tendency towards illness.* 小孩都容易得病.

tend² [tend] *vt* look after; attend to 照顧, 照料; 服侍. *A good farmer tends his land.* (rather *o. f.*) 一個好的農民精心照管他的土地. (相當舊式).

tender¹ ['tendə*] *adj* 1 easily damaged or hurt 脆弱的, 嫩的: *He joined the army at the tender age of 15.* 他在十五歲小小年紀時就參軍了. 2 kind; loving 善良的; 溫柔的; 親切的: *She has a tender heart.* 她心地善良. *He gave her a tender look.* 他含情脈脈地看了她一眼. 3 (with reference to meat) soft; easily cut and eaten (指肉) 柔軟的, 嫩的. 4 painful when touched 一觸即痛的. **tenderly** *adv* **tenderness** *nu.*

tender² ['tendə*] *vt / i* 1 offer; give to be accepted 提供, 提出: *The manager offered his resignation to the committee.* 經理向委員會提出辭呈. 2 offer to do something for a particular price 投標: *Several firms have tendered for building the new school.* 有數家公司已經投標欲建造這所新學校. Also 亦作 *nc* 1 offer of this kind 投標: *We have received tenders from several firms.* 我們已收到數家公司的投標. *The work was put out to tender* i.e. tenders for doing the work were asked for 這項工作已讓公眾投標. 2 railway truck (鐵路) 煤水車. **legal tender** form of money or currency which the law states must be accepted in payment 法定貨幣: *In Britain, Bank of England*

pound notes are legal tender. 在英國, 英格蘭銀行發行的英鎊鈔票是法定貨幣.

tendon ['tendn] *nc* strong substance like string which joins a muscle to a bone 筋, 腱.

tendril ['tendril] *nc* thin part of a climbing plant which helps the plant to grow by fixing itself to a tree, stick, wall etc. 植物的鬚蔓.

tenement ['tenəmənt] *nc* large building divided into separate flats which are rented (often such a building in a poor part of a city) (多位於城市貧民區的)公共住宅, 廉價公寓.

tenet ['tenət] *nc* (often *pl*) belief; principle. (常用複數)信念; 教義; 教條; 原則.

tennis ['tenis] *nu* game played by two or four players in which a ball is hit backwards and forwards across a low net 網球. *Note* 說明: the full name is *lawn tennis,* although it can be played on hard surfaces as well as on grass. 雖然它可在草地也可在堅硬的地面上打, 但是其全稱是 lawn tennis 草地網球.

tenor¹ ['tenə*] 1 *nu* highest male adult voice (in the usual range) 男高音. 2 *nc* person who sings with this kind of voice 男高音歌唱者(家). Also 亦作 *adj.*

tenor² ['tenə*] *n sing* (with **the**) general meaning, direction or course (與 the 連用)大意; 方向; 一般趨向, 進程: *The tenor of his speech was that war would come.* 他講話的大意是戰爭將要發生.

tense¹ [tens] *nc* form of the verb which shows time (動詞的)時態: *present / past / future tense.* 現在/過去/將來式.

tense² [tens] *adj* showing strain 緊張的: *They had tense faces as they waited for the news.* 在等待消息時, 他

們臉上顯出緊張的神情. *There was a tense silence in the room.* 房間裏有一種令人緊張的寂靜. **tensely** *adv* **tenseness** *nu* **tension 1** *nu* state of being stretched tightly 張拉度: *The tension was so great that the wire broke.* 由於張拉度過大,金屬綫斷了. **2** *nc* nervous strain; excitement 緊張; 激動: *We do not like the tensions of life in a big city.* 我們不喜歡大城市裏的緊張生活.

tent [tent] *nc* shelter made of strong cloth (usu. spread over poles and held in position by ropes and pegs) 帳篷.

tentacle ['tentəkl] *nc* long, boneless limb which grows from the head of certain sea animals, used for feeling and holding things, and moving 觸手; 觸角; 觸鬚.

tentative ['tentətiv] *adj* made or done to find out what may happen; experimental; not yet decided 試探性的; 試驗的; 嘗試性的: *I can only give a tentative opinion.* 我只能提出嘗試性的意見. **tentatively** *adv*.

tenterhooks ['tentəhuks] *npl only in* **be on tenterhooks** i. e. be in a state of great anxiety 僅用於 be on tenterhooks, 即: 坐立不安, 焦慮.

tenuous ['tenjuəs] *adj* very thin and fine 纖細的.

tenure ['tenjuə*] *nc / u* length of time, or condition under which, a job is held or land is occupied etc. (職位的)任期; 任職條件; (土地的)佔有期限, 佔有條件: *Tenure of the position of professor is for ten years.* 教授任職的期限爲十年.

tepid ['tepid] *adj* **1** slightly warm 微溫的: *tepid water* 微溫的水. **2** half-hearted 半心半意的: *a tepid welcome* 不太熱情的歡迎.

term [təm] *nc* **1** definite period of time 特定的期間: *He was made secretary for a term of two years.* 他被選用爲秘書, 任期兩年. **2** part of the year at school, college or university 學期: *Our school has two terms a year instead of three.* 我們學校一年兩學期而不是三學期. *I did not like my first term at university.* 我不喜歡我入大學的第一學期. **3** word or phrase with a definite or special meaning 術語: *The term 'death duty' means the tax paid on the property of a person when he dies.* "death duty" 這個術語的意思是人死時所付的個人財產稅. **4** (in *pl*) conditions; agreement (用於複數)條件; 協定: *The terms of service in the company are good* i.e. the conditions of employment. 該公司的工作條件很好. *They have come to terms* i.e. they have reached an agreement. 他們已達成協議. **5** (in *pl*) relations (用於複數)關係: *He is on friendly terms with everybody.* 他與大家友好相處. Also 亦作 *vt* call; name 稱⋯爲, 給⋯取名爲: *This tool is termed a chisel.* 這種工具叫做鑿子.

terminal ['təminl] *nc* **1** place where a railway line, bus route etc ends (**terminus** is more often used for railways and buses); place in town where an airline deals with its passengers on their way to or from an airport 火車、公共汽車等的終點站 (terminus 更常用於火車); (民航)乘客候機室, 終點站(航空公司負責將乘客自此接送至機場, 也負責將下飛機之乘客自機場送至市區以內). **2** piece of metal which connects the ends of all electrical circuit 電路接頭: *The terminals of his car battery are dirty.* 他的汽車蓄電池的接頭很髒. Also 亦作 *adj* coming at the end; final;

approaching death 終端的; 晚期的; 臨終的: *He has a terminal disease.* 他得了絕症. *He is a terminal patient.* 他是個即將去世的病人.

terminate ['tə:mineit] *vt / i* come, bring to an end; finish (使)終止; 結束: *The conference terminated yesterday.* 會議昨天結束. *Most plural nouns terminate in 's'* 大多數複數名詞以"s"結尾. *The letter 's' terminates most plural nouns.* 大多數複數名詞都以字母"s"結尾. **termination** [tə:mi'neiʃən] *nu* act of coming or bringing to an end 終止; 結束.

terminology [tə:mi'nɔlədʒi] *nc / u* words with a special or definite meaning (e.g. those used in a particular branch of knowledge) 術語, 專門用語: *engineering / medical terminology* 工程學/醫學術語.

terminus ['tə:minəs] *nc* place where a journey by air, bus or railway etc ends; station at the end of a railway line 航空, 公共汽車或鐵路等行程的終點站; 鐵路線的終點車站. *pl* 複數 **terminuses** or **termini** ['tə:minai].

termite ['tə:mait] *nc* type of insect, found especially in the tropics, which builds hills and destroys wood 白蟻.

terrace ['terəs] *nc* 1 level piece of ground on a slope or cut from a slope 斜坡上的一塊(挖出來的)水平地面; 台地; 梯田: *The people here grow rice on terraces.* 此地的人們在梯田裏種植水稻. *They were walking on the terrace behind the house* i.e. the raised level ground just outside the back of the house 他們在屋後的台地上行走. 2 row of houses joined together 一排並列的房屋. **terraced** *adj*: *a terraced hill* 有梯層的丘陵; *terraced houses* i.e. houses joined together in a row 成排並列的房屋.

terracotta ['terə'kɔtə] *nu* type of brownish-red pottery 赤土陶器.

terrain [te'rein] *nu* area of land (esp. with reference to its use in war) 地帶; 地勢, 地形: *Before the battle the general studied the terrain.* 戰鬥前將軍研究地形.

terrible ['teribl] *adj* 1 very bad; very annoying 糟糕的; 令人十分討厭的: *She wears terrible clothes.* 她穿着很糟糕的衣服. *They made a terrible noise.* 他們吵吵鬧鬧, 討厭死了. 2 causing fear; dreadful 可怕的; 怕的: *He spoke in a terrible voice.* 他用一種很可怕的聲音說話. **terribly** *adv* 1 *He has been terribly ill.* 他病得很重. 2 very 很, 非常: *They are terribly kind. (informal)* 他們非常和善. (非正式).

terrier ['teriə*] *nc* type of small dog originally used for hunting badgers, foxes etc. 㹴.

terrify ['terifai] *vt* frighten greatly; fill with fear 使嚇壞; 使恐懼. **terrific** [tə'rifik] *adj* 1 very frightening 非常嚇人的. 2 very great; excellent 巨大的; 極好的: *He ate a terrific breakfast. (informal in sense 2)* 他美美地吃了一頓早餐. (義2爲非正式).

territory ['teritəri] *nc / u* area of land under one government (esp. a foreign government) 地區; 領土, 版圖: *The mainland part of Tanzania was once called Tanganyika Territory.* 坦桑尼亞的大陸部份一度叫做坦噶尼卡地區. **territorial** [teri'tɔ:riəl] *adj*.

terror ['terə*] *nu* great fear 恐怖, 十分驚慌: *They screamed with terror.* 她們嚇得尖叫起來. *She ran away in terror.* 她十分驚慌地逃走了. **terrorism** *nu* policy of getting what one wants in politics by using murder etc. 恐怖主義. **terrorist** *nc* person who uses terror in this way 恐怖分子. **terror-**

ize *vt* fill with terror; rule by using terror 威脅; 恫嚇; 使恐懼; 以恐怖手段統治.

terse [təːs] *adj* (with reference to speaking and writing) short; in a few words (指講話和寫作) 簡短的; 言簡意賅的.

tertiary ['təːʃəri] *adj* of the third rank, order, formation etc; third 第三位的; 第三級的; 第三系的; 第三的的; **The Tertiary period** (geology) the third period in the formation of rocks (地質) 岩石形成的第三紀.

test [test] *nc* act or means of measuring or finding out about something; examination 測試, 檢驗; 測驗, 考試; *intelligence test* i. e. one to measure intelligence 智力測驗; *blood test* i.e. one to find out what is in a person's blood 驗血; *driving test* i.e. one to find out if a person can drive 駕駛考試. Also 亦作 *vt* give a test to; examine 測驗; 檢驗: *He is testing the brakes of his car.* 他正在檢驗車子的刹車裝置. *I tested my tea for sugar* i.e. to find out if there was sugar in it. 我檢查茶裏是否有糖; *The long journey tested their patience* i.e. strained it. 長途旅行考驗他們的耐性. **'test pilot** pilot who flies new aircraft to test them 飛機試飛員. **'test tube** glass tube closed at one end in which liquids are tested 試管.

testament ['testəmənt] *nc* **1** (esp. with reference to somebody's wishes about what should happen to his property after his death) written statement. (Often in **last will and testament**) 遺囑 (常見於 last will and testament 遺囑) 2 (**Testament**) one of the two main parts of the Bible 聖經的兩個主要部份之一: *Old / New Testament* 舊 / 新約全書.

testicle ['testikl] *nc* one of the two sex glands of a male 睾丸.

testify ['testifai] *vt / i* give evidence; state solemnly 證明; 作證: *He testified in court that he was abroad at the time of the crime.* 他在法庭作證說, 罪行發生時他在國外. *I can testify to his honesty* i.e. that he is honest 我可以證明他的誠實. *He will not testify against his own brother.* 他不願作不利於他弟弟的證明.

testimonial [testi'mouniəl] *nc* **1** written statement about somebody's character and abilities (有關某人品格和能力的) 推薦書; 證明書; 鑑定書: *When I left school, the headmaster gave me a good testimonial.* 我畢業離校時, 校長給我一份很好的證明書. **2** written statement together with a gift presented to somebody by a group of persons (e.g. when he retires) (在退休時收到的由同事們贈送並有禮品的) 褒揚狀; 感謝狀.

testimony ['testiməni] *nc / u* solemn statement; evidence 證詞; 證明.

testy ['testi] *adj* quick-tempered; impatient 暴躁的; 性急的.

tetanus ['tetənəs] *nu* type of dangerous disease which makes the muscles stiff and painful (esp. those round the mouth) 破傷風 (此疾病會導致肌肉特別是嘴部肌肉僵硬和疼痛). (Also 亦作 **lockjaw**).

tether ['teðə*] *vt* tie an animal with a rope or chain so that it cannot run away 用繩 或 鍊子 拴 (牲畜): *He tethered the horse to a post.* 他把馬拴在木樁上. Also 亦作 *nc* rope or chain used in this way (拴牲畜用的) 繩或鍊子.

tetra- ['tetrə] *prefix* four (e.g. **tetragon** i.e. figure with four sides) 四 (例如 tetragon 四邊形).

text [tekst] **1** *nc* original words of an author or speaker as distinct from reports about them or summaries (文章 或演說的) 原文. **2** *nu* main part of a book as distinct from diagrams, notes, index etc. 正文 (以別於圖表、註解、索引等). **'textbook** book which gives information; book which is studied in a school etc. 教科書; 課本.

textile ['tekstail] *nc* cloth; fabric 布; 織物.

texture ['tekstʃə*] *nc / u* way in which cloth is woven or something is formed; structure of something 布的織法; 某物的結構; 質地; 紋理: *coat with a rough texture* 質地粗糙的上衣. *The weather spoilt the fine texture of her skin.* 風吹日曬使她那細嫩的皮膚變得粗糙了.

than [ðæn, ðən] *conj* used after the *comparative* of an *adj* or *adv* 用於形容詞或副詞比較級之後: *He is quicker than you.* 他比你機敏. *He runs more quickly than you (do).* 他跑得比你快. *Note* 說明: although *He is stronger than I (am)* was once thought more correct, *He is stronger than me* is now much more usual and just as correct. But there can be a difference in meaning after a *vt* (e.g. *He teaches them better than I* i.e. better than I teach them, and *He teaches them better than me* i.e. than he teaches me). With *all* only one form is correct (e.g. *He is stronger than them all*). 雖然 He is stronger than I (am) (他比我強壯)一度被認爲比較正確, 但是 He is stronger than me 如今更爲常見而且也同樣正確. 不過在及物動詞後, 二者意思有差別. (例如 He teaches them better than I. 意即: 他教他們要比我教他們好. He teaches them better than me. 意即: 他教他們要比你教我好). 與 all

連用時只有一種形式是正確的. (例如 He is stronger than them all. 他比他們所有的人都強壯). **other than** besides 除…之外: *Have you any books other than these?* 你除了這些書以外還有甚麼書?

thank [θæŋk] *vt* say that one is grateful 感謝; 謝謝: *He thanked us for our help.* 他感謝我們的幫助. *He thanked us for helping (him).* 他感謝我們對他的幫助. 'Can I help?' 'Thank you' i.e. Yes, you can. "我可以幫忙嗎?" "謝謝你". 即: 行, 你可以幫忙. 'Can I help?' 'No, thank you' i.e. No, you can't. "我可以幫忙嗎?" "不, 謝謝你". 即: 不, 你不用幫忙. *Thank God you arrived in time* i.e. I thank God that you did. 感謝上帝, 你及時到達了. **thanks** *npl: He wrote to express his thanks for our help.* 他寫信對我們的幫助表示謝意. 'Can I help?' 'No, thanks' i.e. No, you can't. "我可以幫忙嗎?" "不, 謝謝". 即: 不, 你不用幫忙. *Thanks to the doctor I am well again* i.e. because of him, owing to his help 多虧了這位大夫, 我的病好了. **thankful** *adj* grateful 感激的, 感謝的: *You should be thankful to be alive / that you are alive.* 你還能活着應當感激才是. **thankfully** *adv* **'thanksgiving** act of expressing thanks (usu. to God in worship or prayer) (通常指對上帝的)感恩的表示; 感恩祈禱.

that¹ [ðæt] *adj / adv / pron / determiner* **1** Who is that man? 那個男人是誰? *I want that book, not this one.* 我想要那本書, 不要這本. **2** Who is that? 那人是誰? *I want that, not this.* 我想要那個, 不要這個. *Don't drink that.* 別喝那個. *pl* 複數 those [ðouz]: *Who are those men?* 那些男人是誰? *I want those, not these.* 我想要那些, 不要這些. **3** so; very 那麼, 非常: *I can't eat *that much.* 我吃不了那麼多。*He is not that fat. (informal in sense 3)* 他不是非常胖。(義 3 爲非正式)。*Note* 說明：*that or those* cannot be used with *my, your, his etc.* Instead one must use of *mine, of yours, of his etc (e.g. I have lost that book of mine. Where are those friends of theirs?) that* 或 *those* 不能與 my, your, his 等連用.但可以與 of mine, of yours. of his 等一起使用。(例如 I have lost that book of mine. 我已經把我那本書弄丢了。Where are those friends of theirs? 他們的那些朋友在哪兒?)

that² [ðət] *relative pron* often used instead of *who, whom, which, when* 常用於替代 who, whom, which, when: *Where is the boy that did it?* 幹這事的男生在哪兒？*I have lost the book that was here.* 我丢失了原先在這兒的那本書。*I stay at home on the days that I am not busy.* 我不忙的時候就呆在家裏。*Note* 說明：**1** when the word before *that* is not the subject of the following clause (as it is in each of the three sentences above), *that* is usually omitted (e.g. *Where is the boy they saw in my room? I have lost the book I bought yesterday. Do you remember the days we spent together?)* **2** *that* is often used instead of *who,* but with *any, only* and superlatives, *that* is more usual. *Any boy that wants to play can do so. She was the only woman that smoked a pipe. He is the bravest man that ever lived.* 1. 如果 *that* 前的詞不是後面從句的主語 (與上列三個句子的每一種情況都不同)，那麼 *that* 通常省略。(例如，Where is the boy they saw in my room? 他們在我房裏見到的那個男孩在哪兒? I have lost the book I bought yesterday. 我把我昨天買的那本書弄丢了。Do you re-

member the days we spent together? 你記得我們一起度過的時光嗎?) 2. *that* 常用來替代 *who,* 但與 *any, only* 以及形容詞最高級連用則更爲常見。Any boy that wants to play can do so. 想玩耍的男生可以去玩。She was the only woman that smoked a pipe. 她是唯一吸烟的婦女。He is the bravest man that ever lived. 他是所有男人中最勇敢的。

that³ [ðət] *conj* at the beginning of a clause, often not used, but understood 用於從句前,常不用,但清楚: *He says (that) he will come.* 他說他會來。*We saw (that) he was tired.* 我們知道他累了。*I wish (that) I were rich.* 但願我很富有。*I hit it so hard (that) it broke.* 我猛擊它,結果它破了。*That I was late is a lie.* 說我遲到那是撒謊。Also 亦作 *interj: Oh that the rain would stop!* i.e. I wish very much that it would *(o.f.* in this sense) 哦,但願雨會停! (本義爲舊式)。

thatch [θætʃ] *nu* roof made of dry straw, leaves, rushes etc. 茅草屋頂。Also 亦作 *vt* put thatch on 以茅草蓋 (屋頂)

thaw [θɔ:] *vt / i* **1** (with reference to snow or anything frozen) melt; become, cause to become, soft (指雪或冰凍物) (使) 融化, (使) 解凍: *The ice on the river will thaw when the weather becomes warmer.* 當天氣暖和些時, 河面上的冰就會融化。*He thawed his frozen hands at the fire.* 他把凍僵的雙手放到爐火上烤火取暖。**2** become, cause to become, more friendly (使) 變得較爲友好: *At first he was angry, but he thawed when we explained what had happened.* 開始他很生氣,不過當我把發生的事情解釋了以後他就變得友善了。Also 亦作 *nu* warmer weather which causes snow, ice etc to thaw 融雪期, 解凍期; *After the storm there was a thaw.* 這場暴風雪過後就是融雪期. *Winter is followed by the thaw.* 冬季之後是融雪期.

the [ðɪ; ðɪ, ðə] *determiner* **1** one that is known or has already been mentioned 已知的人或物; 已提到的人或物: *There's a man at the door.* 門口有位男人. *Is he the man who came yesterday?* 是昨天來過的那個人嗎? *The roads are very busy.* 這些公路交通繁忙. *He has gone to the bank.* 他到那家銀行去了. **2** only one of its kind 唯一的事物: *The sun is shining.* 太陽照耀着. *The weather is cold.* 天氣很冷. *What is the name of this flower?* 這種花叫甚麼名? therefore often used with reference to place names etc. 因此常用來指地名等: *the Indian Ocean* 印度洋; *the Atlantic* 大西洋; *the North Pole* 北極; *the (river) Nile* 尼羅河; *the Sudan* 蘇丹; *the British Isles* 英倫三島. **3** (with *superlatives*) (與形容詞最高級連用): *the biggest house in our village* 我們村莊裏最大的房子; *the last bus* 最後一班公共汽車. **4** all those of a particular kind 特定的一羣: *They look after the poor and the sick.* 他們照料窮人和病人. Also with *n sing* 亦與單數名詞連用: *The African buffalo is very dangerous* (instead of *African buffaloes are very dangerous*). 非洲水牛很危險 (以替代 African buffaloes are very dangerous). *Who invented the steam engine?* 誰發明了蒸汽機? **5** (instead of *a* or *one*) for each one (以替代 *a* 或 *one*) 每一: *It costs fifty pence the pound.* 它價值每磅五十便士. *Our car does thirty miles to the gallon.* 我們的小汽車使用每一加侖汽油可以行駛三十英里. Also 亦作 *adv* by that amount 越, 愈. *The more we are together, the happier we shall be.*

我們越常在一起就會越快活. *Note* 說明: only long practice in English can show when to use and when not to use *the*, *a* or no article at all (e.g. (a) *He has (the) measles. He has a cold. He has fever.* (b) *The buffalo is the most dangerous animal of all* (superlative). *The buffalo is most dangerous. The buffalo is a most dangerous animal* i.e. very dangerous. (c) *The sky above us was beautiful. There was a beautiful blue sky above us.* (d) *He plays the piano / the trumpet / the violin* (musical instruments). *He plays chess / football / tennis* (games) but *He has played pianos in every town in England. He plays the game of chess etc well.*) 只有長期的英語實踐才能弄清楚何時可以使用和何時不可以使用 the, a 或者完全不用冠詞. (例如 (a) He has (the) measles. 他患麻疹. He has a cold. 他感冒. He has fever. 他發燒. (b) The buffalo is the most dangerous animal of all (superlative). 水牛是最危險的動物 (最高級). The buffalo is most dangerous. 水牛是很危險的. The buffalo is a most dangerous animal. 水牛是一種很危險的動物. (c) The sky above us was beautiful. 我們頭上的天空很美麗. There was a beautiful blue sky above us. 我們頭上的藍天很美麗. (d) He plays the piano / the trumpet / the violin (musical instruments). 他彈鋼琴/吹喇叭/拉小提琴 (樂器). He plays chess / football / tennis (games) but he has played pianos in every town in England. 他下棋/踢足球/打網球 (運動), 但是他在英國各鎮演奏過鋼琴. He plays the game of chess etc well. 他棋等下得很好.)

theatre ['θɪətə*] (*US* 美 **theater**) *nc* **1** building where plays, operas etc are acted on a stage 戲院, 劇場. **2** (usu.

with **the**) drama; work in or for a theatre (通常與 the 連用)戲劇; 戲劇活動: *Because he is an actor he knows the theatre very well.* 因爲他是個演員, 所以他對戲劇瞭如指掌. **theatrical** *adj* **1** of the theatre 戲劇的; 戲院的, 劇場的. **2** behaving like an actor on the stage i.e. in an affected, showy manner (舉止)矯揉造作的; 誇張的. **'operating theatre** special room in a hospital where operations are done by doctors 手術室.

theft [θeft] *nc / u* act of stealing 偷盜.

their [ðɛə*] *determiner* belonging to them 他們的: *This is their house.* 這是他們的房子. **theirs** *pron*: *This house is theirs.* 這房子是他們的.

them [ðem, ðəm] *pron* form which **they** takes when it is the object of a verb or preposition 他們的賓格: *You saw them there.* 你看見他們在那兒. *Give it to them.* 把那個東西給他們. **themselves 1** emphatic form of **they** or **them.** they 或 them 的強調式: *They went themselves.* 他們自己去了. **2** reflexive form of **them.** them 的反身式: *They hurt themselves.* 他們傷了自己.

theme [θi:m] *nc* **1** subject of a talk or of writing; essay 話題; (文章的)題目; 論文. **2** (music) tune which is repeated again and again in a piece of music (音樂)主旋律. **'theme song** song which is repeated again and again in a musical play or film (歌劇或電影中的)主題歌.

themselves [ðem'selvz] see 見 **them.**

then [ðen] *adv* **1** at that time in the past (過去)那時, 當時: *We were at school then.* 當時我們在上課. **2** at that time in the future (將來)那時: *As I'll be here on Monday, I'll see you then.* 星期一我將在這兒, 所以那時我會去看你. **3** next; afterwards 接着; 然

後, 後來: *I had supper and then went to bed.* 我用過晚餐, 然後上床睡覺. **4** (put at the beginning or end of a sentence) if that is so; for this reason; therefore (用於句首或句末)倘若如此; 那麼; 因此: *He says that he is hungry. Then he must have some food / He must have some food then.* 他說他餓了. 因此, 他必須吃點東西. *It was decided then, that we would go.* 因此決定我們去. **5** also; in addition 也; 而且: *My mother was there. Then there were my brother and two sisters.* 我母親在那兒. 我哥哥和兩個姐姐也在那兒. Also 亦作 *adj* of that time 當時的: *the then manager* 當時的經理.

theology [θɪ'ɔlədʒɪ] *nu* science of the nature of God and of religion 神學, 宗教學. **theological** [θɪə'lɔdʒɪkl] *adj*.

theorem ['θɪərəm] *nc* (mathematics) statement which has to be proved by reasoning (數學)定理, 命題.

theory ['θɪəri] **1** *nc* reason or argument which is not yet proved, made to explain something 學說: *Many scientists accept the theory that the universe is growing larger.* 許多科學家接受宇宙正在變大的學說. **2** *nc / u* general laws and principles 理論: *In theory this is possible, in practice it is not* i.e. according to general principles it appears to be possible, but when one tries to follow these principles and actually do something, it is not possible. 在理論上這是可能的, 在實踐上卻是不可能的, 即依據一般原理這似乎可行, 但是遵循這些原理並且實際做起來的話, 這卻是不可行的. **theoretical** [θɪə'retikl] *adj* (opp 反義詞 practical). **theoretically** *adv* **theorist** *nc* person who has theories 理論家. **theorize** ['θɪəraiz] *vi* form a theory 建立理論; 推理; 推論: *Man has always* *theorized about how life began.* 人類總是在推論生命的起源.

therapeutic [θerəˈpjuːtik] *adj* concerned with the curing of diseases 治病的: *Many plants have therapeutic qualities* i.e. can be used to cure diseases 許多植物都具有治病性質. 即: 可用以治病.

therapy [ˈθerəpi] *nu* medical treatment 治療; 療法.

there [ðɛə*] *adv* 1 at, in; to that place 在那裏; 去那裏: *I was standing there.* 我站在那兒. *He works there, in that shop.* 他在那裏工作, 在那家商店裏. *Are you going there?* 你準備到那兒去嗎? *Note* 說明: *there* is often used at the beginning of a sentence expressing an exclamation. When it is, the subject of the verb comes *before* the verb if it is a personal pronoun, and *after* the verb if it is a noun. *There they are! There are my books! There he goes! There goes my friend!* It is also used informally in the same way *after* a pronoun or by itself. *You there! Stop talking! There! There! Don't worry!* there 常用於表示驚嘆的句子的開頭.當它處於這種用時,如果動詞主語是人稱代詞的話, 主語就置於動詞之前; 如果動詞主語是名詞的話, 則置於動詞之後. *There they are!* 他們就在那裏! *There are my books!* 瞧, 我的書! *There he goes!* 他走了! *There goes my friends!* 我的朋友走了! 在這一用法中, there 亦可非正式地用於代詞之後或單獨使用. *You there! Stop talking!* 你們哪, 別講話了! *There! There! Don't worry!* 好了! 好了! 別擔心! 2 that place 那兒: *I lived near there.* 我住在靠近那兒或那裏. *The distance from there is a mile.* 距離那兒有一英里遠. 3 used at the beginning of a sentence with a verb (usu. *is, appear* and *seem*) followed by its subject 用

於主語在動詞(通常為 is, appear 和 seem)之後的句子的句首: *There's a dog in your garden.* 你的花園裏有隻狗. *There can be many reasons for this.* 爲此可有許多理由. *There seems to be nobody in the house.* 屋裏似乎沒有人. *Note* 說明: *there's* is often used to express an exclamation and give emphasis. *There's a lovely girl for you!* i.e. look at that lovely girl! *There's a good boy!* i.e. you are a good boy. there's 常用於表示驚嘆和强調. *There's a lovely girl for you!* 瞧, 多可愛的姑娘! *There's a good boy!* 真是個好孩子! **thereabouts** *adv* (usu. with **or**) near that place, number or quantity (通常與 or 連用) 附近; 左右; 大約: *He lives in the village or thereabouts.* 他住在那個村莊附近. *I'll come at 6 o'clock or thereabouts.* 我將在六點左右來. **there'after** *adv* afterwards *(formal)* 後來(正式). **'therefore** *adv* for that reason 因此, 所以. **here and there** see 見 **here.**

thereby [ˌðɛəˈbai] *adv* 1 by that means 由此; 因此: *I gave her my advice; I hope she may profit thereby.* 我已勸她提出勸告, 希望她會由此得到益處. 2 connected with that 與那一點有關係; 在那一方面; 從而: *Thereby hangs a tale.* 其中大有文章. 3 by or near that place; near there 在那地方附近; 在那附近: *A farm lay thereby* 一個農場座落在那地方附近.

therein [ˌðɛərˈin] *adv* 1 in that place, time or thing; into that place or thing 在那裏; 在那時; 在那點上; 在其中: *the case and the books found therein* 箱子和放在箱子裏的書. 2 in that matter, in that way 在那件事上; 那樣: *The captain thought all danger was past; therein he made a mistake.* 隊長認爲危險全都過去; 在那件事上他犯了個錯

誤.

thermal ['θə:ml] *adj* of heat 熱的; *thermal springs* i.e. natural springs of hot water 溫泉.

thermo- ['θə:mou] *prefix* of heat (e.g. **thermostat**) 熱的(例如 thermostat 自動調溫器).

thermometer [θə'mɔmitə*] *nc* instrument for measuring temperature 溫度計.

thermonuclear ['θə:mou'nju:kliə*] *adj* concerned with hydrogen bombs or other bombs of that type 熱核的; *thermonuclear war* 熱核戰爭.

thermos ['θə:məs] ® *nc* trade name for a **vacuum flask** i.e. one consisting of one container inside another with a vacuum between them, so that the contents of the inner container are kept at a constant temperature 熱水瓶. (Also 亦作 **thermos flask**). *pl* 複數 **thermoses.**

thermostat ['θə:moustæt] *nc* device for controlling temperature automatically 自動調溫器.

these [ði:z] pl of **this.** this 的複數.

thesis ['θi:sis] *nc* reasoned argument about a particular subject (esp. a long one written to obtain a university degree) 專題論文(尤指爲獲大學學位而寫的長篇論文). *pl* 複數 **theses** ['θi:si:z]

they [ðei, ði] *pron* 1 pl of **he, she** and **it.** he, she 和 it 的複數形式. 2 people in general or people whom one does not know as individuals (泛指) 大家，人人: *They say that birds know when it is going to rain* i.e. this is what many people believe. 大家都說鳥兒知道何時下雨. *They have decided to build a new road* i.e. the government etc has decided. (*informal* in sense 2). 聽說已決定建一條新路. 即: 政府等

已決定. (義 2 爲非正式). see 見 **them.**

thick [θik] *adj* 1 big from side to side, from front to back or all the way round 厚的; 粗的: *He is a strong man with thick arms.* 他是個雙臂很粗的强壯男子. *He drew a thick line on the paper.* 他在紙上畫了一條粗線. *The book is two inches thick.* 這本書兩英寸厚. 2 placed closely together; dense 密的; 濃的: *She has thick hair.* 她的頭髮濃密. *The crowd was very thick.* 人羣十分擁擠. *It was hidden by a thick mist.* 它被濃霧遮住了. 3 not easily poured (液體)稠的, 濃的: *thick oil* 濃油. (*opp* thin in senses 1, 2 and 3) (義 1, 義 2 和義 3 的反義詞爲 thin). 4 stupid 笨的, 蠢的: *I think he is thickheaded* i.e. stupid (*informal*) 笨頭笨腦的 (非正式). Also 亦作 *nu* thickest part 最粗厚的部份; 最密的部份. *He was hit on the thick of his arm.* 他的胳膊夹被打中了. *There was a large crowd and he was in the thick of it.* 那兒有一大羣人, 他夹在人羣中. **thickness** *nc / u: It is two feet in thickness.* 它二英尺厚. *This wood is sold in two thicknesses.* 這種木材以兩種厚度出售. **thicken** *vt / i* become, cause to become, thick 變濃; (使) 變濃; (使) 變厚. **thickening** *nu* something used to thicken something else 增稠劑. **'thick'set** *adj* (with reference to person) broad and strong (指人)矮胖結實的. **have a thick skin** not likely to be upset by criticism etc; be insensitive (*informal*) 厚臉皮; 麻木不仁. (非正式). **thickskinned** *adj: Being thickskinned he does not care what people say.* (*informal*) 他厚臉皮, 因此不在乎人們說些甚麼. (非正式).

thief [θi:f] *nc* person who steals 竊賊,

小偷. *pl* 複數 **thieves** [θi:vz].

thieve [θi:v] *vt / i* be a thief; steal 作賊;
偷.

thigh [θai] *nc* thick part of leg above
the knee 大腿.

thimble ['θimbl] *nc* small, hard cover
put on the end of the finger to protect
it when using a needle 頂針.

thin [θin] *adj* **1** small from front to
back, from side to side, or all the way
round 薄的; 細的: *thin book* 薄書;
thin sticks 細棍. **2** not close together;
having gaps 稀鬆的; 稀疏的: *His hair
has become very thin.* 他的頭髮已變
得很稀疏. *The game was watched by
a thin crowd* i.e. a few people 這場比
賽觀眾稀少. *The sun was shining
through a thin mist.* 陽光透過薄霧閃
耀. **3** easily poured; watery (液體)稀
的; 水分多的: *thin oil* 清油; *thin soup*
清湯. (*opp* **thick** in senses **1, 2** and
3) (義 1, 義 2 和義 3 的反義詞爲
thick). **4** without much flesh; lean 瘦
的: *The children are thin because
they do not get enough to eat.* (*opp*
fat in sense **4**) 由於沒有足夠的東西
吃, 孩子們很瘦. (義 4 的反義詞爲fat).
comparative 比較級 **thinner.** *superlative* 最高級 **thinnest. thinly** *adv* **thin-
ness** *nu.*

thing [θiŋ] *nc* **1** object which can be
seen or touched 東西(指可見或可觸覺
的物體): *This is the thing I use to cut
wood.* 這就是我用來砍木頭的東西.
What is that thing in your hand? 你手
中那個東西是甚麼? **2** object which
cannot be seen or touched etc but
can be thought or felt 抽象的東西:
Jealousy is a terrible thing. 嫉妒是一
種可怕的東西. *Religion is a thing of
the mind and spirit.* 宗教是心靈的東
西. **3** (in *pl*) possessions; belonging
(用於複數) 擁有物; 所有物: *They lost

all their things in the war.* 戰爭中他們
失去了所有的財產. *Put your things
down here and come inside* i.e. what
you are carrying. 把你的東西放這兒,
然後進來. **4** (in *pl*) events; conditions
(用於複數) 形勢; 情況: *He worries a-
bout things.* 他對形勢感到憂慮.
*Things have been much better for me
since I got a job.* 自從我找到工作以來
情況已大爲改觀. **5** (with **the**) particular act or kind of behaviour (與 the
連用)事, 特定的行爲或舉止: *The best
thing I did was (to) buy this house.* 我
做的最好的事就是買下這座房子. *The
thing to do is to go away.* 要做的事就
是走開. **6** (with **the** and usu. **just** or
very) what is needed (與 the 通常也
與 just 或 very 連用)需要之物: *This
house is just the thing.* 這座房子正合
適. *I have the very thing for mending
your car* i.e. the most suitable 我有修
理你的車子最爲合適的工具. **7** some-
body one is fond of 令人喜歡的人兒:
My aunt is a nice old thing. 我姨媽是
個很好的老人. *She has no money,
poor thing.* (*informal* in sense **7**) 她沒
錢, 可憐的人兒. (義 7 爲非正式). **the
done thing** correct or acceptable behaviour; good manners 正確的或可接
受的行爲; 禮貌: *It's not the done
thing to eat with your fingers here.*
(*informal*) 在這兒用手抓東西吃很不禮
貌. (非正式). **first thing** as soon as
possible 儘快; 儘早: *I'll see you
tomorrow first thing.* 我明天一清早就
來看你. **last thing** after doing everything else at night 晚上要做的最後一
件事: *He locks all the doors last thing
before he goes to bed.* 上床睡覺前他
做的最後一件事就是鎖上所有的門. **a
near thing** narrow escape 僥倖的事;
倖免: *We finished in time but it was a
near thing* i.e. we almost did not fin-

ish. (informal) 我們準時完成了，但這是一件傻倖事. 即: 我們差點兒就完不成. (非正式) **the thing is** the main point is; what must be decided etc is 問題是; 必須決定的是: *The thing is, do you want to come or don't you?* 問題是, 你想來還是不想來?

thingummy ['θiŋəmi] *nc* word used to an object when one does not know its name *(informal)* (當說不上名稱時用) 那麼個東西(非正式)

think [θiŋk] *vt / i* **1** use the mind 思考, 想: *We had to think very quickly.* 我們只好快動腦筋. *It is so noisy here that I can't think.* 這裏太吵了, 我沒法思考. **2** believe; have an opinion; suppose 認為, 以為: *They think (that) I am wrong.* 他們認為我錯了. *He thinks (that) it will rain.* 他認為會下雨. *I thought (that) you would come.* 我原以為你會來. *We don't think them good enough.* 我們並不認為他們好得很. *Do you think it necessary?* 你認為這是必要的嗎? *He was thought stupid to try.* 他的努力被認為是愚蠢的. *past 過去式和過去分詞* **thought** [θɔːt].

thinking *nu* act of thinking 思考: *I did some quick thinking.* 我很快地想了想. *Also 亦作 adj* who thinks in has 有思想的; 思慮的: *Any thinking parent wants education for his children.* 凡有思想的父親都想讓孩子受教育. **think about someone / something 1** turn the mind to 想: *I thought about you all day.* 我成天想你. **2** wonder whether or not to do something 考慮: *Are you thinking about buying a new car?* 你是否正在考慮買一輛新車? **think of someone / something 1** turn the mind to; consider 想; 考慮: *I thought of you all day.* 我成天想你. *Think of all the money that he has!* 想想看他所擁有的錢財! **2** find; suggest

想出; 建議: *I could not think of a suitable reply.* 我想不出一個合適的答覆. *He had to think of some plan to escape.* 他得想出個逃脫的辦法. **3** (*with adv*) have an opinion about; regard. (與副詞連用) 具有…的看法; 認為: *The people think very highly of him.* 人們對他評價很高. *Our work was well thought of.* 我們的工作得到很好的評價. **think something over** consider carefully before deciding (決定前)仔細考慮: *I need a couple of days to think this matter over.* 我需要幾天時間來好好考慮一下這個事情. **think something up** find a way; make a plan 想辦法; 訂計劃: *It is very difficult to do this, but I'll think up a plan.* 雖然做這件事很困難, 但是我會想出個辦法的. **think better of** think about and then decide not to (仔細思考後)決定不: *They have thought better of buying a new car. They are keeping their old one.* 他們已打消買新車的念頭. 他們仍使用原來那輛車. **think nothing of 1** have a poor opinion of 認為…沒甚麼, 看不起: *He thinks nothing of your work.* 他認為你的工作沒甚麼了不起. **2** consider to be quite easy or usual 認為…輕而易舉或平常: *They think nothing of spending £100 a week.* 他們認為一週花費100英鎊很平常.

third [θɜːd] see appendix 見附錄. **'third 'party** (esp. with reference to an insurance policy) person in addition to, but considered by, two persons who make a legal agreement or contract (尤指保險單)第三者: *third-party risks* i.e. risks covered by an insurance policy to include other persons who may be hurt or suffer loss or damage to their property because of something done by the person who is in-

sured. 第三者險. 即: 被保人對他人造成
人身傷害或財産損失時由保險公司賠償
的險種. **third-rate** *adj* of poor quality 低級的,三流的.

thirst [θəːst] *nu* **1** desire to drink; lack
of drink 渴; 口渴: *We satisfied our
thirst with a glass of water.* 我們喝了
一杯水解渴. *I was suffering from
thirst.* 我渴得慌. **2** any strong desire
渴望: *their thirst for news* 他們對消息
的渴望. **thirsty** *adj* feeling or causing
thirst 口渴的; 令人口渴的; 渴望的.

this [ðis] **1** *adj* / *adv* / *pron* / *determiner*: *Who is this man?* 這男人是誰?
I want this book, not that one. 我想要
這本書, 不要那本. **2** *pron*: *Who is
this?* 這是誰? *I want this, not that.* 我
想要這個, 不要那個. *pl* 複數 **these**
[ðiːz]. **3** *adj* of the present time 現在
的, 目前的: *I am going away this month.* 我打
算本月份離開. *He is never at home
these days.* 近來他從未在家呆過. *This
time last year they were in Africa* i.e.
a year ago 去年這個時候他們在非洲.
即: 一年前. **Note** 說明: *this* or *these*
cannot be used with *my, your, his* etc.
Instead one must use *of mine, of
yours, of his* etc. *This room of mine is
too small. These friends of theirs are
very quiet.* this 或 these 不能與 my,
your, his 等連用. 應該用 of mine, of
yours, of his 等. *This room of mine is
too small.* 我這間房間太小. *These
friends of theirs are very quiet.* 他們
這些朋友很文靜. **4** *adv* so; to this degree 這麼; 到這樣程度: *We have
walked this far without stopping* i.e. as
far as here 我們已經不停地走了這麼
遠. 即: 一直到此. *The table is about
this big.* 這張桌子大約這麼大.

thistle [ˈθisl] *nc* type of plant with many
sharp points; emblem of Scotland 薊;
蘇格蘭的國徽.

thong [θɒŋ] *nc* thin piece of leather 皮
帶; 皮條.

thorax [ˈθɔːræks] *nc* **1** in a human or
animal body, the chest (人的) 胸, 胸
部; 動物的胸腔. **2** in an insect's body,
the middle of three main sections 昆
蟲體三部份的中間一節.

thoraxes or **thoraces** [ˈθɔːrəsiːz] *pl* of
thorax. thorax 的複數

thorn [θɔːn] **1** *nc* sharp point growing
from a plant (植物的) 刺: *This tree
has thorns.* 這棵樹有刺. **2** *nc* / *u* / *adj*
(with another word) type of plant or
tree which has thorns (e.g. *hawthorn;
thorn bush*) (與另一個詞連用) 有刺的
植物或樹 (例如 hawthorn 山楂; thorn
bush 刺叢). **thorny** *adj* **1** having
thorns 有刺的. **2** difficult; causing
trouble 困難的; 棘手的; 傷腦筋的:
thorny problem 棘手的問題.

thorough [ˈθʌrə] *adj* complete; careful
and exact 徹底的; 全面的; 周密的; 細
心的; 精確的: *The doctor gave me a
thorough examination.* 大夫爲我做了
徹底的檢查. *She is a thorough
teacher.* 她是個做事細心的教師. thoroughly *adv* **thoroughness** *nu*.

thoroughbred [ˈθʌrəbred] *nc* animal or
person of pure breed 純種的動物; 有
教養的人. Also 亦作 *adj*: *thoroughbred horse* 純種馬.

thoroughfare [ˈθʌrəfɛə*] *nc* road or
street which is open at both ends to
allow traffic to pass through 大道; 大
街. **no thoroughfare** (used as a
notice) this road is closed (用於告示)
此路不通.

those [ðəuz] *pl* of **that**ᴵ. that ᴵ 的複數形
式.

though [ðəu] *conj* even if 即便, 雖然:
*Though the book is difficult to under-
stand, it is interesting.* 雖然這本書難以
理解, 卻很有趣. **Note** 說明: *although*

can usu. be used instead of *though* except: (a) in the phrase *as though* (which has the sense of *as if*) we cannot use *although*. *He behaves as though he were my father* i.e. he behaves like my father but he isn't. (b) *though* but not *although* is sometimes used after a clause to mean what was expected but did not happen. *I went to town. I didn't see John though* i.e. I expected to see him but did not. *(informal).* although 通常可以用來替代 though, 但下列情況除外: (a) 不可在短語 as though (其意義與 as if 同)中用 although 來替代. He behaves as though he were my father. 他表現得 像是我父親一樣. 即: 他表現得像是我父親, 但他不是我父親. (b) though (而不是 although) 有時用於從句之後, 表示所期待的事沒有發生. I went to town. I didn't see John though. 我進城去, 不過我沒見到約翰. 即: 我期待着見到他, 可是沒見着. (非正式式).

thought¹ [θɔ:t] past of **think.** think 的過去式和過去分詞.

thought² [θɔ:t] **1** *nu* act or way of thinking 思想; 思考; 思想方式: *This problem needs great thought.* 這個問題需要認真思考. *Modern thought is against slavery.* 現代的思潮是反對奴隸制的. **2** *nc* what somebody thinks or intends 想法, 念頭; 意圖: *I told him my thoughts.* 我告訴他我的想法. *They have no thought of going away.* 他們並沒有要離開的意思. **thoughtful** *adj* **1** full of thought 富有思想的: *This is a thoughtful book.* 這是一本富有思想內容的書. **2** full of concern for others 關心體貼的; 無微不至的; 設想週到的: *It was thoughtful of them to come and meet us.* 他們來接我們, 真是想得週到. **thoughtless** *adj* without concern for others 不體貼的; 不顧及他人的; 自私

的. **on second thoughts** after thinking about it again 再度考慮後, 進一步思考後. (Also 亦作 have second thoughts about something).

thousand ['θauzənd] see appendix 見附錄.

thrash [θræʃ] **1** *vt* beat; strike 打; 擊: *He thrashed the boy with a stick.* 他用棍子打那男孩. *As he swam, he thrashed the water with his hands.* 游泳時, 他用雙手擊水. *We thrashed them at football* i.e. we beat easily. 我們在足球比賽時輕而易舉地擊敗了他們. **2** *vt / i* see 見 **thresh. thrashing** *nc: He gave the boy a thrashing.* 他痛打那個男孩一頓. **thrash about** move noisily and violently 亂蹦亂跳; 翻騰: *They were thrashing about in the water.* 他們在水裏翻騰游動.

thread [θred] *nc / u* **1** very thin piece of cotton, silk, wool etc (棉花、絲、羊毛等的) 細線: *I sewed on the buttons with thread.* 我用線縫鈕扣. *There are threads of wool on your dress.* 你的衣服上有幾條羊毛線. **2** something which joins or keeps things together 頭緒, 思路: *I have lost the thread of my argument.* 我的論題失了頭緒. **3** spiral part of a screw (螺釘上的) 螺紋. Also 亦作 *vt* **1** pass a thread through 把線穿過: *She threaded her needle.* 她把線穿過針孔. **2** (usu. with **one's way**) go slowly and carefully (通常與 one's way 連用)緩慢而且小心翼翼地走: *I threaded my way through the large crowd.* 我從一大羣人中擠了過去. **threadbare** *adj* (with reference to clothes, carpets etc.) worn so much that the threads are seen (指衣服、地毯等) 磨破, 破到露出線來的.

threat [θret] *nc* **1** statement that one will harm somebody (esp. if he does not agree to do something) 威脅, 恐

嚇: *He was arrested for making threats against the president.* 他因曾對總統進行恐嚇而被捕. **2** danger 危險: *The flood was a threat to our homes.* 這場洪水危及我們的家. **threaten** *vt / i* **1** make a threat against 威脅, 恐嚇: *He threatened them with death.* 他以死來威脅他們. *He threatened to kill them* 他揚言說要殺死他們. **2** be a danger to 危及: *The flood threatened our homes.* 洪水危及我們的家. **3** warn that something is likely to happen 預示…的兆頭; 有…的危險: *The dark clouds threaten a storm.* 烏雲預兆一場暴風雨. **threatening** *adj: a threatening voice* 威脅的語調; *threatening clouds* 預兆風雨的雲層.

three [θri:] see appendix 見附錄.

thresh [θreʃ] *vt / i* **1** separate the grain or seeds from (wheat, rye, or other grain); thresh grain 打 (麥子等); 打穀子: *Nowadays most farmers use a machine to thresh their wheat.* 現在大部份農民使用機器打麥子. **2** toss about; move violently (使) 猛烈擺動; (使) 翻來覆去. **3** strike repeatedly 反覆打擊.

thresher *nc* machine or person that threshes 打穀機; 脫粒機; 打穀者.

threshold ['θreʃhould] *nc* **1** piece of wood or stone under the door of a house 門檻; 門限: *He stood on the threshold for a minute before going into the house.* 他在門檻處站了一會兒才走進房子. **2** place where something ends and something begins 起點, 開端: *We are on the threshold of a great discovery.* 我們將有重大發現.

threw [θru:] past tense of **throw**. throw 的過去式.

thrift [θrift] *nu* careful control of money or property 節儉; 節約; 節省. **thrifty** *adj* using thrift 節儉的, 節省的.

thriftily *adv.*

thrill [θril] *nc* sudden feeling of pleasure or excitement 突然的愉快; 突然的興奮或激動. Also 亦作 *vt / i* have, cause to have, a thrill (使) 感到愉快, (使) 感到興奮或激動; 使緊張: *We were thrilled when we saw the high mountains.* 見到高山時我們興奮極了. *The lovely house thrills her.* 那座可愛的房子使她高興極了. **thriller** *nc* book, play or film etc about detectives, spies etc which thrills those who read or see it (有關偵探、間諜等的) 驚險讀物 (或戲劇, 電影等). **thrilling** *adj* very exciting 非常激動人心的, 驚心動魄的.

thrive [θraiv] *vi* **1** grow well 茁壯生長: *Corn thrives in that climate.* 在那種氣候裏, 小麥長勢良好. **2** be successful 成功: *His business is thriving.* 他的生意興隆.

throat [θrout] *nc / u* front of the neck; passage between the back of the mouth and the lungs and the stomach 喉部, 喉頭; 喉嚨, 咽喉: *He seized me by the throat.* 他扼住我的喉嚨. *He poured the drink down his throat.* 他把酒倒進喉嚨.

throb [θrɔb] *vi* **1** (with reference to the heart) beat more strongly (指心臟) 劇烈跳動: *Her heart throbbed with excitement.* 她興奮得卜卜地跳. **2** beat or work regularly like the heart 悸動; 律動; 顫動: *My head was throbbing with pain.* 我的頭疼得卜卜直跳. *The engine throbbed all night.* 發動機徹夜顫動. *past* 過去式和過去分詞 **throbbed.** Also 亦作 *nc / u: throb of her heart* 她的心的跳動; *throb of the engine* 發動機的顫動.

throes [θrouz] *npl* pain (usu. only in **in the throes of** i.e. suffering the pain or trouble of) 痛苦 (通常僅用於 **in the**

throes of 經歷了…的痛苦或麻煩): *We are in the throes of moving to another house.* 我們正爲搬家忙得團團轉.

thrombosis [θrɔm'bousis] *nu* hardening of some blood in a vein or artery which stops the flow of blood in a living person 血栓症, 血栓形成.

throne [θroun] *nc* official chair of a king, queen or bishop 王, 女王的寶座或御座; 主教的寶座.

throng [θrɔŋ] *nc* crowd (*o. f.*) 羣, 堆(舊式).

throttle ['θrɔtl] *vt / i* prevent from breathing by pressing the hands on somebody's throat; strangle 掐, 扼(某人的脖子); 勒. Also *nc* device which controls the amount of fuel, steam etc passing into an engine 油門; 氣門: *He opened the throttle of his motorbike on the straight road* i.e. to go faster 他在直路上加大摩托車的油門. 即: 開得更快.

through [θru:] **1** *adj / adv / prep* (with reference to place) from one end or side to the other (指地點)穿過; 從一端到一端, 從一邊到另一邊: *The main road goes through the town.* 大道穿過該鎮. *They made a hole through the wall.* 他們在牆上穿了個洞. **2** *prep* (with reference to time) from beginning to end (指時間)從頭到尾, 由始至終: *We sat through the meeting.* 我們從頭到尾都坐着開會. *They worked through the night.* 他們通宵達旦地工作. **Note** 說明: (*US*) sense is up to and including. *Shops are open (from) Monday through Friday* i.e. from Monday morning to Friday evening (美)意爲由至星期五早晨到並且包括. *Shops are open (from) Monday through Friday.* 商店星期一到星期五都營業. **3** *prep* by means of; because of 通過; 由於: *I heard about it through a friend.* 我從一位朋友那兒聽

到這事兒的情況. *He became ill through eating too much.* 由於吃得太多他病了. **4** *adv* from one end or side to the other; from beginning to end 從一端到另一端地; 從一邊到另一邊地; 從頭到尾地: *Can I get through by this road?* 我可以從這條大道穿過去嗎? *They worked the whole night through.* 他們通宵達旦地工作. **5** *adj*: *We took a through train to London* i.e. one which went all the way to London without our having to change trains 我們乘直達火車到倫敦. **be through with 1** be finished with 完成, 結束: *I am just through with (reading) this book.* 我剛看完這本書. **2** be tired of 對…感到厭煩: *He is through with trying to please them. (informal)* 他對想討好他們的做法感到厭煩. (非正式). **get through something 1** finish 結束: *They got through the meal without speaking.* 他們一言不發地吃完了飯. **2** succeed; cause to succeed (使)成功: *Did you get through the examination?* 你考試通過了嗎? **get through to someone / something 1** (usu. with reference to a message, telephone call, radio etc) reach (通常指電報, 電話, 無線電等)與…取得聯繫: *He could not get through to his mother last night* i.e. by telephone. 昨晚他給母親的電話打不通. **2** make someone understand something 使明白, 使理解: *I couldn't get the facts through to him.* 我無法使他明白這些事實. **go through something 1** examine carefully 仔細檢查: *We shall go through the book together.* 我們將一起審閱這本書. **2** spend 花費: *He went through all the money his father gave him.* 他把父親給的錢都花掉了. **3** endure 忍受: *He went through a long illness.* 他長期患病. **go through**

with something do until finished; continue to the end 做完, 完成, 堅持到底: *Can we still go through with this plan?* 我們還能完成這項計劃嗎? **see through something** see that something is wrong; not be deceived by 看透, 看穿, 識破: *He soon saw through their promises.* 他很快就看出他們的許諾是騙人的. **through and through** completely 徹底地, 完全地: *He is cowardly through and through.* 他是個徹頭徹尾的膽小鬼. **through 'out** prep everywhere in; from beginning to end of 遍及; 貫穿: *throughout the world* 世界各地; *throughout his life* 貫穿他的一生. Also 亦作 adv: *The house was painted white throughout.* i. e. everywhere inside 這房子裏頭全部漆成白色.

throw [θrou] vt / i send through the air with a quick movement of the arm 投, 擲, 扔, 拋: *He was throwing stones into the river.* 他正往河裏扔石頭. *I threw the ball to him / I threw him the ball.* 我把球拋給他. past tense 過去式 **threw** [θru:]. past part. 過去分詞 **thrown** [θroun]. Also 亦作 nc act of throwing; distance which something is thrown 投, 擲, 扔, 拋; 投(或擲, 扔, 拋)的距離: *That was a good throw.* 投得很不錯. *It was a throw of about 50 metres.* 投擲的距離大約50米遠. **throw something away** get rid of 除去, 丟棄: *You should throw away these chairs and buy new ones.* 你應當丟掉這些椅子, 然後買新的. **throw oneself into something** begin to do very actively 積極(或起勁)地做做(某事): *She has thrown herself into gardening with great enthusiasm.* 她勁頭十足地栽培起花木來. **throw something off 1** take off quickly 迅速脫掉: *He threw off his coat.* 他忽然脫掉外

衣. **2** get rid of 除掉, 擺脫: *I can't throw off this fever I have.* 我發燒老不退. **throw someone / something over** abandon; give up. 拋棄; 放棄: *Why have you thrown him over? He was your best friend.* 你爲甚麼甩了他? 他以前可是你最好的朋友. **throw together** put, place together 忽忽拼湊成; 使偶然聚合在一起: *The war threw them together in a strange country.* 戰爭使他們在一個陌生的國家裏偶然相遇. **throw something up** vomit; be sick 嘔吐; 作嘔. **throw a fit 1** have a fit 大吃一驚. **2** be very angry *(informal)* 勃然大怒(非正式). **throw a party** give, have a party. *(informal)* 舉行宴會(非正式).

thrush [θrʌʃ] nc one of various types of small songbird (esp. one with a speckled chest) 畫眉鳥.

thrust [θrʌst] vt / i push suddenly and with force 猛推; 衝; 戳, 刺: *He thrust his knife into the man attacking him.* 他用刀子刺進那個攻擊他的人的身體. *I thrust all my books into the box.* 我把所有的書都塞進箱子了. *We thrust (ourselves) through the crowd.* 我們從人羣中衝了出來. past 過去式和過去分詞 **thrust**. Also 亦作 nc: act of thrusting or attacking 戳, 刺; 猛推; 攻擊: *The enemy made a thrust against our troops.* 敵軍對我軍發起攻擊.

thud [θʌd] nc dull sound made by a blow or heavy fall on something soft (打擊或重物落到鬆軟物體上發出的)沉重的聲音, 砰的一聲: *We could hear the thud of their feet as they ran on the grass.* 我們可以聽到他們在草地上奔跑時的沉重的腳步聲. Also 亦作 vi stike with a thud 砰然地打擊. past 過去式和過去分詞 **thudded**.

thug [θʌg] nc person who is violent and dangerous 暴徒, 心狠手辣的人.

thumb [θʌm] *nc* short, thick finger of the hand which is separate from the other four 大拇指. Also 亦作 *vt* use the thumb to do something 用大拇指做(某事): *He thumbed through the book* i. e. he used his thumb to turn over the pages quickly. 他用大拇指快速翻書. *They are trying to thumb a lift* i. e. trying to get a driver to stop and give them a lift by signalling to him with their thumb 他們伸出大拇指打手勢要求搭便車. *The little boy thumbed his nose at me* i. e. put his thumb on his nose with the rest of his fingers stretched out and pointing at me (a rude and insulting sign) 小男孩把大拇指放在鼻子上, 其餘四指張開指着我. (一種粗魯而且帶侮辱性的表示). **'thumbnail** nail of the thumb 大拇指指甲: *thumbnail sketch* i. e. small picture; quick, short description 小畫像; 速寫; 簡短的叙述. **'thumb- tack** (US) drawing pin (美)圖釘. **under somebody's thumb** under the complete control of somebody 在某人的完全控制之下.

thump [θʌmp] *nc* **1** blow (usu. with the closed hand) (通常用拳頭)重擊: *He gave me a friendly thump on the back.* 他親切地在我背上打了一拳. **2** sound made by something heavy falling suddenly (重物突然落地發出的)砰然聲: *The bag hit the ground with a thump.* 袋子砰的一聲掉到地上. Also 亦作 *vt / i* strike hard (usu. with the closed hand) (通常用拳)重擊: *Who is thumping on the door?* 誰在打門? *He thumped me on the nose.* 他猛擊我的鼻子.

thunder ['θʌndə*] *nu* loud noise in the sky which is often accompanied by lightning 雷, 雷聲. Also 亦作 *vt / i*: *Outside it was raining and thundering.* 外頭正下雨打雷. *The sea thundered against the rocks.* 大海咆哮着拍擊岩石. *The speaker thundered against his opponents* i. e. spoke loudly and violently 講演者厲聲指責其對手. **thunderous** *adj* making a sound like thunder; very loud 雷鳴般的; 非常響的: *There was thunderous applause.* 響起了雷鳴般的掌聲. **thundery** *adj* (with reference to the weather) likely to have thunder (指天氣)要打雷的. **'thunderbolt 1** single discharge of electricity followed by a great sound of thunder 電電, 霹靂. **2** something unpleasant which happens suddenly 晴天霹靂(突然發生的令人不快的事情). **'thunderclap** sudden, sharp burst of thunder (突然的尖厲的)雷響. **'thunderstorm** storm of thunder and lightning with heavy rain 雷雨.

Thursday ['θə:zdi] *n* fifth day of the Christian week 星期四, 禮拜四.

thus [ðʌs] *adv* in this way 如此, 這樣.

thwart [θwɔ:t] *vt* prevent somebody doing something he wishes to do 阻撓, 使受挫: *They have thwarted (him in) all his plans.* 他們挫敗了他所有的計劃.

thyme [taim] *nu* type of sweet-smelling plant 麝香草.

thyroid ['θairoid] *nc* one of the glands of the body, found in the neck 甲狀腺. Also 亦作 *adj.*

tiara [ti'ɑ:rə] *nc* circle of jewels worn by a woman on her head (婦女所佩)冕狀頭飾.

tic [tik] *nc* uncontrolled movement of the muscles of the face 面部肌肉的抽搐: *He has a tic under his left eve.* 他左眼下肌肉抽搐.

tick [tik] *nc* **1** small, regular sound made by a clock or watch (鐘或錶)滴嗒聲: *It was so quiet that I could hear* *the tick of the clock on the wall.* 静極了，我可以聽到上掛鐘的滴嗒聲. **2** moment; second 一會兒; 一瞬間, 一剎那: *I'll be ready in a tick.* (informal) 我一會兒就準備好. (非正式). **3** the mark ✓ made to show that something is correct or has been seen (表示正確或驗訖的) 勾號. Also 亦作 *vt / i* **1** make the sound of a tick 發出滴嗒聲: *I could hear the clock on the wall ticking.* 我可以聽到牆上掛鐘發出的滴嗒聲. *The engine was ticking over quietly* i. e. running slowly and smoothly like a clock 發動機緩慢平穩地轉動着. **2** put the mark ✓ after 打勾號於…之後: *The teacher ticked (off) the boys' names in his book as they came into the classroom.* 當男生們走進教室時老師在他們的名字後打勾號. **tick somebody off** speak severely to; rebuke 責備; 斥責: *The teacher ticked him off for being rude.* (informal) 老師責備他粗魯無禮. (非正式).

ticket ['tikit] *nc* **1** small piece of paper or cardboard which shows that the person who has it has paid, or has been given permission, to travel by bus, train etc or to enter a cinema, theatre, sports ground etc. 車票; 電影票, 戲票; 比賽入場券等. **2** small piece of paper or cardboard showing the price of something in a shop (商店裏的) 價格標籤或價目牌. **complimentary ticket** free ticket given to somebody 贈券; 贈送票. **re'turn ticket** (Brit) ticket allowing somebody to travel to a place and back again (英) 來回票. (US 美 **round-trip ticket**). **'season ticket 1** ticket allowing somebody to attend a number of concerts, lectures etc. (音樂會、講座等的) 定期入場券. **2** (Brit) ticket allowing somebody to travel daily for a par-

ticular period of time (英) 月季車票, 長期車票. **'single ticket** see 見 **single**.

tickle ['tikl] *vt / i* **1** touch somebody's skin lightly and make him laugh 搔癢 (使發笑): *She tickled the child under the arms.* 她搔孩子的胳肢窩. **2** amuse; please 逗樂; 使開心; 使高興: *His stories always tickle us.* 他講的故事總是逗我們樂. Also 亦作 *nc* feeling of being tickled 發癢. **ticklish** *adj* **1** (with reference to a person) easily made to laugh when tickled (指人) 怕癢的, 一搔癢就笑的. **2** (with reference to a problem, situation etc.) requiring skill and care in dealing with it (指問題、局勢等) 棘手的, 難對付的: *His tact and good manners enabled him to deal with many ticklish situations.* 他爲人機智而且很有禮貌, 因此能够對付許多棘手的場面.

tidbit ['tidbit] *nc* see 見 **titbit.**

tide [taid] *nc / u* **1** regular rise and fall of the sea twice each day 潮汐: *Today high tide was at 6 a. m. and low tide at midday.* 今天的高潮在上午6點, 低潮在正午. *The tides have worn away the rocks.* 潮水已經把岩石都磨損了. **2** (used only with other words) season (僅與其他詞連用) 季節: *Eastertide* 復活節季節; *eventide* (o. f. in sence **2**) 薄暮, 黃昏 (義 2 爲舊義). Also 亦作 *vt* (with **over**) help for the moment (與 **over** 連用) 使渡過難關. *This money should tide us over until Friday.* 這筆錢能當可以幫助我們渡過星期五之前的這段難關. **tidal** *adj* of, with a tide 潮汐的; 有潮水的: *tidal river* i. e. one which the sea enters and so causes a tide in it 潮水河; 海水可以進入其中並導致其產生潮汐的河流. *tidal wave* i. e. very large wave which can cause damage 海嘯.

tidy ['taidi] *adj* in good order; neat 整齊的; 整潔的: *You must keep your desk tidy.* 你必須保持書桌整潔. *He is a very tidy man.* 他是個很整潔的人. (*opp* 反義詞 **untidy**). Also 亦作 *vt / i* cause to be tidy (使) 整潔: *She tidied (up) the room before going out.* 她離開前把房間收拾整齊. **tidily** *adv* **tidiness** *nu*.

tie [tai] *vt / i* **1** fasten with rope, string, wire etc 捆, 綁, 縛, 拴: *I tied the sticks together.* 我把棍子捆起來. *Please tie (up) this parcel.* 請把這包裹捆起來. **2** join the ends of pieces of rope, string, wire etc together 打結, 繫: *He is tying his shoelaces.* 他正在繫鞋帶. *He tied the two ropes in / with a knot.* 他把兩條繩子打結繫在一起. (*opp* **untie** in senses 1 and 2) (義 1 和義 2 的反義詞為 untie). **3** keep busy; give less freedom 使忙碌; 限制, 束縛: *His work ties him down.* 他的工作把他束縛住了. *He is tied to his work.* 他忙於工作. *They want to tie up the agreement as soon as possible* i. e. make it definite so that it cannot be changed 他們想盡快締結協約. **4** (with reference to games, competitions etc.) get the same score or number of marks (指比賽、競爭等) 得分相同, 不分勝負: *John and James tied in the race.* 約翰與詹姆士在賽跑中不分勝負. *Our team tied with theirs in athletics.* 在田徑比賽中我們隊與他們隊旗鼓相當. *pres part* 現在分詞 **tying**, *past* 過去式和過去分詞 **tied**. Also 亦作 *nc* **1** strip of cloth worn round the neck (usu. by men) 領帶: *He was wearing a white shirt and / with a red tie.* 他穿着一件白襯衫, 繫着一條紅領帶. **2** something which joins something else together 連接物: *These ties hold up the roof* i. e. beams 這些橫樑支撐着屋頂. (US) the ties on

a railroad (*Brit* 英 **sleepers on a railway line**) (美) 鐵路枕木. *We have many ties of friendship with your country.* 我們同貴國有許多友誼的紐帶. **3** equal score or marks 得分相同, 不分勝負: *The result of the competition was a tie.* 競賽結果比分相同.

tier [tiə*] *nc* row (esp. of seats arranged above and behind another row) 一排, 一列, (尤指階梯式的座位): *The tiers in the theatre were full.* 劇院裏一排排的座位都坐滿了人.

tiger ['taigə*] *nc* large striped animal of the cat family found in Asia 虎. (*fem* 陰 **tigress** ['taigris]).

tight [tait] *adj* **1** firm; not easily moved; fitting closely 緊的, 緊的; 緊身的: *The knot is so tight that I cannot unfasten it.* 這個結太緊, 我解不開. *His pockets were tight with papers* i. e. firm because they were full. 他的口袋裏塞滿了文件. *She was wearing a tight dress.* 她穿着一套緊身衣. **2** stretched 張緊的, 繃緊的: *The wires between the poles are very tight.* 兩根電線桿之間的電線繃得很緊. **3** drunk. (*informal* in sense 3) 醉的 (義 3 為非正式). **tightly** *adv*: *He held my hand tight / tightly.* 他緊緊握住我的手. **tightness** *nu* **tighten** *vt / i* become, cause to become, tight or tighter (使) 變緊; (使) 繃緊. **tights** *npl* closely-fitting garment covering the feet, legs, and lower part of the body worn by women and children and also by acrobats and dancers (婦女、小孩、雜技演員和舞蹈演員穿的) 緊身衣. 'tight-'fisted *adj* mean (*informal*) 吝嗇的, 小氣的 (非正式). 'tightrope *nc / u* rope on which acrobats balance and do tricks (雜技演員在上面表演技巧的) 繃緊的鋼絲, 繩索. 'airtight / 'watertight *adj* not allowing air / water to get in or out 不透氣的/不漏水的.

tigress ['taigris] *nc* female tiger 雌虎.

tile [tail] *nc* flat piece of baked clay, plastic, cork etc used on roofs, floors and walls 瓷磚; 貼磚; 瓦, 瓦片. Also 亦作 *vt* cover with tiles 砌瓷磚; 用瓦舖, 舖瓦.

till[1] [til] *conj / prep* **1** up to a certain time 直到 ... 時: *He will stay here till Saturday.* 他將在這兒逗留到星期六. *The office is open from morning till night.* 該辦事處從早開到晚. **2** up to the time when 直到: *They waited till I arrived.* 他們一直等到我來. *I won't go till you tell me.* 我要一直等到你告訴我才走. *Note* 說明: *until* has the same sense as *till* and can be used instead of it in the sentences above. *Until*, however, is more usual when the clause or phrase in which it is used comes first. *Until now we have had good news. Until I arrived I said nothing.* until 與 till 同義, 而且可以在上句子的從句或短語開頭的話, 那麼 until 要比 till 常見. *Until now we have had good news.* 到目前為止我們已經得到好消息了. *Until I arrived I said nothing.* 我到達之前甚麼也沒說.

till[2] [til] *vt* make land ready for planting; cultivate 耕地; 耕作; 耕田.

till[3] [til] *nc* box or drawer where money is kept in a shop (商店裏的)錢櫃, 放錢的抽屜.

tiller ['tilə] *nc* bar by which the rudder of a boat is moved (小船的)舵柄.

tilt [tilt] *vt / i* lean, cause to lean, so as to be no longer level or upright (使)傾斜: *When he tilted the desk the books fell off.* 他掀斜書桌時, 書桌上的書掉到地上. *Her hat is tilted to one side of her head.* 她的帽子歪向腦袋的另一邊. *The boat tilted in the storm.*

船在風暴中傾斜了. **(at) full tilt** very quickly; with great force 全速地; 猛烈地: *He ran into the wall (at) full tilt.* 他猛然撞到牆上.

timber ['timbə] **1** *nu* trees cut down, or about to be cut down and prepared for use in building, carpentry etc. (建築, 木工等用的)木材, 木料: *The roofs and floors of the house are made of timber.* 這座房子的屋頂和地板都是用木材做的. *Half of the land is under timber* i. e. planted with trees which can be cut down and used 這塊土地有一半種了(可作木材的)樹. **2** *nc* large piece of wood prepared for use (e. g. as a beam to hold up a roof) 棟木, 橫木(如支撐屋頂的樑).

time [taim] **1** *nu* (often with **a** or **the**) intervals of minutes, hours, days or years needed to do something (常與 a 或 the 連用)(做某事所需的一段時間)(以分, 小時, 日或年計): *Have you time to look at it?* 你有時間看看它嗎? *Building a house takes a long time.* 建築一座房子耗時很長. *We cannot spare the time for extra work.* 我們騰不出時間去做額外的工作. **2** *nu* (without **a** or **the**) passing of minutes, hours, days etc (不與 a 或 the 連用)流逝的時光, 時間: *Only time will show if he is right.* 只有時間才會表明他是否正確. *Time never stands still.* 時間絕不會靜止不動. **3** *nc / u* particular moment, hour or occasion. (特定的)時刻; 鐘點; 次, 回: *At that time I was abroad.* 當時我在國外. *'What is the time?' / 'What time is it?' 'It is 8 o'clock.'* "幾點了?"/"幾點了?""八點." *Every time he comes here a friend.* 他每次來都帶來一位朋友. **4** *nc* number of occasions 次數: *Two times four are eight.* 二乘四得八. *He has been here many times.* 他已來過這地

多次. **5** *nc* exact measure of passing minutes, hours, days etc. 時間 (對經過時間的準確測定): *His time for (running) the mile was just over 4 minutes.* 他跑完一英里的時間正好超過四分鐘. **6** *nc* life; period; age 生活; 時期; 時代: *This happened before my time* i. e. before I was born or came here 我生在我出生之前(或我來到此地之前). *They had a bad time at school.* 他們在學校生活很不愉快. *In ancient times there were no motorcars.* 古代沒有汽車. **7** *nu* measure or rate of music; rate of moving to music (音樂)節拍, 節奏; 進行速度; *The band is playing the tune in waltz time.* 樂隊正以華爾茲的節奏演奏樂曲. *The soldiers marched in slow time.* 士兵們慢步前進. Also 亦作 *vt* **1** measure the amount of time taken to do something 測定…(做某事)所需的時間: *We timed him for the mile.* 我們測定他跑完一英里所需的時間. **2** choose or follow the correct time for something 選擇或注意(做某事)的正確時機: *They have timed their holidays to miss the busy season.* 他們使假期避開休假旺季. *A good boxer times his punches.* 好拳手注意出拳的時機. **timing** *nc* / *u* choice of, setting to, the correct time 時機的選擇; 調速: *There's something wrong with the timing of this engine.* 這發動機的調速有毛病. **timeless** *adj* never-ending 永恆的. **timely** *adj* happening at the right time 適時的. (*opp* 反義詞 **untimely**). **timekeeper** *nc* person who keeps time or a record of time (e. g. of the arrivals and departures of workers in a factory, of rounds in a boxing match, at a sports meeting etc.) 時間記錄員, 計時員. (如工人上下班時間, 拳擊比賽回合時間, 田徑運動會等的時間的記錄員). **time-**

keeping *nu* **time-lag** interval between two events which are related, delay (兩個相關事件的)時間間隔; 時滯: *There is usually a time-lag between making a plan and carrying it out.* 從擬定計劃到實行計劃通常要有一段間隔時間. **time limit** time allowed for something to end or be completed 時限, 期限: *This ticket has a time limit of 7 days.* 這張票的期限為 7 天. **timetable** *nc* list showing the times of events, of lessons in a school, or arrivals and departures of buses, trains etc. 時間表; 功課表; 時刻表. **all the time 1** always 總是: *He is busy all the time.* 他老是很忙. **2** during the whole period that something was happening 一直, 始終: *All the time we were working he did nothing.* 我們一直都在幹活而他卻無所事事. **at a time** on each occasion 每次: *The children came into the room three at a time.* 孩子們每次三個地走進房間. **at the same time 1** together 一同, 一起. **2** however 不過, 然而: *I think it is his own fault, at the same time, I can't help feeling sorry for him.* 我想這是他的錯, 不過我不禁為他感到難過. **behind the times** old-fashioned; out-of-date 老式的; 過時的. **do time** be in prison (*informal*) 坐牢 (非正式). **from time to time** occasionally. 不時, 偶爾. **in time 1** not late 及時: *He always arrives in time.* 他總是及時到達. **2** after a period of time 將來; 過一段時間後: *The mark on your face will disappear in time.* 你臉上那個斑痕過一陣子就會消失的. **in good time** not late 提早: *We arrived in good time.* 我們提早到達. **keep time 1** follow the correct time of a piece of music (e. g. when singing, dancing or playing a musical instrument) 跟着音

樂節拍，合着拍子(如唱歌、跳舞或演奏樂器時)．**2** (with reference to a clock or watch) go at the correct time (指鐘、錶) 走得準: *My watch keeps (good) time.* 我的錶走得準．**on time** at the expected or correct time 準時．

time and again very often 經常．

timid ['timid] *adj* easily frightened; nervous 易受驚的；膽怯的．**timidly** *adv*. **timidity** [ti'miditi] *nu*.

tin [tin] **1** *nu* type of soft metal 錫；馬口鐵；鍍錫鋼板．**2** *nu* (Brit) container (usu. airtight) made of tinplate i. e. thin sheet of iron covered by a thin sheet of tin (英) 罐(通常密封不透氣): *We bought five tins of fruit and two tins of soup. (US 美 can)* 我們買了五個水果罐頭和兩個湯罐頭．Also 亦作 *vt (Brit)* put food etc in an airtight tin (英)把(食物等)裝於罐中: *tinned fruit (US 美 canned fruit)* 罐頭水果．*past* 過去式和過去分詞 **tinned. tinny** *adj* like tin; making a sound like tin when struck 像錫的；(聲音)不響亮的．**'tin-foil** very thin sheet of tin like paper used for packing food etc. (Often **silver paper** because it has the colour of silver) (用於包裝食品等的錫箔紙(常寫作 silver paper 因爲它是銀色的)．**'tin opener** device used to open tins *(US 美 can opener)* 開罐器，罐頭刀．

tinge [tindʒ] *vt* (with **with**) give a slight colour or suggestion of (與 with 連用)使微染；使微帶: *The sun tinged the sea with yellow.* 陽光使大海一片微黃．*His words were tinged with anger.* 他的話微帶怒意．Also 亦作 *nc: a tinge of yellow / anger* 一絲黃色/怒氣．

tingle ['tingl] *vi* have a slight stinging feeling in the skin (e. g. when the blood comes back to the skin after a person has been cold or has been hit)

感到刺痛: *My face tingled after the walk over the hills.* 爬過山後，我的臉感到刺痛．Also 亦作 *nc: He felt a tingle of excitement.* 他感到極爲興奮．

tinker ['tiŋkə*] *nc* person who repairs pots and pans (esp. one who travels from place to place) (尤指流動的)補鍋匠．Also 亦作 *vi* try to repair (usu. in a clumsy way) (通常指)笨拙地修補或修理: *He likes tinkering with broken clocks.* 他喜歡亂修理壞鐘．

tinkle ['tiŋkl] *vt / i* make, cause to make, small quick sounds like those made by a small bell (使)發出叮璫聲: *The glasses on the tray tinkled.* 盤裏的玻璃杯叮璫作響．Also 亦作 *nc: tinkle of glasses* 玻璃杯的叮璫聲; *tinkle of a bell* 鈴兒的叮璫聲．

tinny ['tini] *adj* see 見 **tin.**

tinsel ['tinsl] *nu* **1** type of thin, bright material used in strips as a decoration or ornament (裝飾用的)發亮金屬薄片，金屬絲．**2** something which is showy, but of little value 華而不實的東西．

tint [tint] *nc* colour which is made paler by mixing it with white; slight colour 淡色；淺色: *There is a tint of red in her hair.* 她的頭髮微帶紅色．Also 亦作 *vt*.

tiny ['taini] *adj* very small 很小的．

tip[1] [tip] *nc* **1** narrow or pointed end of something (某物的)狹端或尖端: *tip of his finger / nose / tongue* 他的指尖/鼻尖/舌尖; *wing tips of an aeroplane* 飛機的翼端．**2** something fixed to the end of something else 裝於末端的東西: *This stick has a metal tip.* 這根手杖裝有金屬頭．*He smokes cigarettes with filter tips.* 他吸煙帶濾嘴的香煙．Also 亦作 *vt* put a tip on …上裝上尖頭: *filter-tipped cigarettes* 帶濾嘴的香煙．*past* 過去式和過去分詞 **tipped**

'**tiptoe** *adv (with* **on**) on the tips of the toes. (與 on 連用)踮起腳尖. *We went very quietly from the room on tiptoe.* 我們踮起腳尖悄悄地走出房間. Also 亦作 *vi* walk in this way 踮起腳尖走. *We tiptoed from the room.* 我們踮起腳尖走出房間. '**tip'top** *adj / adv* excellent *(informal)* 極好的(地) (非正式).

tip² [tip] *vt / i* **1** move easily; cause to move without much effort 容易翻; 使易於翻倒; 把…扔進; 脫(帽)致意: *The small boat tipped over* i. e. went over on its side 小船翻了. *The top of the desk tips up* i. e. can be raised and lowered easily 這桌面可以翻開. *He tipped over the basket.* 他碰翻了籃子. *He tipped the ball into the hole.* 他輕輕一擊把球打進了洞裏. *Shall I tip the water out of the jug?* 我可以把水從壺裏倒出來嗎? *The boy tipped his cap to the headmaster* i. e. touched or moved it slightly instead of raising it from his head 該男生向校長脫帽致意. **2** give a small amount of money to somebody (usu. for doing something) 給(某人)小費: *After paying for our lunch in the hotel, I tipped the waiter.* 付清我們在旅館的午餐費後, 我給侍者小費. *past* 過去式和過去分詞 **tipped**. Also 亦作 *nc* **1** place where rubbish is put (e. g. from a mine or from a town) 堆垃圾(例如礦井或城鎮的垃圾)的地方. **2** small amount of money (usu. given for doing something) 小費: *I gave the waiter a tip.* 我給侍者小費. **3** advice about how to do something 提示, 竅門: *This book has some useful tips about gardening.* 這本書有一些種植花草的竅門. '**tip-off** *nc* advice or warning *(informal)* 警告; 暗示; 提醒. (非正式).

tipple ['tipl] *nu* alcoholic drink 烈酒.

tipsy ['tipsi] *adj* slightly drunk 微醉的.

tirade [tai'reid] *nc* long, angry speech 長篇激烈的演說.

tire¹ ['taiə*] *vt / i* become, cause to become, weary or exhausted (使)疲倦; (使)厭倦; (使)精疲力盡: *Young children tire quickly.* 小孩很容易厭倦. *They soon tired of doing the same thing.* 他們很快就對做同樣的事感到厭倦. *The heavy work tired me.* 這重活使我精疲力盡. **tired** *adj* weary 疲倦的; 厭倦的. **tiredness** *nu* **tireless** *adj* not becoming weary easily; never stopping 不易疲倦的; 孜孜不倦的. **tirelessly** *adv* **tiresome** *adj* dull; annoying 沉悶的, 單調的; 討厭的. **be tired of** be weary with; have too much of 對…感到厭倦; 對…感到厭煩: *I am tired of going to school every day.* 我討厭每天上學.

tire² [taiə*] *nc* see 見 **tyre**.

tissue ['tiʃu:] *nc / u* **1** fine, light cloth or paper 薄絹; 薄紙. **2** piece of such paper 薄紙片. **3** group of cells which form part of an animal or plant (e. g. *muscular tissue*) 動植物的細胞組織(如肌肉組織). '**tissue paper** type of thin, soft paper used in parcels to protect things which are easily damaged etc. 薄而軟的包裝紙.

tit¹ [tit] *nc* see 見 **titmouse**.

tit² [tit] *nc* breast *(informal and impolite)* 乳房(非正式和不禮貌).

tit³ [tit] *nc* only in **tit for tat** i. e. blow for blow 僅用於 tit for tat, 即: 以牙還牙,一報還一報.

titbit ['titbit], **tidbit** ['tidbit] *nc* very pleasant or interesting piece of something 珍品; 珍聞: *titbit of cake* 精美的糕點; *titbits of news* 令人愉快而有趣的新聞.

title ['taitl] *nc* **1** name of a book, film, play, piece of music etc. (書、電影、戲

劇、樂曲等的)名稱, 標題. **2** word put in front of somebody's name to show his position, rank or work (e. g. *Dr, Lord, Professor*) (置於姓名前的)頭銜, 稱號(如博士、勳爵、教授). **3** (with to) legal claim or right (與 to 連用)權益, 權利: *He has the title to all the land here.* 他對此地的所有土地擁有所有權. 'title deed legal document which gives somebody the legal title to land or property 所有權狀; 地契; 房契. 'title role actor's part in a play from which the play takes its name (戲劇中演員扮演的角色的名字被用作劇名的)劇名角色: *He had the title role in Shakespeare's 'Macbeth'* i. e. he played the part of Macbeth in the play called 'Macbeth'. 他在莎劇"麥克白"中扮演劇名角色. 即: 他扮演麥克白這一角色.

titmouse ['titmaus] *nc* type of small bird which often hangs upside down when finding food 小山雀. *pl* **titmice** ['titmais] (usu. 常作 tit).

titter ['titə*] *vi* laugh in a silly way. 傻笑. Also 亦作 *nc*.

tittle-tattle ['titltætl] *nu* gossip; idle talk 無聊閑談; 聊天.

titular ['titjulə*] *adj* having a title without the power suggested by the title 有名無實的, 名義上的: *He is the titular ruler of Ruritania.* 他是盧利塔尼亞的名義統治者.

to [tu:, tə] *prep / adv* **1** towards; in the direction of 往; 向; 去: *Is this the road to the hospital?* 這是去醫院的路嗎? *We turned to the right.* 我們向右拐. *The farm is to the east of the town.* 農場位於該鎮的東面. *You should be kind to animals.* 你對動物應該愛護. **2** as far as 至, 到, 達: *from top to bottom* 從頭到底; *from east to west* 從東到西; *from first to last* 自始至終. *I*

read the book to the end. 我把這本書讀完了. **3** (with reference to time) until; before (指時間)到; 在…之前: *He will be in London from Monday to Friday.* 從星期一到星期五將在倫敦. *The time is five (minutes) to four.* 時間是四點差五分. (*opp past* in sense **3**)(義 **3** 反義詞為 past). **4** compared with 與…比較: *He is fat to what he was as a little boy.* 與孩提時比, 他胖了. *Our team scored three goals to their two.* 我們隊和他們隊的比分爲三比二. *We won by three goals to two.* 我們隊以三比二獲勝. *They prefer tea to coffee.* 茶與咖啡相比, 他們更喜歡茶. **5** showing the indirect object 指示間接賓語: *Please give it to me.* 請把它給我. *It seemed silly to us.* 這在我們看來似乎很愚蠢. **6** showing the infinitive 表示不定式: *to be or not to be* 生存或滅亡. *He wants to help.* 他想幫忙. *I have come to see you.* 我來看了你. *This is difficult to do.* 這很難做. *They were the last to leave.* 他們是最後離開的. **7** showing purpose or result 表示目的或結果: *The pupils rose to greet us.* 學生們起立歡迎我們. **8** in a particular position 處於某種特定位置: *He pushed the door to* i. e. pushed it into the position of being closed or almost closed 他把門推上. 即: 把門推到關閉的位置或幾乎關閉的位置. **to and fro** backwards and forwards 來回地, 往復地.

toad [toud] *nc* small animal like a frog with a dry skin 蟾蜍, 癩蛤蟆. 'toadstool name given to various types of fungus like a mushroom in shape 菌覃.

toast[1] [toust] *vt* **1** make hard and dry by heating 烤, 烘: *She toasted two slices of bread.* 她烤兩片麵包. **2** make warm by putting near a fire 烤火取暖.

We toasted ourselves in front of the big fire. 我們在大火前取暖. Also 亦作 *nu* bread which has been toasted 烤麵包, 烤麵包片. *two slices of toast* 兩片烤麵包. **toaster** *nc* device for toasting bread 烤麵包器.

toast² [toust] *vt* drink to the health of, or in honour of, somebody / something 舉杯祝賀(某人或某事物): *At the dinner they toasted the Queen.* 宴會上他們舉杯爲女王乾杯. Also 亦作 *nc* person / thing toasted; act of toasting 被舉杯祝賀的人/事物; 舉杯祝賀: *They drank a toast to the Queen.* 他們爲女王而乾杯. **toastmaster** person who announces the toasts at a party, formal dinner etc. (在大型聚會, 正式宴會等上)提議舉杯祝賀的人, 祝酒人.

tobacco [tə'bækou] *nc / u* type of plant, the dried leaves of which are smoked in cigars, cigarettes and pipes 煙草, 煙葉. **tobacconist** *nc* person who sells tobacco 煙草商.

toboggan [tə'bɔgən] *nc* type of sledge used for going down hills which are covered with snow (從覆蓋着積雪的山丘上下滑用的)一種雪橇.

today [tə'dei] *nu* this day; the present time 今天; 現代: *Today is Friday* 今天是星期五; *aeroplanes of today* 現代的飛機. Also 亦作 *adv* on this day 在今天, 在今日: *We are meeting today.* 我們要在今天碰頭. *Later today there is a football match.* 今天晚些時候有一場足球賽.

toddle ['tɔdl] *vi* walk with short, unsteady steps as a baby does when learning to walk (如學走路的嬰兒般)蹣跚而行, 搖搖提提地移動腳步. **toddler** *nc* baby who toddles 初學走路的嬰兒.

toddy ['tɔdi] *nc / u* drink made from mixing whisky etc, sugar and hot water 威士忌等酒類加糖和熱水混和而成的飲料.

to-do [tə'du:] *nc / u* excitement; fuss 吵鬧; 騷動; 紛擾: *There was a great to-do about the money which was stolen.* 爲款項被盜發生了一場激烈的爭吵. *He made quite a to-do about it.* (informal) 他爲此大吵大鬧一番. (非正式).

toe [tou] *nc* **1** one of the five parts at the end of the foot 腳趾, 腳指頭: *I've hurt my big toe* i. e. the one on the inner side of the foot which is bigger than the other four 我把自己的大腳指頭弄傷了. **2** front of a shoe. sock etc which covers the toes 鞋, 襪等的腳趾部份: *There is a hole in the toe of your sock.* 你襪子的腳趾部有個洞. **'toehold** space only big enough to put the toes in when climbing a rock, wall etc. (攀登岩石, 牆壁等時只容腳尖踩住的)立腳點. **'toenail** nail growing on a toe 腳趾甲. **toe the line** see 見 **line¹**.

toffee ['tɔfi] *nc / u* (Brit) type of hard sweet made from sugar and butter (英)乳脂糖, 太妃糖. (US 美 **taffy**).

together [tə'geðə*] *adv* **1** in one group; in the company of others 一起, 一塊兒: *Let's go to the shop together.* 咱們一塊兒去商店. *I want to speak to them all together.* 我想對他們全體講話. *Note* 說明: *all together* has the meaning of everybody / everything included; *altogether* has the meaning of completely; entirely; when everything is carefully considered: *an altogether stupid idea. So altogether, I think it would be better to try something else.* all together 意爲"全體地"; altogether 意爲"完全地; 徹底地; 全面認眞考慮地; an altogether stupid idea 十分愚蠢的想法. So altogether, I think it would be better to try something else. 因此 從全局考慮, 我認爲試試其他方法也許 更好. **2** in, to the same place, at the same time 在一起; 一起去; 同時: *Please put the books together on the desk.* 請把這些書一起放到書桌上. *His arrival and my departure happened together.* 他到達時正好我離開. **together with** along with; added to 和⋯一道; 加上: *My money together with his will be enough.* 我的錢加上他的錢就够了.

toggle ['tɔgl] *nc* short piece of wood attached to a piece of string which can be used like a button 木製栓扣.

toil [tɔil] *vi* work hard; move slowly and with difficulty 辛勤工作, 苦幹; 艱難緩慢地走走: *They toiled all day digging the hole.* 他們整天苦幹挖洞. *We toiled across the desert under the hot sun.* 在烈日下我們艱難緩慢地步行穿越沙漠. Also 見 *nu.*

toilet ['tɔilət] *nc* water closet; lavatory 厠所; 盥洗室: *Where is the toilet in this house?* 這房子裏的盥洗室在哪? '**toilet paper** paper used in a lavatory 衛生紙. '**toilet roll** of toilet paper (圓筒狀的) 衛生捲紙. '**toilet soap** scented soap of good quality used when washing the hands and face or when having a bath (盥洗用的) 香皂. '**toilet water** sweet-smelling water put on the skin 化妝水, (花露) 香水.

token ['toukən] *nc* **1** proof of something; sign 表明; 象徵: *We sent her flowers as a token of our gratitude.* 我們送花給她以表示我們的感激之情. **2** disc or card used instead of money for a particular purpose (金屬圓片或紙卡片) 代用幣: *milk token* i.e. a disc used instead of money when paying for milk 購牛奶代用幣; *book token* i.

e. card used instead of money to buy a book 購書代幣卡. Also 亦作 *adj* giving proof of something without doing it completely 象徵性的: *token payment* i. e. payment of a small amount of money to show that one agrees to pay the whole amount 象徵性付款, 即: 付一小筆款項以表明同意付全部款項; *token strike* i. e. strike by workmen which is not complete but is a warning to employers that a real strike may take place 象徵性罷工, 即: 不徹底的, 僅作爲對雇主的一種警告, 即真的罷工將舉行.

told [tould] past of **tell.** tell 的過去式和過去分詞

tolerate ['tɔləreit] *vt* allow something to be done even although one does not like it; endure somebody / something one does not like 容許; 容忍: *The government tolerates smoking and drinking but not taking drugs.* 政府容許吸烟和飲酒, 但不能容忍吸毒. *I can't tolerate the noise any longer.* 我再也無法忍受這種吵鬧聲了. **tolerable** ['tɔlərəbl] *adj* able to be tolerated; quite good 可以忍受的; 還好的. (*opp* 反義詞 **intolerable**). **tolerant** ['tɔlərnt] *adj* ready to allow or endure somebody / something even although one does not like it 寬容的; 容忍的: *The people in this country are very tolerant about / of the strange behaviour of visitors.* 這個國家的人民對來訪者奇怪的舉動是十分寬容的. (*opp* 反義詞 **intolerant**). **tolerance** ['tɔlərns], **toleration** [tɔlə'reifən] *nu.*

toll[1] [toul] *nc* **1** money paid to use a bridge, ferry, road etc. (過橋、過渡、過路等的) 費, 稅. **2** damage; loss 損害; 損失: *toll of malaria in tropical countries* i. e. deaths caused by malaria 瘧疾在熱帶國家造成的損失, 即: 造成的死

亡數.

toll² [toul] *vt / i* (with reference to a bell) ring slowly and deeply (指鐘)緩慢而低沉地響鐘；緩慢低沉地鳴鐘報(時).

tomato [tə'mɑːtou, *US* 美 tə'meitou] *nc* **1** type of plant with soft red or yellow fruit used as a salad vegetable (植物)番茄, 西紅柿. **2** the fruit itself 番茄, 西紅柿. *pl* 複數 **tomatoes.**

tomb [tuːm] *nc* place dug or built in which a dead person is put; grave 墳墓. **'tombstone** stone put above a tomb 墓碑.

tomboy ['tɔmbɔi] *nc* girl who behaves like a boy 男孩子氣的姑娘, 假小子.

tomcat ['tɔmkæt] *nc* male cat 雄貓.

tomorrow [tə'mɔrou] *nu* day after today; the future 明天；將來: *Tomorrow is a holiday.* 明天放假. *The boy of today is the man of tomorrow.* 今日的男孩是明日的男子漢. Also 亦作 *adv* on the day after today 在明天: *I'll see you tomorrow.* 我明天見你. **to'morrow'week, a'week to'morrow** a week from tomorrow i.e. in eight days' time. 下星期的明天, 即: 距今八天時間.

ton [tʌn] *nc* unit of weight equal to 20 hundredweight 噸.

tone [toun] **1** *nc / u* sound made by a musical instrument or voice (樂器發出的)聲音；音調；(嗓子發出的)噪音: *deep tones of the church bells* 教堂大鐘深沉的音響；*I don't like the tone of his voice.* 我不喜歡他的噪音. *She spoke in a high tone.* 她尖聲地說話. **2** *nc* shade of colour; effect caused by colour 色調；色彩效果: *The bright tones of the picture are seen better against the quiet tone of the wall.* 這幅圖畫明亮的色調在牆壁靜謐色調的映襯下更爲好看. **3** *nu* condition; character 狀況；特性: *The tone of a school depends on both the teachers and the*

pupils. 一所學校的風氣取決於教師和學生. Also 亦作 *vt / i* have, cause to have, a certain tone (of sound or colour) (使) 具有某種音調或色調. **2** (with reference to colour) agree with (指顏色) 諧調, 和諧: *Her hat toned (in) well with her dress.* 她的帽子與衣服的顏色很諧調. **'tone-'deaf** *adj* unable to distinguish different musical notes 沒有分辨音調能力的. **tone something down** become or make less loud, bright or strong (使)降低聲調；(使)柔和；(使)緩和: *Please tone down your voice.* 請你小聲點兒.

tongs [tɔŋz] *npl* device or tool for picking up and holding something 夾子, 鑷子, 鉗子: *sugar tongs* 糖夾子；*coal tongs* 煤鉗.

tongue [tʌŋ] **1** *nc* movable piece of flesh in the mouth used for licking, swallowing and tasting and (in humans) for speaking (人的)舌；舌頭. **2** *nc / u* tongue of an animal used as food (作爲食物的)動物的舌頭, 舌: *He was eating boiled tongue.* 他正在吃煮的舌頭. **'tongue-tied** *adj* unable to speak because of embarrassment or surprise 張口結舌的；(因尷尬或驚訝而)說不出話的: *I was tongue-tied with surprise.* 我驚訝得說不出話來. **'tongue twister** word or words difficult to say quickly 繞口令, 急口令. **have one's tongue in one's cheek, say something tongue in cheek** say something which is not meant to be taken seriously *(informal)* 話裏有話, 言不由衷, 說話無誠意. (非正式). **hold one's tongue** keep quiet *(informal)* 住嘴, 保持沉默. (非正式). **put / stick out one's tongue** show one's tongue either to be examined by a doctor or as a sign of rudeness 伸出舌頭(讓醫生檢查), 伸舌頭(無禮的表示): *He put*

out his tongue at me. 他朝我伸舌頭.
on the tip of one's tongue just a-
bout to be said 即將說話, 話到嘴邊: *It
was on the tip of my tongue to tell
him he was wrong. (informal)* 我正要
告訴他是他錯了. (非正式).

tonic ['tɔnik] *nc* something which helps
to bring back health and strength 滋
補品: *The doctor told me to get a
tonic* i. e. type of medicine to make
me healthier and stronger 大夫告訴我
要進補. *Fresh air is a good tonic.* 新
鮮空氣是一種良好的滋補品. '**tonic
water** mixture of water and quinine
水和奎寧的混合物: *gin and tonic (water)* 奎寧杜松子酒.

tonight [tə'nait] *nu* night after this day /
today 今晚, 今夜: *Tonight's concert
will be a good one.* 今晚的音樂會會很
不錯的. Also 亦作 *adv* on the night
after this day / today 在今夜, 在今晚:
I'll see you tonight. 我今晚見你.

tonnage ['tʌnidʒ] *nc / u* **1** space available inside a ship in tons (each ton
=100 cubic feet) 船的體積噸位 (每噸
=100立方英尺). **2** amount of cargo a
ship can actually carry (each ton = 40
cubic feet) 船的載重噸位 (每噸=40立
方英尺).

tonne ['tʌni] *nc* unit of weight equal to
1000 kilograms 噸 (=1000公斤).

tonsil ['tɔnsl] *nc* one of the two small
organs at the back of the throat
which sometimes become diseased
and have to be taken away 扁桃腺.
tonsillitis [tɔnsi'laitis] *nu* disease of
the tonsils 扁桃腺炎.

too [tu:] *adv / intensifier* **1** also; as well
也, 亦: *She went and I went too.* 她去
了, 我也去了. *She used to live in London. Me too.* 她以前住在倫敦. 我以前
也住在那兒. *Note* 說明: *too* is not
used after a negative; either is used

instead (e. g. not *I, too, don't like coffee* but *I don't like coffee either,* and
not *He, too, does not speak English
and French* but *He does not speak
English or French either*) 在否定式後
不用 too, 要用 either (例如, 不能說 I,
too, don't like coffee 而應說 I don't
like coffee either. 不能說 He, too,
does not speak English
and French 而應說 He does not
speak English or French either). **2**
more than is necessary 太, 過於: *He
talks too much.* 他話說得太多了. *The
coat is too big for me.* 這件上衣給我
穿太大了. **3** so very much (that) 太…
(以至於不): *I was too angry to
answer.* 我氣得回答不出來. *Note* 說
明: the difference between *too little*
and *a little too. The coat is too little
for me. The coat is a little too big for
me* i. e. rather too big; big but not by
much. too little 和 a little too 之間存
在差異. *The coat is too little for me.*
這件上衣給我穿太小. *The coat is a
little too big for me.* 這件上衣給我穿
大了一點.

took [tuk] past tense of **take.** take 的過
去式.

tool [tu:l] *nc* instrument held or controlled by the hands or by machinery
(e. g. axe, hammer, hoe, spanner) 手
工工具; 機器工具. (例如, 斧頭、鎚子、鋤
頭、扳手). '**toolbox** box for holding
tools 工具箱.

toot [tu:t] *nc* short but loud sound (e. g.
one made by the horn of a motorcar,
a ship's siren) (如汽車、船等發出的)
短促的鳴笛聲. Also 亦作 *vt / i* make,
cause to make, this sound (使)發出短
促的鳴笛聲.

tooth [tu:θ] *nc* **1** one of the bones
arranged in two rows in the mouth
and used for biting and chewing 牙

齒. 2 something shaped like a tooth 齒狀物: *tooth of a comb / saw* 梳子齒/ 鋸 齒. *pl* 複數 **teeth** [ti:θ]. **'toothache** pain in a tooth or teeth 牙痛. **'toothbrush** brush for cleaning the teeth 牙刷. **'toothpaste, tooth powder** substance used for cleaning the teeth 牙膏; 牙粉. **'toothpick** small pointed stick used for cleaning between the teeth 牙籤. **go through something with a fine-tooth-comb** search something carefully 仔細搜查某物. **in the teeth of** against; in opposition to 面對; 冒著: *The motion was carried in the teeth of fierce opposition.* 儘管遇到激烈的反對, 該提議還是被表決通過. **long in the tooth** (with reference to animals and people) old (*informal* when reference is to people) (指動物和人)老的, 上年紀的. (指人時寫非正式).

top¹ [tɒp] *nc* 1 highest part 頂部, 頂端: *the top of the mountain* 山頂; *tops of the flowers* 花葉. 2 most important position; first in rank 地位最高的; 級別最高的: *He was sitting at the top of the table* i. e. at the end of the table where important persons sit 他坐在桌子的首席. *He is (at the) top of his class* i. e. he is the best boy in it. 他是班裏最好的學生. 3 upper side 上部, 上面: *Put the box here with its top up.* 把箱子面朝上放這兒. *The top of his desk was covered with books.* 他的書桌上擺滿了書. Also 亦作 *adj* highest; most important thing 最高的; 最重要的: *He lives on the top floor.* 他住在最高一層樓. *The train went at top speed.* 火車以高速行駛. *Who is the top man here?* 誰是這兒的頭? **topmost** *adj* highest 最高的. **'topcoat** overcoat 大衣. **'top 'hat** type of tall hat shaped like a cylinder with a rim

禮帽, 圓頂有綠高帽. **'top-'heavy** *adj* too heavy at the top and so-likely to fall over 頭重腳輕的. **'top-'secret** *adj* most secret; secret and very important 絕密的; 非常機密的. **in top (gear)** using the highest gear 掛最高速檔, 全速地. **on top** above the others 在最上面: *I put your bag on top.* 我把你的包放在最上面. **on (the) top of 1** above over 在…之上: *I put your bag on (the) top of mine.* 我把你的包放在我的包上面. 2 also; as well 亦, 也; 除…外還: *He gave me a meal and on top of that, money for my journey.* 他請我吃了一頓飯, 此外還給了我旅費. **at the top of one's voice** as loudly as one can 使勁高聲地. **get on top of 1** be successful in dealing with (something difficult) 成功地處理 (棘手之事): *We are getting on top of the problem at last.* 最後我們會成功地處理好這個問題的. 2 be too much for 使…受不了: *Things are getting on top of me.* 局勢快要使我受不了啦.

top² [tɒp] *vt* 1 cover; have as a top 覆蓋; 以…爲頂部: *She topped the cake with nuts.* 她在這塊蛋糕上放了一層堅果仁. *The mountain was topped with snow.* 山覆蓋著一層雪. 2 be higher or better than 高於; 勝過: *This building tops all the others in the city.* 這座大廈是該市最高的建築物. *past* 過去式和過去分詞 **topped. top something up** fill to the required level 注滿, 裝滿(使達到要求的水準): *top up a battery / petrol tank etc.* 給蓄電池加電瓶水/給汽油箱加油等.

top³ [tɒp] *nc* type of toy which is made to spin on its pointed end 陀螺.

topaz ['toupæz] *nc / u* type of precious stone (usu. yellow in colour) 黃寶石, 黃玉.

topic ['tɒpik] *nc* subject talked or written about 話題; 題目. **topical** *adj* talked or written about now; up-to-date; current 時興話題或題目的; 時新的; 現行的, 當前的.

topple ['tɔpl] *vt / i* (with reference to something high) fall; cause to fall (指高的物體) (使) 倒下: *The tree toppled down / over.* 這棵樹倒了下來.

topsy-turvy ['tɔpsi'tɜːvi] *adj / adv* upside down; in disorder. *(informal)* 顛三倒四, 亂七八糟. (非正式).

torch [tɔːtʃ] *nc* **1** piece of wood or rope soaked in oil or grease and used as a light which can be carried 火炬, 火把. **2** *(Brit)* electric light with battery which can be carried (英) 手電筒. *(US 美 flashlight).*

tore [tɔː] past tense of **tear**². **tear**² 的過去式.

torment ['tɔːment] *nc / u* great pain of body or mind; something which causes this (肉體或心靈的) 劇痛; 折磨; 煎熬; 折磨人的事物: *We suffered torment / torments from thirst.* 我們受到乾渴的折磨. *The flies were a torment.* 蒼蠅是折磨人的東西. Also 亦作 [tɔːment] *vt* cause great pain or annoyance to 令 (人) 十分痛苦; 使苦惱.

torn [tɔːn] past part of **tear**². **tear**² 的過去分詞.

tornado [tɔːneidou] *nc* violent wind which goes round and round 龍捲風, 颶風. *pl* 複數 **tornadoes.**

torpedo [tɔːpiːdou] *nc* long metal container, filled with explosives and travelling below the surface of the sea, which is used against ships by other ships, submarines and aircraft 魚雷. *pl* 複數 **torpedoes.**

torpid ['tɔːpid] *adj* slow; without energy 遲緩的, 有氣無力的. **torpor** ['tɔːpə] *nu.*

torrent ['tɔrnt] *nc* **1** violent flow of liquid (usu. water) (通常指排水) 急流: *The rain fell in torrents.* 大雨滂沱. *We crossed the torrent by a small bridge* i. e. the small, swiftly moving river 我們走小橋跨過急流. **2** violent flow of words (話語的) 接連不斷: *torrent of abuse* 接連不斷的謾罵. **torrential** [tɔːrenʃl] *adj* of, like a torrent 急流的, 急流般的.

torso ['tɔːsou] *nc* human body or statue without head and limbs; human trunk (沒有頭和四肢的) 人體或雕像; 人體軀幹. *pl* 複數 **torsos.**

tortoise ['tɔːtəs] *nc* type of land animal which has a hard shell on its back and moves slowly 烏龜.

tortuous ['tɔːtjuəs] *adj* **1** having many bends and twists 彎彎曲曲的: *tortuous road over the hills* 彎彎曲曲的盤山路. **2** difficult to understand; dishonest 難以理解的, 轉彎抹角的; 不正直的: *He has a tortuous mind.* 他的思想令人難以捉摸.

torture ['tɔːtʃə] *nc / u* act of causing somebody great pain as a punishment or in order to make him confess something; great pain 酷刑; 拷打, 拷問; 折磨; 巨大的痛苦: *They say that in that country the police use torture.* 據說在那個國家裏警察使用酷刑. *I suffered tortures from headaches.* 我蒙受著巨大的痛苦. Also 亦作 *vt* cause great pain 使遭受巨大的痛苦, 折磨; 拷打, 拷問: *In former times they tortured prisoners.* 以前他們拷打犯人.

Tory ['tɔːri] *n* member of the Conservative Party in British politics 英國的保守黨黨員. Also 亦作 *adj.*

toss [tɔs] *vt / i* **1** throw 扔, 投, 拋: *He tossed me the newspaper.* 他把報紙扔給我. **2** move, cause to move, up and down or from side to side (使) 顛簸;

(使) 搖擺: *I tossed about in my bed because I could not sleep.* 我睡不着覺 在床上輾轉反側. *The horse tossed its head.* 這馬搖搖腦袋. Also 亦作 *nc* act of throwing or being thrown; quick movement 扔, 投, 拋; 快速移動: *He had a nasty toss from his horse.* 他從 馬上重重地摔了下來. *He gave an angry toss of his head.* 他生氣地搖搖 腦袋. **toss up** throw a coin into the air to decide something according to which side (heads or tails) falls upwards 擲錢幣(根據落地後向上的一面 —正面或反面—決定某事). **toss-up** *nc* 1 act of tossing a coin 擲錢幣. 2 something which may or may not happen 說不準的事情: *It is a toss-up whether I'll go. (informal* in sense **2**) 很難說是否會去.(義 2 爲非正式).

tot¹ [tɒt] *nc* 1 small child 小孩子. 2 small measure of alcoholic liquor 少 量烈酒.

tot² [tɒt] *vt* / *i* (with **up**) add. (與 up 連 用)加. *past* 過去式或過去分詞 **totted.**

total ['təutl] *adj* complete; full 全部的; 完全的: *What is the total cost of these books?* 這些書總共多少錢? *He was a total stranger to me.* 我對他一無所知. Also 亦作 *nc* the whole; sum after adding everything up 全部; 總和: *If you add 6 and 4, the total is 10.* 如果 你把 6 和 4 相加, 那麼總和就是 10. Also 亦作 *vt* / *i* amount to; add up. 合 計爲; 把…相加: *My money totals only ten pence.* 我的錢總共只有十便士. *Please total this bill for me.* 請爲我結 賬. *past* 過去式及過去分詞 **totalled.** (*US* 美 **totaled**). **totally** *adv* completely 完全地, 全部地. **totality** [təu-ˈtæliti] *nu.*

totalitarian [təutæliˈtɛəriən] *adj* of a government which allows only one political party and no opposition 極權

的, 一黨專政的.

totem ['təutəm] *nc* animal or plant believed by some primitive people to belong to their group and to have special powers in it 圖騰. **'totem pole** thick pole on which a totem is carved 刻有圖騰的粗木柱.

totter ['tɒtə*] *vi* move or walk as if about to fall 搖搖提提地行走.

touch¹ [tʌtʃ] *vt* / *i* 1 come in contact with 接觸: *Her dress is touching the floor.* 她的衣服碰到地板. *His car touched mine as it passed but did no damage.* 他的車子駛過時擦了我的車 子一下, 但是沒有造成損壞. 2 press gently with the hang; feel. 觸; 摸: *I touched him on the shoulder.* 我碰了 碰他的肩膀. *Please don't touch my books.* 請別碰我的書. 3 reach 觸及: *Can you touch your toes?* 你能摸得着 自己的腳趾嗎? 4 (usu. with **not** or **never**) have anything to do with(通常 與 not 或 never連用)與…有聯繫: *He never touches beer.* 他從不喝啤酒. *He hasn't touched his work for weeks.* 他 已經好幾週沒有做工作了. 5 move the feelings; affect感動; 影響: *I was very touched by his kindness.* 他的好意使 我很受感動. *These words touched his pride.* 這些話觸動了他的自尊心. **touching** *adj* moving the feelings 動 人的, 令人感動的: *touching request for help.* 令人感動地請求幫助. **'touchdown** *nc* (with reference to aircraft) landing (飛機的)降落. **touch somebody for something** ask or borrow something from somebody 向 某人求要(或借)某物: *He touched me for fifty pence. (informal)* 他向我高借 50便士. **touch something off** cause to begin suddenly 觸發某 事: *His remark touched off an argument.* 他的話激起了一場爭論. **touch**

on / upon something mention or deal with in a few words 提及, 談到. **touch something up** improve slightly by making a few changes 畧作修改, 修飾: *The artist was touching up the landscape that he had painted.* 畫家正在潤色他畫的風景畫. **touch wood** hope for good luck. *(informal)* 但願好運. (非正式).

touch²[tʌtʃ] **1** *nc* act of coming in contact with 觸, 碰: *He felt a touch on his shoulder.* 他覺得有人在他肩上輕輕拍了一下. **2** *nu* feeling; sensation 觸摸; 觸覺: *A blind man has to use his sense of touch a lot.* 盲人主要得用觸覺. *The child's face was hot to the touch.* 這孩子的臉摸起來很燙. **3** *nc* small amount 少許, 微量: *She added a touch of sugar.* 她加了一點糖. *I have a touch of the cold* i.e. a slight cold 我有點感冒. **4** *nu* style, skill (esp. with the hands) 風格; 技能, 手法: *She played the piano with a light touch.* 她用輕觸法彈鋼琴. **touchy** *adj* easily made angry 易發脾氣的. **touchiness** *nu* **'touchline** sideline of a football pitch (足球場的) 邊線. **in touch with** in communication or correspondence with; informed about 同⋯有聯繫, 與⋯常通信; 了解⋯: *He is in touch with the head office.* 他經常與總部聯繫. *Do you keep in touch with events in Africa?* 你一直在關心非洲的時事嗎? **lose one's touch** no longer have the same skill that one used to have 變得生疏. **touch-and-go** *adj* very uncertain 很不穩定的, 毫無把握的: *It is touch-and-go whether he will pass the exam.* *(informal)* 他能否通過考試還很難說. (非正式).

tough[tʌf] *adj* **1** difficult to bend, break, cut, chew etc. 堅韌的, 堅硬的: *This cloth is tough.* 這種布很耐穿. **tough** *meat* 硬而咬不動的肉. **2** (with reference to persons) difficult to frighten; energetic; able to endure hardship (人) 堅強的; 精力旺盛的; 能吃苦耐勞的: *In an argument he can be very tough.* 他很會強詞奪理. *To be a good runner, you must be tough.* 要跑得好必須是能吃苦耐勞的. **3** difficult 困難的: *This is a tough job.* 這是個棘手的工作. Also 亦作 *nc* person who is rough and violent; criminal 惡棍; 罪犯: *I was attacked on the way home by two toughs.* 我回家時在路上遭到兩個流氓毆打. **toughness** *nu* **toughen** *vt / i* become, cause to become, tough (使) 變堅強; (使) 變堅強; (使) 變困難.

toupee['tu:pei] *nc* piece of false hair worn over a bald part of the head (遮秃的) 假髮.

tour [tuə*] *nc* journey during which one visits several places and then returns to the place where one started 旅遊, 旅行: *They are making a tour of Scotland.* 他們在遊覽蘇格蘭. *He is on tour in Africa.* 他正在非洲旅遊. *The orchestra will be on tour next summer* i.e. it will play in several places. 這支管弦樂隊將於明年夏天進行巡迴演出. Also 亦作 *nc* I make a tour of 旅行; 遊歷; 觀光: *They are touring Scotland.* 他們在蘇格蘭旅行. **touring** *nu* act of touring, being on tour 旅行; 遊覽. **tourist** *nc* person who tours (esp. when on holiday) (尤指度假的) 旅遊者, 觀光者. Also 亦作 *adj* cheaper, of a lower class of travel 較便宜的, 旅遊等級較低的: *We travelled home by tourist class on the ship.* 我們坐經濟艙回家. Also 亦作 *adv*: *We always travel tourist.* 我們旅遊時都是坐經濟艙 (或 座). **tourism** *nu* practice of touring; industry depending on tourists 旅遊, 觀光; 旅遊業: *All countries*

now encourage tourism. 各國現在都鼓
勵發展旅遊業.

tournament ['tuənəmənt] *nc* organized
competition in a sport or game for a
number of players to find out who is
best 比賽, 錦標賽: *golf tournament*.
高爾夫球比賽.

tourniquet ['tuənikei] *nc* band twisted
tightly round the arm, leg etc to stop
bleding 止血帶, 壓脈器.

tousle ['tauzl] *vt* make the hair untidy
by pushing the fingers through it etc.
(用手指)弄亂(頭髮).

tow [tou] *vt* pull along by a rope or
chain (用繩, 鍊)拖, 拉: *The ship was
towed into harbour.* 這船被拖進港口.
Also 亦作 *nc / u* act of towing or
being towed 拖, 拉: *The tug took the
ship in tow.* 拖船拖着那隻船. *He
asked us for a tow.* 他請求我們幫忙拉
一下. **'towline** rope used for towing
拖纜, 繂. **'towpath** path beside a canal or river once used by horses for
towing boats (運河或河流邊的)拖船
路, 繂道.

toward,towards [tə'wɔ:d(z)] *prep.* 1 in
the direction of; 向, 朝: *He came to-
ward(s) me.* 他向我走來. *The window
faces toward(s) the hills.* 這窗戶朝着
丘陵. 2 (with reference to time) near;
just before (指時間)接近; 將近: *We
should arrive toward(s) nine o'clock.*
我們應在將近九點到達. *There was
a storm toward(s) evening.* 黃昏時有
暴雨. *Toward(s) the end of the day I
became tired.* 接近下班時我就疲倦了.
3 with reference to 對於: *I could not
feel angry toward(s) him.* 我不能對
他們生氣. 4 resulting in; in order to
get 導致; 爲了. *These talks are a step
toward(s) agreement.* 這些會談是朝向
達成協議的一步. *They are working
toward(s) peace.* 他們正在爲和平工

作.

towel ['tauəl] *nc* cloth or paper used for
drying something which is wet 毛巾;
手巾; 紙巾. Also 亦作 *vt* dry with a
towel 用毛巾擦. *past* 過去式和過去分
詞 **towelled.** (*US* 美 **toweled).**
towelling *nu* type of soft cloth used
for making towels 毛巾布, 製毛巾的布
料. **'tea towel** small towel used to
dry dishes 擦盤子用的小毛巾.

tower ['tauə*] *nc* tall, narrow building
or part of a building formerly for defence 塔, 高樓; 城堡. Also 亦作 *vi* 1
rise high 高聳: *The hotel towers
above / over the houses round it.* 這家
旅館高高地聳立在它四週的房屋之間.
2 (with reference to persons) very big
or very outstanding (指人)勝過, 超過:
*He is so intelligent that he towers
above all the others in his class.* 他很
聰明, 因此在班上智力超羣. **towering**
adj (used with anger, rage, bad temper etc) very great (與 anger, rage,
bad temper 等連用)極大的, 激烈的.

town [taun] *nc / u* 1 group of houses
and buildings larger than a village 鎮;
城鎮; 市鎮. 2 people who live in a
town 鎮民, 市民: *The whole town is
talking about the news.* 全市都在談論
這則新聞. 3 (without **a** or **the**) centre
of a town where the offices and shops
are (不用冠詞a或the)市區, 城鎮的商
業中心區: *He works in town and lives
in the suburbs.* 他在市區工作, 但住在
郊區. *We took a bus across / down /
up town.* 我們乘公共汽車穿過 / 到 / 去
市區. 4 (without **a** or **the** and esp.
with reference to London, England)
capital; most important town (不用冠
詞a或the,尤指英國倫敦)首府; 最重要
的城市: *I travel up to town from Oxford once a week.* 我每週從牛津上倫
敦一次. 5 (with **the**) towns in general

(用冠詞 the) 城鎮 (通稱): *Prices are higher in the town than in the country.* 城裏的物價比鄉下高. *Note* 說明: *(Brit) town* is used even with reference to a *city*, because *city* tends to give the sense of its official organizations, local government etc. There is little difference in sense between *Manchester is a big town* and *Manchester is a big city*, but one must say *Manchester City Police; City of Manchester's secondary schools.(US) city* is more often used. *Town* there refers more definitely to a smaller place. (英)用 *town* 也用以指 *city*, 因爲 *city* 的意義往往指它的官方組織, 地方政府等. *Manchester is a big town* 和 *Manchester is a big city* 幾乎沒有差別, 但是應該說 *Manchester City Police* (曼徹斯特市警署); *City of Manchester's secondary schools* (曼徹斯特市的中學). (美) *city* 更常用. *town* 更肯定地指較小的地方. **'town 'council** *nc* group of people elected to govern a town 市議會; 鎮議會. **'town 'councillor** *nc* member of a town council 市議會議員; 鎮議會議員. **'town 'hall** building used by the officials of a town and also used for meetings etc. 鎮公所; 市政廳. **'town 'planning** designing of a town to make its streets, housing etc pleasant and efficient 城鎮規劃.

toxic ['tɔksik] *adj* poisonous 有毒的.

toy [tɔi] *nc* something a child plays with 玩具. Also 亦作 *adj: toy train* 玩具火車. Also 亦作 *vt* play with; consider in a casual way 玩弄, 擺弄; 不認真地考慮: *He sat toying with his gloves.* 他坐着擺弄他的手套. *I toyed with the idea of going.* 我想去, 但不大認真. **'toyshop** shop which sells toys 玩具店.

trace [treis] *nc* 1 mark made by something which has passed or has existed. 痕跡; 踪跡; 足跡; 遺跡: *We could not find any trace(s) of the cattle.* 我們找不到牛的任何足跡. 2 small amount 微量, 一點點: *There are traces of gold in this rock.* 這塊岩石含有微量黃金. Also 亦作 *vt* 1 follow marks or signs in order to find something 跟踪, 追踪: *We are trying to trace our cattle.* 我們正跟着痕跡找我們的牛. 2 copy (esp. by putting a thin piece of paper over something) 描, 描摹 (尤指用薄紙蒙在底樣上畫): *They traced the map in the atlas onto a sheet of paper.* 他們把地圖册裏的那幅地圖描在一張紙上. **'tracing paper** thin, transparent paper used for tracing 透明描圖紙.

trachea [trə'ki(:)ə] *nc* 1 windpipe 氣管. 2 conducting tube in a plant (植物的) 導管.

track [træk] *nc* 1 mark left by something as it moves 行踪; 足跡; 軌跡: *The tracks of the car could be seen in the mud* i.e. marks made by its tyres. 在泥淖裏可見到那汽車輪胎的痕跡. *We followed the lion's tracks* i.e. marks made by its paws 我們跟踪獅子的足跡. 2 path made by humans or animals constantly using it (人或動物走出來的) 小道, 小徑: *We walked along the track to the village.* 我們沿小道走進那個村莊. 3 course or way specially prepared for running etc (特殊用途的) 道, 路, 路綫: *racetrack* 跑道; *railway track* 軌道. 4 band of magnetized tape for a tape recorder. (錄音磁帶的) 音軌. Also 亦作 *vt* follow the track of; find by following the track of 跟踪; 追踪找到: *We tracked him to his house.* 我們跟踪到他家找到了他. **trackless** *adj* without paths 無路的. **'sound track** see 見 **sound**[1].

track someone / something down follow someone / something until it is found 追尋到某人／某物. **keep track of** follow the track of; keep informed about 隨時了解…的情況. (*opp* 反義詞 **lose track of**). **make tracks for** set out for; go towards. (*informal*) 向…出發; 朝…去. (非正式).

tract¹ [trækt] *nc* area of land 一片土地, 地帶.

tract² [trækt] *nc* printed article or small book about a particular subject (esp. a religious one) 印刷的文章, 小册子 (尤指宗教性的).

tractor ['træktə*] *nc* vehicle for pulling heavy loads (e.g. machinery used in agriculture) 牽引機, 拖拉機.

trade¹ [treid] **1** *nu* business of buying and selling 貿易, 交易; 買賣: *Trade between Europe and Asia has increased.* 歐亞間的貿易增加了. *They are in the book trade.* 他們開書店. **2** *nc* occupation, work (esp. skilled work in industry etc.) 職業, 行業; 手工藝: *I am a mechanic by trade.* 我的職業是機械工. *Boys leaving school can be trained for many trades.* 男生離校後可以培訓幹許多種行業. **3** *nu* (with **the**) persons working in a particular trade (用冠詞the) 同行, 同業者: *The new tax on clothes is not liked by the trade* i.e. those who make or sell clothes 新服裝稅使服裝行業的人感到不滿. **'tradesman** shopkeeper 店主, (零售)商人. **'trademark** special mark put on goods to show what company made them 商標. **'trade name** special name which is given to a particular article by the company making it and which only that company can use in trade 商品的獨家商標名稱. **'trade 'union** *nc* recognized organization of workers in one or more trades to get

better conditions of work, more pay etc. 工會. **'trade 'unionist** *nc* person who belongs to a trade union 工會會員.

trade² [treid] *vt / i* **1** buy and sell; have as a business. 作買賣; 交易; 經商, 做生意: *In former times the people of this country traded in gold, ivory and slaves.* 這個國家的人以前是做黃金、象牙和奴隸買賣生意的. **2** (*US*) exchange (美) 交換, 換賣: *I'll trade my book for your watch.* 我用書換你的手錶. **trader** *nc* **'trading estate** area of land in which factories are built by the government and then rented to manufacturers 工業區(區內由政府興建工廠, 然後出租給廠商). **trade something in** give an old article as part payment for a new one 用舊物折價(換取新物), 貼換: *I have traded my old radio in for a transistor.* 我以舊收音機貼換了一架晶體管收音機.

tradition [trə'diʃən] *nc / u* belief, custom or story passed down from age to age and not usually written 傳統; 習俗; 傳說: *According to tradition the first king came from another country.* 據傳說, 第一個國王來自別國. *As a child he learnt the tradition of his tribe.* 他從小就學習本部族的傳統習慣. **traditional** *adj.*

traffic ['træfik] *nu* **1** flow of people and vehicles along the roads, of ships over the sea or aircraft through the sky 交通(指路上的行人車輛、海上船隻或空中飛機的來來往往): *There is always a lot of traffic in the centre of a town.* 市中心的交通總是很擁擠; *heavy / light traffic* i.e. a lot of / very little traffic 擁擠／稀疏的交通. **2** (often in a bad sense) trade; commerce. (常貶義) 買賣; 交易: *There was a big traffic in drugs.* 有人在大搞

毒品買賣. **'traffic lights** device fitted with red, orange and green lights to control traffic on the roads 交通燈, 紅綠燈.

tragedy ['trædʒədi] *nc/u* **1** serious play with a sad ending; type of drama of this kind 悲劇; 悲劇體裁. **2** any very sad event 悲劇, 悲慘的事: *The loss of all our money was a tragedy.* 我們的錢都丟了是一大不幸. **tragic** ['trædʒik] *adj* of tragedy; very sad 悲劇的; 悲慘的. **tragically** *adv.*

trail [treil] *nc* **1** lines, marks or scent left by somebody/something that has passed by 痕跡; 足跡; 留下的氣味: *There was a trail of water across the floor from the bucket.* 地板上有一條從桶裏漏出來的水的水跡. **2** rough path through wild country (荒野中的) 崎嶇小道, 小徑. Also 亦作 *vt/i* **1** follow the trail of 跟踪: *The hunter trailed the wounded buffalo through the bush.* 獵人穿過灌木林追獵受傷的水牛. **2** pull, be pulled, along 拖, 拉, 曳: *Her long dress trailed along the floor.* 她的長裙拖在地板上. **3** walk slowly because one is tired 疲倦地走, 緩慢地走: *The children trailed behind their teacher.* 孩子們拖着腳步跟在老師後面走. **trailer 1** vehicle pulled along by another vehicle 拖車, 掛車. **2** short parts of a film shown in a cinema as an advertisement before the complete film is shown later (作為廣告的) 電影預告片.

train¹ [trein] *vt/i* **1** prepare somebody for something by teaching and practice; prepare oneself in this way 培養; 訓練; 鍛鍊, 練習: *My parents trained me to behave properly.* 我父母教育我要守規矩. *Our football team is training for the next game.* 我們的足球隊正在爲下一場比賽進行訓練. **2** aim;

point at 把...對準, 瞄準; 指着: *He trained his binoculars on the ship.* 他把他的望遠鏡對準那條船. **3** (with reference to plants) cause to grow in a certain way 使 (植物) 向某方向生長: *They trained the vines up the wall.* 他們使葡萄藤往牆上爬. **trained** *adj* skilled; fully qualified 熟練的; 完全勝任的: *He is a trained teacher.* 他是個很勝任的教師. (*opp* 反義詞 **untrained**). **trainer** *nc* person who trains athletes, horses etc (esp. for sports, races etc.) 訓練者, 教練員; 馴馬師. **training** *nu* act of preparing somebody for something; act of preparing oneself for something 訓練; 培養; 鍛鍊: *The training of teachers is done at universities and colleges.* 教師的培訓是在大學和學院裏進行的. *He is in training for the school sports.* 他正在爲參加學校運動會而進行訓練.

trainee [treiˈniː] *nc* person who is being trained (esp. in industry) 受訓練的人 (尤指在工業).

train² [trein] *nc* **1** line of carriages or wagons pulled by a railway engine 火車: *We went by train to London* 我們乘火車去倫敦. *Does this train go to Edinburgh?* 這列火車是開往愛丁堡的嗎? **2** back of a long dress which trails behind on the ground (拖在地上的) 長衣裙. **3** number of connected events or ideas 一連串(事件), 一系列(想法): *The train of events led to war.* 這一連串事件導致了戰爭. *I cannot follow the train of his thoughts.* 我不能理解他那套想法.

trait [treit] *nc* special feature (esp. of somebody's character) 特性, 特點; 品質: *One of his traits is complete honesty.* 他的特點之一是十分誠實.

traitor ['treitə*] *nc* person who helps the enemies of his country or is not faithful to his friends etc. 賣國賊, 叛徒: *During the war he was a traitor to his country.* 戰爭時期他是個叛國分子.

tram [træm] *nc (Brit)* public vehicle which is driven by electricity and runs on rails laid on a road 電車.(Also 亦作 **tramcar**, *US* 美 **streetcar**).

tramp [træmp] *vt / i* l walk heavily 用沉重的腳步走; 踩: *They tramped over the carpet in their big boots.* 他們穿着大皮靴在地毯上重步行走. **2** go for a long walk (esp. through fields, over hills etc.) (長距離地)行走, 步行(尤指在野外). Also 亦作 *nc (Brit)* person who has no home and does no work, and travels from place to place (英)流浪漢, 漂泊者. *(US* 美 **hobo; bum.** *(informal)* (非正式) *US* tramp usually has the sense of an immoral woman 美語的tramp通常有"蕩婦"之意).

trample ['træmpl] *vt* walk heavily on, and so damage or crush, somebody / something 踩(壞); 踐踏; 踩躝: *The cows got into the field and trampled (down) the corn.* 一些牛闖進田裏, 踩壞了小麥.

trampoline ['træmpəlin] *nc* strong frame covered with canvas used by acrobats and gymnasts to jump high in the air (雜技演員和體操人員用以高跳的)蹦床, 彈簧墊.

trance [trɑːns] *nc* state of unconsciousness during which a person seems to be asleep but can see or do strange things 出神; 恍惚; 昏睡狀態, 迷睡: *The holy man fell into a trance* i.e. became unconscious in this way 這個聖徒進入出神狀態.

tranquil ['træŋkwil] *adj* quiet; peaceful 安靜的; 寧靜的; 平靜的; 安寧的. **tranquility** [træŋ'kwiliti] *nu* **tranquillizer** *nc* drug which makes a person calm, less worried etc. 鎮靜劑; 鎮定劑.

trans- [træns] *prefix* across; beyond; on the other side of (e.g. **transatlantic**). 橫越; 超越; 在⋯的另一邊(例如: transatlantic).

transact [træn'zækt] *vt* (usu. with reference to business) carry out; do (通常指事務)執行; 辦理; 處理. **transaction** **1** *nc / u* piece of business done; act of transacting business 交易; 事務, 業務; 辦理. **2** *nc* (in *pl*) activities and written records of a club or society (用於複數)(俱樂部或學會的)活動記錄, 會刊, 集刊.

transatlantic ['trænzət'læntik] *adj* across or on the other side of the Atlantic 橫越大西洋的; 在大西洋彼岸的.

transcend [træn'send] *vt* (esp. with reference to the limits of knowledge, experience etc.) go further than; be better than (尤指知識、經驗等範圍)超越, 超出; 優於; 勝過: *The origin of the universe transcends human understanding.* 宇宙的起源是人類無法理解的. **transcendental** [trænsən'dentl] *adj.*

transcribe [træns'kraib] *vt* (esp. with reference to writing out in full notes taken in shorthand) write out again 抄寫(尤指將速記符號轉寫成文).

transcript ['trænskript] *nc* something which has been transcribed 抄本, 謄本, 副本, 錄音; 改編曲. **transcription** [træns'kripʃən] **1** *nu* act of transcribing 抄寫, 謄寫; 轉寫; 改編. **2** *nc* something which has been transcribed or recorded in a particular way (e.g. a piece of music; a broadcast recorded for future use) 抄本, 謄本, 樂曲錄音; 廣播錄音; 改編曲.

transect [træn'sekt] *vt* cut across; divide by passing across 橫切; 橫斷.

transection [træn'sekʃən] *nu* act or

process of transecting; cross section 横切; 横断面.

transfer [træns'fə:*] *vt / i* **1** move from one place to another 转移; 调动: *He transferred the money from the box to his pocket.* 他把盒子裏的钱转放到自己的口袋裏. *I was transferred from the district office to headquarters.* 我从区办公室调到总部工作. **2** copy a design, photograph on one surface to another 转印; 摹绘. **3** change from one type of job to another 变换(工作): *Next term he wants to transfer from history to economics.* 下学期他希望改教经济, 不教历史. *past* 过去式和过去分词 **transferred**. Also 亦作 ['trænsfə:*] *nc* **1** act of transferring or being transferred 转移; (工作)调动; 变换: *I was given a transfer to headquarters.* 我被调往总部. **2** something / someone transferred (e.g. a design, photograph, football player) 转印物 (如图样、照片); 被转调者(如足球运动员). **transferable** *adj* able to be transferred 可转移的; 可调动的; 可变换的; 可转印的.

transform [træns'fɔ:m] *vt* change the form, nature or character of 改变; 改造; 使变样: *Water can transform a desert into a garden.* 水能使沙漠变为花园. **transformation** [trænsfə'meiʃən] *nc / u* **transformer** *nc* something which transforms (esp. a device which changes the voltage of an alternating electric current) 促使变化的东西; 变压器.

transfuse [træns'fju:z] *vt* take blood from one person and put it into another 给 … 输血. **transfusion** [træns'fju:ʒən] *nc / u*: *The doctor gave him a blood transfusion after the accident.* 事故发生后医生给他输血.

transient ['trænziənt] *adj* not lasting or staying long; short in time 一时的; 短暂的; 片刻的; (指人)过路的, 逗留时间很短的: *transient pleasures* 片刻的快乐.

transistor [træn'zistə*] *nc* **1** very small device which is used in radio sets, tape recorders etc. 晶体管. **2** small radio set in which it is used 晶体管收音机.

transit ['trænzit] *nu* act of moving or being moved across or through 通过; 穿过; 运行; 运输: *Transit by ship through the canal is expensive.* 乘船通过运河费用昂贵. *His luggage was lost in transit.* i.e. while being sent from one place to another 他的行李在运送中丢失了.

transition [træn'ziʃən] *nc / u* change from one state or condition to another 转变; 变迁; 过渡: *The transition from home to boarding school is not easy for many boys.* 对许多男孩子来说, 从家裏过渡到寄宿学校是不容易的. **transitional** *adj*.

transitive ['trænzitiv] *adj.* (with reference to a verb) having a direct object (shown in this dictionary by *vt*) (指动词) 及物的 (本词典用 *vt* 表示). (*opp* 反义词 **intransitive**).

transitory ['trænzitəri] *adj* not lasting long; short in time 暂时的, 短暂的; 瞬间的.

translate [trænz'leit] *vt* give the meaning of words of one language in the words of another 翻译: *He translated what I said in English into French.* 他把我用英语讲的话翻译成法语. *This French book is translated from Latin.* 这本法语书译自拉丁文. **translator** *nc* **translation** *nc / u* something which has been translated; act of translation 译文; 译本; 翻译: *Have you a good translation of Plato?* 你有没有柏拉图

著作的好譯本? *I am not very good at English translation* i.e. translating into English. 我英語翻譯得不怎麼好.

transmit [trænz'mit] *vt* send or pass on 傳送; 傳播; 傳染: *The mosquito transmits malaria.* 蚊子傳播瘧疾. *Rubber does not transmit electricity.* 橡膠不導電. *past* 過去式及過去分詞 **transmitted. transmission 1** *nc / u* act of transmitting 傳送; 播送; 傳染. **2** *nc* part of a car which carries the power from the engine to the wheels 傳動器. **transmitter** *nc* instrument for sending out messages by radio; radio broadcasting station (無線電) 發報機; 無線廣播電台.

transparent [træns'pærnt] *adj* **1** able to be seen through 透明的; *Glass is transparent.* 玻璃是透明的. **2** clear; obvious 清楚的; 明顯的; *The meaning is transparent.* 這含義是清楚的. *He laughed at our transparent attempts to deny it.* 他對我們顯然想抵賴的意圖加以嘲笑. **transparency** *nc* picture or photograph put on transparent material (so that it can be shown on a screen) 幻燈片.

transpire [træns'paɪə*] *vt / i* become known slowly 洩露; 漸漸爲人所知: *From our questions it transpired that he had told a lie.* 我們通過提問逐漸發覺他撒了謊.

transplant [træns'plɑːnt] *vt* **1** remove and plant in another place 移植; 移種 (植物). **2** remove an organ from one body and put it in another 移植 (器官). *Also* 亦作 ['trænsplɑːnt] *nc*: *The heart transplant was done by a team of doctors.* 心臟移植手術是由一個醫療小組做的.

transport[1] [træns'pɔːt] *vt* carry from one place to another 運輸; 運送; 搬運: *Coal is usually transported by rail.* 煤通常由鐵路運輸. **transportable** *adj* able to be transported 可運輸的; 可運送的; 可搬運的. **transportation** [trænspɔː'teiʃən] *nu* act of transporting or being transported 運輸; 運送; 搬運.

transport[2] ['trænspɔːt] *nu* carrying of persons or goods from one place to another 運輸; 運送: *The transport of coal is usually done by rail.* 通常用火車運輸煤. *Because of the flood the village is without transport.* 由於洪水, 該村莊的交通中斷. *Note.* 說明: in this sense *transport* is the more usual British word; *transportation* is the American word. 在這個意義上, 英國更常用transport; 美國則用transportation.

transpose [træns'pouz] *vt* **1** change the usual or relative order or position of (two or more things); interchange 改換…的位置; 改變次序; 調換; 變換: *Transpose the two colours to make a better design.* 把這兩種顏色的位置互換一下, 使圖案更加好看. **2** (music) Change the key of (a composition) (音樂) 使換調; 使變調: **be transposed from G to B** 從G調變爲B調. **3** transfer (a term) to the other side of an algebraic equation, changing plus to minus or mimus to plus 移 (項).

transposition [trænspə'ziʃən] *nc / u* **1** action of transposing or condition of being transposed 調換; 變換; 互換位置. **2** (music) composition transposed into a different key (音樂) 變調; 換調; 變調曲. **3** transfer of a term of an algebraic equation from one side to the other with a change of sign 易位; 移項: *transposition of terms of an equation* 方程式的移項.

transversal [trænz'vəːsəl] *adj* lying or passing across; transverse 橫向的; 橫斷的; 橫截的. *Also* 亦作 *nc* line intersecting two or more other lines 截斷綫; 橫斷綫.

transverse ['trænzvə:s] *adj* lying or passing across; placed crosswise; crossing from side to side 橫向的; 橫放的; 橫截的; 橫切的; 橫貫的: *transverse axis* (數學)橫截軸; *transverse beams* 橫樑; *transverse current* 橫向電流, 渦流; *transverse nerve* 橫神經; *transverse section* 橫斷面; *transverse stress* 橫向應力, 彎曲應力. Also 亦作 *nc* **1** transverse part, beam etc 橫向物; 橫向部份; 橫樑. **2** transverse axis; the longer axis of an ellipse 橫軸; 橢圓的長軸. **3** muscle which is transverse to other part of the body 橫肌.

transvestite [trænz'vestait] *nc* person who wears the clothes of the opposite sex. 穿異性服裝的人. Also 亦作 *adj*.

trap [træp] *nc* **1** device for catching animals; trick to catch somebody doing something 捕捉器; 陷阱; 圈套; 詭計. **2** type of small two-wheeled cart pulled by a horse 雙輪輕便馬車. **3** small door in a floor or roof (地板上或屋頂的)活門. (Often 常作 **trap door**). Also 亦作 *vt* catch in a trap or by a trick 用捕捉器或設陷阱捕捉, 誘捕; 使陷入圈套. *past* 過去式和過去分詞 **trapped**. **trapper** *nc* person who traps animals (esp. for their skins) 誘捕動物的人(尤指爲獲取皮毛).

trapeze [trə'pi:z] *nc* horizontal bar which swings on two ropes and is used for gymnastic exercises, and by acrobats in circuses (體操訓練或雜技表演用的)吊架; 高鞦韆.

trappings ['træpiŋz] *npl* ornaments; signs of rank 裝飾物; 官階的標誌: *He was wearing the trappings of an army general.* 他身著陸軍上將的服飾.

trash [træʃ] *nu* rubbish; something of very poor quality (e.g. in music, writ-

ing etc.) 垃圾, 廢物; 廢話; 劣貨; 拙劣的作品. **trashy** *adj* **'trashcan** *nc* (US) container for putting rubbish in (美)垃圾箱. (*Brit* 英 **dustbin**).

trauma ['trɔ:mə] *nc* condition of the body or mind caused by severe injury or shock 外傷; 損傷; 精神創傷. **traumatic** [trɔ:'mætik] *adj*.

travel ['trævl] *vt/i* **1** make a journey or journeys (esp. abroad) 旅行(尤指到國外): *He has travelled all over Africa.* 他已經遊遍非洲. **2** move; move along; go 移動; 運行, 傳開: *Bad news travels quickly.* 壞消息傳得快. *I want a car which can travel* i.e. can move at high speeds 我要一輛能跑得飛快的汽車. *Let your mind travel back to what happened yesterday* i.e. remember; think about 你回憶一下昨天發生的事情吧. **3** make journeys on business (usu. to sell things) 作商務旅行(通常指推銷商品): *My brother travels in furniture.* 我兄弟到各地推銷傢具. *He travels for a firm which makes furniture.* 他爲一家傢具廠商作旅行推銷. *past* 過去式和過去分詞 **travelled**. (US. 美 **traveled**). Also 亦作 *nc/u*: *his travels all over Africa* 他遍及非洲的旅行. *Travel through this country is very slow.* 在這個國家旅遊很費時間. **traveller** (US 美 **traveler**) *nc* **1** person who travels 旅行者, 遊客. **2** commercial traveller 旅行推銷員. see below 見下面. **travelling** (US 美 **traveling**) *adj*: *travelling bag* i.e. one used when travelling 旅行包. **'travel agency** business which arranges journeys, holidays etc for other people 旅行社. **co'mmercial 'traveller** (*Brit*) person employed by a manufacturer to travel about visiting shops in order to persuade the shopkeeper to buy the manufacturer's goods (爲廠商所雇用

到各商店兜售產品的) 旅行推銷員. *(US*
美 **traveling salesman).**

traverse ['træˈvɜːs] *vt* pass across 通過;
穿過; 橫越: *The main road traverses
the plain from north to south.* 這條主
幹道由北向南穿越平原.

travesty ['trævəstɪ] *nc* very poor imitation or false description of something
(often made on purpose) 拙劣的模倣;
曲解, 歪曲: *Your study is a travesty of
the facts.* 你的研究是對事實的曲解.
The trial was a travesty of justice i.e.
it was in no way just. 這一審判是對公
正的歪曲. 即: 一點都不公正.

trawl [trɔːl] *nc* type of very large fishing
net shaped like a bag, dragged along
the bottom of the sea (海上捕魚用的)
拖網. (Also 亦作 **trawl net**). Also 亦
作 *vt / i* fish with a trawl 用拖網捕
(魚). **trawler** *nc* type of ship used
for trawling 拖網漁船.

tray [treɪ] *nc* flat piece of wood or metal
etc with a raised edge round it, used
for carrying things (e.g. dishes), keeping papers (e.g. on a desk) or catching a liquid as it drops (e.g. oil from
an engine) 盤子, 托盤;(書桌上的)文件
盤, 槽.

treacherous ['tretʃərəs] *adj* unfaithful;
not to be trusted or relied upon 背叛
的; 叛逆的; 不忠實的; 不可信的; 靠不住
的: *The treacherous soldier told the
enemy where his friends were.* 那個背
叛的士兵把朋友們所在的地方告訴敵
人. *The sea is very treacherous in
bad weather.* 天氣惡劣時海上是很危
險的. **treachery** *nc / u.*

treacle ['triːkl] *nu* (Brit) thick, dark,
sweet liquid made from sugar (英) 糖
漿; 糖蜜. *(US* 美 **molasses).**

tread [tred] *vt / i* walk; step 走; 踩; 踐
踏: *Please don't tread on the flowers.*
請勿踐踏花草. *past tense* 過去式 **trod**

[trɔd]. *past part* 過去分詞 **trodden**
['trɔdn]. Also 亦作 *nc* **1** act of treading; sound made by treading 步行; 踩;
踏; 腳步聲: *I could hear his heavy
tread on the floor outside my room.*
我聽得到他在我房間外面地板上的沉重
的腳步聲. **2** outside part of a rubber
tyre which has a pattern on it (to prevent skidding) (帶有花紋防止打滑的)
輪胎面. **tread on somebody's toes**
offend somebody *(informal)* 觸怒某
人, 得罪某人. (非正式). **tread water**
keep upright and afloat in deep water
by treading with the feet 踩水.

treason ['triːzn] *nu* disloyalty to, betrayal of, one's own country 叛國; 賣
國. **treasonable** *adj.*

treasure ['treʒə*] *nc / u* collection of
valuable things (e.g. money, gold,
jewels); somebody / something which
is greatly valued 財富, 財寶; 珍品; 寶
藏; 寶貴的人材: *The divers found treasure at the bottom of the sea* 潛水員在
海底發現了寶藏;*the treasures of Eng-
lish¯ literature* 英國文學的財富. *Our
servant is a treasure* 我們的傭人是個
不可多得的人. Also 亦作 *vt* value
greatly 珍視; 珍惜: *He treasures all
his books.* 他珍愛他所有的書.
treasurer *nc* person who looks after
the money of a club, society etc. 財務
員, 司庫. **treasury** *nc* department of
government which is responsible for
collecting and paying out government's money (in Britain **the Treasury**) 財政部 (英國爲 the Treasury).
'**treasuretrove** treasure, the owner of
which is not known, found buried in
the ground 地財, 埋於地下的無主寶
藏.

treat [triːt] *vt* **1** deal with or use in a
particular way, behave towards 處理;
處置; 對待: *They are treating the mat-*

ter seriously. 他們正在認真處理那件事. *They are not treating it as a joke.* 他們不會把它當作笑話. *How did he treat you?* 他怎樣對待你? **2** give medical attention to 醫治, 治療: *The doctor treated me for malaria.* 醫生給我治療瘧疾. *It is difficult to treat a person with cancer* i.e. who has cancer 癌症病人難治. *Nowadays they treat malaria with drugs* i.e. by using drugs 現在他們用藥物治療瘧疾. **3** buy something for somebody; pay for somebody 款待; 請(客): *Our uncle treated us to an ice cream.* 叔叔請我們吃冰淇淋. *I treated myself to a big dinner.* 我飽餐了一頓. Also 亦作 *nc* **1** something unusual which gives pleasure 不尋常的樂趣: *The visit to the seaside was a great treat for us.* 到海邊遊玩是我們最大的樂趣. **2** act of buying something for somebody 款待; 請客: *Our uncle's treat was to give us tickets for the cinema.* 叔叔買票請我們看電影.

treatise ['tri:tiz] *nc* serious book or paper about a particular subject. (專題)論者, (專題)論文.

treatment ['tri:tmənt] *nc/u* **1** particular way of dealing with somebody/something 處理; 待遇: *His treatment of the problem was most interesting.* 他處理那個問題的方法極其有趣. *They were given good treatment by the soldiers.* 他們受到士兵們的良好對待. **2** medical attention 治療: *He has gone to the hospital for treatment.* 他已經去醫院治療. *There are several treatments for a cold.* 治療感冒有好幾種方法. *I was under treatment for two weeks.* 我受過兩週的治療.

treaty ['tri:ti] *nc* agreement(esp. a written one made between countries) 條約; 協議; 協定(尤指國家之間).

treble[1] ['trebl] *adj* three times as much as 三倍的: *Clothes are treble the price (that) they used to be.* 服裝的價格是以前的三倍. Also 亦作 *vt/i* become, cause to become, treble (使)成為三倍, (使)增加兩倍: *Why have the prices trebled?* 為甚麼物價增加了兩倍?

treble[2] ['trebl] *nc* highest notes in music; boy's voice which can sing the highest notes 最高音部; 唱最高音部的童聲. Also 亦作 *adj*.

tree [tri:] *nc* large plant with a trunk, branches and leaves 樹, 樹木. *Note* 說明: a *shrub* or *bush* is much smaller and although it has branches it does not have a trunk. shrub或bush比tree小得多, 雖然它們也有枝, 但沒有樹幹.
'family 'tree see 見 **family.**

trek [trek] *vi* make a long journey (originally in a wagon pulled by oxen in South Africa) 作長途旅行(原指在南非乘坐牛車旅行). *past* 過去式和過去分詞 **trekked.** Also 亦作 *nc* journey of this kind (乘牛車的)長途旅行.

trellis ['trelis] *nc* light frame used for supporting climbing plants, and making doors and screens (支撐攀緣植物的)棚, 架, (門屏的)格子結構.

tremble ['trembl] *vi* shake; shiver 搖動; 哆嗦; 顫抖: *The children were trembling with cold/excitement/fear.* 孩子們冷/激動/害怕得發抖. *His voice trembled as he spoke* 他說話時聲音發抖. Also 亦作 *nc*: *I could feel the tremble in his hands.* 我能感覺到他的手在顫抖. **in fear and trembling** see 見 **fear.**

tremendous [tri'mendəs] *adj* very great 巨大的, 極大的. **tremendously** *adv.*

tremor ['tremə*] *nc* very short, shaking movement; quiver 震動; 震顫; 發抖.
'earth tremor shaking of the earth

which is less severe than an earth-quake (輕微)地震.

trench [trentʃ] *nc* long, narrow hole dug in the earth (e.g. for laying pipes or to protect soldiers from the enemy's fire) 溝, 壕, 塹溝; 戰壕.

trend [trend] *vi* go in a certain direction 走向; 傾向, 趨向. Also *亦作 nc* direction; tendency; inclination 方向; 傾向; 趨勢, 趨向: *Young women are always interested in the trends of fashion.* 年輕婦女總是對時裝趨向感興趣.

trepidation [trepi'deiʃən] *nu* state of being both afraid and excited 又驚又喜的狀態; 惶恐; 戰戰兢兢.

trespass ['trespəs] *vi* **1** go on to somebody's land or property without permission 未經許可進入他人土地; 非法侵入: *You must not trespass on / upon government land.* 你不能非法侵入政府的土地. **2** take too much advantage of 過份利用: *They are always trespassing upon his kindness.* 他們老是利用他心地善良佔便宜, 太過份了. **trespasser** *nc*.

trestle ['tresl] *nc* wooden frame made of two pairs of legs, each pair joined at the top to a horizontal bar (used to support planks, platforms or tables) (用以支撑木板、枱面或桌子的)支架; 枱架. **'trestle table** table with its top resting on a pair of trestles 擱板桌, 枱桌.

tri- [trai] *prefix* three (e.g. **triangle**). 三 (例如: triangle).

triad ['traiæd] *nc* group of three 三個一組.

trial ['traiəl] *nc / u* **1** test to see if somebody / something is suitable etc. 試, 試驗; 試用; 檢驗: *He says he will give the new medicine a trial* i.e. use it and see what it is like 他說他要試一試那

種新藥. *The manager has promised to give me a trial as a clerk.* 經理答應要試用我當文書. *New cars have several severe trials before they are put on the market.* 新汽車在投放市場前要經過好幾道嚴格檢驗. *We went for a trial run in the new car* i.e. in order to test it 我們去試開這輛新車. **2** examination of the facts in a court of law to decide a case 審判, 審訊: *His trial for murder begins tomorrow.* 他的殺人案明天開始審理. **3** somebody / something that gives trouble; nuisance 使人傷腦筋的人或物; 討厭的東西: *He is a great trial to his parents.* 他真叫父母傷透腦筋. **on trial 1** in order to be tested 作爲試用: *The shopkeeper has allowed me to have the radio set on trial.* 店主已允許我試用這台收音機. **2** accused in a court of law 受審: *He is on trial for murder.* 他因謀殺而在受審.

triangle ['traiæŋgl] *nc* **1** figure with three straight sides 三角形. **2** small musical instrument made of a piece of metal shaped like a triangle 三角鐵 (一種小樂器). **triangular** [trai'æŋgjulə*] *adj* having three angles shaped like a triangle 三角(形)的.

tribe [traib] *nc* large group of families having the same language and customs 部落; 部族. **tribal** *adj* of a tribe 部落的; 部族的. **'tribesman** person who belongs to a tribe 部落成員; 同部族的人.

tribulation [tribju'leiʃən] *nc* trouble; hardship 憂患; 苦難; 災難; 艱辛.

tribunal [trai'bjuːnl] *nc* court of law 法庭.

tribune[1] ['tribjuːn] *nc* **1** high official elected by the ordinary people of ancient Rome to defend their rights (古羅馬由平民選出的)護民官. **2**

popular leader; person who defends popular rights and interests 民眾領袖;民權保衛者.

tribune² ['tribju:n] *nc* raised platform or dais for speakers 論壇;講壇.

tribute ['tribju:t] *nc* something said or done to show respect or express thanks 頌辭;讚揚;向⋯致: *I wish to pay tribute to all those who have helped me.* 我要向所有幫助我的人表示謝意. *There were many tributes to him in the newspapers.* 報紙紛紛頌揚他. **tributary** river which flows into a bigger one 支流: *The River Amazon has many tributaries.* 亞馬遜河有許多支流.

trice [trais] *nu* only in **in a trice** i.e. in an instant; very quickly 僅用於 in a trice 即:馬上,立刻;很快地.

trick [trik] *nc* **1** something done to deceive somebody 詭計;騙局;手法: *We used several tricks to make the enemy believe that we were about to attack.* 我們巧施了幾個計謀,使敵人相信我們就要進攻. *They got into the castle by a trick.* 他們用計進入城堡. **2** something done as a joke or in mischief 開玩笑,惡作劇: *These boys like playing tricks on their teacher.* 這些男學生喜歡捉弄他們的老師. **3** something done by skill to deceive but also to amuse; conjuring tricks 戲法,把戲: *I'll show you a trick which you can do with two pennies.* 我來變個戲法給你看,用兩個便士就能變. **4** strange habit 怪習慣;怪癖: *He has a trick of looking at his feet when he talks.* 他有個奇怪的習慣,講話時老看着自己的腳. **5** cards played in one round and taken by the player with the winning card (牌戲的)一墩牌: *We won the game by three tricks.* 這一盤我們贏了三墩牌. *My ace took the trick.* 我的A牌贏了這

墩. Also 亦作 *vt* deceive 欺騙. **trickery** *nu* act of deceiving or cheating 欺騙;詐詐. **tricky** *adj* (with reference to things) requiring great skill; difficult (指事情)極需要技巧的;棘手的;困難的.

trickle ['trikl] *vt/i* flow or move slowly or in small drops (使)徐徐地流;(使)滴;緩慢移動: *The rain trickled down my neck.* 雨水滴在我的脖子上. *The boys trickled into the classroom.* 男孩子們陸陸續續地走進教室. Also 亦作 *nc* very small flow 細流.

tricycle ['traisikl] *nc* cycle with three wheels (often used by young children instead of a bicycle) 三輪(腳踏)車.

tried [traid] past of **try**. try 的過去式及過去分詞.

trier ['traiə*] *nc* see 見 **try**.

trifle ['traifl] **1** *nc* something of little worth or importance 小事;瑣事;微不足道的東西: *Great men do not worry about trifles.* 偉人不會爲瑣事煩惱. **2** *nc/u* type of sweet food made of cake covered with fruit, custard and cream etc 一種蛋糕上有水果、蛋羹、奶油等的甜食;蛋糕. Also 亦作 *vt/i* (with **with**) treat lightly; not be serious about; play with (與 with 連用)輕率地對待;輕視,小看;玩弄: *It is dangerous to trifle with such a fierce animal.* 逗弄這麼兇猛的動物是危險的. *He trifled with his food instead of eating it.* 他撥弄他的食物而不吃. **trifling** *adj* of little importance 瑣碎的,無足輕重的: *a trifling matter* 瑣事. **a trifle** *adv* just a little; rather 一點點;稍微: *He was a trifle too slow to catch me.* 他太慢了點,趕不上我.

trigger ['trigə*] *nc* small lever on a gun which is pulled by the finger to fire it. (槍的)扳機. Also 亦作 *vt* (often with **off**) start suddenly (常與 off 連用)突然

開始；觸發：*The news has triggered (off) a serious crisis.* 這消息觸發了一場嚴重的危機．

trigonometry [trigə'nɔmətri] *nu* branch of mathematics which deals with triangles 三角學．

trilby ['trilbi] *nc* man's soft felt hat (男用)特里比式軟氈帽．

trilogy ['trilədʒi] *nc* group of three books or plays about the same subject 三部曲．

trim [trim] *adj* neat and tidy 整齊的；整潔的．Also 亦作 *nu* condition; readiness 狀況，狀態；準備就緒．*He was in good trim when I saw him.* 我見到他時他身體很好．*An athlete must never get out of trim.* 運動員絕不能準備不足．Also 亦作 *vt / i* 1 decorate; make neat and tidy by adding or taking away something from the edges 裝飾；使整潔；修剪．*She trimmed her hat with flowers.* 她用鮮花裝飾她的帽子．*He trimmed his beard with a pair of scissors.* 他用剪刀修剪他的鬍鬚．2 adjust the sails of a ship or the wings of an aircraft to the wind 調整(船帆或機翼)以適應風向．*past* 過去式和過去分詞 **trimmed. trimming** *nc* 1 something used to trim clothes (衣服的)裝飾品；裝飾物．2 (in *pl*) extra food eaten with other food (用於複數)(食物的)花色配菜：*roast beef with all the trimmings* 烤牛肉加上一切應有的配料．

trinity ['triniti] *nc* group of three: 三個一組，**the Trinity** i.e. Father, Son and Holy Ghost, considered as one in the Christian religion 三位一體，即: 在基督教中，天父、耶穌和聖靈被認爲是一體．

trinket ['triŋkit] *nc* small ornament of little value 不值錢的小裝飾品．

trio ['tri:ou] *nc* group of three persons (esp. three playing music together);

piece of music for three players 三人的一組；三重奏；三部合奏曲．*pl* 複數 **trios.**

trip [trip] *vt / i* 1 strike the foot against something and fall or almost fall; cause somebody to do this 絆；(使)絆倒；(使)失脚：*I tripped over the basket as I ran away.* 我跑開時被籃子絆了一跤．*He put out his foot to trip me (up).* 他伸出脚要把我絆倒．2 walk, run or dance lightly 輕快地走(或跑、跳舞) *past* 過去式和過去分詞 **tripped.** Also 亦作 *nc* 1 journey taken for pleasure 旅遊；遠足：*trip to the seaside* 去海濱的遠足．2 fall, mistake. 絆倒；過失，錯誤．**tripper** *nc* person who makes a journey for pleasure (usu. for a day) 旅遊者，遠足者(通常爲玩一天)．

tripe [traip] *nu* 1 inside part of the stomach of a sheep or an ox used as food (供食用的)羊(或牛)肚．2 worthless talk or writing (*informal* in sense 2). 廢話；無價值的作品(義2爲非正式)．

triple ['tripl] *adj* 1 made up of three parts 由三部份組成的．2 three times as much or as many 三倍的：*Clothes are triple the price they used to be.* 服裝的價格是過去的三倍．Also 亦作 *vt / i* become, cause to become, triple (使)增至三倍：*The population has tripled in three years.* 人口在三年內增加了兩倍．see also 參見 **treble¹.**

triplet ['triplit] *nc* one of three children born at the same time to the same mother 三胞胎孩子中的一個．

triplicate ['triplikət] *nu* (esp. with reference to papers which are typed) third copy made of something (尤指打出的文件)一式三份中的第三份：*Please type this letter in triplicate.* 請把這封信打成一式三份．

tripod ['traipɔd] *nc* table with three legs; stand with three legs on which something can be rested (e.g. a blackboard or camera) 三脚桌; (黑板或攝影機等的)三脚架.

trite [trait] *adj* (with reference to something said or written) used too often; not new (指話語或文章)陳詞濫調的; 陳舊的.

triumph ['traiʌmf] *nc / u* success; victory; happy feeling caused by a great success 成功; 勝利; (因巨大成功而産生的)喜悦: *Winning the football cup was one of their greatest triumphs.* 贏得足球賽獎杯是他們的最大成功之一. *They returned from the match in triumph.* 他們參加比賽後凱旋而歸. Also 亦作 *vi* (with **over**) win a victory; have a happy feeling becuse of success (與over連用) 獲勝, 戰勝; (因成功而)得意揚揚: *We have triumphed over our enemies.* 我們戰勝了敵人. **triumphal** [trai'ʌmfl] *adj* of a triumph 成功的; 勝利的; 凱旋的. **triumphant** [trai'ʌmfənt] *adj* expressing happy feelings because of a triumph (因成功、勝利而)高興的; 得意的: *The triumphant team returned home with the football cup.* 那個得意揚揚的足球隊捧杯而歸. **triumphantly** *adv*.

trival ['triviəl] *adj* not important; ordinary 不重要的; ordinary 平凡的; 瑣細的; 普通的: *trivial complaints* 無關緊要的抱怨. **triviality** [trivi'æliti] *nc / u*: *They complain about trivialities.* 他們埋怨一些鷄毛蒜皮的事. **trivia** *npl* unimportant things 瑣事, 微不足道的事物.

trod [trɔd] past tense of **tread.** tread的過去式.

trodden ['trɔdn] past part of **tread.** tread的過去分詞.

trolley ['trɔli] *nc* **1** small cart with two or four wheels which is pushed by hand (兩輪或四輪的)手推車; *railway porter's trolley* 鐵路搬運工的手推車; *tea trolley* i.e. one on which dishes and food are brought at tea time 送茶具和茶點的小推車. **2** type of truck which can be pushed or driven by hand on a railway 鐵道手搖車. **3** long pole with a small wheel at the end which connects a train or trolley to the electric wire overhead (電車與架空電線連接的)觸輪. **'trolley bus** type of bus with a trolley on top (觸輪式)電車.

trombone [trɔm'boun] *nc* type of musical instrument played by pushing a sliding tube in and out 長號, 拉管 (一種樂器).

troop [tru:p] *nc* **1** large group of people; small company of soldiers (esp. cavalry). 大羣(人); 騎兵隊. **2** (in *pl*) soldiers; army. (用於複數)部隊; 軍隊. Also 亦作 *vt / i* move in a large group 成羣結隊地行動: *All the boys trooped off to see the football match.* 所有的男孩子都涌去看足球賽. **trooper** *nc* soldier in a cavalry regiment 騎兵.

trophy ['troufi] *nc* **1** something which is kept as a reminder of a success or victory (e.g. the horns of an animal which one has shot) (成功的或勝利的)紀念物(如獵獲的動物的角). **2** prize 獎品: *The trophy for winning the race was a gold medal.* 跑贏的獎品是一枚金牌.

tropic ['trɔpik] *nc* one of the two circles round the earth about 23° 30′ north or south of the equator. (The one north of the equator is *the Tropicc of Cancer;* the one south of it *the Tropic of Capricorn*) 回歸線. (赤道以北的稱 the Tropic of Cancer北回歸線; 赤道以南的稱 the Tropic of Capricorn南回歸線). **the tropics** *npl* part of the

world between the two circles 熱帶.
tropical *adj* of, like the tropics; very hot 熱帶的; 像熱帶地區的; 炎熱的: *tropical climate* 熱帶氣候.

trot [trɒt] *vt / i* (usu. with reference to a horse) go, cause to go, faster than walking (通常指馬) 小跑; 使 (馬) 小跑; 慢步跑: *The horse trotted down the road.* 馬沿路小跑而去. *He trotted his horse to the end of the field.* 他騎馬慢跑到田野的盡頭. *We saw the schoolboys trotting home.* 我們看到男生們正慢慢地跑回家. *past* 過去式和過去分詞 **trotted.** Also 亦作 *nu* speed faster than walking 小跑; 慢跑; 快步: *They passed us at a trot.* 他們快步從我們身邊走過.

trouble [ˈtrʌbl] *vt / i* **1** have or cause difficulty, discomfort or worry 麻煩; 使苦難; 使不舒服; (使) 煩惱: *One of my teeth is troubling me.* 我的一顆牙齒在折磨我. **2** (usu. in question or with not) cause oneself discomfort or inconvenience. (通常用於疑問句或與not 連用) 煩勞, 費事: *Why did they trouble to come?* 他們爲甚麼不辭勞苦前來? *Please don't trouble (yourself); I can do it by myself.* 請別麻煩啦, 這我自己會做. **3** as a polite request (作爲禮貌的請求) 麻煩: *May I trouble you for the salt?* i.e. please pass me the salt 麻煩你把鹽遞給我好嗎? Also 亦作 *nc / u* **1** difficulty, discomfort, worry 困難; 辛苦; 煩惱: *One of my teeth is giving me trouble.* 我的一顆牙齒在折磨我. *He has had many troubles since his father died.* 自從他父親去世後, 他碰到了許多困難. **2** special care or attention 特別關心; 費心: *Thank you for all your trouble in looking after me.* 謝謝你這麼費心照顧我. *He went to the trouble of finding out (for) himself.* 他不辭勞苦自己查明原因.

troublesome *adj* causing trouble 令人煩惱的; 討厭的; 麻煩的: *troublesome child* 討厭的孩子; *troublesome tooth* 折騰人的牙齒. **ˈtroubleshooter** person who tries to sort out troubles in an organization 排解(組織)糾紛者. **ask for trouble** see 見 **ask**. **be in trouble 1** be worried 煩惱的: *He is in great trouble because he has no money.* 他很煩惱, 因爲他身無分文. **2** likely to have trouble, be punished etc for doing something wrong (因做錯事) 會有麻煩; 受處罰等: *John is in trouble again for losing his books.* 約翰丟了書又要倒霉了. **get into trouble** do something wrong for which one is likely to be blamed, punished etc. (因做錯事而) 遭到責罵、懲罰等; 倒霉: *He got into trouble with his wife for coming home late.* 他因遲回家而挨妻子的罵. **get somebody into trouble 1** cause somebody to do something for which he may be blamed, punished etc. 使某人惹禍, 使某人遭到責罵、懲罰等. **2** cause an unmarried girl to become pregnant. (*informal* in sense 2) 使未婚女子懷孕(義2爲非正式). **put somebody to trouble** cause somebody trouble 給某人添麻煩: *I am sorry for putting you to so much trouble.* 我這樣麻煩你真對不起. **take trouble over** take special care; give special attention to 對…特別注意; 對…特別關照: *He should take more trouble over his work.* 他應當更加盡力做好工作.

trough [trɒf] *nc* **1** long, narrow container which holds food or water for animals 飼料槽; (牲口喝水的) 水槽. **2** hollow between two waves 兩浪間的凹處, 波谷. **3** (with reference to weather) decrease in the pressure of the atmosphere (指天氣) 低壓槽: *a* *trough of low pressure over the British Isles* 不列顛羣島上空的低壓槽.

trounce [trauns] *vt* beat or defeat thoroughly 徹底打敗.

troupe [tru:p] *nc* group of actors or performers 劇團; 歌唱圈; 舞蹈圈等.

trousers ['trauzəz] *npl* garment with two separate places for the legs which covers the lower part of the body and the legs 褲子, 長褲. **trouser** *adj*: *trouser pockets* 褲袋. **'trouser suit** woman's suit with trousers instead of a skirt 上衣配褲子的女套裝.

trousseau ['tru:sou] *nc* clothes, personal articles etc which a woman collects before she marries 嫁妝, 妝奩. *pl* 複數 **trousseaux** ['tru:souz] or **trousseaus.**

trout [traut] *nc* type of spotted fish often used for food 鮭魚; 鱒魚. *pl* 複數 **trout.**

trove [trouv] *nc* see 見 **treasure.**

trowel ['trauəl] *nc* 1 tool with a flat blade used to spread cement or mortar when building 泥刀, 抹子. 2 tool with a curved blade used when gardening 移植手鏟.

troy [trɔi] *nu* system of weights for gold, silver, precious stones, etc in which one pound equals twelve ounces 金衡, 金衡制 (金、銀、寶石等的衡量制度, 每金衡磅等於十二盎司): *weigh 3 lb 5 oz troy* 計重金衡制 3 磅 5 盎司. Also 亦作 **troy weight.**

truant ['truənt] usu. in **play truant** not attend school when one ought to 通常用於 play truant 逃學.

truce [tru:s] *nc* agreement to stop a war, fighting etc for a short time 休戰協定.

truck [trʌk] *nc* 1 open wagon for carrying heavy goods by rail (鐵路) 敞車, 無蓋貨車. 2 porter's handcart for heavy luggage (搬運工人用的) 手推車. 3 lorry 卡車. *Note* 說明: *(US) truck*, not *lorry*, is always used. *(Brit)* both *truck* and *lorry* are used (美) 總是用 truck, 不用 lorry. (英) truck 和 lorry 通用. **'truck farmer** *(US)* farmer who grows and sells vegetables *(Brit* 英 **market gardener)** (美) 菜農.

truculent ['trʌkjulənt] *adj* fierce; ready to fight 兇猛的; 好戰的.

trudge [trʌdʒ] *vi* walk heavily as one does when tired 跋涉; 步履艱難地走.

true [tru:] *adj* 1 correct in fact 真實的, 確實的: *What I say is true.* 我所說的是真的. *This is a true report of what happened.* 這是所發生情況的確實報告. 2 honest; loyal; faithful 誠實的; 忠誠的; 忠實的: *He is true to his friends.* 他對朋友忠誠. 3 genuine; real 真的; 真正的: *This is not a true Rembrandt.* 這不是倫布蘭特的原畫. *He is not the true son of the chief.* 他不是首領的親生兒子. 4 exact; accurate 確切的; 準確的, 精確的: *Is this a true copy of the letter?* 這是那封信的準確抄本嗎? *Only a skilled worker can build a wall that is true.* 只有熟練工人才能把牆砌得不歪不斜. see 見 **truth. truly** *adv* really; genuinely 真正地; 名副其實地; *I am truly grateful* 我確實非常感謝; *Yours truly* (put at the end of a letter) 您的忠實的 (信末的套語) **come true** happen as had been hoped or wished 實現: *When he passed his exams he felt as if all his dreams had come true.* 他考試合格時感到他的所有夢想似乎都已實現.

truffle ['trʌfl] *nc* type of chocolate or sweet 一種巧克力糖.

truly ['tru:li] *adv* see 見 **true.**

trump [trʌmp] *nc* one of a suit of playing cards which by agreement can take any card of the other three suits

王牌: *In the first game of bridge spades were trumps.* 橋牌比賽的第一局中黑桃是王牌. **trump something up** make up or invent something which is not true 捏造: *He trumped up a story about being ill. (informal)* 他謊稱生病. (非正式). **play one's trump card** make the final move or use the only advantage left to win success 打出王牌, 拿出最後一手.

trumpet ['trʌmpit] *nc* type of wind musical instrument, made of brass and played by blowing through it; sound made by this 喇叭; 小號; 吹喇叭的聲音. Also 亦作 *vt* make a sound like a trumpet; make known by sounding trumpets 發出吹喇叭似的聲音; 以吹喇叭宣告; 象的吼聲 (似喇叭聲); *We heard the elephants trumpeting in the forest.* 我們聽見大象在樹林裏吼叫. *The heralds trumpeted the arrival of the king.* 傳令官吹起喇叭宣告國王駕到. **blow one's own trumpet** boast; praise oneself. *(informal)* 自吹自擂; 自我讚揚. (非正式).

truncate [trʌŋ'keit] *vt* make short by cutting off the end 把⋯截短. **truncated** *adj*.

truncheon ['trʌntʃən] *nc (Brit)* short, heavy stick used by the police *(US 美* **club; night stick)** (英) 警棍.

trundle ['trʌndl] *vt* roll heavily 使 (沉重地) 滾動: *They trundled the barrels into the store.* 他們把那些桶滾進倉庫.

trunk [trʌŋk] *nc* **1** part of a tree between its roots and its branches 樹幹. **2** body without its arms, legs and head (人的) 軀幹. **3** large box with a hinged lid for storing clothes etc or for carrying them when travelling 大衣箱. **4** long nose of an elephant 象鼻. **5** (in *pl*) tight-fitting short trousers worn by men for swimming or

games (用於複數) 男游泳褲; 男運動短褲. **'trunk call** *(Brit)* long-distance call by telephone (英) 長途電話. **'trunk road** main road 幹道.

truss [trʌs] *nc* bundle of hay or straw (乾草或稻草的) 捆. Also 亦作 *vt* (often with **up**) tie (常與up連用) 捆, 紮: *She trussed (up) the chicken* i.e. tied the legs and wings before cooking it. 她把鷄紮緊. 即: 煮鷄之前把鷄腿和翅膀捆好.

trust¹ [trʌst] *vt* **1** believe; have confidence or faith in 相信; 信任: *We trusted everything he said.* 我們相信他說的一切. *You should never trust a stranger.* 你絕對不能相信陌生人. **2** have enough confidence in somebody to allow him to do something 放心讓 (某人) 做 (某事): *Can I trust you to post these letters?* 能讓你去寄這些信嗎? **3** give something to somebody to be cared for 委託; 存放: *He trusted me with his watch.* 他把錶存放在我處. see also 參見 **entrust**. **4** hope 希望: *We trust (that) you are well.* 我們希望你身體健康. **trusting** *adj* ready to believe or have confidence in somebody 信任的. **trust in someone / something** have confidence in 相信: *We trust in God.* 我們信上帝.

trust² [trʌst] **1** *nu* belief; confidence 信任; 信心: *It is safe to put your trust in him* i.e. have confidence in him. 信任他是萬無一失的. *We have no trust in the new medicine.* 我們不相信這種新藥. **2** *nc* property or money which is managed by others for the benefit of somebody / something 託管的財產或款項: *The man set up a trust to educate poor children.* 那人設置了一筆信託金用來教育貧困兒童. **trustee** [trʌs'ti:] *nc* person who is given property or money to manage for others 受託

(管理他人財產款項的)人. **trustful** adj ready to believe or have confidence in somebody 信任某人的. **trustworthy** adj deserving to be trusted; reliable 值得信任的; 可靠的. *(opp 反義詞* **untrustworthy**). **trusty** adj reliable *(o.f. use* **trustworthy**) 可靠的(舊式一現在用 trustworthy). **in trust** managed on behalf of others 受託的, 代管的: *He holds the money in trust for the dead man's children.* 他受託爲死者子女保管這筆錢. **on trust** accepting or believing without enquiry or proof 不加深究地; 不查問證據地: *We took his story on trust.* 我們不加深究便相信了他的說法.

trustee [trʌsˈtiː] *nc* see 見 **trust**[2].

truth [truːθ] *nc / u* something true or believed to be true; state of being true 真相; 人們所認爲的真相; 真實性; *I told him a few truths about his bad behaviour.* 我告訴他有關他品行不軌的一些真相. *There is some truth in the story that he ran away.* 在關於他逃走的說法中有幾分是真的. *Always tell the truth!* 要永遠說實話! see 見 **true**.

try [traɪ] *vt / i* **1** find out what somebody / something is like by doing something with him or it 試用某人 / 某物: *They tried him as goalkeeper but he was too small.* 他們試用他當守門員, 但他個子太矮小. *Try this hat for size* i.e. put it on to see if it fits 試試這頂帽子的大小. 即: 戴上帽子看是否合適. *We tried tying it with string.* 我們試圖用繩子把它捆住. **2** make an attempt 嘗試, 試圖: *It looks difficult but we'll try.* 這事看來不好辦, 但我們會試試. *He always tries his hardest* i.e. makes as great an attempt as he can 他總是盡他的最大努力. *He tried to kill me.* 他企圖殺死我. *Note* 說明: *try and can*

be used instead of *try to* in the imperative. *Try to get some sleep* or *Try and get some sleep.* 在祈使句中, 可以用 try and 來代替 try to. 如 Try to get some sleep 或 Try and get some sleep. (設法入睡一會兒.) **3** examine the facts in a court of law 審問, 審判: *He was tried for murder and found guilty.* 他因殺人罪受審而被判決有罪. **4** make demands on; make tired etc. 對…提出要求; 使疲勞: *That child's behaviour tries my patience.* 那孩子的行爲惹我生氣. *past* 過去式和過去分詞 **tried.** Also 亦作 *nc* **1** attempt; test 試圖; 試驗: *We had a try at doing it.* 我們試做此事一次. *Why don't you give it a try?* i.e. see what it is like 你幹嗎不試一試呢? **2** (rugby football) points gained when a player puts the ball down behind the line of the opponents' goal (橄欖球賽中)在對方球門線後帶球觸地所得的分. **tried** adj reliable; fully tested 可靠的; 受過充分考驗的. *(opp 反義詞* **untried**). **trier** *nc* person who tries hard or works as well as he can 盡力工作的人. **trying** adj tiring; annoying 累人的; 惱人的: *I have had a trying day.* 我度過了好難挨的一天. *Children can be very trying.* 孩子們有時會非常煩人. **try something on** put on to see what it is like 試穿: *I tried on the shoes but they were too big.* 我試穿了, 鞋子太大. **try somebody / something out** find out what somebody / something is like by testing 試驗某人 / 某物.

tsar [zɑː*] ,**tsarina** [zɑːˈriːnə] *nc* see 見 **czer.**

tsetse,tzetze [ˈtsetsi] *nc* type of biting fly found in some parts of Africa 舌蠅, 采采蠅(非洲某些地區的咬人着蠅). (Also 亦作 **tsetse fly, tzetze fly**). *pl* 複數 **tsetse.**

tub [tʌb] *nc* round container (usu. made of wood) for holding liquids 桶, 盆(通常爲木製的).

tuba ['tjuːbə] *nc* type of large, brass musical instrument 大號, 低音號.

tubby ['tʌbi] *adj* (with reference to persons) short and fat (指人)矮胖的.

tube [tjuːb] *nc* 1 pipe made of glass, metal, rubber etc (玻璃、金屬、橡膠等製成的)管子; *test tube* i.e. short, glass pipe closed at one end, used for experiments 試管. *inner tube of a tyre* i.e. rubber tube inside a tyre(輪胎的)內胎. 2 small container made of soft metal and with a top which screws on 有蓋軟管: *tube of toothpaste* 牙膏管. 3 (*Brit*) underground railway. (*US* 美 **subway**) (英)地鐵. **tubing** *nc* piece of tube (esp. rubber tube) 一段管子 (尤指橡膠管). **tubular** ['tjuːbjulə*] *adj* having the shape of a tube 管狀的.

tuber ['tjuːbə*] *nc* growth on the roots of a plant from which new plants can grow (A potato is a tuber) 塊莖(如馬鈴薯).

tuberculosis [tjuːbəːkjuˈlousis] *nu* type of disease (usu. of the lungs and often called T.B.) 結核病(通常指肺結核, 常稱作T.B.).

tubing ['tjuːbiŋ] *nc* see 見 **tube.**

tubular ['tjuːbjulə*] *adj* see 見 **tube.**

tuck [tʌk] *vt* 1 fold a piece of cloth before sewing it (縫之前)把(布)摺疊. 2 put into position; make firm and tidy 放妥; 收緊; 弄整齊: *He tucked the handkerchief into his pocket.* 他把手帕塞進口袋. *The mother tucked her baby into bed.* 母親把嬰孩安頓在床上睡好. *They tucked up their sleeves and began working.* 他們捲起袖子開始幹活. Also 亦作 *nc* fold in a piece of cloth which is sewn into position (衣服的)褶, 襉: *She made a tuck round the bottom of her coat.* 她在上衣的下襬打褶. **tuck in** eat a lot (*informal*) 大吃(非正式).

Tuesday ['tjuːzdi] *n* third day of the Christian week, following Monday 星期二, 禮拜二.

tuft [tʌft] *nc* bunch of something soft (e.g. hair, grass) (頭髮、草等的)一束, 一簇, 一叢.

tug [tʌg] *vt / i* pull hard 用力拉. *past* 過去式以分詞 **tugged.** Also 亦作 *nc* 1 quick, hard pull 猛拉: *He gave the knots a tug to make them tighter.* 他使勁拉了拉, 把那些繩結拉緊些. 2 type of small boat used to pull or push ships (e.g. into or out of harbour) 拖船. '**tug-of-'war** competition between two teams puiling at either end of a rope 拔河(比賽).

tuition [tjuːˈiʃən] *nu* act of teaching (usu. teaching one person or a small group) 教, 講授(通常指教一個人或幾個人).

tulip ['tjuːlip] *nc* type of tall flower with brightly-coloured, cupshaped blooms 鬱金香.

tumble ['tʌmbl] *vt / i* 1 fall, cause to fall, quickly or heavily (使)猛然跌倒, 摔倒; 翻滾下來, (使)沉重地落下: *Babies tumble when they are learning to walk.* 嬰孩學步時常常跌倒. *He tumbled off his bicycle.* 他從自行車上摔下來. *He tumbled his clothes out of his bag on to the ground.* 他把袋子裏的衣服亂扔到地上. 2 (with *to*) get to know; become aware of (與to連用)逐漸明白, 開始意識到: *He hasn't yet tumbled to our plan.* (*informal* in sense 2) 他還不曉得我們的計劃. (義2爲非正式). Also 亦作 *nc* heavy fall 跌倒, 跌落. **tumbler** *nc* drinking glass 玻璃杯. **tumbler dryer** machine that dries clothes by tumbling them in warm air 衣服乾燥機. **'tumbledown** *adj* looking likely to fall down 搖搖欲墜的; 瀕於倒塌的: *a tumbledown old cottage* 要倒塌的舊農舍.

tummy ['tʌmi] *nc* informal form of **stomach.** stomach 的非正式形式.

tumour ['tju:mə*] (*US* 美 **tumor**) *nc* diseased swelling in the body 瘤, 腫瘤.

tumult ['tju:mʌlt] *nc / u* noisy excitement; confusion 吵鬧, 喧嘩; 混亂: *His mind was in a tumult.* 他心煩意亂.

tumultuous [tju:'mʌltjuəs] *adj* noisy and excited 吵鬧的, 喧嘩的; 激動的: *a tumultuous welcome* 亂哄哄的歡迎.

tuna ['tju:nə] *nc* type of very large sea fish, related to the mackerel, used for food. 金槍魚 (Also 亦作 **tunny, tunny fish**). *pl.* 複數版 **tunas** or **tuna.**

tundra ['tʌndrə] *nc / u* vast, nearly level, treeless plain in the arctic regions (北極地區不生樹木的) 苔原, 凍原, 凍土地帶.

tune [tju:n] **1** *nc* number of musical notes which make a pleasant sound. 調子, 曲調: *He played some modern tunes on the piano.* 他在鋼琴上彈了幾首現代曲子. **2** *nu* quality of being musically pleasant; musical harmony 和諧, 協調; 合調: *This song has no tune.* 這首歌沒有聽頭. *His voice and the piano were in tune.* 他的聲音同鋼琴聲很協調. (*opp* 反義語 **out of tune**). Also 亦作 *vt* **1** (with reference to a musical instrument) give the correct musical pitch to 爲(樂器)調音. **2** (with reference to a radio) move the controls to get the correct wavelength (指收音機)調譜; 調準; 調好頻率, 收聽: *We tune in to London every evening.* 我們每晚收聽倫敦的廣播. **3** (with reference to an engine) improve by

making small adjustments 調整, 調校 (發動機). **tuneful** *adj* having a pleasant tune 曲調優美的. **tuner** *nc* person who tunes musical instruments (給樂器)調音的人: *piano tuner* 鋼琴調音師. **tune up** give the correct pitch to a musical instrument 調音: *The orchestra tuned up before the concert.* 管弦樂隊在音樂會之前調音. **to the tune of** (usu. with reference to an amount which is thought to be too great) to the amount of (通常指過大的數)總量達…之多: *For a few repairs to our car we had to pay to the tune of £20.* (*informal*) 因爲修理了幾次汽車, 我們得付出總費二十英鎊. (非正式)

tungsten ['tʌŋstn] *nu* type of metal (W) 鎢.

tunic ['tju:nik] *nc* **1** type of jacket worn by policemen or soldiers 軍, 警制服的短上裝. **2** loose dress worn by women over trousers 穿在褲子外面的寬鬆女服. **3** sleeveless dress worn over a blouse as the uniform at some girls' schools 女學校制服的無袖裙子.

tunnel ['tʌnl] *nc* long passage cut under the ground or through a hill (e.g. for a road or railway line) (公路或鐵路等的) 隧道. Also 亦作 *vi* (with **into** or **through**) make a tunnel (與 **into** 或 **through**連用)開鑿隧道. *past* 過去式和過去分詞 **tunnelled.** (*US* 美 **tunneled**).

tunny ['tʌni] *nc* see 見 **tuna.**

turban ['tə:bən] *nc* covering for a man's head made from a long piece of cloth wound round it 男用纏頭巾.

turbid ['tə:bid] *adj* (with reference to a liquid) muddy; not clear (指液體)渾濁的; 泥濘的; 不清的.

turbine ['tə:bain] *nc* type of engine

which is driven by the force of gas or water striking on a wheel and making it go round 渦輪機.

turbulent ['təːbjulənt] *adj* disturbed; moving violently 騷亂的; 狂暴的; 洶湧的. **turbulence** *nu*.

tureen [tjuˈriːn] *nc* large, deep dish with a lid used for serving soup and vegetables at table (盛湯、菜的大而深的) 蓋碗, 大湯盤.

turf [təːf] *nc / u* earth or pieces of earth thickly covered with grass 草皮. *pl* 複數 **turfs. the turf** *nu* horse-racing; betting on horse-races 跑馬; 賭跑馬. **turf something out** throw out (*informal*) 拋出(非正式).

turgid ['təːdʒid] *adj* foolishly solemn; pompous 煞有介事的; 浮誇的: *He writes in turgid prose.* 他的文章華而不實.

Turk [təːk] *n* native of Turkey 土耳其人.

turkey ['təːki] **1** *nc* large bird with a red featherless head and big flaps under the chin 火鷄. **2** *nu* the meat of this bird, eaten as food 火鷄肉.

Turkish ['təːkiʃ] *nu* language of Turkey 土耳其語. Also 亦作 *adj* of Turkey or its people 土耳其的; 土耳其人的. **Turkish bath** steam bath followed by massage 土耳其浴, 蒸氣(按摩)浴. **Turkish delight** type of sweet 土耳其軟糖.

turmeric ['təːmərik] *nu* **1** perennial low-growing East Indian plant (東印度的) 薑黃, 鬱金. **2** its yellow root, dried and powdered and used esp. in curry powder, for colouring foods 薑黃根; 薑黃根粉; 鬱金根; 鬱金根粉(尤用於製作咖喱粉).

turmoil ['təːmɔil] *nc / u* confusion; disorder 混亂; 動亂; 騷亂.

turn[1] [təːn] *vt / i* **1** go, cause to go,

round (使)轉動; (使)轉: *The wheels of the car were turning quickly.* 汽車輪子在飛快地轉動. *He turned the steering wheel.* 他轉動方向盤. *This machine turns metal* i.e. shapes it as it is turned round quickly (on a lathe). 這車床車削金屬. *The car turned the corner.* 汽車轉過了拐彎處. **2** pass, cause to pass (使)超過: *It has turned 10 o'clock* i.e. it is just after 10 o'clock. 剛過十點鐘. *His son has turned sixteen* i.e. he has passed sixteen. 他的兒子剛滿十六歲. **3** change, cause to change, direction (使)轉變方向: *We turned to the right.* 我們向右轉. *He turned his face towards me.* 他把臉轉向我. *Turn the car and go back.* 把汽車掉個頭回去吧. **4** become, cause to become, different. (使)變樣: *His face turned white.* 他的臉色變白. *He has turned his room into a study.* 他把房間改作書房. *The rain turned the dust into mud.* 雨把塵土變成泥漿. *The leaves are beginning to turn* i.e. change colour 樹葉開始變色. *This milk has turned* i.e. gone sour 這牛奶已經發酸. **turning** *nc* place where a road turns; where one road joins another 轉彎處; 叉路口: *Take the first turning on the left.* 在第一個拐彎處向左轉. **'turncoat** person who betrays his party or his friends 叛徒; 叛黨者; 出賣朋友的人. **'turnpike 1** (*Brit*) gate across a road where a toll was once paid (英) 舊時收路稅的關卡. **2** (*US*) motorway for which a toll is paid (美) 收費公路. **'turnstile** device at the entrance to a sports ground, hall etc which allows only one person at a time to go in or out (入口處每次僅容一人通過的) 旋轉門, 十字轉門. **'turntable** small, round plate on which a gramophone record turns (留聲機的) 轉盤. **'turning point** important point which causes great changes 轉折點: *The battle was a turning point in our history.* 這次戰役是我們歷史上的一個轉折點. **turn about** face, cause to face, the opposite way (使) 向後轉, (使) 轉身. **turn against someone / something** become, cause to become, unfriendly; refuse to obey (使) 與…爲敵; 反目; 背叛; 反抗, 反對: *The people turned against their president.* 人民轉而反對總統. **turn someone away** turn, cause to turn, in another direction (esp. to avoid meeting or receiving somebody) (使) 轉身避開; 拒絕: *He turned away rather than have to meet me.* 他轉過去, 而不是勉強跟我見面. *Because the hall was full, many people were turned away.* 大廳滿座了, 許多人被拒之門外. **turn someone / something down 1** turn, cause to turn, downwards (使) 翻下. **2** make less by turning a tap, knob etc. 調低; 關小 (龍頭, 旋鈕等): *As the radio set was making too much noise, he turned it down.* 收音機太響了, 他把聲音調低些. *He·turned down the oil / gas lamp.* 他把油燈/煤氣燈捻小些. **3** refuse to consider or accept 拒絕考慮; 拒絕接受: *He applied for the job but the firm turned him down.* 他申請這個職位, 但沒被公司錄用. **turn in** go to bed 上床睡覺, 就寢. *I think I'll turn in now. (informal)* 我想我要去睡覺了. (非正式). **turn something in** turn, cause to turn, inwards (使) 向裏彎. **turn off** stop by turning a tap, knob etc. 關掉 (龍頭, 旋鈕等): *He turned off the radio.* 他收音機關掉了. *I forgot to turn off the water.* 我忘了把水龍頭關上. **turn on someone / something 1** turn and attack 轉而攻擊: *The*

wounded lion turned on the hunter.* 受傷的獅子向獵人撲去. **2** start by turning a tap, knob etc. 打開 (龍頭, 旋鈕等): *He turned on the radio.* 他開收音機. *When it became dark, I turned on the lights.* 天黑了, 我打開電燈. **3** cause to like 使喜歡: *This music turns me on. (informal in sense 3)* 這音樂使我很感興趣. (義3爲非正式). **turn (something) out 1** empty (esp. when looking for or tidying something) 倒空, 出清 (尤指尋找或整理某物時): *I turned out my pockets.* 我把口袋都翻出來. *My mother is turning out the bedroom.* 我媽媽正在打掃寢室. **2** come, cause to come, out for a special reason (使) 出來; (使) 出動: *All our friends turned out to meet us.* 我們的所有朋友都出來歡迎我們. *The soldiers were turned out to defend the city.* 士兵們奉命出動保衛這個城市. **3** produce 生產, 製造: *This factory turns out bicycles.* 這家工廠生產自行車. *The college turns out a hundred teachers a year.* 這所學院每年培養出一百名教師. **4** cause somebody to leave against his will 把…趕走, 把…趕出: *He was turned out of the hotel because he was drunk.* 他因醉酒被趕出旅館. **5** stop something burning by turning a tap, knob etc. 關掉 (龍頭, 旋鈕等); 旋熄: *He turend out the gas fire / lights.* 他關掉了煤氣爐/煤氣燈. (Also 亦作 **turn off**). **6** be seen or found out (to be) 看來(是); 結果(是), 證明(是). *The examination turned out (to be) easy.* 考試原來不難. **'turnout** *nc* **1** *My mother gave the bedroom a good turnout.* 我媽媽把寢室徹底打掃了一番. **2** *There was a big turnout of friends to meet us.* 一大批朋友出來歡迎我們. **3** *The college has a turnout of a hundred teachers a*

year. 這所學院每年培養出一百名教師.
4 appearance; way one is dressed 外貌; 穿著方式: *They admired the smart turnout of the soldiers.* 他們羨慕士兵的漂亮裝束. **turn something over** sell in business a certain amount of goods in a certain time 在一段時間內銷售 (一定數量的商品); *This shop turns over no less than £100 a day.* 這家商店每天的銷售額不少於100英鎊. **'turnover** *nc*: *This shop has a turnover of no less than £100 a day.* 這家商店每天的銷售額不少於100英鎊. **turn to someone** ask; expect help from 請求; 求助於: *They always turn to me when they are in trouble.* 他們有困難時總是請我幫忙. **turn (something) up 1** turn, cause to turn, upwards (使) 向上翻; 捲起, 摺起: *He turned up the bottom of his trousers.* 他捲起褲腿. **2** appear, cause to appear or be seen (使) 出現; (使) 被看到: *He turned up late for the game.* 他很遲才出場參加比賽. *We turned up some old books when we were emptying the bookcase.* 我們在清理書櫥時發現了一些舊書. **'turnup** *nc (Brit)*: *These trousers have no turnups* i.e. the bottoms are not turned up and sewn in place. (*US* 美 **cuff**). (英) 這幾條褲的褲腳不摺邊.

turn² [tə:n] *nc* **1** act of turning round 轉動, 旋轉: *This loose screw needs a turn or two.* 這螺絲鬆了, 要轉緊一、兩圈. **2** change of direction 轉向; 轉彎: *We are waiting for the turn of the tide.* 我們在等候轉潮. *Never stop your car at a sharp turn in the road.* 不要在公路急轉彎的地方停住汽車. **3** (with **take**) change in state (與 take 連用) (情況的) 轉變: *The weather has taken a turn for the worse.* 天氣變壞. **4** act or duty of several kinds 行為; 責任; 輪

替: *It is your turn to wash the dishes* i.e. others have done so and it is now the time for you to do so. 輪到你洗盤子了. *He did me a good turn by lending me his bicycle* i.e. he kindly helped me. 他借給我自行車, 幫了我一個大忙. (*opp* 反義語 **bad turn**). *The next turn on the stage was most amusing* i.e. act or performance 台上接下去的一段表演非常有趣. *He has gone for a turn in the garden* i.e. a walk 他已去花園散步. *Seeing him gave me a fright* (*informal* in this sense) 見到他使我大吃一驚. (本義爲非正式). **in turn** one after the other in order 依次, 輪流: *We went in turn to be examined by the doctor.* 我們輪流去讓醫生檢查. **take turns at something** do something in turn 依次, 輪流做某事. **turn of phrase** way of expressing something 口吻, 措辭, 表達方式. **turn a-bout** *adv* (with reference to two persons) alternately; one, then the other (指兩人) 交替地; 輪流地: *We took turn about to stay with the injured man.* 我們輪流陪受傷的人. (*Also* 亦作 **turn and turn about**).

turnip ['tə:nip] *nc / u* type of plant with a round root used as food and to feed animals 蘿蔔.

turnpike ['tə:npaik] *nc* **1** (*US*) road, esp. expressway, for the use of which a toll is charged (美) 徵收通行稅的道路; (尤指) 徵收通行稅的高速公路. **2** gate across a road, which was opened when the traveller paid a toll (昔日的) 收費門; 徵收通行稅的卡門.

turntable ['tə:n,teible] *nc* **1** round, revolving platform of a record player upon which records are played 唱機的轉盤. **2** circular revolving platform for reversing engines (轉換機車方向

的)轉車台.

turpentine ['tə:pəntain] *nu* type of oil used for mixing paint 松節油.(Also 亦作 **turps**).

turquoise ['tə:kwɔiz] *nc* greenish-blue colour 藍綠色, 天藍色, 湖藍色. Also 亦作 *adj.*

turret ['tʌrit] *nc* small tower on a building 塔樓, 角塔.

turtle ['tə:tl] *nc* (Brit) big tortoise which lives in the sea; (US) tortoise or sea tortoise (英)大海龜; 海鱉; (美)龜或海龜.

tusk [tʌsk] *nc* long, pointed tooth which sticks out of the mouth of certain animals (e.g. elephant, walrus, boar) (象、海象、野豬等露出口外的)長尖牙.

tussle ['tʌsl] *vi* (with **with**) struggle; fight (與 with 連用)奪門; 打鬥; 扭打. Also 亦作 *nc.*

tut, tut-tut [tʌt,'tʌt'tʌt] *interj* noise made to show disapproval 噴(表示不贊成的聲音). Also 亦作 *vt / i* make this noise 發"噴"聲. *past* 過去式和過去分詞 **tutted, tut-tutted.**

tutor ['tju:tə*] *nc* **1** private teacher 私人教師. **2** (Brit) university lecturer who is responsible for directing the studies of a group of students (英)大學裏的指導教師, 導師. **tutorial** [tju:'tɔ:riəl] period of instruction and discussion with a tutor 導師的指導時間.

tuxedo [tʌk'si:dou] *nc* (US) dinner jacket (美) 晚禮服. *pl* 複數 **tuxedos.**

twang [twæŋ] *nc* sound made when a tight string or wire is pulled and let go quickly 撥弦聲: *We heard the twang of his bow as he shot an arrow.* 他射箭時我們聽到了弓弦撥動的聲音. Also 亦作 *vt / i* make, cause to make, this sound (使)發出撥弦聲.

tweed [twi:d] *nu* type of woollen cloth 花呢. Also 亦作 *adj*: *tweed jacket* 花

呢短上衣.

tweezers ['twi:zəz] *npl* pair of small pincers used for picking up very small things or pulling out hairs (e.g. *eyebrow tweezers*) 鑷子; 小鉗子(如: eyebrow tweezers修眉鉗).

twelve [twelv] see appendix 見附錄.

twenty ['twenti] see appendix 見附錄.

twice [twais] *adv* two times 兩次; 兩倍: *twice as much / many* 兩倍之多. *He is twice the man you are* i.e. he is twice as good, strong etc. 他比你好一倍或強健一倍等.

twig [twig] *nc* small branch of a tree or shrub 小枝; 細枝. Also 亦作 *vt* understand 領會, 瞭解: *He twigged it.* (informal) 他明白這一點. (非正式).

twilight ['twailait] *nu* half-light just after sunset or just before sunrise 薄暮; 黃昏; 曙光; 黎明.

twin [twin] *nc* one of two children born at the same time to the same mother 孿生兒, 雙胞胎. Also 亦作 *adj* **1** *twin sisters* 孿生姊妹. **2** one of a pair 成對東西之一的: *twin beds* i.e. two single beds which are exactly alike 兩張完全一樣的單人床; *twin carburettors* i.e. two carburettors which are exactly alike and are fitted to the same engine 裝在同一發動機上的兩個相同的汽化器.

twine [twain] *nu* string; wool 線, 細繩; 毛線. Also 亦作 *vt / i* go, cause to go, round (使)纏繞: *The plants twine round the tree as they grow.* 這些植物纏繞着樹木生長. *He twined the wire round the post.* 他把細繩繞在柱子上.

twinge [twindʒ] *nc* short, sharp pain 陣痛; 劇痛.

twinkle ['twiŋkl] *vi* shine with a short, bright, changing light 閃爍; 閃耀: *Stars twinkle.* 星星閃閃發光. *His eyes twinkled with delight.* 他眼裏閃爍着喜

悦的光芒. Also 亦作 *nu: the twinkle of stars* 星星的闪光; *the twinkle in his eyes* 他眼裏闪耀着的光芒.

twirl [twə:l] *vt / i* turn, cause to turn, round and round quickly (使)快速旋轉. Also 亦作 *nc* quick movement round and round 快速的旋转.

twist [twist] *vt / i* **1** turn one thing round another (e.g. thread, string, wire) 捻, 搓, 编织 (线、绳子、金屬線等); (使) 纏绕: *He twisted the three ropes to make one very strong rope.* 他把三根绳子搓成一根很结實的绳子. **2** turn one end of something while the other is held or fixed 扭; 绞; 搾: *I twisted my wet socks to dry them.* 我把濕襪子搾乾. *The big boy twisted my arm* i.e. to cause pain 這大男孩搾我的胳膊. 即: 弄痛我. *If you twist the cork, it will come out of the bottle.* 你把软木塞搾一搾, 就能把它從瓶口拔出来. **3** change direction suddenly 突然改变方向: *The road twists over the hills.* 這條路在小山間蜿蜒迂回. *We had to twist (our way) through the thick forest.* 我们只得在茂密的森林裏曲摺穿行. **4** (with reference to words) change the meaning of (usu. to give them a worse one) (指话、言詞) 歪曲, 曲解: *Your enemies will twist everything you say.* 你的敌人会歪曲你所说的一切. Also 亦作 *nc* act of twisting or being twisted 捻, 搓, 编织; 纏绕; 扭; 绞; 搾; 歪曲, 曲解: *The big boy gave my arm a twist.* 這大男孩搾我的胳膊. *The road has many twists.* 這條路迂回曲摺. *By giving a twist to your words they can make them mean something else.* 用断章取義的办法, 他们能使你的话含義不同.

twit [twit] *nc* foolish person (*informal*). 蠢人; 傻瓜. (非正式).

twitch [twitʃ] *nc* **1** uncontrolled move-

ment of the body 抽動, 顫動, 抽搐. **2** sharp, sudden pull 突然的一扯; 抽走; 搶去. Also 亦作 *vt / i* move, cause to move, in this way (使) 抽動, (使) 顫動, (使) 抽搐; 痙攣: *He can't stop his hands twitching.* 他的雙手抽搐個不停.

twitter ['twitə*] *nc / u* sharp, short sound made by birds when they are excited; excited talk 鸟嘰嘰喳喳的鸣叫聲; 興奮的談話. Also 亦作 *vt / i* make this sound; talk in this way 嘰嘰喳喳地叫; 興奮地嘰嘰喳喳地講.

two [tu:] see appendix 見 附 錄.
'two-'faced not straightforward or honest (*informal*) 口是心非的; 虚偽的. (非正式).
'twofold *adj / adv* double 兩重的; 雙重的.
'two-'piece *adj* having two parts 由兩件配成的; *He was wearing a two-piece suit.* 他穿着兩件式的西裝.
'two-'way *adj* (with reference to a road or a radio) allowing traffic or communication to move in both directions (指路) 雙行的; (指無線電) 收發兩用的.

tycoon [tai'ku:n] *nc* very rich and powerful businessman 有錢有勢的商人, 大亨, (實業界) 鉅頭.

tying ['taiiŋ] pres part of **tie**. tie 的現在分詞.

type [taip] *nc / u* **1** class or kind; example 類; 典型, 樣本: *There are several types of trees in the garden.* 園裏有好幾種樹. *He is not the type of man to tell a lie.* 他不是那種愛撒謊的人. *A woman who seldom talks is not true to type* i.e. is not like all the others of the same type, not like other women 寡言少語的婦女並不典型. 即: 不像其他婦女. **2** piece of metal with a letter or sign on it used in printing; letters or signs printed in this way 鉛字; 鉛印的字母或符號, 字體: *The type in this book is so small* *that it is difficult to read.* 這本書字體太小，讀起來很費勁. Also 亦作 *vt / i* print on paper using a typewriter 打字. **typist** *nc* person who types using a typewriter 打字員. **typical** ['tipikl] *adj* of a type; true to type 具有代表性的；典型的: *He is a typical Englishman.* 他是典型的英國人. (*opp* 反義詞 **untypical**). **typically** *adv* **typify** ['tipifal] *vt* be of a certain type; be an example of 代表；作爲…的典範: *This excellent essay typifies all his work.* 這篇精彩的文章是他的代表作. **'typewriter** machine which prints on paper when the letters or numbers on the keyboard are pressed down by the fingers 打字機.

typhoid ['taifɔid] *nu* type of disease 傷寒.

typhoon [tai'fu:n] *nc* very strong; violent wind 颱風.

typhus ['taifəs] *nu* type of disease (different from typhoid) 斑疹傷寒.

tyrant ['tairnt] *nc* cruel and unjust ruler 暴君，殘酷、專制的統治者. **tyranny** ['tirəni] *nc / u* cruel and unjust rule; country ruled in this way; government of this kind 暴政；殘酷，專制的統治，暴政統治下的國家；施行暴政的政府. **tyrannical** [ti'rænikl] *adj* of, like a tyrant 暴君的；暴虐的: *He has a tyrannical father.* 他父親生性暴虐. **tyrannize** ['tirənaiz] *vt* rule or behave like a tyrant 殘暴統治；虐待.

tyre ['taiə*] *(US* 美 **tire**) *nc* iron or rubber ring round the wheel of a cart, car, bicycle etc. 輪箍；輪胎.

tzar [zɑ:*],**tzarina** [zɑ:ri:nə] *nc* see 見 **czer.**

tzetze ['tsetsi] *nc* see 見 **tsetse.**

U,u

U- [ju:] *prefix* shaped like a U (e.g. **U-bend; U-bolt; U-turn).** U字形的 (如U-bend U形彎頭; U-bolt U形螺栓; U-turn U形轉彎, 180°轉彎).

ubiquitous [ju:'bikwitəs] *adj* existing everywhere at the same time 同時普遍存在的, 同時無處不在的.

udder [ˈʌdə*] *nc* part of a cow, goat etc from which milk comes (牛、羊等的) 乳房.

ugh [ə:h] *interj* expressing feelings of disgust 嘿! 啊! 呸! (表示厭惡).

ugly [ˈʌgli] *adj* **1** not pleasing to look at; badly shaped 難看的; 醜陋的. **2** dangerous 危險的: *an ugly situation* 險惡的局勢. **ugliness** *nu*.

ulcer [ˈʌlsə*] *nc* sore on the skin or inside the body which produces pus. 潰瘍.

ulterior [ʌlˈtiəriə*] *adj* situated on the further side; beyond (most often in **ulterior motive** i.e. motive different from the one actually stated. *He says that he is doing this to help me, but I suspect an ulterior motive* 在那邊的, 較遠的; 藏在背後的 (最常用於ulterior motive, 即: 不可告人的動機. He says that he is doing this to help me, but I suspect an ulterior motive. 他說他這樣做是爲了幫助我, 但我懷疑他別有用心).

ultimate [ˈʌltimət] *adj* furthest; final; original 最遠的; 最終的; 根本的: *the ultimate deterrent* i.e. the atomic bomb 最後威懾力量, 即: 原子彈. **ultimately** *adv* **ultimatum** [ʌltiˈmeitəm] *nc* final demand which must be agreed to (e.g. one sent by one government to another which will cause a war if it is not agreed to) 最後通牒; 哀的美敦書.

ultra- [ˈʌltrə] *prefix* more than is usual; extreme (e.g. **ultramodern** i.e. extremely modern) 超; 極 (如: ultramodern, 即: 極其現代化的; 極其時髦的; 最新的).

ultraviolet [ˈʌltrəˈvaiəlet] *adj* beyond the violet end of the spectrum and so not seen 紫外的: *ultraviolet rays* i.e. invisible rays from the sun or from a special type of lamp which can improve health 紫外線.

umbrella [ʌmˈbrelə] *nc* light frame covered with cloth etc which can be opened or shut and is used as a shelter against the rain or sun 雨傘; 陽傘.

umpire [ˈʌmpaiə*] *nc* person chosen to decide a dispute or quarrel, or to see that the rules of certain games are followed (e.g. cricket, tennis, baseball; for football use **referee**) 公斷人, 仲裁人; (板球、網球、棒球等的) 裁判 (足球裁判用 referee). Also 亦作 *vt / i* act as umpire 當公斷人, 當仲裁人; 當裁判: *Will you umpire (in) our cricket match?* 請你當我們板球比賽的裁判好嗎?

umpteen [ˈʌmpti:n] *adj* many *(informal)* 許多 (非正式).

un- [ʌn] *prefix* **1** (before an *adj, adv* or *n*) not (e.g. **unable; unaffected).** (用於形容詞、副詞或名詞前) 不 (如: unable 不能的; unaffected 不裝腔作勢的; 未受影響的). **2** (before a *verb*) do the opposite of (e.g. **undress; unchain).** (用於動詞前) 做相反的動作 (如: undress 脫衣服; unchain 替…解開鎖鏈).

unabashed [ˌʌnəˈbæʃt] *adj* not abashed or ashamed; knowing what to do or say 不害羞的; 不難爲情的; 不畏懼的; 知道該做或該說甚麼的.

unabated [ˌʌnəˈbeitid] *adj* (usu. with reference to noise, pain, suffering etc.) not becoming less. (通常指噪音、疼痛、苦難等)不減弱的: *The storm continued unabated for several hours.* 暴風雨持續數小時未見減弱.

unable [ʌnˈeibl] *adj* (always with *to*) not able (總是與to連用)不能的, 沒有辦法的.

unaccompanied [ˌʌnəˈkʌmpənid] *adj* not accompanied (e.g. a person travelling alone; (of a song) sung without the help of a musical instrument) (旅行時等)無人作伴的; (唱歌時)無伴奏的.

unaccountable [ˌʌnəˈkauntəbl] *adj* not able to be explained 無法解釋的; 不可理喻的; 莫明其妙的. **unaccountably** *adv.*

unaccustomed [ˌʌnəˈkʌstəmd] *adj* **1** (with *to*) not accustomed (與to連用) 不習慣於…的. **2** new; not usual 新的; 異常的: *They do not know what to do with their unaccustomed wealth.* 他們對從天而降的財富不知所措.

unanimous [juːˈnæniməs] *adj* everybody; agreeing; agreed to by everybody 意見一致的; 一致同意的: *The decision to stop working was unanimous.* 停工的決定得到一致同意. **unanimously** *adv* **unanimity** [ˌjuːnəˈnimiti] *nu.*

unassuming [ˌʌnəˈsjuːmiŋ] *adj* modest; not proud or overbearing 謙遜的; 不傲慢的, 不專橫的.

unattached [ˌʌnəˈtætʃt] *adj* not attached to a particular person or group 不隸屬於某人或某集團的; 未婚的; 尚未訂婚的: *an unattached young man* i.e. one not yet married or engaged to be married 一名未婚或未訂婚的青年男子.

unattended [ˌʌnəˈtendid] *adj* not watched or looked after 無人看守的; 無人照料的: *You should not leave your bicycle unattended in a busy street.* 你不該把自行車留在熱鬧的街上不加看管.

unavoidable [ˌʌnəˈvɔidəbl] *adj* not able to be avoided 不可避免的: *unavoidable delay* 不得已的耽擱. **unavoidably** *adv.*

unaware [ˌʌnəˈwɛə*] *adj* (with *of*) not aware; not knowing (與of連用)未曾意識到的; 不知道的. **unawares** *adv* by surprise 出其不意地, 冷不防地: *We took the enemy unawares by attacking at night.* 我們乘其不意夜襲敵人.

unbalanced [ʌnˈbælənst] *adj* not balanced; not having mental balance; mad 不均衡的; 精神失常的; 瘋的.

unbearable [ʌnˈbɛərəbl] *adj* not able to be endured 難以忍受的, 不能容忍的.

unbeaten [ʌnˈbiːtn] *adj* not beaten; not defeated 未受打擊的; 未被擊敗的: *Our football team was unbeaten last year.* 我們的足球隊去年保持不敗.

unbecoming [ˌʌnbiˈkʌmiŋ] *adj* not suitable; rude 不恰當的, 不相稱的; 粗野的: *an unbecoming dress* i.e. one which does not suit the person wearing it 一件不合身的衣服; *unbecoming behaviour* 有失體統的舉止.

unbeknown [ˌʌnbiˈnoun] *adj* (with *to*) without the knowledge of (與to連用)不爲…所知的: *They arrived unbeknown to us.* 他們到了, 我們還不知道.

unbend [ʌnˈbend] *vt / i* become less stiff; behave in an easier manner; relax 變得不拘謹; 舉止從容; (使)鬆弛;

In public he was very solemn, but in private he unbent. 在公開場合他很嚴肅, 在家裏卻平易近人. **unbending** *adj* 堅定的; 不屈的; 固定在目的上的. **unbiased, unbiassed** [ʌn'baiəst] *adj* without bias; not prejudiced; fair 不偏心的; 沒有偏見的; 公平的.

unbolt [ʌn'boult] *vt* open by drawing a bolt 拉開門; *unbolt a door* 拔開閂開門.

unbounded [ʌn'baundid] *adj* without limit; excessive 無限的; 過多的.

unbridled [ʌn'braidld] *adj* without control or restraint 不受約束的; 不加控制的; 不可遏止的: *He has an unbridled temper.* 他有一種不受羈絆的脾氣.

unbroken [ʌn'broukən] *adj* 1 without a break; continuous 未中斷的; 繼續不斷的. *They had a life of unbroken happiness.* 他們的生活一直很幸福. 2 (with reference to records) not beaten (指記錄) 未打破的: *His time for the mile is still unbroken.* 他跑一英里的時間記錄仍未被打破. 3 (with reference to a horse etc) not tamed or trained (指馬等) 未馴服的; 未受訓練的.

unburden [ʌn'bə:dn] *vt* get rid of a burden; make easier 使卸去負擔; 使輕鬆: *He unburdened his mind by telling me everything that was worrying him.* 他把煩惱的事情全都告訴了我, 解除了思想負擔. *He unburdened himself to me* i.e. he told me what was worrying him. 他向我傾訴衷腸. 即: 他把使他煩惱的事情告訴了我.

unbutton [ʌn'bʌtn] *vt* open the buttons of 解開…的鈕扣: *unbutton a shirt* 解開襯衫的鈕扣.

uncalled [ʌn'kɔ:ld] *adj* (with **for**) necessary; not justified (與for連用) 不必要的; 沒有理由的: *His anger was uncalled for when everybody was*

being very friendly to him. 在大家都對他非常友好時, 他生氣是沒有道理的.

uncanny [ʌn'kæni] *adj* not natural; not usual 不自然的, 不正常的; 不平常的: *The way he was able to predict future events was positively uncanny.* 他能預言未來事件, 這一情況確實非同尋常.

uncertain [ʌn'sə:tn] *adj* 1 not sure; doubtful 不確定的, 拿不準的; 懷疑的: *We are / feel uncertain about / of the future.* 我們不知道將來會怎樣. *The date of his arrival is still uncertain.* 他到達的日期仍未確定. 2 not reliable 靠不住的: *The weather is uncertain.* 天氣變化莫測. **uncertainty** *nc / u* something which is uncertain; state of being uncertain 不確定的事情, 靠不住的事情; 不確定, 靠不住: *Life is full of uncertainties.* 人生變幻多端.

uncharitable [ʌn'tʃæritəbl] *adj* not kind; severe 無情的; 嚴酷的.

uncharted [ʌn'tʃɑ:tid] *adj* not shown on a map; not explored so as to be shown on a map 地圖上未標明的; 未經探查及標圖的.

unchecked [ʌn'tʃekt] *adj* not checked or controlled or restrained 未受制止的; 未加控制的; 未被阻攔的: *the enemy's unchecked advance* 敵人的長驅直入.

uncivilized [ʌn'sivilaizd] *adj* rough, cruel and ignorant in behaviour etc. 粗魯的; 殘酷的; 愚昧無知的; 未開化的.

uncle ['ʌŋkl] *nc* brother of one's father or mother; husband of one's aunt 伯父; 叔父; 舅父; 姑丈; 姨丈.

uncomfortable [ʌn'kʌmfətəbl] *adj* 1 not comfortable 不舒服的: *I feel uncomfortable in this chair.* 我坐這張椅子覺得不舒服. *This chair feels uncomfortable.* 這張椅子坐起來不舒適. 2 (with reference to feelings etc.) uneasy; not content (指感情等) 不安的;

不滿意的: *I have an uncomfortable feeling that we shall be too late.* 我有一種不安的感覺, 我們會太遲了.

uncommon [ʌnˈkɔmən] *adj* not common; rare; extraordinary 不普通的; 罕見的; 非同尋常的. **uncommonly** *adv* unusually; very 不尋常地; 很, 非常: *an uncommonly pretty girl* 一個非常漂亮的女孩.

uncompromising [ʌnˈkɔmprəmaiziŋ] *adj* not compromising; refusing to come to an agreement or to change any of one's opinions 不妥協的; 不肯通融的; 不讓步的: *He is an uncompromising defender of freedom.* 他是堅定的自由衛士.

unconditional [ʌnkənˈdiʃənl] *adj* without conditions; complete 無條件的; 完全的: *They have reached an unconditional agreement.* 他們達成了不附條件的協議.

unconscious [ʌnˈkɔnʃəs] *adj* not conscious; not fully aware 人事的, 失去知覺的; 沒有充分注意到的: *When he was hit on the head he became unconscious.* 他頭部被擊中後不省人事. *Children make unconscious remarks* i.e. remarks which they do not fully understand or think about before they make them 孩子們常說一些不知深淺的話. **unconsciously** *adv* **unconsciousness** *nu* **the unconscious** part of the mind containing ideas of which one is not aware 無意識, 下意識, 潛意識.

unconventional [ʌnkənˈvenʃənl] *adj* not following the normal rules or customs 非常規的; 不從慣例或習俗的: *unconventional clothing* 標新立異的衣著; *an unconventional idea* 不落俗套的想法.

uncouth [ʌnˈkuːθ] *adj* (with reference to a person) having rough manners;

awkward (指人) 粗魯的; 笨拙的.

uncover [ʌnˈkʌvə*] *vt* **1** take the cover from; make known 揭開…的蓋子; 揭露; 暴露. **2** leave undefended 使失去防禦能力; 暴露.

undecided [ʌndiˈsaidid] *adj* not decided; not yet sure 未作決定的; 還沒有把握的: *He is undecided about what he should do.* 他對於他該做些甚麼尚未作出決定. *He is undecided about what to do.* 他對於該做些甚麼尚未作出決定.

undeniable [ʌndiˈnaiəbl] *adj* not able to be denied; certain; obvious 不能否認的; 確實的; 確鑿無疑的; 明顯的. **undeniably** *adv*.

under[1] [ˈʌndə*] *prep* **1** below in place 在…下面: *The box is under the desk.* 盒子在書桌的下面. *Draw a line under your name.* 在你的名字下面劃一條線. *We looked under the bushes.* 我們搜索樹叢下面. **2** below in rank (級別) 低於…的: *I worked under him for seven years.* 我在他手下幹了七年. *The assistant manager is under the manager.* 副經理低於經理. **3** less in number (數量) 少於…的: *Under 100 people were present.* 出席人數不到一百人. *Are you under 21 years of age?* 你還不到二十一歲吧? *He sold it for under £10.* 他把它賣了不到十英鎊. (*opp* 反義詞 **over**). **4** during; while; in the condition of 在…期間; 當…的時候; 在…的條件下: *under discussion* i.e. still being discussed 討論中的; *under repair* i.e. being repaired 修理中的; *under sail* i.e. while sailing 航行中的. *This land is under corn* i.e. is planted with corn 這塊地種着小麥. *He is living in France under a different name* i.e. different from the name he used to be known by 他改名換姓住在法國. **5** during the rule of 在…

的統治下: *France under Napoleon* 拿破崙統治下的法國. Also 亦作 *adv* in or to a lower place 在下面; 到下面去: *The boat went under* i.e. sank 那艘船沉沒了. *You cannot keep people under forever* i.e. oppressed 不可能永遠壓迫人民.

under-² ['ʌndə*] *prefix* **1** (with *n*) below in place; rank, number etc. (與名詞連用) 在…下面; (級別) 低於…; 少於…: *underclothes* 內衣褲; *under-manager* 副經理; *all the under-twelves* i.e. children under twelve years of age 所有十二歲以下的兒童. **2** (with *verb*) not enough (與動詞連用) 不足: *undercook* 煮得半生不熟; 煮得嫩. *underpopulated* 人口稀少的.

undercarriage ['ʌndəkærɪdʒ] *nc* wheels etc on which an aircraft lands 飛機的起落架.

undercharge [ʌndə'tʃɑːdʒ] *vt* not charge enough in price 對…少算了價錢; 對…少要價.

underclothes ['ʌndəkləʊðz] *npl* clothes worn under a suit or dress (esp. those worn next to the skin) 內衣褲; 貼身衣褲.

undercover ['ʌndəkʌvə*] *adj* (esp. with reference to the secret service) secret (尤指特務機關) 秘密的.

undercurrent ['ʌndəkʌrnt] *nc* hidden movement or feeling 暗流; 潛流; 潛在的情緒: *There is an undercurrent of anger in their behaviour.* 他們的舉止中有一種潛在的憤怒情緒.

underdeveloped [ʌndədi'veləpt] *adj* (esp. of countries which need financial help) not fully developed (尤指需要經濟援助的國家) 不發達的.

underdog ['ʌndədɒg] *nc* person who usually loses; one neglected or oppressed by others 常輸的人, 輸家; 失敗者; 被忽視或受壓迫的人.

underdone ['ʌndə'dʌn] *adj* not completely cooked 半生不熟的, 煮得嫩的.

underestimate [ʌndər'estimeit] *vt* not value highly enough; make too low an estimate of 對…估價不足; 對…評價或估計過低.

underfed [ʌndə'fed] *adj* not given enough to eat 未給足夠食物的.

underfoot [ʌndə'fut] *adv* under the feet 在腳下: *The wet ground was soft underfoot.* 濕漉漉的地面踩上去很軟.

undergo [ʌndə'gəu] *vt* suffer; receive 經歷; 遭受: *He has just undergone an operation.* 他剛接受了一次外科手術. *I am undergoing an examination on Monday.* 星期一我要參加一次考試. *past tense* 過去式 **underwent** [ʌndə'went]. *past part* 過去分詞 **undergone** [ʌndə'gɒn].

undergraduate [ʌndə'grædjuit] *nc* student at a university who has not yet got a degree (尚未取得學位的) 大學生. Also 亦作 *adj*.

underground ['ʌndəgraund] *adj* **1** below the ground 地下的, 地面下的: *an underground railway* 地下鐵道. **2** (esp. with reference to resisting a government) secret (尤指反抗政府的活動) 秘密的: *the underground movement to free the country* 解放這個國家的秘密活動. Also 亦作 *adv* below the ground; secretly 在地下; 秘密地. Also 亦作 *nc / u* **1** underground railway 地下鐵道. *Do you travel by the underground or by bus?* 你乘地鐵還是乘公共汽車去? **2** secret movement against a government 反對政府的秘密活動: *After his country was defeated he joined the underground.* 他的國家戰敗後他參加了地下活動.

undergrowth ['ʌndəgrəuθ] *nu* smaller trees or bushes growing among taller trees (長在大樹下的) 小樹或矮樹叢.

underhand ['ʌndəhænd] *adj / adv* secret; secretly; deceitful; deceitfully 秘密的(地); 欺詐的(地): *He gets what he wants in an underhand way.* 他用卑鄙的手段得到了他想得到的東西.

underline [ʌndə'lain] *vt* **1** draw a line under 在…下面劃線. **2** emphasize 強調.

underling ['ʌndəliŋ] *nc* person who works under others (rather *impolite*) 手下, 下屬 (頗爲不禮貌).

underlying [ʌndə'laiiŋ] *adj* under the surface, not easily seen, but important (often in **underlying causes**) 潛在的 (常用於 underlying causes 潛在的原因).

undermine [ʌndə'main] *vt* **1** make a mine or hole below something 在…下挖坑道或挖洞. **2** slowly make weak 慢慢削弱, 慢慢損壞; 傷害: *Lack of food has undermined his strength.* 由於食物不足, 他的體力逐漸衰弱.

underneath [ʌndə'ni:θ] *adv / prep* below; under 在下面; 在底下; 在…下面; 在…底下.

underpass ['ʌndəpɑ:s] *nc* place where one road passes under another 地下通道; 立交橋下的通道. (*opp* 反義詞 **overpass** or **flyover**).

underpay [ʌndə'pei] *vt* not pay enough 少付…的工資; 付給…不足額的工資; 剋扣工資. *past* 過去式和過去分詞 **underpaid. underpayment** *nc / u.*

underprivileged [ʌndə'priviliʒd] *adj* not having as many privileges or benefits as other people in one's own country or other countries; poor (在國內或國外) 享受不到正當權益的; 未享受應有權益的; 貧困的.

underrate [ʌndə'reit] *vt* rate too low; not value highly enough 低估; 貶低; 輕視.

understand [ʌndə'stænd] *vt / i* **1** get the meaning of somebody / something 懂; 理解; 瞭解; 明白; 領會: *They don't understand what we are saying.* 他們聽不懂我們在說甚麼. *They don't understand us.* 他們不瞭解我們. *I understand French.* 我懂法語. *He understood why I had to go.* 他理解爲甚麼我一定得去. *My parents don't understand me* i.e. my personality 我的父母親不瞭解我. 即: 不瞭解我的個性. **2** be informed; learn; assume 被告知; 聽說, 獲悉; 假定, 設想: *I understand that you wish to see me.* 我聽說你想見我. *We understood them to be your friends.* 我們以爲他們是你的朋友. *past* 過去式和過去分詞 **understood** [ʌndə'stud]. **understandable** *adj* able to be understood 可懂的; 可理解的; 可瞭解的. **understandably** *adv* **understanding** *nu* **1** comprehension; knowledge 理解; 認識; 領悟; 理解力: *Have you any understanding of this problem?* 你瞭解這個問題嗎? *He is a teacher of great understanding.* 他是一位頭腦極其清楚的教師. **2** (usu. with **an**) agreement (通常與 an 連用) 協議: *We have an understanding not to meet each other when we are busy.* 我們有協議, 忙時不見面. *They have come to / reached an understanding.* 他們已達成協議. Also 亦作 *adj* able to understand clearly the difficulties, feelings etc of somebody 能諒解別人困難的; 同情別人的; 能理解別人感情的; *My doctor is a very understanding man.* 我的醫生善於諒解別人. **on the understanding that** on condition that 以…爲條件; 如果.

understate ['ʌndə'steit] *vt* not state strongly or fully enough 輕描淡寫地陳述; 打折扣地陳述. **understatement** *nc / u: It is an understatement to say they are not very pleased. They are* *furious.* 說他們不太高興是把話説輕了.他們遺怒不得已呢.

understudy ['ʌndəstʌdi] *vt* study the part in a play taken by another actor in case he is absent; act in the place of another actor 學習(某角色)準備當替角;代替(別的演員)演出. Also 亦作 *nc* person who understudies 預備演員;替角.

undertake [ʌndə'teik] *vt / i* **1** agree or promise to do something 同意, 答應 (做某事): *He undertook to be here before midday.* 他答應在中午之前到這裏的. *I have undertaken the work of cleaning all the rooms.* 我同意打掃所有的房間. **2** promise; guarantee 答應; 保證: *We cannot undertake that we shall finish it in time.* 我們不能保證準時做完這件事. *We cannot undertake to do that.* 我們不能答應做那件事. *past tense* 過去式 **undertook** [ʌndə'tuk]; *past part* 過去分詞 **undertaken.** 'undertaker *nc* (Brit) person who arranges funerals (US 美 **mortician**) (英)殯葬承辦人, 殯儀業者. **undertaking** *nc* work to be done; promise 任務;承諾.

undertone ['ʌndətoun] *nc* **1** quiet tone of voice or colour 低沉的聲調;柔和的色調: *They were speaking in undertones.* 他們正在低聲細語. **2** suggestion; hint 跡象; 暗示: *There was an undertone of anger in his letter.* 他的信中隱含着一份怒意.

undertook [ʌndə'tuk] *past tense of* **undertake.** undertake的過去式.

underwear ['ʌndəweə*] *nu* clothes worn under a suit or dress (esp. those worn next to the skin) 內衣褲;貼身衣褲.

underwent [ʌndə'went] *past tense of* **undergo.** undergo的過去式.

underworld ['ʌndəwə:ld] *nu* **1** place

where it was once believed persons went after death 陰間;地獄. **2** criminal part of a society or community 黑社會.

undesirable [ʌndi'zairəbl] *adj* not desirable; to be avoided; not approved 不合需要的;令人討厭的;不受歡迎的;應當避免的;未被認可的: *Criminals are undesirable people.* 罪犯是令人討厭的人. Also 亦作 *nc* undesirable person 不受歡迎的人.

undid [ʌn'did] *past tense of* **undo.** undo的過去式.

undies ['ʌndiz] *npl* women's underclothes (informal) 婦女的內衣(非正式).

undo [ʌn'du:] *vt* destroy what has been done; unfasten 破壞(已做好之事);解開, 放鬆: *Would you please undo my dress?* i.e. unfasten it 請你解開我的衣服好嗎? *She undid all her sewing.* 她把她縫好的線都拆開了. *This mistake has undone all our good work.* 這次錯誤毀了我們所有良好工作的成果. *past tense* 過去式 **undid** [ʌn'did]. *past part* 過去分詞 **undone** [ʌn'dʌn]. **undoing** *nu* (esp. with reference to a person's character or reputation) ruin (指一個人的名望或聲譽)毀滅: *A passion for gambling proved to be his undoing.* 嗜賭終於導致了他的毀滅. **leave undone** not do 未做.

undoubted [ʌn'dautid] *adj* not doubted; certain 不容置疑的;確實的. **undoubtedly** *adv.*

undress [ʌn'dres] **1** *vi* remove one's clothes 脱去(自己的)衣服. **2** *vt* remove someone's clothes 脱去(別人的衣服): *undress a baby* 把嬰孩的衣服脱下來.

undue [ʌn'dju:] *adj* more than is needed or is suitable 過份的;不適當的: *He gives undue attention to small* *problems.* 他謹小慎微. **unduly** *adv*.

undulate ['ʌndjuleit] *vi* move up and down like waves 像波浪似地起伏;波動.

unearth [ʌn'ə:θ] *vt* dig up; discover 發掘出,挖出;發現.

unearthly [ʌn'ə:θli] *adj* not of this world; very strange and frightening 非塵世的;不屬於現世的;怪異的;可怕的;陰森森的. **at an unearthly hour** at a very early or inconvenient time *(informal)* 過早地;在很不方便的時刻. (非正式).

uneasy [ʌn'i:zi] *adj* not at ease; worried 不舒服的;心神不安的;憂慮的,擔心的. **uneasiness** *nu* **unease** *nu* uneasiness 心神不安;憂慮;擔心.

unemployed [ʌnim'plɔid] *adj* (with reference to a person) without work (指人) 失業的. **the unemployed** all those who are without work (所有的) 失業者. **unemployment** *nu* state of being unemployed; number of unemployed persons 失業;失業人數: *Unemployment has increased because trade is bad.* 由於商業不景氣,失業人數有所增加.

unending [ʌn'endiŋ] *adj* never ending 無終止的,不盡的.

unequal [ʌn'i:kwəl] *adj* 1 not equal 不相等的: *a triangle with unequal sides* 不等邊三角形 2 not good in all parts 不均衡的: *an unequal piece of writing* 一部瑕瑜互見的作品.

unerring [ʌn'ə:riŋ] *adj* sure; accurate 確實的,可靠的;準確的,沒有偏差的.

uneventful [ʌni'ventful] *adj* not eventful; quiet; without any trouble 無重大事件的;平靜的;過程平凡的;沒有麻煩事的: *an uneventful journey* 一路順風.

unfailing [ʌn'feiliŋ] *adj* never failing; always there when needed 經久不衰的;

永久的: *his unfailing cheerfulness* 他那種始終如一的愉快情緒. **unfailingly** *adv*.

unfair [ʌn'fɛə*] *adj* not fair; unjust 不公平的;不公正的. **unfairly** *adv*.

unfaithful [ʌn'feiθful] *adj* not faithful (esp. in marriage by having a love affair with someone not one's husband or wife); not doing what one has promised to do 不忠實的 (尤指婚外戀);不貞潔的;不履行諾言的.

unfamiliar [ʌnfə'miliə*] *adj* 1 (with to) not well-known; strange (與Ｃ連用)陌生的;新奇的: *The new work was unfamiliar to me.* 這新工作對我說來很生疏. 2 (with with) not knowing well (與Ｃ連用)不熟悉的: *I was unfamiliar with the work.* 我不熟悉這工作.

unfasten [ʌn'fɑ:sn] *vt* open by removing a fastening 解開,脫開,鬆開: *unfasten a belt* 解開帶子.

unfeeling [ʌn'fi:liŋ] *adj* without feeling or sympathy 冷酷的;無情的;沒有同情心的.

unfit [ʌn'fit] *adj* (usu. with **for** or **to do**) not fit (通常與for或to do連用) 不合適的;不適宜的: *He is unfit for / to do heavy work.* 他不宜幹重活. *Smoking has made him very unfit* i.e. unhealthy 吸烟已嚴重損害了他的健康.

unflagging [ʌn'flæɡiŋ] *adj* continuing to work hard etc, after a long time, and showing no signs of tiredness 不懈的;不倦的: *He was unflagging in his efforts to help us.* 他爲了幫助我們作了不懈的努力.

unfold [ʌn'fould] *vt / vi* 1 open the folds of 將(摺疊的束西)打開,展開,攤開: *He unfolded the map.* 他攤開了地圖. 2 become, cause to become, known 逐漸表露;闡明: *A strange story unfolded from what he told us.* 從他向我們所講的話中逐漸呈現出一個奇怪的故

事來. *They have unfolded all their secrets to us.* 他們已將自己的秘密向我們全盤托出.

unforeseen [ˈʌnfɔːˈsiːn] *adj* not expected at an earlier time 意想不到的, 意料之外的: *Unforeseen circumstances have forced us to cancel the meeting.* 意料不到的情況已迫使我們取消會議.

unforgettable [ʌnfəˈgetəbl] *adj* making a very strong impression, and so not easily forgotten 不會被遺忘的, 難以忘懷的: *an unforgettable holiday* 難忘的假日.

unfortunate [ʌnˈfɔːtʃənit] *adj* 1 not fortunate 不幸的, 倒霉的: *He was unfortunate not to win the race* i.e. he lost only because of bad luck. 他很不幸, 沒有贏得這場比賽. 即 [因為運氣不好, 輸了]. 2 not suitable and causing difficulty, 不當的, 不得體的; 造成困難的: *That was an unfortunate remark to make.* 那次說的話很不得體. *He came at an unfortunate time.* 他來得不是時候. **unfortunately** *adv.*

unfounded [ʌnˈfaundid] *adj* false; without cause 假的; 沒有理由的; 沒有根據的: *an unfounded allegation* i.e. something said which is not true 沒有根據的辯解, 即: 所說的不是真的.

unfurnished [ʌnˈfɜːniʃt] *adj* (with reference to a house, flat, lodgings etc.) let without furniture (指出租的房子, 套間, 住所等)無傢具的.

ungainly [ʌnˈgeinli] *adj* clumsy; awkward 笨拙的; 難看的.

ungodly [ʌnˈgɔdli] *adj* 1 not godly; sinful 不敬神的; 邪惡的; 罪孽深重的. 2 shocking (*informal* in sense 2) 驚人的, 可怕的(義2爲非正式).

unguarded [ʌnˈgɑːdid] *adj* 1 not guarded 沒有防備的. 2 careless 不留神的, 不謹慎的: *an unguarded remark*

不小心的話.

unhealthy [ʌnˈhelθi] *adj* 1 harmful to the health 對健康有害的: *unhealthy climate* 對健康有害的氣候. 2 not in good health; often ill 不健康的; 常有病的: *unhealthy person* 有病的人. 3 harmful to moral or spiritual health 對道德或精神的健康有害的; 不良的: *unhealthy interest in money* 對金錢的不良嗜好. **unhealthiness** *nu.*

unheard-of [ʌnˈhɜːdɔv] *adj* never known before; most unusual 前所未聞的; 不尋常的. *It was unheard-of for anyone to speak to the headmaster like that.* 對校長那樣講話還是從來沒有聽說過的.

unicorn [ˈjuːnikɔːn] *nc* animal in legend like a horse, having one horn growing from the middle of its head (傳說中的)獨角獸.

uniform [ˈjuːnifɔːm] *adj* always having the same form; not different; never changing 一直不變的; 相同的; 始終如一的: *Bricks must be of uniform size.* 磚塊必須有相同的尺寸. Also 亦作 *nc/u* official dress 制服: *Soldiers wear uniform(s).* 士兵穿軍服. **uniformity** [juːniˈfɔːmiti] *nu* state of being the same 一模一樣, 一律, 同一; 一致性.

unify [ˈjuːnifai] *vt* make into one; join together 統一, 使成一體, 使一致; 使合一, 結合. **unification** [juːnifiˈkeiʃən] *nu.*

unilateral [juːniˈlætərl] *adj* one sided; done by one side or party only 一方的, 單方面的, 片面的; 僅由單方面做的: *The presidents of the two countries promised that they would not take unilateral action on the matter* i.e. that each would consult the other before acting 兩國總統答應將不會就此事採取單方面的行動. 即: 採取行動之前, 一方將同另一方磋商.

union ['juːniən] **1** nc / u act or state of being joined together 聯合, 結合, 合併; 聯邦: *the union of the three companies into one* 三個公司合併為一; *the Union of Soviet Socialist Republics.* 蘇維埃社會主義共和國聯盟, 蘇聯. **2** nc organization for a special purpose (為某一特定目的的組織) 社; 會; 同盟: *trade union* 工會; *customs union* 關稅同盟; *students' union* 學生會.
unionist nc member of a trade union 工會會員.

unique [juːˈniːk] adj only one of its kind; completely different from any other 唯一的, 獨一無二的; 無與倫比的, 獨特的.

unison ['juːnisn] nu agreement 一致. **in unison 1** together 一齊, 一起. **2** (with reference to a choir singing) with all voices singing the same notes (指合唱) 齊唱.

unit ['juːnit] nc **1** single person / thing; groups of persons / things regarded as one. 一人, 一物, 小組; 分部 / 分隊; 單位. *The soldiers returned to their unit* i.e. company, regiment etc to which they belong 士兵們回到了所在的部隊. 即: 他們所屬的連, 團等. **2** fixed amount or length used in measuring 計量 (標準的) 單位: *In France and many other countries the unit of length is the metre.* 在法國和許多其他國家, 長度的單位是米. **3** piece of equipment (something made up of several parts) 組合件, 一套用具: *kitchen unit.* 廚房的成套用具.

unite [juːˈnait] vt / i become, cause to become, one; join together (使) 聯合, 結合; 合併, 團結: *England and Scotland united to become the United Kingdom.* 英格蘭和蘇格蘭合併成為聯合王國. *The people united to overthrow / in overthrowing the govern-*ment. 人民聯合起來推翻政府. **united** adj **unity** ['juːniti] nc / u **1** state of being united; state of forming a complete whole 聯合, 團結; 整體, 統一. **2** agreement; common purpose 一致(性); 契合, 和諧. (opp 反義詞 **disunity**).

universe ['juːnivəːs] nu everything that exists, including all living creatures, the earth, the sun, moon and stars 宇宙, 天地萬物, 世界. **universal** [juːniˈvəːsl] adj of the universe; general; worldwide 宇宙的; 普遍的, 普通的, 一般的; 全世界的: *Football is a universal game.* 足球是一項世界性的運動. **universally** adv.

university [juːniˈvəːsiti] nc place of higher education and research which awards degrees to its students 大學.

unkempt [ʌnˈkempt] adj with untidy hair; untidy 頭髮蓬亂的; 不整潔的.

unleash [ʌnˈliːʃ] vt free from a leash; let go 解開皮帶; 放出; 釋放: *unleash a dog* 把狗的皮帶解開, 放開狗; *unleash nuclear energy* 釋放核能.

unless [ʌnˈles] conj if···not 如果···不, 除非: *I refuse to do it unless you help.* 如果你不幫助, 我拒絕做此事.

unlike [ʌnˈlaik] adj not similar in appearance, behaviour etc. (外表、行為等) 不像; 不同的. Also 亦作 prep: *Unlike me, he doesn't smoke.* 他跟我不同, 他不抽烟. **unlikely** adj **1** not probable 不大可能的: *It is unlikely that he knows the answer.* 他不大可能知道答案. **2** unexpected or difficult to believe 意料不到的; 難以相信的, 未必的: *an unlikely explanation* 靠不住的解釋.

unload [ʌnˈloud] vt / i **1** take the load from 從···卸下貨物, 卸 (貨): *They unloaded the ships in the harbour.* 他們在港口從船上卸貨. *The ships in the* *harbour were unloading.* 港口的船正在卸貨. **2** (with reference to a gun etc.) take out the bullet(s) or shell(s) without firing it 退出(槍、砲等)的子彈或砲彈; 退出子彈或砲彈.

unmanned [ʌn'mænd] *adj* not having anybody inside; without a crew 無人居住的; 無人駕駛的; 遙控的: *an unmanned space rocket* 無人駕駛的宇宙火箭.

unmistakable [ʌnmi'steikəbl] *adj* about which there can be no doubt; clear; certain 不會弄錯的; 不容置疑的; 明白的; 肯定的. **unmistakably** *adv*.

unmitigated [ʌn'mitigeitid] *adj* (usu. with reference to something bad) complete in every way (通常指不好的事物)十足的; 純粹的; (壞)透頂的: *an unmitigated liar* 十足的撒謊者.

unnatural [ʌn'nætʃərəl] *adj* not natural; abnormal 不自然的; 反常的.

unnerve [ʌn'nɜːv] *vt* cause somebody to lose his nerve; weaken somebody's confidence or courage 使失去自制力; 使氣餒, 使失去勇氣.

unpack [ʌn'pæk] *vt / i* take from a box or trunk etc things which have been packed in it 從盒子、皮箱等裏取出(包裝好的東西).

unpick [ʌn'pik] *vt* take out the stitches from 將…的針線拆開: *Her mother unpicked the dress and sewed it again.* 她母親拆開了衣服的針線, 再重新縫上.

unpleasant [ʌn'pleznt] *adj* not pleasant; disagreeable 使人不愉快的; 討厭的; 不合意的. **unpleasantness** *nu* unpleasant feeling; unpleasant quarrel 不愉快; 不愉快的爭執.

unprecedented [ʌn'presidentid] *adj* having no precedent; having no earlier example; first of its kind 無前例的; 空前的, 前所未有的; 首次的.

unpretentious [ʌnpri'tenʃəs] *adj* not

pretending to be important; modest 不自誇的, 不驕傲的, 不擺架子的; 謙虛的.

unqualified [ʌn'kwɒlifaid] *adj* **1** not qualified 不合格的, 無資格的: *an unqualified teacher* 不合格的教師. **2** complete; not limited in any way 完全的, 絕對的; 無限制的: *They have given their unqualified approval* 他們已表示完全同意.

unquote ['ʌn'kwout] *vt / i* used to show the end of a quotation (用以表示)結束引語: *I now quote what he said-'Success depends on hard work', unquote.* 我現在引用他所說的—"成功取決於辛勤的勞動", (引語結束).

unravel [ʌn'rævl] *vt / i* **1** (with reference to something which is knitted, sewn or tied) become, cause to become, separate (指已織、縫、綁之物)(使) 散開, 解開, 拆散: *Can you unravel the knots in this string?* 你能解開這條繩子的結嗎? **2** solve something difficult 解決, 澄清, 闡明; *past* 過去式和過去分詞 **unravelled.** (*US* 美 **unraveled**).

unrelieved [ʌnri'liːvd] *adj* not relieved; not having anything to change its condition or appearance 未被減輕的; 未得緩和的; 無變化的; 單調的: *They had a life of unrelieved poverty.* 他們一直過着貧困的生活.

unrest [ʌn'rest] *nu* dissatisfaction which may lead to trouble or violence 不滿; 不安; 動亂, 騷動: *social / political unrest* 社會/政治動亂.

unruly [ʌn'ruːli] *adj* not easily controlled; refusing to obey 難控制的, 難駕馭的; 不守秩序的, 不守規矩的.

unsaid [ʌn'sed] *adj* not said; understood without being said 未說出的; 秘而不宣的: *Some things are better left unsaid* i.e. it is not always good to express what one feels or thinks. 有些事還是不說為妙. 即: 表達出所感覺的或所想的未必都好.

unsavoury [ʌnˈseivəri] (*US* 美 **unsavory**) *adj* not pleasant; disgusting 令人不快的; 討厭的; 噁心的; 肉麻的.

unscathed [ʌnˈskeiðd] *adj* safe; without injury 未受損傷的; 未遭傷害的.

unscrupulous [ʌnˈskru:pjuləs] *adj* not scrupulous; ruthless 不審慎的; 無恥的; 無情的; 殘忍的.

unseemly [ʌnˈsi:mli] *adj* (esp. with reference to behaviour) not suitable; disgusting (尤指行為)不適宜的; 令人討厭的.

unsightly [ʌnˈsaitli] *adj* not pleasing to the eye; ugly 不悅目的; 難看的; 醜陋的; 不雅觀的. **unsightliness** *nu*.

unsound [ʌnˈsaund] *adj* not perfect; (with reference to the mind) damaged (指身體)不健康的, 不完美的; (指精神)不健全的, 受損害的.

unsparing [ʌnˈspɛəriŋ] *adj* working as hard as possible 盡力工作的; *be unsparing in one's efforts* 不遺餘力.

unspeakable [ʌnˈspi:kəbl] *adj* not fit to be expressed in words 不能以言語表達的, 無法形容的.

unstable [ʌnˈsteibl] *adj* showing great and sudden changes (esp. in a way which is not normal) 易變的, 不穩定的; (尤指非正常的)突變的; *an unstable person* 反覆無常的人; *unstable weather conditions* 不穩定的天氣狀況.

unswerving [ʌnˈswɜ:viŋ] *adj* steady; reliable 堅定的, 不懈的; 可靠的.

untidy [ʌnˈtaidi] *adj* not tidy 不整齊的, 不整潔的. Also 亦作 *vt*.

until [ʌnˈtil] *prep / conj* see 見 **till**[1].

untimely [ʌnˈtaimli] *adj* happening too soon or at the wrong time 過早的; 不適時的, 不合時宜的.

untiring [ʌnˈtaiəriŋ] *adj* not becoming tired; continuing to work hard 不倦的; 繼續努力工作的, 堅持不懈的; *be untiring in one's efforts* 堅持不懈地努力.

unto [ˈʌntu, ˈʌntu:, ˈʌntə] *prep* (rhetoric or archaic) (修辭或古體) 1 to 到; 對; *Do unto him as he does unto others.* 以其人之道, 還治其人之身. 2 till, until 到; 到⋯為止; *unto this day* 直到今日; 至今.

untold [ʌnˈtould] *adj* too great or too many to be counted 數不清的, 無數的; 不可計量的; *untold millions* 千千萬萬; *untold wealth* 數不清的財富.

untoward [ˌʌntəˈwɔ:d] *adj* unlucky; inconvenient (rather *o.f.*) 不幸的; 不便的, 不當的. (頗為舊式)

unveil [ʌnˈveil] *vt* take off a veil; show to the public for the first time (e.g. a statue or memorial) 揭去⋯的面紗(幕布); 首次展示(塑像、紀念碑等), 舉行(塑像、紀念碑等)的揭幕禮.

unwieldy [ʌnˈwi:ldi] *adj* difficult to move or carry 難以移動(搬動)的, 笨拙的; 笨重的.

unwitting [ʌnˈwitiŋ] *adj* not knowing; not intending to 無意的, 非故意的. **unwittingly** *adv*.

up [ʌp] *adj / adv / prep* 1 to a higher place 向高處; *He climbed up the hill.* 他往山上爬. *They ran up the stairs.* 他們跑上樓梯. (*opp* 反義詞 **down**). 2 in or to a higher place or state 在高處, 在上方; 向上, 向高處; *He climbed up by himself.* 他自己爬上來的. *Can you carry it up?* 你能把它提起來嗎? *The price of meat is up.* 肉的價格上漲了. (*opp* 反義詞 **down**). 3 out of bed; on one's feet 起床; 站著; *Are the children up yet?* 孩子們起床了嗎? *He stayed up till 11 o'clock last night.* 昨晚他到十一點才睡. *The boys stood up* *when the teacher came into the class-room.* 老師走進教室時，孩子們都站了起來. **4** to the north 往北: *They sailed up to Iceland* i.e. from the south 他們往北駛向冰島. 即: 從南駛向北. (*opp* 反義詞 **down**). **5** *(Brit)* to a larger or more important place; to a more important person. (英)往較大或較重要的地方; 向較重要的人: *They have gone up to London* (used even if travelling from the north). 他們上倫敦去了 (甚至用於從北方去倫敦). *Are you going up to town?* 你上城裏去嗎? *All the school reports go up to the headmaster.* 學校的所有報告都上報給校長. **6** close to; nearer 靠近; 接近: *They went up to the policeman to ask the way.* 他們走到警察跟前問路. *Go up to that door and knock.* 走到那門口, 然後敲門. **7** completely; more strongly 全部地; 更强地, 更有力地: *They drank up all the beer.* 他們把啤酒喝光了. *Have you tied up the parcel?* 你把包裹捆緊了嗎? *Time's up* i.e. the time allowed for something is over. 時間到了. 即: 供做某事的時間已結束. *Hurry up!* 趕快! *Why doesn't he speak up? I can't hear him.* 他怎麼不講大聲點? 我聽不見. **up-and-coming** *adj* (with reference to a person) likely to be successful; promising (指人) 很可能成功的; 極有前途的. **up and down** *adv* **1** rising and falling 上下, 上上下下: *The boat went up and down on the rough sea.* 船在洶湧的海上顛簸前進. **2** backwards and forwards 來去, 來回, 來來往往: *People were walking up and down in front of the school.* 人們在學校門口走來走去. **ups and downs** *npl* good and bad times; changes in one's luck(指人生的) 順逆, 浮沉, 榮枯, 盛衰: *Life has its ups and downs.* *(informal)* 人生有得意時也有

失意時. (非正式). **up against** meeting difficulties 碰上, 面臨 (困難): *We shall be up against a strong team in the next match.* 下一場比賽, 我們將碰到一支强隊. *Having lost all his money, he is up against it* i.e. he is in difficulties. *(informal)* 他的錢都丟了, 他正處於困境. (非正式). **up to 1** as far as 直到: *Up to now I've been lucky.* 至今我還算幸運. *He has read up to chapter ten.* 他已經讀到第十章. **2** depending on 該由…, 輪到…: *It is now up to them to do it.* 現在該由他們來做此事了. **3** as good as; ready for 及得上; 能作; 勝任, 適於: *His work is not up to the required standard.* 他的作品還達不到所要求的標準. *They are not up to doing it by themselves.* 他們還不能自己幹這件事. **4** intending to do; busy with (often something bad or mischievous) 想做, 想搞; 忙於 (常指壞事或有害的事): *What are these boys up to?* 這些男孩子想搞甚麼鬼? **what's up?** what is the matter? what is happening? *(informal)* 甚麼事? 發生甚麼事了? (非正式).

upbringing ['ʌpbrɪŋɪŋ] *nc / u* training and education of a child (兒童的)教育, 撫育; 教養; 培養.

upgrade [ʌp'greɪd] *vt* put in a higher grade 使升級; 提升.

upheaval [ʌp'hiːvl] *nc* sudden disturbance or change 動亂, 激變.

upheld [ʌp'held] past of **uphold.** *uphold*的過去式和過去分詞.

uphill ['ʌp'hɪl] *adj / adv* **1** going up a hill 往山上的, 向上的; 往上坡: *We walked uphill.* 我們往山上走. **2** difficult 困難的; 費力的: *uphill work* 困難的工作.

uphold [ʌp'həʊld] *vt* approve; support a decision 贊成; 支持(某決定). *past* 過去式和過去分詞 **upheld** [ʌp'held].

upholster [ʌp'houlstə*] *vt* fit chairs and other pieces of furnitur with springs and cover them with cloth, leather etc. 給(椅子和其他傢具)裝上彈簧、套子、墊子等, 做軟墊 **upholsterer** *nc* **upholstery** *nu* business of an upholsterer; materials used to upholster 室內裝潢業; 室內裝潢物品.

upkeep ['ʌpki:p] *nu* act of keeping something in good condition (e.g. a house, car or garden); cost of doing so (房屋, 車, 花園等的)保養, 維修; 維修費, 保養費.

upon [ə'pɒn] *prep* on 和on意義相同. *Note* 說明: *on* and *upon* have the same sense but *on* is by far the more commonly used. There are, however, a few phrases in which only *upon* is used (e.g. *once upon a time*; *put upon somebody* i.e. ask from somebody more than one should). on和upon意義相同, 但on要通用得多. 然而有些短語只能用upon(如: once upon a time 從前; put upon somebody 向某人要求過多).

upper ['ʌpə*] *adj* higher 較高的: *upper lip* 上唇 (*opp* 反義詞 **lower**). superlative 最高級 **uppermost**. **uppermost** *adj / adv* 1 highest 最高的(地). 2 (with reference to thoughts, ideas) receiving more attention; most likely to be carried out (指思想、念頭)得到較大重視的; 最主要的; 最可能實現的: *The uppermost thought in my mind was to escape.* 我心中最主要的念頭就是逃跑. **upper classes** *npl* the rich and powerful people in society 上流社會. **upperclass** *adj*.

upright ['ʌprait] 1 *adj / adv* straight up; vertical, vertically 筆直的(地), 垂直的(地), 直立的(地): *Are these plants upright?* 這些植物是直立的嗎? *The soldier stood upright.* 士兵筆直地站立著. 2 *adj* honest and just 誠實的, 正直的: *He is an upright citizen.* 他是個正直的公民. Also 亦作 *nc* something which is fixed in an upright position 直立的東西, 筆直的東西, 直柱: *The roof was held up by four uprights.* 屋頂由四根直柱支撐著.

uprising ['ʌpraiziŋ] *nc* revolt 叛亂; 變, 起義; 暴動.

uproar ['ʌprɔ:*] *nu* (usu. with **an**) violent and noisy shouting (通常與an連用)喧鬧(聲), 鼓噪(聲), 喧囂(聲): *There was an uproar when he told them they had all failed in the examination.* 他告訴他們說他們考試都不及格, 此時響發出一陣鼓噪聲聲. **uproarious** [ʌp'rɔ:riəs] *adj* noisy but happy 暴笑如雷的, 鬧哄哄的.

uproot [ʌp'ru:t] *vt* pull up by the roots; get rid of 連根拔起, 根除; 根絕, 去除.

upset [ʌp'set] *vt / i* 1 turn over; knock over 打翻, 弄翻, 傾覆, 顛覆: *The boat will upset if you move about in it.* 如果你在船上走來走去, 船會弄翻的. *He upest the teapot.* 他把茶壺打翻了. 2 be, cause to be, distressed or disturbed (使)苦惱; (使)心煩意亂; 打亂: *They were very upset when they heard the news.* 聽到這消息, 他們都心煩意亂. *The news upset them.* 這消息使他們煩惱. *The sudden rain upset our game of tennis.* 突然下起雨來, 我們的網球賽不能舉行. *pres part* 現在分詞 **upsetting**. *past* 過去式和過去分詞 **upset**. Also 亦作['ʌpset] *nc*: *The news was a great upset to them.* 這消息使他們極為不安.

upshot ['ʌpʃɔt] *nu* (with **the**) result (與the連用)結果, 結局: *What was the upshot of the official investigation?* 官方調查的結果如何呢?

upside down ['ʌpsai'daun] *adv* with the top side underneath; in confusion 倒

置(地), 顛倒; 混亂地, 亂七八糟: *That picture is hanging upside down.* 那幅圖畫掛倒了. *He turned the whole room upside down looking for his book.* 他爲了找他的書, 把整個房間弄得亂七八糟.

upstairs [ˈʌpˈstɛəz] *adv* to or on the upper floor 往樓上; 在樓上. Also 亦作 *adj: an upstairs room* 樓上的房間.

upstart [ˈʌpstɑːt] *nc* person who has suddenly become rich or powerful and is unpleasant because of this 暴發戶; 驟起者; 新貴 (因此常招致反感).

upstream [ʌpˈstriːm] *adv* against the flow of water in a river, stream etc. 逆流地: *It is much more difficult to row a boat upstream than downstream.* 逆流划船要比順流划船困難得多.

uptake [ˈʌpteik] *nu* only in **quick / slow on the uptake** i.e. quick / slow to understand *(informal)* 僅用於 quick / slow on the uptake, 即: 理解快/慢, 領悟快/慢 (非正式).

up-to-date [ˈʌptəˈdeit] *adj* of the latest kind; right up to the present 新式的; 時新的; 直到最近的, 最新的: *up-to-date clothes* 時髦的衣服; *up-to-date information* 最新消息. *Note* 說明: as a *pred adj* write up to date without hyphens. *You must keep up to date.* 用作表語形容詞時, 不用連字號, 寫作 up to date. *You must keep up to date.* 你必須跟得上時代.

upward [ˈʌpwəd] *adj* going higher 向上的, 上升的: *an upward movement of the arm* 手臂向上運動. **upwards** *adv* to a higher place 向上地, 上升地: *The path went upwards through the forest.* 路向上穿過森林.

uranium [juːˈreiniəm] *nu* type of radioactive metal(U) 鈾 (放射性金屬, 符號U).

urban [ˈəːbən] *adj* of a town 城市的, 都市的.

urbane [əːˈbein] *adj* very polite; refined 有禮貌的; 溫文有禮的; 文雅的.

urchin [ˈəːtʃin] *nc* **1** small and mischievous boy 小淘氣, 頑童. **2** type of small sea creature with a round spiky shell (usu. **sea urchin**) 海膽 (通常用 sea urchin).

urea [ˈjuəriə] *nu* soluble, crystalline solid, found in urine or produced synthetically; used in making plastics, etc. 脲; 尿素.

urge [əːdʒ] *vt* **1** try hard to make somebody do something; drive 催促; 力勸; 推進; 驅策: *They urged me to go home at once.* 他們催促我馬上回家. *The officer urged his men on.* 軍官催促士兵們前進. **2** (with **upon**) bring strongly to the attention of (與upon連用) 力言, 強調: *They urged upon me the need to escape.* 他們向我強調必需逃跑. Also 亦作 *nu* act of urging; strong desire 推動力, 促動; 衝動; 強烈的慾望: *I resisted an urge to interrupt the speaker.* 我忍住了想要打斷講話者的衝動. **urgent** [ˈəːdʒənt] *adj* requiring immediate attention 緊急的, 急迫的: *I received an urgent message from my father telling me to return home at once.* 我收到了父親的急信, 告訴我馬上回家. **urgently** *adv* **urgency** [ˈəːdʒənsi] *nu: This is a problem of great urgency.* 這是一個極爲緊急的問題.

urine [ˈjuərin] *nu* waste liquid from the body 尿. **urinal** [juəˈrainl] *nc* container for urine; public lavatory for men 尿壺, 盛尿器; 男人公共小便處.

urn [əːn] *nc* **1** tall container with a narrow neck (esp. used for the ashes of the dead after cremation) 甕, 缸 (尤指骨灰甕). **2** large metal container with a tap used for holding liquid (e.g. tea or coffee) 壺(如: 茶壺, 咖啡壺).

us [ʌs] *pron* object form of **we**. we的賓格形式.

use¹ [juːz] *vt* **1** employ for a purpose; do something with something 使用;利用: *They used a rope to tie the boat.* 他們用繩子來拴住船. *Can I use your telephone?* 我能用你的電話嗎? *You must use your own judgment.* 你必須用你自己的判斷力. **2** spend; finish 消耗;用完: *Have we used all the writing paper?* 我們用完了所有的書寫紙嗎? **3** (with **up**) spend or finish completely (與 up 連用) 耗盡;用盡: *They have used up their money.* 他們把錢花光了. **used¹** [juːzd] *adj* already used, so not new or clean 用舊了的: *Please put the used towels in this basket.* 請把用過的毛巾放在這個籃子裏. **used²** [juːst] (with **to**) accustomed to (與to連用) 習慣的, 適應於: *I am not used to getting up early.* 我不習慣早起床. *They are not used to cold weather.* 他們不習慣冷天氣. **used to** part of the verb which has the sense of something happening regularly or often in the past 接動詞, 表示過去常常發生某事: *They used to go to the market every Saturday.* 他們過去通常在星期六到市場買東西. *This is the village where we used to live.* 這就是我們過去常住的村子. *Did you use to play football?* 你過去常踢足球嗎? *He used to play cricket, didn't he?* (less commonly *Usen't he to play cricket?*) *Yes, he did.* 他過去常打板球, 是嗎? (較不常用 Usen't he to play cricket?) 是的, 他常打板球. **usage** [ˈjuːsidʒ] *n* **1** *nu* way in which something is used 用法. **2** *nc / u* established custom; approved way of using or doing something 習俗; 慣例; 慣用法: *The usages of some English words are difficult to learn.* 某

些英語詞的慣用法很難學. **user** *nc* somebody / something that uses 使用者(人或物).

use² [juːs] **1** *nc* purpose; work which can be done by something 用途; 效用; 功能: *Can you find a use for these empty boxes?* 你能設法利用這些空箱子嗎? *A sharp knife has many uses.* 鋒利的刀子有許多用處. **2** *nu* act or condition of using or being used 用, 使用; 利用; 被使用狀況: *This classroom is for the use of young children only.* 這間教室僅供小孩子使用. *The use of the present tense in this sentence is wrong.* 這個句子使用現在時是錯的. **3** *nu* benefit; value 益處; 價值: *What's the use of working so hard?* 這樣努力幹, 有何用呢? *It is no use your running away.* 你跑掉沒有好處. *It is no use for you to run away.* 你跑掉於你是沒有益處的. **useful** *adj* **1** handy; having good results 有用的; 有益的; 實用的; 有幫助的: *I find this pen very useful.* 我覺得這枝筆很好用. **2** (with reference to a person having influence) efficient (指有影響的人)有效率的; 能幹的: *He is a useful friend to have.* 他是一位可交往的能幹的朋友. **usefulness** *nu* **useless** *adj* of no use; not efficient; having no effect 無用的; 無效的; 無價值的; 無益的: *A blunt knife is useless.* 鈍刀是無用的. *These workmen are useless.* 這些工人沒甚麼效率. *It's useless to run away.* 跑掉是無用的. **uselessly** *adv* **uselessness** *nu* **in use** being used 在使用中. **make use of** see 見 **make¹**. **out of use** no longer being used 不使用, 不再使用.

usher [ˈʌʃə*] *nc* person who leads people to their seats in a cinema, theatre, church etc. (電影院, 戲院, 教堂等的)引座員, 招待員. Also 亦作 *vt* lead to a

seat or room 引導…(入座或入房間);
領引: *I was ushered into the head-master's office by my teacher.* 我的老師把我領到校長辦公室. **usherette** [ʌʃəˈret] *nc* woman who leads people to their seats (usu. in a cinema or theatre) (通常在電影院或戲院的)女引座員, 女招待員.

usual [ˈjuːʒl] *adj* often happening or being done; common; normal 通常的, 平常的; 普通的; 慣常的; 慣例的. (*opp* 反義詞 **unusual**). **usually** *adv*.

usurp [juːˈzəːp] *vt* take somebody's position unlawfully or by force 篡奪; 奪取; 侵佔: *He killed the king and usurped the throne.* 他殺了國王, 篡奪了王位. **usurper** *nc*.

usury [ˈjuːʒuri] *nu* practice of lending money and charging interest for doing so; high interest on money lent (放)高利貸; 高利.

utensil [juːˈtensl] *nc* container or instrument of any kind used in the home (esp. in the kitchen) (尤指廚房的)器皿, 器具.

uteri [ˈjuːtərai] *pl* of **uterus.** uterus 的複數.

uterus [ˈjuːtərəs] *nc* womb 子宮.

utilitarian [juːtiliˈteəriən] *adj* of practical use only 功利的; 實利的; 功利主義的; 實利主義的.

utility [juːˈtiliti] **1** *nu* usefulness; quality of being useful 有用; 實用; 效用. **2** *nc* something which is useful to, and is used by, many people 公用事業: *Railways and roads are public utilities.* 鐵路和道路是公用事業.

utilize [ˈjuːtilaiz] *vt* use; make useful 使用; 利用. **utilization** [juːtilaiˈzeiʃən] *nu*.

utmost [ˈʌtmoust] *adj* **1** farthest away 最遠的. **2** greatest 最大的, 極度的: *You must do your work with the utmost care.* 你必須極小心地做工作. Also 亦作 *nu* the most that is possible 最大可能, 極限, 極度: *He tried his utmost to win.* 他竭盡全力去取勝.

utter¹ [ˈʌtə*] *adj* complete 完全的, 十足的: *He is an utter fool.* 他是一個十足的傻瓜. **utterly** *adv*.

utter² [ˈʌtə*] *vt* **1** make a sound with the mouth; speak (用口)發出聲音; 說, 講: *She uttered a sigh.* 她長嘆了一聲. *Don't utter another word.* 別再說了. **2** (with reference to a false cheque) pass for payment (指偽支票)流通, 使用: **utterance** *nc* / *u* something spoken; word 所說的話; 言詞.

V,v

vacant ['veikənt] *adj* **1** empty; not occupied 空的，未被佔用的: *There was not a vacant seat in the hall.* 大廳裏没有一個空座位. **2** not interested; stupid 茫然的；出神的；無表情的；愚蠢的: *He gave us a vacant look.* 他帶着茫然的眼神望了我們一下. **vacancy** [*nc* position or job which has not yet been filled (職位、工作) 空缺，空額: *The school has vacancies for three teachers.* 學校有三名教師的空額.

vacate [və'keit] *vt* leave empty or not occupied 空出；騰出: *They must vacate their rooms in the hotel before Saturday.* 他們必須在星期六之前騰出旅館的房間. **vacation 1** *nc* time when schools, colleges and courts of law are closed (學校的) 假期; (法庭的) 休庭期. **2** *nc/u* holidays 假日: *Where are you spending your vacation?* 你在哪兒度假? Also 亦作 *vi (US)* spend holidays (美) 度假.

vaccine ['væksiːn] *nc/u* substance introduced into a human or animal body to protect it from getting certain diseases (e.g. measles, smallpox) 痘苗，疫苗；菌苗 (如防麻疹，天花). **vaccinate** ['væksineit] *vt* put a vaccine into a human or animal body (esp. the vaccine against smallpox) 給…種牛痘 (以預防天花)，給…種疫苗；給…打預防針. **vaccination** [væksi'nei∫ən] *nc/u* act of vaccinating or being vaccinated 種痘；接種疫苗；預防注射.

vacuous ['vækjuəs] *adj* **1** empty 空的；空洞的. **2** stupid; foolish 愚蠢的，傻的: *the vacuous smile of an idiot* 白癡的傻笑. **3** senseless; idle; indolent 無

意義的；懶散的；無所事事的: *a vacuous life* 無聊的生活.

vacuum ['vækjum] *nc* space completely empty of substance or gas; space from which air or another gas has been removed 真空，真空狀態. **'vacuum cleaner** type of machine which sucks dirt and dust from carpets, curtains etc. 吸塵器. **'vacuum flask** type of container with a smaller container inside it and a vacuum between them, used for keeping the contents at a constant temperature. (usu. **thermos flask**) 保温瓶，熱水瓶 (通常作 thermos flask). *(US* 美 **vacuum bottle).**

vagabond ['vægəbɔnd] *adj* moving from place to place without a home 流浪的，漂泊的. Also 亦作 *nc* person who does this 流浪者，漂泊者.

vagary ['veigəri] *nc* (often *pl*) act or thoughts for which there is no clear reason (常用複數) (無明顯理由的) 古怪的行爲或觀念；奇想；妄想；異想天開: *It is difficult to explain the vagaries of a child's mind.* 很難解釋兒童的奇異念頭.

vagina [və'dʒainə] *nc* membranous passage connecting the outer sex organ of women or female animals to the womb (女人或雌性動物的) 陰道. **vaginae** [və'dʒaini:] pl of **vagina.** vagina 的複數.

vagrant ['veigrnt] *adj* moving from place to place; wandering 流浪的；漂泊不定的. Also 亦作 *nc* person who does this; tramp 流浪者，漂泊者；遊民. **vagrancy** *nu.*

vague [veig] *adj* not certain; not defi-

nite 不肯定的; 含糊的; 模糊的; 不清楚
的. **vaguely** *adv* **vagueness** *nu.*

vain [vein] *adj* **1** useless; worthless;
having no result 無益的; 無效的; 無結
果的; 徒勞的. **2** (with reference to a person) too proud about
oneself; conceited (指人) 自視過高的;
自負的. **vainly** *adv* **vanity** ['vænɪtɪ]
nu too much pride; conceit 自大; 自
負, 虛榮心; *Many beautiful women
are spoilt by vanity*. 許多美貌的女子
都給虛榮心弄壞了. **in vain** *adv* **1**
without result or success 徒勞, 白辛
苦, 無結果, 徒然. *We tried in vain to
see him*. 我們要去見他, 但沒見到. **2**
without proper respect 不尊敬, 輕慢;
Never take God's name in vain. 切勿
輕慢地談論上帝.

vale [veil] *nc* area of low land between
hills (*o.f.* except in place names e.g.
the Vale of York. Use **valley**) 谷, 山谷
(舊式, 用於地名, 如the Vale of York約
克谷. 現在用valley).

valentine ['væləntain] *nc* **1** letter or
card expressing love, sent on St
Valentine's day i.e. 14 February, to a
person of the opposite sex 在聖瓦倫
丁節(2月14日)送給異性的表示愛情的
情書或卡片; 情人卡. **2** person to
whom such a letter or card is sent 在
聖瓦倫丁節被贈送情書或情人卡的人,
情人節愛人, 情人.

valiant ['væliənt] *adj* brave 勇敢的, 英勇
的. **valiantly** *adv* see 見 **valour.**

valid ['vælid] *adj* **1** strong; well supported 健全的, 站得住腳的; *They
have valid reasons for refusing to do
it*. 他們有充分的理由拒絕做此事. **2**
correct according to the law or rules
依法有效的; 有正當手續的; *He has a
valid claim to the property*. 他對財產
的要求是有效的. *Is your passport
valid for travel in the USA?* 在美國旅

行, 你的護照有效嗎? (*opp* 反義詞 **invalid**). **validity** [və'lidɪti] *nu.*

valley ['væli] *nc* area of land between
hills (usu. with a river) 山谷 (通常有河
流).

valour ['vælə*] (*US* 美 **valor**) *nc* bravery 勇敢, 英勇.

value ['vælju:] **1** *nu* importance; usefulness 重要性; 有用性, 價值: *Most pa-
rents know the value of a good education*. 大多數父母知道良好教育的重要
性. *These books are of great / little /
some / no value to somebody learning
English*. 這些書對學習英語的人很有 /
沒甚麼/有些/沒有價值. **2** *nu* worth of
something in money (金錢) 價值; 價
格: *What is the value of your house?*
你的房子的價值是多少? *Gold has re-
cently increased in value*. 黃金價格最
近上漲了. *In this shop you get good
value for your money*. 在這個商店,
(你的)錢花得很值得. *Note* 說明: because *value* has the sense of what
something is considered to be worth,
it does not always have the same
sense as the actual cost or price (e.g.
*Although I paid only fifty pence for
this book, its value is much higher.
The new bridge cost £100,000 but its
value to the people who live near it is
doubtful*. 雖然value表示某物被認爲値
得的價值, 但並不總是表示實際的價值
或價格(如: *Although I paid only fifty
pence for this book, its value is much
higher*. 我雖然只花50便士買這本書,但
其價值要高得多. *The new bridge cost
£100,000 but its value to the people
who live near it is doubtful*. 新橋樑花
費100,000英鎊,但對其附近的人們的價
值卻是令人懷疑). **3** *nc* (in *pl*) rules
or standards; beliefs (用於複數) 價値
標準; 價值觀念: *People behave in certain ways because of their social

values. 人們的社會價值標準決定其行爲方式. Also 亦作 *vt* 1 think important; have great respect for 重視; 尊重: *I value his opinions*. 我尊重他的意見. 2 estimate the value of something in money 估 … 的價格: *He valued the diamond ring at £100*. 他估計這鑽石戒指價值100英鎊. **valuable** *adj* of great value 很有價值的, 值錢的, 貴重的. Also 亦作 *nc* (in *pl*) things which are valuable (e.g. jewels) (用於複數) 值錢的東西 (如: 寶石). **valueless** *adj* having no value 無價值的, 無用的. **valuation** [ˌvælju'eiʃən] 1 *nu* act of valuing 評價, 估價: *experienced in the valuation of paintings* 對評價繪畫有經驗的. 2 *nc* value given to something (esp. by a **valuer**) (尤指由估價者) 估定的價值: *get a valuation for one's house*. 估價自己的房子. **valuer** *nc* person who is skilled in valuing 估價者, 評價者.

valve [vælv] *nc* 1 device which opens and closes to allow gas or liquid to flow in one direction only; part of heart or blood vessel which allows blood to flow in one direction only (控制煤氣或液體流動的) 閥, 活閥 (心臟或血管的) 瓣, 瓣膜. 2 (*Brit*) closed glass tube in which a vacuum has been made, used in radios etc. (英) 真空管, 電子管. (*US* see **tube**).

vampire ['væmpaiə*] *nc* spirit of a dead person believed to suck the blood of living persons while they are asleep 吸血鬼 (迷信所說死人的鬼魂吸食睡眠者的血).

van[1] [væn] *nc* (*Brit*) covered cart, lorry or railway truck used for carrying goods. (英) 有頂蓋的運貨馬 (牛) 車; 運貨汽車; 有頂蓋的鐵路貨車.

van[2] [væn] *nu* 1 leading part of an army or fleet 先頭部隊; 前驅艦隊; 前衛. 2

leaders of any movement or advance (運動或行進的) 領袖, 領導者, 前驅, 先鋒 **vanguard** 1 troops who go ahead of an army to protect it 先頭部隊; 前衛. 2 leading part 先鋒; 前驅; 前導: *in the vanguard of public opinion* 在引導輿論的前列.

vandal ['vændl] *nc* person who damages or destroys something attractive or useful without reason (美妙或有用東西尤指文化藝術的) 摧殘者, 破壞者. **vandalism** *nu* act or behaviour of a vandal (對美妙或有用東西尤指文化藝術的) 故意破壞 (行爲). **vandalize** *vt* destroy or damage for fun or out of spite (爲嬉鬧或出於惡意而) 破壞, 摧殘: *The empty house had been vandalized by a gang of boys*. 這座空房子被一幫男孩故意破壞了.

vane [vein] *nc* 1 piece of metal, or some other device, fixed upon a spire or other high object in such a way as to move with the wind and indicate its direction; weather vane; weather cock 風向標. 2 blade of a windmill, fan, etc. (風車, 風扇等的) 翼; 葉片; 輪葉.

vanilla [və'nilə] 1 *nc* type of plant 香草. 2 *nu* substance obtained from this plant used to flavour food and drink 香草香精. Also 亦作 *adj*: *vanilla ice cream* 香草冰淇淋.

vanish ['væniʃ] *vi* no longer be seen or felt; go out of sight 消散, 消失; 消失不見.

vanity ['væniti] *nu* see **vain**.

vanquish ['væŋkwiʃ] *vt* conquer; defeat; overcome; suppress 征服; 戰勝; 克服; 抑制: *vanquish all enemies* 戰勝一切敵人; *vanquish fear* 克服恐懼心理.

vantage ['vɑːntidʒ] *nu* better chance; advantage 較好機會; 優勢: *The hill was a good vantage point to watch* *the soldiers passing.* 這座山是個有利地勢，可以觀望士兵走過．

vapour ['veipə*] (*US* 美 **vapor**) *nu* substance in a cloudy form (e.g. fog, mist, smoke, steam) (如：霧、靄、烟、汽，水蒸汽)． **vaporize** *vt / i* become, cause to become, vapour (使)蒸發，(使)汽化． **vaporization** [veipərai'zeiʃən] *nu*.

variable ['veəriəbl] *adj* able to change or be changed; not steady or reliable 可變的；易變的；不穩定的；不可靠的：*variable winds* 方向不定的風；*a variable quantity* 不定量，可變量． (*opp* 反義詞 **invariable**)．

variant ['veəriənt] *adj* different 不同的． Also 亦作 *nc* different form (esp. with reference to spellings of one word e.g. *gray* and *grey*) 不同的形式，替換的形式 (尤指詞的拼寫法，如 gray 和 grey)．

variance *nu* difference which causes argument; disagreement 意見不同，分歧；爭論；不和：*He has been at variance with his parents for years.* 他多年來一直與父母不和．

variation [veəri'eiʃən] *nc / u* see 見 **vary**.

varicose ['værikous] *adj* (with reference to veins of the body esp. of the leg) swollen (指靜脈，尤指腿的靜脈)曲張的，腫大的．

varied ['veərid] *adj* see 見 **vary**.

variegate ['veərigeit] *vt* **1** mark, spot or streak with different colours 使成雜色；使斑駁． **2** give variety to 使多樣化．

variegated ['veərigeitid] *adj* **1** marked with patches or spots of different colours; many-coloured 雜色的，斑駁的：*The flowers of pansies are usually variegated.* 紫羅蘭的花通常是雜色的． **2** having variety 多樣化的．

variety [və'raiəti] **1** *nu* state of changing

from time to time, of not always being the same 多變化，多變性，多樣性；變化：*Life at school has plenty of variety.* 學校的生活豐富多彩．*Variety is the spice of life.* 多樣化是生活的調味品． **2** *nu* group of different things 若干不同的事物，種種：*The shop sells a variety of goods.* 商店出售種種貨物．*She went through an amazing variety of different moods.* 她有過種種不同的心情，真是令人驚異． **3** *nc* type which is different from the larger group to which it belongs 變種，異種，種類：*There are several varieties of red roses.* 紅玫瑰有好些不同種類． **4** *nu* (*Brit*) type of entertainment which is a mixture of dancing, singing, acting etc. (英) 雜耍，綜藝節目． Also 亦作 *adj*: *variety show* 雜耍演出；*variety theatre* 雜耍劇場． (*US* 美 **vaudeville**)．

various ['veəriəs] *adj* see 見 **vary**.

varnish ['vɑːniʃ] *nc / u* type of liquid which when dry gives a hard, shining surface to wood, metal etc. 清漆，罩光漆，油漆，凡立水． Also 亦作 *vt* put varnish on 給……塗清漆．

vary ['veəri] *vt / i* change, cause to change; be, cause to be, different (使)改變；變更；修改(使)不同：*Temperatures vary from day to day.* 溫度每天都在變化．*You should vary your lessons to make them more interesting.* 你必須改變你的課程，使之更加有趣．*What's the weather like? It varies.* 天氣如何？常有變化． **variation** [veəri'eiʃən] *nc / u* extent to which something varies; act of varying 變量；變度；偏差；變化，變異：*variations between day and night temperatures* 日夜的溫差．*There are many variations of this story.* 本故事有許多變化．

varied *adj* **1** having many changes 多

變化的: *a varied life* 多變化的生活. **2** of different types; mixed. 各種不同的; 各式各樣的; 雜色的: *The news we get is very varied.* 我們收到的消息是各式各樣的. (*opp* 反義詞 **unvaried**). **various** *adj* different; several 不同的; 幾個的: *I went there at various times.* 我去那裏好幾次了. *He has various excuses for being late.* 他為遲到找了各種各樣的藉口.

vascular ['væskjulə] *adj* of, made up of, containing vessels or ducts through which blood or sap flows 脈管的; 血管的; 導管的; 血管形成的; 含有脈管的: *vascular net* 血管網; *vascular tissue* 脈管組織.

vase [vɑːz] *nc* container for flowers (usu. made of glass or pottery) 花瓶 (通常用玻璃或陶瓷製成).

vaseline ['væsəliːn] ® *nu* type of ointment made from petroleum; petroleum jelly 凡士林; 石油凍, 礦脂.

vassal ['væsəl] *nc* **1** person in the feudal system who held land in return for loyalty, military help, etc to an overlord; tenant in fee (封建時代的) 諸侯; 封臣; 家臣. **2** subordinate; servant; slave 附庸; 部屬; 奴僕; 奴隸.

vast [vɑːst] *adj* very large 巨大的; 廣大的; 遼闊的; 浩瀚的. **vastly** *adv* **vastness** *nu*.

vat [væt] *nc* type of large container for holding liquids 大桶, 大缸.

vaudeville ['vɔːdəvil] *nu* (US) variety show (美) 雜耍演出.

vault¹ [vɔːlt] *nc* **1** arched roof 拱形圓屋頂, 拱頂. **2** underground room; cellar (esp. for keeping wine or money or for burying the dead) 地下室; 地窖 (尤指供存放酒, 金錢或埋葬死人).

vault² [vɔːlt] *vt/i* jump with one or two hands placed on something (以手撐物) 跳躍: *He vaulted over the gate.* 他

跳過門. Also 亦作 *nc* jump made in this way 跳躍; 撐身跳躍; 撐竿跳.

veal [viːl] *nu* meat of a calf (食用的) 小牛肉.

vector ['vektə] *nc* **1** (mathematics) quantity, such as a force or velocity, which has both force and magnitude and which can be represented by a straight line, such as an arrow (數學) 矢量, 向量. **2** mosquito or other organism that transmits disease germs 傳染病媒介 (如蚊子等). **3** course of an aircraft 飛機航線.

veer [viə*] *vi* turn; (esp. with reference to the wind) change direction. 轉變; (尤指風) 轉向.

vegetable ['vedʒitəbl] *adj* of or from plants 植物的; 由植物得來的: *vegetable oil* 植物油. Also 亦作 *nc* plant used for food (e.g. bean, cabbage, potato etc.) 蔬菜(如: 豆, 捲心菜, 馬鈴薯等). **vegetarian** [vedʒi'tɛəriən] *nc* person who does not eat meat 吃素的人; 素食者, 蔬食者.

vegetate ['vedʒiteit] *vi* **1** grow as a plant does 植物似地生長. **2** live an idle, uninteresting life 過散板乏味的生活, 過單調的生活. **vegetation** [vedʒi'teiʃən] *nu* plants in general (泛指一般的) 植物, 草木: *Deserts have very little vegetation.* 沙漠幾乎沒有植物.

vehement ['viəmənt] *adj* (with reference to a person or his behaviour) having great force or strong feelings (指人或其行為) 強烈的, 猛烈的, 感情激烈的, 熱烈的: *He made a vehement speech about drugs.* 他就毒品問題發表了感情激烈的講話. **vehemence** *nu*.

vehicle ['viəkl] *nc* something (usu. with wheels) for carrying person or goods (e.g. car, cart, lorry or truck) 運載工具 (通常有輪子, 如: 車, 馬車, 貨車或卡車). **vehicular** [vi'hikjulə*] *adj*:

vehicular traffic 車輛交通.

veil [veil] *nc* 1 thin piece of cloth used to cover a woman's face and／or head (婦女的) 面紗, 面罩; 頭巾. 2 any cover or disguise 遮蔽物; 掩飾物; 假託, 藉口: *There is a veil of secrecy over their plans.* 一股神秘的氣氛掩蓋着他們的計劃. Also 亦作 *vt* cover with a veil; hide 用面紗掩飾; 掩飾; 遮蔽; 隱蔽: *She veiled her face when the stranger entered the room.* 陌生人入房間時, 她蒙着面紗. *The hills are veiled in mist.* 羣山被霧籠罩着.

vein [vein] *nc* 1 blood vessel which carries blood back to the heart from the rest of the body 靜脈; 血管. 2 line or layer of different material or colour appearing like a vein in something 脈; (不同顏色的) 紋理: *a vein of gold in rock* 石頭內的金礦脈; *the veins in a leaf* 葉脈.

velocity [vi'lɔsiti] *nu* speed 速度; 速率: *the velocity of light* 光的速度.

velvet ['velvit] *nu* type of soft, thick cloth made from silk, cotton, nylon etc. 天鵝絨. Also 亦作 *adj* 1 made of velvet 天鵝絨製的. 2 soft like velvet 天鵝絨似的; 柔軟的. **velvety** *adj* soft like velvet 天鵝絨般柔軟的: *velvety skin* 光滑柔軟的皮膚.

vendetta [ven'detə] *nc* fierce quarrel between families during which members are murdered in revenge; any long, fierce quarrel 家族間的宿怨, 仇殺, 血仇; 深仇, 長年的爭鬥.

vendor ['vendə*] *nc* person who sells something 小販; 賣主: *newsvendor* i.e. person who sells newspapers 報販.

veneer [vi'niə*] *nc／u* 1 thin layer of valuable wood fixed to the surface of cheap wood 黏在廉價木材上的上等木材薄板, 鑲面板. 2 outward appearance which hides something bad beneath (掩蓋醜陋的) 外表, 外飾; 虛飾: *Although he has a veneer of honesty, he is not to be trusted.* 他雖顯得老實, 但不能信賴.

venerate ['venəreit] *vt* admire or respect greatly 崇拜; 尊敬. **veneration** *nu* **venerable** ['venərəbl] *adj* deserving to be venerated (esp. because of age or long experience) 可尊敬的, 可崇敬的.(尤指因年高歷深).

venereal [vi'niəriəl] *adj* caused or spread by sexual acts 因性交而引起或傳染的: *venereal disease* 性病, 花柳病.

Venetian [vi'ni:ʃən] *adj* of Venice 威尼斯的. **venetian blind** type of blind made of thin horizontal pieces of plastic etc which can be moved to allow air and light to pass through 軟百葉簾, 活動百葉簾.

vengeance ['vendʒəns] *nu* act of causing somebody pain or loss in return for a wrong he has done; revenge 報仇; 復仇; 報復. **vengeful** ['vendʒful] *adj* wishing to take vengeance 想報仇的; 謀報復的. **vengefulness** *nu*.

venison ['venisn] *nu* meat of a deer 鹿肉.

venom ['venəm] *nu* 1 poison (esp. that produced by a snake) (尤指蛇的) 毒液. 2 spite; malice 惡意; 怨恨; 惡毒. **venomous** *adj*.

vent [vent] 1 *nc* small hole or outlet for air, smoke etc. (e.g. in a barrel or fireplace) (大桶, 壁爐等供空氣, 烟等進出的) 孔, 口; 通風孔, 烟道, 排氣孔. 2 *nu* expression of an emotion (感情的) 發洩, 吐露: *He gave vent to his anger by striking the boy.* 他打孩子出氣. 3 *nc* opening in the back of a coat or jacket 上衣背部的開口. Also 亦作 *vt* express an emotion 發洩 (情感): *He vented his anger on the boy.* 他把怒氣

發洩在孩子身上.

ventilate ['ventileit] *vt* cause fresh air to enter 使通風, 使通氣: *He opened the window to ventilate the room.* 他打開窗戶, 使房間通風. **ventilation** [venti'leiʃən] *nu* **ventilator** *nc* device which ventilates 通風設備.

ventricle ['ventrikl] *nc* **1** either of the two lower chambers of the heart 心室: *left / right ventricle of the heart* 左/右心室. **2** small cavity in the brain (腦)室: *ventricles of the brain* 腦室.

ventriloquism [ven'trilәkwizәm] *nu* art of speaking which makes it appear that the sound comes not from the speaker but from somebody / something else 口技 (使語音聽起來不是發自說話者, 而似發自他人或他物). **ventriloquist** *nc* person skilled in this art 口技表演者.

venture ['ventʃә*] *nc / u* something which is risky or dangerous to do 冒險, 冒險行動; 冒險事業; 投機. Also 亦作 *vt / i* **1** do something of this kind 冒險: *They should not venture on the river in such a small boat.* 他們不應該乘這麼小的船在河上冒險. **2** dare; go so far as 敢於; 膽敢, 竟敢: *I venture to suggest that you are wrong.* 我冒昧地說, 你是錯的.

venue ['venju:] *nc* place where an event (e.g. a sports meeting) happens (犯罪或審判)地點; 現場; 集合地點, 聚會地點 (如: 運動會).

veranda, verandah [vә'rændә] *nc* passage with a roof along the side of a house (usu. open on one side) 遊廊; 走廊; 陽台.

verb [vә:b] *nc* word or words which tell what somebody / something does or is (e.g. in the sentence *The man bought the house,* bought is *a* verb) 動詞(如: The man bought the house

這句中, bought是動詞). **verbal** *adj* **1** of a verb 動詞的: *verbal noun* (e.g. in *smoking is dangerous, smoking* is a *verbal noun*) 動名詞(如: Smoking is dangerous這句中, smoking是動名詞). **2** spoken not written 口頭的: *verbal promise* 口頭答應. **verbally** *adv* in spoken not written words 口頭上: *He reported to me verbally.* 他向我口頭彙報.

verbatim [vә:'beitim] *adj / adv* word for word; using exactly the same words 逐字的(地); 完全照字面的(地): *a verbatim report of his speech* 逐字地報導他的演說.

verbose [vә:'bous] *adj* using more words than are necessary (措詞) 囉嗦; (說話) 嘮叨的; 冗長的. **verboseness, verbosity** [vә:'bositi] *nu.*

verdict ['vә:dikt] *nc* decision or judgment made after the evidence (esp. by a jury in a court of law) (尤指法庭陪審團的) 評決, 裁決; 判斷; 決定. *The verdict of the jury is that you are guilty.* 陪審團裁決你有罪.

verge [vә:dʒ] *nc* edge; border (esp. the grass edge at the side of a road or bed of flowers) 邊; 邊緣(尤指路邊草或花壇的圍邊草). Also 亦作 *vt* (with **on** or **upon**) come near the edge of; be very close to 接近; 瀕於: *His behaviour verges on madness.* 他的行爲近於發瘋. **be on the verge of** be very close to; be about to 瀕於; 行將: *He was on the verge of telling him the truth.* 他差點兒告訴他真相.

verger ['vә:dʒә*] *nc* person who leads people to their seats in church and acts as caretaker of the church 教堂的司事; 堂守.

verify ['verifai] *vt* **1** test whether something is correct or not 檢驗, 核實; 驗

證. *I looked up the word in a dictionary to verify its spelling.* 我在詞典裏查找了這個詞，以核查其拼寫. **2** show that something is correct; prove 證實; 證明: *Everything he said then was verified by what happened later.* 他所說的話已由後來所發生的事證實了.

verification [verifi'keiʃən] *nc / u* act of verifying or being verified; proof 核對; 驗證; 核實; 證實, 證明; 證據.

verifiable *adj* able to be verified 可檢驗的, 可核實的; 可證實的; 可考證的.

vermilion, vermillion [və'miljən] *n* **1** bright red pigment 硃砂. **2** bright red or scarlet 朱紅色. Also 亦作 *adj* of the colour vermilion 朱紅色的. Also 亦作 *vt* colour or paint with vermilion 塗朱紅色.

vermin ['və:min] *nu / npl* insects or small animals or birds which do damage or harm 害蟲; 害獸; 害鳥.

vernacular [və'nækjulə*] *adj* local language or dialect 本國語的; 方言的, 本地話的土話的; 口語的: *the vernacular press* 當地語報刊. Also 亦作 *nc*: *textbooks written in the vernacular* 用本國語寫的課本.

versatile ['və:sətail] *adj* able to do many different things well 有多方面才能的, 多才多藝的. **versatility** [və:sə'tiliti] *nu*.

verse [və:s] **1** *nu* arrangement of words in lines according to a pattern; poetry 韻文; 詩, 詩歌. (*opp* 反義詞 **prose**). **2** *nc* group of lines or one line of this kind 詩節; 詩句: *This poem has four verses.* 這首詩有四個詩節. **3** *nc* short, numbered part of a chapter of the Bible (聖經的) 節. **versed** *adj* (with in) skilled or experienced in some subject (與in連用) 精通的; 熟練的.

version ['və:ʃən] *nc* description from one particular point of view (根據某一觀點的) 描述, 叙述: *John's version of the accident is different from mine.* 約翰對事故的叙述與我的叙述不同.

versus ['və:səs] *prep* (esp. sport and legal) against (often in short form v or vs) (尤指運動和法律的) 對, 對抗 (常略作v或vs): *England v Italy* 英格蘭對意大利.

vertebra ['və:tibrə] *nc* one of the bones in the backbone 脊骨, 脊椎骨. *pl* 複數 **vertebrae** ['və:tibrei]. **vertebrate** ['və:tibrit] *adj* having a backbone 有脊椎骨的. Also 亦作 *nc* animal with a backbone 脊椎動物 (*opp* 反義詞 **invertebrate**).

vertex ['və:teks] *nc* **1** highest point of something; top 頂, 頂點: *the vertex of a hill* 山的頂點. **2** (anatomy) top or crown of the head (解剖) 頭頂. **3** (astronomy) point in the heavens directly overhead; zenith (天文) 天頂. **4** (mathematics) point opposite to and farthest from the base of a triangle, pyramid, or other figure having a base; point where the two sides of an angle meet (數學) (三角形、角椎形等與底線相對的) 頂點; 角頂: *vertex angle* 頂角; *vertex of a cone* 椎頂; *vertex of a triangle* 三角形的頂點.

vertical ['və:tikl] *adj* straight up and down, perpendicular 垂直的, 直立的, 豎式的: *The walls of a room are vertical, the floor horizontal.* 房間的牆是垂直的, 地板是水平的. (*opp* 反義詞 **horizontal**). **vertically** *adv*.

vertices ['və:tisi:z] *pl* of **vertex.** vertex 的複數.

vertigo ['və:tigou] *nu* dizziness; giddiness 眩暈; 頭暈.

verve [və:v] *nu* energy; enthusiasm 活力; 生氣; 熱情.

very ['veri] *adj / adv / intensifier* **1** used to make stronger or emphasize the *adj* or *adv* which follows 用於形容詞或副詞之前，以加強語氣或強調: *It is very cold today.* 今天很冷. *He drives very slowly.* 他開車開得很慢. *This is the very best way to do it.* 這是做此事的最佳辦法. *She looked very annoyed.* 她看起來很生氣. *I'm feeling very much better today.* 今天我覺得好多了. *The lecture was not very interesting.* 講課不大有趣. Also before own 亦用於 own 之前. *It is good to have a house of our very own.* 有我們自己的房子，那就好了. **2** this and no other; actual 這正是: 恰好: *You are the very man I want to speak to.* 你正是我所要談話的人. *The very thought of going frightens me.* 一想到要去，我就害怕. **3** used to make stronger or emphasize the noun which follows 用於名詞之前，以加強語氣或強調: *the very beginning / middle / end* 最開始/正中間/剛好結束.

vespers ['vespəz] *nu* evening service in a church 晚間禮拜, 晚禱.

vessel ['vesl] *nc* **1** container (esp. for liquids) (尤指供裝液體的桶, 鉢, 杯等) 容器, 器皿. **2** large ship 船, 艦.

vest¹ [vest] *nc* **1** (*Brit*) garment worn next to the skin on the upper part of the body (英) 汗衫; 內衣. (*US 美* **undershirt**). **2** (*US*) short garment fastened with buttons up the front but without sleeves, worn beneath a jacket (美) 馬甲, 背心. (*Brit 英* **waistcoat**).

vest² [vest] *vt* (with **in** or **with**) give the right to use (與 in 或 with 連用) 給予, 授予, 賦予(某人使用某權利): *The government has vested great powers in the Minister of Agriculture.* 政府已把大權授予農業部長. *The government has vested the Minister of Agriculture with great powers.* 政府已授予農業部

長很大的權力. **vested interests 1** interests which are recognized by law and cannot be taken away 既得利益. **2** (sometimes *sing*) selfish interest 自私利益: *Those employers have a vested interest in keeping workers' wages low.* 那些雇主們壓低工人的工資, 這有其私利.

vestibule ['vestibju:l] *nc* small room between an outer and an inner door 前廳, 門廳.

vestige ['vestidʒ] *nc* mark or sign left by something that once existed; trace 遺跡; 形跡; 痕跡.

vestry ['vestri] *nc* room in a church, used by a priest etc for dressing in (教堂的)祭服室, 祭器室; 教士更衣室.

vet¹ [vet] *nc* short informal form of **veterinary surgeon** veterinary surgeon 的非正式縮略式.

vet² [vet] *vt* inspect a plan, proposal etc before giving offical approval to it 細心檢查, 調查. *past* 過去式和過去分詞 **vetted**. (*informal*) (非正式).

veteran ['vetərn] *nc* person who has served a long time (esp. in the armed forces) 資深者, 老手, 老練者(尤指軍隊的老兵). Also 亦作 *adj*: *a veteran soldier* 老兵; *a veteran car* i.e. one built before 1919 老式車, 老爺車, 即: 1919年前製造的車.

veterinary ['vetərinəri] *adj* concerned with diseases of animals 獸醫的, 有關家畜之疾病的. **veterinary surgeon** (*Brit*) person skilled in treating these diseases (informally shortened to **vet**). (英) 獸醫(非正式縮略為vet). (*US 美* **veterinarian** [vetiri'nɛəriən]).

veto ['vi:tou] *nc* power or right to forbid something (esp. the passing of a law, a resolution of UNO etc.) 否決; 禁止; 否決權(尤指否決一項法令, 聯合國某決議等): *Which countries have the veto?*

pl 複數 **vetoes.** Also 亦作 *vt* forbid 禁止, 否決: *The plan was vetoed by two members.* 這項計劃遭到兩名成員的否決.

vex [veks] *vt* make angry; trouble 使惱怒; 使苦惱, 使煩惱.

via ['vaiə] *prep* by way of 經由, 途經, 取道: *He went to New York via Rome.* 他取道羅馬到紐約.

viable ['vaiəbl] *adj* able to exist or develop 能生存的; 能生長發育的; 行得通的: *The economy of the country is not viable.* 這個國家的經濟是行不通的. **viability** [vaiə'biliti] *nu.*

viaduct ['vaiədʌkt] *nc* high bridge carrying a road or railway over a valley 高架橋, 跨線橋, 旱橋.

vibrate [vai'breit] *vt / i* 1 move, cause to move, very quickly from side to side or up and down (使)顫動; (使)振動; (使)震動; (使)擺動: *The skin of a drum vibrates when it is struck.* 鼓面受擊時就會顫動. 2 make a throbbing sound 使發出顫動聲: *The speaker's voice vibrated with emotion.* 講演人的聲音激動得顫抖了. **vibration** *nc / u* **vibrant** ['vaibrnt], **vibrating** *adj.*

vicar ['vikə*] *nc* priest of the Church of England in charge of a parish (英國國教的)教區牧師. **vicarage** *nc* house where a vicar lives 教區牧師的住宅.

vice¹ [vais] *nc / u* wicked behaviour; bad habit 惡行, 不道德行為; 壞習慣: *Gambling and drunkenness are vices.* 賭博和酗酒都是惡習. *He descended to a life of vice.* 他墮落了, 過着邪惡的生活. **vicious** ['viʃəs] *adj* 1 wicked 邪惡的: *He has vicious habits.* 他有許多惡習. 2 spiteful; intending to harm 惡意的; 惡毒的; 有意傷害的: *He gave me a vicious look.* 他惡狠狠地看了我一眼. *This dog has a really vicious bite.* 這條狗咬人真兇狠. **viciously**

adv **viciousness** *nu* **vicious circle** state in which one bad thing produces another which in turn produces the first bad thing again (e.g. poverty causes poor health and poor health then causes more poverty) 惡性循環 (如: 貧困致體弱, 而體弱又致更加貧困).

vice² [vais] *nc* tool which holds firmly a piece of wood or metal etc between two jaws moved by a screw 老虎鉗.

vice-³ [vais] *prefix* acting in place of; second in rank to (e.g. **vice-president; vice-principal**) 代理; 副, 次 (如: vice-president 副總統; vice-principal 副校長).

viceroy ['vaisrɔi] *nc* person ruling a country, colony, or province as the deputy of the sovereign (代表國王或統治者管轄一個國家, 殖民地或行省的)總督: *The Viceroy of India* 印度總督.

vice versa ['vaisə'və:sə] *adv* the other way round 反過來 (也是這樣): *You sent my letter to John, and vice versa* 你也送John's letter to me. 你把我的信送給約翰, 反過來也是這樣. 即: 你也把約翰的信送給我.

vicinity [vi'siniti] *nu* nearness; neighbourhood 附近; 近處; 鄰近. *Is there a hospital in the vicinity?* 附近有沒有醫院?

victim ['viktim] *nc* person who suffers because of the actions of others or because of bad luck, illness etc. 受害者, 罹難者, 受災者, 犧牲者: *They were the victims of a railway accident.* 他們是火車事故的受害者. **victimize** *vt* make a victim of; cause to suffer 使受害, 使犧牲, 使受苦, 使受難. **victimization** [viktimai'zeiʃən] *nu.*

victor ['viktə*] *nc* person who defeats an enemy in battle; person who wins

戰勝者, 勝利者. **victory** *nc / u* defeat of an enemy in battle; success 戰勝; 勝利, 成功: *The general gained / won a victory over the army of the enemy.* 將軍戰勝了敵軍而贏得了勝利. **victorious** [vik'tɔ:riəs] *adj*: *The general was victorious* 將軍勝利了.

Victorian [vik'tɔ:riən] *n* person who lived during the reign of Queen Victoria (1837-1901) 維多利亞女王時代 (1837-1901) 的人. Also 亦作 *adj* of, during that reign 維多利亞女王時代的.

video ['vidiou] *nu (US)* television (美) 電視. **'video tape** special magnetic tape which records television pictures 電視錄影帶, 錄像帶.

vie [vai] *vt* (with **with**) try to do better than somebody else; compete (與**with** 連用) 爭取勝過別人; 爭, 競爭: *They vied with each other in wealth.* 他們在財富方面互相競爭. *pres part* 現在分詞 **vying**. *past* 過去式和過去分詞 **vied.**

view [vju:] **1** *nu* act or power of seeing 看; 視力: *The house was hidden from our view by trees.* 樹林擋住了我們的視線, 使我們看不見那房子. *They climbed the hill to get a good view of the country.* 他們爬上了山, 鄉村的景色盡收眼底. **2** *nc* something which can be seen (esp. from a distance) (尤指從遠處看的) 景色, 風景: *The view from the front of his house is lovely.* 從他房子前面往外看, 景色很美. **3** *nc* way of looking at something; opinion 看法; 觀點, 意見: *In my view he is wrong.* 依我看, 他是錯誤的. *What are your views about the present situation?* 你對目前形勢的看法如何? **4** *nc* aim; purpose 目標; 目的: *He is studying with a view to going to university.* 爲了上大學, 他正在學習.

Also 亦作 *vt* look at; consider 看; 考慮. *We can view the problem in many ways.* 我們可以從多方面來考慮這個問題. **viewer** *nc* **1** person who views (esp. one who watches television) (尤指看電視) 觀衆. **2** small device with a light for looking at photographic transparencies 看底片的設備. **'view-finder** device in a camera which shows what will be in the picture if taken (照相機的) 觀景鏡, 檢像鏡. **'viewpoint 1** place from which something is viewed 觀察點, 視點. **2** opinion about some problem (看法) (point of view in sense 2) 觀點, 看法, 見解 (義2亦作 point of view). **in view of** because of 鑑於, 考慮到; 由於. **in full view of** able to be seen completely 完全被看到: *The teacher fell down in full view of the boys in his class.* 老師跌倒了, 班上的男生全看到. **on view** so as to be seen; open to inspection 展示中, 展覽着, 陳列中: *The handwork of the pupils is on view to the parents.* 小學生的手工藝品正在展示給家長看.

vigil ['vidʒil] *nc / u* act of staying awake at a time when one usually sleeps 守夜, 值夜; 徹夜不眠. **vigilant** *adj* awake and watchful; ready for any danger 警戒着的; 警惕着的. **vigilance** *nu.*

vigour ['vigə*] *(US* 美 **vigor)** *nu* energy; strength 精力; 力量. **vigorous** *adj* **vigorously** *adv.*

vile [vail] *adj* **1** disgusting 卑鄙的, 令人厭惡的. **2** bad 壞的: *He was in a vile temper. (informal* in sense 2) 他那時脾氣不好. (義2爲非正式)

villa ['vilə] *nc* large house with its own garden 別墅.

village ['vilidʒ] *nc* group of houses and shops etc smaller than a town 鄉村,

村莊. Also 亦作 *adj*: *the village church* 鄉村教堂. **villager** *nc* person who lives in a village 村民.

villain ['vilən] *nc* wicked person; rogue 壞人; 惡棍; 歹徒.

vindicate ['vindikeit] *vt* prove to be true or correct; justify 證實, 辨明, 辯護; *I always said that he would be a brilliant writer and his latest book has vindicated my judgment.* 我過去常說過, 他會成為一位卓越的作家, 如今他最近的一本書已證實了我的判斷. **vindication** [vindi'keiʃən] *nc / u* act of vindicating or being vindicated; defence of an act, statement etc. 證實, 辨明, 辯護: *There was no vindication for their outrageous behaviour.* 無法爲他們的暴行辯護.

vindictive [vin'diktiv] *adj* wanting revenge; spiteful 報復性的, 懷恨的.

vine [vain] *nc* type of climbing plant (esp. one on which grapes grow) 蔓生植物, 藤蔓植物 (尤 指 葡 萄 藤). **vineyard** ['vinjɑ:d] piece of land where vines are grown 葡萄園.

vinegar ['vinigə*] *nu* type of weak acid made from beer, wine etc. and used to flavour or preserve food 醋.

vintage ['vintidʒ] **1** *nu* time of year when grapes are gathered to make wine 葡萄收穫期. **2** *nc* wine made in a particular year 由某一年產的葡萄所釀的酒: *Last year's vintage is not yet ready for drinking.* 去年釀的葡萄酒還不能喝. Also 亦作 *adj* made in a good year or a period in the past 在著名年份或過去製造的: *This is a vintage wine* 這是佳釀酒; *a vintage car* 老式的名貴汽車.

vinyl ['vainl] *nu* type of plastic often used for making floor covering 常用於覆蓋地板的塑膠板; 乙烯基.

viola [vi'oulə] *nc* type of stringed

musical instrument larger than a violin 中提琴.

violate ['vaiəleit] *vt* **1** break a promise or treaty 違犯, 違背, 違反. **2** disturb; interrupt rudely 擾亂; 妨礙; 侵犯. **3** rape 強姦. **violation** [vaiə'leiʃən] *nc / u* act of violating or being violated 違犯, 違背, 違反; 擾亂; 妨礙; 侵犯; 強姦.

violent ['vaiələnt] *adj* **1** having great force; powerful 猛烈的; 激烈的; 強烈的: *a violent storm* 狂風暴雨; *a violent blow on the head* 頭上猛烈一擊; *a violent speech* 激烈的講話. **2** caused by great force or an attack 由暴力或攻擊引起的: *Many political leaders have met violent deaths* i.e. they have not died naturally. 許多政治領導人遭到橫死. 即: 不是自然死去. **3** severe 厲害的; 劇烈的: *a violent pain* 劇烈的疼痛. **violence** *nu* state of being violent; violent behaviour 猛烈; 激烈; 強烈; 劇烈; 暴力; 暴行: *the violence of the wind* 風的狂暴. *death by violence* 橫死.

violet ['vaiəlit] **1** *nc* type of very small flower (usu. blue or purple) 紫羅蘭. **2** *nu* blue or purple colour 藍紫色的. Also 亦作 *adj*.

violin [vaiə'lin] *nc* type of stringed musical instrument played with a bow 小提琴. **violinist** *nc* person who plays a violin 小提琴手.

viper ['vaipə*] *nc* type of poisonous snake 蝰蛇, 毒蛇. see 見 **adder.**

virgin ['və:dʒin] *nc* person (esp. a girl or woman) who has not had sexual relations with a member of the opposite sex 處女. Also 亦作 *adj* **1** without sexual experience; pure 無性經驗的, 處女的; 純潔的: *virgin land* i.e. land which has not yet been used by man 處女地, 即: 人類尚未使用過的土地. **virgin-**

ity [vəˈdʒiniti] *nu* state of being virgin 處女的狀態, 童貞; 純潔.

virile [ˈvirail] *adj* of a man; strong; vigorous 男子的; 強有力的; 精力充沛的. **virility** [viˈriliti] *nu*.

virtual [ˈvəːtjuəl] *adj* being something in fact, although it is not openly admitted 事實上的, 實際上的(雖未公開得到承認): *Because the government was weak, the army became the virtual ruler of the country.* 因為政府虛弱, 軍隊實際上統治了國家. **virtually** *adv*.

virtue [ˈvəːtjuː] *nc / u* goodness of character; good quality; excellence. 善品德; 美德; 優點, 長處; 節操: *Honesty is a great virtue.* 誠實是一種美德. *One of his virtues is that he never gets angry.* 他的一個優點是: 他從來不生氣. **virtuous** *adj* **by / in virtue of** because of 因為.

virtuoso [vəːtjuˈouzou] *nc* person who is very skilled in, or has great knowledge of, one of the arts (e.g. music) 藝術上的名家, 藝術大師(如: 音樂演奏大師); 演藝精湛的人. *pl* 複數 **virtuosos**. **virtuosity** [vəːtjuˈositi] *nu* great skill in one of the arts (某項藝術的)精湛技巧.

virulent [ˈvirjulnt] *adj* 1 very poisonous; deadly 劇毒的; 致命的: *a virulent disease* 致命的病. 2 (with reference to feelings etc.) full of hate; bitter (指情緒等)仇恨的; 刻毒的: *He made a virulent speech against the government.* 他發表了一次對政府充滿仇恨的講話.

virus [ˈvaiərəs] *nc* very small thing which spreads certain diseases 病毒, 過濾性病原體. *pl* 複數 **viruses**.

visa [ˈviːzə] *nc* official stamp put on a passport to allow its owner to enter or leave a foreign country 簽證: *entrance visa* 入境簽證; *exit visa* 出境簽

證. *pl* 複數 **visas.**

viscose [ˈviskous] *nu* thick, sticky substance used in manufacturing rayon and cellophane, and for other purposes 黏膠; 黏膠液; 黏膠纖維(製造人造絲、賽璐玢等的原料). Also 亦作 *adj* having to do with or made from viscose 黏性的; 黏膠的; 黏膠製的.

viscount [ˈvaikaunt] *nc* title of nobility lower in rank than an earl 子爵. **viscountess** [ˈvaikauntis] *nc* wife of a viscount 子爵夫人.

viscous [ˈviskəs] *adj* (usu. with reference to liquids e.g. oil) thick; sticky (通常指液體, 如油)黏滯的; 黏性的.

visible [ˈvizibl] *adj* able to be seen 看得見的, 可見的. (*opp* 反義詞 **invisible**). **visibly** *adv* **visibility** [viziˈbiliti] *nu* (esp. with reference to the clearness of the air when travelling etc.) state of being visible (尤指旅行等時空氣的清晰度)能見度: *The poor visibility caused by the fog made driving very difficult.* 由於霧, 能見度很差, 開車變得很困難了.

vision [ˈviʒən] 1 *nu* power of seeing 視力, 視覺: *He wears spectacles because his vision is weak.* 他因為視力差而戴起了眼鏡. 2 *nu* power of imagining; ability to understand clearly what will happen 想像力; 眼光, 遠見: *The educational plan will fail because it has no vision.* 教育計劃沒有遠見, 因而會失敗的. 3 *nc* something believed to have been seen in a dream; something imagined by the mind 幻想; 幻象, 幻影: *When I was a boy I had visions of being a famous actor.* 我小時候曾幻想當一名著名的演員. **visionary** [ˈviʒənəri] *adj* (with reference to a person) seeing visions; having unreal, fanciful ideas (指人)耽於幻想的, 好夢想的; 空想的, 不實際的. Also 亦

作 *nc* person who is visionary 好幻想
的人，幻想家；空想家．

visit ['vizit] *vt* / *i* **1** come or go to see
somebody 訪問，拜訪，探望: *They are
visiting their friends in London*. 他們
正在訪問倫敦的朋友． *The doctor
visits his patients every day*. 醫生每天
探望病人． *She has gone visiting*. 她出
訪了． **2** go to a place for a time 參觀，
遊覽: *Have you ever visited London?*
你遊覽過倫敦嗎? Also 亦作 *nc* act of
visiting; short stay 訪問；參觀，遊覽，逗
留: *They are paying a visit to their
friends*. 他們正在拜訪朋友． *He went
to London on a visit*. 他訪問過倫敦．
visitor *nc* person who visits 訪問者；
參觀者；遊客． **'visiting card** (*Brit*)
card with one's name and address on
it (英) 名片． (*US* 美 **calling card**).

visor ['vaizə*] *nc* part of a helmet which
can be lifted to show the face (頭盔
的) 面罩，臉甲．

vista ['vistə] *nc* view (esp. from a distance and in a particular direction) 遠
景，深景; *We enjoyed the vista of the
mountain as seen from the north*. 我
們欣賞了由北望去的山的遠景．

visual ['vizjuəl] *adj* used in seeing; of or
by sight 用於看的；看的；視覺的;
visual aids i.e. pictures, films etc used
to aid teaching 直觀教具，即：圖片，影
片等用以輔助教學． **visually** *adv*
visualize *vt* make a mental picture of
somebody / something 想像，設想: *I
cannot visualize him as an old man*.
我不能想像他老了會是甚麼樣子．

vital ['vaitl] *adj* **1** concerned with,
necessary to, life 生命的；維持生命所
必需的；生死攸關的． *The heart is a
vital organ*. 心臟是重要的器官． **2** very
necessary or important 必不可少的；
極其重要的． *This letter contains vital
information*. 這封信含有極其重要的情

報． **vitally** *adv* **vitality** [vai'tæliti] *nu*
vital force; liveliness of manner; ability to go on enduring and living 生命
力；生氣，活力． **vital statistics 1** statistics about births, marriages and
deaths etc. (有關生生，婚姻，死亡等
的) 人口動態統計． **2** measurements of
a woman's bust, waist and hips. (*informal* in sense 2) (女人的胸圍，腰圍，
臀圍) 三圍．(義2為非正式).

vitamin ['vitəmin] *nc* chemical substance, found in small amounts in
food and necessary for health and
growth 維生素，維他命．

vivacious [vi'veiʃəs] *adj* full of energy;
lively; gay 生氣勃勃的；活潑的；快活
的． **vivacity** [vi'væsiti] *nu*.

vivid ['vivid] *adj* bright; clear; lively 鮮
明的；鮮艷的；明晰的；生動的；栩栩如生
的；逼真的: *a vivid blue sky* 明朗的藍
天; *a vivid imagination* 生動的想像．
vividly *adv* **vividness** *nu*.

vixen ['viksn] *nc* female fox 雌狐．

vocabulary [vou'kæbjuləri] *nc* **1** list of
words (usu. in alphabetical order,
with explanations of their meanings)
詞彙表(通常依字母順序排列，並有詞義
解釋)． **2** total number of words used
by somebody 詞彙，語
彙，詞彙量: *He has increased his English vocabulary by reading many English books*. 他閱讀了許多英語書，因而
擴大了英語詞彙量．

vocal ['voukl] *adj* of the voice; using the
voice 嗓音的，聲音的；使用嗓音的; (用
語言) 表達出來的: *vocal music*
i.e. singing 聲樂: *They are very vocal
in their demands for more money* i.e.
they say very clearly that they want
more. 他們非常清楚地說，他們要求更
多的錢． **vocalist** *nc* person who sings
歌唱者；歌唱家；聲樂家．

vocation [vou'keiʃən] *nc* / *u* career or

profession (esp. one followed in a spirit of service to others) (尤指本着為別人服務的精神而從事的)事業; 職業. **vocational** *adj: vocational guidance* i.e. advice on what career to choose 就業指導, 職業輔導.

vociferate [vəˈsɪfəreɪt] *vt / i* shout 大聲說, 叫喊. **vociferous** [vəˈsɪfərəs] *adj*.

vodka [ˈvɔdkə] *nu* type of alcoholic liquor made from rye or potatoes 伏特加酒(用黑麥或馬鈴薯釀製)

vogue [voug] *nc* (usu. only *sing*) something which is popular at a particular time either now or in the past (通常僅用單數) 時尚, 流行物, 時髦的事物; *Short skirts are the vogue this year.* 今年流行短裙; *in vogue* in fashion 正在流行; 行時.

voice [vɔɪs] **1** *nc* sound made when speaking or singing; ability to make such a sound 說話聲, 歌唱聲; 發聲力, 嗓子: *We could hear the voices of the people in the next room.* 我們可以聽見隔壁的人聲. *They were speaking in loud voices.* 他們那時正在大聲說話. *Because he has a cold he has lost his voice.* 因爲感冒, 他嗓子啞了. **2** *nu* (grammar) form of the verb which shows the relation of the subject to the action of the verb (語法) 語態; *active voice* 主動語態; *passive voice* 被動語態. Also 亦作 *vt* express in words (用言語) 表達; *He voiced his opinions to everybody.* 他向每一個人表達自己的意見. *with one voice* everybody agreeing and saying so; unanimously 異口同聲地; 一致地.

void [vɔɪd] *adj* **1** empty 空的. **2** having no force or effect 無用的, 無效的, 作廢的; *Your cheque will be void if you do not sign it.* 你不簽名, 你的支票就無效. Also 亦作 *nu* empty space 空處, 空隙, 空間. **void of** empty of; without

沒有; 缺乏; *a life void of excitement.* 沒有刺激的生活. **null and void** see **null.**

volatile [ˈvɔlətaɪl] *adj* **1** (with reference to a liquid) evaporating easily; changing easily into a gas (指液體)易揮發的, 揮發性的. **2** (with reference to a person) changing moods easily; lively (指人)心情變化快的, 反覆無常的; 快活的.

volcano [vɔlˈkeɪnou] *nc* **1** hole in the crust of the earth out of which fire, smoke, and lava come 火山噴口. **2** mountain formed in this way 火山. *pl* 複數 **volcanoes. volcanic** [vɔlˈkænɪk] *adj*.

volition [vəˈlɪʃən] *nu* act of willing or choosing 意志; 意志力, 決斷: *He gave the money of his own volition* i.e. he decided himself to do so. 他是出於自己的意思給這筆錢的. 即: 他自己決定這樣做.

volley [ˈvɔlɪ] *nc* **1** number of shots fired at the same time (槍砲)羣射, 齊射. **2** number of questions, remarks etc made at the same time or very quickly one after the other (質問、言語等的)齊發, 連發. **3** (tennis) act of hitting the ball back to one's opponent before it bounces (網球)(球落地前的)截擊, 飛擊. **volleyball** game played by two teams, who volley a large air-filled ball with their hands until the ball touches the ground 排球.

volt [voult] *nc* unit of electrical force i.e. the force needed to send a current of one amp (ampere) through a resistance of one ohm 伏特(電壓單位). **voltage** *nc / u* electrical force measured in volts 電壓, 電壓量, 伏特數.

voluble [ˈvɔljubl] *adj* speaking quickly and easily 流利的, 流暢的; 健談的; 口若懸河的. **volubly** *adv* **volubility**

[vɔljuˈbiliti] *nu*.

volume [ˈvɔljuːm] **1** *nc* book (esp. one of a set). (尤指一套書中的)一卷,一册,一部. **2** *nc* large amount 大量,大宗,許多: *A volume / volumes of smoke rose from the burning house.* 着火的房子升起了大團大團的烟. **3** *nu* amount of sound 音量,響度: *Your radio is too loud. Turn down the volume.* 你的收音機太響了,把音量調小一點. **4** *nu* amount of space occupied by something (usu. shown in cubic feet, metres etc.); cubic content of something 體積(通常以立方英尺、立方米等表示);容量,容積: *find the volume of a box 4 feet long, 3 feet broad and 2 feet high* 一個箱子,4英尺長,3英尺寬,2英尺高,求其體積. **voluminous** [vəˈljuːminəs] *adj* **1** of great size 體積大的,寬大的: *a voluminous dress* 寬大的女服. **2** in many volumes 卷數多的,大部頭的: *He wrote a voluminous report on education.* 他寫了一部有關教育的大部頭的報告.

voluntary [ˈvɔləntəri] *adj* **1** doing, or done, willingly without being forced or without pay 自願的,志願的: *I am a voluntary helper.* 我是自願幫助的. *He has just finished his voluntary service overseas.* 他剛剛完成在海外的志願服務. **2** helped by private, not government, money 由私人捐助的,非官辦的: *This school belongs to a voluntary organization.* 這所學校屬於一個義務團體. **voluntarily** *adv*.

volunteer [vɔlənˈtiə*] *nc* person who enters a service (esp. military service) of his own free will; person willing to do a job without being forced 志願兵,義勇軍;自願效勞者,自告奮勇者: *Are there any volunteers for cleaning the kitchen?* 有誰願意打掃廚房? Also 亦作 *vt / i* enter a service of one's own free

will; offer (to do) something 自願效勞;自告奮勇;自動提供: *When war broke out, I volunteered.* 戰爭爆發時,我志願參軍了. *They volunteered some interesting suggestions* i.e. made them without being asked. 他們自動提供了一些有趣的建議. 即:没有要求他們提供,而他們卻做了. *She volunteered to help with the washing up.* 她自願幫助洗餐具.

voluptuous [vəˈlʌptjuəs] *adj* causing sensual pleasure 淫慾的;令人銷魂的. *a voluptuous blonde* 令人銷魂的白膚金髮女郎.

vomit [ˈvɔmit] *vt / i* put out through the mouth what is in the stomach 嘔吐,吐出: *The poisoned food made him vomit.* 有毒的食物使他嘔吐. *He vomited all the food he had eaten.* 他吐出了吃下去的所有食物. Also 亦作 *nu* matter which has been vomited 嘔吐物.

voodoo [ˈvuːduː] *nu* type of religion which believes in evil spirits and witchcraft 伏都教,巫毒教,巫術信仰. **voodooism** *nu*.

voracious [vəˈreiʃəs] *adj* very greedy; ready to eat a lot 貪婪的,貪得無厭的,貪吃的,食量驚人的.

vote [vout] *nc / u* act of showing one's choice, opinion or wish (esp. in choosing candidates for government etc.); right to do so (esp. by ballot or by raising one's hand at a meeting) 投票;表決;選舉(尤指選舉政府候選人等);投票權,表決權,選舉權(尤指通過投票或會上舉手表決): *I gave my vote to the first speaker.* 我投票選第一位發言者. *He is too young to have a vote.* 他太年輕了,不能參加投票. *He was elected captain by 20 votes* i.e. 20 votes more than those given to the other persons who wished to become captain. 他以20票之多數當選爲隊長. 即: 比其他愚當隊長的人多出20票. Also 亦作 *vt / i* **1** show one's choice, opinion or wish; allow by a vote 投票; 表決; 選舉: *We voted against / for him. The chairman asked us to vote on the plan.* 主席要求我們就這計劃進行表決. *The National Assembly voted more money to education.* 國民會議通過給教育更多的撥款. **2** propose 建議, 提議: *I vote (that) we stay at home today.* 我提議今天我們呆在家裏. **voter** *nc* person who votes; person who has the right to vote 投票人, 選舉人; 法定選舉人. **vote of confidence** support for a plan, proposal etc shown by the fact that most people vote for it (投票支持某項計劃, 建議等的) 信任票. **vote of thanks** thanks expressed at a meeting by one person on behalf of all the others and usually followed by hand-clapping (在會上某人代表聽衆的) 公開鳴謝 (通常繼以鼓掌).

vouch [vautʃ] *vi* (with **for**) state that somebody / something is correct, reliable etc.; guarantee (與 for 連用) 確定地說; 擔保, 保證: *I can vouch for their honesty.* 我可以保證, 他們是誠實的. **voucher** *nc* document which shows that accounts are correct, money has been paid or that a person has a right to something 證件; 收據; 憑證.

vow [vau] *nc* solemn promise (usu. one made to God or in the name of God) (通常對上帝或以上帝名義所作的) 誓約; 宣誓, 許願: *marriage vows* 婚誓.

Also 亦作 *vt* make a vow 立誓, 發誓, 許願: *He vowed that he would never do it again / He vowed never to do it again.* 他發誓再也不做此事了.

vowel ['vauəl] *nc* vocal sound shown mainly by the letters *a,e, i, o* or *u*; one of these letters (主要由字母 a, e, i, o, u 所表示的) 元音; 元音字母.

voyage ['vɔiidʒ] *nc* long journey by water 航海, 航行: *They have gone on a voyage round Africa.* 他們已出海環繞非洲航行.

vulgar ['vʌlgə*] *adj* **1** coarse; rude; bad-mannered 粗俗的; 粗陋的; 庸俗的; 卑下的: *vulgar jokes* 庸俗的玩笑; *vulgar behaviour* 粗俗的行爲. **2** in common use; of the common people. (rather *o.f.* in sense 2) 通俗的; 普通的, 平民的. (義2爲相當舊式). **vulgarity** [vʌl'gæriti] *nc / u* vulgar act or behaviour 粗野行爲; 粗俗; 庸俗. **vulgar fraction** (mathematics) fractions shown thus: ¾ (as a decimal fraction shown thus: .75) (數學) 普通分數, 如: ¾ (以小數點表示則爲0.75).

vulnerable ['vʌlnərəbl] *adj* easily damaged or injured; open to attack 易受損壞的; 易受傷害的; 易受攻擊的; 脆弱的: *I am vulnerable to headaches when I am tired.* 我累的時候, 容易頭疼. (*opp* 反義詞 **invulnerable**). **vulnerability** [vʌlnərə'biliti] *nu.*

vulture ['vʌltʃə*] *nc* type of large bird which eats the flesh of dead animals 兀鷹; 禿鷲.

vying ['vaiiŋ] *pres part of* **vie**. vie 的現在分詞.

W,w

wad [wɔd] *nc* number of folded bank-notes or papers (鈔票、文件的)一捲，一疊.

waddle ['wɔdl] *vi* walk like a duck i.e. with short steps and swaying from side to side 如鴨子行走，即：搖搖擺擺地走. Also 亦作 *nc / u* a walk with a waddle 搖搖擺擺地走.

wade [weid] *vt / i* walk through something which makes movement difficult (e.g. water or mud) 從阻礙物(如水、泥濘)涉過：*We waded across the river because there was no bridge.* 因爲没有橋，我們涉水過河.

wafer ['weifə*] *nc* very thin, crisp biscuit (often eaten with ice cream) 薄脆餅乾(常與冰淇淋一起吃).

waffle¹ ['wɔfl] *nc* type of cake made of batter and cooked in an iron mould 用麵粉、蛋、牛奶等和成，在鐵模裏烘出的蛋奶餅.

waffle² ['wɔfl] *vi* talk nonsense; talk too much 胡扯；嘮叨：*What is he waffling on about?* 他在嘮叨些甚麼? Also 亦作 *nu* foolish, unnecessary talk or writing 無聊、不必要的談話或文字：*There is too much waffle in this essay.* 這篇散文的無聊話太多了. (both *informal*) (均為非正式).

waft [wɔft] *vt* carry lightly across water or through air 使飄浮；飄送：*The gentle wind wafted the sound of music towards us.* 柔風把樂曲聲傳送給我們.

wag [wæg] *vt / i* move, cause to move, up and down or from side to side quickly and often (使)搖擺，擺動；上下移動：*The dog's tail is wagging / The dog is wagging its tail.* 狗在搖尾巴.

Her tongue is always wagging i.e. she gossips a lot etc. 她老是饒舌. 即：她老是喋喋不休等. *past* 過去式和過去分詞 **wagged.**

wage¹ [weidʒ] *nc* (usu. *pl*) payment made or received for work done (通常用複數)工資；薪水：*My wages are £50 a week.* 我每週薪水五十鎊. *Note* 說明：when payments are made every week the usual word is *wages;* when made every month the word used is *salary.* 週薪通常用wages; 月薪用salary. **'wage earner** somebody who works for wages 靠工作挣工資的人，雇傭勞動者. **'wage freeze** time during which no increase in wages is allowed 工資凍結.

wage² [weidʒ] *vt* (with reference to a war or campaign) fight, carry on (指戰爭、運動)進行，開展.

wager ['weidʒə*] *nc* bet 賭注.

waggle ['wægl] *vt / i* move, cause to move, quickly, up and down or from side to side 擺動；上下移動：*The bird waggled its tail to shake the water off.* 那隻鳥擺動着尾巴，把水抖掉. Also 亦作 *nc.*

waggon, wagon ['wægən] *nc* **1** large four-wheeled vehicle pulled by horses or oxen and used for carrying goods 四輪運貨馬(牛)車. **2** (*Brit*) railway truck (英)鐵路貨車 (*US* 美 **freight car).**

waif [weif] *nc* person (esp. a child) or animal without a home 無家可歸的人；(尤指)流浪兒；無主動物.

wail [weil] *vt / i* express sorrow loudly 哀號，嚎啕大哭，痛哭. Also 亦作 *nc* loud, long cry of sorrow 大哭, 痛哭.

waist [weist] *nc* part of the body just above the hips 腰, 腰部. **waistcoat** ['weiskout] *(Brit)* short garment without sleeves, worn under a jacket (英) 背心. *(US* 美 **vest).** **'waistline** measurement round the waist; shape of the waist 腰圍; 腰身.

wait [weit] *vt / i* **1** stop or stay in a place without doing anything until somebody / something arrives or something happens 等, 等候, 等待: *I waited for him at the gate.* 我在門口等他. *We waited (for) an hour but they did not come.* 我們等了一小時, 他們卻沒來. *Have you been waiting long?* 你等了很久嗎? **2** be ready for; do nothing until something happens 準備好; 等候: *You must wait your turn to see the doctor.* 你必須等輪到你才看病. see also 參見 **await.** Also 亦作 *nc* act of waiting 等待: *We had a long wait before we could see him.* 我們等了好久才能見到他. **waiter** *nc* man who serves food at table in a restaurant or hotel 飯館或旅店的侍者, 侍應生, 服務員. *(fem* 陰 **waitress** ['weitris]).** **'waiting list** list of names of those waiting to get or do something 等候者名單; 候補(申請)人名單. *New houses are very scarce. There is a waiting list for all of them.* 新房子供不應求, 申請者全要了. **'waiting room** room where people wait (e.g. at a railway station for a train or in a doctor's house until the doctor can attend to them) 等候室(如候車室, 候診室). **wait on / upon someone** be a servant to 服侍(某人), 伺候(某人), 侍奉. **wait up for someone / something** not go to bed until someone / something arrives 熬夜等候某人/某事物. **lie in wait for** hide and wait to

attack 埋伏着等待, 伏擊.

waive [weiv] *vt* (with reference to a claim or right) give up; not insist on (指要求, 權利) 放棄, 不堅持.

wake¹ [weik] *vt / i* stop sleeping; cause somebody to stop sleeping 醒; 喚醒: *I always wake (up) at 7 o'clock.* 我總是在七點鐘醒來. *Please wake me (up) earlier tomorrow.* 明天請早些叫醒我. *past tense* 過去式 **woke** [wouk] or **waked.** *past part* 過去分詞 **woken** ['woukən], **woke** or **waked.** *Note* 說明: **1** the verb forms of the following verbs: **2** *wake up* is the most usual of these four and it is the one which is recommended for us with *past tense woke up. past part woken up.* 下列動詞的形式: 2 wake up 是這四者中最常用的, 其過去式宜爲 woke up, 過去分詞宜爲 woken up.

wake² [weik] *nc* (esp. in Ireland) act of staying up all night with a corpse before its burial (尤用於愛爾蘭) 葬禮前夕的守夜, 守靈.

wake³ [weik] *nc* track left by a ship as it moves through water 船的尾波, 航跡. **in the wake of** following or happening immediately after 尾隨, 緊跟 …, 隨之而來.

waken ['weikən] *vt / i* past 過去式和過去分詞 **wakened.** see 見 **wake¹.**

walk [wɔːk] *vt / i* move on the feet (keeping one foot at a time on the ground while doing so) (使) 走, 步行: *Our baby cannot walk yet.* 我們的嬰兒還不會走呢. *I usually walk to school and come home by bus.* 我通常走路上學, 乘公共汽車回家. *They walked four miles in one hour.* 他們一小時走了四英里. Also 亦作 *nc* distance covered, time taken, by walking 走的距離, 花的時間; *We went for a walk after lunch.* 午飯後我們去散步.

Our house is half an hour's walk from the church. 從我們的房子走到教堂有半小時的路程. **2** way of walking 走路的姿態: *I know him by his walk.* 我從他走路的樣子認出他. **'walking stick** stick used when walking (usu. as a support) 手杖. **'walkover** *nc* (sport) event in which there is only one competitor; very easy victory (體育)只有一個對手的競賽, 輕易得勝. **walk of life** kind of work one does; occupation; social position 職業; 行業; 階層: *In the army there were men from every walk of life.* 軍隊裏有來自各行各業的人.

walkie-talkie ['wɔːki'tɔːki] *nc* type of small two-way radio which can be carried and used by one person. *(informal)* 無線電對講機, 步話機. (非正式).

wall [wɔːl] *nc* structure of brick, stone etc built to form a side of a building or room, the boundary of a piece of land, or as a defence against something 牆, 牆壁; 圍牆: *The walls of our house are built of brick.* 我們房子的牆壁是用磚砌成的. *There is a blackboard on one wall of the classroom.* 教室的一堵牆上有一塊黑板. *He climbed over the wall into the garden.* 他爬過牆進入花園. **'wallpaper** *nc* type of paper used to cover the walls of a room 牆紙.

wallet ['wɔlit] *nc* flat, folding case carried in the pocket to hold banknotes, papers etc. 皮夾, 錢包.

wallop ['wɔləp] *vt* hit hard; beat 重擊, 猛打. Also 亦作 *nc* hard blow (both *informal*) 重擊, 痛打. (均為非正式).

wallow ['wɔləu] *vi* **1** roll about in mud or dirty water (在泥、濁水中)打滾, 翻滾. **2** indulge too much in 沉迷: *wallow in money* 沉迷於金錢.

walnut ['wɔːlnʌt] **1** *nc* type of nut with a bumpy shell, divided into two inside 胡桃, 核桃. **2** *nc* the tree on which this nut grows 胡桃樹, 核桃樹. **3** *nc* the wood of this tree 胡桃木, 核桃木.

walrus ['wɔːlrəs] *nc* type of large sea animal with two tusks pointing downwards 海象. *pl* 複數 **walrus** or **walruses.**

waltz [wɔːls] *nc* type of dance in which men and women move round in pairs 華爾茲舞. Also 亦作 *vt / i* dance, cause to dance, in this way (使)跳華爾茲舞.

wan [wɔn] *adj* **1** (with reference to a person) looking tired or ill; pale (指人)有倦容的, 病態的; 蒼白的. **2** (with reference to light) pale and weak (指光)暗淡的, 微弱的.

wand [wɔnd] *nc* thin stick carried in the hand (e.g. by a conjurer or fairy) 短杖, 魔杖(如魔術師或仙女用的).

wander ['wɔndə*] *vi* **1** move about from place to place without any particular purpose 漫遊, 逛, 漫步; 流浪, 漂泊: *We wandered through the town with nothing to do.* 我們在城裏到處閒逛. **2** go away from the correct path 迷路, 脫離正路, 走岔: *Don't wander off the road into the forest.* 別走離道路而誤入森林. **3** go away from the proper course of action; think about other things 離開正道, 心不在焉: *The teacher wandered from the subject of his lesson.* 老師講課離題. *As he spoke, my thoughts wandered.* 他說話的時候, 我心不在焉. **wanderer** *nc.*

wane [wein] *vi* (esp. with reference to the bright part of the moon) become smaller or less bright (尤指月亮之發亮部份)變小, 變暗淡: *Last night there was a full moon. Tonight it begins to wane.* 昨晚滿月. 今晚月開始缺虧.

(*opp* 反義詞 **wax**). Also 亦作 *nu* usu. only in **be on the wane** i.e. decrease in strength or brightness 通常僅用於 be on the wane, 即: 力量或光亮減弱: *The moon is on the wane.* 月亮漸虧. *The king's power was on the wane.* 國王的勢力在衰落.

wangle ['wæŋgl] *vt* get something by clever talk or a trick (以花言巧語或詭計) 騙取: *He wangled free tickets to the concert.* 他用計騙取音樂會免費入場券. Also 亦作 *nc*: *Be careful! This is one of his wangles.* 小心! 這是他的一個狡詐行爲. (both *informal*). (均爲非正式).

want¹ [wɔnt] *vt / i* **1** need; require 需要; 要: *Do you want the car today?* 今天你要車嗎? *I want more money to buy it.* 我需要更多的錢來買它. *This room wants cleaning* i.e. needs to be cleaned. 這房子需要打掃了. **2** desire; wish 希望, 願望: *I want to go home.* 我想回家了. *They want us to help them.* 他們希望我們幫助他們. Note 說明: **1** in sense **2** *wish* can also be used (e.g. *I wish to go home*) but *want* is much more common. **2** *wish for* usu. has the sense of desiring something which is impossible or very difficult to have. *He is wishing for the moon; want* has the sense of desiring what is definite and possible. *He wants £10 before Friday.* 1 義 2 也可用 wish (如: I wish to go home) 但 want 常用得多. 2 wish for 通常表示想要某種無法得到或很難得到的東西. He is wishing for the moon. 他想要月亮, want 表示想要某種明確的、可能的東西. He wants £10 before Friday. 星期五以前他要10鎊.

want² [wɔnt] **1** *nu* state of not having; lack of what is needed 沒有; 缺乏, 缺少: *The children are unhappy from*

want of love. 孩子們缺乏愛, 生活不快樂. *He is ill through want of food.* 他缺乏食物, 生病了. *Many people live in want* i.e. are poor and hungry 許多人過着窮困的日子. 即: 貧窮又飢餓. **2** *nc* (in *pl*) things desired or needed (用於複數) 想要的東西; 必需品: *This shop can supply all your wants.* 這商店可以供應你所需要的一切. *Simple people have few wants.* 樸素的人需要的東西很少.

wanton ['wɔntn] *adj* wild or immoral in behaviour 任性的; 放縱的; 行爲不檢的: *wanton destruction* i.e. without purpose or reason 胡亂的破壞, 即: 沒有理由或沒有目的的: *a wanton woman* 蕩婦.

war [wɔ:*] *nc / u* **1** fight between countries using armed forces 戰爭: *The Second World War began in 1939 and ended in 1945.* 第二次世界大戰於1939年開始, 1945年結束. *Great Britain was at war for six years.* 英國打了六年的仗. *Soldiers are trained for war.* 士兵爲戰爭而受訓練. **2** any fight 戰鬥, 鬥爭: *our war against ignorance, poverty and disease* 我們與無知、貧困和疾病的鬥爭. '**warfare** fighting in war; type of fighting in war 戰爭, 作戰, 鬥爭: *jungle warfare* 叢林戰; *chemical warfare* 化學戰. '**warhead** front of a torpedo or missile which contains explosives 魚雷或水雷彈頭, 導彈彈頭. '**warlike** *adj* ready for, fond of, war. 戰備的, 好戰的. '**warpath** only in **on the warpath** i.e. looking for a fight or quarrel; fighting or quarrelling (*informal* unless with reference to American Indians) 僅用於 on the warpath, 即: 準備作戰或爭吵; 正在作戰或爭吵 (除指美洲印第安人外, 非正式). '**warship** ship armed for war 軍艦, 戰艦. '**wartime** time when there is war

戰時. **civil war** war between people of a country 內戰.

warble ['wɔːbl] *vt / i* (esp. with reference to birds) sing with trembling or quavering notes (鳥) 啼囀; 用顫音唱.

ward¹ [wɔːd] *nc* **1** young person looked after by and under the control of an older person 受監護人: *When his parents died the boy became the ward of his uncle.* 這個男孩的父母去世, 他的舅父便成了他的監護人. **2** (with reference to local elections) part of a town (指地方選舉) 選區. **3** large room in a hospital or prison 大病房; 牢房: *surgical ward* 外科病房.

ward² [wɔːd] *vt* (with **off**) defend; prevent (與 off 連用) 保衛, 保護; 擋住; 防止: *He warded off the blow with his arm.* 他用手臂擋住打擊.

warden ['wɔːdn] *nc* person who is in charge of a building or has particular duties 看守人, 看管員, 管理員; the *warden of a students' hostel* 學生寄宿舍的管理員. '**traffic warden** person who controls the parking of cars in streets and also sometimes directs traffic 交通執勤人員.

warder ['wɔːdə*] *nc* man who guards those in prison, jailer 獄吏, (監獄) 看守. (*fem* 陰 **wardress** ['wɔːdris]).

wardrobe ['wɔːdroub] *nc* **1** tall cupboard or small room for keeping clothes 衣櫥; 藏衣室. **2** clothes belonging to a particular person 個人的全部衣裳: *Her wardrobe must have cost hundreds of pounds.* 他的衣服恐怕值數百鎊.

ware [wɛə*] **1** *nc* (in *pl*) goods for sale (用於複數) 貨品, 商品. **2** *nu* (with other words) particular type of goods (e.g. *earthenware* i.e. pottery; *hardware* i.e. goods made of metal for use in the home; *silverware* i.e. dishes etc

made of silver) (與其他詞連用) 某種貨品, 器皿 (如: earthenware 陶器; hardware 金屬器皿; silverware 銀器). '**warehouse** large building for keeping goods 倉庫.

warfare ['wɔːfɛə*] *nu* see 見 **war.**

warily ['wɛərili] *adv* see 見 **wary.**

warm¹ [wɔːm] *adj* **1** moderately hot; giving a pleasant, comfortable heat 暖和的, 溫暖的: *In England the summers are usually warm but seldom hot.* 英國的夏天通常是暖和的, 很少是熱的. *You should wear warm clothes in cold weather.* 寒冷的天氣你必須穿暖和的衣服. **2** kind; friendly 熱心的, 友好的; 親切的: *They gave us a warm welcome.* 他們熱烈歡迎我們. **3** (with reference to the tracks or scent of an animal when being hunted) recently made; fresh (指獵物的氣味或獸跡) 新近發出的, 強烈的, 新鮮的: *We followed the buffalo through the bush while the scent was still warm.* 趁獸跡還新鮮, 我們通過叢林追野牛. **warmly** *adv* **warmth** [wɔːmθ] *nu* '**warm-hearted** *adj* friendly and kind 熱情的, 親切的.

warm² [wɔːm] *vt / i* become, cause to become, warm or warmer (使) 變暖; (使) 變熱; 暖和起來: *The food was warming near the fire.* 食物在火邊開始變熱了. *They warmed themselves in the sun.* 他們在陽光下取暖. **warm (something) up 1** make something warm 加熱, 熱一熱; 使某物變暖: *Mother warmed up some milk.* 媽媽把一些牛奶熱一熱. **2** make oneself warm and ready for something (esp. a competition or game) (比賽或競賽前) 預備動作; 熱身: *The two teams are warming up for the relay race.* 這兩個隊在做接力賽的準備動作.

warn [wɔːn] *vt* inform or give advice to

somebody about a future danger or difficulty 警告; 告誡: *We warned him of the dangers of driving too quickly.* 我們警告過他, 開車太快是危險的. *My father warned me against strangers* i.e. he told me to be careful with them and avoid them. 我父親要我提防陌生人. 即: 他告訴我, 對他們要小心, 並避開他們. *The headmaster warned them that next time they were late they would be punished.* 校長警告他們, 下次他們若遲到, 將受到處分. *He warned them not to be late again.* 他警告他們, 別再遲到了. **warning** *nc* act or happening which warns 警告; 提醒: *Let this be a warning to you.* 就讓這事作爲對你的警告吧.

warp [wɔːp] *vt / i* **1** (esp. with reference to wood) become twisted, cause to be twisted, out of shape (尤指木頭) 使翹; 彎, 扭曲: *The wooden planks have warped in the sun.* 這木板已被曬得變彎了. *The heavy rain warped the roof.* 大雨把屋頂也弄彎了. **2** (esp. with reference to a person's character, nature etc.) make twisted or evil (尤指人的性格、本性等) 使歪曲, 使不正, 使不良; 乖戾: *This evil deed was planned by a warped mind.* 這件壞事是由存心不良的人想出來的.

warrant ['wɔrnt] *vt* give authority or right to do something 授權: *His wealth does not warrant his rude behaviour.* 他的財富也不能使他粗魯的行爲顯得有理. Also 亦作 *nc* written official authority to do something 令狀; 授權狀; 委任狀; 許可票; 拘票; 逮捕證: *The police have a warrant for his arrest.* 警方有逮捕他的逮捕令. **warranty** *nc* guarantee; authority 保證書; 擔保; 權威; 根據. '**warrant officer** (in the armed forces) officer ranking below a commissioned officer and

above a noncommissioned officer (e.g. sergeant-major in the army) (軍隊)准尉.

warren ['wɔrn] *nc* **1** piece of land in which many rabbits have dug holes and tunnels 許多兔子挖洞、挖地道的地方; 養兔場. **2** any crowded place with narrow streets; slum 街窄擁擠不堪的地方, 陋巷.

warrior ['wɔriə*] *nc* soldier; brave fighter 戰士; 勇士.

wart [wɔːt] *adj* small, hard lump which grows on the skin 疣, 肉贅, 瘊子.

wary ['weəri] *adj* careful; cautious 小心的, 謹慎的. **warily** *adv.*

was [wɔz,wəz] past tense of **be.** be的過去式.

wash¹ [wɔʃ] *vt / i* **1** clean with water or other liquid 洗: *Have you washed (yourself) yet?* 你洗澡了嗎? *She is washing our clothes.* 她在洗我們的衣服. **2** (with reference to the action of water e.g. the sea, a lake, a river, rain etc) move against; carry away (指水的流動, 如海, 湖, 河, 雨等) 拍打, 冲洗: *The west coast of Europe is washed by the Atlantic.* 大西洋拍打着歐洲的西海岸. *The river rose until it was washing the walls of the houses.* 河水漲了, 直至它拍打着房子的牆壁. *The rain washed the dry leaves into the ditch.* 雨水把乾樹葉冲到溝裏. **3** able to be washed without damage 耐洗: *Does this dress wash?* 這件衣服耐洗嗎? **washable** *adj* able to be washed without damage 經洗的, 耐洗的. **washer** *nc* flat ring of metal, rubber etc put below a screw 皮圈; 墊圈. **washing** *nu* **1** act of washing or being washed 洗, 洗滌. **2** clothes washed or to be washed at one time 洗過的或待洗的衣物: *My mother has a lot of washing today.* 我母親今天有很多衣物

要洗. see also **wash²** (in sense 2) 參見 wash² (義2). **'washbasin, 'washhand basin** basin or bowl for washing the hands and face (usu. fixed to a wall and having taps) 洗臉盆. **'wash leather** *nc/u* piece of soft leather used for washing smooth surfaces (e.g. windows, cars etc.) (擦窗或車等的) 軟皮, 擦拭皮. **'washing machine** machine for washing clothes 洗衣機. **wash something away** carry away by the action of water 冲走; 洗掉: *The flood has washed away their fishing nets.* 洪水把他們的漁網冲走了. **wash something down** **1** clean by washing (usu. with water from a hose) 冲洗(通常用水管,軟管): *He is washing down his car.* 他在冲洗汽車. **2** cause to go down into the stomach by drinking liquid 連同液體吞下: *We washed down our food with a glass of water.* 我們用一杯水把食物吞下. **'washout** *nc* complete failure 完全失敗: *The concert was a washout.* 音樂會完全失敗了. *(informal).* (非正式). **wash up** (with reference to a number of dishes, knives, forks, spoons etc.) wash after being used at a meal 洗餐具(指一些碗,盤,刀,叉,湯匙等): *After supper we helped her to wash up.* 晚飯後我們幫她洗碗碟. **washing-'up** *nu: We helped her with the washing-up.* 我們幫她洗碗碟. **feel / look washed out** feel / look very tired or ill *(informal)* 感覺/顯得很累或有病(非正式).

wash² [wɔʃ] *nu* **1** (with **a**) act of washing or being washed (與a連用) 洗, 洗滌: *Have you had a wash yet?* 你洗了嗎? *He gave his hands a good wash.* 他把手好好地洗了洗. **2** clothes washed or to be washed at one time. 洗過的或待洗的衣物: *Is the wash dry*

yet? 洗的衣服乾了嗎? see also 參見 **washing.**

wasp [wɔsp] *nc* type of stinging insect like a bee 黃蜂, 胡蜂, 螞蜂, 細腰蜂.

waste [weist] *vt/i* **1** use badly or wrongly; use more than is needed 糟蹋, 濫用, 浪費: *We are wasting our time by listening to such nonsense.* 聽這樣的廢話就等於浪費我們的時間. *You should not waste food when many people are hungry.* 許多人正在挨餓, 你不應浪費食物. **2** become, cause to become, weak and thin slowly (使)消耗, (使)損耗, (使)消瘦: *The children are wasting away because they do not get enough food.* 孩子們吃得不夠, 消瘦了. *His face was wasted by fever.* 他發燒, 臉消瘦了. **3** (with reference to land, buildings etc.) damage; destroy (指土地, 建築物等)使荒蕪, 糟蹋, 毀壞, 破壞. Also 亦作 *nu* act of wasting or being wasted 糟蹋, 濫用, 浪費; 毀壞, 損壞: *This waste of good food should not be allowed.* 不許浪費好食物. *It's a waste of time.* 這是浪費時間. **2** *nu* material already used and no longer needed; rubbish 廢物, 廢料; 垃圾: *Put all the waste in this bag.* 把廢物都放入這個袋子. **3** *nc* (in *pl*) empty land with little vegetation (用於複數) 荒地, 荒野: *the Arctic wastes* 北極荒地. **wastage** *nu* amount or number lost by waste 損耗量, 浪費量: *The wastage in the universities is high* i.e. many students leave before they have finished the course. 大學的浪費很大. 即: 許多學生未完成學業就離校. **wasteful** *adj* causing to waste; using too much 浪費的, 糟蹋的, 揮霍的. **'wastepaper basket** *(Brit)* container for putting used paper in (英) 廢紙簍, 字紙簍. *(US* 美 **wastebasket).** **go / run to waste** be wasted 浪

費掉. **lay waste** (with reference to land) destroy crops; damage (esp. by the enemy during a war) (指土地) 糟蹋莊稼; (尤指戰爭中受到敵人的) 蹂躪, 毀壞.

watch¹ [wɔtʃ] *vt / i* look at somebody / something to see what is happening or to be on guard against something 觀看, 注視; 監視; 注意: *If you watch how I do it you will be able to do it yourself.* 如果你看我怎麼做, 你自己就會做了. *We sat watching the people pass / passing by.* 我們坐着看走過的人. *They watched for any signs of trouble.* 他們注意出亂子的任何跡象. *Would you please watch these boys while I am away.* 我不在的時候, 請你照管一下這些男孩, 好嗎? *Note* 說明: *watch* usu. has the sense of looking at somebody / something moving or doing something for a period of time or from the beginning to the end of an action (e.g. *I watched him eat / eating his breakfast* i.e. I saw everything he did from beginning to end, but *I saw him eat / eating his breakfast* i.e. I noticed (while I was perhaps doing something else) that he was eating his breakfast). *watch* 通常表示注意看着人或事物一段時間內進行或發生的動作, 或某一行為從開始到結束的整個過程 (如: *I watched him eat / eating his breakfast*, 我看着他吃 / 正在吃早飯. 即: 我看見他自始至終所做的一切, 但 *I saw him / eat / eating his breakfast*, 我注意到 (當我可能在做別的事時) 他正在吃早飯). **watch out for 1** keep watching for 密切注意: *He's been watching out for the postman.* 他一直在等待這個郵差. **2** be careful of 小心, 戒備, 提防: *Watch out for snakes* 當心有蛇.

watch² [wɔtʃ] **1** *nu* act of watching (esp. when on guard against something) 看, 注視 (尤指警戒, 監視): *The police were on the watch for any trouble.* 警方監視着可能出現的騷動. **2** *nc* one of the seven periods of duty on a ship: *the first watch* i.e. 8 p.m. to midnight; *the middle watch* i.e. midnight to 4 a.m.; *the dog watch* i.e. 4 p.m. to 6 p.m. or 6 p.m. to 8 p.m.; members of the crew who are on duty at the same time 船上輪班, 值班 (首班, 即: 夜晚八時至午夜; 中班, 即: 午夜至凌晨四時; 暮更, 即: 下午四時至六時, 或下午六時至八時); 值班的海員. **watchful** *adj* watching carefully; attentive; alert 警惕的, 戒備的, 注意的. **'watchdog** dog kept to guard a building etc. 看門狗, 看家狗等. **'watchman** man who guards a building (esp. at night) 房子的守衛, (尤指看晚) 看更, 更夫.

watch³ [wɔtʃ] *nc* small clock carried in a pocket or worn on the wrist 手錶, 懷錶. **'watch strap** piece of leather etc for fastening a watch around one's wrist 錶帶.

water¹ ['wɔ:tə*] **1** *nu* most common of liquids found in rainfall, rivers, lakes etc. 水: *There is no water in the well.* 井裏沒有水. *Is there enough hot water for a bath?* 熱水夠不夠洗澡? *He jumped into the water and swam away.* 他跳入水中, 游走了. **2** *nc* (in *pl*) waves; large amount of water (用於複數) 波浪; 大片的水: *The waters of the lake beat against the wall of the castle.* 湖水拍打着城堡的圍牆. *Our ship was in enemy waters* i.e. in part of the sea controlled by the enemy 我們的船當時在敵人的水域; 即: 在敵人控制的海域. **watery** *adj* like water; pale; weak 像水的; 淡的; 稀薄的. **'water closet** small room where waste matter from the body is washed down a pipe by water. *Note:* commonly referred to by the initials *W.C.* (有抽水設備的) 厠所. 說明: 通常用首字母縮寫爲 W.C. **'watercolour 1** paint which is mixed with water, not oil 水彩顏料. **2** picture painted with this type of paint 水彩畫. **'watercress** type of green plant which grows in running water and is used as a food in salads 水田芹. **'waterfall** fall of the water of a river over a cliff 瀑布. **'waterfront** land next to the sea, lake or river; part of a town next to the sea, a lake or a river (e.g. its harbour, docks etc.) 海邊; 江邊; 湖邊; 濱水區(如: 其港灣, 港口等). **water hole** (in a desert or arid area) hole in the ground where water collects 水坑, 池. **'water level** level reached by the surface of an amount of water 水平面, 水位, 水準. **waterlogged** *adj* **1** (with reference to the ground) full of water; very wet (指地面) 浸滿水的, 澇的, 泥濘的. **2** (with reference to wood or a ship) full of water but still floating (指木材, 船) 浸飽水仍浮着的. **'waterproof** *adj* not allowing water to enter 防水的, 不透水的: *a waterproof hat* 防水帽. Also 亦作 *nc* coat which is waterproof 雨衣: *You must wear your waterproof when it is raining.* 雨天要穿上雨衣. **'watershed** ridge of ground between two separate rivers and their tributaries 分水嶺. **'watertight** *adj* **1** made so that water cannot get in or out 不滲水的, 不漏水的. **2** so definite that there is no doubt 嚴密的, 無懈可擊的: *a watertight agreement* 完美無缺的協議. **'waterway** channel of water deep enough for ships; canal 航道, 水路. **'waterworks** *npl* (with *a sing* or *pl* verb) reservoirs, storage tanks and pumps etc for supplying water (與單

數或複數動詞連用) 供水系統.

water² ['wɔ:tə*] *vt / i* **1** put water on; give water to plants etc. 灌水, 澆水. **2** weaken by adding water 摻水; 冲淡: *He watered the wine before drinking it.* 他把酒摻水後再喝. **3** (with reference to the eyes or mouth) fill with water (指眼或口) 流淚; 流口水: *The smoke made his eyes water.* 烟熏得他流淚. *The smell of the food made my mouth water.* 食物的味道使我流口水.

watermelon ['wɔ:təmelən] *nc / u* large edible fruit with a hard, green rind and juicy, pink or red pulp having many seeds 西瓜.

watt [wɔt] *nc* unit of electrical power (電力單位) 瓦.

wave [weiv] *nc* **1** moving ridge of water on the surface of the sea, a lake etc. (海, 湖等的) 浪, 波浪: *The boat rose and fell on the high waves.* 船在大浪中顛簸. **2** movement of the hand as a signal or greeting 揮手 (問候): *He gave us a friendly wave as he passed.* 他走過時, 友好地向我們揮手. **3** sudden but temporary increase in feelings, action, heat etc. (情緒, 行動, 熱度等) 突增, 波動: *A wave of anger swept through the crowd.* 一陣憤怒的情緒迅速傳遍人羣; *heatwave* i.e. period when the temperature is much higher than usual 熱浪, 即: 氣溫比平時高得多的時候. **4** something shaped or moving like waves 波狀物; 起伏: *She has lovely waves in her hair.* 她有一頭漂亮的鬈髮. *A wave of soldiers attacked the town.* 士兵們以波浪式攻擊城鎮. *This radio set can receive on short, medium and long waves.* 這收音機可以收到短波、中波和長波. Also 亦作 *vt / i* **1** move, cause to move, from side to side or up and down (使) 飄蕩; (使) 飄揚; (使) 波動; (使) 起伏: *The* *flags waved in the wind.* 旗子迎風飄揚. **2** make a signal, give a greeting by moving the hand or something held in the hand 揮(手中之物)致意, 招手: *They waved me goodbye.* 他們向我揮手告別. *He waved his handkerchief to me.* 他向我揮舞手帕. **3** give something the shape of a wave 使成波浪形, 使鬈曲: *I am told that he waves his hair.* 有人告訴我他捲了頭髮. **wavy** *adj* having curves like a wave. 波(浪)形的, 波紋的; 起伏的: *wavy hair* 鬈髮; *a wavy line* 曲線. **'waveband** group of wavelengths close together, used by a broadcasting station 波段. **'wavelength** (with reference to radio) speed of a wave divided by the number of oscillations (無線電)波長. **(be) on the same wavelength (as someone)** (be) able to understand (someone) 能理解(某人), (和某人)能相互溝通.

waver [ˈweɪvə*] *vi* **1** be unsteady; move from side to side 搖擺; 顫動: *His eyes wavered when he looked at me.* 他看着我時, 眼睛閃爍着. **2** be uncertain; hesitate 猶疑不決, 動搖不定: *They are wavering between agreeing and refusing.* 同意還是拒絕, 他們拿不定主意.

wax[1] [wæks] *nu* **1** substance which is made by bees and used by them for building honeycombs; this substance used by humans (e.g. to make polish or candles) (often **beeswax**) 蜂蠟; 蠟(如用以製擦亮劑或蠟燭)(常作 beeswax) **2** substance which is like beeswax 蠟狀物; *earwax* i.e. substance which collects in the ears 耳垢; *paraffin wax* i.e. type of resin used in making polish 石蠟. Also 亦作 *vt* put wax on; polish 給…打蠟, 用蠟擦 **'waxwork 1** model made from

wax (esp. one of a famous person) 蠟像(尤指名人). **2** (in *pl*) place where these models are shown (用於複數) 蠟像館.

wax[2] [wæks] *vi* (usu. with reference to the moon) become larger (通常指月亮)盈滿, 漸漸變圓; 漸漸變大. (**opp** 反義詞 **wane**).

way [wei] **1** *nc* path; road 道路; 路: *We followed the narrow way between the trees.* 我們沿着樹間狹窄的路走去. *The family across / over the way is on holiday* i.e. the one living on the other side of the road. 路那邊的一家正在度假. **2** *nu* correct path or road to be followed from one place to another 通往某處的正確道, 路: *Is this the way to London?* 這是通往倫敦的路嗎? *They lost their way in the forest.* 他們在森林中迷路了. **3** *nc* direction 方向: *Look both ways before you cross the road.* 看看兩邊再過馬路. *She looked the other way.* 她看另一個方向. *Please come this way.* 請往這邊走. **4** *nu* distance between two places (兩地)距離, 路程: *New York is a long way from London.* 紐約與倫敦的距離很遠. *Our house is only a little way from the school.* 我們的房子離學校很近. *We saw him a long way away / off* i.e. far in the distance. 我們遠遠地看見他. **5** *nu* space for somebody / something to move forward 向前進的空間: *You are standing in my way.* 你擋住了我的路. *Please get out of my way.* 請讓開. *They made way for the bus* i.e. they stood aside to let it pass. 他們給公共汽車讓路. 即: 站在一邊讓它通過. **6** *nc* method; means; habit 方法, 方式; 習慣: *Do it this way.* 照這樣做. *I know a better way of finding out.* 我知道一個更好的方法去查詢. *I don't like their way of blaming other* *people.* 我不喜歡他們那樣責備人家. *My father spoke about the old ways of travelling when he was a boy.* 我父親講起他小時候旅行的老辦法. **7** *nc* condition; state; extent 情形; 狀態; 程度; *He was in a bad way after the accident. (informal)* 事故以後, 他身體很差. (非正式) *In a way he is right* i.e. to some extent 從某種程度上說, 他是對的. **anyway** in any case or circumstances 無論如何. **by the way** (used with reference to a remark brought suddenly into a conversation) incidentally; if I may say so (用於插入語) 順便說, 附帶說說: *We like your new car by the way, how much did it cost?* 我們喜歡你的新車, 順便問問, 多少錢買的? **out-of-the-way** *adj* far from a road; difficult to find 偏僻的, 難找的: *They lived in an out-of-the-way house in the country.* 他們住在鄉村一個偏僻的房子裏. **under way** begun; in the process of being done 開始了; 進行中, 着手了: *Our plans are under way.* 我們的計劃正在進行中. **get / have one's (own) way** get or do what one wishes 爲所欲爲, 隨心所欲. **give way** yield; break 讓步, 屈服; 折斷: *You should give way to traffic coming from the right.* 你必須給右邊來的車輛讓路. *The branch gave way under his weight.* 他把樹枝壓斷了. **go out of one's way to do something** try hard; make a special point of doing something 盡力; 特意: *They went out of their way to help us.* 他們盡力幫助我們.

waylay [weiˈlei] *vt* wait in order to attack, or speak to, somebody passing by 埋伏等候, 伏擊; *past* 過去式和過去分詞 **waylaid** [weiˈleid].

wayward [ˈweiwəd] *adj* liking to do what one wants to do; not easily con-trolled; wilful 任性的; 不易管束的; 故意的.

we [wi:] *pron* people who are speaking; person who is speaking and others 我們; 咱們: *You leave just now and we'll join you later.* 你們現在離開, 我們隨後和你們會合.

weak [wi:k] *adj* **1** not strong; feeble; easily damaged or made useless 不結實; 虛弱的; 易損壞的; 不耐用: *He is very weak after his illness.* 他病後很虛弱. *She has weak eyes.* 她視力弱. *The box is too weak to stand on* 箱子太不結實了, 立不起來. **2** (with at or in) not good at (與at或in連用) 不精, 不擅長於: *They are weak in English grammar.* 他們的英語語法掌握得不好. **3** (with reference to a liquid mixture) having a lot of water; thin (指混合溶液) 多水的; 稀薄的: *weak coffee / tea* 淡咖啡/茶. (*opp* 反義詞 **strong**). **weakness** *nc / u* **weakly** *adv* in a weak manner 弱地, 虛弱地, 脆弱地. **weaken** *vt / i* become, cause to become, weak or weaker (使) 變弱. **weakling** *nc* person or animal that is weak 虛弱的人或動物, 弱者. **have a weakness for** like more than one should 特別喜歡, 過於喜歡: *He has a weakness for chocolate ice cream.* 他特別喜歡吃巧克力雪糕.

wealth [welθ] *nu* **1** riches; large amount of money 財富, 財產, 錢財: *A millionaire is a man of wealth.* 百萬富翁即大富豪. **2** (with a or the) great number of something; abundance (與a或the連用) 大量; 豐富: *The wealth of detail in this report is amazing.* 這篇報告裏的細節之多, 令人驚異. **wealthy** *adj*.

weapon [ˈwepən] *nc* instrument or method used when fighting 武器; 鬥爭工具或手段: *The atomic missile is the* *most modern weapon of war.* 原子導彈是戰爭中最現代的武器. *His weapons are a good brain and a quick tongue.* 他的鬥爭手段是好腦筋及好口才.

wear¹ [wɛə*] *vt / i* **1** have on the body or part of the body 穿；戴；佩；留；著：*He was wearing a brown coat and a black hat.* 他穿着一件棕色大衣, 戴着一頂黑色帽子. *She is wearing a gold ring on her finger.* 她手指上戴着一個金戒指. *She should not wear red* i.e. red clothes 她不應該穿紅色的衣服. **2** become, cause to become, damaged or changed by long use (使)磨損, (使)變舊：*Your shirt is very worn at the collar.* 你的襯衫的衣領已變得很舊了. *He has worn holes in all his shoes.* 他所有的鞋都已穿出洞來了. **3** continue to be useful; last 經用, 耐用：*Leather gloves wear better than cloth ones.* 皮手套比布手套耐用. *This jacket has worn well* i.e. has lasted a long time without becoming damaged 這件夾克很耐穿. 即: 已穿了很久而沒有破損. *past tense* 過去式 **wore** [wɔ:*]. *past part* 過去分詞 **worn** [wɔ:n]. **wearing** *adj* tiring 令人疲倦的, 使人厭煩的：*We've had a wearing day.* 我們過了令人困乏的一天. **wear (something) away** become, cause to become, thin or weak by rubbing; disappear, cause to disappear, in this way (使)磨薄, 磨弱；(使)耗損；磨去, (使)消失：*The name on the door has worn away.* 門上的名字已磨得模糊不清了. *The river has worn away the rocks.* 河水把石頭磨掉了. **wear someone / something down 1** make less by rubbing or use 磨短；磨薄；磨小；因使用而使變短；變薄, 變小：*I have worn down the point of the pencil.* 我已經把鉛筆尖用短了. **2** make weaker by attacking often 經

常攻擊而使衰弱, 削弱：*He wore down the other boxer with strong punches.* 他重重的幾拳把另一個拳擊手擊敗了. **wear off 1** disappear, cause to disappear, by rubbing 磨損, 磨滅, (使)消失：*The polish on your car will soon wear off.* 你車皮上的擦亮劑很快就會消失. **2** gradually disappear or stop 逐漸消失或停止：*My headache is wearing off.* 我的頭疼漸漸消失了. **wear (something) out 1** finish by long use 耗盡；用盡；穿壞, 穿破：*I have worn out this old coat.* 我把這件舊大衣穿破了. *This old coat is worn out.* 這件舊大衣已穿破. **2** become, cause to become, very tired (使)疲乏, (使)筋疲力竭：*Teaching wears her out.* 教學工作把她累壞了.

wear² [wɛə*] *nu* something which is worn on the body 某種衣服：*Do you sell menswear here?* 你們這兒賣男裝嗎? **wear and tear** change or damage caused by normal use (正常使用所造成的)損耗. (also 亦作 **fair wear and tear).** *Any damage will be repaired at our expense, if caused by fair wear and tear.* 正常使用所造成的損壞, 將由我們付費修理.

weary ['wiəri] *adj* tired or tiring 疲倦的；令人厭倦的：*We rested our weary legs.* 我們讓疲倦的雙腿歇一歇. *We are weary of learning English.* 我們對學習英語感到厭倦. Also 亦作 *vt / i* become, cause to become, tired (使)厭倦：*We soon wearied of listening to him.* 聽他的話, 我們很快就厭煩. *past* 過去式和過去分詞 **wearied. wearily** *adv* **weariness** *nu* **wearied** *adj.*

weasel ['wi:zl] *nc* small fierce animal with a thin body, short legs and a long tail, which kills and eats chickens, rabbits etc. 鼬鼠, 黃鼠狼.

weather ['weðə*] *nu* condition of the

air in a particular place at a particular time which causes wind, rain, sunshine, heat, cold etc. 天氣: *What was the weather like in Paris last week?* 上週巴黎的天氣如何? *You should wear thick clothes in cold weather.* 冷天氣你要穿厚衣服. *Note* 說明: *climate* has the sense of the usual condition of the air etc for a long time in a large area. climate表示大地區、長時間的氣候. *The climate of tropical Africa is much warmer than that of Western Europe.* 熱帶非洲的氣候比西歐的氣候熱得多. Also 亦作 *vt / i* 1 become changed and worn because of the weather; cause this to happen 因天氣受損傷, 變質損, 風化; 使風化: *The wind and the waves have weathered the rocks on the shore.* 海濱的岩石已受到風浪的侵蝕. 2 escape safely (e.g. from a storm or difficulty) 安然逃脫, 平安渡過(如暴風雨、難關): *Our country has not yet weathered its financial crisis.* 我國還沒有渡過它的財政危機. '**weather-beaten** *adj* marked or made rough by the weather 受到風吹雨打日曬的, 飽經風霜的: *a sailor with a weather-beaten face* 曬黑了臉的水手. '**weathercock** weather vane shaped like a cock 風標, 風信標. '**weather forecast** statement telling what the future weather should be like 天氣預報. '**weather vane** device which is fixed on top of a building or pole and turns to show the direction of the wind 風向標. **be / feel under the weather** be / feel ill or depressed *(informal)* 不適, 生病; 精神不振的. (非正式).

weave [wi:v] *vt / i* 1 make cloth from threads (用紗線) 織布. 2 make by twisting or forming together 編成: *She is weaving the flowers into a*

wreath. 她正在把花編成花圈. *The old man weaves many interesting stories from his adventures as a young man.* 那位老人根據他年輕時的奇遇編出許多有趣的故事. 3 move from side to side through 迂迴; 穿梭: *He wove in and out of the traffic in his car.* 他開車在車輛中穿出穿入. *past tense* 過去式 **wove** [wouv]. *past part* 過去分詞 **woven** ['wouvən]. **weaver** *nc* person who weaves (in sense 1) 織工, 織者. **weaving** *nu* art of weaving (in sense 1) 織法.

web [web] *nc* 1 something made by weaving threads together 網狀物, 織物: *a web of cloth* 一匹布; *a spider's web* 蜘蛛網. 2 skin between the toes of certain types of water birds and animals (水禽和水生動物的) 蹼. **webbed** *adj* having skin of this kind 有蹼的: *Ducks have webbed feet.* 鴨的爪有蹼.

wed [wed] *vt / i* take as husband or wife; marry 娶; 嫁; 結婚. *past* 過去式和過去分詞 **wedded** or **wed** *(o.f.)* (舊式). **wedding** *nc* ceremony in which a man and woman are married 婚禮.

wedge [wedʒ] *nc* 1 piece of wood or metal shaped like a V which is driven into wood etc to split it, or is used to keep two things firm or separate 楔子, 三角木. 2 something which is V-shaped 楔形物, V形物: *a wedge of cake* 切成楔形的一塊糕餅. Also 亦作 *vt* 1 keep firm or separate with a wedge 用楔木使牢固; 用楔木劈開. 2 push in like a wedge 楔入; 擠進: *The little boy wedged himself between the two big ones.* 這小孩擠在兩個大孩子中間.

Wednesday ['wednzdi] *n* fourth day of the Christian week 星期三, 禮拜三.

wee [wi:] *adj* small; little. *(informal)* 小

的; 少的. (非正式).

weed [wi:d] *nc* plant growing where it is useless or not wanted 雜草, 莠草. Also 亦作 *vt/i* take out weeds 除去…的雜草; 除去雜草: *In this country the men plant the corn and the women later weed it* i.e. take out the weeds growing among the corn 在這個國家裏, 男人種玉米, 女人以後除雜草. 即: 除去長在玉米邊的雜草.

week [wi:k] *nc* period of seven days (usu. from midnight on Saturday to midnight on the next Saturday) 週, 星期, 禮拜(通常從星期六的午夜至下星期六的午夜, 七天). **weekly** *adj/adv* of or for a week; happening once a week 每週, 一週的, 每週的; 每週發生一次的. Also 亦作 *nc* magazine or paper which is published once a week 週刊; 週報. **weekday** any day of the week except Sunday (除星期天外的任何一天) 週日, 平日. **week'end** *nc* period from Friday or Saturday to Monday; holiday during this period 週末(星期五或星期六至星期一); 週末假日. **tomorrow week** eight days from today 距今八天, 一週後的明天.

weep [wi:p] *vt/i* let tears fall; cry 流淚, 哭泣. *past* 過去式和過去分詞 **wept**.

weigh [wei] *vt* **1** find out how heavy somebody/something is (usu. by using scales) 稱…的重量 (通常用秤): *The butcher weighed the meat for me.* 肉商爲我稱肉. **2** be equal in heaviness to have…重: *The meat weighed five and a half pounds.* 這塊肉重五磅半. *How much do you weigh?* 你的體重是多少? **weighbridge** large machine for weighing a lorry etc and its load (稱車輛及其載重用的) 地磅, 台秤, 橋秤. **weigh down 1** push down by being heavy; be too heavy for 重得把…壓下; 對…太重了: *The*

small boy was weighed down with the parcels he was carrying. 那小孩被自己揹着的包裹壓彎了腰. **2** be too much for 對…太過份: *All his troubles are weighing him down.* 他的種種煩惱正把他壓得透不過氣來. **weigh in** be weighed before an event (e.g. a boxer before a fight, a jockey before a horse-race) (拳擊手, 騎師等) 比賽前量體重. **'weigh-in** *nc*: *At the weigh-in he was 110 pounds.* 比賽前他的體重是110磅. **weigh someone/something up** estimate 估量: *I weighed up my chances of winning.* 我估計了取勝的可能性. *A good teacher soon weighs up his pupils.* 優秀的教師很快能評估他的學生. **weigh anchor** raise the anchor of a ship in order to sail away 起錨; 啓航.

weight [weit] **1** *nu* heaviness of something/somebody 重量: *What is your weight?* 你的體重是多少? *The parcel is 2 pounds in weight.* 這包裹重兩磅. **2** *nc* something which is known to weigh a particular amount 砝碼; 秤錘: *He put three one-ounce weights on the scales.* 他在天平上放了三個一英兩的砝碼. *He wrote down the weights of the boxes.* 他寫下了這些箱子的砝碼數. **3** *nc* something heavy 重物: *If you are ill, you should not lift heavy weights.* 如果你病了, 就不要提重物. **4** *nu* importance; effect. 重要性; 影響力: *He has great weight with people.* 他在人民中間很有影響. **weighty** *adj* heavy; important 重的; 重要的. **'over/'under-'weight** (usu. with reference to a person) weighing too much/too little (通常指人) 太重/太輕. **put on weight** (with reference to a person) become heavier or fatter (指人) 體重增加, 長胖.

weir [wiə*] *nc* wall built across a river

to control but not stop the flow of water (攔河而築以控制水流的)堰堤, 攔河壩, 水柵.

weird [wiəd] *adj* strange; unearthly 古怪的; 非人世所有的.

welcome ['welkəm] *adj* causing pleasure; received with pleasure 令人愉快的; 受歡迎的: *This is welcome news.* 這是可喜的消息. *The money was very welcome to them.* 他們很高興收到這筆錢. *You are welcome to try* i.e. there is nothing to stop you trying. 歡迎你試試. 即: 沒甚麽阻止你試一試. *He is welcome to my room while I'm away* i.e. I'll gladly allow him to use it. 我不在時, 歡迎他用我的房間. 即: 我會高興地允許他使用. (*opp* 反義詞 **unwelcome).** Also 亦作 *nc* greeting or reception 歡迎; 接待: *They gave us a great welcome.* 他們給予我們熱烈的歡迎. *He received a cold / warm welcome.* 他受到冷淡/熱情的接待. Also 亦作 *vt* receive with kindness or pleasure 歡迎, 迎接: *He welcomed them when they arrived.* 他們到達時受到他的迎接.

weld [weld] *vt* join pieces of metal by first softening them by heat and then pressing or fixing them together; join anything closely together 焊接, 熔接; 鍛接; 使緊密結合. Also 亦作 *nc* metal joint made in this way 焊接(點), 熔接點, 接頭. **welder** *nc* **welding** *nu.*

welfare ['welfɛə*] *nu* health and comfort; happiness; well-being 康樂; 幸福; 福利: *In every country, child welfare is important.* 每個國家的兒童福利都是重要的. *He works hard for the welfare of the poor.* 他爲窮人的福利而努力工作. **'welfare 'state** country which provides for the security and health of its citizens 福利國家.

well¹ [wel] *nc* deep hole made in the ground to get water or oil 水井; 油井. Also 亦作 *vi* (with reference to a liquid) flow (指液體) 流出來, 湧出: *Tears welled up in her eyes.* 眼淚從她的眼裏湧出.

well² [wel] *adj / adv* **1** in a proper, satisfactory manner 好, 對; 適當地; 令人滿意地: *You speak English well.* 你英語講得好. *I slept well.* 我睡得好. *He treated us well.* 他待我們不錯. **2** carefully; thoroughly 仔細地; 徹底地: *Think well before you answer.* 想好了再回答. *He mixed the drink well before giving it to me.* 他把飲料混合好了再拿給我. **3** with good reason; wisely; probably 有理由地; 明智地; 可能地: *You may well be right.* 你很可能是對的. *I couldn't very well stay.* 我沒甚麽理由呆下去. *Note* 說明: in sense **3** *well* is put in the middle of the verb. 義3well放在動詞之間. **4** to a great degree; considerably 至相當的程度; 頗, 甚: *He sat well back in his chair.* 他坐在椅上, 身體往後靠. *It is now well past two o'clock.* 現在早就過兩點了. **5** in good health; in satisfactory condition 健康的; 令人滿意的: *Are you well?* 你好嗎? *I feel very well.* 我覺得很好. *They are very well where they are.* 他們目前的處境(或位置)很好. (*opp* **unwell** in sense **5)** (義5的反義詞爲unwell). **6** (usu. with **it would be as)** desirable; in one's interest (通常與it would be as連用)可取的, 還是…好; 合…利益: *It would be as well to arrive early.* 還是早到爲好. *It would have been as well to tell him your plans.* 還是把你的計劃告訴他爲好. Also 亦作 *interj*: *Well, here we are!* 啊, 我們到了! *Very well, I'll come.* 很好, 我會來的. *Well, as I was saying, we went away.* 唔, 當時我談到, 我們走開了. **as well** also; in addition 也; 又:

He went away. She went as well. 他走了，她也走了. **as well as** also; in addition to 也;(除…之外)又; *He is learning French as well as English.* 他除了學習英語外，還在學習法語. **just as well** equally suitable; to one's advantage 同樣適合;幸虧; *You might just as well give me the books now as wait till tomorrow.* 你現在把書給我還是等到明天才給我，都可以. *It is just as well (that) he is a kind man* i.e. it is fortunate that he is. 幸虧他是個好心人. **speak well of** praise; approve 稱讚;贊同; *Your teacher speaks well of your work.* 你的老師稱讚你的學業. **wish somebody well** wish somebody success or good luck 祝某人成功或好運.

well-³ [wel] *prefix* **'well-being** health and happiness; welfare 健康和幸福;福利. **'well-known** *adj* known by many; famous 衆所周知的, 著名的. **'well-meaning** *adj* having good intentions; friendly 善意的;友好的. **'well-'meant** *adj* done or said with good intentions 善意的, 好心的. **'well-'off** *adj* rich; having quite a lot of money. *(informal)* 富有的;有錢的. (非正式). **'well-'read** [red] *adj* (with reference to a person) having read many books and so having great knowledge (指人)博覽羣書的, 博學的. **'well-'spoken** *adj* (with reference to a person) speaking well; cultured in speech (指人)談吐令的, 說話得體的. **'well-to-'do** *adj* wealthy 有錢的. **'well-wisher** person who wishes somebody well 表示良好祝願的人, 祝福者.

wellingtons ['weliŋtnz] *npl* type of rubber boots which reach to below the knees 防水長統靴.

wend [wend] *vt* only in **wend one's way** i.e. go *(o.f.)* 僅用於 wend one's way, 即: 走(舊式).

went [went] past tense of **go.** go的過去式.

wept [wept] past of **weep.** weep的過去式和過去分詞.

were [wɜː*] past tense of **be.** be的過去式.

west [west] *nu* (with **the**) part of the sky or direction in which the sun sets (與the連用)西;西方;西邊. Also 亦作 *adj* from or in this direction 從西面來的;在西邊的; *a west wind* i.e. blowing from the west 西風, 即: 從西面來的風; *the west side of the forest* i.e. facing towards the west 森林的西邊, 即: 朝西的. Also 亦作 *adv* towards the west 向西地; *I drove west along the road.* 我沿着路向西開車. (*opp* 反義詞 **east**). **westerly** ['westəli] *adj / adv* **1** from or in the west 從西面來(的); 在西邊的); *a westerly wind* 西風. **2** towards the west 向西的. **western** ['westən] *adj* of or in the west 西方的; 西部的;在西方的; *Western Europe* 西歐; *western civilization* 西方文明. Also 亦作 *nc* film or story about the adventures of cowboys in the western part of the USA (美國西部騎馬牧人奇遇的)西部片, 西部小說. **westward** ['westwəd] *adj / adv* towards the west 向西的;向西.

wet [wet] *adj* **1** covered with water or other liquid 濕的; *The grass was wet after the rain.* 下雨後草濕了. *The paint is still wet.* 油漆仍未乾. **2** rainy 多雨的;下雨的; *wet weather* 多雨的天氣; *the wet season* 雨季. (*opp* 反義詞 **dry**). *comparative* 比較級 **wetter.** *superlative* 最高級 **wettest.** Also 亦作 *vt* make wet 弄濕. *past* 過去式和過去分詞 **wetted. wetness** *nu.*

whack [wæk] *vt* hit hard (usu. causing a

noise when doing so) 用力打, 重擊(通常發出聲來). Also 亦作 *nc* hard, noisy blow 啪的一擊.

whale [weil] *nc* type of very large sea creature 鯨魚.

wharf [wɔːf] *nc* structure built into the water where ships can load and unload 碼頭. *pl* 複數 **wharfs** or **wharves** [wɔːvz].

what [wɔt] *adj / pron / determiner* **1** asking a question with reference to one or more of several (問句中)甚麼; 哪一個或哪幾個: *What country do you come from?* 你從哪個國家來? *What kinds of food do they eat?* 他們吃甚麼樣的食物? *What time is it?* 幾點鐘了? **2** instead of *the;* any / the … that 代替the; 任何…的; …的: *I gave him what money I had.* 我把我當時所有的錢都給了他. *What little I had I gave to him.* 我把僅有的那一點點都給了他. **3** *What a lovely house you have!* 你有一座多麼漂亮的房子啊! *What a strange thing to say!* 要說的事多麼奇怪啊! **4** what thing or things 甚麼, 甚麼東西: *What's worrying you?* 甚麼事使你擔心? *What is your job?* 你做甚麼工作? *What?* i.e. what did you say? 甚麼?即: 你說甚麼? *Note* 說明: in senses **1** and **4** *what* gives a wider choice than *which; which* has the sense of choosing one of two, or one of more from a definite number (e.g. *What coat will you wear?* i.e. you have several to choose from). *Which coat will you wear, the black one or the brown one? Which are˚ yours, these or those?* 義1和義4的what比which有更多的選擇; which表示從二者選一或從一定的數量中選擇其一(如: what coat will you wear? 即: 你穿甚麼大衣?即: 你有幾件可供選擇). *Which coat will you wear, the black one or*

the brown one? 你要穿哪件大衣, 黑色的還是棕色的? *Which are yours, these or those?* 哪些是你的, 這些還是那些? Also 亦作 *relative pron* the thing or things that… 所…的事物: *What he said was very helpful.* 他所說的很有幫助. *He gave me what I wanted.* 他給了我所要的東西. Also 亦作 *interj* (expressing surprise etc.) (表示驚訝等) *What! He's already here!* 甚麼?他已經在這裏了? **what about** asking for information or getting an opinion 問消息或徵求意見. *Dictionaries? What about them?* i.e. tell me about them 詞典? 怎麼樣? 即: 告訴我詞典怎麼樣. *What about going for a walk?* i.e. do you think it is a good idea? 去散散步怎麼樣? 即: 你認為這個主意好嗎? *What about a drink?* i.e. would you like one? 來杯酒如何? 即: 你要喝一杯嗎? **what for** for what purpose? why? 爲甚麼目的? 爲甚麼? *What is this tool (used) for?* 這件工具作甚麼用? *You have come to see me. What for?* 你來見我了. 爲甚麼呢? **what if** what will or would happen if 如果…怎麼樣, 萬一…怎麼辦: *What if I am late?* 要是我遲到了, 怎麼辦? **what…like** asking information about somebody / something 問有關某人／某事物的消息: *What's England like?* 英國怎麼樣? **what with…and** for the following reasons 由於以下原因: *What with plenty of money and good friends, he had a happy life.* 一方面由於有很多金錢, 一方面也由於有很多好朋友, 他過得很幸福.

whatever [wɔtˈevə*] *adj / pron* **1** emphatic form of **what.** what的強調式: *I'll give you whatever help you need.* 你需要甚麼幫助, 我都會幫助你. *You can eat whatever you want.* 你要吃甚麼, 就吃甚麼. **2** emphatic negative after **none** and **no** 用於 none 和 no 之後, 強調否定: *He had no reason whatever for saying this.* 他這樣說是毫無理由的. **3** in spite of what 不論甚麼, 不管甚麼: *Whatever he says, don't go.* 不論他說甚麼, 都不要去. *I am ready to leave whatever the time(is).* 不管現在甚麼時候, 我都準備離開.

whatsoever [ˌwɒtsəu'evə] *pron* whatever 不管甚麼; 無論甚麼; 凡是…的事物. Also 亦作 (used in negative sentences, questions, etc placed immediately after noun) at all (用於否定句, 問句, 緊接在名詞的後面) 任何的: *That's nothing whatsoever with me.* 那件事和我沒有任何關係.

wheat [wi:t] *nu* grain from which flour for making bread is obtained; plant which produces this grain 麥粒; 小麥; 麥子.

wheedle [ˈwi:dl] *vt* get something from somebody, get somebody to do something by being very pleasant to him 騙取(某物); 哄騙(某人幹某事): *They have wheedled a holiday from / out of the headmaster.* 他們用甜言蜜語從校長那裏要准一個假日. *They have wheedled the headmaster into giving them a holiday.* 他們用甜言蜜語使校長給他們一個假日.

wheel [wi:l] *nc* **1** circular device which turns round a central rod or axle and on which bicycles, cars, trains, machines etc move 輪子. **2** device by which a car, ship etc is steered. (often **steering wheel** when reference is to a car) (車等的)駕駛盤(船的)舵輪(駕車時, 常用 steering wheel). Also 亦作 *vt / i* **1** push or pull something which has a wheel or wheels 推動; 拉動(有輪子的東西): *He wheeled his bicycle up the hill* i.e. instead of riding it. 他

把自行車推上了小山. 即: 不是騎車上山. **2** carry somebody / something in a vehicle with wheels 用有輪的車載運(某人 / 某物): *They wheeled him away in an invalid chair.* 他們用輪椅把他推走了. **3** move, cause to move, round like a wheel (使)旋轉; 迴旋: *The soldiers wheeled to the left.* 士兵們向左轉. **'wheelbarrow** type of small cart with one wheel in front and two handles behind 獨輪手推車. **'wheelchair** chair on wheels for a person who cannot walk 輪椅.

wheeze [wi:z] *vt / i* breathe noisily (as one does when one has a cold); make a noise like this 喘氣; 發出呼哧呼哧的喘息聲. Also 亦作 *nc* noise of this kind 喘息聲.

when [wen] **1** *adv* at what time 甚麼時候: *When did you arrive?* 你甚麼時候到的? *I wonder when he'll come.* 我倒想知道他甚麼時候會來. **2** *adv / conj* (with **after, from, since, till** etc.) what time (與 after, from, since, till 等連用)甚麼時候: *Since when have they known him?* 從甚麼時候起他們就認識他了? **3** *rel adv* (after a *n* showing time) (在名詞之後表示時間): *He came last night when I was out.* 昨晚我外出時他來了. *July and August are the months when the weather is hot.* 七月和八月是天氣熱的月份. **4** *conj* at; during; after the time that 當…時; 在…的時候; 在…之後; when did you when he came. 他來的時候我出去了. *When I have finished my work, I will go home.* 我把活幹完後就回家. **5** *conj* if; although 如果; 雖然: *When you cross a main road, you must be careful.* 你過大馬路, 一定要小心. *I'll come when I am needed.* 如果需要我, 我會來的. *He refuses help when he has many friends.* 雖然他有很多朋友, 他還是拒

絕接受幫助. *I'll be here to give you help when necessary* i.e. if it is necessary 如果需要, 我會來這裏幫助你的.

whenever [wen'evə*] *adv* at whatever time; at any time that 在任何時候; 無論何時; *I'll come whenever you want.* 你要我甚麼時候來我就來. *Whenever he speaks, I listen carefully.* 每當他講話時, 我都仔細聽着.

where [weə*] *adv / conj* **1** at, in, to what place 在哪裏; 往哪裏; *Where is my book?* 我的書在哪裏? *Where are you going?* 你上哪兒去? *I don't know where he is.* 我不知道他在哪兒. **2** (with **to, from** etc.) what place (與 to,from等連用) 甚麼地方; *Where are you going (to)?* 你到哪裏去? *Where has he come from?* 他剛從哪裏來? **3** (after a *n* showing place) (在名詞之後表示地點) *The book is on the table where you left it.* 書在你原來放的桌子上. *Where I go for my holidays, there are no shops.* 我去度假的地方, 甚麼商店都沒有. *Go where you like.* 你喜歡到哪兒去就到哪兒去吧. **'whereabouts** *adv* in or near what place 在甚麼地方, 靠近甚麼地方? *Whereabouts does he live?* 他住在甚麼地方? Also 亦作 **'whereabouts** *nc* (with *sing* or *pl* verb) place where somebody / something is (與單數或複數動詞連用) 下落; 去向; *Nobody now knows his whereabouts.* 現在沒有人知道他的去向. **where'as** *conj* on the other hand 而在另一方面, 而, 但是; *He is fat, whereas his brother is thin.* 他很胖, 而他弟弟卻很瘦. **wher'ever** *adv* at, in, to any place 在任何地方; 到任何地方; 不管任何地方; *He goes wherever he wants.* 他愛去哪裏就去哪裏.

whereby [weə'bai] *adv* by what; by which 靠甚麼; 靠哪個; 憑甚麼. *Whereby shall we know her?* 我們靠甚麼認

出她呢? *He devised a plan whereby he might escape.* 他想出一個逃走的辦法.

whereupon [,weərə'pɒn] *adv* **1** upon what; upon which 在甚麼上面; 在那個上面. **2** at which, after which 因此; 於是; 當時; *He insulted her, whereupon she slapped him.* 他侮辱她, 於是她給了他一巴掌.

whet [wet] *vt* often in **whet someone's appetite** i.e. make more hungry or more interested, by giving a little food or a little information etc. 常用於whet someone's appetite, 即: 提供一點食物或消息去刺激某人的胃口, 引起某人的興趣; 使某人更想.... *past* 過去式和過去分詞 **whetted**.

whether ['weðə*] *conj* **1** (in an indirect question) if (用於間接問句) 是否; *I asked him whether he could come.* 我問他能不能來. *He doesn't know whether he can come.* 他不知道他是否能來. *He is not sure whether to come or not* i.e. if he should come or not 他不知道該不該來. *I'll see whether he is at home.* 我看看他是否在家. *Note* 說明: when there are two indirect questions *whether* is used twice (e.g. *We don't know whether our work is finished or whether there is more to be done.* 當有兩個間接問句時, whether用兩次 (如: We don't know whether our work is finished or whether there is more to be done. 我們不知道我們的工作是已經完成了還是有更多的工作要做). **2** (with or in statements, conditions etc which are not indirect questions) if; even if (在陳述句或非間接問句的條件句等中, 與 or 連用) 是否; 無論是不是; 不管; *I am going whether it is raining or not.* 不管下不下雨, 我都要去.

which [witʃ] *adj / adv / pron / determin-*

er **1** asking a question with reference to one or two things / persons, or one or more of a definite number (問句中) 哪個, 哪些 (人, 東西): *Which coat will you wear, the black one or the brown one?* 你要穿哪件大衣, 那件黑的還是那件棕色的? *Which boy did it?* 哪個男孩幹的這事? *Which books are yours?* 哪些書是你的? see also **what. 2** which thing or things; which person or persons 哪個 (些) 東西; 哪個 (些) 人: *Which are your books?* 哪些是你的書? *Which is your brother, John or James?* 哪個是你弟弟, 約翰還是詹姆士? *Which of these boys did it?* 這些男孩中哪一個幹的這事? *He laughed at me, which made me angry.* 他嘲笑我, 弄得我很生氣。 **3** with reference to things only 僅指事物: *The money which is on the table is mine.* 桌上的錢是我的。 *Note* 說明: **1** in this sense *that* can be used instead of *which*, or *which* can be left out. *The money that is on the table is mine. The money on the table is mine.* **2** the sense of *which* as a relative pron changes if commas are put at the beginning and end of its clause (e.g. *Take the key which is on the desk, and open the door* shows what particular key is meant, there being another key or other keys present. But *Take the key, which is on the desk and open the door* merely gives more information about one already known key, there being no others to consider). **3** it is important to remember that *which* as an *adj* and *pron* can be used with reference to things and persons (see senses **1** and **2**); but *which* as a *relative pron* can be used only with reference to things, just as *who* can be used only with reference

to persons. (see sense **3** above). On the other hand, *that* as a *relative pron* can be used with reference to things and persons. see *that²*. **1** 表示本義時, 可用 *that* 代替 *which*, 或將 *which* 省略。*The money that is on the table is mine. The money on the table is mine.* 桌上的錢是我的。**2** *which* 作為關係代詞時, 如果在其從句的前後加上逗號, 其意義不同 (例如 *Take the key which is on the desk and open the door* 拿桌上的鑰匙開門, 表明指那一把鑰匙, 還有另一把或幾把。但 *Take the key, which is on the desk, and open the door* 拿鑰匙開門, 鑰匙就在桌上, 僅對一把已知的鑰匙進一步說明, 並無其他鑰匙需要考慮)。**3** 應記住 *which* 作為形容詞和代詞可指事物和人 (見義 **1**, **2**); 但 *which* 作為關係代詞僅指事物, 正如 *who* 僅指人 (見上述義 **3**)。另一方面, *that* 作為關係代詞可指事物和人。見 *that²*。

whichever [witʃ'evə*] *pron / adj* **1** any one that; any that 隨便哪個; 隨便哪些: *Take whichever you like best.* 你最喜歡哪一個, 就挑哪一個。*Buy whichever hat you like.* 你喜歡哪一頂帽子就買哪一頂。**2** no matter which 無論哪個; 無論哪些: *Whichever side wins, I shall be satisfied.* 無論哪一方獲勝, 我都滿意。

whiff [wif] *nc* slight breath or smell of something 一陣氣味: *a whiff of cigarette smoke* 一股香烟味。

while [wail] *conj* **1** at the time when; during 當…的時候; 在…的時候: *You must keep quiet while he is speaking.* 他講話的時候, 你必須保持安靜。*I met him often while (I was) abroad.* 我在國外期間常常見到他。**2** on the other hand; whereas 另一方面; 而, 卻: *I like tea while she likes coffee.* 我喜歡茶, 而她喜歡咖啡。**3** although 雖然;

While I am ready to help, I hope that others will do so too. 雖然我願意幫忙, 但我希望其他人也來幫忙. Also 亦作 *nu period of time* 一段時間; *I can stay for a little while.* 我可以停留一會兒. *He came here a long time ago.* 他很久以前來過這裏. Also 亦作 *vt* (with **away**) *pass the time, doing a little or nothing* (與away連用) 消磨 (時間), 閒混 (時間); *We whiled away the afternoon sitting on the beach.* 我們坐在海灘上消磨了一個下午.

whilst [waɪlst] *conj* = **while**.

whim [wɪm] *nc sudden idea or wish* (usu. one without a good reason) 忽起的念頭, 一時的興致 (通常是沒有充足理由的).

whimper ['wɪmpə*] *vt / i cry in a weak, frightened manner* (微弱而驚恐地) 抽噎, 啜泣, 嗚咽; (狗等的) 悲嗥. Also 亦作 *nc cry of this kind* 嗚咽; 悲嗥.

whimsy ['wɪmzɪ] *nc sudden strange idea or wish; strange sense of humour* 奇怪念頭, 異想天開; 怪脾氣; 與衆不同的幽默感. **whimsical** *adj*.

whine [waɪn] *vt / i* **1** *make a long moaning or screaming sound* 哀號; *The bullets whined through the air.* 子彈在空中呼嘯而過. **2** *complain in a voice like this* 哀訴, 訴怨. Also 亦作 *nc sound or complaint of this kind* 哀號聲, 哀嗥聲; 哀訴.

whip¹ [wɪp] *nc* **1** *cord or strip of leather fastened to a stick and used for beating* 鞭子. **2** *person who has authority to see that members of a political party who have been elected to parliament obey the rules of the party and attend important meetings and debates in parliament* 國會督導員 (負責敦促跟進國會的黨員遵守黨的紀律並參加國會的重要會議和辯論).

whip² [wɪp] *vt / i* **1** *strike or beat with a*

whip (用鞭子) 鞭打, 抽打. **2** *mix by stirring quickly with a stick, fork etc.* 攪拌; *She whipped the cream to make it thicker.* 她攪打奶油, 使其變稠. **3** *move, cause to move, quickly and suddenly* 迅速又突然移動; *He whipped a gun out of his pocket.* 他突然從口袋裏拔出一枝槍. *past* 過去式和過去分詞 **whipped. whipping** *nc punishment with a whip* 鞭打 (處罰), 笞刑. **whip-round** *collect money for a particular purpose* (usu. to help somebody) (informal) 湊錢, 募捐 (通常用以助人). (非正式). '**whip-round** *nc: We had a whip-round at school to buy something for our friend who was in hospital.* (informal) 我們在學校湊錢給住院的朋友買東西. (非正式).

whip up 1 (with reference to feelings) *make stronger* (指情緒) 激起, 增強; *The news whipped up their anger.* 這消息激起了他們的憤怒. **2** *mix by stirring quickly* 迅速攪打; *My mother whipped up two eggs to put in the cake she was making.* 我母親攪打兩個蛋放進她正在做的蛋糕裏.

whirl [wɜːl] *vt / i move or turn, cause to move or turn, quickly* (使) 飛快移動; 飛跑 (使) 旋轉; *He whirled round to see what was happening.* 他迅速轉過身來看發生了甚麼事. *He whirled his stick above his head.* 他拿着棍子在頭頂上揮舞. *They whirled me away before I could say anything.* 我還來不及說話, 他們就把我飛快地帶走了. *The noise made my head whirl* i.e. *made me dizzy or confused* 那聲音把我弄得暈頭轉向. 即: 使我頭暈或慌亂. Also 亦作 *nc quick movement; confusion* 迅速的活動; 混亂; *the whirl of fast traffic* 車輛交通的繁忙、忙碌. *My thoughts were in a whirl.* 我的思想一片混亂. '**whirlpool** *water which goes*

round and round quickly 漩渦.
'whirlwind wind which blows round
and round instead of in one direction
旋風.

whirr [wə:*] *nu* noise made by something moving quickly in or through
the air 呼呼地飛或旋轉的聲音, 颼颼
聲. Also 亦作 *vi* make this kind of
noise 發出颼颼聲, 作呼呼聲. *past* 過
去式和過去分詞 **whirred.**

whisk [wisk] *vt / i* **1** move, cause to
move, lightly and quickly (使)輕快地
移動, 拂, 揮, 掃, 揮動; 忽忙帶走.
The horse stood whisking its tail. 那匹馬站
着揮動尾巴. *He whisked the dust off
his desk with a cloth.* 他用一塊布把桌
上的灰塵撣掉. *She was whisked away
by her friends before I could speak to
her.* 我還來不及跟她說話, 她的朋友就
把她帶走了. **2** mix by stirring lightly
and quickly 輕快地攪拌, 打: *She
whisked the eggs and milk together.*
她把蛋和牛奶攪拌在一起. Also 亦作
nc device for stirring and mixing food
攪拌器.

whisker ['wiskə*] *nc* (usu. *pl*) (通常用
複數) **1** hair growing on the side of a
man's face 連鬢鬍子, 腮鬚. **2** stiff hair
growing sideways from the face of
some animals (某些動物的)鬚: *a cat's
whiskers* 貓的鬚.

whisky, whiskey ['wiski] *nc / u* type of
alcoholic drink 威士忌酒.

whisper ['wispə*] *vt / i* **1** speak softly,
using only the breath, not the voice
低聲說(話), 耳語, 嘀咕: *He whispered
to me to follow.* 他低聲叫我跟上. *I
whispered my name to him so that the
others would not hear.* 我低聲告訴他
我的名字, 以免別人聽見. **2** make any
soft, gentle sound 發颼颼聲, 沙沙地
響: *The wind whispered through the
trees.* 風穿過樹林颼颼作響. Also 亦作

nc / u: *He spoke to me in a whisper.*
他低聲地對我說. *I hear whispers that
you are getting a new job* i.e. I hear
rumours. 我聽到謠傳說你要得到一份
新的工作.

whist [wist] *nu* type of card game 惠斯
特牌(一種紙牌戲).

whistle ['wisl] *vt / i* **1** make a high, clear
sound by passing air through a small
hole (e.g. by almost closing the lips
and blowing hard through them; or by
blowing through a device with a small
hole in it) 吹口哨; 吹笛; 鳴汽笛. **2**
make this kind of sound in other ways
風的嘯聲; 子彈打出時的颼颼聲等. *The
high wind whistled through the streets.*
大風呼呼吹過街道. *The birds were
whistling in the forest.* 鳥兒在林中囀
鳴. Almost 幾乎 *nc / u* **1** sound of this
kind 口哨聲; 笛聲; 汽笛聲; 哨子聲; 嘯
聲. **2** device which makes this sound
口笛; 哨子; 汽笛: *a policeman's whistle* 警笛; *a referee's whistle* 裁判的哨
子; *a steam whistle* i.e. one which is
blown by steam 汽笛, 即: 蒸汽發出的
笛聲.

white [wait] **1** *nc / u* colour like the
page of a book 白(色): *The boys
wore white.* 男孩子們穿白色衣服. **2**
nc somebody / something that is
white 白種人; 白色的東西: *Few whites
live in West Africa* i.e. white people 很
少白人住在西非. *She used the whites
of six eggs to make the cake* i.e. the
parts round the yellow yolks 她用了六
個蛋的蛋白來做那個蛋糕. *The whites
of his eyes are bloodshot* i.e. the white
parts round the coloured centre of
the eyes. 他的眼白充滿血絲. Also 亦
作 *adj* of this colour; having no colour; very pale 白(色)的; 無色的; 蒼白
的: *Snow is white.* 雪是白色的. *He
was wearing a white shirt.* 他那時穿着

一件白襯衫. *Many old people have white hair.* 許多老人有白頭髮. *West Africa was once ruled by white men* i.e. men with pale skins, from Europe 西非一度由白人統治: 即從歐洲來的白皮膚的人. **whiteness** *nu* **'white-'collar** *adj* with reference to work which is not done with the hands (e.g. a clerk has a white-collar job, a motor mechanic has not) 不從事體力勞動的, 白領階級的, 腦力工作的 (如: 文書是白領職位, 而汽車修理工則不是).

white lie type of lie which is not serious and can be excused (esp. one told to avoid hurting somebody's feelings) 不嚴重並可以原諒的小謊, 圓場謊 (尤指避免傷害某人感情的) **'whitewash** *nu* **1** mixture of water and lime or chalk, used to paint walls, ceilings etc. (粉刷用的) 石灰水. **2** attempt to hide the mistakes made by somebody 掩飾; 粉飾. Also 亦作 *vt* **1** paint with whitewash (用石灰水) 粉刷. **2** try to hide mistakes; try to make somebody appear better than he really is 掩飾(錯誤); 粉飾, 美化.

Whitsun ['witsn] *nc* seventh Sunday after Easter 復活節後的第七個星期天, 聖靈降臨節.

whittle ['witl] *vt* (with **away, down**) cut thin pieces from something (esp. wood); slowly make smaller (與 away,down 連用) 切, 削 (尤指木頭); 使逐漸變小: *He is whittling down the branch with a knife to make a handle for his hoe.* 他正用刀削樹枝做一把鋤頭柄. *The power of the chiefs has been whittled away by the government.* 政府已逐漸削弱了酋長們的權力.

whizz [wiz] *nu* noise made by something moving quickly in／through the air 某物掠過空中的聲音, 颼颼聲. Also

亦作 *vt／i* make this kind of noise 發颼颼聲: *He whizzed past us on his bicycle.* 他騎着自行車颼颼地從我們身邊經過. *past* 過去式和過去分詞 **whizzed.** **'whizz kid** young person who has achieved early success because of his ability *(informal)* (因能幹而早早取得成功的) 傑出青年, 青年才俊, 神童 (非正式).

who [hu:] *pron* **1** used in asking a question with reference to a person or persons (usu. used as a subject but see *Note* below) (用於問句) 誰 (通常用作主語, 見下文說明). **whom** [hu:m] objective form of **who** (but see *Note* below) who的受格 (見以下說明): *Who is your teacher?* 誰是你的老師? *I don't know who he is.* 我不知道他是誰. *Whom did you see yesterday?* 昨天你見到誰了? *With whom are you staying?* 你住在誰家裏? *Note* 說明: although *whom* is more correct as an object and after *a prep, who* is more often used instead in conversation. *Whom did you see yesterday? (formal)／Who did you see yesterday? (informal) With whom are you staying? (formal)／Who are you staying with? (informal)* 作爲賓語或用於介詞之後, whom較爲正確, 但在口語中, who較爲常用. Whom did you see yesterday? (正式)／Who did you see yesterday? (非正式) 昨天你見到誰了? With whom are you staying? (正式) ／Who are you staying with? (非正式) 你住在誰家裏? **2** used to define or identify a person or persons 用以指明某(些)人: *The tall man who is standing over there is my brother.* 站在那裏的那位高個子的人是我的哥哥. *This is the boy who broke the window.* 這就是打破窗子的那個男孩. *The tall man whom you met is my brother.* 你遇見

的那個高個子是我哥哥. *Note* 說明: **1** in this sense of defining or identifying, *that* can be used instead of *who* or *whom*. **2** *who* or *whom* can be left out (e.g. *The tall man standing over there is my brother. The tall man you met is my brother*). **3** when there is a *prep* either *whom* or *that* can be used but *whom* must come immediately after the *prep*. With *that* the *prep* comes at the end (e.g. *The man that you spoke to is my brother* or (leaving out *that*) *The man you spoke to is my brother*). **4** the sense of *who* and *whom* changes if commas are put at the beginning and the end of their clause (e.g. *The tall man who is standing over there is my brother* i.e. without commas *who is standing over there* shows which person is meant, there being others present. *My brother, who is standing over there, is a doctor* i.e. with commas, *who is standing over there*, merely gives more information about somebody already known, there being no need to identify him. In the same way compare *The man whom you met just now is my brother* and *My brother, whom you met just now, is a doctor*). 1. 表示本義即說明或指明時, *that* 可用來代替 *who* 或 *whom*. 2. *who* 或 *whom* 可以省略 (如: The tall man standing over there is my brother. The tall man you met is my brother). 3. 有介詞時, *whom* 或 *that* 都可選用, 但 *whom* 必須緊跟在介詞之後. 用 *that* 時, 介詞放在最後 (如: The man that you spoke to is my brother 或 (省 *that*) The man you spoke to is my brother). 4. 若在其從句的前後加上逗號, *who* 和 *whom* 表示的意義即改變 (如: The tall man who is standing over there is my brother. 即:

沒有逗號, who is standing over there 表示指的是那個人, 還有其他人也在那裏. My brother, who is standing over there, is a doctor. 即: 加上逗號, who is standing over there 僅對已知的那個人加以進一步說明, 因爲不必對他另加以指明. 同樣比較 The man whom you met just now is my brother 和 My brother, whom you met just now, is a doctor). **whose** [hu:z] *pron / determiner* of whom 誰的; 那個 / 些人的; *Whose books are these?* 這些是誰的書? *I wonder whose coat this is?* 我不清楚這是誰的外衣? *The boys whose names were called stood up.* 叫到名字的那些男孩子都站了起來. *Note* 說明: the sense of *whose* as a *relative pron* changes if commas are put at the beginning and end of its clause in the same way as for *who* and *whom* (e.g. *The one whose hair is grey is my brother. My brother, whose hair is grey, is younger than I am*). see who Note **4**. 與 who 和 whom 一樣, 若在其從句前後加上逗號, whose 作爲關係代詞的意義也改變 (如: The one whose hair is grey is my brother. 那位頭髮灰白的人是我弟弟. My brother, whose hair is grey, is younger than I am. 我弟弟比我年輕, 可是頭髮都灰白了). 見 who 說明 4. **whoever** *pron* any person who; no matter who 任何人; 不論誰; *Whoever thinks that is silly.* 那樣想的人都是愚蠢的. *Whoever tries to beat him, he always wins.* 不論誰去打他, 他總是贏的.

whole [houl] *adj / determiner* **1** complete; all 完全; 全部: *I lived here for a whole year.* 我在這裏住了整整一年. *The whole school had a holiday.* 全校放了一天假. *You must give your whole attention to the problem.* 你必須把全部注意力用於解決這個問題. *He* spoke for two whole hours. 他講了整整兩個鐘頭. *Whole cities were destroyed in the earthquake.* 許多城市在地震中被整個毀壞了. **2** not damaged or broken 未損壞的; 未打破的; 完整的: *He escaped with a whole skin.* 他安然脫險了. *I haven't a whole pair of socks left.* 我沒有剩下一雙完好的短襪. *Note* 說明: as the above examples show, *whole* usu. comes just before its noun. When it comes after the *n* it has a different sense (e.g. *He ate the whole egg* i.e. all it, but *He ate the egg whole* i.e. all at once without cutting it into pieces). 上面例子說明, whole 通常僅用於名詞之前, 若用於名詞之後, 則意義不同 (如: He ate the whole egg.他吃了整個一個蛋. 即: 蛋的全部.但 He ate the egg whole. 他一口吞下一個蛋. 即: 沒有分開吃). Also 亦作 *nc / u* (usu. *sing*) (通常用單數): *I lived here for the whole of a year.* 我在這裏住了整整一年. *You must give the whole of your attention to the problem.* 你必須把全部注意力關注這個問題. *The whole of his family was killed.* 他全家都被殺害了. **wholly** ['houli] *adv* completely; altogether 完全地, 全部地: *He is wholly reliable.* 他完全可靠. *I don't wholly trust them.* 我不完全信賴他們. **'whole'hearted** *adj* with all one's power; as well as one can 全力的; 全心全意的. **wholeheartedly** *adv*.

wholesale ['houseil] *nu* sale of goods in large quantities to shopkeepers and traders who then sell them to the public 批發. (*opp* 反義詞 **retail**). Also 亦作 *adj / adv* **1** *They own a wholesale business in clothes.* 他們經營服裝批發生意. *Shopkeepers buy wholesale and sell retail.* 小店主整批買進貨物再零售出去. **2** on a large

scale; including almost everybody / everything 大規模的(地); 大批的(地); 全部的(地): *During the war houses were destroyed wholesale.* 戰爭時期, 大批的房子被摧毀了. **wholesaler** *nc* person who sells wholesale 批發商.

wholesome ['houlsəm] *adj* clean and pleasant; good for the health 合乎衛生的; 有益健康的. (*opp* 反義詞 **unwholesome**).

whom [hu:m] objective form of **who**. who的受格.

whoop [hu:p] *nc* loud cry 大叫, 吶喊. Also 亦作 *vt / i* cry out loudly 大叫, 吶喊.

whore [hɔ:*] *nc* prostitute 娼妓, 妓女.

whose [hu:z] *pron / determiner* see 見 **who**.

why [wai] *adv* **1** for what reason 爲甚麼: *Why did you do it?* 你爲甚麼幹這件事? *I don't know why I did it.* 我不知道爲甚麼我做這件事. *Why not try yourself?* 你爲甚麼不自己試試? **2** *The reason why he left school was to look after his parents.* 他退學的理由是要照顧父母. *That is why I am late.* 那就是我遲到的原因. Also 亦作 *interj* to express surprise or disagreement 表示驚訝或異議: *Why, it's our friend, John!* 咦, 是我們的朋友, 約翰! *It isn't difficult! Why, I have done it many times!* 那不難嘛! 怎麼, 我已經做過好多次了!

wick [wik] *nc* narrow piece of cloth which draws up oil in an oil lamp etc and so, when set alight, continues to burn for a long time; string in the centre of a candle for the same purpose 燈芯, 蠟燭芯.

wicked ['wikid] *adj* (with reference to a person or what he does) wrong; bad (指人或其行爲) 錯的; 邪惡的; 不道德的; 壞的; 頑皮的. **'wickedness** *nu*.

wicker ['wikə*] *nu* sticks crossed over each other as in a basket (usu. used as an *adj*: *a wicker chair*) 編籃子的柳條 (通常用作形容詞: a wicker chair柳條椅). **'wickerwork** things made of wicker 柳條製品.

wicket ['wikit] *nc* three sticks put in the ground for playing cricket; the ground between the two sticks of this (板球的)三柱門; 兩個三柱門之間的球場.

wide [waid] *adj* **1** great in distance from side to side; broad 寬的; 廣闊的: *a wide road* 寬闊的路; *a carpet 3 metres long and 2 metres wide* 三米長、兩米寬的地毯. (*opp* 反義詞 **narrow**). **2** great; including much 廣大的; 廣泛的; 淵博的: *He has a wide knowledge of English.* 他有淵博的英語知識. *We looked across the wide plains.* 我們望着那片廣闊的平原. *The children watched with wide eyes* i.e. big, fully-opened eyes. 孩子們睜大眼睛看着. **3** missing by much what is aimed at or intended 遠離目標的, 差得遠的: *His spear was wide of the man he threw it at.* 他的矛遠離他所投向的那個人. Also 亦作 *adv*: *He left the door wide open.* 他讓門敞開着. *Open your mouth wide.* 張大你的嘴. *His spear fell wide.* 他的矛沒有投中.

widely *adv* greatly; to a great degree 廣大地, 廣闊地, 廣泛地; 相當地, 大大地: *The two books are widely different.* 兩本書大不相同. *It is not widely known that he is a writer.* 很少人知道他是一位作家. **width** [widθ] *nc / u*: *a carpet two metres in length and one metre in width* 長兩米、寬一米的地毯.

widen *vt / i* make, cause to become, wide or wider 加寬, 弄寬, 變寬, 擴展. **'wide-a'wake** *adj* **1** fully awake 清醒的. **2** lively; fully aware of what

is happening 精明的; 機警的. **'widespread** *adj* spread over, found in, a large area 分佈廣的, 遍及各地的; 傳遍各處的; 普遍的, 蔓延的. **far and wide** over a large area; everywhere 廣泛地; 到處: *They looked far and wide for the escaped prisoner.* 他們到處尋找逃犯.

widow ['widou] *nc* woman whose husband is dead 寡婦. **widower** *nc* man whose wife is dead 鰥夫.

width [widθ] *nc / u* see 見 **wide**.

wield [wi:ld] *vt* use in the hand; hold 揮舞, 使用; 支配, 掌握, 行使: *He was wielding a knife.* 他在揮舞着一把刀. *The president wields great power.* 總統行使很大的權力.

wife [waif] *nc* woman to whom a man is married 妻子, 太太, 内人. *pl* 複數 **wives** [waivz].

wig [wig] *nc* covering made of hair or a substance like hair to be worn on the head (e.g. by an actor, judge, bald person or for reasons of fashion) 假髮 (如: 演員, 法官, 禿子或爲時髦裝飾而戴).

wiggle ['wigl] *vt / i* move, cause to move, quickly up and down or from side to side (使快速上下或左右)扭動, 擺動: *He sat wiggling his toes.* 他坐着扭動腳趾. Also 亦作 *nc / u* movement of this kind 扭動; 擺動.

wild [waild] *adj* **1** (with reference to an animal) not tamed by man; free (指動物)野的, 未馴養的; 野居的, 野生的; *Lions are wild animals.* 獅子是野生動物. **2** (with reference to a plant) not planted by man; growing naturally (指植物)非栽植的; 野生的: *The field is full of wild flowers.* 田裏長滿野花. **3** (with reference to a person, country etc.) not civilized; rough (指人, 國家等)未開化的; 野蠻的: *The forest is the* *home of wild tribes.* 森林是野蠻部族居住的地方. *The country outside the town was wild and hilly.* 城外的鄉村荒涼又多山. **4** (with reference to the weather etc.) severe; violent (指天氣等) 強烈的; 狂烈的: *The weather in winter is wild.* 冬天的天氣是狂烈的. *It was impossible to swim in the wild sea.* 在波濤洶湧的大海裏游泳是不可能的. **5** (with reference to feelings, behaviour etc) very excited; not controlled; reckless (指情感, 行爲等) 很激動的; 無節制的; 瘋狂的: *He gave a wild laugh.* 他狂笑了一陣. *His stupid behaviour made me wild* i.e. very angry 他的愚蠢舉動使我氣炸了. 即: 非常憤怒. *He has a wild plan to run away from school.* 他有一個輕率的逃學計劃. **wildly** adv: *He laughed wildly.* 他狂笑了. **the wilds** npl uncultivated or uncivilized areas of land 荒野: *the wilds of Canada* 加拿大的荒野. **'wildcat** adj sudden and reckless; without good reason 莽撞的; 盲目的: *This is a wildcat scheme.* 這是一項冒險的計劃. *The workmen have started a wildcat strike* i.e. one not supported by their trade union 工人們臨時發動了罷工. 即: 未得到工會支持的. **'wildfire** only in **spread like wildfire** (of news etc.) i.e. spread very quickly 僅用於spread like wildfire (指新聞等), 即: 傳播得很快. **wild-'goose chase** useless journey or course of action 白費心機的搜尋或行動: *The false information set us off on a wild-goose chase.* 這個假傳閒讓我們白白地搜尋了一番. **'wildlife** wild animals; animals living in their natural state 野生動物: *He has gone to Africa to photograph wildlife.* 他到過非洲拍攝野生動物.

wilderness ['wildənis] *nu* bare uninhab-

ited land; desert 荒野; 沙漠.

wile [wail] *nc* trick; temptation 詭計; 花言巧語, 騙人的把戲. **wily** adj.

wilful ['wilful] (*US* 美 **willful**) adj **1** (with reference to a person) determined to do what one wants, whether it is good or bad; having a strong will (指人) 任性的; 倔强的. **2** (with reference to an act) done on purpose, not by accident (指行爲) 蓄意的, 故意的: *The wilful killing of a person is murder.* 故意殺人便是謀殺.

will[1] [wil] *aux* **1** showing the future 表示將來: *He will be here tomorrow.* 他明天會到這裏來. *You will meet him later.* 你以後會見到他的. *Next Monday will be a holiday.* 下星期一將是假日. *Note* 說明: **1** to express the idea of the future, some speakers of English use *will* with the second and third persons, and *shall* with the first person. However, many speakers of English use *will* with all persons. **2** *would* is used instead of *will* to show the future in the past or in certain *if* clauses (e.g. *I know (that) he will be here* but *I knew (that) he would be here. If he were your father, you would obey him).* **3** in speech *will* is usu. shortened to *'ll, would* to *'d, will not* to *won't* and *would not* to *wouldn't* (e.g. *You'll meet him later. I knew he'd be there. Next Monday won't be a holiday. He told me next Monday wouldn't be a holiday).* 1.表示將來, 有些說英語的人用*will*於第二人稱和第三人稱, 用shall於第一人稱. 但是, 許多說英語的人用will於所有人稱. 2.表示過去將來或在某些if句中, 用would, 不用will (如: I know (that) he will be here.我(現在)知道他將會到這裏來, 但I knew (that) he would be here. 我(過去)早就知道他會到這裏來.

If he were your father, you would obey him.如果他是你的父親,你就會服從他的). 3.在口語中,will通常畧作'll,would畧作'd, will not畧作won't, would not畧作wouldn't (如: You'll meet him later.你以後會見到他.I knew he'd be there.我早就知道他會到那裏去.Next Monday won't be a holiday. 下星期一不放假.He told me next Monday wouldn't be a holiday.他告訴過我, 下星期一不放假). **2** with the sense of agreeing, promising or being ready to 表示同意, 答應, 意願: *Will you help me? Yes, I will / I'll help you.* 你願意幫助我嗎?願意 / 我願意幫助你. *I promised (that) I would / I'd help you.* 我答應過要幫助你. *Please help me. I won't* i.e. I am not ready to help you; I refuse. 請幫助我吧.我才不哩.即: 我不願意幫助你; 我拒絕幫助你. *He wouldn't come* i.e. he refused to come. 他不肯來. 即: 他拒絕來. *The door won't shut* i.e. it cannot be shut. 門關不上. 即: 没法把門關上. *Note* 說明: the question form *Would you...?* is often used as a polite form of request (e.g. *Would you help me open this window?*) 問句式Would you…?常用作客氣的請求(如: Would you help me open this window?請幫我打開這個窗子, 好嗎?). **3** with the sense of happening regularly or from time to time 表示某事定期或時常發生; *Sometimes their father would bring the children home sweets and sometimes he would not.* 有時候他們的父親會帶些糖果回家給孩子們, 有時候不帶. **4** with the sense of being likely to be or to happen 表示很可能是或很可能會發生: *That will be your friend at the door.* 門外那位大概就是你的朋友. *In most cases this method will get good results.* 在大多數情況下, 這個方法都能

取得良好效果. *Note* 說明: in the past *would* is also used in this sense instead of *will* (e.g. *Sometimes they would agree and sometimes they would refuse. We found that in most cases this method would get good results. He would spend the whole weekend listening to records* i.e. that was his custom). (表示本義時, 也可用過去式would代替will (如: Sometimes they would agree and sometimes they would refuse.有時候他們會同意, 有時候他們卻拒絕. We found that in most cases this method would get good results.我們發現在大多情況下這個方法會獲得好結果.He would spend the whole weekend listening to records.他往往把整個週末用來聽唱片. 即: 那是他的習慣). **would rather** prefer to 寧願; 寧可: *He would rather pay now.* 他寧願現在就付錢. *Would you rather have tea or coffee?* 你願意喝茶還是喝咖啡? *I would rather have gone with my brother but it is too late now.* 我本來想和我弟弟一起去, 可是現在太遲了.

will² [wil] **1** *nc / u* power of the mind; determination; wish 意志; 決心; 願望: *He has a strong will.* 他有堅強的意志. *You can win if you have the will to try hard.* 如果你有決心去努力爭取, 你會取勝的. *It was God's will.* 那是上帝的旨意. **2** *nc* written wish of a person about what should happen to his property and money when he dies 遺囑: *In his will he left all his money to his wife and children.* 他在遺囑中把他所有的錢留給妻子和孩子們. '**will-power** strength to control one's feelings; determination 克制力; 意志力; 決心. **good / ill will** kind / unkind feeling; sympathy / lack of sympathy 善意 / 惡意; 同情 / 缺乏同情. **of one's own free will** because one wants to; without being forced 自願, 甘心情願; 不受強迫.

will³ [wil] *vt* use one's power of mind to do something or get something done 立意要做某事或使某事完成, 想要, 意欲: *He died because God willed it.* 他的死乃是上帝的意旨. *Although I was very tired, I willed myself to keep running.* 雖然我很累, 還是堅持跑下去. **willing** *adj* ready to do something 願意 (做某事): *They are willing to help.* 他們願意幫忙. *He is a very willing student.* 他是一個很好學的學生. (*opp* 反義詞 **unwilling**). **willingly** *adv* **willingness** *nu.*

willow ['wilou] *nc* type of tree with flexible branches and long, thin leaves 柳樹. **willowy** *adj* (with reference to a person) tall and slender (指人) 苗條的.

willy-nilly [wili'nili] *adv* **1** in any fashion 雜亂無章地, 亂七八糟地: *She threw the books willy-nilly into the cupboard.* 她把書往櫥裏亂扔. **2** whether willingly or unwillingly 不管願意不願意: *He'll have to do it willy-nilly.* 不管願意不願意, 他都得做此事.

wilt [wilt] *vi / i* lose strength and hang down loosely (使) 凋謝; 枯萎: *The flowers wilted in the hot sun.* 花在猛烈的陽光下萎謝了.

wily ['waili] *adj* see 見 **wile.**

win [win] *vt / i* **1** get by working hard, by being better than others; be successful 贏; 獲勝, 得到成功: *John has won a scholarship.* 約翰已得了一筆獎學金. *We hope to win (the game).* 我們希望贏. *Which side won the war?* 哪一邊贏啦? **2** get by chance or luck (通過機會或運氣) 贏得: *He won a lot of money by gambling on horses.* 他賭馬贏了很多錢. *pres part* 現在分詞 **winning**. *past* 過去式和過去

分詞 won [wʌn]. Also 亦作 *nc* success or victory (esp. in a game) (尤指遊戲中的) 成功, 勝利. **winner** *nc* person, animal or thing that wins 獲勝的人, 動物或東西. **winning** *adj* successful; that wins 成功的; 獲勝的: *the winning horse in the first race* 在第一場比賽中獲勝的馬. **winnings** *npl* money which has been won (usu. by betting or gambling) 贏得的錢 (通常由打賭或賭博而來). '**winning post** post which marks the end of a race 決勝終點. **win somebody over** persuade somebody to agree 說服某人同意, 爭取某人.

wince [wins] *vi* move the body suddenly, or show signs of pain or fear 趕緊避開, 畏縮: *He winced when the stone hit him.* 石頭打中他的時候, 他哆嗦了一下. Also 亦作 *nc* movement of this kind 避開; 畏縮; 退縮.

winch [wintʃ] *nc* device for pulling or lifting by winding a rope round a wheel or drum 絞盤; 絞車. Also 亦作 *vt* pull or lift by a winch 用絞盤, 絞車拉或吊.

wind¹ [wind] **1** *nc / u* moving air 風. *Note* 說明: **1** wind is usu. used with *a, much, little, no* etc or in *pl* when it refers to the amount or type of moving air. *A gentle wind was blowing over the lake. There is too much wind today. As soon as we left the shore we met strong winds.* **2** wind is usu. used with *the* when it refers to a particular time or to something caused by moving air. *In the evening the wind rose / fell* i.e. increased / lessened. *The wind blew down the trees. His house was damaged by the high winds.* 1. 說明風的大小或種類時, wind通常與a, much, little, no 等連用, 或用複數. *A gentle wind was blowing over the lake.* 微風

吹過湖面．There is too much wind today. 今天風太大了．As soon as we left the shore we met strong winds. 我們一離開海岸就遇到了強風．2. 説明某一時間或由風引起某事物時，wind通常與the連用．In the evening the wind rose / fell. 晚上，風增強／減弱了．The wind blew down the trees. 風把樹颳倒了．His house was damaged by the high winds. 他的房子被強風颳壞了．**2** *nu* ability to breathe properly when doing something strenuous (幹費力的事所需的) 呼吸；喘息：*Football players who do not practise soon lose their wind* i.e. become breathless. 若不作練習，足球運動員很快就沒氣了．即：變得上氣不接下氣．**3** *nu* gas which forms in the stomach 胃裏產生的氣體．*People who eat too quickly often suffer from wind.* 吃得太快的人往往肚子會脹氣．**winded** *adj* breathless; not able to breathe properly 喘不過氣來的；氣促的．**windy** *adj* having much wind 大風的．**'windbreak** fence, hedge etc to protect something from strong winds 防風籬，防風牆等防風設備．**'windfall** good fortune which is not expected 意外的好運．**'wind in-strument** musical instrument which is played by blowing air into it (e.g. a trumpet) 管樂器，吹奏器（如：喇叭）．**'windmill** see 見 **mill¹**. **'windpipe** tube in the throat between the mouth and the lungs 氣管．**'windscreen** (*Brit*) piece of glass in front of the driver of a car (英) (汽車的) 擋風玻璃．(*US* 美 **windshield**). **'windswept** *adj* over which strong winds blow 擋風的．

wind² [waind] *vt / i* **1** move, cause to move, in twists or circles (使) 彎曲移動；迂迴，蜿蜒：*We wound our way through the thick forest.* 我們穿過茂密

的森林迂迴前進．*The river winds across the plain.* 那條河蜿蜒流過平原．**2** put something round somebody / something 用某物纏、繞某人／某物：*The nurse wound a bandage round my finger.* 護士用繃帶把我的手指纏起來．*They are winding the rope onto a pole.* 他們正把繩子繞到一根柱子上．**3** (esp. with reference to the spring of a clock or watch) turn round to make tighter (尤指鐘錶的發條) 轉緊，上緊：*You must wind this clock once a week.* 你必須每週一次給這個鐘上一次發條．*past* 過去式 和 過去分詞 **wound** [waund]. Also 亦作 *nc* twist; turn 彎曲；彎繞；轉動；轉：*There are many winds in this road.* 這條路有許多轉彎．*Give the clock one more wind.* 給這個鐘再上一次發條．**wind something up 1** put something round somebody / something; turn round to make tighter. 用某物纏、繞某人／某物；繞緊：*She is winding up the string into a ball.* 她正把細繩繞成一球．*Have you wound up your watch?* 你給錶上發條了沒有？**2** finish 結束；辦完：*The teacher wound up his lesson by showing some pictures.* 老師出示一些圖畫，結束了一堂課．*The baker is winding up his business here* i.e. is preparing to give it up 麵包師傅正在結束他這裏的生意．即：準備放棄生意．**wound up** tense, emotionally excited 緊張的；興奮的．

window ['windou] *nc* opening (usu. of glass) in the wall or roof of a building, car etc to let in air and light (通常指玻璃的) 窗，窗戶．**'window box** container for plants kept outside a window 吊窗錘箱，(窗台上的) 花盆箱．**'window dressing** *nu* skill in showing goods in a shop window to attract attention 櫥窗裝飾；櫥窗陳列．**win-dow dresser** *nc* **'window pane** piece of glass in a window 窗玻璃. '**window shopping** looking at goods in shop windows without buying anything 只看商店櫥窗而不買貨, 逛商店. '**windowsill** ledge inside and outside a window 窗台, 窗檻.

wine [wain] *nc / u* alcoholic drink (usu. made form grapes or other types of fruit) 酒 (通常用葡萄或其他水果製成).

wing [wiŋ] *nc* **1** one of the two parts of the body which a bird uses to fly; one of the parts used by an insect to fly; part of an aircraft needed by it to fly (鳥, 昆蟲, 飛機等的) 翅膀, 翼. **2** something which stretches to the side like a wing (像翅膀一樣伸出的) 側翼: *the right wing of an army* 軍隊的右翼; *the wing of a house* 廂房. **3** (in a football or hockey team) player or players playing on the left or right side (足球隊, 曲棍球隊的) 邊鋒球員: *The first goal was scored by the left wing.* 左翼球員獲得第一分. Also 亦作 *vt* wound a bird in the wing or a person in the arm 傷 (鳥) 翼; 傷 (人) 臂. '**wingspan,** '**wingspread** distance between the tip of one wing and the tip of the other when they are spread 兩翼展開的寬度, 翼展, 翼幅. **take under one's wing** protect; help 保護; 幫助.

wink [wiŋk] *vt / i* **1** shut and open one eye quickly (usu. as a sign of friendship, amusement etc to somebody) (通常表示對某人的友好, 感到快樂等); 使個眼神, 遞個眼色: *When the teacher dropped his books, John winked at me.* 老師把書掉了的時候, 約翰對我遞了個眼色. **2** (with reference to a light) appear to go on and off quickly (指光) 閃爍, 閃亮: *The stars were winking in the clear sky.* 星星在晴空中閃爍. Also 亦作 *nc* **1** act

of shutting one's eye in this way. 眨眼; *He gave me a friendly wink.* 他向我遞了個友好的眼色. **2** very short period 一眨眼間, 一會兒, 瞬間. *We could not sleep a wink last night because of the noise.* 因爲那種噪音, 昨晚我們一會兒也沒有睡. **forty winks** short sleep *(informal)* 小眠, 小睡. (非正式)

winter ['wintə*] *nc* the cold season of the year 冬天. Also 亦作 *vi* spend this season 過冬: *They usually winter in the south of France.* 他們通常在法國南部過冬. '**wintry** ['wintri] *adj* like winter; very cold 冬天 (似) 的; 寒冷的.

wipe [waip] *vt* rub with a cloth, piece of paper etc in order to clean or dry (用布, 紙等) 擦, 抹, 揩: *She wiped the table with a cloth.* 她用布擦桌子. *He wiped his dirty hands on a rag.* 他在一塊破布上擦他的髒手. Also 亦作 *nc*: *He gave his hands a wipe.* 他把手擦一擦. '**wiper** *nc* something which wipes 擦拭物. *(Brit) windscreen wiper* i.e. device which wipes rain from a windscreen (英) (汽車擋風玻璃上的) 刮水器, 雨刮. *(US 美 windshield wiper).* **wipe someone / something out** destroy, remove, completely 消滅; 清除: *One atom bomb can wipe out thousands of people.* 一顆原子彈可以消滅數以千計的人. *We wiped out the defeat by winning the next game.* 我們贏了下一局而免於失敗.

wire ['waiə*] **1** *nc / u* string or thread made of metal 金屬線; 鐵絲; 電線. **2** *nc* message sent by telegraph wire; telegram 電報. Also 亦作 *vt* **1** fasten by wire 用鐵絲捆綁, 綁. **2** send a telegram 打電報: *I wired him because there was no time to send a letter.* 因爲沒有時間寄信, 我打電報給他. '**wiry** *adj* (with reference to a person) thin but strong (指人) 瘦削而結實的. **'live 'wire 1** wire which carries electrical current 通電的電線. **2** person who is full of energy 精力充沛的人.

wireless ['waiəlis] *nc ∕ u* radio 無線電; 收音機.

wise¹ [waiz] *adj* having, or resulting from, knowledge and intelligence 智慧的; 明智的; 明智的: *No wise man wants war.* 明智的人都不要戰爭. *They were wise to take their friend's advice.* 他們很聰明, 聽取了朋友的勸告. *He gave me a wise look* i.e. showing that he understood or pretending that he understood 看他的樣子, 他是明白的. 即: 他理解了或似乎理解了. (*opp* 反義詞 **unwise**). **wisely** *adv* **wisdom** ['wizdəm] *nu* **'wisecrack** clever and amusing remark (*informal*) 俏皮話; 妙語. (非正式). **'wisdom tooth** one of the four teeth which grow at the back of the jaw of an adult 智齒.

wise² [waiz] *nu* manner; way (*o.f.* except when joined to other words e.g. *lengthwise; otherwise; clockwise* i.e. moving in the same direction as the hands of a clock) 方式; 方法(舊式, 與其他詞結合者例外. 如: lengthwise 直; otherwise 不那樣; clockwise 順時針方向). *Note* 說明: this word is combined with many words in an informal way (e.g. *careerwise; planning-wise* i.e. with regard to one's career, the planning etc.), but it is better not to imitate this usage. 這個詞與許多詞結合, 爲非正式(如: careerwise 就職業來說; planning-wise 就計劃而言等), 但最好不要模倣這種用法.

wish [wiʃ] *vt ∕ i* **1** desire; want 希望; 要: *I wish to see the headmaster.* 我希望見到校長. *He wishes us to listen carefully.* 他要我們細心地聽. *Note* 說明:

in this sense *wish* is more formal; *want* is more usual 表示本義時, wish 較爲正式; want 較爲通用. **2** have or express a hope or desire 渴望; 祝願: *I wished him safe at home.* 我真希望他平安到家. *They wished me good luck.* 他們祝我好運. **3** (without *that* and followed by the *past tense* or *subjunctive*) desire something which is not possible or is not very likely (不用 that,後接過去式或虛擬語氣)盼望無法實現或不大可能的事物; 但願: *I wish I were rich.* 但願我很有錢. *We only wish we could help.* 只盼我們能予以幫助. *He wished he had agreed to go.* 他真希望他已同意要去. **4** (without *that* and followed by **would**) ask or hope that (不用 that,後接 would) 請求或希望: *I wish you would stop talking so much.* 我請求你別談這麼多了. *We wish they would leave us alone.* 我們希望他們別來打攪了. Also 亦作 *nc ∕ u* **1** desire; request 願望; 要求: *They have no wish to work.* 他們不想工作. *Has he told you what his wishes are?* 他有甚麼願望, 告訴你了嗎? **2** something wished for 所願望的事物: *All her wishes have come true.* 她的所有願望都實現了. **'wishbone** V-shaped bone of a hen, sometimes pulled in two by two people who wish for the longer part which is supposed to bring good luck 願望骨, 叉骨 (母雞的V形骨, 有時兩人吃前各持一端拉開, 據信, 扯到較長一端者會帶來好運氣.

wishy-washy ['wiʃiwɔʃi] *adj* watery; thin; weak; uninteresting. (*informal*) 稀稀拉拉的; 稀薄的; 淡的; 乏味的. (非正式).

wisp [wisp] *nc* small amount of grass, hair, smoke etc. 一小束(草), 一綹(頭髮), 一縷(烟)等.

wistful ['wistful] *adj* wanting something

but sad because it is not likely to be obtained 渴望某物但因難以得到而愁悶的: *There was a wistful look on the child's face when he saw all the toys in the shop window.* 那孩子看見商店櫥窗裏所陳列的玩具, 臉上露出了渴望又愁悶的神情.

wit [wit] **1** *nc* (often *pl*) intelligence; quick thinking (常用複數) 理智, 才智; 機智, 機靈: *To solve this problem you must use your wits.* 要解決這個問題, 你必須運用理智. **2** *nu* ability to say clever and amusing things 措辭巧妙的能力: *His talk was full of wit.* 他的講話趣味橫溢. **3** *nc* person who has this ability 富於機智的人, 風趣的人. **witty** *adj* clever and amusing 機敏的; 詼諧的. **wittily** *adv* **witticism** ['witisizəm] *nc* clever and amusing saying or remark 妙語; 俏皮話; 詼諧語; 雋語.

witch [witʃ] *nc* woman who is believed to have magic powers 巫婆, 女巫. **'witchcraft** magic power or skill 魔法; 巫術. **'witch doctor** man who is believed to have magic powers (esp. to cure diseases) 巫醫; 巫師.

with [wið] *prep* **1** in the company of; accompanied by; together; at the same time as 跟; 與, 同; 和…在一起, 與…同時: *We live with our uncle and aunt.* 我們與伯父和伯母住在一起. *He arrived at school with his friends.* 他和朋友一起到校. *We had the English lesson with another class.* 我們和另一班上英語課. *I always have a spare pencil with me.* 我總是帶着一把備用的鉛筆. **2** having 有; 帶着; 顯出: *Who is the man with the long beard?* 那位留着長鬍子的人是誰? *I want a book with all the information.* 我要一本含有這一切資料的書. **3** using; by means of; by 用; 被: *I cut the rope with a knife.* 我用小刀割繩子. *He

writes with his left hand.* 他用左手寫字. *The country is covered with thick frost.* 鄉村被厚霜覆蓋着. *He opened the meeting with a short speech.* 會議以他簡短的講話開始. **4** showing manner 表示方式: *Please drive with care.* 請小心開車. *They did it with great pleasure.* 他們很愉快地做了這件事. *The bomb exploded with a bang.* 炸彈砰地一聲爆炸了. *They agreed with reluctance.* 他們勉強同意了. **5** because of 因為: *He was shaking with fright.* 他驚得發抖. *They are dying with hunger.* 他們快要餓死了. **6** referring to; concerning 對於; 關於: *With most children play is as important as work.* 對於大多數孩子來說, 玩耍像工作一樣重要. *The real aim with him is to make lots of money.* 至於他, 真正的目的是大量挣錢. **7** in spite of; even although having 儘管; 雖然有: *With all his terrible injuries he did not die.* 儘管他的傷勢很重, 他卻沒死. *With the best teachers in the world they cannot pass the examination.* 雖然他們有世界上最好的老師, 他們還是考不及格.

withdraw [wið'drɔ:] *vt / i* **1** move or draw back; take away 後退; 縮回; 取回; 領出: *After being attacked, the army withdrew.* 軍隊受到攻擊後便撤退了. *I am going to withdraw all my money from the bank.* 我要從銀行裏提取我的所有存款. **2** take back; cancel 收回; 取消: *You must withdraw your stupid statement.* 你必須收回你那愚蠢的話. *Why did he withdraw his consent?* 為甚麼他撤銷他的承諾? *past tense* **withdrew** [wið'dru:] *past part* 過去分詞 **withdrawn**. **withdrawal** *nc / u* act of withdrawing or being withdrawn 後退; 縮回; 撤走; 退出; 退回; 收回; 取消. **withdrawn** *adj* (of persons) reserved, unsociable (指

人)退隱的, 遁世的; 離羣的, 孤僻的.

wither ['wiðə*] *vt/i* (often with **away** or **up**) dry up, cause to dry up, and die (常與 away 或 up 連用) (使) 枯萎; 凋零, 凋謝: *The crops withered (away/up) because there was no rain.* 因為沒有下雨, 作物枯萎了. **withering** *adj*: *He gave me a withering look* i.e. one showing great disapproval 他惡狠狠地看了我一眼, 使我畏縮. 即: 表示很不贊同.

withhold [wið'hould] *vt* refuse to give 不給; 扣留: *withhold information from the police* 把消息扣着不報告警察. *past* 過去式和過去分詞 **withheld** [wið'held].

within [wið'in] *prep* inside; in 在…內; 在…裏: *He'll arrive within the next hour.* 不到一小時他就會到. *I live within a mile of the railway station.* 我住在離火車站不到一英里的地方.

without [wið'aut] *prep* not with; not having 缺乏, 沒帶; 沒有: *I have come without (any) money.* 我沒帶錢就來了. *Don't go without your coat.* 帶上大衣走吧. *He is completely without fear.* 他一點也不害怕. *He went away without saying goodbye* i.e. and did not say goodbye 他沒出聲再見就走了. *He cannot argue without losing his temper* i.e. he always loses his temper when he argues. 他不發脾氣就不會爭辯的. 即: 他爭辯時總是發脾氣. **without (a) doubt** see 見 **doubt. do without someone/something** manage without somebody/something 沒有某人/某物也行: *People cannot do without food.* 人沒有食物可不行. *If he has no coat, he will have to do without (it).* 他若沒有大衣, 他就只好不穿了.

withstand [wið'stænd] *vt* stand against; resist successfully 抵抗, 抵擋; 經得起.

past 過去式和過去分詞 **withstood** [wið'stud].

witness ['witnis] *nc* **1** person who has himself seen something happening 目擊者: *Were you a witness to this accident?* 你是這場事故的目擊者嗎? **2** person who is called upon to tell what he knows in a court of law (法庭上的) 證人: *The accused had many witnesses to say that he was not guilty.* 被告有很多證人可以證明他是無罪的. **3** person who signs his name on a document to confirm that another person's signature is genuine (在文件上簽名以證明他人的簽名無誤的) 證人, 連署人. Also 亦作 *vt* **1** see 見: *Did you witness this accident?* 你看見過這場事故嗎? **2** sign a document to confirm that another person has signed it (在文件上) 簽名作證, 連署: *If I sign this document will you witness my signature?* 如果我在這文件上簽名, 你能簽名爲我作證嗎? '**witness box** place where a witness stands in a court of law (法庭上的) 證人席, 證人台. '**eyewitness** see 見 **eye.**

witticism ['witisizəm] *nc* **witty** ['witi] *adj* see 見 **wit¹.**

wives [waivz] *pl* of **wife.** wife 的複數形式.

wizard ['wizəd] *nc* man who is believed to have magic powers 男巫, 術士.

wobble ['wɔbl] *vt/i* shake, cause to shake, because not firmly fixed or placed (使) 搖搖擺擺, 搖擺: *My desk wobbles because one of its legs is too short.* 我的桌子搖搖擺擺, 因爲有一條桌腿太短了.

woe [wou] *nc* (often *pl*) troubles; difficulties (常用複數) 苦痛; 困難: *the woes of being a schoolmaster* 作爲校長的難處. **woeful** *adj* full of sorrow; sad 悲痛的; 悲傷的; 憂傷的.

woke [wouk] past tense of **wake¹**. wake¹的過去式.

wolf [wulf] *nc* type of wild animal like a dog found especially in cold northern regions 狼. *pl* 複數 **wolves** [wulvz].

woman ['wumən] *nc* female adult human being (成年) 女人. *pl* 複數 **women** ['wimin]. Also 亦作 *adj*: *a woman doctor* 女醫生; *a woman lawyer* 女律師. *Note* 說明: in some circumstances it is more polite to use *lady* than *woman* (e.g. if referring to a woman who is present one would say *This lady has come to help us* rather than *This woman etc.*) 在某些情況下, 用lady比用woman較爲客氣(如: 指在場的女人常說 This lady has come to help us.這位女士來幫助我們, 而不用 This woman…).

womb [wu:m] *nc* organ of a woman or female animal inside which a baby grows before it is born 子宮.

women ['wimin] *pl* of **woman**. woman 的複數形式.

won [wʌn] past of **win**. win 的過去式及過去分詞.

wonder [wʌndə*] *vt / i* **1** be anxious to know; ask oneself 急於知道; 自己發問, 想知道: *I wonder why he is late.* 我很想知道他爲甚麼遲到. *We wondered who told you.* 我們想知道誰告訴你. **2** (with **about**) feel curious about, think about (與about連用)對…感到好奇; 掛念: *We were wondering about you before you arrived.* 你到達之前我們一直在掛念你. **3** (with **at** or **that**) be surprised (與 at 或 that 連用)感到奇怪; 驚訝: *I don't wonder at their anger.* 他們很憤怒, 我並不奇怪. *How can they wonder (that) they are hated?* 有人恨他們, 他們怎麼會驚訝呢? **4** (with **whether**) as a polite request (與whether連用)表示客氣的請求: *I wonder whether you would lend me some money.* 我不知道你是否能借我一些錢. *I was wondering whether you might be able to help me.* 我正在想你是否能幫助我. Also 亦作 **1** *nc* somebody / something that causes surprise or admiration 奇跡, 奇觀, 奇事; 奇才: *He told us about the wonders of space travel.* 他給我們講有關太空航行的奇觀. **2** *nu* feeling of surprise or admiration 驚奇; 驚異; 驚嘆: *The children looked at the strange pictures in / with wonder.* 孩子們驚奇地看着奇怪的圖畫. **wonderingly** *adv* in a surprised or doubting manner 驚奇地; 懷疑地. **wonderful** *adj* very good, marvellous 好極了; 精彩的; 了不起的: *a wonderful idea* 極好的主意; *a wonderful holiday* 過得很好的假日; *a wonderful person* 了不起的人. **wonderfully** *adv* **it is a wonder (that)** it is surprising that 奇怪的是, 令人驚奇的是: *It was a wonder (that) they were not killed.* 奇怪的是, 他們竟然沒有被殺死. **it is no wonder (that)** it is not surprising that 並不奇怪, 難怪. *Note* 說明: *it is / was etc* is also often left out in the *negative* (e.g. *No wonder he refused*). 在否定式中, it is / was等也常省略(如: No wonder he refused難怪他拒絕了).

won't [wount] short form of **will not**. will not的縮略形式.

woo [wu:] *vt / i* **1** make love to; seek to marry; court 向…求愛; 向…求婚; 求愛; 求婚. **2** try to win 追求; *woo fame and fortune* 追求名利. **3** try to persuade; urge; to make entreaty 說服; 力勸; 懇求.

wood [wud] **1** *nu* substance of which a tree is made 木材, 木頭: *He is cutting wood to make a door.* 他正在砍木頭做門. *The desks are made of wood.*

桌子是木材做的. **2** *nc* (often *pl*) piece of land which is covered with trees (常用 複數) 樹林: *The path goes through the wood/woods.* 這條路通過樹林. *Note* 說明: *a wood is much smaller than a forest.* wood比forest小得多. **wooded** *adj* covered with trees 樹林遍佈的, 長滿樹木的. **wooden** *adj* made of wood 木製的: *wooden desks* 木桌. **'woodpecker** type of small bird which makes holes in trees with its beak to catch insects 啄木鳥. **'wood-wind** musical instruments which are or once were made of wood and are played by blowing 木管樂器, 管樂. **'woodwork** use of wood for making things 木工活.

wool [wul] *nu* hair of sheep, goats etc either in its natural state or after having been made into threads or clothing 羊毛; 毛線; 毛料衣服: *We wear wool in winter and cotton in summer.* 我們冬天穿毛料衣服, 夏天穿棉料衣服. **woollen** ['wulən] (*US* 美 **woolen**) *adj* made of wool 羊毛製的. **woollens** *npl* things made of wool (e.g. clothing, blankets etc.) 毛織品 (如: 衣服, 毛毯等): *Because the weather is cold you should wear your woollens.* 天氣寒冷, 你必須穿呢絨衣服. **woolly** *adj* covered with wool; looking like wool 蓋滿羊毛的; 生滿絨毛的; 毛茸茸的, 像羊毛的.

word [wə:d] **1** *nc* unit of language either spoken or written 字; 詞; 話; 語詞: *This dictionary gives the meaning of many words.* 這部詞典給很多詞註明意思. *In English 'get' is a very common word.* 英語的'get'是一個很常用的詞. **2** *nc* something said; remark; speech 所說的話; 談話; 講話: *I don't believe a word you say.* 你的話我一句也不相信. *We had a few words with*

him i.e. a short talk with him 我們跟他說了幾句話. 即: 跟他的簡短談話. **3** *nu* (without **a** or **the**) message; news (不用 a 或 the) 訊息; 消息: *They have sent me word of their arrival.* 他們給我送來了他們到達的消息. *I received word of his death this morning.* 我接到消息說他今天早上死了. **4** *nu* (with **my, your, his** etc.) promise (與 **my, your, his** 等連用) 承諾: *I give you my word that I'll help.* 我向你保證我會幫助的. *He always keeps his word.* 他總是信守諾言. *He never breaks his word.* 他從不食言. Also 亦作 *vt* put, or express, in words 措詞; 說; 寫: *You can word this sentence much better if you try.* 如果你試試, 這句話的措詞可以好得多. **wording** *nu* way in which words are used to express meaning 措詞; 用語. **'word-'perfect** *adj* (with reference to a person) able to say something which has been learnt by heart without making any mistakes (指人) 能一字不錯地熟記的, 說得一字不誤的. **for words** (usu. with **too**) to express or describe (通常與 too 連用) 表達 或 描繪: *The sunset was too beautiful for words.* 日落之美是難以用言語形容的. **have words with** argue or quarrel with 與…爭辯或爭吵. *Note* 說明: *have a word with* means talk with. *I'll have a word with him tomorrow.* have a word with 的意思是與…交談. *I'll have a word with him tomorrow.* 明天我要和他談談. **word of honour** promise made on one's honour 以名譽擔保的諾言. **by word of mouth** in words which are spoken, not written 口頭地: *The story was passed on by word of mouth.* 這個故事是口頭傳下來的. **word for word** exactly as said or written 逐詞地, 一字不變地, 原原本本地.

wore [wɔ:*] past tense of **wear¹**. **wear¹** 的過去式.

work¹ [wəːk] **1** *nu* energy of mind or body, or of a machine used for a definite purpose 工作, 勞動, 事: *Learning a foreign language is hard work.* 學習一門外語是艱苦的事. *You will be paid well for your day's work.* 你幹了一天的活, 會得到很好的報酬. *This machine does the work of a hundred men.* 這台機器可幹一百個人的活. **2** *nu* what one must do to make a living; trade; profession (爲謀生所做的) 工作; 行業, 職業: *When you leave school you will have to find work.* 你離開學校就得找份工作. *When does he get home from work?* 他下班後甚麼時候到家? *These men have been without work for months.* 這些人已經失業好幾個月了. *Note* 說明: the word *job* (*nc*) can also be used; *find a job; without a job* 也可用 job: find a job 找到工作; without a job 失業. **3** *nu* something which has to be done 必須做的事: *My mother does all the housework.* 我母親做所有的家務事. *Have you finished your homework?* 你的作業做完了嗎? 即: 必須在家而不是在學校做的功課. **4** *nc / u* something produced by the energy of mind or body 作品; 行爲: *the complete works of Dickens* i.e. all the books which he wrote 狄更斯全集. *The robbery was the work of a clever criminal.* 搶劫是一個精靈的罪犯幹的. **5** *nc* (in *pl*) (often with *sing* verb) building or set of buildings for industry or manufacture; factory; (用於複數) (常用單數動詞連用) 工廠; 工場: *brickworks* 磚廠; *ironworks* 鐵廠. **6** *nc* (in *pl*) moving parts of a machine which make it go (用於

複數) 機器的活動部份, 機件: *The works of a watch are very small.* 手錶的機件很小. **'workman** man who earns his living by using his hands 工人, 勞工. **workmanship** *nu* skill of a good workman 技藝, 手藝. **'workshop** place where things are made or repaired 車間, 廠房, 工作坊; 修理廠. **out of work** unemployed 失業: *be out of work* 失業; *out-of-work miners* 失業的礦工.

work² [wəːk] *vt / i* **1** (with reference to mind, body or a machine) use, cause to use, energy or power for a definite purpose (指腦力, 體力或機器) (使) 工作, (使) 勞動; (使) 運轉: *At school we have to work very hard.* 在學校我們必須努力學習. *Our teacher works us very hard.* 我們的老師促使我們努力學習. *This machine is worked by electricity.* 這台機器是電動的. **2** do what is necessary to make a living; be employed 工作; 勞動; 做事; 做工: *He works in an office.* 他在辦公室工作. *My brother works for a farmer.* 我哥哥給一個農場主幹活. **3** be successful; get a result 成功; 有結果; 行得通: *This new method really works.* 這個新方法真的起作用了. *The medicine has worked wonders* i.e. has had wonderful results 產生非常好的效果. **workable** *adj* able to work or be worked 能動的; 能用的; 行得通的: *Your plan is workable.* 你的計劃是行得通的. *The soil is so poor that it is not workable.* 這土壤已貧瘠得無法耕種了. *(opp* 反義詞 **unworkable**). **worker** *nc* person who works (esp. a member of the working classes) 工作者; 勞動者; 工人, 職工 (尤指工人階級的一員). **work something out 1** finish by using or working 用完, 耗盡: *Many coalmines in Great*

Britain are worked out. 英國的許多煤礦已採完了. **2** find the answer to; solve 找到…的答案; 解決: *Have you worked out this problem yet?* 這個問題你解決了沒有? *We are working out a way to have a cheap holiday.* 我們正在想辦法過一個花費少的假日. '**workout** *nc* practice; exercise; training 練習; 訓練: *Before the race the runners had a workout.* 比賽前, 賽跑的人進行了訓練. **work (something) up 1** cause to grow slowly by working hard (努力工作使)逐漸發展, 拓展: *I worked up this business from nothing.* 我白手起家逐步把這家商店建立起來. **2** make excited 使情緒激動; 煽動; 鼓動: *Why is he so worked up?* 他為甚麼如此激動? **3** slowly reach 逐漸達到, 逐步發展: *The situation has now worked up to the point that nobody will do anything.* 形勢如今已發展到任何人都不要幹甚麼事了.

working ['wə:kiŋ] *adj* of work; having work; useful for work 工作的; 有工作的; 工作用的: *He is wearing his working clothes.* 他穿着工作服. *There are five working days in each week.* 每週有五個工作日. *Before building the ship they made a working model of it.* 造船以前, 他們製作了一個施工模型. **the working class(es)** section of society which works mainly with its hands 工人階級, 勞動階級. Also 亦作 *adj*: *a little working-class house* 勞動階級的小房子. **working man** man who makes his living by working with his hands 工人; 勞動者. **in working order** working well; able to do what it is intended to do 良好的工作狀態; 能正常工作(運轉): *Is the lamp in working order?* 燈會亮嗎?

world [wə:ld] *nc* **1** the earth and all that is in it; planet like our own planet, earth 世界; 地球; 宇宙; 星球, 天體: *He sailed alone round the world.* 他獨自乘船環球航行. *The new invention amazed the world* i.e. countries or people everywhere. 這項新發明驚動了全世界. 即: 所有的國家或人民. *It is possible that there are other worlds.* 還有其他星球, 這是可能的. **2** separate or special part of the earth or of the activities in it 世界某一部份或其活動; 社會, 界, 領域: *the New World* i.e. America 新世界, 即: 美洲; *the animal / vegetable / mineral world* 動物界/植物界/礦物界; *the world of books* 書的世界; *the political world* 政界. **3** life on earth or elsewhere 人間, 現世, 世間, 世上: *He came into the world after the war* i.e. he was born then. 他戰後出生. *Do you believe in the next world?* i.e. another life after death 你相信來世嗎?即: 死後的世間. Also 亦作 *adj* spread over the whole world or most of it. 遍布全世界的: *There have been two world wars in this century.* 本世紀有兩次世界大戰. *English is now a world language.* 英語如今是世界通用的語言. **worldly** *adj* **1** of the world 世間的, 世上的; 世俗的: *worldly pleasures* 俗世的享樂. **2** as a result of knowing the world 老於世故的, 善於處世的: *worldly wisdom* 處世本領, 世故. (*opp* 反義詞 **unworldly**). '**world-wide** *adj* reaching all parts of the world 遍及全世界的: *a world-wide airline* 遍及世界的航線. **in the world** emphatic use 強調用法: *Nobody in the world is better known than he is* i.e. nobody else; nobody at all 世界上誰都不如他聞名. 即: 沒有別人; 根本沒有人. *What in the world has happened?* i.e. whatever? what on earth? 究竟發生了甚麼事? **out of this world** very unusual and very good 特別好

的, 無與倫比的, 舉世無雙的: *The food we ate was out of this world.* (*informal*) 我們吃過的食物好極了. (非正式).

worm [wə:m] *nc* any type of very small creature shaped like a snake 蠕蟲, 蟲, 蛆. Also 亦作 *vt* 1 move slowly and silently like a worm 緩慢, 悄悄地蠕行, 蠕動: *He wormed himself into the front row.* 他慢慢地挪到前排去. *We wormed our way through the crowd.* 我們緩慢地穿過人羣. 2 get with difficulty or effort 好不容易才得到: *I had to worm a reply from him.* 我好不容易才得到他的回答.

worn [wɔ:n] past part of **wear**[1]. **wear**[1] 的過去分詞.

worry ['wʌri] *vt / i* be, cause to be, annoyed, anxious or upset (使)困擾, (使)煩惱; (使)着急; (使)不安, 擔心, 發愁: *My mother worries if I come home late.* 要是我回家晚了, 我母親總是擔心. *Don't worry about the examination. It's easy.* 別爲考試煩惱. 很容易. *Please don't worry him when he is working.* 他工作的時候, 請別打擾他. *His illness worried me.* 他的病使我擔心. *I was worried about by his illness.* 我擔心他的病. Also 亦作 1 *nc* (often *pl*) something which causes anxiety etc. (常用複數)令人着急不安等的事物: *She has all the worries of looking after a large family.* 她有照顧大家庭的一切煩惱. 2 *nu* state of being anxious. 煩惱; 憂慮: *His face showed his worry.* 他的憂慮在神情中流露出來. **worried** *adj*: *He has a worried face.* 他滿面愁容. **worrying** *adj* causing worry 令人煩惱的.

worse [wə:s] 1 *adj* (*comparative* of **bad**) (bad 的比較級): *This road is bad but that one is worse.* 這條路不好, 那條路更糟. *His writing is worse*

than yours. 他的文章比你的差. *He made things worse by telling lies.* 他撒謊, 把事情弄得更糟了. 2 *pred adj* (*comparative* of **ill**) (ill 的比較級): *During the night he became worse.* 夜間他的病情更糟了. *The medicine made me feel worse.* 這藥使我感覺更壞. Also 亦作 *adv* 1 (*comparative* of **badly**) (badly 的比較級): *He writes much worse than you do.* 他寫得比你差得多. 2 more 更猛烈, 更厲害; 更…, 還…: *The wind is blowing worse than it did yesterday* i.e. more strongly 風颳得比昨天更猛烈了. *We hate him worse than ever.* 我們比以前更恨他了. Also 亦作 *nu* something which is worse 更壞的事物: *Life has gone from bad to worse.* 生活變得越來越壞了. *I am quite pleased with your work. I expected worse.* 我對你的工作很滿意. 我沒想到會這麼好. *superlative* 最高級 **worst** [wə:st]. (*opp* 反義詞 **better**). **worsen** *vt / i* become, or cause to become, worse (使)變得更壞; 惡化. **none the worse** 1 not harmed 沒怎麼樣, 安然無恙: *He is none the worse for his terrible journey.* 他雖經歷了那趟可怕的旅行, 卻也安然無恙. 2 no less (of him) 仍然, 還是, 不差: *I think none the worse of him for refusing to work* i.e. I think no less of him. 他雖拒絕去工作, 我對他的看法仍然不錯. 即: 仍然一樣看法, 像以前一樣讚賞他. **worse off** not as prosperous, happy etc as before 不如以前昌盛、幸福等; 惡化, 情況更壞: *My father's death has left me worse off.* 我父親死後, 我的處境更壞了.

worship ['wə:ʃip] *nu* honour and praise to God or to somebody / something that is greatly admired (對上帝或某人/某物的)崇拜, 仰慕; 禮拜: *A church or mosque is a place of worship.* 教堂或

清真寺是禮拜的地方. *Their worship of rich, powerful people is disgusting.* 他們對有錢有勢的人的仰慕令人厭惡. Also 亦作 *vt / i* praise and pray to God; admire greatly 做禮拜; 仰慕, 敬仰. *past* 過去式和過去分詞 **worshipped.** (US 美 **worshiped**). **worshipper** *nc* **your Worship, his Worship** title of respect when addressing or speaking about a mayor or magistrate of a law court (對市長或地方法官的尊稱)閣下: *Not guilty, your Worship.* 無罪, 閣下.

worst [wɜːst] *adj (superlative* of **bad**) (bad 的最高級): *He is the worst boy in the class.* 他是班裏最壞的男生. *It was the worst accident I have ever seen.* 那是我見過的最嚴重的事故了. Also 亦作 *adv (superlative* of **badly**) (badly 的最高級): *During the famine all the people suffered badly, but the poor people living in towns suffered (the) worst.* 饑荒期間, 人人遭殃, 城裏的窮人受苦最深. Also 亦作 *nu* something which is worst 最壞的事物, 最差的事物: *Hope for the best but expect the worst.* 作最好的希望, 作最壞的打算. *The worst that can happen is that you will lose your job.* 可能發生的最壞的事情, 是你將要失業. **at its / one's worst** when something / somebody is in the worst state 在某事/某人情況最壞的時候: *We met him before breakfast when he was at his worst* i.e. hungry and bad-tempered 早飯前他情緒最壞的時候我們見過他. 即: 又餓又脾氣不好. **at (the) worst** even if the worst happens 即使發生了最壞的情況: *At (the) worst you will be delayed for only one hour.* 最糟糕的也不過是你將被耽擱一小時.

worth [wɜːθ] *pred adj* **1** having a particular value 值, 有 … 的價值: *This watch is worth £50.* 這個錶值50鎊. *All your books are not worth more than fifty pence.* 你所有的書的價值不超過五十便士. **2** giving something valuable or satisfying 值得: *The new film is worth seeing.* 這部新電影值得看. *His opinion is not worth considering.* 他的意見不值得考慮. **3** (with reference to a person) having wealth, property etc of a particular value (指人) 有 … 的財產的: *That farmer is worth several thousand pounds.* 那個農場主有數千鎊財產. Also 亦作 *nu* what somebody / something is worth 某人/某物的價值: *I think his ideas are of very little worth.* 我認為他的意見沒甚麼價值. **2** amount obtained for a particular sum of money 值一定金額的數量: *I bought ten pounds' worth of food.* 我買了十鎊錢的食物. **worthless** *adj* having no usefulness 沒有用的, 沒有價值的: 'worth'while, **worth one's while** enjoyable, useful etc considering the time spent 值得花時間的: *The visit to Paris was worthwhile.* 遊覽巴黎是值得的. **worth it** worthwhile 值得的.

worthy ['wɜːði] *adj* **1** (usu. *pred*) deserving (通常用作表語)值得的, 配得上的: *He is a teacher worthy of great respect.* 他是一位很值得尊敬的老師. *Surely the country is worthy of a better president.* 無疑地, 這個國家應該有一個更好的總統. (*opp* 反義詞 **unworthy**). **2** (usu. with a humorous or ironical sense) deserving praise or honour (通常表示幽默或諷刺) 值得讚揚或尊敬的: *Our worthy friends refuse to help us.* 我們可敬的朋友們拒絕幫助我們. *comparative* 比較級 **worthier.** *superlative* 最高級 **worthiest.**

would [wud] *aux* see 見 **will**[1]. 'would-

be *adj* intended but unsuccessful 自稱的, 自命的, 以⋯自居的: *a would-be teacher* i.e. someone who failed to become a teacher, or someone who wishes to be a teacher but is not one yet (*informal*) 自命爲教師的人, 即: 未能成爲教師的人, 或想要成爲教師卻仍還不是的人 (非正式).

wound¹ [wu:nd] *vt* 1 deliberately damage the body by cutting, striking, shooting at it etc. 使受傷, 傷害: *He fired his gun and wounded the thief in the leg.* 他開了槍, 打傷了賊的腿. *In the battle ten soldiers were wounded.* 在交戰中, 十個士兵受了傷. *Note* 說明: *wound* has only this sense of damaging deliberately; when the damage to the body is not caused deliberately *injure* or *hurt* should be used. *In the railway accident ten passengers were injured / hurt.* wound僅表示故意傷害; 若非故意傷害, 須用injure或hurt. *In the railway accident ten passengers were injured / hurt.* 在火車事故中, 十名乘客受了傷. 2 cause a person to have an unpleasant feeling 傷害 (人的感情); 屈辱: *Your remarks have wounded his pride.* 你的話傷了他的自尊心. *We must not wound his feelings.* 我們不應傷他的感情. Also 亦作 *nc* 1 deliberate damage done to the body (故意造成的) 傷, 創傷. 2 painful feeling 痛苦的感覺: *The defeat was a wound to his pride.* 失敗傷了他的自尊心.

wound² [waund] past of **wind**². wind² 的過去式和過去分詞.

wove [wouv] past tense of **weave.** weave的過去式.

wrangle [ˈræŋgl] *vi* argue or quarrel noisily 爭辯, 爭論; 爭吵, 口角. Also 亦作 *nc.*

wrap [ræp] *vt* put round; cover by putting round (esp. using cloth or paper)

(尤指用布或紙) 包; 裹: *I wrapped a blanket round him.* 我用一條毛毯把他包起來. *I wrapped him in a blanket.* 我用一條毛毯把他包起來. *We wrapped the bread in paper.* 我們用紙包麵包. *In very cold weather you must wrap yourself up* i.e. cover yourself with warm clothes 天氣很冷時, 你必須穿得暖暖和和的. 即: 穿暖和的衣服. past 過去式和過去分詞 **wrapped.** Also 亦作 *nc* piece of cloth or clothing worn over clothes to keep warm 圍巾; 披肩; 圍毯; 外套; 大衣. **wrapper** *nc* piece of paper used to cover or put round something (e.g.a book) (書等的) 封皮, 包裝紙. **wrapping** *nc / u* material put round something to cover and protect it (e.g. when it is being sent by post) (郵寄包裹等用的) 包裝材料. **be wrapped up in 1** be covered or hidden in 包在⋯裏; 被包藏: *The dishes were wrapped up in soft paper.* 碟子用柔軟的紙包起來. 2 give all one's attention to 專心於, 全神貫注於: *He is wrapped up in his work.* 他專心於他的工作.

wreath [ri:θ] *nc* circle made from flowers and leaves 花圈; 花環.

wreathe [ri:ð] *vt / i* put round; cover 籠罩; 纏繞: *The burning house was wreathed in smoke.* 燃燒着的房子籠罩在烟霧之中.

wreck [rek] **1** *nc* something (esp. a ship) which has been severely damaged or destroyed; somebody who has been greatly weakened by illness, worry or injury (尤指船的) 殘骸; 失事船(物件); (因疾病、憂慮或受傷而) 健康極度受損的人; 殘廢; 落魄者: *The sailors jumped from the wreck before it sank.* 水手們在船沉沒之前從其殘骸跳出來. *After the examination I was a nervous wreck.* 考試之後, 我緊張得不

成人樣了. **2** *nu* severe damage or destruction 破壞; (船隻)失事; 毀滅, 毀壞; *The captain tried to save his ship from wreck.* 船長努力拯救他的船, 使其免遭毀壞. Also 亦作 *vt* severely damage or destroy (esp. a ship) 使(尤指船)失事, 遇險破壞或毀滅. **wreckage** *nu* parts of something which has been wrecked 殘骸, 破片; 難船殘餘貨物.

wren [ren] *nc* type of very small bird 鷦鷯.

wrench [rentʃ] *vt* **1** pull suddenly and violently 猛拉, 猛扭; *He wrenched the stick from me.* 他從我這裏奪走拐杖. *He wrenched the stick from / out of my hand.* 他從我手裏奪走拐杖. **2** twist suddenly and painfully 扭傷; *When I fell I wrenched my ankle.* 我跌倒時扭傷了腳脖子. Also 亦作 *nc* **1** sudden and violent pull or twist 猛拉, 猛扭. **2** tool for holding and twisting nust and bolts etc.; spanner 扳手; 扳鉗.

wrestle ['resl] *vt / i* fight or compete with somebody by seizing him and trying to throw him to the ground (與…)搏鬥; 摔交, 角力; 格鬥. **wrestler** *nc* **wrestling** *nu* 'all-in 'wrestling type of wrestling in which the wrestlers are allowed to hit as well as hold 允許摔交運動員抓住碰撞的摔交.

wretch [retʃ] *nc* poor, miserable person who is either pitied or despised 可憐的人, 不幸的人; 卑鄙的人, 可恥的人. **wretched** ['retʃid] *adj* poor; miserable; annoying 可憐的; 悲慘的; 討厭的; *The wretched people are starving.* 可憐的人們在捱餓. *The trouble was caused by his wretched pride.* 這麻煩是由他那討厭的傲氣造成的.

wriggle ['rigl] *vt / i* move, cause to move, the body or part of it quickly from side to side (使)扭動, (使)蠕動; *The snake wriggled through the grass.* 蛇蠕蠕着穿過雜草. *He wriggled himself out of my grip.* 我緊緊住他, 他卻扭動掙脫了. Also 亦作 *nc.*

wright [rait] *nc* maker of something (now usually in combinations) (現在通常用以構成複合名詞)工人, 匠, 製造者; *a shipwright* 造船工人; *a wheelwright* 製造車輪的工人; *a playwright* 劇作家.

wring [riŋ] *vt* **1** hold firmly and twist 扭, 擰緊; *He is wringing the chicken's neck* i.e. twisting in order to kill it 他正在擰雞的脖子. 即: 扭緊脖子以便宰殺. **2** remove water from clothes etc in this way. 擰掉(濕衣服的水); 擰乾, 絞乾(衣服); *My socks were so wet that I had to wring them (out).* 我的短襪太濕了, 我得把它擰乾了. *I had to wring the water out of my socks.* 我得把襪子的水擰掉. *past* 過去式和過去分詞 **wrung** [rʌŋ]. **wringer** *nc* device for wringing water from clothes (esp. after they have been washed) (尤指衣服洗後用的)絞乾器. 'wringing 'wet so wet that water can be squeezed out of it 濕淋淋的, 濕得能擰出水來的. **wring one's hands** show sorrow or distress by twisting and moving one's hands together 搓着雙手(表示悲哀或憂傷).

wrinkle ['riŋkl] *nc* fold or line on the surface of something (e.g. of the skin because of age; of a piece of cloth) 皺紋(如: 老人的皮膚, 一塊布); *The old man's face is covered with wrinkles.* 那老人的臉佈滿皺紋. Also 亦作 *vt / i* have, cause to have, wrinkles (使)皺紋; 起皺紋; *Don't wrinkle your new dress.* 別把你的新衣服弄皺了. **wrinkled** *adj* having wrinkles 有皺紋的.

wrist [rist] *nc* joint between the arm

and the hand 手腕. '**wrist watch** small watch held on the wrist by a band of leather, metal etc. 手錶.·

writ [rit] *nc* written order made by a court of law (法院的)令狀, (書面)命令, 傳票.

write [rait] *vt / i* **1** put words, figures or signs on something (usu. on paper with a pen or pencil) 書寫, 寫; 記; 抄: *He can neither read nor write.* 他不會讀, 也不會寫. *I wrote my name and address in the book.* 我把名字和地址寫在書裏. *How many words have you written?* 你寫了多少個詞了? *I am writing an essay.* 我正在寫一篇散文. **2** write and send what has been written 寫並寄出: *Write your friend a note.* 給你的朋友寫封短信吧. *I wrote (to) you from London.* 我從倫敦給你寫過信. **3** be an author; do the work of an author 寫作, 著作: *What does he do? He writes.* 他是幹甚麼的? 他是作家. *He has written for several magazines.* 他已爲幾家雜誌撰寫文章. *past tense* 過去式 **wrote** [rout]. *past part* 過去分詞 **written** ['ritn]. **writer** *nc* person who writes; author 作家; 作者. **writing 1** *nu* act of writing; words etc which have been written 寫作, 著述; 字跡; 筆跡: *I can't read your writing.* 你的字很潦草, 我認不出來. **2** *nc* (in *pl*) work done by an author (用於複數)作品, 著作: *This term we are studying the writings of Dickens.* 本學期我們正在研究狄更斯的作品. '**writing paper** paper for writing letters 信紙. **write something down** make a written note of; put on paper in writing 寫下; 記下: *The policeman wrote down my name and address.* 警察把我的姓名和地址記下來. *If you know the answer write it down.* 你知道答案的話就寫下來吧. **write something off** no longer show something in a written list; remove something from the written record (because it is useless, lost, cannot be recovered etc.) 註銷; 取消: (因無用, 丟失, 無法復原等而)勾銷, 報廢: *The manager told me to write off one of the old pumps in the factory.* 經理告訴我把工廠裏的一台舊抽水機註銷了. *The company has written off the debt* i.e. because it knows the debt will not be paid. 公司已註銷了這筆債款. 即: 因爲公司知道這筆債款將不支付. '**write-off** *nc* something which is so badly damaged that it is useless 破損得無用的物品, 報廢物品: *After the accident his car was a write-off. (informal)* 事故以後他的車報廢了. (非正式). **write something out 1** write completely, in full 全部寫出: *The teacher made me write out the whole essay again.* 老師要我把散文全部再寫一遍. **2** write in order to give or send 寫出, 開出: *He wrote his landlord out a cheque for £20.* 他開出一張20鎊的支票給房東. **write something up 1** write out in a complete form 整理: *I must write up my history notes.* 我必須整理歷史筆記. **2** describe fully (and usu. very favourably) in a newspaper or periodical 在報刊上詳細描述, 報導(通常讚揚). '**write-up** *nc* comment (either favourable or unfavourable) in a newspaper or periodical 報刊上(好或壞)的評論: *The school play was given a very bad write-up in the local paper. (informal)* 學校的戲劇在當地的報紙上評價很壞. (非正式).

wrong [rɔŋ] *adj* **1** sinful, not moral; mistaken or not correct 罪惡的, 不道德的; 錯的, 不對的: *Telling lies is wrong.* 撒謊是不對的. *It is wrong to drink and drive.* 酒後開車是錯誤的.

The man gave the wrong answer. 那個人回答錯了. *We are late because we took the wrong road.* 我們走錯了路, 所以遲到了. *You are quite wrong* i.e. mistaken 你錯了. *He is wrong in thinking this.* 他這樣想是不對的. *It is wrong of him to think this.* 他這樣想是不對的. (*opp* 反義詞 **right**). **2** not working properly; not in order 有毛病的; 不正常工作的; 失常的: *There's something wrong with my watch.* 我的錶有點毛病. *What's wrong with your leg?* 你的腿怎麼啦? Also 亦作 *adv*: *You've done the work wrong.* 你把事情弄錯了. *He never went wrong* i.e. never made a mistake or broke the law 他從來不犯錯誤. 即: 不犯錯誤或不犯法. **wrongful** *adj* not lawful; unjust 非法的; 不法的; 不正當的. **wrongly** *adv*: *You've done the work wrongly.* 你把事情弄錯了. *Note* 說明: *wrong* as an *adv* usu. comes at the end of its sentence; *wrongly* can come either at the end or earlier (esp. before *a past part*) (e.g. *The parcel is tied wrong(ly)* or *The parcel is wrongly tied*). wrong

作爲副詞通常放在句末; wrongly可放在句末或句中(尤其在過去分詞之前) (如: The parcel is tied wrong(ly) 或 The parcel is wrongly tied包裹捆紮錯了).

in the wrong guilty; at fault; mistaken 有罪的; 出毛病; 不正當; 錯的.

wrote [rout] past tense of **write.** write 的過去式.

wrought [rɔːt] (past tense of old verb meaning 'to work') caused (舊式動詞意爲'to work'的過去式) 造成, 引起: *The storm wrought great damage.* 暴風雨造成了巨大的破壞. **'wrought iron** *nu* special kind of iron which resists rust and can be made into different shapes 熟鐵; 鍛鐵; Also 亦作 *adj*: *a wrought-iron gate* 鍛鐵所造的閘.

wrung [rʌŋ] past of **wring.** wring的過去式和過去分詞.

wry [rai] *adj* (with reference to the mouth or face) pulled to one side to express dislike (指嘴唇或臉 扭歪的, 歪斜的) (表示厭惡): *When he tasted the tea he made a wry face.* 他嘗了嘗茶, 做了個苦臉.

X,x

Xmas ['krisməs, 'eksməs] *nc* short written form of **Christmas** *(informal)* Christmas的縮寫形式(非正式).

X-ray ['eksrei] *nc* **1** type of ray which can pass through solids and is therefore used to see into or photograph what is inside them X射線, X光. **2** photograph taken in this way X光照片: *He has gone into hospital for an X-ray.* 他去醫院作X光檢查. Also 亦作 *vt* examine or photograph using X-rays 用X射線檢查或拍照.

xylophone ['zailəfoun] *nc* musical instrument in which wooden bars of different lengths are hit with wooden hammers 木琴.

Y,y

yacht [jɔt] *nc* **1** type of sailing boat used for racing and pleasure (競賽和娛樂用的)快艇,帆船. **2** type of small ship (usu. with an engine, not sails) used by the rich for private travel (富人私人旅遊用的)遊艇(通常以一發動機推動,無帆). **yachting** *nu* skill or sport of sailing a yacht 駕駛快艇(或帆船)的技術;快艇(或帆船)比賽.

yam [jæm] *nc / u* type of tropical plant; its root, like a potato, which is used as food 薯蕷屬植物;山藥.

yank [jæŋk] *vt* pull sharply and suddenly 拽,猛拉,拔: *He yanked away the chair before I could sit on it.* 我還沒有坐下他就猛地把椅子拉走了. Also 亦作 *nc* action of pulling away sharply 突然的猛拉;猛拉: *give something a yank* 突然猛拉某物.

Yank [jæŋk] *nc* American (*informal and rather impolite*) 美國人,美國佬.(非正式,頗不禮貌).

yap [jæp] *vi* (with reference to a dog) bark with a short, sharp sound (指狗)吠叫,汪汪叫. *past* 過去式和過去分詞 **yapped.**

yard[1] [jɑːd] *nc* measure of length equal to 3 feet (.91 metres) 碼(=3英尺或0.91米). **'yardstick** something with which other things are compared (比較的)標準,尺度.

yard[2] [jɑːd] *nc* **1** enclosed space next to a house or building 院子,庭院. *Note* 說明: *(US)* the space next to a house or building is called a yard even if it has grass, trees and flowers. *(Brit* garden*)* (美)房子旁邊長有花草樹木的地方也稱爲

yard. (英爲garden). **2** open space used for a particular purpose 場地;工場;廠: *dockyard* i.e. space where ships are repaired 修船廠; *railway yard* i.e. space where there are many railway lines for keeping wagons and carriages when not used or for making up trains (鐵路)車場,調車場,編車場; *builder's yard* i.e. space where a builder keeps his building materials 營造場

yarn [jɑːn] **1** *nu* type of thread used for knitting; thick thread from which a rope is made 紗;線. **2** *nc* story (often one which is untrue) (*informal*) (常爲非真實的)故事,捏造的話;奇談. (義2爲非正式).

yashmak [ˈjæʃmæk] *nc* (in some Muslim countries) type of veil worn over the face by women (某些穆斯林國家婦女所戴的)面紗.

yawn [jɔːn] *vi* **1** open the mouth widely, as one does when sleepy or weary 打呵欠. **2** be wide open 張得很大,張得很開: *a yawning hole* 張着大口的洞. Also 亦作 *nc* act of this kind (打)呵欠;張開大口: *He gave a yawn and then fell asleep.* 他打了個呵欠,然後睡着了.

yea [jei] *adv / interj* yes (*o.f.*) 然,是(舊式).

yeah [jɛə] *adv / interj* yes (*informal*) 是,嗯.(非正式).

year [jiə*] *nc* **1** period of 365 days or 12 months 年,歲: *He is 17 years of age and is in the sixth year of secondary school.* 他十七歲,在中學六年級學習.

2 period of 365 days or 12 months between 1 January and 31 December 曆年，年度：*Last year I went to London.* 去年我到了倫敦．*In the year 1945, the Second World War ended.* 1945年，第二次世界大戰結束了．**yearly** *adj/adv* happening every year; happening once a year 每年(的)；一年一次(的)．
'leap year see 見 **leap.**

yearn [jə:n] *vt* (with **for** or **after**) greatly desire (esp. somebody / something that one loves) (與for或after連用) 思念；盼望；渴望 (尤指所愛的某人或某事物)：*The sailor yearned for home.* 海員想家了．*They yearned to see their parents again.* 他們渴望再見到父母．**yearning** *nc / u.*

yeast [ji:st] *nu* living substance used in the preparation of bread and beer and other alcoholic drinks. 酵母(菌)．

yell [jel] *vt / i* shout loudly and sharply 大聲叫喊；叫嚷．Also 亦作 *nc* shout of this kind 叫嚷；叫喊．

yellow ['jeləu] *nc / u* colour of butter or the sun 黃色．Also 亦作 *adj* **1** a *yellow ball* 黃色的球．**2** not brave; cowardly. (*informal* in sense 2) 膽小的；沒骨氣的；縮頭縮腦的 (義2爲非正式)．Also 亦作 *vt / i* become, cause to become, yellow (使) 變黃．**yellowish** *adj* rather yellow 淡黃色的，帶黃色的．

yelp [jelp] *vi* cry out suddenly because of fear or pain (由於害怕或疼痛) 突然叫喊，尖叫．Also 亦作 *nc.*

yes [jes] *interj* expressing agreement 是，對．**'yes man** person who always agrees with what is said by his employer etc. (*informal*) 唯唯諾諾的人，應聲蟲 (非正式)．

yesterday ['jestədi] *adv / nu* day before the present one 昨天：*He arrived yesterday.* 他昨天到達．*Today is Friday; yesterday was Thursday.* 今天星期五；昨天星期四．Also 亦作 *adj*: *Yesterday morning / afternoon / evening was fine and dry.* 昨天上午/下午/晚上天晴但乾燥．**Note** 說明：with **night**, **last** must be used; *last night; yesterday night* is not normally used. 與night連用時，必須用last：last night昨晚；yesterday night通常不用．

yet [jet] *adv* **1** (at the end of a question) up to now; so far (問句句末) 到現在，至今：*Has he gone yet?* 他走了沒有？*Are you ready yet?* 你準備好了嗎？**2** (immediately after **not**, **never**, **nothing** etc or at the end of the sentence) up to now; up to then; by now; by then (緊接not, never, nothing等之後或置於句末) 到現在，到那時：*He has not yet gone / He has not gone yet.* 他還沒有走呢．*I am not yet ready / I am not ready yet.* 我還沒有準備好．*Nothing yet is known / Nothing is known yet.* 至今什麼也不知道．*Are you ready to go now? No, not just yet.* 你準備好在走嗎？不，還沒有．**3** (with *affirmative*) still (用於肯定句) 還是；仍然，仍舊；更：*We may yet hear from him / We may hear from him yet.* 我們還會收到他的信息．*This is bad; that is yet worse.* 這不好；那更壞．Also 亦作 *conj* still; but 還，可是；然而；但是；卻．*I gave him ten pounds (and) yet he was not satisfied.* 我給了他十鎊而他還不滿足．*He is a clever, yet lazy man.* 他是個聰明但卻懶惰的人．**as yet** up to now; up to then 到現在，到那時：*As yet we have not met him.* 至今我們還沒有遇見他．

yield [ji:ld] *vt / i* **1** (with **to**) give up; surrender (與to連用) 放棄；讓步；屈服；投降：*Our army refused to yield.* 我軍拒絕投降．*The enemy yielded the town to our forces.* 敵人把城鎮放棄給我們的部隊．**2** produce; give 生產；生

長出: *Fertile land yields good crops.* 肥沃的土地生長出良好的莊稼. Also 亦作 *nc* amount produced 產量, 收獲量: *What is the yield of this ricefield?* 這塊稻田的產量是多少?

yodel ['joudl] *vt / i* change the voice quickly and frequently from low notes to high notes while singing 輪替用常聲和假聲唱, 用岳得爾調唱. *past* 過去式和過去分詞 **yodelled.** (*US* 美 **yodeled.**)

yoga ['jougə] *nu* religious way of life (originally followed mainly by some Hindus) which includes prayer, deep breathing, physical exercises and fasting (主要始於印度教) 瑜伽, 瑜伽修行法.

yoghourt, yoghurt ['jɔgɛt] *nu* thick liquid food made from sour milk 酸乳酪.

yoke [jouk] *nc* **1** frame of wood fitted on the neck of an animal (esp. an ox) so that it can pull a cart or plough 軛, 牛軛. **2** piece of wood fitted on a person's shoulders so that a pail, basket etc can be carried more easily on each side 軛狀扁擔. **3** part of a dress which fits round the shoulders (女服) 上衣的抵肩. Also 亦作 *vt* put a yoke on; join in pairs 用軛套上; 使結合成對, 接合, 連接.

yolk [jouk] *nc / u* the yellow part inside an egg 蛋黃.

yonder ['jɔndə*] *adj / adv* (with reference to somebody / something that can be seen) over there (rather *o.f.* — use **over there**) (指可以看見的某人/某物)那邊的, 那邊 (相當舊式—現在用over there).

you [ju:] *pron* **1** (with reference to a person / persons spoken to) 你, 你們: *Where do you live?* 你住在哪兒? **2** anybody; a person (泛指)任何人; 一個

人: *At our school you soon learn that the headmaster is very strict.* 在我們學校, 任何人很快便會知道校長是很嚴厲的. *What can you do in a situation like that?* 那樣的情況下, 能做甚麼呢?

young [jʌŋ] *adj* recently born or started etc. 年輕的; 幼小的; 幼嫩的; 新興的: *a young man* 年輕人; *young corn* 嫩玉米; *a young nation* 新興的國家. *He is two years younger than his brother.* 他比他哥哥小兩歲. *I am the youngest in the class.* 我是班裏最年輕的. (*opp* 反義詞 **old**). Also 亦作 *nu* young animals or birds 幼小的動物或鳥, 崽, 仔, 雛: *We saw a deer with its young.* 我們看見一隻鹿和它的幼仔. **young-ish** *adj* rather young 還年輕的, 還幼小的. **youngster** ['jʌŋstə*] *nc* young boy or girl 年輕人, 少年, 小孩子.

your [jɔ:*] *adj / determiner* of, belonging to, you 你的; 你們的: *Is this your book?* 這是你的書嗎?

yours [jɔ:z] *pron / pred adj*: *Is this book yours?* 這本書是你的嗎?

yourself [jɔ:'self] **1** *reflexive pron*: *Look at yourself in the mirror.* 從鏡子裏看看你自己吧. **2** (emphatic) (強調): *You yourself said so.* 是你自己這樣說的. **by yourself** without help; alone. 獨力, 靠自己; 獨自, 單獨. *pl* 複數 **yourselves.**

youth [ju:θ] **1** *nu* time of life when one is young 青春; 青年時期, 青少年時期: *In his youth he was a good runner.* 年輕時他是個優秀的賽跑運動員. **2** *nc* young man 年青人, 小伙子: *Who is that youth?* 那個小伙子是誰? *pl* 複數 **youths** [ju:ðz]. **3** *nu* (with **the**) young men and women (與the連用)青年, 青少年: *The youth of today are very lively.* 如今青年很活潑. **youthful** *adj* young; looking young; behaving like a young person 年輕的; 青年的; 富於青

春活力的, 朝氣蓬勃的. **youthfulness** *nu.* **'youth hostel** inexpensive place where young travellers can stay 青年招待所, 青年旅舍.

yule [juːl] *nu* Christmas *(o.f.)* 聖誕節(舊式). **'yuletide** Christmas time *(o.f.)* 聖誕節假期(舊式).

Z, z

zeal [ziːl] *nu* eagerness; enthusiasm 熱心，熱忱；熱情. **zealous** ['zeləs] *adj* **zealously** *adv*.

zebra ['zebrə] *nc* type of wild animal like a horse, with dark brown and white stripes 斑馬.

zenith ['zeniθ] *nu* highest point of something 頂點，頂峯；全盛(時期).

zero ['ziərou] *nc* **1** the figure 0 數字 "零", 0. **2** the figure 0 marked on a scale (esp. on a thermometer) (尤指溫度計上的)零度: *ten degrees above / below zero* 零上／零下十度. *pl* 複數 **zeros**. **'zero hour** exact time fixed for something important to begin (e.g. a battle; the launching of a rocket etc) (如戰役，發射火箭等的)重要事件開始的時刻.

zigzag ['zigzæg] *nc* line or course which turns sharply from side to side 鋸齒形的線或路，之字形. Also 亦作 *adj / adv*: *a zigzag path* 曲曲折折的小路. Also 亦作 *vi go zigzag* 曲曲折折走，取之字形行進；蜿蜒而行: *He zigzagged across the field*. 他曲曲折折地穿過田野. *past* 過去式和過去分詞 **zigzagged**.

zinc [ziŋk] *nu* bluish-white metallic element (**Zn**) 鋅(化學符號 Zn). Also 亦作 *vt* coat or treat with zinc; galvanize 在…上面鍍鋅；用鋅處理；給…鍍鋅；電鍍. *past* 過去式和過去分詞 **zincked** or **zinced**.

zip [zip] *nc* device (made of metal etc) for fastening quickly two pieces of cloth, leather etc, by pulling a tab over two rows of teeth 拉鏈. Also 亦作 *vt / i* fasten or unfasten with a zip 拉開或扣上(…的)拉鏈: *Will you zip up my dress?* 請你扣上我的衣服的拉鏈，好嗎？ *past* 過去式和過去分詞 **zipped. zipper, 'zip 'fastener** *nc* zip.

zodiac ['zoudiæk] *nu* part of the sky extending on either side of the path which the sun seems to take through the sky in a year 黄道帶(天空中每year太陽行經路線向兩側延伸的區域). **signs of the zodiac** the 12 divisions of the zodiac, each named after a constellation of stars, through which the sun and the planets appear to move during one year 黄道十二宫(依星羣命名，分成十二宫，每年太陽及行星運行通過).

zone [zoun] *nc* **1** area of a country or town marked off and used for a special reason or purpose 地區，區域，地帶: *the war zone* i.e. an area where a war is fought 戰區，即：打仗的地區; *traffic zones* 交通區. **2** (*US*) division of the country for postal purposes (美)郵區. (*Brit* 英 **area**). Also 亦作 *vt* **1** divide into zones 將…分區. **2** give a special purpose to 將(某區)劃做…: *This part of the city has been zoned for redevelopment.* 城市的這部份地區已劃做重新開發區.

zoo [zuː] *nc* park where many kinds of animals are kept in captivity 動物園. (Also 亦作 **zoological gardens**).

zoology [zuː'ɔlədʒi] *nu* science of animals 動物學. **zoological** [zuə'lɔdʒikl] *adj* **zoologist** *nc* person who studies zoology 動物學家.

zoom [zuːm] *vi* **1** (with reference to an aircraft) climb quickly; move quickly at a low height (指飛機)陡直上升,迅速上升; 低空迅速移動. **2** (with reference to a camera) move in quickly to a close-up view (指照相機)迅速移近 以獲近景特寫鏡頭: *The camera zoomed in on the man's face.* 攝影機鏡頭迅速移近那人臉部, 來一個特寫.

Appendix   附錄

Numbers
數

Cardinal numbers 基數	Ordinal numbers 序數
one 1	first 1st 第一
two 2	second 2nd 第二
three 3	third 3rd 第三
four 4	fourth 4th 第四
five 5	fifth 5th 第五
six 6	sixth 6th 第六
seven 7	seventh 7th 第七
eight 8	eighth 8th 第八
nine 9	ninth 9th 第九
ten 10	tenth 10th 第十
eleven 11	eleventh 11th 第十一
twelve 12	twelfth 12th 第十二
thirteen 13	thirteenth 13th 第十三
fourteen 14	fourteenth 14th 第十四
fifteen 15	fifteenth 15th 第十五
sixteen 16	sixteenth 16th 第十六
seventeen 17	seventeenth 17th 第十七
eighteen 18	eighteenth 18th 第十八
nineteen 19	nineteenth 19th 第十九
twenty 20	twentieth 20th 第二十
twenty-one 21	twenth-first 21st 第二十一
twenty-two 22	twenty-second 22nd 第二十二
thirty 30	thirtieth 30th 第三十
forty 40	fortieth 40th 第四十
fifty 50	fiftieth 50th 第五十
sixty 60	sixtieth 60th 第六十
seventy 70	seventieth 70th 第七十
eighty 80	eightieth 80th 第八十
ninety 90	ninetieth 90th 第九十
one/a hundred 100	hundredth 100th 第一百
a hundred and one 101	hundred-and-first 101st 第一百零一
two hundred 200	two hundredth 200th 第二百
one/a thousand 1,000	thousandth 1,000th 第一千
two thousand 2,000	two thousandth 2,000th 第兩千
one/a million 1,000,000	millionth 1,000,000th 第一百萬

Vulgar fractions
普通分數

$\frac{1}{2}$ a half $\frac{3}{4}$ three-quarters

$\frac{1}{3}$ a third $\frac{1}{5}$ a fifth

$\frac{2}{3}$ two-thirds $\frac{2}{5}$ two-fifths

$\frac{1}{4}$ a quarter $15\frac{1}{4}$ fifteen and a quarter

5/6	five-sixths	1/20	a twentieth
1/7	a seventh	1/100	a hundredth
1/10	a tenth		

Decimal fractions
小數

0.5   (nought) point five
0.33   (nought) point three three
15.25   fifteen point two five